D0882521

3 2109 00096 5419

WITHDRAWN

TWENTIETH-CENTURY
CRIME AND MYSTERY
WRITERS

Twentieth-Century Writers of the English Language

already published:

Twentieth-Century Children's Writers

Twentieth-Century Crime and Mystery Writers

in preparation:

Twentieth-Century Science-Fiction Writers

TWENTIETH-CENTURY CRIME AND MYSTERY WRITERS

EDITOR
JOHN M. REILLY

© by The Macmillan Press Ltd., 1980

All rights reserved. No part of this publication
may be reproduced or transmitted in any form
or by any means, without permission.

First published 1980 by
THE MACMILLAN PRESS LIMITED
London and Basingstoke
Associated companies in New York, Dublin
Melbourne, Johannesburg and Madras

ISBN 0 333 30107 2

Typeset by Computacomp (UK) Ltd.
Fort William, Scotland.
Printed in Great Britain by
REDWOOD BURN LIMITED
Trowbridge & Esher

CONTENTS

Reference
PR
888
D4
T8

PREFACE

The art of crime and mystery literature conceals a paradox. If we were not so captivated by the entertainment, we might pause to wonder how it can be that stories devoted to the spectacle of violent crime neither disturb nor horrify us. Thomas De Quincey, in his essay "On Murder Considered as One of the Fine Arts," was the first to note the aesthetic value of well-accomplished, and appropriately reported, homicide. Read today, De Quincey's essay confirms more than a century of fiction. Imaginary tales of crime provide a sensation of incongruity when victims meet their death in libraries, clubs, and private houses, or they offer the satisfaction of probability when violence occurs in society's back-alleys; but these accounts of murder engender no anxiety. In the same way, death by poison, strangulation, firearms, the blunt instrument, bladed weapons, explosives, and bizarre devices illustrate the range of human invention available, on the one hand to culprits who spill the blood of family and friends for the simple motives of greed, hate, or lust, and on the other hand to killers who undertake murder as a simple job of work; but, if the writing is skillful, we appreciate the ingenuity more than the perversity. At once predictable in their formulaized representation of crime and resolution and cunning in their craft, stories of crime and mystery could scarcely be more entertaining, and less likely to remind their readers of the sin of Cain.

Evidently, though, reading crime and mystery fiction is one thing, explaining it another. The thrill of danger evaded, ratification of fantasy, satisfaction with a witty or tough style, the grace and idiosyncrasy of character keep us reading, but when challenged to justify a taste for literature that is, after all, devoted to anti-social violence, one reader will speak of the attraction of the riddle to be solved, while another reader, no more or less sophisticated, will say the tale of crime is realistic. The first explanation has the advantage of paying some attention to the special craft of crime fiction, and the second acknowledges a sense of the tale's origin, but neither gives a satisfactory account of the genre.

Authoritative precedence for both of these popular justifications can be found in the words of the genre's ablest writers. Among the so-called Golden Age authors there are R. Austin Freeman whose "The Art of the Detective Story" inveighs against sensationalism that distracts from a controlled effect of a detection puzzle; S. S. Van Dine whose "Twenty Rules for Writing Detective Stories" prescribe rational limits to the means of detection, thereby advancing the dogma of plausibility; Ronald A. Knox whose "Ten Commandments of Detection" anathematizes hackneyed devices and asserts the obligation to challenge a reader with details that, properly arranged, constitute a rational solution to mystery. In support of realism there is Raymond Chandler, a master of narrative artifice, insisting in "The Simple Art of Murder" that his own type of mystery – what we have learned to call hard-boiled – is distinguished by typical murder, actual speech, and normal setting. Evidently, though, the character of the detective may be other than life-like, for Chandler describes him in the remarkable conclusion to his essay as though he were the hero of a medieval romance, armored with honor and pride, searching for hidden truth.

Chandler's effort, or anyone else's for that matter, to champion the crime and mystery story as essentially realistic confuses subject with treatment. With all narrative, mystery and crime fiction shares the necessity of supplying the illusion that the story conforms to a reality other than the text. Just as setting gives the plot a place to happen, and character allows for description of action, a fictional crime and the usually dominant detective are necessities of story-telling more than reflections of actuality. The account of a crime in, say, a newspaper article contrives to establish raw fear of criminal violence. In other words the conventions of reportage function to diminish the distance between readers and the threat of actuality. In contrast, mystery fiction thrills rather than threatens, because such motifs as the perversity of human invention when bent to violence, or the evident similarity of motives shared among likely suspects and the guilty, are contained within a design of plot in which we are always sensitive to the artist's hand. Theme, event, character – all these affirm the literary form rather than reconstruct actuality. Crime and mystery literature, thus, displaces the subject of violence with patterns of story-telling that, even in tales of mean streets, work against our receiving them as direct commentary on real life.

Other reading may urge utilitarian goals. History, current affairs, and biography, like the newspaper report of crime, are to help us understand how the world works. The "classics" are to inform us of life philosophically, or so it is said, and if they do not accomplish that, then they will improve our taste. But we consume crime and mystery stories, apart from a natural curiosity about the outcome of the plot, in the way we exercise for the pleasure of physical activity. If ever there were art read for its own sake, this is it.

Because it has been so often repeated, the claim that the essence of the genre is an intellectual puzzle seems much harder to deny than the allegation of realism. One thinks, for example, of the mystery book reviewers' habit of appraising a novel in terms of the surprises it contains and conspicuously refusing to divulge a book's ending so as not to spoil the reader's encounter with the criminal problem; or of the author Ellery Queen's practice of halting a story to challenge the reader to match wits with the detective Ellery Queen; or of the hundred-and-one times some fellow mystery fan has announced that he knew the killer at least as soon as the fictional detective. The weight of such testimony is intimidating, but it simply cannot be conclusive. Most of the puzzles, if abstracted from their tales, have practically no intrinsic interest, and, what is more, may be as available to ridicule as Chandler found the puzzle in *The Red House Mystery*. Of course ridicule is not the point either. Illogic in the way Mark Ablett (or is it his brother Robert?) is killed makes little difference, for the book interests us above all else because of its good-natured play on the manners and character of Great Detectives; that is to say, the rendering of the tale interests us in the Ablett case despite its flimsy riddle.

The dominance of the tale over its subject was announced as long ago as 1913, in E. C. Bentley's novel *Trent's Last Case*. Bentley has been praised for many contributions to the craft of detective story writing, but so far as I remember never for the implied statement of the writer's business contained in his story of a crime that has three solutions. Readers will remember that the detective Philip Trent first accounts for Sigsbee Manderson's death in an extended analysis that is then overturned by testimony that uses the same facts to produce a different explanation. Later, in the final pages of the book, the facts are once again reinterpreted when the murderer confesses. All three solutions are valid. The third solution contains the same evidence as the first or second and is no truer, even though a fictional character, at Bentley's bidding, certifies its accuracy by owning up to the crime. What, then, is the significance of the puzzle? It is a literary device like any other. What is more, the reduction of the puzzle to a device carries with it the suggestion that our knowledge of the laws of evidence, or of the objective reality on which we base our notions of the truth, becomes decidedly secondary when we read a novel of mystery. Its primary field of reference is literature, the previous experience we have had with similar stories that allows us to see that tales of crime justify themselves.

In denying that crime and mystery fiction is either realistic or an intellectual puzzle, I want to be careful not to endorse a third popular view which holds that the genre is fundamentally a literature of escape designed to be positively irrelevant to real experience. That idea is untenable because in its own non-realistic way crime and mystery fiction bears a definite relationship to history.

With all popular culture crime and mystery literature shares an origin in the technology that makes possible economical reproduction and wide distribution of printed texts to a literate, largely urban audience. Readily acquired in a money market, crime and mystery books, which can be collected in impressive numbers or disposed of after they are read, are examples of culture as commodity. Among the jumble of commodities available to a modern consumer, it has special significance for being the result of the manifestly modern interest in social control. Although literary concern for justice is universal, stories grounded in plots devoted to unraveling the mystery surrounding crimes originate only with the consciousness among the populations of large, urban settings that neither traditional associations of family, clan, and village, nor the ideal of self-reliant individualism are practical means of protecting the peace of all and the property of the privileged. On the streets, as well as in the courts, state power enforces order, more or less with the consent of the governed. Thus, crime has become a social issue, and in the anonymity of the city its solution and control, a problem. This is what is meant when historians of crime fiction remark that its prerequisites were public sympathy for law and order and the creation of official police.

Crime and mystery fiction, however, is no more a problem literature than it is a puzzle literature. It approaches its subject obliquely, conveying attitudes through the contrivance of technique and affirming with the inherent order of plot a myth of the resolution of the criminal issue. Of course, the foundation of the genre is the criminal event, and without minimizing or explaining away the differences among the types of crime story, it can be said that the plot is normally arranged to represent clarification of the mystery surrounding the event; thus, there are, at the very least, two imperatives. One is a character who works as an expositor of crime. The detective, amateur or professional, is the most familiar agent of rationalization, but a group of investigators, as in the police procedural novel, a Raffles-like rogue or his counterparts in the caper story, the spy, even the Gothic heroine – all these have as their literary motive the reduction of threatening events to a rational system of explanation. Inevitably, the implicit effect when this motive becomes plot is the conviction that there is a means to control and direct events, temporarily if not most of the time.

Authors whom the critics classify as classic – the creators of a Golden Age in detective fiction – direct their art to the creation of settings and characters that idealize the achievement of rationality as though it were a norm of civilized society and crime a brief eruption of behavior that, akin to evil, is nevertheless controllable. In contrast to this social conservatism, the later variations manifest in hard-boiled writing and allied types insist by their fictional settings and characters that the social environment is corrupt. Still, they, too, have plots which include an agent who provides a tentative explanation of crime. Therefore, a second generic imperative is met in the "tough" examples of the genre as well as in the comedic classic examples – the effect of closure, an explanation of crime that brings the story to an end with a neat conclusiveness that rarely appears in actual life.

These necessities of plot, together with other conventions of the idealized world of crime and mystery fiction, reveal their origin in a middle-class culture that sees reality in terms of personality. That culture's literature characteristically projects the issues involved in a matter like crime as problems to be managed, that is, solved, by remarkable individuals who will reveal that the predominant motives for everyone's behavior is personal. The genres of middle-class literature, including crime and mystery fiction, thus, provide ways of perceiving reality, ways that interpret also, though in no way revealing themselves through direct social commentary. Development of new varieties in the genre, most strikingly the hard-boiled departure, signal a partial rejection of the received ways of interpreting reality; however, complete repudiation would result in a new genre altogether. Sometime that may happen, but in the meantime the seemingly endless possibilities for character types, the rising fortunes of the thriller, the maturing of the police story, and the insistence of some contemporary authors on writing novels that almost abandon detection characterize a vital form with a long history before it.

Customarily we trace a literary history such as I have been outlining through accounts of the work of significant authors, and that is a major purpose of this book. The critical essays on William Godwin, Edgar Allan Poe, Charles Dickens, Emile Gaboriau, Anna Katharine Green, Arthur Conan Doyle, and others describe the foundation of crime and mystery fiction by discussing the techniques and conventions invented by the parents of the genre. Similarly, analyses of such Golden Age writers as E. C. Bentley, Agatha Christie, Dorothy L. Sayers, Anthony Berkeley, S. S. Van Dine, Ellery Queen, John Dickson Carr, and many more will indicate how the patterns of that version of the mystery story formed. The studies of Carroll John Daly, Erle Stanley Gardner, George Harmon Coxe, Steve Fisher, Bruno Fischer, and, of course, Dashiell Hammett and Raymond Chandler will do the same for the American invention of the hard-boiled or tough guy writing. Essays on John Buchan, Erskine Childers, Ian Fleming, Martha Albrand, Helen MacInnes, Geoffrey Household, Len Deighton, John le Carré and their fellow authors of thrillers and spy stories will illustrate the traditions of that type. The same task is accomplished for the police procedural novel by the essays on Maurice Procter, Hillary Waugh, Ed McBain, Lawrence Treat, and more. And there are other vantage points too. The reader of this volume will find the special significance of the short story illustrated in essays on contributors to the dime weeklies, the pulp magazines, as well as the band of contemporary writers whose work regularly appears in such remaining magazines of short fiction as *Ellery Queen's Mystery Magazine*; the phenomenon of the best-seller described in such essays as those on Edgar Wallace, John Creasey, and Mickey Spillane, to name only a few of these remarkable writers; the appearance of fiction that may be considered as efforts to re-define the genre receives analysis in essays on Patricia Highsmith, Julian Symons, Brian Garfield, and others. These highly selective examples hardly do justice to the information available in the critical essays. They omit, for instance, reference to the authors whose work sustains the genre by creation of freshly compelling series characters, or those who enrich the tradition by inventive variations on the basic conventions, or the authors writing in other languages whose books become English classics in translation. Perhaps the examples are sufficient, though, to show that the more than 600 critical articles, in addition to their value as analyses of individual writers, also constitute a collective essay in literary history. All that leaves to be done here in the preface is to add a few remarks on background.

The great matter of crime first reached a popular audience through the medium of writing that purported to be more or less the truth about thief-catching and criminal investigation. Precedence goes to the French author François Eugène Vidocq whose memoirs appeared in 1829. Evidently the widely circulated English translations of Vidocq encouraged others, and in the later 19th century recollections of detective and police work flooded from the presses. The most familiar of these memoirists is Allan Pinkerton whose name, if not his writing, still has household currency. The veracity of Pinkerton and his contemporaries need not concern us, but the construction of their works must, for the simple reason that they read very much like fiction. The detective author presides over his narrative, imparting the authority of experience to his pronouncements on crime, selecting events to testify about his skill in detection, and dramatizing the achievements of a singular individual in combat with criminals. Typically a memoir contains a sequence of formulaized steps: the detective meets his client, he undertakes an investigation that may require the use of disguises and other ingenuities, he passes through a climactic adventure, and provides a summary that suggests the obligatory scene in fiction where the sleuth assembles suspects and proceeds to retrace the steps of his inquiry. The fact that detective memoirists found a model for their reports in the devices of fiction rather than in the forms of autobiographical writing was lucky, because it meant that, besides meeting a rising interest in the subject of crime and helping to build a consensus on the social importance of the detective, their books also helped to prepare the audience for the entirely imaginative creations that would flower at the end of the century.

Yet another literary type contributing to the development of crime and mystery fiction was the romantic adventure. As Dorothy L. Sayers observed in the introduction to her *Great Short Stories of Detection, Mystery, and Horror* the huge popularity of James Fenimore Cooper, among others, helped to stimulate the intention of adapting the excitement of tracking and hunting to the routine of criminal investigation. "In the 'sixties," she writes, "the generation who had read Fenimore Cooper in boyhood turned, as novelists and readers, to tracing the spoor of the criminal upon their own native heath." An interesting combination of such a source with the memoir appears in the books that Julian Hawthorne, son of the American romancer, wrote in the 1880's about Thomas Byrnes, Chief of New York detectives. The stories purport to be from Byrnes's diaries of day-to-day police experience, but in the plotting they include attenuated love stories and a whirlwind of events surrounding international conspiracies and high society figures. Over all rears Byrnes as an executive armchair detective dispatching his amateur aides to their adventures in criminal apprehension. In its own wonderful way the hodge-podge of forms and types in Hawthorne's stories illustrates the new genre constituting itself out of usable parts of its predecessors. A still clearer portrayal of the significance of romantic adventure to crime and mystery writing might be offered by anyone who recalls the stories about Nick Carter, Sexton Blake, or their brothers in derring-do, Doc Savage and The Shadow, but that is unnecessary, for we have reached the heart of the matter.

Our literature of crime and mystery is a species of adventure tale, the oldest class of narrative. Its central characters whose names – Sherlock Holmes, Perry Mason – rather than the authors' specify the tale, just as Robin Hood or King Arthur specify theirs, are modern heroes. Whether they are sleuths or the pursued, elite or typical, men or women, these characters live in the popular imagination as both representatives of modern life and its ideal. Their narratives, whose plots oscillate between stressing the accomplishments of intellectual force and featuring the protagonist facing tests of physical peril, transform the mundane subject of crime into material with an aura of the extraordinary.

If such descriptions of the crime and mystery story as I have given stress its fixed form, it is because I am intrigued by the idea that when we "discover" a new author our eagerness to read seems to be a desire to see how this new author will solve not criminal problems, but the technical problems involved in telling a crime story. Our enthusiasm for a new detective character, a novel investigative method, setting, or turn in the plot is a response to craft. But despite the repetition of stories that permits one to see their fixed form, the genre of crime and mystery writing is marked by great vigor. This vigor ought to be kept in mind, because it is due to the grand and simple fact that this fiction tells us stories, an ability which in other realms of literature has suffered decline. Mind you, stories need not be new to be interesting. Possibly they need not even be about anything in particular so far as theme goes or what we usually think of as meaning. We tell anecdotes all the time for the purpose of establishing human community; any information the anecdotes contain is secondary. It is the act of the telling that we love.

Finally, then, it is the narrative impulse of crime and mystery writing that accounts for the paradox of violent entertainment and explains how a form that originated in the distinctive circumstances of Victorian middle-class culture retains the power to affect us. Through the ability to simulate compelling experience, writers of crime and mystery fiction have created a nearly autonomous world. As readers we are proprietary about that world, since we know it so well. And we keep reading, sure that world can delight us again. And again.

JOHN M. REILLY

READING LIST

1. General Works

Adams, Donald K., editor, *The Mystery and Detection Annual* (for 1972 and 1973).   Beverly Hills, California, Donald Adams, 1972–74.

Albert, Walter, "Bibliography of Secondary Sources," in *Armchair Detective* (White Bear Lake, Minnesota; Del Mar, California; New York).   (Annual compilation since 1972.)

Allen, Dick, and David Chacko, editors, *Detective Fiction: Crime and Consequences*.   New York, Harcourt Brace, 1974.

Altick, Richard, *Victorian Studies in Scarlet*.   New York, Norton, 1970.

Ball, John, editor, *The Mystery Story*.   San Diego, University of California Extension, 1976; London, Penguin, 1978.

Barnes, Melvyn, *Best Detective Fiction: A Guide from Godwin to the Present*.   London, Clive Bingley, and Hamden, Connecticut, Linnet, 1975.

Barzun, Jacques, editor, *The Delights of Detection*.   New York, Criterion, 1961.

Barzun, Jacques, and Wendell Hertig Taylor, *A Book of Prefaces to Fifty Classics of Crime Fiction 1900–50*. New York, Garland, 1976.

Barzun, Jacques, and Wendell Hertig Taylor, *A Catalogue of Crime*. New York, Harper, 1971.

Becker, Jens Peter, *Der Englische Spionageroman*. Munich, Goldmann, 1973.

Becker, Jens Peter, and Paul G. Buchloh, editors, *Der Detektiverzählung auf der Spur*. Darmstadt, Wissenschaftliche Buchgesellschaft, 1977.

Best Detective Stories of the Year. New York, Dutton, 1945–79. (Annual volumes have been edited by David Coxe Cooke, Brett Halliday, Anthony Boucher, Allen J. Hubin, and Edward D. Hoch.)

Birkhead, Edith, *The Tale of Terror: A Study of the Gothic Romance*. London, Constable, 1921; New York, Russell, 1963.

Boileau-Narcejac, *Le Roman Policier*. Paris, Payot, 1964.

Borowitz, Albert, *Innocence and Arsenic: Studies in Crime and Literature*. New York, Harper, 1977.

Brean, Herbert, editor, *The Mystery Writers Handbook*. New York, Harper, 1956.

Briney, R. E., and Francis M. Nevins, Jr., editors, *Multiplying Villainies: Selected Mystery Criticism 1942–1968*, by Anthony Boucher. Boston, Bouchercon, 1973.

Buchloh, Paul G., and Jens Peter Becker, *Der Detektivroman: Studien zur Geschichte und Form der Englischen und Amerikanischen Detektivliteratur*. Darmstadt, Wissenschaftliche Buchgesellschaft, 1973; revised edition, 1978.

Burack, A. S., editor, *Writing Detective and Mystery Fiction*. Boston, The Writer, 1945; revised edition, 1967.

Butler, William Vivian, *The Durable Desperadoes*. London, Macmillan, 1973.

Byrnes, Thomas, *1886 Professional Criminals of America*. New York, Chelsea House, 1960.

Carter, John, *Books and Book-Collectors*. London, Hart Davis, 1956; Cleveland, World, 1957.

Carter, John, editor, *New Paths in Book-Collecting*. London, Constable, 1934.

Cawelti, John G., *Adventure, Mystery, and Romance: Formula Stories as Art and Popular Culture*. Chicago, University of Chicago Press, 1976.

Champigny, Robert, *What Will Have Happened: A Philosophical and Technical Essay on Mystery Stories*. Bloomington, Indiana University Press, 1977.

Chandler, Frank Wadleigh, *The Literature of Roguery*. London, Constable, and Boston, Houghton Mifflin, 2 vols., 1907.

Cook, Michael L., *Murder by Mail: Inside the Mystery Book Clubs, with Complete Checklist*. Evansville, Indiana, Cook, 1979.

Crime Writers Association of Great Britain, anthologies edited by members, 1953–79.

Davis, David Brian, *Homicide in American Fiction, 1798–1860*. Ithaca, New York, Cornell University Press, 1957.

Depken, F., *Sherlock Holmes, Raffles, und Ihre Vorbilder*. Heidelberg, Winter, 1914.

De Quincey, Thomas, "On Murder Considered as One of the Fine Arts" (1827), in *The Collected Writings of Thomas De Quincey*, edited by David Masson, vol. 13. London, Black, 1889–90.

de Vries, P. H., *Poe and After: The Detective Story Investigated*. Amsterdam, Bakker, 1956.

Disher, M. Willson, *Melodrama: Plots That Thrilled*. New York, Macmillan, and London, Rockliff, 1954.

Donaldson, Betty, and Norman Donaldson, *How Did They Die?* New York, St. Martin's Press, 1979.

Eames, Hugh, *Sleuths, Inc.: Studies of Problem Solvers, Doyle, Simenon, Hammett, Ambler, Chandler*. Philadelphia, Lippincott, 1978.

Epstein, H., *Der Detektivroman der Unterschicht*. Frankfurt, Neuer Frankfurter Verlag, 1930.

Everson, William K., *The Detective in Film*. Secaucus, New Jersey, Citadel, 1972.

Fosca, F., *Histoire et Technique du Roman Policier*. Paris, Editions de la Nouvelle Revue Critique, 1937.

Friedland, Susan, *South African Detective Stories in English and Afrikaans from 1951–1971.* Johannesburg, University of the Witwatersrand, 1972.

Gilbert, Elliot L., editor, *The World of Mystery Fiction.* San Diego, University of California Extension, 1978.

Gilbert, Michael, editor, *Crime in Good Company: Essays on Criminals and Crime-Writing.* London, Constable, 1959.

Glover, Dorothy, and Graham Greene, *Victorian Detective Fiction: A Catalogue.* London, Bodley Head, 1966.

Goulart, Ron, *Cheap Thrills: An Informal History of the Pulp Magazines.* New Rochelle, New York, Arlington House, 1972.

Goulart, Ron, editor, *The Hardboiled Dicks: An Anthology and Study of Pulp Detective Fiction.* Los Angeles, Sherbourne Press, 1965; London, Boardman, 1967.

Graves, Robert, and Alan Hodge, *The Long Week-end.* London, Faber, 1940; New York, Macmillan, 1941.

Greene, Graham, and Hugh Greene, editors, *The Spy's Bedside Book.* London, Hart Davis, 1957.

Greene, Hugh, editor, *The American Rivals of Sherlock Holmes.* London, Bodley Head, and New York, Pantheon, 1976.

Greene, Hugh, editor, *The Crooked Counties.* London, Bodley Head, 1973; as *The Further Rivals of Sherlock Holmes,* New York, Pantheon, 1973.

Greene, Hugh, editor, *More Rivals of Sherlock Holmes: Cosmopolitan Crimes.* London, Bodley Head, 1971; as *Cosmopolitan Crimes: Foreign Rivals of Sherlock Holmes,* New York, Pantheon, 1971.

Greene, Hugh, editor, *The Rivals of Sherlock Holmes.* London, Bodley Head, and New York, Pantheon, 1970.

Gribbin, Lenore S., *Who's Whodunit: A List of 3218 Detective Story Writers and Their 1100 Pseudonyms.* Chapel Hill, University of North Carolina Library, 1968.

Grossvogel, David I., *Mystery and Its Fictions.* Baltimore, Johns Hopkins University Press, 1979.

Gruber, Frank, *The Pulp Jungle.* Los Angeles, Sherbourne Press, 1967.

Hackett, Alice Payne, and James Henry Burke, *80 Years of Best Sellers 1895–1975.* New York, Bowker, 1977.

Hagen, Ordean, *Who Done It? A Guide to Detective, Mystery, and Suspense Fiction.* New York, Bowker, 1969.

Haining, Peter, editor, *The Fantastic Pulps.* London, Gollancz, and New York, St. Martin's Press, 1975.

Haining, Peter, *Mystery!* (on book illustration). London, Souvenir Press, 1977.

Haining, Peter, *The Penny Dreadful.* London, Gollancz, 1975.

Hall, Stuart, and Paddy Whannel, *The Popular Arts.* London, Hutchinson, 1964; New York, Pantheon, 1965.

Harper, Ralph, *The World of the Thriller.* Cleveland, Press of Case Western Reserve University, 1969.

Hart, James D., *The Popular Book: A History of America's Literary Taste.* New York, Oxford University Press, 1950.

Haycraft, Howard, *Murder for Pleasure: The Life and Times of the Detective Story.* New York, Appleton Century, 1941; London, Davies, 1942; revised edition, New York, Biblo and Tannen, 1968.

Haycraft, Howard, editor, *The Art of the Mystery Story: A Collection of Critical Essays.* New York, Simon and Schuster, 1946.

Hedman-Morelius, Iwan, *Deckare och Thrillers pa Svenska, 1864–1973.* Strängäs, Dast, 1974.

Herman, Linda, and Beth Stiel, *Corpus Delicti of Mystery Fiction: A Guide to the Body of the Case.* Metuchen, New Jersey, Scarecrow Press, 1974.

Hersey, Harold, *Pulpwood Editor: The Fabulous World of the Thriller Magazines Revealed by a Veteran Editor and Publisher.* New York, Stokes, 1937.

Highsmith, Patricia, *Plotting and Writing Suspense Fiction.* Boston, The Writer, 1966.
Hogarth, Basil, *Writing Thrillers for Profit: A Practical Guide.* London, Black, 1936.
Hoveyda, Fereydoren, *Histoire du Roman Policier.* Paris, Pavillon, 1955.
Hubin, Allen J., *The Bibliography of Crime Fiction, 1749–1975.* San Diego, University of California Extension, 1979.
Inge, M. Thomas, editor, *Handbook of American Popular Culture.* Westport, Connecticut, Greenwood Press, 1978.
Ivy, Randolph, "The Victorian Sensation Novel" (unpublished dissertation). Chicago, University of Chicago, 1974.
Johannsen, Albert, *The House of Beadle and Adams and Its Dime and Nickel Novels.* Norman, University of Oklahoma Press, 3 vols., 1950.
Jones, Robert Kenneth, *The Shudder Pulps: A History of the Weird Menace Magazines of the 1930's.* West Linn, Oregon, FAX, 1975.
Keating, H. R. F., *Murder Must Appetize.* London, Lemon Tree Press, 1975.
Knox, Ronald A., editor, *The Best Detective Stories of the Year 1928.* London, Faber, 1929; as *The Best English Detective Stories of 1928*, New York, Liveright, 1929.
Lacassin, Francis, *Mythologie du Roman Policier.* Paris, Union Generale d'Editions, 2 vols., 1974.
LaCombe, Alain, *Le Roman Noir Américain.* Paris, 10/18, 1975.
la Cour, Tage, and Harald Mogensen, *The Murder Book: An Illustrated History of the Detective Story.* London, Allen and Unwin, and New York, Herder, 1971.
Lambert, Gavin, *The Dangerous Edge.* London, Barrie and Jenkins, 1975; New York, Grossman, 1976.
Landrum, Larry N., Pat Browne, and Ray B. Browne, editors, *Dimensions of Detective Fiction.* Bowling Green, Ohio, Popular Press, 1976.
Larmoth, Jeanine, *Murder on the Menu.* New York, Scribner, 1972.
Leavis, Q. D., *Fiction and the Reading Public.* London, Chatto and Windus, 1932; New York, Russell, 1965.
Lins, Álvaro, *No Mundo do Romance Policial.* Rio de Janeiro, Ministério do Educacão, 1953.
Lofts, W. O. G., and Derek Adley, *The Men Behind Boys' Fiction.* London, Baker, 1970.
Madden, David, editor, *Tough Guy Writers of the Thirties.* Carbondale, Southern Illinois University Press, 1968.
Marsch, Edgar, *Die Kriminalerzählung: Theorie, Geschichte, Analyse.* Munich, Winkler, 1972.
Martiensen, Anthony, *Crime and the Police.* London, Penguin, 1951.
Mason, Bobbie Ann, *The Girl Sleuth: A Feminist Guide.* Old Westbury, New York, Feminist Press, 1975.
McCormick, Donald, *Who's Who in Spy Fiction.* London, Elm Tree Books, and New York, Taplinger, 1977.
Meet the Detective (broadcasts by 10 authors). London, Allen and Unwin, 1935.
Merry, Bruce, *Anatomy of the Spy Thriller.* Dublin, Gill and Macmillan, 1977.
Messac, Regis, *Le "Detective Novel" et L'Influence de la Pensée Scientifique.* Paris, Champion, 1929.
Mooney, Joan M., "Best-Selling American Detective Fiction," in *Armchair Detective* (White Bear Lake, Minnesota), 9 issues, January 1970–1973.
Morland, Nigel, *How to Write Detective Novels.* London, Allen and Unwin, 1936.
Mott, Frank Luther, *Golden Multitudes: The Story of Best Sellers in the United States.* New York, Macmillan, 1947.
Mundell, E. H., and G. Jay Rausch, *The Detective Short Story: A Bibliography and Index.* Manhattan, Kansas State University Library, 1974.
Murch, A. E., *The Development of the Detective Novel.* London, Peter Owen, and New York, Philosophical Library, 1958.
Murder Manual: A Handbook for Mystery Writers. East San Diego, Wight House, 1936.
Mystery Writers of America, Annual Short Story Collections, edited by members since 1946.

Narcejac, Thomas, *Une Machine à Lire: Le Roman Policier*. Paris, Denoël Gonthier, 1975.

Nevins, Francis M., Jr., editor, *The Mystery Writer's Art*. Bowling Green, Ohio, Popular Press, 1971.

Nieminski, John, *EQMM 350: An Author/Title Index to Ellery Queen's Mystery Magazine, Fall 1941 through January 1973*. White Bear Lake, Minnesota, Armchair Detective Press, 1974.

Noel, Mary, *Villains Galore: The Heyday of the Popular Story Weekly*. New York, Macmillan, 1954.

Nye, Russel B., *The Unembarrassed Muse: The Popular Arts in America*. New York, Dial Press, 1970.

Odell, Robin, *Jack the Ripper in Fact and Fiction*. London, Harrap, 1965.

Ousby, Ian, *Bloodhounds of Heaven: The Detective in English Fiction from Godwin to Doyle*. Cambridge, Masssachusetts, Harvard University Press, 1976.

Overton, Grant, *Cargoes for Crusoes*. New York, Appleton, 1924.

Palmer, Jerry, *Thrillers*. London, Arnold, and New York, St. Martin's Press, 1979.

Panek, Leroy Lad, *Watteau's Shepherds: The Detective Novel in Britain 1914–1940*. Bowling Green, Ohio, Popular Press, 1979.

Pearson, Edmund, *Dime Novels; or, Following an Old Trail in Popular Literature*. Boston, Little Brown, 1929.

Penzler, Otto, *The Private Lives of Private Eyes, Spies, Crime Fighters, and Other Good Guys*. New York, Grosset and Dunlap, 1977.

Penzler, Otto, editor, *The Great Detectives*. Boston, Little Brown, 1978.

Phillips, Walter C., *Dickens, Reade, and Collins, Sensation Novelists*. New York, Columbia University Press, 1919.

Prager, Arthur, *Rascals at Large; or, The Clue in the Old Nostalgia*. New York, Doubleday, 1971.

Quayle, Eric, *The Collector's Book of Detective Fiction*. London, Studio Vista, 1972.

Queen, Ellery, *The Detective Short Story: A Bibliography*. Boston, Little Brown, 1942.

Queen, Ellery, *In the Queen's Parlor and Other Leaves from the Editors' Notebook*. New York, Simon and Schuster, and London, Gollancz, 1957.

Queen, Ellery, *Queen's Quorum: A History of the Detective-Crime Short Story as Revealed by the 106 Most Important Books Published in the Field since 1845*. Boston, Little Brown, 1951; London, Gollancz, 1953; revised edition, New York, Biblo and Tannen, 1969.

Randall, David A., editor, *The First Hundred Years of Detective Fiction, 1841–1941*. Bloomington, Indiana University Lilly Library, 1973.

Reinert, Claus, *Das Unheimliche und die Detektivliteratur: Entwurfe, Poetolog*. Bonn, Bouvier, 1973.

Reynolds, Quentin, *The Fiction Factory; or, From Pulp Row to Quality Street: The Story of 100 Years of Publishing at Street and Smith*. New York, Random House, 1955.

Richardson, Maurice, editor, *Novels of Mystery from the Victorian Age*. London, Pilot Press, 1945.

Rodell, Marie F., *Mystery Fiction: Theory and Technique*. New York, Duell, 1943; revised edition, New York, Hermitage House, 1952; London, Hammond, 1954.

Routley, Erik, *The Puritan Pleasures of the Detective Story: A Personal Monograph*. London, Gollancz, 1972.

Ruehlmann, William, *Saint with a Gun: The Unlawful American Private Eye*. New York, New York University Press, 1974.

Ruhm, Herbert, editor, *The Hard-Boiled Detective: Stories from Black Mask Magazine, 1920–1951*. New York, Vintage, 1977.

Sandoe, James, *The Hard-Boiled Dick: A Personal Checklist*. Chicago, Arthur Lovell, 1952.

Sandoe, James, editor, *Murder: Plain and Fanciful, with Some Milder Malefactions*. New York, Sheridan House, 1948.

Sayers, Dorothy L., editor, *Great Short Stories of Detection, Mystery and Horror*. London, Gollancz, 3 vols., 1928–34; as *The Omnibus of Crime*, New York, Payson and Clarke, 1 vol., 1929, Coward McCann, 2 vols., 1932–35.

Sayers, Dorothy L., editor, *Tales of Detection.* London, Dent, 1936.

Schönhaar, Rainer, *Novelle und Kriminalschema: Ein Strukturmodell Deutscher Erzahlkunst um 1800.* Berlin, Gehlen, 1969.

Schwartz, Saul, *The Detective Story: An Introduction to the Whodunit.* Skokie, Illinois, National Textbook Company, 1976.

Scott, Sutherland, *Blood in Their Ink: The March of the Modern Mystery Novel.* London, Stanley Paul, 1953; Folcroft, Pennsylvania, Folcroft Editions, 1973.

Scribner's Detective Fiction: A Collection of First and a Few Early Editions. New York, Scribner, 1934.

Shaw, Joseph T., editor, *The Hardboiled Omnibus: Early Stories from Black Mask.* New York, Simon and Schuster, 1946.

Slung, Michele, editor, *Crime on Her Mind: Fifteen Stories of Female Sleuths from the Victorian Era to the Forties.* New York, Pantheon, 1975.

Smith, Myron J., Jr., *Cloak-and-Dagger Bibliography: An Annotated Guide to Spy Fiction, 1937–1975.* Metuchen, New Jersey, Scarecrow Press, 1976.

Solmes, Alwyn, *The English Policeman, 1871–1935.* London, Allen and Unwin, 1935.

Steinbrunner, Chris, and others, *Detectionary: A Bibliographical Dictionary of the Leading Characters in Detective and Mystery Fiction.* New York, Hammerhill Paper, 1971; revised edition, New York, Overlook Press, 1977.

Steinbrunner, Chris, and Otto Penzler, *Encyclopedia of Mystery and Detection.* New York, McGraw Hill, 1976.

Stevenson, W. B., *Detective Fiction.* Cambridge, National Book League, 1958.

Symons, Julian, *Bloody Murder.* London, Faber, 1972; as *Mortal Consequences*, New York, Harper, 1972.

Symons, Julian, *Critical Occasions.* London, Hamish Hamilton, 1966.

Symons, Julian, *The Detective Story in Britain.* London, Longman, 1962.

Symons, Julian, *The 100 Best Crime Stories.* London, Sunday Times, 1959.

Talburt, Nancy Ellen, and Lyna Lee Montgomery, editors, *A Mystery Reader.* New York, Scribner, 1975.

Thomas, Gilbert, *How to Enjoy Detective Fiction.* London, Rockliff, 1947.

Thomson, H. Douglas, *Masters of Mystery: A Study of the Detective Story.* London, Collins, 1931; Folcroft, Pennsylvania, Folcroft Editions, 1973.

Turner, Robert, *Some of My Best Friends Are Writers, But I Wouldn't Want My Daughter to Marry One.* Los Angeles, Sherbourne Press, 1970.

Tuska, Jon, *The Detective in Hollywood.* New York, Doubleday, 1978.

Usborne, Richard, *Clubland Heroes: A Nostalgic Study of Some Recurrent Characters in the Romantic Fiction of Dornford Yates, John Buchan and Sapper.* London, Constable, 1953; revised edition, London, Barrie and Jenkins, 1975.

Vogt, Jochen, editor, *Der Kriminalroman: Zur Theorie und Geschichte einer Galtung.* Munich, Fink, 2 vols., 1971.

Watson, Colin, *Snobbery with Violence: Crime Stories and Their Audience.* London, Eyre and Spottiswoode, 1971; New York, St. Martin's Press, 1972; revised edition, London, Eyre Methuen, 1979.

Wells, Carolyn, *The Technique of the Mystery Story.* Springfield, Massachusetts, Home Correspondence School, 1913; revised edition, 1929.

Wilson, Edmund, *A Literary Chronicle, 1920–1950.* New York, Doubleday, 1956.

Winks, Robin W., editor, *The Historian as Detective: Essays on Evidence.* New York, Harper, 1969.

Winn, Dilys, editor, *Murder Ink: The Mystery Reader's Companion.* New York, Workman, 1977.

Wölcken, Fritz, *Der Literaiesche Mord: Eine Untersuchung über die Englisch und Amerikanische Detektivliteratur.* Nuremberg, Nest Verlag, 1953.

Wright, Willard Huntington, editor, *The Great Detective Stories: A Chronological Anthology.* New York, Scribner, 1927.

Wrong, E. M., editor, *Crime and Detection.* London and New York, Oxford University Press, 1926.

Yates, Donald A., editor, *Antologia del Cuento Policial Hispanoamericano*. Mexico City, Ediciones de Andrea, 1964.

Yates, Donald A., editor and translator, *Latin Blood: The Best Crime and Detective Stories of Spanish America*. New York, Herder, 1972.

2. Studies of Individual Authors, Characters, or Works

Amis, Kingsley, *The James Bond Dossier*. London, Cape, and New York, New American Library, 1965.

Aylmer, Felix, *The Drood Case*. London, Hart Davis, 1964.

Baker, Richard M., *The Drood Murder Case*. Berkeley, University of California Press, 1951.

Baring-Gould, William S., *The Annotated Sherlock Holmes*. New York, Potter, 2 vols., 1967.

Baring-Gould, William S., *Nero Wolfe of West Thirty-Fifth Street: The Life and Times of America's Largest Private Detective*. New York, Viking Press, 1969.

Becker, Lucille, *Georges Simenon*. Boston, Twayne, 1977.

Bentley, E. C., *Those Days: An Autobiography*. London, Constable, 1940.

Browne, Nelson, *Sheridan Le Fanu*. London, Barker, 1951.

Cambiaire, C. P., *The Influence of Edgar Allan Poe in France*. New York, Stechert, 1927.

Carr, John Dickson, *The Life of Sir Arthur Conan Doyle*. London, Murray, and New York, Harper, 1949.

Carr, Nick, *America's Secret Service Ace* (Operator No. 5). Oak Lawn, Illinois, Weinberg, 1974.

Creasey, John, *John Creasey – Fact or Fiction? A Candid Commentary in Third Person, With a Bibliography by John Creasey and Robert E. Briney*. White Bear Lake, Minnesota, Armchair Detective Press, 1968; revised edition, 1969.

Daniell, David, *The Interpreter's House: A Critical Assessment of John Buchan*. London, Nelson, 1975.

Davis, Nuel Pharr, *The Life of Wilkie Collins*. Urbana, University of Illinois Press, 1956.

Day Lewis, C., *The Buried Day* (autobiography). London, Chatto and Windus, and New York, Harper, 1960.

De Camara, Mary P., and Stephen Hayes, *Sir Arthur Conan Doyle's Sherlock Holmes: The Short Stories, a Critical Commentary*. New York, Monarch, 1976.

Del Buono, Oreste, and Umberto Eco, *The Bond Affair*. London, Macdonald, 1966.

Derleth, August, *A Praed Street Dossier*. Sauk City, Wisconsin, Mycroft and Moran, 1968.

De Waal, Ronald Burt, *The World Bibliography of Sherlock Holmes and Dr. Watson*. Boston, New York Graphic Society, 1975.

Donaldson, Norman, *In Search of Dr. Thorndyke: The Story of R. Austin Freeman's Great Scientific Investigator and His Creator*. Bowling Green, Ohio, Popular Press, 1971.

Durham, Philip, *Down These Mean Streets a Man Must Go: Raymond Chandler's Knight*. Chapel Hill, University of North Carolina Press, 1963.

Eisgruber, Frank, Jr., *Gangland's Doom: The Shadow of the Pulps*. Oak Lawn, Illinois, Weinberg, 1974.

Fallois, Bernard de, *Simenon*. Paris, Gallimard, 1961.

Farmer, Philip José, *Doc Savage: His Apocalyptic Life*. New York, Doubleday, 1973.

Feinman, Jeffrey, *The Mysterious World of Agatha Christie*. New York, Award, 1975.

For Bond Lovers Only. New York, Dell, 1965.

Gardiner, Dorothy, and Kathrine Sorley Walker, editors, *Raymand Chandler Speaking*. Boston, Houghton Mifflin, and London, Hamish Hamilton, 1962.

Gibson, Walter B., *The Shadow Scrapbook*. New York, Harcourt Brace, 1979.

Girvan, Waveney, editor, *Eden Phillpotts: An Assessment and a Tribute*. London, Hutchinson, 1953.

Gross, Mary, editor, *The World of Raymond Chandler*. London, Weidenfeld and Nicolson, 1977; New York, A and W, 1978.

Hannay, Margaret, editor, *As Her Whimsey Took Her: Critical Essays on the Work of Dorothy L. Sayers*. Kent, Ohio, Kent State University Press, 1979.

Harrison, Michael, *In the Footsteps of Sherlock Holmes*. London, Cassell, 1958; New York, Fell, 1960; revised edition, Newton Abbot, Devon, David and Charles, 1971; New York, Drake, 1972.

Harrison, Michael, *Peter Cheyney: Prince of Hokum*. London, Spearman, 1954.

Hawke, Jessica, *Follow My Dust! A Biography of Arthur Upfield*. London, Heinemann, 1957.

Hellman, Lillian, editor, *The Big Knockover*. New York, Random House, 1966; as *The Hammett Story Omnibus*, London, Cassell, 1966.

Higham, Charles, *The Adventures of Conan Doyle: The Life of the Creator of Sherlock Holmes*. London, Hamish Hamilton, and New York, Norton, 1976.

Hitchman, Janet, *Such a Strange Lady: An Introduction to Dorothy L. Sayers*. London, New English Library, and New York, Harper, 1975.

Hoffman, Daniel, *Poe Poe Poe Poe Poe Poe Poe*. New York, Doubleday, 1972; London, Robson, 1973.

Hone, Ralph E., *Dorothy L. Sayers: A Literary Biography*. Kent, Ohio, Kent State University Press, 1979.

Hughes, Dorothy B., *Erle Stanley Gardner: The Case of the Real Perry Mason*. New York, Morrow, 1978.

Johnston, Alva, *The Case of Erle Stanley Gardner*. New York, Morrow, 1947.

Keating, H. R. F., *Sherlock Holmes: The Man and His World*. London, Thames and Hudson, and New York, Scribner, 1979.

Keating, H. R. F., editor, *Agatha Christie: First Lady of Crime*. London, Weidenfeld and Nicolson, and New York, Holt Rinehart, 1977.

Keating, H. R. F., editor, *Crime Writers: Reflections on Crime Fiction*. London, BBC Publications, 1979.

Lane, Margaret, *Edgar Wallace: The Biography of a Phenomenon*. London, Heinemann, 1938; New York, Doubleday, 1939; revised edition, London, Hamish Hamilton, 1964.

Lofts, W. O. G., and Derek Adley, *The Saint and Leslie Charteris*. London, Hutchinson, 1971; Bowling Green, Ohio, Popular Press, 1972.

Loudenflager, Nancy, "The Life and Works, of Emile Gaboriau" (unpublished dissertation). Lexington, University of Kentucky, 1970.

Ludlam, Harry, *A Biography of Dracula: The Life Story of Bram Stoker*. London, Foulsham, 1962.

Macdonald, Ross, *On Crime Writing*. Santa Barbara, California, Capra Press, 1973.

MacShane, Frank, *The Life of Raymond Chandler*. New York, Dutton, 1976.

Marcus, Steven, editor, *The Continental Op*. New York, Knopf, 1974.

McAleer, John, *Rex Stout*. Boston, Little Brown, 1977.

Milliken, Stephen F., *Chester Himes: A Critical Appraisal*. Columbia, University of Missouri Press, 1976.

Murray, Will, *The Duende History of The Shadow Magazine*. North Quincy, Massachusetts, Odyssey, 1979.

Narcejac, Thomas, *The Art of Georges Simenon*. London, Routledge, 1952.

Nevins, Francis M., Jr., *Royal Bloodline: Ellery Queen, Author and Detective*. Bowling Green, Ohio, Popular Press, 1974.

Nicoll, W. Robertson, *The Problem of Edwin Drood*. London, Hodder and Stoughton, 1912.

Nolan, William F., *Dashiell Hammett: A Casebook*. Santa Barbara, California, McNally and Loftin, 1969.

Nordon, Pierre, *Conan Doyle: A Biography*. London, Murray, 1966; New York, Holt Rinehart, 1967.

Norton, Charles A., *Melville Davisson Post: Man of Many Mysteries*. Bowling Green, Ohio, Popular Press, 1973.

Nyberg, Benjamin M., "The Novels of Mary Elizabeth Braddon: A Reappraisal of the Author of *Lady Audley's Secret*" (unpublished dissertation). Boulder, University of Colorado, 1965.

Pearson, Hesketh, *Conan Doyle: His Life and Art.* London, Methuen, 1943; New York, Walker, 1961.

Pearson, John, *The Life of Ian Fleming.* London, Cape, and New York, McGraw Hill, 1966.

Pearson, John, *007 James Bond.* London, Sidgwick and Jackson, and New York, Morrow, 1973.

Ramsey, G. C., *Agatha Christie: Mistress of Mystery.* New York, Dodd Mead, 1967; revised edition, London, Collins, 1968.

Raymond, John, *Simenon in Court.* London, Hamish Hamilton, and New York, Harcourt Brace, 1969.

Robyns, Gwyn, *The Mystery of Agatha Christie.* New York, Doubleday, 1978.

Sandoe, James, editor, *Lord Peter: A Collection of All the Lord Peter Wimsey Stories.* New York, Harper, 1972; augmented edition, 1972.

Sayers, Dorothy L., *Wilkie Collins: A Critical and Biographical Study,* edited by E. R. Gregory. Toledo, Ohio, Friends of the University of Toledo Libraries, 1977.

Sladen, N. St. Barbe, *The Real Le Queux.* London, Nicholson and Watson, 1938.

Snelling, O. F., *007 James Bond: A Report.* London, Spearman, 1964; New York, New American Library, 1965.

Speir, Jerry, *Ross Macdonald.* New York, Ungar, 1978.

Standish, Robert, *The Prince of Story-Tellers* (on E. Phillips Oppenheim). London, Davies, 1957.

Starrett, Vincent, *The Private Life of Sherlock Holmes.* New York, Macmillan, 1933; London, Nicholson and Watson, 1934; revised edition, Chicago, University of Chicago Press, 1960; London, Allen and Unwin, 1961.

Sturak, John Thomas, "The Life and Writings of Horace McCoy 1897–1955" (unpublished dissertation). Los Angeles, University of California, 1966.

Sullivan, John, editor, *Chesterton: A Centennial Appraisal.* New York, Barnes and Noble, 1974.

Tuska, Jon, with others, *Philo Vance: The Life and Times of S. S. Van Dine.* Bowling Green, Ohio, Popular Press, 1971.

Van Ash, Cay, and Elizabeth Sax Rohmer, *Master of Villainy: A Biography of Sax Rohmer,* edited by R. E. Briney. Bowling Green, Ohio, Popular Press, and London, Stacey, 1972.

Van Dine, S. S., introduction to *The Philo Vance Omnibus.* New York, Scribner, 1936.

Wallace, Edgar, *People: A Short Autobiography.* London, Hodder and Stoughton, 1926; New York, Doubleday, 1929.

Walsh, John, *Poe the Detective: The Curious Circumstances Behind the Mystery of Marie Roget.* New Brunswick, New Jersey, Rutgers University Press, 1968.

Waugh, Evelyn, *The Life of the Right Reverend Ronald Knox.* London, Chapman, 1959; as *Monsignor Ronald Knox,* Boston, Little Brown, 1959.

Weinberg, Robert, editor, *The Man Behind Doc Savage: A Tribute to Lester Dent.* Oak Lawn, Illinois, Weinberg, 1974.

Wolfe, Peter, *Dreamers Who Live Their Dreams: The World of Ross Macdonald's Novels.* Bowling Green, Ohio, Popular Press, 1976.

Wolfe, Peter, *Graham Greene: The Entertainer.* Carbondale, Southern Illinois University Press, 1972.

Wood, C. W., *Memorials of Mrs. Henry Wood.* London, Bentley, 1894.

Wynne, Nancy Blue, *An Agatha Christie Chronology.* New York, Ace, 1976.

Young, Trudee, *Georges Simenon: A Checklist of His "Maigret" and Other Mystery Novels and Short Stories in French and in English Translations.* Metuchen, New Jersey, Scarecrow Press, 1976.

Zeiger, Henry, *Ian Fleming: The Spy Who Came In with the Gold.* New York, Duell, 1966.

EDITOR'S NOTE

The selection of writers included in this book is based upon the recommendations of the advisers listed on page xxiii.

The main part of the book covers English-language writers of crime and mystery fiction whose work appeared during or since the time of Sir Arthur Conan Doyle. Appendices include selective representations of authors preceding Doyle and foreign-language writers whose books have a large audience in English translation.

The entry for each writer in the main part of the book consists of a biography, a bibliography, and a signed critical essay. Living authors were invited to add a comment on their work. The bibliographies list writings according to the categories of crime fiction and other publications. In addition, crime writing is further sub-divided into lists of works published under pseudonyms. Series characters are indicated for novels. Original British and United States editions of all books have been listed; other editions are listed only if they are the first editions. As a rule all uncollected crime short stories published since the entrant's last collection have been listed; exceptions occur when a writer's reputation is based largely on short stories.

Entries include notations of available bibliographies and manuscript collections. Other critical materials appear in the Reading List of secondary works on the genre.

Special thanks are due to Allen J. Hubin whose bibliographical work promises to become legendary among students of crime fiction, Francis M. Nevins, Jr. and Edward D. Hoch who lent their practical knowledge any number of ways, J. Randolph Cox and Bill Pronzini who gave us invaluable suggestions for broadening the book's coverage and the means to accomplish it. In addition, it is a pleasure to acknowledge the generosity with which these critics and scholars shared the results of their research: E. F. Bleiler, Robert E. Briney, Betty and Norman Donaldson, E. R. Hagemann, John Harwood, Stephen Mertz, Will Murray, and John Nieminski. We would also like to thank the entrants for the interest they have taken in a project made possible by their creative work and the contributors for the eagerness with which they helped us compile this book.

ADVISERS

Jane S. Bakerman
John Ball
Melvyn Barnes
Manfred A. Bertram
E. F. Bleiler
Jon L. Breen
Jan Broberg
John G. Cawelti
George N. Dove
George Grella
L. T. Hergenhan

C. Hugh Holman
Allen J. Hubin
A. Norman Jeffares
H. R. F. Keating
H. M. Klein
Dennis Lynds
Francis M. Nevins, Jr.
Robert B. Parker
Michele Slung
Donald A. Yates

CONTRIBUTORS

Alison Susan Adey
Robert C. S. Adey
Derek Adley
Walter Albert
Martha Alderson
Pearl G. Aldrich
Kenneth D. Alley
Arthur Nicholas Athanason
Newton Baird
Jane S. Bakerman
John Ball
Jeff Banks
Melvyn Barnes
Jacques Baudou
Jens Peter Becker
Mary Helen Becker
Jeanne F. Bedell
Carol Ann Bergman
Manfred A. Bertram
E. F. Bleiler
Ellen Bleiler
R. E. Briney
Jan Broberg
Frank Campenni
Peter Caracciolo
Richard C. Carpenter
Steven Carter
Neysa Chouteau
Carol Cleveland
Don Cole
J. Randolph Cox
Patricia Craig
Bill Crider
Harald Curjel
Frank Denton
Betty Donaldson
Norman Donaldson
George N. Dove

Fred Dueren
Elizabeth F. Duke
Jeanne Carter Emmons
Elizabeth Evans
Larry L. French
David J. Geherin
Elliot L. Gilbert
James Gindin
Jane Gottschalk
George Grella
Larry E. Grimes
Mary Ann Grochowski
Mary Groff
E. R. Hagemann
Herbert Harris
John Harwood
Barrie Hayne
Joanne Harack Hayne
Carolyn G. Heilbrun
Reginald Hill
Edward D. Hoch
C. Hugh Holman
Dorothy B. Hughes
Donald C. Ireland
A. Norman Jeffares
David K. Jeffrey
Nancy C. Joyner
H. R. F. Keating
George Kelley
R. Gordon Kelly
Burton Kendle
Donna Rose Casella Kern
Daniel P. King
Margaret J. King
H. M. Klein
Kathleen G. Klein
Marvin Lachman
Donald Lammers

Larry N. Landrum
W. O. G. Lofts
Christopher Lowder
Bo Lundin
Dennis Lynds
Andrew F. Macdonald
Virginia Macdonald
Susan B. MacDougall
Kathleen L. Maio
Ann Massa
James R. McCahery
Frances D. McConachie
Frank D. McSherry, Jr.
Stephen Mertz
Jeffrey Meyerson
Will Murray
Kay J. Mussell
John M. Muste
Francis M. Nevins, Jr.
William F. Nolan
Frank Occhiogrosso
Ian Ousby
Robert B. Parker
Donald J. Pattow
Stuart Piggott
B. A. Pike

Bill Pronzini
Elmer Pry
Katherine M. Restaino
Seymour Rudin
Ray Russell
Joan M. Saliskas
Art Scott
Charles Shibuk
Michele Slung
Dwight C. Smith, Jr.
John Snyder
Katherine Staples
Jane W. Stedman
Carol Simpson Stern
Nancy Ellen Talburt
George J. Thompson
Guy M. Townsend
Donald C. Wall
Carol Washburne
William Weaver
John A. Weigel
John S. Whitley
Neville W. Wood
George Woodcock
Joan Y. Worley
Donald A. Yates

TWENTIETH-CENTURY CRIME AND MYSTERY WRITERS

Edward S. Aarons
Anthony Abbot
Cleve F. Adams
Joan Aiken
Catherine Aird
Martha Albrand
Ted Allbeury
Margery Allingham
Eric Ambler
Kingsley Amis
Frederick Irving Anderson
James Anderson
Evelyn Anthony
Peter Antony
Tom Ardies
Charlotte Armstrong
Frank Arthur
Isaac Asimov
Philip Atlee
Pierre Audemars
John Austwick
Michael Avallone

Marian Babson
Desmond Bagley
H. C. Bailey
John Ball
Willis Todhunter Ballard
Bill S. Ballinger
Edwin Balmer and William MacHarg
John Franklin Bardin
Nina Bawden
George Baxt
Francis Beeding
Noel Behn
Josephine Bell
George Bellairs
Robert Leslie Bellem
Margot Bennett
Ben Benson
E. F. Benson
E. C. Bentley
Nicolas Bentley
Phyllis Bentley
Kenneth Benton
Evelyn Berckman
Andrew Bergman
Anthony Berkeley
Earl Derr Biggers
John Bingham
Gavin Black
Lionel Black
John Blackburn
Charity Blackstock
Algernon Blackwood

Nicholas Blake
Suzanne Blanc
Robert Bloch
Lawrence G. Blochman
Lawrence Block
M. M'Donnell Bodkin
John Boland
John and Emery Bonett
Miriam Borgenicht
Anthony Boucher
Edgar Box
Jack Boyle
Ray Bradbury
Caryl Brahms
Ernest Bramah
Christianna Brand
Max Brand
John G. Brandon
H. C. Branson
Lillian Jackson Braun
Herbert Brean
Simon Brett
Gil Brewer
Ann Bridge
Victor Bridges
William Brittain
Lynn Brock
Carter Brown
Fredric Brown
Leo Bruce
Eric Bruton
John Buchan
John Bude
Gelett Burgess
John Burke
Thomas Burke
W. J. Burley
W. R. Burnett
Rex Burns
Roger Busby
Christopher Bush
Gwendoline Butler

Alan Caillou
James M. Cain
Janet Caird
Edward Candy
Joanna Cannan
Victor Canning
Harry Carmichael
Carol Carnac
A. H. Z. Carr
Glyn Carr
John Dickson Carr
Margaret Carr

Heron Carvic
Vera Caspary
Henry Cecil
John Newton Chance
Raymond Chandler
Leslie Charteris
James Hadley Chase
G. K. Chesterton
Peter Cheyney
Erskine Childers
Agatha Christie
Anna Clarke
Jon Cleary
Brian Cleeve
Francis Clifford
V. C. Clinton-Baddeley
G. Belton Cobb
Octavus Roy Cohen
G. D. H. and Margaret Cole
Manning Coles
John Collier
Michael Collins
Richard Condon
J. J. Connington
Brian Cooper
A. E. Coppard
Alec Coppel
Basil Copper
Mark Corrigan
Desmond Cory
Stephen Coulter
S. H. Courtier
Frances Cowen
George Harmon Coxe
Frances Crane
John Creasey
Michael Crichton
Edmund Crispin
Freeman Wills Crofts
Amanda Cross
Ken Crossen
Guy Cullingford
Marten Cumberland
E. V. Cunningham
Ursula Curtiss

Roald Dahl
Carroll John Daly
Elizabeth Daly
Clemence Dane
Glyn Daniel
Roland Daniel
Jocelyn Davey
Lionel Davidson
L. P. Davies

Dorothy Salisbury Davis
Frederick C. Davis
Amber Dean
Miriam Allen deFord
Len Deighton
Lillian de la Torre
Michael Delving
Ovid Demaris
Richard Deming
Lester Dent
August Derleth
Hugh Desmond
D. M. Devine
Thomas B. Dewey
Frederic Van Rensselaer Dey
Peter Dickinson
Adam Diment
Doris Miles Disney
Dorothy Cameron Disney
David Dodge
Hildegarde Dolson
Dick Donovan
Arthur Conan Doyle
Peter Driscoll
Ivor Drummond
June Drummond
Daphne du Maurier
W. Murdoch Duncan
John Gregory Dunne
Dorothy Dunnett
Francis Durbridge

Mignon G. Eberhart
Dorothy Eden
Clive Egleton
Stanley Ellin
Paul E. Erdman
Margaret Erskine
Robert Eustace
Helen Eustis

Gerard Fairlie
Katharine Farrer
William Faulkner
Kenneth Fearing
Ruth Fenisong
Elizabeth Fenwick
Elizabeth Ferrars
A. Fielding
Robert Finnegan
Jack Finney
Bruno Fischer
Robert L. Fish
Steve Fisher
Mary Fitt

4

Nigel Fitzgerald
Ian Fleming
Joan Fleming
J. S. Fletcher
Lucille Fletcher
Fletcher Flora
Pat Flower
Rae Foley
Hulbert Footner
Stanton Forbes
Leslie Ford
Frederick Forsyth
Sydney Fowler
Dick Francis
Antonia Fraser
Nicolas Freeling
R. Austin Freeman
Brian Freemantle
Celia Fremlin
Roy Fuller
Samuel Fuller
Jacques Futrelle

Reg Gadney
Sarah Gainham
Dorothy Gardiner
Erle Stanley Gardner
John Gardner
Brian Garfield
Andrew Garve
Catherine Gaskin
William Campbell Gault
Walter B. Gibson
Val Gielgud
Thomas Gifford
Anthony Gilbert
Michael Gilbert
Dorothy Gilman
John Godey
Arthur D. Goldstein
The Gordons
Joe Gores
Ron Goulart
Bruce Graeme
Winston Graham
Berkeley Gray
Dulcie Gray
Anna Katharine Green
Graham Greene
Leonard Gribble
Edward Grierson
Frank Gruber

William Haggard
Brett Halliday

Donald Hamilton
Patrick Hamilton
Dashiell Hammett
Joseph Hansen
Thomas W. Hanshew
Cyril Hare
Robert Harling
Joseph Harrington
Joyce Harrington
Herbert Harris
Rosemary Harris
Michael Harrison
Frances Noyes Hart
Simon Harvester
Macdonald Hastings
Joseph Hayes
Matthew Head
Tim Heald
H. F. Heard
Shaun Herron
Georgette Heyer
George V. Higgins
Patricia Highsmith
Wallace Hildick
Reginald Hill
Tony Hillerman
John Buxton Hilton
Chester Himes
Cornelius Hirschberg
Edward D. Hoch
Anne Hocking
William Hope Hodgson
Elisabeth Sanxay Holding
James Holding
C. Hugh Holman
Leonard Holton
Geoffrey Homes
Sydney Horler
E. W. Hornung
S. B. Hough
Geoffrey Household
P. M. Hubbard
Dorothy B. Hughes
Richard Hull
Fergus Hume
Alan Hunter
Elspeth Huxley
Stanley Hyland

Jack Iams
John N. Iannuzzi
Hammond Innes
Michael Innes

Stuart Jackman

5

Shirley Jackson
T. C. H. Jacobs
P. D. James
Cora Jarrett
Charlotte Jay
Roderic Jeffries
Selwyn Jepson
F. Tennyson Jesse
Hamilton Jobson
E. Richard Johnson

Frank Kane
Henry Kane
H. R. F. Keating
Harry Stephen Keeler
Day Keene
Clarence Budington Kelland
Mary Kelly
Harry Kemelman
Baynard H. Kendrick
Milward Kennedy
Tony Kenrick
Michael Kenyon
Gerald Kersh
Richard Keverne
C. Daly King
Rufus King
C. H. B. Kitchin
Henry Klinger
Bill Knox
Ronald A. Knox
Thomas Kyd

Arthur La Bern
Ed Lacy
Emma Lathen
Jonathan Latimer
Hilda Lawrence
James Leasor
John le Carré
Anthony Lejeune
Elizabeth Lemarchand
William Le Queux
Ira Levin
Michael Z. Lewin
Roy Lewis
Elizabeth Linington
Constance and Gwyneth Little
Ivy Litvinov
Richard and Frances Lockridge
Norah Lofts
Philip Loraine
Peter Lovesey
Marie Belloc Lowndes
Robert Ludlum

Edgar Lustgarten
John Lutz
Gavin Lyall

John D. MacDonald
Philip MacDonald
Ross Macdonald
Helen MacInnes
Donald MacKenzie
Alistair MacLean
Arthur Maling
Jessica Mann
Dan J. Marlowe
Derek Marlowe
Hugh Marlowe
Stephen Marlowe
John P. Marquand
Ngaio Marsh
A. E. W. Mason
F. Van Wyck Mason
Harold Q. Masur
Berkely Mather
Robin Maugham
W. Somerset Maugham
Ed McBain
Charles McCarry
Helen McCloy
James McClure
Horace McCoy
Philip McCutchan
Gregory Mcdonald
Patricia McGerr
Edmund McGirr
William P. McGivern
Paul McGuire
Mary McMullen
Mark McShane
L. T. Meade
Brown Meggs
Nicholas Meyer
Laurence Meynell
Margaret Millar
Wade Miller
A. A. Milne
Gladys Mitchell
Gwen Moffat
Anne Morice
Nigel Morland
Arthur Morrison
Patricia Moyes
Max Murray

Frederick Nebel
Margot Neville
Francis M. Nevins, Jr.

Bernard Newman
Beverley Nichols
Helen Nielsen
William F. Nolan
James Norman
Gil North

Lillian O'Donnell
Peter O'Donnell
Lenore Glen Offord
D. B. Olsen
E. Phillips Oppenheim
Baroness Orczy
Roger Ormerod

Frank L. Packard
Emma Page
Marco Page
Stuart Palmer
Robert B. Parker
Elliot Paul
Max Pemberton
Don Pendleton
Hugh Pentecost
Barry Perowne
Ritchie Perry
Elizabeth Peters
Ellis Peters
Ludovic Peters
Rhona Petrie
Eden Phillpotts
Evelyn Piper
Robert Player
Zelda Popkin
Joyce Porter
Melville Davisson Post
Raymond Postgate
Jean Potts
James Powell
Richard S. Prather
Anthony Price
J. B. Priestley
Allan Prior
Maurice Procter
Bill Pronzini
Milton Propper

Ellery Queen
Patrick Quentin

E. and M. A. Radford
Hugh C. Rae
S. S. Rafferty
Marion Randolph
Julian Rathbone

Clayton Rawson
Ishmael Reed
Arthur B. Reeve
Helen Reilly
Ruth Rendell
John Rhode
Craig Rice
Mary Roberts Rinehart
Jack Ritchie
James Hall Roberts
Joel Townsley Rogers
Sax Rohmer
Kelley Roos
Angus Ross
Jonathan Ross
Holly Roth
Kenneth Royce
Martin Russell
Ray Russell
Douglas Rutherford

Richard Sale
Lawrence Sanders
Sapper
Dorothy L. Sayers
Margaret Scherf
R. T. M. Scott
Mabel Seeley
Francis Selwyn
Joseph Shearing
Nevil Shute
Van Siller
Roger L. Simon
Helen Simpson
George Sims
Henry Slesar
Shelley Smith
Bart Spicer
Mickey Spillane
Christopher St. John Sprigg
Vincent Starrett
Aaron Marc Stein
Richard Martin Stern
Mary Stewart
Bram Stoker
Rex Stout
J. F. Straker
John Stephen Strange
T. S. Stribling
Jean Stubbs
Jeremy Sturrock
Margaret Summerton
Julian Symons

Phoebe Atwood Taylor

Josephine Tey
Lee Thayer
Ross Thomas
Basil Thomson
June Thomson
Ernest Tidyman
Arthur Train
Lawrence Treat
John Trench
Trevanian
Elleston Trevor
Glen Trevor
Miles Tripp
Nedra Tyre

Dorothy Uhnak
Michael Underwood
Arthur W. Upfield

John Holbrook Vance
Louis Joseph Vance
S. S. Van Dine
Roy Vickers
C. E. Vulliamy

Henry Wade
John Wainwright
Edgar Wallace
R. A. J. Walling
Thomas Walsh
Joseph Wambaugh
Thurman Warriner

Colin Watson
Hillary Waugh
Patrick Wayland
Jack Webb
John Welcome
Carolyn Wells
Patricia Wentworth
Donald E. Westlake
Carolyn Weston
Dennis Wheatley
Ethel Lina White
Jon Manchip White
Lionel White
Victor L. Whitechurch
Raoul Whitfield
Phyllis A. Whitney
Harry Whittington
William Wiegand
Collin Wilcox
Charles Williams
Valentine Williams
Ted Willis
Cecil M. Wills
Colin Wilson
Clifford Witting
Sara Woods
Cornell Woolrich

Andrew York
Margaret Yorke
P. B. Yuill

Israel Zangwill

NINETEENTH-CENTURY WRITERS

Mary Elizabeth Braddon
Wilkie Collins
Charles Dickens
William Godwin
Sheridan Le Fanu

Edgar Allan Poe
Richmond
Waters
Mrs. Henry Wood

FOREIGN-LANGUAGE WRITERS

Jorge Luis Borges
Pierre Boulle
Michel Butor
Friedrich Dürrenmatt
Emile Gaboriau
Sebastien Japrisot
Hans Hellmut Kirst
Maurice Leblanc

Gaston Leroux
Hubert Monteilhet
Poul Ørum
Alain Robbe-Grillet
Georges Simenon
Janwillem van de Wetering
Robert H. van Gulik
Per Wahlöö and Maj Sjöwall

AARONS, Edward S(idney). Also wrote as Paul Ayres; Edward Ronns. American. Born in Philadelphia, Pennsylvania, in 1916. Educated at Columbia University, New York, degrees in ancient history and literature. Served in the United States Coast Guard, 1941–45. Married 1) Ruth Ives (died); 2) Grace Dyer. Worked as millhand, salesman, fisherman, and as reporter on Philadelphia newspaper. Full-time writer from 1945. Lived in Connecticut. *Died 16 June 1975.*

CRIME PUBLICATIONS

Novels (series character: Sam Durell in all Assignment books)

Nightmare.   Philadelphia, McKay, 1948.
Dead Heat (as Paul Ayres).   Drexel Hill, Pennsylvania, Bell, 1950.
Escape to Love.   New York, Fawcett, 1952; London, Fawcett, 1957.
Come Back, My Love.   New York, Fawcett, 1953; London, Fawcett, 1954.
The Sinners.   New York, Fawcett, 1953; London, Fawcett, 1954.
Girl on the Run.   New York, Fawcett, 1954.
Assignment to Disaster.   New York, Fawcett, 1955; London, Fawcett, 1956.
Assignment – Suicide.   New York, Fawcett, 1956; London, Fawcett, 1958.
Assignment – Treason.   New York, Fawcett, 1956; London, Fawcett, 1957.
Assignment – Budapest.   New York, Fawcett, 1957; London, Fawcett, 1959.
Assignment – Stella Marni.   New York, Fawcett, 1957; London, Fawcett, 1958.
Assignment – Angelina.   New York, Fawcett, 1958; London, Fawcett, 1959.
Assignment – Madeleine.   New York, Fawcett, 1958; London, Muller, 1960.
Assignment – Carlotta Cortez.   New York, Fawcett, 1959; London, Muller, 1960.
Assignment – Helene.   New York, Fawcett, 1959; London, Muller, 1960.
Assignment – Lili Lamaris.   New York, Fawcett, 1959; London, Muller, 1960.
Assignment – Mara Tirana.   New York, Fawcett, 1960; London, Jenkins, 1966.
Hell to Eternity (novelization of screenplay).   New York, Fawcett, and London, Muller, 1960.
Assignment – Zoraya.   New York, Fawcett, and London, Muller, 1960.
Assignment – Ankara.   New York, Fawcett, 1961; London, Muller, 1963.
Assignment – Lowlands.   New York, Fawcett, 1961.
The Defenders (novelization of tv play).   New York, Fawcett, 1961; London, Jenkins, 1962.
Assignment – Burma Girl.   New York, Fawcett, and London, Muller, 1962.
Assignment – Karachi.   New York, Fawcett, 1962; London, Muller, 1963.
Assignment – Sorrento Siren.   New York, Fawcett, and London, Muller, 1963.
Assignment – Manchurian Doll.   New York, Fawcett, 1963; London, Muller, 1964.
Assignment – Sulu Sea.   New York, Fawcett, 1964.
Assignment – The Girl in the Gondola.   New York, Fawcett, 1964; London, Hodder and Stoughton, 1969.
Assignment – The Cairo Dancers.   New York, Fawcett, 1965.
Assignment – Palermo.   New York, Fawcett, 1966; London, Hodder and Stoughton, 1967.
Assignment – Cong Hai Kill.   New York, Fawcett, 1966.
Assignment – School for Spies.   New York, Fawcett, 1966; London, Hodder and Stoughton, 1967.
Assignment – Black Viking.   New York, Fawcett, 1967; London, Hodder and Stoughton, 1968.
Assignment – Moon Girl.   New York, Fawcett, 1967.
Assignment – Nuclear Nude.   New York, Fawcett, 1968; London, Hodder and Stoughton, 1969.

Assignment – Peking. New York, Fawcett, 1969; London, Hodder and Stoughton, 1970.

Assignment – Star Stealers. New York, Fawcett, and London, Hodder and Stoughton, 1970.

Assignment – White Rajah. New York, Fawcett, and London, Hodder and Stoughton, 1970.

Assignment – Tokyo. New York, Fawcett, and London, Hodder and Stoughton, 1971.

Assignment – Bangkok. New York, Fawcett, and London, Hodder and Stoughton, 1972.

Assignment – Golden Girl. New York, Fawcett, and London, Hodder and Stoughton, 1972.

Assignment – Maltese Maiden. New York, Fawcett, 1972; London, Hodder and Stoughton, 1973.

Assignment – Ceylon. New York, Fawcett, 1973; London, Hodder and Stoughton, 1974.

Assignment – Silver Scorpion. New York, Fawcett, 1973; London, Hodder and Stoughton, 1974.

Assignment – Amazon Queen. New York, Fawcett, 1974; London, Hodder and Stoughton, 1975.

Assignment – Sumatra. New York, Fawcett, 1974; London, Hodder and Stoughton, 1975.

Assignment – Black Gold. New York, Fawcett, 1975; London, Hodder and Stoughton, 1977.

Assignment – Quayle Question. New York, Fawcett, 1975; London, Hodder and Stoughton, 1976.

Novels as Edward Ronns

Death in a Lighthouse. New York, Phoenix Press, 1938; as *The Cowl of Doom*, n.p., Hangman's House, 1946.

Murder Money. New York, Phoenix Press, 1938; as *$1,000,000 in Corpses*, n.p., Best Detective Selections, 1943.

The Corpse Hangs High. New York, Phoenix Press, 1939.

No Place to Live. Philadelphia, McKay, 1947; London, Boardman, 1950; as *Lady, The Guy Is Dead*, New York, Avon, 1950.

Terror in the Town. Philadelphia, McKay, 1947.

Gift of Death. Philadelphia, McKay, 1948.

The Art Studio Murders. Kingston, New York, Quin, 1950.

Catspaw Ordeal. New York, Fawcett, 1950.

Dark Memory. Kingston, New York, Quin, 1950.

Million Dollar Murder. New York, Fawcett, 1950; London, Fawcett, 1952.

State Department Murders. New York, Fawcett, 1950; London, Fawcett, 1957.

The Decoy. New York, Fawcett, 1951.

I Can't Stop Running. New York, Fawcett, 1951.

Don't Cry, Beloved. New York, Fawcett, 1952.

Passage to Terror. New York, Fawcett, 1952.

Dark Destiny. Hasbrouck Heights, New Jersey, Graphic, 1953.

The Net. Hasbrouck Heights, New Jersey, Graphic, 1953.

Say It with Murder. Hasbrouck Heights, New Jersey, Graphic, 1954; London, Red Seal, 1960.

They All Ran Away. Hasbrouck Heights, New Jersey, Graphic, 1955.

Point of Peril. New York, Curl, 1956.

Death Is My Shadow. New York, Curl, 1957.

Pickup Alley (novelization of screenplay). New York, Avon, 1957.

Gang Rumble. New York, Avon, 1958.

The Lady Takes a Flyer (novelization of screenplay).   New York, Avon, 1958.
The Big Bedroom.   New York, Pyramid, 1959.
The Black Orchid (novelization of screenplay).   New York, Pyramid, 1959.
But Not for Me (novelization of screenplay).   New York, Pyramid, 1959; London,
    World Distributors, 1960.
The Glass Cage.   New York, Pyramid, 1962.

Uncollected Short Story

"We've Got Time," in *The Saint* (New York), June–July 1953.

                              *   *   *

Edward S. Aarons's most successful creation has been the *Assignment* series, featuring
durable Sam Durell of the CIA "K" section. In the twenty-odd years he has been operative,
Durell has aged little, his thick black hair showing grey at the temples only recently. Early in
the series, he had served with G-2 and the OSS, but of late no mention has been made of
organizations which would date him. Still a Yalie, however, Durell prefers dark blue or gray
suits, white shirts with button-down collars, and solid neckties. He was reared by his
grandfather, a riverboat captain who taught him his gambler's instincts and ways aboard an
old paddlewheeler in the Delta's Bayou Peche Rouge. Thus Durell's code name – Cajun.
    The *Assignment* series is characteristically humorless and tough-minded. Durell claims to
be a coldly objective man, calculating odds and consequences, placing his patriotic duty to job
and country before the lives of his cohorts. His actions, however, contradict these claims;
despite his rhetoric, he has always instinctively and impetuously attempted to rescue his
underlings – at least the women among them – from the villains' schemes and clutches, no
matter the consequences. Violence in the series is frequent, explicit, and brutal. Characters
are tortured and slaughtered by villains in a variety of arcane ways. Durell's violence, by
contrast, is straightforward; he kills quickly with fists, knives, guns, and bombs. Durell
himself absorbs an astonishing amount of punishment. He is beaten and knocked
unconscious at least twice in every novel, coming to a climactic confrontation with the arch-
villain bloody but unbowed, although at the arch-villain's mercy. Indeed, in *The Girl in the
Gondola* Durell allows himself to be tortured in order to buy time for the successful
completion of a mission. There, too, Aarons deals most interestingly with the psychic effects
of violence, linking Durell's apparent emotional coldness with his violence. In that novel, the
scars on Durell's body and on his woman's symbolically measure the losses his job has
caused. As always, however, Durell finds the reservoir of strength necessary to overcome
both his own pain and the enemy.
    The arch-villains of the series represent a threat at least to an entire country – to Algeria,
for example, in *Madeleine*, to the U.S. in *Angelina* and *Stella Marni*, to Thailand in *Cong Hai
Kill*, and to an African nation in *Black Gold* – if not to the world – *The Girl in the Gondola*,
Star Stealers, and *Amazon Queen*. The villains are typically either sadistic barbarians of
incredible physical strength – L'Heureux in *Madeleine*, Slago in *Angelina*, Agpak terrorists in
Black Gold – or the cunning and nasty brains behind such brawn – Dr. Von Handel in *Star
Stealers*, Paio Chu in *Cong Hai Kill*. Occasionally, the villain will be a combination of the two
– Dinov in *The Girl in the Gondola*, Agosto in *Amazon Queen*. Early in the series, the villains
were sometimes women – Jessie Corbin in *Angelina*, and Stella Marni in the book of that
name.
    Of late, however, the women in the series have been pliant and accessible ladies of
considerable class and background or pliant and accessible females of, shall I say, rather less
breeding. Instead of faulting Aarons for what may seem on its face a chauvinistic
divisiveness, I would congratulate him for his creation of women of the first type. His
"ladies," while hardly saintly virgins, are in fact, competent and determined people with
intelligence and power. In various novels such women as Queen Salduva of Pakuru, the
wealthy owner of an electronics industry, and the widow of Italy's Defense Minister have

11

been Durell's lovely and loving helpmates, despite his more or less regular attachment to Deirdre Padgett, also a "lady," coming from a wealthy family on Maryland's Eastern Shore. Deirdre was a newspaper reporter before joining the CIA, and she now figures in occasional novels as a tough and cunning operative who accompanies Durell on his adventures.

The novels are generally as topical as yesterday's newspaper. Aarons has written, for example, of the Algerian conflict, Cold War tensions, the Chinese influence in Albania, spy satellites, the Indo-China wars, and the oil crisis. His formula is to open each novel with a chapter of violence and mystery, introduce Durell, situate him in a foreign country and direct him through a series of false leads and traitors until he meets the arch-villain and emerges triumphantly from his confrontation with a shaky peace and the lady.

—David K. Jeffrey

ABBEY, Kieran.   See REILLY, Helen.

ABBOT, Anthony. Pseudonym for (Charles) Fulton Oursler. American. Born in Baltimore, Maryland, 22 January 1893. Educated in public schools in Baltimore. Married 1) Rose Keller Karger in 1911; one daughter and one son; 2) the writer Grace Perkins in 1925; one daughter and one son. Reporter, 1910–12, and music and drama critic, 1912–18, Baltimore *American*; Managing Editor, New York *Music Trades*, 1920–22; Editor-in-Chief, *Metropolitan* magazine, 1923; Editor, *Liberty* magazine, 1931–42; Vice-President and Editorial Director, Macfadden Publications, 1941; Senior Editor, *Reader's Digest*, 1944; Editor and Publisher, *The Sandalwood Herald*, West Falmouth, Massachusetts. Radio broadcaster in World War II; syndicated columnist, "Modern Parables." Trustee, Andrew Carnegie Fund for Needy Authors; President, Catholic Institute Press; Director, Alcoholics Anonymous Foundation; Vice-President, American Writers Association. *Died 24 May 1952.*

CRIME PUBLICATIONS

Novels (series character: Thatcher Colt)

> *About the Murder of Geraldine Foster* (Colt).   New York, Covici Friede, 1930; London, Collins, 1931.
> *About the Murder of the Clergyman's Mistress* (Colt).   New York, Covici Friede, 1931; as *The Crime of the Century*, London, Collins, 1931.
> *About the Murder of the Night Club Lady* (Colt).   New York, Covici Friede, 1931; London, Collins, 1932.
> *About the Murder of the Circus Queen* (Colt).   New York, Covici Friede, 1932; London, Collins, 1933.
> *About the Murder of a Startled Lady* (Colt).   New York, Farrar and Rinehart, 1935; London, Collins, 1937.
> *The President's Mystery Story*, with others.   New York, Farrar and Rinehart, 1935.

Dark Masquerade (published anonymously).   New York, Furman, 1936.
About the Murder of a Man Afraid of Women (Colt).   New York, Farrar and Rinehart,
   and London, Collins, 1937.
The Creeps (Colt).   New York, Farrar and Rinehart, 1939; as *Murder at Buzzard's Bay*,
   London, Collins, 1940.
The Shudders (Colt).   New York, Farrar and Rinehart, 1943; as *Deadly Secret*,
   London, Collins, 1943.

Short Stories

The Wager, and The House at Fernwood.   New York, Pony, 1946.
These Are Strange Tales.   Philadelphia, Winston, 1948.

Uncollected Short Stories

"About the Disappearance of Agatha King," in *The Mystery Book.*   New York, Farrar
   and Rinehart, 1939.
"About the Perfect Crime of Mr. Digberry," in *To the Queen's Taste*, edited by Ellery
   Queen.   Boston, Little Brown, 1946.
"Hula Homicide," in *The Saint Mystery Library No. 7*, edited by Leslie Charteris.   New
   York, Great American, 1959.

OTHER PUBLICATIONS as Fulton Oursler

Novels

Behold This Dreamer!   New York, Macaulay, and London, Unwin, 1924.
Sandalwood.   New York, Macaulay, 1925; London, Heinemann, 1928.
Stepchild of the Moon.   New York, Harper, 1926; London, Benn, 1927.
Poor Little Fool.   New York, Harper, 1928.
The World's Delight.   New York, Harper, 1929.
The Great Jasper.   New York, Covici Friede, 1930; London, Lane, 1932.
Joshua Todd.   New York, Farrar and Rinehart, and London, Lane, 1935.
A String of Blue Beads.   New York, Doubleday, 1956; Kingswood, Surrey, World's
   Work, 1957.

Plays

The Spider, with Lowell Brentano (produced New York, 1927; revised version by
   Roland Pertwee, produced London, 1928).   New York, French, 1925.
Sandalwood, with Owen Davis, adaptation of the novel by Oursler (produced New
   York, 1926).
Behold This Dreamer, with Aubrey Kennedy, adaptation of the novel by Oursler
   (produced New York, 1927).   New York, French, 1930.
All the King's Men (produced New York, 1929).
The Walking Gentleman, with Grace Perkins Oursler (produced New York, 1942).
The Bridge (produced 1946).

Other

The True Story of Bernarr Macfadden.   New York, Copeland, 1929.
The Flower of the Gods (as Anthony Abbot), with Achmed Abdullah.   New York,
   Furman, 1936.
A Skeptic in the Holy Land.   New York, Farrar and Rinehart, 1936; London, Methuen,
   1937.

The Shadow of the Master (as Anthony Abbot), with 'Abd Allah Ahmad. London, Hurst and Blackett, 1940.

Three Things We Can Believe In. New York, Revell, 1942.

The Precious Secret. Philadelphia, Winston, 1947; Kingswood, Surrey, World's Work, 1948.

The Happy Grotto. New York, McMullen, 1948; Kingswood, Surrey, World's Work, 1957.

Father Flanagan of Boys Town, with Will Oursler. New York, Doubleday, 1949; Kingswood, Surrey, World's Work, 1950.

The Greatest Story Ever Told: A Tale of the Greatest Life Ever Lived. New York, Doubleday, and Kingswood, Surrey, World's Work, 1949.

Why I Know There Is a God. New York, Doubleday, 1950; Kingswood, Surrey, World's Work, 1952.

Modern Parables. New York, Doubleday, 1950; Kingswood, Surrey, World's Work, 1951.

A Child's Life of Jesus. New York, Watts, 1951.

The Greatest Book Ever Written: The Old Testament Story. New York, Doubleday, 1951.

The Reader's Digest Murder Case: A Tragedy in Parole. New York, Farrar Straus, 1952.

The Greatest Faith Ever Known, with April Oursler Armstrong. New York, Doubleday, and Kingswood, Surrey, World's Work, 1953.

Lights along the Shore. New York, Doubleday, 1954; Kingswood, Surrey, World's Work, 1955.

Behold This Dreamer! (autobiography), edited by Fulton Oursler, Jr. Boston, Little Brown, 1964.

Editor and translator, with J.B. Mussey, *Illustrated Magic*, by Ottokar Fischer. New York, Macmillan, 1931.

*   *   *

The classical detective story has several aspects. First and foremost is the bizarre, often impossible, type of crime that was pioneered by Edgar Allan Poe in "The Murders in the Rue Morgue." Other authors, including Conan Doyle, S.S. Van Dine, Ellery Queen, and John Dickson Carr continued this tradition. These stories often featured amateur detectives whose personal mannerisms were as outré as the murders they investigated. A later though important form of the detective story was the police novel as created by Freeman Wills Crofts in *The Cask*. In this type of novel, the detectives were ordinary (sometimes even faceless) human beings, such as Crofts's Inspector French and Henry Wade's Inspector Poole, and dealt with crime as a means of earning a living. Fulton Oursler, a journalist with a deep interest in crime detection, tried to combine these two forms by placing a series character who is police commissioner of New York City, and able to command the full resources of his organization, into situations that would encompass bizarre and impossible murder cases.

Oursler's novels as Anthony Abbot are heavily influenced by the work of S. S. Van Dine and the early Ellery Queen, though fortunately they lack many of the former author's most irritating mannerisms. Most of them are imaginatively conceived, and, though out of print, are well worth seeking out.

Commissioner Thatcher Colt is not too far removed from Van Dine's detective Philo Vance and Queen (in his early years): all are tall, but Colt is more robust. He is also a cold, deeply intellectual, and often verbose person, though unlike the others, Colt is capable of feeling compassion toward his fellow man. Vance and Colt both have secretaries who act as Watsons and bear the names of their creators, but, sad to relate, both have been found guilty on several occasions of failing to put all the evidence before the reader. Critic John L. Breen has stated that Colt was to Vance as R. Austin Freeman's Dr. Thorndyke was to Doyle's

Holmes. He also finds that Colt's exploits have withstood the test of time better than the Vance works.

Abbot's better than average debut, *About the Murder of Geraldine Foster*, is concerned with the victim of an axe murder, and vaguely based on the Lizzie Borden case. *About the Murder of the Clergyman's Mistress* is better. Plotted with all the dexterity of an early Ellery Queen novel, this work was based on the famous Hall-Mills case. A sidelight, of interest in terms of Oursler's later (1943) conversion to Catholicism, is his less than flattering depiction of the clergy. One sequence in *About the Murder of a Startled Lady* wherein a moulder reconstructs the face of a murder victim from her skull is an outstanding example of police science, and worthy of Dr. Thorndyke at his best. *The Creeps* is a minor and straightforward story of crime and investigation that presents a retired and married Colt at a houseparty in Buzzard's Bay that is disrupted by a snowstorm and murder.

The Shudders features a mad scientist who claims to have discovered an untraceable method of murder and promises that his successes will culminate with the death of Commissioner Colt. This is Abbot's best work – a serial-like thriller that is every bit as baffling and bizarre as anything penned by Queen or Carr, and a memorable climax to one of the outstanding series of American mystery novels of the 1930's and early 1940's.

—Charles Shibuk

ADAMS, Cleve F(ranklin). Also wrote as Franklin Charles; John Spain. American. Born in Chicago, Illinois, in 1895. Married: one child. Worked as a copper miner, detective, life insurance executive, art director for films, and operated a chain of candy stores before becoming a full-time writer in the 1930's. *Died 28 December 1949.*

CRIME PUBLICATIONS

Novels (series character: Rex McBride)

And Sudden Death. New York, Dutton, 1940.
Sabotage (McBride). New York, Dutton, 1940; as *Death at the Dam*, London, Cassell, 1946.
The Black Door. New York, Dutton, 1941.
Decoy (McBride). New York, Dutton, 1941.
The Vice Czar Murders (as Franklin Charles; with Robert Leslie Bellem). New York, Funk and Wagnalls, 1941.
The Private Eye. New York, Reynal, 1942.
What Price Murder. New York, Dutton, 1942.
Up Jumped the Devil (McBride). New York, Reynal, 1943; as *Murder All Over*, New York, New American Library, 1950.
The Crooking Finger (McBride). New York, Reynal, 1944.
Contraband. New York, Knopf, 1950; as *Borderline Cases*, London, Cassell, 1952.

No Wings on a Cop, expanded by Robert Leslie Bellem.   Kingston, New York, Quin, 1950.
Shady Lady (McBride).   New York, Ace, 1955.

Novels as John Spain (series character: Bill Rye)

Dig Me a Grave (Rye).   New York, Dutton, 1942; London, Corgi, 1952.
Death Is Like That (Rye).   New York, Dutton, 1943.
The Evil Star.   New York, Dutton, 1944; London, Swan, 1950.

Uncollected Short Stories

"Vision of Violet," in *Clues* (New York), February 1936.
"Important Money," in *Clues* (New York), December 1936.
"Double Shuffle," in *Detective Fiction Weekly* (New York), 11 September 1937.
"Private War," in *Detective Fiction Weekly* (New York), 2 October 1937.
"Money No Object," in *Detective Fiction Weekly* (New York), 13 November 1937.
"Pattern of Panic," in *Double Detective* (New York), November 1937.
"The Heel," in *Detective Fiction Weekly* (New York), 11 December 1937.
"The Girl from Frisco," in *Detective Fiction Weekly* (New York), 1 January 1938.
"Tragedy of Errors," in *Double Detective* (New York), January 1938.
"Traffic Case," in *Detective Fiction Weekly* (New York), 12 February 1938.
"Murder Takes a Trade," in *Detective Fiction Weekly* (New York), 5 March 1938.
"Punk," in *Detective Fiction Weekly* (New York), 19 March 1938.
"This Is Murder," in *Double Detective* (New York), April 1938.
"Jigsaw," in *Detective Fiction Weekly* (New York), 11 June 1938.
"Flatfoot," in *Double Detective* (New York), July 1938.
"Give the Guy Rope," in *Detective Fiction Weekly* (New York), 20 August 1938.
"Song of Hate," in *Double Detective* (New York), August 1938.
"Guardian Angel," in *Detective Fiction Weekly* (New York), 10 September 1938.
"Burn a Feather," in *Detective Fiction Weekly* (New York), 29 October 1938.
"Inside Straight," in *Detective Fiction Weekly* (New York), 5 November 1938.
"Speak No Evil," in *Collier's* (Springfield, Ohio), 26 November 1938.
"Homing Pigeon," in *Detective Fiction Weekly* (New York), 10 December 1938.
"Murder Goes Unshod," in *Detective Fiction Weekly* (New York), 17 December 1938.
"Mannequin for a Morgue," in *Double Detective* (New York), December 1938.
"Help! Murder! Police!" in *Argosy* (New York), 4, 11, and 18 February 1939.
"Cops Are Sissies," in *Detective Tales* (New York), May 1939.
"The Jade Ring," in *Detective Fiction Weekly* (New York), 24 June 1939.
"Smart Guy," in *Detective Fiction Weekly* (New York), 12 August 1939.
"Exit with Bullets," in *Double Detective* (New York), August 1939.
"Contraband," in *Detective Fiction Weekly* (New York), 9 September 1939.
"Exodus," in *Detective Fiction Weekly* (New York), 13 January 1940.
"Death Strikes a Chord," in *Detective Fiction Weekly* (New York), 13 January 1940.
"The Key," in *Black Mask* (New York), July 1940.
"The Dead Can't Vote," in *Detective Fiction Weekly* (New York), 3 August 1940.
"Clean Sweep," in *Detective Fiction Weekly* (New York), 24 August 1940.
"Passage for Satan," in *Argosy* (New York), 14 September 1940.
"That Certain Feeling," in *Black Mask* (New York), September 1940.
"Backfire," in *Detective Fiction Weekly* (New York), 30 November 1940.
"Murder While You Wait," in *Dime Detective* (New York), December 1940.
"Sinners Three," in *Argosy* (New York), 18 January 1941.
"The Aunt of Sigma Chi," in *Black Mask* (New York), January 1941.
"Murder Ad Lib," in *Detective Fiction Weekly* (New York), 17 May 1941.
"Night in Sinaloa," in *Argosy* (New York), 31 May 1941.

"Murder Parade," in *Black Mask* (New York), May 1941.
"Nobody Loves Cops," in *Black Mask* (New York), July 1941.
"Herrings Are Red," in *Black Mask* (New York), March 1942.

OTHER PUBLICATIONS

Other

"Motivation in Mystery Fiction," in *The Writer* (Boston), April 1942.

Bibliography: by Francis M. Nevins, Jr., and William J. Clark, in "The World of Cleve Adams" by Nevins, in *Armchair Detective* (White Bear Lake, Minnesota), May 1975.

*   *   *

After working at a variety of jobs, Cleve F. Adams began writing mystery fiction for the pulp magazines around 1934, almost simultaneously with Raymond Chandler and Cornell Woolrich, and like them he turned to novels at the end of the 1930's and produced most of his books in a frenzy of activity during the early 1940's. Although the books are little read today, in his own style Adams captured the gray and gritty feel of the time as powerfully as Chandler, and created as enduring an image of the private detective.

The Adams private eye – who has many names but is usually called Rex McBride – is a sort of prophecy of the Humphrey Bogart persona. But unlike Bogey, whose apparent hard shell hid a sentimental heart, the Adams protagonist's apparent soft heart is itself a shell concealing a brutal and cynical core. He is slim and dark, with a wolfishly satanic look and a capacity for deep brooding silences, sudden ribald laughter, fierce rages, aloof arrogance. He is a supreme male chauvinist, with a penchant for slapping his girlfriends around and chasing other women. He's a fascist ("An American Gestapo is goddam well what we need"), a racist (throwing around terms like spic, wop, nigger, and kike as casually as he shoots people), a cynic and a hypocrite, but a sentimental ballad can bring tears to his eyes. Chandler said of the private eye that "He is the hero, he is everything," but Adams's aim is to debunk this knightly image and reduce the eye to a royal ass and a cosmic oaf. In Adams's cynical world there is no hero, and the detective is as rotten as everyone else, just tougher and luckier.

Almost all of Adams's novels feature a good girl, a bad girl, a gambling czar, a good gray police captain, a sadistic Homicide dick, a corrupt politician, hired goons, a pompous businessman or government official, and a Runyonesque cabbie who miraculously pops up to pull the eye out of jams. Every book contains a smoke-ring blowing scene, some drunk scenes, at least two beatings, and a confrontation between the detective and each woman in the tale, one of whom is usually the murderer. Adams recycles the same descriptions and lines of dialogue tirelessly, and he was so fond of Dashiell Hammett's novels that he filched the storyline of *Red Harvest* three times and of *The Glass Key* twice, although Adams's versions collapse whenever he tries to explain his chaotic plots. And yet for all his faults he was a genius at juggling disparate groups of shady characters each with a separate greedy objective, and his books boil over with breathless raw readability. His last and best novel, *Shady Lady*, is rich in character sketches and powerfully understated scenes which suggest that, had he lived longer, he might have grown into a writer rivaling Chandler.

—Francis M. Nevins, Jr.

AIKEN, Joan (Delano). British. Born in Rye, Sussex, 4 September 1924; daughter of the poet Conrad Aiken. Educated at Wychwood School, Oxford, 1936–40. Married Ronald George Brown in 1945 (died, 1955); has one son and one daughter. Worked for the BBC, 1942–43; Librarian, United Nations Information Centre, London, 1943–49; Sub-Editor and Features Editor. *Argosy*, London, 1955–60; Copywriter, J. Walter Thompson, London, 1960–61. Recipient: *Guardian Award*, 1969; Mystery Writers of America Edgar Allan Poe Award, 1972. Agent: A. M. Heath, 40–42 William IV Street, London WC2N 4DD; or, Brandt and Brandt, 101 Park Avenue, New York, New York 10017, U.S.A. Address: The Hermitage, East Street, Petworth, Sussex, England.

CRIME PUBLICATIONS

Novels

> *The Silence of Herondale.* New York, Doubleday, 1964; London, Gollancz, 1965.
> *The Fortune Hunters.* New York, Doubleday, 1965.
> *Trouble with Product X.* London, Gollancz, 1966; as *Beware of the Banquet*, New York, Doubleday, 1966.
> *Hate Begins at Home.* London, Gollancz, 1967; as *Dark Interval*, New York, Doubleday, 1967.
> *The Ribs of Death.* London, Gollancz, 1967; as *The Crystal Crow*, New York, Doubleday, 1968.
> *The Embroidered Sunset.* London, Gollancz, and New York, Doubleday, 1970.
> *Died on a Rainy Sunday.* London, Gollancz, and New York, Holt Rinehart, 1972.
> *The Butterfly Picnic.* London, Gollancz, 1972; as *A Cluster of Separate Sparks*, New York, Doubleday, 1972.
> *Last Movement.* London, Gollancz, and New York, Doubleday, 1977.

Short Stories

> *The Windscreen Weepers and Other Tales of Horror and Suspense.* London, Gollancz, 1969

OTHER PUBLICATIONS

Novels

> *Voices in an Empty House.* London, Gollancz, and New York, Doubleday, 1975.
> *Castle Barebane.* London, Gollancz, and New York, Viking Press, 1976.
> *The Five-Minute Marriage.* London, Gollancz, 1977; New York, Doubleday, 1978.
> *The Smile of the Stranger.* London, Gollancz, and New York, Doubleday, 1978.

Plays (for children)

> *Winterthing*, music by John Sebastian Brown (produced Albany, New York, 1977). New York, Holt Rinehart, 1972; included in *Winterthing, and The Mooncusser's Daughter*, 1973.
> *The Mooncusser's Daughter.* New York, Viking Press, 1973; included in *Winterthing, and The Mooncusser's Daughter*, 1973.
> *Winterthing, and The Mooncusser's Daughter.* London, Cape, 1973.
> *Street,* music by John Sebastian Brown (produced London, 1977). New York, Viking Press, 1978.

Television Plays: *The Dark Streets of Kimballs Green*, 1976; *Mortimer's Tie*, 1976; *The Apple of Trouble*, 1977; *Midnight Is a Place* (serial), from her own novel, 1977; *The*

Rose of Puddle Fratrum, 1978; *Armitage, Armitage, Fly Away Home*, from her own novel, 1978.

Verse

The Skin Spinners (juvenile). New York, Viking Press, 1976.

Other (fiction for children)

All You've Ever Wanted and Other Stories. London, Cape, 1953.
More Than You Bargained For and Other Stories. London, Cape, 1955: New York, Abelard Schuman, 1957.
The Kingdom and the Cave. London and New York, Abelard Schuman, 1960.
The Wolves of Willoughby Chase. London, Cape, 1962; New York, Doubleday, 1963.
Black Hearts in Battersea. New York, Doubleday, 1964; London, Cape, 1965.
Nightbirds on Nantucket. London, Cape, and New York, Doubleday, 1966.
The Whispering Mountain. London, Cape, 1968; New York, Doubleday, 1969.
A Necklace of Raindrops and Other Stories. London, Cape, and New York, Doubleday, 1968.
Armitage, Armitage, Fly Away Home. New York, Doubleday, 1968.
A Small Pinch of Weather and Other Stories. London, Cape, 1969.
Night Fall. London, Macmillan, 1969; New York, Holt Rinehart, 1971.
Smoke from Cromwell's Time and Other Stories. New York, Doubleday, 1970.
The Green Flash and Other Tales of Horror, Suspense and Fantasy. New York, Holt Rinehart, 1971.
The Cuckoo Tree. London, Cape and New York, Doubleday, 1971.
The Kingdom under the Sea and Other Stories. London, Cape, 1971.
A Harp of Fishbones and Other Stories. London, Cape, 1972.
Arabel's Raven. London, BBC Publications, 1972; New York, Doubleday, 1974.
The Escaped Black Mamba. London, BBC Publications, 1973.
All But a Few. London, Penguin, 1974.
The Bread Bin. London, BBC Publications, 1974.
Midnight Is a Place. London, Cape, and New York, Viking Press, 1974.
Not What You Expected: A Collection of Short Stories. New York, Doubleday, 1974.
Mortimer's Tie. London, BBC Publications, 1976.
A Bundle of Nerves. London, Gollancz, 1976.
The Faithless Lollybird and Other Stories. London, Cape, 1977; New York, Doubleday, 1978.
The Far Forests: Tales of Romance, Fantasy, and Suspense. New York, Viking Press, 1977.
Go Saddle the Sea. New York, Doubleday, 1977; London, Cape, 1978.
Tale of a One-Way Street and Other Stories. London, Cape, 1978.
Mice and Mendelson. London, Cape, 1978.
Mortimer and the Sword Excalibur. London, BBC Publications, 1979.
The Spiral Stair. London, BBC Publications, 1979.
A Touch of Chill (stories). London, Gollancz, 1979.
Arabel and Mortimer. London, Cape, 1979.

Translator, *The Angel Inn* by Contessa de Segur. London, Cape, 1976; Owings Mills, Maryland, Stemmer House, 1978.

*　　*　　*

Joan Aiken is a highly respected writer of children's fiction who turned to the adult novel in 1964 with excellent results. Her first three gothic romances followed the conventional plot:

the damsels-in-distress won through to happy endings with the right young men. But even in these relatively unremarkable books, there were signs that Aiken would find the form too confining for her imagination, which is full of highly plausible fantasies and horrors. In *Trouble with Product X*, for instance, one of the major secondary characters is a four-month-old baby girl who is the heiress to a fabulous perfume formula which gets eaten by Cornish slugs. *Hate Begins at Home*, her next book, is described on the cover as a "modern novel with gothic suspense," and in fact the elements of horror almost overwhelm the heroine and the book. The issue of the heroine's survival is left in doubt until the last sentence. There followed two of Aiken's best and most characteristic books. They are indefinable as to genre and reach denouements determined only by the logic of the characters she has created and the situations she has placed them in.

The Ribs of Death gives us as heroine a very young novelist who lives with a horrible female saint. This couple is juxtaposed with a psychotic female doctor and her brother, whom she has placed under a false medical death sentence. Several other characters with various mental problems, including schizophrenia and depression, wander about, together with an escaped leopard. The plot proceeds through various quotidian horrors to a final passage of mayhem and a bleak ending. The young innocents have survived the destruction, but their fragile intimacy is dead. *The Embroidered Sunset* has just as diverse and engaging a cast of characters as its predecessor. The heroine is a young woman with a talent for the piano, a nasty step-father, a weak heart, and a dedicated appreciation for the art of Aunt Fennel Culpepper, who may or may not be her companion of many years. Dr. Adnan, a lively young Turkish doctor, and Max Benovek, a dying pianist, both come to the rescue of the heroine, but they arrive an hour after the heroine's heart has worn out.

How Aiken makes these characters and plots both moving and credible is something of a mystery. One attractive quality of Aiken's heroes and heroines is their high threshold for self-pity. They may have a great many burdens to bear, but they don't shift them onto others, and Aiken's incident-filled plots leave them little time for brooding. Her short stories, collected in *The Green Flash* and *The Far Forests*, flash with wit, and fantasy, and the peculiar wisdom of this very individual writer.

—Carol Cleveland

AIRD, Catherine. Pseudonym for Kinn Hamilton McIntosh. British. Born in Huddersfield, Yorkshire, 20 June 1930. Educated at Waverley School and Greenhead High School, both in Huddersfield. Since 1975, Chairman of the Finance Committee, Girl Guides Association, London. Agent: Hughes Massie Ltd., 31 Southampton Row, London WC1B 5HL. Address: Invergordon, Sturry Hill, Sturry, Canterbury, Kent CT2 0NG, England.

CRIME PUBLICATIONS

Novels (series character: Inspector Sloan)

The Religious Body (Sloan). London, Macdonald, and New York, Doubleday, 1966.
A Most Contagious Game. London, Macdonald, and New York, Doubleday, 1967.
Henrietta Who? (Sloan). London, Macdonald, and New York, Doubleday, 1968.
The Complete Steel (Sloan). London, Macdonald, 1969; as *The Stately Home Murder*, New York, Doubleday, 1970.
A Late Phoenix (Sloan). London, Collins, and New York, Doubleday, 1971.

His Burial Too (Sloan).   London, Collins, and New York, Doubleday, 1973.
Slight Mourning (Sloan).   London, Collins, 1975; New York, Doubleday, 1976.
Parting Breath (Sloan).   London, Collins, 1975; New York, Doubleday, 1978.
Some Die Eloquent (Sloan).   London, Collins, 1979.

Uncollected Short Story

"The Scales of Justice," in *Argosy* (London), February 1974.

<small>OTHER PUBLICATIONS</small>

Play

The Story of Sturry (*son et lumière* script) (produced Sturry, 1973).

Other

"Gervase Fen and the Teacake School" and "Benefit of Clergy," in *Murder Ink: The Mystery Reader's Companion*, edited by Dilys Winn.   New York, Workman, 1977.

Editor, *Sturry: The Changing Scene*.   Privately printed, 1972.
Editor, *Fordwich, The Lost Port*.   Privately printed, 1975.
Editor, *Chislet and Westbere, Villages of the Stour Lathe*.   Privately printed, 1979.

*   *   *

Catherine Aird's novels bear as their hallmark an unruffled neatness, a straightforward presentation, a firm grasp of the narrative line. The author creates the convincing world of her story, each time, with admirable economy, whether the setting be a small village (as in *Slight Mourning*) or an eruptive university (*Parting Breath*). But the locale is never downright stark, there are always corroborating details, the necessary touches of colour, and a welcome, quiet wit. Generally speaking, Catherine Aird's books are in the great domestic tradition – the body in the library, the gossip at the vicarage – but they are never conventional or machine-made.

—William Weaver

————————————

ALBRAND, Martha. Pseudonym for Heidi Huberta Freybe; also writes as Katrin Holland; Christine Lambert.   American.   Born in Rostock, Germany, 8 September 1914, emigrated to U.S. in 1937: naturalized, 1947. Educated privately and in public and private schools in Italy, France, Switzerland, and England; attended the University of Zurich. Married 1) Joseph M. Loewengard in 1932 (died); 2) Sydney J. Lamon in 1957 (died). Full-time writer. Recipient: Le Grand Prix de Littérature Policière, 1950. Ph.D.: Colorado State Christian College, 1972. Member, American Academy of Achievement, 1975. Agent: Robert Lantz, 114 East 55th Street, New York, New York 10022. Address: 953 Fifth Avenue, New York, New York 10021, U.S.A.

CRIME PUBLICATIONS

Novels

No Surrender.   Boston, Little Brown, 1942; London, Chatto and Windus, 1943.
Without Orders.   Boston, Little Brown, 1943; London, Chatto and Windus, 1944.
None Shall Know.   Boston, Little Brown, 1945; London, Chatto and Windus, 1946.
Remembered Anger.   Boston, Little Brown, 1946.
After Midnight.   New York, Random House, 1948; London, Chatto and Windus, 1949.
Desperate Moment.   New York, Random House, and London, Chatto and Windus, 1951.
The Hunted Woman.   New York, Random House, 1952; London, Hodder and Stoughton, 1953.
Nightmare in Copenhagen.   New York, Random House, and London, Hodder and Stoughton, 1954.
The Mask of Alexander.   New York, Random House, 1955; London, Hodder and Stoughton, 1956.
The Linden Affair.   New York, Random House, 1956; as *The Story That Could Not Be Told*, London, Hodder and Stoughton, 1956.
A Day in Monte Carlo.   New York, Random House, and London, Hodder and Stoughton, 1959.
Meet Me Tonight.   New York, Random House, 1960; London, Hodder and Stoughton, 1961; as *Return to Terror*, New York, Ace, 1964.
A Call from Austria.   New York, Random House, and London, Hodder and Stoughton, 1963.
A Door Fell Shut.   New York, New American Library, and London, Hodder and Stoughton, 1966.
Rhine Replica.   New York, Random House, 1969; London, Hodder and Stoughton, 1970.
Manhattan North.   New York, Coward McCann, 1971; London, Hodder and Stoughton, 1972.
Zürich AZ/900.   New York, Holt Rinehart, 1974; London, Hodder and Stoughton, 1975.
A Taste of Terror.   London, Hodder and Stoughton, 1976; New York, Putnam, 1977.
Intermission.   London, Hodder and Stoughton, 1978; as *Final Score*, New York, St. Martin's Press, 1978.

OTHER PUBLICATIONS

Novels

Endure No Longer.   Boston, Little Brown, 1944; London, Chatto and Windus, 1945.
Whispering Hill.   New York, Random House, 1947; London, Chatto and Windus, 1948.
Wait for the Dawn.   New York, Random House, and London, Chatto and Windus, 1950.
The Obsession of Emmet Booth.   New York, Random House, 1957; London, Gollancz, 1958.
The Ball (as Christine Lambert).   New York, Atheneum, 1961.
A Sudden Woman (as Christine Lambert).   New York, Atheneum, 1964.

Novels as Katrin Holland

Man Spricht über Jacqueline.   Berlin, Ullstein, 1930.
Wie macht Man das Nur! (juvenile).   Oldenburg, Stalling, 1930.

Indisches Abendteuer.   Ahrbeck, Knorr and Hirth, 1932.
Unterwegs zu Alexander.   Berlin, Ullstein, 1932.
Die Silberne Wolke.   Berlin, Ullstein, 1933; as *The Silver Cloud*, London, Nicholson and Watson, 1936.
Ein Mädchen fiel vom Himmel.   Berlin, Ullstein, 1933; as *Girl Tumbles Out of the Sky*, London, Nicholson and Watson, 1934.
Jutta von Tilseck.   Ahrbeck, Knorr and Hirth, 1933.
Babbett auf Gottes Gnaden.   Berlin, Ullstein, 1934.
Das Frauenhaus.   Zurich, Orell Füssli, 1935; as *Youth Breaks In*, London, Nicholson and Watson, 1935.
Das Mädchen, das niemand Mochte (juvenile).   Berlin, Ullstein, 1935.
Sandro Irrt sich.   Zurich, Orell Füssli, 1936.
Einsamer Himmel.   Zurich, Orell Füssli, 1938.
Carlotta Torrensani.   Zurich, Orell Füssli, 1938.
Vierzehn Tage mit Edith.   Zurich, Orell Füssli, 1939.
Helene.   Zurich, Orell Füssli, 1940.

Play

Television Play: *Nightmare in Copenhagen.*

Manuscript Collection: Mugar Memorial Library, Boston University.

Martha Albrand comments:
My early novels published in Germany reflect the interest and concern of a young female writer with the romantic influences of that period. They were successful because the reading public in Germany wanted, besides a good story, a plot with which they could temporarily exit from reality.

But my first book published in America, *No Surrender*, changed my writing wittingly and unwittingly. It was a story of the Dutch underground fictionalized but basically as I'd known it firsthand. I considered it a novel, but the public again dictated its whims, for they saw the book as a suspense story. Because it was my initial exposure in America, I was labeled a suspense writer and more was expected to follow, particularly since the book was so successful. Therefore, the majority of my books published in America have been in the genre of suspense.

I found the genre to be a workable vehicle for my major concern as an author, namely the theme of personal freedom. Although this concept has frequently been politically realized in many of my books, I do not believe it is the only freedom valuable to the individual and have explored a variety of other freedoms, both in my suspense novels and in my non-suspense works.

Because I have traveled extensively most of my life and lived in many countries, I have always felt it important for people of different nationalities to become more knowledgeable of one another. And I have incorporated this philosophy into my writing.

I am primarily a storyteller. As a storyteller I must first decide if I want to tell the story through sheer development of action or through the development of characters or both. The latter requires the least artificial plot and is the most comfortable for me. I live with my characters – get to know them – before I actually start writing. Once I begin, the characters often dictate their personalities as well as the direction of the story. When I have completed the first draft, I must eliminate the unnecessary. Though all writing is a process of elimination, it is of the utmost importance in a suspense novel.

*   *   *

The strength of Martha Albrand's novels of suspense, most reviewers have agreed, is the superb sense of milieu and background in each of her books, as well as the way in which the setting contributes to the development of believable and interesting characters. Her first few novels in English were timely evocations of the crisis in Europe during World War II. Two novels of the underground were published in 1942 and 1943, although the former, *No Surrender*, was somewhat more favorably reviewed than the latter, *Without Orders*, which was described by the *New York Times* as a long novel "written in a hurry." *Endure No Longer*, a novel of pre-war Germany, analyzes the class structure in order to understand the causes of Germany's disaster. Immediately following the war, Albrand shifted her interest to postwar intrigue, concentrating on the aftermath of Nazism and the growing realization of the threat of Communism to ordinary European citizens.

Albrand has been best known as the author of novels of international intrigue, but she has also evidenced a consistent concern with the issues of domestic mystery; in *Whispering Hill* and *The Obsession of Emmet Booth*, the sensitive portrayal of emotional horrors inflicted in the name of love is especially well realized. Even in her international mysteries, however, the element of subtle torment in personal relationships is a constant theme.

Because Albrand has always been interested in the contemporary world, her novels over the years have changed in theme and focus. Although some of the earlier books are still popular enough to be in print, the later ones do not merely rework her earlier interests. *A Call from Austria* is about the discovery of a long-hidden Nazi treasure, still being used to fund nefarious projects. *Manhattan North* is a mystery about the murder of a Supreme Court Justice. *Zürich AZ/900* is about the attempt to steal an innovative treatment for arteriosclerosis in order to save the life of a Latin American dictator. Although background and situations change, however, most of her novels of suspense delineate the ways in which political considerations and conditions can affect and victimize individuals.

Critics are not always kind to Albrand, citing occasionally her haste and her tendency to melodrama. Readers, however, have responded for years to her fast-paced and complex plots. Consistently offering suspense and intrigue, she rarely repeats herself. Although she always solves the mystery, she does not always end the love story as neatly. Exigencies of plot determine the fate of characters. Taken as a whole, her long career may have produced few classics of the genre, but it has contributed a variety of sophisticated suspense novels for her fans.

—Kay J. Mussell

ALDING, Peter. See JEFFRIES, Roderic.

ALLAN, Dennis. See FOLEY, Rae.

ALLARDYCE, Paula. See BLACKSTOCK, Charity.

ALLBEURY, Ted (Theodore Edward le Bouthillier Allbeury). Also writes as Richard Butler. British. Born in Stockport, Cheshire, 24 October 1917. Educated at Slade Primary School, Erdington, Birmingham; King Edward's Grammar School, Aston, Birmingham. Served in the Intelligence Corps, 1940–47: Lt. Colonel. Married Grazyna Maria Felinska in 1971; has two daughters, and two children by two previous marriages. Foundry worker and junior draughtsman before the war; worked in sales and advertising after the war: Creative Director, E. Walter Lord, London, 1950–57; Managing Director, W. J. Southcombe, London, 1957–62; Managing Director of Pirate Radio Station Radio 390, 1964–67. Since 1964, Co-Founder, Allbeury Coombs & Partners, Tunbridge Wells, Kent. Member, BBC Advisory Council. Agent: Leslie Gardner, London Management, 235–241 Regent Street, London W1A 2JT. Address: Cheriton House, Furnace Lane, Lamberhurst, Kent, England.

CRIME PUBLICATIONS

Novels

>   *A Choice of Enemies.*   New York, St. Martin's Press, 1972; London, Davies, 1973.
>   *Snowball.*   London, Davies, and Philadelphia, Lippincott, 1974.
>   *Palomino Blonde.*   London, Davies, 1975; as *Omega Minus*, New York, Viking Press, 1975.
>   *The Special Collection.*   London, Davies, 1975.
>   *Where All the Girls Are Sweeter* (as Richard Butler).   London, Davies, 1975.
>   *Italian Assets* (as Richard Butler).   London, Davies, 1976.
>   *Moscow Quadrille.*   London, Davies, 1976.
>   *The Only Good German.*   London, Davies, 1976.
>   *The Man with the President's Mind.*   London, Davies, 1977; New York, Simon and Schuster, 1978.
>   *The Lantern Network.*   London, Davies, 1978.
>   *The Alpha List.*   London, Hart Davis MacGibbon, 1979.
>   *Consequence of Fear.*   London, Hart Davis MacGibbon, 1979.

OTHER PUBLICATIONS

Other

>   "Memoirs of an Ex-Spy," in *Murder Ink: The Mystery Reader's Companion*, edited by Dilys Winn. New York, Workman, 1977.

Manuscript Collection: Mugar Memorial Library, Boston University.

Ted Allbeury comments:
   I have tried in my novels to show that people employed in espionage or in intelligence work have private lives, and that their work affects their lives. The man who is tough in his intelligence work may compensate by always picking lame ducks so far as his ladies are concerned. Although so far I have had the nicest of reviews in all countries, there is

sometimes a comment that my books have sad endings. This, of course, is deliberate. I believe that all wars have sad endings for both losers and winners, and that those who are concerned with espionage and counter espionage tend to have sad endings even in peace time. In the real-life recruitment of intelligence agents, to want to do that kind of work would be considered a disadvantage. It is reckoned that it is better to use men who feel some doubt about the morality of what they are doing. This, naturally, has some disadvantages in operational terms, but it also has the advantage of avoiding excessive use of power. I have tried to get this over in my books. Although most of my books are anti-Communist and anti-KGB, I have nevertheless tried to paint a fairly full picture of Russian life and the life of a typical KGB man, and tried also to show their point of view. Reviewers have praised my novels for having authenticity, and I expect that this flows from my having done this type of work. But I hope that the authenticity has been provided in a fairly subtle way, as I dislike undue dwelling on hardware, organisation, and method. I didn't start writing until I was 54, and I had no particular ambition to be a writer, but starting late in life gives one a store of incident, characters, and location which is a great help. Like most writers, I concentrated on plot and action in my early books, and I hope that in my later books the characters themselves are more deeply and better explored. Having a full-time job and writing two novels a year requires a very strict discipline, but each source of income gives me a feeling of independence of the other, and that makes the routine full-time job more tolerable.

*   *   *

Links between real spying and espionage fiction have been a feature of that particular sub-genre of crime writing ever since its earliest modern days, and Ted Allbeury is one of not a few ex-agents to abandon the microdot for the commas and full-stops. Except, however, where the ex-agent was already a writer, like Somerset Maugham and Graham Greene, the resulting fiction generally has been only moderately successful. With Allbeury the case is altered.

An Army Intelligence officer during the 1939–45 War, it was not until 1970 that, quite unexpectedly, the writing bug bit and memories of the planting and detecting of listening bugs among other more alarming things emerged as fiction. Though his first book, *A Choice of Enemies*, was very well received, being chosen by the *New York Times* as one of the ten best thrillers of its year, from an artistic point of view it showed to some extent its origins. The facts tended to get in the way of the fiction, as they do more damagingly with so many ex-agents' novels.

But Allbeury wrote steadily and increasingly demonstrated that he had realised that a work of fiction is a work of fiction, that telling a story is its first and over-riding aim. And certainly by the time he wrote *The Man with the President's Mind*, he was producing work that stood comparison with the best in the field. It is a novel of true imagination which yet reflects its author's special knowledge of the way in which an agent in the field thinks. "Only someone who has done it," he once said, "knows what it feels like to arrest a man, shoot a man, assess a deadly opponent, chase and be chased." All of that remained in his books, but it no longer got in the way.

Not that facts, which can play an essential part in a certain sort of spy fiction, have dropped out of his books. Far from it. *The Man with the President's Mind*, for instance, is full of well-researched material with plenty of convincing detail about how the KGB operates, what it is like inside the White House or the offices of the British Special Branch or, for that matter, outside on the pavements of everyday Moscow. But the end result is not solely to convince us that this is how spying in the late 1970's was actually carried out (a long article in a magazine would do that better) but to make us feel that we have met real people, have inhabited their minds for a little, undergone with them experiences often far more terrible than anything likely to happen to us in our humdrum existences. Allbeury's people are real in the way that Greene's or Maugham's are. So that by the time one has finished this book one has not only lived excitingly and even wept inward tears for the sadness of things, but one has learnt about individuals and even about national consciousnesses. One's understanding of what makes the

Russians tick, for instance, has been quite simply enlarged. And this, though it is not the prime purpose of fiction, fulfils, as other Allbeury books have done, a political purpose in alerting readers in the West to a danger that exists for them.

But the books do more than warn us of political dangers. They tell us about ourselves, about people today, how they feel and how they think. And how they suffer. Because this is something that the spy novel, on the whole, can do much better than, say, the murder mystery. The death or deaths in a mystery often occur at a remove from the experiences of the characters we get to know: in a spy novel death or the threat of death is frequently central to the story (think of le Carré's *The Spy Who Came In from the Cold* or Greene's *The Human Factor*), and Allbeury is a writer who can handle suffering, make us feel the deep misery of tragedy, and even, because he is a writer, a novelist, make us realise that the tragedy is a part of a greater whole. There are not so many others in the suspense field who can do this.

—H.R.F. Keating

ALLEN, John. See **PERRY, Ritchie.**

ALLINGHAM, Margery (Louise). British. Born in London, 20 May 1904; daughter of the writer H. J. Allingham. Educated at Perse High School for Girls, Cambridge; Polytechnic of Speech Training. Married the artist and editor Philip Youngman Carter in 1927. *Died 30 June 1966.*

CRIME PUBLICATIONS

Novels (series character: Albert Campion)

> *The White Cottage Mystery.* London, Jarrolds, 1928.
> *The Crime at Black Dudley* (Campion). London, Jarrolds, 1929; as *The Black Dudley Murder*, New York, Doubleday, 1930.
> *Mystery Mile* (Campion). London, Jarrolds, and New York, Doubleday, 1930.
> *Look to the Lady* (Campion). London, Jarrolds, 1931; as *The Gyrth Chalice Mystery*, New York, Doubleday, 1931.
> *Police at the Funeral* (Campion). London, Heinemann, 1931; New York, Doubleday, 1932.
> *Sweet Danger* (Campion). London, Heinemann, 1933; as *Kingdom of Death*, New York, Doubleday, 1933; as *The Fear Sign*, New York, Macfadden, 1933.
> *Death of a Ghost* (Campion). London, Heinemann, and New York, Doubleday, 1934.
> *Flowers for the Judge* (Campion). London, Heinemann, and New York, Doubleday, 1936; as *Legacy in Blood*, New York, American Mercury, 1949.
> *Six Against the Yard*, with others. London, Selwyn and Blount, 1936; as *Six Against Scotland Yard*, New York, Doubleday, 1936.
> *Dancers in Mourning* (Campion). London, Heinemann, and New York, Doubleday,

1937; as *Who Killed Chloe?*, New York, Avon, 1943.

The Case of the Late Pig (Campion). London, Hodder and Stoughton, 1937.

Mr. Campion, Criminologist (includes *The Case of the Late Pig* and stories). New York, Doubleday, 1937.

The Fashion in Shrouds (Campion). London, Heinemann, and New York, Doubleday, 1938.

Black Plumes. London, Heinemann, and New York, Doubleday, 1940.

Traitor's Purse (Campion). London, Heinemann, and New York, Doubleday, 1941; as *The Sabotage Murder Mystery*, New York, Avon, 1943.

Coroner's Pidgin (Campion). London, Heinemann, 1945; as *Pearls Before Swine*, New York, Doubleday, 1945.

More Work for the Undertaker (Campion). London, Heinemann, 1948; New York, Doubleday, 1949.

Deadly Duo (2 novelets). New York, Doubleday, 1949; as *Take Two at Bedtime*, Kingswood, Surrey, World's Work, 1950.

The Tiger in the Smoke (Campion). London, Chatto and Windus, and New York, Doubleday, 1952.

No Love Lost (2 novelets). Kingswood, Surrey, World's Work, and New York, Doubleday, 1954.

The Beckoning Lady (Campion). London, Chatto and Windus, 1955; as *The Estate of the Beckoning Lady*, New York, Doubleday, 1955.

Hide My Eyes (Campion). London, Chatto and Windus, 1958; as *Tether's End*, New York, Doubleday, 1958; as *Ten Were Missing*, New York, Dell, 1959.

The China Governess (Campion). New York, Doubleday, 1962; London, Chatto and Windus, 1963.

The Mysterious Mr. Campion (omnibus). London, Chatto and Windus, 1963.

The Mind Readers (Campion). London, Chatto and Windus, and New York, Morrow, 1965.

Mr. Campion's Lady (omnibus, with stories). London, Chatto and Windus, 1965.

Cargo of Eagles (Campion; completed by Youngman Carter). London, Chatto and Windus, and New York, Morrow, 1968.

Short Stories

Mr. Campion and Others. London, Heinemann, 1939; augmented edition, London, Penguin, 1950.

Wanted: Someone Innocent (novelet and stories). N.p., Pony Books, 1946.

The Case Book of Mr. Campion, edited by Ellery Queen. New York, American Mercury, 1947.

The Allingham Case-Book. London, Chatto and Windus, and New York, Morrow, 1969.

Other Publications

Novels

Blackkerchief Dick: A Tale of Mersea Island. London, Hodder and Stoughton, and New York, Doubleday, 1923.

Dance of the Years. London, Joseph, 1943; as *The Gallantrys*, Boston, Little Brown, 1943.

Plays

Dido and Aeneas (produced London, 1922).

Water in a Sieve. London, French, 1925.

Other

The Oaken Heart.   London, Joseph, and New York, Doubleday, 1941.

*   *   *

A cook-book phrase perhaps best describes the writings of Margery Allingham: Boil until a rich consistency is reached. To some extent in everything she wrote and in her best books from start to finish she created worlds of her own, rich and romantic yet springing undeniably from the actual world in which she lived.

She had an extraordinary energy of observation that took objects and made them almost into people, forcing life as it is to marry with her high romantic outlook. As early as *Mystery Mile*, she could say of London that it "seemed to be huddled round his hotel room as if it were trying to squeeze the life out of it," and as late as *More Work for the Undertaker* we find the casual phrase "On the desk the telephone squatted patiently." The everyday was surely and simply made into something supercharged.

And if her energy made things into people, of her people it made beings at once recognisable as belonging to the world of which she wrote (chiefly teeming London and the mysterious salt-marshes of Essex) and at the same time demons or gods. Take Campion's faithful valet, Magersfontein Lugg: the very name combines verisimilitude (people were named after battles) and the tuppence, nay fourpence, coloured. Or take that splendid creation, the Scotland Yard man Charlie Luke. Hear him describe a local doctor: "Comes out of his flat nagged to a rag in the mornings and goes down into his surgery-room with a shop front like a laundry. Seven-and-six for a visit, half-a-dollar for a squint at your tonsils or a thorough once-over if he isn't sure, and a bottle of muck which does you good. Stooping. Back like a camel...." Charlie Luke, Margery Allingham continues, "talked with his whole body. When he described Doctor Smith's back his own arched. When he mentioned the shop front he squared it with his hands." It is a marvellously energetic portrait.

Allied to that superabundance of energy was a gift for the topsy-turvy. She had but to make a bishop visit a smart London restaurant (in *Coroner's Pidgin*) to remark, "It was typical of him that at that moment it was not he, but the Minoan, which appeared a little out of place." Such a thought process derived from her strong intuitive intelligence which over the years she came to bring to bear on a widening spectrum of human activity. It seems, in fact, to have been the experience of the 1939–45 war in England, during which she tackled a variety of jobs grimmer than writing, that moved her sympathies a vital layer deeper making her able to write, still within the confines of the crime novel, of evil and the great issues.

As early as 1936, however, she had produced in *Flowers for the Judge* a murder story that kept in all the dull bits that the crime writers of that age (and a good many even forty years later) omitted and, so infusing was her energy, that they read as grippingly as any smelly red herring trailed across lesser pages.

Her development is interestingly reflected in her handling of Albert Campion. Originally he was pretty much of a caricature, a cleverly updated version of Baroness Orczy's Scarlet Pimpernel, the indolent man-about-town who in reality ... (and is as well probably related to the Royal Family). But as the books she wrote became more serious, moving away from the skilfully fabricated romance, that two-dimensional detective became more and more of a hindrance. So gradually she froze him out until he was little more than a pair of observing eyes. Then came the trauma of the war. And in the post-war books Campion is quite a different figure, even physically. "There were new lines on his over-thin face and with their appearance some of his old misleading vacancy of expression had vanished." He became, in fact, Margery Allingham speaking.

In the post-war books her extraordinary energy expressed itself in a splendid certainty that marks every line she wrote. Pen in hand, she was afraid of no one. Cheerfully she labelled a county family as "frightful females who smell like puppies' breath." As confidently, she created a figure of real evil in the criminal Jack Havoc of *The Tiger in the Smoke*. She could write without straining of love and of death, death as a reality rather than that "body with a neat hole in the forehead" beloved of the straightforward whodunit writers.

She could compose a poem to put into the mouth of a character, and it is no bad creation. She could write a *Times* obituary that actually reads like words from that august newspaper (reproducing newspaper extracts is a feat which seems to fox almost every crime writer who tackles it, including those who have been journalists). She could produce a learned lecture joke that was exactly what such a curious piece of humour should be. And in *The Beckoning Lady* she casually invents a remark for Queen Victoria to have made of an ancestor that might have issued primly from the royal lips themselves.

Increasingly in the later books that strong female intelligence enabled her to say much that is penetrating and wise about men and women, perhaps especially women. And it is this which gives to these books (from which, alas, one must except the posthumously published *Cargo of Eagles*) a universality which some thirty years after the earliest of them was written makes them still immensely readable and is likely to make them readable a hundred years after their publication.

—H.R.F. Keating

AMBLER, Eric.   Also writes as Eliot Reed (with Charles Rodda).   British.   Educated at Colfe's Grammar School, London; London University. Served in the Royal Artillery, 1940–46; Assistant Director of Army Kinematography, 1944–46: Bronze Star (USA). Married 1) Louise Crombie in 1939; 2) the writer Joan Harrison in 1958. Engineering apprentice, 1928; advertising copywriter, 1928–37; director of an advertising agency, 1937–38. Recipient: Crime Writers Association Award, 1959, 1962, 1967, 1972; Mystery Writers of America Edgar Allan Poe Award, 1964, and Grand Master Award, 1975; Svenska Deckarakademins Grand Master, 1975. Agent: Linder A G, Jupiterstrasse 1, Postfach CH-8032 Zurich, Switzerland. Address: Chemin de l'Ile de Salagon 1, 1815 Clarens, Switzerland.

CRIME PUBLICATIONS

Novels (series characters: Charles Latimer; Arthur Abdel Simpson)

The Dark Frontier.   London, Hodder and Stoughton, 1936.
Uncommon Danger.   London, Hodder and Stoughton, 1937; as *Background to Danger*, New York, Knopf, 1937.
Epitaph for a Spy.   London, Hodder and Stoughton, 1938; New York, Knopf, 1952.
Cause for Alarm.   London, Hodder and Stoughton, 1938; New York, Knopf, 1939.
The Mask of Dimitrios (Latimer).   London, Hodder and Stoughton, 1939; as *A Coffin for Dimitrios*, New York, Knopf, 1939.
Journey into Fear.   London, Hodder and Stoughton, and New York, Knopf, 1940.
Judgment on Deltchev.   London, Hodder and Stoughton, and New York, Knopf, 1951.
The Schirmer Inheritance.   London, Heinemann, and New York, Knopf, 1953.
The Night-Comers.   London, Heinemann, 1956; as *State of Siege*, New York, Knopf, 1956.
Passage of Arms.   London, Heinemann, 1959; New York, Knopf, 1960.
The Light of Day (Simpson).   London, Heinemann, 1962; New York, Knopf, 1963; as *Topkapi*, New York, Bantam, 1964.

A Kind of Anger. London, Bodley Head, and New York, Atheneum, 1964.
Dirty Story (Simpson). London, Bodley Head, and New York, Atheneum, 1967.
The Intercom Conspiracy (Latimer). New York, Atheneum, 1969; London, Weidenfeld and Nicolson, 1970.
The Levanter. London, Weidenfeld and Nicolson, and New York, Atheneum, 1972.
Doctor Frigo. London, Weidenfeld and Nicolson, and New York, Atheneum, 1974.
Send No More Roses. London, Weidenfeld and Nicolson, 1977; as *The Siege of the Villa Lipp*, New York, Random House, 1977.

Novels as Eliot Reed (with Charles Rodda)

Skytip. New York, Doubleday, 1950; London, Hodder and Stoughton, 1951.
Tender to Danger. New York, Doubleday, 1951; as *Tender to Moonlight*, London, Hodder and Stoughton, 1952.
The Maras Affair. London, Collins, and New York, Doubleday, 1953.
Charter to Danger. London, Collins, 1954.
Passport to Panic. London, Collins, 1958.

Uncollected Short Stories

"The Army of the Shadows," in *The Queen's Book of the Red Cross.* London, Hodder and Stoughton, 1939.
"The Intrusions of Dr. Czissar" ("A Bird in the Tree," The Case of the Emerald Sky," "Case of the Gentleman Poet," "Case of the Landlady's Brother," "Case of the Overheated Flat," "The Case of the Pinchbeck Locket"), in *The Sketch* (London), 1940.
"The Blood Bargain," in *Winter's Crimes 2*, edited by George Hardinge. London, Macmillan, 1970.

Other Publications

Plays

Screenplays: *The Way Ahead*, with Peter Ustinov, 1944; *United States*, 1945; *The October Man*, 1947; *The Passionate Friends (One Woman's Story)*, with David Lean and Stanley Haynes, 1949; *Highly Dangerous*, 1950; *The Clouded Yellow*, 1950; *The Magic Box*, 1951; *Gigolo and Gigolette*, in *Encore*, 1951; *The Card (The Promoter)*, 1952; *Rough Shoot (Shoot First)*, 1953; *The Cruel Sea*, 1953; *Lease of Life*, 1954; *The Purple Plain*, 1954; *Yangtse Incident (Battle Hell)*, 1957; *A Night to Remember*, 1958; *The Wreck of the Mary Deare*, 1960; *Mutiny on the Bounty* (uncredited), with others, 1962; *Topkapi*, 1964; *Love Hate Love*, 1970.

Other

The Ability to Kill and Other Pieces. London, Bodley Head, 1963.
"Introduction" to *The Adventures of Sherlock Holmes*, by Arthur Conan Doyle. London, Murray-Cape, 1974.
"A Better Sort of Rubbish: An Inquiry into the State of the Thriller," in *The Times* (London), 30 November 1974.

Editor, *To Catch a Spy: An Anthology of Favourite Spy Stories.* London, Bodley Head, 1964; New York, Atheneum, 1965.

Bibliography: in *Uber Eric Ambler*, edited by Gerd Haffmans, Zurich, Diogenes Verlag, 1979.

Manuscript Collection: Mugar Memorial Library, Boston University.

*   *   *

Eric Ambler is a master of narrative; he tells his story economically but with all the detail necessary to establish its authenticity effectively; and his stories, which can be either complex or simple, have the essential ingredient of the successful thriller, suspense.

His early stories, notably *Uncommon Danger* and *Cause for Alarm*, set in the 1930's world of power politics, are fast-moving, hard-hitting stories which feature an innocent Englishman caught in a web of German, Italian, and Russian intrigue. They display a knowledge of European scenery, transport, and authoritarian societies which makes the action and the political policies involved seem convincing to the reader.

While these stories rightly established Ambler as an excellent storyteller, *The Mask of Dimitrios* marked a development in his idiosyncratic handling of the revelations of a plot, for here Latimer, a writer of detective stories, becomes intensely curious about the details of the life of a man called Dimitrios whose supposed body he sees in a morgue. The track he follows leads to past incidents of political assassination, drug-trafficking, pimping, double-crossing, and intrigue of many kinds, involving many changes of identity – until he discovers Dimitrios is dangerously alive. Latimer's thoughts, as he makes headway in his search for Dimitrios, are shared with the reader, and neither Dimitrios nor the mysterious Mr. Peters receives any sympathy. Indeed, this is a sordid world to which we are introduced, and its details are built up slowly, so that the life of a crook is revealed in a way which continues to hold our attention while demonstrating clearly to us the ruthless realities involved.

The picture of an ordinary man in the hands of the police had emerged in *Epitaph for a Spy*. In this story an innocent man is arrested and charged with espionage, since negatives apparently taken by his camera show a forbidden military area. But someone in his *pension* took the photographs: and the problem is which of them. The tension mounts steadily, and finally there is a roof-top chase; Ambler is at his best when the resolution of the plot erupts into swift action. The attitudes of Beghin, the man from the Sûreté-Générale, and the local police Commissaire are cold, the atmosphere for the innocent yet vulnerable man caught up in espionage is nightmarish, and the complications convincing.

This nightmarish quality can affect others as well as the innocent. For instance, Arthur Abdel Simpson, a battered adventurer who first appears in *The Light of Day*, is described in an Interpol dossier as an interpreter, chauffeur, waiter, pornographer, and guide. He makes an ill-advised attempt to rob a man who turns out to be a very sophisticated criminal, and is subsequently caught up in the activities of a mysterious heavily armed gang in Istanbul while being forced to act as an undercover agent for the Turkish secret police. In Arthur's subsequent appearance his antecedents are discussed directly by the British vice-consul in *Dirty Story*, to whom Arthur seems to be "a disgusting creature whose life is nothing but a long, dirty story." In this novel his efforts to obtain a passport – by any means – lead him from casting for blue films to becoming a mercenary in Central Africa, eventually escaping to Tangier. Arthur is indeed a rogue in the classical tradition but despite this we begin to sympathise with his predicaments, although the element of absurdity is a welcome touch as things go from bad to worse.

The Night-Comers is a simple story, concentrated and compelling. Ambler's realism brings the predicament of the main protagonists, an English engineer and a Eurasian girl, into sharp focus. They are involved unwillingly in the events of a military coup in an island off Indonesia, since their flat is on top of the local radio station which the rebels make their headquarters. The fighting goes on around the building as the government forces close in, and the engineer is forced to repair a generator so that the rebels' general can broadcast to the outside world. Both the Englishman and the Eurasian girl have acted as spectators, and this gives the story a balanced, double dimension which both sharpens the reader's view of the situation and engages his sympathy for the hapless pair.

In contrast, the plot of *A Kind of Anger* is highly complex, full of cross-purposes. Here a newspaper man is brought into a search for a missing girl, the mistress of a Kurdish conspirator, an Iraqi colonel, whose papers are sought by rival buyers. The newspaper man eventually helps the girl to sell them: this thriller affords a good example of Ambler's ability to create mounting tension as he unfolds the tangled skein of his story.

Complexity blended with the seedy, cynical secrecy of the world of espionage marks *The Intercom Conspiracy*. Ambler's use of Latimer allows him to tell the tale from different points of view. His professional competence is at its best here, with characters drawn sufficiently deeply for the needs of his steadily faster-moving plot. All the way he is working well within his limits, giving the reader exactly the right amount of realism, the right amount of information, none of it to excess, and all of it germane to the basic purpose of telling a story effectively.

In *Doctor Frigo* he allows himself more scope for the creation of character, this time the honesty of an assassinated dictator's son who does not want to return, does not – surprisingly – want power. The Caribbean setting is tawdry and lush, the suspense is kept up, the would-be innocent figure is again in the power of unscrupulous manipulators; as ever Ambler is economical, always efficient, highly evocative, detail matching suspense in superb narrative skill.

—A. Norman Jeffares

AMIS, Kingsley (William).   Also writes as Robert Markham.   British.   Born in London, 16 April 1922. Educated at City of London School; St. John's College, Oxford, M.A. Served in the Royal Corps of Signals, 1942–45. Married 1) Hilary Ann Bardwell in 1948 (marriage dissolved, 1965); 2) the writer Elizabeth Jane Howard in 1965; has three children. Lecturer in English, University College, Swansea, Wales, 1949–61; Fellow in English, Peterhouse, Cambridge, 1961–63. Visiting Fellow in Creative Writing, Princeton University, New Jersey, 1958–59; Visiting Professor, Vanderbilt University, Nashville, Tennessee, 1967. Recipient: Maugham Award, 1955; *Yorkshire Post* Award, 1974; John W. Campbell Memorial Award, for science fiction, 1976. Agent: Jonathan Clowes & Co., 19 Jeffrey's Place, London NW1 9PP, England.

Crime Publications

Novels

> *The Anti-Death League.*   London, Gollancz, and New York, Harcourt Brace, 1966.
> *Colonel Sun: A James Bond Adventure* (as Robert Markham).   London, Cape, and New York, Harper, 1968.
> *The Riverside Villas Murder.*   London, Cape, and New York, Harcourt Brace, 1973.

Short Story

> *The Darkwater Hall Mystery.*   Edinburgh, Tragara Press, 1978.

Other Publications

Novels

> *Lucky Jim.*   London, Gollancz, and New York, Doubleday, 1954.
> *That Uncertain Feeling.*   London, Gollancz, 1955; New York, Harcourt Brace, 1956.
> *I Like It Here.*   London, Gollancz, and New York, Harcourt Brace, 1958.
> *Take a Girl Like You.*   London, Gollancz, 1960; New York, Harcourt Brace. 1961.

One Fat Englishman. London, Gollancz, 1963; New York, Harcourt Brace, 1964.
The Egyptologists, with Robert Conquest. London, Cape, 1965; New York, Random House, 1966.
I Want It Now. London, Cape, 1968; New York, Harcourt Brace, 1969.
The Green Man. London, Cape, 1969; New York, Harcourt Brace, 1970.
Girl, 20. London, Cape, 1971; New York, Harcourt Brace, 1972.
Ending Up. London, Cape, and New York, Harcourt Brace, 1974.
The Alteration. London, Cape, 1976; New York, Viking Press, 1977.
Jake's Thing. London, Hutchinson, 1978; New York, Viking Press, 1979.

Short Stories

My Enemy's Enemy. London, Gollancz, 1962; New York, Harcourt Brace, 1963.
Penguin Modern Stories 11, with others. London, Penguin, 1972.
Dear Illusion. London, Covent Garden Press, 1972.

Plays

Radio Play: *Something Strange,* 1962.

Television Plays: *A Question about Hell,* 1964; *The Importance of Being Harry,* 1971; *Dr. Watson and the Darkwater Hall Mystery,* 1974; *See What You've Done* (*Softly, Softly* series), 1974; *We Are All Guilty* (*Against the Crowd* series), 1975.

Verse

Bright November. London, Fortune Press, 1947.
A Frame of Mind. Reading, Berkshire, Reading School of Art, 1953.
(Poems). Oxford, Fantasy Press, 1954.
A Case of Samples: Poems 1946–1956. London, Gollancz, 1956; New York, Harcourt Brace, 1957.
The Evans Country. Oxford, Fantasy Press, 1962.
Penguin Modern Poets 2, with Dom Moraes and Peter Porter. London, Penguin, 1962.
A Look round the Estate: Poems 1957–1967. London, Cape, 1967; New York, Harcourt Brace, 1968.
Collected Poems 1944–1979. London, Hutchinson, 1979.

Recordings: *Reading His Own Poems,* Listen, 1962; *Poems,* with Thomas Blackburn, Jupiter, 1962.

Other

Socialism and the Intellectuals. London, Fabian Society, 1957.
New Maps of Hell: A Survey of Science Fiction. New York, Harcourt Brace, 1960; London, Gollancz, 1961.
The James Bond Dossier. London, Cape, and New York, New American Library, 1965.
Lucky Jim's Politics. London, Conservative Political Centre, 1968.
What Became of Jane Austen? and Other Questions. London, Cape, 1970; New York, Harcourt Brace, 1971.
On Drink. London, Cape, 1972; New York, Harcourt Brace, 1973.
Kipling and His World. London, Thames and Hudson, 1975; New York, Scribner, 1976.

Editor, with James Michie, *Oxford Poetry 1949.* Oxford, Blackwell, 1949.

Editor, with Robert Conquest, *Spectrum: A Science Fiction Anthology.* London, Gollancz, 1961; New York, Harcourt Brace, 1962. (and later volumes)

Editor, *Selected Short Stories of G. K. Chesterton.* London, Faber, 1972.

Editor, *Tennyson.* London, Penguin, 1973.

Editor, *Harold's Years: The Harold Wilson Era.* New York, Horizon Press, 1977.

Editor, *The New Oxford Book of Light Verse.* London and New York, Oxford University Press, 1978.

Editor, *The Faber Popular Reciter.* London, Faber, 1978.

Bibliography: *Kingsley Amis: A Checklist* by Jack Benoit Cohn, Kent, Ohio, Kent State University Press, 1976.

Manuscript Collection: State University of New York, Buffalo.

*　　*　　*

Although he has made only one venture into the "pure" mystery novel, *The Riverside Villas Murders*, Kingsley Amis has worked around the form for many years. Like many of his characters and like the other "Angry Young Men," he has been a proponent of a variety of popular genres; *New Maps of Hell* is an early study of science fiction, *The Green Man* is an excellent and frightening ghost story, and *The James Bond Dossier* is a useful guide to the works of Ian Fleming. The *Dossier* obviously led to his writing *Colonel Sun* as "Robert Markham," the last James Bond adventure. Despite his enthusiasm for spy thrillers and his knowledge of the Bond novels, *Colonel Sun* is an uncommonly disappointing book, unworthy of its author and his original. Although his *The Anti-Death League* probably should be considered a failure, it does at least suggest some of the possibilities that the espionage novel can generate for thoughtful writers, perhaps the sort of spy novel Amis could write very well if he were to devote more of his considerable ability to the form.

The Riverside Villas Murders, however, is a very fine mystery. Set in the 1930's with a successful comprehension of the drabness of ordinary middle-class life of the time, it creates not only a good puzzle but also a believable cast of characters. Especially interesting is Amis's use of the mystery to introduce his young protagonist to the realities of death, sex, and filial love. The book very unpretentiously demonstrates that solving a murder can be an ambiguous and not entirely happy business and that through it a young, sensitive, decent boy can come of age. The novel makes one wish Amis would practice more in a form worthy of his talents.

—George Grella

ANDERSON, Frederick Irving. American. Born in Aurora, Illinois, 14 November 1877. Educated in public schools; Wharton School, University of Pennsylvania, Philadelphia, graduated 1899. Married Emma Helen de Zouche in 1908 (died, 1937). Worked as a journalist on the Aurora *News*, 1895–96, and New York *World*, 1898–1908. Free-lance writer from 1910. *Died 24 December 1947.*

Crime Publications

Novel

The Notorious Sophie Lang. London, Heinemann, 1925.

Short Stories

The Adventures of the Infallible Godahl. New York, Crowell, 1914.
The Book of Murder. New York, Dutton, 1930.

Uncollected Short Stories

"Madame the Cat," in *Best American Mystery Stories of the Year*, edited by Carolyn
    Wells. New York, Day, 1931.
"The Unknown Man," in *Ellery Queen's Mystery Magazine* (New York), July 1942.
"The Phantom Guest," in *Ellery Queen's Mystery Magazine* (New York), Winter 1942.
"The Jorgensen Plates," in *Female of the Species*, edited by Ellery Queen. Boston,
    Little Brown, 1943; as *Ladies of Crime*, London, Faber, 1947.
"Murder in Triplicate," in *Ellery Queen's Mystery Magazine* (New York), December
    1946.
"The Phantom Alibi," in *Ellery Queen's Mystery Magazine* (New York), November
    1947.
"The Half-Way House," in *Anthology 1963 Mid-Year*, edited by Ellery Queen. New
    York, Davis, 1963.

OTHER PUBLICATIONS

Other

The Farmer of To-morrow. New York, Macmillan, 1913.
Electricity for the Farm. New York, Macmillan, 1915.

*   *   *

Frederick Irving Anderson, although a fairly prolific writer for the American slick
magazines, is represented by only three fiction books, the first and third of which are among
the rarest collector's items.
   The Adventures of the Infallible Godahl narrates six adventures of a remarkable master
thief. An interesting touch is that Godahl employs the unwitting Oliver Armiston, a famous
writer of detective stories, to plan his greatest coup. Because of this, Armiston retired from
authorship. In *The Book of Murder* Armiston is again employed, but now by the great Deputy
Parr of the New York police, for assistance in unusual crimes. Together they work through
eight cases, all of which are characterized by a Baghdadian zest. The two remaining stories in
the book are concerned with crime in a rural setting, with other detective figures. In *The
Notorious Sophie Lang*, an episodic novel, the most brilliantly conceived female criminal in
the literature leads Parr and Armiston a long and frustrating chase through insurance fraud,
murder, a gem robbery, and other crimes. Sophie is always more than a match for them.
   Anderson has never achieved the recognition that he deserves. He was probably the only
detective story writer to capture successfully the pre-Titanic syndrome of ultra-sophistication
mingled with vulgarity, refinement with crude greed, hedonism with a zest for cultural color.
He brought a certain Stevensonian glamor and fairytale quality into even police routine. His
stories are intelligent, original, well-crafted, excellent in characterization, and often brilliant
stylistically.

—E. F. Bleiler

ANDERSON, James. British. Educated at grammar school and at Reading University,
B.A. in history. Has worked as salesman, copywriter, and journalist. Address: 4 Church
Road, Penarth, Glamorgan, Wales.

Crime Publications

Novels

Assassin. London, Constable, 1969; New York, Simon and Schuster, 1970.
The Alpha List. London, Constable, 1972; New York, Walker, 1973.
The Abolition of Death. London, Constable, 1974; New York, Walker, 1975.
The Affair of the Blood-Stained Egg Cosy. London, Constable, 1975; New York, McKay, 1977.
Appearance of Evil. London, Constable, 1977.
Angel of Death. London, Constable, 1978.

*   *   *

The first of James Anderson's novels to be widely reviewed in America was his affectionate variation on the classic British golden-age mystery novel, The Affair of the Blood-Stained Egg Cosy. The light touch Anderson displays in this criminous novel of manners might seem surprising to someone who has read only the three political thrillers, Assassin, The Abolition of Death, and Appearance of Evil, but Anderson's second novel, The Alpha List, which begins as a taut procedural, suddenly loses its leading character halfway through and acquires as a replacement a young woman with the naivety and gift for hard-nosed sleuthing of a contemporary Nancy Drew. She also takes on an assistant, a high-society post-debutante whose flippant attitude toward the vagaries of the upper class strikes an apparently uncharacteristic note which becomes dominant in Affair.

The stylistic incongruity of Alpha List is further compounded by a wildly skewered plot reminiscent of a schizoid Marric/Creasey performance in its awkward mix of procedural sobriety and melodramatic plotting, with a masked master criminal, an underground hideaway with top-secret files, and a final confrontation between heroine and villain in a deserted house in which, in good film serial fashion, a scream or a gunshot appears to lurk around every corner. This fondness for melodrama is also somewhat in evidence in The Abolition of Death, but here, as in Assassin, the monochromatic writing with its restraint in the handling of both plot and characters creates a greater sense of stylistic unity.

Appearance of Evil, Anderson's first post-Affair work, ends with a playful flourish that sabotages the narrative's tenuous credibility. Anderson's humor is more flavorful than his suspense, and it will be interesting to see to what extent he does or does not resolve tonal dissonances in his future work.

—Walter Albert

ANTHONY, Evelyn. Pseudonym for Evelyn Bridget Patricia Ward-Thomas, née Stephens. British. Born in London, 3 July 1928. Educated at Convent of the Sacred Heart, Roehampton, to 1944, and privately. Married Michael Ward-Thomas in 1955; two daughters and four sons. Recipient: Yorkshire Post award, 1973. Agent: A. P. Watt & Son, 26–28 Bedford Row, London WC1R 4HL, England. Address: Castlesize, Sallins, Co. Kildare, Ireland.

Crime Publications

Novels

The Rendezvous. London, Hutchinson, 1967; New York, Coward McCann, 1968.
The Legend. London, Hutchinson, and New York, Coward McCann, 1969.

The Assassin. London, Hutchinson, and New York, Coward McCann, 1970.

The Tamarind Seed. London, Hutchinson, and New York, Coward McCann, 1971.

The Poellenberg Inheritance. London, Hutchinson, and New York, Coward McCann, 1972.

The Occupying Power. London, Hutchinson, 1973; as *Stranger at the Gates*, New York, Coward McCann, 1973.

The Malaspiga Exit. London, Hutchinson, 1974; as *Mission to Malaspiga*, New York, Coward McCann, 1974.

The Persian Ransom. London, Hutchinson, 1975; as *The Persian Price*, New York, Coward McCann, 1975.

The Silver Falcon. London, Hutchinson, and New York, Coward McCann, 1977.

The Return. London, Hutchinson, and New York, Coward McCann, 1978.

The Grave of Truth. London, Hutchinson, 1979.

OTHER PUBLICATIONS

Novels

Imperial Highness. London, Museum Press, 1953; as *Rebel Princess*, New York, Crowell, 1953.

Curse Not the King. London, Museum Press, 1954; as *Royal Intrigue*, New York, Crowell, 1954.

Far Flies the Eagle. New York, Crowell, 1955.

Anne Boleyn. London, Museum Press, and New York, Crowell, 1957.

Victoria and Albert. New York, Crowell, 1958; as *Victoria*, London, Museum Press, 1959.

Elizabeth. London, Museum Press, 1960; as *All the Queen's Men*, New York, Crowell, 1960.

Charles the King. London, Museum Press, and New York, Doubleday, 1961.

Clandara. London, Hurst and Blackett, and New York, Doubleday, 1963.

The Heiress. London, Hurst and Blackett, and New York, Doubleday, 1964.

The French Bride. New York, Doubleday, 1964; London, Arrow, 1966.

Valentina. London, Hurst and Blackett, and New York, Doubleday, 1966.

Anne of Austria. London, Hurst and Blackett, 1968; as *The Cardinal and the Queen*, New York, Coward McCann, 1968.

Evelyn Anthony comments:
I seek only to entertain.

*   *   *

Evelyn Anthony's novels of suspense often begin with a situation out of today's headlines before developing into the type of international love story she writes so well. *The Rendezvous, The Poellenberg Inheritance,* and *The Occupying Power* all concern Nazi war criminals trying to escape punishment. *The Legend* and *The Tamarind Seed* are about Russian spies and defectors. *The Assassin* takes place in the midst of an American election during which a bizarre Russian assassination plot is unwittingly financed by an American millionaire. *The Malaspiga Exit* uncovers an international drug and art smuggling ring. *The Persian Ransom* is about a Palestine Liberation Organization kidnapping. *The Silver Falcon* is a novel of intrigue and sabotage in the world of international horse racing.

Although the initial events of each novel are motivated by current events, the action of the novels often involves more romance than intrigue. The villains may be evil in themselves, but political realities also pose an almost insurmountable threat to the lovers. In *The Rendezvous, The Legend,* and *The Persian Ransom,* one of the lovers is killed; in the other books, they are united, even if it means fleeing respectable society. Anthony's lovers in each novel are immediately identifiable to the reader by the strong and immutable sexual attraction they feel for each other. No matter how the book ends, the characters have no choice but to be motivated and controlled by that attraction.

Anthony is interested in victim psychology, a subject she handles with great skill, often depicting lovers whose relationship develops out of a captor-captive situation. *The Persian Ransom* is the most thorough evocation; the kidnapping victim and one of her captors fall in love, and he turns against his fellows to help her escape. In *The Rendezvous*, a former Nazi has a love affair with a woman he had interrogated during the war; he had been kind to her then and, although she remembers the experience with terror, she loves him. Characters in other Anthony books also find love a stronger motivation than politics.

—Kay J. Mussell

ANTONY, Peter. Pseudonym for the brothers Anthony Shaffer and Peter Shaffer. British. **SHAFFER, Anthony (Joshua):** Born in Liverpool, Lancashire, 15 May 1926. Educated at St. Paul's School, London; Trinity College, Cambridge (Editor, *Granta*), graduated 1950. Married to Carolyn Soley; two daughters. Worked as barrister and journalist. Recipient: Mystery Writers of America Edgar Allan Poe Award, for screenplay, 1973. Lives in Wiltshire. Agent: Fraser and Dunlop Scripts Ltd., 91 Regent Street, London W1R 8RU, England. **SHAFFER, Peter (Levin):** Born in Liverpool, Lancashire, 15 May 1926. Educated at St. Paul's School, London; Trinity College, Cambridge, 1947–50, B.A. 1950. Conscripted: coalminer, 1944–47. Worked in the acquisition department of the New York Public Library, 1951–54; worked for Boosey and Hawkes, music publishers, London, 1954–55; Literary Critic, *Truth*, 1956–57; Music Critic, *Time and Tide*, 1961–62. Recipient: *Evening Standard* award, for drama, 1958; New York Drama Critics Circle Award, 1960, 1975; Tony Award, for drama, 1975. Address: 18 Earl's Terrace, London W.8, England.

CRIME PUBLICATIONS

Novels (series character: Mr. Verity)

> *The Woman in the Wardrobe* (Verity).   London, Evans, 1951.
> *How Doth the Little Crocodile?* (Verity).   London, Evans, 1952; New York, Macmillan, 1957.
> *Withered Murder* (as Anthony and Peter Shaffer).   London, Gollancz, 1955; New York, Macmillan, 1956.
> *Absolution* (by Anthony Shaffer).   London, Severn House, 1979.

OTHER PUBLICATIONS

Novel by Anthony Shaffer

> *The Wicker Man*, with Robin Hardy.   New York, Crown, 1978.

Plays by Anthony Shafer

> *The Savage Parade* (produced London, 1963).

Sleuth (produced London and New York, 1970). New York, Dodd Mead, 1970; London, Calder and Boyars, 1971.
Murderer (produced Brighton and London, 1975). London, Boyars, 1977.
The Case of the Oily Levantine (produced Richmond, Surrey, and London, 1979).

Screenplays: *Black Comedy*; *Mr. Forbush and the Penguins*, 1971; *Frenzy*, 1972; *Sleuth*, 1973; *The Wicker Man*, 1973; *The Goshawk Squadron*, 1973; *Masada*, 1974; *The Moonstone*, 1975; *Evil under the Sun*, 1976; *Absolution*, 1976; *Death on the Nile*, 1977.

Television Play: *Pig in the Middle*.

Plays by Peter Shaffer

Five Finger Exercise (produced London, 1958; New York, 1959). London, Hamish Hamilton 1958; New York, Harcourt Brace, 1959.
The Private Ear and The Public Eye (produced London, 1962; New York, 1963). London, Hamish Hamilton, 1962; New York, Stein and Day, 1964.
The Merry Roosters Panto, with the Theatre Workshop (produced London, 1963).
Sketch in *The Establishment* (produced New York, 1963).
The Royal Hunt of the Sun: A Play Concerning the Conquest of Peru (produced Chichester and London, 1964; New York, 1965). London, Hamish Hamilton, 1964; New York, Stein and Day, 1965.
Black Comedy (produced Chichester, 1965; London, 1966; New York, 1967). Included in *Black Comedy, Including White Lies*, 1967; London, French, 1968.
A Warning Game (produced New York, 1967).
White Lies (produced New York, 1967). Included in *Black Comedy, Including White Lies*, 1967; as *The White Liars* (produced London, 1968), London, French, 1967 (revised version, produced London and New York, 1976), French, 1976.
Black Comedy, Including White Lies: Two Plays. New York, Stein and Day, 1967; as *The White Liars, Black Comedy: Two Plays*, London, Hamish Hamilton, 1968.
It's about Cinderella (produced London, 1969).
Shrivings (as *The Battle of Shrivings*, produced London, 1970). London, Deutsch, 1974; in *Equus and Shrivings*, 1974.
Equus (produced London, 1973; New York, 1974). London, Deutsch, 1973; in *Equus and Shrivings*, 1974.
Equus and Shrivings: Two Plays. New York, Atheneum, 1974.

Screenplays: *Lord of the Flies*, with Peter Brook, 1963; *The Public Eye (Follow Me!)*, 1972.

Radio Play: *The Prodigal Father*, 1957.

Television Plays: *The Salt Land*, 1955; *Balance of Terror*, 1957.

* * *

In the first of their three books, *The Woman in the Wardrobe*, the Shaffer brothers set the scene in a seaside resort and introduce their detective, Mr. Verity. (In the last book his name was inexplicably changed to Fathom.) There is in the literature a long tradition of eccentric detectives, and Verity is true to that tradition. He is described as "an immense man, just tall enough to carry his breadth majestically. His face was sharp, smooth and teak-brown; his blue eyes small and of a startling brilliance. He wore a fine chestnut Van-Dyck and an habitual cloak in winter, all of which lent him in equal proportions the roles of a corpulent

Satyr and an elderly Laughing Cavalier." His passions were twofold, black Cuban cigars and collecting statuary. He made constant use, we are told, of a huge purple bathing costume purchased in 1924 from a fruit merchant in Beirut. But the Shaffers do not maroon their strangely behaved detective in a world of normal people. He is quickly joined by Detective Inspector Rambler, a man almost as large and unusual as himself, and, in the first book only, by the irritating Richard Tudor, a latter-day pretender to the throne. Equally odd characters appear in the later books.

For their main themes the authors also choose from the classical repertory. Two of the books present problems of impossible crime after the manner of Edgar Allan Poe, while the other is concerned with that fine old detective story institution, the Criminologists' Club, established for the discussion of crime considered as a fine art.

It is not then the basic ingredients of the Shaffers' books which make them stand out from the rest; it is the manner in which they handle those ingredients. Take first the plots. Locked-room murders and murder clubs were hardly new departures; indeed the literature of the twenties and thirties abounded with them. Yet most of those books are now forgotten, and deservedly so because they were generally dull, wordy affairs with no vestige of originality in problem or solution. In comparison the Shaffers shine. Their first book somehow manages to invest that hardy perennial, the locked-room murder, with a brilliant original tongue-in-cheek solution which a hundred other authors had overlooked. In fact this book may well be the best locked-room novel written in the last thirty years. Their second contains a devious and diabolical plot of multiple murder to which a solution of equal merit is provided, while their third returns unashamedly to impossible crime and sets down yet another new and ingenious explanation.

Finally in considering the success of the novels there is another major factor which must not be overlooked, their humour. They are witty, full of telling observations and apt descriptions, and best of all they display their writers' rare ability to poke gentle fun at the time-worn form, and incidentally at themselves. There can be no doubt that the authors are devotees of the detective novel, but there can also be no doubt that they have never taken the subject or themselves too seriously. The result is a small but heady brew of the highest quality.

—Robert C. S. Adey

ARCHER, Frank. See **WAYLAND, Patrick.**

ARDEN, William. See **COLLINS, Michael.**

ARDIES, Tom. American. Born in Seattle, Washington, 5 August 1931. Educated at Daniel McIntyre Collegiate Institute, Winnipeg, Manitoba. Served in the United States Air Force. Married Sharon Bernard in 1963; two children. Journalist: reporter, columnist, and editorial writer, Vancouver *Sun*, 1950–64; telegraph editor, *Honolulu Star Bulletin*, 1964–65. Special Assistant to Governor of Guam, 1965–67. Address: 3985 Lakeside Road, Penticton, British Columbia, Canada.

CRIME PUBLICATIONS

Novels (series character: Charlie Sparrow)

Their Man in the White House (Sparrow).   New York, Doubleday, and London, Macmillan, 1971.
This Suitcase Is Going to Explode (Sparrow).   New York, Doubleday, and London, Macmillan, 1972.
Pandemic (Sparrow).   New York, Doubleday, 1973; London, Angus and Robertson, 1974.
Kosygin Is Coming.   New York, Doubleday, 1974; London, Angus and Robertson, 1975.
Russian Roulette.   London, Panther, 1975.
In a Lady's Service.   New York, Doubleday, 1976.
Palm Springs.   New York, Doubleday, 1978.

*   *   *

Tom Ardies's early novels, *Their Man in the White House*, *This Suitcase Is Going to Explode*, and *Pandemic*, are facile tales of counter-espionage whose plots follow a "minutes to midnight" pattern, culminating in dramatic, but implausible, climaxes. Charlie Sparrow is their hero: a handsome, cocky spy, good with women, and always the victor, be it pitting his will against both his superiors, the CIA, and the fanatical enemy to save the nation from World War III, as in one book, or preventing the outbreak of a flu-virus pandemic, as in another. Sparrow descends from the chivalric and outlaw traditions, a kind of modern knight errant and Dick Turpin. Capable of ball-breaking when he needs valuable information fast, a stud with women, he is nonetheless, the democratic hero, an individualist, crude, but governed by a moral code that demands that fanatics who use cloning, lobotomies, or nuclear reactions for evil ends be defeated.

Kosygin Is Coming and *In a Lady's Service*, a spy story and a spoof, are Ardies's best novels. Earlier, detailed accounts of germ warfare and the Manhattan project did not lend plausibility to his plots. In *Kosygin Is Coming*, he used the Warren Commission report to give his story an inferior version of the chilling relevance Robert Ludlum brilliantly accomplishes. In his spoof, his journalistic tidbits yield a Dip Threat, Mission-Impossible-like directives, and a ludicrous parody of his own plots. In both, the plots are tighter, complications more zany, and characters more convincing. Shaver, the bungling cop suspended from the Royal Canadian Mounted police who foils the KGB and CIA, and Buchanan, a ne'er-do-well in Mexico who disguises himself as a pansy, a gigolo, and a remittance man, are among his best characters.

—Carol Simpson Stern

ARMSTRONG, Charlotte. Also wrote as Jo Valentine.   American.   Born in Vulcan, Michigan, in 1905. Educated at the University of Wisconsin, Madison; Barnard College New York, B.A. 1925. Married Jack Lewi; one daughter and two sons. Worked in the *New York Times* advertising department, as a fashion reporter for *Breath of the Avenue* (a buyer's guide), and in an accounting firm. Recipient: Mystery Writers of America Edgar Allan Poe Award, 1956. *Died 18 July 1969.*

CRIME PUBLICATIONS

Novels (series character: MacDougal Duff)

Lay On, Mac Duff! (Duff). New York, Coward McCann, 1942; London, Gifford, 1943.

The Case of the Weird Sisters (Duff). New York, Coward McCann, and London, Gifford, 1943.

The Innocent Flower (Duff). New York, Coward McCann, 1945; as *Death Filled the Glass*, London, Cherry Tree Books, 1945.

The Unsuspected. New York, Coward McCann, 1946; London, Harrap, 1947.

The Chocolate Cobweb. New York, Coward McCann, 1948; London, Davies, 1952.

Mischief. New York, Coward McCann, 1950; London, Davies, 1951.

The Black-Eyed Stranger. New York, Coward McCann, 1951; London, Davies, 1952.

Catch-as-Catch-Can. New York, Coward McCann, 1952; London, Davies, 1953; as *Walk Out on Death*, New York, Pocket Books, 1954.

The Trouble in Thor (as Jo Valentine). New York, Coward McCann, and London, Davies, 1953; as *And Sometimes Death*, New York, Pocket Books, 1954.

The Better to Eat You. New York, Coward McCann, and London, Davies, 1954; as *Murder's Nest*, New York, Pocket Books, 1954.

The Dream Walker. New York, Coward McCann, and London, Davies, 1955; as *Alibi for Murder*, New York, Pocket Books, 1956.

A Dram of Poison. New York, Coward McCann, and London, Davies, 1956.

Mask of Evil. New York, Fawcett, 1958.

The Seventeen Widows of Sans Souci. New York, Coward McCann, and London, Davies, 1959.

Duo: The Girl with a Secret, Incident at a Corner. New York, Coward McCann, 1959; London, Davies, 1960.

Something Blue. New York, Ace, 1962.

Who's Been Sitting in My Chair? New York, Ace, 1962.

Then Came Two Women. New York, Ace, 1962.

A Little Less Than Kind. New York, Coward McCann, 1963; London, Collins, 1964.

The Mark of the Hand. New York, Ace, 1963.

The One-Faced Girl. New York, Ace, 1963.

The Witch's House. New York, Coward McCann, 1963; London, Collins, 1964.

The Turret Room. New York, Coward McCann, and London, Collins, 1965.

Dream of Fair Woman. New York, Coward McCann, and London, Collins, 1966.

The Gift Shop. New York, Coward McCann, and London, Collins, 1967.

Lemon in the Basket. New York, Coward McCann, 1967; London, Collins, 1968.

The Balloon Man. New York, Coward McCann, and London, Collins, 1968.

Seven Seats to the Moon. New York, Coward McCann, and London, Collins, 1969.

The Protege. New York, Coward McCann, and London, Collins, 1970.

Short Stories

The Albatross. New York, Coward McCann, 1957; London, Davies, 1958.

I See You. New York, Coward McCann, 1966.

Uncollected Short Stories

"More Than One Kind of Luck," in *Ellery Queen's Mystery Magazine* (New York), December 1967.

"The Splintered Monday," in *Ellery Queen's All-Star Lineup.* New York, New American Library, 1967.

"The Cool Ones," in *Ellery Queen's Mystery Parade.* New York, New American Library, 1968.

"The Light Next Door," in *Ellery Queen's Mystery Magazine* (New York), January 1969.

"Night Call," in *Ellery Queen's Mystery Magazine* (New York), April 1969.

"From Out of the Garden," in *Ellery Queen's Murder Menu.* Cleveland, World, 1969.

"The Second Commandment," in *Ellery Queen's Aces of Mystery*.   New York, Davis, 1975.

OTHER PUBLICATIONS

Plays

The Happiest Days (produced New York, 1939).
Ring Around Elizabeth (produced New York, 1940).   New York, French, 1942.

Screenplays: *The Unsuspected*, 1947; *Don't Bother to Knock*, 1952.

Manuscript Collection: Mugar Memorial Library, Boston University.

*   *   *

Charlotte Armstrong was one of America's most energetic practical moralists, who masqueraded for 28 years as a successful suspense novelist. The best of her work still packs a high degree of tension into the plot. Armstrong was an expert at creating a situation in which an innocent is threatened, setting a rescue effort in motion, and then manipulating the world of ordinary events into a crescendo of perfectly maddening delays and mishaps. *Catch-as-Catch-Can*, *The Gift Shop*, and *The Witch's House* are good examples of her technique.

As a moralist, she was not insensitive to the psychology of groups or individuals. But she had a distaste for looking at abnormal psychology in as much depth as Margaret Millar or Patricia Highsmith. Armstrong was a competent observer with such insights as are available to the intelligent adult, and a vigorous expositor of her findings. One of her early successes was *The Unsuspected*; it is built around a convincing portrait of a modern Svengali, who hypnotizes by projecting an uncritical love, in a commandingly beautiful voice. Luther Grandison has even convinced the richer of his two wards that she is ugly, so that she will believe that he loves her despite her lack of beauty. *The Witch's House*, though not first rate Armstrong, has a good study of an adolescent girl who has retreated to a world of fantasy because the adults around her don't trouble to introduce her to the real one. Her isolation and self-dramatization are ludicrous and faintly frightening. In *A Little Less Than Kind*, Armstrong reveals a positive dislike of coddling the emotionally ill by giving them too much understanding. The book reworks *Hamlet* by taking the premise that if Hamlet believed on insufficient evidence that his father had been murdered, then he was neurotic, and very destructive. The book is unsuccessful because Ladd Cunningham, the Hamlet figure, is one of Armstrong's flimsiest characters. He reveals her lack of patience with those who, for whatever reason, refuse to *think*.

The kind of psychology that Armstrong did grasp was that of sane and decent people. In most of her best work, it is the people who live as though their behavior mattered who manage to get themselves out of some very tight places, or to save the innocents who are threatened by the forces of evil. Again and again, the good prevail because they come up with the understanding, the courage, the resourcefulness, or the friends that tip the balance. The evil doers include the greedy, the manipulators, the plotters, and, above all, those who lie to themselves as well as others. In *The Seventeen Widows of Sans Souci* one of the characters coins the term "li-ee," to describe those who force others to lie to them by giving the impression that anything but a sanitized version of reality would kill them. The hard core "li-ee" in that novel proves to be a very dangerous friend.

The best of Armstrong's novels and stories discuss practical moral problems, and even philosophical ones, while the plot holds the reader in suspense. In *A Dram of Poison*, one of her best, a group of people discuss the questions of free will and determinism with great relish while trying to find a dose of poison disguised as olive oil before someone cooks dinner with it. The enemy of life and health in this novel is an amateur psychologist who manages to convince her brother and his young wife that they are variously doomed, guilty of destructive impulses, and that the love they have discovered for each other, but not had a chance to declare, is futile. The cast of characters who join this couple in the search for the poison includes a blond nurse who is anything but dumb, a ruminative bus driver, a portly society matron with the mind of a general and the heart of a woman, and several other non-conformists. These good samaritans throw the newlyweds back into each other's arms, after they have settled the hash of irresponsible psychologizers, determinists, and all those who stereotype large or small groups of people.

Armstrong was quite aware of the power of the wealthy and the injustice they can inflict on the poor who get in their way. The hero of *The Turret Room* has already suffered grossly at the hands of his wife's family when he returns to their house at the opening of the book. He walks into trouble, because another crime has just been committed which the Whitman's would love to pin on him, as they did once before, because it is so much more convenient than finding out where the blame really lies. Fortunately, a young woman who does social work and feels for the underdog comes to his rescue. In *The Balloon Man*, the heroine is a young woman who simply wants to get out of a bad marriage with custody of her young son. She is a fine example of the Armstrong heroine, penniless, but bright, resourceful, and determined. The man her father-in-law hires to defame her is shrewd, imaginative, and nervy, but he is just outmatched. Both these novels have convincing casts and plots timed to the split second. And they are largely unmarred by the sentimentality that is the defect of Armstrong's literary virtues. There is a distinct coyness in the handling of dialogue and character in *The Witch's House* and *Lemon in the Basket*, as well as in the earlier gothic romances like *The Chocolate Cobweb* and *The Better to Eat You*.

Although Armstrong's short story "The Enemy" won the *Ellery Queen Mystery Magazine* contest, that story is surpassed by four others in the volume in which it is collected, including the title novelette, "The Albatross." That story, and "Laugh It Off," "Miss Murphy," and "Ride with the Executioner" are all built around encounters with society's misfits. They are shocking, tightly plotted, and very convincing. Two stories from a later collection, "How They Met," and the title story, "I See You," are unconventional and beautiful love stories.

—Carol Cleveland

ARMSTRONG, Raymond. See **CORRIGAN, Mark.**

ARTHUR, Frank. Pseudonym for Arthur Frank Ebert. British. Born in Islington, London, 27 October 1902. Educated at Colfe's Grammar School, London. Served in the Home Guard, 1940–44. Married Eileen Reynolds Clarkson in 1929 (died, 1974); one daughter and one son. Clerk in a leather factory, London, 1919–27; salesman, Auckland, New Zealand, 1928; accountant in the Fiji Islands, 1928–34, and for the New Zealand dairy industry, London, 1935–39; served in the Ministry of Food, later the Ministry of Agriculture, Fisheries, and Food, London, 1939–67. Writes romantic fiction under another pseudonym. Vice-Chairman, 1963–75, and since 1975, Vice-President, Society of Civil Service Authors. Honorary Librarian, Crime Writers Association, 1969–76. M.B.E. (Member, Order of the British Empire), 1947. Address: 106 Southborough Road, Bromley, Kent BR1 2ER, England.

CRIME PUBLICATIONS

Novels (series character: Inspector Spearpoint)

Who Killed Netta Maul? (Spearpoint).   London, Gollancz, 1940; as *The Suva Harbour Mystery*, London, Penguin, 1948.
Another Mystery in Suva (Spearpoint).   London, Heinemann, 1956.
Murder in the Tropic Night (Spearpoint).   London, Jenkins, 1961.
The Throbbing Dark (Spearpoint).   London, Jenkins, 1963.
Confession to Murder.   London, United Writers, 1974.

OTHER PUBLICATIONS

Novel

The Abandoned Woman: The Story of Lucy Walter (1630–1658).   London, Heinemann, 1964.

Plays

The Willsons of Lewis'm (produced London, 1949).
Time's a Thief.   London, French, 1952.
Twenty Minutes with Mrs. Oakentubb.   London, J. Garnett Miller, 1955.
She Would Not Dance.   London, Quekett, 1956.
The Profit from Murder.   London, Hub, 1974.

Other

Captain Rocco Rides to Sheffield (juvenile).   London, Chatto and Windus, 1975.

Frank Arthur comments:
All my *crime* novels are set in the Fiji Islands, where I resided from 1928 to 1934. The first four are straightforward, old-fashioned puzzle detective stories, with a corpse on page 1 and the murderer indicated on the last page; they are told from the point of view of Inspector Spearpoint of the Fiji Constabulary. *Confession to Murder*, which I regard as my best crime novel, is told in the first person by Frank Arthur, writing in old age of how his adulterous wife was murdered many years ago. It is complete fiction.

My most important novel is *The Abandoned Woman*, the autobiography of the mother of the Duke of Monmouth, based on considerable research and only in one place including an incident that could not have happened. I have recently completed a long non-fiction study of the problems arising from the scant records of the career of Lucy Walter.

*   *   *

Frank Arthur's Fijian detective novels are few in number, but Inspector Spearpoint of Suva is in his way an impressive character. Not generally strong on characterisation, Arthur presents Spearpoint as essentially human but one who knows the respect (even fear) in which he is held by so many of the multi-national inhabitants of Fiji. Without the favour expected by the higher-class residents, he steers his bulky frame and intellectual ability in relentless pursuit of evil-doers.

There are certain strands running through all the Spearpoint books, of which the first (*Who Killed Netta Maul?*) is the best. The tropical atmosphere, enough to get tempers running high, is well conveyed if a trifle theatrical. The cast of characters – a steaming mixture of Fijians, Europeans, part-Europeans, and Indians – is superficially drawn, but adequately enough to show the attitudes dividing races and social classes. Their customs and languages, both official and pidgin, are areas in which Arthur is clearly at home. In these respects his books have something in common with the Australian tales of Arthur Upfield, and Spearpoint with Bonaparte. The superiority of the whites, the subjection of the blacks – no doubt a realistic picture at the time – combine with the eerie tropical atmosphere to present a backcloth against which murder seems quite inevitable.

As plots they are not strong or particularly ingenious; suspicion falls upon one character after another, and the murderer is usually revealed to be someone who has made a rather fleeting appearance. Nevertheless, one's disappointment is alleviated by the novelty of the setting and Arthur's easy and occasionally humorous style.

—Melvyn Barnes

ASHDOWN, Clifford.   See FREEMAN, R. Austin.

ASHE, Gordon.   See CREASEY, John.

ASHFORD, Jeffrey.   See JEFFRIES, Roderic.

ASIMOV, Isaac.   Also writes as Paul French.   American.   Born in Petrovichi, Russia, 2 January 1920; emigrated to the United States in 1923; naturalized, 1928. Educated at Columbia University. New York. B.S. 1939. M.A. 1941. Ph.D. 1948. Served in the United States Army, 1945–46. Married 1) Gertrude Blugerman in 1942 (divorced), one son and one daughter; 2) Janet Opal Jeppson in 1973. Instructor in Biochemistry, 1949–51, Assistant Professor, 1951–55, and since 1955 Associate Professor, Boston University School of Medicine. Recipient: Edison Foundation National Mass Media Award, 1958; Blakeslee Award, for non-fiction, 1960; American Chemical Society James T. Grady Award, 1965; American Association for the Advancement of Science-Westinghouse Science Writing Award, 1967; Hugo Award, 1973; Science Fiction Writers Award, 1973. Address: 10 West 66th Street, New York, New York 10023, U.S.A.

CRIME PUBLICATIONS

Novels

The Caves of Steel. New York, Doubleday, and London, Boardman, 1954.
The Naked Sun. New York, Doubleday, 1957; London, Joseph, 1958.
The Death Dealers. New York, Avon, 1958; as A Whiff of Death, New York, Walker,
    and London, Gollancz, 1968.
Murder at the ABA. New York, Doubleday, 1976; as Authorized Murder, London,
    Gollancz, 1976.

Short Stories

Asimov's Mysteries. New York, Doubleday, and London, Rapp and Whiting, 1968.
Tales of the Black Widowers. New York, Doubleday, 1974.
More Tales of the Black Widowers. New York, Doubleday, 1976; London, Gollancz,
    1977.

Uncollected Short Stories

"The Sports Page," in Ellery Queen's Mystery Magazine (New York), April 1977.
"The Thirteenth Day of Christmas," in Ellery Queen's Mystery Magazine (New York),
    July 1977.
"The Next Day," in Ellery Queen's Mystery Magazine (New York), May 1978.
"A Matter of Irridescence," in Ellery Queen's Mystery Magazine (New York), March
    1979.
"None So Blind," in Ellery Queen's Mystery Magazine (New York), June 1979.
"To the Barest," in Ellery Queen's Mystery Magazine (New York), August 1979.

OTHER PUBLICATIONS

Novels

Pebble in the Sky. New York, Doubleday, 1950; London, Sidgwick and Jackson,
    1968.
The Stars, Like Dust. New York, Doubleday, 1951; as The Rebellious Stars, New
    York, Ace, 1954.
Foundation. New York, Gnome Press, 1951; London, Weidenfeld and Nicolson,
    1953; abridgement, as The 1,000-Year Plan, New York, Ace, 1955.
Foundation and Empire. New York, Gnome Press, 1952; London, Panther, 1962; as
    The Man Who Upset the Universe, New York, Ace, 1955.
The Currents of Space. New York, Doubleday, 1952; London, Boardman, 1955.
Second Foundation. New York, Gnome Press, 1953.
The End of Eternity. New York, Doubleday, 1955; London, Panther, 1958.
Fantastic Voyage (novelization of screenplay). Boston, Houghton Mifflin, and London,
    Dobson, 1966.
The Gods Themselves. New York, Doubleday, and London, Gollancz, 1972.
The Collected Fiction: The Far Ends of Time and Earth, Prisoners of the Stars. New
    York, Doubleday, 2 vols., 1979.

Short Stories

I, Robot. New York, Gnome Press, 1950; London, Grayson, 1952.
The Martian Way and Other Stories. New York, Doubleday, 1955; London, Dobson,
    1964.
Earth Is Room Enough. New York, Doubleday, 1957; London, Panther, 1960.

Nine Tomorrows: Tales of the Near Future. New York, Doubleday, 1959; London, Dobson, 1963.
The Rest of the Robots. New York, Doubleday, 1964.
Through a Glass, Clearly. London, New English Library, 1967.
Nightfall and Other Stories. New York, Doubleday, 1969; London, Rapp and Whiting, 1970.
The Early Asimov; or, Eleven Years of Trying. New York, Doubleday, 1972.
The Best of Isaac Asimov (1939–1972). London, Sidgwick and Jackson, 1973; New York, Doubleday, 1974.
Have You Seen These? Cambridge, Massachusetts, NESFA, 1974.
The Heavenly Host. New York, Walker, 1975.
Buy Jupiter and Other Stories. New York, Doubleday, 1975; London, Gollancz, 1976.
The Dream, Benjamin's Dream, Benjamin's Bicentennial Blast. Privately printed, 1976.
The Bicentennial Man and Other Stories. New York, Doubleday, and London, Gollancz, 1976.
Good Taste. Topeka, Kansas, Apocalypse Press, 1976.

Verse

Lecherous Limericks. New York, Walker, 1975; London, Corgi, 1977.
More Lecherous Limericks. New York, Walker, 1976.
Still More Lecherous Limericks. New York, Walker, 1977.
Asimov's Sherlockian Limericks. Yonkers, New York, Mysterious Press, 1978.
Limericks: Too Gross, with John Ciardi. New York, Norton, 1978.

Other as Paul French (juvenile)

David Starr: Spaceranger. New York, Doubleday, 1952; Kingswood, Surrey, World's Work, 1953.
Lucky Starr and the Pirates of the Asteroids. New York, Doubleday, 1953; Kingswood, Surrey, World's Work, 1954.
Lucky Starr and the Oceans of Venus. New York, Doubleday, 1954.
Lucky Starr and the Big Sun of Mercury. New York, Doubleday, 1956.
Lucky Starr and the Moons of Jupiter. New York, Doubleday, 1957.
Lucky Starr and the Rings of Saturn. New York, Doubleday, 1958.

Other

Biochemistry and Human Metabolism, with Burnham Walker and William C. Boyd. Baltimore, Williams and Wilkins, 1952; revised edition, 1954, 1957.
Chemicals of Life: Enzymes, Vitamins, Hormones. New York, Abelard Schuman, 1954; London, Bell, 1956.
Races and People, with William C. Boyd. New York, Abelard Schuman, 1955; London, Abelard Schuman, 1958.
Chemistry and Human Health, with Burnham Walker and M. K. Nicholas. New York, McGraw Hill, 1956.
Inside the Atom. New York, Abelard Schuman, 1956; revised edition, New York and London, Abelard Schuman, 1958, 1961, 1966, 1974.
Building Blocks of the Universe. New York, Abelard Schuman, 1957; London, Abelard Schuman, 1958; revised edition, 1961, 1974.
Only a Trillion. London, Abelard Schuman, 1957; New York, Abelard Schuman, 1958; as *Marvels of Science,* New York, Collier, 1962.
The World of Carbon. New York and London, Abelard Schuman, 1958; revised edition, New York, Collier, 1962.

The World of Nitrogen. New York and London, Abelard Schuman, 1958; revised edition, New York, Collier, 1962.

The Clock We Live On. New York and London, Abelard Schuman, 1959; revised edition, New York, Collier, 1962; Abelard Schuman, 1965.

The Living River. New York and London, Abelard Schuman, 1959; revised edition, as *The Bloodstream: River of Life*, New York, Collier, 1961.

Realm of Numbers. Boston, Houghton Mifflin, 1959; London, Gollancz, 1963.

Words of Science. Boston, Houghton Mifflin, 1959; London, Harrap, 1974.

Breakthroughs in Science (juvenile). Boston, Houghton Mifflin, 1960.

The Intelligent Man's Guide to Science. New York, Basic Books, 2 vols., 1960; revised edition, 1965; London, Nelson, 1967.

The Kingdom of the Sun. New York and London, Abelard Schuman, 1960; revised edition, New York, Collier, 1962; Abelard Schuman, 1963.

Realm of Measure. Boston, Houghton Mifflin, 1960.

Satellites in Outer Space (juvenile). New York, Random House, 1960; revised edition, 1964, 1973.

The Double Planet. New York, Abelard Schuman, 1960; London, Abelard Schuman, 1962; revised edition, 1967.

The Wellsprings of Life. London, Abelard Schuman, 1960; New York, Abelard Schuman, 1961.

Realm of Algebra. Boston, Houghton Mifflin, 1961; London, Gollancz, 1964.

Words from the Myths. Boston, Houghton Mifflin, 1961; London, Faber, 1963.

Fact and Fancy. New York, Doubleday, 1962.

Life and Energy. New York, Doubleday, 1962; London, Dobson, 1963.

The Search for the Elements. New York, Basic Books, 1962.

Words in Genesis. Boston, Houghton Mifflin, 1962.

Words on the Map. Boston, Houghton Mifflin, 1962.

View from a Height. New York, Doubleday, 1963; London, Dobson, 1964.

The Genetic Code. New York, Orion Press, 1963; London, Murray, 1964.

The Human Body: Its Structure and Operation. Boston, Houghton Mifflin, 1963; London, Nelson, 1965.

The Kite That Won the Revolution. Boston, Houghton Mifflin, 1963.

Words from the Exodus. Boston, Houghton Mifflin, 1963.

Adding a Dimension: 17 Essays on the History of Science. New York, Doubleday, 1964; London, Dobson, 1966.

The Human Brain: Its Capacities and Functions. Boston, Houghton Mifflin, 1964; London, Nelson, 1965.

Quick and Easy Math. Boston, Houghton Mifflin, 1964; London, Whiting and Wheaton, 1967.

A Short History of Biology. Garden City, New York, Natural History Press, 1964; London, Nelson, 1965.

Planets for Man, with Stephen H. Dole. New York, Random House, 1964.

Asimov's Biographical Encyclopedia of Science and Technology. New York, Doubleday, 1964; revised edition, 1972; London, Pan, 1975.

An Easy Introduction to the Slide Rule. Boston, Houghton Mifflin, 1965; London, Whiting and Wheaton, 1967.

The Greeks: A Great Adventure. Boston, Houghton Mifflin, 1965.

Of Time and Space and Other Things. New York, Doubleday, 1965; London, Dobson, 1967.

A Short History of Chemistry. New York, Doubleday, 1965; London, Heinemann, 1972.

The Neutrino: Ghost Particle of the Atom. New York, Doubleday, and London, Dobson, 1966.

The Genetic Effects of Radiation. Washington, D.C., Atomic Energy Commission, 1966.

The Noble Gases. New York, Basic Books, 1966.

The Roman Republic. Boston, Houghton Mifflin, 1966.

From Earth to Heaven. New York, Doubleday, 1966.

Understanding Physics. New York, Walker, 3 vols., 1966; London, Allen and Unwin, 1967.

The Universe: From Flat Earth to Quasar. New York, Walker, 1966; London, Allen Lane, 1967.

The Roman Empire. Boston, Houghton Mifflin, 1967.

The Moon (juvenile). Chicago, Follett, 1967.

Is Anyone There? (essays). New York, Doubleday, 1967; London, Rapp and Whiting, 1968.

To the Ends of the Universe. New York, Walker, 1967; revised edition 1976.

The Egyptians. Boston, Houghton Mifflin, 1967.

Mars (juvenile). Chicago, Follett, 1967.

From Earth to Heaven: 17 Essays on Science. New York, Doubleday, 1967; London, Dobson, 1968.

Environments Out There. New York and London, Abelard Schuman, 1968.

Science, Numbers and I: Essays on Science. New York, Doubleday, 1968.

The Near East: 10,000 Years of History. Boston, Houghton Mifflin, 1968.

Asimov's Guide to the Bible: I. *The Old Testament,* II. *The New Testament.* New York, Doubleday, 1968–69.

The Dark Ages. Boston, Houghton Mifflin, 1968.

Galaxies (juvenile). Chicago, Follett, 1968.

Stars (juvenile). Chicago, Follett, 1968.

Words from History. Boston, Houghton Mifflin, 1968.

The Shaping of England. Boston, Houghton Mifflin, 1969.

Photosynthesis. New York, Basic Books, 1969.

Twentieth Century Discovery. New York, Doubleday, 1969.

Opus 100 (selection). Boston, Houghton Mifflin, 1969.

ABC's of Space. New York, Walker, 1969.

Great Ideas of Science (juvenile). Boston, Houghton Mifflin, 1969.

The Solar System and Back. New York, Doubleday, 1970.

Asimov's Guide to Shakespeare: I. *The Greek, Roman and Italian Plays,* II. *The English Plays.* New York, Doubleday, 1969–70.

Constantinople. Boston, Houghton Mifflin, 1970.

ABC's of the Ocean (juvenile). New York, Walker, 1970.

Light (juvenile). Chicago, Follett, 1970.

The Best New Thing (juvenile). Cleveland, World, 1971.

The Stars in Their Courses. New York, Doubleday, 1971; London, White Lion, 1974.

What Makes the Sun Shine. Boston, Little Brown, 1971.

Isaac Asimov Treasury of Humor. Boston, Houghton Mifflin, 1971; London, Vallentine Mitchell, 1972.

The Sensuous Dirty Old Man (as Dr. A.). New York, Walker, 1971.

The Land of Canaan. Boston, Houghton Mifflin, 1971.

ABC's of the Earth (juvenile). New York, Walker, 1971.

More Words of Science. Boston, Houghton Mifflin, 1972.

Electricity and Man. Washington, D.C., Atomic Energy Commission, 1972.

The Shaping of France. Boston, Houghton Mifflin, 1972.

Asimov's Guide to Science. New York, Basic Books, 1972; London, Penguin, 1975.

Asimov's Annotated "Don Juan." New York, Doubleday, 1972.

ABC's of Ecology (juvenile). New York, Walker, 1972.

The Story of Ruth. New York, Doubleday, 1972.

Worlds Within Worlds. Washington, D.C., Atomic Energy Commission, 1972.

Ginn Science Program. Boston, Ginn, 5 vols., 1972–73.

How Did We Find Out about Dinosaurs [*The Earth Is Round, Electricity, Vitamins, Germs, Comets, Energy, Atoms, Nuclear Power, Numbers, Outer Space, Earthquakes, Black Holes, Our Human Roots*] (juvenile).   New York, Walker, 13 vols., 1973–79; 6 vols. published London, White Lion, 1975–76.

The Tragedy of the Moon (essays).   New York, Doubleday, 1973; London, Abelard Schuman, 1974.

Comets and Meteors (juvenile).   Chicago, Follett, 1973.

The Sun (juvenile).   Chicago, Follett, 1973.

The Shaping of North America.   Boston, Houghton Mifflin, 1973.

Please Explain (juvenile).   Boston, Houghton Mifflin, 1973; London, Abelard Schuman, 1975.

Physical Science Today.   Del Mar, California, CRM, 1973.

Jupiter the Largest Planet.   New York, Lothrop, 1973; revised edition, 1976.

Today, Tomorrow, and....   New York, Doubleday, 1973; London, Abelard Schuman, 1974.

The Birth of the United States 1763–1816.   Boston, Houghton Mifflin, 1974.

Earth: Our Crowded Spaceship.   New York, Day, 1974; London, Abelard Schuman, 1975.

Asimov on Chemistry.   New York, Doubleday, 1974; London, Macdonald, 1975.

Asimov on Astronomy.   New York, Doubleday, and London, Macdonald, 1974.

Asimov's Annotated "Paradise Lost."   New York, Doubleday, 1974.

Our World in Space.   Greenwich, Connecticut, New York Graphic Society, and Cambridge, Patrick Stephens, 1974.

The Solar System (juvenile).   Chicago, Follett, 1975.

Birth and Death of the Universe.   New York, Walker, 1975.

The Collapsing Universe: The Story of Black Holes.   New York, Walker, 1975; London, Hutchinson, 1977.

Of Matters Great and Small.   New York, Doubleday, 1975.

Our Federal Union: The United States from 1816 to 1865.   Boston, Houghton Mifflin, and London, Dobson, 1975.

The Ends of the Earth: The Polar Regions of the World.   New York, Weybright and Talley, 1975.

Eyes on the Universe: A History of the Telescope.   Boston, Houghton Mifflin, 1975; London, Deutsch, 1976.

Science Past – Science Future.   New York, Doubleday, 1975.

The Stars in Their Courses.   London, Panther, 1975.

Alpha Centauri, The Nearest Star.   New York, Lothrop, 1976.

I, Rabbi (juvenile).   New York, Walker, 1976.

Asimov on Numbers.   New York, Doubleday, 1976.

Asimov on Physics.   New York, Doubleday, 1976.

Twentieth Century Discovery.   New York, Ace, 1976.

The Planet That Wasn't.   New York, Doubleday, 1976; London, Sphere, 1977.

The Beginning and the End.   New York, Doubleday, 1977.

Familiar Poems Annotated.   New York, Doubleday, 1977.

The Golden Door: The United States from 1865 to 1918.   Boston, Houghton Mifflin, 1977.

The Key Word and Other Mysteries (juvenile).   New York, Walker, 1977.

Mars, The Red Planet (juvenile).   New York, Lothrop, 1977.

Towards Tomorrow.   London, Hodder and Stoughton, 1977.

Isaac Asimov's Masters of Science Fiction, edited by George Scithers.   New York, Dial Press, 1978.

Isaac Asimov's Fantastic Facts.   New York, Grosset and Dunlap, 1978.

Quasar, Quasar, Burning Bright.   New York, Doubleday, 1978.

Animals of the Bible (juvenile).   New York, Doubleday, 1978.

Extraterrestrial Civilizations.   New York, Crown, 1979.

Saturn and Beyond. New York, Lothrop, 1979.

Opus 200 (selection). Boston, Houghton Mifflin, 1979.

In Memory Yet Green: The Autobiography of Isaac Asimov 1920–1954. New York, Doubleday, 1979.

The Road to Infinity. New York, Doubleday, 1979.

Editor, *The Hugo Winners 1, 2.* New York, Doubleday, 1962–71; London, Sphere, 1973; *3*, Doubleday, and London, Dobson, 1977.

Editor, with Groff Conklin, *Fifty Short Science Fiction Tales.* New York, Collier, 1963.

Editor, *Tomorrow's Children: 18 Tales of Fantasy and Science Fiction.* New York, Doubleday, 1966.

Editor, *Where Do We Go from Here?* New York, Doubleday, 1971; London, Joseph, 1973.

Editor, *The Left Hand of the Electron* (stories). New York, Doubleday, 1972; London, Panther, 1978.

Editor, *Nebula Award Stories 8.* New York, Harper, and London, Gollancz, 1973.

Editor, *Before the Golden Age: A Science Fiction Anthology of the 1930's.* New York, Doubleday, and London, Robson, 1974.

Editor, *Familiar Poems.* New York, Doubleday, 1977.

Editor, with Martin Harry Greenberg and Joseph D. Olander, *100 Great Science Fiction Short Short Stories.* New York, Doubleday, and London, Robson, 1978.

Editor, *The Science Fictional Solar System.* New York, Harper, 1979.

Manuscript Collection: Mugar Memorial Library, Boston University.

*   *   *

Both science fiction and detective fiction by Isaac Asimov unite in revealing in the author a fondness for the fact, a delight in reasoning from careful observation, and an absorption in cause and effect. Several different types of mystery occur in his writings.

The Black Widowers tales illustrate the author's inventiveness in meeting the stringent requirements of the armchair formula. At club meetings guests pose problems which are solved by the least likely detective in so distinguished a company, the waiter, Henry. Puzzle is all – club members are characterized only by a few habits, a common misogyny, and a consistent truculence. But with the clever juxtaposition of elaborate false solutions against the simple, correct ones furnished by Henry, the stories please and often surprise. The imaginative variations on the traditional use and misuse of clues are not uniformly surprising, fair, or successful in matching the resolution to the build up, yet the average in quality is high, and particularly good are the simple reversal in "No Smoking," the familiar clue in "The Biological Clock," the Ackroydal note of "The Obvious Factor," and the Sherlockian elements of "The Ultimate Clue."

More than a little of Archie Goodwin flavors the bantam bristlings of Darius Just, the five-foot-five novelist who narrates and does the sleuthing in *Murder at the ABA*. This breezy venture into a parodic approximation of the hard-boiled tradition provides clues for the reader and also exhibits the slangy wise-cracks, sexual adventure, and fuller characterization of that tradition. Direct addresses by Just to the reader, resembling Asimov's earlier Forewords and Afterwords to stories, are part of the chatty and consciously clever texture of the novel in which Asimov himself plays a minor role.

Asimov's most original contribution to mystery fiction is the subject matter of future worlds, worlds containing such denizens as the rabbit-eared, rock-eating *silicony* and the robot. Stories set against this scene include armchair investigations by the extra-terrologist Dr. Wendell Urth; two inverted stories in which the crime is seen by the reader who then follows the efforts of a detective at reconstruction ("The Singing Bell" and "The Dust of Death"); and a handful of other mysteries involving less detection. Among the latter are "The

Billiard Ball," which utilizes the theory of relativity in a murder method, and "I'm at Marsport Without Hilda," which manages to satirize and emulate James Bond-like adventure in a Mars setting.

The Caves of Steel has a startling innovation: the first robot detective. Assigned to partner an Earth policeman, R. Daneel Olivaw might have become the ultimate detective. Instead, the author chose to show human intelligence superior to that of the perfectly logical, but unreasonable, robot. Nevertheless, as a Watson-figure R. Daneel is a superior invention. Detection by Elijah "Lije" Baley and the robot contains classic patterns, following Sherlock Holmes at every turn and resembling the work of such early police detectives as Josephine Tey's Alan Grant rather than that in a police-procedural novel. Biblical allusion and dystopian and even Swiftian elements in the depiction of the earthmen's agoraphobia and the spacers' revulsion at "seeing" complement detection. While *The Caves of Steel* and its sequel, *The Naked Sun*, contain excellent detection, they are primarily utopian science fiction, inasmuch as the solution to the crime is less significant than the reestablishment of the potentiality for Earth's political and cultural vitality.

Consistent with the bulk of detective fiction, that by Isaac Asimov leaves unattempted analyses of emotional and philosophic issues, development of three-dimensional character, and stylistic innovation. Unlike much such writing, however, his is intelligent, varied, sound in construction, and enlivened by humor, energy, and a love of paradox and pun: his works consistently interest and entertain.

—Nancy Ellen Talburt

ATKEY, Philip.   See **PEROWNE, Barry.**

ATLEE, Philip.   Pseudonym for James Atlee Phillips.   Born in 1915.

CRIME PUBLICATIONS

Novels (series character: Joe Gall in all books)

> *The Green Wound.*   New York, Fawcett, 1963; London, Muller, 1964; as *The Green Wound Contract*, New York, Fawcett, 1967.
> *The Silken Baroness.*   New York, Fawcett, 1964: as *The Silken Baroness Contract*, New York, Fawcett, 1966; London, Hodder and Stoughton, 1967.
> *The Death Bird Contract.*   New York, Fawcett, 1966; London, Hodder and Stoughton, 1968.
> *The Irish Beauty Contract.*   New York, Fawcett, 1966: London, Hodder and Stoughton, 1968.
> *The Paper Pistol Contract.*   New York, Fawcett, 1966; London, Hodder and Stoughton, 1968.
> *The Star Ruby Contract.*   New York, Fawcett, 1967; London, Hodder and Stoughton, 1969.

 The Skeleton Coast Contract. New York, Fawcett, 1968.
 The Rockabye Contract. New York, Fawcett, 1968.
 The Ill Wind Contract. New York, Fawcett, 1969.
 The Trembling Earth Contract. New York, Fawcett, 1969; London, Hodder and
  Stoughton, 1970.
 The Fer-de-Lance Contract. New York, Fawcett, 1970.
 The Canadian Bomber Contract. New York, Fawcett, 1971.
 The White Wolverine Contract. New York, Fawcett, 1971.
 The Judah Lion Contract. New York, Fawcett, 1972.
 The Kiwi Contract. New York, Fawcett, 1972.
 The Shankill Road Contract. New York, Fawcett, 1973.
 The Spice Route Contract. New York, Fawcett, 1973.
 The Kowloon Contract. New York, Fawcett, 1974.
 The Underground Cities Contract. New York, Fawcett, 1974.
 The Black Venus Contract. New York, Fawcett, 1975.
 The Last Domino Contract. New York, Fawcett, 1976.

Novels as James Atlee Phillips

 The Case of the Shivering Chorus Girls. New York, Coward McCann, 1942; London,
  Lane, 1950.
 Suitable for Framing. New York, Macmillan, 1949: London, Lane, 1952.
 Pagoda. New York, Macmillan, 1951; London, Lane, 1953.
 The Deadly Mermaids. New York, Dell, 1954.

OTHER PUBLICATIONS

Novels

 The Inheritors. New York, Dial Press, 1940.
 The Naked Year. New York, Lion, 1954.

* * *

When James Atlee Phillips became Philip Atlee for the purpose of selling a paperback original novel about an attempt by Black militants to take over a Southern town in 1963, he brought a lot of his old writing self – the self that had produced in *Suitable for Framing* what many people still regard as the best American crime novel of 1949. He borrowed the opening scene, one of the most spectacular in modern popular fiction, from that book. He borrowed his lead character, Joe Gall, from *Pagoda*, which he had published two years later; finally, he added to Gall's background a considerable amount of details he had created for the unnamed hero of his first real spy book, *The Deadly Mermaids*. Further fleshing out of Gall, who had begun his fictional life as a convincing soldier of fortune, involved a topical reference to the Bay of Pigs incident as an explanation for his forced early retirement from the CIA and a very important switch of point of view so that Gall narrated his own adventure. The overall result was a hero who could be appealing as well as a more believable American equivalent of James Bond.

 Gall returned soon in several later adventures, ending with the aptly named *The Last Domino Contract*. During the thirteen years of the Fawcett Gold Medal series, various gimmicks were tried (such as the brief use of "The Nullifier" as a Gall *nom-de-guerre*), but generally the books centered on character. Beginning as one of the most interesting heroes of action fiction, Gall went on to become even more so. Kelly Wu, the exotic Canadian Chinese heroine of *The White Wolverine Contract* and *The Kowloon Contract*, became Gall's common law wife and presided over the "clapboard castle" in the Arkansas Ozarks which had always been his home-base. Padraic O'Connell, adopted by Gall as an autistic victim of the Northern

Ireland Civil War at the end of *The Shankill Road Contract*, benefitted from a surprisingly near-normal later childhood. Most importantly, this "family" seems to have given Gall a growing maturity and sense of responsibility.

His withdrawal from spying at the end of the particularly bitter "final" book in the series is quite credible, but only because of the gradual development of his socio-political conscience. Thus, while the first half dozen books, with their exotic villains and extravagant gimmickry, remind the reader of Ian Fleming, the last half dozen are more comparable to Deighton and le Carré. Yet Gall is as convincing and compelling at the end as he was at the beginning. Atlee's achievement in this series may well be regarded by future generations as the best American espionage series of the latter half of the 20th century.

—Jeff Banks

AUDEMARS, Pierre. Also writes as Peter Hodemart. British. Born in London, 25 December 1909. Served in the army, 1940–46: Lieutenant. Married to Joan Wood; two sons. Salesman, Louis Audemars & Co., London, 1928–39; Manager, Camerer Cuss & Co., jewellers, London, 1949–56; Sales Manager, Zenith Watch Co. Ltd., London, 1960–76. Agent: Winant Towers Ltd., 14 Clifford's Inn, London EC4A 1DA, England.

CRIME PUBLICATIONS

Novels (series characters: Monsieur Pinaud; Hercule Renard)

Night Without Darkness.   London, Selwyn and Blount, 1936.
Hercule and the Gods.   London, Pilot Press, 1944; New York, Rinehart, 1946.
The Temptations of Hercule.   London, Pilot Press, 1945.
When the Gods Laughed.   Hounslow, Middlesex, Foster, 1946.
The Obligations of Hercule.   London, Sampson Low, 1947.
The Confessions of Hercule.   London, Sampson Low, 1947.
The Thieves of Enchantment.   London, Chambers, 1956.
The Two Imposters (Pinaud).   London, Long, 1958.
The Fire and the Clay (Pinaud).   London, Long, 1959.
The Turns of Time (Pinaud).   London, Long, 1961; New York, Harper, 1962.
The Crown of Night (Pinaud).   London, Long, and New York, Harper, 1962.
The Dream and the Dead (Pinaud).   London, Long, 1963.
The Wings of Darkness (Pinaud).   London, Long, 1963; as *The Street of Grass*, New York, Harper, 1963.
Fair Maids Missing (Pinaud).   London, Long, 1964; New York, Doubleday, 1965.
Dead with Sorrow (Pinaud).   London, Long, 1964; as *A Woven Web*, New York, Doubleday, 1965.
Time of Temptation (Pinaud).   London, Long, and New York, Doubleday, 1966.
A Thorn in the Dust (Pinaud).   London, Long, 1967.
The Veins of Compassion (Pinaud).   London, Long, 1967.
The White Leaves of Death (Pinaud).   London, Long, 1968.
The Flame in the Mist (Pinaud).   London, Long, 1969; New York, Curtis, 1971.
A Host for Dying (Pinaud).   London, Long, 1970; New York, Curtis, 1972.
Stolen Like Magic Away (Pinaud).   London, Long, 1971.
The Delicate Dust of Death (Pinaud).   London, Long, 1973.

No Tears for the Dead (Pinaud).   London, Long, 1974.
Nightmare in Rust (Pinaud).   London, Long, 1975.
And One for the Dead (Pinaud).   London, Long, 1975.
The Healing Hands of Death.   London, Long, 1977.
Now Dead Is Any Man.   London, Long, 1978.
A Sad and Savage Dying.   London, Long, 1978.
Slay Me a Sinner.   London, Long, 1979.

Short Story

Fate and Fernand.   London, Vallancey Press, 1945.

Uncollected Short Story

"Hercule and Jou-Jou," in *Murder Plain and Fanciful*, edited by James Sandoe. New York, Sheridan House, 1948.

OTHER PUBLICATIONS

Novel

Wrath of the Valley (as Peter Hodemart).   London, Rockliff, 1947.

*   *   *

Pierre Audemars has written more than 25 suspense tales. They are set in France, a mythical France created by the author, in which the forces of evil are frequently rooted in ancient families whose character and power were established in the Middle Ages. The mythical quality is underlined by what would otherwise seem to be inexplicable geographical dislocations – placing the Gorges du Tarn, for example, in Haute Savoie.

Audemars invariably writes well, lightly manipulating narrative devices which many writers would hesitate to employ. In *Hercule and the Gods*, an early story, a railway passenger is told a tale by the French laborer Hercule, so that there are two first person narrators. What could be cumbersome and distracting to the reader is instead cleverly handled. Hercule's language is sprinkled with French expressions and consistently seems to have been somewhat awkwardly translated from French. The author manages all this admirably, enhancing the atmosphere as well as the humor, which in this book ranges from broad farce to rather subtle word play. Hercule's cousin, an actor, impersonates Pinaud, "the greatest detective in France."

In most of Audemars's suspense novels, the hero is Inspector Pinaud of the French Sûreté. Pinaud is very fond of good food and fine wine. He loves fast cars and is often shown at the wheel of a powerful Sûreté car or an interesting antique or hand-built model. He is highly susceptible to attractive women, and in practically every adventure encounters a lovely nude female, a bit of fortune much envied by M. le Chef, Pinaud's boss. For all that, Pinaud is the antithesis of a James Bond. He is a conscientious family man who nearly always resists the temptations lavished upon him, despite the torments of his carnal thoughts. He and his wife Germaine have two daughters. They struggle against poverty and are often separated because of his work, reminding the mystery fan, in this respect, of Marric's George Gideon and his Kate. Constantly chafed by the injustice of a system which pays him only a pittance for his brilliance and dedication, Pinaud has, nevertheless, an almost feudal obligation to M. le Chef, though he is well aware that the loyalty is not reciprocated. Our hero is a philosopher, a great sympathizer with all the unfortunate and downtrodden, and a firm believer in a higher law which "worked, granted – but not always, and not often enough, not irrevocably, not consistently, and not inevitably ...," so that Pinaud continues to seek justice. He sometimes sees himself as a medieval knight, rescuing maidens and righting wrongs.

Pinaud's cases are related by a detached, somewhat tongue-in-cheek narrator who refers to the great detective's unpublished (and unpublishable) memoirs. The stories begin in a stylized manner – "In the days when M. Pinaud's fame had grown to such an extent that no one ever dared to question his veracity ...," or "In the days when M. Pinaud was younger and leaner than one would ever have believed possible (considering the gargantuan majesty of his present appearance) and when his utterances and pronouncements rang more with the certainty of his own convictions than with the complacency of universal acclaim...." If Pinaud's cases seem most often to deal with narcotics and white slavery, or the murder of young girls, they are told in such a way that the gruesome details do not offend (not too much, anyway, nor for long). He is characterized by sardonic humor, intrepid self-confidence, and much information – he declares, for instance, that a great detective "must know something about everything. Not everything about everything. And certainly not something about something. But something about everything."

Pierre Audemars, whose sense of humor is delectable, writes suspense fiction that is original and intriguing. Any reader who has not yet met M. Pinaud would do well to make his acquaintance.

—Mary Helen Becker

AUSTWICK, John. Pseudonym for Austin Lee; also wrote as Julian Callender. British. Born in Cowling, Yorkshire, 9 July 1904. Educated at Trinity College, Cambridge, B.A. 1926, M.A. 1928. Ordained, 1928: Royal Navy chaplain, 1931–36; vicar of Pampisford, Cambridgeshire, 1935–38; Chaplain to Middlesex Hospital, London, 1938–39, and to Royal Air Force Motorboats Crew, 1940; rector of Claxby and of Willoughby and Alford, Lincolnshire; vicar of Great Paxton, Huntingdonshire, 1963–65. *Died in 1965.*

CRIME PUBLICATIONS

Novels (series character: Inspector Parker)

Highland Homicide (Parker).   London, Hale, 1957.
The Hubberthwaite Horror.   London, Hale, 1958.
Murder in the Borough Library (Parker).   London, Hale, 1959.
The County Library Murders.   London, Hale, 1962.
The Mobile Library Murders.   London, Hale, 1964.
The Borough Council Murders.   London, Hale, 1965.

Novels as Austin Lee (series character: Miss Hogg)

Sheep's Clothing (Hogg).   London, Cape, 1955.
Call in Miss Hogg.   London, Cape, 1956.
Miss Hogg and the Brontë Murders.   London, Cape, 1956.
Miss Hogg and the Squash Club Murder.   London, Cape, 1957.
Miss Hogg Flies High.   London, Cape, 1958.
Miss Hogg and the Dead Dean.   London, Cape, 1958.
Miss Hogg and the Covent Garden Murders.   London, Cape, 1960.
Miss Hogg and the Missing Sisters.   London, Cape, 1961.
Miss Hogg's Last Case.   London, Cape, 1963.
Corpse Too Many (as Julian Callender).   London, Jenkins, 1965.

OTHER PUBLICATIONS

Novels as Julian Callender

Company of Heaven. London, Wingate, 1956.
St. Dingan's Bones. London, Wingate, 1957; New York, Vanguard Press, 1958.

Other

Round Many a Bend, Being Chapters from the Autobiography of the Reverend A. Lee. London, Cape, 1954.

*   *   *

John Austwick's local government background gave a superficial authenticity to such books as *The Borough Council Murders*, in which the deaths of two senior council officials and the mayor set the police on the track of a killer who apparently has a senseless grudge against the local authority of Bancaster. It is a lively tale which keeps the reader guessing and does not tax his concentration with non-essentials. The same may be said of Austwick's several mysteries in public library settings, but it is interesting to note that such settings have little relevance to the murders themselves; they are merely convenient backcloths, whereas they could have been integral parts of the plots.

The series of novels by Austin Lee featuring Miss Hogg, schoolmistress turned private detective, displays the same easy style but with added humour. There is an attempt at urbanity, but they succeed really as comedy thrillers. Miss Hogg, a little scatty and extremely active, could have been more significant if the author had spent more time building up her character and projecting her personality.

The roots of many of the Austwick/Lee crimes are buried deep in the past, which appears to be a favourite device. He also has his digs at politics and religion, occasionally takes sidelong glances at technology, and adds touches of small-town corruption and bigotry. There is nothing deep or memorable, however, and his works are simply entertaining detective stories of the type which has enabled countless readers to while away a pleasant hour.

—Melvyn Barnes

AVALLONE, Michael (Angelo, Jr.). Also writes as Nick Carter; Troy Conway; Priscilla Dalton; Mark Dane; Jean-Anne de Pre; Dora Highland; Steve Michaels; Dorothea Nile; Edwina Noone; Vance Stanton; Sidney Stuart; Max Walker. American. Born in Manhattan, New York, 27 October 1924. Educated at Theodore Roosevelt High School, Bronx, New York. Served in the United States Army, 1943–46: Sergeant. Married 1) Lucille Asero in 1949; one son, 2) Fran Weinstein in 1960; one daughter and one son. Worked as stationery salesman, 1946–55; editor for Republic Features, New York, 1956–58; editor for Cape Magazines, New York, 1958–60. Since 1955, guest lecturer in New York and New Jersey schools. Chairman, television committee, 1963–65, and movie committee, 1965–70, Mystery Writers of America. Agent: Jay Garon, 415 Central Park West, New York, New York 10025. Address: 80 Hilltop Boulevard, East Brunswick, New Jersey 08816, U.S.A.

CRIME PUBLICATIONS

Novels (series character: Ed Noon)

The Spitting Image (Noon). New York, Holt Rinehart, 1953; London, Barker, 1957.

The Tall Dolores (Noon). New York, Holt Rinehart, 1953; London, Barker, 1956.

Dead Game (Noon). New York, Holt Rinehart, 1954; London, W. H. Allen, 1959.

Violence in Velvet (Noon). New York, New American Library, 1956; London, W. H. Allen, 1958.

The Case of the Bouncing Betty (Noon). New York, Ace, 1957; London, W. H. Allen, 1959.

The Case of the Violent Virgin (Noon). New York, Ace, 1957; London, W. H. Allen, 1960.

The Crazy Mixed-Up Corpse (Noon). New York, Fawcett, 1957; London, Fawcett, 1959.

The Voodoo Murders (Noon). New York, Fawcett, 1957; London, Fawcett, 1959.

Meanwhile Back at the Morgue (Noon). New York, Fawcett, 1960; London, Muller, 1961.

The Alarming Clock (Noon). London, W. H. Allen, 1961; New York, Curtis, 1973.

The Bedroom Bolero (Noon). New York, Belmont, 1963; as *The Bolero Murders*, London, Hale, 1972.

The Main Attraction (novelization of screenplay; as Steve Michaels). New York, Belmont, 1963.

The Living Bomb (Noon). London, W. H. Allen, 1963; New York, Curtis, 1972.

There Is Something about a Dame (Noon). New York, Belmont, 1963.

Shock Corridor (novelization of screenplay). New York, Belmont, 1963.

The Doctor's Wife. Beacon, New York, Beacon Signal, 1963.

Lust Is No Lady (Noon). New York, Belmont, 1964; as *The Brutal Kook*, London, W. H. Allen, 1965.

Felicia (novelization of screenplay; as Mark Dane). New York, Belmont, 1964.

The Thousand Coffins Affair. New York, Ace, and London, New English Library, 1965.

The Birds of a Feather Affair. New York, New American Library, 1966; London, New English Library, 1967.

The Blazing Affair. New York, New American Library, 1966.

The Fat Death (Noon). London, W. H. Allen, 1966; New York, Curtis, 1972.

Kaleidoscope (novelization of screenplay). New York, Popular Library, 1966.

The February Doll Murders (Noon). London, W. H. Allen, 1966; New York, New American Library, 1967.

The Felony Squad. New York, Popular Library, 1967.

The Man from AVON. New York, Avon, 1967.

Assassins Don't Lie in Bed (Noon). New York, New American Library, 1968.

The Coffin Things. New York, Lancer, 1968.

Hawaii Five-O. New York, New American Library, 1968.

The Incident (novelization of screenplay). New York, New American Library, 1968.

The Horrible Man (Noon). London, Hale, 1968; New York, Curtis, 1972.

Mannix. New York, Popular Library, 1968.

The Flower-Covered Corpse (Noon). London, Hale, 1969; New York, Curtis, 1972.

The Doomsday Bag (Noon). New York, New American Library, 1969; as *Killer's Highway*, London, Hale, 1970.

Hawaii Five-O: Terror in the Sun. New York, New American Library, 1969.

The Killing Star. London, Hale, 1969.

Missing! New York, New American Library, 1969.

A Bullet for Pretty Boy (novelization of screenplay). New York, Curtis, 1970.

One More Time (novelization of screenplay). New York, Popular Library, 1970.

Death Dives Deep (Noon). New York, New American Library, and London, Hale, 1971.

Little Miss Murder (Noon). New York, New American Library, 1971; as *The Ultimate Client*, London, Hale, 1971.

When Were You Born? Paris, Gallimard, 1971.

The Night Before Chaos. Paris, Gallimard, 1971.
Shoot It Again, Sam (Noon). New York, Curtis, 1972; as *The Moving Graveyard*, London, Hale, 1973.
The Girl in the Cockpit (Noon). New York, Curtis, 1972; London, Hale, 1974.
London Bloody London. New York, Curtis, 1972; as *Ed Noon in London*, London, Hale, 1974.
Kill Her – You'll Like It (Noon). New York, Curtis, 1973; London, Hale, 1974.
The Hot Body (Noon). New York, Curtis, 1973.
Killer on the Keys (Noon). New York, Curtis, 1973.
The X-Rated Corpse (Noon). New York, Curtis, 1973.
153 Oakland Street (as Dora Highland). New York, Popular Library, 1973.
Death Is a Dark Man (as Dora Highland). New York, Popular Library, 1974.
Fallen Angel. New York, Warner, 1974.
The Werewolf Walks Tonight. New York, Warner, 1974.
Devil, Devil. New York, Warner, 1975; London, New English Library, 1976.
Only One More Miracle. New York, Scholastic, 1975.
The Big Stiffs (Noon). London, Hale, 1977.
Dark on Monday (Noon). London, Hale, 1978.

Novels as Nick Carter

The China Doll. New York, Award, 1964.
Run Spy Run. New York, Award, 1964.
Saigon. New York, Award, 1964.

Novels as Sidney Stuart

The Night Walker (novelization of screenplay). New York, Award, 1964.
Young Dillinger (novelization of screenplay). New York, Belmont, 1965.
The Beast with Red Hands. New York, Popular Library, 1973.

Novels as Priscilla Dalton (Gothics)

The Darkening Willows. New York, Paperback Library, 1965.
90 Gramercy Park. New York, Paperback Library, 1965.
The Silent, Silken Shadows. New York, Paperback Library, 1965.

Novels as Edwina Noone (Gothics)

Corridor of Whispers. New York, Ace, 1965.
Dark Cypress. New York, Ace, 1965.
Heirloom of Tragedy. New York, Lancer, 1965.
Daughter of Darkness. New York, New American Library, 1966.
The Second Secret. New York, Belmont, 1966.
The Victorian Crown. New York, Belmont, 1966.
Seacliffe. New York, New American Library, 1968.
The Cloisonne Vase. New York, Curtis, 1970.
The Craghold Legacy. New York, Beagle, 1971.
The Craghold Creatures. New York, Beagle, 1972.
The Craghold Curse. New York, Beagle, 1972.
The Craghold Crypt. New York, Beagle, 1973.

Novels as Dorothea Nile (Gothics)

The Evil Men Do. New York, Tower, 1966.

Mistress of Farrondale. New York, Tower, 1966.
Terror at Deepcliff. New York, Tower, 1966.
The Vampire Cameo. New York, Lancer, 1968.
The Third Shadow. New York, Avon, 1973.

Novels as Troy Conway (series character: The Coxeman in all books)

Come One, Come All. New York, Paperback Library, 1968.
The Man-Eater. New York, Paperback Library, 1968.
The Big Broad Jump. New York, Paperback Library, 1969.
A Good Peace. New York, Paperback Library, 1969.
Had Any Lately? New York, Paperback Library, 1969.
I'd Rather Fight than Swish. New York, Paperback Library, 1969.
The Blow-Your-Mind Job. New York, Paperback Library, 1970.
The Cunning Linguist. New York, Paperback Library, 1970.
All Screwed Up. New York, Paperback Library, 1971.
The Penetrator. New York, Paperback Library, 1971.
A Stiff Proposition. New York, Paperback Library, 1971.

Novels as Jean-Anne de Pre (Gothics)

A Sound of Dying Roses. New York, Popular Library, 1971.
The Third Woman. New York, Popular Library, 1971; London, Sphere, 1973.
Aquarius, My Evil. New York, Popular Library, 1972.
Die, Jessica, Die. New York, Popular Library, 1972.
Warlock's Woman. New York, Popular Library, 1973.

Novels as Vance Stanton

Keith Partridge, Master Spy. New York, Curtis, 1971.
The Fat and Skinny Murder Mystery. New York, Curtis, 1972.
The Walking Fingers. New York, Curtis, 1972.
Who's That Laughing in the Grave? New York, Curtis, 1972.

Short Stories

Tales of the Frightened. New York, Belmont, 1963.
Edwina Noone's Gothic Sampler. New York, Fawcett, 1966.
Where Monsters Walk. New York, Scholastic, 1978.
Five Minute Mysteries. New York, Scholastic, 1978.

OTHER PUBLICATIONS

Novels

All the Way Home. New York, Midwood, 1960.
The Little Black Book. New York, Midwood, 1961.
Stag Stripper. New York, Midwood, 1961.
Women in Prison. New York, Midwood, 1961.
Flight Hostess Rogers. New York, Midwood, 1962.
Never Love a Call Girl. New York, Midwood, 1962.
The Platinum Trap. New York, Midwood, 1962.
Sex Kitten. New York, Midwood, 1962.
Sinners in White. New York, Midwood, 1962.
Lust at Leisure. Beacon, New York, Beacon Signal, 1963.

And Sex Walked In. Beacon, New York, Beacon Signal, 1963.
Station Six—Sahara (novelization of screenplay). New York, Popular Library, 1964.
Madame X (novelization of screenplay). New York, Popular Library, 1966.
Krakatoa, East of Java (novelization of screenplay). New York, New American Library, 1969.
Beneath the Planet of the Apes (novelization of screenplay). New York, New American Library, 1970.
The Doctors. New York, Popular Library, 1970.
Hornets' Nest (novelization of screenplay). New York, Popular Library, 1970.
The Haunted Hall. New York, Curtis, 1970.
Keith, The Hero. New York, Curtis, 1970.
The Partridge Family. New York, Curtis, 1970.
The Last Escape (as Max Walker). New York, Popular Library, 1970.
Love Comes to Keith Partridge. New York, Curtis, 1973.
The Girls in Television. New York, Ace, 1974.
CB Logbook of the White Knight. New York, Scholastic, 1977.
Carquake. London, Star, 1977.
Name That Movie. New York, Scholastic, 1978.
Son of Name That Movie. New York, Scholastic, 1978.

Bibliography: "Michael Avallone: A Checklist" by Stephen Mertz, in *Armchair Detective* (White Bear Lake, Minnesota), February 1976.

Manuscript Collection: Mugar Memorial Library, Boston University.

Michael Avallone comments:
 A professional writer should be able to write anything from a garden seed catalogue to the Bible. Writing is the Last Frontier of Individualism left in a 1984 world, for it is the art form that demands the *least* collaboration.

*   *   *

 Since 1953 Michael Avallone has ground out countless short stories and over 150 paperback novels – private eye tales, Gothics under female bylines, juveniles, erotics, espionage thrillers, movie and TV tie-in books. But unlike most purveyors of drugstore fiction, Avallone is a true *auteur*, with a unique personality discernible throughout his work.
 He is best known for the thirty-odd novels about his fantasy alter ego, Ed Noon, New York private detective, movie and baseball nut, lover of luscious women and lousy jokes ("Hi, Noon!" his friends greet him), and personal investigator for a disgraced recent president of the United States. The key to the Nooniverse is its creator's passion for old movies. He is so immersed in Hollywood's output of the 1930's and 1940's that fragments from dozens of those flicks leap from his cine-satiated mind to his pages and fill them with jumbled, raucous, and frenetic life. The fun of reading Avallone lies in encountering the most film-intoxicated man alive.
 By normal standards every Nooner is an inept mess. Avallone's chaotic plots, all of them dealing with the quest for some McGuffin or other, are literally improvised as he goes along, and his style is an ungrammatical, misspelled, brain-jangling approximation of English. "My stunned intellect, the one that found death in his own backyard with him standing only feet away, hard to swallow in a hurry, found the answer." "She had tremendous hips and breasts encased in a silly short black fur jacket and calf-high boots." When the plot squeaks to a halt, have a black dwarf enter the room walking on his hands with a .45 in each foot. Make the language do flipflops, mangle the metaphors like a trash compactor, slap down as many allusions to characters and incidents and lines and settings from old movies as the page can hold, spice with gobs of revulsion at hippies, perverts, Commies, pacifists, dissidents, militant

blacks, liberated women, longhairs and pointyheads, and all other traitors to the John Wayne ethos. With this recipe Avallone has inadvertently created a private Nooniverse.

If any of his books is Avallone's testament it's *Shoot It Again, Sam*, in which the President orders Noon to accompany a dead Hollywood star's body on a transcontinental train ride. While the "corpse" sits up in its coffin, Chinese agents raid the train, kidnap Noon, and use brainwashers made up to look like Gable, Cagney, and Lorre to convince Noon that he is none other than Sam Spade (as portrayed by Bogart of course). It's all part of the screwiest assassination plot ever concocted by a movie maniac. Whatever else might be said about Avallone, one must say what Casper Gutman said to Spade in *The Maltese Falcon*: "By Gad, sir, you're a character, that you are!"

—Francis M. Nevins, Jr.

BABSON, Marian. American. Born in Salem, Massachusetts. Has lived in London since 1960; works as temporary secretary. Since 1976, Secretary, Crime Writers Association. Address: c/o Collins, 14 St. James's Place, London SW1A 1PS, England.

CRIME PUBLICATIONS

Novels (series character: Douglas Perkins)

Cover-Up Story (Perkins).   London, Collins, 1971.
Murder on Show (Perkins).   London, Collins, 1972.
Pretty Lady.   London, Collins, 1973.
The Stalking Lamb.   London, Collins, 1974.
Unfair Exchange.   London, Collins, 1974.
Murder Sails at Midnight.   London, Collins, 1975.
There Must Be Some Mistake.   London, Collins, 1975.
Untimely Guest.   London, Collins, 1976.
The Lord Mayor of Death.   London, Collins, 1977; New York, Walker, 1979.
Murder, Murder, Little Star.   London, Collins, 1977.
Tightrope for Three.   London, Collins, 1978.
So Soon Done For.   London, Collins, 1979.
The Twelve Deaths of Christmas.   London, Collins, 1979.

Marian Babson comments:
I have always enjoyed reading mystery novels; I enjoy writing them. (It's even more enjoyable since they started selling.) My favourites are straight suspense and crime-with-comedy, and I alternate between the two. Which is not to say that I might not do something completely different at any time. I don't think writers ought to be too predictable. I also think they ought to let their work speak for them.

*   *   *

It is common to find the crime writer who produces a good first novel followed by many inferior works, and therefore refreshing to find one who goes from strength to strength. Marian Babson is a very clear example of the latter, and has noticeably developed in technique. Her first two books were not far from straight detection, with Douglas Perkins of Perkins and Tate (Public Relations) Limited assigned to a group of hillbilly singers and a cat show respectively; in both cases he encounters jealousy and spite leading to skullduggery and murder, and almost as a self-protective device he turns amateur detective. They were interesting stories, well plotted and with entertaining characters, and Perkins's attempts to hush up the scandals as well as solve the crimes gave them an added dimension, but still there was little to indicate that Marian Babson was a new name to watch.

For her third novel, *Pretty Lady*, she moved away from the traditional form and began to show her true skill. In this tale of a mentally retarded man who becomes involved in murder, she displayed a deft hand at creating suspense and a capacity to treat a difficult subject with sympathy and plausibility. From this point her talent became increasingly obvious. In *The Stalking Lamb*, she presented an absorbing study of a girl in unfamiliar surroundings who is thrust into a criminal situation from which she finds it more and more difficult to escape, and again the line of suspense forces the reader to associate with the central character. In many ways *Unfair Exchange* displayed a lighter touch; fast moving, with a somewhat superficial kidnap and murder plot, it remains memorable for its flawless portrayal of a selfish yet magnetic woman with a childishly transparent tendency to deceive and fantasize.

This ability to produce a web of intrigue, together with skilful character studies which do nothing to slow down the almost breathless pace of the narrative, is used in every Babson novel from *Pretty Lady* onwards. Her inventiveness has been remarkable. On board a luxury liner in *Murder Sails at Midnight*, who is the hired assassin and who is to be his victim? In *There Must Be Some Mistake*, we share the predicament of a woman whose husband has disappeared under suspicion of embezzlement. Examining family relationships in *Untimely Guest*, she produced perhaps her deepest study of character in her exploration of the passions leading to violence. Then she immediately turned to something completely different with *The Lord Mayor of Death*, painting the backcloth of the pageantry and fun and crowds at the City of London Lord Mayor's Show, and placing against it an Irishman using a small child as cover in his plot to bomb the ceremonial coach; the excitement is made intense by successively switching the action between pursuers, pursued, and potential victim.

And so the list of credits has gone on. It is not easy to summarise the qualities of Marian Babson. She displays imagination and versatility of subject, skilful handling of both humour and the more delicate human problems, and a mixture of fine characterisation (especially child studies, by no means a common accomplishment among writers) and crisp action. In short, she must be among the best contemporary writers in the field.

—Melvyn Barnes

BAGBY, George. See **STEIN, Aaron Marc.**

BAGLEY, Desmond. British. Born in Kendal, Westmorland, 29 October 1923. Left school at 14. Married Joan Margaret Brown in 1960. Worked in the aircraft industry, 1940–46; worked in Uganda, 1947, Kenya, 1948, Rhodesia, 1949; worked for the South African Broadcasting Corporation, Durban, 1951–52; editor of house magazine for Masonite (Africa) Ltd., 1953; film critic, Rand *Daily Mail*, Johannesburg, 1958–62; writer for Filmlets Ltd., Johannesburg, 1960–61. Agent: Collins, 14 St. James's Place, London SW1A 1PS, England. Address: Câtel House, Les Rohais de Haut, St. Andrew, Guernsey, Channel Islands.

CRIME PUBLICATIONS

Novels

> *The Golden Keel.* London, Collins, 1963; New York, Doubleday, 1964.
> *High Citadel.* London, Collins, and New York, Doubleday, 1965.
> *Wyatt's Hurricane.* London, Collins, and New York, Doubleday, 1966.
> *Landslide.* London, Collins, and New York, Doubleday, 1967.
> *The Vivero Letter.* London, Collins, and New York, Doubleday, 1968.
> *The Spoilers.* London, Collins, 1969; New York, Doubleday, 1970.
> *Running Blind.* London, Collins, 1970; New York, Doubleday, 1971.
> *The Freedom Trap.* London, Collins, 1971; New York, Doubleday, 1972; as *The Mackintosh Man*, New York, Crest, 1973.
> *The Tightrope Men.* London, Collins, and New York, Doubleday, 1973.
> *The Snow Tiger.* London, Collins, 1974; New York, Doubleday, 1975.
> *The Enemy.* London, Collins, 1977; New York, Doubleday, 1978.
> *Flyaway.* London, Collins, 1978; New York, Doubleday, 1979.

Uncollected Short Stories

> "My Old Man's Trumpet," in *Argosy* (London), January 1957.
> "A Matter of Mouths," in *Winter's Crimes 8*, edited by Hilary Watson. London, Macmillan, 1976.

OTHER PUBLICATIONS

Other

> "The Circumstances Surrounding the Crime," in *I, Witness: True Personal Encounters with Crime by Members of the Mystery Writers of America.* New York, Times Books, 1978.

*   *   *

In the course of fifteen years and almost as many books, Desmond Bagley has climbed into the premier division of British thriller writers and in many ways he can now lay claim to the Number One spot. More consistently lively than Innes, less mechanical than MacLean, he writes fast-moving stories whose action is underpinned, but never overwhelmed, by detailed technical expertise and rich local colour. Like all the great adventure/thriller writers from Haggard via Buchan to the moderns, he is more interested in movement than shape, and occasionally (as for example in *The Spoilers*) the reader may experience a sense almost of dislocation as the narrative is wrenched in an unexpected direction. But the sheer momentum of his writing is always more than enough to carry the reader happily through to the end.

There has to be more than action, of course, and with Bagley the "more" is not just tossed in as a make-weight. His books are as international in their settings as in their success and he has the priceless ability to conjure up the feel of places as various and remote as the Mexican jungle (*The Vivero Letter*), the peaks of the Andes (*High Citadel*), the Icelandic wastes (*Running Blind*), and the mountains of New Zealand's South Island (*The Snow Tiger*). He makes the terrain work for him. What the reader gets is never simply a tourist's-eye view of a place, but the living reality.

The same attention to detail is apparent in the technical backgrounds of the stories. It's reasonable to expect a thriller writer to sound as knowledgeable about weapons as Bagley does in, say, his description of Fleet's rifle in *Running Blind* but it takes a scrupulous craftsman to dig as deep as he has obviously done into such esoteric areas of knowledge as computer technology and genetic engineering (*The Enemy*), the history of bronze mirrors

(*The Vivero Letter*), the causes and behaviour of hurricanes (*Wyatt's Hurricane*), of earth tremors (*Landslide*), and of avalanches (*The Snow Tiger*). And it takes a percipient artist to resist the temptation to overload his book with the results of his researches and instead include precisely that amount which is interesting, informative, and authentic. Bagley has the knack of getting the mix just right, nowhere to more effect than in his two recent books *The Snow Tiger* and *The Enemy*.

These two novels also illustrate Bagley's skill at handling both the main prototypes of thriller hero. In *The Enemy* we meet the professional agent, with all the requisite physical and mental ingenuity of his training; in *The Snow Tiger* we have the (fairly) ordinary man, facing a challenge cast down equally by external circumstances and internal awareness. One or the other appears in all his books, and though characterization is not the most powerful weapon in his armoury, he is adept at whittling out heroes who are both identifiable and identifiable with. His favoured method of story-telling is the first-person narrative which permits him to involve the reader as closely as possible in the excitement of life-or-death decisions and explosive action. But when the occasion demands, as in *The Spoilers* or *The Snow Tiger*, Bagley can work with just as much ease within the conventions of a third-person narrative; indeed, in the latter, set in the framework of a Commission of Enquiry into an avalanche disaster, he has brought off a *tour de force* which is perhaps his most substantial work to date.

Action, authenticity, expertise: these are what make Desmond Bagley's books outstanding in their field.

—Reginald Hill

BAILEY, H(enry) C(hristopher). British. Born in London, 1 February 1878. Educated at City of London School; Corpus Christi College, Oxford (Scholar), B.A. 1901. Married Lydia Haden Janet Guest in 1908; two daughters. Drama critic, war correspondent, and leader writer, *Daily Telegraph*, London, 1901–46. *Died 24 March 1961.*

CRIME PUBLICATIONS

Novels (series characters: Joshua Clunk; Reggie Fortune)

> *Garstons* (Clunk). London, Methuen, 1930; as *The Garston Murder Case*, New York, Doubleday, 1930.
> *The Red Castle* (Clunk). London, Ward Lock, 1932; as *The Red Castle Mystery*, New York, Doubleday, 1932.
> *The Man in the Cape.* London, Benn, 1933.
> *Shadow on the Wall* (Fortune). London, Gollancz, and New York, Doubleday, 1934.
> *The Sullen Sky Mystery* (Clunk). London, Gollancz, and New York, Doubleday, 1935.
> *Black Land, White Land* (Fortune). London, Gollancz, and New York, Doubleday, 1937.
> *Clunk's Claimant.* London, Gollancz, 1937; as *The Twittering Bird Mystery*, New York, Doubleday, 1937.
> *The Great Game* (Fortune; Clunk). London, Gollancz, and New York, Doubleday, 1939.
> *The Veron Mystery.* London, Gollancz, 1939; as *Mr. Clunk's Text*, New York, Doubleday, 1939.
> *The Bottle Party.* New York, Doubleday, 1940.

The Bishop's Crime (Fortune).   London, Gollancz, 1940; New York, Doubleday, 1941.
The Little Captain (Clunk).   London, Gollancz, 1941; as *Orphan Ann*, New York, Doubleday, 1941.
Dead Man's Shoes (Clunk).   London, Gollancz, 1942; as *Nobody's Vineyard*, New York, Doubleday, 1942.
No Murder (Fortune).   London, Gollancz, 1942; as *The Apprehensive Dog*, New York, Doubleday, 1942.
Mr. Fortune Finds a Pig.   London, Gollancz, and New York, Doubleday, 1943.
Slippery Ann (Clunk).   London, Gollancz, 1944; as *The Queen of Spades*, New York, Doubleday, 1944.
The Cat's Whisker (Fortune).   New York, Doubleday, 1944; as *Dead Man's Effects*, London, Macdonald, 1945.
The Wrong Man (Clunk; Fortune).   New York, Doubleday, 1945; London, Macdonald, 1946.
The Life Sentence (Fortune).   London, Macdonald, and New York, Doubleday, 1946.
Honour among Thieves (Fortune).   London, Macdonald, and New York, Doubleday, 1947.
Saving a Rope (Fortune).   London, Macdonald, 1948; as *Save a Rope*, New York, Doubleday, 1948.
Shrouded Death (Clunk).   London, Macdonald, 1950.

Short Stories

Call Mr. Fortune.   London, Methuen, 1920; New York, Dutton, 1921.
Mr. Fortune's Practice.   London, Methuen, 1923; New York, Dutton, 1924.
Mr. Fortune's Trials.   London, Methuen, 1925; New York, Dutton, 1926.
Mr. Fortune, Please.   London, Methuen, 1927; New York, Dutton, 1928.
Mr. Fortune Speaking.   London, Ward Lock, 1929; New York, Dutton, 1931.
Mr. Fortune Explains.   London, Ward Lock, 1930; New York, Dutton, 1931.
Case for Mr. Fortune.   London, Ward Lock, and New York, Doubleday, 1932.
Mr. Fortune Wonders.   London, Ward Lock, and New York, Doubleday, 1933.
Mr. Fortune Objects.   London, Gollancz, and New York, Doubleday, 1935.
A Clue for Mr. Fortune.   London, Gollancz, and New York, Doubleday, 1936.
Mr. Fortune's Case Book (omnibus).   London, Methuen, 1936.
Mr. Fortune Here.   London, Gollancz, and New York, Doubleday, 1940.
Meet Mr. Fortune (selection).   New York, Doubleday, 1942.
The Best of Mr. Fortune.   New York, Pocket Books, 1943.

Uncollected Short Stories

"The Thistle Down," in *The Queen's Book of the Red Cross*.   London, Hodder and Stoughton, 1939.
"A Matter of Speculation," in *Anthology 1968 Mid-Year*, edited by Ellery Queen.   New York, Davis, 1968.

OTHER PUBLICATIONS

Novels

My Lady of Orange.   London and New York, Longman, 1901.
Karl of Erbach.   New York, Longman, 1902; London, Longman, 1903.
The Master of Gray.   London and New York, Longman, 1903.
Rimingtons.   London, Chapman and Hall, 1904.
Beaujeu.   London, Murray, 1905.
Under Castle Walls.   New York, Appleton, 1906; as *Springtime*, London, Murray, 1907.

Raoul, Gentleman of Fortune.   London, Hutchinson, 1907; as *A Gentleman of Fortune*, New York, Appleton, 1907.
The God of Clay.   London, Hutchinson, and New York, Brentano's, 1908.
Colonel Stow.   London, Hutchinson, 1908; as *Colonel Greatheart*, Indianapolis, Bobbs Merrill, 1908.
Storm and Treasure.   London, Methuen, and New York, Brentano's, 1910.
The Lonely Queen.   London, Methuen, and New York, Doran, 1911.
The Suburban.   London, Methuen, 1912.
The Sea Captain.   New York, Doran, 1913; London, Methuen, 1914.
The Gentleman Adventurer.   London, Methuen, 1914; New York, Doran, 1915.
The Highwayman.   London, Methuen, 1915; New York, Dutton, 1918.
The Gamesters.   London, Methuen, 1916; New York, Dutton, 1919.
The Young Lovers.   London, Methuen, 1917; New York, Dutton, 1929.
The Pillar of Fire.   London, Methuen, 1918.
Barry Leroy.   London, Methuen, 1919; New York, Dutton, 1920.
His Serene Highness.   London, Methuen, 1920; New York, Dutton, 1922.
The Fool.   London, Methuen, 1921.
The Plot.   London, Methuen, 1922.
The Rebel.   London, Methuen, 1923.
Knight at Arms.   London, Methuen, 1924; New York, Dutton, 1925.
The Golden Fleece.   London, Methuen, 1925.
The Merchant Prince.   London, Methuen, 1926; New York, Dutton, 1929.
Bonaventure.   London, Methuen, 1927.
Judy Bovenden.   London, Methuen, 1928.
Mr. Cardonnel.   London, Ward Lock, 1931.

Play

The White Hawk, with David Kimball, adaptation of the novel *Beaujeu* by Bailey (produced London, 1909).

Other

Forty Years After: The Story of the Franco-German War, 1870.   London, Hodder and Stoughton, 1914.
The Roman Eagles (juvenile).   London, Gill, 1929

*   *   *

One of the Big Five of British mystery writers of the Golden Age, H. C. Bailey has been praised for his puzzles, and many readers delight in his style and characterization. Readers who do not delight usually dislike his major detectives. Is Reggie Fortune "intolerably facetious and whimsical" (Julian Symons) or engagingly benevolent? Is Joshua Clunk a villainous Christian or do his ends justify the means? Critics take sides: detectives are fair game.

More disturbing is the critical inaccuracy of categorizing the well-known Fortune as an intuitive detective. In mild protest, Bailey's Introduction to *Meet Mr. Fortune* informs readers that Reginald Fortune intended to continue in his father's surburban medical practice after studies at Oxford and Vienna. But his testimony in cases arising from the practice made his powers of inference from "slight obscure facts" known to the CID, which drafted him as scientific advisor. A "natural man," Reginald would disclaim any abnormal powers, insists Bailey. Unfortunately for Fortune, the intuitive label persists. Readers, if not critics, however, recognize Fortune's observation and inference. The Hon. Sidney Lomas is his chief, Supt. Bell his admiring colleague, and Inspector Underwood Fortune's choice for a co-worker. Plump, fair, and clean-shaven, the fastidious Fortune looks cherubically youthful even as he ages. He is fond of children and cats, and enjoys his garden and laboratory. Devoted to his wife, Joan, he is a gourmet who can demand lunch after a gory autopsy with the directness of a child. He knows himself. "That's what I'm for. Compellin' the official mind to think." "I'm on the side of those who are wronged. I'm for the weak." The weak are frequently children. He is also for his own justice – not always the legal one.

No authorial biography is provided for Joshua Clunk, but novels reveal that he continued in Covent Garden family quarters for Clunk & Clunk, a law practice in which he is the only Clunk remaining, "a block off the old chip." He deploys a loyal staff in investigating, and lives cozily with Mrs. Clunk in a suburb. Like Fortune, Clunk is plump and fond of children. His method is similar to Fortune's. "Apply your mind!" However, Clunk is of coarser clay. Prominent gray eyes in an ivory-yellow face match his moustache and whiskers. Quantity rather than quality pleases his palate and sucking sweets is his oral vice (no alcohol). Amiable Fortune quotes literature, but affable Clunk croons hymns, quotes the Bible, and runs Gospel Hall. He has an eye for a fee, though frequently there is none, and he is reputed to thwart justice and keep criminals in business. He is also for his own justice – not always the legal one. Clunk criticism is also misleading, especially concerning his relationship with Superintendent Bell.

Obviously Bailey uses the same police personnel in each series and occasionally Fortune and Clunk appear in the same novel. In *The Great Game*, Reggie's case, Clunk represents a client; squeaking, he establishes doubt about police evidence and gets an open verdict. The lawyer and the doctor exchange greetings after the episode. In *The Wrong Man*, Clunk's case, Inspector Underwood calls Reggie, asking about digitalis. Reggie is plaintive: "I cannot tell you whether an overdose in him was murder, suicide, or accident. Your job." A post-mortem is requested.

The Bailey canon? Rarely is any author's work of uniform calibre, and Bailey's, though readable and fair, has its gems. Anthologists and readers select favorites from the tales of Mr. Fortune. A choice few illustrate different situations. "The Hermit Crab" is atypical, a Wodehousian romp, with working girls of the 1920's discomfitting Reggie. "The Yellow Slugs" is "Not nice. No." Called in by Bell on a case of near-drowned children, Reggie finds poor people; a boy and a girl are the real victims, not the corpse; the title is a physical clue. Initially reluctant to go with his wife to a girls' school for "The Greek Play," Reggie finds snobbery and criminous action, not only on stage. He uses medical knowledge to frustrate murder, and wit and physical exertion to conclude the action. Many readers choose *The Bishop's Crime* as the best Fortune novel, a case begun when Reggie finds a mixture of old mortar, red sandstone, and limestone under the fingernails of a tramp found dead. This leads him to his sister and thence to Badon Cathedral for goings-on he suspects if the Bishop does not. Assisted by Inspector Underwood and later by Bell, Reggie uses his knowledge of Dante to reach the solution, and he confronts the whodunits. In *Slippery Ann*, Clunk gets a client acquitted but immediately initiates additional inquiry. This leads him to Sturton, a seaport town, where he uses his operatives, John Scott, a one-armed veteran, and Miss Jones. Both novels demonstrate the superior wit of the detective, his physical activity, and his own kind of justice. For leisurely reading, Mr. Fortune is good fortune, Joshua Clunk fit the battle of whodunit, and the Hon. Victoria Pumphrey, in a single tale, is victorious as a charming lady detective. Bailey entertains.

—Jane Gottschalk

BALL, John (Dudley, Jr.). American. Born in Schenectady, New York, 8 July 1911. Educated at Carroll College, Waukesha, Wisconsin, B.A. 1934. Served in the United States

Army Air Corps during World War II: Lieutenant Colonel; currently, Command Pilot in the Civil Air Patrol. Worked as commercial pilot; Music Editor, the Brooklyn *Eagle*; columnist, New York *World Telegram*; commentator on WOL radio, Washington, D.C.; Director of Public Relations, Institute of the Aerospace Sciences, Los Angeles; Editor-in-Chief, DMS (aerospace) News Service, Beverly Hills, California; science staff member, *Fortune*, New York; Chairman of the Board and Editor-in-Chief, Mystery Library of the University of California, San Diego Extension. Full-time writer since 1958. Recipient: Mystery Writers of America Edgar Allan Poe Award, 1965; Crime Writers Association Gold Dagger, 1966. D.H.L.: Carroll College, 1978. Agent: (literary) Brandt and Brandt, 101 Park Avenue, New York, New York 10017; (films) Swanson Agency, 8523 Sunset Boulevard, Los Angeles, California 90069. Address: 16401 Otsego Street, Encino, California 91436, U.S.A.

CRIME PUBLICATIONS

Novels (series character: Virgil Tibbs)

In the Heat of the Night (Tibbs). New York, Harper, 1965; London, Joseph, 1966.
The Cool Cottontail (Tibbs). New York, Harper, 1966; London, Joseph, 1967.
Johnny Get Your Gun (Tibbs). Boston, Little Brown, 1969; London, Joseph, 1970; revised edition, as *Death for a Playmate*, New York, Bantam, 1972.
The First Team. Boston, Little Brown, 1971; London, Joseph, 1973.
Five Pieces of Jade (Tibbs). Boston, Little Brown, and London, Joseph, 1972.
The Eyes of the Buddha (Tibbs). Boston, Little Brown, 1976.
Mark One – The Dummy. Boston, Little Brown, 1974.
Police Chief. New York, Doubleday, 1977.
The Killing in the Market, with Bevan Smith. New York, Doubleday, 1978.

Uncollected Short Stories

"One for Virgil Tibbs," in *Ellery Queen's Mystery Magazine* (New York), January 1976.
"Full Circle," in *Ellery Queen's Mystery Magazine* (New York), November 1976.
"Virgil Tibbs and the Cocktail Napkin," in *Ellery Queen's Mystery Magazine* (New York), April 1977.
"The Man Who Liked Baseball," in *Ellery Queen's Mystery Magazine* (New York), October 1977.
"Virgil Tibbs and the Fallen Body," in *Ellery Queen's Mystery Magazine* (New York), September 1978.

OTHER PUBLICATIONS

Novels

Rescue Mission. New York, Harper, 1966.
Miss 1000 Spring Blossoms. Boston, Little Brown, 1968.
Last Plane Out. Boston, Little Brown, 1970.
The Fourteenth Point. Boston, Little Brown, 1973.
The Winds of Mitamura. Boston, Little Brown, 1975.
Phase Three Alert. Boston, Little Brown, 1977.

Other

Operation Springboard (juvenile). New York, Duell, 1958; as *Operation Space*, London, Hutchinson, 1960.
Spacemaster I (juvenile). New York, Duell, 1960.

Edwards: Flight Test Center of the U.S.A.F.   New York, Duell, 1962.
Judo Boy (juvenile).   New York, Duell, 1964.
Arctic Showdown (juvenile).   New York, Duell, 1966.
Dragon Hotel (travel).   New York, Walker Wetherhill, 1969.

Editor, *The Mystery Story.*   San Diego, University of California, 1976; London, Penguin, 1978.
Editor, *Cop Cade.*   New York, Doubleday, 1979.

Manuscript Collection: Mugar Memorial Library, Boston University.

John Ball comments:

For as long as I have been writing, I have been doing the books that I genuinely wanted to create; I have never tried to fit into market trends and I have undertaken some projects that I felt sure would not return the time and research costs I would have to invest. *The Fourteenth Point* is an example: to the best of my knowledge no one had ever written a novel based on the religions of the world. The idea appealed to me immensely and I did it – after two trips around the world and visits with religious leaders and institutions in a great many different countries.

To me research and accuracy are prime essentials. I will never make up facts to suit a plot idea if the actual data are available. If they conflict with the plot idea, then it will have to be modified or abandoned. I have a strong personal distaste for writing, no matter how good in itself, which irresponsibly describes places the author has never seen, or which is totally careless in supplying technical data. People believe what they read in books and I want mine to be as accurately informative as I can make them. I determined on this policy in high school when I found that all of the supposed "science" I had read in the Tom Swift books, and had so carefully learned, was the author's own invention. He let me down and I won't do it to others.

I am not a "message" author, but I believe in building books on ideas. For example, the idea behind *In the Heat of the Night* is that in any group of men a WASP is not necessarily the best qualified person present. *The Cool Cottontail* is built on the theme "Don't judge minorities until you know what you're talking about." This gives me a satisfaction in my work and the sales records seem to indicate that the public approves of this approach.

*   *   *

John Ball has had a many-sided career as everything from flight instructor in the Army Air Corps to music editor, science staff writer, and Sherlock Holmes aficionado, writing mystery and flight adventure in equal abundance. With his first mystery, *In the Heat of the Night*, Ball created an original of the growing league of cross-cultural detectives and the best-known black detective in fiction: homicide detective Virgil Tibbs of the Pasadena Police Department. *Mark One – The Dummy*, a non-Tibbs mystery, introduced Ed Nesbitt in a tale of espionage.

Ball's penchant for the Oriental – in literature, religion, and the martial arts – suggests the cross-cultural perspective which he brings to his picture of American culture divided by issues of region and race. This view of cultures in conflict sets up the terms of interracial confrontation which is at the heart of the Tibbs stories. As a black police officer in a white world, Tibbs himself suffers the humiliations of racial intolerance as he works through the solution to his cases. His shrewd, proud repartee with various white tormentors is a hallmark of Ball's style in characterization, in particular one quick comeback to a Southern police chief: "They call me *Mister* Tibbs."

Personal experience in the South, together with a university education and a career in law and science as detective on the Pasadena police force, gives Tibbs an extra purchase – a double or parallax vision – in his detection techniques. (Early in his career his color gives him a "disguise" – as a menial bootblack – behind which he learns vital information.) A positive version of the marginal or bicultural man, he understands two opposed cultures from the inside, allowing him to mediate between these two groups politically, in addition to using logic and value systems of both to intuit and trace events, causes, and motives to arrive at the truth. However, any racial clash also poses more elaborate problems: for example, *In the Heat of the Night* finds Tibbs as the middle man in a confrontation not only of black and white but by implication also of North and South, rich and poor, urban and rural, sophisticated and unlettered.

Like Kemelman's rabbi-detective David Small and Linington's Inspector Luis Mendoza, Tibbs is a striking example of a new breed of cross-cultural or subcultural detective arising in the wake of the ethnic consciousness of the 1960's and 1970's. These figures and their cases (along with such international characters as Christie's Hercule Poirot and Keating's Inspector Ghote) are part of a larger movement rooted in the encounter of subcultures within larger cultures as well as the meeting of national cultures on every level of personality, action, symbol, and value. Political and social conflict is a mainstay of cross-cultural writing, and Ball's concerns are as sociological and ethical as they are literary. In fact, critics have suggested that Ball's deep social consciousness overwhelms and overbalances the fiction. In their serious preoccupation with questions of race, these works deserve quite legitimately to be considered as novels of social problems. Uncomfortable with the tag of "message author," Ball is nonetheless firmly a believer in the power of ideas in the form of literature, and it is a point of pride with him that his works can be read for information as well as for creative imagination. Extensive research into police procedure, undertaken with the advice and guidance of the Pasadena Police Department itself, in addition to on-the-scene field study at the more exotic locales for the later stories, helps the plotting and characterization, giving his writing firm roots in realism.

Tibbs's bicultural character lends his craft of detection an added edge and interest as the key to understanding interracial and pluralistic situations. He is granted a certain detachment and aloofness in the cause of justice as well as a mobility and effectiveness not permitted other more conventional investigators. The second Tibbs book, *The Cool Cottontail*, deals with another (cultural) minority; Tibbs is called into a California nudist colony after a body is found floating in a swimming pool. In *Johnny Get Your Gun*, racial tensions threaten to explode when a disturbed nine-year-old white boy settles a score by shooting a black classmate, and Ball uses the incident to discuss gun laws and the social implications of gun ownership. In *Five Pieces of Jade* Tibbs travels to Asia to look into the murder of a jade collector, involving an *ainoko*, the illegitimate child of a Japanese woman and an American G. I., along with international drug traffic and Red Chinese politics. And in *The Eyes of Buddha* Tibbs, on the trail of an interlocking double mystery, is finally led to the Monkey Temple of Katmandu.

The Tibbs series testifies to the capacity of the mystery/detective novel to stimulate thought and feeling, to educate, and, by extension, to broaden the awareness of the reader in his relations with the world. The power of this type of "light" reading to go beyond entertainment and diversion is the subject of increasing fascination and research.

—Margaret J. King

BALLARD, K. G. See **ROTH, Holly.**

BALLARD, P. D.   See BALLARD, Willis Todhunter.

BALLARD, Willis Todhunter.   Also writes as P. D. Ballard; Parker Bonner; Nick Carter; Harrison Hunt (with Norbert Davis); John Hunter; Neil MacNeil; John Shepherd.   American.   Born in Cleveland, Ohio, 13 December 1903.   Educated at Westtown Preparatory School; Wilmington College, Ohio, B.S. 1926.   Married Phoebe Dwigging in 1936; one son.   Recipient: Western Writers of America Spur Award, 1956.   Agent: August Lenniger, 437 Fifth Avenue, New York, New York.   Address: Box 1042, Mt. Dora, Florida 32757, U.S.A.

CRIME PUBLICATIONS

Novels (series characters: Lieutenant Max Hunter; Bill Lennox)

> *Say Yes to Murder* (Lennox).   New York, Putnam, 1942; as *The Demise of a Louse* (as John Shepherd), New York, Belmont, 1962.
> *Murder Can't Stop* (Lennox).   Philadelphia, McKay, 1946.
> *Murder Picks the Jury* (as Harrison Hunt, with Norbert Davis).   New York, Curl, 1947.
> *Dealing Out Death* (Lennox).   Philadelphia, McKay, 1948.
> *Walk in Fear.*   New York, Fawcett, 1952; London, Red Seal, 1957.
> *Chance Elson.*   New York, Pocket Books, 1958.
> *Lights, Camera, Murder* (Lennox; as John Shepherd).   New York, Belmont, 1960.
> *Pretty Miss Murder* (Hunter).   New York, Permabooks, 1961.
> *The Seven Sisters* (Hunter).   New York, Permabooks, 1962.
> *Three for the Money* (Hunter).   New York, Permabooks, 1963.
> *Murder Las Vegas Style* (Lennox).   New York, Tower, 1967.
> *The Kremlin File* (as Nick Carter).   New York, Award, 1973.

Novels as Neil MacNeil (series characters: Tony Costaine and Bert McCall in all books)

> *Death Takes an Option.*   New York, Fawcett, 1958; London, Fawcett, 1960.
> *Third on a Seesaw.*   New York, Fawcett, 1959; London, Muller, 1961.
> *Two Guns for Hire.*   New York, Fawcett, 1959; London, Muller, 1960.
> *Hot Dam.*   New York, Fawcett, and London, Muller, 1960.
> *The Death Ride.*   New York, Fawcett, 1960; London, Muller, 1962.
> *Mexican Slay Ride.*   New York, Fawcett, 1962; London, Muller, 1963.
> *The Spy Catchers.*   New York, Fawcett, 1966.

Novels as P. D. Ballard

> *Brothers in Blood.*   New York, Fawcett, 1972.
> *Angel of Death.*   New York, Fawcett, 1973.
> *The Death Brokers.*   New York, Fawcett, 1973.

OTHER PUBLICATIONS

Novels

Two-Edged Vengeance.   New York, Macmillan, 1951.
The Circle C Feud.   London, Sampson Low, 1952.
Incident at Sun Mountain.   Boston, Houghton Mifflin, 1952; London, Rich and Cowan, 1954.
West of Quarantine.   Boston, Houghton Mifflin, 1953; London, Rich and Cowan, 1954.
High Iron.   Boston, Houghton Mifflin, 1953; London, Rich and Cowan, 1955.
Rawhide Gunman.   New York, Popular Library, 1954.
Trigger Trail.   New York, Popular Library, 1955.
The Package Deal.   New York, Appleton Century Crofts, 1956; London, Corgi, 1959.
The Long Trail Back.   New York, Doubleday, 1960; London, Jenkins, 1961.
Gunman from Texas.   New York, Popular Library, 1960.
The Night Riders.   New York, Doubleday, 1961; London, Jenkins, 1962.
Gopher Gold.   New York, Doubleday, 1962; as *Gold Fever in Gopher*, London, Jenkins, 1962.
Westward the Monitors Roar.   New York, Doubleday, and London, Jenkins, 1963; as *Fight or Die*, New York, Belmont, 1977.
Guns of the Lawless.   New York, Popular Library, 1963.
Desperation Valley.   New York, Macmillan, 1964.
Gold in California!   New York, Doubleday, 1965.
Look to Your Guns (as Parker Bonner).   New York, Paperback Library, 1969.
The Californian.   New York, Doubleday, 1971.
Nowhere Left to Run.   New York, Doubleday, 1972.
Outlaw Brand (as Parker Bonner).   New York, Avon, 1972.
Applegate's Gold.   New York, Avon, 1973.
Loco and the Wolf.   New York, Doubleday, 1973.
Trouble on the Massacre.   New York, Avon, 1974.
Home to Texas.   New York, Doubleday, 1974.
Trails of Rage.   New York, Doubleday, 1975.
Sheriff of Tombstone.   New York, Doubleday, 1977.

Novels as John Hunter

West of Justice.   Boston, Houghton Mifflin, 1954.
Ride the Wind South.   New York, Permabooks, 1957.
Badlands Buccaneer.   London, Ward Lock, 1961.

Other

The Man Who Stole a University (juvenile), with Phoebe Ballard.   New York, Doubleday, 1967.
How to Defend Yourself, Your Family, and Your Home.   New York, McKay, 1967.

Editor, *A Western Bonanza.*   New York, Doubleday, 1969.

Manuscript Collection: University of Oregon Library, Eugene.

*   *   *

Willis Todhunter Ballard was one of the original contributors to *Black Mask*, the famous American detective pulp magazine which, during the 1930's under the editorship of Joseph

Shaw, pioneered the then-revolutionary hard-boiled detective genre. Ballard, along with Raymond Chandler, Dashiell Hammett, and Erle Stanley Gardner, was one of that magazine's most popular contributors. His series about Bill Lennox, troubleshooter for General Consolidated Studios, which ran for many years in *Black Mask*, set the tone and laid the ground rules for countless Hollywood-milieu mysteries to follow.

The best of Ballard's novels, such as the first Lennox case, *Say Yes to Murder*, are highlighted by a crisp, clean prose style, vivid characterization, rapid plot development, and a singular humaneness. *The Death Brokers*, written as "P. D. Ballard," is a prime example of Ballard's ability to introduce complex characters with only a minimum of wordage into a twisty, imaginative storyline. Originally packaged by Fawcett to exploit the Mafia fad which infested American paperback publishing during the early 1970's, the book stands on its own as a well-crafted evocation of the all-pervasive fear, treachery, and moral decay that is life in the Brotherhood. *Murder Las Vegas Style*, on the other hand, is neo-*Black Mask*: a beautifully written private eye novel in the Raymond Chandler vein.

Many of Ballard's novels are set either completely or partially in Las Vegas, and he always does a convincing job of portraying this fascinating, seldom utilized desert locale with its wide-open casinos, its moral ambiguity, and the uneasy alliance between gamblers and police.

—Stephen Mertz

BALLINGER, Bill S. (William Sanborn Ballinger). Also writes as Frederic Freyer; B. X. Sanborn. American. Born in Oskaloosa, Iowa, 13 March 1912. Educated at the University of Wisconsin, Madison, B.S. 1934. Married 1) Geraldine Taylor in 1936 (divorced, 1948); 2) Laura Dunham in 1949 (died, 1962); 3) Lucille Rambeau in 1964; has two daughters, two sons, one step-daughter, and one step-son. Worked in advertising; radio and television writer, 1934–77; Associate Professor of Writing, California State University, Northridge, 1977–79. Executive Vice-President, Mystery Writers of America, 1957; Member of the Board of Directors, Health and Welfare Plan and Pension Plan, 1977–78, and President of Federal Credit Union, 1978–79, Writers Guild of America. Recipient: Presses de la Cité Prix Roman Policier, 1953; Mystery Writers of America Edgar Allan Poe Award, for tv play, 1960. LL.D.: Northern Colleges of the Philippines, 1940. Guest of Honor, Bouchercon II writing conference, 1971. Agent: Russell and Volkening Inc., 551 Fifth Avenue, New York, New York 10017. Address: P.O. Box 4034, North Hollywood, California 91607, U.S.A.

CRIME PUBLICATIONS

Novels (series characters: Barr Breed; Joaquin Hawks)

> *The Body in the Bed* (Breed). New York, Harper, 1948; London, World Distributors, 1960.
> *The Body Beautiful* (Breed). New York, Harper, 1949; London, World Distributors, 1960.
> *Portrait in Smoke*. New York, Harper, 1950; London, Reinhardt and Evans, 1951; as *The Deadlier Sex*, London, Corgi, 1958.
> *The Darkening Door*. New York, Harper, 1952.
> *Rafferty*. New York, Harper, and London, Reinhardt and Evans, 1953; as *The Beautiful Trap*, New York, New American Library, 1955.
> *The Black, Black Hearse* (as Frederic Freyer). New York, St. Martin's Press, 1955; London, Hale, 1956; as *The Case of the Black, Black Hearse*, New York, Avon, 1955.

The Tooth and the Nail.   New York, Harper, and London, Reinhardt and Evans, 1955.
The Longest Second.   New York, Harper, 1957; London, Reinhardt and Evans, 1958.
The Wife of the Red-Haired Man.   New York, Harper, and London, Reinhardt and Evans, 1957.
Beacon in the Night.   New York, Harper, 1958; London, Boardman, 1960.
Formula for Murder.   New York, New American Library, 1958.
The Doom-Maker (as B. X. Sanborn).   New York, Dutton, and London, Boardman, 1959; as *The Blonde on Borrowed Time*, Rockville Centre, New York, Zenith, 1960.
The Fourth of Forever.   New York, Harper, and London, Boardman, 1963.
The Chinese Mask (Hawks).   New York, New American Library, 1965.
Not I, Said the Vixen.   New York, Fawcett, 1965.
The Spy in Bangkok (Hawks).   New York, New American Library, 1965.
The Spy in the Jungle (Hawks).   New York, New American Library, 1965.
The Heir Hunters.   New York, Harper, 1966; London, Boardman, 1967.
The Spy at Angkor Wat (Hawks).   New York, New American Library, 1966.
The Spy in the Java Sea (Hawks).   New York, New American Library, 1966.
The Source of Fear.   New York, New American Library, 1968; London, Hale, 1971.
The 49 Days of Death.   Los Angeles, Sherbourne Press, 1969.
Heist Me Higher.   New York, New American Library, 1969; London, Hale, 1971.
The Lopsided Man.   New York, Pyramid, 1969.
Triptych (omnibus).   Los Angeles, Sherbourne Press, 1971.
The Corsican.   New York, Dodd Mead, 1974; London, Hale, 1976.
The Law (novelization of tv play).   New York, Warner, 1975.
The Ultimate Warrior (novelization of screenplay).   New York, Warner, 1975.

Other Publications

Plays

Screenplays: *The Strangler*, 1964; *Operation CIA*, with Peter J. Oppenheimer, 1966.

Television Plays: over 150 scripts.

Other

Lost City of Stone.   New York, Simon and Schuster, 1978.
The California Story.   Dubuque, Iowa, Kendall Hunt, 1979.

Manuscript Collection: Mugar Memorial Library, Boston University.

Bill S. Ballinger comments:
I consider myself, primarily, a story-teller. To me the story *is* the thing. Although I usually try to make a point, as all good stories should, I stay away from moralizing and propaganda. Usually, I also try to include some material – "information" – which may be of extra interest to my reader. I have always enjoyed a good plot, the thrill of plotting. Nothing is more pleasant than to receive a letter saying – "You out-guessed me." Although I have been writing for 50 years – first as a "stringer" for newspapers – I intend to keep on with my books.

*   *   *

Bill S. Ballinger began his career writing conventional and clearly derivative hard-boiled detective fiction. His first novel, *The Body in the Bed*, featured a private eye named Barr Breed, and the resemblances between this book and *The Maltese Falcon* go well beyond the fact that their heroes share tough, alliterative, single-syllable names. They extend to the important presence of an antique wooden statue, and to the central role of a woman who is less innocent than she appears to be; in both novels, incidentally, the novelists violate one of the cardinal unwritten rules of this genre by sending their detectives to bed with the murderess. *The Body in the Bed* is somewhat over-complicated and hides too many clues from the reader, but its Chicago setting, its violence, and its emphasis on sex mark it as a typical example of the hard-boiled novel from the period just after World War II.

Ballinger soon abandoned the conventional detective novel, however, and since the early 1950's has concentrated on novels about many different kinds of crime; he has also moved away from the first-person narration of the private eye genre. Instead, Ballinger has specialized in a multi-leveled kind of narration, typified by what is perhaps his best-known book, *The Wife of the Red-Haired Man*. Beginning with an Enoch Arden situation, this novel involves the murder of the second husband by the first, and the subsequent flight of the murderer and the wife from New York to Williamsburg to Kansas City to New Orleans and finally to a small village in Ireland. Chapters telling this story from an omniscient viewpoint alternate with the first-person narration of the detective who is leading the search for the couple. The wife is the most interesting of the characters; she manages the flight, holds her companion together when his fear would betray them, and in the end arranges for him to be killed to save him from what he fears most, a return to prison. The gimmick in the novel (later copied by others) is that the reader does not know until the final page that the detective, who feels a mystical kinship with the fleeing killer, is black.

The same kind of divided narrative is used in *The Tooth and the Nail*. Here the first-person protagonist is a magician whose wife is murdered and who sets out to find the killer and wreak vengeance. The alternating narrative tells, somewhat tediously, the story of a murder trial in which the identity of the accused is kept hidden from the reader. In the end, we learn that the avenger has faked a murder and successfully framed his wife's murderer for the apparent crime. Like many of Ballinger's novels, this one is flawed by an improbability in the early stages – in this case, the fact that the magician has no good reason for withholding what he knows from the police when his wife is murdered. Later in his career, Ballinger used narratives which shift focus among several different characters; in *Beacon in the Night*, the survivors of a criminal network compete with each other for a map purported to show rich Albanian oil deposits. In spite of a too-conventional love triangle, this novel generates a good deal of suspense.

Ballinger's novels are entertainments which often include a puzzle, but they are seldom mystery stories. Typically, they include a considerable amount of bloodshed but (except for the early private eye stories) very little sex, and there is not much character development: the revelation of the racial background of the detective in *The Wife of the Red-Haired Man* is a surprise because we have been allowed to learn very little about the characters. And all of the novels are flawed by a prose which is characteristically wooden, interspersed occasionally with purple descriptions of scenery or exhaustive details, always irrelevant to the narrative; and there is too much twisted syntax, along with occasional blunders in language. But in the best of his novels, Ballinger does generate considerable suspense.

—John M. Muste

BALMER, Edwin. Collaborated with William MacHarg. American. Born in Chicago, Illinois, 26 July 1883. Educated at Northwestern University, Evanston, Illinois, A.B. 1902 (Phi Beta Kappa); Harvard University, Cambridge, Massachusetts, A.M. 1903. Married 1) Katharine MacHarg in 1909 (died, 1925); two daughters and one son; 2) Grace A. Kee in

1927. Reporter, Chicago *Tribune* 1903; associated with Graham Taylor in publishing *The Commons*, New York, 1904–05; Editor, 1927–49, and Associate Publisher, 1949–53, *Red Book* magazine. *Died 21 March 1959.*

CRIME PUBLICATIONS

Novels with William MacHarg

The Surakarta. Boston, Small Maynard, 1913.
The Blind Man's Eyes. Boston, Little Brown, and London, Nash, 1916.
The Indian Drum. Boston, Little Brown, 1917; London, Stanley Paul, 1919.

Novels by Edwin Balmer

Waylaid by Wireless. Boston, Small Maynard, 1909.
Ruth of the U.S.A. Chicago, McClurg, 1919.
Resurrection Rock. Boston, Little Brown, and London, Hodder and Stoughton, 1920.
Her Great Moment. London, Stanley Paul, 1921.
The Breath of Scandal. Boston, Little Brown, 1922; London, Arnold, 1923.
Keeban. Boston, Little Brown, and London, Arnold, 1923.
That Royle Girl. New York, Dodd Mead, 1925.
Dangerous Business. New York, Dodd Mead, 1927; London, Long, 1928.
Flying Death. New York, Dodd Mead, 1927.
Dragons Drive You. New York, Dodd Mead, 1934.
The Torn Letter. New York, Dodd Mead, 1941; London, Nicholson and Watson, 1943.
The Candle of the Wicked. New York, Longman, 1956.

Novels with Philip Wylie

Five Fatal Words. New York, Land and Smith, 1932; London, Stanley Paul, 1933.
The Golden Hoard. New York, Stokes, 1934.
The Shield of Silence. New York, Stokes, 1936; London, Collins, 1937.

Short Stories with William MacHarg

The Achievements of Luther Trant. Boston, Small Maynard, 1910.

Short Stories by William MacHarg

The Affairs of O'Malley. New York, Dial Press, 1940; as *Smart Guy*, New York, Popular Library, 1951.

Uncollected Short Stories by William MacHarg

"The Important Point," in *Fourth Mystery Companion*, edited by Abraham Louis Furman. New York, Lantern Press, 1946.
"Hidden Evidence," in *Best Detective Stories of the Year 1947*, edited by David Coxe Cooke. New York, Dutton, 1947.
"Information Obtained," in *Fireside Mystery Book*, edited by Frank Owen. New York, Lantern Press, 1947.
"Deceiving Clothes," in *The Saint* (New York), March 1955.
"The Murder Trap," in *The Saint* (New York), July 1955.
"The Murderer's Ring," in *The Saint* (New York), May 1956.

"The Vanishing Man," in *The Saint* (New York), September 1956.
"Green Paint and Neat Knots," in *The Saint* (New York), March 1957.

OTHER PUBLICATIONS

Novels

A Wild-Goose Chase.   New York, Duffield, 1915.
Fidelia.   New York, Dodd Mead, 1924.
In His Hands.   New York, Longman, 1954.
With All the World Away.   New York, Longman, 1958.

Novels with Philip Wylie

When Worlds Collide.   New York, Stokes, and London, Stanley Paul, 1933.
After Worlds Collide.   New York, Stokes, and London, Stanley Paul, 1934.

Other

The Science of Advertising.   Chicago, Wallace Press, 1909.

*   *   *

Edwin Balmer and William MacHarg, one-time reporters on the Chicago *Tribune* and successful career writers of popular fiction, collaborated on several mystery-adventures. The best-remembered of them, *The Achievements of Luther Trant*, introduces psychology as a means of detection when an upright student of "the methods of Freud and Jung" uses word association, memory tests, and several elaborate prototypes of the lie detector to solve crimes. In *The Blind Man's Eyes* an attempt is made on the life of a prominent blind lawyer who depends on his daughter and his secretary as his "eyes." He himself discovers the criminals, one of whom must be one of his trusted "eyes." *The Indian Drum* is a tale of crime, romance, hidden identity, and adventure in a prosperous Great Lakes shipping firm.

The characters and values of the Balmer-MacHarg collaborations much resemble those of other popular adventures of the period. The distinction between good and evil is always clear, despite the development of psychology as a theme. Detective heroes are compassionate, cleancut, and men of action; criminal villains, whether the motivation for their crimes is conscious or unconscious, are self-centered, sneering, and cynical.

—Katherine Staples

BARBETTE, Jay.   See **SPICER, Bart.**

BARDIN, John Franklin. Also writes as Douglas Ashe; Gregory Tree.   American.   Born in Cincinnati, Ohio, 30 November 1916. Educated at Walnut Hills

High School, Cincinnati. Married 1) Rhea Schooler Yalowich in 1943; one daughter and one son; 2) Phyllida Korman in 1966. Vice-President and Director of Edwin Bird Wilson Inc., New York, 1944–63; Instructor, New School for Social Research, New York, 1961–66; Senior Editor, *Coronet* magazine, New York, 1968–72; Managing Editor, *Today's Health* magazine, Chicago, 1972–73; Managing Editor of magazines published by the American Bar Association, 1973–74. Currently full-time writer. Agent: Franklin Clark Bardin, 510–12 East 6th Street, New York, New York 10009, U.S.A.

CRIME PUBLICATIONS

Novels

>*The Deadly Percheron.*   London, Gollancz, and New York, Dodd Mead, 1946.
>*The Last of Philip Banter.*   London, Gollancz, and New York, Dodd Mead, 1947.
>*Devil Take the Blue-Tail Fly.*   London, Gollancz, 1948; New York, Macfadden, 1967.
>*A Shroud for Grandmama* (as Douglas Ashe).   New York, Scribner, and London, Gollancz, 1951; as *The Longstreet Legacy*, New York, Paperback Library, 1970.
>*Purloining Tiny.*   New York, Harper, 1978.

Novels as Gregory Tree (series characters: Bill Bradley and Noel Mayberry in first two books)

>*The Case Against Myself.*   New York, Scribner, 1950; London, Gollancz, 1951.
>*The Case Against Butterfly.*   New York, Scribner, 1951.
>*So Young to Die.*   New York, Scribner, and London, Gollancz, 1953.

OTHER PUBLICATIONS

Novels

>*The Burning Glass.*   New York, Scribner, and London, Gollancz, 1950.
>*Christmas Comes But Once a Year.*   New York, Scribner, 1953; London, Davies, 1954.

John Franklin Bardin comments:
A novel is a detector of mined experience. As a soldier walks a mined field with a contraption in front of him that buzzes when it's over a mine, so a novelist, such as I, elaborates a contraption that when the reader experiences it may warn him of the mines of his own emotions. I draw no distinction between the novel and the detective novel: there are only good and bad novels. I have tried to make each of my novels different from all the rest, better to explore other mine fields.

*   *   *

John Franklin Bardin's career as a writer of mystery stories has been an unusual one. In a three-year period (1946–48) he published three interesting novels, *The Deadly Percheron*, *The Last of Philip Banter*, and *Devil Take the Blue-Tail Fly*. Since then he has written other novels, including several orthodox and rather dull crime novels under the pseudonym of Gregory Tree, but the three earlier novels were long out of print and have only recently been reprinted in England, due to the patient efforts of Julian Symons.

Bardin's three novels have close affinities with the Hollywood "film noir" of the 1940's combining eerily mysterious occurrences with an interest in abnormal psychology and dreams, and an almost Gothic sense of the ways in which the past interpenetrates the present. As Symons points out in his Introduction to the Penguin edition, the first two are flawed by a need to provide a surprise ending which, inevitably, fails to surprise; but the third is a brilliant study of the disintegration of an artist where the mystery elements are effortlessly carried by the confusions inherent in the central character's disturbed mind. As in the film noir, all three novels derive much of their power from a continuing sense that the real, "normal" world is always in danger of being overturned by a parallel shadow world of guilt, perversion, and lack of control, a situation that receives its final, terrifying statement in the use of the "split personality" in the closing pages of *Blue-Tail Fly*. It is a pity that Bardin did not see fit to work this rich vein over a longer period.

—John S. Whitley

BARKER, Dudley.   See BLACK, Lionel.

BAWDEN, Nina (Mary Mabey).   British.   Born in London, 19 January 1925. Educated at Ilford County High School; Somerville College, Oxford, B.A. 1946, M.A. 1951; Salzburg Seminar in American Studies, 1960. Married 1) H. W. Bawden in 1946; 2 sons; 2) A. S. Kark in 1954; one son. Assistant, Town & Country Planning Association, 1946–47. Since 1969, Justice of the Peace for Surrey. Member, P.E.N. Executive Committee, 1968–71. Recipient: *Guardian* Award, 1976. Fellow, Royal Society of Literature, 1970. Address: 22 Noel Road, London N1 8HA, England.

CRIME PUBLICATIONS

Novels

Who Calls the Tune.   London, Collins, 1953; as *Eyes of Green*, New York, Morrow, 1953.
The Odd Flamingo.   London, Collins, 1954.
Change Here for Babylon.   London, Collins, 1955.
The Solitary Child.   London, Collins, 1956; New York, Lancer, 1966.
Devil by the Sea.   London, Collins, 1957; Philadelphia, Lippincott, 1959.

OTHER PUBLICATIONS

Novels

Just Like a Lady.   London, Longman, 1960; as *Glass Slippers Always Pinch*, Philadelphia, Lippincott, 1960.

In Honour Bound. London, Longman, 1961.
Tortoise by Candlelight. London, Longman, and New York, Harper, 1963.
Under the Skin. London, Longman, and New York, Harper, 1964.
A Little Love, A Little Learning. London, Longman, and New York, Harper, 1966.
A Woman of My Age. London, Longman, and New York, Harper, 1967.
The Grain of Truth. London, Longman, and New York, Harper, 1968.
The Birds on the Trees. London, Longman, 1970; New York, Harper, 1971.
Anna Apparent. London, Longman, and New York, Harper, 1972.
George Beneath a Paper Moon. London, Allen Lane, and New York, Harper, 1974.
Afternoon of a Good Woman. London, Macmillan, and New York, Harper, 1976.
Familiar Passions. London, Macmillan, and New York, Morrow, 1979.

Other (fiction for children)

The Secret Passage. London, Gollancz, 1963; as *The House of Secrets*, Philadelphia, Lippincott, 1964.
On the Run. London, Gollancz, 1964; as *Three on the Run*, Philadelphia, Lippincott, 1965.
The White Horse Gang. London, Gollancz, and Philadelphia, Lippincott, 1966.
The Witch's Daughter. London, Gollancz, and Philadelphia, Lippincott, 1966.
A Handful of Thieves. London, Gollancz, and Philadelphia, Lippincott, 1967.
The Runaway Summer. London, Gollancz, and Philadelphia, Lippincott, 1969.
Squib. London, Gollancz, and Philadelphia, Lippincott, 1971.
Carrie's War. London, Gollancz, and Philadelphia, Lippincott, 1973.
The Peppermint Pig. London, Gollancz, and Philadelphia, Lippincott, 1975.
Rebel on a Rock. London, Gollancz, and Philadelphia, Lippincott, 1978.
The Robbers. London, Gollancz, and New York, Lothrop, 1979.

*   *   *

Nina Bawden's most conventional detective stories are novels, several of which are written for children, in which young heroes and heroines catch jewel thieves and get involved with immigrant smuggling. But it is the psychology and the mystery of human relationships, in the contexts of crime and political and social unrest, which concern her most. In *Afternoon of a Good Woman* the focus is less on who sends poison pen letters to Penelope and tries to wreck her car than on her emotional life and the people she meets as a magistrate. Why does the jury in the Crown Court decide, against judge's advice, to proceed with the prosecution of a patently innocent man? Bawden quotes Tolstoy – "Human Law – what a farce" – and her sympathy is often with those who want violent change. Her novels are difficult to categorize: in *George Beneath a Paper Moon* – a comedy/love story/thriller, and as Bawden says, "a bit of a moral tale" – set against the background of student unrest in Istanbul, George falls in love with one of the rebels, a girl who may be his daughter. The fates allow and approve, getting rid of George's inconvenient wife in an earthquake.

Bawden commands a range of detective fiction skills. *The Odd Flamingo* shows her capacity to sustain suspense as the dead body proves not to be the anticipated victim, and a missing person, presumed dead, is surprisingly found. She strikes a good plot balance between the neatly characterised chief police investigator and the amateur detective, the accused's solicitor, who becomes fascinated with the girl his client may have murdered.

—Ann Massa

BAX, Roger.   See **GARVE, Andrew.**

BAXT, George.   American.   Born in Brooklyn, New York, 11 June 1923. Attended City College of New York, 1940; Brooklyn College, 1941.

CRIME PUBLICATIONS

Novels (series characters: Pharoah Love; Sylvia Plotkin and Max Van Larsen)

> *A Queer Kind of Death* (Love).   New York, Simon and Schuster, 1966; London, Cape, 1967.
> *Swing Low, Sweet Harriet* (Love).   New York, Simon and Schuster, 1967.
> *A Parade of Cockeyed Creatures; or, Did Someone Murder Our Wandering Boy?* (Plotkin and Van Larsen).   New York, Random House, 1967; London, Cape, 1968.
> *Topsy and Evil* (Love).   New York, Simon and Schuster, 1968.
> *"I!" Said the Demon* (Plotkin and Van Larsen).   New York, Random House, and London, Cape, 1969.
> *The Affair at Royalties.*   London, Macmillan, 1971; New York, Scribner, 1972.
> *Burning Sappho.*   New York, Macmillan, and London, Macmillan, 1972.

Uncollected Short Story

> "So Much Like Me," in *Winter's Crimes 4* edited by George Hardinge.   London, Macmillan, 1972.

OTHER PUBLICATIONS

Plays

> Screenplays: *Circus of Horrors*, 1960; *The City of the Dead (Horror Hotel)*, 1960; *The Shadow of the Cat*, 1961; *Payroll*, 1961; *Night of the Eagle (Burn Witch Burn)*, with Charles Beaumont and Richard Matheson, 1962; *Strangler's Web*, 1965; *Thunder in Dixie*, 1965.

Manuscript collection: Mugar Memorial Library, Boston University.

*   *   *

George Baxt exploded across the skies of mystery fiction like a particularly bright meteor in 1966 with the launching of an excellent series. His brief career was so brilliant that it will take those of us who seek among more enduring stars for his equal long to forget him.

The pair of good, solid books which detail the adventures of Sylvia Plotkin and Max Van Larsen account for part of his total output, but it is the remainder, the Pharoah (sic) Love trilogy, upon which his fame does and will depend. These began with his first, and best known, work *A Queer Kind of Love*, a quite satisfactory murder-puzzle solved by police detective Love. But the book is no more a police procedural novel than are the *Columbo* television movies. What makes it unique is its verisimilitude-laden portrayal of the homosexual underground of New York City. Victim, murderer, *and* detective all belong to this milieu; the presentation mixes irony and clinical objectivity without losing sympathy, a feat in the realm of style and tone analogous to juggling while walking on eggshells.

That book was universally and deservedly praised by reviewers, but the inevitable sequel was even better. In *Swing Low, Sweet Harriet*, Baxt emerged as one of the finest of modern satirists, with the homosexual scene and Busby Berkeley musicals as the chief of his many targets. In the last series book, *Topsy and Evil*, Love surrendered center stage to another black detective (Satan Stagg), but he remained a major figure nevertheless.

Mystery lovers should read the trilogy in proper sequence if possible, but they *should* read it!

—Jeff Banks

BEEDING, Francis. Pseudonym for John Leslie Palmer and Hilary Adam St. George Saunders; also wrote as David Pilgrim. British. **PALMER, John Leslie:** Born in 1885. Educated at Balliol College, Oxford (Brackenbury Scholar). Married Mildred Hodson Woodfield in 1911; one son and one daughter. Drama Critic and Assistant Editor, *Saturday Review of Literature*, London, 1910–15; Drama Critic, *Evening Standard*, London, 1916–19; served in the War Trade Intelligence Department, 1915–19; Member of the British Delegation to the Paris Peace Conference, 1919; Staff Member, Permanent Secretariat of the League of Nations, 1920–39. *Died 5 August 1944.* **SAUNDERS, Hilary Adam St. George:** Born 14 January 1898. Educated at Balliol College, Oxford. Served in the Welch Guard, 1916–19; Military Cross, 1919; worked for the Air Ministry during World War II. Married 1) Helen Foley (died, 1917); 2) Joan Bedford. Staff Member, Permanent Secretariat of the League of Nations, 1920–37; Private Secretary to Fridtjof Nansen, 1921–23; Librarian of the House of Commons, 1946–50. *Died 16 December 1951.*

CRIME PUBLICATIONS

Novels (series characters: Colonel Alastair Granby; Professor Kreutzemark; Inspector George Martin)

The Seven Sleepers (Kreutzemark). London, Hutchinson, and Boston, Little Brown, 1925.
The Little White Hag. London, Hutchinson, and Boston, Little Brown, 1926.
The Hidden Kingdom (Kreutzemark). London, Hodder and Stoughton, and Boston, Little Brown, 1927.
The House of Dr. Edwardes. London, Hodder and Stoughton, 1927; Boston, Little Brown, 1928; as *Spellbound*, Cleveland, World, 1945.
The Six Proud Walkers (Granby). London, Hodder and Stoughton, and Boston, Little Brown, 1928.
The Five Flamboys (Granby). London, Hodder and Stoughton, and Boston, Little Brown, 1929.
Pretty Sinister (Granby). London, Hodder and Stoughton, and Boston, Little Brown, 1929.
The Four Armourers (Granby). London, Hodder and Stoughton, and Boston, Little Brown, 1930.
The League of Discontent (Granby). London, Hodder and Stoughton, and Boston, Little Brown, 1930.

Death Walks in Eastrepps. London, Hodder and Stoughton, and New York, Mystery League, 1931.
The Three Fishers. London, Hodder and Stoughton, and Boston, Little Brown, 1931.
Murder Intended. London, Hodder and Stoughton, and Boston, Little Brown, 1932.
Take It Crooked (Granby). London, Hodder and Stoughton, and Boston, Little Brown, 1932.
The Emerald Clasp. London, Hodder and Stoughton, and Boston, Little Brown, 1933.
The Two Undertakers (Granby). London, Hodder and Stoughton, and Boston, Little Brown, 1933.
The One Sane Man (Granby). London, Hodder and Stoughton, and Boston, Little Brown, 1934.
Mr. Bobadil. London, Hodder and Stoughton, 1934; as *The Street of the Serpents*, New York, Harper, 1934.
Death in Four Letters. London, Hodder and Stoughton, and New York, Harper, 1935.
The Norwich Victims (Martin). London, Hodder and Stoughton, and New York, Harper, 1935.
The Eight Crooked Trenches (Granby). London, Hodder and Stoughton, and New York, Harper, 1936; as *Coffin for One*, New York, Avon, 1943.
The Nine Waxed Faces (Granby). London, Hodder and Stoughton, and New York, Harper, 1936.
The Erring Under-Secretary. London, Hodder and Stoughton, 1937.
Hell Let Loose (Granby). London, Hodder and Stoughton, and New York, Harper, 1937.
No Fury (Martin). London, Hodder and Stoughton, 1937; as *Murdered: One by One*, New York, Harper, 1937.
The Big Fish. London, Hodder and Stoughton, 1938; as *Heads Off at Midnight*, New York, Harper, 1938.
The Black Arrows (Granby). London, Hodder and Stoughton, and New York, Harper, 1938.
The Ten Holy Terrors (Granby). London, Hodder and Stoughton, and New York, Harper, 1939.
Not a Bad Show (Granby). London, Hodder and Stoughton, 1940; as *The Secret Weapon*, New York, Harper, 1940.
Eleven Were Brave (Granby). London, Hodder and Stoughton, 1940; New York, Harper, 1941.
The Twelve Disguises (Granby). London, Hodder and Stoughton, and New York, Harper, 1942.
There Are Thirteen (Granby). London, Hodder and Stoughton, and New York, Harper, 1946.

Novels as David Pilgrim

So Great a Man. London, Macmillan, and New York, Harper, 1937.
No Common Glory. London, Macmillan, and New York, Harper, 1941.
The Grand Design. London, Macmillan, and New York, Harper, 1944.
The Emperor's Servant. London, Macmillan, 1946.

Novels by John Leslie Palmer

Under the Long Barrow (as Christopher Haddon). London, Gollancz, 1939; as *The Man in the Purple Gown*, New York, Dodd Mead, 1939.
Mandragora. London, Gollancz, 1940; as *The Man with Two Names*, New York, Dodd Mead, 1940.

Novels by Hilary Aidan St. George Saunders

The Devil and X.Y.Z., with Geoffrey Dennis (as Barum Browne). London, Gollancz, and New York, Doubleday, 1931.
The Death-Riders, with John de Vere Loder (as Cornelius Cofyn). London, Gollancz, and New York, Knopf, 1935.
The Sleeping Bacchus. London, Joseph, 1951.

Uncollected Short Stories

"Death by Judicial Hanging," in *My Best Thriller*. London, Faber, 1933.
"Me Ne Frego," in *Detective Stories of Today*, edited by Raymond Postgate. London, Faber, 1940.

OTHER PUBLICATIONS by Palmer

Novels

Peter Paragon: A Tale of Youth. London, Secker, and New York, Dodd Mead, 1915.
The King's Men. London, Secker, and New York, Putnam, 1916.
The Happy Fool. London, Christophers, and New York, Harcourt Brace, 1922.
Looking after Joan. London, Christophers, and New York, Harcourt Brace, 1923.
Jennifer. London, Christophers, and New York, Harcourt Brace, 1926.
Timothy. London, Eyre and Spottiswoode, 1931; New York, Doubleday, 1932.

Play

Over the Hills (produced London, 1912). London, Sidgwick and Jackson, 1914.

Other

The Censor and the Theatres. London, Unwin, 1912; New York, Kennerley, 1913.
The Comedy of Manners. London, Bell, 1913.
The Future of the Theatre. London, Bell, 1913.
Comedy. London, Secker, and New York, Doran, 1914.
Bernard Shaw: An Epitaph. London, Richards, 1915; as *George Bernard Shaw, Harlequin or Patriot?*, New York, Century, 1915.
Rudyard Kipling. London, Nisbet, 1915; New York, Holt, 1925(?).
Studies in the Contemporary Theatre. London, Secker, and Boston, Little Brown, 1927.
Molière: His Life and Works. London, Bell, and New York, Brewer and Warren, 1930.
Ben Jonson. London, Routledge, and New York, Viking Press, 1934.
The Hesperides: A Looking-Glass Fugue. London, Secker and Warburg, 1936.
Political [Comic] Characters of Shakespeare. London, Macmillan, 2 vols., 1945–46; New York, St. Martin's Press, 1961.

OTHER PUBLICATIONS by Saunders

Other

The Battle of Britain, August–October 1940: An Air Ministry Record. London, Ministry of Information, 1941.
Bomber Command: The Air Ministry's Account of Bomber Command's Offensive Against the Axis. London, Ministry of Information, 1941.
Combined Operations, 1940–1942. London, His Majesty's Stationery Office, 1943; as *Combined Operations: The Official Story of the Commandos*, New York, Macmillan, 1943.

Return at Dawn: The Official Story of the New Zealand Bomber Squadron of the R.A.F. Wellington, New Zealand Tourist and Publicity Department, 1943.
Pioneers! O Pioneers! London and New York, Macmillan, 1944.
Per Ardua: The Rise of British Air Power, 1911–1939. London, Oxford University Press, 1944.
Ford at War. London, Harrison, 1946.
The Left Hand Shakes: The Boy Scout Movement During the War. London, Collins, 1948.
Valiant Voyaging: A Short History of the British India Steam Navigation Company in the Second World War. London, Faber, 1948.
The Green Beret: The Story of the Commandos, 1940–1945. London, Joseph, 1949.
The Middlesex Hospital, 1745–1948. London, Parrish, 1949.
The Red Cross and the White: A Short History of the Joint War Organization of the British Red Cross Society and the Order of St. John of Jerusalem. London, Hollis and Carter, 1949.
The Red Beret: The Story of the Parachute Regiment at War. London, Joseph, 1951.
Westminster Hall. London, Joseph, 1951.
Royal Air Force, 1939–1945, with Denis Richards. London, Her Majesty's Stationery Office, 3 vols., 1954.

*   *   *

Francis Beeding and David Pilgrim were the shared pseudonyms of two English writers, John Leslie Palmer and Hilary Aidan St. George Saunders, who met shortly after 1920 in Geneva where they were both serving in the League of Nations Permanent Secretariat. Their acquaintanceship soon developed into a literary collaboration that lasted for years and eventually produced some fifty detective novels and thrillers by which they are best known. When Palmer and Saunders resigned from the League in 1939, they had published as Francis Beeding almost a score of thrillers about the espionage adventures of Colonel Alastair Granby, D.S.O., of the British Intelligence Service and a number of exceptionally fine *romans policiers*. Under the pseudonym of David Pilgrim, they also produced several noteworthy detective novels.

Saunders once explained the success of their collaboration by saying, "Palmer can't be troubled with description and narrative, and I'm no good at creating characters or dialogue." Their literary aim, it has been said, was to take as contemporary a situation as possible and deal with it in a way that did not run absolutely counter to the rules of plausibility. Their pseudonymous anonymity permitted them the freedom to be as extravagant as they wished in their presentation of issues and their invention of incidents.

Of all Palmer and Saunders's collaborative detective novels, *Death Walks in Eastrepps* is today the best known – and by common consent the best written and conceived. Set in the quiet English seacoast village of Eastrepps, this fast-paced detective story of multiple brutal murder is a "page-turner" beyond compare filled with mounting, almost unendurable suspense. Considered by Vincent Starrett "one of the ten greatest detective novels" ever written, *Death Walks in Eastrepps* boasts a unique crime motive, an impressive gallery of engaging characters, a superb and highly satisfying surprise-ending, and a dramatic Old Bailey courtroom sequence that ranks with Agatha Christie's *Witness for the Prosecution*.

Other successes by this talented team are *The House of Dr. Edwardes*, a detective novel filmed by Alfred Hitchcock as *Spellbound*, and *The Norwich Victims*, a thriller, filmed by Emlyn Williams as *Dead Men Tell No Tales*.

—Arthur Nicholas Athanason

BEHN, Noel. American. Born in Chicago, Illinois, 6 January 1928. Educated at the University of Wyoming, Cheyenne, 1946–47; Stanford University, California, B.A. 1950; University of Paris, 1950–51. Served in the United States Army Counter Intelligence, 1952–54. Married Jo Ann Le Compte in 1956 (divorced, 1961). Producer at East Chop Playhouse, Martha's Vineyard, Massachusetts, Summer 1954; Co-Manager, Flint Musical Tent Theatre, Michigan, Summer 1955; Producer and Operator of Cherry Lane Theatre, New York, 1956–61; Producer at Edgewater Beach Playhouse, Chicago, Summers 1957–60. Recipient: Obie Award, 1958. Address: 73 Horatio Street, New York, New York 10014, U.S.A.

CRIME PUBLICATIONS

Novels

> *The Kremlin Letter.* New York, Simon and Schuster, and London, W. H. Allen, 1966.
> *The Shadowboxer.* New York, Simon and Schuster, 1969; London, Hart Davis, 1970.

OTHER PUBLICATIONS

Other

> *Big Stick-Up at Brink's!* New York, Putnam, 1977.

*   *   *

Noel Behn's first espionage thriller, *The Kremlin Letter*, was widely reviewed; the *New York Times* and *Time* magazine harshly condemned Behn's explicit depiction of sex and sadism and remarked on the improbable premise of the plot. That a team of American agents could be put into Russia, make their way unnoticed to Moscow and there live undetected for weeks while they set about locating and retrieving an indiscreet letter sent to a Russian official by Western politicians seems no less improbable now than it did in 1966, although Behn deserves high marks for the novel's circumstantiality of setting and detail. But a decade of revelations about the conduct of covert operations by the FBI and the CIA ought to vindicate Behn from the charge of having exaggerated the conscience-numbing amorality of intelligence operations. Behn's nominal hero, Charles Rone, has two distinguishing qualities: his photographic memory and his alleged willingness to let another person die in his place if need be. His fellow operatives have compatible talents and values. Skilled in motivating betrayal, they routinely resort to violence, sex, drugs – whatever works.

The Shadowboxer, Behn's second thriller, is set in Germany in 1944 and depicts, with the same thumb-in-the-eye realism, characters and scenes that are, if possible, more despicable than those in *The Kremlin Letter*. Eric Spangler, the shadowboxer of the title, is a tormented, enigmatic agent with an uncanny ability to get into and out of concentration camps at will. He is treacherously used by his American masters to further the establishment of a provisional German government. Spangler, however, is less a character in his own right than a device by means of which Behn can make his point: that in their ruthless expediency, the Americans are indistinguishable from their German counterparts who are administering the death camps. *The Kremlin Letter* and *The Shadowboxer* are books infused with undisguised anger and revulsion. When Behn returned to writing in 1977, after an eight-year silence, it was not to the espionage novel but to the non-fiction novel and an account of the Brink's robbery.

—R. Gordon Kelly

BELL, Josephine. Pseudonym for Doris Bell Ball, née Collier. British. Born in Manchester, Lancashire, 8 December 1897. Educated at Godolphin School, 1910–16; Newnham College, Cambridge, 1916–19; University College Hospital, London, M.R.C.S., L.R.C.P., 1922, M.B., B.S. 1924. Married Norman Dyer Ball in 1923 (died, 1936); one son and three daughters. Practiced medicine with her husband in Greenwich and London, 1927–35, and in Guildford, Surrey, 1936–54; Member of the Management Committee, St. Luke's Hospital, 1954–62. Co-Founder, Crime Writers Association, 1953. Agent: Curtis Brown Ltd., 1 Craven Hill, London W2 3EP. Address: Jasmine Cottage, 88 The Street, Puttenham, Surrey GU3 1AU, England.

Crime Publications

Novels (series characters: Dr. Henry Frost; Inspector Steven Mitchell; Claude Warrington-Reeve; Dr. David Wintringham)

Murder in Hospital (Wintringham; Mitchell). London, Longman, 1937.
Death on the Borough Council (Wintringham). London, Longman, 1937.
Fall over Cliff (Wintringham; Mitchell). London, Longman, 1938; New York, Macmillan, 1956.
The Port of London Murders (Mitchell). London, Longman, 1938; New York, Macmillan, 1958.
Death at Half-Term (Wintringham; Mitchell). London, Longman, 1939; as *Curtain Call for a Corpse*, New York, Macmillan, 1965.
From Natural Causes (Wintringham). London, Longman, 1939.
All Is Vanity (Wintringham). London, Longman, 1940.
Trouble at Wrekin Farm (Wintringham). London, Longman, 1942.
Death at the Medical Board (Wintringham). London, Longman, 1944; New York, Ballantine, 1964.
Death in Clairvoyance (Wintringham; Mitchell). London, Longman, 1949.
The Summer School Mystery (Wintringham; Mitchell). London, Methuen, 1950.
To Let, Furnished. London, Methuen, 1952; as *Stranger on a Cliff*, New York, Ace, 1964.
Bones in the Barrow (Wintringham; Mitchell). London, Methuen, 1953; New York, Macmillan, 1955.
Fires at Fairlawn (Wintringham). London, Methuen, 1954.
Death in Retirement (Wintringham). London, Methuen, and New York, Macmillan, 1956.
The China Roundabout (Wintringham; Mitchell). London, Hodder and Stoughton, 1956; as *Murder on the Merry-Go-Round*, New York, Ballantine, 1965.
Double Doom. London, Hodder and Stoughton, 1957; New York, Macmillan, 1958.
The Seeing Eye (Wintringham; Mitchell). London, Hodder and Stoughton, 1958.
The House above the River. London, Hodder and Stoughton, 1959.
Easy Prey (Warrington-Reeve; Mitchell). London, Hodder and Stoughton, and New York, Macmillan, 1959.
A Well-Known Face (Warrington-Reeve; Mitchell). London, Hodder and Stoughton, and New York, Washburn, 1960.
New People at the Hollies. London, Hodder and Stoughton, and New York, Macmillan, 1961.
Adventure with Crime. London, Hodder and Stoughton, 1962.
A Flat Tyre in Fulham (Warrington-Reeve; Mitchell). London, Hodder and Stoughton, 1963; as *Fiasco in Fulham*, New York, Macmillan, 1963; as *Room for a Body*, New York, Ballantine, 1964.
The Hunter and the Trapped. London, Hodder and Stoughton, 1963.
The Upfold Witch (Frost). London, Hodder and Stoughton, and New York, Macmillan, 1964.

No Escape. London, Hodder and Stoughton, 1965; New York, Macmillan, 1966.

Death on the Reserve (Frost). London, Hodder and Stoughton, and New York, Macmillan, 1966.

The Catalyst. London, Hodder and Stoughton, 1966; New York, Macmillan, 1967.

Death of a Con Man. London, Hodder and Stoughton, and Philadelphia, Lippincott, 1968.

The Fennister Affair. London, Hodder and Stoughton, 1969; New York, Stein and Day, 1977.

The Wilberforce Legacy. London, Hodder and Stoughton, and New York, Walker, 1969.

A Hydra with Six Heads. London, Hodder and Stoughton, 1970; New York, Stein and Day, 1977.

A Hole in the Ground. London, Hodder and Stoughton, 1971; New York, Ace, 1973.

Death of a Poison-Tongue. London, Hodder and Stoughton, 1972; New York, Stein and Day, 1977.

A Pigeon among the Cats. London, Hodder and Stoughton, 1974; New York, Stein and Day, 1977.

Victim. London, Hodder and Stoughton, 1975; New York, Walker, 1976.

The Trouble in Hunter Ward. London, Hodder and Stoughton, 1976; New York, Walker, 1977.

Such a Nice Client. London, Hodder and Stoughton, 1977; as *Stroke of Death*, New York, Walker, 1977.

A Swan Song Betrayed. London, Hodder and Stoughton, 1978; as *Treachery in Type*, New York, Walker, 1979.

Wolf! Wolf! London, Hodder and Stoughton, 1979.

Uncollected Short Stories

"The Case of the Faulty Drier," "Gale Warning," "Death in Ambrose Ward," "The Thimble River Murder," and "Death in a Cage," in *The Evening Standard Detective Book.* London, Gollancz, 1950.

"The Packet-Boat Murder," in *The Evening Standard Detective Book*, 2nd series. London, Gollancz, 1951.

"The Sea Decides," in *Planned Departures*, edited by Elizabeth Ferrars. London, Hodder and Stoughton, 1958.

"Wash, Set, and Murder," in *The Mystery Bedside Book*, edited by John Creasey. London, Hodder and Stoughton, 1960.

"Death in a Crystal," in *The Saint* (New York), August 1960.

"A Case of Fugue," in *Crime Writers' Choice*, edited by Roy Vickers. London, Hodder and Stoughton, 1964.

"Murder Delayed," in *Crimes Across the Sea*, edited by John Creasey. London, Longman, and New York, Harper, 1964.

"Experiment," in *The Saint* (New York), October 1965.

"The Commuters," in *John Creasey's Mystery Bedside Book*, edited by Herbert Harris. London, Hodder and Stoughton, 1966.

"The Unfinished Heart," in *John Creasey's Mystery Bedside Book 1974*, edited by Herbert Harris. London, Hodder and Stoughton, 1973.

OTHER PUBLICATIONS

Novels

The Bottom of the Well. London, Longman, 1940.
Martin Croft. London, Longman, 1941.
Alvina Foster. London, Longman, 1943.

Compassionate Adventure. London, Longman, 1946.
Total War at Haverington. London, Longman, 1947.
Wonderful Mrs. Marriott. London, Longman, 1948.
The Whirlpool. London, Methuen, 1949.
Backing Winds. London, Methuen, 1951.
Cage-Birds. London, Methuen, 1953.
Two Ways to Love. London, Methuen, 1954.
Hell's Pavement. London, Methuen, 1955.
The Convalescent. London, Bles, 1960.
Safety First. London, Bles, 1962.
The Alien. London, Bles, 1964.
Tudor Pilgrimage. London, Bles, 1967.
Jacobean Adventure. London, Bles, 1969.
Over the Seas. London, Bles, 1970.
The Dark and the Light. London, Bles, 1971.
To Serve a Queen. London, Bles, 1972.
In the King's Absence. London, Bles, 1973.
A Question of Loyalties. London, Bles, 1974.

Other

Crime in Our Time. London, Nicholas Vane, 1961; New York, Abelard Schuman, 1962.

*   *   *

A requisite of the detective novel is someone who detects. Yet Josephine Bell's novels – traditional, numerous, and a product of the golden age of such fiction – omit the Great Detective. Since characters impressive in their variety, vitality, and realistic naturalism are one of Bell's accomplishments, it is perhaps not unexpected that her works fail to utilize a central series figure. Barzun and Taylor observe that Bell "has written more than she should if she had any hope of becoming a classic," but it is possible that her choice not to use a highly visible continuing figure bears the main responsibility for her lesser reputation.

Josephine Bell is a decidedly competent craftsman. Her writing is seamless (never drawing attention through stylistic eccentricity), quietly ironic, economic without terseness, and mildly flavored with effective humor. Third-person narration is the rule. Authorial comment is seldom intrusive but often foreshadows or underscores. Narrative is more prevalent than dialogue, but the characters' lines, when spoken, ring true. Like Ross Macdonald, whom she does not otherwise resemble, she has a good sense of domestic conflict, effectively sketching out the difficulties of living with tedious, humorless, quarrelsome family members one must not only endure but for whom one tries to care.

Bell's early works are traditional. Dr. David Wintringham appears destined to become a strong detective figure. However, it is Inspector Mitchell of Scotland Yard (who appears in the same novels, as well as those featuring the barrister Warrington-Reeve) who comes up with the crucial clues which are the result of painstaking detection or the correct interpretation of what his amateur colleague has discovered. Early works such as *Death at Half-Term* and *Fall over Cliff* as well as later ones such as *A Flat Tyre in Fulham* and *The China Roundabout* follow this pattern and are effective puzzles, though the last one resembles the thriller.

Consistent throughout the novels is the figure of the young, idealistic, overworked, and underpaid physician. Hospital routine and personnel figure prominently. Also consistent is the love affair involving a young career girl on whom the work, in the absence of a series figure, often focuses. Criminals are usually evil, rather than simply misguided, and include both amateurs and professionals. The strongest passion presented is hatred, and sexual desire is sordid, heartless, and often deadly. The weakest aspect of Bell's art is plotting. Action is sometimes insufficient to sustain the interest and suspects too few to provide the suspense necessary for a strong conclusion.

Josephine Bell writes novels which fit into a number of categories, although in few cases is the fit exact. The isolated heroine with a tragic past and the brooding figure of the principal male character place *To Let, Furnished* squarely in the gothic tradition of *Jane Eyre* and *Rebecca*. Notable departures from this formula, however, include the facts that the heroine is forty, and the mother of two, and that the mansion is in perfect repair. A feature of *Double Doom*, a kind of mystery melodrama, is one of the author's most unusual characters, the thirty-eight-year-old Joyce Morley who has the mental age of twelve.

Two other works of particular interest are *The Catalyst*, a domestic tragedy in which young lovers serve as chorus and detective, and *Death in Retirement*, a classic mystery centering on Dr. Clayton, one of Miss Bell's most fascinating older women. In both, characterization is absorbing, pace good, and conclusion equal to the development. *Bones in the Barrow* is a good example of the unvarnished, even grisly, presentation of the facts of a crime and of the communal method, including police procedure, of getting at the truth. There is an unusual love story, as well. Later novels, especially those of the 1970's, tend to be thrillers rather than puzzles. *Such a Nice Client* is essentially a thesis novel, making a strong indictment of the simplistic views of social workers.

Josephine Bell has a distinctive voice, and among her novels are those whose combination of qualities will please most readers and whose characters will be hard to forget.

—Nancy Ellen Talburt

BELLAIRS, George. Pseudonym for Harold Blundell. British. Born in Heywood, Lancashire, 19 April 1902. Educated at Heywood Grammar School; London School of Economics, B.Sc. 1928. Married Gwladys Mabel Roberts in 1930. Banker: Superintendent of Branches, Manchester, 1949–53, and Chief of the Manchester office, 1953–62, Martin's Bank. Member of the Board, United Manchester Hospitals and Manchester Royal Infirmary. M.A.: University of Manchester, 1958. Agent: John Gifford Ltd., 125 Charing Cross Road, London WC2H 0EB, England. Address: Gat-y-Whing, Colby, Isle of Man.

Crime Publications

Novels (series character: Chief Inspector/Detective Inspector/Superintendent Thomas Littlejohn in all books except *Turmoil in Zion*)

Littlejohn on Leave. London, Gifford, 1941.
The Four Faithful Servants. London, Gifford, 1942.
Death of a Busybody. London, Gifford, 1942; New York, Macmillan, 1943.
The Dead Shall Be Raised. London, Gifford, 1942; as *Murder Will Speak*, New York, Macmillan, 1943.
Turmoil in Zion. London, Gifford, 1943; as *Death Stops the Frolic*, New York, Macmillan, 1944.
The Murder of a Quack. London, Gifford, 1943; New York, Macmillan, 1944.
Calamity at Harwood. New York, Macmillan, 1945; London, Gifford, 1946.
He'd Rather Be Dead. London, Gifford, 1945.
Death in the Night Watches. London, Gifford, 1945; New York, Macmillan, 1946.
The Crime at Halfpenny Bridge. London, Gifford, 1946.

The Case of the Scared Rabbits.   London, Gifford, 1947.
The Case of the Seven Whistlers.   London, Gifford, and New York, Macmillan, 1948.
Death on the Last Train.   London, Gifford, 1948; New York, Macmillan, 1949.
The Case of the Famished Parson.   London, Gifford, and New York, Macmillan, 1949.
Outrage on Gallows Hill.   London, Gifford, 1949.
The Case of the Demented Spiv.   London, Gifford, 1949; New York, Macmillan, 1950.
The Case of the Headless Jesuit.   London, Gifford, 1950; as *Death Brings In the New Year*, New York, Macmillan, 1951.
Dead March for Penelope Blow.   London, Gifford, and New York, Macmillan, 1951.
Death in Dark Glasses.   London, Gifford, and New York, Macmillan, 1952.
Crime in Lepers' Hollow.   London, Gifford, 1952.
A Knife for Harry Dodd.   London, Gifford, 1953.
Half-Mast for the Deemster.   London, Gifford, 1953.
Corpses in Enderby.   London, Gifford, 1954.
The Cursing Stones Murder.   London, Gifford, 1954.
Death in Room Five.   London, Gifford, 1955.
Death Treads Softly.   London, Gifford, 1956.
Death Drops the Pilot.   London, Gifford, 1956.
Death in High Provence.   London, Gifford, 1957.
Death Sends for the Doctor.   London, Gifford, 1957.
Corpse at the Carnival.   London, Gifford, 1958.
Murder Makes Mistakes.   London, Gifford, 1958.
Bones in the Wilderness.   London, Gifford, 1959.
Toll the Bell for Murder.   London, Gifford, 1959.
Death in the Fearful Night.   London, Gifford, 1960.
Death in Despair.   London, Gifford, 1960.
Death of a Tin God.   London, Gifford, 1961.
The Body in the Dumb River.   London, Gifford, 1961.
Death Before Breakfast.   London, Gifford, and New York, British Book Centre, 1962.
The Tormentors.   London, Gifford, 1962.
Death in the Wasteland.   London, Gifford, 1963; New York, British Book Centre, 1964.
Surfeit of Suspects.   London, Gifford, 1964.
Death of a Shadow.   London, Gifford, 1964.
Death Spins the Wheel.   London, Gifford, 1965.
Intruder in the Dark.   London, Gifford, 1966.
Strangers among the Dead.   London, Gifford, 1966.
Death in Desolation.   London, Gifford, 1967.
Single Ticket to Death.   London, Gifford, 1967.
Fatal Alibi.   London, Gifford, 1968.
Murder Gone Mad.   London, Gifford, 1968.
Tycoon's Death-Bed.   London, Gifford, 1970.
The Night They Killed Joss Varran.   London, Gifford, 1970.
Pomeroy, Deceased.   London, Gifford, 1971.
Murder Adrift.   London, Gifford, 1972.
Devious Murder.   London, Gifford, 1973.
Fear round About.   London, Gifford, 1975.
Close All Roads to Sospel.   London, Gifford, 1976.

*   *   *

George Bellairs writes classic British detective fiction laced with comic byplay. Scotland Yard Inspector Thomas Littlejohn, later promoted to Chief Superintendent, is responsible for collecting clues and drawing inferences from them, while the humor is provided by a fantastic collection of eccentrics and colorful figures.

As puzzles, Bellairs's books are fairly typical of their genre. The least likely suspect is often guilty; along these lines, *The Case of the Seven Whistlers* and *Pomeroy, Deceased* are particularly surprising. The mystery's solution often depends on Littlejohn's destroying an apparent alibi; in fact, *Death in the Night Watches* is virtually a study in alibis. Littlejohn's instinctive reactions should also be noted since frequently someone who initially repels him turns out to be guilty of murder. In general, Bellairs plays fair with the reader, enabling him to compete with Littlejohn in unravelling the mystery, although in *The Case of the Famished Parson* we are misled by a deceptive glimpse into the murderer's mind. The one technical flaw which recurs in Bellairs's work is an extended denouement after the killer's identity becomes known both to the reader and to the fictional police. Sometimes this interval is genuinely exciting (*The Case of the Demented Spiv*) or psychologically intriguing (*Calamity at Harwood*), but sometimes it is simply tedious.

Bellairs's books are comic in spirit, and where the humor works minor structural flaws are easily forgiven. Bellairs works in a comic tradition that extends from Ben Jonson through contemporary situation comedies on television. Each character has a particular trait exaggerated to the point of obsession or caricature. Some eccentrics are affectionately drawn – for example, the rather vague, bee-keeping and sherry-drinking Rev. Ethelred Claplady in *Death of a Busybody* and his poignant reappearance in *Dead March for Penelope Blow*. The local police, too, are generally treated sympathetically, and a recurring figure is the earnest young constable (often with a ludicrous name) who earns his sergeant's stripes for good work on Littlejohn's case. Poseurs and hypocrites, on the other hand, are described with satiric bite – Lorrimer and Wynyard in *Death of a Busybody*, for example. Several stock characters recur, including drunken physicians, crotchety coroners, and tyrannic daughters-in-law.

Humorous detective stories can be delightful, but the writer in this difficult genre risks irritating his readers whenever the humor is unsuccessful or when it detracts from development of the central story line. Bellairs's work is markedly uneven for this reason. He is at his best when the eccentricities or comic traits are functional to the plot rather than superfluous additions. Among his successful works in this sense are *Death Before Breakfast*, *The Case of the Demented Spiv*, *The Murder of a Quack*, *The Dead Shall Be Raised*, *Tycoon's Death-Bed*, and *The Night They Killed Joss Varran*.

—Susan B. MacDougall

BELLEM, Robert Leslie. Also wrote as Franklin Charles (with Cleve F. Adams); John A. Saxon. American. Born in 1902. *Died in 1968.*

CRIME PUBLICATIONS

Novels

> *Blue Murder.* New York, Phoenix Press, 1938.
> *The Window with the Sleeping Nude.* Kingston, New York, Quin, 1950.
> *The Vice Czar Murders* (as Franklin Charles; with Cleve F. Adams). New York, Funk and Wagnalls, 1941.
> *Half-Past Mortem* (as John A. Saxon). New York, Mill, 1947; London, Foulsham, 1949.
> *No Wings on a Cop* (expanded by Bellem from story by Cleve F. Adams). Kingston, New York, Quin, 1950.

Uncollected Short Stories

"Gun from Gotham," in *Rue Morgue No. 1*, edited by Rex Stout and Louis
Greenfield. New York, Creative Age Press, 1946.
"Death's Passport," in *The Pulps: Fifty Years of American Pop Culture*, edited by Tony
Goodstone. New York, Chelsea House, 1970.
"The Lake of the Left-Hand Moon," in *The American Detective*, edited by William
Kittredge and Steven M. Krauzer. New York, New American Library, 1978.

OTHER PUBLICATIONS

Plays

Television Plays: for *The Lone Ranger*, *Superman*, *Broken Arrow*, *Perry Mason*, *77
Sunset Strip*, *Death Valley Days*, and *The FBI* series.

Bibliography: "The Further Adventures of Robert Leslie Bellem; or, The Bellem-Adams
Connection" by Stephen Mertz, in *Xenophile* (St. Louis), March-April 1978.

Manuscript Collection: University of California at Los Angeles.

* * *

Robert Leslie Bellem was a prolific writer for the American pulp magazines, producing
over 3,000 published stories between his first sale to *Argosy* in 1925 and the folding of the
pulp markets in 1950. His work appeared in magazines of every conceivable category, from
adventure and sports to westerns and mysteries. Although much of his output was hurriedly
written and hackneyed, his best work was characterized by a colorful, colloquial style, swift
plot development, and a talent for setting the plot in motion full-throttle with the opening
paragraph.

With his series about Dan Turner, Hollywood Detective, begun in 1934, Bellem
established himself as detective fiction's brightest satirist. The series, which ran for sixteen
years in pulps like *Spicy Detective*, *Speed Detective*, and *Dan Turner: Hollywood Detective*
(which for a time was devoted exclusively to Turner's adventures), comprises the longest
running, most inventive parody of the hard-boiled private eye genre ever conceived.
Humorist S. J. Perelman called Turner "the apotheosis of all private detectives ... out of Ma
Barker by Dashiell Hammett's Sam Spade." The stories provided Bellem with an ongoing
vehicle for constantly twisting fresh, irreverent, funny angles out of the Hammett/Chandler
tradition. Turner was always "setting fire to a gasper" or reaching for his "roscoe." He also
had an eye for the fairer sex ("Her bosom surged up and down like buoys in a Catalina
ground-swell").

The series was extremely popular, yet only three of Turner's whacky capers have ever
been anthologized in book form.

William Marshall portrayed Turner in the movie *Blackmail* (1947), the Hollywood dick's
single screen appearance.

Blue Murder and *The Window with the Sleeping Nude* are both representative of his
tongue-in-cheek hard-boiled approach; this approach was to have a strong influence on such
later stylists as Richard S. Prather, Carter Brown, and Mickey Spillane.

—Stephen Mertz

BENNETT, Margot. British. Born in Lenzie, Scotland, in 1912. Educated at schools in Scotland and Australia. Married Richard Bennett in 1938; one daughter and three sons. Worked as an advertising copywriter in Sydney and London in the 1930's. Agent: David Higham Associates Ltd., 5–8 Lower John Street, London W1R 4HA. Address: 2 South Hill Park Gardens, London N.W.3, England.

CRIME PUBLICATIONS

Novels

> Time to Change Hats. London, Nicholson and Watson, 1945; New York, Doubleday, 1946.
> Away Went the Little Fish. London, Nicholson and Watson, and New York, Doubleday, 1946.
> The Widow of Bath. London, Eyre and Spottiswoode, and New York, Doubleday, 1952.
> Farewell Crown and Good-Bye King. London, Eyre and Spottiswoode, 1953; New York, Walker, 1961.
> The Man Who Didn't Fly. London, Eyre and Spottiswoode, 1955; New York, Harper, 1956.
> Someone from the Past. London, Eyre and Spottiswoode, and New York, Dutton, 1958.

Uncollected Short Stories

> "An Old-Fashioned Poker for My Uncle's Head," in Magazine of Fantasy and Science Fiction (New York), 1946.
> "No Bath for the Browns," in Alfred Hitchcock Presents: Stories Not for the Nervous. New York, Random House, 1965.

OTHER PUBLICATIONS

Novels

> The Golden Pebble. London, Nicholson and Watson, 1948.
> The Long Way Back. London, Lane, 1954; New York, Coward McCann, 1955.
> That Summer's Earthquake. London, Eyre and Spottiswoode, 1964.
> The Furious Masters. London, Eyre and Spottiswoode, 1968.

Plays

> Screenplays: The Crowning Touch, 1959; The Man Who Liked Funerals, 1959.

> Television Plays: Emergency Ward Ten series (20 episodes); The Sun Divorce, 1956; The Widow of Bath, from her own novel, 1959; The Third Man series (2 episodes), 1960; Maigret series (8 episodes), 1960–64; They Met in a City series (1 episode), 1961; Killer in the Band, 1962; The Flying Swan series (1 episode), 1965; The Big Spender, 1965; The Tungsten Ring, 1966; Honey Lane series (7 episodes), 1968.

Other

> The Intelligent Woman's Guide to Atomic Radiation. London, Penguin, 1964.

Margot Bennett comments:

When I wrote my first book, *Time to Change Hats*, I tried the novelty of combining comedy with the obligatory murder. This gave me a good start – but the book was too long. *The Widow of Bath* had an entirely plausible and novel plot, but it was low on comedy and had too many twists. My best books were the last two. *The Man Who Didn't Fly* had an unusual plot and a set of people I believed in. In the same way, *Someone from the Past* had five characters that I might have met anywhere. The best of all my people was the girl Nancy. She was kind and cruel, and loyal and bitchy. She was a ready liar, with a sharp tongue, but she was brave and real. All through my books, the best I have done is to make the people real.

*   *   *

Margot Bennett's work is impossible to categorise; indeed not one of her books can be described as classic detection or thriller or psychological suspense story; they each display a rare mixture of these elements, and may be enjoyed as much by the reader who is fascinated by the puzzle as by the reader whose interest mainly lies in the examination of human relationships leading to a criminal situation.

Her early detective novels demonstrated conclusively that the mystery factor need not stifle the social background or the development of strong character studies. The unsettled post-war atmosphere, the desperate struggle to build new relationships between people, and many other nuances show the deft skill of Margot Bennett's writing. Of her work following *Time to Change Hats* and *Away Went the Little Fish*, it is no easy task to decide upon pride of place between *The Widow of Bath* and *The Man Who Didn't Fly*.

The Widow of Bath has as its central character Hugh Everton, betrayed and imprisoned in the past and gradually adjusting his life to a stagnant respectability as a reporter for a restaurant guide. Alternatively, the central character might be Lucy, the wife of Mr. Justice Bath; she is completely without scruples, of a physical perfection which ensnares everyone with whom she comes into contact, and whom Everton has found to be "luxurious, greedy, mercenary, unscrupulous, selfish, faithless, ambitious and lax." Then again, in spite of the fact that the elderly judge is shot in the early pages, his incorruptibility and his need for a legally clear conscience are dominant features of the book. Margot Bennett gives considerable weight to each of her characters; there is not a cardboard figure among them. This applies also to the hangers-on in the judge's retinue, the evil Atkinson who has reappeared with Lucy from Everton's past, and the oily public-school figure of the necrophile Cady. The background and atmosphere of a seedy seaside resort, used as the centre of a vile criminal activity stemming directly from the aftermath of war, is conveyed to perfection. The mystery of the judge's death, and a further murder, exists almost as a parallel plot to the main mystery of what is actually going on in the town. In due course, however, they are beautifully dovetailed.

The Man Who Didn't Fly is, yet again, a novel of character. The fact that four men set off to fly to Ireland, but only three are on the plane when it crashes, is the basis of a most original mystery – which one did not fly? was he murdered? and if so who murdered him? This would in itself have made a sufficiently acceptable plot for many crime writers, but Margot Bennett shows us the events leading up to the flight and portrays the relationships between the principal characters with a dexterity possessed by few novelists.

Throughout her regrettably short list of books, Margot Bennett's technical originality and literary craftsmanship depict love and hate, absurdity and helplessness, humour and suspense. She does it by using a devastating wit, a capacity for crackling dialogue and repartee, and an incredible facility for summing up a person or place or situation with an exquisitely apt stroke of her pen.

—Melvyn Barnes

BENSON, Ben(jamin). American. Born in Boston, Massachusetts, in 1915. Educated at Suffolk University Law School, Boston. Served in the United States Army, 1943–45: Purple Heart, two battle stars: seriously wounded and confined to hospital for three years; began writing as therapy. Married; one daughter. Tea salesman; self-employed writer after 1949. Member, Board of Directors, Mystery Writers of America. *Died 29 April 1959.*

CRIME PUBLICATIONS

Novels (series characters: Trooper Ralph Lindsay; Detective Inspector Wade Paris)

Beware the Pale Horse (Paris). New York, Mill, 1951; London, Muller, 1952.
Alibi at Dusk (Paris). New York, Mill, 1951; London, Corgi, 1952.
Lily in Her Coffin (Paris). New York, Mill, 1952; London, Boardman, 1954.
Stamped for Murder (Paris). New York, Mill, 1952; London, Gannet, 1955.
Target in Taffeta (Paris). New York, Mill, 1953; London, Collins, 1955.
The Venus Death (Lindsay). New York, Mill, 1953; London, Muller, 1954.
The Girl in the Cage (Lindsay). New York, Mill, 1954; London, Collins, 1955.
The Burning Fuse (Paris). New York, Mill, 1954; London, Collins, 1956.
Broken Shield (Lindsay). New York, Mill, 1955; London, Collins, 1957.
The Silver Cobweb (Lindsay). New York, Mill, 1955; London, Collins, 1956.
The Ninth Hour (Paris). New York, Mill, 1956; London, Collins, 1957.
The Black Mirror. New York, Mill, 1957; London, Collins, 1958.
The Running Man (Lindsay). New York, Mill, 1957; London, Collins, 1958.
The Affair of the Exotic Dancer (Paris). New York, Mill, 1958.
The Blonde in Black (Paris). New York, Mill, 1958; London, Collins, 1959.
The End of Violence (Lindsay). New York, Mill, and London, Collins, 1959.
Seven Steps East (Lindsay). New York, Mill, 1959.
The Frightened Ladies (novelets). New York, Mill, 1960.
The Huntress Is Dead (Paris). New York, Mill, 1960.

Uncollected Short Stories

"Killer in the House," in *Butcher, Baker, Murder-Maker.* New York, Knopf, 1954.
"The Big Kiss-Off," in *Eat, Drink, and Be Buried*, edited by Rex Stout. New York, Viking Press, 1956; as *For Tomorrow We Die*, London, Macdonald, 1958.
"Somebody Has to Make a Move," in *The Second Mystery Bedside Book*, edited by John Creasey. London, Hodder and Stoughton, 1961.

OTHER PUBLICATIONS

Other

Hoboes of America: Sensational Life Story and Epic of Life on the Road, by Hobo Benson. New York, Hobo News, 1942.

* * *

Writers of police procedural mysteries – e.g., Ed McBain, Elizabeth Linington, and John Creasey – have written mostly of urban crime. Ben Benson is an exception, generally avoiding the city in his two series about Wade Paris and Ralph Lindsay of the Massachusetts State Police. Benson's protagonists even appear uncomfortable in cities. In *Stamped for Murder* Paris is uncharacteristically careless, obeying the instructions of an anonymous phone caller in "Eastern City" (Benson's Boston) to go to a crowded nightclub, where he is stabbed. Lindsay seems out of place in Times Square where he trails a suspect during *The Running Man*.

It was more than his rural settings that set Benson apart from his competitors. They adopted a documentary approach, often including facsimiles of police records – e.g., fingerprint cards and arrest sheets. They used criminal argot and usually had their detectives juggle several cases at the same time. Though Benson had done considerable research (with the full cooperation of the Massachusetts Police), he never attempted to overwhelm the reader with details. His realism was achieved more subtly by authentic bits of dialogue and shared thoughts that rang true, what Anthony Boucher called "a sympathetic comprehension of the policeman-as-human being," praising *Target in Taffeta* for its "reader-character intimacy." If it was less realistic of Benson to have his policemen work on only one case at a time, it also allowed the reader to care more about its resolution.

Benson was especially good at depicting young people, and the immaturity and vulnerability of his rookie State trooper, Ralph Lindsay, adds to the interest of this series. He is quick to lose his temper and become emotionally involved with suspects, permitting himself in *The End of Violence* to be accused of police brutality. He is occasionally rebellious against authority, and intolerant of the older trooper who does not wear his uniform as smartly as he does. But he is always brave and dedicated, willingly posing as a juvenile delinquent in *The Girl in the Cage* to get evidence against a brutal young gang.

Dubbed "Old Icewater" by his colleagues, Wade Paris is much more mature and almost invulnerable. He is very cool under stress, as in *The Ninth Hour*, in which he must free hostages taken during an attempted prison break, and "Somebody Has to Make a Move," where he keeps vigil outside a house in which a cop-killer is trapped. In addition to being patient and fearless, Paris seldom shows fatigue. He is careful not to become involved with suspects, thus appearing immune to the charms of attractive females. His traits led the critic Avis De Voto to say, "We'd enjoy seeing Paris develop a few human weaknesses."

Yet, Paris is not without emotion, either personally or professionally. True, his sex life is treated discreetly, in keeping with his times. He reacts angrily to political pressure and the argument that, since the "people" pay his salary, he must treat them obsequiously rather than with his customary firm politeness.

It would have been interesting to see how Paris and Lindsay might have developed. However, Benson's untimely death ended a career of considerable achievement and even greater promise.

—Marvin Lachman

BENSON, E(dward) F(rederic).   British.   Born at Wellington College, Shropshire, 24 July 1867; son of E. W. Benson, afterwards Archbishop of Canterbury; brother of the writer A. C. Benson. Educated at Marlborough College (Editor of the *Marlburian*); King's College, Cambridge (exhibitioner, 1888; scholar, 1890; Wortz Student; Prendergast and Craven Student), first-class honours degree, 1891. Member of the staff of the British School of Archaeology, Athens, 1892–95, and the Society for the Promotion of Hellenic Studies, in Egypt, 1895; full-time writer from 1895; Editor, with "Celt," *The Imperial and Colonial Magazine and Review*, London, 1900–01; settled in Rye, Sussex: Mayor of Rye, 1934–37. Honorary Fellow, Magdalene College, Cambridge, 1938. *Died 29 February 1940.*

CRIME PUBLICATIONS

Novel

The Blotting Book. London, Heinemann, and New York, Doubleday, 1908.

Short Stories

The Room in the Tower and Other Stories. London, Mills and Boon, 1912; New York, Knopf, 1929.
The Countess of Lowndes Square and Other Stories. London and New York, Cassell, 1920.
Visible and Invisible. London, Hutchinson, 1923; New York, Doubleday, 1924.

OTHER PUBLICATIONS

Novels

Dodo: A Detail of the Day. London, Methuen, 2 vols., and New York, Appleton, 1893.
The Rubicon. London, Methuen, 2 vols., and New York, Appleton, 1893.
The Judgment Books. London, Osgood McIlvaine, and New York, Harper, 1895.
Limitations. London, Innes, and New York, Harper, 1896.
The Babe, B.A. New York, Putnam, 1896; London, Putnam, 1897.
The Vintage. London, Methuen, and New York, Harper, 1898.
The Money Market. Bristol, Arrowsmith, and Philadelphia, Biddle, 1898.
The Capsina. London, Methuen, and New York, Harper, 1899.
Mammon and Co. London, Heinemann, and New York, Appleton, 1899.
The Princess Sophia. London, Heinemann, and New York, Harper, 1900.
The Luck of the Vails. London, Heinemann, and New York, Appleton, 1901.
Scarlet and Hyssop. London, Heinemann, and New York, Appleton, 1902.
The Book of Months. London, Heinemann, and New York, Harper, 1903.
The Valkyries. London, Dean, 1903; Boston, Page, 1905.
The Relentless City. London, Heinemann, and New York, Harper, 1903.
An Act in a Backwater. London, Heinemann, and New York, Appleton, 1903.
The Challoners. London, Heinemann, and Philadelphia, Lippincott, 1904.
The Angel of Pain. Philadelphia, Lippincott, 1905; New York, Heinemann, 1906.
The Image in the Sands. London, Heinemann, and Philadelphia, Lippincott, 1905.
Paul. London, Heinemann, and Philadelphia, Lippincott, 1906.
The House of Defence. New York, Authors and Newspapers Association, 1906; London, Heinemann, 1907.
Sheaves. New York, Doubleday, 1907; London, Heinemann, 1908.
The Climber. London, Heinemann, 1908; New York, Doubleday, 1909.
A Reaping. London, Heinemann, and New York, Doubleday, 1909.
Daisy's Aunt. London, Nelson, 1910; as The Fascinating Mrs. Halton, New York, Doubleday, 1910.
Margery. New York, Doubleday, 1910.
The Osbornes. London, Smith and Elder, and New York, Doubleday, 1910.
Juggernaut. London, Heinemann, 1911.
Account Rendered. London, Heinemann, and New York, Doubleday, 1911.
Mrs. Ames. London, Hodder and Stoughton, and New York, Doubleday, 1912.
The Weaker Vessel. London, Heinemann, and New York, Dodd Mead, 1913.
Dodo's Daughter. New York, Century, 1913.
Thorley Weir. London, Smith and Elder, and Philadelphia, Lippincott, 1913.
Dodo the Second. London, Hodder and Stoughton, 1914.
Arundel. London, Unwin, 1914; New York, Doran, 1915.

The Oakleyites.   London, Hodder and Stoughton, and New York, Doran, 1915.
David Blaize.   London, Hodder and Stoughton, and New York, Doran, 1916.
Mike.   London, Cassell, 1916; as *Michael*, New York, Doran, 1916.
The Freaks of Mayfair.   London, Foulis, 1916; New York, Doran, 1917.
An Autumn Sowing.   London, Collins, 1917; New York, Doran, 1918.
Mr. Teddy.   London, Unwin, 1917; as *The Tortoise*, New York, Doran, 1917.
Up and Down.   London, Hutchinson, and New York, Doran, 1918.
David Blaize and the Blue Door.   London, Hodder and Stoughton, 1918; New York,
    Doran, 1919.
Robin Linnet.   London, Hutchinson, and New York, Doran, 1919.
Across the Stream.   London, Murray, and New York, Doran, 1919.
Queen Lucia.   London, Hutchinson, and New York, Doran, 1920.
Lovers and Friends.   London, Unwin, and New York, Doran, 1921.
Dodo Wonders.   London, Hutchinson, and New York, Doran, 1921.
Miss Mapp.   London, Hutchinson, 1922; New York, Doran, 1923.
Peter.   London, Cassell, and New York, Doran, 1922.
Colin.   London, Hutchinson, and New York, Doran, 1923.
David of King's.   London, Hodder and Stoughton, 1924; as *David Blaize of King's*,
    New York, Doran, 1924.
Alan.   London, Unwin, 1924; New York, Doran, 1925.
Rex.   London, Hodder and Stoughton, and New York, Doran, 1925.
Colin II.   London, Hutchinson, and New York, Doran, 1925.
Mezzanine.   London, Cassell, and New York, Doran, 1926.
Pharisees and Publicans.   London, Hutchinson, 1926; New York, Doran, 1927.
Lucia in London.   London, Hutchinson, 1927; New York, Doubleday, 1928.
Paying Guests.   London, Hutchinson, and New York, Doubleday, 1929.
The Inheritor.   London, Hutchinson, and New York, Doubleday, 1930.
Mapp and Lucia.   London, Hodder and Stoughton, and New York, Doubleday, 1931.
Secret Lives.   London, Hodder and Stoughton, and New York, Doubleday, 1932.
As We Are: A Modern Revue.   London and New York, Longman, 1932.
Travail of Gold.   London, Hodder and Stoughton, and New York, Doubleday, 1933.
Ravens' Brood.   London, Barker, and New York, Doubleday, 1934.
Lucia's Progress.   London, Hodder and Stoughton, 1935; as *The Worshipful Lucia*,
    New York, Doubleday, 1935.
Old London.   New York, Appleton Century, 4 vols., 1937.
Trouble for Lucia.   London, Hodder and Stoughton, and New York, Doubleday, 1939.

Short Stories

A Double Overture.   Chicago, Sergel, 1894.
And the Dead Spake –, and The Horror-Horn.   New York, Doran, 1923.
Expiation, and Naboth's Vineyard.   New York, Doran, 1924.
The Face.   New York, Doran, 1924.
Spinach and Reconciliation.   New York, Doran, 1924.
A Tale of an Empty House, and Bagnell Terrace.   New York, Doran, 1925.
The Temple.   New York, Doran, 1925.
Spook Stories.   London, Hutchinson, 1928.
The Step.   London, Marrot, 1930.
More Spook Stories.   London, Hutchinson, 1934.
The Horror Horn and Other Stories, edited by Alexis Lykiard.   London, Panther, 1974.

Plays

Aunt Jeannie (produced New York, 1902).
Dodo, from his own novel (produced London, 1905).

The Friend in the Garden (produced London, 1907).
Dinner for Eight (produced London, 1915).
The Luck of the Vails, from his own novel (produced Eastbourne and London, 1928).

Other

Six Common Things.   London, Osgood McIlvaine, 1893.
Daily Training, with E. H. Miles.   London, Hurst and Blackett, 1902; New York, Dutton, 1903.
Two Generations.   London, Daily Mail, 1904.
Diversions Day by Day, with E. H. Miles.   London, Hurst and Blackett, 1905.
English Figure Skating.   London, Bell, 1908.
Bensoniana.   London, Humphreys, 1912.
Winter Sports in Switzerland.   London, Allen, and New York, Dodd Mead, 1913.
Thoughts from E. F. Benson, edited by Elsie E. Morton.   London, Harrap, 1913.
Thoughts from E. F. Benson, edited by H. B. Elliott.   London, Holden and Hardingham, 1917.
Deutschland über Allah.   London, Hodder and Stoughton, 1917.
Poland and Mittel-Europa.   London and New York, Hodder and Stoughton, 1918.
The White Eagle of Poland.   London, Hodder and Stoughton, 1918; New York, Doran, 1919.
Crescent and Iron Cross.   London, Hodder and Stoughton, and New York, Doran, 1918.
Our Family Affairs 1867–1896.   London, Cassell, 1920; New York, Doran, 1921.
Mother (on Mary Benson).   London, Hodder and Stoughton, and New York, Doran, 1925.
Sir Francis Drake.   London, Lane, and New York, Harper, 1927.
The Life of Alcibiades.   London, Benn, 1928; New York, Appleton, 1929.
Ferdinand Magellan.   London, Lane, 1929; New York, Harper, 1930.
The Male Impersonator.   London, Mathews and Marrot, 1929.
As We Were: A Victorian Peep-Show (autobiography).   London and New York, Longman, 1930.
Charlotte Brontë.   London and New York, Longman, 1932.
King Edward VII: An Appreciation.   London and New York, Longman, 1933.
The Outbreak of War 1914.   London, Davies, 1933; New York, Putnam, 1934.
Queen Victoria.   London and New York, Longman, 1935.
The Kaiser and English Relations.   London and New York, Longman, 1936.
Queen Victoria's Daughters.   New York, Appleton Century, 1938; as *Daughters of Queen Victoria*, London, Cassell, 1939.
Final Edition: Informal Autobiography.   London, Longman, and New York, Appleton Century, 1940.

Editor, with E. H. Miles, *A Book of Golf.*   London, Hurst and Blackett, and New York, Dutton, 1903.
Editor, with E. H. Miles, *The Cricket of Abel, Hirst, and Shrewsbury.*   London, Hurst and Blackett, 1903.
Editor, with E. H. Miles, *The Mad Annual.*   London, Richards, 1903.
Editor, *Henry James: Letters to A. C. Benson and Auguste Monod.*   London, Mathews and Marrot, and New York, Scribner, 1930.

*   *   *

The nearest E. F. Benson came to writing a detective story was *The Blotting Book*. In the early pages of this mystery it gradually emerges that Taynton, the old family lawyer, has embezzled the entire fortune of Morris Assheton, and that, if the young man's projected marriage takes place, Taynton and his partner must flee the country. The old hypocrite is smoothly portrayed, and up to a point his double standard of morality is convincing; but the author's attempt to share Taynton's thoughts with us while hiding his murderous plans is at once unsuccessful and dishonest. Despite this flaw the short novel is worth reading by anyone with the patience to disentangle the ill-punctuated sentences.

Benson's many tales of the macabre are too mild to set today's more sophisticated readers shuddering. An odd *frisson* or two may be evoked by "Mrs. Amworth" (a vampire story) from *Visible and Invisible*, and "Caterpillars" (in which a horde of these insects besieges the narrator) from *The Room in the Tower*. "Mr. Tilly's Séance," from the former collection, is unusual in its farcical approach. That Benson, a life-long bachelor, created as the central figure of many of these stories a large cheery woman with a secret depravity is not without interest.

—Norman Donaldson

BENTLEY, E(dmund) C(lerihew). British. Born in Shepherds Bush, London, 10 July 1875. Educated at St. Paul's School, London; Merton College, Oxford (scholar; President, Oxford Union, 1898), B.A.; Inner Temple, London, called to the Bar, 1902. Married Violet Boileau in 1902 (died, 1949); two sons, including Nicolas Bentley, *q.v.* Journalist: staff member, *Daily News*, London, 1902–12; leader writer, *Daily Telegraph*, 1912–34; retired in 1934, but returned as Chief Literary Critic, *Daily Telegraph*, 1940–47. *Died 30 March 1956.*

CRIME PUBLICATIONS

Novels (series character: Philip Trent)

> *Trent's Last Case.* London, Nelson, 1913; as *The Woman in Black*, New York, Century, 1913; revised edition, New York and London, Knopf, 1929.
> *Trent's Own Case*, with H. Warner Allen. London, Constable, and New York, Knopf, 1936.
> *Elephant's Work: An Enigma.* London, Hodder and Stoughton, and New York, Knopf, 1950; as *The Chill*, New York, Dell, 1953.

Short Stories

> *Trent Intervenes.* London, Nelson, and New York, Knopf, 1938.

Uncollected Short Stories

> "Greedy Night," in *Stories of Detection*, edited by R. W. Jepson. London, Longman, 1939.
> "The Ministering Angel," in *To the Queen's Taste*, edited by Ellery Queen. Boston, Little Brown, 1946.
> "The Feeble Folk," in *Ellery Queen's Mystery Magazine* (New York), March 1953.

OTHER PUBLICATIONS

Verse

Biography for Beginners (as E. Clerihew).   London, Laurie, 1905.
More Biography.   London, Methuen, 1929.
Baseless Biography.   London, Constable, 1939.
Clerihews Complete.   London, Laurie, 1951.

Other

Peace Year in the City, 1918–1919: An Account of the Outstanding Events in the City of London During Peace Year.   Privately printed, 1920.
Those Days: An Autobiography.   London, Constable, 1940.
Far Horizon: A Biography of Hester Dowden, Medium and Psychic Investigator.   London and New York, Rider, 1951.

Editor, *More Than Somewhat*, by Damon Runyon.   London, Constable, 1937.
Editor, *Damon Runyon Presents Furthermore.*   London, Constable, 1938.
Editor, *The Best of Runyon.*   New York, Stokes, 1938.
Editor, *The Second Century of Detective Stories.*   London, Hutchinson, 1938.

*   *   *

Most writers who attempt novels usually improve their skills with time and experience. E. C. Bentley, with over a decade of professional journalism and a book of nonsense verse behind him, reversed this process with his first novel, *Trent's Last Case.* I venture to suggest that not only is this work the best "first" produced by anyone writing in the mystery genre, but that it is also one of the ten best mystery novels of all time.

The detective story in those days – particularly in the novel form – was in a virtual state of wilderness. In his autobiography, *Those Days*, Bentley stated that *Trent's Last Case* was a conscious reaction against the sterility and artificiality into which much of the detection writing of the day had sunk. "It does not seem to have been noticed that *Trent's Last Case* is not so much a detective story as an exposure of detective stories ... it should be possible, I thought, to write a detective story in which the detective was recognizable as a human being." Bentley's attempt to "expose" the detective story was ineffective and ignored by most commentators, who have viewed this novel in a serious and straightforward manner. In terms of the characterizations in *Trent's Last Case*, Bentley was closer to the mark. His central character, Philip Trent, a youngish, untidy-looking artist, has been retained by a prominent London newspaper to investigate the sensational murder of a wealthy financier. Trent, unlike Dupin or Sherlock Holmes, is fallible. During his investigation he falls in love with the victim's widow – who is also the chief suspect. When he concludes his efforts, he discovers that his ingenious solution is completely wrong.

The popularity of *Trent's Last Case* through the years has been awesome. It has generated 3 film versions, a radio dramatization, and many reprints. Now, after the passage of over 60 years, Bentley's unprecedented masterpiece remains mint-fresh, witty, literate, immensely appealing, and an exhilarating reading experience. Unquestionably, *Trent's Last Case* is a great and enduring detective novel.

Bentley's demanding journalistic career, unfortunately, left little opportunity for further crime fiction efforts for too many years. A breakthrough came with a short story "Greedy Night," a take-off on Dorothy L. Sayers's novel *Gaudy Night*, and features Lord Peter Wimsey. Ellery Queen called it "the finest detective parody of our time." A long awaited and hoped for sequel to *Trent's Last Case* was finally published in 1936. *Trent's Own Case* was written in collaboration with H(erbert) Warner Allen – a writer with several minor mystery novels to his credit. It starts with the discovery of an elderly philanthropist found shot in the back in his bedroom, and the only clue points straight to Philip Trent. *Trent's Own Case*, it must be admitted, is hardly the equal of its illustrious predecessor, but it is an excellent detective novel of considerable skill and depth. *Trent Intervenes* is a collection of 12 short stories that displays its author's ability to perform notable work in the short form. Several of these stories have become anthology favorites. "The Ministering Angel" is an uncollected Trent short story which Ellery Queen thought one of Bentley's most satisfying efforts.

Bentley's last novel, *Elephant's Work*, concerns a protagonist whose pursuit of a master criminal is complicated by his own amnesia. Its creation was inspired by John Buchan in 1916, and is dedicated to his memory. Many detective story writers, including Allingham, Blake, and Innes, turned their attention to the thriller form at the start of World War II. Here, belatedly, is Bentley's sole essay in this genre. Most of the reviewers thought it was below standard, but it is a literate, exciting, and highly readable thriller that is not unworthy of Bentley's talent.

—Charles Shibuk

BENTLEY, Nicolas (Clerihew). British. Born in Highgate, London, 14 June 1907; son of E. C. Bentley, *q.v.* Educated at University College School, London; Hatherley School of Art, London. Served in the Fire Service during World War II. Married Barbara Hastings in 1934; one daughter. Circus clown and film extra for a short period; then worked in the publicity department for Shell in the 1920's; illustrator from 1930, and cartoonist for the *Daily Mail*, London, in the 1960's; Director, André Deutsch, publishers, London, in the 1950's, and Editor, Thomas Nelson & Son, London. Fellow, Royal Society of Arts, and Society of Industrial Artists. *Died 14 August 1978.*

CRIME PUBLICATIONS

Novels

    Gammon and Espionage. London, Cresset Press, 1938.
    The Tongue-Tied Canary. London, Joseph, 1948; New York, Duell, 1949.
    The Floating Dutchman. London, Joseph, 1950; New York, Duell, 1951.
    Third Party Risk. London, Joseph, 1953.
    The Events of That Week. London, Collins, and New York, St. Martin's Press, 1972.
    Inside Information. London, Deutsch, 1974; New York, Penguin, 1978.

Uncollected Short Stories

    "Double Exposure," in *Evening Standard Detective Book*, 2nd series. London, Gollancz, 1951.
    "The Look-Out Man," in *The Saint* (New York), April 1955.

OTHER PUBLICATIONS

Verse

    Second Thoughts on First Lines and Other Poems. London, Joseph, 1939.

Other

Die? I Thought I'd Laugh: A Book of Pictures.   London, Methuen, 1936.
The Time of My Life.   London, Joseph, 1937.
Ballet-Hoo.   London, Cresset Press, 1937; revised edition, London, Joseph, 1948.
Le Sport.   London, Gollancz, 1939.
Animal, Vegetable, and South Kensington: A Book of Bentley's Pictures.   London, Methuen, 1940.
How Can You Bear to Be Human?   London, Deutsch, 1957; New York, Dutton, 1958.
A Choice of Ornaments.   London, Deutsch, 1959.
A Version of the Truth.   London, Deutsch, 1960.
Book of Birds: An Avian Alphabet.   London, Deutsch, 1965.
The Victorian Scene: A Picture Book of the Period 1837–1901.   London, Weidenfeld and Nicolson, 1968.
Don't Do-It-Yourself: A Fantasy for Exporters.   London, British National Export Council, 1970.
Golden Sovereigns, and Some of Lesser Value, from Boadicea to Elizabeth II.   London, Mitchell Beazley, 1970; New York, Simon and Schuster, 1973.
Tales from Shakespeare.   London, Mitchell Beazley, 1972; New York, Simon and Schuster, 1973.
Edwardian Album: A Photographic Excursion into a Lost Age of Innocence.   London, Weidenfeld and Nicolson, and New York, Viking Press, 1974.
Pay Bed.   London, Deutsch, 1976.
The History of the Circus.   London, Joseph, 1977.

Editor, *All Fall Down! or, The Nonsense Fanciers' Assistant.*   London, Nicholson and Watson, 1932.
Editor, *The Beastly Birthday Book.*   London, Methuen, 1934.
Editor, *Ready Refusals; or, The White Liar's Engagement Book.*   London, Methuen, 1935.
Editor, *The Week-End Wants of a Guest [Worries of a Hostess]: A Memorandum Book.*   London, Cobden Sanderson, 2 vols., 1938.
Editor, with Leonard Russell, *The English Comic Album.*   London, Joseph, 1948.
Editor, *Fred Bason's Diary.*   London, Wingate, 1950.
Editor, *The Treasury of Humorous Quotations,* edited by Evan Esar.   London, Phoenix House, 1951.
Editor, *The Pick of Punch.*   London, Deutsch, 3 vols., 1955–57.
Editor, *Comfortable Words,* by Bergen Evans.   New York, Random House, 1962; London, Deutsch, 1963.
Editor, *Despatches from the Crimea, 1854–56,* by Sir William Russell.   London, Panther, 1970; New York, Hill and Wang, 1976.
Editor, *The Shell Book of Motoring Humour.*   London, Joseph, 1976.

*   *   *

Nicolas Bentley is best known for his often humorous literary illustrations. However, like his father, E. C. Bentley, creator of the famous Trent, he is also the author of several works of detective fiction. His first thriller, *Gammon and Espionage,* which he illustrated himself, is a delightful spoof of the novel of international intrigue. It features agents from Scotland Yard and the Secret Service who set out in pursuit of a stolen plan in whose margins are scrawled their Chief's chess problems. The style and setting of *Gammon and Espionage* parody the work of Sax Rohmer and other popular adventure novelists. Bentley took the formula, settings, and characters of detective fiction much more seriously in *The Tongue-Tied Canary,* *Third Party Risk,* and *The Floating Dutchman.* These novels successfully build suspense around light plots, witty dialogue, and accurate use of detail. *The Events of That Week* concerns the adventures of a hapless English tourist involved in a Sicilian Mafia drug ring, and *Inside Information* is an account of the perfect crime, a jailbreak and gold bullion heist, detected only because one of the gang rebels against the crime's tyrannical mastermind.

—Katherine Staples

BENTLEY, Phyllis (Eleanor).   British.   Born in Halifax, Yorkshire, 19 November 1894. Educated at Cheltenham Ladies' College; University of London, B.A. 1914. Taught briefly, 1914; worked for Ministry of Munitions in World War I and for the Ministry of Information in World War II. Vice-President, P.E.N. English centre. D.Litt.: University of Leeds, 1949. Fellow, Royal Society of Literature, 1958. O.B.E. (Member, Order of the British Empire), 1970. *Died 27 June 1977.*

CRIME PUBLICATIONS

Novels

> *The House of Moreys.*   London, Gollancz, and New York, Macmillan, 1953.
> *Gold Pieces.*   London, Macdonald, 1968; as *Forgery!*, New York, Doubleday, 1968.

Uncollected Short Stories (series character: Miss Phipps)

> "The Way Round," in *Ellery Queen's Mystery Magazine* (New York), August 1953.
> "Conversations at an Inn," in *Ellery Queen's Mystery Magazine* (New York), February 1954.
> "Chain of Witnesses," in *Ellery Queen's Mystery Magazine* (New York), May 1954.
> "A Telegram for Miss Phipps," in *Ellery Queen's Mystery Magazine* (New York), June 1954.
> "The Tuesday and Friday Thefts," in *Ellery Queen's Mystery Magazine* (New York), July 1954.
> "The Crooked Figures," in *Ellery Queen's Mystery Magazine* (New York), October 1954.
> "The Spirit of the Place," in *Ellery Queen's Mystery Magazine* (New York), December 1954.
> "The Significant Letter," in *Ellery Queen's Mystery Magazine* (New York), February 1955.
> "The Incongruous Letter," in *Ellery Queen's Mystery Magazine* (New York), August 1955.
> "Author in Search of a Character," in *Anthology 1962*, edited by Ellery Queen.   New York, Davis, 1961.
> "Miss Phipps Improvises," in *To Be Read Before Midnight*, edited by Ellery Queen.   New York, Random House, 1962; London, New English Library, 1967.
> "Message in a Bottle," in *Ellery Queen's Mystery Magazine* (New York), May 1962.
> "Miss Phipps Discovers America," in *Ellery Queen's Mystery Magazine* (New York), March 1963.
> "Miss Phipps Jousts with the Press," in *Ellery Queen's Mystery Magazine* (New York), December 1963.
> "The Man on the Back Seat," in *The Saint* (New York), December 1963.
> "Miss Phipps in the Hospital," in *Ellery Queen's Mystery Magazine* (New York), July 1964.

"Miss Phipps Considers the Cat," in *Ellery Queen's Mystery Magazine* (New York), April 1965.
"Miss Phipps and the Invisible Murderer," in *Best Detective Stories of the Year 1967*, edited by Anthony Boucher. New York, Dutton, 1967.
"Miss Phipps Goes to the Hairdresser," in *Ellery Queen's Mystery Magazine* (New York), December 1967.
"The Secret," in *Ellery Queen's Murder Menu.* Cleveland, World, 1969.
"Miss Phipps and the Nest of Illusion," in *Ellery Queen's Mystery Magazine* (New York), August 1969.
"Miss Phipps Is Too Modest," in *Ellery Queen's Mystery Magazine* (New York), December 1971.
"A Midsummer Night's Crime," in *Grande Dames of Detection*, edited by Seon Manley and Gogo Lewis. New York, Lothrop, 1973.
"Miss Phipps Meets a Dog," in *Best Detective Stories of the Year 1975*, edited by Allen J. Hubin. New York, Dutton, 1975.
"Miss Phipps Exercises Her Métier," in *Ellery Queen's Magicians of Mystery.* New York, Davis, 1976.

Other Publications

Novels

Environment. London, Sidgwick and Jackson, 1922; New York, Curl, 1935.
Cat-in-the-Manger. London, Sidgwick and Jackson, 1923.
The Spinner of the Years. London, Unwin, 1928; New York, Henkle, 1929.
The Partnership. London, Benn, 1928; Boston, Little Brown, 1929.
Carr. London, Benn, 1929; New York, Macmillan, 1933.
Trio. London, Gollancz, 1930.
Inheritance. London, Gollancz, and New York, Macmillan, 1932.
A Modern Tragedy. London, Gollancz, and New York, Macmillan, 1934.
Freedom, Farewell! London, Gollancz, and New York, Macmillan, 1936.
Sleep in Peace. London, Gollancz, and New York, Macmillan, 1938.
Take Courage. London, Gollancz, 1940; as *The Power and the Glory*, New York, Macmillan, 1940.
Manhold. London, Gollancz, and New York, Macmillan, 1941.
The Rise of Henry Morcar. London, Gollancz, and New York, Macmillan, 1946.
Life Story. London, Gollancz, and New York, Macmillan, 1948.
Quorum. London, Gollancz, 1950; New York, Macmillan, 1951.
Noble in Reason. London, Gollancz, and New York, Macmillan, 1955.
Crescendo. London, Gollancz, and New York, Macmillan, 1958.
A Man of His Time. London, Gollancz, and New York, Macmillan, 1966.
Ring in the New. London, Gollancz, 1969.

Short Stories

The World's Bane and Other Stories. London, Unwin, 1918.
The Whole of the Story. London, Gollancz, 1935.
Panorama: Tales of the West Riding. London, Gollancz, and New York, Macmillan, 1952.
Love and Money: Seven Tales of the West Riding. London, Gollancz, and New York, Macmillan, 1957.
Kith and Kin: Nine Tales of Family Life. London, Gollancz, and New York, Macmillan, 1960.
Tales of the West Riding. London, Gollancz, 1965.
More Tales of the West Riding. London, Gollancz, 1974.

Play

Sounding Brass.   Halifax, Stott, 1930.

Other

Pedagomania; or, The Gentle Art of Teaching (as A Bachelor of Arts).   London, Unwin, 1918.
Here Is America.   London, Gollancz, 1941.
The English Regional Novel.   London, Allen and Unwin, 1941; Folcroft, Pennsylvania, Folcroft Editions, 1973.
Some Observations on the Art of Narrative.   London, Home and Van Thal, 1946; New York, Macmillan, 1947.
Colne Valley Cloth from the Earliest Times to the Present Day.   Huddersfield, Huddersfield and District Woollen Export Group, 1947.
The Brontës.   London, Home and Van Thal, 1947; Denver, Swallow, 1948.
The Brontë Sisters.   London, Longman, 1950; revised edition, 1954.
The Young Brontës (juvenile).   London, Parrish, and New York, Roy, 1961.
"O Dreams, O Destinations": An Autobiography.   London, Gollancz, and New York, Macmillan, 1962.
Committees.   London, Collins, 1962.
Enjoy Books: Reading and Collecting.   London, Gollancz, 1964.
Public Speaking.   London, Collins, 1964.
The Adventures of Tom Leigh Macdonald (juvenile).   London, Macdonald, 1964; New York, Doubleday, 1966.
Ned Carver in Danger (juvenile).   London, Macdonald, 1967.
Oath of Silence (juvenile).   New York, Doubleday, 1967.
The Brontës and Their World.   London, Thames and Hudson, and New York, Viking Press, 1969.
Sheep May Safely Graze (juvenile).   London, Gollancz, 1972.
The New Venturers (juvenile).   London, Gollancz, 1973.

Editor, *The Brontës* (works).   London, Wingate, 1949.
Editor, *The Professor, Tales from Angria, Emma: A Fragment by Charlotte Brontë, Together with a Selection of Poems by Charlotte, Emily, and Anne Brontë.*   London, Collins, 1954.

*   *   *

The 1890's was productive of women writers who would shape detective fiction. Phyllis Bentley, while a minor figure, may be compared with such others as Christie, Tey, Sayers, and Marsh. Only she and Christie wrote of women − an extremely small class − whose investigative efforts are the focus of a series. Her Miss Phipps shares views with Tey's Miss Pym, and the profession of mystery writer with Sayers's Harriet Vane. They have in common with Marsh's Agatha Troy (Alleyn) the satisfactions of a career.

Bentley's mysteries represent an interest of her later writing career and consist of stories featuring Miss Marian Phipps and two minor mystery novels. The stories, short puzzles of detection, usually begin with an event unusual in Miss Phipps's otherwise quiet existence, and center on her perceptiveness and analysis. Crimes in them range from the negligible misdemeanor to murder. Stylistically, the stories are economically told and share a quiet humor and misleading simplicity of statement with the works of Christie. Miss Phipps's almost prim, highly self-conscious, and nearly fussy manner − often the feminine equivalent of the classic detective's eccentricity − is warmed by an interest in the problems of the young and animals and enlivened by career activities and movement through a range of locales that goes beyond the traditional village.

Bentley's contribution is small but not slight, her work informed and consistent with the classic traditions of the mystery.

—Nancy Ellen Talburt

BENTON, Kenneth (Carter).   British.   Born in Sutton Coldfield, Warwickshire, 4 March 1909. Educated at Wolverhampton Grammar School, 1919–25; University of London, B.A. in modern languages 1936. Married Peggie Pollock Lambert in 1938; one son and two stepsons. Teacher in England, then language student and teacher in Florence and Vienna, 1930–37; joined Foreign Office in 1937: Assistant Passport Control Officer, Vienna, 1937–38; Vice Consul, Riga, 1938–40; 3rd Secretary, Madrid, 1941–43; 2nd Secretary, later 1st Secretary, Rome, 1944–48; in London, 1948–50; 1st Secretary, Rome, 1950–53; in Madrid, 1953–56; in London, 1956–62; 1st Secretary and Consul, Lima, 1962–63; in London, 1964–65; Counsellor of Embassy, Rio de Janeiro, 1966–68; retired in 1968. Vice-Chairman, 1973–74, and Chairman, 1974–75, Crime Writers Association. C.M.G. (Companion, Order of St. Michael and St. George), 1966. Agent: Gerald Pollinger, Laurence Pollinger Ltd., 18 Maddox Street, London W1R 0EU. Address: Vine House, Appledore, Ashford, Kent, England.

CRIME PUBLICATIONS

Novels (series character: Peter Craig)

> *Twenty-Fourth Level* (Craig).   London, Collins, 1969; New York, Dodd Mead, 1970.
> *Sole Agent* (Craig).   London, Collins, 1970; New York, Walker, 1974.
> *Spy in Chancery* (Craig).   London, Collins, 1972; New York, Walker, 1973.
> *Craig and the Jaguar*.   London, Macmillan, 1973; New York, Walker, 1974.
> *Craig and the Tunisian Tangle*.   London, Macmillan, 1974; New York, Walker, 1975.
> *Craig and the Midas Touch*.   London, Macmillan, 1975; New York, Walker, 1976.
> *A Single Monstrous Act*.   London, Macmillan, 1976.
> *The Red Hen Conspiracy*.   London, Macmillan, 1977.

Uncollected Short Stories

> "Flotsam," in *Winter's Crimes 6*, edited by George Hardinge.   London, Macmillan, 1974.
> "Gifted Amateurs," in *John Creasey's Crime Collection 1978*, edited by Herbert Harris.   London, Gollancz, 1978.
> "The Watertight D.L.B.," in *John Creasey's Crime Collection 1979*, edited by Herbert Harris.   London, Gollancz, 1979.

OTHER PUBLICATIONS

Novel

> *Death on the Appian Way*.   London, Chatto and Windus, 1974.

Other

Peru's Revolution from Above.   London, Institute for the Study of Conflict, 1970.

Kenneth Benton comments:
   Until the year before I retired from the Diplomatic Service I had not written any fiction since boyhood, but I had always been a crime fiction fan, and the places in which I had been posted during my career provided backgrounds and local colour which I thought would be of interest to readers. So I began to write stories about the countries and cities my wife and I knew well (Rio de Janeiro, Rome, Lisbon, etc.). Later, I introduced more esoteric aspects of espionage work, of which I had a close knowledge from the official angle. *A Single Monstrous Act* is based to some extent on the research I carried out for a handbook on subversion and counter-subversion.

*   *   *

   Kenneth Benton's policeman hero, Peter Craig, reflects the background of his creator, a former British intelligence head during World War II and a diplomat for thirty years after. Craig is a Diplomatic Corps Overseas Police Advisor, a methodical, upright policeman by training but also, when circumstances demand, a tough man of action ready to ignore procedure and fight the enemy on his own brutal terms. Craig is skilful at manipulating the official fictions so necessary to the police discourse of nations while doing what must be done. He is young enough for credible physical heroics but far more wordly than the naive young idealists whose blindness to the real motives of spies, terrorists, and other miscreants makes them self-righteous pawns. A professional, Craig understands the amoral diplomatic underworld, but retains a decent empathy with the humanity of his antagonists.
   Craig's adventures follow the author's diplomatic postings. Benton carefully integrates terrain, cuisine, history, politics, language, and customs with plot. While making gold mining fascinating, the coincidence-ridden *Twenty-Fourth Level* cleverly and cynically undercuts a seemingly romantic Brazilian idyll. Craig joins the British ambassador to battle a Soviet spy in the Rome embassy (*Spy in Chancery*), the Peruvian Army to prevent a vindictive patrón and Tupamaros from undamming a glacial lake (*Craig and the Jaguar*), and embassy staff to rescue a naive, irresponsible diplomat's daughter (*Sole Agent*). In *Craig and the Midas Touch*, he confronts the PLO, an irresponsible Arab prince, and the primitive Islamic judicial system to save a multi-million dollar oil rig and an innocent American. In all the novels, tackling his foes involves exciting chase scenes, personality clashes, conflicts with local authorities, and grotesque injuries and deaths, including a near asphyxiation at the bottom of a gold mine, an overdose of truth serum, a neck run over by a car, and a suicide crash into the Andes resulting in a human snowball.

—Andrew F. Macdonald

BERCKMAN, Evelyn (Domenica).   American.   Born in Philadelphia, Pennsylvania, 18 October 1900. Educated at Columbia University, New York. Concert pianist and composer: compositions include the ballets *From the Odyssey* and *County Fair* and other works. Lived in London after 1960. *Died 18 September 1978.*

CRIME PUBLICATIONS

Novels

> *The Evil of Time.* New York, Dodd Mead, 1954; London, Eyre and Spottiswoode, 1955.
> *The Beckoning Dream.* New York, Dodd Mead, 1955; London, Eyre and Spottiswoode, 1956; as *Worse Than Murder*, New York, Dell, 1957.
> *The Strange Bedfellow.* New York, Dodd Mead, 1956; London, Eyre and Spottiswoode, 1957; as *Jewel of Death*, New York, Pyramid, 1968.
> *The Blind Villain.* New York, Dodd Mead, and London, Eyre and Spottiswoode, 1957; as *House of Terror*, New York, Dell, 1960.
> *The Hovering Darkness.* New York, Dodd Mead, 1957; London, Eyre and Spottiswoode, 1958.
> *No Known Grave.* New York, Dodd Mead, 1958; London, Eyre and Spottiswoode, 1959.
> *Lament for Four Brides.* New York, Dodd Mead, 1959; London, Eyre and Spottiswoode, 1960.
> *Do You Know This Voice?* New York, Dodd Mead, 1960; London, Eyre and Spottiswoode, 1961.
> *Blind-Girl's-Buff.* New York, Dodd Mead, and London, Eyre and Spottiswoode, 1962.
> *A Thing That Happens to You.* New York, Dodd Mead, 1964; as *Keys from a Window*, London, Eyre and Spottiswoode, 1965.
> *A Simple Case of Ill-Will.* London, Eyre and Spottiswoode, 1964; New York, Dodd Mead, 1965.
> *Stalemate.* London, Eyre and Spottiswoode, and New York, Doubleday, 1966.
> *A Case in Nullity.* London, Eyre and Spottiswoode, 1967; New York, Doubleday, 1968.
> *The Heir of Starvelings.* New York, Doubleday, 1967; London, Eyre and Spottiswoode, 1968.
> *The Long Arm of the Prince.* London, Hale, 1968.
> *She Asked for It.* New York, Doubleday, 1969; London, Hamish Hamilton, 1970.
> *The Voice of Air.* New York, Doubleday, 1970; London, Hale, 1971.
> *A Finger to Her Lips.* London, Hale, and New York, Doubleday, 1971.
> *The Stake in the Game.* London, Hamish Hamilton, 1971; New York, Doubleday, 1973.
> *The Fourth Man on the Rope.* London, Hamish Hamilton, and New York, Doubleday, 1972.
> *The Victorian Album.* London, Hamish Hamilton, and New York, Doubleday, 1973.
> *Wait.* London, Hamish Hamilton, 1973; as *Wait, Just You Wait*, New York, Doubleday, 1973.
> *Indecent Exposure.* London, Hamish Hamilton, 1975; as *The Nightmare Chase*, New York, Doubleday, 1975.
> *The Blessed Plot.* London, Hamish Hamilton, 1976.
> *The Crown Estate.* New York, Doubleday, 1976.
> *Be All and End All.* London, Hamish Hamilton, 1976.
> *Journey's End.* New York, Doubleday, 1977.

OTHER PUBLICATIONS

Other

> *Nelson's Dear Lord: A Portrait of St. Vincent.* London, Macmillan, 1962.
> *The Hidden Navy.* London, Hamish Hamilton, 1973.
> *Creators and Destroyers of the English Navy.* London, Hamish Hamilton, 1974.

Victims of Piracy: The Admiralty Court 1575–1678.   London, Hamish Hamilton, 1979.

Manuscript Collection: Mugar Memorial Library, Boston University.

*   *   *

Evelyn Berckman's modest output has been a most acceptable mixture of the classic style and the psychological thriller, with attention to detail and careful literary craftsmanship. She has shown herself at home with the more conventional detective themes – one recalls *A Simple Case of Ill-Will*, where quarrels at a bridge club lead to foul play, with some neat character sketches along the way. She is equally at home in the gothic style – *The Heir of Starvelings*, with her genteel heroine surrounded by an atmosphere of menace, not only displays her ability to out-write many of today's so-called gothic novelists, but shows very clearly the painstaking research which is one of her most enduring features.

The Victorian Album, perhaps her most interesting work, illustrates her multi-faceted talents; in a strange and eerie mixture of detection and the supernatural, combined with a strong line of suspense, we share the innermost thoughts of a latent medium impelled by an old album she finds in her attic to delve back into a Victorian murder. We see initial curiosity turn into inexorable pursuit of truth, leading to a disturbing climax.

A consistent feature of Evelyn Berckman's novels has been her ability to present credible characters. In some she explores complex emotional relationships, like the ménage of the ageing actress in *She Asked for It*, while some others stem from her interest in art, history, and archaeology without leaving an impression of mustiness.

Evelyn Berckman's multiplicity of talents and styles makes it impossible to "type-cast" her in any one area of crime fiction, which might account for her undeserved neglect by historians of the genre.

—Melvyn Barnes

BERGMAN, Andrew.   American.

CRIME PUBLICATIONS

Novels (series character: Jack LeVine in both books)

> *The Big Kiss-Off of 1944.*   New York, Holt Rinehart, 1974; London, Hutchinson, 1975.
> *Hollywood and LeVine.*   New York, Holt Rinehart, 1975; London, Hutchinson, 1976.

OTHER PUBLICATIONS

Other

> *James Cagney.*   New York, Pyramid, 1975.

*   *   *

Andrew Bergman, well-known as a commentator on American movies, has written two novels, *The Big Kiss-Off of 1944* and *Hollywood and LeVine*, both featuring a fat, balding private detective, Jack LeVine, who describes himself in the first novel as a "basic model 1944 prole." Both novels are well-plotted and witty, and model their barbed similes on those of Raymond Chandler. Both novels were written after Watergate and, in addition to the wealth of period detail, they bring their hero into contact with important public events, respectively the Presidential Election of 1944 and the beginnings of the McCarthy "witch-hunt" in Hollywood as early as 1947. In order to achieve credibility, Bergman introduces Dewey into the first novel and Nixon into the second: neat portraits whose ironies are increased through the reader's hindsight. The private eye of the inter-war years occupied a small, claustrophobic world, but Bergman has ingeniously adapted the formula to include a view of large-scale corruption and distrust which, in the post-war years, have been very much the province of the thriller and investigative journalism. Credulity is, however, strained by the extent to which LeVine is attractive to beautiful women, and Bergman's admiration for Bogart leads him, in *Hollywood and LeVine*, to have his detective join forces with the actor in overcoming evil with a sentimental heroism much more in keeping with Bulldog Drummond than a supposedly tough and cynical private eye: "The pursuit of a beautiful and good woman held captive by a two-time killer was the clearest and simplest thing I had done in a long time." Hammett and Chandler would scarcely have approved.

—John S. Whitley

BERKELEY, Anthony. Pseudonym for A(nthony) B(erkeley) Cox; also wrote as Francis Iles. British. Born in Watford, Hertfordshire, in July 1893. Educated at Sherborne School; University College, London. Served in the army during World War I. Married Helen Macgregor in 1932 (died). Journalist: contributor to *Punch*, London, and, as Francis Iles, reviewer for *Daily Telegraph*, London, from the 1930's, and for the *Sunday Times*, London, after World War II. Founder, and first Honorary Secretary, Detection Club, 1928. *Died 9 March 1971.*

CRIME PUBLICATIONS

Novels (series character: Roger Sheringham)

> *The Layton Court Mystery* (Sheringham). London, Jenkins, 1925; New York, Doubleday, 1929.
> *The Wychford Poisoning Case* (Sheringham). London, Collins, 1926; New York, Doubleday, 1930.
> *Roger Sheringham and the Vane Mystery.* London, Collins, 1927; as *The Mystery at Lovers' Cave*, New York, Simon and Schuster, 1927.
> *Mr. Priestley's Problem* (as A. B. Cox). London, Collins, 1927; as *The Amateur Crime*, New York, Doubleday, 1928.
> *The Silk Stocking Murders* (Sheringham). London, Collins, and New York, Doubleday, 1928.
> *The Piccadilly Murder.* London, Collins, 1929; New York, Doubleday, 1930.
> *The Poisoned Chocolates Case* (Sheringham). London, Collins, and New York, Doubleday, 1929.
> *The Second Shot* (Sheringham). London, Hodder and Stoughton, 1930; New York, Doubleday, 1931.

Top Storey Murder (Sheringham).   London, Hodder and Stoughton, and New York, Doubleday, 1931.

The Floating Admiral, with others.   London, Hodder and Stoughton, 1931; New York, Doubleday, 1932.

Murder in the Basement (Sheringham).   London, Hodder and Stoughton, and New York, Doubleday, 1932.

Ask a Policeman, with others.   London, Barker, and New York, Morrow, 1933.

Jumping Jenny (Sheringham).   London, Hodder and Stoughton, 1933; as *Dead Mrs. Stratton*, New York, Doubleday, 1933.

Panic Party (Sheringham).   London, Hodder and Stoughton, 1934; as *Mr. Pidgeon's Island*, New York, Doubleday, 1934.

Six Against the Yard, with others.   London, Selwyn and Blount, 1936; as *Six Against Scotland Yard*, New York, Doubleday, 1936.

Trial and Error.   London, Hodder and Stoughton, and New York, Doubleday, 1937.

Not to Be Taken.   London, Hodder and Stoughton, 1938; as *A Puzzle in Poison*, New York, Doubleday, 1938.

Death in the House.   London, Hodder and Stoughton, and New York, Doubleday, 1939.

Novels as Francis Iles

Malice Aforethought.   London, Gollancz, and New York, Harper, 1931.

Before the Fact.   London, Gollancz, and New York, Doubleday, 1932; revised edition, London, Pan, 1958.

As for the Woman.   London, Jarrolds, and New York, Doubleday, 1939.

Uncollected Short Stories as Anthony Berkeley

"The Avenging Chance," in *The Best Detective Stories of the Year 1929.*   London, Faber, 1930; as *The Best English Detective Stories of the Year*, New York, Liveright, 1930.

"White Butterfly," in *Fifty Famous Detectives of Fiction.*   London, Odhams Press, 1938.

"The Wrong Jar," in *Detective Stories of Today*, edited by Raymond Postgate.   London, Faber, 1940.

"Mr. Mimpson Goes to the Dogs," in *Ellery Queen's Mystery Magazine* (New York), February 1946.

"Mr. Bearstowe Says," in *Anthology 1965 Mid-Year*, edited by Ellery Queen.   New York, Davis, 1965.

Uncollected Short Stories as Francis Iles

"It Takes Two to Make a Hero," in *Collier's* (Springfield, Ohio), 4 September 1943.

"The Lost Diary of Th*m*s A. Ed*s*n," in *The Saturday Book 6*, edited by Leonard Russell.   London, Hutchinson, 1946.

"Dark Journey," in *To the Queen's Taste*, edited by Ellery Queen.   Boston, Little Brown, 1946.

"Outside the Law," in *Ellery Queen's Mystery Magazine* (New York), June 1949.

"The Coward," in *Ellery Queen's Mystery Magazine* (New York), January 1953.

OTHER PUBLICATIONS as A. B. COX

Novels

The Family Witch: An Essay in Absurdity.   London, Jenkins, 1925.

The Professor on Paws.   London, Collins, 1926; New York, Dial Press, 1927.

Short Stories

Brenda Entertains.   London, Jenkins, 1925.

Play

Mr. Priestley's Adventure, adaptation of his own novel (produced Brighton, 1928; as
Mr. Priestley's Night Out, produced London, 1928; also produced as *Mr. Priestley's
Problem* and *Handcuffs for Two*).

Other

Jugged Journalism (sketches).   London, Jenkins, 1925.
O England!   London, Hamish Hamilton, 1934.
A Pocketful of One Hundred New Limericks.   Privately printed, 1960.

*   *   *

A. B. Cox wrote as both Anthony Berkeley and Francis Iles, in the latter case producing
work which ensured him a distinguished place in the history of the crime novel as we know
it today.

The typical detective novel of the 1920's was, on the whole, somewhat staid. It contained
all the expected ingredients of systematic investigation, methodical questioning of suspects,
examination of small clues, and so on. In this scene, like a herald of the Golden Age of
detection, came "Anthony Berkeley" with his detective Roger Sheringham. His debut in 1925
with *The Layton Court Mystery* (published anonymously, but soon followed by many others
under the Berkeley name) was praised by Howard Haycraft as bringing a "naturalistic quality
that was a welcome and needed relief." In Roger Sheringham, Berkeley introduced an
amateur detective who was loquacious, conceited, occasionally downright offensive, on good
terms with the police, and something of a man-about-town with contacts in all the right
places.

Infallibility was not one of Sheringham's virtues. In *The Poisoned Chocolates Case*, Chief
Inspector Moresby of Scotland Yard (a regular Berkeley character) recounts a murder case to
the assembled members of the Crimes Circle, who then in turn produce alternative solutions.
Berkeley developed the novel from his short story "The Avenging Chance," a brilliant model
of construction which has appeared in many anthologies. The novel stands on its own,
however, as a clear demonstration of Berkeley's ingenious mind. It also shows his satirical
bent, as he lampoons the Great Detective syndrome and pokes gentle fun at the London
Detection Club (of which he was Honorary Secretary). The debunking of Sheringham is a
nice touch, it being unusual for writers of the time to portray their detective heroes as
anything other than invincible, and the triumph of the hen-pecked little Ambrose Chitterwick
is nothing short of a brainwave. Chitterwick appeared in other Berkeley novels, but never to
such magnificent effect. *The Poisoned Chocolates Case* is a classic.

Berkeley's tendency to laugh behind his hand at the rather stuffy conventions of detective
fiction was evident throughout his books. So too was his penchant for the farcical, as seen in
Mr. Priestley's Problem or in that delicious scene toward the end of *Trial and Error* when
mild-mannered Mr. Lawrence Todhunter punches the hangman on the chin. To such
examples may be added the pastiche short story "Holmes and the Dasher" (*Jugged
Journalism*) and his collaboration with other members of The Detection Club in *Ask a
Policeman*.

There are many admirable facets to Berkeley. One recalls his ability to enlist our sympathy
for the murderer, often by creating murder victims so disagreeable that we feel bumping-off
to be too good for them. He was also able to portray chinless young men and flappers, so

shallow and superficial in many novels and plays of the time, yet inject into them such life that they emerged from the pages as credible characters. His talent sometimes extended to producing a moving study which we feel to be an "inverted" crime novel, then stunning the reader with an entirely unpredictable ending which turns the whole thing into a "whodunit." His sound knowledge of police procedure, and his mastery of legal points, indicated an interest in criminology which showed through many of the novels, and was evident also in his reconstructions of famous crimes. Particularly noteworthy are his second novel, *The Wychford Poisoning Case* (based on the Florence Maybrick affair), and his analysis of the Rattenbury case in *The Anatomy of Murder* (1937).

It was in 1930, in his preface to *The Second Shot*, that Berkeley asserted his significant views on the likely future pattern of crime fiction. He felt that "the detective story is in the process of developing into the novel ... holding its readers less by mathematical than by psychological ties. The puzzle element will no doubt remain, but it will become a puzzle of character rather than a puzzle of time, place, motive, and opportunity." *The Second Shot* was not itself a particularly good example of what Berkeley was suggesting, but his ideas were fully developed one year later (as Francis Iles) with the masterpiece *Malice Aforethought*. From the first page, we know that Dr. Bickleigh intends to murder his wife – just as on the first page of Iles's second book, *Before the Fact*, we are told that Lina Aysgarth's husband is a murderer.

This was something different, with the mind of the murderer established as more important that his identity. We are shown murder not as a sensational subject, but planned in the cosy drawing-rooms of English suburbia or at tennis parties. With a nice mixture of cynicism and realism Iles allows us to accompany the murderer, or the victim, through a succession of twists and turns which make his plots even more enthralling than those of the classic detective novel. The reader finds it impossible not to identify himself with the protagonist – certainly in Bickleigh's case – and not to feel personally the pressures and fears. The Iles novels are, however, very far from the documentary crime novel or the police procedural story which later writers developed from his ideas. He shows, with stunning panache, that there are countless ways of shocking the reader while completely eliminating the "whodunit" element.

Iles was the innovator, the father of those techniques so evident in much of today's crime fiction; Berkeley was the dry-humoured, literary, clever exponent of detective novels in which he rebelled against the stolid conventions. Cox, the man behind both, will for long remain a key figure in the history of the genre.

—Melvyn Barnes

BETTERIDGE, Don. See **NEWMAN, Bernard.**

BIGGERS, Earl Derr. American. Born in Warren, Ohio, 26 August 1884. Educated at Harvard University, Cambridge, Massachusetts, B.A. 1907. Married Eleanor Ladd in 1912; one son. Began career in journalism as staff member, Boston *Traveler*, 1907. *Died 5 April 1933.*

CRIME PUBLICATIONS

Novels (series character: Detective Sergeant/Inspector Charlie Chan)

Seven Keys to Baldpate. Indianapolis, Bobbs Merrill, 1913; London, Mills and Boon, 1914.
Love Insurance. Indianapolis, Bobbs Merrill, 1914.
Inside the Lines, with Robert Welles Ritchie. Indianapolis, Bobbs Merrill, 1914.
The Agony Column. Indianapolis, Bobbs Merrill, 1916; as *Second Floor Mystery*, New York, Grosset and Dunlap, 1930.
The House Without a Key (Chan). Indianapolis, Bobbs Merrill, 1925; London, Harrap, 1926.
The Chinese Parrot (Chan). Indianapolis, Bobbs Merrill, 1926; London, Harrap, 1927.
Fifty Candles. Indianapolis, Bobbs Merrill, 1926.
Behind That Curtain (Chan). Indianapolis, Bobbs Merrill, and London, Harrap, 1928.
The Black Camel (Chan). Indianapolis, Bobbs Merrill, 1929; London, Cassell, 1930.
Charlie Chan Carries On. Indianapolis, Bobbs Merrill, 1930; London, Cassell, 1931.
Keeper of the Keys (Chan). Indianapolis, Bobbs Merrill, and London, Cassell, 1932.

Short Stories

Earl Derr Biggers Tells Ten Stories. Indianapolis, Bobbs Merrill, 1933.

OTHER PUBLICATIONS

Plays

If You're Only Human (produced 1912).
Inside the Lines (produced Baltimore and New York, 1915; London, 1917). Indianapolis, Bobbs Merrill, 1915; London, French, 1924.
A Cure for Curables, with Lawrence Whitman, adaptation of a story by Cora Harris (produced New York, 1918).
See-Saw, music by Louis A. Hirsch (produced New York, 1919).
Three's a Crowd, with Christopher Morley (produced New York, 1919; London, 1923).
The Ruling Passion, in *Reference Scenarios.* Hollywood, Palmer Institute of Authorship, 1924.

*   *   *

Earl Derr Biggers began as a newspaper columnist and playwright, and wrote his first successful mystery novel, *Seven Keys to Baldpate*, in 1913, followed by other mystery-romances cast in the melodramatic mold. But his contribution to the mystery-detective genre is his detective, Charlie Chan. Based on an actual Honolulu police detective, Chan was introduced in 1925 as a marked departure from the clichés of the sinister Chinese villain with *A House Without a Key* (often considered the best of the series), followed by five additional Chan novels, all initially published as serials in *The Saturday Evening Post*. The unassuming sleuth and his adventures were immediately successful and a sizeable "industry" of radio dramas, comic strips, and films grew up around the Chan character, manners, and methods. Chan soon acquired international repute, becoming, for better or for worse, the household name for any Chinese.

A member of the Honolulu Police Department, Chan works both in and away from Hawaii to build his reputation of tenacious sagacity in solving his baffling cases, crowded with suspects of every description. The pudgy, keen-eyed sleuth is a student of Chinese philosophy and in his terse, stilted, pidgin style quotes Confucian aphorisms to fit every occasion: "Eggs shouldn't dance with stones"; "The fool in a hurry drinks his tea with the fork." Chan's hybrid cultural character of race and national affiliation (Chinese, Chinese-Hawaiian, and assimilated American) brings to these puzzles – themselves compounds of national, cultural, ethnic, and generational elements – resources of cross-cultural acumen going beyond the more obvious Asian-American connections. In *The Chinese Parrot* Chan goes to California to look into the murder of a Chinese cook on a ranch. *Behind That Curtain* connects two killings sixteen years apart – one in London, one in San Francisco – through the only clue: a pair of Chinese slippers embroidered with Chinese characters. The setting of *The Black Camel* is Waikiki Beach, the scene of the crime in the stabbing of a famous film actress. *Charlie Chan Carries On* features ship-board suspense as Chan pursues a murderer on a round-the-world cruise in its final lap between San Francisco and Honolulu. The final adventure, *Keeper of the Keys*, takes Chan to Lake Tahoe where a flamboyant opera prima donna has been murdered; in this story Chan is able to discern motives because of his familiarity with differences between Chinese and American codes of justice.

Chan lore has recently begun to take on new meaning with the emergence of the study of popular culture as an academic subject. As a Chinese on the side of law and order, Chan was in part designed to counteract the image of the sinister or deviously clever Oriental which had dominated foreign adventure novels from the 19th century: E. Harcourt Burrage's Chinese Ching Ching, Sax Rohmer's Dr. Fu Manchu, and the Yellow Menace figures of *Detective Comics*. Chan's amiable if enigmatic persona prepared the way for other favorable images of the Oriental, which included Hugh Wiley's James Lee Wong, John Marquand's Mr. Moto, and Robert van Gulik's revival of the 7th century magistrate Judge Dee. Chan is a well-rounded figure, mediating and discoursing on questions of justice, liberty, right, tradition, and cultural identity, as well as on a range of ethical problems which often focus on racism. But it is the persistent polarity of Eastern and Western values that makes Chan such an intriguing man in terms of cross-cultural interaction. His cases interweave with the ambiguity and ambivalence of his cultural identity as an Americanized Chinese, and his struggle to maintain his traditional heritage under pressure of demands from a modern Western environment. The cross-cultural detective, manifest in such new creations as Harry Kemelman's Rabbi David Small, Arthur Upfield's Aboriginal police inspector Napoleon Bonaparte, and H. R. F. Keating's Indian C.I.D. Inspector Ghote have in common a venerable ancestor in Charlie Chan.

—Margaret J. King

BINGHAM, John (Michael Ward, Lord Clanmoris).   British.   Born in York, 3 November 1908. Educated at Cheltenham College, and in France and Germany. Served in the Royal Engineers, 1939–40. Married Madeleine Ebel in 1934; one son and one daughter, the writer Charlotte Bingham. Worked in the War Office, 1940–46, with the Control Commission in Germany, 1946–48, and in the Ministry of Defence, 1950–77. Reporter, Hull *Daily Mail*, after 1931, and picture editor and feature writer for *Sunday Dispatch*, London. Lives in London. Agent: A. D. Peters & Co. Ltd., 10 Buckingham Street, London WC2N 6BU, England.

CRIME PUBLICATIONS

Novels

   My Name Is Michael Sibley.   London, Gollancz, and New York, Dodd Mead, 1952.

Five Roundabouts to Heaven.   London, Gollancz, 1953; as *The Tender Poisoner*, New York, Dodd Mead, 1953.

The Third Skin.   London, Gollancz, and New York, Dodd Mead, 1954; as *Murder Is a Witch*, New York, Dell, 1957.

The Paton Street Case.   London, Gollancz, 1955; as *Inspector Morgan's Dilemma*, New York, Dodd Mead, 1956.

Murder off the Record.   New York, Dodd Mead, 1957; as *Marion*, London, Gollancz, 1958.

Murder Plan Six.   London, Gollancz, 1958; New York, Dodd Mead, 1959.

Night's Black Agent.   London, Gollancz, and New York, Dodd Mead, 1961.

A Case of Libel.   London, Gollancz, 1963.

A Fragment of Fear.   London, Gollancz, 1965; New York, Dutton, 1966.

The Double Agent.   London, Gollancz, 1966; New York, Dutton, 1967.

I Love, I Kill.   London, Gollancz, 1968; as *Good Old Charlie*, New York, Simon and Schuster, 1969.

Vulture in the Sun.   London, Gollancz, 1971.

God's Defector.   London, Macmillan, 1976; as *Ministry of Death*, New York, Walker, 1977.

The Marriage Bureau Murders.   London, Macmillan, 1977.

Uncollected Short Stories

"Murderer at Large," in *Ellery Queen's Mystery Magazine* (New York), January 1961.
"The Hangman's Fish," in *Ellery Queen's Mystery Magazine* (New York), March 1965.

OTHER PUBLICATIONS

Play

Radio Play: *Not My Pigeon*, 1977.

Other

The Hunting Down of Peter Manuel, Glasgow Multiple Murderer, with William Muncie.   London, Macmillan, 1973.

John Bingham comments:
I am not so much interested in who committed, say, the murder, but in the psychological build-up, whether the murder will, in fact, be committed, and whether the criminal will be caught. I do not describe sadistic scenes in detail, since I think this is pandering to only a section of the reading public, probably offends and upsets a larger section, and may spark off imitative action among some. Similarly, I do not describe sexual matters for the first two of the above reasons, and in any case it is better to imply certain events and allow the reader to use his or her own imagination: a description which might excite one reader may bore another. This assumption is based on the reasonable theory that the readers know what sex is all about.

Any small contribution I may have made in the crime novel field is partly due, I think, to fairly new and accurate descriptions of some police interrogation methods and indeed of police officers. It has been said that the book *My Name Is Michael Sibley*, and certain others, were a breakthrough from stereotyped characters and interrogation methods, and set a trend which was subsequently developed and bore fruit in some well-known and popular television series and characterisations, showing police officers and their methods as they often are. I have evolved no brilliant amateur detectives who solve crimes better than the police, because they do not exist, and, not having the same organisation, scientific equipment, and records, could not exist; nor are my detectives bumbling, amusing, sadistic, stupid, or whimsical. Most of them are over-worked and human, and involved in normal hopes for promotion and normal family life.

*   *   *

"The world's full of people taking chances," a spymaster called Vandoren remarks sardonically to one of his agents in the closing pages of *God's Defector*. Vandoren, who appears earlier as Ducane in *The Double Agent* and *Vulture in the Sun*, is John Bingham's version of the chief of Britain's Secret Intelligence Service – the counterpart of Maugham's "R," Fleming's "M," and le Carré's "Control." "A concentrated force of pure ferocity, easily misinterpreted as malevolence," Vandoren is engaged in plotting the death of a Conservative MP turned traitor. His retort, meant to rebuke the agent who objects to his plan, is a particularly apt gloss on Bingham's work as a whole; for in his dozen crime novels and espionage thrillers written over a twenty-five year period, Bingham has drawn a compelling picture of a dangerous world full of people taking chances. Life, Bingham's novels suggest, is an exceedingly dangerous business – and not just for traitorous MP's. Especially for the unwary, the foolish, or those inclined to take the seemingly easy way out – but for the cunning, the cautious, and the farsighted as well – destruction lies all too close at hand. Unlike most mystery writers, who celebrate the sufficiency of rationality in a deceptive and dangerous world, Bingham explores the limits, the vulnerability of rational procedures.

The world of Bingham's fiction is a menacing one, in part, because there are some very nasty predators abroad in it. Men like Green, the blackmailing villain of *Night's Black Agent*, and Robert Draper, the murderer in *The Paton Street Case*, are quintessentially evil – brutal, vicious, cunning, sadistic, preternaturally alert both to potential danger and to the weaknesses of their prey. Both are nondescript in appearance – epitomizing the "banality of evil" – and utterly conscienceless; their criminality is simply a given. In other cases Bingham makes a gesture in the direction of explanation: in *The Marriage Bureau Murders* Shaw's criminal aggression can be traced to a destructive marriage. In other novels, the predators are foreign intelligence agents out to protect themselves from exposure, whether at the hands of persistent curious amateurs or opposing agents. Explicit in *A Fragment of Fear*, the division of the world into the hunters and the hunted is implicit throughout Bingham's work, especially since *Night's Black Agent*, published in 1961.

Bingham's is a dangerous world, too, because of the unsettling ease with which hatred, malice, or treachery can dissemble, even among friends of long standing, as in Bingham's first novel, *My Name Is Michael Sibley*, where the narrator successfully conceals for years his hatred of a bullying former schoolmate. In *I Love, I Kill*, the narrator comes to hate Paul King, who has stolen his girl from him and married her, but he feigns friendship for King and devotes himself to furthering King's acting career, convinced that if King becomes successful he will eventually divorce his wife, leaving her free to marry Charlie. In *Five Roundabouts to Heaven*, a married man plots the poisoning of his wife so that he can be free to marry a younger woman.

Throughout Bingham's fiction, the most trivial or ordinary acts turn out to have dangerous, even fatal, consequences. Sometimes it is years before the danger is precipitated; on other occasions the slip leads immediately to trouble. In *The Marriage Bureau Murders*, Sidney Shaw's ex-wife continues to carry his picture in her purse – and as a direct result Shaw is murdered. In *The Paton Street Case*, Chief Detective Inspector David Morgan decides, out of consideration for the person, to delay the arrest of a suspect until the last possible moment – and it leads to two unnecessary deaths. In *Five Roundabouts to Heaven*, a woman, stirring in her sleep and reaching out for her husband, precipitates his decision to poison her. An indiscreet conversation in a pub years earlier leads the police to suspect Charles Maither of murder in *Good Old Charlie*. A boy, bullied at school, buys a knuckleduster and continues to carry it as a talisman into manhood but is seen disposing of it in a trash container following the fatal bludgeoning of a friend (*My Name Is Michael Sibley*).

The act becomes a damaging bit of circumstantial evidence as the police build a plausible but false case against him.

In Bingham's world, the police are more likely to be part of what threatens the individual rather than a source of aid and protection. In *The Paton Street Case* Inspector Morgan, though portrayed sympathetically, disastrously mishandles the case. In *A Fragment of Fear*, however, it is stolid, suspicious, unimaginative policemen who endanger the narrator by refusing him needed protection, and in *My Name Is Michael Sibley* the narrator finds himself interrogated by officers whose principal interest is in closing out cases rather than discovering the truth of the matter. The murder in that novel remains unsolved at the end.

Luck has a great deal to do, finally, with survival in Bingham's world. Few characters, by means of their own exertions, can evade the determined efforts of the predators. James Compton (in *A Fragment of Fear*) survives only because Special Branch agents happen to pick up his captors before they can dispose of him. "We live in dangerous times," Compton concludes, reflecting on his ordeal. "All one can do is to keep the spear ready, and a feeble thing it is, touch an amulet, and hope for the best, and trust that, as in my case, the tribe can after all protect not only the tribe but the individual."

Bingham is one of the more original writers of suspense fiction to appear in the last twenty-five years. He is also one of the most varied. His absorption with character, his interest in the effects of crime, and his stunning descriptions of police interrogations, at which he must be acknowledged a master, distinguish his work. And equally to his credit, his novels do little to celebrate or perpetuate the exaggerated claims for functional rationality and the abductive method that characterize mystery fiction as a whole, particularly that part that is misleadingly termed "detection."

—R. Gordon Kelly

BLACK, Gavin. Pseudonym for Oswald (Morris) Wynd. Scottish. Born in Tokyo, Japan, 4 July 1913. Educated at American School, Tokyo; Atlantic City High School, New Jersey; Edinburgh University. Served in the British army, 1940–45: Lieutenant, mentioned in despatches. Married Janet Muir. Since 1946, free-lance writer. Agent: Curtis Brown Ltd., 575 Madison Avenue, New York, New York 10022, U.S.A. Address: St. Adrian's, Crail, Fife KY10 3SU, Scotland.

CRIME PUBLICATIONS

Novels (series character: Paul Harris in all books)

Suddenly, At Singapore.... London, Collins, 1961.
Dead Man Calling. London, Collins, and New York, Random House, 1962.
A Dragon for Christmas. London, Collins, and New York, Harper, 1963.
The Eyes Around Me. London, Collins, and New York, Harper, 1964.
You Want to Die, Johnny? London, Collins, and New York, Harper, 1966.
A Wind of Death. London, Collins, and New York, Harper, 1967.
The Cold Jungle. London, Collins, and New York, Harper, 1969.
A Time for Pirates. London, Collins, and New York, Harper, 1971.
The Bitter Tea. New York, Harper, 1972; London, Collins, 1973.
The Golden Cockatrice. London, Collins, 1974; New York, Harper, 1975.

A Big Wind for Summer.   London, Collins, and New York, Harper, 1975; as *Gale Force*, London, Fontana, 1978.
A Moon for Killers.   London, Collins, 1976; as *Killer Moon*, London, Fontana, 1977.
Night Run from Java.   London, Collins, 1979.

Novels as Oswald Wynd

When Ape Is King.   London, Home and Van Thal, 1949.
Stars in the Heather.   Edinburgh, Blackwood, 1956.
A Wall in the Long Dark Night.   London, Cassell, 1962.
Death the Red Flower.   London, Cassell, and New York, Harcourt Brace, 1965.
Walk Softly, Men Praying.   London, Cassell, and New York, Harcourt Brace, 1967.
Sumatra Seven Zero.   London, Cassell, and New York, Harcourt Brace, 1968.
The Forty Days.   London, Collins, 1972; New York, Harcourt Brace, 1973.

OTHER PUBLICATIONS

Novels

Black Fountains.   New York, Doubleday, 1947; London, Home and Van Thal, 1948.
Red Sun South.   New York, Doubleday, 1948.
The Stubborn Flower.   London, Joseph, 1949; as *Friend of the Family*, Doubleday, 1949.
The Gentle Pirate.   New York, Doubleday, 1951.
Moon of the Tiger.   London, Cassell, and New York, Doubleday, 1958.
Summer Can't Last.   London, Cassell, 1960.
The Devil Came on Sunday.   London, Cassell, and New York, Doubleday, 1961.
The Hawser Pirates.   London, Cassell, and New York, Harcourt Brace, 1970.
The Ginger Tree.   London, Collins, and New York, Harper, 1977.

Plays

Radio Plays: *Tomorrow All My Hopes*, 1951; *Satan and a House in the Country*, 1951; *Anna from the Jungle*, 1952; *A Medal for the Poachers*, 1954.

Television Play: *Killer Lie Waiting*, 1963.

Manuscript Collection: Mugar Memorial Library, Boston University.

Gavin Black comments:
I really can't think of much to say about my suspense product; you either like it or you don't. Fortunately quite a few people seem to like it, but I can't do the bang bang action stuff which makes for the really big sales. Can't read the products of the boys who do it so successfully. I like characters who at least vaguely resemble human beings.

*   *   *

Gavin Black is a Scotsman who knows and writes of the Far East quite as if he were a native of Malaysia. In *A Dragon for Christmas*, one of the most entertaining as well as thought-provoking mysteries of its year, Gavin Black took the reader into Red China, not with spies and counter-spies, but with a nice, sensible young fellow, Paul Harris, whose project was to sell to the Chinese engines for their river boats. Another salesman, the pragmatic and mysterious Mr. Kishimura, is also on his way to China. However, he has another reason for his voyage: his partner has vanished there and he intends to find out why.

The story moves at a quick pace, and is witty, wise, and quietly probing without interrupting the suspense.

A like pattern was followed in subsequent books. The Scotsman in a foreign place was always basic, whether being harried in Hong Kong as in *The Eyes Around Me*, or taking Malaysian citizenship as his business prospered and he made his home there. In these years, newsmen covering the Far East were aware of the undercurrents marking troubles to come, and other novelists, like William J. Lederer, Eugene Burdick, and Graham Greene, were writing about the Far East. Meanwhile Gavin Black was adroitly educating his readers as to what was happening and about to happen.

In *A Big Wind for Summer* Paul Harris has returned to Scotland. Instead of the islands of Malaysia, he was travelling to the Outer Hebrides, which could become just as well known and as beautifully explored as the others.

Hopefully, Harris is launched on a new series of meaningful adventures.

—Dorothy B. Hughes

BLACK, Lionel. Pseudonym for Dudley Barker; also writes as Anthony Matthews. British. Born in London, 25 March 1910. Educated at Bournemouth School, 1920–29; Oriel College, Oxford, B.A. 1933. Served in the Royal Air Force, 1941–45: Wing Commander, mentioned in despatches. Married Muriel Irene Griffiths in 1935; one son and one daughter. Reporter and News Editor, *Evening Standard*, London, 1933–39; Reporter and Features Editor, *Daily Herald*, London, 1940–41, 1945–54; Associate Editor, *John Bull*, London, 1954–59; staff member of Curtis Brown Ltd., literary agents, London, 1960–65. Since 1965, free-lance writer and broadcaster. Address: French Court, Pett, Sussex TN35 4JA, England.

CRIME PUBLICATIONS

Novels (series characters: Emma Greaves; Kate Theobald)

A Provincial Crime. London, Cassell, 1960.
Chance to Die (Greaves). London, Cassell, 1965.
The Bait (Greaves). London, Cassell, 1966; New York, Paperback Library, 1968.
Two Ladies in Verona (Greaves). London, Cassell, 1967; as *The Lady Is a Spy*, New York, Paperback Library, 1969.
Outbreak. London, Cassell, and New York, Stein and Day, 1968.
Swinging Murder (Theobald). London, Cassell, 1969; (as Anthony Matthews) New York, Walker, 1969.
Breakaway. London, Collins, 1970; as *Flood*, New York, Stein and Day, 1971.
Death Has Green Fingers (Theobald). London, Collins, 1971; (as Anthony Matthews) New York, Walker, 1971.
Ransom for a Nude. London, Collins, and New York, Stein and Day, 1972.
The Life and Death of Peter Wade. London, Collins, 1973; New York, Stein and Day, 1974.
Death by Hoax (Theobald). London, Collins, 1974; New York, Avon, 1978.
Arafat Is Next! New York, Stein and Day, 1975.
A Healthy Way to Die (Theobald). London, Collins, 1976; New York, Avon, 1979.

The Foursome. London, Collins, 1978.
The Penny Murders (Theobald).   London, Collins, and New York, Avon, 1979.

OTHER PUBLICATIONS as Dudley Barker

Novels

A Few of the People.   London, Jarrolds, 1946.
Grandfather's House.   London, Heinemann, 1951.
The Voice.   London, Heinemann, 1953.
Green and Pleasant Land.   London, Heinemann, 1955; as *This Green and Pleasant Land*, New York, Holt, 1956.
Toby Pinn.   London, Heinemann, 1956.
Private Company.   London, Longman, 1959.
The Ladder.   London, Cassell, 1968.
A Pillar of Rest.   London, Cassell, 1970.

Plays

Radio Plays: *Visiting Airman*, 1960; *Obedience Test*, 1961.

Other

Laughter in Court (sketches).   London, Methuen, 1935.
Palmer, The Rugeley Poisoner.   London, Duckworth, 1935.
Lord Darling's Famous Cases.   London, Hutchinson, 1936.
Coastal Command at War, with Gordon Campbell and Tom Guthrie (as Tom Dudley-Gordon).   Cairo, Schindler, and London, Jarrolds, 1943; as *I Seek My Prey in the Waters*, New York, Doubleday, 1943.
Harvest Home: The Official Story of the Great Floods of 1947 and Their Sequel.   London, His Majesty's Stationery Office, 1947.
People for the Commonwealth: The Case for Mass Migration.   London, Werner Laurie, 1958.
Berlin Air Lift: An Account of the British Contribution.   London, His Majesty's Stationery Office, 1949.
Grivas: Portrait of a Terrorist.   London, Cresset Press, 1959; New York, Harcourt Brace, 1960.
The Commonwealth We Live In.   London, Her Majesty's Stationery Office, 1960.
The Young Man's Guide to Journalism.   London, Hamish Hamilton, 1963.
The Man of Principle: A View of John Galsworthy.   London, Heinemann, and New York, British Book Centre, 1963.
British Aid to Developing Nations.   London, Her Majesty's Stationery Office, 1964.
Swaziland.   London, Her Majesty's Stationery Office, 1965.
Writer by Trade: A View of Arnold Bennett.   London, Allen and Unwin, and New York, Atheneum, 1966.
Prominent Edwardians.   London, Allen and Unwin, and New York, Atheneum, 1969.
G. K. Chesterton: A Biography.   London, Constable, and New York, Stein and Day, 1973.

Lionel Black comments:
I write as well as I can, and hope that, at least, it's always a professional job.

* * *

Lionel Black has established himself as a leading crime writer with his 15 novels published since 1960. Although he introduced a series character – Emma Greaves – in his earlier novels, and he has used Kate Theobald in some later ones, his books without a recurring character seem more appropriate to his fluent and easy style.

The settings are always very English and deal in depth with the area concerned. In *Breakaway*, the action was set in the Fens and the reader was left with a deep impression of Eastern England in all its moods. He has the knack of varying his themes so that there is no standardisation; whether he is writing about the planning and carrying out of an attack on a security van or the more racy semi-classic English detective story featuring roses and murder, the attention to detail and authenticity is always complete.

A natural story-teller, he can involve the reader completely with his description of a flood scene geographically complete, and his dialogue adds much to the hatching of the plot. A good detective story must rely upon the prose rather than purely on an ingenious plot. When he gets an author who can combine both, the "whodunit" lover is left with a feeling of euphoria. *Death Has Green Fingers* is such a book. It has all the ingredients of a good detective story, being entirely readable, carefully plotted, and, above all, believable. This summing up could apply to all of Black's books.

—Donald C. Ireland

BLACK, Mansell. See **TREVOR, Elleston.**

BLACKBURN, John (Fenwick). British. Born in Corbridge on Tyne, Northumberland, 26 June 1923; brother of the writer Thomas Blackburn. Educated at Haileybury College, 1937–40; Durham University, B.A. 1949. Served as a radio officer in the merchant navy, 1942–45. Married Joan Mary Clift in 1950. Worked as a lorry driver, schoolmaster in London, 1949–51, and Berlin, 1951–52; Director, Red Lion Books, London, 1952–59. Ran a book shop with his wife in Richmond, Surrey. Agent: A. M. Heath & Co. Ltd., 40–42 William IV Street, London WC2N 4DD, England.

CRIME PUBLICATIONS

Novels

    A Scent of New-Mown Hay. London, Secker and Warburg, and New York, Mill, 1958; as *The Reluctant Spy*, London, Lancer, 1966.
    A Sour Apple Tree. London, Secker and Warburg, 1958; New York, Mill, 1959.

Broken Boy.   London, Secker and Warburg, 1959; New York, Mill, 1962.
Dead Man Running.   London, Secker and Warburg, 1960; New York, Mill, 1961.
The Gaunt Woman.   London, Cape, and New York, Mill, 1962.
Blue Octavo.   London, Cape, 1963; as *Bound to Kill*, New York, Mill, 1963.
Colonel Bogus.   London, Cape, 1964; As *Packed for Murder*, New York, Mill, 1964.
The Winds of Midnight.   London, Cape, 1964; as *Murder at Midnight*, New York, Mill, 1964.
A Ring of Roses.   London, Cape, 1965; as *A Wreath of Roses*, New York, Mill, 1965.
Children of the Night.   London, Cape, 1966; New York, Putnam, 1969.
The Flame and the Wind.   London, Cape, 1967.
Nothing But the Night.   London, Cape, 1968.
The Young Man from Lima.   London, Cape, 1968.
Bury Him Darkly.   London, Cape, 1969; New York, Putnam, 1970.
Blow the House Down.   London, Cape, 1970.
The Household Traitors.   London, Cape, 1971.
Devil Daddy.   London, Cape, 1972.
For Fear of Little Men.   London, Cape, 1972.
Deep among the Dead Men.   London, Cape, 1973.
Our Lady of Pain.   London, Cape, 1974.
Mister Brown's Bodies.   London, Cape, 1975.
The Face of the Lion.   London, Cape, 1976.
The Cyclops Goblet.   London, Cape, 1977.
Dead Man's Handle.   London, Cape, 1978.
The Sins of the Father.   London, Cape, 1978.

Uncollected Short Stories

"Johnny Cut-Throat," in *The Devil's Kisses*.   London, Corgi, 1976.
"The Final Trick," in *The Taste of Fear*, edited by Hugh Lamb.   New York, Taplinger, 1976.
"Dad," in *Return from the Grave*, edited by Hugh Lamb.   New York, Taplinger, 1977.

Manuscript Collection: Mugar Memorial Library, Boston University.

*   *   *

John Blackburn has gained, over a period of twenty years, a solid reputation in the mystery, suspense, and espionage field. He is known as a stylish, genuinely chilling author. He has successfully wed the thriller with aspects of the super-scientific or the supernatural. His characters must directly confront objects of horror. These evils do not loom vaguely in the background, but seem unstoppable and are among the most malevolent portrayals in the genre.

Blackburn's first novel, *A Scent of New-Mown Hay*, creates a sustained nightmare in which the survivor of a Nazi concentration camp looses a biological weapon which threatens both Russia and England. What begins as a routine investigation turns into a matter of life and death. The novel has been praised for its explicit detail, but criticized for having too much science and not enough detection. General Kirk and the British Foreign Office Intelligence, featured in several other novels, appear here for the first time.

In *Children of the Night*, Blackburn has a tightly plotted story of nature-gone-daft. The setting of the Yorkshire moors is suitably forbidding. *Dead Man Running* begins with the protagonist taking a prosaic business trip to Russia. It quickly turns into a nightmare: he is accused of murder, branded as a traitor, and becomes a hunted man. This novel also introduces the engaging J. Moldon Mott, explorer and big-game hunter turned amateur detective.

Broken Boy is a sinister and macabre tale involving underground rituals, the revival of an unholy religion, and a cult of women seeking revenge. Here, too, Blackburn weaves in espionage. In *Colonel Bogus*, Blackburn uses his first-hand knowledge of the used book business in a tale of intrigue and assassination.

The author uses a contemporary version of the Black Death in *A Ring of Roses*. A small English boy lost in East Germany is infected with the bubonic plague and carries it to West Germany and England. Countries suspect each other until intelligence departments cooperate to track down the scientist-priest responsible.

Bury Him Darkly is a supernatural horror story which is one of Blackburn's most successful novels. An unremarkable 18th-century gentleman had a period of intense creativity in his last years, and commanded that his last journals be buried with him. Events leading to the opening of his tomb make a remarkable story, a gripping, elemental confrontation of good and evil, though the climax does not reach the level of the build-up.

Blackburn has achieved a substantial following. He can be depended upon to sustain swift, sure, exciting, and absorbing stories with some characters who are off-beat and bizarre. They will almost assuredly deal with super-science of the supernatural, often verging on the occult. They have been labelled science fiction as often as thriller or mystery. Critics occasionally feel that the climaxes do not live up to the rest of the book, that essential clues sometimes come much too late, or that the author has not been totally fair in his misdirection. His faults, however, are far outweighed by his accomplishments. In style, Blackburn has been compared to John Buchan and Geoffrey Household, in plot to John Creasey. No matter the comparisons, John Blackburn is undoubtedly England's best practicing novelist in the tradition of the thriller/fantasy novel.

—Frank Denton

BLACKSTOCK, Charity. Pseudonym for Ursula Torday; also writes as Paula Allardyce. British. Born in London. Educated at Kensington High School, London; Lady Margaret Hall, Oxford, B.A. in English; London School of Economics, social science certificate. Worked as a typist at the National Central Library, London. Agent: Anna Cooper, John Johnson, 45–47 Clerkenwell Green, London EC1R 0HT. Address: 23 Montagu Mansions, London W1H 1LD, England.

CRIME PUBLICATIONS

Novels

> *Dewey Death.* London, Heinemann, 1956; with *The Foggy, Foggy Dew*, New York, British Book Centre, 1959.
> *Miss Fenny.* London, Hodder and Stoughton, 1957; as *The Woman in the Woods*, New York, Doubleday, 1958.
> *The Foggy, Foggy Dew.* London, Hodder and Stoughton, 1958; with *Dewey Death*, New York, British Book Centre, 1959.
> *All Men Are Murderers.* New York, Doubleday, 1958; as *The Shadow of Murder*, London, Hodder and Stoughton, 1959.

The Bitter Conquest. London, Hodder and Stoughton, 1959.
The Briar Patch. London, Hodder and Stoughton, 1960; as *Young Lucifer*, Philadelphia, Lippincott, 1960.
The Exorcism. London, Hodder and Stoughton, 1961; as *A House Possessed*, Philadelphia, Lippincott, 1962.
The Gallant. London, Hodder and Stoughton, 1962; New York, Ballantine, 1966.
Mr. Christopoulos. London, Hodder and Stoughton, 1963; New York, British Book Centre, 1964.
The Factor's Wife. London, Hodder and Stoughton, 1964; as *The English Wife*, New York, Coward McCann, 1964.
When the Sun Goes Down. London, Hodder and Stoughton, 1965; as *Monkey on a Chain*, New York, Coward McCann, 1965.
The Knock at Midnight. London, Hodder and Stoughton, 1966; New York, Coward McCann, 1967.
Party in Dolly Creek. London, Hodder and Stoughton, 1967; as *The Widow*, New York, Coward McCann, 1967.
The Melon in the Cornfield. London, Hodder and Stoughton, 1969; as *The Lemmings*, New York, Coward McCann, 1969.
The Encounter. New York, Coward McCann, 1971.
I Met Murder on the Way. London, Hodder and Stoughton, 1977; as *The Shirt Front*, New York, Coward McCann, 1977.

Novels as Paula Allardyce

After the Lady. London, Ward Lock, 1954.
The Doctor's Daughter. London, Ward Lock, 1955.
A Game of Hazard. London, Ward Lock, 1955.
Adam and Evelina. London, Ward Lock, 1956.
The Man of Wrath. London, Ward Lock, 1956.
The Lady and the Pirate. London, Ward Lock, 1957.
Southarn Folly. London, Ward Lock, 1957.
Beloved Enemy. London, Ward Lock, 1958.
My Dear Miss Emma. London, Ward Lock, 1958.
Death My Lover. London, Ward Lock, 1959.
A Marriage Has Been Arranged. London, Ward Lock, 1959.
Johnny Danger. London, Ward Lock, 1960.
Witches' Sabbath. London, Ward Lock, 1961; New York, Macmillan, 1962.
The Gentle Highwayman. London, Ward Lock, 1961.
Adam's Rib. London, Hodder and Stoughton, 1963.
The Respectable Miss Parkington-Smith. London, Hodder and Stoughton, 1964.

OTHER PUBLICATIONS

Novels

The Daughter. New York, Coward McCann, 1970; London, Hodder and Stoughton, 1971.
The Jungle. London, Hodder and Stoughton, and New York, Coward McCann, 1972.
The Lonely Strangers. New York, Coward McCann, 1972; London, Hodder and Stoughton, 1973.
People in Glass Houses. London, Hodder and Stoughton, and New York, Coward McCann, 1975.
Ghost Town. London, Hodder and Stoughton, and New York, Coward McCann, 1976.
Miss Charley. London, Hodder and Stoughton, 1979.

Novels as Ursula Torday

> *The Ballad-Maker of Paris.* London, Allan, 1935.
> *No Peace for the Wicked.* London, Nelson, 1937.
> *The Mirror of the Sun.* London, Nelson, 1938.

Novels as Paula Allardyce

> *Octavia; or, The Trials of a Romantic Novelist.* London, Hodder and Stoughton, 1965.
> *The Moonlighters.* London, Hodder and Stoughton, 1966.
> *Six Passengers for the "Sweet Bird."* London, Hodder and Stoughton, 1967.
> *Waiting at the Church.* London, Hodder and Stoughton, 1968.
> *Miss Jonas's Boy.* London, Hodder and Stoughton, 1972.
> *The Gentle Sex.* London, Hodder and Stoughton, 1974.
> *Miss Philadelphia Smith.* London, Hodder and Stoughton, 1977.

Other

> *The Children.* Boston, Little Brown, 1966; as *Wednesday's Children,* London, Hutchinson, 1967.

* * *

Emotions are important in the mysteries written by Charity Blackstock, and quite often hold a higher place in her interests than the deaths or the motives. While full of misplaced passions and well-placed hatreds, it could never be said that these works are packed with logical conclusions: the scenes sometimes seem to shake with frustration, loathing, or fear, and hatred is present nearly all the time in each character's heart.

In *Miss Fenny* there is a mixture of personalities living and dying in Braxham Parva, and tension reigns, touching even the innocent and crippled child belonging to the heroine. Naturally the child has no organic disability and is able, in a crisis, to escape. The ghost of the murdered woman seems more alive than the living and leaves messages in people's minds and ears when necessary. The child's mother and her slightly overweight boy-friend are touched too by the village hatreds while suffering endlessly from frustrated passions. The life of this formerly placid village is in such upheaval that the tourists cease to visit the fourteenth-century church; this puts quite a dent in the collective pocket until the murder is cleaned up and the villain brought to justice.

There is an unusual approach to chapter headings in *Dewey Death,* chapter 1 being "Male and Female Employees. 647.22 and 647.23" and the final chapter "Shades and Shadows 515.7." This time a library is rocked by hatred, by drug smuggling and book theft with a spiteful and blackmailing clerk; there are plenty of inefficient typists and a librarian who writes best-sellers of bloodlust, duelling, and mild sexuality. A complement of two bodies provides one well-deserved death and one that is sinfully sad. In neither *Dewey Death* nor *Miss Fenny* are the police particularly effective or even efficient.

Some of the mysteries wear an isolated and brooding air, as in *The Exorcism* which is set in one of those uncomfortable private hotels haunted by a ghost. The ghost is much beloved by a visiting child who is as lonely in his life as the long-dead girl was in her unhappy existence 150 years before. The Catholic owner of the house insists upon an exorcism which releases long-dead emotions in the hearts of the guests, and a mixture of good and bad incidents results. The ending does not really solve any of the living, human problems, even if it minimizes the ghost's. *All Men Are Murderers* is another brooder, set again in Scotland but in a freezing and inhospitable winter. Two murders, one executed in London, do very little to heat up the climate or the atmosphere. The most appealing of the characters here is a huge horse with a lust for apples, oats, and biscuits. It is reputed to carry the soul of a Scottish chieftain who, it must be hoped, also enjoys the snacks freely handed out by the admirers.

Romantic intrigue as well as mystery feature in many of Blackstock's books. *I Met Murder on the Way* is based upon spies, counterspies, and international suspicion. There is a lover named Zoltan, always more appealing than the Freds and Dicks more usually available to womankind. Mirek, a Czech, is the prize offered in *The Encounter*, although he is pledged to avenge the deaths of his brothers. This is another chilly international situation.

Unfortunately there are often too many pages in Charity Blackstock's books before a suitable crisis or murder appears. The passions in *Miss Fenny* are the most consistent, and the murder starts from the first chapter. This book is one of the better ones. The humour is often delightful in *Dewey Death* but there is not enough of it, and fear and tension are sadly missing.

—Mary Groff

BLACKWOOD, Algernon (Henry).   British.   Born in Kent, 14 March 1869. Educated at Moravian School, Germany; Wellington College; Edinburgh University. Ran a hotel and was a farmer in Canada; staff member, *Canadian Methodist Magazine*, Toronto, New York *Evening Sun* and New York *Times*; private secretary to James Speyer, New York; returned to England in 1899, and worked briefly in the dried milk business; appeared on television, 1947–51. Recipient: Television Society Silver Medal, 1948. C.B.E. (Commander, Order of the British Empire), 1949. *Died 10 December 1951.*

CRIME PUBLICATIONS

Short Stories (series character: John Silence)

   John Silence, Physician Extraordinary.   London, Nash, 1908; Boston, Luce, 1909.
   Day and Night Stories (Silence).   London, Cassell, and New York, Dutton, 1917.

OTHER PUBLICATIONS

Novels

   Jimbo: A Fantasy.   London and New York, Macmillan, 1909.
   The Human Chord.   London and New York, Macmillan, 1910.
   The Centaur.   London and New York, Macmillan, 1911.
   Julius Le Vallon.   London, Cassell, and New York, Dutton, 1916.
   The Wave: An Egyptian Aftermath.   London, Macmillan, and New York, Dutton, 1916.
   The Garden of Survival.   London, Macmillan, and New York, Dutton, 1918.
   The Promise of Air.   London, Macmillan, and New York, Dutton, 1918.
   The Bright Messenger.   London, Cassell, 1921; New York, Dutton, 1922.
   Dudley and Gilderoy: A Nonsense.   London, Benn, and New York, Dutton, 1929.

Short Stories

   The Empty House and Other Ghost Stories.   London, Nash, 1906; New York, Vaughan, 1915.
   The Listener and Other Stories.   London, Nash, 1907; New York, Vaughan, 1914.

The Lost Valley and Other Stories.   London, Nash, 1910; New York, Vaughan, 1914.
Pan's Garden.   London and New York, Macmillan, 1912.
Incredible Adventures.   London and New York, Macmillan, 1914.
Ten Minute Stories.   London, Murray, and New York, Dutton, 1914.
The Wolves of God and Other Fey Stories, with Wilfred Wilson.   London, Cassell, and
   New York, Dutton, 1921.
Tongues of Fire and Other Sketches.   London, Jenkins, 1924; New York, Dutton,
   1925.
The Dance of Death and Other Tales.   London, Jenkins, 1927; New York, Dial Press,
   1928.
Ancient Sorceries and Other Tales.   London, Collins, 1927.
Full Circle (story).   London, Mathews and Marrot, 1929.
Strange Stories.   London, Heinemann, 1929.
(Stories).   London, Harrap, 1930.
The Willows and Other Queer Tales.   London, Collins, 1932.
Shocks.   London, Grayson, 1935; New York, Dutton, 1936.
The Tales of Algernon Blackwood.   London, Secker and Warburg, 1938; New York,
   Dutton, 1939.
Selected Tales: Stories of the Supernatural and the Uncanny.   London, Penguin, 1942.
The Doll and One Other.   Sauk City, Wisconsin, Arkham House, 1946.
Tales of the Uncanny and Supernatural.   London, Nevill, 1949.
In the Realm of Terror: 8 Haunting Tales.   New York, Pantheon, 1957.
Selected Tales.   London, Baker, 1964; as *Tales of Terror and the Unknown*, New York,
   Dutton, 1965; as *The Insanity of Jones and Other Stories*, London, Penguin, 1966.
Ancient Sorceries and Other Stories.   London, Penguin, 1968.
Tales of the Mysterious and Macabre.   London, Spring, 1968.

Plays

The Starlight Express, with Violet Pearn, adaptation of the story *A Prisoner in
   Fairyland* by Blackwood (produced London, 1915).
Karma: A Re-incarnation Play, with Violet Pearn.   London, Macmillan, and New
   York, Dutton, 1918.
Through the Crack, with Violet Pearn (produced London, 1920).   London and New
   York, French, 1920.
The Crossing, with Bertram Forsyth (produced London, 1920).
The Halfway House, with Elaine Ainley (produced London, 1921).
Max Hensig, with Kinsey Peile (produced London, 1929).

Other (juvenile)

The Education of Uncle Paul.   London, Macmillan, 1909; New York, Holt, 1910.
A Prisoner in Fairyland: The Book That "Uncle Paul" Wrote.   London and New York,
   Macmillan, 1913.
The Extra Day.   London and New York, Macmillan, 1915.
Episodes Before Thirty (autobiography).   London, Cassell, 1923; New York, Dutton,
   1924; as *Adventures Before Thirty*, London, Cape, 1934.
Sambo and Snitch.   Oxford, Blackwell, and New York, Appleton, 1927.
Mr. Cupboard.   Oxford, Blackwell, 1928.
By Underground.   Oxford, Blackwell, 1930
The Italian Conjuror.   Oxford, Blackwell, 1932.
Maria − of England − in the Rain.   Oxford, Blackwell, 1933.

The Fruit Stoners.   London, Grayson, 1934; New York, Dutton, 1935.
Sergeant Poppett and Policeman James.   Oxford, Blackwell, 1934.
How the Circus Came to Tea.   Oxford, Blackwell, 1936.

*   *   *

Algernon Blackwood was a writer whose early popularity in the first decade of this century faded into an unjustified neglect. It was ironic that, when his tales of ghostly visitations underwent a revival in the last years of his long life, it should have been through a medium so visually definite as television.

Born in 1869, Blackwood left England as a wandering adventurer when he was 20, roaming for a decade around Canada and the United States. All the time he was gathering the kind of impressions and listening to the kind of tales that fitted his personal interest in the psychic and the supernatural. Many years later he described these wanderings in a lively book, *Episodes Before Thirty.*

In 1899 Blackwood returned to England, and began to write the kind of stories of the borderland between the natural and the supernatural that became his special genre. In his first book of stories, *The Empty House*, Blackwood already showed his special ability to magnify spiritual terror with controlled understatement. Some of the best of his stories in this and later volumes are those in which one cannot say definitely what has happened and yet is aware that in some occult way the world has been transformed.

Blackwood was always at his best as a short story writer, a tale-teller creating an episode in which the reader half-wittingly becomes aware of a sudden opening into another sphere of consciousness, with consequences that may be delightful but usually are fearful. He wrote novels, like *Jimbo* and *The Centaur*, but the elaborate structure of a long narrative usually defeated his ability to sustain the necessary suspense.

Blackwood published ten volumes of short stories about ghostly hauntings and stranger psychic phenomena. Apart from *The Empty House*, the best are probably *The Listener* and *Pan's Garden.* Blackwood was not a writer who developed perceptibly after his first decade of publication. He seemed content with the kind of story, the level of writing, he had achieved in these early works, and perhaps the reason why his considerable popularity was not sustained is the lack of new depths of understanding, as distinct from fresh details of plot (in which Blackwood was always ingenious), in the stories contained in volumes of the 1920's and 1930's like *The Wolves of God* and *Shocks.* It is true that in 1908 Blackwood made one interesting experiment, a collection of interlinked stories, *John Silence*, which joined two different kinds of literary mystery, since its central figure was a detective working through extrasensory perceptions; he went no farther in this promising direction, though Silence reappears in *Day and Night Stories.*

Blackwood's eventual revival, which took place when he was almost eighty, was due to the fact that television could provide a stage on which he appeared as he really was – a teller of tales rather than a novelist; it is to this late era that belongs the volume of selected stories, *Tales of the Uncanny and Supernatural*, which contains most of Blackwood's best writings.

—George Woodcock

BLAISDELL, Anne.   See LININGTON, Elizabeth.

BLAKE, Nicholas. Pseudonym for C(ecil) Day Lewis. British. Born in Ballintubber, Ireland, 27 April 1904. Educated at Sherborne School, Dorset: Wadham College, Oxford, M.A. Served as an Editor in the Ministry of Information, London, 1941–46. Married 1) Mary King in 1928 (divorced, 1951); two sons; 2) Jill Balcon in 1951; one son and one daughter. Assistant Master, Summerfields School, Oxford, 1927–28; Larchfield, Helensburgh, 1928–30; Cheltenham College, Gloucestershire, 1930–35; Professor of Poetry, Oxford University, 1951–56; Norton Professor of Poetry, Harvard University, Cambridge, Massachusetts, 1964–65. Clark Lecturer, 1946, and Sidgwick Lecturer, 1956, Cambridge University; Warton Lecturer, British Academy, London, 1951; Byron Lecturer, University of Nottingham, 1952; Chancellor Dunning Lecturer, Queen's University, Kingston, Ontario, 1954; Compton Lecturer, University of Hull, Yorkshire, 1968. Director of Chatto and Windus Ltd., publishers, London, 1954–72. Member of the Arts Council of Great Britain, 1962–67. Honorary Fellow, Wadham College, Oxford, 1968. D.Litt.: University of Exeter, 1965; University of Hull, 1969; Litt.D.: Trinity College, Dublin, 1968. Fellow, 1944, Vice-President, 1958, and Companion of Literature, 1964, Royal Society of Literature; Honorary Member, American Academy of Arts and Letters, 1966; Member, Irish Academy of Letters, 1968. C.B.E. (Commander, Order of the British Empire), 1950. Poet Laureate, 1968. *Died 22 May 1972.*

CRIME PUBLICATIONS

Novels (series character: Nigel Strangeways)

A Question of Proof (Strangeways).   London, Collins, and New York, Harper, 1935.
Thou Shell of Death (Strangeways).   London, Collins, 1936; as *Shell of Death*, New York, Harper, 1936.
There's Trouble Brewing (Strangeways).   London, Collins, and New York, Harper, 1937.
The Beast Must Die (Strangeways).   London, Collins, and New York, Harper, 1938.
The Smiler with the Knife (Strangeways).   London, Collins, and New York, Harper, 1939.
Malice in Wonderland (Strangeways).   London, Collins, 1940; as *The Summer Camp Mystery*, New York, Harper, 1940; as *Malice with Murder*, New York, Pyramid, 1964.
The Case of the Abominable Snowman (Strangeways).   London, Collins, 1941; as *The Corpse in the Snowman*, New York, Harper, 1941.
Minute for Murder (Strangeways).   London, Collins, 1947; New York, Harper, 1948.
Head of a Traveller (Strangeways).   London, Collins, and New York, Harper, 1949.
The Dreadful Hollow (Strangeways).   London, Collins, and New York, Harper, 1953.
The Whisper in the Gloom (Strangeways).   London, Collins, and New York, Harper, 1954; as *Catch and Kill*, New York, Bestseller, 1955.
A Tangled Web.   London, Collins, and New York, Harper, 1956; as *Death and Daisy Bland*, New York, Dell, 1960.
End of Chapter (Strangeways).   London, Collins, and New York, Harper, 1957.
A Penknife in My Heart.   London, Collins, 1958; New York, Harper, 1959.
The Window's Cruise (Strangeways).   London, Collins, and New York, Harper, 1959.
The Worm of Death (Strangeways).   London, Collins, and New York, Harper, 1961.
The Deadly Joker.   London, Collins, 1963.
The Sad Variety (Strangeways).   London, Collins, and New York, Harper, 1964.
The Morning after Death (Strangeways).   London, Collins, and New York, Harper, 1966.
The Private Wound.   London, Collins, and New York, Harper, 1968.

Uncollected Short Stories

"A Slice of Bad Luck," in *Detection Medley*, edited by John Rhode. London, Hutchinson, 1939; abridged edition, as *Line Up*, New York, Dodd Mead, 1940.
"The Assassin's Club," in *Murder for the Millions*, edited by Frank Owen. New York, Fell, 1946.
"It Fell to Earth," in *Armchair Detective Reader*, edited by Ernest Dudley. London, Boardman, 1948.
"A Study in White," in *Queen's Awards*, 4th series, edited by Ellery Queen. Boston, Little Brown, and London, Gollancz, 1949.
"Mr. Prendergast and the Orange," in *Great Stories of Detection*, edited by R. C. Bull. London, Barker, 1960.
"Conscience Money," in *Ellery Queen's Mystery Magazine* (New York), January 1962.
"Sometimes the Blind," in *The Saint* (New York), January 1964.
"Long Shot," in *Twentieth Anniversary Annual*, edited by Ellery Queen. New York, Random House, 1965.

Other Publications

Novels

The Friendly Tree. London, Cape, 1936; New York, Harper, 1937.
Starting Point. London, Cape, 1937; New York, Harper, 1938.
Child of Misfortune. London, Cape, 1939.

Verse

Beechen Vigil and Other Poems. London, Fortune Press, 1925.
Country Comets. London, Martin Hopkinson, 1928.
Transitional Poem. London, Hogarth Press, 1929.
From Feathers to Iron. London, Hogarth Press, 1931.
The Magnetic Mountain. London, Hogarth Press, 1933.
Collected Poems, 1929–1933. London, Hogarth Press, 1935; with *A Hope for Poetry*, New York, Random House, 1935.
A Time to Dance and Other Poems. London, Hogarth Press, 1935.
Noah and the Waters. London, Hogarth Press, 1936.
A Time to Dance, Noah and the Waters and Other Poems, with an Essay, Revolution in Writing. New York, Random House, 1936.
Overtures to Death and Other Poems. London, Cape, 1938.
Poems in Wartime. London, Cape, 1940.
Selected Poems. London, Hogarth Press, 1940.
Word over All. London, Cape, 1943; New York, Transatlantic, 1944.
(Poems). London, Eyre and Spottiswoode, 1943
Short Is the Time: Poems, 1936–1943 (includes *Overtures to Death* and *Word over All*). New York, Oxford University Press, 1945.
Poems, 1943–1947. London, Cape, and New York, Oxford University Press, 1948.
Collected Poems, 1929–1936. London, Hogarth Press, 1948.
Selected Poems. London, Penguin, 1951; revised edition, 1957, 1969.
An Italian Visit. London, Cape, and New York, Harper, 1953.
Collected Poems. London, Cape-Hogarth Press, 1954.
Christmas Eve. London, Faber, 1954.
The Newborn: D.M.B., 29th April, 1957. London, Favil Press of Kensington, 1957.
Pegasus and Other Poems. London, Cape, 1957; New York, Harper, 1958.
The Gate and Other Poems. London, Cape, 1962.
Requiem for the Living. New York, Harper, 1964.

On Not Saying Anything. Cambridge, Massachusetts, privately printed, 1964.
A Marriage Song for Albert and Barbara. Cambridge, Massachusetts, privately printed, 1965.
The Room and Other Poems. London, Cape, 1965.
C. Day Lewis: Selections from His Poetry, edited by Patric Dickinson. London, Chatto and Windus, 1967.
Selected Poems. New York, Harper, 1967.
The Abbey That Refused to Die: A Poem. County Mayo, Ireland, Ballintubber Abbey, 1967.
The Whispering Roots. London, Cape, 1970; as *The Whispering Roots and Other Poems*, New York, Harper, 1970.
Going My Way. London, Poem-of-the-Month Club, 1970.
The Poems of C. Day Lewis, edited by Ian Parsons. London, Cape, 1977.

Recording; *Poems*, Argo, 1974.

Other

Dick Willoughby (juvenile). Oxford, Blackwell, 1933; New York, Ramdom House, 1938.
A Hope for Poetry. Oxford, Blackwell, 1934; with *Collected Poems*, New York, Random House, 1935.
Revolution in Writing. London, Hogarth Press, 1935; New York, Ramdom House, 1936.
Imagination and Thinking, with L. Susan Stebbing. London, British Institute of Adult Education, 1936.
We're Not Going to Do Nothing: A Reply to Mr. Aldous Huxley's Pamphlet "What Are You Going to Do about It?" London, Left Review, 1936; Folcroft, Pennsylvania, Folcroft Editions, 1970.
Poetry for You: A Book for Boys and Girls on the Enjoyment of Poetry. Oxford, Blackwell, 1944; New York, Oxford University Press, 1947.
The Poetic Image. London, Cape, and New York, Oxford University Press, 1947.
Enjoying Poetry: A Reader's Guide. London, National Book League, 1947.
The Colloquial Element in English Poetry. Newcastle upon Tyne, Literary and Philosophical Society, 1947.
The Otterbury Incident (juvenile). London, Putnam, 1948; New York, Viking Press, 1949.
The Poet's Task. Oxford, Clarendon Press, 1951; Folcroft, Pennsylvania, Folcroft Editions, 1970.
The Grand Manner. Nottingham, University of Nottingham, 1962.
The Lyrical Poetry of Thomas Hardy. London, Oxford University Press, 1953; Folcroft, Pennsylvania, Folcroft Editions, 1970.
Notable Images of Virtue: Emily Brontë, George Meredith, W. B. Yeats. Toronto, Ryerson Press, 1954; Folcroft, Pennsylvania, Folcroft Editions, 1969.
The Poet's Way of Knowledge. Cambridge, University Press, 1957.
The Buried Day (autobiography). London, Chatto and Windus, and New York, Harper, 1960.
The Lyric Impulse. Cambridge, Massachusetts, Harvard University Press, and London, Chatto and Windus, 1965.
Thomas Hardy, with R. A. Scott-James. London, Longman, 1965.
A Need for Poetry? Hull, University of Hull, 1968.
On Translating Poetry: A Lecture. Abingdon-on-Thames, Berkshire, Abbey Press, 1970.

Editor, with W. H. Auden, *Oxford Poetry 1927.* Oxford, Blackwell, 1927.

Editor, with others, *A Writer in Arms*, by Ralph Fox.   London, Lawrence and Wishart, 1937.

Editor, *The Mind in Chains: Socialism and the Cultural Revolution.*   London, Muller, 1937; Folcroft, Pennsylvania, Folcroft Editions, 1972.

Editor, *The Echoing Green: An Anthology of Verse.*   Oxford, Blackwell, 3 vols., 1937.

Editor, with Charles Fenby, *Anatomy of Oxford: An Anthology.*   London, Cape, 1938.

Editor, with L. A. G. Strong, *A New Anthology of Modern Verse, 1920–1940.*   London, Methuen, 1941.

Editor, with others, *Orion 2* and *3*.   London, Nicholson and Watson, 1945–46.

Editor, *The Golden Treasury of the Best Songs and Lyrical Poems in the English Language*, by Francis Turner Palgrave.   London, Collins, 1954.

Editor, with John Lehmann, *The Chatto Book of Modern Poetry, 1915–1955.*   London, Chatto and Windus, 1956.

Editor, with Kathleen Nott and Thomas Blackburn, *New Poems 1957.*   London, Joseph, 1957.

Editor, *A Book of English Lyrics.*   London, Chatto and Windus, 1961; as *English Lyric Poems, 1500–1900*, New York, Appleton Century Crofts, 1961.

Editor, *The Collected Poems of Wilfred Owen.*   London, Chatto and Windus, 1964; revised edition, New York, New Directions, 1964.

Editor, *The Midnight Skaters: Poems for Young Readers*, by Edmund Blunden.   London, Bodley Head, 1968.

Editor, *The Poems of Robert Browning.*   Cambridge, Limited Editions Club, 1969; New York, Heritage Press, 1971.

Editor, *A Choice of Keats's Verse.*   London, Faber, 1971.

Editor, *Crabbe.*   London, Penguin, 1973.

Translator, *The Georgics of Virgil.*   London, Cape, 1940; New York, Oxford University Press, 1947.

Translator, *The Graveyard by the Sea*, by Paul Valéry.   London, Secker and Warburg, 1947.

Translator, *The Aeneid of Virgil.*   London, Hogarth Press, and New York, Oxford University Press, 1952.

Translator, *The Eclogues of Virgil.*   London, Cape, 1963; with *The Georgics*, New York, Doubleday, 1964.

Translator, with Mátyás Sárközi, *The Tomtit in the Rain: Traditional Hungarian Rhymes*, by Erzsi Gazdas.   London, Chatto and Windus, 1971.

Bibliography: *C. Day Lewis, The Poet Laureate: A Bibliography* by Geoffrey Handley-Taylor and Timothy d'Arch Smith, London and Chicago, St. James Press, 1968.

Manuscript Collections: New York Public Library; State University of New York at Buffalo; British Museum, London; University of Liverpool.

*   *   *

Under the pseudonym of Nicholas Blake, Cecil Day Lewis, the poet and novelist who was Poet Laureate from 1968 until his death in 1972, wrote 20 detective novels. His detective, the urbane, cultivated, amateur Nigel Strangeways, an Oxford graduate of many skills and no profession, through his many acquaintances just happens to be on or familiar with the scene before the crime is committed. Strangeways works well, with mutual respect, with Inspector Blount, the blunt hard-headed Scotsman in charge of the investigations for Scotland Yard. The novels are full of literary references, ranging from Shakespeare and the classics to more recent poetry like that of Blake, Keats, Arthur Hugh Clough, and A. E. Housman. Puns and literary digressions are frequent, particularly in the more heavily written early novels. One of these, *Thou Shell of Death*, set in a country house on a cold Christmas week-end, even updates a famous and intricate literary plot. A former First World War flying ace, embittered by his past, and ill, stages his own suicide to look like murder to incriminate enemies from his distant Irish past, enemies themselves destroyed in the course of the novel. This is a contemporary version of Cyril Tourneur's gory 1607 play, *The Revenger's Tragedy*. Themes are frequently those central to classical and Elizabethan literature. Plots, often complicated with multiple murders or with murders faked to look like suicide, gradually reveal the past, dig down to discover basic corruptions of the family unit or sibling rivalries. There is, over the course of the novels published between 1935 and 1968, a gradual, uneven progression from the novels based on one sibling protecting the other to preserve a sense of family to one sibling destroying another out of jealousy. In the best of the novels, *The Case of the Abominable Snowman*, set in a country house, *Minute for Murder*, which takes place in the government ministry for propaganda at the end of the Second World War, and *End of Chapter*, set in a publishing house, the murderer is a complex and tragic figure, torn between protection and revenge or unable to choose between what represents active life and what represents peaceful death.

The novels pay strict attention to the passing of years. Nigel Strangeways ages and changes, and the texture of topical reference, like comments on Marx Brothers films in the 1930's, dates each novel fairly accurately. In the novels from the 1930's, possible psychological explanations are likely to be put down as accounting for behavior by "glands," and the few characters of proletarian origin are straightforwardly defiant of arid convention and admirably honest. Over the years, Nigel Strangeways gradually becomes more hospitable to deepening psychological explanations, and the defiant artists from the working classes, although never maimed enough to become the criminals, are seen less idealistically. A novel from the mid-1950's, *The Whisper in the Gloom*, centers on saving talks, designed to assuage the Cold War, between the Russians and the British from the murderous plots of an unscrupulous leader of cartels who makes millions from the Cold War. This novel, like some of the others, is more a story of action and adventure than an exercise in detection; others, like *Minute for Murder* or, another novel set in a country house owned by a complicated poet, *Head of a Traveller*, advance the story through a more intricately executed series of clues and events. Sometimes, the characters are stereotypes, like the academic Americans in *The Morning after Death*; often, the typology is only a superficial view and the characters grow into more complex figures, particularly the gentle poets, the thwarted intellectuals, the repressed siblings, and the sexy and forward women. The range and variety of characters, all seen through the sensitive, shrewd, and sophisticated judgment of Nigel Strangeways, is, perhaps, the fiction's principal fascination.

—James Gindin

BLAKE, Sexton. See **BRANDON, John G.**

BLANC, Suzanne. American. Recipient: Mystery Writers of America Edgar Allan Poe Award, 1961.

CRIME PUBLICATIONS

Novels (series character: Inspector Miguel Menendes in all books except *The Sea Troll*)

The Green Stone. New York, Harper, 1961; London, Cassell, 1962.
The Yellow Villa. New York, Doubleday, 1964; London, Cassell, 1965.
The Rose Window. New York, Doubleday, 1967; London, Cassell, 1968.
The Sea Troll. New York, Doubleday, 1969.

Uncollected Short Stories

"Amateur Standing," in *Merchants of Menace*, edited by Hillary Waugh. New York, Doubleday, 1969.
"An Inside Straight," in *Men and Malice*, edited by Dean Dickensheet. New York, Doubleday, 1973.

*   *   *

All of Suzanne Blanc's novels, including the least successful, *The Sea Troll* (set aboard a passenger-cargo ship sailing the Pacific), study characters suffering from a sense of isolation. This motif, applied to victims, villains, and hero alike, is particularly effective set against a realistic portrait of Mexico: lush, lovely, povery-stricken, rich, hot, and, for her protagonists, foreign.

Blanc's protagonists, potential victims all, are American women, unused to foreign travel, who come to Mexico to try to work through some personal crisis. Each of the women is aware of having reached a turning point in her life; each is thoughtful and sensitive; and each, thus, is an appealing character. Their personal problems and their progress toward solutions of them provide interesting and realistic sub-plots for the crime stories.

The villains are also interesting characters, for Blanc goes to some trouble to dramatize – but never to excuse or to rationalize – their motivations. The identity of the killers is known to the readers from the outset, and, in defining their backgrounds so clearly, Blanc is not only delineating character but also offering a second sub-plot as well as enlarging her theme, for these men are isolated by their backgrounds and by their crimes.

Miguel Menendes, the continuing character of *The Green Stone*, *The Yellow Villa*, and *The Rose Window*, is both a bureaucrat and a family man; he works for the Bureau of Tourism as an investigator, and has a wife, a daughter, and in-laws. Yet he is alone, for Menendes is an Indian and so an anomaly among his colleagues and within his family, and the plots make good capital of the irony arising from Menendes's representing and restoring a social order which will always reject him because Indians are not valued citizens in the Mexican culture Blanc paints.

The books provide some social criticism, for the Indian is ever mindful of the discrimination around him. He realizes, for instance, that other characters repress any awareness of their own Indian blood. He notes that unpopular schedules accrue to men with Indian blood, and he empathizes with one victim, for he knows that many of his colleagues will find it appropriate that she, an Indian, died a violent death. Because Blanc reports these concerns in even, cool tones, the commentary is powerful; the presence of injustice among the symbols of justice is very effective.

The Menendes marriage is not a happy one. His mother-in-law opposed it from the start and seizes every chance to increase the tension between Miguel and Teresa. The situation is exacerbated by Menendes's scorn for Teresa's religious devotion and by his preoccupation with his work. Though he adores his daughter, that love and his occasional propitiative gestures toward Teresa are not enough to resolve the situation. Blanc's treatment, compassionate, realistic, honest, lends depth to the novels, and the relationship provides continuity as well as a third sub-plot for the books.

Menendes, then, is the center of these novels, and Blanc's characterization of him coupled with her deft treatment of murder and the isolation motif guarantee interesting, compelling works. She is a good writer whose canon, though slender, is strong.

—Jane S. Bakerman

BLEECK, Oliver.   See **THOMAS, Ross.**

BLOCH, Robert.   Also writes as Collier Young.   American.   Born in Chicago, Illinois, 5 April 1917. Educated in public schools. Married 1) Marion Holcombe; 2) Eleanor Alexander; one daughter. Worked as copywriter, Gustav Marx Advertising Agency, Milwaukee, Wisconsin, 1943–53. President, Mystery Writers of America, 1970–71. Recipient: E. E. Evans Memorial Award for Fantasy and Science Fiction, 1959; Hugo short story award, 1959; Ann Radcliffe Award for Literature, 1960, for Television, 1966; Mystery Writers of America Edgar Allan Poe Award, 1960; Third Trieste Film Festival Award, 1965; Convention du Cinéma Fantastique de Paris Prize, 1973; World Fantasy Convention Award, 1975. Guest of Honor: World Science Fiction Convention, 1948, 1973; World Fantasy Convention, 1975; Bouchercon I writing conference, 1971. Agent: Scott Meredith, 845 Third Avenue, New York, New York 10022. Address: 2111 Sunset Crest Drive, Los Angeles, California 90046, U.S.A.

CRIME PUBLICATIONS

Novels

    The Scarf.   New York, Dial Press, 1947; as *The Scarf of Passion*, New York, Avon, 1948; revised edition, New York, Fawcett, 1966; London, New English Library, 1972.
    The Kidnapper.   New York, Lion, 1954.
    Spiderweb.   New York, Ace, 1954.
    The Will to Kill.   New York, Ace, 1954.
    Shooting Star.   New York, Ace, 1958.
    Psycho.   New York, Simon and Schuster, 1959; London, Hale, 1960.
    The Dead Beat.   New York, Simon and Schuster, 1960; London, Hale, 1961.
    Firebug.   Evanston, Illinois, Regency, 1961; London, Corgi, 1977.
    The Couch (novelization of screenplay).   New York, Fawcett, 1962.
    Terror.   New York, Belmont, 1962; London, Corgi, 1964.
    The Star Stalker.   New York, Pyramid, 1968.
    The Todd Dossier (as Collier Young).   New York, Delacorte Press, and London, Macmillan, 1969.
    Night-World.   New York, Simon and Scuster, 1972; London, Hale, 1974.

American Gothic. New York, Simon and Schuster, 1974; London, W. H. Allen, 1975.
The Serpent Was Cunning. New York, Zebra, 1979.

Short Stories

Terror in the Night and Other Stories. New York, Ace, 1958.
Blood Runs Cold. New York, Simon and Schuster, 1961; London, Hale, 1963.
Tales in a Jugular Vein. New York, Pyramid, 1965; London, Sphere, 1970.
Chamber of Horrors. New York, Award, 1966; London, Corgi, 1977.
Cold Chills. New York, Doubleday, 1977; London, Hale, 1978.
The King of Terrors. Yonkers, New York, Mysterious Press, 1977; London, Hale, 1978.
Out of the Mouths of Graves. Yonkers, New York, Mysterious Press, 1978.

OTHER PUBLICATIONS

Novels

It's All in Your Mind. New York, Curtis, 1971.
Sneak Preview. New York, Paperback Library, 1971.
Strange Eons. Browns Mills, New Jersey, Whispers Press, 1979.

Short Stories

Sea-Kissed. London, Utopian, 1945.
The Opener of the Way. Sauk City, Wisconsin, Arkham House, 1945; London, Spearman, 1974.
Pleasant Dreams – Nightmares. Sauk City, Wisconsin, Arkham House, 1959; London, Whiting, 1967.
Nightmares. New York, Belmont, 1961.
More Nightmares. New York, Belmont, 1961.
Yours Truly, Jack the Ripper: Tales of Horror. New York, Belmont, 1962; as *The House of the Hatchet and Other Tales of Horror*, London, Tandem, 1965.
The Eighth Stage of Fandom: Selections from 25 Years of Fan Writing, edited by Earl Kemp. Chicago, Advent, 1962.
Atoms and Evil. New York, Fawcett, 1962; London, Muller, 1963.
Horror-7. New York, Belmont, 1963; as *Torture Garden*, London, New English Library, 1965.
Bogey Men. New York, Pyramid, 1963.
The Skull of the Marquis de Sade and Other Stories. New York, Pyramid, 1965; London, Hale, 1972.
The Living Demons. New York, Belmont, 1967; London, Sphere, 1970.
Ladies Day/This Crowded Earth. New York, Belmont, 1968.
Dragons and Nightmares. Baltimore, Mirage Press, 1969.
Bloch and Bradbury. New York, Tower, 1969; as *Fever Dream and Other Fantasies*, London, Sphere, 1970.
Fear Today – Gone Tomorrow. New York, Award, 1971.
The Best of Robert Bloch. New York, Ballantine, 1977.
Such Stuff as Screams Are Made Of. New York, Ballantine, 1979.
Mysteries of the Worm. New York, Zebra, 1979.

Plays

Screenplays: *The Couch*, with Owen Crump and Blake Edwards, 1962; *The Cabinet of Caligari*, 1962; *Strait-Jacket*, 1964; *The Night Walker*, 1964; *The Psychopath*, 1966;

The Deadly Bees, with Anthony Marriott, 1967; *Torture Garden*, 1967; *The House That Dripped Blood*, 1970; *Asylum*, 1972.

Radio Plays: *Stay Tuned for Terror* series (39 scripts), 1944–45.

Television Plays: contributions to *Lock-Up*, 1960; *Alfred Hitchcock Presents*, 1960–64; *Thriller*, 1961–62; *I Spy*, 1964; *Run for Your Life*, 1965; *Star Trek*, 1966–67; *Journey to the Unknown*, 1968; *Night Gallery*, 1971.

Other

The Laughter of a Ghoul.   West Warwick, Rhode Island, Necronomicon Press, 1977.

Editor, *The Best of Fredric Brown.*   New York, Ballantine, 1977.

Bibliography: in *The Robert Bloch Fanzine* (Los Altos, California), 1973.

Manuscript Collection: University of Wyoming Library, Laramie.

Robert Bloch comments:

I have been a professional writer since the age of 17 and it's too late for me to reform now. About all I can do is to scrawl on the wall in red letters, "Stop me before I write more!"

But, judging from current production, the output will continue – which statement can be regarded either as a promise or a warning.

There's very little to be said about – or for – my work. I consider my writing to be an "entertainment," as Graham Greene so aptly designated his novels in the genre. What the reader considers it to be is his problem.

*   *   *

One of Robert Bloch's most frequently quoted lines is his claim "I have the heart of a small boy; I keep it in a jar on my desk." This gruesome word-play is characteristic of a large part of Bloch's writing. Many of his stories stem from a stock phrase or cliché carried to a grisly extreme, or a pun given a macabre new interpretation. Bloch's ability to generate chills when playing things straight (if that is the appropriate word) is just as impressive. Many of his stories deal with one or another form of psychopathology, and their impact is in no way diminished by the author's disclaimer of specialized knowledge in this area.

Robert Bloch began writing stories while still in high school, and at the age of 17 made his first professional sale, to *Weird Tales* magazine. Many of his early stories (such as those collected in *The Opener of the Way*) show the unmistakable influence of the weird-fiction writer H. P. Lovecraft, with whom Bloch had corresponded since 1932. Gradually Bloch developed a voice of his own. He branched out into humorous fantasy, science fiction, and stories of crime and suspense, although *Weird Tales* continued to publish much of his best work. A very successful story from that magazine was "Yours Truly, Jack the Ripper," which told of the search for Jack the Ripper, believed to have preserved his youth through supernatural means and to be haunting the streets of modern Chicago.

Bloch's first novel appeared in 1947. *The Scarf* is the first-person narrative of a psychopathic strangler. It is told in a terse, conversational style far removed from the mannered prose of the Lovecraft imitations or the manic slang of Bloch's humorous fantasies. In its original version, the conclusion shows the narrator coming to a realization of his condition, and generates a certain sympathy for him. In 1966 a revised version of the novel was prepared for paperback publication. Here the last few pages were replaced by new text, tightening up the original ending and putting the narrator's obsession in an altogether more chilling perspective.

Seven years passed before the publication of Bloch's next book. In 1954 three novels appeared. The best of these, and one of the author's own favorites among his work, is *The Kidnapper*, another first-person narrative of a psychopath, cold, clinical, and unsparingly honest in treatment. *Spiderweb* is the story of a phony California cult, and *The Will to Kill* tells of a Korean War veteran searching for the secret of his periodic mental blackouts. *Shooting Star* is a Hollywood private eye novel.

The watershed of Bloch's career came in 1959: a novel whose impact (helped in no small measure by Alfred Hitchcock's stunning film version) has caused Bloch to become permanently labeled as "the author of *Psycho*." This story of Norman Bates and the odd events at his isolated motel has had a profound effect on both written and filmed suspense stories ever since. By the time of the film's release, Bloch had already moved to Hollywood and was at work on a number of television and film assignments but the success of *Psycho* undoubtedly opened further doors for him. Since 1959 he has supplied stories or scripts for a dozen films and some seventy-five teleplays, as well as ten novels and many stories.

Bloch's first novel after *Psycho* was, understandably, something of a let-down. *The Dead Beat* told of an attractive but dangerous young con-man and his effect on the family that befriended him. *Firebug* was the story of a murderous pyromaniac; *The Couch* was the novelization of a screenplay about a mass murderer; *Terror* was a tale of Indian Thuggee in contemporary Chicago. *Night-World* is a story of the search for an escaped madman. *American Gothic* is based on the murderous career of Herman W. Mudgett in Chicago in the 1890's. Not quite a part of the crime genre, despite its title, is *The Star Stalker*, an excellent novel set in Hollywood during the last days of silent movies.

—R. E. Briney

BLOCHMAN, Lawrence G(oldtree). American. Born in San Diego, California, 17 February 1900. Educated at the University of California, Berkeley, A.B. 1921; Armed Forces Institute of Pathology, Certificate in Forensic Pathology 1952. Worked in the Office of War Information, 1941–46. Married Marguerite Maillard in 1926. Assistant night editor, *Japan Advertiser*, Tokyo, 1921; staff writer, *South China Morning Post*, Hong Kong, 1922; feature writer, *Englishman*, Calcutta, 1922–23; assistant night editor and editor of Riviera supplement, Chicago *Tribune*, European edition, 1923–25; editorial writer, Paris *Times*, 1925–27; free-lance writer, 1928–33; script writer, Universal Pictures, 1933–34; free-lance writer from 1946. Consultant, Commission on Government Security, 1957, and United States Information Agency, 1962–67. President, Mystery Writers of America, 1948–49. Recipient: Mystery Writers of America Edgar Allan Poe Award, 1950, Special Award, 1958. *Died 22 January 1975.*

CRIME PUBLICATIONS

Novels (series character: Inspector Leonidas Prike)

> *Bombay Mail* (Prike).   Boston, Little Brown, and London, Collins, 1934.
> *Bengal Fire* (Prike).   London, Collins, 1937; New York, Dell, 1948.
> *Red Snow at Darjeeling* (Prike).   London, Collins, 1938; New York, Great American Publications, 1960.
> *Midnight Sailing.*   New York, Harcourt Brace, 1938; London, Collins, 1939.
> *Blow-Down.*   New York, Harcourt Brace, 1939; London, Collins, 1940.

Wives to Burn. New York, Harcourt Brace, and London, Collins, 1940.
See You at the Morgue. New York, Duell, 1941; London, Cassell, 1946.
Death Walks in Marble Halls. New York, Dell, 1951.
Pursuit. Kingston, New York, Quin, 1951; as *Menace*, London, Comyns, 1951.
Rather Cool for Mayhem. Philadelphia, Lippincott, 1951; London, Cassell, 1952.
Recipe for Homicide. Philadelphia, Lippincott, 1952; London, Hammond, 1954.

Short Stories

Diagnosis: Homicide. Philadelphia, Lippincott, 1950.
Clues for Dr. Coffee. Philadelphia, Lippincott, 1964.

Uncollected Short Stories

"Red Wine," in *Eat, Drink and Be Buried*, edited by Rex Stout. New York, Viking Press, 1956; as *For Tomorrow We Die*, London, Macdonald, 1958.
"Death by Drowning," in *Ellery Queen's Mystery Magazine* (New York), April 1965.
"The Man Who Lost His Taste," in *Ellery Queen's Anthology 1966.* New York, Davis, 1965.
"Toast to Victory," in *The Saint Magazine Reader*, edited by Leslie Charteris and Hans S. Santesson. New York, Doubleday, 1966.
"Dr. Coffee and the Philanderer's Brain," in *Ellery Queen's All-Star Lineup.* New York, New American Library, 1967.
"The Case of Poetic Justice," in *Ellery Queen's Mid-Year Anthology, 1968.* New York, Davis, 1968.
"Reprieve," in *The Locked Room Reader*, edited by Hans S. Santesson. New York, Random House, 1968.
"Dr. Coffee and the Amateur Angel," in *Ellery Queen's Mystery Magazine* (New York), October 1971.
"Dr. Coffee and the Pardell Case," in *Ellery Queen's Mystery Magazine* (New York), June 1972.
"Dr. Coffee and the Whiz Kid," in *Killers of the Mind*, edited by Lucy Freeman. New York, Random House, 1974.
"Missing: One Stage-Struck Hippie," in *Ellery Queen's Aces of Mystery.* New York, Davis, 1975.

OTHER PUBLICATIONS

Play

Screenplay: *Quiet, Please, Murder*, with John Larkin, 1943.

Other

Here's How! A Round-the-World Bar Book. New York, New American Library, 1957.
Doctor Squibb: The Life and Times of a Rugged Idealist. New York, Simon and Schuster, 1958.
My Daughter Maria Callas, with Evangelia Callas. New York, Fleet, 1960; London, Freivin, 1967.
Alone No Longer, with Stanley Stein. New York, Funk and Wagnalls, 1963.
Are You Misunderstood?, with Harlan Logan. New York, Funk and Wagnalls, 1965.
The Power of Life or Death, with Michael V. Di Salle. New York, Random House, 1965.
Second Choice, with Michael V. Di Salle. New York, Hawthorn, 1966.

Understanding Your Body. New York, Crowell Collier, 1968.
Wake Up Your Body. New York, McKay, 1969.
Help Without Psychoanalysis, with Herbert Fensterheim. New York, Stein and Day, 1971.
Mister Mayor, with A. J. Cervantes. Los Angeles, Nash, 1974.

Translator, *The Unknown Warriors: A Personal Account of the French Resistance*, by Pierre Guillain de Bénouville. New York, Simon and Schuster, 1949.
Translator, *In Search of Man*, by André Missenard. New York, Hawthorn, 1957.
Translator, *The Heroes of God*, by Henri Daniel-Rops. Kingswood, Surrey, World's Work, 1959.
Translator, *The Shorter Cases of Inspector Maigret*, by Simenon. New York, Doubleday, 1959.

Manuscript Collection: University of Wyoming Library, Laramie.

*   *   *

Lawrence G. Blochman was a journalist first and a mystery novelist second. It would require the most serious of mystery scholars to recall Mr. Blochman's fictional sleuths. Anthony Boucher noted, however, that "Blochman has single-handed created enough series detectives to fill an anthology by themselves." Blochman's specialties were the knowledge of police routine and an intimate acquaintance with India, and his very first published mystery short story ("The Fifty-Carat Jinx") contained both elements. He credited the mechanics of the detective story to the Charles G. Booth, though neither Booth nor Blochman is mentioned in Haycraft's *Murder for Pleasure* or Symons's *Bloody Murder*.

The foregoing is not intended to diminish the quality and value of a Blochman mystery novel, but to emphasize the point that the man never attained the fame he deserved. He is perhaps best known for his first mystery novel, *Bombay Mail*. It featured Inspector Leonidas Prike of the C.I.D., British Secret Service in India, who was described as small, dynamic, efficient, and, when on a case, interested only in the facts. The story features one of the more famous mystery motifs, a railroad train carrying a host of interesting characters.

Blochman's most famous detective, however, was Dr. Daniel Webster Coffee, a famous pathologist, who appeared in only one novel, *Recipe for Homicide*, but in a large number of short stories. A television series, *Diagnosis: Unknown*, also featured him. Blochman's most famous short story is "Red Wine," in which the temperature of the table wine served at a jungle outpost is a vital point.

—Larry L. French

BLOCK, Lawrence. Also writes as Chip Harrison; Paul Kavanagh. American. Born in Buffalo, New York, 24 June 1938. Educated at Antioch College, Yellow Springs, Ohio, 1955–59. Married Loretta Ann Kallett in 1960; two children. Editor, Scott Meredith Inc., New York, 1957–58. Since 1958, self-employed writer. Associate editor, *Whitman Numismatic Journal*. Agent: Kelly Bramhall and Ford, 463 Commonwealth Avenue, Boston, Massachusetts 02115, U.S.A.

CRIME PUBLICATIONS

Novels (series characters: Chip Harrison; Bernie Rhodenbarr; Matthew Scudder; Evan
    Tanner)

Death Pulls a Double Cross.   New York, Fawcett, 1961.
Mona.   New York, Fawcett, 1961; London, Muller, 1963.
The Case of the Pornographic Photos (novelization of tv play).   New York, Belmont,
    1961; as *Markham: The Case of the Pornographic Photos*, London, Consul, 1965.
The Girl with the Long Green Heart.   New York, Fawcett, 1965; London, Muller,
    1967.
The Cancelled Czech (Tanner).   New York, Fawcett, 1966.
The Thief Who Couldn't Sleep (Tanner).   New York, Fawcett, 1966.
Deadly Honeymoon.   New York, Macmillan, 1967.
Tanner's Twelve Swingers.   New York, Fawcett, 1967.
Two for Tanner.   New York, Fawcett, 1967.
Here Comes a Hero (Tanner).   New York, Fawcett, 1968.
Tanner's Tiger.   New York, Fawcett, 1968.
After the First Death.   New York, Macmillan, 1969.
The Specialists.   New York, Fawcett, 1969.
Me Tanner, You Jane.   New York, Macmillan, 1970.
Make Out with Murder (as Chip Harrison).   New York, Fawcett, 1974.
The Topless Tulip Caper (as Chip Harrison).   New York, Fawcett, 1975.
In the Midst of Death (Scudder).   New York, Dell, 1976; London, Hale, 1979.
Sins of the Fathers (Scudder).   New York, Dell, 1977; London, Hale, 1979.
Time to Murder and Create (Scudder).   New York, Dell, 1977; London, Hale, 1979.
Burglars Can't Be Choosers (Rhodenbarr).   New York, Random House, 1977.
The Burglar in the Closet (Rhodenbarr).   New York, Random House, 1978.
The Burglar Who Liked to Quote Kipling (Rhodenbarr).   New York, Random House,
    1979.

Novels as Paul Kavanagh

Such Men Are Dangerous.   New York, Macmillan, 1969; London, Hodder and
    Stoughton, 1971.
The Triumph of Evil   Cleveland, World, 1971; London, Hodder and Stoughton, 1972.
Not Comin' Home to You.   New York, Putnam, 1974; London, Hodder and Stoughton,
    1976.

Uncollected Short Stories

"Death Wish," in *Alfred Hitchcock Presents: A Month of Mystery.*   New York, Random
    House, 1969.
"The Gentle Man," in *Best Detective Stories of the Year 1975*, edited by Allen J.
    Hubin.   New York, Dutton, 1975.
"The Dangerous Game," in *Ellery Queen's Mystery Magazine* (New York), June 1976.
"Gentleman's Agreement," in *Ellery Queen's Mystery Magazine* (New York), April
    1977.
"Like a Dog in the Street," in *Alfred Hitchcock's Mystery Magazine* (New York), April
    1977.
"This Crazy Business," in *Alfred Hitchcock's Mystery Magazine* (New York), May 1977.
"The Dettweiler Solution," in *Alfred Hitchcock's Tales to Take Your Breath Away*,
    edited by Eleanor Sullivan.   New York, Davis, 1977.
"Out of the Window," in *Alfred Hitchcock's Mystery Magazine* (New York), September
    1977.

147

"The Ehrengraf Method," in *Ellery Queen's Mystery Magazine* (New York), February 1978.
"The Ehrengraf Presumption," in *Ellery Queen's Mystery Magazine* (New York), May 1978.
"The Ehrengraf Experience," in *Ellery Queen's Mystery Magazine* (New York), August 1978.
"Life after Life," in *Alfred Hitchcock's Mystery Magazine* (New York), October 1978.
"The Books Always Balance," in *Alfred Hitchcock's Tales to Scare You Stiff*, edited by Eleanor Sullivan.   New York, Davis, 1978.
"The Ehrengraf Obligation," in *Ellery Queen's Mystery Magazine* (New York), March 1979.

OTHER PUBLICATIONS

Novels

No Score (as Chip Harrison).   New York, Fawcett, 1970.
Ronald Rabbit Is a Dirty Old Man.   New York, Geis, 1971.
Chip Harrison Scores Again (as Chip Harrison).   New York, Fawcett, 1971.

Other

A Guide Book to Australian Coins.   Racine, Wisconsin, Whitman, 1965.
Swiss Shooting Talers and Medals, with Delbert Ray Krause.   Racine, Wisconsin, Whitman, 1965.
Writing the Novel: From Plot to Print.   Cincinnati, Writer's Digest, 1979.

Bibliography: "Lawrence Block: Annotated Checklist of Tanner Series Books," by Jeff Banks in *Mystery Nook* (Wheaton, Maryland), May 1975.

*   *   *

Lawrence Block is a journeyman genre writer of considerable talent. The majority of his work has been for the paperback original market, under his own name and several pseudonyms; and he has produced a body of work of exceptional diversity and appeal. He has done spy and detective series, pastiche, tv tie-ins, and suspense and caper novels (*Deadly Honeymoon, The Specialists*).

The spy novels featuring Evan Tanner form a particularly enjoyable series. The likable and somewhat reluctant hero, who works for one of those nameless supersecret agencies which proliferated during the James Bond craze, has a unique gimmick. A shrapnel wound in the brain has made him unable to sleep, thus allowing him to tend to his espionage chores on a round-the-clock basis. The Tanner books are done with considerable wit and humor, and are populated with sharply drawn, oddball characters – a Block specialty.

A particular treat for mystery aficionados is to be found in two books under the Chip Harrison pseudonym, *Make Out with Murder* and *The Topless Tulip Caper*. Two earlier novels were Holden Caulfieldish sex romps related by the adolescent Chip, but with the third book the series turned into mystery parody-pastiche, with Chip hiring on as assistant to Leo Haig – a fat private detective who collects tropical fish and admires Nero Wolfe. Chip plays Archie to Haig's Nero, and the books are loaded with in-jokes relating to Rex Stout's great characters, as well as to the exigencies of the paperback market (Chip is always arguing with his editor at Fawcett Gold Medal, who want him to put more sex in his books).

More recently, Block has launched two new series: the Matt Scudder books, which relate the rather nasty contemporary cases handled by a humane New York ex-cop, and a more lightweight series featuring a professional thief named Bernie Rhodenbarr.

—Art Scott

BODKIN, M(atthias) M'Donnell. Irish. Born in Ireland, 8 October 1850. Educated at Tullabeg Jesuit College; Catholic University (Exhibitioner). Married Arabella Norman in 1885. Barrister: King's Counsel; County Court Judge for Clare, 1907–24. Member of Parliament (Nationalist) for North Roscommon, 1892–95. *Died 7 June 1933.*

CRIME PUBLICATIONS

Novels

> *White Magic.* London, Chapman and Hall, 1897.
> *A Stolen Life.* London, Ward Lock, 1898.
> *The Capture of Paul Beck.* London, Unwin, 1909; Boston, Little Brown, 1911.
> *His Brother's Keeper.* London, Hurst and Blackett, 1913.
> *The Test.* London, Everett, 1914.
> *Behind the Picture.* London, Ward Lock, 1914.
> *Pigeon Blood Rubies.* London, Nash, 1915.
> *Old Rowley.* London, Holden and Hardingham, 1916.
> *Kitty the Madcap.* Dublin, Talbot Press, 1927.
> *Guilty or Not Guilty?* Dublin, Talbot Press, 1929.

Short Stores (series character: Paul Beck)

> *Pat o' Nine Tales and One Over.* Dublin, Gill, and New York, Benzinger, 1894.
> *Paul Beck, The Rule of Thumb Detective.* London, Pearson, 1898.
> *Dora Myrl, The Lady Detective.* London, Chatto and Windus, 1900.
> *A Modern Robin Hood.* London, Ward Lock, 1903.
> *The Quests of Paul Beck.* London, Unwin, 1908; Boston, Little Brown, 1910.
> *Young Beck: A Chip of the Old Block.* London, Unwin, 1911; Boston, Little Brown, 1912.
> *Paul Beck, Detective.* Dublin, Talbot Press, 1929.

OTHER PUBLICATIONS

Novels

> *Lord Edward Fitzgerald.* London, Chapman and Hall, 1896.
> *The Rebels.* London, Ward Lock, 1899.
> *A Bear Squeeze; or, Her Second Self.* London, Ward Lock, 1901.
> *A Modern Miracle.* London, Ward Lock, 1902.
> *Shillelagh and Shamrock.* London, Chatto and Windus, 1902.
> *In the Days of Goldsmith.* London, Long, 1903.
> *Patsey the Omadawn.* London, Chatto and Windus, 1904.

A Madcap Marriage. London, Long, 1905.
True Man and Traitor; or, The Rising of Emmet. London, Unwin, 1910.

Plays

Hunt the Hare. Dublin, Duffy, 1926.
The Lottery (as Crom a Boo). Dublin, Duffy, 1927.

Other

Poteen Punch, Strong, Hot, and Sweet, Being a Succession of Irish After-Dinner Stories (as Crom a Boo). Dublin, Gill, 1890.
A Trip Through the States and a Talk with the President. Dublin, Duffy, 1907.
Grattan's Parliament, Before and After. London, Unwin, 1912.
Recollections of an Irish Judge: Press, Bar, and Parliament. London, Hurst and Blackett, and New York, Dodd Mead, 1914.
Famous Irish Trials. Dublin, Maunsell, 1918.
When Youth Meets Youth. Dublin, Talbot Press, London, Unwin, and New York, Kenedy, 1920.
Another Considered Judgment: Second Report of Judge Bodkin. Dublin, Talbot Press, 1921.

*   *   *

M. M'Donnell Bodkin, Irish barrister and author of detective stories, flourished as a writer of popular fiction during the early decades of this century. He was one of literally dozens of British authors who were stimulated to create detective series characters in response to the extraordinary vogue inspired by the unprecedented success of the adventures of Sherlock Holmes. Among these legions he was one of the most persistent and, unfortunately, one of the least remembered. Despite his books having gone into popular editions in England, Ireland, France, Germany, and Sweden, none of his seven mystery titles is in print.

Bodkin, gifted with a sprightly turn of mind, seemed to have had an enjoyable time with his literary creations. He fashioned his Paul Beck, "the rule of thumb detective," in 1897 for the pages of *Pearson's Magazine*, which in its heyday competed very successfully with the *Strand Magazine* for mass audiences. The Beck stories were collected in 1898, and in 1900 he brought out a volume of stories about Dora Myrl, one of the earliest distaff detectives. It was his pleasure to bring his two characters together to the chase and then to the altar in *The Capture of Paul Beck*. Predictably, he later published a book accounting the first detections of the offspring of this charming union – *Young Beck: A Chip of the Old Block*.

—Donald A. Yates

BOLAND, (Bertram) John. British. Born in Birmingham, Warwickshire, 12 February 1913. Educated privately. Served in the Royal Artillery, 1939–45. Married Philippa Carver in 1952. Worked as a farm labourer, deckhand, lumberjack, railroad and factory worker, and salesman, 1930–38; advertising signs and automobile parts salesman, 1946–55; Chairman, Writers Summer School, 1958–60. Chairman, Associates Branch, 1960–61, and Radio

Committee, 1966–70, Writers Guild of Great Britain; Chairman, Crime Writers Association, 1963. Recipient: Writers Guild of Great Britain Zita Award, for radio play, 1968. *Died 9 November 1976.*

CRIME PUBLICATIONS

Novels (series characters: The Gentlemen; Kim Smith)

White August. London, Joseph, and New York, Arcadia House, 1955.
No Refuge. London, Joseph, 1956.
Queer Fish. London, Boardman, 1958.
The League of Gentlemen. London, Boardman, 1958.
Mysterious Way. London, Boardman, 1959.
Bitter Fortune. London, Boardman, 1959.
Operation Red Carpet. London, Boardman, 1959.
The Midas Touch. London, Boardman, 1960.
Negative Value. London, Boardman, 1960.
The Gentlemen Reform. London, Boardman, 1961; New York, Macmillan, 1964.
Inside Job. London, Boardman, 1961.
Vendetta. London, Boardman, 1961.
The Golden Fleece. London, Boardman, 1961.
The Gentlemen at Large. London, Boardman, 1962.
Fatal Error. London, Boardman, 1962.
Counterpol (Smith). London, Harrap, 1963; New York, Walker, 1965.
The Catch. London, Harrap, 1964; New York, Holt Rinehart, 1966.
Counterpol in Paris (Smith). London, Harrap, 1964; New York, Walker, 1965.
The Good Citizens. London, Harrap, 1965.
The Disposal Unit. London, Harrap, 1966.
The Gusher. London, Harrap, 1967.
Painted Lady. London, Cassell, 1967.
Breakdown. London, Cassell, 1968.
The Fourth Grave. London, Cassell, 1969.
The Shakespeare Curse. London, Cassell, 1969; New York, Walker, 1970.
Kidnap. London, Cassell, 1970.
The Big Job. London, Cassell, 1970.
The Trade of Kings. Crowborough, Sussex, Forest House Books, 1972.

Uncollected Short Stories

"Suddenly Each Summer," in *John Creasey's Mystery Bedside Book*, edited by Herbert Harris. London, Hodder and Stoughton, 1966.
"Death Be My Friend," in *John Creasey's Mystery Bedside Book*, edited by Herbert Harris. London, Hodder and Stoughton, 1967.
"I.O.U.," in *John Creasey's Mystery Bedside Book 1969*, edited by Herbert Harris. London, Hodder and Stoughton, 1968.
"So Long to Remember," in *John Creasey's Mystery Bedside Book 1970*, edited by Herbert Harris. London, Hodder and Stoughton, 1969.

OTHER PUBLICATIONS

Plays

Swag (produced London, 1971).
Gottle (produced London, 1972).

Murder in Company, with Philip King (produced Bexhill, Sussex, 1972). London, French, 1973.

Elementary, My Dear, with Philip King (produced Worthing, Sussex, 1976). London, French, 1975.

Who Says Murder?, with Philip King (produced Cheltenham, 1978). London, French, 1975.

Radio Plays: *Bait*, 1962; *The Character*, 1965; *The Gentlemen Back in League* (serial), 1967; *Uncle Guy*, 1968; *The Burden*, 1969.

Television Plays: *The Fifth Victim*; *The Smoke Boys*, 1963.

Other

Free-Lance Journalism. London, Boardman, 1960.

Short-Story Writing. London, Boardman, 1960; revised edition, as *Short Story Technique*, Crowborough, Sussex, Forest House Books, 1973.

*   *   *

John Boland, the author of some 30 suspense novels and hundreds of short stories, has also written for the theater, for films, and for television, as well as two books on writing. Boland's own fiction is original and witty. The "Gentlemen," a group of former army officers whose escapades are related in three books, are among Boland's most delightful characters. Still operating with military discipline, they devise strategies which, though against the law, are daring and brilliant and win them the admiration of the criminal element. In prison for the bank robbery committed in *The League of Gentlemen*, ex-Colonel John George Norman Hyde considers the fate of his men as *The Gentlemen Reform* begins. "A war is not lost simply because one battle is not won," he declares, keeping in mind that "it was never policy to let the troops see the leadership wavering." Comic effects are achieved by the juxtaposition of honorable military attitudes and cunning criminal activity. For Hyde, escape is as much a duty as if he were a prisoner of war, although the prison is not so very awful: "The bare, austere surroundings didn't bother him in the least; he'd spent plenty of his Service time in less comfortable quarters. But what he did find unpleasant was the smell that pervaded the place, an odour compounded of a mixture of carbolic soap, watery vegetable soup and something else which was best ignored."

"Counterpol," a sort of clandestine consulting firm, acts against a background of international events. In *Counterpol in Paris*, the group is commissioned to steal the French crown jewels from the Louvre and the loot is shot out a window piece by piece with a catapult. The plot develops from the hatred and bitterness resulting from the Algerian conflict and contains some grim incidents. At the end of the adventure, the members of Counterpol decide that thereafter they will act only on behalf of "honest" crooks, not politicians.

The Catch, a tale of a family of psychopaths who revenge themselves on society by imprisoning and murdering rich victims whose wealth they appropriate, is set in a remote part of Scotland. Boland's macabre humor is given full play here in what could be considered a parody of the Gothic horror tale. This bizarre story is both scary and grotesquely comic, surely a virtuoso performance. *The Shakespeare Curse* reveals Boland's talent for the detective story embellished by details of literary history. Gravediggers in a country churchyard near Stratford discover an emaciated young woman who claims to have known Shakespeare. A cult develops around the woman while those involved in the "resurrection" die off.

It is ironic that in the United States Boland's books on writing are easier to come by than his fiction, when beginning writers might learn better from his example. John Boland has a fertile imagination and a rare sense of humor, qualities he uses to advantage in his entertaining suspense fiction.

—Mary Helen Becker

BONETT, John and Emery. Pseudonyms for John H. A. Coulson and Felicity Winifred Carter. British.` **COULSON, John H(ubert) A(rthur)**: Born in Benton, Northumberland, 10 August 1906. Educated at Durham School. Served in the Admiralty, 1940–45. Married Felicity Carter in 1939; one son. Banker, 1924–37, company secretary, 1937–39, and sales promotion executive, 1945–63. **CARTER, Felicity Winifred**: Born in Sheffield, Yorkshire, 2 December 1906. Agent: Curtis Brown Ltd., 1 Craven Hill, London W2 3EP, England.

CRIME PUBLICATIONS

Novels (series characters: Inspector Borges; Professor Mandrake)

Dead Lion (Mandrake).   London, Joseph, and New York, Doubleday, 1949
A Banner for Pegasus (Mandrake).   London, Joseph, 1951; as *Not in the Script*, New York, Doubleday, 1951.
No Grave for a Lady (Mandrake).   New York, Doubleday, 1959; London, Joseph, 1960.
Better Dead (Borges).   London, Joseph, 1964; as *Better Off Dead*, New York, Doubleday, 1964.
The Private Face of Murder (Borges).   London, Joseph, and New York, Doubleday, 1966.
This Side Murder? (Borges).   London, Joseph, 1967; as *Murder on the Costa Brava*, New York, Walker, 1968.
The Sound of Murder (Borges).   London, Harrap, 1970; New York, Walker, 1971.
No Time to Kill (Borges).   London, Harrap, and New York, Walker, 1972.

Novels by Emery Bonett

Never Go Dark (as Felicity Carter).   London, Heinemann, 1940.
Make Do with Spring.   London, Heinemann, 1941.
High Pavement.   London, Heinemann, 1944; as *Old Mrs. Camelot*, Philadelphia, Blakiston, 1944.

OTHER PUBLICATIONS by Emery Bonett

Novel

A Girl Must Live.   London, Barker, 1936.

Plays

One Fine Day (broadcast 1944).   Published in *Radio Theatre*, edited by Val Gielgud, London, Macdonald, 1946.

The Puppet Master, in *5 Radio Plays*.   London, Vox Mundi Books, 1948.

Screenplays: *The Glass Mountain*, with others, 1949; *Children Galore*, with John Bonett and Peter Plaskett, 1954.

Radio Play: *One Fine Day*, 1944.

*   *   *

John and Emery Bonett are mystery writers who have been too engaged in their other literary activities, in particular films, to devote full time to the novel. But the books which they have produced are noted for their charm, wit, and light-handed sophistication.

The early Bonett mysteries had an English background. There is no better example than *A Banner for Pegasus*, in which a motion picture company is on location in the small town of Steeple Tottering in the west country. The working relations between the press, the picture company, and the locals give an inside picture of English film-making in the provinces. With their move to the Costa Brava, the Bonetts began a series of mysteries using that locale. In these, the color of native Spanish life played against the character of English expatriates or holiday visitors added dimension to the plots. In *Better Dead* they introduced Inspector Borges, a deceptively casual Spanish detective whose charm equals his ability. The writing of the Bonetts is as deceptively casual as their Inspector. However, they are professionals; everything in their books is measured with a craftsman's eye before it is put into words.

—Dorothy B. Hughes

BORGENICHT, Miriam.   American.   Born in 1915.

CRIME PUBLICATIONS

Novels

A Corpse in Diplomacy.   New York, Mill, 1949; London, Panther, 1956.
Ring and Walk in.   New York, Harper, and London, Hamish Hamilton, 1952.
Don't Look Back.   New York, Doubleday, 1956; London, Hale, 1958.
To Borrow Trouble.   New York, Doubleday, 1965; London, Hale, 1966.
Extreme Remedies.   New York, Doubleday, 1967; London, Hale, 1968.
Margin for Doubt.   New York, Doubleday, 1968; London, Hale, 1969.
The Tomorrow Trap.   New York, Doubleday, 1969; London, Hale, 1970.
A Very Thin Line.   New York, Doubleday, 1970; London, Hale, 1972.
Roadblock.   Indianapolis, Bobbs Merrill, 1973.
No Bail for Dalton.   Indianapolis, Bobbs Merrill, 1974.

*   *   *

One of Miriam Borgenicht's books is entitled *A Very Thin Line*, used first to indicate the thin line between legal and illegal, then between sanity and madness. However, the phrase can also be applied to the books themselves. They tread a very thin line, each wavering back and forth from competent to inept, credible to ridiculous, interesting to boring. Her main theme is the effect of fear, but cause and effect are frequently unequal. The terror she strives to create and sustain is never really frightening because both motivation and characters are absurd. The children, particularly – and there are too many – fail as people and as fiction.

To her credit, Borgenicht tries hard to reflect social issues. Her early novels involve women with college educations happily rearing children in the suburbs with loving, if self-engrossed, husbands. She moves to a talented woman sculptor with an unloving husband, to an affair between a white woman and a black man, to a cause of judicial injustice, and she changes her women into professionals such as architects and city planners. These latter women are among her best-realized characters, bright and dynamic, while their men are passive, fuzzy-minded, and blinkered. In fact, the only mystery in those books is why these women would bother with such men.

A major concern in all Borgenicht's books is rendering the thoughts of the emotionally disturbed and/or retarded adolescents who people every novel. These kids are unbelievable. Not only are they cardboard figures, but the author details their thoughts in language foreign to them and clumsy in this kind of fiction. For example, in *To Borrow Trouble*, an emotionally disturbed 13-year-old girl is wondering whether or not adults will believe her reasons for kidnapping a 6-month-old child when they had already labelled her a daydreamer: "You just keep on this silly dreaming, they would say, and then stop, voices quivering, eyes ominous, as though the results were too horrendous for them to delineate." In *The Tomorrow Trap*, a retarded adolescent boy uses the purest of literary language inside his head, while an emotionally disturbed 13-year-old boy who is failing in school, told to take extra care of his 6-year-old brother, holds the following internal monologue: "Extra care ... what unaccustomed attributes were thereby called for? What largeness of spirit and breadth of responsibility was [sic] in order?" Borgenicht is obviously very sympathetic to these adolescents, but, as characters, they do not create the same sympathy in the reader. The best developed adolescent in all her books is vicious and ruthless, his actions and motivations stemming from the same warp as all the others.

Borgenicht's narrative technique is based on multiple viewpoints manipulated by the omniscient author, with much of the plot revealed by dialogue alone. One in each of several groups of people knows some part of the situation, but only the reader knows all. Unfortunately for maintaining interest in poorly motivated plots, the groups involve so many foolish parents, disobedient children, unpleasant passers-by, and determinedly obtuse neighbors that what was supposed to be mounting terror dissolves into irritating domestic bickering. At the end of several of the books, the protagonist has all the facts, but in only a few is the denouement complete within the text.

The main interest of Borgenicht's books lies in observing the tricky balancing acts she performs by her chosen techniques, but, sadly, in over 30 years of writing her techniques have not improved. The same flaws and virtues appear in all the books.

—Pearl G. Aldrich

BOUCHER, Anthony. Pseudonym for William Anthony Parker White; also wrote as H. H. Holmes. American. Born in Oakland, California, 21 August 1911. Educated at Pasadena Junior College, California, 1928–30; University of Southern California, Los Angeles, B.A. 1932; University of California, Berkeley, M.A. 1934. Married Phyllis May Price in 1938; two sons. Theatre and music critic, *United Progressive News*, Los Angeles, 1935–37; science fiction and mystery reviewer, San Francisco *Chronicle*, 1942–47; mystery reviewer, *Ellery Queen's Mystery Magazine*, 1948–50 and 1957–68, and *New York Times Book Review*, 1951–68; fantasy book reviewer, as H. H. Holmes, for Chicago *Sun-Times*,

1949–50, and New York *Herald Tribune*, 1951–63; reviewer for *Opera News*, 1961–68. Editor, *Magazine of Fantasy and Science Fiction*, 1949–58, and *True Crime Detective*, 1952–53; edited the Mercury Mysteries, 1952–55, Dell Great Mystery Library, 1957–60, and Collier Mystery Classics, 1962–68, for publishing houses. Originated *Great Voices* program of historical recordings, Pacifica Radio, Berkeley, 1949–68. President, Mystery Writers of America, 1951. Recipient: Mystery Writers of America Edgar Allan Poe Award, for criticism, 1946, 1950, 1953. *Died 31 October 1968.*

CRIME PUBLICATIONS

Novels (series character: Fergus O'Breen)

> *The Case of the Seven of Calvary.* New York, Simon and Schuster, and London, Hamish Hamilton, 1937.
> *The Case of the Crumpled Knave* (O'Breen). New York, Simon and Schuster, and London, Harrap, 1939.
> *The Case of the Baker Street Irregulars* (O'Breen). New York, Simon and Schuster, 1940; as *Blood on Baker Street*, New York, Mercury, 1953.
> *The Case of the Solid Key* (O'Breen). New York, Simon and Schuster, 1941.
> *The Case of the Seven Sneezes* (O'Breen). New York, Simon and Schuster, 1942; London, United Authors, 1946.
> *The Marble Forest* (as Theo Durrant with others). New York, Knopf, and London, Wingate, 1951; as *The Big Fear*, New York, Popular Library, 1953.

Novels as H. H. Holmes (series character: Sister Ursula in both books)

> *Nine Times Nine.* New York, Duell, 1940.
> *Rocket to the Morgue.* New York, Duell, 1942.

Uncollected Short Stories

> "Coffin Corner," in *The Female of the Species*, edited by Ellery Queen. Boston, Little Brown, 1943; as *Ladies in Crime*, London, Faber, 1947.
> "The Adventure of the Illustrious Imposter," in *The Misadventures of Sherlock Holmes*, edited by Ellery Queen. Boston, Little Brown, 1944.
> "Code Zed," in *World's Great Spy Stories*, edited by Vincent Starrett. Cleveland, World, 1944.
> "QL 696.C9," in *Best Stories from Ellery Queen's Mystery Magazine*. Roslyn, New York, Detective Book Club, 1944.
> "Arsène Lupin Versus Colonel Linnaus," in *Ellery Queen's Mystery Magazine* (New York), November 1944.
> "Rumor, Inc.," in *Ellery Queen's Mystery Magazine* (New York), January 1945.
> "Black Murder," in *Great American Detective Stories*, edited by Anthony Boucher. Cleveland, World, 1945.
> "Trick-or-Treat," in *Murder Cavalcade*, edited by Ken Crossen. New York, Duell, 1946; London, Hammond, 1953.
> "Elsewhen," in *Murder: Plain and Fanciful*, edited by James Sandoe. New York, Sheridan House, 1948.
> "The Stripper," in *Twentieth Century Detective Stories*, edited by Ellery Queen. Cleveland, World, 1948.
> "Retired Hangman," in *Best Detective Stories of the Year 1948*, edited by David C. Cooke. New York, Dutton, 1948.
> "Screwball Division," in *Four and Twenty Bloodhounds*, edited by Anthony Boucher. New York, Simon and Schuster, 1950; London, Hammond, 1951.

"Nine-Finger Jack," in *20 Great Tales of Murder*, edited by Helen McCloy and Brett Halliday. New York, Random House, 1951; London, Hammond, 1952.

"Threnody," in *Maiden Murders*, edited by John Dickson Carr. New York, Harper, 1952.

"Public Eye," in *Best Detective Stories of the Year 1953*, edited by David C. Cooke. New York, Dutton, 1953.

"Anomaly of the Empty Man," in *Crooks' Tour*, edited by Bruno Fischer. New York, Dodd Mead, 1953; London, Macdonald, 1954.

"The Girl Who Married a Monster," in *Butcher, Baker, Murder-Maker*. New York, Knopf, 1954.

"Mystery for Christmas," in *Crime for Two*, edited by Frances and Richard Lockridge. Philadelphia, Lippincott, 1955; London, Macdonald, 1957.

"Murder Was Their Business," in *Ellery Queen's Mystery Magazine* (New York), November 1955.

"Crime Must Have a Stop," in *Eat, Drink and Be Buried*, edited by Rex Stout. New York, Viking Press, 1956; as *For Tomorrow We Die*, London, Macdonald, 1958.

"Like Count Palmieri," in *Planned Departures*, edited by Elizabeth Ferrars. London, Hodder and Stoughton, 1958.

"A Matter of Scholarship," in *A Choice of Murders*, edited by Dorothy Salisbury Davis. New York, Scribner, 1958; London, Macdonald, 1960.

"The Ultimate Clue," in *Ellery Queen's 16th Mystery Annual*. New York, Random House, 1961; London, Gollancz, 1962.

"The Pink Caterpillar," in *Tales for a Rainy Night*, edited by David Alexander. New York, Holt Rinehart, 1961; London, Dobson, 1967.

"Death Can Be Beautiful," in *Ellery Queen's Mystery Magazine* (New York), April 1962.

"The Numbers Man," in *A Pride of Felons*, edited by The Gordons. New York, Macmillan, 1963; London, Dobson, 1964.

"The Clue of the Knave of Diamonds," in *Ellery Queen's Mystery Magazine* (New York), May 1963.

"The Last Hand," in *Masters of Mayhem*, edited by Edward D. Radin. New York, Morrow, 1965.

"A Little Honest Stud," in *Masters of Mayhem*, edited by Edward D. Radin. New York, Morrow, 1965.

"Command Performance," in *With Malice Towards All*, edited by Robert L. Fish. New York, Putnam, 1968; London, Macmillan, 1969.

"The Smoke-Filled Locked Room," in *The Locked Room Reader*, edited by Hans S. Santesson. New York, Random House, 1968.

"A Kind of Madness," in *Ellery Queen's Crookbook*. New York, Random House, and London, Gollancz, 1974.

"You Can Get Used to Anything," in *Tricks and Treats*, edited by Joe Gores and Bill Pronzini. New York, Doubleday, 1976; as *Mystery Writers' Choice*, London, Gollancz, 1977.

OTHER PUBLICATIONS

Short Stories

Far and Away: Eleven Fantasy and Science-Fiction Stories. New York, Ballantine, 1955.

The Compleat Werewolf and Other Stories of Fantasy and Science Fiction. New York, Simon and Schuster, 1969; London, W. H. Allen, 1970.

Plays

Radio Plays: for *Sherlock Holmes* and *The Case Book of Gregory Hood* series, 1945–48.

Other

Ellery Queen: A Double Profile.   Boston, Little Brown, 1951.
Multiplying Villainies: Selected Mystery Criticism, 1942–1968.   Boston, Bouchercon, 1973.
Sincerely, Tony/Faithfully, Vincent: The Correspondence of Anthony Boucher and Vincent Starrett, edited by Robert W. Hahn.   Chicago, Catullus Press, 1975.

Editor, *The Pocket Book of True Crime Stories.*   New York, Pocket Books, 1943.
Editor, *Great American Detective Stories.*   Cleveland, World, 1945.
Editor, *Four and Twenty Bloodhounds.*   New York, Simon and Schuster, 1950; London, Hammond, 1951.
Editor, *The Best from Fantasy and Science Fiction.*   Boston, Little Brown, 2 vols., 1952–53; New York, Doubleday, 6 vols., 1954–59.
Editor, *A Treasury of Great Science Fiction.*   New York, Doubleday, 1959.
Editor, *The Quality of Murder.*   New York, Dutton, 1962.
Editor, *The Quintessence of Queen: Best Prize Stories from 12 Years of Ellery Queen's Mystery Magazine.*   New York, Random House, 1962; as *A Magnum of Mysteries,* London, Gollancz, 1963.
Editor, *Best Detective Stories of the Year: 18th* [through *23rd*] *Annual Collection.*   New York, Dutton, and London, Boardman, 6 vols., 1963–68.

Bibliography: "Anthony Boucher Bibliography" by J. R. Christopher, Dean W. Dickensheet, and R. E. Briney, in *Armchair Detective* (White Bear Lake, Minnesota), nos. 2, 3, 4, 1969.

*   *   *

Anthony Boucher's twin careers as author and as critic of mystery fiction are remarkable not only for their duration and quality but also for the fact that they represented only half of the activities of this productive and versatile man. He was equally active in the fields of science fiction and fantasy (being one of the founding editors of *The Magazine of Fantasy and Science Fiction*), and was an authority on opera and other vocal music, a teacher, and a radio and TV personality.

Boucher made his first professional sale (at 16) to *Weird Tales* magazine: a short ghost story parody. The first of his seven mystery novels, *The Case of the Seven of Calvary*, appeared in 1937. Like its successors, this is a fair-play puzzle story in the classic pattern of John Dickson Carr and Ellery Queen, intricately constructed and told with wit and style. It is, unfortunately, the only recorded case of armchair detective Dr. John Ashwin, Professor of Sanskrit at the University of California. *The Case of the Crumpled Knave* introduced the brash and very Irish private detective Fergus O'Breen and Detective Lt. Jackson of the Los Angeles police. Separately or together, O'Breen and Jackson appeared in three further novels. In *The Case of the Baker Street Irregulars* a screen-writer working on a Sherlock Holmes film is murdered. The identity of the person who solves the crime is of almost as much interest here as the identity of the murderer. *The Case of the Solid Key* is a locked-room murder among a crowd of Hollywood personalities. *The Case of the Seven Sneezes* is an isolated-house-party murder with roots in an ugly crime 25 years in the past.

In the early 1940's Boucher's interest in fantasy fiction revived, and soon he was writing stories for the fantasy and science fiction magazines along with his detective novels. He delighted in mixing genres, and characters from his crime fiction pop up frequently in his fantasy stories: Fergus O'Breen in "The Compleat Werewolf" and Martin Lamb (from *The Case of the Seven of Calvary*) in "The Anomaly of the Empty Man."

With the Boucher name tied up by contractual obligations, the author chose the byline H. H. Holmes (the alias of a notorious 19th-century mass murderer) for *Nine Times Nine*. This is a locked-room murder investigated by Sister Ursula of the (fictional) Order of Martha of Bethany. It contains a discussion of locked-room methods building on the famous "Locked

Room Lecture" in John Dickson Carr's *The Three Coffins*. The only other H. H. Holmes novel is *Rocket to the Morgue*, another locked room mystery and a *roman à clef* in which many of Boucher's science fiction writer friends appear in disguise.

Among Boucher's finely crafted mystery short stories, the best remembered are those featuring Nick Noble, an ex-policeman and dipsomaniac who served as armchair detective in some very odd problems.

Boucher's twenty-six year span of reviewing mystery fiction began in 1941. In 1951 he began writing the "Criminals at Large" column in the Sunday *New York Times Book Review*. In this widely circulated forum he built up the remarkable record of more than 850 weekly columns, notable for his breadth of taste and his attention to new writers and to paperback as well as hardcover books. During these years he was surely the most influential as well as the most popular American critic of mystery and detective fiction.

After his death, Boucher's friends and admirers established the tradition of sponsoring in his memory an annual convention of mystery enthusiasts. The fourth of these "Bouchercons," held in Boston in 1973, published a memorial volume of his mystery criticism under the title *Multiplying Villainies*.

—R. E. Briney

BOWEN, Marjorie. See **SHEARING, Joseph**.

BOX, Edgar. Pseudonym for Gore Vidal. American. Born in West Point, New York, 3 October 1925. Educated at Phillips Exeter Academy, New Hampshire. Served in the United States Army, 1943–46. Full-time writer since 1944. Member, Advisory Board, *Partisan Review*, New Brunswick, New Jersey, 1960–71. Democratic-Liberal Candidate for Congress, 1960. Member, President's Advisory Committee on the Arts, 1961–63. Co-Chairman, The New Party, 1968–71. Address: 21 Via di Torre Argentina, Rome, Italy.

CRIME PUBLICATIONS

Novels (series character: Peter Cutler Sargeant in all books)

> *Death in the Fifth Postion.* New York, Dutton, 1952; London, Heinemann, 1954.
> *Death Before Bedtime.* New York, Dutton, 1953; London, Heinemann, 1954.
> *Death Likes It Hot.* New York, Dutton, 1954; London, Heinemann, 1955.

OTHER PUBLICATIONS as Gore Vidal

Novels

> *Williwaw.* New York, Dutton, 1946; London, Panther, 1965.
> *In a Yellow Wood.* New York, Dutton, 1947; London, New English Library, 1967.

The City and the Pillar. New York, Dutton, 1948; London, Lehmann, 1949; revised
  edition, Dutton, and London, Heinemann, 1965.
The Season of Comfort. New York, Dutton, 1949.
Dark Green, Bright Red. New York, Dutton, and London, Lehmann, 1950.
A Search for the King: A Twelfth Century Legend. New York, Dutton, 1950; London,
  New English Library, 1967.
The Judgment of Paris. New York, Dutton, 1952; London, Heinemann, 1953; revised
  edition, Boston, Little Brown, 1965; London, Heinemann, 1966.
Messiah. New York, Dutton, 1954; London, Heinemann, 1955; revised edition,
  Boston, Little Brown, 1965; London, Heinemann, 1968.
Three: Williwaw, A Thirsty Evil, Julian the Apostate. New York, New American
  Library, 1962.
Julian. Boston, Little Brown, and London, Heinemann, 1964.
Washington, D.C. Boston, Little Brown, and London, Heinemann, 1967.
Myra Breckinridge. Boston, Little Brown, and London, Blond, 1968.
Two Sisters: A Memoir in the Form of a Novel. Boston, Little Brown, and London,
  Heinemann, 1970.
Burr. New York, Random House, 1973; London, Heinemann, 1974.
Myron. New York, Random House, 1974; London, Heinemann, 1975.
1876. New York, Random House, and London, Heinemann, 1976.
Kalki. New York, Random House, and London, Heinemann, 1978.

Short Stories

A Thirsty Evil: Seven Short Stories. New York, Zero Press, 1956; London,
  Heinemann, 1958.

Plays

Visit to a Small Planet (televised, 1955).   Included in *Visit to a Small Planet and Other
  Television Plays,* 1956; revised version (produced New York, 1957; London, 1960),
  Boston, Little Brown, 1957; in *Three Plays,* 1962.
Honor (televised, 1956).   Published in *Television Plays for Writers: Eight Television
  Plays,* edited by A. S. Burack, Boston, The Writer, 1957; revised version, as *On the
  March to the Sea: A Southron Comedy* (produced Bonn, Germany, 1962), in *Three
  Plays,* 1962.
Visit to a Small Planet and Other Television Plays (includes *Barn Burning, Dark
  Possession, The Death of Billy the Kid, A Sense of Justice, Smoke, Summer Pavilion,
  The Turn of the Screw*).   Boston, Little Brown, 1956.
The Best Man: A Play about Politics (produced New York, 1960).   Boston, Little
  Brown, 1960; in *Three Plays,* 1962.
Three Plays (Visit to a Small Planet, The Best Man, On the March to the Sea).   London,
  Heinemann, 1962.
Romulus: A New Comedy, adaptation of a play of Friedrich Dürrenmatt (produced New
  York, 1962).   New York, Dramatists Play Service, 1962.
Weekend (produced New York, 1968).   New York, Dramatists Play Service, 1968.
An Evening with Richard Nixon and ... (produced New York, 1972).   New York,
  Random House, 1972.

Screenplays: *The Catered Affair,* 1956; *I Accuse,* 1958; *The Scapegoat,* with Robert
Hamer, 1959; *Suddenly Last Summer,* with Tennessee Williams, 1960; *The Best Man,*
1964; *Is Paris Burning?,* with Francis Ford Coppola, 1966; *Last of the Mobile Hot-Shots,*
1970.

Television Plays: *Barn Burning*, 1954; *Dark Possession*, 1954; *Smoke*, 1954; *Visit to a Small Planet*, 1955; *The Death of Billy the Kid*, 1955; *A Sense of Justice*, 1955; *Summer Pavilion*, 1955; *The Turn of the Screw*, 1955; *Honor*, 1956; *The Indestructible Mr. Gore*, 1960.

Other

Rocking the Boat (essays).   Boston, Little Brown, 1962; London, Heinemann, 1963.
Sex, Death and Money.   New York, Bantam, 1968.
Reflections upon a Sinking Ship (essays).   Boston, Little Brown, and London, Heinemann, 1969.
Homage to Daniel Shays: Collected Essays, 1952–1972.   New York, Random House, 1972; as *Collected Essays, 1952–1972*, London, Heinemann, 1974.
Matters of Fact and of Fiction, Essays 1973–1976.   New York, Random House, and London, Heinemann, 1977.
Great American Families, with others.   New York, Norton, and London, Times Books, 1977.

Editor, *Best Television Plays*.   New York, Ballantine, 1956.

*   *   *

In the early 1950's, at the end of his first period as a novelist and the beginning of his career as a writer of live television drama, Gore Vidal turned briefly to the detective story. Under the pseudonym Edgar Box he published a trilogy of mystery novels narrated by and starring Peter Cutler Sargeant II, young public relations expert, sexual gymnast (exclusively hetero), and amateur sleuth. The books were reprinted regularly in paperback over the next quarter century, often with a glowing encomium from Vidal himself emblazoned on their covers. Judged as formal detective novels all three are mediocre, but Vidal's guided tour through the worlds of art, politics, and high society entertains us royally with countless gleefully sardonic jabs at every target in sight.

In *Death in the Fifth Position* Peter is hired to procure favorable media coverage for a ballet company which is being harassed by a right-wing veterans' group for having a "Communist" choreographer. Then the company's prima ballerina is murdered onstage, and we are treated to pages of superb satire about professional dancers and their hangers-on and much tedious speculation about homicidal motives, interspersed with two more gruesome deaths. *Death Before Bedtime* finds Peter in Washington as public relations adviser to an ultra-conservative senator angling for the Presidential nomination – until he's blown to bits by a gunpowder charge in his fireplace. Once again a lackluster detective plot is saved by Vidal's mocking gibes at politics, journalism, sex, and society. And in *Death Likes It Hot* Peter is invited to a weekend house party at a Long Island beachfront mansion and encounters tangled emotions and murder among a cast of ludicrous plutocrats and talentless pseudo-artists. Its fairly complex plot, a few deft clues and a dramatic climax make this the best mystery of the trio, but as usual it's the pungent satire that brings the book to life.

Clever deductions, fair play with the reader, and the Christie-Queen bag of tricks are not Vidal's strong points. But his mastery of the language did not fail him even in these mysteries that he himself regarded merely as potboilers, and his tone of cynical good-humored tolerance towards an America populated exclusively by crooks, opportunists, and buffoons is the closest approximation to the authentic spirit of H. L. Mencken that readers of mystery fiction are ever likely to experience.

—Francis M. Nevins, Jr.

BOYLE, Jack.   American.

Crime Publications

Short Stores

   Boston Blackie.   New York, H. K. Fly, 1919.

Uncollected Short Story

   "Boston Blackie's Mary," in *For Men Only*, edited by James M. Cain.   Cleveland,
     World, 1944.

Other Publications

Plays

   Screenplays: *The Silent Accuser*, with Chester M. Franklin and Frank O'Connor, 1924;
   The Sporting Chance, with John P. Bernard, 1925.

*   *   *

Jack Boyle is remembered today for only one story, in which he created a character made far more famous by other writers in nearly twenty films and a series of radio plays – Boston Blackie. As often happens, the hero of the films – a light-hearted ex-convict turned crime fighter – has little in common with the hero of the story.

Written about the time of World War I, this short story, "Boston Blackie's Mary," is almost unknown. Which is a shame, for it is a powerful and engrossing prison-escape story. A young college-educated safe-blower, Boston Blackie leads a mutiny in a California prison, forcing the authorities to release fellow inmates being tortured by the guards – and draws upon himself the insane hatred of the intelligent but sadistic Deputy Warden Sherwood, who has hated convicts ever since his wife left him for one years ago. Tricked into striking a guard when the one thing he lives for – the visits of his wife Mary – are forbidden, Blackie nearly dies from the hours of resulting torture – and decides to escape from a prison so well-guarded that no one has ever escaped from it in the fifty years of its existence. Ingenious, grimly authentic, the story was one of several revealing the concentration-camp practices of many American prisons then, including the use of a strait-jacket as a torture device.

Stylistically, the story is an interesting example of a hard-boiled tale told in the days before the hard-boiled style was born, and is flawed only by a sentimental ending typical of the times.

—Frank D. McSherry, Jr.

BRADBURY, Ray (Douglas).   American.   Born in Waukegan, Illinois, 22 August 1920. Educated at Los Angeles High School. Married Marguerite Susan McClure in 1947; four children. Full-time writer since 1943. President, Science-Fantasy Writers of America, 1951–53. Member of the Board of Directors, Screen Writers Guild of America, 1957–61. Recipient: O. Henry Prize, 1947, 1948; Benjamin Franklin Award, 1954; National Institute of Arts and Letters Grant, 1954; Boys' Clubs of America Junior Book Award, 1956; Golden Eagle Award, for screenplay, 1957. Address: 10265 Cheviot Drive, Los Angeles, California 90064, U.S.A.

CRIME PUBLICATIONS

Novel

> *Something Wicked This Way Comes.* New York, Simon and Schuster, 1962; London, Hart Davis, 1963.

Short Stories

> *The Martian Chronicles.* New York, Doubleday, 1950; as *The Silver Locusts*, London, Hart Davis, 1951.
> *The Illustrated Man.* New York, Doubleday, 1951; London, Hart Davis, 1952.
> *The October Country.* New York, Ballantine, 1955; London, Hart Davis, 1957.
> *The Small Assassin.* London, New English Library, 1962; New York, New American Library, 1973.
> *The Machineries of Joy: Short Stories.* New York, Simon and Schuster, and London, Hart Davis, 1964.
> *Long after Midnight.* New York, Knopf, 1976; London, Hart Davis MacGibbon, 1977.

Uncollected Short Stories

> "The Fruit at the Bottom of the Bowl," in *Ellery Queen's Mystery Magazine* (New York), January 1953.
> "And So Died Riabouchinska," in *The Saint* (New York), June–July 1953.
> "The Whole Town's Sleeping," in *Ellery Queen's Mystery Magazine* (New York), June 1954.
> "At Midnight, In the Month of June," in *Ellery Queen's Mystery Magazine* (New York), June 1954.
> "Shopping for Death," in *The Saint* (New York), February 1955.
> "The Screaming Woman," in *The Saint* (New York), September 1955.
> "The Town Where No One Got Off," in *Ellery Queen's Mystery Magazine* (New York), October 1958.

OTHER PUBLICATIONS

Novels

> *Fahrenheit 451.* New York, Ballantine, 1953; London, Hart Davis, 1963.
> *The Halloween Tree.* New York, Knopf, 1972; London, Hart Davis MacGibbon, 1973.

Short Stories

> *Dark Carnival.* Sauk City, Wisconsin, Arkham House, 1947; London, Hamish Hamilton, 1948.
> *The Golden Apples of the Sun.* New York, Doubleday, and London, Hart Davis, 1953.
> *Dandelion Wine.* New York, Doubleday, and London, Hart Davis, 1957.
> *A Medicine for Melancholy.* New York, Doubleday, 1959; as *The Day It Rained Forever*, London, Hart Davis, 1959.
> *The Vintage Bradbury.* New York, Random House, 1965.
> *The Autumn People.* New York, Ballantine, 1965.
> *Tomorrow Midnight.* New York, Ballantine, 1966.
> *I Sing the Body Electric!* New York, Knopf, 1969; London, Hart Davis, 1970.

Plays

The Meadow, in *Best One-Act Plays of 1947–48*.   New York, Dodd Mead, 1948.
The Anthem Sprinters and Other Antics (produced Los Angeles, 1968).   New York, Dial
   Press, 1963.
The World of Ray Bradbury (produced Los Angeles, 1964; New York, 1965).
The Wonderful Ice-Cream Suit (produced Los Angeles, 1965).   Included in *The
   Wonderful Ice-Cream Suit and Other Plays*, 1972.
The Day It Rained Forever.   New York, French, 1966.
The Pedestrian.   New York, French, 1966.
Christus Apollo, music by Jerry Goldsmith (produced Los Angeles, 1969).
The Wonderful Ice-Cream Suit and Other Plays (includes *The Veldt* and *To the Chicago
   Abyss*).   New York, Bantam, 1972; London, Hart Davis MacGibbon, 1973.
Leviathan 99 (produced Los Angeles, 1972).
Pillar of Fire and Other Plays.   London, Bantam, 1976.

Screenplays: *It Came from Outer Space*, with David Schwartz, 1952; *Moby Dick*, with
John Huston, 1956; *Icarus Montgolfer Wright*, 1961; *The Picasso Summer*, 1967.

Verse

*When Elephants Last in the Dooryard Bloomed: Celebrations for Almost Any Day of the
   Year*.   New York, Knopf, 1972; London, Hart Davis MacGibbon, 1975.
*Where Robot Mice and Robot Men Run Round in Robot Towns: New Poems Both Light
   and Dark*.   New York, Knopf, 1977; London, Granada, 1979.

Other

Switch on the Night (juvenile).   New York, Pantheon, and London, Hart Davis, 1955.
R Is for Rocket (juvenile).   New York, Doubleday, 1962; London, Hart Davis, 1968.
S Is for Space (juvenile).   New York, Doubleday, 1966; London, Hart Davis, 1968.
Old Ahab's Friend, and Friend to Noah, Speaks His Piece: A Celebration.   Privately
   printed, 1971.
Mars and the Mind of Man.   New York, Harper, 1973.
Zen and the Art of Writing.   Santa Barbara, California, Capra Press, 1973.
That Son of Richard III.   Glendale, California, Roy Squires Press, 1974.

Editor, *Timeless Stories for Today and Tomorrow*.   New York, Ballantine, 1952.
Editor, *The Circus of Dr. Lao*.   New York, Bantam, 1956.

Bibliography: *Ray Bradbury Companion: A Life and Career History, Photolog, and
Comprehensive Checklist of Writings* by William F. Nolan, Detroit, Gale, 1975.

*   *   *

Though primarily known for his science fiction, Ray Bradbury is also a master of that type
of mystery in the Poe-Bierce-Lovecraft vein known as the weird tale. In such collections as
Long after Midnight and *The October Country* he clearly demonstrates that he is the rightful
heir of his great predecessors in tales that range from the merely bizarre to the horrifying and
from peaceful small town settings to the far reaches of space. Many readers are familiar with
the eerie grotesqueness of "The Veldt" where the electronic lions become real and devour the
parents who would turn off the playroom, or with "The Third Expedition" in *The Martian
Chronicles* and the "hometown" that masks the sinister intentions of the Martians toward
their visitors from Earth. But there are dozens of other creepy stories to satisfy the taste of
those who like to shiver as they read.

The most effective of these are the tales which might be termed "incursions," where a situation that appears as mundane as Sunday in Iowa takes on a strange tilt that reveals a macabre world lurking around the corner. A businessman becomes concerned over his aching bones, progresses to obsession with the skeleton which inhabits his body, and has that skeleton gobbled up by a demoniac "psychologist" who slides down his throat and absorbs his bones, leaving him a mass of jelly ("Skeleton"). A faithful dog who brings a sick boy all the neighborhood news disappears for days, returning with the odor of grave-mold on his muzzle and the dragging footsteps of Miss Haight, the boy's dead teacher, on the stairs behind him – shades of "Ligeia" ("The Emissary"). The crowds that appear almost instantaneously at accidents are really composed of the dead, themselves killed in accidents, and deciding whether or not to recruit new members by moving the victims ("The Crowd"). And in a full-length novel (*Something Wicked This Way Comes*) the Devil runs a black-magic carnival which transmutes people into sideshow freaks with rides on a carousel that realizes their desire to be older or younger. Uncharacteristically but happily the Devil is defeated in this story, a change from those stories that end on the note of evil about to appear. Yet the quiet midwestern town into which evil intrudes epitomizes that "October country" where the eerie and the terrifying are just down the street from the malt shop. Bradbury's mysteries are in this find old Gothic tradition and should be better known.

—Richard C. Carpenter

BRAHMS, Caryl. Pseudonym for Doris Caroline Abrahams. British. Born in Surrey in 1901. Educated at the Royal Academy of Music, London. Recipient: Ivor Novello award, 1966. Address: 3 Cambridge Gate, London N.W. 1, England.

CRIME PUBLICATIONS

Novels with S. J. Simon (series character: Inspector Adam Quill)

A Bullet in the Ballet (Quill). London, Joseph, 1937; New York, Doubleday, 1938.
Casino for Sale (Quill). London, Joseph, 1938; as Murder à la Stroganoff, New York, Doubleday, 1938.
Envoy on Excursion (Quill). London, Joseph, 1940.
Six Curtains for Stroganova. London, Joseph, 1945; as Six Curtains for Natasha, Philadelphia, Lippincott, 1946.
Stroganoff at the Ballet (omnibus). London, Joseph, 1975.

Uncollected Short Story

"A Bishop in the Ballet," in Alfred Hitchcock's Mystery Magazine (New York), September 1979.

OTHER PUBLICATIONS

Novels

The Elephant Is White, with S. J. Simon. London, Joseph, 1939; New York, Farrar and Rinehart, 1940.

Don't Mr. Disraeli!, with S. J. Simon. London, Joseph, 1940; New York, Putnam, 1941.
No Bed for Bacon, with S. J. Simon. London, Joseph, 1941; New York, Crowell, 1950.
No Nightingales, with S. J. Simon. London, Joseph, 1944.
Titania Has a Mother, with S. J. Simon. London, Joseph, 1944.
Trottie True, with S. J. Simon. London, Joseph, 1946; Philadelphia, Lippincott, 1947.
You Were There, with S. J. Simon. London, Joseph, 1950.
Away Went Polly. London, Heinemann, 1952.
Cindy-Ella, with Ned Sherrin. London, W. H. Allen, 1962.
No Castanets. London, W. H. Allen, and New York, Macmillan, 1963.
Rappel 1910, with Ned Sherrin. London, W. H. Allen, 1964.
Benbow Was His Name, with Ned Sherrin. London, Hutchinson, 1967.
A Mutual Pair (omnibus), with S. J. Simon. London, Joseph, 1976.
Enter a Dragon, Stage Centre. London, Hodder and Stoughton, 1979.

Short Stories

To Hell with Hedda! and Other Stories, with S. J. Simon. London, Joseph, 1947.
Ooh! La-la!, with Ned Sherrin. London, W. H. Allen, 1973.
After You, Mr. Feydeau!, with Ned Sherrin. London, W. H. Allen, 1975.

Plays

Cindy-Ella; or, I Gotta Shoe, with Ned Sherrin (broadcast, 1957); revised version, additional music by Peter Knight and Ron Grainer (produced London, 1963).
No Bed for Bacon, with Ned Sherrin, adaptation of the novel by Brahms and S. J. Simon (produced Bristol, 1959).
Benbow Was His Name, with Ned Sherrin (televised, 1964; produced Worthing, Sussex, 1969).
The Spoils, with Ned Sherrin, adaptation of the novel *The Spoils of Poynton* by Henry James (produced Watford, Hertfordshire, 1968).
Sing a Rude Song, with Ned Sherrin, additional material by Alan Bennett, music by Ron Grainer (produced London, 1969).
Fish Out of Water, with Ned Sherrin, adaptation of a play by Feydeau (produced London, 1971).
Liberty Ranch (concept and lyrics only, with Ned Sherrin), book by Dick Vosburgh, music by John Cameron, adaptation of the play *She Stoops to Conquer* by Goldsmith (produced London, 1972).
Paying the Piper, with Ned Sherrin, adaptation of a play by Feydeau (televised, 1973). London, Davis Poynter, 1972.
Nickleby and Me, with Ned Sherrin (produced Stratford upon Avon and London, 1975).
Hush and Hide, with Ned Sherrin (produced Billingham, Cleveland, 1978).

Screenplays: *One Night with You*, with S. J. Simon, 1948; *Girl/Stroke/Boy*, 1971.

Radio Plays: *Don't Mr. Disraeli*, with S. J. Simon, from their own novel, 1943; *Thank You, Mrs. Siddons*, with Simon, 1944; *A Bullet at the Ballet*, with Simon, from their own novel, 1945; *Shorty and Goliath*, with Simon, 1946; *Trottie True*, with Simon, from their own novel, 1955; *Tomorrow Mr. Tompion*, with Christopher Hassell, 1956; *The Little Beggars*, with Simon, 1956; *Look Back to Lyttletoun*, with Simon, 1957; *Away Went Polly*, with Simon, 1957; *Cindy-Ella*, with Ned Sherrin, 1957; *Nymphs and Shepherds Go Away*, with Simon, 1958; *Duchess Don't Allow*, with Sherrin, 1958; *The Haven*, with Sherrin, 1958; *Bigger Beggars*, with Sherrin, 1958; *Titania Has a Mother*, with Simon, from their own novel, 1959; *Shut Up and Sing*, with Sherrin, 1960; *The Hanger On's Tale*, 1960; *Mr. Tooley Tried*, with Sherrin, 1960; *The Italian Straw Hat*, with Sherrin, from the play by Labiche and Michel, 1960; *The Sunday Market*, with Sherrin, 1961; *Justice for Johnny*, with Sherrin, 1962; *The People in the Park*, with Sherrin, 1963; *Those Cowardly Captains!*, with Sherrin, 1963; *Variations on a Theme by Tchekov*, with Simon, 1976.

Television Plays: *And Talking of Tightropes*, with S. J. Simon, 1947; *Take It Away*, with Ned Sherrin, 1955; *Steam, Sanctity, and Song*, 1963; *Benbow Was His Name*, with Sherrin, 1964; *Take a Sapphic*, music by Ron Grainer, 1966; *Ooh La La!* (3 series), with Sherrin, from plays by Feydeau, 1968–73; *The Great Inimitable Mr. Dickens*, with Sherrin, 1970.

Other

The Moon on My Left (juvenile verse). London, Gollancz, 1930.
Sung Before Six (as Oliver Linden; juvenile verse). London, Newnes, 1931.
Curiouser and Curiouser (juvenile verse). London, Harrap, 1932.
Robert Helpmann, Choreographer. London, Batsford, 1943.
Coppélia: The Story of the Ballet Told for the Young. London, Haverstock, 1946.
A Seat at the Ballet. London, Evans, 1951.
The Rest of the Evening's My Own. London, W. H. Allen, 1964.
Gilbert and Sullivan: Lost Chords and Discords. London, Weidenfeld and Nicolson, and Boston, Little Brown, 1975.
Reflections in a Lake: A Study of Chekhov's Greatest Plays. London, Weidenfeld and Nicolson, 1976.

Editor, *Footnotes to the Ballet*. London, Lovat Dickson, and New York, Holt, 1936.

*   *   *

Most of the books which Caryl Brahms wrote in collaboration with S. J. Simon are in no sense of the word mysteries, being instead witty period pastiches such as *No Bed for Bacon* and *Don't Mr. Disraeli* or comic balletic plots filled with humour characters such as *Six Curtains for Stroganova*. Brahms and Simon together had an extravagant but shrewd sense of the ridiculous in the arts, history, government, and life in general. Their style exploited juxtaposition, intercutting, running gags, parody, and a constant play of allusions so varied that reading a Brahms and Simon novel is like playing several memory games simultaneously.

These qualities also characterize their mystery novels beginning with *A Bullet in the Ballet*, in which three successive Petroushkas are murdered. The Brahms-Simon sleuth, Inspector Adam Quill, accompanied by Sergeant Banner, is attractive, "not supernaturally intelligent," and given to consulting the *Detective's Handbook* ("Means, Motive, Opportunity"). In the wartime *Envoy on Excursion*, bound beside a ticking bomb, Quill reflects that "It was a pity perhaps that he had never solved a case...." Murderers confess before he can accuse them. This detective's "unemotional manner" contrasts amusingly with the frenzied world of ballet into which he is periodically plunged, for *A Bullet in the Ballet* created the Stroganoff troupe which proliferated into other novels. It is typical of Brahms and Simon that their characters wander happily from book to book: e.g., the impresario Vladimir Stroganoff with his eternal optimism and his universal comment ("Poof!"); Nicholas Nevjano, choreographer of the future, with his "small scheques" to be changed; Arenskaya, ex-ballerina and elderly tempest of erotic ego; Hannibal the Hothead, *bon vivant* King of Insomnia.

Brahms and Simon preferred deliberate anti-climax to suspense (*Envoy on Excursion* is a shaggy dog story with a Labrador having the last word), but occasionally they achieved a brief grotesque spookiness as when Quill searches an air-raid shelter and finds a hanging corpse. It is likely, however, that readers of these works find less pleasure in clues and unravelment than in the ebullient collision of fantastically comic characters.

—Jane W. Stedman

BRAMAH, Ernest (Ernest Bramah Smith).   British.   Facts of his life are uncertain: born near Manchester, Lancashire, 20 March 1868. Attended Manchester Grammar School. Farmer for 3 years; journalist: worked on a provincial newspaper, then secretary to Jerome K. Jerome, and staff member on Jerome's magazine *To-day*; Editor, *The Minster*, London, 1895–96. *Died 27 June 1942.*

CRIME PUBLICATIONS

Novel (series character: Max Carrados)

> *The Bravo of London* (Carrados).   London, Cassell, 1934.

Short Stories (series character: Max Carrados in all books)

> *Max Carrados.*   London, Methuen, 1914.
> *The Eyes of Max Carrados.*   London, Grant Richards, 1923; New York, Doran, 1924.
> *The Specimen Case.*   London, Hodder and Stoughton, 1924; New York, Doran, 1925.
> *Max Carrados Mysteries.*   London, Hodder and Stoughton, 1927.
> *Best Max Carrados Detective Stories,* edited by E. F. Bleiler.   New York, Dover, 1972.

OTHER PUBLICATIONS

Novel

> *What Might Have Been: The Story of a Social War.*   London, Murray, 1907; as *The Secret of the League,* London, Nelson, 1909.

Short Stories

> *The Wallet of Kai Lung.*   London, Grant Richards, and Boston, Page, 1900.
> *The Mirror of Kong Ho.*   London, Chapman and Hall, 1905; New York, Doubleday, 1930.
> *Kai Lung's Golden Hours.*   London, Grant Richards, 1922; New York, Doran, 1923.
> *The Story of Wan and the Remarkable Shrub and The Story of Ching-Kwei and the Destinies.*   New York, Doubleday, 1927; in *Kai Lung Unrolls His Mat,* 1928.
> *Kai Lung Unrolls His Mat.*   London, Richards Press, and New York, Doubleday, 1928.
> *A Little Flutter.*   London, Cassell, 1930.
> *The Moon of Much Gladness.*   London, Cassell, 1932; as *The Return of Kai Lung,* New York, Sheridan House, 1938.
> *Kai Lung Beneath the Mulberry Tree.*   London, Richards Press, 1940.

Other

> *English Farming and Why I Turned It Up.*   London, Leadenhall, 1894.

A Guide to the Varieties and Rarity of English Regal Copper Coins: Charles II–Victoria, 1671–1860. London, Methuen, 1929.

Bibliography: "Some Uncollected Authors," in *Book Collector 13* (London), 1964, and "A Bramah Biographer's Dilemma," in *American Book Collector 15* (Chicago), 1965, both by William White.

Manuscript Collection: Humanities Research Center, University of Texas, Austin.

*   *   *

The reclusive creator of fiction's most successful blind detective, Ernest Bramah made his mark with his first Kai Lung book, which has been praised by a small but distinguished band of readers ever since. It and its successors concern an itinerant story-teller and are written with great felicity in a mock-Chinese idiom, but the books featuring Kai Lung are quite rich, and too long an exposure being not unlike a surfeit of wedding-cake. By contrast, the stories about the blind detective, Max Carrados, are among the most readable in the genre. Ellery Queen rated the first collection as one of the ten best volumes in the field, and a *Times* reviewer of the final collection recommended it be read "twice running – the first time quickly to reach the solution, the second, slowly, to appreciate neatness of adjustments and subtleties of diction."

The single Carrados tale, "The Bunch of Violets," included in *The Specimen Case* is of indifferent quality, and the Carrados novel, *The Bravo of London*, is uneven and disappointing, exhibiting the hero in a quite unmemorable way. The best works occur in the three volumes of short stories.

"The Coin of Dionysius," the opening episode of *Max Carrados*, finds Louis Carlyle, the capable, unimaginative inquiry agent, appealing for help to the blind amateur. Carlyle is surprised to recognize him as an old acquaintance, Max Wynn, who, in the years since their last meeting, has had the misfortune to be struck blind but the good luck to inherit – on condition he change his name to that of his American benefactor – enough money to make him independent. Carrados is able to solve Carlyle's case without leaving his study. And so the partnership is born.

"The Knight's Cross Signal Problem" concerns a railway crash in which 27 people have died. The engine driver has been suspended, but Carrados clears his name, unmasks the real culprit, and dispenses his own justice. The third case, "The Tragedy at Brookbend Cottage," is perhaps the best of all. Max foils a husband's elaborate plot to electrocute his wife, only to have the affair end – quite plausibly – in utter tragedy. "The Clever Mrs. Straithwaite" shows us that Carrados is very much at ease in a domestic setting especially when, as here, cross-currents must be navigated and cross-purposes resolved. In this tale of a make-believe jewel theft the dialogue of the spoiled wife is a delight. In "The Tilling Shaw Mystery" Bramah again succeeds in breaking new ground. Carrados, upon investigation, declines to aid an attractive young client. Yet he solves her wider problem, rearranges her life, and gains a devoted friend. In this affair, as in most others, the detection is less important than the atmosphere, the characterization, and the fine writing.

The Eyes of Max Carrados opens with a long introduction in which Bramah defends the plausibility of his character's exploits by cataloguing those of real blind persons. But he is not quite convincing. That Carrados can read the morning headlines with his fingertips we may perhaps accept, but not that he can instantly recognize acquaintances before they speak and discover vital hairs on a raspberry cane. It would have been well if more use had been made of Parkinson, the butlerine servant with outstanding powers of observation. E. F. Bleiler has sapiently described Max as "a blind man who can see perfectly well." Such is the impression he makes. Reminders of his supposed handicap do nevertheless remind us how important the other four senses can be, especially when highly developed.

This collection of stories is less successful that its predecessor. Bramah's lack of scientific knowledge reduces him to inventing a new anaesthetic and a new toadstool poison. The best of the nine tales is "The Ghost of Massingham Mansions," the opening of which displays the disparate temperaments of the satirical Carrados and the naive Carlyle to excellent effect. Of the eight stories in *Max Carrados Mysteries*, the best are perhaps "The Holloway Flat Tragedy," a rare homicide case, and "The Vanished Petition Crown," in which the blind sleuth brings a crooked coin-dealer to book. But a choice is difficult; all the tales are dominated by Carrados's personality, and every line is marked by the meticulous touch of a rare literary craftsman.

—Norman Donaldson

BRAND, (Mary) Christianna (Milne).   Also writes as Mary Anne Ashe; Annabel Jones; Mary Roland; China Thompson.   British.   Born in Malaya, 17 December 1909; lived in India as a child. Educated at a Franciscan convent, Taunton, Somerset. Married Roland S. Lewis in 1939; one daughter. Worked as governess, receptionist, dancer, model, salesperson, secretary. Recipient: two Mystery Writers of America awards for short stories. Agent: A. M. Heath, 40–42 William IV Street, London WC2N 4DD. Address: 88 Maida Vale, London W9 1PR, England.

CRIME PUBLICATIONS

Novels (series character: Inspector Cockrill)

Death in High Heels.   London, Lane, 1941; New York, Scribner, 1954.
Heads You Lose (Cockrill).   London, Lane, 1941; New York, Dodd Mead, 1942.
Green for Danger (Cockrill).   New York, Dodd Mead, 1944; London, Lane, 1945.
The Crooked Wreath (Cockrill).   New York, Dodd Mead, 1946; as *Suddenly at His Residence*, London, Lane, 1947.
Death of Jezebel (Cockrill).   New York, Dodd Mead, 1948; London, Lane, 1949.
Cat and Mouse.   London, Joseph, and New York, Knopf, 1950.
London Particular (Cockrill).   London, Joseph, 1952; as *Fog of Doubt*, New York, Scribner, 1953.
Tour de Force (Cockrill).   London, Joseph, and New York, Scribner, 1955.
The Three-Cornered Halo (Cockrill).   London, Joseph, and New York, Scribner, 1957.
Starrbelow (as China Thompson).   London, Hutchinson, and New York, Scribner, 1958.
Court of Foxes.   London, Joseph, 1969; Northridge, California, Brooke House, 1977.
A Ring of Roses (as Mary Ann Ashe).   London, Star, 1976.

Short Stories

What Dread Hand?   London, Joseph, 1968.
Brand X.   London, Joseph, 1974.

Uncollected Short Stories

"Upon Reflection," in *Ellery Queen's Mystery Magazine* (New York), August 1977.
"Over My Dead Body," in *Ellery Queen's Mystery Magazine* (New York), August 1979.

OTHER PUBLICATIONS

Novels

>*The Single Pilgrim* (as Mary Roland). London, Sampson Low, and New York, Crowell, 1946.
>*The Radiant Dove* (as Annabel Jones). London, Joseph, 1974; New York, St. Martin's Press, 1975.

Plays

>*Secret People* (screenplay), with others, in *Making a Film*, edited by Lindsay Anderson. London, Allen and Unwin, and New York, Macmillan, 1952.

>Screenplays: *Death in High Heels*, 1947; *The Mark of Cain*, with W. P. Lipscomb and Francis Cowdry, 1948; *Secret People*, with others, 1952.

Other

>*Danger Unlimited* (juvenile). New York, Dodd Mead, 1948; as *Welcome to Danger*, London, Foley House Press, 1950.
>*Heaven Knows Who.* London, Joseph, and New York, Scribner, 1960.
>*Nurse Matilda* (juvenile). Leicester, Brockhampton Press, and New York, Dutton, 1964.
>*Nurse Matilda Goes to Town* (juvenile). Leicester, Brockhampton Press, 1967; New York, Dutton, 1968.
>*Nurse Matilda Goes to Hospital* (juvenile). London, Hodder and Stoughton, and New York, Dutton, 1974.
>*Alas for Her That Met Me!* (as Mary Ann Ashe). London, Star, 1976.
>*The Honey Harlot.* London, W. H. Allen, 1978.
>"Inspector Cockrill," in *The Great Detectives*, edited by Otto Penzler. Boston, Little Brown, 1978.

>Editor, *Naughty Children: An Anthology.* London, Gollancz, 1962; New York, Dutton, 1963.

Bibliography: "The Works of Christianna Brand" by Otto Penzler, in *Green for Danger*, San Diego, University of California Extension, 1978.

Christianna Brand comments:
  I have written in all eight detective stories of which I can say that I am really proud. I write a few "mainstream" novels also, but crime novels are my real interest. I write them for no reason more pretentious than simply to entertain. I try to include, with the regulation puzzle form, good and interesting characterization, dialogue, and background: having written a scene containing the necessary "clues," I will go back over it and try to make it interesting in itself, so that readers not interested in crime fiction might read the books for their own sakes, as novels. I write with enormous respect for correctness and style, endlessly altering and fiddling with my work, and with scrupulous fairness in the puzzle aspect. But all that being said, I make no claim to do anything other than entertain.

*   *   *

  Perhaps best known for her detective stories featuring Inspector Cockrill of the Kent County Police, Christianna Brand is the author of a number of mystery or suspense stories and novels. *The Three-Cornered Halo*, described by the author as a "mystery-comedy," takes place on an imaginary island (also the setting for *Tour de Force*) and features Inspector Cockrill's sister, Henrietta. This novel, which contains strong fantasy elements, embodies the essence of the author's claim to distinction: a sense of humour, conveyed in a witty style which allows the reader to see the absurdities of human behaviour without losing track of the essential seriousness of the plot. *Green for Danger*, set in a military hospital during World War II, presents one of the most ingenious murders ever devised: a patient is killed on the operating table under the eyes of seven witnesses. *Heads You Lose*, in which Inspector Cockrill made his first appearance, is the story of a jealous spinster who declares that she "wouldn't be caught dead in a ditch" wearing a particular hat. She is murdered, and her severed head, complete with hat, is found in a ditch.

Brand's lightness of touch should not be confused with a lack of seriousness. *Cat and Mouse* is included in Julian Symons's list of the 100 best crime stories because, he says, "the author seems here to take her characters just a little more seriously than usual." In fact, she invariably takes her characters seriously; it is the absurdity of their situations which she observes and documents with telling irony. Her surprise endings, reminiscent of the final "turn of the screw" in an O. Henry story, are much admired; *London Particular* reveals the criminal's method in the last line. It is a tribute to the author's skill at characterization that her endings are as convincing as they are ingenious.

Inspector Cockrill is in the tradition of the eccentric, omniscient private detective rather than that of the realistic police procedural. Shrewd, irascible, and shabbily dressed, his fingers stained dark from rolling cigarettes, Cockrill is a *deus ex machina* who manages, by virtue of acute powers of observation, to ferret out the real criminal from a confusing collection of suspects. The reader derives great satisfaction from trying to outwit the Inspector; that he rarely succeeds in doing so is the result of the author's subtlety in planting false clues, dropping apparent red herrings in unlikely places, and providing a convincing cast of Least Likely Persons from which to choose.

In her shorter mystery fiction, collected in *What Dread Hand?* and *Brand X* the author is particularly adept at the intricate plotting for which she is well known. The stories are almost uniformly satisfying, whether or not they feature Inspector Cockrill. Of her long suspense novels without the serial detective, *Death in High Heels*, about murder in a chic London fashion house, and *Cat and Mouse*, a gothic suspense story, are especially noteworthy.

—Joanne Harack Hayne

BRAND, Max. Pseudonym for Frederick Faust; also wrote as Frank Austin; George Owen Baxter; Walter C. Butler; George Challis; Evan Evans; John Frederick; Frederick Frost; David Manning; Peter Henry Morland; Nicholas Silver. American. Born in Seattle, Washington, 29 May 1892. Educated in schools in Modesto, California; University of California, Berkeley. Married Dorothy Schillig in 1917; two daughters and one son. Freelance writer from 1917; lived in Italy, 1926–36; war correspondent in Italy for *Harper's*, 1944. *Died 12 May 1944*.

CRIME PUBLICATIONS

Novels

    Cross Over Nine (as Walter C. Butler). New York, Macaulay, 1935.

The Night Flower (as Walter C. Butler).   New York, Macaulay, 1936; London, Stanley
  Paul, 1937.
Six Golden Angels.   New York, Dodd Mead, 1937; London, Hodder and Stoughton,
  1938.
Big Game.   New York, Paperback Library, 1973.
The Granduca.   New York, Paperback Library, 1973.
The Phantom Spy.   New York, Dodd Mead, 1973; London, White Lion, 1975.
Dead Man's Treasure.   London, White Lion, 1975.

Novels as Frederick Frost (series character: Anthony Hamilton in all books)

Secret Agent Number One.   Philadelphia, Macrae Smith, 1936; London, Harrap, 1937.
Spy Meets Spy.   Philadelphia, Macrae Smith, and London, Harrap, 1937.
The Bamboo Whistle.   Philadelphia, Macrae Smith, 1937.

OTHER PUBLICATIONS

Novels

The Untamed.   New York, Putnam, 1919; London, Hodder and Stoughton, 1952.
Trailin'.   New York, Putnam, 1920.
The Night Horseman.   New York, Putnam, 1920.
The Seventh Man.   New York, Putnam, 1921.
Children of Night.   London, Hodder and Stoughton, 1923.
Alcatraz.   New York, Putnam, 1923.
Dan Barry's Daughter.   New York, Putnam, 1924.
Clung.   London, Hodder and Stoughton, 1924; New York, Dodd Mead, 1969.
The Guide to Happiness.   London, Hodder and Stoughton, 1924.
Gun Gentlemen.   London, Hodder and Stoughton, 1924; as *The Gentle Gunman*, New
  York, Dodd Mead, 1964.
His Third Majesty.   London, Hodder and Stoughton, 1925.
Beyond the Outpost (as Peter Henry Morland).   New York, Putnam, 1925.
Fire-Brain.   New York, Putnam, 1926.
The White Wolf.   New York, Putnam, 1926.
Fate's Honeymoon.   London, Hodder and Stoughton, 1926.
Luck.   London, Hodder and Stoughton, 1926.
Black Jack.   London, Hodder and Stoughton, 1926; New York, Dodd Mead, 1970.
Harrigan.   London, Hodder and Stoughton, 1926; New York, Dodd Mead, 1971.
The Stranger at the Gate.   London, Hodder and Stoughton, 1926.
The Blue Jay.   New York, Dodd Mead, and London, Hodder and Stoughton, 1927.
The Garden of Eden.   London, Hodder and Stoughton, 1927; New York, Dodd Mead,
  1963.
Pride of Tyson.   London, Hodder and Stoughton, 1927.
Border Guns.   New York, Dodd Mead, 1928; London, Hodder and Stoughton, 1954.
Lost Wolf (as Peter Henry Morland).   New York, Vanguard Press, 1928.
Pillar Mountain.   New York, Dodd Mead, 1928; London, Hodder and Stoughton,
  1929.
Pleasant Jim.   New York, Dodd Mead, and London, Hodder and Stoughton, 1928.
The Galloping Bronchos.   New York, Dodd Mead, 1929; London, Hodder and
  Stoughton, 1953.
The Gun Tamer.   New York, Dodd Mead, 1929; London, Hodder and Stoughton,
  1951.
Mistral.   New York, Dodd Mead, 1929; London, Hodder and Stoughton, 1930.
Destry Rides Again.   New York, Dodd Mead, 1930; London, Hodder and Stoughton,
  1931.

The Outlaw of Buffalo Flat. New York, Dodd Mead, 1930.

Mystery Ranch. New York, Dodd Mead, 1930; as *Mystery Valley*, London, Hodder and Stoughton, 1930.

The Happy Valley. New York, Dodd Mead, 1931; London, Hodder and Stoughton, 1932.

Smiling Charlie. New York, Dodd Mead, and London, Hodder and Stoughton, 1931.

The Jackson Trail. New York, Dodd Mead, 1932; London, Hodder and Stoughton, 1933.

Twenty Notches. New York, Dodd Mead, and London, Hodder and Stoughton, 1932.

Valley Vultures. New York, Dodd Mead, and London, Hodder and Stoughton, 1932.

The False Rider. New York, Dodd Mead, 1933; London, Hodder and Stoughton, 1950.

The Longhorn Feud. New York, Dodd Mead, and London, Hodder and Stoughton, 1933.

The Outlaw. New York, Dodd Mead, 1933.

Slow Joe. New York, Dodd Mead, and London, Hodder and Stoughton, 1933.

Valley Thieves. New York, Grosset and Dunlap, 1933; London, Hodder and Stoughton, 1949.

Brothers on the Trail. New York, Dodd Mead, 1934; London, Hodder and Stoughton, 1935.

War Party. New York, Dodd Mead, 1934.

Timbal Gulch Trail. New York, Dodd Mead, and London, Hodder and Stoughton, 1934.

Crooked Horn. London, Hodder and Stoughton, 1934.

The Rancher's Revenge. New York, Dodd Mead, 1934; London, Hodder and Stoughton, 1935.

Hunted Riders. New York, Dodd Mead, 1935; London, Hodder and Stoughton, 1936.

Dead Man's Treasure. New York, Dodd Mead, 1935.

Rustlers of Beacon Creek. New York, Dodd Mead, 1935; London, Hodder and Stoughton, 1936.

Frontier Feud. New York, Dodd Mead, 1935.

The Seven of Diamonds. New York, Dodd Mead, and London, Hodder and Stoughton, 1935.

Happy Jack. New York, Dodd Mead, and London, Hodder and Stoughton, 1936.

The King Bird Rides. New York, Dodd Mead, and London, Hodder and Stoughton, 1936.

South of Rio Grande. New York, Dodd Mead, 1936; London, Hodder and Stoughton, 1937.

Six Golden Angels. New York, Dodd Mead, 1937; London, Hodder and Stoughton, 1938.

The Streak. New York, Dodd Mead, and London, Hodder and Stoughton, 1937.

Trouble Trail. New York, Dodd Mead, and London, Hodder and Stoughton, 1937.

Dead or Alive. New York, Dodd Mead, 1938.

The Iron Trail. New York, Dodd Mead, 1938, as *Riding the Iron Trail*, London, Hodder and Stoughton, 1938.

Singing Guns. New York, Dodd Mead, and London, Hodder and Stoughton, 1938.

Fightin' Fool. New York, Dodd Mead, 1939; as *A Fairly Slick Guy*, London, Hodder and Stoughton, 1940.

Gunman's Gold. New York, Dodd Mead, and London, Hodder and Stoughton, 1939.

Marbleface. New York, Dodd Mead, 1939; as *Poker Face*, London, Hodder and Stoughton, 1939.

Lanky for Luck. London, Hodder and Stoughton, 1939.

Calling Dr. Kildare (as Frederick Faust). New York, Dodd Mead, 1940.

Danger Trail. New York, Dodd Mead, and London, Hodder and Stoughton, 1940.

The Dude. New York, Dodd Mead, 1940.

Riders of the Plains. New York, Dodd Mead, 1940; London, Hodder and Stoughton, 1941.

The Secret of Dr. Kildare (as Frederick Faust). New York, Dodd Mead, 1940.

Cleaned Out. London, Hodder and Stoughton, 1940.

The Border Kid. New York, Dodd Mead, and London, Hodder and Stoughton, 1941.

Dr. Kildare Takes Charge. New York, Dodd Mead, 1941; London, Hodder and Stoughton, 1942.

The Long Chance. New York, Dodd Mead, 1941.

Vengeance Trail. New York, Dodd Mead, 1941.

Young Dr. Kildare. New York, Dodd Mead, and London, Hodder and Stoughton, 1941.

Silvertip. New York, Dodd Mead, and London, Hodder and Stoughton, 1942.

Dr. Kildare's Crisis. New York, Dodd Mead, 1942; London, Hodder and Stoughton, 1943.

Dr. Kildare's Trial. New York, Dodd Mead, 1942; London, Hodder and Stoughton, 1944.

The Man From Mustang. New York, Dodd Mead, 1942; London, Hodder and Stoughton, 1943.

Silvertip's Strike. New York, Dodd Mead, 1942; London, Hodder and Stoughton, 1944.

The Safety Killer. London, Hodder and Stoughton, 1942.

Striking Eagle. London, Hodder and Stoughton, 1942.

Dr. Kildare's Search, and Dr. Kildare's Hardest Case. New York, Dodd Mead, 1943; London, Hodder and Stoughton, 1945.

Silvertip's Roundup. New York, Dodd Mead, 1943; London, Hodder and Stoughton, 1945.

Silvertip's Trap. New York, Dodd Mead, 1943; London, Hodder and Stoughton, 1946.

The Fighting Four. New York, Dodd Mead, 1944; London, Hodder and Stoughton, 1948.

Silvertip's Chase. Philadelphia, Blakiston, 1944; London, Hodder and Stoughton, 1946.

Silvertip's Search. New York, Dodd Mead, 1945; London, Hodder and Stoughton, 1948.

The Stolen Stallion. New York, Dodd Mead, 1945; London, Hodder and Stoughton, 1949.

Mountain Riders. New York, Dodd Mead, 1946; London, Hodder and Stoughton, 1949.

Valley of Vanishing Men. New York, Dodd Mead, 1947; London, Hodder and Stoughton, 1949.

The False Rider. New York, Dodd Mead, 1947; London, Hodder and Stoughton, 1950.

Flaming Irons. New York, Dodd Mead, 1948; London, Hodder and Stoughton, 1951.

Hired Hands. New York, Dodd Mead, 1948; London, Hodder and Stoughton, 1951.

The Bandit of the Black Hills. New York, Dodd Mead, and London, Hodder and Stoughton, 1949.

Seven Trails. New York, Dodd Mead, 1949; London, Hodder and Stoughton, 1952.

Single Jack. New York, Dodd Mead, 1950; London, Hodder and Stoughton, 1953.

The Hair-Trigger Kid. New York, Dodd Mead, 1951.

Tragedy Trail. New York, Dodd Mead, 1951; London, Hodder and Stoughton, 1954.

The Gambler. New York, Dodd Mead, 1952; London, Hodder and Stoughton, 1956.

Smiling Desperado. New York, Dodd Mead, 1952; London, Hodder and Stoughton, 1955.

The Tenderfoot. New York, Dodd Mead, 1952; London, Hodder and Stoughton, 1955.

The Invisible Outlaw. New York, Dodd Mead, 1954; London, Hodder and Stoughton, 1956.

Outlaw Breed. New York, Dodd Mead, 1955; London, Hodder and Stoughton, 1957.
Speedy. New York, Dodd Mead, 1955; London, Hodder and Stoughton, 1957.
The Big Trail. New York, Dodd Mead, 1956; London, Hodder and Stoughton, 1958.
Trail Partners. New York, Dodd Mead, 1956; London, Hodder and Stoughton, 1958.
Blood on the Trail. New York, Dodd Mead, 1957; London, Hodder and Stoughton, 1959.
Lucky Larribee. New York, Dodd Mead, 1957; London, Hodder and Stoughton, 1960.
The Long Chase. New York, Dodd Mead, 1960; London, Hodder and Stoughton, 1961.
The White Cheyenne. New York, Dodd Mead, 1960; London, Hodder and Stoughton, 1961.
Mighty Lobo. New York, Dodd Mead, 1962.
Tamer of the Wild. New York, Dodd Mead, 1962; London, Hodder and Stoughton, 1963.
The Stranger. New York, Dodd Mead, 1963; London, Panther, 1964.
Golden Lightning. New York, Dodd Mead, 1964; London, Hodder and Stoughton, 1965.
The Guns of Darking Hollow. New York, Dodd Mead, 1965; London, Hodder and Stoughton, 1966.
Torture Trail. New York, Dodd Mead, 1965.
Larramee's Ranch. New York, Dodd Mead, 1966.
Ride the Wild Trail. New York, Dodd Mead, 1966.
Rippon Rides Double. New York, Dodd Mead, 1968.
The Stingaree. New York, Dodd Mead, 1968.
Thunder Moon. New York, Dodd Mead, 1969.
Gunman's Reckoning. New York, Dodd Mead, 1970.
Trouble Kid. New York, Dodd Mead, 1970.
Ambush at Torture Canyon. New York, Dodd Mead, 1971.
Cheyenne Gold. New York, Dodd Mead, 1972.
Drifter's Vengeance. New York, Dodd Mead, 1972.
The Luck of the Spindrift. New York, Dodd Mead, 1972.
Storm on the Range. London, Hale, 1979.

Novels as John Frederick

Riders of the Silences. New York, H. K. Fly, 1920.
The Bronze Collar. New York, Putnam, 1925.
The Sword Lover. New York, Waterson, 1927.

Novels as George Owen Baxter

Free Range Lanning. New York, Chelsea House, 1921; London, Hodder and Stoughton, 1923.
The Gauntlet. London, Lloyd, 1922.
Donnegan. New York, Chelsea House, 1923; London, Hodder and Stoughton, 1924.
The Long, Long Trail. New York, Chelsea House, 1923; London, Hodder and Stoughton, 1924.
The Range-Land Avenger. New York, Chelsea House, 1924; London, Hodder and Stoughton, 1925.
King Charlie. London, Hodder and Stoughton, 1925.
The Shadow of Silver Tip. New York, Chelsea House, 1925; London, Hodder and Stoughton, 1926.
Wooden Guns. New York, Chelsea House, 1925; London, Hodder and Stoughton, 1927.

Train's Trust. New York, Chelsea House, 1926; London, Hodder and Stoughton, 1927; as *Steve Train's Ordeal* (as Max Brand), New York, Dodd Mead, 1967.

The Whispering Outlaw. New York, Chelsea House, 1926; London, Hodder and Stoughton, 1927.

The Trail to San Triste. New York, Chelsea House, 1927; London, Hodder and Stoughton, 1928.

Tiger Man. New York, Macaulay, and, London, Hodder and Stoughton, 1929.

The Killers. New York, Macaulay, and London, Hodder and Stoughton, 1931.

Call of the Blood. New York, Macaulay, and London, Hodder and Stoughton, 1934.

Red Devil of the Range. New York, Macaulay, 1934; London, Hodder and Stoughton, 1935.

Brother of the Cheyennes. New York, Macaulay, 1936.

Rusty. London, Hodder and Stoughton, 1937.

Novels as David Manning

Bill Hunter's Romance. New York, Chelsea House, 1924; London, Hutchinson, 1926.

Jerry Peyton's Notched Inheritance. New York, Chelsea House, 1924.

The Brute. New York, Chelsea House, 1925.

Jim Curry's Test. New York, Chelsea House, 1925; London, Hutchinson, 1927.

King Charlie's Riders. New York, Chelsea House, 1925.

Blackie and Red. New York, Chelsea House, 1926.

Ronicky Doone's Treasure. New York, Chelsea House, 1926.

Bandit's Honor. New York, Chelsea House, 1927.

On the Trail of Four. New York, Chelsea House, 1927.

The Outlaw Tamer. New York, Chelsea House, 1927.

Trap at Comanche Bend. New York, Chelsea House, 1927.

Novels as George Challis

The Splendid Rascal. Indianapolis, Bobbs Merrill, 1926; London, Cassell, 1927.

Monsieur. Indianapolis, Bobbs Merrill, and London, Cassell, 1926.

The Golden Knight. New York, Greystone Press, 1937; London, Cassell, 1938.

The Naked Blade. New York, Greystone Press, 1938; London, Cassell, 1939.

The Firebrand. New York, Harper, 1950.

The Bait and the Trap. New York, Harper, 1951.

Novels as Evan Evans

The Border Bandit. New York, Harper, 1926.

The Rescue of Broken Arrow. New York, Harper, 1930.

Montana Rides! New York, Harper, 1933; London, Penguin, 1957.

Montana Rides Again. New York, Harper, 1934.

The Song of the Whip. New York, Harper, 1936; London, Penguin, 1957.

Gunman's Legacy. New York, Harper, 1949.

Smuggler's Trail. New York, Harper, 1949; as *Lone Hand*, New York, Bantam, 1951.

Sawdust and Sixguns. New York, Harper, 1950.

Strange Courage. New York, Harper, 1952; London, Jenkins, 1953.

Outlaw Valley. New York, Harper, 1953; London, Hale, 1954.

Outlaw's Code. New York, Harper, 1953; London, Hale, 1955.

Novels as Frank Austin

The Return of the Rancher. New York, Dodd Mead, 1933; London, Lane, 1934.

The Sheriff Rides. New York, Dodd Mead, 1934; London, Lane, 1935.

King of the Range.   New York, Dodd Mead, 1935; London, Lane, 1936.

Short Stories

Wine on the Desert and Other Stories.   New York, Dodd Mead, 1940; London, Hodder and Stoughton, 1941.
Max Brand's Best Stories, edited by Robert Easton.   New York, Dodd Mead, 1967.

Plays

The Gate (oratorio), with Mirza Ahmad Sohrab and Julie Chanler, music by Brand.   New York, Associated Music Publishers, 1944.

Screenplays: *Calling Dr. Kildare*, with Harry Ruskin and Willis Goldbeck, 1939; *Dr. Kildare's Strange Case*, with Ruskin, 1940; *Dr. Kildare Goes Home*, with Ruskin and Goldbeck, 1940; *Dr. Kildare's Crisis*, with Ruskin and Goldbeck, 1940; *The People vs. Dr. Kildare*, with others, 1941; *The Desperadoes*, with Robert Carson, 1942; *Uncertain Glory*, with Laszlo Ladnay and Joe May, 1944.

Verse as Frederick Faust

The Village Street and Other Poems.   New York, Putnam, 1922.
Dionysius in Hades.   Oxford, Blackwell, 1931.
The Thunderer.   New York, Berrydale Press, 1933.

Other

The Ten Foot Chain; or, Can Love Survive the Shackles?, with others.   New York, Reynolds, 1920.
The Notebooks and Poems of Max Brand, edited by John Schoolcraft.   New York, Dodd Mead, 1957.

Bibliography: *Max Brand: The Man and His Work, Critical Appreciation and Bibliography*, by Darrell C. Richardson, Los Angeles, Fantasy, 1952.

*   *   *

Between 1917 and 1944, when he died as a European war correspondent, Frederick Faust used at least twenty pen-names to publish 125 novels and over 350 magazine stories and novelettes. His many pseudonyms did not really distinguish style or genres or purposes; instead they allowed Faust to run several stories in a single issue of a magazine or have several longer books published in a single month by different publishers – with the public unaware that they were all by the same author. Although best known as Max Brand, author of popular westerns, Faust also wrote entertaining mystery fiction, particularly in the 1930's when he published a half-dozen novels and many shorter pieces in some of America's most popular pulps, including *Black Mask*.

In the mysteries, Faust expertly mixes the ingredients of popular fiction – humor, adventure, romance, suspense. One series of 1935–36 tales in *Detective Fiction Weekly*, for example, introduces two comical police sergeants in conflict with one another – the sober Scotsman Angus Campbell and the cheerful Irishman Patrick O'Rourke. Of the longer fiction, *Big Game* (republished in book form 37 years after its *Argosy* serialization, an indication of Brand's continuing popularity) typifies Faust's hard-boiled crime stories: ex-safari hunter Terence Radway encounters New York City underworld violence and political corruption; he meets romance and mystery in a beautiful and fragile young woman named Helen Forman; and he lives dangerously by his own Hemingway code: even in confronting vicious murderers, a code of conduct applies – "It's a rule of the game." As usual, Faust's mystery is intriguing, his plot complex and suspenseful, and his drama and romance satisfying.

—Elmer Pry

BRANDON, John G(ordon). Australian. Born in 1879. Married; at least one son, the writer Gordon Brandon. Heavy-weight boxer in his youth; lived in England, after 1923; organized a syndicate of popular writers in the 1930's. *Died in 1941.*

CRIME PUBLICATIONS

Novels (series characters: Sexton Blake; Sergeant/Detective Inspector Patrick Aloysius McCarthy; Arthur Stukeley Pennington).

The Big Heart. London, Methuen, and New York, Brentano's 1923.
Young Love. London, Methuen, 1925; New York, Brentano's, 1926.
The Joy Ride. London, Methuen, and New York, Dial Press, 1927.
Red Altars (McCarthy). London, Cassell, 1928.
The Secret Brotherhood. New York, Dial Press, 1928.
The Silent House (novelization of stage play). London, Cassell, and New York, Dial Press, 1928.
Nighthawks! London, Methuen, 1929; New York, Brentano's, 1930.
Th' Big City. London, Methuen, and New York, Brentano's, 1930.
The Black Joss (McCarthy). London, Methuen, 1931.
West End! (McCarthy; Pennington). London, Methuen, 1933.
The Taxi-Cab Murder (Blake). London, Amalgamated Press, 1933.
The Survivor's Secret (Blake). London, Amalgamated Press, 1933.
The Tragedy of the West End Actress (Blake). London, Amalgamated Press, 1933.
The Championship Crime (Blake). London, Amalgamated Press, 1934.
The Chink's Victim (Blake). London, Amalgamated Press, 1934.
The Case of the Gangster's Moll (Blake). London, Amalgamated Press, 1934.
The Glass Dagger (Blake). London, Amalgamated Press, 1934.
Murder in Mayfair. London, Methuen, 1934.
Murder on the Stage (Blake). London, Amalgamated Press, 1934.
Under Police Protection (Blake). London, Amalgamated Press, 1934.
The Mystery of the Three City's (Blake). London, Amalgamated Press, 1934.
On the Midnight Beat (Blake). London, Amalgamated Press, 1934.
The One-Minute Murder (McCarthy; Pennington). London, Methuen, 1934; New York, Dial Press, 1935.
The Yellow Mask (Blake). London, Amalgamated Press, 1935.
By Order of the Tong (Blake). London, Amalgamated Press, 1935.
The Case of the Murdered Commissionnaire (Blake). London, Amalgamated Press, 1935.
The Riverside Mystery (McCarthy; Pennington). London, Methuen, 1935.
The Red Boomerang (Blake). London, Amalgamated Press, 1935.
The Downing Street Discovery (Blake). London, Amalgamated Press, 1935.
Murder in Y Division (Blake). London, Amalgamated Press, 1935.

The Victim of the Thieves' Den (Blake).   London, Amalgamated Press, 1936.
The Pawnshop Murder (McCarthy; Pennington).   London, Methuen, 1936.
The Mystery of the Murdered Blonde (Blake).   London, Amalgamated Press, 1936.
The Mystery of the Three Acrobats (Blake).   London, Amalgamated Press, 1936.
The Case of the Night Club Queen (Blake).   London, Amalgamated Press, 1936.
Dead Man's Evidence (Blake).   London, Amalgamated Press, 1936.
Murder on the Fourth Floor (Blake).   London, Amalgamated Press, 1936.
The "Snatch" Game (McCarthy; Pennington).   London, Wright and Brown, 1936.
The Case of the Withered Hand.   London, Wright and Brown, 1936.
Death Tolls the Gong (McCarthy; Pennington).   London, Wright and Brown, 1936.
The Dragnet (McCarthy).   London, Wright and Brown, 1936.
McCarthy, C.I.D.   London, Wright and Brown, 1936.
Murder at "the Yard" (McCarthy).   London, Wright and Brown, 1936.
The Girl Who Knew Too Much (Blake).   London, Amalgamated Press, 1936.
The Bond Street Murder (McCarthy; Pennington).   London, Wright and Brown, 1937.
The Bond Street Raiders (Blake).   London, Amalgamated Press, 1937.
The Crime in the Kiosk (Blake).   London, Amalgamated Press, 1937.
Death in Downing Street (McCarthy; Pennington).   London, Wright and Brown, 1937.
The Diamond of Ti Lingo (Blake).   London, Amalgamated Press, 1937.
The Mystery of the Murdered Sentry (Blake).   London, Amalgamated Press, 1937.
The Mystery of X20 (Blake).   London, Amalgamated Press, 1937.
The Spy from Spain (Blake).   London, Amalgamated Press, 1937.
The Tattooed Triangle (Blake).   London, Amalgamated Press, 1937.
The Victim of the Secret Service (Blake).   London, Amalgamated Press, 1937.
The Hand of Seeta (McCarthy).   London, Wright and Brown, 1937.
The Mail-Van Mystery (McCarthy).   London, Wright and Brown, 1937.
The Man from Italy (Blake).   London, Amalgamated Press, 1937.
The Melbourne Mystery (Blake).   London, Amalgamated Press, 1937.
Murder in Soho.   London, Wright and Brown, 1937.
Murder on the High Seas (Blake).   London, Amalgamated Press, 1938.
The Mystery of the Dead Man's Wallet (Blake).   London, Amalgamated Press, 1938.
The Mystery of the Murdered Ice Cream Man (Blake).   London, Amalgamated Press, 1938.
The Mystery of the Street Musician (Blake).   London, Amalgamated Press, 1938.
The Night Club Murder (McCarthy).   London, Wright and Brown, 1938.
The Pigeon Loft Crime (Blake).   London, Amalgamated Press, 1938.
The Regent Street Raid (McCarthy; Pennington).   London, Wright and Brown, 1938.
The Roadhouse Mystery (Blake).   London, Amalgamated Press, 1938.
Bonus for Murder.   London, Wright and Brown, 1938.
The Clue of the Tattooed Man (Blake).   London, Amalgamated Press, 1938.
The Cork Street Crime (McCarthy; Pennington).   London, Wright and Brown, 1938.
The False Alibi (Blake).   London, Amalgamated Press, 1938.
The £50 Marriage Case.   London, Wright and Brown, 1938; as *The £250 Marriage Case*, London, Mellifont Press, 1954.
The Frame-Up (McCarthy).   London, Wright and Brown, 1938.
The Mark of the Tong (McCarthy).   London, Wright and Brown, 1938.
The Crooked Five! (McCarthy).   London, Wright and Brown, 1939.
Death on Delivery (McCarthy).   London, Wright and Brown, 1939.
Fatal Forgery (Blake).   London, Amalgamated Press, 1939.
Finger-Prints Never Lie! (McCarthy).   London, Wright and Brown, 1939.
The Great Taxi-Cab Ramp (Blake).   London, Amalgamated Press, 1939.
In the Hands of Spies (Blake).   London, Amalgamated Press, 1939.
The Gunboat Mystery (Blake).   London, Amalgamated Press, 1939.
The Man from Singapore (Blake).   London, Amalgamated Press, 1939.
The Man with Jitters (Blake).   London, Amalgamated Press, 1939.

Mr. Pennington Comes Through (McCarthy; Pennington). London, Wright and Brown, 1939.

Murder on the Ice Rink (Blake). London, Amalgamated Press, 1939.

The Mystery of the Green Bottle (Blake). London, Amalgamated Press, 1939.

The Riddle of the Greek Financier (Blake). London, Amalgamated Press, 1940.

The Riddle of the Dead Man's Bay (Blake). London, Amalgamated Press, 1940.

On Ticket of Leave (Blake). London, Amalgamated Press, 1940.

A Scream in Soho. London, Wright and Brown, 1940.

The Terror of the Pacific (Blake). London, Amalgamated Press, 1940.

Yellow Gods (McCarthy). London, Wright and Brown, 1940.

The Black Swastika (Blake). London, Amalgamated Press, 1940.

Crook's Cargo (Blake). London, Amalgamated Press, 1940.

Death in the Ditch! (Pennington). London, Wright and Brown, 1940.

Gang War! London, Wright and Brown, 1940.

Mr. Pennington Goes Nap (McCarthy; Pennington). London, Wright and Brown, 1940.

The Death in the Quarry (McCarthy). London, Wright and Brown, 1941.

Mr. Pennington Barges In (McCarthy; Pennington). London, Wright and Brown, 1941.

Under Secret Orders (Blake). London, Amalgamated Press, 1941.

The Transport Murders (McCarthy). London, Wright and Brown, 1942.

The Blue-Print Murders (McCarthy). London, Wright and Brown, 1942.

Murder for a Million. London, Wright and Brown, 1942.

Mr. Pennington Sees Red (McCarthy; Pennington). London, Wright and Brown, 1942.

Death in Jermyn Street (McCarthy; Pennington). London, Wright and Brown, 1942.

Death in "D" Division (McCarthy; Pennington). London, Wright and Brown, 1943.

Death in Duplicate. London, Wright and Brown, 1945.

Candidate for a Coffin! (McCarthy). London, Wright and Brown, 1946.

"M" for Murder. London, Wright and Brown, 1949.

The Case of the Would-Be Widow! (Pennington). London, Wright and Brown, 1950.

The Corpse Rode On (McCarthy; Pennington). London, Wright and Brown, 1952.

Murderer's Stand-In (McCarthy; Pennington). London, Wright and Brown, 1953.

The Call Girl Murders (McCarthy; Pennington). London, Wright and Brown, 1954.

Death of a Greek (McCarthy; Pennington). London, Wright and Brown, 1955.

Murder on the Beam (McCarthy; Pennington). London, Wright and Brown, 1956.

Death of a Socialite (McCarthy; Pennington). London, Wright and Brown, 1957.

Murder in Pimlico (McCarthy; Pennington). London, Wright and Brown, 1958.

The Corpse from "the City"! (McCarthy; Pennington). London, Wright and Brown, 1958.

Death Stalks in Soho! (McCarthy; Pennington). London, Wright and Brown, 1959.

Death Comes Swiftly (McCarthy). London, Wright and Brown, n.d.

The Espionage Killings (McCarthy). London, Wright and Brown, n.d.

OTHER PUBLICATIONS

Play

The Silent House, with George Pickett (produced London, 1927).

*   *   *

An extremely prolific writer, John G. Brandon wrote over 120 novels between 1923 and his death in 1941. His most well-known character was The Honourable Arthur Stukeley Pennington, whose adventures were combined with Inspector McCarthy of Scotland Yard. (Superintendent Burman, another policeman invariably featured, is portrayed as a bucolic character.) Inspector McCarthy was, in fact, featured on his own in *Red Altars*, but no doubt Brandon thought that Pennington would provide more substance to his stories. The extra length of 1930's novels gave far more scope for characterisation and the development of sub-plots.

An interesting innovation used by Brandon was the titling of chapters (e.g., "Which Concerns a Telephone Conversation" or "A Payment for a Commission"). This ploy, no doubt considered rather old-fashioned now, gave the reader a clear foretaste of the novel's format. The influence of Sax Rohmer was also shown in several of his books; the "sinister Chinese threat" was the main theme in such stories as *Death Tolls the Gong* and *The Yellow Mask*. Brandon's works for the Amalgamated Press were concerned with the Sexton Blake library. (Many of these books were later rewritten without Sexton Blake for a more adult audience, and re-issued by Wright and Brown.) One very much suspects that Brandon originated the Sexton Blake character – "The Aristocratic Amateur Sleuth" – whose relationship with New Scotland Yard was good, and that several well-known authors of today have just varied the theme. The foil for Blake (Pennington in the rewritten versions) was his manservant, Flash George Wibley, "the ace of high-class cracksmen," now suitably reformed, aided by Big Bill Withers, the taxi driver who provided suitable back-up. Explicit violence and sex, obvious features of today's thrillers, are noticeably missing, as is romance. What violence there is consists of good wholesome crash-bang-wallop, with the villain receiving his due deserts. Although a gentleman adventurer with his aristocratic friends may perhaps date the novels, the plots are strong enough and the prose good enough to make the books very acceptable reading today. Well worth having a look at are *The Mail-Van Mystery*, *Mr. Pennington Goes Nap*, and *Murder in Y Division*.

—Donald C. Ireland

BRANSON, H(enry) C(lay).   American.   Born in Battle Creek, Michigan. Educated at Princeton University, New Jersey, 1924; University of Michigan, Ann Arbor, B.A. 1937. Married; three daughters.

CRIME PUBLICATIONS

Novels (series character: John Bent in all books)

> *I'll Eat You Last.*   New York, Simon and Schuster, 1941; London, Lane, 1943; as *I'll Kill You Last*, New York, Mystery Novel of the Month, 1942.
> *The Pricking Thumb.*   New York, Simon and Schuster, 1942; London, Lane, 1949.
> *Case of the Giant Killer.*   New York, Simon and Schuster, 1944; London, Lane, 1949.
> *The Fearful Passage.*   New York, Simon and Schuster, 1945; London, Lane, 1950.
> *Last Year's Blood.*   New York, Simon and Schuster, 1947; London, Lane, 1950.
> *The Leaden Bubble.*   New York, Simon and Schuster, 1949; London, Lane, 1951.
> *Beggar's Choice.*   New York, Simon and Schuster, 1953.

OTHER PUBLICATIONS

Novel

Salisbury Plain.   New York, Dutton, 1965.

*   *   *

Henry Clay Branson derived from his father not only his substantial American name but also a solid midwestern upbringing. Branson had read Doyle as a boy, followed Philo Vance's cases in Paris in the pages of *Scribner's Magazine*, and was one of the most familiar of card-holders at the Ann Arbor Public Library, where he withdrew and consumed hundreds of mystery stories. Following a period of physical and emotional crisis, he considered: perhaps he could write detective fiction.

John Bent, Branson's series detective, is a physician by training, but does not practice in the stories. He is low-keyed, humane, likeable, self-assured, and wise. He is singularly observant and frank to the point of being out-spoken – this being perhaps his only vice outside the pleasures of drinking and smoking to which he is openly devoted. We know little more about him. Branson takes a similar approach to the locales of his books. One is never sure precisely where the action is taking place. In his mind, Branson sees all of his stories laid out in and around Battle Creek, Jackson, and Kalamazoo, Michigan. But geography is always vague for his readers. Praise for most of Branson's work has been general and widespread. People and the tangles they involve themselves in are what interest Branson, and consequently the stress in the Bent novels is on plotting. Analyzing behavior and discerning motivations are the detective's strong suits. In these respects he has won his place among the best.

—Donald A. Yates

BRAUN, Lillian Jackson.   American.

CRIME PUBLICATIONS

Novels (series character: Jim Qwilleran in all books)

> *The Cat Who Could Read Backwards.*   New York, Dutton, 1966; London, Collins, 1967.
> *The Cat Who Ate Danish Modern.*   New York, Dutton, 1967; London, Collins, 1968.
> *The Cat Who Turned On and Off.*   New York, Dutton, and London, Collins, 1968.

Uncollected Short Stories

> "The Sin of Madame Phloi," in *Best Detective Stories of the Year*, edited by Anthony Boucher.   New York, Dutton, and London, Boardman, 1963.
> "Phut Phat Concentrates," in *Best Detective Stories of the Year*, edited by Anthony Boucher.   New York, Dutton, and London, Boardman, 1964.
> "SuSu and the 8:30 Ghost," in *Ellery Queen's Mystery Magazine* (New York), April 1964.
> "The Dark One," in *Ellery Queen's Mystery Magazine* (New York), July 1966.

"Tragedy on New Year's Day," in *Ellery Queen's Mystery Magazine* (New York), March 1968.

*   *   *

"It will be read with equal interest by both ailurophiles and ailurophobes," said Ellery Queen of Lillian Jackson Braun's "The Sin of Madame Phloi" (*The Best Detective Stories of the Year 1963*). It concerns Madame Phloi, an aristocratic seal-pointed Siamese, the dreadful fate of her amiable son Thapthim, and Madame's retribution. When Mrs. Braun's "Phut Phat Concentrates" was published in the following year's collection, Anthony Boucher described the author as a "fabulous fabricator of felonious feline fiction."

The author followed these successes with three witty and imaginative full-length murder mysteries involving a newspaper man called Jim Qwilleran and a Siamese cat. In *The Cat Who Could Read Backwards*, the cat Kao K'o-Kung lives with the controversial art critic George Bonifield Mountclemens III. After Mountclemens has told the newspaper man that he "would gladly trade one ear and one eye for a full set of cat's whiskers...." Qwilleran confesses he has a weird feeling that his own moustache makes him "more – more aware!" In this book Kao K'o-Kung (known as Koko) and Qwilleran investigate and solve three murders. In *The Cat Who Ate Danish Modern* the author uses her specialized knowledge of art and interior decorating to provide an authentic background. The cat is lonely and Qwilleran brings home an adorable female Siamese called Yum Yum. She joins Koko and Qwilleran when they are investigating, in *The Cat Who Turned On and Off*, some scary murders among the antiques in Junktown. In this story Koko saves Qwilleran's life and at the end helps along his romance.

—Betty Donaldson

BREAN, Herbert. American. Born in Detroit, Michigan, 10 December 1907. Educated at University of Detroit High School; University of Michigan, Ann Arbor, A.B. 1929. Married Dorothy Skeman in 1934; two daughters. Journalist: staff member, United Press, New York, 1929, and in Detroit an assistant bureau manager; writer for Detroit *Times*, for ten years; Detroit *Time* and *Life* news bureau chief, 1943–44, then in New York as a *Life* editor, and staff writer, 1953–62. Public Relations consultant to General Motors. President of Mystery Writers of America, 1967. Fellow, International Institute of Arts and Letters. *Died 7 May 1973*.

CRIME PUBLICATIONS

Novels (series characters: William Deacon; Reynold Frame)

Wilders Walk Away (Frame).   New York, Morrow, 1948; London, Heinemann, 1949.
The Darker the Night (Frame).   New York, Morrow, 1949; London, Heinemann, 1950.
Hardly a Man Is Now Alive (Frame).   New York, Morrow, 1950; London, Heinemann, 1952; as *Murder Now and Then*, London, Macmillan, 1965.
The Clock Strikes Thirteen (Frame).   New York, Morrow, 1952; London, Heinemann, 1954.

A Matter of Fact. New York, Morrow, 1956; as *Collar for the Killer*, London, Heinemann, 1957; as *Dead Sure*, New York, Dell, 1958.
The Traces of Brillhart (Deacon). New York, Harper, 1960; London, Heinemann, 1961.
The Traces of Merrilee (Deacon). New York, Morrow, 1966.

Uncollected Short Stories

"Nine Hours Late on Opening Run," in *Ellery Queen's Mystery Magazine* (New York), December 1957.
"Then They, Came Running," in *Ellery Queen's 14th Mystery Annual.* New York, Random House, 1959; London, Collins, 1961.
"Something White in the Night," in *Crimes Across the Sea*, edited by John Creasey. New York, Harper, and London, Longman, 1964.

OTHER PUBLICATIONS

Other

How to Stop Smoking. New York, Vanguard Press, 1951; Kingswood, Surrey, World's Work, 1952; revised edition, Vanguard Press, 1958.
How to Stop Drinking. New York, Holt Rinehart, 1958; as *A Handbook for Drinkers – and for Those Who Want to Stop,* New York, Collier, 1963.
The Life Treasury of American Folklore. New York, Time, 1961.
The Music of Life, with the editors of *Life.* New York, Time, 1962.
The Only Diet that Works. New York, Morrow, 1965.

Editor, *The Mystery Writers' Handbook.* New York, Harper, 1956.

Manuscript Collection: Mugar Memorial Library, Boston University.

*   *   *

Herbert Brean, newspaperman, magazine writer, and author of thirteen books, perfected his craft throughout his professional life. During his years on the Detroit *Times*, he began to write detective stories for pulp magazines. After moving to New York to work on *Life* magazine, he fulfilled his ambition to write a mystery novel with *Wilders Walk Away* in 1948, the first of seven he was to produce.

Part of Brean's boyhood was spent in Vermont, his father's home territory, and the setting for his first mystery. The narrator Reynold Frame, a magazine free-lancer in the town of Wilders Lane to do a story, meets the town's oldest family, who still live in their ancestral home surrounded by heirlooms. Plagued with vanishing menfolk since the 1775 disappearance of Jonathan Wilder, the family is in trouble again when Constance Wilder's young sister goes missing, as does an aunt soon after. Secret compartments and passages, murder both contemporary and remote, and a Revolutionary War treasure are parts of this story.

Frame appears again in *Hardly a Man Is Now Alive*, set in Concord, Massachusetts. Frame finds himself among an odd group, and in an atmosphere seemingly conducive to supernatural manifestations. Once again present-day crimes are mixed up with old ones. A mystery of the American Revolution is cleared up, a nineteenth-century literary puzzle is solved, and a modern murderer is exposed. A venerable citizen of 104 who knew Emerson and who had heard about the battles of Lexington and Concord from an eyewitness is a pivotal character. Concord lore from the Revolutionary period and from its literary heyday of the next century are cleverly interwoven to create a delightful tale.

The Clock Strikes Thirteen, another Frame novel, takes place on an island off the coast of

Maine where a team of scientists is engaged in research on germ warfare. When the book appeared it contained information that was only beginning to be known to the public. *A Matter of Fact* is an excellent police procedural in which the attitudes and motivations of several officers are explored in depth. A young detective is tormented by guilt because of evidence tampered with by an unlucky colleague about to retire. The New York setting and the climate in which the police must work are thoughtfully portrayed.

In *The Traces of Brillhart*, the narrator-hero is journalist William Deacon. Deacon's girl friend (an independent young woman with a Phi Beta Kappa key and a Ph.D. in chemistry) and their friends the Dolans help him straighten things out. Supposedly murdered, Brillhart, a contemptible character from the popular music industry, returns from the dead only to be murdered definitively. *The Traces of Merrilee* is set on a luxury liner on which Deacon, his girl, and the Dolans share an elegant suite. Deacon has been hired to look after Merrilee Moore, an insecure but legendary movie star reminiscent of Marilyn Monroe. A campaign of terror is waged to keep her from making a movie. In this last crime novel, Brean is at his best. Deacon, modest and slightly self-mocking, is a thoroughly likable fellow. His encounters with the lovely Merrilee – every man's fantasy – are done with just the right touch.

Many mystery authors have used quotations from other works as chapter headings, and Brean follows this tradition. An original feature of his books, however, is his use of footnotes to provide additional information bearing on his story, to illuminate background, and to distinguish fact from fiction. Intelligent, with a lively curiosity and an unusual fund of knowledge about many things, Brean includes much fascinating material in his mysteries. His interests in music, travel, and good food are obvious, as is that in scientific developments in such fields as parapsychology and microbiology. Herbert Brean was witty, urbane, civilized, and created characters worthy of their author.

—Mary Helen Becker

BRETT, Michael. See **TRIPP, Miles.**

BRETT, Simon (Anthony Lee). British. Born in Worcester Park, Surrey, 28 October 1945. Educated at Dulwich College, London, 1956–64; Wadham College, Oxford (President, Oxford University Dramatic Society), B.A. (honours) in English 1967. Married Lucy Victoria McLaren in 1971; one daughter and one son. Radio Producer, BBC, London, 1967–77. Since 1977, Producer, London Weekend Television. Recipient: Writers Guild of Great Britain radio award, 1973. Agent: Michael Motley Ltd., 78 Gloucester Terrace, London W2 3HH. Address: 7 Graemesdyke Avenue, London S.W. 14, England.

CRIME PUBLICATIONS

Novels (series character: Charles Paris in all books)

   Cast, In Order of Disappearance.   London, Gollancz, 1975; New York, Scribner, 1976.

So Much Blood.   London, Gollancz, 1976; New York, Scribner, 1977.
Star Trap.   London, Gollancz, 1977; New York, Scribner, 1978.
An Amateur Corpse.   London, Gollancz, and New York, Scribner, 1978.
A Comedian Dies.   London, Gollancz, and New York, Scribner, 1979.

OTHER PUBLICATIONS

Plays

Mrs. Gladys Moxon (produced London, 1970).
Did You Sleep Well, and A Good Day at the Office (produced London, 1971).
Third Person (produced London, 1972).
Drake's Dream, music and lyrics by Lynne and Richard Riley (produced Worthing,
    Sussex, and London, 1977).

Other

Frank Muir Goes into ....   London, Robson Books, 1978.
A Second Frank Muir Goes into....   London, Robson Books, 1979.

Manuscript Collection: Mugar Memorial Library, Boston University

Simon Brett comments:
   Interested in the theatre from an early age, I pursued this hobby while at Oxford. All my
mysteries have had the same main character, Charles Paris, a middle-aged actor. He is
separated from his wife; his interests include drink and women, but do not include showbiz
affectation. The aim of the Charles Paris books is solely to entertain.

                              *   *   *

   Cast, In Order of Disappearance heralded the arrival of a promising newcomer, Simon
Brett, on the detective fiction scene. It had a relaxed humour, unpretentious plot, neat puzzle,
and real characters rather than cardboard cut-outs. There was also a welcome and credible
newcomer to the detective ranks called Charles Paris, a middle-aged and unsuccessful radio
actor whose vices appeared to have little effect upon the sharpness of his mind.
   Now that further Paris novels have appeared, there is little doubt that Simon Brett has
considerable talent, and makes excellent use of his theatrical knowledge. From the
unravelling in his first novel of the affairs of a theatrical tycoon, he turned his attention in *So
Much Blood* to the relationships of Paris's acquaintances on the fringe of the Edinburgh
Festival; Brett, with his own Festival experience to draw upon, paints a realistic picture of the
city in high season. Then in *Star Trap* Paris continues his tradition of getting work where he
can and meeting actors and actresses just as faded as he, when he appears in a new musical
which is beset by calamities too frequent to be coincidental.
   One recalls Ngaio Marsh's skilful portrayals of murder in theatrical settings, but Alleyn is a
gentlemanly intruder whereas Paris is a somewhat debauched protagonist; then again, Brett
is poking gentle fun at the acting fraternity whereas Miss Marsh is often matter-of-fact. All in
all, one can pay Simon Brett the greatest compliment by suggesting that he is capable of
making this area very much his own.

                                                                    —Melvyn Barnes

BREWER, Gil. American. Served in the United States Army during World War II. Worked as warehouseman, gas station attendant, cannery worker, and book seller. Lives in Florida. Agent: Scott Meredith Literary Agency, 845 Third Avenue, New York, New York 10022, U.S.A.

CRIME PUBLICATIONS

Novels

13 French Street. New York, Fawcett, 1951; London, New Fiction Press, 1952.
Satan Is a Woman. New York, Fawcett, 1951; London, New Fiction Press, 1952.
So Rich, So Dead. New York, Fawcett, 1951; London, New Fiction Press, 1952.
Flight to Darkness. New York, Fawcett, 1952.
Hell's Our Destination. New York, Fawcett, 1953; London, Fawcett, 1955.
A Killer Is Loose. New York, Fawcett, 1954; London, Moring, 1956.
Some Must Die. New York, Fawcett, 1954; London, Moring, 1956.
The Squeeze. New York, Ace, 1955.
77 Rue Paradis. New York, Fawcett, 1955; London, Red Seal, 1959.
And the Girl Screamed. New York, Fawcett, 1956; London, Fawcett, 1959.
The Angry Dream. New York, Bouregy, 1957; as *The Girl from Hateville*, Rockville Centre, New York, Zenith, 1958.
The Brat. New York, Fawcett, 1957; London, Fawcett, 1958.
Little Tramp. New York, Fawcett, 1957; London, Red Seal, 1959.
The Bitch. New York, Avon, 1958.
The Red Scarf. New York, Bouregy, 1958; London, Digit, 1959.
The Vengeful Virgin. New York, Fawcett, 1958; London, Muller, 1960.
Wild. New York, Fawcett, 1958; London, Fawcett, 1959.
Sugar. New York, Avon, 1959.
Wild to Possess. Derby, Connecticut, Monarch, 1959.
Angel. New York, Avon, 1960.
The Three-Way Split. New York, Fawcett, 1960.
Backwoods Teaser. New York, Fawcett, 1960.
Nude on Thin Ice. New York, Avon, 1960.
Appointment in Hell. Derby, Connecticut, Monarch, 1961.
A Taste of Sin. New York, Berkley, 1961.
Memory of Passion. New York, Lancer, 1963.
Play It Hard. Derby, Connecticut, Monarch, 1964.
The Hungry One. New York, Fawcett, 1966.
Sin for Me. New York, Banner, 1967.
The Tease. New York, Banner, 1967.
The Devil in Davos (novelization of tv play). New York, Ace, 1969.
Mediterranean Caper (novelization of tv play). New York, Ace, 1969.
Appointment in Cairo (novelization of tv play). New York, Ace, 1970.

Uncollected Short Stories

"With This Gun," in *Detective Tales*, March 1951.
"Final Appearance," in *Detective Tales*, October 1951.
"Moonshine," in *Manhunt* (New York), March 1955.
"I Saw Her Die," in *Manhunt* (New York), October 1955.
"Fog," in *Manhunt* (New York), February 1956.
"The Gesture," in *The Saint* (New York), March 1956.
"Home," in *Accused*, March 1956.

"Die, Darling, Die," in *The Hardboiled Lineup*, edited by Harry Widmer.   New York, Lion, 1956.

"On a Sunday Afternoon," in *Manhunt* (New York), January 1957.

"Prowler!," in *Manhunt* (New York), May 1957.

"Meet Me in the Dark," in *Manhunt* (New York), February 1958.

"Sauce for the Goose," in *Bad Girls*, edited by Leo Margulies.   New York, Fawcett, 1958.

"Teen-Age Casanova," in *Young and Deadly*, edited by Leo Margulies.   New York, Fawcett, 1959.

"This Petty Pace," in *Mystery Tales* (New York), June 1959.

"Cop," in *Mike Shayne Mystery Magazine* (New York), July 1968.

"Sympathy," in *Mike Shayne Mystery Magazine* (New York), June 1969.

"Trick," in *Alfred Hitchcock's Mystery Magazine* (North Palm Beach, Florida), November 1969.

"Small Bite," in *Alfred Hitchcock's Mystery Magazine* (North Palm Beach, Florida), February 1970.

"Goodbye, Now," in *Alfred Hitchcock's Get Me to the Wake on Time*.   New York, Dell, 1970.

"Token," in *Mike Shayne Mystery Magazine* (Los Angeles), June 1972.

"Blue Moon," in *Mike Shayne Mystery Magazine* (Los Angeles), April 1974.

"Deadly Little Green Eyes," in *Mike Shayne Mystery Magazine* (Los Angeles), February 1975.

"Cave in the Rain," in *87th Precinct* (New York), April 1975.

"Love-Lark," in *Executioner* (Los Angeles), April 1975.

"The Getaway," in *Mystery Monthly* (New York), June 1976.

"The Thinking Child," in *Mystery Monthly* (New York), September 1976.

"Swamp Tale," in *Mystery Monthly* (New York), December 1976.

"Hit," in *Alfred Hitchcock's Mystery Magazine* (New York), June 1977.

"Family," in *Alfred Hitchcock's Mystery Magazine* (New York), March 1978.

"The Closed Room," in *Alfred Hitchcock's Mystery Magazine* (New York), April 1979.

*   *   *

With the publication of his first novel, *13 French Street*, in 1951, Gil Brewer began a successful career as one of the leading writers of paperback originals.

Most of his thirty crime novels for Fawcett Gold Medal, Avon, Monarch, and others are built around a similar and classic theme: an ordinary man who becomes involved with, and is often corrupted and destroyed by, an evil or designing woman. (Most of his books – just as most of those by softcover "rivals" John D. MacDonald, Harry Whittington, and Day Keene – are set in the cities, small towns, and back-country areas of Florida.) His style is simple and direct, with sharp dialogue and considerable passion and intensity; at times it takes on an almost Hemingwayesque flavor, as in one of his best works, *The Three-Way Split*, where it is so reminiscent of Hemingway's *To Have and Have Not* that it approaches pastiche.

Other well-crafted Brewer books include *13 French Street*, *A Killer Is Loose*, *Some Must Die*, and *And the Girl Screamed*. But his most accomplished work is one of two hardcovers, *The Red Scarf* – a tense story of a motel owner caught up in a web of greed, treachery, and violence made all the more complex by his own weaknesses.

While he was producing novels Brewer also found time to write many short stories for the last of the detective pulps in the early 1950's and for later magazines.

—Bill Pronzini

BRIDGE, Ann. Pseudonym for Lady Mary Dolling O'Malley, née Sanders. British. Born in Shenley, Hertfordshire, 11 September 1889. Educated at the London School of Economics, diploma 1913. Married Sir Owen St. Clair O'Malley in 1913; two daughters and one son. Secretary, Charity Organization Society, London, 1911–13; British Red Cross representative in Hungary, 1940–41; worked with the Polish Red Cross, 1944–45, and did relief work in France after World War II. Fellow, Society of Antiquaries in Scotland. *Died 9 March 1974.*

CRIME PUBLICATIONS

Novels (series character: Julia Probyn in all books)

The Lighthearted Quest. London, Chatto and Windus, and New York, Macmillan, 1956.
The Portuguese Escape. London, Chatto and Windus, and New York, Macmillan, 1958.
The Numbered Account, with Susan Lowndes. London, Chatto and Windus, and New York, McGraw Hill, 1960.
Julia Involved (omnibus). New York, McGraw Hill, 1962.
The Tightening String. London, Chatto and Windus, and New York, McGraw Hill, 1962.
The Dangerous Islands. New York, McGraw Hill, 1963; London, Chatto and Windus, 1964.
Emergency in the Pyrenees. London, Chatto and Windus, and New York, McGraw Hill, 1965.
The Episode at Toledo. New York, McGraw Hill, 1966; London, Chatto and Windus, 1967.
The Malady in Madeira. New York, McGraw Hill, 1969; London, Chatto and Windus, 1970.
Julia in Ireland. New York, McGraw Hill, 1973.

OTHER PUBLICATIONS

Novels

Peking Picnic. London, Chatto and Windus, and Boston, Little Brown, 1932.
The Ginger Griffin. London, Chatto and Windus, and Boston, Little Brown, 1934.
Illyrian Spring. London, Chatto and Windus, and Boston, Little Brown, 1935.
Enchanter's Nightshade. London, Chatto and Windus, and Boston, Little Brown, 1937.
Four-Part Setting. London, Chatto and Windus, and Boston, Little Brown, 1939.
Frontier Passage. London, Chatto and Windus, and Boston, Little Brown, 1942.
Singing Waters. London, Chatto and Windus, 1945; New York, Macmillan, 1946.
And Then You Came. London, Chatto and Windus, 1948; New York, Macmillan, 1949.
The Dark Moment. London, Chatto and Windus, 1951; New York, Macmillan, 1952.
A Place to Stand. London, Chatto and Windus, and New York, Macmillan, 1953.

Short Stories

The Song in the House. London, Chatto and Windus, 1936.

Other

The Selective Traveller in Portugal, with Susan Lowndes. London, Evans, 1949; New
York, Knopf, 1952; revised edition, London, Chatto and Windus, 1958, 1967; New
York, McGraw Hill, 1961.
The House at Kilmartin (juvenile). London, Evans, 1951.
Portrait of My Mother. London, Chatto and Windus, 1955; as *A Family of Two Worlds*,
New York, Macmillan, 1955.
Facts and Fictions: Some Literary Recollections. London, Chatto and Windus, and
New York, McGraw Hill, 1968.
*Moments of Knowing: Some Personal Experiences Beyond Normal
Knowledge.* London, Hodder and Stoughton, and New York, McGraw Hill, 1970.
Permission to Resign: Goings-On in the Corridors of Power. London, Sidgwick and
Jackson, 1971.

*   *   *

Ann Bridge had a flair for the secret service adventure story. Her novels are in no sense
psychological studies of crime but rattling good tales of the activities, abroad and in the
Hebrides, of British Intelligence. In an Ann Bridge novel there is rarely any elaborate
espionage; her upper-class heroes are more likely to find themselves safeguarding mineral
deposits from Communist agents or securing weapons' blueprints which are rightfully
British. Comedy and tension come from the fact that Ann Bridge often has the difference
branches of intelligence working with vastly different methods, if not at cross purposes.

The high point of her fiction is her amateur agent, Julia Probyn, who, in *The Lighthearted
Quest*, accidentally discovers her powers of detection and deception when she goes to
Morocco to look for her missing cousin Colin Monro (who has deliberately "disappeared" –
he's a Secret Service agent) and uncovers not only Colin but a good deal else. Julia looks like a
dumb blonde – natural camouflage – but has wit, intelligence, charm, money, contacts, and
jet-set assurance. The professionals are never quite as good as the resourceful Julia; who else,
if a telephone is tapped, can switch to Gaelic?

Ann Bridge's settings – among them Portugal, Switzerland, and Peking – are always well-
researched, and she has a real sense of political tension, be it Spain in the 1930's or North
Africa in the 1950's. The international climate is such, she suggests, that the Secret Service is
a fact of life, not an exercise in fantasy.

—Ann Massa

BRIDGES, Victor (George de Freyne). British. Born in Clifton, Bristol, 14 March 1878.
Educated at Haileybury College. Married Margaret Lindsay Mackay in 1920 (died, 1957).
Worked in a bank, and as an actor in repertory before becoming a full-time writer. *Died 29
November 1972.*

<small>CRIME PUBLICATIONS</small>

Novels

Another Man's Shoes. London, Hodder and Stoughton, and New York, Doran, 1913.

The Man from Nowhere.   London, Mills and Boon, 1913.
A Rogue by Compulsion.   London and New York, Putnam, 1915.
Mr. Lyndon at Liberty.   London, Mills and Boon, 1915.
The Lady from Long Acre.   London, Mills and Boon, 1918; New York, Putnam, 1919.
Greensea Island.   London, Mills and Boon, and New York, Putnam, 1922.
The Red Lodge.   London, Mills and Boon, and New York, Doubleday, 1926.
The Girl in Black.   London, Mills and Boon, 1926; Philadelphia, Lippincott, 1927.
The King Comes Back.   London, Hodder and Stoughton, 1930.
The Secret of the Creek.   London, Hodder and Stoughton, and Boston, Houghton Mifflin, 1930.
Three Blind Mice.   London, Hodder and Stoughton, 1933; as *I Did Not Kill Osborne*, Philadelphia, Penn, 1934.
The Happy Murderers.   London, Hodder and Stoughton, 1933.
Peter in Peril.   London, Hodder and Stoughton, and Philadelphia, Penn, 1935.
Blue Silver.   London, Hodder and Stoughton, 1936.
It Happened in Essex.   London, Hodder and Stoughton, 1938.
The Seven Stars.   London, Hodder and Stoughton, 1939.
Dusky Night.   London, Hodder and Stoughton, 1940.
The House on the Saltings.   London, Hodder and Stoughton, 1941.
The Man Who Butted In.   London, Hodder and Stoughton, 1942.
The Gulls Fly Low.   London, Hodder and Stoughton, 1943.
It Never Rains –.   London, Macdonald, 1944.
Trouble on the Thames.   London, Macdonald, 1945.
The Man Who Limped.   London, Macdonald, 1947.
Accidents Will Happen.   London, Macdonald, 1948.
Quite Like Old Days.   London, Macdonald, 1949.
The Tenth Commandment.   London, Macdonald, 1951.
We Don't Want to Lose You.   London, Macdonald, 1952.
All Very Irregular.   London, Macdonald, 1953.
The Man Who Vanished.   London, Macdonald, 1954.
The Secret of the Saltings.   London, Macdonald, 1955.
What the Doctor Ordered.   London, Macdonald, 1956.
Exit Mr. Marlowe.   London, Macdonald, 1957.
The Creaking Gate.   London, Macdonald, 1958.
Secrecy Essential.   London, Macdonald, 1959.
The Girl from Belfast.   London, Macdonald, 1961.

Short Stories

Jetsam.   London, Mills and Boon, 1914; as *The Cruise of the "Scandal" and Other Stories*, New York, Putnam, 1920.

Uncollected Short Story

"White Violets," in *My Best Thriller.*   London, Faber, 1933.

OTHER PUBLICATIONS

Plays

Cleopatra (produced London, 1907).
Deadman's Pool, with T. C. Bridges (produced London, 1921).   London, Deane, 1929.
Another Pair of Spectacles.   London, French, 1923.
The Green Monkey (produced Northampton, 1929).   London, Deane, 1929.

Verse

A Handful of Verses.   London, Mills and Boon, 1924.
Edward FitzGerald and Other Verses.   London, Hodder and Stoughton, 1932.

Other

Camping Out, for Boy Scouts and Others.   London, Pearson, 1910.

*   *   *

Victor Bridges has a secure place among the writers of light fiction between the 1910's and the 1950's. He wrote adventure stories rather than mystery/thrillers, and referred to his works as such. His impressive output of novels included many varied backgrounds, but the real "Victor Bridges Country" lies among the tidal estuaries and creeks of Kent, Essex, and Suffolk between the North Foreland and Orford Ness. Here he created for us a "Tir-Nan-Og."

Greensea Island, an early success, was Osea Island in Essex, but his real love was the River Deben in Suffolk. Thinly disguised place-names of the Deben Valley – Bredbridge, Martlesea, etc. – abound.

The heroes are bachelors who invariably marry the heroines. They tend to be writers, artists, bibliophiles or inventors and belong to friendly Bohemian clubs. They have rooms in Chelsea or Hampstead with devoted landladies. Parents are never mentioned, but they sometimes have unpleasant double-crossing cousins. They and their friends can afford to own straight-stemmed, gaff-rigged yachts, old and shabby, but very seaworthy. Having become involved in the mystery the hero and his friend sail off to solve it. Heroines have slim, boyish figures, short curly hair, and grey or blue eyes. They are expert swimmers and sailors and good cooks. They, too, are generally orphans, but sometimes have half-brothers who are weak and crooked. They live in old abbeys or cottages with devoted old housekeepers. They are sweet and kind to everyone, especially to the mentally afflicted. The goodies behave impeccably in country inns but the villains often betray themselves by boorish bad habits. They have names like Dimitri, Orloff, or Van Doren.

The heroes generally get coshed or thrown overboard from yachts at sea. The heroines often have to swim to save either themselves or the heroes. Always there is a thrilling chase down river after the villains or to escape from them. They generally run aground due to faulty navigation and are wrecked, and the stolen jewels, Abbey Plate, or formulae for new explosives or alloys are invariably recovered intact.

Victor Bridges's plots are fairly and adroitly woven and his prose is crisp and flowing in the John Buchan style. All minor characters, even dogs, are lovingly drawn and we meet them as real people.

We are tantalised by frequent descriptions of food, whether recherché restaurant meals, tea and home-made cakes in cottages, or Fortnum and Mason hampers in the cabin.

It has been said that, if Holmes and Watson left Baker Street in a ghostly hansom-cab, there would never be wanting a crowd to follow that cab. Similarly at Liverpool Street Station, there will always be a queue to take tickets for Greensea Island, Fenwell Quay, and the Breden River to cruise with Victor Bridges in these enchanted waters.

—Harald Curjel

BRITTAIN, William.   American.   Born in Rochester, New York, 16 December 1930. Educated at Colgate University, Hamilton, New York; Brockport State Teachers College (now State University College), New York, B.S. 1952; Hofstra University, Hempstead, New York, M.S. 1959. Married Virginia Connorton in 1954; one daughter and one son. Teacher, Leroy Central Schools, New York, 1952–54. Since 1954, English Teacher, Lawrence Junior High School, New York. Address: 395 South Long Beach Avenue, Freeport, New York 11520, U.S.A.

CRIME PUBLICATIONS

Uncollected Short Stories

"Joshua," in *Alfred Hitchcock's Mystery Magazine* (North Palm Beach, Florida), October 1964.

"The Man Who Read John Dickson Carr" and "The Man Who Read Ellery Queen," in *Ellery Queen's Crime Carousel.*   New York, New American Library, 1966.

"The Man Who Didn't Read," in *Ellery Queen's Mystery Magazine* (New York), May 1966.

"Mr. Lightning" (as James Knox), in *Ellery Queen's Mystery Magazine* (New York), July 1966.

"The Woman Who Read Rex Stout," in *Ellery Queen's Mystery Magazine* (New York), July 1966.

"The Boy Who Read Agatha Christie," in *Ellery Queen's Mystery Magazine* (New York), December 1966.

"Mr. Strang Gives a Lecture," in *Ellery Queen's Mystery Magazine* (New York), March 1967.

"Mr. Strang Performs an Experiment," in *Ellery Queen's Mystery Parade.*   New York, New American Library, 1968.

"Mr. Strang Sees a Play," in *Ellery Queen's Mystery Magazine* (New York), March 1968.

"The Zaretski Chain," in *Ellery Queen's Mystery Magazine* (New York), June 1968.

"The Last Word" (as James Knox), in *Ellery Queen's Mystery Magazine* (New York), June 1968.

"Mr. Strang Takes a Field Trip," in *Ellery Queen's Mystery Magazine* (New York), December 1968.

"The Man Who Read Sir Arthur Conan Doyle," in *Ellery Queen's Murder Menu.*   Cleveland, World, 1969.

"The Second Sign in the Melon Patch," in *Ellery Queen's Mystery Magazine* (New York), January 1969.

"Mr. Strang Pulls a Switch," in *Ellery Queen's Mystery Magazine* (New York), June 1969.

"That Day on the Knob," in *Ellery Queen's Mystery Magazine* (New York), September 1969.

"Hand," in *Alfred Hitchcock's Mystery Magazine* (North Palm Beach, Florida), October 1969.

"Mr. Strang Finds the Answers," in *Rogue's Gallery*, edited by Walter Gibson.   New York, Doubleday, 1970.

"Just About Average," in *Alfred Hitchcock's Mystery Magazine* (North Palm Beach, Florida), June 1970.

"A Gallon of Gas," in *Alfred Hitchcock's Mystery Magazine* (North Palm Beach, Florida), April 1971.

"Mr. Strang Lifts a Glass," in *Ellery Queen's Mystery Magazine* (New York), May 1971.

"Mr. Strang Finds an Angle," in *Ellery Queen's Mystery Magazine* (New York), June 1971.

"Mr. Strang Hunts a Bear," in *Ellery Queen's Mystery Magazine* (New York), November 1971.

"Falling Object," in *Ellery Queen's Mystery Bag.*   Cleveland, World, 1972.

"The Driver," in *Alfred Hitchcock's Mystery Magazine* (North Palm Beach, Florida), January 1972.

"Mr. Strang Checks a Record," in *Ellery Queen's Mystery Magazine* (New York), February 1972.

"Wynken, Blynken and Nod," in *Ellery Queen's Mystery Magazine* (New York), April 1972.

"The Artificial Liar," in *Alfred Hitchcock's Mystery Magazine* (North Palm Beach, Florida), April 1972.

"Mr. Strang Finds a Car," in *Ellery Queen's Mystery Magazine* (New York), July 1972.

"Mr. Strang Makes a Snowman," in *Ellery Queen's Mystery Magazine* (New York), December 1972.

"Mr. Strang Amends a Legend," in *Ellery Queen's Mystery Magazine* (New York), February 1973.

"The Sonic Boomer," in *Alfred Hitchcock's Mystery Magazine* (North Palm Beach, Florida), February 1973.

"The Scarab Ring," in *Alfred Hitchcock's Mystery Magazine* (North Palm Beach, Florida), May 1973.

"Mr. Strang Invents a Strange Device," in *Ellery Queen's Mystery Magazine* (New York), June 1973.

"A State of Preparedness," in *Alfred Hitchcock's Mystery Magazine* (North Palm Beach, Florida), September 1973.

"Mr. Strang Follows Through," in *Ellery Queen's Mystery Magazine* (New York), September 1973.

"The Button," in *Alfred Hitchcock's Mystery Magazine* (North Palm Beach, Florida), October 1973.

"The Platt Avenue Irregulars," in *Alfred Hitchcock's Mystery Magazine* (North Palm Beach, Florida), November 1973.

"Mr. Strang Discovers a Bug," in *Ellery Queen's Mystery Magazine* (New York), November 1973.

"Mr. Strang under Arrest," in *Ellery Queen's Mystery Magazine* (New York), February 1974.

"He Can't Die Screaming," in *Ellery Queen's Mystery Magazine* (New York), February 1974.

"Waiting for Harry," in *Alfred Hitchcock's Mystery Magazine* (North Palm Beach, Florida), March 1974.

"The Man Who Read Dashiell Hammett," in *Ellery Queen's Mystery Magazine* (New York), May 1974.

"The Impossible Footprint," in *Alfred Hitchcock's Mystery Magazine* (North Palm Beach, Florida), November 1974.

"I'm Back, Little Sister," in *Alfred Hitchcock's Mystery Magazine* (North Palm Beach, Florida), December 1974.

"The Man Who Read Georges Simenon," in *Ellery Queen's Mystery Magazine* (New York), January 1975.

"The Girl Who Read John Creasey," in *Ellery Queen's Mystery Magazine* (New York), March 1975.

"Aunt Abigail's Wall Safe," in *Alfred Hitchcock's Mystery Magazine* (North Palm Beach, Florida), May 1975.

"Mr. Strang and the Cat Lady," in *Ellery Queen's Mystery Magazine* (New York), May 1975.

"Yellowbelly," in *Alfred Hitchcock's Mystery Magazine* (North Palm Beach, Florida), October 1975.

"Mr. Strang, Armchair Detective," in *Ellery Queen's Mystery Magazine* (New York), December 1975.

"Mr. Strang Picks Up the Pieces," in *Best Detective Stories of the Year 1976*, edited by Edward D. Hoch.   New York, Dutton, 1976.

"Historical Errors," in *Alfred Hitchcock's Mystery Magazine* (New York), February 1976.

"A Private Little War," in *Alfred Hitchcock's Mystery Magazine* (New York), May 1976.

"Mr. Strang Battles a Deadline," in *Ellery Queen's Mystery Magazine* (New York), June 1976.

"One Big Happy Family," in *Alfred Hitchcock's Mystery Magazine* (New York), September 1976.

"Mr. Strang Accepts a Challenge," in *Ellery Queen's Mystery Magazine* (New York), November 1976.

"The Second Reason," in *Alfred Hitchcock's Mystery Magazine* (New York), February 1977.

"The Ferret Man," in *Antaeus* (New York), Spring–Summer 1977.

"The Man Who Read G. K. Chesterton," in *Ellery Queen's Who's Who of Whodunits*. New York, Davis, 1977.

"Mr. Strang Takes a Hand," in *Masterpieces of Mystery – Part II*, edited by Ellery Queen. New York, Davis, 1978.

"Mr. Strang Buys a Big H," in *Ellery Queen's Mystery Magazine* (New York), April 1978.

"The Men Who Read Isaac Asimov," in *Ellery Queen's Mystery Magazine* (New York), May 1978.

OTHER PUBLICATIONS

Other

Survival Outdoors. Derby, Connecticut, Monarch, 1977.
All the Money in the World (juvenile). New York, Harper, 1979.

William Brittain comments:

Much of my mystery writing consists of two series, "The Man Who Read ..." and the Mr. Strang stories. Both series first appeared in the *Ellery Queen's Mystery Magazine*, and they were begun with the help and encouragement of Frederic Dannay. Since Mr. Strang, like me, is a teacher, I often find the germ of a story idea coming from commonplace happenings during my teaching day. However, unlike Aldershot High school, where Mr. Strang holds sway, the school where I teach can hardly be considered a hotbed of crime.

One of the fringe benefits of my writing has been the opportunity to meet other mystery writers, primarily through the Mystery Writers of America. And in total antithesis to the literary violence they so lovingly create, they're some of the friendliest and most helpful and obliging people it has been my pleasure to know.

*   *   *

William Brittain's mystery writing has thus far been confined to the short story field, where he has produced two series of interest. The earliest of these, which might be called "The Man Who Read ..." series, began with "The Man Who Read John Dickson Carr." A pastiche of Carr's plots and style, it involves a murderer who is inspired to devise an intricate locked-room problem. He kills his victim and escapes from the room, but makes one mistake. The story is one of Brittain's best. It was followed by other stories using a similar technique and involving sleuths or criminals who were readers of Ellery Queen, Agatha Christie, Arthur Conan Doyle, Rex Stout, G. K. Chesterton, Isaac Asimov, and others. There was even one story titled "The Man Who Didn't Read."

A longer series with greater potential has been built around Mr. Strang, a high school science teacher in a school which must be fashioned just a bit after the one in which Brittain himself teaches. The first of these stories was "Mr. Strang Gives a Lecture," in which the teacher's car is used in a holdup. Mr. Strang examines the car and finds evidence of the criminal's identity. In "Mr. Strang Picks Up the Pieces" the teacher discovers how the window of a jewelry store could be broken by a seemingly invisible weapon. Often in his cases Mr. Strang comes to the aid of a student falsely accused of a crime. The result is a portrait of modern high school life combined with a solid mystery plot.

—Edward D. Hoch

BROCK, Lynn. Pseudonym for Alister McAllister; also wrote as Anthony Wharton. Irish. Born in Dublin in 1877. Educated at the National University of Ireland, Dublin, B.A. Served in British intelligence and in the machine gun corps, 1915–18. Chief Clerk, National University of Ireland, 1908–14. *Died 6 April 1943.*

CRIME PUBLICATIONS

Novels (series character: Colonel Gore)

> *The Deductions of Colonel Gore.* London, Collins, 1924; New York, Harper, 1925; as *The Barrington Mystery*, Collins, 1932.
> *Colonel Gore's Second Case.* London, Collins, 1925; New York, Harper, 1926.
> *Colonel Gore's Third Case: The Kink.* London, Collins, 1925; New York, Harper, 1927.
> *The Two of Diamonds.* London, Collins, 1926.
> *The Slip-Carriage Mystery* (Gore). London, Collins, and New York, Harper, 1928.
> *The Dagwort Combe Murder.* London, Collins, 1929; as *The Stoke Silver Case*, New York, Harper, 1929.
> *The Mendip Mystery* (Gore). London, Collins, 1929; as *Murder at the Inn*, New York, Harper, 1929.
> *Q.E.D.* (Gore). London, Collins, 1930; as *Murder on the Bridge*, New York, Harper, 1930.
> *Nightmare.* London, Collins, 1932.
> *The Silver Sickle Case.* London, Collins, 1938.
> *Fourfingers.* London, Collins, 1939.
> *The Riddle of the Roost.* London, Collins, 1939.
> *The Stoat.* London, Collins, 1940.

OTHER PUBLICATIONS as Anthony Wharton

Novels

> *Joan of Overbarrow.* New York, Doran, 1921; London, Duckworth, 1922.
> *The Man on the Hill.* London, Unwin, 1923.
> *Be Good, Sweet Maid.* London, Unwin, and New York, Boni and Liveright, 1924.
> *Evil Communications.* London, Unwin, 1926.

Plays

> *Irene Wycherley* (produced London, 1907; New York, 1908).

Nocturne (produced London, 1908; New York, 1918).   London and New York, French, 1913.

At the Barn (produced London, 1912; New York, 1914).   London, Joseph Williams, and New York, French, 1912.

Sylvia Greer (produced London, 1912).

13, Simon Street (produced London, 1913; as *The House in Simon Street*, produced London, 1913).   London and New York, French, 1913.

A Guardian Angel (produced London, 1915).

The Riddle, with Morley Roberts (produced London, 1916).

Needles and Pins (produced London, 1929).

*   *   *

Under the pseudonym Lynn Brock, the Irish author Alister McAllister created the memorable Colonel Gore in a series of often reprinted and widely translated detective novels that won the praise of even the exacting Dorothy L. Sayers.

A member of a military family and a graduate of Harrow, Colonel Warwick Gore was stationed in India before serving a year on the Rhine in World War I. After resigning his commission, he spent a year on a film-making expedition to Central Africa followed by six years in business in Rhodesia. He returns to England (and, unknowingly, to a career of detection) in 1922 to claim a small legacy, just in time to help "Pickles" Melhuish, the stalwart, pert, and attractive sweetheart of his youth now married to a taciturn London physician. In the first novel of the series, *The Deductions of Colonel Gore*, Gore extricates Mrs. Melhuish from an awkward and involved series of crimes centering around blackmail, murder, and a set of African daggers Gore had given the couple as a wedding gift. Gore establishes a detective agency in *Colonel Gore's Second Case*, an agency which later solves the seemingly motiveless murder of Pickles's husband in *Q.E.D.*

Like all of Brock's detective fiction, the Gore novels display a complexity of plot and style which some readers find confusing. All begin with a crime, often minor and seemingly easily explained, which leads to a baffling number of esoteric clues, red herrings, unusual suspects, and bizarre motives. However, Gore's direct approach to ratiocination and his bluffly good-humored willingness to share his discoveries with slow-witted associates and policemen usually make the novels both intelligible and interesting. Even so, *Colonel Gore's Second Case* provides a 25-page supplement to make its solution clear to the reader.

McAllister's preference for rural settings and unusual crimes further complicates his works. These can range from a burking in a disreputable rural roadhouse (in *The Mendip Mystery*) to a stabbing in a moving railroad car (in *The Slip-Carriage Mystery*) and a drowning in an artificial lake near an isolated pleasure pagoda (in *The Kink*). Colonel Gore must usually cover a lot of physical territory to solve a case.

Finest of the Colonel Gore series, *The Kink* represents McAllister's talents at their best. While investigating the theft of some family letters for a distinguished statesman and peer, Gore discovers that his employer's family suffers from a depravity partly hereditary, partly in keeping with the decadent nature of the times. The distinguished statesman is in fact concerned about the theft of a pornographic film of which he is the star, and his beautiful daughter stages elaborate Beardsleyesque orgies on the pleasure grounds of her father's estate. When the peer is murdered, Gore uncovers a squalid web of family history, jealousy, blackmail, cruelty, and insanity. As in the American hard-boiled detective novel, the noble are secretly base, the pure secretly foul. Unlike the American detective, however, Gore can purge the family's social ills, saving future victims and restoring order. Gore's detective abilities and Brock's literary ones appear at their finest.

—Katherine Staples

BROWN, Carter. Pseudonym for Alan Geoffrey Yates. British. Born in London, 1 August 1923. Educated at schools in Essex. Served in the Royal Navy, 1942–46: Lieutenant. Married Denise Sinclair Mackellar; one daughter and three sons. Sound Recordist, Gaumont-British Films, London, 1946–48; salesman in Sydney, Australia, 1948–51; public relations staff member, Qantas Empire Airways, Sydney, 1951–53. Since 1953, full-time writer. Agent: Scott Meredith Literary Agency, 580 Fifth Avenue, New York, New York 10036, U.S.A. Address: 254 Vale Road, Sydney, New South Wales, Australia.

CRIME PUBLICATIONS

Novels as Carter Brown, Peter Carter Brown, and Peter Carter-Brown (series characters: Larry Baker; Danny Boyd; Paul Donavan; Rick Holman; Andy Kane; Randy Roberts; Mavis Seidlitz; Al Wheeler)

Venus Unarmed. Sydney, Transport, 1953.
The Mermaid Murmurs Murder. Sydney, Transport, 1953.
The Lady Is Chased. Sydney, Transport, 1953.
The Frame Is Beautiful. Sydney, Transport, 1953.
Fraulein Is Feline. Sydney, Transport, 1953.
Wreath for Rebecca. Sydney, Transport, 1953(?).
The Black Widow Weeps. Sydney, Transport, 1953(?).
Penthouse Passout. Sydney, Transport, 1953(?); as *Hot Seat for a Honey*, Sydney, Horwitz, 1956.
Shady Lady. Sydney, Transport, 1953(?).
Strip Without Tease. Sydney, Transport, 1953(?).
Trouble Is a Dame. Sydney, Transport, 1953(?).
Lethal in Love. Sydney, Transport, 1953(?); as *The Minx Is Murder*, Sydney, Horwitz, 1957.
Murder – Paris Fashion. Sydney, Transport, 1954.
Nemesis Wore Nylons. Sydney, Transport, 1954.
Maid for Murder. Sydney, Transport, 1954.
Murder Is My Mistress. Sydney, Associated General Publications, 1954; revised edition, as *The Savage Salome* (Boyd), Sydney, Horwitz, and New York, New American Library, 1961.
Homicide Hoyden. Sydney, Horwitz, 1954.
A Morgue Amour. Sydney, Horwitz, 1954.
The Killer Is Kissable. Sydney, Horwitz, 1954.
Curtains for a Chorine. Sydney, Horwitz, 1955.
Shamus, Your Slip Is Showing. Sydney, Horwitz, 1955.
Cutie Cashed His Chips. Sydney, Horwitz, 1955; revised edition, as *The Million Dollar Babe*, New York, New American Library, 1961.
Honey, Here's Your Hearse! (Seidlitz). Sydney, Horwitz, 1955.
The Two-Timing Blonde. Sydney, Horwitz, 1955.
Sob-Sister Cries Murder. Sydney, Horwitz, 1955.
The Blonde (Wheeler). Sydney, Horwitz, 1955; New York, New American Library, 1958; London, New English Library, 1964.
Curves for the Coroner. Sydney, Horwitz, 1955.
Miss Called Murder. Sydney, Horwitz, 1955.
Swan Song for a Siren. Sydney, Horwitz, 1955; revised edition, as *Charlie Sent Me!* (Baker), Horwitz, and New York, New American Library, 1963; London, New English Library, 1965.
A Bullet for My Baby (Seidlitz). Sydney, Horwitz, 1955.
Kiss and Kill. Sydney, Horwitz, 1955.
Kiss Me Deadly. Sydney, Horwitz, 1955.
The Wench Is Wicked. Sydney, Horwitz, 1955.

Shroud for My Sugar.   Sydney, Horwitz, 1955.
Lead Astray.   Sydney, Horwitz, 1955.
Lipstick Larceny.   Sydney, Horwitz, 1955.
The Hoodlum Was a Honey.   Sydney, Horwitz, 1956.
Murder by Miss-Demeanor.   Sydney, Horwitz, 1956.
Darling You're Doomed.   Sydney, Horwitz, 1956.
No Halo for Hedy.   Sydney, Horwitz, 1956.
Donna Died Laughing.   Sydney, Horwitz, 1956.
Blonde, Beautiful, and – Blam!   Sydney, Horwitz, 1956.
Strictly for Felony.   Sydney, Horwitz, 1956.
Booty for a Babe.   Sydney, Horwitz, 1956.
Delilah Was Deadly.   Sydney, Horwitz, 1956.
Blonde Verdict (Wheeler).   Sydney, Horwitz, 1956.
The Eve of His Dying.   Sydney, Horwitz, 1956.
Model of No Virtue.   Sydney, Horwitz, 1956.
My Darling Is Deadpan.   Sydney, Horwitz, 1956.
The Bribe Was Beautiful.   Sydney, Horwitz, 1956.
Death of a Doll.   Sydney, Horwitz, 1956; revised edition (Holman), 1960; as *The Ever-Loving Blues*, New York, New American Library, 1961.
The Lady Has No Convictions.   Sydney, Horwitz, 1956.
Baby, You're Guilt-Edged.   Sydney, Horwitz, 1956.
No Harp for My Angel.   Sydney, Horwitz, 1956.
Hi-Jack for a Jill.   Sydney, Horwitz, 1956.
Bid the Babe By-By.   Sydney, Horwitz, 1956.
Meet Murder, My Angel.   Sydney, Horwitz, 1956.
Caress Before Killing.   Sydney, Horwitz, 1956.
Sweetheart, This Is Homicide.   Sydney, Horwitz, 1956.
That's Piracy, My Pet.   Sydney, Horwitz, 1957; revised edition, as *Bird in a Guilt-Edged Cage* (Kane), 1963; as *The Guilt-Edged Cage*, New York, New American Library, 1962; London, New English Library, 1963.
Last Note for a Lovely.   Sydney, Horwitz, 1957.
Blonde, Bad, and Beautiful.   Sydney, Horwitz, 1957(?); revised edition, as *The Hong Kong Caper* (Kane), Horwitz, and New York, New American Library, 1962; London, New English Library, 1963.
Doll for the Big House.   Sydney, Horwitz, 1957; revised edition, as *The Bombshell* (Wheeler), Horwitz, and New York, New American Library, 1960; London, New English Library, 1968.
Stripper, You've Sinned.   Sydney, Horwitz, 1957(?).
Madam, You're Mayhem.   Sydney, Horwitz, 1957.
Good Morning, Mavis (Seidlitz).   Sydney, Horwitz, 1957(?).
Sinner, You Slay Me!   Sydney, Horwitz, 1957.
No Law Against Angels.   Sydney, Horwitz, 1957; revised edition, as *The Body* (Wheeler), New York, New American Library, 1958; London, New English Library, 1963.
Wreath for a Redhead.   Sydney, Horwitz, 1957.
The Unorthodox Corpse.   Sydney, Horwitz, 1957; revised edition (Wheeler), Horwitz, and New York, New American Library, 1961.
Ten Grand Tallulah and Temptation.   Sydney, Horwitz, 1957.
Cutie Wins a Corpse.   Sydney, Horwitz, 1957; revised edition, as *Graves, I Dig!*, Horwitz, and New York, New American Library, 1960.
Eve, It's Extortion.   Sydney, Horwitz, 1957; revised edition, as *Walk Softly Witch!* (Wheeler), Horwitz, 1959; as *The Victim*, New York, New American Library, 1959.
Bella Donna Was Poison.   Sydney, Horwitz, 1957.
Murder Wears a Mantilla.   Sydney, Horwitz, 1957; revised edition (Seidlitz), New York, New American Library, and London, New English Library, 1962.

Chorine Makes a Killing (Wheeler).   Sydney, Horwitz, 1957.

So Lovely She Lies.   Sydney, Horwitz, 1958.

Ice-Cold in Ermine.   Sydney, Horwitz, 1958.

Goddess Gone Bad.   Sydney, Horwitz, 1958.

No Body She Knows.   Sydney, Horwitz, 1958; with *Slaughter in Satin*, 1960.

Cutie Takes the Count.   Sydney, Horwitz, 1958.

No Future, Fair Lady.   Sydney, Horwitz, 1958.

Hi-Fi Fadeout.   Sydney, Horwitz, 1958.

Widow Bewitched.   Sydney, Horwitz, 1958.

Luck Was No Lady.   Sydney, Horwitz, 1958(?).

A Siren Sounds Off.   Sydney, Horwitz, 1958; with *Moonshine Momma*, 1960; revised
    edition, as *The Myopic Mermaid*, New York, New American Library, 1961.

Tempt a Tigress.   Sydney, Horwitz, 1958(?).

The Charmer Chased.   Sydney, Horwitz, 1958(?).

High Fashion in Homicide.   Sydney, Horwitz, 1958.

Deadly Miss.   Sydney, Horwitz, 1958.

Sinfully Yours.   Sydney, Horwitz, 1958(?).

Death on the Downbeat.   Sydney, Horwitz, 1958; revised edition, as *The Corpse*
    (Wheeler), New York, New American Library, 1958; London, New English Library,
    1963.

The Lover (Wheeler).   Sydney, Horwitz, 1958; New York, New American Library,
    1959; London, New English Library, 1963.

The Mistress (Wheeler).   Sydney, Horwitz, 1958; New York, New American Library,
    1959; London, New English Library, 1963.

The Loving and the Dead (Seidlitz).   Sydney, Horwitz, and New York, New American
    Library, 1959; London, New English Library, 1966.

So Deadly, Sinner! (Boyd).   Sydney, Horwitz, 1959; as *Walk Softly, Witch*, New York,
    New American Library, 1959; London, New English Library, 1965.

The Passionate (Wheeler).   Sydney, Horwitz, and New York, New American Library,
    1959; London, New English Library, 1966.

None But the Lethal Heart (Seidlitz).   Sydney, Horwitz, and New York, New American
    Library, 1959; London, New English Library, 1967; as *The Fabulous*, Horwitz, 1961.

The Wanton (Wheeler).   Sydney, Horwitz, and New York, New American Library,
    1959; London, New English Library, 1968.

Suddenly by Violence (Boyd).   Sydney, Horwitz, and New York, New American
    Library, 1959.

The Dame (Wheeler).   Sydney, Horwitz, and New York, New American Library,
    1959; London, New English Library, 1966.

Terror Comes Creeping (Boyd).   Sydney, Horwitz, and New York, New American
    Library, 1959; London, New English Library, 1967.

The Desired (Wheeler).   Sydney, Horwitz, 1959; New York, New American Library,
    1960; London, New English Library, 1966.

The Wayward Wahine (Boyd).   Sydney, Horwitz, and New York, New American
    Library, 1960; London, New English Library, 1966; as *The Wayward*, Horwitz,
    1962.

Tomorrow Is Murder (Seidlitz).   Sydney, Horwitz, and New York, New American
    Library, 1960.

The Temptress (Wheeler).   Sydney, Horwitz, and New York, New American Library,
    1960; London, New English Library, 1964.

The Brazen (Wheeler).   Sydney, Horwitz, and New York, New American Library,
    1960; London, New English Library, 1962.

The Dream Is Deadly (Boyd).   Sydney, Horwitz, and New York, New American
    Library, 1960; London, New English Library, 1962.

Lament for a Lousy Lover (Seidlitz, Wheeler).   New York, New American Library,
    1960; London, New English Library, 1968.

The Stripper (Wheeler). Sydney, Horwitz, and New York, New American Library, 1961; London, New English Library, 1962.

The Tigress (Wheeler). Sydney, Horwitz, and New York, New American Library, 1961; as *Wildcat*, London, New English Library, 1962.

The Exotic (Wheeler). Sydney, Horwitz, and New York, New American Library, 1961; London, New English Library, 1962.

The Seductress (Boyd). Sydney, Horwitz, 1961; as *The Sad-Eyed Seductress*, New York, New American Library, 1961; London, New English Library, 1962.

Zelda (Holman). Sydney, Horwitz, and New York, New American Library, 1961; London, New English Library, 1962.

Angel! (Wheeler). Sydney, Horwitz, New York, New American Library, and London, New English Library, 1962.

The Ice-Cold Nude (Boyd). Sydney, Horwitz, New York, New American Library, and London, New English Library, 1962.

The Hellcat (Wheeler). Sydney, Horwitz, New York, New American Library, and London, New English Library, 1962.

Murder in the Harem Club (Holman). Sydney, Horwitz, 1962; as *Murder in the Key Club*, New York, New American Library, and London, New English Library, 1962.

The Lady Is Transparent (Wheeler). Sydney, Horwitz, and New York, New American Library, 1962; London, New English Library, 1963.

The Dumdum Murder (Wheeler). Sydney, Horwitz, and New York, New American Library, 1962; London, New English Library, 1963.

Lover, Don't Come Back! (Boyd). Sydney, Horwitz, and New York, New American Library, 1962; London, New English Library, 1963.

The Murder among Us (Holman). Sydney, Horwitz, and New York, New American Library, 1962; London, New English Library, 1964.

Blonde on the Rocks (Holman). Sydney, Horwitz, and New York, New American Library, 1963; London, New English Library, 1964.

Girl in a Shroud (Wheeler). Sydney, Horwitz, and New York, New American Library, 1963; London, New English Library, 1964.

The Sinners (Wheeler). Sydney, Horwitz, 1963; as *The Girl Who Was Possessed*, New York, New American Library, and London, New English Library, 1963.

The Jade-Eyed Jinx (Holman). Sydney, Horwitz, 1963; as *The Jade-Eyed Jungle*, New York, New American Library, 1963; London, New English Library, 1964.

The Lady Is Not Available (Wheeler). Sydney, Horwitz, 1963; as *The Lady Is Available*, New York, New American Library, 1963; London, New English Library, 1964.

Nymph to the Slaughter (Boyd). Sydney, Horwitz, and New York, New American Library, 1963; London, New English Library, 1964.

The Passionate Pagan (Boyd). Sydney, Horwitz, and New York, New American Library, 1963; London, New English Library, 1964.

The Ballad of Loving Jenny (Holman). Sydney, Horwitz, 1963; as *The White Bikini*, New York, New American Library, 1963; London, New English Library, 1965.

The Scarlet Flush. Sydney, Horwitz, and New York, New American Library, 1963; London, New English Library, 1965.

The Silken Nightmare (Boyd). Sydney, Horwitz, and New York, New American Library, 1963; London, New English Library, 1964.

The Wind-Up Doll (Holman). Sydney, Horwitz, 1963; New York, New American Library, 1964; London, New English Library, 1965.

The Dance of Death (Wheeler). Sydney, Horwitz, and New York, New American Library, 1964; London, New English Library, 1965.

The Never-Was Girl (Holman). Sydney, Horwitz, and New York, New American Library, 1964; London, New English Library, 1965.

The Vixen (Wheeler). Sydney, Horwitz, 1964; as *The Velvet Vixen*, New York, New American Library, 1964; London, New English Library, 1965.

The Bump and Grind Murders (Seidlitz).   New York, New American Library, 1964;
London, New English Library, 1965.

Murder Is a Package Deal (Holman).   Sydney, Horwitz, and New York, New
American Library, 1964; London, New English Library, 1965.

Who Killed Dr. Sex? (Holman).   New York, New American Library, 1964; London,
New English Library, 1965.

Catch Me a Phoenix! (Boyd).   Sydney, Horwitz, and New York, New American
Library, 1965; London, New English Library, 1966.

Yogi Shrouds Yolanda, and Poison Ivy.   Sydney, Horwitz, 1965.

A Corpse for Christmas (Wheeler).   Sydney, Horwitz, and New York, New American
Library, 1965; London, New English Library 1966.

No Blonde Is an Island (Baker).   Sydney, Horwitz, New York, New American Library,
and London, New English Library, 1965.

Nude – with a View (Holman).   Sydney, Horwitz, and New York, New American
Library, 1965; London, New English Library, 1966.

The Girl from Outer Space (Holman).   New York, New American Library, 1965;
London, New English Library, 1966.

Homicide Harem, and Felon Angel.   Sydney, Horwitz, 1965.

The Sometime Wife (Boyd).   New York, New American Library, 1965; London, New
English Library, 1966.

The Hammer of Thor (Wheeler).   New York, New American Library, 1965.

Blonde on a Broomstick (Holman).   Sydney, Horwitz, New York, New American
Library, and London, New English Library, 1966.

So What Killed the Vampire? (Baker).   Sydney, Horwitz, and New York, New America
Library, 1966; London, New English Library, 1967.

Play Now – Kill Later (Holman).   Sydney, Horwitz, and New York, New American
Library, 1966.

The Black Lace Hangover (Boyd).   Sydney, Horwitz, and New York, New American
Library, 1966; London, New English Library, 1969.

No Tears from the Widow (Holman).   Sydney, Horwitz, and New York, New American
Library, 1966; London, New English Library, 1968.

Target for Their Dark Desire (Wheeler).   New York, New American Library, 1966;
London, New English Library, 1968.

The Deadly Kitten (Holman).   New York, New American Library, 1967.

House of Sorcery (Boyd).   New York, New American Library, 1967; London, New
English Library, 1968.

No Time for Leola (Holman).   Sydney, Horwitz, and New York, New American
Library, 1967.

The Plush-Lined Coffin (Wheeler).   Sydney, Horwitz, and New York, New American
Library, 1967; London, New English Library, 1968.

Seidlitz and the Super-Spy.   Sydney, Horwitz, and New York, New American Library,
1967; as *The Super-Spy*, London, New English Library, 1968.

Until Temptation Do Us Part (Wheeler).   Sydney, Horwitz, and New York, New
American Library, 1967; London, New English Library, 1968.

The Deep Cold Green (Wheeler).   Sydney, Horwitz, and New York, New American
Library, 1968.

The Mini-Murders (Boyd).   Sydney, Horwitz, and New York, New American Library,
1968.

Had I But Groaned (Baker).   Sydney, Horwitz, and New York, New American Library,
1968; as *The Witches*, London, New English Library, 1969.

Die Anytime, After Tuesday! (Holman).   Sydney, Horwitz, and New York, New
American Library, 1969.

The Flagelator (Holman).   Sydney, Horwitz, and New York, New American Library,
1969.

Murder Is the Message (Boyd).   New York, New American Library, 1969.

Only the Very Rich? (Boyd). Sydney, Horwitz, and New York, New American Library, 1969.

The Streaked-Blonde Slave (Holman). New York, New American Library, 1969.

The Up-Tight Blonde (Wheeler). New York, New American Library, 1969.

Burden of Guilt (Wheeler). New York, New American Library, 1970.

The Coffin Bird (Boyd). New York, New American Library, 1970.

A Good Year for Dwarfs? (Holman). New York, New American Library, 1970.

The Hang-Up Kid (Holman). Sydney, Horwitz, and New York, New American Library, 1970.

True Son of the Beast! (Baker). New York, New American Library, 1970.

Where Did Charity Go? (Holman). New American Library, 1970.

The Coven (Holman). Sydney, Horwitz, and New York, New American Library, 1971.

The Creative Murders (Wheeler). Sydney, Horwitz, and New York, New American Library, 1971.

The Invisible Flamini (Holman). New York, New American Library, 1971.

Murder in the Family Way (Roberts). New York, New American Library, 1971.

The Sex Clinic (Boyd). Sydney, Horwitz, 1971; New York, New American Library, 1972.

W.H.O.R.E. (Wheeler). New York, New American Library, 1971.

The Clown (Wheeler). New York, New American Library, 1972.

The Angry Amazons (Roberts, Boyd). Sydney, Horwitz, and New York, New American Library, 1972.

The Aseptic Murders (Wheeler). Sydney, Horwitz, and New York, New American Library, 1972.

Murder Is So Nostalgic (Seidlitz). New York, New American Library, 1972.

The Pornbroker (Holman). Sydney, Horwitz, and New York, New American Library, 1972.

The Seven Sirens (Roberts). Sydney, Horwitz, and New York, New American Library, 1972.

The Born Loser (Wheeler). Sydney, Horwitz, and New York, New American Library, 1973.

Manhattan Cowboy (Boyd). Sydney, Horwitz, and New York, New American Library, 1973.

The Master (Holman). Sydney, Horwitz, and New York, New American Library, 1973.

Murder on High (Roberts). Sydney, Horwitz, and New York, New American Library, 1973.

So Move the Body (Boyd). Sydney, Horwitz, and New York, New American Library, 1973.

Donavan. Sydney, Horwitz, and New York, New American Library, 1974.

And the Undead Sing (Seidlitz). New York, New American Library, 1974.

Negative in Blue (Holman). New York, New American Library, 1974.

The Star-Crossed Lover (Holman). New York, New American Library, 1974.

Wheeler Fortune. New York, New American Library, 1974.

Donavan's Day. Sydney, Horwitz, and New York, New American Library, 1975.

The Early Boyd. Sydney, Horwitz, and New York, New American Library, 1975.

The Iron Maiden (Baker). Sydney, Horwitz, and New York, New American Library, 1975.

Night Wheeler. New York, New American Library, 1975.

Phreak-Out! (Holman). Sydney, Horwitz, and New York, New American Library, 1975.

Ride the Roller Coaster (Holman). Sydney, Horwitz, and New York, New American Library, 1975.

Wheeler, Dealer! Sydney, Horwitz, and New York, New American Library, 1975.

OTHER PUBLICATIONS

Novel

The Cold Dark Hours (as A. G. Yates).   Sydney, Horwitz, New York, New American Library, and London, Barker, 1958.

*   *   *

The astonishingly prolific Australian paperback writer Alan G. Yates, writing as Carter Brown, has produced a series of books which for some twenty years have been happily devoured by a huge and faithful reading public. At the same time, however, the Brown books have been consistently ignored by most critics of the mystery genre, despite their status as a genuine publishing phenomenon, with sales in the tens – perhaps hundreds – of millions of copies. That the Brown books have been slighted is not too surprising, since they exhibit no pretentions of being other than lightweight, breezy mystery entertainment, to be read in one sitting and forgotten. They also suffer the stigma of being paperback originals, and their sheer number invites easy dismissal as hack potboilers. Only Anthony Boucher, that most exceptional and unstuffy mystery critic, gave the Carter Brown books a fair hearing in his review columns.

That the Brown books were and are so popular with a large segment of the mystery reading public is testimony to the durability of a mystery sub-genre which seemingly perished in the late 1940's, with the demise of the pulp magazines. The Brown books are the direct descendants of the "spicy" detective pulps like *Hollywood Detective* and *Spicy Detective*, which occupied the opposite end of the respectability scale from the revered *Black Mask*. Yates hews to the conventions of that school closely, following in the footsteps of Robert Leslie Bellem, master of that particular style of pulp writing; Brown's private eye heroes are, likewise, close cousins to Bellem's creation, Dan Turner, the ultimate "Hollywood dick." Richard S. Prather's Shell Scott series – like the Browns, hugely popular and critically slighted – belongs to this same school.

The hallmarks of the Carter Brown style are brevity, simple plotting, fast pace, much breezy slang (Yates exhibited a rather shaky grasp of American slang in the early books), broad humor, lots of action and liberal strewing of corpses. Above all there is the spicy element: lots of girls, all gorgeous and impossibly endowed (no female is introduced in a Brown book without her breasts being also introduced and described in the same paragraph). The sex is lighthearted, of the "leer and lights out" variety – up to 1973 at least, when explicit sex scenes were incorporated to disastrous effect. The settings are invariably among the rich and glamorous, most often denizens of the Hollywood film colony. No "mean streets" are to be found in a Carter Brown book.

Brown has worked this formula with a varied cast of series characters, the most noteworthy of which are Al Wheeler, a homicide lieutenant with the sheriff's department of the fictional Pine City, near Los Angeles; Rick Holman, a Hollywood private eye and saviour of blackmailed film starlets; Randy Roberts, lawyer and skirt-chaser based in San Francisco; and Larry Baker, Hollywood scriptwriter, who, accompanied by his perpetually drunk partner Boris Slivka, is saddled with the most bizarre cases to be found in all of Brown, usually involving strange cultists of some sort. There is also a female lead character, private detective Mavis Seidlitz, a sort of cross between Gracie Allen and Candy Christian, whose pulchritudinous assets far outweigh her mental equipment.

The Carter Brown books are indeed formula potboilers, and can be cruelly picked apart on grounds of sloppy plotting, minimal characterization, uninspired prose and, of course, unbelievability (the plots and characters have tended to become sillier over the years). Yet the formula has proven consistently popular; this canny mixture of action, sex, and humor, with its attendant refusal to be taken at all seriously, is escapism pure and simple.

—Art Scott

BROWN, Fredric. American. Born in Cincinnati, Ohio, 29 October 1906. Educated at the University of Cincinnati; Hanover College, Indiana. Married Elizabeth Chandler (second wife); two children by first marriage. Office worker, 1924–36; journalist on Milwaukee *Journal*; free-lance writer after 1947. Recipient: Mystery Writers of America Edgar Allan Poe Award, 1948. *Died 11 March 1972.*

CRIME PUBLICATIONS

Novels (series characters: Ed and Am Hunter)

The Fabulous Clipjoint (Hunter). New York, Dutton, 1947; London, Boardman, 1949.
The Dead Ringer (Hunter). New York, Dutton, 1948; London, Boardman, 1950.
Murder Can Be Fun. New York, Dutton, 1948; London, Boardman, 1951; as *A Plot for Murder*, New York, Bantam, 1949.
The Bloody Moonlight (Hunter). New York, Dutton, 1949; as *Murder in the Moonlight*, London, Boardman, 1950.
The Screaming Mimi. New York, Dutton, 1949; London, Boardman, 1950.
Compliments of a Fiend (Hunter). New York, Dutton, 1950; London, Boardman, 1951.
Here Comes a Candle. New York, Dutton, 1950; London, Boardman, 1951.
Night of the Jabberwock. New York, Dutton, 1950; London, Boardman, 1951.
The Case of the Dancing Sandwiches. New York, Dell, 1951.
Death Has Many Doors (Hunter). New York, Dutton, 1951; London, Boardman, 1952.
The Far Cry. New York, Dutton, 1951; London, Boardman, 1952.
The Deep End. New York, Dutton, 1952; London, Boardman, 1953.
We All Killed Grandma. New York, Dutton, 1952; London, Boardman, 1953.
Madball. New York, Dell, 1953; London, Muller, 1962.
His Name Was Death. New York, Dutton, 1954; London, Boardman, 1955.
The Wench Is Dead. New York, Dutton, 1955.
The Lenient Beast. New York, Dutton, 1956; London, Boardman, 1957.
One for the Road. New York, Dutton, 1958; London, Boardman, 1959.
Knock Three-One-Two. New York, Dutton, and London, Boardman, 1959.
The Late Lamented (Hunter). New York, Dutton, and London, Boardman, 1959.
The Murderers. New York, Dutton, 1961; London, Boardman, 1962.
The Five-Day Nightmare. New York, Dutton, and London, Boardman, 1963.
Mrs. Murphy's Underpants (Hunter). New York, Dutton, 1963; London, Boardman, 1965.

Short Stories

Mostly Murder: Eighteen Stories. New York, Dutton, 1953; London, Boardman, 1954.
Nightmares and Geezenstacks: 47 Stories. New York, Bantam, 1961.
The Shaggy Dog and Other Murders. New York, Dutton, 1963; London, Boardman, 1964.

Uncollected Short Stories

"Why, Benny, Why?," in *Ellery Queen's 20th Anniversary Annual.* New York, Random House, 1965; London, Gollancz, 1966.
"Town Wanted," in *Crimes and Misfortunes*, edited by J. Francis McComass. New York, Random House, 1970.

OTHER PUBLICATIONS

Novels

What Mad Universe. New York, Dutton, 1949; London, Boardman, 1951.
The Lights in the Sky Are Stars. New York, Dutton, 1953; as *Project Jupiter*, London, Boardman, 1954.
Martians, Go Home. New York, Dutton, 1955.
Rogue in Space. New York, Dutton, 1957; London, Boardman, 1958.
The Office. New York, Dutton, 1958.
The Mind Thing. New York, Bantam, 1961.

Short Stories

Space on My Hands. Chicago, Shasta, 1951; London, Boardman, 1952.
Angels and Spaceships. New York, Dutton, 1954; London, Gollancz, 1955; as *Star Shine*, New York, Bantam, 1956.
Honeymoon in Hell. New York, Bantam, 1958.
Daymares. New York, Lancer, 1968.
Paradox Lost and Twelve Other Great Science Fiction Stories. New York, Random House, 1973.
The Best of Fredric Brown, edited by Robert Bloch. New York, Ballantine, 1977.

Plays

Television Plays: for *Alfred Hitchcock* series.

Other

"Where Do You Get Your Plot?," in *The Mystery Writers' Handbook*, edited by Herbert Brean. New York, Harper, 1956.
Mitkey Astromouse (juvenile). New York, Harlan Quist, 1971.

Editor, with Mack Reynolds, *Science-Fiction Carnival*. Chicago, Shasta, 1953.

Bibliography: "Paradox and Plot: The Fiction of Fredric Brown" by Newton Baird, in *Armchair Detective* (San Diego, California), October 1976–January 1978.

*   *   *

The essence of the work of Fredric Brown is uniqueness. One of the most ingenious writers of his time, he wrote mysteries with a lucid style that disguised complex plots and themes. Sometimes he wrote science fiction, he said, to overcome the "too real" aspect of detective fiction. Fantasy, mystery, psychology, and science are often mixed in his stories, along with uses of classic literature, like that of Lewis Carroll in *Night of the Jabberwock. The Office*, his only "straight" novel, is a blend of realism and mystery, based on his experiences in a Cincinnati office. "Star Spangled Night," his only "straight" short work, is an inspiring tale of an ancestor's role in the War of 1812.

Self-taught, he wrote for the pulps. His first full-length mystery, *The Fabulous Clipjoint*, one of seven books dealing with Ed and Am Hunter, an amateur detective team, combines youthful idealism with the logic of a retired circus performer. Other mysteries go beyond the series in invention, especially *The Deep End, The Screaming Mimi, Knock Three-One-Two*, and *The Far Cry*, but *The Fabulous Clipjoint* remained his favorite. A forerunner in plot and theme of later work, the title expresses a paradox that he projected in much of his work. Chicago, the setting, is both "clipjoint" and "fabulous" in its hero's perception. Ayn Rand thought Brown ingenious, but commented on his "malevolent sense of life." Anthony Boucher praised him, but noted this novel was "sordidly compelling." Sometimes Brown brought his experience to a positive resolution: when Ed Hunter solves his father's murder, he no longer sees a clipjoint, but the skyline "looking like fingers reaching to the sky."

My own study of Brown traces the conflict of the romantic versus the naturalistic in his work. This conflict may have influenced him to experiment frequently with point-of-view to improve everyday perception. One experiment with narrative point-of-view is *The Lenient Beast*, with five first person points-of-view. A procedural novel about a killer who murders out of his own perception of "mercy," it makes the conventional procedural detective plot seem tame and static. One novel has ten third person points-of-view. The paradoxical aesthetics in his work may have been responsible for his mix of hero and anti-hero, and his inability to create a viable romantic detective.

A story of extreme malevolence, set in a mental institution, is "Come and Go Mad," which creates an intolerable state of existence in which human volition is a fallacy. Crag, in the novel *Rogue in Space*, is half-hero, half-criminal. He creates an uncorrupted new planet in order to reconcile the dichotomy in his nature.

The Screaming Mimi, his best known work, uses symbolic horror to heighten the suspense of a reporter's search for a "ripper" killer. A revision of the beauty and beast allegory, beauty and beast succumb together to evil. *The Deep End* begins with the death of a boy under the wheels of a roller coaster car, and penetrates both the detective's and the killer's disturbed minds in a Conradian duality. Trauma is symbolized in the ascending and descending roller coaster "deep end" that haunts the reporter-detective's mind. *The Far Cry* is his *tour de force*. It probes a love/hate perplex to one of mystery writing's most startling endings, but the horror almost spoils the achievement.

Knock Three-One-Two is a mystery about a liquor salesman with a gambling habit who happens to observe a killer who terrorizes an entire city. The reader is kept guessing as to the identity of the killer. Competent and incompetent characters are woven into plot and subplot, including a mentally retarded news vendor who wants to be identified as a killer. The novel's theme, derived from the irrationality or rationality of eight points-of-view, is that objectivity brings light (reason or good) to darkness (irrationality or evil) when disturbed perceptions are brought into focus. In fact, the overall theme of much of Brown's fiction concerns the struggle to understand existence and achieve happiness. His larger meaning is the end benefit of his easy-to-read entertainments.

The best expressions of his ingenuity and imagination are in some of his short stories, particularly the collection *Nightmares and Geezenstacks*, a delightful potpourri of innocent and ribald humor, expectation and surprise. Other collections are mixed in quality, but *The Shaggy Dog and Other Murders*, containing stories like "Little Boy Lost" and "Good Night, Good Knight," deserves attention. "Knock," his most famous story, and many others among his best can be found in the collections *Paradox Lost* and *The Best of Fredric Brown*.

Every day characters and conventional villainy dominate his lesser work, like *Murder Can Be Fun* or a failed experiment, *Here Comes a Candle*, but plot invention removes them from the conventional, and a "thinking-ahead" pace makes them highly readable. A sense of unlimited invention comes from a reading of his varied work, and one is reminded of O. Henry and his mind of a million inventions. But Fredric Brown is really one of a kind. His view of a paradoxical existence is capsulated in the science fiction story "Paradox Lost," set in a classroom of bewildering modern philosophy. A student crosses over from reality to fantasy and fulfills his dreams in an invisible world. Brown portrayed a world that always betrayed and terrified idealists, making them yearn for a place that inspired rather than suppressed freedom and adventure. In his detective novels and mysteries his characters sometimes found that what they had hoped for proved more horrifying than what they had to begin with. In his fantasies, through "loopholes in reality," happiness is achieved. So this unique writer wrote for his own time and the future.

—-Newton Baird

BRUCE, Leo. Pseudonym for Rupert Croft-Cooke. British. Born in Edenbridge, Kent, 20 June 1903. Educated at Tonbridge School, Kent; Wellington College, now Wrekin College; University of Buenos Aires, 1923–26. Served in Field Security, 1939–46: Captain; British Empire Medal. Founding Editor, *La Estrella*, Buenos Aires, 1923–24; antiquarian bookseller, 1929–31; Lecturer, Institute Montana, Zugerberg, Switzerland, 1931; Book Critic, *The Sketch*, London, 1946–53. Agent: A. M. Heath & Co. Ltd., 40–42 William IV Street, London WC2N 4DD, England. *Died 10 June 1979.*

CRIME PUBLICATIONS

Novels (series characters: Sergeant William Beef; Carolus Deene)

Case for Three Detectives (Beef). London, Bles, 1936; New York, Stokes, 1937.
Case Without a Corpse (Beef). London, Bles, and New York, Stokes, 1937.
Case with Four Clowns (Beef). London, Davies, and New York, Stokes, 1939.
Case with No Conclusion (Beef). London, Bles, 1939.
Case with Ropes and Rings (Beef). London, Nicholson and Watson, 1940.
Case for Sergeant Beef. London, Nicholson and Watson, 1947.
Neck and Neck (Beef). London, Gollancz, 1951.
Cold Blood (Beef). London, Gollancz, 1952.
At Death's Door (Deene). London, Hamish Hamilton, 1955.
Dead for a Ducat (Deene). London, Davies, 1956.
Death of Cold (Deene). London, Davies, 1956.
Dead Man's Shoes (Deene). London, Davies, 1958.
A Louse for the Hangman (Deene). London, Davies, 1958.
Our Jubilee Is Death (Deene). London, Davies, 1959.
Furious Old Women (Deene). London, Davies, 1960.
Jack on the Gallows Tree (Deene). London, Davies, 1960.
Die All, Die Merrily (Deene). London, Davies, 1961.
A Bone and a Hank of Hair (Deene). London, Davies, 1961.
Nothing Like Blood (Deene). London, Davies, 1962.
Crack of Doom (Deene). London, Davies, 1963; as *Such Is Death*, New York, British
    Book Centre, 1963.
Death in Albert Park (Deene). London, W. H. Allen, 1964; New York, Scribner, 1979.
Death at Hallows End (Deene). London, W. H. Allen, 1965.
Death on the Black Sands (Deene). London, W. H. Allen, 1966.
Death of a Commuter (Deene). London, W. H. Allen, 1967.
Death at St. Asprey's School (Deene). London, W. H. Allen, 1967.
Death on Romney Marsh (Deene). London, W. H. Allen, 1968.
Death with Blue Ribbon (Deene). London, W. H. Allen, 1969.
Death on Allhallowe'en (Deene). London, W. H. Allen, 1970.
Death by the Lake (Deene). London, W. H. Allen, 1971.
Death in the Middle Watch (Deene). London, W. H. Allen, 1974.
Death of a Bovver Boy (Deene). London, W. H. Allen, 1974.

Novels as Rupert Croft-Cooke

Seven Thunders. London, Macmillan, and New York, St. Martin's Press, 1955.
Thief. London, Eyre and Spottiswoode, 1960; New York, Doubleday, 1961.
Clash by Night. London, Eyre and Spottiswoode, 1962.
Paper Albatross. London, Eyre and Spottiswoode, 1965; New York, Abelard
    Schuman, 1968.
Three in a Cell. London, Eyre and Spottiswoode, 1968.
Nasty Piece of Work. London, Eyre Methuen, 1973.

Short Stories as Rupert Croft-Cooke

> *Pharaoh and His Waggons and Other Stories.* London, Jarrolds, 1937.

Uncollected Short Stories

> "Bloody Moon," in *Giant Detective Annual.* New York, Best Books, 1950.
> "Death in the Garden," in *The Evening Standard Detective Book.* London, Gollancz, 1950.
> "Murder in Miniature," in *The Evening Standard Detective Book*, 2nd series. London, Gollancz, 1951.

OTHER PUBLICATIONS as Rupert Croft-Cooke

Novels

> *Troubadour.* London, Chapman and Hall, 1930.
> *Give Him the Earth.* London, Chapman and Hall, 1930; New York, Knopf, 1931.
> *Night Out.* London, Jarrolds, and New York, Dial Press, 1932.
> *Cosmopolis.* London, Jarrolds, 1932; New York, Dial Press, 1933.
> *Release the Lions.* London, Jarrolds, 1933; New York, Dodd Mead, 1934.
> *Her Mexican Lover.* London, Mellifont Press, 1934.
> *Picaro.* London, Jarrolds, and New York, Dodd Mead, 1934.
> *Shoulder the Sky.* London, Jarrolds, 1934.
> *Blind Gunner.* London, Jarrolds, 1935.
> *Crusade.* London, Jarrolds, 1936.
> *Kingdom Come.* London, Jarrolds, 1936.
> *Rule, Britannia.* London, Jarrolds, 1938.
> *Same Way Home.* London, Jarrolds, 1939; New York, Macmillan, 1940.
> *Glorious.* London, Jarrolds, 1940.
> *Ladies Gay.* London, Macdonald, 1946.
> *Octopus.* London, Jarrolds, 1946; as *Miss Allick*, New York, Holt, 1947.
> *Wilkie.* London, Macdonald, 1948; as *Another Sun, Another Home*, New York, Holt, 1949.
> *The White Mountain.* London, Falcon Press, 1949.
> *Brass Farthing.* London, Laurie, 1950.
> *Three Names for Nicholas.* London, Macmillan, 1951.
> *Nine Days with Edward.* London, Macmillan, 1952.
> *Harvest Moon.* London, Macmillan, and New York, St. Martin's Press, 1953.
> *Fall of Man.* London, Macmillan, 1955.
> *Barbary Night.* London, Eyre and Spottiswoode, 1958.
> *Wolf from the Door.* London, W. H. Allen, 1969.
> *Exiles.* London, W. H. Allen, 1970.
> *Under the Rose Garden.* London, W. H. Allen, 1971.
> *While the Iron's Hot.* London, W. H. Allen, 1971.
> *Conduct Unbecoming.* London, W. H. Allen, 1975.

Short Stories

> *A Football for the Brigadier and Other Stories.* London, Laurie, 1950.

Plays

> *Banquo's Chair.* London, Deane, 1930.
> *Tap Three Times.* London, French, 1934.

Deliberate Accident (produced London, 1934).
Gala Night at "The Willows," with G. B. Stern.   London, Deane, 1950.

Radio Plays: *You Bet Your Life*, with Beverley Nichols, 1938; *Peter the Painter*, 1946; *Theft*, 1963.

Verse

Songs of a Sussex Tramp.   Steyning, Sussex, Vine Press, 1922.
Tonbridge School.   Tonbridge, Kent, Free Press, 1923.
Songs South of the Line.   London, Lincoln Torrey, 1925.
The Viking.   Privately printed, 1926.
Some Poems.   Rochester, Kent, Galleon Press, 1929.
Tales of a Wicked Uncle.   London, Cape, 1963.

Other

How Psychology Can Help.   London, Daniel, 1927.
Darts.   London, Bles, 1936.
God in Ruins: A Passing Commentary.   London, Fortune Press, 1936.
The World Is Young.   London, Hodder and Stoughton, 1937; as *Escape to the Andes*, New York, Messner, 1938.
How to Get More Out of Life.   London, Bles, 1938.
The Man in Europe Street (travel).   London, Rich and Cowan, and New York, Putnam, 1938.
The Circus Has No Home.   London, Methuen, 1941; revised edition, London, Falcon Press, 1950.
How to Enjoy Travel Abroad.   London, Rockliff, 1948.
The Moon in My Pocket: Life with the Romanies.   London, Sampson Low, 1948.
Rudyard Kipling.   London, Home and Van Thal, and Denver, Swallow, 1948.
Cities, with Noël Barber.   London, Wingate, 1951.
The Sawdust Ring, with W. S. Meadmore.   London, Odhams Press, 1951.
Buffalo Bill: The Legend, The Man of Action, The Showman, with W. S. Meadmore.   London, Sidgwick and Jackson, 1952.
The Life for Me (memoirs).   London, Macmillan, 1952; New York, St. Martin's Press, 1953.
The Blood-Red Island (memoirs).   London, Staples Press, 1953.
A Few Gypsies.   London, Putnam, 1955.
Sherry.   London, Putnam, 1955; New York, Knopf, 1956.
The Verdict of You All (memoirs).   London, Secker and Warburg, 1955.
The Tangerine House (memoirs).   London, Macmillan, and New York, St. Martin's Press, 1956.
Port.   London, Putnam, 1957.
The Gardens of Camelot (memoirs).   London, Putnam, 1958.
The Quest for Quixote.   London, Secker and Warburg, 1959; as *Through Spain with Don Quixote*, New York, Knopf, 1960.
Smiling Damned Villain: The True Story of Paul Axel Lund.   London, Secker and Warburg, 1959.
The Altar in the Loft (memoirs).   London, Putnam, 1960.
English Cooking: A New Approach.   London, W. H. Allen, 1960.
The Drums of Morning (memoirs).   London, Putnam, 1961.
Madeira.   London, Putnam, 1961.
The Glittering Pastures (memoirs).   London, Putnam, 1962.
Wine and Other Drinks.   London, Collins, 1962.
Bosie: The Story of Lord Alfred Douglas, His Friends and Enemies.   London, W. H. Allen, 1963; Indianapolis, Bobbs Merrill, 1964.

Cooking for Pleasure. London, Collins, 1963.
The Numbers Came (memoirs). London, Putnam, 1963.
The Last of Spring (memoirs). London, Putnam, 1964.
The Wintry Sea (memoirs). London, W. H. Allen, 1964.
The Gorgeous East: One Man's India. London, W. H. Allen, 1965.
The Purple Streak (memoirs). London, W. H. Allen, 1966.
The Wild Hills (memoirs). London, W. H. Allen, 1966.
Feasting with Tigers: A New Consideration of Some Late Victorian Writers. London,
    W. H. Allen, 1967; New York, Holt Rinehart, 1968.
The Happy Highways (memoirs). London, W. H. Allen, 1967.
The Ghost of June: A Return to England and the West. London, W. H. Allen, 1968.
Exotic Food: Three Hundred of the Most Unusual Dishes in Western Cookery. London,
    Allen and Unwin, 1969; New York, Herder, 1971.
The Licentious Soldiery (memoirs). London, W. H. Allen, 1971.
The Unrecorded Life of Oscar Wilde. London, W. H. Allen, and New York, McKay,
    1972.
The Dogs of Peace (memoirs). London, W. H. Allen, 1973.
The Caves of Hercules (memoirs). London, W. H. Allen, 1974.
The Long Way Home (memoirs). London, W. H. Allen, 1974.
Circus: A World History, with Peter Cotes. London, Elek, 1976; New York,
    Macmillan, 1977.
The Green, Green Grass (memoirs). London, W. H. Allen, 1977.

Editor, *Major Road Ahead: A Young Man's Ultimatum.* London, Methuen, 1939.
Editor, *The Circus Book.* London, Sampson Low, 1948.

Translator, *The Last Days of Madrid: The End of the Second Spanish Republic,* by
    Segismundo Casado. London, Davies, 1939.

Manuscript Collection: Humanities Research Center, University of Texas, Austin.

*   *   *

Leo Bruce (pseudonym of Rupert Croft-Cooke) is a major British detective story writer of salient merit. His fertility of invention in devising puzzles that reach totally unexpected conclusions is exceptional. His subtlety is outstanding, and his efforts at misdirection are worthy of Agatha Christie.

Bruce's highly-praised debut, *Case for Three Detectives,* pits his first series detective, the plebeian Sergeant William Beef, against Lord Simon Plimsoll, M. Amer Picon, and Monsignor Smith (alias Wimsey, Poirot, and Brown) in a problem involving a locked-room murder. Beef solves this, and other cunningly devised crime problems such as those told in *Case Without a Corpse, Case with Ropes and Rings,* and *Neck and Neck.* His early successes persuade Beef to leave the police force and set up on his own as a private inquiry agent.

His exploits are chronicled by the irascible Lionel Townsend, who would much rather work with and narrate the exploits of a more aristocratic sleuth such as Lord Peter Wimsey. Townsend's patience is often tried when Beef abandons his interest in a crime problem in favor of drinking copious amounts of beer and indulging in a few innocent games of darts at any nearby pub. The friction and byplay (which is not up to the highest level of Stout's Wolfe-Goodwin team) will often go too far and cut to the bone. Bruce continued this series until *Cold Blood,* in which Beef places his life in jeopardy in order to solve the murder of a millionaire who is dispatched by a croquet mallet. Beef solves this case, but is abandoned by his creator for no explicable reason.

Bruce tightened his prose style, dispensed with a Watson-narrator, and introduced the less colorful Carolus Deene in *At Death's Door.* Deene (who is preferred to Beef by Jacques Barzun and Wendell Hertig Taylor) is a laconic ex-commando who serves as Senior History

Master at Queen's School, Newminster, and solves crime problems as a hobby. During his investigations, Deene often has to cope with the efforts of his headmaster and his housekeeper who try to dissuade him, and his least-favorite student, the odious Rupert Priggley, who always seeks to encourage him. *A Bone and a Hank of Hair*, *Furious Old Women*, *Jack on the Gallows Tree*, and *Nothing Like Blood* are among the best Deene narratives.

—Charles Shibuk

BRUTON, Eric (Moore). British. Born in 1915. Served as an engineering officer in the Royal Air Force, 1940–46. Married Anne Valerie Britton. Ran a riding school; visiting lecturer, Sir John Cass College, London; jeweller: Director, Diamond Boutique Ltd. and Things and Ideas Ltd.; Director, N.A.G. Press Ltd.; Publisher, *Retail Jeweller*, London. Liveryman, Company of Clockmakers and Company of Turners; Freeman, Company of Goldsmiths; Fellow, British Horological Institute and Gemmological Association of Great Britain. Agent: Elaine Greene Ltd., 31 Newington Green, London N16 9PU. Address: White House, Widmer End, Buckinghamshire, England.

CRIME PUBLICATIONS

Novels (series character: Inspector George Judd)

> *Death in Ten Point Bold.* London, Jenkins, 1957.
> *Die, Darling, Die.* London, Boardman, 1959.
> *Violent Brothers.* London, Boardman, 1960.
> *The Hold Out.* London, Boardman, 1961.
> *King Diamond.* London, Boardman, 1961.
> *The Devil's Pawn.* London, Boardman, 1962.
> *The Laughing Policeman* (Judd). London, Boardman, 1963.
> *The Finsbury Mob* (Judd). London, Boardman, 1964.
> *The Smithfield Slayer* (Judd). London, Boardman, 1965.
> *The Wicked Saint* (Judd). London, Boardman, 1965.
> *The Firebug* (Judd). London, Boardman, 1967.

Uncollected Short Story

> "Waxing of a Drone," in *John Creasey's Mystery Bedside Book*, edited by Herbert Harris. London, Hodder and Stoughton, 1966.

OTHER PUBLICATIONS

Other

> *The True Book about Clocks* (juvenile). London, Muller, 1957.
> *The True Book about Diamonds* (juvenile). London, Muller, 1961.
> *Automation* (juvenile). London, Muller, 1962.
> *Dictionary of Clocks and Watches.* London, Arco, 1962; New York, Archer House, 1963.

The Longcase Clock. London, Arco, 1964; New York, Praeger, 1968; revised edition, London, Hart Davis MacGibbon, 1977.

Clocks and Watches 1400–1900. London, Barker, and New York, Praeger, 1967.

Clocks and Watches. London, Hamlyn, 1968.

Diamonds. London, N.A.G. Press, 1970; Philadelphia, Chilton, 1971; revised edition, 1978.

Hallmarks and Date Letters on Gold and Silver, revised edition. London, N.A.G. Press, 1970.

Antique Clocks and Clock Collecting. London, Hamlyn, 1974.

The History of Clocks and Watches. London, Orbis, 1979.

*   *   *

Eric Bruton drew upon his experiences in magazine publishing to write his first crime novel, *Death in Ten Point Bold,* about a murder in the Fleet Street office of *Woman's Post. The Hold Out* was the first of his crime books to be based on the City of London Police. Subsequently, helped by the professional procedural knowledge supplied by his friend Detective Chief Inspector Tom Grealey (who was associated with City Police training-films and himself a crime-writer under the name of Louis Southworth), Bruton produced a whole series of City of London police novels, including *The Laughing Policeman, The Finsbury Mob,* and *The Firebug.*

Bruton, an expert on diamonds and antique clocks, turned to writing books on diamonds and clocks, and found little time to write more crime novels, although he is always hoping to return to this field.

—Herbert Harris

BUCHAN, John; 1st Baron Tweedsmuir of Elsfield. Scottish. Born in Broughton Green, Peebles-shire, 26 August 1875. Educated at the University of Glasgow; Brasenose College, Oxford (scholar, 1895; Stanhope Prize, 1897; Newdigate Prize, 1898; President of the Union, 1899), B.A. (honours) 1899; Middle Temple, London, called to the Bar, 1901. Served on the Headquarters Staff of the British Army in France, as temporary Lieutenant Colonel, 1916–17; Director of Information under the Prime Minister, 1917–18. Married Susan Charlotte Grosvenor in 1907; three sons and one daughter. Private Secretary to the High Commissioner for South Africa, Lord Milner, 1901–03; Director of Nelson, publishers, London, from 1903; Conservative Member of Parliament for the Scottish Universities, 1927–35; Lord High Commissioner to the Church of Scotland, 1933, 1934; Governor-General of Canada, 1935–40; Privy Councillor, 1937. Curator, Oxford University Chest, 1924–30; President, Scottish History Society, 1929–33; Bencher of the Middle Temple, 1935; Chancellor of the University of Edinburgh, 1937–40; Justice of the Peace, Peebles-shire and Oxfordshire. Recipient: Black Memorial Prize, 1929. D.C.L.: Oxford University; LL.D.: University of Glasgow; University of St. Andrews; University of Edinburgh; McGill University, Montreal; University of Toronto; University of Manitoba, Winnipeg; Harvard University, Cambridge, Massachusetts; Yale University, New Haven, Connecticut; D.Litt.: Columbia University, New York; University of British Columbia, Vancouver; McMaster University, Hamilton, Ontario. Honorary Fellow, Brasenose College, Oxford. Companion of Honour, 1932; created Baron Tweedsmuir, 1935; G.C.M.G. (Knight Grand Cross, Order of St. Michael and St. George), 1935; G.C.V.O. (Knight Grand Cross, Royal Victorian Order), 1939. *Died 11 February 1940.*

CRIME PUBLICATIONS

Novels (series characters: Richard Hannay; Sir Edward Leithen; Dickson Mc'Cunn)

The Thirty-Nine Steps (Hannay).   Edinburgh, Blackwood, and New York, Doran, 1915.
The Power-House (Leithen).   Edinburgh, Blackwood, and New York, Doran, 1916.
Greenmantle (Hannay).   London, Hodder and Stoughton, and New York, Doran, 1916.
Mr. Standfast (Hannay).   London, Hodder and Stoughton, and New York, Doran, 1919.
Huntingtower (Mc'Cunn).   London, Hodder and Stoughton, and New York, Doran, 1922.
The Three Hostages (Hannay).   London, Hodder and Stoughton, and Boston, Houghton Mifflin, 1924.
John Macnab (Leithen).   London, Hodder and Stoughton, and Boston, Houghton Mifflin, 1925.
The Dancing Floor (Leithen).   London, Hodder and Stoughton, and Boston, Houghton Mifflin, 1926.
The Courts of the Morning.   London Hodder and Stoughton, and Boston, Houghton Mifflin, 1929.
Castle Gay (Mc'Cunn).   London, Hodder and Stoughton, and Boston, Houghton Mifflin, 1929.
A Prince of the Captivity.   London, Hodder and Stoughton, and Boston, Houghton Mifflin, 1933.
The House of the Four Winds (Mc'Cunn).   London, Hodder and Stoughton, and Boston, Houghton Mifflin, 1935.
The Island of Sheep.   London, Hodder and Stoughton, 1936; as *The Man from the Norlands*, Boston, Houghton Mifflin, 1936.
Sick Heart River (Leithen).   London, Hodder and Stoughton, 1941; as *Mountain Meadow*, Boston, Houghton Mifflin, 1941.

Short Stories

The Watcher by the Threshold and Other Tales.   Edinburgh, Blackwood, 1902; augmented edition, New York, Doran, 1918.
The Moon Endureth: Tales and Fancies.   Edinburgh, Blackwood, and New York, Sturgis, 1912.
The Runagates Club.   London, Hodder and Stoughton, and Boston, Houghton Mifflin, 1928.
The Gap in the Curtain.   London, Hodder and Stoughton, and Boston, Houghton Mifflin, 1932.

OTHER PUBLICATIONS

Novels

Sir Quixote of the Moors, Being Some Account of an Episode in the Life of the Sieur de Rohaine.   London, Unwin, and New York, Holt, 1895.
John Burnet of Barns.   London, Lane, and New York, Dodd Mead, 1898.
A Lost Lady of Old Years.   London, Lane, 1899.
The Half-Hearted.   London, Isbister, and Boston, Houghton Mifflin, 1900.
Salute to Adventurers.   London, Nelson, and Boston, Houghton Mifflin, 1915.
The Path of the King.   London, Hodder and Stoughton, and New York, Doran, 1921.
Midwinter: Certain Travellers in Old England.   London, Hodder and Stoughton, and New York, Doran, 1923.

Witch Wood.   London, Hodder and Stoughton, and Boston, Houghton Mifflin, 1927.
The Blanket of the Dark.   London, Hodder and Stoughton, and Boston, Houghton Mifflin, 1931.
The Free Fishers.   London, Hodder and Stoughton, and Boston, Houghton Mifflin, 1934.
The Long Traverse.   London, Hodder and Stoughton, 1941; as *Lake of Gold*, Boston, Houghton Mifflin, 1941.

Short Stories

Grey Weather: Moorland Tales of My Own People.   London, Lane, 1899.
Ordeal by Marriage: An Eclogue.   London, R. Clay, 1915.

Play

Screenplay: *The Battles of Coronel and Falkland Islands,* with Harry Engholm and Merritt Crawford, 1927.

Verse

The Pilgrim Fathers.   Oxford, Blackwell, 1898.
Poems, Scots and English.   London, Jack, 1917; revised edition, London, Nelson, 1936.

Other

Scholar Gipsies.   London, Lane, and New York, Macmillan, 1896.
Sir Walter Raleigh.   Oxford, Blackwell, 1897.
Brasenose College.   London, Robinson, 1898.
The African Colony: Studies in the Reconstruction.   Edinburgh, Blackwood, 1903.
The Law Relating to the Taxation of Foreign Income.   London, Stevens, 1905.
A Lodge in the Wilderness.   Edinburgh, Blackwood, 1906.
Some Eighteenth Century Byways and Other Essays.   Edinburgh, Blackwood, 1908.
Sir Walter Raleigh (juvenile).   London, Nelson, and New York, Holt, 1911.
What the Home Rule Bill Means (speech).   Peebles, Smythe, 1912.
The Marquis of Montrose.   London, Nelson, and New York, Scribner, 1913.
Andrew Jameson, Lord Ardwall.   Edinburgh, Blackwood, 1913.
Britain's War by Land.   London, Oxford University Press, 1915.
Nelson's History of the War.   London, Nelson, 24 vols., 1915–19; as *A History of the Great War*, 4 vols., 1921–22.
The Achievement of France.   London, Methuen, 1915.
The Future of the War (speech).   London, Boyle Son and Watchurst, 1916.
The Purpose of War (speech).   London, Dent, 1916.
These for Remembrance.   Privately printed, 1919.
The Island of Sheep, with Susan Buchan (as Cadmus and Harmonia).   London, Hodder and Stoughton, 1919; Boston, Houghton Mifflin, 1920.
The Battle-Honours of Scotland 1914–1918.   Glasgow, Outram, 1919.
The History of the South African Forces in France.   London, Nelson, 1920.
Francis and Riversdale Grenfell: A Memoir.   London, Nelson, 1920.
A Book of Escapes and Hurried Journeys.   London, Nelson, 1922; Boston, Houghton Mifflin, 1923.
The Last Secrets: The Final Mysteries of Exploration.   London, Nelson, 1923; Boston, Houghton Mifflin, 1924.
The Memoir of Sir Walter Scott (speech).   Privately printed, 1923.
Days to Remember: The British Empire in the Great War, with Henry Newbolt.   London, Nelson, 1923.

Some Notes on Sir Walter Scott (speech). London, Oxford University Press, 1924.

Lord Minto: A Memoir. London, Nelson, 1924.

The History of the Royal Scots Fusiliers (1678–1918). London, Nelson, 1925.

The Man and the Book: Sir Walter Raleigh. London, Nelson, 1925.

Two Ordeals of Democracy (lecture). Boston, Houghton Mifflin, 1925.

Homilies and Recreations. London, Nelson, 1926; Freeport, New York, Books for Libraries, 1969.

To the Electors of the Scottish Universities (speech). Glasgow, Anderson, 1927.

The Fifteenth – Scottish – Division 1914–1919, with John Stewart. Edinburgh, Blackwood, 1926.

The Causal and the Casual in History (lecture). Cambridge, University Press, and New York, Macmillan, 1929.

What the Union of the Churches Means to Scotland. Edinburgh, McNivern and Wallace, 1929.

Montrose and Leadership (lecture). London, Oxford University Press, 1930.

The Revision of Dogmas (lecture). Ashridge, Wisconsin, Ashridge Journal, 1930.

Lord Rosebery 1847–1930. London, Oxford University Press, 1930.

The Novel and the Fairy Tale. London, Oxford University Press, 1931.

Sir Walter Scott. London, Cassell, and New York, Coward McCann, 1932.

The Magic Walking-Stick (juvenile). London, Hodder and Stoughton, and Boston, Houghton Mifflin, 1932.

Julius Caesar. London, Davies, and New York, Appleton, 1932.

The Massacre of Glencoe. London, Davies, and New York, Putnam, 1933.

Andrew Lang and the Border (lecture). London, Oxford University Press, 1933.

The Margins of Life (speech). London, Birkbeck College, 1933.

The Principles of Social Service (lecture). Glasgow, Glasgow Society of Social Service, 1934(?).

The Scottish Church and the Empire (speech). Glasgow, Church of Scotland Commission on Colonial Churches, 1934.

Gordon at Khartoum. London, Davies, 1934.

Oliver Cromwell. London, Hodder and Stoughton, and Boston, Houghton Mifflin, 1934.

Men and Deeds. London, Davies, 1935; Freeport, New York, Books for Libraries, 1969.

The King's Grace 1910–35 (on George V). London, Hodder and Stoughton, 1935; as *The People's King*, Boston, Houghton Mifflin, 1935.

An Address [The Western Mind]. Montreal, McGill University, 1935.

Address [A University's Bequest to Youth]. Toronto, Victoria University, 1936.

Augustus. London, Hodder and Stoughton, and Boston, Houghton Mifflin, 1937.

The Interpreter's House (speech). London, Hodder and Stoughton, 1938.

Presbyterianism Yesterday, Today, and Tomorrow. Edinburgh, Church of Scotland, 1938.

Memory Hold-the-Door. London, Hodder and Stoughton, 1940; as *Pilgrim's War: An Essay in Recollection*, Boston, Houghton Mifflin, 1940.

Comments and Characters, edited by W. Forbes Gray. London, Nelson, 1940; Freeport, New York, Books for Libraries, 1970.

Canadian Occasions (lectures). London, Hodder and Stoughton, and New York, Musson, 1940.

The Clearing House: A Survey of One Man's Mind, edited by Lady Tweedsmuir. London, Hodder and Stoughton, 1946.

Life's Adventure: Extracts from the Works of John Buchan, edited by Lady Tweedsmuir. London, Hodder and Stoughton, 1947.

Editor, *Essays and Apothegms*, by Francis Bacon. London, Scott, 1894.

Editor, *Musa Piscatrix*. London, Lane, and Chicago, McClurg, 1896.

Editor, *The Compleat Angler*, by Izaak Walton. London, Methuen, 1901.

Editor, *The Long Road to Victory*. London, Nelson, 1920.

Editor, *Great Hours in Sport*. London, Nelson, 1921.

Editor, *Miscellanies, Literary and Historical*, by Archibald Primrose, Earl of Rosebery. London, Hodder and Stoughton, 1921.

Editor, *A History of English Literature*. London, Nelson, 1923; New York, Ronald Press, 1938.

Editor, *The Nations of Today: A New History of the World*. London, Hodder and Stoughton, and Boston, Houghton Mifflin, 12 vols., 1923–24.

Editor, *The Northern Muse: An Anthology of Scots Vernacular Poetry*. London, Nelson, 1924.

Editor, *Modern Short Stories*. London, Nelson, 1926.

Editor, *Essays and Studies 12*. Oxford, Clarendon Press, 1926.

Editor, *South Africa*. London, British Empire Educational Press, 1928.

Editor, *The Teaching of History*. London, Nelson, 11 vols., 1928–30.

Editor, *The Poetry of Neil Munro*. Edinburgh, Blackwood, 1931.

Bibliography: *John Buchan: A Bibliography* by Archibald Hanna, Jr., Hamden, Connecticut, Shoe String Press, 1953; by J. Randolph Cox, in *English Literature in Transition* (Tempe, Arizona), 1966–67.

*   *   *

In recent years the critical biographies of Janet Adam Smith and David Daniell have gone a long way towards separating John Buchan from such less enduringly serious writers as Sapper and E. Phillips Oppenheim; but to claim a place for Buchan beside his fellow Scotsmen Walter Scott and Stevenson is to go too far. Buchan writes a good literary English, there is nothing of the "racism" and jingoism which is so strong in Sapper, and his narrative gift is at least commensurate with his and Oppenheim's. But he continues to be read primarily as a writer of thrillers ("shockers," as he himself called them), however literate, well-constructed, and intellectual they may be.

Buchan's life was acted out on an even larger stage than his fictional heroes trod. One of Lord Milner's Young Men reconstructing South Africa after the Boer War, Buchan held various high intelligence postings during the Great War, and died as Governor-General of Canada during the Second World War. He wrote history and biography, literary criticism (most notably his work on Scott), historical fiction, and at the end a very moving autobiography, *Memory Hold-the-Door*. His best thrillers divide between those featuring Richard Hannay and those featuring the lawyer Edward Leithen. Into these two most lasting of his character creations Buchan put the two sides of himself: the man of action and the man of contemplation. While Hannay's novels are some of the finest examples of the novel of intrigue, Leithen's, in their greater psychological depth and their distillation of Buchan's own thought, may ultimately be the more rewarding.

One quality Buchan does have in common with the thriller writers of his generation, those who mixed snobbery with violence (and there is little of either in Buchan), is his presentation of his heroes as men's men, reserved in female company. Leithen is a bachelor, and Hannay professes to know about as much of woman's ways "as I know about the Chinese language" (Buchan himself said that he could as well fly to the moon as draw a fictional woman). While the good heroines are maternal, such a woman as Hilda von Einem in *Greenmantle*, akin to Doyle's Irene Adler, is both idealized and terrifying. It is the very feminine qualities of Buchan's most convincing villain, Dominic Medina in *The Three Hostages*, which make him so threatening, and charge the relationship between him and Hannay with the same kind of power as binds Holmes to Moriarty, Bulldog Drummond to Carl Peterson, Nayland Smith to Fu Manchu, and so on.

The real antagonists in Buchan's fiction are the forces of irrationality, wherever embodied, which stalk a fragile civilization, and so far is Buchan from mere national hatred that he drew a sympathetic portrait of the Kaiser in *Greenmantle*, at the height of the War. His principal villains are those who seek to subject the minds and wills of others to theirs, like the protean villain of *The Thirty-Nine Steps*, Hilda von Einem, and Dominic Medina.

Buchan is an acute commentator on contemporary public affairs, even in his shockers. Such a seeming excursion into the supernatural as *The Gap in the Curtain* (a number of people are given a glimpse of the *Times*, a year hence) has much to teach about coming to terms with death, as well as being laden with some sharp satire of politics and business. Finally, while it is right to be wary of absolutely equating the dying Leithen in *Sick Heart River* with Buchan himself, it is in this last novel that one finds his final thoughts distilled; it is the last testament of a supremely humane man.

—Barrie Hayne

BUDE, John. Pseudonym for Ernest Carpenter Elmore. British. Born in 1901. Married; one daughter. Stage director and producer. Co-Founder, Crime Writers Association, 1953. *Died in 1957.*

CRIME PUBLICATIONS

Novels (series character: Superintendent Meredith)

> *The Cornish Coast Murder.*   London, Skeffington, 1935.
> *The Lake District Murder* (Meredith).   London, Skeffington, 1935.
> *The Sussex Downs Murder* (Meredith).   London, Skeffington, 1936.
> *The Cheltenham Square Murder* (Meredith).   London, Skeffington, 1937.
> *Loss of a Head.*   London, Skeffington, 1938.
> *Hand on the Alibi.*   London, Skeffington, 1939.
> *Death of a Cad.*   London, Hale, 1940.
> *Death on Paper.*   London, Hale, 1940.
> *Slow Vengeance.*   London, Hale, 1941.
> *Death Knows No Calendar.*   London, Cassell, 1942.
> *Death Deals a Double.*   London, Cassell, 1943.
> *Death in White Pyjamas.*   London, Cassell, 1944.
> *Death in Ambush* (Meredith).   London, Macdonald, 1945.
> *Trouble A-Brewing* (Meredith).   London, Macdonald, 1946.
> *Death Makes a Prophet* (Meredith).   London, Macdonald, 1947.
> *Dangerous Sunlight.*   London, Macdonald, 1948.
> *Murder in Montparnasse.*   London, Brown Watson, 1949.
> *A Glut of Red Herrings.*   London, Macdonald, 1949.
> *Death Steals the Show* (Meredith).   London, Macdonald, 1950.
> *The Constable and the Lady* (Meredith).   London, Macdonald, 1951.
> *When the Case Was Opened.*   London, Macdonald, 1952.
> *Death on the Riviera.*   London, Macdonald, 1952.
> *Twice Dead.*   London, Macdonald, 1953.
> *So Much in the Dark.*   London, Macdonald, 1954.
> *Two Ends to the Town.*   London, Macdonald, 1955.
> *A Shift of Guilt.*   London, Macdonald, 1956.

A Telegram from Le Touquet. London, Macdonald, 1956.
Another Man's Shadow. London, Macdonald, 1957.
A Twist of the Rope. London, Macdonald, 1958.
The Night the Fog Came Down. London, Macdonald, and New York, Washburn, 1958.

OTHER PUBLICATIONS as Ernest Elmore

Novels

The Steel Grubs. London, Selwyn and Blount, 1928.
This Siren Song. London, Collins, 1930.
The Baboon and the Fiddle. London, Hurst and Blackett, 1932.
Green in Judgement. London, Jarrolds, 1939.
Christmas in Gillybrook. London, Quality Press, 1949.
The Lumpton Gobbelings. London, Putnam, 1954.

Other

Snuffly Snorty Dog (juvenile). London, Collins, 1946.

*   *   *

John Bude came into crime writing at a time when thrillers were tremendously in vogue, the 1920's and early 1930's, the period of Edgar Wallace and Sydney Horler. His work as stage director and producer gave him a great sense of theatre. His work was highly descriptive of backgrounds, one of his earliest, *The Lake District Murder*, being freshly original in that the reader was taken step by step along the road of detection with views of the Lake District on the way. *A Twist of the Rope*, the story of a homicidal maniac at large in a country town, was his most convincing novel. Others that deserve attention are *A Telegram from Le Touquet*, *Slow Vengeance*, *Death on Paper*, *Death in Ambush*, *Trouble A-Brewing*, and *Death Makes a Prophet*.

—Herbert Harris

BURGESS, (Frank) Gelett. American. Born in Boston, Massachusetts, 30 January 1866. Educated at Massachusetts Institute of Technology (Editor, *Tech*), Cambridge, B.S. 1887. Married Estelle Loomis in 1914. Draughtsman, Southern Pacific Railway, 1887–90; Instructor in topographical drawing at the University of California, Berkeley, 1891–94; designer and associate editor, *Wave* magazine, 1894–95, and *Lark*, 1895–97, and other experimental printing and design magazines; associate editor, *Ridgeway's* magazine, 1906. *Died 18 September 1951.*

CRIME PUBLICATIONS

Novels

The White Cat. Indianapolis, Bobbs Merrill, 1907; London, Chapman and Hall, 1908.

Find the Woman. Indianapolis, Bobbs Merrill, 1911.
Two O'Clock Courage. Indianapolis, Bobbs Merrill, and London, Nicholson and Watson, 1934.
Ladies in Boxes. New York, Alliance, 1942.

Short Stories

The Picaroons, with Will Irwin. New York, McClure, and London, Chatto and Windus, 1904.
The Master of Mysteries (published anonymously). Indianapolis, Bobbs Merrill, 1912.
A Murder at the Dôme. San Francisco, Book Club of California, 1937.

Uncollected Short Stories

"Up the Spout," in *Best American Mystery Stories of the Year,* edited by Carolyn Wells. New York, Day, 1931.
"Murder at the Monde," in *Best American Mystery Stories of the Year,* edited by Carolyn Wells. New York, Day, 1932.
"Just What Happened," in *Murder for the Millions,* edited by Frank Owen. New York, Fell, 1946.

OTHER PUBLICATIONS

Novels

Vivette; or, The Memoirs of the Romance Association. Boston, Copeland and Day, 1897.
The Reign of Queen Isyl, with Will Irwin. New York, McClure, 1903.
A Little Sister of Destiny. Boston, Houghton Mifflin, 1906.
The Heart Line. Indianapolis, Bobbs Merrill, 1907; London, Richards, 1908.
Lady Méchante; or, Life as It Should Be. New York, Stokes, 1909.
Love in a Hurry. Indianapolis, Bobbs Merrill, 1913.
Mrs. Hope's Husband. New York, Century, 1917.
Ain't Angie Awful! Philadelphia, Dorrance, 1923.
Too Good Looking: The Romance of Flossidoodle Darlo. Indianapolis, Bobbs Merrill, 1936.

Plays

The Cave Man (produced New York, 1911).
The Purple Cow, with Carolyn Wells (produced Washington, D.C., 1924).

Verse

Chant-Royal of California. San Francisco, Channing Auxiliary, 1899.
A Gage of Youth, Lyrics from the Lark, and Other Poems. Boston, Small Maynard, 1901.
The Rubaiyat of Omar Cayenne. New York, Stokes, 1904.
The Cat's Elegy, with Burges Johnson. Chicago, McClurg, 1913.
Ballad of the Hyde Street Grip: A San Francisco Rhapsody. Privately printed, 1937.
The Goop Song Book, music by Elizabeth Merz Butterfield. Cincinnati, Willis Music Company, 1941.
Ballade of Fog in the Cañon. San Mateo, California, Book Club of California, 1947.
The Purple Cow and Other Nonsense. New York, Dover, 1961.

Other

> *The Lively City o' Ligg* (juvenile).   New York, Stokes, 1899; London, Methuen, 1900.
> *Goops and How to Be Them.*   New York, Stokes, and London, Methuen, 1900.
> *The Nonsense Almanac.*   New York, Stokes, 1900.
> *The Burgess Nonsense Book.*   New York, Stokes, 1901; London, Simpkin Marshall, 1914.
> *The Romance of the Commonplace.*   San Francisco, Elder and Shepard, 1902.
> *More Goops and How Not to Be Them.*   New York, Stokes, 1903.
> *Goop Tales Alphabetically Told.*   New York, Stokes, 1904.
> *Are You a Bromide?*   New York, Huebsch, 1906.
> *The Maxims of Methuselah.*   New York, Stokes, and London, Bird, 1907.
> *Blue Goops and Red.*   New York, Stokes, 1909.
> *The Goop Directory of Juvenile Offenders.*   New York, Stokes, 1913.
> *The Maxims of Noah.*   New York, Stokes, 1913; London, Simpkin Marshall, 1914.
> *Burgess Unabridged.*   New York, Stokes, and London, Simpkin Marshall, 1914.
> *The Goop Encyclopedia.*   New York, Stokes, 1916.
> *War the Creator.*   New York, Huebsch, 1916.
> *Have You an Educated Heart?*   New York, Boni and Liveright, 1923.
> *Why Be a Goop?*   New York, Stokes, 1924.
> *Why Men Hate Women.*   New York, Payson and Clarke, and London, Brentano, 1927.
> *The Bromide and Other Theories.*   New York, Viking Press, 1933.
> *Look Eleven Years Younger.*   New York, Simon and Schuster, 1937.
> *Short Words Are Words of Might.*   Privately printed, 1939.
> *New Goops and How to Know Them.*   New York, Random House, 1951.
> *Bayside Bohemia: Fin de Siècle San Francisco and Its Little Magazines.*   San Francisco, Book Club of California, 1954.

Editor, *My Maiden Effort.*   New York, Doubleday, 1921.

*   *   *

Gelett Burgess, journalist and humorist, attempted to spoof the reading public with *The Master of Mysteries*, a collection of stories about Astrogon Kerby, a fraudulent crystal-ball medium who sometimes acts as a detective. It was published anonymously, but ingenious publicity soon revealed its authorship: the first letter of each chapter spelled "Gelett Burgess is the author," while the last letters read, "False to life and false to art." The introduction hints at a third cipher, but it has not been found. The Kerby stories are tongue-in-cheek members of the sentimental detective story which had a short vogue in the pre-Titanic world. They display the Gibson Girl syndrome, what with frothy subject matter, lightness of mood and language, meretricious eroticism, and social snobbery.

In a somewhat similar vein is the lesser-known *Find the Woman*, which knowingly introduces a succession of fictional clichés into an absurd robbery and murder plot. With lost babies who turn out to be heirs, fate-linked characters, and irrelevant intercalated stories, it is best taken as a self-parody of the Stevensonian fantasy, translated into the lightly ironic sentimentalism of the day.

In later life Burgess returned to the detective story with *Two O'Clock Courage*, a novel of amnesia and murder, and *Ladies in Boxes*, a medley of murder, fetichism, and fifth-column activities. Both are conventional and undistinguished, although *Ladies in Boxes* occasionally shows flashes of Burgess's early verbal brilliance.

Burgess's finest crime work is *A Murder at the Dôme*, in which irony, dissociated personality elements, and Bohemian life in Paris all build up to a strange murder.

—E. F. Bleiler

BURKE, John (Frederick).   Also writes as Jonathan Burke; Owen Burke; Harriet Esmond (in collaboration with his wife); Jonathan George; Joanna Jones; Sara Morris; Martin Sands. British. Born in Rye, Sussex, 8 March 1922. Educated at Holt High School, Liverpool. Served in the Royal Air Force, Royal Electrical and Mechanical Engineers, and Royal Marines during World War II: Sergeant. Married Jean Williams in 1963; two sons; five daughters from a previous marriage. Associate Editor, 1953–56, and Production Manager, 1956–57, Museum Press, London; Editorial Manager, Books for Pleasure Group, London, 1957–58; Public Relations and Publications Executive, Shell International Petroleum, London, 1959–63; Story Editor, Twentieth Century-Fox, London, 1963–65; Director, Low Associates Ltd., literary agency, London, 1965. Since 1966, free-lance writer. Recipient: Rockefeller Foundation Atlantic Award, 1949. Agent: David Higham Associates Ltd., 5–8 Lower John Street, London W1R 4HA. Address: 8 North Parade, Southwold, Suffolk, England.

CRIME PUBLICATIONS

Novels as John and Jonathan Burke (series character: Dr. Caspian)

Swift Summer.   London, Laurie, 1949.
Another Chorus.   London, Laurie, 1949.
These Haunted Streets.   London, Laurie, 1950.
The Outward Walls.   London, Laurie, 1952.
Chastity House.   London, Laurie, 1952.
The Poison Cupboard.   London, Secker and Warburg, 1956.
Corpse to Copenhagen.   London, Amalgamated Press, 1957.
Echo of Barbara.   London, Long, 1959.
Fear by Instalments.   London, Long, 1960.
The Angry Silence (novelization of screenplay).   London, Hodder and Stoughton, 1961.
Teach Yourself Treachery.   London, Long, 1962.
Deadly Downbeat.   London, Long, 1962.
The Man Who Finally Died (novelization of screenplay).   London, Pan, 1963.
Guilty Party (novelization of stage play).   London, Elek, 1963.
The Twisted Tongues.   London, Long, 1964; as *Echo of Treason*, New York, Dodd Mead, 1966.
Only the Ruthless Can Play.   London, Long, 1965.
The Weekend Girls.   London, Long, 1966; New York, Doubleday, 1967; as *Goodbye, Gillian*, New York, Ace, n.d.
The Trap (novelization of screenplay).   London, Pan, 1966.
Gossip to the Grave.   London, Long, 1967; as *The Gossip Truth*, New York, Doubleday, 1968.
The Jokers (novelization of screenplay; as Martin Sands).   London, Pan, 1967.
Maroc 7 (novelization of screenplay; as Martin Sands).   London, Pan, 1967.
Privilege (novelization of screenplay).   London, Pan, and New York, Avon, 1967.
Someone Lying, Someone Dying.   London, Long, 1968.
Rob the Lady.   London, Long, 1969.
Four Stars for Danger.   London, Long, 1970.
Strange Report (novelization of tv play).   London, Hodder and Stoughton, and New York, Lancer, 1970.
The Killdog, with George Theiner (as Jonathan George).   London, Macmillan, and New York, Doubleday, 1970.
Dead Letters (as Jonathan George).   London, Macmillan, 1972.
The Devil's Footsteps (Caspian).   London, Weidenfeld and Nicolson, and New York, Coward McCann, 1976.

The Black Charade (Caspian).   London, Weidenfeld and Nicolson, and New York, Coward McCann, 1977.

Ladygrove (Caspian).   London, Weidenfeld and Nicolson, and New York, Coward McCann, 1978.

Novels as Harriet Esmond

Darsham's Tower.   New York, Delacorte Press, 1973; as *Darsham's Folly*, London, Collins, 1974.

The Eye Stones.   London, Collins, and New York, Delacorte Press, 1975.

The Florian Signet.   London, Collins, 1977.

Uncollected Short Stories

"Party Games," in *6th Pan Book of Horror Stories*, edited by Herbert Van Thal.   London, Pan, 1965.

"The Calculated Nightmare," in *John Creasey's Mystery Bedside Book*, edited by Herbert Harris.   London, Hodder and Stoughton, 1967.

"Miss Mouse and Mrs. Mouse," in *Ellery Queen's Mystery Magazine* (New York), November 1968.

"Don't You Dare," in *Splinters*, edited by Alex Hamilton.   London, Hutchinson, 1968; New York, Walker, 1969.

"A Comedy of Terrors," in *9th Pan Book of Horror Stories*, edited by Herbert Van Thal.   London, Pan, 1968.

"Be Our Guest," in *More Tales of Unease*, edited by John Burke.   London, Pan, 1969.

"The Tourists," in *Tandem Horror 3*.   London, Tandem, 1969.

"Casualty," in *The Sixth Ghost Book*.   London, Barrie and Jenkins, 1971.

"Flitting Tenant," in *The Seventh Ghost Book*.   London, Barrie and Jenkins, 1971.

"The Loiterers," in *The Eighth Ghost Book*.   London, Barrie and Jenkins, 1972.

"False Harmonic," in *The Ninth Ghost Book*, edited by Rosemary Timperley.   London, Barrie and Jenkins, 1973.

"Leave of Absence," in *The Tenth Ghost Book*, edited by Aidan Chambers.   London, Barrie and Jenkins, 1974.

"The Custodian," in *The Eleventh Ghost Book*, edited by Aidan Chambers.   London, Barrie and Jenkins, 1975.

"And Cannot Come Again," in *New Tales of Unease*, edited by John Burke.   London, Pan, 1976.

"Lucille Would Have Known," in *New Terrors*.   London, Pan, 1979.

OTHER PUBLICATIONS

Novels as John and Jonathan Burke

Dark Gateway.   London, Panther, 1953.

The Echoing World.   London, Panther, 1954.

Twilight of Reason.   London, Panther, 1954.

Pattern of Shadows.   London, Panther, 1954.

Hotel Cosmos.   London, Panther, 1954.

Deep Freeze.   London, Panther, 1955.

Revolt of the Humans.   London, Panther, 1955.

Pursuit Through Time.   London, Ward Lock, 1956.

The Entertainer (novelization of stage play).   London, Four Square, 1960.

Look Back in Anger (novelization of stage play).   London, Four Square, 1960.

A Widow for the Winter (as Sara Morris).   London, Barker, 1961.

The Lion of Sparta (novelization of screenplay).   London, Pan, 1961; as *The 300 Spartans*, New York, New American Library, 1961.

Flame in the Streets (novelization of screenplay).   London, Four Square, 1961.
The Boys (novelization of screenplay).   London, Pan, 1962.
Private Potter (novelization of screenplay).   London, Pan, 1962.
The World Ten Times Over (novelization of screenplay).   London, Pan, 1962.
The System (novelization of screenplay).   London, Pan, 1964.
A Hard Day's Night (novelization of screenplay).   New York, Dell, 1964.
That Magnificent Air Race (novelization of screenplay).   London, Pan, 1965; as *Those Magnificent Men and Their Flying Machines*, New York, Pocket Books, 1965.
The Suburbs of Pleasure.   London, Secker and Warburg, and New York, Delacorte Press, 1967.
Till Death Us Do Part (novelization of tv play).   London, Pan, 1967.
Chitty Chitty Bang Bang: The Story of the Film.   London, Pan, 1968.
Smashing Time (novelization of screenplay).   London, Pan, 1968.
Moon Zero Two: The Story of the Film.   London, Pan, 1969.
The Smashing Bird I Used to Know (novelization of screenplay).   London, Pan, 1969.
All the Right Noises (novelization of screenplay).   London, Hodder and Stoughton, 1970.
Expo 80.   London, Cassell, 1972.
Luke's Kingdom (novelization of tv play).   London, Fontana, 1976.
The Prince Regent (novelization of tv play).   London, Fontana, 1979.
The Figurehead (as Owen Burke).   London, Collins, and New York, Coward McCann, 1979.

Novels as Joanna Jones

Nurse Is a Neighbour.   London, Joseph, 1958.
Nurse on the District.   London, Joseph, 1959.
The Artless Flat-Hunter.   London, Pelham, 1963.
The Artless Commuter.   London, Pelham, 1965.

Short Stories as John and Jonathan Burke

Alien Landscape: Science Fiction Stories.   London, Museum Press, 1955.
Dr. Terror's House of Horrors (adaptation of screenplay).   London, Pan, 1965.
The Hammer Horror Omnibus.   London, Pan, 1966.
The Power Game (adaptation of screenplays).   London, Pan, 1966.
The Second Hammer Horror Film Omnibus.   London, Pan, 1967.

Plays

Screenplay: *The Sorcerers*, with Michael Reeves and Tom Baker, 1967.

Radio Plays: *The Prodigal Pupil*, 1949; *The Man in the Ditch*, 1958; *Across Miss Desmond's Desk*, 1961.

Television Plays: *Safe Conduct*, 1965; *Calculated Nightmare*, from his own story, 1970; *Miss Mouse*, from his own story, 1972.

Other

The Happy Invaders: A Picture of Denmark in Springtime, with William Luscombe.   London, Hale, 1956.
Suffolk.   London, Batsford, 1971.
England in Colour.   London, Batsford, and New York, Hastings House, 1972.
Sussex.   London, Batsford, 1974.

225

An Illustrated History of England.   London, Collins, 1974; New York, McKay, 1976.
English Villages.   London, Batsford, 1975.
South East England (juvenile).   London, Faber, 1975.
Suffolk in Photographs, photographs by Anthony Kersting.   London, Batsford, 1976.
Beautiful Britain.   London, Batsford, 1976.
Czechoslovakia.   London, Batsford, 1976.
Historic Britain.   London, Batsford, 1977.
Life in the Castle in Mediaeval England.   London, Batsford, and Totowa, New Jersey, Rowan and Littlefield, 1978.
Life in the Villa in Roman Britain.   London, Batsford, 1978.

Editor, *Tales of Unease.*   London, Pan, 1966; New York, Doubleday, 1969.
Editor, *More Tales of Unease.*   London, Pan, 1969.
Editor, *New Tales of Unease.*   London, Pan, 1976.

Translator, *The West Face*, by Guido Magnone.   London, Museum Press, 1955.
Translator, *The Spark and the Flame*, by F. B. Muus.   London, Museum Press, 1957.
Translator, with Eiler Hansen, *The Moon of Beauty*, by Jørgen Andersen-Rosendal.   London, Museum Press, 1957.
Translator, with Eiler Hansen, *The Happy Lagoons: The World of Queen Salote*, by Jørgen Andersen-Rosendal.   London, Jarrolds, 1961.

John Burke comments:

Coming as I do from a long line of master carpenters, I have always considered it complimentary rather than derogatory to be called a "competent craftsman." This does not mean that I have ever consciously devoted myself to hack-work. A good carpenter should be able to make, for the pleasure and use of the people who want to buy it, a good kitchen table which will stand without wobbling and which is free from awkward corners or splintered edges. He may now and then, by refining his craft, aspire to become a Chippendale; but should remain proud of his well-proportioned kitchen tables. In writing thrillers and science-fiction I have rarely used extravagant ideas but tried rather to produce a tightly-knit, credible narrative. And in my other novels – which I refuse to refer to as "straight" or "serious," since I don't think of crime fiction or science-fiction as bent or frivolous – I have planned ahead just as carefully.

I cannot start a story of any kind until I know the setting in which the characters are to live and move. My wife and I cannot write our Victorian Gothic suspense novels (in collaboration as Harriet Esmond) without having stayed in, and explored, the region concerned.

I have always been more interested in the psychological suspense story rather than the detective, spy, or thick-ear picaresque rampage. The element of suspense should, I think, be present in other fictional genres as well: self-indulgent semi-autobiographical novelists insult their readers by supposing that their own personal problems are enough in themselves to carry a story. No matter what its theme, every novel, modern or historical, should to some extent be a mystery story – mysterious to the reader, but not to the carpenter who is planing and polishing the last raw snags off it.

*   *   *

John Burke, man of many aliases, is both prolific and versatile, a writer of thrillers, science fiction, Victorian romantic suspense, novelizations of plays and films, an anthologist, and a short-story writer (his best story, "The Calculated Nightmare," becoming a TV play). His memorable crime novel *Echo of Barbara* became a successful motion-picture, and other thrillers, such as *Deadly Downbeat, Fear by Instalments, The Twisted Tongues, The Weekend Girls, Four Stars for Danger*, and *The Killdog*, followed. These novels were for the most part suspense stories and psychological thrillers, and one, *The Twisted Tongues*, was a thriller in the international-political-power-game genre some years ahead of others in similar vein. Some of his recent novels feature a Victorian psychic investigator, Dr. Caspian.

—Herbert Harris

BURKE, Thomas. British. Born in London, in 1886. Educated at an orphanage after age 9. Served in the American division of the Ministry of Information during World War I. Married Winifred Wells (i.e., the writer Clare Cameron) in 1918. Left school at 14: worked in a boarding house and in an office, age 15–19; secretary in a theatre; bookseller's assistant; worked in Frank Casenove's literary agency, 1907–14. *Died 22 September 1945.*

CRIME PUBLICATIONS

Novels

> *Murder at Elstree; or, Mr. Thurtell and His Gig.* London, Longman, 1936.
> *Abduction: A Story of Limehouse.* London, Jenkins, 1939.

Short Stories (series character: Quong Lee)

> *Limehouse Nights: Tales of Chinatown* (Quong). London, Richards, 1916; New York, McBride, 1917; selections, as *Broken Blossoms*, Richards, 1920, and *In Chinatown*, Richards, 1921.
> *Whispering Windows: Tales of the Waterside.* London, Richards, 1921; as *More Limehouse Nights*, New York, Doran, 1921.
> *The Wind and the Rain: A Book of Confessions.* London, Butterworth, and New York, Doran, 1924.
> *East of Mansion House.* New York, Doran, 1926; London, Cassell, 1928.
> *The Bloomsbury Wonder.* London, Mandrake Press, 1929.
> *The Pleasantries of Old Quong.* London, Constable, and New York, Macmillan, 1931; as *A Tea-Shop in Limehouse*, Boston, Little Brown, 1931.
> *Night Pieces: Eighteen Tales.* London, Constable, 1935; New York, Appleton, 1936.
> *Dark Nights.* London, Jenkins, 1944.
> *The Best Stories of Thomas Burke*, edited by John Gawsworth. London, Phoenix House, 1950.

OTHER PUBLICATIONS

Novels

> *Twinkletoes: A Tale of Chinatown.* London, Richards, 1917; New York, McBride, 1918.
> *The Sun in Splendour.* New York, Doran, 1926; London, Constable, 1927.
> *The Flower of Life.* London, Constable, 1929; New York, Doubleday, 1930.
> *The Winsome Wench: The Story of a London Inn, 1825–1900.* London, Routledge, 1938.

Play

Radio Play: *The Hands of Mr. Ottermole.*

Verse

Verses. Privately printed, 1910.
Pavements and Pastures: A Book of Songs. Privately printed, 1912.
London Lamps: A Book of Songs. London, Richards, 1917; New York, McBride, 1919.
The Song Book of Quong Lee of Limehouse. London, Allen and Unwin, and New York
 Holt, 1920.

Other

Kiddie Land (juvenile verse), with Margaret G. Hays. London, Dean, 1913.
Nights in Town: A London Autobiography (essays). London, Allen and Unwin, 1915;
 as *Nights in London,* New York, Holt, 1916.
Out and About: A Note-Book of London in War-Time. London, Allen and Unwin,
 1919; as *Out and About in London,* New York, Holt, 1919.
The Outer Circle: Rambles in Remote London. London, Allen and Unwin, and New
 York, Doran, 1921.
The London Spy: A Book of Town Travels. London, Butterworth, and New York,
 Doran, 1922.
(Essays). London, Harrap, 1928.
The English Inn. London, Longman, 1930; revised edition, London, Jenkins, 1947.
Go, Lovely Rose. New York, Sesphra Library, 1931.
The Maid's Head, Norwich. London, True Temperance Association, 1931.
An Old London Alehouse: The Anchor, at Bankside. London, True Temperance
 Association, 1932.
City of Encounters: A London Divertissement. London, Constable, and Boston, Little
 Brown, 1932.
The Real East End. London, Constable, 1932.
The Beauty of England. London, Harrap, 1933; New York, McBride, 1934.
London in My Time. London, Rich and Cowan, 1934; New York, Loring and Mussey,
 1935.
Billy and Beryl in Chinatown [Old London, Soho] (juvenile). London, Harrap, 3 vols.,
 1935–36.
Vagabond Minstrel: The Adventures of Thomas Dermody. London, Longman, 1936.
*Will Someone Lead Me to a Pub? Being a Note upon Certain of the Taverns, Old and
 New, of London.* London, Routledge, 1936.
Dinner Is Served! or, Eating round the World in London. London, Routledge, 1937.
Living in Bloomsbury. London, Allen and Unwin, 1939.
The Streets of London Through the Centuries. London, Batsford, and New York,
 Scribner, 1940.
The First Noel. London, Wakeham, 1940.
English Night-Life, From Norman Curfew to Present Black-Out. London, Batsford,
 1941; New York, Scribner, 1946.
Victorian Grotesque. London, Jenkins, 1941.
Travel in England from Pilgrim to Pack-Horse to Light Car and Plane. London,
 Batsford, 1943; New York, Scribner, 1946.
English Inns. London, Collins, 1943.
The English and Their Country. London, Longman, 1945.
The English Townsman, As He Was and as He Is. London, Batsford, 1946; New York,
 Scribner, 1947.
Son of London. London, Jenkins, 1946.

Editor, *The Small People: A Little Book of Verse about Children for Their Elders.* London, Chapman and Hall, 1910.

Editor, *An Artist's Day Book: A Treasury of Good Counsel from the Great Masters in the Arts for Their Disciples.* London, Herbert and Daniel, 1911; selections, as *Life and Art* and *Truth and Beauty*, London, Cape, 2 vols., 1921; Boston, Humphries, 2 vols., 1937.

Editor, *The Charm of the West Country.* Bristol, Arrowsmith, 1913.

Editor, *Children in Verse: Fifty Songs of Playful Childhood.* London, Duckworth, 1913.

Editor, *The Contented Mind: An Anthology of Optimism.* London, Truslove and Hanson, 1914.

Editor, *The Charm of England.* London, Truslove and Hanson, 1914.

Editor, *The German Army from Within*, by B. G. Baker. London, Hodder and Stoughton, and New York, Doran, 1914.

Editor, *The Book of the Inn.* London, Constable, and New York, Doran, 1927.

Editor, *The Ecstasies of Thomas De Quincey.* London, Harrap, 1928; New York, Doubleday, 1929.

Bibliography: in *Ten Contemporaries*, 2nd series, by John Gawsworth, London, Benn, 1933.

*   *   *

Although best known for his exotic tales of London's Chinatown, *Limehouse Nights* and its sequels, Thomas Burke wrote over thirty books, many of them evocative descriptions of London, its streets, its inns, and particularly its East End where he grew up. Orphaned in infancy, Burke lived the first nine years of his life with an uncle in the London working-class district of Poplar, not far from Limehouse and the teeming Thames River docks. Fascinated at an early age with the life of the East End streets, he gained more of an education from observing the flotsam and jetsam of humanity there than he did from books and formal schooling. During those years, his best friend was an elderly Chinaman, the original model for the character of Quong Lee, the Chinatown philosopher in *Limehouse Nights*, whose tea-shop in Limehouse he would visit in secret to receive bits of ginger and a knowledge of "all the beauty and all the evil of the heart of Asia; its cruelty, its grace and its wisdom." "In that shop," Burke wrote, "I knew what some people seek in church and others seek in taverns." Several years later, when his aged friend was deported for having operated an opium den, Burke was inspired to write the first of his collection of short stories about Limehouse. To Burke, whose literary credo was "to tell a story as ably as Ambrose Bierce and to see and write as clearly as Stephen Crane," *Limehouse Nights* was "admittedly violent stuff written hastily," as a means of "simply telling tales." But it firmly established his literary reputation in Britain, and the film adaptation of the first tale in the collection under the title of *Broken Blossoms* extended the boundaries of his reputation internationally.

Among Burke's many tales of terror, superstition, human passion, and borderline mystery-detection, at least three are genuine and noteworthy contributions to detective fiction: "The Hands of Mr. Ottermole" and "Murder under the Crooked Spire," two short stories with anonymous detectives, and *Murder at Elstree; or, Mr. Thurtell and His Gig*, a novelette based on the murder of Mr. William Weare in 1821 by Messrs. Thurtell and Hunt, chronicled in George Borrow's *Celebrated Trials and Remarkable Cases of Criminal Jurisprudence.* Undoubtedly, however, "The Hands of Mr. Ottermole," a fictional reworking *par excellence* of the Jack-the-Ripper story in the original East End setting, replete with foggy, gaslit streets and strangled corpses, is Burke's detective fiction masterpiece. In this multiple murder tale of rushing terror, Burke conjures an air of black magic mixed with mass paranoia and transforms a pair of human hands – "those appendages that are a symbol for our moments of trust and affection and salutation" – into two "five-tentacled members" of brutal and wanton murder. In 1949, a board of eminent critics including Anthony Boucher, John Dickson Carr, and Ellery Queen selected "The Hands of Mr. Ottermole" as the "greatest mystery story of all time."

—Arthur Nicholas Athanason

BURLEY, W(illiam) J(ohn).   British.   Born in Falmouth, Cornwall, 1 August 1914. Educated at County Technical School; trained as gas engineer (Keam Scholar), qualified 1936; Balliol College, Oxford (Herbertson Prize, 1952), 1950–53, M.A. 1953. Married Muriel Wolsey in 1938; two sons. Engineer and manager for South Western Gas and Water Corporation Ltd, in southwest England, 1936–50; Head of Biology Department, Richmond Grammar School, Surrey, 1953–55; Head of Biology, 1955–59, and Tutor, 1959–74, Newquay School, Cornwall. Since 1974, full-time writer. Agent: Victor Gollancz Ltd, 14 Henrietta Street, London WC2E 8QJ. Address: St. Patricks, Holywell, Newquay, Cornwall, England.

CRIME PUBLICATIONS

Novels (series characters: Henry Pym; Superintendent Charles Wycliffe)

A Taste of Power (Pym).   London, Gollancz, 1966.
Three-Toed Pussy (Wycliffe).   London, Gollancz, 1968.
Death in Willow Pattern (Pym).   London, Gollancz, 1969; New York, Walker, 1970.
To Kill a Cat (Wycliffe).   London, Gollancz, and New York, Walker, 1970.
Guilt Edged (Wycliffe).   London, Gollancz, 1971; New York, Walker, 1972.
Death in a Salubrious Place (Wycliffe).   London, Gollancz, and New York, Walker, 1973.
Death in Stanley Street (Wycliffe).   London, Gollancz, and New York, Walker, 1974.
Wycliffe and the Pea-Green Boat.   London, Gollancz, and New York, Walker, 1975.
Wycliffe and the Schoolgirls.   London, Gollancz, and New York, Walker, 1976.
The Schoolmaster.   London, Gollancz, and New York, Walker, 1977.
Wycliffe and the Scapegoat.   London, Gollancz, 1978; New York, Doubleday, 1979.
Charles and Elizabeth.   London, Gollancz, 1979.
Wycliffe in Paul's Court.   London, Gollancz, 1979.

OTHER PUBLICATIONS

Novel

The Sixth Day.   London, Gollancz, 1978.

Other

Centenary History of the City of Truro.   Truro, Blackford, 1977.

W. J. Burley comments:
I started to write crime fiction in 1966 after being greatly impressed by a belated introduction to the work of Simenon. My first three novels were attempts to find my feet and

a publisher. I was lucky, for all three were published by Gollancz. In my fourth – *To Kill a Cat* – I tried to establish my detective, Charles Wycliffe, as a recognizable character round whom I could write a series of novels. I wanted him to be diligent but compassionate, earnest but with a wry sense of humour, and sufficiently idiosyncratic to be interesting. My next five books exploited the Wycliffe character and three of them, *Guilt Edged*, *Wycliffe and the Pea-Green Boat*, and *Wycliffe and the Schoolgirls*, adopted a more psychological approach. This trend culminated in *The Schoolmaster*, a non-Wycliffe crime story which tells how a sensitive, introspective schoolmaster with a load of guilt finds his way to some sort of salvation. Wycliffe, however, continued to thrive in *Wycliffe and the Scapegoat*, which relies a great deal on its Cornish setting.

I have never felt very happy with my books – they seemed rather too derivative, following too closely an established pattern – so in *Charles and Elizabeth* I resolved to break new ground, and for the first time I feel that I have written a book which offers something a little different in the way of crime stories. At least it has in it more of *me* than anything else I have written.

*   *   *

W. J. Burley has written some dozen mystery novels, several of them featuring Superintendent Wycliffe, an unconventional policeman who hates routine and authority, and proceeds about his murder investigations by the gestalt method. He immerses himself in the victim's history and circle of acquaintances until he feels his way to a conclusion. Burley plots competently and writes well, if rather humorlessly. His forte is examining the effect of the psychologically aberrant on those around them. The murder victim in *To Kill a Cat* is a young woman who was as amoral as she was intelligent and beautiful. Wycliffe discovers that she had corrupted her own brother and maimed several other men in a career that culminates in suicide by proxy. The portrait of Pussy Welles is arresting, but not fully convincing.

Burley is fascinated by the figure of the young and beautiful girl who dooms the men around her, and she appears in several later books. Her most satisfying appearance is in *The Schoolmaster*, a balanced, convincing study of guilt. Here, she is reduced to a schoolgirl with advanced sexual tastes who dies young, but gravely alters the life of the young teacher who had been involved with her. Wycliffe does not appear in this book or in *Death in Willow Pattern*, whose hero is Henry Pym, Professor of Zoology and criminologist. Here, murder occurs in a family haunted by fear of hereditary insanity, and Burley handles the theme gently and satisfactorily.

—Carol Cleveland

BURNETT, W(illiam) R(iley). Also writes as John Monahan; James Updyke. American. Born in Springfield, Ohio, 25 November 1899. Educated at Miami Military Institute, Germantown, Ohio; Ohio State University, Columbus, 1919–20. Married Whitney Forbes Johnston in 1943 (second wife); two children. Statistician, State of Ohio, 1921–27; full-time writer since 1927. Recipient: O Henry Memorial Award, 1930; Mystery Writers of America Edgar Allan Poe Award, for screenplay, 1951; Writers Guild of America award, for screenplay, 1963. Agent: H. N. Swanson Inc., 8523 Sunset Boulevard, Hollywood, California; or Scott Meredith Literary Agency Inc., 845 Third Avenue, New York, New York 10022. Address: 1610 San Remo Drive, Pacific Palisades, California, U.S.A.

CRIME PUBLICATIONS

Novels

Little Caesar. New York, Dial Press, and London, Cape, 1929.
The Silver Eagle. New York, Dial Press, 1931; London, Heinemann, 1932.
Dark Hazard. New York, Harper, 1933; London, Heinemann, 1934.
King Cole. New York, Harper, 1936; as *Six Days' Grace*, London, Heinemann, 1937.
High Sierra. New York, Knopf, and London, Heinemann, 1940.
The Quick Brown Fox. New York, Knopf, 1942; London, Heinemann, 1943.
Nobody Lives Forever. New York, Knopf, 1943; London, Heinemann, 1944.
Tomorrow's Another Day. New York, Knopf, 1945; London, Heinemann, 1946.
Romelle. New York, Knopf, 1946; London, Heinemann, 1947.
The Asphalt Jungle. New York, Knopf, 1949; London, Macdonald, 1950.
Little Men, Big World. New York, Knopf, 1951; London, Macdonald, 1952.
Vanity Row. New York, Knopf, 1952; London, Macdonald, 1953.
Big Stan (as John Monahan). New York, Fawcett, 1953; London, Fawcett, 1955.
Underdog. New York, Knopf, and London, Macdonald, 1957.
Conant. New York, Popular Library, 1961.
Round the Clock at Volari's. New York, Fawcett, 1961.
The Widow Barony. London, Macdonald, 1962.
The Cool Man. New York, Fawcett, 1968.

Uncollected Short Stories

"Dressing Up," in *O. Henry Memorial Award Prize Stories of 1930.* New York,
    Doubleday, 1930.
"Ivory Tower," in *Best American Short Stories of 1946*, edited by Martha
    Foley. Boston, Houghton Mifflin, 1946.
"Round Trip," in *Ellery Queen's Mystery Magazine* (New York), December 1950.
"Traveling Light," in *Ellery Queen's Mystery Magazine* (New York), September 1951.
"Nobody's All Bad," in *Ellery Queen's Mystery Magazine* (New York), December 1953.
"The Night of the Gran Baile Mascara," in *Ellery Queen's Mystery Magazine* (New
    York), July 1965.

OTHER PUBLICATIONS

Novels

Iron Man. New York, Dial Press, and London, Heinemann, 1930.
Saint Johnson. New York, Dial Press, 1930; London, Heinemann, 1931.
The Giant Swing. New York, Harper, 1932; London, Heinemann, 1933.
Goodbye to the Past: Scenes from the Life of William Meadows. New York, Harper,
    1934; London, Heinemann, 1935.
The Goodhues of Sinking Creek. New York, Harper, 1934.
The Dark Command: A Kansas Iliad. New York, Knopf, and London, Heinemann,
    1938.
Stretch Dawson. New York, Fawcett, 1950; London, Muller, 1960.
Adobe Walls. New York, Knopf, 1953; London, Macdonald, 1954.
Captain Lightfoot. New York, Knopf, 1954; London, Macdonald, 1955.
It's Always Four O'Clock (as James Updyke). New York, Random House, 1956.
Pale Moon. New York, Knopf, 1956; London, Macdonald, 1957.
Bitter Ground. New York, Knopf, and London, Macdonald, 1958.
Mi Amigo. New York, Knopf, 1959; London, Macdonald, 1960.
The Goldseekers. New York, Doubleday, 1962; London, Macdonald, 1963.

The Winning of Mickey Free. New York, Bantam, 1965.

Plays

Screenplays: *The Finger Points*, with John Monk Saunders, 1931; *The Beast of the City*, 1932; *Some Blondes Are Dangerous*, with Lester Cole, 1937; *King of the Underworld*, with George Bricker and Vincent Sherman, 1938; *High Sierra*, with John Huston, 1941; *This Gun for Hire*, with Albert Maltz, 1941; *The Get-Away*, with Wells Root and J. Walter Ruben, 1941; *Wake Island*, with Frank Butler, 1942; *Crash Dive*, with Jo Swerling, 1943; *Action in the North Atlantic*, with others, 1943; *Background to Danger*, 1943; *San Antonio*, with Allan LeMay, 1945; *Nobody Lives Forever*, 1946; *Belle Starr's Daughter*, 1948; *Yellow Sky*, with Lamar Trotti, 1949; *The Iron Man*, with George Zuckerman and Borden Chase, 1951; *Vendetta*, with Peter O'Crotty, 1951; *The Racket*, with William Wister Haines, 1951; *Dangerous Mission*, with others, 1954; *Captain Lightfoot*, with Oscar Brodney, 1955; *Illegal*, with James R. Webb and Frank Collins, 1955; *I Died a Thousand Deaths*, 1955; *Accused of Murder*, with Robert Creighton Williams, 1957; *September Storm*, with Steve Fisher, 1961; *Sergeants 3*, 1962; *The Great Escape*, with James Clavell, 1963.

Other

The Roar of the Crowd (on baseball). New York, Potter, 1965.

*   *   *

If his novels were to be judged solely for their influence, W. R. Burnett would undeniably be numbered among the most important writers of his time. His works may fall short of greatness, but they deserve more critical attention than they now receive. Three were transformed into major genre movies, pictures that either established or extended the possibilities of their particular kind – *Little Caesar*, *High Sierra*, and *The Asphalt Jungle*. His novels are not mysteries, but crime novels, powerful, accurate, cynical explorations of criminals in their own environment; at their best they are important additions to the honor roll of hard-boiled fiction that includes such writers as Dashiell Hammett, Horace McCoy, and James M. Cain, as well as Hemingway and the early Faulkner. Their terse, clipped style, their close attention to the observed reality of modern urban society, their concentration on the hard surfaces of things, and especially their cinematic urgency and immediacy not only make them easily adaptable to the screen, but place them squarely in the tradition of Thirties naturalism.

Little Caesar and *The Asphalt Jungle*, separated by two decades, are Burnett's major achievements. The first, for all practical purposes, created the gangster as the appropriate figure for his time; the second did for the big caper novel what Walpole did for the Gothic romance. *Little Caesar*, the story of the rise and fall of Rico Cesare Bandello, introduced the major and minor elements that soon became commonplace in the form – the ambitious Italian who rises from petty hoodlum to leader of a gang through ruthlessness and treachery, the world of urban violence that fosters criminal activity, the necessary defeat of the protagonist at the peak of his success. He established the dominant iconography of sleek cars and flashy clothes, bootleg liquor and tommyguns, the atmospheres of dance halls and saloons, brothels and speakeasies, the gilded seediness of city life in what used to be called the underworld. Most of all, *Little Caesar* made the gangster one of the generative symbols of the 1930's – the small, dark, menacingly self-controlled man whose parabolic trajectory and anarchic rebellion against the existing social order reflected ironically the aspirations and dissatisfactions of Americans everywhere in a harsh and difficult time. As a novel, *Little Caesar* influenced William Faulkner's *Sanctuary* and Graham Greene's *Brighton Rock*. As a film, it turned the gangster movie into one of the richest and most significant American genres, engendering some remarkable offspring – *Public Enemy*, *The Roaring Twenties*,

233

White Heat, and *The Godfather* – and energizing the careers of, for example, Edward G. Robinson, Jimmy Cagney, George Raft, and Humphrey Bogart.

Although it lacks some of the relentless pacing and the bleak atmospherics of *Little Caesar*, *The Asphalt Jungle* may be even more original as a fictional achievement. It is generally credited with being the first work built around the complicated crime involving an enormous quantity of loot. It focuses less on one dominating figure and more on the collective entity required to pull off the crime. In the process of showing the necessary interactions of a team of specialists working together, the book comments on the changes in American society between 1929 and 1949; the movement from individualism to group endeavor indicates the evolution of crime from a relatively simple act of free enterprise to a complex corporate action. Crime, we understand, parallels its culture, a much more sophisticated and intricate business than in the days of Little Caesar and more insidious in its evolution from rebellion to cooperation. The big caper novel revolves around the inevitable collision of two organizations – the criminals and the policemen – which, though in some ways similar, must ultimately be opposed; the intercutting between the two sets up the tension and ambivalence that cause the reader to divide his loyalties and at some point root for the bad guys. The novel also originated that important sense of mechanism – the caper as a brilliant, thoroughly planned, rigidly timed scheme depending on absolute adherence to its details. Burnett's novel, and all the big capers that follow it, shows the folly of such schemes – technology cannot triumph over the imponderable absurdities of human behavior: someone acts unpredictably or some trivial chance occurrence intervenes, and the whole structure of delusion collapses.

W. R. Burnett is an important and original writer whose credentials must be recognized and respected: he may be the single most successful writer on the notion of the criminal as the emblem of an era. He provides some of the most dynamic and apposite metaphors for the life of America in the twentieth century. The fact that his metaphors derive from a context of violence and treachery, rebellion and disorder, the violation and corruption of the law, should not shock any alert, informed observer; his world demonstrates Burnett's profound and accurate insight into his country and his age.

—George Grella

BURNS, Rex (Raoul Stephen Schler).   American, Born in San Diego, California, 13 June 1935. Educated at Stanford University, California, B.A. 1958; University of Minnesota, Minneapolis, M.A. 1963, Ph.D. 1965. Served in the United States Marine Corps, 1958–61: Captain. Married Emily Sweitzer in 1959; three sons. Assistant Professor, Central Missouri State University, Warrensburg, 1965–68. Since 1969, Professor, University of Colorado, Denver. Fulbright lecturer in Greece, 1969–70, and Argentina, 1977. Recipient: Mystery Writers of America Edgar Allan Poe Award, 1976. Agent: Brandt and Brandt, 101 Park Avenue, New York, New York 10017. Address: 357 Hollyberry Lane, Boulder, Colorado 80303, U.S.A.

Crime Publications

Novels (series character: Gabriel Wager in all books)

The Alvarez Journal.   New York, Harper, 1975; London, Hale, 1976.
The Farnsworth Score.   New York, Harper, 1977; London, Hale, 1978.

Speak for the Dead.   New York, Harper, 1978; London, Hale, 1979.
Angle of Attack.   New York, Harper, 1979.

OTHER PUBLICATIONS

Other

Success in America: The Yeoman Dream and the Industrial Revolution.   Amherst,
   University of Massachusetts Press, 1975.
"Writing the Police Procedural," in *The Writer* (Boston), July 1977.
"The Reality of the Lie," in *Colorado Quote* (Denver), December 1978.

Rex Burns comments:
I try to do two things: create life and make the reader ask, "What happens next?"
Anything else – themes, patterns, etc. – is of lesser importance, and primarily for my own
pleasure.

*   *   *

Detective Gabriel Wager of the Denver Police Department is the creation of Rex Burns.
Wager belongs among the considerable number of fictional police detectives who are able to
maintain their professional integrity in spite of their own internal suffering. A Chicano cop
caught between the world of white policemen who think of him as a greaser and the Chicano
community who consider him a traitor, Wager is most concerned with his own self-respect,
even when Anglos with no greater ability than his are promoted above him.

Wager's commitment to his job comes into sharp focus in the second novel of his series,
The Farnsworth Score, in which the theme is police corruption. Cops don't cheat, Wager
reflects; they don't make accusations against each other on the basis of circumstantial
evidence. A policeman must expect more from the men he works with than he expects from
a marriage. Practical-minded cop that he is, Wager also knows that erosion of trust in the
police force will hurt relationships with informants, without whose confidence no
department can function.

One of the special strengths of the Wager series is Rex Burns's first-hand knowledge of
police attitudes and the police sub-culture. He knows the frustrations of the mountains of
paper-work, the intense dedication of policemen that is usually not reciprocated by the public
or their own superiors, and the constant temptation of graft as a result of a policeman's low
pay.

—George N. Dove

BURTON, Miles.   See **RHODE, John.**

BUSBY, Roger (Charles). British. Born in Leicester, 24 July 1941. Educated at Bishop Vesey's Grammar School for Boys; Aston University, Birmingham, qualified in journalism. Married Maureen-Jeanette Busby in 1968. Journalist, Caters News Agency, Birmingham, 1959–66, and Birmingham *Evening Mail*, 1966–73. Since 1973, Force Information Officer, Devon and Cornwall Constabulary, Exeter. Address: Sunnymoor, Bridford, near Exeter, Devon, England.

CRIME PUBLICATIONS

Novels (series character: Detective Inspector Leric)

Main Line Kill, with Gerald Holtham. London, Cassell, and New York, Walker, 1968.
Robbery Blue (Leric). London, Collins, 1969.
The Frighteners (Leric). London, Collins, 1970.
Deadlock (Leric). London, Collins, 1971.
A Reasonable Man (Leric). London, Collins, 1972.
Pattern of Violence (Leric). London, Collins, 1973.
New Face in Hell. London, Collins, 1976.
Garvey's Code. London, Collins, 1978.

Roger Busby comments:
My novels are police stories through which I endeavour to produce the authentic flavour of criminal investigation. I hope that they give the reader an insight into the world of the British police within the dramatic framework of crime fiction. For any chronicle of police work would be a pale shadow without drawing upon the character and psychology of both the detectives and the criminals, the principal protagonists of the drama. My emphasis, therefore, is on characterisation rather than the mechanics of the plot. If, on reaching the last page, the reader feels he or she has experienced the unique atmosphere of the police environment, then I have achieved my purpose.

*   *   *

Roger Busby is one of the best practitioners of the police procedural novel. A journalist-crime reporter for many years, he has obviously used his experience to provide very accurate background information. Although the reader has little detection to do, he is kept alert by taut plots; Busby's characters are very believable and the portrayals well-written.

Busby's first novel, *Main Line Kill*, was written in collaboration with Gerald Holtham and received general acclaim. The first novel under his own name was *Robbery Blue*, and he kept to a subject well known to him. The narrative of this book is exciting and the portrayal of characters, be they police or villains, convincing. Inspector Leric made his first appearance in *Robbery Blue*, and his down-to-earth appraisal of both villains and his own superiors made him an obvious character for featuring in future books.

Unlike those of some writers, Busby's books seem to get better and better, and, although still concentrating upon police procedurals, he varies his themes sufficiently to satisfy even the most demanding of readers. Although most of his books are set in the midlands, his stories both north and south of this location do not lose their authenticity. *Pattern of Violence* and *The Frighteners* are good examples of his works.

—Donald C. Ireland

BUSH, Christopher. Pseudonym for Charlie Christmas Bush; also wrote as Michael Home. British. Born in East Anglia, in 1888(?): birth date unrecorded. Educated at Thetford Grammar School, Norfolk; King's College, London, B.A. (honours) in modern languages. Served in both world wars: Major. Schoolmaster before becoming a full-time writer. *Died 21 September 1973.*

<small>CRIME PUBLICATIONS</small>

Novels (series character: Ludovic Travers in all books)

The Plumley Inheritance. London, Jarrolds, 1926.
The Perfect Murder Case. London, Heinemann, and New York, Doubleday, 1929.
Murder at Fenwold. London, Heinemann, 1930; as *The Death of Cosmo Revere*, New York, Doubleday, 1930.
Dead Man Twice. London, Heinemann, and New York, Doubleday, 1930.
Dancing Death. London, Heinemann, and New York, Doubleday, 1931.
Dead Man's Music. London, Heinemann, 1931; New York, Doubleday, 1932.
Cut Throat. London, Heinemann, and New York, Morrow, 1932.
The Case of the Unfortunate Village. London, Cassell, 1932.
The Case of the Three Strange Faces. London, Heinemann, 1933; as *The Crank in the Corner*, New York, Morrow, 1933.
The Case of the April Fools. London, Cassell, and New York, Morrow, 1933.
The Case of the Dead Shepherd. London, Cassell, 1934; as *The Tea Tray Murders*, New York, Morrow, 1934.
The Case of the 100% Alibis. London, Cassell, 1934; as *The Kitchen Cake Murder*, New York, Morrow, 1934.
The Case of the Chinese Gong. London, Cassell, and New York, Holt, 1935.
The Case of the Bonfire Body. London, Cassell, 1936; as *The Body in the Bonfire*, New York, Morrow, 1936.
The Case of the Monday Murders. London, Cassell, 1936; as *Murder on Mondays*, New York, Holt, 1936.
The Case of the Hanging Rope. London, Cassell, 1937; as *The Wedding Night Murder*, New York, Holt, 1937.
The Case of the Missing Minutes. London, Cassell, 1937; as *Eight O'Clock Alibi*, New York, Holt, 1937.
The Case of the Tudor Queen. London, Cassell, and New York, Holt, 1938.
The Case of the Leaning Man. London, Cassell, 1938; as *The Leaning Man*, New York, Holt, 1938.
The Case of the Green Felt Hat. London, Cassell, and New York, Holt, 1939.
The Case of the Flying Ass. London, Cassell, 1939.
The Case of the Climbing Rat. London, Cassell, 1940.
The Case of the Murdered Major. London, Cassell, 1941.
The Case of the Fighting Soldier. London, Cassell, 1942.
The Case of the Kidnapped Colonel. London, Cassell, 1942.
The Case of the Magic Mirror. London, Cassell, 1943.
The Case of the Running Mouse. London, Cassell, 1944.
The Case of the Platinum Blonde. London, Cassell, 1944; New York, Macmillan, 1949.
The Case of the Corporal's Leave. London, Cassell, 1945.
The Case of the Second Chance. London, Cassell, 1946; New York, Macmillan, 1947.
The Case of the Missing Men. London, Macdonald, 1946; New York, Macmillan, 1947.
The Case of the Curious Client. London, Macdonald, 1947; New York, Macmillan, 1948.

The Case of the Haven Hotel. London, Macdonald, 1948.

The Case of the Housekeeper's Hair. London, Macdonald, 1948; New York, Macmillan, 1949.

The Case of the Seven Bells. London, Macdonald, 1949; New York, Macmillan, 1950.

The Case of the Purloined Picture. London, Macdonald, 1949; New York, Macmillan, 1951.

The Case of the Happy Warrior. London, Macdonald, 1950; as *The Case of the Frightened Mannequin*, New York, Macmillan, 1951.

The Case of the Fourth Detective. London, Macdonald, 1951.

The Case of the Corner Cottage. London, Macdonald, 1951; New York, Macmillan, 1952.

The Case of the Happy Medium. London, Macdonald, and New York, Macmillan, 1952.

The Case of the Counterfeit Colonel. London, Macdonald, 1952; New York, Macmillan, 1953.

The Case of the Burnt Bohemian. London, Macdonald, 1953; New York, Macmillan, 1954.

The Case of the Silken Petticoat. London, Macdonald, 1953; New York, Macmillan, 1954.

The Case of the Three Lost Letters. London, Macdonald, 1954; New York, Macmillan, 1955.

The Case of the Red Brunette. London, Macdonald, 1954; New York, Macmillan, 1955.

The Case of the Amateur Actor. London, Macdonald, 1955; New York, Macmillan, 1956.

The Case of the Benevolent Bookie. London, Macdonald, 1955; New York, Macmillan, 1956.

The Case of the Extra Man. London, Macdonald, 1956; New York, Macmillan, 1957.

The Case of the Flowery Corpse. London, Macdonald, 1956; New York, Macmillan, 1957.

The Case of the Russian Cross. London, Macdonald, 1957; New York, Macmillan, 1958.

The Case of the Treble Twist. London, Macdonald, 1958; as *The Case of the Triple Twist*, New York, Macmillan, 1958.

The Case of the Running Man. London, Macdonald, 1958; New York, Macmillan, 1959.

The Case of the Careless Thief. London, Macdonald, 1959; New York, Macmillan, 1960.

The Case of the Sapphire Brooch. London, Macdonald, 1960; New York, Macmillan, 1961.

The Case of the Extra Grave. London, Macdonald, 1961; New York, Macmillan, 1962.

The Case of the Dead Man Gone. London, Macdonald, and New York, Macmillan, 1962.

The Case of the Three-Ring Puzzle. London, Macdonald, 1962; New York, Macmillan, 1963.

The Case of the Heavenly Twin. London, Macdonald, 1963; New York, Macmillan, 1964.

The Case of the Grand Alliance. London, Macdonald, 1964; New York, Macmillan, 1965.

The Case of the Jumbo Sandwich. London, Macdonald, 1965; New York, Macmillan, 1966.

The Case of the Good Employer. London, Macdonald, 1966; New York, Macmillan, 1967.

The Case of the Deadly Diamonds.   London, Macdonald, 1967; New York, Macmillan,
   1969.
The Case of the Prodigal Daughter.   London, Macdonald, 1968; New York,
   Macmillan, 1969.

Novels as Michael Home

The Questing Man.   London, Rich and Cowan, 1936.
The Harvest Is Past.   London, Rich and Cowan, 1937.
July at Fritham.   London, Rich and Cowan, 1938.
City of the Soul.   London, Methuen, 1943.
The Cypress Road.   London, Methuen, 1945.
The Strange Prisoner.   London, Methuen, 1947.
No Snow in Latching.   London, Methuen, 1949.
The Soundless Years.   London, Methuen, 1951.
The Auber File.   London, Methuen, 1953.
That Was Yesterday.   London, Methuen, 1955.

Uncollected Short Stories

"The Hampstead Murder," in *A Century of Detective Stories.*   London, Hutchinson,
   1935.
"A Drop Too Much," in *Fifty Famous Detectives of Fiction.*   London, Odhams Press,
   1938.
"The Holly Bears a Berry: A Ludovic Travers Story," in *Illustrated London News*, 15
   November 1951.
"Tears for the Jury," in *The Saint* (New York), June 1956.
"Wings of Death," in *The Saint* (New York), October 1956.
"Murder of a Maharajah," in *The Saint* (New York), February 1957.

OTHER PUBLICATIONS as Michael Home

Novels

Return.   New York, Morrow, 1933; as *God and the Rabbit*, London, Rich and Cowan,
   1934.
This String First.   London, Rich and Cowan, 1935.
The Place of Little Birds.   London, Methuen, 1941; as *Attack in the Desert*, New York,
   Morrow, 1942.
The House of Shade.   London, Methuen, and New York, Morrow, 1942.
Grain of the Wood.   London, Methuen, 1950; New York, Macmillan, 1951.
The Brackenford Story.   London, Methuen, and New York, Macmillan, 1952.

Other

David.   London, Rich and Cowan, 1937.
Autumn Fields.   London, Methuen, 1944.
Spring Sowing.   London, Methuen, 1946.
Winter Harvest: A Norfolk Boyhood.   London, Macdonald, 1967.

*   *   *

Christopher Bush, during his 40-year writing career, produced over 80 books. His leisurely
English is easy to read; within their limits – and he wrote very much to a pattern – his novels
satisfy because the puzzle is clever, the story not stereotyped. Essentially they are alibi stories,

but their complexity is often more ingenious than Crofts's. They nearly always fall into three parts, sometimes with a prologue: always the crime, generally murder, is followed by the investigation, which results in a long pause, with a number of well-alibied suspects; the third part generally follows after a gap of some months, when some fortuitous incident starts a new train of thoughts or suggests an inconsistency in earlier evidence.

Of course there are maps and plans, an essential of his period of writing. He had the best of both worlds with his detective. Ludovic (Kim) Travers, part-owner of a detective agency, is also a nephew of the Commissioner for Scotland Yard, thus providing a useful link with Superintendent Wharton. Travers and Wharton work happily together, with neither concealing much from the other, and Wharton often using Travers as a stalking horse in the last stages of the case, though often Travers has the break-through idea.

The Perfect Murder Case does not quite live up to its dramatic beginning but has an ingenious alibi. *The Case of the Dead Shepherd* and *The Case of the Treble Twist* are tricky. Even his last, *The Case of the Prodigal Daughter*, very up-to-date with Soho vice, is well-constructed, though not as complex as those of his middle and war periods. From earlier days, the best are *The Case of the Burnt Bohemian*, *The Case of the Seven Bells*, and *The Case of the Murdered Major*.

—Neville W. Wood

BUTLER, Gwendoline (née Williams). Also writes as Jennie Melville. British. Born in London. Educated at Haberdashers' Aske's Hatcham Girls' School, London, 1939–42; Lady Margaret Hall, Oxford, 1944–49, B.A. in modern history 1949. Married Lionel Butler in 1949; one daughter. Taught at two Oxford colleges for a short time. Recipient: Crime Writers Association Silver Dagger, 1973. Agent: John Farquharson Ltd., 8 Bell Yard, London WC2A 2JU. Address: The Principal's House, Royal Holloway College, Egham, Surrey, England.

CRIME PUBLICATIONS

Novels as Gwendoline Butler (series character: Inspector John Coffin)

Receipt for Murder. London, Bles, 1956.
Dead in a Row (Coffin). London, Bles, 1957.
The Dull Dead. London, Bles, 1958; New York, Walker, 1962.
The Murdering Kind. London, Bles, 1958; New York, Roy, 1964.
The Interloper. London, Bles, 1959.
Death Lives Next Door (Coffin). London, Bles, 1960; as *Dine and Be Dead*, New York, Macmillan, 1960.
Make Me a Murderer (Coffin). London, Bles, 1961.
Coffin in Oxford. London, Bles, 1962.
Coffin for Baby. London, Bles, and New York, Walker, 1963.
Coffin Waiting. London, Bles, 1963; New York, Walker, 1965.
Coffin in Malta. London, Bles, 1964; New York, Walker, 1965.
A Nameless Coffin. London, Bles, 1966; New York, Walker, 1967.
Coffin Following. London, Bles, 1968.
Coffin's Dark Number. London, Bles, 1969.
A Coffin from the Past. London, Bles, 1970.

A Coffin for Pandora. London, Macmillan, 1973; as *Olivia,* New York, Coward McCann, 1974.

A Coffin for the Canary. London, Macmillan, 1974; as *Sarsen Place,* New York, Coward McCann, 1974.

The Vesey Inheritance. New York, Coward McCann, 1975; London, Macmillan, 1976.

The Brides of Friedberg. London, Macmillan, 1977; as *Meadowsweet,* New York, Coward McCann, 1977.

Novels as Jennie Melville (series character: Charmian Daniels)

Come Home and Be Killed (Daniels). London, Joseph, 1962; New York, British Book Centre, 1964.

Burning Is a Substitute for Loving (Daniels). London, Joseph, 1963; New York, British Book Centre, 1964.

Murderers' Houses (Daniels). London, Joseph, 1964.

There Lies Your Love (Daniels). London, Joseph, 1965.

Nell Alone. London, Joseph, 1966.

A Different Kind of Summer. London, Hodder and Stoughton, 1967.

The Hunter in the Shadows. London, Hodder and Stoughton, 1969; New York, McKay, 1970.

A New Kind of Killer, An Old Kind of Death. London, Hodder and Stoughton, 1970; as *A New Kind of Killer,* New York, McKay, 1971.

Ironwood. London, Hodder and Stoughton, and New York, McKay, 1972.

Nun's Castle. New York, McKay, 1973; London, Hodder and Stoughton, 1974.

Raven's Forge. London, Macmillan, and New York, McKay, 1975.

Dragon's Eye. New York, Simon and Schuster, 1976; London, Macmillan, 1977.

Axwater. London, Macmillan, 1978; as *Tarot's Tower,* New York, Simon and Schuster, 1978.

The Wages of Zen. London, Secker and Warburg, 1979.

Uncollected Short Stories

"The Sisterhood," in *Ellery Queen's Murder Menu.* Cleveland, World, 1969.

"Time Bomb," in *Winter's Crimes 4,* edited by George Hardinge. London, Macmillan, 1972.

"Older Than the Rocks," in *Winter's Crimes 6,* edited by George Hardinge. London, Macmillan, 1974.

"Hand in Glove" (as Jennie Melville), in *Winter's Crimes 6,* edited by George Hardinge. London, Macmillan, 1974.

OTHER PUBLICATIONS

Play

Radio Play: *Nell Alone,* from her own novel, 1968.

* * *

In British crime-writing, Gwendoline Butler is regarded as a considerable find, and her work deserved its 1973 Silver Dagger. Her prize-winning book, *A Coffin for Pandora,* was set in Oxford (where she lived for some time both as university student and teacher), but the Oxford of the 1880's, the formative years of the British CID, in which a young governess becomes involved in a kidnapping and a murder. It was one of several Victorian mysteries which she has written about, brilliantly evoking the sights and sounds of the turn-of-the-century period.

Strangely enough, *A Coffin for Pandora* had nothing to do with the popular character she created, Inspector Coffin, a contemporary policeman with his "manor" in South London. Coffin is an excellent and unusual creation, a tough, self-educated man with a habit of getting involved in bizarre cases involving elderly women. Coffin and his unimaginative assistant, Sergeant Dove, are memorable characters. They appear in many of her crime novels, including *A Coffin from the Past* (an ingenious story of the murder of an M.P. and his secretary in a house where murder was committed in another century) and *A Coffin for the Canary* (with a numbing shock ending). She is able to create an atmosphere of subliminal evil and corruption (the "smell of something nasty") while achieving an intimate chatty style. Her earlier novels were all able to haunt readers with a chilling and eerie unreality. With *A Coffin for Pandora* Butler proved that she could be a "gothic" novelist of considerable power as well as the author of the popular Inspector Coffin detective stories with their devious twists. Since her debut in 1958 she has produced well over thirty novels, and has seen much of her work serialised in magazines and dramatised.

—Herbert Harris

As Jennie Melville, Gwendoline Butler writes novels in two categories: the straightforward detective stories featuring policewoman Charmian Daniels and the neo-Gothic thrillers, each with its first-person narrator and romantic setting. In the latter, the protagonist is usually a young girl in threatened circumstances, caught up in a sequence of mysterious events, under a near-fatal misapprehension about her own affairs, unable to locate the true source of menace. Someone wishes her ill, generally for economic reasons; someone else has nothing but her good at heart, and often she is hopelessly confused between the two. The lover/killer figure is a favourite motif of Melville's: naturally, since it provides a focus for the tensions of the plot and takes to its most obvious extreme the concept of fear as an erotic force ("You could say for those weeks I was two people; one screaming, the other hopelessly in love," the heroine of *Ironwood* remarks, making an apt comment on the genre). It is used most effectively, however, in an early (1964) detective novel, *Murderers' Houses*, in which the apparent roles of the central characters are reversed, with a great deal of subtlety and low-key humour.

The romantic thrillers are competent and interesting but lack the more original qualities of the Charmian Daniels stories with their flippant narrative tone, their quirks and eccentricities of plot and characterization. Homicidal madness is brought down to suburban level and given a squalid, ludicrous, or grotesque form. Character is established economically, usually by means of a half-mocking assessment – often one of the subject's own phrases which is taken over by the author and repeated until its implications are embedded in the reader's consciousness: for instance Charmian's assistant Chris is a girl who lives "a life and a half." The stories are not without defects: the narrative occasionally reads like a television script and the jaunty, joking style can easily shade into glibness. But they are always cleverly constructed, grounded in an acute sense of the sinister possibilities inherent in the most common-place situations, and presented with assurance.

—Patricia Craig

CAILLOU, Alan. Pseudonym for Alan Lyle-Smythe. British. Born in Redhill, Surrey, 9 November 1914. Studied acting at the Oscar Lewis Academy. Served in the army, 1939–41, and the Intelligence Corps in Africa, Italy, and Yugoslavia, 1941–45; captured and escaped twice: M.B.E. (Member, Order of the British Empire), Military Cross. Married Aliza Sverdlova in 1939; one daughter. Commissioner for the Reserved Areas Police in Ethiopia and Somalia, 1945–47; guide-interpreter, hunter, and trapper in Africa, 1947–52. Actor and writer in Canada, 1952–57, and since 1957 in California. Recipient: Mystery Writers of America Edgar Allan Poe Award, 1970. Agent: Reece Halsey Agency, 8733 Sunset Boulevard, Los Angeles, California 90069; or, Scott Meredith Literary Agency Inc., 845 Third Avenue, New York, New York 10022. Address: 5085 Avenida Oriente, Tarzana, California 91356, U.S.A.

CRIME PUBLICATIONS

Novels (series characters: Mike Benasque; Cabot Cain; Colonel Tobin).

Rogue's Gambit. London, Davies, 1955.
Alien Virus. London, Davies, 1957; as *Cairo Cabal*, New York, Pinnacle, 1974.
The Mindanao Pearl. London, Davies, 1959; New York, Pinnacle, 1973.
The Plotters. London, Davies, and New York, Harper, 1960.
Marseilles (Benasque). New York, Pocket Books, 1964.
A Journey to Orassia. New York, Doubleday, 1965; London, W. H. Allen, 1966.
Who'll Buy My Evil? (Benasque). New York, Pocket Books, 1966.
Assault on Kolchak (Cain). New York, Avon, 1969.
Assault on Loveless (Cain). New York, Avon, 1969.
Assault on Ming (Cain). New York, Avon, 1970.
The Dead Sea Submarine (Tobin). New York, Pinnacle, 1971; London, New English Library, 1973.
Terror in Rio (Tobin). New York, Pinnacle, 1971; London, New English Library, 1973.
Congo War-Cry (Tobin). New York, Pinnacle, 1971.
Afghan Onslaught (Tobin). New York, Pinnacle, 1971.
Assault on Fellawi (Cain). New York, Avon, 1972.
Assault on Agathon (Cain). New York, Avon, 1972.
Swamp War (Tobin). New York, Pinnacle, 1973.
Death Charge (Tobin). New York, Pinnacle, 1973.
The Garonsky Missile. New York, Pinnacle, 1973.
Assault on Aimata (Cain). New York, Avon, 1975.
Diamonds Wild. New York, Avon, 1979.

OTHER PUBLICATIONS

Novels

The Walls of Jolo. New York, Appleton Century Crofts, 1960; London, Davies, 1961.
Rampage. New York, Appleton Century Crofts, 1961; London, Davies, 1962.
Field of Women. New York, Appleton Century Crofts, 1963.
The Hot Sun of Africa. New York, New American Library, 1964; London, W. H. Allen, 1965.
Khartoum (novelization of screenplay). New York, New American Library, 1966.
Charge of the Light Brigade. New York, Pyramid, 1968.
Bichu the Jaguar. Cleveland, World, 1969; London, Hodder and Stoughton, 1970.
The Cheetahs. Cleveland, World, 1970; London, Hodder and Stoughton, 1972.

Plays

Screenplays: *The Plotters*, 1962; *Village of the Giants*, with Bert I. Gordon, 1965;

Clarence, The Cross-Eyed Lion, with Art Arthur and Marshall Thompson, 1965; *The Losers*, 1970; *Evel Knievel*, 1971; *Assault on Agathon*, 1974; *Thermoliath*, 1975; *Kingdom of the Spiders*, 1977; *Tennessee Work Farm*, 1978; *Devilfish*, with Bert I. Gordon, 1978.

Television Plays and Documentaries: about 80 in Canada and the US, including episodes for *The 6 Billion Dollar Man*, *The Man from U.N.C.L.E.*, *The Rogues*, *Voyage to the Bottom of the Sea*, *Thriller*, *Behind Closed Doors*, *The Man from Atlantis*, *The Fugitive*, and *Flipper* series.

Other

The Shakespeare Festival: A Short History of Canada's First Shakespeare Festival, 1949–54, with Arnold M. Walter and Frank Chappell. Toronto, Ryerson Press, 1954.

The World Is Six Feet Square (autobiography). London Davies, 1954; New York, Norton, 1955.

Sheba Slept Here (autobiography). New York, Abelard Schuman, 1973.

South from Khartoum: The Story of Emin Pasha. New York, Hawthorn, 1974.

Theatrical Activities:

Director: **Films** − *The Star of Life*; *The Good Life*.

Actor: **Films** − *The Fiercest Heart*, 1961; *Pirates of Tortuga*, 1961; *Five Weeks in a Balloon*, 1962; *It Happened in Athens*, 1962; *Clarence, The Cross-Eyed Lion*, 1965; *The Rare Breed*, 1966; *Hellfighters*, 1968; *Sole Survivor*, 1969; *Search for Eden*, 1979; *Centennial*, 1979; **Television** − in some 80 plays.

Alan Caillou comments:

Many years ago, in a period of doubt (I suppose all writers suffer this once in a while), I asked the then head of New American Library, Victor Weybright, "What kind of market am I really writing for − or *should* I be writing for?" I did not know at the time that the question was a foolish one, and he took me up on it immediately: "Write what you enjoy writing," he said. "If enough people are of similar persuasion, you will make a living of some sort.... "

The effect of this sound advice, which of course I took, was that I never really specialised in any particular type of writing. I derive most pleasure, perhaps, from working on the kind of book that is loosely classed as "mystery-adventure-suspense." But following my personal tastes in other directions as well, I find that I have written at least one love story, two autobiographies, a biography, and three novels about animals, as well as an historical novel once in a while. This does have its disadvantages. It must be that on occasion a reader picks up a book by a writer he knows to write in his own preferred category, and, finding the book is outside that category, therefore feels cheated; and this is regrettable.

Over the years that sound advice referred to above may have lost some of its value. There seems a tendency − at least in America − to take a peek at the current market before starting work. Today, it seems, one is expected to ask "Would you like a book about this or that?" One even finds oneself submitting *outlines* − and I am quite sure that this is not a healthy trend. I do not believe Victor Hugo ever asked his public (represented by the Sales Department and the Distributors), "Should I kill off Jean Valjean around chapter 27? Or shall

I let him live happily ever after?" But that's the kind of thing we are headed for, if we don't fight it.

*   *   *

Alan Caillou's best work has been in paperback novels of intrigue and adventure, beginning with the Mike Benasque novels (*Marseilles*, *Who'll Buy My Evil?*). The well-rendered international settings, the smooth first-person narratives, and the occasional telling insights into human nature and politics combine to make the stories quite entertaining. But Benasque, a journalist by profession, is caught up in intrigue and violence more or less against his will, unlike Cabot Cain of Caillou's very good *Assault* series. Cain is a huge (6 feet 7 inches, 210 pounds) athletic genius (degrees in microbiology, petrology, automotive engineering, etc.). He is also an engaging adventurer who deals in likelihoods rather than facts, usually very successfully, and – though always his own man – works closely with Interpol and his good friend Colonel Matthias Fenrek. Cain's exploits take him all over the globe, and as usual Caillou's use of local color is excellent. Customs, historical background, landmarks, and even linguistic niceties are described with seemingly easy familarity.

Caillou's most recent series, subtitled "The Private Army of Colonel Tobin," allows him to make full use of his knowledge of history and military tactics. The books feature a group of mercenary soldiers, under the direction of Colonel Tobin, which fights only for the right causes. Again the settings range over the world, from the Sinai Desert to Cambodia. In the sixth book of the series, *Death Charge*, Caillou pulls the unusual stunt of having several major characters killed; and for the subsequent novel, *The Garonsky Missile*, the subtitle was changed to "Tobin's Commando," with the Colonel's son taking charge of the remainder of the troops.

—Bill Crider

CAIN, James M(allahan). American. Born in Annapolis, Maryland, 1 July 1892. Educated at Washington College, Chesterton, Maryland, B.A. 1910, M.A. 1917. Served in the United States Army during World War I (Editor-in-Chief of *Lorraine Cross*, 79th Division newspaper). Married 1) Mary Rebecca Clough in 1920 (divorced, 1923); 2) Elina Sjösted Tyszecha in 1927 (divorced, 1942); 3)Aileen Pringle in 1944 (divorced, 1945); 4) Florence Macbeth Whitwell in 1947 (died, 1966). Reporter, Baltimore *American*, 1917–18; Baltimore *Sun*, 1919–23; Professor of Journalism, St. John's College, Annapolis, 1923–24; editorial writer, New York *World*, 1924–31; screenwriter, 1932–48. Recipient: Mystery Writers of America Grand Master Award. *Died 27 October 1977.*

CRIME PUBLICATIONS

Novels

    The Postman Always Rings Twice. New York, Knopf, and London, Cape, 1934.
    Serenade. New York, Knopf, 1937; London, Cape, 1938.
    Mildred Pierce. New York, Knopf, 1941; London, Hale, 1943.
    Love's Lovely Counterfeit. New York, Knopf, 1942.
    Three of a Kind: Career in C Major, The Embezzler, Double Indemnity. New York,
        Knopf, 1943; London, Hale, 1945.

Past All Dishonor. New York, Knopf, 1946.
Sinful Woman. New York, Avon, 1947.
The Butterfly. New York, Knopf, 1947.
The Moth. New York, Knopf, 1948; London, Hale, 1950.
Three of Hearts (omnibus). London, Hale, 1949.
Jealous Woman. New York, Avon, 1948; London, Hale, 1955.
The Root of His Evil. New York, Avon, 1951; London, Hale, 1954; as *Shameless*, New York, Avon, 1958.
Galatea. New York, Knopf, 1953; London, Hale, 1954.
Mignon. New York, Dial Press, 1962; London, Hale, 1963.
The Magician's Wife. New York, Dial Press, 1965; London, Hale, 1966.
Rainbow's End. New York, Mason Charter, and London, W. H. Allen, 1975.
The Institute. New York, Mason Charter, 1976; London, Hale, 1977.

Short Stories

Career in C Major and Other Stories. New York, Avon, 1943.

Uncollected Short Stories

"The Girl in the Story," in *For Men Only*, edited by James M. Cain. Cleveland, World, 1944.
"It Was the Cat," in *Continent's End: A Collection of California Writing*, edited by J. H. Jackson. New York, McGraw Hill, 1944.
"The Baby in the Icebox," in *Half-a-Hundred: Tales by Great American Writers*, edited by Charles Grayson. Garden City, New York, Garden City Publishing Company, 1945.
"Pastorale," in *To the Queen's Taste*, edited by Ellery Queen. Boston, Little Brown, 1946; London, Faber, 1949.
"Brush Fire," in *Fourth Round*, edited by Charles Grayson. New York, Holt Rinehart, 1952.
"Pay-Off Girl," in *Ellery Queen's Mystery Magazine* (New York), February 1955.
"Visitor," in *Esquire* (New York), September 1961.

OTHER PUBLICATIONS

Plays

Hero; *Hemp*; *Red, White and Blue*; *Trial by Jury*; *Theological Interlude*; *Citizenship*; *Will of the People* in *American Mercury* (New York), 1926–29.
The Postman Always Rings Twice, adaptation of his own novel (produced New York, 1936).

Other

Our Government. New York, Knopf, and London, Allen and Unwin, 1930.

Editor, *79th Division Headquarters Troop: A Record*, with Malcolm Gilbert. Privately printed, 1919.
Editor, *For Men Only: A Collection of Short Stories.* Cleveland, World, 1944.

*   *   *

James M. Cain once remarked that he belonged "to no school, hard-boiled or otherwise, and I believe these so-called schools exist mainly in the imagination of critics." Be that as it may, Cain's first novel, *The Postman Always Rings Twice*, is generally taken to be a high point of hard-boiled writing, partly because of its frank treatment of sex and violence and partly because of its spare, basic style which, like Hemingway's, eschews abstractions and adjectival modification. Its immediacy is enhanced by the directness of its first-person narrative, which is confessional in a specific as well as general sense, since its hero, Frank Chambers, is writing his story in a death cell, and which possesses the sleeve-holding, hypnotic power of an Ancient Mariner's tale.

Unlike a number of his tough-writing contemporaries, Cain offers the reader little direct social criticism. Exceptions might include *Love's Lovely Counterfeit*, with a brutal picture of a corrupt, crime-ridden town in the manner of Hammett's *Red Harvest* and McCoy's *No Pockets in a Shroud*; his historical novels, *Past All Dishonour* and *Mignon*, which both deal in some ways with conflicts between social duties and personal desires; and *Mildred Pierce*, which offers fascinating observations on the lacunae between myth and reality in the American view of the middle-class woman. Yet if there is little direct social comment the very insistence of Cain's plot patterns carries a set of popular mythic meanings which, in a Jungian sense, may offer readers as telling a series of truths about American society as the more obvious social realism of Dreiser and Sinclair Lewis.

The Postman Always Rings Twice can be seen, alongside McCoy's *They Shoot Horses, Don't They?* and O'Hara's *Hope of Heaven*, as a Depression-view of the end of an American dream. Cora has come to California from a small Iowa town to become a Hollywood star; Frank is a bum with no more horizons to reach. Their sordid story provides an ironic comment on their desire for love and respectability. The plot pattern of *Postman* is one that Cain has endlessly modified and reused in his subsequent fiction. A man meets a woman, succumbs to her charms, becomes involved in dangerous, often criminal activity as a result and is frequently destroyed or, at least, loses the woman. This is the pattern of *Serenade*, *Double Indemnity*, *The Butterfly*, *The Magician's Wife*, and *The Institute*, as well as several others. While his men may try to act out large Romantic notions, his women frequently represent earthy reality, and confront the hero with basic, primitive urges involving sex, money, violence, and food. Sex and violence are inextricably linked in *Postman* when Frank and Cora make love beside the body of the murdered Greek; sex and food coalesce in a remarkable scene in the church in *Serenade*, and sex fuels the murderous fraud which unites Walter Huff and Phyllis Nirdlinger in *Double Indemnity*. Like Daisy Buchanan in *The Great Gatsby*, these women represent a bedrock of reality against which the romantic dream must fall, and, like Brigid O'Shaughnessy in Hammett's *The Maltese Falcon*, they can also demonstrate a bewildering unpredictability and dishonesty. In other words, Cain's repeated plot patterns emphasize the basic conflicts in the American psyche between the dream of Romance and the dream of realistic success.

Cain rarely writes mystery novels (perhaps only *Jealous Woman* properly comes into this category) so that murder and crime become, in his work, not something which can be solved and hence disposed of in a cleansing motion, but part of the unalterable series of events usually set in motion by a meeting between man and woman which can exert the same relentless grip (on both protagonists and readers) as Fate in Greek tragedy or Chance in the novels of Thomas Hardy. Part of Cain's power comes from his ability to show the fragility of order and common-sense.

James M. Cain has had a long writing career (despite being over forty when his first novel was published) and the repetitive nature of his plots and language has worked against his overall achievement. His novels are usually well-researched but there is little interaction between his central protagonists and their social setting, and he is so concerned with the way in which characters show themselves in action that he pays much less attention to motivation than he should. Despite these caveats, Cain *was* a prime influence on Camus's *L'Etranger* and has shown himself to be one of the foremost storytellers in American popular literature, demonstrating from the outset of his career a mastery of place, set scenes, and first-person narrative.

—John S. Whitley

CAIRD, Janet (Hinshaw). British. Born in Livingstonia, Malawi, 24 April 1913. Educated at Dollar Academy, Clackmannan; Edinburgh University, 1931–35, M.A. (honours) in English literature 1935; University of Grenoble and the Sorbonne, Paris (Stevenson Exchange Scholar), 1935–36; St. George's Training College, Edinburgh, 1936–37. Married James Bowman Caird in 1938; two daughters. English and Latin teacher, Park School for Girls, Glasgow, 1937–38, Royal High School, Edinburgh, 1940–41, and Dollar Academy, 1941–43. Agent: A. M. Heath & Co. Ltd., 40–42 William IV Street, London WC2N 4DD, England. Address: 1 Drummond Crescent, Inverness IV2 4QW, Scotland.

CRIME PUBLICATIONS

Novels

Murder Reflected. London, Bles, 1965; as In a Glass Darkly, New York, Morrow, 1966.
Perturbing Spirit. London, Bles, and New York, Doubleday, 1966.
Murder Scholastic. London, Bles, 1967; New York, Doubleday, 1968.
The Loch. London, Bles, 1968; New York, Doubleday, 1969.
Murder Remote. New York, Doubleday, 1973; as The Shrouded Way, New York, New American Library, 1973.

OTHER PUBLICATIONS

Verse

Some Walk a Narrow Path. Edinburgh, Ramsay Head Press, 1977.

Other

Angus the Tartan Partan (juvenile). London, Nelson, 1961.

Manuscript Collection: Mugar Memorial Library, Boston University.

Janet Caird comments:
I have always written verse and stories since I was a child, but I did not publish until I was middle-aged, and then only because my husband insisted I must make the effort. Writing is the most satisfying occupation I know, and I am also a voracious reader.

*   *   *

Janet Caird is the author of five mystery tales, all set in Scotland. The earliest, *Murder Reflected*, billed in at least one edition as a Gothic, recounts the adventures of a young woman reporter researching small Scottish towns. She witnesses a murder being committed, reflected in a *camera obscura*. Good characters hold the reader's interest despite the somewhat overpopulated and over-complicated plot. *Murder Scholastic*, a traditional whodunit set in a school, and *Murder Remote*, a thriller in which an isolated coastal village is held hostage on account of sunken treasure, show better technique.

Perturbing Spirit and *The Loch* cannot be considered crime fiction in the usual sense, though both are excellent suspense narratives. In the former, a festival in a small border town is taken over by a compelling and enigmatic stranger who reorganizes the little local celebration into an elaborate production which attracts international folklorists. Affected by an ancient and hypnotic tune and entranced by the ritual, and principal figures in the ceremony are seized by a peculiar exhilaration which spreads to the crowd. When archaeologists excavate a Bronze Age barrow known as Merlin's Mound, the focus of the festival, they find a curious clue to the visitor's identity. *The Loch*, in which crime and violence play a part, is a highly unusual tale of natural disaster and the discovery of a primative tribe which inhabits caves revealed to the modern world by the loch's receding waters. The author's fascination with archaeology is evident in both of these remarkable tales.

Janet Caird's exceptionally good settings and atmosphere, her well-sketched, sympathetic characters, her occasional irony and subtle humor, and her fine eye for detail distinguish her works.

—Mary Helen Becker

CANADAY, John. See **HEAD, Matthew.**

CANDY, Edward. Pseudonym for Barbara Alison Neville, née Boodson. British. Born in London, 22 August 1925. Educated at Hampstead High School for Girls, 1929–43; University College, London, 1943–45; University College Hospital Medical School, 1945–48, M.B., B.S. 1948; D.C.H. 1950; University of East Anglia, Norwich, M.A. 1975. Married Joseph Godfrey Neville in 1946; three sons and two daughters. Worked in hospitals in Norwich, Sheffield, Northwood, and Liverpool; reviewer for *The Times* and *The Sunday Times*, London, 1967–76. Recipient: Arts Council award, 1967. Agent: John Farquharson Ltd., 8 Bell Yard, London WC2A 2JU. Address: 2 Mile End Road, Newmarket Road, Norwich NR4 7QY, England.

CRIME PUBLICATIONS

Novels (series characters: Burnivel in all books)

    Which Doctor. London, Gollancz, 1953; New York, Rinehart, 1954.
    Bones of Contention. London, Gollancz, 1954.
    Words for Murder, Perhaps. London, Gollancz, 1971.

OTHER PUBLICATIONS

Novels

    The Graver Tribe. London, Gollancz, 1958.
    A Lady's Hand. London, Gollancz, 1959.
    A Season of Discord. London, Gollancz, 1964.
    Strokes of Havoc. London, Gollancz, 1966.
    Parents' Day. London, Gollancz, 1967.

Doctor Amadeus. London, Gollancz, 1969.
Scene Changing. London, Gollancz, 1977.
Voices of Children. London, Gollancz, 1980.

Edward Candy comments:

I don't really feel I belong in this book at all. I enormously enjoy reading and writing detective stories, but most of my own work has virtually no suspense/puzzle/violent element whatever, and I can't believe any reader has ever had the least doubt about who did it, why, when, and how, after about page five. What I most delight in, in my own and other writers' detective fiction, is the detailed filling in of a mildly esoteric background, which is why I like *Words for Murder, Perhaps,* which is set in the extra-mural department of a Midlands university, best of the three I've written. For the same reason, I toy with the idea of one day locating a murder in an electroencephalography department, this being my own speciality in my other profession.

*   *   *

Edward Candy is the pseudonym of a woman doctor whose ten novels to date include three crime stories. Each book derives its special character from an exact environment: a children's hospital, the Royal College of Paediatricians, an adult education institute. Because the author likes to observe her doctors and teachers at work, they are often seen more as professional than as private persons, drawn with an attractive blend of irony and sympathy, sharp insight, and sensitive concern. In all three books an unheroic hero survives persecution and murderous attack to begin a promising new life.

Which Doctor is virtually an all-male preserve: even its children are boys. The title is properly a question, since killer, victim, and suspects are all medical men whose rivalries and researches serve both as background and motive for blackmail and murder. An intrusive skeleton sets the tone for *Bones of Contention,* a swifter, darker book, which quickly makes its killer known. Sober, chilling, spare in texture but rich in resonances, it recalls the mode of Ivy Compton-Burnett. *Words for Murder, Perhaps* contrives an elegant, fantastical pattern of murder from elegies by Cowley, Milton, Tennyson, and others: a cat's death justifies Gray's inclusion.

A volatile policeman named Burnivel officiates throughout, though absent till the end from *Bones of Contention.* Fabian Honeychurch, as befits his resounding name, is a more substantial character, similar in appearance and temper to Father Christmas. An eminent paediatrician who wears his dignities lightly, he investigates the first mystery and oversees the second.

—B. A. Pike

CANNAN, Joanna (Maxwell).   British.   Born in Oxford, in 1898. Educated at Wychwood School, Oxford, and in Paris. Married H. J. Pullein-Thompson in 1918 (died, 1957); three daughters, the writers Diana, Christine, and Josephine Pullein-Thompson. *Died 22 April 1961.*

CRIME PUBLICATIONS

Novels (series characters: Inspector Guy Northeast; Inspector Ronald Price)

No Walls of Jasper. London, Benn, 1930; New York, Doubleday, 1931.
Under Proof. London, Hodder and Stoughton, 1934.
A Hand to Burn. London, Hodder and Stoughton, 1936.
They Rang Up the Police (Northeast). London, Gollancz, 1939.
Death at The Dog (Northeast). London, Gollancz, 1940; New York, Reynal, 1941.
Murder Included (Price). London, Gollancz, 1950; as *Poisonous Relations*, New York,
    Morrow, 1950; as *The Taste of Murder*, New York, Dell, 1951.
Body in the Beck (Price). London, Gollancz, 1952.
Long Shadows (Price). London, Gollancz, 1955.
And Be a Villain (Price). London, Gollancz, 1958.
All Is Discovered (Price). London, Gollancz, 1962.

OTHER PUBLICATIONS

Novels

The Misty Valley. London, First Novel Library, 1922; New York, Doran, 1924.
Wild Berry Wine. London, Unwin, and New York, Stokes, 1925.
The Lady of the Heights. London, Unwin, 1926.
Sheila Both-Ways. London, Benn, 1928; New York, Stokes, 1939.
The Simple Pass On. London, Benn, 1929; as *Orphan of Mars*, Indianapolis, Bobbs
    Merrill, 1930.
Ithuriel's Hour. London, Hodder and Stoughton, 1931; New York, Doubleday, 1932.
High Table. London, Benn, and New York, Doubleday, 1931.
Snow in Harvest. London, Hodder and Stoughton, 1932.
North Wall. London, Hodder and Stoughton, 1933.
The Hills Sleep On. London, Hodder and Stoughton, 1935.
Frightened Angels. London, Gollancz, and New York, Harper, 1936.
Pray Do Not Venture. London, Gollancz, 1937.
Princes in the Land. London, Gollancz, 1938.
Idle Apprentice. London, Gollancz, 1940.
Blind Messenger. London, Gollancz, 1941.
Little I Understood. London, Gollancz, 1948.
The Hour of the Angel; Ithuriel's Hour. London, Pan, 1949.
And All I Learned. London, Gollancz, 1952.
People to Be Found. London, Gollancz, 1956.

Other

A Pony for Jean (juvenile). London, Lane, 1936; New York, Scribner, 1937.
We Met Our Cousins (juvenile). London, Collins, 1937; New York, Dodd Mead, 1938.
Another Pony for Jean (juvenile). London, Collins, 1938.
London Pride (juvenile). London, Collins, 1939.
More Ponies for Jean (juvenile). London, Collins, 1943.
They Bought Her a Pony (juvenile). London, Collins, 1944.
Hamish: The Story of a Shetland Pony (juvenile). London, Penguin, 1944.

I Wrote a Pony Book.   London, Collins, 1950.
Gaze at the Moon (juvenile).   London, Collins, 1957.

*   *   *

Joanna Cannan has written some detective fiction as well as many novels and a number of pony books for girls. "The trouble about detective stories is that they're not the least like life. People find a corpse and make no more fuss than if it was a dead rabbit," says Delia Cathcart on the first page of *They Rang Up the Police*; it is a significant remark since the corpse found later in the story is Delia's own, and certainly its discovery leaves no one broken-hearted. Four women, a mother and three middle-aged daughters, live at Marley Grange in the usual state of cloying emotional dependence that can only lead to disaster. Underneath the façade of sweetness and affection a great deal of nastiness is secreting. The perpetrator of the murderous attack on Delia is her younger sister, "the home bird," "the poor baby," "silly timid me." The narrative irony is just a little too emphatic to be convincing.

Guy Northeast is the C.I.D. Inspector who solves the mystery of Marley Grange. His next case (*Death at The Dog*) takes him to a country pub in wartime England where he proceeds to develop a profitless infatuation for one of his suspects. Crescy Hardwick is a writer, spirited, humane, and just sufficiently disreputable to captivate the plodding young detective. It is Crescy who clarifies one of the author's policies when she declares: "I believe I know what my mistake was now... I mean, in my detective novel. I tried to make my detective a brilliant kind of person – like Dr. Priestley, only young and attractive.... "

This is a mistake that Joanna Cannan never makes. In fact there is something subversive and interesting about her refusal to glorify her detectives, though the impulse towards realism is in the end self-defeating, largely because it isn't carried far enough. The fantasy-detectives – Sayers's Lord Peter Wimsey, Allingham's Albert Campion and so on – have a quality of style that balances the obvious exaggerations; industrious, painstaking policemen like Freeman Wills Crofts's Inspector French depend for their impact upon a detailed and meticulous narrative approach. Joanna Cannan, however, has lumbered her sleuths somewhat gratuitously with many squalid defects and deficiencies. The mundane workings of their minds are revealed to the reader as they go through the process of suspecting the wrong people, antagonizing their colleagues, and generally making themselves obnoxious. Guy Northeast isn't exactly a dashing figure, but Cannan's Inspector Ronald Price is positively shoddy and unprepossessing. To complete the picture he is provided with an intolerable wife and a couple of awful children; and one novel at least (*All Is Discovered*) is taken up with low-key observations of domestic friction: "Valerie's rat-like face appeared at a window in the thatch. 'Your dinner's in the oven and if it's all dried up it's your own fault,' she screamed."

"The cankerous malignity of the domestically oppressed" is a quality that interests the author as a source of criminal derangement. The phrase occurs in what is probably her best detective novel, *Murder Included*, where the usual sequence of crimes is reversed, with unquestionable logic. The book contains another version of the only character who merits narrative approval: the slightly jaded, fastidious woman writer with inner resources of vitality and subtle charm. On the whole, the novels are competent rather than brilliant but they do show an admirable grasp of the technical principles of the genre.

—Patricia Craig

CANNING, Victor.   Also wrote as Alan Gould.   British.   Born in Plymouth, Devon, 16 June 1911. Educated at Plymouth Technical College and Oxford University. Served in the

Royal Artillery, 1939–45: Major. Married Phyllis McEwen in 1934. Agent: Curtis Brown Ltd., 1 Craven Hill, London W2 3EP, England.

CRIME PUBLICATIONS

Novels (series character: Rex Carver)

The Chasm. London, Hodder and Stoughton, and New York, Mill, 1947.
Panthers' Moon. London, Hodder and Stoughton, and New York, Mill, 1948.
The Golden Salamander. London, Hodder and Stoughton, and New York, Mill, 1949.
A Forest of Eyes. London, Hodder and Stoughton, and New York, Mill, 1950.
Venetian Bird. London, Hodder and Stoughton, 1951; as *Bird of Prey*, New York, Mill, 1951.
The House of the Seven Flies. London, Hodder and Stoughton, and New York, Mill, 1952.
The Man from the "Turkish Slave." London, Hodder and Stoughton, and New York, Sloane, 1954.
A Handful of Silver. New York, Sloane, 1954; as *Castle Minerva*, London, Hodder and Stoughton, 1955.
His Bones Are Coral. London, Hodder and Stoughton, 1955; as *Twist of the Knife*, New York, Sloane, 1955; as *The Shark Run*, London, New English Library, 1968.
The Hidden Face. London, Hodder and Stoughton, 1956; as *Burden of Proof*, New York, Sloane, 1956.
The Manasco Road. London, Hodder and Stoughton, and New York, Sloane, 1957; as *The Forbidden Road*, New York, Permabooks, 1959.
The Dragon Tree. London, Hodder and Stoughton, and New York, Sloane, 1958; as *The Captives of Mora Island*, New York, Permabooks, 1959.
The Burning Eye. London, Hodder and Stoughton, and New York, Sloane, 1960.
A Delivery of Furies. London, Hodder and Stoughton, and New York, Sloane, 1961.
Black Flamingo. London, Hodder and Stoughton, 1962; New York, Sloane, 1963.
The Limbo Line. London, Heinemann, 1963; New York, Sloane, 1964.
The Scorpio Letters. London, Heinemann, and New York, Sloane, 1964.
The Whip Hand (Carver). London, Heinemann, and New York, Sloane, 1965.
Doubled in Diamonds (Carver). London, Heinemann, 1966; New York, Morrow, 1967.
The Python Project (Carver). London, Heinemann, 1967; New York, Morrow, 1968.
The Melting Man (Carver). London, Heinemann, 1968; New York, Morrow, 1969.
Queen's Pawn. London, Heinemann, 1969; New York, Morrow, 1970.
The Great Affair. London, Heinemann, 1969; New York, Morrow, 1970.
Firecrest. London, Heinemann, 1971; New York, Morrow, 1972.
The Runaways. London, Heinemann, and New York, Morrow, 1972.
The Rainbird Pattern. London, Heinemann, 1972; New York, Morrow, 1973; as *Family Plot*, New York, Award, 1976.
Flight of the Grey Goose. London, Heinemann, and New York, Morrow, 1973.
The Finger of Saturn. London, Heinemann, 1973; New York, Morrow, 1974.
The Painted Tent. London, Heinemann, and New York, Morrow, 1974.
The Mask of Memory. London, Heinemann, 1974; New York, Morrow, 1975.
The Kingsford Mark. London, Heinemann, 1975; New York, Morrow, 1976.
The Crimson Chalice. London, Heinemann, 1976; New York, Morrow, 1978.
The Doomsday Carrier. London, Heinemann, 1976; New York, Morrow, 1977.
Charlie in Summertime. London, Heinemann, 1976.
The Circle of the Gods. London, Heinemann, 1977.
The Immortal Wound. London, Heinemann, 1978.

Birdcage. London, Heinemann, 1978; New York, Morrow, 1979.
The Satan Sampler. London, Heinemann, 1979.

Short Stories

Young Man on a Bicycle and Other Stories. London, Hodder and Stoughton, 1958; as
  Oasis Nine: Four Short Novels, New York, Sloane, 1959.
Delay on Turtle and Other Stories. London, New English Library, 1962.

Uncollected Short Stories

"Star Stuff," in *Ellery Queen's Mystery Magazine* (New York), June 1962.
"The Sunday Fishing Club," in *To Be Read Before Midnight,* edited by Ellery Queen.
  New York, Random, 1962; London, New English Library, 1967.
"The Carnation Mystery," in *Ellery Queen's Mystery Magazine* (New York), January
  1963.
"A Stroke of Genius," in *Ellery Queen's Mystery Magazine* (New York), February 1965.
"Baskets of Apples and Roses," in *Ellery Queen's Mystery Magazine* (New York),
  October 1965.
"Flint's Diamonds," in *Alfred Hitchcock Presents: Stories That Scared Even Me.* New
  York, Random House, 1967.
"A Question of Character," in *John Creasey's Mystery Bedside Book 1970,* edited by
  Herbert Harris. London, Hodder and Stoughton, 1969.
"The Botany Pattern," in *Anthology 1970 Mid-Year,* edited by Ellery Queen. New
  York, Davis, 1970.
"Disappearing Trick," in *John Creasey's Mystery Bedside Book 1971,* edited by Herbert
  Harris. London, Hodder and Stoughton, 1970.

OTHER PUBLICATIONS

Novels

Polycarp's Progress. London, Hodder and Stoughton, 1935.
Mr. Finchley Discovers His England. London, Hodder and Stoughton, 1934; as *Mr.
  Finchley's Holiday,* New York, Reynal, 1935.
Fly Away Paul. London, Hodder and Stoughton, and New York, Reynal, 1936.
Matthew Silverman. London, Hodder and Stoughton, 1937.
Mr. Finchley Goes to Paris. London, Hodder and Stoughton, and New York, Carrick
  and Evans, 1938.
Fountain Inn. London, Hodder and Stoughton, 1939.
Mr. Finchley Takes the Road. London, Hodder and Stoughton, 1940.
Green Battlefield. London, Hodder and Stoughton, 1943.

Novels as Alan Gould

Two Men Fought. London, Collins, 1936.
Mercy Lane. London, Collins, 1937.
Sanctuary from the Dragon. London, Collins, 1938.
Every Creature of God Is Good. London, Hodder and Stoughton, 1939.
The Viaduct. London, Hodder and Stoughton, 1939.
Atlantic Company. London, Hodder and Stoughton, 1940.

Plays

Screenplays: *Golden Salamander*, with Ronald Neame, 1950; *Venetian Bird* (*The Assassin*), 1952.

Television Plays: *Curtain of Fear*, 1964; *Breaking Point*, 1966; *This Way to Murder*, 1967; *Cuculus Canorum*, 1972.

Other

Everyman's England. London, Hodder and Stoughton, 1936.

*   *   *

Victor Canning has written over 50 novels. He began his career as a skillful writer about the countryside, an aspect which continues in his work today. After World War II he turned his attention almost exclusively to spy and espionage thrillers. The reputation he has gained is solidly established on his ability as a story teller. An inveterate traveler with an eye for local color and detail, Canning has used many locales for his stories, never using the same setting twice. Canning's essential ingredients are excitement, suspense, and realism. His conflicts of personality are always convincing. His characters are real people involved in a steadily moving story, and he has a fine ear for dialogue. Although some stories may be quieter than others, they are always full of contrasts and reverses. Occasionally Canning is accused of inplausibility of plot, but he writes with such skill that it is often overlooked. He also uses a generous dollop of humor, a trait not often found in spy and espionage stories.

In *Panthers' Moon*, two magnificent black panthers are loose in the Alps. In one's collar is a precious microfilm, and the hunters become the hunted. In *The House of the Seven Flies* the secret of a quarter of a million pounds worth of diamonds is contained in the cryptic phrase of the title. One man is given the phrase but no clue to its meaning. *The Dragon Tree* shows Canning at his best with human relationships. The English wife of a Cyrenian exile finds herself with conflicting loyalties, and holds the fate of her companions in her decisions. In *The Burning Eye* Canning used a smelly Somali port, a conglomeration of marooned passengers, and an American engineer facing the local sultan in a struggle for oil. Canning juggles two plots in *The Rainbird Pattern*, the principle one concerning the kidnapping of the Archbishop of Canterbury. In *The Finger of Saturn* a country squire's wife returns after a two-year disappearance with no memory. The squire reverts to a calculating primitive as he uncovers a conspiracy to establish a world supremacy.

Canning's private investigator, Rex Carver, works both for himself and for British Intelligence in trailing two women across Europe in *The Whip Hand*. Settings abound again, with Canning using Paris, the Dalmatian Coast, and Austria. Carver appears in several other novels. A more serious book is *The Great Affair*. Even though this is a mystery–espionage story, it is totally unpredictable. The protagonist is a defrocked Anglican priest with a lopsided morality and the villain is the cynical and enchanting Archbishop of Bakata.

Dorothy Hughes, the noted mystery critic, called Canning the post-war successor to Eric Ambler in writing about the confidential agent. Victor Canning's name is synonymous with the best in international intrigue.

—Frank Denton

CARMICHAEL, Harry. Pseudonym for Leopold Horace Ognall; also wrote as Hartley Howard. British. Born in Montreal, Canada, 20 June 1908. Educated at Rutherglen Academy, Lanarkshire, to age 13. Married Cecilia Jacobson in 1932; two sons and one daughter. Journalist in Glasgow, Leeds, and Manchester, and worked as an efficiency engineer and in a mail order firm before 1939. *Died in April 1979.*

CRIME PUBLICATIONS

Novels (series characters: John Piper; Quinn)

Death Leaves a Diary (Piper; Quinn).   London, Collins, 1952.
The Vanishing Track (Piper).   London, Collins, 1952.
Deadly Night-Cap (Piper; Quinn).   London, Collins, 1953.
School for Murder (Piper).   London, Collins, 1953.
Death Counts Three (Piper).   London, Collins, 1954; as *The Screaming Rabbit*, New York, Simon and Schuster, 1955.
Why Kill Johnny? (Piper; Quinn).   London, Collins, 1954.
Noose for a Lady (Piper; Quinn).   London, Collins, 1955.
Money for Murder (Piper; Quinn).   London, Collins, 1955.
Justice Enough (Piper).   London, Collins, 1956.
The Dead of the Night (Piper; Quinn).   London, Collins, 1956.
Emergency Exit (Piper).   London, Collins, 1957.
Put Out That Star (Piper; Quinn).   London, Collins, 1957; as *Into Thin Air*, New York, Doubleday, 1958.
A Question of Time.   London, Collins, 1958.
James Knowland, Deceased.   London, Collins, 1958.
... Or Be He Dead (Piper; Quinn).   New York, Doubleday, 1958; London, Collins, 1959.
Stranglehold (Piper; Quinn).   London, Collins, 1959; as *Marked Man*, New York, Doubleday, 1959.
The Seeds of Hate.   London, Collins, 1959.
Requiem for Charles (Quinn).   London, Collins, 1960; as *The Late Unlamented*, New York, Doubleday, 1961.
Alibi (Piper; Quinn).   London, Collins, 1961; New York, Macmillan, 1962.
Confession.   London, Collins, 1961.
The Link.   London, Collins, 1962.
Of Unsound Mind (Piper; Quinn).   London, Collins, and New York, Doubleday, 1962.
Vendetta (Piper; Quinn).   London, Collins, and New York, Macmillan, 1963.
Flashback.   London, Collins, 1964.
Safe Secret (Piper; Quinn).   London, Collins, 1964; New York, Macmillan, 1965.
Post Mortem (Piper; Quinn).   London, Collins, 1965; New York, Doubleday, 1966.
Suicide Clause (Piper; Quinn).   London, Collins, 1966.
Murder by Proxy (Piper; Quinn).   London, Collins, 1967.
The Condemned.   London, Collins, 1967.
A Slightly Bitter Taste (Quinn).   London, Collins, 1968.
Remote Control (Piper; Quinn).   London, Collins, 1970; New York, McCall, 1971.
Death Trap (Piper; Quinn).   London, Collins, 1970; New York, McCall, 1971.
Most Deadly Hate (Piper; Quinn).   London, Collins, 1971; New York, Saturday Review Press, 1974.
The Quiet Woman (Piper; Quinn).   London, Collins, 1971; New York, Saturday Review Press, 1972.
Naked to the Grave (Piper; Quinn).   London, Collins, 1972; New York, Saturday Review Press, 1973.

Too Late for Tears (Piper; Quinn).   London, Collins, 1973; New York, Saturday Review Press, 1975.
Candles for the Dead (Piper; Quinn).   London, Collins, 1973; New York, Saturday Review Press, 1976.
The Motive (Piper; Quinn).   London, Collins, 1974; New York, Dutton, 1977.
False Evidence.   London, Collins, 1976; New York, Dutton, 1977.
A Grave for Two.   London, Collins, 1977.
Life Cycle.   London, Collins, 1978.

Novels as Hartley Howard (series characters: Glenn Bowman; Philip Scott)

The Last Appointment (Bowman).   London, Collins, 1951.
The Last Deception (Bowman).   London, Collins, 1951.
The Last Vanity (Bowman).   London, Collins, 1952.
Death of Cecilia (Bowman).   London, Collins, 1952.
The Other Side of the Door.   London, Collins, 1953.
Bowman Strikes Again.   London, Collins, 1953.
Bowman on Broadway.   London, Collins, 1954.
Bowman at a Venture.   London, Collins, 1954.
Sleep for the Wicked (Bowman).   London, Collins, 1955.
No Target for Bowman.   London, Collins, 1955.
The Bowman Touch.   London, Collins, 1956.
A Hearse for Cinderella (Bowman).   London, Collins, 1956.
The Long Night (Bowman).   London, Collins, 1957.
Key to the Morgue (Bowman).   London, Collins, 1957.
The Big Snatch.   London, Collins, 1958.
Sleep, My Pretty One (Bowman).   London, Collins, 1958.
Deadline (Bowman).   London, Collins, 1959.
The Armitage Secret (Bowman).   London, Collins, 1959.
Fall Guy (Bowman).   London, Collins, 1960.
Extortion (Bowman).   London, Collins, 1960.
Time Bomb (Bowman).   London, Collins, 1961.
I'm No Hero (Bowman).   London, Collins, 1961.
Count-Down (Bowman).   London, Collins, 1962.
Double Finesse.   London, Collins, 1962.
The Shelton Case.   London, Collins, 1963.
Department K (Scott).   London, Collins, 1964; as *Assignment K*, New York, Pyramid, 1968.
Out of the Fire.   London, Collins, 1965.
Portrait of a Beautiful Harlot (Bowman).   London, Collins, 1966.
Counterfeit.   London, Collins, 1966.
Routine Investigation (Bowman).   London, Collins, 1967.
The Eye of the Hurricane (Scott).   London, Collins, 1968.
The Secret of Simon Cornell (Bowman).   London, Collins, 1969.
Cry on My Shoulder (Bowman).   London, Collins, 1970.
Room 37 (Bowman).   London, Collins, 1970.
Million Dollar Snapshot (Bowman).   London, Collins, 1971.
Murder One.   London, Collins, 1971.
Epitaph for Joanna.   London, Collins, 1972.
Nice Day for a Funeral.   London, Collins, 1972.
Highway to Murder.   London, Collins, 1973.
Dead Drunk (Bowman).   London, Collins, 1974.
Treble Cross.   London, Collins, 1975.
Payoff.   London, Collins, 1976.

One-Way Ticket. London, Collins, 1978.
The Sealed Envelope (Bowman). London, Collins, 1979.

Harry Carmichael comments:
It is difficult for me to make any valid statement on my own work. I am a slave to accuracy of detail, prefer the classic type of detective fiction to the cops-and-robbers type, and labour hard in the interests of originality. Because I have written so many novels, my main problem nowadays is to avoid self-plagiarization.

*   *   *

Although he has been steadily producing mysteries for over 25 years, Harry Carmichael has written his best work in the last decade. He uses all the tricks of deception and misdirection to produce highly British, traditional works in a modern setting. Insurance assessor John Piper and crime reporter Quinn are his series detectives. Once they are introduced into a story virtually everything is seen from their viewpoint, sometimes resulting in a stiff, dry narrative of events.

In the late 1950's and 1960's Carmichael concentrated on building the characters and personalities of Piper and Quinn. Quinn has never been a particularly likeable person. He's brash, obnoxious, drinks too much, always has a flippant reply. His clothes need pressing, his hair is uncombed. He started as a general reporter for the *Morning Post*, and eventually earned a daily spot with "Quinn's Column on Crime." By the 1970's his unpleasantness had been toned down — he drinks less and is more responsible — and he became the primary detective, calling on Piper for consultation. In contrast, Piper is always neat, polite, quiet: a perfect gentleman. Quinn's inferiority complex is sharpened by Piper's assurance and outward infallibility. But Piper has his own problems — the death of his wife, and his consequent guilt — in the earlier books. Finally, in *Death Trap*, he remarried and settled down to a normal life.

Piper and Quinn's relationship is very close; they understand and tolerate each other in a perfect stereotype of masculine comradeship and solidarity. That relationship plays a strong part in their work as investigators. They work individually, then meet to discuss their findings and continually rehash and rearrange the pieces of the puzzle. They both act more as agitators and catalysts than as detectives. They question and prod endlessly, often unwilling to accept a police solution of accident or suicide. The killer frequently gives himself away while trying to avoid their questions and traps. On the cases that they do work together, they usually arrive at the solution at the same time, but by different routes, Quinn by physical aggression, Piper by psychological cornering.

Carmichael's plots present a consistently pessimistic view of married life. What appears to be a proper, content, happy life is a mask for greed, infidelity, jealousy, and duplicity. *Put Out That Star, Candles for the Dead, False Evidence, Most Deadly Hate, The Quiet Woman*, and others follow this pattern. One spouse is plotting an escape from an intolerable situation. A secondary motive of monetary gain is often involved. Just as often there is a complication: the spouse's new lover is planning his own double-cross, the unwanted spouse learns of the scheme, or an outside force throws the plan off track. A life of sordid cheapness, selfishness, and vindictiveness underlies the placid London suburbs.

Based on ratiocination rather than adventure, Carmichael's books are a holdover from the late Golden Age. There are no bizarre or impossible crimes, but an elaborate scheme and series of events build up to a puzzle story that will, more often than not, deceive the reader.

—Fred Dueren

CARNAC, Carol. Pseudonym for Edith Caroline Rivett; also wrote as E. C. R. Lorac. British. Born in Hendon, London, in 1894. Educated at South Hampstead High School; Central School of Arts and Crafts, London. Member of the Detection Club. *Died 2 July 1958.*

CRIME PUBLICATIONS

Novels (series characters: Chief Inspector Julian Rivers; Inspector Ryvet)

    Triple Death. London, Butterworth, 1936.
    The Missing Rope (Ryvet). London, Skeffington, 1937.
    Murder at Mornington. London, Skeffington, 1937.
    When the Devil Was Sick (Ryvet). London, Davies, 1939.
    The Case of the First-Class Carriage (Ryvet). London, Davies, 1939.
    Death in the Diving-Pool (Ryvet). London, Davies, 1940.
    A Double for Detection (Rivers). London, Macdonald, 1945.
    The Striped Suitcase (Rivers). London, Macdonald, 1946; New York, Doubleday, 1947.
    Clue Sinister (Rivers). London, Macdonald, 1947.
    Over the Garden Wall (Rivers). London, Macdonald, 1948; New York, Doubleday, 1949.
    Upstairs, Downstairs (Rivers). London, Macdonald, 1950; as *Upstairs and Downstairs,* New York, Doubleday, 1950.
    Copy for Crime (Rivers). London, Macdonald, 1950; New York, Doubleday, 1951.
    It's Her Own Funeral (Rivers). London, Collins, 1951; New York, Doubleday, 1952.
    Crossed Skies (Rivers). London, Collins, 1952.
    Murder as a Fine Art (Rivers). London, Collins, 1953.
    A Policeman at the Door (Rivers). London, Collins, 1953; New York, Doubleday, 1954.
    Impact of Evidence (Rivers). London, Collins, and New York, Doubleday, 1954.
    Murder among Members (Rivers). London, Collins, 1955.
    Rigging the Evidence (Rivers). London, Collins, 1955.
    The Double Turn. London, Collins, 1956; as *The Late Miss Trimming,* New York, Doubleday, 1957.
    The Burning Question. London, Collins, 1957.
    Long Shadows (Rivers). London, Collins, 1958; as *Affair at Helen's Court,* New York, Doubleday, 1958.
    Death of a Lady Killer. London, Collins, 1959.

Novels as E. C. R. Lorac (series character: Inspector/Superintendent MacDonald)

    The Murder on the Burrows (MacDonald). London, Sampson Low, 1931; New York, Macaulay, 1932.
    The Affair at Thor's Head (MacDonald). London, Sampson Low, 1932.
    The Greenwell Mystery (MacDonald). London, Sampson Low, 1932; New York, Macaulay, 1934.
    Death on the Oxford Road (MacDonald). London, Sampson Low, 1933.
    The Case of Colonel Marchand (MacDonald). London, Sampson Low, and New York, Macaulay, 1933.
    Murder in St. John's Wood (MacDonald). London, Sampson Low, and New York, Macaulay, 1934.
    Murder in Chelsea (MacDonald). London, Sampson Low, 1934; New York, Macaulay, 1935.

The Organ Speaks (MacDonald).   London, Sampson Low, 1935.

Death of an Author. London, Sampson Low, 1935; New York, Macaulay, 1937.

Crime Counter Crime (MacDonald). London, Collins, 1936.

A Pall for a Painter (MacDonald). London, Collins, 1936.

Post after Post-Mortem (MacDonald). London, Collins, 1936.

These Names Make Clues (Macdonald). London, Collins, 1937.

Bats in the Belfry (MacDonald). London, Collins, and New York, Macaulay, 1937.

The Devil and the C.I.D. (MacDonald). London, Collins, 1938.

Slippery Staircase (MacDonald). London, Collins, 1938.

Black Beadle. London, Collins, 1939.

John Brown's Body (MacDonald). London, Collins, 1939.

Tryst for a Tragedy (MacDonald). London, Collins, 1940.

Death at Dyke's Corner (MacDonald). London, Collins, 1940.

Case in the Clinic (MacDonald). London, Collins, 1941.

Rope's End, Rogue's End (MacDonald). London, Collins, 1942.

The Sixteenth Stair (MacDonald). London, Collins, 1942.

Death Came Softly. London, Collins, and New York, Arcadia House, 1943.

Fell Murder (MacDonald). London, Collins, 1944.

Checkmate to Murder (MacDonald).   London, Collins, and New York, Arcadia House, 1944.

Murder by Matchlight (MacDonald). London, Collins, 1945; New York, Arcadia House, 1946.

Fire in the Thatch (MacDonald). London, Collins, and New York, Arcadia House, 1946.

The Theft of the Iron Dogs (MacDonald). London, Collins, 1946; as *Murderer's Mistake*, New York, Curl, 1947.

Relative to Poison (MacDonald). London, Collins, 1947; New York, Doubleday, 1948.

Death Before Dinner (MacDonald). London, Collins, 1948; as *A Screen for Murder*, New York, Doubleday, 1948.

Part for a Poisoner (MacDonald). London, Collins, 1948; as *Place for a Poisoner*, New York, Doubleday, 1949.

Still Waters (MacDonald). London, Collins, 1949.

Policeman in the Precinct (MacDonald). London, Collins, 1949; as *And Then Put Out the Light*, New York, Doubleday, 1950.

Accident by Design (MacDonald). London, Collins, 1950; New York, Doubleday, 1951.

Murder of a Martinet (MacDonald). London, Collins, 1951; as *I Could Murder Her*, New York, Doubleday, 1951.

The Dog It Was That Died (MacDonald). London, Collins, and New York, Doubleday, 1952.

Murder in the Mill-Race (MacDonald). London, Collins, 1952; as *Speak Justly of the Dead*, New York, Doubleday, 1953.

Crook o' Lune (MacDonald). London, Collins, 1953; as *Shepherd's Crook*, New York, Doubleday, 1953.

Let Well Alone (MacDonald). London, Collins, 1954.

Shroud of Darkness (MacDonald). London, Collins, and New York, Doubleday, 1954.

Ask a Policeman (MacDonald). London, Collins, 1955.

Murder in Vienna (MacDonald). London, Collins, 1956.

Dangerous Domicile (MacDonald). London, Collins, 1957.

Picture of Death (MacDonald). London, Collins, 1957.

Murder on a Monument (MacDonald). London, Collins, 1958.

Death in Triplicate (MacDonald). London, Collins, 1958; as *People Will Talk*, New York, Doubleday, 1958.

Dishonour among Thieves (MacDonald). London, Collins, 1959; as *The Last Escape*, New York, Doubleday, 1959.

Uncollected Short Story as E. C. R. Lorac

"A Bit of Wire-Pulling," in *The Evening Standard Detective Book*, 2nd series.   London, Gollancz, 1951.

OTHER PUBLICATIONS

Novels as Carol Rivett

Outer Circle.   London, Hodder and Stoughton, 1939.
Time Remembered.   London, Hodder and Stoughton, 1940.

*   *   *

Edith Caroline Rivett published more than 70 books under the pseudonyms of Carol Carnac and E. C. R. Lorac.

The Murder on the Burrows, published under the Lorac pseudonym, was her first novel, and introduced Inspector MacDonald, a "London Scot" whose father was a newspaper man. After serving with the first battalion of the London Scottish from 1914 to 1919, MacDonald joined the Metropolitan Police. A bachelor, he lived with an old batman. Although MacDonald appears in many Lorac novels, there is little physical description of him. It can be gleaned from a careful reading that he is physically active, lean, tall, with a penchant for walking the English countryside though a most expert driver when the occasion demands one. His assistant, Reeves, is a bit more colorful, dark, married, easy-going, less dignified, able to disguise himself as one of the "common" folk, and a very able detective. The pair make a formidable team capable of unscrambling even the most twisted circumstances and finding the most well hidden motives.

Inspector Julian Rivers, in the Carnac series, is remarkably like Inspector MacDonald, although more meditative and less inclined to romping through the bush. He leaves that task to his lively assistant, Inspector Lancing, who was a student of "home accidents" which were of the "you never can tell" category. Rivers is from a genteel family; he is an art connoisseur and a romantic. Lancing, a commoner by birth, energetic and enthusiastic, is a perfect complement to Rivers. Other novels written under the Carnac pseudonym which do not feature Inspector Rivers are less interesting with little detection and more obscure plotting.

The author's chief weakness lies in the lack of description given to her characters. They emerge virtually faceless and consequently are quite easily forgotten. In contrast, surprisingly vivid descriptions are always given to the villians, who are promptly murdered off. Usually, the first person murdered in the novels is an embodiment of evil, a hypocritical religious fanatic in several instances, such as *The Double Turn, Murder in the Mill-Race*, or *Policeman in the Precinct*. Subsequent murders of innocent people are only necessitated to cover up the first crime. Another frequent plot device is to take a supposedly accidental death and have MacDonald, or Inspector Rivers, with the aid of their respective assistants, deduce through a complex system of circumstances and plot twists that the death was actually due to murder. Although the manner in which the CID becomes involved in these "accidental deaths" seems a trifle farfetched at times, the plotting and detection which subsequently follow are consistently well done.

—Mary Ann Grochowski

CARPENTER, Duffy. See **RAFFERTY, S. S.**

CARR, A. H. Z. (Albert Zotalkoff Carr). Also wrote as A. B. Carbury. American. Born in Chicago, Illinois, 15 January 1902. Educated at the University of Chicago, B.S. 1921; Columbia University, New York, M.A. 1927; London School of Economics. Married Anne Kingsbury. Assistant to the president, Tradeways Inc., business consultants, New York, 1927–34; assistant to the chairman, War Production Board, Washington, D.C., 1942–44; economic adviser on White House staff, 1944–46; consultant to President Truman, 1948–52; Vice-President, Caravel Films, New York, 1953–56; Vice-President and Director, Cape Lands Inc., 1957–71. Special consultant to American Paper Institute and business firms. Member, government missions to England, 1943; China, 1944, 1945; Inter-Allied Reparations mission to Germany, 1947. Recipient: *Ellery Queen's Mystery Magazine* prize, 1955; Mystery Writers of America Edgar Allan Poe Award, 1971. *Died 28 October 1971.*

CRIME PUBLICATIONS

Novels

The Girl with the Glorious Genes (as A. B. Carbury). New York, Bantam, 1968.
Finding Maubee. New York, Putnam, 1970; as The Calypso Murders, London, Hale, 1973.

Uncollected Short Stories

"The Hunch," in *Best Short Stories of 1936*, edited by Edward J. O'Brien. Boston, Houghton Mifflin, 1936.
"The Trial of John Nobody," in *Queen's Awards, Fifth Series*, edited by Ellery Queen. Boston, Little Brown, 1950; London, Gollancz, 1952.
"Murder at City Hall," in *Queen's Awards, Sixth Series*, edited by Ellery Queen. Boston, Little Brown, 1951; London, Gollancz, 1953.
"Hit and Run," in *Ellery Queen's Mystery Magazine* (New York), July 1952.
"Tyger! Tyger!" in *Queen's Awards, Seventh Series*, edited by Ellery Queen. Boston, Little Brown, 1952; London, Gollancz, 1954.
"If a Body ...," in *Queen's Awards, Eighth Series*, edited by Ellery Queen. Boston, Little Brown, 1953; London, Gollancz, 1955.
"A Case of Catnapping," in *Queen's Awards, Ninth Series*, edited by Ellery Queen. Boston, Little Brown, 1954; London, Collins, 1956.
"A Sudden Dread of ... Nothing," in *Ellery Queen's Mystery Magazine* (New York), January 1955.
"The Black Kitten," in *Queen's Awards, Eleventh Series*, edited by Ellery Queen. New York, Simon and Schuster, 1956; London, Collins, 1958.
"Payment in Kind," in *Ellery Queen's Mystery Magazine* (New York), March 1957.
"The Man Who Understood Women," in *Ellery Queen's Mystery Magazine* (New York), January 1960.
"The Crucial Twist," in *Ellery Queen's Mystery Magazine* (New York), May 1961.
"A Handful of Dust," in *To Be Read Before Midnight*, edited by Ellery Queen. New York, Random House, 1962; London, Gollancz, 1963.

"The Washington Tea Party Murder," in *Ellery Queen's 20th Anniversary Annual*. New York, Random House, 1965; London, Gollancz, 1966.

"The Numerology Murder," in *Ellery Queen's Crime Carousel*. New York, New American Library, 1966; London, Gollancz, 1967.

"The Options of Timothy Merkle," in *Ellery Queen's Grand Slam*. Cleveland, World, 1970; London, Gollancz, 1971.

OTHER PUBLICATIONS

Other

Juggernaut: The Path of Dictatorship. New York, Viking Press, 1939; London, Hutchinson, 1940.

America's Last Chance. New York, Crowell, 1940.

Men of Power: A Book of Dictators. New York, Viking Press, 1941; revised edition, 1956.

Truman, Stalin, and Peace. New York, Doubleday, 1950.

How to Attract Good Luck. New York, Simon and Schuster, 1952; revised edition, New York, Cornerstone Library, 1965.

The Coming of War: An Account of the Remarkable Events Leading to the War of 1812. New York, Doubleday, 1960.

John D. Rockefeller's Secret Weapon. New York, McGraw Hill, 1962.

The World and William Walker (biography). New York, Harper, 1963.

A Matter of Life and Death: How Wars Get Started or Are Prevented. New York, Viking Press, 1966; London, Gollancz, 1967.

Business as a Game. New York, New American Library, 1968.

Translator, *Napoleon Speaks*, by Julia Van Huele. New York, Viking Press, 1942.

*   *   *

A. H. Z. Carr's most significant contribution to the detective-mystery form is his novel *Finding Maubee*. Set on the fictitious island of St. Caro replete with Caribbean color, which Carr was inspired to concoct after a series of visits off the tourist track, the novel is a study in multi-cultural intrigue and suspense in working out the solution to the voodoo murder of a wealthy American tourist. The story introduces a new figure to the lists of cross-cultural detectives: the native West Indian (but American-educated) Chief of Police Xavier Brooke. His unusual detective and setting are appropriate for the novel which, as Carr himself said (*Library Journal*, 1 February 1971), "deals with the ways in which a diversity of men and women try to cope with the hazards and confusions of a fast-changing world."

—Margaret J. King

CARR, Glyn. Pseudonym for Frank Showell Styles. British. Born in Four Oaks, Warwickshire, 14 March 1908. Educated at Bishop Vesey's Grammar School, Sutton Coldfield. Served in the Royal Navy, 1939–46: Commander. Married Kathleen Jane Humphreys in 1954; two daughters and one son. Clerk, 1924–34; tramp, 1934–37; free-lance journalist, 1937–39. Since 1946, full-time writer. Fellow, Royal Geographical Society. Agent: Curtis Brown Ltd., 1 Craven Hill, London W2 3EP, England. Address: Borth y Gest, Porthmadog, Gwynedd LL49 9TW, Wales.

CRIME PUBLICATIONS

Novels (series character: Sir Abercrombie Lewker in all books)

>*Death on Milestone Buttress*. London, Bles, 1951.
>*Murder on the Matterhorn*. London, Bles, 1951; New York, Dutton, 1953.
>*The Youth Hostel Murders*. London, Bles, 1952; New York, Dutton, 1953.
>*The Corpse in the Crevasse*. London, Bles, 1952.
>*Death under Snowdon*. London, Bles, 1952.
>*A Corpse at Camp Two*. London, Bles, 1954.
>*Murder of an Owl*. London, Bles, 1956.
>*The Ice Axe Murders*. London, Bles, 1958.
>*Swing Away, Climber*. London, Bles, and New York, Washburn, 1959.
>*Holiday with Murder*. London, Bles, 1960.
>*Death Finds a Foothold*. London, Bles, 1961.
>*Lewker in Norway*. London, Bles, 1963.
>*Death of a Weirdy*. London, Bles, 1965.
>*Lewker in Tirol*. London, Bles, 1967.
>*Fat Man's Agony*. London, Bles, 1969.

Novels as Showell Styles (series character: Sir Abercrombie Lewker)

>*Traitor's Mountain* (Lewker). London, Selwyn and Blount, 1945; New York, Macmillan, 1946.
>*Kidnap Castle*. London, Selwyn and Blount, 1947.
>*Hammer Island* (Lewker). London, Selwyn and Blount, 1947.
>*Dark Hazard*. London, Selwyn and Blount, 1948.

OTHER PUBLICATIONS

Novels

>*The Rising of the Lark*. London, Selwyn and Blount, 1948.
>*Sir Devil*. London, Selwyn and Blount, 1949.
>*Path to Glory*. London, Faber, 1951.
>*Land from the Sea*. London, Faber, 1952.
>*Mr. Nelson's Ladies*. London, Faber, 1953.
>*The Frigate Captain*. London, Faber, 1954; New York, Vanguard Press, 1956; as *The Sea Lord*, New York, Ballantine, n.d.
>*His Was the Fire*. London, Faber, 1956.
>*Tiger Patrol*. London, Collins, 1957.
>*The Admiral's Fancy*. London, Faber, 1958.
>*Tiger Patrol Wins Through*. London, Collins, 1958.
>*The Tiger Patrol at Sea*. London, Collins, 1959.
>*Wolfe Commands You*. London, Faber, 1959.
>*Shadow Buttress*. London, Faber, 1959.
>*The Flying Ensign*. London, Faber, 1960; as *Greencoats Against Napoleon*, New York, Vanguard Press, 1960.
>*The Sea Officer*. London, Faber, 1961; New York, Macmillan, 1962.
>*Tiger Patrol Presses On*. London, Collins, 1961.

Gentleman Johnny. London, Faber, 1962.

Byrd of the 95th. London, Faber, 1962; as *Thunder over Spain*, New York, Vanguard Press, 1962.

H.M.S. Diamond Rock. London, Faber, 1963.

A Necklace of Glaciers. London, Gollancz, 1963.

Number Two-Ninety. London, Faber, 1966; as *Confederate Raider*, New York, Washburn, 1967.

A Tent on Top. London, Gollancz, 1971.

"Vincey Joe" at Quiberon. London, Faber, 1971.

Admiral of England. London, Faber, 1973.

A Sword for Mr. Fitton. London, Faber, 1975.

Mr. Fitton's Commission. London, Faber, 1977.

The Baltic Convoy. London, Faber, 1979.

A Kiss for Captain Hardy. London, Faber, 1979.

Plays

Two Longer Plays for Juniors (*Prince George's Dragon* and *May Eve*). London, Blackie, 1938.

Radio Play: *The Shop in the Mountain*, from his own novel, 1966.

Other

Walks and Climbs in Malta. Valetta, Progressive Press, 1944.

A Climber in Wales. Birmingham, Cornish Brothers, 1949.

The Mountaineer's Week-End Book. London, Seeley Service, 1951.

Mountains of the Midnight Sun. London, Hurst and Blackett, 1954.

Introduction to Mountaineering. London, Seeley Service, 1955.

The Moated Mountain. London, Hurst and Blackett, 1955.

The Lost Glacier (juvenile). London, Hart Davis, 1955; New York, Vanguard Press, 1956.

Kami the Sherpa (juvenile). Leicester, Brockhampton Press, 1957; as *Sherpa Adventure*, New York, Vanguard Press, 1960.

Midshipman Quinn (juvenile). London, Faber, and New York, Vanguard Press, 1957.

The Camper's and Tramper's Weekend Book. London, Seeley Service, 1957.

How Mountains Are Climbed. London, Routledge, 1958.

Introduction to Caravanning. London, Seeley Service, 1958.

How Underground Britain Is Explored. London, Routledge, 1958.

Getting to Know Mountains, edited by Jack Cox. London, Newnes, 1958.

Quinn of the "Fury" (juvenile). London, Faber, 1958; New York, Vanguard Press, 1961.

The Battle of Cotton (juvenile). London, Constable, 1959.

The Battle of Steam (juvenile). London, Constable, 1960.

The Lost Pothole (juvenile). Leicester, Brockhampton Press, 1961.

The Shop in the Mountain (juvenile). London, Gollancz, and New York, Vanguard Press, 1961.

Midshipman Quinn Wins Through (juvenile). London, Faber, 1961; as *Midshipman Quinn and Denise the Spy*, New York, Vanguard Press, 1961.

The Ladder of Snow (juvenile). London, Gollancz, 1962.

Look at Mountains. London, Hamish Hamilton, 1962.

Greenhorn's Cruise (juvenile). Leicester, Brockhampton Press, and Princeton, New Jersey, Van Nostrand, 1964.

The Camp in the Hills (juvenile). London, Benn, 1964.

Modern Mountaineering. London, Faber, 1964.

Blue Remembered Hills.   London, Faber, 1965.

Quinn at Trafalgar (juvenile).   London, Faber, and New York, Vanguard Press, 1965.

Red for Adventure (juvenile).   Leicester, Brockhampton Press, 1965.

Mr. Fiddle (juvenile).   London, Hamish Hamilton, 1965.

The Foundations of Climbing.   London, Stanley Paul, 1966; as *The Arrow Book of Climbing*, London, Arrow, 1967.

Wolf Club Island (juvenile).   Leicester, Brockhampton Press, 1966.

The Pass of Morning (juvenile).   London, Gollancz, and New York, Washburn, 1966.

Mr. Fiddle's Pig (juvenile).   London, Hamish Hamilton, 1966.

Mallory of Everest.   London, Hamish Hamilton, and New York, Macmillan, 1967.

The Sea Cub (juvenile).   Leicester, Brockhampton Press, 1967.

On Top of the World: An Illustrated History of Mountaineering and Mountaineers.   London, Hamish Hamilton, and New York, Macmillan, 1967.

Mr. Fiddle's Band (juvenile).   London, Hamish Hamilton, 1967.

Rock and Rope.   London, Faber, 1967.

Indestructible Jones (juvenile).   London, Faber, 1967; New York, Washburn, 1969.

The Climber's Bedside Book.   London, Faber, 1968.

Sea Road to Camperdown (juvenile).   London, Faber, 1968.

Journey with a Secret (juvenile).   London, Gollancz, 1968; New York, Meredith Press, 1969.

A Case for Mr. Fiddle (juvenile).   London, Hamish Hamilton, 1969.

Jones's Private Navy (juvenile).   London, Faber, 1969.

First on the Summits.   London, Gollancz, 1970.

First Up Everest.   London, Hamish Hamilton, and New York, Coward McCann, 1970.

The Forbidden Frontiers: A Survey of India from 1765 to 1949.   London, Hamish Hamilton, 1970.

Welsh Walks and Legends.   Cardiff, John Jones, 1972.

Snowdon Range.   Reading, Berkshire, Gaston's Alpine Books, 1973.

The Mountains of North Wales.   London, Gollancz, 1973.

Glyder Range.   Reading, Berkshire, Gaston's Alpine Books, 1974.

Backpacking: A Comprehensive Guide.   London, Macmillan, 1976; New York, McKay, 1977.

Backpacking in Alps and Pyrenees.   London, Gollancz, 1976.

Backpacking in Wales.   London, Hale, 1977.

Welsh Walks and Legends: South Wales.   Cardiff, John Jones, 1977.

Editor, *Men and Mountaineering: An Anthology of Writings by Climbers.*   London, Hamish Hamilton, and New York, David White, 1968.

Translator, *White Fury*, by Raymond Lambert and Claude Kogan.   London, Hurst and Blackett, 1956.

Glyn Carr comments:

My pompous actor-manager detective Sir Abercrombie Lewker stumped and boomed his way through fifteen novels almost by accident. By predilection I am a writer of historical novels and children's books, but my lifelong recreation has been mountaineering and rock-climbing. One day on a particular "pitch" of the classic rock-climb called Milestone Buttress, it struck me how easy it would be to arrange an undetectable murder in that place, and by way of experiment I worked out the system and wove a thinnish plot round it. Bles published the book and wanted more of the same sort. So a further fourteen novels under the pseudonym Glyn Carr were written and published – until, ways of slaughtering people on steep rock-faces being limited, they had to stop.

I enjoy the whodunits of other writers (particularly those of Michael Innes, Margery Allingham, and William Haggard), but I have not myself the whodunit mind. I believe the people who read my Glyn Carr books are people who themselves know the mountains and climbs I described – always with assiduous care for topography and mountain atmosphere – and enjoy a fictional, and perhaps exciting, return to their old haunts.

*   *   *

Glyn Carr is the pseudonym of Frank Showell Styles, a noted explorer and author of many works on the subject of mountaineering. Many of Carr's detective novels are set in exotic locales such as the Nepal Himalayas (*A Corpse at Camp Two*), Innsbruck (*The Corpse in the Crevasse*), Wales (*Death under Snowdon, Murder of an Owl, Death of a Weirdy, Swing Away, Climber*), and Majorca (*Holiday with Murder*); *Lewker in Tirol, Lewker in Norway*, and *Murder on the Matterhorn* speak for themselves. Many also feature mountaineering as an integral part of their plot and puzzle. This is especially true of *A Corpse at Camp Two, Murder of an Owl*, and *Swing Away, Climber*.

Carr's series detective, Sir Abercrombie Lewker (nicknamed "Filthy"), is a famous actor-manager and interpreter of Shakespeare. He is bald and squat, with heavy jowls and a pouchy face. A pompous, perhaps unattractive person, his most impressive feature is his voice which booms constantly – often with a Shakespearean quotation. He seems the least likely person to have climbed Chomolu, a 24,000 foot peak in the Himalayas, when he was over 50 years of age. Lewker has been a passionate mountain climber for many years, and his flair for detection may have been acquired as the result of his training in the Special Commando Branch of Intelligence during World War Two. Obviously, Lewker's interest and ability make him the right man to solve crime problems set in mountainous regions.

Carr's narratives are well-written and characterized. His puzzles usually involve maps, timetables, and "perfect" alibis in the demanding tradition of Freeman Wills Crofts. Clues may be found among rocks, cliffs, precipices, and crevasses. Mountaineering equipment such as nailed boots, pitons, climbing ropes, and snaplinks must also be carefully scrutinized.

In *Murder of an Owl*, Lewker sums up a murderer he had encountered in *Death on Milestone Buttress* by stating, "He even had the effrontery to use the hills themselves as the means and mechanism of murder." This statement might also be applicable to Glyn Carr himself.

—Charles Shibuk

CARR, John Dickson. Also wrote as Carr Dickson; Carter Dickson; Roger Fairbairn. American. Born in Uniontown, Pennsylvania, 30 November 1906. Educated at the Hill School; Haverford College, 1928; studied abroad. Married Clarice Cleaves in 1931; three children. Lived in England, 1932–48, wrote for the BBC during World War II. Reviewer, *Ellery Queen's Mystery Magazine*, 1969–77. President, Mystery Writers of America, 1949. Recipient: *Ellery Queen's Mystery Magazine* award (twice); Mystery Writers of America Edgar Allan Poe Award, 1949, 1969, and Grand Master Award, 1962. *Died 27 February 1977.*

CRIME PUBLICATIONS

Novels (series characters: Henri Bencolin; Patrick Butler; Dr. Gideon Fell)

It Walks by Night (Bencolin).   New York, Harper, 1930.
Castle Skull (Bencolin).   New York, Harper, 1931; London, Severn House, 1976.
The Lost Gallows (Bencolin).   New York, Harper, 1931; London, Severn House, 1976.
Poison in Jest.   New York, Harper, and London, Hamish Hamilton, 1932.
The Corpse in the Waxworks (Bencolin).   New York, Harper, 1932; as *The Waxworks Murder*, London, Hamish Hamilton, 1932.
Hag's Nook (Fell).   New York, Harper, and London, Hamish Hamilton, 1933.
The Mad Hatter Mystery (Fell).   New York, Harper, and London, Hamish Hamilton, 1933.
The Blind Barber (Fell).   New York, Harper, and London, Hamish Hamilton, 1934.
The Eight of Swords (Fell).   New York, Harper, and London, Hamish Hamilton, 1934.
Devil Kinsmere (as Roger Fairbairn).   New York, Harper, and London, Hamish Hamilton, 1934; revised edition, as *Most Secret*, 1964.
Death-Watch (Fell).   New York, Harper, and London, Hamish Hamilton, 1935.
The Three Coffins (Fell).   New York, Harper, 1935; as *The Hollow Man*, London, Hamish Hamilton, 1935.
The Arabian Nights Murder (Fell).   New York, Harper, and London, Hamish Hamilton, 1936.
The Burning Court.   New York, Harper, and London, Hamish Hamilton, 1937.
The Four False Weapons, Being the Return of Bencolin.   New York, Harper, 1937; London, Hamish Hamilton, 1938.
To Wake the Dead (Fell).   New York, Harper, and London, Hamish Hamilton, 1938.
The Crooked Hinge (Fell).   New York, Harper, and London, Hamish Hamilton, 1938.
The Problem of the Green Capsule (Fell).   New York, Harper, 1939; as *The Black Spectacles*, London, Hamish Hamilton, 1939.
The Problem of the Wire Cage (Fell).   New York, Harper, 1939; London, Hamish Hamilton, 1940.
The Man Who Could Not Shudder (Fell).   New York, Harper, and London, Hamish Hamilton, 1940.
The Case of the Constant Suicides (Fell).   New York, Harper, and London, Hamish Hamilton, 1941.
Death Turns the Tables (Fell).   New York, Harper, 1941; as *The Seat of the Scornful*, London, Hamish Hamilton, 1942.
The Emperor's Snuffbox.   New York, Harper, 1942; London, Hamish Hamilton, 1943.
Till Death Do Us Part (Fell).   New York, Harper, and London, Hamish Hamilton, 1944.
He Who Whispers (Fell).   New York, Harper, and London, Hamish Hamilton, 1946.
The Sleeping Sphinx (Fell).   New York, Harper, and London, Hamish Hamilton, 1947.
The Dead Man's Knock (Fell).   New York, Harper, and London, Hamish Hamilton, 1948.
Below Suspicion (Fell, Butler).   New York, Harper, 1949; London, Hamish Hamilton, 1950.
The Bride of Newgate.   New York, Harper, and London, Hamish Hamilton, 1950.
The Devil in Velvet.   New York, Harper, and London, Hamish Hamilton, 1951.
The Nine Wrong Answers.   New York, Harper, and London, Hamish Hamilton, 1952.
Captain Cut-Throat.   New York, Harper, and London, Hamish Hamilton, 1955.
Patrick Butler for the Defense.   New York, Harper, and London, Hamish Hamilton, 1956.
Fire, Burn!   New York, Harper, and London, Hamish Hamilton, 1957.
Scandal at High Chimneys: A Victorian Melodrama.   New York, Harper, and London, Hamish Hamilton, 1959.
In Spite of Thunder (Fell).   New York, Harper, and London, Hamish Hamilton, 1960.

The Witch of the Lowtide: An Edwardian Melodrama. New York, Harper, and London, Hamish Hamilton, 1961.

The Demoniacs. New York, Harper, and London, Hamish Hamilton, 1962.

The House at Satan's Elbow (Fell). New York, Harper, and London, Hamish Hamilton, 1965.

Panic in Box C (Fell). New York, Harper, and London, Hamish Hamilton, 1966.

Dark of the Moon (Fell). New York, Harper, 1967; London, Hamish Hamilton, 1968.

Papa La-Bas. New York, Harper, 1968; London, Hamish Hamilton, 1969.

The Ghosts' High Noon. New York, Harper, 1969; London, Hamish Hamilton, 1970.

Deadly Hall. New York, Harper, and London, Hamish Hamilton, 1971.

The Hungry Goblin: A Victorian Detective Novel. New York, Harper, and London, Hamish Hamilton, 1972.

Novels as Carter Dickson (series character: Sir Henry Merrivale)

The Bowstring Murders (as Carr Dickson). New York, Morrow, 1933; London, Heinemann, 1934.

The Plague Court Murders (Merrivale). New York, Morrow, 1934; London, Heinemann, 1935.

The White Priory Murders (Merrivale). New York, Morrow, 1934; London, Heinemann, 1935.

The Red Widow Murders (Merrivale). New York, Morrow, and London, Heinemann, 1935.

The Unicorn Murders (Merrivale). New York, Morrow, 1935; London, Heinemann, 1936.

The Magic Lantern Murders (Merrivale). London, Heinemann, 1936; as *The Punch and Judy Murders*, New York, Morrow, 1937.

The Third Bullet (novelet). London, Hodder and Stoughton, 1937.

The Peacock Feather Murders (Merrivale). New York, Morrow, 1937; as *The Ten Teacups*, London, Heinemann, 1937.

Death in Five Boxes (Merrivale). New York, Morrow, and London, Heinemann, 1938.

The Judas Window (Merrivale). New York, Morrow, and London, Heinemann, 1938; as *The Crossbow Murder*, New York, Berkley, 1964.

Drop to His Death, with John Rhode. London, Heinemann, 1939; as *Fatal Descent*, New York, Dodd Mead, 1939.

The Reader Is Warned (Merrivale). New York, Morrow, and London, Heinemann, 1939.

And So to Murder (Merrivale). New York, Morrow, 1940; London, Heinemann, 1941.

Nine – and Death Makes Ten (Merrivale). New York, Morrow, 1940; as *Murder in the Submarine Zone*, London, Heinemann, 1940; as *Murder in the Atlantic*, Cleveland, World, 1959.

Seeing Is Believing (Merrivale). New York, Morrow, 1941; London, Heinemann, 1942; as *Cross of Murder*, Cleveland, World, 1959.

The Gilded Man (Merrivale). New York, Morrow, and London, Heinemann, 1942; as *Death and the Gilded Man*, New York, Pocket Books, 1947.

She Died a Lady (Merrivale). New York, Morrow, and London, Heinemann, 1943.

He Wouldn't Kill Patience (Merrivale). New York, Morrow, and London, Heinemann, 1944.

The Curse of the Bronze Lamp (Merrivale). New York, Morrow, 1945; as *Lord of the Sorcerers*, London, Heinemann, 1946.

My Late Wives (Merrivale). New York, Morrow, 1946; London, Heinemann, 1947.

The Skeleton in the Clock (Merrivale). New York, Morrow, 1948; London, Heinemann, 1949.

A Graveyard to Let (Merrivale). New York, Morrow, 1949; London, Heinemann, 1950.

Night at the Mocking Widow (Merrivale). New York, Morrow, 1950; London, Heinemann, 1951.
Behind the Crimson Blind (Merrivale). New York, Morrow, and London, Heinemann, 1952.
The Cavalier's Cup (Merrivale). New York, Morrow, 1953; London, Heinemann, 1954.
Fear Is the Same. New York, Morrow, and London, Heinemann, 1956.

Short Stories

The Department of Queer Complaints (as Carter Dickson). New York, Morrow, and London, Heinemann, 1940.
Dr. Fell, Detective, and Other Stories. New York, Spivak, 1947.
The Third Bullet and Other Stories. New York, Harper, and London, Hamish Hamilton, 1954.
The Exploits of Sherlock Holmes, with Adrian Conan Doyle. New York, Random House, and London, Murray, 1954.
The Men Who Explained Miracles. New York, Harper, 1963; London, Hamish Hamilton, 1964.

OTHER PUBLICATIONS

Plays

Radio Plays: *Appointment with Fear* series, 1940's, and *Suspense* series.

Other

The Murder of Sir Edmund Godfrey. New York, Harper, and London, Hamish Hamilton, 1936.
The Life of Sir Arthur Conan Doyle. New York, Harper, 1949.

Editor, *Maiden Murders*. New York, Harper, 1952.
Editor, *Great Stories*, by Arthur Conan Doyle. London, Murray, and New York, British Book Centre, 1959.

Bibliography: "The Books of John Dickson Carr/Carter Dickson" by R. E. Briney, in *The Crooked Hinge*, San Diego, University of California Extension, 1976.

*   *   *

In John Dickson Carr's first novel, *It Walks by Night*, there is a passage from a play ascribed to one of the characters: "The art of the murderer, my dear Maurot, is the same as the art of the magician. And the art of the magician does not lie in any such nonsense as 'the hand is quicker than the eye,' but consists simply in directing your attention to the wrong place. He will cause you to be watching one hand, while with the other hand, unseen though in full view, he produces his effect." This is also the art of the mystery writer as practiced for more than forty years by John Dickson Carr. Additional facets of his talent were perfected through the years – the meticulous historical reconstructions; the broad, sometimes farcical humor; the expert deployment of bizarre incident and eerie atmosphere; the occasional touch of outright fantasy – but the fundamental framework was always the same: the ingeniously plotted murder puzzle, set forth with all the illusionist's skill at deception. Carr's particular *forte* was the "miracle problem" or "impossible crime," with its primary sub-category, the locked-room murder. He compiled a longer list of variations on this theme than any other author, and even included an analytical lecture on the subject in one of his novels (the famous "Locked Room Lecture" in *The Three Coffins*.

Fifty out of Carr's seventy mystery novels belong to series featuring one of three continuing detective characters. The first of these detectives, introduced in *It Walks by Night*, was the flamboyant Parisian *juge d'instruction*, Henri Bencolin. Bencolin's cases include an impossible murder in a gambling club – the victim, seen to enter an empty room with all entrances under observation, is subsequently found there, beheaded; the stabbing of a young girl in a wax museum; and multiple deaths in a macabre castle on the Rhine. The books do not have the discipline and polish of Carr's best mysteries, and lack the overt humor often present in later work. But all of the author's other hallmarks are present, including his fondness for "bad" women in place of *ingénues*.

Four Bencolin novels and one non-series mystery, *Poison in Jest*, appeared in rapid succession. It became obvious that Carr's output was more than his original publishers were prepared to handle. A second publisher was more than happy to take the overflow, under a new byline. Carr's most durable detective, the bulky and bibulous Dr. Gideon Fell, was introduced in *Hag's Nook*. Modelled in appearance and mannerisms on G. K. Chesterton, whom Carr admired, Dr. Fell appeared in some twenty-three novels. Among the notable Dr. Fell novels are *The Blind Barber*, an all-stops-out farce about murder on an ocean liner; *The Three Coffins*, which contains two "impossible" murders and the celebrated "Locked Room Lecture"; *The Crooked Hinge*, one of the most audacious mystery puzzles ever written; *The Problem of the Wire Cage*, in which a man is found strangled in the middle of a wet clay tennis court, with only his own footprints leading out to the body; *He Who Whispers*, with its brooding atmosphere and hints of vampires; and *Below Suspicion*, in which murder is mixed with modern Satanism. Dr. Fell's last appearance was in *Dark of the Moon*, in which he unmasked a murderer in Carr's adopted city of Charleston, South Carolina.

A year after the introduction of Dr. Fell, the equally imposing bulk of Sir Henry Merrivale ("H.M.") hove into view in *The Plague Court Murders* under the Carter Dickson byline. More broadly drawn than Gideon Fell, and prone to fits of childishness and ill-temper, H.M. was equally astute at unravelling intricate crimes. Almost all of his cases are "impossible" crimes. *The Peacock Feather Murders* and *The Judas Window* are justly regarded as classics of the locked-room story. In *The Curse of the Bronze Lamp* and *A Graveyard to Let* there are miraculous disappearances to rival any produced by stage illusionists. H.M. is an openly comic figure, but even in the midst of the funny scenes the author keeps the demands of his plots in mind. In one story, H.M.'s majestic progress along the pavement comes to an abrupt halt when he slips on a banana peel. His classic prat-fall is funny in context, but it also serves to distract the reader's attention from a revealing conversation taking place in the foreground. One of the funniest scenes in all of Carr/Dickson's books occurs in the opening pages of *Night at the Mocking Widow* when H.M.'s suitcase on wheels gets away from him and is chased down a village street by a pack of dogs. This is pure slapstick, like something from a Laurel and Hardy comedy; but the climax of the scene provides H.M. with a significant clue to later crimes. H.M. ultimately bows out (at least in book length) in a blaze of comic glory in *The Cavalier's Cup*, which reads like a cross between P. G. Wodehouse and Thorne Smith, but still has a substantial crime puzzle at its core.

A small number of Carr's contemporary detective novels fall outside his established series. Of these, undoubtedly the best is *The Burning Court*. In this astonishing tour de force, the narrator discovers that his wife has the name and the appearance of a notorious poisoner, executed some seventy-five years previously. What is he to think when new deaths by poison begin to occur?

In 1928, before he turned to detective fiction, Carr had written a historical romance "with lots of Gadzookses and swordplay." The story was never published, and the manuscript was destroyed. But in 1934, while the Fell and H.M. series were just getting off the ground, he published a historical novel called *Devil Kinsmere* under the pseudonym Roger Fairbairn. Thirty years later, the book was rewritten and published as *Most Secret* under Carr's own name. Carr published no historical fiction, as such, between 1934 and 1950, although in 1936 he wrote *The Murder of Sir Edmund Godfrey*, a fascinating account of an actual crime from the late seventeenth century. In 1950, Carr produced *The Bride of Newgate*, the first of a series of historical romances that were also detective novels. The second of these, *The Devil in Velvet*, sold better than any of Carr's other novels. Here the historical setting and the murder puzzle were augmented by deal-with-the-Devil and time-travel fantasy themes. Two subsequent historical mysteries, *Fear Is the Same* and *Fire, Burn!*, also involved time-travel, much in the manner of John Balderston's stage drama *Berkeley Square*. Carr's historical novels culminated with *The Hungry Goblin*, a Victorian mystery in which the role of the detective was played by the writer Wilkie Collins.

In addition to his novels, Carr wrote a highly successful *Life of Sir Arthur Conan Doyle*, as well as numerous short stories and radio plays. His short fiction ranged from pulp-magazine melodrama to classic puzzle stories, from the fantasy of "New Murders for Old" to the prize-winning and often reprinted "The Gentleman from Paris." Nine of the short stories featured another series detective, Colonel March of the Department of Queer Complaints. Carr also collaborated with Adrian Conan Doyle, Sir Arthur's youngest son, on six Sherlock Holmes pastiches, *The Exploits of Sherlock Holmes*.

—R. E. Briney

CARR, Margaret.   Also writes as Martin Carroll; Carole Kerr.   British.   Born in Salford, Lancashire, in 1935. Educated at Pendleton High School. Works as local government secretary. Address: Waverley, Wavering Lane, Gillingham, Dorset, England.

CRIME PUBLICATIONS

Novels

> *Tread Warily at Midnight.*   London, Hale, 1971.
> *Sitting Duck.*   London, Hale, 1972.
> *Who's the Target?*   London, Hale, 1974.
> *Wait for the Wake.*   London, Hale, 1974.
> *Too Close for Comfort.*   London, Hale, 1974.
> *Blood Will Out.*   London, Hale, 1975.
> *Blindman's Bluff.*   London, Hale, 1976.
> *Out of the Past.*   London, Hale, 1976.
> *Dare the Devil.*   London, Hale, 1976.
> *Twin Tragedy.*   London, Hale, 1977.
> *The Witch of Wykham.*   London, Hale, 1978.

Novels as Martin Carroll

> *Begotten Murder.*   London, Hale, 1967.
> *Blood Vengeance.*   London, Hale, 1968.
> *Dead Trouble.*   London, Hale, 1968.
> *Goodbye Is Forever.*   London, Hale, 1968.
> *Too Beautiful to Die.*   London, Hale, 1969.
> *Bait.*   London, Hale, 1970.
> *Miranda Said Murder.*   London, Hale, 1970.
> *Hear No Evil.*   London, Hale, 1971.

OTHER PUBLICATIONS

Novels

Spring into Love. London, Hale, 1967.
Sharendel. London, Hale, 1976.

Novels as Carole Kerr

Not for Sale. London, Hale, 1975.
Shadow of the Hunter. London, Hale, 1975.
A Time to Surrender. London, Hale, 1975.
Love All Start. London, Hale, 1977.
Lamb to the Slaughter. London, Hale, 1978.
An Innocent Abroad. London, Hale, 1979.

*   *   *

Margaret Carr brings a lighthearted touch to the romantic thriller, taking an ordinary girl (secretary, teacher, bookseller, clerk) out of her normal orbit and putting her down in places like Spain, the Balearic Isles, Crete, or the Channel Islands, sometimes striking out on a new job or new life-style, or trying to find out what happened to a relative or friend, or helping someone in trouble. She trips over dead bodies, is confronted with a variety of mysteries, is thwarted and aided in turn by a strong, masterful hero, deceived by a smooth-tongued villain, usually has a good friend to provide a secondary romance, and ends up happily in the hero's arms after numerous perils and alarms.

Margaret Carr published her early books under the male name of Martin Carroll, but as her work has always been aimed at female readers, particularly the young and unsophisticated, she reverted to her real name.

—Herbert Harris

CARROLL, Martin. See **CARR, Margaret.**

CARTER, Nick. See **DEY, Frederic Van Rensselaer; AVALLONE, Michael; BALLARD, Willis Todhunter; COLLINS, Michael.**

CARVIC, Heron.   British.   Born in London. Educated at Eton College. Married the actress Phyllis Neilson-Terry in 1958 (died, 1977). Radio and stage actor; also worked at many other jobs. Lives in Kent. Agent: Curtis Brown Ltd., 1 Craven Hill, London W2 3EP, England.

CRIME PUBLICATIONS

Novels (series character: Miss Seeton)

Picture Miss Seeton.   London, Bles, and New York, Harper, 1968.
Miss Seeton Draws the Line.   London, Bles, 1969; New York, Harper, 1970.
Miss Seeton Bewitched.   London, Bles, 1971; as *Witch Miss Seeton*, New York, Harper, 1971.
Miss Seeton Sings.   New York, Harper, 1973; London, Davies, 1974.
Odds on Miss Seeton.   New York, Harper, 1975; London, Davies, 1976.

OTHER PUBLICATIONS

Plays

The Widow of 40 (also director: produced London, 1944).
Beggars' Union (also director: produced London, 1947).

Other

"Little Old Ladies," in *Murder Ink: The Mystery Reader's Companion*, edited by Dilys Winn.   New York, Workman, 1977.

Theatrical Activities:

Director: both his own plays.
Actor: **Plays** – Richard Fleming, in *The Bat* by Mary Roberts Rinehart and Avery Hopwood, London, 1937; Jack Norman, in *Young England* by Walter Reynolds, London, 1939; Hortensio, in *The Taming of the Shrew*, and Feste, in *Twelfth Night*, both London, 1941; John Blister, in *The Widow of 40*, London, 1944. **Radio** – Latimer Lord, in *One Fine Day* by Emery Bonett, 1944, and other roles.

*   *   *

Heron Carvic's contribution to the detective genre is a character – the Miss Seeton whose name appears in the books' titles. She is an unlikely combination of the quintessential Victorian lady who is also fey. Of course, she keeps the latter characteristic sternly suppressed, but people still feel disoriented with her. They see the real world while she marches to her own drummer. The result is chaos; however, chaos useful to Scotland Yard after the perceptive Superintendent Delphick accidentally discovers her talents while investigating a murder that she witnessed. And thereby hang several tales.

The first book established characters and setting: Miss Seeton, an eccentric art mistress on the verge of retirement; the English village of Plummergen to which she retires; and an engaging collection of villagers ranging from the normal Squire and his family through those with mild, endearing eccentricities such as the Vicar, to the two malicious old maids known as The Nuts. Delphick, and his minions and superiors, complete the cast of continuing characters. Each succeeding book attempts to reinforce Miss Seeton's talents and eccentricities while extending her range of activities, but with mixed and uneven success.

Carvic's viewpoint is necessarily multiple, otherwise readers would never know what was happening; however, his pompous ironic voice unnecessarily intrudes in every book. Satire about village life is so heavy-handed that little humor and poignance remain after he pounds the point home. Frequently, too, plot becomes farce, lessening credibility and denigrating all concerned. The characters, however, are consistently fascinating.

—Pearl G. Aldrich

CASPARY, Vera. American. Born in Chicago, Illinois, 13 November 1904. Educated in public schools in Chicago. Married I. G. Goldsmith in 1949 (died). Worked as stenographer; copy writer; director of mail order school; editor of *Dance* magazine, 1925–27. Free-lance author and screen writer after 1927. Recipient: Screen Writers Guild Award, 1948, 1967. Agent: Monica McCall Inc., 667 Madison Avenue, New York, New York 10021. Address: 1454 Blue Ridge Drive, Beverly Hills, California, U.S.A.

CRIME PUBLICATIONS

Novels

> *Laura.* Boston, Houghton Mifflin, 1943; London, Eyre and Spottiswoode, 1944.
> *Bedelia.* Boston, Houghton Mifflin, and London, Eyre and Spottiswoode, 1945.
> *The Murder in the Stork Club.* New York, Black, 1946; as *The Lady in Mink*, London, Gordon Martin, 1946.
> *Stranger Than Truth.* New York, Random House, 1946; London, Eyre and Spottiswoode, 1947.
> *The Weeping and the Laughter.* Boston, Little Brown, 1950; as *The Death Wish*, London, Eyre and Spottiswoode, 1951.
> *Thelma.* Boston, Little Brown, 1952; London, W. H. Allen, 1953.
> *False Face.* London, W. H. Allen, 1954.
> *The Husband.* New York, Harper, and London, W. H. Allen, 1957.
> *Evvie.* New York, Harper, and London, W. H. Allen, 1960.
> *A Chosen Sparrow.* New York, Putnam, and London, W. H. Allen, 1964.
> *The Man Who Loved His Wife.* New York, Putnam, and London, W. H. Allen, 1966.
> *The Rosecrest Cell.* New York, Putnam, 1967; London, W. H. Allen, 1968.
> *Final Portrait.* London, W. H. Allen, 1971.
> *Ruth.* New York, Pocket Books, 1972.

Uncollected Short Story

"Sugar and Spice," in *Ellery Queen's Mystery Magazine* (New York), October 1948.

OTHER PUBLICATIONS

Novels

> *The White Girl.* New York, Sears, 1929.
> *Ladies and Gents.* New York, Century, 1929.
> *Music in the Street.* New York, Sears, 1930.

Thicker Than Water. New York, Liveright, 1932.
The Dreamers. New York, Pocket Books, 1975.

Plays

Blind Mice, with Winifred Lenihan (produced New York, 1930).
Geraniums in My Window, with Samuel Ornitz (produced New York, 1934).
Laura, with George Sklar, adaptation of the novel by Caspary (produced London, 1945; New York, 1947). New York, Dramatists Play Service, 1945.
Wedding in Paris, music by Hans May, lyrics by Sonny Miller (produced London, 1954). New York, French, 1956.

Screenplays: *I'll Love You Always*, 1935; *Easy Living*, with Preston Sturges, 1937; *Scandal Street*, with Bertram Millhauser and Eddie Welch, 1938; *Service Deluxe*, with others, 1938; *Sing, Dance, Plenty Hot*, with others, 1940; *Lady from Louisiana*, with others, 1941; *Lady Bodyguard*, with Edmund L. Hartmann and Art Arthur, 1942; *Claudia and David*, with Rose Franken and William Brown Meloney, 1946; *Bedelia*, with others, 1946; *Out of the Blue*, with Walter Bullock and Edward Eliscu, 1947; *A Letter to Three Wives*, with Joseph L. Mankiewicz, 1949; *Three Husbands*, with Edward Eliscu, 1950; *I Can Get It for You Wholesale*, with Abraham Polonsky, 1951; *The Blue Gardenia*, with Charles Hoffman, 1953; *Give a Girl a Break*, with Albert Hackett and Frances Goodrich, 1954; *Les Girls*, with John Patrick, 1957; *Bachelor in Paradise*, with Valentine Davies and Hal Kanter, 1961.

Other

The Secrets of Grown-Ups (autobiography). New York, McGraw Hill, 1979.

*   *   *

Best known for her mystery novels, Vera Caspary has also written screenplays and non-mysteries. In all her fiction, she employs a taut, gritty style whose even, unjudgmental tone is almost Naturalistic. All the novels reveal her accurate ear for clipped, brisk dialogue, one of her strongest techniques, for this device conveys clearly and without burdensome modifiers the tone, mood, and tension of men and women under threat. Another Caspary strength is her understanding of the herd instinct of frightened human beings. The books explore the likely and unlikely alliances her characters make in the face of terror or in response to police investigations. The impulse to resist the investigator, to protect one's own circle, is strong in her mystery protagonists, and this impulse lends a realistic complication to the plots.

Evvie is a good example of all these factors and, as is typical of Caspary's mysteries, is essentially a personality study. Both the victim, Evvie Ashton, and the narrator, Louise Goodman, consider themselves emancipated women, and the two range through widely varied social levels of prohibition-era Chicago, believing their friendship to be the one constant in a world of shifting familial and sexual alliances. When Evvie takes a lover whose identity she keeps secret, however, new pressures threaten their relationship. Evvie's murder, while certainly central to the plot, is but one incident in Louise's sustained attempt to come to terms with herself, her friend, and with Evvie's lover. The results are greatly satisfying to both the mystery fan and to the general reader.

Caspary's best known work, *Laura*, is also a personality study. Here, the policeman-detective is a sympathetic character who falls in love with the victim during the investigation. As in *Stranger Than Truth*, *Final Portrait*, and *The Husband*, Caspary effectively employs multiple points of view. *Laura* is brilliantly constructed, and the reader shares the characters' fascination with Laura's vivid, appealing personality. Actually, *Laura* examines the American Dream from a new, revealing angle. The unreality of the Dream is clearly symbolized by the novel's cleverly constructed double climax. Deservedly, *Laura* is a mystery classic.

The plots of *Bedelia* and *The Man Who Loved His Wife* hinge on personalities which lack some civilizing factor, for each centers around a person who allows one emotion to govern his behavior and to overshadow concern for family and friends. In *Bedelia*, Charlie Horst seeks to discover the true character of his seemingly ideal wife. Equally fascinating are the alterations in Charlie himself as he changes from enchanted lover to judge. In *The Man Who Loved His Wife*, jealous Fletcher Strode plans his suicide to look like murder. By means of a carefully crafted diary in which his fantasies are recorded as fact, he posthumously accuses his wife of infidelity, always considered a strong motive for murder. The strange crime is in itself a powerful complication, but Caspary's sure touch with personality development and revelation carries the novel.

Equally compelling is *False Face*, the story of the abduction of Nina Redfield who, though a successful teacher and seemingly a mature, competent adult, is emotionally adolescent. Nina has remained entranced with her school beau, Nick Brazza, a dangerous criminal whom she romanticizes. The plot moves briskly along, aided by the portrait of Nina's friend, brassy Flo Allen, who contrasts nicely with the protagonist. As usual, the novel is flavored by a new romance. In this variation of the maturation tale, Caspary deftly creates an intriguing mystery.

A careful writer who vividly depicts both character and setting, Caspary achieves powerful plots with unusual climaxes in her excellent novels. Despite her consistent use of similar themes, motifs, and devices, each plot is a unique contribution to the genre.

—Jane S. Bakerman

CASSELS, John. See **DUNCAN, W. Murdoch.**

CAUDWELL, Christopher. See **SPRIGG, Christopher St. John.**

CECIL, Henry. Pseudonym for Henry Cecil Leon. British. Born in London, 19 September 1902. Educated at St. Paul's School, London; King's College, Cambridge; Gray's Inn, London: called to the Bar 1923. Served in the 1/5 Queen's Regiment, 1939–45: Military Cross, 1942. Married 1) Lettice Mabel Apperly in 1935 (died, 1950); 2) Barbara Jeanne Ovenden in 1954; one step-son. County Court Judge, 1949–67. Chairman, British Copyright Council, 1973–76. *Died in May 1976.*

CRIME PUBLICATIONS

Novels (series characters: Colonel Brain; Ambrose Low; Roger Thursby)

The Painswick Line. London, Chapman and Hall, 1951.
No Bail for the Judge (Brain; Low). London, Chapman and Hall, and New York, Harper, 1952.
Ways and Means. London, Chapman and Hall, 1952.
Natural Causes (Brain). London, Chapman and Hall, 1953.
According to the Evidence (Brain; Low). London, Chapman and Hall, and New York, Harper, 1954.
Brothers in Law (Thursby). London, Joseph, and New York, Harper, 1955.
Friends at Court (Thursby). London, Joseph, 1956; New York, Harper, 1957.
Much in Evidence. London, Joseph, 1957; as *The Long Arm*, New York, Harper, 1957.
Sober as a Judge (Thursby). London, Joseph, and New York, Harper, 1958.
Settled Out of Court. London, Joseph, and New York, Harper, 1959.
Alibi for a Judge. London, Joseph, 1960.
Daughters in Law. London, Joseph, and New York, Harper, 1961.
Unlawful Occasions. London, Joseph, 1962.
Independent Witness. London, Joseph, 1963.
Fathers in Law. London, Joseph, 1965; as *A Child Divided*, New York, Harper, 1965.
The Asking Price. London, Joseph, and New York, Harper, 1966.
A Woman Named Anne. London, Joseph, and New York, Harper, 1967.
No Fear or Favour. London, Joseph, 1968; as *The Blackmailers*, New York, Simon and Schuster, 1969.
Tell You What I'll Do. London, Joseph, and New York, Simon and Schuster, 1969.
The Buttercup Spell. London, Joseph, 1971.
The Wanted Man. London, Joseph, 1972.
Truth with Her Boots On. London, Joseph, 1974.
Cross Purposes. London, Joseph, 1976.
Hunt the Slipper. London, Joseph, 1977.

Short Stories

Full Circle. London, Chapman and Hall, 1948.
Portrait of a Judge and Other Stories. London, Joseph, 1964; New York, Harper, 1965.
Brief Tales from the Bench. London, BBC Publications, 1968; New York, Simon and Schuster, 1972.

OTHER PUBLICATIONS

Plays

Brothers-in-Law, with Ted Willis, adaptation of the novel by Cecil (produced Wimbledon, Surrey, 1959). London, French, 1959.
Settled Out of Court, with William Saroyan, adaptation of the novel by Cecil (produced London, 1960). London, French, 1962.
Alibi for a Judge, with Felicity Douglas and Basil Dawson, adaptation of the novel by Cecil (produced London, 1965). London, French, 1967.
According to the Evidence, with Felicity Douglas and Basil Dawson, adaptation of the novel by Cecil (produced London, 1967). London, French, 1968.
No Fear or Favour (produced Birmingham, 1967).
Hugo, with C. E. Webber (produced London, 1969).

A Woman Named Anne, adaptation of his own novel (produced Edinburgh, 1969; London, 1970).
The Tilted Scales (produced Guildford, Surrey, 1971).

Radio Plays: *Independent Witness*, 1958; *A Matter for Speculation*, 1965; *Fathers in Law*, from his own novel, 1965; *Brief Tales from the Bench*, 1967; *Contempt of Court*, 1967; *The Buttercup Spell*, from his own novel, 1972.

Television Plays: *The Painswick Line*, from his own novel, 1963; *Mr. Justice Duncannon* (series), with Frank Muir and Denis Nordern, 1963.

Other

Brief to Counsel.   London, Joseph, 1958; New York, Harper, 1959.
I Married the Girl (as Clifford Maxwell).   London, Joseph, 1960.
Not Such an Ass.   London, Hutchinson, 1961.
Tipping the Scales.   London, Hutchinson, 1964.
Know about English Law.   London, Blackie, 1965; revised edition, as *Learn about English Law*, London, Luscombe Press, 1974.
A Matter of Speculation: The Case of Lord Cochrane.   London, Hutchinson, 1965.
The English Judge.   London, Stevens, 1970; revised edition, London, Arrow, 1972.
Just Within the Law (autobiography).   London, Hutchinson, 1975.

Editor, *Trial of Walter Graham Rowland.*   Newton Abbot, Devon, David and Charles, 1975.

Manuscript Collection: McMaster University, Hamilton, Ontario.

*   *   *

Mystery literature abounds with excellent writers who, because they are stereotyped as "mystery writers," fail to acquire the larger audience they deserve. Henry Cecil is one of these writers. Cecil has written a number of works, of which almost all manage to keep a fine balance; while they are thoughtful and thought-provoking, they maintain a healthy view of society's more curious foibles. Though one might not always agree with Cecil's views, he is always provocative and entertaining.

Cecil's fiction deals with the law, though not all of his works are mysteries. And the mysteries are not all of a piece. Some are suspense novels, some are puzzling murder mysteries, and some are just puzzles. *Tell You What I'll Do* is a typical (if any Cecil novel can be called typical) suspense story about a con-man who commits crimes in order to be put *in* prison. Though it is one of Cecil's lighter works, it is stylish and incorporates both humor and social criticism in an attempt to argue for prison reform.

Cecil's murder mysteries are equally distinguished by skillful style, appropriate comic relief, an uncanny ear for dialogue and the rhythms of speech, deftly handled detail, and a consistently unique (and often refreshing) perspective.

Some of Cecil's more memorable murder mysteries are those starring Ambrose Low, an ex-criminal, and Colonel Brain, an ex-army officer. In the inverted tale *No Bail for the Judge*, the unframing of Sir Edwin Prout provides the basis for an enlightening story. An even stronger work, also involving Low and Brain, is *According to the Evidence*, in which Cecil raises fundamental questions about the legal system while telling a good story. It is fascinating to watch Low get Alec Morland acquitted of murdering a murderer – and even more fascinating to find out who did it.

Those murder mysteries not including Low and Brain are also skilfully crafted and entertaining. In *The Asking Price*, for example, 52-year-old Ronald Holbrook is accused of murdering his seventeen year old fiancée. The detail is superb, the character study of

Holbrook is concise, and the humorous anecdotes are both amusing *and* relevant to the story. This novel does seem to be more cynical than Cecil's earlier works; the social criticism is more biting, there are no heroes, the solution is very sardonic.

As effective and fascinating as Cecil's mysteries are, it is his marginal mysteries, his puzzles, that are truly extraordinary. In *A Woman Named Anne*, for example, there is no detection, no murder, no violence – yet the novel is absolutely spellbinding. Almost all the story takes place in a courtroom, where Michael Amberley is being divorced by his wife. The exchanges crackle, the dialogue is witty and quick, the plot is inspired. The characters are colorful, three-dimensional, and seemingly sketched with ease.

Henry Cecil is an excellent model for a would-be writer, or for many already established writers. He is a skilful author who clearly cares for the language. He has a good eye for detail, he often has strong female characters, and, though he is obviously very knowledgeable about law and the legal system, he is never (well, almost never) pedantic. Though he has strong feelings, they are tempered with a humaneness and humor that are rare today. He should be read.

—Donald J. Pattow

CHABER, M. E.   See **CROSSEN, Ken.**

CHANCE, John Newton. Also writes as J. Drummond; John Lymington. British. Born in London, in 1911. Educated at Streatham Hill College and privately. Served in the Royal Air Force during World War II. Address: c/o Robert Hale Ltd., 45–47 Clerkenwell Green, London EC1R 0HT, England.

CRIME PUBLICATIONS

Novels (series characters: Superintendent Black; Jonathan Blake; Chance; Mr. DeHavilland; Jason)

Murder in Oils.   London, Gollancz, 1935.
Wheels in the Forest (DeHavilland; Black).   London, Gollancz, 1935.
The Devil Drives.   London, Gollancz, 1936.
Maiden Possessed.   London, Gollancz, 1937.
Rhapsody in Fear.   London, Gollancz, 1937.
Death of an Innocent (DeHavilland; Black).   London, Gollancz, 1938.
The Devil in Greenlands.   London, Gollancz, 1939.
The Ghost of Truth (Black).   London, Gollancz, 1939.
Screaming Fog (Chance).   London, Macdonald, 1944; as *Death Stalks the Cobbled Square*, New York, McBride, 1946.
The Red Knight (Chance; Black; DeHavilland).   London, Macdonald, and New York, Macmillan, 1945.

The Eye in Darkness (Chance). London, Macdonald, 1946.
The Knight and the Castle (DeHavilland). London, Macdonald, 1946.
The Black Highway (DeHavilland). London, Macdonald, 1947.
Coven Gibbet. London, Macdonald, 1948.
The Brandy Pole (DeHavilland). London, Macdonald, 1949.
The Night of the Full Moon (DeHavilland). London, Macdonald, 1950.
Aunt Miranda's Murder. London, Macdonald, and New York, Dodd Mead, 1951.
The Man in My Shoes (Chance). London, Macdonald, 1952.
The Twopenny Box. London, Macdonald, 1952.
The Jason Affair. London, Macdonald, 1953; as *Up to Her Neck*, New York, Popular
     Library, 1955.
The Randy Inheritance. London, Macdonald, 1953.
Jason and the Sleep Game. London, Macdonald, 1954.
The Jason Murders. London, Macdonald, 1954.
Jason Goes West. London, Macdonald, 1955.
The Last Seven Hours. London, Macdonald, 1956.
A Shadow Called Janet. London, Macdonald, 1956.
Dead Man's Knock. London, Hale, 1957.
The Little Crime. London, Hale, 1957.
Affair with a Rich Girl. London, Hale, 1958.
The Man with Three Witches. London, Hale, 1958.
The Fatal Fascination. London, Hale, 1959.
The Man with No Face. London, Hale, 1959.
Alarm at Black Brake. London, Hale, 1960.
Lady in a Frame. London, Hale, 1960.
Import of Evil. London, Hale, 1961.
The Night of the Settlement. London, Hale, 1961.
Triangle of Fear. London, Hale, 1962.
The Man Behind Me. London, Hale, 1963.
The Forest Affair. London, Hale, 1963.
Commission for Disaster. London, Hale, 1964.
Death under Desolate. London, Hale, 1964.
Stormlight. London, Hale, 1965.
The Affair at Dead End (Blake). London, Hale, 1966.
The Double Death. London, Hale, 1966.
The Case of the Death Computer. London, Hale, 1967.
The Case of the Fear Makers. London, Hale, 1967.
The Death Women (Blake). London, Hale, 1967.
The Hurricane Drift (Blake). London, Hale, 1967.
The Mask of Pursuit (Blake). London, Hale, 1967.
The Thug Executive. London, Hale, 1967.
Dead Man's Shoes (Blake). London, Hale, 1968.
Death of the Wild Bird. London, Hale, 1968.
Fate of the Lying Jade. London, Hale, 1968.
The Halloween Murders. London, Hale, 1968.
Mantrap. London, Hale, 1968.
The Rogue Aunt (Blake). London, Hale, 1968.
The Abel Coincidence (Blake). London, Hale, 1969.
The Ice Maidens (Blake). London, Hale, 1969.
Involvement in Austria. London, Hale, 1969.
The Killer Reaction (Blake). London, Hale, 1969.
The Killing Experiment (Blake). London, Hale, 1969.
The Mists of Treason (Blake). London, Hale, 1970.
A Ring of Liars. London, Hale, 1970.
Three Masks of Death (Blake). London, Hale, 1970.

The Mirror Train. London, Hale, 1970.
The Cat Watchers. London, Hale, 1971.
The Faces of a Bad Girl. London, Hale, 1971.
A Wreath of Bones. London, Hale, 1971.
A Bad Dream of Death. London, Hale, 1972.
Last Train to Limbo. London, Hale, 1972.
The Man with Two Heads. London, Hale, 1972.
The Dead Tale-Tellers. London, Hale, 1972.
The Farm Villains. London, Hale, 1973.
The Grab Operators. London, Hale, 1973.
The Love-Hate Relationship. London, Hale, 1973.
The Girl in the Crime Belt. London, Hale, 1974.
The Shadow of the Killer. London, Hale, 1974.
The Starfish Affair. London, Hale, 1974.
The Canterbury Killgrims. London, Hale, 1974.
Hill Fog (Blake). London, Hale, 1975.
The Devil's Edge. London, Hale, 1975.
The Monstrous Regiment. London, Hale, 1975.
The Murder Makers. London, Hale, 1976.
Return to Death Alley. London, Hale, 1976.
A Fall-Out of Thieves. London, Hale, 1976.
The Frightened Fisherman. London, Hale, 1977.
The House of the Dead Ones. London, Hale, 1977.
Motive for a Kill. London, Hale, 1977.
The Ducrow Folly. London, Hale, 1978.
End of an Iron Man. London, Hale, 1978.
A Drop of Hot Gold. London, Hale, 1978.
Thieves' Kitchen. London, Hale, 1979.
The Guilty Witnesses. London, Hale, 1979.
A Place Called Skull. London, Hale, 1979.

Novels as J. Drummond (series character: Sexton Blake in all books)

The Essex Road Crime. London, Amalgamated Press, 1944.
The Manor House Menace. London, Amalgamated Press, 1944.
The Painted Dagger. London, Amalgamated Press, 1944.
The Riddle of the Leather Bottle. London, Amalgamated Press, 1944.
The Tragic Case of the Station Master's Legacy. London, Amalgamated Press, 1944.
At Sixty Miles an Hour. London, Amalgamated Press, 1945.
The House on the Hill. London, Amalgamated Press, 1945.
The Riddle of the Mummy Case. London, Amalgamated Press, 1945.
The Mystery of the Deserted Camp. London, Amalgamated Press, 1948.
The Town of Shadows. London, Amalgamated Press, 1948.
The Case of the "Dead" Spy. London, Amalgamated Press, 1949.
The Riddle of the Receiver's Hoard. London, Amalgamated Press, 1949.
The Secret of the Living Skeleton. London, Amalgamated Press, 1949.
The South Coast Mystery. London, Amalgamated Press, 1949.
The Case of the L. A. C. Dickson. London, Amalgamated Press, 1950.
The Mystery of the Haunted Square. London, Amalgamated Press, 1950.
The House in the Woods. London, Amalgamated Press, 1950.
The Secret of the Sixty Steps. London, Amalgamated Press, 1951.
The Case of the Man with No Name. London, Amalgamated Press, 1951.
Hated by All! London, Amalgamated Press, 1951.
The Mystery of the Sabotaged Jet. London, Amalgamated Press, 1951.
The House on the River. London, Amalgamated Press, 1952.

The Mystery of the Five Guilty Men. London, Amalgamated Press, 1954.
The Case of the Two-Faced Swindler. London, Amalgamated Press, 1955.

OTHER PUBLICATIONS

Novels as John Lymington

Night of the Big Heat. London, Corgi, 1959; New York, Dutton, 1960.
The Giant Stumbles. London, Hodder and Stoughton, 1960.
The Grey Ones. London, Hodder and Stoughton, 1960.
The Coming of the Strangers. London, Hodder and Stoughton, 1961.
A Sword above the Night. London, Hodder and Stoughton, 1962.
The Screaming Face. London, Hodder and Stoughton, 1963.
Froomb! London, Hodder and Stoughton, 1964; New York, Doubleday, 1966.
The Star Witches. London, Hodder and Stoughton, 1965.
The Green Drift. London, Hodder and Stoughton, 1965.
Ten Million Years to Friday. London, Hodder and Stoughton, 1967.
The Nowhere Place. London, Hodder and Stoughton, 1969.
Give Daddy the Knife, Darling. London, Hodder and Stoughton, 1969.
The Year Dot. London, Hodder and Stoughton, 1972.
The Sleep Eaters. London, Hodder and Stoughton, 1973.
The Hole in the World. London, Hodder and Stoughton, 1974.
A Spider in the Bath. London, Hodder and Stoughton, 1975.
The Laxham Haunting. London, Hodder and Stoughton, 1976.
Starseed on Eye Moor. London, Hodder and Stoughton, 1977.
The Waking of the Stone. London, Hodder and Stoughton, 1978.

Short Stories

The Night Spiders (as John Lymington). London, Corgi, 1964; New York, Doubleday, 1967.

Other

The Black Ghost (juvenile; as David C. Newton). London, Oxford University Press, 1947.
The Dangerous Road (juvenile; as David C. Newton). London, Oxford University Press, 1948.
Bunst and the Brown Voice [*the Bold, and the Secret Six, and the Flying Eye*] (juvenile). London, Oxford University Press, 4 vols., 1950–53.
The Jennifer Jigsaw (juvenile), with Shirley Newton Chance. London, Oxford University Press, 1951.
Yellow Belly (autobiography). London, Hale, 1959.
The Crimes at Rillington Place: A Novelist's Reconstruction. London, Hodder and Stoughton, 1961.

*   *   *

Under a variety of pseudonyms, John Newton Chance is one of the more prolific detective-thriller writers of the mid-20th Century. His early novels gained much critical acclaim, yet his work as a whole has been largely shunned by later commentators, who, if they mention him at all, usually relegate him to a footnote on "pot-boilers." Possibly the later work can be placed in this category, but to ignore the books published from the 1930's to the 1950's would be a mistake; the thrillers of the 1940's are particularly rich in atmosphere.

Eerie and bizarre situations abound: the flight through the plague-pits in *Screaming Fog*;

the entrance of the garrulous vicar through the French windows in *The Red Knight*; the discovery of a body among the dismembered figures in a waxworks modelling-room at night in *The Eye in Darkness*. To offset this, Chance injects much lively dialogue into his stories, and fills them with a host of Dickensian (indeed, Chaucerian) characters, many of whom are not what they seem.

Probably his most sustained creative effort is to be found in the 25 thrillers he wrote (1944–55) for the Sexton Blake Library under the name J. Drummond. Especially good are *The Manor House Menace*, *The Town of Shadows*, *The Mystery of the Haunted Square*, and *The House on the River* – though all are worth reading.

In recent years, he has channelled his energies into a series of excellent psychological SF novels. Also of interest are a reconstruction of the Christie/Evans case *The Crimes at Rillington Place*; *The Night Spiders*, a collection of weird stories under the John Lymington pseudonym; and the highly readable account of his wartime and writing experiences, *Yellow Belly*.

—Christopher Lowder

CHANDLER, Raymond (Thornton). American. Born in Chicago, Illinois, 23 July 1888; moved to England with his mother: naturalized British subject, 1907; again became an American citizen, 1956. Educated in a local school in Upper Norwood, London; Dulwich College, London, 1900–05; studied in France and Germany, 1905–07. Served in the Gordon Highlanders, Canadian Army, 1917–18, and in the Royal Air Force, 1918–19. Married Pearl Cecily Hurlburt in 1924 (died, 1954). Worked in the supply and accounting departments of the Admiralty, London, 1907; Reporter for the *Daily Express*, London, and the *Western Gazette*, Bristol, 1908–12; returned to the United States, 1912; worked in St. Louis, then on a ranch and in a sporting goods firm in California; accountant and bookkeeper at the Los Angeles Creamery, 1912–17; worked in a bank in San Francisco, 1919; worked for the *Daily Express*, Los Angeles, 1919; Bookkeeper, then Auditor, Dabney Oil Syndicate, Los Angeles, 1922–32; full-time writer from 1933. President, Mystery Writers of America, 1959. Recipient: Mystery Writers of America Edgar Allan Poe Award, for screenplay, 1946, for novel, 1954. *Died 26 March 1959.*

CRIME PUBLICATIONS

Novels (series character: Philip Marlowe in all books)

  The Big Sleep. New York, Knopf, and London, Hamish Hamilton, 1939.
  Farewell, My Lovely. New York, Knopf, and London, Hamish Hamilton, 1940.
  The High Window. New York, Knopf, 1942; London, Hamish Hamilton, 1943.
  The Lady in the Lake. New York, Knopf, 1943; London, Hamish Hamilton, 1944.
  The Little Sister. London, Hamish Hamilton, and Boston, Houghton Mifflin, 1949; as
    Marlowe, New York, Pocket Books, 1969.
  The Long Goodbye. London, Hamish Hamilton, 1953; Boston, Houghton Mifflin, 1954.
  Playback. London, Hamish Hamilton, and Boston, Houghton Mifflin, 1958.
  Poodle Springs (unfinished), in *Raymond Chandler Speaking.* 1964.

Short Stories

  Five Murderers. New York, Avon, 1944.

Five Sinister Characters. New York, Avon, 1945.
Finger Man and Other Stories. New York, Avon, 1946.
Red Wind. Cleveland, World, 1946.
Spanish Blood. Cleveland, World, 1946.
The Simple Art of Murder. Boston, Houghton Mifflin, and London, Hamish Hamilton,
   1950; as *Trouble Is My Business*, *Pick-Up on Noon Street*, and *The Simple Art of
   Murder*, New York, Pocket Books, 3 vols., 1951–53.
Smart Aleck Kill. London, Hamish Hamilton, 1953.
Pearls Are a Nuisance. London, Hamish Hamilton, 1953.
Killer in the Rain, edited by Philip Durham. Boston, Houghton Mifflin, and London,
   Hamish Hamilton, 1964.
The Smell of Fear. London, Hamish Hamilton, 1965.
The Midnight Raymond Chandler (omnibus), edited by Joan Kahn. Boston, Houghton
   Mifflin, 1971.

Uncollected Short Stories

"The Bronze Door," in *Unknown* (New York), November 1939.
"Professor Bingo's Snuff," in *Park East* (New York), June–August 1951.

OTHER PUBLICATIONS

Plays

Double Indemnity, with Billy Wilder, in *Best Film Plays 1945*, edited by John Gassner
   and Dudley Nichols. New York, Crown, 1946.
The Blue Dahlia (screenplay), edited by Matthew J. Bruccoli. Carbondale, Southern
   Illinois University Press, 1976.

Screenplays: *And Now Tomorrow*, with Frank Partos, 1944; *Double Indemnity*, with
Billy Wilder, 1944; *The Unseen*, with Hagar Wilde and Ken Englund, 1945; *The Blue
Dahlia*, 1946; *Strangers on a Train*, with Czenzi Ormonde and Whitfield Cook, 1951.

Other

Raymond Chandler Speaking, edited by Dorothy Gardiner and Kathrine Sorley
   Walker. Boston, Houghton Mifflin, and London, Hamish Hamilton, 1962.
Chandler Before Marlowe, edited by Matthew J. Bruccoli. Columbia, University of
   South Carolina Press, 1973.
The Notebooks of Raymond Chandler, and English Summer: A Gothic Romance, edited
   by Frank MacShane. New York, Ecco Press, 1976; London, Weidenfeld and
   Nicolson, 1977.
"Farewell My Hollywood," in *Antaeus* (New York), Autumn 1976.
Raymond Chandler and James M. Fox: Letters. Privately printed, 1979.

Bibliography: *Raymond Chandler: A Descriptive Bibliography* by Matthew J. Bruccoli,
Pittsburgh, University of Pittsburgh Press, 1979.

Manuscript Collection: Department of Special Collections, University of California Research
Library, Los Angeles.

*   *   *

I was fourteen when I first read *The Big Sleep*. I have never gotten over it. Growing up, I
saw in Marlowe an icon of manhood to which everyone should aspire. The result was

sometimes disheartening to my parents, and, in truth, I have had to learn from others. But there was quality in Marlowe, and if I had it to do over again I would.

I learned to write from Raymond Chandler. I learned how to use the concrete phenomena of the story's setting to advance the story. I learned how to characterize the narrator protagonist by the way he reports those phenomena. I learned the place of wit in a serious story. And I learned that a good story could be sentimental, and a good writer, romantic. I learned also that the evocation of place lends resonance to the work.

The second paragraph of *The Little Sister* reads this way: "It was one of those clear, bright summer mornings we get in the early spring in California before the high fog sets in. The rains are over. The hills are still green and in the valley across the Hollywood Hills you can see snow on the high mountains. The fur stores are advertising their annual sales. The call houses that specialize in sixteen-year-old virgins are doing a land office business. And in Beverly Hills the jacaranda trees are beginning to bloom."

It is quintessential Chandler. The careful juxtaposition of things gives us both a visual and a moral sense of place. We are reminded of the green land where promise once abounded, and we are reminded of what's become of it. We are also given a clear image of the kind of man we're meeting: one who sees the prostitution and the flowers; one who knows the range of society represented by each; one sensitive to the seasons; one at once romantic and cynical.

Marlowe can't prevent the prostituting of children. If we conceive his mission as setting right what Auden called "the Great Wrong Place" then we are forced to agree with Auden that Chandler's books, though "powerful" are "extremely depressing." But I think we must understand, as Auden did not, that the books are also triumphant. Marlowe's triumph is not that he prevents the call houses. It is that he sees the jacaranda. In a world of corruption and schlock Marlowe is tough enough and brave enough to maintain a system of values that is humanistic, romantic, sentimental, and chivalric. He is a man of honor.

Honor has several virtues. It may be maintained in defeat as well as in triumph. It is inner-directed. And it proves as permanent a stay against confusion as one is likely to come across in the post-Christian age. In a dishonorable world, to persist in honorable behavior is to court adversity. But since adversity serves to authenticate honorable behavior it provides meaning, or a substitute for meaning. We are in an unobliging universe. Whether or not we admire Marlowe's ideals, his willingness to incur injury and risk death rather than forsake them invests both his ideals and his behavior with moral seriousness.

And so I learned too from Raymond Chandler that the form in which he worked was a form in which one could do serious work. All his life Chandler was annoyed at the critics who were inclined to take his work less seriously than he did because he wrote about a detective. I share Auden's belief that Chandler's "books should be read and judged, not as escape literature, but as works of art." Chandler was in earnest. Most of us are.

—Robert B. Parker

CHARTERIS, Leslie. Born Leslie Charles Bowyer Yin; adopted the name Charteris legally in 1926. American. Born in Singapore 12 May 1907; naturalized American citizen, 1946. Educated privately; Falconbury School, Purley, Surrey, 1919–22; Rossall School, Fleetwood, Lancashire, 1922–24; King's College, Cambridge, 1925–26. Married 1) Pauline Schishkin in 1931 (divorced, 1937); one daughter; 2) Barbara Meyer in 1938 (divorced, 1943); 3) Elizabeth Bryant Borst in 1943 (divorced, 1951); 4) Audrey Long in 1952. Worked at odd jobs in England, France, and Malaya until 1935; lived in America after 1935. Writer and journalist: wrote syndicated comic strip *Secret Agent X-9*, in mid-1930's, and *Saint*, 1945–55; Editor, *Suspense* magazine, 1946–47, and *The Saint Detective Magazine*, later *The Saint Mystery Magazine*, 1953–67; Columnist, *Gourmet Magazine*, 1966–68. Fellow, Royal Society of Arts. Address: c/o Thompson Levett & Co., 8 Southampton Row, London W.C.1, England.

Crime Publications

Novels (series character: Simon Templar, The Saint)

X Esquire.   London, Ward Lock, 1927.
Meet the Tiger (Saint).   London, Ward Lock, 1928; New York, Doubleday, 1929.
The White Rider.   London, Ward Lock, 1928; New York, Doubleday, 1930.
Daredevil.   London, Ward Lock, and New York, Doubleday, 1929.
The Bandit.   London, Ward Lock, and New York, Doubleday, 1929.
The Last Hero.   London, Hodder and Stoughton, and New York, Doubleday, 1930; as *The Saint Closes the Case*, New York, Sun Dial Press, 1941.
Enter the Saint (3 novelets).   London, Hodder and Stoughton, 1930; New York, Doubleday, 1931.
Knight Templar.   London, Hodder and Stoughton, 1930; as *The Avenging Saint*, New York, Doubleday, 1931.
Featuring the Saint (3 novelets).   London, Hodder and Stoughton, 1931.
Alias the Saint (3 novelets).   London, Hodder and Stoughton, 1931.
Wanted for Murder (combines *Featuring the Saint* and *Alias the Saint*).   New York, Doubleday, 1931.
She Was a Lady.   London, Hodder and Stoughton, 1931; as *Angels of Doom*, New York, Doubleday, 1932; as *The Saint Meets His Match*, New York, Sun Dial Press, 1941.
The Holy Terror (3 novelets).   London, Hodder and Stoughton, 1932; as *The Saint Versus Scotland Yard*, New York, Doubleday, 1932.
Getaway.   London, Hodder and Stoughton, 1932; as *The Saint's Getaway*, New York, Doubleday, 1933.
Once More the Saint (3 novelets).   London, Hodder and Stoughton, 1933; as *The Saint and Mr. Teal*, New York, Doubleday, 1933.
The Misfortunes of Mr. Teal (3 novelets).   London, Hodder and Stoughton, and New York, Doubleday, 1934; as *The Saint in London*, New York, Sun Dial Press, 1941.
The Saint Goes On (3 novelets).   London, Hodder and Stoughton, 1934; New York, Doubleday, 1935.
The Saint in New York.   London, Hodder and Stoughton, and New York, Doubleday, 1935.
The Saint Overboard.   London, Hodder and Stoughton, and New York, Doubleday, 1936; as *The Pirate Saint*, New York, Triangle, 1941.
The Ace of Knaves (3 novelets).   London, Hodder and Stoughton, and New York, Doubleday, 1937; as *The Saint in Action*, New York, Sun Dial Press, 1938.
Thieves' Picnic.   London, Hodder and Stoughton, and New York, Doubleday, 1937; as *The Saint Bids Diamonds*, New York, Triangle, 1942.
Prelude for War.   London, Hodder and Stoughton, and New York, Doubleday, 1938; as *The Saint Plays with Fire*, New York, Triangle, 1942.
Follow the Saint (3 novelets).   New York, Doubleday, 1938; London, Hodder and Stoughton, 1939.
The Saint in Miami.   New York, Doubleday, 1940; London, Hodder and Stoughton, 1941.
The Saint Goes West.   New York, Doubleday, and London, Hodder and Stoughton, 1942.
The Saint Steps In.   New York, Doubleday, 1943; London, Hodder and Stoughton, 1944.

The Saint on Guard (2 novelets).   New York, Doubleday, 1944; London, Hodder and
Stoughton, 1945; 1 novelet published as *The Saint and the Sizzling Saboteur*, New
York, Avon, 1956.
The Saint Sees It Through.   New York, Doubleday, 1946; London, Hodder and
Stoughton, 1947.
Call for the Saint (2 novelets).   New York, Doubleday, and London, Hodder and
Stoughton, 1948.
Arrest the Saint (omnibus).   New York, Avon, 1956.
Vendetta for the Saint.   New York, Doubleday, 1964; London, Hodder and Stoughton,
1965.
The Saint in Pursuit (novelization of comic strip).   New York, Doubleday, 1970;
London, Hodder and Stoughton, 1971.
Send for the Saint.   London, Hodder and Stoughton, 1977; New York, Doubleday,
1978.
The Saint and the Templar Treasure.   London, Hodder and Stoughton, 1978; New
York, Doubleday, 1979.

Short Stories

The Brighter Buccaneer.   London, Hodder and Stoughton, and New York, Doubleday,
1933.
Boodle.   London, Hodder and Stoughton, 1934; as *The Saint Intervenes*, New York,
Doubleday, 1934.
The Happy Highwayman.   New York, Doubleday, and London, Hodder and
Stoughton, 1939.
The Saint at Large.   New York, Sun Dial Press, 1943.
Saint Errant.   New York, Doubleday, 1948; London, Hodder and Stoughton, 1949.
The Saint in Europe.   New York, Doubleday, 1953; London, Hodder and Stoughton,
1954.
The Saint on the Spanish Main.   New York, Doubleday, and London, Hodder and
Stoughton, 1955.
The Saint Around the World.   New York, Doubleday, 1956; London, Hodder and
Stoughton, 1957.
Thanks to the Saint.   New York, Doubleday, 1957; London, Hodder and Stoughton,
1958.
Señor Saint.   New York, Doubleday, 1958; London, Hodder and Stoughton, 1959.
Concerning the Saint.   New York, Avon, 1958.
The Saint to the Rescue.   New York, Doubleday, 1959; London, Hodder and
Stoughton, 1961.
The Saint Cleans Up.   New York, Avon, 1959.
Trust the Saint.   New York, Doubleday, and London, Hodder and Stughton, 1962.
The Saint in the Sun.   New York, Doubleday, 1963; London, Hodder and Stoughton,
1964.

OTHER PUBLICATIONS

Plays

Screenplays: *Midnight Club*, with Seton I. Miller, 1933; *The Saint's Double Trouble*,
with Ben Holmes, 1940; *The Saint's Vacation*, with Jeffrey Dell, 1941; *The Saint in
Palm Springs*, with Jerry Cady, 1941; *Lady on a Train*, with Edmund Beloin and Robert
O'Brien, 1945; *River Gang*, with others, 1945; *Two Smart People*, with others, 1946;
Tarzan and the Huntress, with Jerry Grushkind and Rowland Leigh, 1947.

Radio Plays: *Sherlock Holmes* series, with Denis Green.

Other

Spanish for Fun.   London, Hodder and Stoughton, 1964.
Paleneo: A Universal Sign Language.   London, Hodder and Stoughton, 1972.

Editor, *The Saint's Choice of Humorous Crime.*   Los Angeles, Shaw Press, 1945.
Editor, *The Saint's Choice of Impossible Crime.*   Los Angeles, Bond Charteris, 1945.
Editor, *The Saint's Choice of Hollywood Crime.*   Los Angeles, Saint Enterprises, 1946.
Editor, *The Saint Mystery Library.*   New York, Great American Publications, 13 vols.,
   1959–60.
Editor, with Hans Santesson, *The Saint Magazine Reader.*   New York, Doubleday,
   1966; as *The Saint's Choice,* London, Hodder and Stoughton, 1967.

Translator, *Juan Belmonte, Killer of Bulls: The Autobiography of a Matador,* by
   Belmonte and Manuel Chaves Nogales.   New York, Doubleday, and London,
   Heinemann, 1937.

Bibliography: *Leslie Charteris och Helgonet under 5 Decennium* by Jan Alexandersson and
Iwan Hedman, Strängnäs, DAST Magazine, 1972.

Manuscript Collection: Mugar Memorial Library, Boston University.

*   *   *

Thriller fiction in England in the 1920's and early 1930's was full of rich young men of the
officer class, who returned from the War, found peace too peaceful, gathered their old trench-
mates around them, and declared themselves Gentleman Outlaws at war with boredom,
officialdom, and – more often than not – democracy. There is a strong smell of latent fascism
in their exploits: they had put themselves not only outside, but above, the law, were self-
proclaimed judges and enthusiastic executioners of unwanted foreigners, communists, Jews,
and other possible enemies of Good Old England as it once was and forever should be.

Leslie Charteris started his Saint saga, about the brilliant buccaneer Simon Templar, in that
literary climate when, after a couple of false starts, he began writing Saint stories for *The
Thriller* in 1930. He conformed to most of the unspoken rules of the genre when he wrote
about dealing out private justice, making fun of Scotland Yard (personified by Inspector
Claude Eustace Teal), and collecting wealth – "boodle" – from people not fit to be so filthy
rich. But, like the Saint, Leslie Charteris in those days was a bit of an outlaw and an outsider,
never quite at home among the clubland gentlemen, and wryly modifying the clichés of the
popular thriller to suit his own, sometimes surprising, ends. The Saint has no war record, a
classless, romantic past only hinted at, and nothing but caustic contempt for chauvinism,
pride of birth, public schools, and the ruling classes.

Sapper's Bulldog Drummond flogged Jews "within an inch of their lives," but Charteris
lets the Saint use the whip on an underpaying and knighted lorry magnate to teach him
respect for work. He praises Roosevelt's New Deal, and once he even exposes a fox-hunting
and noble sportsman as the murderer of a pale, left-wing poet. There is no doubt about his
sympathies – and still less doubt that they were not shared by the majority of thriller writers
of the day. Yet he kept himself within the limits of the society around him, and was never a
revolutionary. Charteris enjoyed himself by tickling the feet of the upright citizen with furled
umbrella (as he once defined his readers), but he was never ready to cut off his head.

Charteris's prose in those days was carefree, lighthearted, sometimes Wodehousian. The
stories are full not only of an outsider's social comments, but of experiments by a self-
confident and amused writer in how far he can lead his reader by the nose. The tongue-in-
cheek commentaries often have little to do with the plot, and include long nonsense poems
and extemporized limericks – but the reader tended to fall under the Charteris charm.

In the 1930's Charteris moved to the United States, and in *The Saint in Miami* (1940), he moved the whole group, Templar and his loyal gang, across the Atlantic. But hereafter we meet a new Saint. If being the center of a group of idle, rich, and admiring followers is a British ideal, the hard-working, half-anonymous lone ranger is an American one. During the War, the Saint worked as an undercover agent for a government department, and his loyalties are more to democracy than to economic systems. After the War, Charteris for nearly 30 years sent the Saint around the world as a lonely, solitary traveller with a new hotel room, a new heroine, and a new adventure in each short story, and in the single full-length novel from the period, *Vendetta for the Saint*. The timeless, always 35-year-old Gentleman Outlaw is still an outlaw, but depends more on his own legend than on actual lawbreaking to keep alive. He accepts rather than seeks out adventure, seemingly more interested in good food and luxury surroundings than in the adventure itself; the caustic comments have disappeared. Many of the stories based on the tv series were written by Fleming Lee and others, and merely touched up by Charteris before publication; for an old Saint fan, reading them is like chewing plastic beef: an artificial product only superficially similar to the real thing. *The Saint in Pursuit*, based on an old comic strip, was slightly better.

The literary idea of a hero outside the law is an old and honored one: Robin Hood is a venerable ancestor, Raffles, Arsène Lupin, and Chesterton's Flambeau older cousins, and Spillane's Mike Hammer a young relative. In the best Charteris stories, that tradition is free from its fascist overtones and loaded with witty humor, fast story-telling, and a refreshing outlook on the world of crime, the ruling classes, and romantic heroes. "Maybe I am a crook," said the Saint once; "But in between times I'm something more. In my simple way I am a kind of justice...." There was a time when one could almost believe him.

—Bo Lundin

CHASE, James Hadley. Pseudonym for René Brabazon Raymond; also writes as James L. Docherty; Ambrose Grant; Raymond Marshall. British. Born in London, 24 December 1906. Educated at King's School, Rochester, Kent. Editor of Royal Air Force journal: Squadron Leader. Married Sylvia Ray; one son. Agent: David Higham Associates Ltd., 5–8 Lower John Street, London W1R 4HA. Address: c/o Robert Hale Ltd., 45–47 Clerkenwell Green, London EC1R 0HT, England.

CRIME PUBLICATIONS

Novels (series characters: Al Barney; Dave Fenner; Mark Girland; Steve Harmas; Tom Lepski; Vic Malloy; Herman Radnitz; Helga Rolfe; Lu Silk)

No Orchids for Miss Blandish (Fenner). London, Jarrolds, 1939; New York, Howell Soskin, 1942; as *The Villain and the Virgin*, New York, Avon, 1948; revised edition, London, Panther, and Avon, 1961.
The Dead Stay Dumb. London, Jarrolds, 1939; as *Kiss My Fist!*, New York, Eton, 1952.
He Won't Need It Now (as James L. Docherty). London, Rich and Cowan, 1939.
Twelve Chinks and a Woman (Fenner). London, Jarrolds, 1940; New York, Howell Soskin, 1941; revised edition, as *12 Chinamen and a Woman*, London, Novel Library, 1950; as *The Doll's Bad News*, London, Panther, 1970.
Miss Callaghan Comes to Grief. London, Jarrolds, 1941.
Miss Shumway Waves a Wand. London, Jarrolds, 1944.
Eve. London, Jarrolds, 1945.

More Deadly Than the Male (as Ambrose Grant). London, Eyre and Spottiswoode, 1946.

I'll Get You for This. London, Jarrolds, 1946; New York, Avon, 1951.

The Flesh of the Orchid. London, Jarrolds, 1948; New York, Pocket Books, 1972.

You Never Know with Women. London, Jarrolds, 1949; New York, Pocket Books, 1972.

You're Lonely When You're Dead (Malloy). London, Hale, 1949; New York, Duell, 1950.

Figure It Out for Yourself (Malloy). London, Hale, 1950; New York, Duell, 1951; as *The Marijuana Mob*, New York, Eton, 1952.

Lay Her among the Lilies (Malloy). London, Hale, 1950; as *Too Dangerous to Be Free*, New York, Duell, 1951.

Strictly for Cash. London, Hale, 1951; New York, Pocket Books, 1973.

The Fast Buck. London, Hale, 1952.

The Double Shuffle (Harmas). London, Hale, 1952; New York, Dutton, 1953.

This Way for a Shroud. London, Hale, 1953.

I'll Bury My Dead. London, Hale, 1953; New York, Dutton, 1954.

Tiger by the Tail. London, Hale, 1954.

Safer Dead. London, Hale, 1954; as *Dead Ringer*, New York, Ace, 1955.

You've Got It Coming. London, Hale, 1955; New York, Pocket Books, 1973; revised edition, Hale, 1975.

There's Always a Price Tag (Harmas). London, Hale, 1956; New York, Pocket Books, 1973.

The Guilty Are Afraid. London, Hale, 1957; New York, New American Library, 1959.

Not Safe to Be Free. London, Hale, 1958; as *The Case of the Strangled Starlet*, New York, New American Library, 1958.

Shock Treatment (Harmas). London, Hale, and New York, New American Library, 1959.

The World in My Pocket. London, Hale, 1959; New York, Popular Library, 1962.

What's Better Than Money? London, Hale, 1960; New York, Pocket Books, 1972.

Come Easy – Go Easy. London, Hale, 1960; New York, Pocket Books, 1974.

A Lotus for Miss Quon. London, Hale, 1961.

Just Another Sucker. London, Hale, 1961; New York, Pocket Books, 1974.

I Would Rather Stay Poor. London, Hale, 1962; New York, Pocket Books, 1974.

A Coffin from Hong Kong. London, Hale, 1962.

Tell It to the Birds (Harmas). London, Hale, 1963; New York, Pocket Books, 1974.

One Bright Summer Morning. London, Hale, 1963; New York, Pocket Books, 1974.

The Soft Centre (Lepski). London, Hale, 1964.

This Is for Real (Girland; Radnitz). London, Hale, 1965; New York, Walker, 1967.

The Way the Cookie Crumbles (Lepski). London, Hale, 1965; New York, Pocket Books, 1974.

You Have Yourself a Deal (Girland). London, Hale, 1966; New York, Walker, 1968.

Well Now, My Pretty – (Lepski). London, Hale, 1967; New York, Pocket Books, 1972.

Have This One on Me (Girland). London, Hale, 1967.

An Ear to the Ground (Barney; Harmas; Lepski). London, Hale, 1968.

Believed Violent (Girland; Radnitz; Silk; Lepski). London, Hale, 1968.

The Vulture Is a Patient Bird. London, Hale, 1969.

The Whiff of Money (Girland; Radnitz; Silk). London, Hale, 1969.

There's a Hippie on the Highway (Lepski). London, Hale, 1970.

Like a Hole in the Head. London, Hale, 1970.

Want to Stay Alive? London, Hale, 1971.

An Ace up My Sleeve (Rolfe). London, Hale, 1971.

Just a Matter of Time. London, Hale, 1972.

You're Dead Without Money (Barney; Radnitz). London, Hale, 1972.

Knock, Knock! Who's There? London, Hale, 1973.

Have a Change of Scene. London, Hale, 1973.
Three of Spades (omnibus). London, Hale, 1974.
Goldfish Have No Hiding Place. London, Hale, 1974.
So What Happens to Me? London, Hale, 1974.
Believe This, You'll Believe Anything. London, Hale, 1975.
The Joker in the Pack (Rolfe). London, Hale, 1975.
Do Me a Favour – Drop Dead. London, Hale, 1976.
I Hold the Four Aces (Rolfe). London, Hale, 1977.
Meet Mark Girland (omnibus). London, Hale, 1977.
My Laugh Comes Last. London, Hale, 1977.
Consider Yourself Dead. London, Hale, 1978.
You Must Be Kidding. London, Hale, 1979.
Can of Worms. London, Hale, 1979.

Novels as Raymond Marshall (series characters: Brick-Top Corrigan; Don Micklem)

Lady – Here's Your Wreath. London, Jarrolds, 1940.
Just the Way It Is. London, Jarrolds, 1944.
Blondes' Requiem. London, Jarrolds, 1945; New York, Crown, 1946.
Make the Corpse Walk. London, Jarrolds, 1946.
No Business of Mine. London, Jarrolds, 1947.
Trusted Like the Fox. London, Jarrolds, 1948.
The Paw in the Bottle. London, Jarrolds, 1949.
Mallory (Corrigan). London, Jarrolds, 1950.
In a Vain Shadow. London, Jarrolds, 1951.
But a Short Time to Live. London, Jarrolds, 1951.
Why Pick on Me? (Corrigan). London, Jarrolds, 1951.
The Wary Transgressor. London, Jarrolds, 1952.
The Things Men Do. London, Jarrolds, 1953.
Mission to Venice (Micklem). London, Hale, 1954.
The Sucker Punch. London, Jarrolds, 1954.
Mission to Siena (Micklem). London, Hale, 1955.
You Find Him – I'll Fix Him. London, Hale, 1956.
Hit and Run. London, Hale, 1958.

OTHER PUBLICATIONS

Plays

Get a Load of This, with Arthur Macrea, music and lyrics by Manning Sherwin and Val Guest (produced London, 1941).
No Orchids for Miss Blandish, with Robert Nesbitt, adaptation of the novel by Chase (produced London, 1942).
Last Page (produced London, 1946). London, French, 1947.

Other

Editor (as René Raymond), with David Langdon, *Slipstream: A Royal Air Force Anthology.* London, Eyre and Spottiswoode, 1946.

James Hadley Chase comments:
There are authors who like to talk about themselves and their work. I don't. If an author's work sells steadily and well, world-wide, he should not need to waste time giving press interviews, writing introductions, or bothering about what critics have to say. My job is to

write a book for a wide variety of readers. I do this job conscientiously. An introduction to my work would certainly not be of use to my general readers. They couldn't care less. All they are asking for is a good read: that is what I try to give them.

*   *   *

James Hadley Chase has the dubious distinction of being a very prolific English author who has written more than 80 novels almost exclusively about American characters in American settings in spite of having made very few trips to the United States, and then visiting only the atypical locales of Florida and New Orleans. Most of the author's knowledge of America has been derived from encyclopedias, detailed maps, and slang dictionaries. Often referred to in the past as "the king" of thriller writers by both English and Continental critics, Chase propels the reader through complex, intricate plots with gaudy, explosive characters and a fast-moving, hard-boiled style.

Chase was working for a book wholesaler in London when he wrote his first extremely popular mystery novel, *No Orchids for Miss Blandish*. An heiress is kidnapped by a mob of ruthless gangsters. Dave Fenner, an ex-reporter turned private eye, is the hero of this tale. Fenner stars again in *Twelve Chinks and a Woman*.

The world of the novels written as Raymond Marshall, sometimes about Brick-Top Corrigan, an unscrupulous private eye, or Don Micklem, a millionaire playboy, is the same hard-boiled, explosive, violent, and fast-paced world of the Chase novels.

Two of the prominent Chase characters are Vic Malloy, a California private eye, and Mark Girland, a former CIA agent who sells his services to support his tastes in women. Girland is occasionally engaged by the head of the Paris branch of the CIA; in *You Have Yourself a Deal*, the appearance of a beautiful amnesiac with three Chinese symbols tattooed on her left buttock signals the involvement of Girland in a dangerous caper fraught with Russian and Chinese agents, brutal methods of information seeking, and beautiful girls.

Ingeniously plotted insurance frauds are the subjects of the Chase novels starring Maddux and his chief investigator Steve Harmas, whose beautiful wife, Helen, often provides valuable assistance. In *Tell It to the Birds* Harmas uncovers an intricate murder scheme involving a sadistic husband, a prostitute, a pimp, and an amoral insurance salesman. In *The Double Shuffle* Harmas and his wife investigate two unusual insurance policies which could cost Harmas's company, National Fidelity, 650,000 dollars. Twins, one of whom is an exotic dancer who enjoys "kissing" a pet cobra, a kidnapped movie star, an ex-con, and a snake island make intriguing ingredients for a chilling thriller. The facts that the insurance frauds are highly questionable, that the settings do not much resemble the California locale on which they are based, and that the characters retain a 1930's image can all be overlooked when the reader has been captured by the fast-paced action and thrill-a-minute dialogue of the Chase style.

—Mary Ann Grochowski

CHESTERTON, G(ilbert) K(eith).   British.   Born in London, 28 May 1874. Educated at Colet Court School, London; St. Paul's School, London (Editor, *The Debater*, 1891–93), 1887–92; Slade School of Art, London 1893–96. Married Frances Blogg in 1901. Worked for the London publishers Redway, 1896, and T. Fisher Unwin, 1896–1902; weekly contributor to the *Daily News*, London, 1901–13, and the *Illustrated London News*, 1905–36; Co-Editor, *Eye Witness*, London, 1911–12, and Editor, *New Witness*, 1912–23; regular contributor to the *Daily Herald*, London, 1913–14; leader of the Distributist movement after the war, and subsequently President of the Distributist League; convert to Roman Catholicism, 1922; Editor, with H. Jackson and R. B. Johnson, Readers' Classics series, 1922; Editor, *G. K.'s Weekly*, 1925–36; Lecturer, Notre Dame University, Indiana, 1930; radio broadcaster in the 1930's. Also an illustrator: illustrated some of his own works and books by Hilaire Belloc and E. C. Bentley. Honorary degrees: Edinburgh, Dublin, and Notre Dame universities. Fellow, Royal Society of Literature. Knight Commander with Star, Order of St. Gregory the Great, 1934. *Died 14 June 1936.*

CRIME PUBLICATIONS

Novel

> *The Man Who Was Thursday: A Nightmare.*   Bristol, Arrowsmith, and New York, Dodd Mead, 1908.

Short Stories (series character: Father Brown)

> *The Tremendous Adventures of Major Brown.*   London, Shurmer Sibthorp, 1903.
> *The Club of Queer Trades.*   London and New York, Harper, 1905.
> *The Innocence of Father Brown.*   London, Cassell, and New York, Lane, 1911.
> *The Wisdom of Father Brown.*   London, Cassell, 1914; New York, Lane, 1915.
> *The Man Who Knew Too Much and Other Stories.*   London, Cassell, and New York, Harper, 1922.
> *The Incredulity of Father Brown.*   London, Cassell, and New York, Dodd Mead, 1926.
> *The Secret of Father Brown.*   London, Cassell, and New York, Harper, 1927.
> *The Poet and the Lunatic: Episodes in the Life of Gabriel Gale.*   London, Cassell, and New York, Dodd Mead, 1929.
> *The Moderate Murderer, and The Honest Quack.*   New York, Dodd Mead, 1929.
> *The Ecstatic Thief.*   New York, Dodd Mead, 1930.
> *Four Faultless Felons.*   London, Cassell, and New York, Dodd Mead, 1930.
> *The Floating Admiral*, with others.   London, Hodder and Stoughton, 1931; New York, Doubleday, 1932.
> *The Scandal of Father Brown.*   London, Cassell, and New York, Dodd Mead, 1935.
> *The Paradoxes of Mr. Pond.*   London, Cassell, 1936; New York, Dodd Mead, 1937.
> *The Vampire of the Village.*   Privately printed, 1947.
> *Father Brown: Selected Stories*, edited by Ronald Knox.   London, Oxford University Press, 1955.

Uncollected Short Story

> "Dr. Hyde, Detective" ["The White Pillar Murders"], in *To the Queen's Taste*, edited by Ellery Queen.   Boston, Little Brown, 1946.

OTHER PUBLICATIONS

Novels

> *The Napoleon of Notting Hill.*   London and New York, Lane, 1904.
> *The Ball and the Cross.*   New York, Lane, 1909; London, Wells Gardner, 1910.
> *Manalive.*   London, Nelson, and New York, Lane, 1912.
> *The Flying Inn.*   London, Methuen, and New York, Lane, 1914.
> *The Return of Don Quixote.*   London, Chatto and Windus, and New York, Dodd Mead, 1927.

Short Stories

The Perishing of the Pendragons. New York, Paget, 1914.
Tales of the Long Bow. London, Cassell, and New York, Dodd Mead, 1925.
The Sword of Wood. London, Elkin Mathews, 1928.
(Stories). London, Harrap, 1928.
Selected Stories, edited by Kingsley Amis. London, Faber, 1972.

Plays

Magic: A Fantastic Comedy (produced Eastbourne and London, 1913; New York,
    1917). London, Martin Secker, and New York, Putnam, 1913.
The Judgment of Dr. Johnson (produced London, 1932). London, Sheed and Ward,
    1927; New York, Putnam, 1928.
The Surprise (produced Hull, 1953). London, Sheed and Ward, 1953.

Verse

*Greybeards at Play: Literature and Art for Old Gentlemen: Rhymes and
    Sketches.* London, R. Brimley Johnson, 1900.
The Wild Knight and Other Poems. London, Richards, 1900; revised edition, London,
    Dent, and New York, Dutton, 1914.
The Ballad of the White Horse. London, Methuen, and New York, Lane, 1911.
Poems. London, Burns Oates, 1915; New York, Lane, 1916.
Wine, Water, and Song. London, Methuen, 1915.
A Poem. Privately printed, 1915.
Old King Cole. Privately printed, 1920.
The Ballad of St. Barbara and Other Verses. London, Palmer, 1922; New York,
    Putnam, 1923.
(Poems). London, Benn, and New York, Stokes, 1925.
The Queen of Seven Swords. London, Sheed and Ward, 1926.
The Collected Poems of G. K. Chesterton. London, Palmer, 1927; revised edition, New
    York, Dodd Mead, 1932.
Gloria in Profundis. London, Faber and Gwyer, and New York, Rudge, 1927.
Ubi Ecclesia. London, Faber, 1929.
The Grave of Arthur. London, Faber, 1930.
Greybeards at Play and Other Comic Verse, edited by John Sullivan. London, Elek,
    1974.

Other

The Defendant. London, R. Brimley Johnson, 1901; New York, Dodd Mead, 1902.
Twelve Types. London, Humphreys, 1902; augmented edition, as *Varied Types*, New
    York, Dodd Mead, 1903; selections as *Five Types*, Humphreys, 1910; New York,
    Holt, 1911; and as *Simplicity and Tolstoy*, Humphreys, 1912.
Thomas Carlyle. London, Hodder and Stoughton, 1902; New York, Pott, n.d.
Robert Louis Stevenson, with W. Robertson Nicoll. London, Hodder and Stoughton,
    and New York, Pott, 1903.
Leo Tolstoy, with G. H. Perris and Edward Garnett. London, Hodder and Stoughton,
    and New York, Pott, 1903.
Charles Dickens, with F. G. Kitton. London, Hodder and Stoughton, and New York,
    Pott, 1903.
Robert Browning. London and New York, Macmillan, 1903.
Tennyson, with Richard Garnett. London, Hodder and Stoughton, 1903; New York,
    Pott, n.d.

Thackeray, with Lewis Melville. London, Hodder and Stoughton, and New York, Pott, 1903.

G. F. Watts. London, Duckworth, and New York, Dutton, 1904.

Heretics. London and New York, Lane, 1905.

Charles Dickens. London, Methuen, and New York, Dodd Mead, 1906.

All Things Considered. London, Methuen, and New York, Lane, 1908.

Orthodoxy. London and New York, Lane, 1908.

George Bernard Shaw. London and New York, Lane, 1909; revised edition, London, Lane, 1935.

Tremendous Trifles. London, Methuen, and New York, Dodd Mead, 1909.

What's Wrong with the World. London, Cassell, and New York, Dodd Mead, 1910.

Alarms and Discursions. London, Methuen, 1910; New York, Dodd Mead, 1911.

William Blake. London, Duckworth, and New York, Dutton, 1910.

The Ultimate Lie. Privately printed, 1910.

A Chesterton Calendar. London, Kegan Paul, 1911; as *Wit and Wisdom of G. K. Chesterton*, New York, Dodd Mead, 1911; as *Chesterton Day by Day*, Kegan Paul, 1912.

Appreciations and Criticisms of the Works of Charles Dickens. London, Dent, and New York, Dutton, 1911.

A Defence of Nonsense and Other Essays. New York, Dodd Mead, 1911.

The Future of Religion: Mr. G. K. Chesterton's Reply to Mr. Bernard Shaw. Privately printed, 1911.

The Conversion of an Anarchist. New York, Paget, 1912.

A Miscellany of Men. London, Methuen, and New York, Dodd Mead, 1912.

The Victorian Age in Literature. London, Williams and Norgate, and New York, Holt, 1913.

Thoughts from Chesterton, edited by Elsie E. Morton. London, Harrap, 1913.

The Barbarism of Berlin. London, Cassell, 1914.

London, photographs by Alvin Langdon Coburn. Privately printed, 1914.

Prussian Versus Belgian Culture. Edinburgh, Belgian Relief and Reconstruction Fund, 1914.

Letters to an Old Garibaldian. London, Methuen, 1915; with *The Barbarism of Berlin*, as *The Appetite of Tyranny*, New York, Dodd Mead, 1915.

The So-Called Belgian Bargain. London, National War Aims Committee, 1915.

The Crimes of England. London, Palmer and Hayward, 1915; New York, Lane, 1916.

Divorce Versus Democracy. London, Society of SS. Peter and Paul, 1916.

Temperance and the Great Alliance. London, True Temperance Association, 1916.

The G. K. Chesterton Calendar, edited by H. Cecil Palmer. London, Palmer and Hayward, 1916.

A Shilling for My Thoughts, edited by E. V. Lucas. London, Methuen, 1916.

Lord Kitchener. Privately printed, 1917.

A Short History of England. London, Chatto and Windus, and New York, Lane, 1917.

Utopia of Usurers and Other Essays. New York, Boni and Liveright, 1917.

How to Help Annexation. London, Hayman Christy and Lilly, 1918.

Irish Impressions. London, Collins, and New York, Lane, 1920.

The Superstition of Divorce. London, Chatto and Windus, and New York, Lane, 1920.

Charles Dickens Fifty Years After. Privately printed, 1920.

The Uses of Diversity: A Book of Essays. London, Methuen, 1920; New York, Dodd Mead, 1921.

The New Jerusalem. London, Hodder and Stoughton, 1920; New York, Doran, 1921.

Eugenics and Other Evils. London, Cassell, 1922; New York, Dodd Mead, 1927.

What I Saw in America. London, Hodder and Stoughton, and New York, Dodd Mead, 1922.

Fancies Versus Fads. London, Methuen, and New York, Dodd Mead, 1923.

St. Francis of Assisi. London, Hodder and Stoughton, 1923; New York, Dodd Mead, 1924.

The End of the Roman Road: A Pageant of Wayfarers. London, Classic Press, 1924.
The Superstitions of the Sceptic (lecture). Cambridge, Heffer, and St. Louis, Herder, 1925.
The Everlasting Man. London, Hodder and Stoughton, and New York, Dodd Mead, 1925.
William Cobbett. London, Hodder and Stoughton, 1925; New York, Dodd Mead, 1926.
The Outline of Sanity. London, Methuen, 1926; New York, Dodd Mead, 1927.
The Catholic Church and Conversion. New York, Macmillan, 1926; London, Burns Oates, 1927.
Selected Works (Minerva Edition). London, Methuen, 9 vols., 1926.
A Gleaming Cohort, Being Selections from the Works of G. K. Chesterton, edited by E. V. Lucas. London, Methuen, 1926.
Social Reform Versus Birth Control. London, Simpkin Marshall, 1927.
Culture and the Coming Peril (lecture). London, University of London Press, 1927.
Robert Louis Stevenson. London, Hodder and Stoughton, 1927; New York, Dodd Mead, 1928.
Generally Speaking: A Book of Essays. London, Methuen, and New York, Dodd Mead, 1928.
(Essays). London, Harrap, 1928.
Do We Agree? A Debate, with G. B. Shaw. London, Palmer, and Hartford, Connecticut, Mitchell, 1928.
A Chesterton Catholic Anthology, edited by Patrick Braybrooke. London, Burns Oates, and New York, Kenedy, 1928.
The Thing (essays). London, Sheed and Ward, 1929.
G.K.C. as M.C., Being a Collection of Thirty-Seven Introductions, edited by J. P. de Fonseka. London, Methuen, 1929.
The Resurrection of Rome. London, Hodder and Stoughton, and New York, Dodd Mead, 1930.
Come to Think of It: A Book of Essays. London, Methuen, 1930; New York, Dodd Mead, 1931.
The Turkey and the Turk. Ditchling, Sussex, St. Dominic's Press, 1930.
At the Sign of the World's End. Palo Alto, California, Harvest Press, 1930.
Is There a Return to Religion?, with E. Haldeman-Julius. Girard, Kansas, Haldeman Julius, 1931.
All Is Grist: A Book of Essays. London, Methuen, 1931; New York, Dodd Mead, 1932.
Chaucer. London, Faber, and New York, Farrar Rinehart, 1932.
Sidelights on New London and Newer York and Other Essays. London, Sheed and Ward, and New York, Dodd Mead, 1932.
Christendom in Dublin. London, Sheed and Ward, 1932; New York, Sheed and Ward, 1933.
All I Survey: A Book of Essays. London, Methuen, and New York, Dodd Mead, 1933.
St. Thomas Aquinas. London, Hodder and Stoughton, and New York, Sheed and Ward, 1933.
G. K. Chesterton (selected humour), edited by E. V. Knox. London, Methuen, 1933; as *Running after One's Hat and Other Whimsies,* New York, McBride, 1933.
Avowals and Denials: A Book of Essays. London, Methuen, 1934; New York, Dodd Mead, 1935.
The Well and the Shallows. London and New York, Sheed and Ward, 1935.
Explaining the English. London, British Council, 1935.
Stories, Essays, and Poems. London, Dent, 1935.
As I Was Saying: A Book of Essays. London, Methuen, and New York, Dodd Mead, 1936.
Autobiography. London, Hutchinson, and New York, Sheed and Ward, 1936.
The Man Who Was Chesterton, edited by Raymond T. Bond. New York, Dodd Mead, 1937.

The Coloured Lands (miscellany). London and New York, Sheed and Ward, 1938.
Essays, edited by John Guest. London, Collins, 1939.
The End of the Armistice, edited by F. J. Sheed. London and New York, Sheed and Ward, 1940.
Selected Essays, edited by Dorothy Collins. London, Methuen, 1949.
The Common Man. London and New York, Sheed and Ward, 1950.
Essays, edited by K. E. Whitehorn. London, Methuen, 1953.
A Handful of Authors: Essays on Books and Writers, edited by Dorothy Collins. London and New York, Sheed and Ward, 1953.
The Glass Walking-Stick and Other Essays from the Illustrated London News 1905–1936, edited by Dorothy Collins. London, Methuen, 1955.
G. K. Chesterton: An Anthology, edited by D. B. Wyndham Lewis. London and New York, Oxford University Press, 1957.
Essays and Poems, edited by Wilfrid Sheed. London, Penguin, 1958.
Lunacy and Letters (essays), edited by Dorothy Collins. London and New York, Sheed and Ward, 1958.
Where All Roads Lead. London, Catholic Truth Society, 1961.
The Man Who Was Orthodox: A Selection from the Uncollected Writings of G. K. Chesterton, edited by A. L. Maycock. London, Dobson, 1963.
The Spice of Life and Other Essays, edited by Dorothy Collins. Beaconsfield, Buckinghamshire, Finlayson, 1964; Philadelphia, Dufour, 1966.
G. K. Chesterton: A Selection from His Non-Fictional Prose, edited by W. H. Auden. London, Faber, 1970.
Chesterton on Shakespeare, edited by Dorothy Collins. Henley on Thames, Oxfordshire, and Chester Springs, Pennsylvania, Dufour, 1971.
The Apostle and the Wild Ducks, and Other Essays, edited by Dorothy Collins. London, Elek, 1975.

Editor, *Thackeray* (selections). London, Bell, 1909.
Editor, with Alice Meynell, *Samuel Johnson* (selections). London, Herbert and Daniel, 1911.
Editor, *Essays by Divers Hands 6.* London, Oxford University Press, 1926.
Editor, *G. K.'s* (miscellany from *G. K.'s Weekly*). London, Rich and Cowan, 1934.

Bibliography: *Chesterton: A Bibliography* by John Sullivan, London, University of London Press, 1958, supplement, 1968.

Manuscript Collection: Humanities Research Center, University of Texas, Austin.

*   *   *

G. K. Chesterton once said of the Charles Dickens that "he decided to abandon the picaresque type of work in which he excelled," and he showed his disapproval of the author of such serious and sombre novels as *Bleak House* and *Edwin Drood* by adding, "the unique purveyor of comical eccentrics had become a commonplace novelist." These remarks tell us a great deal more about Chesterton than they do about Dickens. Chesterton's preference, in poetry and fiction alike, was always for the racy, the vigorous, the picaresque. He preferred eccentrics to commonplace human beings (as distinct from "the common man" whom he regarded as eccentric by nature) whether he encountered them in real life or put them into his novels. He was far from being a realist in any known definition of the term, since his aim in writing novels seems to have been to demonstrate how much of the miraculous and of the wonderful human life can sustain. Chesterton had a cavalier way of dealing with probabilities and even actualities, and, as Graham Greene put it, a tendency to play on words as "fanatical" as James Joyce's.

These qualities can be seen in every kind of writing that Chesterton undertook. He was a relentlessly paradoxical journalist, a rumbustiously undisciplined poet who always scanned perfectly, and a fiction writer bent on taking any situation to the farthest edge of absurdity before he drew it back with a masterful swing into the world of commonsense.

The essential paradox of Chesterton lay in the fact that he was writing fantasy directed at the triumph of reason. He was a man of the same generation as H. G. Wells and George Bernard Shaw, and his popularity waxed and waned with theirs. He was as concerned as Wells and Shaw over questions of social justice, even though he gave them a Christian tinge which his contemporaries rejected. He sustained a lifelong devotion to the common man, and especially to the "rolling English drunkard" who made "the rolling English road." For all the wilfulness with which he seemed intent on turning fact into fantasy, he wrote nothing without the purpose of posing some idea. The ideas were often as extreme as the fantasy, and sometimes the logical substructure seemed singularly rickety, so that there was more than a little justification in T. S. Eliot's remark, "Mr. Chesterton's brain swarms with ideas; I see no evidence that it thinks."

These qualities of Chesterton are emphatically demonstrated in those of his writings which one can regard as prose mysteries – notably his early (and perhaps his best) novel, *The Man Who Was Thursday*, and the series of stories in which Father Brown, modelled on the Father O'Connor who was Chesterton's friend and who took him into the Roman Catholic Church in 1922, figures as an unusual (though clearly not unorthodox) detective.

Though Chesterton's formal conversion came in 1922, he was already deeply involved in religious matters when he wrote *The Man Who Was Thursday*, in some ways a predecessor of later and more enigmatic works of the maverick Catholic tradition like Beckett's *Waiting for Godot*; the opening plot of a revolutionary conspiracy involving anarchists and secret service agents is transformed in the end into a parable concerning the known yet unknowable God. Similarly, the Father Brown cycle, which, on the level of a mundane yet naive priest solving mundane mysteries, might be taken as a spoofing of the whole genre of the detective novel, on another level becomes not only an exposition of Chesterton's ideas on the nature of human community but also a disguised chronicle of his own spiritual progress, loaded with Christian symbolism, heavy with homiletic wisdom and Thomistic rationality. When one talks of Chesterton as a mystery writer it has to be understood in two ways; there is indeed a crime to be solved, and in each of his books that basic task is completed, but in the process one becomes aware of the author plucking one's sleeve, and whispering urgently, "Behold, I show you a mystery," and revealing one of those ideas of which – as Eliot remarked – Chesterton's head was so abundantly full.

Chesterton's fiction, and especially the Father Brown cycle, exploit – I suggest – a vulnerable aspect of the orthodox detective novel. It is essentially a rationalist form, based on the application of the intelligence to a group of given facts plus whatever further data may emerge from the interaction of mind and situation. But it is also a moral form, concerned with motivation as a spur to and an explanation of action. As such it is open to the introduction of other forms of rationalism and morality; it is as vulnerable to Thomistic as to Cartesian reasoning, and eminently adaptable to the service of social criticism and religio-moral edification. Chesterton, who was in no sense an aestheticist, a respecter of forms, used the detective story for both these didactic purposes.

—George Woodcock

CHEYNEY, Peter. British. Born in London in 1896. Trained as a lawyer; worked as songwriter, bookmaker, journalist, and politician. *Died 26 June 1951.*

Novels (series characters: Lemmy Caution; Slim Callaghan; Michael Kells; Johnny
Vallon)

This Man Is Dangerous (Caution). London, Collins, 1936; New York, Coward
McCann, 1938.
Poison Ivy (Caution). London, Collins, 1937.
Dames Don't Care (Caution). London, Collins, 1937; New York, Coward McCann,
1938.
Can Ladies Kill? (Caution). London, Collins, 1938.
The Urgent Hangman (Callaghan). London, Collins, 1938; New York, Coward
McCann, 1939.
Don't Get Me Wrong (Caution). London, Collins, 1939.
Dangerous Curves. London, Collins, 1939; as *Callaghan*, New York, Belmont, 1973.
Another Little Drink. London, Collins, 1940; as *A Trap for Bellamy*, New York, Dodd
Mead, 1941; as *Premeditated Murder*, New York, Avon, 1943.
You'd Be Surprised (Caution). London, Collins, 1940.
You Can't Keep the Change (Callaghan). London, Collins, 1940; New York, Dodd
Mead, 1944.
Your Deal, My Lovely (Caution). London, Collins, 1941.
It Couldn't Matter Less (Callaghan). London, Collins, 1941; New York, Arcadia
House, 1943.
Never a Dull Moment (Caution). London, Collins, 1942.
Dark Duet. London, Collins, 1942; New York, Dodd Mead, 1943; as *The Counter Spy
Murders*, New York, Avon, 1944.
Sorry You've Been Troubled (Callaghan). London, Collins, 1942; as *Farewell to the
Admiral*, New York, Dodd Mead, 1943.
The Unscrupulous Mr. Callaghan. New York, Handi-Books, 1943.
You Can Always Duck (Caution). London, Collins, 1943.
The Stars Are Dark. London, Collins, and New York, Dodd Mead, 1943; as *The
London Spy Murders*, New York, Avon, 1944.
They Never Say When (Callaghan). London, Collins, 1944; New York, Dodd Mead,
1945.
The Dark Street. London, Collins, and New York, Dodd Mead, 1944; as *The Dark
Street Murders*, New York, Avon, 1946.
Sinister Errand (Kells). London, Collins, and New York, Dodd Mead, 1945; as
Sinister Murders, New York, Avon, 1957.
I'll Say She Does! (Caution). London, Collins, 1945; New York, Dodd Mead, 1946.
Dark Hero. London, Collins, and New York, Dodd Mead, 1946.
Uneasy Terms (Callaghan). London, Collins, 1946; New York, Dodd Mead, 1947.
The Curiosity of Etienne MacGregor. London, Locke, 1947; as *The Sweetheart of the
Razors*, London, New English Library, 1962.
Dark Interlude. London, Collins, and New York, Dodd Mead, 1947; as *The Terrible
Night*, New York, Avon, 1959.
Dance Without Music. London, Collins, 1947; New York, Dodd Mead, 1948.
Try Anything Twice. London, Collins, and New York, Dodd Mead, 1948; as
Undressed to Kill, New York, Avon, 1959.
Dark Wanton. London, Collins, 1948; New York, Dodd Mead, 1949.
You Can Call It a Day (Vallon). London, Collins, 1949; as *The Man Nobody Saw*, New
York, Dodd Mead, 1949.
One of Those Things. London, Collins, 1949; New York, Dodd Mead, 1950; as
Mistress Murder, New York, Avon, 1951.
Lady, Behave! (Vallon). London, Collins, 1950; as *Lady Beware*, New York, Dodd
Mead, 1950.

Dark Bahama (Vallon).   London, Collins, 1950; New York, Dodd Mead, 1951; as *I'll Bring Her Back*, New York, Eton, 1952.
Set Up for Murder.   New York, Pyramid, 1950.
Ladies Won't Wait (Kells).   London, Collins, and New York, Dodd Mead, 1951; as *Cocktails and the Killer*, New York, Avon, 1957.

Short Stories

You Can't Hit a Woman and Other Stories.   London, Collins, 1937.
Knave Takes Queen.   London, Collins, 1939.
Mister Caution − Mister Callaghan.   London, Collins, 1941.
Adventures of Alonzo MacTavish.   London, Todd, 1943.
Alonzo MacTavish Again.   London, Todd, 1943.
Love with a Gun and Other Stories.   London, Todd, 1943.
The Murder of Alonzo.   London, Todd, 1943.
Account Rendered.   London, Vallancey Press, 1944.
The Adventures of Julia.   Brighton, Poynings Press, 1945; as *The Adventures of Julia and Two Other Spy Stories*, London, Todd, 1954; as *The Killing Game*, New York, Belmont, 1975.
Dance Without Music.   London, Vallancey Press, 1945.
Escape for Sandra.   Brighton, Poynings Press, 1945.
Night Club.   Brighton, Poynings Press, 1945; as *Dressed to Kill*, London, Todd, 1952.
A Tough Spot for Cupid and Other Stories.   London, Vallancey Press, 1945.
G Man at the Yard.   Brighton, Poynings Press, 1946.
Date after Dark and Other Stories.   London, Todd, 1946.
He Walked in Her Sleep and Other Stories.   London, Todd, 1946; as *MacTavish*, New York, Belmont, 1973.
The Man with Two Wives and Other Stories.   London, Todd, 1946.
A Spot of Murder and Other Stories.   London, Todd, 1946.
Time for Caution.   Hounslow, Middlesex, Foster, 1946.
Vengeance with a Twist and Other Stories.   London, Vallancey Press, 1946.
You Can't Trust a Duchess and Other Stories.   London, Vallancey Press, 1946.
Lady in Green and Other Stories.   London, Bantam, 1947.
A Matter of Luck and Other Stories.   London, Bantam, 1947.
Cocktail for Cupid and Other Stories.   London, Bantam, 1948.
Cocktail Party and Other Stories.   London, Bantam, 1948.
Fast Work and Other Stories.   London, Bantam, 1948.
Information Received and Other Stories.   London, Bantam, 1948.
The Unhappy Lady and Other Stories.   London, Bantam, 1948.
The Lady in Tears and Other Stories.   London, Bantam, 1949.
Velvet Johnnie and Other Stories.   London, Collins, 1952.
Calling Mr. Callaghan.   London, Todd, 1953.
The Best Stories of Peter Cheyney, edited by Viola G. Garvin.   London, Faber, 1954.

OTHER PUBLICATIONS

Plays

Screenplay: *Wife of General Ling*, with others, 1937.

Radio Plays: *The Adventures of Alonzo MacTavish* (serial), 1939; *The Callaghan Touch* (serial), 1941; *Knave Takes Queen*, 1941; *The Key*, 1941; *The Lady Talks*, 1942; *Again − Callaghan*, 1942; *The Perfumed Murder*, 1943; *Concerto for Crooks*, 1943; *Parisian Ghost*, 1943; *The Callaghan Come-Back* (serial), 1943; *The Adventures of Julia*, 1945; *Way Out*, 1945; *Pay-Off for Cupid*, 1946; *Duet for Crooks*, 1946.

Other

Three Character Sketches. London, Reynolds, 1927.
"I Guarded Kings": The Memoirs of a Political Police Officer (as Harold Brust). London, Stanley Paul, 1935.
In Plain Clothes: Further Memoirs of a Political Police Officer (as Harold Brust). London, Stanley Paul, 1937.
Making Crime Pay (miscellany). London, Faber, 1944.
No Ordinary Cheyney (stories and sketches). London, Faber, 1948.

Editor, *Best Stories of the Underworld.* London, Faber, 1942.

*   *   *

Peter Cheyney was an Englishman whose specialty was ersatz hard-boiled "American" style thrillers aimed primarily at British and European audiences, although by the mid-1940's he had acquired a considerable following in America as well.

Cheyney's earliest fiction works were short stories and serials for British magazines and newspapers in the early 1930's. His initial series character, who never appeared in a novel, was a debonair rogue named Alonzo MacTavish. The MacTavish tales offer early, well-done examples of Cheyney's affinity for intricate plots concerning opposing criminal factions who try to outwit each other through an intricate web of double- and triple-crosses. This became a common plot element throughout the Cheyney canon. The character and style of the MacTavish stories were more than a little influenced by the Saint adventures by Leslie Charteris, and were gathered together in a volume entitled *He Walked In Her Sleep.*

For his first novel, *This Man Is Dangerous,* Cheyney turned to the American detective pulp magazines for his inspiration, primarily to the work of Carroll John Daly and Robert Leslie Bellem, with an occasional nod to Jonathan Latimer. Cheyney's first novel introduced Lemmy Caution, a tough American G-man who narrates his own adventures in the present tense. Caution went on to appear in several more novels as well as a handful of short stories and radio dramas, with the plotting mannerisms of the MacTavish stories now set against the constant rattling of pistols and tommyguns. Unfortunately, Cheyney's American underworld milieu in most of these books is far from convincing; his attempts at tough guy dialogue are uniformly unintentionally hilarious, far closer to Damon Runyon than anything actually spoken by such hard-boiled types ("Carson, a New York 'G' man, was takin' it all down in shorthand, after which this palooka passes out and hands in his dinner pail before he comes around again, an' so that is that, an' where do you go from there?").

Cheyney was the first British thriller writer to attempt to write in a purely American vein, and the cynicism and graphic violence of the Caution books, which far exceeded even that of the earlier Bulldog Drummond tales by Sapper, both shocked and dismayed many British readers and critics. Yet the best of the Caution books – such as the first, as well as *Can Ladies Kill?* and *You'd Be Surprised* – serve as interesting examples of Cheyney's singular gifts for breakneck pace, colorful characterization, wit, and intricacy of plotting. The Caution series also served to launch Cheyney's career as one of the most popular storytellers of his time, and his success inspired a long line of British hard-boiled writers such as James Hadley Chase, Hartley Howard, Peter Chambers, Hank Janson, and Carter Brown.

For his next series, about private eye Slim Callaghan, Cheyney again switched influences, this time to two more American detective writers, borrowing the understated prose style of Dashiell Hammett and the slightly tipsy humor of Cleve F. Adams. Cheyney also wisely shifted the setting of the Callaghan books to London, drawing on his first-hand knowledge of that city's West End gambling club and crime scene which he had acquired during his years as a journalist before turning to fiction. The Callaghan books were every bit as popular as the Caution tales and indicated a maturing of Cheyney's talents as a writer, with the frantic nonstop action of the Caution novels giving way to a more subtle approach. *The Urgent Hangman* and *Dangerous Curves* are both fine examples of the Callaghan series. Cheyney also employed a similar tone and style in a number of non-series private eye books, the best of these being *Another Little Drink* and *Dance Without Music*.

Cheyney's most original, and most critically acclaimed, work was his so-called "Dark" series of espionage novels, all of which feature the word dark in the title, concerning a top secret British counter-intelligence unit operating against Nazi agents in wartime England and abroad. Cheyney's cross-doublecross plotting technique reached its zenith in these uncompromising studies of the cold-blooded world of spies and double agents. With their vivid characterizations, effective low-key writing style, and well-maintained building of suspense, the first two books of this series, *Dark Duet* and *The Stars Are Dark*, represent Peter Cheyney at the very top of his form.

—Stephen Mertz

CHILDERS, (Robert) Erskine. British. Born in London, 25 June 1870. Educated at Haileybury College; Trinity College, Cambridge, B.A. 1893. Married Mary Alden Osgood c. 1904. Served in the City Imperial Volunteer Battery of the Honourable Artillery Company during the Boer War; in the Royal Naval Air Service during World War I: Lieutenant-Commander; mentioned in despatches; Distinguished Service Cross. Clerk in the House of Commons, 1895–1910; settled in Dublin in 1919, and fought for Home Rule; elected to the Dail Eireann, for County Wicklow, 1921; Principal Secretary to delegation for Irish-UK treaty; joined the Irish Republican Army after the establishment of the Irish Free State: court-martialled and executed, 1922. *Died 24 November 1922.*

CRIME PUBLICATIONS

Novel

> *The Riddle of the Sands: A Record of Secret Service Recently Achieved.* London, Smith Elder, 1903; New York, Dodd Mead, 1915.

OTHER PUBLICATIONS

Other

> *In the Ranks of the C.I.V.: A Narrative and Diary of Personal Experiences with the C.I.V. Battery (Honourable Artillery Company) in South Africa.* London, Smith Elder, 1900.
> *War and the Arme Blanche.* London, Arnold, 1910.
> *German Influence on British Cavalry.* London, Arnold, 1911.
> *The Framework of Home Rule.* London, Arnold, 1911.
> *The Form and Purpose of Home Rule: A Lecture.* Dublin, Ponsonby, 1912.
> *Military Rule in Ireland.* Dublin, Talbot Press, 1920.
> *Is Ireland a Danger to England?* Dublin, Woodgrange Press, 1921.
> *What the Treaty Means.* Dublin, Republic of Ireland, 1922.
> *Clause by Clause: A Comparison Between the "Treaty" and Document No. 2.* Dublin, Republic of Ireland, 1922.

Editor, with Basil Williams, *The H.A.C. in South Africa: A Record of the Services Rendered in the South African War by Members of the Honourable Artillery Company.* London, Smith Elder, 1903.

Editor, *The Times History of the War in South Africa*, vol. 5. London, Sampson Low, 1907.

Editor, with Alfred O'Rahilly, *Who Burnt Cork City? A Tale of Arson, Loot, and Murder.* Dublin, Irish Labour Party and Trade Union Congress, 1921.

Bibliography: *A Bibliography of the Books of Erskine Childers* by P. S. O'Hegarty, privately printed, 1948.

*   *   *

Erskine Childers's *The Riddle of the Sands* is narrated by Carruthers, a sociable, smart young man from the Foreign Office who spends a holiday with his friend Davies in the cramped quarters of the latter's 7-ton yacht, the *Dulcibella*, a converted lifeboat, cruising among the Frisian islands. The pair are complementary, Davies being socially diffident, but a skilled navigator and yachtsman. The story moves slowly, the detail builds up its authenticity, and the tension gradually mounts as the pair prove the shallow channels between the sands, and eventually discover the German plans to assemble fleets of small ships and barges for an invasion of England.

The local characters are well-drawn and, like all the sailing details, are founded upon the author's experiences (recorded in his log-book) of cruising his yacht *Vixen* in the area in 1897–98. The romantic element, "spatchcocked" into the story as Childers put it, is weak, and the Royal Naval officer who has become a German spy is not convincing: but what Childers aimed at was not "sensation, only what is meant to be convincing fact." Though the book appeals to yachtsmen, though its picture of grey northern skies, yeasty seas and the wet sands fringing the "feathery line" of the Frisian coast seemed to John Buchan to equal Conrad's mastery, its prime purpose was to draw attention to a national danger. In doing so it has become a classic; the author's epilogue and postscript confirm its realism.

—A. Norman Jeffares

CHRISTIE, Dame Agatha (Mary Clarissa, née Miller). Also wrote as Mary Westmacott. British. Born in Torquay, Devon, 15 September 1890. Educated privately at home; studied singing and piano in Paris. Married 1) Colonel Archibald Christie in 1914 (divorced, 1928), one daughter; 2) the archaeologist Max Mallowan in 1930. Served as a Voluntary Aid Detachment nurse in a Red Cross Hospital in Torquay during World War I, and worked in the dispensary of University College Hospital, London, during World War II; also assisted her husband on excavations in Iraq and Syria and on the Assyrian cities. President, Detection Club. Recipient: Mystery Writers of America Grand Master Award, 1954; New York Drama Critics Circle Award, 1955. D.Litt.: University of Exeter, 1961. Fellow, Royal Society of Literature, 1950. C.B.E. (Commander, Order of the British Empire), 1956; D.B.E. (Dame Commander, Order of the British Empire), 1971. *Died 12 January 1976.*

Crime Publications

Novels (series characters: Superintendent Battle; Tuppence and Tommy Beresford; Jane
    Marple; Hercule Poirot)

The Mysterious Affair at Styles (Poirot).   London, Lane, 1920; New York, Dodd Mead,
    1927.
The Secret Adversary (Beresfords).   London, Lane, and New York, Dodd Mead, 1922.
The Murder on the Links (Poirot).   London, Lane, and New York, Dodd Mead, 1923.
The Man in the Brown Suit.   London, Lane, and New York, Dodd Mead, 1924.
The Secret of Chimneys (Battle).   London, Lane, and New York, Dodd Mead, 1925.
The Murder of Roger Ackroyd (Poirot).   London, Collins, and New York, Dodd Mead,
    1926.
The Big Four (Poirot).   London, Collins, and New York, Dodd Mead, 1927.
The Mystery of the Blue Train (Poirot).   London, Collins, and New York, Dodd Mead,
    1928.
The Seven Dials Murder (Battle).   London, Collins, and New York, Dodd Mead, 1929.
The Murder at the Vicarage.   London, Collins, and New York, Dodd Mead, 1930.
The Floating Admiral, with others.   London, Hodder and Stoughton, 1931; New York,
    Doubleday, 1932.
The Sittaford Mystery.   London, Collins, 1931; as *The Murder at Hazelmoor*, New
    York, Dodd Mead, 1931.
Peril at End House (Poirot).   London, Collins, and New York, Dodd Mead, 1932.
Lord Edgware Dies (Poirot).   London, Collins, 1933; as *Thirteen at Dinner*, New York,
    Dodd Mead, 1933.
Why Didn't They Ask Evans?   London, Collins, 1934; as *The Boomerang Clue*, New
    York, Dodd Mead, 1935.
Murder on the Orient Express (Poirot).   London, Collins, 1934; as *Murder on the Calais
    Coach*, New York, Dodd Mead, 1934.
Murder in Three Acts.   New York, Dodd Mead, 1934; as *Three Act Tragedy*, London,
    Collins, 1935.
Death in the Clouds (Poirot).   London, Collins, 1935; as *Death in the Air*, New York,
    Dodd Mead, 1935.
The A.B.C. Murders (Poirot).   London, Collins, and New York, Dodd Mead, 1936; as
    The Alphabet Murders, New York, Pocket Books, 1966.
Cards on the Table (Battle; Poirot).   London, Collins, 1936; New York, Dodd Mead,
    1937.
Murder in Mesopotamia (Poirot).   London, Collins, and New York, Dodd Mead, 1936.
Death on the Nile (Poirot).   London, Collins, 1937; New York, Dodd Mead, 1938.
Dumb Witness.   London, Collins, 1937; as *Poirot Loses a Client*, New York, Dodd
    Mead, 1937.
Appointment with Death (Poirot).   London, Collins, and New York, Dodd Mead, 1938.
Hercule Poirot's Christmas.   London, Collins, 1938; as *Murder for Christmas*, New
    York, Dodd Mead, 1939; as *A Holiday for Murder*, New York, Avon, 1947.
Murder Is Easy (Battle).   London, Collins, 1939; as *Easy to Kill*, New York, Dodd
    Mead, 1939.
Ten Little Niggers.   London, Collins, 1939; as *And Then There Were None*, New York,
    Dodd Mead, 1940; as *Ten Little Indians*, New York, Pocket Books, 1965.
One, Two, Buckle My Shoe (Poirot).   London, Collins, 1940; as *The Patriotic Murders*,
    New York, Dodd Mead, 1941; as *An Overdose of Death*, New York, Dell, 1953.
Sad Cypress (Poirot).   London, Collins, and New York, Dodd Mead, 1940.
Evil under the Sun (Poirot).   London, Collins, and New York, Dodd Mead, 1941.
N or M? (Beresfords).   London, Collins, and New York, Dodd Mead, 1941.
The Body in the Library (Marple).   London, Collins, and New York, Dodd Mead, 1942.
The Moving Finger (Marple).   New York, Dodd Mead, 1942; London, Collins, 1943.

Five Little Pigs (Poirot).   London, Collins, 1942; as *Murder in Retrospect*, New York, Dodd Mead, 1942.

Death Comes as the End.   New York, Dodd Mead, 1944; London, Collins, 1945.

Towards Zero (Battle).   London, Collins, and New York, Dodd Mead, 1944.

Sparkling Cyanide.   London, Collins, 1945; as *Remembered Death*, New York, Dodd Mead, 1945.

The Hollow (Poirot).   London, Collins, and New York, Dodd Mead, 1946; as *Murder after Hours*, New York, Dell, 1954.

Taken at the Flood (Poirot).   London, Collins, 1948; as *There Is a Tide ...*, New York, Dodd Mead, 1948.

Crooked House.   London, Collins, and New York, Dodd Mead, 1949.

A Murder Is Announced (Marple).   London, Collins, and New York, Dodd Mead, 1950.

They Came to Baghdad.   London, Collins, and New York, Dodd Mead, 1951.

They Do It with Mirrors (Marple).   London, Collins, 1952; as *Murder with Mirrors*, New York, Dodd Mead, 1952.

Mrs. McGinty's Dead (Poirot).   London, Collins, and New York, Dodd Mead, 1952.

After the Funeral (Poirot).   London, Collins, 1953; as *Funerals Are Fatal*, New York, Dodd Mead, 1953; as *Murder at the Gallop*, London, Fontana, 1963.

A Pocket Full of Rye (Marple).   London, Collins, 1953; New York, Dodd Mead, 1954.

Destination Unknown.   London, Collins, 1954; as *So Many Steps to Death*, New York, Dodd Mead, 1955.

Hickory, Dickory, Dock (Poirot).   London, Collins, 1955; as *Hickory, Dickory, Death*, New York, Dodd Mead, 1955.

Dead Man's Folly (Poirot).   London, Collins, and New York, Dodd Mead, 1956.

4:50 from Paddington (Marple).   London, Collins, 1957; as *What Mrs. McGillicuddy Saw!*, New York, Dodd Mead, 1957; as *Murder She Said*, New York, Pocket Books, 1961.

Ordeal by Innocence.   London, Collins, 1958; New York, Dodd Mead, 1959.

Cat among the Pigeons (Poirot).   London, Collins, 1959; New York, Dodd Mead, 1960.

The Pale Horse.   London, Collins, 1961; New York, Dodd Mead, 1962.

The Mirror Crack'd from Side to Side (Marple).   London, Collins, 1962; as *The Mirror Crack'd*, New York, Dodd Mead, 1963.

The Clocks (Poirot).   London, Collins, 1963; New York, Dodd Mead, 1964.

A Caribbean Mystery (Marple).   London, Collins, 1964; New York, Dodd Mead, 1965.

At Bertram's Hotel (Marple).   London, Collins, 1965; New York, Dodd Mead, 1966.

Third Girl (Poirot).   London, Collins, 1966; New York, Dodd Mead, 1967.

Endless Night.   London, Collins, 1967; New York, Dodd Mead, 1968.

By the Pricking of My Thumbs (Beresfords).   London, Collins, and New York, Dodd Mead, 1968.

Hallowe'en Party (Poirot).   London, Collins, and New York, Dodd Mead, 1969.

Passenger to Frankfurt.   London, Collins, and New York, Dodd Mead, 1970.

Nemesis (Marple).   London, Collins, and New York, Dodd Mead, 1971.

Elephants Can Remember (Poirot).   London, Collins, and New York, Dodd Mead, 1972.

Postern of Fate (Beresfords).   London, Collins, and New York, Dodd Mead, 1973.

Murder on Board (omnibus).   New York, Dodd Mead, 1974.

Curtain: Hercule Poirot's Last Case.   London, Collins, and New York, Dodd Mead, 1975.

Sleeping Murder (Marple).   London, Collins, and New York, Dodd Mead, 1976.

Short Stories

Poirot Investigates.   London, Lane, 1924; New York, Dodd Mead, 1925.

Partners in Crime.   London, Collins, and New York, Dodd Mead, 1929; reprinted in part as *The Sunningdale Mystery*, Collins, 1933.

The Under Dog. London, Readers Library, 1929.

The Mysterious Mr. Quin. London, Collins, and New York, Dodd Mead, 1930.

The Thirteen Problems. London, Collins, 1932; as *The Tuesday Club Murders*, New York, Dodd Mead, 1933 selection, as *The Mystery of the Blue Geraniums and Other Tuesday Club Murders*, New York, Bantam, 1940.

The Hound of Death and Other Stories. London, Odhams Press, 1933.

Parker Pyne Investigates. London, Collins, 1934; as *Mr. Parker Pyne, Detective*, New York, Dodd Mead, 1934.

The Listerdale Mystery and Other Stories. London, Collins, 1934.

Murder in the Mews and Other Stories. London, Collins, 1937; as *Dead Man's Mirror and Other Stories*, New York, Dodd Mead, 1937.

The Regatta Mystery and Other Stories. New York, Dodd Mead, 1939.

The Mystery of the Baghdad Chest. London, Bantam, 1943.

The Mystery of the Crime in Cabin 66. London, Bantam, 1943.

Poirot and the Regatta Mystery. London, Bantam, 1943.

Poirot on Holiday. London, Todd, 1943.

Problem at Pollensa Bay, and Christmas Adventure. London, Todd, 1943.

The Veiled Lady, and The Mystery of the Baghdad Chest. London, Todd, 1944.

Poirot Knows the Murderer. London, Todd, 1946.

Poirot Lends a Hand. London, Todd, 1946.

The Labours of Hercules. London, Collins, and New York, Dodd Mead, 1947.

The Witness for the Prosecution and Other Stories. New York, Dodd Mead, 1948.

The Mousetrap and Other Stories. New York, Dell, 1949; as *Three Blind Mice and Other Stories*, New York, Dodd Mead, 1950.

The Under Dog and Other Stories. New York, Dodd Mead, 1951.

The Adventures of the Christmas Pudding, and Selection of Entrées. London, Collins, 1960.

Double Sin and Other Stories. New York, Dodd Mead, 1961.

13 for Luck! A Selection of Mystery Stories for Young Readers. New York, Dodd Mead, 1961; London, Collins, 1966.

Surprise! Surprise! A Collection of Mystery Stories with Unexpected Endings. New York, Dodd Mead, 1965.

13 Clues for Miss Marple. New York, Dodd Mead, 1966.

The Golden Ball and Other Stories. New York, Dodd Mead, 1971.

Poirot's Early Cases. London, Collins, and New York, Dodd Mead, 1974.

Miss Marple's Final Cases and Others. London, Collins, 1979.

OTHER PUBLICATIONS

Novels as Mary Westmacott

Giants' Bread. London, Collins, and New York, Doubleday, 1930.

Unfinished Portrait. London, Collins, and New York, Doubleday, 1934.

Absent in the Spring. London, Collins, and New York, Farrar and Rinehart, 1944.

The Rose and the Yew Tree. London, Heinemann, and New York, Rinehart, 1948.

A Daughter's a Daughter. London, Heinemann, 1952.

The Burden. London, Heinemann, 1956.

Short Stories

Star over Bethlehem and Other Stories (as Agatha Christie Mallowan). London, Collins, and New York, Dodd Mead, 1965.

Plays

Black Coffee (produced London, 1930). London, Ashley, and Boston, Baker, 1934.
Ten Little Niggers, adaptation of her own novel (produced Wimbledon and London, 1943). London, French, 1944; as Ten Little Indians (produced New York, 1944), New York, French, 1946.
Appointment with Death, adaptation of her own novel (produced Glasgow and London, 1945). London, French, 1945; in The Mousetrap and Other Plays, 1978.
Murder on the Nile, adaptation of her novel Death on the Nile (as Little Horizon, produced Wimbledon, 1945; as Murder on the Nile, produced London and New York, 1946). London and New York, French, 1948.
The Hollow, adaptation of her own novel (produced Cambridge and London, 1951; Princeton, New Jersey, 1952; New York, 1978). London and New York, French, 1952.
The Mousetrap, adaptation of her story "Three Blind Mice" (broadcast, 1952; produced Nottingham and London, 1952; New York, 1960). London and New York, French, 1954.
Witness for the Prosecution, adaptation of her own story (produced Nottingham and London, 1953; New York, 1954). London and New York, French, 1954.
Spider's Web (produced Nottingham and London, 1954; New York, 1974). London and New York, French, 1957.
Towards Zero, with Gerald Verner, adaptation of the novel by Christie (produced Nottingham and London, 1956). New York, Dramatists Play Service, 1957; London, French, 1958.
Verdict (produced Wolverhampton and London, 1958). London, French, 1958; in The Mousetrap and Other Plays, 1978.
The Unexpected Guest (produced Bristol and London, 1958). London, French, 1958; in The Mousetrap and Other Plays, 1978.
Go Back for Murder, adaptation of her novel Five Little Pigs (produced Edinburgh and London, 1960). London, French, 1960; in The Mousetrap and Other Plays, 1978.
Rule of Three: Afternoon at the Seaside, The Patient, The Rats (produced Aberdeen and London, 1962; The Rats produced New York, 1974; The Patient produced New York, 1978). London, French, 3 vols., 1963.
Fiddlers Three (produced Southsea, 1971; London, 1972).
Akhnaton (as Akhnaton and Nefertiti, produced New York, 1979). London, Collins, and New York, Dodd Mead, 1973.
The Mousetrap and Other Plays (includes Witness for the Prosecution, Ten Little Indians, Appointment with Death, The Hollow, Towards Zero, Verdict, Go Back for Murder). New York, Dodd Mead, 1978.

Radio Plays: The Mousetrap, 1952; Personal Call, 1960.

Verse

The Road of Dreams. London, Bles, 1925.
Poems. London, Collins, and New York, Dodd Mead, 1973.

Other

Come, Tell Me How You Live (travel). London, Collins, and New York, Dodd Mead, 1946.

An Autobiography.   London, Collins, and New York, Dodd Mead, 1977.

*   *   *

Shortly after the end of World War One an aspirant to the then increasingly popular ranks of detective-story writers sent a manuscript to a London publisher. It was returned. Five more times it went off, and five more times it came back. But at last a seventh publisher, John Lane at the Bodley Head, accepted it and in 1920 *The Mysterious Affair at Styles* by Agatha Christie first introduced the world to Hercule Poirot. The book was a modest success. Others followed. Gradually Christie began to emerge as a leader in the genre, and eventually the regular stream of Christie books took off (about the time of the Second World War). By the end of her life she had become a name known from China (where they were apt to call her a running-dog of imperialism) to Nicaragua (where the magnificent moustaches of Hercule Poirot decorated a postage stamp) and she was selling more books than anyone in the genre. But to acknowledge the hugeness of her sales is not to disparage her achievement. A vessel that can take such a hurricane in her sails and keep upright must be a sturdy barque, and Agatha Christie's books – set aside some weak performances in a total of over 80 – are well-built craft indeed.

She developed and continued to keep a wonderful ingenuity of plot. She knew the rules of the game and worked out every possible variation of them delightfully to trick her readers. The least likely person, the very least likely person, the person already cleared, the apparently unbreakable alibi, the unimpeachable witness who for a very good reason proves not to be, the murder committed after the "corpse" has been seen – all these, and more, she cunningly employed. She had a dazzling ingenuity in the planting of clues and the trailing of red herrings, the basis of her particular patch in the great field of crime-writing. Does she need to establish that the butler is short-sighted (and so did not see the person he swore he had)? Poirot makes great play over asking whether a date has been torn off a wall-calendar. The butler crosses the room to give him his answer. Poor deluded readers puzzle away about the significance of dates while the true clue has been quietly dropped into their laps.

But if she was a mistress of complication, she was also a mistress of simplicity. The actual writing of her complicated stories was always marvellously simple. A great deal of what she had to tell her reader she told in dialogue. She had a good ear (she had had an excellent musical education, good enough to consider – had she not been a very private person – concert careers both as pianist and singer) and she catches exactly the tone of her middle-class English characters, though with servants and lower-class "extras" she is a little apt to caricature. And here is another clue to her success. She was an upper-middle-class English lady and, almost always, she wrote only about upper-middle-class English life. She had the modesty to know her limits, and the sense to stick to them.

But despite this social limitation her books are loved world-wide. This is because she was an ordinary person herself and took for her characters what was ordinary, shared-by-everyone about them. Miss Marple is the most ordinary of old ladies, triumphing as a detective frequently by seeing the ordinary (the butcher boy's deceit) in the act of murder or by finding clues during the everyday process of gossip and tittle-tattle. Poirot, who on the surface might appear quite extraordinary, is in fact no more than a gathering together of all the simple eccentricities the ordinary person would expect, though they are seen with a warm enjoyment.

In short, Agatha Christie's prime virtue is her unoriginality in everything bar plot. But hers is an unoriginality presented always with exceptional rightness. Other unoriginal crime writers produce books in which uninteresting people say uninteresting things and try to make up for it often by frantic activity. Agatha Christie gives us ordinary, not wildly exciting, people, but by describing them with exact rightness she makes them clear and clean to every reader. Nothing clogs. Her timing is unostentatiously right. This is what makes her such a good storyteller: you get the right piece of information at exactly the right moment. And you never get digressions, those bits of cleverness that tempt other writers.

I see her as a clown in the circus, an entertainer connected to her audience by an invisible magic link. She produces for them things that are quite simple but are nonetheless welcome, welcome to the ordinary spectator and welcome to the spectator more used to the complexities of the drama (provided only that he is willing to sink some prejudices). Out of the conical white cap with its big black bobbles comes the expected, long waited-for check silk handkerchief – at exactly the right moment, and in neatly the *unexpected* colour. We burst out clapping. And so we should.

—H. R. F. Keating

CLARKE, Anna. British. Born in Cape Town, South Africa, 28 April 1919. Educated at schools in Cape Town, Oxford, and Montreal; University of London external B.Sc. in economics 1945; Open University, 1971–74; University of Sussex, Brighton, M.A. 1975. Divorced. Private Secretary, Victor Gollancz, publishers, London, 1947–50, and Eyre and Spottiswoode, publishers, London, 1951–53; Administrative Secretary, British Association for American Studies, London, 1956–63. Agent: Collins, 14 St. James's Place, London SW1A 1PS. Address: 12 Franklin Road, Brighton, Sussex, England.

CRIME PUBLICATIONS

Novels

> *The Darkened Room.* London, Long, 1968.
> *A Mind to Murder.* London, Chatto and Windus, 1971.
> *The End of a Shadow.* London, Chatto and Windus, 1972.
> *Plot Counter-Plot.* London, Collins, 1974; New York, Walker, 1975.
> *My Search for Ruth.* London, Collins, 1975.
> *Legacy of Evil.* London, Collins, 1976.
> *The Deathless and the Dead.* London, Collins, 1976; as *This Downhill Path*, New York, McKay, 1977.
> *The Lady in Black.* London, Collins, 1977; New York, McKay, 1978.
> *Letter from the Dead.* London, Collins, 1977.
> *One of Us Must Die.* London, Collins, 1978.
> *The Poisoned Web.* London, Collins, 1979.
> *Poison Parsley.* London, Collins, 1979.

Anna Clarke comments:

It is difficult to say anything about my own writing because I have never taken it very seriously except as a source of income and a mental release from the frustrations of life. I have turned into an obsessional spinner of stories, going on with them in my own mind even when not writing them down, but I only started writing late in life and should never have done so if a very long and severe illness had not destroyed my chosen career. I should have been a mathematician, and am even now more interested in maths than in fiction. I don't know whether the love of pattern and order and an eye for similarities that form the love of mathematics have any influence on what I write. I never plan a novel and have no idea when I start how it is going to develop and end. This is the only way I can keep up my interest enough to finish it – not knowing myself "whodunit"! But it always seems to fall into some sort of pattern and to conclude at about the same length, so there must be a connection. There is certainly a connection between what I write and the fact that I was cured of my illness by a long and deep Freudian analysis and that I have done a lot of work on psycho-analytical writings. As far as I have any conscious feeling about writing novels at all beyond the obsessional story-telling, I am interested in the workings of the human mind and their effect on character and action. And I only took to writing mystery and suspense stories because nobody wanted to publish the straight novels that I was writing.

*   *   *

Anna Clarke's crime fiction gives the whole genre an interesting twist for she moves detecting away from the mystery of the criminal mind to the mystery of writing itself. It is the wonder of writing and not of thinking that thrills the reader of Clarke's works.

Plot Counter-Plot is about a novel whose plot is itself the action of the book, in the manner of James M. Cain's *The Postman Always Rings Twice*. An established and successful suspense novelist, Helen Mitchell, engages in a literary and love affair with a young, unsuccessful author named Brent Ashwood. As their lives merge together, so does their literary activity, and they begin to write separate novels.

The "plot" passes from plotting in the literary sense to plotting in the criminal sense. Brent quickly realizes that he lacks the discipline or the talent necessary to complete his work. Therefore, he resolves to steal Helen's novel (after all, it is about him and so, in a fashion, is his) and to pass it off as an autobiographical novel of his own. Helen discovers his plot to steal her plot and decides to kill Brent. The plot thickens, and the counter-plot grows bolder; the denouement is superb.

For Clarke, aesthetic considerations and the literary act become one with the presentation and solution of the crime.

My Search for Ruth is particularly interesting as an illustration of the way in which literary activity yields the subtle mysteries of self to those possessed of literary sensibility. Ruth writes for us a chronicle of her search for identity. Like Hitchcock's Marnie, Ruth follows a single image through a maze of violence and death, until that image is so embellished as to show forth the truth of her identity. The image is presented on the first page of the novel:

> The head in the wall; that was the first of my memories. It had a grinning red face, surrounded by hair sticking up in all directions like Shockheaded Peter, and it shot out of the shadows by the side of the fireplace in my Aunt Bessie's little living room and remained twisting about as if it belonged to some monstrous being that was striving to break through the brown wallpaper and run rampant through the house, leaving in its wake a horror beyond what the timid mind could bear.

Ruth possesses a fine literary sense and was raised and educated by literary people; but her search for her parents and her attempt to understand the image that contains the essential truth about her life cause her to reject a university education and life as a scholar in favor of a compulsive, personal, primary encounter with the stuff of literature itself – image, character, plot.

The Deathless and the Dead continues Clarke's pattern of building crime fiction from the literary act, though here the agent of action is the scholar and not the creative artist. The novel, set in Oxford, is rich in character and scene. Both are handled with a flare for texture and tone that readers of crime fiction have come to expect from such writers as Edmund Crispin and Dorothy Sayers. Clarke lets setting feed character and plot in an organic way. John Broom, a young scholar, is studying the life and tragic death of a minor nineteenth-century poetess, Emily Witherington. His girl friend, Alice, arranges an interview for him with a great-uncle, Sir Roderick Heron, who knew the poet before her untimely death in a cycling accident on Boar's Hill. In pursuit of a ribbon-tied cache of old letters, the literary detectives, John and Alice, find a new angle of vision on the old mystery plot of manners and manors, while the mysteries of Emily's life and death, the criminal mind, and literary research all unfold. The tale of crime and its detection is a roaring good one, but the better mystery is the one which unfolds as the literary sensibility gives life and order to the world by shaping fact, fear, and fantasy into a complete and coherent biography.

The talent of Anna Clarke, then, is immense. She breathes a true creator's breath into old conventions and clichés precisely because, as a writer of mysteries, she is bold enough to fashion them from the mystery of writing itself.

—Larry E. Grimes

CLEARY, Jon (Stephen). Australian. Born in Sydney, 22 November 1917. Educated at Marist Brothers School, Randwick, New South Wales, 1924–32. Served in the Australian Imperial Forces in the Middle East and New Guinea, 1940–45. Married Constantine Lucas in 1946; two children. Prior to 1939 worked as a commercial traveller, bush worker and commercial artist. Full-time Writer since 1945. Journalist, Government of Australia News and Information Bureau, in London, 1948–49, and in New York, 1949–51. Recipient: Australian Broadcasting Commission Prize, for radio drama, 1944; Second Prize, *Sydney Morning Herald* Novel Contest, 1946; Australian Section Prize, *New York Herald Tribune* World Short Story Contest, 1950; Mystery Writers of America Edgar Allan Poe Award, 1974. Lives in New South Wales. Address: c/o John Farquharson Ltd., 8 Bell Yard, London WC2A 2JU, England.

CRIME PUBLICATIONS

Novels (series character: Scobie Malone)

> *You Can't See Around Corners.* New York, Scribner, 1947; London, Eyre and Spottiswoode, 1949.
> *The Long Shadow.* London, Laurie, 1949.
> *Just Let Me Be.* London, Laurie, 1950.
> *The Climate of Courage.* London, Collins, 1954; as *Naked in the Night*, New York, Popular Library, 1955.
> *Justin Bayard.* London, Collins, 1955; New York, Morrow, 1956; as *Dust in the Sun*, New York, Popular Library, 1957.
> *Forests of the Night.* New York, Morrow, and London, Collins, 1963.
> *A Flight of Chariots.* New York, Morrow, 1963; London, Collins, 1964.
> *The Fall of an Eagle.* New York, Morrow, 1964; London, Collins, 1965.
> *The Pulse of Danger.* New York, Morrow, and London, Collins, 1966.
> *The High Commissioner* (Malone). New York, Morrow, and London, Collins, 1966.
> *The Long Pursuit.* New York, Morrow, and London, Collins, 1967.
> *Season of Doubt.* New York, Morrow, and London, Collins, 1968.
> *Helga's Web* (Malone). New York, Morrow, and London, Collins, 1970.
> *The Liberators.* New York, Morrow, 1971; as *Mask of the Andes*, London, Collins, 1971.
> *Ransom* (Malone). New York, Morrow, and London, Collins, 1973.
> *Peter's Pence.* New York, Morrow, and London, Collins, 1974.
> *The Safe House.* New York, Morrow, and London, Collins, 1975.
> *A Sound of Lightning.* New York, Morrow, and London, Collins, 1976.
> *High Road to China.* New York, Morrow, and London, Collins, 1977.
> *Vortex.* London, Collins, 1977; New York, Morrow, 1978.

The Beaufort Sisters.   New York, Morrow, and London, Collins, 1979.

Short Stories

These Small Glories.   Sydney, Angus and Robertson, 1946.
Pillar of Salt.   Sydney, Horwitz, 1963.

OTHER PUBLICATIONS

Novels

The Sundowners.   New York, Scribner, and London, Laurie, 1952.
The Green Helmet.   London, Collins, 1957; New York, Morrow, 1958.
Back of Sunset.   New York, Morrow, and London, Collins, 1959.
North from Thursday.   London, Collins, 1960; New York, Morrow, 1961.
The Country of Marriage.   New York, Morrow, and London, Collins, 1962.
Remember Jack Hoxie.   New York, Morrow, and London, Collins, 1969.
The Ninth Marquess.   New York, Morrow, 1972; as *Man's Estate*, London, Collins,
   1972.

Plays

Strike Me Lucky (produced Bromley, Kent, 1963).

Screenplays: *The Siege of Pinchgut*, with Harry Watt and Alexander Baron, 1959; *The
Green Helmet*, 1961; *The Sundowners*, 1961; *The Sidecar Boys*, 1975.

Radio Play: *Safe Horizon*, 1944.

Television Play: *Just Let Me Be* (UK), 1957.

*   *   *

Jon Cleary is one of the finest novelists of our day. Before he turned to mystery, he had
already achieved distinction in general fiction. Among his early books was *The Sundowners*,
a broad canvas of his native Australia, and which was to become one of the classics of the
cinema.

The Cleary suspense novels explore the entire globe, wherever there is the unusual scene
and the challenge of character. He has been a mountain climber, and mountains are one of
his particular interests. In *The Pulse of Danger*, he wrote of an unforgettable chase over the
Himalayas. For *The Liberators*, he explored the almost inaccessible Bolivian village atop the
Andes.

In 1974 he was awarded an Edgar for the most unusual of all his works, *Peter's Pence*.
Most of the action in the story takes place in the Vatican, whose art treasures are the target of
a group of thieves of varied nationalities. How Cleary discovered and studied the architectural
plan of St. Peter's, with its subterranean passages, has not been revealed.

Cleary never seems an outsider to the scene he is entering. *Vortex* is a prime example. It is
set in the cyclone country of rural Missouri, and even a native would find it hard to believe
that the Australian Cleary was not one of them, and had not been there during a high wind
disaster.

The most important element of Cleary's serious stories is his moral indignation at the
injustices he observes. In *The Safe House* he has written of the displaced Jews in the post-
Nazi period, denied Palestine by the mandate but determining to find a way to reach the
homeland, while the defeated Nazis are trying to reach the safety of South America. *The
Liberators*, which some consider the finest of Cleary's works, has for its theme the

awakening of the Bolivian Indians to their human and cultural rights. A young American priest and an agronomist from the United Nations defy the *ricos*, the *politicos*, and the hierarchy of the church in their attempt to make a beginning at righting the wrongs long burdening the natives. As a sociological study the book is superb, but equally superb is the excitement of the suspense story in which the theme is interwoven.

Jon Cleary has never rested on his laurels. Each year there is another major novel from him, and each one stands on its own with no echoes of its forerunners.

—Dorothy B. Hughes

CLEEVE, Brian (Talbot). Irish. Born in Thorpe Bay, Essex, England, 22 November 1921. Educated at Selwyn House, Broadstairs, Kent, 1930–35; St. Edward's School, Oxford, 1935–38; University of South Africa, Pretoria, 1951–53, B.A. 1953; National University of Ireland, Dublin, 1954–56, Ph.D. 1956. Served in the British Merchant Navy, 1939–45. Married Veronica McAdie in 1945; two daughters. Free-lance journalist in South Africa, 1948–54, and in Ireland since 1954. Broadcaster, Radio Telefis Eireann, Dublin, 1962–72. Address: 60 Heytesbury Lane, Ballsbridge, Dublin 4, Ireland.

CRIME PUBLICATIONS

Novels (series character: Sean Ryan)

> *Birth of a Dark Soul.* London, Jarrolds, 1953; as *The Night Winds*, Boston, Houghton Mifflin, 1954.
> *Assignment to Vengeance.* London, Hammond, 1961.
> *Death of a Painted Lady.* London, Hammond, 1962; New York, Random House, 1963.
> *Death of a Wicked Servant.* London, Hammond, 1963; New York, Random House, 1964.
> *Vote X for Treason* (Ryan). London, Collins, 1964; New York, Random House, 1965; as *Counterspy*, London, Lancer, 1966.
> *Dark Blood, Dark Terror* (Ryan). New York, Random House, 1965; London, Hammond, 1966.
> *The Judas Goat* (Ryan). London, Hammond, 1966; as *Vice Isn't Private*, New York, Random House, 1966.
> *Violent Death of a Bitter Englishman* (Ryan). New York, Random House, 1967; London, Corgi, 1969.
> *You Must Never Go Back.* New York, Random House, 1968.
> *Exit from Prague.* London, Corgi, 1970; as *Escape from Prague*, New York, Pinnacle, 1973.

Uncollected Short Stories

> "Foxer," in *Best Detective Stories of the Year 1966*, edited by Anthony Boucher. New York, Dutton, 1966.
> "The Devil Finds Work for Jake O'Hara," in *Ellery Queen's Mystery Magazine* (New York), December 1969.

OTHER PUBLICATIONS

Novels

The Far Hills.   London, Jarrolds, 1952.
Portrait of My City.   London, Jarrolds, 1952.
Birth of a Dark Soul.   London, Jarrolds, 1953; as The Night Winds, Boston, Houghton
     Mifflin, 1954.
Cry of Morning.   London, Joseph, 1971; as The Triumph of O'Rourke, New York,
     Doubleday, 1972.
Tread Softly in This Place.   London, Cassell, and New York, Day, 1972.
The Dark Side of the Sun.   London, Cassell, 1973.
A Question of Inheritance.   London, Cassell, 1974; as For Love of Crannagh Castle,
     New York, Dutton, 1975.
Sara.   London, Cassell, and New York, Coward McCann, 1976.
Kate.   London, Cassell, and New York, Coward McCann, 1977.
Judith.   London, Cassell, and New York, Coward McCann, 1978.
Hester.   London, Cassell, 1979.

Short Stories

The Horse Thieves of Ballysaggert and Other Stories.   Cork, Mercier Press, 1966.

Other

Colonial Policies in Africa.   Johannesburg, St. Benedict's House, 1954.
Dictionary of Irish Writers.   Cork, Mercier Press, 3 vols., 1967–71.

Editor, W. B. Yeats and the Designing of Ireland's Coinage.   Dublin, Dolmen Press,
     1972.

Manuscript Collection: Mugar Memorial Library, Boston University.

Brian Cleeve comments:
   Crime and thriller stories have always appealed to me for the same reason that fairy stories
do, and folk tales and myths. They deal directly with the conflict between good and evil, and
for that reason touch the most fundamental levels of human experience. In my own crime
and thriller novels I tried — I only wish I had succeeded — to deal with this theme as seriously
as it should be dealt with. I wish that publishers and novel readers were willing to accept
serious work in these categories — and I wish too that the whole concept of categories for
fiction could be thrown away.

                              *   *   *

   Brian Cleeve's Irish novels put to rest romanticized myths of an idyllic Ireland with Seal
Queens and Martyrs, yet show how these have shaped modern Irish goals and actions. Cleeve
sees inevitable contradictions and self-destructive extremes in the Irish character: legendary
ancestry versus present economic deprivation, repressive puritanical training versus
retaliatory drunkenness and lechery, rigid conservative Catholicism versus socialist/
communist sympathies, an ancient system of clans and feuds versus modern community and
democracy, tight-lips to strangers versus continual gossip and rumor among friends, a
xenophobic love of rural Ireland and its ancient manor houses versus a desire for the wealth
foreign developers bring. Cleeve's digressive sagas suggest the subtle class and racial tensions
that influence the thoughts, actions, goals, and transformations of a number of families or

individuals from diverse social levels: itinerants (particularly tinkers), gentry, clergy, Anglo-Irish, peasant families with noble ancestry. In *Tread Softly in This Place* developers blame a costly prank by local xenophobes on IRA commandos and expect plots everywhere, which causes local radicals to mount a real raid. *Death of a Painted Lady*, a more traditional tale of promiscuity, drunkenness, and sadism in the art world that lead to rape, murder, robbery, and the conviction of an innocent man, focuses on the hypocrisies of Dublin characters from tramp to art critic – all in or around the scene of the crime at the crucial moment.

Cleeve's spy series follow the checkered career of Sean Ryan, an impetuous ex-Irish revolutionary turned cynic, recruited from prison by Major Courtney of British Intelligence to infiltrate and investigate groups whose plans threaten the security of England. Usually these are large-scale operations to seize or keep power: a Home Secretary who destroys his own agents to conceal his kinky sex habits (*The Judas Goat*); a group of reactionary Lords and MP's who use commandos and teddy boys trained in health clubs and a secret oil agreement with Iraq to precipitate a change of government (*Vote X for Treason*); another fascist organization that plots to seize power on a racist wave to eliminate coloreds in England on funds extorted from them by protection rackets (*Violent Death of a Bitter Englishman*); an Afrikaner task force using Ryan's agency as a front for their plot to assassinate the South African Prime Minister (*Dark Blood, Dark Terror*). The sadistic directors of these diabolical schemes employ hideous physical punishment to break and eliminate opponents: crucifixion, castration, electroshock, drugs. To counter his own deep-seated fear of torture and personal injury, Ryan resorts to equally violent methods with the tools at hand – a tank of boiling coffee in the face, gasoline to produce a human torch, deadly karate chops, sudden blows with spike, mace, or board. But the villains' violence is planned and savoured while Ryan's is a spontaneous instinct to save himself and the innocents he seeks to protect (usually a pliable, clinging female). Always Ryan suffers from guilt about his cruel temper, and doubts the worth of his cause since another evil group quickly replaces the one destroyed; he also questions his status in an organization in which, as an Irishman, he can never fully belong.

Cleeve's other short stories and novels vary from straightforward adventure like *You Must Never Go Back*, in which a young man returns to the scene of his parents' murder to put to rest childhood nightmares, only to find Italian murderers ready to finish the job, to romantic intrigue like *Kate*, *Sara*, and *Judith*, Regency novels focusing on women who survive revolution, prison, poverty, and heartbreak.

—Virginia Macdonald

CLIFFORD, Francis. Pseudonym for Arthur Leonard Bell Thompson. British. Born in Bristol, 1 December 1917. Educated at Christ's Hospital, Horsham, Sussex, 1928–35. Served in the Burma Rifles, 1939–43, and as Special Operations Executive, 1943–45: Distinguished Service Order. Married 1) Marjorie Bennett in 1944 (marriage dissolved), one son; 2) Josephine Bridget Devereux in 1955, one son. Commercial Assistant in the rice trade, London, 1935–38, and Burma, 1938–39; Industrial Journalist in the steel industry, London, 1946–59. Recipient: Crime Writers Association Silver Dagger, 1969. *Died 24 August 1975.*

CRIME PUBLICATIONS

Novels

   The Trembling Earth.   London, Hamish Hamilton, 1955.

Overdue.   London, Hamish Hamilton, 1957; New York, Dutton, 1958.

Act of Mercy.   London, Hamish Hamilton, and New York, Coward McCann, 1960; as
    Guns of Darkness, New York, Dell, 1962.

Time Is an Ambush.   London, Hodder and Stoughton, 1962.

The Green Fields of Eden.   London, Hodder and Stoughton, and New York, Coward
    McCann, 1963.

The Hunting-Ground.   London, Hodder and Stoughton, and New York, Coward
    McCann, 1964.

The Third Side of the Coin.   London, Hodder and Stoughton, and New York, Coward
    McCann, 1965.

The Naked Runner.   London, Hodder and Stoughton, and New York, Coward
    McCann, 1966.

Spanish Duet: Two Novels of Suspense (includes *The Trembling Earth* and *Time Is an
    Ambush*).   New York, Coward McCann, 1966.

All Men Are Lonely Now.   London, Hodder and Stoughton, and New York, Coward
    McCann, 1967.

Another Way of Dying.   London, Hodder and Stoughton, 1968; New York, Coward
    McCann, 1969.

The Blind Side.   London, Hodder and Stoughton, and New York, Coward McCann,
    1971.

A Wild Justice.   London, Hodder and Stoughton, and New York, Coward McCann,
    1972.

Amigo, Amigo.   London, Hodder and Stoughton, and New York, Coward McCann,
    1973.

The Grosvenor Square Goodbye.   London, Hodder and Stoughton, 1974; as *Goodbye
    and Amen*, New York, Coward McCann, 1974.

Drummer in the Dark.   London, Hodder and Stoughton, and New York, Harcourt
    Brace, 1976.

Short Stories

Ten Minutes on a June Morning and Other Stories.   London, Hodder and Stoughton,
    1977.

OTHER PUBLICATIONS

Novels

Honour the Shrine.   London, Cape, 1953.

Something to Love.   London, Hamish Hamilton, 1958.

A Battle Is Fought to Be Won.   London, Hamish Hamilton, 1960; New York, Coward
    McCann, 1961.

Other

Desperate Journey.   London, Hodder and Stoughton, 1979.

*   *   *

"Only during strain − a moral, a physical, or a psychological strain − do you get to know
your own character; that's my experience from the war − it is only under such circumstances
that the right character of a man emerges." These remarks were made by Francis Clifford
when I interviewed him in London more than ten years ago, and they explain very much in
his novels.

Clifford's first novels were war novels set in Southeast Asia, and they are still very readable, especially as they seem based on his own adventures during the Second World War, when he belonged to the Special Operations Executive, first in India and later in London. His favourite among these books was *A Battle Is Fought to Be Won*, which he considered as his most honest war novel.

But there is no doubt that his later thrillers are of much greater importance, for example, *The Green Fields of Eden* with its portrait of an Englishman with a serious disease living on a tropical island where he is confronted with a hired killer, and *The Naked Runner*, which is written in the same vein as the novels by Len Deighton and John le Carré. In my opinion however, the most ambitious novels by Clifford are *All Men Are Lonely Now*, *The Blind Side*, and *Amigo, Amigo*. These form a trilogy in which he deals with the moral dilemmas of man varied in three extremely fascinating ways. The courses of events in the books are different, as are the geographical backgrounds – England, Biafra, and Central America – but the theme is the same: the demands of loyalty and the stress that loyalty may lead to.

Ernest Hemingway was among Clifford's literary favourites and also – naturally enough – Graham Greene. Clifford, in fact, is the only thriller writer of the 1960's and 1970's who continues the tradition of Graham Greene as seen in such works as *The Power and the Glory* and *The Heart of the Matter*. Religion is a recurrent theme in some of the novels of Clifford – and it is probably not mere chance that, like Greene, he converted to catholicism.

To be sure, some of Clifford's novels are somewhat superficial, with rather impersonally constructed scenes of suspense, but this can not conceal the fact that in many ways he is a greater artist that most of his contemporaries.

—Jan Broberg

CLINTON-BADDELEY, V(ictor Vaughan Reynolds Geraint) C(linton). Born in Budleigh Salterton, Devon, in 1900. Educated at Sherborne School, Dorset; Jesus College, Cambridge, M.A. Editor in the moderm history section of the Encyclopaedia Britannica; actor: toured in the U.S.A. with Ben Greet Company; gave many poetry readings and ran Jupiter Records which specialised in poetry recordings. *Died 6 August 1970.*

CRIME PUBLICATIONS

Novels (series character: Dr. R. V. Davie in all books)

Death's Bright Dart. London, Gollancz, 1967; New York, Morrow, 1970.
My Foe Outstretch'd Beneath the Tree. London, Gollancz, and New York, Morrow, 1968.
Only a Matter of Time. London, Gollancz, 1969; New York, Morrow, 1970.
No Case for the Police. London, Gollancz, and New York, Morrow, 1970.
To Study a Long Silence. London, Gollancz, 1972.

OTHER PUBLICATIONS

Plays

Behind the Beyond, adaptation of the story by Stephen Leacock (produced London, 1926). London, Gowans and Gray, and Boston, Baker, 1932.
The Cup That Cheers, with Joyce Dennys (produced 1927). London, Gowans and Gray, and Boston, Baker, 1934.

Aladdin; or, Love Will Find Out the Way, music by Walter Leigh (produced London, 1931). London, Westminster Press, 1931.
The Split in the Cabinet, adaptation of a story by Stephen Leacock (produced London, 1931). London, Gowans and Gray, 1938.
The Billiard Room Mystery; or, Who D'You Think Did It?, adaptation of a story by Stephen Leacock (produced Cambridge, 1931). London, Gowans and Gray, and Boston, Baker, 1934.
The Pride of the Regiment; or, Cashiered for His Country: An Operetta, with Scobie Mackenzie, music by Walter Leigh (also director: produced London, 1932). London, Westminster Press, 1932.
Winsome Winnie: A Romantic Drama, adaptation of the story by Stephen Leacock (broadcast, 1944). London, Gowans and Gray, 1932.
Jolly Roger; or, The Admiral's Daughter: A Comic Opera, with Scobie Mackenzie, music by Walter Leigh (produced London, 1933). London, Boosey, 1933.
Nichevo, with Scobie Mackenzie (produced London, 1934). London, French, 1938.
Cinderella: A Cynical Pantomine, music by Walter Leigh. London, French, 1935.
The Babes in the Wood: A Cynical Pantomime. London, French, 1935.
Sherborne Story: A Chronicle Play. Winchester, Warren, 1950.
Jack and the Beanstalk; or, Love Conquers All, music by Gavin Gordon (broadcast, 1952). London, French, 1953.
Dick Whittington; or, Love Is the Key That Opens Every Door, music by Gavin Gordon. London, French, 1959.
Sleeping Beauty, music by Julian Leigh and Courtney Kenny. London, French, 1959.

Screenplay: *Born That Way*, with Diana Bourbon, 1936.

Radio Plays: *Nicholas Nickleby*, from the novel by Dickens, 1929; *Mr. Pickwick's a Hundred Years Old*, 1936; *Up the Garden* (parts 2 and 3), 1938; *Mr. Pickwick*, 1939; *Winsome Winnie*, 1944; *Stephen Leacock*, 1944; *Bardell v. Pickwick*, from *The Pickwick Papers* by Dickens, 1945; *Thomas Campion*, 1946; *A Tale of Two Cities*, from the novel by Dickens, 1947; *Jack and the Beanstalk*, 1952; *Benevolent Teachers of Youth 1820–1840*, 1955.

Verse

Songs from the Festival Revue. Cambridge, Arliss, 1931.

Other

Devon. London, A. and C. Black, 1935.
Words for Music (essays). Cambridge, University Press, 1941.
The Burlesque Tradition in the English Theatre after 1660. London, Methuen, 1952; New York, Bloom, 1971.
All Right on the Night (on the Georgian theatre). London, Putnam, 1954.
Some Pantomime Pedigrees. London, Society for Theatre Research, 1963.

Editor, *The What D'Ye Call It: An Opera by Phyllis Tate, based on the Tragi-Comi-Pastoral Farce by John Gay*. London, Oxford University Press, 1966.

Theatrical Activities:

Director: **Play** – *The Pride of the Regiment*, London, 1932.
Actor: **Plays** – John Williams in *Water* by Molly Marshall-Hale, London, 1929; Francisco and Rosencrantz in *Hamlet* by Shakespeare, London, 1930; Perriton in *The Split in the Cabinet*, London, 1931; Pontius Pilate in *Judas* by R. V. Ratti, London, 1931; Abanazar in

Aladdin, London, 1931; General Sir Joshua Blazes in *The Pride of the Regiment*, London, 1932; Jens Schelotrup in *The Witch* by John Masefield, London, 1933; Julian Cleveland in *Cock Robin* by Elmer Rice and Philip Barry, London, 1933; The Abbot in *Montebanks* by Frank Birch, London, 1934; Semyon Semyonitch Kristoffy in *Nichevo*, London, 1934; roles in *Victoria Regina* by Laurence Housman, London, 1935.

*   *   *

The five mysteries that V. C. Clinton-Baddeley wrote are special treats. At a time when many writers were turning away from the classical, fair-play detective story, Clinton-Baddeley was demonstrating that the form still had considerable life left in it. More than that, however, mystery readers should be thankful to Clinton-Baddeley for creating one of the most personable, believable, and downright likeable amateur detectives in the history of the genre. Indeed, Dr. R. V. Davie of St. Nicholas College, Cambridge, is so delightful that the reader easily overlooks the occasional flaws in the stories as detective tales. In his seventies, Dr. Davie is blessed with good health, a superb memory, and an ever-active mind which puzzles out patterns in wallpaper and carpets when it is not busy remembering how things were and how they have changed. He is ever being reminded of sights and events of his long-distant youth, not in the manner of one hungering disconsolately after a never-again-to-be-experienced past, but, rather, in the manner of a collector, for whom the possession of memories is a pleasure second only to the making of them. Dr. Davie uses the experiences of his seven decades, his understanding of human nature and behavior, and his keen intelligence to ferret out solutions to problems which have baffled the police or, in one instance, have been dismissed by the police as not being crimes at all. Clinton-Baddeley writes delightful dialogue, and this, combined with his knack for creating entertaining characters, insures a pleasant read from first page to last. His books are witty, literate, and superb.

—Guy M. Townsend

COBB, G(eoffrey) Belton. British. Born in Tunbridge Wells, Kent, in 1892. Sales Director, Longman, publishers, London, before World War II; during the war worked for the British Council. Regular contributor to *Punch* and other magazines. *Died 15 August 1971.*

CRIME PUBLICATIONS

Novels (series characters: Bryan Armitage; Inspector Cheviot Burmann; Superintendent Manning)

> *No Alibi* (Burmann). London, Longman, 1936.
> *The Poisoner's Mistake* (Burmann). London, Longman, 1936.
> *Fatal Dose* (Burmann). London, Longman, 1937.
> *Quickly Dead* (Burmann). London, Longman, 1937.
> *The Fatal Holiday* (Burmann). London, Longman, 1938.
> *Like a Guilty Thing* (Burmann). London, Longman, 1938; New York, British Book Centre, 1959.
> *Death Defies the Doctor* (Burmann). London, Longman, 1939.
> *Inspector Burmann's Busiest Day.* London, Longman, 1939.
> *Sergeant Ross in Disguise.* London, Longman, 1940.

Home Guard Mystery.   London, Longman, 1941.
Inspector Burmann's Black-Out.   London, Longman, 1941.
Double Detection (Burmann).   London, Longman, 1945.
Death in the 13th Dose (Burmann).   London, Longman, 1946.
Early Morning Poison (Manning).   London, Longman, 1947.
The Framing of Carol Woan (Manning).   London, Longman, 1948.
The Secret of Superintendent Manning.   London, Longman, 1948.
No Last Words (Manning).   London, Longman, 1949.
Stolen Strychnine (Manning).   London, Longman, 1949.
The Lunatic, The Lover.   London, Methuen, 1950.
No Charge for Poison (Manning).   London, Methuen, 1950.
Next-Door to Death (Burmann).   London, Methuen, 1952.
No Mercy for Margaret (Burmann).   London, Methuen, 1952.
Corpse Incognito.   London, Methuen, 1953.
Detective in Distress (Burmann).   London, Methuen, 1953.
Need a Body Tell? (Burmann).   London, W. H. Allen, 1954.
The Willing Witness (Burmann).   London, W. H. Allen, 1955.
Corpse at Casablanca (Burmann).   London, W. H. Allen, and New York, Abelard
   Schuman, 1956.
Drink Alone and Die (Burmann).   London, W. H. Allen, 1956.
Doubly Dead (Burmann).   London, W. H. Allen, 1956.
Poisoner's Base (Burmann).   London, W. H. Allen, 1957; New York, British Book
   Centre, 1958.
The Missing Scapegoat (Burmann).   London, W. H. Allen, 1958.
With Intent to Kill.   London, W. H. Allen, and New York, British Book Centre, 1958.
Death with a Difference (Burmann).   London, W. H. Allen, 1960.
Don't Lie to the Police (Burmann).   London, W. H. Allen, 1960.
Corpse in the Cargo (Burmann).   London, W. H. Allen, 1961.
Search for Sergeant Baxter (Burmann).   London, W. H. Allen, 1961.
Murder: Men Only (Burmann).   London, W. H. Allen, 1962.
Death of a Peeping Tom (Burmann).   London, W. H. Allen, 1963.
Dead Girl's Shoes (Burmann).   London, W. H. Allen, 1964.
No Shame for the Devil (Burmann).   London, W. H. Allen, 1964.
I Never Miss Twice (Burmann, Armitage).   London, W. H. Allen, 1965.
Last Drop (Burmann).   London, W. H. Allen, 1965.
Some Must Watch (Burmann).   London, W. H. Allen, 1966.
A Stone for His Head (Burmann).   London, W. H. Allen, 1966.
Lost Without Trace (Burmann).   London, W. H. Allen, 1967.
Security Secrets Sold Here.   London, W. H. Allen, 1967.
Secret Enquiry (Burmann, Armitage).   London, W. H. Allen, 1968.
Silence under Threat.   London, W. H. Allen, 1968.
Scandal at Scotland Yard (Armitage).   London, W. H. Allen, 1969.
Food for Felony (Armitage).   London, W. H. Allen, 1969.
Catch Me – If You Can.   London, W. H. Allen, 1970.
The Horrible Man in Heron's Wood.   London, W. H. Allen, 1970.
I Fell among Thieves.   London, W. H. Allen, 1971.
Suspicion in Triplicate.   London, W. H. Allen, 1971.

Uncollected Short Story

   "Mr. Flexman's Boast," in *Detective Stories of Today*, edited by Raymond
      Postgate.   London, Faber, 1940.

OTHER PUBLICATIONS

Novels

Stand to Arms. London, Wells Gardner, 1916.
Island Adventurers. London, Wells Gardner, 1927.

Other

A Price on Their Heads (juvenile). London, A. and C. Black, 1930.
Critical Years at the Yard: The Career of Frederick Williamson of the Detective Department and the C.I.D. London, Faber, 1956.
The First Detectives and the Early Career of Richard Mayne, Commissioner of Police. London, Faber, 1958.
Criminals Confess. London, Faber, 1959.
Murdered on Duty: A Chronicle of the Killing of Policemen. London, W. H. Allen, 1961.
Trials – and Errors: 11 Miscarriages of Justice. London, W. H. Allen, 1962.

*   *   *

G. Belton Cobb was an English editor, journalist, and novelist who wrote some thirty-five detective novels, including a half dozen on Scotland Yard. Cheviot Burmann is his major series character. *Corpse at Casablanca*, while lacking in logic and "fairness" as a detective story, is remarkably light and fast in style. Inspector Cheviot Burmann and his bride are on their honeymoon on a cruise ship along the North African coast when a body calls him to duty. In *Poisoner's Base*, the Inspector is on vacation in Dartmoor when he encounters a clever method of prison escape. Again the writing is fast-paced and lightweight and the puzzle this time is well-conceived. *Like a Guilty Thing* is generally considered his best work. Inspector Burmann's specialty, poisoning, is again used in a neat plot. Cobb's characterization of a middle-aged nurse who is not sure whether she committed the murder is engrossing. His *With Intent to Kill*, on the other hand, is a poorly plotted story in which the Inspector ploddingly appears, tediously questioning witness after witness about the oxalic acid in the hangover "preventative." Belton Cobb's earlier books are the better; as his output increased, his style seemed increasingly pedestrian and dreary.

—Daniel P. King

COE, Tucker. See **WESTLAKE, Donald E.**

COHEN, Octavus Roy. American. Born in Charleston, South Carolina, 26 June 1891. Educated at Porter Military Academy, Charleston; Clemson Agricultural College, South Carolina, B.S. 1911; studied law in his father's office, and admitted to the South Carolina Bar,

1913. Served in the United States Naval Reserve, 1939–40: Lieutenant. Married Inez Lopez in 1914; one son. Civil engineer, Tennessee Coal Iron and Railroad Company, 1909–10; newspaperman for Birmingham *Ledger*, Charleston *News and Courier*, Bayonne *Times*, New Jersey, and Newark *Morning Star*, before practising law, Charleston, 1913–15. Self-employed writer after 1915. Litt. D.: Birmingham Southern College, 1927. *Died 6 January 1959.*

CRIME PUBLICATIONS

Novels (series characters: David Carroll; Jim Hanvey)

The Other Woman, with J. U. Giesy. New York, Macaulay, 1917; London, Wells Gardner, 1920.
The Crimson Alibi. New York, Dodd Mead, and London, Nash, 1919.
Gray Dusk (Carroll). New York, Dodd Mead, and London, Nash, 1920.
Six Seconds of Darkness (Carroll). New York, Dodd Mead, and London, Nash, 1921.
Midnight (Carroll). New York, Dodd Mead, and London, Nash, 1922.
The Iron Chalice. Boston, Little Brown, 1925; London, Cassell, 1926.
The Outer Gate. Boston, Little Brown, and London, Hodder and Stoughton, 1927.
The May Day Mystery (Hanvey). New York, Appleton, 1929.
The Backstage Mystery (Hanvey). New York, Appleton, 1930; as *Curtain at Eight*, New York, Grossett and Dunlap, 1933.
Lilies of the Alley. New York, Appleton, 1931.
Star of Earth. New York, Appleton, 1932.
The Townsend Murder Mystery (novelization of radio play). New York, Appleton Century, 1933.
Child of Evil. New York, Appleton Century, 1936.
I Love You Again. New York, Appleton Century, 1937; as *There's Always Time to Die*, New York, Popular Library, 1949.
East of Broadway. New York, Appleton Century, 1938.
Romance in Crimson. New York, Appleton Century, 1940; as *Murder in Season*, New York, Popular Library, 1946.
Lady in Armor. New York, Appleton Century, 1941.
Sound of Revelry. New York, Macmillan, 1943; London, Hale, 1945.
Romance in the First Degree. New York, Macmillan, 1944; London, Hale, 1951.
Danger in Paradise. New York, Macmillan, 1945; London, Hale, 1949.
Dangerous Lady. New York, Macmillan, 1946; London, Barker, 1948.
Love Has No Alibi. New York, Macmillan, 1946; London, Hale, 1952.
Don't Ever Love Me. New York, Macmillan, 1947; London, Barker, 1948.
My Love Wears Black. New York, Macmillan, 1948; London, Barker, 1949.
More Beautiful Than Murder. New York, Macmillan, 1948; London, Barker, 1950.
A Bullet for My Love. New York, Macmillan, 1950; London, Barker, 1951.
The Corpse That Walked. New York, Fawcett, 1951; London, Red Seal, 1957.
Lost Lady. New York, Fawcett, 1951; London, Fawcett, 1953.
Love Can Be Dangerous. New York, Macmillan, and London, Barker, 1955; as *The Intruder*, Hasbrouck Heights, New Jersey, Graphic, 1956.

Short Stories

Jim Hanvey, Detective. New York, Dodd Mead, 1923; London, Nash, 1924.
Detours. Boston, Little Brown, 1927.
Florian Slappey Goes Abroad. Boston, Little Brown, 1928.
Cameos. New York, Appleton, 1931.

Scrambled Yeggs.   New York, Appleton Century, 1934.
Florian Slappey.   New York, Appleton Century, 1938.

Uncollected Short Stories

"Always Trust a Cop," in *Queen's Awards, Seventh Series*, edited by Ellery
Queen.   Boston, Little Brown, 1952; London, Gollancz, 1954.
"Let Me Kill You Sweetheart," in *The Saint* (New York), October–November 1953.
"The Midway Murder," in *The Saint* (New York), May 1954.
"Sweet Music and Murder," in *The Saint* (New York), January 1955.
"The Bridal-Night Murder," in *The Saint* (New York), September 1956.
"Double Jeopardy," in *The Saint* (New York), December 1957.

OTHER PUBLICATIONS

Novels

Polished Ebony.   New York, Dodd Mead, 1919.
Come Seven.   New York, Dodd Mead, 1920.
Sunclouds.   New York, Dodd Mead, 1924; London, Hodder and Stoughton, 1925.
The Other Tomorrow.   New York, Appleton, 1927.
The Light Shines Through.   Boston, Little Brown, 1928.
Spring Tide.   New York, Appleton, 1928.
The Valley of Olympus.   New York, Appleton, 1929.
Epic Peters, Pullman Porter.   New York, Appleton, 1930.
Scarlet Woman.   New York, Appleton Century, 1934.
Transient Lady.   New York, Appleton Century, 1934.
Back to Nature.   New York, Appleton Century, 1935.
With Benefit of Clergy.   New York, Appleton Century, 1935.
Strange Honeymoon.   New York, Appleton Century, 1939.
Kid Tinsel.   New York, Appleton Century, 1941.
Borrasca.   New York, Macmillan, 1953; London, Barker, 1954.

Short Stories

Highly Colored.   New York, Dodd Mead, 1921.
Assorted Chocolates.   New York, Dodd Mead, 1922; London, Hodder and Stoughton,
1925.
Dark Days and White Knights.   New York, Dodd Mead, 1923.
Bigger and Blacker.   Boston, Little Brown, 1925.
Black and Blue.   Boston, Little Brown, 1926.
Carbon Copies.   New York, Appleton, 1932.

Plays

The Crimson Alibi (produced New York, 1919).
Come Seven, adaptation of his own novel (produced New York, 1920).   New York,
Longman, 1927.
The Melancholy Dane, in *The Appleton Book of Short Plays*, 2nd series, edited by Kenyon
Nicholson.   New York, Appleton, 1927.

Other plays: *The Scourge*, 1920; *Shadows*, 1920; *Every Saturday Night*, 1921; *Alias Mrs. Roberts*, 1928.

Radio Plays: *Amos 'n' Andy* series, 1945–46.

* * *

A prolific American author of countless short stories and many detective novels, Octavus Roy Cohen is best known for the creation of his extremely soft-hearted and amiable detective, Jim Hanvey, who first appeared in *Jim Hanvey, Detective*. This book was later nominated by Ellery Queen as a book of historical value with a high quality of literary style.

A man of immense proportions, wearing clothes that always seemed too large, Jim Hanvey had remarkable fishlike eyes and always sported a gold toothpick attached to his vest by a long gold chain. It had been given to him as a token of good will by a crook he had sent up for a long stretch. Reformed criminals were some of Hanvey's closest allies, but he was relentless in their pursuit should they ever go astray.

One other noteworthy character introduced by Cohen was Florian Slappey, the opposite of Jim Hanvey in almost every respect, the Black Beau Brummell of Birmingham, Alabama, meticulous in dress, and manner. His witty and humorous adventures are related in two collections of stories, *Florian Slappey Goes Abroad* and *Florian Slappey*.

Cohen's literary style is smooth, his characters romanticized but credible, and his suspenseful plots are varied. The settings range from Broadway to Hollywood with a few like *I Love You Again*, set in Cohen's native South.

—Mary Ann Grochowski

COLE, G. D. H. and Margaret.　British.　**COLE, G(eorge) D(ouglas) H(oward):**　Born 25 September 1889. Educated at St. Paul's School, London; Balliol College, Oxford (Domus and Jenkyns exhibitioner). Head of Research Department, Amalgamated Society of Engineers, 1914–18, and trade union economic adviser during World War I; Head of Nuffield College Social Reconstruction Survey during World War II. Married Margaret Isabel Postgate in 1918; one son and two daughters. Fellow, Magdalen College, Oxford, 1912–19; Deputy Professor of Philosophy, Armstrong College, University of Durham, 1913–14; Head of Tutorial Classes Department, University of London, 1919–25; Fellow, University College, Oxford, and University Reader in Economics, 1925–44; Fellow, All Souls College, Oxford, 1944–57; Chichele Professor of Social and Political Theory, Oxford University, 1944–57; Sub-Warden, later Fellow, and from 1957, Research Fellow, Nuffield College, Oxford. Associated from 1912 with the Workers' Educational Association: vice-president for some years, and acting president for one year; Director of Labour Party Research from 1918; staff member, *New Statesman*, London, 1918 to the 1940's; General Editor, Oxford Studies in Economics and Hutchinson's University Library. President, University Socialist Federation; Founding President, Association of Tutors in Adult Education; Chairman, 1939–46 and 1948–50, and President, 1952–59, Fabian Society. Honorary Fellow, University College and Balliol College, Oxford. *Died 15 January 1959.*　**COLE, Margaret (Isabel, née Postgate):**　Born in Cambridge, 6 May 1893; sister of Raymond Postgate, *q.v.* Educated at Roedean School, Brighton; Girton College, Cambridge, B.A. (honours) in classics 1914. Married G. D. H. Cole in 1918 (died, 1959); one son and two daughters. Classical Mistress, St. Paul's Girls' School, London, 1914–16; Assistant Secretary, Labour Research Department, London, 1917–25; Lecturer, University Tutorial classes,

London, 1925–49, and Cambridge, 1941–44. Honorary Secretary, New Fabian Research Bureau, 1935–39; Honorary Secretary, 1939–53, Chairman, 1955, and President from 1963, Fabian Society; Member of the Education Committee, 1943–65 (Chairman, Further Education Committee, 1951–60 and 1961–65), and Alderman, 1952–65, London County Council; Member of the Education Committee and Vice-Chairman of the Further and Higher Education Sub-Committee, Inner London Education Authority, 1965–67; Chairman, Geffrye Museum, Sidney Webb College of Education, and Battersea College of Education, all London. Honorary Fellow, London School of Economics. Fellow, Royal Historical Society. O.B.E. (Officer, Order of the British Empire), 1965; D.B.E. (Dame Commander, Order of the British Empire), 1970. Address: 4 Ashdown, Cliveden Court, London W13 8DR, England. The Coles: Editor, *The Guildsman*, later *The Guild Socialist*, London, 1916–23.

CRIME PUBLICATIONS

Novels (series characters: Superintendent Henry Wilson; Everard Blatchington; Dr. Tancred)

The Brooklyn Murders (Wilson; by G. D. H. Cole alone).   London, Collins, 1923; New York, Seltzer, 1924.

The Death of a Millionaire (Wilson).   London, Collins, and New York, Macmillan, 1925.

The Blatchington Tangle (Blatchington, Wilson).   London, Collins, and New York, Macmillan, 1926.

The Murder at Crome House.   London, Collins, and New York, Macmillan, 1927.

The Man from the River (Wilson).   London, Collins, and New York, Macmillan, 1928.

Poison in the Garden Suburb (Wilson).   London, Collins, and New York, Payson and Clarke, 1929.

Burglars in Bucks (Wilson).   London, Collins, 1930; as *The Berkshire Mystery*, New York, Brewer and Warren, 1930.

Corpse in Canonicals (Wilson).   London, Collins, 1930; as *Corpse in the Constable's Garden*, New York, Morrow, 1931; Collins, 1933.

The Great Southern Mystery (Wilson).   London, Collins, 1931; as *The Walking Corpse*, New York, Morrow, 1931.

The Floating Admiral, with others.   London, Hodder and Stoughton, 1931; New York, Doubleday, 1932.

Dead Man's Watch.   London, Collins, 1931; New York, Doubleday, 1932.

Death of a Star.   London, Collins, 1932; New York, Doubleday, 1933.

The Affair at Aliquid.   London, Collins, 1933.

End of an Ancient Mariner (Wilson).   London, Collins, 1933; New York, Doubleday, 1934.

Death in the Quarry (Wilson, Blatchington).   London, Collins, and New York, Doubleday, 1934.

Murder in Four Parts.   London, Collins, 1934.

Big Business Murder.   London, Collins, and New York, Doubleday, 1935.

Dr. Tancred Begins; or, The Pendexter Saga, First Canto.   London, Collins, and New York, Doubleday, 1935.

Scandal at School (Blatchington).   London, Collins, 1935; as *The Sleeping Death*, New York, Doubleday, 1936.

Last Will and Testament; or, The Pendexter Saga, Second (and Last) Canto (Tancred).   London, Collins, and New York, Doubleday, 1936.

The Brothers Sackville (Wilson).   London, Collins, 1936; New York, Macmillan, 1937.

Disgrace to the College.   London, Hodder and Stoughton, 1937.

The Missing Aunt.   London, Collins, 1937; New York, Macmillan, 1938.

Off with Her Head! (Wilson).   London, Collins, 1938; New York, Macmillan, 1939.

Double Blackmail (Wilson).   London, Collins, and New York, Macmillan, 1939.
Greek Tragedy (Wilson).   London, Collins, 1939; New York, Macmillan, 1940.
Murder at the Munition Works (Wilson).   London, Collins, and New York, Macmillan, 1940.
Counterpoint Murder (Wilson).   London, Collins, 1940; New York, Macmillan, 1941.
Knife in the Dark.   London, Collins, 1941; New York, Macmillan, 1942.
Toper's End (Wilson).   London, Collins, and New York, Macmillan, 1942.

Short Stories

Superintendent Wilson's Holiday.   London, Collins, 1928; New York, Payson and Clarke, 1929.
A Lesson in Crime and Other Stories.   London, Collins, 1933.
Mrs. Warrender's Profession.   London, Collins, 1938; New York, Macmillan, 1939.
Wilson and Some Others.   London, Collins, 1940.
Death in the Tankard (story).   London, Todd, 1943.
Strychnine Tonic, and A Dose of Cyanide.   London, Todd, 1943.
Birthday Gifts and Other Stories.   London, Todd, 1946.

OTHER PUBLICATIONS by G. D. H. Cole

Verse

The Record.   Privately printed, 1912.
New Beginnings, and The Record.   Oxford, Blackwell, 1914.
The Crooked World.   London, Gollancz, 1933.

Other

The Greater Unionism, with William Mellor.   Manchester, National Labour Press, 1913.
The World of Labour: A Discussion of the Present and Future of Trade Unionism.   London, Bell, 1913; revised edition, 1915.
Labour in War Time.   London, Bell, 1915.
Trade Unionism in War Time, with William Mellor.   London, Limit, 1915(?).
Some Problems of Urban and Rural Industry, with others.   Oxford, Council of Ruskin College, 1917.
The Principles of Socialism: A Syllabus, revised edition.   London, University Socialist Federation, 1917.
Self-Government in Industry.   London, Bell, 1917; revised edition, 1920; Freeport, New York, Books for Libraries, 1971.
The British Labour Movement: A Syllabus for Study Circles.   London, University Socialist Federation, 1917; revised edition, 1922; New York, Workers Education Bureau of America, 1924.
Trade Unionism on the Railways: Its History and Problems, with R. Page Arnot.   London, Allen and Unwin, 1917.
An Introduction to Trade Unionism.   London, Allen and Unwin, 1918; as *Organised Labour*, 1924; revised edition, 1929.
Labour in the Commonwealth: A Book for the Younger Generation.   London, Headley, 1918; New York, Huebsch, 1920.
The Meaning of Industrial Freedom, with William Mellor.   London, Allen and Unwin, 1918.
The Payment of Wages: A Study in Payment by Results under the Wage-System.   London, Allen and Unwin, 1918; revised edition, 1928.
Workers' Control in Industry.   London, Independent Labour Party, 1919.

Chaos and Order in Industry. London, Methuen, and New York, Stokes, 1920.
Democracy in Industry (lecture). Manchester, Manchester University Press, 1920.
Guild Socialism. London, Fabian Publications, 1920.
Guild Socialism Re-Stated. London, Parsons, 1920.
Social Theory. London, Methuen, and New York, Stokes, 1920; revised edition, Methuen, 1921.
Unemployment and Industrial Maintenance. London, Labour Publishing Company, 1921.
The Future of Local Government. London, Cassell, 1921.
Guild Socialism: A Plan for Economic Democracy. New York, Stokes, 1921.
English Economic History. London, Labour Research Department, 1922(?).
Labour in the Coal-Mining Industry 1914–1921. Oxford, Clarendon Press, 1923.
Unemployment: A Study Syllabus. London, Labour Research Department, 1923.
Out of Work: An Introduction to the Study of Unemployment. London, Labour Publishing Company, and New York, Knopf, 1923.
National Government and Inflation: Six Little Talks on Politics. London, Society for Socialist Inquiry, n.d.
Trade Unionism and Munitions. Oxford, Clarendon Press, 1923.
Rents, Rings, and Houses, with Margaret Cole. London, Labour Publishing Company, 1923.
Workshop Organisation. Oxford, Clarendon Press, 1923.
British Trade Unionism: Problems and Policy. London, Labour Research Department, 1923.
The Life of William Cobbett. London, Collins, and New York, Harcourt Brace, 1924; revised edition, London, Home and Van Thal, 1947; New York, Russell and Russell, 1971.
The Place of the Workers' Educational Association in Working Class Education. Leicester, Blackfriars Press, 1924(?).
Robert Owen. London, Benn, and Boston, Little Brown, 1925; as *The Life of Robert Owen*, London, Macmillan, 1930; Hamden, Connecticut, Archon Books, 1966.
William Cobbett. London, Fabian Publications, 1925; Folcroft, Pennsylvania, Folcroft Editions, 1973.
A Short History of the British Working Class Movement. London, Allen and Unwin, 3 vols., 1925–27; New York, Macmillan, 2 vols., 1927; revised edition, Allen and Unwin, 1937, 1948; Macmillan, 1938.
Industrial Policy for Socialists: A Syllabus. London, Independent Labour Party Information Committee, 1926.
A Select List of Books on Economic and Social History, with H. L. Beales. London, Tutors' Association, 1927.
The Economic System. London, Longman, 1927.
What to Read on English Economic History. Leeds, Leeds Public Libraries, 1928.
The Next Ten Years of British Social and Economic Policy. London, Macmillan, 1929.
Politics and Literature. London, Hogarth Press, and New York, Harcourt Brace, 1929.
Gold, Credit and Employment: Four Essays for Laymen. London, Allen and Unwin, 1930; New York, Macmillan, 1931.
Unemployment Problems in 1931, with others. Geneva, International Labour Organisation, 1931.
The Bank of England. London, Society for Socialist Inquiry and Propaganda, 1931(?).
How Capitalism Works. London, Society for Socialist Inquiry and Propaganda, 1931(?).
The Crisis: What It Is, How It Arose, What to Do, with Ernest Bevin. London, New Statesman and Nation, 1931.
British Trade and Industry, Past and Future. London, Macmillan, 1932.
Banks and Credit. London, Society for Socialist Inquiry and Propaganda, 1932.
Economic Tracts for the Times. London, Macmillan, 1932.

The Essentials of Socialisation. London, New Fabian Research Bureau, 1932.
Scope and Method in Social and Political Theory (lecture). Oxford, Clarendon Press, 1932.
What to Read on Economic Problems of Today and Tomorrow. Leeds, Leeds Public Libraries, 1932.
War Debts and Reparations: What They Are, Why They Must Be Cancelled, with Richard Seymour Postgate. London, New Statesman and Nation, 1932.
The Intelligent Man's Guide Through World Chaos. London, Gollancz, 1932; as *A Guide Through World Chaos*, New York, Knopf, 1932.
Some Essentials of Socialist Propaganda. London, Fabian Society, 1932.
Modern Theories and Forms of Industrial Organisation. London, Gollancz, 1932.
The Gold Standard. London, Society for Socialist Inquiry and Propaganda, 1932.
Theories and Forms of Political Organisation. London, Gollancz, 1932.
Saving and Spending; or, The Economics of "Economy." London, New Statesman and Nation, 1933.
Socialism in Pictures and Figures, with J. F. Horrabin. London, Socialist League, 1933.
The Intelligent Man's Guide to Europe Today, with Margaret Cole. London, Gollancz, and New York, Knopf, 1933.
A Plan for Britain. London, Clarion Press, 1933.
What Is This Socialism? Letters to a Young Inquirer. London, Gollancz, 1933.
A Study-Guide to Socialist Policy. London, Socialist League, 1934(?).
A Guide to Modern Politics, with Margaret Cole. London, Gollancz, and New York, Knopf, 1934.
Some Relations Between Political and Economic Theory. London, Macmillan, 1934.
Planning International Trade, with *Self-Sufficiency*, by Walter Lippmann. New York, Carnegie Endowment, 1934.
Studies in World Economics. London, Macmillan, 1934; Freeport, New York, Books for Libraries, 1967.
What Marx Really Meant. London, Gollancz, and New York, Knopf, 1934.
Marxism, with others. London, Chapman and Hall, 1935.
The Need for a Socialist Programme, with Dick Mitchison. London, Socialist League, 1935(?).
Principles of Economic Planning. London, Macmillan, 1935; as *Economic Planning*, New York, Knopf, 1935.
The Simple Case for Socialism. London, Gollancz, 1935.
Fifty Propositions about Money and Production. London, Nott, 1936.
The Condition of Britain, with Margaret Cole. London, Gollancz, 1937.
The People's Front. London, Gollancz, 1937.
What Is Ahead of Us?, with others. London, Allen and Unwin, 1937.
Practical Economics; or, Studies in Economic Planning. London, Penguin, 1937.
The Common People 1746–1938, with Raymond Postgate. London, Methuen, 1938; revised edition, 1946; as *The British Common People*, New York, Knopf, 1939; revised edition, as *The British People*, Knopf, 1947.
Living Wages: The Case for a New Minimum Wage Act. London, Gollancz, 1938.
The Machinery of Socialist Planning. London, Hogarth Press, 1938.
Economic Prospects: 1938 and After. London, Fact, 1938.
Persons and Periods: Studies. London, Macmillan, 1938; New York, Kelley, 1969.
Etude du Statut de la Production et du Rôle du Capital, with Thomas Nixon Carver and Carl Brinkmann. Paris, Librarie du Recueil Sirey, 1938.
Socialism in Evolution. London, Penguin, 1938.
British Trade-Unionism Today: A Survey, with the Collaboration of Thirty Trade Union Leaders and Other Experts. London, Gollancz, 1939; revised edition, as *An Introduction to Trade Unionism*, London, Allen and Unwin, 1953; New York, Barnes and Noble, 1955.

Plan for Democratic Britain.   London, Labour Book Service, 1939.
War Aims.   London, New Statesman and Nation, 1939.
British Working Class Politics 1834–1914.   London, Routledge, 1941.
James Keir Hardie.   London, Gollancz, 1941.
Chartist Portraits.   London, Macmillan, 1941; New York, St. Martin's Press, 1965.
A Letter to an Industrial Manager.   London, Fabian Publications, 1941.
Europe, Russia and the Future.   London, Gollancz, 1941; New York, Macmillan, 1942.
The War on the Home Front.   London, Fabian Society, 1941.
Victory or Vested Interest?   London, Routledge, 1942.
A Memorandum on the Reorganization of Local Government in England.   New York, Committee on Public Administration, 1942.
Great Britain in the Post-War World.   London, Gollancz, 1942.
Beveridge Explained: What the Beveridge Report on Social Security Means.   London, New Statesman and Nation, 1942.
The Fabian Society, Past and Present.   London, Fabian Society, 1942; revised edition, with Margaret Cole, London, Fabian Publications, 1952.
Richard Carlile, 1790–1843.   London, Gollancz, 1943.
John Burns.   London, Gollancz, 1943.
Building Societies and the Housing Problem.   London, Dent, 1943.
Fabian Socialism.   London, Allen and Unwin, 1943.
Monetary Systems and Theories.   London, Rotary International, 1943.
When the Fighting Stops.   London, National Peace Council, 1943.
The Means to Full Employment.   London, Gollancz, 1943.
How to Obtain Full Employment.   London, Odhams Press, 1944.
The Planning of World Trade.   London, Odhams Press, 1944.
A Century of Co-Operation (history of the Co-Operative movement).   London, Allen and Unwin, 1944.
The British Working-Class Movement: An Outline and Study-Guide.   London, Fabian Publications, 1944; revised edition, 1949.
Money: Its Present and Future.   London, Cassell, 1944; revised edition, 1947; revised edition, as *Money, Trade, and Investment,* 1954.
Reparations and the Future of German Industry.   London, Fabian Publications, 1945.
Welfare and Peace, with John Boyd Orr.   London, National Peace Council, 1945.
The Co-Ops and Labour.   London, London Co-Operative Society, 1945.
Building and Planning.   London, Cassell, 1945.
Banks and Credit.   London, Society for Socialist Inquiry and Propaganda, 1946(?).
Labour's Foreign Policy.   London, New Statesman and Nation, 1946.
The Intelligent Man's Guide to the Post-War World.   London, Gollancz, 1947.
A Guide to the Elements of Socialism.   London, Labour Party, 1947.
Local and Regional Government.   London, Cassell, 1947.
The Rochdale Principles: Their History and Application (lecture).   London, London Co-Operative Society, 1947.
Samuel Butler and The Way of All Flesh.   London, Home and Van Thal, 1947; as *Samuel Butler,* Denver, Swallow, 1948.
The National Coal Board: Its Tasks, Its Organisation, and Its Prospects.   London, Fabian Publications, 1948.
A History of the Labour Party from 1914.   London, Routledge, 1948; New York, Kelley, 1969.
British Social Services.   London, Longman, 1948.
The Meaning of Marxism.   London, Gollancz, 1948; Ann Arbor, University of Michigan Press, 1964.
Europe and the Problem of Democracy.   London, National Peace Council, 1948.
Why Nationalise Steel?   London, New Statesman and Nation, 1948; revised edition, 1948.

World in Transition: A Guide to the Shifting Political and Economic Forces of Our Time. New York, Oxford University Press, 1949.

Facts for Socialists, revised edition. London, Fabian Publications, 1949.

Labour's Second Term. London, Fabian Publications, 1949.

Consultation or Joint Management? A Contribution to the Discussion of Industrial Democracy, with J. M. Chalmers and Ian Mikardo. London, Fabian Publications, 1949.

Essays in Social Theory. London, Macmillan, 1950.

Socialist Economics. London, Gollancz, 1950.

Weakness Through Strength: The Economics of Re-Armament. London, Union of Democratic Control, 1951.

The British Co-Operative Movement in a Socialist Society: A Report. London, Allen and Unwin, 1951.

British Labour Movement: Retrospect and Prospect (lecture). London, Gollancz, 1951.

Samuel Butler. London, Longman, 1952; revised edition, 1961.

Introduction to Economic History 1750–1950. London, Macmillan, 1952; New York, St. Martin's Press, 1960.

The Development of Socialism During the Past Fifty Years (lecture). London, Athlone Press, 1952.

A History of Socialist Thought. London, Macmillan, 5 vols., and New York, St. Martin's Press, 5 vols., 1953–60.

Attempts at General Union: A Study in British Trade Union History 1818–1834. London, Macmillan, 1953.

Is This Socialism? London, New Statesman and Nation, 1954.

Studies in Class Structure. London, Routledge, 1955.

World Socialism Restated. London, New Statesman and Nation, 1956; revised edition, 1957.

The Post-War Condition of Britain. London, Routledge, and New York, Praeger, 1956.

What Is Wrong with Trade Unions? London, Fabian Society, 1956.

The Case for Industrial Partnership. London, Macmillan, and New York, St. Martin's Press, 1957.

William Morris as a Socialist (lecture). London, William Morris Society, 1960; Folcroft, Pennsylvania, Folcroft Editions, 1973.

Editor, with G. P. Dennis and Sherard Vines, *Oxford Poetry 1910–13.* Oxford, Blackwell, 1913.

Editor, with Sherard Vines, *Oxford Poetry 1914.* Oxford, Blackwell, 1914.

Editor, with T. W. Earp, *Oxford Poetry 1915.* Oxford, Blackwell, 1915.

Editor, *The Library of Social Studies.* London, Methuen, 4 vols., 1920–21.

Editor, with Margaret Cole, *The Bolo Book* (political songs). London, Allen and Unwin, 1921.

Editor, with Margaret Cole, *The Ormond Poets.* London, Noel Douglas, 16 vols., 1927–28.

Editor, *The Life and Adventures of Peter Porcupine, with Other Records of His Early Career in England and America,* by William Cobbett. London, Nonesuch Press, 1927.

Editor, with Margaret Cole, *Rural Rides in Southern, Western, and Eastern Counties of England, Together with Tours in Scotland and the Northern and Midland Counties of England and Letters from Ireland,* by William Cobbett. London, Davies, 3 vols., 1930.

Editor, with William Mellor, *Workers' Control and Self-Government in Industry.* London, Gollancz, 1933.

Editor, *What Everybody Wants to Know about Money: A Planned Outline of Monetary Problems by Nine Economists from Oxford.* London, Gollancz, 1933.

Editor, *Stories in Verse, Stories in Prose, Shorter Poems, Lectures and Essays*, by William Morris. London, Nonesuch Press, and New York, Random House, 1934.

Editor, *Studies in Capital and Investment*. London, Gollancz, 1935.

Editor, *The Rights of Man*, by Thomas Paine. London, Watts, 1937.

Editor, *Letters to Edward Thornton Written in the Years 1797 to 1800*, by William Cobbett. London, Oxford University Press, 1937.

Editor, with Margaret Cole, *The Opinions of William Cobbett*. London, Cobbett Publishing Company, 1944.

Editor, *The Essential Samuel Butler*. London, Cape, 1950.

Editor, with A. W. Filson, *British Working Class Movements: Selected Documents 1789–1875*. London, Macmillan, 1951; New York, St. Martin's Press, 1965.

Editor, with André Philip, *A Report on the Unesco La Brévière Seminar on Workers' Education*. Paris, Unesco, 1953.

Translator, *The Social Contract and Discourse*, by Rousseau. London, Dent, 1913; New York, Dutton, 1935.

Translator, *Planned Socialism*, by Henri de Man. London, Gollancz, 1935.

OTHER PUBLICATIONS by Margaret Cole

Verse

Bits of Things, with others. Cambridge, Heffer, 1914.

Poems. London, Allen and Unwin, 1918.

Other

A Story of Santa Claus for Little People. London, Bell, 1920.

The Control of Industry. London, Labour Publishing Company, 1921.

Rents, Rings, and Houses, with G. D. H. Cole. London, Labour Publishing Company, 1923.

An Introduction to World History for Classes and Study Circles. London, Labour Research Department, 1923.

Local Government for Beginners. London, Longman, 1927.

A Book List of Local Government. London, Tutors' Association, 1933.

The Intelligent Man's Guide to Europe Today, with G. D. H. Cole. London, Gollancz, and New York, Knopf, 1933.

A Guide to Modern Politics, with G. D. H. Cole. London, Gollancz, and New York, Knopf, 1934.

The Condition of Britain, with G. D. H. Cole. London, Gollancz, 1937.

The New Economic Revolution. London, Fact, 1937.

Books and the People. London, Hogarth Press, 1938.

Women of Today. London, Nelson, 1938.

Marriage, Past and Present. London, Dent, 1938; New York, AMS Press, 1975.

Wartime Billeting. London, Gollancz, 1941.

A Letter to a Student. London, Fabian Society, 1942.

Education for Democracy. London, Allen and Unwin, 1942.

The General Election, 1945, and After. London, Gollancz, 1945.

Beatrice Webb. London, Longman, 1945; New York, Harcourt Brace, 1946.

The Rate for the Job. London, Gollancz, 1946.

The Social Services and the Webb Tradition. London, Fabian Publications, 1946.

Makers of the Labour Movement. London, Longman, 1948.

Growing Up into Revolution (autobiography). London, Longman, 1949.

Miners and the Board. London, Fabian Publications, 1949.

The Fabian Society, Past and Present, revised edition, with G. D. H. Cole. London, Fabian Publications, 1952.

Robert Owen of New Lanark. London, Batchworth Press, and New York, Oxford University Press, 1953.

What Is a Comprehensive School? The London Plan in Practice. London, London Labour Party, 1953.

Beatrice and Sidney Webb. London, Fabian Society, 1955.

Servant of the County (on local government). London, Dobson, 1956.

Plan for Industrial Pensions. London, Fabian Society, 1956.

The Story of Fabian Socialism. London, Heinemann, and Stanford, California, Stanford University Press, 1961.

Robert Owen: Industrialist, Reformer, Visionary: Four Essays, with others. London, Robert Owen Bi-Centenary Association, 1971.

The Life of G. D. H. Cole. London, Macmillan, and New York, St. Martin's Press, 1971.

Editor, with G. D. H. Cole, *The Bolo Book* (poltiical songs). London, Allen and Unwin, 1921.

Editor, with G. D. H. Cole, *The Ormond Poets.* London, Noel Douglas, 16 vols., 1927–28.

Editor, with G. D. H. Cole, *Rural Rides in Southern, Western, and Eastern Counties of England, Together with Tours in Scotland and the Northern and Midland Counties of England and Letters from Ireland*, by William Cobbett. London, Davies, 3 vols., 1930.

Editor, *Twelve Studies in Soviet Russia.* London, Fabian Research Bureau, 1933.

Editor, *The Road to Success: Twenty Essays on the Choice of a Career for Women.* London, Methuen, 1936.

Editor, with Charles Smith, *Democratic Sweden: A Volume of Studies Prepared by Members of the New Fabian Research Bureau.* London, Routledge, 1938; New York, Greystone Press, 1939.

Editor, with Richard Padley, *Evacuation Survey: A Report to the Fabian Society.* London, Routledge, 1940.

Editor, *Our Soviet Ally.* London, Labour Book Service, 1943.

Editor, with G. D. H. Cole, *The Opinions of William Cobbett.* London, Cobbett Publishing Company, 1944.

Editor, with Barbara Drake, *Our Partnership*, by Beatrice Webb. London, Longman, 1948.

Editor, *The Webbs and Their Work.* London, Muller, 1949; New York, Barnes and Noble, 1974.

Editor, *Beatrice Webb: Diaries 1912–1924* and *1924–1932.* London, Longman, 2 vols., 1952–56.

*   *   *

In *The Life of G. D. H. Cole*, Dame Margaret Cole dismisses in two pages the detective fiction she and her husband co-authored. Both viewed the detective stories as a pleasant, undemanding sideline, and Dame Margaret's view that the books are "competent but not more" is accurate. Generally undistinguishable from dozens of other detective novels written during the interwar period, the Coles' work is marred by serious deficiencies in characterization and by slow-moving plots in which details are recapitulated at far-too-frequent intervals. G. D. H. Cole's reputation will, of course, rest upon his studies in social and economic history, especially the classic five-volume *History of Socialist Thought*, while Dame Margaret's is secured by her biography of Beatrice Webb and her edition of Mrs. Webb's journals. The detective stories provide only an interesting footnote to the lesiure-time activities of two eminent social historians.

The first Cole novel, *The Brooklyn Murders*, was written by G. D. H. alone. Subsequent novels appeared under a joint by-line, even though one author was usually responsible for an entire volume. In only a handful of books, most notably *Murder at the Munition Works*, is the Coles' socio-economic knowledge used to advantage. Country house and university settings, upper-class characters, and virtual absence of references to contemporary events are typical of the Coles' novels, as they are of others of the period. All the detectives, including Everard Blatchington, James Warrender, and the Coles' principal detective, Superintendent Henry Wilson, lack memorable personalities; Wilson, in fact, is surely one of the most colorless detectives ever created.

Of the country house novels, *Murder at Crome House* and *Double Blackmail* are perhaps the best. Casual amateur detection, light romantic interest, an unusual alibi, and clever unmasking of identity distinguish the first, while the second is a well-plotted account of blackmail and murder in a wealthy, respectable English family. In Amelia Selvidge, the family matriarch, and her son Brian, Bishop of Silchester, the Coles have created two characters who possess sufficient individuality to make their actions psychologically valid; and they have provided a delightfully satiric account of the political maneuvers by which Brian, a comfort-loving windbag, achieves his bishopric.

The Coles devoted a collection of short stories, *Mrs. Warrender's Profession*, to Warrender's mother. Other collections of short stories feature Wilson, who appears to advantage in the shorter form in which his methods of detection can be viewed without obscuring detail.

Of the Coles' remaining novels, *Counterpoint Murder*, *End of an Ancient Mariner*, and *Murder at the Munition Works* are worthy of attention. *Counterpoint Murder*, one of Wilson's best cases, has a skilfully worked out plot in which two men exchange victims in order to secure alibis and avoid suspicion. Sound police work eventually links the two apparently unrelated murders through a series of fairly presented clues. *End of an Ancient Mariner*, in which the villain is an appealing confidence man, contains careful reconstruction of past events by Wilson and an appealing character in Philip Blakway. *Murder at the Munition Works* is the one novel in which the Coles make extensive use of their knowledge of trade unionism and the working class. Set in a factory during an industrial dispute, the novel features a large cast of characters drawn from both management and labor. The Coles work out the solution to murder by traditional methods with careful attention to alibis, time-tables, and diagrams, while simultaneously offering fresh subject matter and characters unusual to the genre. It is to be regretted that they did not do so more often.

—Jeanne F. Bedell

COLES, Manning. Pseudonym for Cyril Henry Coles and Adelaide Frances Oke Manning. British. **COLES, Cyril Henry:** Born in London, 11 June 1899. Educated at a school in Petersfield, Hampshire. Served in the Hampshire Regiment and later with British Intelligence during World War I; also served with British Intelligence during World War II. Married Dorothy Cordelia Smith in 1934; two sons. Apprentice at John I. Thornycroft, shipbuilders, Southampton, after World War I; worked in Australia during the 1920's as a railwayman, garage manager, and columnist on a Melbourne newspaper; returned to England, 1928. Lived in East Meon, Hampshire. *Died 9 October 1965.* **MANNING, Adelaide Frances Oke:** Born in London. Educated at the High School for Girls, Tunbridge Wells, Kent. Worked in a munitions factory and at the War Office, London, during World War I. Lived in East Meon, Hampshire. *Died 25 September 1959.*

CRIME PUBLICATIONS

Novels (series character: Tommy Hambledon in all books except *This Fortress*)

Drink to Yesterday. London, Hodder and Stoughton, 1940; New York, Knopf, 1941.
Pray Silence. London, Hodder and Stoughton, 1940; as *A Toast for Tomorrow*, New York, Doubleday, 1941.
They Tell No Tales. London, Hodder and Stoughton, 1941; New York, Doubleday, 1942.
This Fortress. New York, Doubleday, 1942.
Without Lawful Authority. London, Hodder and Stoughton, and New York, Doubleday, 1943.
Green Hazard. London, Hodder and Stoughton, and New York, Doubleday, 1945.
The Fifth Man. London, Hodder and Stoughton, and New York, Doubleday, 1946.
Let the Tiger Die. New York, Doubleday, 1947; London, Hodder and Stoughton, 1948.
A Brother for Hugh. London, Hodder and Stoughton, 1947; as *With Intent to Deceive*, New York, Doubleday, 1947.
Among Those Absent. London, Hodder and Stoughton, and New York, Doubleday, 1948.
Diamonds to Amsterdam. New York, Doubleday, 1949; London, Hodder and Stoughton, 1950.
Not Negotiable. London, Hodder and Stoughton, and New York, Doubleday, 1949.
Dangerous by Nature. London, Hodder and Stoughton, and New York, Doubleday, 1950.
Now or Never. London, Hodder and Stoughton, and New York, Doubleday, 1951.
Alias Uncle Hugo. New York, Doubleday, 1952; London, Hodder and Stoughton, 1953; as *Operation Manhunt*, New York, Spivak, 1954.
Night Train to Paris. London, Hodder and Stoughton, and New York, Doubleday, 1952.
A Knife for the Juggler. London, Hodder and Stoughton, 1953; New York, Doubleday, 1964; as *The Vengeance Man*, New York, Pyramid, 1967.
Not for Export. London, Hodder and Stoughton, 1954; as *All That Glitters*, New York, Doubleday, 1954; as *The Mystery of the Stolen Plans*, New York, Berkley, 1960.
The Man in the Green Hat. London, Hodder and Stoughton, and New York, Doubleday, 1955.
The Basle Express. London, Hodder and Stoughton, and New York, Doubleday, 1956.
Birdwatcher's Quarry. New York, Doubleday, 1956; as *The Three Beans*, London, Hodder and Stoughton, 1957.
Death of an Ambassador. London, Hodder and Stoughton, and New York, Doubleday, 1957.
No Entry. London, Hodder and Stoughton, and New York, Doubleday, 1958.
Crime in Concrete. London, Hodder and Stoughton, 1960; as *Concrete Crime*, New York, Doubleday, 1960.
Search for a Sultan. London, Hodder and Stoughton, and New York, Doubleday, 1961.
The House at Pluck's Gutter. London, Hodder and Stoughton, 1963; New York, Pyramid, 1968.

Novels as Francis Gaite (series characters: Charles and James Latimer; published as Manning Coles in US)

Brief Candles (Latimers). London, Hodder and Stoughton, and New York, Doubleday, 1954.

Happy Returns (Latimers). New York, Doubleday, 1955; as *A Family Matter*, London, Hodder and Stoughton, 1956.
The Far Traveller. New York, Doubleday, 1956; London, Hodder and Stoughton, 1957.
Come and Go (Latimers). London, Hodder and Stoughton, and New York, Doubleday, 1958.
Duty Free. London, Hodder and Stoughton, and New York, Doubleday, 1959.

Short Stories

Nothing to Declare. New York, Doubleday, 1960.

Uncollected Short Story

"Death Keeps a Secret," in *The Mystery Bedside Book*, edited by John Creasey. London, Hodder and Stoughton, 1960.

OTHER PUBLICATIONS

Novel

Half-Valdez (by Manning alone). London, Hodder and Stoughton, 1939.

Other

Great Caesar's Ghost (juvenile). New York, Doubleday, 1943; as *The Emperor's Bracelet*, London, University of London Press, 1947.

*   *   *

The best-known longer works of the Manning Coles writing team are the Tommy Hambledon stories, featuring Thomas Elphinstone Hambledon of the British Intelligence Service. Tommy's adventures were based on Cyril Coles's own war experiences with the Nazis, and his characterization on a much-admired professor of Coles's. Tommy, like Coles, has a talent for emerging unscathed from behind enemy lines. And, like the professor, he has an uncanny knack at mastering foreign languages.

Drink to Yesterday and *Pray Silence* cover Tommy's experiences from the end of World War I until shortly before World War II. He is a victim of amnesia, but as the second novel draws to a close he discovers his real identity and looks forward to using his talents in the future to help Scotland Yard. However, as the 1940's ended, the public taste for spy fiction about Nazis declined, and the team attempted to adapt Tommy's adventures to the international scene of the 1950's. It was at this point that their reputation began to slip, with reviewers commenting on the formulaic nature of both settings and plots.

At about the same time, the team turned to a second type of fiction, loosely categorized as "novels." In reality they are thinly disguised ghost stories laced with a good bit of social satire, and, like the Tommy Hambledon series, were received at first with high praise.

In the first book in this series, *Brief Candles*, James and Charles Latimer – two cousins, the former English, the latter from Virginia – are killed and buried near each other alongside their pet monkey, Ulysses, who died with them in 1870 in the Franco–Prussian Wars. Later in the book, and in later books, the Latimers come back from the grave, accompanied by Ulysses, and help their descendant Richard Scroby through a number of hair-raising scrapes. *Brief Candles* was highly praised for its whimsical humor and charm; people seemed to enjoy reading about a crook named Pepi the Crocodile (he had a wide smile) and a thief named Finger Dupre. But even as early as the second book, reviewers began complaining that this kind of whimsical satire wears pretty thin.

And so, in 1959, the team tried a kind of fiction that could be termed a satiric romance, *Duty Free*. It did not feature Tommy Hambledon, but had lots of international skullduggery mingled with European urbanity. In short fiction, the team showed a similar pattern of running out of imaginative energy. In the mid-1940's they published a dozen short stories featuring Tommy Hambledon under the title *Nothing to Declare*. Threaded among the intrigue and adventure episodes are farcical characters like Superintendent Bagshott of Scotland Yard, Mr. Heaven, an undertaker, Joseph Joseph, a fence for stolen goods, and Butler Harry, a housebreaker. The stories are also full of ghosts, missing jewels, stolen tombstones and other predictable elements of whimsy.

—Elizabeth F. Duke

COLLIER, John (Henry Noyes). British. Born in London, 3 May 1901. Educated privately. Married 1) Shirley Lee Palmer in 1936 (divorced, 1943); 2) Margaret Elizabeth Eke in 1945. Poetry Editor, *Time and Tide*, London, in the 1920's and 1930's. Scriptwriter in the United States; lived in France. Now lives in London. Recipient: Mystery Writers of America Edgar Allan Poe Award, 1951; International Fantasy Award, 1952. Agent: A. D. Peters and Company Ltd., 10 Buckingham Street, London WC2N 6BU, England.

CRIME PUBLICATIONS

Short Stories

> *No Traveller Returns.* London, White Owl Press, 1931.
> *An Epistle to a Friend.* London, Ulysses Bookshop, 1931.
> *Green Thoughts.* London, Joiner and Steele, 1932.
> *The Devil and All.* London, Nonesuch Press, 1934.
> *Variation on a Theme.* London, Grayson, 1935.
> *Witch's Money.* New York, Viking Press, 1940.
> *Presenting Moonshine: Stories.* London, Macmillan, and New York, Viking Press, 1941.
> *The Touch of Nutmeg and More Unlikely Stories.* New York, Readers Club, 1943.
> *Green Thoughts and Other Strange Tales.* New York, Editions for the Armed Services, 1943.
> *Fancies and Goodnights.* New York, Doubleday, 1951; abridged version, as *Of Demons and Darkness*, London, Corgi, 1965.
> *Pictures in the Fire.* London, Hart Davis, 1958.

OTHER PUBLICATIONS

Novels

> *His Monkey Wife; or, Married to a Chimp.* London, Davies, 1930; New York, Appleton, 1931.
> *Tom's A-Cold.* London, Macmillan, 1933; as *Full Circle*, New York, Appleton Century, 1933.
> *Defy the Foul Fiend; or, The Misadventures of a Heart.* London, Macmillan, and New York, Knopf, 1934.

Plays

Wet Saturday (produced New York).   New York, One-Act, n.d.

His Monkey Wife, music by Sandy Wilson, adaptation of the novel by Collier (produced London, 1971).

Milton's "Paradise Lost": Screenplay for Cinema of the Mind.   New York, Knopf, 1973.

Screenplays: *Sylvia Scarlett*, with Gladys Unger and Mortimer Offner, 1936; *Elephant Boy* with Akos Tolnay and Marcia de Sylva, 1937; *Her Cardboard Lover*, with Anthony Veiller and William H. Wright, 1942; *Deception*, with Joseph Than, 1946; *Roseanna McCoy*, 1949; *The Story of Three Loves*, with others, 1953; *I Am a Camera*, 1955; *The War Lord*, with Millard Kaufman, 1965.

Verse

Gemini: Poems.   London, Ulysses Bookshop, 1931.

Other

Just the Other Day: An Informal History of Britain since the War, with Iain Lang.   London, Hamish Hamilton, and New York, Harper, 1932.

The John Collier Reader.   New York, Knopf, 1972; London, Souvenir Press, 1975.

Editor, *The Scandal and Credulities of John Aubrey.*   London, Davies, and New York, Appleton, 1931.

*   *   *

The short stories of John Collier have been favorites of fantasy and mystery anthologists for nearly fifty years, ever since Dashiell Hammett reprinted *Green Thoughts* (about a sinister orchid) in his 1931 horror anthology *Creeps by Night*. The reason for their popularity with editors and readers is easy to understand. Collier has the knack of writing about the fantastic and the bizarre with a special quality that often approaches whimsey. It's doubtful if any reader was ever terrified or revolted by the horrors of John Collier. A more likely reaction would be a quiet chuckle of satisfaction.

Collier's two novels, *His Monkey Wife* and *Defy the Foul Fiend*, are both fantasies, as are many of his sixty or more short stories. But several stories dealing with murder are of special interest to mystery readers. Two of the most familiar are "De Mortuis" and "Back for Christmas," both included in Collier's mammoth collection *Fancies and Goodnights*. It's safe to say that most stories about a husband killing his wife and burying her body in the basement are variations on one or the other of these definitive tales. Yet another variation on the husband as wife-killer can be found in Collier's uncollected story "Anniversary Gift," in which the husband brings home a poisonous snake, with surprising results.

Other Collier stories deal with poison or the hint of poison, as in "Over Insurance" and "The Chaser." An elixir of youth figures in the non-criminous "Youth from Vienna," which could have been written by O. Henry. Another murder story, "Wet Saturday," was successfully presented on television by Alfred Hitchcock, and Hitchcock expressed regret at not being able to televise Collier's "The Lady on the Grey," a fantasy about a man transformed into a dog by a beautiful woman with whom he has fallen in love. Many of Collier's stories lend themselves quite well to television, and "Evening Primrose" – about people who live by night in a large department store – was even transformed into a television musical.

A recurring theme in Collier's fantasy is a deal with the devil, or with some sort of evil spirit. In "Bottle Party" the traditional jinn in the bottle manages to change places with the man who buys the bottle. In "Pictures in the Fire" the devil is a movie producer, and much of "The Devil George and Rosie" is set in Hell.

John Collier's success with the short story owes much to his early days as a poet and his later experience as a screenwriter. His stories combine visual perfection with a perfect choice of words – especially in his endings, where the most shocking denouements are often rendered in a style that brings a smile to the reader's lips.

—Edward D. Hoch

COLLINS, Michael. Pseudonym for Dennis Lynds; also writes as William Arden; Nick Carter; John Crowe; Carl Dekker; Maxwell Grant; Mark Sadler. American. Born in St. Louis, Missouri, 15 January 1924. Educated at Brooklyn Technical High School; Cooper Union, New York, 1942–43; Texas Agricultural and Mechanical College, College Station, 1943–44; Hofstra University, Hempstead, New York, B.A. 1949; Syracuse University, New York, M.A. 1951. Served with the United States Army Infantry, 1943–46: Purple Heart, three battle stars. Married 1) Doris Flood in 1949 (divorced, 1956); 2) Sheila McErlean in 1961; two daughters. Assistant chemist, Charles Pfizer and Company, Brooklyn, 1942–43; Assistant Editor, *Chemical Week*, New York, 1951–52; Editorial Director, American Institute of Management, New York, 1952–53; Associate Editor, then Managing Editor, *Chemical Engineering Progress*, New York, 1954–60; Editor, *Chemical Equipment* and *Laboratory Equipment*, New York, 1962–66; Instructor, Santa Barbara City College Adult Education Division, California, 1966–67. Self-employed writer since 1960. Recipient: Mystery Writers of America Edgar Allan Poe Award, 1968. Agent: Harold Ober Associates, 40 East 49th Street, New York, New York 10017. Address: 633 Chelham Way, Santa Barbara, California 93108, U.S.A.

CRIME PUBLICATIONS

Novels (series character: Dan Fortune in all books)

Act of Fear. New York, Dodd Mead, 1967; London, Joseph, 1968.
The Brass Rainbow. New York, Dodd Mead, 1969; London, Joseph, 1970.
Night of the Toads. New York, Dodd Mead, 1970; London, Hale, 1972.
Walk a Black Wind. New York, Dodd Mead, 1971; London, Hale, 1973.
Shadow of a Tiger. New York, Dodd Mead, 1972; London, Hale, 1974.
The Silent Scream. New York, Dodd Mead, 1973; London, Hale, 1975.
Woman in Marble (as Carl Dekker). Indianapolis, Bobbs Merrill, 1973.
Blue Death. New York, Dodd Mead, 1975; London, Hale, 1976.
The Blood-Red Dream. New York, Dodd Mead, 1976; London, Hale, 1977.
The Nightrunners. New York, Dodd Mead, 1978; London, Hale, 1979.

Novels as Maxwell Grant (series character: The Shadow in all books)

The Shadow Strikes. New York, Belmont, 1964.
Shadow Beware. New York, Belmont, 1965.
Cry Shadow. New York, Belmont, 1965.
The Shadow's Revenge. New York, Belmont, 1965.
Mark of the Shadow. New York, Belmont, 1966.

Shadow – Go Mad! New York, Belmont, 1966.
The Night of the Shadow. New York, Belmont, 1966.
The Shadow – Destination: Moon. New York, Belmont, 1967.

Novels as William Arden (series character: Kane Jackson in all books)

A Dark Power. New York, Dodd Mead, 1968; London, Hale, 1970.
Deal in Violence. New York, Dodd Mead, 1969; London, Hale, 1971.
The Goliath Scheme. New York, Dodd Mead, 1971; London, Hale, 1973.
Die to a Distant Drum. New York, Dodd Mead, 1972; as *Murder Underground*,
London, Hale, 1974.
Deadly Legacy. New York, Dodd Mead, 1973; London, Hale, 1974.

Novels as Mark Sadler (series character: Paul Shaw in all books)

The Falling Man. New York, Random House, 1970.
Here to Die. New York, Random House, 1971.
Mirror Image. New York, Random House, 1972.
Circle of Fire. New York, Random House, 1973.

Novels as John Crowe

Another Way to Die. New York, Random House, 1972.
A Touch of Darkness. New York, Random House, 1972.
Bloodwater. New York, Dodd Mead, 1974.
Crooked Shadows. New York, Dodd Mead, 1975.
When They Kill Your Wife. New York, Dodd Mead, 1977.
Close to Death. New York, Dodd Mead, 1979.

Novels as Nick Carter (series character: Nick Carter in all books)

The N3 Conspiracy. New York, Award, 1974.
The Green Wolf Connection. New York, Award, 1976.
Triple Cross. New York, Award, 1976.

Novels as Dennis Lynds

Charlie Chan Returns (novelization of tv play). New York, Bantam, 1974.
S.W.A.T. – Crossfire (novelization of tv play). New York, Pocket Books, 1975.

Uncollected Short Stories

"Death, My Love" (as John Douglas), in *Mink Is for a Minx: The Best from Mike
Shayne's Mystery Magazine.* New York, Dell, 1964.
"Murder from Inside," in *Mike Shayne Mystery Magazine* (New York), March 1968.
"Hot Night Homicide," in *Mike Shayne Mystery Magazine* (New York), August 1968.
"No One Likes to Be Played for a Sucker," in *Ellery Queen's Mystery Magazine* (New
York), July 1969.
"Scream All the Way," in *Alfred Hitchcock's Mystery Magazine* (North Palm Beach,
Florida), October 1969.
"Freedom Fighter," in *Crime Without Murder*, edited by Dorothy Salisbury
Davis. New York, Scribner, 1970.
"Long Shot," in *Alfred Hitchcock's Mystery Magazine* (North Palm Beach, Florida), July
1972.

"Who?," in *Alfred Hitchcock's Mystery Magazine* (North Palm Beach, Florida), August 1972.

"Occupational Hazard" (as John Crowe), in *Alfred Hitchcock's Mystery Magazine* (North Palm Beach, Florida), September 1972.

"The Choice" (as Mark Sadler), in *Alfred Hitchcock's Mystery Magazine* (North Palm Beach, Florida), February 1973.

Uncollected Short Stories as Dennis Lynds

"It's Whisky or Dames," in *Mike Shayne Mystery Magazine* (New York), August 1962.

"The Bodyguard," in *Mike Shayne Mystery Magazine* (New York), October 1962.

"Accidents Will Happen," in *Mike Shayne Mystery Magazine* (New York), November 1962.

"Carrier Pigeon," in *Mike Shayne Mystery Magazine* (New York), February 1963.

"The Blue Hand," in *Mike Shayne Mystery Magazine* (New York), April 1963.

"The Price of a Dollar," in *Mike Shayne Mystery Magazine* (New York), June 1963.

"Harness Bull," in *Mike Shayne Mystery Magazine* (New York), July 1963.

"Even Bartenders Die," in *Mike Shayne Mystery Magazine* (New York), August 1963.

"Death for Dinner," in *Mike Shayne Mystery Magazine* (New York), October 1963.

"Nobody Frames Big Sam," in *Alfred Hitchcock's Mystery Magazine* (North Palm Beach, Florida), October 1963.

"The Heckler," in *Mike Shayne Mystery Magazine* (New York), November 1963.

"A Better Murder," in *Mike Shayne Mystery Magazine* (New York), January 1964.

"No Way Out," in *Mike Shayne Mystery Magazine* (New York), February 1964.

"Silent Partner," in *Alfred Hitchcock's Mystery Magazine* (North Palm Beach, Florida), April 1964.

"The Sinner," in *Alfred Hitchcock's Mystery Magazine* (North Palm Beach, Florida), May 1964.

"Winner Pay Off," in *Mike Shayne Mystery Magazine* (New York), May 1964.

"Hard Cop," in *Mike Shayne Mystery Magazine* (New York), July 1964.

"Homecoming," in *Mike Shayne Mystery Magazine* (New York), September 1964.

"No Loose Ends," in *Mike Shayne Mystery Magazine* (New York), November 1964.

"Man on the Run," in *Mink Is for a Minx: The Best from Mike Shayne's Mystery Magazine.* New York, Dell, 1964.

"Full Circle," in *Mike Shayne Mystery Magazine* (New York), January 1965.

"The Hero," in *Mike Shayne Mystery Magazine* (New York), May 1965.

"A Well-Planned Death," in *Mike Shayne Mystery Magazine* (New York), December 1965.

"No Way Out," in *Best Detective Stories of the Year, 19th Annual Collection*, edited by Anthony Boucher. New York, Dutton, and London, Boardman, 1965.

"Viking Blood," in *Manhunt* (New York), April–May 1966.

"The DirkJune 1966.

"Climate of Immorality," in *Shell Scott Mystery Magazine* (New York), 1967.

Uncollected Short Stories as William Arden

"Success of a Mission," in *Argosy* (New York), April 1968.

"The Savage," in *Argosy* (New York), January 1970.

"The Bizarre Case Expert," in *Ellery Queen's Mystery Magazine* (New York), June 1970.

"Clay Pigeon," in *Argosy* (New York), March 1971.

OTHER PUBLICATIONS

Novels

   Combat Soldier (as Dennis Lynds).   New York, New American Library, 1962.
   Uptown Downtown (as Dennis Lynds).   New York, New American Library, 1963.
   Lukan War.   New York, Belmont, 1969.
   The Planets of Death.   New York, Berkley, 1970.

Other as Wirlliam Arden (juvenile)

   The Mystery of the Moaning Cave.   New York, Random House, 1968; London, Collins,
      1969.
   The Mystery of the Laughing Shadow.   New York, Random House, 1969; London,
      Collins, 1970.
   The Secret of the Crooked Cat.   New York, Random House, 1970; London, Collins,
      1971.
   The Mystery of the Shrinking House.   New York, Random House, 1972; London,
      Collins, 1973.
   The Mystery of the Blue Condor.   Lexington, Massachusetts, Ginn, 1973.
   The Secret of the Phantom Lake.   New York, Random House, 1973; London, Collins,
      1974.
   The Mystery of the Dead Man's Riddle.   New York, Random House, 1974; London,
      Collins, 1975.
   The Mystery of the Dancing Devil.   New York, Random House, 1976; London, Collins,
      1977.
   The Mystery of the Headless Horse.   New York, Random House, 1977; London,
      Collins, 1978.
   The Mystery of the Deadly Double.   New York, Random House, 1978; London, Collins,
      1979.
   The Secret of Shark Reef.   New York, Random House, 1979; London, Collins, 1980.

Manuscript Collection: Center for the Study of Popular Culture, Bowling Green State
University, Ohio.

Michael Collins comments:
   I write about people driven to violent actions by forces from inside and outside. The forces
of the world in which they live. A real world. Our world. If anything distinguishes my books
particularly from other books, it is that I write what could be called *socio-dramas*. I want to
understand and show what made these people as they are, what created the pressures that
will explode within them. What made them, then, act in a crisis as they acted, and what made
violence their ultimate solution.
   A novel is a novel; suspense novels are no less novels than sonnets are poems. The basic
mark of a "crime" novel is exactly that – it centers on an overt crime, a specific moment of
violence at a particular time and place. I chose to write "crime" novels precisely for this
reason – I think a society and its people can be seen in sharp outline at such moments of
violence.
   I hope my books excite, thrill, and entertain, but what I try to give is the excitement of
truth, the thrill of understanding our own world as it is, the entertainment of living a real
experience with real people. Still, I do not write primarily to thrill or entertain, but to know

what makes our world tick – your world and mine – in all its strengths and its weaknesses, its hopes and its horrors, its everyday streets and its hidden corners.

*　　*　　*

Michael Collins is the most successful pseudonym of Dennis Lynds. Lynds has done several books under each of several pseudonyms. The Buena Costa County stories (John Crowe) and the Mark Sadler mysteries are good journeyman work, but it is only in the "Collins" books that Lynds manages to write tales distinguished by a strong personal flavor and originality. Although he is usually allied to the "hard-boiled school" of contemporary sensibility he has his own habits and perspectives, which are most effectively represented in the stories centered on Dan Fortune, the one-armed, passive, compassionate, and philosophical private eye of the Collins series.

The least profitable of Lynds's habits is elaborate plotting with too many characters, murders and assaults, sub-plots and interconnections. A minor problem – the disappearance of a grandfather, a struggling actress dead from an abortion, a parking-lot operator who cannot get his lease renewed – is the thread that leads to a vast, entangling web of greed, obsessions, hidden crimes that involve up to fifteen or more concatenated characters. The initial problem escalates into assaults and murders, one after another, for Lynds's world is a brutal and violent one. The plots are ingenious and precisely crafted, the motives credible in terms of character and situation, the solutions surprising but satisfying. But they are too tightly packed into short books and devilishly hard to follow.

Love of plot for its sake is not, however, the real reason for these intricate networks, for they are the proper outcome of Lynds's concern with the ways in which people's lives are interconnected on ethnic, regional, economic, and professional levels. In the California stories of John Crowe and William Arden, and the California episodes in Mark Sadler, we meet wealthy business families, hippies, Indians, sadistic policemen, venal politicians, and theatrical types – a cross-section of provincial California as Lynds sees it. New York, much more exotic and diversified, gives Lynds the chance to examine the seedy denizens of the Chelsea district where Dan Fortune grew up and still lives; ethnic Lithuanians and partly assimilated Norwegians; ex-French maquis trading on false laurels; gamblers, mobsters, and exotic dancers; corporation vice-presidents and other wealthy businessmen; up-state, gut-fighting politicians; and youth gangs in the ghetto. Michael Collins, who is, according to Lynds, his authentic New York alter ego, knows all these groups and types inside out, and in particular is aware of the multiple, inter-weaving relationships that link them up, down, and across social barriers. Less sociologist than philosopher of culture he is primarily interested in the common humanity of these interwoven lives – how the same motives of ambition, obsession, revenge, or self-protection drive corporation executives and minor mobsters, displaced Manchurians and Lithuanian nationalists.

In *Blue Death*, for example, Collins explores the world of big business, where Franklin Weaver, chief executive officer of International Metals and Refining, and a Great Man of the Ayn Rand persuasion, is instrumental in the deaths of four people in order to protect his ambitions and his corporation. But the threads of the plot reach out into the lives of a parking-lot operator, his belly-dancer wife, street gangs in Newark, a research and development scientist with a wife-and-drinking problem; to seedy bars, near-deserted shore hotels, and the Passaic River, where Dan Fortune takes an enforced swim. By thus spreading his web over a large chunk of the New York scene, Collins is able to demonstrate his thesis that the violence and crime in American society are pervasive and endemic. Similarly, in *The Blood-Red Dream* Lithuanian nationalists are sold out by their own leader, just for money; in *Shadow of a Tiger*, Jimmy Sung, crazily dreaming of a glorious China he never knew, kills the wrong man in seeking revenge for the French spoliation in Indo-China; in *Night of the Toads* deaths accumulate around Emory Foxx who has for years been nursing plans of vengeance on Rey Vega for fingering him during the McCarthy era.

The social philosophy in the Collins books would, however, be only mildly interesting if it were not for Dan Fortune. If Collins is to be recognized as a fine mystery writer, it will

343

undoubtedly be because of his one-armed protagonist. For although Fortune might be classed with other seedy anti-heroes of modern fiction, he has qualities that set him apart. A traumatized drop-out from the main stream, a maverick in a pea-jacket and beret, he is nevertheless not merely an angry rebel. Essentially he is a thinker, a contemplator of human weaknesses drawn into whirlpools of crime and violence almost against his will. Although he has chosen his profession and prefers it to any other, it is not in order to fight criminals or wield the sword of vengeance that he is a private detective; he is never the aggressor, and he never fires his ancient .45, partly because he is such a poor shot.

His being one-armed is more than a gimmick, a diversion like Columbo's raincoat designed to mislead the wicked into underestimating him, although it often has that effect; it is a symbol of his alienation and the prime reason for his physical passivity. He is the wounded man whose wound makes him fearful – the thought that something might happen to his remaining arm fills him with dread – yet conversely makes him expose himself to danger in order to prove he exists. And he is the determined man bent on carrying out his mission no matter what the cost. This exposure and this determination lead to insult, injury, loneliness solaced only by brief love affairs, and the risk of sudden death. In every novel he is beaten, harassed, or sometimes shot.

This is his ultimate commitment: he has become a detective because in that role above all others he has the freedom and the responsibility to *know*. He is not interested in abstract justice; the criminals are never brought to book; they suffer in other ways and sometimes escape the law completely. For him the ruling principle of life is chance, which rules the wicked as well as the good and which can only be countered by an active effort to choose – basically he is an existentialist. He is well described in these respects by Franklin Weaver: "... You believe in absolute truth. I can see it in everything you say and do. Your shabby clothes, your maverick manner. You reject conventions, creature comforts, success in your contemporary world. You prefer to be *right* rather than powerful, to *know* rather than to act, to understand, not manage."

Such a man might well, of course, be a kind of monster, concerned only with Truth, and what saves Dan from this fate and humanizes him into the sympathetic character he is is his own sympathy, his profound intuition of human weakness. It is this quality that lifts him above the ruck of hard-boiled detectives. Sometimes it leads him to preach too much (there are too many philosophical musings); sometimes it seems sentimental. But on the whole it is what rounds Dan Fortune out into one of the most fully-realized detectives in recent mystery fiction and helps to make the novels in which he appears achievements which should continue to add luster to the work of Dennis Lynds.

—Richard C. Carpenter

CONDON, Richard (Thomas). American. Born in New York City, 18 March 1915. Educated in public schools in New York. Married Evelyn Hunt in 1938; two children. Publicist in the American film industry for 21 years; Theatrical Producer, New York, 1951–52. Lives in Ireland. Agent: Harold Matson, 30 Rockefeller Plaza, New York, New York 10020, U.S.A.; or, A. D. Peters and Company, 10 Buckingham Street, London WC2N 6BU, England.

CRIME PUBLICATIONS

Novels

> *The Oldest Confession.* New York, Appleton Century Crofts, 1958; London, Longman, 1959; as *The Happy Thieves*, New York, Bantam, 1962.
> *The Manchurian Candidate.* New York, McGraw Hill, 1959; London, Joseph, 1960.

An Infinity of Mirrors.   New York, Random House, 1964; London, Heinemann, 1967.
Any God Will Do.   New York, Random House, 1964; London, Heinemann, 1967.
Mile High.   New York, Dial Press, and London, Heinemann, 1969.
The Vertical Smile.   New York, Dial Press, 1971; London, Weidenfeld and Nicolson, 1972.
Arigato.   New York, Dial Press, and London, Weidenfeld and Nicolson, 1972.
Winter Kills.   New York, Dial Press, and London, Weidenfeld and Nicolson, 1974.
The Whisper of the Axe.   New York, Dial Press, and London, Weidenfeld and Nicolson, 1976.
Death of a Politician.   New York, Marek, 1978.

OTHER PUBLICATIONS

Novels

Some Angry Angel: A Mid-Century Faerie Tale.   New York, McGraw Hill, 1960; London, Joseph, 1961.
A Talent for Loving; or, The Great Cowboy Race.   New York, McGraw Hill, 1961; London, Joseph, 1963.
The Ecstasy Business.   New York, Dial Press, and London, Heinemann, 1967.
The Star-Spangled Crunch.   New York, Bantam, 1974.
Money Is Love.   New York, Dial Press, and London, Weidenfeld and Nicolson, 1975.
The Abandoned Woman.   New York, Dial Press, 1977; London, Hutchinson, 1978.
Bandicoot.   New York, Dial Press, and London, Hutchinson, 1978.

Plays

Men of Distinction (produced New York, 1953).

Screenplays: *A Talent for Loving,* 1965; *The Summer Music,* 1969; *The Long Loud Silence,* 1969.

Other

And Then We Moved to Rossenarra; or, The Art of Emigrating.   New York, Dial Press, 1973.
The Mexican Stove: A History of Mexican Food, with Wendy Bennett.   New York, Doubleday, 1973.

Editor, with Burton O. Kurth, *Writing from Experience.*   New York, Harper, 1960.

Manuscript Collection: Mugar Memorial Library, Boston University.

*   *   *

Richard Condon would be more comprehensible if he were two different writers. Although consistencies of style preclude this possibility it may still be helpful to think of him in that light. His literary schizophrenia began after the huge success of his second novel – and *The Manchurian Candidate* must still be regarded as the definitive psychological thriller – assured him of a publisher for anything he turned out. One side of Richard Condon has continued to write books with considerable popular appeal. *Mile High,* a skewed and gangster-dominated fictional history of Prohibition, *Winter Kills,* a fictional study of the Kennedy family, and the more recent *The Whisper of the Axe* are all books of this type. The reader can relate to them, for all that he may resent a satire of his particular sacred cow.

On the other hand, an even larger group of Condon books, many of them at least related to the mystery field, are as murky and uncommunicative as the most self-absorbed modern poetry. These include *Any God Will Do*, a psychological study of an opportunistic bankrobber who believes himself descended from European royalty and makes himself into a great chef; *The Vertical Smile*, primarily a satire on the human sex drive, but peopled with a good many characters familiar to the mystery reader; *Arigato*, a "big caper" novel which satirizes several of Condon's favorite targets. The latter work is probably the masterpiece of the obscurantist books, although the author himself is the only reader who understands the works in this group well enough to rate them.

Both groups of books reveal Condon as a fine satirist. The tragedy of his later career is mitigated for mystery readers by the fact that his most affected later works include most of his non-mystery fiction.

—Jeff Banks

CONNINGTON, J. J. Pseudonym for Alfred Walter Stewart. British. Born in 1880. Educated at the University of Glasgow; University of Marburg; University College, London, D.Sc. Married Jessie Lily Courts in 1916; one daughter. Mackay-Smith Scholar, 1901, 1851 Exhibition Scholar, 1903–05, Carnegie Research Fellow, 1905–08, and Lecturer in Organic Chemistry, 1909–14, Queen's University, Belfast; Lecturer in Physical Chemistry and Radioactivity, University of Glasgow, 1914–19; Professor of Chemistry, 1919–44, and Dean of Faculties, Queen's University, Belfast. *Died 1 July 1947.*

CRIME PUBLICATIONS

Novels (series characters: Mark Brand; Sir Clinton Driffield; Superintendent Ross)

> *Death at Swaythling Court.* London, Benn, and Boston, Little Brown, 1926.
> *The Dangerfield Talisman.* London, Benn, 1926; Boston, Little Brown, 1927.
> *Murder in the Maze* (Driffield). London, Benn, and Boston, Little Brown, 1927.
> *Tragedy at Ravensthorpe* (Driffield). London, Benn, 1927; Boston, Little Brown, 1928.
> *The Case with Nine Solutions* (Driffield). London, Gollancz, 1928; Boston, Little Brown, 1929.
> *Mystery at Lynden Sands* (Driffield). London, Gollancz, and Boston, Little Brown, 1928.
> *Nemesis at Raynham Parva* (Driffield). London, Gollancz, 1929; as *Grim Vengeance*, Boston, Little Brown, 1929.
> *The Eye in the Museum* (Ross). London, Gollancz, 1929; Boston, Little Brown, 1930.
> *The Two Tickets Puzzle* (Ross). London, Gollancz, 1930; as *The Two Ticket Puzzle*, Boston, Little Brown, 1930.
> *The Boat-House Riddle* (Driffield). London, Gollancz, and Boston, Little Brown, 1931.
> *The Sweepstake Murders* (Driffield). London, Hodder and Stoughton, 1931; Boston, Little Brown, 1932.
> *The Castleford Conundrum* (Driffield). London, Hodder and Stoughton, and Boston, Little Brown, 1932.
> *Tom Tiddler's Island.* London, Hodder and Stoughton, 1933; as *Gold Brick Island*, Boston, Little Brown, 1933.
> *The Ha-Ha Case* (Driffield). London, Hodder and Stoughton, 1934; as *The Brandon Case*, Boston, Little Brown, 1934.

In Whose Dim Shadow (Driffield). London, Hodder and Stoughton, 1935; as *The Tau Cross Mystery*, Boston, Little Brown, 1935.

A Minor Operation (Driffield). London, Hodder and Stoughton, and Boston, Little Brown, 1937.

For Murder Will Speak (Driffield). London, Hodder and Stoughton, 1938; as *Murder Will Speak*, Boston, Little Brown, 1938.

Truth Comes Limping (Driffield). London, Hodder and Stoughton, and Boston, Little Brown, 1938.

The Counsellor (Brand). London, Hodder and Stoughton, and Boston, Little Brown, 1939.

The Four Defences (Brand). London, Hodder and Stoughton, and Boston, Little Brown, 1940.

The Twenty-One Clues (Driffield). London, Hodder and Stoughton, and Boston, Little Brown, 1941.

No Past Is Dead (Driffield). London, Hodder and Stoughton, and Boston, Little Brown, 1942.

Jack-in-the-Box (Driffield). London, Hodder and Stoughton, and Boston, Little Brown, 1944.

Common Sense Is All You Need (Driffield). London, Hodder and Stoughton, 1947.

Uncollected Short Stories

"Before Insulin," in *Fifty Masterpieces of Mystery*. London, Odhams Press, 1935.
"A Criminologist's Bookshelf," in *Detective Medley*, edited by John Rhode. London, Hutchinson, 1939.
"The Thinking Machine," in *My Best Mystery Story*. London, Faber, 1939.

OTHER PUBLICATIONS

Novels

Nordenholt's Millions. London, Constable, 1923.
Almighty Gold. London, Constable, 1924.

Other as A. W. Stewart

Stereochemistry. London, Longman, 1907.
Recent Advances in Organic Chemistry. London, Longman, 1908.
Recent Advances in Physical and Inorganic Chemistry. London, Longman, 1909.
A Manual of Practical Chemistry for Public Health Students. London, Bale and Danielsson, 1913.
Chemistry and Its Borderland. London, Longman, 1914.
Some Physico-Chemical Themes. London, Longman, 1922.
Alias J. J. Connington (essays). London, Hollis and Carter, 1947.

*   *   *

J. J. Connington possessed the British flavour of Freeman Wills Crofts and others, the same rather humourless approach, the same pedantic and sometimes stilted use of language, and the same ingenuity of murder methods and alibis. He also displayed certain characteristics of his own – his scientific background was often put to good use, including the medical aspects of crime such as poisons and blood tests, and his occasional whiff of the occult was achieved competently and unsensationally. He was inclined to introduce more physical action than the cerebral exponents of the Crofts school, including some good chases, as in *The Eye in the Museum.*

Like those of Crofts, Connington's first books contained no series detective. *Death at Swaythling Court* was not an auspicious start to his career, but it is possible to muster a certain affection for his second, *The Dangerfield Talisman*. Here Connington managed the difficult task of producing an exciting and intellectually satisfying detective novel without a real detective, and without even a murder. The disappearance of a family heirloom, with its dark history a closely guarded secret, is combined with a chess problem against the well-worn background of a country house-party to present a readable story with little to complain about.

In spite of some competent non-series novels during his career, one tends to associate Connington (like so many other writers) with his series characters. Together, Chief Constable Sir Clinton Driffield and Squire Wendover investigated a considerable number of cases. Although Connington used another series character, Mark Brand ("The Counsellor"), it is for the Driffield/Wendover books that historians of the genre tend to remember him. By giving these two men a somewhat uneasy relationship, Connington hit upon a good idea. It was no Holmes/Watson combination, for it is often unclear as to who is the detective and who is playing second fiddle. The two frequently disagree, but are thrown together time after time by the fact that murders and strange happenings abound in the county of which Wendover is principal landlord and Driffield is top policeman. Of the many Driffield/Wendover cases, it is possible to single out for special commendation *Murder in the Maze*, *The Boat-House Riddle*, *The Sweepstake Murders* (perhaps the best), and *A Minor Operation*. Of the non-series novels, one must particularly mention again *The Eye in the Museum*; the title refers to a camera obscura, and this book was quoted for some time as the only appearance of this type of equipment in detective fiction. (This claim, incidentally, has now been invalidated by at least one book, Janet Caird's *Murder Reflected*.)

It is unaccountable that Connington has not achieved the place in the genre's history afforded to similar writers such as Crofts. He told a good tale, broke many an "unbreakable" alibi, displayed the customary plot-before-characterisation priority of his contemporaries, conveyed the atmosphere of classy county life most acceptably, and laced his crime with ballistics, footprints, maps of the scene, railway timetables in a sometimes ingenious but always meticulous manner. He just didn't have the benefit of Crofts's Inspector French.

—Melvyn Barnes

CONRAD, Brenda. See **FORD, Leslie**.

CONWAY, Troy. See **AVALLONE, Michael**.

COOKE, M. E.   See CREASEY, John.

COOPER, Brian (Newman).   British.   Born in Stockport, Cheshire, 15 September 1919. Educated at Jesus College, Cambridge, M.A. 1945, Dip.Ed. 1947. Served in the Bedfordshire and Hertfordshire Regiment, 1940–42, and in the Intelligence Corps, 1942–45. Married Ellen Martin in 1942; one son and one daughter. History Assistant, County Grammar School, Bromley, Kent, 1947–48; Senior History Master, Selective Central School, Shirebrook, Derbyshire, 1948–55. Since 1955, Senior History Master, Bolsover School, Derbyshire. Address: 43 Parkland Close, Southlands, Mansfield, Nottinghamshire, England.

CRIME PUBLICATIONS

Novels

Where the Fresh Grass Grows.   London, Heinemann, 1955; as Maria, New York, Vanguard Press, 1956.
A Path to the Bridge.   London, Heinemann, 1958; as Giselle, New York, Vanguard Press, 1958.
The Van Langeren Girl.   London, Heinemann, and New York, Vanguard Press, 1960.
A Touch of Thunder.   London, Heinemann, 1961; New York, Vanguard Press, 1962.
A Time to Retreat.   London, Heinemann, and New York, Vanguard Press, 1963.
Genesis 38.   London, Heinemann, 1965; as The Murder of Mary Steers, New York, Vanguard Press, 1966.
A Mission for Betty Smith.   London, Heinemann, 1967; as Monsoon Murder, New York, Vanguard Press, 1968.

Brian Cooper comments:
I am, purely and simply, a teller of stories, and, despite the deeper meanings that reviewers persistently find in my work, I prefer that my novels should be regarded as nothing more than, I hope, well-told tales.
I have not written a novel of suspense since 1967, and I doubt if I will ever write another. Since then, I have devoted myself to a lifelong interest in the history of the industrial revolution and its archaeological remains. I am writing a book to be called Transformation of a Valley: The Derbyshire Derwent.

*   *   *

Brian Cooper has written novels of suspense that have that special ring of authenticity about them. In fact, some readers might pick up a book such as Genesis 38 and, without reading the author's note, perceive it to be true fact. Cooper in other cases has based his fiction on fact, but these novels seem limited in scope. The court of inquiry in A Time to Retreat, for instance, is in essence the entire book. But this is not to say that Cooper has a tendency to dawdle in his approach. Cooper has a crisp, fast-paced delivery; the details unfold quickly. His forte is in his great talent for dialogue. He has that special ability to have his characters talk in real and believable terms. His descriptive abilities do not quite match up to the dialogue. Also missing in many of his books is the one central character that we can identify with. In solving the puzzle, we must meet all involved and become acquainted with their part in the scheme of things.

Cooper's books are well thought out and excellently written. He finds a puzzle that must be unraveled and then lets the reader join in as he unwinds it from the beginning, through court martial or narrative. First, the facts of what happened, and then the post mortem. Cooper does not write what can be called a fast-paced thriller, but indeed a fictional documentary. He can be very sensitive at times to the subtleties of the circumstances surrounding the basic story line, an effective approach. *The New York Times* Sunday Magazine said: "one thinks of thrillers as rushing like runners doing a hundred yard race. Mr. Cooper is a miler and runs a memorable race." To read Brian Cooper is to be curious: to hear of something happening, and wonder why.

—Don Cole

COPPARD, A(lfred) E(dgar). British. Born in Folkestone, Kent, 4 January 1878. Educated at Lewes Road Boarding School, Brighton, Sussex, 1883–87; apprenticed to a tailor in Whitechapel, London, 1887–90. Married 1) Lily Annie Richardson in 1905 (died); 2) Winifred May de Kok; one son and one daughter. Messenger for Reuters, London, 1890–92; also worked as a paraffin vendor's assistant, auctioneer, cheesemonger, and soap-agent; worked for several years in the office of an engineering firm; Confidential Clerk, Eagle Ironworks, Oxford, 1907 until he became full-time writer in 1919; Reviewer, *Manchester Guardian*, 1919–24. *Died 13 January 1957.*

CRIME PUBLICATIONS

Short Stories

>   *Adam and Eve and Pinch Me: Tales.*   Waltham Saint Lawrence, Berkshire, Golden Cockerel Press, 1921; New York, Knopf, 1922; augmented edition, Knopf, 1922.
>   *Clorinda Walks in Heaven: Tales.*   Waltham Saint Lawrence, Berkshire, Golden Cockerel Press, 1922.
>   *The Black Dog and Other Stories.*   London, Cape, and New York, Knopf, 1923.
>   *Fishmonger's Fiddle: Tales.*   London, Cape, and New York, Knopf, 1925.
>   *The Field of Mustard: Tales.*   London, Cape, 1926; New York, Knopf, 1927.
>   *Silver Circus: Tales.*   London, Cape, 1928; New York, Knopf, 1929.
>   *Count Stefan.*   Waltham Saint Lawrence, Berkshire, Golden Cockerel Press, 1928.
>   *The Gollan.*   Privately printed, 1929.
>   *The Hundredth Story of A. E. Coppard.*   Waltham Saint Lawrence, Berkshire, Golden Cockerel Press, 1930.
>   *Pink Furniture: A Tale for Lonely Children with Noble Natures.*   London, Cape, and New York, Cape and Smith, 1930.
>   *Nixey's Harlequin: Tales.*   London, Cape, 1931; New York, Knopf, 1932.
>   *Crotty Shinkwin, The Beauty Spot.*   Waltham Saint Lawrence, Berkshire, Golden Cockerel Press, 1932.
>   *Cheefoo.*   Privately printed, 1932.
>   *Dunky Fitlow: Tales.*   London, Cape, 1933.
>   *Ring the Bells of Heaven.*   London, White Owl Press, 1933.
>   *Emergency Exit.*   New York, Random House, 1934.

Good Samaritans. New York, Spiral Press, 1934.
Polly Oliver: Tales. London, Cape, 1935.
Ninepenny Flute: Twenty-One Tales. London, Macmillan, 1937.
Tapster's Tapestry. London, Golden Cockerel Press, 1938.
You Never Know, Do You? and Other Tales. London, Methuen, 1939.
Ugly Anna and Other Tales. London, Methuen, 1944.
Selected Tales. London, Cape, 1946.
Fearful Pleasures. Sauk City, Wisconsin, Arkham House, 1946; London, Peter Nevill, 1952.
Dark-Eyed Lady: Fourteen Tales. London, Methuen, 1947.
The Collected Tales of A. E. Coppard. New York, Knopf, 1948.
Lucy in Her Pink Jacket. London, Peter Nevill, 1954.
Selected Stories. London, Cape, 1972.

OTHER PUBLICATIONS

Verse

Hips and Haws. Waltham Saint Lawrence, Berkshire, Golden Cockerel Press, 1922.
Pelagea and Other Poems. Waltham Saint Lawrence, Berkshire, Golden Cockerel Press, 1926.
Yokohama Garland and Other Poems. Philadelphia, Centaur Press, 1926.
The Collected Poems of A. E. Coppard. London, Cape, and New York, Knopf, 1928.
Easter Day. London, Ulysses Bookshop, 1931.
These Hopes of Heaven. London, Blue Moon Press, 1934.
Cherry Ripe. Chepstow, Monmouthshire, Tintern Press, and Windham, Connecticut, Hawthorn House, 1935.

Other

Rummy, That Noble Game, Expounded in Prose, Poetry, Diagram, and Engraving, illustrated by Robert Gibbings. Waltham Saint Lawrence, Berkshire, Golden Cockerel Press, 1932; Boston, Houghton Mifflin, 1933.
It's Me, O Lord! An Abstract and Brief Chronicle of Some of the Life with Some of the Opinions of A. E. Coppard. London, Methuen, 1957.

Editor, *Songs from Robert Burns.* Waltham Saint Lawrence, Berkshire, Golden Cockerel Press, 1925.

Bibliography: *The Writings of A. E. Coppard: A Bibliography* by Jacob Schwartz, London, Ulysses Bookshop, 1931.

*   *   *

The numerous volumes of tales by A. E. Coppard, from *Adam and Eve and Pinch Me* to *Polly Oliver*, are wrought with the natural suspense of life. Occasionally, as in the title story to *Adam and Eve* and in "The Bogey Man" (*The Field of Mustard*), Coppard experiments with the fantastic, the supernatural. All of his tales are well-constructed and low-keyed; among his prevalent themes are man's loneliness and frustration in a secretive world where the unknown is common.

"Adam and Eve" is the most anthologized and the most stylistically effective of Coppard's tales. Gilbert, the central character of the tale, is allowed a glimpse of the future on one brilliant afternoon when he is invisible to everyone around him. Gilbert fancies seeing his wife, conducting her daily business, and three children, two his own. In this fantasy world, he can communicate with no one but the child who is not his, Gabriel. At the tale's close, the reader learns that Gilbert's wife will have a child; Gilbert decides to name him Gabriel.

The satisfying ending of "Adam and Eve" is in sharp contrast to the uncertainty of "The Bogey Man." As in many of Coppard's tales, good and evil are undefineable in this tale. Sheila, the protagonist, agonizes after stealing a black box for her ill godmother. Torn by the righteousness of the deed, she is forced to repent to a little droll, perhaps God, perhaps Satan, who lives inside the box. Sheila fears the unknown and resists the droll's temptations. At the conclusion, she is rewarded for her endurance with beauty, the health of her godmother, and the joy of many suitors. But in her long life, she never marries and her happiness is questionable.

Coppard's other tales also explore the "inexplicable." The young boy's punishment in "Communion" (*Adam and Eve*) seems grossly unfair. The young man in "Dusky Ruth," another tale from this collection, never learns the nature of his lover's "strange sorrow." In the title story from *The Black Dog* the main character is left with the baffling question: did Lizzie kill herself out of loneliness or was she the victim of Orianda, her lover's jealous daughter. The title story from *The Field of Mustard* also explores loneliness as two women, Rose and Dinah, find relief from their sorrows in the exchange of friendship.

Coppard skillfully exposed every facet of human sorrow and joy. Many of his tales border on the tragic, but his characters, in their ability to endure, rise above a threatening and unsettling environment.

—Donna Rose Casella Kern

COPPEL, Alec.   Australian.   Born in 1909(?). *Died 22 January 1972.*

CRIME PUBLICATIONS

Novels

> *I Killed the Count* (novelization of stage play).   London, Blackie, 1939.
> *A Man about a Dog.*   London, Harrap, 1947; as *Over the Line*, New York, Doubleday, 1947; as *Obsession,* London, Corgi, 1953.
> *Mr. Denning Drives North.*   London, Harrap, 1950; New York, Dutton, 1951.
> *The Last Parable.*   London, Barker, 1953.
> *Moment to Moment* (novelization of screenplay).   New York, Fawcett, 1966.
> *Tweedledum and Tweedledee.*   London, Bles, 1967.

OTHER PUBLICATIONS

Plays

> *Short Circuit* (produced London, 1935).
> *The Stars Foretell* (produced London, 1936).
> *I Killed the Count* (produced London, 1937; New York, 1942).   London, Heinemann, 1938.
> *Let's Pretend*, with Steve Geray, music by Nicholas Brodsky, lyrics by Lynton Hudson and Sonny Miller (produced London, 1938).
> *Believe It or Not* (produced London, 1940).

My Friend Lester (produced London, 1947).

A Man about a Dog (produced London, 1949).

The Genius and the Goddess, with Aldous Huxley and Beth Wendel, adaptation of the novel by Huxley (produced New York, 1957; London, 1962).

The Joshua Tree, adaptation of a story by Myra and Alec Coppel (produced London, 1958).

The Gazebo, adaptation of a story by Myra and Alec Coppel (produced New York, 1958; London, 1960). New York, Dramatists Play Service, 1959; London, English Theatre Guild, 1962.

The Captain's Paradise. New York, French, 1961.

Not in My Bed, You Don't, with Myra Coppel (produced Richmond, Surrey, 1968).

Cadenza (produced Leatherhead, Surrey, 1973). Hornchurch, Essex, Ian Henry, 1977.

Screenplays: *Over the Moon*, with Anthony Pelissier and Arthur Wimperis, 1937; *Just Like a Woman*, 1938; *I Killed the Count (Who Is Guilty?)*, with Laurence Huntington, 1939; *Pacific Adventures*, with others, 1947; *The Brass Monkey*, with Thornton Freeland and C. Denis Freeman, 1948; *Woman Hater*, with Robert Westerby and Nicholas Phipps, 1948; *Obsession (The Hidden Room)*, 1949; *Smart Alex*, 1951; *No Highway (No Highway in the Sky)*, with Oscar Millard and R. C. Sherriff, 1951; *Two on the Tiles*, 1951; *Mr. Denning Drives North*, 1951; *The Captain's Paradise*, with Nicholas Phipps and Anthony Kimmins, 1953; *Hell below Zero*, with Max Trell and Richard Maibaum, 1953; *The Black Knight*, with Bryan Forbes and Dennis O'Keefe, 1954; *Vertigo*, with Samuel Taylor, 1958; *Appointment with a Shadow*, with Norman Jolley, 1959; *Swordsman of Siena*, with others, 1962; *Moment to Moment*, with John Lee Mahin, 1966; *The Bliss of Mrs. Blossom*, with Denis Norden, 1968; *The Statue*, with Denis Norden, 1970.

Television Plays (UK): *Two on the Tiles*, 1969; *A Kiss Is Just a Kiss*, 1971.

*   *   *

Alec Coppel's name may well go down to posterity for something he seems not to have done: he is credited as screenwriter for Alfred Hitchcock's *Vertigo*, though Hitchcock, according to Donald Spoto, rejected Coppel's script as "unshootable." Yet many of Coppel's trademarks remain on *Vertigo*, and Hitchcock may be the closest analogue to Coppel as an artist. One of the running gags in Coppel's play *The Gazebo* (written about the time of *Vertigo*) has the hero repeatedly telephoning Hitchcock himself with more and more bizarre plans for the murder he is planning ("I thought you'd like it, Hitch"). In both Coppel and Hitchcock there is the characteristic movement between titillation and reassurance; the same striking misanthropy, more particularly misogyny, in both.

Coppel's crime fictions are of a mordantly cynical kind: the recurrent plot, with variations, concerns the outwardly normal and respected character who commits a crime which is arguably to be justified – the killing of a blackmailer, a daughter's would-be seducer, a wife's lover. He escapes the consequences of his crime so long as he had not crossed the bounds of human decency, as Coppel rather liberally delineates them, more liberally for the wronged husband or father than for the erring wife. This formula appears in almost all his work, with brilliant suspense in his best novel, *Mr. Denning Drives North*, and with no less brilliant comedy in his best play, *The Captain's Paradise*, and persists even in the lesser work that rounds off his career, the film *Moment to Moment* (a redoing of *Mr. Denning*) and the disagreeably prurient sex comedy film *The Statue*.

Coppel's writing is brisk and witty, and his control of suspense at its best, as in *Mr. Denning Drives North*, superb. But his gift for invention is slight, and his psychological penetration as flashily superficial as Hitchcock's, without Hitchcock's ability to transfer psychological data to symbol and so transcend direct exposition.

—Barrie Hayne

COPPER, Basil. Also writes as Lee Falk. British. Born in 1924. Educated at a grammar school and a private commercial college. Married to Annie Renée Guerin. Journalist for 30 years, including 14 years as News Editor with the Kent County Newspaper. Address: Stockdoves, South Park, Sevenoaks, Kent TN13 1EN, England.

CRIME PUBLICATIONS

Novels (series character: Mike Faraday in all books)

The Dark Mirror. London, Hale, 1966.
Night Frost. London, Hale, 1966.
No Flowers for the General. London, Hale, 1967.
Scratch on the Dark. London, Hale, 1967.
Die Now, Live Later. London, Hale, 1968.
Don't Bleed on Me. London, Hale, 1968.
The Marble Orchard. London, Hale, 1969.
Dead File. London, Hale, 1970.
No Letters from the Grave. London, Hale, 1971.
The Big Chill. London, Hale, 1972.
Strong-Arm. London, Hale, 1972.
A Great Year for Dying. London, Hale, 1973.
Shock-Wave. London, Hale, 1973.
The Breaking Point. London, Hale, 1973.
A Voice from the Dead. London, Hale, 1974.
Feedback. London, Hale, 1974.
Ricochet. London, Hale, 1974.
The High Wall. London, Hale, 1975.
Impact. London, Hale, 1975.
A Good Place to Die. London, Hale, 1975.
The Lonely Place. London, Hale, 1976.
Crack in the Sidewalk. London, Hale, 1976.
Tight Corner. London, Hale, 1976.
The Year of the Dragon. London, Hale, 1977.
Death Squad. London, Hale, 1977.
Murder One. London, Hale, 1978.
A Quiet Room in Hell. London, Hale, 1979.
The Big Rip-Off. London, Hale, 1979.

Short Stories

The Dossier of Solar Pons. Los Angeles, Pinnacle, 1979.
The Further Adventures of Solar Pons. Los Angeles, Pinnacle, 1979.

OTHER PUBLICATIONS

Novels

The Phantom (as Lee Falk).   New York, Avon, 1972.
The Phantom and the Scorpia Menace (as Lee Falk).   New York, Avon, 1972.
The Phantom and the Slave Market of Mucar (as Lee Falk).   New York, Avon, 1972.
The Great White Space.   London, Hale, 1974; New York, St. Martin's Press, 1975.
The Curse of the Fleers.   London, Harwood Smart, 1976; New York, St. Martin's Press, 1977.
Necropolis.   Sauk City, Wisconsin, Arkham House, 1979.

Short Stories

Not after Nightfall.   London, New English Library, 1967.
From Evil's Pillow.   Sauk City, Wisconsin, Arkham House, 1973.
When Footsteps Echo: Tales of Terror and the Unknown.   London, Hale, and New York, St. Martin's Press, 1975.
And Afterward, the Dark: Seven Tales.   Sauk City, Wisconsin, Arkham House, 1977.
Here Be Daemons.   London, Hale, 1978; New York, St. Martin's Press, 1979.

Other

The Vampire: In Legend, Fact, and Art.   London, Hale, 1973.
The Werewolf: In Legend, Fact, and Art.   London, Hale, and New York, St. Martin's Press, 1977.

Basil Copper comments:

My most important work lies in the macabre and fantasy fields, but, so far as crime and mystery are concerned, my Mike Faraday novels, set in Los Angeles, may be considered an homage to Ring Lardner, Dashiell Hammett, Raymond Chandler, and the hard-boiled school of thriller writing.

Among those things that have given me most pleasure in recent years is my editing of the Solar Pons series by the late August Derleth. I have been commissioned to write several new Pons collections, for which I intend to combine the traditional detective form pioneered by Poe and Conan Doyle with the atmospheric and macabre themes that lie closest to my heart.

*   *   *

Basil Copper has established himself as a master of the macabre and the fantastic. Macabre books like *And Afterward, The Dark*, *From Evil's Pillow*, and *No Letters from the Grave* show by their titles the type of story in which he excels. There is another side to Copper, however. He is the creator of the private eye Mike Faraday, who has appeared in almost 30 novels. In the traditional detective field Copper has produced new volumes of Solar Pons adventures, Pons being the character created by August Derleth in homage to Sherlock Holmes.

—Herbert Harris

CORRIGAN, Mark. Pseudonym for Norman Lee; also wrote as Raymond Armstrong; Robertson Hobart. British. Born in 1905. *Died in 1962.*

CRIME PUBLICATIONS

Novels (series character: Mark Corrigan in all books)

Bullets and Brown Eyes. London, Laurie, 1948.
Sinner Takes All. London, Laurie, 1949.
The Wayward Blonde. London, Laurie, 1950.
The Golden Angel. London, Laurie, 1950.
Lovely Lady. London, Laurie, 1950.
Madame Sly. London, Laurie, 1951.
Shanghai Jezebel. London, Laurie, 1951.
Lady of China Street. London, Laurie, 1952.
Baby Face. London, Laurie, 1952.
All Brides Are Beautiful. London, Laurie, 1953.
Sweet and Deadly. London, Laurie, 1953.
I Like Danger. London, Laurie, 1954.
Love for Sale. London, Laurie, 1954.
The Naked Lady. London, Laurie, 1954.
Madam and Eve. London, Laurie, 1955.
The Big Squeeze. London, Angus and Robertson, 1955.
Big Boys Don't Cry. London, Angus and Robertson, 1956.
Sydney for Sin. London, Angus and Robertson, 1956.
The Cruel Lady. London, Angus and Robertson, 1957.
Dumb as They Come. London, Angus and Robertson, 1957.
Honolulu Snatch. London, Angus and Robertson, 1958.
Menace in Siam. London, Angus and Robertson, 1958.
The Girl from Moscow. London, Angus and Robertson, 1959.
Singapore Downbeat. London, Angus and Robertson, 1959.
Sin of Hong Kong. London, Angus and Robertson, 1960.
Lady from Tokyo. London, Angus and Robertson, 1961.
Riddle of Double Island. London, Angus and Robertson, 1962.
Danger's Green Eyes. London, Angus and Robertson, 1962.
Why Do Women ...? London, Angus and Robertson, 1963.
The Riddle of the Spanish Circus. London, Angus and Robertson, 1964.

Novels as Raymond Armstrong (series characters: Laura Scudamore; J. Rockingham Stone)

Dangerous Limelight. London, Long, 1947.
Sinister Playhouse. London, Long, 1949.
The Sinister Widow (Scudamore). London, Long, 1951.
They Couldn't Go Wrong. London, Long, 1951.
The Sinister Widow Again (Scudamore). London, Long, 1952.
The Sinister Widow Returns (Scudamore). London, Long, 1953.
The Midnight Cavalier (Stone). London, Long, 1954.
Cavalier of the Night (Stone). London, Long, 1956.
The Widow and the Cavalier. London, Long, 1956.
The Sinister Widow Comes Back (Scudamore). London, Long, 1957.
The Sinister Widow Down Under (Scudamore). London, Long, 1958.
The Sinister Widow at Sea (Scudamore). London, Long, 1959.
Murder of a Marriage. London, Long, 1960.

Novels as Robertson Hobart (series character: Grant Vickary)

Case of the Shaven Blonde (Vickary).   London, Hale, 1959.
Dangerous Cargoes (Vickary).   London, Hale, 1960.
Death of a Love.   London, Hale, 1961.
Blood on the Lake.   London, Hale, 1961.

OTHER PUBLICATIONS as Norman Lee

Novels

The Four Winds Mystery.   Dublin, McCann, 1945; London, Mitre Press, 1946.
Deputy Wife.   Dublin, McCann, and London, Mitre Press, 1946.
Peril at Journey's End.   Hounslow, Middlesex, Foster, 1947.

Play

Lifeline, with Barbara Toy (as Norman Armstrong) (produced London and New York,
    1942).   London, French, 1943.

Other

Money for Film Stories.   London, Pitman, 1937.
Action on the Rolling Road (juvenile).   London, Oxford University Press, 1945.
*A Film Is Born: How 40 Film Fathers Bring a Modern Talking Picture into
    Being.*   London, Jordan, 1945.
Landlubber's Log: 25,000 Miles with the Merchant Navy.   London, Quality Press,
    1945.
The Hoodoo Ship (juvenile).   London, Hollis and Carter, 1946.
Amateur Dramatics (juvenile).   London, Oxford University Press, 1947.
*I Want to Go to Sea: For the Boy Who Wants to Join the British Merchant
    Service.*   London, Jordan, 1947.
My Personal Log: The Autobiography of an Amateur Sailor.   London, Quality Press,
    1947.
The Terrified Village: A Tale of Kent and Sussex Smugglers (juvenile).   London,
    Lutterworth Press, 1947.
The Legion of the Eagle (juvenile).   London, Lutterworth Press, 1948.
The Ship of the Missing Men (juvenile).   London, Oxford University Press, 1948.
Ship of Adventure (juvenile).   London, Skilton, 1948.
The Green Chateau (juvenile).   London, Lutterworth Press, 1949.
The Phantom Buccaneer (juvenile).   London, Lutterworth Press, 1949.
Log of a Film Director.   London, Quality Press, 1949.
Johnny Carew (juvenile).   London, Ward Lock, 1951.
Seaway to Adventure (juvenile).   London, Ward Lock, 1956.
Australian Adventure (as Mark Corrigan).   London, Hale, 1960.

*   *   *

Norman Lee wrote some 50 novels under a variety of pseudonyms between 1945 and
1962. Raymond Armstrong and Robertson Hobart are two of the pseudonyms, but Mark
Corrigan (as author-hero) is the name that became most popular, and Lee concentrated on his
Corrigan books.

The Mark Corrigan books, written in the first person, suit his particular form of thriller.
The hero was born on the wrong side of the tracks, and as a youngster gravitates, via private
sleuthing, to U.S. Intelligence. Accompanied by Tucker Maclean, his glamorous assistant,

Corrigan survives numerous assaults on his person in locations as far apart as Australia and South America, with Singapore and Honolulu as stopping-off places in between.

Lee's style is light in these books, with a vein of romantic adventure, but the action is swift, and the dialogue forceful. The verve and repartee are enough to make *The Big Squeeze, The Naked Lady*, and *Bullets and Brown Eyes* highly recommended.

—Donald C. Ireland

CORY, Desmond. Pseudonym for Shaun Lloyd McCarthy; also writes as Theo Callas. British. Born in Lancing, Sussex, 16 February 1928. Educated at Steyning Grammar School, Sussex, 1938–44; St. Peter's College, Oxford, 1948–51, B.A. (honours) in English 1951, M.A. 1960; University of Wales, Cardiff, Ph.D. 1976. Served in the 45 Commando Unit, Royal Marines, 1944–48. Married Blanca Rosa Poyatos in 1956; four sons. Free-lance journalist and translator in Europe, 1951–54; language teacher in Spain and Sweden, 1954–60; Lecturer, University of Wales Institute of Science and Technology, Cardiff, 1960–77. Since 1977, Lecturer, University of Qatar, Doha, Arabian Gulf. Agent: George Greenfield, John Farquharson Ltd., Bell House, 8 Bell Yard, London WC2A 2JU, England. Address: 65 Westbourne Road, Penarth, South Glamorgan, Wales; or, P.O. Box 5585, Doha, Qatar, Arabian Gulf.

CRIME PUBLICATIONS

Novels (series characters: Mr. Dee; Johnny Fedora; Lindy Grey; Mr. Pilgrim)

Secret Ministry (Fedora).   London, Muller, 1951; as *The Nazi Assassins*, New York, Award, 1970.
Begin, Murderer! (Grey).   London, Muller, 1951.
This Traitor, Death (Fedora).   London, Muller, 1952; as *The Gestapo File*, New York, Award, 1971.
This Is Jezebel (Grey).   London, Muller, 1952.
Dead Man Falling (Fedora).   London, Muller, 1953; as *The Hitler Diamonds*, New York, Award, 1979.
Lady Lost (Grey).   London, Muller, 1953.
Intrigue (Fedora).   London, Muller, 1954; as *Trieste*, New York, Award, 1968.
The Shaken Leaf (Grey).   London, Muller, 1955.
Height of Day (Fedora).   London, Muller, 1955; as *Dead Men Alive*, New York, Award, 1969.
City of Kites (as Theo Callas).   London, Muller, 1955; New York, Walker, 1964.
The Phoenix Sings.   London, Muller, 1955.
High Requiem (Fedora).   London, Muller, 1956; New York, Award, 1969.
Johnny Goes North (Fedora).   London, Muller, 1956; as *The Swastika Hunt*, New York, Award, 1969.
Pilgrim at the Gate.   London, Muller, 1957; New York, Washburn, 1958.
Johnny Goes East (Fedora).   London, Muller, 1958; as *Mountainhead*, London, New English Library, 1966; New York, Award, 1968.
Johnny Goes West (Fedora).   London, Muller, 1959; New York, Walker, 1967.
Johnny Goes South (Fedora).   London, Muller, 1959; New York, Walker, 1964; as *Overload*, London, New English Library, 1964.

Pilgrim on the Island. London, Muller, 1959; New York, Walker, 1961.
The Head (Fedora). London, Muller, 1960.
Stranglehold (Dee). London, Muller, 1961.
Undertow (Fedora). London, Muller, 1962; New York, Walker, 1963.
Hammerhead (Fedora). London, Muller, 1963; as *Shockwave*, New York, Walker, 1964; London, New English Library, 1966.
The Name of the Game (Dee). London, Muller, 1964.
Deadfall. London, Muller, and New York, Walker, 1965.
Feramontov (Fedora). London, Muller, and New York, Walker, 1966.
Timelock (Fedora). London, Muller, and New York, Walker, 1967.
The Night Hawk. London, Hodder and Stoughton, and New York, Walker, 1969.
Sunburst (Fedora). London, Hodder and Stoughton, and New York, Walker, 1971.
Take My Drum to England. London, Hodder and Stoughton, 1971; as *Even If You Run*, New York, Doubleday, 1972.
A Bit of a Shunt up the River. New York, Doubleday, 1974.
The Circe Complex. London, Macmillan, and New York, Doubleday, 1975.
Bennett. London, Macmillan, and New York, Doubleday, 1977.

Uncollected Short Stories

"The Crime of Prince Milo," in *Winter's Crimes 7*, edited by George Hardinge. London, Macmillan, 1975.
"The Story of Stumblebum, The Wizard," in *Winter's Crimes 8*, edited by George Hardinge. London, Macmillan, 1976.

OTHER PUBLICATIONS

Novel

Lucky Ham (as Shaun McCarthy). London, Macmillan, 1977.

Play

Radio Play: *Orbit One*, 1961.

Other

Ann and Peter in Southern Spain (juvenile; as Theo Callas). London, Muller, 1959.
Jones on the Belgrade Express (juvenile). London, Muller, 1960.

Manuscript Collection: Mugar Memorial Library, Boston University.

Desmond Cory comments:
I published my first novel in 1951. I was then 23. My earliest ambition was to write the kind of books I most enjoyed reading. I did this for quite a few years, and they were very good years, because other (and better) writers were doing the same thing and I could feel I was taking part in a splendid post-war spree. We spy-writers gave pleasure to millions of people, and while it lasted it was all the greatest of fun. But then Fleming took our small success beyond all reasonable measure and our carnival floats were replaced by the noisy band-wagons of the mass media.
For the past ten years or so the questions for me, as for many others, have been What comes next? Which way should it go? Toward more documentary realism? Or towards more imaginative fantasy? Back to detective-story-style ingenuity? Or maybe comedy? Or political satire? You can find all these things in the vintage-years secret agent story, and it's

hard to explain why the problem is so difficult to solve. It is easy enough to convince oneself of the rightness of any particular solution – but good stories aren't written out of that kind of a conviction, and any number of clever bad books exist to prove it.

So since 1970 I've probed this way and that, trying to carry along enough readers with me to make the process worth their while as well as worth mine. It's exciting, but in a different way. In a sense, every experienced writer builds books out of the books that he has written before, moving them effortfully towards the books that he didn't write. In my case it's a slow, slow business. Thirty-odd years of books take a lot of shifting. But at 52 years of age one feels one has a goodish way still to go.

*　　*　　*

Shaun McCarthy, whose thrillers are written under the name Desmond Cory, is a prolific and versatile stylist. In the past 15 years, Cory has experimented with various narrative techniques. His broad range of knowledge and his inventiveness have also led him to write several types of suspense fiction—espionage, detective, and crime novels with an emphasis on psychological portraits of the characters. Skillful at creating atmosphere, he frequently uses Spain, a country he knows well, as a setting for his tales.

In five books called the "Feramontov quintet" – *Undertow, Hammerhead, Feramontov, Timelock,* and *Sunburst* – Cory matches the British agent Johnny Fedora, hero of earlier adventures, against Feramontov, formerly a Soviet agent. Feramontov is now a renegade, and all the more dangerous. A worthy opponent, Fedora's arch-enemy is intellectually gifted, physically powerful, and a creative genius who manipulates people and events like moves on a chessboard. Fedora and Laura Alonso, a beautiful Spanish agent, make time for interludes of passionate love-making. Political intrigue and corruption do not bring nuclear annihilation – only horrible deaths, often preceded by all-too-well described scenes of sadism and torture. The action is complicated, but well told.

Another political tale set in Spain is *Take My Drum to England,* in which a young Englishman gets involved with aging Spanish revolutionaries. An author's note at the end of the book, warning readers attempting to detonate gelignite by means of the telephone (because "I don't have all that many readers I can spare"), is disarming. The atmosphere is good, but perhaps the author's talent is wasted on what is rather a sordid little story after all. *Deadfall,* also set in Spain, examines the psychology of a jewel thief, Michael Jeye, an acrobatic burglar working with a Spanish couple. Jeye falls in love with the young wife and learns that her husband, an elderly homosexual, is also her father. True love is as elusive as a fortune in jewels.

Cory has an impressive command of psychiatric theory and jargon. In one of his best novels, *A Bit of a Shunt up the River,* Bony Wright, an escaped killer, is called by the prison psychiatrist an "affective schizoid sociopath," and we are told that "Bony thought that he himself was perfectly normal and that the psychiatrist was a bearded weirdie who couldn't have told him breakfast time from Thursday." Bony is matched against Tracy, a former racing driver, in a superb auto chase. Depth of character and Cory's fine wit set this tale far above the average suspense story. *The Circe Complex* is also excellent, both a thoroughly good tale and a satire of psychology and psychiatry. A hapless prison psychologist, beguiled by the wife of a patient (she also ensnares an Irish terrorist and a policeman), finds himself in prison for the same crimes committed by his former patient. He writes a scientific paper, complete with footnotes, describing the "Circe complex."

Bennett, a book within a book, is sophisticated and clever, but may be too much of a literary game to entertain most crime fiction fans. Low-key, amusing, and very *nouveau roman,* it should be compared with the works of Alain Robbe-Grillet. One wonders why *Bennett* was not published under the author's own name, since he published *Lucky Ham* as Shaun McCarthy. *Lucky Ham* is a literary spoof, a brilliant take-off on practically everybody – Shakespeare, Kingsley Amis, Lévi-Strauss, Joyce, Conrad, Beckett, and Sir Thomas Malory, to name a few. The hero Hamilton Biggs, called Hamlet or Ham for short, is called home from his anthropological researches in South America when his father, the president of an

Oxford college, is murdered by his uncle who then married his mother. A parody of *Hamlet* which goes on for 217 pages is scarcely to be imagined, but McCarthy interweaves pastiches of the classics with shots at contemporaries, and brings it off.

Shaun McCarthy/Desmond Cory has enormous talent and an especially keen sense of humor. Readers who do not yet know his works will do well to read them.

—Mary Helen Becker

COULTER, Stephen. Also writes as James Mayo. British. Born in 1914. Educated in England and France. Served in the Royal Navy Intelligence during World War II. Newspaper reporter in British home counties; joined Reuters as Parliamentary staff correspondent in 1937; staff correspondent for Kemsley Newspapers, Paris, 1945–65.

CRIME PUBLICATIONS

Novels

> *The Loved Enemy.* London, Deutsch, 1962.
> *Threshold.* London, Heinemann, and New York, Morrow, 1964.
> *Offshore!* London, Heinemann, 1965; New York, Morrow, 1966.
> *A Stranger Called the Blues.* London, Heinemann, 1968; as *Players in a Dark Game*,
> New York, Morrow, 1968; as *Death in the Sun*, London, Pan, 1970.
> *Embassy.* London, Heinemann, and New York, Coward McCann, 1969.
> *An Account to Render.* London, Heinemann, 1970.

Novels as James Mayo (series character: Charles Hood)

> *The Quickness of the Hand.* London, Deutsch, 1952.
> *Rebound.* London, Heinemann, 1961.
> *A Season of Nerves.* London, Heinemann, 1962.
> *Hammerhead* (Hood). London, Heinemann, and New York, Morrow, 1964.
> *Let Sleeping Girls Lie* (Hood). London, Heinemann, 1965; New York, Morrow, 1966.
> *Shamelady* (Hood). London, Heinemann, and New York, Morrow, 1966.
> *Once in a Lifetime* (Hood). London, Heinemann, 1968; as *Sergeant Death*, New York,
> Morrow, 1968.
> *The Man above Suspicion* (Hood). London, Heinemann, 1969.
> *Asking for It.* London, Heinemann, 1971.

OTHER PUBLICATIONS

Novels

> *Damned Shall Be Desire: The Loves of Guy de Maupassant.* London, Cape, 1958; New
> York, Doubleday, 1959.
> *The Devil Inside: A Novel of Dostoevsky's Life.* London, Cape, and New York,
> Doubleday, 1960.

Other

The Chateau. New York, Simon and Schuster, and London, Heinemann, 1974.

*   *   *

Stephen Coulter, who was in the Royal Navy during World War II and later assigned to special intelligence work in Europe, applies his knowledge to bring his readers realism in several exciting novels. *Threshold* tells of the attempted rescue of the 29 survivors of a British nuclear submarine sunk in Russian territorial waters. *Offshore!* is a suspenseful yarn concerning a monstrous oil rig in the North sea, winter weather, sabotage, and a fanatic boss who cares only about himself – "a notable thriller" says Anthony Boucher. In *A Stranger Called the Blues*, the tough American Ed Murray is unwillingly detailed in Calcutta, smuggles in Nepal, and has a run-in with the Chinese on the Nepalese border, during all of which he is haunted by an English nanny. In *Embassy*, Semyon Gorenko, sweating profusely, seeks political asylum in Paris, promising vital secrets in return. The story deals with the upheaval caused by his presence in the U.S. Embassy. This is a fast-paced novel told by an expert. The author has been compared with Eric Ambler in a review of *An Account to Render* for his excellent characterization in this thriller, which is a study of corruption set in South America. Mr. Coulter writes in a more serious vein under his own name than when he uses his Mayo pseudonym.

As James Mayo, Coulter writes novels often centering on tall, handsome, cosmopolitan Charles Hood, elegantly dressed, a gourmet and connoisseur of beautiful girls. Hood would seem to be just a wealthy dealer in objets d'art, but often, as in *Hammerhead*, he works on British Government missions for Special Intelligence. Hood, introduced in this book, is based on Ian Fleming's James Bond, but the violence is accented to the point of sadism, as noted by Anthony Boucher in his review of Hood's second case: "*Let Sleeping Girls Lie* has loads of sex, sadism and snobbery, and no sense at all of plot or structure; and Charles Hood's performance as a secret agent makes James Bond look realistic and intelligent." However, Boucher adds that the vivid action is excellently depicted and the sex scenes are amusingly written. In *Shamelady* a computer programmed not only to torture and kill Hood but to record his dying screams is foiled in a battle of wits. The best Mayo suspense story is *Once in a Lifetime*, in which Hood, investigating some incredibly good art forgeries, follows the trail from London through Paris to Teheran, where, in a final explosive climax, he is matched against dangerous U.S.A.F. Master-Sergeant Lloyd Bannion. James Mayo has a wild imagination; his exciting, fast-paced books are not for the squeamish.

—Betty Donaldson

COURTIER, S(idney) H(obson). Australian. Born in Kangaroo Flat, Victoria, 28 January 1904. Educated at the University of Melbourne, Cert. Ed. (honours). Married Audrey Jennie George in 1932; two sons and one daughter. Primary school teacher; later principal in Melbourne schools for teacher training for 12 years; retired in 1969. President, Melbourne branch, International P.E.N., 1954–57, 1958–61. *Died in 1974.*

CRIME PUBLICATIONS

Novels (series characters: Inspector "Digger" Haig; Ambrose Mahon)

The Glass Spear (Mahon).   New York, Wyn, 1950; London, Dakers, 1952.
One Cried Murder.   New York, Rinehart, 1954; London, Hammond, 1956.
Come Back to Murder (Mahon).   London, Hammond, 1957.
Now Seek My Bones (Haig).   London, Hammond, 1957.
A Shroud for Unlac (Mahon).   London, Hammond, 1958.
Death in Dream Time (Haig).   London, Hammond, 1959.
Gently Dust the Corpse.   London, Hammond, 1960; as *Softly Dust the Corpse*, London, Corgi, 1961.
Let the Man Die (Mahon).   London, Hammond, 1961.
Swing High, Sweet Murder (Haig).   London, Hammond, 1962.
Who Dies for Me?   London, Hammond, 1962.
A Corpse Won't Sing (Mahon).   London, Hammond, 1964.
Mimic a Murderer (Mahon).   London, Hammond, 1964.
The Ringnecker (Haig).   London, Hammond, 1965.
A Corpse at Least (Mahon).   London, Hammond, 1966.
Murder's Burning.   London, Hammond, and New York, Random House, 1967.
See Who's Dying.   London, Hammond, 1967.
No Obelisk for Emily (Haig).   London, Jenkins, 1970.
Ligny's Lake.   London, Hale, and New York, Simon and Schuster, 1971.
Some Village Borgia.   London, Hale, 1971.
Dead If I Remember.   London, Hale, 1972.
Into the Silence.   London, Hale, 1973.
Listening to the Mocking Bird.   London, Hale, 1974.
A Window in Chungking.   London, Hale, 1975.

Uncollected Short Stories

"Run for Your Life," in *Argosy Book of Adventure Stories*, edited by Rogers Terrill.   New York, A. S. Barnes, 1952.
"Island of No Escape," in *John Creasey's Mystery Bedside Book*, edited by Herbert Harris.   London, Hodder and Stoughton, 1966.

OTHER PUBLICATIONS

Novels

Gold for My Fair Lady.   New York, Wyn, 1951.
The Mudflat Million, with R. G. Campbell.   Sydney, Angus and Robertson, 1955.

*   *   *

For more than a dozen years before his first book, *The Glass Spear*, was published in 1950, S. H. Courtier supplied articles, stories, and serials to Australian periodicals, and also wrote radio scripts. During this period his work also appeared under the name Rui Chestor in the American magazines *Argosy* and *Short Stories*. All but two of Courtier's novels are mysteries. The two exceptions, both eminently worth reading, are *Gold for My Fair Lady*, a historical novel of the gold diggings at Kangaroo Flat, where the author was born, and *The Mudflat Million*, a wild comic novel written with Ronald G. Campbell.

In the London *Sunday Times* in 1959, Julian Symons wrote, "S. H. Courtier writes as well as the highly-praised Arthur Upfield, and is a good deal more ingenious." The ingenuity of plot is combined with an exceptionally skillful use of physical settings. Much of the action in

Come Back to Murder takes place in the tunnels of a worked-out gold mine. *Now Seek My Bones* is set in the crocodile- and snake-infested environs of McGorrie's Island on the Queensland coast. Brought to life with vividness and economy, these and other settings are not mere exotic backdrops, but are fully integrated into the plot and action of the books.

Two of the best Courtier novels are *Death in Dream Time* and *Murder's Burning*. The former is an extended set-piece, taking up less than twenty-four hours of time, set in Dream Time Land, an entertainment park built around themes from aboriginal creation myths. The latter novel chronicles the investigation of a mysterious fire that had ravaged a remote valley, killing a friend of the hero. The scenes in the subterranean passages beneath the valley are hair-raising.

Not all of Courtier's novels uphold his usual high standard. *See Who's Dying* is a strained James Bond-ish adventure, filled with unconvincing heroics and unbelievable impersonations. In *Some Village Borgia* the unappealing characters and the author's determination to have a surprise ending at all costs undercut the interest and consistency of the plot.

—R. E. Briney

COWEN, Frances.   Also writes as Eleanor Hyde.   British.   Born in Oxford, 27 December 1915. Educated at Ursuline Convent, Oxford, 1920–28; Milham Ford School, Oxford, 1928–35. Married George Heinrich Munthe in 1938 (died, 1941); one daughter. Worked for Blackwell, publishers, Oxford 1938–39; member of Air Raid Precautions staff, Dartmouth, 1940–44; Assistant Secretary, Royal Literary Fund, London, 1955–66. Agent: Hughes Massie Ltd., 69 Great Russell Street, London WC1B 3DH. Address: Flat One, 13 Thornton Hill, Wimbledon, London S.W. 19, England.

CRIME PUBLICATIONS

Novels

The Little Heiress.   London, Gresham, 1961.
The Balcony.   London, Gresham, 1962.
A Step in the Dark.   London, Gresham, 1962.
The Desperate Holiday.   London, Gresham, 1962.
The Elusive Quest.   London, Gresham, 1965.
The Bitter Reason.   London, Gresham, 1966.
Scented Danger.   London, Gresham, 1966.
The One Between.   London, Hale, 1967.
The Gentle Obsession.   London, Hale, 1968.
The Fractured Silence.   London, Hale, 1969.
The Daylight Fear.   London, Hale, 1969.
The Shadow of Polperro.   London, Hale, 1969.
Edge of Terror.   London, Hale, 1970.
The Hounds of Carvello.   London, Hale, 1970.
The Nightmare Ends.   London, Hale, 1970.
The Lake of Darkness.   London, Hale, 1971; New York, Ace, 1974.
The Unforgiving Moment.   London, Hale, 1971.
The Curse of the Clodaghs.   London, Hale, 1973; New York, Ace, 1974.

Shadow of Theale.   London, Hale, and New York, Ace, 1974.
The Village of Fear.   New York, Ace, 1974; London, Hale, 1975.
The Secret of Weir House.   London, Hale, 1975.
The Dangerous Child.   London, Hale, 1975.
The Haunting of Helen Farley.   London, Hale, 1976.
The Medusa Connection.   London, Hale, 1976.
Sinister Melody.   London, Hale, 1976.
The Silent Pool.   London, Hale, 1977.
The Lost One.   London, Hale, 1977.

OTHER PUBLICATIONS

Novels

Gateway to Nowhere.   London, Hale, 1978.
The House Without a Heart.   London, Hale, 1978.
The Princess Passes.   London, Hale, 1979.

Novels as Eleanor Hyde

Tudor Maid.   London, Hale, 1972.
Tudor Masquerade.   London, Hale, 1972.
Tudor Mayhem.   London, Hale, 1973.
Tudor Mystery.   London, Hale, 1974.
Tudor Myth.   London, Hale, 1976.
Tudor Mausoleum.   London, Hale, 1977.
Tudor Murder.   London, Hale, 1977.
Tudor Mansion.   London, Hale, 1978.
Tudor Menace.   London, Hale, 1979.

Other (juvenile)

In the Clutch of the Green Hand.   London, Nelson, 1929.
The Wings That Failed.   London, Collins, 1931; abridged, as *The Plot That Failed,*
    1933.
The Milhurst Mystery.   London, Blackie, 1933.
The Conspiracy of Silence.   London, Sheldon Press, 1935.
The Perilous Adventure.   London, Queensway Press, 1936.
Children's Book of Pantomimes.   London, Cassell, 1936.
Laddie's Way: The Adventures of a Fox Terrier.   London, Lutterworth Press, 1939.
The Girl Who Knew Too Much.   London, Lutterworth Press, 1940.
Mystery Tower.   London, Lutterworth Press, 1945.
Honor Bound.   London, Lutterworth Press, 1946.
Castle in Wales.   Huddersfield, Schofield and Sims, 1947.
The Secret of Arrivol.   Huddersfield, Schofield and Sims, 1947.
Mystery at the Walled House.   London, Lutterworth Press, 1951.
The Little Countess.   London, Thames, 1954.
The Riddle of the Rocks.   London, Lutterworth Press, 1956.
Clover Cottage.   London, Blackie, 1958.
The Secret of Grange Farm.   London, Children's Press, 1961.
The Secret of the Loch.   London, Children's Press, 1963.

*   *   *

Frances Cowen's first book was a boy's adventure yarn with the title *In the Clutch of the Green Hand*, and she went on writing other children's adventure stories. When she turned to writing for adults, she continued with her characteristic horrific suspense, made apparent by such recent titles as *The Haunting of Helen Farley*, *Sinister Melody*, *The Village of Fear*, and *The Secret of Weir House*. Her novels frequently have in their titles the words "Danger," "Fear," "Shadow," "Terror," "Secret," or "Curse." Her formula is the distinctly "gothic" one of placing a woman character in a desperate and threatened situation and subjecting her to terrifying ordeals.

Writing as Eleanor Hyde, she has produced several historical works set in the Tudor period. Despite her prolific output, she is a careful, methodical writer of well-rounded plots, and keeps her followers supplied with the type of story they expect from her.

—Herbert Harris

COXE, George Harmon. American. Born in Olean, New York, 23 April 1901. Educated at Purdue University, West Lafayette, Indiana, 1919–20; Cornell University, Ithaca, New York, 1920–21. Married Elizabeth Fowler in 1929; one daughter and one son. Reporter, Santa Monica *Outlook*, California, Los Angeles *Express*, Utica *Observer Dispatch*, New York, *Commercial & Financial Chronicle*, New York, and Elmira *Star-Gazette*, New York, 1922–27; advertising salesman, Cambridge, Massachusetts, 1927–32. Member of the Board of Directors, 1946–48, 1969–70, and President, 1952, Mystery Writers of America. Recipient: Mystery Writers of America Grand Master Award, 1964. Agent: Brandt and Brandt, 101 Park Avenue, New York, New York 10017. Address: Deepledge, Old Lyme, Connecticut 06371; or, 13 Painted Bunting Road, Hilton Head Island, South Carolina 29928, U.S.A.

CRIME PUBLICATIONS

Novels (series characters: Flash Casey; Sam Crombie; Jack Fenner; Max Hale; Kent Murdock)

> *Murder with Pictures* (Murdock). New York, Knopf, 1935; London, Heinemann, 1937.
> *The Barotique Mystery* (Murdock). New York, Knopf, 1936; London, Heinemann, 1937; as *Murdock's Acid Test*, New York, Dell, 1977.
> *The Camera Clue* (Murdock). New York, Knopf, 1937; London, Heinemann, 1938.
> *Four Frightened Women* (Murdock; Fenner). New York, Knopf, 1939; as *The Frightened Woman*, London, Heinemann, 1939.
> *Murder for the Asking* (Hale). New York, Knopf, 1939; London, Heinemann, 1940.
> *The Glass Triangle* (Murdock). New York, Knopf, 1940.
> *The Lady Is Afraid* (Hale). New York, Knopf, and London, Heinemann, 1940.
> *Mrs. Murdock Takes a Case* (Murdock). New York, Knopf, 1941; London, Swan, 1949.
> *No Time to Kill.* New York, Knopf, 1941.
> *Assignment in Guiana.* New York, Knopf, 1942; London, Macdonald, 1943.
> *The Charred Witness* (Murdock). New York, Knopf, 1942; London, Swan, 1949.
> *Silent Are the Dead* (Casey). New York, Knopf, 1942.
> *Alias the Dead.* New York, Knopf, 1943; London, Hammond, 1945.
> *Murder for Two* (Casey). New York, Knopf, 1943; London, Hammond, 1944.
> *Murder in Havana.* New York, Knopf, 1943; London, Hammond, 1945.
> *The Groom Lay Dead.* New York, Knopf, 1944; London, Hammond, 1946.

The Jade Venus (Murdock).   New York, Knopf, 1945; London, Hammond, 1947.
Woman at Bay.   New York, Knopf, 1945; London, Hammond, 1948.
Dangerous Legacy.   New York, Knopf, 1946; London, Hammond, 1949.
Fashioned for Murder.   New York, Knopf, 1947; London, Hammond, 1950.
The Fifth Key (Murdock).   New York, Knopf, 1947; London, Hammond, 1950.
The Hollow Needle (Murdock).   New York, Knopf, 1948; London, Hammond, 1952.
Venturous Lady.   New York, Knopf, 1948; London, Hammond, 1951.
Inland Passage.   New York, Knopf, 1949; London, Hammond, 1953.
Lady Killer (Murdock).   New York, Knopf, 1949; London, Hammond, 1952.
Eye Witness (Murdock).   New York, Knopf, 1950; London, Hammond, 1953.
The Frightened Fiancée (Crombie).   New York, Knopf, 1950; London, Hammond,
    1953.
The Man Who Died Twice.   New York, Knopf, 1951; London, Hammond, 1955.
The Widow Had a Gun (Murdock).   New York, Knopf, 1951; London, Hammond,
    1954.
Never Bet Your Life.   New York, Knopf, 1952; London, Hammond, 1955.
The Crimson Clue (Murdock).   New York, Knopf, 1953; London, Hammond, 1955.
Uninvited Guest.   New York, Knopf, 1953; London, Hammond, 1956.
Death at the Isthmus.   New York, Knopf, 1954; London, Hammond, 1956.
Focus on Murder (Murdock).   New York, Knopf, 1954; London, Hammond, 1956.
Top Assignment.   New York, Knopf, 1955; London, Hammond, 1957.
Man on a Rope.   New York, Knopf, 1956; London, Hammond, 1958.
Suddenly a Widow.   New York, Knopf, 1956; London, Hammond, 1957.
Murder on Their Minds (Murdock).   New York, Knopf, 1957; London, Hammond,
    1958.
One Minute Past Eight.   New York, Knopf, 1957; London, Hammond, 1959.
The Big Gamble (Murdock).   New York, Knopf, 1958; London, Hammond, 1960.
The Impetuous Mistress (Crombie).   New York, Knopf, 1958; London, Hammond,
    1959.
Slack Tide.   New York, Knopf, 1959; London, Hammond, 1960.
Triple Exposure (omnibus).   New York, Knopf, 1959.
The Last Commandment (Murdock).   New York, Knopf, 1960; London, Hammond,
    1961.
One Way Out.   New York, Knopf, 1960; London, Hammond, 1961.
Error of Judgment (Casey).   New York, Knopf, 1961; London, Hammond, 1962; as
    One Murder Too Many, New York, Pyramid, 1969.
Moment of Violence.   New York, Knopf, 1961; London, Hammond, 1962.
The Man Who Died Too Soon (Casey).   New York, Knopf, 1962; London, Hammond,
    1963.
Mission of Fear.   New York, Knopf, 1962; London, Hammond, 1963.
The Hidden Key (Murdock).   New York, Knopf, 1963; London, Hammond, 1964.
One Hour to Kill.   New York, Knopf, 1963; London, Hammond, 1964.
Deadly Image (Casey).   New York, Knopf, and London, Hammond, 1964.
The Reluctant Heiress (Murdock).   New York, Knopf, 1965; London, Hammond,
    1966.
With Intent to Kill.   New York, Knopf, and London, Hammond, 1965.
The Ring of Truth.   New York, Knopf, 1966; London, Hammond, 1967.
The Candid Imposter.   New York, Knopf, 1968; London, Hale, 1969.
An Easy Way to Go (Murdock).   New York, Knopf, and London, Hale, 1969.
Double Identity.   New York, Knopf, 1970; London, Hale, 1971.
Fenner (Fenner, Murdock).   New York, Knopf, 1971; London, Hale, 1973.
Woman with a Gun.   New York, Knopf, 1972; London, Hale 1974.
The Silent Witness (Fenner).   New York, Knopf, 1973; London, Hale, 1974.
The Inside Man.   New York, Knopf, 1974; London, Hale, 1975.
No Place for Murder (Fenner).   New York, Knopf, 1975; London, Hale, 1976.

Short Stories

Flash Casey, Detective.   New York, Avon, 1946.

Uncollected Short Stories

"No Provisions for Picnics," in *Street & Smith's Detective Story Magazine* (New York), 1 April 1922.
"Time to a T," in *Street & Smith's Detective Story Magazine* (New York), 21 April 1923.
"Special Delivery," in *Top Notch* (New York), 15 July 1932.
"No Work, No Pay," in *Top Notch* (New York), 15 August 1932.
"Stop Sign," in *Top Notch* (New York), 1 September 1932.
"Bad Medicine," in *Complete Stories* (New York), 15 December 1932.
"Hot Hunches," in *Clues* (New York), February 1933.
"Mad Masquerade," in *Clues* (New York), April 1933.
"Full Payment," in *Argosy* (New York), 1 April 1933.
"Face Value," in *Complete Stories* (New York), 15 April 1933.
"Murder at Eight," in *Dime Mystery Book* (New York), May 1933.
"Ahead of Death," in *Street & Smith's Detective Story Magazine* (New York), 10 May 1933.
"Fifteen a Week," in *Detective Fiction Weekly* (New York), 10 June 1933.
"Counter-Evidence," in *Detective Fiction Weekly* (New York), 10 June 1933.
"Trustworthy," in *Argosy* (New York), 24 June 1933.
"The Weakest Link," in *Complete Stories* (New York), 1 August 1933.
"Planned Luck," in *Detective Fiction Weekly* (New York), 30 September 1933.
"Cyclops," in *Complete Stories* (New York), 1 October 1933.
"Material Witness," in *Detective Fiction Weekly* (New York), 28 October 1933.
"Slay Ride," in *Dime Detective* (New York), 1 November 1933.
"Special Messenger," in *Complete Stories* (New York), 1 November 1933.
"Testimonial," in *Argosy* (New York), 4 November 1933.
"Alias the Killer," in *Complete Stories* (New York), 15 November 1933.
"The Perfect Frame," in *Thrilling Detective* (New York), December 1933.
"Protection Promised," in *Complete Stories* (New York), 1 December 1933.
"The Last Witness," in *Detective Fiction Weekly* (New York), 9 December 1933.
"The Death Club," in *Complete Stories* (New York), 15 December 1933.
"Touch System," in *Complete Stories* (New York), 1 January 1934.
"Turn About," in *Complete Stories* (New York), 15 January 1934.
"Psychology Stuff," in *Thrilling Detective* (New York), February 1934.
"Return Engagement," in *Black Mask* (New York), March 1934.
"The Missing Man," in *Phantom Detective* (New York), March 1934.
"A Letter of Death," in *Complete Stories* (New York), 15 March 1934.
"Special Assignment," in *Black Mask* (New York), April 1934.
"Blackmail Incorporated," in *Complete Stories* (New York), 1 April 1934.
"Clip Killer," in *Dime Detective* (New York), 1 April 1934.
"Licorice Drops," in *Complete Stories* (New York), 30 April 1934.
"Two-Man Job," in *Black Mask* (New York), May 1934.
"Solo!," in *Clues* (New York), May 1934.
"Jailed," in *Thrilling Detective* (New York), May 1934.
"Push-Over," in *Black Mask* (New York), June 1934.
"The Twelfth Woman," in *Complete Stories* (New York), 11 June 1934.
"Hot Delivery," in *Black Mask* (New York), July 1934.
"Easy Money," in *Complete Stories* (New York), 1 July 1934.
"Final Appeal," in *Detective Fiction Weekly* (New York), 7 July 1934.
"Party Murder," in *Detective Fiction Weekly* (New York), 14 July 1934.
"One-Buck Pay-Off," in *Dime Detective* (New York), 15 July 1934.

"Mixed Drinks," in *Black Mask* (New York), August 1934.
"Pinch-Hitters," in *Black Mask* (New York), September 1934.
"It's Teamwork That Counts," in *Complete Stories* (New York), 24 September 1934.
"The Murder Schedule," in *Clues* (New York), November 1934.
"Stuffed Shirts," in *Complete Stories* (New York), 5 November 1934.
"When a Cop's a Good Cop," in *The Mystery Magazine* (New York), December 1934.
"Murder Picture," in *Black Mask* (New York), January 1935.
"Greed Crazy," in *Detective Fiction Weekly* (New York), 5 January 1935.
"The Murder Bridge," in *Thrilling Detective* (New York), February 1935.
"Earned Reward," in *Black Mask* (New York), March 1935.
"Hot Assignment," in *Clues-Detective* (New York), March 1935.
"Reprisal," in *Complete Stories* (New York), 8 March 1935.
"One-Man Job," in *Complete Stories* (New York), 22 April 1935.
"Murder Date," in *Dime Detective* (New York), 1 May 1935.
"Thirty Tickets to Win," in *Black Mask* (New York), June 1935.
"When a Lady's Involved," in *The Mystery Magazine* (New York), June 1935.
"The Seventy Grand Bullet," in *Detective Fiction Weekly* (New York), 1 June 1935.
"Unfair Bargain," in *Maclean's* (Toronto), 1 June 1935.
"Buried Evidence," in *Black Mask* (New York), July 1935.
"Guiana Gold," in *Blue Book* (Chicago), August 1935.
"Mr. Casey Flashguns Murder," in *Black Mask* (New York), October 1935.
"Murder Set-Up," in *Detective Fiction Weekly* (New York), 9 November 1935.
"Murder Touch," in *Detective Fiction Weekly* (New York), 9 November 1935.
"The Dead Can't Hide," in *Detective Fiction Weekly* (New York), 23 November 1935.
"The Isle of New Fortunes," in *Blue Book* (Chicago), December 1935.
"Ungallant Evidence," in *Complete Magazine* (New York), December 1935.
"Portrait of Murder," in *Black Mask* (New York), February 1936.
"You Gotta Be Tough," in *Black Mask* (New York), March 1936.
"Letters Are Poison," in *Black Mask* (New York), April 1936.
"Murder Mix-Up," in *Black Mask* (New York), May 1936.
"Fall Guy," in *Black Mask* (New York), June 1936.
"Trouble for Two," in *Black Mask* (New York), July 1936.
"Head-Work Payoff," in *Ten Detective Aces* (New York), August 1936.
"Double or Nothing," in *Black Mask* (New York), November 1936.
"The Camera Clue," in *American Magazine* (Springfield, Ohio), February 1937.
"Peril Afloat," in *Thrilling Detective* (New York), July 1937.
"Death Is a Gamble," in *American Magazine* (Springfield, Ohio), October 1939.
"Casey and the Blonde Wren," in *Black Mask* (New York), August 1940.
"Vigilance," in *Collier's* (Springfield, Ohio), 19 April 1941.
"All Routes Covered," in *Coronet* (Chicago), October 1941.
"Boy, Are You Lucky," in *Liberty* (New York), 29 November 1941.
"Surprise in a Bottle," in *This Week* (New York), 1 February 1942.
"Intelligence from the Reich," in *American Magazine* (Springfield, Ohio), April 1942.
"Murder in the Red," in *Black Mask* (New York), June 1942.
"Alias the Killer," in *Collier's* (Springfield, Ohio), 26 August 1944.
"The Unloved Corpse," in *Mystery Book Magazine* (New York), December 1945.
"Three Guesses to Guilt," in *Mystery Book Magazine* (New York), March 1946.
"Murder to Music," in *Liberty* (New York), 7 September 1946.
"Post Mortem," in *Liberty* (New York), 16 November 1946.
"The Fourth Visitor," and "The Canary Sang," in *Murder for the Millions*, edited by
    Frank Owen. New York, Fell, 1946.
"The Doctor Makes It Murder," in *Murder Cavalcade*, edited by Ken Crossen. New
    York, Duell, 1946; London, Hammond, 1953.
"The Painted Nail," in *Fourth Mystery Companion*, edited by Abraham Louis
    Furman. New York, Lantern Press, 1946.

"Cause for Suspicion," in *Liberty* (New York), 1 February 1947.

"Death Certificate," in *Four and Twenty Bloodhounds*, edited by Anthony Boucher. New York, Simon and Schuster, 1950; London, Hammond, 1951.

"One for the Book," in *Giant Detective Annual*. New York, Best Books, 1950.

"Invited Witness," in *As Tough As They Come*, edited by Will Oursler. New York, Doubleday, 1951.

"Black Target," in *American Magazine* (Springfield, Ohio), March 1951.

"The Doctor Takes a Case," in *20 Great Tales of Murder*, edited by Helen McCloy and Brett Halliday. New York, Random House, 1951; London, Hammond, 1952.

"The Fatal Hour," in *American Magazine* (Springfield, Ohio), November 1951.

"Weapon of Fear," in *American Magazine* (Springfield, Ohio), May 1952.

"The Captive-Bride Murders," in *American Magazine* (Springfield, Ohio), July 1953.

"No Loose Ends," in *Eat, Drink, and Be Buried*, edited by Rex Stout. New York, Viking Press, 1956; as *For Tomorrow We Die*, London, Macdonald, 1958.

"Courage Isn't Everything," in *For Love or Money*, edited by Dorothy Gardiner. New York, Doubleday, 1957; London, Macdonald, 1959.

"Two Minute Alibi," in *Ellery Queen's Mystery Magazine* (New York), August 1958.

"There's Still Tomorrow," in *Ellery Queen's 15th Mystery Annual*. New York, Random House, 1960; London, Gollancz, 1961.

"The Barbados Beach House," in *Cosmopolitan* (New York), May 1961.

"The Girl in the Melody Lounge," in *Cosmopolitan* (New York), December 1963.

"Circumstantial Evidence," in *Anthology 1965*, edited by Ellery Queen. New York, Davis, 1964.

"When a Wife Is Murdered," in *Anthology 1965 Mid-Year*, edited by Ellery Queen. New York, Davis, 1965.

"A Routine Night's Work," in *Anthology 1968*, edited by Ellery Queen. New York, Davis, 1967.

"A Neat and Tidy Job," in *Anthology 1969*, edited by Ellery Queen. New York, Davis, 1968.

"The Cop Killer," in *Anthology 1970*, edited by Ellery Queen. New York, Davis, 1969.

"Seed of Suspicion," in *Anthology 1971*, edited by Ellery Queen. New York, Davis, 1970.

OTHER PUBLICATIONS

Plays

Screenplays: *Arsene Lupin Returns*, 1938; *The Hidden Eye*, with Harry Ruskin, 1946.

Radio Plays: *Crime Photographer* series, 1943–52; *The Commandos* series.

Television Plays: *Kraft Television Theatre*, 1957.

Other

Editor, *Butcher, Baker, Murder-Maker*. New York, Knopf, 1954; London, Macdonald, 1956.

Bibliography: "Mystery Master: A Survey and Appreciation of the Fiction of George Harmon Coxe" by J. Randolph Cox, in *Armchair Detective* (White Bear Lake, Minnesota), February to November 1973.

Manuscript Collection: Beinecke Rare Book and Manuscript Library, Yale University, New Haven, Connecticut.

* * *

George Harmon Coxe has been called "the professional's professional" by Anthony Boucher and "a master of the art of the detective novel" by William Lyon Phelps. Erle Stanley Gardner referred to his books as "uniformly entertaining, gripping, and exciting."

His earliest stories in the pulps were told from the point of view of the crook. He avoided the clichés of the locked-room mystery; instead he concentrated on ordinary characters who were killed by gun or knife (whichever was most plausible), and then followed the other characters to see what would happen. He soon shifted to third-person narratives from the point of view of the police or the detective (his private detectives were often men who had been on the police force).

The strictly deductive story in the Sherlock Holmes tradition was not among Coxe's stock of material, as he himself has admitted. Since writers are told to write what they know, Coxe concentrated on the newspaper business.

The Coxe hero, even in the early years, was often a college educated man who clashed with the rough, self taught street educated character. Sometimes there was a degree of cooperation, opposites definitely attracting. The humor arising from such a situation was never forced. Some of his best work was done for *Black Mask*, where his stories of Flash Casey first appeared. Casey was created to fill a gap in the fictional detective field: in the early 1930's there were plenty of reporters who doubled as sleuths, but there was no photographer. Casey originally worked for the Boston *Globe*, but soon transferred to the *Express*, the paper with which he is commonly associated. Jack (Flashgun, or Flash) Casey is a large, rumpled man with a touch of gray at the temples. He may curse at being dragged out of bed in the morning, but will do anything to help a colleague or anyone else in genuine trouble. He has a distaste for people who are too smooth and too clever. His eyes are dark, his fists are big, and he weighs 210 pounds under the sweat-stained felt hat he jams onto his head. A Casey plot can be summed up as a triple conflict: Casey is after a news story in pictures, the opposition (the criminals) don't want him to get those pictures, and the police don't want him to interfere. Casey's interference, of course, delivers the criminals to the police. Casey is a figure from American folklore – the sentimental tough guy – and this may account for much of his appeal. Coxe was never a truly hard-boiled writer, preferring to substitute character for action and violence. He used Casey in several novels after the *Black Mask* days. (Another *Black Mask* character, Paul Baron, did not have the appeal of Casey and appeared in only four stories.)

When Coxe began to write books he replaced Casey with photographer Kent Murdock of the *Courier-Herald*. Murdock is more sophisticated than Casey and is more socially at ease. Murdock knows people on all levels of society and his first case (*Murder with Pictures*) is easily among Coxe's best novels with its multiple conflicts. One of the most interesting characters in the series was Murdock's wife, Joyce, confident, self-reliant, intelligent – just the sort of woman the cynical sentimentalist, Kent Murdock, would have married. She was too strong a character, however, and was dropped before she could take over the series. There is a certain amount of pleasant predictability about the Murdock stories. This familiarity may have helped the reader who expected and wanted a story much like the last one. Murdock was expected to stumble over bodies in closets; it was part of his job and part of his character. Murdock's colleague in some of the novels was Jack Fenner. In 1971 he branched out on his own. Flippant and good-natured, there was something hard and unyielding about his character. He was unafraid and, at times, merciless.

Coxe's third major series centers on the medical examiner Paul Standish. The medical background is as authentic in this series as the newspaper background in the Casey and Murdock series. Coxe also wrote books about Sam Crombie (a large man in a seersucker suit and Panama hat, who plods along and does his job) and Maxfield Chauncey Hale (detective in spite of himself).

Nearly half of Coxe's published novels have not been part of any series at all. The heroes and villains resemble ones in his series books, but there is more freedom for the author to develop characters, tell different kinds of stories, and use varying backgrounds. One of the obvious advantages in writing a mystery about a character who does not have to survive unchanged for another book is the way the reader is allowed to get inside his skin. The feelings of Murdock and Casey could not be described in the same way as those of Spence Rankin in *Dangerous Legacy*. The settings vary for the non-series books, but within the group are 16 which take place in the Caribbean, an area their author knows well.

To some readers Coxe may seem dull. There is little explicit violence, just tales of people caught up in webs of their own spinning, told in a deceptively simple formal style. For others – that's entertainment.

—J. Randolph Cox

CRANE, Frances (née Kirkwood). American. Born in Lawrenceville, Illinois, in 1896. Educated at the University of Illinois, Urbana, B.A. (Phi Beta Kappa). Married Ned Crane (died); one daughter. Address: c/o Robert E. Mills, 156 East 52nd Street, New York, New York 10022, U.S.A.

CRIME PUBLICATIONS

Novels (series characters; Pat and Jean Abbott in all books except those without color references in the title)

The Turquoise Shop. Philadelphia, Lippincott, 1941; London, Hammond, 1943.
The Golden Box. Philadelphia, Lippincott, 1942; London, Hammond, 1944.
The Yellow Violet. Philadelphia, Lippincott, 1942; London, Hammond, 1944.
The Applegreen Cat. Philadelphia, Lippincott, 1943; London, Hammond, 1945.
The Pink Umbrella. Philadelphia, Lippincott, 1943; London, Hammond, 1944.
The Amethyst Spectacles. New York, Random House, 1944; London, Hammond, 1946.
The Indigo Necklace. New York, Random House, 1945; London, Hammond, 1947.
The Cinnamon Murder. New York, Random House, 1946; London, Hammond, 1948.
The Shocking Pink Hat. New York, Random House, 1946; London, Hammond, 1948.
Murder on the Purple Water. New York, Random House, 1947; London, Hammond, 1949.
Black Cypress. New York, Random House, 1948; London, Hammond, 1950.
The Flying Red Horse. New York, Random House, and London, Hammond, 1950.
The Daffodil Blonde. New York, Random House, 1950; London, Hammond, 1951.
Murder in Blue Street. New York, Random House, 1951; as *Death in the Blue Hour*, London, Hammond, 1952.
The Polkadot Murder. New York, Random House, 1951; London, Hammond, 1952.
Murder in Bright Red. New York, Random House, 1953; London, Hammond, 1954.
13 White Tulips. New York, Random House, and London, Hammond, 1953.
The Coral Princess Murders. New York, Random House, 1954; London, Hammond, 1955.

Death in Lilac Time. New York, Random House, and London, Hammond, 1955.
Horror on the Ruby X. New York, Random House, and London, Hammond, 1956.
The Ultraviolet Widow. New York, Random House, 1956; London, Hammond, 1957.
The Buttercup Case. New York, Random House, and London, Hammond, 1958.
The Man in Gray. New York, Random House, 1958; as *The Gray Stranger,* London, Hammond, 1958.
Death-Wish Green. New York, Random House, and London, Hammond, 1960.
The Reluctant Sleuth. London, Hammond, 1961.
The Amber Eyes. New York, Random House, and London, Hammond, 1962.
Three Days in Hong Kong. London, Hammond, 1965.
Body Beneath a Mandarin Tree. London, Hammond, 1965.
A Very Quiet Murder. London, Hammond, 1966.
Worse Than a Crime. London, Hale, 1968.

Uncollected Short Story

"The Blue Hat," in *Queen's Awards 1946,* edited by Ellery Queen. Boston, Little Brown, 1946; London, Gollancz, 1948.

OTHER PUBLICATIONS

Novel

The Tennessee Poppy; or, Which Way Is Westminster Abbey. New York, Farrar and Rinehart, 1932.

*   *   *

Primarily a formula mystery writer, Frances Crane wrote mysteries for over two decades, moving from the conventions of the late Golden Age "Had-I-But-Known" school to the fringes of modern crime novels. Jean Abbott (Holly in her pre-marriage books) narrates the stories while her husband, Pat, is the strong silent detective. Though they live in San Francisco, many of the Abbotts' cases occur while they are on vacation: in fact, the books are often travelogues, but only occasionally successful in using local color to create atmosphere.

Crane's work is mostly in the mystery field. As in *The Yellow Violet*, hints of spies or gangsters are usually kept vague. A murder occurs, usually off-stage, and Jean becomes involved; Pat, in charge of the final scenes, catches the villain and explains how and why the murder occurred. His solution is based largely on points learned or discussed by Jean, but his reasoning process to uncover the murderer's identity is not given. The earlier books used Had-I-But-Known teasers to evoke suspense, but Crane dropped most of those by the late 1950's. And Crane moved with the times in other ways, introducing more naturalistic elements, drugs in *Death-Wish Green* and *Coral Princess* and a retarded child in *The Amber Eyes*.

Crane tried to achieve characterization by bizarreness. Her books often drop the reader into the middle of a situation and then backtrack to show how the Abbotts got into it. A large eccentric family or close-knit group makes up the list of suspects, often not clearly differentiated. There is often a pair of young lovers toward whom Jean is sympathetic, even though at least one of them acts suspiciously. Pat seems to accept them at face value, forcing Jean to withhold some incriminating information.

As a husband and wife team, the Abbotts don't provide the humor or oddity of the Lockridges' Norths, Roos's Jeff and Haila Troy, or Christie's Tommy and Tuppence Beresford. Because we never know what Pat is really thinking, he never becomes truly alive. In the earlier books Jean is a prominent character. Her style is almost chatty, including detailed reporting of clothes and make-up. Later, she is primarily an observer.

Crane's popularity is based on competent working of familiar themes, taking her readers to exotic places, and presenting a non-taxing, unthreatening tale where all ends as it should.

—Fred Dueren

CRAWFORD, Robert.   See RAE, Hugh C.

CREASEY, John.   Also wrote as Gordon Ashe; M. E. Cooke; Margaret Cooke; Henry St. John Cooper; Norman Deane; Elise Fecamps; Robert Caine Frazer; Patrick Gill; Michael Halliday; Charles Hogarth; Brian Hope; Colin Hughes; Kyle Hunt; Peter Manton; J. J. Marric; Richard Martin; Rodney Mattheson; Anthony Morton; Ken Ranger; William K. Reilly; Tex Riley; Jeremy York.   British.   Born in Southfields, Surrey, 17 September 1908. Educated at Fulham Elementary School and Sloane School, both in London. Married 1) Margaret Elizabeth Cooke in 1935; 2) Evelyn Jean Fudge in 1941; 3) Jeanne Williams; three sons. Worked in various clerical posts, 1923–35; full-time writer from 1935: Editor and Publisher, *John Creasey Mystery Magazine*, 1956–65; Publisher, Jay Books, 1957–59. Co-founder, Crime Writers Association, 1953; Member of the Board, 1957–60, and President, 1966–67, Mystery Writers of America. Liberal Party Parliamentary Candidate for Bournemouth, 1950; Founded All Party Alliance Movement, 1967, and Parliamentary Candidate at Nuneaton, 1967, Brierley Hill, April 1967, Gorton, Manchester, 1967, and Oldham West, 1968. Recipient: Mystery Writers of America Edgar Allan Poe Award, 1962. M.B.E. (Member, Order of the British Empire), 1946. *Died 9 June 1973.*

CRIME PUBLICATIONS

Novels (series characters: Sexton Blake; Department Z; Dr. Palfrey; the Hon. Richard Rollison, "The Toff"; Roger West)

Seven Times Seven.   London, Melrose, 1932.
Men, Maids, and Murder.   London, Melrose, 1933; revised edition, London, Long, 1973.
Redhead (Department Z).   London, Hurst and Blackett, 1933.
The Death Miser (Department Z).   London, Melrose, 1933.
First Came a Murder (Department Z).   London, Melrose, 1934; revised edition, London, Long, 1969; New York, Popular Library, 1972.
Death round the Corner (Department Z).   London, Melrose, 1935; revised edition, London, Long, 1971; New York, Popular Library, 1972.
The Mark of the Crescent (Department Z).   London, Melrose, 1935; revised edition, London, Long, 1970; New York, Popular Library, 1972.
The Dark Shadow (as Rodney Mattheson).   London, Fiction House, n.d.
Thunder in Europe (Department Z).   London, Melrose, 1936; revised edition, London, Long, 1970; New York, Popular Library, 1972.

The Terror Trap (Department Z). London, Melrose, 1936; revised edition, London, Long, 1970; New York, Popular Library, 1972.

The House of Ferrars (as Rodney Mattheson). London, Fiction House, n.d.

Carriers of Death (Department Z). London, Melrose, 1937; revised edition, London, Arrow, 1968; New York, Popular Library, 1972.

The Case of the Murdered Financier (Blake). London, Amalgamated Press, 1937.

Days of Danger (Department Z). London, Melrose, 1937; revised edition, London, Long, 1970; New York, Popular Library, 1972.

Four Motives for Murder (as Brian Hope). London, Newnes, 1938.

Death Stands By (Department Z). London, Long, 1938; revised edition, London, Arrow, 1966; New York, Popular Library, 1972.

Introducing the Toff. London, Long, 1938; revised edition, 1954.

Menace! (Department Z). London, Long, 1938; revised edition, Long, and New York, Popular Library, 1972.

The Great Air Swindle (Blake). London, Amalgamated Press, 1939.

Murder Must Wait (Department Z). London, Melrose, 1939; revised edition, London, Long, 1969; New York, Popular Library, 1972.

Panic! (Department Z). London, Long, 1939; New York, Popular Library, 1972.

The Toff Goes On. London, Long, 1939; revised edition, 1955.

The Toff Steps Out. London, Long, 1939; revised edition, 1955.

Triple Murder (as Colin Hughes). London, Newnes, 1940.

Death by Night (Department Z). London, Long, 1940; revised edition, 1971; New York, Popular Library, 1972.

Here Comes the Toff! London, Long, 1940; New York, Walker, 1967.

The Island of Peril (Department Z). London, Long, 1940; revised edition, 1970; New York, Popular Library, 1976.

The Man from Fleet Street (Blake). London, Amalgamated Press, 1940.

The Toff Breaks In. London, Long, 1940; revised edition, 1955.

Sabotage (Department Z). London, Long, 1941; revised edition, 1972; New York, Popular Library, 1976.

Go Away Death (Department Z). London, Long, 1941; New York, Popular Library, 1976.

Salute the Toff. London, Long, 1941; New York, Walker, 1971.

The Toff Proceeds. London, Long, 1941; New York, Walker, 1968.

The Case of the Mad Inventor (Blake). London, Amalgamated Press, 1942.

The Day of Disaster (Department Z). London, Long, 1942.

Inspector West Takes Charge. London, Stanley Paul, 1942; revised edition, London, Pan, 1963; New York, Scribner, 1972.

Prepare for Action (Department Z). London, Stanley Paul, 1942; revised edition, London, Arrow, 1966; New York, Popular Library, 1975.

The Toff Goes to Market. London, Long, 1942; New York, Walker, 1967.

The Toff Is Back. London, Long, 1942; New York, Walker, 1974.

Traitors' Doom (Palfrey). London, Long, 1942; New York, Walker, 1970.

Inspector West Leaves Town. London, Stanley Paul, 1943; as *Go Away to Murder*, London, Lancer, 1972.

The Legion of the Lost (Palfrey). London, Long, 1943; New York, Daye, 1944; revised edition, New York, Walker, 1974.

No Darker Crime (Department Z). London, Stanley Paul, 1943; New York, Popular Library, 1976.

Private Carter's Crime (Blake). London, Amalgamated Press, 1943.

The Toff among the Millions. London, Long, 1943; revised edition, London, Panther, 1964; New York, Walker, 1976.

The Valley of Fear (Palfrey). London, Long, 1943; as *The Perilous Country*, 1949; revised edition, London, Arrow, 1966; New York, Walker, 1973.

Accuse the Toff. London, Long, 1943; New York, Walker, 1975.

The Toff on the Trail. London, Everybody's Books, n.d.

Murder on Largo Island, with Ian Bowen (as Charles Hogarth). London, Selwyn and Blount, 1944.

Dangerous Quest (Department Z). London, Long, 1944; revised edition, London, Arrow, 1965; New York, Walker, 1974.

Dark Peril (Department Z). London, Stanley Paul, 1944; revised edition, London, Long, 1969; New York, Popular Library, 1975.

Inspector West at Home. London, Stanley Paul, 1944; New York, Scribner, 1973.

The Toff and the Curate. London, Long, 1944; New York, Walker, 1969; as *The Toff and the Deadly Parson,* London, Lancer, 1970.

The Toff and the Great Illusion. London, Long, 1944; New York, Walker, 1967.

Death in the Rising Sun (Palfrey). London, Long, 1945; revised edition, 1970; New York, Walker, 1976.

The Hounds of Vengeance (Palfrey). London, Long. 1945; revised edition, 1969.

Inspector West Regrets –. London, Stanley Paul, 1945; revised edition, Hodder and Stoughton, 1965.

Feathers for the Toff. London, Long, 1945; revised edition, London, Hodder and Stoughton, 1964; New York, Walker, 1970.

Holiday for Inspector West. London, Stanley Paul, 1946.

The Peril Ahead (Department Z). London, Stanley Paul, 1946; revised edition, London, Long, 1969; New York, Popular Library, 1974.

Shadow of Doom (Palfrey). London, Long, 1946; revised edition, 1970.

The Toff and the Lady. London, Long, 1946; New York, Walker, 1975.

The Toff on Ice. London, Long, 1946; as *Poison for the Toff,* New York, Pyramid, 1965; revised edition, London, Corgi, 1976.

The House of the Bears (Palfrey). London, Long, 1946; revised edition, London, Arrow, 1962; New York, Walker, 1975.

Dark Harvest (Palfrey). London, Long, 1947; revised edition, London, Arrow, 1962; New York, Walker, 1977.

Hammer the Toff. London, Long, 1947.

The League of Dark Men (Department Z). London, Stanley Paul, 1947; revised edition, London, Arrow, 1965; New York, Popular Library, 1975.

Keys to Crime (as Richard Martin). Bournemouth, Earl, 1947.

Vote for Murder (as Richard Martin). Bournemouth, Earl, 1948.

Battle for Inspector West. London, Stanley Paul, 1948.

The Toff in Town. London, Long, 1948; revised edition, New York, Walker, 1977.

The Toff Takes Shares. London, Long, 1948; New York, Walker, 1972.

Triumph for Inspector West. London, Stanley Paul, 1948; as *The Case Against Paul Raeburn,* New York, Harper, 1958.

The Wings of Peace (Palfrey). London, Long, 1948; New York, Walker, 1978.

Sons of Satan (Palfrey). London, Long, 1948.

The Dawn of Darkness (Palfrey). London, Long, 1949.

The Department of Death (Department Z). London, Evans, 1949.

Inspector West Kicks Off. London, Stanley Paul, 1949; as *Sport for Inspector West,* London, Lancer, 1971.

The League of Light (Palfrey). London, Evans, 1949.

The Toff and Old Harry. London, Long, 1949; revised edition, London, Hodder and Stoughton, 1964; New York, Walker, 1970.

The Toff on Board. London, Evans, 1949; revised edition, New York, Walker, 1973.

The Enemy Within (Department Z). London, Evans, 1950; New York, Popular Library, 1977.

Fool the Toff. London, Evans, 1950; New York, Walker, 1966.

Inspector West Alone. London, Evans, 1950; New York, Scribner, 1975.

Inspector West Cries Wolf. London, Evans, 1950; as *The Creepers,* New York, Harper, 1952.

Kill the Toff. London, Evans, 1950; New York, Walker, 1966.

The Man Who Shook the World (Palfrey). London, Evans, 1950.

A Case for Inspector West. London, Evans, 1951; as *The Figure in the Dusk*, New York, Harper, 1952.

Dead or Alive (Department Z). London, Evans, 1951; New York, Popular Library, 1974.

A Knife for the Toff. London, Evans, 1951; New York, Pyramid, 1964.

The Prophet of Fire (Palfrey). London, Evans, 1951; New York, Walker, 1978.

Puzzle for Inspector West. London, Evans, 1951; as *The Dissemblers*, New York, Scribner, 1967.

The Toff Goes Gay. London, Evans, 1951; as *A Mask for the Toff*, New York, Walker, 1966.

The Children of Hate (Palfrey). London, Evans, 1952; as *The Children of Despair*, New York, Jay, 1958; revised edition, London, Long, 1970; as *The Killers of Innocence*, New York, Walker, 1971.

Inspector West at Bay. London, Evans, 1952; as *The Blind Spot*, New York, Harper, 1954; as *The Case of the Acid Throwers*, New York, Avon, 1960.

Hunt the Toff. London, Evans, 1952; New York, Walker, 1969.

Call the Toff. London, Hodder and Stoughton, 1953; New York, Walker, 1969.

A Gun for Inspector West. London, Hodder and Stoughton, 1953; as *Give a Man a Gun*, New York, Harper, 1954.

Send Inspector West. London, Hodder and Stoughton, 1953; revised edition, as *Send Superintendent West*, London, Pan, 1965; New York, Scribner, 1976.

The Toff Down Under. London, Hodder and Stoughton, 1953; New York, Walker, 1969; as *Break the Toff*, London, Lancer, 1970.

A Beauty for Inspector West. London, Hodder and Stoughton, 1954; as *The Beauty Queen Killer*, New York, Harper, 1956; as *So Young, So Cold, So Fair*, New York, Dell, 1958.

A Kind of Prisoner (Department Z). London, Hodder and Stoughton, 1954; New York, Popular Library, 1975.

The Toff at Butlin's. London, Hodder and Stoughton, 1954; New York, Walker, 1976.

The Toff at the Fair. London, Hodder and Stoughton, 1954; New York, Walker, 1968.

The Touch of Death (Palfrey). London, Hodder and Stoughton, 1954; New York, Walker, 1969.

Inspector West Makes Haste. London, Hodder and Stoughton, 1955; as *The Gelignite Gang*, New York, Harper, 1956; as *Night of the Watchman*, New York, Berkley, n.d.

The Mists of Fear (Palfrey). London, Hodder and Stoughton, 1955; New York, Walker, 1977.

A Six for the Toff. London, Hodder and Stoughton, 1955; New York, Walker, 1969; as *A Score for the Toff*, London, Lancer, 1972.

The Toff and the Deep Blue Sea. London, Hodder and Stoughton, 1955; New York, Walker, 1967.

Two for Inspector West. London, Hodder and Stoughton, 1955; as *Murder: One, Two, Three*, New York, Scribner, 1960; as *Murder Tips the Scales*, New York, Berkley, 1962.

Make-Up for the Toff. London, Hodder and Stoughton, 1956; New York, Walker, 1967; as *Kiss the Toff*, London, Lancer, 1971.

The Flood (Palfrey). London, Hodder and Stoughton, 1956; New York, Walker, 1969.

Parcels for Inspector West. London, Hodder and Stoughton, 1956; as *Death of a Postman*, New York, Harper, 1957.

A Prince for Inspector West. London, Hodder and Stoughton, 1956; as *Death of an Assassin*, New York, Scribner, 1960.

The Toff in New York. London, Hodder and Stoughton, 1956; New York, Pyramid, 1964.

Accident for Inspector West. London, Hodder and Stoughton, 1957; as *Hit and Run*, New York, Scribner, 1959.

The Black Spiders (Department Z).   London, Hodder and Stoughton, 1957; New York, Popular Library, 1975.

Find Inspector West.   London, Hodder and Stoughton, 1957; as *The Trouble at Saxby's*, New York, Harper, 1959; as *Doorway to Death*, New York, Berkley, 1961.

Model for the Toff.   London, Hodder and Stoughton, 1957; New York, Pyramid, 1965.

The Toff on Fire.   London, Hodder and Stoughton, 1957; New York, Walker, 1966.

Murder, London – New York (West).   London, Hodder and Stoughton, 1958; New York, Scribner, 1961.

The Plague of Silence (Palfrey).   London, Hodder and Stoughton, 1958; New York, Walker, 1968.

Strike for Death (West).   London, Hodder and Stoughton, 1958; as *The Killing Strike*, New York, Scribner, 1961.

The Toff and the Stolen Tresses.   London, Hodder and Stoughton, 1958; New York, Walker, 1965.

The Toff on the Farm.   London, Hodder and Stoughton, 1958; New York, Walker, 1964; as *Terror for the Toff*, New York, Pyramid, 1965.

Death of a Racehorse (West).   London, Hodder and Stoughton, 1959; New York, Scribner, 1962.

Double for the Toff.   London, Hodder and Stoughton, 1959; New York, Walker, 1965.

The Drought (Palfrey).   London, Hodder and Stoughton, 1959; New York, Walker, 1967; as *Dry Spell*, London, New English Library, 1967.

The Toff and the Runaway Bride.   London, Hodder and Stoughton, 1959; New York, Walker, 1964.

The Case of the Innocent Victims (West).   London, Hodder and Stoughton, 1959; New York, Scribner, 1966.

The Mountain of the Blind.   London, Hodder and Stoughton, 1960.

Murder on the Line (West).   London, Hodder and Stoughton, 1960; New York, Scribner, 1963.

A Rocket for the Toff.   London, Hodder and Stoughton, 1960; New York, Pyramid, 1964.

The Toff and the Kidnapped Child.   London, Hodder and Stoughton, 1960; New York, Walker, 1965.

Death in Cold Print (West).   London, Hodder and Stoughton, 1961; New York, Scribner, 1962.

Follow the Toff.   London, Hodder and Stoughton, 1961; New York, Walker, 1967.

The Foothills of Fear.   London, Hodder and Stoughton, 1961; New York, Walker, 1966.

The Scene of the Crime (West).   London, Hodder and Stoughton, 1961; New York, Scribner, 1963.

The Toff and the Teds.   London, Hodder and Stoughton, 1961; as *The Toff and the Toughs*, New York, Walker, 1968.

Policeman's Dread (West).   London, Hodder and Stoughton, 1962; New York, Scribner, 1964.

The Terror: The Return of Dr. Palfrey.   London, Hodder and Stoughton, 1962; New York, Walker, 1966.

The Depths (Palfrey).   London, Hodder and Stoughton, 1963; New York, Walker, 1966.

A Doll for the Toff.   London, Hodder and Stoughton, 1963; New York, Walker, 1965.

Hang the Little Man (West).   London, Hodder and Stoughton, and New York, Scribner, 1963.

Leave It to the Toff.   London, Hodder and Stoughton, 1963; New York, Pyramid, 1965.

Look Three Ways at Murder (West).   London, Hodder and Stoughton, 1964; New York, Scribner, 1965.

The Sleep! (Palfrey).   London, Hodder and Stoughton, 1964; New York, Walker, 1968.

The Inferno (Palfrey).   London, Hodder and Stoughton, 1965; New York, Walker, 1966.

Murder, London – Australia (West).   London, Hodder and Stoughton, and New York, Scribner, 1965.

The Toff and the Spider.   London, Hodder and Stoughton, 1965; New York, Walker, 1966.

Danger Woman (as Abel Mann).   New York, Pocket Books, 1966.

Murder, London – South Africa (West).   London, Hodder and Stoughton, and New York, Scribner, 1966.

The Toff in Wax.   London, Hodder and Stoughton, and New York, Walker, 1966.

A Bundle for the Toff.   London, Hodder and Stoughton, 1967; New York, Walker, 1968.

The Executioners (West).   London, Hodder and Stoughton, and New York, Scribner, 1967.

The Famine (Palfrey).   London, Hodder and Stoughton, 1967; New York, Walker, 1968.

The Blight (Palfrey).   London, Hodder and Stoughton, and New York, Walker, 1968.

So Young to Burn (West).   London, Hodder and Stoughton, and New York, Scribner, 1968.

Stars for the Toff.   London, Hodder and Stoughton, and New York, Walker, 1968.

Murder, London — Miami (West).   London, Hodder and Stoughton, and New York, Scribner, 1969.

The Oasis (Palfrey).   London, Hodder and Stoughton, 1969; New York, Walker, 1970.

The Toff and the Golden Boy.   London, Hodder and Stoughton, and New York, Walker, 1969.

A Part for a Policeman (West).   London, Hodder and Stoughton, and New York, Scribner, 1970.

The Smog (Palfrey).   London, Hodder and Stoughton, 1970; New York, Walker, 1971.

The Toff and the Fallen Angels.   London, Hodder and Stoughton, and New York, Walker, 1970.

Alibi (West).   London, Hodder and Stoughton, and New York, Scribner, 1971.

The Unbegotten (Palfrey).   London, Hodder and Stoughton, 1971; New York, Walker, 1972.

Vote for the Toff.   London, Hodder and Stoughton, and New York, Walker, 1971.

The Insulators (Palfrey).   London, Hodder and Stoughton, 1972; New York, Walker, 1973.

The Masters of Bow Street.   London, Hodder and Stoughton, 1972; New York, Simon and Schuster, 1973.

A Splinter of Glass (West).   London, Hodder and Stoughton, and New York, Scribner, 1972.

The Toff and the Trip-Trip-Triplets.   London, Hodder and Stoughton, and New York, Walker, 1972.

The Toff and the Terrified Taxman.   London, Hodder and Stoughton, and New York, Walker, 1973.

The Theft of Magna Carta (West).   London, Hodder and Stoughton, and New York, Scribner, 1973.

The Voiceless Ones (Palfrey).   London, Hodder and Stoughton, 1973; New York, Walker, 1974.

The Extortioners (West).   London, Hodder and Stoughton, 1974; New York, Scribner, 1975.

The Toff and the Sleepy Cowboy.   London, Hodder and Stoughton, 1974; New York, Walker, 1975.

The Thunder-Maker (Palfrey).   London, Hodder and Stoughton, and New York, Walker, 1976.

The Toff and the Crooked Copper.   London, Hodder and Stoughton, 1977.

The Toff and the Dead Man's Finger. London, Hodder and Stoughton, 1978.
A Sharp Rise in Crime (West). New York, Scribner, 1978.

Novels as M. E. Cooke

Fire of Death. London, Fiction House, 1934.
The Black Heart. London, Gramol, 1935.
The Casino Mystery. London, Mellifont Press, 1935.
The Crime Gang. London, Mellifont Press, 1935.
The Death Drive. London, Mellifont Press, 1935.
Number One's Last Crime. London, Fiction House, 1935.
The Stolen Formula Mystery. London, Mellifont Press, 1935.
The Big Radium Mystery. London, Mellifont Press, 1936.
The Day of Terror. London, Mellifont Press, 1936.
The Dummy Robberies. London, Mellifont Press, 1936.
The Hypnotic Demon. London, Fiction House, 1936.
The Moat Farm Mystery. London, Fiction House, 1936.
The Secret Formula. London, Fiction House, 1936.
The Successful Alibi. London, Mellifont Press, 1936.
The Hadfield Mystery. London, Mellifont Press, 1937.
The Moving Eye. London, Mellifont Press, 1937.
The Raven. London, Fiction House, 1937.
The Mountain Terror. London, Mellifont Press, 1938.
For Her Sister's Sake. London, Fiction House, 1938.
The Verrall Street Affair. London, Newnes, 1940.

Novels as Michael Halliday (series characters: Dr. Emmanuel Cellini; Martin and Richard
    Fane; Cellini books published as Kyle Hunt in U.S.)

Four Find Adventure. London, Cassell, 1937.
Three for Adventure. London, Cassell, 1937.
Two Meet Trouble. London, Cassell, 1938.
Murder Comes Home. London, Stanley Paul, 1940.
Heir to Murder. London, Stanley Paul, 1940.
Murder by the Way. London, Stanley Paul, 1941.
Who Saw Him Die? London, Stanley Paul, 1941.
Foul Play Suspected. London, Stanley Paul, 1942.
Who Died at the Grange? London, Stanley Paul, 1942.
Five to Kill. London, Stanley Paul, 1943.
Murder at King's Kitchen. London, Stanley Paul, 1943.
Who Said Murder? London, Stanley Paul, 1944.
No Crime More Cruel. London, Stanley Paul, 1944.
Crime with Many Voices. London, Stanley Paul, 1945.
Murder Makes Murder. London, Stanley Paul, 1946.
Murder Motive. London, Stanley Paul, 1947; New York, McKay, 1974.
Lend a Hand to Murder. London, Stanley Paul, 1947.
First a Murder. London, Stanley Paul, 1948; New York, McKay, 1972.
No End to Danger. London, Stanley Paul, 1948.
Who Killed Rebecca? London, Stanley Paul, 1949.
The Dying Witnesses. London, Evans, 1949.
Dine with Murder. London, Evans, 1950.
Murder Week-End. London, Evans, 1950.
Quarrel with Murder. London, Evans, 1951; revised edition, London, Corgi, 1975.
Take a Body (Fanes). London, Evans, 1951; revised edition, London, Hodder and
    Stoughton, 1964; Cleveland, World, 1972.

Lame Dog Murders (Fanes). London, Evans, 1952; Cleveland, World, 1972.

Murder in the Stars (Fanes). London, Hodder and Stoughton, 1953.

Murder on the Run (Fanes). London, Hodder and Stoughton, 1953; Cleveland, World, 1972.

Death Out of Darkness. London, Hodder and Stoughton, 1954; Cleveland, World, 1971.

Out of the Shadows. London, Hodder and Stoughton, 1954; Cleveland, World, 1971.

Cat and Mouse. London, Hodder and Stoughton, 1955; as *Hilda, Take Heed*, New York, Scribner, 1957.

Murder at End House. London, Hodder and Stoughton, 1955.

Death of a Stranger. London, Hodder and Stoughton, 1957; as *Come Here and Die*, New York, Scribner, 1959.

Runaway. London, Hodder and Stoughton, 1957; Cleveland, World, 1971.

Murder Assured. London, Hodder and Stoughton, 1958.

Missing from Home. London, Hodder and Stoughton, 1959; as *Missing*, New York, Scribner, 1960.

Thicker Than Water. London, Hodder and Stoughton, 1959; New York, Doubleday, 1962.

Go Ahead with Murder. London, Hodder and Stoughton, 1960; as *Two for the Money*, New York, Doubleday, 1962.

How Many to Kill? London, Hodder and Stoughton, 1960; as *The Girl with the Leopard-Skin Bag*, New York, Scribner, 1961.

The Edge of Terror. London, Hodder and Stoughton, 1961; New York, Macmillan, 1963.

The Man I Killed. London, Hodder and Stoughton, 1961; New York, Macmillan, 1963.

Hate to Kill. London, Hodder and Stoughton, 1962.

The Quiet Fear. London, Hodder and Stoughton, 1963; New York, Macmillan, 1968.

The Guilt of Innocence. London, Hodder and Stoughton, 1964.

Cunning as a Fox (Cellini). London, Hodder and Stoughton, and New York, Macmillan, 1965.

Wicked as the Devil (Cellini). London, Hodder and Stoughton, and New York, Macmillan, 1966.

Sly as a Serpent (Cellini). London, Hodder and Stoughton, and New York, Macmillan, 1967.

Cruel as a Cat (Cellini). London, Hodder and Stoughton, and New York, Macmillan, 1968.

Too Good to Be True (Cellini). London, Hodder and Stoughton, and New York, Macmillan, 1969.

A Period of Evil (Cellini). London, Hodder and Stoughton, 1970; Cleveland, World, 1971.

As Lonely as the Damned (Cellini). London, Hodder and Stoughton, 1971; Cleveland, World, 1972.

As Empty as Hate (Cellini). London, Hodder and Stoughton, and Cleveland, World, 1972.

As Merry as Hell (Cellini). London, Hodder and Stoughton, 1973; New York, Stein and Day, 1974.

This Man Did I Kill? (Cellini). London, Hodder and Stoughton, and New York, Stein and Day, 1974.

The Man Who Was Not Himself (Cellini). London, Hodder and Stoughton, and New York, Stein and Day, 1976.

Novels as Peter Manton

Murder Manor. London, Wright and Brown, 1937.

Stand By for Danger.   London, Wright and Brown, 1937.
The Circle of Justice.   London, Wright and Brown, 1938.
Three Days' Terror.   London, Wright and Brown, 1938.
The Crime Syndicate.   London, Wright and Brown, 1939.
Death Looks On.   London, Wright and Brown, 1939.
Murder in the Highlands.   London, Wright and Brown, 1939.
Policeman's Triumph.   London, Wright and Brown, 1948.
Thief in the Night.   London, Wright and Brown, 1950.
No Escape from Murder.   London, Wright and Brown, 1953.
The Crooked Killer.   London, Wright and Brown, 1954.

Novels as Anthony Morton (series character: John Mannering, The Baron [Blue Mask])

Meet the Baron.   London, Harrap, 1937; as *The Man in the Blue Mask*, Philadelphia,
  Lippincott, 1937.
The Baron Returns.   London, Harrap, 1937; as *The Return of Blue Mask*, Philadelphia,
  Lippincott, 1937.
The Baron Again.   London, Sampson Low, 1938; as *Salute Blue Mask!*, Philadelphia,
  Lippincott, 1938.
The Baron at Bay.   London, Sampson Low, 1938; as *Blue Mask at Bay*, Philadelphia,
  Lippincott, 1938.
Alias the Baron.   London, Sampson Low, 1939; as *Alias Blue Mask*, Philadelphia,
  Lippincott, 1939.
The Baron at Large.   London, Sampson Low, 1939; as *Challenge Blue Mask!*,
  Philadelphia, Lippincott, 1939.
Versus the Baron.   London, Sampson Low, 1940; as *Blue Mask Strikes Again*,
  Philadelphia, Lippincott, 1940.
Call for the Baron.   London, Sampson Low, 1940; as *Blue Mask Victorious*,
  Philadelphia, Lippincott, 1940.
The Baron Comes Back.   London, Sampson Low, 1943.
Mr. Quentin Investigates.   London, Sampson Low, 1943.
Introducing Mr. Brandon.   London, Sampson Low, 1944.
A Case for the Baron.   London, Sampson Low, 1945; New York, Duell, 1949.
Reward for the Baron.   London, Sampson Low, 1945.
Career for the Baron.   London, Sampson Low, 1946; New York, Duell, 1950.
The Baron and the Beggar.   London, Sampson Low, 1947; New York, Duell, 1950.
Blame the Baron.   London, Sampson Low, 1948; New York, Duell, 1951.
A Rope for the Baron.   London, Sampson Low, 1948; New York, Duell, 1949.
Books for the Baron.   London, Sampson Low, 1949; New York, Duell, 1952.
Cry for the Baron.   London, Sampson Low, 1950; New York, Walker, 1970.
Trap the Baron.   London, Sampson Low, 1950; New York, Walker, 1971.
Attack the Baron.   London, Sampson Low, 1951.
Shadow the Baron.   London, Sampson Low, 1951.
Warn the Baron.   London, Sampson Low, 1952.
The Baron Goes East.   London, Sampson Low, 1953.
The Baron in France.   London, Hodder and Stoughton, 1953; New York, Walker,
  1976.
Danger for the Baron.   London, Hodder and Stoughton, 1953; New York, Walker,
  1974.
The Baron Goes Fast.   London, Hodder and Stoughton, 1954; New York, Walker,
  1972.
Nest-Egg for the Baron.   London, Hodder and Stoughton, 1954; as *Deaf, Dumb, and
  Blonde*, New York, Doubleday, 1961.
Help from the Baron.   London, Hodder and Stoughton, 1955; New York, Walker,
  1977.

Hide the Baron.   London, Hodder and Stoughton, 1956; New York, Walker, 1978.

Frame the Baron.   London, Hodder and Stoughton, 1957; as *The Double Frame*, New York, Doubleday, 1961.

Red Eye for the Baron.   London, Hodder and Stoughton, 1958; as *Blood Red*, New York, Doubleday, 1960.

Black for the Baron.   London, Hodder and Stoughton, 1959; as *If Anything Happens to Hester*, New York, Doubleday, 1962.

Salute for the Baron.   London, Hodder and Stoughton, 1960; New York, Walker, 1973.

A Branch for the Baron.   London, Hodder and Stoughton, 1961; as *The Baron Branches Out*, New York, Scribner, 1967.

Bad for the Baron.   London, Hodder and Stoughton, 1962; as *The Baron and the Stolen Legacy*, New York, Scribner, 1967.

A Sword for the Baron.   London, Hodder and Stoughton, 1963; as *The Baron and the Mogul Swords*, New York, Scribner, 1966.

The Baron on Board.   London, Hodder and Stoughton, 1964; New York, Walker, 1968.

The Baron and the Chinese Puzzle.   London, Hodder and Stoughton, 1965; New York, Scribner, 1966.

Sport for the Baron.   London, Hodder and Stoughton, 1966; New York, Walker, 1969.

Affair for the Baron.   London, Hodder and Stoughton, 1967; New York, Walker, 1968.

The Baron and the Missing Old Masters.   London, Hodder and Stoughton, 1968; New York, Walker, 1969.

The Baron and the Unfinished Portrait.   London, Hodder and Stoughton, 1969; New York, Walker, 1970.

Last Laugh for the Baron.   London, Hodder and Stoughton, 1970; New York, Walker, 1971.

The Baron Goes A-Buying.   London, Hodder and Stoughton, 1971; New York, Walker, 1972.

The Baron and the Arrogant Artist.   London, Hodder and Stoughton, 1972; New York, Walker, 1973.

The Baron, King-Maker.   London, Hodder and Stoughton, and New York, Walker, 1975.

Love for the Baron.   London, Hodder and Stoughton, 1979.

Novels as Gordon Ashe (series character: Patrick Dawlish in all books except *The Man Who Stayed Alive* and *No Need to Die*)

Death on Demand.   London, Long, 1939.

The Speaker.   London, Long, 1939; as *The Croaker*, New York, Holt Rinehart, 1972.

Who Was the Jester?   London, Newnes, 1940.

Terror by Day.   London, Long, 1940.

Secret Murder.   London, Long, 1940.

'Ware Danger!   London, Long, 1941.

Murder Most Foul.   London, Long, 1942; revised edition, London, Corgi, 1973.

There Goes Death.   London, Long, 1942; revised edition, London, Corgi, 1973.

Death in High Places.   London, Long, 1942.

Death in Flames.   London, Long, 1943.

Two Men Missing.   London, Long, 1943; revised edition, London, Corgi, 1971.

Rogues Rampant.   London, Long, 1944; revised edition, London, Corgi, 1973.

Death on the Move.   London, Long, 1945.

Invitation to Adventure.   London, Long, 1945.

Here Is Danger!   London, Long, 1946.

Give Me Murder.   London, Long, 1947.

Murder Too Late.   London, Long, 1947.

Dark Mystery. London, Long, 1948.
Engagement with Death. London, Long, 1948.
A Puzzle in Pearls. London, Long, 1949; revised edition, London, Corgi, 1971.
Kill or Be Killed. London, Evans, 1949.
Murder with Mushrooms. London, Evans, 1950; revised edition, London, Corgi, 1971; New York, Holt Rinehart, 1974.
Death in Diamonds. London, Evans, 1951.
Missing or Dead? London, Evans, 1951.
Death in a Hurry. London, Evans, 1952.
The Long Search. London, Long, 1953; as *Drop Dead*, New York, Ace, 1954.
Sleepy Death. London, Long, 1953.
Double for Death. London, Long, 1954; New York, Holt Rinehart, 1969.
Death in the Trees. London, Long, 1954; as *No Need to Die*, New York, Ace, 1957.
The Kidnapped Child. London, Long, 1955; New York, Holt Rinehart, 1971; as *The Snatch*, London, Corgi, 1965.
The Man Who Stayed Alive. London, Long, 1955.
No Need to Die. London, Long, 1956.
Day of Fear. London, Long, 1956; New York, Holt Rinehart, 1978.
Wait for Death. London, Long, 1957; New York, Holt Rinehart, 1972.
Come Home to Death. London, Long, 1958; as *The Pack of Lies*, New York, Doubleday, 1959.
Elope to Death. London, Long, 1959; New York, Holt Rinehart, 1977.
The Crime Haters. New York, Doubleday, 1960; London, Long, 1961.
The Dark Circle. London, Evans, 1960.
Don't Let Him Kill. London, Long, 1960; as *The Man Who Laughed at Murder*, New York, Doubleday, 1960.
Rogues' Ransom. New York, Doubleday, 1961; London, Long, 1962.
Death from Below. London, Long, 1963; New York, Holt Rinehart, 1968.
The Big Call. London, Long, 1964; New York, Holt Rinehart, 1975.
A Promise of Diamonds. New York, Dodd Mead, 1964; London, Long, 1965.
A Taste of Treasure. London, Long, and New York, Holt Rinehart, 1966.
A Clutch of Coppers. London, Long, 1967; New York, Holt Rinehart, 1969.
A Shadow of Death. London, Long, 1968; New York, Holt Rinehart, 1976.
A Scream of Murder. London, Long, 1969; New York, Holt Rinehart, 1970.
A Nest of Traitors. London, Long, 1970; New York, Holt Rinehart, 1971.
A Rabble of Rebels. London, Long, 1971; New York, Holt Rinehart, 1972.
A Life for a Death. London, Long, and New York, Holt Rinehart, 1973.
A Herald of Doom. London, Long, 1974; New York, Holt Rinehart, 1975.
A Blast of Trumpets. London, Long, and New York, Holt Rinehart, 1975.
A Plague of Demons. London, Long, 1976; New York, Holt Rinehart, 1977.

Novels as Norman Deane (series characters: The Liberator; Bruce Murdoch)

Secret Errand (Murdoch). London, Hurst and Blackett, 1939; New York, McKay, 1974.
Dangerous Journey (Murdoch). London, Hurst and Blackett, 1939; New York, McKay, 1974.
Unknown Mission (Murdoch). London, Hurst and Blackett, 1940; revised edition, London, Arrow, and New York, McKay, 1972.
The Withered Man (Murdoch). London, Hurst and Blackett, 1940; New York, McKay, 1974.
I Am the Withered Man (Murdoch). London, Hurst and Blackett, 1941; revised edition, London, Long, 1972; New York, McKay, 1973.
Where Is the Withered Man? (Murdoch). London, Hurst and Blackett, 1942; revised edition, London, Arrow, and New York, McKay, 1972.

Return to Adventure (Liberator).   London, Hurst and Blackett, 1943; revised edition, London, Long, 1974.

Gateway to Escape (Liberator).   London, Hurst and Blackett, 1944.

Come Home to Crime (Liberator).   London, Hurst and Blackett, 1945; revised edition, London, Long, 1974.

Play for Murder.   London, Hurst and Blackett, 1946; revised edition, London, Arrow, 1975.

The Silent House.   London, Hurst and Blackett, 1947; revised edition, London, Arrow, 1973.

Why Murder?   London, Hurst and Blackett, 1948; revised edition, London, Arrow, 1975.

Intent to Murder.   London, Hurst and Blackett, 1948; revised edition, London, Arrow, 1975.

The Man I Didn't Kill.   London, Hurst and Blackett, 1950; revised edition, London, Hutchinson, 1973.

No Hurry to Kill.   London, Hurst and Blackett, 1950; revised edition, London, Arrow, 1973.

Double for Death.   London, Hurst and Blackett, 1951; revised edition, London, Hutchinson, 1973.

Golden Death.   London, Hurst and Blackett, 1952.

Look at Murder.   London, Hurst and Blackett, 1952.

Murder Ahead.   London, Hurst and Blackett, 1953.

Death in the Spanish Sun.   London, Hurst and Blackett, 1954.

Incense of Death.   London, Hurst and Blackett, 1954.

Novels as Jeremy York (series character in revised versions only: Superintendent Folly)

By Persons Unknown.   London, Bles, 1941.

Murder Unseen.   London, Bles, 1943.

No Alibi.   London, Melrose, 1943.

Murder in the Family.   London, Melrose, 1944; New York, McKay, 1976.

Yesterday's Murder.   London, Melrose, 1945.

Find the Body (Folly).   London, Melrose, 1945; revised edition, New York, Macmillan, 1967.

Murder Came Late (Folly).   London, Melrose, 1946; revised edition, New York, Macmillan, 1969.

Wilful Murder.   Los Angeles, McNaughton, 1946.

Let's Kill Uncle Lionel.   London, Melrose, 1947; revised edition, London, Corgi, 1973; New York, McKay, 1976.

Run Away to Murder.   London, Melrose, 1947; New York, Macmillan, 1970.

Close the Door on Murder (Folly).   London, Melrose, 1948; revised edition, New York, McKay, 1973.

The Gallows Are Waiting.   London, Melrose, 1949; New York, McKay, 1973.

Death to My Killer.   London, Melrose, 1950; New York, Macmillan, 1966.

Sentence of Death.   London, Melrose, 1950; New York, Macmillan, 1964.

Voyage with Murder.   London, Melrose, 1952.

Safari with Fear.   London, Melrose, 1953.

So Soon to Die.   London, Stanley Paul, 1955; New York, Scribner, 1957.

Seeds of Murder.   London, Stanley Paul, 1956; New York, Scribner, 1958.

Sight of Death.   London, Stanley Pual, 1956; New York, Scribner, 1958.

My Brother's Killer.   London, Long, 1958; New York, Scribner, 1959.

Hide and Kill.   London, Long, 1959; New York, Scribner, 1960.

To Kill or to Die.   London, Long, 1960; New York, Macmillan, 1965.

Novels as J. J. Marric (series character: Commander George Gideon)

Gideon's Day. London, Hodder and Stoughton, and New York, Harper, 1955; as
   Gideon of Scotland Yard, New York, Berkley, 1958.
Gideon's Week. London, Hodder and Stoughton, and New York, Harper, 1956.
Gideon's Night. London, Hodder and Stoughton, and New York, Harper, 1957.
Gideon's Month. London, Hodder and Stoughton, and New York, Harper, 1958.
Gideon's Staff. London, Hodder and Stoughton, and New York, Harper, 1959.
Gideon's Risk. London, Hodder and Stoughton, and New York, Harper, 1960.
Gideon's Fire. London, Hodder and Stoughton, and New York, Harper, 1961.
Gideon's March. London, Hodder and Stoughton, and New York, Harper, 1962.
Gideon's Ride. London, Hodder and Stoughton, and New York, Harper, 1963.
Gideon's Vote. London, Hodder and Stoughton, and New York, Harper, 1964.
Gideon's Lot. New York, Harper, 1964; London, Hodder and Stoughton, 1965.
Gideon's Badge. London, Hodder and Stoughton, and New York, Harper, 1966.
Gideon's Wrath. London, Hodder and Stoughton, and New York, Harper, 1967.
Gideon's River. London, Hodder and Stoughton, and New York, Harper, 1968.
Gideon's Power. London, Hodder and Stoughton, and New York, Harper, 1969.
Gideon's Sport. London, Hodder and Stoughton, and New York, Harper, 1970.
Gideon's Art. London, Hodder and Stoughton, and New York, Harper, 1971.
Gideon's Men. London, Hodder and Stoughton, and New York, Harper, 1972.
Gideon's Press. London, Hodder and Stoughton, and New York, Harper, 1973.
Gideon's Fog. New York, Harper, 1974; London, Hodder and Stoughton, 1975.
Gideon's Drive. London, Hodder and Stoughton, and New York, Harper, 1976.

Novels as Kyle Hunt

Kill Once, Kill Twice. New York, Simon and Schuster, 1956; London, Barker, 1957.
Kill a Wicked Man. New York, Simon and Schuster, 1957; London, Barker, 1958.
Kill My Love. New York, Simon and Schuster, 1958; London, Barker, 1959.
To Kill a Killer. London, Boardman, and New York, Random House, 1960.

Novels as Robert Caine Frazer (series character: Mark Kirby in all books)

Mark Kirby Solves a Murder. New York, Pocket Books, 1959; as *R.I.S.C.*, London,
   Collins, 1962; as *The Timid Tycoon*, London, Fontana, 1966.
Mark Kirby and the Secret Syndicate. New York, Pocket Books, 1960; London,
   Collins, 1963.
Mark Kirby and the Miami Mob. New York, Pocket Books, 1960; with *Mark Kirby
   Stands Alone*, London, Collins, 1965.
The Hollywood Hoax. New York, Pocket Books, 1961; London, Collins, 1964.
Mark Kirby Stands Alone. New York, Pocket Books, 1962; with *The Miami Mob*,
   London, Collins, 1965; as *Mark Kirby and the Manhattan Murders*, London, Fontana,
   1966.
Mark Kirby Takes a Risk. New York, Pocket Books, 1962.

Short Stories

The Toff on the Trail. London, Everybody's Books, n.d.
Murder Out of the Past, and Under-Cover Man (Toff). Leigh-on-Sea, Essex, Barrington
   Gray, 1953.

Uncollected Short Stories

"Hair of His Head," in *The Evening Standard Detective Book.* London, Gollancz, 1950.

"Piece of Cake," in *Eat, Drink, and Be Buried*, edited by Rex Stout.   New York, Viking Press, 1956; as *For Tomorrow We Die*, London, Macdonald, 1958.

"Betrayal of the Hopeless," in *Ellery Queen's Mystery Magazine* (New York), February 1957.

"Inspector West Triumphs," in *Ellery Queen's Mystery Magazine* (New York), August 1957.

"The Chief Witness," in *Planned Departures*, edited by Elizabeth Ferrars.   London, Hodder and Stoughton, 1958.

"The Book of Honour," in *The Sixth Mystery Bedside Book*, edited by John Creasey.   London, Hodder and Stoughton, 1965.

"Shadow of the Noose," in *The Saint* (New York), August 1966.

"The Greyling Crescent Mystery," in *Ellery Queen's All-Star Lineup*.   New York, New American Library, 1967.

OTHER PUBLICATIONS

Novels

One-Shot Marriott (as Ken Ranger).   London, Sampson Low, 1938.
Roaring Guns (as Ken Ranger).   London, Sampson Low, 1939.
Adrian and Jonathan (as Richard Martin).   London, Hodder and Stoughton, 1954.

Novels as Margaret Cooke

For Love's Sake.   N.p., Northern News Syndicate, 1934.
Troubled Journey.   London, Fiction House, 1937.
False Love or True.   N.p., Northern News Syndicate, 1937.
Fate's Playthings.   London, Fiction House, 1938.
Web of Destiny.   London, Fiction House, 1938.
Whose Lover?   London, Fiction House, 1938.
A Mannequin's Romance.   London, Fiction House, 1938.
Love Calls Twice.   London, Fiction House, 1938.
The Road to Happiness.   London, Fiction House, 1938.
The Turn of Fate.   London, Fiction House, 1939.
Love Triumphant.   London, Fiction House, 1939.
Love Comes Back.   London, Fiction House, 1939.
Crossroads of Love.   London, Mellifont Press, 1939.
Love's Journey.   London, Fiction House, 1940.

Novels as Elise Fecamps

Love of Hate.   London, Fiction House, 1936.
True Love.   London, Fiction House, 1937.
Love's Triumph.   London, Fiction House, 1937.

Novels as Henry St. John Cooper

Chains of Love.   London, Sampson Low, 1937.
Love's Pilgrimage.   London, Sampson Low, 1937.
The Tangled Legacy.   London, Sampson Low, 1938.
The Greater Desire.   London, Sampson Low, 1938.
Love's Ordeal.   London, Sampson Low, 1939.
The Lost Lover.   London, Sampson Low, 1940.

Novels as Tex Riley

Two-Gun Girl. London, Wright and Brown, 1938.
Gun-Smoke Range. London, Wright and Brown, 1938.
Gunshot Mesa. London, Wright and Brown, 1939.
The Shootin' Sheriff. London, Wright and Brown, 1940.
Rustler's Range. London, Wright and Brown, 1940.
Masked Riders. London, Wright and Brown, 1940.
Death Canyon. London, Wright and Brown, 1941.
Guns on the Range. London, Wright and Brown, 1942.
Range Justice. London, Wright and Brown, 1943.
Outlaw Hollow. London, Wright and Brown, 1944.
Hidden Range. Bournemouth, Earl, 1946.
Forgotten Range. Bournemouth, Earl, 1947.
Trigger Justice. Bournemouth, Earl, 1948.
Lynch Hollow. Bournemouth, Earl, 1949.

Novels as William K. Reilly

Range War. London, Stanley Paul, 1939.
Two Gun Texan. London, Stanley Paul, 1939.
Gun Feud. London, Stanley Paul, 1940.
Stolen Range. London, Stanley Paul, 1940.
War on Lazy-K. London, Stanley Paul, 1941; New York, Phoenix Press, 1946.
Outlaw's Vengeance. London, Stanley Paul, 1941.
Guns over Blue Lake. London, Jenkins, 1942.
Rivers of Dry Gulch. London, Jenkins, 1943.
Long John Rides the Range. London, Jenkins, 1944.
Miracle Range. London, Jenkins, 1945.
The Secrets of the Range. London, Jenkins, 1946.
Outlaw Guns. Bournemouth, Earl, 1949.
Range Vengeance. London, Ward Lock, 1953.

Plays

Gideon's Fear, adaptation of his novel *Gideon's Week* (produced Salisbury, 1960). London, Evans, 1967.
Strike for Death (produced Salisbury, 1960).
The Toff. London, Evans, 1963.
Hear Nothing, Say All (produced Salisbury, 1964).

Other

Ned Cartwright − Middleweight Champion (juvenile; as James Marsden). London, Mellifont Press, 1935.
The Men Who Died Laughing (juvenile). Dundee, Thompson, 1935.
The Killer Squad (juvenile). London, Newnes, 1936.
Our Glorious Term (juvenile). London, Sampson Low, n.d.
The Captain of the Fifth (juvenile). London, Sampson Low, n.d.
Blazing the Air Trail (juvenile). London, Sampson Low, 1936.
The Jungle Flight Mystery (juvenile). London, Sampson Low, 1936.
The Mystery 'plane (juvenile). London, Sampson Low, 1936.
Murder by Magic (juvenile). London, Amalgamated Press, 1937.
The Mysterious Mr. Rocco (juvenile). London, Mellifont Press, 1937.
The S.O.S. Flight (juvenile). London, Sampson Low, 1937.

The Secret Aeroplane Mystery (juvenile).   London, Sampson Low, 1937.
The Grey Vale School Mystery (juvenile; as Peter Manton).   London, Sampson Low, 1937.
The Treasure Flight (juvenile).   London, Sampson Low, 1937.
The Air Marauders (juvenile).   London, Sampson Low, 1937.
The Black Biplane (juvenile).   London, Sampson Low, 1937.
The Mystery Flight (juvenile).   London, Sampson Low, 1937.
The Double Motive (juvenile).   London, Mellifont Press, 1938.
The Doublecross of Death (juvenile).   London, Mellifont Press, 1938.
The Missing Hoard (juvenile).   London, Mellifont Press, 1938.
Mystery at Manby House (juvenile).   N.p., Northern News Syndicate, 1938.
Fighting Was My Business, by Jimmy Wilde (ghost written by Creasey).   London, Joseph, 1938.
The Fighting Flyers (juvenile).   London, Sampson Low, 1938.
The Flying Stowaways (juvenile).   London, Sampson Low, 1938.
The Miracle 'plane (juvenile).   London, Sampson Low, 1938.
Dixon Hawke, Secret Agent (juvenile).   Dundee, Thompson, 1939.
Documents of Death (juvenile).   London, Mellifont Press, 1939.
The Hidden Hoard (juvenile).   London, Mellifont Press, 1939.
Mottled Death (juvenile).   Dundee, Thompson, 1939.
The Blue Flyer (juvenile).   London, Mellifont Press, 1939.
The Jumper (juvenile).   N.p., Northern News Syndicate, 1939.
The Mystery of Blackmoor Prison (juvenile).   London, Mellifont Press, 1939.
The Sacred Eye (juvenile).   Dundee, Thompson, 1939.
The Ship of Death (juvenile).   Dundee, Thompson, 1939.
Peril by Air (juvenile).   London, Newnes, 1939.
The Flying Turk (juvenile).   London, Sampson Low, 1939.
The Monarch of the Skies (juvenile).   London, Sampson Low, 1939.
The Fear of Felix Corder (juvenile).   London, Fleetway Press, n.d.
John Brand, Fugitive (juvenile).   London, Fleetway Press, n.d.
The Night of Dread (juvenile).   London, Fleetway Press, n.d.
Dazzle – Air Ace No. 1 (juvenile).   London, Newnes, 1940.
Dazzle and the Red Bomber (juvenile).   London, Newnes, n.d.
Five Missing Men (juvenile).   London, Newnes, 1940.
The Poison Gas Robberies (juvenile).   London, Mellifont Press, 1940.
The Midget Marvel (juvenile; as Peter Manton).   London, Mellifont Press, 1940.
Log of a Merchant Airman, with John H. Lock.   London, Stanley Paul, 1943.
Heroes of the Air: A Tribute to the Courage, Sacrifice, and Skill of the Men of the R.A.F.   Dorchester, Dorset Wings for Victory Committee, 1943.
The Printers' Devil: An Account of the History and Objects of the Printers' Pension, Almshouse, and Orphan Asylum Corporation, edited by Walter Hutchinson.   London, Hutchinson, 1943.
The Crimea Crimes (juvenile).   Manchester, Pemberton, 1945.
The Missing Monoplane (juvenile).   London, Sampson Low, 1947.
Man in Danger.   London, Hutchinson, 1949.
Round the World in 465 Days, with Jean Creasey.   London, Hale, 1953.
Round Table: The First Twenty-Five Years of the Round Table Movement.   London, National Association of Round Tables of Great Britain and Ireland, 1953.
Let's Look at America, with others.   London, Hale, 1956.
They Didn't Mean to Kill: The Real Story of Road Accidents.   London, Hodder and Stoughton, 1960.
Optimists in Africa, with others.   Cape Town, Timmins, 1963.
African Holiday, drawings by Martin Creasey.   Cape Town, Timmins, 1963.
Good, God, and Man: An Outline of the Philosophy of Self-ism.   London, Hodder and Stoughton, 1967; New York, Walker, 1971.

Evolution to Democracy.   London, Hodder and Stoughton, 1969.

Editor, *Action Stations! An Account of the H.M.S. Dorsetshire and Her Earlier Namesakes.*   London, Long, 1942.
Editor, *The First [Second, Third, Fourth, Fifth, Sixth] Mystery Bedside Book.*   London, Hodder and Stoughton, 6 vols., 1960–65.
Editor, *Crimes Across the Sea: The 19th Annual Anthology of the Mystery Writers of America 1964.*   New York, Harper, and London, Longman, 1964.

Other as Patrick Gill (juvenile)

The Fighting Footballers.   London, Mellifont Press, 1937.
The Laughing Lightweight.   London, Mellifont Press, 1937.
The Battle for the Cup.   London, Mellifont Press, 1939.
The Fighting Tramp.   London, Mellifont Press, 1939.
The Mystery of the Centre-Forward.   London, Mellifont Press, 1939.
The £10,000 Trophy Race.   London, Mellifont Press, 1939.
The Secret Super-Charger.   London, Mellifont Press, 1940.

Bibliography: "A John Creasey Bibliography" by R. E. Briney and John Creasey, in *The Armchair Detective* (White Bear Lake, Minnesota), October 1968.

*   *   *

The phenomenal John Creasey wrote some 560 novels under more than twenty names. Over sixty million copies of his books have been sold throughout the world, and they continue to sell steadily today. Although his early novels gave little evidence of the good standard of his work to come, he was later to show that he possessed a well of ideas which was never to run dry, a facility to keep countless readers enthralled with action as well as mystery, and the ability to improve upon the literary quality of his actual writing as his career progressed.

Of Creasey's series characters, The Hon. Richard Rollison ("The Toff") and Roger West of Scotland Yard present an interesting contrast. Rollison, rich and gentlemanly, is a larger-than-life character who encounters more than his share of damsels in distress and is a stickler for fair play. The stories are fast-moving, with a succession of twists and crises; they are straight thrillers, far from the detective stories of so many of Creasey's contemporaries, although the identity of the master criminal is sometimes well concealed until the finale. The Toff is portrayed as a glamorous adventurer on the lines of Charteris's The Saint, in a series of books entirely unpretentious, typically British, thoroughly readable, apparently seeking only to entertain yet being prepared to wrestle with the occasional social problem. When we turn to the Roger West books, we find something more solid, not only a competent picture of life and relationships at Scotland Yard, but good examples of detection and pursuit. West may be a little too much the romantic figure, and his domestic life may be somewhat intrusive in those books where it has little bearing upon the investigation in hand. Nevertheless Creasey produced some quite excellent West books in structure (*Look Three Ways at Murder*), in topicality (*Strike for Death*), and in variety of background. Although most of West's cases are set in London, those with international connections and titles are particularly good.

Creasey's "Department Z" and Dr. Palfrey books also have a large following. The former are craftsmanlike counter-espionage stories featuring tough Scotsman Gordon Craigie and his agents, which well convey the wartime atmosphere. Dr. Palfrey was similarly active during the hostilities, and the tales of his organisation pitted against spies or those seeking world domination are enjoyable if a little sensational. The later development of the Palfrey series into the science fiction field is most interesting – on the surface they might appear to be thrillers concerning evil attempts to plague the world into submission, but the underlying messages are frightening and prophetic.

Creasey's pseudonymous series are many, and comments must therefore be selective. As Gordon Ashe, his tales of Patrick Dawlish and "The Crime Haters" are brisk and tough thrillers but unmemorable; much the same may be said about Norman Deane's books featuring Bruce Murdoch and "The Liberator," although Murdoch's wartime adventures are further evidence of Creasey's skill in weaving a good spy yarn. There is much confusion surrounding the novels Creasey wrote as Michael Halliday, as they have also been published in the United States variously as by Jeremy York and by Kyle Hunt. Of these, the straight non-series thrillers concerning people enmeshed in murder have a tense and psychological quality which is most satisfying. The Halliday (or Hunt) series featuring Dr. Emmanuel Cellini, with their ingenious uniformity of title – *Cunning as a Fox, Cruel as a Cat*, etc. – are perhaps the author's most successful forays into the realm of psychology, whereas the Superintendent Folly novels by Jeremy York are the nearest he comes to classical detection. In the books by Anthony Morton, central character John Mannering ("The Baron") is a reformed jewel thief and man-about-town who is always ready to turn his expertise to good use on the side of the angels; his relationship with Superintendent Bristow, who is forever suspicious that Mannering is capable of returning to his old trade, is one of the more entertaining aspects of these adventures.

Pride of place must be given to the novels written under the J. J. Marric pseudonym, which are police procedural novels of a considerable standard. Gideon of Scotland Yard was a major breakthrough for Creasey in terms of the critics' approbation, a character of greater credibility than any of Creasey's other heroes. In their almost documentary coverage of Gideon's professional life, the books give the impression that this is the real Scotland Yard, and the police officers surrounding Gideon have a welcome ring of authenticity. In the skilful inter-twining of the strands of various investigations, and in the unobtrusive scenes from Gideon's domestic life, there are both naturalism and suspense. By switching from case to case and back again, the result is not confusion but a satisfying and well-rounded picture of the life of a busy detective. They are the best things Creasey produced, which is intended as no empty compliment – there is little doubt that Gideon *is* the British police procedural novel.

No attempt need be made to examine Creasey's huge output for philosophical messages or sociological import, although these can be found if one feels them to be essential attributes before deeming a crime novelist respectable. Suffice it to say that his reported belief, that the crime novel is almost the only novel worth reading today, was amply justified by the tremendous public response to the sheer entertainment value of his books. In spite of his easy style, the historians of the genre will be very stuffy if they choose to ignore him.

—Melvyn Barnes

CRICHTON, (John) Michael.   Also writes as Michael Douglas (with Douglas Crichton); Jeffery Hudson; John Lange.   American.   Born in Chicago, Illinios, 23 October 1942. Educated at Harvard University, Cambridge, Massachusetts, A.B. (summa cum laude) 1965 (Phi Beta Kappa); Harvard Medical School, M.D. 1969; Salk Institute, La Jolla, California, 1969–70. Married Joan Radam in 1965. Recipient: Mystery Writers of America Edgar Allan Poe Award, 1968; Association of American Medical Writers Award, 1970. Address: c/o Alfred A. Knopf Inc., 201 East 50th Street, New York, New York 10022, U.S.A.

CRIME PUBLICATIONS

Novels

A Case of Need (as Jeffery Hudson). Cleveland, World, and London, Heinemann, 1968.
The Andromeda Strain. New York, Knopf, and London, Cape, 1969.
Dealing; or, The Berkeley-to-Boston Forty-Brick Lost-Bag Blues, with Douglas Crichton (as Michael Douglas). New York, Knopf, 1971; London, Talmy Franklin, 1972.
The Terminal Man. New York, Knopf, and London, Cape, 1972.
Westworld. New York, Bantam, 1975.
The Great Train Robbery. New York, Knopf, and London, Cape, 1975.
Eaters of the Dead. New York, Knopf, and London, Cape, 1976.

Novels as John Lange

Odds On. New York, New American Library, 1966.
Scratch One. New York, New American Library, 1967.
Easy Go. New York, New American Library, 1968; London, Sphere, 1972; as The Last Tomb (as Michael Crichton), New York, Bantam, 1974.
Zero Cool. New York, New American Library, 1969; London, Sphere, 1972.
Drug of Choice. New York, New American Library, 1970; as Overkill, New York, Centesis, 1970; London, Sphere, 1972.
Binary. New York, Knopf, and London, Heinemann, 1972.
Grave Descend. New York, New American Library, 1973.

OTHER PUBLICATIONS

Plays

Screenplays: Westworld, 1973; Coma, 1978; The Great Train Robbery, 1979.

Other

Five Patients: The Hospital Explained. New York, Knopf, 1970; London, Cape, 1971.
Jasper Johns. New York, Abrams, and London, Thames and Hudson, 1977.

Theatrical Activities:

Director: Films – Westworld, 1973; Coma, 1978. Television – Pursuit, 1972.

*   *   *

Michael Crichton began writing thrillers in the late 1960's, a period of proliferating fiction probably largely inspired by the success of Ian Fleming. He seems to epitomize that group of popular writers who were financially successful but failed to achieve any lasting artistic accomplishments. His prime goal (and his achievement) seems to have been technical virtuosity. His best work has a stylistic ease and pace that make writers like Chandler and Hammett, on a technical level, seem like work horses.

He is a complex writer, but not the simplistic "computer" that some critics have tried to reduce him to. He has written fiction under several names, a weak collaboration with his brother on the drug-traffic among youth, and a non-fiction work about hospital life. He has both written and directed for the screen.

His best-selling science-documentary thrillers, The Andromeda Strain and The Terminal Man, have earned him the widest attention, but are not his most successful literary achievements. George Stewart (*Fire, Storm, Earth Abides*) could teach him something about naturalism in dealing with the environment, and Jack London handled the pathology of psychological obsession in a way that makes his "terminal man" look like the stereotype he is.

His plots – the hallmark of the mystery-thriller – are weak. His early thrillers, written as John Lange, contain some good plot ideas but only a modicum of ingenuity in execution. Some of his best touches – the snake containers concealing a compartment for a double deal in underground traffic, an exciting chase through Spain's Alhambra, or the bureaucratic entrapments that inspire a skilled crook into almost heroic endeavor to loot an Egyptian tomb – are largely wasted on characters of the "who cares" variety.

His characterizations, with villains only a shade more villainous (but sometimes more interesting) than his heroes, hardly merit discussion, except for his women, sophisticated with an out-of-the ordinary intelligence that makes them attractive. An underappreciated strength is his excellent ability to pace the shorter novel; the best example is *Binary*.

His best work is *A Case of Need*, written as Jeffery Hudson. The appeal of this entertaining mystery is in the focus of the hero pathologist's mind tracking down the evidence of death in a way that is both engrossing and believable. The plot is itself somewhat helter-skelter, but the angle of approach draws it together. Pace, sytle, and characterizations are integrated.

Lately, in *The Great Train Robbery*, he has gone to the historical documentary novel, a hybrid form which has a built-in contradiction to his forte of fast-paced action by substituting history for plot.

Ironically, it is Crichton's obvious ability and technical achievements which have been either ignored or attacked by critics. On his scientific knowledge: "[it] reads as though it were written by a computer, and there may be no Michael Crichton at all." On his commercial success: "One reliable approach to writing a novel that will sell is to select a topic of gut-level public concern and fictionalize it." But the disappointment about writers of Mr. Crichton's promise and ability has little to do with the market place. In his thriller *Binary* he seemed to try to construct a metaphor for modern man's philosophical dilemma. Man (he almost seemed to say), unlike the stars, numbers, and gases defined in the book's foreword, has volition, but still seems of a binary, destructive nature. Crichton assigns his central characters this duality, the body/mind dichotomy between reason or science and ideas. See it, for instance, in the pathologist's conclusion on the guilt or innocence of the evil acts of death in *A Case of Need*. To integrate that split, to channel creativity into a rational, moral course, is the "case of need" of not only Michael Crichton, but an entire culture.

—Newton Baird

CRISPIN, Edmund. Pseudonym for Robert Bruce Montgomery. British. Born in Chesham Bois, Buckinghamshire, 2 October 1921. Educated at the Merchant Taylors' School, London; St. John's College, Oxford, B.A. 1943. Schoolmaster, Shrewsbury School, 1943–45; composer of choral and orchestral works, songs, and film music. *Died 15 September 1978.*

CRIME PUBLICATIONS

Novels (series character: Gervase Fen in all books)

The Case of the Gilded Fly. London, Gollancz, 1944; as Obsequies at Oxford, Philadelphia, Lippincott, 1945.
Holy Disorders. London, Gollancz, 1945; Philadelphia, Lippincott, 1946.
The Moving Toyshop. London, Gollancz, and Philadelphia, Lippincott, 1946.
Swan Song. London, Gollancz, 1947; as Dead and Dumb, Philadelphia, Lippincott, 1947.
Love Lies Bleeding. London, Gollancz, and Philadelphia, Lippincott, 1948.
Buried for Pleasure. London, Gollancz, 1948; Philadelphia, Lippincott, 1949.
Frequent Hearses. London, Gollancz, 1950; as Sudden Vengeance, New York, Dodd Mead, 1950.
The Long Divorce. London, Gollancz, and New York, Dodd Mead, 1951; as A Noose for Her, New York, Spivak, 1952.
The Glimpses of the Moon. London, Gollancz, 1977; New York, Walker, 1978.

Short Stories

Beware of the Trains: Sixteen Stories. London, Gollancz, 1953; New York, Walker, 1962.
Fen Country. London, Gollancz, 1979.

OTHER PUBLICATIONS

Play

Screenplay: Raising the Wind, 1961.

Other

Editor, Best SF: Science Fiction Stories. London, Faber, 7 vols., 1955–70.
Editor, Best Detective Stories. London, Faber, 2 vols, 1959–64.
Editor, Best Tales of Terror. London, Faber, 2 vols, 1962–65.
Editor, The Stars and Under: A Selection of Science Fiction. London, Faber, 1968.
Editor, Best Murder Stories 2. London, Faber, 1973.
Editor, Outwards from Earth: A Selection of Science Fiction. London, Faber, 1974.

Published music includes An Ode on the Resurrection of Christ, 1947; Mary Ambree, 1948; Four Shakespeare Songs, 1948; Two Suites for Chorus and Strings: Venus' Praise (1951), and Christ's Birthday, 1948; Concertino for String Orchestra, 1950; An Oxford Requiem, 1950; Concerto Waltz for Two Pianos, 1952; John Barleycorn: An Opera for Children, 1962. Unpublished work includes music for 38 films.

Edmund Crispin comments:
I have no great liking for spy stories, or, come to that, for the more so-called "realistic" type of crime story. I believe that crime stories in general and detective stories in particular should be essentially imaginative and artificial in order to make their best effect. Another way

of putting it would be to say that I make Jacques Barzun's distinction between the novel and the tale, and think that you try to mix the two things at your peril.

*   *   *

After Edmund Crispin published his short story collection *Beware of the Trains* in 1953, there was a long silence: year after year and no new novels. Finally, in 1977, *The Glimpses of the Moon* was published with Gervase Fen as fit as ever.

Crispin is one of the most original detective fiction writers. He is a product of the University of Oxford, and among his friends during his university years was Kingsley Amis. In a way Crispin's detective novels are closely related to the works of Amis: what is Gervase Fen if not something of a neo-picaresque hero just as Lucky Jim? Fen is an Oxford professor of literature who prefers being an amateur detective. His sense of logic is no doubt very impressive but his esprit and wit even more so. Like John Appleby – the hero in Michael Innes's novels – he very often uses literary allusions in his small talk, and it's not always very easy for a reader to follow him in all his associations.

Anthony Boucher once described Crispin as a blend of John Dickson Carr, Michael Innes, M. R. James, and the Marx Brothers. I think that it is a brilliant characterization. Like Carr he has the capacity to construct flawless plots of great suggestive power, like Innes he is a superb stylist who specializes in entertaining dialogues – it's a compliment to Michael Innes that he uses the pen-name Edmund Crispin and has baptized his hero Gervase Fen (see Innes's *Hamlet, Revenge!*) – like M. R. James he can be slightly macabre and frightening, and like the Marx Brothers he has a fabulous talent to create hilarious scenes with a surrealistic quality. There is, for example, really no difference between the extremely funny finale in *The Moving Toyshop* and that of *A Night at the Opera*. But Crispin's sense of humour has many shades; he can also be most satirical, as in *Buried for Pleasure* where he deals with local politics.

His plots are in most cases masterworks of finesse and ingenuity – he is at his best in *The Case of the Gilded Fly* and *The Long Divorce* with its clever use of a poisoned pen letters theme. Many of his short stories also tend to be small masterpieces, especially when he constructs locked-room or dying message puzzles.

Even if Crispin's detective novels now and then tend to be a little flippant and rather lightweight, there is no doubt that he is a strikingly original writer, one of the few really important newcomers of the forties. Julian Symons appropriately calls him "the last and most charming of the farceurs."

—Jan Broberg

CROFT-COOKE, Rupert.   See **BRUCE, Leo.**

CROFTS, Freeman Wills.   British.   Born in Dublin, Ireland, in June 1879. Educated at Methodist and Campbell colleges, Belfast. Married Mary Bellas Canning in 1912. Apprenticed at 17 to Berkeley D. Wise, Belfast and North Countries Railway; Junior Assistant Engineer, 1899; District Engineer, Coleraine, 1900; Chief Assistant Engineer,

Belfast, 1923; resigned, 1929, to become full-time writer. Fellow, Royal Society of Arts, 1939. *Died 11 April 1957.*

CRIME PUBLICATIONS

Novels (series character: Inspector Joseph French)

The Cask. London, Collins, 1920; New York, Seltzer, 1924.
The Ponson Case. London, Collins, 1921; New York, Boni, 1927.
The Pit-Prop Syndicate. London, Collins, 1922; New York, Seltzer, 1925.
The Groote Park Murder. London, Collins, 1924; New York, Seltzer, 1925.
Inspector French's Greatest Case. London, Collins, and New York, Seltzer, 1925.
Inspector French and the Starvel Tragedy. London, Collins, 1927; as *The Starvel Hollow Tragedy*, New York, Harper, 1927.
The Sea Mystery (French). London, Collins, and New York, Harper, 1928.
Double Death, with others. London, Gollancz, 1929.
The Box Office Murders (French). London, Collins, 1929; as *The Purple Sickle Murders*, New York, Harper, 1929.
Sir John Magill's Last Journey (French). London, Collins, and New York, Harper, 1930.
Mystery in the Channel (French). London, Collins, 1931; as *Mystery in the English Channel*, New York, Harper, 1931.
The Floating Admiral, with others. London, Hodder and Stoughton, 1931; New York, Doubleday, 1932.
Sudden Death (French). London, Collins, and New York, Harper, 1932.
Death on the Way (French). London, Collins, 1932; as *Double Death*, New York, Harper, 1932.
The Hog's Back Mystery (French). London, Hodder and Stoughton, 1933; as *The Strange Case of Dr. Earle*, New York, Dodd Mead, 1933.
The 12:30 from Croydon (French). London, Hodder and Stoughton, 1934; as *Wilful and Premeditated*, New York, Dodd Mead, 1934.
Mystery on Southampton Water (French). London, Hodder and Stoughton, 1934; as *Crime on the Solent*, New York, Dodd Mead, 1934.
Crime at Guildford (French). London, Collins, 1935; as *The Crime at Nornes*, New York, Dodd Mead, 1935.
The Loss of the "Jane Vosper" (French). London, Collins, and New York, Dodd Mead, 1936.
Six Against the Yard, with others. London, Selwyn and Blount, 1936; as *Six Against Scotland Yard*, New York, Doubleday, 1936.
Man Overboard! (French). London, Collins, and New York, Dodd Mead, 1936; abridged, as *Cold-Blooded Murder*, New York, Avon, 1947.
Found Floating (French). London, Hodder and Stoughton, and New York, Dodd Mead, 1937.
The End of Andrew Harrison (French). London, Hodder and Stoughton, 1938; as *The Futile Alibi*, New York, Dodd Mead, 1938.
Antidote to Venom (French). London, Hodder and Stoughton, 1938; New York, Dodd Mead, 1939.
Fatal Venture (French). London, Hodder and Stoughton, 1939; as *Tragedy in the Hollow*, New York, Dodd Mead, 1939.
Golden Ashes (French). London, Hodder and Stoughton, and New York, Dodd Mead, 1940.
James Tarrant, Adventurer (French). London, Hodder and Stoughton, 1941; as *Circumstantial Evidence*, New York, Dodd Mead, 1941.

The Losing Game (French).   London, Hodder and Stoughton, and New York, Dodd
   Mead, 1941.
Fear Comes to Chalfont (French).   London, Hodder and Stoughton, and New York,
   Dodd Mead, 1942.
The Affair at Little Wokeham (French).   London, Hodder and Stoughton, 1943; as
   Double Tragedy, New York, Dodd Mead, 1943.
Enemy Unseen (French).   London, Hodder and Stoughton, and New York, Dodd Mead,
   1945.
Death of a Train (French).   London, Hodder and Stoughton, 1946; New York, Dodd
   Mead, 1947.
Silence for the Murderer (French).   New York, Dodd Mead, 1948; London, Hodder
   and Stoughton, 1949.
Dark Journey.   New York, Dodd Mead, 1951; as *French Strikes Oil*, London, Hodder
   and Stoughton, 1952.
Anything to Declare (French).   London, Hodder and Stoughton, 1957.

Short Stories

The Hunt Ball Murder.   London, Todd, 1943.
Mr. Sefton, Murderer.   London, Vallancey Press, 1944.
Murderers Make Mistakes.   London, Hodder and Stoughton, 1947.
Many a Slip.   London, Hodder and Stoughton, 1955.
The Mystery of the Sleeping Car Express and Other Stories.   London, Hodder and
   Stoughton, 1956.

OTHER PUBLICATIONS

Plays

   Radio Plays: *The Nine-Fifty Up Express*, 1942; *Chief Inspector's Cases* (series), 1943;
   Mr. Pemberton's Commission, from his own story, 1952; *The Greuze*, 1953; *East Wind*,
   1953.

Other

   Bann and Lough Neagh Drainage.   Belfast, His Majesty's Stationery Office, 1930.
   Young Robin Brand, Detective (juvenile).   London, University of London Press, 1947;
      New York, Dodd Mead, 1948.
   The Four Gospels in One Story.   London, Longman, 1949.

*   *   *

Purity of plot construction is the principal feature for which Freeman Wills Crofts will be
remembered. In all but a handful of his books the ramifications of the criminal investigation
fit together in a most satisfying manner. His ability to break down the supposedly
unbreakable alibi is almost legendary. This automatically means that as whodunits, in the
Agatha Christie sense, his novels fail; look for the person with the cast-iron alibi, and you
have your murderer. For this reason, if one knows his style, one tends not to regard a Crofts
novel as the time-honoured duel between author and reader. There is little pleasure in
attempting to guess or to deduce the murderer's identity, but every satisfaction in trying to
outpace the detective in deciding how the murder was committed and how the murderer
covered his tracks.
Crofts's first detective novel, *The Cask*, remained his masterpiece. It has been generally

regarded by experts as the finest first novel in the field, and as a significant landmark in the history of the genre, with Anthony Boucher describing it as "the definitive novel" in its use of alibis and timetables. The solid, plodding, logical detective work and almost fanatical attention to detail were to become the hallmark of Crofts. From the moment the cask at the London docks is found to contain gold coins and a woman's hand instead of statuary, an enthralling trail leads to Paris and engages the attention of detectives on both sides of the Channel. Anyone wishing to experience the quintessence of Crofts should turn to *The Cask*.

Of Crofts's highly competent books following *The Cask*, but preceding the introduction of his famous series detective Inspector French, perhaps *The Pit-Prop Syndicate* is the most interesting. Although none of Crofts's plots could be described as racy or fast moving, this one goes close to combining the elements of the thriller and the detective novel; the action alternates between France and England (a favourite device of Crofts), and two amateur detectives find themselves out of their depth (another favourite device), from which point the professionals take over.

Inspector French's Greatest Case was the first in a long line of investigations by French, in which he was consistently meticulous, perhaps a skilful plodder, with the cases as neatly dovetailed as the railway timetables which were so often his stock-in-trade. The stories were the product of a brilliantly logical mind, a mind with a background of engineering and mathematics. It may well be pedantic, it may well be mechanical, it may well be too ponderous for the reader requiring faster action, but it is tremendously enjoyable to accompany French on the job. We accompany him rather than follow him, for Crofts is the epitome of fair play; the reader is with French each step of the way, sharing his every thought, his disappointing leads and his lucky breaks, and being presented with each clue at the same moment as the detective. Not until late in his career did Crofts become a little wearisome in his technique, stemming either from his pool of ideas running dry or the fact that he was by then competing with far livelier writers.

Although Crofts was at home mainly in the novel, it being the best medium for the systematic development of an investigation, he also wrote some very creditable short stories and radio plays. Of the former, the volume entitled *The Mystery of the Sleeping Car Express* shows him to be adept at the concise detective plot with a quick twist; in *Murderers Make Mistakes* there are examples of the "inverted" type, in which the criminal's actions are first described and then French reveals how he established the truth.

Various devices and stylistic techniques are common to some or all of Crofts's novels. There is never, for example, any attempt to present a murderer whose culpability is in question — quite often the motive is sheer monetary gain, and indeed murder is often connected with either a financial swindle or a robbery. Time and again we find a strong railway interest (*Death of a Train*, *Sir John Magill's Last Journey*) or shipping interest (*The Loss of the "Jane Vosper," Found Floating*) where Crofts puts his technical knowledge to excellent use. Then again, although Crofts's characters occasionally fall in love, this is treated most clinically and is rarely developed as an integral part of the stories, a facet of a wider criticism often made of him — he seldom attempts to explore character. His books are peopled with ciphers, existing merely as the links in a criminal investigation, and when toward the end of his career he attempted more complex characterisation (*Silence for the Murderer*) he failed at it. One book, *The 12:30 from Croydon*, can be regarded as a successful attempt to go rather deeper, and to show us the workings of a murderer's mind; in most of his other books, crime is seen purely in black and white terms, the mechanics of the investigation being paramount.

In spite of all this, or perhaps because of it, Freeman Wills Crofts remains the supreme exponent of his type of detective fiction. He created arguably the greatest police detective, whose solid and tireless work enabled countless readers to identify with his triumphs and frustrations. Even the moral — crime is wrong, and criminals will be caught by the inexorable machinery of the law — was something with which, though not always fashionable today, readers could associate. His method of telling a tale was ordinary and straightforward, and he seldom strayed from the confines of his set pattern. Perhaps, as Julian Symons suggests, he was the best of what may be termed "the Humdrum School"; to be entirely complimentary, he was, in Raymond Chandler's words, "the soundest builder of them all."

—Melvyn Barnes

CROSS, Amanda. Pseudonym for Carolyn G(old) Heilbrun. American. Born in East Orange, New Jersey, 13 January 1926. Educated at Wellesley College, Massachusetts, B.A. 1947 (Phi Beta Kappa); Columbia University, New York, M.A. 1951, Ph.D. 1959. Married James Heilbrun; two daughters and one son. Instructor, Brooklyn College, 1959–60. Instructor, 1960–62, Assistant Professor, 1962–67, and since 1972, Professor of English, Columbia University. Visiting Lecturer, Union Theological Seminary, New York, 1968–70, Swarthmore College, Pennsylvania, 1970, Yale University, New Haven, Connecticut, 1974, and University of California, Santa Cruz, 1979. Recipient: Guggenheim Fellowship; Rockefeller Fellowship; Radcliffe Institute Fellowship. Agent: Curtis Brown Ltd., 575 Madison Avenue, New York, New York 10022. Address: 613 Philosophy Hall, Columbia University, New York, New York 10027, U.S.A.

CRIME PUBLICATIONS

Novels (series character: Kate Fansler in all books)

In the Last Analysis. New York, Macmillan, and London, Gollancz, 1964.
The James Joyce Murder. New York, Macmillan, and London, Gollancz, 1967.
Poetic Justice. New York, Knopf, and London, Gollancz, 1970.
The Theban Mysteries. New York, Knopf, 1971; London, Gollancz, 1972.
The Question of Max. New York, Knopf, and London, Gollancz, 1976.

OTHER PUBLICATIONS as Carolyn G. Heilbrun

Other

The Garnett Family. New York, Macmillan, and London, Allen and Unwin, 1961.
Christopher Isherwood. New York, Columbia University Press, 1970.
Towards a Recognition of Androgyny: Aspects of Male and Female in Literature. New York, Harper, 1973; as *Towards Androgyny*, London, Gollancz, 1973.
Reinventing Womanhood. New York, Norton, and London, Gollancz, 1979.

Editor, *Lady Ottoline's Album.* New York, Knopf, 1976; London, Joseph, 1977.

Amanda Cross comments:
I began writing the Amanda Cross novels in 1963 because I could not find any detective fiction that I enjoyed reading. Alas, the situation (except for the work of P. D. James) is largely unchanged since then. I expect that I represent an old style of detective fiction, perhaps even anachronistic. From the number of sales, the letters I receive, paperback reprints, and the infrequency with which my out-of-print novels turn up in the second-hand market, I conclude that I have some following. At the same time, I have been largely ignored by those who now dominate the mystery field, and I feel as though I do not rightfully belong, for example, to the MWA.
What was it I wanted in detective fiction and could no longer find? First of all,

conversation, and an ambiance in which violence was unexpected and shocking. In short, the exact opposite of what Chandler wanted (or said he wanted) in "The Simple Art of Murder." Second of all, I like literary mysteries, not necessarily with a quotation at the head of every chapter, though I don't mind that, but with a cast of characters comprising those who may not now know much literature only because they have forgotten it. Also, I like fiction in which women figure as more than decoration and appendages, domestic machinery, or sex objects. In short, I like the women in my novels to be people, as they were in Nicholas Blake's early works, and in a novel like Edward Grierson's *The Second Man.*

My sort of detective fiction will always be accused of snobbery. This, I have decided, is inevitable. I myself am that apparently rare anomaly, an individual who likes courtesy and intelligence, but would like to see the end of reaction, stereotyped sex-roles, and convention that arises from the fear of change, and the anxiety change brings. I loathe violence, and do not consider sex a spectator sport. I like humor, but fear unkindness, and the cruelty of power.

One day Kate Fansler, therefore, sprang from by brain to counter these things I loathe, to talk all the time, occasionally with wit, and to offer to those who like it the company of people I consider civilized, and a plot, feeble, perhaps, but reflecting a moral universe.

*   *   *

Amanda Cross is the pseudonym of an American academic who found herself in possession of more wit than could be gracefully accommodated in the average scholarly monograph, and of a conviction that literature illuminates life, even the apparent chaos of American campus life in the 1960's. Knowing how commodious the genre of detective fiction is, Carolyn Heilbrun began writing novels of manners with strong detective sub-plots. There is a murder, or at least a death that requires concealment, in each of her novels, and each crime is unravelled by the series heroine, Professor Kate Fansler.

Kate is a strong and likeable character – fastidious without being cold, thoughtful without pedantry, and able to appreciate and communicate with a wide variety of people. She is the central consciousness in a picture of American university life that calmly flouts the modern literary fashion for demeaning satires of self-deluded professors. Heilbrun insists on describing the university with charity as well as clarity, and with considerable elegance of style. Some early reviewers of Kate's conversation find it "pompous," "lecture-talky," and "peppered with the kind of erudite quotation that truly academic people would consider show-off." One may also feel that Kate simply has the courage of the syntax that she is capable of, and that she is asking, in her usual straightforward way, whether William F. Buckley, Jr., should have all the fun.

Heilbrun gives us a cross section of the types of *homo academicus*: the great humane scholar, the cliché-ridden administrator with a heart of gold, the hungry graduate student and the brilliant one, the scholar harmlessly crazed by devotion to his minor poet, the teacher who can also do, the facile and the snobbish. All of these characters are believable as types and often as individuals. Heilbrun involves them in situations that range from the farcical to the tragic, and most of them emerge with considerable dignity. Her academic community manages to hold to its ideals while tolerating the inevitable proportion of fools and knaves.

Three of Heilbrun's novels are built around major writers or works of literature, the first around Freud. *In the Last Analysis* is one of her most satisfying puzzles. When a friend of Kate's who is a psychoanalyst becomes a murder suspect, Kate sets to work to clear him. She comes up with a brilliant, nearly unprovable, hypothesis about the murderer's identity. In the process, she demonstrates that the mind of the literary critic can also decipher dreams and piece together apparently unrelated incidents and slips of the tongue, but has less tendency to ignore the obvious than the psychoanalytic mind does. One scene, a conversation between Kate's neophyte assistant detective and a suspect from Madison Avenue, demonstrates Heilbrun's fine talent for social comedy, which she rightly gives rein to in later books.

The James Joyce Murder is one of her less successful mysteries, containing some startling implausibilities in the murderer's actions and one flagrant error in Kate's reasoning. But the book should not be missed for the success of its translation of the paralytic characters from *The Dubliners* to the modern Berkshires and its zestful deflation of certain popular myths about country life.

Heilbrun's next two books, *Poetic Justice* and *The Theban Mysteries*, take their themes from the political disorders of the 1960's as they affect a proud old university and a proud old private girl's school, respectively. The university is found to be a bit stiffer in the knees and its faculty a bit more fragile than that of the girl's school. *Poetic Justice* examines the ways in which some worthwhile people react to a frontal assault on the value of what they have given their lives to. Fatigue, rather than lack of justice or commitment, is found to be the major obstacle to reformation. The book is chock full of Auden's poetry, and if the poet were not Auden, there would be too much of it. *The Theban Mysteries* demonstrates the relevance of the *Antigone* to the moral position of the Vietnam draft resister. Heilbrun's contemporary Creon is entirely convincing, though some elements of the plot are not.

In *The Question of Max*, the plot is tight and plausible as Kate and the reader are presented with an apparent double mystery. Kate first comes up with the wrong solution because she is a feminist as well as a detective, and because research scholars can be over-imaginative. But because scholarship demands thoroughness, Kate arrives at the right answer, and brings a convincing villain to justice.

—Carol Cleveland

* * *

CROSSEN, Ken(dell Foster). Also writes as Bennett Barlay; M. E. Chaber; Richard Foster; Christopher Monig; Clay Richards. American. Born in Albany, Ohio, 25 July 1910. Educated at Rio Grande College, Ohio. Worked as insurance investigator in Cleveland, and on WPA Writers' Project, New York; Editor, *Detective Fiction Weekly*, New York, 1936. Self-employed writer. Agent: Elaine Greene Ltd., 31 Newington Green, London N16 9PU, England. Address: 520 South Burnside Avenue, Apartment 8-D, Los Angeles, California U.S.A.

CRIME PUBLICATIONS

Novels (series character: Kim Locke)

The Case of the Curious Heel. New York, Vulcan, 1944.
The Case of the Phantom Fingerprints. New York, Vulcan, 1945.
Murder Out of Mind. New York, Green, 1945.
Satan Comes Across (as Bennett Barlay). New York, Eerie, 1945.
The Tortured Path (Locke; as Kendell Foster Crossen). New York, Dutton, 1957; London, Eyre and Spottiswoode, 1958.
The Big Dive (Locke; as Kendell Foster Crossen). New York, Dutton, and London, Eyre and Spottiswoode, 1959.
The Conspiracy of Death, with George Redston. Indianapolis, Bobbs Merrill, 1965.

Novels as Richard Foster (series characters: Pete Draco; Chin Kwang Kham)

The Laughing Buddha Murders (Chin). New York, Vulcan, 1944.
The Invisible Man Murders (Chin). New York, Green, 1945.
The Girl from Easy Street. New York, Popular Library, 1952.

Blonde and Beautiful.   New York, Popular Library, 1955.
Bier for a Chaser (Draco).   New York, Fawcett, 1959; London, Muller, 1960.
The Rest Must Die.   New York, Fawcett, 1959; London, Muller, 1960.
Too Late for Mourning (Draco).   New York, Fawcett, 1960; London, Muller, 1961.

Novels as M. E. Chaber (series character: Milo March in all books except *The Green Lama*)

Hangman's Harvest.   New York, Holt, 1952; as *Don't Get Caught*, New York, Popular Library, 1953.
No Grave for March.   New York, Holt, 1953; London, Eyre and Spottiswoode, 1954; as *All the Way Down*, New York, Popular Library, 1953.
As Old as Cain.   New York, Holt, 1954; as *Take One for Murder*, New York, Spivak, 1955.
The Man Inside.   New York, Holt, 1954; London, Eyre and Spottiswoode, 1955; as *Now It's My Turn*, New York, Popular Library, 1954.
The Splintered Man.   New York, Holt, 1955; London, Boardman, 1957.
A Lonely Walk.   New York, Holt, 1956; London, Boardman, 1957.
The Gallows Garden.   New York, Holt, and London, Boardman, 1958; as *The Lady Came to Kill*, New York, Pocket Books, 1959.
A Hearse of Another Color.   New York, Holt, 1958; London, Boardman, 1959.
So Dead the Rose.   New York, Holt Rinehart, 1959; London, Boardman, 1960.
Jade for a Lady.   New York, Holt Rinehart, and London, Boardman, 1962.
Softly in the Night.   New York, Holt Rinehart, and London, Boardman, 1963.
Six Who Ran.   New York, Holt Rinehart, 1964; London, Boardman, 1965.
Uneasy Lies the Dead.   New York, Holt Rinehart, and London, Boardman, 1964.
Wanted: Dead Men.   New York, Holt Rinehart, 1965; London, Boardman, 1966.
The Day It Rained Diamonds.   New York, Holt Rinehart, 1966; London, Macdonald, 1968.
A Man in the Middle.   New York, Holt Rinehart, 1967.
Wild Midnight Falls.   New York, Holt Rinehart, 1968.
The Flaming Man.   New York, Holt Rinehart, 1969; London, Hale, 1970.
Green Grow the Graves.   New York, Holt Rinehart, 1970; London, Hale, 1971.
The Bonded Dead.   New York, Holt Rinehart, 1971; London, Hale, 1973.
Born to Be Hanged.   New York, Holt Rinehart, 1973.
The Green Lama.   Chicago, Pulp Press, 1976.

Novels as Christopher Monig (series character: Brian Brett in all books)

The Burned Man.   New York, Dutton, 1956; London, Boardman, 1957; as *Don't Count the Corpses*, New York, Dell, 1958.
Abra-Cadaver.   New York, Dutton, and London, Boardman, 1958.
Once upon a Crime.   New York, Dutton, 1959; London, Boardman, 1960.
The Lonely Graves.   New York, Dutton, 1960; London, Boardman, 1961.

Novels as Clay Richards (series character: Grant Kirby)

The Marble Jungle (Kirby).   New York, Obolensky, 1961; London, Cassell, 1963.
Death of an Angel (Kirby).   Indianapolis, Bobbs Merrill, 1963.
The Gentle Assassin.   Indianapolis, Bobbs Merrill, 1964; London, Boardman, 1965.
Who Steals My Name.   Indianapolis, Bobbs Merrill, 1964; London, Boardman, 1965.

Uncollected Short Stories

"The Aaron Burr Murder Case," in *Detective Fiction Weekly* (New York), September 1939.

"John Brown's Body," in *Detective Fiction Weekly* (New York), 16 December 1939.

"The Bowman of Mons," in *Argosy* (New York), 25 January 1940.

"Satan Comes Across" (as Bennett Barlay), in *Detective Fiction Weekly* (New York), 16 March 1940.

"The Red Rooster of Death," in *Detective Fiction Weekly* (New York), 10 August 1940.

"A Vision of Murder," in *Stirring Detective and Western Stories*, October 1940.

"A Shield and a Club," in *Stirring Detective and Western Stories*, November 1940.

"The Cat and the Foil," in *Detective Fiction Weekly* (New York), 14 December 1940.

"The Parson Returns," in *Detective Fiction Weekly* (New York), 22 March 1941.

"Presto-Chango Murder," in *Detective Fiction Weekly* (New York), 12 April 1941.

"The Earl of Loretta," in *Detective Fiction Weekly* (New York), 19 April 1941.

"Fifty to One Is Murder," in *Detective Fiction Weekly* (New York), 26 April 1941.

"The Miniature Murders," in *Detective Fiction Weekly* (New York), 17 May 1941.

"The Crime in the Wastebasket," in *Detective Fiction Weekly* (New York), 31 May 1941.

"Three on a Murder," in *Detective Fiction Weekly* (New York), June 1941.

"Too Late for Murder," in *Detective Fiction Weekly* (New York), 14 June 1941.

"Murder Is a Fine Art," in *Detective Fiction Weekly* (New York), June 1941.

"Trouble with Twins," in *Detective Fiction Weekly* (New York), 19 June 1941.

"Ax for the Parson," in *Detective Fiction Weekly* (New York), 21 June 1941.

"And So to Murder," in *Detective Fiction Weekly* (New York), 2 August 1941.

"The Case of the Curious Heel," "An Angle to Murder," "Death's Key Ring," in *Baffling Mysteries* (Mt. Morris, Illinois), May 1943.

"The Crime in the Envelope," in *Murder Cavalcade*, edited by Ken Crossen. New York, Duell, 1946; London, Hammond, 1953.

"Too Late for Murder," in *Four and Twenty Bloodhounds*, edited by Anthony Boucher. New York, Simon and Schuster, 1950; London, Hammond, 1951.

"The Murder Trap," in *Stories Annual*, 1955.

"The Closed Door," in *Space Police*, edited by Andre Norton. Cleveland, World, 1956.

Uncollected Short Stories as Richard Foster

"The Green Lama," in *Double Detective* (New York), April 1940.

"Croesus of Crime," in *Double Detective* (New York), May 1940.

"Babies for Sale," in *Double Detective* (New York), June 1940.

"The Wave of Death," in *Double Detective* (New York), July 1940.

"The Man Who Wasn't There," in *Double Detective* (New York), August 1940.

"The Man with the Death's Head Face," in *Double Detective* (New York), September 1940.

"The Clown Who Laughed," in *Double Detective* (New York), October 1940.

"The Invisible Enemy," in *Double Detective* (New York), December 1940.

"The Case of the Mad Maji," in *Double Detective* (New York), February 1941.

"The Case of the Vanishing Ships," in *Double Detective* (New York), April 1941.

"The Case of the Fugitive Fingerprints," in *Double Detective* (New York), June 1941.

"The Case of the Crooked Cane," in *Double Detective* (New York), August 1941.

"The Case of the Hollywood Ghost," in *Double Detective* (New York), October 1941.

"The Case of the Beardless Corpse," in *Double Detective* (New York), March 1943.

Uncollected Short Stories as M. E. Chaber

"Assignment: Red Berlin," in *Blue Book* (Chicago), December 1952.

"Hair the Color of Blood," in *Blue Book* (Chicago), July 1953.

"The Hot Ice Blues," in *Blue Book* (Chicago), September 1953.

"The Man Inside," in *Blue Book* (Chicago), December 1953.

"Murder on the Inside," in *Blue Book* (Chicago), January 1954.

"The Red, Red Flower," in *Blue Book* (Chicago), February 1961.
"The Twisted Trap," in *Blue Book* (Chicago), June 1961.

OTHER PUBLICATIONS

Novels

Once upon a Star. New York, Holt, 1953.
Year of Consent. New York, Dell, 1954.
The Acid Nightmare (as M. E. Chaber). New York, Holt Rinehart, 1967.

Other

Comeback: The Story of My Stroke, by Robert E. Van Rosen as told to Ken
   Crossen. Indianapolis, Bobbs Merrill, 1963.

Editor, *Murder Cavalcade.* New York, Duell, 1946; London, Hammond, 1953.
Editor, *Adventures in Tomorrow.* New York, Greenberg, 1951; London, Lane, 1953.
Editor, *Future Tense: New and Old Tales of Science Fiction.* New York, Greenberg,
   1952; London, Lane, 1954.

Manuscript Collection: Mugar Memorial Library, Boston University.

*   *   *

Detective fiction is often formula fiction. Writers employ formulas in the creation of their
plots to facilitate composition, but the formula can also be applied to the development of
characters. Ken Crossen is one such writer. He has, after several decades of writing,
discovered a successful plot and character which he has polished to an artful smoothness.
Crossen writes under a variety of aliases which helps to disguise the commonalities in his
writing, but he is best known as M. E. Chaber.

   It is under that name that Crossen developed his formula as typified by his Milo March
novels. March is an unusual character in that he operates as an investigator for the
Intercontinental Insurance Company and as a sometime CIA agent. As such, his adventures
are divisible into the separate categories of the tough private detective novel (*Softly in the
Night*) and the espionage adventure (*So Dead the Rose*). Regardless of story type, March's
adventures follow a formula pattern in which he is employed to locate a missing person or
object. He may be in pursuit of stolen jade in Hong Kong (*Jade for a Lady*) or a defector in
East Berlin (*The Splintered Man*). The particulars may vary, but the essentials of plot and its
development are the same.

   There is little suspense to be found in March's CIA assignments and less actual detection
present in his insurance investigations. March is a hedonist, albeit a tough hedonist, who
dislikes legwork or violence and prefers large expense accounts, fine restaurants, good drink,
and at least two women per novel. He spends a great deal of each novel indulging himself,
while his presence actuates violent events among his quarry. He sometimes pushes the latter,
whom he usually identifies early and with a minimum of effort, until they incriminate
themselves, as in *The Bonded Dead*. When he chooses, he will play his suspects against one
another (*Six Who Ran*) until attrition reduces his quarry to a manageable number. Through it
all, he is wry and philosophical, but as unconcerned with justice as he is uninvolved with the
people he meets.

   Codified within the March novels are most of the elements of Crossen's fiction. His other
characters strongly resemble March in part, but never in totality. Under the name
Christopher Monig, Crossen writes about another insurance investigator, Brian Brett, and a
third series, published as Richard Foster, concerned an insurance investigator of the future,
Pete Draco. Another character, Kim Locke, is a virtual twin of March's CIA incarnations.

The Gentle Assassin, written as Clay Richards, is essentially a Milo March novel in which the lead character is assisted by a trained dog as a gesture to innovation.

Such reliance upon formula is the signature of the pulp-magazine writer. Ken Crossen still favors the devices he learned writing for those magazines. (As Richard Foster, he wrote a series of novelettes for *Double Detective* about a character named the Green Lama and a later variation on that character, the Tibetan detective Chin Kwang Kham, appeared in such novels as *The Laughing Buddha Murders* and *The Invisible Man Murders*.) But he has mastered those devices and made them work for him. Further, Crossen has invested those formulas with the lustre of craft and fine writing, a not inconsiderable accomplishment.

—Will Murray

CROWE, John. See **COLLINS, Michael**.

CULLINGFORD, Guy. Pseudonym for Constance Lindsay Taylor. British. Born in 1907.

CRIME PUBLICATIONS

Novels

> *Murder with Relish* (as C. Lindsay Taylor). London, Skeffington, 1948.
> *If Wishes Were Hearses*. London, Hammond, 1952; Philadelphia, Lippincott, 1953.
> *Post Mortem*. London, Hammond, and Philadelphia, Lippincott, 1953.
> *Conjurer's Coffin*. London, Hammond, and Philadelphia, Lippincott, 1954.
> *Framed for Hanging*. London, Hammond, and Philadelphia, Lippincott, 1956.
> *The Whipping Boys*. London, Hammond, 1958.
> *A Touch of Drama*. London, Hammond, 1960.
> *Third Party Risk*. London, Bles, 1962.
> *Brink of Disaster*. London, Bles, 1964; New York, Roy, 1966.
> *The Stylist*. London, Bles, 1968.

Uncollected Short Stories

> "Kill and Cure," in *Planned Departures*, edited by Elizabeth Ferrars. London, Hodder and Stoughton, 1958.
> "My Unfair Lady," in *Alfred Hitchcock Presents: My Favorites in Suspense*. New York, Random House, 1959.
> "Mr. Mowbray's Predecessor," in *Ellery Queen's Mystery Magazine* (New York), December 1961.
> "Something to Get at Quick," in *Ellery Queen's Mystery Magazine* (New York), July 1967.

"Locals Should Know Best," in *Ellery Queen's Mystery Magazine* (New York), October 1968.

"The Incurable Complaint," in *Ellery Queen's Mystery Magazine* (New York), May 1969.

OTHER PUBLICATIONS

Novel

The Bread and Butter Miss.   London, Hale, 1979.

Plays

Television Plays: *Sarah*, 1973; *Little Boy Dave*, 1975; *The Winter Ladies*, 1979.

*   *   *

Guy Cullingford has written a group of interesting, even unusual books, set firmly in what everybody (including the English themselves) consider to be most typically English settings. A London boarding house in a wet summer, or the timelessness of an East Anglian village holding almost feudal attitudes and trying to come to grips, not too successfully, with today and now.

A good start could be made by examining *Post Mortem*, a most unusual novel where an account of the murder is given to us by the victim himself. Gilbert Worth, a writer with an adequate private income, is shot while asleep at his desk. One moment he is sitting comfortably inside his skin and the next he is outside and viewing his own corpse, wondering, along with the police, "whodunit." There are many suspects, as he is generally loathed by family, servants, and neighbours. Not too shocked to find his children hate him (he disliked them heartily), he is not very pleased to learn that after death duties they will go their own ways. His least favourite child is planning to become a clergyman and to marry his own ex-mistress. Worth feels a vague desire for revenge and, feeling the detectives are not particularly interested, he decides to do the investigation himself.

Conjurer's Coffin is about the sudden disappearance of a magician's help with worse to come. A damp Coronation year at the Bellevue Hotel where Madame hopes to put everything in the black with all those foreigners bashing down the door eager for bed and breakfast in Soho. The Gormans are well-used to the grimy and uncomfortable rooms with unwilling service provided. They are not dismayed to see another new face at the desk as they have never seen the same one twice. Miss Jessie Milk, a devoted and dutiful daughter, is now realizing a life's ambition to live and work in London. Travelling salesmen, unstable actors, a fat bad-tempered dog, and nice village-bred old ladies up for a thrilling week in The Big City: all enjoying themselves or suffering in their own manner until death spoils the Coronation celebrations for them.

If Wishes Were Hearses is a step back to The Golden Age, although it is set in the 1950's. The scene is an isolated, almost feudal, village. George White is the owner of the old-fashioned chemist's where he mixes his own remedies for most things and does not possess a telephone. While short on both culture and entertainment the village does possess two inns, one run by Miss Death who is a strict teetotaller. The young may be leaving hastily for the thrills of Camden Town or Bayswater but the old folk left behind are also having a few thrills when the Major dies suddenly. His wife is amusing herself with the doctor and nobody seems to regret the man's death as he was considered "slightly difficult" or "damned impossible" according to temperament. Much more sad is the fire that destroys the oldest village building.

A speech written by an aggravating and bossy husband blows out of a lady's hand and starts a new political party for the benefit of women in *Third Party Risk*. The benefits are short-lived as deadly disagreements begin between the various organizers. *Framed for*

Hanging looks backwards to the days after the Maybrick trial when death was much more respectable than divorce.

If Guy Cullingford has a fault, it is perhaps that all the characterizations are so entertaining that one can lose sight of the crime and the victim.

—Mary Groff

CUMBERLAND, Marten. Also wrote as Kevin O'Hara. British. Born in London, 23 July 1892. Educated at Cranleigh School, Surrey. Served in the British merchant navy, 1914–18. Married Kathleen Walsh in 1928. Worked on the London Stock Exchange; trained as wireless operator, and went to sea, 1913; Assistant Editor, *New Illustrated*, London, 1918–19; staff member, *Harmsworth Encyclopaedia*, London, 1919–20; Assistant Fiction Editor, Hulton Press, later Allied Newspapers, London, 1922–24; free-lance journalist and writer from 1924; regular contributor to *New Age*, *New English Weekly*, *Ideas*, *Truth*, and *Dublin Magazine*; columnist ("Paris Letter") for *Daily Dispatch*, Manchester, 1930–31; lived in Dublin in later life. *Died in 1972.*

CRIME PUBLICATIONS

Novels (series character: Saturnin Dax)

Loaded Dice, with B. V. Shann. London, Methuen, 1926.
The Perilous Way. London, Jarrolds, 1926.
The Dark House. London, Gramol, 1935.
Devil's Snare. London, Gramol, 1935.
The Imposter. London, Gramol, 1935.
Murder at Midnight, with B. V. Shann. London, Mellifont Press, 1935.
Shadowed. London, Mellifont Press, 1936.
Birds of Prey. London, Gramol, 1937.
Someone Must Die (Dax). London, Hurst and Blackett, 1940.
Questionable Shape (Dax). London, Hurst and Blackett, 1941.
Quislings over Paris (Dax). London, Hurst and Blackett, 1942.
The Testing of Tony. London, Macdonald, 1943.
The Knife Will Fall (Dax). London, Hurst and Blackett, 1943; New York, Doubleday, 1944.
Everything He Touched. London, Macdonald, 1945.
Not Expected to Live (Dax). London, Hurst and Blackett, 1945.
Steps in the Dark (Dax). London, Hurst and Blackett, and New York, Doubleday, 1945.
A Dilemma for Dax. New York, Doubleday, 1946; as *Hearsed in Death*, London, Hurst and Blackett, 1947.
A Lovely Corpse (Dax). London, Hurst and Blackett, 1946.
Darkness as a Bride. London, Hurst and Blackett, 1947.
Hate Will Find a Way (Dax). New York, Doubleday, 1947; as *And Worms Have Eaten Them*, London, Hurst and Blackett, 1948.
And Then Came Fear (Dax). New York, Doubleday, 1948; London, Hurst and Blackett, 1949.
The Crime School London, Eldon Press, 1949.

The Man Who Covered Mirrors (Dax).   New York, Doubleday, 1949; London, Hurst and Blackett, 1951.

Policeman's Nightmare (Dax).   New York, Doubleday, 1949; London, Hurst and Blackett, 1950.

The House in the Forest (Dax).   New York, Doubleday, 1950; as *Confetti Can Be Red*, London, Hurst and Blackett, 1951.

On the Danger List (Dax).   London, Hurst and Blackett, 1950.

Fade Out the Stars (Dax).   London, Hurst and Blackett, and New York, Doubleday, 1952.

Booked for Death (Dax).   London, Hurst and Blackett, 1952; as *Grave Consequences*, New York, Doubleday, 1952.

One Foot in the Grave (Dax).   London, Hurst and Blackett, 1952.

Etched in Violence (Dax).   London, Hurst and Blackett, 1953.

Which of Us Is Safe? (Dax).   London, Hurst and Blackett, 1953; as *Nobody Is Safe*, New York, Doubleday, 1953.

The Charge Is Murder (Dax).   London, Hurst and Blackett, 1953.

The Frightened Brides (Dax).   London, Hurst and Blackett, 1954.

Unto Death Utterly (Dax).   London, Hurst and Blackett, 1954.

Lying at Death's Door (Dax).   London, Hurst and Blackett, 1956.

Far Better Dead! (Dax).   London, Hutchinson, 1957.

Hate for Sale (Dax).   London, Hutchinson, and New York, British Book Centre, 1957.

Out of This World (Dax).   London, Hutchinson, 1958; New York, British Book Centre, 1959.

Murmurs in the Rue Morgue (Dax).   London, Hutchinson, and New York, British Book Centre, 1959.

Remains to Be Seen (Dax).   London, Hutchinson, 1960.

There Must Be Victims (Dax).   London, Hutchinson, 1961.

Attention! Saturnin Dax!   London, Hutchinson, 1962.

Postscript to a Death (Dax).   London, Hutchinson, 1963.

Hate Finds a Way (Dax).   London, Hutchinson, 1964.

The Dice Were Loaded (Dax).   London, Hutchinson, 1965.

No Sentiment in Murder (Dax).   London, Hutchinson, 1966.

Novels as Kevin O'Hara (series character: Chico Brett in all books)

The Customer's Always Wrong.   London, Hurst and Blackett, 1951.

Exit and Curtain.   London, Hurst and Blackett, 1952.

Sing, Clubman, Sing!   London, Hurst and Blackett, 1952.

Always Tell the Sleuth.   London, Hurst and Blackett, 1953.

It Leaves Them Cold.   London, Hurst and Blackett, 1954.

Keep Your Fingers Crossed.   London, Hurst and Blackett, 1955.

The Pace That Kills.   London, Hurst and Blackett, 1955.

Women Like to Know.   London, Jarrolds, 1957.

Danger: Women at Work!   London, Long, 1958.

Well, I'll Be Hanged!   London, Long, 1958.

And Here Is the Noose!   London, Long, 1959.

Taking Life Easy.   London, Long, 1961.

If Anything Should Happen.   London, Long, 1962.

Don't Tell the Police.   London, Long, 1963.

Don't Neglect the Body.   London, Long, 1964.

It's Your Funeral.   London, Long, 1966.

Uncollected Short Stories

"The Diary of Death," in *The Best Detective Stories of the Year 1928*, edited by Ronald Knox and H. Harrington. London, Faber, 1929; as *The Best English Detective Stories of 1928*, New York, Liveright, 1929.
"Mate in Three Moves," in *The Best Detective Stories of the Year*, edited by Ronald Knox. London, Faber, 1930; as *The Best English Detective Stories of 1929*, New York, Liveright, 1930.
"One False Note," in *The Fourth Mystery Bedside Book*, edited by John Creasey. London, Hodder and Stoughton, 1963.
"Or Not to Be ...," in *The Fifth Mystery Bedside Book*, edited by John Creasey. London, Hodder and Stoughton, 1964.
"Red for Death," in *John Creasey's Mystery Bedside Book*, edited by Herbert Harris. London, Hodder and Stoughton, 1966.
"The Voice," in *Tales of Unease*, edited by John Burke. London, Pan, 1966; New York, Doubleday, 1969.
"Unsound Move," in *John Creasey's Mystery Bedside Book*, edited by Herbert Harris. London, Hodder and Stoughton, 1967.

OTHER PUBLICATIONS

Novels

Behind the Scenes: A Novel of the Stage, with B. V. Shann. London, Palmer, 1923.
The Sin of David. London, Selwyn and Blount, 1932.

Plays

Inside the Room (produced London, 1934).
No Ordinary Lady, adaptation of a play by Louis Verneuil (produced London, 1936).
Climbing (produced London, 1937). London, Deane, and Boston, Baker, 1937.
Men and Wife (produced London, 1937).
Believe It or Not (produced London, 1938).
Baxter's Second Wife, with Claude Houghton (produced London, 1949).

Ballet Scenario: *The Golden Bell of Ko*, music by Aloys Fleischmann.

Other

The New Economics, with Raymond Harrison. London, Palmer, 1922.
How to Write Serial Fiction, with Michael Joseph. London, Hutchinson, and New York, Holt, 1928.

*   *   *

Marten Cumberland is a noted English journalist and prolific author. His Dax series have won the most praise from critics, though, under the pseudonym of Kevin O'Hara, he wrote a series featuring an equally intriguing hero, Chico Brett.

Classified as intellectual puzzlers involving shrewd deduction and perceptive police work, the novels about French Commissaire Saturnin Dax are entertaining, challenging, and well-written. The earlier novels are better plotted, with the interplay between Commissaire Dax and his half-English assistant, Brigadier Felix Norman, providing the reader with amusing red herrings and intimate portrayals of French nightclubs and countryside. The plots are convoluted and intricate, unraveling slowly and containing few action scenes. The characters are remarkably similar, with journalists and actors playing vital parts in many of the stories.

A total contrast in style are the Kevin O'Hara thrillers – fast-paced, action-packed, and loaded with dialogue. Chico Brett, red-heared, half-Argentinian, half-Irish, vermouth swilling, intense, intuitive, and compassionate, is a hard-boiled private eye investigating the seamy side of London's elegant theatres and nightclubs. Starting with deceptively simple cases involving pilferage or missing persons, Chico Brett inevitably finds himself embroiled in a tangled web of passionate crime.

—Mary Ann Grochowski

CUNNINGHAM, E. V. Pseudonym for Howard (Melvin) Fast; also writes as Walter Ericson. American. Born in New York City, 11 November 1914. Educated at George Washington High School, and the National Academy of Design, New York. Served with the Office of War Information, 1942–43, and the Army Film Project, 1944. Married Bette Cohen in 1937; two children. War Correspondent in the Far East for *Esquire* and *Coronet* magazines, New York, 1945. Taught at Indiana University, Bloomington, Summer 1947. Imprisoned for contempt of Congress, 1947. Founder of the World Peace Movement, and member of the World Peace Council, 1950–55. Operated Blue Heron Press, New York, 1952–57. Currently, Member of The Fellowship for Reconciliation. American-Labor Party candidate for Congress for the 23rd District of New York, 1952. Recipient: Bread Loaf Writers Conference Award, 1933; Schomburg Race Relations Award, 1944; Newspaper Guild Award, 1947; Jewish Book Council of America Award, 1948; Stalin International Peace Prize (now Soviet International Peace Prize), 1954; Screenwriters Award, 1960; National Association of Independent Schools Award, 1962. Agent: Paul Reynolds Inc., 599 Fifth Avenue, New York, New York 10017. Address: 1401 Laurel Way, Beverly Hills, California 90210, U.S.A.

CRIME PUBLICATIONS

Novels (series characters: Harvey Krim; Masao Masuto)

Fallen Angel (as Walter Ericson).   Boston, Little Brown, 1952; as *The Darkness Within*, New York, Ace, 1953; as *Mirage* (as Howard Fast), New York, Fawcett, 1965.
The Winston Affair (as Howard Fast).   New York, Crown, 1959; London, Methuen, 1960.
Sylvia.   New York, Doubleday, 1960; London, Deutsch, 1962.
Phyllis.   New York, Doubleday, and, London, Deutsch, 1962.
Alice.   New York, Doubleday, 1963; London, Deutsch, 1965.
Lydia (Krim).   New York, Doubleday, 1964; London, Deutsch, 1965.
Shirley.   New York, Doubleday, and London, Deutsch, 1964.
Penelope.   New York, Doubleday, 1965; London, Deutsch, 1966.
Helen.   New York, Doubleday, 1966; London, Deutsch, 1967.
Margie.   New York, Morrow, 1966; London, Deutsch, 1968.
Sally.   New York, Morrow, and London, Deutsch, 1967.
Samantha (Masuto).   New York, Morrow, 1967; London, Deutsch, 1968.
Cynthia (Krim).   New York, Morrow, 1968; London, Deutsch, 1969.
The Assassin Who Gave Up His Gun.   New York, Morrow, 1969; London, Deutsch, 1970.
Millie.   New York, Morrow, 1973; London, Deutsch, 1975.

The Case of the One-Penny Orange (Masuto). New York, Holt Rinehart, 1977; London, Deutsch, 1978.

The Case of the Russian Diplomat (Masuto). New York, Holt Rinehart, 1978; London, Deutsch, 1979.

The Case of the Poisoned Eclairs (Masuto). New York, Holt Rinehart, 1979.

OTHER PUBLICATIONS as Howard Fast

Novels

Two Valleys. New York, Dial Press, 1933; London, Dickson, 1934.

Strange Yesterday. New York, Dodd Mead, 1934.

Place in the City. New York, Harcourt Brace, 1937.

Conceived in Liberty: A Novel of Valley Forge. New York, Simon and Schuster, and London, Joseph, 1939.

The Last Frontier. New York, Duell, 1941; London, Lane, 1948.

The Unvanquished. New York, Duell, 1942; London, Lane, 1947.

The Tall Hunter. New York, Harper, 1942.

Citizen Tom Paine. New York, Duell, 1944; London, Lane, 1945.

Freedom Road. New York, Duell, 1944; London, Lane, 1946.

The American: A Middle Western Legend. New York, Duell, 1946; London, Lane, 1949.

The Children. New York, Duell, 1947.

Clarkton. New York, Duell, 1947.

My Glorious Brothers. Boston, Little Brown, 1948; London, Lane, 1952.

The Proud and the Free. Boston, Little Brown, 1950; London, Lane, 1952.

Spartacus. Privately printed, 1951; London, Lane, 1952.

Silas Timberman. New York, Blue Heron Press, 1954; London, Lane, 1955.

The Story of Lola Gregg. New York, Blue Heron Press, 1956; London, Lane, 1957.

Moses, Prince of Egypt. New York, Crown, 1958; London, Methuen, 1959.

The Golden River, in *The Howard Fast Reader.* New York, Crown, 1960.

April Morning. New York, Crown, and London, Methuen, 1961.

Power. New York, Doubleday, 1962; London, Methuen, 1963.

Agrippa's Daughter. New York, Doubleday, 1964; London, Methuen, 1965.

Torquemada. New York, Doubleday, 1966; London, Methuen, 1967.

The Hunter and the Trap. New York, Dial Press, 1967.

The General Zapped an Angel. New York, Morrow, 1970.

The Crossing. New York, Morrow, 1971; London, Eyre Methuen, 1972.

The Hessian. New York, Morrow, 1972; London, Hodder and Stoughton, 1973.

The Immigrants. Boston, Houghton Mifflin, and London, Hodder and Stoughton,1978.

Second Generation. Boston, Houghton Mifflin, 1978; London, Hodder and Stoughton, 1979.

The Establishment. Boston, Houghton Mifflin, 1979; London, Hodder and Stoughton, 1980.

Short Stories

Patrick Henry and the Frigate's Keel and Other Stories of a Young Nation. New York, Duell, 1945.

Departures and Other Stories. Boston, Little Brown, 1949.

The Last Supper and Other Stories. New York, Blue Heron Press, 1955; London, Lane, 1956.

The Edge of Tomorrow. New York, Bantam, 1961.

A Touch of Infinity: Thirteen Stories of Fantasy and Science Fiction. New York, Morrow, 1973; London, Hodder and Stoughton, 1975.
Time and the Riddle: Thirty-One Zen Stories. Pasadena, California, Ward Ritchie Press, 1975.

Plays

The Hammer (produced New York, 1950).
Thirty Pieces of Silver (produced Melbourne, 1951). New York, Blue Heron Press, and London, Lane, 1954.
George Washington and the Water Witch. London, Lane, 1956.
The Crossing (produced Dallas, 1962).
The Hill (screenplay). New York, Doubleday, 1964.

Screenplay: *The Hessian,* 1971.

Other

The Romance of a People. New York, Hebrew Publishing Company, 1941.
Lord Baden-Powell of the Boy Scouts. New York, Messner, 1941.
Haym Solomon, Son of Liberty. New York, Messner, 1941.
The Picture-Book History of the Jews, with Bette Fast. New York, Hebrew Publishing Company, 1942.
Goethals and the Panama Canal. New York, Messner, 1942.
The Incredible Tito. New York, Magazine House, 1944.
Never to Forget: The Story of the Warsaw Ghetto, with William Gropper. New York, Book League of the Jewish People Fraternal Order, 1946.
Intellectuals in the Fight for Peace. New York, Masses and Mainstream, 1949.
Tito and His People. Winnipeg, Manitoba, Contemporary Publishers, 1950.
Literature and Reality. New York, International Publishers, 1950.
Peekskill, U.S.A.: A Personal Experience. New York, Civil Rights Congress, and London, International Publishing Company, 1951.
Spain and Peace. New York, Joint Anti-Fascist Refugee Committee, 1952.
The Passion of Sacco and Vanzetti: A New England Legend. New York, Blue Heron Press, 1953; London, Lane, 1954.
The Naked God: The Writer and the Communist Party. New York, Praeger, 1957; London, Bodley Head, 1958.
The Howard Fast Reader. New York, Crown, 1960.
The Jews: Story of a People. New York, Dial Press, 1968.
The Art of Zen Meditation. Culver City, California, Peace Press, 1977.

Editor, *The Selected Works of Tom Paine.* New York, Modern Library, 1946.
Editor, *Best Short Stories of Theodore Dreiser.* Cleveland, World, 1947.

Manuscript Collection: University of Pennsylvania Library, Philadelphia.

*   *   *

Between 1960 and 1968, E. V. Cunningham produced eleven mystery novels, each with the one-word title of its heroine's first name. These were followed by *The Assassin Who Gave Up His Gun,* then one last woman's mystery, *Millie,* before a new series was begun about Masao Masuto, a Japanese-American attached to the Beverly Hills Police Department. Cunningham's prolific and successful output is particularly impressive because he is actually Howard Fast, who has produced fifteen books under his own name during that same period of less than twenty years.

In the first few of his high-heeled thrillers, Cunningham's style resembled Ian Fleming's in some, and a cross between Dashiell Hammett's and Rex Stout's in others. The "given" conditions strained plausibility: in *Sylvia* a multi-millionaire hires a small-time investigator to find out, almost on the eve of the wedding, who his prospective bride really is; in *Alice* a stranger, just before jumping into the path of a subway train, slips a safe-deposit key into the narrator's pocket; *Phyllis* works the tired atom-bomb theme of guilt-ridden scientists and the desperate crisis of getting to the villain before he can blow up the world. In *Sally* a young woman, mistakenly told she has leukemia, hires a gunman to kill her without warning; when she discovers that she is really well, the chain of communication has been snapped and she is the unwilling prey in the "contract" she has purchased.

Cunningham's gimmick of building each novel around an "ordinary" woman violated both the private-eye tradition of male domination and the lesser genre of girl-detective. His women, usually the victims of bizarre situations, are pluckier, cleverer, and more honest than the men they meet; perhaps by discovering deeper resources in themselves than they or others suspected, they foreshadowed the women's liberation novels of the 1960's. In about half of these thrillers (e.g., *Penelope, Margie, Cynthia*) the author's touch is light, with liberal use of "screwball comedy" heroines and situations reminiscent of the 1930's film comedies of Carole Lombard or Claudette Colbert. In others, such as *Helen* and *Samantha*, there is a somber, brooding quality in what are essentially mysteries of character and motivation rather than plot. These latter suggest the allegorical explorations of the "entertainments" of Graham Greene, a writer whom Cunningham has always admired. (Perhaps the most Greene-like of this author's mysteries, however, is *Fallen Angel*, written under the pseudonym of Walter Ericson.)

Nisei detective Masao Masuto first appeared as a character in *Samantha* and has "spun-off" into his own series. He is a Zen Buddhist (as is his creator), aloof in philosophy but socially involved as detective and family man. A karate expert, lover of roses, and possessor of caustic wit, Masuto moves coolly among the richly corrupt of Beverly Hills and Los Angeles. In *The Case of the One-Penny Orange*, he chases down the rare one-penny orange stamp that has occasioned murder, while in *The Case of the Russian Diplomat* an apparent drowning in the Beverly Glen hotel leads to a Russian diplomat, an East German spy, and Masuto's kidnapped daughter. In both, Masuto's personality and his relations with colleagues and family are as appealing as the plot; his Charlie Chan put-on before bigots is especially beguiling.

—Frank Campenni

CURTIS, Peter. See **LOFTS, Norah**.

CURTISS, Ursula (née Reilly). American. Born in Yonkers, New York, 8 April 1923; daughter of Helen Reilly, *q.v.*, and the artist Paul Reilly; sister of Mary McMullen, *q.v.* Educated at Staples High School, Westport, Connecticut. Married John Curtiss, Jr., in 1947; two daughters and three sons. Columnist for Fairfield *News*, Connecticut, 1942–43; fashion copywriter, Gimbels, 1944, Macy's, 1944–45, Bates Fabrics Inc., 1945–47. Self-employed

writer. Agent: Brandt and Brandt Inc., 101 Park Avenue, New York, New York 10017.
Address: 8408 Rio Grande Boulevard N.W., Albuquerque, New Mexico 87114, U.S.A.

CRIME PUBLICATIONS

Novels

Voice Out of Darkness. New York, Dodd Mead, 1948; London, Evans, 1949.
The Second Sickle. New York, Dodd Mead, 1950; as *The Hollow House*, London, Evans, 1951.
The Noonday Devil. New York, Dodd Mead, 1951; London, Eyre and Spottiswoode, 1953; as *Catch a Killer*, New York, Pocket Books, 1952.
The Iron Cobweb. New York, Dodd Mead, and London, Eyre and Spottiswoode, 1953.
The Deadly Climate. New York, Dodd Mead, 1954; London, Eyre and Spottiswoode, 1955.
Widow's Web. New York, Dodd Mead, and London, Eyre and Spottiswoode, 1956.
The Stairway. New York, Dodd Mead, 1957; London, Eyre and Spottiswoode, 1958.
The Face of the Tiger. New York, Dodd Mead, 1958; London, Eyre and Spottiswoode, 1960.
So Dies the Dreamer. New York, Dodd Mead, and London, Eyre and Spottiswoode, 1960.
Hours to Kill. New York, Dodd Mead, 1961; London, Eyre and Spottiswoode, 1962.
The Forbidden Garden. New York, Dodd Mead, 1962; London, Eyre and Spottiswoode, 1963; as *Whatever Happened to Aunt Alice?*, New York, Ace, 1969.
The Wasp. New York, Dodd Mead, 1963; London, Eyre and Spottiswoode, 1964.
Out of the Dark. New York, Dodd Mead, 1964; as *Child's Play*, London, Eyre and Spottiswoode, 1965.
Danger: Hospital Zone. New York, Dodd Mead, 1966; London, Hodder and Stoughton, 1967.
Don't Open the Door. New York, Dodd Mead, 1968; London, Hodder and Stoughton, 1969.
Letter of Intent. New York, Dodd Mead, 1971; London, Macmillan, 1972.
The Birthday Gift. New York, Dodd Mead, 1975; as *Dig a Little Deeper*, London, Macmillan, 1976.
In Cold Pursuit. New York, Dodd Mead, 1977; London, Macmillan, 1978.
The Menace Within. New York, Dodd Mead, and London, Macmillan, 1979.

Uncollected Short Stories

"Snowball," in *The Lethal Sex*, edited by John D. MacDonald. New York, Dell, 1959; London, Collins, 1962.
"The Stone House," in *Toronto Star*, 1960.
"The Old Barn on the Pond," in *Ellery Queen's Crime Carousel.* New York, New American Library, 1966; London, Gollancz, 1967.
"The Good Neighbor," in *Ellery Queen's All-Star Lineup.* New York, New American Library, 1967; as *Ellery Queen's 22nd Mystery Annual*, London, Gollancz, 1968.
"Tiger by the Tail," in *Anthology 1968 Mid-Year*, edited by Ellery Queen. New York, Davis, 1968.
"Change of Climate," in *Ellery Queen's Mystery Parade.* New York, New American Library, 1968; London, Gollancz, 1969.
"A Judicious Half Inch," in *Ellery Queen's Murdercade.* New York, Random House, 1975; London, Gollancz, 1976.
"The Pool Sharks," in *Ellery Queen's Mystery Magazine* (New York), October, 1976.

"The Right Perspective," in *Ellery Queen's Searches and Seizures.* New York, Davis, 1977.

Manuscript Collection: Mugar Memorial Library, Boston University.

* * *

For over thirty years, Ursula Curtiss has been successfully blending elements of the gothic and the detective genres into popular suspense stories. She is a master at creating intriguing chapter endings and swiftly paced plots, and the portraits of even relatively minor characters – Kate Clemence of *So Dies the Dreamer* or Barney Maynard of *The Wasp*, for example – are sharply and memorably drawn.

In several novels, the protagonist undertakes some seemingly simple task, only to find herself caught up in intrigue. In *The Birthday Gift*, Lydia Peel is put at risk by simply agreeing to deliver a present. A more arduous favor is undertaken by Harriet Crewe, in *The Forbidden Garden*; when she brings her sickly little nephew to the Southwest, she encounters a deadly elderly woman who is perfectly willing to murder to ensure her own comfort. In both books, the contrast between the mundaneness of the errand and the deadliness of the hidden dangers proves very effective. *The Forbidden Garden*, like *Letter of Intent*, is an "inverted" mystery, for the murderer is known from the outset. In *Letter of Intent*, the killer exchanges other people's lives for her own upward mobility. In these novels, Curtiss contrasts utterly selfish, untamed personalities with ordinary people who practice decent self-restraint. The portrayals are among her best.

Another pattern studies young women whose peace and security are threatened by the re-emergence of some old crime. A good measure of the tension arises from the sense that innocence is no protection from calumny or danger for Lou Fabian (*The Face of the Tiger*), or Katy Meredith (*Voice Out of Darkness*). Unable to trust anyone else, each turns amateur sleuth; the results are satisfying to the reader.

Coincidence figures largely in two novels which represent a third pattern. In the splendid *Out of the Dark*, children's random telephone pranks trigger danger and death. When Caroline Emmett (*The Deadly Climate*) accidentally witnesses a murder, she immediately becomes a potential victim. These novels illustrate the old saw that even the most sedate-seeming people have much to hide, and Curtiss makes full use of the irony inherent in each situation. Further, the sense of terrorizing isolation felt by Caroline Emmett, a total stranger in the community and uncertain of the identity of her pursuer, is remarkably well drawn; the reader is wholly convinced that the protagonist is drawing on the deepest reserves of her strength and courage.

Another set of novels depicts protagonists who deliberately seek vengeance. Both Nick Sentry (*The Noonday Devil*) and Torrant (*Widow's Web*) discover evidence which satisfies them that murders have been committed. Because of deep personal loyalties, the men undertake to avenge the victims, only to become entangled in danger and – as always in a Curtiss work – romance. *The Noonday Devil*'s evocation of World War II prison camps is extremely effective, as is the portrayal of the postwar period.

Curtiss is adept at several patterns, each successfully wrought. Refusing to romanticize her characters, she produces works which are a satisfying blend of the expected and the surprising. Often, the surprise arises not only from a variation of a familiar pattern but also from startling and effective endings. *The Wasp* and *Letter of Intent* are good examples of this device. In each instance, the reader is at first shocked and then gratified. The conclusions seem grimly appropriate, and they testify to Curtiss's skill.

—Jane S. Bakerman

DAHL, Roald.   British.   Born in Llandaff, Glamorgan, 13 September 1916. Educated at Repton School, Yorkshire. Served in the Royal Air Force, 1939–45: in Nairobi and Habbanyah, 1939–40; with a Fighter Squadron in the Western Desert, 1940 (wounded); in Greece and Syria, 1941; Assistant Air Attaché, Washington, D.C., 1942–43; Wing Commander, 1943; with British Security Co-ordination, North America, 1943–45. Married the actress Patricia Neal in 1953; one son and four daughters (one deceased). Member of the Public Schools Exploring Society expedition to Newfoundland, 1934; Member of the Eastern Staff, Shell Company, London, 1933–37, and Shell Company of East Africa, Dar-es-Salaam, 1937–39. Recipient: Mystery Writers of America Edgar Allan Poe Award, 1953, 1959. Agent: Murray Pollinger, 4 Garrick Street, London WC2E 9BH. Address: Gipsy House, Great Missenden, Buckinghamshire HP16 0PB, England.

CRIME PUBLICATIONS

Short Stories

> *Over to You: 10 Stories of Flyers and Flying.*   New York, Reynal, 1946; London, Hamish Hamilton, 1947.
> *Someone Like You.*   New York, Knopf, 1953; London, Secker and Warburg, 1954; revised edition, London, Joseph, 1961.
> *Kiss, Kiss.*   New York, Knopf, and London, Joseph, 1960.
> *Twenty-Nine Kisses.*   London, Joseph, 1969.
> *Selected Stories.*   New York, Random House, 1970.
> *Penguin Modern Stories 12*, with others.   London, Penguin, 1972.
> *Switch Bitch.*   New York, Knopf, and London, Joseph, 1974.
> *The Best of Roald Dahl.*   New York, Vintage Books, 1978.
> *Tales of the Unexpected.*   London, Joseph, 1979.

OTHER PUBLICATIONS

Novels

> *Sometime Never: A Fable for Supermen.*   New York, Scribner, 1948; London, Collins, 1949.
> *My Uncle Oswald.*   London, Joseph, 1979.

Plays

> *The Honeys* (produced New York, 1955).

> Screenplays: *You Only Live Twice*, 1965; *Chitty-Chitty-Bang-Bang*, 1967; *The Night-Digger*, 1970; *The Lightning Bug*, 1971; *Willie Wonka and the Chocolate Factory*, 1971.

Other (fiction for children)

> *The Gremlins.*   New York, Random House, 1943; London, Collins, 1944.
> *James and the Giant Peach.*   New York, Knopf, 1961; London, Allen and Unwin, 1967.
> *Charlie and the Chocolate Factory.*   New York, Knopf, 1964; London, Allen and Unwin, 1967.
> *The Magic Finger.*   New York, Harper, 1966; London, Allen and Unwin, 1968.

Fantastic Mr. Fox. New York, Knopf, and London, Allen and Unwin, 1970.
Charlie and the Great Glass Elevator: The Further Adventures of Charlie Bucket and
    Willy Wonka, Chocolate-Maker Extraordinary. New York, Knopf, 1972; London,
    Allen and Unwin, 1973.
Danny, The Champion of the World. London, Cape, and New York, Knopf, 1975.
The Wonderful Story of Henry Sugar and Six More. London, Cape, and New York,
    Knopf, 1977.
The Enormous Crocodile. London, Cape, and New York, Knopf, 1978.

*   *   *

> It is a minor talent, not a great one, but I am
> nonetheless thankful to have had it bestowed
> upon me, and I have done my best at all times
> to see that it has not been wasted.
>
> ("The Visitor," *Switch Bitch*)

Like the narrator of "The Visitor," Roald Dahl seems early in his career to have recognized his own talent for playful horror rooted in a teasingly circumstantial reality that both supports and mocks bizarre narratives. "A Piece of Cake," a typical early story from *Over to You*, explores the psychological and moral implications of war through the sufferings of a pilot whose nose has been destroyed. Though competent, the story seems primarily a rehearsal for the more comic treatments of mutilation, actual or threatened, in Dahl's later fiction: the fate of the beggar on whose back Soutine painted a portrait produces only a pleasurable *frisson* ("Skin"). At his best, Dahl makes the reader an eager voyeur: "Something extremely unpleasant was about to happen – I was sure of that. Something sinister and cruel and ratlike, and perhaps it really would make me sick. But I had to see it now" ("Claud's Dog").

Dahl's early novel *Sometime Never* attempted to blend whimsy and anti-war parable, but lacked the tight plot control of later stories, though the book demonstrated the talent for fantasy he was to push to grotesque extremes. Dahl's tales tempt the reader with outré characters and situations: a brain that survives the body's death ("William and Mary"); a sickly baby that becomes a bee-like monster through feedings of "Royal Jelly." Though the stories often inflict sadistic punishments on guilty and innocent alike, Dahl's tone softens the horror, since the supporting reality is clearly a canard, and the fiction raises none of the disturbing questions that define the horror in works like *Frankenstein*.

The stories perversely reinforce traditional morality, as unethical protagonists attempt to win bets or contests and sometimes lose their lives ("Dip in the Pool"), or more usually their professional reputations and considerable money (the gourmet whose "mouth is like a large wet keyhole" in "Taste"). Dahl immerses the reader in presumably authentic details about wine-tasting or painting-restoration to mock the lore of experts which is powerless to protect them against their own greed and the uncomprehending practicality of louts who violate a Chippendale commode to make a quick sale ("Parson's Pleasure"): in Dahl's universe mutilated furniture is as horrific as flayed humanity.

This contest motif reinforces Dahl's stories of sexual mismatches, physically intimidating women frequently dwarfing their males. Typical is the fate of the clergyman in "Georgy Porgy," pathologically afraid of the touch of a woman's skin because of his botched sex education. Both his upbringing and chosen profession make him fair game when overwhelming female parishioners besiege him; Dahl's comedy insures the destiny the cleric most fears, a conviction that he has been swallowed by his seducer's "great mouth," and now resides in her interior: "It is all a trifle bizarre for a man of conservative tastes like myself. Personally, I prefer oak furniture and parquet flooring...." Unlike Thurber, Dahl often favors the woman: the wife triumphs over her dead husband's surviving brain in "William and

Mary." Such struggles depend on apparently fortuitous shifts of strength which reveal the workings of a comic Providence; death makes the husband's unimpaired intellect ludicrously dependent upon a wife he had mistreated. The irony of the husband's comeuppance undercuts the story's sadism, though stories like "The Last Act" (*Switch Bitch*) reveal cruelty too strong for Dahl's comedy, too unsubstantial for serious horror.

Dahl's best story, "The Visitor," makes the protagonist's fate doubly appropriate: the world's supreme seducer, Oswald courts the destruction a mocking providence reserves for his hubris; the ultimate hypochondriac, he is an obvious target for every disease in the universe, inevitably leprosy. (Like the fastidious Absalom in "The Miller's Tale," Oswald allows his sexual vanity to override his caution.) Instead of punishing Oswald with venereal disease, Dahl characteristically intensifies the horror while maintaining the form of a bawdy joke. This fusion of diverse elements which teases the reader's credulity marks Dahl's finest work.

—Burton Kendle

DALTON, Priscilla. See **AVALLONE, Michael.**

DALY, Carroll John. American. Born in Yonkers, New York, 14 September 1889. Educated at Yonkers High School; De La Salle Institute and American Academy of Dramatic Arts, New York. Married Margaret G. Blakley in 1913; one son. Theatre manager: owner/operator of theatres in Atlantic City, Asbury Park, New Jersey; Averne, New York; Yonkers. Writer from 1922. *Died 16 January 1958.*

CRIME PUBLICATIONS

Novels (series characters: Vee Brown; Satan Hall; Race Williams)

The White Circle. New York, Clode, 1926; London, Hutchinson, 1927.
The Snarl of the Beast (Williams). New York, Clode, 1927; London, Hutchinson, 1928.
The Man in the Shadows. New York, Clode, 1928; London, Hutchinson, 1929.
The Hidden Hand (Williams). New York, Clode, 1929; London, Hutchinson, 1930.
The Tag Murders (Williams). New York, Clode, 1930; London, Hutchinson, 1931.
Tainted Power (Williams). New York, Clode, and London, Hutchinson, 1931.
The Third Murderer (Williams). New York, Farrar and Rinehart, 1931; London, Hutchinson, 1932.
The Amateur Murderer (Williams). New York, Washburn, and London, Hutchinson, 1933.
Murder Won't Wait (Brown). New York, Washburn, 1933; London, Hutchinson, 1934.
Murder from the East (Williams). New York, Stokes, and London, Hutchinson, 1935.

Mr. Strang. New York, Stokes, 1936; London, Hale, 1937.
The Mystery of the Smoking Gun (Hall). New York, Stokes, 1936; as *Death's Juggler*, London, Hutchinson, 1935.
Emperor of Evil (Brown). London, Hutchinson, 1936; New York, Stokes, 1937.
Better Corpses (Williams). London, Hale, 1940.
The Legion of the Living Dead. Toronto, Popular Publications, 1947.
Murder at Our House. London, Museum Press, 1950.
Ready to Burn (Hall). London, Museum Press, 1951.

Uncollected Short Stories

"Dolly," in *Black Mask* (New York), October 1922.
"It's All in the Game," in *Black Mask* (New York), 15 May 1923.
"Three Gun Terry," in *Black Mask* (New York), 15 May 1923.
"Three Thousand to the Good," in *Black Mask* (New York), 15 July 1923.
"Action! Action!," in *Black Mask* (New York), 1 January 1924.
"One Night of Frenzy," in *Black Mask* (New York), 15 April 1924.
"The Red Peril," in *Black Mask* (New York), June 1924.
"Them That Lives by Their Guns," in *Black Mask* (New York), August 1924.
"Devil Cat," in *Black Mask* (New York), November, 1924.
"The Face Behind the Mask," in *Black Mask* (New York), February 1925.
"Conceited, Maybe," in *Black Mask* (New York), April 1925.
"Say It with Lead," in *Black Mask* (New York), June 1925.
"I'll Tell the World," in *Black Mask* (New York), August 1925.
"Alias, Buttercup," in *Black Mask* (New York), October 1925.
"Under Cover," in *Black Mask* (New York), December 1925–January 1926.
"South Sea Steel," in *Black Mask* (New York), May 1926.
"The False Clara Burkhart," in *Black Mask* (New York), July 1926.
"The Super Devil," in *Black Mask* (New York), August 1926.
"The Code of the House," in *Detective Story* (New York), October 1926.
"Half-Breed," in *Black Mask* (New York), November 1926.
"Twenty Grand," in *Black Mask* (New York), January 1927.
"Blind Alleys," in *Black Mask* (New York), April 1927.
"The Egyptian Lure," in *Black Mask* (New York), March 1928.
"The Law of Silence," in *Black Mask* (New York), April–May 1928.
"The House of Crime," in *Detective Fiction Weekly* (New York), 10 November 1928.
"Gun Law," in *Complete Stories* (New York), February 1929.
"The Silver Eagle," in *Black Mask* (New York), October–November 1929.
"Shooting Out of Turn," in *Black Mask* (New York), October 1930.
"The Crime Machine," in *Dime Detective* (New York), January 1931.
"Murder by Mail," in *Black Mask* (New York), March 1931.
"The Flame and Race Williams," in *Black Mask* (New York), June–August 1931.
"Death for Two," in *Black Mask* (New York), September 1931.
"Satan Sees Red," in *Detective Fiction Weekly* (New York), 25 June 1932.
"Satan's Law," in *Detective Fiction Weekly* (New York), 6 August 1932.
"Satan's Kill," in *Detective Fiction Weekly* (New York), 19 November 1932.
"Merger with Death," in *Black Mask* (New York), December 1932.
"The Death Drop," in *Black Mask* (New York), May 1933.
"If Death Is Respectable," in *Black Mask* (New York), July 1933.
"The Sign of the Rat," in *Detective Fiction Weekly* (New York), 2 September 1933.
"Murder in the Open," in *Black Mask* (New York), October 1933.
"Blood on the Curtain," in *Dime Detective* (New York), 1 December 1933.
"Answered in Blood," in *Dime Detective* (New York), 1 March 1934.
"The Killer in the Hood," in *Detective Fiction Weekly* (New York), 14 April 1934.
"Make Your Own Corpse," in *Dime Detective* (New York), 15 April 1934.

"Six Have Died," in *Black Mask* (New York), May 1934.
"Flaming Death," in *Black Mask* (New York), June 1934.
"Behind the Black Hood," in *Detective Fiction Weekly* (New York), 23 June 1934.
"The Mexican Legion," in *Frontier Stories* (New York), July 1934.
"Death Drops In," in *Dime Detective* (New York), 1 July 1934.
"Murder Book," in *Black Mask* (New York), August 1934.
"Red Friday," in *Dime Detective* (New York), 1 September 1934.
"Satan Returns," in *Detective Fiction Weekly* (New York), 8 September 1934.
"The Clawed Killer," in *Dime Detective* (New York), 15 October 1934.
"The Eyes Have It," in *Black Mask* (New York), November 1934.
"Satan Laughed," in *Detective Fiction Weekly* (New York), 15 December 1934.
"Excuse to Kill," in *Dime Detective* (New York), 15 December 1934.
"Ready to Burn," in *Detective Fiction Weekly* (New York), 16 February 1935.
"The Bridal Bullet," in *Dime Detective* (New York), 1 May 1935.
"Some Die Hard," in *Dime Detective* (New York), September 1935.
"Dead Hands Reaching," in *Dime Detective* (New York), November 1935.
"The Mark of the Raven," in *Dime Detective* (New York), January 1936.
"Corpse & Company," in *Dime Detective* (New York), February 1936.
"Satan's Vengeance," in *Detective Fiction Weekly* (New York), 7 March–25 April 1936.
"Just Another Stiff," in *Dime Detective* (New York), April 1936.
"Red Dynamite," in *Dime Detective* (New York), July 1936.
"City of Blood," in *Dime Detective* (New York), October 1936.
"The Tongueless Men," with William E. Barrett and others, in *Dime Detective* (New York), November 1936.
"The Morgue's Our Home," in *Dime Detective* (New York), December 1936.
"Monogram in Lead," in *Dime Detective* (New York), February 1937.
"Dead Men Don't Kill," in *Dime Detective* (New York), August 1937.
"Anyone's Corpse!" in *Dime Detective* (New York), October 1937.
"The $1,000,000 Corpse," in *Dime Detective* (New York), December 1937.
"The Book of the Dead," in *Dime Detective* (New York), January 1938.
"I Am the Law," in *Black Mask* (New York), March 1938.
"Wrong Street," in *Black Mask* (New York), May 1938.
"A Corpse for a Corpse," in *Dime Detective* (New York), July 1938.
"Men in Black," in *Dime Detective* (New York), October 1938.
"The Quick and the Dead," in *Dime Detective* (New York), December 1938.
"Hell with the Lid Lifted," in *Dime Detective* (New York), March 1939.
"Murder Made Easy," in *Black Mask* (New York), May 1939.
"A Corpse in the Hand," in *Dime Detective* (New York), June 1939.
"The White-Headed Corpse," in *Dime Detective* (New York), November 1939.
"Mr. Sinister," in *Detective Fiction Weekly* (New York), 11 November–25 November 1939.
"Beauty and the Feast," in *Argosy* (New York), 25 May 1940.
"Victim for Vengeance," in *Clues* (New York), September 1940.
"No Sap for Murder," in *Black Mask* (New York), November 1940.
"The Strange Case of Iva Grey," in *Dime Detective* (New York), December 1940.
"Five Minutes for Murder," in *Black Mask* (New York), January 1941.
"Too Dead to Pay," in *Clues* (New York), March 1941.
"Clay Holt, Detective," in *Detective Story* (New York), February 1942.
"City of the Dead," in *Detective Fiction* (New York), June 1944.
"Murder Theme," in *Black Mask* (New York), July 1944.
"Body, Body – Who's Got the Body?" in *Detective Story* (New York), October 1944.
"A Corpse Loses Its Head," in *Detective Story* (New York), March 1945.
"I'll Be Killing You," in *New Detective Magazine* (New York), September 1945.
"The Seventh Murderer," in *Detective Story* (New York), November 1945.
"The Giant Has Fleas," in *Detective Story* (New York), February 1947.

"This Corpse on Me," in *Thrilling Detective* (New York), June 1947.
"Dead Man's Street," in *New Detective* (New York), September 1947.
"I'll Feel Better When You're Dead," in *Thrilling Detective* (New York), December 1947.
"Not My Corpse," in *Thrilling Detective* (New York), June 1948.
"Race Williams' Double Date," in *Dime Detective* (New York), August 1948.
"The Law of the Night," in *New Detective* (New York), September 1948.
"The Wrong Corpse," in *Thrilling Detective* (New York), February 1949.
"Half a Corpse," in *Dime Detective* (New York), May 1949.
"Race Williams Cooks a Goose," in *Dime Detective* (New York), October 1949.
"The $100,000 Corpse," in *Popular Detective* (New York), March 1950.
"Cash for a Killer," in *The Evening Standard Detective Book.*   London, Gollancz, 1950.
"The Strange Case of Alta May," in *Thrilling Detective* (New York), April 1950.
"If I Go in a Hearse," in *Phantom Detective* (New York), Spring 1950.
"Little Miss Murder," in *Smashing Detective* (New York), June 1952.
"This Corpse Is Free," in *Smashing Detective* (New York), September 1952.
"Gas," in *Smashing Detective* (New York), June 1953.
"The Cops Came at Seven," in *Famous Detective* (New York), August 1953.
"Lantern in the Mind" (as John D. Carroll), in *Famous Detective* (New York), August 1953.
"Avenging Angel," in *Famous Detective* (New York), February 1954.
"Manhunter," in *Famous Detective* (New York), August 1954.
"Murder Yet to Come," in *Famous Detective* (New York), December 1954.
"With a Bullet in You," in *Smashing Detective* (New York), March 1955.
"Head over Homicide," in *Smashing Detective* (New York), May 1955.
"The False Burton Combs," in *The Hard-Boiled Detective: Stories from Black Mask Magazine (1920–1951),* edited by Herbert Ruhm.   New York, Vintage, 1977.
"Knights of the Open Palm," in *The Great American Detective,* edited by William Kittredge and Steven M. Krauzer.   New York, New American Library, 1978.

OTHER PUBLICATION

Other

Two-Gun Gerta, with C. C. Waddell.   New York, Chelsea House, 1926.

*   *   *

It is universally accepted that the hard-boiled school of detective fiction originated in the American pulp magazine *Black Mask* during the early 1920's. An outgrowth of the lawless prohibition era, the writers who embodied this new kind of mystery writing explored the realism and violence of modern society through the professional detective, be he private or police. These stories, which embraced an odd sentimentality and a signature toughness of characterization and prose, were written often in the first person and always in the vernacular.

Carroll John Daly initiated the movement away from the traditional tale of ratiocination which had been the staple of the mystery field and toward the story of urban violence. Daly accomplished this neither deliberately nor spontaneously in his 1922 *Black Mask* story "The False Burton Combs," which is considered to be the first hard-boiled detective story. Although its protagonist is not a detective, his attitudes are those of the later Daly detectives. The story's narrator is a nameless adventurer for hire who operates in the shady half-world between the criminal and the police, and is willing to risk his life – or to kill – for a fee.

This character prefigures Race Williams, who, like Daly's other characters – Satan Hall, Vee Brown, Clay Holt, and others – is a fictional cowboy transferred to the modern streets.

Williams is a pragmatic cynical gunman who lives by his gun and trades on his reputation as a killer of criminals. He is a private investigator, often at odds with the law, who describes himself as "a middleman – just a half-way house between the cops and the crooks" and who boasts that he "never bumped off a guy what didn't need it." He is an uncomplicated figure who believes in a simple code of ethics which demands that he earn his fee and remain loyal to his client, though he will forego payment for a friend ("Death for Two") or gun down a treacherous client if he "deserves it" (*The Amateur Murderer*).

Williams, like Daly's other characters, is an aggressive investigator who accomplishes his aims through violence. He espouses a kind of frontier retribution which equates justice with a bullet in the brain of the malefactor. Aware of public antagonism toward his pragmatic philosophy, he is unconcerned and unapologetic, though when a woman adopts his cold-blooded attitude toward criminals he is both sickened and horrified, indicating lingering moral reservations ("Anyone's Corpse").

Carroll John Daly's stories are marked by a curious strain of melodrama which undermines their illusion of realism. Race Williams uses the affected speech of the dime-novel hero as much as he does the hard-boiled idiom. His cases often take him into the unremitting grimness of underworld life ("Not My Corpse"), but they also find him in opposition to dime-novel master criminals (*The Hidden Hand*). Essentially, Daly was a transitional writer who was not above placing one of his hard-boiled protagonists in a more traditional mystery (*The Man in the Shadows*), and who did not find his direction until later, more gifted writers legitimized his ideas, thereby showing him the way.

—Will Murray

DALY, Elizabeth. American. Born in New York City, 15 October 1878. Educated at Miss Baldwin's School; Bryn Mawr College, Pennsylvania, B.A. 1901; Columbia University, New York, M.A. 1902. Reader in English, Bryn Mawr College, 1904–06; tutor in French and English; producer of amateur theatre. Recipient: Mystery Writers of America Edgar Allan Poe Award, 1960. *Died 2 September 1967.*

Crime Publications

Novels (series character: Henry Gamadge in all books)

Unexpected Night. New York, Farrar and Rinehart, and London, Gollancz, 1940.
Deadly Nightshade. New York, Farrar and Rinehart, 1940; London, Hammond, 1948.
Murders in Volume 2. New York, Farrar and Rinehart, 1941; London, Eyre and Spottiswoode, 1943.
The House Without the Door. New York, Farrar and Rinehart, 1942; London, Hammond, 1945.
Evidence of Things Seen. New York, Farrar and Rinehart, 1943; London, Hammond, 1946.
Nothing Can Rescue Me. New York, Farrar and Rinehart, 1943; London, Hammond, 1945.
Arrow Pointing Nowhere. New York, Farrar and Rinehart, 1944; London, Hammond, 1946; as Murder Listens In, New York, Bantam, 1949.
The Book of the Dead. New York, Farrar and Rinehart, 1944; London, Hammond, 1946.

Any Shape or Form. New York, Farrar and Rinehart, 1945; London, Hammond, 1949.

Somewhere in the House. New York, Rinehart, 1946; London, Hammond, 1949.

The Wrong Way Down. New York, Rinehart, 1946; London, Hammond, 1950; as *Shroud for a Lady*, New York, Spivak, 1956.

Night Walk. New York, Rinehart, 1947; London, Hammond, 1950.

The Book of the Lion. New York, Rinehart, 1948; London, Hammond, 1951.

And Dangerous to Know. New York, Rinehart, 1949; London, Hammond, 1952.

Death and Letters. New York, Rinehart, 1950; London, Hammond, 1953.

The Book of the Crime. New York, Rinehart, 1951; London, Hammond, 1954.

OTHER PUBLICATIONS

Novel

The Street Has Changed. New York, Farrar and Rinehart, 1941.

*   *   *

When asked the name of her favorite American mystery writer, Agatha Christie replied that it was Elizabeth Daly. It isn't too difficult to explain this phenomenon because Daly has transposed most of the apparatus of the cozy British Golden Age detective story, as written by Christie, to a New York setting in the 1940's. Here are crime problems among the well-to-do classes who spend most of their time observing the social conventions in a closed circle that is isolated from much of the reality of World War II, crime, and the struggle for existence among the lower classes.

Daly's series detective, Henry Gamadge, lives in an old but respectable house in the fashionable Murray Hill district of New York City. He doesn't work for a living, but is an author and bibliophile. He accepts commissions as a consultant on old books, manuscripts, inks, or autographs – all of which fall within his expertise. On many occasions his bibliographic skills become intertwined with crime problems that include theft, forgery, and murder. Gamadge's blunt features and poor posture rule out a role as the conventionally suave and handsome detective of Golden Age fiction. He has a wife, a son, a cat named Martin, and an assistant, Harold Bantz. He numbers among his hobbies bridge, golf, music, and the conservation of the transitive verb. Anthony Boucher stated that he "is a man so well-bred as to make Lord Peter Wimsey seem a trifle coarse."

Gamadge tries to live a quiet, civilized life and pursue his literary interests, but his tranquillity is disrupted by a series of disquieting incidents that often lead to murder investigations. In *Unexpected Night* a million dollar legacy results in its recipient's demise. *Deadly Nightshade* is set in Maine, and deals with several cases of poisoning caused by a wild flower. *Murders in Volume 2* concerns a girl who claims to be the reincarnation of a missing 19th-century governess, and a volume of Lord Byron's poems that seems to have disappeared. *Nothing Can Rescue Me* presents Gamadge's Aunt Florence's attempt to write a novel, but she finds additional material added to her manuscript during the night. Gamadge is in the army in *Evidence of Things Seen*, but his wife Clara, vacationing in the Berkshires, is troubled when she sees an apparition on a hill at sunset. *Arrow Pointing Nowhere* presents Gamadge with a strangely marked railroad timetable.

The Book of the Dead might be solved by a clue in a copy of Shakespeare's *The Tempest.* This is one of the few Daly works (excluding the non-mystery *The Street Has Changed*) to display her vast theatrical expertise. A far-from-subtle rifle shot explodes the serenity of a rose garden in *Any Shape or Form.* An elderly caretaker uses the wrong door and takes *The Wrong Way Down* to the street with lethal consequences. The local library in the village of Fraser Mills is troubled by a prowler in *Night Walk. The Book of the Lion* concerns a lost Chaucer manuscript, and a recently deceased poet-playwright. A young woman leaves her home and vanishes into thin air for no explicable reason in *And Dangerous to Know* – recalling the famous Dorothy Arnold case. A crossword puzzle contains a message from a widow being held against her will and threatened with institutionalization in *Death and Letters*.

Daly's youthful fondness for games and puzzles led to a lifetime interest in detective fiction which she considered to be a high form of literary art. Her own work is unsensational, and conceived with subtle skill. It is always both civilized and literate.

—Charles Shibuk

DANE, Clemence. Pseudonym for Winifred Ashton. British. Born in Blackheath, London, in 1887. Educated at private schools, and at the Slade School of Art, London, 1904–06; studied art in Dresden, 1906–07. Taught French in Geneva, 1903, and in Ireland, 1907–13; taught at a girls' school during World War I; actress, as Diana Portis, 1913–18. General Editor, Novels of Tomorrow series, Michael Joseph, publishers, London, from 1955. President, Society of Women Journalists, 1941. C.B.E. (Commander, Order of the British Empire), 1953. *Died 28 March 1965.*

CRIME PUBLICATIONS

Novels (series character: Sir John Saumarez)

Enter Sir John, with Helen Simpson.   London, Hodder and Stoughton, and New York, Cosmopolitan, 1928.
Printer's Devil, with Helen Simpson.   London, Hodder and Stoughton, 1930; as *Author Unknown*, New York, Cosmopolitan, 1930.
The Floating Admiral, with others.   London, Hodder and Stoughton, 1931; New York, Doubleday, 1932.
Re-Enter Sir John, with Helen Simpson.   London, Hodder and Stoughton, and New York, Farrar and Rinehart, 1932.

OTHER PUBLICATIONS

Novels

Regiment of Women.   London, Heinemann, and New York, Macmillan, 1917.
First the Blade: A Comedy of Growth.   London, Heinemann, and New York, Macmillan, 1918.
Legend.   London, Heinemann, 1919; New York, Macmillan, 1920.
Wandering Stars, Together with The Lover.   London, Heinemann, and New York, Macmillan, 1924.
The Dearly Beloved of Benjamin Cobb.   London, Benn, 1927.
The Babyons: A Family Chronicle.   London, Heinemann, and New York, Doubleday, 1928.
Broome Stages.   London, Heinemann, and New York, Doubleday, 1931.
The Moon Is Feminine.   London, Heinemann, and New York, Doubleday, 1938.
The Arrogant History of White Ben.   London, Heinemann, and New York, Doubleday, 1939.
He Brings Great News.   London, Heinemann, 1944; New York, Random House, 1945.
The Flower Girls.   London, Joseph, 1954; New York, Norton, 1955.

Short Stories

The King Waits. London, Heinemann, 1929.
Fate Cries Out: Nine Tales. London, Heinemann, and New York, Doubleday, 1935.

Plays

A Bill of Divorcement (produced London and New York, 1921). London, Heinemann, and New York, Macmillan, 1921.
The Terror (produced Liverpool, 1921).
Will Shakespeare: An Invention (produced London, 1921; New York, 1923). London, Heinemann, 1921; New York, Macmillan, 1922.
The Way Things Happen: A Story, adaptation of her own novel *Legend* (produced Newark, New Jersey, 1923; New York and London, 1924). London, Heinemann, and New York, Macmillan, 1924.
Shivering Shocks; or, The Hiding Place: A Play for Boys. London, French, 1923.
Naboth's Vineyard. London, Heinemann, 1925; New York, Macmillan, 1926.
Granite (produced London, 1926; New York, 1927). London, Heinemann, and New York, Macmillan, 1926.
Mariners (produced New York, 1927; London, 1929). London, Heinemann, and New York, Macmillan, 1927.
Mr. Fox: A Play for Boys. London, French, 1927.
A Traveller Returns. London, French, 1927.
Adam's Opera, music by Richard Addinsell (produced London, 1928). London, Heinemann, 1928; New York, Doubleday, 1929.
Gooseberry Fool, with Helen Simpson (produced London, 1929).
Wild Decembers (produced London, 1933). London, Heinemann, and New York, Doubleday, 1932.
Come of Age, music by Richard Addinsell (produced New York, 1934). New York, Doubleday, 1934; London, Heinemann, 1938.
L'Aiglon, music by Richard Addinsell, adaptation of the play by Rostand (produced New York, 1934). New York, Doubleday, 1934.
Moonlight Is Silver (also director: produced London, 1934). London, Heinemann, 1934.
Richard of Bordeaux (produced New York, 1934).
The Laughing Woman (produced New York, 1936).
The Happy Hypocrite, adaptation of the story by Max Beerbohm (produced London, 1936).
Herod and Mariamne, adaptation of the play by Friedrich Hebbel (produced Pittsburgh, 1938). New York, Doubleday, 1938; London, Heinemann, 1939.
England's Darling, music by Richard Addinsell. London, Heinemann, 1940.
Cousin Muriel (produced London, 1940). London, Heinemann, 1940.
The Saviours: Seven Plays on One Theme (includes *Merlin, The Hope of Britain, England's Darling, The May King, The Light of Britain, Remember Nelson, The Unknown Soldier*), music by Richard Addinsell (broadcast, 1940–41). London, Heinemann, and New York, Doubleday, 1942.
The Golden Reign of Queen Elizabeth (produced York, 1941). London, French 1941.
Cathedral Steps (produced London, 1942).
Alice's Adventures in Wonderland and Through the Looking-Glass, music by Richard Addinsell, adaptation of the novels by Lewis Carroll (produced London, 1943). London, French, 1948.
The Lion and the Unicorn. London, Heinemann, 1943.
Call Home the Heart (produced London, 1947). London, Heinemann, 1947.
Scandal at Coventry (broadcast, 1958). Included in *The Collected Plays*, 1961

Eighty in the Shade (produced Newcastle, 1958; London, 1959).   London, Heinemann, 1959.

Till Time Shall End (televised, 1958).   Included in *The Collected Plays*, 1961.

The Collected Plays of Clemence Dane (includes *Scandal at Coventry, Granite, A Bill of Divorcement, Till Time Shall End*).   London, Heinemann, 1961 (one vol. only published).

The Godson: A Fantasy.   London, Joseph, and New York, Norton, 1964.

Screenplays: *The Lame Duck*, 1921; *The Tunnel (Transatlantic Tunnel)*, with Curt Siodmak and L. DuGarde Peach, 1935; *Anna Karenina*, 1935; *The Amateur Gentleman*, with Edward Knoblock, 1936; *Fairwell Again (Troopship)*, with Patrick Kirwan, 1937; *Fire over England*, with Sergei Nolbandov, 1937; *St. Martin's Lane (Sidewalks of London)*, 1938; *Salute John Citizen*, with Elizabeth Baron, 1942; *Perfect Strangers (Vacation from Marriage)*, with Anthony Pelissier, 1945; *Bonnie Prince Charlie*, 1948; *Bride of Vengeance*, with Cyril Hume and Michael Hogan, 1949; *The Angel with the Trumpet*, with Karl Hartl and Franz Tassie, 1950.

Radio Plays: *The Scoop* (serial), with others, 1931; *The Saviours* (7 plays), 1940–41; *Henry VIII*, from the play by Shakespeare, 1954; *Don Carlos*, from the play by Schiller, 1955; *Scandal at Coventry*, 1958.

Television Play: *Till Time Shall End*, 1958.

Verse

Trafalgar Day 1940.   London, Heinemann, 1940; New York, Doubleday, 1941.

Christmas in War-Time.   New York, Doubleday, 1941.

Other

The Women's Side.   London, Jenkins, 1926; New York, Doran, 1927.

Tradition and Hugh Walpole.   New York, Doubleday, 1929; London, Heinemann, 1930.

Recapture: A Clemence Dane Omnibus.   London, Heinemann, 1932.

Claude Houghton: Appreciations, with Hugh Walpole.   London, Heinemann, 1935.

Mozart's Cosi fan Tutte: Essays, with Edward J. Dent and Eric Blom.   London, Lane, 1945.

Approaches to Drama (address).   London, English Association, 1961.

London Has a Garden (on Covent Garden).   London, Joseph, and New York, Norton, 1964.

Editor, *A Hundred Enchanted Tales*.   London, Joseph, 1937.

Editor, *The Shelter Book: A Gathering of Tales, Poems, Essays, Notes and Notions for Use in Shelters, Tubes, Basements and Cellars in War-Time*.   London, Longman, 1940.

Editor, *The Nelson Touch: An Anthology of Lord Nelson's Letters*.   London, Heinemann, 1942.

Theatrical Activities:

Director: **Play** – *Moonlight Is Silver*, London, 1934.

Actress (as Diana Portis): **Plays** – Vera Lawrence, in *Eliza Comes to Stay* by H. V. Esmond, London, 1913; Baroness des Herbettes, in *This Way* by Sydney Blow and

Douglas Hoare, London, 1913; Sidonie in *Oh, I Say!* by Sydney Blow and Douglas Hoare, toured 1914.

See essay on Helen Simpson.

DANIEL, Glyn (Edmund). Also writes as Dilwyn Rees. British. Born in Lampeter Velfrey, Pembrokeshire, 23 April 1914. Educated at Barry County School, 1925–31; University College of South Wales, Cardiff, 1931–32; St. John's College, Cambridge (Scholar; Strathcona Student, 1936; Allen Scholar, 1937; Wallenberg Prizeman, 1937), 1932–38, B.A. (honours) in archaeology 1935, Ph.D., 1938, M.A. 1939. Served as an Intelligence Officer in the Royal Air Force, 1940–45; in charge of Photographic Interpretation, India and Southeast Asia, 1942–45; Wing Commander, 1943; mentioned in despatches. Married Ruth Langhorne in 1946. Research Fellow, 1938–46, and Steward, 1946–54, St. John's College. Teaching Fellow and Director of Studies in Archaeology and Anthropology, 1946–75, University Lecturer in Archaeology, 1946–74, and since 1975, Disney Professor of Archaeology and Head of the Department of Archaeology, Cambridge University. Munro Lecturer in Archaeology, 1954, and O'Donnell Lecturer, 1956, University of Edinburgh; Rhys Lecturer, British Academy, 1954; Josiah Mason Lecturer, University of Birmingham, 1956; Gregynog Lecturer, University College, Cardiff, 1968; Ballard-Matthews Lecturer, University College of North Wales, Bangor, 1968; Visiting Professor, University of Aarhus, Denmark, 1968; Ferrens Professor, University of Hull, Yorkshire, 1969; George Grant MacCurdy Lecturer, Harvard University, Cambridge, Massachusetts, 1971. Since 1957, Director of Anglia Television, Director and Trustee of the Arts Theatre, Cambridge, and Director and Editor, *Antiquity*, Cambridge; since 1958, General Editor, Ancient Peoples and Places series, Thames and Hudson, publishers, London. President, Royal Anthropological Institute, 1977–79. Litt.D.: Cambridge University, 1962. Fellow, Society of Antiquaries; Knight (First Class) of the Danebrog, 1961. Agent: Curtis Brown Ltd., 1 Craven Hill, London W2 3EP. Address: The Flying Stag, 70 Bridge Street, Cambridge, England.

CRIME PUBLICATIONS

Novels (series character: Sir Richard Cherrington in both books)

The Cambridge Murders (as Dilwyn Rees). London, Gollancz, 1945.
Welcome Death. London, Gollancz, 1954; New York, Dodd Mead, 1955.

OTHER PUBLICATIONS

Other

The Three Ages: An Essay on Archaeological Method. Cambridge, University Press, 1943.
A Hundred Years of Archaeology. London, Duckworth, 1950.
The Prehistoric Chamber Tombs of England and Wales. Cambridge, University Press, 1950.
A Picture Book of Ancient British Art, with Stuart Piggott. Cambridge, University Press, 1951.

427

Lascaux and Carnac. London, Lutterworth Press, 1955; revised edition, as *The Hungry Archaeologist in France: A Travelling Guide to Caves, Graves, and Good Living in the Dordogne and Brittany*, London, Faber, 1963.

Myth or Legend? (broadcast), with others. London, Bell, and New York, Macmillan, 1955.

Barclodiad y Gawres: The Excavation of a Megalithic Chamber Tomb in Angelsey 1952–53, with T. G. E. Powell. Liverpool, Liverpool University Press, 1956.

The Megalith Builders of Western Europe. London, Hutchinson, 1958; New York, Praeger, 1959.

The Prehistoric Chamber Tombs of France: A Geographical, Morphological, and Chronological Survey. London, Thames and Hudson, 1960.

The Pen of My Aunt. Cambridge, privately printed, 1961.

The Idea of Prehistory (lectures). London, C. A. Watts, 1962; Cleveland, World, 1963.

New Grange and the Bend of the Boyne, with Seán P. O Ríordáin. London, Thames and Hudson, and New York, Praeger, 1964.

Oxford Chicken Pie. Cambridge, privately printed, 1965.

Man Discovers His Past. London, Duckworth, 1966; New York, Crowell, 1968.

The Origins and Growth of Archaeology. London, Penguin, 1967; New York, Crowell, 1968.

The Western Mediterranean, with J. D. Evans. Cambridge, University Press, 1967.

The First Civilisations: The Archaeology of Their Origins. London, Thames and Hudson, and New York, Crowell, 1968.

Archaeology and the History of Art (lecture). Hull, University of Hull, 1970.

Megaliths in History. London, Thames and Hudson, 1972.

A Hundred and Fifty Years of Archaeology. Cambridge, Massachusetts, Harvard University Press, 1976.

Cambridge and the Back-Looking Curiosity: An Inaugural Lecture. Cambridge, University Press, 1976.

Editor, with I. Ll. Foster, *Prehistoric and Early Wales.* London, Routledge, 1965.
Editor, with others, *France Before the Romans.* London, Thames and Hudson, 1974.
Editor, with others, *The Illustrated Encyclopedia of Archaeology.* New York, Crowell, 1977; London, Macmillan, 1978.

Glyn Daniel comments:

I wrote my two detective stories for fun. The first one came at the end of the war: Professor Stuart Piggott and I had been travelling about in the Near East and after reading one detective story I said, "What rubbish," and threw it out the window of a Cairo hotel. "Surely," I said, "if we bothered and had the time we could do better." His reply was, "Why not try?" So I did. To my great surprise Gollancz took the book at once and demanded that I write another, which I did.

But from then to now the cares of academe and research have prevented me from writing any more. Those cares disappear in 1981 and then I will be back in the market. My third detective story is called *Trumpets on the Other Side* and is again set in Cambridge.

*   *   *

Glyn Daniel has written two works of detective fiction, *The Cambridge Murders* and *Welcome Death*. The first is the more successful and has an engaging authenticity, since the writer is a Cambridge don and sets his fiction among undergraduates and Fellows in an imaginary college with convincing topographical and social detail. The book then presents the classic "closed community" context, and falls into the category of Oxbridge detective fantasies, a genre exploited by Michael Innes and Edmund Crispin. *The Cambridge Murders* is urbane and entertaining, and the affectionate references to good food and wine in and out of college made agreeable reading in the days of post-war austerity and rationing. The amateur detective, Sir Richard Cherrington, is Professor of Prehistory and combines features of the late Sir Mortimer Wheeler and of the author himself. The setting is wholly Cambridge with a brisk French episode at the end.

In *Welcome Death* the setting is Welsh, in South Glamorgan, the author's home country. Here, although Sir Richard's sister lives in Llanddewi, and he is on the scene by Chapter 7, the atmosphere is non-academic, and centres on the tensions in a small village community intensified by the return of two of its young men at the end of the war. The scene, the jealousies, the snobbery and inverted snobbery are nicely observed, but Sir Richard is not at his best. Perhaps he is thinking wistfully of crème brulée for dinner in Fisher College.

—Stuart Piggott

DANIEL, (William) Roland. Also wrote as Sonia Anderson. British. Born in Wandsworth, London, 14 August 1880; grew up in Florida. Educated at Madras House, Eastbourne, Sussex. Served with the Canadian Scouts in the Boer War, and the Royal Navy during World War I. Married Pearl Daniel in 1919; one daughter. Manager, Theatre Royal, Croydon, Surrey, after the war; toured England in acting companies in the 1920's. *Died 20 March 1969.*

CRIME PUBLICATIONS

Novels (series characters: Michael Grant; John Hopkins; Buddy Mustard; Brian O'Malley; Jack Pearson; The Remover; Brian Saville; Michael Wallace; Wu Fang)

The Society of the Spiders (Saville). London, Brentano's, 1928.
Wu Fang (Wu Fang and Saville). London, Brentano's, 1929.
The Brown Murder Case. London, Shaylor, 1930.
The Rosario Murder Case (Hopkins). London, Brentano's, 1930.
Dead Man's Vengeance. London, Shaylor, 1931.
The Shooting of Sergius Leroy (Hopkins). London, Modern Publishing Company, 1931.
The Mystery of Mary Hamilton. London, Modern Publishing Company, 1931.
Ann Turns Detective. London, Wright and Brown, 1932.
The Crackswoman (Pearson). London, Wright and Brown, 1932.
Dead Man's Corner. London, Wright and Brown, 1932.
The Gangster. London, Wright and Brown, 1932.
The Green Jade God. London, Wright and Brown, 1932.
Husky Voice. London, Wright and Brown, 1932.
The Yellow Devil (Wu Fang). London, Wright and Brown, 1932.
The Arch-Criminal. London, Wright and Brown, 1933.
The Princess' Own. London, Wright and Brown, 1933.
The Remover (The Remover and Saville). London, Wright and Brown, 1933.
Ruby of a Thousand Dreams (Wu Fang). London, Wright and Brown, 1933.
The Signal. London, Wright and Brown, 1933.
White Eagle. London, Wright and Brown, 1933.
The Blackmailer (The Remover and Saville). London, Wright and Brown, 1934.

The Dragon's Claw. London, Wright and Brown, 1934.
The Jail-Breakers. London, Wright and Brown, 1934.
The Murphy Gang. London, Wright and Brown, 1934.
Sally of the Underworld. London, Wright and Brown, 1934.
Scarthroat. London, Wright and Brown, 1934; New York, Godwin, 1935.
Wu Fang's Revenge. London, Wright and Brown, 1934.
Amber Eyes. London, Wright and Brown, 1935.
The Crimson Shadow (Pearson). London, Wright and Brown, 1935.
The Killer. London, Wright and Brown, 1935.
The 'Lo Sweeny Gang. London, Wright and Brown, 1935.
The Man Who Sought Trouble. London, Wright and Brown, 1935.
The Remover Returns (The Remover and Saville). London, Wright and Brown, 1935.
The Son of Wu Fang. London, Wright and Brown, 1935.
Red Murchison. London, Wright and Brown, 1936.
The Secret Hand. London, Wright and Brown, 1936.
The Slayer. London, Wright and Brown, 1936.
Slick-Fingered Kate. London, Wright and Brown, 1936.
Snake Face. London, Wright and Brown, 1936.
The Stedman Gang. London, Wright and Brown, 1936.
The Stool Pigeon. London, Wright and Brown, 1936.
The Buddha's Secret. London, Wright and Brown, 1937.
The Missing Lady. London, Wright and Brown, 1937.
The Return of Wu Fang. London, Wright and Brown, 1937.
The Snide Man. London, Wright and Brown, 1937.
The Tipster. London, Wright and Brown, 1937.
At the Silver Butterfly. London, Wright and Brown, 1938.
The Langley Murder Case. London, Wright and Brown, 1938.
The Man with the Magnetic Eyes. London, Wright and Brown, 1938.
The River Gang. London, Wright and Brown, 1938.
Again the Remover (The Remover and Saville). London, Wright and Brown, 1939.
The Black Raven. London, Wright and Brown, 1939.
The Blonde Murder Case. London, Wright and Brown, 1939.
The Gangster's Last Shot (Pearson). London, Wright and Brown, 1939.
Human Vultures. London, Wright and Brown, 1939.
The Big Squeal. London, Wright and Brown, 1940.
Slant Eye. London, Wright and Brown, 1940.
This Woman Is Wanted. London, Wright and Brown, 1940.
The Crawshay Jewel Mystery (Mustard). London, Wright and Brown, 1941.
The Death House. London, Wright and Brown, 1941.
Shattered Hopes. London, Wright and Brown, 1941.
The Doublecrosser. London, Wright and Brown, 1942.
Evil Eyes. London, Wright and Brown, 1942.
The Girl by the Roadside. London, Wright and Brown, 1942.
The Missing Heiress. London, Wright and Brown, 1942.
The Twenty-Two Windows. London, Wright and Brown, 1942.
The Black Market. London, Wright and Brown, 1943.
The Hunchback of Soho. London, Wright and Brown, 1943.
Singapore Kate. London, Wright and Brown, 1943.
The Spider's Web. London, Wright and Brown, 1943.
Evil Shadows (Mustard). London, Wright and Brown, 1944.
The Millionaire Crook. London, Wright and Brown, 1944.
The Professor. London, Wright and Brown, 1944.
The Girl in the Dark. London, Wright and Brown, 1945.
A Bunch of Crooks. London, Wright and Brown, 1946.
The Desert Crime. London, Wright and Brown, 1946.

Murder at Little Malling (Pearson).   London, Wright and Brown, 1946.
The Haughton Diamond Robbery.   London, Wright and Brown, 1947.
The Lady in Scarlet (Mustard).   London, Wright and Brown, 1947.
Mrs. Graystone – Murdered.   London, Wright and Brown, 1947.
The Z Case.   London, Wright and Brown, 1947.
The Kenya Tragedy.   London, Wright and Brown, 1948.
The Man Who Sold Secrets.   London, Wright and Brown, 1948.
A Dead Man Sings (Mustard).   London, Wright and Brown, 1949.
The Man from Prison.   London, Wright and Brown, 1949.
Spencer Blair, G-Man.   London, Wright and Brown, 1949.
Murder at a Cottage (Mustard).   London, Wright and Brown, 1949.
The Stop-at-Nothing Man.   London, Wright and Brown, 1950.
Murder in Piccadilly.   London, Wright and Brown, 1950.
The Little Old Lady.   London, Wright and Brown, 1950.
Arrested for Murder (O'Malley).   London, Wright and Brown, 1951.
The Arrow of Death (Mustard).   London, Wright and Brown, 1951.
The Black Eagle.   London, Wright and Brown, 1951.
The Undercover Girl.   London, Wright and Brown, 1951.
It Happened at Night.   London, Wright and Brown, 1952.
Three Sundays to Live (Mustard).   London, Wright and Brown, 1952.
The Case of the King of Montavia.   London, Wright and Brown, 1953; as *The Case of the Blackmailed King*, London, Mellifont Press, 1955.
Murder of a Bookmaker.   London, Wright and Brown, 1953.
Quicksilver.   London, Wright and Brown, 1953.
Trouble at the Inn.   London, Wright and Brown, 1953.
The Murder Gang (Mustard).   London, Wright and Brown, 1954.
Murder Goes Free.   London, Wright and Brown, 1954.
The Stolen Necklace.   London, Wright and Brown, 1954.
The Big Racket.   London, Wright and Brown, 1955.
Killers Must Die.   London, Wright and Brown, 1955.
On the Run.   London, Wright and Brown, 1955.
Frightened Eyes (Grant).   London, Wright and Brown, 1956.
Murder of Guy Thorpe.   London, Wright and Brown, 1956.
Suicide Can Be Murder.   London, Wright and Brown, 1956.
Dangerous Moment.   London, Wright and Brown, 1957.
Murder in Dawson City.   London, Wright and Brown, 1957.
Special Agent.   London, Wright and Brown, 1957.
All Thugs Are Dangerous.   London, Wright and Brown, 1958.
The Great Secret.   London, Wright and Brown, 1958.
The Man from Paris (Mustard).   London, Wright and Brown, 1958.
Dangerous Mission.   London, Wright and Brown, 1959.
A Double-Crossing Traitor.   London, Wright and Brown, 1959.
The Kidnappers (Grant).   London, Wright and Brown, 1959.
Brunettes Are Dangerous (Grant).   London, Wright and Brown, 1960.
Lovely but Dangerous (Wallace).   London, Wright and Brown, 1960.
Red-Headed Dames and Murder (Grant).   London, Wright and Brown, 1960.
Deadly Mission (O'Malley).   London, Wright and Brown, 1961.
The Lady Turned Traitor.   London, Wright and Brown, 1961.
The Missing Body (Mustard).   London, Wright and Brown, 1961.
The Big Shot (Mustard).   London, Wright and Brown, 1962.
The Lady Was a Spy (Wallace).   London, Wright and Brown, 1962.
Women – Dope – and Murder (Grant).   London, Wright and Brown, 1962.
Death by the Lake.   London, Wright and Brown, 1963.
The Hangman Waits (Mustard).   London, Wright and Brown, 1963.
Night Club Murder (Wallace).   London, Wright and Brown, 1963.

The Devil Woman (O'Malley).   London, Wright and Brown, 1964.
The Female Spy (O'Malley).   London, Wright and Brown, 1964.
Murder in Ocean Drive.   London, Wright and Brown, 1964.
The Gangster's Daughter (Mustard).   London, Wright and Brown, 1965.
Kidnapped Wife.   London, Wright and Brown, 1965.
The Prisoner (Wallace).   London, Wright and Brown, 1965.
The Secret Service Girl.   London, Wright and Brown, 1966.

OTHER PUBLICATIONS

Novels as Sonia Anderson

Blind Love.   London, Wright and Brown, 1953.
Red Sands.   London, Wright and Brown, 1953.
A Woman Deceived.   London, Wright and Brown, 1954.
Jean Burchell's Ordeal.   London, Wright and Brown, 1955.
The Naughty Widow.   London, Wright and Brown, 1955.
Secret Sands.   London, Wright and Brown, 1955.
Stella Munday.   London, Wright and Brown, 1956.
Between Two Women.   London, Wright and Brown, 1957.
Faithful Lover.   London, Wright and Brown, 1957.
The Flame.   London, Wright and Brown, 1957.
For Rose with Love.   London, Wright and Brown, 1957.
Affair in Malaya.   London, Wright and Brown, 1958.
New Love for Nina.   London, Wright and Brown, 1958.
Imprudent Interlude.   London, Wright and Brown, 1959.
Road to Happiness.   London, Wright and Brown, 1959.
Lovely Lady.   London, Wright and Brown, 1960.
Lover Come Back to Me.   London, Wright and Brown, 1960.
Stardom for Diana.   London, Wright and Brown, 1960.
Malayan Interlude.   London, Wright and Brown, 1961.
Scandal for Susie.   London, Wright and Brown, 1961.
Riding to Love.   London, Wright and Brown, 1962.
Dreams Must Wait.   London, Wright and Brown, 1963.
The Lady in Scarlet.   London, Wright and Brown, 1963.
Love from Odini.   London, Wright and Brown, 1964.
The Love Trap.   London, Wright and Brown, 1964.
Elusive Husband.   London, Wright and Brown, 1965.
Lady in Love.   London, Wright and Brown, 1965.
Love on an Island.   London, Wright and Brown, 1965.

Plays

The Princess's Own (produced Brighton and London, 1924).
The Signal: A Mystery Play (produced Eastbourne, Sussex, and London, 1925).
A Wife or Two, with Clifford B. Poultney (produced Portsmouth, Hampshire, 1927).
Who's Who, with Clifford B. Poultney (produced London, 1928).

*   *   *

The most striking thing about the work of Roland Daniel is his incredible change of style depending on whether the locale of the plot was England or America. We have, on the one hand, the typical English hero of the 1930's with his apologetic mannerisms, and on the other that slicker style of dialogue commonly associated with the American hard-boiled pulp, "I was thinking of a quiet evening reading with a bottle of Bourbon on the table beside me...."

It is doubtful whether this latter style owed anything to Daniel's early American background; it was more likely designed to appeal to a transatlantic readership, but certainly from the contrasting differences one could be forgiven for believing there were two Roland Daniels.

Daniel uses a variety of detectives and private eyes, many of whom became series characters. Brian O'Malley, Buddy Mustard, Michael Wallace, and Michael Grant are just a few of the regulars. Very often a hint of the Orient would creep into his stories, whether it was merely a Chinese servant or a tale of opium trafficking in London's East End.

At times one needed an interpreter to translate the almost laughable pidgin English that his Eastern characters spoke. "Then I glo and see mistress and tell her blother is safe, you glo to blothers and get girl." His major villain, Wu Fang, was an obvious attempt to create another Dr. Fu Manchu but, though a good try, he was never quite a household name and certainly never as insidious.

While the novels of Roland Daniel were not of a high literary quality, they were extremely popular with those who liked thrillers and exciting narration.

—Derek Adley

DANNAY, Frederic. See QUEEN, Ellery.

DAVEY, Jocelyn. Pseudonym for Chaim Raphael. British. Born in Middlesbrough, Yorkshire, 14 July 1908. Educated at Portsmouth Grammar School, 1921–27; University College, Oxford (history scholar), 1927–30, B.A. in philosophy, politics and economics 1930, M.A. 1933; James Mew Graduate Scholar in Hebrew, 1931; Kennicott Fellow in Hebrew, 1934–37. Married Diana Rose in 1934 (marriage dissolved, 1964); one son and one daughter. Cowley Lecturer in Post-Biblical Hebrew, Oxford University, 1932–39; engaged in government work, 1939–70: Liaison Officer for Internment Camps, 1939–42; Economics Adviser, 1942–45, and Economics Director, British Information Services, New York; Deputy Head, 1957–59, and Head of the Information Division, 1959–69, Department of the Treasury; Head of the Information Division, Civil Service Department, 1969–70. Since 1970, Research Fellow in Jewish Social History, University of Sussex, Brighton. O.B.E. (Officer, Order of the British Empire), 1951; C.B.E. (Commander, Order of the British Empire), 1965. Agent: A. P. Watt and Son, 26–28 Bedford Row, London WC1R 4HL. Address: 27 Langdale Road, Hove, East Sussex, England.

CRIME PUBLICATIONS

Novels (series character: Ambrose Usher in all books)

> The Undoubted Deed.   London, Chatto and Windus, 1956; as A Capitol Offense, New York, Knopf, 1956.
> The Naked Villainy.   London, Chatto and Windus, and New York, Knopf, 1958.
> A Touch of Stagefright.   London, Chatto and Windus, 1960.

433

A Killing in Hats.   London, Chatto and Windus, 1965.
A Treasury Alarm.   London, Chatto and Windus, 1976.

OTHER PUBLICATIONS as Chaim Raphael

Other

Memoirs of a Special Case.   London, Chatto and Windus, and Boston, Little Brown, 1962.
The Walls of Jerusalem: An Excursion into Jewish History.   London, Chatto and Windus, and New York, Knopf, 1968.
A Feast of History: Passover Through the Ages as a Key to Jewish Experience.   London, Weidenfeld and Nicolson, and New York, Simon and Schuster, 1972.
A Coat of Many Colours: Memoirs of Jewish Experience.   London, Chatto and Windus, 1979; as *Encounters with the Jewish People*, New York, Behrman House, 1979.

Jocelyn Davey comments:
My mysteries are diversions in which the central character, Ambrose Usher, an Oxford philosophy don who is intended to be both erudite and entertaining, finds himself in various parts of the world, roped in on some mysterious project by the British government. Reviewers (and, I hope, the public) have found the books satisfyingly light-hearted. They all echo personal experience in some degree.

*   *   *

Under the pseudonym Jocelyn Davey, Chaim Raphael has written a series of detective novels, which he describes as "entertainments." These feature the ratiocinations of Ambrose Usher, the most learned, sophisticated, and literary detective since Dorothy L. Sayers's Lord Peter Wimsey.

A witty and amorous bachelor of middle age, Ambrose Usher is an Oxford don specializing in philosophy, a fluent speaker of several languages, an avid reader of ancient and modern classics, and a connoisseur of music and music manuscripts. He is often assigned ill-defined advisory duties at foreign Embassies, duties which often involve him in international intrigue and always with murder. Usher particularly relishes his assignments to the United States, the setting for two of the works in which he appears.

The "entertainments" are complicated novels; all develop crowds of characters in clusters of subplots. While the discovery of the criminal ties these subplots together, the murder itself often seems less important than the events, people, and researches between which Usher must dash, cocktail in hand, in order to solve it. Needless to say, a scholarly diplomat-detective operates with brain rather than brawn. In *The Naked Villainy* the clue appears in Usher's interpretation of the Bible story of Jacob and Esau. In *A Touch of Stagefright* a series of telephone calls and a bit of research at the New York Public Library solve the crime.

While some critics object to Davey's far-fetched murders and complicated plots, far more admire his playfully allusive style and variety of entertaining characters in bizarre situations. Flat-footed FBI agents, English treasury agents, svelte Russian émigrés, eccentric aristocrats, anti-vivisectionists, fashionable ladies, loyal retainers, self-made industrialists, and bookish dons throng his tales whose unifying element tends to be theme rather than plot. Davey succeeds almost more as a novelist than as a detective novelist.

The career and interests of Chaim Raphael parallel those of his detective hero. Like Usher, he is amused and intrigued by America, which he describes as his "recreation." He has a university teaching background and has published a variety of serious non-fiction works, notably on Judaica. Raphael also served as Intelligence Advisor in the United States and in

Canada during World War II and as a Treasury and Civil Service Officer. Raphael's experience, learning and wit all appear in crafted "entertainments."

—Katherine Staples

DAVIDSON, Lionel. British. Born in Hull, Yorkshire, 31 March 1922. Served in the Royal Naval Submarine Service, 1941–46. Married Fay Jacobs in 1949; two sons. Free-lance magazine journalist and editor, 1946–59. Recipient: Crime Writers Association Golden Dagger, 1961, 1967, 1979. Agent: Curtis Brown Ltd., 1 Craven Hill, London W2 3EP, England.

CRIME PUBLICATIONS

Novels

> The Night of Wenceslas. London, Gollancz, 1960; New York, Harper, 1961.
> The Rose of Tibet. London, Gollancz, and New York, Harper, 1962.
> A Long Way to Shiloh. London, Gollancz, 1966; as The Menorah Men, New York, Harper, 1966.
> Making Good Again. London, Cape, and New York, Harper, 1968.
> Smith's Gazelle. London, Cape, and New York, Knopf, 1971.
> The Sun Chemist. London, Cape, and New York, Knopf, 1976.
> The Chelsea Murders. London, Cape, 1978; as Murder Games, New York, Coward McCann, 1978.

*   *   *

Lionel Davidson is a crime writer whose career has taken a by no means common path. Instead of finding a successful formula and sticking to it with perhaps some gradual expansion he has bounded from sub-genre to sub-genre, each bound taking him usually yet higher.

Beginning with *The Night of Wenceslas*, an espionage thriller that won him deserved prizes for its uncluttered sharpness of tone and its memorable vividness (all the more remarkable since Davidson had never visited Czechoslovakia, where most of the story takes place), he went on at once to write quite a different sort of book, a novel of pure adventure, *The Rose of Tibet*. This perhaps falls outside our brief here, but it is worth noting that Graham Greene said of its extraordinary evocation of the forbidden, exotic land of Tibet, "I hadn't realised how much I had missed the genuine adventure story," and Daphne du Maurier asked, "Is Lionel Davidson today's Rider Haggard?"

Four years later – he is by no means a prolific author – he gave her her answer. And it was "No." *A Long Way to Shiloh* has stunning adventure in it, as well as excellent jokes and a sophisticated strain of sex, but it is a good deal more than "the genuine adventure story." It is not only ceaselessly gripping with its account of a hunt for the centuries-lost true Menorah from the Temple at Jerusalem, but it has a setting that is not merely an exotic or unusual background, a mere commercial additive. In it the background, Israel in the 1960's, becomes a major character in its own right. This makes the book, whatever your political allegiance and despite the sad events of later days, a joy to devour, a hymn to hopefulness. Not that it is all lyrical. Davidson's gift of vividness and his ability to be immensely funny are not forgotten.

Making Good Again is perhaps not dissimilar in intention, though in method it largely eschews adventure in favour of a complex, gradual unravelling. Set in post-war Germany (with a sombre chapter at the Auschwitz memorial), it tackles head-on one of the great themes of our times, a theme that would have challenged our mightiest novelists, the meaning of the phenomenon of Nazism. And to do this Davidson employs to the full the methods of the novelist, those layers of ever richer meaning. But again he did not abandon humour.

The complex novel *Smith's Gazelle* has about it something of the world-creating myth, which has made it a treasured book among young people. Its story of the chances and determinations that preserve a herd of almost extinct deer take it, again, out of the strict confines of these pages. But it had all the immense vividness that is perhaps Davidson's chief hallmark.

The novel that followed, *The Sun Chemist*, falls, however, squarely into the espionage bracket with its excellent plot-spring, the supposed existence among the forgotten papers of the scientist-statesman Chaim Weizmann of a formula that will free any nation possessing it of dependence on oil. The whole is told with Davidson's characteristic combination of cleverness and warmth, a rare enough blend. But the cleverness is not used just to make good jokes, but to dig with jokes the long needles of the acupuncturist deep into the body politic.

Finally, after another long gap, we have had *The Chelsea Murders*, a book whose title exactly describes it, a mystery story set in the bohemian world of London's art district and a dazzling send-up of the conventional whodunnit. Where Davidson will go after that is anybody's guess, but wherever it is it will be well worth going too.

—H. R. F. Keating

DAVIES, L(eslie) P(urnell).   Also writes as Leslie Vardre.   British.   Born in Crewe, Cheshire, 20 October 1914. Educated at Manchester College of Science and Technology, University of Manchester, qualified as optometrist 1939 (Fellow, British Optical Association). Served in the British Army Medical Corps in France, North Africa, and Italy, 1939–45. Married Winifred Tench in 1940. Dispensing pharmacist, Crewe, Cheshire, 1930–39; freelance artist in Rome, 1945–46; postmaster, West Heath, Birmingham, 1946–56; Optician in private practice, and gift shop owner, Deganwy, North Wales, 1956–75. Since 1975, has lived in Tenerife. Agent: Howard Moorpark, 444 East 82nd Street, New York, New York 10028, U.S.A.; or, Carl Routledge, Charles Lavell Ltd., 176 Wardour Street, London W1V 3AA, England. Address: Apartment K-1, Edificio Alondra, El Botanico, Puerto de la Cruz, Tenerife, Canary Islands, Spain.

CRIME PUBLICATIONS

Novels

The Paper Dolls.   London, Jenkins, 1964; New York, Doubleday, 1966.
Man Out of Nowhere.   London, Jenkins, 1965; as *Who Is Lewis Pinder?*, New York, Doubleday, 1966.
The Artificial Man.   London, Jenkins, 1965; New York, Doubleday, 1967.
The Lampton Dreamers.   London, Jenkins, 1966; New York, Doubleday, 1967.

Tell It to the Dead (as Leslie Vardre).   London, Long, 1966; as *The Reluctant Medium*, as L. P. Davies, New York, Doubleday, 1967.
Twilight Journey.   London, Jenkins, 1967; New York, Doubleday, 1968.
The Nameless Ones (as Leslie Vardre).   London, Long, 1967; as *A Grave Matter*, as L. P. Davies, New York, Doubleday, 1968.
Stranger to Town.   London, Jenkins, and New York, Doubleday, 1969.
The White Room.   New York, Doubleday, 1969; London, Barrie and Jenkins, 1970.
The Shadow Before.   New York, Doubleday, 1970; London, rrie and Jenkins, 1971.
Give Me Back Myself.   New York, Doubleday, 1971; London, Barrie and Jenkins, 1972.
What Did I Do Tomorrow?   London, Barrie and Jenkins, 1972; New York, Doubleday, 1973.
Assignment Abacus.   London, Barrie and Jenkins, and New York, Doubleday, 1975.
Possession.   London, Hale, and New York, Doubleday, 1976.
The Land of Leys.   New York, Doubleday, 1979; London, Hale, 1980.

Uncollected Short Story

"The Unknown Factor," in *The Sixth Mystery Bedside Book*, edited by John Creasey.   London, Hodder and Stoughton, 1965.

OTHER PUBLICATIONS

Novels

Psychogeist.   London, Jenkins, 1966; New York, Doubleday, 1967.
The Alien.   London, Jenkins, 1968; New York, Doubleday, 1971.
Dimension A.   London, Jenkins, and New York, Doubleday, 1969.
Genesis Two.   London, Jenkins, 1969; New York, Doubleday, 1970.
Adventure Holidays Ltd.   New York, Doubleday, 1970.
The Silver Man (in Swedish).   Stockholm, Wahlströms Bokförlag, 1972.

L. P. Davies comments:
Although I think I have written every type of material available, I have mainly concentrated on what I call "Psycho fiction" and my American editor calls "Tomorrow fiction." It has proved remunerative – this fiction based on the workings of the human mind – but has had its drawbacks. My first novel, *The Paper Dolls*, was rejected by four publishers because it didn't fit into any of their categories. I try to puzzle my readers; I have no axes to grind; I think I have always played fair with my readers when offering them what I hope may seem like an unsolvable mystery. I try to offer entertainment only.

*   *   *

An author who has written under other names, L. P. Davies writes science fiction and thrillers in his own name. Fascinated with psychic phenomena and the supernatural, he has based most of his suspense novels on these themes. Some of his books published as mystery or crime fiction have science fiction elements so that classification is not always clear.
The Paper Dolls, Davies's first thriller, is considered a crime novel, though it could just as well be shelved with the science fiction. The story opens and closes in a school with a class of boys reading from *A Midsummer Night's Dream*. Two young teachers, Gordon Seacombe and Joan Grey, determined to discover the truth about some peculiar happenings in their school which seem to revolve about one boy, learn that, instead of one boy, brothers are involved. The brothers seem able to induce terrifying psychic states in other people. Seacombe, after one such experience, says: "I think that in some way he reached a mental

437

finger into our minds, pressing the button labeled 'fear.' The things we saw we each made up ourselves. The things we have the greatest horror of." The explanation deals with a condition said to be abnormal, as opposed to supernatural. The story is out of the ordinary and well executed. In addition to the romantic interest between the two teachers, the feelings of a grandfather for his grandson are nicely evoked.

The Artificial Man is Davies's earliest tale in which the protagonist is uncertain of his identity, a situation frequently exploited by the author, though from different angles. A political struggle between the army and the Bureau of Counter-Psycho-conflict underlies the hero's personal diffculties. *Tell It to the Dead*, perhaps Davies's least interesting yarn, debunks fraudulent fortune-tellers while managing to suggest that there is such a thing as a real medium. *Man Out of Nowhere* is a thriller in which the central character does not know who he is, although he is "positively" identified, more or less vehemently, as four different individuals, all of whom are thought to be dead and buried.

From the late 1960's to the present, L. P. Davies has turned out some dozen thrillers, each dealing with some aspect of psychic disturbance – caused by drugs, brain tumor, amnesia, hypnosis, or deception. The depersonalization or disorientation of the hero, or the seemingly supernatural goings-on are satisfactorily – sometimes ingeniously – explained. In *Stranger to Town*, a widow who belongs to the "Return" church is befriended by a man who appears to be the recipient of thought transference from her late husband. She, of course, thinks her husband has somehow come back in another man's body. A good plot and some successful detection by the "stranger" enliven this book. The hero of *The White Room*, Axel Champlee, who suffers from a curious form of depersonalization, believes he is being drugged and subtly driven to murder. Romance is part of the plot, as it often is in Davies's thrillers.

The Shadow Before, *Give Me Back Myself*, and *What Did I Do Tomorrow?*, all very clever narratives, represent Davies at his best, and also reveal his own obsessive concern with characters who are disoriented in time or space, victims of their own delusions as well as of the evil designs of those around them; each is a variation on the theme. In *Assignment Abacus*, a businessman is whisked away to an isolated house in Scotland and subjected to some confusing tests, one of which is to figure out why he has been brought there. *Possession* contains a weird cult, an unethical scientist, and a rich old man who wishes to take over the body of a healthy young person.

L. P. Davies can surely be considered the master of the suspenseful identity crisis – one character after another must confront reality (or apparent reality) with a disordered perception. The author is proficient at sketching English villages and rural scenes for background, and adroitly constructs thrillers which are unusual and entertaining.

—Mary Helen Becker

DAVIOT, Gordon.   See TEY, Josephine.

DAVIS, Dorothy Salisbury. American. Born in Chicago, Illinois, 26 April 1916. Educated at Holy Child High School, Waukegan, Illinois; Barat College, Lake Forest, Illinois, A.B. 1938. Married Harry Davis in 1946. Past President, Mystery Writers of America. Agent: McIntosh and Otis Inc., 475 Fifth Avenue, New York, New York 10017. Address: Snedens Landing, Palisades, New York 10964, U.S.A.

Crime Publications

Novels (series characters: Mrs. Norris and Jasper Tully)

The Judas Cat. New York, Scribner, 1949; London, Corgi, 1952.
The Clay Hand. New York, Scribner, 1950; London, Corgi, 1952.
A Gentle Murderer. New York, Scribner, 1951; London, Corgi, 1953.
A Town of Masks. New York, Scribner, 1952.
Death of an Old Sinner (Norris and Tully). New York, Scribner, 1957; London, Secker and Warburg, 1958.
A Gentleman Called (Norris and Tully). New York, Scribner, and London, Secker and Warburg, 1958.
Old Sinners Never Die (Norris). New York, Scribner, 1959; London, Secker and Warburg, 1960.
Black Sheep, White Lamb. New York, Scribner, 1963; London, Boardman, 1964.
The Pale Betrayer. New York, Scribner, 1965; London, Hodder and Stoughton, 1967.
Enemy and Brother. New York, Scribner, 1966; London, Hodder and Stoughton, 1967.
God Speed the Night, with Jerome Ross. New York, Scribner, 1968; London, Hodder and Stoughton, 1969.
Where the Dark Streets Go. New York, Scribner, 1969; London, Hodder and Stoughton, 1970.
Shock Wave. New York, Scribner, 1972; London, Hodder and Stoughton, 1974.
The Little Brothers. New York, Scribner, 1973; London, Barker, 1974.
A Death in the Life. New York, Scribner, 1976; London, Gollancz, 1977.

Uncollected Short Stories

"Sweet William," in *Ellery Queen's Mystery Magazine* (New York), April 1953.
"Backward, Turn Backward," in *Queen's Awards, Ninth Series,* edited by Ellery Queen. Boston, Little Brown, 1954; London, Collins, 1956.
"A Matter of Public Notice," in *Queen's Awards, Twelfth Series,* edited by Ellery Queen. New York, Simon and Schuster, 1957; London, Collins, 1959.
"Mrs. Norris Visits the Library," in *Ellery Queen's Mystery Magazine* (New York), April 1959.
"Meeting at the Crossroad," in *Ellery Queen's Mystery Magazine* (New York), July 1959.
"Spring Fever," in *Alfred Hitchcock Presents: My Favorites in Suspense.* New York, Random House, 1959.
"By the Scruff of the Soul," in *Ellery Queen's Mystery Mix.* New York, Random House, 1963; London, Gollancz, 1964.
"The Purple Is Everything," in *Ellery Queen's 20th Anniversary Annual.* New York, Random House, 1965; London, Gollancz, 1966.
"Lost Generation," in *Mirror, Mirror, Fatal Mirror,* edited by Hans S. Santesson. New York, Doubleday, 1973.
"Born Killer," in *When Last Seen,* edited by Arthur Maling. New York, Harper, 1977.
"Old Friends," in *Ellery Queen's Searches and Seizures.* New York, Davis, 1977.

OTHER PUBLICATIONS

Novels

Men of No Property.   New York, Scribner, 1956.
The Evening of the Good Samaritan.   New York, Scribner, 1961.

Other

"Mystery Writers: A Think Tank for Police?" in *Murder Ink: The Mystery Reader's Companion*, edited by Dilys Winn.   New York, Workman, 1977.

Editor, *A Choice of Murders.*   New York, Scribner, 1958; London, Macdonald, 1960.
Editor, *Crime Without Murder.*   New York, Scribner, 1970.

Manuscript Collection: Brooklyn College Library, City Universty of New York.

Dorothy Salisbury Davis comments:

I am a restless and sometimes troubled writer. Although I am content at this point in my life, and indeed proud, to be a crime writer, I have often wondered why I am in the field. I have not been able to develop a running character – except perhaps myself and I do not mean to be facetious – I think because my own interest flags after he or she has finished one good job; also because detection, per se, is not my strong point. My detectives almost always turn out to be straight men to a lot of character actors. I am fonder of my villains, if the truth be told; and I suppose that is it: the pursuit of truth which shines best in the dark excesses of human behavior. I am at my best in *A Gentle Murderer*, *The Pale Betrayer*, and *God Speed the Night* where the villains are known, and the police less spectacular. But I should dearly love to have been able to create an Inspector Maigret, my all time favorite among the detectives of fiction. I think I could have lived happily with him through many more books than I have written.

*   *   *

That Dorothy Salisbury Davis is equally skilled at writing novels and short stories can be seen by the fact that her seven Edgar nominations include four for novels and three for short stories.

Though her second novel, *The Clay Hand*, drew critical attention for its sympathetic view of the poor in a Kentucky coal mining area, it was Davis's third novel, *A Gentle Murderer*, which established her as a major suspense writer. It remains a novel central to her work, the one which best explains the themes of religious crisis and an opposition to violence which recur in later books. The murderer of the title, truly a gentle man, confesses his crime to a priest, who must then track him down to prevent further violence. The insight into the characters of these two men raises the book far above the level of the usual suspense novel. Davis's dislike of violence, almost unique among modern mystery writers, led her to edit a 1970 anthology called *Crime Without Murder*. In its introduction she attempts to come to grips with the problem of violence in the mystery, and to explain why she and others continue to write of it.

Her fourth novel, *A Town of Masks*, deals with the impact of murder on a small midwestern town, and especially upon the life of a middle-aged spinster who attempts to solve it. *Death of an Old Sinner* is about a retired general whose blackmail activities lead to his murder. The author was so fond of her victim that she revived him two years later in *Old Sinners Never Die*, a "prequel" to the prior book.

Davis once again chose a priest as her protagonist in *Where the Dark Streets Go*, a return to the American scene following two novels set in Europe, *Where the Dark Streets Go* is very much a New York story, and Father McMahon's slum parish has all the problems of violence and despair one would expect. But the priest's problems are not merely with his parish but also with himself, and with a girl he meets while investigating a murder case.

Shock Wave deals with murder at a midwestern university during the student unrest of the early 1970's. *The Little Brothers* tells of a murdered shopkeeper in New York's Little Italy, and of a group of boys who may be involved in the crime. In each case Davis has perfectly captured the atmosphere of the times, and the feelings of people trapped by events around them. In a sense these books were a form of preparation for *A Death in the Life*, the best of her recent novels and one which speaks directly to the problems of city life today. Its tale of young Julie Hayes, who opens a storefront fortune-telling service in the heart of New York's pornography-prostitution district, tells us much about the real lives of the people who exist there – and tells it with an understanding and compassion which are Davis's hallmark.

Among her short stories, "Born Killer," an excellent psychological study of a midwestern farm boy, is most typical. "Backward, Turn Backward" is one of her rare detective short stories, in which Sheriff Willets solves a small town murder involving two families. Again, psychology plays a large part in the outcome. "The Purple Is Everything" deals with a woman who rescues a valuable painting during a museum fire and finds herself becoming a criminal against her will.

Dealing as they do with both small town and big city life, with both male and female protagonists, the novels and stories of Dorothy Salisbury Davis may seem difficult to categorize. But they are all marked by an awareness of the stress of modern living on the individual, and by a deeply felt compassion for both victim and criminal alike which is rare in mystery fiction today.

—Edward D. Hoch

DAVIS, Frederick C(lyde). Also wrote as Murdo Coombs; Stephen Ransome; Curtis Steele. American. Born in 1902. Educated at Dartmouth College, Hanover, New Hampshire, 1924–25. Married. Professional writer from 1924. Wrote 20 to 30 novels as Curtis Steele for *Secret Operator No. 5* in the 1930's. Lived in later life in Pennsylvania. *Died in 1977.*

CRIME PUBLICATIONS

Novels (series characters: Schyler Cole and Luke Speare; Professor Cyrus Hatch; published as Stephen Ransome in UK)

Coffins for Three (Hatch). New York, Doubleday, 1938; as *One Murder Too Many*, London, Heinemann, 1938.
He Wouldn't Stay Dead (Hatch). New York, Doubleday, and London, Heinemann, 1939.
Poor, Poor Yorick (Hatch). New York, Doubleday, 1939; as *Murder Doesn't Always Out*, London, Heinemann, 1939.
The Graveyard Never Closes (Hatch). New York, Doubleday, 1940.
Deep Lay the Dead. New York, Doubleday, 1942.
Let the Skeletons Rattle (Hatch). New York, Doubleday, 1944.
Detour to Oblivion (Hatch). New York, Doubleday, 1947.
A Moment of Need (as Murdo Coombs). New York, Dutton, 1947.

Thursday's Blade (Hatch).   New York, Doubleday, 1947.

Gone Tomorrow (Hatch).   New York, Doubleday, 1948.

The Deadly Miss Ashley (Cole and Speare).   New York, Doubleday, and London, Gollancz, 1950.

Lilies in Her Garden Grew (Cole and Speare).   New York, Doubleday, and London, Gollancz, 1951.

Tread Lightly, Angel (Cole and Speare).   New York, Doubleday, and London, Gollancz, 1952.

Drag the Dark (Cole and Speare).   New York, Doubleday, 1953; London, Gollancz, 1954.

Another Morgue Heard From (Cole and Speare).   New York, Doubleday, 1954; as *Deadly Bedfellows*, London, Gollancz, 1955.

Night Drop (Cole and Speare).   New York, Doubleday, 1955; London, Gollancz, 1956.

High Heel Homicide.   New York, Ace, 1961.

Novels as Stephen Ransome (series characters: Lee Barcello; Steve Ransome).

Death Checks In.   New York, Doubleday, 1939; as *Whose Corpse?*, London, Davies, 1939.

A Shroud for Shylock.   New York, Doubleday, 1939.

Hearses Don't Hurry.   New York, Doubleday, 1941.

False Bounty.   New York, Doubleday, 1948; London, Gollancz, 1949; as *I, The Executioner*, New York, Ace, 1953.

Hear No Evil (Ransome).   New York, Doubleday, 1953; London, Gollancz, 1954.

The Shroud Off Her Back (Ransome).   New York, Doubleday, and London, Gollancz, 1953.

The Frazier Acquittal.   New York, Doubleday, and London, Gollancz, 1955.

The Men in Her Death.   New York, Doubleday, 1956; London, Gollancz, 1957.

So Deadly My Love.   New York, Doubleday, 1957; London, Gollancz, 1958.

I'll Die for You.   New York, Doubleday, and London, Gollancz, 1959.

The Unspeakable.   New York, Doubleday, and London, Gollancz, 1960.

Warning Bell.   New York, Doubleday, and London, Gollancz, 1960.

Some Must Watch.   New York, Doubleday, and London, Gollancz, 1961.

Without a Trace.   New York, Doubleday, and London, Gollancz, 1962.

The Night, The Woman.   New York, Dodd Mead, and London, Gollancz, 1963.

Meet in Darkness.   New York, Dodd Mead, and London, Gollancz, 1964.

One-Man Jury (Barcello).   New York, Dodd Mead, 1964; London, Gollancz, 1965.

Alias His Wife (Barcello).   New York, Dodd Mead, and London, Gollancz, 1965.

The Sin File (Barcello).   New York, Dodd Mead, 1965; London, Gollancz, 1966.

The Hidden Hour (Barcello).   New York, Dodd Mead, and London, Gollancz, 1966.

Trap No. 6 (Barcello).   New York, Doubleday, 1971; London, Gollancz, 1972.

Crucibles of the Damned.   Chicago, Pulp Press, 1976.

Calling Car 13.   Chicago, Pulp Press, 1977.

Novels as Curtis Steele (series character: James Christopher, Operator No. 5 in all books)

The Invisible Empire.   New York, Corinth, 1966.

The Army of the Dead.   New York, Corinth, 1966.

Blood Reign of the Dictator.   New York, Corinth, 1966.

Hosts of the Flaming Death.   New York, Corinth, 1966.

Invasion of the Yellow Warlords.   New York, Corinth, 1966.

Legions of the Death Master.   New York, Corinth, 1966.

March of the Flame Marauders.   New York, Corinth, 1966.

Master of Broken Men.   New York, Corinth, 1966.

The Masked Invasion. N.p., Freeway, 1974.
The Yellow Scourge. N.p., Freeway, 1974.

Short Stories

The Moon Man. Chicago, Pulp Press, 1974.

Uncollected Short Stories

"Blood on the Block." in *Dime Detective* (New York), 15 December 1933.
"Skeleton Without Arms," in *Dime Detective* (New York), 1 February 1934.
"Death Lights the Candle," in *Dime Detective* (New York), 15 June 1934.
"Death on Delivery," in *Dime Detective* (New York), 1 September 1934.
"The Green Ghoul," in *Dime Detective* (New York), 15 June 1935.
"Doorway to Doom," in *Dime Detective* (New York), 1 July 1935.
"Dynamite Friendship," in *Detective Tales*, August 1935.
"Death's Flaming Hour," in *Detective Tales*, September 1935.
"Guardian Against the Law," in *Detective Tales*, December 1935.
"The Smiling Killer," in *Dime Mystery* (New York), January 1936.
"The Case of the Smiling Giantess," in *Dime Detective* (New York), March 1936.
"Crime Crusader," in *Detective Tales*, May 1936.
"Suicide Sweepstakes," in *Ace G-Man* (New York), May–June 1936.
"Four Alarm Murder," in *Ace Detective* (New York), August 1936.
"Princess of Death's Desire," in *Ace Mystery* (New York), September 1936.
"Poison Plunder," in *Ace Detective* (New York), October 1936.
"The Case of the Terrified Twins," in *Dime Detective* (New York), March 1937.
"The Trail of the Thirteenth Brain," in *Detective Tales*, April 1937.
"Murder Made Easy," in *Dime Detective* (New York), May 1937.
"Mistress of Satan's Hounds," in *Terror Tales*, May–June 1938.
"Seven Knocks at My Door," in *Black Mask* (New York), August 1938.
"Nameless Brides of Forbidden City," in *Uncanny Tales*, April–May 1939.
"The Premature Obituary," in *Ten Detective Aces* (Springfield, Massachusetts), October 1941.
"The Case of the Gambling Corpse," in *New Detective*, January 1942.
"I'm the Corpse," in *Detective Tales*, January 1942.
"No Appeal for the Dead," in *Detective Tales*, October 1942.
"Pick Your Casket," in *Detective Tales*, December 1942.
"More Deadly than the Male," in *Dime Detective* (New York), December 1942.
"Home Sweet Homicide," in *Dime Detective* (New York), May 1943.
"Blood on My Doorstep," in *Detective Tales*, July 1943.
"Hostage," in *New Detective*, September 1943.
"Clinic for Corpses," in *Dime Detective* (New York), October 1943.
"I'll See You at the Morgue," in *Detective Tales*, April 1944.
"Boomerang Scoop," in *Dime Detective* (New York), June 1944.
"Little Green Door of Doom," in *Dime Mystery* (New York), July 1944.
"Death Wears Red Heels," in *Dime Detective* (New York), December 1944.
"The Killer Waits," in *New Detective*, May 1945.
"The Corpse Takes a Wife," in *Dime Detective* (New York), June 1945.
"Assignment — Death," in *New Detective*, January 1946.
"Some Like 'em Dead," in *Dime Detective* (New York), March 1946.
"Murder in Two-Time," in *Dime Detective* (New York), July 1947.
"Nine Toes Up," in *Dime Detective* (New York), March 1948.
"Death Is a Dame," in *Shock* (New York), March 1948.
"Dicks Die Hard," in *Dime Detective* (New York), May 1948.
"I'll Marry a Killer," in *Shock* (New York), July 1948.

"Kill-and-Run Blonde," in *Dime Detective* (New York), January 1949.
"Hide Behind Homicide," in *F.B.I. Detective*, February 1949.
"Flaming Angel," in *Black Mask* (New York), March 1949.
"Up in Murder's Room," in *Dime Detective* (New York), June 1949.
"Sinner Take All," in *Dime Detective* (New York), September 1949.
"Swing Low, Sweet Casket," in *Black Mask* (New York), March 1950.
"So Dead the Rogue," in *15 Story Detective*, August 1950.
"Kill Me, Kate," in *Dime Detective* (New York), August 1950.
"Guns Across the Table," in *Dime Detective* (New York), June 1951.
"Lenore," in *Manhunt* :(New York), May 1956.
"Goddess of Evil Revelry," in *Weird Menace No. 1*. Chicago, Pulp Press, 1977.

OTHER PUBLICATIONS

Other

Making Your Camera Pay. New York, McBride, 1922.
"Why Did She Shoot Him?," in *Writer's Digest* (Cincinnati), March 1942.
"Synopses Without Sorrow," in *Writer's Digest* (Cincinnati), October 1942.
"Mysteries Plus," in *Writing Detective and Mystery Fiction*, edited by A. S. Burack. Boston, The Writer, 1945.
"How to Organize a Book," in *The Mystery Writer's Handbook*, edited by Herbert Brean. New York, Harper, 1956.

*　　*　　*

There were many writers in the heyday of the pulp magazines whose total published wordage reached staggering proportions, writers like Max Brand, Arthur J. Burks, H. Bedford Jones, Walter B. Gibson, Norman Daniels, and Frederick C. Davis. For more than 25 years Davis's byline appeared on at least 1000 pulp stories. Early 1930's issues of *Dime Detective* featured his long-running "casebook" series about Doctor Carter Cole; later issues introduced additional series characters, among them newspaper columnist Bill Brent. Other top-line pulps such as *Black Mask*, *Detective Tales*, and *Dime Mystery* were also regular showcases for his work.

Under the house name Curtis Steele he was also the author of dozens of Operator No. 5 novels for the *Shadow*-rival "hero pulp" of the same title. While a large percentage of pulp stories seem dated and somewhat juvenile by today's fictional standards, Davis's fiction was among the most literate and entertaining of its day and stands up well to the test of time. The Carter Cole "cases" in *Dime Detective* are of a particularly high quality.

In 1938 Davis began writing novels for Doubleday and he published a total of 16 under his own name. Many of these features the deductive abilities of Professor Cyrus Hatch and of the semi-hard-boiled detective team of Schyler Cole and Luke Speare. A memorable non-series book is *Deep Lay the Dead*, which is fashioned around the classic mystery situation of murder and intrigue among a group of people trapped in a snowbound country house.

Davis wrote one novel as Murdo Coombs, but it was his mysteries as by Stephen Ransome which were perhaps the most successful of all his longer works, as evidenced by the fact that he continued to write novels with the Ransom byline for ten years after retiring his own name. *The Unspeakable* involves a brutal and heinous crime in a small Pennsylvania town, and is notable for its sensitive handling and excellent characterization.

—Bill Pronzini

DAY LEWIS, C.   See BLAKE, Nicholas.

DEAN, Amber.   American.   Born in Depew, New York, 4 December 1902. Married Norman J. Getzin in 1926; one child. Self-employed writer. Agent: James Brown Associates Inc., 22 East 60th Street, New York, New York 10022. Address: Meadowood, West Rush, New York, U.S.A.

CRIME PUBLICATIONS

Novels (series character: Albie Harris)

Dead Man's Float (Harris).   New York, Doubleday, 1944.
Chanticleer's Muffled Crow (Harris).   New York, Doubleday, 1945.
Call Me Pandora (Harris).   New York, Doubleday, 1946; as *The Blonde Is Dead*, New York, Mystery Novel Classic, n.d.
Wrap It Up (Harris).   New York, Doubleday, 1946.
Foggy Foggy Dew.   New York, Doubleday, 1947.
No Traveller Returns (Harris).   New York, Doubleday, 1948.
Snipe Hunt (Harris).   New York, Doubleday, 1949.
August Incident.   New York, Doubleday, 1951.
Ticket to Buffalo.   New York, Doubleday, 1951.
Collectors' Item.   New York, Doubleday, 1953.
The Devil Threw Dice.   New York, Doubleday, 1954.
Something for the Birds.   New York, Doubleday, 1959.
Bullet Proof.   New York, Doubleday, 1960.
Encounter with Evil.   New York, Doubleday, 1961.
Deadly Contact.   New York, Doubleday, 1963; London, Hale, 1964.
The Dower Chest.   New York, Putnam, 1970; London, Hale, 1971.
Be Home by Eleven.   New York, Putnam, 1973; London, Hale, 1974

Manuscript Collection: University of Rochester Library, New York.

*   *   *

Amber Dean is best at creating suspense novels with interesting and unusual characters in a variety of plot settings, ranging from bank robbers who tangle with bird watchers and rich old aunts who die of unusual diseases to electrocution at the Rochester Post Office. Using the third-person narrative and flashbacks, the author tends to shift storylines from the victim's viewpoint, to the criminal's, to the hero's, and back to the victim's again. This is done in a consistent and efficient manner using each chapter as a transitional device.

One series of novels centers on Albie Harris, and a few of the author's best novels, such as *Foggy Foggy Dew* and *The Devil Threw Dice*, involve detection either by an amateur detective or a police officer, or a combination of both. In all of Dean's novels a strong element of romance is as an integral part of the plot. In fact, who will end up with whom is as much a mystery, in some cases, as "who done it?"

The author's major fault lies in an overdose of melodrama, girls fainting, lying trussed in a bathtub filling slowly with water, or having premonitions of danger which, of course, are never heeded.

—Mary Ann Grochowski

DEANE, Norman. See **CREASEY, John.**

DECOLTA, Ramon. See **WHITFIELD, Raoul.**

---

deFORD, Miriam Allen. American. Born in Philadelphia, Pennsylvania, 21 August 1888. Educated at Wellesley College, Massachusetts; Temple University, Philadelphia, A.B. 1911; University of Pennsylvania, Philadelphia. Married 1) Armistead Collier in 1915 (divorced, 1921); 2) Maynard Shipley in 1921 (died, 1934). Feature writer, Philadelphia *North American*, 1906–11; editorial staff member, Associated Advertising, 1913–14; Editor of house organ, Pompeiian Oil Company, Baltimore, 1917; Claims Adjuster, 1918–23; Staff Correspondent, Federated Press, 1921–56; Editor, Federal Writers Project, 1936–39; Staff Correspondent, *Labor's Daily*, California, 1956–58. Lecturer and Member of the Board, San Francisco Senior Citizens Center, 1952–58. Member of the Board, Mystery Writers of America, 1960, 1963. Recipient: Committee for Economic Development Essay Prize, 1958; Mystery Writers of America Edgar Allan Poe Award, 1961. *Died in 1975.*

CRIME PUBLICATIONS

Short Stories

    The Theme Is Murder. New York, Abelard Schuman, 1967.
    Elsewhere, Elsewhen, Elsehow: Collected Stories. New York, Walker, 1971.

Uncollected Short Stories

    "Turnabout," in *Ellery Queen's Mystery Magazine* (New York), January 1972.
    "April Story," in *Ellery Queen's Mystery Magazine* (New York), May 1972.
    "Number One Suspect," in *Ellery Queen's Mystery Magazine* (New York), August 1972.
    "A Queer Sad Story," in *Killers of the Mind*, edited by Lucy Freeman. New York, Random House, 1974.

OTHER PUBLICATIONS

Novel

Shaken with the Wind. New York, Doubleday, 1942.

Verse

Penultimates. New York, Fine Editions Press, 1962.

Other

Cicero as Revealed in His Letters. Girard, Kansas, Haldeman Julius, 1925.
The Life and Poems of Catullus. Girard, Kansas, Haldeman Julius, 1925.
The Augustan Poets of Rome. Girard, Kansas, Haldeman Julius, 1925.
The Facts about Fascism. Girard, Kansas, Haldeman Julius, 1926.
Latin Self Taught. Girard, Kansas, Haldeman Julius, 1926.
The Truth about Mussolini. Girard, Kansas, Haldeman Julius, 1926.
Love Children: A Book of Illustrious Illegitimates. New York, Dial Press, 1931.
Children of Sun. New York, League to Support Poetry, 1939.
Who Was When? A Dictionary of Contemporaries. New York, Wilson, 1940; revised
    edition, 1950; revised edition, with Joan S. Jackson, 1976.
They Were San Franciscans. Caldwell, Idaho, Caxton, 1941; revised edition, 1947.
The Meaning of All Common Given Names. Girard, Kansas, Haldeman Julius, 1943.
The Facts about Basic English. Girard, Kansas, Haldeman Julius, 1944.
Facts You Should Know about California. Girard, Kansas, Haldeman Julius, 1945.
Psychologist Unretired: The Life Pattern of Lillien J. Martin. Palo Alto, California,
    Stanford University Press, 1948.
Uphill All the Way: The Life of Maynard Shipley. Yellow Springs, Ohio, Antioch Press,
    1956.
The Overbury Affair: The Murder That Rocked the Court of James I. Philadelphia,
    Chilton, 1960.
Stone Walls: Prisons from Fetters to Furloughs. Philadelphia, Chilton, 1962.
*Murderers Sane and Mad: Case Histories in the Motivation and Rationale of
    Murder.* London and New York, Abelard Schuman, 1965.
Thomas Moore. New York, Twayne, 1967.
The Old Worker Comes Back. San Francisco, Old Age Counselling Center, n.d.
On Being Concerned: The Vanguard Years of Carl and Laura Brannin. Privately
    printed, 1969.
Ma Barker. New York, Ace, 1970.

Editor, *Space, Time, and Crime.* New York, Paperback Library, 1964.

*   *   *

Miriam Allen deFord distinguished herself in two particular categories of crime writing –
the true crime documentary, and the short story of crime, often perverse and always marked
by a surprise ending. In the first category, her writings range from an account of the
mysterious murder of Sir Thomas Overbury in the Tower of London in 1613 to a history (in
the wake of Arthur Penn's film) of the *real* Bonnie and Clyde. This category of her writing is
marked by the social conscience which involved her always in civil rights issues (she was for
many years a labor reporter, and wrote a number of monitory pamphlets in the "Little Blue
Book" series, most notably *The Truth about Mussolini* and *The Facts about Fascism*). But her
chief contribution to crime writing lies in the 28 short stories she published over three
decades in *Ellery Queen's Mystery Magazine*, starting with "Mortmain" in 1944. Some of her

characteristic originality lies in the setting and choice of detective – "The Judgment of En-Lil" is set in the Sumeria of 2500 years ago, and "The Ptarmigan Knife" in the valley of the Dordogne in the Cro-Magnon era, with "the first detective in human history." Thus deFord goes herself twice better than in the earlier "De Crimine," where Cicero is the detective, and in "The Mystery of the Vanished Brother," where the detective, well animated from scholarly sources, though not unmarred by a certain archness, is Edgar Allan Poe. These last two stories, moreover, draw upon the author's well-established skill in historical reconstruction.

Some of her best stories – "The Oleander," "Farewell to the Faulkners" – are concerned with twisted relationships within families, suppressed but virulent sibling feelings which burst forth into murder; her use of Faulkner as surname is suggestive. Many of her stories are marked by the typical surprise ending: her most memorable final sentence may be the one which reveals that two characters, one referred to throughout the story by his first name, the other by his surname, are in fact the same person.

Retribution is a major force in deFord's fiction, either accidental or by human agency; often the agent is a spouse, lover, or sibling whose forebearance is at an end, as in "The Oleander," "The Crack," or (with its chilling final sentence) "Beyond the Sea of Death." The retribution is sometimes levied by impartial irony – a man carefully plans and carries out the murder of his wife, timed to the last minute, only to find that his car, essential to his alibi, has been stolen; a woman hires killers to murder her husband, but is apprehended after a tape recorder in his pocket is activated during the crime. Yet the retribution is sometimes thwarted by the same impartial irony.

There is often a neatness about deFord's stories which makes the reader feel "sold" by the trick ending – but that is a risk undertaken by the most accomplished writers of such stories, and not always successfully avoided even by de Maupassant. Her best story may indeed be "Beyond the Sea of Death," where the primary criminal energies are channelled into the main plot, and the last sentence, however shocking, has an effect unrelated to the principal crime; or "Homecoming," an uncharacteristically bitter story, where the ending follows, without surprise, from the dark view of human nature presented in the story.

—Barrie Hayne

DEIGHTON, Len (Leonard Cyril Deighton). British. Born in London, 18 February 1929. Educated at Marylebone Grammar School, St. Martin's School of Art, and Royal College of Art, all London. Served in the Royal Air Force. Married Shirley Thompson in 1960. Has worked as a railway lengthman, pastry cook, dress factory manager, waiter, illustrator, teacher, and photographer; art director of advertising agencies in London and New York; steward, British Overseas Airways Corporation, 1956–57; wrote a weekly comic strip on cooking for *The Observer*, London, in the 1960's; founder of Continuum One literary agency, London. Lives in Ireland. Address: c/o Jonathan Cape Ltd., 30 Bedford Square, London WC1B 3EL, England.

CRIME PUBLICATIONS

Novels

   The Ipcress File. London, Hodder and Stoughton, 1962; New York, Simon and
      Schuster, 1963.

Horse under Water. London, Cape, 1963; New York, Putnam, 1968.
Funeral in Berlin. London, Cape, 1964; New York, Putnam, 1965.
Billion-Dollar Brain. London, Cape, and New York, Putnam, 1966.
An Expensive Place to Die. London, Cape, and New York, Putnam, 1967.
Spy Story. London, Cape, and New York, Harcourt Brace, 1974.
Yesterday's Spy. London, Cape, and New York, Harcourt Brace, 1975.
Twinkle, Twinkle, Little Spy. London, Cape, 1976; as *Catch a Falling Spy*, New York,
    Harcourt Brace, 1976.

OTHER PUBLICATIONS

Novels

Only When I Larf. London, Joseph, 1968.
Bomber. London, Cape, and New York, Harper, 1970.
Close-Up. London, Cape, and New York, Atheneum, 1972.
SS-GB: Nazi-Occupied Britain 1941. London, Cape, 1978; New York, Knopf, 1979.

Short Stories

Declarations of War. London, Cape, 1971; as *Eleven Declarations of War*, New York,
    Harcourt Brace, 1975.

Plays

Screenplay: *Oh! What a Lovely War*, 1969.

Television Plays: *Long Past Glory*, 1963; *It Must Have Been Two Other Fellows*, 1977.

Other

Action Cook Book: Len Deighton's Guide to Eating. London, Cape, 1965; as *Cookstrip
    Cook Book*, New York, Geis, 1966.
Où Est le Garlic; or, Len Deighton's French Cook Book. London, Penguin, 1965; New
    York, Harper, 1977; revised edition, as *Basic French Cooking*, London, Cape, 1978.
*Len Deighton's Continental Dossier: A Collection of Cultural, Culinary, Historical,
    Spooky, Grim and Preposterous Fact*, compiled by Victor and Margaret
    Pettitt. London, Joseph, 1968.
Fighter: The True Story of the Battle of Britain. London, Cape, 1977; New York,
    Knopf, 1978.
Airshipwreck, with Arnold Schwartzman. London, Cape, 1978; New York, Holt
    Rinehart, 1979.
Blitzkrieg: From the Rise of Hitler to the Fall of Dunkirk. London, Cape, 1979.

Editor, *London Dossier.* London, Cape, 1967.
Editor, with Michael Rund and Howard Loxton, *The Assassination of President
    Kennedy.* London, Cape, 1967.

*   *   *

In a succession of stylish, witty, well-crafted novels beginning with *The Ipcress File* in
1962, Len Deighton has proved himself a master of modern spy fiction and one of the most
innovative writers in the short but eventful history of the form. He brings to the novel of
espionage some highly relevant interests and concerns, most of which had never troubled the
minds of previous practitioners; along with his brilliant contemporary, John le Carré, he

sketches a convincingly detailed picture of the world of espionage while carefully examining the ethics and morality of that world. The darker aspects of his novels, however seriously intended, are frequently illuminated by understated irony and humor. His prose is bright and breezy, clearly influenced by Raymond Chandler, with a somewhat Chandleresque taste for metaphors and wisecracks. In some ways, in fact, he seems rather a mid-atlantic writer − he is just about the only English writer who can create credible Americans who speak credible American. Another of his strengths lies in his ability to provide his best works with powerfully elliptical structures: his architecture never seems fully clear until the books end, revealing themselves as intricate and solid creations. Together with their structures, the plots of his novels usually entangle his protagonist in difficult enough knots of double- and triple-crosses to satisfy even the most finicky connoisseur of spy fiction. He has contributed substantially to the genre and, in the process, to the education of a large reading public in the realities of espionage. An air of authenticity permeates his books. Whether he is describing a sunset in Lebanon, cocktails in a Berlin nightclub, the food in a Helsinki restaurant, an automobile chase through the Sahara, or a journey under the North Atlantic in a nuclear submarine, Deighton convincingly captures the atmosphere of a real place − he has been there and he takes his reader with him. The authenticity extends to the actual business of espionage; his novels display a thorough and intimate knowledge of spies and spying, demonstrated in their action and in their detailed attention to the particulars of a specialized profession − documents, memos, technical data, learned appendices. The attention to the minutiae of all aspects of spying not only lends considerable realism to his books but also suggests some of the further truths of the practice of espionage. Spies, we see, are real people, a special kind of bureaucrat or civil servant; their activities represent a kind of institutionalized deceit, the normal practice of modern government in the modern world. The intricate puzzles of Deighton's novels, full of deceptions and betrayals, are made entirely believable by Deighton's careful and interesting documentation, and at the same time made aptly symbolic of our time by their apparent universality. Espionage, a battle in the shadows, appropriately symbolizes the crepuscular morality of today's vague alliances and complicated struggles.

His protagonist, significantly, is a man without a name, or rather, a man of many names; although he is the same person throughout the books, he uses a variety of pseudonyms and aliases, as if identity itself were a shifting, unknowable, or meaningless concept in the world of espionage. The anonymous narrator frequently discovers that his enemy is as difficult to identify as his friend or himself; the enemy is as likely to be German as Russian, since the fear and hatred of Nazism still haunts Europe. More disturbing, the most serious enemy may turn out to be English, often a traitor from his own department, sometimes a respected and privileged citizen; Deighton's agent is frequently endangered by the incompetence or the malevolence of impassioned ideologues. He usually expresses a wry recognition of the state of his nation and profession, debilitated by the futility of rank and class, the Old Boy network, the collection of ninnies, dolts, and eccentrics who appear to control his life: "what chance did I stand between the Communists on one side and the Establishment on the other" (*The Ipcress File*). In fact, Deighton is the Angry Young Man of the espionage novel, with precisely the same mixture of humor and outrage as his literary predecessors over his society and its problems. The constant class battle he wages provides a considerable amount of the wit, tension, danger, complexity, and charm of the novels.

Thematically and architecturally supporting the ambiguity and intricacy of the novels, the labyrinthine plots and unusual structures suggest genuine literary sophistication. *The Ipcress File* shows the hero constantly a jump behind several elaborate schemes while counterpointing his adventures with his daily horoscope; *Horse under Water* underlines its confusing puzzles with chapter headings that, put together, make up one of those punning crosswords that one must be British to solve. Deighton's finest novel, *Funeral in Berlin*, explores the Cold War, neo-Nazism, German guilt, complicated treacheries, unifying all themes with epigraphs from a chess book; the agent is clearly a pawn moving among the conflicting spaces of a vast board, his job determined by the turns and counterturns of competing organizations, the schemes of traitors, the guilt and greed of his antagonists. He succeeds in that and other novels mostly through his dedication to professionalism and through maintaining his personal integrity in the midst of betrayal and deception.

Deighton's wry and ironic recognition of the realities of espionage and the crackling energy that motivates his fiction place him in the first rank of spy novelists. He writes thrillers that are witty, thoughtful, authentic, and entertaining, a rare combination of merits. Together with his "straight" novels, his thrillers deserve careful reading and rereading: his work rewards study and inspires affection. He is a writer to be cherished and enjoyed, one of the most interesting novelists in England today.

—George Grella

de la **TORRE, Lillian.** Pseudonym for Lillian McCue, née Bueno. American. Born in New York City, 15 March 1902. Educated at College of New Rochelle, New York, A.B. 1921; Columbia University, New York, M.A. 1927; University of Munich, 1928; Harvard University, Cambridge, Massachusetts, M.A. 1933; University of Colorado, Boulder, 1934–35. Married George S. McCue in 1932. High school teacher, New York City, 1923–34; Instructor, Colorado College, Colorado Springs, 1937, and University of Colorado (Extension), 1937–41. Technical advisor, Twentieth Century-Fox, 1945. Since 1942, self-employed writer. Agent: Harold Ober Associates, 40 East 49th Street, New York, New York 10017. Address: 16 Valley Place, Apartment 302, Colorado Springs, Colorado 80903, U.S.A.

CRIME PUBLICATIONS

Novels

> *Elizabeth Is Missing.* New York, Knopf, 1945; London, Joseph, 1947.
> *The Heir of Douglas.* New York, Knopf, 1952; London, Joseph, 1953.
> *The Truth about Belle Gunness.* New York, Fawcett, 1955; London, Muller, 1960.

Short Stories

> *Dr. Sam: Johnson, Detector.* New York, Knopf, 1946; London, Joseph, 1948.
> *The Detections of Dr. Sam: Johnson.* New York, Doubleday, 1960.

Uncollected Short Stories

> "A Fool for a Client," in *Dear Dead Days*, edited by Edward D. Hoch. New York, Walker, 1972.
> "The Virtuosi Venus," in *Ellery Queen's Mystery Magazine* (New York), June 1973.
> "The Westcombe Witch," in *Ellery Queen's Mystery Magazine* (New York), October 1973.
> "The Resurrection Man," in *Ellery Queen's Crookbook*. New York, Random House, and London, Gollancz, 1974.
> "The Blackamoor Unchain'd," in *Ellery Queen's Mystery Magazine* (New York), June 1974.
> "The Bedlam Bam," in *Best Detective Stories of the Year 1976*, edited by Edward D. Hoch. New York, Dutton, 1976.
> "The Aerostatick Globe," in *Ellery Queen's Mystery Magazine* (New York), June 1976.

"The Spirit of the '76," in *Ellery Queen's Mystery Magazine* (New York), January 1977.

"The Lost Heir," in *When Last Seen*, edited by Arthur Maling.   New York, Harper, 1977.

"Milady Bigamy," in *Ellery Queen's Mystery Magazine* (New York), July 1978.

OTHER PUBLICATIONS

Plays

Goodbye, Miss Lizzie Borden (produced Colorado Springs, 1948).   Published in *Murder Plain and Fanciful*, edited by James Sandoe, New York, Sheridan House, 1948.

Cheat the Wuddy (produced Colorado Springs, 1948).

Remember Constance Kent (produced Colorado Springs, 1949).

The Sally Cathleen Claim (produced Cripple Creek, Colorado, 1952).

The Coffee Cup (produced Willimantic, Connecticut, 1955).   Published in *Butcher, Baker, Murder Maker*, edited by George Harmon Coxe, New York, Knopf, 1954; London, Macdonald, 1956.

The Queen's Choristers, music by J. Julius Baird (juvenile; produced Colorado Springs, 1961).

The Jester's Apprentice, music by J. Julius Baird (juvenile; produced Colorado Springs, 1962).

The Bar-Room Floor (produced Central City, Colorado, 1964).

The Stroller's Girl, music by J. Julius Baird (juvenile; produced Colorado Springs, 1966).

Other

The 60 Minute Chef, with Carol Truax.   New York, Macmillan, 1947.

Villainy Detected.   New York, Appleton Century, 1947.

The White Rose of Stuart (juvenile).   New York, Nelson, 1954.

The Actress (juvenile).   New York, Nelson, 1957.

"The Scholar as Sherlock," in *New York Times Book Review*, 9 June 1963.

The New 60 Minute Chef, with Carol Truax.   New York, Bantam, 1975.

"The Pleasures of Histo-Detection," in *Armchair Detective* (San Diego), May 1976.

Bibliography: "Blood on the Periwigs" by James Mark Purcell, in *Mystery Readers Newsletter* (Melrose, Massachusetts), July–August 1971.

Lillian de la Torre comments:

I call myself a "histo-detector." The name comes from the funny papers, but the calling is a serious one, the craft of solving mysteries of the long-ago. I began "histo-detecting" for fun when in 1942 I was inspired to write mystery fiction featuring as "detector" Dr. Johnson, the real-life eighteenth-century lexicographer and sage, narrated by his biographer, the fascinating rake, James Boswell. The crime scene in their time was rich and raffish, and afforded many an intriguing mystery to be fictitiously unravelled. Twenty-nine "Dr. Sam: Johnson" mystery short stories have appeared. The mysteries, characters, and settings are real, but the solutions only rarely make any pretence of being other than fiction.

Once in a while, it may become apparent to me that I have lit on the truth of one of those old cases in sober earnest. Then a book results, exhaustively researched and definitive. Such are my books on Elizabeth Canning, Belle Gunness, and the disputed Douglas claim. "Sir, I think such a publication does good," said Dr. Johnson of an earlier book on the Douglas Cause, "as it does good to show us the possibilities of human life."

I agree. Thoughtful consideration of such mysterious moments in history, in my opinion, is uniquely fitted to illuminate the human condition, probing as it does man's behavior under stress, brilliantly flood-lighted in the glare of public curiosity. Thus in serious "histo-detection," the humane value will equal or transcend the usual amusement values of sensational narrative and puzzle-solving.

*   *   *

Best known as the creator of the "Dr. Sam: Johnson" stories, Lillian de la Torre is a writer of considerable range. Her contributions to mystery/detective literature include three historical mystery novels, several plays based on historical crimes, and two articles which present convincing arguments in favour of the seriousness of crime literature as a means of probing human motivation.

Goodbye, Miss Lizzie Borden, a one-act play, exemplifies de la Torre's method at its best. She is able to take a well-known historical case and present it in a form which is both viable dramatically and believable in realistic terms. The surprise ending is not contrived, and the play as a whole is infinitely more touching than many historical dramas which attempt simply to recreate known events.

De la Torre calls herself a "histo-detector," and her 29 published stories featuring Dr. Johnson, narrated by the ideal "Watson," James Boswell, are successful examples of histo-detection. Having fastened upon an historical period rich in criminal possibilities, the author concentrates upon the presentation of character, setting, and atmosphere, with little pretence at providing an original or ingenious puzzle. The tone of the stories, which gracefully reflects the style of Dr. Johnson and his period, allows the author to point a moral, explain an historical mystery, or otherwise indulge in a didacticism which might be out of place in a contemporary crime story. Julian Symons has referred to these stories as "pastiches," a description which fails to suggest the author's originality. In such historical novels as *Elizabeth Is Missing* or *The Heir of Douglas*, de la Torre exhibits a combination of careful attention to historical detail and a humane interest in justice as the result of a proper understanding of human behaviour. Like the Dr. Johnson stories, the novels present thoughtful but lively considerations of mysterious moments in history as these reveal universal human traits.

—Joanne Harack Hayne

DELVING, Michael. Pseudonym for Jay Williams. American. Born in Buffalo, New York, 31 May 1914. Educated at the University of Pennsylvania, Philadelphia, 1931–32; Columbia University, New York, 1933–34. Served in the United States Army, 1941–45: Purple Heart. Married Barbara Girdansky in 1941; one daughter and one son. Comedian, upstate New York; press agent, 1936–41; full-time writer after 1945. Recipient: Guggenheim Fellowship, 1949; Boys' Club of America Award, 1949; Bank Street College of Education Irma Black Award, 1977. *Died 12 July 1978.*

CRIME PUBLICATIONS

Novels (series characters: Dave Cannon; Bob Eddison)

    Smiling, The Boy Fell Dead (Cannon).   New York, Scribner, and London, Macdonald, 1967.

The Devil Finds Work (Cannon, Eddison). New York, Scribner, 1969; London, Collins, 1970.
Die Like a Man (Cannon). New York, Scribner, and London, Collins, 1970.
A Shadow of Himself (Eddison). New York, Scribner, and London, Collins, 1972.
Bored to Death (Cannon). New York, Scribner, 1975; as *Wave of Fatalities*, London, Collins, 1975.
The China Expert. London, Collins, 1976; New York, Scribner, 1977.
No Sign of Life. New York, Doubleday, 1979.

OTHER PUBLICATIONS as Jay Williams

Novels

The Good Yeoman. New York, Appleton Century Crofts, 1948; London, Macdonald, 1956.
The Rogue from Padua. Boston, Little Brown, 1952; London, Macdonald, 1954.
The Siege. Boston, Little Brown, and London, Macdonald, 1955.
The Witches. New York, Random House, 1957; London, Macdonald, 1958.
Solomon and Sheba. New York, Random House, and London, Macdonald, 1959.
The Forger. New York, Atheneum, and London, Macdonald, 1961.
Tomorrow's Fire. New York, Atheneum, 1964; London, Macdonald, 1965.
Uniad. New York, Scribner, 1968; London, Murray, 1969.

Other

Fall of the Sparrow. New York, Oxford University Press, 1951.
A Change of Climate (on Majorca). New York, Random House, and London, Macdonald, 1956.
The World of Titian. New York, Time, 1968.
Stage Left. New York, Scribner, 1974.

Other (juvenile)

The Stolen Oracle. New York, Oxford University Press, 1943.
The Counterfeit African. New York and London, Oxford University Press, 1944.
The Sword and the Scythe. New York, Oxford University Press, 1946.
The Roman Moon Mystery. New York, Oxford University Press, 1948.
The Magic Gate. New York, Oxford University Press, 1949.
Eagle Jake and Indian Pete. New York, Rinehart, 1947.
Augustus Caesar. Evanston, Illinois, Row Peterson, 1952.
Danny Dunn and the Antigravity Paint [on a Desert Island, and the Homework Machine, and the Weather Machine, on the Ocean Floor, and the Fossil Cave, and the Heat Ray, Time Traveler, and the Automatic House, and the Voice from Space, and the Smallifying Machine, and the Swamp Monster, Invisible Boy, Scientific Detective, and the Universal Glue], with Raymond Abrashkin. New York, McGraw Hill, 15 vols., 1956–77; Leicester, Brockhampton Press, 2 vols., 1956, 1960; London, Macdonald, 13 vols., 1965–78.
The Battle for the Atlantic. New York, Random House, 1959.
The Tournament of the Lions. New York, Walck, 1960.
Medusa's Head. New York, Random House, 1960; London, Muller, 1963.
Knights of the Crusades. New York, American Heritage Press, 1962; London, Cassell, 1963.
Puppy Pie. New York, Crowell Collier, 1962.
I Wish I Had Another Name (verse). New York, Atheneum, 1962.
Joan of Arc. New York, American Heritage Press, 1963; London, Cassell, 1964.

The Question Box. New York, Norton, 1965.

Leonardo da Vinci. New York, American Heritage Press, 1965; London, Cassell, 1966.

The Spanish Armada. New York, American Heritage Press, and London, Cassell, 1966.

Life in the Middle Ages. New York, Random House, 1966; London, Nelson, 1967.

Philbert the Fearful. New York, Norton, 1966.

What Can You Do with a Word? New York, Macmillan, 1966.

The Cookie Tree. New York, Parents' Magazine Press, 1967.

To Catch a Bird. New York, Crowell Collier, 1968.

The Sword of King Arthur. New York, Crowell, 1968.

The Horn of Roland. New York, Crowell, 1968.

The King with Six Friends. New York, Parents' Magazine Press, 1968.

The Good-for-Nothing Prince. New York, Norton, 1969.

The Practical Princess. New York, Parents' Magazine Press, 1969.

School for Sillies. New York, Parents' Magazine Press, 1969.

A Box Full of Infinity. New York, Norton, 1970.

Stupid Marco. New York, Parents' Magazine Press, 1970.

The Silver Whistle. New York, Parents' Magazine Press, 1971.

A Present from a Bird. New York, Parents' Magazine Press, 1971.

The Hawkstone. New York, Walck, 1971; London, Gollancz, 1972.

The Youngest Captain. New York, Parents' Magazine Press, 1972.

Magical Storybook. New York, American Heritage Press, 1972.

The Hero from Otherwhere. New York, Walck, 1972.

Seven at One Blow. New York, Parents' Magazine Press, 1972.

Petronella. New York, Parents' Magazine Press, 1973.

Forgetful Fred. New York, Parents' Magazine Press, 1974.

The People of the Ax. New York, Walck, 1974; London, Macdonald and Jane's, 1975.

A Bag Full of Nothing. New York, Parents' Magazine Press, 1974.

Moon Journey (based on works by Jules Verne). London, Macdonald and Jane's, 1976; New York, Crown, 1977.

Everyone Knows What a Dragon Looks Like. New York, Scholastic, 1976.

The Burglar Next Door. New York, Scholastic, 1976; as *Daylight Robbery*, London, Penguin, 1977.

The Reward Worth Having. New York, Scholastic, 1977.

The Time of the Kraken. New York, Scholastic, and London, Gollancz, 1977.

Pettifur. New York, Scholastic, 1977.

The Practical Princess and Other Liberating Fairy Tales. New York, Parents' Magazine Press, 1978; London, Chatto and Windus, 1979.

The Wicked Tricks of Tyl Uilenspiegel. New York, Scholastic, 1978.

The Magic Grandfather. New York, Scholastic, and London, Macdonald and Jane's, 1979.

Unearthly Beasts and Other Strange People. London, Macmillan, 1979.

The City Witch and the Country Witch. New York, Macmillan, 1979.

Manuscript Collection: Mugar Memorial Library, Boston University.

*   *   *

Under the pseudonym Michael Delving, the versatile and prolific author Jay Williams wrote seven crime novels. His protagonists in five of them, two American antique dealers and rare-booksellers, discover murder and mystery, both ancient and modern, as well as stock for their Connecticut shop on their buying trips to England. The sixth book, *The China Expert*, features an American specialist in Chinese porcelain who becomes embroiled in espionage in a comic tale in which Delving's accustomed expertise in the antiques trade is displayed. The author's knowledge of history and folklore, as shown in his historical works set in the Middle Ages, is used to great advantage in his crime fiction. Delving, who maintained homes on both sides of the Atlantic, was also well-qualified to record the observations of his American heroes on Britain and British life which enrich these books; in their turn, the British characters have their say about America and Americans.

Dave Cannon, a Connecticut Yankee, and his partner Bob Eddison, a Cherokee Indian, are unusual and interesting heroes. They appear together or separately in Delving's first five novels, set in rural Gloucestershire and in Wales. In the course of their adventures, both fall in love with and eventually marry English women. The romantic element is well-handled and adds dimension to Delving's cast of characters. Though only amateur sleuths, Cannon and Eddison are adepts at their own trade, and use their powers of observation, energy, and curiosity, as well as their uninhibited American "brashness," in their search for assorted artifacts. At first, Cannon has problems with a Scotland Yard inspector who, quite understandably, objects to their "incorrigible" interference in his case. Subsequently they become friends and the police make use of the Americans' facility for obtaining information.

Delving makes the modern crimes plausible and his plotting is solid. Suspense is sustained in every instance. What sets Delving's books apart from other well-written, witty, and civilized mystery novels is his remarkable ability to integrate folklore and literature into the structure of the stories. An outstanding example is *Die Like a Man*, in which betrayal and murder result from the pursuit of a gold-rimmed wooden bowl said to be the Holy Grail. The modern "wasteland" of industrialization and nationalism is superimposed on the mythical wasteland of Percival and the Maimed King. Quotes from Sir Thomas Malory and George Borrow's *Wild Wales* are deftly woven into the plot. Cannon, the skeptical and self-mocking hero, wonders if he should declare "one dish from the Last Supper" in customs. The symbolism and literary allusions do not slow the action or become oppressive, but combine with humor and excitement to make a tale that comes off delightfully. Fans of literate crime fiction will find much to enjoy in Michael Delving's books, which have practically everything – action, romance, humor, imaginative situations, well-developed characters, and a wealth of fascinating lore.

—Mary Helen Becker

DEMARIS, Ovid (Ovide E. Desmarais). American. Born in Biddeford, Maine, 6 September 1919. Educated at the College of Idaho, Caldwell, A.B. 1948; Syracuse University Law School, New York; Boston University, M.S. 1950. Served in the United States Army Air Forces: warrant officer. Married Inez E. Frakes in 1942; two children. Reporter, Quincy *Patriot Ledger*, Massachusetts, 1949–50, and United Press, Boston, 1950–52; advertising copy chief, Los Angeles *Times*, 1953–59; self-employed writer since 1959. Address: P. O. Box 6071, Santa Barbara, California 93111, U.S.A.

CRIME PUBLICATIONS

Novels

> *The Hoods Take Over.*   New York, Fawcett, 1957; London, Fawcett, 1959.
> *Ride the Gold Mare.*   New York, Fawcett, 1957.
> *The Lusting Drive.*   New York, Fawcett, 1958; London, Muller, 1961.
> *The Long Night.*   New York, Avon, 1959.

The Slasher. New York, Fawcett, 1959.
The Enforcer. New York, Fawcett, 1960.
The Extortioners. New York, Fawcett, 1960; London, Muller, 1961.
The Gold-Plated Sewer. New York, Avon, 1960.
Candyleg. New York, Fawcett, 1961; London, Muller, 1962; as *Machine Gun McCain*, New York, Fawcett, and London, Hodder and Stoughton, 1970.
The Parasite. New York, Berkley, 1963.
The Organization. New York, Tower, 1965; as *The Contract*, New York, Belmont, 1970; London, Sphere, 1971.
The Overlord. New York, New American Library, 1972.

OTHER PUBLICATIONS

Other

Lucky Luciano. Derby, Connecticut, Monarch, 1960.
The Lindbergh Kidnapping Case. Derby, Connecticut, Monarch, 1961.
The Dillinger Story. Derby, Connecticut, Monarch, 1961.
The Green Felt Jungle, with Edward Reid. New York, Trident Press, 1963; London, Heinemann, 1965.
Jack Ruby, with Garry Wills. New York, New American Library, 1968.
Captive City: Chicago in Chains. New York, Stuart, 1969.
America the Violent. New York, Cowles, 1970.
Poso del Mundo: Inside the Mexican-American Border. Boston, Little Brown, 1970.
Dirty Business: The Corporate-Political Money-Power Game. New York, Harper's Magazine Press, 1974.
The Director: An Oral Biography of J. Edgar Hoover. New York, Harper's Magazine Press, 1975.
Brothers in Blood: The International Terrorist Network. New York, Scribner, 1977.
My Story, by Judith Exner as told to Demaris. New York, Grove Press, 1977.

*   *   *

The early work of Ovid Demaris exemplifies the hard-boiled genre in paperback form. Centered on a California-based private eye, Vince Slader, his first novels featured a series of crime scenes representative of a mid-century world of dope-running, blackmail, and gangland killings. Action was complex and rapid; and, though his plot outlines were not novel, Demaris established a modest reputation for fast tempo and an economic way of interweaving complex counterplots. This early period culminated in *Candyleg*, his most widely-known novel, later to become a movie called *Machine Gun McCain*. Now focusing on a gangster-hero, Demaris evoked a Dillinger-style bank-robber, sprung from a life sentence on Alcatraz to pull a $2 million casino holdup in Las Vegas. McCain soon learns that he is involved in a gangland double-cross, and organizes his own triple-cross; the robbery is successful, but is followed by the inevitable collapse of each private plan. McCain survives, but his girl – his hope for the future – is one of 19 victims in what has become largely a tale of violence and death.

Even in its success, *Candyleg* presaged a new theme that served Demaris less well than the hard-boiled message of his early work. He discovered the Mafia; and in his attempts to portray a bureaucratic gangdom he lost his sense of pace and his ability to tell a good story. Only three novels followed, of considerably less literary value, as Demaris shifted his interest to criminal conspiracies in a non-fiction world.

—Dwight C. Smith, Jr.

DEMING,   Richard.   Also   writes   as   Max   Franklin;   Emily   Moor;   Nick
Morino.   American.   Born in Des Moines, Iowa, 25 April 1915. Educated at Central
College, Fayette, Missouri, 1933–35; Washington University, St. Louis, B.A. 1937; State
University of Iowa, Iowa City, M.A. 1939. Served in the United States Army, 1941–45:
Captain. Married Ruth DuBois in 1948; three daughters. Self-employed writer. Since 1976,
member of the Board of Directors, Mystery Writers of America. Agent: Scott Meredith
Literary Agency, 845 Third Avenue, New York, New York 10022. Address: P.O. Box 3129,
Ventura, California 93003, U.S.A.

Crime Publications

Novels (series character: Manville "Manny" Moon; Matt Rudd)

The Gallows in My Garden (Moon).   New York, Rinehart, 1952; London, Boardman,
1953.
Tweak the Devil's Nose (Moon).   New York, Rinehart, and London, Boardman, 1953;
as Hand-Picked to Die, New York, Spivak, 1956.
Whistle Past the Graveyard (Moon).   New York, Rinehart, 1954; London, Boardman,
1955; as Give the Girl a Gun, New York, Spivak, 1955.
Juvenile Delinquent (Moon).   London, Boardman, 1958.
Dragnet: The Case of the Courteous Killer.   New York, Pocket Books, 1958.
City Limits (as Nick Morino).   New York, Pyramid, 1958.
Dragnet: The Case of the Crime King.   New York, Pocket Books, 1959.
Fall Girl.   Rockville Centre, New York, Zenith, 1959; as Walk a Crooked Mile,
London, Boardman, 1959.
Kiss and Kill.   Rockville Centre, New York, Zenith, 1960; London, Digit, 1961.
Edge of the Law.   New York, Berkley, 1960.
Hit and Run.   New York, Pocket Books, 1960.
Vice Cop (Rudd).   New York, Belmont, 1961.
This Is My Night.   Derby, Connecticut, Monarch, 1961.
Body for Sale.   New York, Pocket Books, 1962.
The Careful Man.   London, W. H. Allen, 1962.
She'll Hate Me Tomorrow.   Derby, Connecticut, Monarch, 1963.
Anything But Saintly (Rudd).   New York, Pocket Books, 1963.
Death of a Pusher (Rudd).   New York, Pocket Books, 1964.
This Game of Murder.   Derby, Connecticut, Monarch, 1964.
The Mod Squad: The Greek God Affair.   New York, Pyramid, 1968.
The Mod Squad: A Groovy Way to Die.   New York, Pyramid, 1968.
The Mod Squad: The Sock-It-to-Em Murders.   New York, Pyramid, 1969.
The Mod Squad: Spy-In.   New York, Pyramid, 1969.
The Mod Squad: Assignment, The Arranger.   Racine, Wisconsin, Whitman, 1969.
The Mod Squad: The Hit.   New York, Pyramid, 1970.
The Mod Squad: Assignment, The Hideout.   Racine, Wisconsin, Whitman, 1970.
What's the Matter with Helen?   New York, Beagle, 1971.
The Shadowed Porch (as Emily Moor).   New York, Beagle, 1972.

Novels as Max Franklin

Justice Has No Sword.   New York, Rinehart, 1953; London, Boardman, 1954; as
Murder Muscles In, New York, Spivak, 1956.
Hell Street.   New York, Rinehart, 1954.
99 44/100% Dead (novelization of screenplay).   New York, Award, 1974.
The Destructors (novelization of screenplay).   New York, Ballantine, 1974.

The 5th of November (novelization of screenplay). New York, Ballantine, 1975; as *Hennessy*, London, Futura, 1975.

Starsky and Hutch (novelization of tv play). New York, Ballantine, 1975.

Starsky and Hutch: Kill Huggy Bear (novelization of tv play). New York, Ballantine, 1976.

Starsky and Hutch: Death Ride (novelization of tv play). New York, Ballantine, 1976.

Starsky and Hutch: Bounty Hunter (novelization of tv play). New York, Ballantine, 1977.

Starsky and Hutch: Terror on the Docks (novelization of tv play). New York, Ballantine, 1977.

Charlie's Angels (novelization of tv play). New York, Ballantine, 1977.

Charlie's Angels: The Killing Kind (novelization of tv play). New York, Ballantine, 1977.

Charlie's Angels: Angels on a String (novelization of tv play). New York, Ballantine, 1977.

Charlie's Angels: Angels in Chains (novelization of tv play). New York, Ballantine, 1977.

Starsky and Hutch: The Setup (novelization of tv play). New York, Ballantine, 1978.

Starsky and Hutch: Murder on Playboy Island (novelization of tv play). New York, Ballantine, 1978.

Good Guys Wear Black. New York, New American Library, 1978.

The Dark. New York, New American Library, 1978.

Vega$ (novelization of tv play). New York, Ballantine, 1978.

Short Stories

Dragnet: Case Histories from the Popular Television Series. Racine, Wisconsin, Western, 1970.

Uncollected Short Stories

"For Value Received," in *Best Detective Stories of the Year 1953*, edited by David Coxe Cooke. New York, Dutton, and London, Boardman, 1953.

"Mugger Murder," in *Best Detective Stories of the Year 1954*, edited by David Coxe Cooke. New York, Dutton, and London, Boardman, 1954.

"The Choice," in *Best Detective Stories of the Year 1955*, edited by David Coxe Cooke. New York, Dutton, and London, Boardman, 1956.

"I Want It Foolproof," in *The Saint* (New York), August 1957.

"Custody," in *Best Detective Stories of the Year 1956*, edited by David Coxe Cooke. New York, Dutton, and London, Boardman, 1957.

"The Front," in *The Saint* (New York), May 1959.

"Ultimate Terror," in *The Saint* (New York), November 1959.

"Optical Illusion," in *Dames, Danger, and Death*, edited by Leo Margulies. New York, Pyramid, 1960.

"The Hard Man," in *The Saint* (New York), December 1961.

"The Blood Oath," in *The Saint* (New York), March 1962.

"A Medal for Don Carlos," in *The Saint* (New York), July 1962.

"Homicide, Inc.," in *The Saint* (New York), November 1962.

"Second Honeymoon," in *Best Detective Stories of the Year: 17th Annual Collection*, edited by Brett Halliday. New York, Dutton, 1962.

"Death at Midnight," in *The Saint* (New York), July 1963.

"The Man Who Chose the Devil," in *The Saint* (New York), October 1963.

"Red Herring," in *Best Detective Stories of the Year*, edited by Anthony Boucher. New York, Dutton, and London, Boardman, 1963.

"Uncle Willie," in *The Saint* (New York), July 1964.

"Errand Boy," in *The Saint* (New York), March 1965.

"The Shakedown," in *Come Seven, Come Death*, edited by Henry Morrison. New York, Pocket Books, 1965.

"The Most Ethical Man in the Business," in *Ellery Queen's Crime Carousel*. New York, New American Library, 1966; London, Gollancz, 1967.

"Open File," in *Anthology 1967*, edited by Ellery Queen. New York, Davis, 1966.

"The Jolly Jugglers, Retired," in *Ellery Queen's Mystery Magazine* (New York), March 1967.

"The Competitors," in *Crimes and Misfortunes*, edited by J. Francis McComas. New York, Random House, 1970.

"Black Belt," in *Mirror, Mirror, Fatal Mirror*, edited by Hans S. Santesson. New York, Doubleday, 1973.

"Bunco Game," in *Men and Malice*, edited by Dean Dickensheet. New York, Doubleday, 1973.

"The Man Who Was Two," in *Killers of the Mind*, edited by Lucy Freeman. New York, Random House, 1974.

OTHER PUBLICATIONS

Novels

Baby Blue Marine (as Max Franklin). New York, New American Library, 1976.
The Last of the Cowboys (as Max Franklin). New York, New American Library, 1977.

Other

American Spies. Racine, Wisconsin, Whitman, 1960.
Famous Investigators. Racine, Wisconsin, Whitman, 1963.
The Police Lab at Work. Indianapolis, Bobbs Merrill, 1967.
Heroes of the International Red Cross. New York, Meredith Press, 1969.
Man and Society: Criminal Law at Work. New York, Hawthorn, 1970.
Man Against Man: Civil Law at Work. New York, Hawthorn, 1972.
Sleep, Our Unknown Life. New York, Nelson, 1972.
Man and the World: International Law at Work. New York, Hawthorn, 1974.
Metric Power: Why and How We Are Going Metric. New York, Nelson, 1974; as *Metric Now*, New York, Dell, 1976.
Women: The New Criminals. New York, Nelson, 1977.

*   *   *

Richard Deming is rather typical of that generation of crime writers who began writing during the latter days of the pulp magazine era. When the pulps expired, he moved to writing short stories for the digest-sized mystery magazines (*Manhunt, Alfred Hitchcock's Mystery Magazine, Mike Shayne Mystery Magazine*, etc.) and original paperback novels. The new post-pulp markets required much the same skills as the pulps: the ability to write crisp, realistic dialogue; to plot competently, without over-elaboration; to know how to blend sex, violence, and sensationalism for maximum sales appeal without getting in trouble with the censors. Drawbacks to this sort of career included generally unspectacular pay, short deadlines, and a fast-changing market, where magazines and paperback houses were formed and dissolved, and a writer frequently did not know who his next publisher would be.

Some writers working in this field eventually achieved notable popular and critical success – John D. MacDonald is the prime example – usually by virtue of having happened on a steady publisher and a series character of broad appeal. Others, like Deming, never quite broke out of the paperback ghetto; nevertheless, his work is interesting, varied, thoroughly professional, and very much worth the attention of those who love good crime writing.

He did try his hand at a series detective, Manville "Manny" Moon, who appeared in three early novels and in many short stories. Manny is tough, honest, quick-witted, fast with the wisecracks, and equipped with an artificial leg. His home base is the El Patio Cafe; his girlfriend is Fausta Moreni, the proprietress. The plot material is the familiar sort of nastiness that keeps the hard-boiled genre alive: vice, racketeering, blackmail, and casual murder. The Moon books have strong atmosphere, crackling dialogue, and considerable forward momentum, very much in the Hammett-Chandler tradition. That the Moon series never caught on while less appealing and well-crafted private eye series enjoyed great success is one of those baffling mysteries of the paperback market.

Deming's non-series works in the suspense field display the same virtues as the Moon novels. Such books as *Edge of the Law* and *She'll Hate Me Tomorrow* are rousing reworkings of the classic hard-boiled theme of the man on the run from the Syndicate; money, mayhem, and sex are stirred together with considerable skill. *Hit and Run* is noteworthy for Deming's dedication: "For the Bureau of Internal Revenue" – a reminder of the driving force behind the work of the journeyman crime writer.

Deming launched another short-lived series in 1963. *Anything But Saintly* and *Death of a Pusher* are hard-boiled procedural novels featuring Matt Rudd (Mateusz Rudowski), a vice cop in the fictional Southern California town of St. Cecilia – a corrupt and violence-ridden city reminiscent of Chandler's Bay City.

Deming has also done many tv novelizations, most recently a series of books based on the *Mod Squad* series. The tv tie-in has become an increasingly important market for experienced and versatile writers like Deming. In the late 1950's Deming also did two *Dragnet* books, in which he displayed a fine feel for the modern police procedural novel; his personal approach to dialogue, however, was sacrificed to the peculiar style associated with the tv series.

—Art Scott

DENT, Lester. Also wrote as Kenneth Robeson; Tim Ryan. American. Born in La Plata, Missouri, 12 October 1904. Studied telegraphy at Chillicothe Business College, Missouri, 1923–24. Married Norma Gerling in 1925. Taught at Chillicothe Business College, 1924; telegrapher, Western Union, Carrolton, Missouri, 1924, and Empire Oil and Gas Company, Ponca City, Oklahoma, 1925; telegrapher, then teletype operator, Associated Press, Tulsa, 1926; journalist for Tulsa *World*; house-writer for Dell, publishers, 1930; free-lance writer from 1930, and also dairy farmer and aerial photographer. *Died 11 March 1959.*

CRIME PUBLICATIONS

Novels (series character: Chance Malloy)

> *Dead at the Take-Off* (Malloy). New York, Doubleday, 1946; London, Cassell, 1948; as *High Stakes*, New York, Ace, 1953.
> *Lady to Kill* (Malloy). New York, Doubleday, 1946; London, Cassell, 1949.
> *Lady Afraid.* New York, Doubleday, 1948; London, Cassell, 1950.
> *Lady So Silent.* London, Cassell, 1951.
> *Cry at Dusk.* New York, Fawcett, 1952; London, Fawcett, 1959.
> *Lady in Peril.* New York, Ace, 1959.
> *Hades and Hocus Pocus,* edited by Robert Weinberg. Chicago, Pulp Press, 1979.

461

Novels as Kenneth Robeson (series character: Doc Savage in all books)

Quest of the Spider. New York, Street and Smith, 1933.
The Man of Bronze. New York, Street and Smith, 1933.
The Land of Terror. New York, Street and Smith, 1933.
The Thousand-Headed Man. New York, Bantam, 1964.
Meteor Menace. New York, Bantam, 1964.
The Polar Treasure. New York, Bantam, 1965.
Brand of the Werewolf. New York, Bantam, 1965.
The Lost Oasis. New York, Bantam, 1965.
The Monsters. New York, Bantam, 1965.
The Land of Terror. New York, Bantam, and London, Tandem, 1965.
Quest of Qui. London, Bantam, 1965; New York, Bantam, 1966.
The Mystic Mullah. New York, Bantam, 1965; London, Bantam, 1966.
The Phantom City. New York, Bantam, 1966.
Fear Cay. New York, Bantam, 1966.
Land of Always-Night. New York, Bantam, 1966.
The Fantastic Island. New York, Bantam, 1966; London, Bantam, 1967.
The Spook Legion. New York, Bantam, 1967.
The Red Skull. New York, Bantam, 1967.
The Sargasso Ogre. New York, Bantam, 1967.
Pirate of the Pacific. New York, Bantam, 1967.
The Secret of the Sky. New York, Bantam, 1967; London, Bantam, 1968.
The Czar of Fear. New York, Bantam, 1968.
Fortress of Solitude. New York, Bantam, 1968.
The Green Eagle. New York, Bantam, 1968.
Death in Silver. New York, Bantam, 1968.
The Mystery under the Sea. New York, Bantam, 1968; London, Bantam, 1969.
The Deadly Dwarf. New York, Bantam, 1968.
The Other World. New York, Bantam, 1968; London, Bantam, 1969.
The Flaming Falcons. New York, Bantam, 1968; London, Bantam, 1969.
The Annihilist. New York, Bantam, 1968; London, Bantam, 1969.
Hex. London, Bantam, 1968; New York, Bantam, 1969.
The Squeaking Goblins. New York, Bantam, 1969.
Mad Eyes. New York, Bantam, 1969.
The Terror in the Navy. New York, Bantam, 1969.
Dust of Death. New York, Bantam, 1969.
Resurrection Day. New York, Bantam, 1969.
Red Snow. New York, Bantam, 1969.
World's Fair Goblin. New York, Bantam, 1969.
The Dagger in the Sky. New York, Bantam, 1969.
Merchants of Disaster. New York, Bantam, 1969.
The Gold Ogre. New York, Bantam, 1969.
The Man Who Shook the Earth. New York, Bantam, 1969.
The Sea Magician. New York, Bantam, 1970.
The Midas Man. New York, Bantam, 1970.
The Feathered Octopus. New York, Bantam, 1970.
The Sea Angel. New York, Bantam, 1970.
Devil on the Moon. New York, Bantam, 1970.
The Vanisher. New York, Bantam, 1970.
The Mental Wizard. New York, Bantam, 1970.
He Could Stop the World. New York, Bantam, 1970.
The Golden Peril. New York, Bantam, 1970.
The Giggling Ghosts. New York, Bantam, 1971.
Poison Island. New York, Bantam, 1971.

The Munitions Master. New York, Bantam, 1971.
The Yellow Cloud. New York, Bantam, 1971.
The Majii. New York, Bantam, 1971.
The Living Fire Menace. New York, Bantam, 1971.
The Pirate's Ghost. New York, Bantam, 1971.
The Submarine Mystery. New York, Bantam, 1971.
The Motion Menace. New York, Bantam, 1971.
The Green Death. New York, Bantam, 1971.
Mad Mesa. New York, Bantam, 1972.
The Freckled Shark. New York, Bantam, 1972.
The Mystery of the Snow. New York, Bantam, 1972.
Spook Hole. New York, Bantam, 1972.
The Mental Monster. New York, Bantam, 1973.
The Seven Agate Devils. New York, Bantam, 1973.
The Derrick Devil. New York, Bantam, 1973.
Land of Fear. New York, Bantam, 1973.
The South Pole Terror. New York, Bantam, 1974.
The Crimson Serpent. New York, Bantam, 1974.
The Devil Ghengis. New York, Bantam, 1974.
The King Maker. New York, Bantam, 1975.
The Stone Man. New York, Bantam, 1976.
The Evil Gnome. New York, Bantam, 1976.
The Red Terrors. New York, Bantam, 1976.
The Mountain Monster. New York, Bantam, 1976.
The Boss of Terror. New York, Bantam, 1976.
The Angry Ghost. New York, Bantam, 1977.
The Spotted Men. New York, Bantam, 1977.
The Roar Devil. New York, Bantam, 1977.
The Magic Island. New York, Bantam, 1977.
The Flying Goblin. New York, Bantam, 1977.
The Purple Dragon. New York, Bantam, 1978.
The Awful Egg. New York, Bantam, 1978.
Tunnel Terror. New York, Bantam, 1979.
The Hate Genius. New York, Bantam, 1979.
The Red Spider. New York, Bantam, 1979.

Uncollected Novels as Kenneth Robeson (series character: Doc Savage)

"The Men Vanished," in *Doc Savage* (New York), December 1940.
"The All-White Elf," in *Doc Savage* (New York), March 1941.
"The Golden Man," in *Doc Savage* (New York), April 1941.
"The Pink Lady," in *Doc Savage* (New York), May 1941.
"Mystery Island," in *Doc Savage* (New York), August 1941.
"Birds of Death," in *Doc Savage* (New York), October 1941.
"The Invisible Box Monsters," in *Doc Savage* (New York), November 1941.
"Peril in the North," in *Doc Savage* (New York), December 1941.
"Men of Fear," in *Doc Savage* (New York), February 1942.
"The Too-Wise Owl," in *Doc Savage* (New York), March 1942.
"Pirate Isle," in *Doc Savage* (New York), May 1942.
"The Speaking Stone," in *Doc Savage* (New York), June 1942.
"The Man Who Fell Up," in *Doc Savage* (New York), July 1942.
"The Three Wild Men," in *Doc Savage* (New York), August 1942.
"The Fiery Menace," in *Doc Savage* (New York), September 1942.
"The Laugh of Death," in *Doc Savage* (New York), October 1942.
"They Died Twice," in *Doc Savage* (New York), November 1942.

"The Devil's Black Rock," in *Doc Savage* (New York), December 1942.
"The Time Terror," in *Doc Savage* (New York), January 1943.
"Waves of Death," in *Doc Savage* (New York), February 1943.
"The Black, Black Witch," in *Doc Savage* (New York), March 1943.
"The King of Terror," in *Doc Savage* (New York), April 1943.
"The Talking Devil," in *Doc Savage* (New York), May 1943.
"The Running Skeletons," in *Doc Savage* (New York), June 1943.
"Mystery on Happy Bones," in *Doc Savage* (New York), July 1943.
"Hell Below," in *Doc Savage* (New York), September 1943.
"The Goblins," in *Doc Savage* (New York), October 1943.
"The Secret of the Su," in *Doc Savage* (New York), November 1943.
"The Spook of Grandpa Eben," in *Doc Savage* (New York), December 1943.
"According to Plan of a One-Eyed Mystic," in *Doc Savage* (New York), January 1944.
"Death Had Yellow Eyes," in *Doc Savage* (New York), February 1944.
"The Derelict of Skull Shoal," in *Doc Savage* (New York), March 1944.
"The Whisker of Hercules," in *Doc Savage* (New York), April 1944.
"The Three Devils," in *Doc Savage* (New York), May 1944.
"The Pharaoh's Ghost," in *Doc Savage* (New York), June 1944.
"The Man Who Was Scared," in *Doc Savage* (New York), July 1944.
"The Shape of Terror," in *Doc Savage* (New York), August 1944.
"Weird Valley," in *Doc Savage* (New York), September 1944.
"Jiu San," in *Doc Savage* (New York), October 1944.
"Satan Black," in *Doc Savage* (New York), November 1944.
"The Lost Giant," in *Doc Savage* (New York), December 1944.
"Violent Night," in *Doc Savage* (New York), January 1945.
"Strange Fish," in *Doc Savage* (New York), February 1945.
"Ten Ton Snakes," in *Doc Savage* (New York), March 1945.
"Cargo Unknown," in *Doc Savage* (New York), April 1945.
"Rock Sinister," in *Doc Savage* (New York), May 1945.
"The Terrible Stork," in *Doc Savage* (New York), June 1945.
"King Joe Cay," in *Doc Savage* (New York), July 1945.
"The Wee Ones," in *Doc Savage* (New York), August 1945.
"Terror Takes Seven," in *Doc Savage* (New York), September 1945.
"The Thing That Pursued," in *Doc Savage* (New York), October 1945.
"Trouble on Parade," in *Doc Savage* (New York), November 1945.
"The Screaming Man," in *Doc Savage* (New York), December 1945.
"Measure for a Coffin," in *Doc Savage* (New York), January 1946.
"Se-Pah-Poo," in *Doc Savage* (New York), February 1946.
"Terror and the Lonely Widow," in *Doc Savage* (New York), March 1946.
"Five Fathoms Dead," in *Doc Savage* (New York), April 1946.
"Death Is a Round Black Spot," in *Doc Savage* (New York), May 1946.
"Colors for Murder," in *Doc Savage* (New York), June 1946.
"The Exploding Lake," in *Doc Savage* (New York), September 1946.
"The Devil Is Jones," in *Doc Savage* (New York), November 1946.
"Danger Lies East," in *Doc Savage* (New York), March 1947.
"No Light to Die By," in *Doc Savage* (New York), May 1947.
"The Monkey Suit," in *Doc Savage* (New York), July 1947.
"Let's Kill Ames," in *Doc Savage* (New York), September 1947.
"Once Over Lightly," in *Doc Savage* (New York), November 1947.
"I Died Yesterday," in *Doc Savage* (New York), January 1948.
"The Pure Evil," in *Doc Savage* (New York), March 1948.
"Terror Wears No Shoes," in *Doc Savage* (New York), May 1948.
"The Angry Canary," in *Doc Savage* (New York), July 1948.
"The Swooning Lady," in *Doc Savage* (New York), September 1948.
"The Green Master," in *Doc Savage* (New York), Winter 1949.

"Return from Cormoral," in *Doc Savage* (New York), Spring 1949.
"Up from Earth's Center," in *Doc Savage* (New York), Summer 1949.

Uncollected Short Stories

"Pirate Cay," in *Top-Notch* (New York), 1 September 1929.
"Death Zone," in *Top-Notch* (New York), 1 April 1930.
"Buccaneers of the Midnight Sun," in *Top-Notch* (New York), 1 May 1930.
"The Thirteen Million Dollar Robbery," in *The Popular Magazine* (New York), 1 May 1930.
"The Devil's Derelict," in *Action Stories* (New York), December 1930.
"Wildcat," in *Scotland Yard* (New York), March 1931.
"One Day to Live," in *Scotland Yard* (New York), April 1931.
"Teeth of Revenge," "Out China Way," in *Scotland Yard* (New York), May 1931.
"One Billion Gold," in *Scotland Yard* (New York), June 1931.
"Diamond Death," in *Scotland Yard* (New York), August 1931.
"The Sinister Ray," in *Detective-Dragnet* (Springfield, Massachusetts), March 1932.
"Terror, Inc.," in *Detective-Dragnet* (Springfield, Massachusetts), May 1932.
"The Devil's Cargo," in *Detective-Dragnet* (Springfield, Massachusetts), July 1932.
"The Invisible Horde," in *Detective-Dragnet* (Springfield, Massachusetts), September 1932.
"The Mummy Murders," in *Detective-Dragnet* (Springfield, Massachusetts), December 1932.
"The Whistling Death," in *Ten Detective Aces* (Springfield, Massachusetts), March 1933.
"The Hang String," in *The Shadow* (New York), 1 March 1933.
"The Cavern of Heads," in *Ten Detective Aces* (Springfield, Massachusetts), April 1933.
"The Stamp Murders," in *The Shadow* (New York), 1 April 1933.
"Murder Street," in *Ten Detective Aces* (Springfield, Massachusetts), June 1933.
"The Death Blast," in *Ten Detective Aces* (Springfield, Massachusetts), July 1933.
"The Skeleton's Clutch," in *Ten Detective Aces* (Springfield, Massachusetts), August 1933.
"The Diving Dead," in *Ten Detective Aces* (Springfield, Massachusetts), September 1933.
"The Tank of Terror," in *Ten Detective Aces* (Springfield, Massachusetts), October 1933.
"The Flaming Mask," in *Ten Detective Aces* (Springfield, Massachusetts), December 1933.
"Hell in Boxes," in *All-Detective* (New York), February 1934.
"White-Hot Corpses," in *All-Detective* (New York), March 1934.
"Murder by Circles," in *All-Detective* (New York), May 1934.
"The Finger," in *All-Detective* (New York), December, 1934.
"Talking Toad," in *Crime Busters* (New York), November 1937.
"Death in Boxes," in *Crime Busters* (New York), December 1937.
"Genius Jones," in *Argosy* (New York), 28 November; 4, 11, 18, 25 December 1937; 1 January 1938.
"Funny Faces," in *Crime Busters* (New York), January 1938.
"The Scared Swamp," in *Crime Busters* (New York), February 1938.
"Windjam," in *Crime Busters* (New York), March 1938.
"The Little Mud Men," in *Crime Busters* (New York), April 1938.
"The Hairless Wonders," in *Crime Busters* (New York), May 1938.
"Run, Actor, Run," in *Crime Busters* (New York), June 1938.
"A Man and a Mess," in *Crime Busters* (New York), July 1938.
"The Wild Indians," in *Crime Busters* (New York), August 1938.
"Ring Around a Rosey," in *Crime Busters* (New York), August 1938.
"The Dancing Dog," in *Crime Busters* (New York), September 1938.
"The Itching Men," in *Crime Busters* (New York), October 1938.
"The Queer Bees," in *Crime Busters* (New York), November 1938.

"The Devils Smelled Nice," in *Crime Busters* (New York), December 1938.
"The Foolish Whales," in *Crime Busters* (New York), January 1939.
"Six White Horses," in *Crime Busters* (New York), February 1939.
"The Poet's Bones," in *Crime Busters* (New York), March 1939.
"The Mysterious Jugs," in *Crime Busters* (New York), April 1939.
"The Horse's Egg," in *Crime Busters* (New York), July 1939.
"The Remarkable Zeke," in *Crime Busters* (New York), August 1939.
"The Frightened Yachtsmen," in *Crime Busters* (New York), September 1939.
"The Green Birds," in *Mystery* (New York), December 1939.
"Death Wore Skis," in *The Star Weekly* (Toronto), 25 October 1941.
"Sail," in *Hard-Boiled Omnibus: Early Stories from Black Mask*, edited by Joseph T. Shaw.   New York, Simon and Schuster, 1946.
"Smith Is Dead," in *Shadow Mystery* (New York), February 1947.
"V Marks the Spot," in *Ellery Queen's Mystery Magazine* (New York), November 1952.
"Angelfish," in *The Hardboiled Dicks*, edited by Ron Goulart. Los Angeles, Sherbourne Press, 1965; London, Boardman, 1967.

OTHER PUBLICATIONS

Play

Screenplay: *Bowery Buckaroos* (as Tim Ryan), with Edmond Seward, 1947.

Bibliography: "The Secret Kenneth Robesons" and "The *Duende* Doc Savage Index" by Will Murray, in *Duende 2* (North Quincy, Massachusetts), 1977.

                                        *   *   *

The contributors to the American pulp magazines were not concerned, by and large, with craft but with production. Except in the rare instance of a *Black Mask*, their editors did not pay well enough to insure quality and, as Raymond Chandler has pointed out elsewhere, they actively discouraged it. As a result, these writers either became word-production drudges or considered the pulps as a training ground for better fields. Despite their talent, many pulp authors were too long writing for these markets ever fully to escape them.

Lester Dent, who enjoys a curious dual reputation in the mystery field, falls into this latter category. Dent is best known for the nearly two-hundred Doc Savage pulp adventure novels which he wrote under the pseudonym Kenneth Robeson and for his unusual detectives – Click Rush, the Gadget Man; Lee Nace, the Blond Adder; and Foster Fade, the Crime Spectacularist – all of the Craig Kennedy type.

At the same time, Dent is considered to be one of the major exponents of the *Black Mask* school of detective fiction, despite the fact that he contributed only two stories, "Sail" and "Angelfish," to the magazine. While these are fine examples of that school's craftsmanship, they are grounded in the same themes which characterize his *Doc Savage* work. His protagonist, Oscar Sail, is a physically unusual investigator who exists apart from society and whose principal techniques involve violence and deception. The plots are largely treasure hunts in which the characters move at cross-purposes and no one is to be trusted.

Dent's later mystery novels are both extensions of his *Black Mask* work and reactions against the kind of fiction he had previously written, and they represent the by-products of the more sophisticated writing he was applying to *Doc Savage*. These are novels of intrigue and psychological interaction in which realistic characters and emotions dominate. Violence and mystery are subordinated to conflict and tension between individuals and their ambitions.

Dent is partial to protagonists who are larger than life. In his non-pulp work their greatness is bounded by their maturity and moral rectitude as measured against a real world, and not by their *physical* prowess. They are capable men who are drawn into conflict because their lives, friends, or positions in society are imperiled. Chance Malloy (*Dead at the Take-Off*) resorts to unsavory tactics only because his airline company has become the victim of such tactics. Mitchell Loneman (*Lady in Peril*) is a lobbyist for a food co-operative whose need to identify a killer stems from his desire to protect his wife and exonerate his employer. Women are often the focus of the conflict, the catalysts who themselves are transmuted (*Lady to Kill*).

Murder is incidental to Dent's plots and his formula treasure hunt is replaced by the hidden secret which murder conceals. The dead man and his killer are less crucial than the buried complexities of human failings and ambitions which threaten the characters in *Lady So Silent*. While the kidnapped child may be the focus of *Lady Afraid*, the deeper motives of the kidnapper are decidedly more significant. In *Cry at Dusk*, Johnny Marks's search for his uncle's killer is less important than his struggle against an evil which threatens to absorb him spiritually.

In spite of their skill and craft, Dent's novels are marred by a self-concious stiffness indicative of a writer not fully at ease with his material and one who, in attempting to purge the stylistics of the pulp magazines from his prose, goes too far because their formula has become inextricable with his own style.

—Will Murray

DENTINGER, Stephen. See **HOCH, Edward D.**

---

de PRE, Jean-Anne. See **AVALLONE, Michael.**

DERLETH, August (William). Also wrote as Stephen Grendon; Tally Mason. American. Born in Sauk City, Wisconsin, 24 February 1909. Educated at the University of Wisconsin, Madison, B.A. 1930. Married Sandra Winters in 1953 (divorced, 1959); two children. Editor, Fawcett Publications, Minneapolis, 1930–31; Editor, *The Midwesterner*, Madison, 1931; Lecturer in American Regional Literature, University of Wisconsin, 1940–43. Owner and Co-Founder, with Donald Wandrei, Arkham House Publishers (including the imprints Mycroft and Moran, and Stanton and Lee), Sauk City, 1939–71. Literary Editor and Columnist for the Madison *Capital Times*, 1941–71; Editor, *The Arkham Sampler*, Sauk City, 1948–49, and *Hawk and Whippoorwill*, Sauk City, 1960–63; Editor, *The Arkham Collector*, Sauk City, 1967–71. Recipient: Guggenheim Fellowship, 1938; Midland Authors Golden Anniversary Award for Poetry, 1965. *Died 4 July 1971.*

CRIME PUBLICATIONS

Novels (series characters: Judge Ephraim Peck; Solar Pons)

Murder Stalks the Wakely Family (Peck).   New York, Loring and Mussey, 1934; as
   Death Strikes the Wakely Family, London, Newnes, 1937.
The Man on All Fours (Peck).   New York, Loring and Mussey, 1934; London, Newnes,
   1936.
Three Who Died (Peck).   New York, Loring and Mussey, 1935.
Sign of Fear (Peck).   New York, Loring and Mussey, 1935; London, Newnes, 1936.
Sentence Deferred (Peck).   New York, Scribner, and London, Heinemann, 1939.
The Narracong Riddle (Peck).   New York, Scribner, 1940.
The Seven Who Waited (Peck).   New York, Scribner, 1943; London, Muller, 1945.
Mischief in the Lane (Peck).   New York, Scribner, 1944; London, Muller, 1948.
No Future for Luana (Peck).   New York, Scribner, 1945; London, Muller, 1948.
The Lurker at the Threshold, with H. P. Lovecraft.   Sauk City, Wisconsin, Arkham
   House, 1945.
Death by Design.   New York, Arcadia House, 1953.
Fell Purpose (Peck).   New York, Arcadia House, 1953.
The Trail of Cthulhu.   Sauk City, Wisconsin, Arkham House, 1962.
The Adventure of the Orient Express (Pons).   Sauk City, Wisconsin, Mycroft and
   Moran, 1965.
Mr. Fairlie's Final Journey (Pons).   Sauk City, Wisconsin, Mycroft and Moran, 1968.
The Adventure of the Unique Dickensians (Pons).   Sauk City, Wisconsin, Mycroft and
   Moran, 1968.

Short Stories

Someone in the Dark.   Sauk City, Wisconsin, Arkham House, 1941.
Something Near.   Sauk City, Wisconsin, Arkham House, 1945.
In Re: Sherlock Holmes — The Adventure of Solar Pons.   Sauk City, Wisconsin, Mycroft
   and Moran, 1945; as *The Adventures of Solar Pons*, London, Robson, 1975.
Not Long for This World.   Sauk City, Wisconsin, Arkham House, 1948.
The Memoirs of Solar Pons.   Sauk City, Wisconsin, Mycroft and Moran, 1951.
Three Problems for Solar Pons.   Sauk City, Wisconsin, Mycroft and Moran, 1952.
The Survivor and Others, with H. P. Lovecraft.   Sauk City, Wisconsin, Arkham House,
   1957.
The Return of Solar Pons.   Sauk City, Wisconsin, Mycroft and Moran, 1958.
The Mask of Cthulhu.   Sauk City, Wisconsin, Arkham House, 1958.
The Reminiscences of Solar Pons.   Sauk City, Wisconsin, Mycroft and Moran, 1961.
Lonesome Places.   Sauk City, Wisconsin, Arkham House, 1962.
Mr. George and Other Odd Persons (as Stephen Grendon).   Sauk City, Wisconsin,
   Arkham House, 1963.
The Casebook of Solar Pons.   Sauk City, Wisconsin, Mycroft and Moran, 1965.
Praed Street Papers.   New York, Candlelight Press, 1965.
Colonel Markesan and Less Pleasant People, with Mark Schorer.   Sauk City,
   Wisconsin, Arkham House, 1966.
A Praed Street Dossier.   Sauk City, Wisconsin, Mycroft and Moran, 1968.
The Shadow Out of Time and Other Tales of Horror, with H. P. Lovecraft.   London,
   Gollancz, 1968.
The Chronicles of Solar Pons.   Sauk City, Wisconsin, Mycroft and Moran, 1972;
   London, Robson, 1975.
The Watchers Out of Time, with H. P. Lovecraft.   Sauk City, Wisconsin, Arkham
   House, 1974.
Harrigan's File.   Sauk City, Wisconsin, Arkham House, 1975.

Dwellers in Darkness.   Sauk City, Wisconsin, Arkham House, 1976.

OTHER PUBLICATIONS

Novels

 Still Is the Summer Night.   New York, Scribner, 1937.
 Wind over Wisconsin.   New York, Scribner, 1938.
 Restless Is the River.   New York, Scribner, 1939.
 Bright Journey.   Sauk City, Wisconsin, Arkham House, 1940.
 Evening in Spring.   New York, Scribner, 1941.
 Sweet Genevieve.   New York, Scribner, 1942.
 Shadow of Night.   New York, Scribner, 1943.
 The Shield of the Valiant.   New York, Scribner, 1945.
 The House on the Mound.   New York, Duell, 1958.
 The Hills Stand Watch.   New York, Duell, 1960.
 The Shadow in the Glass.   New York, Duell, 1963.
 The Prince Goes West.   Des Moines, Iowa, Meredith Press, 1968.
 The Wind Leans West.   New York, Candlelight Press, 1969.

Short Stories

 Place of Hawks.   New York, Loring and Mussey, 1935.
 Country Growths.   Sauk City, Wisconsin, Arkham House, 1940.
 Sac Prairie People.   Sauk City, Wisconsin, Stanton and Lee, 1948.
 Wisconsin in Their Bones.   New York, Duell, 1961.
 The House of Moonlight.   Iowa City, Prairie Press, 1963.

Verse

 Hawk on the Wind.   Philadelphia, Ritten House, 1938.
 Man Track Here.   Philadelphia, Ritten House, 1939.
 Here on a Darkling Plain.   Philadelphia, Ritten House, 1940.
 Wind in the Elms.   Philadelphia, Ritten House, 1941.
 Rind of Earth.   Prairie City, Illinois, Decker Press, 1942.
 Selected Poems.   Prairie City, Illinois, Decker Press, 1944.
 And You, Thoreau!   New York, New Directions, 1944.
 The Edge of Night.   Prairie City, Illinois, Decker Press, 1945.
 Psyche.   Iowa City, Prairie Press, 1953.
 Country Poems.   Iowa City, Prairie Press, 1956.
 West of Morning.   Francestown, New Hampshire, Golden Quill Press, 1960.
 This Wound.   Iowa City, Prairie Press, 1962.
 Country Places.   Iowa City, Prairie Press, 1965.
 The Only Place We Live.   Iowa City, Prairie Press, 1966.
 By Owl Light.   Iowa City, Prairie Press, 1967.
 Collected Poems, 1937–1967.   New York, Candlelight Press, 1967.
 Caitlin.   Sauk City, Wisconsin, Arkham House, 1969.
 The Landscape of the Heart.   Iowa City, Prairie Press, 1970.
 Listening to the Wind.   New York, Candlelight Press, 1971.
 Last Light.   New York, Candlelight Press, 1971.

Recordings: *Psyche: A Sequence of Love Lyrics*, Cuca, 1960; *Sugar Bush by Moonlight and Other Poems of Man and Nature*, Cuca, 1962; *Caitlin*, Cuca, 1971.

Other

Consider Your Verdict: Ten Coroner's Cases for You to Solve (as Tally Mason).   New York, Stacpole, 1937.
Any Day Now.   Chicago, Normandie House, 1938.
Atmosphere of Houses.   Muscatine, Iowa, Prairie Press, 1939.
Still Small Voice: The Biography of Zona Gale.   New York, Appleton Century, 1940.
Village Year: A Sac Prairie Journal.   New York, Coward McCann, 1941.
The Wisconsin: River of a Thousand Isles.   New York, Farrar and Rinehart, 1942.
H.P.L.: A Memoir.   New York, Ben Abramson, 1945.
Oliver, The Wayward Owl (juvenile), with Clare Victor Dwiggins. Sauk City, Wisconsin, Stanton and Lee, 1945.
Writing Fiction.   Boston, The Writer, 1946.
The Habitant of Dusk: A Garland for Cassandra.   Boston, Walden Press, 1946.
Village Daybook: A Sac Prairie Journal.   Chicago, Pelligrini and Cudahy, 1947.
A Boy's Way: Poems (juvenile).   Sauk City, Wisconsin, Stanton and Lee, 1948.
Sauk County: A Centennial History.   Baraboo, Wisconsin, Sauk County Centennial Committee, 1948.
It's a Boy's World: Poems (juvenile).   Sauk City, Wisconsin, Stanton and Lee, 1948.
The Milwaukee Road: Its First 100 Years.   New York, Creative Age Press, 1948.
The Captive Island (juvenile).   New York, Aladdin, 1952.
The Country of the Hawk (juvenile).   New York, Aladdin, 1952.
Empire of Fur: Trading in the Lake Superior Region (juvenile).   New York, Aladdin, 1953.
The Land of Grey Gold: Lead Mining in Wisconsin (juvenile).   New York, Aladdin, 1954.
Father Marquette and the Great Rivers (juvenile).   New York, Farrar Straus, 1955; London, Burns Oates, 1956.
Land of Sky Blue Water (juvenile).   New York, Aladdin, 1955.
St. Ignatius and the Company of Jesus (juvenile).   New York, Farrar Straus, and London, Burns Oates, 1956.
Columbus and the New World (juvenile).   New York, Farrar Straus, and London, Burns Oates, 1957.
The Moon Tenders (juvenile).   New York, Duell, 1958.
The Mill Creek Irregulars (juvenile).   New York, Duell, 1959.
Wilbur, The Trusting Whippoorwill (juvenile).   Sauk City, Wisconsin, Stanton and Lee, 1959.
Arkham House: The First Twenty Years – 1939–1959.   Sauk City, Wisconsin, Arkham House, 1959.
Some Notes on H. P. Lovecraft.   Sauk City, Wisconsin, Arkham House, 1959.
The Pinkertons Ride Again (juvenile).   New York, Duell, 1960.
The Ghost of Black Hawk Island (juvenile).   New York, Duell, 1961.
Walden West (autobiography).   New York, Duell, 1961.
Sweet Land of Michigan (juvenile).   New York, Duell, 1962.
Concord Rebel: A Life of Henry D. Thoreau.   Philadelphia, Chilton, 1962.
Countryman's Journal.   New York, Duell, 1963.
The Tent Show Summer (juvenile).   New York, Duell, 1963.
The Irregulars Strike Again (juvenile).   New York, Duell, 1964.
The Forest Orphans (juvenile).   New York, Ernest, 1964.
Wisconsin Country: A Sac Prairie Journal.   New York, Candlelight Press, 1965.
The House by the River (juvenile).   New York, Duell, 1965.
The Watcher on the Heights (juvenile).   New York, Duell, 1966.
A House above Cuzco.   New York, Candlelight Press, 1967.
Wisconsin: Consultant: Russell Mosely.   New York, Coward McCann, 1967.
Vincennes: Portal to the West.   Englewood Cliffs, New Jersey, Prentice Hall, 1968.

Walden Pond: Homage to Thoreau. Iowa City, Prairie Press, 1968.
Wisconsin Murders. Sauk City, Wisconsin, Arkham House, 1968.
The Three Straw Men (juvenile). New York, Candlelight Press, 1970.
Return to Walden West. New York, Candlelight Press, 1970.
Love Letters to Caitlin. New York, Candlelight Press, 1971.

Editor, with R. E. Larsson, *Poetry Out of Wisconsin.* New York, Harrison, 1937.
Editor, with Donald Wandrei, *The Outsider and Others*, by H. P. Lovecraft. Sauk City, Wisconsin, Arkham House, 1939.
Editor, *Sleep No More: Twenty Masterpieces of Horror for the Connoisseur.* New York, Farrar and Rinehart, 1944.
Editor, *Who Knocks? Twenty Masterpieces of the Spectral for the Connoisseur.* New York, Rinehart, 1946.
Editor, *The Night Side: Masterpieces of the Strange and Terrible.* New York, Rinehart, 1947.
Editor, *The Sleeping and the Dead.* Chicago, Pelligrini and Cudahy, 1947.
Editor, *Dark of the Moon: Poems of Fantasy and the Macabre.* Sauk City, Wisconsin, Arkham House, 1947.
Editor, *Strange Ports of Call.* New York, Pelligrini and Cudahy, 1948.
Editor, *The Other Side of the Moon.* New York, Pelligrini and Cudahy, 1949; London, Grayson, 1956.
Editor, *Something about Cats and Other Pieces*, by H. P. Lovecraft. Sauk City, Wisconsin, Arkham House, 1949.
Editor, *Beyond Time and Space.* New York, Pelligrini and Cudahy, 1950.
Editor. *Far Boundaries: 20 Science-Fiction Stories.* New York, Pelligrini and Cudahy, 1951.
Editor, *The Outer Reaches: Favorite Science-Fiction Tales Chosen by Their Authors.* New York, Pelligrini and Cudahy, 1951.
Editor, *Beachheads in Space.* New York, Pelligrini and Cudahy, 1952; London, Weidenfeld and Nicolson, 1954.
Editor, *Rendezvous in a Landscape.* New York, Fine Editions Press, 1952.
Editor, *Night's Yawning Peal: A Ghostly Company.* Sauk City, Wisconsin, Arkham House, 1952.
Editor, *Worlds of Tomorrow: Science Fiction with a Difference.* New York, Pelligrini and Cudahy, 1953; London, Weidenfeld and Nicolson, 1954.
Editor, *Time to Come: Science-Fiction Stories of Tomorrow.* New York, Farrar Straus, 1954.
Editor, *Portals of Tomorrow: The Best Tales of Science Fiction and Other Fantasy.* New York, Rinehart, 1954; London, Cassell, 1956.
Editor, *The Shuttered Room and Other Pieces by H. P. Lovecraft and Divers Hands.* Sauk City, Wisconsin, Arkham House, 1959.
Editor, *Fire and Sleet and Candlelight.* Sauk City, Wisconsin, Arkham House, 1961.
Editor, *Dark Mind, Dark Heart.* Sauk City, Wisconsin, Arkham House, 1962.
Editor, *When Evil Wakes: A New Anthology of the Macabre.* London, Souvenir Press, 1963.
Editor, *The Dunwich Horror and Others: The Best Supernatural Stories by H. P. Lovecraft.* Sauk City, Wisconsin, Arkham House, 1963.
Editor, *Over the Edge.* Sauk City, Wisconsin, Arkham House, 1964; London, Gollancz, 1967.
Editor, *At the Mountains of Madness and Other Novels*, by H. P. Lovecraft. Sauk City, Wisconsin, Arkham House, 1964.
Editor, *Dagon and Other Macabre Tales*, by H. P. Lovecraft. Sauk City, Wisconsin, Arkham House, 1965.
Editor, with Donald Wandrei, *Selected Letters, 1925–1929*, by H. P. Lovecraft. Sauk City, Wisconsin, Arkham House, 1968.

Editor, *New Poetry Out of Wisconsin*. Sauk City, Wisconsin, Arkham House, 1969.
Editor, *Tales of the Cthulhu Mythos*, by H. P. Lovecraft and others. Sauk City, Wisconsin, Arkham House, 1969.
Editor, *The Horror in the Museum and Other Revisions*, by H. P. Lovecraft. Sauk City, Wisconsin, Arkham House, 1970.
Editor, with Donald Wandrei, *Selected Letters, 1929–1931*, by H. P. Lovecraft. Sauk City, Wisconsin, Arkham House, 1971.

Bibliography: *100 Books by August Derleth*, Sauk City. Wisconsin, Arkham House, 1962.

Manuscript Collection: State Historical Society of Wisconsin Library, Madison.

*   *   *

On the dust jacket of his second novel, *The Man on All Fours*, August Derleth's publishers described him as "this astonishing young author." Throughout his life, Derleth continued to astonish publishers and readers alike with the volume and diversity of his writing. Among his more than 150 books are contemporary novels, historical novels, biographies, personal journals, compilations of nature observations, poetry, mystery fiction, true crime essays, macabre tales, science fiction, regional history, pastiches, and children's books. As an editor and publisher, he was an active champion of weird and macabre fiction. He was almost single-handedly responsible for the preservation and popularization of the works by H. P. Lovecraft, and his Arkham House publishing firm issued the first books of such authors as Ray Bradbury, Fritz Leiber, and A. E. Van Vogt.

Derleth sold his first fiction, a weird story called "Bat's Belfry," when he was 15 years old. Weird fiction continued to occupy a large part of his attention. His stories in this vein were eventually collected in eleven volumes, from *Someone in the Dark* to the posthumously issued *Dwellers in Darkness*. The least effective of these stories are the ones written in imitation of Lovecraft; but others such as "Mrs. Manifold" and "The Lonesome Place," have a definite power to chill.

Derleth's contributions to mystery fiction began when he was 19 years old. He had read and re-read the Sherlock Holmes stories, and was finally impelled to write to Sir Arthur Conan Doyle to ask if there would ever be any more of them. Receiving a non-committal reply, he determined to fill the void himself. In the autumn of 1928 he wrote "The Adventure of the Black Narcissus," the first of some 70 stories featuring Solar Pons of 7B Praed Street, London, and his companion Dr. Lyndon Parker. In the words of Vincent Starrett, "Solar Pons is – as it were – an ectoplasmic emanation of his great prototype, and his adventures are pure pastiche.... He is ... a clever impersonator, with a twinkle in his eye, which tells us that he is not Sherlock Holmes, and knows that *we* know it, but that he hopes we will like him anyway for what he symbolizes." This hope was certainly fulfilled. The appearance of that first story in the February 1929 issue of *The Dragnet* magazine led eventually to the publication of six volumes of stories (a pastiche not only of the Holmes character but of the Holmesian canon as a whole), one novel, and a volume of miscellaneous commentary. It also inspired the formation of an organization called The Praed Street Irregulars, in imitation of The Baker Street Irregulars, and the publication of a journal, *The Pontine Dossier*. As might be expected in so extended a series, the Pons stories are variable in quality and in their effectiveness as echoes of the original model; but the average is high, as exemplified in such stories as "The Adventure of the Norcross Riddle," "The Adventure of the Remarkable Worm," and "The Adventure of the Unique Dickensians."

Derleth's most ambitious literary creation was his Sac Prairie Saga, a multivolume project designed to portray life in the fictional Sac Prairie (based on the Sauk City-Prairie du Sac region of Wisconsin where Derleth was born and spent most of his life) from the early nineteenth century up to the present day. In addition to its more serious uses in the furtherance of his Saga, Derleth employed Sac Prairie as the setting for his series of ten detective novels featuring Judge Ephraim Peabody Peck. The Judge, a shrewd, elderly small-town lawyer, was introduced in *Murder Stalks the Wakely Family*, followed in the same year by *The Man on All Fours*. The latter book is typical of the early Judge Peck novels; it has all the trappings of the formal puzzle novel, with floor plans, an annotated list of characters, a plot centering around multiple murders in an isolated country house, and the John Dickson Carr-like touch of a mysterious barefooted figure who prowls the house and environs on all fours. Later in the series, Derleth changed from third person to first person narration, telling the stories through the medium of a smart-talking young assistant to the Judge. The change of tone jarred against the leisurely pace and rural setting. And a narrator who could accost a female witness (in *Mischief in the Lane*) with the words "Come on, Mouse Eyes, out with it!" wore out his welcome rapidly. By the author's own admission, the Judge Peck books were written in ten days each. The consequent lack of polish and the internal inconsistencies are regrettable, but the generally clever plots and the well-realized small-town setting and incidental characters make the books worth sampling. Sac Prairie is also the setting for a series of "junior mysteries" featuring a pair of teen-age detectives, Steve Grendon and Sim Jones.

Not part of a series, though similar in its characters and small-town setting to the Judge Peck books, was *Consider Your Verdict: Ten Coroner's Cases for You to Solve*. This was a collection of ten short murder mysteries, each in the form of the transcript of a coroner's inquest. In each case, a particular mis-statement by one of the witnesses pointed the way to the solution of the crime, and the reader was invited to identify the crucial bit of testimony. In fact, the book's Introduction suggested that it could be used as the basis of a parlor game. The solutions were given in a sealed section at the end of the book.

—R. E. Briney

DESMOND, Hugh. British.

<small>CRIME PUBLICATIONS</small>

Novels (series character: Alan Fraser)

The Slasher. London, Wright and Brown, 1939.
Highways of Death. London, Wright and Brown, 1940.
The Misty Pathway. London, Wright and Brown, 1940.
The Secret of the Moat. London, Wright and Brown, 1940.
Murder Run Wild. London, Hale, 1941.
Intent to Kill. London, Hale, 1942.
The Secret Voice. London, Wright and Brown, 1942.
Death Strikes at Dawn. London, Wright and Brown, 1943.
The Mystery Killer. London, Wright and Brown, 1943.
The Fuehrer Dies. London, Wright and Brown, 1944.
Terror Walks by Night. London, Wright and Brown, 1944.
The Hand of Vengeance (Fraser). London, Wright and Brown, 1945.
They Lived with Death. London, Wright and Brown, 1945.
A Desperate Gamble. London, Wright and Brown, 1946.
His Reverence the Rogue. London, Wright and Brown, 1946.
Lady in Peril. London, Wright and Brown, 1946.
The Viper's Sting (Fraser). London, Wright and Brown, 1946.

Bluebeard's Wife.   London, Wright and Brown, 1947.
Overture to Death.   London, Wright and Brown, 1947.
The Strangler.   London, Wright and Brown, 1947.
Blood Cries for Vengeance.   London, Wright and Brown, 1948.
Death in the Shingle.   London, Wright and Brown, 1948.
Death Walks in Scarlet.   London, Wright and Brown, 1948.
A Wife in the Dark.   London, Wright and Brown, 1948.
Gallows' Fruit.   London, Wright and Brown, 1949.
A Clear Case of Murder.   London, Wright and Brown, 1950.
The Edge of Horror.   London, Wright and Brown, 1950.
Calling Alan Fraser.   London, Wright and Brown, 1951.
Fear Walks the Island.   London, Wright and Brown, 1951.
The Jacaranda Murders.   London, Wright and Brown, 1951.
Murder Is Justified.   London, Wright and Brown, 1951.
Dark Deeds.   London, Wright and Brown, 1952.
A Pact with the Devil (Fraser).   London, Wright and Brown, 1952.
Reign of Terror.   London, Wright and Brown, 1952.
Deliver Us from Evil (Fraser).   London, Wright and Brown, 1953.
Night of Terror.   London, Wright and Brown, 1953.
The Night of the Crime.   London, Wright and Brown, 1953.
Breath of Suspicion.   London, Wright and Brown, 1954.
The Death Parade (Fraser).   London, Wright and Brown, 1954.
Murderer's Bride.   London, Wright and Brown, 1954.
Destination — Death (Fraser).   London, Wright and Brown, 1955.
The Hangman Waits.   London, Wright and Brown, 1955.
A Scream in the Night.   London, Wright and Brown, 1955.
Death Let Loose.   London, Wright and Brown, 1956.
She Met Murder (Fraser).   London, Wright and Brown, 1956.
Stella Shall Die.   London, Wright and Brown, 1956.
Appointment at Eight (Fraser).   London, Wright and Brown, 1957.
Lady, Where Are You? (Fraser).   London, Wright and Brown, 1957.
No Reprieve.   London, Wright and Brown, 1957.
Look Upon the Prisoner.   London, Wright and Brown, 1958.
Poison Pen (Fraser).   London, Wright and Brown, 1958.
Doorway to Death (Fraser).   London, Wright and Brown, 1959.
Suicide Fleet.   London, Wright and Brown, 1959.
A Strong Dose of Poison.   London, Wright and Brown, 1959.
The Wicked Shall Flourish.   London, Wright and Brown, 1959.
Death at My Elbow.   London, Wright and Brown, 1960.
In Fear of the Night (Fraser).   London, Wright and Brown, 1960.
Turn Back from Death.   London, Wright and Brown, 1960.
The Case of the Blue Orchid (Fraser).   London, Wright and Brown, 1961.
Fanfare for Murder (Fraser).   London, Wright and Brown, 1961.
Stranger than Fiction.   London, Wright and Brown, 1961.
Murder at Midnight.   London, Wright and Brown, 1962.
Put Out the Light.   London, Wright and Brown, 1962.
Stay of Execution (Fraser).   London, Wright and Brown, 1962.
Bodies in a Cupboard (Fraser).   London, Wright and Brown, 1963.
The Silent Witness (Fraser).   London, Wright and Brown, 1963.
A Slight Case of Murder (Fraser).   London, Wright and Brown, 1963.
Condemned (Fraser).   London, Wright and Brown, 1964.
Hostage to Death (Fraser).   London, Wright and Brown, 1964.
Someday I'll Kill You (Fraser).   London, Wright and Brown, 1964.
The Dark Shadow (Fraser).   London, Wright and Brown, 1965.
Murder Strikes at Dawn (Fraser).   London, Wright and Brown, 1965.

Not Guilty, My Lord (Fraser). London, Wright and Brown, 1965.
The Lady Has Claws (Fraser). London, Wright and Brown, 1966.
Murder on the Moor (Fraser). London, Wright and Brown, 1967.
Escape. London, Wright and Brown, 1968.
Mask of Terror (Fraser). London, Wright and Brown, 1968.
We Walk with Death (Fraser). London, Wright and Brown, 1968.

*   *   *

The writer of some 80 novels between 1940 and 1968, Hugh Desmond fits very easily into the category of a good library author. This is possibly an under-valuation of his work, for certainly two of his novels, *A Scream in the Night* and *Death Let Loose*, are much sought after by collectors.

About 30 of his books feature Alan Fraser, once an "Ace" detective who now runs a Private Enquiry Bureau. Although he may be the catalyst that unites the elements which solve the crime, he is not necessarily the main character. All too often he seems to solve the mystery without fully explaining to the reader the deduction processes used. Many of his books are based upon true life crimes. *Stay of Execution*, for instance, is based upon a famous Scottish murder trial of the 1880's, and *Murder at Midnight* is based upon two horrific murders in Britain in 1946.

His detective work is well leavened with romance, and many of his books fall into the category of romantic adventure novels rather than that of true thrillers. He also wrote several spy thrillers, and though his background knowledge of Europe is useful, these books are rather ordinary. Two books which are good examples of his work are *Murder Is Justified* and *The Strangler.*

—Donald C. Ireland

DEVINE, D(avid) M(cDonald). Also writes as Dominic Devine. British. Born in Greenock, Renfrew, 16 August 1920. Educated at Greenock Academy, 1925–38; University of Glasgow, M.A. 1945; University of London, LL.B. 1953. Married Betsy Findlay Munro in 1946; one daughter. Assistant Secretary, North West Engineering Employers Association, Glasgow, 1944–46. Assistant Secretary, 1946–61, Deputy Secretary, 1961–72, and since 1972, Secretary and Registrar, University of St. Andrews, Fife. Agent: John Johnson, Clerkenwell House, 45–47 Clerkenwell Green, London EC1R 0HT, England. Address: Melvaig, 6 Lade Braes, St. Andrews, Fife KY16 9ET, Scotland.

CRIME PUBLICATIONS

Novels

My Brother's Killer. London, Collins, 1961; New York, Dodd Mead, 1962.
Doctors Also Die. London, Collins, 1962; New York, Dodd Mead, 1963.
The Royston Affair. London, Collins, 1964; New York, Dodd Mead, 1965.
His Own Appointed Day. London, Collins, 1965; New York, Walker, 1966.
Devil at Your Elbow. London, Collins, 1966; New York, Walker, 1967.
The Fifth Cord. London, Collins, and New York, Walker, 1967.

Novels as Dominic Devine

The Sleeping Tiger.   London, Collins, and New York, Walker, 1968.
Death Is My Bridegroom.   London, Collins, and New York, Walker, 1969.
Illegal Tender.   London, Collins, and New York, Walker, 1970.
Dead Trouble.   London, Collins, and New York, Doubleday, 1971.
Three Green Bottles.   London, Collins, and New York, Doubleday, 1972.
Sunk Without Trace.   London, Collins, and New York, St. Martin's Press, 1978.

OTHER PUBLICATIONS

Play

Radio Play (as David Munro): *Degree of Guilt,* 1965.

D. M. Devine comments:
Writer of detective stories which attempt to combine good characterisation with the traditional puzzle element.

*   *   *

People who like mysteries that slide down effortlessly, providing comfort and familiarity during an evening's relaxation, will welcome D. M. Devine's novels and return to them frequently. Indeed, a fringe benefit from reading these books is that you *can* return to them frequently and reread them as though you had never seen them before. Devine's writing style is brisk, businesslike, concise, and undistinguished. Every time he introduces a character, he gives the character's family history at tedious length, much of it unimportant to the story. This is not to say that Devine's novels are inept, or even dull while you are reading. They're not. They're journeyman productions written to a familiar formula.

Devine's characters from book to book are cut from the same patterns: fathers are irresponsible; mothers, self-centered; daughters, neurotic if single; heroines, vapid; heroes, average but tenacious; and murderers, mad. The setting is usually a medium-sized Scottish town, and the men are professionals such as lawyers, physicians, school teachers, college professors, government administrators, and a few tradesmen and realtors. The women are usually from the traditional mold: housewives, students, school teachers, clerks, secretaries, and shop assistants. Occasionally Devine produces a grotesque – a character so extreme in his or her madness as to be temporarily shocking.

With his long background in university administration, Devine's novels set on a university campus should be the most believable, ringing with authenticity. Unfortunately, they're not. Both faculty and students in *Death Is My Bridegroom* are artificial, though the characters in *His Own Appointed Day*, set mainly in a school, and *Illegal Tender*, about urban administrators, are human, with understandable problems and reactions.

In *Illegal Tender*, the one book in which he attempted to create a woman as a person and elevated her professionally above a motherly high school teacher, he creates a woman lawyer, bright, competent, and strong, but then has her react in a soppy, traditionally "feminine" way to expiate her "crime" of having an affair with a ruthless, selfish, ambitious administrator who is promoted at her expense. Devine's characters usually remain truer to type than this, but he is much better devising men and wives, mothers, daughters, and secretaries than he is women-as-people.

Devine's contribution to the genre is to give readers many evenings of relaxation and pleasure.

—Pearl G. Aldrich

DEWEY, Thomas B(lanchard). Also writes as Tom Brandt; Cord Wainer. American. Born in Elkhart, Indiana, 6 March 1915. Educated at Kansas State Teachers College, B.S. 1936; University of Iowa, Iowa City, 1937–38; University of California, Los Angeles, Ph.D. 1973. Married Maxine Morley Sorensen (second wife) in 1951; 3) Doris L. Smith in 1972; two children by first marriage. Clerical worker, Harding Market Company, Chicago, 1936–37; Editor, Storycraft Inc., correspondence school, Hollywood, 1938–42; Administrative and Editorial Assistant, Department of State, Washington, D.C., 1942–45; worked in advertising, Los Angeles, 1945–52. Self-employed writer, 1952–71, and since 1977. Professor, Arizona State University, Tempe, 1971–77. Address: c/o Simon and Schuster, 1230 Avenue of the Americas, New York, New York 10020, U.S.A.

CRIME PUBLICATIONS

Novels (series characters: Singer Batts; Mac; Pete Schofield)

Hue and Cry (Batts). New York, Jefferson House, 1944; as *The Murder of Marion Mason*, London, Dakers, 1951; as *Room for Murder*, New York, New American Library, 1950.
As Good as Dead (Batts). New York, Jefferson House, 1946; London, Dakers, 1952.
Draw the Curtain Close (Batts). New York, Jefferson House, 1947; London, Dakers, 1951; as *Dame in Danger*, New York, New American Library, 1958.
Mourning After (Batts). New York, Mill, 1950; London, Dakers, 1953.
Handle with Fear (Batts). New York, Mill, 1951; London, Dakers, 1955.
Every Bet's a Sure Thing. New York, Simon and Schuster, and London, Dakers, 1953.
Mountain Girl (as Cord Wainer). New York, Fawcett, 1953.
Kiss Me Hard (as Tom Brandt). New York, Popular Library, 1954.
Run, Brother, Run! (as Tom Brandt). New York, Popular Library, 1954; London, Consul, 1961.
Prey for Me (Mac). New York, Simon and Schuster, and London, Boardman, 1954; as *The Case of the Murdered Model*, New York, Avon, 1955.
The Mean Streets (Mac). New York, Simon and Schuster, and London, Boardman, 1955.
The Brave, Bad Girls (Mac). New York, Simon and Schuster, 1956; London, Boardman, 1957.
My Love Is Violent. New York, Popular Library, 1956; London, Consul, 1961.
And Where She Stops (Schofield). New York, Popular Library, 1957; as *I.O.U. Murder*, London, Boardman, 1958.
You've Got Him Cold (Mac). New York, Simon and Schuster, 1958; London, Boardman, 1959.
The Case of the Chased and the Unchaste (Mac). New York, Random House, 1959; London, Boardman, 1960.
Go to Sleep Jeannie (Schofield). New York, Popular Library, 1959; London, Boardman, 1960.
The Girl Who Wasn't There (Schofield). New York, Simon and Schuster, and London, Boardman, 1960; as *The Girl Who Never Was*, New York, Mayflower, 1962.
Too Hot for Hawaii (Schofield). New York, Popular Library, 1960; London, Boardman, 1963.
The Golden Hooligan (Schofield). New York, Dell, 1961; as *Mexican Slayride*, London, Boardman, 1961.
Hunter at Large. New York, Simon and Schuster, 1961; London, Boardman, 1962.
Go, Honeylou (Schofield). New York, Dell, and London, Boardman, 1962.
How Hard to Kill (Mac). New York, Simon and Schuster, 1962; London, Boardman, 1963.

The Girl with the Sweet Plump Knees (Schofield). New York, Dell, and London,
   Boardman, 1963.
A Sad Song Singing (Mac). New York, Simon and Schuster, 1963; London,
   Boardman, 1964.
Don't Cry for Long (Mac). New York, Simon and Schuster, 1964; London, Boardman,
   1965.
The Girl in the Punchbowl (Schofield). New York, Dell, 1964; London, Boardman,
   1965.
Only on Tuesdays (Schofield). New York, Dell, and London, Boardman, 1964.
Nude in Nevada (Schofield). New York, Dell, 1965; London, Boardman, 1966.
Can a Mermaid Kill? New York, Tower, 1965.
Portrait of a Dead Heiress (Mac). New York, Simon and Schuster, 1965; London,
   Boardman, 1966.
Deadline (Mac). New York, Simon and Schuster, 1966; London, Boardman, 1967.
A Season for Violence. New York, Fawcett, 1966.
Death and Taxes (Mac). New York, Putnam, 1967; London, Hale, 1969.
The King-Killers (Mac). New York, Putnam, 1968; as *Death Turns Right*, London,
   Hale, 1969.
The Love-Death Thing (Mac). New York, Simon and Schuster, 1969.
The Taurus Trip (Mac). New York, Simon and Schuster, 1970.

Uncollected Short Stories

"Thorn in the Flesh," in *Cosmopolitan* (New York), January 1953.
"Never Send to Know," in *Ellery Queen's Mystery Magazine* (New York), January 1965.
"The Prevalence of Monsters," in *Ellery Queen's Mystery Magazine* (New York), April
   1965.
"The Big Job," in *Best Detective Stories of the Year*, edited by Anthony Boucher.   New
   York, Dutton, and London, Boardman, 1966.
"Lucien's Nose," in *Ellery Queen's Mystery Magazine* (New York), July 1966.

OTHER PUBLICATIONS

Other

What Women Want to Know, with Harold M. Imerman. New York, Crown, 1958;
   London, Hammond, 1960.

Editor, *Sleuths and Consequences*. New York, Simon and Schuster, 1966.

Manuscript Collection: Mugar Memorial Library, Boston University.

*   *   *

Thomas B. Dewey has been a prolific writer of crime fiction. He has written about a
troubled but honest District Attorney (in *A Season for Violence*), an avenging cop whose wife
was killed by mistake (*Hunger at Large*), and a Los Angeles private eye named Pete Schofield,
whose chief distinction among such characters is that he is married. But Dewey has written
most often and most successfully about a Chicago private detective whose first and last names
are a carefully guarded secret; he is known always only as "Mac."
   Mac is very much in the Sam Spade/Philip Marlowe/Lew Archer tradition of private eyes.
He is always, if sometimes reluctantly, on the side of the underdog; he tells his own stories,
and he seems to have no life apart from his activities as a detective; he lives alone, and his
existence is spartan; he is tough, but partial to children; gorgeous women throw themselves,
or are thrown, into his path, but with rare exceptions he is chaste; and he always solves his

cases before the police do. Mac differs from the other famous detectives of his type in a few ways. For one thing, until late in his career, when he goes to Los Angeles, he operates in Chicago, and while the novels in which he appears are not burdened with local color, he is more likely to encounter gangsters of the old school than are the West Coast operatives. For another, Mac almost always works with a veteran police officer named Donovan, who had trained him as a cop and who either helps him with cases or pushes him into situations which policemen are supposed to avoid; Donovan is always a somewhat shadowy, if bulky, figure, since we see him only in his official role. The other variant on the standard pattern is that Mac is ageless; he was still the same robust man in early middle age in 1970 that he had been in his earliest appearances in the early 1950's.

In his typical cases, Mac is approached by an old friend, or a friend of a friend, who has run afoul of the law. There is almost always, early in the novel, a murder; Mac's client is either a suspect, in which case Mac's job is to solve the puzzle and get the client off the hook, or the client becomes the victim, and Mac's job is to ease his conscience by tracking down the killer. At least twice during the course of the action, Mac will find himself isolated with one or two tough opponents, usually gangsters and usually armed when he is not; although he occasionally loses the first fight, Mac usually wins, and he always wins the last fight. Apart from these encounters, Dewey's novels are not particularly gruesome or violent, and there are seldom spectacular death scenes. The cases with which Mac becomes involved often include kidnapped children or adolescent girls; the latter are in some way lost and helpless, but they never prove to be criminals and they almost always find reasonably happy endings. None of the kidnapped children is ever seriously harmed. In the end, Mac sorts out the clues and, with the help of Donovan, apprehends the culprits.

Dewey's novels combine the classic private-eye pattern with the equally classic mystery pattern. During the course of his narration, Mac provides the reader with the clues which, if put together properly, will point to the criminal. Properly, such clues are not highlighted when they are first presented, but they do afford the reader the opportunity to solve the mystery before it is explained to him. Fortunately, the solution is seldom given away early in the novel.

Dewey's novels are interesting and successful, and Mac is a memorable private eye, even if he too often exemplifies the "White Knight" referred to in several of these stories. Dewey is less tough than Hammett, and his stories lack both the pungent local color which makes Chandler's and Ross Macdonald's novels distinctive and the moral ambiguity which tantalizes Philip Marlowe and Lew Archer. But Dewey belongs at the head of the second rank of the hard-boiled writers.

—John M. Muste

DEY, Frederic (Merrill) Van Rensselaer. Wrote as Nicholas and Nick Carter; Marmaduke Dey; Frederic Ormond; Varick Vanardy. American. Born in Watkins Glen, New York, 10 February 1865. Educated at Havana Academy, New York; Columbia University Law School, New York. Married 1) Annie Shepard in 1885; two children; 2) Hattie Hamblin Cahoon in 1898. Practiced law. Engaged by the publishers Street and Smith in 1891 to continue Carter stories originated by John R. Coryell. *Died 26 April 1922.*

Crime Publications

Novels as Nicholas Carter (series character: Nicholas Carter in all books except *Harrison Keith, Sleuth* and *Two Plus Two*)

The Piano Box Mystery. New York, Street and Smith, 1892.
A Stolen Identity. New York, Street and Smith, 1892.
The Great Enigma. New York, Street and Smith, 1892.
The Gamblers' Syndicate. New York, Street and Smith, 1892.
Caught in the Toils. New York, Street and Smith, 1894.
Playing a Bold Game. New York, Street and Smith, 1894.
Tracked Across the Atlantic. New York, Street and Smith, 1894.
The Mysterious Mail Robbery. New York, Street and Smith, 1895.
A Chance Discovery. New York, Street and Smith, 1895.
A Deposit Vault Puzzle. New York, Street and Smith, 1895.
Evidence by Telephone. New York, Street and Smith, 1895.
Among the Counterfeiters. New York, Street and Smith, 1898.
Two Plus Two. New York, Street and Smith, 1899.
A Dead Man's Grip. New York, Street and Smith, 1899.
Nick Carter and the Green Goods Men. New York, Street and Smith, 1899.
The Great Money Order Swindle. New York, Street and Smith, 1899.
Sealed Orders. New York, Street and Smith, 1899.
Gideon Drexel's Millions. New York, Street and Smith, 1899.
The Missing Cotton King. New York, Street and Smith, 1901.
The Price of a Secret. New York, Street and Smith, 1901.
Weaving the Web. New York, Street and Smith, 1902.
Run to Earth. New York, Street and Smith, 1902.
The Toss of a Coin. New York, Street and Smith, 1902.
A Double-Headed Game. New York, Street and Smith, 1902.
Behind a Mask. New York, Street and Smith, 1902.
The Vial of Death. New York, Street and Smith, 1902.
Man Against Man. New York, Street and Smith, 1902.
The Chain of Evidence. New York, Street and Smith, 1902.
Driven from Cover. New York, Street and Smith, 1904.
The Criminal Link. New York, Street and Smith, 1904.
Against Desperate Odds. New York, Street and Smith, 1904.
The Mystic Diagram. New York, Street and Smith, 1904.
An Ingenious Strategem. New York, Street and Smith, 1904.
In the Gloom of the Night. New York, Street and Smith, 1904.
A Scientific Terror. New York, Street and Smith, 1904.
Trapped in His Own Net. New York, Street and Smith, 1905.
The Price of Treachery. New York, Street and Smith, 1905.
Down and Out. New York, Street and Smith, 1905.
With Links of Steel. New York, Street and Smith, 1905.
Under a Black Veil. New York, Street and Smith, 1905.
Nick Carter's Double Catch. New York, Street and Smith, 1905.
The Boulevard Mutes. New York, Street and Smith, 1905.
The Four-Fingered Glove. New York, Street and Smith, 1905.
A Victim of Deceit. New York, Street and Smith, 1905.
The Bloodstone Terror. New York, Street and Smith, 1905.
A Triple Identity. New York, Street and Smith, 1905.
The Terrible Thirteen. New York, Street and Smith, 1905.
The Crime of the Camera. New York, Street and Smith, 1906.
The Sign of the Dagger. New York, Street and Smith, 1906.
Marked for Death. New York, Street and Smith, 1906.

The "Limited" Hold-Up. New York, Street and Smith, 1906.
Through the Cellar Wall. New York, Street and Smith, 1906.
Under the Tiger's Claws. New York, Street and Smith, 1906.
Behind a Throne. New York, Street and Smith, 1906.
The Lure of Gold. New York, Street and Smith, 1906.
From a Prison Cell. New York, Street and Smith, 1906.
Dr. Quartz, Magician. New York, Street and Smith, 1906.
The Broadway Cross. New York, Street and Smith, 1906.
The Death Circle. New York, Street and Smith, 1906.
Doctor Quartz's Quick Move. New York, Street and Smith, 1906.
Trapped by a Woman. New York, Street and Smith, 1906.
Nick Carter's Masterpiece. New York, Street and Smith, 1906.
A Plot Within a Plot. New York, Street and Smith, 1906.
In the Lap of Danger. New York, Street and Smith, 1906.
Captain Sparkle, Pirate. New York, Street and Smith, 1906.
Out of Death's Shadow. New York, Street and Smith, 1906.
Nick Carter's Fall. New York, Street and Smith, 1906.
A Voice from the Past. New York, Street and Smith, 1906.
Accident or Murder? New York, Street and Smith, 1906.
The Unaccountable Crook. New York, Street and Smith, 1906.
The Man Who Was Cursed. New York, Street and Smith, 1906.
Baffled, But Not Beaten. New York, Street and Smith, 1906.
A Case Without a Clue. New York, Street and Smith, 1906.
Done in the Dark. New York, Street and Smith, 1907.
The Demon's Eye. New York, Street and Smith, 1907.
The Man Without a Conscience. New York, Street and Smith, 1907.
The Finger of Suspicion. New York, Street and Smith, 1907.
The Chain of Clues. New York, Street and Smith, 1907.
The Dynamite Trap. New York, Street and Smith, 1907.
Harrison Smith, Sleuth. New York, Street and Smith, 1907.
The Woman of Evil. New York, Street and Smith, 1907.
A Legacy of Hate. New York, Street and Smith, 1907.
The Brotherhood of Death. New York, Street and Smith, 1907.
The Demons of the Night. New York, Street and Smith, 1907.
A Cry for Help. New York, Street and Smith, 1907.
A Bargain in Crime. New York, Street and Smith, 1907.
The Man of Iron. New York, Street and Smith, 1907.
The Woman of Steel. New York, Street and Smith, 1907.
A Fight for a Throne. New York, Street and Smith, 1907.
An Amazing Scoundrel. New York, Street and Smith, 1907.
The Silent Guardian. New York, Street and Smith, 1907.
The Bank Draft Puzzle. New York, Street and Smith, 1907.
The Human Fiend. New York, Street and Smith, 1907.
A Chase in the Dark. New York, Street and Smith, 1907.
Nick Carter's Close Call. New York, Street and Smith, 1907.
A Game of Plots. New York, Street and Smith, 1907.
The Red League. New York, Street and Smith, 1907.
Nick Carter's Chinese Puzzle. New York, Street and Smith, 1907.
Without a Clue. New York, Street and Smith, 1908.
In Death's Grip. New York, Street and Smith, 1908.
A Ring of Rascals. New York, Street and Smith, 1908.
A Hunter of Men. New York, Street and Smith, 1908.
Into Nick Carter's Web. New York, Street and Smith, 1908.
Hand to Hand. New York, Street and Smith, 1908.
From Peril to Peril. New York, Street and Smith, 1908.

The Girl in the Case. New York, Street and Smith, 1908.
When the Trap Was Sprung. New York, Street and Smith, 1908.
Nick Carter's Promise. New York, Street and Smith, 1908.
Tangled Threads. New York, Street and Smith, 1908.
The Crime and the Motive. New York, Street and Smith, 1908.
A Game Well Played. New York, Street and Smith, 1908.
The Silent Partner. New York, Street and Smith, 1908.
A Trap of Tangled Wire. New York, Street and Smith, 1908.
Nick Carter's Cipher. New York, Street and Smith, 1908.
Nabob and Knave. New York, Street and Smith, 1908.
A Fight with a Fiend. New York, Street and Smith, 1908.
The Hand That Won. New York, Street and Smith, 1908.
A Strike for Freedom. New York, Street and Smith, 1908.
An Artful Schemer. New York, Street and Smith, 1908.
A Blindfold Mystery. New York, Street and Smith, 1909.
A Plaything of Fate. New York, Street and Smith, 1909.
A Master of Deviltry. New York, Street and Smith, 1909.
When the Wicked Prosper. New York, Street and Smith, 1909.
A Woman at Bay. New York, Street and Smith, 1909.
The Temple of Vice. New York, Street and Smith, 1909.
A Plot Uncovered. New York, Street and Smith, 1909.
Death at the Feast. New York, Street and Smith, 1909.
A Double Plot. New York, Street and Smith, 1909.
In Search of Himself. New York, Street and Smith, 1909.
Saved by a Ruse. New York, Street and Smith, 1909.
Nick Carter's Swim to Victory. New York, Street and Smith, 1909.
A Man to Be Feared. New York, Street and Smith, 1909.
The Last Move in the Game. New York, Street and Smith, 1910.
A Carnival of Crime. New York, Street and Smith, 1910.
Nick Carter's Auto Trail. New York, Street and Smith, 1910.
Nick Carter's Wildest Chase. New York, Street and Smith, 1910.
A Nation's Peril. New York, Street and Smith, 1910.
The Rajah's Ruby. New York, Street and Smith, 1910.
The Trail of a Human Tiger. New York, Street and Smith, 1910.
The Disappearing Princess. New York, Street and Smith, 1910.
The Lost Chittendens. New York, Street and Smith, 1910.
The Crystal Mystery. New York, Street and Smith, 1910.
The King's Prisoner. New York, Street and Smith, 1910.
Talika, The Geisha Girl. New York, Street and Smith, 1910.
The Doom of the Reds. New York, Street and Smith, 1910.
The Lady of Shadows. New York, Street and Smith, 1911.
The Mysterious Castle. New York, Street and Smith, 1911.
The Senator's Plot. New York, Street and Smith, 1911.
Pauline – A Mystery. New York, Street and Smith, 1911.
The Confidence King. New York, Street and Smith, 1911.
A Chase for Millions. New York, Street and Smith, 1911.
Shown on the Screen. New York, Street and Smith, 1911.
The Streaked Peril. New York, Street and Smith, 1911.
The Room of Mirrors. New York, Street and Smith, 1911.
A Plot for an Empire. New York, Street and Smith, 1911.
A Call on the Phone. New York, Street and Smith, 1911.
A Fatal Bargain. New York, Street and Smith, 1911.
A Masterly Trick. New York, Street and Smith, 1911.
For a Madman's Millions. New York, Street and Smith, 1911.
An Elusive Knave. New York, Street and Smith, 1911.

The Four Hoodoo Charms. New York, Street and Smith, 1911.
At Face Value. New York, Street and Smith, 1911.
A Vain Sacrifice. New York, Street and Smith, 1912.
The Vanishing Heiress. New York, Street and Smith, 1912.
The Red Triangle. New York, Street and Smith, 1912.
Nick Carter's Subtle Foe. New York, Street and Smith, 1912.
Nick Carter's Chance Clue. New York, Street and Smith, 1912.
Nick Carter's Last Card. New York, Street and Smith, 1912.
The Taxicab Riddle. New York, Street and Smith, 1912.
A Stolen Name. New York, Street and Smith, 1912.
A Play for Millions. New York, Street and Smith, 1912.
A Woman of Mystery. New York, Street and Smith, 1912.
The Dead Accomplice. New York, Street and Smith, 1912.
Nick Carter's Counterplot. New York, Street and Smith, 1912.
The Seven Schemers. New York, Street and Smith, 1912.
The Mysterious Cavern. New York, Street and Smith, 1912.
The Crime of a Century. New York, Street and Smith, 1912.
A Double Identity. New York, Street and Smith, 1913.
The Babbington Case. New York, Street and Smith, 1913.
The Midnight Message. New York, Street and Smith, 1913.
The Turn of a Card. New York, Street and Smith, 1913.
The Unfinished Letter. New York, Street and Smith, 1913.
Nick Carter and the Red Button. New York, Street and Smith, 1913.
Nick Carter's New Assistant. New York, Street and Smith, 1913.
The Kregoff Necklace. New York, Street and Smith, 1913.
The Sign of the Coin. New York, Street and Smith, 1913.
A Riddle of Identities. New York, Street and Smith, 1913.
Pointers to Crime. New York, Street and Smith, 1913.
The Spider's Parlor. New York, Street and Smith, 1913.

Novels as Marmaduke Dey

Captain Ironnerve, The Counterfeiter Chief. New York, Beadle, 1881.
Muertalma; or, The Poisoned Pen. New York, Street and Smith, 1888.
The Magic Word. New York, Street and Smith, 1899.
A Gentleman of Quality (as Frederic Dey). Boston, Page, 1909.
The Three Keys (as Frederic Ormond). New York, Watt, 1909.

Novels as Varick Vanardy (series characters: Crewe; Bingham Harvard)

Alias the Night Wind (Harvard). New York, Dillingham, 1913.
The Return of the Night Wind (Harvard). Chicago, Donohue, 1914.
The Night Wind's Promise (Harvard). Chicago, Donohue, 1914.
The Girl by the Roadside. New York, Macaulay, 1917; London, Jarrolds, 1923.
The Two-Faced Man (Crewe). New York, Macaulay, 1918; London, Jarrolds, 1920.
Something Doing (Crewe). New York, Macaulay, 1919.
The Lady of the Night Wind (Harvard). New York, Macaulay, 1919; London, Skeffington, 1926.
Up Against It. New York, Macaulay, 1920.

Short Stories as Nicholas Carter

The Queen of Knaves and Other Stories. New York, Street and Smith, 1901.

Uncollected Short Stories as Nicholas Carter

"A Witch City Mystery," in *Black Cat* (New York), August 1901.
"Nick Carter, Detective" and "Nick Carter's Mysterious Clue," in *Nick Carter, Detective*, edited by Robert Clurman. New York, Macmillan, 1963.

Uncollected Short Stories as Varick Vanardy

"By Process of Elimination," in *Detective Story* (New York), 24 June 1919.
"The Holbrook Forgery," in *Detective Story* (New York), 22 July 1919.
"A Message in Punctures," in *Detective Story* (New York), 12 August 1919.

OTHER PUBLICATIONS

Other

The Magic Story. New York, Success, 1903.

Plays as F. Marmaduke Dey

Passions. Clyde, Ohio, Ames, 1881.
H.M.S. Plum. Clyde, Ohio, Ames, 1883.

*   *   *

Had Frederic Van Rensselaer Dey not written so many of the Nick Carter stories it is doubtful that his name would be remembered today. Because of the quantity of those stories and their anonymous publication it has always been difficult to determine just how many he wrote. In an article for the *American Magazine* in 1920 he claimed to have written 1,000 of them and the statistic stuck. In fact, he wrote only 437, but it probably seemed like 1,000. (He perpetuated another error by referring to Nick Carter's father as Seth Carter when it should have been Sim Carter.)

Dey wrote his first Nick Carter in 1891, following John Russell Coryell's original trilogy of serials, and using most of the same characters. Nick's wife, Ethel, was never as prominent a figure in Dey's stories as she had been in Coryell's. That editorial supervision was lax is evident from the fact that one of the writers who substituted for Dey in 1901 renamed her Edith and no one seemed to notice. When Dey returned to writing the stories full time in 1904 he wrote her out of the series by having her murdered by gangsters. Dey added characters like Chick; Patsy Murphy Garvan; Ten-Ichi, the son of the Mikado; Ida Jones; Mrs. Peters, the housekeeper; Joseph, the butler; and Patsy's wife, Adelina de Mendoza. Over the years Nick met such villains as the arch-villain Dr. Quartz, Morris, Livingston, and Maitland Carruthers, Dan Derrington, the Unaccountable Crook, Bare-faced Jimmy, the gentleman burglar, and the Criminal Trust.

Dey's original Nick Carter stories appeared in the *Nick Carter Library*, 1891–93; the *Nick Carter Weekly*, 1904–12; *Nick Carter Stories*, 1912–13; and in Street & Smith's *New York Weekly* in two series, 1892–94 and 1901–06. He published a number of stories under his own name and several pseudonyms. In an 1899 serial for *Argosy* he gave his hero the same name as one Nick Carter sometimes assumed while disguised, Felix Parsons. He stopped writing about Nick Carter shortly before the end of the dime-novel era and published several mystery adventure novels under the name Varick Vanardy. In one of them, *The Two-Faced Man*, he anticipated some of the underworld style of the hard-boiled detective story. His Lady Kate of the Police (in the "Night Wind" stories) was a strong-willed heroine in an age of shrinking violets.

But it is for Nick Carter that Dey will be remembered. He took the format created by Old Sleuth and Old Cap. Collier and developed it into an American institution. Equally at home writing of the Bowery and waterfront, baronial mansion and exotic palace, he varied from stories of routine crime investigation to tales of lost civilizations and mechanized smugglers. Dey was never a great writer, but he was a good story-teller. His imagination often overcame any flaws in his style. His early work contained loose threads, unresolved problems, and disorganized sequences. By 1904 he had mastered his craft enough to make his reader want to finish the story. His work was filled with recognizable traits, including a fondness for the name Madge and names beginning with the letter Q. He liked bizarre settings for murders – particularly piano boxes and box cars fitted out as living quarters with the victim displayed in a natural tableau. During the Golden Age of Nick Carter he kept a generation of readers, young and old, eager to know what would happen next.

—J. Randolph Cox

DEY, Marmaduke. See **DEY, Frederic Van Rensselaer.**

DICKINSON, Peter. British. Born in Livingstone, Zambia, 16 December 1927. Educated at Eton College, Buckinghamshire, 1941–46; King's College, Cambridge (exhibitioner), B.A. 1951. Served in the British Army (national service), 1946–48. Married Mary Rose Barnard in 1953; two daughters and two sons. Assistant Editor, and reviewer, *Punch* magazine, London, 1952–69. Recipient: Crime Writers Association Golden Dagger, for novel, 1968, 1969; *Guardian* Award, for children's book, 1977; *Boston Globe-Horn Book* Award, for children's book, 1977. Agent: A. P. Watt and Son, 26–28 Bedford Row, London WC1R 4HL. Address: 33 Queensdale Road, London W11 4SB, England.

CRIME PUBLICATIONS

Novels (series character: Superintendent James Pibble)

> *Skin Deep* (Pibble). London, Hodder and Stoughton, 1968; as *The Glass-Sided Ants' Nest*, New York, Harper, 1968.
> *A Pride of Heroes* (Pibble). London, Hodder and Stoughton, 1969; as *The Old English Peep Show*, New York, Harper, 1969.
> *The Seals* (Pibble). London, Hodder and Stoughton, 1970; as *The Sinful Stones*, New York, Harper, 1970.
> *Sleep and His Brother* (Pibble). London, Hodder and Stoughton, and New York, Harper, 1971.
> *The Lizard in the Cup* (Pibble). London, Hodder and Stoughton, and New York, Harper, 1972.
> *The Green Gene*. London, Hodder and Stoughton, and New York, Pantheon Books, 1973.
> *The Poison Oracle*. London, Hodder and Stoughton, and New York, Pantheon Books, 1974.

The Lively Dead. London, Hodder and Stoughton, and New York, Pantheon Books, 1975.

King and Joker. London, Hodder and Stoughton, and New York, Pantheon Books, 1976.

Walking Dead. London, Hodder and Stoughton, 1977.

One Foot in the Grave (Pibble). London, Hodder and Stoughton, 1979.

OTHER PUBLICATIONS

Plays

Television Plays (for children): *Mandog* series, 1972; *The Changes*, 1975.

Other (fiction for children)

The Weathermonger. London, Gollancz, 1968; Boston, Little Brown, 1969.

Heartsease. London, Gollancz, and Boston, Little Brown, 1969.

The Devil's Children. London, Gollancz, and Boston, Little Brown, 1970.

Emma Tupper's Diary. London, Gollancz, and Boston, Little Brown, 1971.

The Dancing Bear. London, Gollancz, and Boston, Little Brown, 1972.

The Iron Lion. Boston, Little Brown, 1972; London, Allen and Unwin, 1973.

The Gift. London, Gollancz, 1973; Boston, Little Brown, 1974.

Chance, Luck, and Destiny (miscellany). London, Gollancz, 1975; Boston, Little Brown, 1976.

The Blue Hawk. London, Gollancz, and Boston, Little Brown, 1976.

Annerton Pit. London, Gollancz, and Boston, Little Brown, 1977.

"The Lure of the Reichenbach," in *Murder Ink: The Mystery Reader's Companion,* edited by Dilys Winn. New York, Workman, 1977.

Hepzibah. Twickenham, Middlesex, Eel Pie, 1978.

Tulku. London, Gollancz, and New York, Dutton, 1979.

The Flight of the Dragons. London, Pierrot, and New York, Harper, 1979.

Editor, *Presto! Humorous Bits and Pieces.* London, Hutchinson, 1975.

Peter Dickinson comments:

I think of myself as writing science fiction with the science left out. I try to write proper detective stories, with clues and solutions, which work in the traditional way, but also provide something extra by way of ideas, without getting portentous about it. My books have tended to deal with closed worlds – partly because that makes it easier to limit suspects, etc. (as in the good old snowbound country house), and partly because it allows me to give the inhabitants of that closed world a definite twist which sets them apart from the outside world. For my main characters I like competent women and weedy men, and tend to overpopulate my books with grotesques.

*   *   *

Peter Dickinson's gift to the crime story has been an imagination of unusual, even extraordinary, forcefulness. Think of the settings of some of his books – a New Guinea tribe living in the attics of a row of London houses, a home for children suffering from a disease which turns them into sleepily charming psychic sensitives, an oil-sheik's desert palace where a chimpanzee is learning grammar. Each is put before you with such conviction, such vividness, such coherence that you come easily to believe that they actually exist. In his power to create new worlds Dickinson is the Tolkien of the crime novel.

Yet all the while he has, with perhaps only one exception, kept rigidly to the form of the old classical detective story. There is a mystery; there is a detective to solve it (for the first five books a Scotland Yard superintendent, James Pibble, reticent, quiet, very British, almost wanting to be done down, yet an excellent policeman, a getter of his man); there is a murderer; you suspect various people; there are clues to be picked up and seen for what they are, if you are clever enough. Dickinson plainly likes the sub-genre. Not for nothing did he review crime for years in *Punch*.

But each of his classical mysteries has had its extraordinary "background," its small odd world. Note the smallness. If Pibble was typically British, so is Dickinson, an eccentric, a romantic, and nowhere more so than in his careful keeping within limits. Yet inside this smallness he has become increasingly willing to go for the big themes, all the more successfully for not trying to echo them in grandeur of gesture.

He has, however, tackled subjects as formidably large as all that can be summed up in the word ecology. *The Poison Oracle* is the book that deals with this, besides of course having a complex murder plot with a splendidly gripping climactic scene where the murderer, in true classical fashion (Poirot might have gathered the suspects in a library), is exposed. Here the poison of the title is both murder means and the process that is blotting out in the name of civilisation whole tracts of nature. But Dickinson takes no simple stance in this. Like a true novelist, he lets all the implications of the situation percolate through his imagination to emerge as differing characters, as contradictory aspects of the book's setting. And the characters, each vividly presented, range from a sympathetic and entirely likely intelligent chimpanzee, through a formidably clever psycho-linguist who is yet delightfully naive and an Oxford-veneered sheik, truly charming, believably ruthless, to half a dozen differing tribesmen living in almost inaccessible marshland, credibly primitive and at the same time recognisably fellow humans to us twentieth-century sophisticated readers.

The fantastic background, the sheik's desert castle built upside-down (for the good practical reason that this provides maximum shade), the marshes, even the hobby zoo inside the castle − all not only create a literally marvellous atmosphere but also contribute to the theme that underlies the whole, even down to the smallest detail like a croaking sound which is heard at a moment of suspense in the marshes, "the ugly noise of the lungfish adapting themselves over thousands of generations to live in an altered world."

There is perhaps a substratum common to all Dickinson's lively, suspenseful detection tales − and that is a plea for the instincts as opposed to the intellect. *The Poison Oracle* ends with the balance in favour of the slow processes of nature rather than the corner-cutting, though often beneficial, ways of civilising man. *Walking Dead*, set in a Haiti-like tropical island, explores the relationship between id, mind, and soul, and comes down in favour of those mysterious, almost forgotten powers that humans, in the western world at least, have often done their best to suppress. *The Lively Dead*, set in an ordinary London house that is yet as extraordinary as any of the other settings I have mentioned, makes a plea for us to look askance at empty dreams of a future or at a past that is finished in favour of acknowledging and welcoming the life that is, with "its green blade thrusting through."

Finally it should be said that Dickinson writes extremely well. Not only are those characters wonderfully vivid and his settings such that you remember them for years afterwards, but the actual prose is excellent. Phrases leap out, sending sharp images into the distant reader's mind. Yet occasionally, it must be admitted, words do go to Dickinson's head. He has an immense vocabulary and is himself as intelligent as a table quorum of dons. And sometimes the checks that ought to be put on these qualities flick off. Once he described somebody's nose as "less accipitrine than columbaceous." This is a small blemish, but the phrase does signal a quality in Dickinson's work that will not appeal to everyone. He is formidably intelligent, and he feels no need to conceal this. So for the less learned reader he is perhaps at times heavy-going, even too heavy-going. But reach up to his level, and the rewards are far greater than the mere feeling that you too have been bright today.

—H.R.F. Keating

DICKSON, Carter.   See CARR, John Dickson.

DIMENT, Adam.

CRIME PUBLICATIONS

Novels (series character: Philip McAlpine in all books)

> *The Dolly Dolly Spy.*   London, Joseph, and New York, Dutton, 1967.
> *The Bang Bang Birds.*   London, Joseph, and New York, Dutton, 1968.
> *The Great Spy Race.*   London, Joseph and New York, Dutton, 1968.
> *Think Inc.*   London, Joseph, 1971.

*   *   *

The 1960's witnessed a boom in spy fiction after President Kennedy declared himself a James Bond fan. Adam Diment successfully mixed the trends of the era into the anti-establishment spy. Philip McAlpine, Diment's hero, is no agent of the old school, but a chatty, long-haired, pot-smoking youngster in his twenties, with frilled shirt and white Levis, and a keen expert with the fair – and always willing – sex. He is blackmailed into working for Rupert "The Swine" Quine and his spy department, and uses his considerable expertise in flying, killing, and getting out of jams to keep alive for the good life at the end of the caper.

His patriotism is peripheral – as it probably was for the young, hip, and swinging male audience aimed at. The scene is international, the pace smooth and fast. The first two novels give us McAlpine as a younger, smarter, meaner, and, despite all this, rather more likeable version of Ashenden or Bond. Soon, though, it was all over: the 1960's ended, pink shirts were out, and the hippies gave way to anti-war demonstrators. The last novel shows McAlpine working as an international crook, on the run from Quine, and somewhat desperately trying to adjust to the new times. Evidently, he never quite made it.

—Bo Lundin

DISNEY, Doris Miles.   American.   Born in Glastonbury, Connecticut, 22 December 1907. Educated at schools in Glastonbury. Married George J. Disney in 1936 (died); one daughter. Worked in an insurance office and did publicity for social agencies. *Died 9 March 1976.*

CRIME PUBLICATIONS

Novels (series characters: Jeff DiMarco; David Madden; Jim O'Neill)

A Compound for Death (O'Neill).   New York, Doubleday, 1943.
Murder on a Tangent (O'Neill).   New York, Doubleday, 1945.
Dark Road (DiMarco).   New York, Doubleday, 1946; London, Nimmo, 1947; as *Dead Stop*, New York, Dell, 1956.
Who Rides a Tiger.   New York, Doubleday, 1946; as *Sow the Wind*, London, Nimmo, 1948.
Appointment at Nine (O'Neill).   New York, Doubleday, 1947.
Enduring Old Charms.   New York, Doubleday, 1947; as *Death for My Beloved*, New York, Spivak, 1949.
Testimony by Silence.   New York, Doubleday, 1948.
That Which Is Crooked.   New York, Doubleday, 1948.
Count the Ways.   New York, Doubleday, 1949.
Family Skeleton (DiMarco).   New York, Doubleday, 1949.
Fire at Will (O'Neill).   New York, Doubleday, 1950.
Look Back on Murder.   New York, Doubleday, 1951.
Straw Man (DiMarco).   New York, Doubleday, 1951; London, Foulsham, 1958.
Heavy, Heavy Hangs.   New York, Doubleday, 1952.
Do unto Others.   New York, Doubleday, 1953.
Prescription: Murder.   New York, Doubleday, 1953.
The Last Straw (O'Neill).   New York, Doubleday, 1954; as *Driven to Kill*, London, Foulsham, 1957.
Room for Murder.   New York, Doubleday, 1955; London, Foulsham, 1959.
Trick or Treat (DiMarco).   New York, Doubleday, 1955; as *The Halloween Murder*, London, Foulsham, 1957.
Unappointed Rounds (Madden).   New York, Doubleday, 1956; as *The Post Office Case*, London, Foulsham, 1957.
Method in Madness.   New York, Doubleday, 1957; as *Quiet Violence*, London, Foulsham, 1959; as *Too Innocent to Kill*, New York, Avon, 1957.
My Neighbor's Wife.   New York, Doubleday, 1957; London, Foulsham, 1958.
Black Mail (Madden).   New York, Doubleday, 1958; London, Foulsham, 1960.
Did She Fall or Was She Pushed? (DiMarco).   New York, Doubleday, 1959; London, Hale, 1962.
No Next of Kin.   New York, Doubleday, 1959; London, Foulsham, 1961.
Dark Lady.   New York, Doubleday, 1960; as *Sinister Lady*, London, Hale, 1962.
Mrs. Meeker's Money (Madden).   New York, Doubleday, 1961; London, Hale, 1963.
Find the Woman (DiMarco).   New York, Doubleday, 1962; London, Hale, 1964.
Should Auld Acquaintance.   New York, Doubleday, 1962; London, Hale, 1963.
Here Lies.   New York, Doubleday, 1963; London, Hale, 1964.
The Departure of Mr. Gaudette.   New York, Doubleday, 1964; as *Fateful Departure*, London, Hale, 1965.
The Hospitality of the House.   New York, Doubleday, 1964; as *Unsuspected Evil*, London, Hale, 1965.
Shadow of a Man.   New York, Doubleday, 1965; London, Hale, 1966.
At Some Forgotten Door.   New York, Doubleday, 1966; London, Hale, 1967.
The Magic Grandfather.   New York, Doubleday, 1966; as *Mask of Evil*, London, Hale, 1967.
Night of Clear Choice.   New York, Doubleday, 1967; as *Flame of Evil*, London, Hale, 1968.
Money for the Taking.   New York, Doubleday, and London, Hale, 1968.
Voice from the Grave.   New York, Doubleday, 1968; London, Hale, 1969.

Two Little Children and How They Grew. New York, Doubleday, 1969; as *Fatal Choice*, London, Hale, 1970.

Do Not Fold, Spindle, or Mutilate. New York, Doubleday, 1970; as *Death by Computer*, London, Hale, 1971.

The Chandler Policy (DiMarco). New York, Putnam, 1971; London, Hale, 1973.

Three's a Crowd. New York, Doubleday, 1971; London, Hale, 1972.

The Day Miss Bessie Lewis Disappeared. New York, Doubleday, 1972; London, Hale, 1973.

Only Couples Need Apply. New York, Doubleday, 1973; London, Hale, 1974.

Don't Go into the Woods Today. New York, Doubleday, 1974.

Cry for Help. New York, Doubleday, 1975; London, Hale, 1976.

Uncollected Short Story

"Ghost of a Chance," in *American Magazine* (Springfield, Ohio), October 1954.

Manuscript Collection: Mugar Memorial Library, Boston University.

*   *   *

Investigation into fictional murders usually causes the reader to *care* only on an intellectual level. Because Doris Miles Disney so often wrote of crimes involving the most vulnerable members of society, the old and the very young, she created an emotional nexus between writer and reader that was rare in crime fiction. The wealthy elderly, traditional victims in mysteries, are presented in depth and with considerable sympathy – e.g., Mrs. Carroll, placed in a nursing home by greedy relatives in *Method in Madness*, and the title character of *Mrs. Meeker's Money*, subjected to mail fraud and murder. We care when another titular character vanishes mysteriously on the eve of his retirement in *The Departure of Mr. Gaudette*.

Often the young and the old interact in Disney books, as in *The Magic Grandfather*, and her observations are acute, especially of the devices lonely old people use to gain the attention and affection of children.

The impact of murder on the victim's survivors is another neglected area – even among authors who stress characterization. At her best, Disney did a superb job of presenting this. A young mother dies at the start of *Heavy, Heavy Hangs*, possibly by suicide. Disney carefully integrates in her plot the impact of this death on her young son. Convincing scenes about the necessity of notifying next-of-kin are adroitly used to advance the plot and introduce characters. Another small boy and his mother are central to Disney's best book, *No Next of Kin*, and she successfully creates shock and outrage in the reader.

No one has used New England's suburbs and small towns as often and effectively as Disney. She possessed a special knack for weaving the area's past with its present as in one of her earliest, and best, works, *Who Rides a Tiger*. The reading of an old lady's will in 1945 discloses roots and conflicts in a northern Connecticut town going back to 1879. She depicted (and probably reflected) middle class values and was at her best when her characters, including her murderers, were "nice" people. She conveyed quite believably the stresses that could lead "the people next door" to commit murder.

Though most of her books were not part of any series, she did use three continuing characters. Each had integrity and dedication to the task of crime-solving; none had unusual idiosyncrasies. Almost forgotten is Jim O'Neill, a policeman in a small Connecticut city who appeared in three early books. Slightly better remembered is David Madden who also appeared three times in a series of procedural novels about a Postal Inspector.

The best-known Disney character is insurance investigator Jeff DiMarco; he is also the most believable. In his first appearance, *Dark Road*, he falls in love with a murderess. In *Method in Madness* his sympathies are better directed as he becomes convinced that the old lady in the nursing home is the victim of a murderous scheme. DiMarco ages believably during the series, exhibiting understandable concern as his hair grows gray and his waistline thickens.

Unfortunately, there is often a bewildering change of viewpoint or style in her work. For example, the heroine of *Heavy, Heavy Hangs* is initially depicted as having enough intellectual and emotional resources to discover the solution to her sister's death. But the last quarter of the book takes on elements of a standard Gothic novel, and Disney offers a patchwork solution and gratuitous violence to conclude a very promising book. The switch in *Straw Man* was even more disconcerting as, at mid-point, she changes focus from a DiMarco detective puzzle to an inverted mystery, disclosing the identity of the murderer.

If individual books showed changes that did not seem wise, Disney's entire body of work suffered a disappointing shift in her last decade. She abandoned the "decent" people inadvertently involved in crime and changed her viewpoint. *Money for the Taking* is told from the perspective of Donna Jenner, a young bank teller driven by her love for an amoral man to help him in a bank robbery. Unfortunately, the book contains no virtues like careful plotting or depth of characterization to offset the completely unsympathetic protagonist. *Voice from the Grave, Only Couples Need Apply,* and *Cry for Help* suffer from similar defects.

Though occasionally disappointing, especially at the end of a career that spanned more than three decades, Disney's legacy is an impressive one: a body of work with a strong narrative drive, believable characters, and considerable emotional impact, with seldom a descent into bathos.

—Marvin Lachman

DISNEY, Dorothy Cameron.   American.   Born in the Indian Territory, now Oklahoma, in 1903. Educated at Barnard College, New York, B.A. Married Milton MacKaye. Worked as stenographer, nightclub hostess, copy writer, film extra; Marriage Editor, *Ladies' Home Journal,* New York.

CRIME PUBLICATIONS

Novels

> *Death in the Back Seat.*   New York, Random House, 1936; London, Hale, 1937.
> *The Golden Swan Murder.*   New York, Random House, 1939; London, Hale, 1940.
> *Strawstack.*   New York, Random House, and London, Hale, 1939.
> *The Balcony.*   New York, Random House, 1940; London, Hale, 1941.
> *Thirty Days Hath September,* with George Sessions Perry.   New York, Random House, 1942; London, Hale, 1950.
> *Crimson Friday.*   New York, Random House, 1943; London, Hale, 1945.
> *The Seventeenth Letter.*   New York, Random House, 1945; London, Hale, 1948.
> *Explosion.*   New York, Random House, 1948.
> *The Hangman's Tree.*   New York, Random House, 1949.

OTHER PUBLICATIONS

Other

Guggenheim, with Milton MacKaye. New York, Boni, 1927.
Mary Roberts Rinehart, with Milton MacKaye. New York, Rinehart, 1948.
Can This Marriage Be Saved?, with Paul Popenoe. New York, Macmillan, 1960.

*   *   *

Dorothy Cameron Disney's novels remain quite fresh and readable, not only because they are fast-paced but also because the major characters are fully drawn and believable. As is appropriate for books by the *Ladies' Home Journal* Marriage Editor, most of Disney's works feature a tightly knit group, either a family or a small group bound by work or community ties. The members of the group are forced to realize that one of them is a murderer. In several books, the motive for murder is directly related to a family situation. The murderer kills to protect a family, to protect a marriage, or to get out of a marriage. The protagonists are either young married couples or spinsters with strong family ties. The families are often upper-middle-class and afflicted or strengthened by a strong case of ancestor worship. Inherited family money, dissipated or unfairly distributed, figures in several of the novels.

In spite of such beginnings as "it seems to me now ... I could have prevented the dreadful series of crimes which so hideously involved us all," (*Strawstack*) which sets a tone of horror, the novels are actually realistic. Disney manipulates the episodes so that strategic moments are chilling without being terrifying. In *Strawstack*, Margaret Tilbury allows herself but a "thin scream" upon finding a body in a shower. Immediately she begins to worry about the impression the ugly scene might have upon her approaching niece.

The surprising note for the period, and for the white-collar, upper-middle-class milieu Disney favors, is that the women of the novels, in spite of hats, gloves, dresses, and apparently conventional attitudes, are liberated. Her females are actresses, doctors, successful businesswomen, civil servants – and villains. In fact, the strongest aspect of Disney's novels is her characterization of women. Three distinct types stand out. One type includes strong spinsters, often leading characters and narrators. Although Disney pokes mild fun at their unworldliness and set ways, she draws deft and sympathetic portraits of strong-willed women who move with intelligence, boldness, and fierceness to protect their loved ones. Less prominent but commonly used women characters are the attractive, self-centered, hard-working businesswomen. The third type appears most frequently and in the most varied forms. These are the really wicked women. They are usually young and attractive. If they love, the love is poisonous and all-possessive. Often, they love only themselves. Their strength is in managing to appear something they are not. The author plays fair, planting clues consistently, but these are easy to overlook as the characters steadily build a deceptive facade.

Dorothy Cameron Disney presents interesting characters, lots of action, and cleverly devised plots that will still interest readers who cannot themselves make a nickel phone call or ride in a rumble seat. It would be easy to slight Disney as a writer of "women's stories." She deserves revisiting as a writer of people stories.

—Neysa Chouteau and Martha Alderson

DODGE, David (Francis). American. Born in Berkeley, California, in August 1910. Attended high school in Los Angeles. Served in the United States Naval Reserve, 1941–45. Married Elva Keith in 1936; one child. Bank clerk, ship's fireman, social worker, San Francisco; accountant, 1935–42. Self-employed author. Address: 706 Kingston Road, Princeton, New Jersey, U.S.A.

CRIME PUBLICATIONS

Novels (series characters: Al Colby; John Abraham Lincoln; Whit Whitney)

Death and Taxes (Whitney). New York, Macmillan, 1941; London, Joseph, 1947.
Shear the Black Sheep (Whitney). New York, Macmillan, 1942; London, Joseph, 1949.
Bullets for the Bridegroom (Whitney). New York, Macmillan, 1944; London, Joseph, 1948.
It Ain't Hay (Whitney). New York, Simon and Schuster, 1946; as *A Drug on the Market*, London, Joseph, 1949.
The Long Escape (Colby). New York, Random House, 1948; London, Joseph, 1950.
Plunder of the Sun (Colby). New York, Random House, 1949; London, Joseph, 1950.
The Red Tassel (Colby). New York, Random House, 1950; London, Joseph, 1951.
To Catch a Thief. New York, Random House, 1952; London, Joseph, 1953.
The Lights of Skaro. New York, Random House, and London, Joseph, 1954.
Angel's Ransom. New York, Random House, 1956; London, Joseph, 1957.
Loo Loo's Legacy. London, Joseph, 1960; Boston, Little Brown, 1961.
Carambola. Boston, Little Brown, 1961; as *High Corniche*, London, Joseph, 1961.
Hooligan (Lincoln). New York, Macmillan, 1969; as *Hatchetman*, London, Joseph, 1970.
Troubleshooter (Lincoln). New York, Macmillan, 1971; London, Joseph, 1972.

Uncollected Short Story

"Murder Is No Accident," in *Ellery Queen's Mystery Magazine* (New York), September 1953.

OTHER PUBLICATIONS

Other

How Green Was My Father: A Sort of Travel Diary. New York, Simon and Schuster, 1947; London, Home and Van Thal, 1950.
How Lost Was My Weekend: A Greenhorn in Guatemala. New York, Random House, 1948; London, Home and Van Thal, 1949.
The Crazy Glasspecker; or, High Life in the Andes. New York, Random House, 1949; as *High Life in the Andes*, London, Barker, 1951.
20,000 Leagues Behind the 8 Ball. New York, Random House, 1951.
With a Knife and Fork down the Amazon. London, Barker, 1952.
The Poor Man's Guide to Europe. New York, Random House, 1953 (and later editions).
Time Out for Turkey. New York, Random House, 1955; as *Talking Turkey*, London, Barker, 1955.
The Rich Man's Guide to the Riviera. Boston, Little Brown, 1962; London, Cassell, 1963.

The Poor Man's Guide to the Orient. New York, Simon and Schuster, 1965.
Fly Down, Drive Mexico. New York, Macmillan, 1968; revised edition, as *The Best of Mexico by Car*, 1969.

*   *   *

Prior to becoming a writer, David Dodge was an accountant, and he drew on this background in creating his first series character, Whit Whitney, a tax accountant and unwilling investigator of assorted murders. The first Whitney novel, *Death and Taxes*, is very much in the tradition of the screwball comedy mystery style which began with Dashiell Hammett's *The Thin Man* and reached an apex in the Bill Crane novels of Jonathan Latimer. There is a good bit of action and a medium-hard-boiled atmosphere, but the focus is on sharp, witty dialogue, with much attendant consumption of cocktails. Whitney is a likeable, generally bemused hero, not particularly happy with having to solve murders, but not lacking in brains and courage when called for. Kitty MacLeod, Whitney's girlfriend (and later his wife), plays the Nora Charles role to Whit's Nick in fine fashion. The four Whitney books are consistently well-crafted and entertaining examples of the screwball style.

Dodge became a world traveler, and began a second career as writer of humorous travel books. He dropped the Whitney series and thereafter drew on his familiarity with exotic locales for his later books. The Cote d'Azur is the setting for both *Angel's Ransom*, a crackling suspense yarn involving the kidnapping of the kept woman of a rich American wastrel, and *To Catch a Thief*, Dodge's best-known book, which Hitchcock made into a memorable movie with Cary Grant and Grace Kelly.

Central and South America was Dodge's favorite locale, and the scenery figures prominently in the three continent-spanning adventures of Al Colby, a hard-boiled private investigator based in Mexico City. In contrast to Whitney, Colby is a cynical tough-guy detective-adventurer; the light touch of the Whitney novels is consequently absent in the Colby novels, but the crisp dialogue, fast pace, and thoroughly professional plotting are not.

—Art Scott

DOLSON, Hildegarde. American. Born in Franklin, Pennsylvania, 31 August 1908. Educated at Allegheny College, Meadville, Pennsylvania, 1926–29. Married Richard Lockridge, *q.v.*, in 1965. Advertising Copywriter, Gimbels, Macy's, Franklin Simon, Bamberger department stores, New York, 1933–38. Since 1938, self-employed writer. D.Litt.: Allegheny College. Agent: James Brown Associates, 25 West 43rd Street, New York, New York 10036. Address: 206 Hillside Court, Tryon, North Carolina 28782, U.S.A.

CRIME PUBLICATIONS

Novels (series character: Lucy Ramsdale in all books)

To Spite Her Face. Philadelphia, Lippincott, 1971.
A Dying Fall. Philadelphia, Lippincott, 1973.
Please Omit Funeral. Philadelphia, Lippincott, 1975.
Beauty Sleep. Philadelphia, Lippincott, 1977; London, Hale, 1979.

OTHER PUBLICATIONS

Novels

The Husband Who Ran Away. New York, Random House, 1948.
The Form Divine. New York, Random House, and London, Hammond, 1951.
A Growing Wonder. New York, Random House, and London, Hammond, 1957.
Guess Whose Hair I'm Wearing? New York, Random House, 1963; as Adventures of
  a Light-Headed Blonde, London, Hammond, 1964.
Open the Door. Philadelphia, Lippincott, 1966.
Heat Lightning. Philadelphia, Lippincott, 1970.

Other

How about a Man. Philadelphia, Lippincott, and London, Duckworth, 1938.
We Shook the Family Tree (autobiography). New York, Random House, 1946;
  London, Hammond, 1954.
My Brother Adlai, with Elizabeth Stevenson Ives. New York, Morrow, 1956.
The Great Oildorado. New York, Random House, 1959; as They Struck Oil, London,
  Hammond, 1959.
William Penn, Quaker Hero (juvenile). New York, Random House, 1961.
Disaster at Johnstown: The Great Flood (juvenile). New York, Random House, 1965.

*   *   *

Hildegarde Dolson writes delightful, charming mysteries set in the small Connecticut town of Wingate. Her detectives are the widowed artist Lucy Ramsdale, a beautiful, petite, and spunky woman in her sixties who is sometimes bossy, imperious, egocentric, arrogant, and selfish, but just as often generous, feeling, sensitive, and thoughtful; Inspector James MacDougal, who comes to Wingate seeking peace after resigning as head of the Connecticut State Police homicide division in the wake of a humiliating divorce; and Nicky Terrizi, a rising young policeman who had disappointed Lucy by leaving her employ as a gardener to follow his present profession and who regards MacDougal with a mixture of respect and affection.

When murder occurs in Wingate the local authorities, woefully undermanned and inexperienced in homicidal matters, are delighted to enlist the aid of the newly arrived inspector. Because of her personality and her acquaintance with most of Wingate's residents, Lucy also gets involved in the investigations, frequently crossing paths with the inspector, not always to their mutual satisfaction. In each novel these characters develop, as do their relations with each other. They are believable and likeable, and the attraction of the series lies as much in the affection the reader develops for them as in the interesting cases in which they are involved. Indeed, it is fair to say that the mystery in these novels, though competent, is subordinate to the characters themselves.

—Guy M. Townsend

DOMINIC, R. B. See **LATHEN, Emma.**

DONAVAN, John. See **MORLAND, Nigel.**

DONOVAN, Dick. Pseudonym for Joyce Emmerson Preston Muddock. British. Born in Southampton, Hampshire, 28 May 1842. Educated at a collegiate school in Cheshire, and in India. Married; two sons. Worked for the British Government in India; employed for a time at a gun foundry at Cossipore, near Calcutta; special correspondent for the *Hour* in Asia and the Pacific for several years; Swiss correspondent for the London *Daily News* for five years; attached to the Special Constabulary, London, during World War I. *Died 23 January 1934.*

CRIME PUBLICATIONS

Novels

> *From the Bosom of the Deep* (as J. E. Muddock). London, Swan Sonnenschein, 1886.
> *The Man from Manchester.* London, Chatto and Windus, 1890; New York, Street and Smith, 1900.
> *Tracked to Doom.* London, Chatto and Windus, 1891.
> *Eugene Vidocq, Soldier, Thief, Spy, Detective: A Romance Founded on Facts.* London, Hutchinson, 1895.
> *The Mystery of Jamaica Terrace.* London, Chatto and Windus, 1896.
> *Deacon Brodie; or, Behind the Mask.* London, Chatto and Windus, 1901.
> *Jim the Penman.* London, Newnes, 1901.
> *Whose Was the Hand?* (as J. E. Muddock). London, Digby Long, 1901.
> *The Scarlet Seal: A Tale of the Borgias.* London, Long, 1902.
> *The Crime of the Century.* London, Long, 1904.
> *The Fatal Ring.* London, Hurst and Blackett, 1905.
> *A Knight of Evil.* London, White, 1905.
> *Thurtell's Crime.* London, Laurie, 1906.
> *The Knutsford Mystery.* London, White, 1906.
> *The Gold-Spinner.* London, White, 1907.
> *The Shadow of Evil.* London, Everett, 1907.
> *In the Queen's Service.* London, Long, 1907.
> *A Gilded Serpent.* London, Ward Lock, 1908.
> *In the Face of the Night.* London, Long, 1908.
> *The Sin of Preaching Jim.* London, Everett, 1908; as *Preaching Jim*, London, Aldine Publishing Company, 1919.
> *Tangled Destinies.* London, Laurie, 1908.
> *A Wild Beauty.* London, White, 1909.
> *Lil of the Slums.* London, Laurie, 1909.

For Honour or Death. London, Ward Lock, 1910.
The Naughty Maid of Mitcham. London, White, 1910.
The Fatal Woman. London, White, 1911.
The Trap: A Revelation. London, White, 1911.
The Rich Man's Wife, with E. W. Elkington. London, Ham Smith, 1912.
The Turning Wheel. London, White, 1912.
Out There: A Romance of Australia. London, Everett, 1922.

Short Stories (series character: Dick Donovan)

The Man-Hunter: Stories from the Note-Book of a Detective (Donovan). London,
   Chatto and Windus, 1888; New York, Lovell, 1889.
Caught at Last! Leaves from the Note-Book of a Detective. London, Chatto and
   Windus, and New York, Lovell, 1889.
Who Poisoned Hetty Duncan? and Other Detective Stories. London, Chatto and
   Windus, 1890.
Tracked and Taken: Detective Sketches. London, Chatto and Windus, and New York,
   Lovell, 1890.
A Detective's Triumphs. London, Chatto and Windus, 1891.
Wanted! A Detective's Strange Adventures (Donovan). London, Chatto and Windus,
   1892.
In the Grip of the Law (Donovan). London, Chatto and Windus, 1892.
From Information Received. London, Chatto and Windus, 1893.
Link by Link (Donovan). London, Chatto and Windus, 1893.
From Clue to Capture (Donovan). London, Hutchinson, 1893.
Suspicion Aroused (Donovan). London, Chatto and Windus, 1893.
Found and Fettered (Donovan). London, Hutchinson, 1894.
Dark Deeds (Donovan). London, Chatto and Windus, 1895.
Riddles Read (Donovan). London, Chatto and Windus, 1896.
The Chronicles of Michael Danevitch of the Russian Secret Service. London, Chatto
   and Windus, 1897.
The Records of Vincent Trill of the Detective Service. London, Chatto and Windus,
   1899.
Tales of Terror (Donovan). London, Chatto and Windus, 1899.
The Adventures of Tyler Tatlock, Private Detective. London, Chatto and Windus, 1900.
Startling Crimes and Notorious Criminals. London, Pearson, 1908.
The Great Turf Fraud and Other Notable Crimes. London, Pearson, 1909.
Scarlet Sinners: Stories of Notorious Criminals and Crimes. London, Newnes, 1910.
The Triumphs of Fabian Field, Criminologist. London, White, 1912.

OTHER PUBLICATIONS as J. E. Muddock

Novels

Grace O'Malley. London, People's Pocket Story Books, 1873.
A False Heart. London, Tinsley, 3 vols., 1873.
A Wingless Angel. London, Virtue, 1875.
As the Shadows Fall. London, Tinsley, 3 vols., 1876.
*"Doll": A Dream of Haddon Hall, Being the Story of Dorothy Vernon's Wooing and
   Flight.* London, Heywood, 1880.
Snowdrops: A Story of Three Christmas Eves. London, Wyman, 1887.
The Shadow Hunter. London, Unwin, 1887.
Stormlight. London, Ward Lock, 1888.
The Dead Man's Secret; or, The Valley of Gold. London, Chatto and Windus, 1889.
For God and the Czar. London, Newnes, 1892.

Maid Marian and Robin Hood. London, Chatto and Windus, and Philadelphia, Lippincott, 1892.
Only a Woman's Heart. London, Newnes, 1893.
The Star of Fortune. London, Chapman and Hall, 2 vols., 1894.
Stripped of the Tinsel. London, Digby Long, 1896.
Young Lochinvar. London, Chatto and Windus, 1896.
The Great White Hand; or, The Tiger of Cawnpore. London, Hutchinson, 1896.
Without Faith or Fear. London, Digby Long, 1896.
Basile the Jester. London, Chatto and Windus, 1896; New York, New Amsterdam Book Company, 1897.
The Lost Laird. London, Digby Long, 1898.
In the King's Favour. London, Digby Long, 1899.
The Golden Idol. London, Chatto and Windus, 1899.
The Sting of the Scorpion. London, Simpkin Marshall, 1899.
Kate Cameron of Brux; or, The Feud. London, Digby Long, 1900.
Fair Rosalind. London, Long, 1902.
A Woman's Checkmate. London, Long, 1902.
Liz. London, White, 1903.
Sweet "Doll" of Haddon Hall. London, Long, 1903; revised edition, 1905.
In the Red Dawn. London, Long, 1904.
The Sunless City. London, White, 1905.
Jane Shore. London, Long, 1905.
From the Clutch of the Sea: The Story of Some Real Lives. London, Long, 1905.
For the White Cockade. London, Long, 1905.
The Alluring Flame. London, Long, 1906.

Short Stories

Stories Weird and Wonderful. London, Chatto and Windus, 1889.
For Love of Lucille and Other Stories. London, White, 1905.

Other

Did Dorothy Vernon Elope? A Rejoinder. London, Drane, 1907.
Pages from an Adventurous Life (as Dick Donovan). London, Laurie, and New York, Kennerley, 1907.
The Romance and History of the Crystal Palace. London, Gill, 1911.
A Patriotic American (on Harold Shaw; as Dick Donovan). London, Baldwin, 1916.
All Clear: A Brief Record of the Work of the London Special Constabulary 1914-1919. London, Everett, 1920.

Editor, *The "J. E. M." Guide to Davos-Platz.* London, Simpkin Marshall, 1881.
Editor, *The "J. E. M." Guide to Switzerland.* London, Simpkin Marshall, 1882.
Editor, *Pocket Guide to Geneva and Chamounix.* London, Wyman, 1886.
Editor, *For Valour: The V.C.: A Record of the Brave and Noble Deeds for Which Her Majesty Has Bestowed the Victoria Cross.* London, Hutchinson, 1895.
Editor, *The Savage Club Papers.* London, Hutchinson, 1895.

*   *   *

In the 1880's and 1890's Dick Donovan (Joyce Emmerson Preston Muddock) was one of the most prolific and popular British mystery writers. With well over 200 short stories to his credit in newspapers and periodicals, he was as well-known on the lower reading levels as Sherlock Holmes later became on higher levels.

Dick Donovan appeared as both author and police detective in *The Man-Hunter*, a collection reprinted from earlier newspaper publications. The name Donovan, according to Muddock's memoirs, was that of an 18th-century Bow Street Runner; the stories themselves, however, were all modern in setting. Dick Donovan remained the central figure in succeeding short story collections until *The Chronicles of Michael Danevitch*, in which Muddock wrote about a Czarist police official and Peter Brodie, an English detective. Later volumes are concerned with private detectives Fabian Field, Tyler Tatlock, and Vincent Trill.

Although Donovan is remembered today primarily as a writer of short stories, he also wrote much incidental journalism and many novels. Of his mystery novels, *The Man from Manchester* is generally considered the best. He also worked in the area of fictionalized factual crime. Here *Eugene Vidocq, Jim the Penman*, and *Thurtell's Crime* are best-known.

Muddock's work is marked by a strong conservatism and an archaic quality which seem to have been matched by his political and social views. Just as he retained the mid-Victorian practice of coincident detective and author, his Dick Donovan stories are undramatic, first-person narratives in the manner of "Waters." His subject matter came partly from factual crime and partly from the romantic themes of the day – anarchist plots, Oriental vengeance. *The Man from Manchester*, which attempts a character portrayal as well as a crime, might have been written a generation earlier, while *The Mystery of Jamaica Terrace* often reads like a stage melodrama. In his later fiction Muddock attempted to write a more contemporary story, but without too much success.

—E. F. Bleiler

DOWNES, Quentin. See **HARRISON, Michael.**

DOYLE, Arthur Conan. British. Born in Edinburgh, 22 May 1859. Educated at the Hodder School, Lancashire, 1868–70, Stonyhurst College, Lancashire, 1870–75, and the Jesuit School, Feldkirch, Austria, 1875–76; studied medicine at the University of Edinburgh, 1876–81, M.B. 1881, M.D. 1885. Served as Senior Physician to a field hospital in South Africa during the Boer War, 1899–1902: knighted, 1902. Married 1) Louise Hawkins in 1885 (died, 1906), one daughter and one son; 2) Jean Leckie in 1907, two sons and one daughter. Practised medicine in Southsea, 1882–90; full-time writer from 1891; stood for Parliament as Unionist candidate for Central Edinburgh, 1900, and tariff reform candidate for the Hawick Burghs, 1906. LL.D.: University of Edinburgh, 1905. Knight of Grace of the Order of St. John of Jerusalem. *Died 7 July 1930.*

Crime Publications

Novels (series character: Sherlock Holmes)

   A Study in Scarlet (Holmes).   London, Ward Lock, 1888; Philadelphia, Lippincott, 1890.

The Mystery of Cloomber. London, Ward and Downey, 1888; New York, Fenno, 1895.

The Sign of Four (Holmes). London, Blackett, 1890; Philadelphia, Lippincott, 1893.

The Doings of Raffles Haw. London, Cassell, and New York, Lovell, 1892.

The Hound of the Baskervilles (Holmes). London, Newnes, and New York, McClure, 1902.

The Valley of Fear (Holmes). New York, Doran, 1914; London, Smith Elder, 1915.

Short Stories (series character: Sherlock Holmes)

Mysteries and Adventures. London, Scott, 1889; as *The Gully of Bluemansdyke and Other Stories*, 1893.

The Captain of the Polestar and Other Tales. London, Longman, 1890; New York, Munro, 1894.

The Adventures of Sherlock Holmes. London, Newnes, and New York, Harper, 1892.

My Friend the Murderer and Other Mysteries and Adventures. New York, Lovell, 1893.

The Great Keinplatz Experiment and Other Stories. Chicago, Rand McNally, 1894.

The Memoirs of Sherlock Holmes. London, Newnes, and New York, Harper, 1894.

Round the Red Lamp, Being Facts and Fancies of Medical Life. London, Methuen, and New York, Appleton, 1894.

The Green Flag and Other Stories of War and Sport. London, Smith Elder, and New York, McClure, 1900.

The Return of Sherlock Holmes. London, Newnes, and New York, McClure, 1905.

Round the Fire Stories. London, Smith Elder, and New York, McClure, 1908.

The Last Galley: Impressions and Tales. London, Smith Elder, and New York, Doubleday, 1911.

His Last Bow: Some Reminiscences of Sherlock Holmes. London, Murray, and New York, Doran, 1917.

Danger! and Other Stories. London, Murray, and New York, Doran, 1918.

The Black Doctor and Other Tales of Terror and Mystery (selection). New York, Doran, 1925.

The Case-Book of Sherlock Holmes. London, Murray, and New York, Doran, 1927.

Great Stories, edited by John Dickson Carr. London, Murray, and New York, London House and Maxwell, 1959.

The Annotated Sherlock Holmes, edited by William S. Baring-Gould. New York, Clarkson N. Potter, 2 vols., 1967; London, Murray, 2 vols., 1968.

OTHER PUBLICATIONS

Novels

Micah Clarke. London, Longman, and New York, Harper, 1889.

The Firm of Girdlestone. London, Chatto and Windus, and New York, Lovell, 1890.

The White Company. London, Smith Elder, 3 vols., 1891; New York, Lovell, 1 vol., 1891.

The Great Shadow. New York, Harper, 1893.

The Great Shadow, and Beyond the City. Bristol, Arrowsmith, 1893; New York, Ogilvie, 1894.

The Refugees. London, Longman, 3 vols., 1893; New York, Harper, 1 vol., 1893.

The Parasite. London, Constable, 1894; New York, Harper, 1895.

The Stark Munro Letters. London, Longman, and New York, Appleton, 1895.

Rodney Stone. London, Smith Elder, and New York, Appleton, 1896.

Uncle Bernac: A Memory of Empire. London, Smith Elder, and New York, Appleton, 1897.

The Tragedy of Korosko. London, Smith Elder, 1898; as *A Desert Drama*,
    Philadelphia, Lippincott, 1898.
A Duet, with an Occasional Chorus. London, Grant Richards, and New York,
    Appleton, 1899; revised edition, London, Smith Elder, 1910.
Sir Nigel. London, Smith Elder, and New York, McClure, 1906.
The Lost World. London, Hodder and Stoughton, and New York, Doran, 1912.
The Poison Belt. London, Hodder and Stoughton, and New York, Doran, 1913.
The Land of Mist. London, Hutchinson, and New York, Doran, 1926.

Short Stories

The Exploits of Brigadier Gerard. London, Newnes, and New York, Appleton, 1896.
The Man from Archangel and Other Stories. New York, Street and Smith, 1898.
The Adventures of Gerard. London, Newnes, and New York, McClure, 1903.
The Dealings of Captain Sharkey and Other Tales of Pirates. New York, Doran, 1925.
The Last of the Legions and Other Tales of Long Ago. New York, Doran, 1925.
The Man from Archangel and Other Tales of Adventure. New York, Doran, 1925.
The Maracot Deep and other Stories. London, Murray, and New York, Doran, 1929.
The Conan Doyle Historical Romances. London, Murray, 2 vols., 1931–32.
The Professor Challenger Stories. London, Murray, 1952.
Strange Studies from Life, Containing Three Hitherto Uncollected Tales, edited by Peter
    Ruber. New York, Candlelight Press, 1963.

Plays

Jane Annie; or, The Good Conduct Prize, with J. M. Barrie, music by Ernest Ford
    (produced London, 1893). London, Chappell, 1893.
Foreign Policy (produced London, 1893).
Waterloo (as *A Story of Waterloo*, produced Bristol, 1894; London, 1895; as *Waterloo*,
    produced New York, 1899). London, French, 1919(?).
Halves (produced Aberdeen and London, 1899).
Sherlock Holmes, with William Gillette, adaptation of works by Doyle (produced New
    York, 1899; Liverpool and London, 1901). London, French, 1922; New York,
    Doubleday, 1935.
A Duet. London, French, 1903.
Brigadier Gerard, adaptation of his own stories (produced London and New York,
    1906).
The Fires of Fate: A Modern Morality, adaptation of his own novel *The Tragedy of
    Korosko* (produced London and New York, 1909).
The House of Temperley, adaptation of his own novel *Rodney Stone* (produced London,
    1909).
The Pot of Caviare, adaptation of his own story (produced London, 1910). London,
    French, 1912.
The Speckled Band (produced London and New York, 1910). London, French, 1912.
The Crown Diamond (produced London, 1921).
It's Time Something Happened. New York, Appleton, 1925.

Verse

Songs of Action. London, Smith Elder, and New York, Doubleday, 1898.
Songs of the Road. London, Smith Elder, and New York, Doubleday, 1911.
The Guards Came Through and Other Poems. London, Murray, 1919; New York,
    Doran, 1920.
The Poems: Collected Edition. London, Murray, 1922.

Other

The Great Boer War. London, Smith Elder, and New York, McClure, 1900.

The War in South Africa: Its Cause and Conflict. London, Smith Elder, and New York, McClure, 1902.

Works. London, Smith Elder, 12 vols., 1903.

Through the Magic Door (essays). London, Smith Elder, 1907; New York, McClure, 1908.

The Case of Mr. George Edalji. London, Blake, 1907.

The Crime of the Congo. London, Hutchinson, and New York, Doubleday, 1909.

The Case of Oscar Slater. London, Hodder and Stoughton, 1912; New York, Doran, 1913.

Great Britain and the Next War. Boston, Small Maynard, 1914.

In Quest of Truth, Being a Correspondence Between Sir Arthur Conan Doyle and Captain H. Stansbury. London, Watts, 1914.

The German War: Some Sidelights and Reflections. London, Hodder and Stoughton, 1914; New York, Doran, 1915.

To Arms! London, Hodder and Stoughton, 1914.

Western Wanderings (travel in Canada). New York, Doran, 1915.

The Origin and Outbreak of the War. New York, Doran, 1916.

A Petition to the Prime Minister on Behalf of Roger Casement. Privately printed, 1916(?).

The British Campaign in France and Flanders. London, Hodder and Stoughton, 6 vols., 1916–19; New York, Doran, 6 vols., 1916–20; revised edition, as *The British Campaigns in Europe 1914–1918*, London, Bles, 1 vol., 1928.

A Visit to Three Fronts. London, Hodder and Stoughton, and New York, Doran, 1916.

The New Revelation; or, What Is Spiritualism? London, Hodder and Stoughton, and New York, Doran, 1918.

The Vital Message (on spiritualism). London, Hodder and Stoughton, and New York, Doran, 1919.

Our Reply to the Cleric. London, Spiritualists' Union, 1920.

A Debate on Spiritualism, with Joseph McCabe. London, Watts, 1920; Girard, Kansas, Haldeman Julius, 1922.

Spiritualism and Rationalism. London, Hodder and Stoughton, 1920.

Fairies Photographed. New York, Doran, 1921.

The Evidence for Fairies. New York, Doran, 1921.

The Wanderings of a Spiritualist. London, Hodder and Stoughton, and New York, Doran, 1921.

The Case for Spirit Photography, with others. London, Hutchinson, 1922; New York, Doran, 1923.

The Coming of the Fairies. London, Hodder and Stoughton, and New York, Doran, 1922.

Three of Them: A Reminiscence. London, Murray, 1923.

Our American Adventure. London, Hodder and Stoughton, and New York, Doran, 1923.

Memories and Adventures. London, Hodder and Stoughton, and Boston, Little Brown, 1924.

Our Second American Adventure. London, Hodder and Stoughton, and Boston, Little Brown, 1924.

Psychic Experiences. London and New York, Putnam, 1925.

The Early Christian Church and Modern Spiritualism. London, Psychic Press, 1925.

The History of Spiritualism. London, Cassell, 2 vols., and New York, Doran, 2 vols., 1926.

Pheneas Speaks: Direct Spirit Communications. London, Psychic Press, and New York, Doran, 1927.

What Does Spiritualism Actually Teach and Stand For?   London, Psychic Press, 1928.
A Word of Warning.   London, Psychic Press, 1928.
An Open Letter to Those of My Generation.   London, Psychic Press, 1929.
Our African Winter.   London, Murray, 1929.
The Roman Catholic Church: A Rejoinder.   London, Psychic Press, 1929.
The Edge of the Unknown.   London, Murray, and New York, Putnam, 1930.

Editor, *D. D. Home: His Life and Mission*, by Mrs. Douglas Home.   London, Paul
   Trench Trubner, and New York, Dutton, 1921.
Editor, *The Spiritualist's Reader.*   Manchester, Two Worlds Publishing Company,
   1924.

Translator, *The Mystery of Joan of Arc*, by Léon Denis.   London, Murray, 1924.

Bibliography: *A Bibliographical Catalogue of the Writings of Sir Arthur Conan Doyle* by
Harold Locke, Tunbridge Wells, Kent, Webster, 1928.

Manuscript Collection: Humanities Research Center, University of Texas, Austin.

*   *   *

The young impecunious doctor who invented, without at first much success, Sherlock
Holmes may be said to have in doing so brought about crime literature as a distinct entity.
Had it not been for the extraordinary eventual triumph of his character, it is quite possible
that what we now call crime writing would not be considered as a separate category at all.
   What was it that was so right about Holmes that it had this effect? First, that he was a
human being, a person, a man, not a mere single walking attribute nor even a cunning
collection of attributes. Wherever he came from – a little from Dr. Joseph Bell, remarkable
medical diagnostician, more from someone hidden in the stolid body of Arthur Conan Doyle
– he was a person whose opposing qualities, extreme mental and physical agility as against
drug-induced opting-out, all that is summed up by the phrase "an English gentleman" as
against a "decadent" aesthete dreaming over his violin, somehow complemented each other
to make one single, extraordinarily believable person. Second, Holmes was a scientist in an
age that was just ready to acknowledge a scientist as hero. General education had just reached
the point, when the first Holmes stories appeared in the *Strand* magazine, of providing
enough readers armed with some idea of the scientific attitude to make this figure, first seen
just after discovering a way of testing for minute quantities of blood, set a chord humming in
thousands of minds. Third, Doyle made two valuable technical writing discoveries. There
was the series character, which he believed he was the first to hit on. And there was the
Watson, the person through whom the average reader can see a superman operating and yet
feel comfortable, a pair of eyes to see a clue and miss its meaning.
   To these major innovations Doyle was able to add other extremely useful qualities. He
could create a memorable character with remarkable economy. A page and a half suffices for
the evilly menacing Dr. Grimesby Roylott. And indeed often much of his character creation
is done by his simple genius for hitting on the right name (Bartholomew Sholto, Mr. Hall
Pycroft, even John H. Watson, M.D.). He found, too, plots that are excellent and stories that
would intrigue even if Holmes were absent. He had a gift for laying down some initial oddity
that hardly a reader can resist, like the whole conception of the Red-headed League, or he
could put in, with just the right judgment, some eerily outré touch, like the two severed ears
in the story to which he gave (how rightly) the flat title "The Cardboard Box." And, though
by no means all the stories are in the pure puzzle pattern, he was enormously skilful with
that, as in the whodunit "Silver Blaze," paving the way for all the puzzle stories of the Golden
Age of detection.
   Doyle was, too, a splendid writer in the sheer writing. He got his dialogue marvellously
right, swiftly economical without any feeling of thinness or austerity, illuminating character

in a hundred tiny touches, and when called on wonderfully trenchant ("Mr. Holmes, they were the footsteps of a gigantic hound"). He is equally successful in narrative. He tells his readers just what they need to know just when they need to know it. Seldom indeed does he allow the least digression, and when he does, as in Holmes's sudden discussion of the German essayist Jean-Paul Richter in *The Sign of Four*, it is barely noticeable, totally in character, and put to good service with that sudden jump back into the story proper, "You have not a pistol, have you?"

Always his English is simple and direct, though perfectly naturally so and perfectly capable of rising to a polysyllabic word where a polysyllabic word is called for. And every now and again he produces a phrase that is telling indeed without any appearance of striving to be so. This he was able to do right from the beginning with that description (it is only one of scores as good) in *A Study in Scarlet* of the houses in a Brixton street all with vacant windows on which "here and there a To Let card had developed like a cataract upon the bleared pane."

It is from touches like this as well as from more developed evil characters like the blackmailer Charles Augustus Milverton (another splendid name) that Doyle built up the sense of evil which it gives us so much interior satisfaction to watch Holmes vanquishing. And it is from other phrases quietly rising from the general level that he builds up the necessary counterpoise to that streak of evil, the surrounding cushion of pure cosiness, "the hall-light shining through stained glass, the barometer, and the bright stair rods" (*The Sign of Four*).

But the stories and yet more the novels are not without fault. The four novels are really too long for the Holmes formula to work properly, and indeed in all of them Holmes disappears from the action for long (and generally pretty dull) periods. In the stories the logic can sometimes be found wanting; occasionally the end hardly lives up to the beginning; we are not invariably given the clues Holmes has seen. There are, too, feeble repetitions of particularly successful devices. Holmes even was not always as up-to-date scientifically as he might have been (hot though he was on footprints, fingerprints, with the single exception of an unlikely sealing-wax transfer, are ignored). There are unlikelinesses, generally to do with impenetrable disguises.

But none of these matter. Doyle's extraordinary gifts, for story-telling, for the sounding in us of primeval depths that respond to the mystery of the tale, for the creation of characters, sweep away all criticisms. Sherlock Holmes lives, and will live as long as there are books, or films, or television series, or feelies, or telethinks.

—H. R. F. Keating

DRESSER, Davis. See **HALLIDAY, Brett.**

DRISCOLL, Peter. British. Born in London, 4 February 1942. Educated at St. David's Marist College, Johannesburg, 1955–58; University of the Witwatersrand, Johannesburg, 1964–66, B.A. 1967. Served in the South Africa Army, intermittently 1961–66. Married Angela Hennessy in 1967; two daughters. Reporter, *Rand Daily Mail*, Johannesburg, 1959–67; News Editor, Post Newspapers, Johannesburg, 1967–68; Scriptwriter and Sub-

Editor, Independent Television News, London, 1969–73. Agent: Campbell Thomson and McLaughlin Ltd., 31 Newington Green, London N16 9PU, England. Address: Castlecrest, Killincarrig, Delgany, County Wicklow, Ireland.

CRIME PUBLICATIONS

Novels

> *The White Lie Assignment.*   London, Macdonald, 1971; Philadelphia, Lippincott, 1975.
> *The Wilby Conspiracy.*   Philadelphia, Lippincott, 1972; London, Macdonald, 1973.
> *In Connection with Kilshaw.*   Philadelphia, Lippincott, and London, Macdonald, 1974.
> *The Barboza Credentials.*   Philadelphia, Lippincott, and London, Macdonald and Jane's, 1976.
> *Pangolin.*   Philadelphia, Lippincott, and London, Macdonald and Jane's, 1979.

Manuscript Collection: Mugar Memorial Library, Boston University.

Peter Driscoll comments:
  I have always considered a good crime novel/suspense story/thriller to be an achievement at least as solid as a mediocre serious novel. This is truer than ever today, when novelists, in their search for new horizons, have moved into the realms of surrealism; crime writers are increasingly filling the gap to meet the demand for good old-fashioned story-telling, and some have achieved a depth and insight worthy of the best "straight" novelists. So, while I accept the limitations imposed by the genre, I hope one day to be able to extend them.
  The starting point for all the books I have written – and perhaps the key by which any one of them might be described – is a setting. Often it is a place with a background of some political or social instability which I like to examine in some detail and which gives an undertone of tension to the narrative. One critic (writing in the St. Louis *Post-Dispatch*) said, "Driscoll weaves a tight drama of suspense and adventure around an existing social-political situation." My first book, *The White Lie Assignment*, was set in the Greek-Albanian border country; the story of *The Wilby Conspiracy* unfolded against the background of apartheid in South Africa; *In Connection with Kilshaw* dealt with the troubles in Northern Ireland; *The Barboza Credentials* was set in newly-independent Mozambique.
  Beyond the obvious elements of action, conflict, and suspense, what I try hardest to communicate are authenticity, atmosphere, and – an elusive but essential ingredient – the quality of fear. That, after all, is what every thriller ought to be about.

                        *   *   *

  The Wilby Conspiracy showed Peter Driscoll to be a first-rate practitioner of the type of thriller, developed by Buchan and perfected by Ambler, in which an individual inadvertently becomes enmeshed in a dangerous bit of international intrigue. Driscoll's hero, James Keogh, resembles Richard Hannay more than a little. A mining engineer on holiday in Cape Town, Keogh suddenly finds himself on the run from the South African police, accompanied by a black nationalist fugitive recently escaped from prison. Gradually Keogh discovers that he and his companion are being used by the South African secret police in a complicated plot to kidnap a black revolutionary leader living in exile in Botswana since his escape from South Africa several years earlier. Driscoll successfully individualizes Keogh, in part by creating a romantic sub-plot, and he is particularly effective at creating and sustaining suspense through a well-paced chase sequence that takes up the central portion of the book. *The Wilby Conspiracy*, however, is something more than a well-executed variation of a formula thriller. Driscoll offers a devastating portrait of the South African secret police – cunning, brutal, sadistic – who are the linchpin of apartheid.

In Connection with Kilshaw is equally accomplished in technique and political statement. Harry Finn, the central character, is a burnt-out case, a British army intelligence officer who has barely survived massive radiation treatments for throat cancer. Attached to a high-ranking Home Office civil servant with vaguely defined responsibilities, Finn agrees to go into Northern Ireland, ostensibly to collect damaging information about a Protestant demagogue, James Kilshaw, who is moving openly toward civil war. Gradually Finn realizes that he has been set up to play an unwitting part in a conspiracy to assassinate Kilshaw in such a way as to leave no trace of British complicity. A tough, resourceful, but basically decent man, Finn is appalled to discover that the price of Kilshaw's death, agreed to by Finn's superior, is a shipment of M-16 rifles delivered into the hands of an IRA faction for use in a future revolution in the south of Ireland.

The White Lie Assignment, his first novel, is a merely competent, routine thriller. To the character of Michael Mannis, a naturalized British citizen of Greek ancestry, Driscoll gives perfunctory attention. Mannis, a free-lance photographer rather than a trained agent, agrees to go into Albania on a one-shot contract to photograph a secret missile site established by the Chinese. He succeeds in getting the photographs but is double-crossed and spends the second half of the book extricating himself from his erstwhile employer. A workmanlike but hardly stylish effort, *The White Lie Assignment* lacks the originality and the intensity of the later two books. The fourth novel *The Barboza Credentials*, too, lacks their brilliance. The central character, Joe Hickey, is a former Kenyan police officer turned mining machinery salesman and engaged in evading the United Nation's sanctions against Rhodesia. Vulnerable to blackmail, he finds himself compelled to aid Mozambique officials in their search for the "Barboza credentials," documents that will permit a notorious Portuguese former secret police officer to flee the country. Though Driscoll shows himself adept at contriving a complicated conspiracy, the story lacks the sustained tension of *Wilby* or the skillful evocation of place that enriches *Kilshaw*. And Joe Hickey, while more substantially characterized than Michael Mannis, is not as convincing as Keogh or Finn. Given the quality of his middle two books, *The Barboza Credentials* may represent Driscoll's temporary decline to the level of creditable but not remarkable competency.

—R. Gordon Kelly

DRUMMOND, Charles. See **McGIRR, Edmund.**

DRUMMOND, Ivor. Pseudonym for Roger Erskine Longrigg; also writes as Rosalind Erskine. British. Born in Edinburgh, 1 May 1929. Educated privately and at Magdalen College, Oxford, B.A. in modern history, 1952. Served in the British Army, 1947–49: Captain, Territorial and Army Volunteer Reserve. Married Jane Chichester in 1957; three daughters. Agent: Curtis Brown Ltd., 1 Craven Hill, London W2 3EP, England.

CRIME PUBLICATIONS

Novels (series characters: Lady Jennifer Norrington, Count Alessandro di Ganzarello, and
Coleridge Tucker, III, in all books)

The Man with the Tiny Head. London, Macmillan, 1969; New York, Harcourt Brace,
1970.
The Priests of the Abomination. London, Macmillan, 1970; New York, Harcourt
Brace, 1971.
The Frog in the Moonflower. London, Macmillan, 1972; New York, St. Martin's Press,
1973.
The Jaws of the Watchdog. London, Macmillan, and New York, St. Martin's Press,
1973.
The Power of the Bug. London, Macmillan, and New York, St. Martin's Press, 1974.
The Tank of Sacred Eeels. London, Joseph, and New York, St. Martin's Press, 1976.
The Necklace of Skulls. London, Joseph, and New York, St. Martin's Press, 1977.
A Stench of Poppies. London, Joseph, and New York, St. Martin's Press, 1978.

Uncollected Short Stories

"Death in the Private Dining Room," in *Compleat Imbiber 11* (London), 1970.
"The Five-Million-Dollar Baby," in *Winter's Crimes 2*, edited by George
Hardinge. London, Macmillan, 1970.
"Lock-up," in *Woman's Journal* (London), June 1974.
"The Chair," in *Winter's Crimes 6*, edited by George Hardinge. London, Macmillan,
1974.

OTHER PUBLICATIONS as Roger Longrigg

Novels

A High-Pitched Buzz. London, Faber, 1956.
Switchboard. London, Faber, 1957.
Wrong Number. London, Faber, 1959.
Daughters of Mulberry. London, Faber, 1961.
The Passion-Flower Hotel (as Rosalind Erskine). London, Cape, and New York, Simon
and Schuster, 1962.
The Paper Boats. London, Faber, and New York, Harper, 1963.
Passion Flowers in Italy (as Rosalind Erskine). London, Cape, 1963; New York, Simon
and Schuster, 1964.
Passion Flowers in Business (as Rosalind Erskine). London, Cape, 1965.
Love among the Bottles. London, Faber, 1967.
The Sun on the Water. London, Macmillan, 1969.
The Desperate Criminals. London, Macmillan, 1971.
The Jevington System. London, Macmillan, 1973.
Their Pleasing Sport. London, Macmillan, 1975.

Plays

Radio Play: *The Chair*, 1976.

Television Plays: *A High-Pitched Buzz*, from his own novel, 1967; *Arson*, 1974; *Firing
Point*, 1974; *Dead Connection*, 1974; *Contempt of Court*, 1975.

Other

The Artless Gambler.   London, Pelham, 1964.
The History of Horse Racing.   London, Macmillan, and New York, Stein and Day, 1972.
The English Squire and His Sport.   London, Joseph, and New York, St. Martin's Press, 1977.

Ivor Drummond comments:

The late Ian Fleming was quoted as saying that his highest ambition as a writer of thrillers was to make the reader want to turn over the page to see what happened next. I disagreed with Fleming about many things (especially his dislike of Italy), but in this I wholly agree with him. The reader's curiosity is sharpened, I think, by credible and attractive characters – villains as well as heroes – and the escapism of exotic settings accurately described.

*   *   *

Ivor Drummond writes books that are, above all, fun. He is in the tradition of James Bond, that is to say there is in his books some large looming international plot and the hero (in his case a triple figure, three heroic personae acting as one) after falling into a number of impossibly tight corners – only this is a hero – escapes and rounds up the villains. The Drummond heroes are Lady Jennifer Norrington, deceptively debutante-like but really jolly tough, Count Sandro di Ganzarello, a maxi-masculine bear-shaped Italian, and Colly Tucker, III, a Pimpernel American playboy millionaire. Both men are permanently in love with Lady Jennifer, but, though she cherishes the warmest friendship for them, she can give love to neither.

Their adventures, in which they are always up against a reeking evil of some sort, are made into the easiest and smoothest of reads, but behind this there is always a well thought-out plot with adroitly managed climaxes and generally just a touch of feeling. Drummond contrives always, too, at least one thoroughly exotic and romantic setting, and sometimes two or three in a book. Since, too, his heroes are, all three, very upper-class people indeed, they move naturally in a world of glamorous sophistication, though Drummond is clever enough not to have them fall for that glamour themselves however much they swim in it.

Only in *A Stench of Poppies* have there been signs that the formula was prevailing over the fun.

—H. R. F. Keating

DRUMMOND, J.   See CHANCE, John Newton.

DRUMMOND, June. South African. Born in Durban, Natal, 15 November 1923. Educated at the University of Cape Town, B.A. 1944. Journalist, *Woman's Weekly* and *Natal*

Mercury, both Durban, 1946–48; secretary in London, 1948–50, and with Durban Civic Orchestra, 1950–53; Assistant Secretary, Church Adoption Society, London, 1954–60; Chairman, Durban Adoption Committee, Indian Child Welfare Society, 1963–74. Address: 24-A Miller Grove, Durban, Natal, South Africa.

CRIME PUBLICATIONS

Novels

The Black Unicorn. London, Gollancz, 1959.
Thursday's Child. London, Gollancz, 1961.
A Time to Speak. London, Gollancz, 1962; Cleveland, World, 1963.
A Cage of Humming-Birds. London, Gollancz, 1964.
Welcome, Proud Lady. London, Gollancz, 1964; New York, Holt Rinehart, 1968.
Cable-Car. London, Gollancz, 1965; New York, Holt Rinehart, 1967.
The Saboteurs. London, Gollancz, 1967; New York, Holt Rinehart, 1969.
The Gantry Episode. London, Gollancz, 1968; as *Murder on a Bad Trip*, New York, Holt Rinehart, 1968.
The People in Glass House. London, Gollancz, 1969; New York, Simon and Schuster, 1970.
Farewell Party. London, Gollancz, 1971; New York, Dodd Mead, 1973.
Bang! Bang! You're Dead. London, Gollancz, 1973.
The Boon Companions. London, Collins, 1974; as *Drop Dead*, New York, Walker, 1976.
Slowly the Poison. London, Gollancz, 1975; New York, Walker, 1976.
Funeral Urn. London, Gollancz, 1976; New York, Walker, 1977.
The Patriots. London, Gollancz, 1979.
I Saw Him Die. London, Gollancz, 1979.

*   *   *

June Drummond, a native of South Africa, has written some 15 novels. *Cable-Car* is representative of her work. Set in an Alpine village, it spins an admirably contrived tale of several suspenseful days when a famous engineer, Paul Roman, and his daughter, Lisa, are held in a cable car stuck midway in the air to prevent a dam being built. Steve Talbot, Lisa's fiancé and the bodyguard and secretary of Roman, and Anton Dominic, Commissioner of Police, struggle to save their lives in an atmosphere of intrigue and an impending political election. Seeking clues about the identity of the conspirators holding Roman, Talbot and Dominic delve into Roman's past when his beautiful wife, believed dead, and he were partisans. Ultimately, Talbot recalls an illusionist's trick and realizes that Roman's wife is not dead, but is a defector from the West, bent on revenge upon her husband's name and upon the town whose future he was shaping to capitalistic ends. The story reaches its climax when Marthe Roman is captured, and Talbot realizes that an imposter, not Roman, is in the cable car.

The elements in this novel recur in various forms in all the other Drummond tales. In *Cable-Car*, Marthe Roman is the liar, saboteur, and traitor to her country, the beautiful but deadly goddess who bewitches men to destroy them. In *The People in Glass House*, two women shape the tale: Grace Villier, the president of a vast industrial empire, who uses blackmail and putative bastardy to guarantee that her son shall assume her place in the business, and Emma Salt, the mysterious claimant of half this empire, who, too, resorts to blackmail and guerilla tactics to ensure that her story is heard and her identity determined. In *Farewell Party* Drummond creates two women enchantresses: Kate Falconer, a vibrant, reckless woman artist whose mysterious disappearance amid rumors of scandal, murder, and suicide must be unravelled if the lives of the inhabitants of Kolumbe and Michael Crescent are to be secure, and a half-mad keeper of a secret garden, Gretha Corbitt, who knows the truth about Kate. *Welcome, Proud Lady* features a brilliant female student who fears that the frequent accidents in her family's past are part of a dark design in which her sanity is being tested. In both *The Gantry Episode* and *The Saboteurs* the estranged wife of the powerful protagonist figures prominently in the mystery. Drummond seems fond of weaving tales that distantly descend from gothic horror stories. Half-mad women, mistaken identities, women moon-goddesses who destroy those near them, all appear in her pages.

The settings in her novels are of two kinds: the imaginary village in a changing world, fraught by factions, or real cities, London or Durban, populated by powerful, socially elite individuals who struggle to maintain their inheritances, be it an industrial empire or a personal legacy. Drummond's failure in novels like *Cable-Car* and *The Gantry Episode* to locate her story in real places mars the credibility of her tales. It is as though she asks us to believe there is a convenient Transylvania-Chinese border where her story can be set.

Finally, Drummond's fascination with men of money and power who are rendered helpless by a beautiful, but destructive, woman, usually either their mother, mistress, or wife, is a recurring element. Too, there is frequently a hint of love interest. In *Farewell Party*, the first-person narrator, who works to unravel the mystery of her aunt's disappearance, finds herself drawn to a young man who also has inordinate interest in her aunt's history. In *Cable-Car*, Lisa and Steve Talbot are courting one another; in *The People in Glass House*, the heir apparent of the industrial empire is drawn to the mysterious claimant who turns out to be his half-sister. In many of Drummond's more recent novels, especially *Farewell Party* and *Funeral Urn*, the cast of characters and the mode of narration are reminiscent of Mary Robert Rinehart's. And like Rinehart, Drummond seems to be unable to resist involving her characters in moral dilemmas and using the suspense tale as a novel of character development. This impulse is strongest in her treatment of the moral redemption of Casper Douglas in *The Saboteurs*.

Drummond is weakest in her invention of characters. Too many of her stories seem to belong in *The Reader's Digest*. The characters are trivial, the situation stock, and the moralizing and sentimentality too obtrusive. Occasionally, Drummond creates a genuinely chilling scene. She is a story-teller who works best in shaping convoluted tales of the personal past of her protagonists and slowly unravelling them.

—Carol Simpson Stern

DUDLEY-SMITH, T. See **TREVOR, Elleston.**

---

du MAURIER, Daphne. British. Born in London, 13 May 1907; daughter of the actor/ manager Sir Gerald du Maurier; grand-daughter of the writer George du Maurier. Educated privately and in Paris. Married Lieutenant-General Sir Frederick Browning in 1932 (died, 1965); two daughters and one son. Recipient: Mystery Writers of America Grand Master Award, 1977. Fellow, Royal Society of Literature, 1952. D.B.E. (Dame Commander, Order of the British Empire), 1969. Address: Kilmarth, Par, Cornwall, England.

CRIME PUBLICATIONS

Novels

Jamaica Inn. London, Gollancz, and New York, Doubleday, 1936.
Rebecca. London, Gollancz, and New York, Doubleday, 1938.
My Cousin Rachel. London, Gollancz, 1951; New York, Doubleday, 1952.
The Scapegoat. London, Gollancz, and New York, Doubleday, 1957.
The Flight of the Falcon. London, Gollancz, and New York, Doubleday, 1965.
The House on the Strand. London, Gollancz, and New York, Doubleday, 1969.

Short Stories

The Apple Tree: A Short Novel, and Some Stories. London, Gollancz, 1952; as *Kiss Me Again, Stranger: A Collection of Eight Stories, Long and Short*, New York, Doubleday, 1953; as *The Birds and Other Stories*, London, Penguin, 1968.
The Breaking Point: Eight Stories. London, Gollancz, and New York, Doubleday, 1959; as *The Blue Lenses and Other Stories*, London, Penguin, 1970.
Not after Midnight and Other Stories. London, Gollancz, 1971; as *Don't Look Now*, New York, Doubleday, 1971.

OTHER PUBLICATIONS

Novels

The Loving Spirit. London, Heinemann, and New York, Doubleday, 1931.
I'll Never Be Young Again. London, Heinemann, and New York, Doubleday, 1932.
The Progress of Julius. London, Heinemann, and New York, Doubleday, 1933.
Frenchman's Creek. London, Gollancz, 1941; New York, Doubleday, 1942.
Hungry Hill. London, Gollancz, and New York, Doubleday, 1943.
The King's General. London, Gollancz, and New York, Doubleday, 1946.
The Parasites. London, Gollancz, 1949; New York, Doubleday, 1950.
Mary Anne. London, Gollancz, and New York, Doubleday, 1954.
Castle Dor, by Arthur Quiller-Couch, completed by du Maurier. London, Dent, and New York, Doubleday, 1962.
The Glass-Blowers. London, Gollancz, and New York, Doubleday, 1963.
Rule Britannia. London, Gollancz, 1972; New York, Doubleday, 1973.

Short Stories

Happy Christmas (story). New York, Doubleday, 1940; London, Todd, 1943.
Come Wind, Come Weather. London, Heinemann, 1940; New York, Doubleday, 1941.
Nothing Hurts for Long, and Escort. London, Todd, 1943.
Consider the Lilies (story). London, Todd, 1943.
Spring Picture (story). London, Todd, 1944.
Leading Lady (story). London, Vallancey Press, 1945.
London and Paris (two stories). London, Vallancey Press, 1945.
Early Stories. London, Bantam, 1954.
The Treasury of du Maurier Short Stories. London, Gollancz, 1960.
Echoes from the Macabre: Selected Stories. London, Gollancz, 1976; New York, Doubleday, 1977.

Plays

Rebecca, adaptation of her own novel (produced Manchester and London, 1940; New York, 1945). London, Gollancz, 1940; New York, Dramatists Play Service, 1943.
The Years Between (produced Manchester, 1944; London, 1945). London, Gollancz, 1945; New York, Doubleday, 1946.
September Tide (produced Oxford and London, 1948). London, Gollancz, 1949; New York, Doubleday, 1950.

Screenplay: Hungry Hill, with Terence Young and Francis Crowdry, 1947.

Television Play: The Breakthrough, 1976.

Other

Gerald: A Portrait (on Gerald du Maurier). London, Gollancz, 1934; New York, Doubleday, 1935.
The du Mauriers. London, Gollancz, and New York, Doubleday, 1937.
The Infernal World of Branwell Brontë. London, Gollancz, 1960; New York, Doubleday, 1961.
Vanishing Cornwall, photographs by Christian Browning. London, Gollancz, and New York, Doubleday, 1967.
Golden Lads: Sir Francis Bacon, Anthony Bacon, and Their Friends. London, Gollancz, and New York, Doubleday, 1975.
The Winding Stair: Francis Bacon, His Rise and Fall. London, Gollancz, 1976; New York, Doubleday, 1977.
Growing Pains: The Shaping of a Writer (autobiography). London, Gollancz, 1977; as Myself When Young, New York, Doubleday, 1977.

Editor, The Young George du Maurier: A Selection of His Letters 1860–1867. London, Davies, 1951; New York, Doubleday, 1952.
Editor, Best Stories, by Phyllis Bottome. London, Faber, 1963.

* * *

Among Daphne du Maurier's excellent studies in suspense are four novels which focus upon the beautifully paced delineation of an unusually powerful personality. Also portrayed is a less glamorous but equally fascinating protagonist who recounts a plot complicated by jealousy and misconception. The impact of some criminal act, real or imagined, affects each situation, and the novels end on notes of ironic justice.

The unnamed protagonist of Rebecca is kept from full happiness by her lack of self-confidence and because she lives under the ghostly shadow of a brilliant, headstrong first wife. The mounting tension surrounding Rebecca's mysterious death combines with a vividly evoked setting to achieve the novel's remarkable and deserved success. The title character of My Cousin Rachel is beloved by two cousins, Ambrose and Philip Ashley. Rachel may be a true gentlewoman or a merciless poisoner, and this mystery is enhanced by Philip's convincingly dramatized search for maturity. The Scapegoat makes probable a wild coincidence when the narrator is tricked into temporarily living the life of Jean de Gué whom he strikingly resembles. Much of the impact stems from his developing sense of himself as he learns to wield the power de Gué customarily exercises. The Flight of the Falcon contrasts Armino and Aldo Donati in a compelling examination of the hunger for personal and political power of both modern and Renaissance man.

These, like many of du Maurier's works, raise serious questions about the nature of good and of evil – then enticingly leave the answers to the reader's imagination.

—Jane S. Bakerman

DUNCAN, Robert L.   See **ROBERTS, James Hall.**

DUNCAN, W(illiam) Murdoch.   Also wrote as John Cassells; John Dallas; Neill Graham; Martin Locke; Peter Malloch; Lovat Marshall.   British.   Born in Glasgow, Lanark, 18 November 1909. Educated at Windsor and Waterville Collegiate Institutes; University of Glasgow, M.A. in history 1934. Served in the British Army, 1940–41. Married Marion Hughes; one son and one daughter. *Died 19 April 1976.*

CRIME PUBLICATIONS

Novels (series characters: The Dreamer [Superintendent D. Reamer]; Superintendent Gaylord; Mr. Gilly; Laurie Hume; Superintendent MacNeill)

The Doctor Deals with Murder.   London, Melrose, 1944.
Death Wears a Silk Stocking.   London, Melrose, 1945.
Mystery on the Clyde.   London, Melrose, 1945.
Murder at Marks Caris.   London, Melrose, 1945.
Death Beckons Quietly.   London, Melrose, 1946.
Killer Keep.   London, Melrose, 1946.
Straight Ahead for Danger.   London, Melrose, 1946.
The Tiled House Mystery.   London, Melrose, 1947.
The Blackbird Sings of Murder.   London, Melrose, 1948.
The Puppets of Father Bouvard.   London, Melrose, 1948.
The Cult of the Queer People.   London, Melrose, 1949.
The Brothers of Judgement.   London, Melrose, 1950.
The Black Mitre.   London, Melrose, 1951.
The Company of Sinners.   London, Melrose, 1951.
The Blood Red Leaf.   London, Melrose, 1952.
Death Comes to Lady's Steps.   London, Melrose, 1952.
The Deathmaster.   London, Hutchinson, 1953.
Death Stands round the Corner (MacNeill).   London, Rich and Cowan, 1955.
A Knife in the Night (MacNeill).   London, Rich and Cowan, 1955.
Pennies for His Eyes.   London, Rich and Cowan, 1956.
Murder Calls the Tune (Hume).   London, Long, 1957.
The Joker Deals with Death.   London, Long, 1958.
The Murder Man (Hume).   London, Long, 1959.
The Whispering Man (Hume).   London, Long, 1959.

The Hooded Man (Gaylord).   London, Long, 1960.
The House in Spite Street.   London, Long, 1961.
The Vengeance of Mortimer Daly (as Martin Locke).   London, Ward Lock, 1961.
The Night of the Storm (as John Dallas).   London, Jenkins, 1961.
The Nighthawk (Gaylord).   London, Long, 1962.
Redfingers.   London, Long, 1962.
The Crime Master (Gilly).   London, Long, 1963.
Meet the Dreamer.   London, Long, 1963.
The Green Knight.   London, Long, 1963.
The Hour of the Bishop.   London, Long, 1964.
The House of Wailing Winds.   London, Long, 1965.
Again the Dreamer.   London, Long, 1965.
Presenting the Dreamer.   London, Long, 1966.
Case for the Dreamer.   London, Long, 1966.
The Council of Comforters.   London, Long, 1967.
Problem for the Dreamer.   London, Long, 1967.
Salute the Dreamer.   London, Long, 1968.
The Dreamer Intervenes.   London, Long, 1968.
Cord for a Killer.   London, Long, 1969.
Challenge for the Dreamer.   London, Long, 1969.
The Green Triangle.   London, Long, 1969.
The Dreamer Deals with Murder.   London, Long, 1970.
The Whisperer.   London, Long, 1970.
Detail for the Dreamer.   London, Long, 1971.
The Breath of Murder.   London, Long, 1972.
The Dreamer at Large.   London, Long, 1972.
The Big Timer.   London, Long, 1973.
Red Ice (as John Dallas).   London, Hale, 1973.
Prey for the Dreamer.   London, Long, 1974.
Death and Mr. Gilly.   London, Long, 1974.
Laurels for the Dreamer.   London, Long, 1975.
Murder of a Cop.   London, Long, 1976.

Novels as John Cassels (series characters: Inspector/Superintendent Flagg; The Picaroon
    [Ludovic Saxon])

The Sons of Morning.   London, Melrose, 1946.
The Bastion of the Damned.   London, Melrose, 1946.
Murder Comes to Rothesay.   London, Melrose, 1946.
The Mark of the Leech.   London, Melrose, 1947.
Master of the Dark.   London, Melrose, 1948.
The League of Nameless Men.   London, Melrose, 1948.
The Castle of Sin.   London, Melrose, 1949.
The Clue of the Purple Asters (Flagg).   London, Melrose, 1949.
The Waters of Sadness.   London, Melrose, 1950.
The Circle of Dust (Flagg).   London, Melrose, 1950.
The Grey Ghost (Flagg).   London, Melrose, 1951.
Exit Mr. Shane (Flagg).   London, Melrose, 1951.
The Second Mrs. Locke.   London, Melrose, 1952.
The Rattler (Flagg).   London, Melrose, 1952.
Salute Inspector Flagg.   London, Muller, 1953.
Case for Inspector Flagg.   London, Muller, 1954.
Enter the Picaroon.   London, Muller, 1954.
Inspector Flagg and the Scarlet Skeleton.   London, Muller, 1955.
The Avenging Picaroon.   London, Muller, 1956.

Again Inspector Flagg. London, Muller, 1956.
Beware! The Picaroon. London, Muller, 1956.
Meet the Picaroon. London, Long, 1957.
Presenting Inspector Flagg. London, Muller, 1957.
Case 29 (Flagg). London, Long, 1958.
The Engaging Picaroon. London, Long, 1958.
Enter Superintendent Flagg. London, Long, 1959.
The Enterprising Picaroon. London, Long, 1959.
Score for Superintendent Flagg. London, Long, 1960.
Salute the Picaroon. London, Long, 1960.
Problem for Superintendent Flagg. London, Long, 1961.
The Brothers of Benevolence (Flagg). London, Long, 1962.
The Picaroon Goes West. London, Long, 1962.
Prey for the Picaroon. London, Long, 1963.
The Council of the Rat (Flagg). London, Long, 1963.
Blue Mask. London, Long, 1964.
Challenge for the Picaroon. London, Long, 1964.
Grey Face (Flagg). London, Long, 1965.
The Benevolent Picaroon. London, Long, 1965.
Plunder for the Picaroon. London, Long, 1966.
Blackfingers (Flagg). London, Long, 1966.
The Audacious Picaroon. London, Long, 1967.
The Room in Quiver Court (Flagg). London, Long, 1967.
The Elusive Picaroon. London, Long, 1968.
Call for Superintendent Flagg. London, Long, 1968.
Night of the Picaroon. London, Long, 1969.
The Double-Crosser (Flagg). London, Long, 1969.
Quest for the Picaroon. London, Long, 1970.
The Grafter (Flagg). London, Long, 1970.
The Picaroon Collects. London, Long, 1970.
The Hatchet Man (Flagg). London, Long, 1971.
Profit for the Picaroon. London, Long, 1972.
The Enforcer (Flagg). London, Long, 1973.
The Picaroon Laughs Last. London, Long, 1973.
Killer's Role (Flagg). London, Long, 1974.
Action for the Picaroon. London, Long, 1975.
Quest for Superintendent Flagg. London, Long, 1975.
The Picaroon Gets the Run-Around. London, Long, 1976.

Novels as Neill Graham (series characters: James "Solo" Malcolm; Mr. Sandyman)

The Symbol of the Cat (Sandyman). London, Melrose, 1948.
Passport to Murder (Sandyman). London, Melrose, 1949.
The Temple of Slumber. London, Melrose, 1950.
The Quest of Mr. Sandyman. London, Jarrolds, 1951.
Murder Walks on Tiptoe. London, Melrose, 1951.
Again, Mr. Sandyman. London, Jarrolds, 1952.
Amazing Mr. Sandyman. London, Jarrolds, 1952.
Salute Mr. Sandyman. London, Jarrolds, 1953.
Play It Solo (Malcolm). London, Jarrolds, 1955.
Murder Makes a Date (Malcolm). London, Jarrolds, 1955; New York, Roy, 1956.
Say It with Murder (Malcolm). London, Jarrolds, 1956.
You Can't Call It Murder (Malcolm). London, Jarrolds, 1957.
Salute to Murder (Malcolm). London, Long, 1958.
Hit Me Hard (Malcolm). London, Long, 1958.

Murder Rings the Bell (Malcolm).   London, Jarrolds, 1959.
Killers Are on Velvet (Malcolm).   London, Long, 1960.
Murder Is My Weakness (Malcolm).   London, Long, 1961.
Murder on the "Duchess" (Malcolm).   London, Long, 1961.
Make Mine Murder (Malcolm).   London, Long, 1962.
Label It Murder (Malcolm).   London, Long, 1963.
Graft Town (Malcolm).   London, Long, 1963.
Murder Makes It Certain (Malcolm).   London, Long, 1963.
Murder Made Easy (Malcolm).   London, Long, 1964.
Murder of a Black Cat (Malcolm).   London, Long, 1964.
Murder on My Hands (Malcolm).   London, Long, 1965.
Murder's Always Final (Malcolm).   London, Long, 1965.
Money for Murder (Malcolm).   London, Long, 1966.
Murder on Demand (Malcolm).   London, Long, 1966.
Murder Makes the News (Malcolm).   London, Long, 1967.
Murder Has Been Done (Malcolm).   London, Long, 1967.
Pay Off (Malcolm).   London, Long, 1968.
Candidate for a Coffin (Malcolm).   London, Long, 1968.
Death of a Canary (Malcolm).   London, Long, 1968.
Murder Lies in Waiting (Malcolm).   London, Long, 1969.
Blood on the Pavement (Malcolm).   London, Long, 1970.
One for the Book (Malcolm).   London, Long, 1970.
A Matter for Murder (Malcolm).   London, Long, 1971.
Murder, Double Murder (Malcolm).   London, Long, 1971.
Frame-Up (Malcolm).   London, Long, 1972.
Cop in a Tight Frame (Malcolm).   London, Long, 1973.
Murder in a Dark Room (Malcolm).   London, Long, 1973.
Assignment, Murder (Malcolm).   London, Long, 1974.
Murder on the List (Malcolm).   London, Long, 1975.

Novels as Peter Malloch

11:20 Glasgow Central.   London, Rich and Cowan, 1955.
Sweet Lady Death.   London, Rich and Cowan, 1956.
Tread Softly, Death.   London, Rich and Cowan, 1957.
Walk In, Death.   London, Long, 1957.
Fly Away, Death.   London, Long, 1958.
My Shadow, Death.   London, Long, 1959.
Hardiman's Landing.   London, Long, 1960.
Anchor Island.   London, Long, 1962.
Blood Money.   London, Long, 1962.
Break-Through.   London, Long, 1963.
Fugitive's Road.   London, Long, 1963.
Cop-Lover.   London, Long, 1964.
The Nicholas Snatch.   London, Long, 1964.
The Sniper.   London, Long, 1965.
Lady of No Compassion.   London, Long, 1966.
The Big Steal.   London, Long, 1966.
Murder of the Man Next Door.   London, Long, 1966.
Die, My Beloved.   London, Long, 1967.
Johnny Blood.   London, Long, 1967.
Murder of a Student.   London, Long, 1968.
Death Whispers Softly.   London, Long, 1968.
Backwash.   London, Long, 1969.
Blood on Pale Fingers.   London, Long, 1969.

The Adjustor. London, Long, 1970.
The Grab. London, Long, 1970.
The Slugger. London, Long, 1971.
Two with a Gun. London, Long, 1971.
Write-Off. London, Long, 1972.
Kickback. London, Long, 1973.
The Delinquents. London, Long, 1974.
The Big Killing. London, Long, 1974.
Killer's Blade. London, Long, 1975.
The Big Deal. London, Long, 1977.

Novels as Lovat Marshall (series character: Sugar Kane in all books)

Sugar for the Lady. London, Hurst and Blackett, 1955.
Sugar on the Carpet. London, Hurst and Blackett, 1956.
Sugar Cuts the Corners. London, Long, 1957.
Sugar on the Target. London, Long, 1958.
Sugar on the Cuff. London, Hale, 1960.
Sugar on the Kill. London, Hale, 1961.
Sugar on the Loose. London, Hale, 1962.
Sugar on the Prowl. London, Hale, 1962.
Murder in Triplicate. London, Hale, 1963.
Murder Is the Reason. London, Hale, 1964.
Ladies Can Be Dangerous. London, Hale, 1964.
Death Strikes in Darkness. London, Hale, 1965.
The Dead Are Silent. London, Hale, 1966.
The Dead Are Dangerous. London, Hale, 1966.
Murder of a Lady. London, Hale, 1967.
Blood on the Blotter. London, Hale, 1968.
Money Means Murder. London, Hale, 1968.
Death Is For Ever. London, Hale, 1969.
Murder's Out of Season. London, Hale, 1970.
Murder's Just for Cops. London, Hale, 1971.
Death Casts a Shadow. London, Hale, 1972.
Moment for Murder. London, Hale, 1972.
Loose Lady Death. London, Hale, 1973.
Date with Murder. London, Hale, 1973.
Murder Town. London, Hale, 1974.
The Strangler. London, Hale, 1974.
Key to Murder. London, Hale, 1975.
Murder Mission. London, Hale, 1975.
Murder to Order. London, Hale, 1975.

*   *   *

I suppose there are but a handful of British thriller or mystery writers who have been automatically on publishers' lists for the past thirty years with their reputations untarnished. Success is only consistent for a very few years, and even fewer remain authors in this field for a very long time. W. Murdoch Duncan wrote over 200 books, under his own name and several pseudonyms. He was a writer who paid as much attention to his characters as to his plots, and was able to create atmosphere and pace, as well as providing the reader with a real problem in detection. Perhaps the real value of him as an author is summed up by these two criteria. Are his books un-put-downable, and can they be read more than once and still be enjoyed? The answer to both these questions is a resounding yes.

Duncan wrote his books in three different styles, grouping his thrillers in his major bye-line Duncan and Cassells (A), Graham and Marshall (B), Malloch and Dallas (C). The Duncan stories are basically ones of detection, often featuring organised crime. Murders here are incidental rather than essential to the main plot. Part of the fascination established in his earlier books are the intricacies of the sub-plots which give great scope for the development of characters. The Graham-Marshall books use private detectives, but with a Duncan touch. Those written as Malloch and Dallas are basically thrillers rather than detection and are of the "true to life" type.

Duncan started writing in the early 1930's, and wrote several hundred short stories for the pre-war magazines *The Detective*, *The Thriller*, and *Tit-Bits*. His novels ran to 80–90,000 words, and this length enabled him to develop his characters and include sub-plots. Such emphasis on strong characterisation naturally produced recurring series characters, such as Superintendent Flagg and his redoubtable henchman Newell, Solo Malcolm, and the Picaroon and his ex-wrestler assistant McNab. Only in the 1960's did Duncan introduce "The Dreamer" (Superintendent Donald Reamer), a complete contrast to Flagg, both in character and in physique. The Dreamer is helped by Sergeant Kettle, a policeman of the old school, who is as insubordinate as he is efficient, but in his insubordination gives many opportunities for laconic humour.

For straight mysteries with an intricate measure of intrigue, plenty of action, and an unexpected solution, Duncan's books are to be recommended, particularly *Murder at Marks Caris*, *Mystery on the Clyde*, *Bastion of the Damned*, and *Circle of Dust*.

—Donald C. Ireland

DUNNE, John Gregory. American. Born in Hartford, Connecticut, 25 May 1932. Educated at Princeton University, New Jersey, A.B. 1954. Married the writer Joan Didion in 1964; one daughter. Self-employed writer. Agent: Lynn Nesbit, International Creative Management, 40 West 57th Street, New York, New York 10019, U.S.A.

CRIME PUBLICATIONS

Novel

True Confessions.   New York, Dutton, 1977.

OTHER PUBLICATIONS

Novel

Vegas: A Memoir of a Dark Season.   New York, Random House, 1974.

Plays

Screenplays (with Joan Didion): *Panic in Needle Park*, 1971; *Play It as It Lays*, 1972.

Other

Delano: The Story of the California Grape Strike.   New York, Farrar Straus, 1967; revised edition, 1971.

The Studio. New York, Farrar Straus, 1969.

Quintana and Friends (essays). New York, Dutton, and London, Weidenfeld and Nicolson, 1979.

* * *

The naked and severed body of a young woman is discovered in a vacant lot in Los Angeles in the 1940's, and Detective Tom Spellacy is called in to investigate. Thus begins John Gregory Dunne's mystery novel *True Confessions*, and before the case of "The Virgin Tramp" (as the tabloids dub it) is solved, far more than anyone had bargained for is revealed.

The search for the girl's killer provides an interesting picture of police investigation, but the real business of the novel is elsewhere: Dunne's primary interest is the fraternal rivalry between Detective Spellacy and his brother, the Right Reverend Monsignor Desmond Spellacy, Chancellor of the Roman Catholic diocese of Los Angeles, and the incestuous relationship between the police department and the Irish hierarchy of the Church as both are drawn into a tangled web of crime, corruption, and complicity. The investigation into the murder uncovers information that implicates practically everyone, but not in the murder. The damaging truths are revealed unnecessarily since, in an ironic twist, it turns out that the girl's murderer was himself killed in an accident even before her body was discovered.

As a mystery writer, Dunne echoes many others: Raymond Chandler in his depiction of the seamy side of L.A. in the forties; Ross Macdonald in his tracing of the multiple reverberations touched off by a crime; Joseph Wambaugh in his no-holds-barred picture of the policeman at work and play; George Higgins in his ear for lusty Irish-American vernacular speech. But *True Confessions* is more than merely echoes; it is a highly original novel distinguished for its vitality and wit, for its brilliant characterizations, and for its hard-boiled style that is a unique blend of Irish idiom, scatological and blasphemous humor, and mordant wit. Dunne has taken the police procedural novel and made it simultaneously more serious and more humorous than anyone before him. The novel is a most inventive contribution to contemporary crime fiction.

—David J. Geherin

DUNNETT, Dorothy (née Halliday). British. Born in Dunfermline, Fife, 25 August 1923. Educated at James Gillespie's High School, Edinburgh; Edinburgh College of Art; Glasgow School of Art. Married Alastair M. Dunnett in 1946; two sons. Worked in the Public Relations Department of the Secretary of State for Scotland, Edinburgh, 1940–46, and the Research Department, Board of Trade, Glasgow, 1946–55. Professional Portrait Painter: has exhibited at the Royal Scottish Academy, Edinburgh, since 1950. Director, Scottish Television Ltd. Since 1976, Panel Member, Scottish Arts Council. Recipient: Scottish Arts Council award, 1976. Agent: Curtis Brown Ltd., 1 Craven Hill, London W2 3EP, England. Address: 87 Colinton Road, Edinburgh EH10 5DF, Scotland.

CRIME PUBLICATIONS

Novels (series character: Johnson Johnson in all books; published as Dorothy Halliday in
UK)

Dolly and the Singing Bird. London, Cassell, 1968; as *The Photogenic Soprano*, Boston,
Houghton Mifflin, 1968.
Dolly and the Cookie Bird. London, Cassell, 1970; as *Murder in the Round*, Boston,
Houghton Mifflin, 1970.
Dolly and the Doctor Bird. London, Cassell, 1971; as *Match for a Murderer*, Boston,
Houghton Mifflin, 1971.
Dolly and the Starry Bird. London, Cassell, 1973; as *Murder in Focus*, Boston,
Houghton Mifflin, 1973.
Dolly and the Nanny Bird. London, Joseph, 1976.

OTHER PUBLICATIONS

Novels

The Game of Kings. New York, Putnam, 1961; London, Cassell, 1962.
Queens' Play. London, Cassell, and New York, Putnam, 1964.
The Disorderly Knights. London, Cassell, and New York, Putnam, 1966.
Pawn in Frankincense. London, Cassell, and New York, Putnam, 1969.
The Ringed Castle. London, Cassell, 1971; New York, Putnam, 1972.
Checkmate. London, Cassell, and New York, Putnam, 1975.

Dorothy Dunnett comments:

My crime books are fast fun-thrillers about a portrait painter called Johnson Johnson who
sails his own yacht, the *Dolly*, to a series of glamorous posts as a cover for a world-wide
Intelligence job. The narrator of each book is a pretty girl – the "bird" of the title: each one
quite different, and with a distinctive job of her own. Which of them gets Johnson in the end
will not be apparent until the series finishes.

*   *   *

Dorothy Dunnett has produced a series of detective/suspense novels loosely united by the
presence of their hero, Johnson Johnson, an international portrait painter and spy. Johnson,
whose baggy sweaters and bifocals camouflage a first-rate mind, owes a great deal to
Allingham's early Albert Campion, including his generous capacity to keep to the
background while some remarkable heroines occupy center stage and narrate their
adventures. There is little to choose between the heroines for intelligence, competence, or
charm, but perhaps the most impressive, in different ways, are Tina Rossi, the coloratura of
Dolly and the Singing Bird, and Dr. Beltanno Douglas Mac Rannoch of *Dolly and the Doctor
Bird*. Tina Rossi is a portrait whose full tragic dimensions are concealed until almost the last
page. Dr. Mac Rannoch must be brought to accept her sexuality before she can take charge of
her own destiny, and Dunnett handles the theme with as much delicacy as humor.

The basic genre of the novels is the suspense story: each is full of action, including at least
one superb chase sequence. In *Dolly and the Doctor Bird*, Johnson's ketch *Dolly* only
narrowly escapes an explosive small boat with a homing device. In *Dolly and the Starry Bird*,
there is a car chase with explosive balloons along Roman roads in rush-hour traffic that
modulates from the chilling to the farcical. All of this is rendered in a sophisticated prose
which is elegantly constructed, idiomatic, and thick with detail from the worlds of music,
medicine, astronomy, and gastronomy.

—Carol Cleveland

DURBRIDGE, Francis (Henry).   British.   Born in Hull, Yorkshire, 25 November 1912. Educated at Bradford Grammar School; Wylde Green College; Birmingham University, 1933. Married Norah Lawley in 1940; two sons. Worked briefly in a stockbroker's office before becoming full-time writer. Agent: Harvey Unna and Stephen Durbridge Ltd., 14 Beaumont Mews, Marylebone High Street, London W1N 4HE, England.

CRIME PUBLICATIONS

Novels (series characters: Tim Frazer; Paul Temple)

Send for Paul Temple (novelization of radio serial).   London, Long, 1938.
Paul Temple and the Front Page Men (novelization of radio serial), with Charles Hatton.   London, Long, 1939.
News of Paul Temple.   London, Long, 1940.
Paul Temple Intervenes.   London, Long, 1944.
Send for Paul Temple Again!   London, Long, 1948.
The Back Room Girl.   London, Long, 1950.
Beware of Johnny Washington.   London, Long, 1951.
Design for Murder.   London, Long, 1951.
The Tyler Mystery (Temple), with Douglas Rutherford (as Paul Temple).   London, Hodder and Stoughton, 1957.
The Other Man.   London, Hodder and Stoughton, 1958.
East of Algiers (Temple), with Douglas Rutherford (as Paul Temple).   London, Hodder and Stoughton, 1959.
A Time of Day.   London, Hodder and Stoughton, 1959.
The Scarf.   London, Hodder and Stoughton, 1960; as *The Case of the Twisted Scarf*, New York, Dodd Mead, 1961.
Portrait of Alison.   London, Hodder and Stoughton, and New York, Dodd Mead, 1962.
The World of Tim Frazer.   London, Hodder and Stoughton, and New York, Dodd Mead, 1962.
My Friend Charles.   London, Hodder and Stoughton, 1963.
Tim Frazer Again.   London, Hodder and Stoughton, 1964.
Another Woman's Shoes.   London, Hodder and Stoughton, 1965.
The Desperate People.   London, Hodder and Stoughton, 1966.
Dead to the World.   London, Hodder and Stoughton, 1967.
My Wife Melissa.   London, Hodder and Stoughton, 1967.
The Pig-Tail Murder.   London, Hodder and Stoughton, 1969.
Paul Temple and the Kelby Affair.   London, Hodder and Stoughton, 1970.
Paul Temple and the Harkdale Robbery.   London, Hodder and Stoughton, 1970.
A Man Called Harry Brent (novelization of tv series).   London, Hodder and Stoughton, 1970.
The Geneva Mystery (Temple).   London, Hodder and Stoughton, 1971.
Bat Out of Hell.   London, Hodder and Stoughton, 1972.
The Curzon Case (Temple).   London, Coronet, 1972.
A Game of Murder.   London, Hodder and Stoughton, 1975.
The Passenger.   London, Hodder and Stoughton, 1977.
Tim Frazer Gets the Message.   London, Hodder and Stoughton, 1978.

OTHER PUBLICATIONS

Plays

Suddenly at Home (produced London, 1971).   London, French, 1973.
The Gentle Hook (produced London, 1974).   London, French, 1975.
Murder with Love (produced Windsor, 1976).   London, French, 1977.

Screenplays: *Send for Paul Temple*, with John Argyle, 1946; *Calling Paul Temple*, with A. R. Rawlinson, 1948; *Paul Temple Returns*, 1952; *The Teckman Mystery*, with James Matthews, 1954; *The Vicious Circle (The Circle)*, 1957.

Radio Plays: *Promotion*, 1937; *Paul Temple*, 1938; *Information Received*, 1938; *And Anthony Sherwood Laughed*, 1940; *We Were Strangers*, 1941; *Send for Paul Temple*, 1941; *Mr. Hartington Died Tomorrow* (as Lewis Middleton Harvey), 1942; *Paul Temple Intervenes*, 1942; *The Essential Heart*, 1943; *Farewell Leicester Square* (as Lewis Middleton Harvey), 1943; *News of Paul Temple*, 1944; *Send for Paul Temple Again*, 1945; *Over My Dead Body*, 1946; *Paul Temple and the Gregory Affair*, 1946; *The Case for Paul Temple*, 1946; *Paul Temple and Steve*, 1947; *Paul Temple and the Sullivan Mystery*, 1947; *Mr. and Mrs. Paul Temple*, 1947; *Paul Temple and the Curzon Case*, 1948; *Paul Temple and the Madison Mystery*, 1949; *Johnny Washington Esquire* (series), 1949; *Paul Temple and the Vandyke Affair*, 1950; *Paul Temple and the Jonathan Mystery*, 1951; *Paul Temple and Steve Again*, 1953; *Paul Temple and the Lawrence Affair*, 1956; *Paul Temple and the Spencer Affair*, 1957; *Paul Temple and the Conrad Case*, 1959; *Paul Temple and the Margot Mystery*, 1961; *What Do You Think?*, 1962; *Paul Temple and the Geneva Mystery*, 1965; *La Boutique*, 1967; *Paul Temple and the Alex Affair*, 1968.

Television Plays (all serials): *The Broken Horseshoe*, 1952; *Operation Diplomat*, 1952; *The Teckman Biography*, 1953; *Portrait of Alison*, 1955; *My Friend Charles*, 1956; *The Other Man*, 1956; *A Time of Day*, 1957; *The Scarf*, 1959; *The World of Tim Frazer*, with others, 1960; *The Desperate People*, 1963; *Melissa*, 1964, 1974; *A Man Called Harry Brent*, 1965; *A Game of Murder*, 1966; *Bat Out of Hell*, 1966; *The Passenger*, 1971; *The Doll*, 1975; *Breakaway*, 1979.

*   *   *

The name of Francis Durbridge will always be associated with the BBC radio serials featuring the novelist-detective Paul Temple and his wife Steve. Durbridge was the master of the cliff-hanger, albeit verbal rather than unpleasantly physical; his radio serials were produced and re-produced from the 1930's onwards. Temple cases also appeared as novels, and Durbridge later brought his character to life by collaborating with Douglas Rutherford in writing two books "by Paul Temple." Today, millions are aware of Durbridge as one of the most successful writers for television. His television serials have been produced sparingly, which has enabled him to maintain a freshness within a type of mystery he has made very much his own. The compulsive viewing of his serials throughout a large part of the world speaks greatly for his power as a storyteller.

Many of the television serials have been transferred by Durbridge to the printed page. They have no series character like Temple – perhaps the inter-linked adventures of Tim Frazer come closest – but this enables Durbridge each time to make his central character a protagonist rather than an onlooker, either an anti-hero or a suspect who is attempting to extricate himself from a web which enmeshes him more securely at every turn. Although he has freed himself from the Temple strait-jacket, Durbridge appears to know precisely what his readers and viewers expect of him, and he works almost exclusively within his own particular niche. The cast is normally drawn from what is popularly termed the gin-and-tonic set – upper-middle-class estate agents, photographers, and antique dealers abound, as do others who appear to have ample time to indulge in deception and criminal intrigue.

Followers of Durbridge must be so well acquainted with his style that the twists and turns of his plots become somewhat predictable. As a master of his craft, however, he is capable of springing a surprise or two and revealing a totally unexpected murderer – one recalls, for example, *The Other Man*. Transferred to the printed page, his serials tend to betray their origin by a succession of cliff-hangers throughout, and the shortage of descriptive passages and predominance of dialogue indicate that his real skill lies in creating scripts rather than novels. Other areas of predictability may be mentioned, not necessarily as adverse criticism but as examples of the Durbridge milieu and style. His plots are frequently populated with pals of the hero or hail-fellows who turn out to be something completely different. Then there are his settings – switching from London to Thames-side commuter country, and back again. When the hero is lured to a cottage at Marlow or a houseboat on the river, we can be sure he will find a door ajar and a corpse just beyond. We can also expect, more often than not, that the murder victims will be women and the master criminal will turn out to be a man; a strange point this, but the whole atmosphere surrounding Durbridge's plots tends to be one of male chauvinism.

Durbridge has no special message, no mission to examine the springs of violence or the motivation which leads a man to murder, and seemingly no purpose other than to present to his audience one piece of craftsmanlike escapism after another. Nevertheless, whether in adaptations from the screen or original novels – *The Pig-Tail Murder* is a competent example of the latter – Durbridge's ability as a skilful weaver of webs and a typically British exponent of the guessing-game has maintained his position as one of the most consistently entertaining crime writers.

—Melvyn Barnes

DURHAM, David.   See **VICKERS, Roy C.**

EBERHART, Mignon G(ood).   American.   Born in University Place, Nebraska, 6 July 1899. Educated in local schools; Nebraska Wesleyan University, Lincoln, 1917–20. Married 1) John P. Hazen Perry (divorced); 2) Alanson C. Eberhart in 1923. Self-employed writer since 1930. Past President, Mystery Writers of America. Recipient: Scotland Yard Prize, 1931; Mystery Writers of America Grand Master Award, 1970. D.Litt.: Nebraska Wesleyan University, 1935. Agent: Brandt and Brandt, 101 Park Avenue, New York, New York 10017. Address: c/o Popular Library, 355 Lexington Avenue, New York, New York 10017, U.S.A.

CRIME PUBLICATIONS

Novels (series characters: Sarah Keate and Lance O'Leary)

   The Patient in Room 18 (Keate and O'Leary).   New York, Doubleday, and London, Heinemann, 1929.

The Mystery of Hunting's End (Keate and O'Leary). New York, Doubleday, 1930; London, Heinemann, 1931.

While the Patient Slept (Keate and O'Leary). New York, Doubleday, and London, Heinemann, 1930.

From This Dark Stairway (Keate and O'Leary). New York, Doubleday, 1931; London, Heinemann, 1932.

Murder by an Aristocrat (Keate and O'Leary). New York, Doubleday, 1932; as *Murder of My Patient*, London, Lane, 1934.

The Dark Garden. New York, Doubleday, 1933; as *Death in the Fog*, London, Lane, 1934.

The White Cockatoo. New York, Doubleday, and London, Falcon Books, 1933.

The House on the Roof. New York, Doubleday, and London, Collins, 1935.

Fair Warning. New York, Doubleday, and London, Collins, 1936.

Danger in the Dark. New York, Doubleday, 1937; as *Hand in Glove*, London, Collins, 1937.

The Pattern. New York, Doubleday, and London, Collins, 1937; as *Pattern of Murder*, New York, Popular Library, 1948.

The Glass Slipper. New York, Doubleday, and London, Collins, 1938.

Hasty Wedding. New York, Doubleday, 1938; London, Collins, 1939.

Brief Return. London, Collins, 1939.

The Chiffon Scarf. New York, Doubleday, 1939; London, Collins, 1940.

The Hangman's Whip. New York, Doubleday, 1940; London, Collins, 1941.

Strangers in Flight. Los Angeles, Bantam, 1941.

Speak No Evil. New York, Random House, and London, Collins, 1941.

With This Ring. New York, Random House, 1941; London, Collins, 1942.

Wolf in Man's Clothing (Keate). New York, Random House, 1942; London, Collins, 1943.

The Man Next Door. New York, Random House, 1943; London, Collins, 1944.

Unidentified Woman. New York, Random House, 1943; London, Collins, 1945.

Escape the Night. New York, Random House, 1944; London, Collins, 1945.

Five Passengers from Lisbon. New York, Random House, and London, Collins, 1946.

Wings of Fear. New York, Random House, 1945; London, Collins, 1946.

The White Dress. New York, Random House, 1946; London, Collins, 1947.

Another Woman's House. New York, Random House, 1947; London, Collins, 1948.

House of Storm. New York, Random House, and London, Collins, 1949.

Hunt with the Hounds. New York, Random House, 1950; London, Collins, 1951.

Never Look Back. New York, Random House, and London, Collins, 1951.

Dead Men's Plans. New York, Random House, 1952; London, Collins, 1953.

The Unknown Quantity. New York, Random House, and London, Collins, 1953.

Man Missing (Keate). New York, Random House, and London, Collins, 1954.

Postmark Murder. New York, Random House, and London, Collins, 1956.

Another Man's Murder. New York, Random House, 1957; London, Collins, 1958.

Melora. New York, Random House, 1959; London, Collins, 1960; as *The Promise of Murder*, New York, Dell, 1961.

Jury of One. New York, Random House, 1960; London, Collins, 1961.

The Cup, The Blade, or the Gun. New York, Random House, 1961; as *The Crime at Honotassa*, London, Collins, 1962.

Enemy in the House. New York, Random House, 1962; London, Collins, 1963.

Run Scared. New York, Random House, 1963; London, Collins, 1964.

Call after Midnight. New York, Random House, 1964; London, Collins, 1965.

R.S.V.P. Murder. New York, Random House, 1965; London, Collins, 1966.

Witness at Large. New York, Random House, 1966; London, Collins, 1967.

Woman on the Roof. New York, Random House, and London, Collins, 1968.

Message from Hong Kong. New York, Random House, and London, Collins, 1969.

El Rancho Rio. New York, Random House, 1970; London, Collins, 1971.

Two Little Rich Girls. New York, Random House, 1972.
The House by the Sea. New York, Pocket Books, 1972.
Murder in Waiting. New York, Random House, 1973; London, Collins, 1974.
Danger Money. New York, Random House, and London, Collins, 1975.
Family Fortune. New York, Random House, 1976; London, Collins, 1977.
Nine O'Clock Tide. New York, Random House, 1978.
The Bayou Road. New York, Random House, 1979.

Short Stories

The Cases of Susan Dare. New York, Doubleday, 1934; London, Lane, 1935.
Deadly Is the Diamond. New York, Dell, 1942.
*Five of My Best: Deadly Is the Diamond, Bermuda Grapevine, Murder Goes to Market,
Strangers in Flight, Express to Danger.* London, Hammond, 1949.
*Deadly Is the Diamond and Three Other Novelettes of Murder: Bermuda Grapevine, The
Crimson Paw, Murder in Waltz Time.* New York, Random House, 1958.
The Crimson Paw. London, Hammond, 1959.

Uncollected Short Stories

"The E-String Murder," in *The Saint* (New York), Spring 1953.
"The Wagstaff Pearls," in *Best Detective Stories of the Year 1953*, edited by David Coxe
Cooke. New York, Dutton, and London, Boardman, 1953.
"No Cry of Murder," in *Ellery Queen's Mystery Magazine* (New York), August 1955.
"Dangerous Widows," in *Ellery Queen's Mystery Magazine* (New York), April 1956.
"Murder in the Rain," in *Ellery Queen's Mystery Magazine* (New York), June 1956.
"The Hound of the Wellingtons," in *Ellery Queen's Mystery Magazine* (New York), June
1957.
"Mr. Wickwire's 'Gun Moll,'" in *A Choice of Murders*, edited by Dorothy Salisbury
Davis. New York, Scribner, 1958; London, Macdonald, 1960.
"Mr. Wickwire Adds and Subtracts," in *Ellery Queen's Mystery Magazine* (New York),
December 1959.
"Date to Die," in *Anthology 1961*, edited by Ellery Queen. New York, Davis, 1960.
"Murder on St. Valentine's Day," in *Anthology 1966 Mid-Year*, edited by Ellery
Queen. New York, Davis, 1966.
"Murder at the Dog Show," in *Anthology 1968*, edited by Ellery Queen. New York,
Davis, 1967.
"Mr. Wickwire's Widow," in *With Malice Toward All*, edited by Robert L. Fish. New
York, Putnam, 1968; London, Macmillan, 1969.

OTHER PUBLICATIONS

Plays

320 College Avenue, with Fred Ballard. New York, French, 1938.
Eight O'Clock Tuesday, with Robert Wallsten, adaptation of a novel by Eberhart
(produced New York, 1941). New York, French, 1941.

Manuscript Collection: Mugar Memorial Library, Boston University.

*   *   *

The author of more than 50 mystery novels and numerous short stories, Mignon G.
Eberhart is usually associated with the school of suspense fiction founded by Mary Roberts
Rinehart. Certainly her early works, particularly those featuring nurse Sarah Keate and

detective Lance O'Leary, are reminiscent of Rinehart at her most mediocre, presenting a succession of events experienced by a spinster heroine who combines the pluckiness and stupidity which are characteristic of the worst of the "Had-I-But-Known" narrators. The stories featuring Susan Dare, a writer of mystery fiction, are rather more successful, as are those concerning the banker James Wickwire. However, Eberhart's contribution to mystery fiction does not lie in her creation of serial detectives; to the tradition of the eccentric private eye, she adds little that is noteworthy. Rather, her best works, and the most popular, are those which combine elements of the gothic romance with those of the classic mystery story. She has many imitators, particularly in the field of pure romance, but few of them exhibit the assurance of the Eberhart style.

Typical of the Eberhart mystery/romance is its insistence upon an exotic locale, and its attention to details of local color. Careful presentation of the milieu in which the mystery unfolds is evident in her serial detective stories (it is perhaps this feature which has attracted film makers to Eberhart's works). In the mystery/romances, the exotic locale corresponds to the strange events which must take place before the heroine can be united with her true love. Unlike the novels of Mary Roberts Rinehart, which take place in a cozily normal world, Eberhart's are set in a world replete with mystery at the outset, so that the heroine – together with the reader – is catapulted into an environment which is strange and vaguely threatening.

The presentation of exotic setting is typical of the gothic romance. What distinguishes an Eberhart novel is the presence of a crime – usually murder, often associated with shady financial dealings – for which the heroine is suspect. Typically, she is an orphan (again, emphasizing her relative helplessness) married to a man about whom she knows relatively little. The husband may be an alcoholic (*Speak No Evil*) or an invalid (*With This Ring*); he is often the first murder victim, making his wife a prime suspect. In the course of her investigations, which are usually undertaken in order to prove her own innocence, the heroine comes to realize that her interest in a family friend is far from innocent. She also begins to suspect that she herself has overheard or involuntarily discovered a vital clue to the identity of the criminal. She identifies the murderer just at the moment of peril, from which she is rescued by the masterful hero, who reconstructs the crime and claims her for his own.

Eberhart's originality lies in her compelling studies of the psychological processes of her characters, particularly the heroines. Her dialogue, especially in scenes of emotional crisis, is sometimes overwrought ("Elizabeth, the world is wide. And war changes things. So the real things – love and time – are so terribly important. Elizabeth, I want you ..." – *Speak No Evil*), but her treatment of sexual motivation is generally free from the coyness associated with the more pedestrian modern romances. The perilous situations are believable precisely because the heroines are depicted in the midst of them, rather than being narrated by them in retrospect. The stories are escape fantasy/adventures, from which the heroines emerge wiser women than they were at the beginning. Within the confines of formula fiction, the novels of Mignon G. Eberhart embody an unusual degree of clarity and intelligence.

—Joanne Harack Hayne

EDEN, Dorothy.   Also writes as Mary Paradise.   British.   Born near Christchurch, New Zealand, 3 April 1912. Educated at a village school and a secretarial college. Secretary, 1929–39. Lives in London. Agent: David Higham Associates Ltd., 5–8 Lower John Street, London W1R 4HA, England.

Crime Publications

Novels

The Laughing Ghost. London, Macdonald, 1943; New York, Ace, 1968.
We Are for the Dark. London, Macdonald, 1944.
Summer Sunday. London, Macdonald, 1946.
Walk into My Parlour. London, Macdonald, 1947.
The Schoolmaster's Daughters. London, Macdonald, 1948; as *The Daughters of Ardmore Hall*, New York, Ace, 1968.
Crow Hollow. London, Macdonald, 1950; New York, Ace, 1967.
The Voice of the Dolls. London, Macdonald, 1950; New York, Ace, 1971.
Cat's Prey. London, Macdonald, 1952; New York, Ace, 1967.
Lamb to the Slaughter. London, Macdonald, 1953; as *The Brooding Lake*, New York, Ace, 1966.
Bride by Candlelight. London, Macdonald, 1954; New York, Ace, 1972.
Darling Clementine. London, Macdonald, 1955; as *Night of the Letter*, New York, Ace, 1967; Leicester, Ulverscroft, 1976.
Death Is a Red Rose. London, Macdonald, 1956; New York, Ace, 1970.
The Pretty Ones. London, Macdonald, 1957; New York, Ace, 1966.
Listen To Danger. London, Macdonald, 1958; New York, Ace, 1967.
The Deadly Travellers. London, Macdonald, 1959; New York, Ace, 1966.
The Sleeping Bride. London, Macdonald, 1959; New York, Ace, 1969.
Samantha. London, Hodder and Stoughton, 1960; as *Lady of Mallow*, New York, Coward McCann, 1962.
Sleep in the Woods. London, Hodder and Stoughton, 1960; New York, Coward McCann, 1961.
Face of an Angel (as Mary Paradise). London, Hale, 1961; New York, Ace, 1966.
Shadow of a Witch (as Mary Paradise). London, Hale, 1962; New York, Ace, 1966.
Whistle for the Crows. London, Hodder and Stoughton, 1962; New York, Ace, 1964.
Afternoon for Lizards. London, Hodder and Stoughton, 1962; as *The Bridge of Fear*, New York, Ace, 1966.
The Bird in the Chimney. London, Hodder and Stoughton, 1963; as *Darkwater*, New York, Coward McCann, 1964.
Bella. London, Hodder and Stoughton, 1964; as *Ravenscroft*, New York, Coward McCann, 1965.
The Marriage Chest. London, Hodder and Stoughton, 1965; (as Mary Paradise), New York, Coward McCann, 1966.
Winterwood. London, Hodder and Stoughton, and New York, Coward McCann, 1967.
The Shadow Wife. London, Hodder and Stoughton, and New York, Coward McCann, 1968.
Waiting for Willa. London, Hodder and Stoughton, and New York, Coward McCann, 1970.
Afternoon Walk. London, Hodder and Stoughton, and New York, Coward McCann, 1971.

Short Stories

Yellow Is for Fear and Other Stories. New York, Ace, 1968; London, Coronet, 1976.
The House on Hay Hill and Other Stories. London, Coronet, and New York, Fawcett, 1976.

OTHER PUBLICATIONS

Novels

Singing Shadows. London, Stanley Paul, 1940.
Never Call It Loving. London, Hodder and Stoughton, and New York, Coward McCann, 1966.
Siege in the Sun. London, Hodder and Stoughton, and New York, Coward McCann, 1967.
The Vines of Yarrabee. London, Hodder and Stoughton, and New York, Coward McCann, 1969.
Melbury Square. London, Hodder and Stoughton, 1970; New York, Coward McCann, 1971.
A Linnet Singing. New York, Pocket Books, 1972.
Speak to Me of Love. London, Hodder and Stoughton, and New York, Coward McCann, 1972.
The Millionaire's Daughter. London, Hodder and Stoughton, and New York, Coward McCann, 1974.
The Time of the Dragon. London, Hodder and Stoughton, and New York, Coward McCann, 1975.
The Salamanca Drum. London, Hodder and Stoughton, and New York, Coward McCann, 1977.
The Storrington Papers. New York, Coward McCann, 1978; London, Hodder and Stoughton, 1979.
Depart in Peace. London, Hodder and Stoughton, 1979.

Manuscript Collection: Mugar Memorial Library, Boston University.

Dorothy Eden comments:
I regard myself purely as a story-teller, and having become adept at that form of writing, I have never abandoned it nor desired to do anything else.

*   *   *

Although born and raised on a farm in New Zealand, Dorothy Eden, the versatile and prolific author of more than 40 novels, has long been a resident of London. Alternating between historical novels and Gothic adventures of romantic suspense, Eden provides the reader with rich atmosphere, exotic settings, and haunting characters.

Predictable as only a Gothic novel can be, with the sinister, brooding husband, and the innocent young heroine valiantly struggling to save their love in spite of the sinister spell of the haunted old mansion, housed with evil forces by which they find themselves trapped, Miss Eden's works contain all these elements but a few redeeming ones as well. Intricate plotting, rich description, and climactic action scenes help to move Miss Eden's novels to a step above the usual Gothic romance.

One of her more memorable novels involving some elements of detection is *Waiting for Willa*, in which an almost forgotten school-girl code for danger alerts Grace Asherton that her cousin Willa is in danger. Following this summons, Grace follows her not so innocent cousin to Stockholm where she learns that Willa had unwittingly become involved in the perilous world of international espionage. Grace's futile efforts to rescue Willa do succeed in the capture of Willa's abductors, however, and the amorous prize of the hero for Grace.

—Mary Ann Grochowski

EGAN, Leslie. See LININGTON, Elizabeth.

EGLETON, Clive. Also writes as Patrick Blake; John Tarrant. British. Born in South Harrow, Middlesex, 25 November 1927. Educated at Haberdashers' Aske's School, London, 1938–44; Army Staff College, Camberley, Surrey, graduated 1957. Married Joan Evelyn in 1949; two sons. Served in the British Army, rising to the rank of Lieutenant Colonel, 1945–75; had many appointments throughout the world dealing with logistics operations and law; did intelligence work in Cyprus, 1955–56, the Persian Gulf, 1958–59, and East Africa, 1964. Agent: George Greenfield, John Farquharson Ltd., 8 Bell Yard, London WC2A 2JU. Address: Dolphin House, Beach House Road, Bembridge, Isle of Wight PO35 5TA, England.

CRIME PUBLICATIONS

Novels (series character: David Garnett)

A Piece of Resistance (Garnett). London, Hodder and Stoughton, and New York, Coward McCann, 1970.
Last Post for a Partisan (Garnett). London, Hodder and Stoughton, and New York, Coward McCann, 1971.
The Judas Mandate (Garnett). London, Hodder and Stoughton, and New York, Coward McCann, 1972.
Seven Days to a Killing. London, Hodder and Stoughton, and New York, Coward McCann, 1973; as The Black Windmill, New York, Fawcett, 1974.
The October Plot. London, Hodder and Stoughton, 1974; as The Bormann Brief, New York, Coward McCann, 1974.
Skirmish. London, Hodder and Stoughton, and New York, Coward McCann, 1975.
State Visit. London, Hodder and Stoughton, 1976.
The Rommel Plot (as John Tarrant). London, Macdonald and Jane's, and Philadelphia, Lippincott, 1977.
The Mills Bomb. London, Hodder and Stoughton, and New York, Atheneum, 1978.
The Clauber Trigger (as John Tarrant). London, Macdonald and Jane's, 1978; New York, Atheneum, 1979.
Backfire. London, Hodder and Stoughton, and New York, Atheneum, 1979.
Escape to Athena (as Patrick Blake). London, Fontana, and New York, Berkley, 1979.

Manuscript Collection: Mugar Memorial Library, Boston University.

Clive Egleton comments:
My field is the crime and suspense novel. I hope the story I tell is good enough to make the reader want to turn over to the next page to see what happens next.

*   *   *

Clive Egleton has a growing reputation as a writer of tough, realistic terror and espionage novels. They are often bitter and bruising.
In A Piece of Resistance, Last Post for a Partisan, and The Judas Mandate, Egleton

chronicles the efforts of members of a resistance movement in a near-future England occupied by the Russians. The writing is crisp, often ironic; the dialogue, taut. While the action and characters are vivid, critics complain that the background is neither integral nor sufficiently detailed. These novels might have been set anywhere. *Seven Days to a Killing* is a tale of treachery, violence, and espionage with the hero's son as pawn. It is as gripping as a Hitchcock thriller. *The October Plot* may be Egleton's best work. A Commando intrigues with the German High Command to shorten the war by assassinating Martin Bormann. The story is told with documentary efficiency and displays Egleton's penchant for treachery and deviousness. In *Skirmish* the Department of Subversive Warfare confronts the KGB. When a sheik is killed, a boy photographs the assassins. He and his mother must be protected. London, Paris, and the south of France provide settings for Egleton's explosive story and its ironic conclusion.

Egleton writes excellent dialogue and creates tension from beginning to end. His stories are filled with intrigue, violence, double-dealing, and treachery. His backgrounds tend to be less important than the action he presents, and he may rely upon assassination too often, running the danger of becoming predictable.

—Frank Denton

ELLIN, Stanley (Bernard). American. Born in New York City, 6 October 1916. Educated at Brooklyn College, New York, B.A. 1936. Served in the United States Army, 1944–45. Married Jeanne Michael in 1937; one daughter. Worked as teacher, steelworker, dairy farmer. Full-time writer since 1946. Past President, Mystery Writers of America. Recipient: Mystery Writers of America Edgar Allan Poe Award, for short story, 1954, 1956, for novel, 1958; Le Grand Prix de Littérature Policière, 1975. Agent: Curtis Brown Ltd., 575 Madison Avenue, New York, New York 10022, U.S.A.

CRIME PUBLICATIONS

Novels

    Dreadful Summit. New York, Simon and Schuster, 1948; London, Boardman, 1958; as *The Big Night*, New York, New American Library, 1966.
    The Key to Nicholas Street. New York, Simon and Schuster, 1952; London, Boardman, 1953.
    The Eighth Circle. New York, Random House, 1958; London, Boardman, 1959.
    House of Cards. New York, Random House, and London, Macdonald, 1967.
    The Valentine Estate. New York, Random House, and London, Macdonald, 1968.
    The Bind. New York, Random House, 1970; as *The Man from Nowhere*, London, Cape, 1970.
    Mirror, Mirror on the Wall. New York, Random House, 1972; London, Cape, 1973.
    Stronghold. New York, Random House, and London, Cape, 1975.
    The Luxembourg Run. New York, Random House, 1977.
    Star Light, Star Bright. New York, Random House, 1979.

Short Stories

> *Mystery Stories.*   New York, Simon and Schuster, 1956; London, Boardman, 1957; as
> *Quiet Horror*, New York, Dell, 1959; as *The Speciality of the House and Other Stories*,
> London, Penguin, 1967.
> *The Blessington Method and Other Strange Tales.*   New York, Random House, 1964;
> London, Macdonald, 1965.
> *Kindly Dig Your Grave and Other Wicked Stories*, edited by Ellery Queen.   New York,
> Davis, 1975.

Uncollected Short Stories

> "Generation Gap," in *Ellery Queen's Mystery Magazine* (New York), September 1976.
> "The Family Circle," in *Ellery Queen's Mystery Magazine* (New York), December 1977.

OTHER PUBLICATIONS

Novels

> *The Winter after This Summer.*   New York, Random House, 1960; London,
> Boardman, 1961.
> *The Panama Portrait.*   New York, Random House, 1962; London, Macdonald, 1963.

Play

> Screenplay: *The Big Night*, with Joseph Losey, 1951.

Manuscript Collection: Mugar Memorial Library, Boston University.

Stanley Ellin comments:
The crime fiction genre offers the writer infinite diversity of theme and treatment. I like to take advantage of that diversity.

*   *   *

Stanley Ellin's career has been blessed with a first story that everyone remembers and many consider the finest of the three dozen or so short stories he's produced in the past thirty-odd years. But in truth even without "The Specialty of the House" Ellin would be one of the modern masters of the genre, with a reputation built firmly upon novels and some of the most imaginative stories in the mystery-suspense field.

Ellin's second novel, *The Key to Nicholas Street*, is of special interest, with its viewpoint shifting among the five members of the Ayres household. The woman next door has been found dead at the bottom of the cellar stairs, and her death is to affect the members of the Ayres household as much as her life had. It is a book of near-classic stature, curiously overlooked by most critics, and one of Ellin's three best novels.

The Eighth Circle is an attempt at a long, serious novel about a modern private detective. It succeeds admirably. Murray Kirk is far removed from the standard private eye, yet there is a hard-edged sentimentality about him that recalls the best of his predecessors. His case is a good one, and the reader regrets he has never made a second appearance in an Ellin novel. The third of Stanley Ellin's top trio is undoubtedly *Mirror, Mirror on the Wall*, a breakthrough novel that carries the mystery into psycho-sexual areas where it had previously feared to tread.

Slightly behind these three are a group of mystery-adventure novels in which the protagonist, a young man, somehow becomes involved with wealthy and glamorous people

531

in Miami Beach or Europe. Often an estate or a legacy is involved, and the action is fast and deadly. Fitting generally into this group are *House of Cards*, *The Valentine Estate*, *The Bind*, and *The Luxembourg Run*. Another recent novel is *Stronghold*, which portrays a family of non-violent Quakers at the mercy of four murderous criminals bent on holding them for ransom.

Despite his achievements in the novel, it is by his short stories that Stanley Ellin is best known. Beginning with the unforgettable "The Specialty of the House" (1948), about a New York restaurant with a special treat for gourmets, Ellin produced a remarkable series of tales collected as *Mystery Stories*. The volume has been hailed by Julian Symons as "the finest collection of stories in the crime form published in the past half century."

Many of these first ten stories deserve special mention. "The Cat's-Paw" is a neat variation on the situation in Doyle's "The Red-Headed League." "The Orderly World of Mr. Appleby" is about a wife-murderer who seems to have the formula for the perfect crime. "The House Party" (Edgar-winner) is one of Ellin's rare fantasies. "Broker's Special" is his contribution to the sub-genre combining crime and trains. And "The Moment of Decision," a stunning riddle story about a magician, comes very close to equaling "The Specialty of the House" in its impact.

"The Blessington Method" (Edgar-winner) became the title story of Ellin's second collection. Again, many of the ten stories deserve special mention. "You Can't Be a Little Girl All Your Life" is the story of a rape, with the identity of the rapist revealed only at the end. It is one of Ellin's few attempts at a whodunit in the short form, and one of the best stories in the volume. "The Day of the Bullet" tells of the murder of a Brooklyn rackets boss, with a flashback to an incident in his boyhood. "The Nine-to-Five Man" is a memorable tale of a typical working day in the life of a man who just happens to be a professional arsonist. And "The Question" is also about a professional man – an executioner who must face his son's question about the work he does.

If the stories in Ellin's third collection, *Kindly Dig Your Grave*, seem a bit less remarkable it is only because of the high standards he has set with the previous books. Even so, there are at least two more small masterpieces here. "The Crime of Ezechiele Coen" is set in Rome, with roots going back to World War II. And "The Last Bottle in the World" could easily be one of the half-dozen best short stories about wine. There is more detection in Ellin's later short stories, and more foreign settings as in the later novels. Though some may lack the stunning surprises of the earlier work, they are solid professional jobs.

—Edward D. Hoch

ERDMAN, Paul E(mil). American. Born in Stratford, Ontario, Canada, 19 May 1932. Educated at Concordia College, Fort Wayne, Indiana (later St. Louis), B.A.; Georgetown University School of Foreign Service, Washington, D.C., B.S.F.S.; University of Basel, Switzerland, M.A., Ph.D. Married Helly Erdman in 1954; two daughters. Economist, Stanford Research Institute, Menlo Park, California, 1958–61; Executive Vice-President, Electronics International Capital, Hamilton, Bermuda, 1961–64; President and Vice Chairman, United California Bank, Basel, 1964–70. Self-employed writer. Recipient: Mystery Writers of America Edgar Allan Poe Award, 1973. Agent: Ziegler Diskant, 9255 Sunset Boulevard, Los Angeles, California. Address: 126 Madrona Avenue, Belvedere, California 94920, U.S.A.

CRIME PUBLICATIONS

Novels

The Billion Dollar Sure Thing. New York, Scribner, 1973; as The Billion Dollar
   Killing, London, Hutchinson, 1973.
The Silver Bears. New York, Scribner, and London, Hutchinson, 1975.
The Crash of '79. New York, Simon and Schuster, 1976; London, Secker and
   Warburg, 1977.

OTHER PUBLICATIONS

Other

Swiss-American Economic Relations. Tuebingen, Mohr and Siebeck, 1958.
Die Europaeische Wirtschaftsgemeinschaft und die Drittlaender. Tuebingen, Mohr and
   Siebeck, 1959.

                              *   *   *

Entering a new field and becoming an immediate star performer is not a usual pattern,
though Paul E. Erdman accomplished it. A one-time banker in California and Switzerland,
Erdman was jailed in a Swiss prison, and there he wrote his first novel, the best-selling
mystery about banking in Switzerland, The Billion Dollar Sure Thing. Even a person who
can't add a row of figures could understand Erdman's story, and speak in superlatives about
its plot machinations. He followed it the next year with The Silver Bears, another story of
international banking in Switzerland. Without any hinting by the author, The Silver Bears
would seem to be the story, somewhat fictionalized, of how Erdman managed to get himself
into the Swiss prison, almost inadvertently and certainly with no criminal intent.
   His third book repeated the familiar success story. The Crash of '79 is that paradox, an
upbeat story of complete disaster. What it relates is the logical ending to the oil situation of
the late 20th century, spelling the end of the civilized world as modern man has known it.
One need not accept Erdman's conclusion, but one must admit its logic.
   Erdman writes with pace and panache. Each of his books is as intellectually amusing as it
is instructive.

                                                            —Dorothy B. Hughes

---

ERSKINE, Margaret. Pseudonym for Margaret Wetherby Williams. British. Born in
Kingston, Ontario, Canada; grew up in Devon. Educated privately. Agent: A. M. Heath and
Company Ltd., 40–42 William IV Street, London WC2N 4DD, England.

CRIME PUBLICATIONS

Novels (series character: Inspector Septimus Finch in all books)

And Being Dead. London, Bles, 1938; as The Limping Man, New York, Doubleday,
   1939; as The Painted Mask, New York, Ace, 1972.

The Whispering House. London, Hammond, 1947; as *The Voice of the House*, New York, Doubleday, 1947.

I Knew MacBean. London, Hammond, and New York, Doubleday, 1948; as *Caravan of Night*, New York, Ace, 1972.

Give Up the Ghost. London, Hammond, and New York, Doubleday, 1949.

The Disappearing Bridegroom. London, Hammond, 1950; as *The Silver Ladies*, New York, Doubleday, 1951.

Death of Our Dear One. London, Hammond, 1952; as *Look Behind You, Lady*, New York, Doubleday, 1952; as *Don't Look Behind You*, New York, Ace, 1972.

Dead by Now. London, Hammond, 1953; New York, Doubleday, 1954; revised edition, New York, Ace, 1972.

Fatal Relations. London, Hammond, 1955; as *Old Mrs. Ommanney Is Dead*, New York, Doubleday, 1955; as *The Dead Don't Speak*, Roslyn, New York, Detective Book Club, 1955.

The Voice of Murder. London, Hodder and Stoughton, and New York, Doubleday, 1956.

Sleep No More. London, Hodder and Stoughton, 1958; New York, Ace, 1969.

The House of the Enchantress. London, Hodder and Stoughton, 1959; as *A Graveyard Plot*, New York, Doubleday, 1959.

The Woman at Belguardo. London, Hodder and Stoughton, and New York, Doubleday, 1961.

The House in Belmont Square. London, Hodder and Stoughton, 1963; as *No. 9 Belmont Square*, New York, Doubleday, 1963.

Take a Dark Journey. London, Hodder and Stoughton, 1965; as *The Family at Tammerton*, New York, Doubleday, 1966.

Case with Three Husbands. London, Hodder and Stoughton, and New York, Doubleday, 1967.

The Ewe Lamb. London, Hodder and Stoughton, and New York, Doubleday, 1968.

The Case of Mary Fielding. London, Hodder and Stoughton, and New York, Doubleday, 1970.

The Brood of Folly. London, Hodder and Stoughton, and New York, Doubleday, 1971.

Besides the Wench Is Dead. London, Hodder and Stoughton, and New York, Doubleday, 1973.

Harriet Farewell. London, Hodder and Stoughton, and New York, Doubleday, 1975.

The House in Hook Street. New York, Doubleday, 1977; London, Hale, 1978.

*   *   *

Mysteries by Margaret Erskine began to appear in the late 1930's, and over the years there have been over 20 of them. Miss Erskine's hero is Septimus (a seventh son, of course) Finch of the CID. In *The House of the Enchantress* Finch is described: "... he was large, bland, and solemn-looking. His walk was deceptively lazy. His voice was small and soft as a woman's. From his mother he had inherited a sensitiveness to his surroundings that amounted almost to a sixth sense. With his aunt Lilian he shared an immense but impersonal curiosity. People fascinated him even though, in the course of years, he had lost the capacity to be surprised." When his creator forgets about lending him distinguishing features and idiosyncrasies, he is quite acceptable as the investigator in charge of a case. Finch doesn't always do a lot of detecting, and at times, he seems to relish the problems of other people. Finch's delight mirrors that of his author.

Margaret Erskine likes creepy old houses with sliding panels and secret rooms, strange art works and curios which conceal information bearing on the crime at hand; she is interested in witchcraft and psychic phenomena; but, most of all, she likes large eccentric families. Several generations of loonies under one roof, with assorted – and ill-assorted – in-laws, relics of past marriages, and odd connections too remote to keep track of fascinate her, and she revels in bright and breathless descriptions of their antics. *Case with Three Husbands* contains just such a bunch – two elderly brothers, one of whom renounced his military rank and gave back his medals when India got independence, and the twin sister of one of them, who live, along with three younger generations of the same tribe, in a house whose front gates have not been opened since the abdication of Edward VIII. Other books have clans just as unfathomable. One wishes that Erskine would exercise population control in regard to casts of characters, since masses of them, while amusing in the aggregate, confuse the reader and are detrimental to neat plotting. Also, after the initial sketch, the author usually neglects to develop them into separate personalities, leaving the scene strewn with cartoon – if not cardboard – characters.

While certain aspects of Margaret Erskine's mystery fiction are predictable, the overall success of any particular book is not. *Give Up the Ghost*, a fairly early effort with a Jack-the-Ripper theme, holds together rather well; although there are too many characters, motivations are clear. *Dead by Now*, a slightly later book, does not come off as well. Set in an old theater, it has ghosts, ancient tragedy, and multiple murder, but the spooky atmosphere shows up as fake. *The Woman at Belguardo*, typically convoluted, is well worked out, and the truth is discovered because a jade figurine is not cracked – a nice touch. *The Ewe Lamb*, set in a sixteenth-century house filled with musical instruments, is one of Erskine's best. The house, a museum as well as a family home, is satisfactorily described and the situation is suspenseful. *The Case of Mary Fielding*, shorter than most of Erskine's tales, with fewer but better-drawn characters, is a good story, tight and well-written. Other recent books are also entertaining.

Margaret Erskine writes conventional crime fiction. She is perhaps a paradigm of the female English mystery writer. Not really in the first rank, she is nevertheless better than many, and hers is a dependable product. Horrible things happen but they are packaged for polite society. The traditional trappings are all here, and are rearranged to make new but ever familiar puzzles.

—Mary Helen Becker

ESMOND, Harriet. See **BURKE, John.**

EUSTACE, Robert. Pseudonym for Eustace Robert Barton; also wrote as Eustace Robert Rawlins. British. Born in 1854. Served in the Royal Army Medical Corps. *Died in 1943.*

CRIME PUBLICATIONS

Novels

The Lost Square, with L. T. Meade. London, Ward Lock, 1902.
The Stolen Pearl: A Romance of London, with Gertrude Warden. London, Ward Lock, 1903.
A Human Bacillus: The Story of a Strange Character. London, Long, 1907.

The Documents in the Case, with Dorothy L. Sayers.   London, Benn, and New York, Brewer and Warren, 1930.

Short Stories with L. T. Meade

A Master of Mysteries.   London, Ward Lock, 1898.
The Gold Star Line.   London, Ward Lock, 1899; New York, New Amsterdam Book Company, n.d.
The Brotherhood of the Seven Kings.   London, Ward Lock, 1899.
The Sanctuary Club.   London, Ward Lock, 1900.
The Sorceress of the Strand.   London, Ward Lock, 1903.

Uncollected Short Stories

"The Face in the Dark," with L. T. Meade, and "Mr. Belton's Immunity," with Edgar Jepson, in *Great Short Stories of Detection, Mystery and Horror*, vol. 1, edited by Dorothy L. Sayers.   London, Gollancz, 1928; as *The Omnibus of Crime*, New York, Payson and Clarke, 1929.
"The Tea-Leaf," with Edgar Jepson, in *Tales of Detection*.   London, Dent, 1936.

OTHER PUBLICATIONS

Novel

The Hidden Treasures of Egypt: A Romance.   London, Simpkin Marshall, 1925; New York, Stratford Press, 1926.

Play

The Brotherhood of the Seven Kings, with L. T. Meade and Max Elgin, adaptation of the story by Meade and Eustace (produced South Shields, County Durham, 1900).

*   *   *

One of the more enigmatic writers of mysteries, Robert Eustace had a hand in a large number of stories but co-authored virtually all of them. Though many stories were written with L. T. Meade, Eustace also collaborated with Clifford Halifax, Gertrude Warden, Edgar Jepson, and Dorothy L. Sayers. It is impossible to determine precisely what Eustace's contribution to the various partnerships was, though both Sayers, in *The Omnibus of Crime*, and Barzun and Taylor, in *A Catalogue of Crime*, suggest that Eustace provided the raw material that others formed into finished products.

If Sayers and Barzun/Taylor are correct, and they probably are since the writing styles vary so greatly, then the raw material Eustace provided was most likely exotic and detailed medical information. Besides the fact that Eustace was a medical doctor, almost all of the works he is associated with involve medicine in general and poison in particular.

"Madame Sara," for example (from *The Sorceress of the Strand*, written with L. T. Meade) is a well-told tale of a puzzling murder by poison. The hero, a police surgeon, discovers the means of administering a rare poison, thereby saving the life of a beautiful and wealthy bride. In "Mr. Belton's Immunity" (written with Edgar Jepson), Belton traps an enemy agent by having himself injected with anti-toxin in order to combat an inevitable dose of daboia venom. Unlike "Madame Sara," the writing in "Mr. Belton's Immunity" is heavy-handed and often very melodramatic.

In *The Documents in the Case* (written with Dorothy L. Sayers), poison is again the means of murder. Sayers, however, appears to have used Eustace's particular talents to a greater degree than anyone before. This fascinating novel, which is mostly a series of letters, includes a variety of medical ingredients: there are the psychoanalytic ramblings of Agatha Milsom on repressions, which offer a devastating portrait of a sexually repressed middle-aged spinster whose doctor is apparently filling her head with simplified Freud; there is a rather detailed description of *rigor mortis*; there is a seemingly knowledgeable discussion of the results of muscarine poisoning; and there is a highly technical presentation of various aspects of organic chemistry. As in most of Sayers, the characterizations are excellent.

Though Eustace probably played a relatively minor role in most collaborations, his unique contribution to the mystery story was in providing the kind of expertise that helped foster what has become an important sub-genre, the medical mystery story.

—Donald J. Pattow

EUSTIS, Helen (White). American. Born in Cincinnati, Ohio, 31 December 1916. Educated at Hillsdale School, Cincinnati; Smith College, Northampton, Massachusetts, B.A. 1938; Columbia University, New York. Married 1) Alfred Young Fisher; one son; 2) Martin Harris (divorced). Worked briefly as copywriter. Recipient: Mystery Writers of America Edgar Allan Poe Award, 1947.

CRIME PUBLICATIONS

Novels

> *The Horizontal Man.* New York, Harper, 1946; London, Hamish Hamilton, 1947.
> *The Fool Killer.* New York, Doubleday, 1954; London, Secker and Warburg, 1955.

OTHER PUBLICATIONS

Short Stories

> *The Captains and the Kings Depart and Other Stories.* New York, Harper, 1949.

Other

> Translator, *When I Was Old*, by Georges Simenon. New York, Harcourt Brace, 1971; London, Hamish Hamilton, 1972.

*   *   *

A writer who has attracted considerable critical acclaim as the result of a single work, Helen Eustis owes her permanent place in the history of detective fiction to her first novel, the Edgar Award-winning *The Horizontal Man*. In addition, she has published *The Fool Killer*, a mystery novel for both children and adults, somewhat self-consciously imitative of Mark Twain; and numerous short stories, some of which are collected in the volume *The Captains and the Kings Depart*. The stories are not, generically, mysteries, but they are informed by an almost gothic interest in human psychology and motivation.

A similar, though more specifically psychoanalytic, sensibility characterizes *The Horizontal Man*. Connoisseurs of detective fiction praise the unique use of the "least likely person" device, which has been compared, in its originality and impact, to that used by Agatha

537

Christie in *The Murder of Roger Ackroyd*. The novel is set in Hollymount College, an Eastern American girl's school (modelled, perhaps, on Smith College, the author's *alma mater*). Several "private detectives," including a young newspaper reporter, a homely but witty student, and a beleaguered college president become involved in the murder of handsome English professor Kevin Boyle. It is the staff psychiatrist who finally puts the pieces together.

Unlike many detective stories set in academe, *The Horizontal Man* is not in the least self-conscious in its use of literary allusions or intellectual puns. The story, which contains an element of the bizarre, is told with a charming combination of sophistication and humour, and the author's presentation of both locale and characters is so realistic that what might be regarded as artificial or "symbolic" always arises naturally from the action. It is this essential realism which distinguishes the novel from the category of merely clever pastiches of detective story devices. Its originality lies both in its honest treatment of sexual motivation, and in its use of such traditional devices as shifting narrative point of view in an uncompromisingly realistic context.

—Joanne Harack Hayne

FAIR, A. A. See **GARDNER, Erle Stanley.**

FAIRLIE, Gerard. British. Born in London, 1 November 1899. Educated in Brussels, 1906–11; Downside School, 1912–17; Royal Military College, Camberley, Surrey, 1917--18. Served in the Scots Guards, 1918–24 (Army heavyweight boxer, 1919); Lieutenant-Colonel, Royal Sussex Regiment, 1939–45: Croix de Guerre; Bronze Star. Married Joan Roskell in 1923; two daughters and one son. Assistant to Bernard Darwin, Golf Correspondent of *The Times*, London, 1924–25; Golf Correspondent, *Bystander*, 1925–30, and *Britannia*, 1930, both London; Screenwriter for British and American film companies, 1931–49. Member, British Olympic Bobsleigh Team, Chamonix, France, 1924. Agent: Michael Horniman, A. P. Watt and Son, 26–28 Bedford Row, London WC1R 4HL. Address: Rose Cottage, East Lavington, Petworth, Sussex, England.

CRIME PUBLICATIONS

Novels (series characters: Victor Caryll; Bulldog Drummond; Johnny Macall; Mr. Malcolm)

  Scissors Cut Paper (Caryll).   London, Hodder and Stoughton, 1927; Boston, Little Brown, 1928.
  The Man Who Laughed (Caryll).   London, Hodder and Stoughton, and Boston, Little Brown, 1928.
  Stone Blunts Scissors (Caryll).   London, Hodder and Stoughton, 1928; Boston, Little Brown, 1929.

The Exquisite Lady.   London, Hodder and Stoughton, 1929; as *Yellow Munro*, Boston, Little Brown, 1929.
The Reaper.   Boston, Little Brown, 1929.
The Muster of Vultures.   London, Hodder and Stoughton, 1929; Boston, Little Brown, 1930.
Suspect.   London, Hodder and Stoughton, and New York, Doubleday, 1930.
Unfair Lady.   London, Hodder and Stoughton, 1931.
The Man with Talent.   London, Hodder and Stoughton, 1931.
Shot in the Dark (Malcolm).   London, Hodder and Stoughton, and New York, Doubleday, 1932.
The Rope Which Hangs.   London, Hodder and Stoughton, 1932.
Mr. Malcolm Presents.   London, Hodder and Stoughton, 1932.
Birds of Prey.   London, Hodder and Stoughton, 1932.
Men for Counters (Malcolm).   London, Hodder and Stoughton, 1933.
The Treasure Nets.   London, Hodder and Stoughton, 1933.
That Man Returns (Caryll).   London, Hodder and Stoughton, 1934.
Copper at Sea.   London, Hodder and Stoughton, 1934.
Bulldog Drummond on Dartmoor.   London, Hodder and Stoughton, 1938; New York, Curl, 1939.
The Pianist Shoots First.   London, Hodder and Stoughton, 1938.
Bulldog Drummond Attacks.   London, Hodder and Stoughton, 1939; New York, Gateway, 1940.
Captain Bulldog Drummond.   London, Hodder and Stoughton, 1945.
They Found Each Other.   London, Hodder and Stoughton, 1946.
Bulldog Drummond Stands Fast.   London, Hodder and Stoughton, 1947.
Hands Off Bulldog Drummond.   London, Hodder and Stoughton, 1949.
Calling Bulldog Drummond.   London, Hodder and Stoughton, 1951.
Winner Take All (Macall).   London, Hodder and Stoughton, and New York, Dodd Mead, 1953.
The Return of the Black Gang (Drummond).   London, Hodder and Stoughton, 1954.
No Sleep for Macall.   London, Hodder and Stoughton, 1955.
Deadline for Macall.   London, Hodder and Stoughton, and New York, Mill, 1956.
Double the Bluff (Macall).   London, Hodder and Stoughton, 1957.
Macall Gets Curious.   London, Hodder and Stoughton, 1959.
Please Kill My Cousin (Macall).   London, Hodder and Stoughton, 1961.

Uncollected Short Story

"The Ghost of a Smile," in *Fifty Masterpieces of Mystery*.   London, Odhams Press, 1935.

OTHER PUBLICATIONS

Novels

Moral Holiday.   London, Hutchinson, 1936.
Approach to Happiness.   London, Hutchinson, 1939.
The Mill of Circumstance: A Novelized History of the Life and Times of General Wolfe.   London, Hutchinson, 1941.

Plays

Bulldog Drummond Hits Out, with Sapper (produced Brighton and London, 1937).
Number Six, with Guy Bolton, adaptation of a novel by Edgar Wallace (produced London, 1938).

Screenplays: *Jack Ahoy!*, with others, 1934; *Open All Night*, 1934; *Lazybones*, 1935; *The Lad*, 1935; *The Ace of Spades*, 1935; *Bulldog Jack (Alias Bulldog Drummond)*, with Sapper and J. O. C. Orton, 1935; *Brown on Resolution (Born for Glory)*, with Michael Hogan, 1935; *Troubled Waters*, 1936; *The Big Noise*, 1936; *The Lonely Road (Scotland Yard Commands)*, with James Flood and Anthony Kimmins, 1936; *Chick*, with others, 1936; *Conspirator*, with Sally Benson, 1949; *Calling Bulldog Drummond*, with Howard Emmett Rogers and Arthur Wimperis, 1951.

Other

With Prejudice: Almost an Autobiography. London, Hodder and Stoughton, 1952.
Flight Without Wings: The Biography of Hannes Schneider. London, Hodder and Stoughton, and New York, A. S. Barnes, 1957.
The Reluctant Cop: The Story, and the Cases, of Superintendent Albert Webb. London, Hodder and Stoughton, 1958.
The Fred Emney Story. London, Hutchinson, 1960.
The Life of a Genius (biography of Sir George Cayley), with Elizabeth Cayley. London, Hodder and Stoughton, 1965.

Gerard Fairlie comments:
I met Lieutenant-Colonel H. C. McNeile (Sapper) at the end of the First World War. We were soon helping each other – he helping me far more than I was helping him. The relationship was master-pupil except when it came to writing dialogue. His has been the greatest influence on me in my now long and varied career. Both of us wrote to entertain, not to impress.

*   *   *

Gerard Fairlie's fame is linked to Sapper's: he was, by Sapper's own account, the original for Bulldog Drummond, and on Sapper's death in 1937 he took over the Drummond series. In Fairlie's hands Drummond mellows, becomes a more likeable character, is more at ease with women, who become more believable; even Irma is referred to, in *Bulldog Drummond Stands Fast* (we may allow for irony) as a "peach." Much of the sadism and the jingoistic hostility has gone, but so has much of Sapper's narrative gift, and the sense of Drummond as a figure larger than life. (In Fairlie's autobiography, *With Prejudice*, it is Fairlie himself, not Sapper – though the older writer is treated barely this side idolatry – who comes across as the more mature and balanced personality, and the difference is felt in the two Drummonds.)

Fairlie has written more than twenty novels outside Sapper's shadow; he also worked as a screenwriter, both in England and Hollywood. As samples of his fiction, one may take an early novel, *The Muster of Vultures*, and *They Found Each Other*. The first is a thriller, not without relevance for the 1970's, in which high officials are kidnapped and ransomed by a gang of criminals – and take the view that their lives are insignificant when set against the public good. The second presumably draws upon Fairlie's very distinguished service with the French Resistance (for which he was decorated), and is set in occupied Paris at the time of D-Day. Fairlie mixes exciting incident – crime and espionage – with a love story. The ultimate difference between him and Sapper is that Fairlie does not fuse a racial or national belief with an imaginative character creation, and so does not, as Sapper however disagreeably does, rise to a level of myth and archetype.

—Barrie Hayne

FALLON, Martin. See **MARLOWE, Hugh.**

FARR, John. See **WEBB, Jack.**

FARRER, Katharine (Dorothy, née Newton). British. Born in Chippenham, Wiltshire, 27 September 1911. Educated at St. Anne's College, Oxford, diploma in education 1933. Married Austin Farrer in 1937; one daughter. Teacher of Latin and Greek, 1933–37. Agent: David Higham Associates Ltd., 5–8 Lower John Street, London W1R 4HA, England.

CRIME PUBLICATIONS

Novels (series character: Inspector Richard Ringwood in all books)

> *The Missing Link.* London, Collins, 1952.
> *The Cretan Counterfeit.* London, Collins, 1954.
> *Gownsman's Gallows.* London, Hodder and Stoughton, 1957.

OTHER PUBLICATIONS

Novel

> *At Odds with Morning.* London, Hodder and Stoughton, 1960.

Other

> Translator, *Being and Having*, by Gabriel Marcel. London, Dacre Press, 1949.
> Translator, *The Church Which Presides in Love* (symposium). London, Faith Press, 1962.
> Translator, *The Primacy of Peter*, by Jean Meyendorff and others. London, Faith Press, 1963.

*   *   *

Katharine Farrer's mysteries are set among highly educated people in Oxford or elsewhere. Richard Ringwood of Scotland Yard is an Oxford man who is aware of classical mythology and archaeology, who is fluent in French and uses Norman understanding of dog-training on his own bloodhound, and feels, like most Englishmen, no particular pressures to conform.

In *The Missing Link* a six-week-old baby girl is kidnapped from the front garden of her Oxford home. The Links, her parents, have tedious ideas about child-rearing based on routine and unbreakable schedules. One feels almost sorry for the baby when it is learnt that she must be taught to recognize and deal with her own problems. One slips into the idea that the baby is lucky to be rescued from her very humourless and unattractive parents. Ringwood feels otherwise and, quite flowing with poetic quotations, paces around Oxford interviewing both dons and dustmen in an effort to restore the child to her rightful owners. For a few bleak pages it looks as if the child was taken by gypsies, and even the innocent nanny of the next-door children is suspected. When the child is retrieved the motive turns out to be a most unusual one. Intellectual reasons for crimes are not the norm either in fiction or in true crime.

In *The Cretan Counterfeit* a well-known archaeologist, who sups most freely from the minds of his assistants, dies suddenly and unexpectedly. The woman who has helped him the most in his Cretan discoveries is stabbed as she walks through Soho; then it is discovered that Sir Alban Worrall died from hydrochloric acid and not from a gastric ulcer. Most of the suspects are a part of the Crete expedition, and the forgery and selling of faked Cretan jewelry to the unsuspecting public is, to some of them, far more serious than any mere murder. Their reputations are at stake, their chances of being included on other expeditions are seriously eroded and money worries, purity of thought and opinion and other motives place themselves before Ringwood's eyes for inspection. As well as the archaeologists there is also a cast of Greeks living and working in London; these men are obsessed not with antiquities but the more mundane matters of family and national honour.

In *Gownsman's Gallows*, Ringwood can provide his own bloodhound to track down a victim and a murderer. A body, found in Oxford, is disposed of and then a fire in a haystack leaves merely a foot as a small memento of a man. As the victim is French, most of the action takes place across the Channel and naturally Ringwood can adapt himself and fit into French family life immediately. The victim had posed as a rich and aristocratic Frenchman, but blackmail, prostitution, social snobbery, and treachery are all involved. The views of life in a small town in a southern region of France are pleasant, even charming.

Katharine Farrer's detective is not of the usual mould. Richard Ringwood is as equally comfortable with sonnets as with fingerprints and he has no trouble at all spelling words of more than two syllables. The only question is why should such an adept and able man wish to be a policeman?

—Mary Groff

FAST, Howard. See **CUNNINGHAM, E. V.**

FAULKNER, William. American. Born William Cuthbert Falkner in New Albany, Mississippi, 25 September 1897; moved with his family to Oxford, Mississippi, 1902. Educated at local schools in Oxford, and at the University of Mississippi, 1919–20. Served in the Royal Canadian Air Force, 1918. Married Estelle Oldham Franklin in 1929; one daughter. Worked in the University Post Office, Oxford, 1921–24; lived in New Orleans briefly, and wrote for the New Orleans *Times-Picayune*, then lived in Paris, and travelled in Italy, Switzerland, and England, 1925; returned to Oxford, 1926: thereafter a full-time writer; screenwriter for Metro-Goldwyn-Mayer, 1932–33, 20th Century Fox, 1935–37, and Warner Brothers, 1942–45; Writer-in-Residence, University of Virginia, Charlottesville, 1957, and part of each year thereafter until his death. Recipient: O. Henry Award, 1939, 1949; Nobel Prize for Literature, 1950; Howells Medal, 1950; National Book Award, 1951,

1955; Pulitzer Prize, 1955, 1963; American Academy of Arts and Letters Gold Medal, 1962. Member, National Institute of Arts and Letters, 1939. *Died 6 July 1962.*

CRIME PUBLICATIONS

Novels

> *Sanctuary.* New York, Cape and Smith, and London, Chatto and Windus, 1931.
> *Light in August.* New York, Smith and Haas, 1932; London, Chatto and Windus, 1933.
> *Absalom, Absalom!* New York, Random House, 1936; London, Chatto and Windus, 1937.
> *Intruder in the Dust.* New York, Random House, 1948; London, Chatto and Windus, 1949.

Short Stories

> *Knight's Gambit.* New York, Random House, and London, Chatto and Windus, 1949.

OTHER PUBLICATIONS

Novels

> *Soldiers' Pay.* New York, Boni and Liveright, 1926; London, Chatto and Windus, 1930.
> *Mosquitoes.* New York, Boni and Liveright, 1927; London, Chatto and Windus, 1964.
> *Sartoris.* New York, Harcourt Brace, 1929; London, Chatto and Windus, 1932.
> *The Sound and the Fury.* New York, Cape and Smith, 1929; London, Chatto and Windus, 1931.
> *As I Lay Dying.* New York, Cape and Smith, 1930; London, Chatto and Windus, 1935.
> *Pylon.* New York, Smith and Haas, and London, Chatto and Windus, 1935.
> *The Wild Palms.* New York, Random House, and London, Chatto and Windus, 1939.
> *The Hamlet.* New York, Random House, and London, Chatto and Windus, 1940; excerpt, as *The Long Hot Summer*, New York, New American Library, 1958.
> *A Fable.* New York, Random House, 1954; London, Chatto and Windus, 1955.
> *The Town.* New York, Random House, 1957; London, Chatto and Windus, 1958.
> *The Mansion.* New York, Random House, and London, Chatto and Windus, 1959.
> *The Rievers: A Reminiscence.* New York, Random House, and London, Chatto and Windus, 1962.
> *Flags in the Dust*, edited by Douglas Day. New York, Random House, 1973.

Short Stories

> *These 13.* New York, Cape and Smith, 1931; London, Chatto and Windus, 1933.
> *Idyll in the Desert.* New York, Random House, 1931.
> *Miss Zilphia Gant.* Dallas, Book Club of Texas, 1932.
> *Doctor Martino and Other Stories.* New York, Smith and Haas, and London, Chatto and Windus, 1934.
> *The Unvanquished.* New York, Random House, and London, Chatto and Windus, 1938.
> *Go Down, Moses, and Other Stories.* New York, Random House, and London, Chatto and Windus, 1942.

Collected Stories of William Faulkner. New York, Random House, 1950; London, Chatto and Windus, 1951.
Notes on a Horsethief. Greenville, Mississippi, Levee Press, 1950.
Big Woods. New York, Random House, 1955.
Faulkner County. London, Chatto and Windus, 1955.
Jealousy, and Episode: Two Stories. Minneapolis, Faulkner Studies, 1955.
Uncle Willy and Other Stories. London, Chatto and Windus, 1958.
Selected Short Stories. New York, Modern Library, 1961.
Barn Burning and Other Stories. London, Chatto and Windus, 1977.
Uncollected Stories, edited by Joseph L. Blotner. New York, Random House, 1979.

Plays

Requiem for a Nun (produced London, 1957; New York, 1959). New York, Random House, 1951; London, Chatto and Windus, 1953.
The Big Sleep, with Leigh Brackett and Jules Furthman, in *Film Scripts One*, edited by George P. Garrett, O. B. Harrison, Jr., and Jane Gelfmann. New York, Appleton Century Crofts, 1971.

Screenplays: *Today We Live*, with Edith Fitzgerald and Dwight Taylor, 1933; *The Road to Glory*, with Joel Sayre, 1936; *Slave Ship*, with others, 1937; *Air Force* (uncredited), with Dudley Nichols, 1943; *To Have and Have Not*, with Jules Furthman, 1945; *The Big Sleep*, with Leigh Brackett and Jules Furthman, 1945; *Land of the Pharaohs*, with Harry Kurnitz and Harold Jack Bloom, 1955.

Verse

The Marble Faun. Boston, Four Seas, 1924.
Salmagundi (includes prose), edited by Paul Romaine. Milwaukee, Casanova Press, 1932.
This Earth. New York, Equinox, 1932.
A Green Bough. New York, Smith and Haas, 1933.

Other

Mirror of Chartres Street. Minneapolis, Faulkner Studies, 1953.
New Orleans Sketches, edited by Ichiro Nishizaki. Tokyo, Hokuseido, 1955; revised edition, edited by Carvel Collins, New Brunswick, New Jersey, Rutgers University Press, 1958; London, Sidgwick and Jackson, 1959.
On Truth and Freedom. Manila (?), Philippine Writers Association, 1955(?).
Faulkner in the University (interviews), edited by Frederick L. Gwynn and Joseph L. Blotner. Charlottesville, University Press of Virginia, 1959.
University Pieces, edited by Carvel Collins. Tokyo, Kenkyusha, 1962.
Early Prose and Poetry, edited by Carvel Collins. Boston, Little Brown, 1962; London, Cape, 1963.
Faulkner at West Point (interviews), edited by Joseph L. Fant and Robert Ashley. New York, Random House, 1964.
The Faulkner-Cowley File, edited by Malcolm Cowley. New York, Viking Press, and London, Chatto and Windus, 1966.
Essays, Speeches, and Public Letters, edited by James B. Merewether. New York, Random House, 1966; London, Chatto and Windus, 1967.
The Wishing Tree (juvenile). New York, Random House, and London, Chatto and Windus, 1967.
Lion in the Garden (interviews), edited by James B. Merewether and Michael Millgate. New York, Random House, 1968.

Bibliography: *The Literary Career of William Faulkner: A Bibliographical Study* by James B. Merewether, Princeton, New Jersey, Princeton University Library, 1961.

*   *   *

William Faulkner, one of America's greatest novelists, and the winner of the 1950 Nobel Prize for literature, was a writer of great power and imaginative energy whose work often hovered on the edge of crime and detective fiction and sometimes fully spilled over, with two of his works, *Intruder in the Dust* and *Knight's Gambit*, unmistakably mystery fiction, two others, *Sanctuary* and *Light in August*, clearly, among other things, crime stories, and *Absalom, Absalom!* deeply informed by the structure of the classic detective novel.

Faulkner was a reader and admirer of the detective novel; in his libraries were the works of thirty-one detective story writers, including Carr, Christie, Queen, Sayers, and Stout. As early as 1930 he wrote a detective short story, "Smoke," and continued to write them until 1949. In 1946 his story "An Error in Chemistry" won second place in the *Ellery Queen Mystery Magazine* contest, missing first place by only one vote. In 1945 he wrote the screenplay for Raymond Chandler's *The Big Sleep*, and while working on it began to write what he called "a murder-mystery," in which a Negro man, while he is in jail, solves the crime of which he is accused. This story grew into *Intruder in the Dust*, in which Charles Mallison and Gavin Stevens, following instructions from the jailed Lucas Beauchamp, solve the crime and free him. In the writing, however, Faulkner's primary interest shifted from producing the detective story he originally planned to using this detective story to comment on the relationships of white and black in a segregated society.

In 1949 he assembled five detective stories, including "Smoke" and "An Error in Chemistry," added a novelette, and published the collection as *Knight's Gambit*. In these stories Gavin Stevens functions as the detective and Charles Mallison as the Watson-like narrator. The title story, a novelette, was written to tie the other stories together into a loosely constructed novel, but it leaves them a collection of tales.

In his famous horror story *Sanctuary*, Faulkner dealt with gangsters, rape, murder, and a murder trial – the materials of the crime story, although he made no effort to conceal the identity of the criminals. In *Light in August* the central plot hinges on a brutal murder, but the story is told from the murderer's viewpoint. Although these novels deal profoundly with great problems of the human heart, they employ the materials of the crime story for their basic structure.

In *Absalom, Absalom!*, one of his greatest works, Faulkner used the double plot and time structure of the detective story to give form to a serious inquiry into the meaning of southern history and the reliability of history itself. In the classic detective story the dramatic action is in the present and consists of the effort to uncover the meaning of actions taken in the past. Thus it tells two stories in a complexly inter-involved way. *Absalom, Absalom!* has a past plot, dealing with the violent career of Thomas Sutpen, before, during, and after the Civil War. But the forward action of the novel is concerned with two characters, neither of whom had ever seen Sutpen, who are attempting to piece together out of the recollections of others, fragments of letters, and similar clues, what Sutpen's history had truly been, and how to understand it. This, the most complex of Faulkner's novels, uses detective story devices extensively for its structure and meaning, and forces its readers to recognize and use the detective's method, if they are to understand the story.

Thus William Faulkner knew detective story conventions, on occasion wrote conventional detective stories, but most often used elements of them significantly to his own purposes in some of his finest work.

—C. Hugh Holman

FEARING, Kenneth (Flexner). American. Born in Oak Park, Illinois, 28 July 1902. Educated at the University of Wisconsin, Madison, B.A. 1924. Married the painter Nan Lurie in 1945; one son by previous marriage. Reporter, Chicago; staff writer, *Time* magazine, New York. Self-employed writer. Recipient: Guggenheim Fellowship, 1936, 1939. *Died 26 June 1961.*

CRIME PUBLICATIONS

Novels

> *The Hospital.* New York, Random House, 1939; London, Thorpe and Porter, 1962.
> *Dagger of the Mind.* New York, Random House, and London, Lane, 1941; as *Cry Killer!*, New York, Avon, 1958.
> *Clark Gifford's Body.* New York, Random House, 1942; London, Lane, 1943.
> *The Big Clock.* New York, Harcourt Brace, 1946; London, Lane, 1947.
> *Loneliest Girl in the World.* New York, Harcourt Brace, 1951; London, Lane, 1952; as *The Sound of Murder*, New York, Spivak, 1952.
> *The Generous Heart.* New York, Harcourt Brace, 1954; London, Lane, 1955.
> *The Crozart Story.* New York, Doubleday, 1960.

Uncollected Short Story

> "Three Wives Too Many," in *Best Detective Stories of the Year 1957*, edited by David Coxe Cooke. New York, Dutton, and London, Boardman, 1957.

OTHER PUBLICATIONS

Novel

> *John Barry* (as H. Bedford Jones, with Donald Freide as Donald F. Bedford). New York, Creative Age Press, 1947.

Verse

> *Angel Arms.* New York, Coward McCann, 1929.
> *Poems.* New York, Dynamo, 1935.
> *Dead Reckoning.* New York, Random House, 1938.
> *Collected Poems.* New York, Random House, 1940.
> *Afternoon of a Pawnbroker and Other Poems.* New York, Harcourt Brace, 1943.
> *Stranger at Coney Island and Other Poems.* New York, Harcourt Brace, 1948.
> *New and Selected Poems.* Bloomington, University of Indiana Press, 1956.

*   *   *

Better known as a post-Depression era American poet, Kenneth Fearing also wrote seven novels, between 1939 and 1960, several of them qualifying in the thriller or intrigue categories. They are distinguished by their use of the technique of multiple and recurrent narrators, which Fearing borrowed from Faulkner and which he used brilliantly in at least one novel, *The Big Clock*. He also used the technique effectively in his first novel, *The Hospital*; he was still using it in the interesting though labored *Crozart Story*, published just a year before his death in 1961. But I agree with Julian Symons that *The Big Clock* is Fearing's principal contribution to crime fiction.

In this novel Fearing excels, not only as the teller or a gripping suspense thriller but also as the creator of a number of convincingly drawn psychological character portraits. The chief of these is the novel's protagonist, George Stroud, who is depicted as an intelligent, sensitive individual chafing under the collar of conformity imposed upon him by life in the big city magazine publishing game, but whose flight from conformity is also perceptively shown by his creator to contain an element of the reckless and self-destructive as well. Which makes the plight he ultimately finds himself in perfect. Stroud's boss, the magazine mogul Earl Janoth, commits a murder but is seen leaving the scene of the crime by an unidentified observer. Janoth then puts Stroud at the head of an investigative unit of crime writers to find the unknown witness, whom Janoth has marked for destruction. What Stroud alone knows, the moment that the situation is described to him, is that the man they're all seeking is Stroud himself. Extraordinary suspense follows, as each piece of new information brought in to the command post at the magazine offices tightens the net around Stroud, who must use his wits to keep those working for him from making the connection and realizing *he* is their mystery witness.

But Fearing adds still another element to this novel to elevate it even further above the level of the average crime thriller. In the center of things he places a symbol, The Big Clock. Representing as it does the constantly moving hand of time, the clock is an obviously apt symbol for the plight of Stroud, for whom time must sooner or later run out. But the symbol also operates in a larger sphere; it serves as a constant reminder to Stroud of his mortality, and in doing so becomes sufficiently universalized to speak to us as well. In having his protagonist rebel against the conformity of the rat-race while all the time confronting the Big Clock, Fearing reminds his protagonist – and us – that there is one kind of conformity from which all of us have ultimately no escape.

The Big Clock is, because of its gripping story, a classic of thriller fiction. But because of the masterful way in which he also uses narrative technique, characterization, and symbolism, Kenneth Fearing lays legitimate claim, in at least this one novel, to being a serious and significant writer of fiction without any further qualifying label.

—Frank Occhiogrosso

FENISONG, Ruth. American.

CRIME PUBLICATIONS

Novels (series character: Gridley Nelson)

Murder Needs a Face (Nelson).   New York, Doubleday, 1942.
Murder Needs a Name (Nelson).   New York, Doubleday, 1942; London, Swan, 1950.
The Butler Died in Brooklyn (Nelson).   New York, Doubleday, 1943; London, Aldor, 1946.
Murder Runs a Fever (Nelson).   New York, Doubleday, 1943.
Jenny Kissed Me.   New York, Doubleday, 1944; as *Death Is a Lovely Lady*, New York, Popular Library, 1949.
The Lost Caesar.   New York, Doubleday, 1945; London, Aldor, 1946; as *Death Is a Gold Coin*, New York, Popular Library, 1950.
Desperate Cure.   New York, Doubleday, 1946.
Snare for Sinners.   New York, Doubleday, 1949; London, Foulsham, 1951.
Grim Rehearsal (Nelson).   New York, Doubleday, 1950; London, Foulsham, 1951.
Ill Wind.   New York, Doubleday, 1950; London, Foulsham, 1952.

Dead Yesterday (Nelson). New York, Doubleday, 1951.

Deadlock (Nelson). New York, Doubleday, 1952.

The Wench Is Dead (Nelson). New York, Doubleday, 1953.

Miscast for Murder (Nelson). New York, Doubleday, 1954; as *Too Lively to Live*, New York, Spivak, 1955.

Widows' Plight. New York, Doubleday, 1955; as *Widow's Blackmail*, London, Foulsham, 1957.

Bite the Hand (Nelson). New York, Doubleday, 1956; as *The Blackmailer*, London, Foulsham, 1958.

The Schemers. New York, Doubleday, 1957; as *The Case of the Gloating Landlord*, London, Foulsham, 1958.

Death of the Party (Nelson). New York, Doubleday, 1958.

But Not Forgotten (Nelson). New York, Doubleday, 1960; as *Sinister Assignment*, London, Foulsham, 1960.

Dead Weight (Nelson). New York, Doubleday, 1962; London, Hale, 1964.

Villainous Company. New York, Doubleday, 1967; London, Hale, 1968.

The Drop of a Hat. New York, Doubleday, 1970; London, Hale, 1971.

*   *   *

Ruth Fenisong contrives tidy plots with an action climax; character types, sometimes overblown and clichéd but necessary to the plot, invariably include a beautiful woman for romance. True love triumphs. Quick reading, her mystery novels are fairly clued if detection is involved. Many are set in New York City, the world of her series detective, the olive-skinned, prematurely white-haired Lieutenant (later Captain) Gridley Nelson of Homicide. Fenisong explains but does not dramatize Nelson's Princeton education and sundry jobs before his becoming a rookie, his inherited wealth, and his liking for people. Nelson claims that his cases yield by-products, one a honey-colored maid from New Orleans, another his ash-blond wife: "He never had any difficulty in conjuring up the image of Kyrie, no matter how much physical distance lay between them" (*Deadlock*). Nelson investigates Manhattan homicides, mostly bludgeonings, in *Grim Rehearsal*, *Dead Yesterday*, and *Miscast for Murder*. Neighbor-friends of his young son involve him in a blackmail case in *Bite the Hand*. Without Nelson, New York City is the setting for *The Lost Caesar*, and for the suspense novels *Widows' Plight* and *The Drop of a Hat*. Outside of New York City, types continue, from a Mysterious Stranger (*Snare for Sinners*) to hoods (*Villainous Company*), and American and British stereotypes near Genoa, Italy (*The Schemers*). An elderly Gothic heroine, a widow-mother transplanted from the South to New York City, makes *Widows' Plight* Fenisong's most successful entertainment.

—Jane Gottschalk

FENWICK, Elizabeth (Elizabeth Fenwick Way). Also writes as E. P. Fenwick. American. Born in 1920.

CRIME PUBLICATIONS

Novels

The Inconvenient Corpse (as E. P. Fenwick).   New York, Farrar and Rinehart, 1943.
Murder in Haste (as E. P. Fenwick).   New York, Farrar and Rinehart, 1944.
Two Names for Death (as E. P. Fenwick).   New York, Farrar and Rinehart, 1945;
   London, Wells Gardner, 1949.
Poor Harriet.   New York, Harper, 1957; London, Gollancz, 1958.
A Long Way Down.   New York, Harper, and London, Gollancz, 1959.
A Friend of Mary Rose.   New York, Harper, 1961; London, Gollancz, 1962.
A Night Run.   London, Gollancz, 1961.
The Silent Cousin.   London, Gollancz, 1962; New York, Atheneum, 1966.
The Make-Believe Man.   New York, Harper, and London, Gollancz, 1963.
The Passenger.   New York, Atheneum, and London, Gollancz, 1967.
Disturbance on Berry Hill.   New York, Atheneum, and London, Gollancz, 1968.
Goodbye, Aunt Elva.   New York, Atheneum, 1968; London, Gollancz, 1969.
Impeccable People.   London, Gollancz, 1971.
The Last of Lysandra.   London, Gollancz, 1973.

OTHER PUBLICATIONS

Novels

The Long Wing.   New York, Rinehart, 1947.
Afterwords.   New York, Rinehart, 1950.
Days of Plenty.   New York, Harcourt Brace, 1956.
Cockleberry Castle (juvenile).   New York, Pantheon, 1963.

Manuscript Collection: Mugar Memorial Library, Boston University.

*   *   *

Elizabeth Fenwick's suspense novels are remarkable for the degree of horror they can extract from minimal materials. Each novel deals with a closed or isolated community, or records a collision between families of very different kinds. The psychology of these small groups is exposed with fastidious authority. Fenwick can describe the best and worst of a character in one sentence, and can make a single gesture tell of years of accumulated pain or madness. In *The Passenger*, the destruction of a woman's garden halfway through the book is unexpectedly shocking in itself, and foreshadows the tragedy to come. In *Goodbye, Aunt Elva*, an elderly woman's years of harmless vanity are exposed by her hysteria when it is suggested that a dying woman looks like her.

Fenwick's novels are all beautifully plotted studies in human intimacy. The depraved families in *Poor Harriet* and *Goodbye, Aunt Elva* draw extra strength for wickedness from their kin. The tragic family in *The Silent Cousin* has seen its great strenth deteriorate into madness. The sound families in *Poor Harriet*, *The Make-Believe Man*, and *Disturbance on Berry Hill* are causes for celebration.

Fenwick's characters are highly individual and often memorable. A woman in *A Long Way Down* is a masterpiece of manipulative menace, even though she never appears in person. And the same novel gives us an elderly bachelor college professor whose isolation has not stunted his charity or understanding.

—Carol Cleveland

FERRARS, Elizabeth. Pseudonym for Morna Doris Brown (née MacTaggart); also writes as E. X. Ferrars. British. Born in Rangoon, Burma, 7 September 1907. Educated at Bedales School, Petersfield, Hampshire, 1918–24; University College, London, 1925–28, diploma in journalism 1928. Married Robert Brown in 1940. Founding Member, Crime Writers Association, 1953. Agent: David Higham Associates Ltd., 5–8 Lower John Street, London W1R 4HA, England. Address: 15-A Corrennie Drive, Edinburgh EH10 6EG, Scotland.

CRIME PUBLICATIONS

Novels (series character: Toby Dyke; published as E. X. Ferrars in US)

Give a Corpse a Bad Name (Dyke). London, Hodder and Stoughton, 1940.
Remove the Bodies (Dyke). London, Hodder and Stoughton, 1940; as *Rehearsals for Murder*, New York, Doubleday, 1941.
Death in Botanist's Bay (Dyke). London, Hodder and Stoughton, 1941; as *Murder of a Suicide*, New York, Doubleday, 1941.
Don't Monkey with Murder (Dyke). London, Hodder and Stoughton, 1942; as *The Shape of a Stain*, New York, Doubleday, 1942.
Your Neck in a Noose (Dyke). London, Hodder and Stoughton, 1942; as *Neck in a Noose*, New York, Doubleday, 1943.
I, Said the Fly. London, Hodder and Stoughton, and New York, Doubleday, 1945.
Murder among Friends. London, Collins, 1946; as *Cheat the Hangman*, New York, Doubleday, 1946.
With Murder in Mind. London, Collins, 1948.
The March Hare Murders. London, Collins, and New York, Doubleday, 1949.
Hunt the Tortoise. London, Collins, and New York, Doubleday, 1950.
Milk of Human Kindness. London, Collins, 1950.
The Clock That Wouldn't Stop. London, Collins, and New York, Doubleday, 1952.
Alibi for a Witch. London, Collins, and New York, Doubleday, 1952.
Murder in Time. London, Collins, 1953.
The Lying Voices. London, Collins, 1954.
Enough to Kill a Horse. London, Collins, and New York, Doubleday, 1955.
Always Say Die. London, Collins, 1956; as *We Haven't Seen Her Lately*, New York, Doubleday, 1956.
Murder Moves In. London, Collins, 1956; as *Kill or Cure*, New York, Doubleday, 1956.
Furnished for Murder. London, Collins, 1957.
Count the Cost. New York, Doubleday, 1957; as *Unreasonable Doubt*, London, Collins, 1958.
Depart This Life. New York, Doubleday, 1958; as *A Tale of Two Murders*, London, Collins, 1959.
Fear the Light. London, Collins, and New York, Doubleday, 1960.
The Sleeping Dogs. London, Collins, and New York, Doubleday, 1960.
The Busy Body. London, Collins, 1962; as *Seeing Double*, New York, Doubleday, 1962.
The Wandering Widows. London, Collins, and New York, Doubleday, 1962.
The Doubly Dead. London, Collins, and New York, Doubleday, 1963.
The Decayed Gentlewoman. New York, Doubleday, 1963; as *A Legal Fiction*, London, Collins, 1964.

Ninth Life. London, Collins, 1965.
No Peace for the Wicked. London, Collins, and New York, Harper, 1966.
Zero at the Bone. London, Collins, 1967; New York, Walker, 1968.
The Swaying Pillars. London, Collins, 1968; New York, Walker, 1969.
Skeleton Staff. London, Collins, and New York, Walker, 1969.
The Seven Sleepers. London, Collins, and New York, Walker, 1970.
A Stranger and Afraid. London, Collins, and New York, Walker, 1971.
Breath of Suspicion. London, Collins, and New York, Doubleday, 1972.
Foot in the Grave. New York, Doubleday, 1972; London, Collins, 1973.
The Small World of Murder. London, Collins, and New York, Doubleday, 1973.
Hanged Man's House. London, Collins, and New York, Doubleday, 1974.
Alive and Dead. London, Collins, 1974; New York, Doubleday, 1975.
Drowned Rat. London, Collins, and New York, Doubleday, 1975.
The Cup and the Lip. London, Collins, 1975; New York, Doubleday, 1976.
Blood Flies Upward. London, Collins, 1976; New York, Doubleday, 1977.
The Pretty Pink Shroud. London, Collins, and New York, Doubleday, 1977.
Murders Anonymous. London, Collins, 1977; New York, Doubleday, 1978.
Last Will and Testament. London, Collins, and New York, Doubleday, 1978.
In at the Kill. London, Collins, 1978; New York, Doubleday, 1979.

Uncollected Short Stories

"After Death the Deluge," in *Detective Stories of Today*, edited by Raymond
Postgate. London, Faber, 1940.
"The Truthful Witness," in *Choice of Weapons*. London, Hodder and Stoughton,
1958.
"Drawn into Error," in *Planned Departures*, edited by Elizabeth Ferrars. London,
Hodder and Stoughton, 1958.
"The Case of the Two Questions," in *Ellery Queen's Mystery Magazine* (New York),
August 1959.
"The Case of the Blue Bowl," in *Ellery Queen's Mystery Magazine* (New York), October
1959.
"Playing with Fire," in *Ellery Queen's Mystery Magazine* (New York), January 1960.
"The Case of the Auction Catalogue," in *Ellery Queen's Mystery Magazine* (New York),
March 1960.
"The Case of the Left Hand," in *Ellery Queen's Mystery Magazine* (New York),
December 1960.
"Suicide?," in *The Saint* (New York), October 1964.
"Look for Trouble," in *The Saint* (New York), May 1965.
"Scatter His Ashes," in *Winter's Crimes 2*, edited by George Hardinge. London,
Macmillan, 1970.
"The Long Way Round," in *Winter's Crimes 4*, edited by George Hardinge. London,
Macmillan, 1972.
"Undue Influence," in *Winter's Crimes 6*, edited by George Hardinge. London,
Macmillan, 1974.
"Ashes to Ashes," in *Ellery Queen's Giants of Mystery*. New York, Davis, 1976.
"Sequence of Events," in *Winter's Crimes 9*, edited by George Hardinge. London,
Macmillan, 1977.
"The Rose Murders," in *Ellery Queen's Mystery Magazine* (New York), May 1977.
"A Very Small Clue," in *Ellery Queen's Mystery Magazine* (New York), June 1977.
"The Forgotten Murder," in *Ellery Queen's Mystery Magazine* (New York), January
1978.

OTHER PUBLICATIONS

Other

Editor, *Planned Departures.*   London, Hodder and Stoughton, 1958.

*   *   *

Morna Brown, whose thrillers appear under the name Elizabeth Ferrars or E. X. Ferrars, is a prolific writer of well-made traditional suspense fiction. Even a nervous reader alone on a dark night may enjoy the tales concocted by this competent British writer. Anything gruesome or horrible is treated in such a way that the reader is spared nightmares or undue distress. Ferrars writes about nice people who inhabit a world in which good manners predominate. Her educated, upper-middle-class characters, unused to the intrusion of violence or crime into their lives, at times exclaim that murder and things like that simply don't happen to them. The author excels at creating sympathetic and natural types whose personalities are convincingly delineated and whose involvement in murder does not fail to arouse interest.

Her protagonists are often writers or artists, scholars or graduate students. Her female characters are politely feminist, independent young women who do not submerge their work or their professional identity in a quest for romance. Ferrars admirably rejects trite "happily-ever-after" solutions to the love affairs which usually figure in her tales. Even an early book like *I, Said the Fly*, set in wartime London, features a self-reliant heroine whose sentimental difficulties are not neatly resolved on the last page.

Backgrounds for the tales range from Greece to Australia, from Africa to Madeira, but most frequently are English villages or Scottish locales. In several books the author has developed the town of Helsington with its surrounding villages, creating a fabric of communities that add charm and familiarity to her fictional world. Though they may be played out in exotic places, the plots tends to be domestic intrigues. Murder in a household or among friends, though sometimes a bit claustrophobic, gives the author an occasion to explore the feelings and motivations of ordinary people. *The Small World of Murder*, which contains a kidnapping and a complex conspiracy among intimates, rather ironically unfolds while the participants travel around the world, from London to Mexico to Fiji to Australia. The foreign scenery is integrated into the plot and is sketched as seen by one member of the party, a bystander who is, at the same time, inextricably involved.

The author incorporates enough specialized information into her stories to add dimension but not enough to overwhelm the reader who, it is presumed, has picked up the book to be entertained and not to be treated to a dissertation on falconry or the art market. Although Miss Ferrars is obviously familiar with university and literary milieux, her books are never marred by excessive academic jargon or too many literary allusions. She is sometimes quite witty, and her subtle, gentle humor enhances many passages in her fiction.

Her readers expect good plotting and ingenious situations and are not often disappointed. In *Breath of Suspicion*, a scientist mixed up in espionage reveals his whereabouts to a deadly enemy by writing a successful thriller. In *Ninth Life*, a crime reporter turned gourmet cook unwisely taunts a criminal from his past and gets himself murdered. In *The Decayed Gentlewoman*, the ownership of a painting, long unrecognized as by Rubens, depends upon an obscure point of law. A group of women who enjoy travelling together harbor a swindler and murderer in their midst in *The Wandering Widows*, a cleverly constructed tale set in the Inner Hebrides, on Iona and Mull. A Helsington story, *Alive and Dead*, revolves around an agency for unwed mothers, and contains a pair of Ferrars's best characters, an elderly woman volunteer and her cantankerous male boarder whose gruff exterior hides a kindly nature.

Elizabeth Ferrars combines fine craftsmanship with skillful plotting and likable people to provide first-rate entertainment. She is one of the best contemporary writers of civilized murder mysteries.

—Mary Helen Becker

FIELDING, A. Pseudonym for Dorothy Feilding; also wrote as A. E. Fielding. British. Born in 1884.

CRIME PUBLICATIONS

Novels (series character: Chief Inspector Pointer in all books except *Deep Currents* and *Murder in Suffolk*)

The Eames-Erskine Case. London, Collins, 1924; New York, Knopf, 1925.
Deep Currents. London, Collins, 1924.
The Charteris Mystery. London, Collins, and New York, Knopf, 1925.
The Footsteps That Stopped. London, Collins, and New York, Knopf, 1926.
The Clifford Affair. London, Collins, and New York, Knopf, 1927; as *The Clifford Mystery*, Collins, 1933.
The Net Around Joan Ingilby. London, Collins, and New York, Knopf, 1928.
The Cluny Problem. London, Collins, 1928; New York, Knopf, 1929.
The Mysterious Partner. London, Collins, and New York, Knopf, 1929.
Murder at the Nook. London, Collins, 1929; New York, Knopf, 1930.
The Craig Poisoning Mystery. London, Collins, and New York, Cosmopolitan, 1930.
The Wedding-Chest Mystery. London, Collins, 1930; New York, Kinsey, 1932.
The Upfold Farm Mystery. London, Collins, 1931; New York, Kinsey, 1932.
Death of John Tait. London, Collins, and New York, Kinsey, 1932.
The Westwood Mystery. London, Collins, 1932; New York, Kinsey, 1933.
The Tall House Mystery. London, Collins, and New York, Kinsey, 1933.
The Paper Chase. London, Collins, 1934; as *The Paper-Chase Mystery*, New York, Kinsey, 1935.
The Cautley Conundrum. London, Collins, 1934; as *The Cautley Mystery*, New York, Kinsey, 1934.
The Case of the Missing Diary. London, Collins, 1935; New York, Kinsey, 1936.
Tragedy at Beachcroft. London, Collins, and New York, Kinsey, 1935.
The Case of the Two Pearl Necklaces. London, Collins, 1936; (as A. E. Fielding), New York, Kinsey, 1936.
Mystery at the Rectory. London, Collins, 1936; (as A. E. Fielding), New York, Kinsey, 1937.
Scarecrow. London, Collins, 1937; (as A. E. Fielding), New York, Kinsey, 1937.

Black Cats Are Lucky.   London, Collins, 1937; (as A. E. Fielding), New York, Kinsey, 1938.
Murder in Suffolk.   London, Collins, 1938; (as A. E. Fielding), New York, Kinsey, 1938.
Pointer to a Crime.   London, Collins, 1944; New York, Arcadia House, 1945.

                              *   *   *

A. Fielding wrote some 25 books. It is not unfair to say that her intricately involved stories, lengthy and slow moving, were what the readers of the period wanted. But none of her stories was outstanding or even very memorable. However even now they can provide an interesting read on a wet day at a seaside hotel. Her detective, Chief Inspector Pointer of Scotland Yard, was rather a grey character who methodically took pains to be thorough. Many of her books were located in the country so that quite often interesting village relationships could be established. She often used two main plots, each rather complicated but not necessarily related, merely impinging. Such is *The Eames-Erskine Case*, her first story, which starts in nice style with a young man's body locked in a hotel bedroom wardrobe. But *Mystery at the Rectory*, published some 11 years later, is a much more readable story: the criminal is well concealed, though the motivation is good. Another of her early books, *The Footsteps That Stopped*, is complex, well-clued, and with a surprise twist solution. *Death of John Tait* has the usual plethora of suspects but is interesting. It is surprising also how often Pointer has to follow his suspects to the Continent. The Yard writ runs wide if somewhat unorthodoxly.

                                                                  —Neville W. Wood

                              _____

FINNEGAN, Robert. Pseudonym for Paul William Ryan; also wrote as Mike Quin. American. Born in San Francisco, California, in 1906. Left school at age 15. Married Mary King O'Donnell in 1944; one daughter. Worked in shops and offices until becoming a sailor, 1925–29; worked in book store in Hollywood; joined the John Reed Club of Hollywood, and contributed to the club magazine, *Partisan*; returned to San Francisco in 1934, became active in the labor movement writing for the International Longshoreman and Warehouseman's Union's *The Waterfront Worker* and *The Dispatcher*, and *Western Worker* (later *People's World*); employed on WPA Writers' Project; Public Relations Director, Congress of Industrial Organizations in California in the 1940's: "CIO Reporter on the Air," 1943–45, columnist, *Daily People's World*, 1946–47, and produced broadcasts for National Maritime Union and others; active member of the Communist Party. *Died 14 August 1947.*

CRIME PUBLICATIONS

Novels (series character: Dan Banion in all books)

The Lying Ladies.   New York, Simon and Schuster, 1946; London, Lane, 1949.
The Bandaged Nude.   New York, Simon and Schuster, 1946; London, Boardman, 1949.
Many a Monster.   New York, Simon and Schuster, 1948; London, Boardman, 1950.

OTHER PUBLICATIONS as Paul W. Ryan

Other

And We Are Millions: The League of Homeless Youth (as Mike Quin).   Hollywood,
   John Reed Club, 1933.
The C.S. Case Against Labor.   San Francisco, International Labor Defense, 1936.
Ashcan the M-Plan (as Mike Quin).   San Francisco, Yanks Are Not Coming
   Committee, 1938.
Dangerous Thoughts.   San Francisco, People's World, 1940.
The Yanks Are Not Coming.   San Francisco, Maritime Federation of the Pacific, 1940.
The Enemy Within.   San Francisco, People's World, 1941.
More Dangerous Thoughts.   San Francisco, People's World, 1941.
On the Drumhead: A Selection from the Writings of Mike Quin, edited by Henry
   Carlisle.   San Francisco, Pacific Publishing Foundation, 1948.
The Big Strike (as Mike Quin).   Olema, California, Olema Publishing Company, 1949.

*   *   *

Robert Finnegan died young, having produced a handful of books demonstrating a very
real talent. Of these, perhaps *The Bandaged Nude* has remained the best known. Finnegan
painted his backgrounds and characters, whether of low or high life, with a sure touch. The
whole post-war atmosphere is there, which journalist Dan Banion feels even within himself
as he drifts around following his discharge from the army. In the people he meets, he "could
see it in their eyes and sense it in their conversation. Restlessness. Dissatisfaction. An
uncertainty about the world and about themselves. The war had left everybody on edge." So
Banion ends up in San Francisco, and in a bar learns of the painting of a bandaged nude; the
artist, just back from the war, tries to trace it and becomes a corpse in a lorry-load of bad
spaghetti. Banion invades artistic circles in his quest for the killer, and Finnegan presents
some nice character sketches and a line in wisecracking dialogue worthy of Raymond
Chandler. Complex relationships are conveyed clearly and with a standard of writing not
always evident in the semi-tough detective field; Finnegan's dry humour is used to good
effect. The story twists and turns toward a satisfying climax with more murders en route, and
Banion finds both the murderer and himself.

It is a tragedy that Banion, with his streak of social conscience, could not have appeared in
a longer series. There have been too few writers as good as Finnegan.

—Melvyn Barnes

FINNEY, Jack (Walter Braden Finney).   American.   Born in Milwaukee, Wisconsin, in
1911. Educated at Knox College, Galesburg, Illinois. Married Marguerite Guest; one
daughter and one son. Self-employed writer. Agent: Harold Matson Co. Inc., 22 East 40th
Street, New York, New York 10016, U.S.A.

CRIME PUBLICATIONS

Novels

Five Against the House.   New York, Doubleday, and London, Eyre and Spottiswoode,
   1954.

The House of Numbers. New York, Dell, and London, Eyre and Spottiswoode, 1957.
Assault on a Queen. New York, Simon and Schuster, 1959; London, Eyre and Spottiswoode, 1960.
The Night People. New York, Doubleday, 1977.

Uncollected Short Stories

"The Widow's Walk," in *Queen's Award's 1947*, edited by Ellery Queen. Boston, Little Brown, 1947; London, Gollancz, 1949.
"Contents of the Dead Man's Pockets," in *Collier's* (Springfield, Ohio), 26 October 1954.
"The Other Arrow," with F. M. Barratt, in *Ellery Queen's Mystery Magazine* (New York), January 1956.
"House of Numbers," in *Cosmopolitan* (New York), July 1956.
"It Wouldn't Be Fair," in *The Comfortable Coffin*, edited by Richard S. Prather. New York, Fawcett, 1960.

OTHER PUBLICATIONS

Novels

The Body Snatchers. New York, Dell, and London, Eyre and Spottiswoode, 1955.
Good Neighbor Sam. New York, Simon and Schuster, and London, Eyre and Spottiswoode, 1963.
The Woodrow Wilson Dime. New York, Simon and Schuster, 1968.
Time and Again. New York, Simon and Schuster, 1970.
Marion's Wall. New York, Simon and Schuster, 1973.

Short Stories

The Third Level. New York, Rinehart, 1957; as *The Clock of Time*, London, Eyre and Spottiswoode, 1958.
I Love Galesburg in the Springtime. New York, Simon and Schuster, 1963; London, Eyre and Spottiswoode, 1965.

Play

Telephone Roulette. Chicago, Dramatic Publishing Company, 1956.

*   *   *

Though none of Jack Finney's nine novels is primarily concerned with the investigation and solution of crime, he has a place in the history of American mystery fiction. From *Five Against the House* to *The Night People*, Finney has dealt with bizarre, sensational, and often criminal aspects of American life in a continuing effort to contrast ugly contemporary realities with his romantic vision of the gracious past. In *Assault on a Queen*, a band of adventurers plot to refloat a sunken World War I U-Boat as part of an elaborate plot – fully revealed only at the conclusion – to rob the *Queen Mary*. In *Time and Again*, his best-known work, a young artist becomes involved in a secret government project, in the course of which he literally travels back in time to the New York of the 1880's. In *Marion's Wall*, a young couple who move into an old California house make contact with the spirit of a 1920's starlet who once lived there. In *The Night People*, a group of San Francisco pranksters bedevil the police and amaze fellow Californians by a series of bizarre events culminating in a monster film-showing-cum-traffic-jam on the Golden Gate Bridge. In these and other writings, including the science fiction novel *The Body Snatchers* and two short-story collections, Finney creates ingenious, suspenseful narratives, treats regretfully, though sometimes humorously, the tensions and conflicts in mid-20th-century America, and contrasts the latter, though not always explicitly, with a romantically imagined pre-modern age.

Some of Finney's novels have been adapted as films, Don Siegel's *Invasion of the Body Snatchers*, a science-fiction classic, being the most highly regarded among them. Though short stories of his have been included in collections of detective fiction much of his work lies beyond the bounds of any strict definition of detective or mystery fiction. He continues to use fictional form to create, often with apparent light-heartedness, images of the grim contemporary American scene and to set them – in actuality or by implication – against his sense of the past.

—Seymour Rudin

FISCHER, Bruno. Also writes as Russell Gray. American. Born in Berlin, Germany, 29 June 1908; emigrated to the United States in 1913. Educated at Richmond Hill High School, Long Island, New York; Rand School of Social Sciences, New York. Married Ruth Miller in 1934; one daughter and one son. Journalist and editor: Editor, *Socialist Call*, 1936; Executive Editor, Collier Books, New York; Education Editor, Arco Publishing Company, New York, in the 1960's. Agent: Lenniger Literary Agency, 437 Fifth Avenue, New York, New York 10016. Address: Three Arrows, R.D. 3, Putnam Valley, New York, 10579, U.S.A.

CRIME PUBLICATIONS

Novels (series characters: Ben Helm; Rick Train)

> *So Much Blood.* New York, Greystone Press, 1939; as *Stairway to Death*, New York, Pyramid, 1951.
> *The Hornet's Nest* (Train). New York, Morrow, 1944; London, Quality Press, 1947.
> *Quoth the Raven.* New York, Doubleday, 1944; as *Croaked the Raven*, London, Quality Press, 1947; as *The Fingered Man*, New York, Ace, 1953.
> *The Dead Men Grin* (Helm). Philadelphia, McKay, 1945; London, Quality Press, 1947.
> *Kill to Fit* (Train). New York, Green, 1946; London, Instructive Arts, 1951.
> *The Pigskin Bag.* New York, Ziff Davis, 1946; London, Foulsham, 1951.
> *The Spider Lily.* Philadelphia, McKay, 1946; London, Quality Press, 1953.
> *More Deaths Than One* (Helm). New York, Ziff Davis, 1947; London, Foulsham, 1950.
> *The Bleeding Scissors.* New York, Ziff Davis, 1948; as *The Scarlet Scissors*, London, Foulsham, 1950.
> *The Restless Hands* (Helm). New York, Dodd Mead, 1949; London, Foulsham, 1950.
> *The Lustful Ape* (as Russell Gray). New York, Lion, 1950; as Bruno Fischer, New York, Fawcett, and London, Red Seal, 1959.
> *The Angels Fell.* New York, Dodd Mead, 1950; London, Boardman, 1951; as *The Flesh Was Cold*, New York, New American Library, 1951.
> *House of Flesh.* New York, Fawcett, 1950; London, Red Seal, 1958.
> *The Silent Dust* (Helm). New York, Dodd Mead, 1950; London, Boardman, 1951.
> *Fools Walk In.* New York, Fawcett, 1951; London, Red Seal, 1958.
> *The Lady Kills.* New York, Fawcett, 1951.

The Paper Circle (Helm).   New York, Dodd Mead, 1951; London, Boardman, 1952; as
  Stripped for Murder, New York, New American Library, 1953.
The Fast Buck.   New York, Fawcett, 1952; London, Red Seal, 1959.
Run for Your Life.   New York, Fawcett, 1953; London, Fawcett, 1954.
So Wicked My Love.   New York, Fawcett, 1954; London, Fawcett, 1957.
Knee-Deep in Death.   New York, Fawcett, 1956; London, Fawcett, 1957.
Murder in the Raw.   New York, Fawcett, 1957; London, Fawcett, 1959.
Second-Hand Nude.   New York, Fawcett, 1959; London, Muller, 1960.
The Girl Between.   New York, Fawcett, 1960.
The Evil Days.   New York, Random House, 1974; London, Hale, 1976.

Uncollected Short Stories

"The Light That Killed," in *Dime Mystery* (New York), August 1940.
"The Sign of the Skull," in *Dime Mystery* (New York), September 1940.
"Bubbles of Death," in *Dime Mystery* (New York), October 1940.
"The Death Dolls," in *Horror Stories*, October 1940.
"The Body I Stole," in *Terror Tales*, November 1940.
"Death Has Three Sisters," in *Dime Mystery* (New York), November 1940.
"The Mummy Men," in *Dime Mystery* (New York), November 1940.
"Death Comes Crawling," in *Dime Mystery* (New York), December 1940.
"Beware the Blind Killer," in *Strange Detective*, January 1941.
"Inn of Shipwrecked Corpses," in *Dime Mystery* (New York), January 1941.
"We Who Are Lost," in *Terror Tales*, January 1941.
"Home of the Headless Ones," in *Horror Stories*, February 1941.
"Which One of Us?" in *Dime Mystery* (New York), February 1941.
"Death's Old Women," in *Dime Mystery* (New York), March 1941.
"Satan's Theme Song," in *Detective Tales*, April 1941.
"Satan's Watch Fob," in *Dime Mystery* (New York), May 1941.
"City under Fire," in *Five Novels*, September 1941.
"His Good Angel," in *Dime Mystery* (New York), September 1941.
"They Can't Kill Us," in *Dime Mystery* (New York), September 1941.
"Death Hitch-Hikes South," in *Dime Mystery* (New York), January 1942.
"Murder Is News," in *Big Book Detective*, February 1942.
"Homicide Jest," in *10-Story Detective*, March 1942.
"They Knew Dolly," in *10-Story Mystery*, April 1942.
"The Dead Hang High," in *Dime Mystery* (New York), May 1942.
"The Female of the Species," in *The Avenger* (New York), May 1942.
"Waldo Jones and the Killers," in *Big Book Detective*, June 1942.
"But I Call It Murder," in *Detective Short Stories*, July 1942.
"Homicide Can't Happen Here," in *Detective Short Stories*, July 1942.
"Satan's Scandal Sheet," in *10-Story Detective*, July 1942.
"Murder Has Seven Guests," in *10-Story Mystery*, August 1942.
"Bring 'em Back Dead," in *New Detective*, September 1942.
"Suicide Circus," in *New Detective*, September 1942.
"Come to My Dying," in *10-Story Mystery*, October 1942.
"Daughter of Murder," in *10-Story Mystery*, October 1942.
"Death Is a Saboteur," in *Detective Short Stories*, November 1942.
"The Dead Laugh Last," in *10-Story Mystery*, October 1942.
"Bargain Day for Corpses," in *Strange Detective*, November 1942.
"The Caricature Murders," in *Dime Mystery* (New York), November 1942.
"Happy Death Day to You," in *New Detective*, November 1942.
"Call the Cops," in *Detective Short Stories*, January 1943.
"Death's Black Bag," in *Strange Detective*, January 1943.
"Kill and Run," in *New Detective*, January 1943.

"Murder Begins at Midnight," in *The Spider*, January 1943.
"Murder Is Where you Find It," in *New Detective*, January 1943.
"Murder Man," in *Read*, January 1943.
"Murder Mask," in *10-Story Mystery*, February 1943.
"Nine Dead Men and a Girl," in *Big Book Detective*, February 1943.
"The Riddle House," in *10-Story Mystery*, February 1943.
"Death Lives on the Lake," in *Strange Detective*, March 1943.
"The Killer Waits," in *Dime Mystery* (New York), March 1943.
"Locket for a Lady," in *Mammoth Detective*, March 1943.
"Me, My Coffin, and My Killer," in *Strange Detective*, March 1943.
"Satan's Servant," in *10-Story Mystery*, April 1943.
"Secret Weapons Murders," in *Detective Short Stories*, April 1943.
"The Woman in the Case," *Detective Fiction* (New York), April 1943.
"Cold Is the Grave," in *Strange Detective*, May 1943.
"A Friend of Goebbels," in *Detective Fiction* (New York), May 1943.
"One Thousand Ways to Die," in *Dime Mystery* (New York), May 1943.
"Death Is the Wedding Guest," in *Dime Mystery* (New York), July 1943.
"Killers' Tournament," in *Dime Mystery* (New York), July 1943.
"Sing a Song of Death," in *New Detective*, July 1943.
"The Coward," in *Mammoth Detective*, August 1943.
"The Night Is for Dying," in *Detective Fiction* (New York), August 1943.
"The Lady Smiles at Fate," in *Crack Detective* (New York), September 1943.
"Murder Is Simple," in *Detective Fiction* (New York), September 1943.
"Murder on Wheels," in *Dime Mystery* (New York), September 1943.
"Ride for Mr. Two-by-Four," in *10-Story Detective*, September 1943.
"This Girl, Miss Murder," in *Detective Short Stories*, October 1943.
"The Gift," in *Mammoth Detective*, November 1943.
"I'll Slay You Later," in *Dime Mystery* (New York), November 1943.
"The League of Little Men," in *Detective Fiction* (New York), November 1943.
"Murder Is Unlucky," in *Detective Fiction* (New York), November 1943.
"Seven Doorways to Death," in *Crack Detective* (New York), November 1943.
"A Female on the Squad," in *Detective Story*, December 1943.
"Case of the Handless Corpse," in *Dime Mystery* (New York), January 1944.
"The House That Wasn't There," in *Crack Detective* (New York), January 1944.
"Kill Without Murder," in *Black Mask* (New York), January 1944.
"The Lady of Death," in *Detective Fiction* (New York), January 1944.
"Death on the Beach," in *Mammoth Detective*, February 1944.
"Little Men, What Now?," in *Detective Fiction* (New York), February 1944.
"My Problem Is – Murder," in *10 Detective Aces* (Springfield, Massachusetts), February 1944.
"X Marks the Redhead," in *Crack Detective* (New York), March 1944.
"Fatally Yours," in *New Detective*, May 1944.
"I'll Bury You Deeper," in *Dime Mystery* (New York), May 1944.
"The Man Who Would Be Hitler," in *Dime Mystery* (New York), May 1944.
"The Twelfth Bottle," in *Detective Story*, May 1944.
"Murder Takes No Furlough," in *Crack Detective* (New York), July 1944.
"Anything But the Truth," in *Mammoth Detective*, August 1944.
"I Am Thinking of Murder," in *The Shadow* (New York), August 1944.
"The Little Things," in *Detective Fiction* (New York), August 1944.
"The Bride Wore Black," in *Dime Mystery* (New York), September 1944.
"Death's Secret Agent," in *Crack Detective* (New York), September 1944.
"My Friend – The Killer," in *Dime Mystery* (New York), September 1944.
"Come Home to Murder," in *Mammoth Detective*, November 1944.
"The Man Who Wasn't Himself," in *New Detective*, November 1944.
"Blood on My Doorstep," in *New Detective*, January 1945.

"Death Paints a Picture," in *Crack Detective* (New York), January 1945.
"Ike Walsh and the Boy Wonder," in *The Shadow* (New York), January 1945.
"Bones Will Tell," in *Mammoth Mystery*, February 1945.
"Murder Throws One Stone," in *The Shadow* (New York), February 1945.
"Scream Theme," in *10 Detective Aces* (Springfield, Massachusetts), March 1945.
"Deadlier Than the Male," in *Dime Mystery* (New York), May 1945.
"Smart Guy," in *Mystery Quarterly*, May 1945.
"Wrap Up the Corpse," in *Detective Story*, May 1945.
"TNT for Two," in *10-Story Detective*, June 1945.
"Ask a Body," in *New Detective*, July 1945.
"Mind Your Own Murder," in *Mammoth Detective*, August 1945.
"Night Race," in *Doc Savage* (New York), September 1945.
"Killing the Goose," in *Detective Story*, October 1945.
"Come to My Funeral," in *Dime Mystery* (New York), November 1945.
"Night Time Is Murder Time," in *New Detective*, November 1945.
"Give a Dog the Name," in *Mammoth Detective*, January 1946.
"Murder – My Aunt," in *Dime Mystery* (New York), January 1946.
"Two Mice for a Cat," in *Crack Detective* (New York), January 1946.
"The Enemy," in *Doc Savage* (New York), May 1946.
"A Copy with Wings," in *Mammoth Detective*, July 1946.
"Don't Bury Him Deep," in *Doc Savage* (New York), July 1946.
"Two's Company, 22's a Shroud," in *10-Story Detective*, September 1946.
"Case of the Sleeping Doll," in *Detective Story*, October 1946.
"Death's Bright Red Lips," in *Mammoth Mystery*, December 1946.
"The Man Who Lost His Head," in *Best Detective Stories of the Year 1945*, edited by
    David Coxe Cooke.   New York, Dutton, 1946.
"Double Deadline," in *Detective Book*, 1946.
"I'll Slay You in My Dreams," in *Rue Morgue No. 1*, edited by Rex Stout and Louis
    Greenfield.   New York, Creative Age Press, 1946.
"A Killer in the Crowd," in *Black Mask* (New York), July 1947.
"Killers Leave Me Cold," in *Dime Mystery* (New York), October 1947.
"The Face of Fear," in *New Detective*, November 1947.
"Homicide Homework," in *Detective Tales*, November 1947.
"Middleman for Murder," in *Black Mask* (New York), November 1947.
"Smile, Corpse, Smile," in *Dime Mystery* (New York), February 1948.
"Homicidal Homestead," in *Shock* (New York), March 1948.
"The Trap," in *Detective Tales*, March 1948.
"Guest from the Grave," in *10 Detective Aces* (Springfield, Massachusetts), May 1948.
"Silent as a Shiv," in *Detective Tales*, May 1948.
"The Mam'selle Means Murder," in *10 Detective Aces* (Springfield, Massachusetts), June
    1948.
"I Thought I'd Die," in *New Detective*, September 1948.
"Murder Turns the Curve," in *Popular Detective* (New York), September 1948.
"Terror Had Two Faces," in *New Detective*, September 1948.
"The Green Vest," in *The Shadow* (New York), Fall 1948.
"Strange Man, Strange Murder," in *Crack Detective* (New York), November 1948.
"The Hour of the Rat," in *Dime Mystery* (New York), December 1948.
"Pickup on Nightmare Road," in *10-Story Detective* (New York), December 1948.
"The Hands of Mr. Prescott," in *Popular Detective* (New York), March 1949.
"The Dead Don't Die," in *Popular Detective* (New York), November 1949.
"Lady in Distress," in *Thrilling Detective* (New York), December 1949.
"The Dream," in *Male*, July 1950.
"Hotel Murder," in *Giant Detective Annual*.   New York, Best Books, 1950.
"The Dog Died First," in *Best Detective Stories of the Year 1950*, edited by David Coxe
    Cooke.   New York, Dutton, 1950.

"The Deep, Dark Grave," in *Giant Detective*, Winter 1951.

"No Escape," in *As Tough As They Come*, edited by Will Oursler. New York, Doubleday, 1951.

"Kiss the Dead Girl," in *Popular Detective* (New York), May 1952.

"Stop Him," in *Manhunt* (New York), March 1953.

"Say Good-Bye to Janie," in *Manhunt* (New York), July 1953.

"Coney Island Incident," in *Manhunt* (New York), November 1953.

"Nobody's Business," in *Crooks' Tour*, edited by Bruno Fischer. New York, Dodd Mead, 1953; London, Macdonald, 1954.

"Double," in *Manhunt* (New York), April 1954.

"My Aunt Cecilia," in *Butcher, Baker, Murder-Maker*, edited by George Harmon Coxe. New York, Knopf, 1954; London, Macdonald, 1956.

"The Quiet Woman," in *Dell Mystery Novels* (New York), January–March 1955.

"Hang That Husband High," in *Dangerous Dames*, edited by Brett Halliday. New York, Dell, 1955.

"The Shallow Grave," in *Suspect*, February 1956.

"They Came with Guns," in *Manhunt* (New York), July 1957.

"Sam Rall's Private Ghost," in *For Love or Money*, edited by Dorothy Gardiner. New York, Doubleday, 1957; London, Macdonald, 1959.

"The Portraits of Eve," in *Manhunt* (New York), February 1958.

"The Wind Blows Death," in *Murder in Miami*, edited by Brett Halliday. New York, Dodd Mead, 1959.

"Bugged," in *Manhunt* (New York), August 1961.

"Service Call," in *Best Detective Stories of the Year, 17th Annual Collection*, edited by David Coxe Cooke. New York, Dutton, 1962.

"Five O'Clock Menace," in *The Hard-Boiled Detective: Stories from Black Mask Magazine 1920–1950*, edited by Herbert Ruhm. New York, Vintage, 1977.

OTHER PUBLICATIONS

Other

Editor, *Crooks' Tour*. New York, Dodd Mead, 1953; London, Macdonald, 1954.

*　　*　　*

Like many other mystery and suspense writers, Bruno Fischer began his career in the pages of the pulp magazines. In the late 1930's, under the pseudonym of Russell Gray, he appeared regularly in most of the mystery-horror (or "shudder") pulps; later, he graduated to the detective magazines and began signing his work with his real name. He is the author of hundreds of short stories, including "The Man Who Lost His Head," considered by some to be a minor classic, "The Dog Died First," and "Service Call."

Fischer's first novel, *So Much Blood*, appeared in 1939; but it was not until 1944 that he turned in earnest to the full-length mystery with two above-average books, *Quoth the Raven* and *The Hornet's Nest*. In 1945 one of his best novels, *The Dead Men Grin*, introduced Ben Helm, a likable private detective who depends more on his wits than on his fists and who stars in several other adventures.

With the rise of the paperback in the early 1950's, Fischer turned to that medium and wrote several books for the house generally considered to have published the best of the early soft-cover originals, Fawcett Gold Medal; among his noteworthy Gold Medal novels are *House of Flesh* and *So Wicked My Love*.

Much of Fischer's work deals with shocking and gruesome crimes, a good percentage of which take place in small upstate New York communities; but his handling of this material is deft and restrained, with emphasis on detection and characterization rather than on the lurid aspects. One of his recurring themes is the morality play: ordinary people thrust into extraordinary situations in which their moral standards are tested and sometimes corrupted. An example is his most recent novel, *The Evil Days* – a mordant tale of thievery, kidnapping, murder, and adultery.

—Bill Pronzini

FISH, Robert L. Also writes as Robert L. Pike; Lawrence Roberts. American. Born in Cleveland, Ohio, 21 August 1912. Educated at Case School of Applied Science (now Case-Western Reserve University), Cleveland, B.S. 1933. Served three years in the National Guard, Ohio 37th Division. Married Mamie Kates in 1935; two daughters. Managerial positions in many companies, including Firestone Tire and Rubber; for past 20 years has been a consulting engineer on vinyl plastics in Brazil, Argentina, England, Korea, Taiwan, Colombia, Mexico, Venezuela. President, Mystery Writers of America, 1978. Recipient: Mystery Writers of America Edgar Allan Poe Award for novel, 1962, short story, 1971. Address: 143 Sterling Road, Trumbull, Connecticut 06611, U.S.A.

CRIME PUBLICATIONS

Novels (series characters: Carruthers, Simpson, and Briggs; Captain José da Silva; Kek Huuygens)

> *The Fugitive* (da Silva). New York, Simon and Schuster, 1962; London, Boardman, 1963.
> *The Assassination Bureau* (completion of Jack London story). New York, McGraw Hill, and London, Deutsch, 1963.
> *Isle of the Snakes* (da Silva). New York, Simon and Schuster, 1963; London, Boardman, 1964.
> *The Shrunken Head* (da Silva). New York, Simon and Schuster, 1963; London, Boardman, 1965.
> *Brazilian Sleigh Ride* (da Silva). New York, Simon and Schuster, 1965; London, Boardman, 1966.
> *The Diamond Bubble* (da Silva). New York, Simon and Schuster, and London, Boardman, 1965.
> *Trials of O'Brien* (novelization of tv play). New York, New American Library, 1965.
> *Always Kill a Stranger* (da Silva). New York, Putnam, 1967.
> *The Hochmann Miniatures* (Huuygens). New York, New American Library, 1967.
> *The Bridge That Went Nowhere* (da Silva). New York, Putnam, 1968; London, Long, 1970.
> *The Murder League* (Carruthers *et al.*) New York, Simon and Schuster, 1968; London, New English Library, 1970.
> *The Xavier Affair* (da Silva). New York, Putnam, 1969; London, Hale, 1974.
> *Whirligig* (Huuygens). New York, Putnam, 1970.
> *The Green Hell Treasure* (da Silva). New York, Putnam, 1971.
> *Rub-a-Dub-Dub* (Carruthers *et al.*). New York, Simon and Schuster, 1971; as *Death Cuts the Deck*, New York, Ace, 1972.
> *The Tricks of the Trade* (Huuygens). New York, Putnam, 1972; London, Hale, 1974.
> *Weekend '33*, with Bob Thomas. New York, Doubleday, 1972.

A Handy Death, with Henry Rothblatt. New York, Simon and Schuster, 1973; London, Hale, 1975.
The Wager (Huuygens). New York, Putnam, 1974; London, Hale, 1976.
Trouble in Paradise (da Silva). New York, Doubleday, 1975.
Pursuit. New York, Doubleday, 1978.
A Gross Carriage of Justice (Carruthers *et al.*). New York, Doubleday, 1979.

Novels as Robert L. Pike (series characters: Lieutenant Clancy; Lieutenant Jim Reardon)

Mute Witness (Clancy). New York, Doubleday, 1963; London, Deutsch, 1965; as *Bullitt*, New York, Avon, 1968.
The Quarry (Clancy). New York, Doubleday, 1964.
Police Blotter (Clancy). New York, Doubleday, 1965; London, Deutsch, 1966.
Reardon. New York, Doubleday, 1970.
The Gremlin's Grampa (Reardon). New York, Doubleday, 1972.
Bank Job (Reardon). New York, Doubleday, 1974; London, Hale, 1975.
Deadline 2 A.M. New York, Doubleday, 1976; London, Hale, 1977.

Short Stories

The Incredible Schlock Homes. New York, Simon and Schuster, 1966.
The Memoirs of Schlock Homes. Indianapolis, Bobbs Merrill, 1974.
Kek Huuygens, Smuggler. Yonkers, New York, Mysterious Press, 1976.

Uncollected Short Stories

"One of the Oldest Con Games," in *Ellery Queen's Mystery Magazine* (New York), March 1977.
"Stranger in Town," in *Antaeus* (New York), Spring–Summer 1977.
"The Adventure of the Elite Type," in *Ellery Queen's Mystery Magazine* (New York), July 1977.
"The Adventures of the Odd Lotteries," in *Ellery Queen's Searches and Seizures.* New York, Davis, 1977.
"The Adventure of the Animal Fare," in *Ellery Queen's Mystery Magazine* (New York), October 1977.
"No Rough Stuff," in *Ellery Queen's Faces of Mystery.* New York, Davis, 1977.
"The Art of Deduction," in *Ellery Queen's Mystery Magazine* (New York), June 1979.
"The Adventure of the Common Code," in *Ellery Queen's Mystery Magazine* (New York), September 1979.

OTHER PUBLICATIONS

Other

The Break In (as Lawrence Roberts). New York, Scholastic, 1974.
Big Wheels (as Lawrence Roberts). New York, Scholastic, 1977.
Pele: My Life and a Wonderful Game, with Pele. New York, Doubleday, 1978.
Alley Fever (as Lawrence Roberts). New York, Scholastic, 1979.

Editor, *With Malice Toward All.* New York, Putnam, 1968; London, Macmillan, 1969.
Editor, *Every Crime in the Book.* New York, Putnam, 1975; London, Macmillan, 1976.

Manuscript Collection: Mugar Memorial Library, Boston University.

Robert L. Fish comments:

I write to entertain; if it is possible to inform at the same time, all the better, but entertainment comes first. I like to write using places I have been and enjoyed as the background location for my stories and books. I write the kind of stories and books I like to read, and if I can get a reader to turn the page, I feel I have succeeded in what I started out to do.

*   *   *

Although Robert L. Fish did not begin his writing career until he was in his late forties, he has made up for his late start by the quality and versatility of his talents. Ranging from Sherlockian parodies to fascinatingly realistic police procedural novels, Fish's short stories and novels are witty and well-plotted, alternating between expertly crafted humor and breath-taking suspense.

In 1960, *Ellery Queen Mystery Magazine* published the first of a series of Sherlockian parodies by Robert Fish, "The Adventure of the Ascot Tie," introducing the remarkably inept Schlock Homes and his enthusiastically tolerant assistant, Dr. Watney. Since then, over 25 of the Schlock Homes stories have been published. Although the adventures of Schlock Homes have received disparaging criticism from Barzun and Taylor, who in their *A Catalogue of Crime* describe the parodies as "distressing" and "indifferent attempts at parody," the reception by both Doyle scholars and mystery fans in general has been very favorable. Utilizing hilarious puns, extremely astute misobservations, and outrageously illogical solutions, Fish dares to invade the austere Sherlockian's den with rampant comedy.

The Brazilian climate of Rio de Janeiro where Fish was employed as an engineering consultant to a Brazilian plastics firm must have been particularly conducive to mystery-plotting since not only Schlock Homes, but several other notable characters were conceived there, such as Kek Huuygens, the smuggler, and José da Silva, a liaison officer between the Brazilian police and Interpol. Kek Huuygens, an international smuggler extraordinaire, with tastes in wine, women, and entertainment which match his aesthetic taste in the fine arts, appears in a number of novels and stories.

Fish's best-known character, the swarthy, vibrant, Captain José da Silva, as much at home in the Brazilian jungles as on the streets of Manhattan, first appeared in the Edgar-winning novel *The Fugitive*. Since then, a wealth of adventure has befallen this intuitive, witty, romantic, and extremely courageous character. Da Silva has tangled with swarms of poisonous snakes (*Isle of the Snakes*), bands of head-shrinking Indians, Brazilian revolutionaries (*The Shrunken Head*), and even New York's gambling syndicate (*Brazilian Sleigh Ride*). Usually accompanied by his own faithful Watson in the form of the often amusing, sometimes harrowing, Mr. Wilson of the American Embassy in Rio de Janeiro, da Silva always gets his "man," even when the ultimate culprit turns out to be feminine in nature.

Writing under the name of Robert L. Pike, Fish portrays the demanding, frustrating, and occasionally rewarding life of an American policeman. In *Mute Witness* (the basis of the film *Bullitt*) the astute deductive reasoning of the indefatigable Lieutenant Clancy, whose sidekicks Kaproski and Stanton prowl the streets of Manhattan's 52nd precinct, devises a daring rescue of a famous underworld figure from gang execution. *Police Blotter* finds the same trio in a race against time and professional killers who are determined to assassinate one of the U.N. delegates.

On the other side of the continent, roaming the hilly streets of San Francisco is Pike's amorous and resourceful Lieutenant Jim Reardon.

—Mary Ann Grochowski

FISHER, Steve (Stephen Gould Fisher). Also writes as Stephen Gould; Grant Lane. American. Born in 1912. Served in the United States Navy, 1928–32. Wrote for Navy publications; settled in New York City to write for pulp magazines; worked in Hollywood as screenwriter and television writer.

CRIME PUBLICATIONS

Novels

Spend the Night (as Grant Lane). New York, Phoenix Press, 1935.
Satan's Angel. New York, Macaulay, 1935.
Forever Glory. New York, Macaulay, 1936.
Murder of the Admiral (as Stephen Gould). New York, Macaulay, 1936.
Murder of the Pigboat Skipper. New York, Curl, 1937.
The Night Before Murder. New York, Curl, 1939.
Homicide Johnny (as Stephen Gould). New York, Arcadia House, 1940; London, Pemberton, 1946.
I Wake Up Screaming. New York, Dodd Mead, 1941; London, Hale, 1943; revised edition, New York, Bantam, 1960.
Winter Kill. New York, Dodd Mead, 1946.
The Sheltering Night. New York, Fawcett, 1952.
Giveaway. New York, Random House, 1954.
Take All You Can Get. New York, Random House, 1955.
No House Limit. New York, Dutton, 1958.
Image of Hell. New York, Dutton, 1961.
Saxon's Ghost. Los Angeles, Sherbourne Press, 1969.
The Big Dream. New York, Doubleday, 1970.
The Hell-Black Night. Los Angeles, Sherbourne Press, 1970.

Uncollected Short Stories

"If Christmas Comes," in Ellery Queen's Mystery Magazine (New York) January 1944.
"Goodbye Hannah," in To the Queen's Taste, edited by Ellery Queen. Boston, Little Brown, 1946; London, Faber, 1949.
"Day Never Came," in Ellery Queen's Mystery Magazine (New York), October 1953.
"Me and Mickey Mouse," in The Saint (New York), May 1954.
"Lucky Cop," in Ellery Queen's Mystery Magazine (New York), March 1956.
"Cinderella Wore Black," in The Saint (New York), June 1956.
"Wait for Me," in The Saint (New York), May 1964.

OTHER PUBLICATIONS

Novels

Destroyer. New York, Appleton Century, 1941.
Destination Tokyo. New York, Appleton Century, 1943.

Plays

Susan Slept Here, with Alex Gottlieb (produced New York, 1961). New York, French, 1956.

Screenplays: *Typhoon*, with Allen Rivkin and Leonard Lee, 1940; *To the Shores of Tripoli*, with Lamar Trotti, 1942; *Berlin Correspondent*, with Jack Andrews, 1942; *Destination Tokyo*, with Delmer Daves and Albert Maltz, 1943; *Johnny Angel*, with Frank Gruber, 1945; *Lady in the Lake*, 1946; *Dead Reckoning*, with others, 1946; *That's My Man*, with Bradley King, 1947; *Song of the Thin Man*, with others, 1947; *The Hunted*, 1948; *I Wouldn't Be in Your Shoes*, 1948; *Tokyo Joe*, with others, 1949; *A Lady Without Passport*, with others, 1950; *Roadblock*, with others, 1951; *Battle Zone*, 1952; *Flat Top*, 1952; *San Antone*, 1953; *Woman They Almost Lynched*, 1953; *The Man from the Alamo*, with others, 1953; *The Big Frame*, with others, 1953; *City That Never Sleeps*, 1953; *Sea of Lost Ships*, with Norman Reilly Raine, 1953; *Terror Street*, 1953; *Night Freight*, 1953; *Hell's Half Acre*, 1954; *The Shanghai Story*, with Seton I. Miller and Lester Yard, 1954; *The Big Tip-Off*, 1955; *Las Vegas Shakedown*, 1955; *Top Gun*, with Richard Schayer, 1955; *Silent Fear*, 1955; *Toughest Man Alive*, 1956; *Betrayed Women*, with Paul L. Peil, 1956; *The Restless Breed*, 1957; *Courage of Black Beauty*, 1957; *I, Mobster*, 1959; *September Storm*, with W. R. Burnett, 1961; *Law of the Lawless*, 1964; *The Quick Gun*, with Robert E. Kent, 1964; *Young Fury*, with A. C. Lyles, 1965; *Black Spurs*, 1965; *Johnny Reno*, with Andrew Craddock, 1966; *Waco*, 1966; *Red Tomahawk*, with Andrew Craddock, 1967; *Fort Utah*, with Andrew Craddock, 1967; *Hostile Guns*, with Sloane Nibley and James Edward Grant, 1968; *Arizona Bushwhackers*, with Andrew Craddock, 1968; *Rogue's Gallery*, with A. C. Lyles, 1968.

*   *   *

The career of Steve Fisher was launched in 1928, when he ran away from a California military academy to begin a four-year tenure in the U.S. Navy. He utilized this background in such novels as *Murder of the Admiral* and *Murder of the Pigboat Skipper*.

Fisher's melodramatic style, an emotionally-charged mixture of toughness and open sentimentality, is reflected in his best-known novel, *I Wake Up Screaming* (filmed with Victor Mature and Betty Grable). The narrative deals with an unlucky sports promoter, accused of murdering the young film starlet he helped promote, who finds himself being tracked relentlessly by a hard-nosed police detective. The mystery fiction of Steve Fisher is swift and unsubtle, typical of its period, reflecting the gaudy pulps which formed its roots. But it has emotion. As his friend, the writer Frank Gruber, once declared, "Steve was never afraid to put his heart on a printed page."

—William F. Nolan

FITT, Mary. Pseudonym for Kathleen Freeman; also wrote as Stuart Mary Wick. British. Born 22 June 1897. Educated at University College of South Wales and Monmouthshire, Cardiff, B.A. 1918, M.A. 1922. Lecturer in Greek, University College of South Wales and Monmouthshire, 1919–46. Lecturer for the Ministry of Information and the National Scheme for Education, 1939–45. D.Litt.: University College of South Wales and Monmouthshire, 1940. *Died 21 February 1959.*

CRIME PUBLICATIONS

Novels (series character: Inspector Mallett)

Murder Mars the Tour. London, Nicholson and Watson, 1936.
Three Sisters Flew Home. London, Nicholson and Watson, and New York, Doubleday, 1936.
The Three Hunting Horns. London, Nicholson and Watson, 1937.
Bulls Like Death. London, Nicholson and Watson, 1937.
Expected Death. London, Nicholson and Watson, 1938.
Sky-Rocket (Mallett). London, Nicholson and Watson, 1938.
Death at Dancing Stones (Mallett). London, Nicholson and Watson, 1939.
Murder of a Mouse. London, Nicholson and Watson, 1939.
Death Starts a Rumour. London, Nicholson and Watson, 1940.
Death and Mary Dazill (Mallett). London, Joseph, 1941; as *Aftermath of Murder*, New York, Doubleday, 1941.
Death on Herons' Mere (Mallett). London, Joseph, 1941; as *Death Finds a Target*, New York, Doubleday, 1942.
Requiem for Robert (Mallett). London, Joseph, 1942.
Clues for Christabel (Mallett). London, Joseph, and New York, Doubleday, 1944.
Death and the Pleasant Voices (Mallett). London, Joseph, and New York, Putnam, 1946.
A Fine and Private Place (Mallett). London, Macdonald, and New York, Putnam, 1947.
Death and the Bright Day (Mallett). London, Macdonald, 1948.
And Where's Mr. Bellamy? (as Stuart Mary Wick). London, Hutchinson, 1948.
The Banquet Ceases (Mallett). London, Macdonald, 1949.
The Statue and the Lady (as Stuart Mary Wick). London, Hodder and Stoughton, 1950.
Pity for Pamela. London, Macdonald, 1950; New York, Harper, 1951.
An Ill Wind (Mallett). London, Macdonald, 1951.
Death and the Shortest Day (Mallett). London, Macdonald, 1952.
The Night-Watchman's Friend. London, Macdonald, 1953.
Love from Elizabeth (Mallett). London, Macdonald, 1954.
Sweet Poison (Mallett). London, Macdonald, 1956.
The Late Uncle Max. London, Macdonald, 1957.
Case for the Defense. London, Macdonald, and New York, British Book Centre, 1958.
Mizmaze (Mallett). London, Joseph, 1958; New York, British Book Centre, 1959.
There Are More Ways of Killing.... London, Joseph, and New York, British Book Centre, 1960.

Short Stories

The Man Who Shot Birds and Other Tales of Mystery-Detection. London, Macdonald, 1954.

Uncollected Short Story

"Highlight," in *Choice of Weapons.* London, Hodder and Stoughton, 1958.

OTHER PUBLICATIONS as Kathleen Freeman

Novels

Martin Hanner: A Comedy. London, Cape, and New York, Harcourt Brace, 1926.

Quarrelling with Lois. London, Cape, 1928.
This Love. London, Cape, 1929.
The Huge Shipwreck. London, Dent, 1934.
Adventure from the Grave. London, Davies, 1936.
Gown and Shroud. London, Macdonald, 1947.
Doctor Underground (as Caroline Cory). London, Macdonald, 1956.

Short Stories

The Intruder and Other Stories. London, Cape, 1926.

Other

The Work and Life of Solon. Cardiff, University of Wales Press, 1926.
Voices of Freedom. London, Muller, 1943.
*What They Said at the Time: A Survey of the Causes of the Second World War and the
    Hopes for a Lasting Peace as Exhibited in the Utterances of the World's Leaders and
    Some Others from 1917–1944.* London, Muller, 1945.
*The Pre-Socratic Philosophers: A Companion to Diels, Fragmente der
    Vorsokratiker.* Oxford, Blackwell, 1946; Cambridge, Massachusetts, Harvard
    University Press, 1948.
The Murder of Herodes and Other Trials from the Athenian Law Courts. London,
    Macdonald, 1946; New York, Norton, 1963.
Greek City-States. London, Macdonald, and New York, Norton, 1950.
God, Man and State: Greek Concepts. London, Macdonald, and Boston, Beacon Press,
    1952.
The Paths of Justice. London, Lutterworth Press, 1954; New York, Roy, 1957(?).
T'other Miss Austen (on Jane Austen). London, Macdonald, 1956.
If Any Man Build: The History of the Save the Children Fund. London, Hodder and
    Stoughton, 1965.

Editor and Translator, *It Has All Happened Before: What the Greeks Thought of Their
    Nazis.* London, Muller, 1941.
Editor and Translator, *The Greek Way: An Anthology.* London, Macdonald, 1947.
Editor and Translator, *Fighting Words from the Greeks for Today's Struggle.* Boston,
    Beacon Press, 1952.
Editor, *Everyday Things in Ancient Greece*, revised edition, by Marjorie and C. H. B.
    Quennell. London, Batsford, 1954.

Translator, *Ancilla to the Pre-Socratic Philosophers: A Complete Translation of the
    Fragments in Diels, Fragmente der Vorsokratiker.* Oxford, Blackwell, and
    Cambridge, Massachusetts, Harvard University Press, 1948.
Translator, *The Philoctetes of Sophocles: A Modern Version.* London, Muller, 1948.
Translator, *The Sophists*, by Mario Untersteiner. Oxford, Blackwell, 1954.

Other as Mary Fitt (juvenile)

The Island Castle. London, Nelson, 1953.
Annabella at the Lighthouse. London, Nelson, 1955.
Annabella Takes a Plunge. London, Nelson, 1955.
Annabella to the Rescue. London, Nelson, 1955.
Pomeroy's Postscript. London, Nelson, 1955.
The Turnip Watch. London, Nelson, 1956.
Annabella and the Smugglers. London, Nelson, 1957.
Man of Justice: The Story of Solon. London, Nelson, 1957.

Vendetta. London, Nelson, 1957.
Alfred the Great. London, Nelson, 1958.
The Shifting Sands. London, Nelson, 1958.
The Great River. London, Nelson, 1959.

*   *   *

As might be expected from a lecturer in Classical Greek, the novels of Mary Fitt are patently the products of a cultivated mind. A character in them is likely to comment on a situation with the words "as in Turgeniev," and the reader is expected to pick up the allusion. But her books were designed for the sort of reader who could, or who could nearly, recognise such a glancing hint and derive satisfaction from it. And to that sort of reader they will still give considerable pleasure.

Although the last of her many novels did not come out till 1960, it is not unfair to say that she was a writer of the 1930's in the intelligent tradition of Dorothy L. Sayers. Indeed, even a book like the fine *Death and the Pleasant Voices* (1946) seems to have been set in pre-1939 Britain where large country houses had immaculate gardens, where servants (though mildly complained about) were taken for granted and performed their duties with silent efficiency, where people could expect not to have to work for their living. And Mary Fitt wrote very much in the style of the best sort of 1930's British women novelists, of, say, someone like Elizabeth Bowen, supple, intelligent, quiet.

Perhaps in the crime novel this is, if not a fault, at least a weakness (perhaps it is so even in the mainstream novel). Mary Fitt lacked that touch of bravura, that insistence, which pulls Dorothy L. Sayers out of the ruck. She never created a hero that a large public could identify easily with and come to worship. In many of her books a stolidly efficient Scottish Superintendent Mallett appears, but even when he does so he does not necessarily take the hero's role and brilliantly solve the case. Instead often one detects for oneself, by seeing character slowly revealed. It is a method worth trying.

—H. R. F. Keating

FITZGERALD, Nigel. Irish. Born in Charleville, County Cork, in 1906. Educated at Mount St. Benedict School; Clongowes Wood College, Dublin; King's Inns, Trinity College, Dublin. Married to Clodagh Garratt; one son and two daughters. Former President, Irish Actors' Equity Association.

C RIME P UBLICATIONS

Novels (series characters: Inspector/Superintendent Duffy; Alan Russell)

Midsummer Malice (Duffy). London, Collins, 1953; New York, Macmillan, 1959.
The Rosy Pastor (Duffy). London, Collins, 1954.
The House Is Falling (Duffy). London, Collins, 1955.
Imagine a Man (Duffy). London, Collins, 1956.
The Student Body (Duffy). London, Collins, 1958.
Suffer a Witch (Duffy). London, Collins, 1958.
This Won't Hurt You. London, Collins, 1959; New York, Macmillan, 1960.

The Candles Are All Out (Russell).   London, Collins, 1960; New York, Macmillan, 1961.
Ghost in the Making (Russell).   London, Collins, 1960.
Black Welcome (Duffy).   London, Collins, 1961; New York, Macmillan, 1962.
The Day of the Adder (Duffy).   London, Collins, 1963; as *Echo Answers Murder*, New York, Macmillan, 1965.
Affairs of Death (Duffy).   London, Collins, 1967.

*   *   *

Nigel Fitzgerald sets most of his novels in remote pockets of Ireland where the atmosphere is charged with popular superstition, ancient ritual, and not-so-well-kept secrets. Into these rural settings, he introduces murders of unusual violence: stabbings with pickaxes (*The Candles Are All Out*) and pitchforks (*Affairs of Death*) and, in one case, the injection of the corrosive phenol into the jaw of a dental patient (*This Won't Hurt You*). The horror of the crimes, however, takes second place to Fitzgerald's strong characterization and polished style. And the gothic atmospheres dissipate under the objective scrutiny of his detectives, Alan Russell, the urbane actor-manager, and Superintendent Duffy, whose impassivity belies his acute perception.

Fitzgerald's protagonists are sophisticated characters who indulge weaknesses for women and Irish whiskey but invariably reaffirm, through the sobering effects of murder, a latent sense of individual integrity. Fitzgerald's juxtaposition of an old-fashioned world view with the modern laissez-faire morality, and the final resolution of the two, are primary themes of his work.

Fitzgerald's novels belong among the best of classic detective fiction. They are intricately plotted, suspenseful, and full of wit.

—Jeanne Carter Emmons

FLEMING, Ian (Lancaster).   British.   Born in London, 28 May 1908. Educated at Eton College; Royal Military Academy, Sandhurst, Kent; studied languages at the University of Munich and the University of Geneva. Served in the Royal Naval Volunteer Reserve, as personal assistant to the Director of Naval Intelligence, 1939–45: Lieutenant. Married Anne Geraldine Charteris in 1952; one son. Moscow Correspondent, Reuters news agency, London, 1929–33; worked for Cull and Company, merchant bankers, London, 1933–35; stockbroker, Rowe and Pitman, London, 1935–39; Moscow Correspondent, *The Times*, London, 1939; Foreign Manager, Kemsley, later Thomson, Newspapers, 1945–49. Publisher, *Book Collector*, London, 1949–64. Order of the Dannebrog, 1945. *Died 12 August 1964.*

Crime Publications

Novels (series character: James Bond in all books)

Casino Royale.   London, Cape, and New York, Macmillan, 1954; as *You Asked for It*, New York, Popular Library, 1955.
Live and Let Die.   London, Cape, 1954; New York, Macmillan, 1955.

Moonraker. London, Cape, and New York, Macmillan, 1955; as *Too Hot to Handle*, New York, Permabooks, 1957.
Diamonds Are Forever. London, Cape, and New York, Macmillan, 1956.
From Russia, With Love. London, Cape, and New York, Macmillan, 1957.
Doctor No. London, Cape, and New York, Macmillan, 1958.
Goldfinger. London, Cape, and New York, Macmillan, 1959.
Thunderball. London, Cape, and New York, Viking Press, 1961.
The Spy Who Loved Me. London, Cape, and New York, Viking Press, 1962.
On Her Majesty's Secret Service. London, Cape, and New York, New American Library, 1963.
You Only Live Twice. London, Cape, and New York, New American Library, 1964.
The Man with the Golden Gun. London, Cape, and New York, New American Library, 1965.

Short Stories

For Your Eyes Only: Five Secret Occasions in the Life of James Bond. London, Cape, and New York, Viking Press, 1960.
Octopussy, and The Living Daylights. London, Cape, and New York, New American Library, 1966.

OTHER PUBLICATIONS

Novel

The Diamond Smugglers. London, Cape, 1957; New York, Macmillan, 1958.

Play

Screenplay: *Thunderball*, with others, 1965.

Other

Thrilling Cities. London, Cape, 1963; New York, New American Library, 1964.
Chitty-Chitty-Bang-Bang (juvenile). London, Cape, 3 vols., 1964–65; New York, Random House, 1 vol., 1964; collected edition, Cape, 1971.
Ian Fleming Introduces Jamaica, edited by Morris Cargill. London, Deutsch, 1965; New York, Hawthorn, 1966.

Bibliography: *Ian Fleming: A Catalogue of a Collection: Preliminary to a Bibliography* by Iain Campbell, privately printed, 1978.

*   *   *

Whatever his present standing among readers and critics, Ian Fleming accomplished an extraordinary amount in the history of the thriller. Almost singlehandedly, he revived popular interest in the spy novel, spawning legions of imitations, parodies, and critical and fictional reactions, thus indirectly creating an audience for a number of novelists who followed him in the form. Through the immense success of the filmed versions of his books, his character James Bond became the best known fictional personality of his time and Fleming the most famous writer of thrillers since Sir Arthur Conan Doyle. Everybody tried to jump on the Bondwagon – there were Bond-style books, films, comic strips, and television shows; children played with 007 games, toys, dolls, and puzzles; one could munch bread endorsed by Bond or anoint oneself with toiletries that guaranteed the virility and sex appeal of Bond to the user. Whatever Fleming's merits or defects, he created more than novels of action and adventure, sex and violence – he created a phenomenon. Such an achievement is eminently worthy of attention.

Fleming's enormous popularity – which actually came late in his career, after most of his work had been done – and the phenomenon of James Bond have always troubled both his admirers and his detractors, who have great difficulty simply accounting for it. Although it may require the passage of time to evaluate Fleming's achievement fully, the major sources of his appeal are not entirely obscure. For one thing, the James Bond novels are a perfect example of the right thing at the right time, as appropriate an expression and index of their age as, for example, the Sherlock Holmes stories or the novels of Dashiell Hammett. Fleming caught the *Zeitgeist* and grasped it firmly.

The initial reactions to Fleming – especially the negative responses – involved the sex and violence in the novels. Violence, though perhaps not so spectacularly presented, had always appeared prominently in thrillers, but readers had forgotten about the kinds of novels that Fleming's works imitated and were not accustomed to villains so grotesquely presented as Hugo Drax or Blofeld or Doctor No. Sex, especially in an English writer, was something new for the thriller, which had previously concerned itself with juvenile adventures or cerebral puzzles; to a hard-bitten reader of American popular fiction, a non-traditionalist (fans of the genre tend to be very conservative in their literary tastes), or anyone vaguely aware of the facts of life, of course, the sexuality of the James Bond novels was tame, minor, and not at all pornographic. To any sophisticated reader it hardly seemed likely that Fleming's success was based on an erotic appeal.

Like any writer of any level of quality, Fleming burglarized from the past. The closest source for his novels was the sensational thriller of such writers as Erskine Childers, John Buchan, and Sapper, who initiated the notion of espionage as a jolly, healthy, outdoor activity for patriotic public-school graduates. James Bond's world is the world of British gentlemen and the gentlemanly code; despite his ostensibly professional status and his vaunted license to kill, he is an amateur in the grand tradition, a jazzed-up Richard Hannay or Bulldog Drummond giving his all for dear old England. His caste-consciousness, his snobbishness, his racism, his unmitigated delight in the perquisites of wealth, class, and privilege place him squarely in the ranks of the gentleman amateurs who dominate a large area of English popular fiction.

In addition to updating the rather motheaten material of the Childers-Buchan-Sapper school, Fleming skillfully combined it with the perennially new forms and patterns of a far more distant past, the folklore, fairy tales, legends, and myths that give his books their often outrageously unreal atmosphere. *Goldfinger*, for example, is built upon the Midas myth; *Moonraker* uses the story of St. George and the dragon; *Doctor No* and *You Only Live Twice* present two versions (or perversions) of the universal fertility myth that lies behind much literature, including *The Waste Land*. Fleming's audacity in placing his rather humdrum hero in situations out of a primordial past is astonishing; even more astonishing, he gets away with it, which is the final key to the puzzle of his success. He supports his essentially implausible works with a special sort of surface authenticity, derived from a minute (though not always accurate) attention to both the ordinary and the extraordinary details of places, objects, and experience. He paints a broad and garish canvas but varnishes it with a glossy layer of glamorous materialism and knowing archness, what Kingsley Amis dubbed the "Fleming effect." Thus we are told more than we could ever want to know about cars, airplanes, weapons, resort hotels, casinos, private clubs, high-stakes card games, skindiving, jewelry, perfume, hairbrushes, shampoos, colognes, luggage. Possessing the talent of a born copywriter, Fleming probably did more for names like Guerlain, Lanvin, Yardley, Rolex, and Cartier than a century of advertising in slick magazines. But the instruction of the reader in the arcana of twentieth-century consumer goods and luxuries, the author's own unabashed enjoyment of material reality, and the reader's vicarious participation in the six-page meals, the special Martinis, and the vintage champagne combine to give the novels a glittering superficial reality that was both seductive and convincing.

Ian Fleming in his own way mastered one of the most enviable and admirable feats in all of literature – the mingling of the barely credible, the utterly incredible, and the specifically identifiable in an excitingly sustained narrative fiction. In literary circles the product of such a mixture is often referred to as the concrete universal; it is no mean accomplishment, and is shared by writers like Chaucer, Fielding, Dickens, Melville, and Faulkner. Whatever the final quality of Fleming's achievement, his undeniable popularity and financial success, his powerful influence over the writers who follow him, and his union of the fantastic and the absolutely real deserve serious and careful study. It may be a very long time before that study reaches its proper point, but it may eventually establish Ian Fleming as one of the most appropriate writers of his time.

—George Grella

FLEMING, Joan (Margaret). British. Born in Horwich, Lancashire, 27 March 1908. Educated at Brighthelmston School, Southport, Lancashire; Grand Belle Vue, Lausanne; Lausanne University. Married Norman Bell Beattie Fleming in 1932 (died, 1968); three daughters and one son. Secretary to a doctor, London, 1928–32. Recipient: Crime Writers Association Golden Dagger, 1962, 1970. Agent: David Higham Associates Ltd., 5–8 Lower John Street, London W1R 4HA. Address: Kylsant House, Broadway, Worcestershire WR12 7AE, England.

CRIME PUBLICATIONS

Novels (series character: Nuri Iskirlak)

Two Lovers Too Many. London, Hutchinson, 1949.
A Daisy-Chain for Satan. London, Hutchinson, and New York, Doubleday, 1950.
The Gallows in My Garden. London, Hutchinson, 1951.
The Man Who Looked Back. London, Hutchinson, 1951; New York, Doubleday, 1952; as *A Cup of Cold Poison*, London, Hamish Hamilton, 1969.
Polly Put the Kettle On. London, Hutchinson, 1952.
The Good and the Bad. London, Hutchinson, and New York, Doubleday, 1953.
He Ought to Be Shot. London, Hutchinson, and New York, Doubleday, 1955.
The Deeds of Dr. Deadcert. London, Hutchinson, 1955; New York, Washburn, 1957.
You Can't Believe Your Eyes. London, Collins, and New York, Washburn, 1957.
Maiden's Prayer. London, Collins, 1957; New York, Washburn, 1958.
Malice Matrimonial. London, Collins, and New York, Washburn, 1959.
Miss Bones. London, Collins, 1959; New York, Washburn, 1960.
The Man from Nowhere. London, Collins, 1960; New York, Washburn, 1961.
In the Red. London, Collins, and New York, Washburn, 1961.
When I Grow Rich (Iskirlak). London, Collins, and New York, Washburn, 1962.
Death of a Sardine. London, Collins, 1963; New York, Washburn, 1964.
The Chill and the Kill. London, Collins, and New York, Washburn, 1964.
Nothing Is the Number When You Die (Iskirlak). London, Collins, and New York, Washburn, 1965.
Midnight Hag. London, Collins, and New York, Washburn, 1966.
No Bones about It. London, Collins, and New York, Washburn, 1967.
Kill or Cure. London, Collins, and New York, Washburn, 1968.
Hell's Belle. London, Collins, 1968; New York, Washburn, 1969.
Young Man, I Think You're Dying. London, Collins, and New York, Putnam, 1970.

Screams from a Penny Dreadful. London, Hamish Hamilton, 1971.
Grim Death and the Barrow Boys. London, Collins, 1971; as *Be a Good Boy*, New York, Putnam, 1972.
Alas Poor Father. London, Collins, 1972; New York, Putnam, 1973.
Dirty Butter for Servants. London, Hamish Hamilton, 1972.
You Won't Let Me Finish. London, Collins, 1973; as *You Won't Let Me Finnish*, New York, Putnam, 1974.
How to Live Dangerously. London, Collins, 1974; New York, Putnam, 1975.
Too Late! Too Late! the Maiden Cried: A Gothick Novel. London, Hamish Hamilton, and New York, Putnam, 1975.
To Make an Underworld. London, Collins, and New York, Putnam, 1976.
Every Inch a Lady. London, Collins, 1977; New York, Putnam, 1978.
The Day of the Donkey Derby. London, Collins, and New York, Putnam, 1978.

Uncollected Short Stories

"Cat on the Trail," in *The Saint* (New York), June 1964.
"Gone Is Gone," in *Tales of Unease*, edited by John Burke. London, Pan, 1966; New York, Doubleday, 1969.
"Still Waters," in *Winter's Crimes 1*, edited by George Hardinge. London, Macmillan, 1969.
"The Bore," in *Winter's Crimes 4*, edited by George Hardinge. London, Macmillan, 1972.

OTHER PUBLICATIONS

Other

Dick Brownie and the Zaga Bog (juvenile). London, Fairston, 1944.
Mulberry Hall (juvenile). Bognor Regis, Sussex, Crowther, 1945.
The Riddle in the River (juvenile). London, Hammond, 1946.
Button Jugs (juvenile). London, Hammond, 1947.
The Jackdaw's Nest (juvenile). London, Hammond, 1949.
Quonian Quartet (includes the 4 previous books). London, Hutchinson, 1949.
Shakespeare's Country in Colour. London, Batsford, 1960.

Manuscript Collection: Mugar Memorial Library, Boston University.

*   *   *

Often the crime novels of Joan Fleming concentrate on the psychological reactions of her characters rather than the detective's investigation. In this way, they are somewhat less complex versions of the works of Patricia Highsmith. Fleming is less demanding in her consideration of the criminal while nonetheless writing competently. Her interest in the mental and emotional reactions of the crime's victims – either direct or indirect victims – is always in line with contemporary trends.

The Man from Nowhere is one of the best examples of her probing the psychological aspects of crime's victims as she examines the reaction by a small closed community to murder and the presence of a birthmarked stranger. The man Rockambole first disconcerts by his appearance and later by his ideas: he is quiet about his past; he is unconcerned about possession; he does not overvalue money. Fleming demonstrates how the villagers, including the cleric whose fiancée was attracted to Rock, turn these traits to suspicious motives, despite their difficulty in doing so. Although the novel ends on an ironic note, the conclusion is an unsettling rather than a unifying one. Much the same motif, with an even more tragic consequence, is employed in *Midnight Hag*. Fleming again demonstrates the malice of a small town which can destroy an innocent person while the guilty prosper. As in *The Man from Nowhere*, a quiet love story between two mature people who had never expected to find someone to love adds poignancy to the plot's unfolding.

In other examples of Fleming's work it is possible to see the opposite side of this psychological investigation, as a kind of flippancy comes to the foreground. Miss Maiden (her name bettered only by the implications of her mother's – Mrs. Maiden) is connivingly wooed by a Mr. Alladin who hopes to cheat her of her inheritance and finally plots to kill her. The conclusion of *Maiden's Prayer*, so unlike that of *The Man from Nowhere* or *Midnight Hag*, almost denies the possibility of successful villainy in the world. What the *San Francisco Chronicle* calls Fleming's "charming oddities" can be clearly seen here, as well as in the burglar-detective exchanges in *Miss Bones*, an otherwise grim tale of dual identities and a skeleton exhumed from the shop court-yard.

In an unusual pair of detective novels featuring the Turkish philosopher Nuri bey, Fleming alternates Eastern and Western attitudes even as Nuri bey frequently crosses the Bosphorus from Europe to Asia. *When I Grow Rich* draws an English girl into a Turkish opium smuggling attempt and *Nothing Is the Number When You Die* takes Nuri bey to Oxford to find a friend's missing son and again be involved in opium smuggling. With the cultural differences accentuated by the outsider in each novel and the contrast between Nuri bey's contemplative, bookish way of life and the active, criminal world into which he enters, a variety of tensions are produced. Adaptation to the changing demands of time and circumstance are described in the portraits of Mme. Miasma of Turkey and Lady Mercia Mossops of England as well as in the destruction of Nuri bey's home and library, and the difference between the Oxford of his expectation and of reality. These and the cultural distinctions dominate the novels more than the suspense and detection: the opium selling is never explicitly horrible; killers only menace; the deaths of even Mme. Miasma, Rhonda, and Hadji are secondary. Tamara Yenish's destruction of her dead husband's opium field is too easily accomplished in view of the potential danger. Nevertheless, the descriptions of Turkish life in the Sultan's time and Nuri bey's understandable but amusing misconceptions at Oxford make these multi-cultural explorations fascinating.

Fleming's enormous variety in plots and concerns makes it impossible to generalize about her works. She can generally be expected to produce a slightly different approach to the mystery novel with each new book. These unexpected "oddities" are always carefully written and interestingly oriented, although seldom outstanding.

—Kathleen G. Klein

FLETCHER, J(oseph) S(mith). British. Born in Halifax, Yorkshire, 7 February 1863. Educated privately and at Silcoates School. Married Rosamond Langbridge; one son. Sub-Editor, *Practical Teacher* magazine, London, 1881–83; free-lance journalist in London, 1883–90; staff member, Leeds *Mercury*, 1890–1900; columnist ("A Son of the Soil") on rural life for several newspapers. Fellow, Royal Historical Society, 1918. *Died 30 January 1935.*

CRIME PUBLICATIONS

Novels (series character: Ronald Camberwell)

   Andrewlina. London, Kegan Paul, 1889.
   The Winding Way. London, Kegan Paul, 1890.

Old Lattimer's Legacy. London, Jarrolds, 1892; New York, Clode, 1929.

The Three Days' Terror. London, Long, 1901; New York, Clode, 1927.

The Golden Spur. London, Long, 1901; New York, Dial Press, 1928.

The Investigators. London, Long, 1902; New York, Clode, 1930.

The Secret Way. London, Digby Long, 1903; Boston, Small Maynard, 1925.

The Diamonds. London, Digby Long, 1904; as *The Diamond Makers*, New York, Dodd Mead, 1929.

The Threshing-Floor. London, Unwin, 1905.

The Queen of a Day. London, Unwin, 1907; New York, Doubleday, 1929.

Paradise Court. London, Unwin, 1908; New York, Doubleday, 1929.

The Harvest Moon. London, Nash, 1908; New York, McBride, 1909.

The Mantle of Ishmael. London, Nash, 1909.

Marchester Royal. London, Everett, 1909; New York, Doran, 1926.

Hardican's Hollow. London, Everett, 1910; New York, Doran, 1927.

The Bartenstein Case. London, Long, 1913.

Perris of the Cherry-Trees. London, Nash, 1913; New York, Doubleday, 1930.

The Secret Cargo. London, Ward Lock, 1913.

The Ransom for London. London, Long, 1914; New York, Dial Press, 1929.

The Shadow of Ravenscliffe. London, Digby Long, 1914; New York, Clode, 1928.

The Marriage Lines. London, Nash, 1914.

The Wolves and the Lamb. London, Ward Lock, 1914; New York, Knopf, 1925.

The King Versus Wargrave. London, Ward Lock, 1915; New York, Knopf, 1924.

The Annexation Society. London, Ward Lock, 1916; New York, Knopf, 1925.

Families Repaired. London, Allen and Unwin, 1916.

The Lynne Court Spinney. London, Ward Lock, 1916; as *The Mystery of Lynne Court*, Baltimore, Norman Remington, 1923.

Malvery Hold. London, Ward Lock, 1917; as *The Mystery of the Hushing Pool*, New York, Curl, 1938.

The Perilous Crossways. London, Ward Lock, 1917; New York, Curl, n.d.

The Rayner-Slade Amalgamation. London, Allen and Unwin, 1917; New York, Knopf, 1922.

The Amaranth Club. London, Ward Lock, 1918; New York, Knopf, 1926.

The Chestermarke Instinct. London, Allen and Unwin, 1918; New York, Knopf, 1921.

The Borough Treasurer. London, Ward Lock, 1919; New York, Knopf, 1921.

Droonin' Watter. London, Allen and Unwin, 1919; as *Dead Men's Money*, New York, Knopf, 1920; Allen and Unwin, 1928.

The Middle Temple Murder. London, Ward Lock, and New York, Knopf, 1919.

The Seven Days' Secret. London, Jarrolds, 1919; New York, Clode, 1930.

The Talleyrand Maxim. London, Ward Lock, 1919; New York, Knopf, 1920.

The Valley of Headstrong Men. London, Hodder and Stoughton, 1919; New York, Doran, 1924.

The Herapath Property. London, Ward Lock, 1920; New York, Knopf, 1921.

The Lost Mr. Linthwaite. London, Hodder and Stoughton, 1920; New York, Knopf, 1923.

The Orange-Yellow Diamond. London, Newnes, 1920; New York, Knopf, 1921.

Scarhaven Keep. London, Ward Lock, 1920; New York, Knopf, 1922.

The Paradise Mystery. New York, Knopf, 1920; as *Wrychester Paradise*, London, Ward Lock, 1921.

The Markenmore Mystery. London, Jenkins, 1921; New York, Knopf, 1923.

The Root of All Evil. London, Hodder and Stoughton, 1921; New York, Doran, 1924.

The Heaven-Kissed Hill. London, Hodder and Stoughton, 1922; New York, Doran, 1924.

In the Mayor's Parlour. London, Lane, 1922; as *Behind the Panel*, London, Collins, 1931.

The Mazaroff Murder.   London, Jenkins, 1922; as *The Mazaroff Mystery*, New York, Knopf, 1924.

The Middle of Things.   London, Ward Lock, and New York, Knopf, 1922.

Ravensdene Court.   London, Ward Lock, and New York, Knopf, 1922.

The Ambitious Lady.   London, Ward Lock, 1923; as *And Sudden Death*, New York, Curl, 1938; as *Pedigreed Murder Case*, New York, Detective Novel Classics, n.d.

The Charing Cross Mystery.   London, Jenkins, and New York, Putnam, 1923.

The Copper Box.   London, Hodder and Stoughton, and New York, Doran, 1923.

The Million-Dollar Diamond.   London, Jenkins, 1923; as *The Black House in Harley Street*, New York, Doubleday, 1928.

The Mysterious Chinaman.   London, Jenkins, 1923; as *Rippling Ruby*, New York, Putnam, 1923.

The Cartwright Gardens Murder.   London, Collins, 1924; New York, Knopf, 1926.

False Scent.   London, Jenkins, 1924; New York, Knopf, 1925.

The Kang-He Vase.   London, Collins, 1924; New York, Knopf, 1926.

The Safety Pin.   London, Jenkins, and New York, Putnam, 1924.

The Time-Worn Town.   New York, Knopf, 1924; London, Collins, 1929.

The Bedford Row Mystery.   London, Hodder and Stoughton, 1925; as *The Strange Case of Mr. Henry Marchmont*, New York, Knopf, 1927.

The Great Brighton Mystery.   London, Hodder and Stoughton, 1925; New York, Knopf, 1926.

Sea Fog.   London, Jenkins, and New York, Knopf, 1925.

The Mill of Many Windows.   London, Collins, and New York, Doran, 1925.

The Mortover Grange Mystery.   London, Jenkins, 1926; as *The Mortover Grange Affair*, New York, Knopf, 1927.

The Stolen Budget.   London, Hodder and Stoughton, 1926; as *The Missing Chancellor*, New York, Knopf, 1927.

The Green Rope.   London, Jenkins, and New York, Knopf, 1927.

The Murder in the Pallant.   London, Jenkins, 1927; New York, Knopf, 1928.

The Passenger to Folkestone.   London, Jenkins, and New York, Knopf, 1927.

Cobweb Castle.   London, Jenkins, and New York, Knopf, 1928.

The Double Chance.   London, Nash and Grayson, and New York, Dodd Mead, 1928.

The Wrist Mark.   New York, Knopf, 1928; London, Jenkins, 1929.

The Box Hill Murder.   New York, Knopf, 1929; London, Jenkins, 1931.

The House in Tuesday Market.   New York, Knopf, 1929; London, Jenkins, 1930.

The Matheson Formula.   New York, Knopf, 1929; London, Jenkins, 1930.

The Secret of Secrets.   New York, Clode, 1929.

The Dressing-Room Murder.   London, Jenkins, 1930; New York, Knopf, 1931.

The Borgia Cabinet.   New York, Knopf, 1930; London, Jenkins, 1932.

The South Foreland Murder.   London, Jenkins, and New York, Knopf, 1930.

The Yorkshire Moorland Murder.   London, Jenkins, and New York, Knopf, 1930.

The Guarded Room.   London, Long, and New York, Clode, 1931.

Murder at Wrides Park (Camberwell).   London, Harrap, and New York, Knopf, 1931.

Murder in Four Degrees (Camberwell).   London, Harrap, and New York, Knopf, 1931.

The Burma Ruby.   London, Benn, 1932; New York, Dial Press, 1933.

Murder in the Squire's Pew (Camberwell).   London, Harrap, and New York, Knopf, 1932.

Murder of the Ninth Baronet (Camberwell).   London, Harrap, and New York, Knopf, 1932.

The Solution of a Mystery.   London, Harrap, and New York, Doubleday, 1932.

Murder of the Only Witness (Camberwell).   London, Harrap, and New York, Knopf, 1933.

The Mystery of the London Banker (Camberwell).   London, Harrap, 1933; as *Murder of a Banker*, New York, Knopf, 1933.

Who Killed Alfred Snowe? (Camberwell).   London, Harrap, 1933; as *Murder of the Lawyer's Clerk*, New York, Knopf, 1933.

Murder of the Secret Agent (Camberwell). London, Harrap, and New York, Knopf, 1934.
The Ebony Box (Camberwell). London, Butterworth, and New York, Knopf, 1934.
The Eleventh Hour (Camberwell). London, Butterworth, and New York, Knopf, 1935.
Todmanhawe Grange, completed by Torquemada. London, Butterworth, 1937; as *The Mill House Murder, Being the Last of the Adventures of Ronald Camberwell*, New York, Knopf, 1937.

Short Stories

Pasquinado. London, Ward Lock, 1898.
The Death That Lurks Unseen. London, Ward Lock, 1899.
The Air-Ship and Other Stories. London, Digby Long, 1903.
The Fear of the Night. London, Routledge, 1903.
The Ivory God and Other Stories. London, Murray, 1907.
The Adventures of Archer Dawe, Sleuth-Hound. London, Digby Long, 1909; as *The Contents of the Coffin*, London, London Book Company, 1928.
The Wheatstack and Other Stories. London, Nash, 1909.
Paul Campenhaye, Specialist in Criminology. London, Ward Lock, 1918; as *The Clue of the Artificial Eye*, New York, Curl, 1939.
Exterior to the Evidence. London, Hodder and Stoughton, 1920; New York, Knopf, 1923.
Many Engagements. London, Long, 1923.
The Secret of the Barbican and Other Stories. London, Hodder and Stoughton, 1924; New York, Doran, 1925.
Green Ink and Other Stories. London, Jenkins, and Boston, Small Maynard, 1926.
The Massingham Butterfly and Other Stories. London, Jenkins, and Boston, Small Maynard, 1926.
Behind the Monocle and Other Stories. London, Jarrolds, 1928; New York, Doubleday, 1930.
The Ravenswood Mystery and Other Stories. London, Collins, 1929; as *The Canterbury Mystery*, London, Collins, 1933.
The Heaven-Sent Witness. New York, Doubleday, 1930.
The Malachite Jar and Other Stories. London, Collins, 1930; as *The Flamstock Mystery*, 1932; abridged edition, as *The Manor House Mystery*, 1933.
The Marrendon Mystery and Other Stories of Crime and Detection. London, Collins, 1930.
The Man in No. 3 and Other Stories. London, Collins, 1931.
Safe Number Sixty-Nine and Other Stories. Boston, International Pocket Library, 1931.
The Man in the Fur Coat and Other Stories. London, Collins, 1932.
The Murder in Medora Mansions and Other Stories of Crime and Mystery. London, Collins, 1933.
Find the Woman. London, Collins, 1933.
The Carrismore Ruby and Other Stories. London, Jarrolds, 1935.

Uncollected Short Story

"Bickmore Deals with the Duchess," in *Ellery Queen's Mystery Magazine* (New York), November 1951.

OTHER PUBLICATIONS

Novels

Frank Carisbroke's Stratagem; or, Lost and Won.   London, Jarrolds, 1888.
Mr. Spivey's Clerk.   London, Ward and Downey, 1890.
Through Storm and Stress.   London, Chambers, 1892.
When Charles the First Was King.   London, Bentley, 1892; Chicago, McClurg, 1895.
The Remarkable Adventure of Walter Trelawney.   London, Chambers, 1893.
The Quarry Farm: A Country Tale.   London, Ward and Downey, 1893.
In the Days of Drake.   London, Blackie, 1895; Chicago, Rand McNally, 1897.
Where Highways Cross.   London and New York, Macmillan, 1895.
At the Gate of the Fold.   London, Ward and Downey, and New York, Macmillan, 1896.
Life In Arcadia.   London, Lane, and New York, Macmillan, 1896.
Mistress Spitfire.   London, Dent, 1896.
The Making of Matthias.   London, Lane, 1897.
The Builders.   London, Methuen, 1897; New York, Mansfield, 1898; as *The Furnace of Youth*, London, Pearson, 1914.
The Paths of the Prudent.   London, Methuen, and New York, Page, 1899.
The Harvesters.   London, Long, 1900.
Morrison's Machine.   London, Hutchinson, 1900.
Bonds of Steel.   London, Digby Long, 1902.
Anthony Everton.   London, Chambers, 1903.
The Arcadians: A Whimsicality.   London, Long, 1903.
Lucian the Dreamer.   London, Methuen, 1903.
David March.   London, Methuen, 1904.
The Pigeon's Cave.   London, Partridge, 1904.
Grand Relations.   London, Unwin, 1905.
Highcroft Farm.   London, Cassell, 1906; as *The Harringtons of Highcroft Farm*, 1907.
A Maid and Her Money.   London, Digby Long, 1906; New York, Doubleday, 1929.
Daniel Quayne.   London, Murray, 1907; New York, Doran, 1926.
Mr. Poskitt.   London, Nash, 1907.
Mothers in Israel: A Study in Rustic Amenities.   London, Murray, and New York, Moffat, 1908.
The Pinfold.   London, Everett, 1911; New York, Doran, 1928.
The Fine Air of Morning: A Pastoral Romance.   London, Nash, 1912; Boston, Estes, 1913.
The Golden Venture.   London, Nash, 1912.
I'd Venture All for Thee.   London, Nash, 1913; New York, Doubleday, 1928.
Both of This Parish.   London, Nash, 1914.
Heronshaw Main: The Story of a Yorkshire Colliery.   London, Ward Lock, 1918.
The Wild Oat.   London, Jarrolds, 1928; New York, Doubleday, 1929.
The Grocer's Wife.   London, Hutchinson, 1933.

Short Stories

One of His Little Ones and Other Tales in Prose and Verse.   London, Washbourne, 1888.
The Wonderful Wapentake.   London, Lane, 1894; Chicago, McClurg, 1895.
God's Failures.   London, Lane, 1897.
At the Blue Bell Inn.   Chicago, Rand McNally, 1898.
From the Broad Acres: Stories Illustrative of Rural Life in Yorkshire.   London, Grant Richards, 1899.
For Those Were Stirring Times and Other Stories.   London, Everett, 1904.

Mr. Poskitt's Nightcaps: Stories of a Yorkshire Farmer. London, Nash, 1910.
The Clue of the Artificial Eye. New York, Curl, 1939.

Play

Hearthstone Corner (produced Leeds, 1926).

Verse

The Bride of Venice. London, Poole, 1879.
The Juvenile Poems of Joseph S. Fletcher. Dartford, Kent, Snowden, 1879.
Songs after Sunset. London, Poole, 1881.
Early Poems. London, Poole, 1882.
Anima Christi. Bradford, Yorkshire, Fletcher, 1884.
Deus Homo. London, Washbourne, 1887.
Poems, Chiefly Against Pessimism. London, Ward and Downey, 1893.
Ballads of Revolt. London, Lane, 1897.
Leet-Livvy: A Verse-Story in the Dialect of Osgoodcross. London, Simpkin Marshall, 1915.
Verses Written in Early Youth. Privately printed, 1931.
Collected Verse 1881-1931. London, Harrap, 1931.

Other

Jesus Calls Thee! Thoughts for One in Indecision. London, Washbourne, 1887.
Our Lady's Month: A Manual of Devotion for the Month of May. London, Washbourne, 1887.
A Short Life of Cardinal Newman. London, Ward and Downey, 1890.
Where Shall We Go for a Holiday? York, Waddington, 1894.
A Picturesque History of Yorkshire. London, Dent, 3 vols., 1899-1900.
Roberts of Pretoria: The Story of His Life. London, Methuen, 1900.
Baden-Powell of Mafeking. London, Methuen, 1900.
The History of the St. Leger Stakes 1776-1901. London, Hutchinson, 1902; revised edition, as *The History of the St. Leger Stakes 1776-1926*, 1927.
Owd Poskitt: His Opinions on Mr. Chamberlain in Particular and on English Trade in General. London and New York, Harper, 1903.
A Book about Yorkshire. London, Methuen, and New York, McClure, 1908.
The Enchanting North. London, Nash, 1908.
Recollections of a Yorkshire Village. London, Digby Long, 1910.
Nooks and Corners of Yorkshire. London, Nash, 1911.
Memories of a Spectator. London, Nash, 1912.
The Adventures of Turco Bullworthy, His Dog Shrimp, and His Friend Dick Wynyard (juvenile). London, Washbourne, 1912.
The Town of Crooked Ways. London, Nash, and Boston, Estes, 1912.
Memorials of a Yorkshire Parish: A Historical Sketch of the Parish of Darrington. London, Lane, 1917.
The Making of Modern Yorkshire 1750-1914. London, Allen and Unwin, 1918.
The Cistercians of Yorkshire. London, S.P.C.K., and New York, Macmillan, 1919.
Sheffield. London, S.P.C.K., and New York, Macmillan, 1919.
Leeds. London, S.P.C.K., and New York, Macmillan, 1919.
Pontefract. London, S.P.C.K., and New York, Macmillan, 1920.
Harrogate and Knaresborough. London, S.P.C.K., and New York, Macmillan, 1920.
Yorkshiremen of the Restoration. London, Allen and Unwin, 1921.
Halifax. London, S.P.C.K., and New York, Macmillan, 1923.

The Life and Work of St. Wilfrid of Ripon, Apostle of Sussex (lecture).   Chichester, Thompson, 1925.
The Reformation in Northern England: Six Lectures.   London, Allen and Unwin, 1925; Port Washington, New York, Kennikat Press, 1971.

*   *   *

J. S. Fletcher's works are little known today, yet at the height of his fame he was one of the most popular detective novelists on both sides of the Atlantic. He produced at an incredible rate during the 1920's and early 1930's, at which time his only rival in terms of quantity was Edgar Wallace, and like Wallace his best books were submerged in a torrent of mediocre work.

It is an oft-recorded fact by historians of the genre that Fletcher was "discovered" by President Woodrow Wilson, a compulsive reader of detective fiction. *The Middle Temple Murder* was the book in question, and it still holds together well today; from the moment journalist Frank Spargo is involved in the discovery of a body in Middle Temple Lane, the pace is faster than many detective novels of the period, and the atmosphere of London is well conveyed. Fletcher was adept at London settings, and *The Charing Cross Mystery* deserves to stand with *The Middle Temple Murder* as the best examples. Hetherwick is an eager young barrister, of a type appearing regularly in Fletcher's stories; when he catches the last train at Sloane Square, and is faced with the body of a fellow passenger at Charing Cross, we are treated to a lively tale of some gusto and a nicely contrived mystery which bears re-reading.

Fletcher by no means confined his settings to London. Not only do his detectives frequently have to hare about the English countryside in pursuit of leads, but he also excelled in mysteries with rural settings. A Yorkshireman himself, he was able to depict the wide open spaces with some skill. His long list contains many in which the background is the best feature, and such books as *Scarhaven Keep* are sufficiently atmospheric for us to overlook the trivial nature of some of his plots.

It must be said that the largest proportion of Fletcher's work falls outside the field of pure detective fiction. Although there is often a mystery to be solved, his detectives are in many cases young men who are fortuitously involved in the mystery and pursue its solution with little professional dedication. The equivalent of Crofts's Inspector French or Freeman's Dr. Thorndyke is not to be found in Fletcher. On the credit side, the fact that his stories border on the thriller form is inclined to make them more readable and sometimes less pedantic than those of some of his contemporaries. His occasional carelessness over details, his almost total lack of characterisation, and the melodramatic nature of many of the mysteries were all overlooked by the many readers who found the pace of his narratives completely enthralling. During the 1920's he epitomised for many people all that was best in the field.

In retrospect, it is a pity that a writer so influential in popularising detective fiction throughout two continents, and possessing the innate craftsmanship of a real storyteller, should produce such a mass of hastily conceived second-class work that his genuine contributions to detective fiction are now almost forgotten. His only significant series character, Ronald Camberwell, appeared in some poor novels toward the end of Fletcher's career. It must be recalled, however, that he had the talent to produce some good novels approaching the classic form (*The Middle Temple Murder* and *The Charing Cross Mystery*) and some excellent short stories of detection (*The Adventures of Archer Dawe, Sleuth-Hound* and *Paul Campenhaye, Specialist in Criminology*), all in the early part of his career, presumably before the public's voracious appetite had brought about a parallel rise in output and reduction in quality.

—Melvyn Barnes

FLETCHER, Lucille. American. Born in Brooklyn, New York, 28 March 1912. Educated in public schools in Brooklyn; Vassar College, Poughkeepsie, New York, B.A. 1933. Married 1) Bernard Herrmann in 1939; 2) John Douglass Wallop, III, in 1949; two daughters. Employed by the Columbia Broadcasting System as music librarian, copyright clerk, and publicity writer, 1934–39. Self-employed writer. Recipient: Mystery Writers of America Edgar Allan Poe Award, 1959. Agent: William Morris Agency, 1340 Avenue of the Americas, New York, New York 10019. Address: Avon Light, Oxford, Maryland 21654, U.S.A.

CRIME PUBLICATIONS

Novels

Blindfold. New York, Random House, and London, Eyre and Spottiswoode, 1960.
... and Presumed Dead. New York, Random House, and London, Eyre and Spottiswoode, 1963.
The Strange Blue Yawl. New York, Random House, 1964; London, Eyre and Spottiswoode, 1965.
The Girl in Cabin B54. New York, Random House, 1968; London, Hodder and Stoughton, 1969.
Eighty Dollars to Stamford. New York, Random House, 1975; London, Hale, 1977.

OTHER PUBLICATIONS

Novel

The Daughter of Jasper Clay. New York, Holt Rinehart, 1958.

Plays

My Client Curley, with Norman Corwin (broadcast, 1940). Published in Best Broadcasts of 1939–1940, edited by Max Wylie, New York, Whittlesey House, 1940.
The Hitch-Hiker (broadcast, 1941). Included in Sorry, Wrong Number, 1952.
Sorry, Wrong Number (broadcast, 1944). New York, Dramatists Play Service, 1952.

Screenplay: Sorry, Wrong Number, 1948.

Radio Plays: My Client Curley, 1940; The Hitch-Hiker, 1941; Sorry, Wrong Number, 1944; Remodeled Brownstone, The Furnished Floor, The Diary of Sophronia Winters, The Search for Henri Le Fevre, and other contributions to Suspense and Mercury Theatre on the Air series; Bad Dreams.

*   *   *

The typical suspense novel of Lucille Fletcher is less concerned with the solution of a mystery than with the anticipation and fear which the protagonist and the reader experience. Both are misdirected by the events while even a careful reverse accounting of the clues does not always demonstrate how the solution was reached. Since the police force is uninvolved, the protagonist's apprehensiveness and isolation can be emphasized to control mood, the primary focus of the novels. The hallmark of Fletcher's work is that the solution of the mystery is only the first part of a two fold conclusion. The second climax of each story provides an unexpected twist – a new murder is committed, a disguise penetrated, a motive revealed. Even with foreknowledge of Fletcher's style, the reader becomes absorbed in the tension of the plot and is unlikely to anticipate the specific ending.

Fletcher's best known work, *Sorry, Wrong Number* (adapted for various media), demonstrates the mounting terror and hysteria of an apparent invalid, alone in her apartment, who hears the details of a murder plot over the telephone when she tries to call her husband's office. Without friends, she calls the police to report her suspicion and her doctor to ask him to make a house call; neither of these societal caretakers gives her story much credence and both refuse to humor her desire for "protection" – actually companionship. The rejection of requests for assistance, the anticipation of a rejection, or the fear of being disbelieved and suspected often traumatizes Fletcher's protagonists. They become increasingly isolated from society, suspicious of others, and easily frightened by their lack of knowledge. As a consequence they often reject safe and trustworthy assistance which could save them from the problems they fear. This reversal is the dramatic twist at the conclusion of *Sorry, Wrong Number* where ironically every attempt to cope with the terror has contradictory results.

Because of its first person narration, *The Strange Blue Yawl* (involving boats and waterways, as do several other Fletcher novels) is especially fascinating and misleading. The "artist"-narrator relays the information gathered by his wife's investigation while he tries to compose the music which will win him fame and assure their fortune. To discover if an unknown woman whose screams she'd heard from a blue yawl docked near their home had been murdered, the wife investigates every blue-painted boat and every recently repainted yawl in the Maryland-Virginia vicinity. However, it is the narrator who solves the mystery in one instant of inspiration. As in Fletcher's other novels, this is only the apparent climax for, while strange as the discovery is, it is followed by a predictable but shocking twist.

The recent *Eighty Dollars to Stamford* provides a slight departure from the previous suspense novels. The recently widowed protagonist, driving a cab to occupy his mind, is framed for the murder of his wife's alleged hit-and-run killer. To extricate himself, he decides to solve the mystery himself; this independent detective work is a variation for Fletcher but allows the manipulation of suspense by having him avoid the police investigation which would charge him to uncover the real killer and the motives for both the murder and the frame attempt. This case is also different in allowing the suspect-detective a trusted family and a friend who can shield him from the police and assist in the investigation besides offering advice, support, and reassurance. As a result, the sheer terror and fear of the unknown are subordinated here to detection – despite the improbable collection of clues and unlikely conclusion.

Lucille Fletcher's competently written suspense-mystery novels seldom vary from a predictable pattern: fear of the unknown, followed by relief of the tension, concluded with a disturbing revelation which provides a distinctive twist to the plot. Nevertheless, they are generally satisfying examples of this variation of the genre.

—Kathleen G. Klein

FLORA, Fletcher. American. Born in Parsons, Kansas, 20 May 1914. Educated at Parsons Junior College, A.A. 1934; Kansas State College, Manhattan, B.S. 1938; University of Kansas, Lawrence, 1938–40. Served in the United States Army Infantry in New Guinea, Leyte, Luzon, 1943–45: Sergeant. Married Betty Ogden in 1940; three children. Teacher in public schools of Golden City, 1939–41, and Fairview High School, Missouri, 1941–42; Education Adviser, Department of the Army, Fort Leavenworth, Kansas, 1945–63. *Died in 1968.*

CRIME PUBLICATIONS

Novels

Strange Sisters. New York, Lion, 1954.
Desperate Asylum. New York, Lion, 1955; as Whisper of Love, New York, Pyramid, 1959.
The Hot Shot. New York, Avon, 1956.
The Brass Bed. New York, Lion, 1956; London, Miller, 1959.
Let Me Kill You, Sweetheart. New York, Avon, 1958.
Leave Her to Hell. New York, Avon, 1958.
Whispers of the Flesh. New York, New American Library, 1958.
Park Avenue Tramp. New York, Fawcett, 1958; London, Fawcett, 1959.
Take Me Home. Derby, Connecticut, Monarch, 1959.
Wake Up with a Stranger. New York, New American Library, 1959.
Killing Cousins. New York, Macmillan, 1960; London, Cape, 1961.
Most Likely to Love. Derby, Connecticut, Monarch, 1960.
The Seducer. Derby, Connecticut, Monarch, 1961.
The Irrepressible Peccadillo. New York, Macmillan, 1962; London, Boardman, 1963.
Skuldoggery. New York, Belmont, 1967.
Hildegarde Withers Makes the Scene, with Stuart Palmer. New York, Random House, 1969.

Uncollected Short Stories

"The Two-Faced Corpse," in New Detective, April 1952.
"Tall Guys Come High," in Detective Story (Kokomo, Indiana), November 1952.
"Torrid Zone," in The Queen's Awards: 7th Series, edited by Ellery Queen. Boston, Little Brown, 1952.
"So Lovely – and So Dead," in Detective Tales, December 1952.
"The Heat Is Killing Me," in Dime Detective (New York), February 1953.
"As I Lie Dead," in Manhunt (New York), February 1953.
"Pursued," in Ellery Queen's Mystery Magazine (New York), April 1953.
"Death in Waiting," in Fifteen Detective Stories (Kokomo, Indiana), December 1953.
"Heels Are for Hating," in Manhunt (New York), February 1954.
"Death Lives Here," in Fifteen Detective Stories (Kokomo, Indiana), June 1954.
"Points South," in Manhunt (New York), June 1954.
"Tough," in Pursuit (New York), July 1954.
"The Day It Began Again," in Manhunt (New York), April 1955.
"The Silent One," in Hunted (Holyoke, Massachusetts), December 1955.
"Handy Man," in Manhunt (New York), February 1956.
"Late Date with Death," in Mike Shayne Mystery Magazine (New York), October 1956.
"Three Gallons of Gas," in Mike Shayne Mystery Magazine (New York), August 1957.
"A Husband Is Missing," in Alfred Hitchcock's Mystery Magazine (North Palm Beach, Florida), August 1957.
"Setup," in Manhunt (New York), November 1957.
"Loose Ends," in Manhunt (New York), August 1958.
"The Collector Comes after Payday," in The Best from Manhunt, edited by Scott and Sidney Meredith. New York, Pocket Books, 1958.
"Of the Five Who Came," in Alfred Hitchcock's Mystery Magazine (North Palm Beach, Florida), March 1959.
"Nine, Ten, and Die," in Mystery Tales (New York), June 1959.
"The Witness Was a Lady," in Alfred Hitchcock's Mystery Magazine (North Palm Beach, Florida), March 1960.
"Sounds and Smells," in Ed McBain's Mystery Book (New York), 1962.

"The Spent Days," in *To Be Read Before Midnight*, edited by Ellery Queen. New York, Random House, 1962; London, Gollancz, 1963.

"Most Agreeably Poisoned," in *Alfred Hitchcock Presents: Hangman's Dozen*. New York, Dell, 1962.

"Dinner Will Be Cold," in *Alfred Hitchcock's Mystery Magazine* (North Palm Beach, Florida), August 1963.

"Homicide and Gentlemen," in *Alfred Hitchcock Presents: 16 Skeletons from My Closet*. New York, Dell, 1963.

"Mrs. Dearly's Special Day," in *Ellery Queen's Double Dozen*. New York, Random House, 1964; as *19th Mystery Annual*, London, Gollancz, 1965.

"Cool Swim on a Hot Day," in *Alfred Hitchcock's Once upon a Dreadful Time*. New York, Dell, 1964.

"Six Reasons for Murder," in *Ellery Queen's Mystery Magazine* (New York), March 1964.

"The Invisible Gauntley," in *Ellery Queen's Mystery Magazine* (New York), July 1964.

"How? When? Who?," in *Ellery Queen's Mystery Magazine* (New York), September 1964.

"The Satin-Quilted Box," in *Ellery Queen's Mystery Magazine* (New York), December 1964.

"The Tool," in *Alfred Hitchcock's Mystery Magazine* (North Palm Beach, Florida), December 1964.

"The Capsule," in *Mike Shayne Mystery Magazine* (New York), December 1964.

"My Father Died Young," in *Ellery Queen's Mystery Magazine* (New York), July 1965.

"Tune Me In," in *Alfred Hitchcock's Anti-Social Register*. New York, Dell, 1965.

"Hink Dink," in *Mike Shayne Mystery Magazine* (New York), August 1965.

"Something Very Special," in *Alfred Hitchcock's Mystery Magazine* (North Palm Beach, Florida), September 1965.

"Not Exactly Love," in *Alfred Hitchcock's Mystery Magazine* (North Palm Beach, Florida), December 1965.

"Wait and See," in *The Saint* (New York), December 1965.

"Darling, You Deserve Me," in *Shell Scott Mystery Magazine* (New York), March 1966.

"Obituary," in *Man from U.N.C.L.E.* (New York), March 1966.

"Affair of the Gander's Shoes," in *Mike Shayne Mystery Magazine* (New York), April 1966.

"A Lesson in Reciprocity," in *Alfred Hitchcock's Mystery Magazine* (North Palm Beach, Florida), August 1966.

"For Money Received," in *Alfred Hitchcock: Meet Death at Night*. London, New English Library, 1967.

"The Seasons Come, The Seasons Go," in *Ellery Queen's All-Star Lineup*. New York, New American Library, 1967; as *22nd Mystery Annual*, London, Gollancz, 1968.

"I'll Be Loving You," in *Alfred Hitchcock's Mystery Magazine* (North Palm Beach, Florida), December 1967.

"The Scrap of Knowledge," in *Ellery Queen's Mystery Magazine* (New York), May 1968.

"Handle of the Pump," in *Mike Shayne Mystery Magazine* (New York), December 1968.

"A Word for Murder," in *Homicide Department*, edited by Ed McBain. London, New English Library, 1968.

"Where's Milo?," in *Alfred Hitchcock's Mystery Magazine* (North Palm Beach, Florida), May 1969.

"Tutored to Death," in *Mike Shayne Mystery Magazine* (New York), July 1969.

"I'll Race You," in *Alfred Hitchcock's Mystery Magazine* (North Palm Beach, Florida), August 1969.

"Two Bits Worth of Luck," in *Alfred Hitchcock's Mystery Magazine* (North Palm Beach, Florida), May 1970.

"Bach in a Few Minutes," in *Alfred Hitchcock's Get Me to the Wake on Time*. New York, Dell, 1970.

"In the Shade of the Old Apple Tree," in *Crimes and Misfortunes*, edited by J. Francis
  McComas.   New York, Random House, 1970.
"Beside a Flowering Wall," in *Alfred Hitchcock's Death Can Be Beautiful.*   New York,
  Dell, 1972.

OTHER PUBLICATIONS

  Other

  "Six Burrs in the Blanket," in *The Writer* (Boston), August 1967.

*   *   *

Fletcher Flora was a talented writer whose work received regrettably little attention during
his lifetime. Although his short stories earned him considerable stature among editors,
writers, and magazine readers, his novels – with one exception – were unsuccessful. Part of
the reason for this was his emphasis on style and characterization rather than on intricate
plotting; but a much greater part seems to have been disinterested agents and publishers and
poor advice. A case in point is *Skuldoggery*, a marvelously witty and clever mystery which
was sold to one of the lesser paperback houses and given such poor distribution that few
people have read it or even know that it exists. It deserves a far better fate.

Flora began writing for the detective pulps in the early 1950's and soon graduated to *Ellery
Queen's Mystery Magazine, Manhunt, Alfred Hitchcock's Mystery Magazine*, and other digest
crime periodicals. His only successful novel, *Killing Cousins* (Macmillan Cock Robin Award)
is a delightful tongue-in-cheek story of a lethal lady named Willie, and a fine example of
Flora's literate, urbane, and sometimes lyrical style. Additional books of note are *Strange
Sisters, The Hot Shot, The Irrepressible Peccadillo*, and the above-mentioned *Skuldoggery*.

Ironically, since Flora's death in 1968 a small cult following of his work has formed, but
the fact that he was never able to realize his full potentiality is a tragic one.

—Bill Pronzini

FLOWER, Pat(ricia Mary Bryson).   British.   Born in 1914. Lived in Australia. *Died in
1978.*

CRIME PUBLICATIONS

  Novels (series character: Inspector Swinton)

  Wax Flowers for Gloria (Swinton).   Sydney, Ure Smith, and London, Angus and
    Robertson, 1958.
  Goodbye, Sweet William (Swinton).   London, Angus and Robertson, 1959.
  A Wreath of Water-Lilies (Swinton).   Sydney, Ure Smith, and London, Angus and
    Robertson, 1960.
  One Rose Less (Swinton).   London, Angus and Robertson, 1961.
  Hell for Heather (Swinton).   London, Hale, 1962.
  Term of Terror (Swinton).   London, Hale, 1963.
  Fiends of the Family (Swinton).   London, Hale, 1966.

Hunt the Body. London, Hale, 1968.
Cobweb. London, Collins, 1972; New York, Stein and Day, 1978.
Cat's Cradle. London, Collins, 1973; New York, Stein and Day, 1977.
Slyboots. London, Collins, 1974; New York, Stein and Day, 1977.
Odd Job. London, Collins, 1974; New York, Stein and Day, 1978.
Vanishing Point. London, Collins, 1975; New York, Stein and Day, 1977.
Crisscross. London, Collins, 1976; New York, Stein and Day, 1977.
Shadow Show. London, Collins, 1976; New York, Stein and Day, 1978.

OTHER PUBLICATIONS

Plays

Radio and Television Plays: *This Seems as Good a Time as Any,* 1948; *Love Returns to Umbrizi,* 1949, and *From the Tropics to the Snow,* 1965, both with Cedric Flower; *The Tape Recorder,* 1966; *The Lace Counter,* 1966; *Marleen,* 1966; *The V.I.P.P.,* 1966; *Easy Terms,* 1966; *The Prowler,* 1966; *Anonymous,* 1966; *The Empty Day,* 1966; *Done Away With,* 1966; *Tilley Landed on Our Shore,* 1968.

Verse

Pistils for Two. Newnham, Tasmania, Wattle Grove Press, 1963.

*   *   *

Pat Flower, who plays on her name in titles and in characters' names (Miss Applejohn, Miss Plant, Heather, Rose), writes highly competent mysteries that hinge on character study, ironic twists of plot, and credible surprise endings: a husband whose murderous attempts on his wife result in her accidental death while trying to murder him (*Hell for Heather*), another who murders his wife only to learn she was dying of leukemia and to find himself inexorably trapped in a web spun by her sister (*Cobweb*), three independent murderers of the same man – none of whom can be legally convicted because of a further ironic twist (*Goodbye, Sweet William*). Flower is interested in pathological liars, the meanness and insularity of the rich, and cases of *folie à deux*.

Although her narrative view varies from that of neurotic criminal or unsuspecting victim to wary detective, Inspector Swinton and Sergeant Primrose, her blunt, hearty Australian detectives, are always on call, with the young intellectual Primrose as foil to the more intuitive Swinton. Stodgy, fortyish, a happily married suburbanite and obsessive consumer of Australian meat pies, Swinton uses long silences to unnerve suspects, and usually experiences a sudden intuitive flash whereby all the pieces of the problem suddenly fit together in an unexpected way. He has a close eye for detail – a woman casually eating poached eggs before her so-called suicide, a highly competent head mistress suddenly forgetting minor duties, a solitary admirer of a hated boss. Swinton's investigations involve understanding human motives and character in terms of environment and past, for the crimes he deals with grow out of human psychology, particularly of the abused or pampered child who fails to mature emotionally, but also of the hypocritical religious fanatic, the sexually repressed, the congenitally insane (a family of murderers in *Fiends of the Family*).

Flower's mysteries often involve the sane man who thinks he is going mad (Clinton, in *One Rose Less,* witnesses a murder whose victim seems very much alive), or the insane who feel superior to humanity despite their continual confusion and forgetfulness. In *Odd Job* an aging paranoid junkman with delusions of grandeur speculates about stuffing his butchered wife in a sofa, only to find he has lost the line between reality and illusion and must murder her again and maybe again, while in *Term of Terror* a young artist rapes and murders young girls in a posh private school, while courting the gullible head mistress. Flower convincingly describes the sly ways paranoiacs try to control reality and explain incongruities in themselves and their victims. Her portraits of women are skillful and poignant: the naive trust of a spinster for a stranger, the loneliness of a single career woman, the surprising strengths of the crippled or ill, the suspicions of wives for husbands they have loved and trusted for years, the hatefulness of a domineering termagant.

—Virginia Macdonald

FOLEY, Rae. Pseudonym for Elinore Denniston; also wrote as Dennis Allan. American. Born in 1900. *Died 24 May 1978.*

CRIME PUBLICATIONS

Novels (series characters: John Harland; Hiram Potter)

No Tears for the Dead. New York, Dodd Mead, 1948; London, Cherry Tree Books, 1949.
Girl from Nowhere (Harland). New York, Dodd Mead, 1949.
Bones of Contention. New York, Dodd Mead, 1950.
The Hundredth Door. New York, Dodd Mead, 1950; London, Boardman, 1951.
An Ape in Velvet (Harland). New York, Dodd Mead, 1951; London, Boardman, 1952.
Wake the Sleeping Wolf. New York, Dodd Mead, 1952; London, Boardman, 1953; as *Don't Kill, My Love,* New York, Spivak, 1953.
The Man in the Shadow. New York, Dodd Mead, 1953; London, Boardman, 1954.
Dark Intent. New York, Dodd Mead, 1954; London, Boardman, 1955.
Death and Mr. Potter. New York, Dodd Mead, and London, Boardman, 1955; as *The Peacock Is a Bird of Prey,* New York, Dell, 1976.
The Last Gamble (Potter). New York, Dodd Mead, 1956; London, Boardman, 1957.
Run for Your Life (Potter). New York, Dodd Mead, 1957; London, Boardman, 1958.
Where Is Nancy Bostwick (Potter). New York, Dodd Mead, 1958; as *Where Is Mary Bostwick?,* London, Boardman, 1958.
Dangerous to Me (Potter). New York, Dodd Mead, 1959; London, Hammond, 1960.
It's Murder, Mr. Potter. New York, Dodd Mead, and London, Hammond, 1961; as *Curtain Call,* New York, Dell, 1976.
Repent at Leisure (Potter). New York, Dodd Mead, 1962; as *The Deadly Noose,* London, Hammond, 1963.
Back Door to Death (Potter). New York, Dodd Mead, and London, Boardman, 1963; as *Nightmare Honeymoon,* New York, Dell, 1976.
Fatal Lady (Potter). New York, Dodd Mead, and London, Boardman, 1964.
Call It Accident (Potter). New York, Dodd Mead, 1965; London, Hale, 1966.
Suffer a Witch. New York, Dodd Mead, 1965; London, Hale, 1966.
Scared to Death. New York, Dodd Mead, 1966; London, Hale, 1967.
Wild Night. New York, Dodd Mead, 1966; London, Hale, 1967.
Fear of a Stranger. New York, Dodd Mead, 1967; London, Hale, 1968.
The Shelton Conspiracy. New York, Dodd Mead, 1967; London, Hale, 1968.
Malice Domestic. New York, Dodd Mead, 1968; London, Hale, 1969.
Nightmare House. New York, Dodd Mead, 1968; London, Hale, 1969.
Girl on a High Wire. New York, Dodd Mead, 1969; London, Hale, 1971.
No Hiding Place. New York, Dodd Mead, 1969; London, Hale, 1970.

A Calculated Risk. New York, Dodd Mead, 1970; London, Hale, 1972.
This Woman Wanted. New York, Dodd Mead, 1971; London, Hale, 1972.
Ominous Star. New York, Dodd Mead, 1971; London, Hale, 1973.
Sleep Without Morning. New York, Dodd Mead, 1972; London, Hale, 1974.
The First Mrs. Winston. New York, Dodd Mead, 1972; Bath, Chivers, 1974.
Trust a Woman? New York, Dodd Mead, 1973.
Reckless Lady. New York, Dodd Mead, 1973; London, Hale, 1975.
The Brownstone House. New York, Dodd Mead, 1974; as *Murder by Bequest*, London,
   Hale, 1976.
One O'Clock at the Gotham. New York, Dodd Mead, 1974; London, Hale, 1975.
The Barclay Place. New York, Dodd Mead, 1975; London, Hale, 1976.
The Dark Hill. New York, Dodd Mead, 1975; London, Hale, 1976.
Where Helen Lies. New York, Dodd Mead, 1976.
Put Out the Light. New York, Dodd Mead, 1976.
The Girl Who Had Everything. New York, Dodd Mead, 1977.
The Slippery Step. New York, Dodd Mead, 1977.

Novels as Dennis Allan

House of Treason. New York, Greystone Press, 1936.
Brandon Is Missing. London, John Hamilton, 1938; New York, Mill, 1940.
Born to Be Murdered. New York, Mill, 1945; London, Hammond, 1952.
The Case of the Headless Corpse. New York, Mill, 1945.
Dead to Rights. New York, Mill, 1946; London, Hammond, 1953.

OTHER PUBLICATIONS

Novel

Madness in the Spring. New York, Dodd Mead, 1954.

Other

Portraits with Backgrounds (as Elinore Denniston), with Catherine Barjansky. New
   York, Macmillan, 1947.
Famous American Spies (juvenile). New York, Dodd Mead, 1962.
Famous Makers of America (juvenile). New York, Dodd Mead, 1963.
*America's Silent Investigators: The Story of the Postal Inspectors Who Protect the United
   States Mail.* New York, Dodd Mead, 1964.

Translator (as Elinore Denniston), *Gouverneur Morris, Witness of Two Revolutions*, by
   Daniel Walther. New York, Funk and Wagnalls, 1934.

*   *   *

Rae Foley is one of the most prolific and successful of America's "romantic suspense"
novelists, with some 40 such novels to her credit, admired as much in the United Kingdom as
in the United States. She writes very much with her own sex in mind, specialising in the
nerve-tingling Gothic type of story which has for its principal character a woman in a
dangerous and frightening situation, usually, of course, in sinister surroundings.

Typical of her work is *The Barclay Place*, which begins with a girl returning home to claim
an inheritance following the death of her parents and discovering that she is menaced by
people she previously trusted. The setting is New York, and heroin smuggling and murder
come into the plot. Another much admired book by Rae Foley is *Sleep Without Morning*,
excellent for its suspense, while earlier novels like *Run for Your Life* and *Where Is Nancy*

Bostwick? were no less lacking in a sure professional touch which grew more practised with the years.

—Herbert Harris

FOOTNER, (William) Hulbert. Canadian. Born in Hamilton, Ontario, 2 April 1879. Educated in evening high school in New York City. Married Gladys Marsh in 1916; three daughters and two sons. Journalist: in New York, 1905, and Calgary, 1906; then free-lance writer. Lived in Maryland. *Died 25 November 1944.*

Crime Publications

Novels (series characters: Amos Lee Mappin; Rosika Storey)

The Fugitive Sleuth. London, Hodder and Stoughton, 1918.
Thieves' Wit. New York, Doran, 1918; London, Hodder and Stoughton, 1919.
The Substitute Millionaire. New York, Doran, 1919; London, Collins, 1921.
The Owl Taxi. New York, Doran, 1921; London, Collins, 1922.
The Deaves Affair. New York, Doran, and London, Collins, 1922.
Ramshackle House. New York, Doran, 1922; London, Collins, 1923; as *Mystery at Ramshackle House,* London, Collins, 1932.
Officer! New York, Doran, and London, Collins, 1924.
The Chase of the "Linda Belle." London, Hodder and Stoughton, 1925.
The Under Dogs (Storey). New York, Doran, and London, Collins, 1925.
Queen of Clubs. New York, Doran, 1927; London, Collins, 1928.
The Doctor Who Held Hands (Storey). New York, Doubleday, and London, Collins, 1929; as *The Murderer's Challenge,* London, Collins, 1932.
A Self-Made Thief. New York, Doubleday, and London, Collins, 1929.
Anybody's Pearls. London, Hodder and Stoughton, 1929; New York, Doubleday, 1930.
The Mystery of the Folded Paper (Mappin). New York, Harper, and London, Collins, 1930.
Trial by Water. London, Hodder and Stoughton, 1930; New York, Farrar and Rinehart, 1931.
Easy to Kill (Storey). New York, Harper, and London, Collins, 1931.
Dead Man's Hat. New York, Harper, and London, Collins, 1932.
The Ring of Eyes. New York, Harper, and London, Collins, 1933.
Dangerous Cargo (Storey). New York, Harper, and London, Collins, 1934.
Murder Runs in the Family. New York, Harper, and London, Collins, 1934.
Scarred Jungle. New York, Harper, and London, Cassell, 1935.
The Whip-Poor-Will Mystery. New York, Harper, 1935; as *The New Made Grave,* London, Collins, 1935.
Murder of a Bad Man. London, Collins, 1935; New York, Harper, 1936.
The Island of Fear. New York, Harper, and London, Cassell, 1936.
The Dark Ships. New York, Harper, and London, Collins, 1937.
The Obeah Murders. New York, Harper, 1937; as *Murder in the Sun,* London, Collins, 1938.
The Death of a Celebrity (Mappin). New York, Harper, and London, Collins, 1938.

The Murder That Had Everything (Mappin).   New York, Harper, and London, Collins, 1939.
The Nation's Missing Guest (Mappin).   New York, Harper, and London, Collins, 1939.
Murderer's Vanity (Mappin).   New York, Harper, 1940; London, Collins, 1941.
Sinfully Rich.   New York, Harper, and London, Collins, 1940.
Who Killed the Husband? (Mappin).   New York, Harper, 1941; London, Collins, 1942.
The House with the Blue Door (Mappin).   New York, Harper, 1942; London, Collins, 1943.
Death of a Saboteur (Mappin).   New York, Harper, 1943; London, Collins, 1944.
Unneutral Murder (Mappin).   New York, Harper, and London, Collins, 1944.
Orchids to Murder (Mappin).   New York, Harper, and London, Collins, 1945.

Short Stories

Madame Storey.   New York, Doran, and London, Collins, 1926.
The Velvet Hand: New Madame Storey Mysteries.   New York, Doubleday, and London, Collins, 1928.
The Viper.   London, Collins, 1930.
The Casual Murderer.   London, Collins, 1932; Philadelphia, Lippincott, 1937; as *The Kidnapping of Madame Storey and Other Stories*, London, Collins, 1936.
The Almost Perfect Murder: More Madame Storey Mysteries.   London, Collins, 1933; Philadelphia, Lippincott, 1937.
Tortuous Trails.   London, Collins, 1937.

OTHER PUBLICATIONS

Novels

Two on the Trail: A Story of the Far Northwest.   New York, Doubleday, and London, Methuen, 1911.
Jack Chanty: A Story of Athabasca.   New York, Doubleday, 1913; London, Hodder and Stoughton, 1917.
The Sealed Valley.   New York, Doubleday, 1914; London, Hodder and Stoughton, 1915.
The Fur-Bringers: A Tale of Athabasca.   London, Hodder and Stoughton, 1916; New York, Coward McCann, 1920.
The Huntress.   London, Hodder and Stoughton, 1917; New York, Coward McCann, 1922.
On Swan River.   London, Hodder and Stoughton, 1919; as *The Woman from Outside*, New York, Coward McCann, 1921.
Country Love.   London, Hodder and Stoughton, 1921.
The Wild Bird.   New York, Doran, and London, Hodder and Stoughton, 1923.
Roger Manion's Girl.   London, Hodder and Stoughton, 1925.
The Shanty Sled.   London, Hodder and Stoughton, 1925; New York, Doran, 1926.
A Backwoods Princess.   New York, Doran, and London, Hodder and Stoughton, 1926.
Antennae.   New York, Doran, 1926; as *Rich Man, Poor Man*, London, Faber, 1928.
Cap'n Sue.   London, Hodder and Stoughton, 1927; New York, Doubleday, 1928.
A New Girl in Town.   London, Hodder and Stoughton, 1927.
More Than Bread.   Philadelphia, Lippincott, and London, Faber, 1938.

Play

Shirley Kaye (produced New York, 1916).

Other

> *New Rivers of the North.* New York, Outing, 1912; London, Unwin, 1913.
> *New York, City of Cities.* Philadelphia, Lippincott, 1937.
> *Charles' Gift: Salute to a Maryland House of 1650.* New York, Harper, 1939; London, Faber, 1940.
> *Sailor of Fortune: The Life and Adventures of Commodore Barney, U.S.N.* New York, Harper, 1940.
> *Maryland Main and the Eastern Shore.* New York, Appleton Century, 1942.
> *Rivers of the Eastern Shore.* New York, Farrar and Rinehart, 1944.

*　　*　　*

Hulbert Footner, Canadian-born author, actor, playwright, and journalist, had an undistinguished literary style, with characters common to the detective thrillers of the 1920's and 1930's. His first books were adventure novels of the Canadian northwest, but he soon began writing thrillers and detective novels, usually set in New York, but occasionally in London, as in *Anybody's Pearls.*

The sleuths which Footner created were interesting and diversified although not always the hero or heroine of the yarn. The first was the youthful B. Enderby, then Amos Lee Mappin, who resembled Dickens's Mr. Pickwick, and finally the voluptuous but cool-headed Mme. Rosika Storey. Mme. Storey is portrayed in *The Under Dogs* as having deliberately cultivated a faculty of inspiring awe in other people. But, alone, with her assistant Bella she was "keen, human, lovable, and full of laughter." Amos Lee Mappin, wealthy author and criminologist, is the brains behind the solution of many of Footner's mysteries, although he rarely does any of the actual sleuthing himself, leaving the "dirty work" to his many friends and associates. Footner, an admirer and friend of the writer Christopher Morley, featured Morley as one of his main characters in *The Mystery of the Folded Paper.* In return, Christopher Morley wrote a touching biographical tribute to Footner in *Orchids to Murder*, published after Footner's death.

—Mary Ann Grochowski

FORBES, (Deloris Florine) Stanton. Also writes as De Forbes (D. E. Forbes); Forbes Rydell (with Helen Rydell); Tobias Wells. American. Born in Kansas City, Missouri, 10 July 1923. Educated at Wichita High School North, Kansas; Oklahoma A. and M. (now Oklahoma State University), Stillwater; University of Chicago. Married William J. Forbes, Jr., in 1948; one daughter and two sons. Assistant Editor, Wellesley *Townsman*, Massachusetts, 1960–73; Broadcaster, De Forbes talk show, Station PJD2, St. Martin, French West Indies, 1974–75. Owner and operator, with husband, of Pierre Lapin clothing shop and workshop, Grand Case, Fat Cat, fashion shop, Marigot and Goetz House, resort apartments, St. Martin. Address: Goetz House, Grand Case, St. Martin, French West Indies.

CRIME PUBLICATIONS

Novels

> *Grieve for the Past.* New York, Doubleday, 1963; London, Gollancz, 1964.

The Terrors of the Earth. New York, Doubleday, 1964; as *The Long Hate*, London, Hale, 1966; as *Melody of Terror*, New York, Pyramid, 1967.
Relative to Death. New York, Doubleday, 1965; London, Hale, 1966.
Terror Touches Me. New York, Doubleday, and London, Hale, 1966.
A Business of Bodies. New York, Doubleday, 1966; London, Hale, 1967.
Encounter Darkness. New York, Doubleday, 1967; London, Hale, 1968.
If Two of Them Are Dead. New York, Doubleday, and London, Hale, 1968.
Go to Thy Death Bed. New York, Doubleday, 1968; London, Hale, 1969.
The Name's Death, Remember Me? New York, Doubleday, 1969; London, Hale, 1970.
She Was Only the Sheriff's Daughter. New York, Doubleday, and London, Hale, 1970.
If Laurel Shot Hardy the World Would End. New York, Doubleday, 1970; as *Murder Runs Riot*, London, Hale, 1971.
The Sad, Sudden Death of My Fair Lady. New York, Doubleday, and London, Hale, 1971.
All for One and One for Death. New York, Doubleday, 1971; London, Hale, 1972.
A Deadly Kind of Lonely. New York, Doubleday, 1971; London, Hale, 1973.
But I Wouldn't Want to Die There. New York, Doubleday, 1972; London, Hale, 1973.
Welcome, My Dear, to Belfrey House. New York, Doubleday, 1973; London, Hale, 1974.
Some Poisoned by Their Wives. New York, Doubleday, 1974; London, Hale, 1975.
Bury Me in Gold Lamé. New York, Doubleday, 1974; London, Hale, 1975.
Buried in So Sweet a Place. New York, Doubleday, 1977; London, Hale, 1978.
The Will and Last Testament of Constance Cobble. New York, Doubleday, 1980.

Novels as Forbes Rydell (with Helen Rydell)

Annalisa. New York, Dodd Mead, 1959; London, Gollancz, 1960.
If She Should Die. New York, Doubleday, and London, Gollancz, 1961.
They're Not Home Yet (by Forbes alone). New York, Doubleday, and London, Gollancz, 1962.
No Questions Asked. New York, Doubleday, and London, Gollancz, 1963.

Novels as Tobias Wells (series character: Knute Severson in all books)

A Matter of Love and Death. New York, Doubleday, and London, Gollancz, 1966.
What Should You Know of Dying? New York, Doubleday, and London, Gollancz, 1967.
Dead by the Light of the Moon. New York, Doubleday, 1967; London, Gollancz, 1968.
Murder Most Fouled Up. New York, Doubleday, 1968; London, Hale, 1969.
Die Quickly, Dear Mother. New York, Doubleday, and London, Hale, 1969.
The Young Can Die Protesting. New York, Doubleday, 1969; London, Hale, 1970.
Dinky Died. New York, Doubleday, and London, Hale, 1970.
The Foo Dog. New York, Doubleday, 1971; as *The Lotus Affair*, London, Hale, 1973.
What to Do Until the Undertaker Comes. New York, Doubleday, 1971; London, Hale, 1973.
How to Kill a Man. New York, Doubleday, 1972; London, Hale, 1973.
A Die in the Country. New York, Doubleday, 1972; London, Hale, 1974.
Brenda's Murder. New York, Doubleday, 1973; London, Hale, 1974.
Have Mercy upon Us. New York, Doubleday, 1974; London, Hale, 1975.
Hark, Hark, The Watchdogs Bark. New York, Doubleday, 1975; London, Hale, 1976.
A Creature Was Stirring. New York, Doubleday, and London, Hale, 1977.

Uncollected Short Stories as De Forbes (D. E. Forbes)

"Suffer Little Children" in *Manhunt* (New York), 1956.
"So I Can Forget," in *Ellery Queen's Mystery Magazine* (New York), May 1957.
"In a Neat Package," in *Mike Shayne Mystery Magazine* (New York), June 1957.
"The Fifth One," in *Mike Shayne Mystery Magazine* (New York), December 1957.
"Flora Africana," in *Alfred Hitchcock's Mystery Magazine* (North Palm Beach, Florida), April 1962.
"The Courtship of Jingoe Moon," in *Alfred Hitchcock's Mystery Magazine* (North Palm Beach, Florida), November 1966.
"Quetzelcoatl," in *Murder in Mind*, edited by Lawrence Treat. New York, Dutton, 1967.
"The Day of the Inchworms," in *Alfred Hitchcock's Mystery Magazine* (North Palm Beach, Florida), April 1968.
"My Sister Annabelle," in *Best of the Best Detective Stories*, edited by Allen J. Hubin. New York, Dutton, 1971.

Manuscript Collection: Mugar Memorial Library, Boston University.

Stanton Forbes comments:
Writing has been, for me, a distinct pleasure, a privilege, a duty, the Hyde to my Jekyll or vice versa. Often asked when and/or how did you begin to write mysteries I answer, "I didn't *begin*, it was always there" (no answer at all, but the truth). When asked where do you get your ideas, I answer, "From a question, 'What If?' " (again perhaps no answer at all). At any rate, to the powers that be who gave me the desire and the will and a certain natural aptitude with words I say, "Thank you!" That I didn't (so far – who knows?) do a better job with my tools is my fault.

*   *   *

The lady who publishes under the names of Stanton Forbes and Tobias Wells, among others, is one of the most prolific of American women in mystery. It follows that she is also one of the most proficient. She writes of people, everyday people, not rich and not poor, not famous or infamous, just people who find themselves involved in ordinary murders arising out of the troubles in their own neighborhoods. More often than not the narrator is an author who must get on with her fictional problems while helping to discover the cause of real ones.

For the most part her background is the small town, sometimes in the midwest, sometimes New England, and recently the Caribbean island of St. Martin. Tobias Wells has moved there as has her writer character, Constance Cobble. Although her Massachusetts detective, Knute Severson, is on deck in *Hark, Hark, The Watchdogs Bark*, island customs and its people are the plot movers.

As Stanton Forbes, she wrote one of the finest mysteries of the sixties, *Grieve for the Past*. It is a beautifully crafted story, told with the quiet simplicity that intensifies impact. The time is the 1930's, an ordinary summer in the "small town city" of Wichita, Kansas. It is the fifteenth summer of Ramona, the narrator. In the heat which characterizes a Kansas summer, an extraordinary double murder takes place in the neighborhood. How she divines the murderer is written with a gifted hand, moving to a climax wherein one feels that even a breath will topple its perfection.

It is unfortunate that the prolific writer more often than not is taken for granted. That Tobias Wells and Stanton Forbes can write better than many of her less active peers has been evident over and again. There is always an engrossing story in her books, each with its well-made plot and its characters who are real, not puppets.

—Dorothy B. Hughes

FORD, Leslie. Pseudonym for Zenith Brown, née Jones; also writes as Brenda Conrad; David Frome. American. Born in Smith River, California, 8 December 1898. Educated at the University of Washington, Seattle, 1917–21. Married Ford K. Brown in 1921 (died, 1977); one daughter. Assistant, departments of Greek and Philosophy, 1918–21, and Instructor and Teaching Assistant, Department of English, 1921–23, University of Washington; Assistant to Editor and Circulation Manager, *Dial* magazine, New York, 1922–23. Since 1927, free-lance writer. Correspondent for United States Air Force in the Pacific and England during World War II. Agent: Brandt and Brandt, 101 Park Avenue, New York, New York 10017. Address: 235 King George Street, Annapolis, Maryland 21401, U.S.A.

CRIME PUBLICATIONS

Novels (series characters: Lieutenant Joseph Kelly; Grace Latham; Colonel John Primrose)

The Sound of Footsteps. New York, Doubleday, 1931; as *Footsteps on the Stairs*, London, Gollancz, 1931.
By the Watchman's Clock. New York, Farrar and Rinehart, 1932.
Murder in Maryland (Kelly). New York, Farrar and Rinehart, 1932; London, Hutchinson, 1933.
The Clue of the Judas Tree (Kelly). New York, Farrar and Rinehart, 1933.
The Strangled Witness (Primrose). New York, Farrar and Rinehart, 1934.
Burn Forever. New York, Farrar and Rinehart, 1935; as *Mountain Madness*, London, Hutchinson, 1935.
Ill Met by Moonlight (Latham; Primrose). New York, Farrar and Rinehart, and London, Collins, 1937.
The Simple Way of Poison (Latham; Primrose). New York, Farrar and Rinehart, 1937; London, Collins, 1938.
Three Bright Pebbles (Latham). New York, Farrar and Rinehart, and London, Collins, 1938.
Reno Rendezvous (Latham; Primrose). New York, Farrar and Rinehart, 1939; as *Mr. Cromwell Is Dead*, London, Collins, 1939.
False to Any Man (Latham; Primrose). New York, Scribner, 1939; as *Snow-White Murder*, London, Collins, 1940.
The Town Cried Murder. New York, Scribner, and London, Collins, 1939.
Old Lover's Ghost (Latham; Primrose). New York, Scribner, 1940.
Road to Folly. New York, Scribner, 1940; London, Collins, 1941.
The Murder of a Fifth Columnist (Latham; Primrose). New York, Scribner, 1941; as *The Capital Crime*, London, Collins, 1941.
Murder in the O.P.M. (Latham; Primrose). New York, Scribner, 1942; as *The Priority Murder*, London, Collins, 1943.
Murder with Southern Hospitality. New York, Scribner, 1942; as *Murder Down South*, London, Collins, 1943.
Siren in the Night (Latham; Primrose). New York, Scribner, 1943; London, Collins, 1944.
All for the Love of a Lady (Latham; Primrose). New York, Scribner, 1944; as *Crack of Dawn*, London, Collins, 1945.
The Philadelphia Murder Story (Latham; Primrose). New York, Scribner, and London, Collins, 1945.
Honolulu Story (Latham; Primrose). New York, Scribner, 1946; as *Honolulu Murder Story*, London, Collins, 1947; as *Honolulu Murders*, New York, Popular Library, 1967.

The Woman in Black (Latham; Primrose). New York, Scribner, 1947; London, Collins, 1948.

The Devil's Stronghold (Latham; Primrose). New York, Scribner, and London, Collins, 1948.

Date with Death. New York, Scribner, 1949; as *Shot in the Dark*, London, Collins, 1949.

Murder Is the Pay-Off. New York, Scribner, and London, Collins, 1951.

The Bahamas Murder Case. New York, Scribner, and London, Collins, 1952.

Washington Whispers Murder (Latham; Primrose). New York, Scribner, 1953; as *The Lying Jade*, London, Collins, 1953.

Invitation to Murder. New York, Scribner, 1954; London, Collins, 1955.

Murder Comes to Eden. New York, Scribner, 1955; London, Collins, 1956.

The Girl from the Mimosa Club. New York, Scribner, and London, Collins, 1957.

Trial by Ambush. New York, Scribner, 1962; as *Trial from Ambush*, London, Collins, 1962.

Novels as David Frome (series characters: Major Gregory Lewis; Evan Pinkerton)

The Murder of an Old Man (Lewis). London, Methuen, 1929.

In at the Death. London, Skeffington, 1929; New York, Longman, 1930.

The Hammersmith Murders (Pinkerton). New York, Doubleday, and London, Methuen, 1930.

The Strange Death of Martin Green (Lewis). New York, Doubleday, 1931; as *The Murder on the Sixth Hole*, London, Methuen, 1931.

Two Against Scotland Yard (Pinkerton). New York, Farrar and Rinehart, 1931; as *The By-Pass Murder*, London, Longman, 1932.

The Man from Scotland Yard (Pinkerton). New York, Farrar and Rinehart, 1932; as *Mr. Simpson Finds a Body*, London, Longman, 1933.

The Eel Pie Murders (Pinkerton). New York, Farrar and Rinehart, and London, Longman, 1933.

Scotland Yard Can Wait! New York, Farrar and Rinehart, 1933; as *That's Your Man, Inspector!*, London, Longman, 1934.

Mr. Pinkerton Goes to Scotland Yard. New York, Farrar and Rinehart, 1934; as *Arsenic in Richmond*, London, Longman, 1934.

Mr. Pinkerton Finds a Body. New York, Farrar and Rinehart, 1934; as *The Body in the Turl*, London, Longman, 1935.

Mr. Pinkerton Grows a Beard. New York, Farrar and Rinehart, 1935; as *The Body in Bedford Square*, London, Longman, 1935.

Mr. Pinkerton Has the Clue. New York, Farrar and Rinehart, and London, Longman, 1936.

The Black Envelope: Mr. Pinkerton Again. New York, Farrar and Rinehart, 1937; as *The Guilt Is Plain*, London, Longman, 1938.

Mr. Pinkerton at the Old Angel. New York, Farrar and Rinehart, and London, Longman, 1939.

Homicide House: Mr. Pinkerton Returns. New York, Rinehart, 1950; as *Murder on the Square*, London, Hale, 1951.

Novels as Brenda Conrad

The Stars Give Warning. New York, Scribner, 1941.

Caribbean Conspiracy. New York, Scribner, 1942.

Girl with a Golden Bar. New York, Scribner, 1944.

Uncollected Short Stories

"Visitor in the Night," in *American Magazine* (Springfield, Ohio), July 1939.
"Death Stops at a Tourist Camp," in *The Mystery Book*. New York, Farrar and Rinehart, 1939.
"The Clock Strikes," in *The Second Mystery Book*. New York, Farrar and Rinehart, 1940.
"The Farewell Party," in *The Third Mystery Book*. New York, Farrar and Rinehart, 1941.
"Story of Jenny Wingate" (novel), in *Collier's* (Springfield, Ohio), 17 February–10 March 1945.
"Jealousy" (novel), in *Collier's* (Springfield, Ohio), 6 April–27 April 1946.
"The Collapsing Clues," in *My Favorite True Mystery*, edited by Ernest V. Heyn. New York, Coward McCann, 1954.
"Death of a Quiet Girl," in *American Weekly* (New York), 21 February 1954.
"The Lonely Hearts Case," in *American Weekly* (New York), 14 March 1954.
"The Lively Corpse," in *American Weekly* (New York), 9 May 1954.

Uncollected Short Stories as David Frome

"Mr. Pinkerton Is Present," in *American Magazine* (Springfield, Ohio), October 1936.
"Passage for One," in *The Mystery Book*. New York, Farrar and Rinehart, 1939.
"Mr. Pinkerton Lends a Hand," in *The Second Mystery Book*. New York, Farrar and Rinehart, 1940.
"The Policeman's Cape," in *The Third Mystery Book*. New York, Farrar and Rinehart, 1941.

OTHER PUBLICATIONS

Other

"Why Murder Fascinates Me," in *Good Housekeeping* (New York), May 1940.

Manuscript Collection: St. John's College Library, Annapolis, Maryland.

*   *   *

The hallmark of Mrs. Zenith Brown (under her Leslie Ford and David Frome pseudonyms) was the use of a variety of interesting places with accurate descriptions of local scenery, manners, and mores. Her earliest mysteries date from a time when her husband was doing research in Oxford, and she had extra time to devote to writing.

Accepting the conventional wisdom of the time that mysteries by men sold better than those of women, she adopted the name David Frome for her first book *The Murder of an Old Man*. She continued to write as Frome, and Ellery Queen wrote, "She soaked in so much local color and acquired so much familiarity with English idiom that ... no one dreamed she was an American." When the Browns returned to the United States, Mrs. Brown began to write books with American backgrounds, adopting a second, androgynous pseudonym, Leslie Ford, which eventually became far better known than "Frome."

At first Ford described the Maryland scene, basing the college town in *By the Watchman's Clock* on Annapolis, the site of St. John's College. Other early mysteries with Maryland settings include *Murder in Maryland* and *Ill Met by Moonlight*. Roaming only slighter farther afield, she used Washington D.C.'s Georgetown in *The Simple Way of Poison* and the Supreme Court Building in the 1935 novelet "The Clock Strikes."

As Ford became more successful she was able to combine a love of travel with the opportunity to do research at different locations, Frome mysteries like *Mr. Pinkerton Finds a*

Body and *Mr. Pinkerton Grows a Beard* reflect visits to Oxford and the British Museum. More often, she travelled in the United States, where she described restored colonial Williamsburg, Virginia, in *The Town Cried Murder*, Yellowstone National Park in *Old Lover's Ghost*, the historic Garden Club Pilgrimage of Natchez, Mississippi, in *Murder with Southern Hospitality*, and Hawaii in *Honolulu Story*. One of her best was *Siren in the Night*, a portrait of an attractive city, San Francisco, as well as a good description of attitudes, especially toward those of Japanese ancestry, shortly after the attack on Pearl Harbor. Washington politics and gossip were often used, most notably in *Murder in the O.P.M.*, *The Woman in Black*, and *Washington Whispers Murder*, the last named one of the few mystery stories about McCarthyism.

Holding a belief contrary to Raymond Chandler's of restricting murder mysteries to "the mean streets," Brown wrote of murder as committed by the wealthy, urbane, and intelligent. She once said she was only interested in "murder done by people I can understand – people I might play bridge with or dine with. That kind of murder is a powerfully compelling, even primitive impulse that lies deep, dormant in every one of us."

Though she created two famous detective teams, the detection in her novels does not measure up to the backgrounds. As Frome she wrote of the rabbity Mr. Pinkerton and his friend Sergeant Bull. Deduction is minimal, with Pinkerton literally stumbling over dead bodies and figuratively stumbling into solutions. As Ford she wrote of middle-aged Colonel Primrose, ex-U.S. Army Intelligence who continues his career as an investigator, assisted by his loyal army aide Sergeant Buck. In *Ill Met by Moonlight* Ford introduced Grace Latham, an attractive Georgetown widow, to the team. Though Latham is a fairly sensible, independent person, Brown apparently felt that the conventions of her era required her to wander senselessly into danger, and the Colonel shows up to rescue her and solve the case. His solutions are often without air-tight detection and may involve information withheld from the reader. The Primrose–Latham relationship grows warmer, but never beyond the platonic state.

Ford was extremely popular, especially with readers of *The Saturday Evening Post* where much of her work was originally serialized. She received her best reviews for such non-series books as *The Bahamas Murder Case* and her last book, *Trial by Ambush*, which, in anticipation of another era, dealt (albeit discreetly) with rape. Her series books suffered by comparison because she had too many sleuths in each, thus diffusing reader identification.

—Marvin Lachman

FORSYTH, Frederick. British. Born in Ashford, Kent, in 1938. Educated at Tonbridge School, Kent. Served in the Royal Air Force. Married; has children. Journalist: with *Eastern Daily Press*, Norwich, and later in King's Lynn, Norfolk, 1958–61; reporter for Reuters, London, Paris, and East Berlin, 1961; reporter, BBC Radio, London, 1965–67; Assistant Diplomatic Correspondent, BBC Television, 1967; free-lance journalist in Nigeria, 1967–68. Recipient: Mystery Writers of America Edgar Allan Poe Award, 1971. Lives in Ireland. Address: c/o Hutchinson Publishing Group Ltd., 3 Fitzroy Square, London W1P 6JD, England.

CRIME PUBLICATIONS

Novels

>The Day of the Jackal. London, Hutchinson, and New York, Viking Press, 1971.
>The Odessa File. London, Hutchinson, and New York, Viking Press, 1972.
>The Dogs of War. London, Hutchinson, and New York, Viking Press, 1974.
>The Devil's Alternative. London, Hutchinson, 1979.

Uncollected Short Story

>"No Comebacks," in Best Detective Stories of the Year 1974, edited by Allen J.
>Hubin. New York, Dutton, 1974.

OTHER PUBLICATIONS

Novel

>The Shepherd. London, Hutchinson, 1975; New York, Viking Press, 1976.

Other

>The Biafra Story. London, Penguin, 1969; as The Making of an African Legend: The
>Biafra Story, 1977.

*   *   *

In Frederick Forsyth's three great suspense thrillers, *The Day of the Jackal*, *The Odessa File*, and *The Dogs of War*, a thirty-ish, highly professional man of action is pitted against an establishment bureaucracy or organization. The hero, while ruthless and socially unacceptable, lives up to his own high professional standards; the established organization, though seemingly highly respectable, uses its legal identity to impose its will on others with a brutality the general populace is unaware of. The novels' scenes shift back and forth from the hero to the organization; a collision course is set up early and the action gradually quickens to the inevitable confrontation. The main characters travel constantly; if their movements were represented on road maps, the opponents would begin in widely separated locations, zig-zag with increasing rapidity across the map, sometimes ironically crossing paths, and then finally head inexorably toward one another for the denouement. Forsyth's technique suggests a hidden pattern governing great events, a pattern not always obvious even to the participants, much less to newspaper readers, who receive only a sanitized version of current history.

Forsyth comes to suspense fiction from journalism, his other major work being reportage, non-fiction (*The Biafra Story*), and *The Shepherd*, a finely crafted yarn about a modern jet pilot in trouble, guided to safety by a ghost airplane from World War II. Authenticity in his novels comes from journalistic writing at its best: concrete, immediate, and immensely well-informed. A reserved authorial persona confines himself to precise, thorough description about how illegal actions and transactions are managed (the construction of the special rifle in *The Day of the Jackal*, the bomb-making in *The Odessa File*, gun-running in *Dogs of War* are all marvels of technical description). This journalistic precision is enhanced by the use of real people, places, and events in the immediate background; the ultimate effect is less that of fiction than of a fictional projection into the lives of the real makers of history, not the great leaders but their lieutenants, details about whom never make the front page.

The Day of the Jackal contrasts the professional and amateur – the professional assassin with the OAS amateur terrorist, the professional gun maker with the amateur forger, the professional detective with political appointees – with only a true professional capable of appreciating the subtlety and thoroughness of a fellow professional, since each pays close attention to trivial details, checks remote angles and contingency plans, and deals with situations intellectually rather than emotionally. Thus only a Lebel is capable of keeping up with the Jackal's calculated attempt to assassinate de Gaulle, and both men know it. In *The Odessa File*, Peter Miller, a highly competent crime reporter, tracks down a former SS concentration camp commandant (a real person, Captain Eduard Roschmann, whose story is historically accurate); Miller's investigative expertise serves him well until he runs up against the professionalism of the Odessa (the organization of former SS) and of the anti-Nazi underground. *The Dogs of War* concerns the efforts of a brilliant mercenary leader, Cat Shannon, to topple an Idi Amin-like African tyrant on behalf of Sir James Manson, director of a British mining company, who has discovered a mountain of platinum in the tyrant's country. Shannon and a handful of mercenaries are engaged to install a puppet government which will turn over mining rights to Manson, but the values of the professional mercenary and the amateur king-maker ultimately conflict, with results highly satisfactory to the reader. The three suspense novels are thus fine depictions of the political underworlds of our times, packed with technical detail, set against real characters and events, and focusing on tough, competent professionals who defy bureaucracies but achieve a measure of success, at least on their own terms.

—Andrew F. Macdonald

FOSTER, Richard. See **CROSSEN, Ken.**

FOWLER, Sydney. Pseudonym for Sydney Fowler Wright. Born 6 January 1874. Educated at King Edward VI School, Birmingham. Married 1) Nellie Ashbarry in 1895 (died, 1918), three sons and three daughters; 2) Truda Hancock in 1920, one son and three daughters. Accountant in Birmingham from 1895. Editor *Poetry* (later *Poetry and the Play*) magazine, Birmingham, 1920–32. *Died 25 February 1965.*

CRIME PUBLICATIONS

Novels (series characters: Professor Blinkwell; Inspector Cauldron; Inspector Cleveland; Mr. Jellipot)

The King Against Anne Bickerton. London, Harrap, 1930; as *The Case of Anne Bickerton*, New York, Boni, 1930; as *Rex v. Anne Bickerton*, London, Penguin, 1947.
The Bell Street Murders (Jellipot; Blinkwell). London, Harrap, and New York, Macaulay, 1931.
By Saturday (Cleveland). London, Lane, 1931.
The Hanging of Constance Hillier (Cleveland). London, Jarrolds, 1931; New York, Macaulay, 1932.
Crime & Co. (Cleveland). New York, Macaulay, 1931; as *The Hand-Print Mystery*, London, Jarrolds, 1932.

Arresting Delia (Cleveland).   London, Jarrolds, and New York, Macaulay, 1933.
The Secret of the Screen (Blinkwell).   London, Jarrolds, 1933.
Who Else But She?   London, Jarrolds, 1934.
Three Witnesses.   London, Butterworth, 1935.
The Attic Murder (Jellipot).   London, Butterworth, 1936.
Was Murder Done?   London, Butterworth, 1936.
Post-Mortem Evidence (Jellipot).   London, Butterworth, 1936.
Four Callers in Razor Street (Jellipot).   London, Jenkins, 1937.
The Jordans Murder (Jellipot).   London, Jenkins, 1938; New York, Curl, 1939.
The Murder in Bethnal Square (Jellipot).   London, Jenkins, 1938.
The Wills of Jane Kanwhistle.   London, Jenkins, 1939.
The Rissole Mystery.   London, Rich and Cowan, 1941.
A Bout with the Mildew Gang (Cauldron).   London, Eyre and Spottiswoode, 1941.
Second Bout with the Mildew Gang (Cauldron).   London, Eyre and Spottiswoode, 1942.
Dinner in New York (Jellipot).   London, Eyre and Spottiswoode, 1943.
The End of the Mildew Gang (Cauldron).   London, Eyre and Spottiswoode, 1944.
Too Much for Mr. Jellipot.   London, Eyre and Spottiswoode, 1945.
The Adventure of the Blue Room.   London, Rich and Cowan, 1945.
Who Murdered Reynard? (Blinkwell).   London, Jarrolds, 1947.
With Cause Enough (Jellipot).   London, Harvill Press, 1954.

Short Stories

The New Gods Lead.   London, Jarrolds, 1932.

OTHER PUBLICATIONS as S. Fowler Wright

Novels

The Amphibians: A Romance of 500,000 Years Hence.   London, Merton Press, 1925.
Deluge.   London, Fowler Wright, 1927; New York, Cosmopolitan, 1928.
The Island of Captain Sparrow.   London, Gollancz, and New York, Cosmopolitan, 1928.
The World Below (includes *The Amphibians*).   London, Collins, 1929; New York, Longman, 1930; *The World Below* published as *The Dwellers*, London, Panther, 1954.
Dawn.   New York, Cosmopolitan, 1929; London, Harrap, 1930.
Elfwin.   London, Harrap, and New York, Longman, 1930.
Dream; or, The Simian Maid.   London, Harrap, 1931.
Seven Thousand in Israel.   London, Jarrolds, 1931.
Red Ike, with J. M. Denwood.   London, Hutchinson, 1931; as *Under the Brutchstone*, New York, Coward McCann, 1931.
Beyond the Rim.   London, Jarrolds, 1932.
Lord's Right in Languedoc.   London, Jarrolds, 1933.
Power.   London, Jarrolds, 1933.
David.   London, Butterworth, 1934.
Prelude in Prague: A Story of the War of 1938.   London, Newnes, 1935; as *The War of 1938*, New York, Putnam, 1936.
Four Days War.   London, Hale, 1936.
The Screaming Lake.   London, Hale, 1937.
Megiddo's Ridge.   London, Hale, 1937.
The Hidden Tribe.   London, Hale, 1938.
The Adventure of Wyndham Smith.   London, Jenkins, 1938.
Ordeal of Barata.   London, Jenkins, 1939.

The Siege of Malta: Founded on an Unfinished Romance by Sir Walter Scott. London, Muller, 1942.
Vengeance of Gwa. London, Books of Today, 1945.
Spiders' War: A Fantasy Novel. New York, Abelard Schuman, 1954.

Short Stories

Justice, and The Rat. London, Books of Today, 1945.
The Witchfinder. London, Books of Today, 1946.
The Throne of Saturn. Sauk City, Wisconsin, Arkham House, 1949; London, Heinemann, 1951.

Verse

Scenes from the Morte d'Arthur (as Alan Seymour). London, Erskine MacDonald, 1919.
Some Songs of Bilitis. Birmingham, Poetry, 1921.
The Song of Songs and Other Poems. London, Merton Press, 1925; New York, Cosmopolitan, 1929.
The Ballad of Elaine. London, Merton Press, 1926.
The Riding of Lancelot: A Narrative Poem. London, Fowler Wright, 1929.

Other

Police and Public: A Political Pamphlet. London, Fowler Wright, 1929.
The Life of Walter Scott: A Biography. London, Poetry League, 1932; New York, Haskell House, 1971.
Should We Surrender Colonies? London, Readers' Library, 1939.

Editor, *Voices on the Wind: An Anthology of Contemporary Verse.* London, Merton Press, 3 vols., 1922–24.
Editor, *Poets of Merseyside: An Anthology of Present-Day Liverpool Poetry.* London, Merton Press, 1923.
Editor, with R. Crompton Rhodes, *Poems: Chosen by Boys and Girls.* Oxford, Blackwell, 4 vols., 1923–24.
Editor, *Birmingham Poetry 1923–1924.* London, Merton Press, 1924.
Editor, *From Overseas: An Anthology of Contemporary Dominion and Colonial Verse.* London, Merton Press, 1924.
Editor, *Some Yorkshire Poets.* London, Merton Press, 1924.
Editor, *A Somerset Anthology of Modern Verse 1924.* London, Merton Press, 1924.
Editor, *The County Series* (verse anthologies). London, Fowler Wright, 13 vols., 1927–30.
Editor, *The Last Days of Pompeii: A Redaction*, by Edward Bulwer-Lytton. London, Vision Press, 1948.

Translator, *The Inferno*, by Dante. London, Fowler Wright, 1928.
Translator, *Marguerite de Valois*, by Dumas père. London, Temple, 1947.
Translator, *The Purgatorio*, by Dante. Edinburgh, Oliver and Boyd, 1954.

*   *   *

S. Fowler Wright was one of the giants of science-fiction: *The World Below* and *Deluge* place him in the company of the later Wells, Huxley, and Olaf Stapledon. His mystery fiction (written mostly as by Sydney Fowler) is not, however, on this same level. Sydney Fowler was a somewhat uneven writer, whose work varied from flimsy *romans du moment* to competent, well-plotted legalistic detective stories that respect the reader's intelligence.

Much of Fowler's work breaks down into story chains, which sometimes overlap slightly. Two important sequences, the novels concerned with the Mildew Gang and those with Professor Blinkwell, are criminal mastermind and gang stories in the manner of the 1930's. If they lack the verve and drive of Edgar Wallace's work, they often have greater depth and more solid writing.

Fowler's strongest stories are in the classical fair-play tradition. These center mostly around Mr. Jellipot, who is not exactly a detective, but an extremely astute (if intuitive) solicitor, around whom solutions jell. The Jellipot stories often embody ideas, such as the legal difficulties in handling multiple guilt, the morality of murdering vicious people, the principles for disguising culpability. The better Jellipot books include *The Murder in Bethnal Square, Four Callers in Razor Street,* and *Too Much for Mr. Jellipot.*

A lesser grouping of novels (*Crime & Co, Arresting Delia,* and *By Saturday*) describes adventures of bright young English people who lightheartedly circumvent bumbling police or incredible Americans. Since Fowler was essentially humorless, these are his least successful work.

Wright was an idiosyncratic writer, with a peculiarly cold and cerebral style (with many sarcastic asides) which some readers find repellent, others piquant. Related to this was his skill at portraying men of intellect, like Jellipot, the hanging judge Ackling (*The King Against Anne Bickerton*), or such gifted scoundrels as Professor Blinkwell. Wright was one of the very few writers who could render convincingly the amoral, passionless egotist of genius.

Wright's serious science-fiction (as distinguished from his thrillers) often served as a vehicle for his philosophical system. This was a paradoxical, somewhat inconsistent mixture of rationalism and anti-scientism, anarchism and elitism, often with a coldly surreptitious romantic note. These ideas sometimes operate in the background of his mystery fiction, but are particularly strong in the occasional excellent crime stories (with science-fiction elements) that appear in *The New Gods Lead.*

—E. F. Bleiler

FOXX, Jack. See **PRONZINI, Bill.**

FRANCIS, Dick (Richard Stanley Francis). British. Born in Tenby, Pembrokeshire, 31 October 1920. Educated at Maidenhead County Boys' School, Berkshire. Served as a Flying Officer in the Royal Air Force, 1940–45. Married Mary Margaret Brenchley in 1947; two sons. Amateur National Hunt (steeplechase) Jockey, 1946–48; Professional, 1948–57; National Hunt Champion, 1953–54. Racing Correspondent, *Sunday Express,* London, 1957–73. Recipient: Crime Writers Association Silver Dagger, 1965; Mystery Writers of America Edgar Allan Poe Award, 1969. Agent: John Johnson, 45–47 Clerkenwell Green, London EC1R 0HT. Address: Penny Chase, Blewbury, Didcot, Oxfordshire OX11 9NH, England.

CRIME PUBLICATIONS

Novels (series character: Sid Halley)

Dead Cert. London, Joseph, and New York, Holt Rinehart, 1962.
Nerve. London, Joseph, and New York, Harper, 1964.
For Kicks. London, Joseph, and New York, Harper, 1965.
Odds Against (Halley). London, Joseph, 1965; New York, Harper, 1966.
Flying Finish. London, Joseph, 1966; New York, Harper, 1967.
Blood Sport. London, Joseph, 1967; New York, Harper, 1968.
Forfeit. London, Joseph, and New York, Harper, 1969.
Enquiry. London, Joseph, and New York, Harper, 1969.
Rat Race. London, Joseph, 1970; New York, Harper, 1971.
Bonecrack. London, Joseph, 1971; New York, Harper, 1972.
Smokescreen. London, Joseph, and New York, Harper, 1972.
Slay-Ride. London, Joseph, 1973; New York, Harper, 1974.
Knock-Down. London, Joseph, 1974; New York, Harper, 1975.
High Stakes. London, Joseph, 1975; New York, Harper, 1976.
In the Frame. London, Joseph, 1976; New York, Harper, 1977.
Risk. London, Joseph, 1977; New York, Harper, 1978.
Trial Run. London, Joseph, 1978; New York, Harper, 1979.
Whip Hand (Halley). London, Joseph, 1979.

Uncollected Short Stories

"A Day of Wine and Roses," in *Sports Illustrated* (New York), May 1973.
"The Gift," in *Winter's Crimes 5*, edited by Virginia Whitaker. London, Macmillan, 1973.
"A Carrot for a Chestnut," in *Stories of Crime and Detection*, edited by Joan D. Berbrich. New York, McGraw Hill, 1974.
"The Big Story," in *Ellery Queen's Crime Wave.* New York, Putnam, 1976.
"Nightmare," in *Ellery Queen's Searches and Seizures.* New York, Davis, 1977.

OTHER PUBLICATIONS

Play

Screenplay: *Dead Cert*, 1974.

Other

The Sport of Queens: The Autobiography of Dick Francis. London, Joseph, 1957; revised edition, 1968, 1974; New York, Harper, 1969.

Editor, with John Welcome, *Best Racing and Chasing Stories 1–2.* London, Faber, 2 vols., 1966–69.
Editor, with John Welcome, *The Racing Man's Bedside Book.* London, Faber, 1969.

*   *   *

It is rare indeed for a writer to win both wide popular success as well as critical acclaim. Yet Dick Francis, who until he was approaching forty had never thought of putting pen to paper, has achieved just that. He began with an autobiography, written at the casual suggestion of a friend when he had ended his career as a top jockey in British racing. Then, in need he says of the price of a new carpet, he thought he would try his hand at a thriller and produced *Dead Cert*, an immediate success. Each year afterwards a new adventure tale generally with a turf setting has appeared, and their standard is always remarkably high.

His method is to write a first version and then to read it aloud on to tape. I suspect that it is this process that accounts for the first of his virtues, the extreme easiness of his style. But easy reading generally comes from hard work first, and Francis has said that producing a novel is "just as tiring" as race riding. Besides the style, there are solid plots underneath the whole, the way whatever turns out to have happened in the end has its reasonable and likely cause. There is the continuing pull of the story, so that you are all the time wanting to know what will happen next. You get told what you want to know, too, and not something just a little bit different as often with less skilled authors. And at the same time you are made to want to know some new thing.

Then there is the language. Francis never succumbs to the temptation to use a long or complex word where a simple one exists, something that writers with high reputations are often guilty of. Francis chooses straightforward words and never wastes them. This virtue comes perhaps from his sense of timing, a gift he brought with him from racing to writing. The art of judging at just what moment to put a new fact into the reader's head, whether the fact is as important as the discovery of a body (most adroitly done in *Slay-Ride*) or just some necessary detail, is one that Francis shares with the masters of his craft, figures as outwardly different as Agatha Christie or the subtle Simenon.

But more important than the pacing of a book or than its plot, more even than a well-told story, are the people that the writer invents for it. It is through people that the story-teller affects his audience. The people in the Francis books are as real as real-life people. Perhaps the best example of the kind of human being to be found in the Francis books is the girl the hero either loves or comes to love. There is not one in every book (Francis has succeeded in bringing considerable variety to thrillers that might with their customary turf setting and action plots have become very much formula affairs), but she has featured often enough to be easily identifiable as a certain sort of person. She will have some grave handicap, needing to live in an iron lung or having been crippled or simply being recently widowed. Many thriller writers would not dare use such people because the reality of their situation would show up the tinsel world around them. But Francis is tough enough, and compassionate enough, to be able to write about such things.

His knowledge of the effects of tragedy comes from his own experience. While his own wife was expecting their first child, she was struck down by poliomyelitis and confined to an iron lung. It is from personal experience, too, that the typically stoic Francis hero springs. One of the few complaints made about the books is that the heroes (a different one each time, a jockey, a horse-owner, a trainer, a painter, a private detective, a film star, an accountant) are too tough to be credible. But the fact is that most critics are not used to taking actual physical hard knocks: Francis, the jockey, was. So if you look carefully at what he says happens when one of his heroes gets beaten up, you find that, unlike many a pseudo-Bond or carbon-copy private eye, he gets really hurt and recovers only as fast as a physically fit and resilient man could in real life.

A Francis hero will have another characteristic as well as bodily toughness. He will be a man not scared of judging. He weighs up the characters he meets and sees them for what they are, tough men, good men, nasty men, weak men, tough women, greedy women, sensitive women. And, more than this, the Francis books make judgments on a wider scale. Each book is about something. From its particular choice of hero it tackles some particular human dilemma. *Slay-Ride*, for instance, though it might seem on the surface to be no more than a good story about dirty work on the Norwegian race-courses, is in fact a book about what it is like to be the parent of children, to give these hostages to fortune, to be taking part in the continuing pattern of all human existence. Similarly, *Blood Sport* was about failure of the will to advance, *Rat Race* about being on top of circumstances or permanently underneath them. It is such themes which give the Francis books the weight that lifts them right out of the run of good but ordinary thrillers.

—H. R. F. Keating

FRANKLIN, Max.   See DEMING, Richard.

FRASER, (Lady) Antonia.   British.   Born in London, 27 August 1932; daughter of the writer Lord Longford. Educated at the Dragon School, Oxford, 1940–44; St. Mary's Convent, Ascot, Berkshire, 1946–48; Lady Margaret Hall, Oxford, 1950–53, B.A. in history 1953, M.A. Married Hugh Fraser in 1956 (divorced, 1977); three daughters and three sons. General Editor, Kings and Queens of England series, Weidenfeld and Nicolson, publishers, London. Chairman, Society of Authors, 1974–75. Recipient: Black Memorial Prize, for biography, 1970. Lives in London. Agent: Curtis Brown Ltd., 1 Craven Hill, London W2 3EP, England.

CRIME PUBLICATIONS

Novels (series character: Jemima Shore in both books)

> *Quiet as a Nun.*   London, Weidenfeld and Nicolson, and New York, Viking Press, 1977.
> *The Wild Island.*   London, Weidenfeld and Nicolson, and New York, Norton, 1978.

Uncollected Short Stories

> "Death of an Old Dog," in *Winter's Crimes 10*, edited by Hilary Watson.   London, Macmillan, 1978.
> "The Case of the Parr Children," in *The Fourth Bedside Book of Great Detective Stories*, edited by Herbert Van Thal.   London, Barker, 1979.

OTHER PUBLICATIONS

Plays

> Radio Plays: *On the Battlements*, 1975; *The Heroine*, 1976; *Penelope*, 1976.

> Television Play: *Charades*, 1977.

Other

> *King Arthur and the Knights of the Round Table* (juvenile).   London, Weidenfeld and Nicolson, 1954; New York, Knopf, 1970.
> *Robin Hood* (juvenile).   London, Weidenfeld and Nicolson, 1957; New York, Knopf, 1971.
> *Dolls.*   London, Weidenfeld and Nicolson, and New York, Putnam, 1963.
> *A History of Toys.*   London, Weidenfeld and Nicolson, and New York, Delacorte Press, 1966.
> *Mary, Queen of Scots.*   London, Weidenfeld and Nicolson, and New York, Delacorte Press, 1969.
> *Cromwell Our Chief of Men.*   London, Weidenfeld and Nicolson, 1973; as *Cromwell, The Lord Protector*, New York, Knopf, 1973.
> *Mary, Queen of Scots, and the Historians.*   Ilford, Essex, Royal Stuart Society, 1974.

King James: VI of Scotland, I of England.   London, Weidenfeld and Nicolson, 1974;
  New York, Knopf, 1975.
King Charles II.   London, Weidenfeld and Nicolson, 1979.

Editor, *The Lives of the Kings and Queen of Scotland.*   London, Weidenfeld and
  Nicolson, and New York, Knopf, 1975.
Editor, *Scottish Love Poems: A Personal Anthology.*   Edinburgh, Canongate, 1975;
  New York, Viking Press, 1976.
Editor, *Love Letters: An Anthology.*   London, Weidenfeld and Nicolson, 1976; New
  York, Knopf, 1977.

Translator, *Martyrs in China*, by Jean Monsterleet.   London, Longman, 1956.
Translator, *Dior by Dior: The Autobiography of Christian Dior.*   London, Weidenfeld
  and Nicolson, 1957.

Antonia Fraser comments:
  I aim to produce a straightforward mystery story (if that is not a contradiction in terms!) in
the tradition of those writers I most admire, as it happens principally women. They include
Dorothy L. Sayers, Emma Lathen, Ruth Rendell, and P. D. James, as well as the great
Patricia Highsmith. I have a horror of blood dripping from the page in the books I read,
thinking effects are better achieved with more subtlety; my books are therefore aimed at
readers who feel likewise. I am very interested in the possibilities of my amateur sleuth,
Jemima Shore, Investigator, the celebrated TV reporter, and hope to explore them further in
future books – against a variety of backgrounds other than Catholic convents and the
Highlands of Scotland, which I have already considered.

                                  *   *   *

  Antonia Fraser is the author of two mystery stories located respectively in a convent and
on a Scottish island. Her heroine, Jemima Shore, is one of the latest additions to a long line of
amateur women sleuths and not an especially creditable one: she manages to elucidate partly
the cause of disturbances at Blessed Eleanor's convent but is baffled completely by the strange
occurrences on Eilean Fas, "the wild island." On each occasion, at the climax of the action
Jemima is involved in a confrontation with a person whom she has failed to suspect, her life
is endangered and it is only the intervention of a third character that gets her out of a nasty
spot.
  As a heroine, however, Jemima is stylish and intelligent: a television personality whose
detecting is incidental. She observes the antics of distraught nuns with a certain amount of
coolness and detachment; lays a ghost and restores order to the disrupted convent and school
life. The plot has a kind of Gothic exuberance which is balanced to an extent by the author's
forthright tone. The second novel, however, is less self-contained and this robs the events of a
great deal of plausibility. A group of crackpot royalists, a number of doomed or demented
individuals, a princess, and a flamboyant M.P. are included in the cast. Many of the
ingredients of melodrama are thrown in, and the narrative hovers uneasily between parody –
for Antonia Fraser is thoroughly familiar with all the relevant genres – and complete
seriousness, which is hard to take. Suspension of disbelief is necessary; but once it is effected,
the novels' entertainment value is high.

                                                                          —Patricia Craig

FRAZER, Robert Caine. See **CREASEY, John.**

FREELING, Nicolas. British. Born in London in 1927. Educated in local primary and secondary schools. Served in the British military forces. Married Cornelia Termes in 1954; four sons and one daughter. Worked as a hotel and restaurant cook, throughout Europe, 1945–60. Recipient: Crime Writers Association Golden Dagger, 1964; Grand Prix de Roman Policier, 1964; Mystery Writers of America Edgar Allan Poe Award, 1966. Address: 28 Rue de Fréland, 67100 Strasbourg, France.

CRIME PUBLICATIONS

Novels (series characters: Henri Castang; Inspector Van der Valk; Arlette Van der Valk)

Love in Amsterdam (Van der Valk). London, Gollancz, and New York, Harper, 1962; as *Death in Amsterdam*, New York, Ballantine, 1964.
Because of the Cats (Van der Valk). London, Gollancz, 1963; New York, Harper, 1964.
Gun Before Butter (Van der Valk). London, Gollancz, 1963; as *Question of Loyalty*, New York, Harper, 1963.
Valparaiso (as F. R. E. Nicolas). London, Gollancz, 1964; as Nicolas Freeling, New York, Harper, 1965.
Double-Barrel (Van der Valk). London, Gollancz, 1964; New York, Harper, 1965.
Criminal Conversation (Van der Valk). London, Gollancz, 1965; New York, Harper, 1966.
The King of the Rainy Country (Van der Valk). London, Gollancz, and New York, Harper, 1966.
The Dresden Green (Van der Valk). London, Gollancz, 1966; New York, Harper, 1967.
Strike Out Where Not Applicable (Van der Valk). London, Gollancz, and New York, Harper, 1967.
This Is the Castle. London, Gollancz, and New York, Harper, 1968.
Tsing-Boum (Van der Valk). London, Hamish Hamilton, 1969; as *Tsing-Boom!*, New York, Harper, 1969.
Over the High Side (Van der Valk). London, Hamish Hamilton, 1971; as *The Lovely Ladies*, New York, Harper, 1971.
A Long Silence (Van der Valk; Arlette Van der Valk). London, Hamish Hamilton, 1972; as *Auprès de ma Blonde*, New York, Harper, 1972.
Dressing of Diamond (Castang). London, Hamish Hamilton, and New York, Harper, 1974.
What Are Bugles Blowing For? (Castang). London, Heinemann, 1975; as *The Bugles Blowing*, New York, Harper, 1976.
Lake Isle. London, Heinemann, 1976; as *Sabine*, New York, Harper, 1977.
Gadget. London, Heinemann, and New York, Coward McCann, 1977.
The Night Lords. London, Heinemann, and New York, Pantheon, 1978.
The Widow (Arlette Van der Valk). London, Heinemann, and New York, Pantheon, 1979.

Uncollected Short Stories

"Van der Valk and the Beach Number," in *Ellery Queen's Mystery Magazine* (New York), May 1969.
"Van der Valk and the Old Seaman," in *Ellery Queen's Mystery Magazine* (New York), August 1969.
"Van der Valk and the Four Mice," in *Ellery Queen's Mystery Magazine* (New York), November 1969.
"Van der Valk and the Young Man," in *Ellery Queen's Mystery Magazine* (New York), December 1969.
"Van der Valk and the High School Riot," in *Ellery Queen's Mystery Magazine* (New York), March 1970.
"Van der Valk and the Great Pot Problem," in *Ellery Queen's Mystery Magazine* (New York), April 1970.
"Van der Valk and the Wolfpack," in *Ellery Queen's Mystery Magazine* (New York), August 1970.
"Van der Valk and the False Caesar," in *Ellery Queen's Mystery Magazine* (New York), February 1972.
"Van der Valk and the Man from Nowhere," in *Ellery Queen's Mystery Magazine* (New York), May 1972.
"Van der Valk and the Cavalier," in *Ellery Queen's Mystery Magazine* (New York), January 1974.
"Van der Valk and the Spanish Galleon," in *Ellery Queen's Mystery Magazine* (New York), August 1975.
"Van der Valk and the Two Pigeons," in *Ellery Queen's Magicians of Mystery*. New York, Davis, 1976.

OTHER PUBLICATIONS

Other

Kitchen Book. London, Hamish Hamilton, 1970; as *The Kitchen*, New York, Harper, 1970.
Cook Book. London, Hamish Hamilton, and New York, Harper, 1971.

*   *   *

Nicolas Freeling rightly relates fact and form in his stories of crime and its common companions, destruction, anxiety, guilt, and cruelty. From the start he has written out of a sharp awareness of the need for reality. *Love in Amsterdam* conveys convincingly the general feeling of the Dutch city and the particular attitudes of its inhabitants, whose actions take place not so much against a backdrop as within a locale. *Because of the Cats* builds upon his achievement in adumbrating the life of the city of Amsterdam; now he has moved his action to a new town, "the pride of Dutch building and planning," half an hour by train from Amsterdam. Here by the peaceful seaside a gang of teenagers behave with brutality, with a cunning ruthlessness. Their actions are probed by Freeling's Dutch detective Van der Valk, who carries Freeling's commentary upon crime unobtrusively; he is compassionate, but sceptical; he has no illusions but he has an intense intellectual curiosity which compels him to the solution of the puzzles which crime presents, the oddities of human behaviour under stress.

Van der Valk is a character who shares his thoughts with Freeling's readers; he is sufficiently unorthodox to be attractively human, sufficiently intuitive to lift these stories above the mechanically commercial. In the initial stages of his investigation Van der Valk gets to know the nature of the new town, and conveys the uneasy relationships between parents and children in it. Then the story speeds up, with a horrifying inevitability, while the policeman, long stripped of illusions, comments sceptically but in the process paradoxically reveals his own humanity.

The atmosphere of place permeates *Valparaiso*; it is a mediterranean novel, set in Porquerolles, where a Parisian film star meets and energises Raymond into attempting his dream of crossing the Atlantic in his boat, the *Olivia*. But money is needed to refit her, and crime seems to promise its quick acquisition. Here the mood shifts from easy timeless drifting into urgent activity, and the story moves faster to its climax, the encounter between Raymond and the French patrol-boat. The action is well and economically described, and the characters are established effectively, rather in the manner of a Simenon story.

There is a move away from the genre of the *roman policier* in *This Is the Castle* where Freeling develops his techniques further, where his narrative art encompasses a larger less precise dimension where the imagination can create its own apparent reality. Here the novelist living in Switzerland is neurotic; his menage of adoring wife, secretary-mistress, sons, and teenage daughter is visited by a publisher and an American journalist when a macabre shooting takes place: we see the tensions, the eccentricities through the eyes of the novelist and his wife, and the strange strains of the successful writer's life are explored with sensitive understanding.

Tsing-Boum develops the Van der Valk story to deeper levels, to a balanced view of the human motives behind the machine-gunning of the wife of a Dutch sergeant in her municipal flat while a television gangster serial is proceeding. Van der Valk is led into the after effects of the French surrender at Dien Bien Phu, but the way to violence goes through cowardice and revenge, blackmail, and jealousy. The Dutch police Commissaire is older, wiser – suffering from wounds incurred in an action described in an earlier novel – and more tolerant; he finds himself regarding the best as well as the worst of human behaviour, and the dullness of the surroundings of the crime makes the strange, but universal nature of human activities unfolded seem completely acceptable in their variety.

Freeling has not wanted to become set in any mould; he killed off Van der Valk as a clear indication of this, but kept his sense of experiment alive and in the process he has become more capable of creating character. Take, for instance, Colette Delavigne, the children's Judge, a French examining magistrate who seems secure in her cosy little world until Rachel, her child, is kidnapped. Through her sufferings we are reminded of the emptiness brought by the disappearance. Freeling's skill in guiding his readers unobtrusively enough with his comments ("flatly," "with sarcastic emphasis," "mildly," "carefully," "thoughtfully") is effective because he largely relies on dialogue or conversation presented without adverbial or other guidance. And the speech presented has the genuineness of ordinary speech, not the strange syntax we hear from a tape recording or ourselves, but speech produced by literary art to seem that of casual or intense conversation.

Whereas the reader is often reminded of Simenon – and Freeling is obviously conscious of his technique; he is mentioned twice in *Tsing-Boum*, for instance – the difference between the novelists is that Freeling is allowing his characters more time for reflection, he is taking pains to provide suggestions, in order to bring home ethical ideas, and to convey them effectively through the form of his writing. He is using pattern, narrative rhythm, counterpointing to give coherence to the human condition he creates and analyses. His art is to leave questions in the reader's mind by showing the disruptive effects of crime upon all those who are involved in the action, as well as upon society as a whole. His policemen may be Dutch or French, his scenes may be in Amsterdam, Paris, Geneva, or Cannes; but his policemen are representative of decent, honest policemen anywhere, under stress, like the public he describes, who can stand as the modern Everyman or Everywoman. This generalising ability, this capacity for understanding what it is like to live anywhere, here and now, raises him above mere mechanical practitioners of the form of the crime novel, because, while presenting his stories with increasing subtlety in shape and style, he develops and deepens his view of human nature.

—A. Norman Jeffares

FREEMAN, Kathleen. See **FITT, Mary.**

FREEMAN, R(ichard) Austin. Also wrote as Clifford Ashdown (with J. J. Pitcairn). British. Born in London, 11 April 1862. Apprenticed as apothecary; studied at Middlesex Hospital, London; qualified as Physician and Surgeon, 1887. Served in Royal Army Medical Corps, 1915–19: Captain. Married Annie Elizabeth Edwards in 1887; two sons. Assistant Colonial Surgeon, Accra, Gold Coast (now Ghana), 1887–91; appointed Boundary Commissioner, 1891; invalided home 1891; Assistant Medical Officer, Holloway Prison, 1900; Port of London Authority physician. Settled in Gravesend, 1903; worked as private tutor, then after 1919 as self-employed writer. Member of the Council, Eugenics Society. *Died 28 September 1943.*

CRIME PUBLICATIONS

Novels (series character: Dr. John Evelyn Thorndyke)

The Red Thumb Mark (Thorndyke). London, Collingwood, 1907; New York, Newton, 1911.
The Eye of Osiris: A Detective Romance (Thorndyke). London, Hodder and Stoughton, 1911; as *The Vanishing Man*, New York, Dodd Mead, 1912.
The Mystery of 31, New Inn (Thorndyke). London, Hodder and Stoughton, 1912; Philadelphia, Winston, 1913.
The Uttermost Farthing: A Savant's Vendetta. Philadelphia, Winston, 1914; as *A Savant's Vendetta*, London, Pearson, 1920.
A Silent Witness (Thorndyke). London, Hodder and Stoughton, 1914; Philadelphia, Winston, 1915.
The Exploits of Danby Croker, Being Extracts from a Somewhat Disreputable Autobiography. London, Duckworth, 1916.
Helen Vardon's Confession (Thorndyke). London, Hodder and Stoughton, 1922.
The Cat's Eye (Thorndyke). London, Hodder and Stoughton, 1923; New York, Dodd Mead, 1927.
The Mystery of Angelina Frood (Thorndyke). London, Hodder and Stoughton, 1924; New York, Dodd Mead, 1925.
The Shadow of the Wolf (Thorndyke). London, Hodder and Stoughton, and New York, Dodd Mead, 1925.
The D'Arblay Mystery (Thorndyke). London, Hodder and Stoughton, and New York, Dodd Mead, 1926.
A Certain Dr. Thorndyke. London, Hodder and Stoughton, 1927; New York, Dodd Mead, 1928.
As a Thief in the Night (Thorndyke). London, Hodder and Stoughton, and New York, Dodd Mead, 1928.
Mr. Pottermack's Oversight (Thorndyke). London, Hodder and Stoughton, and New York, Dodd Mead, 1930.
Pontifex, Son and Thorndyke. London, Hodder and Stoughton, and New York, Dodd Mead, 1931.
When Rogues Fall Out. London, Hodder and Stoughton, 1932; as *Dr. Thorndyke's Discovery*, New York, Dodd Mead, 1932.

Dr. Thorndyke Intervenes. London, Hodder and Stoughton, and New York, Dodd
Mead, 1933.

For the Defence: Dr. Thorndyke. London, Hodder and Stoughton, and New York,
Dodd Mead, 1934.

The Penrose Mystery (Thorndyke). London, Hodder and Stoughton, and New York,
Dodd Mead, 1936.

Felo De Se? (Thorndyke). London, Hodder and Stoughton, 1937; as *Death at the Inn*,
New York, Dodd Mead, 1937.

The Stoneware Monkey (Thorndyke). London, Hodder and Stoughton, 1938; New
York, Dodd Mead, 1939.

Mr. Polton Explains (Thorndyke). London, Hodder and Stoughton, and New York,
Dodd Mead, 1940.

Dr. Thorndyke's Crime File (omnibus). New York, Dodd Mead, 1941.

The Jacob Street Mystery (Thorndyke). London, Hodder and Stoughton, 1942; as *The
Unconscious Witness*, New York, Dodd Mead, 1942.

Short Stories

John Thorndyke's Cases. London, Chatto and Windus, 1909; as *Dr. Thorndyke's
Cases*, New York, Dodd Mead, 1931.

The Singing Bone. London, Hodder and Stoughton, 1912; New York, Dodd Mead,
1923; as *The Adventures of Dr. Thorndyke*, New York, Popular Library, 1947.

The Great Portrait Mystery. London, Hodder and Stoughton, 1918.

Dr. Thorndyke's Case Book. London, Hodder and Stoughton, 1923; as *The Blue
Scarab*, New York, Dodd Mead, 1924.

The Puzzle Lock. London, Hodder and Stoughton, 1925; New York, Dodd Mead,
1926.

The Magic Casket. London, Hodder and Stoughton, and New York, Dodd Mead,
1927.

The Famous Cases of Dr. Thorndyke. London, Hodder and Stoughton, 1929; as *The
Dr. Thorndyke Omnibus*, New York, Dodd Mead, 1932.

Dr. Thorndyke Investigates. London, University of London Press, 1930.

Short Stories as Clifford Ashdown (with J. J. Pitcairn)

The Adventures of Romney Pringle. London, Ward Lock, 1902; Philadelphia, Oswald
Train, 1968.

The Further Adventures of Romney Pringle. Philadelphia, Oswald Train, 1970.

The Queen's Treasure. Philadelphia, Oswald Train, 1975.

From a Surgeon's Diary. London, Ferret Fantasy, 1975; Philadelphia, Oswald Train,
1977.

Other Publications

Novels

The Golden Pool: A Story of a Forgotten Mine. London, Cassell, 1905.

The Unwilling Adventurer. London, Hodder and Stoughton, 1913.

The Surprising Adventures of Mr. Shuttlebury Cobb. London, Hodder and Stoughton,
1927.

Flighty Phyllis. London, Hodder and Stoughton, 1928.

Other

Travels and Life in Ashanti and Jaman. London, Constable, 1898.

Social Decay and Regeneration. London, Constable, and Boston, Houghton Mifflin, 1921.

Bibliography: *In Search of Dr. Thorndyke* by Norman Donaldson, Bowling Green, Ohio, Popular Press, 1971.

*   *   *

Dr. John Evelyn Thorndyke remains the only convincing scientific investigator of detective fiction. That is the measure of R. Austin Freeman's achievement, and it rests not particularly on the accuracy of the technical details presented – accurate though they are – but on the impact of "scientific method" as a way of thought brought to bear in convincing fashion on the essentially romantic materials of the detective story. On the one hand, Freeman was a leisurely, old-fashioned writer, tending to platitudes, though Raymond Chandler found his style achieved "an even suspense that is quite unexpected." On the other, whether his materials were drawn from marine zoology or tropical medicine, Thorndyke's impact on non-scientists was always sharp and unequivocal. "Precise measurements don't seem to matter much," said an old lawyer in one story. "On the other hand," retorted Thorndyke, "inexact measurements are of no use at all."

Freeman achieved a second breakthrough. With his fictional investigator's career only just launched – in *The Red Thumb Mark* – he wrote for *Pearson's Magazine* a series of "inverted" stories, in which he forfeited the element of surprise by identifying the criminal and letting us see him at his nefarious work. As he put it himself, "the usual circumstances are reversed; the reader knows everything, the detective knows nothing, and the interest focuses on the unexpected significance of trivial circumstances." As television viewers watch the *Colombo* series and other examples of this form, how many of them know who originated it? John Adams, reviewing the first collection, *The Singing Bone*, admitted them to be "beyond the range of the ordinary devourer of 'sleuth' novels.... A very obvious and natural criticism of the stories is that they are too clever; they ask too much of the reader. But unlike some clever writers, Mr. Freeman is clever enough to carry off his cleverness. His exposition is so clear, his arrangement of events so methodical, that the reader is led along with the minimum amount of effort consistent with a very definite exercise of the reason."

The short stories and novels of the Freeman canon, however, are dominated by the handsome, usually impassive medical jurist of 5A King's Bench Walk in London's Inner Temple, Dr. Thorndyke. In the short tales the narrator is almost always his chief associate, Christopher Jervis, M.D., but several of the novels open with the discovery of a crime by a young physician who subsequently becomes romantically involved in the investigation. *The Red Thumb Mark*, which has to do with forged finger-prints, ends with Jervis's marriage. A finer example is *A Silent Witness*, with its persuasive description of the laboratory upstairs at No. 5A, lighted by the glow of the furnace and alive with workers, including Thorndyke's factotum, the diminutive, crinkly Nathaniel Polton.

The Cat's Eye has perhaps the most complex plot of all the novels, and is entirely successful. In *The Mystery of Angelina Frood* the author takes a scientific fallacy from Dickens's unfinished *Mystery of Edwin Drood* and weaves a lighthearted mystery around it. *The Shadow of the Wolf* is an expanded version of a two-part inverted magazine story published in 1914; the indispensable clue is a marine worm. Only occasionally did Freeman write a classic "whodunit," in which one of the main characters is identified as the criminal; *As a Thief in the Night* is a fine example – a dramatic novel rich in deep-felt emotions. *Mr. Pottermack's Oversight*, a general favorite, is an inverted novel that shows the good Doctor at his most amiable in dealing with the murderer of a blackmailer. *Dr. Thorndyke Intervenes* uses as its basis the real-life Druce-Portland Case of 1907, whereas a fictitious excavation in *The Penrose Mystery* was instrumental in bringing about a real "dig" at the same site a little later.

Although some falling off in quality is evident in Freeman's writing as he approached his eighties, his ability to ring the changes from one Thorndyke case to the next is almost as remarkable a feat as his original conception of the great medical jurist.

—Norman Donaldson

FREEMANTLE, Brian (Harry). Also writes as John Maxwell. British. Born in Southampton, Hampshire, 10 June 1936. Educated at Bitterne Park Secondary Modern School, Southampton. Married Maureen Hazel Tipney in 1956; three daughters. Reporter, New Milton *Advertiser*, Hampshire, 1953–58, Bristol *Evening World*, 1958, and *Evening News*, London, 1958–60; Reporter, later Assistant Foreign Editor, *Daily Express*, London, 1960–69; Foreign Editor, *Daily Sketch*, London, 1969–70, and *Daily Mail*, London, 1970–75; as a foreign correspondent worked in 30 countries. Agent: Jonathan Clowes Ltd., 19 Jeffrey's Place, London NW1 9PP, England.

CRIME PUBLICATIONS

Novels (series character: Charlie Muffin)

Goodbye to an Old Friend. London, Cape, and New York, Putnam, 1973.
Face Me When You Walk Away. London, Cape, 1974; New York, Putnam, 1975.
The Man Who Wanted Tomorrow. London, Cape, and New York, Stein and Day, 1975.
The November Man. London, Cape, 1976.
Charlie Muffin. London, Cape, 1977; as *Charlie M*, New York, Doubleday, 1977; London, Sphere, 1978.
Clap Hands, Here Comes Charlie. London, Cape, 1978; as *Here Comes Charlie M*, New York, Doubleday, 1978.
The Inscrutable Charlie Muffin. London, Cape, 1979.

OTHER PUBLICATIONS

Novels

The Touchables (novelization of screenplay). London, Hodder and Stoughton, 1969.
H.M.S. Bounty (as John Maxwell). London, Cape, 1977.
The Mary Celeste (as John Maxwell). London, Cape, 1979.

Brian Freemantle comments:
Although I write spy fiction, I have always tried to make my novels good *as novels*, and I rely heavily upon characterisation. I am happiest with the traditional type of plot line, and, through the use of strong plots and strong characterisation, I try to create a "rooftop" effect in my stories.

*   *   *   *

Brian Freemantle writes espionage thrillers in the tradition of John le Carré. In Freemantle's fiction, the intelligence service works more for self-aggrandizement than for patriotism. The "good" and the "bad" characters are blurred. For instance, in *The Man Who Wanted Tomorrow*, the Israelis are as vicious as the former Nazis upon whom they seek revenge. And like Altmann of *The November Man*, who is caught between the KGB and the CIA, the agents are weak characters who are used as pawns by their superiors.

At the same time, however, Freemantle plays variations on the conventions of the espionage tale. He adds the puzzle element of the mystery story. For example, both *Goodbye to an Old Friend* and *Charlie Muffin* center around the discovery of the true motives for the defections of famous Russians. Freemantle also emphasizes psychology more than violent action, often giving his protagonists psychological doubles. This doubling is especially prominent in *Face Me When You Walk Away*: the Russian Josef Bultova must "face" that part of himself which he has seen – and rejected – in a Jew whom he left behind in a concentration camp, as well as in the Nobel-Prize author whom he conducts on a tour to the West. Finally, Freemantle shows his cowardly characters refusing to be the conventional pawns; as the epigraph to *Goodbye to an Old Friend* says, cowards at times "adapt themselves to courage." But only *Charlie Muffin* depicts courage as completely triumphant. Charlie cunningly effects revenge upon his snobbish superiors in a surprise ending which, although rather contrived, leaves us anticipating Freemantle's promised further adventures of this "new kind of spy."

—Joan M. Saliskas

FREMLIN, Celia. British. Born in Ryarsh, Kent, 20 June 1914. Educated at Berkhamsted School for Girls, Hertfordshire; Somerville College, Oxford, B.A. in classics 1936, B.Litt. in philosophy 1937. Served as an air raid warden during World War II. Married Elia Goller in 1942 (died); one son and two daughters. Recipient: Mystery Writers of America Edgar Allan Poe Award, 1960. Address: 50 South Hill Park, London N.W.3, England.

CRIME PUBLICATIONS

Novels

The Hours Before Dawn. London, Gollancz, 1958; Philadelphia, Lippincott, 1959.
Uncle Paul. London, Gollancz, 1959; Philadelphia, Lippincott, 1960.
Seven Lean Years. London, Gollancz, 1961; as *Wait for the Wedding*, Philadelphia, Lippincott, 1961.
The Trouble-Makers. London, Gollancz, and Philadelphia, Lippincott, 1963.
The Jealous One. London, Gollancz, and Philadelphia, Lippincott, 1965.
Prisoner's Base. London, Gollancz, and Philadelphia, Lippincott, 1967.
Possession. London, Gollancz, and Philadelphia, Lippincott, 1969.
Appointment with Yesterday. London, Gollancz, and Philadelphia, Lippincott, 1972.
The Long Shadow. London, Gollancz, 1975; New York, Doubleday, 1976.
The Spider-Orchid. London, Gollancz, 1977; New York, Doubleday, 1978.

Short Stories

Don't Go to Sleep in the Dark. London, Gollancz, and Philadelphia, Lippincott, 1970.
By Horror Haunted. London, Gollancz, 1974.

Uncollected Short Stories

"The Coldness of a Thousand Suns," in *Ellery Queen's Crookbook*. New York, Random House, 1974.
"The Magic Carpet," in *Ellery Queen's Mystery Magazine* (New York), February 1975.
"If It's Got Your Number," in *Ellery Queen's Murdercade*. New York, Random House, 1975.
"Accomodation Vacant," in *Winter's Crimes 7*, edited by George Hardinge. London, Macmillan, 1975.
"Don't Be Frightened," in *MS Mysteries*, edited by Arthur Liebman. New York, Washington Square Press, 1976.
"Dangerous Sport," in *Ellery Queen's Mystery Magazine* (New York), September 1976.
"Etiquette for Dying," in *Ellery Queen's Mystery Magazine* (New York), January 1977.
"A Case of Maximum Need," in *Ellery Queen's Mystery Magazine* (New York), March 1977.
"Golden Tuesday," in *Ellery Queen's Champions of Mystery*. New York, Davis, 1977.
"The Woman Who Had Everything," in *John Creasey's Crime Collection*, edited by Herbert Harris. London, Hodder and Stoughton, 1977.
"The Postgraduate Thesis," in *Verdict of Thirteen*, edited by Julian Symons. London, Faber, and New York, Harper, 1979.

OTHER PUBLICATIONS

Other

The Seven Chars of Chelsea (on domestic service). London, Methuen, 1940.
War Factory. London, Gollancz, 1943.
Living Through the Blitz, with Tom Harrisson. London, Collins, 1976.

Manuscript Collection: Mugar Memorial Library, Boston University.

Celia Fremlin comments:
   The kind of crime novels I write are usually listed as "novels of suspense," since there are no policemen, no detectives, and (quite often) no murder: just some sort of mysterious threat hanging over someone and escalating (or so I hope!) chapter by chapter.
   What first launched me on writing this sort of book was simply the fact that this was the sort of book I wanted to read, and there seemed to be terribly few of them. What I aim at, I think, is an exciting and terrifying plot set against a very ordinary sort of humdrum domestic background, with a heroine beset by all the day-to-day problems of husband and children, as well as the mysterious outside threat. I find that by this juxtaposition I can throw across my characters a lurid sort of illumination which enables me to explore them in much greater depth than I could by any other means.

*   *   *

   Celia Fremlin's novels, especially the more recent ones, are notable for their elegant, even fastidious detachment. She brings a light touch to crime fiction, along with an admirable clarity and concision. Characteristically, she is one of today's few really successful practitioners of the thriller short story; and her volumes of collected stories contain, in fact, some of her finest work. She moves, as a rule, within a self-imposed, deliberately restricted frame: the characters are usually literate and articulate; the settings are urban, middle-class, apparently normal. Fremlin's great gift is to see horror in the ordinary. Thus, on the opening page of *The Spider-Orchid*, the protagonist looks at a pile of coat-hangers and sees them as a "dreadful glittering threat ... to the very core of his comfortable, self-sufficient existence."

Critics have justly underlined the excellence of Celia Fremlin's prose. In a genre where careless, even ungrammatical writing is more the rule than the exception, her graceful, polished style shines like a good deed.

—William Weaver

FROME, David. See **FORD, Leslie.**

FROST, Frederick. See **BRAND, Max.**

FULLER, Roy (Broadbent). British. Born in Failsworth, Lancashire, 11 February 1912. Educated at Blackpool High School, Lancashire; qualified as a solicitor, 1934. Served in the Royal Navy, 1941–46; Lieutenant, Royal Naval Volunteer Reserve. Married Kathleen Smith in 1936; one son, the poet John Fuller. Assistant Solicitor, 1938–58, Solicitor, 1958–69, and since 1969, Director, Woolwich Equitable Building Society, London. Chairman of the Legal Advisory Panel, 1958–69, and since 1969, a Vice-President, Building Societies Association. Professor of Poetry, Oxford University, 1968–73. Chairman, Poetry Book Society, London, 1960–68; Governor, BBC, 1972–79; Member, Arts Council of Great Britain, and Chairman of the Literature Panel, 1976–77 (resigned). Recipient: Arts Council Poetry Award, 1959; Duff Cooper Memorial Prize, for poetry, 1968; Queen's Gold Medal for Poetry, 1970. M.A.: Oxford University. Fellow, Royal Society of Literature, 1958. C.B.E. (Companion, Order of the British Empire), 1970. Address: 37 Langton Way, Blackheath, London S.E.3, England.

CRIME PUBLICATIONS

Novels

> *The Second Curtain.* London, Verschoyle, 1953; New York, Macmillan, 1956.
> *Fantasy and Fugue.* London, Verschoyle, 1954; New York, Macmillan, 1956.
> *Image of a Society.* London, Deutsch, 1956; New York, Macmillan, 1958.
> *The Ruined Boys.* London, Deutsch, 1959; as *That Distant Afternoon*, New York, Macmillan, 1959.
> *The Father's Comedy.* London, Deutsch, 1961.
> *The Perfect Fool.* London, Deutsch, 1963.
> *My Child, My Sister.* London, Deutsch, 1965.
> *The Carnal Island.* London, Deutsch, 1970.

617

OTHER PUBLICATIONS

Verse

Poems. London, Fortune Press, 1940.
The Middle of a War. London, Hogarth Press, 1942.
A Lost Season. London, Hogarth Press, 1944.
Epitaphs and Occasions. London, Lehmann, 1949.
Counterparts. London, Verschoyle, 1954.
Brutus's Orchard. London, Deutsch, 1957; New York, Macmillan, 1958.
Collected Poems, 1936–1961. London, Deutsch, and Chester Springs, Pennsylvania, Dufour, 1962.
Buff. London, Deutsch, and Chester Springs, Pennsylvania, Dufour, 1965.
New Poems. London, Deutsch, and Chester Springs, Pennsylvania, Dufour, 1968.
Pergamon Poets 1, with R. S. Thomas, edited by Evan Owen. Oxford, Pergamon Press, 1968.
Off Course. London, Turret Books, 1969.
Penguin Modern Poets 18, with A. Alvarez and Anthony Thwaite. London, Penguin, 1970.
To an Unknown Reader. London, Poem-of-the-Month Club, 1970.
Song Cycle from a Record Sleeve. Oxford, Sycamore Press, 1972.
Tiny Tears. London, Deutsch, 1973.
An Old War. Edinburgh, Tragara Press, 1974.
Waiting for the Barbarians: A Poem. Richmond, Surrey, Keepsake Press, 1974.
From the Joke Shop. London, Deutsch, 1975.
The Joke Shop Annexe. Edinburgh, Tragara Press, 1975.
An Ill-Governed Coast: Poems. Sunderland, Ceolfrith Press, 1976.
Re-treads. Edinburgh, Tragara Press, 1979.

Other

Savage Gold (juvenile). London, Lehmann, 1946.
With My Little Eye (juvenile). London, Lehmann, 1948; New York, Macmillan, 1957.
Catspaw (juvenile). London, Alan Ross, 1966.
Owls and Artificers: Oxford Lectures on Poetry. London, Deutsch, and La Salle, Illinois, Library Press, 1971.
Seen Grandpa Lately? (juvenile). London, Deutsch, 1972.
Professors and Gods: Last Oxford Lectures on Poetry. London, Deutsch, 1973; New York, St. Martin's Press, 1974.
Poor Roy (juvenile). London, Deutsch, 1977.
The Other Planet (juvenile). Richmond, Keepsake Press, 1979.

Editor, *Byron for Today.* London, Porcupine Press, 1948.
Editor, with Clifford Dyment and Montagu Slater, *New Poems 1952.* London, Joseph, 1952.
Editor, *The Building Societies Acts 1874–1960: Great Britain and Northern Ireland*, 5th edition. London, Frayney, 1961.
Editor, *Supplement of New Poetry.* London, Poetry Book Society, 1964.

*   *   *

Roy Fuller is best known as a poet who developed in the 1930's and whose work has since retained those concerns with the relationship between the individual and the collectivity that were characteristic of that decade. His novels all belong to later decades, and the difference between them and his poetry of the 1930's lies in the extent to which the collective has assumed a negative and hostile role. The novels are really moral thrillers, in which there is sometimes an actual crime that the central character finds himself forced to attempt to solve, but in which the real mystery lies in how the individual, who cannot command the strength needed to defeat powerful institutions, may still himself retain some shred of undefeated integrity.

It is perhaps in *The Second Curtain* that the two sides are most clearly demarcated, for the Power Industries Protection Corporation is in the most literal sense a criminal organization which operates on behalf of industrial interests generally regarded as pillars of society. Drawn into conflict with it is George Garner, a minor writer who lives largely by the drudgery of reading for publishers, an untidy and no more than ordinarily courageous man unwittingly involved in a web of violence and treachery when a friend mysteriously dies and he sets out, with no detective's training, to find out why and how. What Garner does find, to his consternation, is that the very patrons who propose to make him editor of a new literary magazine, and so liberate him from Grub Street drudgery, are in fact responsible for his friend's death. In the end, faced with naked brutality, the experience of violence, the threat of death, Garner gives up. He has learnt the truth about power. He cannot make his knowledge work effectively.

Individuals overshadowed by yet defying collectivities recur in Fuller's novels. In *Image of a Society* the collectivity is a Building Society like that in which Fuller himself worked for three decades; in *The Ruined Boys* it is a near-bankrupt private school. In *My Child, My Sister* the collectivity does not take institutional form, but an ageing man sexually stirred by his wife's daughter by another marriage finds himself facing and judging the whole structure of moral convention and its relevance to his own life. None of these books is a "mystery" in the same literal way as *The Second Curtain*, yet in their essential moral flavour, in their central opposition of the individual and the collectivity they belong in the same world.

This particularly applies to Fuller's fifth and perhaps most ambitious novel, *The Father's Comedy*, in which Colmore, an ambitious and successful civil servant employed by the mysterious "Authority," which is really an image for society as a whole, finds himself in a moral dilemma when his son rebels against the repression of the army and faces a court martial from which he can only be saved by the father's revelation of his own left-wing past. Colmore allows the call of human distress to overcome that of duty, and gains his son's acquittal, but when he returns "to show himself to the Authority," we know that what may happen in the future is less significant than the present, in which Colmore is able to accept that his planned career may be ruined when he declares for human love. In so far as in modern thrillers this kind of basic social conflict is one of the imponderable but necessary issues, one of the mysteries, all of Roy Fuller's fiction is essentially mysterious.

—George Woodcock

FULLER, Samuel (Michael). American. Born in Worcester, Massachusetts, 12 August 1911. Served in the 1st Infantry Division in World War II: Bronze Star, Silver Star, Purple Heart. Married Christa Lang in 1965. Journalist from 1924: copy-boy to Arthur Brisbane on New York *Journal*; staff member, New York *Graphic*; crime reporter for San Diego *Sun*. Since 1936, film writer, producer, and director. Recipient: Venice Film Festival Bronze Lion, 1953.

CRIME PUBLICATIONS

Novels

> *The Dark Page.* New York, Duell, 1944; as *Murder Makes a Deadline*, New York, Spivak, 1952.
> *The Naked Kiss* (novelization of screenplay). New York, Belmont, 1964.
> *Crown of India.* New York, Award, 1966.
> *144 Piccadilly.* New York, Baron, 1971; London, New English Library, 1972.
> *Dead Pigeon on Beethoven Street* (novelization of screenplay). New York, Pyramid, 1974.

OTHER PUBLICATIONS

Novels

> *Burn, Baby, Burn!* New York, Phoenix Press, 1935.
> *Test Tube Baby.* New York, Godwin, 1936.
> *Make Up and Kiss.* New York, Godwin, 1938.
> *The Rifle.* N.p., Simon and Flynn, 1969.

Plays

> Screenplays: *Hats Off*, with Edmund Joseph, 1937; *It Happened in Hollywood (Once a Hero)*, with others, 1937; *Adventure in Sahara*, with Maxwell Shane, 1938; *Federal Man-Hunt*, with Maxwell Shane and William Lively, 1938; *Gangs of New York*, with Wellyn Totman and Charles Francis Royal, 1938; *Bowery Boy*, with others, 1941; *Confirm or Deny*, with Jo Swerling and Henry Wales, 1941; *Power of the Press*, with Robert Hardy Andrews, 1942; *Gangs of the Waterfront*, with Albert Bleich, 1945; *Shockproof*, with Helen Deutsch, 1948; *I Shot Jesse James*, with Robert W. Gardner, 1949; *The Baron of Arizona*, 1950; *The Steel Helmet*, 1951; *Fixed Bayonets*, 1951; *The Tanks Are Coming*, with Robert Hardy Andrews, 1951; *Park Row*, 1952; *Pickup on South Street*, with Dwight Taylor, 1953; *The Command*, with Russell Hughes, 1954; *Hell and High Water*, with Jesse L. Lasky, Jr., and David Hempstead, 1954; *House of Bamboo*, with Harry Kleiner, 1955; *Run of the Arrow*, 1957; *China Gate*, 1957; *Forty Guns*, 1957; *Verboten!*, 1959; *The Crimson Kimono*, 1959; *Underworld U.S.A.*, 1961; *Merrill's Marauders*, with Milton Sperling, 1962; *Shock Corridor*, 1963; *The Naked Kiss*, 1964; *Cape Town Affair*, with Harold Medford, 1968; *Shark!*, with John Kingsbridge, 1969; *Dead Pigeon on Beethoven Street*, 1972.

> Television Plays: *The Virginian* series (1 episode), 1963; *The Iron Horse* series (5 episodes), 1966.

Theatrical Activities:

> Director: **Films** – *I Shot Jesse James*, 1949; *The Baron of Arizona*, 1950; *The Steel Helmet*, 1951; *Fixed Bayonets*, 1951; *Park Row*, 1952; *Pickup on South Street*, 1953; *Hell and High Water*, 1954; *House of Bamboo*, 1955; *Run of the Arrow*, 1957; *China Gate*, 1957; *Forty Guns*, 1957; *Verboten!*, 1959; *The Crimson Kimono*, 1959; *Underworld U.S.A.*, 1961; *Merrill's Marauders*, 1962; *Shock Corridor*, 1963; *The Naked Kiss*, 1964; *Shark!*, 1969; *Dead Pigeon on Beethoven Street*, 1972.

Actor: **Films** – *House of Bamboo*, 1955; *Pierrot le Fou*, 1965; *Brigitte et Brigitte*, 1966; *The Last Movie*, 1970; *The American Friend*, 1977.

*   *   *

Samuel Fuller, the movie director, has been the subject of two full-length studies and numerous articles in film journals. Fuller, responsible for several film classics, is a prolific writer of novels, screenplays, and tv plays, many of which remain unpublished and unproduced.

Fuller began his career as a copy-boy and, later, a crime reporter. His apprenticeship introduced him simultaneously to the worlds of journalism and crime. As a crime reporter he encountered scenes of violence, people of the streets, gangsters, and the corrupt politicians who were later to people his books and his films. One of his early novels, *The Dark Page*, was made into the film *Scandal Sheet*. *Park Row*, written, directed, and produced by Fuller, reflects the early days of his career.

Fuller has always been drawn to themes of sadism and violence, and his novels and films have always been associated with a realism almost grotesque in nature. In *The Naked Kiss* Fuller tells the story of a prostitute turned nurse who looks for the normal things of life, i.e., marriage, and who, in nearly achieving normalcy, almost marries an upright, cultured citizen who is a child molester. The film version of the story characterizes Fuller's obsession with absolutes – black/white, right/wrong – and shows everything turned upside down. The pristine white of the sets cannot purify the prostitute/nurse, nor can it disguise the sickness of the child molester. In a recent interview, Fuller described violence as "not an abnormal but a normal way of life." Elsewhere he analyzed "hookers as the dullest and most miserable people in the world." They may be miserable, but they are not dull in a Fuller work.

—Katherine M. Restaino

FUTRELLE, Jacques. American. Born in Pike County, Georgia, 9 April 1875. Married the writer L. May Peel in 1895. Theatrical manager; staff member, Boston *American. Died on the Titanic 15 April 1912*.

CRIME PUBLICATIONS

Novels (series character: Professor S. F. X. Van Dusen, The Thinking Machine)

The Chase of the Golden Plate (Van Dusen). New York, Dodd Mead, 1906.
The Simple Case of Susan. New York, Appleton, 1908; expanded by May Futrelle as *Lieutenant What's-His-Name*, Indianapolis, Bobbs Merrill, 1915.
Elusive Isabel. Indianapolis, Bobbs Merrill, 1909; as *The Lady in the Case*, London, Nelson, 1910.
The High Hand. Indianapolis, Bobbs Merrill, 1911; as *The Master Hand*, London, Hodder and Stoughton, 1914.
My Lady's Garter. Chicago, Rand McNally, 1912; London, Hodder and Stoughton, 1913.
Blind Man's Buff. London, Hodder and Stoughton, 1914.

Short Stories

The Thinking Machine.   New York, Dodd Mead, and London, Chapman, 1907; as *The Problem of Cell 13*, New York, Dodd Mead, 1918.
The Thinking Machine on the Case.   New York, Appleton, 1908; as *The Professor on the Case*, London, Nelson, 1909.
The Diamond Master.   Indianapolis, Bobbs Merrill, 1909; London, Holden, 1912; collected with *The Haunted Bell*, New York, Burt, 1915.
Best Thinking Machine Detective Stories, edited by E. F. Bleiler.   New York, Dover, 1973.

Uncollected Short Story

"The Mystery of Room 666," in *The Crooked Counties*, edited by Sir Hugh Greene.   London, Bodley Head, 1973; as *The Further Rivals of Sherlock Holmes*, New York, Pantheon, 1973.

*   *   *

The most popular story in mystery literature, with the possible exception of certain adventures of Sherlock Holmes, is probably Jacques Futrelle's "The Problem of Cell 13," which first appeared serially as a contest in a Boston newspaper in 1905. It was eventually followed by 42 other short stories about The Thinking Machine (Professor Augustus S. F. X. Van Dusen), in which the Professor continued his joust against the impossible. In the same series is a short novel, *The Haunted Bell*, which contains a note of the supernatural, and a longer work, *The Chase of the Golden Plate*, which is an automobile and society novel with mystery elements.

The essence of The Thinking Machine stories, which first appeared in newspapers, is that they were stories of idea at a time when most detective short stories were concerned with incident or situation. Most of Futrelle's earlier stories were built upon scientific concepts that permitted "impossible" situations; the later stories, on the other hand, were explications of weirdly colorful events in terms of ordinary circumstances.

Excellent characterization, ingenious ideas, fast-moving journalistic prose and amusing small touches make Futrelle's better stories outstanding in their period, but it must be admitted that his work is uneven. Futrelle was prolific in other areas of fiction, and in his later years he concentrated on frothy Edwardian romances. His mystery novels *Elusive Isabel*, *My Lady's Garter*, and *Blind Man's Buff* are in this vein. Futrelle also wrote a few miscellaneous detective stories which have not been collected; these are on the trivial side. Apart from the better stories about The Thinking Machine, Futrelle's finest work is *The Diamond Master*, a puzzling mystery with a small element of science-fiction.

—E. F. Bleiler

GADNEY, Reg.   British.   Born in Cross Hills, Yorkshire, 20 January 1941. Educated at Stowe School, Buckinghamshire; St. Catharine's College, Cambridge, 1962–66, M.A. 1966. Served in the Coldstream Guards, 1959–62. Married Annette Margot Kobak in 1966; one son and one daughter. Research Fellow and Instructor, School of Architecture and Planning, Massachusetts Institute of Technology, Cambridge, 1966–67; Deputy Controller, National Film Theatre, London, 1967–68. Senior Tutor, 1968–78, and since 1978, Pro-Rector, Royal College of Art, London. Regular contributor of articles on crime fiction for *London Magazine*, 1964–78. Recipient: Josephine de Kārmān Trust Scholarship, 1966. Fellow, Royal

College of Art, 1978. Agent: A. D. Peters and Company Ltd., 10 Buckingham Street, London
WC2N 6BU, England.

CRIME PUBLICATIONS

Novels

> *Drawn Blanc.*   London, Heinemann, 1970; New York, Coward McCann, 1972.
> *Somewhere in England.*   London, Heinemann, 1971; New York, St. Martin's Press,
> 1972.
> *Seduction of a Tall Man.*   London, Heinemann, 1972.
> *Something Worth Fighting For.*   London, Heinemann, 1974.
> *The Last Hours Before Dawn.*   London, Heinemann, 1975; as *Victoria*, New York,
> Coward McCann, 1975.
> *The Champagne Marxist.*   London, Hutchinson, 1977; as *The Cage*, New York,
> Coward McCann, 1977.

Uncollected Short Story

> "The Democratic Murder," in *Winter's Crimes 10*, edited by Hilary Watson.   London,
> Macmillan, 1978.

OTHER PUBLICATIONS

Other

> *Constable and His World.*   London, Thames and Hudson, and New York, Norton,
> 1976.
> *A Catalogue of Drawings and Watercolours by John Constable, R. A., with a Selection of
> Mezzotints by David Lucas after Constable for "English Landscape Scenery" in the
> Fitzwilliam Museum, Cambridge.*   London, Arts Council, 1976.

Manuscript Collection: Mugar Memorial Library, Boston University.

*   *   *

Reg Gadney has been called "a master of tightly-packed prose and fast-moving narrative"
by the *New York Times Review of Books*. It is, in fact, the swift narrative and sinewy prose
style which characterise his books. His subjects include international espionage, blackmail,
protection rackets, the war in Europe, and American Intelligence. The books are mostly set in
the underbelly of Europe, nearer to its thoroughfares of vice or its high society than the
respectable bourgeois territory which is more frequently found in the realms of British crime-
writing.

His audience is largely to be found among the younger generation of crime-fiction readers,
but, despite the high quality of his well-spaced output, he remains comparatively little known
in his native country.

—Herbert Harris

GAINHAM, Sarah. Pseudonym for Sarah Rachel Ames, née Stainer. British. Born 1 October 1922. Educated at Newbury High School for Girls, Berkshire. Married 1) Antony Terry; 2) Kenneth Ames in 1964 (died, 1975). From 1947 travelled in Eastern and Central Europe: Central Europe Correspondent for the *Spectator*, London, 1956–66. Lives in Austria. Address: c/o Macmillan London Ltd., 4 Little Essex Street, London WC2R 3LF, England.

CRIME PUBLICATIONS

Novels

  Time Right Deadly.   London, Barker, 1956; New York, Walker, 1961.
  The Cold Dark Night.   London, Barker, 1957; New York, Walker, 1961.
  The Mythmaker.   London, Barker, 1957; as *Appointment in Vienna*, New York, Dutton, 1958.
  The Stone Roses.   London, Eyre and Spottiswoode, and New York, Dutton, 1959.
  The Silent Hostage.   London, Eyre and Spottiswoode, and New York, Dutton, 1960.
  Night Falls on the City.   London, Collins, and New York, Holt Rinehart, 1967.

OTHER PUBLICATIONS

Novels

  A Place in the Country.   London, Weidenfeld and Nicolson, and New York, Holt Rinehart, 1969.
  Takeover Bid.   London, Weidenfeld and Nicolson, 1970; New York, Holt Rinehart, 1972.
  Private Worlds.   London, Weidenfeld and Nicolson, and New York, Holt Rinehart, 1971.
  Maculan's Daughter.   London, Macmillan, 1973; New York, Putnam, 1974.
  To the Opera Ball.   London, Macmillan, 1975; New York, Doubleday, 1977.

Other

  The Habsburg Twilight: Tales from Vienna.   London, Weidenfeld and Nicolson, and New York, Atheneum, 1979.

*   *   *

Sarah Gainham is now a well-known author in the field of the general novel. However, before abandoning the mystery/thriller, she was one of the most important of espionage-suspense writers. The first of her novels to lift her into the upper ranks of suspense was the brilliant *The Mythmaker*. The story unfolded against the background of the postwar years, when the once glittering city was under the occupation of the four allied powers, Russia, England, France, and the United States. Espionage was indigenous to the time and Gainham handled the material with authority and grace.

Time Right Deadly played against the same background. Its catalyst was the finding of the body of a London news correspondent in the Russian zone. Gainham was married to a London *Sunday Times* correspondent and with him traveled to all the trouble spots of Continental Europe. They were in Hungary for the abortive revolution there. All of her material was personally observed and translated later with invention into her books. One of the most intriguing of her novels was *The Silent Hostage*, which took place in Yugoslavia in its revolutionary period. Hungarian refugees, an English husband of one of the protagonists, and the partisans were all central to the plot. Whether writing of cities or the countryside,

Gainham brought a sensitivity to the scene as well as a special understanding of characters during political upheaval.

—Dorothy B. Hughes

GAITE, Francis. See **COLES, Manning.**

GALWAY, Robert Conington. See **McCUTCHAN, Philip.**

GARDINER, Dorothy. American. Born in Naples, Italy, 5 November 1894. Educated at the University of Colorado, Boulder. Executive Secretary, Mystery Writers of America, 1950–57. Address: 900 Delaware Avenue, Buffalo, New York, 14209, U.S.A.

CRIME PUBLICATIONS

Novels (series characters: Sheriff Moss Magill; Mr. Watson)

> *The Transatlantic Ghost* (Watson).   New York, Doubleday, and London, Harrap, 1933.
> *A Drink for Mr. Cherry* (Watson).   New York, Doubleday, 1934; as *Mr. Watson Intervenes*, London, Hurst and Blackett, 1935.
> *Beer for Psyche.*   New York, Doubleday, 1946; London, Hurst and Blackett, 1948.
> *What Crime Is It?* (Magill).   New York, Doubleday, 1956; as *The Case of the Hula Clock*, London, Hammond, 1957.
> *The Seventh Mourner* (Magill).   New York, Doubleday, 1958; London, Hammond, 1960.
> *Lion in Wait* (Magill).   New York, Doubleday, 1963; as *Lion? or Murder?*, London, Hammond, 1964.

Uncollected Short Story

> "Not a Lack of Sense," in *Big Times Mysteries*, edited by Brett Halliday.   New York, Dodd Mead, 1958.

OTHER PUBLICATIONS

Novels

The Golden Lady. New York, Doubleday, and London, Hurst and Blackett, 1936.
Snow-Water. New York, Doubleday, and London, Hurst and Blackett, 1939.
The Great Betrayal. New York, Doubleday, 1949; London, Hammond, 1956.

Other

West of the River. New York, Crowell, 1941.

Editor, *For Love or Money.* New York, Doubleday, 1957; London, Macdonald, 1959.
Editor, with Kathrine Sorley Walker, *Raymond Chandler Speaking.* Boston, Houghton Mifflin, and London, Hamish Hamilton, 1962.

*   *   *

The regional mystery is not common. Most mysterious activities seem to take place in the big cities, New York, London, Los Angeles, or their near countryside, but Dorothy Gardiner, one of the most proficient of regional writers, went far from the metropolitan centers for her books. She returned to her old home state of Colorado, not only for background material but for her characters, most important of whom was Sheriff Moss Magill. Colorado is a state which combines homely country atmosphere with ranching background, and both these regional elements feature in Gardiner's books.

Sheriff Magill is a country-and-western type, easy going but shrewd, with an authoritative sense of detection. He is a natural law man. Although he is customarily on his home ground, Gardiner did take him to the Scottish Highlands, which she knows well, for *The Seventh Mourner,* his most unusual adventure. Her contrasting the Highlands with the Rockies of Colorado, through the Sheriff's impressions, make this perhaps the best of the series.

For all of Gardiner's prowess as a writer, she made an even more important mark on the mystery scene as Executive Secretary of the Mystery Writers of America. No one was more important in shaping the organization and advancing it to its present high stature. From a handful of mystery writers and editors in the 1940's, standing together beneath the banner "Crime Does Not Pay – Enough," the MWA today is known and respected internationally for its championship of mystery writers. No small part of the present standing came through Dorothy Gardiner's eagle eye and forthright tongue. (When John Creasey initiated the Crime Writers Association in England, he had the assistance of Miss Gardiner.) She also helped prepare the first writings of Raymond Chandler to be published after his death, *Raymond Chandler Speaking.*

—Dorothy B. Hughes

GARDNER, Erle Stanley. Also wrote as A. A. Fair; Carleton Kendrake; Charles J. Kenny. American. Born in Malden, Massachusetts, 17 July 1889. Educated at Palo Alto High School, California, graduated 1909; Valparaiso University, Indiana, 1909; studied in law offices and admitted to the California Bar, 1911. Married 1) Natalie Talbert in 1912 (separated, 1935; died, 1968), one daughter; 2) Agnes Jean Bethell in 1968. Lawyer, Oxnard, California, 1911–18; salesman, Consolidated Sales Company, 1918–21; Lawyer, Ventura,

California, 1921–33. Contributed hundreds of stories, often under pseudonyms, to magazines, 1923–32; self-employed writer after 1933. Founder and member of the Court of Last Resort (now the Case Review Committee), 1948–60; frequent reporter on criminal trials; Founder of Paisano Productions, 1957. Honorary Life Member, American Polygraph Association. Recipient: Mystery Writers of America Edgar Allan Poe Award, 1952; Grand Master Award, 1961. Honorary alumnus: Kansas City University, 1955; D. L.: McGeorge College of Law, Sacramento, California, 1956. *Died 11 March 1970.*

CRIME PUBLICATIONS

Novels (series characters: Terry Clane; Sheriff Bill Eldon; Perry Mason; Doug Selby; Gramps Wiggins)

The Case of the Velvet Claws (Mason).   New York, Morrow, and London, Harrap, 1933.

The Case of the Sulky Girl (Mason).   New York, Morrow, 1933; London, Harrap, 1934.

The Case of the Lucky Legs (Mason).   New York, Morrow, and London, Harrap, 1934.

The Case of the Howling Dog (Mason).   New York, Morrow, 1934; London, Cassell, 1935.

The Case of the Curious Bride (Mason).   New York, Morrow, 1934; London, Cassell, 1935.

The Clew of the Forgotten Murder (as Carleton Kendrake).   New York, Morrow, and London, Cassell, 1935.

This Is Murder (as Charles J. Kenny).   New York, Morrow, 1935; London, Methuen, 1936.

The Case of the Counterfeit Eye (Mason).   New York, Morrow, and London, Cassell, 1935.

The Case of the Caretaker's Cat (Mason).   New York, Morrow, 1935; London, Cassell, 1936.

The Case of the Sleepwalker's Niece (Mason).   New York, Morrow, and London, Cassell, 1936.

The Case of the Stuttering Bishop (Mason).   New York, Morrow, 1936; London, Cassell, 1937.

The D.A. Calls It Murder (Selby).   New York, Morrow, and London, Cassell, 1937.

The Case of the Dangerous Dowager (Mason).   New York, Morrow, and London, Cassell, 1937.

The Case of the Lame Canary (Mason).   New York, Morrow, and London, Cassell, 1937.

Murder up My Sleeve (Clane).   New York, Morrow, 1937; London, Cassell, 1938.

The Case of the Substitute Face (Mason).   New York, Morrow, and London, Cassell, 1938.

The Case of the Shoplifter's Shoe (Mason).   New York, Morrow, 1938; London, Cassell, 1939.

The D.A. Holds a Candle (Selby).   New York, Morrow, 1938; London, Cassell, 1939.

The Case of the Perjured Parrot (Mason).   New York, Morrow, and London, Cassell, 1939.

The Case of the Rolling Bones (Mason).   New York, Morrow, 1939; London, Cassell, 1940.

The D.A. Draws a Circle (Selby).   New York, Morrow, 1939; London, Cassell, 1940.

The Case of the Baited Hook (Mason).   New York, Morrow, and London, Cassell, 1940.

The D.A. Goes to Trial (Selby).   New York, Morrow, 1940; London, Cassell, 1941.

The Case of the Silent Partner (Mason).   New York, Morrow, 1940; London, Cassell, 1941.

The Case of the Haunted Husband (Mason).   New York, Morrow, 1941; London, Cassell, 1942.

The Case of the Turning Tide (Wiggins).   New York, Morrow, 1941; London, Cassell, 1942.

The Case of the Empty Tin (Mason).   New York, Morrow, 1941; London, Cassell, 1943.

The D.A. Cooks a Goose (Selby).   New York, Morrow, 1942; London, Cassell, 1943.

The Case of the Drowning Duck (Mason).   New York, Morrow, 1942; London, Cassell, 1944.

The Case of the Careless Kitten (Mason).   New York, Morrow, 1942; London, Cassell, 1944.

The Case of the Smoking Chimney (Wiggins).   New York, Morrow, 1943; London, Cassell, 1945.

The Case of the Buried Clock (Mason).   New York, Morrow, 1943; London, Cassell, 1945.

The Case of the Drowsy Mosquito (Mason).   New York, Morrow, 1943; London, Cassell, 1946.

The D.A. Calls a Turn (Selby).   New York, Morrow, 1944; London, Cassell, 1947.

The Case of the Crooked Candle (Mason).   New York, Morrow, 1944; London, Cassell, 1947.

The Case of the Black-Eyed Blonde (Mason).   New York, Morrow, 1944; London, Cassell, 1948.

The Case of the Golddigger's Purse (Mason).   New York, Morrow, 1945; London, Cassell, 1948.

The Case of the Half-Wakened Wife (Mason).   New York, Morrow, 1945; London, Cassell, 1949.

The D.A. Breaks a Seal (Selby).   New York, Morrow, 1946; London, Cassell, 1950.

The Case of the Backward Mule (Clane).   New York, Morrow, 1946; London, Heinemann, 1955.

The Case of the Borrowed Brunette (Mason).   New York, Morrow, 1946; London, Cassell, 1951.

Two Clues (novelets; Eldon).   New York, Morrow, 1947; London, Cassell, 1951.

The Case of the Fan Dancer's Horse (Mason).   New York, Morrow, 1947; London, Heinemann, 1952.

The Case of the Lazy Lover (Mason).   New York, Morrow, 1947; London, Heinemann, 1954.

The Case of the Lonely Heiress (Mason).   New York, Morrow, 1948; London, Heinemann, 1952.

The Case of the Vagabond Virgin (Mason).   New York, Morrow, 1948; London, Heinemann, 1952.

The D.A. Takes a Chance (Selby).   New York, Morrow, 1948; London, Heinemann, 1956.

The Case of the Dubious Bridegroom (Mason).   New York, Morrow, 1949; London, Heinemann, 1954.

The Case of the Cautious Coquette (Mason).   New York, Morrow, 1949; London, Heinemann, 1955.

The D.A. Breaks an Egg (Selby).   New York, Morrow, 1949; London, Heinemann, 1957.

The Case of the Negligent Nymph (Mason).   New York, Morrow, 1950; London, Heinemann, 1956.

The Case of the Musical Cow.   New York, Morrow, 1950; London, Heinemann, 1957.

The Case of the One-Eyed Witness (Mason).   New York, Morrow, 1950; London, Heinemann, 1956.

The Case of the Fiery Fingers (Mason). New York, Morrow, 1951; London, Heinemann, 1957.

The Case of the Angry Mourner (Mason). New York, Morrow, 1951; London, Heinemann, 1958.

The Case of the Moth-Eaten Mink (Mason). New York, Morrow, 1952; London, Heinemann, 1958.

The Case of the Grinning Gorilla (Mason). New York, Morrow, 1952; London, Heinemann, 1958.

The Case of the Hesitant Hostess (Mason). New York, Morrow, 1953; London, Heinemann, 1959.

The Case of the Green-Eyed Sister (Mason). New York, Morrow, 1953; London, Heinemann, 1959.

The Case of the Fugitive Nurse (Mason). New York, Morrow, 1954; London, Heinemann, 1959.

The Case of the Runaway Corpse (Mason). New York, Morrow, 1954; London, Heinemann, 1960.

The Case of the Restless Redhead (Mason). New York, Morrow, 1954; London, Heinemann, 1960.

The Case of the Glamorous Ghost (Mason). New York, Morrow, 1955; London, Heinemann, 1960.

The Case of the Sun Bather's Diary (Mason). New York, Morrow, 1955; London, Heinemann, 1961.

The Case of the Nervous Accomplice (Mason). New York, Morrow, 1955; London, Heinemann, 1961.

The Case of the Terrified Typist (Mason). New York, Morrow, 1956; London, Heinemann, 1961.

The Case of the Demure Defendant (Mason). New York, Morrow, 1956; London, Heinemann, 1962.

The Case of the Gilded Lily (Mason). New York, Morrow, 1956; London, Heinemann, 1962.

The Case of the Lucky Loser (Mason). New York, Morrow, 1957; London, Heinemann, 1962.

The Case of the Screaming Woman (Mason). New York, Morrow, 1957; London, Heinemann, 1963.

The Case of the Daring Decoy (Mason). New York, Morrow, 1957; London, Heinemann, 1963.

The Case of the Long-Legged Models (Mason). New York, Morrow, 1958; London, Heinemann, 1963.

The Case of the Foot-Loose Doll (Mason). New York, Morrow, 1958; London, Heinemann, 1964.

The Case of the Calendar Girl (Mason). New York, Morrow, 1958; London, Heinemann, 1964.

The Case of the Deadly Toy (Mason). New York, Morrow, 1959; London, Heinemann, 1964.

The Case of the Mythical Monkeys (Mason). New York, Morrow, 1959; London, Heinemann, 1965.

The Case of the Singing Skirt (Mason). New York, Morrow, 1959; London, Heinemann, 1965.

The Case of the Waylaid Wolf (Mason). New York, Morrow, 1960; London, Heinemann, 1965.

The Case of the Duplicate Daughter (Mason). New York, Morrow, 1960; London, Heinemann, 1965.

The Case of the Shapely Shadow (Mason). New York, Morrow, 1960; London, Heinemann, 1966.

The Case of the Spurious Spinster (Mason). New York, Morrow, 1961; London, Heinemann, 1966.

The Case of the Bigamous Spouse (Mason). New York, Morrow, 1961; London, Heinemann, 1967.

The Case of the Reluctant Model (Mason). New York, Morrow, 1962; London, Heinemann, 1967.

The Case of the Blonde Bonanza (Mason). New York, Morrow, 1962; London, Heinemann, 1967.

The Case of the Ice-Cold Hands (Mason). New York, Morrow, 1962; London, Heinemann, 1968.

The Case of the Mischievous Doll (Mason). New York, Morrow, 1963; London, Heinemann, 1968.

The Case of the Stepdaughter's Secret (Mason). New York, Morrow, 1963; London, Heinemann, 1968.

The Case of the Amorous Aunt (Mason). New York, Morrow, 1963; London, Heinemann, 1969.

The Case of the Daring Divorcee (Mason). New York, Morrow, 1964; London, Heinemann, 1969.

The Case of the Phantom Fortune (Mason). New York, Morrow, 1964; London, Heinemann, 1970.

The Case of the Horrified Heirs (Mason). New York, Morrow, 1964; London, Heinemann, 1971.

The Case of the Troubled Trustee (Mason). New York, Morrow, 1965; London, Heinemann, 1971.

The Case of the Beautiful Beggar (Mason). New York, Morrow, 1965; London, Heinemann, 1972.

The Case of the Worried Waitress (Mason). New York, Morrow, 1966; London, Heinemann, 1972.

The Case of the Queenly Contestant (Mason). New York, Morrow, 1967; London, Heinemann, 1973.

The Case of the Careless Cupid (Mason). New York, Morrow, 1968; London, Heinemann, 1972.

The Case of the Fabulous Fake (Mason). New York, Morrow, 1969; London, Heinemann, 1974.

The Case of the Fenced-In Woman (Mason). New York, Morrow, 1972; London, Heinemann, 1976.

The Case of the Postponed Murder (Mason). New York, Morrow, 1973; London, Heinemann, 1977.

Novels as A. A. Fair (series characters: Bertha Cool and Donald Lam in all books)

The Bigger They Come. New York, Morrow, 1939; as *Lam to the Slaughter*, London, Hamish Hamilton, 1939.
Turn On the Heat. New York, Morrow, and London, Hamish Hamilton, 1940.
Gold Comes in Bricks. New York, Morrow, 1940; London, Hale, 1942.
Spill the Jackpot. New York, Morrow, 1941; London, Hale, 1948.
Double or Quits. New York, Morrow, 1941; London, Hale, 1949.
Owls Don't Blink. New York, Morrow, 1942; London, Hale, 1951.
Bats Fly at Dusk. New York, Morrow, 1942; London, Hale, 1951.
Cats Prowl at Night. New York, Morrow, 1943; London, Hale, 1949.
Give 'em the Ax. New York, Morrow, 1944; as *An Axe to Grind*, London, Heinemann, 1951.
Crows Can't Count. New York, Morrow, 1946; London, Heinemann, 1953.
Fools Die on Friday. New York, Morrow, 1947; London, Heinemann, 1955.
Bedrooms Have Windows. New York, Morrow, 1949; London, Heinemann, 1956.
Top of the Heap. New York, Morrow, 1952; London, Heinemann, 1957.
Some Women Won't Wait. New York, Morrow, 1953; London, Heinemann, 1958.

Beware the Curves. New York, Morrow, 1956; London, Heinemann, 1957.
You Can Die Laughing. New York, Morrow, 1957; London, Heinemann, 1958.
Some Slips Don't Show. New York, Morrow, 1957; London, Heinemann, 1959.
The Count of Nine. New York, Morrow, 1958; London, Heinemann, 1959.
Pass the Gravy. New York, Morrow, 1959; London, Heinemann, 1960.
Kept Women Can't Quit. New York, Morrow, 1960; London, Heinemann, 1961.
Bachelors Get Lonely. New York, Morrow, 1961; London, Heinemann, 1962.
Shills Can't Cash Chips. New York, Morrow, 1961; as *Stop at the Red Light*, London,
   Heinemann, 1962.
Try Anything Once. New York, Morrow, 1962; London, Heinemann, 1963.
Fish or Cut Bait. New York, Morrow, 1963; London, Heinemann, 1964.
Up for Grabs. New York, Morrow, 1964; London, Heinemann, 1965.
Cut Thin to Win. New York, Morrow, 1965; London, Heinemann, 1966.
Widows Wear Weeds. New York, Morrow, and London, Heinemann, 1966.
Traps Need Fresh Bait. New York, Morrow, 1967; London, Heinemann, 1968.
All Grass Isn't Green. New York, Morrow, and London, Heinemann, 1970.

Short Stories

The Case of the Murderer's Bride and Other Stories, edited by Ellery Queen. New
   York, Davis, 1969.
The Case of the Crimson Kiss. New York, Morrow, 1971; London, Heinemann, 1975.
The Case of the Crying Swallow. New York, Morrow, 1971; London, Heinemann,
   1974.
The Case of the Irate Witness. New York, Morrow, 1972; London, Heinemann, 1975.

OTHER PUBLICATIONS

Other

"The Coming Fiction Trend," in *Writer's Digest* (Cincinnati), September 1936.
"Doing It the Hard Way," in *Writer's Digest Year Book* (Cincinnati), 1937.
"Within Quotes," in *Writer's Digest* (Cincinnati), August 1938.
"They Wanted Horror," in *Writer's Digest* (Cincinnati), August 1939.
"The Greatest Detectives I Know," in *McClurg Book News* (Chicago), January–February
   1944.
"A Method to Mystery" (as A. A. Fair), in *The Writer* (Boston), August 1944.
"The Case of the Early Beginning," in *The Art of the Mystery Story*, edited by Howard
   Haycraft. New York, Simon and Schuster, 1946.
"Come Right In, Mr. Doyle," in *Atlantic Monthly* (Boston), September 1947.
"Is Clarence Boggie Innocent?" in *Argosy* (New York), September 1948 (first of the
   Court of Last Resort series: 75 articles between 1948 and October 1958).
The Land of Shorter Shadows. New York, Morrow, 1948.
The Court of Last Resort. New York, Morrow, 1952.
Neighborhood Frontiers. New York, Morrow, 1954.
"My Casebook of True Crime – Introduction," in *American Weekly* (New York), 4
   September 1955 (first of 28 articles between 1955 and 3 November 1957).
*The Case of the Boy Who Wrote "The Case of the Missing Clue" with Perry
   Mason.* New York, Morrow, 1959.
Hunting the Desert Whale. New York, Morrow, 1960.
Hovering over Baja. New York, Morrow, 1961.
The Hidden Heart of Baja. New York, Morrow, 1962.
The Desert Is Yours. New York, Morrow, 1963.
The World of Water. New York, Morrow, 1964.
Hunting Lost Mines by Helicopter. New York, Morrow, 1965.

"Getting Away with Murder," in *Atlantic Monthly* (Boston), January 1965.
Off the Beaten Track in Baja. New York, Morrow, 1967.
Gypsy Days on the Delta. New York, Morrow, 1967.
Mexico's Magic Square. New York, Morrow, 1968.
Drifting Down the Delta. New York, Morrow, 1969.
Host with the Big Hat. New York, Morrow, 1970.
Cops on Campus and Crime in the Streets. New York, Morrow, 1970.

Bibliography: "Bibliography of Erle Stanley Gardner" by Ruth Moore, in *The Case of the Real Perry Mason: A Biography* by Dorothy B. Hughes, New York, Morrow, 1978.

Manuscript Collection: Humanities Research Center, University of Texas, Austin.

*   *   *

Erle Stanley Gardner spent much of his childhood traveling with his mining-engineer father through the remote regions of California, Oregon, and the Klondike. In his teens he not only boxed for money but promoted a number of unlicensed matches. Soon after entering college he was, by his own account, expelled for slugging a professor. But in the practice of law he found the form of combat he seemed born to master. He was admitted to the California bar in 1911 and opened an office in Oxnard, where he represented the Chinese community and gained a reputation for flamboyant trial tactics. In one case, for instance, he had dozens of Chinese merchants exchange identities so that he could discredit a policeman's identification of a client. In the early 1920's he began to write western and mystery stories for magazines, and eventually he was turning out and selling the equivalent of a short novel every three nights while still lawyering during the business day. With the sale of his first novel in 1933 he gave up the practice of law and devoted himself to full-time writing, or more precisely to dictating. Thanks to the popularity of his series characters – lawyer-detective Perry Mason, his loyal secretary Della Street, his private detective Paul Drake, and the foxy trio of Sergeant Holcomb, Lieutenant Tragg and District Attorney Hamilton Burger – Gardner became one of the wealthiest mystery writers of all time.

The 82 Mason adventures from *The Case of the Velvet Claws* (1933) to the posthumously published *The Case of the Postponed Murder* (1973) contain few of the literary graces. Characterization and description are perfunctory and often reduced to a few lines that are repeated in similar situations book after book. Indeed virtually every word not within quotation marks could be deleted and little would be lost. For what vivifies these novels is the sheer readability, the breakneck pacing, the involuted plots, the fireworks displays of courtroom tactics (many based on gimmicks Gardner used in his own law practice), and the dialogue, where each line is a jab in a complex form of oral combat.

The first nine Masons are steeped in the hardboiled tradition of *Black Mask* magazine, their taut understated realism leavened with raw wit, sentimentality, and a positive zest for the dog-eat-dog milieu of the free enterprise system during its worst depression. The Mason of these novels is a tiger in the social-Darwinian jungle, totally self-reliant, asking no favors, despising the weaklings who want society to care for them, willing to take any risk for a client no matter how unfairly the client plays the game with him. Asked what he does for a living, he replies: "I fight!" or "I am a paid gladiator." He will bribe policemen for information, loosen a hostile witness's tongue by pretending to frame him for a murder, twist the evidence to get a guilty client acquitted and manipulate estate funds to prevent a guilty non-client from obtaining money for his defense. Besides *Velvet Claws*, perhaps the best early Mason novels are *The Case of the Howling Dog* and *The Case of the Curious Bride* (both 1934).

From the late 1930's to the late 1950's the main influence on Gardner was not *Black Mask* but the *Saturday Evening Post*, which serialized most of the Masons before book publication. In these novels the tough-guy notes are muted, "love interest" plays a stronger role, and Mason is less willing to play fast and loose with the law. Still the oral combat remains breathlessly exciting, the pace never slackens and the plots are as labyrinthine as before, most of them centering on various sharp-witted and greedy people battling over control of capital. Mason of course is Gardner's alter ego throughout the series, but in several novels of the second period another author-surrogate arrives on the scene in the person of a philosophical old desert rat or prospector who delights in living alone in the wilderness, discrediting by his example the greed of the urban wealth- and power-hunters. Among the best cases of this period are *Lazy Lover*; *Hesitant Hostess* which deals with Mason's breaking down a single prosecution witness; and *Lucky Loser* and *Foot-Loose Doll* with their spectacularly complex plots.

Gardner worked without credit as script supervisor for the long-running *Perry Mason* television series (1957–66), starring Raymond Burr, and within a few years television's restrictive influence had infiltrated the new Mason novels. The lawyer evolved into a ponderous bureaucrat mindful of the law's niceties, just as Burr played him, and the plots became chaotic and the courtroom sequences mediocre, as happened all too often in the TV scripts. But by the mid-1960's the libertarian decisions of the Supreme Court under Chief Justice Earl Warren had already undermined a basic premise of the Mason novels, namely that defendants menaced by the sneaky tactics of police and prosecutors needed a pyrotechnician like Mason in their corner. Once the Court ruled that such tactics required reversal of convictions gained thereby, Mason had lost his *raison d'etre*.

Several other detective series sprang from Gardner's dictating machine during his peak years. The 29 novels he wrote under the byline of A. A. Fair about diminutive private eye Donald Lam and his huge irascible partner Bertha Cool are often preferred over the Masons because of their fusion of corkscrew plots with fresh writing, characterizations, and humor, the high spots of the series being *The Bigger They Come* and *Beware the Curves*. And in his nine books about small-town district attorney Doug Selby, Gardner reversed the polarities of the Mason series, making the prosecutor his hero and the defense lawyer the oft-confounded trickster. But most of Gardner's reputation stems from Perry Mason, and his best novels in both this and his other series offer abundant evidence of his natural storytelling talent, which is likely to retain its appeal as long as people read at all.

—Francis M. Nevins, Jr.

GARDNER, John (Edmund). British. Born in Seaton Delaval, Northumberland, 20 November 1926. Educated at Cottham's Preparatory School, Newcastle on Tyne, 1931–34; King Alfred's School, Wantage, Berkshire, 1934–43; St. John's College, Cambridge, 1947–50, B.A. in theology 1950, M.A. 1951; St. Stephen's House, Oxford, 1950–52. Served in the Royal Navy and the Royal Marines, 1943–47: Commando Service in the Far and Middle East. Married Margaret Mercer in 1952; one daughter and one son. Entertainer, American Red Cross Entertainments Department, London, 1943; Clerk in Holy Orders, Church of England, 1952–58: spent some time as a Chaplain in the Royal Air Force; Theatre and Cultural Reviewer, Stratford upon Avon *Herald*, 1959–67. Lives in Wiltshire. Agent: Jonathan Clowes Ltd., 19 Jeffrey's Place, London NW1 9PP, England.

CRIME PUBLICATIONS

Novels (series characters: Professor Moriarty; Boysie Oakes; Derek Torry)

The Liquidator (Oakes). London, Muller, and New York, Viking Press, 1964.

The Understrike (Oakes).   London, Muller, and New York, Viking Press, 1965.
Amber Nine (Oakes).   London, Muller, and New York, Viking Press, 1966.
Madrigal (Oakes).   London, Muller, 1967; New York, Viking Press, 1968.
Founder Member (Oakes).   London, Muller, 1969.
A Complete State of Death (Torry).   London, Cape, and New York, Viking Press, 1969;
    as *The Stone Killer*, New York, Award, 1973.
Traitor's Exit (Oakes).   London, Muller, 1970.
The Airline Pirates (Oakes).   London, Hodder and Stoughton, 1970; as *Air Apparent*,
    New York, Putnam, 1971.
The Return of Moriarty.   London, Weidenfeld and Nicolson, and New York, Putnam,
    1974; as *Moriarty*, London, Pan, 1976.
The Corner Men (Torry).   London, Joseph, 1974; New York, Doubleday, 1976.
A Killer for a Song (Oakes).   London, Hodder and Stoughton, 1975.
The Revenge of Moriarty.   London, Weidenfeld and Nicolson, and New York, Putnam,
    1975.
To Run a Little Faster.   London, Joseph, 1976.
The Werewolf Trace.   London, Hodder and Stoughton, and New York, Doubleday,
    1977.
The Dancing Dodo.   London, Hodder and Stoughton, and New York, Doubleday, 1978.
The Nostradamus Traitor.   London, Hodder and Stoughton, and New York,
    Doubleday, 1979.

Short Stories

Hideaway.   London, Corgi, 1968.
The Assassination File.   London, Corgi, 1974.

OTHER PUBLICATIONS

Novels

The Censor.   London, New English Library, 1970.
Every Night's a Bullfight.   London, Joseph, 1971; as *Every Night's a Festival*, New
    York, Morrow, 1973.

Other

Spin the Bottle: The Autobiography of an Alcoholic.   London, Muller, 1964.
"Smiley at the Circus: Cold War Espionage," in *Murder Ink: The Mystery Reader's
    Companion*, edited by Dilys Winn.   New York, Workman, 1977.

John Gardner comments:
   To write a personal statement introducing one's work, seems to me to be an act of wanton
folly. Everything you say or write about yourself can, in turn, be written down and may be
used in evidence – colouring future critical comment and clouding more important issues. I
wince because I am still marked down by some people as being politically of the far left,
because of an interview with the *Morning Star* in the mid-sixties. In fact I am a political
observer with no allegiance to any one party or creed. The world, attitudes, economies, and
societies change with the rapidity of a scorpion's sting – and sometimes with as much pain
and danger. So, naturally, the work, if not the aim, of a suspense writer's fiction changes:
relevant one year; passé the next.
   For instance, the "Boysie Oakes" series of books was born in the hope of being an amusing
counter-irritant to the excesses of 007. They were meant to be irreverent, glossy black
comedies, edged with tight plotting, overloaded with belly laughs and vulgar schoolboy

humour. This seemed to be the way to provide an antidote to the snobby pseudo-sophistication of the Bond business. Looking back on it, that aim seems pretentious and, happily, Bond changed direction, the books becoming amusing send-ups of themselves when transferred to film. As for the Oakes books, they were a shade naughty at the time they were written. Now they seem tame, though my mail tells me they are still enjoyed.

So also, the two Derek Torry books were more of a comment on criminal violence, and the unpleasant side effects of that violence on those who have to deal with it. The Moriarty Journals were a different business: a peep into the past, and an attempt to recreate a fictional character – the arch-enemy of the stuffy Sherlock Holmes – within the framework of a factual reconstruction of the Victorian underworld. Here, the fun for me (and, one hopes, the reader) came in the creation of a secret criminal world, together with the language and methods of nineteenth-century crime.

In recent years, I have sought to combine the classic suspense story, together with espionage and detection of a different kind. At the time of writing, my last three books have – while grounded in the present – been aimed at the most recent past: World War II and its effect on contemporary characters.

The future? I think that, after one more attempt to recreate a classic suspense style from the past (this time, Shanghai of the early thirties in the style of Hollywood c.1945) it is probably ripe for the suspense story to take off into the future: not in terms of science fiction, but in political, military, and espionographical content.

The classic, "who-done-it?" detective story does not appeal to me, though there must always be more than a hint of mystery about suspense: certainly a maze to be entered, a puzzle to be solved. My main passions lie in the secret worlds of security services, politics, crime, and police agencies. Above everything else, however, I am convinced that these interests must be harnessed to one purpose as far as suspense fiction is concerned: the purpose of entertainment – in the fullest sense of the word. Through that one word the writer of suspense should bring to his readers both horror and laughter, joy and fear, delight and terror. If there is any merit in my past work – and, I trust, in work to come – then I would wish it to be no more than the merit of being entertaining.

*   *   *

John Gardner is one of those writers (Victor Canning is another) who are far more interested in the story they have to tell than the genre to which it might belong. His fictional debut, *The Liquidator*, is a good example of this: a spy story, clearly; equally clearly a comedy in a farcical (indeed, Rabelaisian) vein. Boysie Oakes (anti-hero of the book, and the subsequent series) was a risk that paid off handsomely: he embodied the missing ingredient (the belly-laugh) in spy stories up to that date. He was stupid, lecherous, a blunderer and a coward, who only made it to the end of each adventure by the skin of his teeth. The ironical jumping-off point of the series – that Boysie the government-hired hitman couldn't stand killing and had to hire someone else to do the dirty work – clearly couldn't last too long as a plot-device, but while it did Gardner extracted a good deal of black farce out of the situations into which he plunged his hapless hero. Perhaps most representative is *Amber Nine*, with a nicely complex plot played out on the shores of Lake Maggiore and involving plague-rockets and a splendid bunch of bizarre characters, including a demonic Javan killer-dwarf and a lady who might or might not be Hitler's daughter.

Cleverly, Gardner soon lifted his oafish hero out of the Intelligence service and turned him into a free-lance. Then, in 1970, he took five years' leave-of-absence from him – which is probably why the final book in the series, *A Killer for a Song*, is so good. The plot was well-worn (shadows from the past reaching out to threaten Boysie) but entertainingly handled, and that special blend of sex, farce, and tension peculiar to a Boysie book seemed all the more fresh after the lay-off.

Meanwhile, Gardner had diversified. There were two straight novels – one of which, the vastly entertaining *Every Night's a Bullfight*, was based on his intimate knowledge of the Royal Shakespeare Company – and two tightly-plotted tough-cop thrillers, *A Complete State of Death* and the superior *The Corner Men*, both featuring the sharply drawn Derek Torry, a Scotland Yard detective with religious problems. Two volumes of short stories, though readable enough, showed that Gardner was perhaps happier using a broader canvas, and this was certainly achieved with his two Moriarty books, superbly researched and written thrillers set in the late-19th Century and featuring the arch-criminal of the Sherlock Holmes saga.

After immersing himself in Victorian London for so long, he returned to the straight thriller with the under-rated Munich-era story *To Run a Little Faster. The Werewolf Trace* showed him to be in cracking form. A compulsively readable thriller with delicately-handled paranormal undertones and a bitter ending (the destruction of an innocent man by the monolithic and ruthless forces of the State), this is possibly his most flawless book to date.

What at first seems to be an astonishingly good horror novel – *The Dancing Dodo* – falls apart badly when the supernatural elements are rationalised in a slightly absurd and definitely long-winded (unusual for Gardner) explanation. A gripping climax doesn't quite save the book, though there are some fine characterisations. Happily *The Nostradamus Traitor* found him back on form with a vengeance, with an ingenious plot set once more in the world of Intelligence. Now, however, the style was sparer; the tone dry and witty rather than raucous. The characters were more ambiguous: the "villain" (just as in *The Werewolf Trace*) was shown to be not entirely villainous, and was allowed to escape in the end. Thus, under the cover of a rattling good yarn (something at which Gardner is an expert) there are often to be found moral statements – again, there's more to *Flamingo* (forthcoming) than merely a full-blooded tip of the hat to the Bogart-Greenstreet-Lorre films of the 1940's – and one invariably leaves the Gardner world stimulated as well as entertained.

—Christopher Lowder

GARFIELD, Brian (Francis Wynne). Also writes as Bennett Garland; Alex Hawk; Drew Mallory; Frank O'Brian; Brian Wynne; Frank Wynne; Jonas Ward. American. Born in New York City, 26 January 1939. Educated at Southern Arizona School, Tucson, graduated 1955; University of Arizona, Tucson, B.A. 1959, M.A. 1963. Served in the United States Army and Army Reserve, 1957–65. Married 1) Virve Sein in 1962 (divorced, 1965); 2) Shan Willson Botley in 1969. Musician and Bandleader, "The Palisades," 1959–63; Teaching Assistant in English, University of Arizona, 1962–63. Since 1963, self-employed writer. Since 1974, President, Shan Productions Company. Advertising Manager, Director, and Vice-President, 1965–69, and President, 1967–68, Western Writers of America; Director, Mystery Writers of America, 1974–78; Co-Organizer, Second International Congress of Crime Writers, New York, 1978. Lives part of each year in England. Recipient: Mystery Writers of America Edgar Allan Poe Award, 1976. Agent: Henry Morrison Inc., 58 West 10th Street, New York, New York 10011. Address: P.O. Box 376, Alpine, New Jersey 07620, U.S.A.

CRIME PUBLICATIONS

Novels (series characters: Paul Benjamin; Sam Watchman)

The Rimfire Murders (as Frank O'Brian).   New York, Bouregy, 1962.
The Last Bridge.   New York, McKay, 1966.
The Villiers Touch.   New York, Delacorte Press, 1970.

The Hit. New York, Macmillan, 1970.
What of Terry Coniston? Cleveland, World, 1971; London, Hodder and Stoughton, 1976.
Deep Cover. New York, Delacorte Press, 1971; London, Hodder and Stoughton, 1972.
Relentless (Watchman). Cleveland, World, 1972; London, Hodder and Stoughton, 1973.
Line of Succession. New York, Delacorte Press, 1972; London, Hodder and Stoughton, 1974.
Death Wish (Benjamin). New York, McKay, 1972; London, Hodder and Stoughton, 1973.
Tripwire. New York, McKay, 1973; London, Hodder and Stoughton, 1976.
Kolchak's Gold. New York, McKay, and London, Macmillan, 1974.
The Romanov Succession. New York, Evans, and London, Macmillan, 1974.
The Threepersons Hunt (Watchman). New York, Evans, 1974; London, Hodder and Stoughton, 1975.
Hopscotch. New York, Evans, and London, Macmillan, 1975.
Target Manhattan (as Drew Mallory). New York, Putnam, 1975.
Death Sentence (Benjamin). New York, Evans, 1975; London, Macmillan, 1976.
Recoil. New York, Morrow, and London, Macmillan, 1977.
Wild Times. London, Macmillan, 1979.

Uncollected Short Stories

"The Toll at Yaeger's Ferry," in *Toronto Star Weekly*, 17 July 1965.
"Ends and Means," in *Alfred Hitchcock's Mystery Magazine* (New York), February 1977.
"The Gun Law," in *Alfred Hitchcock's Mystery Magazine* (New York), March 1977.
"Hunting Accident," in *Ellery Queen's Mystery Magazine* (New York), June 1977.
"The Glory Hunter," in *Ellery Queen's Mystery Magazine* (New York), September 1977.
"Charlie's Shell Game," in *Ellery Queen's Mystery Magazine* (New York), February 1978.
"Joe Cutter's Game," in *Alfred Hitchcock's Anthology, Spring-Summer 1978*. New York, Davis, 1978.
"Checkpoint Charlie," in *Ellery Queen's Mystery Magazine* (New York), May 1978.
"Trust Charlie," in *Ellery Queen's Mystery Magazine* (New York), June 1978.
"Charlie's Vigorish," in *Ellery Queen's Mystery Magazine* (New York), August 1978.
"Challenge for Charlie," in *Ellery Queen's Mystery Magazine* (New York), October 1978.
"Charlie in Moscow," in *Ellery Queen's Mystery Magazine* (New York), November 1978.
"Jode's Last Hunt," in *Best Detective Stories of the Year 1978*, edited by Edward D. Hoch. New York, Dutton, 1978.
"Charlie in the Tundra," in *Ellery Queen's Mystery Magazine* (New York), January 1979.
"Charlie's Dodge," in *Ellery Queen's Mystery Magazine* (New York), March 1979.
"Passport for Charlie," in *Ellery Queen's Mystery Magazine* (New York), June 1979.

OTHER PUBLICATIONS

Novels

Range Justice. New York, Bouregy, 1960; as *Justice at Spanish Flat*, New York, Ace, 1961.
The Arizonans. New York, Bouregy, 1961.
The Lawbringers. New York, Macmillan, 1962; London, Long, 1963.

Trail Drive. New York, Bouregy, 1962.

Vultures in the Sun. New York, Macmillan, 1963; London, Long, 1964.

Apache Canyon. New York, Bouregy, 1963.

The Vanquished. New York, Doubleday, 1964.

Buchanan's Gun (as Jonas Ward). New York, Fawcett, and London, Hodder and Stoughton, 1968.

Savage Guns (as Alex Hawk). New York, Paperback Library, 1968.

Valley of the Shadow. New York, Doubleday, 1970; London, White Lion, 1973.

Sliphammer. New York, Dell, 1970.

Gun Down. New York, Dell, 1971; as *The Last Hard Men* (as Frank Wynne), London, Hodder and Stoughton, 1974.

Sweeny's Honor. New York, Dell, 1971; as Frank Wynne, London, Hodder and Stoughton, 1974.

Gangway!, with Donald E. Westlake. New York, Evans, 1973; London, Barker, 1975.

Wild Times. New York, Simon and Schuster, 1978; London, Macmillan, 1979.

Novels as Bennett Garland

Seven Brave Men. Derby, Connecticut, Monarch, 1962.

High Storm, with Theodore V. Olsen. Derby, Connecticut, Monarch, 1963.

The Last Outlaw. Derby, Connecticut, Monarch, 1964.

Rio Chama. New York, Award, 1968.

Novels as Frank O'Brian

Bugle and Spur. New York, Ballantine, 1966; as Brian Garfield, London, Sphere, 1968.

Arizona. New York, Ballantine, 1969.

Act of Piracy. New York, Dell, 1975.

Novels as Brian Wynne

Mr. Sixgun. New York, Ace, 1964.

The Night It Rained Bullets. New York, Ace, 1965.

The Bravos. New York, Ace, 1966.

The Proud Riders. New York, Ace, 1967.

A Badge for a Badman. New York, Ace, 1967.

Brand of the Gun. New York, Ace, 1968.

Gundown. New York, Ace, 1969.

Big Country, Big Men. New York, Ace, 1969.

Gunslick Territory. New York, Ace, 1973.

Novels as Frank Wynne

Massacre Basin. New York, Bouregy, 1961.

The Big Snow. New York, Bouregy, 1962.

Arizona Rider. New York, Bouregy, 1962.

Dragoon Pass. New York, Bouregy, 1963.

Rio Concho. New York, Bouregy, 1964.

Rails West. New York, Bouregy, 1964.

Lynch Law Canyon. New York, Ace, 1965.

The Wolf Pack. New York, Ace, 1966.

Call Me Hazard. New York, Ace, 1966.

The Lusty Breed. New York, Bouregy, 1966; London, Hale, 1974.

Other

The Thousand-Mile War: World War II in Alaska and the Aleutians. New York,
Doubleday, 1969.
"Suspense Is Where the Action Is," in *The Writer* (Boston), December 1976.
"Dear Mr. Garfield: An Author Opens His Mail," in *Murder Ink: The Mystery Reader's
Companion,* edited by Dilys Winn. New York, Workman, 1977.

Editor, *War Whoop and Battle Cry.* New York, Scholastic, 1968.
Editor, *I, Witness: True Personal Encounters with Crime by Members of the Mystery
Writers of America.* New York, Times Books, 1978.

Manuscript Collection: University of Oregon Library, Eugene.

Brian Garfield comments:
   I grew up in Arizona accustomed to having writers about the house, since a number of our
neighbors were writers and my mother was the cover-artist for *Saturday Review*; her job
entailed painting authors' portraits from life. By the time I was 12 or so I had concluded that
writing was not only an honorable calling but perhaps the only palatable one. Under the
tutelage of a sympathetic high-school English teacher and the late Western writer Frederick
D. Glidden ("Luke Short") I wrote dozens of short stories in my teens, but each time I sent
one to a pulp magazine the magazine died; this caused a bit of paranoia but finally I managed
to write a novel when I was 18 and, after three years' rejections from publishers, it appeared
in print in 1960 and after that I did not look back.
   For the next ten years I wrote mainly Westerns, most of them for fringe publishers and
paperback-original outfits; it was ephemeral apprenticeship work and I have retired nearly all
those books from circulation by repossessing the publication rights. The books don't
embarrass me but I'd rather not confuse the present book-buying world with relics.
   At the same time, however, I began to make tentative forays into crime fiction, war novels,
and historical stories. In my twenties I traveled extensively about the Western world, from
Helsinki to Tangier, from Istanbul to Loch Ness, from Berlin to Anchorage, from Montreal to
Tijuana; it became apparent there were things of interest in the world other than cowboys.
The sort of writing I do is rather a follow-your-nose operation; I become interested in an
idea, a place, a character, an event or a question, and proceed to write a book about it. This
seems to have induced apoplexy in several of my publishers over the past decade because they
find it impossible to type-cast me; I sympathize with their public-relations dilemma but
remain impatient with writers who keep writing the same book time and again. (One
suspects, sometimes, that they may plan to keep writing until they get it right.) Writers are
dreamers; dreamers are children; perhaps I am the sort of child whose attention-span is
limited; in any case each book I write tends to be quite different – in kind and in subject-
matter – from its predecessor; otherwise I risk boredom – and if the writer is bored how can
the reader be enthralled?
   As a result I do not particularly think of myself as a mystery-writer, a Western-writer, a
thriller-writer or any other sort of hyphenate. I'm simply a teller of tales. What they have in
common, I suppose, is a sense of dramatic conflict – they tend to be stories of action rather
than ratiocination or introspection, but I must hedge the word "action" a bit because usually I
tend to eschew extreme violence, both because of an aversion to it (a matter of taste) and
because I believe it is improper to confuse violence with suspense (a matter of judgment).
   Because of a popular film made from one of my books I seem to be known, if at all, as "the
author of *Death Wish*," and while the popularity and commercial success has been gratifying,
I nevertheless dislike the film and tend to resent the distorted public-image of my work that
Death Wish seems to have caused. That novel is the only modern urban crime thriller I've
written, and it is one of the very few books I've attempted in which there is not a heroic

protagonist. Unlike *Death Wish*, most of my novels are romances (in the old sense); I'm not at heart a cynic.

My claim to categorization as a "mystery writer" is tenuous. Normally my stories do not emphasize the unraveling of mysteries. Stanley Ellin defines the difference between mysteries and thrillers by pointing out that in the mystery a crime takes place at the beginning; in the thriller if there is a crime at all, it is more likely to take place at the end rather than the beginning. By that definition I suppose I'm a thriller writer. As a reader I find "pure" detective stories dehumanized and sterile and mathematical; insufficiently dramatic. Finally, in the matter of literacy: it seems to me we have reached a point in the history of popular literature at which the division is greater than ever before between writers and storytellers. Those who spin exciting yarns seem to be those who are incapable of writing good prose; those who write well are, by and large, incompetent or boring storytellers. In the main I find most contemporary fiction unreadable because either it has nothing to say or it has a great deal to say but says it badly. The stylists have turned inward; the yarnspinners disdain style. And this sorry state of affairs seems to have been compounded by the arrival on Publishers' Row of a new generation of editors whose sense of style and literacy is no greater than that of the yarnspinners. I suppose all this can be blamed on failures in our educational system but it is not a question of fixing blame; it is a question of curing an illness. We must re-join the divided art of popular literature; we must encourage new generations of writers who know the good and proper uses of language.

*   *   *

A prolific writer skillful in a variety of genres (ranging from westerns and historical tales – generally excluded from this discussion – to spy thrillers), Brian Garfield has produced only a few works, such as *The Hit* and *The Threepersons Hunt*, that fit the description of conventional mysteries. He has created no single sleuth, no Poirot or Maigret, whose continuing adventures fill most of his pages. A few characters, such as CIA operative Charlie Dark, do enjoy serial treatment, but their stories form only a small portion of Garfield's works; most characters play out their roles within a single book. In the few conventional mysteries, the main characters are busy tracking clues to a murder committed before the time of the novel's action; in the thrillers, they are busily trying to avoid becoming the victim of an impending crime. The American southwest is a favorite setting, but Garfield's characters also turn up in such diverse locations as Moscow's GUM, New York's Wall Street, and the bomb-shattered floor of the U.S. Senate.

While the players and places change, the world they define remains generally recognizable from novel to novel. It is a world threatened by such power-greedy organizations as the Mafia, FBI, CIA, and KGB; even the police threaten Garfield's world, although less by their villainy than by their institutional incompetence. Yet it is from the ranks of the agencies that many of Garfield's protagonists spring. By the time of their stories' action, however, they have become alienated and disillusioned. Simon Crane in *The Hit* (as much a thriller as a mystery, since Crane must solve the mystery to save his own life) is an ex-cop retired early, to his superiors' relief, because of an injury from a fellow policeman's gun. After having to battle both the Mafia and the police to solve the mystery, Crane trusts no official authorities to parcel out either justice or the loot: "the system thinks a lot about the rules of the game but never asks whether the game itself has any meaning." Even Sam Watchman in *Relentless* and *The Threepersons Hunt*, always working within the law as an Arizona State Trooper, is outside the full blessing of his force: he is repeatedly passed over for promotion because of his Navajo blood. In both novels, fellowship with victimized Indians more than blind professional loyalty keeps Watchman on the trail of justice.

Despite the menaces, however, Garfield's world is seldom hopeless. In it, strident but generally principled individualists can succeed in fighting off their foes, sometimes skirting but rarely defying conventional law. Paul Benjamin, the vigilante murderer in *Death Wish* and its sequel *Death Sentence*, is an exception: by far the most defiant of Garfield's characters, he is also the least effective in making peace with his world. In the end, he gives up his private brand of justice, rehabilitated in part by a remedy common in Garfield's novels: love. Never officially punished, Benjamin is nonetheless made to suffer; his penance is to give up the woman whose love brought him to reason and to live out his life imprisoned in loneliness. Love is frequently risky in Garfield's world, but it is just as frequently worth the risk, often swerving evil-doers, as in *Recoil* and *Deep Cover*, from their paths of violence.

Revenge motivates many of Garfield's characters, who spend much of their time pursued or in pursuit: "The hunting way of life is the only one natural to man" (*Hopscotch*). In Garfield's fundamentally moral world, however, the hunt need not climax in the kill. Charlie Dark is emphatic: "I flatly refuse to kill" ("Trust Charlie"). In fact, Fred Mathieson in *Recoil* squirms free of the Mafia without even harming anyone, although he does resort to blackmail and kidnapping. Garfield's world recognizes a difference between moral and written law, tolerating violations of certain written laws for the sake of moral justice. Murder, however, is intolerable, as even Paul Benjamin learns.

Occasionally, as in *Recoil*, the characters themselves take time to debate the moral issues their actions raise. More often, and more successfully, Garfield stops for nothing in the telling of his tales, and with simple and powerful language builds suspense well designed to keep the pages turning.

—Carol Ann Bergman

GARNETT, Roger.   See MORLAND, Nigel.

GARVE, Andrew.   Pseudonym for Paul Winterton; also writes as Roger Bax; Paul Somers.   British.   Born in Leicester, 12 February 1908. Educated at the London School of Economics; University of London, B.Sc. 1928. Staff Member, *Economist*, London, 1929–33; Reporter, Leader Writer, and Foreign Correspondent, London *News Chronicle*, 1933–46: in Moscow, 1942–45. Founding Member, and first Joint Secretary, Crime Writers Association, 1953. Address: c/o William Collins Sons and Company Ltd., 14 St. James's Place, London SW1A 1PS, England.

CRIME PUBLICATIONS

Novels

No Tears for Hilda.   London, Collins, and New York, Harper, 1950.
No Mask for Murder.   London, Collins, 1950; as *Fontego's Folly*, New York, Harper, 1950.
Murder in Moscow.   London, Collins, 1951; as *Murder Through the Looking Glass*, London, Harper, 1952.
A Press of Suspects.   London, Collins, 1951; as *By-Line for Murder*, New York, Harper, 1951.
A Hole in the Ground.   London, Collins, and New York, Harper, 1952.

The Cuckoo Line Affair. London, Collins, and New York, Harper, 1953.
Death and the Sky Above. London, Collins, 1953; New York, Harper, 1954.
The Riddle of Samson. London, Collins, 1954; New York, Harper, 1955.
The End of the Track. London, Collins, and New York, Harper, 1956.
The Megstone Plot. London, Collins, 1956; New York, Harper, 1957.
The Narrow Search. London, Collins, 1957; New York, Harper, 1958.
The Galloway Case. London, Collins, and New York, Harper, 1958.
A Hero for Leanda. London, Collins, and New York, Harper, 1959.
The Far Sands. New York, Harper, 1960; London, Collins, 1961.
The Golden Deed. London, Collins, and New York, Harper, 1960.
The House of Soldiers. New York, Harper, 1961; London, Collins, 1962.
Prisoner's Friend. London, Collins, and New York, Harper, 1962.
The Sea Monks. London, Collins, and New York, Harper, 1963.
Frame-Up. London, Collins, and New York, Harper, 1964.
The Ashes of Loda. London, Collins, and New York, Harper, 1965.
Murderer's Fen. London, Collins, 1966; as *Hide and Go Seek*, New York, Harper, 1966.
A Very Quiet Place. London, Collins, and New York, Harper, 1967.
The Long Short Cut. London, Collins, and New York, Harper, 1968.
The Ascent of D-13. London, Collins, and New York, Harper, 1969.
Boomerang. London, Collins, 1969; New York, Harper, 1970.
The Late Bill Smith. London, Collins, and New York, Harper, 1971.
The Case of Robert Quarry. London, Collins, and New York, Harper, 1972.
The File on Lester. London, Collins, 1974; as *The Lester Affair*, New York, Harper, 1974.
Home to Roost. London, Collins, and New York, Crowell, 1976.
Counterstroke. London, Collins, and New York, Crowell, 1978.

Novels as Roger Bax

Death Beneath Jerusalem. London, Nelson, 1938.
Red Escapade. London, Skeffington, 1940.
Disposing of Henry. London, Hutchinson, 1946; New York, Harper, 1947.
Blueprint for Murder. London, Hutchinson, 1948; as *The Trouble with Murder*, New York, Harper, 1948.
Came the Dawn. London, Hutchinson, 1949; as *Two If by Sea*, New York, Harper, 1949.
A Grave Case of Murder. London, Hutchinson, and New York, Harper, 1951.

Novels as Paul Somers (series character: Hugh Curtis)

Beginner's Luck (Curtis). London, Collins, and New York, Harper, 1958.
Operation Piracy (Curtis). London, Collins, 1958; New York, Harper, 1959.
The Shivering Mountain (Curtis). London, Collins, and New York, Harper, 1959.
The Broken Jigsaw. London, Collins, and New York, Harper, 1961.

Uncollected Short Stories

"The Downshire Terror," in *Ellery Queen's Mystery Magazine* (New York), June 1957.
"The Man Who Wasn't Scared," in *A Choice of Murders*, edited by Dorothy Salisbury Davis. New York, Scribner, 1958; London, Macdonald, 1960.
"Revenge," in *The Saint* (New York), September 1963.
"The Last Link," in *Best Detective Stories of the Year*, edited by Anthony Boucher. New York, Dutton, 1963.

"Who Would Steal a Mailbox?," in *John Creasey's Mystery Bedside Book 1969*, edited by Herbert Harris. London, Hodder and Stoughton, 1968.
"Line of Communication," in *Ellery Queen's Mystery Parade.* New York, New American Library, 1968.
"A Case of Blackmail," in *John Creasey's Mystery Bedside Book 1972*, edited by Herbert Harris. London, Hodder and Stoughton, 1971.
"A Glass of Port," in *Winter's Crimes 7*, edited by George Hardinge. London, Macmillan, 1975.

OTHER PUBLICATIONSas Paul Winterton

Other

A Student in Russia. Manchester, Co-operative Union, 1931.
Russia − with Open Eyes. London, Lawrence and Wishart, 1937.
Mending Minds: The Truth about our Mental Hospitals. London, Davies, 1938.
Eye-Witness on the Soviet War-Front. London, Russia Today Society, 1943.
Report on Russia. London, Cresset Press, 1945.
Inquest on an Ally (on Soviet foreign policy). London, Cresset Press, 1948.

Manuscript Collection: Mugar Memorial Library, Boston University.

*   *   *

Paul Winterton has used the pseudonym Andrew Garve for most of his suspense novels, though he has published several books as Roger Bax and Paul Somers. A fine craftsman, he is prolific as well as proficient, having turned out some 40 thrillers over the past four decades. What is most impressive about this productivity is the amazing variety that distinguishes it. Winterton does not rely on a familiar detective or recurring cast of characters − each new book is separate and discrete, each tale seeming to arise inevitably from the concurrence of personalities and settings. What does carry over from book to book is a straightforward, transparent writing style, and a certain type of hero, to all appearances ordinary, but whose perseverance and courage in crisis prove to be extraordinary. The diversity of the settings − English villages, the Scilly Isles, Ireland, France, Australia, Russia, the Baltic Sea and the Gulf of Finland, Africa, the Indian Ocean − is equalled by that of the sub-genres of suspense fiction this author handles with ease − detection, mystery, espionage, adventure, romance, and combinations thereof. Winterton's Russian experience, including his stint as a newspaper correspondent in Moscow during World War II, has been turned to good advantage in several stories, notably *Came the Dawn* (Bax), *Murder in Moscow*, *The Ashes of Loda*, *The Ascent of D-13*, and *The Late Bill Smith*. His knowledge of the Russians and the Soviet government lend these tales an unusual authenticity. His acquaintance with archaeology adds background for *The Riddle of Samson* and *The House of Soldiers*. Themes which reappear most frequently in the Winterton books, however, are small boats and the sea. The author has the knack of providing a wealth of information on these favorite topics in such an appealing way that even the most confirmed landlubber is fascinated. Two splendid sailing yarns, where the heroes overcome apparently insuperable odds, are *Came the Dawn* (Bax) and *A Hero for Leanda*. His sailors find adventure not only on the high seas, but in coastal waters, as in *The Megstone Plot* and *The File on Lester*. Other protagonists ply the waterways of England in canal boats, houseboats, dinghies, and other small craft. Only P. M. Hubbard among contemporary English thriller writers is so preoccupied with seamanship and other nautical matters.

Scotland Yard inspectors and assorted policemen figure in Winterton's stories, and they are not fools. Policemen gone bad make formidable villains: Stratton, for example, in *The Broken Jigsaw* (Somers), or Parker in *The End of the Track*. Some of Winterton's wrongdoers, when they are the central characters, arouse considerable sympathy because of the author's skill in portraying their feelings and motives, making them seem human, not so much worse than other people, exceptional only because of their ingenuity and boldness. In *The Megstone Plot*, the lustful and cynical ex-war hero Clive Easton, whose plotting is indisputably dishonorable, nevertheless retains some scruples, is physically courageous, and is a quite disarming narrator. Still more engaging outlaws are to be found in *The Long Short Cut* and *Boomerang*.

Most often, however, Winterton's heroes are private individuals forced by circumstances to use whatever strengths they have. When confronted by a situation which everybody else, including officialdom, accepts, these heroes achieve their ends – a daring rescue, the removal of an intolerable threat, the exoneration of a loved one – by persistence. In Winterton's detective stories this hero becomes the detective, an amateur indefatigably pursuing facts, testing theories, and finally arriving at a solution. *The Cuckoo Line Affair* contains just such a stubborn hero, doggedly determined to clear his father of a ruinous indictment. In *The Narrow Search*, the kidnapping of a baby is solved by clever reasoning and relentless investigation. Sometimes the police do the detecting, as in *Murderer's Fen* and *Frame-Up*.

Winterton excels at domestic murders, especially triangles of husband, wife, and lover. Although critics say that he never writes the same book – as indeed he does not – he explores certain themes such as the triangle from all different angles, each time constructing an absorbing book: *The Case of Robert Quarry*, for instance, or the ingenious *Home to Roost*. His classic *No Tears for Hilda*, in which a husband is charged with the murder of a really obnoxious wife, reveals his talent for depicting married couples and lovers in various combinations, connections which result in murder, with a typically satisfactory denouement. Families threatened from without, taking desperate action to survive, are shown in *The End of the Track*, *The Golden Deed*, and *The House of Soldiers*. The author, though occasionally writing about libertines, in numerous tales creates chivalrous romantic heroes, made more attractive because of their all too human doubts and imperfections. The unfolding of a love story often provides a more gentle suspense as counterpoint to the violent excitement of the adventure.

Winterton, so skilled at detailing domestic drama and familial felony, also concocts first-rate tales of high adventure. *The Sea Monks*, which recounts the confrontation between a group of murderous young hoodlums and a team of lighthouse keepers, is a good example. The evocation of the storm at sea and its devastating effects inside the lighthouse is memorable. A most admirable tale is *The Ascent of D-13*, a compelling account of mountain climbing on the Turkish-Russian frontier. The hazards of blizzard, avalanche, and East-West romance, combined with an eloquent passage in praise of mountaineering in general, and the superiority of freedom over totalitarianism, make a story that is Garve of the first order.

Paul Winterton by any other name would write as well! Not surprisingly, several of his books have been turned into successful films. Some of his earlier tales are more complicated than those of recent years. Simple, even austere, in regard to incident and number of characters, they are nevertheless gripping stories, forceful and fascinating. Winterton's suspense fiction is tasteful, discriminating, intelligent, at times ironic, and often witty. It is hard to praise him too highly, as he is surely one of the finest contemporary practitioners of the art.

—Mary Helen Becker

GASKIN, Catherine. Irish. Born in Dundalk, County Louth, 2 April 1929. Educated at Holy Cross College, Sydney, Australia. Married Sol Cornberg in 1955. Lived in London, 1948–55, and in New York, 1955–67. Address: Ballymacahara, Wicklow, County Wicklow, Ireland.

CRIME PUBLICATIONS

Novels

The Tilsit Inheritance. London, Collins, and New York, Doubleday, 1963.
The File on Devlin. London, Collins, and New York, Doubleday, 1965.
Edge of Glass. London, Collins, and New York, Doubleday, 1967.
Fiona. London, Collins, and New York, Doubleday, 1970.
A Falcon for a Queen. London, Collins, and New York, Doubleday, 1972.
The Property of a Gentleman. London, Collins, and New York, Doubleday, 1974.
The Lynmara Legacy. London, Collins, 1975; New York, Doubleday, 1976.
The Summer of the Spanish Woman. London, Collins, and New York, Doubleday, 1977.

OTHER PUBLICATIONS

Novels

This Other Eden. London, Collins, 1947.
With Every Year. London, Collins, 1949.
Dust in the Sunlight. London, Collins, 1950.
All Else Is Folly. London, Collins, and New York, Harper, 1951.
Daughter of the House. London, Collins, 1952; New York, Harper, 1953.
Sara Dane. London, Collins, 1954; Philadelphia, Lippincott, 1955.
Blake's Reach. London, Collins, and Philadelphia, Lippincott, 1958.
Corporation Wife. London, Collins, and New York, Doubleday, 1960.
I Know My Love. London, Collins, and New York, Doubleday, 1962.

*   *   *

Catherine Gaskin's novels of suspense have won for her an increasingly appreciative audience, in addition to the readers of her romances and historical novels. Gaskin's suspense fiction is usually of the gothic type, its typical old house and proud but tormented family providing the mystery. She has, however, her own specialty as she focuses upon a different art or craft in each of her books, with the details of her subject each time integral to the suspense plot. In *The Tilsit Inheritance*, she explores the making of fine bone china; in *Edge of Glass*, her subject is Irish glassblowing; *A Falcon for a Queen*, set in the Scottish highlands, concerns the making of fine malt whisky; *The Property of a Gentleman* is about the business of auctioning fine arts; in *The Summer of the Spanish Woman*, the family makes sherry in Jerez. In *The File on Devlin*, her one novel of international intrigue, a Nobel Prize-winning author disappears on a flight near Russia. It is left to his daughter and a British agent to discover what happened to him, partly by using clues in an unpublished manuscript. Often in Gaskin's books, the details of the artistic process provide evidence for the unfolding of the mystery, although she is less interested in detection and punishment than are many other gothic writers. In some books, the mystery is left unresolved; in others, there may be a suspected crime rather than a real one. In each book, however, the atmosphere of mystery and terror is strong.

Most of Gaskin's other works are romantic novels, a few with historical settings. These include two especially fine novels of early Australia, *Sara Dane* and *I Know My Love*. A recent novel, *The Lynmara Legacy*, a revision of an earlier book, is a sensitive domestic drama of World War II.

—Kay J. Mussell

GAULT, William Campbell. Also writes as Will Duke. American. Born in Milwaukee, Wisconsin, 9 March 1910. Educated at the University of Wisconsin, Madison, 1929. Served with the 166th Infantry, 1943–45. Married Virginia Kaprelian in 1942; one daughter and one son. Manager and part-owner, Blatz Hotel, Milwaukee, 1932–39. Since 1939 self-employed writer. Recipient: Mystery Writers of America Edgar Allan Poe Award 1953; Boys Club of America Junior Book Award, 1957. Agent: Harold Matson Company, 22 East 40th Street, New York, New York 10016. Address: 482 Vaquero Lane, Santa Barbara, California 93111, U.S.A.

Crime Publications

Novels (series characters: Brock Callahan; Joe Puma)

Don't Cry for Me. New York, Dutton, and London, Boardman, 1952.
The Bloody Bokhara. New York, Dutton, 1952; as *The Bloodstained Bokhara*, London, Boardman, 1953.
The Canvas Coffin. New York, Dutton, and London, Boardman, 1953.
Blood on the Boards. New York, Dutton, 1953; London, Boardman, 1954.
Run, Killer, Run. New York, Dutton, 1954; London, Boardman, 1955.
Ring Around Rosa (Callahan). New York, Dutton, and London, Boardman, 1955; as *Murder in the Raw*, New York, Dell, 1956.
Square in the Middle. New York, Random House, 1956; London, Boardman, 1957.
Day of the Ram (Callahan). New York, Random House, 1956; London, Boardman, 1958.
Fair Prey (as Will Duke). Hasbrouck Heights, New Jersey, Graphic, 1956; London, Boardman, 1958.
The Convertible Hearse (Callahan). New York, Random House, 1957; London, Boardman, 1958.
The Atom and Eve. New York, Fawcett, 1958; London, Boardman, 1959.
End of a Call Girl (Puma). New York, Fawcett, 1958; as *Don't Call Tonight*, London, Boardman, 1960.
Night Lady (Puma). New York, Fawcett, 1958; London, Boardman, 1960.
Death Out of Focus. New York, Random House, and London, Boardman, 1959.
Sweet Wild Wench (Puma). New York, Fawcett, 1959; London, Boardman, 1961.
The Wayward Widow (Puma). New York, Fawcett, 1959; London, Boardman, 1960.
Come Die with Me (Callahan). New York, Random House, 1959; London, Boardman, 1961.
Million Dollar Tramp (Puma). New York, Fawcett, 1960; London, Boardman, 1962.
The Hundred-Dollar Girl (Puma). New York, Dutton, 1961; London, Boardman, 1963.
Vein of Violence (Callahan). New York, Simon and Schuster, 1961; London, Boardman, 1962.
County Kill (Callahan). New York, Simon and Schuster, 1962; London, Boardman, 1963.
Dead Hero (Callahan). New York, Dutton, 1963; London, Boardman, 1964.

Uncollected Short Stories

"Marksman," in *Maiden Murders*, edited by John Dickson Carr. New York, Harper, 1952.
"Sweet Rolls and Murder," in *The Saint* (New York), October–November 1953.
"Night Work," in *The Saint* (New York), July 1954.
"The Sacrificial Lamb," in *The Saint* (New York), August 1955.
"Who's Buying Murder?" in *The Saint* (New York), December 1955.

"Be Smart, Really Smart," in *The Saint* (New York), December 1956.
"Don't Crowd Your Luck," in *Ellery Queen's Mystery Magazine* (New York), May 1957.
"Blood of the Innocent," in *The Saint* (New York), July 1957.
"Million Dollar Gesture," in *Best Detective Stories of the Year*, edited by David Coxe Cooke. New York, Dutton, and London, Boardman, 1958.
"Nobody Wants to Kill," in *The Saint* (New York), October 1959.
"The Cackle Bladder," in *Ellery Queen's Mystery Magazine* (New York), November 1960.

OTHER PUBLICATIONS

Other (juvenile fiction)

Thunder Road. New York, Dutton, 1952.
Mr. Fullback. New York, Dutton, 1953.
Gallant Colt. New York, Dutton, 1954.
Mr. Quarterback. New York, Dutton, 1955.
Speedway Challenge. New York, Dutton, 1956.
Bruce Benedict, Halfback. New York, Dutton, 1957.
Dim Thunder. New York, Dutton, 1958.
Rough Road to Glory. New York, Dutton, 1958.
Drag Strip. New York, Dutton, 1959.
Dirt Track Summer. New York, Dutton, 1961.
Through the Line. New York, Dutton, 1961.
Road-Race Rookie. New York, Dutton, 1962.
Two-Wheeled Thunder. New York, Dutton, 1962.
Little Big Foot. New York, Dutton, 1963.
Wheels of Fortune: Four Racing Stories. New York, Dutton, 1963.
The Checkered Flag. New York, Dutton, 1964.
The Karters. New York, Dutton, 1965.
The Long Green. New York, Dutton, 1965.
Sunday's Dust. New York, Dutton, 1966.
Backfield Challenge. New York, Dutton, 1967.
The Lonely Mound. New York, Dutton, 1967.
The Oval Playground. New York, Dutton, 1968.
Stubborn Sam. New York, Dutton, 1969.
Quarterback Gamble. New York, Dutton, 1970.
The Last Lap. New York, Dutton, 1972.
Trouble at Second. New York, Dutton, 1973.
Gasoline Cowboy. New York, Dutton, 1974.
Wild Willie, Wide Receiver. New York, Dutton, 1974.
The Big Stick. New York, Dutton, 1975.
Underground Skipper. New York, Dutton, 1975.
Showboat in the Backcourt. New York, Dutton, 1976.
Cut-Rate Quarterback. New York, Dutton, 1977.
Thin Ice. New York, Dutton, 1978.
Sunday Cycles. New York, Dodd Mead, 1979.

William Campbell Gault comments:
There isn't much I can say about my mystery novels. I sold all that I wrote through the years I was actively in the field. Ten years after I had left it, in 1962, I tried another mystery novel, but nobody wanted it (though it has recently been accepted for publication). I started to . concentrate on the juvenile novels in 1962. Though they weren't as much fun to write, they

stayed in print much longer, earning me considerably more money. My Edgar winner – *Don't Cry for Me* – came out in 1952 and was out of print two months later. In 1952, I also wrote a juvenile novel, *Thunder Road*, which is still in print. So, one has to eat.... My only mystery fame lately has been in someone else's novel – Ross Macdonald dedicated *The Blue Hammer* to me.

*   *   *

William Campbell Gault's detective and suspense novels are representative of the high standard of professionalism that marks the work of many of the genre writers who learned their trade in the pulp magazines and turned to the hardcover and paperback original market when the pulps folded. His work has been undeservedly neglected and long out of print, lost in the mass of mostly mediocre private-eye fiction that flooded the mystery field in the 1950's. His two series private eyes, Brock Callahan and Joe Puma, are memorable, believable characters, notable for their directness, integrity and – atypically for most 1950's private eyes – healthy, non-satyr-like relationships with women.

The usual scene is Southern California, and Gault covers that overworked territory with keen observation, coherent plotting, and fresh, direct writing. The familiar subjects for Los Angeles hardboiled novels are to be found in Gault's work: cars (Callahan versus hot car racketeers in *The Convertible Hearse*), cults (*Sweet Wild Wench*, with Puma), and the movie industry (*Death Out of Focus*); but the handling of these topics is far from hackneyed. Gault's primary career has been as a writer of juvenile sports fiction, and this interest surfaces in *Day of the Ram*, in which Callahan, an ex-football player himself, investigates the blackmailing of a pro football star. *The Canvas Coffin* is a gritty novel about boxing. Gault's one major departure from the California venue is *The Bloody Bokhara*, which involves murder among Armenian rug dealers in Milwaukee.

Anthony Boucher was a consistent champion of Gault's work, calling it "consistently rewarding and refreshing."

—Art Scott

GIBBS, Henry.   See **HARVESTER, Simon.**

GIBSON, Walter B.   Also writes as Ishi Black; Douglas Brown; Maxwell Grant; Maborushi Kineji.   American.   Born in 1897. Married to Litzka R. Gibson. Free-lance writer: wrote The Shadow stories for *The Shadow* magazine and Norgil stories for *Crime Busters*; wrote *The Shadow* comic books, 1941–47. Lives in Kingston, New York.

CRIME PUBLICATIONS

Novels

A Blonde for Murder. Chicago, Atlas, 1948.
Looks that Kill. Chicago, Atlas, 1948.
Anne Bonny, Pirate Queen. Derby, Connecticut, Monarch, 1962.

Novels as Maxwell Grant (series character: Lamont Cranston, The Shadow, in all books)

The Living Shadow. New York, Street and Smith, 1931; London, New English Library, 1976.
Eyes of the Shadow. New York, Street and Smith, 1931.
The Shadow Laughs. New York, Street and Smith, 1931.
The Shadow and the Voice of Murder. Los Angeles, Bantam, 1945.
Return of the Shadow. New York, Belmont, 1963.
The Weird Adventures of the Shadow: Grove of Doom, Voodoo Death, Murder by Moonlight. New York, Grosset and Dunlap, 1966.
The Death Tower. New York, Bantam, 1969.
Gangdom's Doom. New York, Bantam, 1970.
The Ghost Makers. New York, Bantam, 1970.
Hidden Death. New York, Bantam, 1970.
The Mobsmen on the Spot. New York, Pyramid, 1974; London, New English Library, 1976.
The Black Master. New York, Pyramid, 1974; London, New English Library, 1975.
The Red Menace. New York, Pyramid, 1975.
The Crime Oracle and The Teeth of the Dragon: Two Adventures of the Shadow. New York, Dover, and London, Constable, 1975.
The Shadow: The Mask of Mephisto and Murder by Magic. New York, Doubleday, 1975.
Mox: From the Shadow's Private Annals. New York, Pyramid, 1975.
The Romanoff Jewels. New York, Pyramid, 1975.
The Crime Cult. New York, Pyramid, 1975.
The Silent Seven. New York, Pyramid, 1975.
Double Z. New York, Pyramid, 1975.
Hands in the Dark. New York, Pyramid, 1975; London, New English Library, 1977.
Kings of Crime. New York, Pyramid, n.d.
Shadowed Millions. New York, Pyramid, n.d.
Green Eyes. New York, Pyramid, n.d.
The Creeping Death. New York, Pyramid, n.d.
Gray Fist. New York, Pyramid, n.d.
The Shadow's Shadow. New York, Pyramid, n.d.
Fingers of Death. New York, Pyramid, n.d.
Murder Trail. New York, Pyramid, n.d.
Zemba. New York, Pyramid, n.d.
Charg, Monster. New York, Pyramid, n.d.
The Wealth Seeker. New York, Pyramid, n.d.
The Silent Death. New York, Pyramid, n.d.
The Shadow: A Quarter of Eight and The Freak Show Murders. New York, Doubleday, 1978.
The Death Giver. New York, Harcourt Brace, 1978.
The Shadow: Crime over Casco and The Mother Goose Murders. New York, Doubleday, 1979.

Short Stories

Norgil the Magician. Yonkers, New York, Mysterious Press, 1976.
Norgil: More Tales of Prestidigitation. Yonkers, New York, Mysterious Press, 1979.

Uncollected Novels as Maxwell Grant (series character: Lamont Cranston, The Shadow in all works; all works appeared in *The Shadow* magazine, New York)

"The Blackmail Ring," August 1932; "The Five Chameleons," 1 November 1932; "Dead Men Live," 15 November 1932; "Six Men of Evil," 15 February 1933; "The Shadow's Justice," 15 April 1933; "The Golden Grotto," 1 May 1933; "The Red Blot," 1 June 1933; "The Ghost of the Manor," 15 June 1933; "The Living Joss," 1 July 1933; "The Silver Scourge," 15 July 1933; "The Black Hush," 1 August 1933; "The Isle of Doubt," 15 August 1933; "Master of Death," 15 September 1933; "Road of Crime," 1 October 1933; "The Death Triangle," 15 October 1933; "The Killer," 1 November 1933; "The Crime Clinic," 1 December 1933; "Treasures of Death," 15 December 1933; "The Embassy Murders," 1 January 1934; "The Black Falcon," 1 February 1934; "The Circle of Death," 1 March 1934; "The Green Box," 15 March 1934; "The Cobra," 1 April 1934; "Crime Circus," 15 April 1934; "Tower of Death," 1 May 1934; "Death Clew," 15 May 1934; "The Key," 1 June 1934; "The Crime Crypt," 15 June 1934; "Chain of Death," 15 July 1934; "The Crime Master," 1 August 1934; "Gypsy Vengeance," 15 August 1934; "Spoils of The Shadow," 1 September 1934; "The Garaucan Swindle," 15 September 1934; "Murder Marsh," 1 October 1934; "The Death Sleep," 15 October 1934; "The Chinese Disks," 1 November 1934; "Doom on the Hill," 15 November 1934; "The Unseen Killer," 1 December 1934; "Cyro," 15 December 1934; "The Four Signets," 1 January 1935; "The Blue Sphinx," 15 January 1935; "The Plot Master," 1 February 1935; "The Dark Death," 15 February 1935; "Crooks Go Straight," 1 March 1935; "Bells of Doom," 15 March 1935; "Lingo," 1 April 1935; "The Triple Trail," 15 April 1935; "The Golden Quest," 1 May 1935; "The Third Skull," 15 May 1935; "Murder Every Hour," 1 June 1935; "The Condor," 15 June 1935; "The Fate Joss," 1 July 1935; "Atoms of Death," 15 July 1935; "The Man from Scotland Yard," 1 August 1935; "The Creeper," 15 August 1935; "The Mardi Gras Mystery," 1 September 1935; "The London Crimes," 15 September 1935; "The Ribbon Clues," 1 October 1935; "The House That Vanished," 15 October 1935; "The Chinese Tapestry," 1 November 1935; "The Python," 15 November 1935; "The Case of Congressman Coyd," 15 December 1935; "The Ghost Murders," 1 January 1936; "Castle of Doom," 15 January 1936; "Death Rides the Skyway," 1 February 1936; "The North Woods Mystery," 15 February 1936; "The Voodoo Master," 1 March 1936; "The Third Shadow," 15 March 1936; "The Salamanders," 1 April 1936; "The Man from Shanghai," 15 April 1936; "The Gray Ghost," 1 May 1936; "The City of Doom," 15 May 1936; "Murder Town," 15 June 1936; "The Yellow Door," 1 July 1936; "The Broken Napoleons," 15 July 1936; "The Sledge Hammer Crimes," 1 August 1936; "Terror Island," 15 August 1936; "The Golden Masks," 1 September 1936; "Jibaro Death," 15 September 1936; "City of Crime," 1 October 1936; "Death by Proxy," 15 October 1936; "The Strange Disappearance of Joe Cardona," 15 November 1936; "The Seven Drops of Blood," 1 December 1936; "Intimidation, Inc.," 15 December 1936; "Vengeance Is Mine," 1 January 1937; "Loot of Death," 1 February 1937; "Quetzal," 15 February 1937; "Death Token," 1 March 1937; "Murder House," 15 March 1937; "Washington Crime," 1 April 1937; "The Masked Headsman," 15 April 1937; "Treasure Trail," 15 May 1937; "Brothers of Doom," 1 June 1937; "The Shadow's Rival," 15 June 1937; "Crime, Insured," 1 July 1937; "House of Silence," 15 July 1937; "The Shadow Unmasks," 1 August 1937; "The Yellow Band," 15 August 1937; "Buried Evidence," 1 September 1937; "The Radium Murders," 15 September 1937; "The Keeper's Gold," 15 October 1937; "Death Turrets," 1

November 1937; "The Sealed Box," 1 December 1937; "Racket Town," 15 December 1937; "The Crystal Buddha," 1 January 1938; "Hills of Death," 15 January 1938; "The Murder Master," 15 February 1938; "The Golden Pagoda," 1 March 1938; "Face of Doom," 15 March 1938; "Serpents of Siva," 15 April 1938; "Cards of Death," 1 May 1938; "The Hand," 15 May 1938; "Voodoo Trail," 1 June 1938; "The Rackets King," 15 June 1938; "Murder for Sale," 1 July 1938; "The Golden Vulture" with Lester Dent, 15 July 1938; "Death Jewels," 1 August 1938; "The Green Hoods," 15 August 1938; "Crime over Boston," 15 September 1938; "The Dead Who Lived," 1 October 1938; "Vanished Treasure," 15 October 1938; "The Voice," 1 November 1938; "Chicago Crime," 15 November 1938; "Shadow over Alcatraz," 1 December 1938; "Silver Skull," 1 January 1939; "Crime Rides the Sea," 15 January 1939; "Realm of Doom," 1 February 1939; "The Lone Tiger," 15 February 1939; "The Vindicator," 15 March 1939; "Death Ship," 1 April 1939; "Battle of Greed," 15 April 1939; "The Three Brothers," 15 May 1939; "Smugglers of Death," 1 June 1939; "City of Shadows," 15 June 1939; "Death from Nowhere," 15 July 1939; "Isle of Gold," 1 August 1939; "Wizard of Crime," 15 August 1939; "The Crime Ray," 1 September 1939; "The Golden Master," 15 September 1939; "Castle of Crime," 1 October 1939; "The Masked Lady," 15 October 1939; "Ships of Doom," 1 November 1939; "City of Ghosts," 15 November 1939; "Shiwan Khan Returns," 1 December 1939; "House of Shadows," 15 December 1939; "Death Premium," 1 January 1940; "The Hooded Circle," 15 January 1940; "The Getaway Ring," 1 February 1940; "Voice of Death," 15 February 1940; "The Invincible Shiwan Khan," 1 March 1940; "The Veiled Prophet," 15 March 1940; "The Spy Ring," 1 April 1940; "Death in the Stars," 1 May 1940; "Masters of Death," 15 May 1940; "The Scent of Death," 1 June 1940; "Q," 15 June 1940; "Gems of Doom," 15 July 1940; "Crime at Seven Oaks," 1 August 1940; "The Fifth Face," 15 August 1940; "Crime County," 1 September 1940; "The Wasp," 1 October 1940; "Crime over Miami," 1 November 1940; "Xitli, God of Fire," 1 December 1940; "The Shadow, The Hawk, and the Skull," 15 December 1940; "Forgotten Gold," 1 January 1941; "The Wasp Returns," 1 February 1941; "The Chinese Primrose," 15 February 1941; "Mansion of Crime," 1 March 1941; "The Time Master," 1 April 1941; "The House on the Ledge," 15 April 1941; "The League of Death," 1 May 1941; "Crime under Cover," 1 June 1941; "The Thunder King," 15 June 1941; "The Star of Delhi," 1 July 1941; "The Blur," 15 July 1941; "The Shadow Meets the Mask," 15 August 1941; "The Devil-Master," 15 September 1941; "Garden of Death," 1 October 1941; "Dictator of Crime," 15 October 1941; "The Blackmail King," 1 November 1941; "Temple of Crime," 15 November 1941; "Murder Mansion," 1 December 1941; "Crime's Stronghold," 15 December 1941; "Alibi Trail," 1 January 1942; "The Book of Death," 15 January 1942; "Death Diamonds," 1 February 1942; "Vengeance Bay," 1 March 1942; "Formula for Crime," 15 March 1942; "Room of Doom," 1 April 1942; "The Jade Dragon," 15 April 1942; "The Northdale Mystery," 1 May 1942; "Twins of Crime," 1 June 1942; "The Devil's Feud," 15 June 1942; "Five Ivory Boxes," 1 July 1942; "Death about Town," 15 July 1942; "Legacy of Death," 1 August 1942; "Judge Lawless," 15 August 1942; "The Vampire Murders," 1 September 1942; "Clue for Clue," 15 October 1942; "Trail of Vengeance," 1 November 1942; "The Murdering Ghost," 15 November 1942; "The Hydra," 1 December 1942; "The Money Master," 15 December 1942; "The Museum Murders," 1 January 1943; "Death's Masquerade," 15 January 1943; "The Devil Monsters," 1 February 1943; "Wizard of Crime," 15 February 1943; "The Black Dragon," 1 March 1943; "The Robot Master," May 1943; "Murder Lake," June 1943; "Messenger of Death," August 1943; "House of Ghosts," September 1943; "King of the Black Market," October 1943; "The Muggers," November 1943; "The Crystal Skull," January 1944; "Syndicate of Death," February 1944; "The Toll of Death," March 1944; "Crime Caravan," April 1944; "Town of Hate," July 1944; "Death in the Crystal," August 1944; "The Chest of Chu-Chan," September 1944;

"Fountain of Death," November 1944; "No Time for Murder," December 1944; "Guardian of Death," January 1945; "Merry Mrs. Macbeth," February 1945; "Five Keys to Crime," March 1945; "Death Has Gray Eyes," April 1945; "Teardrops of Buddha," May 1945; "Three Stamps of Death," June 1945; "The Taiwan Joss," September 1945; "The White Skulls," November 1945; "The Stars Promise Death," December 1945; "The Banshee Murders," January 1946; "Crime Out of Mind," February 1946; "The Curse of Thoth," May 1946; "Alibi Trail," June 1946; "Malmordo," July 1946; "Jade Dragon," August–September 1948; "Dead Man's Chest," Fall 1948; "The Magigal's Mystery," Winter 1949; "The Black Circle," Spring 1949; "The Whispering Eyes," Summer 1949.

OTHER PUBLICATIONS

Other

After Dinner Tricks. Columbus, Ohio, Magic Publishing Company, 1921.
Practical Card Tricks. Hika, Wisconsin, Mill, 1921.
The Book of Secrets, Miracles Ancient and Modern. Scranton, Pennsylvania, Personal Arts, 1927.
The Bunco Book. Privately printed, 1927.
The Magic Square. New York, Scully, 1927.
The Mystic Fortune Teller. New York, Scully, 1927.
The Science of Numerology. New York, Scully, 1927.
The World's Best Book of Magic. Philadelphia, Penn, 1927.
Popular Card Tricks. New York, E.I., 1928.
Brain Tests. Boston, Page, 1930.
Houdini's Escapes. New York, Harcourt Brace, 1930.
Houdini's Magic. New York, Harcourt Brace, 1932.
Magic Made Easy. Springfield, Massachusetts, McLoughlin, 1932.
Magician's Manual. New York, Magician's League of America, 1933.
The New Magician's Manual. New York, Kemp, 1936.
Secrets of Magic. New York, Popper, 1945.
Professional Magic for Amateurs. New York, Prentice Hall, 1947; London, Kaye, 1948.
Magic Explained. New York, Doubleday, 1949.
The Key to Hypnotism. Baltimore, Oppenheimer, 1956.
What's New in Magic? New York, Hanover House, 1956.
The Key to Astronomy. New York, Key, 1958.
The Key to Judo and Jiujitsu (as Ishi Black). New York, Key, 1958.
The Key to Yoga. New York, Key, 1958.
Magic Explained. New York, Vista House, 1958.
Astrology Explained. New York, Vista House, 1959.
Fell's Official Guide to Knots and How to Tie Them. New York, Fell, 1961.
Houdini's Fabulous Magic, with Morris N. Young. Philadelphia, Chilton, 1961.
Hypnotism Through the Ages. New York, Vista House, 1961.
Judo: Attack and Defense (as Maborushi Kineji). New York, Vista House, 1961.
Fell's Guide to Papercraft Tricks, Games, and Puzzles. New York, Fell, 1963.
Magic Made Simple. New York, Doubleday, 1963.
Hoyle's Simplified Guide to the Popular Card Games. New York, Doubleday, 1963; revised edition, 1971.
How to Win at Solitaire. New York, Doubleday, 1964.
Hoyle Card Games: Reference Crammer. New York, Ken, 1964.
The Complete Illustrated Book of the Psychic Sciences, with Litzka R. Gibson. New York, Doubleday, 1966; London, Souvenir Press, 1967.
How to Bet the Harness Races. New York, Doubleday, 1966.

The Key to Solitaire (as Douglas Brown).   New York, Bell, 1966.
The Master Magicians: Their Lives and Most Famous Tricks.   New York, Doubleday, 1966.
Secrets of Magic, Ancient and Modern.   New York, Grosset and Dunlap, 1967.
Winning the $2 Bet.   New York, Doubleday, 1967.
Magic with Science.   New York, Grosset and Dunlap, 1968.
How to Develop an Exceptional Memory, with Morris N. Young.   Hollywood, Wilshire, 1968.
Dreams.   New York, Constellation International, 1969.
The Mystic and Occult Arts, with Litzka R. Gibson.   West Nyack, New York, Parker, 1969.
The Complete Illustrated Book of Card Magic.   New York, Doubleday, 1969.
Family Games America Plays.   New York, Doubleday, 1970.
Hypnotism.   New York, Grosset and Dunlap, 1970.
What Are the Odds?, with Melvin Evans.   New York, Western, 1972.
Witchcraft.   New York, Grosset and Dunlap, 1973.
The Complete Illustrated Book of Divination and Prophecy, with Litzka R. Gibson.   London, Souvenir Press, 1974; New York, New American Library, 1975.
Hoyle's Modern Encyclopedia of Card Games.   New York, Doubleday, and London, Hale, 1974.
Fell's Guide to Winning Backgammon.   New York, Fell, 1974.
Pinochle Is the Name of the Game.   New York, Barnes and Noble, 1974.
Poker Is the Name of the Game.   New York, Harper, 1974.
Fell's Beginner's Guide to Magic.   New York, Fell, 1976.
Walter Gibson's Encyclopedia of Magic and Conjuring.   New York, Drake, 1976.
Mastering Magic.   New York, Fell, 1977.
How to Win at Backgammon.   New York, Grosset and Dunlap, 1978.

Editor, *Houdini on Magic.*   New York, Dover, 1953.
Editor, *The Fine Art of Murder* [*Spying, Robbery, Swindling*].   New York, Grosset and Dunlap, 4 vols., 1965–66.
Editor, *Rogue's Gallery: A Variety of Mystery Stories.*   New York, Doubleday, 1969.
Editor, *The Original Houdini Scrapbook.*   New York, Corwin Sterling, 1976.
Editor, *The Shadow Scrapbook.*   New York, Harcourt Brace, 1979.

Bibliography: *Gangland's Doom* by Frank Eisgruber, Jr., Oaklawn, Illinois, Robert Weinberg, 1974; *Duende History of The Shadow Magazine* by Will Murray, New York, Odyssey, 1979.

*   *   *

The mystery story writer and the professional stage magician share many of the same techniques in the execution of their respective crafts. Whether it be the creation of a successful illusion or the crafting of an intricate mystery, the professional in each case intends to create a precise *effect* while concealing from his audience the mechanisms by which he achieves that effect. Mystery, drama, deception, and misdirection are the essential techniques employed. Unlike the magician who will never reveal his secrets for fear of destroying his illusions, the mystery writer must reveal all for his story to succeed.

Many writers have consciously applied the illusionist's techniques to the mystery story but few have done so with greater ability than has Walter B. Gibson, himself a magician and a confidant of Houdini, Thurston, and Dunninger. Gibson was conversant with all aspects of the Black Arts, having written several books and articles on magic and its modern practitioners, when he was asked to create the lead character for the Street and Smith pulp, *The Shadow Magazine.* Under the pseudonym Maxwell Grant, he wrote nearly 300 Shadow novels.

The Shadow is Gibson's signal contribution to the detective story genre and to popular literature. He is a Machiavellian creation, a crepuscular version of Sherlock Holmes garbed in a magician's cloak. The Shadow, like Holmes, is an analytical, passionless intellect engaged in the pursuit of criminals for reasons which are intrinsic to his nature but extrinsic of the published stories. He appears, however, to regard the processes of suppressing criminal activity as a game, rather like chess, but one in which there are no set rules. Like Leblanc's Arsène Lupin, whom The Shadow also resembles, he flagrantly disregards the law in favor of his own ideal of justice. Unlike his predecessors, The Shadow relies equally upon deduction and gunplay.

Gibson infused his Shadow mysteries with magician's lore. Although few Shadow stories had as their background the world of the professional magician, as do *Murder by Magic* and *The Magigals Mystery*, illusionist's paraphernalia pervade the novels. The basis of The Shadow's "invisibility" is the ancient Black Art Illusion, and he is a master of the Houdiniesque escape (Gibson wrote a book titled *Houdini's Escapes*). The Shadow's antagonists also applied magician's equipment to crime, as they do in *The Unseen Killer*, *The Blur*, *Room of Doom*, and others.

Gibson's genius, however, lies in his application of the techniques of misdirection and illusion to his plots. He manipulates his readers with the same deftness that a magician controls his audience. Facts are withheld, or made ambiguous. Characters are presented in false lights which cloud their motives (*The Green Box*). The Shadow himself is enwrapped in a cloak of obfuscation in which his actions are rendered but his thoughts are hidden. Thus, he may have several incarnations in a given story (*Lingo* or *Zemba*) without the other characters or Gibson's audience being aware of it. The Shadow may see through misleading actions and clues, while Gibson leads the reader to believe them valid. Misdirection is employed so freely that one is hard-pressed to accept any character or event at face value.

Such controlled techniques were common to the Golden Age mystery story and, despite their violence, the Shadow novels fall into this category. The plots possess the same artificial ingeniousness, bizarre murder devices, arraying of suspects and occasional costumed villains. Such manipulations of convention, no matter how artful, do have their limitations, however. Whether Gibson is writing about The Shadow, Norgil, Valdor, Ardini or any of his other stage-magician detectives, the reader knows, in the end, that the illusions generated are not those of reality, but of invention.

—Will Murray

GIELGUD, Val (Henry). British. Born in Earl's Court, London, 28 April 1900; brother of the actor Sir John Gielgud. Educated at Hillside School, Godalming, Surrey; Rugby School, Warwickshire; Trinity College, Oxford. Married 1) Natalie Mamontoff in 1921 (marriage dissolved, 1925); 2) Barbara Druce in 1928 (marriage dissolved), one son; 3) Rita Vale in 1946 (marriage dissolved); 4) Monica Grey in 1955 (marriage dissolved); 5) Vivienne June Bailey in 1960. Worked as a secretary to an M.P., a sub-editor for a comic paper, and an actor, in the 1920's; staff member, *Radio Times*, London, 1928–29; appointed Dramatic Director, BBC, London, 1929, and worked in the Drama Department until 1963; retired as Head of Drama (Sound). O.B.E. (Officer, Order of the British Empire), 1942; C.B.E. (Commander, Order of the British Empire), 1958. Agent: David Higham Associates Ltd., 5–8 Lower John Street, London W1R 4HA. Address: Wychwood, Barcombe, near Lewes, East Sussex, England.

CRIME PUBLICATIONS

Novels (series characters: Antony Havilland; Inspector Gregory Pellew and Viscount Clymping; Inspector Simon Spears)

Imperial Treasure. London, Constable, and Boston, Houghton Mifflin, 1931.
The Broken Men. London, Constable, 1932; Boston, Houghton Mifflin, 1933.
Under London, with Holt Marvell. London, Rich and Cowan, 1933.
Gravelhanger (Havilland). London, Cassell, 1934; as *The Ruse of the Vanished Women,* New York, Doubleday, 1934.
Death at Broadcasting House (Spears), with Holt Marvell. London, Rich and Cowan, 1934; as *London Calling,* New York, Doubleday, 1934.
Death as an Extra (Spears), with Holt Marvell. London, Rich and Cowan, 1935.
Death in Budapest (Spears), with Holt Marvell. London, Rich and Cowan, 1937.
Outrage in Manchukuo (Havilland). London, Cassell, 1937.
The Red Account. London, Rich and Cowan, 1938.
The First Television Murder, with Eric Maschwitz. London, Hutchinson, 1940.
Confident Morning. London, Collins, 1943.
Fall of a Sparrow (Havilland). London, Collins, 1949; as *Stalking Horse,* New York, Morrow, 1950.
Special Delivery (Havilland). London, Collins, 1950.
The High Jump. London, Collins, 1953; as *Ride for a Fall,* New York, Morrow, 1953.
Cat. London, Collins, 1956; New York, Random House, 1957.
Gallows' Foot (Pellew and Clymping). London, Collins, 1958.
To Bed at Noon. London, Collins, 1960.
And Died So? (Pellew and Clymping). London, Collins, 1961.
The Goggle-Box Affair (Pellew and Clymping). London, Collins, 1963; as *Through a Glass Darkly,* New York, Scribner, 1963.
Prinvest-London (Pellew and Clymping). London, Collins, 1965.
Conduct of a Member (Pellew and Clymping). London, Collins, 1967.
A Necessary End (Pellew and Clymping). London, Collins, 1969.
The Candle-Holders (Pellew and Clymping). London, Macmillan, 1970.
The Black Sambo Affair (Pellew and Clymping). London, Macmillan, 1972.
In Such a Night ... (Pellew and Clymping). London, Macmillan, 1974.
A Fearful Thing (Pellew and Clymping). London, Macmillan, 1975.

Short Stories

Beyond Dover, Announcer's Holiday, Africa Flight. London, Hutchinson, 1940.

Uncollected Short Stories

"Hot Water," in *The Great Book of Thrillers,* edited by H. Douglas Thomson. London, Odhams Press, n.d.
"Who Killed the Drama Critic?," in *The Saint* (New York), January 1964.
"To Make a Holiday," in *Winter's Crimes 2,* edited by George Hardinge. London, Macmillan, 1970.
"A Policeman's Lot," in *Winter's Crimes 6,* edited by George Hardinge. London, Macmillan, 1974.

OTHER PUBLICATIONS

Novels

Black Gallantry. London, Constable, 1928; as *Old Swords,* Boston, Houghton Mifflin, 1928.

Gathering of Eagles: A Story of 1812. London, Constable, 1929; as *White Eagles*, Boston, Houghton Mifflin, 1929.

Plays

Self (produced London, 1926).

The Job (produced London, 1928).

Chinese White (produced London, 1929). Published in *Five Three-Act Plays*, London, Rich and Cowan, 1933.

Red Triangle, adaptation of the novel *Special Providence* by Mary Agnes Hamilton (produced London, 1932).

Red Tabs, *Exiles*, and *Friday Morning*, in *How to Write Broadcast Plays*. London, Hurst and Blackett, 1933.

I May Be Old-Fashioned (produced London, 1934).

Fours into Seven — Won't Go, with Stephen King-Hall, in *Twelve One-Act Plays*, edited by Geoffrey Whitworth. London, Sidgwick and Jackson, 1934.

Punch and Judy (also director: produced London, 1937).

Mr. Pratt's Waterloo, with Philip Wade (broadcast, 1937). Included in *Radio Theatre*, edited by Gielgud. London, Macdonald, 1946.

Music at Dusk (broadcast, 1939). Included in *Radio Theatre*, edited by Gielgud. London, Macdonald, 1946.

Africa Flight (produced Richmond, Surrey, 1939).

Man's Company (produced Northampton, 1942).

Away from It All (produced London, 1946). Published in *Embassy Successes 3*, London, Sampson Low, 1948.

Party Manners (produced London, 1950). London, Muller, 1950.

A Shadow of Death, from a translation by Alan Blair of a play by Stig Dagerman (broadcast, 1950; as *Condemned to Live*, produced London, 1952).

Iron Curtain (produced London, 1951).

The Bombshell (produced Croydon, Surrey, and London, 1954).

Mediterranean Blue (produced Northampton, 1956).

Not Enough Tragedy (produced Colchester, Essex, 1959).

Screenplays: *Royal Cavalcade*, with others, 1935; *Cafe Colette (Danger in Paris)*, with others, 1937; *Inspector Silence Takes the Air*, 1942; *Thirteen to the Gallows*, 1945.

Radio Plays: *Exiles*, 1928; *Red Tabs*, 1930; *Waterloo*, with Norman Edwards, 1932; *Gallipoli*, 1935; *The Sergeant Major*, 1936; *Mr. Pratt's Waterloo*, with Philip Wade, 1937; *Death of a Queen*, from a work by Hilaire Belloc, 1937; *Hassan*, with Dulcima Glasby, from the play by James Elroy Flecker, 1938; *Ending It*, 1938; *Music at Dusk*, 1939; *Scott in the Antarctic*, with Peter Cresswell, 1940; *Valiant for Truth*, with Igar Vinogradoff, 1940; *The Field of Kings*, with Cynthia Pughe, from a work by Thiery Maulnier, 1947; *Roman Holiday*, 1949; *A Shadow of Death*, from a translation by Alan Blair of a work by Stig Dagerman, 1950; *Unhurrying Chase*, with Margaret Gore Browne, 1954; *The Lanchester Tradition*, from a work by G. F. Bradley, 1956; *Mr. Justice Raffles*, from works by E. W. Hornung, 1964; *The Goggle-Box Affair*, from his own novel, 1964; *The Crimson Star*, from a novel by Anthony Hope, 1964; *Fog*, 1964; *The Gentleman* (serial), from a work by Aldred Olivant, 1965; *They Were So Few*, from a work by W. S. Davis, 1966; *The Bad Samaritan*, 1966; *Porto Bello Gold*, from a work by A. D. M. Smith, 1967; *Too Clever by Half*, 1967; *The Tents of Kedar*, from a work by H. Seton Merriman, 1967; *So Easy to Forget*, 1968; *The Hornblower Story*, from works by C. S. Forester, 1968; *The Fall of Edward Barnard*, *Flotsam and Jetsam*, *Gigolo and Gigolette*, *Sanitorium*, and *Dark Eagle*, from stories by W. S. Maugham, 1968–70; *Hornblower and the Crisis*, from a story by C. S. Forester, 1970; *The Time of My Life*, 1970; *The Tumbled House*, from a story by Winston Graham, 1971; *Conscience Doth*

Make Cowards, 1971; *Cry Wolf*, from stories by Saki, 1971; *A Necessary End*, from his own novel, 1972; *Broome Stages*, from the novel by Clemence Dane, 1975; *Les Misérables*, with B. Campbell and C. Cox, from the novel by Victor Hugo, 1976; *Mr. Perrin and Mr. Traill*, from the novel by Hugh Walpole, 1978.

Other

How to Write Broadcast Plays (includes *Friday Morning, Red Tabs, Exiles*).   London, Hurst and Blackett, 1932.
Years of the Locust (autobiography).   London, Nicholson and Watson, 1947.
The Right Way to Radio Playwriting.   Kingswood, Surrey, Andrew George Eliot, 1948.
One Year of Grace: A Fragment of Autobiography.   London, Longman, 1950.
British Radio Drama 1922–1956: A Survey.   London, Harrap, 1957.
Years in a Mirror (autobiography).   London, Bodley Head, 1965.
My Cats and Myself: A Fragment of Autobiography.   London, Joseph, 1972.

Editor, *Radio Theatre: Plays Specially Written for Broadcasting.*   London, Macdonald, 1946.
Editor, *Cats: A Personal Anthology.*   London, Newnes, 1966.

Theatrical Activities:

Director: **Plays** – *Tread Softly* by Peter Traill, London, 1935; *The Road to Ruin* by Thomas Holcroft, London, 1937; *Punch and Judy*, London, 1937; *Home and Beauty* by W. S. Maugham, Wimbledon and London, 1942; *This Land Is Ours* by Lionel Brown, London, 1945; *Autumn Gold* by Lionel Brown, London, 1948.

Actor: **Plays** – Mr. Malakoff in *For First-Class Passengers Only* by Osbert and Sacheverell Sitwell, London, 1927; Ronald Keith in *The Eldest Son* by John Galsworthy, London, 1928; Karl Starck in *Comrades* by Strindberg, London, 1928; Mr. Veal in *The Last Man In* by W. B. Maxwell, London, 1928; Pongo Hodge in *Flies and Treacle* by C. Dudley Ward, London, 1928. **Film** – *Men Are Not Gods*, 1936.

*   *   *

Val Gielgud has been producing a varied group of mystery novels for almost five decades. Two unexceptional novels in the late 1920's were followed by a short (1933–40) but fruitful collaboration with Holt Marvell (pseudonym of Eric Maschwitz). Their detective novels featured the young and ambitious Detective-Inspector Simon Spears of Scotland Yard who is frequently assisted by BBC executive Julian Caird. Their best effort, *Death at Broadcasting House*, concerns the murder of an actor during a radio broadcast. This novel's plot, puzzle, characterizations, and especially its radio background are beautifully combined, and Gielgud's experience as head of sound drama for the BBC was a special asset in the creation of this minor masterpiece.

A later but minor series featured Inspector Gregory Pellew and Viscount Humphrey Clymping. They eventually become partners in a private enquiry agency called Prinvest, after the former's retirement from the CID, and are aided by the latter's wife and mother. Of more than passing interest is the non-series *Cat*, an acronym for its protagonist Charles Adolphus Trent. The first short chapter deals with the discovery of a murder and the punishment of its perpetrator. The bulk of this inverted novel outlines the life of its central character and details the events leading to the crime. This is a flawed effort that might have been notable if it were more deeply felt by its author. *A Necessary End* has been lavishly praised by Jacques Barzun and Wendell Hertig Taylor as one of the best shipboard stories for its first-class detection and its amusing sidelights cast on the United States by a Londoner.

—Charles Shibuk

GIFFORD, Thomas (Eugene). American. Born in Dubuque, Iowa, 16 May 1937. Educated at Harvard University, Cambridge, Massachusetts, A.B. 1959. Married 1) Kari Sandven (divorced); 2) Camille d'Ambrose; two children. Textbook Salesman, Minneapolis, Minnesota, 1960–68; Editor-in-Chief, *Twin Citian*, Minneapolis, 1968–69; Director of Public Relations, Tyrone Guthrie Theatre, Minneapolis, 1970; Editor and Columnist, Sun Newspapers, Minneapolis, 1971–75. Since 1975, self-employed writer. Agent: Julian Bach Literary Agency Inc., 3 East 48th Street, New York, New York 10017, U.S.A.

CRIME PUBLICATIONS

Novels

> *The Wind Chill Factor.* New York, Putnam, and London, Hamish Hamilton, 1975.
> *The Cavanaugh Quest.* New York, Putnam, 1976.
> *The Man from Lisbon.* New York, McGraw Hill, 1977.
> *The Glendower Experiment.* New York, Putnam, 1978; London, Hamish Hamilton, 1979.
> *Hollywood Gothic.* New York, Putnam, 1979.

OTHER PUBLICATIONS

Other

> *Benchwarmer Bob* (juvenile). Blue Earth, Minnesota, Piper, 1974.

*   *   *

Thomas Gifford's first book, *The Wind Chill Factor*, is, at first glance, yet another tale of resurgent Nazis. It is distinguished, however, by the quality of the writing, the excellent descriptive passages, the superb sense of place, and the fine characterization. The book takes its hero John Cooper to South America and Europe in an attempt to unravel the Nazi conspiracy, and keeps the reader enthralled.

Gifford's knowledge of Minneapolis and the rest of Minnesota, scene of the early part of *The Wind Chill Factor*, comes through to an even greater extent in his second book, *The Cavanaugh Quest*. A man commits suicide, and Paul Cavanaugh is asked to find out why. Motivated only by curiosity at first, he finds himself drawn deeper into the case by his attraction to the man's ex-wife. The case has roots in a hunting and fishing club of the 1930's, whose members start dying in rapid succession as Cavanaugh gets closer to the answer. The brilliantly realized characters and settings and the fine writing make the book engrossing reading, even though the solution is clear to the reader long before Cavanaugh sees it.

The Man from Lisbon is a departure from Minnesota and the character types of the earlier books. It is an interesting novelization of a true crime of the twenties, when a man swindled the Bank of Portugal out of five million dollars.

—Jeffrey Meyerson

GILBERT, Anthony. Pseudonym for Lucy Beatrice Malleson; also wrote as J. Kilmeny Keith; Anne Meredith. British. Born in Upper Norwood, London, 15 February 1899. Educated at St. Paul's Girls' School, Hammersmith, London. Worked as a secretary for the Red Cross, Ministry of Food, and Coal Association. Founding Member, and General Secretary, Detection Club. *Died 9 December 1973.*

CRIME PUBLICATIONS

Novels (series characters: Arthur G. Crook; M. Dupuy; Scott Egerton)

The Man Who Was London (as J. Kilmeny Keith).   London, Collins, 1925.
The Sword of Harlequin (as J. Kilmeny Keith).   London, Collins, 1927.
The Tragedy at Freyne (Egerton).   London, Collins, and New York, Dial Press, 1927.
The Murder of Mrs. Davenport (Egerton).   London, Collins, and New York, Dial Press, 1928.
The Mystery of the Open Window (Egerton).   London, Gollancz, 1929; New York, Dodd Mead, 1930.
Death at Four Corners (Egerton).   London, Collins, and New York, Dial Press, 1929.
The Night of the Fog (Egerton).   London, Gollancz, and New York, Dial Press, 1930.
The Case Against Andrew Fane.   London, Collins, and New York, Dodd Mead, 1931.
The Body on the Beam (Egerton).   London, Collins, and New York, Dodd Mead, 1932.
The Long Shadow (Egerton).   London, Collins, 1932.
The Musical Comedy Crime (Egerton).   London, Collins, 1933.
Death in Fancy Dress.   London, Collins, 1933.
Portrait of a Murderer (as Anne Meredith).   London, Gollancz, 1933; New York, Reynal, 1934.
The Man in Button Boots (Dupuy).   London, Collins, 1934; New York, Holt, 1935.
An Old Lady Dies (Egerton).   London, Collins, 1934.
The Man Who Was Too Clever (Egerton).   London, Collins, 1935.
Murder by Experts (Crook).   London, Collins, 1936; New York, Dial Press, 1937.
Courtier to Death (Dupuy).   London, Collins, 1936; as *The Dover Train Mystery*, New York, Dial Press, 1936.
The Man Who Wasn't There (Crook).   London, Collins, 1937.
Murder Has No Tongue (Crook).   London, Collins, 1937.
Treason in My Breast (Crook).   London, Collins, 1938.
The Clock in the Hat Box (Crook).   London, Collins, 1939; New York, Arcadia House, 1943.
The Bell of Death.   London, Collins, 1939.
Dear Dead Woman (Crook).   London, Collins, 1940; New York, Arcadia House, 1942; as *Death Takes a Redhead*, New York, Arrow Editions, 1944.
The Vanishing Corpse (Crook).   London, Collins, 1941; as *She Vanished in the Dawn*, New York, Arcadia House, 1941.

There's Always Tomorrow (as Anne Meredith).   London, Faber, 1941; as *Home Is the Heart*, New York, Howell Soskin, 1942.

The Woman in Red (Crook).   London, Collins, 1941; New York, Smith and Durrell, 1943; as *The Mystery of the Woman in Red*, New York, Quin, 1944.

Something Nasty in the Woodshed (Crook).   London, Collins, 1942; as *Mystery in the Woodshed*, New York, Smith and Durrell, 1942.

The Case of the Tea-Cosy's Aunt (Crook).   London, Collins, 1942; as *Death in the Blackout*, New York, Smith and Durrell, 1943.

The Mouse Who Wouldn't Play Ball (Crook).   London, Collins, 1943; as *Thirty Days to Live*, New York, Smith and Durrell, 1944.

A Spy for Mr. Crook.   New York, A. S. Barnes, 1944.

He Came by Night (Crook).   London, Collins, 1944; as *Death at the Door*, New York, Smith and Durrell, 1945.

The Scarlet Button (Crook).   London, Collins, 1944; New York, Smith and Durrell, 1945; as *Murder Is Cheap*, New York, Bantam, 1949.

The Black Stage (Crook).   London, Collins, 1945; New York, A. S. Barnes, 1946; as *Murder Cheats the Bride*, New York, Bantam, 1948.

Don't Open the Door (Crook).   London, Collins, 1945; as *Death Lifts the Latch*, New York, A. S. Barnes, 1946.

The Spinster's Secret (Crook).   London, Collins, 1946; as *By Hook or Crook*, New York, A. S. Barnes, 1947.

Death in the Wrong Room (Crook).   London, Collins, and New York, A. S. Barnes, 1947.

Die in the Dark (Crook).   London, Collins, 1947; as *The Missing Widow*, New York, A. S. Barnes, 1948.

Lift Up the Lid.   London, Collins, 1948; as *The Innocent Bottle*, New York, A. S. Barnes, 1949.

Death Knocks Three Times (Crook).   London, Collins, 1949; New York, Random House, 1950.

Murder Comes Home (Crook).   London, Collins, 1950; New York, Random House, 1951.

A Nice Cup of Tea (Crook).   London, Collins, 1950; as *The Wrong Body*, New York, Random House, 1951.

Lady-Killer (Crook).   London, Collins, 1951.

Miss Pinnegar Disappears.   London, Collins, 1952; as *A Case for Mr. Crook*, New York, Random House, 1952.

Footsteps Behind Me (Crook).   London, Collins, 1953; as *Black Death*, New York, Random House, 1953; as *Dark Death*, New York, Pyramid, 1963.

Snake in the Grass (Crook).   London, Collins, 1954; as *Death Won't Wait*, New York, Random House, 1954.

A Question of Murder (Crook).   New York, Random House, 1955; as *Is She Dead Too?*, London, Collins, 1956.

Riddle of a Lady (Crook).   London, Collins, 1956; New York, Random House, 1957.

And Death Came Too (Crook).   London, Collins, and New York, Random House, 1956.

Give Death a Name (Crook).   London, Collins, 1957.

Death Against the Clock (Crook).   London, Collins, and New York, Random House, 1958.

Death Takes a Wife (Crook).   London, Collins, 1959; as *Death Casts a Long Shadow*, New York, Random House, 1959.

Third Crime Lucky (Crook).   London, Collins, 1959; as *Prelude to Murder*, New York, Random House, 1959.

Out for the Kill (Crook).   London, Collins, and New York, Random House, 1960.

Uncertain Death (Crook).   London, Collins, 1961; New York, Random House, 1962.

She Shall Die (Crook).   London, Collins, 1961; as *After the Verdict*, New York, Random House, 1961.

No Dust in the Attic (Crook).   London, Collins, 1962; New York, Random House, 1963.

Ring for a Noose (Crook).   London, Collins, 1963; New York, Random House, 1964.

Knock, Knock, Who's There? (Crook).   London, Collins, 1964; as *The Voice*, New York, Random House, 1965.

The Fingerprint (Crook).   London, Collins, and New York, Random House, 1964.

Passenger to Nowhere (Crook).   London, Collins, 1965; New York, Random House, 1966.

The Looking Glass Murder (Crook).   London, Collins, 1966; New York, Random House, 1967.

The Visitor (Crook).   London, Collins, and New York, Random House, 1967.

Night Encounter (Crook).   London, Collins, 1968; as *Murder Anonymous*, New York, Random House, 1968.

Missing from Her Home (Crook).   London, Collins, and New York, Random House, 1969.

Death Wears a Mask.   London, Collins, 1970; as *Mr. Crook Lifts the Mask*, New York, Random House, 1970.

Tenant for the Tomb (Crook).   London, Collins, and New York, Random House, 1971

Murder's a Waiting Game (Crook).   London, Collins, and New York, Random House, 1972.

A Nice Little Killing (Crook).   London, Collins, and New York, Random House, 1974.

Uncollected Short Stories

"The Cockroach and the Tortoise" and "Horsehoes for Luck," in *Detection Medley*, edited by John Rhode.   London, Hutchinson, 1939; as *Line Up*, New York, Dodd Mead, 1940.

"You Can't Hang Twice," in *To the Queen's Taste*, edited by Ellery Queen.   Boston, Little Brown, 1946; London, Faber, 1949.

"Black for Innocence," in *The Evening Standard Detective Book*.   London, Gollancz, 1950.

"What Would You Have Done?," in *The Evening Standard Detective Book*, 2nd series.   London, Gollancz, 1951.

"Over My Dead Body," in *Ellery Queen's Mystery Magazine* (New York), July 1952.

"Remember Madame Clementine," in *Ellery Queen's Mystery Magazine* (New York), October 1955.

"Give Me a Ring," in *Illustrated London News*, 11 November 1955.

"Once Is Once Too Many," in *Ellery Queen's Mystery Magazine* (New York), December 1955.

"Sequel to Murder," in *Eat, Drink, and Be Buried*, edited by Rex Stout.   New York, Viking Press, 1956; as *For Tomorrow We Die*, London, Macdonald, 1958.

"Blood Will Tell," in *A Choice of Murders*, edited by Dorothy Salisbury Davis.   New York, Scribner, 1958; London, Macdonald, 1960.

"The Goldfish Button," in *Ellery Queen's Mystery Magazine* (New York), February 1958.

"The Blackmailer," in *The Second Mystery Bedside Book*, edited by John Creasey.   London, Hodder and Stoughton, 1961.

"A Nice Little Mare Called Murder," in *Crime Writers' Choice*, edited by Roy Vickers.   London, Hodder and Stoughton, 1964.

"Evan a Woman," in *The Saint* (New York), July 1964.

"He Found Out Too Late," in *The Saint* (New York), May 1966.

"Cat among the Pigeons," in *Ellery Queen's Mystery Magazine* (New York), October 1966.

"The Eternal Chase," in *Ellery Queen's Crime Carousel.*   New York, New American Library, 1966.

"Sleep Is the Enemy," in *Ellery Queen's All-Star Lineup*.   New York, New American Library, 1967.

"Point of No Return," in *Ellery Queen's Mystery Magazine* (New York), May 1968.

"The Intruders," in *Ellery Queen's Mystery Parade*.   New York, New American Library, 1968.

"The Puzzled Heart," in *Ellery Queen's Mystery Magazine* (New York), March 1969.

"The Mills of God," in *Ellery Queen's Mystery Magazine* (New York), April 1969.

"Who Cares about an Old Woman?," in *Ellery Queen's Murder Menu*.   Cleveland, World, 1969.

"Tiger on the Premises," in *Ellery Queen's Mystery Magazine* (New York), September 1969.

"The Funeral of Dendy Watt," in *Ellery Queen's Mystery Magazine* (New York), January 1970.

"The Quiet Man," in *Ellery Queen's Grand Slam*.   Cleveland, World, 1970.

"Door to a Different World," in *Ellery Queen's Headliners*.   Cleveland, World, 1971; London, Gollancz, 1972.

"When Suns Collide," in *Ellery Queen's Mystery Bag*.   Cleveland, World, 1972.

"A Day of Encounters," in *Ellery Queen's Crookbook*.   New York, Random House, 1974.

"Fifty Years After," in *Ellery Queen's Murdercade*.   New York, Random House, 1975.

"The Invisible Witness," in *Ellery Queen's Crime Wave*.   New York, Putnam, 1976.

OTHER PUBLICATIONS

Novels as Anne Meredith

The Coward.   London, Gollancz, 1934.
The Gambler.   London, Gollancz, 1937.
The Showman.   London, Faber, 1938.
The Stranger.   London, Faber, 1939.
The Adventurer.   London, Faber, 1940.
The Family Man.   London, Faber, and New York, Howell Soskin, 1942.
Curtain, Mr. Greatheart.   London, Faber, 1943.
The Beautiful Miss Burroughes.   London, Faber, 1945.
The Rich Woman.   London, Faber, and New York, Random House, 1947.
The Sisters.   London, Faber, 1948; New York, Random House, 1949.
The Draper of Edgecumbe.   London, Faber, 1950; as *The Unknown Path*, New York, Random House, 1950.
A Fig for Virtue.   London, Faber, 1951.
Call Back Yesterday.   London, Faber, 1952.
The Innocent Bride.   London, Hodder and Stoughton, 1954.
The Day of the Miracle.   London, Hodder and Stoughton, 1955.
Impetuous Heart.   London, Hodder and Stoughton, 1956.
Christine.   London, Hodder and Stoughton, 1957.
A Man in the Family.   London, Hodder and Stoughton, 1959.
The Wise Child.   London, Hodder and Stoughton, 1960.
Up Goes the Donkey.   London, Hodder and Stoughton, 1962.

Plays

Mrs. Boot's Legacy.   London, French, 1941.

Radio Plays: *The Plain Woman*, 1940; *Death at 6:30*, 1940; *A Cavalier in Love*, 1940; *The Bird of Passage*, 1941; *There's Always Tomorrow*, 1941; *Calling Mr. Brown*, 1941;

He Came by Night, 1941; *The Adventurer*, 1941; *Footprints*, 1941; *Thirty Years Is a Long Time*, 1941; *A Bird in a Cage*, 1942; *His Professional Conscience*, 1942; *Find the Lady*, 1942; *The Home-Coming*, 1944; *Mystery Man of New York*, 1945; *Of Brides in Baths*, 1945; *Full Circle*, 1946; *Hard Luck Story*, 1947; *The Sympathetic Table*, 1948; *A Nice Cup of Tea*, 1948; *Profitable Death*, 1950; *After the Verdict*, 1952; *Now You Can Sleep*, 1952; *My Guess Would Be Murder*, 1954; *I Love My Love with an "A,"* 1957; *No One Will Ever Know*, 1960; *Black Death*, from her own novel, 1960; *And Death Came Too*, from her own novel, 1962.

Other

Three-a-Penny (autobiography; as Anne Meredith).   London, Faber, 1940.
"The British or the American Story," in *The Mystery Writers' Handbook*, edited by
    Herbert Brean.   London, Harper, 1956.

*   *   *

Although Lucy Beatrice Malleson also wrote as J. Kilmeny Keith and Anne Meredith, and though she also created other series characters, it is as Anthony Gilbert, the creator of lawyer-detective Arthur G. Crook, one of the most interesting fictional detectives yet to solve a case, that she enjoyed the greatest success.

From Gilbert's originally rather unattractive creation (*Murder by Experts*), Crook developed into an irrepressible Cockney who earns his living by dilligent work, constant watchfulness, and occasional lapses from standing professionalism, for "The Criminals' Hope and The Judges' Despair" frequents pubs, drinking beer and distributing his oversized business cards to chance acquaintances. A colorful, cheeky, confident man of perpetual middle age, Crook is addicted to bright brown, off-the-rack suits which, like his chaotic office at the top of a shabby building in a disreputable part of town, reflect his personality and serve to reassure his clients (usually young women) and to mislead his opponents. Mistaking Crook's cover for foolishness, murderers remain off-guard – until Crook's trap has sprung.

Generally, Crook is not the protagonist of the novels. Rather, Gilbert uses either the frame technique or the rider-to-the-rescue method. *And Death Came Too* is a good example of the frame story, for readers meet Crook when a fellow lawyer confides his fear that trouble is destined to haunt Ruth Appleyard. The plot then shifts to explore Ruth's personality, love affairs, and adventures. But when she becomes involved in a third questionable death, Crook is called in, and, having met him in the frame, the reader is prepared to accept his intervention. Gilbert has suspended disbelief and coincidence becomes destiny.

In *A Question of Murder*, however, Crook arrives on the scene much later in the story. The early chapters focus on the deadly conflict between Edward Poulden and his boarder. Caught up in the struggle is young Margaret Reeve, the protagonist. When Poulden eliminates the boarder and attempts to implicate Margaret, a mutual friend summons Crook to exonerate her. Though here Crook's appearance comes about more naturally than in *And Death Came Too*, both novels, like the others of their types, succeed handily. These books also reveal that Gilbert is adroit at both the conventionally ordered mystery and the "inverted" mystery in which the criminal is known from the outset and the suspense depends on the reader's concern lest the murderer succeed.

Another of Gilbert's strengths is splendid development of supporting characters. Two of the best are headstrong, independent divorcée Margaret Ross, the blackmailed protagonist of *The Visitor*, and her neighbor, Angela Muir, seemingly a sterotypical spinster who emerges as a humorous, determined companion in crisis. And perhaps Gilbert's most charming supporting figure is May Forbes in *Death Wears a Mask*, a brisk, capable, middle-aged woman worthy of Crook's respect. There is no hint of romance between the two, but instead a beautifully depicted friendship.

Though the novels center around murder, Gilbert substitutes Crook's ebullience for violent action, and, using his adoration of his autos (the Scourge and then the Superb) as a trigger, creates some remarkably vivid and gripping car chases.

For skillful plotting, lively characterization, and clever action, then, Anthony Gilbert can be highly ranked among mystery writers, and for her creation of Arthur Crook, she cannot be faulted.

—Jane S. Bakerman

GILBERT, Michael (Francis). British. Born in Billinghay, Lincolnshire, 17 July 1912. Educated at St. Peter's School, Seaford, Sussex; Blundell's School, 1926–31; University of London, LL.B. (honours) 1937. Served in the Royal Horse Artillery in North Africa and Europe, 1939–45; mentioned in despatches. Married Roberta Mary Marsden in 1947; five daughters and two sons. Articled Clerk, Ellis Bickersteth Aglionby and Hazel, London, 1938–39. Solicitor, 1947–51, and since 1952, Partner, Trower Still and Keeling, London. Legal Adviser, Government of Bahrain, 1960. Series Editor, Classics of Detection and Adventure, Hodder and Stoughton, publishers, London. Founding Member, Crime Writers Association, 1953. Agent: Curtis Brown Ltd., 1 Craven Hill, London W2 3EP. Address: Luddesdown Old Rectory, Cobham, Gravesend, Kent, England.

CRIME PUBLICATIONS

Novels (series character: Inspector Hazelrigg)

> *Close Quarters* (Hazelrigg). London, Hodder and Stoughton, 1947; New York, Walker, 1963.
> *They Never Looked Inside* (Hazelrigg). London, Hodder and Stoughton, 1948; as *He Didn't Mind Danger*, New York, Harper, 1949.
> *The Doors Open* (Hazelrigg). London, Hodder and Stoughton, 1949; New York, Walker, 1962.
> *Smallbone Deceased* (Hazelrigg). London, Hodder and Stoughton, and New York, Harper, 1950.
> *Death Has Deep Roots* (Hazelrigg). London, Hodder and Stoughton, 1951; New York, Harper, 1952.
> *Death in Captivity.* London, Hodder and Stoughton, 1952; as *The Danger Within*, New York, Harper, 1952.
> *Fear to Tread* (Hazelrigg). London, Hodder and Stoughton, and New York, Harper, 1953.
> *Sky High.* London, Hodder and Stoughton, 1955; as *The Country-House Burglar*, New York, Harper, 1955.
> *Be Shot for Sixpence.* London, Hodder and Stoughton, and New York, Harper, 1956.
> *Blood and Judgement.* London, Hodder and Stoughton, and New York, Harper, 1959.
> *After the Fine Weather.* London, Hodder and Stoughton, and New York, Harper, 1963.
> *The Crack in the Teacup.* London, Hodder and Stoughton, and New York, Harper, 1966.
> *The Dust and the Heat.* London, Hodder and Stoughton, 1967; as *Overdrive*, New York, Harper, 1968.

The Etruscan Net. London, Hodder and Stoughton, 1969; as *The Family Tomb*, New York, Harper, 1969.
The Body of a Girl. London, Hodder and Stoughton, and New York, Harper, 1972.
The 92nd Tiger. London, Hodder and Stoughton, and New York, Harper, 1973.
Flash Point. London, Hodder and Stoughton, and New York, Harper, 1974.
The Night of the Twelfth. London, Hodder and Stoughton, and New York, Harper, 1976.
The Empty House. London, Hodder and Stoughton, 1978; New York, Harper, 1979.

Short Stories

Game Without Rules. New York, Harper, 1967; London, Hodder and Stoughton, 1968.
Stay of Execution and Other Stories of Legal Practice. London, Hodder and Stoughton, 1971.
Amateur in Violence. New York, Davis, 1973.
Petrella at Q. London, Hodder and Stoughton, and New York, Harper, 1977.

Uncollected Short Stories

"The Decline and Fall of Mr. Behrens," in *John Creasey's Crime Collection 1978*, edited by Herbert Harris. London, Gollancz, 1978.
"Verdict of Thirteen," in *Verdict of Thirteen*, edited by Julian Symons. London, Faber, and New York, Harper, 1979.
"The Man in the Middle," in *Ellery Queen's Mystery Magazine* (New York), May 1979.
"The Man at the Top," in *Ellery Queen's Mystery Magazine* (New York), June 1979.

OTHER PUBLICATIONS

Plays

A Clean Kill (produced London, 1959). London, Constable, 1961.
The Bargain (produced London, 1961). London, Constable, 1961.
The Shot in Question (produced Brighton and London, 1963). London, Constable, 1963.
Windfall (produced Liverpool and London, 1963). London, Constable, 1963.

Radio Plays: *Death in Captivity*, 1953; *The Man Who Could Not Sleep*, 1955; *Crime Report*, 1956; *Doctor at Law*, 1956; *The Waterloo Table*, 1957; *You Must Take Things Easy*, 1958; *Stay of Execution*, 1965; *Game Without Rules* series, 1968; *The Last Chapter*, 1970; *Black Light*, 1972; *Flash Point*, 1974; *Petrella* series, 1976.

Television Plays: *The Crime of the Century* (serial), 1956; *Wideawake* (serial), 1957; *The Body of a Girl*, 1958; *Fair Game* (serial), 1958; *Crime Report* (documentary), 1958; *Blackmail Is So Difficult*, 1959; *Dangerous Ice*, 1959; *A Clean Kill*, 1961; *The Men from Room 13* (serial), from a work by Stanley Firmin, 1961; *Scene of the Accident*, 1961; *The Betrayers*, from a work by Stanley Ellin, 1962; *Trial Run*, 1963; *The Blackmailing of Mr. S.*, 1964; *The Mind of the Enemy* (serial), 1965; *The Man in Room 17* series (1 episode), 1966; *Misleading Cases* series, with Christopher Bond, from work by A. P. Herbert, 1971; *Hadleigh* series (1 episode), 1971; *Money to Burn*, from the novel by Margery Allingham, 1974; *Where There's a Will*, 1975.

Other

Dr. Crippen. London, Odhams Press, 1953.
"Technicalese," in *The Mystery Writers' Handbook*, edited by Herbert Brean. New York, Harper, 1956.
The Claimant. London, Constable, 1957.
The Law. Newton Abbot, Devon, David and Charles, 1977.
"The Invisible Bond," in *Murder Ink: The Mystery Reader's Companion*, edited by Dilys Winn. New York, Workman, 1977.

Editor, *Crime in Good Company: Essays on Criminals and Crime-Writing.* London, Constable, 1959.
Editor, *Best Detective Stories of Cyril Hare.* London, Faber, 1959; New York, Walker, 1961.

Manuscript Collections: University of California, Berkeley; Mugar Memorial Library, Boston University.

Michael Gilbert comments:

It is impossible in a brief space to make any useful summary of an output that spans forty years (my first book was actually written in 1930), and that comprises twenty novels, three collections of short stories, three or four hundred other short stories, four stage plays, and a good number of television and radio plays. I can best introduce my crime writing with two quotations. One is from Julian Symons's compendium *Bloody Murder.* He says (in a section headed "Entertainers"), "In our time there are many writers who put into their books little or nothing of their own personalities. Now that the old rules no longer apply they are able to treat lightly and amusingly many subjects that would not have been touched 30 years ago." Under this heading he mentions my name and Emma Lathen's, a coupling I appreciate.

So I am an entertainer? A fact that Harry Keating, in his review of one of my recent books, found "disappointing." In fact he went on to say that he found this book less disappointing, in this respect, than earlier ones. I find the whole thing puzzling. What is a writer to do if he is not allowed to entertain?

*   *   *

Michael Gilbert, a London solicitor, has written strict intellectual puzzles, romantic thrillers, espionage, and police procedural novels. All are done with equal skill and a high level of artistic achievement. Gilbert is a master of complex plotting and well-rounded characters. With a penchant for detail and a special feel for the places he uses as settings, he delivers stories which are compelling and engage the reader immediately.

Gilbert has also written short stories and plays with equal success. Anthony Boucher, critic for the *New York Times*, called Gilbert's collection of spy stories *Game Without Rules* "the second best volume of spy short stories ever published": he ranked only *Ashenden*, by Somerset Maugham, higher.

While his early novels, beginning in 1947 with *Close Quarters*, are now considered somewhat weak, it is only by comparison. Experience brought maturity of writing. Combining a humor rarely found in the genre with layers of plotting, clues, and suspects, Gilbert can always be depended upon to deliver solid reading entertainment. He has created several exceptional series characters, the chief of whom is Patrick Petrella. Followers have watched Petrella deal with blackmail, arson, theft and murder, while rising steadily from constable to Detective Chief Inspector with the Metropolitan Police. Calder and Behrens are Counter-Intelligence agents who appear in a number of short stories, and Inspector Hazelrigg was featured in six early novels. Mercer is a highly individualistic inspector in *The Body of a*

Girl, who quits the force for a job in the Middle East, but has recently returned in several short stories.

Gilbert has also written many non-series novels. *Sky High* has as its amateur detective Liz, a bass in the church choir. In *The Etruscan Net* the amateur is an art gallery owner. *Death in Captivity* is a classic of escape of prisoners of war in Italy, and may be partially autobiographical, as Gilbert was captured in North Africa and imprisoned in Tunis and in Italy in World War II. In his latest novel, *The Empty House*, Gilbert has created yet another engaging character, Peter Manciple, an insurance investigator. Set on Exmoor, it is a fine example of Gilbert's knowledge and utilization of place in his novels. At the story's end, Manciple accepts a position at Blundell's school, but the reader hopes that Gilbert might chronicle his further adventures.

Gilbert's legal background has contributed to excellent novels concerning law firms, young solicitors as protagonists and courtroom style, technique, procedure, and drama.

Gilbert's novels and short stories mark him as a careful writer rather than a prolific one. Such care has contributed believable plots, characters with whom we can identify, and details of setting and geography. Wit and humor used judiciously add greatly to the reader's enjoyment. Gilbert's novels are not only plausible but of unusual substance.

—Frank Denton

GILES, Kenneth.   See **McGIRR, Edmund.**

GILMAN, Dorothy.   American.   Born in New Brunswick, New Jersey, 25 June 1923. Educated at Pennsylvania Academy of Fine Arts, Philadelphia (William Emlen Cresson European Scholarship, 1944); Art Students' League, New York, 1964. Married Edgar A. Butters, Jr., in 1945 (divorced, 1965); two sons. Instructor in Drawing, Samuel Fleischer Art Memorial, Philadelphia, for two years. Self-employed writer. Agent: McIntosh and Otis Inc., 475 Fifth Avenue, New York, New York 10017, U.S.A. Address: Lower East Pubnico, Nova Scotia B0W 2AO, Canada.

CRIME PUBLICATIONS

Novels (series character: Mrs. Pollifax)

> *The Unexpected Mrs. Pollifax.*   New York, Doubleday, 1966; London, Hale, 1967; as *Mrs. Pollifax, Spy*, London, Tandem, 1971.
> *Uncertain Voyage.*   New York, Doubleday, 1967; London, Hale, 1968.
> *The Amazing Mrs. Pollifax.*   New York, Doubleday, 1970; London, Hale, 1971.
> *The Elusive Mrs. Pollifax.*   New York, Doubleday, 1971; London, Hale, 1973.
> *A Palm for Mrs. Pollifax.*   New York, Doubleday, 1973; London, Hale, 1974.
> *A Nun in the Closet.*   New York, Doubleday, 1975; as *A Nun in the Cupboard*, London, Hale, 1976.

The Clairvoyant Countess. New York, Doubleday, 1975; London, Prior, 1976.
Mrs. Pollifax on Safari. New York, Doubleday, 1977.
The Tightrope Walker. New York, Doubleday, 1979.

OTHER PUBLICATIONS as Dorothy Gilman Butters

Other (juvenile)

Enchanted Caravan. Philadelphia, Macrae Smith, 1949.
Carnival Gypsy. Philadelphia, Macrae Smith, 1950.
Ragamuffin Alley. Philadelphia, Macrae Smith, 1951.
The Calico Year. Philadelphia, Macrae Smith, 1953.
Four-Party Line. Philadelphia, Macrae Smith, 1954.
Papa Dolphin's Table. New York, Knopf, 1955.
Girl in Buckskin. Philadelphia, Macrae Smith, 1956.
Heartbreak Street. Philadelphia, Macrae Smith, 1958.
Witch's Silver. Philadelphia, Macrae Smith, 1959.
Masquerade. Philadelphia, Macrae Smith, 1961.
Ten Leagues to Boston Town. Philadelphia, Macrae Smith, 1962.
The Bells of Freedom. Philadelphia, Macrae Smith, 1963.
A New Kind of Country (for adults). New York, Doubleday, 1978.

Manuscript Collection: Mugar Memorial Library, Boston University.

*   *   *

After more than a decade of writing for magazines and producing books for young readers, Dorothy Gilman began to write suspense fiction for an adult audience in the 1960's. *The Unexpected Mrs. Pollifax* is the first of a series which has wide appeal to young and old alike.

In her first adventure, Mrs. Pollifax is a sweet, elderly widow whose life has settled into a routine of volunteer work, garden club and women's associations, and comfortable monotony. Her children and grandchildren live far away and no longer need her. She feels useless and depressed. Not a personality to succumb in such a crisis, she remembers a childhood dream of becoming a spy, travels to CIA headquarters, and applies for a job. By a series of coincidences that would seem merely absurd were it not for the author's charming and delightful way of telling a tale, Emily Pollifax is taken on as a courier for a single mission. She is hired because she looks and acts so completely unlike an agent, and becomes a part-timer whose brilliant improvisations and stunning successes are nothing short of fantastic.

In her various adventures, Mrs. Pollifax rescues a Chinese scientist from a seemingly impregnable fortress in Albania; joins a gypsy caravan in Turkey to rescue a woman whose career in espionage dates from World War II, at the same time exposing a dangerous double agent; smuggles passports and counterfeit money into Bulgaria; inspires an audacious raid on a maximum security prison; and prevents the assassination of an African leader. In *A Palm for Mrs. Pollifax*, she substitutes canned peaches for cannisters of plutonium and foils Arab terrorists. Dorothy Gilman recounts her heroine's exploits with such liveliness, optimism, and humor that disbelief is willingly suspended. Warmhearted and open minded, Mrs. Pollifax is without prejudice and is always sympathetic to those in trouble. Disarmingly self-mocking, whenever she is in a tight spot, Mrs. Pollifax imagines what would happen in the movies and acts accordingly, all the while regretting her own clichés. After her first triumph, she studies karate, a skill put to good use in subsequent adventures. She makes friends of all ages and even finds romance. A Bulgarian patriot, grown fond of her, exclaims: "If only you were born Bulgarian, Amerikanski, we would change the world!" In Africa, an attractive American widower proposes marriage. In perilous circumstances as she and her companions attempt to escape from Albania, Mrs. Pollifax feels "a stirring in her that was almost mystical; an exhilarating sense of freedom that she had never known before...." At another crucial moment, she considers that she is at "exactly the age ... when life ought to be spent, not hoarded. There had been enough years of comfortable living, and complacency was nothing but delusion. One could not always change the world, she felt, but one could change oneself."

In Dorothy Gilman's other suspense novels, the heroines are young women who rise above psychiatric problems and surmount personal danger to become strong individuals; cloistered nuns who take on some of the difficult problems of the modern world; and a psychic who overcomes prejudice against "fortunetellers" and solves crimes for the police. Two young nuns shelter a gangster with three bullet holes in him, run headlong into the Mafia, the FBI, crooked lawmen, a commune with its own guru, and some oppressed migrant workers. They manage to sort things out and "mend a little of the world" in a comic morality play. *The Tightrope Walker* features an allegorical fairy tale, a lost manuscript, and a young woman recovering from emotional illness who solves a murder committed years earlier.

Gilman creates appealing characters whose "ordinary" lives are changed by their encounters with danger. Naive and innocent to begin with, apparently handicapped by age, poverty, or emotional problems, they pit their courage, perseverance, and resourcefulness (fortified by inner strength discovered in time of need), against the organized powers of evil. Gilman is interested in mysticism, psychic phenomena, and Oriental philosophies, and incorporates them into her fiction. Her readers will enjoy *A New Kind of Country*, an inspirational account of her quest for self-understanding and for harmony in her own nature and with her environment.

Dorothy Gilman's action-filled plots unfold amidst the upheavals of world events – power politics, cold war struggles, oil shortages, the arms race, and the problems of emerging nations, complicated in the personal sphere by greed, prejudice, dishonesty, and cruelty. The achievements of her heroines are made more plausible by the matter-of-fact tone of the narration, by the author's sense of humor and skillful use of topical detail. Goodness and kindness prevail in these tales which show things the way we wish they were. Dorothy Gilman's suspense fiction is wholesome, up-beat entertainment for readers of all ages.

—Mary Helen Becker

GODEY, John. Pseudonym for Morton Freedgood; also writes as Stanley Morton. American. Born in Brooklyn, New York, in 1912. Educated at City College of New York; New York University. Served in the United States Army, 1943. Public Relations Agent for United Artists, Twentieth Century-Fox, Paramount.

CRIME PUBLICATIONS

Novels (series character: Jack Albany)

   The Gun and Mr. Smith. New York, Doubleday, 1947; London, Hodder and
     Stoughton, 1976.
   The Blue Hour. New York, Doubleday, 1948; London, Boardman, 1949; as *Killer at
     His Back,* New York, Spivak, 1955; as *The Next to Die,* London, Tandem, 1975.
   The Man in Question. New York, Doubleday, 1951; London, Boardman, 1953; as *The
     Blonde Betrayer,* New York, Spivak, 1955.

This Year's Death. New York, Doubleday, and London, Boardman, 1953.
The Clay Assassin. London, Boardman, 1959.
The Fifth House. London, Boardman, 1960; New York, Berkley, 1973.
The Reluctant Assassin. London, Hale, 1966.
A Thrill a Minute with Jack Albany. New York, Simon and Schuster, 1967.
Never Put Off till Tomorrow What You Can Kill Today (Albany). New York, Random House, 1970.
The Three Worlds of Johnny Handsome. New York, Random House, 1972; London, Hodder and Stoughton, 1973.
The Taking of Pelham One Two Three. New York, Putnam, and London, Hodder and Stoughton, 1973.
Talisman. New York, Putnam, 1976.
The Snake. New York, Putnam, 1978.

OTHER PUBLICATIONS

Novels

Yankee Trader (as Stanley Morton), with Stanley Freedgood. New York, Sheridan House, 1947.
The Wall-to-Wall Trap (as Morton Freedgood). New York, Simon and Schuster, 1957; London, Jarrolds, 1958.

Other

The Crime of the Century and Other Misdemeanors (autobiography). New York, Putnam, 1973.

*   *   *

Although he is the author of numerous short stories, John Godey's most memorable claim to fame is his best-selling novel *The Taking of Pelham One Two Three.* In this alarmingly realistic and breathtakingly tense novel, four armed men hijack a New York subway train containing 16 passengers and hold them for a ransom of one million dollars. Godey's intimate knowledge of New York City, where he has spent most of his life, enables him to bring to life the interworkings of the city's political leaders, news reporters, police force, and subway authorities in a cooperative effort to capture the ruthless kidnappers who have threatened to kill the hostages if the money is not delivered.

Godey's characters are vivid, particularly in his later novels. A good example of this is *Talisman*, the tense, fast-paced story of a revolutionary group which steals the remains of the unknown soldier. The climax is scorchingly ironic. Godey frequently switches the narrative viewpoint from character to character, adding depth to the story in the transition. He is also adept in the wise use of "street language" which adds another dimension of credibility to his characters. Although Godey's novels could not really be classified as typically hard-boiled or gangster stories, they do involve ex-cons, prostitutes, crooked cops, grafting politicians, and crimes methodically planned, motivated primarily by greed rather than by passion.

Somewhat lacking in the credibility of their plotting, Godey's earlier novels rely heavily on characterization, and, in some instances, on humor. The Albany series, *A Thrill a Minute* and *Never Put Off till Tomorrow What You Can Kill Today*, for instance are farcical thrillers involving Jack Albany, a bit-part character actor, with intricate plots which allow plenty of room for Albany's blustery bungling. Both novels start off with a case of mistaken identity, since Albany looks too much like a crook should look. Of course, when the actor in Albany cannot resist playing the role in which he has been mistakenly cast, the real action starts, and the comedic errors are compiled in a witty and amusing romp.

—Mary Ann Grochowski

GOLDSTEIN, Arthur D(avid). Also writes as Albert Ross. American. Born in Brooklyn, New York, 21 May 1937. Educated at Ohio University, Athens, B.A. 1958. Served in the United States Army, 1961–63. Married Lynne Milstein in 1967 (divorced, 1975). Editor, Marine Engineers Beneficial Association, Brooklyn, 1963–65; Account Executive, Hal Leyshon and Associates, public relations, 1965–67 and Gilbert A. Robinson Inc., 1967–68; Editor, *Securities*, New York, 1968–70; member of the American Stock Exchange, New York, 1970–75. Since 1975, self-employed author. Agent: Henry Morrison Inc., 68 West 10th Street, New York, New York 10011, U.S.A.

CRIME PUBLICATIONS

Novels (series character: Max Guttman)

> *A Person Shouldn't Die Like That* (Guttman). New York, Random House, 1972; London, Prior, 1977.
> *Your're Never Too Old to Die* (Guttman). New York, Random House, 1974.
> *If I Knew What I Was Doing* (as Albert Ross). New York, Random House, 1974.
> *Nobody's Sorry He Got Killed* (Guttman). New York, Random House, 1976.

* * *

A Person Shouldn't Die Like That, Arthur D. Goldstein's first mystery, was a memorable one. It was, furthermore, an immediate success. The story is of an elderly man, Max Guttman, who has lived for many years in an old-fashioned apartment on the lower East Side of New York City. Since the death of his wife, he has resisted the pressure of his married daughter to move him to California where she lives. He is content with his familiar ways, visiting with his old cronies in the park, deploring the criminal tendencies of too many of the young people. Curious about one old friend who hasn't been seen recently, he finds the man murdered in his own rooms. Max then decides a person shouldn't die like that, and sets out to find why and by whom. So perfectly has Arthur Goldstein created the old man that it comes as a surprise to find the author to be a young man. He has also avoided the stereotyped sayings and philosophies usually put into the mouth of a man like Guttman. The full flavor of the old Jew's world, his environs and his personal relationships, are without cliché.

There have been two more books about Max, *You're Never Too Old to Die*, and *Nobody's Sorry He Got Killed*. In the second of these, his daughter has had her way, and Max is doing his best to retain his identity in a strange environment. But Goldstein should transport Max back to his own little pond and the kindness of old friends. A room in his daughter's home isn't good enough for Max.

—Dorothy B. Hughes

THE GORDONS: Mildred Gordon and Gordon Gordon. American. **GORDON, Mildred** (née Nixon): Born in Eureka, Kansas, 24 July 1905. Educated at the University of Arizona, Tucson, B.A. 1930. Married Gordon Gordon in 1932. Teacher, Carrillo School, Tucson, 1931–32; Editor, *Arizona* magazine, 1932–34; Correspondent, United Press, 1935; self-employed author after 1935. *Died 3 February 1979.* **GORDON, Gordon:** Born in Anderson, Indiana, 12 March 1906. Educated at the University of Arizona, Tucson, B.A. 1929. Reporter, 1930–31, and Managing Editor, 1931–35, Tucson *Daily Citizen*; Publicist, Twentieth Century-Fox, Hollywood, 1935–42; Counter-Espionage Agent, Federal Bureau of Investigation, Washington, D.C., and Chicago, 1942–45. Self-employed author after 1945. Joint Recipients: Book Society of Great Britain Award, 1954; Writers Guild of America Award, 1965; American Humor Society Award, 1965; University of Arizona Achievement Award, 1970. Agent: William Morris Agency, 151 El Camino, Beverly Hills, California 90212. Address: 22556 Marlin Place, Canoga Park, California 91307, U.S.A.

CRIME PUBLICATIONS

Novels (series characters: D. C. Randall, The Cat; John Ripley)

The Little Man Who Wasn't There (as Mildred Gordon).   New York, Doubleday, 1946.
Make Haste to Live.   New York, Doubleday, 1950.
FBI Story (Ripley).   New York, Doubleday, 1950; London, Corgi, 1957.
Campaign Train.   New York, Doubleday, and London, Wingate, 1952; as *Murder Rides the Campaign Train*, New York, Bantam, 1976.
Case File: FBI (Ripley).   New York, Doubleday, 1953; London, Macdonald, 1954.
The Case of the Talking Bug.   New York, Doubleday, 1955; as *Playback*, London, Macdonald, 1955.
The Big Frame.   New York, Doubleday, and London, Macdonald, 1957.
Captive (Ripley).   New York, Doubleday, 1957; London, Macdonald, 1958.
Tiger on My Back.   New York, Doubleday, and London, Macdonald, 1960.
Operation Terror (Ripley).   New York, Doubleday, and London, Macdonald, 1961; as *Experiment in Terror*, New York, Bantam, 1962.
Menace.   New York, Doubleday, 1962; as *Journey with a Stranger*, London, Macdonald, 1963.
Undercover Cat.   New York, Doubleday, 1963; London, Macdonald, 1964; as *That Darn Cat*, New York, Bantam, and London, Corgi, 1966.
Power Play.   New York, Doubleday, 1965; London, Macdonald, 1966.
Undercover Cat Prowls Again.   New York, Doubleday, 1966; London, Macdonald, 1967.
Night Before the Wedding.   New York, Doubleday, and London, Macdonald, 1969.
The Tumult and the Joy.   New York, Doubleday, 1971.
The Informant (Ripley).   New York, Doubleday, and London, Macdonald, 1973.
Catnapped: The Further Adventures of Undercover Cat.   New York, Doubleday, 1974; London, Macdonald, 1975.
Ordeal.   New York, Doubleday, 1976; London, Macdonald, 1977.
Night after the Wedding.   New York, Doubleday, 1979.

Uncollected Short Story

"The Terror Racket," in *Ellery Queen's Mystery Magazine* (New York), August 1967.

OTHER PUBLICATIONS

Plays

Screenplays: *Down Three Dark Streets*, with Bernard C. Schoenfeld, 1954; *Experiment in Terror*, 1962; *That Darn Cat*, with Bill Walsh, 1965.

Other

With This Ring, with Judge Louis H. Burke. New York, McGraw Hill, 1958.
"A Marriage of Minds," in *Murder Ink: The Mystery Reader's Companion*, edited by Dilys Winn. New York, Workman, 1977.

Editor, *A Pride of Felons*. New York, Macmillan, 1963; London, Dobson, 1964.

Manuscript Collection: Mugar Memorial Library, Boston University.

Gordon Gordon comments:
In twenty novels we tried to write the kind of stories that we ourselves enjoyed reading. Fast moving ones with excitement and surprises, flashes of humor, and about very ordinary people, much like ourselves.

Usually the tales were about an innocent person – someone struggling to make a living – who was caught up unexpectedly in a kidnapping, extortion, or blackmail. He was caught up because he just happened to be standing in a certain spot at a certain time, a facet of everyday living that keeps increasing with terrifying regularity. During our newspaper and FBI days we encountered much of this and marveled at the innate courage and jaw-setting of even the quietest victims.

We liked characters who never gave up, no matter the odds, who struggled to live decent lives, who knew there is a God and tomorrow will be better, who loved deeply, and who rose above the sordid world in which many of them lived. We have been told by critics that there are no such people, that we were romanticists hiding in the suspense and excitement of very real situations and settings. We admit that our violence was brief, our sex never explicit, and our bad people often had signs of being redeemable. We thank the critics for granting that the stories possessed realism. Because we enjoyed backgrounds in the novels we read, we worked long and hard over the ones in our own books.

Since our third or fourth novel, we have used a "continuous suspense situation," a single crime that unfolds in its creation and detection quickly with many logical tangents and twists. Most of our books were morality plays, in that good triumphed over evil. Not a squashy kind of good but that of courage, strength, and high intentions.

We collaborated in our work as well as marriage for almost a half century. We loved furiously and deeply, went everywhere, did everything, and had a terrific time in one of the most exciting jobs in the world, writing "entertainments" about characters we liked and often loved.

Oh, what the hell, maybe we were romanticists – in fiction as well as in life.

*   *   *

The Gordons write first-rate escapist suspense fiction. Their best books adhere to a definite formula, but it is a good one and skillfully handled. This formula can be summed up as *the girl, the crook, the cop, and the clock*. Take one spunky, not-beautiful-but-pertly-attractive heroine, and place her in acute danger; bring to her aid a determined, not-handsome-but-ruggedly-attractive cop who is conscientious and competent; create a deadline before which the crook must be caught or the girl will be killed, and delay the resolution to the last possible moment before time runs out. Although capturing the criminal depends on the hero's accurate deductions, the emphasis is not on a process of detection, but rather on the steadily ticking clock. The formula is standard, but the Gordons exploit to the fullest its emotional potential.

This formula works because it sharply excites but ultimately assuages feelings of helplessness and vulnerability. The Gordons use several techniques to intensify both halves of this response. First of all, a Gordons heroine rarely brings her trouble on herself; rather, the threat to her safety intrudes suddenly, apparently out of nowhere: in *Operation Terror* Kelly is thrust into a nightmare simply because she works in a bank; *Menace* is half over before we discover why Sheri is being persecuted. The reader's sense of the heroine's vulnerability is compounded by an ever-present possibility of sexual violence. Furthermore, the heroine is often responsible for a younger person who is also in danger, thus limiting her freedom to deal with her tormentor. The Gordons emphasize the psychological pressures on the heroine of terror, vulnerability, and the tension of waiting. With a feral viciousness, the criminal threatens not just her life but also her sanity. Thus the reader's question becomes not just "Will she survive?" but "Will she survive psychically intact?" The psychological battle of the heroine parallels the hero's battle of wits with the criminal. The hero commands the tools of modern scientific detection, but finally he must outwit the crook. And to do so he is willing to act independently of the procedural rules he should officially follow. When the criminal is foiled, then, the reader is reassured that the forces of good have the psychic strength, the intellectual resources, and the flexibility necessary to defeat a threatened evil.

The formula outlined above can be varied considerably without destroying its impact. In *The Informant* and *Power Play*, not just a single girl but our whole society is in jeopardy. *Undercover Cat* successfully presents a humorous version of the formula by displacing the danger onto someone we know less well than the attractive heroine. Tension is thus diffused, and the audience freed to laugh. (The sequels to *Undercover Cat*, particularly *Catnapped*, suffer from being too obviously constructed as sequences of cute scenes suitable for filming.)

Within their narrow genre, the Gordons write effectively and responsibly. As is appropriate to escapist fiction, they do not dwell on their material's implicit moral issues – such as the ethics of wiretapping or the ambiguous morality of using or being an informant – but neither do they evade or oversimplify them. (Indeed, *The Case of the Talking Bug* reveals a surprisingly early concern with wiretapping.) Mr. Gordon's background as an ex-FBI agent lends authenticity to portrayals of investigative procedures, and the settings for all the Gordons's books are drawn with care. In general, a novel by the Gordons can be relied upon to provide an evening of suspenseful entertainment.

—Susan B. MacDougall

GORES, Joe (Joseph N. Gores). American. Born in Rochester, Minnesota, 25 December 1931. Educated at the University of Notre Dame, Indiana, A.B. 1953; Stanford University, California, M.A. 1961. Served in the United States Army, 1958–59. Married Dori Gould in 1976. Worked as laborer, logger, clerk, driver, carnival helper, assistant motel manager; Instructor, Floyd Page's Gymnasium, Palo Alto, 1953–55; Private Investigator, L.A. Walker Company, 1955–57, and David Kikkert and Associates, 1959–62, 1965–67, both San Francisco; English Teacher, Kakamega Boys Secondary School, Kenya, 1963–64; Manager and Auctioneer, Automobile Auction Company, San Francisco, 1968. Self-employed writer. Secretary, 1966, 1968, Vice-President, 1967, 1969–70, Member of the Board of Directors, 1967–70, 1975–76, and General Awards Chair, 1976–77, Mystery Writers of America.

Recipient: Mystery Writers of America Edgar Allan Poe Award, for novel, 1969, for short story, 1969, for tv series, 1975. Agent: Henry Morrison Inc., 58 West 10th Street, New York, New York 10011. Address: P.O. Box 446, Fairfax, California 94930, U.S.A.

CRIME PUBLICATIONS

Novels (series characters: Dan Kearney Associates)

A Time of Predators.   New York, Random House, 1969; London, W. H. Allen, 1970.
Dead Skip (Kearney).   New York, Random House, 1972; London, Gollancz, 1973.
Final Notice (Kearney).   New York, Random House, 1973; London, Gollancz, 1974.
Interface.   New York, Evans, 1974; London, Futura, 1977.
Hammett: A Novel.   New York, Putnam, 1975; London, Macdonald, 1976.
Gone, No Forwarding (Kearney).   New York, Random House, 1978; London, Gollancz, 1979.

Uncollected Short Stories

"Darl I Luv U," in *Ellery Queen's Mystery Mix.*   New York, Random House, 1963; London, Gollancz, 1964.
"A Sad and Bloody House," in *Ellery Queen's Mystery Magazine* (New York), April 1965.
"The Seeker of Ultimates," in *Ellery Queen's Mystery Magazine* (New York), November 1965.
"The Second Coming," in *Murder in Mind*, edited by Lawrence Treat.   New York, Dutton, 1967.
"File No. 3: The Pedretti Case," in *Ellery Queen's Mystery Magazine* (New York), July 1968.
"File No. 1: The Mayfield Case," in *Best Detective Stories of the Year*, edited by Anthony Boucher.   New York, Dutton, 1968.
"File No. 5: The Maria Navarro Case," in *Ellery Queen's Mystery Magazine* (New York), June 1969.
"South of Market," in *Alfred Hitchcock Presents: A Month of Mystery.*   New York, Random House, 1969.
"File No. 2: Stakeout on Page Street," in *Ellery Queen's Murder Menu.*   Cleveland, World, and London, Gollancz, 1969.
"File No. 4: Lincoln Sedan Deadline," in *Crimes and Misfortunes*, edited by J. Francis McComas.   New York, Random House, 1970.
"O Black and Unknown Bard," in *Best Detective Stories of the Year 1970*, edited by Allen J. Hubin.   New York, Dutton, 1970.
"Odendahl," in *Murder Most Foul*, edited by Harold Q. Masur.   New York, Walker, 1971.
"The Andrech Samples," in *Best Detective Stories of the Year 1971*, edited by Allan J. Hubin.   New York, Dutton, 1971.
"The O'Bannon Blarney File," in *Men and Malice*, edited by Dean Dickensheet.   New York, Doubleday, 1973.
"Watch for It," in *Mirror, Mirror, Fatal Mirror*, edited by Hans S. Santesson.   New York, Doubleday, 1973.
"You're Putting Me On – Aren't You?" in *Killers of the Mind*, edited by Lucy Freeman.   New York, Random House, 1974.
"Goodbye, Pops," in *Every Crime in the Book*, edited by Robert L. Fish.   New York, Putnam, 1975.
"File No. 10: The Maimed and the Halt," in *Ellery Queen's Mystery Magazine* (New York), January 1976.

"File No. 6: Beyond the Shadow," in *Ellery Queen's Magicians of Mystery.* New York, Davis, 1976.

"Rope Enough," in *Tricks and Treats*, edited by Joe Gores and Bill Pronzini. New York, Doubleday, 1976; as *Mystery Writers' Choice*, London, Gollancz, 1977.

"The Three Halves," in *When Last Seen*, edited by Arthur Maling. New York, Harper, 1977.

OTHER PUBLICATIONS

Plays

Television Plays: *No Immunity for Murder* (*Kojak* series), 1976, and others.

Other

Marine Salvage. New York, Doubleday, 1971; Newton Abbot, Devon, David and Charles, 1972.

Editor, *Honolulu: Port of Call.* New York, Ballantine, 1974.

Editor, with Bill Pronzini, *Tricks or Treats.* New York, Doubleday, 1976; as *Mystery Writers' Choice*, London, Gollancz, 1977.

*   *   *

The San Francisco author Joe Gores is the only writer to have won the Mystery Writers of America Edgars in three categories: short story, television drama, and novel. He has written over a hundred short stories, a number of television and movie scripts, and six quite varied crime novels.

The first, *A Time of Predators*, concerns a sociology professor, Curt Halstead, who abandons his academic theories about violence when his wife, the only witness to a vicious assault, commits suicide after having been gang-raped by the four young thugs she can identify. Halstead gradually reverts to the "bloody-mindedness" he had learned as a young man in a British Commando unit, and seeks his own vengeance on the rapists when the law fails. The book is flawed (particularly in characterization), but its strong, well-paced narrative showed a promise that has been realized in subsequent novels.

Three of them are procedural novels involving a team of auto repossessors, Dan Kearney Associates, in the San Francisco area. Gores, himself a private detective for a dozen years, uses that experience well: this is perhaps the best procedural series written, as far as attention to actual detective practices is concerned. The first "DKA File" novel, *Dead Skip*, involves the efforts of Dan Kearney and Larry Ballard to track down the man who attempted to kill their colleague, Bart Heslip, and disguise it as an accident. Heslip had discovered something odd in one of the repossessions he had been working on; the DKA men, while Heslip is in a coma, work through his current cases to discover the guilty person. In the process, the reader is introduced to a sad spectrum of broken and damaged lives in a vividly-described variety of squalid circumstances before the DKA men catch a kinky killer. In *Final Notice*, the DKA men are drawn into an investigation which uncovers the attempted blackmail of a Mafia boss, power struggle within that organization, and two murders. They unravel the complicated plot but are unable to provide enough hard evidence to turn the clever killer over to the police. Kearney, acting on his own, tips the mob off to the fact that the killer murdered the top Mafia boss to gain power himself, and it is intimated that he won't escape syndicate punishment.

Early in Gores's latest book, *Gone, No Forwarding*, we see that punishment enacted. Most of the book, however, concerns someone's efforts to get Kearney's license revoked. The harassment, it turns out, is to provide an alibi for a mob assassin. In breaking the case against Kearney and uncovering a murderer, the DKA men range over the country tracking down witnesses. The same vivid portrayal of the underbelly of humanity enlivens this DKA novel also, as is true of a different kind of book, *Interface*. Here a mysterious killer known only as Docker weaves a complicated plot against several mob figures. Docker has been hired by Neil Fargo, a tough, shady private investigator, to import heroin for the mobsters, but Docker runs amok for his own unfathomable reasons. Revolving around a cleverly concealed false-identity, the book is a fast-paced, violent, sordid tale of chase and revenge as Fargo and the gangsters try to catch and destroy the elusive Docker before he destroys them.

Different from all the above is *Hammett*, Gores's most ambitious and successful book to date. Gores combines Hammett the writer and Hammett the detective, recreates San Francisco in 1928, and invents a plausible, action-filled plot in which Hammett, to avenge the murder of a detective-friend, leads a reform committee investigation of corruption. It is a difficult task to reconstruct a city and an era and to dramatize such a well-known figure at work as writer-detective; Gores, as San Franciscan, scholar, writer, and ex-detective, is uniquely suited for this demanding job and carries it off superbly.

Gores has established himself securely as one of the best and most versatile authors of crime novels.

—Donald C. Wall

GOULART, Ron(ald Joseph). Also writes as Josephine Kains; Howard Lee; Kenneth Robeson; Frank S. Shawn; Con Steffanson. American. Born in Berkeley, California, 13 January 1933. Educated at the University of California, Berkeley, B.A. 1955. Married Frances Sheridan in 1964; two sons. Advertising Copywriter, Guild Bascom and Bonfigci, San Francisco, Alan Alch Inc., Hollywood, and Hoefer Dietrich and Brown, San Francisco. Self-employed writer since 1968. Since 1977, author of science fiction comic strip *Star Hawks*, with Gil Kane. Recipient: Mystery Writers of America Edgar Allan Poe Award, 1971. Address: 232 Georgetown Road, Weston, Connecticut 06883, U.S.A.

CRIME PUBLICATIONS

Novels (series character: John Easy)

The Sword Swallower. New York, Doubleday, 1968.
After Things Fell Apart. New York, Ace, 1970.
If Dying Was All (Easy). New York, Ace, 1971.
Hawkshaw. New York, Doubleday, 1972.
Too Sweet to Die (Easy). New York, Ace, 1972.
The Same Lie Twice (Easy). New York, Ace, 1973.
Cleopatra Jones (novelization of screenplay). New York, Warner, 1973.
One Grave Too Many (Easy). New York, Ace, 1974.
Cleopatra Jones and the Casino of Gold (novelization of screenplay). New York, Warner, 1975.
Spacehawk, Inc. New York, Daw Books, 1975.
The Enormous Hourglass. New York, Award, 1976.
Calling Dr. Patchwork. New York, Daw Books, 1978.

Novels as Kenneth Robeson (series character: the Avenger in all books)

The Man from Atlantis. New York, Warner, 1974.

Red Moon. New York, Warner, 1974.
The Purple Zombie. New York, Warner, 1974.
Dr. Time. New York, Warner, 1974.
The Nightwitch Devil. New York, Warner, 1974.
Black Chariots. New York, Warner, 1974.
The Cartoon Crimes. New York, Warner, 1974.
The Iron Skull. New York, Warner, 1974.
The Death Machine. New York, Warner, 1975.
The Blood Countess. New York, Warner, 1975.
The Glass Man. New York, Warner, 1975.
Demon Island. New York, Warner, 1975.

Short Stories

What's Become of Screwloose and Other Stories. New York, Scribner, and London, Sidgwick and Jackson, 1971.
Ghost Breaker. New York, Ace, 1971.
Odd Job No. 101 and Other Future Crimes and Intrigues. New York, Scribner, 1975; London, Hale, 1976.

Uncollected Short Stories

"You Have to Stay Dead So Long," in *Mystery Monthly* (New York), September 1976.
"They're Gonna Kill You after Awhile," in *Mystery Monthly* (New York), January 1977.
"Please Don't Help the Bear," in *Ellery Queen's Mystery Magazine* (New York), January 1977.
"Now He Thinks He's Dead," in *Ellery Queen's Mystery Magazine* (New York), November 1977.
"The Laughing Chef," in *Ellery Queen's Who's Who of Whodunits.* New York, Davis, 1977.
"And the Winner Is," in *Ellery Queen's Mystery Magazine* (New York), April 1978.
"Out of the Inkwell," in *Alfred Hitchcock's Mystery Magazine* (New York), September 1978.
"How Come My Dog Don't Bark," in *Ellery Queen's Mystery Magazine* (New York), September 1978.
"Running," in *Alfred Hitchcock's Mystery Magazine* (New York), November 1978.
"News from Nowhere," in *Alfred Hitchcock's Tales to Scare You Stiff*, edited by Eleanor Sullivan. New York, Davis, 1978.
"Ninety-Nine Clop Clop," in *Ellery Queen's Mystery Magazine* (New York), January 1979.

Other Publications

Novels

Gadget Man. New York, Doubleday, 1971; London, New English Library, 1977.
The Fire Eater. New York, Ace, 1970.
Death Cell. New York, Beagle Books, 1971.
Clockwork's Pirates. New York, Ace, 1971.
Plunder. New York, Beagle Books, 1972.
Wildsmith. New York, Ace, 1972.
Shaggy Planet. New York, Lancer, 1973.
A Talent for the Invisible. New York, Daw Books, 1973.
Superstition (novelization of tv play; as Howard Lee). New York, Warner, 1973.
The Tin Angel. New York, Daw Books, 1973.

Flux. New York, Daw Books, 1974.
When the Waker Sleeps. New York, Daw Books, 1975.
The Tremendous Adventures of Bernie Wine. New York, Warner, 1975.
Bloodstalk (novelization of comic strip). New York, Warner, 1975.
On Alien Wings (novelization of comic strip). New York, Warner, 1975.
The Hellhound Project. New York, Doubleday, 1975.
A Whiff of Madness. New York, Daw Books, 1975.
Quest of the Gypsy. New York, Daw Books, 1976.
Deadwalk (novelization of comic strip). New York, Warner, 1976.
Crackpot. New York, Doubleday, and London, Hale, 1977.
The Emperor of the Last Days. New York, Popular Library, 1977.
The Panchronicon Plot. New York, Daw Books, 1977.
Nemo. New York, Berkley, 1977; London, Hale, 1979.
Eye of the Vulture. New York, Pyramid, 1977.
The Wicked Cyborg. New York, Daw Books, 1978.
The Devil Mask Mystery (as Josephine Kains). New York, Zebra, 1978.
Cowboy Heaven. New York, Doubleday, 1979.
Dr. Scofflaw, in *Binary Star No. 3*, with Isidore Haiblum. New York, Dell, 1979.

Novels as Frank S. Shawn (series character: The Phantom in all books)

The Veiled Lady. New York, Avon, 1973.
The Golden Circle. New York, Avon, 1973.
The Mystery of the Sea Horse. New York, Avon, 1973.
The Hydra Monster. New York, Avon, 1974.
The Goggle-Eyed Pirates. New York, Avon, 1974.
The Swamp Rats. New York, Avon, 1974.

Novels as Con Steffanson (series character: Flash Gordon)

The Lion Men of Mongo (Gordon). New York, Avon, 1974.
The Plague of Sound (Gordon). New York, Avon, 1974.
The Space Circus (Gordon). New York, Avon, 1974.
Laverne and Shirley: Teamwork (novelization of tv play). New York, Warner, 1976.
Laverne and Shirley: Easy Money (novelization of tv play). New York, Warner, 1976.
Laverne and Shirley: Gold Rush (novelization of tv play). New York, Warner, 1976.

Short Stories

Broke Down Engine. New York, Macmillan, 1971.
The Chameleon Corps. New York, Macmillan, 1972.
Nutzenbolts. New York, Macmillan, 1975.

Other

The Assault on Childhood. Los Angeles, Sherbourne Press, 1969; London, Gollancz, 1970.
Cheap Thrills: An Informal History of the Pulp Magazines. New Rochelle, New York, Arlington House, 1972.
An American Family. New York, Warner, 1973.
The Adventurous Decade: Comic Strips in the Thirties. New Rochelle, New York, Arlington House, 1975.

Editor, *The Hardboiled Dicks: An Anthology and Study of Pulp Detective Fiction.* Los Angeles, Sherbourne Press, 1965; London, Boardman, 1967.
Editor, *Lineup Tough Guys.* Los Angeles, Sherbourne Press, 1966.

Ron Goulart comments:

The fact that I am, to the best of my knowledge, the only writer ever to win a Mystery Writers of America award for a science fiction novel indicates my dual fascination with both detective stories and fantasies. I had the good fortune to study with Anthony Boucher in my youth, and he also practiced in both genres and sometimes mixed them. It isn't only the opportunity to construct puzzles and extrapolations which drew me to these two areas. I also discovered quite early that both fields allowed you to be funny. This is important to me and I plan to keep mixing murder, bugeyed monsters and satire for as long as I can get away with it.

*   *   *

Ron Goulart's fictional world bears only a superficial resemblance to our own. His science-fiction is usually set in the Barnum System which exists far beyond our own Solar System and contains as many planets as the current story may call for. To anyone's knowledge, no one has ever charted or mapped the Barnum System. His mysteries are often set in Southern California, a state which exists far beyond mortal imagination and contains whatever the current story may call for. Sometimes, reading one genre example next to another, there is a sudden feeling of time warp *déjà vu*: his science-fiction often has a mystery in its basic plot, and his mysteries have a touch of fantasy. Even in his straightest, most deadpan, serious mysteries there is a glimpse of glee.

Some of his earliest contributions to the genre were parodies of well known crime writers: Ross Macdonald, Raymond Chandler, John D. MacDonald, Richard Stark, and Ed McBain. His first John Easy story, "The Tin Ear," was a subtle spoof on parts of *The Maltese Falcon.*

The stories of Max Kearny, amateur occult detective, in *Ghost Breaker* are concerned more with fantasy than detection though some might consider them a border-line category. *The Enormous Hourglass* is a science-fiction novel about a "time-detective" named Sam Brimmer, while "Monte Cristo Complex" (in *What's Become of Screwloose*) features a psychiatric detective named Vincent Hawthorn.

He has used only a few series characters. Hilda and Jake Pace of Odd Jobs, Inc. investigate cases no sane detective would touch. The stories are also set in the future. His short stories narrated by an anonymous account executive for an advertising agency present a satiric commentary on the jealousies between actors, writers, directors, and other artists in the motion picture and television industry. Since Goulart has never given his narrator a name, it is tempting to think of him as a sort of Hollywood Op, although he merely observes and does not really participate in the action. Perhaps he should just be called the Hollywood Ad Man. Goulart's most solid contribution to the literature of the private eye is his Hollywood Dick, John Easy, who seems to specialize in missing-persons cases, especially women. The minor characters in the Easy novels are even more wildly unconventional than the usual Hollywood detective story calls for. Hagopian, the writer for *TV Look* who opens his files to Easy, has choice criticism for the city and its inhabitants, but he is as cockeyed as any of them. John Easy is the one sane man in an insane world. His story is his attempt to restore sanity, while maintaining his own. (Easy was named after Roy Crane's newspaper cartoon strip hero.)

There is an air of the unreal in much of Goulart, as though the story were being told at a party where the reader's attention was being constantly diverted. The story is carried largely by the dialogue; the physical background and characters are sketched in lightly. Much of his style and content can be traced to his experience as an advertising copywriter; his stories often begin with a sentence designed to hold the reader's interest. He is probably not breaking new ground in the detective field, but he is holding up the Hollywood scene for a fresh and not completely cynical scrutiny.

—J. Randolph Cox

GRAEME, Bruce. Pseudonym for Graham Montague Jeffries; also writes as Peter Bourne; David Graeme. British. Born in London, 23 May 1900. Educated privately. Served in the Queen's Westminster Rifles, 1918. Married Lorna Hélène Louch in 1925; one son, Roderic Jeffries, *q.v.*, and one daughter. Film producer in 1919 and in the 1940's; Reporter, *Middlesex County Times*, Ealing, in the 1920's; entered Gray's Inn, London, 1930. Founding Member, Crime Writers Association, 1953. Address: Gorse Field Cottage, Aldington Frith, near Ashford, Kent TN25 7AR, England.

CRIME PUBLICATIONS

Novels (series characters: Detective Sergeant Robert Mather; Superintendent William Stevens and Inspector Pierre Allain; Theodore I. Terhune)

La Belle Laurine. London, Unwin, 1926; revised edition, as *Laurine*, London, Philip Allan, 1935.
The Trail of the White Knight. London, Harrap, 1926; New York, Doran, 1927.
Hate Ship! London, Hutchinson, and New York, Dodd Mead, 1928.
Trouble! London, Harrap, and Philadelphia, Lippincott, 1929.
Through the Eyes of the Judge. London, Hutchinson, and Philadelphia, Lippincott, 1930.
The Penance of Brother Alaric. London, Hutchinson, 1930.
A Murder of Some Importance (Stevens and Allain). London, Hutchinson, and Philadelphia, Lippincott, 1931.
Unsolved. London, Hutchinson, 1931; Philadelphia, Lippincott, 1932.
Gigins Court. London, Hutchinson, 1932.
The Imperfect Crime (Stevens and Allain). London, Hutchinson, 1932; Philadelphia, Lippincott, 1933.
Impeached! London, Hutchinson, 1933.
Epilogue (Stevens and Allain). London, Hutchinson, 1933; Philadelphia, Lippincott, 1934.
An International Affair (Stevens and Allain). London, Hutchinson, 1934.
Public Enemy – No. 1. London, Hutchinson, 1934; as *John Jenkin, Public Enemy*, Philadelphia, Lippincott, 1935.
Madame Spy. London, Philip Allan, 1935.
Satan's Mistress (Stevens and Allain). London, Hutchinson, 1935.
Not Proven (Stevens and Allain). London, Hutchinson, 1935.
Cardyce for the Defence. London, Hutchinson, 1936.
Mystery on the Queen Mary (Stevens and Allain). London, Hutchinson, 1937; Philadelphia, Lippincott, 1938.
Disappearance of Roger Tremayne. London, Hutchinson, 1937.
Racing Yacht Mystery. London, Hutchinson, 1938.
The Man from Michigan (Stevens and Allain). London, Hutchinson, 1938; as *The Mystery of the Stolen Hats*, Philadelphia, Lippincott, 1939.

Body Unknown (Stevens and Allain).   London, Hutchinson, 1939.

Poisoned Sleep (Stevens and Allain).   London, Hutchinson, 1939.

Thirteen in a Fog.   London, Hutchinson, 1940.

The Corporal Died in Bed, Being the Swan-Song of Pierre Allain (Stevens and Allain).   London, Hutchinson, 1940.

Seven Clues in Search of a Crime (Terhune).   London, Hutchinson, 1941.

Encore Allain! (Stevens and Allain).   London, Hutchinson, 1941.

House with Crooked Walls (Terhune).   London, Hutchinson, 1942.

News Travels by Night (Stevens and Allain).   London, Hutchinson, 1943.

A Case for Solomon (Terhune).   London, Hutchinson, 1943.

Work for the Hangman (Terhune).   London, Hutchinson, 1944.

Ten Trails to Tyburn (Terhune).   London, Hutchinson, 1944.

The Coming of Carew.   London, Hutchinson, 1945.

A Case of Books.   London, Hutchinson, 1946.

Without Malice.   London, Hutchinson, 1946.

No Clues for Dexter.   London, Hutchinson, 1948.

And a Bottle of Rum (Terhune).   London, Hutchinson, 1949.

Tigers Have Claws.   London, Hutchinson, 1949.

Cherchez la Femme.   London, Hutchinson, 1951.

Dead Pigs at Hungry Farm (Terhune).   London, Hutchinson, 1951.

Lady in Black.   London, Hutchinson, 1952.

Mr. Whimset Buys a Gun.   London, Hutchinson, 1953.

Suspense.   London, Hutchinson, 1953.

The Way Out.   London, Hutchinson, 1954.

So Sharp the Razor.   London, Hutchinson, 1955.

Just an Ordinary Case.   London, Hutchinson, 1956.

The Accidental Clue.   London, Hutchinson, 1957.

The Long Night.   London, Hutchinson, 1958.

Boomerang.   London, Hutchinson, 1959.

Fog for a Killer.   London, Hutchinson, 1960.

The Undetective.   London, Hutchinson, 1962; New York, London House and Maxwell, 1963.

Almost Without Murder.   London, Hutchinson, 1963.

Holiday for a Spy.   London, Hutchinson, 1963.

Always Expect the Unexpected.   London, Hutchinson, 1965.

The Devil Was a Woman.   London, Hutchinson, 1966.

Much Ado about Something.   London, Hutchinson, 1967.

Never Mix Business with Pleasure.   London, Hutchinson, 1968.

Some Geese Lay Golden Eggs.   London, Hutchinson, 1968.

Blind Date for a Private Eye.   London, Hutchinson, 1969.

The Quiet Ones (Mather).   London, Hutchinson, 1970.

The Lady Doth Protest.   London, Hutchinson, 1971.

Tomorrow's Yesterday.   London, Hutchinson, 1972.

Two and Two Make Five (Mather).   London, Hutchinson, 1973.

The D Notice (Mather).   London, Hutchinson, 1974.

The Snatch (Mather).   London, Hutchinson, 1976.

Two-Faced (Mather).   London, Hutchinson, 1977.

Double Trouble (Mather).   London, Hutchinson, 1978.

Mather Again.   London, Hutchinson, 1979.

Invitation to Mather.   London, Hale, 1979.

Novels as David Graeme (series character: Monsieur Blackshirt)

Monsieur Blackshirt.   London, Harrap, and Philadelphia, Lippincott, 1933.

The Vengeance of Monsieur Blackshirt. London, Harrap, 1934; Philadelphia, Lippincott, 1935.

The Sword of Monsieur Blackshirt. London, Harrap, and Philadelphia, Lippincott, 1936.

The Inn of Thirteen Swords (Monsieur Blackshirt). London, Harrap, 1938.

The Drums Beat Red. London, Harrap, 1963.

Short Stories (series characters: Blackshirt; Lord Blackshirt)

Blackshirt. London, Unwin, and New York, Dodd Mead, 1925; revised edition, London, Benn, 1930.

The Return of Blackshirt. London, Unwin, and New York, Dodd Mead, 1927; revised edition, London, Benn, 1927.

Blackshirt Again. London, Hutchinson, 1929; as *Adventures of Blackshirt*, New York, Dodd Mead, 1929.

Alias Blackshirt. London, Harrap, and New York, Dodd Mead, 1932.

Blackshirt the Audacious. London, Hutchinson, 1935; Philadelphia, Lippincott, 1936.

Blackshirt the Adventurer. London, Hutchinson, 1936.

Blackshirt Takes a Hand. London, Hutchinson, 1937.

Blackshirt, Counter-Spy. London, Hutchinson, 1938.

Blackshirt Interferes. London, Hutchinson, 1939.

Blackshirt Strikes Back. London, Hutchinson, 1940.

Son of Blackshirt (Lord Blackshirt). London, Hutchinson, 1941.

Lord Blackshirt: The Son of Blackshirt Carries On. London, Hutchinson, 1942.

Calling Lord Blackshirt. London, Hutchinson, 1943.

A Battle for O'Leary and Two Other Episodes in His Career. London, Hutchinson, 1947.

Uncollected Short Stories

"Hand of Steele," in *My Best Thriller.* London, Faber, 1933.

"Miss Mystery," in *A Century of Spy Stories*, edited by Dennis Wheatley. London, Hutchinson, 1938.

"The Empty House," in *My Best Mystery Story.* London, Faber, 1939.

"Chequemate," in *The Saint* (New York), May 1958.

"Unseen Alibi," in *Murder in Mind*, edited by Lawrence Treat. New York, Dutton, 1967.

OTHER PUBLICATIONS

Novels as Peter Bourne

When the Bells Ring (as Bruce Graeme), with Anthony Armstrong. London, Harrap, 1943.

Black Saga. London, Hutchinson, 1947; as *Drums of Destiny*, New York, Putnam, 1947.

Flames of Empire. New York, Putnam, 1949; as *Dupe of Destiny*, London, Hutchinson, 1950.

Ten Thousand Shall Die. London, Hutchinson, 1951; as *The Golden Road*, New York, Putnam, 1951.

Gateway to Fortune. London, Hutchinson, and New York, Putnam, 1952.

Twilight of the Dragon. London, Hutchinson, and New York, Putnam, 1954.

When Gods Slept. London, Hutchinson, and New York, Putnam, 1956.

The Court of Love. London, Hutchinson, and New York, Putnam, 1958.

Soldiers of Fortune. London, Hutchinson, 1962; New York, Putnam, 1963.

Black Gold.   London, Hutchinson, 1964.
Fall of the Eagle.   London, Hutchinson, 1967.
And Bay the Moon.   London, Hutchinson, 1975.

Other

Passion, Murder and Mystery.   London, Hutchinson, and New York, Doubleday, 1928.
The Story of Buckingham Palace.   London, Hutchinson, 1928; revised edition, London, Howard Baker, 1970.
The Story of St. James's Palace.   London, Hutchinson, 1929.
A Century of Buckingham Palace 1837–1937.   London, Hutchinson, 1937.
The Story of Windsor Castle.   London, Hutchinson, 1937.
Danger in the Channel (juvenile).   London, Kaye and Ward, 1973.

*   *   *

Bruce Graeme (pseudonym of Graham Montague Jeffries) is noted for his literary longevity, his production (averaging almost 2 books per year), and his series characters. Graeme is an extremely competent professional storyteller whose best work is worth revival today.

Graeme's first attempt to write a novel ended in fiasco, but he hit the jackpot on his next try with a series of short stories that were later published in book form as *Blackshirt*. This volume and its successor, *The Return of Blackshirt*, went on to sell a million copies. Blackshirt is a well-known and respected mystery writer named Richard Verrell. By night he becomes a gentleman thief who disguises himself by dressing completely in black. He commits his thefts for the sheer love and excitement of the game. Blackshirt went on to become, in William Vivian Butler's words, "the most durable desperado of them all." The length of Blackshirt's career (1923–69) has been exceeded only by that of Charteris's the Saint. Graeme provided a successor in 1941; *Son of Blackshirt* was the first of these novels detailing the adventures of Verrell's son Anthony, who eventually becomes Lord Blackshirt. Graeme had also created a series of four novels about a Monsieur Blackshirt, a 17th-century ancestor of Verrell, whose adventures were set in France; these books were published under the pseudonym David Graeme. (But that wasn't all. Graeme's son, Roderic Graeme Jeffries, continued the original Blackshirt series with some 20 novels published as Roderic Graeme.)

Bruce Graeme's best series started in 1931 with *A Murder of Some Importance*, which introduced the conservative and very British Superintendent William Stevens of Scotland Yard, and the fiery Inspector Pierre Allain of the Sûreté who is noted for his prowess in detection as well as love. This series of some dozen novels featured some of Graeme's best writing and detective puzzles. Among the best is *The Imperfect Crime* with its deceptive clues and its neat (though not unprecedented) variation of the least-likely suspect gambit that is only solved by a slip of the murderer's tongue. Not as effective is *Not Proven*, a partially inverted tale that starts with a murder by a policeman who is subsequently placed in charge of the investigation, anticipating Kenneth Fearing's *The Big Clock*. Stevens and Allain finally discover the murderer's identity – but can't prove it.

Another series centers on Theodore I. Terhune, a young bookseller in a small British town whose desire to live a quiet life is often interrupted by murder problems. Graeme's most recent character, Detective-Sergeant Robert Mather of the Bretton Police, was introduced in *The Quiet Ones*; his investigations are more concerned with adventure than detection.

Graeme has also written many non-series novels. *The Undetective* has a mystery writer as its protagonist. He seeks material that will expose police methods, but finds trouble instead. An early and lucid section on the economic perils of mystery writing is of interest.

Graeme's voyage on the Queen Mary's initial outing provided the inspiration for *Mystery on the Queen Mary*. It's one of the best shipboard mysteries ever written, intensely entertaining, and a thorough delight. In *Epilogue* Superintendent Stevens goes back through time and finds himself obliged to solve the mystery of Edwin Drood, which Dickens left unfinished. Several of Graeme's efforts contain legal problems. His masterpiece, *Through the Eyes of the Judge*, is a long, detailed courtroom novel whose ironic ending is a challenge to the British legal system. It had some influence on one of Richard Hull's novels, and the work of his son.

—Charles Shibuk

GRAEME, David. See **GRAEME, Bruce.**

GRAEME, Roderic. See **JEFFRIES, Roderic.**

GRAHAM, Jack. See **MARLOWE, Hugh.**

GRAHAM, Neill. See **DUNCAN, W. Murdoch.**

GRAHAM, Winston. British. Born in Victoria Park, Manchester, Lancashire, in 1909. Married Jean Mary Williamson in 1939; one son and one daughter. Chairman, Society of Authors, London, 1967–69. Recipient: Crime Writers Association prize, 1956. Fellow, Royal Society of Literature, 1968. Address: Abbotswood House, Buxted, East Sussex, England.

CRIME PUBLICATIONS

Novels

The House with the Stained-Glass Windows. London, Ward Lock, 1934.
Into the Fog. London, Ward Lock, 1935.
The Riddle of John Rowe. London, Ward Lock, 1935.
Without Motive. London, Ward Lock, 1936.
The Dangerous Pawn. London, Ward Lock, 1937.
The Giant's Chair. London, Ward Lock, 1938.
Strangers Meeting. London, Ward Lock, 1939.
Keys of Chance. London, Ward Lock, 1939.
No Exit: An Adventure. London, Ward Lock, 1940.
Night Journey. London, Ward Lock, 1941; New York, Doubleday, 1968.
My Turn Next. London, Ward Lock, 1942.
The Merciless Ladies. London, Ward Lock, 1944; revised edition, London, Bodley
    Head, 1979.
The Forgotten Story. London, Ward Lock, 1945; as *The Wreck of The Grey Cat*, New
    York, Doubleday, 1958.
Take My Life. London, Ward Lock, 1947; New York, Doubleday, 1967.
Night Without Stars. London, Hodder and Stoughton, and New York, Doubleday,
    1950.
Fortune Is a Woman. London, Hodder and Stoughton, and New York, Doubleday,
    1953.
The Little Walls. London, Hodder and Stoughton, and New York, Doubleday, 1955;
    abridged edition, as *Bridge to Vengeance*, New York, Spivak, 1957.
The Sleeping Partner. London, Hodder and Stoughton, and New York, Doubleday,
    1956.
Greek Fire. London, Hodder and Stoughton, and New York, Doubleday, 1958.
The Tumbled House. London, Hodder and Stoughton, 1959; New York, Doubleday,
    1960.
Marnie. London, Hodder and Stoughton, and New York, Doubleday, 1961.
The Grove of Eagles. London, Hodder and Stoughton, 1963; New York, Doubleday,
    1964.
After the Act. London, Hodder and Stoughton, 1965; New York, Doubleday, 1966.
The Walking Stick. London, Collins, and New York, Doubleday, 1967.
Angell, Pearl and Little God. London, Collins, and New York, Doubleday, 1970.
Woman in the Mirror. London, Bodley Head, and New York, Doubleday, 1975.

Short Stories

The Japanese Girl and Other Stories. London, Collins, 1971; New York, Doubleday,
    1972.

Uncollected Short Story

"The Circus," in *Winter's Crimes 6*, edited by George Hardinge. London, Macmillan,
    1974.

OTHER PUBLICATIONS

Novels

Ross Poldark: A Novel of Cornwall 1783–1787. London, Ward Lock, 1945; as *The
    Renegade*, New York, Doubleday, 1951; as *Ross Poldark*, New York, Ballantine,
    1977.

Demelza: A Novel of Cornwall 1788–1790. London, Ward Lock, 1946; New York, Doubleday, 1953.

Cordelia. London, Ward Lock, 1949; New York, Doubleday, 1950.

Jeremy Poldark: A Novel of Cornwall 1790–1791. London, Ward Lock, 1950; as *Venture Once More*, New York, Doubleday, 1954; as *Jeremy Poldark*, New York, Ballantine, 1977.

Warleggan: A Novel of Cornwall 1792–1793. London, Ward Lock, 1953; as *The Last Gamble*, New York, Doubleday, 1955; as *Warleggan*, New York, Ballantine, 1977.

The Grove of Eagles. London, Hodder and Stoughton, 1963; New York, Doubleday, 1964.

The Black Moon: A Novel of Cornwall 1794–1795. London, Collins, 1973; New York, Doubleday, 1974.

The Four Swans: A Novel of Cornwall 1795–1797. London, Collins, 1976; New York, Doubleday, 1977.

The Angry Tide: A Novel of Cornwall 1798–1799. London, Collins, 1977; New York, Doubleday, 1978.

Plays

Shadow Play (produced Salisbury, 1978).

Screenplays: *Take My Life*, with Valerie Taylor, 1947; *Night Without Stars*, 1951.

Radio Play: *Little Walls*, 1956.

Other

The Spanish Armadas. London, Collins, and New York, Doubleday, 1972.

*   *   *

The novels of Winston Graham cover a wide generic range, including the spy story *Night Journey*, the psychological thriller *Marnie*, several historical novels, and a number of detective stories. In his mysteries, the influence of the other genres is apparent, and this versatility helps to ensure against the formulaic and the merely conventional.

In Graham's novels the detective is usually an amateur: a lawyer or a young boy (*The Forgotten Story*); an insurance claims adjuster (*Fortune Is a Woman*); and even an opera singer (*Take My Life*). The amateur status of these sleuths lends itself to an emotional atmosphere which is characteristic of Graham's work. The "detective" is personally involved with the suspected party or is himself the suspect; his motives are seldom unmixed. The result is that Graham's stories place less emphasis upon methods of detection than they do upon the interplay of suspicion and guilt, of love and revenge, within his cast of characters.

In the "Prologue" to *The Forgotten Story*, a historical mystery, Graham raises an issue which may be considered a primary theme of his work, the relation of the past to the present. Speaking of the difficulty of reconstructing real events from newspaper accounts, he observes that we are "like palaeontologists trying to reconstruct an extinct animal." Graham's characters are frequently beset by the difficulties of extrapolating the truth from mere remnants of fact or from the often deceptive surfaces of things.

The discovery of and response to the past is a theme central to what is probably Graham's finest novel, *Marnie*. In it, the protagonist, like Oedipus, is at once the core of the mystery, a criminal, and the detective. Marnie's reluctant journey into the secret of her past is a fascinating example of the fusion of the psychological novel with the mystery genre.

Graham's interest in human psychology is observable throughout his career and is reflected in his preference for first-person narration. He gives his readers access to the thought processes of his protagonists, their delusions, fears, and moral struggles. In doing so, he

687

avoids mere riddle-making and produces intriguing character studies. These serious concerns in Graham's work, along with the finesse of his style and his careful handling of description and atmosphere, place him among the best of contemporary mystery writers.

—Jeanne Carter Emmons

GRANDOWER, Elissa.   See WAUGH, Hillary.

GRANT, Maxwell.   See GIBSON, Walter B.; COLLINS, Michael.

GRAY, Berkeley. Pseudonym for Edwy Searles Brooks; also wrote as Robert W. Comrade; Victor Gunn; Carlton Ross.   British.   Born in Hackney, London, 11 November 1889. Educated at Banham Manor School, Norfolk. Married Frances Brooks. Wrote many Sexton Blake stories and serial fiction. *Died in December 1965.*

Crime Publications

Novels (series character: Norman Conquest in all books except *Three Frightened Men* and those by Carlton Ross)

Three Frightened Men.   London, Amalgamated Press, 1938.
Mr. Mortimer Gets the Jitters.   London, Collins, 1938.
Vultures Ltd.   London, Collins, 1938.
Conquest Marches On.   London, Collins, 1939.
Leave It to Conquest.   London, Collins, 1939.
Miss Dynamite.   London, Collins, 1939.
Conquest Takes All.   London, Collins, 1940.
Convict 1066.   London, Collins, 1940.
Meet the Don.   London, Collins, 1940.
Six to Kill.   London, Collins, 1940.
Thank You, Mr. Conquest.   London, Collins, 1941.
Six Feet of Dynamite.   London, Collins, 1941.
The Black Skull Murders (as Carlton Ross).   London, Swan, 1942.
Blonde for Danger.   London, Collins, 1943.
Cavalier Conquest.   London, Collins, 1944.
The Gay Desperado.   London, Collins, 1944.

Alias Norman Conquest. London, Collins, 1945.
Mr. Ball of Fire. London, Collins, 1946.
Killer Conquest. London, Collins, 1947.
Racketeers of the Turf (as Carlton Ross). London, Swan, 1947.
The Spot Marked X. London, Collins, 1948.
The Conquest Touch. London, Collins, 1948.
Duel Murder. London, Collins, 1949.
Dare-Devil Conquest. London, Collins, 1950.
Seven Dawns to Death. London, Collins, 1950.
Operation Conquest. London, Collins, 1951.
Conquest in Scotland. London, Collins, 1951.
The Lady Is Poison. London, Collins, 1952.
Target for Conquest. London, Collins, 1953.
The Half-Open Door. London, Collins, 1953.
Conquest Goes West. London, Collins, 1954.
Follow the Lady. London, Collins, 1954.
Turn Left for Danger. London, Collins, 1955.
Conquest in Command. London, Collins, 1956.
The House of the Lost. London, Collins, 1956.
Conquest after Midnight. London, Collins, 1957.
Conquest Goes Home. London, Collins, 1957.
Conquest in California. London, Collins, 1958.
Death on the Hit Parade. London, Collins, 1958.
The Big Brain. London, Collins, 1959.
Murder & Co. London, Collins, 1959.
Nightmare House. London, Collins, 1960.
Conquest on the Run. London, Collins, 1960.
Call Conquest for Danger. London, Collins, 1961.
Get Ready to Die. London, Collins, 1961.
Conquest in the Underworld. London, Collins, 1962.
Count Down for Conquest. London, Collins, 1963.
Castle Conquest. London, Collins, 1964.
Conquest Overboard. London, Collins, 1964.
Calamity Conquest. London, Collins, 1965.
Conquest Likes It Hot. London, Collins, 1965.
Curtains for Conquest? London, Collins, 1966.
Conquest Calls the Tune. London, Hale, 1968.
Conquest in Ireland. London, Hale, 1969.

Novels as Edwy Searles Brooks (series characters: Sexton Blake, in all books except those
    featuring Chief Detective-Inspector William Beeke [The Grouser])

The Case of the Twin Detectives. London, Amalgamated Press, 1916.
Midst Balkan Perils. London, Amalgamated Press, 1916.
The Peril of the Prince. London, Amalgamated Press, 1916.
The Red Spider. London, Amalgamated Press, 1916.
The House with the Double Moat. London, Amalgamated Press, 1917.
On the Bed of the Ocean. London, Amalgamated Press, 1922.
The Green Eyes. London, Amalgamated Press, 1923.
The Boarding-House Mystery. London, Amalgamated Press, 1924.
The Brixham Manor Mystery. London, Amalgamated Press, 1924.
The Case of the Sleeping Partner. London, Amalgamated Press, 1924.
The Human Bloodhound. London, Amalgamated Press, 1924.
The Mystery of Rodney's Cove. London, Amalgamated Press, 1924.
In the Night Watch. London, Amalgamated Press, 1925.

The Impersonators.   London, Amalgamated Press, 1926.
The Black Dagger.   London, Amalgamated Press, 1933.
The Strange Case of the Antlered Man (Grouser).   London, Harrap, 1935.
The Grouser Investigates.   London, Harrap, 1936.
The Midnight Lorry Crime.   London, Amalgamated Press, 1937.
The Riddle of the Body in the Road.   London, Amalgamated Press, 1941.

Novels as Victor Gunn (series character: Bill "Ironsides" Cromwell in all books)

Footsteps of Death.   London, Collins, 1939.
Ironsides of the Yard.   London, Collins, 1940.
Ironsides Smashes Through.   London, Collins, 1940.
Death's Doorway.   London, Collins, 1941.
Ironsides' Lone Hand.   London, Collins, 1941.
Mad Hatter's Rock.   London, Collins, 1942.
The Dead Man Laughs.   London, Collins, 1944.
Nice Day for a Murder.   London, Collins, 1945.
Death on Shivering Sand.   London, Collins, 1946.
Ironsides Smells Blood.   London, Collins, 1946.
Three Dates with Death.   London, Collins, 1947.
Ironsides on the Spot.   London, Collins, 1948.
Dead Man's Warning.   London, Collins, 1949.
Road to Murder.   London, Collins, 1949.
Alias the Hangman.   London, Collins, 1950.
The Borgia Head Mystery.   London, Collins, 1951.
Murder on Ice.   London, Collins, 1951.
The Body Vanishes.   London, Collins, 1952.
Death Comes Laughing.   London, Collins, 1952.
The Whistling Key.   London, Collins, 1953.
The Crippled Canary.   London, Collins, 1954.
The Crooked Staircase.   London, Collins, 1954.
The Laughing Grave.   London, Collins, 1955.
The Painted Dog.   London, Collins, 1955.
Dead Men's Bells.   London, Collins, 1956.
The Golden Monkey.   London, Collins, 1957.
Castle Dangerous.   London, Collins, 1957.
Ironsides Sees Red.   London, Collins, 1957.
The 64 Thousand Murder.   London, Collins, 1958.
The Treble Chance Murder.   London, Collins, 1958.
Dead in a Ditch.   London, Collins, 1958.
The Next One to Die.   London, Collins, 1959.
Death at Traitors' Gate.   London, Collins, 1960.
Death on Bodmin Moor.   London, Collins, 1960.
Devil in the Maze.   London, Collins, 1961.
Sweet Smelling Death.   London, Collins, 1961.
All Change for Murder.   London, Collins, 1962.
The Body in the Boot.   London, Collins, 1963.
Murder with a Kiss.   London, Collins, 1963.
Murder at the Motel.   London, Collins, 1964.
The Black Cap Murder.   London, Collins, 1965.
Murder on Whispering Sands.   London, Collins, 1965.
The Petticoat Lane Murders.   London, Collins, 1966.

OTHER PUBLICATIONS

Novel

   Ghost Gold (as Robert W. Comrade).   London, Rich and Cowan, 1925.

Other (juvenile) as Edwy Searles Brooks

   The Schoolboy Treasure Seekers.   London, Amalgamated Press, 1925.
   The Black Sheep of the Remove.   London, Amalgamated Press, 1925.
   The Tyrant of St. Frank's.   London, Amalgamated Press, 1926.
   The Boy from Bermondsey.   London, Amalgamated Press, 1926.
   The Bullies of St. Frank's.   London, Amalgamated Press, 1926.
   Expelled!   London, Amalgamated Press, 1926.
   'Neath African Skies.   London, Amalgamated Press, 1926.
   St. Frank's in London.   London, Amalgamated Press, 1926.
   The Boy from the "Bush"; or, The Brand of the Twin Stars.   London, Amalgamated
      Press, 1926.
   The Spendthrift of St. Frank's.   London, Amalgamated Press, 1926.
   The Barring-Out at St. Frank's.   London, Amalgamated Press, 1926.
   The Mystery Master.   London, Amalgamated Press, 1926.
   The Voyage of the "Wanderer."   London, Amalgamated Press, 1926.
   The Ghost of the Bannington Grange.   London, Amalgamated Press, 1926.
   The Boy Who Vanished.   London, Amalgamated Press, 1927.
   St. Frank's on the Spree.   London, Amalgamated Press, 1927.
   Prisoners of the Mountains.   London, Amalgamated Press, 1927.
   The Remove in the Wild West.   London, Amalgamated Press, 1927.
   Rebels of the Remove.   London, Amalgamated Press, 1927.
   The Lost World of Everest (for adults; as Berkeley Gray).   London, Collins, 1941.

                              *   *   *

Edwy Searles Brooks was one of the most prolific writers of boys stories in the twentieth century. Under his own name he wrote school and adventure stories for the *Nelson Lee Library* (1915–33) and 125 stories about Sexton Blake for the *Union Jack* (1912–34), *Sexton Blake Library* (1916–41), and *Detective Weekly* (1933–40). In 1938 he began writing adult thrillers under the names Berkeley Gray and Victor Gunn.

His stories are full of the Romance of Detection and he rings the changes on all the clichés in the English school. His light-hearted style and sympathetic characters carry the reader along with disbelief cheerfully suspended. His work is imaginative and full of humor and he shifts points of view with skill. Some of his plots are expanded versions of his older Sexton Blake stories, and many of his characters are variations on ones he has used before. His detectives are often a team of opposites. As Victor Gunn: Chief Inspector Bill ("Ironsides") Cromwell is disheveled and grumpy while Sgt. Johnny Lister is a fashion-conscious college graduate. (For an earlier version see the detectives in *The Grouser Investigates*.) As Berkeley Gray: Norman Conquest is another Simon Templar, a high-spirited optimist and knight errant whose exploits are meant to be taken with tongue in cheek. With knock-out gas in his cigarette-case, file blades in his watch-band, and luck up both sleeves, he goes to face Battle, Murder, and Sudden Death.

                                                            —J. Randolph Cox

GRAY, Dulcie. Pseudonym for Dulcie Winifred Catherine Denison, née Bailey. British. Born in Kuala Lumpur, Malaya, 20 November 1920. Educated at schools in England and Malaya, and at the Academy des Beaux Arts, London, and the Webber-Douglas Dramatic School, London. Married the actor Michael Denison in 1939. Actress from 1939. Recipient: *Times Educational Supplement* award, for non-fiction, 1976. Agent: Douglas Rae (Management) Ltd., 28 Charing Cross Road, London W.C.2. Address: Shardeloes, Amersham, Buckinghamshire, England.

CRIME PUBLICATIONS

Novels (series character: Inspector Cardiff)

> *Murder on the Stairs.* London, Barker, 1957; New York, British Book Centre, 1958.
> *Murder in Melbourne.* London, Barker, 1958.
> *Baby Face.* London, Barker, 1959.
> *Epitaph for a Dead Actor* (Cardiff). London, Barker, 1960.
> *Murder on a Saturday.* London, Barker, 1961.
> *Murder in Mind.* London, Macdonald, 1963.
> *The Devil Wore Scarlet.* London, Macdonald, 1964.
> *No Quarter for a Star.* London, Macdonald, 1964.
> *The Murder of Love.* London, Macdonald, 1967.
> *Died in the Red* (Cardiff). London, Macdonald, 1968.
> *Murder on Honeymoon.* London, Macdonald, 1969.
> *For Richer for Richer.* London, Macdonald, 1970.
> *Deadly Lampshade.* London, Macdonald, 1971.
> *Understudy to Murder.* London, Macdonald, 1972.
> *Dead Give Away.* London, Macdonald, 1974.
> *Ride on a Tiger.* London, Macdonald and Jane's, 1975.
> *Dark Calypso.* London, Macdonald and Jane's, 1979.

Short Stories

> *Stage Door Fright.* London, Macdonald and Jane's, 1977.

OTHER PUBLICATIONS

Plays

> *Love Affair* (produced Birmingham, 1955; London, 1956).

> Radio Plays (from her own novels): *Murder in Melbourne*, 1961; *The Devil Wore Scarlet*, 1964; *No Quarter for a Star*, 1965; *The Happy Honeymoon*, 1966; *Self Defense*, 1970.

Other

> *The Actor and His World: A Young Person's Guide*, with Michael Denison. London, Gollancz, 1964.
> *Death in Denims* (juvenile). London, Everest, 1977.
> *Butterflies on My Mind: Their Life and Conservation in Britain Today.* Brighton, Angus and Robertson, 1978.

Theatrical Activities:

Actress: **Plays** – Sorrel Bliss in *Hay Fever* by Noël Coward, Aberdeen, 1939; in repertory with H. M. Tennent company, Edinburgh and Glasgow, 1940, and with Harrogate Repertory Company, 1940–41; Maria in *Twelfth Night*, Hermia in *A Midsummer Night's Dream*, and Bianca in *The Taming of the Shrew*, London, 1942; Alexandra Giddens in *The Little Foxes* by Lillian Hellman, London, 1942; Rose Wilson in *Brighton Rock* by Frank Harvey, London, 1943; Vivien in *Landslide* by Dorothy Albertyn and David Peel, London, 1943; Greta in *Lady from Edinburgh* by Aimée Stuart and L. Arthur Rose, London, 1945; Ruth Wilkins in *Dear Ruth* by Norman Krasna, London, 1946; Jean Ritchie in *The Wind Is Ninety* by Ralph Nelson, London, 1946; in *Fools Rush In* by Kenneth Horne, toured, 1946; Nurse Ransome in *Rain on the Just* by Peter Watling, London, 1948; Norah Fuller in *Queen Elizabeth Slept Here* by Talbot Rothwell, London, 1949; Agnes in *The Four-Poster* by Jan de Hartog, London, 1950, and toured South Africa, 1954–55; in *See You Later* (revue) by Sandy Wilson, London, 1951; Nina in *Dragon's Mouth* by J. B. Priestley and Jacquetta Hawkes, London, 1952; Robina Jevons in *Sweet Peril* by Mary Orr and Reginald Denham, London, 1952; Anna Lutcar in *The Distant Hill* by James Parish, London and tour, 1953; Toni Oberon in *We Must Kill Toni* by Ian Stuart Black, London, 1954; Mrs. Pooter in *The Diary of a Nobody* by Basil Dean and Richard Blake, London, 1954; the White Queen in *Alice Through the Looking-Glass* by Felicity Douglas, London, 1955, and Croydon, Surrey, 1972; Marion Field in *Love Affair*, Birmingham, 1955, and London, 1956; Lady Shotter in *South Sea Bubble* by Noël Coward, and Laura Reynolds in *Tea and Sympathy* by Robert Anderson, toured South Africa and Australia, 1956–57; Sarah Banning in *Double Cross* by John O'Hare, Richmond, Surrey, and London, 1958; title role in *Candida* by G. B. Shaw, Oxford, 1958, and Bath and London, 1960; Duchess of Hampshire in *Let Them Eat Cake* by Frederick Lonsdale, London, 1959; Mary in *The Bald Prima Donna*, and Old Woman in *The Chairs*, both by Eugène Ionesco, Oxford, 1961; Lady Utterword in *Heartbreak House* by Shaw, Oxford and London, 1961; Z in *A Village Wooing* by G. B Shaw (also London, 1970, and tour, 1971), and Lady Aline in *A Marriage Has Been Arranged* by Alfred Sutro, Hong Kong, 1962; in a Shakespeare Recital, Berlin, 1962; Katerina of Aragon in *Royal Gambit* by Hermann Gressieker, Croydon, Surrey, 1962; Caroline Abbott in *Where Angels Fear to Tread* by Elizabeth Hart, London, 1963; in *Merely Players* Shakespeare programme, toured, 1964; Madame Arkadina in *The Seagull* by Chekhov, Birmingham, 1964; Lady Chiltern in *An Ideal Husband* by Oscar Wilde, London, 1965; Maria Wislack in *On Approval* by Frederick Lonsdale, London, 1966, and in repertory with role of Susan in *Happy Family* by Giles Cooper, London, 1967; Julia Pyrton in *Number Ten* by Ronald Millar, London, 1967; May in *Vacant Possession* by Maisie Mosco, and Yulya Glebova in *Confession at Night* by Alexei Arbuzov, Nottingham, 1968; Celia Pilgrim in *Out of the Question* by Ira Wallach, London, 1968; Mrs. Banger in *Press Cuttings* by G. B Shaw, 1970; Gina Ekdal in *The Wild Duck* by Ibsen, London, 1970; Mrs. Heidelberg in *The Clandestine Marriage* by George Colman the Elder and David Garrick, toured, 1971; in *Ghosts* by Ibsen, York, 1972; Ellen Blake in *The Dragon Variation* by Robert King, Windsor, 1972, and tour, 1973; Mabel Jackson in *At the End of the Day* by William Douglas Home, London, 1973; Grace Bishop in *The Sack Race* by George Ross and Campbell Singer, London, 1974; Olivia Cameron in *The Pay-Off* by William Fairchild, London, 1974 and 1975; Mrs. Conway in *Time and the Conways* by J. B. Priestley, toured, 1976; Ellen Creed in *Ladies in Retirement* by Reginald Denham and Edward Percy, toured, 1976; Lady Twombley in *The Cabinet Minister* by A. W. Pinero, toured, 1977; Miss Marple in *A Murder Is Announced* by Agatha Christie, London, 1977; Delia in *Bedroom Farce* by Alan Ayckbourn, London, 1979. **Films** – *Victory Wedding*, 1944; *2,000 Women*, 1944; *Madonna of the Seven Moons*, 1944; *A Place of One's Own*, 1945; *They Were Sisters*, 1945; *Wanted for Murder (A Voice in the Night)*, 1946; *The Years Between*, 1946; *A Man about the House*, 1947; *Mine Own Executioner*, 1947; *My Brother Jonathan*, 1948; *The Glass Mountain*, 1949; *The Franchise Affair*, 1951; *Angels One Five*, 1952;

There Was a Young Lady, 1953; *A Man Could Get Killed*, 1965. **Radio** – *Front Line Family* serial, 1941, and other plays. Has appeared in several television plays.

Dulcie Gray comments:

I started writing detective stories because I enjoyed reading them, and also because I admired Agatha Christie (as who does not?). I started by writing "whodunits." By my third book, *Baby Face*, however, I found I was becoming less interested in providing a puzzle to be solved than in attempting to delve into the mind of my "criminal," and so began writing what might be called "whydunits." Of my 17 crime books, 11 are whodunits, one an adventure story, and five are crime novels (the last group involving careful character analysis). These five books – *Baby Face, Murder in Mind , The Murder of Love, For Richer for Richer*, and *Ride on a Tiger* – are all violent and perhaps horrifying. I find sick minds, whatever compassion I feel toward their owners, alarming when they destroy the innocent. Of the more conventional books, *Murder on a Saturday* is a horror story and the rest are fairly straightforward puzzles. *Butterflies on My Mind*, a carefully researched study of British butterflies and their conservation, was the book I most wanted to write.

*   *   *

Even if you did not know that Dulcie Gray is a star of the London stage (Agatha Christie's Miss Marple is among her many leading roles) you might perhaps guess at it from her crime books. Some, of course, reflect that background, like *No Quarter for a Star* and *Epitaph for a Dead Actor*. But, first, her extraordinarily speakable dialogue indicates that it has been written by someone used to putting over words aloud. Yet this might be no more than a small-part actress writing. It is another quality that indicates the star: her zest and energy. Sometimes this is a little larger than life and careless even of everyday rules, so that in her pages it is no surprise to find a bank manager happily telling the police all about a client's affairs, though a real British bank manager finding himself doing that would be surprised indeed. She will, too, on occasion pile up necessary information, and sometimes more information than is strictly necessary, with a fine disregard for the proper methods of fiction.

But the zest is the main thing. It has enabled her to produce as many books as some full-time writers while simultaneously having a busy and successful theatrical career. And the books have not been throwaway efforts. They are in principle murder puzzles, but generally they are more. *The Murder of Love*, for instance, tackles the decidedly difficult theme of the relation between violence and sexual attraction. *Dead Give Away* probes the greed and jealousies of a family, and even shows the characters coming to see themselves for what they are.

—H. R. F. Keating

GREEN, Anna Katharine.   American.   Born in Brooklyn, New York, 11 November 1846. Educated in public schools in New York City and Buffalo; Ripley Female College, Poultney, Vermont, B.A. 1867. Married Charles Rohlfs in 1884; one daughter and two sons. Lived most of her life in Buffalo. *Died 11 April 1935.*

CRIME PUBLICATIONS

Novels (series characters: Amelia Butterworth; Ebenezer Gryce)

The Leavenworth Case: A Lawyer's Story (Gryce). New York, Putnam, 1878; London, Routledge, 1884.
A Strange Disappearance (Gryce). New York, Putnam, 1880; London, Routledge, 1884.
The Sword of Damocles: A Story of New York. New York, Putnam, 1881; London, Ward Lock, 1884.
XYZ. New York, Putnam, and London, Ward Lock, 1883.
Hand and Ring (Gryce). New York, Putnam, 1883; London, Ward Lock, 1884.
The Mill Mystery. New York, Putnam, and London, Routledge, 1886.
7 to 12. New York, Putnam, and London, Routledge, 1887.
Behind Closed Doors (Gryce). New York, Putnam, and London, Routledge, 1888.
The Forsaken Inn. New York, Bonner, and London, Routledge, 1890.
A Matter of Millions (Gryce). New York, Bonner, and London, Routledge, 1890.
Cynthia Wakeham's Money. New York, Putnam, 1892; London, Ward Lock, 1904.
Marked "Personal." New York, Putnam, 1893; London, Ward Lock, 1904.
Miss Hurd: An Enigma. New York, Putnam, 1894.
The Doctor, His Wife, and the Clock (Gryce). New York, Putnam, and London, Allen and Unwin, 1895.
Doctor Izard. New York, Putnam, and London, Cassell, 1895.
That Affair Next Door (Gryce; Butterworth). New York, Putnam, 1897; London, Nash, 1903.
Lost Man's Lane: A Second Episode in the Life of Amelia Butterworth (Gryce; Butterworth). New York, Putnam, 1898.
Agatha Webb. New York, Putnam, 1899; London, Ward Lock, 1900.
The Circular Study (Gryce; Butterworth). New York, McClure, 1900; London, Ward Lock, 1902.
One of My Sons (Gryce; Butterworth). New York, Putnam, 1901; London, Ward Lock, 1904.
Three Women and a Mystery. New York, Lovell, 1902.
The Filigree Ball. Indianapolis, Bobbs Merrill, 1903; London, Allen and Unwin, 1904.
The Millionaire Baby. Indianapolis, Bobbs Merrill, and London, Chatto and Windus, 1905.
The Amethyst Box. Indianapolis, Bobbs Merrill, and London, Chatto and Windus, 1905.
The Woman in the Alcove. Indianapolis, Bobbs Merrill, and London, Chatto and Windus, 1906.
The Chief Legatee. New York, Authors and Newspapers Association, 1906; as *A Woman of Mystery*, London, Collier, 1909.
The Mayor's Wife. Indianapolis, Bobbs Merrill, 1907; London, Daily Mail, 1909.
The House of the Whispering Pines. New York, Putnam, and London, Nash, 1910.
Three Thousand Dollars. Boston, Badger Gorham Press, 1910.
Initials Only (Gryce; Butterworth). New York, Dodd Mead, 1911; London, Nash, 1912.
Dark Hollow. New York, Dodd Mead, and London, Nash, 1914.
The Mystery of the Hasty Arrow (Gryce; Butterworth). New York, Dodd Mead, 1917.
The Step on the Stair. New York, Dodd Mead, and London, Lane, 1923.

Short Stories

The Old Stone House and Other Stories. New York, Putnam, 1891.

A Difficult Problem and Other Stories.   New York, Lupton, 1900; London, Ward Lock, 1903.
The House in the Mist.   Indianapolis, Bobbs Merrill, 1905.
Masterpieces of Mystery.   New York, Dodd Mead, 1913; as *Room Number 3 and Other Stories*, 1919.
The Golden Slipper and Other Problems for Violet Strange.   New York, Putnam, 1915.
To the Minute and Scarlet and Black: Two Tales of Life's Perplexities.   New York, Putnam, 1916.

OTHER PUBLICATIONS

Play

Risifi's Daughter.   New York, Putnam, 1887.

Verse

The Defense of the Bride and Other Poems.   New York, Putnam, 1882.

Manuscript Collection: Humanities Research Center, University of Texas, Austin.

*   *   *

A contemporary British review said of Anna Katharine Green that she had "proved herself able to write an interesting story of mysterious crime as well as any man living." However, tastes change, and Green's books no longer appeal to many modern readers. She is a prime example of the author who, for much of her career, was a household word; now, her name is known only by scholars of popular fiction and by superannuated library-goers. When Green published her first book, *The Leavenworth Case*, the New York papers assumed the author was a man. This was in 1878 and Wilkie Collins, for one, was still producing novels. She published simultaneously with Doyle, Bailey, Rohmer, Freeman, Rinehart, and the early Christie. Yet we read Collins and Doyle and Rohmer today and Green is forgotten. For one thing, Green, for all her mechanical skills, lacked both divine genius and the genius of immutable schlock. Her books reveal a talent that is *too* hardworking, *too* earnest, *too* grounded in the tradition of heavy-breathing melodramas in which orphans and wills and madness are the primary ingredients, and in which pale, beautiful women are always giving low, thrilling laughs from beneath dark veils. There *are* crimes and clues aplenty, as well as a respectable amount of deduction, but, by modern standards, these elements are tainted and slowed down by pathos and sentimentality.

Nonetheless, this genteel woman is a significant figure in the history of the genre. Odd as it may seem, *The Leavenworth Case* brought middle-class respectability and a wider readership to the mystery novel. For this achievement – perhaps more of a social than a strictly professional one – Green is often referred to as the "mother of the detective story." *The Leavenworth Case* introduces Green's best-known detective, Ebenezer Gryce, of the New York police force. It makes use of a number of devices that were to become staples of the genre: a map of the scene of the crime, lists of deductions and possibilities, headlines to show the developments of the case. The young lawyer-narrator, in a foreshadowing of the amorous susceptibilities of Watson and Hastings, falls in love with one of the comely suspects. With its treatment of a murder amid polite Manhattan society (the same milieu which provides the background of a novelist to whom Anthony Boucher has compared Green – Edith Wharton), its refined luridness caused it to become a bestseller and launched Green as a writer to be imitated.

In addition to the "portly comfortable" Gryce, Green created two other sleuths worthy of note. Both are women: one, the elderly and excessively nosy Miss Amelia Butterworth, first appears in *The Affair Next Door*, joining Gryce in his investigation; the other, Violet Strange, is a dainty girl detective whose cases are chronicled in *The Golden Slipper and Other Problems for Violet Strange*. Moreover, both can be seen as prototypes, Miss Butterworth for the Jane Marples and Maud Silvers, and Violet Strange for the Nancy Drews.

With regard to Mr. Gryce, it is interesting to pay attention to the changing manner in which Green presents him as the years pass. In *The Circular Study*, twenty-two years after his debut, he is said to be needing fresh challenges to keep him from retiring to a farm. By 1917, in *The Mystery of the Hasty Arrow*, he arrives on the scene in an automobile, being physically weak but with his mental powers undimmed. Like Green's own, Mr. Gryce's was a long and honorable career. (Here, the similarities to Christie and to Poirot must be noted.)

For all of her longevity and productivity, Green left behind a legacy that is now dimmed in the light of her many successors. But one evocative sentence, uttered by Miss Butterworth, is an inheritance for which all mystery fans should be grateful: "For though I have had no adventures, I feel capable of them."

—Michele Slung

GREENE, Graham. British. Born in Berkhamsted, Hertfordshire, 2 October 1904. Educated at Berkhamsted School; Balliol College, Oxford. Served in the Foreign Office, London, 1941–44. Married Vivien Dayrell-Browning in 1927; one son and one daughter. Staff Member, *The Times*, London 1926–30; Movie Critic, 1937–40, and Literary Editor, 1940–41, *Spectator*, London. Director, Eyre and Spottiswoode, publishers, London, 1944–48, and The Bodley Head, publishers, London, 1958–68. Recipient: Hawthornden Prize, 1941; Black Memorial Prize, 1949; Shakespeare Prize, Hamburg, 1968; Thomas More Medal, 1973. Litt.D.: Cambridge University, 1962; D.Litt.: Edinburgh University, 1967. Honorary Fellow, Balliol College, 1963. Companion of Honour, 1966. Chevalier of the Legion of Honour, 1967. Address: c/o The Bodley Head, 9 Bow Street, London WC2E 7AL, England.

CRIME PUBLICATIONS

Novels

The Man Within. London, Heinemann, and New York, Doubleday, 1929.
The Name of Action. London, Heinemann, 1930; New York, Doubleday, 1931.
Rumour at Nightfall. London, Heinemann, 1931; New York, Doubleday, 1932.
Stamboul Train: An Entertainment. London, Heinemann, 1932; as *Orient Express: An Entertainment*, New York, Doubleday, 1933.
It's a Battlefield. London, Heinemann, and New York, Doubleday, 1934; revised edition, London, Heinemann, 1948; New York, Viking Press, 1952.
England Made Me. London, Heinemann, and New York, Doubleday, 1935; as *The Shipwrecked*, New York, Viking Press, 1953.
A Gun for Sale: An Entertainment. London, Heinemann, 1936; as *This Gun for Hire: An Entertainment*, New York, Doubleday, 1936.
Brighton Rock. London, Heinemann, 1938; as *Brighton Rock: An Entertainment*, New York, Viking Press, 1938.
The Confidential Agent. London, Heinemann, and New York, Viking Press, 1939.
The Power and the Glory. London, Heinemann, 1940; as *The Labyrinthine Ways*, New York, Viking Press, 1940.

The Ministry of Fear: An Entertainment.   London, Heinemann, and New York, Viking
   Press, 1943.
The Heart of the Matter.   London, Heinemann, and New York, Viking Press, 1948.
The Third Man: An Entertainment.   New York, Viking Press, 1950.
The Third Man and The Fallen Idol.   London, Heinemann, 1950.
The End of the Affair.   London, Heinemann, and New York, Viking Press, 1951.
Loser Takes All: An Entertainment.   London, Heinemann, 1955; New York, Viking
   Press, 1957.
The Quiet American.   London, Heinemann, 1955; New York, Viking Press, 1956.
Our Man in Havana: An Entertainment.   London, Heinemann, and New York, Viking
   Press, 1958.
A Burnt-Out Case.   London, Heinemann, and New York, Viking Press, 1961.
The Comedians.   London, Bodley Head, and New York, Viking Press, 1966.
Travels with My Aunt.   London, Bodley Head, 1969; New York, Viking Press, 1970.
The Honorary Consul.   London, Bodley Head, and New York, Simon and Schuster,
   1973.
The Human Factor.   London, Bodley Head, and New York, Simon and Schuster, 1978.

Short Stories

The Basement Room and Other Stories.   London, Cresset Press, 1935.
Nineteen Stories.   London, Heinemann, 1947; New York, Viking Press, 1949;
   augmented edition, as *Twenty-One Stories*, London, Heinemann, 1954; New York,
   Viking Press, 1962.
A Sense of Reality.   London, Bodley Head, and New York, Viking Press, 1963.

Other Publications

Short Stories

The Bear Fell Free.   London, Grayson, 1935; Folcroft, Pennsylvania, Folcroft
   Editions, 1977.
Twenty-Four Stories, with James Laver and Sylvia Townsend Warner.   London,
   Cresset Press, 1939.
A Visit to Morin.   Privately printed, 1959.
May We Borrow Your Husband? and Other Comedies of the Sexual Life.   London,
   Bodley Head, and New York, Viking Press, 1967.
The Collected Stories of Graham Greene.   London, Bodley Head-Heinemann, 1972;
   New York, Viking Press, 1973.

Plays

The Living Room (produced London, 1953, New York, 1954).   London, Heinemann,
   1953; New York, Viking Press, 1954.
The Potting Shed (produced New York, 1957; London, 1958).   New York, Viking
   Press, 1957; London, Heinemann, 1958.
The Complaisant Lover (produced London, 1959; New York, 1961).   London,
   Heinemann, 1959; New York, Viking Press, 1961.
Carving a Statue (produced London, 1964; New York, 1968).   London, Bodley Head,
   1964.
The Third Man: A Film, with Carol Reed.   New York, Simon and Schuster, 1968;
   London, Lorrimer Films, 1969.
Alas, Poor Maling, adaptation of his own story (televised, 1975).   Published in *Shades
   of Greene*, London, Bodley Head-Heinemann, 1975.

The Return of A. J. Raffles: An Edwardian Comedy Based Somewhat Loosely on E. W. Hornung's Characters in "The Amateur Cracksman" (produced London, 1975). London, Bodley Head, 1975; New York, Simon and Schuster, 1976.

Screenplays: *The First and the Last (21 Days)*, 1937; *The New Britain*, 1940; *Brighton Rock (Young Scarface)*, with Terence Rattigan, 1947; *The Fallen Idol*, with Lesley Storm and William Templeton, 1948; *The Third Man*, with Carol Reed, 1950; *The Stranger's Hand*, with Guy Elmes and Giorgino Bassani, 1954; *Loser Takes All*, 1956; *Saint Joan*, 1957; *Our Man in Havana*, 1960; *The Comedians*, 1967.

Television Play: *Alas, Poor Maling*, 1975.

Verse

Babbling April: Poems. Oxford, Blackwell, 1925.
For Christmas. Privately printed, 1951.

Other

Journey Without Maps: A Travel Book. London, Heinemann, and New York, Doubleday, 1936.
The Lawless Roads: A Mexican Journey. London, Longman, 1939; as *Another Mexico*, New York, Viking Press, 1939.
British Dramatists. London, Collins, 1942; included in *The Romance of English Literature*, New York, Hastings House, 1944.
The Little Train (juvenile). London, Eyre and Spottiswoode, 1946; New York, Lothrop, 1958.
Why Do I Write: An Exchange of Views Between Elizabeth Bowen, Graham Greene, and V. S. Pritchett. London, Marshall, and New York, British Book Centre, 1948.
After Two Years. Privately printed, 1949.
The Little Fire Engine (juvenile). London, Parrish, 1950; as *The Little Red Fire Engine*, New York, Lothrop, 1952.
The Lost Childhood and Other Essays. London, Eyre and Spottiswoode, 1951; New York, Viking Press, 1952.
The Little Horse Bus (juvenile). London, Parrish, 1952; New York, Lothrop, 1954.
The Little Steam Roller: A Story of Mystery and Detection (juvenile). London, Parrish, 1953; New York, Lothrop, 1955.
Essais Catholiques, translated by Marcelle Sibon. Paris, Editions de Deuil, 1953.
In Search of a Character: Two African Journals. London, Bodley Head, 1961; New York, Viking Press, 1962.
The Revenge: An Autobiographical Fragment. Privately printed, 1963.
Victorian Detective Fiction: A Catalogue of the Collection Made by Dorothy Glover and Graham Greene, Introduced by John Carter. London, Bodley Head, 1966.
Collected Essays. London, Bodley Head, and New York, Viking Press, 1969.
A Sort of Life (autobiography). London, Bodley Head, and New York, Simon and Schuster, 1971.
The Pleasure-Dome: The Collected Film Criticism, 1935–40, of Graham Greene, edited by John Russell Taylor. London, Secker and Warburg, 1972; as *The Pleasure-Dome: Graham Greene on Film: Collected Film Criticism, 1935–40*, New York, Simon and Schuster, 1972.
The Portable Graham Greene, edited by Philip Stratford. New York, Viking Press, 1973; London, Penguin, 1977.
Lord Rochester's Monkey: Being the Life of John Wilmot, Second Earl of Rochester. London, Bodley Head, and New York, Viking Press, 1974.

Editor, *The Old School: Essays by Divers Hands.*   London, Cape, and New York, Peter Smith, 1934.

Editor, *The Best of Saki.*   London, British Publishers Guild, 1950.

Editor, with Hugh Greene, *The Spy's Bedside Book: An Anthology.*   London, Hart Davis, 1957.

Editor, *The Bodley Head Ford Madox Ford.*   London, Bodley Head, 4 vols., 1962, 1963.

Editor, *An Impossible Woman: The Memories of Dottoressa Moor of Capri.*   London, Bodley Head, 1975; New York, Viking Press, 1976.

Bibliography: by N. Brennan, in *Graham Greene: Some Critical Considerations*, edited by Robert O. Evans, Lexington, University of Kentucky Press, 1963.

Manuscript Collection: Humanities Research Center, University of Texas, Austin.

*   *   *

Crime is a dominant element in most of Graham Greene's fictions, whether he calls them "entertainments" or "novels." In fact, the boundary between the two kinds of books is as ambiguous as the real frontiers that figure in so many of them. For Greene in all his books is a superb storyteller, which is one of the reasons why he has a considerable popular appeal as well as being regarded as one of the most important serious writers of his period. Adventure and suspense are constant elements in his novels as well as his entertainments, and in both of them his characters usually find their way into difficult physical predicaments that parallel moral crises. In everything he writes Greene is a master at creating memorable backgrounds drawn from the memories of a life of restless travel; the Cuba of *Our Man in Havana*, the Mexico of *The Power and the Glory*, the Vietnam of *The Quiet American*, the Argentina-Paraguay frontier of *The Honorary Consul*, and, no less striking is the exotic feeling Greene can give with his unerring eye for the seedy and the eccentric to the strange places he makes out of familiar ones, like the Brighton of *Brighton Rock* and the London of *The Ministry of Fear*. Always, whether it is manifest in action or merely thickens the air, one is aware of evil as a constant presence in Greene's worlds; "Hell lay about them in their infancy," he remarked in his travel book on Mexico, *The Lawless Roads*, and his writings lead one to assume that for his characters its presence is lifelong.

Perhaps the main difference between the novels and the entertainments, of which *Stamboul Train*, *A Gun for Sale*, and *The Confidential Agent* are typical, is that in these books action is dominant and constant. They are authentic thrillers in the sense that in them we become involved in the plights of hunted men who in one way or another are social outcasts, whether they are criminals in the literal sense of being professional killers, like the gunman in *A Gun for Sale*, or in the legalistic sense of being leaders of revolutionary groups or of wrong sides in civil wars, like Dr. Czinner in *Stamboul Train* and D. in *The Confidential Agent*. The moral issue is there, as it always is in Graham Greene's books; he was a typical man of the Thirties in the way he symbolized political or ethical conflicts in terms of frontiers and police, of gun-battles and no less lethal betrayals, of life on the run, and his entertainments can indeed be read for their excitement alone.

It is a different matter with the books he calls novels. They too involve one in action, often in pursuit, and usually with crime and criminals, though the latter are not always the main characters. In *Brighton Rock* a stool pigeon is murdered by a petty race-track gang dominated by a teenage boy driven by evil. In *The Power and the Glory* a drunken priest continues to pursue his vocation in a Mexican state where practicing Christianity is forbidden under penalty of death, and he is eventually caught and shot. In *The Heart of the Matter* a British police chief in a wartime West African town, tempted by bribing smugglers, connives at a murder, commits adultery, and finally kills himself. In *England Made Me* a group of English semi-innocents in Sweden find themselves pitted against a ruthless gang of criminal capitalists. Very few of Greene's novels lack these elements of pervading violence and looming evil, and often they are emphasized to the verge of melodrama.

But what cannot be ignored in the novels, as it can in the entertainments, is that behind the melodramatic facade a genuine moral drama is always being enacted, and not merely a moral drama but a religious one, for Greene is perpetually concerned with the problem of grace, with the shape of God's mercy. It is at this point that crime shades off into sin, the burden which the practicing Christian bears in order that by the exercise of his free will he may rise above it. In this context it is impossible to forget that Greene is a Catholic; he was converted two years before he published his first novel, *The Man Within*, in 1929. But he has never been a Catholic apologist in the dogmatic manner of writers like G. K. Chesterton and Hilaire Belloc. Given his dark view of the human condition, he sees Catholicism not as a creed for the triumphant, but rather for the desperate, and he shares with his atheist contemporaries, the existentialists, the tendency to lead his characters to self-knowledge by driving them into life-and-death situations where they learn of God's mercy, as it were, "between the saddle and the ground." And perhaps, if we are to consider Graham Greene a mystery writer, the central mystery lies precisely there. As the priest in *The Heart of the Matter*, Father Rank, says to the dead police chief's widow, "For goodness sake, Mrs. Scobie, don't imagine you – or I – know a thing about God's mercy." In this sense, of acknowledging that the central mystery of Christianity is unknowable, Greene has been justified in calling himself "a Catholic agnostic."

In the more technical sense that they involve plots or betrayals or criminal conspiracies that are gradually revealed to us through a good deal of thrilling action, Greene's books – both entertainments and novels – can be classed as mysteries. Detection is also an element in them, particularly when, like *The Third Man*, *Our Man in Havana*, or *The Human Factor*, they involve the kind of intelligence operations in which Greene was himself employed as a British secret agent during World War II. But the solution of a problem by a detective is never a dominant element; the interest is likely to lie in the pursuit rather than in the detection itself, as in *The Human Factor*, in which we learn very quickly that an apparently impeccable employee of British Intelligence has been corrupted by a sense of gratitude into becoming a double agent. The drama lies not in the reader's being eventually enlightened about the facts, but in the suspenseful time when the investigators are sorting out the clues relating to the leak they have discovered, while the reader enters the guilty man's mind and sees how love led him into a situation that, even if he escapes physically – as he does – must morally destroy him. The criminal rather than the crime, the sinner rather than the sin, are Greene's ultimate concerns.

—George Woodcock

GREGORY, Stephan. See **PENDLETON, Don.**

GREX, Leo. See **GRIBBLE, Leonard.**

GRIBBLE, Leonard (Reginald). Also writes as Sterry Browning; Landon Grant; Leo Grex; Louis Grey; Dexter Muir. British. Born in London, 1 February 1908. Educated at schools in England. Served in the Press and Censorship Division of the Ministry of Information, London, 1940–45. Married Nancy Mason in 1932; one daughter. Has worked as a literary adviser to several publishers; started the Empire Bookshelf series, BBC Radio, London. Founding Member, Crime Writers Association, 1953. Address: Chandons, Firsdown Close, High Salvington, Worthing, West Sussex, England.

CRIME PUBLICATIONS

Novels (series character: Superintendent Anthony Slade)

The Case of the Marsden Rubies (Slade). London, Harrap, 1929; New York, Doubleday, 1930.
The Gillespie Suicide Mystery (Slade). London, Harrap, 1929; as *The Terrace Suicide Mystery*, New York, Doubleday, 1929.
The Grand Modena Murder (Slade). London, Harrap, 1930; New York, Doubleday, 1931.
Is This Revenge? (Slade). London, Harrap, 1931; as *The Serpentine Murder*, New York, Dodd Mead, 1932.
The Stolen Home Secretary (Slade). London, Harrap, 1932; as *The Stolen Statesman*, New York, Dodd Mead, 1932.
The Secret of Tangles (Slade). London, Harrap, 1933; Philadelphia, Lippincott, 1934.
The Yellow Bungalow Mystery (Slade). London, Harrap, 1933.
The Death Chime. London, Harrap, 1934.
The Riddle of the Ravens (Slade). London, Harrap, 1934.
The Signet of Death (as Louis Grey). London, Nicholson and Watson, 1934.
Mystery at Tudor Arches (Slade). London, Harrap, 1935.
The Case of the Malverne Diamonds (Slade). London, Harrap, 1936; New York, Greenberg, 1937.
Riley of the Special Branch. London, Harrap, 1936.
Who Killed Oliver Cromwell? (Slade). London, Harrap, 1937; New York, Greenberg, 1938.
Tragedy in E Flat (Slade). London, Harrap, 1938; New York, Curl, 1939.
The Arsenal Stadium Mystery (Slade). London, Harrap, 1939; revised edition, London, Jenkins, 1950.
Atomic Murder (Slade). London, Harrap, and Chicago, Ziff Davis, 1947.
Hangman's Moon (Slade). London, W. H. Allen, 1950.
They Kidnapped Stanley Matthews (Slade). London, Jenkins, 1950.
The Frightened Chameleon (Slade). London, Jenkins, 1951; New York, Roy, 1957.
Mystery Manor. London, Goulden, 1951.
Crime at Cape Folly (as Sterry Browning). London, Clerke and Cockeran, 1951.
The Glass Alibi (Slade). London, Jenkins, 1952; New York, Roy, 1956.
Murder Out of Season. London, Jenkins, 1952.
She Died Laughing (Slade). London, Jenkins, 1953.
Murder Mistaken, with Janet Green. London, W. H. Allen, 1953.
Sex Marks the Spot (as Sterry Browning). London, Long, 1954.
The Inverted Crime (Slade). London, Jenkins, 1954.
Sally of Scotland Yard, with Geraldine Laws. London, W. H. Allen, 1954.
Death Pays the Piper (Slade). London, Jenkins, 1956; New York, Roy, 1958.
Stand-In for Murder (Slade). London, Jenkins, 1957; New York, Roy, 1958.
Don't Argue with Death (Slade). London, Jenkins, and New York, Roy, 1959.
Wantons Die Hard. London, Jenkins, 1961; New York, Roy, 1962.
Heads You Die (Slade). London, Jenkins, 1964.

The Violent Dark (Slade).   London, Jenkins, 1965.
Strip-Tease Macabre (Slade).   London, Jenkins, 1967.
A Diplomat Dies.   London, Jenkins, 1969.
Alias the Victim.   London, Hale, 1971.
Programmed for Death.   London, Hale, 1973.
You Can't Die Tomorrow.   London, Hale, 1975.
The Cardinal's Diamonds.   London, Hale, 1976.
Midsummer Slay Ride.   London, Hale, 1976.
The Deadly Professionals.   London, Long, 1976.
Compelled to Kill.   London, Long, 1977.
Crime on Her Hands.   London, Hale, 1977.
The Dead End Killers.   London, Long, 1978.
Death Needs No Alibi.   London, Hale, 1979.
They Came to Kill.   London, Long, 1979.

Novels as Leo Grex (series characters: Paul Irving; Phil Sanderson)

The Tragedy at Draythorpe.   London, Hutchinson, 1931.
The Nightborn.   London, Hutchinson, 1931.
The Lonely Inn Mystery (Irving).   London, Hutchinson, 1933.
The Madison Murder (Irving).   London, Hutchinson, 1933.
The Man from Manhattan.   London, Hutchinson, 1934; New York, Doubleday, 1935.
Murder in the Sanctuary (Irving).   London, Hutchinson, 1934.
Crooner's Swan Song.   London, Hutchinson, 1935.
Stolen Death.   London, Hutchinson, 1936.
Transatlantic Trouble.   London, Hutchinson, 1937.
The Carlent Manor Crime.   London, Hutchinson, 1939.
The Black-Out Murders.   London, Harrap, 1940.
The Stalag Mites.   London, Harrap, 1947.
King Spiv.   London, Harrap, 1948.
Crooked Sixpence.   London, Harrap, 1949.
Ace of Danger (Irving).   London, Hutchinson, 1952.
Thanks for the Felony.   London, Long, 1958.
Larceny in Her Heart.   London, Long, 1959.
Terror Wears a Smile.   London, Long, 1962.
The Brass Knuckle.   London, Long, 1964.
Violent Keepsake (Sanderson).   London, Long, 1967.
The Hard Kill (Sanderson).   London, Long, 1969.
Kill Now − Pay Later.   London, Long, 1971.
Die − as in Murder.   London, Hale, 1974.
Death Throws No Shadow.   London, Hale, 1976.
Mix Me a Murder.   London, Hale, 1978.

Novels as Dexter Muir

The Pilgrims Meet Murder.   London, Jenkins, 1948.
The Speckled Swan.   London, Jenkins, 1949.
Rosemary for Death.   London, Jenkins, 1953.

Short Stories

The Case-Book of Anthony Slade.   London, Quality Press, 1937.
The Velvet Mask and Other Stories.   London, W. H. Allen, 1952.
Superintendent Slade Investigates.   London, Jenkins, 1956; New York, Roy, 1957.

OTHER PUBLICATIONS

Novels

  Coastal Commandoes (as Sterry Browning).   London, Nicholson and Watson, 1946.
  Santa Fé Gunslick (as Sterry Browning).   London, Clerke and Cockeran, 1951.
  Dangerous Mission.   London, Brown and Watson, 1957.

Novels as Landon Grant

  Rustlers' Gulch.   London, Rich and Cowan, 1935.
  Wyoming Deadline.   London, Rich and Cowan, 1939.
  Texas Buckaroo.   London, Sampson Low, 1948.
  Ramrod of the Bar X.   London, Sampson Low, 1949.
  Scar Valley Bandit.   London, Sampson Low, 1951.
  The Rawhide Kid.   London, Burke, 1951.
  Gunsmoke Canyon.   London, Sampson Low, 1952.
  Outlaws of Silver Spur.   London, Stanley Paul, 1953.
  Marshall of Mustang.   London, Macdonald, 1954.
  Thunder Valley Deadline.   London, Stanley Paul, 1956.

Play

  Screenplay: *Death by Design*, 1943.

Verse

  Toy Folk and Nursery People.   London, Jenkins, 1945.

Other

  Queens of Crime.   London, Hurst and Blackett, 1932.
  Famous Feats of Detection and Deduction.   London, Harrap, 1933; New York,
      Doubleday, 1934.
  All the Year Round Stories, with Nancy Gribble.   London, Hutchinson, 1935.
  Heroes of the Fighting R.A.F.   London, Harrap, 1941.
  Epics of the Fighting R.A.F.   London, Harrap, 1943.
  Heroes of the Merchant Navy.   London, Harrap, 1944.
  Battle Stories of the R.A.F.   London, Burke, 1945.
  Great Detective Feats.   London, Burke, 1946.
  Murder First Class.   London, Burke, 1946.
  On Secret Service.   London, Burke, 1946.
  The Secret of the Red Mill (juvenile).   London, Burke, 1948.
  The Missing Speed Ace (juvenile).   London, Burke, 1950.
  The Riddle of the Blue Moon (juvenile).   London, Burke, 1950.
  Speed Dermot, Junior Reporter (juvenile).   London, Burke, 1951.
  Famous Manhunts: A Century of Crime.   London, Long, 1953; New York, Roy, 1955.
  Adventures in Murder Undertaken by Some Notorious Killers in Love.   London, Long,
      1954; New York, Roy, 1955.
  Triumphs of Scotland Yard: A Century of Detection.   London, Long, 1955.
  Famous Judges and Their Trials: A Century of Justice.   London, Long, 1957.
  The True Book about Scotland Yard (juvenile).   London, Muller, 1957.
  Great Detective Exploits.   London, Long, 1958.
  Murders Most Strange.   London, Long, 1959.

The True Book about the Old Bailey.   London, Muller, 1959; New Rochelle, New York, Sportshelf, 1960.
Hands of Terror: Notable Assassinations of the Twentieth Century.   London, Muller, 1960.
The True Book about the Mounties.   London, Muller, 1960; New Rochelle, New York, Sportshelf, 1961.
Clues That Spelled Guilty.   London, Long, 1961.
The True Book about Great Escapes.   London, Muller, 1962.
When Killers Err.   London, Long, 1962.
Stories of Famous Detectives.   London, Barker, and New York, Hill and Wang, 1963.
They Challenged the Yard.   London, Long, 1963.
The True Book about Smugglers and Smuggling.   London, Muller, 1963.
The True Book about the Spanish Main.   London, Muller, 1963.
Stories of Famous Spies.   London, Barker, 1964.
Such Women Are Deadly.   London, Long, 1965; New York, Arco, 1969.
Great Manhunters of the Yard.   London, Long, and New York, Roy, 1966.
Stories of Famous Explorers.   London, Barker, 1966.
Famous Stories of the Wild West (juvenile).   London, Barker, 1967.
They Had a Way with Women.   London, Long, 1967; New York, Roy, 1968.
Stories of Famous Conspirators.   London, Barker, 1968.
Famous Stories of Police and Crime.   London, Barker, 1968.
Famous Historical Mysteries.   London, Muller, 1969.
Stories of Famous Scientific Detection.   London, Barker, 1969.
Stories of Famous Modern Trials.   London, Barker, 1970; as *Justice?*, New York, Abelard Schuman, 1971.
Strange Crimes of Passion.   London, Long, 1970.
Famous Detective Feats.   London, Barker, 1971.
They Got Away with Murder.   London, Long, 1971.
More Famous Historical Mysteries.   London, Muller, 1972.
Sisters of Cain.   London, Long, 1972.
Famous Feats of Espionage.   London, Barker, 1972.
The Hallmark of Horror.   London, Long, 1973.
Stories of Famous Master Criminals.   London, Barker, 1973.
Such Was Their Guilt.   London, Long, 1974.
Famous Stories of the Murder Squad.   London, Barker, 1974.
They Conspired to Kill.   London, Long, 1975.
Murder Stranger than Fiction (as Leo Grex).   London, Hale, 1975.
Famous Mysteries of Detection.   London, Barker, 1976.
Famous Mysteries of Modern Times.   London, Muller, 1976.
Detection Stranger than Fiction (as Leo Grex).   London, Hale, 1977.
Compelled to Kill.   London, Long, 1977.

Editor, *A Christmas Treasury in Prose and Verse.*   London, SPCK, and New York, Macmillan, 1929.
Editor, *The Jesus of the Poets: An Anthology.*   London, Student Christian Movement Press, and New York, R. R. Smith, 1930.
Editor, *Best Children's Stories of the Year.*   London, Burke, 4 vols., 1946–49.
Editor, *Fifty Famous Stories for Boys.*   London, Burke, 1948.
Editor, *Fifty Famous Stories for Girls.*   London, Burke, 1949.
Editor, *Fifty Famous Animal Stories* (juvenile).   London, Burke, 1949.
Editor, *The Story Trove: A Collection of the Best Stories of Today for Boys and Girls.*   London, Burke, 1950.
Editor, *Stories for Boys.*   London, Spring Books, 1961.
Editor, *Stories for Girls.*   London, Spring Books, 1961.

Editor, *Famous Stories of High Adventure* (juvenile). London, Barker, 1962; New York, Hill and Wang, 1964.

Editor, *Famous Stories of the Sea and Ships* (juvenile). London, Barker, 1962; New York, Hill and Wang, 1964.

Editor, *Great War Adventures.* London, Barker, 1966.

*   *   *

A prolific writer of detective fiction under at least six names, Leonard Gribble is probably best known for his long series of cases featuring Anthony Slade of Scotland Yard, and for his factual studies of detection and crime.

Slade followed in the footsteps of such investigators as Crofts's Inspector French by pursuing his cases in a solid and dependable manner. There is little of the hero-worship surrounding such figures as Creasey's Inspector West, and there is none of the way-out unconventionality displayed by many of Edgar Wallace's Scotland Yard men. Nevertheless it is possible to draw parallels between Gribble and Wallace; one detects occasional similarities of style, frequent touches of London background, and over all an impression that for most of the time the police are pitted against professional criminals and organised crime rather than the cosy drawing-room murderers depicted in so many detective novels. Gribble does not ignore the domestic murder, but it seems not to play a significant part in his work, although it must be emphasised that throughout his career he has shown a versatility of subject and a stamina in his output that few detective novelists have equalled.

His sometimes stilted manner of writing, and the almost total lack of characterisation, combine to make Gribble's books a little less readable than one would wish. This is a pity, for many of them are well constructed stories and in some the suspense is well built up. He has a good knowledge of police procedures, and gives an impression of authenticity which contrasts with the heavily fictionalised and sensational exploits of the police in many other authors' books. His settings, too, are often original as are his plot ideas – one recalls, for example, *The Arsenal Stadium Mystery* and *They Kidnapped Stanley Matthews.* He has also shown a deft hand at the short story form in *Superintendent Slade Investigates.*

Gribble's detective novels are pieces of escapism rather than police procedural stories as such, although it is understood that his accurately described police techniques are the product of a lifetime's association with friends at Scotland Yard. One wishes, however, that he had managed to inject a little more personality into Slade, that he had sometimes conveyed a more ambitious message than that Crime Does Not Pay, and that he had made the occasional attempt to paint more complex relationships between his police officers in the manner of the best J. J. Marric and John Wainwright novels.

His books of true criminal cases are clearly aimed at the general reader rather than those with a deep interest in criminology. The latter would do better to turn to Lustgarten, Furneaux, Jesse, or a host of others. The most appropriate description of Gribble's non-fiction would be that it is enthralling and entertaining; concentrating as they often do upon the stranger aspects of crime and the more bizarre cases of murder, these books certainly hold the imagination. Written in a non-intellectual and straightforward style, with many of the volumes reflecting police and judicial procedures throughout the world, they make a welcome change from detailed examination of every nuance of criminal behaviour and provide ample evidence that detective fact is often more incredible than detective fiction.

—Melvyn Barnes

GRIERSON, Edward (Dobbyn). Also wrote as Brian Crowther; John P. Stevenson. British. Born in Bedford, 9 March 1914. Educated at St. Paul's School, London, 1927–32; Exeter College, Oxford, 1932–35, B.A. (honours) in jurisprudence 1935; Inner Temple, London: called to the Bar, 1937. Served in the British Army Infantry, 1939–46: Lieutenant Colonel. Married Helen D. Henderson in 1938; one daughter. Barrister, Bradford, Yorkshire, 1938–39; Announcer, Australian Broadcasting Commission, Sydney, 1948–49; Justice of the Peace, Northumberland, 1957–75; Chairman of Petty Sessions, Bellingham, Northumberland, 1960–75; Deputy-Chairman, Northumberland Quarter Sessions, 1960–71; Deputy Traffic Commissioner, Northern Traffic Area, 1974–75. *Died 24 May 1975.*

CRIME PUBLICATIONS

Novels

> *Shall Perish with the Sword* (as Brian Crowther).   London, Quality Press, 1949.
> *Reputation for a Song.*   London, Chatto and Windus, and New York, Knopf, 1952.
> *The Second Man.*   London, Chatto and Windus, and New York, Knopf, 1956.
> *The Massingham Affair.*   London, Chatto and Windus, 1962; New York, Doubleday, 1963.
> *A Crime of One's Own.*   London, Chatto and Windus, and New York, Putnam, 1967.

OTHER PUBLICATIONS

Novels

> *The Lilies and the Bees.*   London, Chatto and Windus, 1953; as *The Hastening Wind*, New York, Knopf, 1953; as *The Royalist*, New York, Bantam, 1956.
> *Far Morning.*   London, Chatto and Windus, and New York, Knopf, 1955.
> *The Captain General* (as John P. Stevenson).   New York, Doubleday, 1956; as Edward Grierson, London, Chatto and Windus, 1958.
> *Dark Torrent of Glencoe.*   New York, Doubleday, 1960; London, Chatto and Windus, 1961.

Plays

> *His Mother's Son,* with Raymond Lulham (produced Harrogate, Yorkshire, 1953).
>
> Radio Plays: *The Ninth Legion,* 1956; *The Second Man,* 1956; *Mr. Curtis's Chambers,* 1959.

Other

> *Storm Bird: The Strange Life of Georgina Weldon.*   London, Chatto and Windus, 1959.
> *The Fatal Inheritance: Philip II and the Spanish Netherlands.*   London, Gollancz, and New York, Doubleday, 1969.
> *The Imperial Dream: The British Commonwealth and the Empire 1775–1969.*   London, Collins, 1972; as *The Death of the Imperial Dream,* New York, Doubleday, 1972.
> *Confessions of a Country Magistrate.*   London, Gollancz, 1972.

King of Two Worlds: Philip II of Spain.   London, Collins, and New York, Putnam, 1974.
The Companion Guide to Northumbria.   London, Collins, 1976.

*   *   *

The books of Edward Grierson are not detective fiction but crime fiction. To claim that he is a descendant of the realistic school of Francis Iles would be to deny him his individuality, yet the development of crime fiction appears to be obligatorily segmented into this or that school by historians of the genre. To compare him too closely with Iles would also be to overlook the fact that with Grierson we are outsiders observing the relationships between his characters, whereas with Iles we identify with the protagonist and follow his or her every thought.

It is really Grierson's novel *Reputation for a Song* which caused him to be categorised with the movement towards modern crime fiction as a novel of character. The book is so good that it can stand on its own. Far removed from classic detective fiction, it is at once a supremely competent study of domestic murder and a perfect example of courtroom drama. The tempestuous family relationships at the home of the stolid and respectable small-town solicitor are skilfully conveyed. Gradually, with apparent ease, Grierson shows us resentment building to hatred, and eventually to murder. By detective fiction standards, it is a simple case. The murderer is soon arrested. The point of the book then becomes apparent, as we are left in little doubt that the simplest case is open to distortion by those inside and outside the legal system. It would be wrong to reveal why the title of the book, from Omar Khayyam, is so apt. Suffice it to say that many readers might unfortunately fail to observe the deftness of Grierson's touch in presenting his characters, and the power of his dialogue throughout some of the best courtroom scenes in modern fiction, in their eager pursuit of the answer to one question – not the identity of the murderer, but whether he will hang. That answer is given at the climax, but we are left with more worrying questions still unanswered after closing the book.

With *The Second Man*, Grierson gives an authentic study of a woman barrister. In this novel he also makes good use of his own legal background so that the atmosphere of the courts can be positively felt. Marion Kerrison fights two battles – to assert her position as a woman in a predominantly male profession, and to clear a man accused of murder who appears to be his own worst enemy – and the two are knitted together so adroitly that the book fully justifies the award made to it as the best British crime novel of 1956.

The Massingham Affair presented further evidence of his talent. Concerning the ceaseless efforts of two men to reconstruct a Victorian *cause célèbre*, and to question the evidence against those convicted, it has the combined qualities of the historical thriller and the perfectly constructed detective story. *A Crime of One's Own*, with the young and romantic bookseller who suspects that a spy ring is mis-using his establishment, does not attain the standard of Grierson's earlier work, although it suggests that he can produce a spirited and witty romp which will keep many readers entertained.

In short, although Grierson has produced other books, *Reputation for a Song, The Second Man*, and *The Massingham Affair*, are the quintessence of his very real contribution to the field of crime fiction.

—Melvyn Barnes

GRUBER, Frank. Also wrote as Stephen Acre; Charles K. Boston; John K. Vedder. American. Born in Elmer, Minnesota, 2 February 1904. Attended high school. Served in the United States Army, 1920–21. Married Lois Mahood in 1931; one son. Editor of trade journals; teacher in correspondence schools; self-employed writer from 1934. *Died 9 December 1969.*

CRIME PUBLICATIONS

Novels (series characters: Otis Beagle; Johnny Fletcher and Sam Cragg; Simon Lash)

The French Key (Fletcher and Cragg). New York, Farrar and Rinehart, 1940; London, Hale, 1941; as *Once Over Deadly*, New York, Spivak, 1956.

The Laughing Fox (Fletcher and Cragg). New York, Farrar and Rinehart, 1940; London, Nicholson and Watson, 1942.

The Hungry Dog (Fletcher and Cragg). New York, Farrar and Rinehart, 1941; London, Nicholson and Watson, 1950; as *The Hungry Dog Murders*, New York, Avon, 1943; as *Die Like a Dog*, New York, Spivak, 1957.

The Navy Colt (Fletcher and Cragg). New York, Farrar and Rinehart, 1941; London, Nicholson and Watson, 1942.

Simon Lash, Private Detective. New York, Farrar and Rinehart, 1941; as *Simon Lash, Detective*, London, Nicholson and Watson, 1943.

The Silver Jackass (Beagle; as Charles K. Boston). New York, Reynal, 1941; London, Cherry Tree, 1952.

The Talking Clock (Fletcher and Cragg). New York, Farrar and Rinehart, 1941; London, Nicholson and Watson, 1942.

The Last Doorbell (as John K. Vedder). New York, Holt, 1941; as *Kiss the Boss Goodbye* (as Frank Gruber), New York, Spivak, 1954.

The Buffalo Box (Lash). New York, Farrar and Rinehart, 1942; London, Nicholson and Watson, 1944.

The Gift Horse (Fletcher and Cragg). New York, Farrar and Rinehart, 1942; London, Nicholson and Watson, 1943.

The Yellow Overcoat (as Stephen Acre). New York, Dodd Mead, 1942; London, Boardman, 1945; as *Fall Guy for a Killer* (as Frank Gruber), New York, Spivak, 1955.

The Mighty Blockhead (Fletcher and Cragg). New York, Farrar and Rinehart, 1942; London, Nicholson and Watson, 1948; as *The Corpse Moved Upstairs*, New York, Belmont, 1964.

The Silver Tombstone (Fletcher and Cragg). New York, Farrar and Rinehart, 1945; London, Nicholson and Watson, 1949.

Beagle Scented Murder. New York, Rinehart, 1946; as *Market for Murder*, New York, New American Library, 1947.

The Fourth Letter. New York, Rinehart, 1947.

The Honest Dealer (Fletcher and Cragg). New York, Rinehart, 1947.

The Whispering Master (Fletcher and Cragg). New York, Rinehart, 1947.

The Lock and the Key. New York, Rinehart, 1948; Kingswood, Surrey, World's Work, 1950; as *Too Tough to Die*, New York, Spivak, 1954; as *Run Thief Run*, New York, Fawcett, 1955.

Murder '97 (Lash). New York, Rinehart, 1948; London, Barker, 1956; as *The Long Arm of Murder*, New York, Spivak, 1956.

The Scarlet Feather (Fletcher and Cragg). New York, Rinehart, 1948; London, Cherry Tree, 1951; as *The Gamecock Murders*, New York, New American Library, 1949.

The Leather Duke (Fletcher and Cragg). New York, Rinehart, 1949; Manchester, Pemberton, 1950; as *A Job of Murder*, New York, New American Library, 1950.

The Limping Goose (Fletcher and Cragg). New York, Rinehart, 1954; London, Barker, 1955; as *Murder One*, New York, Belmont, 1973.

The Lonesome Badger (Beagle). New York, Rinehart, 1954; as *Mood for Murder*, Hasbrouck Heights, New Jersey, Graphic, 1956.

Twenty Plus Two. New York, Dutton, and London, Boardman, 1961.

Brothers of Silence. New York, Dutton, and London, Boardman, 1962.

Bridge of Sand. New York, Dutton, 1963; London, Boardman, 1964.

The Greek Affair. New York, Dutton, 1964; London, Boardman, 1965.

Swing Low Swing Dead (Fletcher and Cragg). New York, Belmont, 1964.

Little Hercules. New York, Dutton, 1965; London, Boardman, 1966.

Run, Fool, Run. New York, Dutton, 1966; London, Hale, 1967.

The Twilight Man. New York, Dutton, and London, Hale, 1967.

The Gold Gap. New York, Dutton, and London, Hale, 1968.

The Etruscan Bull. New York, Dutton, 1969; London, Hale, 1970.

The Spanish Prisoner. New York, Dutton, 1969; London, Hale, 1970.

Short Stories

Brass Knuckles. Los Angeles, Sherbourne Press, 1966.

OTHER PUBLICATIONS

Novels

Peace Marshall. New York, Morrow, 1939; London, Barker, 1957.

Outlaw. New York, Farrar and Rinehart, 1941; London, Wright and Brown, 1942.

Gunsight. New York, Dodd Mead, 1942; London, Wright and Brown, 1943.

Fighting Man. New York, Rinehart, 1948; London, Wright and Brown, 1951.

Broken Lance. New York, Rinehart, 1949; London, Wright and Brown, 1952.

Smoky Road. New York, Rinehart, 1949; London, Wright and Brown, 1952; as *Lone Gunhawk*, Derby, Connecticut, Monarch, 1964.

Fort Starvation. New York, Rinehart, 1953.

Quantrell's Raiders. New York, Ace, 1953.

Bitter Sage. New York, Rinehart, 1954; London, Wright and Brown, 1955.

Bugles West. New York, Rinehart, 1954; London, Barker, 1956.

Johnny Vengeance. New York, Rinehart, 1954; London, Wright and Brown, 1956.

The Highwayman. New York, Rinehart, 1955; London, Barker, 1957.

Buffalo Grass. New York, Rinehart, 1956; London, Barker, 1957.

Lonesome River. New York, Rinehart, 1957; London, Barker, 1958.

The Marshall. New York, Rinehart, 1958; London, Barker, 1959.

Town Tamer. New York, Rinehart, and London, Barker, 1958.

The Bushwackers. New York, Rinehart, 1959; London, New English Library, 1960.

Short Stories

Tales of Wells Fargo. New York, Bantam, and London, Corgi, 1958.

Plays

Screenplays: *Northern Pursuit*, with Alvah Bessie, 1943; *Mask of Dimitrios*, 1944; *Johnny Angel*, with Steve Fisher, 1945; *The French Key*, 1946; *Terror by Night*, 1946; *Accomplice*, with Irving Elman, 1946; *In Old Sacramento*, with Frances Hyland and Jerome Odlum, 1946; *Dressed to Kill*, with Leonard Lee, 1946; *Bulldog Drummond at Bay*, 1947; *The Challenge*, with Irving Elman, 1948; *Fighting Man of the Plains*, 1949;

The Cariboo Trail, with John Rhodes Sturdy, 1950; Dakota Lil, with Maurice Geraghty, 1950; The Texas Rangers, with Richard Schayer, 1950; The Great Missouri Raid, 1951; Warpath, 1951; Silver City, 1951; Flaming Feather, with Gerald Drayson Adams, 1952; The Denver and Rio Grande, 1952; Hurricane Smith, 1952; Pony Express, with Charles Marquis Warren, 1953; Rage at Dawn, with Horace McCoy, 1955; Twenty Plus Two, 1961; Town Tamer, 1965; Arizona Raiders, with others, 1965.

Television Plays: creator of Tales of Wells Fargo, The Texan, and Shotgun Slade series; author of some 200 scripts.

Other

Horatio Alger, Jr.: A Biography and Bibliography.   Privately printed, 1961.
The Pulp Jungle (autobiography).   Los Angeles, Sherbourne Press, 1967.
Zane Grey: A Biography.   Cleveland, World, 1970.

*   *   *

Frank Gruber's production of popular fiction has been immense. About half of his many short stories, novels, and film and television scripts are concerned with detectives and crime. In the 1930's his Oliver Quade stories, along with a variety of others appeared regularly in the pulp magazines. During the 1940's and 1950's his detective novels appeared sometimes at the rate of three or four a year, interspersed with more short stories, and westerns. The Quade stories emphasized the encyclopedic knowledge of its hero, and his exploits with his partner, Charlie Boston. Beginning with The French Key, the Johnny Fletcher novels were produced at a furious pace and signalled a shift from the classic detective hero to Gruber's version of the representative man – an adventurer, however reluctantly, who lives by his wits in an often topsy-turvy world. Johnny Fletcher is mildly hard-boiled and street-wise, often without money except for the sale of books promoting the great strength of his sidekick, Sam Cragg. The brief Otis Beagle series features a detective with the opposite tendencies: flashy clothes and imitation diamonds in his rings and stickpin. In addition to the short Simon Lash series, more than a dozen further novels feature central characters who are caught in circumstances that force them into detection. The odyssey of Gruber's detectives takes them from the relatively mannered world of the classical detective in the early stories, through the witty decencies of the 1940's and early 1950's, into the hard picaresque intrigues of the late 1960's. In The Gold Gap the genteel assumptions of the earliest stories have become polished deceptions that mask the successful psychopath at the center of an international plot.

Anthony Boucher credits Gruber's success to the fast pace of his fiction and his incredibly fertile imagination. Certainly he could be compared in this respect with such prolific pulp writers as Frederick Faust, with whom he also shared an astute market sense and an instinct for light, entertaining plots. In The Pulp Jungle, however, Gruber traced his success with mystery stories to his discovery in the 1930's of an eleven-point plot formula. The successful story, Gruber argued, had to have a colorful hero, a theme that contains information the reader is not likely to have, a villain more powerful than the hero, a colorful background for the action, an unusual murder method or unusual circumstances surrounding the murder, unusual variations on the motives of hate and greed, a concealed clue, the trick that extricates the hero from certain defeat, moving and carefully paced action, a smashing climax, and a hero who is personally involved. In practice Gruber also relied on another element that might be traced to his fondness for Horatio Alger: the play of chance lends a juvenile innocence to many of his stories. On their way through Death Valley in The Honest Dealer, Fletcher and Cragg happen across a dying man who gives them a deck of cards that proves to be the key to the mystery; as they approach Las Vegas they give a ride to the key woman; a colorful policeman finds them a room next to hers when a bribe has failed to turn one up in the entire city; and Fletcher parlays his last dollar into twenty thousand at the gambling tables. Yet after the formula, or in the midst of it, comes the story-teller who has been able to hold his readers' attention regardless of the mechanical thinness of his plots and characters. Few writers have been so consistently successful.

—Larry N. Landrum

GUNN, Victor.   See **GRAY, Berkeley.**

HAGGARD, William.   Pseudonym for Richard Henry Michael Clayton.   British.   Born in Croydon, Surrey, 11 August 1907. Educated at Lancing College, Sussex; Christ Church, Oxford, B.A. 1929. Served in the Indian Army, 1939–45: Staff Lieutenant in Intelligence. Married Barbara Myfanwy Sant in 1936; one son and one daughter. Served in the Indian Civil Service, 1931–39; worked for the Board of Trade, 1947–69: Controller of Enemy Property, 1965–69. M.A.: Oxford University, 1947. Address: 15 Court Gardens, Firlands Avenue, Camberley, Surrey GU15 2HY, England.

CRIME PUBLICATIONS

Novels (series characters: Paul Martiny; Colonel Charles Russell)

 Slow Burner (Russell).   London, Cassell, and Boston, Little Brown, 1958.
 The Telemann Touch.   London, Cassell, and Boston, Little Brown, 1958.
 Venetian Blind (Russell).   London, Cassell, and New York, Washburn, 1959.
 Closed Circuit.   London, Cassell, and New York, Washburn, 1960.
 The Arena (Russell).   London, Cassell, and New York, Washburn, 1961.
 The Unquiet Sleep (Russell).   London, Cassell, and New York, Washburn, 1962.
 The High Wire (Russell).   London, Cassell, and New York, Washburn, 1963.
 The Antagonists (Russell).   London, Cassell, and New York, Washburn, 1964.
 The Powder Barrel (Russell).   London, Cassell, and New York, Washburn, 1965.
 The Hard Sell (Russell).   London, Cassell, 1965; New York, Washburn, 1966.
 The Power House (Russell).   London, Cassell, 1966; New York, Washburn, 1967.
 The Conspirators (Russell).   London, Cassell, 1967; New York, Walker, 1968.
 A Cool Day for Killing (Russell).   London, Cassell, and New York, Walker, 1968.
 The Doubtful Disciple (Russell).   London, Cassell, 1969.
 The Hardliners (Russell).   London, Cassell, and New York, Walker, 1970.
 The Bitter Harvest (Russell).   London, Cassell, 1971; as *Too Many Enemies*, New York, Walker, 1972.
 The Protectors (Martiny).   London, Cassell, and New York, Walker, 1972.
 The Old Masters (Russell).   London, Cassell, 1973; as *The Notch on the Knife*, New York, Walker, 1973.
 The Kinsmen (Martiny).   London, Cassell, and New York, Walker, 1974.
 The Scorpion's Tail (Russell).   London, Cassell, and New York, Walker, 1975.

Yesterday's Enemy. London, Cassell, and New York, Walker, 1976.
The Poison People. London, Cassell, 1978; New York, Walker, 1979.
Visa to Limbo (Russell). London, Cassell, 1978; New York, Walker, 1979.
The Median Line. London, Cassell, 1979.

Uncollected Short Stories

"Night Train to Milan," in *Best Secret Service Stories 2*, edited by John
Welcome. London, Faber, 1965.
"Why Beckett Died," in *Blood on My Mind.* London, Macmillan, 1972.
"The Hirelings," in *Winter's Crimes 4*, edited by George Hardinge. London,
Macmillan, 1972.
"Timeo Danaos," in *Winter's Crimes 8*, edited by Hilary Watson. London, Macmillan,
1976.

OTHER PUBLICATIONS

Other

The Little Rug Book. London, Cassell, 1972.

*   *   *

The flavour of William Haggard: it is one of the pleasures left in life. Bread today is made of bouncy plastic; beer is fizzed-up by chemicals; but the taste of a Haggard book is unique, inimitable (though not too hard to parody, I hazard), and delightful. His view of the world, his tone of voice, enter almost all his characters' heads and certainly permeate every phrase he writes as narrator or describer. He cannot put pen to paper without showing in every word an unchippable top-level view of the world. Even when he chances to reflect on the Almighty this view comes banging across. Listen to a typical Haggard character (from *The Doubtful Disciple*) musing: he "hadn't expected his God would be a fool. He'd be a senior administrator.... He wouldn't hold it against a colleague that he'd simply done his duty." Even the use of that "He'd" is typical, indicating a brusque disregard for the conventional usage of the middle classes, a *droit de seigneur* of grammar.

Whatever story Haggard embarks on he takes you with superb unconcern straight into the highest of high places in the stacked hierarchy of British life (and occasionally into what he sees as the equally hierarchic life of Soviet Russia). It is an entrancing process, because the highest places are of their nature very small places. There is not room at the very top for all of us. But in Haggard we have a proxy in the seats of power. And, note, these highest places are not your mere Cabinet Rooms or Prime Ministers' studies. They are the rooms behind these, the rooms occupied by the people who view prime ministers as simply the awkward and temporary holders of an office. They are the less grandiloquent rooms of those who have acquired, or semi-inherited, the duty of protecting the children of Demos from themselves. I do not know whether in drab real life they actually exist, but while I am reading the pages of a book by Haggard they certainly do.

To descend to details: William Haggard writes what might be called action novels of international power politics. Generally, but not invariably, their hero is Colonel Russell of the Security Executive (a fictitious body). The books work in terms of realpolitik, that is to say their plots are designed to show that it is the realities of any situation that dictate its final outcome. But, though the flavour is always (and savoursomely) the same, the books themselves have been admirably varied. Russell in the course of them retired as Head of the Security Executive and there have been books in which he did not appear at all, or only briefly. Once (in *The Protectors*) he was replaced by a sort of gentleman master-criminal, an investor in the directly criminal activities of others, a man motivated to a large extent by a desire to kick the pompous part of the Establishment, the prating Ministers and others, on the backside.

This desire to tumble tin gods is a strong strain in all the books. Haggard is no mean iconoclast. He it was who had the temerity to draw a portrait (in *The Power House*) of an actual Prime Minister then in office, easily recognisable and cast in vigorously contemptuous terms. Another book had to be withdrawn on the eve of publication while a portrait of a well-known extreme leftist was hurriedly disguised.

Of course, this attitude, full of flavour though it be, is not necessarily to everybody's taste. The conventional are apt to be shocked. To many readers, unable to put themselves in the shoes of Haggard Sahib, his books will be disquieting, or even occasionally downright repulsive. This may be so especially with women readers confronting his treatment of sex. Increasingly (as it has become more and more possible, or even desirable, to put explicit sex into fiction), he has introduced sexual events into his pages, always certainly illuminating character if not advancing the action. He has eschewed those minutely descriptive passages that other, and generally younger, writers have come to use, but he has written of sexual acts with a direct, if generalised, brutality. It was the realpolitik of the bedsheets, and as such certainly offensive to the romantic.

A Haggard novel is, as I have indicated, always politically firmly oriented to the right, though he is not so slavishly attached to current dogma as to make all his villains soft lefties and all his heroes straight-thinking men (and women) of the right. He is quite capable of bestowing his praise – and that is how it comes across – on a socialist, provided he is a socialist who in power will exercise that power with a feeling for its reality rather than by idealistic criteria. So the books were front-runners in a trend that was noticeable in both British and American crime writing from the late 1960's onwards, a turning of the tide to flow to the right. After the revolution carried out in the late 1930's by Eric Ambler in the espionage field and, less markedly, by writers such as Nicholas Blake in detection – a revolution which swung crime writing generally to the left (something to be seen in a host of tiny judgments in any text) – there had been little change. With the Haggard books the first signs of a silent swing began to show.

—H. R. F. Keating

HALL, Adam. See **TREVOR, Elleston**.

HALLIDAY, Brett. Pseudonym for Davis Dresser; also wrote as Asa Baker; Matthew Blood (with Ryerson Johnson); Kathryn Culver; Don Davis; Hal Debrett (with Kathleen Rollins); Anthony Scott; Anderson Wayne. American. Born in Chicago, Illinois, 31 July 1904. Raised in Texas; joined the United States Army Cavalry at 14; returned to Texas to finish high school; educated at Tri-State College, Angola, Indiana, Certificate in Civil Engineering. Married 1) Helen McCloy, *q.v.*, in 1946 (divorced, 1961), one daughter; 2) Kathleen Rollins; 3) Mary Savage. Writer from 1927, contributing stories under many pseudonyms to mystery, western, and adventure pulps; Co-Founder, with Helen McCloy, Torquil Publishing Company, and Halliday and McCloy Literary Agency, 1953–64;

Founding Editor, *Mike Shayne Mystery Magazine*, 1956 (magazine still carries works by-lined Brett Halliday). Recipient: Mystery Writers of America Edgar Allan Poe Award, for criticism, 1953. *Died 4 February 1977.*

CRIME PUBLICATIONS

Novels (series character: Michael Shayne is all books as Halliday)

Mum's the Word for Murder (as Asa Baker). New York, Stokes, 1938; London, Gollancz, 1939.
The Kissed Corpse (as Asa Baker). New York, Carlyle, 1939.
Dividend on Death. New York, Holt, 1939; London, Jarrolds, 1941.
The Private Practice of Michael Shayne. New York, Holt, 1940; London, Jarrolds, 1941.
The Uncomplaining Corpses. New York, Holt, 1940; London, Jarrolds, 1942.
Tickets for Death. New York, Holt, 1941; London, Jarrolds, 1942.
Bodies Are Where You Find Them. New York, Holt, 1941.
Michael Shayne Takes Over (omnibus). New York, Holt, 1941.
The Corpse Came Calling. New York, Dodd Mead, 1942; as *The Case of the Walking Corpse*, Kingston, New York, Quin, 1943.
Murder Wears a Mummer's Mask. New York, Dodd Mead, 1943; as *In a Deadly Vein*, New York, Dell, 1956.
Blood on the Black Market. New York, Dodd Mead, 1943; as *Heads You Lose*, New York, Dell, 1958.
Michael Shayne Investigates (omnibus). London, Jarrolds, 1943.
Michael Shayne Takes a Hand (omnibus). London, Jarrolds, 1944.
Michael Shayne's Long Chance. New York, Dodd Mead, 1944; London, Jarrolds, 1945.
Murder and the Married Virgin. New York, Dodd Mead, 1944; London, Jarrolds, 1946.
Murder Is My Business. New York, Dodd Mead, and London, Jarrolds, 1945.
Marked for Murder. New York, Dodd Mead, 1945; London, Jarrolds, 1950.
Dead Man's Diary, and Dinner at Dupre's. New York, Dell, 1945.
Blood on Biscayne Bay. Chicago, Ziff Davis, 1946; London, Jarrolds, 1950.
Counterfeit Wife. Chicago, Ziff Davis, 1947; London, Jarrolds, 1950.
Blood on the Stars. New York, Dodd Mead, 1948; as *Murder Is a Habit*, London, Jarrolds, 1951.
Michael Shayne's Triple Mystery (*Dead Man's Diary, A Taste for Cognac, Dinner at Dupre's*). New York, Ziff Davis, 1948.
A Taste for Violence. New York, Dodd Mead, 1949; London, Jarrolds, 1952.
Call for Michael Shayne. New York, Dodd Mead, 1949; London, Jarrolds, 1951.
Before I Wake (as Hal Debrett, with Kathleen Rollins). New York, Dodd Mead, 1949; London, Jarrolds, 1953.
A Lonely Way to Die (as Hal Debrett, with Kathleen Culver). New York, Dodd Mead, 1950; London, Jarrolds, 1954.
This Is It, Michael Shayne. New York, Dodd Mead, 1950; London, Jarrolds, 1952.
Framed in Blood. New York, Dodd Mead, 1951; London, Jarrolds, 1953.
When Dorinda Dances. New York, Dodd Mead, 1951; London, Jarrolds, 1953.
What Really Happened. New York, Dodd Mead, 1952; London, Jarrolds, 1953.
Charlie Dell (as Anderson Wayne). New York, Coward McCann, 1952; London, Hale, 1953; as *A Time to Remember*, New York, Popular Library, 1959.
The Avenger (as Matthew Blood, with Ryerson Johnson). New York, Fawcett, 1952.
One Night with Nora. New York, Torquil, 1953; as *The Lady Came by Night*, London, Jarrolds, 1954.

She Woke to Darkness. New York, Torquil, 1954; London, Jarrolds, 1955.

Death Is a Lovely Dame (as Matthew Blood, with Ryerson Johnson). New York, Fawcett, 1954.

Death Has Three Lives. New York, Torquil, and London, Jarrolds, 1955.

Stranger in Town. New York, Torquil, 1955; London, Jarrolds, 1956.

The Blonde Cried Murder. New York, Torquil, 1956; London, Jarrolds, 1957.

Weep for a Blonde. New York, Torquil, 1957; London, Long, 1958.

Shoot the Works. New York, Torquil, 1957; London, Long, 1958.

Murder and the Wanton Bride. New York, Torquil, 1958; London, Long, 1959.

Fit to Kill. New York, Torquil, 1958; London, Long, 1959.

Date with a Dead Man. New York, Torquil, 1959; London, Long, 1960.

Target: Mike Shayne. New York, Torquil, 1959; London, Long, 1960.

Die Like a Dog. New York, Torquil, 1959; London, Long, 1961.

Murder Takes No Holiday. New York, Torquil, 1960.

Dolls Are Deadly. New York, Torquil, 1960.

The Homicidal Virgin. New York, Torquil, 1960; London, Mayflower, 1963.

Killers from the Keys. New York, Torquil, 1961.

Murder in Haste. New York, Torquil, 1961; London, Mayflower, 1963.

The Careless Corpse. New York, Torquil, 1961.

Michael Shayne's Torrid Twelve. New York, Dell, 1961.

Pay-Off in Blood. New York, Torquil, 1962.

Murder by Proxy. New York, Torquil, 1962; London, Mayflower, 1968.

Never Kill a Client. New York, Torquil, 1962.

Too Friendly, Too Dead. New York, Torquil, 1963; London, Mayflower, 1964.

The Corpse That Never Was. New York, Torquil, 1963.

The Body Came Back. New York, Torquil, 1963.

A Redhead for Mike Shayne. New York, Torquil, 1964.

Shoot to Kill. New York, Torquil, 1964.

Michael Shayne's 50th Case. New York, Torquil, 1964.

Dangerous Dames. New York, Dell, 1965.

The Violent World of Michael Shayne. New York, Dell, 1965.

Nice Fillies Finish Last. New York, Dell, 1965.

Murder Spins the Wheel. New York, Dell, 1966.

Armed ... Dangerous.... New York, Dell, 1966.

Mermaid on the Rocks. New York, Dell, 1967.

Guilty as Hell. New York, Dell, 1967.

So Lush, So Deadly. New York, Dell, 1968.

Violence Is Golden. New York, Dell, 1968.

Lady Be Bad. New York, Dell, 1969.

Six Seconds to Kill. New York, Dell, 1970.

Fourth Down to Death. New York, Dell, 1970.

Count Backwards to Zero. New York, Dell, 1971.

I Come to Kill You. New York, Dell, 1971.

Caught Dead. New York, Dell, 1972.

Kill All the Young Girls. New York, Dell, 1973.

Blue Murder. New York, Dell, 1973.

Last Seen Hitchhiking. New York, Dell, 1974.

At the Point of a .38. New York, Dell, 1974.

Million Dollar Handle. New York, Dell, 1976.

Win Some, Lose Some. New York, Dell, 1976.

Uncollected Short Stories

"The Million-dollar Motive," in *Murder Cavalcade*, edited by Ken Crossen. New York, Duell, 1946; London, Hammond, 1953.

"Human Interest Stuff," in *Ellery Queen's Murder by Experts.* Chicago, Ziff Davis, 1947; London, Sampson Low, 1950.

"Big Shot," in *Ellery Queen's Mystery Magazine* (New York), August 1947.

"Extradition," in *Queen's Awards*, edited by Ellery Queen. Boston, Little Brown, 1948; London, Gollancz, 1950.

"Murder Before Midnight," in *Popular Detective* (New York), March 1950.

"Women Are Poison," in *The Saint* (New York), November 1954.

"The Reluctant Client," in *Manhunt* (New York), June 1955.

"Dead Man's Code," in *Crime for Two*, edited by Frances and Richard Lockridge. Philadelphia, Lippincott, 1955.

"Not – Tonight – Danger," in *Ellery Queen's Mystery Magazine* (New York), September 1957.

"Second Honeymoon," in *Ellery Queen's Mystery Magazine* (New York), July 1959.

"Death Goes to the Post," in *Dames, Danger, and Death*, edited by Leo Margulies. New York, Pyramid, 1960.

"Pieces of Silver," in *Alfred Hitchcock Presents: Stories for Late at Night.* New York, Random House, 1961.

"I'm Tough," in *Best Detective Stories of the Year*, edited by Brett Halliday. New York, Dutton, 1962.

"Death of a Dead Man," in *Mink Is for Minx*, edited by Leo Margulies. New York, Dell, 1964.

"Murder in Miami," in *Ellery Queen's Mystery Magazine* (New York), May 1970.

OTHER PUBLICATIONS

Novels as Anthony Scott

Mardi Gras Madness. New York, Godwin, 1934.
Test of Virtue. New York, Godwin, 1934.
Ten Toes Up. New York, Godwin, 1935.
Virgin's Holiday. New York, Godwin, 1935.
Stolen Sins. New York, Godwin, 1936.
Ladies of Chance. New York, Godwin, 1936.
Satan Rides the Night. New York, Godwin, 1938.
Temptation. New York, Godwin, 1938.

Novels as Kathryn Culver

Love Is a Masquerade. New York, Phoenix Press, 1935.
Too Smart for Love. New York, Curl, 1937.
Million Dollar Madness. New York, Curl, 1937.
Green Paths to the Moon. New York, Curl, 1938.
Once to Every Woman. New York, Godwin, 1938.
Girl Alone. New York, Grammercy, 1939.

Novels as Davis Dresser

Let's Laugh at Love. New York, Curl, 1937.
Romance for Julie. New York, Curl, 1938.
Death Rides the Pecos. New York, Morrow, and London, Ward Lock, 1940.
The Hangmen of Sleepy Valley. New York, Morrow, 1940; as *The Masked Riders of Sleepy Valley*, London, Ward Lock, 1941.
Gun Smoke on the Mesa. New York, Carlton, and London, Ward Lock, 1941.
Lynch-Rope Law. New York, Morrow, 1941; London, Ward Lock, 1942.
Murder on the Mesa. London, Ward Lock, 1953.

Novels as Don Davis

Return of the Rio Kid. New York, Morrow, 1940; London, Ward Lock, 1950.
Death on Treasure Trail. London, Hutchinson, 1940; New York, Morrow, 1941.
Rio Kid Justice. New York, Morrow, 1941.
Two-Gun Rio Kid. New York, Morrow, 1941.

Other

Editor, with Helen McCloy, *20 Great Tales of Murder.* New York, Random House, 1951; London, Hammond, 1952.
Editor, *Dangerous Dames.* New York, Dell, 1955.
Editor, *Big Time Mysteries.* New York, Dodd Mead, 1958.
Editor, *Murder in Miami.* New York, Dodd Mead, 1959.
Editor, *Best Detective Stories of the Year (16th* [and *17th*] *Annual Collection).* New York, Dutton, 2 vols., 1961–62.

*   *   *

Beginning in 1939 with a book no publisher wanted, and ending in 1976 with a book that would be sure to sell in the hundreds of thousands, Brett Halliday wrote more than 60 mystery novels that featured private detective Mike Shayne. In the intervening years those books sold in the millions, were translated into seven languages and published all across the world, were made into motion pictures and a television series, placed their hero into a magazine of his own that is still being published every month, and established the big, raw-boned, redhead Michael Shayne as one of the few really immortal fictional detectives.

In a long and often stormy career, Davis Dresser wrote many books under many names, but it is on the Mike Shayne novels he wrote as Brett Halliday that his fame and reputation will rest. The fame is probably secure, but the reputation has sometimes been tarnished by critics. It is true that Halliday was not a literary stylist, a penetrating psychologist, or a keen analyzer of current society. But he was a writer who knew a good story when he found one, and who knew how to tell that story. He knew how to catch the reader's interest from the opening page. He knew how people act with each other both day to day and at violent moments. He knew that a good suspense novel is not an abstract puzzle, but is people acting one way or another. Above all he knew something more important than everything else – he knew that his audience did not want literary style, or unique plot, or dazzling psychology – they wanted to see their hero in action. It is Mike Shayne the audience wants to read about: Mike, and his crony Tim Rourke, his good friend Chief Will Gentry, his faithful secretary/girlfriend Lucy Hamilton, and, yes, his arch-antagonist Miami Beach Chief of Detectives Peter Painter. The writing and the plot don't really matter any more than they do in a successful television series; the hero is the book – Mike Shayne in action, with the crime there only for Mike to solve, the criminal there for Mike to defeat.

Halliday was also an honest writer, and Mike Shayne is a real person – complete, accurate, uniquely American, and the personification of one facet of the American dream. He shapes and dominates each book. We see and understand each adventure through his eyes and his eyes only. We do not see people objectively, or as they see themselves, but as Mike sees them, and he is a man with a firm, steady, totally confident view of everything. He knows what he is, what he wants, and why he acts. He knows right from wrong, morality from immorality, justice from law, and has no hesitation in either action or judgment if his principles conflict with others'. He has no qualms about breaking either law or custom in the name of justice, and he will die for the truth as he sees it. In a time of chaos and confusion he is a man with his own code and no doubts at all. Halliday may not have delved too deeply into the psychology of the other characters in his books, but he knew Mike Shayne's psychology completely, and never wrote a line or scene that wasn't totally accurate and honest to Shayne.

Davis Dresser grew up in the early years of this century in the rugged, vast, barren deserts and mountains of West Texas. He lost an eye to barbed wire as a boy. He rode with Pershing after Pancho Villa. He was one of the last of a generation that grew up on the closing frontier, and it shaped him into a man who knew who and what he was, with a definite view of just about everything, a man like Mike Shayne. Both men stood for a simpler, more confident, less confused time in America. They are loners because they rely on no one but themselves in either action or thought. Wrong they may be, from time to time, but it will never be because of anyone but themselves, because of any code but their own. And that code is in essence the code of the old frontier, of a rugged individualist populism. If they are wrong, as another folk hero used to say, they'll apologize, but they will never hesitate to follow their own code and judgment wherever it takes them, and they will judge harshly any man who fails either their code or his own.

—Dennis Lynds

HALLIDAY, Dorothy.   See **DUNNETT, Dorothy**

HALLIDAY, Michael.   See **CREASEY, John.**

HAMILTON, Donald (Bengtsson).   American.   Born in Uppsala, Sweden, 24 March 1916; emigrated to the United States in 1924. Educated at the University of Chicago, B.S. 1938. Served in the United States Naval Reserve: Lieutenant. Married Kathleen Stick in 1941; two daughters and two sons. Since 1946, self-employed writer and photographer. Agent: Leah Salisbury Inc., 234 West 44th Street, New York, New York 10036. Address: 984 Acequia Madre, P.O. Box 1045, Santa Fe, New Mexico, U.S.A.

CRIME PUBLICATIONS

Novels (series character: Matt Helm)

> Date with Darkness.   New York, Rinehart, 1947; London, Wingate, 1951.
> The Steel Mirror.   New York, Rinehart, 1948; London, Wingate, 1950.
> Murder Twice Told.   New York, Rinehart, 1950; London, Wingate, 1952.
> Night Walker.   New York, Dell, 1954; as Rough Company, London, Wingate, 1954.
> Line of Fire.   New York, Dell, 1955; London, Wingate, 1956.

Assignment: Murder. New York, Dell, 1956; as *Assassins Have Starry Eyes*, New York, Fawcett, 1966.
Death of a Citizen (Helm). New York, Fawcett, and London, Muller, 1960.
The Wrecking Crew (Helm). New York, Fawcett, 1960; London, Muller, 1961.
The Removers (Helm). New York, Fawcett, 1961; London, Muller, 1962.
Murderer's Row (Helm). New York, Fawcett, 1962; London, Muller, 1963.
The Silencers (Helm). New York, Fawcett, 1962; London, Hodder and Stoughton, 1966.
The Ambushers (Helm). New York, Fawcett, 1963; London, Hodder and Stoughton, 1967.
The Ravagers (Helm). New York, Fawcett, 1964.
The Shadowers (Helm). New York, Fawcett, and London, Muller, 1964.
The Devastators (Helm). New York, Fawcett, 1965; London, Hodder and Stoughton, 1967.
The Betrayers (Helm). New York, Fawcett, 1966; London, Hodder and Stoughton, 1968.
The Menacers (Helm). New York, Fawcett, and London, Hodder and Stoughton, 1968.
The Interlopers (Helm). New York, Fawcett, and London, Hodder and Stoughton, 1969.
The Poisoners (Helm). New York, Fawcett, and London, Hodder and Stoughton, 1971.
The Intriguers (Helm). New York, Fawcett, and London, Hodder and Stoughton, 1973.
The Intimidators (Helm). New York, Fawcett, and London, Hodder and Stoughton, 1974.
The Terminators (Helm). New York, Fawcett, 1975; London, Hodder and Stoughton, 1976.
The Retaliators (Helm). New York, Fawcett, 1976.
The Terrorizers (Helm). New York, Fawcett, 1977.

OTHER PUBLICATIONS

Novels

Smoky Valley. New York, Dell, 1954.
Mad River. New York, Dell, 1956; London, Wingate, 1957.
The Big Country. New York, Dell, 1957; London, Panther, 1958.
The Man from Santa Clara. New York, Dell, 1960; as *The Two-Shoot Gun*, New York, Fawcett, 1971.
Texas Fever. New York, Fawcett, 1960; London, Muller, 1961.

Play

Screenplay: *Five Steps to Danger*, with Henry S. Kesler and Turnley Walker, 1957.

Other

On Guns and Hunting. New York, Fawcett, 1970.

*   *   *

"The American James Bond" is Matt Helm, Donald Hamilton's series hero and the subject of all his fiction since 1960. Both Bond and Helm are government-sponsored assassins working primarily in counter-espionage, single, physically attractive, and have numerous other common characteristics. Since Bond came first and remains one of the half-dozen most potent fictional heroes, Helm is often dismissed as a copy. Film treatment, with Dean Martin appearing as Helm, can be interpreted as belonging to the genre of Bond parody and has tended to further the belief that Helm is a copy. This is far from the real story. The first successful American spy hero after World War II was CIA operative Sam Durell, whose adventures were written by Edward S. Aarons until his death and then continued by Will B. Aarons. When the publisher elected to begin a second spy series, Hamilton was selected to write it, for very good reasons. He had established a reputation with half a dozen non-series suspense novels and his popular westerns. Since assassination had been a frequent feature of Hamilton's suspense fiction, and since Durell worked directly as a spy and usually in exotic foreign locations, the companion series was developed about a hero who was primarily a counterspy (and the ultimate way to counter a spy is to kill him), operating usually within the continental United States. There was no need for "an American James Bond" in 1960, for Bond was little known in the United States before 1962 when a genuinely "major movie" launching and a Kennedy family endorsement sparked the beginning of a decade-long Bond boom. By that time, Helm was firmly established with half a dozen of his adventures in print, and the best ones (starting with *The Ambushers*) ready to begin appearing. Undoubtedly, Bond helped increase Helm sales, and Hamilton repaid the compliment by including some Bond parody in several of the later books.

Helm was introduced in the memorable *Death of a Citizen* (and rebirth of a counterspy). The hero, whose background had included assassinations of important Nazis in World War II, was reactivated at the expense of a middle-class family life and a promising career as a western novelist and "field and stream" photographer-writer. As with Bond, relations between the hero and the shadowy father-figure of his spy master (usually called only "Mac," but rather fully revealed in *The Intriguers*) have been a major focal point. Helm is Mac's most trusted agent, and Helm's respect for his boss (mitigated by half-humorous, behind-the-back denigration) borders upon feudal fealty. The agency is never named in the books (in the films it is called I.C.E. with the acronym – like I.A.T.S. in Spillane's Tiger Mann books – never explained). The best villains tend to recur once or twice before being dispatched. "Message" content is often repetitive – Hamilton's dislike of the automobile industry, Women's Lib, and other targets is too often expressed.

Among the best of the pre-Helm Hamilton suspense novels are *The Steel Mirror*, *Assignment: Murder* (more familiar under the later title *Assassins Have Starry Eyes*), and *Line of Fire*. *Line of Fire*, probably the author's best single work, deals with a political assassination that succeeds too well and features a credibly unheroic (yet not anti-heroic) central character. This is the ideal book with which to discover Hamilton. The Helm books should be read in the order written. The film series, even seen free on television, is not recommended.

—Jeff Banks

HAMILTON, Patrick.   British.   Born in Hassocks, Sussex, 17 March 1904. Educated at Holland House School, Hove, Sussex; Colet Court, London; Westminster School, London (Vincent Prize, 1918), 1918–19. Married 1) Lois Martin in 1930 (divorced, 1953); 2) Ursula Stewart in 1953. Actor and assistant stage manager to Andrew Melville in the 1920's. *Died 23 September 1962.*

CRIME PUBLICATIONS

Novels (series character: Ernest Ralph Gorse)

Hangover Square; or, The Man with Two Minds: A Story of Darkest Earl's Court in the
Year 1939. London, Constable, 1941; New York, Random House, 1942.
The West Pier (Gorse). London, Constable, 1951; New York, Doubleday, 1952.
Mr. Stimpson and Mr. Gorse. London, Constable, 1953.
Unknown Assailant (Gorse). London, Constable, 1955.

OTHER PUBLICATIONS

Novels

Monday Morning. London, Constable, and Boston, Houghton Mifflin, 1925.
Craven House. London, Constable, 1926; Boston, Houghton Mifflin, 1927; revised
edition, Constable, 1943.
Twopence Coloured. London, Constable, and Boston, Houghton Mifflin, 1928.
The Midnight Bell: A Love Story. London, Constable, 1929; Boston, Little Brown,
1930.
The Siege of Pleasure. London, Constable, and Boston, Little Brown, 1932.
The Plains of Cement. London, Constable, 1934; Boston, Little Brown, 1935.
Impromptu in Moribundia. London, Constable, 1939.
The Slaves of Solitude. London, Constable, 1947; as Riverside, New York, Random
House, 1947.

Plays

Rope: A Play with a Preface on Thrillers (produced London, 1929). London,
Constable, 1929; as Rope's End (produced New York, 1929), New York, R. R. Smith,
1930.
The Procurator of Judea, adaptation of a work by Anatole France (produced London,
1930).
John Brown's Body (produced London, 1930).
Gas Light: A Victorian Thriller (produced Richmond, Surrey, 1938; London,
1939). London, Constable, 1939; as Angel Street (produced New York, 1941), New
York, French, 1942.
Money with Menaces and To the Public Danger: Two Radio Plays. London, Constable,
1939.
This Is Impossible (broadcast, 1941). London, French, 1942.
The Duke in Darkness (produced Edinburgh and London, 1942; New York,
1944). London, Constable, 1943.
The Governess (produced London, 1946).
The Man Upstairs (produced Blackpool, 1953). London, Constable, 1954.

Radio Plays: Money with Menaces, 1937; To the Public Danger, 1939; This Is
Impossible, 1941; Caller Anonymous, 1952; Miss Roach, from his novel The Slaves of
Solitude, 1958; Hangover Square, from his own novel, 1965.

*   *   *

Various critics, including Carolyn Wells, S. S. Van Dine, and Ronald Knox have
promulgated rules for writing the mystery-detective-suspense story, but Patrick Hamilton
ignored them and maintained his own individualistic approach to crime story-telling. Starting
as a Dickensian novelist in the mid-1920's, Hamilton turned to the crime drama with Rope

which was vaguely based on the notorious Loeb-Leopold case. A better-known play is *Gas Light*, wherein a man tries to drive his wife insane in order to recover jewels he had hidden in her house.

Hamilton's best-known crime novel, *Hangover Square*, is a grim and powerful study of a schizophrenic named George Harvey Bone who lives in the lower depths of Earl's Court, London. His miserable existence and mental deterioration are worsened by his love for a feckless whore who is flagrantly unfaithful to him, and this situation can only be resolved by violence. This novel is possibly the most valid fictional study of a disordered mind.

Much less popular, and little known today, is the Ernest Ralph Gorse series. Gorse is represented as a great villain, but he really doesn't do too much except manipulate other characters, Iago-fashion, and not very much actually happens in the books. Unfortunately, and frustratingly, Hamilton's actual design is obscure because he died before he could write what should have been the fourth and final volume of this proposed quartet.

—Charles Shibuk

HAMMETT, (Samuel) Dashiell. Also wrote as Peter Collinson. American. Born in St. Mary's County, Maryland, 27 May 1894. Educated at Baltimore Polytechnic Institute to age 13. Served with the Motor Ambulance Corps of the United States Army, 1918–19: Sergeant; also served in the United States Army Signal Corps in the Aleutian Islands, 1942–45. Married Josephine Annas Dolan in 1920 (divorced, 1937); two daughters. Worked as a clerk, stevedore, advertising manager; private detective for the Pinkerton Agency, 1908–22; full-time writer from 1922, working in Hollywood 1930–42. Instructor of creative writing, Jefferson School of Social Science, New York, 1946–47. Convicted of contempt of Congress and sentenced to six months in prison, 1951. President, League of American Writers, 1942; President, Civil Rights Congress of New York, 1946–47; Member, Advisory Board, *Soviet Russia Today*. Died 10 January 1961.

CRIME PUBLICATIONS

Novels (series character: The Continental Op)

Red Harvest (Op). New York, Knopf, and London, Cassell, 1929.
The Dain Curse (Op). New York, Knopf, and London, Cassell, 1929.
The Maltese Falcon. New York, Knopf, and London, Cassell, 1930.
The Glass Key. New York, Knopf, and London, Cassell, 1931.
The Thin Man. New York, Knopf, and London, Barker, 1934.
$106,000 Blood Money (Op). New York, Spivak, 1943; as *Blood Money*, Cleveland, World, 1943; as *The Big Knock-Over*, New York, Spivak, 1948.

Short Stories

The Adventures of Sam Spade and Other Stories, edited by Ellery Queen. New York, Spivak, 1944; as *They Can Only Hang You Once*, 1949.
The Continental Op, edited by Ellery Queen. New York, Spivak, 1945.
The Return of the Continental Op, edited by Ellery Queen. New York, Spivak, 1945.
Hammett Homicides, edited by Ellery Queen. New York, Spivak, 1946.
Dead Yellow Women, edited by Ellery Queen. New York, Spivak, 1947.

Nightmare Town, edited by Ellery Queen. New York, Spivak, 1948.
The Creeping Siamese, edited by Ellery Queen. New York, Spivak, 1950.
Woman in the Dark, edited by Ellery Queen. New York, Spivak, 1951.
A Man Named Thin and Other Stories, edited by Ellery Queen. New York, Ferman, 1962.
The Big Knockover: Selected Stories and Short Novels, edited by Lillian Hellman. New York, Random House, 1966; as *The Hammett Story Omnibus*, London, Cassell, 1966; as *The Big Knockover* and *The Continental Op*, New York, Dell, 2 vols., 1967.

OTHER PUBLICATIONS

Plays

Watch on the Rhine (screenplay), with Lillian Hellman, in *Best Film Plays of 1943–44*, edited by John Gassner and Dudley Nichols. New York, Crown, 1945.

Screenplays: *City Streets*, with Oliver H. P. Garrett, 1931; *Mister Dynamite*, with Doris Malloy and Harry Clork, 1935; *After the Thin Man*, with Frances Goodrich and Albert Hackett, 1936; *Another Thin Man*, with Frances Goodrich and Albert Hackett, 1939; *Watch on the Rhine*, with Lillian Hellman, 1943.

Radio Plays: contributed scripts to *The Thin Man*, 1942; *The Adventures of Sam Spade*, 1946; *The Fat Man* (created by Hammett), 1946.

Other

"From the Memoirs of a Private Detective," in *Smart Set* (New York), March 1923.
"Tempo in the Novel," in *Fighting Words*, edited by Donald Ogden Stewart. New York, Harcourt Brace, 1940.
The Battle of the Aleutians, with Robert Colodny. Privately printed, 1944.
Secret Agent X-9 (syndicated comic strip), with Alex Raymond. Philadelphia, McKay, 2 vols., 1934.

Editor, *Creeps by Night*. New York, Day, 1931; as *Modern Tales of Horror*, London, Gollancz, 1932; as *The Red Brain*, New York, Belmont, 1961.

Bibliography: *Dashiell Hammett: A Casebook* by William F. Nolan, Santa Barbara, California, McNally and Loftin, 1969; *Dashiell Hammett: A Descriptive Bibliography* by Richard Layman, Pittsburgh, University of Pittsburgh Press, 1979.

Manuscript Collection: Humanities Research Center, University of Texas, Austin.

*   *   *

What is there in Dashiell Hammett's work that makes it a standard for judging the work of other writers? His output was surprisingly small. He wrote some short stories for the pulps, and between 1929 and 1934 wrote all the novels he was ever to write: *Red Harvest*, *The Dain Curse*, *The Maltese Falcon*, *The Glass Key*, and *The Thin Man*. He left the fragment of another novel, *Tulip*, but there's enough to show that he was trying to go in another direction.

Some of the short stories are very good ("The Gutting of Couffignal"), some are not ("Corkscrew"), but none benefits from comparison to, say, Hemingway's; and, despite the arguments of Steven Marcus, they do not form the basis of Hammett's reputation. The novels do.

And what are the novels about? They are about men who persist in the face of adversity until they do what they set out to do. They are about men who have few friends and no permanent social context. Except for Ned Beaumont in *The Glass Key* these men are detectives. Except for Nick Charles in *The Thin Man* they are alone. They have no family. Their allegiance is not to law but to something else, call it order, a sense of the way things ought to be. They are not of the police any more than they are of the mob. They are of the people. But they are immune to the things that compel the people. They do not succumb to the temptations of money or sex. They are not hostage to the fear of death. They are beset with no illusions. In these ways they are larger than we are; they are supermen, giants of autonomy. Despite the hard-edged vernacular in which the stories are told, and the mean streets in which they take place, Hammett is not writing realistic fiction, he is writing romance. He is writing of heroes who are superior in degree to ordinary men.

Taken as a whole, and chronologically, the novels may be seen to speculate on the way a man should deal with disorder, on the things to which he should give allegiance. In *Red Harvest*, the Continental Op is motivated by what appears to be a work ethic. He finds Personville corrupt and he cleans it up for no better reason than that it's his job (though not his assignment). In *The Dain Curse* the work ethic may be muted by compassion. The Op finds a young woman beset by neurosis, drugs, and lineage. He saves her. In *The Maltese Falcon* Sam Spade's partner is killed. A valuable statue is sought. Spade solves the murder, turns in the seekers. In *The Glass Key* Ned Beaumont endures great pain on behalf of a friend. At the end of the novel he severs the friendship. *The Thin Man* is unfortunate. Let us not speak of it.

The motivation for the behavior of these men is always murky. But in *The Maltese Falcon*, Spade tells Brigid O'Shaughnessy a story while they wait, in Spade's apartment, for Joel Cairo. It is the story of a man named Flitcraft (Hammett was always fond of suggestive names) who was nearly killed by a beam falling from a half-built building as Flitcraft was going to lunch. The beam missed, but "he felt like somebody had taken the lid off life and let him look at the works." Flitcraft discovered that "life could be ended for him at random by a falling beam: he would change his life at random by simply going away." The story is casually told and Brigid pays it little heed. It appears to her a time-killer. But it is not. It is a parable, and it is the code that Spade lives by. In fact, the vision of life embodied in Flitcraft's story is the central spring in Hammett's work. It gives motion to his protagonists. The novels suggest a random universe in which a man may impose his own order if he is tough enough (and has seen under life's lid). The cost of that is probably isolation. But the alternative is chaos.

All of this is, of course, very much in the American grain, and very much of Hammett's time (*Red Harvest* was published in the same year as *A Farewell to Arms*). For Hammett the matters of crime and detection served simply as metaphors for life (for Hemingway it was hunting and war that served). "The essential American soul," D. H. Lawrence wrote, "is hard, isolate, stoic, and a killer.... A man who keeps his moral integrity hard and intact. An isolate, almost selfless, stoic enduring man who lives by death, by killing.... This is the very intrinsic-most American."

—Robert B. Parker

HANSEN, Joseph. Also writes as Rose Brock; James Colton. American. Born in Aberdeen, South Dakota, 19 July 1923. Married Jane Bancroft in 1943; one daughter. Self-employed writer. Teaches mystery and other fiction writing, University of California Extension Programs. Recipient: National Endowment for the Arts Fellowship, 1974; British

Arts Council Grant, 1975. Agent: Collier Associates, 280 Madison Avenue, New York, New York 10016. Address: 2638 Cullen Street, Los Angeles, California 90034, U.S.A.

CRIME PUBLICATIONS

Novels (series character: Dave Brandstetter in all books)

Fadeout. New York, Harper, 1970; London, Harrap, 1972.
Death Claims. New York, Harper, and London, Harrap, 1973.
Troublemaker. New York, Harper, and London, Harrap, 1975.
The Man Everybody Was Afraid Of. New York, Holt Rinehart, and London, Faber, 1978.
Skinflick. New York, Holt Rinehart, 1979; London, Faber, 1980.

Uncollected Short Stories

"Mourner," in *South Dakota Review* (Vermillion), Winter 1971–72.
"The Dog," in *Killers of the Mind*, edited by Lucy Freeman. New York, Random House, 1974.
"Murder on the Surf," in *Mystery Monthly* (New York), December 1976.

OTHER PUBLICATIONS

Novels as James Colton

Lost on Twilight Road. Fresno, California, National Library, 1964.
Strange Marriage. Los Angeles, Argyle Books, 1965.
Known Homosexual. Los Angeles, Brandon House, 1968; as *Stranger to Himself*, Los Angeles, Major Books, 1978.
Cocksure. San Diego, Greenleaf, 1969.
Hang-Up. Los Angeles, Brandon House, 1969.
Gard. New York, Award, 1969.
Tarn House (as Rose Brock). New York, Avon, 1971; London, Harrap, 1975.
The Outward Side. New York, Olympia Press, 1971.
Todd. New York, Olympia Press, 1971.
Longleaf (as Rose Brock). New York, Harper, and London, Harrap, 1974.

Short Stories as James Colton

The Corrupter and Other Stories. San Diego, Greenleaf, 1968.

Verse

One Foot in the Boat. Los Angeles, Momentum Press, 1977.

Other

"The New Mystery," in *The Writer* (Boston), September 1973.
"The Fag as Pop Art Target," in *New Review* (London), March 1975.
"What's Wrong with Your Story?," in *The Writer* (Boston), October 1976.
"Plotting a Murder," in *The Writer* (Boston), October 1979.

Joseph Hansen comments:

Homosexuals have commonly been treated shabbily in detective fiction – vilified, pitied, at best patronized. This was neither fair nor honest. When I sat down to write *Fadeout* in 1967 I wanted to write a good, compelling whodunit, but I also wanted to right some wrongs. Almost all the folksay about homosexuals is false. So I had some fun turning clichés and stereotypes on their heads in that book. It was easy. I gather from the reviews that it worked. But before there were reviews there had to be a published book. And that took some doing. It also took three years. Publishers were leery of my matter-of-fact, non-apologetic approach to a subject that the rule book said had to be treated sensationally or not at all. At last a brave lady named Joan Kahn, mystery editor at Harper and Row, took a chance on me. Brandstetter, shrewd, cool, tough-minded, and, in spite of this (!), a homosexual, now has readers in Britain, France, Holland, and Japan as well. Peter Preston of the London *Guardian* asked me once if it was right for Dave always to be mixed up in mystery plots involving homosexuals and homosexuality. I said it seemed to me there were plenty of mystery plots involving heterosexuals and heterosexuality, weren't there? And Julian Symons has been kind enough to remark somewhere that Dave's special bent gives him insights into areas of everyday life the common reader ordinarily wouldn't see, or if he did see, wouldn't understand. The message that homosexuals are no different from other people hardly seems earth shaking – at least not to men and women of goodwill and commonsense. Alas, such men and women make up a breed small in numbers. I hope the Dave Brandstetter novels can add to them.

*   *   *

Joseph Hansen has written several Dave Brandstetter mysteries. Dave is a middle-aged, somewhat world-weary investigator of insurance death claims. In private life, Dave is a homosexual, and has problems keeping a lover. Many of the people he runs into in his work are homosexual. In fact, Joseph Hansen, by means of the mystery and the detective, strives to universalize the fact of homosexuality.

Hansen's style is strong in description and dialogue. He knows his way around Los Angeles and creates compelling atmosphere. He parallels the antagonisms and love relationships in his murder-mystery plots with those of his detective. In *Fadeout*, Brandstetter's lover is dead of cancer. Investigating a murder, Dave clears a young man of the crime, and the young man at the end becomes his new lover. One lover fades out; another fades in. The victim fades out; by way of investigation the motive behind the murder fades in. The title fits the radio *mise en scène*, as well as plot.

In *Death Claims*, Dave and the new lover are "coming apart." Each has a dead lover in his memory, and "the dead crept cold between them." Dave investigates the death of a bookseller who fought to stay alive through torturous skin-graft surgery, sustained by the love of a younger girl. Finding the murderer, Dave restores the girl's faith in herself and her ability to survive. Dave and his own lover bury the past and their relationship is restored. Again, the title doubles plots and theme.

Troublemaker deals with interlopers. One is the murderer of a gay-bar operator. Sorting out the man's associates, Dave finds the killer. A parasite, meanwhile, tries to break up Dave's relationship with his lover. Dave kicks the interloper out and brings the other, the killer, to justice.

The parallels between private and detective worlds integrate best in *Death Claims*. The theme of loss and restoration universalizes the particular problems of the victims and the hero. But the detective plots (the clues and the ratiocination), the core of any mystery, lack ingenuity and are sidetracked, often weakened, by an over-emphasis upon the esoterics of the gay world and weary nature of the detective. Thus, the main thrust of the Brandstetter series, universalizing sexuality and character, is weakened.

Hansen has chosen a difficult route to travel and done it resolutely in a time when the mystery genre in veering (from debasement) away from its own purpose. The idealized characters in his work are the young, whether in mysteries, his more experimental stories, or his early, sex-oriented paperbacks. *Lost on Twilight Road*, a slight, obscurely published novel, follows a youth who, with the help of an older man, overcomes poverty, matures, and defeats his and his mentor's enemies. The man sets the direction; the youth wins for himself. Hansen's writing career spans several genres, including obscurantist literature and the rational detective world. The mixture, unfortunately, is substantive in the character of Dave Brandstetter and is unresolved. Sex is not his problem; philosophy is. Dave helps youth find themselves, but his own happiness is past-determined. Dave Brandstetter knows that sex is an essential part of happiness, but that it is the other part, as well, that sustains the whole. That is the mystery in his future.

—Newton Baird

HANSHEW, Thomas W. Also wrote as Charlotte Mary Kingsley. American. Born in 1857. Married Mary E. Hanshew. An actor for some years. *Died 3 March 1914.*

CRIME PUBLICATIONS

Novels (series character: Hamilton Cleek)

> *Beautiful But Dangerous; or, The Heir of Shadowdene.* New York, Street and Smith, 1891.
> *The World's Finger.* London, Ward Lock, and New York, Irwin, 1901; as *The Horton Mystery*, New York, Ogilvie, 1905.
> *The Mallison Mystery.* London, Ward Lock, 1903.
> *The Great Ruby.* London, Ward Lock, 1905.
> *The Shadow of a Dead Man.* London, Ward Lock, 1906.
> *Fate and the Man.* London, Cassell, 1910.
> *Cleek of Scotland Yard.* London, Cassell, and New York, Doubleday, 1914.
> *Cleek's Greatest Riddles.* London, Simpkin Marshall, 1916; as *Cleek's Government Cases*, New York, Doubleday, 1917 (possibly not by Hanshew).

Short Stories

> *The Man of the Forty Faces.* London, Cassell, 1910; revised (novel) version, as *Cleek, The Man of the Forty Faces*, Cassell, 1913; short story version as *Cleek, The Master Detective*, New York, Doubleday, 1918.

OTHER PUBLICATIONS

Novels

> *Young Mrs. Charnleigh.* New York, Carleton, 1883.
> *Leonie; or, The Sweet Street Singer of New York.* New York, Munro, 1884.
> *A Wedded Widow; or, The Love That Lived.* New York, Street and Smith, 1887.
> *Arrol's Engagement* (as Charlotte Mary Kingsley). London, Ward Lock, 1903.

Plays

>The Forty-Niners; or, The Pioneer's Daughter, adaptation of his own story (also director:
>   produced). Clyde, Ohio, Ames, n.d.
>Oath Bound; or, Faithful unto Death (produced Chicago).   Clyde, Ohio, Ames, n.d.
>Will-o'-the-Wisp; or, The Shot in the Dark. Clyde, Ohio, Ames, n.d.

*   *   *

The reader who is unprepared or unable to suspend disbelief will never be able to read Thomas W. Hanshew with pleasure. Some have called him an obscure writer who deserves obscurity. Admittedly, he is a "period author" who must be read in the context of his times and the tradition from which he came. Hanshew was an American dime novelist who found his niche in detective history with a long series of stories about Hamilton Cleek, the man of the forty faces. According to tradition he was one of the writers of the Nick Carter stories, but this has never been proved. His use of the pseudonym Bertha M. Clay is also in doubt; both his family and his publishers denied the attribution.

Some three dozen of the more than 80 Cleek stories had been published when their author died; the remaining stories, after an initial magazine appearance, were edited by Hanshew's daughter, Hazel, into collections disguised as novels. The books were published as by Hanshew and his widow, Mary. The Cleek stories have many weaknesses, not the least of which are the melodramatic style and improbable situations. Read with the right approach, though, they can be enjoyed in spite of themselves. At the core of most are some ingenious ideas which tantalize and mystify and disappoint only for the reason many mysteries disappoint: the solution is never as ingenious as the mystery itself. A magician's trick is only as good as his art of misdirection. There are a nine-fingered skeleton, a death on the tenth of each month, inexplicable footprints, a tell-tale tattoo that can be removed only at the expense of an arm, a person who vanishes in plain view, and other mysteries.

Behind the individual stories of detection is the mystery of Cleek himself, which is used to bind episodes into longer stories. Once he was known to the police as the Vanishing Cracksman, his main attribute the ability to disguise himself. He didn't need putty or false whiskers, for he possessed the talent to alter his features by sheer will power. Because of his love for Ailsa Lorne, Cleek resolved to go straight and became Scotland Yard's chief riddle solver. Cleek had forty faces and reserved his real one for the people close to him: Superintendent Maverick Narkom, Dollops (his cockney associate), and Ailsa Lorne. His real identity was that of the true king of Maurevania (bounded, no doubt, on the North by Ruritania and on the South by Graustark), and for Ailsa he renounced the throne. Cleek is continually pursued through the stories by the ghosts of his past, both criminal and regal. This creates a tension which can be enjoyed along with the puzzles.

It is argued that Hanshew knew little of Scotland Yard and less of the mysterious East, both of which play major roles in the chronicles of Cleek. But Cleek is not a real person and his world is not the real one. This is the world of Romance and High Adventure. With tongue in cheek and child-like acceptance of fantasy, the reader of Hanshew can truly escape the mundane. On one level the books may even be read as a burlesque of Edwardian detective stories and all the works of romance which their author once spun for his American publishers. Hanshew's significance may lie in the influence he had on some later writers, like John Dickson Carr, who also had an interest in ingenious situations and intricate plots. Cleek's method of disguise was adapted by Paul Ernst for his novels about Richard Benson in The Avenger magazine (1939–42).

—J. Randolph Cox

HARBAGE, Alfred B.   See KYD, Thomas.

HARE, Cyril. Pseudonym for Alfred Alexander Gordon Clark. British. Born in Mickleham, Surrey, 4 September 1900. Educated at Rugby School, Warwickshire; New College, Oxford, B.A. (honours) in history; Inner Temple, London: called to the Bar, 1924. Married Mary Barbara Lawrence in 1933; one son and two daughters. Joined firm of Ronald Oliver and practiced in civil and criminal courts; Temporary Officer, Ministry of Economic Warfare, 1940, and Temporary Legal Assistant, Director of Public Prosecutions Department, 1940–45; County Court Judge, Surrey, 1950–58. *Died 25 August 1958.*

CRIME PUBLICATIONS

Novels (series characters: Inspector Mallett; Francis Pettigrew)

> *Tenant for Death* (Mallett).   London, Faber, and New York, Dodd Mead, 1937.
> *Death Is No Sportsman* (Mallett).   London, Faber, 1938.
> *Suicide Excepted* (Mallett).   London, Faber, 1939; New York, Macmillan, 1954.
> *Tragedy at Law* (Mallett; Pettigrew).   London, Faber, 1942; New York, Harcourt Brace, 1943.
> *With a Bare Bodkin* (Mallett; Pettigrew).   London, Faber, 1946.
> *When the Wind Blows* (Pettigrew).   London, Faber, 1949; as *The Wind Blows Death*, Boston, Little Brown, 1950.
> *An English Murder.*   London, Faber, and Boston, Little Brown, 1951; as *The Christmas Murder*, New York, Spivak, 1953.
> *That Yew Tree's Shade* (Pettigrew).   London, Faber, 1954; as *Death Walks the Woods*, Boston, Ltttle Brown, 1954.
> *He Should Have Died Hereafter* (Mallett; Pettigrew).   London, Faber, 1958; as *Untimely Death*, New York, Macmillan, 1958.

Short Stories

> *Best Detective Stories of Cyril Hare*, edited by Michael Gilbert.   London, Faber, 1959; New York, Walker, 1961.

Uncollected Short Stories

> "The Boldest Course," in *Ellery Queen's Mystery Magazine* (New York), November 1960.
> "The Homing Wasp," in *Ellery Queen's Mystery Magazine* (New York), March 1961.
> "Blenkinsop's Biggest Boner," in *Ellery Queen's Mystery Magazine* (New York), September 1961.
> "I Never Forget a Face," in *The Saint* (New York), June 1966.

OTHER PUBLICATIONS

Play

> *The House of Warbeck* (produced Margate, Kent, 1955).

Other

The Magic Bottle (juvenile).   London, Faber, 1946.

Editor (as A. A. Gordon Clark), with Alan Garfitt, *Roscoe's Criminal Evidence*, 16th
edition, by Henry Roscoe.   London, Stevens, 1952.
Editor (as A. A. Gordon Clark), *Leith Hill Musical Festival 1905–1955: A Record of Fifty
Years of Music-Making in Surrey.*   Epsom, Surrey, Pullingers, 1955.

*   *   *

The legal profession has attracted some highly talented writers of crime fiction. One of the
first and most noteworthy examples is Melville Davisson Post (his lawyer-protagonist is
Randolph Mason). Other prominent lawyer-authors with legal sleuths include Erle Stanley
Gardner (Perry Mason), and Harold Q. Masur (Scott Jordan). Several authors without legal
training such as H. C. Bailey and Anthony Gilbert created, respectively, shyster-lawyer
Joshua Clunk and Arthur Crook – a lawyer who is much more honest than his name would
indicate, and whose clients are never guilty anyway. There are also Dr. R. Austin Freeman's
Dr. Thorndyke who qualified as both doctor and lawyer, and specialized in forensic science,
and Francis M. Nevins, Jr., who graduated (as did his creation Loren Mensing) from practice
to theory and become professor of law.

And there is Cyril Hare, the pseudonym of Alfred Alexander Gordon Clark, who became
county court judge in Surrey in 1950. His series detective Francis Pettigrew, however, is an
aging and unsuccessful lawyer who is barely making a living. He originally showed great
promise and aptitude for the law, but a series of misfortunes prevented his career from
reaching fruition, and left him a bitter and unhappy person.

Neither Pettigrew nor his creator is well-known, especially in America, and Hare's
reputation as a mystery writer lapsed into obscurity for a decade after his death in 1958, but
recent critical revaluation has established him as a master with at least four major novels and
a notable collection of short stories to his credit. *Tenant for Death* introduced Inspector
Mallett, a Scotland Yard detective who is tall and stout, and not unlike Freeman Wills
Crofts's Inspector Joseph French. This novel and its successor, *Death Is No Sportsman*, are
good, solid detective stories, very typical of the work being turned out during the 1930's, but
neither of them drew to any great extent on Hare's legal expertise. *Suicide Excepted* is about
three amateurs who play detective in order to change a verdict of suicide to murder. It
showed an advance over previous work, was lighter in tone, more entertaining, had more
detailed characterizations, and an unexpected ending.

Hare's own favorite novel, *Tragedy at Law*, is completely unorthodox, brilliantly
characterized, and a masterpiece. It is a lovingly detailed story of a judge on a second-rate
circuit who falls on the wrong side of the law when, while he is far from sober, his car hits a
pedestrian. Very near the end of the novel, a murder problem arises, and Pettigrew (in his
debut) matches wits with Inspector Mallett and bests him.

Tragedy at Law, which was based on Hare's tour as a judge's marshall, received rave
reviews. Henry Cecil, a jurist whose legal farces fall within the mystery genre, later stated,
"This book is acknowledged by many lawyers to be the classic detective story with a legal
background. It has stood the test of time. ... [It was] written with a master's hand and wit of a
very high order, and I have no reason to doubt the correctness of the opinion ... that in
detective fiction it is a work of the highest class." *Tragedy at Law* and Hare's three
subsequent major novels placed him at the top of his literary profession.

Hare's service with the Ministry of Economic Warfare during World War II provided the
inspiration for *With a Bare Bodkin*, which detailed a murder, committed with a spiked paper
holder, in a government office. The collaboration between Mallett and Pettigrew is more
conventional than in *Tragedy at Law*; it bears comparison to Nicholas Blake's *Minute for
Murder* (1947). Even better was *When the Wind Blows* which begins with the death of
England's foremost violinist before he can perform with a local music society. This solo

investigation by Pettigrew was highly praised by Anthony Boucher, and Barzun and Taylor consider it to be Hare's masterpiece. Hare's great interest in music lent authenticity to this novel's vivid background.

Hare's last major work, *An English Murder*, involves a typical English Christmas house party in a castle that becomes snowbound. Czech refugee Dr. Bottwink does the honors here in solving three murders. Much more entertaining than the earlier books, this is a completely unexpected and absolutely delightful work. *An English Murder* is my favorite Hare novel, a model of the British fair-play school, and a "must" item for anyone who likes Agatha Christie. I have encountered very few mysteries that are as sheerly likable as *An English Murder*. Its only flaw is the absence of Frank Pettigrew. Hare's subsequent work declined, but found Pettigrew happily married to a girl half his age. The last novel, *He Should Have Died Hereafter*, is short and fragmentary.

Hare's great friend Michael Gilbert edited the posthumous *Best Detective Stories of Cyril Hare* – an excellent collection of 30 crime stories. Gilbert's introduction to Hare's life and work is illuminating, and serves as an excellent memorial tribute by a fellow lawyer and mystery writer.

—Charles Shibuk

HARLING, Robert. British. Born in 1910. Editor, *Image: A Quarterly of the Visual Arts*, London, in the 1950's; former design consultant, *Times Literary Supplement* and *Sunday Times*, both London. Since 1957, Editor, *House and Garden* magazine, London. Address: c/o House and Garden, Vogue House, Hanover Square, London W1R 0AD, England.

CRIME PUBLICATIONS

Novels

The Paper Palace. London, Chatto and Windus, and New York, Harper, 1951.
The Dark Saviour. London, Chatto and Windus, 1952; New York, Harper, 1953.
The Enormous Shadow. London, Chatto and Windus, 1955; New York, Harper, 1956.
The Endless Colonnade. London, Chatto and Windus, 1958; New York, Putnam, 1959.
The Hollow Sunday. London, Chatto and Windus, 1967.
The Athenian Widow. London, Chatto and Windus, 1974.

OTHER PUBLICATIONS

Novel

The Summer Portrait. London, Chatto and Windus, 1979.

Other

The London Miscellany: A Nineteenth-Century Scrapbook. London, Heinemann, 1937; New York, Oxford University Press, 1938.
Home: A Victorian Vignette. London, Constable, 1938; New York, Appleton Century, 1939.

Amateur Sailor (as Nicholas Drew).   London, Constable, 1944.

Notes on the Wood-Engravings of Eric Ravilious.   London, Faber, 1946.

The Steep Atlantick Stream (wartime autobiography).   London, Chatto and Windus, 1946.

Edward Bawden.   London, Art and Technics, 1950.

The Letter Forms and Type Designs of Eric Gill.   Westerham, Kent, Swensson, 1976.

Editor, *House and Garden's Interiors and Colour.*   London, Condé Nast, 1959.

Editor, with others, *Small Houses.*   London, Condé Nast, 1961.

Editor, *House and Garden Book of Interiors.*   London and New York, Condé Nast, 1962.

Editor, *House and Garden Book of Cottages.*   London, Condé Nast, 1963; New York, Condé Nast, 1964.

Editor, *The Modern Interior.*   London, Condé Nast, 1964; New York, St. Martin's Press, 1965.

Editor, *House and Garden Garden Book.*   London, Condé Nast, 1965; New York, St. Martin's Press, 1966.

Editor, *House and Garden First Cook Book.*   London, Condé Nast, 1965.

Editor, *House and Garden Book of Modern Houses and Conversions.*   London, Condé Nast, 1966.

Editor, *House and Garden Guide to Interior Decoration.*   London, Condé Nast, and New York, St. Martin's Press, 1967.

Editor, *House and Garden Book of Holiday and Weekend Houses.*   London, Condé Nast, and New York, St. Martin's Press, 1968.

Editor, *Historical Houses: Conversations in Stately Homes.*   London, Condé Nast-Collins, 1969; as *The Great Houses and Finest Rooms in England*, New York, Viking Press, 1969.

Editor, *House and Garden Modern Furniture and Decoration.*   London, Condé Nast-Collins, 1971; as *Modern Furniture and Decoration*, New York, Viking Press, 1971.

Editor, *House and Garden Dictionary of Design and Decoration.*   London, Condé Nast-Collins, 1973; as *Studio Dictionary of Design and Decoration*, New York, Viking Press, 1973.

*   *   *

Robert Harling has used his long experience in journalism and advertising to produce six novels memorable for their accurate, lively details about newsmaking, their interest in the moral ambiguities of reporting, and their focus on grudging admiration between men whose different ideologies compel them to conflict. Harling humanizes his villains by their dreams, weaknesses, and unexpected strengths, but suggests that surface changes never touch the unchanging core. His first-person narrator is usually an established, wordly-wise newspaperman, often divorced, susceptible to feminine allure but obsessed by the lone pursuit of "a story." Always his editor's placid façade hides a tough, cynical inner core, a sharp nose for a story, a dual commitment to making money from news and to seeking truth and justice. Harling explores the reporter/editor relationship, the differences between the finished article and the writer's total views, the potentially destructive power of rhetorically manipulated news.

The Hollow Sunday traces a cautious investigation of scandal involving an M.P.'s wife. *The Athenian Widow* portrays the painful, vacillating process a newspaper goes through to decide whether to publish a controversial exposé. *The Dark Saviour* raises the question of moral responsibility, as a journalist discovers his paper's Caribbean man-on-the-spot providing communist support for a black take-over and, despite his sympathy for the "dark saviour," prints a misleading picture that results in death and violence and the end of a potential revolution. In *The Enormous Shadow* a journalist discovers a conservative British M.P.'s strong communist attachments, and, despite his understanding of the man's idealistic commitment, precipitates an exciting midnight chase down the Thames. In the heavily ironic *The Endless Colonnade*, a British psychiatrist on holiday in Italy (detailed sightseeing) fails to take seriously a traitorous young physicist's misplaced idealism, and by procrastinating causes the death of his closest friend. *The Paper Palace*, Harling's first book and perhaps his most ingenious, dramatizes the slow, tedious investigative techniques of a journalist who seeks patterns in obscure details about what a dead man did and why, until they add up to a horrifying story of a wealthy English communist's atrocities and the ironic twist of blackmail producing blackmail.

—Virginia Macdonald

HARRINGTON, Joseph (James). American. Born in Newark, New Jersey, in 1903. Journalist: copyboy at age 14, New York *American*, then reporter; later a free-lance writer.

CRIME PUBLICATIONS

Novels (series character: Lieutenant Francis X. Kerrigan in all books)

The Last Known Address. Philadelphia, Lippincott, 1965; London, Hale, 1966.
Blind Spot. Philadelphia, Lippincott, 1966; London, Hale, 1967.
The Last Doorbell. Philadelphia, Lippincott, 1969; London, Hale, 1970.

Uncollected Short Stories

"Groper in the Dark," in *Saturday Evening Post Stories 1938*, edited by W. W. Stout. New York, Random House, 1939.
"Subway Fire," in *Saturday Evening Post Stories 1939*, edited by W. W. Stout. New York, Random House, 1940.
"Painted Faces," in *Ellery Queen's Mystery Magazine* (New York), February 1949.

OTHER PUBLICATIONS

Novels

Hawaiian Lover. New York, Macaulay, 1932.
Scandal Rag. New York, Smith and Durrell, 1942.

Manuscript Collection: Mugar Memorial Library, Boston University.

*   *   *

Joseph Harrington's splendid procedural novels offer realistic but sympathetic portraits of police officers coping with heavy workloads and an often unsympathetic public. The emphasis is on the frustrating, exacting detail work of investigation, and the protagonist, Frank Kerrigan, so masters that detail that he unassumingly solves crimes which have defeated other capable investigators.

Kerrigan is a slow, deliberate, pragmatic man in his early thirties, frozen in rank because of an unfair charge of roughness toward a prisoner. He serves as mentor for quick, bright, college-educated Jane Boardman, who is rising rapidly in the New York Police Department by a combination of her ability and Frank's tutelage. The growing respect and affection between the two is beautifully drawn, and they are effective models for the "old" and the "new" kinds of police officers. *The Last Known Address* and *The Last Doorbell* show them as a team, but perhaps the strongest novel is *Blind Spot* in which Kerrigan works alone. Political pressure results in his examining a closed case, and the detective's willingness to go to any length to uncover even the smallest fact has amazing results.

Harrington's skill at characterization is considerable; for instance, as Kerrigan reads pages of testimony, the witnesses come alive through their manners of speech, and the portrayal of Eva Midnight is remarkably adroit and persuasive.

Harrington's attention to characterization, setting, and procedure results in smoothly written, compelling, enjoyable novels that rank among the finest in the genre.

—Jane S. Bakerman

HARRINGTON, Joyce. American. Born in Jersey City, New Jersey, in the 1930's. Studied at Pasadena Playhouse, California. Married Phillip A. Harrington in 1960; two sons. Has worked for United States Army Quartermaster Corps; in factories, bank, and insurance company in California; department story in Cincinnati; American Institute of Graphic Arts, American Society of Magazine Photographers; presently employed at Foote Cone and Belding, advertising agency, New York. Recipient: Mystery Writers of America Edgar Allan Poe Award, for short story, 1973. Agent: Scott Meredith Literary Agency Inc., 845 Third Avenue, New York, New York 10022. Address: 91 Rugby Road, Brooklyn, New York 11226 U.S.A.

CRIME PUBLICATIONS

Uncollected Short Stories

"Things Change," in *Ellery Queen's Mystery Magazine* (New York), July 1974.
"Vienna Sausage," in *Alfred Hitchcock's Mystery Magazine* (North Palm Beach, Florida), October 1974.
"The Purple Shroud," in *Ellery Queen's Crookbook.* New York, Random House, and London, Gollancz, 1974.
"The Tomato Man's Daughter," in *Ellery Queen's Mystery Magazine* (New York), May 1975.
"The Green Patch," in *Ellery Queen's Mystery Magazine* (New York), June 1975.
"It Never Happened," in *Ellery Queen's Mystery Magazine* (New York), September 1975.
"The Garage Apartment," in *Alfred Hitchcock's Mystery Magazine* (North Palm Beach, Florida), September 1975.
"Death of a Princess," in *Ellery Queen's Mystery Magazine* (New York), November 1975.
"What My Left Hand Does," in *Alfred Hitchcock's Mystery Magazine* (North Palm Beach, Florida), December 1975.
"The Plastic Jungle," in *Every Crime in the Book*, edited by Robert L. Fish. New York, Putnam, 1975.

"The Pretty Lady Passes By," in *Ellery Queen's Mystery Magazine* (New York), January 1976.

"The Season Ticket Holder," in *Ellery Queen's Mystery Magazine* (New York), March 1976.

"Gemini and the Missing Mother," in *Alfred Hitchcock's Mystery Magazine* (New York), June 1976.

"The Couple Next Door," in *Ellery Queen's Mystery Magazine* (New York), August 1976.

"My Neighbor, Ay" and "The Cabin in the Hollow," in *Ellery Queen's Crime Wave.* New York, Putnam, and London, Gollancz, 1976.

"The Two Sisters," in *Ellery Queen's Mystery Magazine* (New York), December 1976.

"Don't Wait for Me," in *Alfred Hitchcock's Mystery Magazine* (New York), December 1976.

"Grass," in *Ellery Queen's Mystery Magazine* (New York), March 1977.

"August Is a Good Time for Killing," in *Alfred Hitchcock's Mystery Magazine* (New York), April 1977.

"Night Crawlers," in *Ellery Queen's Searches and Seizures.* New York, Davis, 1977.

"The Thirteenth Victim," in *Antaeus* (New York), Spring-Summer 1977.

"When Push Comes to Shove," in *Alfred Hitchcock's Mystery Magazine* (New York), November 1977.

"Looking for Milliken Street," in *Alfred Hitchcock's Anthology, Spring-Summer 1978.* New York, Davis, 1978.

"Blue Monday," in *Ellery Queen's A Multitude of Sins.* New York, Davis, 1978.

"The Old Gray Cat," in *Best Detective Stories of the Year 1978*, edited by Edward D. Hoch. New York, Dutton, 1978.

"Happy Birthday Darling," in *Ellery Queen's Mystery Magazine* (New York), February 1979.

"A Place of Her Own," in *Ellery Queen's Mystery Magazine* (New York), September 1979.

*   *   *

Though her output to date consists of about two dozen short stories and no published novels, Joyce Harrington has already established herself as one of the 1970's brightest discoveries in the crime-suspense field.

Her first story, the Edgar-winning "The Purple Shroud," is a quiet tale of a summer art instructor and the wife he has betrayed; it gradually builds into a murder story of understated terror. Harrington's second story, "The Plastic Jungle," is in some ways even better – a macabre story of a girl and her mother living in today's plastic society. Two of her 1974 stories, "My Neighbor, Ay" and "The Cabin in the Hollow," offered settings as different as Brooklyn and rural West Virginia. "Night Crawlers" presented a memorable portrait of a woman worm-farmer and a hidden treasure. "Blue Monday" offered a gripping study of a murderer and his victim.

Three Harrington stories published during 1977 best illustrate her many moods. "Grass" is a domestic drama of conflict between a husband and wife. "The Old Gray Cat" is a tantalizing mood piece full of deft surprises for the unwary reader. And "The Thirteenth Victim" is a horror story about a man who constructs art works around the bodies of dead people. In each of them, as in most of her writings, Joyce Harrington is examining the human condition. Her viewpoint is sometimes natural, sometimes bizarre – but always fascinating.

—Edward D. Hoch

HARRIS, Herbert. British. Born in London, 25 August 1911. Educated at Clapham College, London. Married Bonney Genn in 1944. Has published more than 3000 short stories in newspapers and magazines under his own name and a number of psuedonyms including Michael Moore, Frank Bury, Peter Friday, and Jerry Regan. Founding Editor, *Red Herrings*, bulletin of the Crime Writers Association, London, 1956–65, and Chairman of the Association, 1969–70. Recipient: Crime Writers Association award, 1965. Address: 26 Castle Court, Ventnor, Isle of Wight PO38 1UE, England.

CRIME PUBLICATIONS

Novels

> *Who Kill to Live.* London, Jenkins, 1962.
> *Painted in Blood.* New York, King Features, 1972.
> *Serpents in Paradise.* London, W. H. Allen, 1975.
> *The Angry Battalion.* London, W. H. Allen, 1976.

Uncollected Short Stories (selection)

"The Big Teddy Bears," in *Choice of Weapons*, edited by Michael Gilbert. London, Hodder and Stoughton, 1958.
"Detective's Wife," in *The First Mystery Bedside Book*, edited by John Creasey. London, Hodder and Stoughton, 1960.
"Budding Sleuth," in *The Second Mystery Bedside Book*, edited by John Creasey. London, Hodder and Stoughton, 1961.
"Death of a Tramp," in *The Third Mystery Bedside Book*, edited by John Creasey. London, Hodder and Stoughton, 1962.
"Link with the Locals," in *The Fifth Mystery Bedside Book*, edited by John Creasey. London, Hodder and Stoughton, 1964.
"Hate-in-the-Mist," in *Crime Writers' Choice*, edited by Roy Vickers. London, Hodder and Stoughton, 1964.
"Danny's Real Talent," in *The Sixth Mystery Bedside Book*, edited by John Creasey. London, Hodder and Stoughton, 1965.
"A Long Rest for Rosie," in *John Creasey's Mystery Bedside Book*, edited by Herbert Harris. London, Hodder and Stoughton, 1966.
"A Nice Cup of Tea," in *John Creasey's Mystery Bedside Book*, edited by Herbert Harris. London, Hodder and Stoughton, 1967.
"Saviour of San Fernando," in *John Creasey's Mystery Bedside Book*, edited by Herbert Harris. London, Hodder and Stoughton, 1968.
"The Dumb Friend," in *Best Underworld Stories*, edited by Douglas Rutherford. London, Faber, 1969.
"The Escort," in *More Tales of Unease*, edited by John Burke. London, Pan, 1969.
"The Chee Min Vase," in *John Creasey's Mystery Bedside Book 1970*, edited by Herbert Harris. London, Hodder and Stoughton, 1969.
"Revenge Is Sweet," in *John Creasey's Mystery Bedside Book 1971*, edited by Herbert Harris. London, Hodder and Stoughton, 1970.
"The Wall Game," in *John Creasey's Mystery Bedside Book 1972*, edited by Herbert Harris. London, Hodder and Stoughton, 1971.
"Low Marks for Murder," in *John Creasey's Mystery Bedside Book 1973*, edited by Herbert Harris. London, Hodder and Stoughton, 1972.
"The Athlete and the Necktie," in *John Creasey's Mystery Bedside Book 1974*, edited by Herbert Harris. London, Hodder and Stoughton, 1973.
"Dogs of Peace," in *John Creasey's Mystery Bedside Book 1975*, edited by Herbert Harris. London, Hodder and Stoughton, 1974.

"Reprieve," in *John Creasey's Mystery Bedside Book 1976*, edited by Herbert Harris. London, Hodder and Stoughton, 1975.

"Mind over Blackmail," in *John Creasey's Crime Collection 1977*, edited by Herbert Harris. London, Gollancz, 1977.

"The Big Fix," in *John Creasey's Crime Collection 1978*, edited by Herbert Harris. London, Gollancz, 1978.

"The Way of Release," in *John Creasey's Crime Collection 1979*, edited by Herbert Harris. London, Gollancz, 1979.

OTHER PUBLICATIONS

Play

Radio Play: *Detective's Wife*, from his own story, 1961.

Other

Editor, *John Creasey's Mystery Bedside Book*. London, Hodder and Stoughton, 11 vols., 1966–76.

Editor, *John Creasey's Crime Collection*. London, Gollancz, 3 vols., 1977–79.

Editor, *Great Short Stories of Scotland Yard*. London, Reader's Digest, 1978; as *Great Cases of Scotland Yard*, New York, Norton, 1978.

Herbert Harris comments:

My speciality has been the short-short story of 1000–2000 words aimed principally at magazines and newspapers, and nearly always containing a surprise sting in the tail. Through writing such a very large number of short-shorts, with their taut economy of words, I have always found writing full-length novels difficult and have thus produced only a few, three of them specially commissioned.

*   *   *

Herbert Harris is very unusual as a crime writer of the post-1945 period in that his work has been exclusively in the short story. Even in the short story field he has kept his best efforts for the short-short. Perhaps for this reason there is not even a collection of his work: a volume consisting entirely of the sort of story which lives by making a quick, snappy impression would be like a meal of plate after plate of cocktail snacks. To a fair extent, however, it may be said that to read one Harris story is to have read them all, though naturally when an author has written more stories – it is believed – than anyone else living there are bound to be so many exceptions to any one rule that they will perhaps form a considerable body of writing on their own.

That being said, let us look at what would seem to be the typical Harris story. First, it is a crime story. Crime seems particularly to suit a writer who depends for his effects on actions, on things being done and being seen (sometimes only in the outcome) to have been done. So not for Harris the sort of story that depends on some subtle change in relations between people, something that might be expressed by a handshake or the raising of an eyebrow or even the omission of a handshake, an eyebrow not raised. With Harris it is much more likely that someone will have been murdered, though by no means all his stories depend on murder.

Second, the Harris story is, as we have said, short. Characters do not change in them, except from alive to dead, from free to arrested. So within the very short length that particularly suits his talent he cannot put over as fiction all the facts necessary to a particular tale. He cannot afford to devote perhaps two or three pages to describing some incident that simply reflects character. He has brutally to tell you that such-and-such a person is as he is. "The English detective-sergeant from the Hong Kong police was an old-stager with sour cynicism written all over his face." That and no more.

The quotation – it is the first sentence of a story called "The Chee Min Vase" – tells us one other thing about the Harris story: it can be set anywhere in the world, and probably in some exotic place. Harris is adept at seizing on some flavoursome setting and using it to give an "extra" to his tale. And he is skilful, given any particular setting, in flicking in just one or two details that give to the reader the impression that the author is writing from that particular location itself. "In gutter Cantonese," the narrator says casually in "The Chee Min Vase" and, at the other extreme of the world almost, in a second-rank British boarding school a master goes up to his room to fetch (ostensibly) a volume of Racine for his class.

Finally, and rather surprisingly, the Harris story is not markedly ingenious, though it may, as in his Sicily-set Mafia tale "Reprieve," have a neat final reversal. But he does not, as does a short-story writer like Edmund Crispin, go in for the dazzling piece of legerdemain. Instead he gives you a quick series of hard-thought clickings into place, of turns as opposed to twists. And the result provides the casual reader with just what he is looking for.

—H. R. F. Keating

HARRIS, Rosemary (Jeanne). British. Born in London, 20 February 1923. Educated at Thorneloe School, Weymouth: St. Martin's, Central, and Chelsea schools of art, London; Department of Technology, Courtauld Institute, London. Served in the Red Cross Nursing Auxiliary, Westminster Division, London, 1941–45. Picture Restorer, 1949; Reader, Metro-Goldwyn-Mayer, 1951–52; Children's Book Reviewer, *The Times*, London, 1970–73. Recipient: Library Association Carnegie Medal, 1969; Arts Council grant 1971. Agent: Michael Horniman, A. P. Watt and Son, 26/28 Bedford Row, London WC1R 4HL. Address: 33 Cheyne Court, Flood Street, London SW3 5TR, England.

CRIME PUBLICATIONS

Novels

> *All My Enemies.* London, Faber, 1967; New York, Simon and Schuster, 1973.
> *The Nice Girl's Story.* London, Faber, 1968; as *Nor Evil Dreams*, New York, Simon and Schuster, 1974.
> *A Wicked Pack of Cards.* London, Faber, 1969; New York, Walker, 1970.
> *The Double Snare.* London, Faber, 1974; New York, Simon and Schuster, 1975.
> *Three Candles for the Dark.* London, Faber, 1976.

OTHER PUBLICATIONS

Novels

> *The Summer-House.* London, Hamish Hamilton, 1956.
> *Voyage to Cythera.* London, Bodley Head, 1958.
> *Venus with Sparrows.* London, Faber, 1961.

Play

Television Play: *Peronik*, 1976.

Other (juvenile)

The Moon in the Cloud.   London, Faber, 1968; New York, Macmillan, 1969.
The Shadow on the Sun.   London, Faber, and New York, Macmillan, 1970.
The Seal-Singing.   London, Faber, and New York, Macmillan, 1971.
The Child in the Bamboo Grove.   London, Faber, 1971; New York, S. G. Phillips, 1972.
The Bright and Morning Star.   London, Faber, and New York, Macmillan, 1972.
The King's White Elephant.   London, Faber, 1973.
The Lotus and the Grail: Legends from East to West.   London, Faber, 1974; abridged
    edition, as *Sea Magic and Other Stories of Enchantment*, New York, Macmillan, 1974.
The Flying Ship.   London, Faber, 1975.
The Little Dog of Fo.   London, Faber, 1976.
I Want to Be a Fish.   London, Penguin, 1977.
A Quest for Orion.   London, Faber, 1978.
Green Finger House.   Twickenham, Middlesex, Eel Pie Books, 1979.
Beauty and the Beast.   London, Faber, 1979.

Rosemary Harris comments:

Probably I'm happiest and most at ease in work that has a strong visual element – like
myth or fantasy – a legacy of my training as a painter. I found this aspect of work particularly
fascinating when I was writing the television play and trying to create action that would
translate effectively into visual images.

*   *   *

Rosemary Harris, a prize-winning author of children's books, has also turned her hand to
suspense fiction. Her romantic thrillers probably appeal primarily to a feminine audience.
While Miss Harris writes smoothly and invents some terrifying situations for her characters,
her plots sometimes falter. *All My Enemies*, which begins well – the once rich and happy
heroine, surrounded by enemies set on by her evil twin sister, loses her husband and then,
haunted by her memory of the *Alexandria Quartet*, follows her kidnapped daughter to Egypt
– but, after a violent climax, ends with a lengthy explanation which might have been avoided
by more careful plotting.

The author's penchant for first-person narrative, which can lend a certain immediacy to
accounts of anxiety-ridden scenes, is at times unfortunate. In *The Nice Girl's Story* a gushing
girlish style at the beginning (the narrator fatuously tells us: "I combed out my long blond
hair") turns grim and matter-of-fact to indicate her growing awareness. Although this
stylistic transformation parallels the heroine's changing attitude, presumably it is the older,
wiser one telling the whole story. This tale deals with the problem of the neo-Nazis which
still infects society on both sides of the Atlantic.

A Wicked Pack of Cards is a traditional murder mystery, though it contains no detection.
One of the victims is a fortune-teller who uses tarot cards and is considered by everybody to
be a thorough nuisance. Her (unlamented) death may have been witnessed by a quite
charming, precocious child whose safety becomes the central issue. The murderer is revealed
when the heroine, previously unable to choose between two suitors, is nearly done in by one
of them, who explains his earlier crimes before falling into the sea. An attempt to exploit the
atmosphere of Tintagel, the Tristan myth, and the Wagnerian version of it, is unconvincing.
Of the ruined castle one character says: "Awe-inspiring, isn't it?... No legend does it justice
on a day like this. It's pure Wagner. If you lay down on that stone, Jane, and flames were lit
around you, it would come straight out of *Siegfried*." Instead of the subtle and artistic use of

740

literary motifs and cultural history found, for example, in the novels of Michael Delving, or the fine settings of Janet Caird, we have here the diligent notes of an eager tourist. Nevertheless, the book offers pleasant reading. Suspense is maintained and the characters are well-depicted, unusual, and sympathetic.

The literary allusions in *The Double Snare* – Shakespearean this time – are much more effectively used than those mentioned above. The heroine, half-Italian and bilingual, suffers from amnesia, and finds herself the pawn in first one scheme and then another. The action is in Italy with some flashbacks to England as she recalls fragments of the past. Taken from a hospital and kept secluded in a villa where she is called Giulia and is importuned to marry the son of the house, she receives clandestine visits from a handsome neighbor who climbs to the balcony of her bedroom and declares she is not Giulia. Her name, she thinks, is Silvia (the opportunity to ask "Who is Silvia, what is she?" is not lost), and she absconds to join a company of travelling players performing Shakespeare in Italy. Art thefts, forgeries, and violence are all part of the past which pursues her.

In *Three Candles for the Dark*, a troubled young woman undergoing Jungian analysis is approached by another patient, a repulsive type, who entices her to take a job with his family in an isolated house in New England. There she finds a delightful child in the midst of a frightful ménage, and the stage is set for ghastly goings-on.

Love interest, imaginatively drawn personages, and some contemporary social problems mixed in with the "gothic" elements characterize the thrillers of Rosemary Harris. She has a talent for portraying children which is uncommon in suspense fiction. Each new tale improves on the earlier ones, and though they do not lend themselves to rereading as do some of the classics of the genre, they are entertaining and decidedly above average.

—Mary Helen Becker

HARRISON, Michael. Also writes as Quentin Downes. Irish. Born in Milton, Kent, England, 25 April 1907. Educated at King's College, and the School of Oriental and African Studies, University of London. Married Maryvonne Aubertin in 1950 (died). Editor (founding editor, *The British Ink Maker* and *Valvology*), market research executive, and industrial and technical consultant; creative director of advertising agency, now retired. Address: 5A Palmeira Court, Palmeira Square, Hove, Sussex BN3 2JP, England.

Crime Publications

Novels as Quentin Downes (series character: Detective Inspector Abraham Kozminski in all books by Downes)

The Darkened Room (as Michael Harrison).   London, Home and Van Thal, 1952.
No Smoke, No Fire.   London, Wingate, 1952; New York, Roy, 1956.
Heads I Win.   London, Wingate, 1953; New York, Roy, 1955.
They Hadn't a Clue.   London, Arco, 1954.

Short Stories

The Exploits of Chevalier Dupin.   Sauk City, Wisconsin, Mycroft and Moran, 1968; expanded version, as *Murder in the Rue Royale*, London, Stacey, 1972.

Uncollected Short Stories

"Wit's End," in *Best Detective Stories of the Year 1971*, edited by Allen J. Hubin.   New
    York, Dutton, 1971.
"The Jewel of Childeric," in *Ellery Queen's Faces of Mystery*.   New York, Davis, 1977.

OTHER PUBLICATIONS

Novels

Weep for Lycidas.   London, Barker, 1934.
Spring in Tartarus: An Arabesque.   London, Barker, 1935.
All the Trees Were Green.   London, Barker, 1936.
What Are We Waiting For?   London, Rich and Cowan, 1939.
Vernal Equinox.   London, Collins, 1939.
Battered Caravanserai.   London, Rich and Cowan, 1942.
Reported Safe Arrival: The Journal of a Voyage to Port X.   London, Rich and Cowan,
    1943.
So Linked Together.   London, Macdonald, 1944.
Higher Things.   London, Macdonald, 1945.
The House in Fishergate.   London, Macdonald, 1946.
Treadmill.   London, Langdon Press, 1947.
Sinecure.   London, Laurie, 1948.
There's Glory for You!   London, Laurie, 1949.
Things Less Noble: A Modern Love Story.   London, Laurie, 1950.
Long Vacation.   London, Laurie, 1951.
The Brain.   London, Cassell, 1953.
The Dividing Stone.   London, Cassell, 1954.
A Hansom to St. James's.   London, Cassell, 1954.

Short Stories

Transit of Venus.   London, Fortune Press, 1936.

Other

Dawn Express: There and Back.   London, Collins, 1938.
Gambler's Glory: The Story of John Law of Lauriston.   London, Rich and Cowan,
    1940.
Count Cagliostro, Nature's Unfortunate Child.   London, Rich and Cowan, 1942.
They Would Be King.   London, Somers, 1947.
Post Office, Mauritius 1847: The Tale of Two Stamps.   London, Stamp Collecting, 1947.
The Story of Christmas: Its Growth and Development from Earliest Times.   London,
    Odhams Press, 1951.
*Airborne at Kitty Hawk: The Story of the First Heavier-than-Air Flight Made by the
    Wright Brothers*.   London, Cassell, 1953.
*Charles Dickens: A Sentimental Journey in Search of an Unvarnished
    Portrait*.   London, Cassell, 1953; New York, Haskell House, 1976.
A New Approach to Stamp Collecting, with Douglas Armstrong.   London, Batsford,
    1953; New York, Hanover House, 1954.
Beer Cookery: 101 Traditional Recipes.   London, Spearman Calder, 1954.
Peter Cheyney, Prince of Hokum: A Biography.   London, Spearman, 1954.
In the Footsteps of Sherlock Holmes.   London, Cassell, 1958; New York, Fell, 1960;
    revised edition, Newton Abbot, Devon, David and Charles, 1971; New York, Drake,
    1972.

The History of the Hat. London, Jenkins, 1960.

London Beneath the Pavement. London, Davies, 1961; revised edition, 1971.

Rosa (biography of Rosa Lewis). London, Davies, 1962.

Painful Details: Twelve Victorian Scandals. London, Parrish, 1962.

London by Gaslight 1861–1911. London, Davies, 1963.

London Growing: The Development of a Metropolis. London, Hutchinson, 1965.

Mulberry: The Return in Triumph. London, W. H. Allen, 1965.

Lord of London: A Biography of the Second Duke of Westminster. London, W. H. Allen, 1966.

Technical and Industrial Publicity. London, Business Publications, 1968.

"A Study in Surmise," in *Ellery Queen's Mystery Magazine* (New York), February 1971.

The London That Was Rome: The Imperial City Recreated by the New Archaeology. London, Allen and Unwin, 1971.

Fanfare of Strumpets. London, W. H. Allen, 1971.

Clarence: The Life of H.R.H. the Duke of Clarence and Avondale 1864–1892. London, W. H. Allen, 1972; as *Clarence: Was He Jack the Ripper?*, New York, Drake, 1974.

The London of Sherlock Holmes. Newton Abbot, Devon, David and Charles, and New York, Drake, 1972.

The Roots of Witchcraft. London, Muller, 1973; Secaucus, New Jersey, Citadel Press, 1974.

The World of Sherlock Holmes. London, Muller, 1973; New York, Dutton, 1975.

Theatrical Mr. Holmes: The World's Greatest Consulting Detective, Considered Against the Background of the Contemporary Theatre. London, Covent Garden Press, 1974.

Fire from Heaven; or, How Safe Are You from Burning? (on spontaneous combustion). London, Sidgwick and Jackson, 1976; revised edition, London, Pan, 1977; New York, Methuen, 1978.

I, Sherlock Holmes. New York, Dutton, 1977.

Editor, *Under Thirty* (anthology of short stories). London, Rich and Cowan, 1939.

Editor, *Beyond Baker Street: A Sherlockian Anthology.* Indianapolis, Bobbs Merrill, 1976.

Michael Harrison comments:

The preference for – indeed, perhaps, the real need for – violence in thriller fiction, has greatly influenced the novel of pure detection, and has almost obscured the essential difference which ought to exist between the novel of detection (what Poe called "of ratiocination") and the novel in which violence is more important than the solving of those problems arising from that violence. That there is every excuse for this confusion between the two forms is understandable; indeed, it seems to have been inevitable, since the tendency to confuse exists at the very beginning of the detective story, as in the four stories of the writer, Poe, who invented the detective story, violence – and very violent violence it is – occurs to originate the problem that the "ratiocinator" has to solve. (In three cases it is Dupin; in the fourth, the solver is unnamed.)

But no matter how much blood-and-thunder is now regarded as an essential ingredient of even the "novel of pure detection," the difference between the thriller and the novel of detection ought rigidly to be maintained – as I have tried to maintain it. There isn't much violence in my novels or stories of detection – there isn't even much blood. But each begins with the clear statement of a problem that intentional crime or unintentional misadventure has left to be solved, and, to the best of my ability, I explain to the reader how the solver arrived at his solution. Such "surprises" as I use are reserved for the criminal, rather than for the detective, though in my now many pastiches of Poe's Dupin tales, I am forced to retain for Dupin those characteristics that his brilliant and immortal creator gave him when inventing the detective story.

*   *   *

Michael Harrison's contributions to mystery and crime writing fall into several areas. His nonfiction books about Holmes and Watson, starting with *In the Footsteps of Sherlock Holmes*, recreate the London of Victorian times. Another work of nonfiction, *Clarence*, offers speculation on the identity of Jack the Ripper. Harrison has also published ghost stories and, under the pseudonym of Quentin Downes, three minor mystery novels.

But Harrison's major contribution has been his short stories, with a series of excellent pastiches of Edgar Allan Poe's detective C. Auguste Dupin. Mystery readers who have long bemoaned the fact that Poe wrote only three Dupin tales can take heart from the work of Michael Harrison, who created twelve new adventures, collected in *Murder in the Rue Royale* (*The Exploits of the Chevalier Dupin* contains only seven). Of the stories themselves at least six deserve special mention. "The Vanished Treasure" finds Dupin solving a 50-year-old mystery involving missing Spanish gold. The discovery of some old Roman ruins masks a crime in "The Man in the Blue Spectacles." "The Fires in the Rue St. Honoré" reveals an ingenious method of arson. A diplomat who vanishes in an empty street provides the mystery in "The Facts in the Case of the Missing Diplomat." Another type of seemingly impossible crime is presented in "The Assassination of Sir Ponsonby Brown." "The Clew of the Single Word" is a clever spy tale. Mention should also be made of a non-Dupin detective story, "Wit's End," a clever tale in the classic tradition.

—Edward D. Hoch

HART, Frances (Newbold) Noyes. American. Born in Silver Springs, Maryland, 10 August 1890. Educated in private schools, and in Italy; the Sorbonne and Collège de France, Paris; Columbia University, New York. Married Edward Henry Hart in 1921; two daughters. Translator for Naval Intelligence, 1917–18; YMCA canteen worker in France, 1918–19. *Died 25 October 1943.*

CRIME PUBLICATIONS

Novels

    The Bellamy Trial. New York, Doubleday, and London, Heinemann, 1927.
    Hide in the Dark. New York, Doubleday, and London, Heinemann, 1929.
    The Crooked Lane. New York, Doubleday, and London, Heinemann, 1934.

Short Stories

    Contact and Other Stories. New York, Doubleday, 1923.

OTHER PUBLICATIONS

Novel

Mark.   New York, Clode, 1913.

Play

The Bellamy Trial, with Frank E. Carstarphen, adaptation of the novel by Hart
(produced New York, 1931).   New York, French, 1932.

Other

My A.E.F.: A Hail and Farewell.   New York, Stokes, 1920.
Pigs in Clover (travel).   New York, Doubleday, 1931; as *Holiday*, London, Heinemann,
1931.

*   *   *

Frances Noyes Hart's mother was a Newbold, as was Edith Wharton's, and Hart writes of
the same classes, by now more in decline. Her *Hide in the Dark* presents a group of bright
young things who meet at Hallowe'en for a game party which rapidly degenerates into an
accusing match as an old suicide is recalled, a number of bitter truths are exchanged, and a
further murder takes place. Rather more agreeable, though darker in its detailing of twisted
emotions and family insanity, is *The Crooked Lane*, told from the point of view of a young
Viennese police official who renews a childhood acquaintance in Washington, informally
investigates a murder, and finds himself at the end of a very dark alley indeed. Both these
novels create effectively an atmosphere of leisured, if certainly decadent, social life in and
around the Washington of 1930, within a class yet untouched by the Depression.

But Hart's fame is primarily attached to *The Bellamy Trial*. Here the locale is the
courtroom throughout, and the novel derives much of its immediacy and conviction from
being told through the consciousnesses of a young woman on her first reporting assignment
and a more cynical and experienced reporter, who fall in love over the eight days of the trial.
Based on the famous Hall-Mills case, *The Bellamy Trial* unfolds the totally absorbing story of
the misalliances and crossed lives of two couples from the gentry of upstate New York: one
wife has been murdered, and her husband and the other wife are the accused. During the trial
sensations occur – a key witness commits suicide; a dilatory witness, in compromising
circumstances, appears at the last moment; the solution is finally revealed only in a letter the
judge receives in his chambers. But these sensational elements in no way detract from the
verisimilitude of what is the best of all crime novels told within the format of a court
procedure.

—Barrie Hayne

HARVESTER, Simon.   Pseudonym for Henry St. John Clair Rumbold-Gibbs; also writes
as Henry Gibbs.   British.   Born in 1910.   Educated at Marlborough College, Wiltshire;
studied painting in London, Paris, and Venice.   Served in the Royal Corps of Signals, 1941.
Married three times, lastly to Mary Elizabeth Hutchings; one son from first marriage.

Worked as a journalist, publisher's reader, and farmer. Recipient: Anisfield-Wolf Award, 1950. *Died in April 1975.*

Crime Publications

Novels (series characters: Malcolm Kenton; Heron Murmur; Dorian Silk)

Let Them Prey. London, Rich and Cowan, 1942.
Epitaphs for Lemmings. London, Rich and Cowan, 1943; New York, Macmillan, 1944.
Maybe a Trumpet. London, Rich and Cowan, 1945.
A Lantern for Diogenes. London, Rich and Cowan, 1946.
Whatsoever Things Are True. London, Rich and Cowan, 1947.
The Sequins Lost Their Lustre. London, Rich and Cowan, 1948.
A Breastplate for Aaron. London, Rich and Cowan, 1949.
Good Men and True. London, Rich and Cowan, 1949.
Sheep May Safely Graze. London, Rich and Cowan, 1950.
Obols for Charon. London, Jarrolds, 1951.
The Vessel May Carry Explosives. London, Jarrolds, 1951.
Witch Hunt. London, Jarrolds, 1951.
Cat's Cradle. London, Jarrolds, 1952.
Traitor's Gate. London, Jarrolds, 1952.
Lucifer at Sunset. London, Jarrolds, 1953.
Spiders' Web. London, Jarrolds, 1953.
Arrival in Suspicion. London, Jarrolds, 1953.
Delay in Danger. London, Jarrolds, 1954.
The Bamboo Screen (Kenton). London, Jarrolds, 1955; New York, Walker, 1968.
Tiger in the North. London, Jarrolds, 1955; New York, Walker, 1963.
Dragon Road (Silk). London, Jarrolds, 1956; New York, Walker, 1969.
The Paradise Men (Kenton). London, Jarrolds, 1956.
The Copper Butterfly (Kenton). London, Jarrolds, 1957; New York, Walker, 1962.
The Golden Fear (Kenton). London, Jarrolds, 1957.
The Yesterday Walkers. London, Jarrolds, 1958.
An Hour Before Zero. London, Jarrolds, 1959.
Unsung Road (Silk). London, Jarrolds, 1960; New York, Walker, 1961.
The Chinese Hammer (Murmur). London, Jarrolds, 1960; New York, Walker, 1961.
The Moonstone Jungle. London, Jarrolds, 1961.
Silk Road (Silk). London, Jarrolds, 1962; New York, Walker, 1963.
Troika (Murmur). London, Jarrolds, 1962; as *The Flying Horse*, New York, Walker, 1964.
Red Road (Silk). London, Jarrolds, 1963; New York, Walker, 1964.
Flight in Darkness. London, Jarrolds, 1964; New York, Walker, 1965.
Assassins Road (Silk). London, Jarrolds, and New York, Walker, 1965.
Shadows in a Hidden Land. London, Jarrolds, and New York, Walker, 1966.
Treacherous Road (Silk). London, Jarrolds, 1966; New York, Walker, 1967.
Battle Road (Silk). London, Jarrolds, and New York, Walker, 1967.
Zion Road (Silk). London, Jarrolds, and New York, Walker, 1968.
Nameless Road (Silk). London, Jarrolds, 1969; New York, Walker, 1970.
Moscow Road (Silk). London, Jarrolds, 1970; New York, Walker, 1971.
Sahara Road (Silk). London, Jarrolds, and New York, Walker, 1972.
A Corner of the Playground. London, Jarrolds, 1973.
Forgotten Road (Silk). London, Hutchinson, and New York, Walker, 1974.
Siberian Road (Silk). London, Hutchinson, and New York, Walker, 1976.

Novels as Henry Gibbs

At a Farthing's Rate. London, Jarrolds, 1943.
Not to the Swift. London, Jarrolds, 1944.
From All Blindness. London, Jarrolds, 1944.
Blue Days and Fair. London, Jarrolds, 1946.
Know Then Thyself. London, Jarrolds, 1947.
Children's Overture: A Study of Juvenile Delinquency in London Slums. London, Jarrolds, 1948.
Ten-Thirty Sharp. London, Jarrolds, 1949.
Withered Garland. London, Jarrolds, 1950.
Taps, Colonel Roberts. London, Jarrolds, 1951.
Cream and Cider. London, Jarrolds, 1952.
The Six-Mile Face. London, Jarrolds, 1952.
Disputed Barricade. London, Jarrolds, 1952.
Cape of Shadows. London, Jarrolds, 1954.
The Splendour and the Dust. London, Jarrolds, 1955.
The Winds of Time. London, Jarrolds, 1956.
Thunder at Dawn. London, Jarrolds, 1957.
The Tumult and the Shouting. London, Jarrolds, 1958.
The Bamboo Prison. London, Jarrolds, 1961.
The Mortal Fire. London, Jarrolds, 1963.

OTHER PUBLICATIONS as Henry Gibbs

Novels

Pawns in Ice. London, Jarrolds, 1948.
Man about Town (as Simon Harvester), with Cyril Campion. London, Rich and Cowan, 1948.
The Crimson Gate. New York, Walker, 1963.

Other

Affectionately Yours, Fanny: Fanny Kemble and the Theatre. London, Jarrolds, 1947.
Theatre Tapestry. London, Jarrolds, 1949.
Twilight in South Africa. London, Jarrolds, and New York, Philosophical Library, 1950.
Crescent in Shadow (on the Middle East). London, Jarrolds, 1952.
Italy on Borrowed Time. London, Jarrolds, 1953.
Background to Bitterness: The Story of South Africa 1652–1954. London, Muller, and New York, Philosophical Library, 1954.
Africa on a Tightrope. London, Jarrolds, 1954.
The Masks of Spain. London, Muller, 1955.
The Hills of India. London, Jarrolds, 1961.

*   *   *

If you are pining for an adventure in an exotic setting but don't want to plow through the red tape of obtaining a passport, or are squeamish about the required immunizations, Simon Harvester can effortlessly transport you to the country of your dreams. Adventure, romance, suspense, and intrigue can all be yours, and all you have to do is turn the pages. Harvester has sampled the hospitality of even the most remote areas about which he writes. The authenticity of descriptions, the insightful analysis of political structures, and the portrayal of idiosyncratic characters make each novel a journey well worth making. His knowledge of six languages, his wealth of experience as a war reporter, and his background as a portrait painter all contribute to the richness of his literary style and his ability to portray realistically the political and aesthetical intrigue of the countries visited by his daring espionage agents.

Dorian Silk, Harvester's most popular spy, a ruggedly human character, has appeared in some dozen novels traveling from his native London to Moscow, China, Japan, North Africa, Egypt, and Israel. Like a chameleon, Silk has the ability to assume an unpretentious local identity complete with native coloring and dialect, no matter where he finds himself. His knowledge of regional customs is undeniably complete. Silk's women also leave little to be desired. They are wily, seductive, sometimes petulant, flamboyant, and, above all, cunning. Their shapes and nationalities, and, certainly, their political loyalties, may change from adventure to adventure, but never their essential importance in Silk's mission. Silk's enemies are varied depending upon his assignment – communists, renegades, revolutionists, or, occasionally, counterspies.

The series of novels about Dorian Silk is recognizable by the appearance of the word Road in each title. *Red Road*, set in the bleak Russian hills along the Soviet frontier, finds Silk, having completed his mission, disguised as an old Turkoman, complete with lice, spouting communist doctrine to Arab peasant children and trying vainly to cross the last few miles to freedom. *Zion Road* varies from the usual Silk adventure since he has a personal interest involved. Fathiya, Silk's glamorous Egyptian girlfriend, is kidnapped. A Russian agent comments to Silk, "I figure you imagine yourself a John Buchan hero maybe. Was it Richard Hanoi and the thirty-eight steps?" Harvester's sense of humor and dry wit are frequently apparent in Silk's sardonic philosophy when he is placed in difficult circumstances. In *Sahara Road* Silk, in the interests of his mission, is forced to submit to the amorous designs of a Saharan female informant. After some delaying tactics, Silk succumbs. "He saw no future in treating her like an Agatha Christie heroine or one of the neurotic females dreamed up by the Brontës. Her hand strayed on him. The Prisoner of Zenda was nothing like this."

Those novels not featuring Dorian Silk are also inviting excursions to exotic lands. Dorian Silk's co-worker, Giles Priest, is featured in *Shadows in a Hidden Land* which is set in the bitter Sinkiang terrain, the site of China's nuclear tests. *The Bamboo Screen* is a tense, action-packed story of a nuclear engineer plagued by murderous "accidents" in Hong Kong.

Harvester is sometimes compared to other superior espionage writers, such as Graham Greene, Eric Ambler, Victor Canning, and Alistair MacLean. He is, indeed, a master of the trade and a superb storyteller.

—Mary Ann Grochowski

HASTINGS, Macdonald. British. Born in London, 6 October 1909; son of the dramatist Basil Macdonald Hastings. Educated at Stonyhurst College, Lancashire, 1917–27. Married 1) the writer Anne Scott-James in 1944 (marriage dissolved), one son and one daughter; 2) Anthea Joseph in 1963, one daughter. War Correspondent and feature writer, *Picture Post*, London, 1939–45; Editor, *Strand Magazine*, London, 1946–49; Founding Editor, *Country Fair* magazine, London, 1951–58. Columnist ("Lemuel Gulliver"), *Lilliput* magazine, London, 1940–45; regular contributor to many British periodicals, and frequent radio and television broadcaster. Agent: Curtis Brown Ltd., 1 Craven Hill, London W2 3EP, England; or, John Cushman Associates Inc., 25 West 43rd Street, New York, New York 10036, U.S.A. Address: Brown's Farm, Old Basing, Hampshire, England.

CRIME PUBLICATIONS

Novels (series character: Montague Cork)

Cork on the Water. London, Joseph, and New York, Random House, 1951; as *Fish and Kill,* New York, Spivak, 1952.
Cork in Bottle. London, Joseph, 1953; New York, Knopf, 1954.
Cork and the Serpent. London, Joseph, 1955.
Cork in the Doghouse. London, Joseph, 1957; New York, Knopf, 1958.
Cork on the Telly. London, Joseph, 1966; as *Cork on Location,* New York, Walker, 1967.

OTHER PUBLICATIONS

Novel

A Glimpse of Arcadia: A Story of Nineteenth-Century England. London, Joseph, 1960; New York, Coward McCann, 1961.

Plays

Screenplay: *Flame of Persia,* 1973.

Television Series: *Call the Gun Expert,* 1964.

Other

Passed as Censored. London, Harrap, 1941.
Rolls Royce: The Story of a Name. N.p., Rolls Royce, 1950.
Eagle Special Investigator (juvenile). London, Joseph, 1953.
Adventure Calling (juvenile). London, Hulton Press, 1955.
The Search for the Little Yellow Men (juvenile). London, Hulton Press, and New York, Knopf, 1956.
Men of Glory (juvenile). London, Hulton Press, 1958.
More Men of Glory (juvenile). London, Hulton Press, 1959.
The Other Mr. Churchill: A Lifetime of Shooting and Murder (on Robert Churchill). London, Harrap, 1963; New York, Dodd Mead, 1965.
London Observed, photographs by John Gay. London, Joseph, and New York, Day, 1964.
How to Shoot Straight: A Manual for Newcomers to the Field. London, Pelham, 1967; New York, A. S. Barnes, 1970.
English Sporting Guns and Accessories. London, Ward Lock, 1969.
Jesuit Child (autobiography). London, Joseph, 1971; New York, St. Martin's Press, 1972.
Mary Celeste: A Centenary Record. London, Joseph, 1972.
Sydney the Sparrow (juvenile). London, Ward Lock, 1973.
Wheeler's Fish Cookery Book, with Carole Walsh. London, Joseph, 1974.
Diane: A Victorian (on Diane Chasseresse). London, Joseph, 1974.
After You, Robinson Crusoe: A Practical Guide for a Desert Islander. London, Pelham, 1975.
Shooting – Why We Miss: Questions and Answers on the Successful Use of the Shotgun. London, Pelham, 1976; New York, McKay, 1977.
Game Book: Sporting round the World. London, Joseph, 1979.

Editor, *Country Book: A Personal Anthology.* London, Newnes, 1961.

Editor, *Game Shooting: A Textbook on the Successful Use of the Modern Shotgun*, by Robert Churchill. London, Joseph, 1963; Harrisburg, Pennsylvania, Stackpole, 1967; revised edition, Joseph, 1970; Stackpole, 1972.

Manuscript Collection: Mugar Memorial Library, Boston University.

Macdonald Hastings comments:

For the record, Mr. Montague Cork, the hero of my series of thrillers, was a real person. His name was Claude Wilson, and he was managing director of the Cornhill Insurance Company in London. Almost nothing happened to him in real life in the way I have told in my books, but, as a man, he was exactly as I have described him.

*   *   *

The detective story, as a literary form, involves a situation in which a crime has been committed and in which the motive and means of the crime and the identity of the criminal are in doubt. Murder is the most usual crime, and the reader engages in a battle of wits with the author, sorting through the clues, answering the questions of who, why, when, and how, until he is rewarded in a manner akin to one who solves a crossword puzzle.

Macdonald Hastings is not a conventional writer of detective novels. While murder peripherally appears, it is not the primary crime. Often the reader has solved the mystery within the first 20 pages and the reward is a richly and artfully crafted travelogue full of the atmosphere of the out-of-doors: salmon fishing in Scotland, the countryside of East Anglia, or the excitement of an illegal dogfight. Hastings is a lover of the open air – of shooting and fishing, hunting and gardening. His books reflect the joys of a country life. A close friend of the late Robert Churchill, he edited a book by that great London shotgun maker and wrote an engrossing biography of him, as well as other books for sportsmen.

As a mystery writer, his reputation is based upon a series of five novels about Montague Cork, the general manager of the Anchor Insurance Company. Cork, an elderly and somewhat stuffy gentleman, is richly endowed with an uncanny skill to spot a false insurance claim. The novels, written between 1951 and 1966, range from the trite to the noble.

In *Cork on the Water* the engaging detective investigates a murder and insurance fraud in Scotland; while the plot is sketchy and obvious, the fishing atmosphere is superb. Hastings's perception of the sly and humorous British character is fresh and original. The plot seems simply a pretext for a fine essay on salmon fishing. *Cork in Bottle* is more the straight detective story. It is a tongue-in-cheek Gothic involving an isolated squirearchy in the countryside of East Anglia. The author's keen interest in guns shows through in the rather extensive description of forensic ballistics techniques.

Cork in the Doghouse presents the shrewd and proper detective at his best, and is a noble example of the novel of detection minus murder. Dog lovers will like its realistic portrayal of the savagery of illegal dog fighting. *Cork and the Serpent* is not Hastings at his best; it is a slow moving tale with much muddling about, but, for the Cork enthusiast, it provides entertainment, detection, and Hastings's usual good characterization. *Cork on the Telly*, the last of the series, draws on the author's broadcasting experiences and provides a satirical and revealing look at British television. There is little else to recommend it. Cork recovers some one million pounds in stolen jewels, but the reader knows from the beginning the location of the jewelry and the story is short on suspense and excitement.

As a writer of mysteries, Macdonald Hastings is not particularly noteworthy, although many have found his characterization and creation of atmosphere appealing. He is obviously at home out-of-doors and he is at his best when describing such scenes.

—Daniel P. King

HAYES, Joseph (Arnold). Also writes as Joseph H. Arnold. American. Born in Indianapolis, Indiana, 2 August 1918. Educated at Indiana University, Bloomington, 1938–41. Married Marrijane Johnston in 1938; three children. Assistant Editor, Samuel French, publishers, New York, 1941–43. Since 1954, Partner, Erskine and Hayes, theatrical producers, New York. Chairman, Sarasota Community Theatre for the Performing Arts, Florida. Chairman, Sarasota Chapter, American Civil Liberties Union. Recipient: Sergel Drama Prize, University of Chicago, 1948; Grand Prix de Littérature Policière; Tony Award, for drama, 1956; Mystery Writers of America Edgar Allan Poe Award, for screenplay, 1956. D.H.L.: Indiana University, 1970. Address: Obtuse Hill, Brookfield Center, Connecticut 06805; or, 1168 Westway Drive, Sarasota, Florida, U.S.A.

CRIME PUBLICATIONS

Novels

The Desperate Hours. New York, Random House, and London, Deutsch, 1954.
The Hours after Midnight. New York, Random House, 1958; London, Deutsch, 1959.
Don't Go Away Mad. New York, Random House, 1962; London, W. H. Allen, 1964.
The Third Day. New York, McGraw Hill, 1964; London, W. H. Allen, 1965.
The Deep End. New York, Viking Press, and London, W. H. Allen, 1967.
Like Any Other Fugitive. New York, Dial Press, 1971; London, Deutsch, 1972.
The Long Dark Night. New York, Putnam, and London, Deutsch, 1974.
Missing and Presumed Dead. New York, Putnam, 1975; London, Deutsch, 1977.
Island on Fire. New York, Grosset and Dunlap, and London, Deutsch, 1979.

OTHER PUBLICATIONS

Novel

Bon Voyage, with Marrijane Hayes. New York, Random House, and London, Deutsch, 1957.

Plays

And Came the Spring, with Marrijane Hayes. New York, French, 1942.
Christmas at Home. New York, French, 1943.
The Thompsons. New York, French, 1943.
The Bridegroom Waits. New York, French, 1943.
Kidnapped, in *On the Air*, edited by Garrett H. Leverton. New York, French, 1944.
Sneak Date (as Joseph H. Arnold). New York, Peterson, 1944.
Come Rain or Shine, with Marrijane Hayes. New York, French, 1944.
Life of the Party, with Marrijane Hayes. New York, French, 1945.
Ask for Me Tomorrow, with Marrijane Hayes. New York, French, 1946.
Where's Laurie (as Joseph H. Arnold). New York, French, 1946.
Come Over to Our House, with Marrijane Hayes. New York, French, 1946.
Home for Christmas. New York, French, 1946.
A Woman's Privilege. New York, French, 1947.
Quiet Summer, with Marrijane Hayes. New York, French, 1947.
Change of Heart, with Marrijane Hayes. New York, French, 1948.
Leaf and Bough (produced New York, 1949).
Too Many Dates, with Marrijane Hayes. New York, French, 1950.
Curtain Going Up, with Marrijane Hayes. New York, French, 1950.
Turn Back the Clock, with Marrijane Hayes. New York, French, 1950.
June Wedding, with Marrijane Hayes. New York, French, 1951.

Once in Every Family, with Marrijane Hayes. New York, French, 1951.
Penny, with Marrijane Hayes. New York, French, 1951.
Too Young, Too Old. Boston, Baker, 1952.
Mister Peepers, with Marrijane Hayes. New York, French, 1952.
Head in the Clouds, with Marrijane Hayes. New York, French, 1952.
The Desperate Hours, adaptation of his own novel (produced New York and London,
    1955). New York, Random House, 1955.
The Midnight Sun (produced New Haven, Connecticut, 1959).
Calculated Risk (produced New York, 1962). New York, French, 1963.
Is Anyone Listening? (produced Tallahassee, Florida, 1970).
Impolite Comedy. New York, French, 1977.

Screenplays: *The Desperate Hours*, 1955; *The Young Doctors*, 1962.

Radio Play: *Kidnapped.*

Manuscript Collection: Lilly Library, Indiana University, Bloomington.

*   *   *

Joseph Hayes has enjoyed a varied career as a novelist, playwright, and theatrical producer. He was born in Indianapolis, a locale he used in *The Desperate Hours*, his first and best-known novel. *The Desperate Hours* was an immediate best seller; it was adapted as a Broadway play and a screenplay in 1955. The story of *The Desperate Hours*, based on factual circumstances, is a gripping one. Readers of the novel become fully involved in the nightmare of suspense in which Dan Hilliard, his wife, and children find themselves enmeshed. Hayes uses the plot of three escaped convicts holding a family hostage to demonstrate various levels of tension: the tension of a family who must function under such extraordinary circumstances, the tension among the three escapees, the tension as well as the bonds of mutual respect developed during the ordeal between the Hilliards and the convicts.

The three convicts, Glenn Griffin, his younger brother Hank, and their companion Robish, represent very different personalities. Glenn, the leader of the group, demonstrates operational reason to the degree possible under such circumstances. Hank has followed his brother's lead, from the commission of crime to imprisonment; he differs from Hank in having a faint sense of humanity. Robish, on the other hand, symbolizes the criminal pushed beyond the bounds; he is happiest when he is able to kill. The conflict among the three, the urgency with which Glenn Griffin must control Robish, and the doubt facing Hank about his brother escalate the tension that develops once they take over the Hilliard home.

Hayes poses the questions we all would ask: How does the ordinary man protect his family? How does he deal with minds so alien to his? How does he choose between heroic impulsive action and what might appear to be cowardly but more thoughtful and safer alternatives? Much of the drama of *The Desperate Hours* derives from the familiarity of the scene for the principals. Glenn Griffin returns to the Indianapolis area for revenge against the sheriff, Jesse Webb, who made the arrest leading to his imprisonment. Through a series of hunches, which Webb describes as the essence of police work, Webb is able to free the Hilliard family of their nightmare.

Of Hayes's other novels, two bear close analysis – *Like Any Other Fugitive* and *The Long Dark Night*. *Like Any Other Fugitive*, a sharply drawn psychological portrait of two young people on the run, is a picaresque novel whose comedy is erased by the burden placed on the protagonists by society and paranoid parents. Written in a quasi-stream-of-consciousness manner, the novel deals with a young couple, one a Vietnam veteran, placed at odds with the law by those close to them – a sister and a right-wing father. A cross-country pursuit brings the two youngsters, B. C. Chadwicke and Laurel Taggart, into the lives of ordinary people – old men from the Midwest who run motels, rancher couples, ladies who own general stores. Hayes draws unforgettable portraits of the American Gothic in these characters. Through their actions they reveal their trust, or suspicion, of the strange young couple touching their lives. Throughout the novel, B. C. and Laurel also confront the same questions of trust, suspicion, and betrayal. Each time they are betrayed, they experience genuine shock and hurt because at heart they are innocents.

In *The Long Dark Night* Hayes tells a gruesome, violent story of revenge. The protagonist, a criminal psychopath, Boyd Ritchie, revisits a New England town and avenges the wrongful conviction and eight-year imprisonment he endured. Systematically Ritchie visits the home of each person who affected his life eight years before. Upon each one he inflicts extreme physical torture (eye gouging, sodomy, etc.), and causes some of his victims to murder others. The physical horrors are graphic and unrelieved, and the novel is paced on a strict timetable – from victim to victim and horror to horror. Hayes creates a tapestry of characters ranging from an innocent teenager to a nymphomaniac and a slightly off-kilter retired Texas Ranger. As in *The Desperate Hours*, Hayes aptly contrasts normality with manic behavior. The race against the clock in *The Long Dark Night* is reminiscent of the pace of *Night of the Juggler* by William P. McGivern.

—Katherine M. Restaino

* * *

HEAD, Matthew. Pseudonym for John (Edwin) Canaday. American. Born in Fort Scott, Kansas, 1 February 1907. Educated at the University of Texas, Austin, B.A. 1925; Yale University, New Haven, Connecticut, M.A. 1932. Served in the United States Marine Corps, 1943–45: First Lieutenant. Married Katherine Hoover in 1935; two children. Teacher of Art History, University of Virginia, Charlottesville, 1938–50; Head, School of Art at Newcomb College of Tulane University, New Orleans, Louisiana, 1950–52; Chief, Division of Education, Philadelphia Museum of Art, 1952–59. Since 1959, Art Critic, and Restaurant Critic, 1974–77, New York *Times*. Member of Mission to the Congo, U.S. Board of Economic Warfare, 1943. Recipient: Athenaeum Library Award, 1959. Address: c/o New York Times, 229 West 43rd Street, New York, New York 10036, U.S.A.

CRIME PUBLICATIONS

Novels (series character: Dr. Mary Finney)

The Smell of Money. New York, Simon and Schuster, 1943.
The Devil in the Bush (Finney). New York, Simon and Schuster, 1945.
The Accomplice. New York, Simon and Schuster, 1947.
The Cabinda Affair (Finney). New York, Simon and Schuster, 1949; London, Heinemann, 1950.
The Congo Venus (Finney). New York, Simon and Schuster, 1950; London, Garland, 1976.
Another Man's Life. New York, Simon and Schuster, 1953.
Murder at the Flea Club (Finney). New York, Simon and Schuster, 1955; London, Heinemann, 1957.

Uncollected Short Story

"Three Strips of Flesh," in *Four and Twenty Bloodhounds*, edited by Anthony Boucher. New York, Simon and Schuster, 1950; London, Hammond, 1951.

OTHER PUBLICATIONS as John Canaday

Other

> *Metropolitan Seminars in Art.* New York, Metropolitan Museum of Art, 12 vols.,
> 1958; 2nd series, 12 vols., 1959.
> *Mainstreams of Modern Art: David to Picasso.* New York, Simon and Schuster, and
> London, Thames and Hudson, 1959.
> *Embattled Critic: Views on Modern Art.* New York, Farrar Straus, 1962.
> *Keys to Art*, with Katherine H. Canaday. New York, Tudor, 1963; as *Look; or, The
> Keys to Art*, London, Methuen, 1964.
> *The Lives of the Painters.* New York, Norton, and London, Thames and Hudson, 4
> vols., 1969.
> *Culture Gulch: Notes on Art and Its Public in the 1960's.* New York, Farrar Straus,
> 1969.
> *Baroque Painters.* New York, Norton, 1972.
> *Late Gothic to Renaissance Painters.* New York, Norton, 1972.
> *Neoclassic to Post-Impressionist Painters.* New York, Norton, 1972.
> *The New York Guide to Dining Out in New York.* New York, Atheneum, 1972; revised
> edition, 1976.
> *The Artful Avocado.* New York, Doubleday, 1973.
> *Richard Estes: The Urban Landscape.* Boston, New York Graphic Society, 1979.

Editor, *Western Painting Illustrated: Giotto to Cézanne.* New York, Norton, 1972.

*   *   *

In 1943 Matthew Head published his first mystery, *The Smell of Money.* Particularly interesting were the descriptive passages of the great house and estate which "smelled of money." But it was with his second book that Head made his name as a mystery writer – since then he has never been overlooked by connoisseurs.

The Devil in the Bush was published in 1945, predating by a good many years Nicholas Monsarrat's *The Tribe That Lost Its Head.* It was perhaps the first modern view in fiction of emerging Africa. There is autobiographical background to the story, which relates the experiences of a young man sent to the Congo on a government mission. Head wrote two more African books, *The Cabinda Affair* and *The Congo Venus*, both as engaging and as revealing as his first African book. With subtlety he foreshadowed a time of change on the African continent. Head has also written several mysteries with a European background, using his artist's eye to convey the enchantment of Paris and Venice.

—Dorothy B. Hughes

HEALD, Tim(othy Villiers). British. Born in Dorchester, Dorset, 28 January 1944. Educated at Connaught House School, Bishops Lydeard, Somerset, 1952–57; Sherborne School, Dorset, 1957–62; Balliol College, Oxford (Galpin Scholar), 1962–65, B.A. (honours) in modern history 1965. Married Alison Martina Leslie in 1968; two daughters and two sons. Reporter, "Atticus" column, *Sunday Times*, London, 1965–67; Feature Editor, *Town* magazine, London, 1967; Feature Writer, *Daily Express*, London, 1967–72; free-lance writer and journalist, London, 1972–77; Associate Editor, *Weekend Magazine*, Toronto, 1977–78.

Agent: Richard Scott Simon Ltd., 32 College Cross, London N1 1PR. Address: 305 Sheen Road, Richmond, Surrey TW10 5AW, England.

CRIME PUBLICATIONS

Novels (series character: Simon Bognor in all books)

> *Unbecoming Habits.* London, Hutchinson, and New York, Stein and Day, 1973.
> *Blue Blood Will Out.* London, Hutchinson, and New York, Stein and Day, 1974.
> *Deadline.* London, Hutchinson, and New York, Stein and Day, 1975.
> *Let Sleeping Dogs Die.* London, Hutchinson, and New York, Stein and Day, 1976.
> *Just Desserts.* London, Hutchinson, 1977; New York, Scribner, 1979.

Uncollected Short Story

"The Case of the Frozen Diplomat," in *Weekend Magazine* (Toronto), 17 June 1978.

OTHER PUBLICATIONS

Other

> *It's a Dog's Life.* London, Elm Tree Books, 1971.
> *The Making of Space 1999.* New York, Ballantine, 1976.
> *John Steed: An Authorized Biography.* London, Weidenfeld and Nicolson, 1977.
> *H.R.H.: The Man Who Will Be King*, with Mayo Mohs. New York, Arbor House, 1979.

Tim Heald comments:

All five of the mysteries are meant to be light (not to say comic) and, as mysteries go, not as mysterious as they might be. They star Simon Bognor who is a special investigator from the Board of Trade, and silly with it. He moves from an Anglican friary to the English stately home business, Fleet Street, dogbreeding, and, finally, food. I know about all of these from personal experience. Bognor always gets his man but is not entirely faithful to Monica who is plain but long-suffering. He smokes, drinks, and takes no exercise.

*   *   *

The appeal of Tim Heald's mystery novels is based on the anti-heroic qualities of their hero, their relentlessly irreverent prose, and a solid core of social satire. Simon Bognor of the Board of Trade's investigative arm is cousin to other fallible, physically unimpressive heroes of the 1970's. Bognor, "mindful as ever of the idiocy of his job," is introduced unwillingly into various modern institutions chosen for their qualities of flamboyance, or anachronism, or both. He then passes through adventures that range from the pathetic to the ludicrous and back again.

Fr. Xavier, the priest-spy whom Bognor just manages to capture at the end of *Unbecoming Habits*, retains the dignity of his conflicting convictions, and the monastery whose ranks he has depleted prays for him and itself with imperfect and appealing faith. The villain in *Blue Blood Will Out*, set in various stately homes that have been opened to the public, is a less interesting human being than Fr. Xavier. But the reader is compensated for this deficiency by Heald's portrait of the marketing mind at work upon Tradition, and Bognor's hairbreadth escape from a herd of stampeding bison. Bognor investigates the world of dog shows in *Let Sleeping Dogs Lie*, and finds that the villains are vicious; one secondary character is actually rabid. In *Deadline*, Bognor infiltrates a modern newspaper after a gossip columnist is murdered for having kept the juiciest bits for himself.

—Carol Cleveland

HEARD, Gerald. See **HEARD, H.F.**

HEARD, H(enry) F(itzgerald). Also wrote as Gerald Heard. British. Born in London, 6 October 1889. Educated at Gonville and Caius College, Cambridge, B.A. (honours) in history 1911, graduate work 1911–12. Worked with the Agricultural Co-operative Movement in Ireland, 1919–23, and in England, 1923–27; Editor, *Realist*, London, 1929; Lecturer, Oxford University, 1929–31; science commentator, BBC Radio, London, 1930–34; settled in the United States, 1937; Visiting Lecturer, Washington University, St. Louis, 1951–52, 1955–56; Haskell Foundation Lecturer, Oberlin College, Ohio, 1958. Recipient: Bollingen grant, 1955; British Academy Hertz award. *Died 14 August 1971.*

CRIME PUBLICATIONS

Novels (series character: Mr. Mycroft in all books except *Murder by Reflection*)

> *A Taste for Honey.* New York, Vanguard Press, 1941; London, Cassell, 1942; as *A Taste for Murder*, New York, Avon, 1955.
> *Reply Paid.* New York, Vanguard Press, 1942; London, Cassell, 1943.
> *Murder by Reflection.* New York, Vanguard Press, 1942; London, Cassell, 1945.
> *Doppelgangers: An Episode of the Fourth, the Psychological Revolution, 1997.* New York, Vanguard Press, 1947; London, Cassell, 1948.
> *The Notched Hairpin.* New York, Vanguard Press, 1949; London, Cassell, 1952.

Short Stories

> *The Great Fog and Other Weird Tales.* New York, Vanguard Press, 1944; London, Cassell, 1947.
> *The Lost Cavern and Other Tales of the Fantastic.* New York, Vanguard Press, 1948; London, Cassell, 1949.

Uncollected Short Stories

> "The President of the U.S., Detective," in *The Queen's Awards 1946*, edited by Ellery Queen. Boston, Little Brown, 1946.
> "Mr. Montalba, Obsequist," in *To the Queen's Taste*, edited by Ellery Queen. Boston, Little Brown, 1946; London, Faber, 1949.

OTHER PUBLICATIONS as Gerald Heard

Other

Narcissus: An Anatomy of Clothes. London, Kegan Paul, and New York, Dutton, 1924.
The Ascent of Humanity: An Essay on the Evolution of Civilization. London, Cape, and New York, Harcourt Brace, 1929.
The Emergence of Man. London, Cape, 1931; New York, Harcourt Brace, 1932.
Social Substance of Religion: An Essay on the Evolution of Religion. London, Allen and Unwin, and New York, Harcourt Brace, 1931.
This Surprising World: A Journalist Looks at Science. London, Cobden Sanderson, 1932.
These Hurrying Years: An Historical Outline 1900–1933. London, Chatto and Windus, and New York, Oxford University Press, 1934.
Science in the Making. London, Faber, 1935.
The Source of Civilisation. London, Cape, 1935; New York, Harper, 1937.
The Significance of the New Pacifism, with *Pacifism and Philosophy*, by Aldous Huxley. London, Headley, 1935.
Exploring the Stratosphere. London, Nelson, 1936.
Science Front 1936. London, Cassell, 1937.
The Third Morality. London, Cassell, and New York, Morrow, 1937.
Pain, Sex, and Time: A New Hypothesis of Evolution. New York, Harper, and London, Cassell, 1939.
The Creed of Christ: An Interpretation of the Lord's Prayer. New York, Harper, 1940; London, Cassell, 1941.
A Quaker Meditation. Wallingford, Pennsylvania, Pendle Hill, 1940(?).
The Code of Christ: An Interpretation of the Beatitudes. New York, Harper, 1941; London, Cassell, 1943.
Training for the Life of the Spirit. London, Cassell, 2 vols., 1941–44; New York, Harper, 1 vol, n.d.
Man the Master. New York, Harper, 1941; London, Faber, 1942.
A Dialogue in the Desert. London, Cassell, and New York, Harper, 1942.
A Preface to Prayer. New York, Harper, 1944; London, Cassell, 1945.
The Recollection. Stanford, California, Delkin, 1944.
The Gospel According to Gamaliel. New York, Harper, 1945; London, Cassell, 1946.
Militarism's Post-Mortem. London, P.P.U., 1946.
The Eternal Gospel. New York, Harper, 1946; London, Cassell, 1948.
Is God Evident? An Essay Toward a Natural Theology. New York, Harper, 1948; London, Faber, 1950.
Is God in History? An Inquiry into Human and Pre-Human History in Terms of the Doctrine of Creation, Fall, and Redemption. New York, Harper, 1950; London, Faber, 1951.
Morals since 1900. London, Dakers, and New York, Harper, 1950.
The Riddle of the Flying Saucers. London, Carroll and Nicholson, 1950; as *Is Another World Watching?*, New York, Harper, 1951; revised edition, New York, Bantam, 1953.
Ten Questions on Prayer. Wallingford, Pennsylvania, Pendle Hill, 1951.
Gabriel and the Creatures. New York, Harper, 1952; as *Wishing Well: An Outline of the Evolution of the Mammals Told as a Series of Stories about How Animals Got Their Wishes*, London, Faber, 1953.
The Human Venture. New York, Harper, 1955.
Kingdom Without God: Road's End for the Social Gospel, with others. Los Angeles, Foundation for Social Research, 1956.
Training for a Life of Growth. Santa Monica, California, Wayfarer Press, 1959.

The Five Ages of Man: The Psychology of Human History. New York, Julian Press, 1964.

Editor, *Prayers and Meditations.* New York, Harper, 1949.

*   *   *

H. F. Heard (Gerald Heard), despite his many serious books on social thought and his later works on mysticism, occultism, and pseudoscience, is now remembered mostly for his delightful novel *A Taste for Honey.* It tells of the experiences of Mr. Mycroft (detective) and Mr. Silchester (narrator) against a criminal who "sends" bees with hypertrophied stinging apparatus. Set in the British countryside, ably characterized, with a leisurely pace, it is perhaps the finest novel-length pastiche of Sherlock Holmes – even though Holmes is not mentioned by name.

In *Reply Paid* Mycroft and Silchester are relocated in California, where they are now concerned with a mystery involving a cryptogram, supernatural phenomena, bacterial murder, and a radioactive meteorite. A third novel, *The Notched Hairpin,* and two short stories, "Mr. Montalba, Obsequist" and "The Enchanted Garden," complete the Mycroft canon. The consensus is that none of these stories matches the first novel.

Heard's other mystery material includes *Murder by Reflection,* a fairly routine mystery; *Doppelgangers,* about crime and politico-mystical intrigue in 1997; and several of the stories in the mixed collections *The Great Fog* and *The Lost Cavern.* In all of these, good, original ideas are likely to be overburdened by meandering development and garrulity.

—E. F. Bleiler

HEILBRUN, Carolyn G. See **CROSS, Amanda**.

HEXT, Harrington. See **PHILLPOTTS, Eden**.

HERRON, Shaun. Canadian. Born in Northern Ireland in 1912. Educated at Queen's University, Belfast; Edinburgh University; Princeton University, New Jersey. Served in the British Army during World War II. Married Marganita Bourdon; two daughters and one son. Editor, *British Weekly,* London, 1950–57. Senior Editorial Writer and now Columnist, Winnipeg *Free Press,* Manitoba; since 1976, Columnist, Montreal *Star;* also radio writer. Recipient: Canada Council Award, 1972. Agent: Curtis Brown Ltd., 575 Madison Avenue,

New York, New York 10022, U.S.A.; or, A. P. Watt & Son, 26/28 Bedford Row, London WC1R 4HL, England.

CRIME PUBLICATIONS

Novels (series character: Miro)

> *Miro.* New York, Random House, 1969; London, Hale, 1971.
> *The Hound and the Fox and the Harper.* New York, Random House, 1970; as *The Miro Papers*, London, Hale, 1972.
> *Through the Dark and Hairy Wood* (Miro). New York, Random House, 1972; London, Cape, 1973.
> *The Whore-Mother.* New York, Evans, and London, Cape, 1973.

OTHER PUBLICATIONS

Novels

> *The Bird in Last Year's Nest.* New York, Evans, and London, Cape, 1974.
> *The Ruling Passion.* New York, New American Library, 1978; as *The MacDonnell*, London, Cape, 1978.
> *Aladale.* New York, Summit, and London, Cape, 1979.

Shaun Herron comments:

I began as an entertainer (a story teller) with my first three books. They were thrillers of a sort – I don't know what sort – with moral undertones. I am still an entertainer though I now write "serious" novels which I hope are still thrillers. Why not? Homer did. So did Shakespeare. Who am I to pretend? I take my craft very seriously, myself less so, therefore it is hard to write an introduction to one's work that pretends to explain what one's up to. I try to write well and think I do. As each book is published I see its faults and hope I don't repeat them (and sometimes do). When I think about it my Miro books were serious books. By that I mean that they had two serious purposes. The first was to make enough money to support my wife and children and give the children a generous education in their own country and abroad. I did and do. The second purpose is harder to define, but since the books are written for readers who define these things for themselves no matter what the author says, why clutter things up with my explanation of my purpose? If I laid it all out, the reader would say: I saw that, or I didn't get that impression. So let him/her decide. As it is, I'm happy. My first two books were nominated for Edgars. They didn't get them, but that didn't matter. People read them. I'm fond of my readers and my books. Together, they have enabled me and mine to live the year out in Canada, Ireland and Spain. So, I'm a story teller. Like the old Gaelic story tellers of my Scots and Irish ancestors whose place was around the turf fire on a cold and windy night? It's an honorable calling.

*   *   *

Whether set in Ireland, Spain, Scotland, or America, Shaun Herron's novels are concerned with the anonymous, stifling, and destructive power of large organizations, the cruelty, prejudice and ignorance of feuding factions, and racial and cultural patterns that seem impervious to time. *The Bird in Last Year's Nest* focuses on a close-knit Spanish family torn apart by the revolutionary deeds of youth (grandfather, father, and son in turn), and the relentless dominance and pursuit of the Spanish Civil Guard, which negates friendship and humanity and forces people into destructive patterns. The Miro series, uneven in quality and credibility, depicts the plight of Miro, a stodgy, middle-aged spy and assassin, who in his

759

youth turned to the American "Firm" (a CIA-type intelligence service) to prove his manhood and to escape the frustrations of a frigid wife, and who now, after 25 years' service brutally manipulating and liquidating as the Firm required, feels he is "a cast-iron jelly," expendable, betrayed, pushed to the limit. The series begins with an impossible mission single-handedly to expose a network of terrorist bombers; it quickly proves double-edged as this worn-out agent finds his most trusted colleague treacherous, the enemy agents more subtle than he predicted, and the woman decoy, despite his own past cynical womanizing, someone he can love and trust. His bumbling and often incompetent fight for love and life leads to pain, violence, death, and a book that blows the whistle on the Firm. *The Hound and the Fox and the Harper* follows the turns and complications produced by his on-going exposé, as Miro and his pregnant new wife are kidnapped, attacked, and nearly killed only to escape again and again from the Firm and Russian agents – helpless individuals assaulted on every side by anonymous and arrogant power, preserved only by luck and warm-hearted Irish friends. When Herron begins to focus specifically on Irish landscapes and Irish conflicts, the series improves in credibility and in the sense of character and place. In *Through the Dark and Hairy Wood* Miro, now a mellowed family man and landowner in Ireland, finds that a cattle-buying trip to Northern Ireland enmeshes him in tribal conflict and Irish rage, trouble from which his sense of decency and honor will not let him walk away. Aided by Catholic and Protestant alike, all outraged by and fearful of terrorist threats despite their own deep-seated prejudices, Miro fights to rescue children, women, and old men who are kidnapped and abused by Irish revolutionaries, envious thugs whose motives are more social and personal than patriotic.

Herron's concern with Irish conflicts continues in *The Hound and the Fox and the Harper*, *The Whore-Mother*, and *The Ruling Passion*, all of which depict Ireland as a "whore-mother" that both suckles and destroys, and all of which confirm Bernard Shaw's adage, "Put an Irishman on the spit, and you can always get another Irishman to turn him." The books expose Irish cordiality as "cold at the centre," a "silent, smiling derision ... which so often looks like charm and friendship"; they attack Celtic "irresponsibility"; they deride causes "invalidated by their own [Irish] excesses"; they depict incest and sexual hysteria as commonplace; always they include a young man initiated into manhood by an older, monumental woman who defies conservative tradition, but who is as loving and gentle as the hills and valleys of Ireland. In *The Whore-Mother* a middle-class Irish Catholic adolescent, schooled in the idealistic legends of Irish patriotism, finds past loyalty will not save him from the ire of the power-mad, lower-class sadists who dominate the IRA, strutting, petty men who not only indiscriminately shoot and bomb Protestants, but who also abuse fellow Catholics – tar and feathering and raping young women, torturing and killing youngsters, beating up old women, and assassinating past members whose only betrayal is a desire to escape violence. *The Ruling Passion* tries to analyze the tensions and differences that have intensified the modern Irish situation; using an historical approach, a saga of the lives and loves of two Ulster-Scot brothers and their families, 19th-century aristocrats with both Protestant and Fenian connections, it focuses on their domestic and political conflicts as they turn from Irish cruelty and stagnation to American opportunity and democracy. *Aladale* takes a similar dynastic approach, following the struggles of a Scottish Highland family of "tackmen" and smugglers, who traffic in illegal whisky to forward their dream of immigration to America. As usual Herron combats romanticized views of Irish and Scots, focusing on the "cold, primitive, squalid" conditions of tenants, and the cruelty or indifference of landlords who depend on tenant poverty to sustain their wealth. Often in Herron the message about prejudice and class conflict determines plot and character.

—Virginia Macdonald

HEYER, Georgette. Also wrote as Stella Martin. British. Born 16 August 1902. Educated ateminary schools and Westminster College, London. Married George Ronald Rougier in 1925; one son. Lived in East Africa, 1925–28, and in Yugoslavia, 1928–29. *Died 5 July 1974.*

CRIME PUBLICATIONS

Novels (series characters: Superintendent Hannasyde; Inspector Hemingway)

Footsteps in the Dark. London, Longman, 1932.
Why Shoot the Butler? London, Longman, 1933; New York, Doubleday, 1936.
The Unfinished Clue. London, Longman, 1934; New York, Doubleday, 1937.
Death in the Stocks (Hannasyde). London, Longman, 1935; as *Merely Murder*, New York, Doubleday, 1935.
Behold, Here's Poison! (Hannasyde). London, Hodder and Stoughton, and New York, Doubleday, 1936.
They Found Him Dead (Hannasyde). London, Hodder and Stoughton, and New York, Doubleday, 1937.
A Blunt Instrument (Hannasyde). London, Hodder and Stoughton, and New York, Doubleday, 1938.
No Wind of Blame (Hemingway). London, Hodder and Stoughton, and New York, Doubleday, 1939.
Envious Casca (Hemingway). London, Hodder and Stoughton, New York, Doubleday, 1941.
Penhallow. London, Heinemann, 1942; New York, Doubleday, 1943.
Duplicate Death (Hemingway). London, Heinemann, 1951; New York, Dutton, 1969.
Detection Unlimited (Hemingway). London, Heinemann, 1953; New York, Dutton, 1969.

OTHER PUBLICATIONS

Novels

The Black Moth. London, Constable, and Boston, Houghton Mifflin, 1921.
The Great Roxhythe. London, Hutchinson, 1922; Boston, Small Maynard, 1923.
The Transformation of Philip Jettan (as Stella Martin). London, Mills and Boon, 1923; as *Powder and Patch*, as Georgette Heyer, London, Heinemann, 1930; New York, Dutton, 1968.
Instead of the Thorn. London, Hutchinson, 1923; Boston, Small Maynard, 1924.
Simon the Coldheart. London, Heinemann, and Boston, Small Maynard, 1925.
These Old Shades. London, Heinemann, and Boston, Small Maynard, 1926.
Helen. London and New York, Longman, 1928.
The Masqueraders. London, Heinemann, 1928; New York, Longman, 1929.
Beauvallet. London, Heinemann, 1929; New York, Longman, 1930.
Pastel. London and New York, Longman, 1929.
Barren Corn. London and New York, Longman, 1930.
The Conqueror. London, Heinemann, 1931; New York, Dutton, 1966.
The Convenient Marriage. London, Heinemann, 1934; New York, Dutton, 1966.
Devil's Cub. London, Heinemann, 1934; New York, Dutton, 1966.
Regency Buck. London, Heinemann, 1935; New York, Dutton, 1966.
The Talisman Ring. London, Heinemann, 1936; New York, Doubleday, 1937.
An Infamous Army. London, Heinemann, 1937; New York, Doubleday, 1938.
Royal Escape. London, Heinemann, 1938; New York, Doubleday, 1939.
The Spanish Bride. London, Heinemann, and New York, Doubleday, 1940.

The Corinthian. London, Heinemann, 1940; New York, Dutton, 1966.
Faro's Daughter. London, Heinemann, 1941; New York, Doubleday, 1942.
Beau Wyndham. New York, Doubleday, 1941.
Friday's Child. London, Heinemann, 1944; New York, Putnam, 1946.
The Reluctant Widow. London, Heinemann, and New York, Putnam, 1946.
The Foundling. London, Heinemann, and New York, Putnam, 1948.
Arabella. London, Heinemann, and New York, Putnam, 1949.
The Grand Sophy. London, Heinemann, and New York, Putnam, 1950.
The Quiet Gentleman. London, Heinemann, 1951; New York, Putnam, 1952.
Cotillion. London, Heinemann, and New York, Putnam, 1953.
The Toll-Gate. London, Heinemann, and New York, Putnam, 1954.
Bath Tangle. London, Heinemann, and New York, Putnam, 1955.
Sprig Muslin. London, Heinemann, and New York, Putnam, 1956.
April Lady. London, Hienemann, and New York, Putnam, 1957.
Sylvester; or, The Wicked Uncle. London, Heinemann, and New York, Putnam, 1957.
Venetia. London, Heinemann, 1958; New York, Putnam, 1959.
The Unknown Ajax. London, Heinemann, 1959; New York, Putnam, 1960.
A Civil Contract. London, Heinemann, 1961; New York, Putnam, 1962.
The Nonesuch. London, Heinemann, 1962; New York, Dutton, 1963.
False Colours. London, Bodley Head, 1963; New York, Dutton, 1964.
Frederica. London, Bodley Head, and New York, Dutton, 1965.
Black Sheep. London, Bodley Head, 1966; New York, Dutton, 1967.
Cousin Kate. London, Bodley Head, 1968; New York, Dutton, 1969.
Charity Girl London, Bodley Head, and New York, Dutton, 1970.
Lady of Quality. London, Bodley Head, and New York, Dutton, 1972.
My Lord John. London, Bodley Head, and New York, Dutton, 1975.

Short Stories

Pistols for Two and Other Stories. London, Heinemann, 1960; New York, Dutton, 1964.

Play

Radio Play: *The Toll-Gate*, from her own novel, 1974.

*   *   *

The dozen detective novels of Georgette Heyer illustrate perfectly the development of the mystery genre in the Golden Age of the 1920's and 1930's. Usually operating within the closed world of a country house or a London party with the addition of extended family groups as major suspects and inheritance eventually revealed as the primary motive for murder, the novels rely on stock plots and characters so deftly handled and so cleverly written as to seem unique.

Although the plotting is successful in individual novels, when all of them are read in close succession their similarities become apparent. Shootings, hair-trigger devices, poisons, and daggers are repeated; identical methods for second murders are used several times in the novels, although each use is different. Heyer's unusual plot accessories include an ancient pair of stocks and a police truncheon.

The Scotland Yard detectives called in to solve several of the crimes are the unremarkable Superintendent Hannasyde and his subordinate Inspector Hemingway. In later novels the principal detective, Hemingway, is distinguished by his penchant for psychology and the theatre, his good-natured ribbing of subordinates, his claim to "flair," and a firm conviction that, when a case seems impossibly confused, he is close to a solution.

Among a plethora of suspects, Heyer creates a remarkable group of comic characters whose eccentric behavior often thwarts the serious investigation. Kenneth and Antonia Verker, who will inherit their step-brother's estate, cheerfully calculate for Hannasyde the many ways they might easily have murdered Arnold and still established their alibis (*Death in the Stocks*). Rosemary Kane, whose limited Russian ancestry provides her with a "tortured soul," is mocked by the characters in the novel and by Heyer in *They Found Him Dead*, but even more improbable is the self-centered, flamboyant, practical cabaret dancer Lola de Silva who arrives at Sir Arthur Billington-Smythe's proper house party as his son's fiancée (*The Unfinished Clue*). The most delightful figure is Vicky Fanshawe who costumes herself for various roles played out hourly for any audience in *No Wind of Blame*; as "Innocent Girl Suspected of Murder," "Mystery Woman," or "Tragic Muse," she annoys and amuses Hemingway whose psychological and theatrical interests are strongly tested.

In a regular subplot, Heyer includes a romance quite clearly patterned on her Regency love stories. The man, hero and sometimes also rake, is arrogant, intelligent, handsome, and often able to control the investigation despite being under suspicion himself. The heroine, generally spunky, is astonished by his declaration and proposal, having believed herself disliked and overlooked.

Heyer's most unusual mystery is *Penhallow* in which the wife of a bullying tyrant is shown plotting and executing his murder with ease. Suspicion falls on almost everyone else in the family and she begins to wish she could undo the murder. Eventually Penhallow's eldest son commits suicide for reasons known only to the reader, but the local police and the family assume that guilt for patricide was responsible. Unable to effect any change by a confession, the murderer keeps silent and remains undiscovered. The novel is rare in removing all internal suspicion from the wife and allowing only the reader to know the whole truth; the convention of "justice done" is forcefully challenged.

Although not so popular as her Regency romances, Georgette Heyer's detective novels are better crafted and more enduring. They illustrate the style of mystery writing in her time while being sufficiently original to carry her unmistakable signature.

—Kathleen G. Klein

HIGGINS, George V(incent). American. Born in Brockton, Massachusetts, 13 November 1939. Educated at Rockland High School, Massachusetts; Boston College, A.B. in English 1961; Stanford University, California, 1961–62, M.A. 1965; Boston College Law School, Brighton, Massachusetts, J.D. 1967: Admitted to the Massachusetts Bar, 1967. Divorced; two children. Reporter, *Journal* and *Evening Bulletin*, Providence, Rhode Island, 1962–63; Bureau Correspondent, Springfield, Massachusetts, 1963–64, and Newsman, Boston, 1964, Associated Press; Researcher, Guterman Horvitz and Rubin, attorneys, Boston, 1966–67; Legal Assistant, Administrative Division and Organized Crime Section, 1967, Deputy Assistant Attorney General, 1967–69, and Assistant Attorney General, 1969–70, Commonwealth of Massachusetts; Assistant U.S. Attorney for the District of Massachusetts, 1970–73, and Special Assistant U.S. Attorney, 1973–74; President, George V. Higgins Inc., Boston, 1973–78. Since 1978, Partner, Griffin and Higgins, Boston. Consultant, National Institute of Law Enforcement and Criminal Practice, Washington, D.C., 1970–71; Instructor in Trial Practice, Boston College Law School, 1973–74 and 1978–79; Columnist, Boston *Herald American*, 1977–79. Address: 50 Staniford Street, Boston, Massachusetts 02114, U.S.A.

CRIME PUBLICATIONS

Novels

The Friends of Eddie Coyle. New York, Knopf, and London, Secker and Warburg, 1972.
The Digger's Game. New York, Knopf, and London, Secker and Warburg, 1973.
Cogan's Trade. New York, Knopf, and London, Secker and Warburg, 1974.
The Judgment of Deke Hunter. Boston, Little Brown, and London, Secker and Warburg, 1976.
Kennedy for the Defense. New York, Knopf, 1980.

Uncollected Short Stories

"All Day Was All There Was," in *Arizona Quarterly* (Tucson), Spring 1963.
"Something of a Memoir," in *Massachusetts Review* (Amherst), Summer 1969.
"Mass in Time of War," in *Cimarron Review* (Stillwater, Oklahoma), September 1969.
"Something Dirty You Could Keep," in *Massachusetts Review* (Amherst), Autumn 1969.
"Dillon Explained That He Was Frightened," in *North American Review* (Cedar Falls, Iowa), Autumn 1970.
"The Habits of Animals, The Progress of the Seasons," in *North American Review* (Cedar Falls, Iowa), Winter 1972.
"Two Cautionary Tales: Donnelly's Uncle and The Original Watercourse," in *North American Review* (Cedar Falls, Iowa), Winter 1974.
"The Judge Who Tried Harder," in *Atlantic Monthly* (Boston), April 1974.

OTHER PUBLICATIONS

Novels

A City on a Hill. New York, Knopf, and London, Secker and Warburg, 1975.
Dreamland. Boston, Little Brown, 1977.

Other

The Friends of Richard Nixon. Boston, Little Brown, 1975.
A Year or So with Edgar. New York, Harper, 1979.

*   *   *

In 1971 a first novel by an Assistant United States Attorney for the District of Massachusetts created what is usually called an immediate sensation. The book was *The Friends of Eddie Coyle* by George V. Higgins, and it was a powerful, raw, fast-paced, implacably grim novel of the underbelly world of the small-time professional criminal and the equally small-time professional law officers who often catch him, and sometimes use him to catch bigger fish, in today's Boston. It is an unvarnished and unsparing picture of small, sordid, devious men in a dirty and devious world, a world where the only rule is self-interest, and there is no absolute morality at all – everything is advantage and convenience.

The story of Eddie Coyle's world was continued in *The Digger's Game*, and both books gathered the highest acclaim: "An exciting book, composed of hard, clean prose about hard, rough characters," "The most powerful and frightening crime novel I have read this year," "The most penetrating glimpse yet into what seems the real world of crime ... positively reeking with authenticity," "He can write dialogue so authentic it spits," "Crackles with the most convincing dialogue of the season." These two books present, in authentic detail, the way it is, day by day and year by year, in the milieu of the professional criminal. We learn what it is like, how it works, and we believe it. It is real, and it is true.

Beyond the mechanics of professional crime, we learn how these shadow-people act, we see their "attitudes" toward their society. Eddie Coyle, the Digger, and their friends live with crime as a matter of daily routine. What to most of us is crime and horror is to them a normal life. Prison, assault, crippling, even murder are taken as a matter of course – business reverses, everyday hazards, the normal risks of living. They act, in essence, very much as we all do, except that they act in crime. As we go to the office, buy and sell, they rob, hijack, burgle, fence, and even murder. They have their careers as we have ours.

What Higgins does not do is show us *why* they are what they are, do what they do, and relate to the world beyond the books. The books are like reports from an alien land. In a documentary report our interest is in the data of that unknown or unfamiliar alien world. But Higgins is not writing reports. The "crackling dialogue" and "authenticity" are not tape-recorder accurate but are clearly stylized set-impressions giving a "truth" greater than any tape-recorder. Higgins is writing novels, and a novel must relate its people and view to the world beyond the book. Despite an implied sense in much of the praise that these books are "unique," they are not. Higgins is writing in a tradition strong in American letters. His predecessors include James M. Cain, W. R. Burnett, Dashiell Hammett, James T. Farrell, and Nelson Algren. In various guises, Eddie Coyle and his friends live in all the novels of these writers.

Basically, they are all people trapped and limited by birth, education, economics. They exist outside the mainstream of a larger America, and in their dark and narrow worlds the legitimate options are pitifully few and always inadequate to their hopes and dreams. We have stacked the deck against them. We have given them all our needs and few of our opportunities. A man does what his world gives him to do, unless he is exceptional, and few men are.

Nelson Algren's *The Man with the Golden Arm* offers us much the same people. Eddie Coyle and Frankie Machine are cousins; Dillon the killer and Nifty Louie the junkie who kicked the habit and now peddles dope to others are brother monsters preying on their own kind. But Algren makes us know and understand these people – what they feel, what they dream, what they suffer, why they are what they are. He relates them to *us*, with compassion. Eddie Coyle and the Digger never move beyond the books they are in. We observe them, but we do not live with them. They are a drama that never moves off its stage, never reaches beyond the footlights, never sends us home with the sense of having witnessed something that has meaning in our own lives, or in the larger world where we must live. But George Higgins is a fine writer, and I have little doubt that the books he has for us in the future will be books we will want to read even more than these two brilliant but limited first works.

—Dennis Lynds

HIGGINS, Jack. See **MARLOWE, Hugh**.

HIGHSMITH, (Mary) Patricia (née Plangman). American. Born in Fort Worth, Texas, 19 January 1921; grew up in New York. Educated at Barnard College, New York, B.A.

1942. Has lived in Europe since 1963. Recipient: Grand Prix de Littérature Policière, 1957; Crime Writers Association Silver Dagger, 1964. Address: 21 Boissière, 77 880 Moncourt, France.

Crime Publications

Novels (series character: Tom Ripley)

Strangers on a Train. New York, Harper, and London, Cresset Press, 1950.
The Blunderer. New York, Coward McCann, 1954; London, Cresset Press, 1956; as *Lament for a Lover*, New York, Popular Library, 1956.
The Talented Mr. Ripley. New York, Coward McCann, 1955; London, Cresset Press, 1957.
Deep Water. New York, Harper, 1957; London, Heinemann, 1958.
A Game for the Living. New York, Harper, 1958; London, Heinemann, 1959.
This Sweet Sickness. New York, Harper, 1960; London, Heinemann, 1961.
The Cry of the Owl. New York, Harper, 1962; London, Heinemann, 1963.
The Two Faces of January. New York, Doubleday, and London, Heinemann, 1964.
The Glass Cell. New York, Doubleday, 1964; London, Heinemann, 1965.
The Story-Teller. New York, Doubelday, 1965; as *A Suspension of Mercy*, London, Heinemann, 1965.
Those Who Walk Away. New York, Doubleday, and London, Heinemann, 1967.
The Tremor of Forgery. New York, Doubleday, and London, Heinemann, 1969.
Ripley under Ground. New York, Doubelday, 1970; London, Heinemann, 1971.
A Dog's Ransom. New York, Knopf, and London, Heinemann, 1972.
Ripley's Game. New York, Knopf, and London, Heinemann, 1974.
Edith's Diary. New York, Simon and Schuster, and London, Heinemann, 1977.

Short Stories

The Snail-Watcher and Other Stories. New York, Doubleday, 1970; as *Eleven*, London, Heinemann, 1970.
Little Tales of Misogny (in German). Zurich, Diogenes Verlag, 1974; (in English) London, Heinemann, 1977.
The Animal Lover's Book of Beastly Murder. London, Heinemann, 1975.
Slowly, Slowly in the Wind. London, Heinemann, 1979.

Other Publications

Other

Miranda the Panda Is on the Veranda, with Doris Sanders (juvenile). New York, Coward McCann, 1958.
Plotting and Writing Suspense Fiction. Boston, The Writer, 1966.

*   *   *

Patricia Highsmith writes fiction that is intriguing, thought-provoking, and sometimes hard to classify. Some of her books fit easily into the category of suspense fiction, a few are considered "serious," and others aren't easily agreed upon. The author is wary of classifications, noting in *Plotting and Writing Suspense Fiction*: "In France and England, I am not particularly categorized as a suspense novelist, just as a novelist, and I fare much better as to prestige, quality of reviewing and – proportionally speaking – in sales than in America....

My advice to young and beginning writers, if they wish to stay free agents, is to keep as clear of the suspense label as possible."

Unpretentious about her writing, and considering herself primarily a storyteller, Highsmith is, nevertheless, as "serious" as any contemporary fiction writer. After the success of her first published book, *Strangers on a Train*, which was made into a film by Alfred Hitchcock and has become a classic in the suspense field, she resolved to do no more "hack" writing, no matter how precarious her finances. She believes that a suspense writer "should throw some light on his characters' minds; he should be interested in justice or the absence of it in the world we live in; he should be interested in the morality, good or bad, that exists today; he should be interested in human cowardice or courage." She adheres to these principles in her own books, creating characters whose personalities are evoked with great subtlety. Her psychological portraits and her refusal to employ the traditional formulas of suspense fiction – her originality and seriousness, in fact – are qualities which set her books apart from ordinary examples of the genre.

Patricia Highsmith explores guilt – or its absence – in her characters. Often her protagonists are highly individual, even abnormal, but in her hands they take on life and are consistent and believable. Her examination of guilt in all of its manifestations does not always result in the commonplace fictional order of crime followed by punishment. Her "heroes" engage the reader's interest, if not always every reader's wholehearted sympathy.

A favorite book of the author's is *The Talented Mr. Ripley* (filmed as *Purple Noon*). Tom Ripley is unique in crime fiction. When introduced to the world, he is a sensitive, unstable young man with a grudge against the world. He feels guilty and afraid when he is telling the truth or acting correctly, only losing his nervousness when he is up to no good. Offered an expense-paid trip by the father of an acquaintance, Ripley goes to Italy to convince Dickie Greenleaf to come home. Tom likes the life in Italy, but realizes after a few weeks that Dickie wants to be rid of him: "He had failed with Dickie in every way. He hated Dickie, because, however he looked at what had happened, his failing had not been his fault, not due to anything he had done, but due to Dickie's inhuman stubbornness.... If he killed him on this trip, Tom thought, he could simply say that some accident had happened. He could – He had just thought of something brilliant: he could become Dickie Greenleaf himself." Ripley, who had been nobody, finds an identity by adopting one ready-made. After two murders and a series of close calls, Ripley finally has to resume his own name and passport, but by that time he is a changed man. The charming psychopath is next observed several years later in *Ripley under Ground*, now the owner of a small chateau near Paris where he lives with his lovely French wife. Still engaged in disreputable enterprises, he must save an art business he and some cronies founded upon the forged works of a dead painter, Derwatt. The scheme is threatened by a collector with an ingenious theory which seems to prove that his "Derwatt" is a forgery. The irony of Ripley, whose whole existence is a forgery, trying to persuade anyone that the fake paintings are genuine, adds dimension to the outrageous tale of Ripley's horrible improvisations. At one point, he is left for dead in the grave of one of his own victims. He reappears in *Ripley's Game*, still enjoying the rewards of his misdeeds, but beginning to develop an unsavory reputation. To avenge an insulting remark made about him by an Englishman, Ripley involves the man in a plot to murder two Mafiosi. Ripley is not completely without conscience – he eventually feels remorse for his treatment of the Englishman, but none for killing the killers. Likeable and monstrous at the same time, comic and frightening, Ripley is a proper hero for dark comedy in suspense fiction.

Another of Highsmith's lighter works is *The Story-Teller*, in which a young American writer attempts to experience guilt by pretending he has murdered his wife. His elaborate charade backfires when the journal containing a record of his imagined emotions falls into the hands of the police. Highsmith plays with mirrors as she shows imaginary guilt for a crime never committed, guilt and responsibility for an unintended death, and a lack of guilt for a purposeful killing.

Highsmith states that a major pattern in her work is the "relationship between two men, usually quite different in make-up, sometimes obviously the good and the evil, sometimes merely ill-matched friends" – as seen, for example, in *Strangers on a Train. The Blunderer*, and *A Game for the Living. The Two Faces of January* shows the compulsion of a young man to pursue a criminal who resembles his dead father. The criminal is generous and kind, but the morally upright father had been harsh and cruel. There is a fine balance between past and present, good and evil, crime and punishment. A flawed hero, a mythic symmetry, and tragic overtones, make this book the antithesis of the Ripley tales in the Highsmith canon.

Deep Water shows the marriage of a poorly matched pair. The husband prefers the company of his pet snails to that of his unfaithful wife. Apparently tolerant of her infidelity, he nevertheless starts a rumor that he murdered one of her boyfriends. The disintegration of his personality is one of Highsmith's most chilling tales. In *The Glass Cell*, the horrifying consequences of an unjust imprisonment are an eloquent condemnation of the barbarous conditions in many prisons. The fictional portrayal of police brutality in *A Dog's Ransom* misses the mark and is merely depressing. *The Tremor of Forgery*, set in North Africa and at times reminiscent of Gide, is an ambiguous book in which violence and disregard for human life have a profound effect on a young writer. Painstaking dissection of motivations for the most part replaces action. Highsmith has published several volumes of short stories. The stories vary in quality, but reflect many of the themes explored in her novels. Her fascination with snails furnishes the subject for two ghastly little tales.

Edith's Diary is a devastating portrayal of a woman, deserted by her husband, who tries to care for their mentally aberrant son and the husband's senile uncle. In this powerful novel (which is not considered a suspense book), Highsmith again employs the theme of a writer who mixes fiction with reality, but unlike Sydney Bartleby in *The Story-Teller* Edith is a tragic figure whose fabrications parallel her retreat into insanity.

Highsmith's settings, whether American or foreign, are depicted in convincing detail and add to the brooding, menacing atmosphere in which her characters await or precipitate the violent fate their author intends. Her books represent to a sizeable group of readers the standard for intelligent suspense fiction. A perceptive critic of her own work, she has provided a wealth of information about her writing in *Plotting and Writing Suspense Fiction*, a book which will interest her readers even if they are not potential writers. In his "Foreword" to *The Snail-Watchers* Graham Greene writes that "Miss Highsmith is a crime novelist whose books one can reread many times. There are very few of whom one can say that. She is a writer who has created a world of her own – a world claustrophobic and irrational which we enter each time with a sense of personal danger...." Calling her work an "acquired taste," Julian Symons says that "there are no more genuine agonies in modern literature than those endured by the couples in her books, who are locked together in a dislike and even hatred that often strangely contains love" (*Bloody Murder*). He declares that Patricia Highsmith is "the most important crime novelist at present in practice."

—Mary Helen Becker

HILDICK, (Edmund) Wallace. British. Born in Bradford, Yorkshire, 29 December 1925. Educated at Wheelwright Grammar School, Dewsbury, Yorkshire, 1937–41; City of Leeds Training College, Yorkshire, 1948–50, Teachers Certificate. Served in the Royal Air Force, 1946–48. Married Doris Clayton in 1950. Junior Assistant, Dewsbury Public Library, 1941–42; clerk, truck repair depot, Leeds, 1942–43; Laboratory Assistant, Signals Establishment, Haslemere, Surrey, and Sowerby Bridge, Yorkshire, 1943–46; teacher, Dewsbury Secondary Modern School, 1950–54. Since 1954, self-employed writer. Visiting Critic and Associate Editor, *Kenyon Review*, Kenyon College, Gambier, Ohio, 1966–67. Recipient: Tom-Gallon Trust Award, for short story, 1957; Mystery Writers of America

Edgar Allan Poe Award, 1979. Agent: Mrs. J. S. Luithlen, 36 Highgate Drive, Knighton, Leicester. Address: c/o Coutts and Company Ltd., 59 The Strand, London W.C.2, England.

CRIME PUBLICATIONS

Novels

Bracknell's Law.   New York, Harper, 1975; London, Hamish Hamilton, 1976.
The Weirdown Experiment.   New York, Harper, and London, Hamish Hamilton, 1976.
Vandals.   London, Hamish Hamilton, 1977.
The Loop.   London, Hamish Hamilton, 1977.

OTHER PUBLICATIONS

Novels

Bed and Work.   London, Faber, 1962.
A Town on the Never.   London, Faber, 1963.
Lunch with Ashurbanipal.   London, Faber, 1965.

Fiction for Children as E. W. Hildick

Jim Starling.   London, Chatto and Windus, 1958.
Jim Starling and the Agency.   London, Chatto and Windus, 1958.
Jim Starling and the Colonel.   London, Heinemann, 1960; New York, Doubleday, 1968.
Jim Starling's Holiday.   London, Heinemann, 1960.
The Boy at the Window.   London, Chatto and Windus, 1960.
Jim Starling Takes Over.   London, Blond, 1963; revised edition, London, New English Library, 1971.
Jim Starling and the Spotted Dog.   London, Blond, 1963.
Jim Starling Goes to Town.   London, Blond, 1963.
Meet Lemon Kelly.   London, Cape, 1963; as *Lemon Kelly*, New York, Doubleday, 1968.
Birdy Jones.   London, Faber, 1963; Harrisburg, Pennsylvania, Stackpole, 1969.
Mapper Mundy's Treasure Hunt.   London, Blond, 1963.
Lemon Kelly Digs Deep.   London, Cape, 1964.
Louie's Lot.   London, Faber, 1965; New York, David White, 1968.
The Questers.   Leicester, Brockhampton Press, 1966; New York, Hawthorn Books, 1970.
Calling Questers Four.   Leicester, Brockhampton Press, 1967.
The Questers and the Whispering Spy.   Leicester, Brockhampton Press, 1967.
Lucky Les: The Adventures of a Cat of Five Tales.   London, Blond, 1967.
Lemon Kelly and the Home-Made Boy.   London, Dobson, 1968.
Louie's S.O.S.   London, Pan, 1968; New York, Doubleday, 1970.
Birdy and the Group.   London, Pan, 1968; Harrisburg, Pennsylvania, Stackpole, 1969.
Here Comes Parren.   London, Macmillan, 1968; Cleveland, World, 1972.
Back with Parren.   London, Macmillan, 1968.
Birdy Swings North.   London, Pan, 1969; Harrisburg, Pennsylvania, Stackpole, 1971.
Manhattan Is Missing.   New York, Doubleday, 1969; London, Stacey, 1972.
Top Boy at Twisters Creek.   New York, David White, 1969.
Birdy in Amsterdam.   London, Pan, 1970; Harrisburg, Pennsylvania, Stackpole, 1971.
Ten Thousand Golden Cockerels.   London, Evans, 1970.
The Dragon That Lived under Manhattan.   New York, Crown, 1970.

The Secret Winners. New York, Crown, 1970.

The Secret Spenders. New York, Crown, 1971.

The Prisoners of Gridling Gap: A Report, With Expert Comments from Doctor Ranulf Quitch. New York, Doubleday, 1971; London. Stacey, 1973.

My Kid Sister. Cleveland, World, 1971; Leicester, Brockhampton Press, 1973.

The Doughnut Dropout. New York, Doubleday, 1972.

Kids Commune. New York, David White, 1972.

The Active-Enzyme Lemon-Freshened Junior High School Witch. New York, Doubleday, 1973.

The Nose Knows. New York, Grosset and Dunlap, 1973; London, Hodder and Stoughton, 1974.

Birdy Jones and the New York Heads. New York, Doubleday, 1974.

Dolls in Danger. London, Hodder and Stoughton, 1974; as *Deadline for McGurk*, New York, Macmillan, 1975.

Louie's Snowstorm. New York, Doubleday, 1974; London, Deutsch, 1975.

The Menaced Midget. London, Hodder and Stoughton, 1975.

The Case of the Condemned Cat. London, Hodder and Stoughton, and New York, Macmillan, 1975.

Time Explorers Inc. New York, Doubleday, 1976.

A Cat Called Amnesia. New York, David White, 1976; London, Deutsch, 1977.

The Case of the Nervous Newsboy. London, Hodder and Stoughton, and New York, Macmillan, 1976.

The Great Rabbit Robbery. London, Hodder and Stoughton, 1976; as *The Great Rabbit Rip-Off*, New York, Macmillan, 1977.

The Top-Flight Fully-Automated Junior High School Girl Detective. New York, Doubleday, 1977; as *The Top-Flight Fully-Automated Girl Detective*, London, Deutsch, 1979.

The Case of the Invisible Dog. London, Hodder and Stoughton, and New York, Macmillan, 1977.

Louie's Ransom. New York, Knopf, 1978; London, Deutsch, 1979.

The Case of the Secret Scribbler. London, Hodder and Stoughton, and New York, Macmillan, 1978.

The Case of the Phantom Frog. New York, Macmillan, and London, Hodder and Stoughton, 1979.

Other

Word for Word: A Study of Authors' Alterations, with Exercises. London, Faber, 1965; abridged edition, as *Word for Word: The Rewriting of Fiction*, New York, Norton, 1966.

A Close Look at Newspapers [*Magazines and Comics, Television, Advertising*] (juveniles; as E. W. Hildick). London, Faber, 4 vols., 1966–69.

Writing with Care: 200 Problems in the Use of English. London, Weidenfeld and Nicolson, and New York, David White, 1967.

Thirteen Types of Narrative. London, Macmillan, 1968; New York, Clarkson N. Potter, 1970.

Monte Carlo or Bust! London, Sphere, 1969; as *Those Daring Young Men in Their Jaunty Jalopies*, New York, Berkley, 1969.

Children and Fiction: A Critical Study in Depth of the Artistic and Psychological Factors Involved in Writing Fiction for and about Children. London, Evans, 1970; Cleveland, World, 1971; revised edition, Evans, 1974.

Cokerheaton (textbook; as E. W. Hildick). London, Evans, 1971.

Rushbrook (textbook; as E. W. Hildick). London, Evans, 1971.

Storypacks: A New Concept in English Teaching (as E. W. Hildick). London, Evans, 1971.
Only the Best: Six Qualities of Excellence. New York, Clarkson N. Potter, 1973.

* * *

Hildick writes two kinds of mysteries for two kinds of audiences. As E. W. Hildick he writes mysteries for young people; as Wallace Hildick he writes mysteries for adults. Curiously, the juveniles come off better than the adult books.

Two typical juveniles are *Louie's S.O.S.* and *The Case of the Condemned Cat.* In *Louie's S.O.S.* the mystery begins when Louie the milkman's customers begin to find odd things in their milk (cigarette butts, gum, dead goldfish, false teeth). Louie's young helpers, along with some of Louie's older ex-helpers, trap the real perpetrators into confessing. This is a credible juvenile police procedural novel. The narrative is quick-paced, with a lot of humor and offbeat wit. As in most literature for young people, the characterizations are weak, the conflict is clear-cut, and there is very little ambiguity. In *The Case of the Condemned Cat*, one of a series featuring 11-year-old Jack McGurk and his "organization" (Willie, Wanda, and Joey), the characterization is fuller, the conflict is not quite so clear-cut, and there is at least the suspicion of ambiguity. In this story the McGurk Organization proves that Whiskers the cat is innocent of killing a neighbor's dove. How they prove it is entertaining and clever, even involving some good detection. Though McGurk is a bit too precocious, the writing is concise, the author is not condescending, and the first-person narrative is effective.

Hildick's adult works, however, tend to be wordy, contrived, and slow moving. In *Bracknell's Law*, for example, Pat Bracknell finds a notebook in her husband Ron's toolbox that outlines a number of "laws" about killing people. The notebooks also offer both the details of murders Ron claims to have committed and newspaper clippings of the deeds. The story is told entirely in diary form (Pat's entries and *verbatim* excerpts from the notebooks). Though this purports to be a psychological thriller, character analysis/development is minimal. There are flashes of humor, and the novel does move more quickly near the end of the story — but it failed to hold this reader's interest.

—Donald J. Pattow

HILL, Reginald. Also writes as Dick Morland; Patrick Ruell; Charles Underhill. British. Born in Hartlepool, County Durham, 3 April 1936. Educated at the Grammar School, Carlisle, Cumberland, 1947–55; St. Catherine's College, Oxford, 1957–60, B.A. (honours) in English 1960. Served in the Border Regiment, British Army, 1955–57. Married Patricia Ruell in 1960. Student Officer, British Council, Edinburgh, 1960–61; Schoolmaster, Essex, 1962–67. Since 1967, Lecturer, Doncaster College of Education, Yorkshire. Agent: Caradoc King, A. P. Watt and Son, 26–28 Bedford Row, London WC1R 4HL. Address: 89 Armthorpe Road, Doncaster, Yorkshire DN2 5LY, England.

CRIME PUBLICATIONS

Novels (series character: Superintendent Andrew Dalziel)

A Clubbable Woman (Dalziel). London, Collins, 1970.
Fell of Dark. London, Collins, 1971.

An Advancement of Learning (Dalziel).   London, Collins, 1971.
A Fairly Dangerous Thing.   London, Collins, 1972.
Ruling Passion (Dalziel).   London, Collins, 1973; New York, Harper, 1977.
A Very Good Hater.   London, Collins, 1974.
An April Shroud (Dalziel).   London, Collins, 1975.
Another Death in Venice.   London, Collins, 1976.
A Pinch of Snuff (Dalziel).   London, Collins, and New York, Harper, 1978.

Novels as Patrick Ruell

The Castle of the Demon.   London, Long, 1971; New York, Hawthorn, 1973.
Red Christmas.   London, Long, 1972; New York, Hawthorn, 1974.
Death Takes the Low Road.   London, Hutchinson, 1974.
Urn Burial.   London, Hutchinson, 1975.

Short Stories

Pascoe's Ghost.   London, Collins, 1979.

OTHER PUBLICATIONS

Novels

Heart Clock (as Dick Morland).   London, Faber, 1973.
Albion! Albion! (as Dick Morland).   London, Faber, 1974.
Captain Fantom (as Charles Underhill).   London, Hutchinson, 1978.
The Forging of Fantom (as Charles Underhill).   London, Hutchinson, 1979.

Play

Television Play: *An Affair of Honour*, 1972.

Other

"The Educator: The Case of the Screaming Spires," in *Murder Ink: The Mystery Reader's Companion*, edited by Dilys Winn.   New York, Workman, 1977.
"Sherlock Holmes: The Hamlet of Crime Fiction," in *Crime Writers*, edited by H. R. F. Keating.   London, BBC Publications, 1978.

Reginald Hill comments:
The crime fiction I write under my own name divides easily into two categories. First there are those books that feature my two police detectives Superintendent Dalziel (pronounced Dee-ell) and Sergeant (later Inspector) Pascoe. They are set mainly in Yorkshire and are concerned with the official investigations of crimes by two men who are absolutely contrasted in background, attitudes, and approach, but are forced to admit grudging respect for each other.
The second category covers the rest: individual novels with no connection. They all contain crime but not all contain detection. They are about characters into whose lives crime comes, sometimes tragically, sometimes comically, often both.
Both categories, I hope, share one thing – well-shaped plots. Plot is the basis of narrative

interest, that force that drives a reader along paths which ahead seem totally mysterious, but behind appear clear as day. It is easy to mystify. The good mystery writer's real skill lies in clarification which must be done without evasion, without dishonesty, and above all without the tedium of long-windedness. So here I'll stop!

*   *   *

The creator of the popular Inspector Dalziel novels, Reginald Hill has also written mystery/suspense stories under the name Patrick Ruell. His first novel, *A Clubbable Woman*, was widely praised as a book which defied classification into any of the genres or sub-genres of crime fiction. Introducing the fat, Yorkshire detective superintendent Andrew Dalziel and his Sergeant Peter Pascoe, the novel combines something of the bawdiness of Joyce Porter's Inspector Dover books with the more sober vision of recent continental crime novelists. In successive Dalziel novels, Hill's vision becomes increasingly dark, as Sergeant Pascoe, questioning the methods of his own profession from the standpoint of a liberal, university-educated man of the 20th century, becomes embroiled in increasingly sordid and confusing crimes.

The dominant quality of Hill's works, particularly of the Dalziel novels, is their literateness; they are, however, saved from donnishness by the robust character of Dalziel himself. Peter Pascoe's introspective, intellectual approach to his job is balanced by the blunt vulgarity of his North Country boss. The blending of humour and philosophy is nowhere so apparent as in *A Fairly Dangerous Thing*, in which Pascoe gets married and Dalziel falls in love. The sheer human interest and topicality of the Dalziel books is complemented by the author's skill with plot; solution of the crime is both interesting in itself and significant in its effect on the development of the character of Peter Pascoe. The total effect is light, but penetrating, providing satisfaction of a very high order.

Of the books which do not feature Dalziel and Pascoe, a noteworthy example is *A Very Good Hater*, subtitled "A Tale of Revenge." It is the story of Goldsmith, a local politician with a future in national politics, and Templewood, an ebullient salesman. The two men meet every year at their regimental reunion. On one of these occasions, they encounter a man who resembles Hebbel, a Nazi war criminal both men have sworn to kill. From this point, the novel unfolds with twist after twist, revealing secret after secret of the two pursuers, as well as of their quarry. Goldsmith, in particular, becomes deeply involved with the family of the man who resembles Hebbel, and his career, his freedom, his very existence are threatened before the novel reveals Hill's final turn of the screw. As in the Dalziel books, Hill is particularly acute in portraying the conflicts between public and private life, and the potentiality for corruption which lurks behind the most seemingly transparent public mask.

The Reginald Hill novels are difficult to classify, but they are a combination of detective and crime stories. Those written as Patrick Ruell are more formulaic: they are suspense stories with a strong romantic interest. There is in each of them an element of espionage which adds to the confusion as identities become revealed and crimes occur. The novels are characterised by a literate, light touch which masks admirable plot construction. Like many espionage thrillers, these are essentially fantasies, but the author is so deft that we believe in them without reservation. In *Red Christmas* a group of holiday-makers descend upon Dingley Dell, a country hotel designed with an outrageous Dickensian motif. In the midst of fancy-dress activities on Christmas Eve, two murders occur. The guests are all trapped in the hotel by a blizzard. And Miss Arabella Allen discovers that her hotel room has a peephole in the ceiling. Each chapter is prefaced by an appropriate quotation from Dickens, lending a charming air to what is, nevertheless, an exciting thriller. In *Death Takes the Low Road*, William Blake Hazlitt, an up-and-coming Deputy Registrar at the University of Lincoln, disappears under suspicious circumstances; it is only after a terrifying three-way chase through Scotland that he is united with Caroline Nevis, an American student. Ruell's portrayal of espionage at a university is both convincing and amusing. All the Patrick Ruell novels contain heroines of special vivacity and intelligence, making these the most intellectually satisfying of modern romance/thrillers. His unique blend of the elements of the romance, crime thriller, and spy story is both original and versatile, even as the combination of Andrew Dalziel and Peter Pascoe reflects the same qualities in his detective fiction.

—Joanne Harack Hayne

HILLERMAN, Tony. American. Born in Sacred Heart, Oklahoma, 27 May 1925. Raised among Pottawatomie and Seminole Indians; attended Indian boarding school for eight years; Oklahoma State University, Stillwater; University of Oklahoma, Norman, B.A. in journalism 1948; University of New Mexico, Albuquerque, M.A. in English 1965. Served in the United States Army Infantry during World War II: Silver Star, Bronze Star, Purple Heart. Married Marie E. Unzner in 1948; three daughters and three sons. Reporter, *News Herald*, Borger, Texas, 1948; News Editor, *Morning Press*, 1949, and City Editor, *Constitution*, 1950, Lawton, Oklahoma; Political Reporter, United Press, Oklahoma City, 1952; Bureau Manager, United Press, Santa Fe, New Mexico, 1953; Executive Editor, *The New Mexican*, Santa Fe, 1954. Associate Professor 1965–66, since 1966, Professor of Journalism and Chairman of Department, and since 1975, Assistant to the President, University of New Mexico. Recipient: Burrows Award, for journalism; Shaffer Award, for reporting, 1952; Mystery Writers of America Edgar Allan Poe Award, 1974. Agent: Curtis Brown Ltd., 575 Madison Avenue, New York, New York 10022. Address: 2729 Texas N.E., Albuquerque, New Mexico 87110, U.S.A.

CRIME PUBLICATIONS

Novels (series character: Lieutenant Joe Leaphorn)

> *The Blessing Way* (Leaphorn). New York, Harper, and London, Macmillan, 1970.
> *The Fly on the Wall.* New York, Harper, 1971.
> *Dance Hall of the Dead* (Leaphorn). New York, Harper, 1973.
> *The Listening Woman* (Leaphorn). New York, Harper, 1978.

OTHER PUBLICATIONS

Other

> *The Great Taos Bank Robbery and Other Affairs of Indian Country* (essays). Albuquerque, University of New Mexico Press, 1970.
> *The Boy Who Made Dragonfly* (juvenile). New York, Harper, 1972.
> *New Mexico.* Portland, Oregon, Graphic Arts Center Press, 1975.
> *Rio Grande.* Portland, Oregon, Graphic Arts Center Press, 1976.

Editor, *The Spell of New Mexico.* Albquerque, University of New Mexico Press, 1977.

Tony Hillerman comments:
  Novels of mystery and suspense seem to be an ideal way to engage readers in a subject of life-long interest to me – the religions, cultures, and value systems of Navajo and Pueblo Indians. To play the game as it should be played, I think the setting must be genuine – the reader must be shown the Indian reservation as it is today. More important, my Navajo tribal

policeman's knowledge of his people, their customs, and their values must be germane to the plot. More than that, the details must be exactly accurate – from the way a hogan is built, to the way a sweat bath is taken, to the way it looks, and sounds, and smells at an Enemy Way Ceremonial at 2:00 A.M. on a wintry morning.

It has been a great source of pleasure to me that both Navajos and Zuñis have recognized themselves and their society in my books. They are heavily used in schools on both reservations and – for that matter – throughout the Indian world by other tribes. In fact, the authenticity of ceremonial details in *Dance Hall of the Dead* caused Zuñi elders to cross-examine me about whether members of their kiva societies had revealed secrets to me.

The background must be authentic. *But*, the name of the game is mystery and suspense. What's really important is the narration which moves against the authentic background. I feel strongly that in our genre, the reader must be caught up quickly and moved rapidly along. I like to keep my novels in a very tight time frame.

*   *   *

Tony Hillerman, after finishing one career as a journalist and taking up another as a Professor of Journalism, set up shop as a detective novelist in 1970 with *The Blessing Way*, the first of three novels featuring Navaho police lieutenant Joe Leaphorn. All three have won consistently, and deservedly, high praise, because there are three novels compacted into every Leaphorn chronicle. There is a taut suspense story, a highly competent police procedural novel, and a traditional western adventure, in which nature sets the atmosphere and tests the character of resourceful, but not superhuman, people. The special appeal of these novels is the fascinating background of Navaho and Zuñi religion that Hillerman interweaves with character and plot.

Joe Leaphorn polices the 25,000 square miles of the Navaho reservation in Arizona. He embodies the best detective skills of the white and Indian worlds: he takes pleasure in logic, he exhibits an Indian patience in unraveling physical and psychological clues, and he is a first-rate tracker. The reader shares the hunt with Leaphorn, and is the more impressed by him because he has so few of the support systems of the modern urban policeman. Communications are not instant on the reservation, information arrives late and full of holes, and when Leaphorn needs fast information from an Indian, he has to allow for the preliminary half hour of small talk that courtesy demands.

These obstacles make Leaphorn's pursuit of an elusive witness or a faceless killer the more exciting. And Leaphorn's hunt is never the only one going on: there are usually two or three hunts in progress, and all but Leaphorn's are to the death. In *The Blessing Way*, while Leaphorn searches for the murderer of a young fugitive, anthropologist Bergen McKee looks for sociological explanations for Navaho Wolf rumors, until a modern Navaho wolf turns the hunt on him. McKee has almost lost his grip on the goodness of life, and his story is typical of Hillerman's normal method of character development: the test by ordeal. McKee passes his, and survives an encounter with one of the deracinated modern killers that Hillerman portrays with chilling authority. In *Dance Hall of the Dead*, Leaphorn hunts a 14-year-old Zuñi boy who witnessed the apparently motiveless murder of his friend. The killer is also after young George Bowlegs, and Leaphorn gets help from a young woman hippie, who proves that her head is much clearer than that of her graduate student fiancé. Leaphorn finds the killer, but insufficient proof for an arrest. The Zuñi people, however, whose gods have been profaned, also find the killer. In *The Listening Woman*, as in *The Blessing Way*, the villain is a young Navaho who has been cut off from the traditional life of his people. Frank Tso, armed with revolutionary tactics and perhaps the scariest dog since the Hound of the Baskervilles, makes a formidable opponent for Leaphorn.

Several solid journalistic virtues adorn these books: a clean disciplined style, a respect for fact, and lucid exposition of whatever is relevant to the story, from Indian mythology, to the formation of limestone caves, to the tangle of conflicting police jurisdictions. In *Fly on the Wall*, a story of political corruption set in a Midwestern city, the hero is a political reporter who wrestles with the ethical problems of modern journalism while trying to stay alive long enough to file his story. As with the Leaphorn books, this one works twice as hard as most suspense novels and makes it look twice as easy.

—Carol Cleveland

HILTON, James. See **TREVOR, Glen**.

HILTON, John Buxton. British. Born in Buxton, Derbyshire, 8 June 1921. Educated at The College, Buxton, 1931–39; Pembroke College, Cambridge, 1939–41, 1946, B.A. in modern and medieval languages 1943, M.A. and Cert. Ed. 1946. Served in the Royal Artillery, 1941–43, and the Intelligence Corps, 1943–46: mentioned in despatches. Married 1) Mary Skitmore in 1943 (died, 1968), three daughters; 2) Rebecca Adams in 1969. Language Teacher, Royds Hall School, Huddersfield, Yorkshire, 1946–47; Language Teacher, Chatham House School, Ramsgate, Kent, 1947–53; Head of the Languages Department, King Edward VI School, Chelmsford, Essex, 1953–57; Headmaster, Chorley Grammar School, Lancashire, 1957–64; Inspector of Schools, Department of Education and Science, London, 1964–70; part-time Tutor-Counsellor, Open University, Milton Keynes, Buckinghamshire, 1971–78. Agent: Curtis Brown Ltd., 1 Craven Hill, London W2 3EP. Address: The White House, West Church Street, Kenninghall, Norfolk NR16 2EN, England.

CRIME PUBLICATIONS

Novels (series characters: Inspector Thomas Brunt; Superintendent Simon Kenworthy)

Death of an Alderman (Kenworthy). London, Cassell, and New York, Walker, 1968.
Death in Midwinter (Kenworthy). London, Cassell, and New York, Walker, 1969.
Hangman's Tide (Kenworthy). London, Macmillan, and New York, St. Martin's Press, 1975.
No Birds Sang (Kenworthy). London, Macmillan, 1975; New York, St. Martin's Press, 1976.
Rescue from the Rose (Brunt). London, Macmillan, and New York, St. Martin's Press, 1976.
Gamekeeper's Gallows (Brunt). London, Macmillan, 1976; New York, St. Martin's Press, 1977.
Dead-Nettle (Brunt). London, Macmillan, and New York, St. Martin's Press, 1977.
Some Run Crooked (Kenworthy). London, Macmillan, and New York, St. Martin's Press, 1978.
The Anathema Stone (Kenworthy). London, Collins, and New York, St. Martin's Press, 1980.

Uncollected Short Stories

"Taken at the Ebb," in *Winter's Crimes 7*, edited by George Hardinge. London, Macmillan, 1975.
"Bellany's Bus," in *Winter's Crimes 8*, edited by Hilary Watson. London, Macmillan, 1976.

"Saskja," in *Winter's Crimes 10*, edited by Hilary Watson.   London, Macmillan, 1978.

OTHER PUBLICATIONS

Other

The Language Laboratory in School.   London, Methuen, 1964.
Language Teaching: A Systems Approach.   London, Methuen, 1973.

John Buxton Hilton comments:
I suppose I am less interested in puzzles – and certainly less in violence – than in character, local colour, folk-lore, social history, and historical influences, most of which loom large in most of my books. With these ingredients I try to write the sort of books that I wish I could find to read. I believe that the distinction between suspense fiction and the "literary" novel is an unreal one and my effort is to bridge the gap. Consequently I believe that my books should appeal to readers of some literary sensitivity who do not normally read "thrillers."

*   *   *

John Buxton Hilton's greatest talent is his ability to evoke the essence of a turn-of-the-century northern English mountain village where a few families have lived in isolation for centuries, some on the same land. From that situation flow the tangled love-hate relationships between villagers and gentry that generations later cause murder. In book after book, Hilton brings to life the villagers' inbred suspiciousness, their pervasive secretiveness, primitive tribesmanship, convoluted loyalties, twisted intolerance, and arrogant ignorance. "I suppose there might be circumstances under which they could be tolerant of what they do not understand," ironically comments CID Sergeant Thomas Brunt, narrator of *Dead-Nettle*, about the men of Margreave.

The three novels featuring Brunt, set in 1877 (*Gamekeeper's Gallows*), 1904 (*Dead-Nettle*), and 1911 (*Rescue from the Rose*), are Hilton's best to date. In addition to solid historical information and well-wrought situations, they have a flow of language that is compelling. There's no way of knowing with accuracy what late 19th-century language among the partially educated such as Brunt might have been, but the author's imaginative transcription makes more of it than reality likely would have provided – giving it not only direction, but also dignity and rhythm.

Of the three, *Dead-Nettle* achieves distinction. For the first half of the book Brunt reconstructs events before a murder from his interviews after it. The second half takes place after Brunt is called in to investigate. A village near abandoned lead mines in the Derbyshire hills is the locale, with the standard complement of villagers. Frank Lomas, an outsider come to mine after his Army discharge, is surely a most hapless hero, while his lover, the daughter of a new and unaccepted local "squire," is surely the most modern heroine among late Victorians, with appealing directness and courage. The telling clue is handled rather clumsily, but this is not a major flaw.

All Hilton's novels span wide ranges of time. After his first, *Death of an Alderman*, he abandoned immediate reasons for murder in favor of those from the increasingly distant past – 30 years removed, 50 years removed, to 200 years removed in *Some Run Croooked*. This book covers three murders: one was committed in 1758, one in 1940, and one in present time. In each of the three, Hilton duplicates situation, characters, place, motivation, and method, finishing in a string-tying blaze of glory, complete with sufficient remains of the 1758 corpse to solve *that* murder, too. Agatha Christie didn't strain her readers' loyal credulity quite that much even in her last pathetic, backward-looking novels.

Scotland Yard's Inspector Simon Kenworthy is Hilton's contemporary detective: unorthodox, quixotic, mercurial, apparently inattentive and sloppy in his methods, but actually surefooted and incisive. He drives his sergeants up the wall, but gets results. Finally, though, it is the villages, their inhabitants, the local lore, the winter scenes, and, in one or two books, the quality of language – as well as solid detection – that constitute Hilton's contribution to the genre.

—Pearl G. Aldrich

HIMES, Chester (Bomar). American. Born in Jefferson City, Missouri, 29 July 1909. Educated at Ohio State University, Columbus, 1926–28. Married Jean Lucinda Johnson in 1937. Worked with the Works Progress Administration (WPA) Writers' Project in Ohio. Served seven years in prison. Recipient: Rosenwald Fellowship, 1944; Grand Prix de Littérature Policière, 1958. Address: c/o William Morrow and Company, 105 Madison Avenue, New York, New York 10016, U.S.A.

CRIME PUBLICATIONS

Novels (series characters: Coffin Ed Johnson and Grave Digger Jones in all books except *Run Man Run* and *Une Affaire de Viol*; all books except *Blind Man with a Pistol* originally published in French by Gallimard, Paris)

> *For Love of Imabelle.* New York, Fawcett, 1959; as *A Rage in Harlem*, New York, Avon, 1965; London, Panther, 1969.
> *The Crazy Kill.* New York, Avon, 1959; London, Panther, 1968.
> *The Real Cool Killers.* New York, Avon, 1959; London, Panther, 1969.
> *All Shot Up.* New York, Avon, 1960; London, Panther, 1969.
> *The Big Gold Dream.* New York, Avon, 1960; London, Panther, 1968.
> *Cotton Comes to Harlem.* New York, Putnam, and London, Muller, 1965.
> *The Heat's On.* New York, Putnam, and London, Muller, 1966; as *Come Back, Charleston Blue*, New York, Berkley, 1970.
> *Run Man Run.* New York, Putnam, 1966; London, Muller, 1967.
> *Une Affaire de Viol.* Paris, Les Yeux Ouverts, 1968.
> *Blind Man with a Pistol.* New York, Morrow, and London, Hodder and Stoughton, 1969; as *Hot Day, Hot Night*, New York, Dell, 1970.

OTHER PUBLICATIONS

Novels

> *If He Hollers Let Him Go.* New York, Doubleday, 1945; London, Falcon Press, 1947.
> *Lonely Crusade.* New York, Knopf, 1947; London, Grey Walls Press, 1950.
> *Cast the First Stone.* New York, Coward McCann, 1953.
> *The Third Generation.* Cleveland, World, 1954.
> *The Primitive.* New York, New American Library, 1955.
> *Pinktoes.* Paris, Olympia Press, 1961; New York, Putnam, and London, Barker, 1965.

Other

> *The Quality of Hurt* (autobiography). New York, Doubleday, 1972; London, Joseph, 1973.

Black on Black, Baby Sister, and Selected Writings. New York, Doubleday, and London, Joseph, 1975.
My Life of Absurdity (autobiography). New York, Doubleday, 1976.

*   *   *

Like Raymond Chandler, Chester Himes was nearly fifty when he began to write detective novels. But the careers of those two leading American writers of crime fiction were quite different: Chandler, with his English gentleman's upbringing, was a director of oil companies, whereas Himes, after seven years in the Ohio State Penitentiary, became an aggressive Negro novelist and after his first success was down and out in Paris. Himes once claimed some connection with the hard-boiled school in an interview: "When I could see the end of my time inside I bought myself a typewriter and taught myself touch typing. I'd been reading stories by Dashiell Hammett in *Black Mask* and I thought I could do them just as well. When my stories finally appeared, the other convicts thought exactly the same thing. There was nothing to it. All you had to do was tell it like it is."

Yet he became a writer of detective novels purely by chance. He accepted the proposal of Marcel Duhamel – editor of the famous *Série Noire* of Gallimard – to write a detective novel in the American style, for the French in the 1950's were very impressed by the American hard-boiled school. His first book, *La Reine des pommes* (later called *For Love of Imabelle* and *A Rage in Harlem*) was an instant success. It secured the "Grand Prix de Littérature Policière" of 1958 for Himes. With the exception of *Run Man Run* Himes kept to his successful formula, creating a violent and funny microcosm in nine novels which he later ironically named "Harlem domestic detective stories." In France (and later in Germany) Himes was accepted as a serious novelist who wrote sociological crime novels (Chandler once protested against this labelling), but America was wary. After the success of the sex satire *Pinktoes* his novels were sold in the "sex and soul" category, promising the reader "lush sex and stark violence, colored Black and served up raw by a great Negro writer." Once again, as so often in America, commercialism was taking over, selling literature under an incorrect label. Of course, there are sex and violence in Himes's novels, but this doesn't make him a disciple of Mickey Spillane.

In discussing the merits of Himes it would be too easy to state that he has augmented the world of fictional detectives by creating two unforgettable characters: Grave Digger Jones and Coffin Ed Johnson. They are tough and violent, and (though they are not private eyes, but official Harlem policemen) they are still in some way "the cowboys adapted to life on the city streets," as Leslie Fiedler once phrased it. But Jones and Johnson are no flat characters like so many fictional detectives; they are in some way tragic heroes: fighting for the law against their corrupt soul brothers, becoming more cynical and disillusioned with every successive novel, their compassion gradually turning into emptiness and cynicism. At the end of *Blind Man with a Pistol* there is a scene where in a world of chaos they are shooting rats with their famous nickel-plated 38's. Himes once stated that "the only way the American Negro will ever be able to participate in the American way of life is by a series of acts of violence. It's tragic, but it's true," and he wanted to end his series with "a final book" in which his heroes get killed, trying to prevent a black revolution: "But I had to stop. The violence shocks even me."

Violence as an American experience becomes an artistic form in the novels of Chester Himes. Like Hammett and Chandler (or Hemingway) he presents violence without any emotional attachment, acting as a sort of camera eye. But he adds a special finesse to this technique, the qualities of the grotesque and absurd. The moral element, the clear division of the fictional world into goodies and baddies, is missing. People die by chance, walking through Harlem with knives in their backs, knives in their heads, burning to death in a church, driving along on a motorcycle and beheaded by a truck carrying steel blades. As one critic has stated, this is nearer to the world of Hieronymous Bosch than to any conventional treatment of violence. Though Himes always maintained that he stayed within the tradiiton – "I haven't created anything whatsoever; I just made the faces black, that's all" – he clearly gave a new quality to the American detective novel. Superficially he stayed within the limits of the detective novel by employing clearly defined heroes, elements of detection, fast moving action, and the denouement at the end. But even with the loving description of his soul brothers, his gentle humour is deceptive: like his heroes, Himes becomes more and more bitter and cynical. Even if he claims that he is telling it as it is, he transcends the genre (as Hammett and Chandler did in their best novels), writing no longer formula stories but sociological crime novels. "To tell it like it is," to have a message, means the end of the orthodox detective novel.

"To accept a mediocre form and make something like literature out of it": Raymond Chandler wrote in a letter two years before his death, the very year Himes published his first detective novel. And here Himes is a true follower of Chandler, for he made literature out of a mediocre form, or as Raymond Nelson phrased it in his essay on Himes (*Virginia Quarterly Review 48*, 1972):

> we may be grateful for the substantial achievement he has already wrung from an improbable genre, and salute both the integrity and the force of the imagination that conceived it. If the vehicle itself is small, Himes's accomplishments within it are not, and the residual portrait left by these books – of Coffin Ed and Grave Digger outlined against the dull, lurid light of a criminal city – is one of the compelling images of our time.

—Jens Peter Becker

HIRSCHBERG, Cornelius. American. Born in Mt. Vernon, New York, 28 March 1901. Educated in public schools through age fourteen. Married in 1925; one daughter. Held many jobs in retail business, 1915–73; the last with Yormark Watch Company, 1959–73. Recipient: Franklin Society award; Mystery Writers of America Edgar Allan Poe Award, 1964. Agent: John Schaffner Literary Agency, 425 East 51st Street, New York, New York 10022. Address: 64 Hawthorne Place, Montclair, New Jersey 07042, U.S.A.

CRIME PUBLICATIONS

Novel

Florentine Finish. New York, Harper, 1963; London, Gollancz, 1964.

OTHER PUBLICATIONS

Other

The Priceless Gift (autobiography). New York, Simon and Schuster, 1959.

*   *   *

At age 62, Cornelius Hirschberg published his only crime story, *Florentine Finish*, a swiftly paced murder tale which richly brings to life the jewelry market on New York's West 47th Street, a market Hirschberg learned working many years as a jewelry salesman. His use of the commercial setting is as intriguing, as informed and informing, and as central to his story as Wall Street's banking milieu is to any of Emma Lathen's Judge Thatcher stories, although Hirschberg's style is closer to the hard-boiled mode, with its colloquial language, violence, and isolated and cynical, but finally somehow sentimental, hero.

The book's narrator, Saul Handy, an ex-Chicago policeman turned New York jewelry salesman, begins his story with a simple "private deal" – an off-the-job diamond sale. That sale leads Handy into the intrigues of black-market jewelry and finally into three brutal murders, with Handy the fall guy until he unravels the mysteries. The story's violence itself may seem at times a bit coy: Handy unknowingly drags a bloody body, half in the back seat of his car and half out, along the street for blocks before a police-man stops him and asks, "Who's your friend?" And the book has its stock hard-boiled characters and situations: Rose, the "blonde (at least to the eye), round, solid, and mature" waitress at the White Lily tavern is Handy's confidante; beautiful Lily Moselle, wife of a rich New York jeweler, tries to seduce Handy, but he lives by his code: "I could see Moselle ready to cover me to do the right thing" – and so escapes with his virtue.

And as the story closes, the rootless hero (he lives in a hotel room) sentimentally recalls that "it was time to go home; a destination I had failed to provide." In sum, *Florentine Finish* is both an exciting addition to the hard-boiled canon and an intriguing picture of New York's jewelry trade.

—Elmer Pry

HITCHENS, Bert.   See **OLSEN, D. B.**

HITCHENS, Dolores.   See **OLSEN, D. B.**

HOBART, Robertson.   See **CORRIGAN, Mark**.

HOCH, Edward D(entinger).   Also writes as Irwin Booth; Stephen Dentinger; Pat McMahon; R. L. Stevens; Mr. X.   American.   Born in Rochester, New York, 22 February 1930. Educated at the University of Rochester, New York, 1947–49. Served in the United

States Army, 1950–52. Married Patricia A. McMahon in 1957. Worked at Rochester Public Library, 1949–50; Pocket Books, New York City, 1952–54; Hutchins Advertising Company, Rochester, 1954–68. Since 1968, self-employed writer. Member, Board of Directors, Mystery Writers of America. Recipient: Mystery Writers of America Edgar Allan Poe Award, for short story, 1968. Agent: Larry Sternig, 742 Robertson Street, Milwaukee, Wisconsin 53213. Address: 2941 Lake Avenue, Rochester, New York 14612, U.S.A.

CRIME PUBLICATIONS

Novels (series characters: Carl Crader and Earl Jazine)

The Shattered Raven. New York, Lancer, 1969; London, Hale, 1970.
The Transvection Machine (Crader and Jazine). New York, Walker, 1971; London, Hale, 1974.
The Fellowship of the Hand (Crader and Jazine). New York, Walker, 1973; London, Hale, 1976.
The Frankenstein Factory (Crader and Jazine). New York, Warner, 1975; London, Hale, 1976

Short Stories

The Judges of Hades and Other Simon Ark Stories. North Hollywood, California, Leisure Books, 1971.
City of Brass and Other Simon Ark Stories. North Hollywood, California, Leisure Books, 1971.
The Spy and the Thief. New York, Davis, 1971.
The Thefts of Nick Velvet. Yonkers, New York, Mysterious Press, 1978.

Uncollected Short Stories

"The Man from Nowhere," in *Famous Detective* (New York), June 1956.
"Getaway," in *Murder!* (New York), September 1956.
"The Wolves of Werclaw," in *Famous Detective* (New York), October 1956.
"The Chippy" (as Irwin Booth), in *Guilty Detective* (New York), November 1956.
"Inspector Fleming's Last Case," in *Crime and Justice* (New York), January 1957.
"Blood in the Stands," in *Terror Detective* (New York), February 1957.
"Jealous Lover," in *Crime and Justice* (New York), March 1957.
"The Naked Corpse," in *Killers Mystery Story* (New York), March 1957.
"Execution on Clover Street," in *Murder!* (New York), March 1957.
"Serpent in Paradise," in *Crack Detective* (New York), April 1957.
"Killer Cop" (as Irwin Booth), in *Terror Detective* (New York), April 1957.
"Twelve for Eternity," in *Crack Detective* (New York), July 1957.
"The Last Darkness," in *Fast Action Detective* (New York), August 1957.
"Darkness for Dawn Stevens," in *Fast Action Detective* (New York), February 1958.
"Desert of Sin," in *Double-Action Detective* (New York), May 1958.
"Traynor's Cipher," in *The Saint* (New York), July 1958.
"The Dragon Murders," in *Double-Action Detective* (New York), September 1958.
"Street of Screams," in *Double-Action Detective* (New York), January 1959.
"Journey to Death," in *Mystery Digest* (New York), February 1959.
"The Case of the Sexy Smugglers," in *Double-Action Detective* (New York), July 1959.
"The Case of the Naked Niece," in *Double-Action Detective* (New York), September 1959.
"The Case of the Vanished Virgin," in *Double-Action Detective* (New York), November 1959.

"The Case of the Ragged Rapist," in *Double-Action Detective* (New York), January 1960.

"The Long Count," in *The Saint* (New York), January 1960.

"Flame at Twilight," in *The Saint Mystery Library* (New York), January 1960.

"The Case of the Mystic Mistress," in *Double-Action Detective* (New York), May 1960.

"The Passionate Phantom," in *Off Beat Detective* (New York), May 1960.

"The Clouded Venus," in *Tightrope Detective* (New York), June 1960.

"Sisters of Slaughter," in *Web Detective* (New York), June 1960.

"A Blade for the Chicken," in *Two-Fisted Detective* (New York), August 1960.

"Murder Is Eternal!" in *Web Detective* (New York), August 1960.

"The Man Who Knew Everything," in *Shock* (New York), September 1960.

"Don't Laugh at Murder," in *Off Beat Detective* (New York), January 1961.

"Drive My Hearse, Darling," in *Two-Fisted Detective* (New York), January 1961.

"The Night People," in *Web Detective* (New York), May 1961.

"Lust Loves the Dark," in *Off Beat Detective* (New York), July 1961.

"Hell's Handmaiden," in *Off Beat Detective* (New York), September 1961.

"The Valley of Arrows," in *The Saint* (New York), September 1961.

"To Serve the Dead," in *Web Detective* (New York), September 1961.

"Frontier Street," in *The Saint* (New York), February 1962.

"Dial 120 for Survival," in *Alfred Hitchcock's Mystery Magazine* (North Palm Beach, Florida), March 1962.

"Lovely Lady of Lust," In *Keyhole Detective* (New York), April 1962.

"Setup for Murder," in *Off Beat Detective* (New York), May 1962.

"Layout for Murder," in *Off Beat Detective* (New York), July 1962.

"The Flying Man," in *The Saint* (New York), July 1962.

"A Corpse Can Love," in *Off Beat Detective* (New York), September 1962.

"Madman's Hotel," in *Off Beat Detective* (New York), November 1962.

"Death in the Harbor," in *Ellery Queen's Mystery Magazine* (New York), December 1962.

"Ghost Town," in *The Saint* (New York), January 1963.

"The Picnic People," in *Alfred Hitchcock's Mystery Magazine* (North Palm Beach, Florida), March 1963.

"The Man in the Alley," in *The Saint* (New York), June 1963.

"The Man Who Was Everywhere," in *Alfred Hitchcock Presents: Stories My Mother Never Told Me.* New York, Random House, 1963.

"The Maze and the Monster," in *Magazine of Horror* (New York), August 1963.

"Day of the Wizard," in *The Saint* (London), August 1963.

"The Faceless Thing," in *Magazine of Horror* (New York), November 1963.

"Shattered Rainbow," in *Alfred Hitchcock's Mystery Magazine* (North Palm Beach, Florida), January 1964.

"Where There's Smoke," in *Manhunt* (New York), March 1964.

"The Wolfram Hunters," in *The Saint* (New York), March 1964.

"The Patient Waiter," in *Alfred Hitchcock's Mystery Magazine* (North Palm Beach, Florida), May 1964.

"Walk with a Wizard," in *Alfred Hitchcock's Mystery Magazine* (North Palm Beach, Florida), July 1964.

"I'd Know You Anywhere," in *Ellery Queen's Double Dozen.* New York, Random House, 1964; London, Gollancz, 1965.

"Too Long at the Fair," in *Alfred Hitchcock's Mystery Magazine* (North Palm Beach, Florida), October 1964.

"The Crime of Avery Mann," in *Ellery Queen's Mystery Magazine* (New York), October 1964.

"Secret Ballot," in *Alfred Hitchcock's Mystery Magazine* (North Palm Beach, Florida), November 1964.

"Winter Run," in *Alfred Hitchcock's Mystery Magazine* (North Palm Beach, Florida), January 1965.

"The Clever Mr. Carton," in *Ellery Queen's Mystery Magazine* (New York), January 1965.

"Snow in Yucatan," in *The Saint* (New York), January 1965.

"Dreaming Is a Lonely Thing," in *Alfred Hitchcock's Mystery Magazine* (North Palm Beach, Florida), March 1965.

"Reunion," in *Best Detective Stories of the Year*, edited by Anthony Boucher. New York, Dutton, 1965.

"In Some Secret Place," in *The Saint* (New York), August 1965.

"The Way of Justice," in *Alfred Hitchcock's Mystery Magazine* (North Palm Beach, Florida), September 1965.

"The Empty Zoo," in *Magazine of Horror* (New York), November 1965.

"They Never Came Back," in *Alfred Hitchcock's Mystery Magazine* (North Palm Beach, Florida), February 1966.

"The Only Girl in His Life," in *Signature* (New York), February 1966.

"Game of Skill," in *Sleuths and Consequences*, edited by Thomas B. Dewey. New York, Simon and Schuster, 1966.

"The Long Way Down," in *Best Detective Stories of the Year*, edited by Anthony Boucher. New York, Dutton, 1966.

"The House by the Ferris," in *The Saint* (New York), May 1966.

"The Fifth Victim," in *Signature* (New York), May 1966.

"Children of Judas," in *The Saint* (New York), October 1966.

"A Girl Like Cathy," in *Signature* (New York), October 1966.

"The Spy Who Walked Through Walls," in *Ellery Queen's Mystery Magazine* (New York), November 1966.

"The Spy Who Did Nothing," in *Spies and More Spies*, edited by Robert Arthur. New York, Random House, 1967.

"The People of the Peacock," in *Spies and More Spies*, edited by Robert Arthur. New York, Random House, 1967.

"A Gift of Myrrh," in *Alfred Hitchcock's Mystery Magazine* (North Palm Beach, Florida), January 1967.

"Fall of Zoo," in *The Saint* (New York), January 1967.

"After the Verdict," in *Alfred Hitchcock's Mystery Magazine* (North Palm Beach, Florida), April 1967.

"The Spy Who Came Out of the Night," in *Ellery Queen's Mystery Magazine* (New York), April 1967.

"Stop at Nothing," in *Alfred Hitchcock's Mystery Magazine* (North Palm Beach, Florida), May 1967.

"The Girl with the Dragon Kite," in *Alfred Hitchcock's Mystery Magazine* (North Palm Beach, Florida), June 1967.

"The Dying Knight," in *Signature* (New York), June 1967.

"It Could Get Warmer," in *Alfred Hitchcock's Mystery Magazine* (North Palm Beach, Florida), July 1967.

"The Spy Who Worked for Peace," in *Ellery Queen's Mystery Magazine* (New York), August 1967.

"The Eye of the Pigeon," in *Alfred Hitchcock's Mystery Magazine* (North Palm Beach, Florida), October 1967.

"Another War," in *Alfred Hitchcock's Mystery Magazine* (North Palm Beach, Florida), December 1967.

"The Spy Who Didn't Exist, in *Ellery Queen's Mystery Magazine* (New York), December 1967.

"The Spy Who Clutched a Playing Card," in *Ellery Queen's Mystery Magazine* (New York), February 1968.

"The Oblong Room," in *Best Detective Stories of the Year*, edited by Anthony Boucher. New York, Dutton, 1968.

"After the Fact," in *Alfred Hitchcock's Mystery Magazine* (North Palm Beach, Florida), March 1968.

"Cold Cognisance," in *Alfred Hitchcock's Mystery Magazine* (North Palm Beach, Florida), May 1968.

"Something for the Dark," in *Alfred Hitchcock's Mystery Magazine* (North Palm Beach, Florida), June 1968.

"Hawk in the Valley," in *Alfred Hitchcock's Mystery Magazine* (North Palm Beach, Florida), August 1968.

"The Spy Who Read Latin," in *Ellery Queen's Mystery Magazine* (New York), August 1968.

"A Certain Power," in *Alfred Hitchcock's Mystery Magazine* (North Palm Beach, Florida), October 1968.

"No Good at Riddles," in *Alfred Hitchcock's Mystery Magazine* (North Palm Beach, Florida), December 1968.

"Cassidy's Saucer," in *Flying Saucers in Fact and Fiction*, edited by Hans S. Santesson. New York, Lancer, 1968.

"The Ring with the Velvet Ropes," in *With Malice Toward All*, edited by Robert L. Fish. New York, Putnam, 1968.

"Poor Sport," in *Alfred Hitchcock's Mystery Magazine* (North Palm Beach, Florida), February 1969.

"Homecoming," in *Alfred Hitchcock's Mystery Magazine* (North Palm Beach, Florida), April 1969.

"Emergency," in *Alfred Hitchcock's Mystery Magazine* (North Palm Beach, Florida), May 1969.

"The Tomb at the Top of the Tree," in *Mike Shayne Mystery Magazine* (New York), June 1969.

"The Dictator's Double," in *Alfred Hitchcock's Mystery Magazine* (North Palm Beach, Florida), July 1969.

"The Spy and the Shopping List Code," in *Ellery Queen's Mystery Magazine* (New York), July 1969.

"The Vanishing of Velma," in *Alfred Hitchcock's Mystery Magazine* (North Palm Beach, Florida), August 1969.

"Dead Man's Song," in *Mike Shayne Mystery Magazine* (New York), September 1969.

"The Impossible 'Impossible' Crime," in *Ellery Queen's Murder Menu.* Cleveland, World, 1969.

"The Secret Savant," in *Alfred Hitchcock's Mystery Magazine* (North Palm Beach, Florida), October 1969.

"Picnic at Midnight," in *Mike Shayne Mystery Magazine* (New York), October 1969.

"The Murder Parade, in *Mike Shayne Mystery Magazine* (New York), November 1969.

"Unnatural Act," in *Gentle Invaders*, edited by Hans S. Santesson. New York, Belmont, 1969.

"Computer Cops," in *Crime Prevention in the 30th Century*, edited by Hans S. Santesson. New York, Walker, 1969.

"The Magic Bullet," in *Best Detective Stories of the Year*, edited by Allen J. Hubin. New York, Dutton, 1970.

"The Theft of the Laughing Lions," in *Ellery Queen's Mystery Magazine* (New York), February 1970.

"The Uttering Man," in *Alfred Hitchcock's Mystery Magazine* (North Palm Beach, Florida), March 1970.

"The Seventh Assassin," in *Ellery Queen's Mystery Magazine* (New York), March 1970.

"The Seventieth Number," in *Ellery Queen's Mystery Magazine* (New York), March 1970.

"Flapdragon," in *Alfred Hitchcock's Mystery Magazine* (North Palm Beach, Florida), April 1970.

"A Place to See the Dark," in *Alfred Hitchcock's Mystery Magazine* (North Palm Beach, Florida), May 1970.

"Zone," in *Mike Shayne Mystery Magazine* (Los Angeles), June 1970.

"Murder Offstage," in *Ellery Queen's Grand Slam.* Cleveland, World, 1970.

"Every Fifth Man," in *Ellery Queen's Grand Slam.* Clevelend, World, 1970.

"The Nile Cat," in *Ellery Queen's Grand Slam.* Cleveland, World, 1970.

"The Afternoon Ear," in *Mike Shayne Mystery Magazine* (Los Angeles), September 1970.

"Verdict of One," in *Alfred Hitchcock's Mystery Magazine* (North Palm Beach, Florida), October 1970.

"The Spy Who Traveled with a Coffin," in *Ellery Queen's Mystery Magazine* (New York), October 1970.

"Bag of Tricks," in *Alfred Hitchcock's Mystery Magazine* (North Palm Beach, Florida), November 1970.

"The Athanasia League," in *Alfred Hitchcock's Mystery Magazine* (North Palm Beach, Florida), December 1970.

"Twist of the Knife," in *Mike Shayne Mystery Magazine* (Los Angeles), December 1970.

"The Spy and the Diplomat's Daughter," in *Ellery Queen's Mystery Magazine* (New York), January 1971.

"Die Hard," in *Mike Shayne Mystery Magazine* (Los Angeles), February 1971.

"A Little More Rope," in *Alfred Hitchcock's Mystery Magazine* (North Palm Beach, Florida), March 1971.

"The Theft of the Dinosaur's Tail," in *Ellery Queen's Mystery Magazine* (New York), March 1971.

"The Poison Man," in *Mike Shayne Mystery Magazine* (Los Angeles), March 1971.

"The Way Out," in *Ellery Queen's Mystery Magazine* (New York), April 1971.

"Blow-Up!" in *Adventure* (Glendale, California), April 1971.

"Siege Perilous," in *Mike Shayne Mystery Magazine* (Los Angeles), April 1971.

"Climax Alley," in *Alfred Hitchcock's Mystery Magazine* (North Palm Beach, Florida), May 1971.

"The Spy and the Nile Mermaid," in *Ellery Queen's Mystery Magazine* (New York), May 1971.

"The Theft of the Satin Jury," in *Ellery Queen's Mystery Magazine* (New York), June 1971.

"The Sugar Man," in *Mike Shayne Mystery Magazine* (Los Angeles), June 1971.

"Dead on the Pavement," in *Alfred Hitchcock's Mystery Magazine* (North Palm Beach, Florida), July 1971.

"The Thing in Lovers' Lane," in *Mike Shayne Mystery Magazine* (Los Angeles), July 1971.

"The Spy Who Knew Too Much," in *Ellery Queen's Mystery Magazine* (New York), August 1971.

"The League of Arthur," in *Argosy* (New York), September 1971.

"Blood Money," in *Mike Shayne Mystery Magazine* (Los Angeles), September 1971.

"The Jersey Devil," in *Alfred Hitchcock's Mystery Magazine* (North Palm Beach, Florida), October 1971.

"Lady with a Cat," in *Alfred Hitchcock's Mystery Magazine* (North Palm Beach, Florida), November 1971.

"The Theft of the Leather Coffin," in *Ellery Queen's Mystery Magazine* (New York), November 1971.

"Twilight Thunder," in *Alfred Hitchcock's I Am Curious Bloody.* New York, Dell, 1971.

"The Rusty Rose," in *Alfred Hitchcock's Rolling Gravestones.* New York, Dell, 1971.

"The Sound of Screaming," in *Mike Shayne Mystery Magazine* (Los Angeles), November 1971.

"Rubber Bullets," in *Alfred Hitchcock's Mystery Magazine* (North Palm Beach, Florida), December 1971.

"Captain Leopold Does His Job," in *Ellery Queen's Mystery Magazine* (New York), December 1971.

"The Zap Effect," in *Mike Shayne Mystery Magazine* (Los Angeles), December 1971.

"The Man at the Top," in *Alfred Hitchcock's Mystery Magazine* (North Palm Beach, Florida), February 1972.

"The Spy Without a Country," in *Ellery Queen's Mystery Magazine* (New York), February 1972.

"The Lost Pilgrim," in *Mike Shayne Mystery Magazine* (Los Angeles), February 1972.

"A Country Like the Sun," in *Mike Shayne Mystery Magazine* (Los Angeles), March 1972.

"A Melee of Diamonds," in *Alfred Hitchcock's Mystery Magazine* (North Palm Beach, Florida), April 1972.

"The Spy Who Didn't Remember," in *Ellery Queen's Mystery Magazine* (New York), April 1972.

"End of the Day," in *Best Detective Stories of the Year*, edited by Allen J. Hubin.   New York, Dutton, 1972.

"The Spy and the Reluctant Courier," in *Ellery Queen's Mystery Magazine* (New York), June 1972.

"The Soft Asylum," in *Alfred Hitchcock's Mystery Magazine* (North Palm Beach, Florida), July 1972.

"The Ripper of Storyville," in *Dear Dead Days*, edited by Edward D. Hoch.   New York, Walker, 1972; London, Gollancz, 1974.

"Suicide," in *Mike Shayne Mystery Magazine* (Los Angeles), August 1972.

"The Leopold Locked Room," in *Ellery Queen's Mystery Bag.* Cleveland, World, 1972.

"Leopold at Best," in *Alfred Hitchcock's Mystery Magazine* (North Palm Beach, Florida), September 1972.

"The Holy Witch," in *Mike Shayne Mystery Magazine* (Los Angeles), September 1972.

"The Spy in the Pyramid," in *Ellery Queen's Mystery Magazine* (New York), September 1972.

"Day of the Vampire," in *Alfred Hitchcock's Mystery Magazine* (North Palm Beach, Florida), November 1972.

"The Theft of the Foggy Film," in *Ellery Queen's Mystery Magazine* (New York), November 1972.

"The Spy Who Was Expected," in *Ellery Queen's Mystery Magazine* (New York), December 1972.

"Bullets for Two," in *Mike Shayne Annual* (Los Angeles), 1972.

"Leopold on Edge," in *Alfred Hitchcock's Mystery Magazine* (North Palm Beach, Florida), January 1973.

"The Million-Dollar Jewel Caper," in *Ellery Queen's Mystery Magazine* (New York), January 1973.

"Burial Monuments Three," in *Best Detective Stories of the Year*, edited by Allen J. Hubin.   New York, Dutton, 1973.

"The Case of the Third Apostle," in *Ellery Queen's Mystery Magazine* (New York), February 1973.

"Captain Leopold Gets Angry," in *Ellery Queen's Mystery Magazine* (New York), March 1973.

"The Man Who Came Back," in *Alfred Hitchcock's Mystery Magazine* (North Palm Beach, Florida), May 1973.

"Captain Leopold Saves a Life," in *Ellery Queen's Anthology: Spring Summer.* New York, Davis, 1973.

"The Plastic Man," in *Alfred Hitchcock's Mystery Magazine* (North Palm Beach, Florida), June 1973.

"The Case of the November Club," in *Ellery Queen's Mystery Magazine* (New York), June 1973.

"Home Movies," in *Mike Shayne Mystery Magazine* (Los Angeles), June 1973.

"Funeral in the Fog," in *Weird Tales* (Los Angeles), Summer 1973.

"The Spy with the Knockout Punch," in *Ellery Queen's Mystery Magazine* (New York), August 1973.

"The Theft of the Cuckoo Clock," in *Ellery Queen's Mystery Magazine* (New York), September 1973.

"The Day We Killed the Madman," in *Alfred Hitchcock's Mystery Magazine* (North Palm Beach, Florida), October 1973.

"Captain Leopold Swings a Bat," in *Ellery Queen's Mystery Magazine* (New York), October 1973.

"Snowsuit," in *Alfred Hitchcock's Mystery Magazine* (North Palm Beach, Florida), November 1973.

"The Case of the Modern Medusa," in *Ellery Queen's Mystery Magazine* (New York), November 1973.

"The Serpent in the Sky," in *Ellery Queen's Anthology: Fall–Winter.* New York, Davis, 1973.

"The Gold Buddha Caper," in *Ellery Queen's Mystery Magazine* (New York), December 1973.

"Night of the Millenium," in *The Other Side of Tomorrow*, edited by Roger Elwood. New York, Random House, 1973.

"The Witch of Westwood," in *Alfred Hitchcock's Mystery Magazine* (North Palm Beach, Florida), January 1974.

"The Spy and the Intercepted Letters," in *Ellery Queen's Mystery Magazine* (New York), January 1974.

"The Infernal Machine," in *Mike Shayne Mystery Magazine* (Los Angeles), January 1974.

"Dinner with the Boss," in *Charlie Chan Mystery Magazine* (Los Angeles), February 1974.

"The Case of the Musical Bullet," in *Ellery Queen's Mystery Magazine* (New York), March 1974.

"The Spy at the End of the Rainbow," in *Ellery Queen's Mystery Magazine* (New York), April 1974.

"The Lollipop Cop," in *Ellery Queen's Mystery Magazine* (New York), June 1974.

"The Theft of the Legal Eagle," in *Ellery Queen's Mystery Magazine* (New York), July 1974.

"Captain Leopold and the Ghost Killer," in *Ellery Queen's Mystery Magazine* (New York), August 1974.

"The Choker," in *Alfred Hitchcock's Mystery Magazine* (North Palm Beach, Florida), September 1974.

"The Perfect Time for the Perfect Crime," in *Killers of the Mind*, edited by Lucy Freeman. New York, Random House, 1974.

"The Case of the Lapidated Man," in *Ellery Queen's Mystery Magazine* (New York), September 1974.

"Story for an October Issue," in *Alfred Hitchcock's Mystery Magazine* (North Palm Beach, Florida), October 1974.

"The Credit Card Caper," in *Ellery Queen's Mystery Magazine* (New York), October 1974.

"Captain Leopold Finds a Tiger," in *Alfred Hitchcock's Mystery Magazine* (North Palm Beach, Florida), November 1974.

"The Spy and the Talking House," in *Ellery Queen's Mystery Magazine* (New York), November 1974.

"The Problem of the Covered Bridge," in *Ellery Queen's Mystery Magazine* (New York), December 1974.

"The Boy Who Bought Love," in *Crisis*, edited by Roger Elwood. New York, Nelson, 1974.

"Captain Leopold Drops a Bomb," in *Alfred Hitchcock's Mystery Magazine* (North Palm Beach, Florida), January 1975.

"The Kindergarten Witch," in *Ellery Queen's Mystery Magazine* (New York), January 1975.

"Captain Leopold Goes Home," in *Ellery Queen's Mystery Magazine* (New York), January 1975.

"The Neptune Fund," in *Mike Shayne Mystery Magazine* (Los Angeles), January 1975.

"The Case of the Broken Wings," in *Ellery Queen's Mystery Magazine* (New York), February 1975.

"The Problem of the Old Gristmill," in *Ellery Queen's Mystery Magazine* (New York), March 1975.

"Bodyguard," in *Executioner* (Los Angeles), April 1975.

"The Spy Who Took a Vacation," in *Ellery Queen's Mystery Magazine* (New York), April 1975.

"The Rainy-Day Bandit," in *Ellery Queen's Anthology, Spring–Summer*. New York, Davis, 1975.

"The Enchanted Tooth," in *Ellery Queen's Mystery Magazine* (New York), May 1975.

"Captain Leopold and the Arrow Murders," in *Ellery Queen's Mystery Magazine* (New York), July 1975.

"One Eden Too Many," in *87th Precinct* (Los Angeles), August 1975.

"The Case of the Terrorists," in *Ellery Queen's Mystery Magazine* (New York), August 1975.

"Twine," in *Mike Shayne Mystery Magazine* (Los Angeles), August 1975.

"The Odor of Melting," in *Alfred Hitchcock Presents: Stories to Be Read with the Door Locked*. New York, Random House, 1975.

"Christmas Is for Cops," in *Ellery Queen's Anthology, Spring–Summer*. New York, Davis, 1975.

"The Problem of the Lobster Shack," in *Ellery Queen's Mystery Magazine* (New York), September 1975.

"Arbiter of Uncertainties," in *Alfred Hitchcock's Murderer's Row*. New York, Dell, 1975.

"The Spy and the Mysterious Card," in *Ellery Queen's Mystery Magazine* (New York), October 1975.

"Man in Hiding," in *Nugget* (Coral Gables, Florida), October 1975.

"Two Days in Organville," in *Alfred Hitchcock's Speak of the Devil*. New York, Dell, 1975.

"The Theft of the Venetian Window," in *Ellery Queen's Mystery Magazine* (New York), November 1975.

"The Death of Lame Jack Lincoln," in *Alfred Hitchcock's Mystery Magazine* (North Palm Beach, Florida), December 1975.

"No Crime for Captain Leopold," in *Ellery Queen's Mystery Magazine* (New York), December 1975.

"The Basilisk Hunt," in *Alfred Hitchcock's Mystery Magazine* (New York), January 1976.

"The Problem of the Haunted Bandstand," in *Ellery Queen's Mystery Magazine* (New York), January 1976.

"The Case of the Flying Graveyard," in *Alfred Hitchcock's Mystery Magazine* (New York), February 1976.

"The Man Who Knew the Method," in *Nugget* (Coral Gables, Florida), February 1976.

"The Spy Who Collected Lapel Pins," in *Ellery Queen's Mystery Magazine* (New York), March 1976.

"The Theft of the Admiral's Snow," in *Ellery Queen's Mystery Magazine* (New York), April 1976.

"Captain Leopold Tries Again," in *Ellery Queen's Mystery Magazine* (New York), June 1976.

"The Bank Job," in *Mystery Monthly* (New York), June 1976.

"The Theft of the Wooden Egg," in *Ellery Queen's Mystery Magazine* (New York), July 1976.

"The Centennial Assassin," in *Ellery Queen's Mystery Magazine* (New York), August 1976.

"The Problem of the Little Red Schoolhouse," in *Ellery Queen's Mystery Magazine* (New York), September 1976.

"The Murder of Captain Leopold," in *Ellery Queen's Mystery Magazine* (New York), October 1976.

"The Spy at the Crime Writers Congress," in *Ellery Queen's Mystery Magazine* (New York), November 1976.

"Captain Leopold and the Impossible Murder," in *Ellery Queen's Mystery Magazine* (New York), December 1976.

"Day of Judgement," in *Mike Shayne Mystery Magazine* (Los Angeles), December 1976.

"The Problem of the Christmas Steeple," in *Ellery Queen's Mystery Magazine* (New York), January 1977.

"The Theft of the Sherlockian Slipper," in *Ellery Queen's Mystery Magazine* (New York), February 1977.

"A Touch of Red," in *Mike Shayne Mystery Magazine* (Los Angeles), February 1977.

"The Problem of Cell 16," in *Ellery Queen's Mystery Magazine* (New York), March 1977.

"Web," in *Dude* (Coral Gables, Florida), March 1977.

"The Wooden Dove," in *Mike Shayne Mystery Magazine* (Los Angeles), March 1977.

"The Case of the Devil's Triangle," in *Ellery Queen's Mystery Magazine* (New York), April 1977.

"A Simple Little Thing," in *Alfred Hitchcock's Mystery Magazine* (New York), May 1977.

"The Theft of Nothing at All," in *Ellery Queen's Mystery Magazine* (New York), May 1977.

"The Case of the Battered Wives," in *Ellery Queen's Mystery Magazine* (New York), June 1977.

"The Spy Who Died Twice," in *Ellery Queen's Mystery Magazine* (New York), July 1977.

"Money on the Skull," in *Antaeus* (New York), Spring–Summer 1977.

"All Knives are Sharp," in *Alfred Hitchcock's Mystery Magazine* (New York), August 1977.

"No Holiday for Captain Leopold," in *Ellery Queen's Mystery Magazine* (New York), August 1977.

"The Problem of the Country Inn," in *Ellery Queen's Mystery Magazine* (New York), September 1977.

"The Theft of the Child's Drawing," in *Ellery Queen's Mystery Magazine* (New York), October 1977.

"Captain Leopold Looks for the Cause," in *Ellery Queen's Mystery Magazine* (New York), November 1977.

"The Lady or the Lion?," in *Alfred Hitchcock's Mystery Magazine* (New York), November 1977.

"The Problem of the Voting Booth," in *Ellery Queen's Mystery Magazine* (New York), December 1977.

"The Spy in the Toy Business," in *Ellery Queen's Mystery Magazine* (New York), January 1978.

"The Problem of the County Fair," in *Ellery Queen's Mystery Magazine* (New York), February 1978.

"The Theft of the Family Portrait," in *Ellery Queen's Mystery Magazine* (New York), March 1978.

"The Case of the Five Coffins," in *Ellery Queen's Mystery Magazine* (New York), April 1978.

"Captain Leopold Incognito," in *Ellery Queen's Mystery Magazine* (New York), May 1978.

"The Nameless Crime," in *Mike Shayne Mystery Magazine* (Los Angeles), May 1978.

"The Spy and the Cats of Rome," in *Ellery Queen's Mystery Magazine* (New York), June 1978.

"Home Is the Hunter," in *Alfred Hitchcock's Mystery Magazine* (New York), June 1978.

"Warrior's Farewell," in *Alfred Hitchcock's Tales to Scare You Stiff*, edited by Eleanor Sullivan. New York, Davis, 1978.

"Captain Leopold Plays a Hunch," in *Ellery Queen's Masters of Mystery*. New York, Davis, 1978.

"The Problem of the Old Oak Tree," in *Ellery Queen's Mystery Magazine* (New York), July 1978.

"The Theft of the Turquoise Elephant," in *Ellery Queen's Mystery Magazine* (New York), August 1978.

"The Pact of the Five,"in *Alfred Hitchcock's Mystery Magazine* (New York), August 1978.

"Captain Leopold and the Three Hostages," in *Ellery Queen's Mystery Magazine* (New York), September 1978.

"A Man Could Get Killed," in *Mike Shayne Mystery Magazine* (Los Angeles), September 1978.

"The Treasure of Jack the Ripper," in *Ellery Queen's Mystery Magazine* (New York), October 1978.

"Memory in the Dark," in *Alfred Hitchcock's Mystery Magazine* (New York), October 1978.

"The Obsession of Officer O'Rourke," in *Alfred Hitchcock's Mystery Magazine* (New York), November 1978.

"After Class," in *Mike Shayne Mystery Magazine* (Los Angeles), November 1978.

"The Problem of the Revival Tent," in *Ellery Queen's Mystery Magazine* (New York), November 1978.

"Three Weeks in a Spanish Town," in *Alfred Hitchcock's Mystery Magazine* (New York), December 1978.

"The Spy in the Labyrinth," in *Ellery Queen's Mystery Magazine* (New York), December 1978.

"Captain Leopold on the Spot," in *Ellery Queen's Mystery Magazine* (New York), January 1979.

"In a Foreign City," in *Mike Shayne Mystery Magazine* (Los Angeles), January 1979.

"The Mummy from the Sea," in *Alfred Hitchcock's Mystery Magazine* (New York), January 1979.

"The Man Who Shot the Werewolf," in *Ellery Queen's Mystery Magazine* (New York), February 1979.

"The Theft of Yesterday's Newspaper," in *Ellery Queen's Mystery Magazine* (New York), March 1979.

"The Gun," in *Mike Shayne Mystery Magazine* (Los Angeles), March 1979.

"Three Hot Days," in *Mike Shayne Mystery Magazine* (Los Angeles), April 1979.

"The Problem of the Whispering House," in *Ellery Queen's Mystery Magazine* (New York), April 1979.

"Captain Leopold and the Murderer's Son," in *Alfred Hitchcock's Mystery Magazine* (New York), May 1979.

"The Spy Who Had a List," in *Ellery Queen's Mystery Magazine* (New York), May 1979.

"The Theft of the Firefighter's Hat," in *Ellery Queen's Mystery Magazine* (New York), June 1979.

"Tough Cop's Girl," in *Mike Shayne Mystery Magazine* (Los Angeles), June 1979.

"Captain Leopold Incognito," in *Best Detective Stories of the Year*, edited by Edward D. Hoch. New York, Dutton, 1979.

"Captain Leopold and the Vanishing Men," in *Ellery Queen's Mystery Magazine* (New York), July 1979.

"The Rattlesnake Man," in *Alfred Hitchcock's Mystery Magazine* (New York), July 1979.

"The Problem of the Boston Common," in *Ellery Queen's Mystery Magazine* (New York), August 1979.

"The Paris Strangler," in *Alfred Hitchcock's Mystery Magazine* (New York), August 1979.

"The Spy Who Was Alone," in *Ellery Queen's Mystery Magazine* (New York), September 1979.

"Where Is Danny Storm?," in *Mike Shayne Mystery Magazine* (Los Angeles), September 1979.

"Second Chance," in *Women's Wiles*, edited by Michele B. Slung. New York, Harcourt Brace, 1979.

"The Avenger from Outer Space," in *Ellery Queen's Mystery Magazine* (New York), October 1979.

"The Problem of the General Store," in *Ellery Queen's Mystery Magazine* (New York), November 1979.

"The Theft of Sahara's Water," in *Ellery Queen's Mystery Magazine* (New York), December 1979.

Uncollected Short Stories as Stephen Dentinger

"Dark Campus," in *Smashing Detective* (New York), March 1956.

"The Late Sports," in *Crack Detective* (New York), December 1956.

"The Last Night of Her Life," in *Fast Action Detective* (New York), May 1957.

"Circus," in *The Saint* (New York), January 1962.

"The Night My Friend," in *The Saint* (London), July 1962.

"Festival in Black," in *The Saint* (London), August 1962.

"The Tattooed Priest," in *The Saint* (London), November 1962.

"The Demon at Noon," in *The Saint* (New York), February 1963.

"The Freech Case," in *The Saint* (New York), May 1964.

"A Stranger Came to Reap," in *The Saint* (New York), September 1964.

"A Question of Punishment," in *The Saint* (New York), September 1965.

"To Slay an Eagle," in *The Award Espionage Reader*, edited by Hans S. Santesson. New York, Award, 1965.

"It Happens, Sometimes," in *The Saint* (New York), April 1966.

"Ring the Bell Softly," in *The Saint* (New York), July 1966.

"What's It All About," in *The Saint* (New York), January 1967.

"Recruitment," in *The Saint* (New York), October 1967.

"God of the Playback," in *Gods for Tomorrow*, edited by Hans S. Santesson. New York, Award, 1967.

"First Offense," in *Ellery Queen's Mystery Magazine* (New York), January 1968.

"The Future Is Ours," in *Crime Prevention in the 30th Century*, edited by Hans S. Santesson. New York, Walker, 1969.

"Fifty Bucks by Monday," in *Mike Shayne Mystery Magazine* (Los Angeles), November 1971.

"The Judas Kiss," in *Alfred Hitchcock's Mystery Magazine* (New York), July 1976.

"A Place for Bleeding," in *Cop Cade*, edited by John Ball. New York, Doubleday 1978.

Uncollected Short Stories as Pat McMahon

"The Suitcase," in *The Saint* (New York), September 1962.

"Day for a Picnic," in *The Saint* (New York), November 1963.

"Uncle Max," in *The Saint* (New York), September 1965.

"The Authentic Death of Cotton Clark," in *The Saint* (New York), May 1966.

Uncollected Short Stories as Mr. X

> *The Will-o'-the-Wisp Mystery* ("The Pawn," "The Rook," "The Knight," "The Bishop," "The Queen," "The King"), in *Ellery Queen's Mystery Magazine* (New York), April–September 1971.

Uncollected Short Stories as R. L. Stevens

> "Thirteen," in *Ellery Queen's Mystery Magazine* (New York), December 1971.
> "The Physician and the Opium Fiend," in *Ellery Queen's Mystery Bag.* Cleveland, World, 1972.
> "Just Something That Happened," in *Ellery Queen's Mystery Magazine* (New York), February 1972.
> "Lot 721/XY258," in *Ellery Queen's Mystery Magazine* (New York), May 1972.
> "The Legacy," in *Ellery Queen's Mystery Magazine* (New York), August 1972.
> "The Lot's Wife Caper," in *Ellery Queen's Anthology, Spring–Summer.* New York, Davis, 1973.
> "King's Knight's Gambit Declined," in *Ellery Queen's Mystery Magazine* (New York), July 1973.
> "Nothing to Chance," in *Ellery Queen's Mystery Magazine* (New York), January 1974.
> "The Most Dangerous Man," in *Ellery Queen's Murdercade.* New York, Random House, 1975.
> "The Great American Novel," in *Ellery Queen's Mystery Magazine* (New York), April 1975.
> "A Deal in Diamonds," in *Ellery Queen's Mystery Magazine* (New York), July 1975.
> "The Three Travellers," in *Ellery Queen's Mystery Magazine* (New York), January 1976.
> "Here Be Dragons," in *Alfred Hitchcock's Mystery Magazine* (New York), May 1976.
> "EQMM Number 400," in *Ellery Queen's Mystery Magazine* (New York), March 1977.
> "The Crime of the Century," in *Ellery Queen's Mystery Magazine* (New York), August 1977.
> "Innocent Victim," in *Ellery Queen's Mystery Magazine* (New York), January 1978.
> "The Missing Money," in *Ellery Queen's Mystery Magazine* (New York), July 1978.
> "Five Rings in Reno," in *A Multitude of Sins*, edited by Ellery Queen. New York, Davis, 1978.
> "The Price of Wisdom," in *Best Detective Stories of the Year*, edited by Edward D. Hoch. New York, Dutton, 1978.
> "The Forbidden Word," in *Mysterious Visions.* New York, St. Martin's Press, 1979.

OTHER PUBLICATIONS

Other

> "Writing the Mystery Short Story," in *The Writers' Handbook*, edited by A. S. Burack. Boston, The Writer, 1975.
> "The Cryptography Bureau: How to Tell a Vigenère from a Pigpen," in *Murder Ink: The Mystery Reader's Companion*, edited by Dilys Winn. New York, Workman, 1977.
> *The Monkey's Clue, and The Stolen Sapphire* (juvenile). New York, Grosset and Dunlap, 1978.

> Editor, *Dear Dead Days.* New York, Walker, 1972; London, Gollancz, 1974.
> Editor, *Best Detective Stories of the Year.* New York, Dutton, 4 volumes, 1976–79.

Bibliography: "Edward D. Hoch: A Checklist," by William J. Clark, Edward D. Hoch, and

Francis M. Nevins, Jr., in *Armchair Detective* (White Bear Lake, Minnesota), February 1976; revised edition, by Nevins and Hoch, privately printed, 1979.

Edward D. Hoch comments:

I work mainly in the short story because I find that form most satisfying to me, and amenable to the type of formal detective story I like to do best. Series characters work especially well for me within the framework of a short story. Writing a novel has always been, to me, a task to be finished as quickly as possible. Writing a short story is a pleasure one can linger over, with delight in the concept and surprise at the finished product.

*   *   *

If ever there was a member of an endangered species it's Ed Hoch, the sole surviving professional writer of short mysteries. Since his debut in 1955, in addition to five novels, he has published nearly five hundred such tales, including numerous non-series stories and a total of 15 separate series. Among his recurring characters are an occult detective who claims to be two centuries old, a private eye, a Western drifter who may be the reincarnation of Billy the Kid, a priest, a British cryptographer-sleuth, a science-fictional Computer Investigation Bureau, a con man, two Interpol agents reminiscent of the stars of TV's *The Avengers*, a Lollipop Cop, and a New England physician-detective of the 1920's. His longest-running and perhaps best series are those dealing with Nick Velvet, the thief who steals only valueless objects and often has to detect while thieving, and Captain Leopold, the tough but sensitive violent-crime specialist on the force of a large northeastern city.

In the stories of Hoch's pre-1960 apprenticeship the ideas are occasionally quite original (e.g., the murder of one of a sect of Penitentes while the cult members are hanging on crucifixes in a dark cellar) but the execution tends to be crude and naive and the Roman Catholic viewpoint somewhat obtrusive. As his work matured it came to reflect the influence of several of his own favorite writers, including Graham Greene, Jorge Luis Borges, and especially John Dickson Carr and Ellery Queen. Such Hoch stories as "The Long Way Down" (*Alfred Hitchcock's Mystery Magazine*, February 1965), in which a man leaps from a skyscraper window but doesn't hit the ground until hours later, and "The Vanishing of Velma" (*Alfred Hitchcock's Mystery Magazine*, August 1969), in which a woman disappears without trace from a moving ferris wheel, are among the finest modern works in the tradition of Carr's impossible-crime tales.

Some of Hoch's most vividly written stories appeared in the *Alfred Hitchcock* and *Saint* mystery magazines during the Sixties, among them his Edgar-winning "The Oblong Room" (*The Saint*, June 1967), in which Captain Leopold investigates a college campus murder with bizarre religious overtones. But from 1965 to the present his most consistent market has been *Ellery Queen's Mystery Magazine*, which with very few exceptions has featured at least one Hoch story a month for the past dozen years. Although his *EQMM* work is usually written in the plainest nuts-and-bolts style, the story concepts are generally stimulating, and his best efforts for the magazine are lovely miniaturizations of the classical fair-play detective novels for which Queen himself is famous.

—Francis M. Nevins, Jr.

HOCKING, (Mona Naomi) Anne (Messer).   Also wrote as Mona Messer.   British.   Born in the 1890's; daughter of the writer Joseph Hocking.

CRIME PUBLICATIONS

Novels (series character: Inspector/Superintendent William Austen)

Mouse Trap (as Mona Messer).   London, Jarrolds, and New York, Putnam, 1931.
Cat's Paw.   London, Stanley Paul, 1933.
Death Duel.   London, Stanley Paul, 1933.
Walk into My Parlour.   London, Stanley Paul, 1934.
The Hunt Is Up.   London, Stanley Paul, 1934.
Without the Option.   London, Stanley Paul, 1935.
Stranglehold.   London, Stanley Paul, 1936.
The House of En-Dor.   London, Stanley Paul, 1936.
As I Was Going to St. Ives.   London, Stanley Paul, 1937.
What a Tangled Web.   London, Stanley Paul, 1937.
Ill Deeds Done.   London, Bles, 1938.
The Little Victims Play.   London, Bles, 1938.
So Many Doors.   London, Bles, 1939.
Old Mrs. Fitzgerald (Austen).   London, Bles, 1939; as *Deadly Is the Evil Tongue*, New
   York, Doubleday, 1940.
The Wicked Flee.   London, Bles, 1940.
Miss Milverton (Austen).   London, Bles, 1941; as *Poison Is a Bitter Brew*, New York,
   Doubleday, 1942.
Night's Candles.   London, Bles, 1941.
One Shall Be Taken (Austen).   London, Bles, 1942.
Death Loves a Shining Mark (Austen).   New York, Doubleday, 1943.
Nile Green (Austen).   London, Bles, 1943.
Six Green Bottles.   London, Bles, 1943.
The Vultures Gather (Austen).   London, Bles, 1945.
Death at the Wedding (Austen).   London, Bles, 1946.
Prussian Blue (Austen).   London, Bles, 1947; as *The Finishing Touch*, New York,
   Doubleday, 1948.
At The Cedars (Austen).   London, Bles, 1949.
Death Disturbs Mr. Jefferson (Austen).   New York, Doubleday, 1950; London, Bles,
   1951.
The Best Laid Plans (Austen).   New York, Doubleday, 1950; London, Bles, 1952.
Mediterranean Murder (Austen).   London, Evans, 1951; as *Killing Kin*, New York,
   Doubleday, 1951.
There's Death in the Cup.   London, Evans, 1952.
Death among the Tulips (Austen).   London, W. H. Allen, 1953.
The Evil That Men Do.   London, W. H. Allen, 1953.
And No One Wept (Austen).   London, W. H. Allen, 1954.
Poison in Paradise (Austen).   London, W. H. Allen, and New York, Doubleday, 1955.
A Reason for Murder (Austen).   London, W. H. Allen, 1955.
Murder at Mid-Day (Austen).   London, W. H. Allen, 1956.
Relative Murder (Austen).   London, W. H. Allen, 1957.
The Simple Way of Poison (Austen).   London, W. H. Allen, and New York, Washburn,
   1957.
Epitaph for a Nurse (Austen).   London, W. H. Allen, 1958; as *A Victim Must Be Found*,
   New York, Doubleday, 1959.
Poisoned Chalice (Austen).   London, Long, 1959.
To Cease upon the Midnight (Austen).   London, Long, 1959.
The Thin-Spun Life (Austen).   London, Long, 1960.
Candidates for Murder (Austen).   London, Long, 1961.
He Had to Die (Austen).   London, Long, 1962.
Murder Cries Out (Austen), completed by Evelyn Healey.   London, Long, 1968.

OTHER PUBLICATIONS as Mona Messer

Novels

A Castle for Sale. London, Methuen, and New York, Dial Press, 1930.
Eternal Compromise. London, Stanley Paul, and New York, Putnam, 1932.
A Dinner of Herbs. London, Stanley Paul, 1933.
The End of the Lane. London, Stanley Paul, 1933.
Playing Providence. London, Stanley Paul, 1934.
Wife of Richard. London, Stanley Paul, 1934.
Cuckoo's Brood. London, Stanley Paul, 1935.
Life Owes Me Something. London, Stanley Paul, 1936.
Tomorrow Also. London, Stanley Paul, 1937.
Marriage Is Like That. London, Stanley Paul, 1938.
Stranger's Vineyard. London, Stanley Paul, 1939.
The Gift of a Daughter. London, Stanley Paul, 1940.

*   *   *

That Mona Messer supplemented her career as a "straight" novelist with over 40 mysteries written as Anne Hocking should surprise no one. Her father, Joseph Hocking, although a religious novelist, was well versed in the use of suspense. And her sister, Elizabeth Nisot, also wrote thrillers – first under the pseudonym William Penmare, and later under her own name. Anne Hocking's own career began in the early 1930's with a series of mysteries containing little detection, but a great many arch-villains, cultured innocents, and obligatory brave-and-beautiful career-girl heroines. Her evolution toward classic detection culminated in the creation, in the late 1930's, of Chief Inspector (later Superintendent) William Austen of Scotland Yard. Thereafter, virtually all of Hocking's mysteries feature Austen. One notable, and appealing, exception is *Night's Candles* in which the co-sleuths are the commandant of the Famagusta Police and his wife, a detective novelist.

Austen is a policeman of the Roderick Alleyn school. He is tall, impeccably dressed, and possessed of a vague military air. He is Oxford educated, "with a charming voice and delightful manners." Suspects often admit that he shatters their stereotyped image of a policeman. Unlike Alleyn, Austen ("a lonely man") never marries. But he does eventually acquire two Watsons: Inspector Curtis and Sergeant Flyte. Neither is highly developed as a character. They do, however, fulfill their major function – as sounding boards for Austen's theories.

Scotland Yard notwithstanding, Austen detects very little in London. Instead, he pursues murderers in such exotic locales as Cyprus, Egypt, South Africa, and the Costa Brava of Spain. And some of Hocking's most effective novels are set in Cornwall.

Like many prolific mystery writers, Hocking displays a certain repetitiousness in her novels. Murder victims tend to be either sadistic older husbands or blackmailers. As to murder methods, a great many barbituate poisonings are punctuated by an occasional fall or bashing. And murderers tend to be so sympathetic that, if they are not saved from the gallows by madness, Austen (always the gent) allows a suicide exit. Suspects often drop a suitable quotation. Unfortunately, the same source may be quoted by different characters in different novels.

This is not to say that Hocking is all cardboard and contrivance. She will often produce a highly satisfying murder method – as in *Prussian Blue* – or a compelling character – as in *Old Mrs. Fitzgerald* and *Miss Milverton*. And she always produces a quiet, amiable mystery, of a type now classic.

—Kathleen L. Maio

HODGSON, William Hope. British. Born in Blackmore End, Essex, 15 November 1877. Went to sea at age 17; became an officer in the Mercantile Marine; later taught physical culture. Joined University of London Officer Training Corps, 1914; commissioned in Royal Field Artillery, 1915; left service because of injury, 1916; recommissioned, 1917, and died at Ypres. Recipient: Royal Humane Society Medal. *Died 17 April 1918.*

CRIME PUBLICATIONS

Short Stories

> *Carnacki, The Ghost Finder, and a Poem.* New York, Reynolds, 1910.
> *Carnacki, The Ghost Finder* (collection). London, Nash, 1913; augmented edition, Sauk City, Wisconsin, Mycroft and Moran, 1947.
> *Captain Gault, Being the Exceedingly Private Log of a Sea-Captain.* London, Nash, 1917; New York, McBride, 1918.

OTHER PUBLICATIONS

Novels

> *The Boats of the "Glen Carrig."* London, Chapman and Hall, 1907.
> *The House on the Borderland.* London, Chapman and Hall, 1908.
> *The Ghost Pirates.* London, Stanley Paul, 1909.
> *The Night Land.* London, Nash, 1912.

Short Stories

> *The Ghost Pirates, A Chaunty, and Another Story.* New York, Reynolds, 1909.
> *Men of the Deep Waters.* London, Nash, 1914.
> *The Luck of the Strong.* London, Nash, 1916.
> *Deep Waters.* Sauk City, Wisconsin, Arkham House, 1967.
> *Out of the Storm: Uncollected Fantasies*, edited by Sam Moskowitz. West Kingston, Rhode Island, Grant, 1975.

Verse

> *Poems and The Dream of X.* London, Watt, and New York, Paget, 1912.
> *Cargunka and Poems and Anecdotes.* London, Watt, and New York, Paget, 1914.
> *The Calling of the Sea.* London, Selwyn and Blount, 1920.
> *The Voice of the Ocean.* London, Selwyn and Blount, 1921.
> *Poems of the Sea.* London, Ferret Fantasy, 1977.

Bibliography: by A. L. Searles, in *The House on the Borderland and Other Novels*, 1946.

*   *   *

William Hope Hodgson was a frequent contributor to the British variety magazines of the early 20th century. He worked in many areas of fiction and non-fiction, and much of his material (including stories with crime elements) is still uncollected.

Captain Gault contains ten adventures of a merchant marine captain who is modelled after C. J. Cutcliffe Hyne's then-popular Captain Kettle. These stories are concerned mostly with outwitting customs authorities in various criminal ways. Much more important are Hodgson's excursions into supernatural fiction, where he is a major figure. His novels *The House on the Borderland, The Ghost Pirates,* and *The Night Land* are visionary accounts that have no real parallels in English literature. Related to them are the adventures of Carnacki, an occult detective.

Carnacki, The Ghost-Finder contains six cases set among the haunts of England and Ireland. While some of these cases are rationalized, others are truly supernatural. These stories embody a mythology which they share with the novels mentioned above: that humanity lives in a state of spiritual and physical peril, surrounded by supernatural forces of utmost malignancy. To further Carnacki's accomplishments Hodgson invented a body of suppositious literature and lore to deal with this hostile universe. In this the influence of Arthur Machen (*The Great God Pan*, "The White People") is probable. The 1947 edition of *Carnacki, The Ghost-Finder* adds three hitherto uncollected stories, two supernatural, and one a rational detective story. Carnacki's adventures, along with those of Le Fanu's Dr. Hesselius and Algernon Blackwood's John Silence, constitute the three great classics in this interesting subdivision of the detective story, where the detective really amounts to a white magician.

—E. F. Bleiler

HOLDING, Elisabeth Sanxay.   American.   Born in Brooklyn, New York, 8 June 1889. Educated at Miss Whitcombe's School; Packer Institute; Miss Botsford's School; Staten Island Academy. Married George E. Holding in 1913 (died, 1943); one daughter and one son. Traveled widely in South America and lived in Bermuda where her husband was a British government officer. *Died 7 February 1955.*

CRIME PUBLICATIONS

Novels (series character: Lieutenant Levy)

Miasma.   New York, Dutton, 1929.
Dark Power.   New York, Vanguard Press, 1930.
The Death Wish.   New York, Dodd Mead, 1934; London, Nicholson and Watson, 1935.
The Unfinished Crime.   New York, Dodd Mead, 1935; London, Newnes, 1936.
The Strange Crime in Bermuda.   New York, Dodd Mead, 1937; London, Lane, 1938.
The Obstinate Murderer.   New York, Dodd Mead, 1938; as *No Harm Intended*, London, Lane, 1939.
The Girl Who Had to Die.   New York, Dodd Mead, 1940.
Who's Afraid?   New York, Duell, 1940; as *Trial by Murder*, New York, Novel Selections, n.d.
Speak of the Devil.   New York, Duell, 1941.
Kill Joy.   New York, Duell, 1942; as *Murder Is a Kill-Joy*, New York, Dell, 1946.
Lady Killer.   New York, Duell, 1942.
The Old Battle Ax.   New York, Simon and Schuster, 1943.
Net of Cobwebs.   New York, Simon and Schuster, 1945; London, Corgi, 1952.
The Innocent Mrs. Duff.   New York, Simon and Schuster, 1946.
The Blank Wall (Levy).   New York, Simon and Schuster, 1947.
Too Many Bottles (Levy).   New York, Simon and Schuster, 1951; London, Muller, 1953; as *The Party Was the Pay-Off*, New York, Spivak, 1952.
The Virgin Huntress.   New York, Simon and Schuster, 1951.

Widow's Mite (Levy).   New York, Simon and Schuster, 1953; London, Muller, 1954.

Uncollected Short Stories

"Kiskadee Bird," in *Third Mystery Companion*, edited by Abraham Louis
Furman.   New York, Gold Label Books, 1945.
"The Blue Envelope," in *Murder for the Millions*, edited by Frank Owen.   New York,
Frederick Fell, 1946.
"Unbelievable Baroness," in *Fourth Mystery Companion*, edited by Abraham Louis
Furman.   New York, Lantern Press, 1946.
"People Do Fall Downstairs," in *Queen's Awards 1947*, edited by Ellery
Queen.   Boston, Little Brown, and London, Gollancz, 1947.
"Farewell, Big Sister," in *Ellery Queen's Mystery Magazine* (New York), July 1952.
"Glitter of Diamonds," in *Ellery Queen's Mystery Magazine* (New York), March 1955.
"Very, Very Dark Mink," in *The Saint* (New York), December 1956.
"The Blank Wall," in *Alfred Hitchcock Presents: My Favorites in Suspense*.   New York,
Random House, 1959.

OTHER PUBLICATIONS

Novels

Invincible Minnie. New York, Doran, and, London, Hodder and Stoughton, 1920.
Rosaleen among the Artists. New York, Doran, 1921.
Angelica. New York, Doran, 1921.
The Unlit Lamp. New York, Dutton, 1922.
The Shoals of Honor. New York, Dutton, 1926.
The Silk Purse. New York, Dutton, 1928.

Other

Miss Kelly. New York, Morrow, 1947.

*   *   *

Best known as a mystery writer, Elisabeth Sanxay Holding also wrote romantic novels and
short stories. All reveal deep interest in psychology and are personality studies flavored with
social criticism or murder. Holding was especially intrigued by middle-aged people under
stress, and she was more concerned with justice than with the letter of the law. Her
continuing character, Lieutenant Levy, is an experienced, clever policeman, unfailingly
decent, courteous, and thoughtful – but not infallible. Levy is never the protagonist; instead,
he symbolizes social order as opposed to the chaos generated by violence.
  This pattern is especially effective in two of Holding's best works. In *The Old Battle Ax*,
Charlotte Herriott allows others to control her life until murder forces her to reevaluate
herself and her extended family circle. In *The Blank Wall*, Lucia Holley's preoccupation with
ration stamps and supportive letters to her serviceman husband is interrupted by murder and
the unsought affection of a criminal. Both women's portraits are clear and realistic; the
symbolism is sound, and the treatment of the generation gap is vivid.
  Lady Killer and *Too Many Bottles* study unwise marriages; *Net of Cobwebs* examines a
damaged personality under extreme pressure. For these protagonists, murder triggers honest
appraisals of midlife situations which are ultimately set right. *The Virgin Huntress* is a
compelling portrait of a cowardly, vain, self-indulgent, and deadly man. Less realistic, *Dark
Power* and *Miasma* are essentially gothics.

A careful, able writer, Holding experimented with many forms within the genre; the works are good, stimulating reading.

—Jane S. Bakerman

HOLDING, James. Also writes as Ellery Queen, Jr. American. Born in Pittsburgh, Pennsylvania, 27 April 1907. Educated at Yale University, New Haven, Connecticut (Editor, *Yale Record*; John Masefield Poetry Prize; John Hubbard Curtis Poetry Prize – twice), B.A. 1928. Married Janet Spice in 1931; two sons. Firebrick salesman, Harbison-Walker, Pittsburgh, 1929–30; Copywriter, 1930–45, Copy Chief, 1945–49, Vice-President, 1949–57, and Consultant, 1958–68, Batten Barten Dun and Osborne Advertising Agency, Pittsburgh. Agent: Scott Meredith Literary Agency Inc., 845 Third Avenue, New York, New York 10022. Address: 1251 Southport Drive, Sarasota, Florida 33581, U.S.A.

CRIME PUBLICATIONS

Uncollected Short Stories

"The Treasure of Pachacamac," in *Ellery Queen's Mystery Magazine* (New York), June 1960.
"The Norwegian Apple Mystery," in *Ellery Queen's Mystery Magazine* (New York), November 1960.
"The African Fish Mystery," in *Ellery Queen's Mystery Magazine* (New York), April 1961.
"The Italian Tile Mystery," in *Ellery Queen's Mystery Magazine* (New York), September 1961.
"A Question of Ethics," in *Best Detective Stories of the Year*, edited by Brett Halliday. New York, Dutton, 1961.
"Do-It-Yourself Escape Kit," in *Ellery Queen's Mystery Magazine* (New York), March 1962.
"Diagnosis: Death," in *The Saint* (New York), July 1962.
"The Photographer and the Undertaker," in *Ellery Queen's Mystery Magazine* (New York), November 1962.
"The Hong Kong Jewel Mystery," in *Ellery Queen's Mystery Magazine* (New York), November 1963.
"The Zanzibar Shirt Mystery," in *Ellery Queen's Mystery Magazine* (New York), December 1963.
"The Photographer and the Policeman," in *Ellery Queen's Mystery Magazine* (New York), April 1964.
"The Tahitian Powder Box Mystery," in *Ellery Queen's Mystery Magazine* (New York), October 1964.
"The Queen's Jewel," in *Crimes Across the Sea*, edited by John Creasey. New York, Harper, 1964.
"Live and Let Live," in *Ellery Queen's Mystery Magazine* (New York), January 1965.

"The Japanese Card Mystery," in *Ellery Queen's Mystery Magazine* (New York), October 1965.

"An Exercise in Insurance," in *Masters of Mayhem*, edited by Edward D. Radin. New York, Morrow, 1965.

"Grounds for Divorce," in *Ellery Queen's Mystery Magazine* (New York), March 1966.

"The Photographer and the Jeweler," in *Ellery Queen's Mystery Magazine* (New York), May 1966.

"The Toothpick Murder," in *Ellery Queen's Mystery Magazine* (New York), July 1966.

"The Photographer and the Professor," in *Ellery Queen's Mystery Magazine* (New York), September 1966.

"The New Zealand Bird Mystery," in *Ellery Queen's Mystery Magazine* (New York), January 1967.

"The Photographer and the Columnist," in *Ellery Queen's Mystery Magazine* (New York), June 1967.

"The Inquisitive Butcher of Nice," in *With Malice Toward All*, edited by Robert L. Fish. New York, Putnam, 1968; London, Macmillan, 1969.

"Cause for Alarm," in *Ellery Queen's Mystery Magazine* (New York), April 1970.

"Test Run," in *Ellery Queen's Mystery Magazine* (New York), July 1970.

"The Photographer and the Servant Problem," in *Ellery Queen's Mystery Magazine* (New York), October 1970.

"Mystery Fan," in *Ellery Queen's Mystery Magazine* (New York), May 1971.

"Second Talent," in *Alfred Hitchcock Presents: Stories to Stay Awake By*. New York, Random House, 1971.

"The Borneo Snapshot Mystery," in *Ellery Queen's Mystery Magazine* (New York), January 1972.

"Cornerback," in *Killers of the Mind*, edited by Lucy Freeman. New York, Random House, 1974.

"Library Fuzz," in *Ellery Queen's Magicians of Mystery*. New York, Davis, 1976.

"The Photographer: Lisbon Assignment," in *Ellery Queen's Mystery Magazine* (New York), February 1976.

"The Mutilated Scholar," in *Ellery Queen's Mystery Magazine* (New York), April 1976.

"Hand in Glove," in *Tricks and Treats*, edited by Joe Gores and Bill Pronzini. New York, Doubleday, 1976; London, Gollancz, 1977.

"The Fund-Raisers," in *Best Detective Stories of the Year 1976*, edited by Edward D. Hoch. New York, Dutton, 1976.

"The Photographer and the Unknown Victim," in *Ellery Queen's Mystery Magazine* (New York), April 1977.

"The Henchman Case," in *Alfred Hitchcock's Mystery Magazine* (New York), May 1977.

"The Philippine Key Mystery," in *When Last Seen*, edited by Arthur Maling. New York, Harper, 1977.

"The Contract," in *Alfred Hitchcock's Mystery Magazine* (New York), August 1977.

"Reason Enough," in *Alfred Hitchcock's Mystery Magazine* (New York), September 1977.

"Rediscovery," in *Best Detective Stories of the Year 1977*, edited by Edward D. Hoch. New York, Dutton, 1977.

"The Swap Shop," in *Alfred Hitchcock's Mystery Magazine* (New York), February 1978.

"One for the Road," in *Mike Shayne Mystery Magazine* (Los Angeles), February 1978.

"The Photographer and the B.L.P.," in *Ellery Queen's Mystery Magazine* (New York), March 1978.

"Once Upon a Bank Floor," in *Alfred Hitchcock's Tales to Scare You Stiff*, edited by Eleanor Sullivan. New York, Davis, 1978.

"The Baby Bit," in *Ellery Queen's Mystery Magazine* (New York), June 1978.

"The Young Runners," in *Ellery Queen's Mystery Magazine* (New York), July 1978.

"In the Presence of Death," in *Ellery Queen's Mystery Magazine* (New York), June 1979.

Other (juvenile)

The Lazy Little Zulu. New York, Morrow, 1962; Kingswood, Surrey, World's Work, 1963.
Cato the Kiwi Bird. New York, Putnam, 1963.
Mr. Moonlight and Omar. New York, Morrow, 1963; Kingswood, Surrey, World's Work, 1964.
The King's Contest and Other North African Tales. London, Abelard Schuman, 1964.
The Mystery of the False Fingertips. New York, Harper, 1964.
Sherlock on the Trail. New York, Morrow, 1964.
The Purple Bird Mystery (as Ellery Queen, Jr.). New York, Putnam, 1965.
The Three Wishes of Hu. New York, Putnam, 1965.
The Sky-Eater and Other South Sea Tales. London, Abelard Schuman, 1966.
Poko and the Golden Demon. London, Abelard Schuman, 1968.
The Robber of Featherbed Lane. New York, Putnam, 1968.
The Mystery of the Dolphin Inlet. New York, Macmillan, 1968.
A Bottle of Pop. New York, Putnam, 1972.
The Watchcat. Middletown, Connecticut, Xerox Educational Publications, 1975.

Manuscript Collection: University of Minnesota Library, Minneapolis.

*   *   *

Retiring from a successful career in advertising, James Holding launched a second career, as a mystery writer, in 1960 with "The Treasure of Pachacamac," a short story about ancient archaeology and modern Peru. He next wrote a series of pastiches in which Ellery Queen the author rather than the detective was the subject. Holding writes of King Danforth and Martin Leroy (names based on Frederic Dannay and Manfred Lee), creators of Leroy King. They are on a round-the-world cruise in which they encounter murder at sea and in almost every port. This permits Holding to present and solve some fine mysteries, using time-tested Queenian devices like the dying message and the locked room. His titles add to the charm of the series, evoking the early Queen – e.g., "The Norwegian Apple Mystery," "The Hong Kong Jewel Mystery," and "The Tahitian Powder Mystery," best in the series.

A second Holding series is entirely different but equally clever. Manuel Andradas is a Brazilian who uses photography to hide his main occupation: professional assassin for "The Big Ones," Brazil's organized crime group. The stories are well plotted, with unexpected complications invariably arising to make Andradas's job more difficult.

In addition to some good (albeit not very deep) views of life in Rio de Janeiro, Holding provides some humorous touches which counter-balance the sense of amorality which the stories convey. Andradas uses the euphemism "nullification" to refer to his work. His discussion of fees with his employers is a parody of labor-management negotiations as a professional killer talks about base pay and his lack of a retirement plan and fringe benefits.

A third series by Holding is less exotic but still depicts an unusual type of detective. Hal Johnson, the titular "Library Fuzz" of the first story in 1972, has the job of recovering stolen and long overdue books from the public library. Inevitably, he comes across more serious crimes, like murder, which he solves using his prior experience as a homicide detective. Though Holding never makes it clear how (or why) a capable detective could be transferred from homicide to library work, his idea is interesting and appealing to mystery fans and book lovers.

—Marvin Lachman

HOLMAN, C(larence) Hugh. Also writes as Clarence Hunt. American. Born in Cross Anchor, South Carolina, 24 February 1914. Educated at Presbyterian College, Clinton, South Carolina, B.S. in chemistry 1936; B.A. in English 1938 (Phi Beta Kappa); New York University, 1939; University of North Carolina, Chapel Hill, Ph.D. 1949. Served as Academic Coordinator in the United States Army Air Corps. Married Verna Virginia McLeod in 1938; one daughter and one son. Instructor, 1939–42, and Academic Dean, 1945–46, Presbyterian College. Instructor, 1946–49, Assistant Professor, 1949–51, Associate Professor, 1951–56, Dean of Arts and Sciences, 1955–56, Professor, 1956–59, Chairman of the English Department, 1957–62, since 1959, Kenan Professor, Dean of the Graduate School, 1963–66, Provost, 1966–68, and since 1972, Special Assistant to the Chancellor, University of North Carolina. Vice-President, 1976–79, and since 1979, President, National Humanities Center. Recipient: Guggenheim Fellowship, 1967; Thomas Jefferson Award, 1975; Mayflower Cup Award, 1976; O. Max Gardner Award, 1977. D.Litt.: Presbyterian College, 1963; L.H.D.: Clemson University, South Carolina, 1969. Address: P.O. Box 2056, Chapel Hill, North Carolina 27514, U.S.A.

CRIME PUBLICATIONS

Novels (series character: Sheriff Macready)

Death Like Thunder. New York, Phoenix Press, 1942.
Trout in the Milk (Macready). New York, Mill, 1945; London, Boardman, 1951.
Slay the Murderer (Macready). New York, Mill, 1946; London, Foulsham, 1950.
Up This Crooked Way (Macready). New York, Mill, 1946; London, Foulsham, 1951.
Another Man's Poison (Macready). New York, Mill, 1947; London, Foulsham, 1950.
Small Town Corpse (as Clarence Hunt). New York, Phoenix Press, 1951.

OTHER PUBLICATIONS

Plays

Thirty-Seven Octobers (produced Chapel Hill, North Carolina, 1969).

Radio Plays: 200 plays for *Forum of the Air* series, 1938–41.

Other

A Handbook to Literature. New York, Odyssey Press, 1960; 4th edition, 1980.
Thomas Wolfe. Minneapolis, University of Minnesota Press, 1960.
John P. Marquand. Minneapolis, University of Minnesota Press, 1965.
Three Modes of Modern Southern Fiction. Athens, University of Georgia Press, 1966.
The Roots of Southern Writing. Athens, University of Georgia Press, 1972.
"Detective Fiction as American Realism," in *Popular Literature in America*, edited by James C. Austin and Donald A. Koch. Bowling Green, Ohio, Bowling Green University Press, 1972.
The Loneliness at the Core: Studies in Thomas Wolfe. Baton Rouge, Louisiana State University Press, 1975.
The Immoderate Past. Athens, University of Georgia Press, 1977.
Windows on the World. Knoxville, University of Tennessee Press, 1979.

Editor, *The Short Novels of Thomas Wolfe.* New York, Scribner, 1961.
Editor, *The Thomas Wolfe Reader.* New York, Scribner, 1962.
Editor, *The World of Thomas Wolfe.* New York, Scribner, 1962.

Editor, *Views and Reviews in American Literature, History and Fiction*, by William Gilmore Simms. Cambridge, Massachusetts, Harvard University Press, 1962.

Editor, *The American Novel Through Henry James* (bibliography). New York, Appleton Century Crofts, 1966; revised edition, 1979.

Editor, *Ten Nights in a Bar-Room*, by T. S. Arthur, and *In His Steps*, by Charles M. Sheldon. New York, Odyssey Press, 1966.

Editor, with Sue Fields Ross, *The Letters of Thomas Wolfe to His Mother*. Chapel Hill, University of North Carolina Press, 1968.

Editor, with Richard Beale Davis and Louis D. Rubin, Jr., *Southern Writing 1585–1920*. New York, Odyssey Press, 1970.

Editor, *The Partisan Leader*, by Nathaniel Beverley Tucker. Chapel Hill, University of North Carolina Press, 1971.

Editor, with Louis D. Rubin, Jr. *Southern Literary Study: Problems and Possibilities*. Chapel Hill, University of North Carolina Press, 1975.

C. Hugh Holman comments:

My detective stories are the sins of my literary youth; sins not in the sense that the form is not noble but that I worked in it no better than I did. My lifetime involvement with literature has always found its own relief in the detective story, which, as a boy, I learned to love in the works of Poe, Doyle, and Anna Katharine Green, and which I have continued to relish throughout my life. In many respects my highest admiration is for the constructors of complex and elaborate plots and impossible crimes – for S. S. Van Dine, the *early* Ellery Queen, and, above all, John Dickson Carr (I am inordinately proud that Carr dedicated his last novel, *The Hungry Goblin*, to me). I have always enjoyed the comic element in detective fiction, too (another reason for admiring Carr). So, when I began to try to write the detective story as an avocation, I found in Percival Wilde's *Inquest* and *Tinsley's Bones* a kind of comic character that appealed to me greatly and that I tried to unite with the Carr-like impossible crime. I have recently read again – after many years – the Sheriff Macready stories, and I found them young, very dated, and sometimes awkward, but re-reading them brought back memories of the happiness I got from writing them, and renewed my hope that their readers also got pleasure from them, whether they were the Americans I set out to address, or the English, Argentinians, French, and Italians who, to my surprise, seemed to like them better than Americans did.

*   *   *

C. Hugh Holman, best known as a critic and historian of southern American literature, has scholarly publications that more than triple the number of his detective novels. Nevertheless, the high calibre of his mystery fiction warrants his being recognized as a practitioner as well as a theorist of the genre. In his article "Detective Fiction as American Realism" he says that "the detective story is often a cross between the novel of manners ... and the local color story." His own novels fit his definition admirably.

Set in the fictional college town of Abeton, South Carolina, Holman's novels deal with social mores as well as social problems appropriate to the provincial southern locale. In *Death Like Thunder*, for example, "Carolina justice" is excoriated by the native son who takes on the defense of the hapless Yankee falsely accused of a crime. The classic plots, complex but logical, generally involve the exoneration of an innocent outsider through the joint efforts of a local resident, usually the sheriff, and the suspect himself.

Holman's most notable creation is Sheriff Macready, the affable, "countrified" law officer who is given to literary quotation and good grammar when matters get tense. Macready makes the first of this four appearances in *Trout in the Milk*, where he quotes the Thoreauvian source of the title and explains, "Ain't no harm in a sheriff reading, is there, as long as he don't tell the voters he's doing it?" Like Michael Innes, Holman does not escape his own erudition in his escapist novels: each title is a quotation and each novel is liberally sprinkled with literary references.

—Nancy C. Joyner

HOLMES, H. H. See **BOUCHER, Anthony.**

HOLTON, Leonard. Pseudonym for Leonard (Patrick O'Connor) Wibberley; also writes as Patrick O'Connor; Christopher Webb. Irish. Born in Dublin, 9 April 1915. Educated at Ring College, Waterford, Ireland; Abbey House, Romsey, Hampshire; Cardinal Vaughan's School, London, 1925–30; El Camino College, Torrance, California. Served in the Trinidad Artillery Volunteers, 1938–40: Lance Bombardier. Married Katherine Hazel Holton in 1948; two daughters and four sons. Reporter, *Sunday Dispatch*, 1931–32, *Sunday Express*, 1932–34, and *Daily Mirror*, 1935–36, all London; Editor, Trinidad *Evening News*, 1936; oilfield worker, Trinidad, 1936–43; Cable Editor, Associated Press, New York, 1943–44; New York Correspondent and Bureau Chief, London *Evening News*, 1944–46; Editor, *Independent Journal*, San Rafael, California, 1947–49; Reporter and Copy Editor, Los Angeles *Times*, 1950–54. Agent: McIntosh and Otis Inc., 475 Fifth Avenue, New York, New York 10017. Address: Box 522, Hermosa Beach, California 90254, U.S.A.

CRIME PUBLICATIONS

Novels (series character: Father Joseph Bredder in all books)

The Saint Maker. New York, Dodd Mead, 1959; London, Hale, 1960.
A Pact with Satan. New York, Dodd Mead, 1960; London, Hale, 1961.
Secret of the Doubting Saint. New York, Dodd Mead, 1961.
Deliver Us from Wolves. New York, Dodd Mead, 1963.
Flowers by Request. New York, Dodd Mead, 1964.
Out of the Depths. New York, Dodd Mead, 1966; London, Hammond, 1967.
A Touch of Jonah. New York, Dodd Mead, 1968.
A Problem in Angels. New York, Dodd Mead, 1970.
The Mirror of Hell. New York, Dodd Mead, 1972.
The Devil to Play. New York, Dodd Mead, 1974.
A Corner of Paradise. New York, St. Martin's Press, 1977.

OTHER PUBLICATIONS as Leonard Wibberley

Novels

Mrs. Searwood's Secret Weapon. Boston, Little Brown, 1954; London, Hale, 1955.

The Mouse That Roared. Boston, Little Brown, 1955; as *The Wrath of Grapes*, London, Hale, 1955.

McGillicuddy McGotham. Boston, Little Brown, 1956; London, Hale, 1957.

Take Me to Your President. New York, Putnam, 1957.

Beware of the Mouse. New York, Putnam, 1958.

The Quest of Excalibur. New York, Putnam, 1959.

The Hands of Cormac Joyce. New York, Putnam, 1960; London, Muller, 1962.

Stranger at Killknock. New York, Putnam, 1961; London, Muller, 1963.

The Mouse on the Moon. New York, Morrow, 1962; London, Muller, 1963.

A Feast of Freedom. New York, Morrow, 1964.

The Island of the Angels. New York, Morrow, 1965.

The Centurion. New York, Morrow, 1966.

The Road from Toomi. New York, Morrow, 1967.

Adventures of an Elephant Boy. New York, Morrow, 1968.

The Mouse on Wall Street. New York, Morrow, 1969.

Meeting with a Great Beast. New York, Morrow, 1971; London, Chatto and Windus, 1972.

The Testament of Theophilus. New York, Morrow, 1973; as *Merchant of Rome*, London, Cassell, 1974.

The Last Stand of Father Felix. New York, Morrow, 1974.

One in Four. New York, Morrow, 1977.

Plays

Black Jack Rides Again. Chicago, Dramatic Publishing Company, 1971.

1776 – And All That. New York, Morrow, 1975.

Once, In a Garden. Chicago, Dramatic Publishing Company, 1975.

Verse

The Ballad of the Pilgrim Cat (juvenile). New York, Washburn, 1962.

The Shepherd's Reward (juvenile). New York, Washburn, 1963.

Other

The King's Beard (juvenile). New York, Farrar Straus, 1952; London, Faber, 1954.

The Coronation Book: The Dramatic Story as History and Legend (juvenile). New York, Farrar Straus, 1953.

The Secret of the Hawk (juvenile). New York, Farrar Straus, 1953; London, Faber, 1956.

Deadmen's Cave (juvenile). New York, Farrar Straus, and London, Faber, 1954.

The Epics of Everest (juvenile). New York, Farrar Straus, 1954; London, Faber, 1955.

The Wound of Peter Wayne (juvenile). New York, Farrar Straus, 1955; London, Faber, 1957.

The Life of Winston Churchill (juvenile). New York, Farrar Straus, 1956; revised edition, 1965.

The Trouble with the Irish (or the English, Depending on Your Point of View). New York, Holt Rinehart, 1956; London, Muller, 1958.

John Barry, Father of the Navy (juvenile). New York, Farrar Straus, 1957.

Kevin O'Connor and the Light Brigade (juvenile). New York, Farrar Straus, 1957; London, Harrap, 1959.

Wes Powell, Conquerer of the Grand Canyon (juvenile). New York, Farrar Straus, 1958.

The Coming of the Green. New York, Holt Rinehart, 1958.

John Treegate's Musket (juvenile). New York, Farrar Straus, 1959.

No Garlic in the Soup (on Portugal).   New York, Washburn, 1959; London, Faber, 1960.
Peter Treegate's War (juvenile).   New York, Farrar Straus, 1960.
The Land That Isn't There: An Irish Adventure.   New York, Washburn, 1960.
Sea Captain from Salem (juvenile).   New York, Farrar Straus, 1961.
Yesterday's Land: A Baja California Adventure.   New York, Washburn, 1961.
Zebulon Pike, Soldier and Explorer (juvenile).   New York, Funk and Wagnalls, 1961.
The Time of the Lamb (juvenile).   New York, Washburn, 1961.
Ventures into the Deep: The Thrill of Scuba Diving.   New York, Washburn, 1962.
Treegate's Raiders (juvenile).   New York, Farrar Straus, 1962.
Ah Julian! A Memoir of Julian Brodetsky.   New York, Washburn, 1963.
Fiji: Islands of the Dawn.   New York, Washburn, 1964.
Toward a Distant Island: A Sailor's Odyssey.   New York, Washburn, 1966.
Something to Read.   New York, Washburn, 1967.
Encounter near Venus (juvenile).   New York, Farrar Straus, 1967; London, Macdonald, 1968.
Man of Liberty: A Life of Thomas Jefferson (juvenile).   New York, Farrar Straus, 1968.
   1. *Young Man from the Piedmont: The Youth of Thomas Jefferson.*   New York, Farrar Straus, 1963.
   2. *A Dawn in the Trees: Thomas Jefferson, The Years 1776 to 1789.*   New York, Farrar Straus, 1964.
   3. *The Gales of Spring: Thomas Jefferson, The Years 1789 to 1801.*   New York, Farrar Straus, 1965.
   4. *Time of the Harvest: Thomas Jefferson, The Years 1801 to 1826.*   New York, Farrar Straus, 1966.
Attar of the Ice Valley (juvenile).   New York, Farrar Straus, and London, Macdonald, 1969.
Hound of the Sea.   New York, Washburn, 1969.
Journey to Untor (juvenile).   New York, Farrar Straus, 1970; London, Macdonald, 1971.
Leopard's Prey (juvenile).   New York, Farrar Straus, 1971.
Voyage by Bus.   New York, Morrow, 1971.
The Shannon Sailors: A Voyage to the Heart of Ireland.   New York, Morrow, 1972.
Flint's Island (juvenile).   New York, Farrar Straus, 1972; London, Macdonald, 1973.
Red Pawns (juvenile).   New York, Farrar Straus, 1973.
Guarneri, Violin Maker of Genius (juvenile).   New York, Farrar Straus, 1974; London, Macdonald and Jane's, 1976.
The Last Battle (juvenile).   New York, Farrar Straus, 1976.

Other as Patrick O'Connor (juvenile)

The Lost Harpooner.   New York, Washburn, 1947; London, Harrap, 1959.
The Flight of the Peacock.   New York, Washburn, 1954.
The Society of Foxes.   New York, Washburn, 1954.
The Watermelon Mystery.   New York, Washburn, 1955.
Gunpowder for Washington.   New York, Washburn, 1956.
The Black Tiger.   New York, Washburn, 1956.
Mexican Road Ace.   New York, Washburn, 1957.
Black Tiger at Le Mans.   New York, Washburn, 1958.
The Five-Dollar Watch.   New York, Washburn, 1959.
Black Tiger at Bonneville.   New York, Washburn, 1960.
Treasure at Twenty Fathoms.   New York, Washburn, 1961.
Black Tiger at Indianapolis.   New York, Washburn, 1962.
The Raising of the Dubhe.   New York, Washburn, 1964.
Seawind from Hawaii.   New York, Washburn, 1965.

South Swell.   New York, Washburn, 1967; London, Macdonald, 1968.
Beyond Hawaii.   New York, Washburn, 1969; London, Macdonald, 1970.
A Car Called Camellia.   New York, Washburn, 1970.

Other as Christopher Webb (juvenile)

Matt Tyler's Chronicle.   New York, Funk and Wagnalls, 1958; London, Macdonald, 1966.
Mark Toyman's Inheritance.   New York, Funk and Wagnalls, 1960.
The River of Pee Dee Jack.   New York, Funk and Wagnalls, 1962.
The "Ann and Hope" Mutiny.   New York, Funk and Wagnalls, 1966; London, Macdonald, 1967.
Eusebius, The Phoenician.   New York, Funk and Wagnalls, 1969; London, Macdonald, 1970.

Manuscript Collection: University of Southern California, Los Angeles.

*   *   *

Leonard Wibberley, probably best known as the author of *The Mouse That Roared*, uses the pseudonym Leonard Holton for publishing his series of mystery novels featuring a detective-priest, Father Joseph Bredder, OFM. Father Bredder, ex-marine, skilled boxer, and chaplain for the Convent of Holy Innocents, solves mysteries with well-drawn backgrounds as diverse as the worlds of scuba-diving, professional baseball, and rare violins. He most often works with his friend Lieutenant Minardi of the police, and the novels include a cast of recurring colorful characters from the seamy section of east Los Angeles.

Holton handles well the technical problems of classic puzzle mystery stories. Father Bredder's status as a priest eliminates the mildly distasteful undercurrent of officious meddling that often taints fiction's amateur detectives. His vocation inherently demands a real concern with sin and sinners, and his interest in identifying criminals is an extension of his commitment to save souls and combat evil. Holton's priest has other advantages as a plausible series detective: his work naturally involves him with people of all classes and backgrounds; his clerkly poverty explains his odd bits of out-of-the-way knowledge, since he can afford only those randomly assorted books sold two-for-a-quarter at bookstalls; people readily confide in and trust him, and years of hearing confessions have honed his sense of human motives. Moreover, since Father Bredder and Lieutenant Minardi frequently solve a case almost simultaneously – one relying on "spiritual fingerprints," the other on more conventional methods of detection – the requisite exposition of the puzzle's solution is gracefully motivated by their mutual explanations of how they reached the same conclusion by different routes. This double chain of evidence also reinforces the reader's sense of the appropriateness of the offered solution.

While each of the Holton books presents a perfectly adequate puzzle in detection, the books are equally enjoyable for the delineation of Father Bredder's personality and his approach to the problems he encounters. Bredder's chief characteristic, as both priest and detective, is his spiritually derived sense of the deep connectedness of superficially disparate things. Sometimes this quality leads him to perceive relationships between a current mystery and events of long ago. In *Flowers by Request*, for example, he solves the puzzle of a mobster's murder by comparing it with the killing of William Rufus, son of William the Conqueror, in 1100. Similarly, in *Deliver Us from Wolves*, his investigation of apparent outbreaks of lycanthropy in a rural Portuguese village reveals the answers to two mysteries, one highly contemporary, one unsolved since the early 18th century. Father Bredder more than once intuits a connection between present-day crimes the police are treating as unrelated (e.g., in *Out of the Depths* and *A Problem in Angels*).

Characteristically, the Bredder books contain two corollary plots, one involving criminal detection, the other Father Bredder's clerical activities. This strategy of double plotting is successful largely because each of the novels is informed by a single spiritual concern. *Secret of the Doubting Saint*, for example, turns on the importance of doubt as a path to truth; the solution of the mystery through active doubting on the part of Bredder and Minardi thus becomes emblematic of this larger principle. Similarly, *A Corner of Paradise* involves multiple instances of racial prejudice; indeed, prejudice, in a surprising variation, turns out to have motivated the novel's murder. This technique of pervading each novel with a single informing theme gives Holton's books a structural coherence both rare in detective fiction and persuasively suited to the nature of their protagonist.

—Susan B. MacDougall

HOME, Michael. See **BUSH, Christopher.**

HOMES, Geoffrey. Pseudonym for Daniel Mainwaring. American. Born in Dunlap, California in 1902. Educated at Fresno State College, California. Office boy, itinerant fruit picker, salesman, private detective, teacher, and reporter for 10 years on San Francisco *Chronicle*. Self-employed writer, later employed as screenwriter and publicist for Warner Brothers and scenarist for Paramount; produced and recorded unusual sound effects for rental to film studios in the 1930's and 1940's. *Died in 1978.*

CRIME PUBLICATIONS

Novels (series characters: Robin Bishop; Humphrey Campbell; Jose Manuel Madero)

> *One Against the Earth* (as Daniel Mainwaring). New York, Long and Smith, 1933.
> *The Doctor Died at Dusk* (Bishop). New York, Morrow, 1936.
> *The Man Who Murdered Himself* (Bishop). New York, Morrow, and London, Lane, 1936.
> *The Man Who Didn't Exist* (Bishop). New York, Morrow, 1937; London, Eyre and Spottiswoode, 1939.
> *The Man Who Murdered Goliath* (Bishop). New York, Morrow, 1938; London, Eyre and Spottiswoode, 1940.
> *Then There Were Three* (Bishop and Campbell). New York, Morrow, 1938; London, Cherry Tree, 1945.
> *No Hands on the Clock* (Campbell). New York, Morrow, 1939.
> *Finders Keepers* (Campbell). New York, Morrow, 1940.
> *Forty Whacks* (Campbell). New York, Morrow, 1941; as *Stiffs Don't Vote*, New York, Bantam, 1947.
> *The Street of the Crying Woman* (Madero). New York, Morrow, 1942; as *Seven Died*, London, Cherry Tree, 1943; as *The Case of the Mexican Knife*, New York, Bantam, 1948.

The Hill of the Terrified Monk (Madero). New York, Morrow, 1943; as *Dead as a Dummy*, New York, Bantam, 1949.

Six Silver Handles (Campbell). New York, Morrow, 1944; London, Cherry Tree, 1946; as *The Case of the Unhappy Angels*, New York, Bantam, 1950.

Build My Gallows High. New York, Morrow, 1946.

Uncollected Short Story

"The Judge Finds the Body," in *The Mystery Companion*, edited by Abraham Louis Furman. New York, Gold Label, 1943.

OTHER PUBLICATIONS

Plays

Screenplays: *Secrets of the Underworld*, with Robert Tasker, 1943; *Dangerous Passage*, 1945; *Scared Stiff*, with Maxwell Shane, 1945; *Swamp Fire*, 1946; *Tokyo Rose*, with Maxwell Shane and Whitman Chambers, 1946; *Hot Cargo*, 1946; *They Made Me a Killer*, with others, 1946; *Big Town*, with Maxwell Shane, 1947; *Out of the Past*, with Frank Fenton, 1947; *Roughshod*, with Hugo Butler and Peter Viertel, 1949; *The Big Steal*, with Gerald Drayson Adams, 1949; *The Eagle and the Hawk*, with Lewis R. Foster and Jess Arnold, 1950; *The Lawless*, 1950; *The Last Outpost*, with others, 1950; *Roadblock*, with others, 1951; *The Tall Target*, with others, 1951; *This Woman Is Dangerous*, with George Worthing Yates and Bernard Girard, 1952; *Bugles in the Afternoon*, with Harry Brown, 1952; *Powder River*, with Sam Hellman, 1953; *Those Redheads from Seattle*, with Lewis R. Foster and George Worthing Yates, 1953; *Alaska Seas*, with Walter Doniger, 1954; *Black Horse Canyon*, with David Lang, 1954; *Southwest Passage*, with Harry Essex, 1954; *The Desperado*, 1954; *The Annapolis Story*, with Daniel Ullman, 1955; *A Bullet for Joey*, with A. I. Bezzerides and James Benson Nablo, 1955; *The Phenix City Story*, with Crane Wilbur, 1955; *Invasion of the Body Snatchers*, 1956; *Thunderstorm*, with George St. George, 1956; *Baby Face Nelson*, with Robert Adler and Irving Shulman, 1957; *Cole Younger, Gunfighter*, 1957; *Space Master X-7*, with George Worthing Yates, 1958; *The Gun Runners*, with Paul Monash, 1958; *Walk Like a Dragon*, with James Clavell, 1960; *Atlantis, The Lost Continent*, 1961; *The Minotaur*, with S. Continenza and G. P. Calligari, 1961; *Revolt of the Slaves* (English dialogue), with Duccio Tessaria and Stefano Strucchi, 1961; *East of Kilimanjaro*, with Arnold Belgard and Richard Goldstone, 1962; *Convict Stage*, with Donald Barry, 1966; *The Woman Who Wouldn't Die*, 1966.

*   *   *

There is a body of mystery writers whose work is of consistently high quality, but who, for unexplainable reasons, have received little attention among students and aficionados of the genre. Geoffrey Homes is one of these writers. Between 1936 and 1946, Homes published 12 detective and suspense novels set primarily in the valleys and foothills of north-central California. Each is distinguished by clever plotting, semi-hard-boiled realism, fast-paced action, witty and remarkably good dialogue, and some of the finest and most vivid descriptive passages in mystery fiction. Each also offers an excellent portrait of rural and small-town life in California during the Depression and World War II years.

His first five books feature the adventures of newspaperman Robin Bishop; the best of these are *The Doctor Died at Dusk* and *The Man Who Didn't Exist*. His most memorable series character, however, is his second: Humphrey Campbell, an unconventional private detective who, with his fat, lazy, and corrupt partner Oscar Morgan, appears in one of the Robin Bishop novels and four of his own. *Finders Keepers* is perhaps the most effective of the Campbell sagas, although *No Hands on the Clock* and *Forty Whacks* rank as close seconds.

The best of the other novels – and his best book overall – is his last, *Build My Gallows High*. This is a powerful suspense tale, strong on mood and characterization, which tells the story of a man named Red Bailey who is haunted and ultimately destroyed by events in his past. It was transferred to the screen as *Out of the Past*, starring Robert Mitchum and Kirk Douglas – a film which is considered by many to be a crime classic.

Mainwaring began to write "B" pictures in Hollywood in 1942, and abandoned novels in 1946 to become a full-time scriptwriter.

—Bill Pronzini

HORLER, Sydney. British. Born in Leytonstone, Essex, 18 July 1888. Educated at Redcliffe and Colston schools, Bristol. Served in the Propaganda Section of Air Intelligence, 1918. Married. Journalist: Reporter, *Western Daily Press*, Bristol, 1905–11; special writer, E. Hulton Ltd., Manchester, and on staffs of *Daily Mail* and *Daily Citizen*, both London, before 1918; worked for Newnes publications, London, and sub-editor, *John O'London's Weekly*, 1919. *Died 27 October 1954.*

CRIME PUBLICATIONS

Novels (series characters: The Ace; Bunny Chipstead; H. Emp; Sir Brian Fordinghame; Gerald Lissendale; Chief Constable Meatyard; Nighthawk [Gerald Frost]; Sebastian Quin; Peter Scarlett; Tiger Standish; Baron Veseloffsky; Paul Vivanti; Robert Wynnton)

The Breed of the Beverleys. London, Odhams Press, 1921.
Love, The Sportsman. London, Hodder and Stoughton, 1923; as *The Man with Two Faces*, London, Collins, 1934.
The Mystery of No. 1 (Vivanti). London, Hodder and Stoughton, 1925; as *The Order of the Octopus*, New York, Doran, 1926.
False-Face (Veseloffsky; Fordinghame). London, Hodder and Stoughton, and New York, Doran, 1926.
The House of Secrets. London, Hodder and Stoughton, 1926; New York, Doran, 1927.
The Black Heart. London, Hodder and Stoughton, 1927; New York, Doubleday, 1928.
In the Dark (Chipstead). London, Hodder and Stoughton, 1927; as *A Life for Sale*, New York, Doubleday, 1928.
Vivanti. London, Hodder and Stoughton, and New York, Doran, 1927.
Chipstead of the Lone Hand. London, Hodder and Stoughton, 1928; New York, Holt, 1929.
The 13th Hour. London, Readers' Library, 1928.
The Curse of Doone. London, Hodder and Stoughton, 1928; New York, Mystery League, 1930.
Miss Mystery (Veseloffsky). London, Hodder and Stoughton, 1928; Boston, Little Brown, 1935.
The Secret Service Man (Lissendale). London, Hodder and Stoughton, 1929; New York, Knopf, 1930.
Heart Cut Diamond. London, Hodder and Stoughton, 1929.

Lady of the Night. London, Hodder and Stoughton, 1929; New York, Knopf, 1930.

Peril! New York, Mystery League, 1930; as *Cavalier of Chance*, London, Hodder and Stoughton, 1931.

Checkmate. London, Hodder and Stoughton, 1930.

Danger's Bright Eyes. London, Hodder and Stoughton, 1930; New York, Harper, 1932.

The Evil Chateau. London, Hodder and Stoughton, 1930; New York, Knopf, 1931.

The Murder Mask. London, Readers' Library, 1930.

Adventure Calling! London, Hodder and Stoughton, 1931.

The Man Who Walked with Death. New York, Knopf, 1931; London, Hodder and Stoughton, 1942.

Princess after Dark. London, Hodder and Stoughton, 1931; as *The False Purple*, New York, Mystery League, 1932.

The Spy. London, Hodder and Stoughton, 1931.

The Temptation of Mary Gordon. London, Newnes, 1931.

Wolves of the Night. London, Readers' Library, 1931.

Vivanti Returns. London, Hodder and Stoughton, 1931.

Gentleman-in-Waiting. London, Benn, 1932.

High Stakes (Fordinghame). London, Collins, 1932; Boston, Little Brown, 1935.

Horror's Head (Emp). London, Hodder and Stoughton, 1932.

My Lady Dangerous. London, Collins, 1932; New York, Harper, 1933.

Tiger Standish. London, Long, 1932; New York, Doubleday, 1933.

The Formula. London, Long, 1933; as *The Charlatan*, Boston, Little Brown, 1934; London, Marshall, 1949.

Harlequin of Death. London, Long, and Boston, Little Brown, 1933.

Huntress of Death. London, Hodder and Stoughton, 1933.

The Menace. London, Collins, and Boston, Little Brown, 1933.

The Man from Scotland Yard. London, Hutchinson, 1934.

The Secret Agent (Chipstead). London, Collins, and Boston, Little Brown, 1934.

S.O.S. London, Hutchinson, 1934.

The Prince of Plunder (Fordinghame). London, Hodder and Stoughton, and Boston, Little Brown, 1934.

Tiger Standish Comes Back. London, Hutchinson, 1934.

The Lessing Murder Case. London, Collins, 1935.

Lord of Terror (Vivanti). London, Collins, 1935; New York, Curl, 1937.

The Mystery of the Seven Cafés: The Novel of the Famous Wireless Play (Standish). London, Hodder and Stoughton, 1935.

The Vampire. London, Hutchinson, 1935; New York, Bookfinger, 1974.

Death at Court Lady. London, Collins, 1936.

The Grim Game (Standish). London, Collins, and Boston, Little Brown, 1936.

The Traitor. London, Collins, and Boston, Little Brown, 1936.

The Hidden Hand. London, Collins, 1937.

Instruments of Darkness. London, Hodder and Stoughton, 1937.

They Called Him Nighthawk. London, Hodder and Stoughton, 1937.

The Destroyer, and The Red-Haired Death. London, Hodder and Stoughton, 1938.

The Evil Messenger (Quin). London, Hodder and Stoughton, 1938.

Dark Journey. London, Hodder and Stoughton, 1938.

A Gentleman for the Gallows. London, Hodder and Stoughton, and New York, Curl, 1938.

The Phantom Forward. London, Hodder and Stoughton, 1939.

Terror on Tip-Toe. London, Hodder and Stoughton, 1939.

Tiger Standish Takes the Field. London, Hodder and Stoughton, 1939.

Here Is an S.O.S. (Meatyard). London, Hodder and Stoughton, 1939.

The Man Who Died Twice. London, Hodder and Stoughton, 1939.

The Enemy Within the Gates (Chipstead). London, Hodder and Stoughton, 1940.

The Return of Nighthawk.   London, Hodder and Stoughton, 1940.
Tiger Standish Steps on It.   London, Hodder and Stoughton, 1940.
Enter the Ace.   London, Hodder and Stoughton, 1941.
Nighthawk Strikes to Kill.   London, Hodder and Stoughton, 1941.
Tiger Standish Does His Stuff (2 novelets).   London, Hodder and Stoughton, 1941.
Danger Preferred.   London, Hodder and Stoughton, 1942.
Fear Walked Behind (Quin).   London, Hale, 1942.
The Man in White.   London, Staples Press, 1942.
The Night of Reckoning.   London, Eyre and Spottiswoode, 1942.
The Hostage.   London, Quality Press, 1943.
High Hazard.   London, Hodder and Stoughton, 1943.
The Man Who Preferred Cocktails.   London, Crowther, 1943.
Murder Is So Simple.   London, Eyre and Spottiswoode, 1943.
The Lady with the Limp (Standish).   London, Hodder and Stoughton, 1944.
The Man with Dry Hands.   London, Eyre and Spottiswoode, 1944.
Nighthawk Mops Up.   London, Hodder and Stoughton, 1944.
A Bullet for the Countess.   London, Quality Press, 1945.
Virus X (Vivanti).   London, Quality Press, 1945.
Dark Danger.   New York, Mystery House, 1945.
Terror Comes to Twelvetrees.   London, Eyre and Spottiswoode, 1945.
Great Adventure, and Out of a Dark Sky (2 novelets).   London, Hale, 1946.
Corridors of Fear.   London, Quality Press, 1947.
Ring Up Nighthawk.   London, Hodder and Stoughton, 1947.
The Closed Door (Lissendale).   London, Pilot Press, 1948.
Exit the Disguiser (Standish).   London, Hodder and Stoughton, 1948.
The House with the Light.   London, Hodder and Stoughton, 1948.
The Man Who Did Not Hang.   London, Quality Press, 1948.
The Man Who Loved Spiders (Meatyard).   London, Barker, 1949.
They Thought He Was Dead (Standish).   London, Hodder and Stoughton, 1949.
Whilst the Crowd Roared.   Stoke on Trent, Archer Press, 1949.
A Man of Affairs.   London, Pilot Press, 1949.
Master of Venom (Emp).   London, Hodder and Stoughton, 1949.
The Blanco Case.   London, Quality Press, 1950.
The High Game.   London, Redman, 1950.
The House of the Uneasy Dead.   London, Barker, 1950.
Nap on Nighthawk.   London, Hodder and Stoughton, 1950.
Scarlett − Special Branch.   London, Foulsham, 1950.
The Devil Comes to Bolobyn.   London, Marshall, 1951.
The Man in the Cloak (Wynnton).   London, Eyre and Spottiswoode, 1951.
The House of Jackals (Standish).   London, Hodder and Stoughton, 1951.
The Man of Evil.   London, Barker, 1951.
Murderer at Large (Emp).   London, Hodder and Stoughton, 1951.
The Mystery of Mr. X.   London, Foulsham, 1951.
Scarlett Gets the Kidnapper.   London, Foulsham, 1951.
These Men and Women.   London, Museum Press, 1951.
The Blade Is Bright.   London, Eyre and Spottiswoode, 1952.
The Face of Stone.   London, Barker, 1952.
Hell's Brew (Ace).   London, Hodder and Stoughton, 1952.
The Man Who Used Perfume (Wynnton).   London, Wingate, 1952.
The Mocking Face of Murder.   London, Hale, 1952.
The Web.   London, Redman, 1952.
The Cage.   London, Hale, 1953.
The Dark Night (Ace).   London, Hodder and Stoughton, 1953.
Death of a Spy.   London, Museum Press, 1953.
The Secret Hand.   London, Barker, 1954.

Nighthawk Swears Vengeance. London, Hodder and Stoughton, 1954.
The Man in the Hood. London, Redman, 1955.
The Man in the Shadows. London, Hale, 1955.
The Dark Hostess. London, Eyre and Spottiswoode, 1955.

Short Stories

The Worst Man in the World. London, Hodder and Stoughton, 1929.
The Screaming Skull and Other Stories. London, Hodder and Stoughton, 1930.
The Mystery Mission and Other Stories. London, Hodder and Stoughton, 1931.
The Man Who Shook the Earth. London, Hutchinson, 1933.
Beauty and the Policeman. London, Hutchinson, 1933.
Dying to Live and Other Stories. London, Hutchinson, 1935.
The House in Greek Street. London, Hodder and Stoughton, 1935; revised edition,
    London, Crowther, 1946.
The Stroke Sinister and Other Stories. London, Hutchinson, 1935.
Knaves & Co. London, Collins, 1938.
Tiger Standish Has a Party. London, Todd, 1943.
Murder for Sale. London, Vallancey Press, 1945.

OTHER PUBLICATIONS

Novels

Standish of the Rangeland: A Story of Cowboy Pluck and Daring. London, Newnes,
    1916.
Goal! A Romance of the English Cup Ties. London, Odhams Press, 1920.
A Legend of the League. London, Hodder and Stoughton, 1922.
McPhee. London, Jenkins, 1922; as *The Great Game*, London, Collins, 1935.
The Ball of Fortune. London, Aldine Press, 1925.
School! School! London, Partridge, 1925.
On the Ball! London, Blackie, 1926.
The Man Who Saved the Club. London, Aldine Press, 1926.
The Fellow Hagan! London, Cassell, 1927.
The House of Wingate (as Martin Heritage). London, Hurst and Blackett, 1928; as *A
    House Divided*, New York, Macaulay, 1929.
Romeo and Julia (as Peter Cavendish). London, Hodder and Stoughton, 1928.
A Pro's Romance. London, Newnes, 1930.
The Exploits of Peter. London, Collins, 1930.
Song of the Scrum. London, Hutchinson, 1934.
The Man Who Stayed to Supper: A Comedy. London, Jenkins, 1941.
Now Let Us Hate. London, Quality Press, 1942.
Springtime Comes to William. London, Jenkins, 1943.
Marry the Girl. London, Jenkins, 1945.
High Pressure. London, Jenkins, 1946.
Oh, Professor! London, Jenkins, 1946.
The Man with Three Wives. London, Jenkins, 1947.
Man Alive. London, Jenkins, 1948.
Haloes for Hire. London, Jenkins, 1949.
The Beacon Light. London, Jenkins, 1949.
Wedding Bells. London, Jenkins, 1950.
Dr. Cupid. London, Jenkins, 1951.
Girl Trouble. London, Jenkins, 1951.

Plays

The House of Secrets, adaptation of his own novel (produced London, 1927).
Oh! My Aunt (produced Birmingham, 1928).
Midnight Love (produced London, 1931). London, Jenkins, 1931.
Death at Court Lady (produced London, 1934).
The Man Who Died Twice. London, Nelson, 1941.
The Man Who Mislaid the War. London, Muller, 1943.

Other

Black Soul. London, Jarrolds, 1931.
Writing for Money. London, Nicholson and Watson, 1932.
Excitement: An Impudent Autobiography. London, Hutchinson, 1933.
Strictly Personal: An Indiscreet Diary. London, Hutchinson, 1934.
London's Underworld: The Record of a Month's Sojourn in the Crime Centres of the Metropolis. London, Hutchinson, 1934.
More Strictly Personal: Six Months of My Life. London, Rich and Cowan, 1935.
Malefactors' Row: A Book of Crime Studies. London, Hale, 1940.
I Accuse the Doctors, Being a Candid Commentary on the Hostility Shown by the Leaders of the Medical Profession Towards the Healing Art of Osteopathy, and How the Public Suffers in Consequence. London, Redman, 1949.

* * *

Sydney Horler competed for the same audience as Edgar Wallace, though the latter, an equally prolific writer, had the advantage of having appeared much earlier. Each specialized in the thriller; Horler's publisher advertised his books with the phrase "Horler for Excitement." After Wallace's untimely death in 1932, Horler acquired many of his readers. Never reticent, Horler ignored few opportunities for self-advertisement, even stressing the number of words (25,000) he dictated weekly. Once Horler announced that, having purchased the machine Edgar Wallace had used, he was shocked to discover the late owner's voice appearing on a *new* cylinder he had dictated. Though many were skeptical, no one was able to prove or disprove Horler's allegations.

A man of strong likes and dislikes, Horler wrote five books in which he combined autobiography, personal opinion, and advice to the reader. His fiction does an equally good job of conveying his tastes. Horler greatly respected British royalty, and his most famous series character is an aristocrat, the Honourable Timothy Overbury "Tiger" Standish. Horler invested Standish with some of his own prejudices against non-Anglo-Saxons. Thus, we find Standish referring to Jews in a derogatory manner and using expressions such as "stinking Italianos."

A self-proclaimed moralist, Horler was critical of much of the post-World War I behavior in Europe. He especially abhorred the French Riviera, an implied criticism of another competitor, E. Phillips Oppenheim, whose high living there was well-known. Horler probably let his own moral code influence him most in his series about Gerald Frost, better known as Nighthawk. In such books as *They Called Him Nighthawk* and *The Return of Nighthawk*, Frost is a cracksman who steals jewelry only from society women he feels are of loose morality. He writes "wanton" on their pillowslips, with their own lipsticks, at the conclusions of his burglaries.

Horler was repelled by homosexuality, taking care to describe his heroes in terms that would leave no doubts in the reader's mind. Thus, of the hero of the non-crime book *The House of Wingate* Horler says, "no one could have mistaken him for being anything but a virile man." He described Standish as possessing "all the attributes of a thoroughly likable fellow ... he likes his glass of beer, he is a confirmed pipe smoker, he is always ready to smile back into the face of danger."

Creator of larger-than-life heroes, Horler himself is recognizable in some of his supporting characters. In *The Curse of Doone* secret agent Ian Heath is aided by Jerry Hartsell, a farmer with poor eyesight, who enjoys writing. Horler's own visual impairment prevented him from achieving his ambition to become an RAF pilot, limiting his wartime service to propaganda writing. The hero's best friend in *The House of Wingate*, the brave and loyal Selby Fowne, is described as a "stout comfortable tub of a man," an accurate picture of the author, according to available photographs.

Horler's considerable narrative skill gained him enormous popularity with a relatively undemanding public. This story-telling ability was able to overcome his recurring tendency to, in his own words, "give old man coincidence's arm a frightful twist." Characters constantly meet, disappear, and reappear in his books, with little thought of credibility. As a result of these coincidences and Horler's lack of subtlety in plotting and characterization, time has not treated his work very well. At present hardly anyone reads Horler, while his contemporaries such as Christie, Sayers, Blake, Allingham, and even Edgar Wallace, remain popular.

—Marvin Lachman

HORNUNG, E(rnest) W(illiam).   British.   Born in Middlesbrough, Yorkshire, 7 June 1866. Educated at Uppingham School. Married Constance Doyle, sister of Arthur Conan Doyle, in 1893; one son. Tutor at Mossgiel Station, Riverina, Australia, 1884–86; worked for the YMCA in France during World War I. *Died 22 March 1921.*

CRIME PUBLICATIONS

Novels

A Bride from the Bush.   London, Smith Elder, and New York, United States Book Company, 1890.
Tiny Luttrell.   London and New York, Cassell, 2 vols., 1893.
The Boss of Taroomba.   London, Bliss, 1894; New York, Scribner, 1900.
The Rogue's March.   London, Cassell, and New York, Scribner, 1896.
Irralie's Bushranger.   London, Beeman, and New York, Scribner, 1896.
My Lord Duke.   London, Cassell, and New York, Scribner, 1897.
Young Blood.   London, Cassell, and New York, Scribner, 1898.
Dead Men Tell No Tales.   London, Methuen, and New York, Scribner, 1899.
The Belle of Toorak.   London, Richards, 1900; as *The Shadow of a Man*, New York, Scribner, 1901.
Peccavi.   London, Richards, and New York, Scribner, 1900.
At Large.   New York, Scribner, 1902.
Denis Dent.   London, Isbister, 1903; New York, Stokes, 1904.
The Camera Fiend.   London, Unwin, and New York, Scribner, 1911.
The Thousandth Woman.   London, Nash, and Indianapolis, Bobbs Merrill, 1913.

Short Stories (series character: A. J. Raffles)

Under Two Skies.   London, A. and C. Black, 1892; New York, Macmillan, 1895.
Some Persons Unknown.   London, Cassell, and New York, Scribner, 1898.

The Amateur Cracksman. London, Methuen, and New York, Scribner, 1899; as
   Raffles, The Amateur Cracksman, London, Nash, 1906.
The Black Mask. London, Richards, 1901; as *Raffles: Further Adventures of the
   Amateur Cracksman,* New York, Scribner, 1901.
The Shadow of the Rope (Raffles). London, Chatto and Windus, and New York,
   Scribner, 1902.
Stingaree. London, Chatto and Windus, and New York, Scribner, 1905.
A Thief in the Night (Raffles). London, Chatto and Windus, and New York, Scribner,
   1905.
Mr. Justice Raffles. London, Smith Elder, and New York, Scribner, 1909.
Witching Hill. London, Hodder and Stoughton, and New York, Scribner, 1913.
The Crime Doctor. London, Nash, and Indianapolis, Bobbs Merrill, 1914.
Old Offenders and a Few Old Scores. London, Murray, 1923.

OTHER PUBLICATIONS

Novels

The Unbidden Guest. London and New York, Longman, 1894.
No Hero. London, Smith Elder, and New York, Scribner, 1903.
Fathers of Men. London, Smith Elder, and New York, Scribner, 1912.

Plays

Raffles, The Amateur Cracksman, with Eugene W. Presbrey, adaptation of stories by
   Hornung (produced New York, 1903; London, 1906).
Stingaree, The Bushranger, adaptation of his own stories (produced London, 1908).
A Visit from Raffles, with Charles Sansom, adaptation of stories by Hornung (produced
   London, 1909).

Verse

The Ballad of Ensign Joy. New York, Dutton, 1917.
Wooden Crosses. London, Nisbet, 1918.
The Young Guard. London, Constable, 1919.

Other

Trusty and Well Beloved: The Little Record of Arthur Oscar Hornung (as E. W.
   H.). Colchester, Essex, privately printed, 1915.
Notes of a Camp-Follower on the Western Front. London, Constable, and New York,
   Dutton, 1919.
E. W. Hornung and His Young Guard, 1914 (poems and addresses), edited by Shane R.
   Chichester. Crowthorne, Berkshire, Wellington College Press, 1941.

*   *   *

I put E. W. Hornung's linked stories about A. J. Raffles, gentleman cracksman, squarely
beside the Holmes tales of Conan Doyle (curiously, Hornung's brother-in-law). Both sets of
stories seem to me to have that feeling of absolute rightness, perhaps the surest way of
distinguishing that hard to define thing "the classic." There are blemishes in the Raffles
stories, as there are (whisper it not) in the Holmes tales. But the faults in the end seem no
more than flakes of rust on engines that work with smooth perfection.
   There is certainly no need to make more allowances than that for Hornung's stories.
Although they date from the turn of the century, they can be read today with shining

pleasure. And this comes not simply from their period atmosphere, strong and delightful though that is. Unless you remember them exceptionally well, they can be re-read and still provide genuine surprises. Hornung had grasped the secret of the adventure tale, which is not only to make your reader ask "What next? What next?" but also to make him cry out "How on earth will he wriggle out of it this time?"

For Hornung was a fine craftsman, and craftsmanship is a quality more necessary within the tight limits of the short story than it is in the novel where there is room for diversions to conceal basic machinery inclined to clank. Look, however, at the way in which Hornung adroitly varies a basic formula (a gentleman who is a thief and who gets away with it despite odds) which on the face of it one would think could hardly bear repetition more than two or three times. Sometimes he takes Raffles out of the snug, snobby private flats of the Albany to a different location; sometimes he gives him a tinge of being a righter of wrongs; sometimes he makes a story a duel with the formidable Inspector Mackenzie; sometimes he shows Raffles as a master of disguise. Finally, he showed his craftsmanship to the utmost in killing Raffles off and, bar writing a few "posthumous" tales, refusing more firmly than this brother-in-law to bring an immensely popular figure back to life.

But what ingenuity he showed in working the formula while there was still life in it. I quote only one instance – but it must stand for many. In the story "Out of Paradise" Raffles's friend Bunny, artless as ever, tells him about a goodies-crammed house owned by one Hector Carruthers with whose niece Bunny is in love. Of course, it is taboo to burgle a place Bunny has got to know in these circumstances. Ah, but, says Raffles, the present owner is not Mr. Carruthers but Lord Lochmaben. Oh, replies Bunny, reader of nothing in the papers but the cricket and the racing news, that's all right then. And, whether we know in advance or not that Mr. Carruthers has recently been made Lord Lochmaben, the trick delights us.

Yet Hornung was more than merely clever. He had all the sensitivity of the good writer. It was George Orwell who pointed out that a lesser writer would have crudely made his gentleman-burglar a lord or a baronet to get the maximum showy contrast. Hornung made Raffles no more than a gentleman pure and simple. Time and again in the stories one comes across not the brutally obvious (and dull), but the next-to-obvious and truth-stamped.

The reason, ultimately, why Raffles has lived when other creations using much the same contrast formula have vanished is that Raffles is far more than a walking formula. He is a person. I have already said that instead of being a stuffed aristocrat he is no more than a gentleman. But note how precisely Hornung placed him in society: a gentleman, yes, but one always strapped for money. And what other attributes he gives him. Yes, he is a cricketer of renown (an easy, but not too easy way of giving him heroic qualities) but he is no sporting hearty. On the walls of the Albany apartment are pre-Raphaelite etchings, the arty okay painters of that day.

Compare him here to Sherlock Holmes who also had a strain of the art-lover in him under the outer shell of the scientific, emotionless detective. There is yet more, in fact, to this comparison. Both Holmes and Raffles were apt to act from motives that brought them not great rewards but rather the satisfaction of exercising their arts. And both too had a similar relationship with the fictitious person who presented them to the public. For Doyle's stolid, mildly obtuse Watson, Hornung gave us Bunny, not the brightest of intellects but brave and all too loyal, a puppy to the bulldog Watson. Add, too, that to redeem anti-social traits (Holmes's cocaine) both heroes were ardent patriots in the days when this was a natural feeling among the great body of the public. Holmes has a pock-marked "VR" in honour of Queen Victoria on his walls; Raffles sent the Queen a (stolen) gold cup for her Jubilee declaring, "For sixty years, Bunny, we've been ruled over by absolutely the finest sovereign the world has ever seen." Like Doyle, one might add, Hornung could capture to a T the right way for his hero to speak.

Finally, if Sherlock Holmes went from rough conception in his creator's mind to become first a recognisable human being and then a figure of myth, exactly the same process happened with A. J. Raffles. It happened perhaps on a lesser scale, but it happened securely nevertheless. Raffles is an abiding hero.

—H. R. F. Keating

HOSKEN, Clifford.   See KEVERNE, Richard.

––––––––––––––

HOUGH,   S(tanley)   B(ennett). Also   writes   as   Rex   Gordon;   Bennett Stanley.   British.   Born in Preston, Lancashire, 25 February 1917.   Educated at Preston Grammar School; Radio Officers College, Preston; attended classes of the Workers Educational Association. Married Justa E. C. Wodschow in 1938. Radio Operator, Marconi Radio Company, 1936–38; Radio Officer, International Marine Radio Company, 1939–45; ran a yachting firm, 1946–51. Recipient: Infinity Award, for science fiction, 1957. Agent: A. M. Heath and Company Ltd., 40–42 William IV Street, London WC2N 4DD. Address: 21 St. Michael's Road, Ponsanooth, Truro, Cornwall, England.

CRIME PUBLICATIONS

Novels (series character: Inspector Brentford)

Frontier Incident.   London, Hodder and Stoughton, 1951; New York, Crowell, 1952.
Moment of Decision.   London, Hodder and Stoughton, 1952.
Mission in Guemo.   London, Hodder and Stoughton, 1953; New York, Walker, 1964.
The Alscott Experiment (as Bennett Stanley).   London, Hodder and Stoughton, 1954.
Government Contract (as Bennett Stanley).   London, Hodder and Stoughton, 1956.
Extinction Bomber.   London, Lane, 1956.
The Bronze Perseus (Brentford).   London, Secker and Warburg, 1959; New York, Walker, 1962; as *The Tender Killer*, New York, Avon, 1963.
Dear Daughter Dead (Brentford).   London, Gollancz, 1965; New York, Walker, 1966.
Sweet Sister Seduced (Brentford).   London, Gollancz, 1968.
Fear Fortune, Father (Brentford).   London, Gollancz, 1974.

OTHER PUBLICATIONS

Novels

Sea Struck (as Bennett Stanley).   New York, Crowell, 1953; as *Sea to Eden*, London, Hodder and Stoughton, 1954.
The Seas South.   London, Hodder and Stoughton, 1953.
The Primitives.   London, Hodder and Stoughton, 1954.
Beyond the Eleventh Hour.   London, Hodder and Stoughton, 1961.

Novels as Rex Gordon

Utopia 239.   London, Heinemann, 1955.
No Man Friday.   London, Heinemann, 1956; as *First on Mars*, New York, Ace, 1957.
First to the Stars.   New York, Ace, 1959; as *The Worlds of Eclos*, London, Consul, 1961.
First Through Time.   New York, Ace, 1962; as *The Time Factor*, London, Tandem, 1964.
Utopia minus X.   New York, Ace, 1967; as *The Paw of God*, London, Tandem, 1967.
The Yellow Fraction.   New York, Ace, 1969; London, Dobson, 1972.

Other

A Pound a Day Inclusive: The Modern Way to Holiday Travel.   London, Hodder and
Stoughton, 1957.
*Expedition Everyman: Your Way on Your Income to All the Desirable Places of
Europe.*   London, Hodder and Stoughton, 1959.
Expedition Everyman 1964.   London, Hodder and Stoughton, 1964.
*Where? An Independent Report on Holiday Resorts in Britain and the
Continent.*   London, Hodder and Stoughton, 1964.

S. B. Hough comments:
   Much of the literature of our time is formless and shapeless; the detective story on the
other hand can and frequently does have a form as demanding as that of a Mozart symphony,
while, at the same time, offering the literary artist a medium of inquiry into human folly and
psychology and the life of his times. I am honoured to have made a small contribution to this
major art-form which, in other hands than mine, uses the simplest of literary devices to
explore the depths of human motivation; but I would rather that readers approached my
work anticipating what they have a right to expect – an entertaining story.

*   *   *

   Readers of S. B. Hough's fiction quickly become aware that Hough is a crime writer with a
purpose. His purpose is twofold and clearly set forth in the fiction itself. First, Hough uses
crime writing to chart the "human character as a whole." He does this because, as a surgeon
says in *Dear Daughter Dead*, "you can't throw up surgery and take to the study of the
brain.... We know nothing about the subject. Who studies the human character as a whole?
We leave it to novelists and playwrights." Second, Hough puts crime fiction to the task of
exploring the "modern predicament," modern meaning existential. Morality in such a world
is personal and situational. Hence, as Hough himself suggests in an author's apology to *Sweet
Sister Seduced*, his works are more appropriately called "did-he-do-its" than "whodunits."
Even when we know that a Hough character "did it" (literally), we are not sure he "did it"
morally. The converse is also true.
   Hough pursues the task of studying the human character as a whole and exploring the
modern predicament through two distinct types of crime writing. On the one hand, he writes
novels of the criminal mind in the tradition of Dostoevsky, Patricia Highsmith, and Julian
Symons. Two of the better novels in this mode are *The Bronze Perseus* and *Fear Fortune,
Father*. On the other hand, he presents a more reflective, distanced view of the human
character in police procedural novels, featuring Chief Detective Inspector Brentford.
Brentford serves as both a filter and a focus for further studies of the criminal mind.
   Hough is at his best when he makes the reader sympathetic with the criminal's moral
world. This is done boldly in *Fear Fortune, Father*. There Hough presents a criminal mind
sans filter. Told in first-person, the whole of the novel is a chronicle of Dalby Pearson's
journey from unemployed technical manager to master criminal. Since the reader is locked
into the narrative perspective of Dalby, Dalby's moral world becomes the reader's own. That
moral world is cynical and existential. And it is the subject of the novel. Dalby's world is
almost convincing, almost acceptable. His anger toward the established business order is
made understandable. His compassion for a crippled girl, Delicia, is admirable. And his
activity as a criminal is non-violent, victimless. Nevertheless, the story refuses to resolve itself
into the happy ending Dalby's move to Penfolds (an exclusive seaside retreat) betokens. In the
final pages, Dalby comes to realize that his inventions now have a history and a will of their
own. His nicely created world is threatened by his own history as a thief, his wife's
unpunished crimes, and the emergence of Delicia as his "Lolita." The web he has spun may
become his own death trap, or at least spell the end of his good fortune. Then we discover
that the tale he has told is both his novel (for money's sake) and his last testament (for

conscience's sake). The book is Dalby's hedge against a future he now doubts he can either posit or control.

The world presented in Hough's procedural novels is but a step from his psychological, existential crime novels. Inspector Brentford is a likeable detective – dedicated, plodding, right-headed, middle-class. At his best, Brentford is both foil to and investigator of the criminal mind. In *Sweet Sister Seduced*, Brentford's own happy marriage and middle-class success clash with the failed middle-class world of one Mr. Milham. Like Dalby in *Fear Fortune, Father*, Milham lives in a fragile world spun from his own mind. Milham's family, in a fit of Victorian rage, disowns Elizabeth (his sister) because she is pregnant out of wedlock. Milham resolves to help her. And through a series of strange, unforeseeable events he finds it necessary to pose as her husband. Once struck, the pose lasts for decades, ending only with his sister/wife's death. Elizabeth's death is investigated by Brentford. During the investigation, Brentford, his wife, and the reader are forced to contemplate the relativity and fragility of the morality and reality as they are understood by the "average person." The entire investigation takes place under a shadow cast by the works of Freud and Kafka. And the final solution does little to erase the terror inherent in the case.

Hough is a crime writer who places the crime story into the philosophical and moral web Dostoevsky wove for it and which existentialism stretched into "truth." At bottom, though, Hough is a stern critic of the existentialist world-view – but he can make it perform a dazzling death dance across the surface of his narratives.

—Larry E. Grimes

HOUSEHOLD, Geoffrey (Edward West). British. Born in Bristol, 30 November 1900. Educated at Clifton College, Bristol, 1914–19; Magdalen College, Oxford, 1919–22, B.A. (honours) in English 1922. Served in the Intelligence Corps, 1939–45: Lieutenant Colonel; Territorial Decoration; mentioned in despatches. Married Ilona M. J. Zsoldos-Gutmán in 1942; one son and two daughters. Engaged in commerce abroad, 1922–35. Address: Church Headland, Whitchurch, Aylesbury, Buckinghamshire, England.

CRIME PUBLICATIONS

Novels

> *The Third Hour.* London, Chatto and Windus, 1937; Boston, Little Brown, 1938.
> *Rogue Male.* London, Chatto and Windus, and Boston, Little Brown, 1939; as *Man Hunt*, New York, Triangle, 1942.
> *Arabesque.* London, Chatto and Windus, and Boston, Little Brown, 1948.
> *The High Place.* London, Joseph, and Boston, Little Brown, 1950.
> *A Rough Shoot.* London, Joseph, and Boston, Little Brown, 1951.
> *A Time to Kill.* Boston, Little Brown, 1951; London, Joseph, 1952.
> *Fellow Passenger.* London, Joseph, and Boston, Little Brown, 1955; as *Hang the Man High*, New York, Spivak, 1957.
> *Watcher in the Shadows.* London, Joseph, and Boston, Little Brown, 1960.
> *Thing to Love.* London, Joseph, and Boston, Little Brown, 1963.
> *Olura.* London, Joseph, and Boston, Little Brown, 1965.
> *The Courtesy of Death.* London, Joseph, and Boston, Little Brown, 1967.
> *Dance of the Dwarfs.* London, Joseph, and Boston, Little Brown, 1968.

Doom's Caravan.   London, Joseph, and Boston, Little Brown, 1971.
The Three Sentinels.   London, Joseph, and Boston, Little Brown, 1972.
The Lives and Times of Bernardo Brown.   London, Joseph, 1973; Boston, Little Brown, 1974.
Red Anger.   London, Joseph, and Boston, Little Brown, 1975.
Hostage — London: The Diary of Julian Despard.   London, Joseph, and Boston, Little Brown, 1977.
The Last Two Weeks of Georges Rivac.   London, Joseph, and Boston, Little Brown, 1978.

Short Stories

The Salvation of Pisco Gabar and Other Stories.   London, Chatto and Windus, 1938; augmented edition, Boston, Little Brown, 1940.
Tales of Adventurers.   London, Joseph, and Boston, Little Brown, 1952.
The Brides of Solomon and Other Stories.   London, Joseph, and Boston, Little Brown, 1958.
Sabres on the Sand and Other Stories.   London, Joseph, and Boston, Little Brown, 1966.
The Cats to Come.   London, Joseph, 1975.
The Europe That Was.   Newton Abbot, Devon, David and Charles, and New York, St. Martin's Press, 1979.

OTHER PUBLICATIONS

Other

The Terror of Villadonga (juvenile).   London, Hutchinson, 1936; revised edition, as *The Spanish Cave*, Boston, Little Brown, 1936; London, Chatto and Windus, 1940.
The Exploits of Xenophon (juvenile).   New York, Random House, 1955; as *Xenophon's Adventure*, London, Bodley Head, 1961.
Against the Wind (autobiography).   London, Joseph, 1958; Boston, Little Brown, 1959.
Prisoner of the Indies (juvenile).   London, Bodley Head, and Boston, Little Brown, 1967.
Escape into Daylight (juvenile).   London, Bodley Head, and Boston, Little Brown, 1976.

Manuscript Collection: Lilly Library, Indiana University, Bloomington.

*   *   *

The lost list of Geoffrey Household's books is varied in both nature and quality, but it includes at least three thrillers of the first order: *Rogue Male, Watcher in the Shadows,* and *Dance of the Dwarfs.* The subject and sustaining interest of these three works is the same: the human hunt or chase. As a chase novelist Household deserves to rank with Buchan, Greene, and the wartime Michael Innes; he occupies an especially interesting place in the history of the genre because of his knack of combining the atmosphere of open-air virility that distinguishes Buchan's work with the interest in political anxiety and private terrors that characterize more recent contributions to the form.

All of Household's heroes are to some degree descendants of Buchan's Richard Hannay. They are slightly raffish gentleman-adventurers, deeply involved in the world of English blood sports and imbued with a public-school code of honour, chivalry, and sportsmanship. Their adventures are frequently conducted against the background of the English counties; in *Rogue Male,* for example, the hero finally confronts his enemy on the territory of the Cattistock Hunt in Dorset. Yet at the same time the stories are impregnated with modern political turmoil. *Rogue Male* begins with the hero's attempt to assassinate an unnamed

European dictator (presumably Hitler), continues with his torture by Gestapo-like interrogators, and ends with his return to the task of assassination, promising, "I shall not miss." In *Watcher in the Shadows* the hero is pursued by a man who mistakenly believes him to have participated in Nazi artrocities. The hero of *Dance of the Dwarfs* is a research scientist living in the South American jungle on terms of uneasy truce with the local Marxist guerillas.

Although both genteel sportsmanship and modern politics are part of the essential background of Household's stories, they rarely predominate. His main interest is in the psychology of his heroes, their reactions to accumulating fears and dangers. His favourite story-telling device (and he handles it like a master) is the first-person narrative, the confessional diary in which the writer attempts to understand and order the experiences he is undergoing. "I have recently noted a tendency to talk to myself," begins Dr. Owen Dawnay in *Dance of the Dwarfs*. "I start on this exercise book again, for I dare not leave my thoughts uncontrolled," explains the nameless narrator of *Rogue Male*.

Viewed in thriller terms, the stories that these men tell are a series of artfully contrived shocks and reversals in which hunter and hunted stalk each other, lay elaborate false scents and exchange roles, before eventually confronting each other in a life-and-death struggle. In psychological terms, the stories show the heroes shedding, first, the appurtenances of civilized life and, finally, some of the attributes of human identity itself. Their narratives have the isolated and desperate quality of Poe's "MS Found in a Bottle" or William Godwin's *Caleb Williams*. Toward the end of *Rogue Male* the hero has himself become a hunted animal, quite literally going to earth in a hole in the ground. Dr. Dawnay of *Dance of the Dwarfs* is drawn into a complex intimacy with the sinister jungle animals whom he hunted and who now hunt him. Such books are sophisticated and gripping revelations of the animal beneath the veneer of civilized life. And Household clearly sees that animal state to which his heroes are reduced not as a form of debasement but as a condition of stubborn courage and integrity – a final manifestation of grace under pressure.

—Ian Ousby

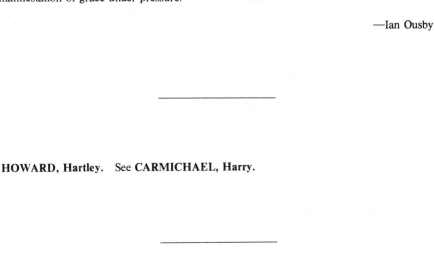

HOWARD, Hartley.   See CARMICHAEL, Harry.

HUBBARD, P(hilip) M(aitland).   British.   Born in Reading, Berkshire, 9 November 1910. Educated at Elizabeth College, Guernsey, 1919–29; Jesus College, Oxford (Newdigate Prize, 1933), 1929–34. Has three children. Worked in the Indian Civil Service in the Punjab, 1934–47; worked for the British Council, 1948–51; free-lance writer, 1951–55; worked for the National Union of Manufacturers, 1955–60. Agent: A. P. Watt and Son, 26–28 Bedford Row, London WC1R 4HL, England.

CRIME PUBLICATIONS

Novels

Flush as May. London, Joseph, and New York, British Book Centre, 1963.
Picture of Millie. London, Joseph, and New York, British Book Centre, 1964.
A Hive of Glass. London, Joseph, and New York, Atheneum, 1965.
The Holm Oaks. London, Joseph, 1965; New York, Atheneum, 1966.
The Tower. New York, Atheneum, 1967; London, Bles, 1968.
The Country of Again. New York, Atheneum, 1968; as *The Custom of the Country*, London, Bles, 1969.
Cold Waters. New York, Atheneum, 1969; London, Bles, 1970.
High Tide. New York, Atheneum, 1970; London, Macmillan, 1971.
The Dancing Man. New York, Atheneum, and London, Macmillan, 1971.
The Whisper of the Glen. New York, Atheneum, and London, Macmillan, 1972.
A Rooted Sorrow. New York, Atheneum, and London, Macmillan, 1973.
A Thirsty Evil. New York, Atheneum, and London, Macmillan, 1974.
The Graveyard. New York, Atheneum, and London, Macmillan, 1975.
The Causeway. London, Macmillan, 1976; New York, Doubleday, 1978.
The Quiet River. London, Macmillan, and New York, Doubleday, 1978.
Kill Claudio. London, Macmillan, 1979.

Uncollected Short Stories

"The Running of the Deer," in *Winter's Crimes 6*, edited by George Hardinge. London, Macmillan, 1974.
"The Altar Tomb," in *Scottish Short Stories 1977*. London, Collins, 1977.
"Leave It to the River," in *Scottish Short Stories 1978*. London, Collins, 1978.

OTHER PUBLICATIONS

Play

Radio Play: *Dead Man's Bay*, 1966.

Verse

Ovid among the Goths. Oxford, Blackwell, 1933.

Other (juvenile)

Anna Highbury. London, Cassell, 1963.
Rat-Trap Island. London, Cassell, 1964.

*   *   *

Since 1963 P. M. Hubbard has produced a fine suspense novel almost every year. His writing is singular in its simplicity and elegance. A survey of his crime fiction reveals that there is, in fact, quite a variety of settings and situations, but an impression remains of almost mythic conflict between few characters, of elemental struggle acted out in a lonely world of brooding landscapes and cold waters. Protagonists, some merely odd or whimsical, others clearly abnormal, are driven by their compulsions.

Hubbard's first two novels, *Flush as May* and *Picture of Millie*, are decidedly different from those that follow. The former is a traditional mystery in which two Oxford undergraduates discover why a body found by the heroine early one May morning disappears. The Old

Religion is alive and well in some remote villages. Perhaps less successful, and certainly unrepresentative, is *Picture of Millie*, a tale with numerous characters and an unexpected ending which does not quite hold together.

The central character in *A Hive of Glass*, more rogue than hero, is a passionate collector of old glass. His collecting mania drives him to extraordinary action when a peculiar household on an isolated tidal island seems to invite violence. In a sense, *The Holm Oaks* sets the pattern for what is to evolve as the Hubbard model: a solitary hero is compelled by circumstances or his own needs to commit acts which, once begun, must continue to a climax, either satisfactory or disastrous. A menacing atmosphere overshadows eroticism and violence, the more powerful for being understated. A matter-of-fact recital of information about seemingly ordinary people, as it accumulates, turns into a very threatening narrative. Occasionally Hubbard misses his mark, as in, some may think, *A Rooted Sorrow* or *The Graveyard*. When he succeeds the results are memorable.

In *The Holm Oaks* the stark setting and dark deeds are lightened by humor. Jake Haddon, the narrator, meets Dennis Wainwright, a sinister type, and muses: "He was a very tall, stiff man, and curiously neat. In a place and weather which sent me naturally to superimposed jerseys, he wore a solid dark suit with a collar and tie. I wondered whether he had been somebody's butler." Wainwright seeks obliquely to learn Haddon's interests, and Haddon notes: "I hesitated between necromancy and numismatics." Ironically, Elizabeth, Jake's unloved wife, is delighted with the dismal woods. A fanatic bird-watcher, she hopes to identify a night heron which her husband calls a "queer tern."

The Country of Again, a fine and original novel set in Pakistan, charts the resolution of a crime which took place twenty years earlier when the protagonist was a magistrate in the Indian Civil Service. In *The Dancing Man*, Hubbard portrays a remote place in Wales where the ruins of a Cistercian abbey rest uneasily atop a prehistoric site similar to the one at Avebury. Centuries ago, vandals destroyed the abbey and changed the image of a cross, incised on the only stone left standing, into a cavorting ithyphallic figure, mocking the intrusion of the monks. An archeologist who comes to visit the owner of the site, a medievalist with an excessive pride of possession, disappears. *A Thirsty Evil*, one of Hubbard's best, concerns an artificial lake, deep and always cold, a peculiar stone pillar which sticks up from the bottom of the lake, and an odd family. The hero arrives in search of Julia, a woman he loves almost at first sight. Her brother and sister, beautiful and golden, seem like sea creatures in the water, but the brother is insane and the sister is a nymphomaniac whom the hero likens to Cressida. The text is sprinkled with Shakespearean allusions, and the hero is, in Julia's words, intent on "his proper bane."

P. M. Hubbard is easily one of the best contemporary writers of suspense fiction. His "thrillers" are, in psychological complexity and literary quality, comparable to the novels of Patricia Highsmith. His fascination with water, sailing, and adventure invites comparison with Andrew Garve's, but while Garve is basically optimistic and upbeat, Hubbard deals with a darker aspect of these subjects. Most crime novels are quickly read and as quickly forgotten, but P. M. Hubbard's books linger in the memory and in the imagination.

—Mary Helen Becker

HUGHES, Dorothy B(elle, née Flanagan). American. Born in Kansas City, Missouri, 10 August 1904. Educated at the University of Missouri, Columbia, B.J. 1924; University of New Mexico, Albuquerque; Columbia University, New York. Married Levi Allen Hughes, Jr., in 1932 (died, 1975); two daughters and one son. Teaching Fellow, University of New Mexico; reporter and woman's editor in the 1920's. Crime reviewer since the 1930's: for the

Albuquerque *Tribune*, Los Angeles *News* and *Mirror*, New York *Herald-Tribune*, and since 1961, Los Angeles *Times*. Recipient: Mystery Writers of America Edgar Allan Poe Award, for criticism, 1950, Grand Master Award, 1978. Agent: Blanche Gregory, 2 Tudor City Place, New York, New York. Address: 113 Zia Road West, Santa Fe, New Mexico 87501, U.S.A.

CRIME PUBLICATIONS

Novels (series character: Inspector Tobin)

The So Blue Marble (Tobin).   New York, Duell, 1940.
The Cross-Eyed Bear (Tobin).   New York, Duell, 1940; London, Nicholson and Watson, 1943.
The Bamboo Blonde.   New York, Duell, 1941.
The Fallen Sparrow (Tobin).   New York, Duell, 1942; London, Nicholson and Watson, 1943.
The Blackbirder.   New York, Duell, 1943; London, Nicholson and Watson, 1948.
The Delicate Ape.   New York, Duell, 1944.
Johnnie.   New York, Duell, 1944; London, Nicholson and Watson, 1946.
Dread Journey.   New York, Duell, 1945; London, Nicholson and Watson, 1948.
Ride the Pink Horse.   New York, Duell, 1946.
The Scarlet Imperial.   New York, Mystery Book, 1946; as *Kiss for a Killer*, New York, Spivak, 1954.
In a Lonely Place.   New York, Duell, 1947; London, Nicholson and Watson, 1950.
The Candy Kid.   New York, Duell, 1950.
The Davidian Report.   New York, Duell, 1952; as *The Body on the Bench*, New York, Dell, 1955.
The Expendable Man.   New York, Random House, 1963; London, Deutsch, 1964.

Uncollected Short Stories

"You Killed Miranda," in *The Saint* (New York), August 1958.
"The Granny Woman," in *Gamma* (North Hollywood), 1963.
"Danger at Deerfawn," in *Ellery Queen's Mystery Magazine* (New York), August 1964.
"Everybody Needs a Mink," in *The Saint* (New York), July 1965.

OTHER PUBLICATIONS

Novel

The Big Barbecue.   New York, Random House, 1949.

Verse

Dark Certainty.   New Haven, Connecticut, Yale University Press, 1931.

Other

Pueblo on the Mesa: The First Fifty Years of the University of New Mexico.   Albuquerque, University of New Mexico Press, 1939.
Erle Stanley Gardner: The Case of the Real Perry Mason.   New York, Morrow, 1978.

Dorothy B. Hughes comments:

I always intended to write books from when I was six years old and learned to write words. I wrote poetry, then short stories, before writing novels. It is true indeed that one learns to write by writing, and it takes time to learn to handle your material.

*   *   *

Dorothy B. Hughes has distinguished herself as a critic and historian of the mystery genre as well as an author of mystery fiction. For her reviews she received an Edgar in 1950 and has gained the approbation of Julian Symons, who names her in *Mortal Consequences* as one of the three contemporary Americans who review detective fiction as competently as he does himself. The decade of the forties was her most prolific period as a novelist: 11 of her 14 novels appeared then. Three of them, *The Fallen Sparrow*, *Ride the Pink Horse*, and *In a Lonely Place*, have been made into major films.

Her first novel, *The So Blue Marble*, concerns a fashion designer who discovers that she is the principal agent through which a ruthless pair of European outlaws are attempting to gain possession of a mysterious priceless treasure. Complications arise when she tries to protect her sisters and her estranged husband from the wrath of the outlaws and the rigors of the law. Most of Hughes's other novels are felicitous variatons on this single, unusual formula: domestic thrillers in which the accomplished and upper-class protagonist becomes innocently involved in a situation of evil intrigue, finally resolved through the hero's cunning, character, and sheer luck. The reviewer Will Cuppy called *The Cross-Eyed Bear* "glittering, but not hard-boiled."

Her most recent novel, *The Expendable Man*, is not a domestic spy thriller but a novel of detection, although it resembles her earlier formula in that the protagonist is both innocent of the crimes he is charged with and a member of the upper class. In this case, however, the crimes are abortion as well as murder, and the hero, Hugh Densmore, is a black intern from UCLA. The theme here is bigotry and the disadvantages of coping with the prejudices of law enforcement officers when one is both black and a stranger.

One of Hughes's most significant contributions to the genre is her masterful re-creation of setting. Streets are named, hotels are placed precisely, descriptions of transit from one place to another are so carefully written that the reader feels he has received directions to join the group. While she employs a variety of locales, such as New York and other cities on the East coast, her novels are most typically set in the Southwest. For instance, detailed descriptions of Juarez, Mexico, and Los Alamos, New Mexico, are featured in *The Candy Kid*. Action in *The Expendable Man* is centered in the Phoenix–Scottsdale area of Arizona. Through this attention to place, Hughes gives to her tales of romantic adventure an impressive verisimilitude.

—Nancy C. Joyner

HULL, Richard.   Pseudonym for Richard Henry Sampson.   British.   Born in London, 6 September 1896. Educated at Rugby School, Warwickshire. Served as an officer in an infantry battalion and in the Machine Gun Corps in World War I; on active list until 1929; also served 1939–40. Worked for a firm of chartered accountants in the early 1920's, then set up his own practice; chartered accountant with the Admiralty, London, during World War II and until the mid-1950's. Fellow, Institute of Chartered Accountants. *Died in 1973.*

Novels

The Murder of My Aunt.   London, Faber, and New York, Minton Balch, 1934.
Keep It Quiet.   London, Faber, and New York, Putnam, 1935.
Murder Isn't Easy.   London, Faber, and New York, Putnam, 1936.
The Ghost It Was.   London, Faber, 1936; New York, Putnam, 1937.
The Murderers of Monty.   London, Faber, and New York, Putnam, 1937.
Excellent Intentions.   London, Faber, 1938; as Beyond Reasonable Doubt, New York,
    Messner, 1941.
And Death Came Too.   London, Collins, 1939; New York, Messner, 1942.
My Own Murderer.   London, Collins, and New York, Messner, 1940.
The Unfortunate Murderer.   London, Collins, 1941; New York, Messner, 1942.
Left-Handed Death.   London, Collins, 1946.
Last First.   London, Collins, 1947.
Until She Was Dead.   London, Collins, 1949.
A Matter of Nerves.   London, Collins, 1950.
Invitation to an Inquest.   London, Collins, 1950.
The Martineau Murders.   London, Collins, 1953.

Uncollected Short Story

"Mrs. Brierly Supplies the Evidence," in Evening Standard Detective Book, 2nd
    series.   London, Gollancz, 1951.

*   *   *

Richard Hull was one of the most notable and inventive crime novelists of the 1930's, and
a major practitioner of the inverted school. Hull was deeply influenced by the work of
Francis Iles – especially the inverted Malice Aforethought (1931) which told its story from the
murderer's point of view. Iles's work was infused with mordant wit, and his important
characters were less than admirable. The Hull narratives contain an acid bite ("brilliantly
vicious" one critic stated), and many of his characters are extremely unpleasant because Hull
thought he had a great deal more to say about such characters, and found them very amusing.
Hull, himself, was noted for his kind-hearted qualities.
    Hull's debut and masterpiece, The Murder of My Aunt, is told by a worthless and
unpleasant young man who wishes to kill his equally detestable aunt in order to inherit her
fortune. His first two attempts fail resoundingly, but he finally thinks he has discovered the
perfect method. This classic inverted tale is an accomplishment of a high order, and deserves
comparison with the best of Iles, Vulliamy, and Bruce Hamilton. Christopher Morley called it
"Really brilliant savage comedy with the coldest and most deliberate cruelty beneath the
highly amusing surface."
    Hull had a great deal more to contribute to the mystery novel. Keep It Quiet details the
efforts of a club secretary to hide a poisoning incident, while a blackmailer tries to take
advantage of his difficulties. Closer to the detective novel is Murder Isn't Easy which tells of
the murder of a company director from the points of view of several of the people involved –
anticipating the narrative structure of Vera Caspary's Laura (1943). The Murderers of Monty
concerns a group of people who form a company to kill Monty as part of an elaborate
practical joke, but the joke turns sour when Monty is found murdered. Excellent Intentions is
a long courtroom novel with more detection than usual. The victim is utterly worthless, and
the murderer has acted from the most unselfish of motives. How can the judge temper justice
with mercy? My Own Murderer details an elaborate conspiracy in which an unwitting
substitute is supposed to take the place of a murderer, and die in his place. One of the most
unpleasant characters in this story is named Richard Henry Sampson (after his creator) in

order to underline a "but for the grace of God" message. Jacques Barzun thought it the most gripping and best written of the Hull's novels. *The Unfortunate Murderer* is a straightforward detective story about the murder of an executive in a munitions factory.

Literary inactivity during most of World War Two was followed by a group of six novels that were published only in England. The creative spark was gone. The acid bite had turned sour and corrosive. The police interrogation of witnesses in *Invitation to an Inquest* makes similar material in Julian Symons's *The Progress of a Crime* or the more powerful *My Name Is Michael Sibley* by John Bingham seem warm and pleasant by comparison. But some of the old inventiveness remained. The otherwise dull *Last First* places its final chapter at the start of this book which is dedicated to "those who habitually read the last chapter first." Possibly Hull's best post-war novel is *A Matter of Nerves* which purports to be the diary of a murderer that relates how he committed his crime, and the events of its aftermath, but conceals the murderer's identity.

—Charles Shibuk

HUME, Fergus(on Wright). British. Born in England, 8 July 1859. Educated at Dunedin High School, and University of Otago, both New Zealand. Admitted to the New Zealand Bar in 1885, and worked as a barrister's clerk; lived in Melbourne, Australia, 1885–88; moved to England in 1888 and settled in Thundersley, Essex. *Died 13 July 1932.*

CRIME PUBLICATIONS

Novels (series character: Octavius Fanks)

> *The Mystery of a Hansom Cab.* Melbourne, Kemp and Boyce, 1886; London, Hansom Cab Company, and New York, Munro, 1888; revised edition, London, Jarrolds, 1896.
> *Professor Brankel's Secret.* Melbourne, Baird's Railway Bookstall, 1886.
> *Madame Midas.* London, Hansom Cab Company, and New York, Munro, 1888.
> *The Girl from Malta.* London, Hansom Cab Company, and New York, Lovell, 1889.
> *The Gentleman Who Vanished: A Psychological Phantasy.* London, White, 1890; as *The Man Who Vanished*, New York, Liberty Book Company, 1892.
> *The Man with a Secret.* London, White, 3 vols., 1890.
> *Miss Mephistopheles.* London, White, and New York, Lovell, 1890.
> *Who God Hath Joined.* London, White, 3 vols., 1891.
> *The Year of Miracle: A Tale of the Year One Thousand Nine Hundred.* London, Routledge, and New York, Lovell, 1891.
> *A Creature of the Night: An Italian Enigma.* London, Sampson Low, and New York, Lovell, 1891.
> *The Fever of Life.* New York, Lovell, 1891; London, Sampson Low, 2 vols., 1892.
> *Monsieur Judas* (Fanks). London, Blackett, and New York, Waverly, 1891.
> *The Black Carnation.* London, Gale and Polden, and New York, United States Book Company, 1892.
> *Aladdin in London.* London, A. and C. Black, and Boston, Houghton Mifflin, 1892.
> *Dowker – Detective.* New York, Seaside, 1892.
> *A Speck of the Motley.* London, Innes, 1893.

The Harlequin Opal.   London, W. H. Allen, 3 vols., 1893; Chicago, Rand McNally, 1893.
The Chinese Jar (Fanks).   London, Sampson Low, 1893.
The Best of Her Sex.   London, W. H. Allen, 2 vols., 1894.
The Gates of Dawn.   London, Sampson Low, and New York, Neely, 1894.
The Lone Inn.   London, Jarrolds, 1894; New York, Cassell, 1895.
A Midnight Mystery.   London, Gale and Polden, 1894.
The Mystery at Landy Court.   London, Jarrolds, 1894.
The Cruise of the 'Liza Jane.   London, Ward Lock, 1895.
The Masquerade Mystery.   London, Digby Long, 1895.
The Third Volume.   New York, Cassell, 1895.
The Unwilling Bride.   New York, Ogilvie, 1895.
The White Prior.   London, Warne, 1895.
The Carbuncle Clue (Fanks).   London, Warne, 1896.
A Marriage Mystery, Told from Three Points of View.   London, Digby Long, 1896.
Tracked by a Tattoo.   London, Warne, 1896.
Claude Duval of the Ninety-Five: A Romance of the Road.   London, Digby Long, and New York, Dillingham, 1897.
The Tombstone Treasure.   London, Jarrolds, 1897.
The Clock Struck One.   London, Warne, 1898.
The Devil-Stick.   London, Downey, 1898.
For the Defense.   Chicago, Rand McNally, 1898.
Lady Jezebel.   London, Pearson, and New York, Mansfield, 1898.
The Rainbow Feather.   London, Digby Long, and New York, Dillingham, 1898.
The Indian Bangle.   London, Sampson Low, 1899.
The Red-Headed Man.   London, Digby Long, 1899.
The Silent House in Pimlico.   London, Long, 1899; as *The Silent House*, New York, Doscher, 1907; London, Long, 1912.
The Bishop's Secret.   London, Long, 1900; as *Bishop Pendle*, Chicago, Rand McNally, 1900.
The Crimson Cryptogram.   London, Long, 1900; New York, New Amsterdam Book Company, 1901.
Shylock of the River.   London, Digby Long, 1900.
A Traitor in London.   London, Long, and New York, Buckles, 1900.
The Lady from Nowhere.   London, Chatto and Windus, and New York, Brentano's, 1900.
The Vanishing of Tera.   London, White, 1900.
The Crime of the Crystal.   London, Digby Long, 1901.
The Golden Wang-Ho.   London, Long, 1901; as *The Secret of the Chinese Jar*, Cleveland, Westbrook, 1928.
The Millionaire Mystery.   London, Chatto and Windus, and New York, Buckles, 1901.
The Pagan's Cup.   London, Digby Long, and New York, Dillingham, 1902.
The Turnpike House.   London, Long, 1902.
Woman: The Sphinx.   London, Long, 1902.
The Jade Eye.   London, Long, 1903.
The Miser's Will.   London, Treherne, 1903.
The Silver Bullet.   London, Long, 1903.
The Guilty House.   London, White, 1903.
The Yellow Holly.   London, Digby Long, and New York, Dillingham, 1903.
The Coin of Edward VII.   London, Digby Long, and New York, Dillingham, 1903.
The Mandarin's Fan.   London, Digby Long, 1904; New York, Dillingham, 1905.
The Lonely Church.   London, Long, 1904.
The Red Window.   London, Digby Long, and New York, Dillingham, 1904.
The Wheeling Light.   London, Chatto and Windus, 1904.
The Wooden Hand.   London, White, 1904.

The Fatal Song. London, White, 1905.
Lady Jim of Curzon Street. London, Laurie, 1905; New York, Dillingham, 1906.
The Opal Serpent. London, Long, and New York, Dillingham, 1905.
The Scarlet Bat. London, White, 1905.
The Secret Passage. London, Long, and New York, Dillingham, 1905.
The Black Patch. London, Long, 1906.
Jonah's Luck. London, White, 1906.
The Mystery of the Shadow. London, Cassell, and New York, Dodge, 1906.
Flies in the Web. London, White, 1907.
The Purple Fern. London, Everett, 1907.
The Sealed Message. New York, Dillingham, 1907; London, Digby Long, 1908.
The Yellow Hunchback. London, White, 1907.
The Amethyst Cross. London, Cassell, 1908.
The Crowned Skull. London, Laurie, 1908; as *The Red Skull*, New York, Dodge, 1908.
The Green Mummy. London, Long, and New York, Dillingham, 1908.
The Mystery of a Motor Cab. London, Everett, 1908.
The Sacred Herb. London, Long, and New York, Dillingham, 1908.
The Devil's Ace. London, Everett, 1909.
The Disappearing Eye. London, Digby Long, and New York, Dillingham, 1909.
The Top Dog. London, White, 1909.
The Solitary Farm. London, Ward Lock, and New York, Dillingham, 1909.
The Lonely Subaltern. London, C. H. White, 1910.
The Mikado Jewel. London, Everett, 1910.
The Peacock of Jewels. London, Digby Long, and New York, Dillingham, 1910.
The Spider. London, Ward Lock, 1910.
High Water Mark. London, White, 1910.
The Jew's House. London, Ward Lock, 1911.
The Pink Shop. London, White, 1911.
The Rectory Governess. London, White, 1911.
Red Money. New York, Dillingham, 1911; London, Ward Lock, 1912.
The Steel Crown. London, Digby Long, and New York, Dillingham, 1911.
Across the Footlights. London, White, 1912.
The Blue Talisman. London, Laurie, 1912; New York, Clode, 1925.
Mother Mandarin. London, White, 1912.
The Mystery Queen. London, Ward Lock, and New York, Dillingham, 1912.
The Curse. London, Laurie, 1913.
The Queer Street. London, White, 1913.
The Thirteenth Guest. London, Ward Lock, 1913.
Seen in the Shadow. London, White, 1913.
The 4 P.M. Express. London, White, 1914.
Not Wanted. London, White, 1914.
The Lost Parchment. London, Ward Lock, and New York, Dillingham, 1914.
Answered: A Spy Story. London, White, 1915.
The Caretaker. London, Ward Lock, 1915.
The Red Bicycle. London, Ward Lock, 1916.
The Silent Signal. London, Ward Lock, 1917.
The Grey Doctor. London, Ward Lock, 1917.
The Black Image. London, Ward Lock, 1918.
Heart of Ice. London, Hurst and Blackett, 1918.
Next Door. London, Ward Lock, 1918.
Crazy-Quilt. London, Ward Lock, 1919.
The Master-Mind. London, Hurst and Blackett, 1919.
The Dark Avenue. London, Ward Lock, 1920.
The Other Person. London, White, 1920.

The Singing Head. London, Hurst and Blackett, 1920.
The Woman Who Held On. London, Ward Lock, 1920.
Three. London, Ward Lock, 1921.
The Unexpected. London, Odhams Press, 1921.
A Trick of Time. London, Hurst and Blackett, 1922.
The Moth-Woman. London, Hurst and Blackett, 1923.
The Whispering Lane. London, Hurst and Blackett, 1924; Boston, Small Maynard, 1925.
The Caravan Mystery. London, Hurst and Blackett, 1926.
The Last Straw. London, Hutchinson, 1932.
The Hurton Treasure Mystery. London, Mellifont Press, 1937.

Short Stories

The Piccadilly Puzzle. London, White, and New York, Lovell, 1889.
The Dwarf's Chamber and Other Stories. London, Ward Lock, 1896.
Hagar of the Pawn-Shop. London, Skeffington, 1898; New York, Buckles, 1899.
The Dancer in Red and Other Stories. London, Digby Long, 1906.

OTHER PUBLICATIONS

Novels

The Island of Fantasy. London, Griffith Farran, 3 vols., 1892; New York, Lovell, 1892.
When I Lived in Bohemia: Papers Selected from the Portfolio of Peter ———, Esq. Bristol, Arrowsmith, and New York, Tait, 1892.
The Expedition of Captain Flick. London, Jarrolds, 1895; New York, New Amsterdam Book Company, 1899.
The Mother of Emeralds. London, Hurst and Blackett, 1901.
The White Room. London, White, 1905.
A Son of Perdition. London, Rider, 1912.

Short Stories

The Chronicles of Faeryland. London, Griffith Farran, 1892; Philadelphia, Lippincott, 1893.

Plays

The Mystery of a Hansom Cab, with Arthur Law (produced London, 1888).
Indiscretion (produced Folkestone, Kent, 1888).
Madame Midas, The Gold Queen, with P. Beck (produced Exeter, 1888).
The Fool of the Family (produced London, 1896).
Teddy's Wives (produced Eastbourne, Sussex, and London, 1896).
Honours Divided (produced Margate, Kent, 1902).
A Scotch Marriage (produced London, 1907).
The Mystery of the Red Web, with Newman Harding (produced Liverpool and London, 1908).

*   *   *

Fergus Hume, so the conventional wisdom has it, is a one-book author, the book being his first, *The Mystery of a Hansom Cab*, the other nearly 150 of his novels being "unreadable." This is far from the truth. Certainly none of his other novels achieved the circulation of his first, which is one of the great bestsellers of history. But there are at least 20 of Hume's novels, mostly written before 1910, which are eminently readable, more readable than the melodramatic Victorian romances of, say, Mary Elizabeth Braddon.

Hume, indeed, aims at realism. One of the characters in his famous novel describes the events in which he finds himself as "a romance in real life, which beats Miss Braddon hollow." "Truth is stranger than fiction" is an adage repeatedly stated in Hume's novels, as though to justify his breaches of *vraisemblance*. But as the scene moves from high society to the mean streets of the great Victorian metropolis (usually London, but in the first novel Melbourne), one sees Hume's sure grasp of a documentary realism. The stories are scarcely realistic, however, and Hume's novels suffer from the overplotting of late Victorian fiction. The last half of a typical novel is frequently a gradual disclosure of familial and marital relationships hitherto unguessed at. In *The Piccadilly Puzzle* there are two women who look alike (they turn out to be sisters); one elopes with the murder suspect, the other is murdered. But there has been a substitution, and Hume keeps us guessing until the end as to which is which. In *The Bishop's Secret*, the children of A, after much suspense, turn out to be legitimate, because though A's former husband proves to have been still alive at the time of her second marriage, he had been previously married, and so her marriage to him was invalid! In *A Coin of Edward VII*, the central character, in the midst of the *éclaircissement* which forms one of the climaxes in any novel of Hume's, finds his brain "in a whirl," and later has to ask his interlocutor to repeat the intricate account of marriages, remarriages, and changes of identity she has just provided.

Though it was Gaboriau who was supposed to have given Hume the impetus to write, it is Wilkie Collins who is his principal master: wills (Hume was trained as a lawyer) are often important, especially eccentrically drawn wills; there are occasional inset narratives; and many of the criminals confess in written documents duly reproduced by the author. Moreover, again after Collins, several of Hume's novels deal with stolen precious stones: as late as *The Blue Talisman* (1925) he wrote a novel about a man who steals a gem from an idol in Africa, and is pursued by the curse of its custodians. Hume is as concerned as Collins in seeing fate as the embodiment of the victim's past crimes, now catching up with him, as in *The Red Skull*. The scenes of Hume's characters' pasts are often exotic – Australia, South Africa, Mexico – and yet are realistically evoked.

Hume's method of initial exposition is often contrived, given in a colloquy between characters otherwise of no importance (though in one notable case the character who receives the opening information turns out to be the murderer). Hume's detectives, in so large a body of novels, are legion, often merely interested parties seeking to clear themselves or those dear to them. One detective, Octavius Fanks, appears several times, and may be seen to best advantage in *Monsieur Judas* or *The Carbuncle Clue*. He is an "idler" in the salon, but a brilliant detective in the streets. In this ingenious way he overcomes the disabilities of such "lower-class" detectives as Cuff or Ebenezer Gryce.

The Mystery of a Hansom Cab, finally: for on its fame Hume's reputation will continue to stand or fall. The plot is as complicated as those which come later: the murdered man's mistress turns out to be the former wife of his prospective father-in-law. The sense of the metropolis is omnipresent, and in the scene of the murder, the apprehension of the criminal, and the weight of the past upon the present the book (though the question of influence does not arise) anticipates *A Study in Scarlet*. That, for better or worse, may be the lasting epitaph for this fluent, readable, and literate novelist.

—Barrie Hayne

HUNT, Kyle.   See CREASEY, John.

HUNTER, Alan (James Herbert).   British.   Born in Hoveton, Norfolk, 25 June 1922. Educated at Wroxham School, Norfolk, 1927–36; studied advertising, B.Ins. 1939. Served as an aircraft electrician in the Royal Air Force Volunteer Reserve, 1940–46. Married Adelaide Cubitt in 1944; one daughter. Poultry farmer, Norfolk, 1936–40; manager of antiquarian books department, Charles Cubitt, booksellers, Norwich, 1946–49; owner, Maddermarket Bookshop, Norwich, 1950–57. Regular contributor since 1955, and crime fiction reviewer, 1955–71, *Eastern Daily Press*, Norwich. Address: 3 St. Laurence Avenue, Brundall, Norwich, Norfolk NR13 5QH, England.

CRIME PUBLICATIONS

Novels (series character: Inspector/Chief Superintendent George Gently in all books)

> *Gently Does It.*   London, Cassell, and New York, Rinehart, 1955.
> *Gently by the Shore.*   London, Cassell, and New York, Rinehart, 1956.
> *Gently down the Stream.*   London, Cassell, 1957; New York, Roy, 1960.
> *Landed Gently.*   London, Cassell, and New York, British Book Centre, 1957.
> *Gently Through the Mill.*   London, Cassell, 1958; included in *Gently in an Omnibus*, New York, St. Martin's Press, 1971.
> *Gently in the Sun.*   London, Cassell, 1959; New York, Berkley, 1964.
> *Gently with the Painters.*   London, Cassell, 1960; New York, Macmillan, 1976.
> *Gently to the Summit.*   London, Cassell, 1961; New York, Berkley, 1964.
> *Gently Go Man.*   London, Cassell, 1961; New York, Berkley, 1964.
> *Gently Where the Roads Go.*   London, Cassell, 1962; included in *Gently in Another Omnibus*, New York, St. Martin's Press, 1972.
> *Gently Floating.*   London, Cassell, 1963; New York, Berkley, 1964.
> *Gently Sahib.*   London, Cassell, 1964.
> *Gently with the Ladies.*   London, Cassell, 1965; New York, Macmillan, 1974.
> *Gently North-West.*   London, Cassell, 1967; as *Gently in the Highlands*, New York, Macmillan, 1975.
> *Gently Continental.*   London, Cassell, 1967.
> *Gently Coloured.*   London, Cassell, 1969.
> *Gently with the Innocents.*   London, Cassell, 1970; New York, Macmillan, 1974.
> *Gently at a Gallop.*   London, Cassell, 1971.
> *Vivienne: Gently Where She Lay.*   London, Cassell, 1972.
> *Gently French.*   London, Cassell, 1973.
> *Gently in Trees.*   London, Cassell, 1974; as *Gently Through the Woods*, New York, Macmillan, 1975.
> *Gently with Love.*   London, Cassell, 1975.
> *Gently Where the Birds Are.*   London, Cassell, 1976.
> *Gently Instrumental.*   London, Cassell, 1977.
> *Gently to a Sleep.*   London, Cassell, 1978.

OTHER PUBLICATIONS

Plays

The Wolf, adaptation of a play by Terence (produced Norwich, 1952).
The Thunderbird (produced Norwich, 1953).
Don't Make Passes at Theo (produced Norwich, 1953?).

Verse

The Norwich Poems 1943–44. Norwich, Soman Wherry Press, 1945.

Alan Hunter comments:
My instincts are those of a playwright, and in consequence I tend to arrange my books so that the time covered is kept to the minimum, and the narrative proceeds in a succession of taut confrontations.

In effect my investigator, Chief Superintendent Gently, comes into a situation which has arisen over months, perhaps years, at its moment of crisis, and acts as a catalyst to bring it to a climax. To understand what is happening he must understand those involved and their relations during the previous development of the situation. Only then can he make a correct interpretation of circumstance and evidence. Needless to say, the enquiry proceeds without flashback, a device artistically suspect. The past is to be understood through the present, and by moment to moment response.

I find the environment of a dramatic situation a critical factor in its evocation: this time, this place, belong to these characters, this mystery. And so I choose a location which is directly familiar to me, usually one I have known for many years. As a result my books are set mostly in East Anglia, though two have Scottish backgrounds, two London, and one Wales.

I have experimented a little with narrative method. The three books *Go Man*, *Where the Roads Go* and *Floating* are successive attempts to write a completely objective style. Conversely, with *Continental*, I chose a strongly subjective style, a serious matter in these post-Hemingway times. A few critics liked it very much, most did not. Now I tend to an objective style with subjective overtones. In three books I have switched from third to first-person narrative. They are not the worst.

A note on Gently's genealogy. At the time I was planning my first crime novel, Anthony Martienssen's *Crime and the Police* had just appeared in paperback. In it he gives thumb-nail sketches of four top-ranking detectives; I amalgamated traits from these and built them into my own concept. Some were phased out later. The character was not, as some people assume, based on myself. Or not entirely.

*   *   *

If a Zen-Buddhist ex-poultry farmer turned crime novelist and critic seems improbable, the existence of Alan Hunter proves it possible. Hunter has written some 20 suspense stories starring Scotland Yard Superintendent George Gently whose name appears in every title. Gently, about 50 years old in his first adventure, does not change much over the years, except for abandoning his passion for peppermint creams, so insistently emphasized in the early books.

In the first tale, *Gently Does It*, the setting is a sawmill. Its proprietor, a Dutchman, is found murdered. His disinherited son rides a motorcycle in a carnival and his "nun-like" daughter is discovered to be pregnant by the chauffeur. Gently comes upon this rather dismal scene and more or less sets things right, though the story is only mildly (gently?) interesting. In the second yarn, *Gently by the Shore*, the hero suffers some anxiety about his diminishing supply of peppermints, but carries on to solve a case involving a secret society and some vague elements of espionage. Hunter's poor ear for American speech is exposed in this second book, but even more obviously in *Landed Gently*, in which American military men are portrayed. In that book, a young American lieutenant, successfully courting an aristocratic Englishwoman, is murdered (though perhaps readers are supposed to sympathize with the killer for doing away with someone who speaks the Queen's English so atrociously). The humor in the book may not always be what the author had in mind. *Gently to the Summit*, much of which is set in Wales near Mount Snowdon, contains the intriguing problem of whether a lone climber could descend Everest to return home and find new adventures.

Alan Hunter introduces experimental techniques and avant-garde mannerisms into his crime fiction, not always with favorable results. *Gently Floating*, in which there is quite a bit of sailing lore, is one of the less effective examples – the experimental aspects are anomalous and the sparse punctuation is an innovation more annoying than exciting. The author is fascinated by dialects, some of which are more felicitously represented than others.

Gently with the Ladies is loaded with literary influences. In it Gently meets Brenda Marryn and a romantic attachment develops which reappears in later books. Gently is pulled into the plot when a distant connection of his sister's is accused of murder. Each appearance of the murdered woman's maid, Albertine – who is from Illiers (Combray)! – is fraught with Proustian allusions.

In *Gently at the Highlands*, Gently and Brenda head for a Scottish holiday and become involved in their adventure while still on the road. A band of Scottish nationalists and a lot of romantic atmosphere add to the tale. In *Gently Coloured* Hunter deals with the race problem in Britain, showing a prejudiced policeman who bullies coloured suspects. That Gently bullies them only in order to solve the murder is hardly less distasteful. *Gently with the Innocents* is one of Hunter's best, containing a dilapidated Elizabethan mansion surrounded by urban decay, some priceless gold coins, and a band of young hoodlums. *Vivienne: Gently Where She Lay* is an odd story involving sado-masochism, orgies, and the corruption of school girls. In *Gently with Love*, Hunter resumes the tale of some of his earlier characters when he sends Gently on a nostalgic adventure in Scotland. The author's interest in Oriental philosophy is reflected in *Gently with Love*, and also in *Gently in Trees*.

As the series progresses, the author improves, making settings and characters more interesting; the early books are adequately written but a bit dull. The affectation of Hunter's titles mirrors his somewhat self-conscious experimentation which at times produces pretentiousness and stylistic oddity and sometimes reveals wit and sophistication. Alan Hunter's books usually offer something to catch the reader's fancy.

—Mary Helen Becker

HUNTER, Evan.   See McBAIN, Ed.

HUXLEY, Elspeth (Josceline, née Grant).   British.   Born in London, 23 July 1907; lived in Kenya, 1912–25. Educated at the European School, Nairobi; Reading University, Berkshire, Diploma in Agriculture; Cornell University, Ithaca, New York. Married Gervas Huxley in 1931 (died, 1971); one son. Assistant Press Officer, Empire Marketing Board,

London, 1929–32; News Talks Assistant, 1941–43, and Colonial Office Liaison, 1943–44, BBC, London; farmer in Wiltshire, 1950–65. Member of the BBC Advisory Council, 1954–60; Independent Member, Monckton Advisory Commission on Central Africa, 1959–61. Justice of the Peace for Wiltshire, 1947–77. C.B.E. (Commander, Order of the British Empire), 1962. Address: Green End, Oaksey, near Malmesbury, Wiltshire, England.

CRIME PUBLICATIONS

Novels (series character: Superintendent Vachell)

Murder at Government House (Vachell).   London, Methuen, and New York, Harper, 1937.
Murder on Safari (Vachell).   London, Methuen, and New York, Harper, 1938.
Death of an Aryan (Vachell).   London, Methuen, 1939; as *The African Poison Murders*, New York, Harper, 1940.
The Merry Hippo.   London, Chatto and Windus, 1963; as *The Incident at the Merry Hippo*, New York, Morrow, 1964.
A Man from Nowhere.   London, Chatto and Windus, and New York, Morrow, 1964.

OTHER PUBLICATIONS

Novels

Red Strangers.   London, Chatto and Windus, and New York, Harper, 1939.
The Walled City.   London, Chatto and Windus, 1948; Philadelphia, Lippincott, 1949.
I Don't Mind If I Do.   London, Chatto and Windus, 1950.
A Thing to Love.   London, Chatto and Windus, 1954.
The Red Rock Wilderness.   London, Chatto and Windus, and New York, Morrow, 1957.

Other

White Man's Country: Lord Delamere and the Making of Kenya.   London, Macmillan, 2 vols., 1935; New York, Praeger, 1968.
Atlantic Ordeal: The Story of Mary Cornish.   London, Chatto and Windus, 1941; New York, Harper, 1942.
East Africa.   London, Collins, 1941.
The Story of Five English Farmers.   London, Sheldon Press, 1941.
English Woman.   London, Sheldon Press, 1942.
Brave Deeds of the War.   London, Sheldon Press, 1943.
Race and Politics in Kenya: A Correspondence Between Elspeth Huxley and Margery Perham.   London, Faber, 1944; revised edition, 1956; Westport, Connecticut, Greenwood Press, 1975.
Colonies: A Reader's Guide.   Cambridge, University Press, 1947.
Settlers of Kenya.   Nairobi, Highway Press, and London, Longman, 1948; Westport, Connecticut, Greenwood Press, 1975.
The Sorcerer's Apprentice: A Journey Through East Africa.   London, Chatto and Windus, 1948; Westport, Connecticut, Greenwood Press, 1975.
African Dilemmas.   London, Longman, 1948.
Four Guineas: A Journey Through West Africa.   London, Chatto and Windus, 1954; Westport, Connecticut, Greenwood Press, 1974.
Kenya Today.   London, Lutterworth Press, 1954.
What Are Trustee Nations?   London, Batchworth Press, 1955.

No Easy Way: A History of the Kenya Farmers' Association and Unga Limited. Nairobi, East African Standard, 1957(?).
The Flame Trees of Thika: Memories of an African Childhood. London, Chatto and Windus, and New York, Morrow, 1959.
A New Earth: An Experiment in Colonialism. London, Chatto and Windus, and New York, Morrow, 1960.
The Mottled Lizard. London, Chatto and Windus, 1962; as *On the Edge of the Rift: Memories of Kenya*, New York, Morrow, 1962.
Forks and Hope: An African Notebook. London, Chatto and Windus, 1964; as *With Forks and Hope*, New York, Morrow, 1964.
Back Street New Worlds: A Look at Immigrants in Britain. London, Chatto and Windus, 1964; New York, Morrow, 1965.
Suki: A Little Tiger, photographs by Laelia Goehr. London, Chatto and Windus, and New York, Morrow, 1964.
Brave New Victuals: An Inquiry into Modern Food Production. London, Chatto and Windus, 1965.
Their Shining Eldorado: A Journey Through Australia. London, Chatto and Windus, and New York, Morrow, 1967.
Love among the Daughters: Memories of the Twenties in England and America. London, Chatto and Windus, and New York, Morrow, 1968.
The Challenge of Africa. London, Aldus, 1971.
Livingstone and His African Journeys. London, Weidenfeld and Nicolson, and New York, Saturday Review Press, 1974.
Florence Nightingale. London, Weidenfeld and Nicolson, 1975.
Gallipot Eyes: A Wiltshire Diary. London, Weidenfeld and Nicolson, 1976.
Scott of the Antarctic. London, Weidenfeld and Nicolson, 1977; New York, Atheneum, 1978.
Nellie: Letters from Africa. London, Weidenfeld and Nicolson, 1980.

Editor, *The Kingsleys: A Biographical Anthology.* London, Allen and Unwin, 1973.
Editor, *Travels in West Africa*, by Mary Kingsley. London, Folio Society, 1976.

Elspeth Huxley comments:
In the 1930's my husband's job took us both on many journeys, in those days mainly by sea, and I took to writing crime stories to pass the time on shipboard and avoid playing bridge. After the 1939–45 War I specialized on African subjects, and abandoned crime fiction, but returned to it again after serving on the Monckton Commission in central Africa, which provided a background for *The Merry Hippo*. In fact all my crime stories have an African setting. Despite Africa's immensity, diversity, and richness in crime, I don't know of any specifically African detective story writers.

*   *   *

Elspeth Huxley's whodunits are set in mythical and not so mythical parts of British Africa. A cross between P. G. Wodehouse and Evelyn Waugh, Mrs. Huxley is gifted in portraying, with a mixture of comedy and satire, the reality and the mentality of Whitehall, Africa, and the criminal. Her gift is well demonstrated in *The Merry Hippo*, in which a Royal Commission is sent to Hapana to take advice on constitutional arrangements for the independence of that colony. A number of vested interests – tapioca growers, the sterilisation lobby, the copper barons – offer evidence and threats to the Commission; and Mrs. Huxley's skill is such that it is almost impossible to guess which member of the Commission is leaking information to the press and who is killing off members of the Commission. Two engaging policemen add much to this novel – John Jacey, the British Colonial, and his mercurial assistant and pending replacement, Chisango. The two have quite different, and ethnically distinct, methods of interrogation and detection. Equally comic and serious are two murder victims, Lord and Lady Bagpus, pig-breeders named to the Commission in error.

Where it serves to thicken her plot, Mrs. Huxley is adept at using the whole range of African detail from politics to big-game hunting. She strews her novels with red herrings; she achieves disconcerting endings; and she does not shrink from brutal physical detail. *Death of an Aryan* is as memorable for its mutilated animals as for another appearance by Mrs. Huxley's attractive Canadian detective, Vachell, head of the Chanian CID.

—Ann Massa

HYLAND, (Henry) Stanley. British. Born in Shipley, Yorkshire, 26 January 1914. Educated at Bradford Grammar School, Yorkshire; Birkbeck College, University of London, B.A. 1946. Served in the Royal Naval Volunteer Reserve during World War II: Lieutenant. Married Nora Hopkinson in 1940; two sons. Research Librarian, House of Commons, London; Producer, BBC-TV, London.

CRIME PUBLICATIONS

Novels

> *Who Goes Hang?* London, Gollancz, 1958; New York, Dodd Mead, 1959.
> *Green Grow the Tresses-O.* London, Gollancz, 1965; Indianapolis, Bobbs Merrill, 1967.
> *Top Bloody Secret.* London, Gollancz, and Indianapolis, Bobbs Merrill, 1969.

OTHER PUBLICATIONS

Other

> *Curiosities from Parliament.* London, Wingate, 1955; New York, De Graff, 1956.

> Editor, *King and Parliament: A Selected List of Books.* Cambridge, University Press, 1951.

*   *   *

In *Who Goes Hang?* Stanley Hyland presented a perfect detective novel set against a specialised background, the whole wrapped up in a manner of which Dorothy L. Sayers would have approved. Hyland had inside knowledge of the House of Commons, its geography and procedures, but it says much for his literary ability that he so ably conveyed this as an enhancement of and not a substitute for the basic whodunit element of his plot. The House of Commons, it might be said, was the principal character in the book. Several critics described it as the best first detective novel they had ever read, and twenty years later it is unlikely that anything has appeared to make them radically revise their views. A body is discovered in the Big Ben tower during repairs, one in a long line of touches showing Hyland's inventiveness and his ability to fuse fictional situations with actual historical and contemporary events.

He turned his attention to M.I.5 in *Green Grow the Tresses-O*, and thrashed that organisation with a wicked wit. Then he aimed his barbs at both parliament and M.I.5 again in *Top Bloody Secret*, which has a plot that jumps from the House of Commons (with another body) to Europe and Turkey and back. By the time the murderer is exposed, one may have received an overall impression of disjointedness but will have had fun along the way at the expense of Britain's most cherished institutions.

Throughout these books Hyland displayed a sense of humour and irreverence in the true Innes, Blake, and (particularly) Crispin tradition. They signified a brilliant career in the field; alas, it was to be too short.

—Melvyn Barnes

IAMS, Jack (Samuel H. Iams, Jr.). American. Born in Baltimore, Maryland, 15 November 1910. Educated in public schools in Waynesburg, Pennsylvania; St. Paul's School, Concord, New Hampshire; Princeton University, New Jersey, A.B. 1932. Married Dorothy Aveling in 1934; three children. Journalist: with London *Daily Mail*, 1932–34, Baltimore *News-Post*, 1934–37, Pittsburgh *Press*, 1937–38, and New York *Daily News* in early 1940's; overseas bureau head in Brazzaville, Congo, Lisbon, and Brussels for Office of War Information, 1942–45. Free-lance writer after 1945.

CRIME PUBLICATIONS

Novels (series character: Rocky Rockwell)

> *The Body Missed the Boat.* New York, Morrow, 1947; London, Rich and Cowan, 1949.
> *Girl Meets Body.* New York, Morrow, 1947; London, Rich and Cowan, 1951.
> *Death Draws the Line.* New York, Morrow, 1949; London, Rich and Cowan, 1951.
> *Do Not Murder Before Christmas* (Rockwell). New York, Morrow, 1949.
> *A Shot of Murder* (Rockwell). New York, Morrow, 1950; London, Gollancz, 1952.
> *What Rhymes with Murder?* (Rockwell). New York, Morrow, 1950; London, Gollancz, 1951.
> *Into Thin Air.* New York, Morrow, 1952; London, Gollancz, 1953.
> *A Corpse of the Old School.* London, Gollancz, 1955.

OTHER PUBLICATIONS

Novels

> *Nowhere with Music.* New York, Longman, 1938.
> *Table for Four.* New York, Simon and Schuster, 1939.
> *The Countess to Boot.* New York, Morrow, 1941; London, Rich and Cowan, 1942.
> *Prophet by Experience.* New York, Morrow, 1943; London, Rich and Cowan, 1944.
> *Prematurely Gay.* New York, Morrow, 1948; London, Rich and Cowan, 1951.

Manuscript Collection: Princeton University Library, New Jersey.

*   *   *

Jack Iams's only literary ambition is to provide a fast-moving mystery story that should interest and entertain the reader who will enter into the spirit of his fun and games. The reader should forget all his problems and have an enjoyable evening as he follows an Iams novel to its happy conclusion.

Iams's first mystery novel, *The Body Missed the Boat*, was based on his experience while employed by the Office of War Information and while serving with the Free French Forces in Africa during World War II. As could be expected from an author with a number of successful comic novels to his credit, this mystery was extremely entertaining.

Iams's second effort, *Girl Meets Body*, set near his home in Bay Head, New Jersey, is routine, and was not as successful as its predecessor. His next work, *Death Draws the Line*, is his best and most entertaining novel. It is set in a cartoon-strip factory, and offers Iams's most accomplished attempt at crime writing. *Do Not Murder Before Christmas* is a brisk, romantic, and delightful novel with several engaging characters, and a deceptive (but not really fair) puzzle that can still provide entertainment for the holiday or any other season.

—Charles Shibuk

IANNUZZI, John N(icholas). American. Born in 1935. Lawyer. Address: c/o Doubleday & Company Inc., 245 Park Avenue, New York, New York 10017, U.S.A.

CRIME PUBLICATIONS

Novels

What's Happening? New York, Barnes, and London, Yoseloff, 1963.
Part 35. New York, Baron, 1970.
Sicilian Defense. New York, Baron, 1972; London, W. H. Allen, 1973.
Courthouse. New York, Doubleday, 1975.

*   *   *

Of the four books John N. Iannuzzi has written to date, only *Sicilian Defense* belongs strictly to the genre of suspense writing. The others, *What's Happening?*, *Part 35*, and *Courthouse*, are novels about lawyers, the police, and the criminal courts in New York. They are not concerned with discovering the perpetrator of the crime; they are concerned with winning aquittal for an accused. In New York, homicide cases are heard in court sections numbered Part 30 or higher. *Part 35* and *Courthouse* offer vivid accounts of the investigative techniques and legal resources the protagonists use to win an acquittal for one defendant (*Courthouse*) and to secure a hung jury for two Puerto Rican drug addicts accused of killing a cop (*Part 35*).

Iannuzzi, a New York trial lawyer, draws heavily upon his own experience defending clients against homicide charges to fund his books. In addition to recounting testimony and cross-examination on pivotal points in murder trials, Iannuzzi acquaints his reader with the vagaries of the legal system, the corruption in the courts, and a lesson in the adversary system in law. He is particularly sympathetic to the plight of the disadvantaged defendant, the black or Puerto Rican in New York, whose want of money tends to make him unequal in the eyes of the law.

In *Courthouse*, Marc Conte, an enterprising New York lawyer of Italian extraction, represents, among others, a bitchy, wealthy, woman accused of killing her estranged husband, an ex-policeman facing a felony charge for bribing an officer, a young, white radical female charged with supplying guns used in a courtroom shoot-out to escaped black political prisoners, and a mafioso character whose Boss has been killed. As Marc, often accompanied by his beautiful, sexy wife, works through the courts and private detectives to aid his clients, Iannuzzi educates us to the law's inconsistencies. That a Grand Jury hearing leading to an indictment is as "secret a proceeding as Henry the Eighth's Court of Star Chamber" and just as antiquated is but one of his complaints. He is also quick to point out the ways money and influence shape the court's actions, and the way shoddy and inaccurate testimony, often on ballistics, is accepted as gospel. Iannuzzi's novels are full of the kind of information that a street-wise trial lawyer in a corrupt city is bound to know. Legal, not moral, guilt is a lawyer's concern in Iannuzzi's books.

Sicilian Defense leaves the arena of the courtroom and goes to the streets and their law. It tells the story, largely through dialogue, of the kidnapping of Sal Angeletti, an Italian Boss, by rival black racketeers who are trying to gain control of Harlem money. The story tracks the maneuvers of Angeletti's men, led by Frankie the Pig, as they seek to get their Don back and secure their position in organized crime. Their efforts are masterminded by Gianni Aquilino, once the big Boss, but now in legitimate business, still hounded by inept and sanctimonious Senate investigatory committees. Aquilino works cunningly side-by-side with Frankie, his old enemy, to bring Angeletti back safely and discredit Frankie. The police, who have been tapping the phone at Angeletti's hangout (which figures in Iannuzzi's other books) are outsmarted by Aquilino who plots the pay-off and uses them as his pawns only when he is ready to let the law step in to complete his revenge. *Sicilian Defense* reads much like Mario Puzo's *The Godfather*. The talk is raunchy; prostitution, loan-sharking, and drugs are the businesses these men know; and loyalty to the Brotherhood is the bond these men honor.

Iannuzzi's talent lies in combining courtroom accounts reminiscent of those of F. Lee Bailey or Louis Nizer with taut stories of life in New York's underworld or the Harlem tenements where poverty, drugs, and fear combine to make the people animals.

—Carol Simpson Stern

ILES, Francis. See **BERKELEY, Anthony.**

INNES, (Ralph) Hammond. Also writes as Ralph Hammond. British. Born in Horsham, Sussex, 15 July 1913. Educated at Cranbrook School, Kent, graduated 1931. Served in the British Army Artillery, 1940–46: Major. Married Dorothy Mary Lang in 1937. Staff Member, *Financial News*, London, 1934–40. C.B.E. (Commander, Order of the British Empire), 1978. Address: Ayres End, Kersey, Ipswich, Suffolk IP7 6EB, England.

CRIME PUBLICATIONS

Novels

The Doppelganger.   London, Jenkins, 1937.
Air Disaster.   London, Jenkins, 1937.
Sabotage Broadcast.   London, Jenkins, 1938.
All Roads Lead to Friday.   London, Jenkins, 1939.
Wreckers Must Breathe.   London, Collins, 1940; as *Trapped*, New York, Putnam, 1940.
The Trojan Horse.   London, Collins, 1940.
Attack Alarm.   London, Collins, 1941; New York, Macmillan, 1942.
Dead and Alive.   London, Collins, 1946.
The Killer Mine.   London, Collins, and New York, Harper, 1947; as *Run by Night*, New York, Bantam, 1951.
The Lonely Skier.   London, Collins, 1947; as *Fire in the Snow*, New York, Harper, 1947.
Maddon's Rock.   London, Collins, 1948; as *Gale Warning*, New York, Harper, 1948.
The Blue Ice.   London, Collins, and New York, Harper, 1948.
The White South.   London, Collins, 1949; as *The Survivors*, New York, Harper, 1950.
The Angry Mountain.   London, Collins, 1950; New York, Harper, 1951.
Air Bridge.   London, Collins, 1951; New York, Knopf, 1952.
Campbell's Kingdom.   London, Collins, and New York, Knopf, 1952.
The Strange Land.   London, Collins, 1954; as *The Naked Land*, New York, Knopf, 1954.
The Mary Deare.   London, Collins, 1956; as *The Wreck of the Mary Deare*, New York, Knopf, 1956.
The Land God Gave to Cain.   London, Collins, and New York, Knopf, 1958.
The Doomed Oasis.   London, Collins, and New York, Knopf, 1960.
Atlantic Fury.   London, Collins, and New York, Knopf, 1962.
The Strode Venturer.   London, Collins, and New York, Knopf, 1965.
Levkas Man.   London, Collins, and New York, Knopf, 1971.
Golden Soak.   London, Collins, and New York, Knopf, 1973.
North Star.   London, Collins, 1974; New York, Knopf, 1975.
The Big Footprints.   London, Collins, and New York, Knopf, 1977.

OTHER PUBLICATIONS

Novel

The Last Voyage: Captain Cook's Lost Diary.   London, Collins, 1978; New York, Knopf, 1979.

Plays

Screenplay: *Campbell's Kingdom*, with Robin Estridge, 1957.

Television Play: *The Story of Captain James Cook*, 1975.

Other

Cocos Gold (juvenile; as Ralph Hammond).   London, Collins, and New York, Harper, 1950.
Isle of Strangers (juvenile; as Ralph Hammond).   London, Collins, 1951; as *Island of Peril*, Philadelphia, Westminster Press, 1953.

Saracen's Tower (juvenile; as Ralph Hammond).   London, Collins, 1952; as *Cruise of Danger*, Philadelphia, Westminster Press, 1954.
Black Gold on the Double Diamond (juvenile; as Ralph Hammond).   London, Collins, 1953.
Harvest of Journeys.   London, Collins, and New York, Knopf, 1960.
Scandinavia, with the editors of *Life.*   New York, Time, 1963.
Sea and Islands.   London, Collins, and New York, Knopf, 1967.
The Conquistadors.   London, Collins, and New York, Knopf, 1969.
Hammond Innes Introduces Australia, edited by Clive Turnbull.   London, Deutsch, and New York, McGraw Hill, 1971.

Editor, *Tales of Old Inns*, by Richard Keverne, revised edition.   London, Collins, 1947.

*   *   *

Hammond Innes has long been an important author of suspense novels. His tales are unique in the genre. He writes of the conflict of man against man, good against evil, but this is no more than an undercurrent to his main theme, that of man against the overpowering force of implacable nature. The initial Innes books pitted his protagonists against varied natural disasters, volcanic eruptions, mine explosions, mountain avalanches, but since *The Mary Deare*, he has repeatedly used the sea as a force in his stories.

Innes himself is a seaman. After his first success as a writer he bought a boat and took to ocean racing: "I ploughed my earnings back into travel." For some twenty years he has maintained a pattern of "six months traveling, six months writing," and has used his travels to provide settings for his books. He sailed to Antarctica for *The White South*, to the islands of Greece for *Levkas Man*, and to the Indian ocean for *The Strode Venturer*. On land he has traveled the wastes of Labrador for *The Land God Gave to Cain*, the emptiness of the Arabian sands for *The Doomed Oasis*, and the deserts of Australia for *Golden Soak*.

As have most of the best writers, Innes served an apprenticeship before becoming a novelist; he was in newspaper work before World War II. He knew he would in time be a novelist and worked at his writing mornings and nights, before and after work. His early novels caused little stir, but the ones he wrote after the war were instantly successful. He writes strong, clear prose and instils it with an excitement that makes for compulsive reading.

There is no one comparable to Hammond Innes. No one has the material he has gathered, and the craftsmanship to transport his readers to the far-flung places of the earth. In a Hammond Innes book, you do not read of the adventures, you experience them. As a reader who has followed Hammond Innes with heart and mind for many years, my personal opinion is that his stature as a novelist has not yet been fully recognized. There is a greatness in his work which should lead to the books becoming classics, to be rediscovered by future generations.

—Dorothy B. Hughes

INNES, Michael.   Pseudonym for John Innes Mackintosh Stewart.   British.   Born in Edinburgh, 30 September 1906. Educated at Edinburgh Academy; Oriel College, Oxford (Matthew Arnold Memorial Prize, 1929; Bishop Fraser's Scholar, 1930), B.A. (honours) in English 1928. Married Margaret Hardwick in 1932; three sons and two daughters. Lecturer in English, University of Leeds, Yorkshire, 1930–35; Jury Professor of English, University of Adelaide, South Australia, 1935–45; Lecturer, Queen's University, Belfast, 1946–48;

Student (i.e., Fellow) of Christ Church, Oxford, 1949–73, now Emeritus; Reader in English Literature, Oxford University, 1969–73. Walker-Ames Professor, University of Washington, Seattle, 1961. D.Litt.: University of New Brunswick, Fredericton, 1962. Address: Fawler Copse, Fawler, Wantage, Oxfordshire, England.

CRIME PUBLICATIONS

Novels (series character: John Appleby)

Death at the President's Lodging (Appleby). London, Gollancz, 1936; as *Seven Suspects*, New York, Dodd Mead, 1937.

Hamlet, Revenge! (Appleby). London, Gollancz, and New York, Dodd Mead, 1937.

Lament for a Maker (Appleby). London, Gollancz, and New York, Dodd Mead, 1938.

Stop Press (Appleby). London, Gollancz, 1939; as *The Spider Strikes*, New York, Dodd Mead, 1939.

The Secret Vanguard (Appleby). London, Gollancz, 1940; New York, Dodd Mead, 1941.

There Came Both Mist and Snow (Appleby). London, Gollancz, 1940; as *A Comedy of Terrors*, New York, Dodd Mead, 1940.

Appleby on Ararat. London, Gollancz, and New York, Dodd Mead, 1941.

The Daffodil Affair (Appleby). London, Gollancz, and New York, Dodd Mead, 1942.

The Weight of the Evidence (Appleby). New York, Dodd Mead, 1943; London, Gollancz, 1944.

Appleby's End. London, Gollancz, and New York, Dodd Mead, 1945.

From London Far. London, Gollancz, 1946; as *The Unsuspected Chasm*, New York, Dodd Mead, 1946.

What Happened at Hazelwood? London, Gollancz, and New York, Dodd Mead, 1946.

A Night of Errors (Appleby). New York, Dodd Mead, 1947; London, Gollancz, 1948.

The Journeying Boy. London, Gollancz, 1949; as *The Case of the Journeying Boy*, New York, Dodd Mead, 1949.

Operation Pax (Appleby). London, Gollancz, 1951; as *The Paper Thunderbolt*, New York, Dodd Mead, 1951.

A Private View (Appleby). London, Gollancz, 1952; as *One-Man Show*, New York, Dodd Mead, 1952; as *Murder Is an Art*, New York, Avon, 1959.

Christmas at Candleshoe. London, Gollancz, and New York, Dodd Mead, 1953; as *Candleshoe*, London, Penguin, 1978.

The Man from the Sea. London, Gollancz, and New York, Dodd Mead, 1955; as *Death by Moonlight*, New York, Avon, 1957.

Old Hall, New Hall. London, Gollancz, 1956; as *A Question of Queens*, New York, Dodd Mead, 1956.

Appleby Plays Chicken. London, Gollancz, 1957; as *Death on a Quiet Day*, New York, Dodd Mead, 1957.

The Long Farewell (Appleby). London, Gollancz, and New York, Dodd Mead, 1958.

Hare Sitting Up (Appleby). London, Gollancz, and New York, Dodd Mead, 1959.

The New Sonia Wayward. London, Gollancz, 1960; as *The Case of Sonia Wayward*, New York, Dodd Mead, 1960; as *The Last of Sonia Wayward*, 1962.

Silence Observed (Appleby). London, Gollancz, and New York, Dodd Mead, 1961.

A Connoisseur's Case (Appleby). London, Gollancz, 1962; as *The Crabtree Affair*, New York, Dodd Mead, 1962.

Money from Holme. London, Gollancz, 1964; New York, Dodd Mead, 1965.

The Bloody Wood (Appleby). London, Gollancz, and New York, Dodd Mead, 1966.

A Change of Heir. London, Gollancz, and New York, Dodd Mead, 1966.

Appleby at Allington. London, Gollancz, 1968; as *Death by Water*, New York, Dodd Mead, 1968.

A Family Affair (Appleby).   London, Gollancz, 1969; as *Picture of Guilt*, New York, Dodd Mead, 1969.
Death at the Chase (Appleby).   London, Gollancz, and New York, Dodd Mead, 1970.
An Awkward Lie (Appleby).   London, Gollancz, and New York, Dodd Mead, 1971.
The Open House (Appleby).   London, Gollancz, and New York, Dodd Mead, 1972.
Appleby's Answer.   London, Gollancz, and New York, Dodd Mead, 1973.
Appleby's Other Story.   London, Gollancz, and New York, Dodd Mead, 1974.
The Mysterious Commission.   London, Gollancz, 1974; New York, Dodd Mead, 1975.
The Gay Phoenix.   London, Gollancz, 1976; New York, Dodd Mead, 1977.
Honeybath's Haven.   London, Gollancz, 1977; New York, Dodd Mead, 1978.
The Ampersand Papers (Appleby).   London, Gollancz, 1978; New York, Dodd Mead, 1979.
Going It Alone.   London, Gollancz, 1979.

Short Stories

Appleby Talking: Twenty-Three Detective Stories.   London, Gollancz, 1954; as *Dead Man's Shoes*, New York, Dodd Mead, 1954.
Appleby Talks Again: Eighteen Detective Stories.   London, Gollancz, 1956; New York, Dodd Mead, 1957.
The Appleby File.   London, Gollancz, 1975; New York, Dodd Mead, 1976.

OTHER PUBLICATIONS as J. I. M. Stewart

Novels

Mark Lambert's Supper.   London, Gollancz, 1954.
The Guardians.   London, Gollancz, 1955; New York, Norton, 1957.
A Use of Riches.   London, Gollancz, and New York, Norton, 1957.
The Man Who Won the Pools.   London, Gollancz, and New York, Norton, 1961.
The Last Tresilians.   London, Gollancz, and New York, Norton, 1963.
An Acre of Grass.   London, Gollancz, 1965; New York, Norton, 1966.
The Aylwins.   London, Gollancz, 1966; New York, Norton, 1967.
Vanderlyn's Kingdom.   London, Gollancz, 1967; New York, Norton, 1968.
Avery's Mission.   London, Gollancz, and New York, Norton, 1971.
A Palace of Art.   London, Gollancz, and New York, Norton, 1972.
Mungo's Dream.   London, Gollancz, and New York, Norton, 1973.
The Gaudy.   London, Gollancz, 1974; New York, Norton, 1975.
Young Pattullo.   London, Gollancz, 1975; New York, Norton, 1976.
A Memorial Service.   London, Gollancz, and New York, Norton, 1976.
The Madonna of the Astrolabe.   London, Gollancz, and New York, Norton, 1977.
Full Term.   London, Gollancz, 1978; New York, Norton, 1979.

Short Stories

Three Tales of Hamlet (as Michael Innes), with Rayner Heppenstall.   London, Gollancz, 1950.
The Man Who Wrote Detective Stories and Other Stories.   London, Gollancz, and New York, Norton, 1959.
Cucumber Sandwiches and Other Stories.   London, Gollancz, and New York, Norton, 1969.
Our England Is a Garden and Other Stories.   London, Gollancz, 1979.

Play as Michael Innes

Strange Intelligence (broadcast, 1947). Published in *Imaginary Conversations*, edited by Rayner Heppenstall, London, Secker and Warburg, 1948.

Radio Play: *Strange Intelligence*, 1947.

Other

Educating the Emotions. Adelaide, New Education Fellowship, 1944.

Character and Motive in Shakespeare: Some Recent Appraisals Examined. London, Longman, 1949; New York, Barnes and Noble, 1966.

James Joyce. London, Longman, 1957; revised edition, 1960.

Thomas Love Peacock. London, Longman, 1963.

Eight Modern Writers. London and New York, Oxford University Press, 1963.

"Death as a Game" (as Michael Innes), in *Ellery Queen's Mystery Magazine* (New York), November 1965.

Rudyard Kipling. London, Gollancz, and New York, Dodd Mead, 1966.

Joseph Conrad. London, Longman, and New York, Dodd Mead, 1968.

Thomas Hardy: A Critical Biography. London, Longman, and New York, Dodd Mead, 1971.

Shakespeare's Lofty Scene (lecture). London, Oxford University Press, 1971.

Editor, *Montaigne's Essays: John Florio's Translation.* London, Nonesuch Press, and New York, Random House, 1931.

Editor, *The Moonstone*, by Wilkie Collins. London, Penguin, 1966.

Editor, *Vanity Fair*, by Thackeray. London, Penguin, 1968.

*   *   *

In one Michael Innes novel a character says of a painting that "the Englishness is unchallengeable ... and the whole effect a landscape in the fullest sense of the word." This statement can be applied equally well to the entire body of Innes's fiction. And it is hard to resist, in describing the persona of Innes himself as he comes through in his books, a portrayal of the title figure in the novella *The Man Who Wrote Detective Stories* (by Stewart): "He loved tumbling out scraps of poetry from a ragbag collection in his mind – and particularly in absurd and extravagant contexts. There was a strong vein of fantasy in him." What could be more mischievously autobiographical than that, from a man whose own thrillers are land-mined with literary allusions and quotations, practical jokes, and elaborate hoaxes?

Thus, the flavor of Innes is very strong and very idiosyncratic: English, bookish, jokey, and bizarre. (In fact, it could be said that certain Innes stories are the ones in the genre best suited for light opera, in the manner of Gilbert and Sullivan.) Over the years there has come to be a word appended to just this sort of mystery, and that word is *donnish*. Not surprisingly, J. I. M. Stewart was an Oxford don, and though not all of his books have university settings, the piquant spirit of an enlightened pedantry hovers over each one.

Hardly a colorful figure, Appleby is of the breed of "noble" policemen; with his good manners, empathy, and erudition, he is a gentleman not by birth but by consensus. He is introduced casually in *Death at the President's Lodging* as a man of "contemplative habit and a tentative mind, poise as well as force, reserve rather than wariness." He is that rare being (in the mid-1930's, anyway) – a policeman with a liberal education. And, as he rises over the years at Scotland Yard, from inspector to detective inspector to commissioner of the metropolitan police, the qualities that serve him the best are his curiosity, his irony, and his love of books, with patience, good nature, and egalitarianism following close behind. Appleby, who along the way acquires a charming wife and eventually a not-so-charming son, does finally retire but continues detecting as he "stumbles" into cases. He accepts a knighthood but refuses to be impressed with himself.

There are basically four sorts of Innes/Appleby tales, each of which is overlaid with the donnish sensibility. One type involves "pursuit and flight"; these tales follow the best John Buchan tradition. In these stories, which include *The Secret Vanguard, Operation Pax, From London Far, The Journeying Boy,* and *The Man from the Sea,* Appleby is not always a primary figure; when he does appear, he performs as an avuncular rescuer representing sanity and authority. Innes is quite skilled at presenting the traumas of the fugitive who, like Richard Hannay in *The Thirty-Nine Steps,* finds that there is a darker side to the everyday world and that not every good samaritan is to be trusted.

The second type contains the novels and stories which deal satirically with the world of art. Many of these are marked by the presence of the egregious Hildebert Braunkopf, an art dealer who labels his old masters in "an orgy of scepticism." *Private View* and *A Family Affair* are in this category, in which Appleby is seen to treat the proprietor of the DaVinci Gallery with affectionate disrespect.

The third kind of Innes plot has as its milieu the university itself, with dons and tutors and undergraduates moving sedately amid mayhem and madness. *The Weight of the Evidence* is one of these, presenting a wicked look at high table and the senior common-room.

The last variety, to which Innes has returned again and again, can only be called pure farce. He has favored this approach especially in his most recent books, although his delightful *Appleby's End,* in which villages are named Drool, Sneak, and Snarl, is an earlier example of his comic talents at their most ditheringly droll. His early novel *Stop Press* is somewhat manically humorous, showing more of the playfulness and whimsy that were to come than did his very first books. But the elements of farce and mystery, more balanced in the middle years, are now weighted in favor of the former and the books are beginning to seem exasperatingly self-indulgent.

Still, Innes devotees have had their rewards, not the least of which has been Innes's productivity. As the progenitor and popularizer of the donnish school, he has given quantity as well as quality to those readers who have become addicted to such fare.

—Michele Slung

IRISH, William.   See WOOLRICH, Cornell.

JACKMAN, Stuart (Brooke).   British.   Born in Manchester, Lancashire, 29 July 1922. Educated at William Hulme's Grammar School; University of Edinburgh; Yorkshire Independent College, Bradford. Served in the Royal Air Force during World War II. Married Sheena Harrow Grierson in 1948; three sons and one daughter. Congregational Minister, Barnstaple, Devon, 1948–52; Pretoria, South Africa, 1952–55; Caterham, Surrey, 1955–61; Auckland, New Zealand, 1961–65; Upminster, Essex, 1965–67; and since 1969, Oxted, Surrey. Editor, Council for World Mission, London, 1967–71. Agent: Curtis Brown Ltd., 1 Craven Hill, London W2 3EW. Address: 36 Chichele Road, Oxted, Surrey, England.

CRIME PUBLICATIONS

Novels

Portrait in Two Colours.   London, Faber, 1948; New York, Scribner, 1949.
The Daybreak Boys.   London, Faber, 1961.
The Davidson Affair.   London, Faber, and Grand Rapids, Michigan, Eerdmans, 1966.
The Golden Orphans.   London, Pan, 1968.
Guns Covered with Flowers.   London, Faber, 1973.
Slingshot.   London, Faber, 1974.
The Burning Men.   London, Faber, 1976.
Operation Catcher.   London, Hamish Hamilton, 1980.

OTHER PUBLICATIONS

Plays

But They Won't Lie Down: Three Plays (includes The Backyard Miracle, The Prototype,
    The Blindman) (produced London, 1954).   London, SCM Press, 1955.
Angels Unawares.   London, SCM Press, 1956.
My Friend, My Brother.   London, London Missionary Society, 1958.

Radio Play: Post Mortem, 1977.

Other

The Numbered Days.   London, SCM Press, 1954.
One Finger for God.   London, Independent Press, 1957.
The Waters of Dinyanti.   London, London Missionary Society, 1959.
The Lady T.V. and Other Stories (juvenile).   London, Independent Press, 1961.
This Desirable Property.   London, Edinburgh House Press, 1966.

Stuart Jackman comments:
   I do not really consider myself to be a writer of detective fiction but of general fiction (with
the accent on adventure). Guns Covered with Flowers and The Golden Orphans are off-shoots
of my main work. The Davidson trilogy (The Davidson Affair, Slingshot, The Burning Men)
sets the New Testament events from Holy Week through to Whitsun in a 20th-century
context. I am now writing adventure novels with a 1939–45 war background as well as
several radio scripts. In short, I would describe myself as a novelist and playwright exploring
the behaviour of human beings under stress conditions.

*   *   *

   Stuart Jackman's works are varied and uneven. At their best they reflect an effective
journalist with an eye for gruesome detail and an instinctive empathy for the pain and hopes
of the oppressed; at their worst they reflect a sentimental moralist, obsessed by man's
limitations and cruelty, compelled to preach about Christianity, international conflict, and
brotherhood. Jackman's forte is manipulation of time sequence to heighten the impact of a
single scene or to contrast different views of the same events.
   The Daybreak Boys, a tough, cynical look at Apartheid, focuses on potential violence at a
kaffir club, and flashes between the building tensions in the club and the individual tragedies
of each of the entertainers – stories of abuse, degradation, and shattered hopes: a mother
raped, a proud father reduced to menial slave, a thank-you returned with beating and
imprisonment, and, ironically, black power turned against itself in petty squabbles and

personal lusts. *Portrait in Two Colours*, narrated by a soldier who returns home to experience the familiar turned alien, focuses on the frustrations of readjustment as it alternates between placid English village life and the animal alertness of desert warfare, with the last two-thirds vividly replaying the narrator's war experiences to explain why normality is disconcerting after years of death and abnormality. *Guns Covered with Flowers* alternates between an idealistic Englishman's view of his assignment behind the Iron Curtain and a skeptical diplomat's interpretation of those same events: religious freedom fighters or counterfeiters? A trilogy, *The Davidson Affair, Slingshot*, and *The Burning Men*, disconcertingly mixes ancient and modern (Roman empire and Hassidic law with helicopters and TV) to retell the story of Jesus and the early Christian movement through contemporary witnesses (Barabbas, a revolutionary leader; Mary Magdala, a belly dancer; Saul, a government prosecutor). *Slingshot* vividly describes the tactics and combat action of revolutionary forces, but its sequels resort to heavy-handed religiosity that undercuts the immediacy of reporter Cass Tennel's investigation and of Jackman's exposé of manipulative TV rhetoric at odds with reality.

—Virginia Macdonald

JACKS, Oliver.   See **ROYCE, Kenneth.**

JACKSON, Shirley.   American.   Born in San Francisco, California, 14 December 1919. Educated at Syracuse University, New York, B.A. 1940. Married the writer Stanley Edgar Hyman in 1940: two daughters and two sons. Recipient: Mystery Writers of America Edgar Allan Poe Award, 1965. *Died 8 August 1965.*

CRIME PUBLICATIONS

Novels

> *The Road Through the Wall.*   New York, Farrar Straus, 1948; as *The Other Side of the Street*, New York, Pyramid, 1956.
> *Hangsaman.*   New York, Farrar Straus, and London, Gollancz, 1951.
> *The Bird's Nest.*   New York, Farrar Straus, 1954; London, Joseph, 1955; as *Lizzie*, New York, New American Library, 1957.
> *The Sundial.*   New York, Farrar Straus, and London, Joseph, 1958.
> *The Haunting of Hill House.*   New York, Viking Press, 1959; London, Joseph, 1960.
> *We Have Always Lived in the Castle.*   New York, Viking Press, 1962; London, Joseph, 1963.

Short Stories

The Lottery; or, The Adventures of James Harris.   New York, Farrar Straus, 1949; London, Gollancz, 1950.

OTHER PUBLICATIONS

Play

The Bad Children: A Play in One Act for Bad Children.   Chicago, Dramatic Publishing Company, 1959.

Other

Life among the Savages.   New York, Farrar Straus, 1953; London, Joseph, 1954.
The Witchcraft of Salem Village (juvenile).   New York, Random House, 1956.
Raising Demons.   New York, Farrar Straus, and London, Joseph, 1957.
Special Delivery: A Useful Book for Brand-New Mothers....   Boston, Little Brown, 1960; as *And Baby Makes Three ...,* New York, Grosset and Dunlap, 1960.
9 Magic Wishes (juvenile).   New York, Crowell Collier, 1963.
Famous Sally (juvenile).   New York, Harlin Quist, 1966.
The Magic of Shirley Jackson, edited by Stanley Edgar Hyman.   New York, Farrar Straus, 1966.
Come Along with Me: Part of a Novel, Sixteen Stories, and Three Lectures, edited by Stanley Edgar Hyman.   New York, Viking Press, 1968.

*   *   *

Although Shirley Jackson's fiction draws on many elements of classic Gothicism (madness, mansions, and murder *inter alia*), the mysteries with which she deals are those of the mind, of reality, and of truth. *The Haunting of Hill House* begins: "No live organism can continue for long to exist sanely under conditions of absolute reality." In *The Bird's Nest*, Dr. Victor Wright says, "Equipped with no magic device beyond a not overly sharp intelligence ... the human creature finds it tempting to endeavor to control its surroundings through manipulated symbols of sorcery, arbitrarily chosen, and frequently ineffectual."

These are crucial circumstances in plots where characters conceal their secrets even from themselves or, like Merricat in *We Have Always Lived in the Castle*, seek protection in burying blue marbles and silver dollars and in eating a word of power written in apricot jam. Jackson's characters often seek safety through psychic disorders as does Elizabeth-Beth-Betsy-Bess, the disintegrated personality of *The Bird's Nest*, or by yielding to the supernatural as does Eleanor in Hill House, changing from haunted to haunter. In each case, the reader must piece together or fill in the hidden past which motivates Jackson's characters: Elizabeth's premature sexual experience with her drunken mother's lover, Merricat's poisoning her family, Eleanor's refusal to hear her dying mother, Natalie's seduction at her first cocktail party (*Hangsaman*). Sometimes chance words are the clues; sometimes the reader is never completely sure that he has understood the mystery; occasionally a character admits the answer.

Only in *The Haunting of Hill House* with its horrifying manifestations, in *The Sundial*, where Aunt Fanny's dead father announces the destruction of the world, and perhaps in the unfinished *Come Along with Me* are there accepted supernatural personages or powers. Nevertheless, menace is an important element in all Jackson's novels as well as in such short stories as "The Lottery" and "The Summer People." Sometimes the threat is internal, as it is in the self-demonic possession of Elizabeth; sometimes it comes from an outsider as when Cousin Charles breaks into the tenuously safe world of Merricat and her sister. Often the danger comes from supposedly ordinary people: the villagers who stone the lottery victim to death; the hateful townspeople who riot destructively through the Blackwood house, drunk with malice. In creating these men, women, and children of ill-will, Jackson repeats the theme of many of her short stories, which depict "decent" or "normal" persons as covertly or overtly racist, doggedly hostile to all outsiders.

Although Jackson rarely describes acts of open violence (even "The Lottery" ends: "and then they were upon her"), she achieves shock through images of disgust and disorientation. Elizabeth's aunt opens the refrigerator and finds it full of mud in which a half-frozen worm stirs; she bites into a sandwich spread with mud. Eleanor and Theodora follow an evil path in a landscape like a photographic negative; in "the churning darkness" of Hill House the room rocks and dances. Aunt Fanny is lost in a maze through which her father's voice resounds; Natalie writes a secret journal to herself as if she were someone else.

Jackson's style, like that of her favorite eighteenth century, is formal and exact, a style which intensifies the horror of her novels by seeming to contain and thus to concentrate it. The children's rituals and word play so amusingly presented in her family chronicles, *Life among the Savages* and *Raising Demons*, become in her novels the rituals, rhymes, and games that protect against, forecast, or engender terror. A student of mythology and of witchcraft, Jackson used elements of both to reach man's oldest fears and motives. Behind "The Lottery" is *The Golden Bough*. But her word games may also be playful and freshly inventive, producing the delight of wit, which temporarily stabilizes the characters and reader by giving them a controllable pattern. In Jackson's plots comedy is not relief but part of the structure that supports horror.

If Jackson's works have any relationship to those of other American novelists, it must be to Henry James's *The Turn of the Screw*, but her style – lucidity overlaying terror – is uniquely her own.

—Jane W. Stedman

JACOBS, T. C. H. Pseudonym for Jacques Pendower; also wrote as Kathleen Carstairs; Tom Curtis; Penn Dower; Marilyn Pender; Anne Penn. British. Born in Plymouth, Devon, 30 December 1899. Educated at a grammar school in Plymouth. Served in the British Army, 1918–21: Second Lieutenant. Married Muriel Newbury in 1925; one son. Worked as a revenue investigating officer prior to 1950. Founding Member, 1953, and Chairman, 1960–61, Crime Writers Association. *Died in 1976.*

CRIME PUBLICATIONS

Novels (series characters: Chief Inspector Barnard; Detective Superintendent John Bellamy; Temple Fortune; Jim Malone; Mike Seton)

The Terror of Torlands. London, Stanley Paul, 1930.
The Bronkhorst Case. London, Stanley Paul, 1931; as *Documents of Murder*, New York, Macaulay, 1933.
Scorpion's Trail (Barnard). London, Stanley Paul, 1932; New York, Macaulay, 1934.
The Kestrel House Mystery (Barnard). London, Stanley Paul, 1932; New York, Macaulay, 1933.
Sinister Quest (Barnard). London, Stanley Paul, and New York, Macaulay, 1934.
The 13th Chime (Barnard). London, Stanley Paul, and New York, Macaulay, 1935.
Silent Terror (Barnard). London, Stanley Paul, 1936; New York, Macaulay, 1937.

Appointment with the Hangman. London, Stanley Paul, and New York, Macaulay, 1936.
The Laughing Men (Barnard). London, Hodder and Stoughton, 1937.
Identity Unknown (Barnard). London, Stanley Paul, 1938.
Traitor Spy (Barnard). London, Stanley Paul, 1939.
Brother Spy (Barnard). London, Stanley Paul, 1940.
The Broken Knife (Barnard). London, Stanley Paul, 1941.
The Grensen Murder Case (Bellamy). London, Stanley Paul, 1943.
Reward for Treason (Barnard). London, Stanley Paul, 1944.
The Black Box (Barnard). London, Stanley Paul, 1946.
The Curse of Khatra (Bellamy). London, Stanley Paul, 1947.
With What Motive? (Bellamy). London, Stanley Paul, 1948.
Dangerous Fortune (Fortune). London, Stanley Paul, 1949.
The Red Eyes of Kali (Fortune). London, Stanley Paul, 1950.
Lock the Door, Mademoiselle (Fortune). London, Stanley Paul, 1951.
Blood and Sun-Tan (Fortune). London, Stanley Paul, 1952.
Lady, What's Your Game? (Fortune). London, Stanley Paul, 1952.
No Sleep for Elsa (Fortune). London, Stanley Paul, 1953.
The Woman Who Waited. London, Stanley Paul, 1954.
Good Knight, Sailor (Fortune). London, Stanley Paul, 1954.
Results of an Accident (Bellamy). London, Stanley Paul, 1955.
Death in the Mews (Fortune). London, Stanley Paul, 1955.
Cause for Suspicion. London, Stanley Paul, 1956.
Broken Alibi (Bellamy). London, Stanley Paul, and New York, Roy, 1957.
Deadly Race (Fortune). London, Long, 1958.
Black Trinity (Bellamy). London, Long, 1959.
Women Are Like That (Fortune). London, Hale, 1960.
Let Him Stay Dead (Malone). London, Hale, 1961.
The Tattooed Man. London, Hale, 1961.
Target for Terror (Seton and Fortune). London, Hale, 1961.
The Red Net (Malone). London, Hale, 1962.
Murder Market (Fortune). London, Hale, 1962.
The Secret Power. London, Hale, 1963.
Danger Money (Fortune). London, Hale, 1963.
The Elusive Monsieur Drago (Seton). London, Hale, 1964.
Final Payment (Fortune). London, Hale, 1965.
Ashes in the Cellar (Fortune). London, Hale, 1966.
Sweet Poison (Fortune). London, Hale, 1966.
Death of a Scoundrel (Fortune). London, Hale, 1967.
Wild Week-End. London, Hale, 1967.
House of Horror (Fortune). London, Hale, 1969.
The Black Devil (Fortune). London, Hale, 1969.
Security Risk. London, Hale, 1972.

Novels as Jacques Pendower (series character: Slade McGinty)

The Dark Avenue. London, Ward Lock, 1955.
Hunted Woman. London, Ward Lock, 1955.
Mission in Tunis. London, Hale, 1958; New York, Paperback Library, 1967.
Double Diamond. London, Hale, 1959.
The Long Shadow. London, Hale, 1959.
Anxious Lady. London, Hale, 1960.
The Widow from Spain. London, Hale, 1961; as *Betrayed*, New York, Paperback Library, 1967.
Death on the Moor. London, Hale, 1962.

The Perfect Wife (McGinty).   London, Hale, 1962.
Operation Carlo.   London, Hale, 1963.
Sinister Talent (McGinty).   London, Hale, 1964.
Master Spy (McGinty).   London, Hale, 1964.
Spy Business.   London, Hale, 1965.
Out of This World.   London, Hale, 1966.
Traitor's Island (McGinty).   London, Hale, 1967.
Try Anything Once.   London, Hale, 1967.
A Trap for Fools.   London, Hale, 1968.
The Golden Statuette.   London, Hale, 1969.
Diamonds for Danger.   London, Hale, 1970.
She Came by Night.   London, Hale, 1971.
Cause for Alarm.   London, Hale, 1971.
Date with Fear.   London, Hale, 1974.

Uncollected Short Stories

"In Full View," in *John Creasey's Mystery Bedtime Book 1970*, edited by Herbert
   Harris.   London, Hodder and Stoughton, 1969.
"In the Surgery," in *John Creasey's Mystery Bedtime Book 1974*, edited by Herbert
   Harris.   London, Hodder and Stoughton, 1973.

OTHER PUBLICATIONS

Novels as Penn Dower

Lone Star Ranger.   London, Long, 1952.
Bret Malone, Texas Marshal.   London, Long, 1953.
Gunsmoke over Alba.   London, Long, 1953.
Texas Stranger.   London, Long, 1954.
Indian Moon.   London, Long, 1954.
Malone Rides In.   London, Long, 1955.
Two-Gun Marshal.   London, Long, 1956.
Desperate Venture.   London, Long, 1956.
Guns in Vengeance.   London, Long, 1957.
Frontier Marshal.   London, Long, 1958.
Bandit Brothers.   London, New English Library, 1964.

Novels as Tom Curtis

Bandit Gold.   London, Stanley Paul, 1953.
Gunman's Glory.   London, Stanley Paul, 1954.
Trail End.   London, Stanley Paul, 1954.
Frontier Mission.   London, Stanley Paul, 1955.
Border Justice.   London, Stanley Paul, 1955.
Ride and Seek.   London, Stanley Paul, 1957.
Phantom Marshal.   London, Long, 1957.
Gun Business.   London, Long, 1958.
Lone Star Law.   London, Long, 1959.

Novels as Kathleen Carstairs

It Began in Spain.   London, Gresham, 1960.
Third Time Lucky.   London, Gresham, 1962.
Shadows of Love.   London, Gresham, 1966.

Novels as Marilyn Pender

The Devouring Flame. London, Gresham, 1960.
A Question of Loyalty. London, Gresham, 1961.
The Golden Vision. London, Gresham, 1962.
Rebel Nurse. London, Gresham, 1962.
Dangerous Love. London, Gresham, 1966.

Novels as Anne Penn

Dangerous Delusion. London, Gresham, 1960.
Prove Your Love. London, Gresham, 1961.
Mystery Patient. London, Gresham, 1966.

Play

Radio Play: *The Grensen Murder Case*, from his own novel, 1946.

Other

Cavalcade of Murder. London, Stanley Paul, 1955.
Pageant of Murder. London, Stanley Paul, 1956.
Aspects of Murder. London, Stanley Paul, 1956.

*   *   *

A prolific writer of easy-reading detective/adventure/spy novels, Jacques Pendower tended to write spy novels under his own name and detective stories under his more famous pseudonym, T. C. H. Jacobs.

Jacobs's main series character was Temple Fortune, assisted by Sailor Mulligan; other recurring characters were Superintendent John Bellamy and, in his earlier books, Chief Inspector Barnard. His novels are fast-moving, and his heroes fall easily into the category of Berkeley Gray's Norman Conquest and John Creasey's The Toff, often with a romantic interest. His heroes are all capable of prodigious feats and seemingly possessed of a lucky charm – chance and luck rarely go against them. *Broken Alibi* was based on the real story of the Brighton trunk murder; another to be recommended is *Good Knight, Sailor.*

In keeping with changing taste, his thriller/adventure stories inevitably gave way to the spy thriller, perhaps less appealing to the discerning reader. One heartily regrets the passing of the prolific writers of the 1930's and 1940's.

—Donald C. Ireland

JAMES, P(hyllis) D(orothy). British. Born in Oxford, 3 August 1920. Educated at Cambridge Girls' High School, 1931–37. During World War II worked as a Red Cross nurse and at the Ministry of Food. Married Ernest C. B. White in 1941 (died, 1964); two daughters. Prior to World War II, Assistant Stage Manager, Festival Theatre, Cambridge; Principal Administrative Assistant, North West Regional Hospital Board, London, 1949–68. Since 1968, senior civil servant in the Home Office, London: currently in the criminal department. Fellow, Institute of Hospital Administrators. Recipient: Crime Writers Association prize,

1967. Agent: Elaine Greene Ltd., 31 Newington Green, London N16 9PU. Address: 31 Dorset Square, London N.W.1, England.

CRIME PUBLICATIONS

Novels (series character: Commander Adam Dalgliesh in all books)

Cover Her Face. London, Faber, 1962; New York, Scribner, 1966.
A Mind to Murder. London, Faber, 1963; New York, Scribner, 1967.
Unnatural Causes. London, Faber, and New York, Scribner, 1967.
Shroud for a Nightingale. London, Faber, and New York, Scribner, 1971.
An Unsuitable Job for a Woman. London, Faber, 1972; New York, Scribner, 1973.
The Black Tower. London, Faber, and New York, Scribner, 1975.
Death of an Expert Witness. London, Faber, and New York, Scribner, 1977.

Uncollected Short Stories

"Moment of Power," in *Ellery Queen's Murder Menu.* Cleveland, World, 1969.
"The Victim," in *Winter's Crimes 5*, edited by Virginia Whitaker. London, Macmillan, 1973.
"Murder, 1986," in *Ellery Queen's Masters of Mystery.* New York, Davis, 1975.
"A Very Desirable Residence," in *Winter's Crimes 8*, edited by Hilary Watson. London, Macmillan, 1976.

OTHER PUBLICATIONS

Other

The Maul and the Pear Tree: The Ratcliffe Highway Murders, 1811, with Thomas A. Critchley. London, Constable, 1971.
"Ought Adam to Marry Cordelia?" and "A Fictional Prognosis," in *Murder Ink: The Mystery Reader's Companion*, edited by Dilys Winn. New York, Workman, 1977.
"Dorothy L. Sayers: From Puzzle to Novel," in *Crime Writers*, edited by H. R. F. Keating. London, BBC Publications, 1978.

*   *   *

P. D. James was complimented in 1974 by an anonymous reviewer in the *Times Literary Supplement* for the success with which "she has revitalized a genre considered by many thriller-readers to be past its prime." Practised at its height by Sayers, Tey, Marsh, and Christie, this genre concerns itself with educated people, among whom murder is uncommon and the detective a genius. It has been almost banished from the field by the other sort of thriller, concerned with violent people, where murder is quotidian and the detective, if any, is scraping a precarious livelihood. The great popularity which P. D. James has found with her seven detective novels suggests that the lack is less in reader interest than in skilled practitioners of her revitalized art.

Together with her only living colleagues in the genre, Ngaio Marsh and Patricia Moyes, P. D. James employs a detective from Scotland Yard who is, like his amateur predecessors Wimsey and Poirot, committed to justice for its own sake. Adam Dalgliesh does not draw his gun at the name of culture. Indeed, he is a poet, whose publisher is "as incapable of providing poor sherry as ... of publishing poor work," a widower who is capable of loving a woman without demeaning her, a policeman who, like his confreres Alleyn and Tibbett, has a flair for the truth, a passion for the preservation of innocence, and a melancholy and fastidious brilliance about his job.

The best of P. D. James's detective novels raise the genre to new heights. *A Mind to Murder, Shroud for a Nightingale,* and *An Unsuitable Job for a Woman* preserve all the glories of the earlier detective fiction while adding a modernity of detail and setting, and a concern with contemporary problems that does more than resurrect a past genre: it both recreates and strengthens it.

Apparently in *A Mind to Murder* as in *Shroud for a Nightingale* P. D. James drew on her experience with the National Health Service. *A Mind to Murder* is set in an autonomous psychiatric outpatient clinic in London, and allows the author all possible fun with arguments between Freudians and those who employ electric convulsive therapy for more direct results, as well as sympathetic analysis of the unhappily married and the unmarried and passionate. The brilliance of the setting, and the steady pace of the plot, avoiding what Jacques Barzun has called "plateaus" of dullness, are expertly handled.

Shroud for a Nightingale, which the *TLS* critic calls her masterpiece, takes place in a private mansion converted to a training college for nurses. The means of death and the solution are alike original and satisfying, and Dalgliesh's involvement with the characters is well handled, as is the love one woman can form for another, ranging from possessive passion to a marvelously comfortable camaraderie.

In *An Unsuitable Job for a Woman,* which many others consider not only P. D. James's masterpiece, but the first truly original detective novel in years, the author provides for the first and, alas, apparently the last time, a satisfying portrait of a woman private detective who is a rare creature even in a genre notable for its interesting women. Cordelia Gray is independent, autonomous, self-supporting, and intelligent; she is, moreover, as Dalgliesh, who makes only a brief appearance in this book puts it, absolutely without guilt. "I don't think that young woman deludes herself about anything." The two novels which followed *An Unsuitable Job for a Woman, The Black Tower* and *Death of an Expert Witness,* while highly competent and intelligent, employ a somewhat more routine Dalgliesh, as though P. D. James had tired a bit of the detective form and was straining to write a novel. The result suggests, however, that she is more successful when she is more distanced from her subject.

Her earlier novels, *Cover Her Face* and *Unnatural Causes,* had suffered from too great revelation of the consciousness of the characters. In *Unnatural Causes,* for example, which takes place in a writers' colony by the sea, all the characters' thoughts are given: it is unlikely that the murderer would fail to think of the murder recently committed. In these works also, as in the last two novels, there is an air of sleazy horror, of nasty sex and nastier habits, which, while more in keeping, certainly, with the subject matter of contemporary fiction, suggests a danger to P. D. James in her explorations of human motives seen from the inside. *Death of an Expert Witness,* her most recent novel, has too many characters; these, while they fascinate the reader for a time, eventually become confusing and muddled in his mind, so that the solution appears arbitrary and not wholly satisfying. Here again, however, the relationship between two women is handled with an originality not always evident in the sexual relations between men and women. This suggests that P. D. James's great talents are better served in the presentation of situations in which she is an observer, without emotional commitment. Cordelia Gray and Adam Dalgliesh, quite rightly, are allowed neither perfervid emotion nor the lengthy expression of uncontrollable passion. They do their proper job, and entrance us.

There can be little question in the minds of those readers, in England and America, for whom the genre of Sayers and Tey remains as attractive as it is now rare, that P. D. James is the best writer of the 1960's and 1970's in that difficult art. One hopes that her achievement will extend into the 1980's and beyond. She has, in any case, provided as much intelligent satisfaction to as many intelligent readers as any writer currently at work.

—Carolyn G. Heilbrun

JARRETT, Cora (née Hardy). Also wrote as Faraday Keene. American. Born in Norfolk, Virginia, 21 February 1877. Educated at Pollock-Stephens Institute, Birmingham, Alabama, 1890–94; Miss Baldwin's School, Bryn Mawr, Pennsylvania, 1894–95; Bryn Mawr College, B.A. 1899; the Sorbonne and Collège de France, Paris; Oxford University. Married Edwin Seton Jarrett in 1906; one daughter and two sons. Taught English and Greek, Ward-Belmont Seminary, Nashville, 1903–04; taught English at St. Timothy's School, Catonsville, Maryland, 1904–07. *Died 19?.*

CRIME PUBLICATIONS

Novels

Night over Fitch's Pond. Boston, Houghton Mifflin, and London, Barker, 1933.
Pattern in Black and Red (as Faraday Keene). Boston, Houghton Mifflin, and London, Barker, 1934.
The Ginkgo Tree. New York, Farrar and Rinehart, and London, Barker, 1935.
Strange Houses. New York, Farrar and Rinehart, 1936; London, Heinemann, 1937.

Short Stories

Peccadilloes (as Faraday Keene). New York, Day, 1929; London, Noel Douglas, 1930.

Uncollected Short Story

"The Little Dry Sticks" (as Faraday Keene) in *Ellery Queen's Murder by Experts.* Chicago, Ziff Davis, 1947; London, Sampson Low, 1950.

OTHER PUBLICATIONS

Novels

Strange Houses. New York, Farrar and Rinehart, 1936; London, Heinemann, 1937.
The Silver String. New York, Farrar and Rinehart, 1937; London, Heinemann, 1938.
Return in December. New York, Rinehart, 1951.

Short Stories

I Asked No Other Thing. New York, Farrar and Rinehart, 1937; London, Heinemann, 1939.

Play

The Cross Goes Westward: A Mystery Play for Children. New York, Board of Missions, n.d.

*   *   *

Cora Jarrett was born in Virginia and lived much of her life in the South, mostly in academic circles. Her novels are truly Southern Gothic wherever they may be set, and the geographical range is wide: a Southern mansion in *Pattern in Red and Black*; a New England lake cabin in *Night over Fitch's Pond*; a brilliantly evoked Manhattan, which Camus or Ralph Ellison would find congenial, in *Strange Houses*. Her novels are deep probings into abnormal psychology which finally, in *Return in December*, move across the boundary they have often hedged, into the supernatural. Even her principal "detective" novel (written as Faraday

Keene), *Pattern in Black and Red*, has the same emphasis, and places little upon mystery solving. Similarly, *I Asked No Other Thing* and *The Silver String* are close – too close! – studies of women fighting to save their marriages, and *The Ginkgo Tree*, shifting the same theme to a man's point of view, lays emphasis as well upon the central character's convoluted, hostile relationship with his father. *Strange Houses* deals with an experiment in rejuvenation which ends in a bizarre personality exchange.

Jarrett's characteristic themes of masked hatred and covert psychological manipulation are best seen in her most accomplished novel, *Night over Fitch's Pond*. As a timid narrator pieces together the tortured relationships involving him with two married couples (one of the wives "an Iago in petticoats"), we have mystery, detection, and solution. But the mood, a nasty one, is more that of Ford's *The Good Soldier* than Christie's *The Murder of Roger Ackroyd*.

—Barrie Hayne

JAY, Charlotte. Pseudonym for Geraldine Mary Jay; also writes as Geraldine Halls. Australian. Born in Adelaide, South Australia, 17 December 1919. Educated at Girton School, Adelaide, 1926–37; University of Adelaide, 1939–41. Married to Albert James Halls. Worked as a secretary in Adelaide, Sydney, Melbourne, and London during the 1940's; Court Stenographer, Court of Papua New Guinea, 1949; lived in Pakistan, Thailand, Lebanon, India, and France, 1950–58. With her husband operated an oriental antique business in Somerset, 1958–71, and since 1971, in Adelaide. Recipient: Mystery Writers of America Edgar Allan Poe Award, for novel, 1953. Agent: Richard Scott Simon Ltd., 32 College Cross, London N1 1PR, England. Address: 21 Commercial Road, Hyde Park, South Australia 5061, Australia.

CRIME PUBLICATIONS

Novels

> *The Knife Is Feminine.* London, Collins, 1951.
> *Beat Not the Bones.* London, Collins, 1952; New York, Harper, 1953.
> *The Fugitive Eye.* London, Collins, 1953; New York, Harper, 1954.
> *The Yellow Turban.* London, Collins, and New York, Harper, 1955.
> *The Feast of the Dead* (as G. M. Jay). London, Hale, 1956; as *The Brink of Silence*, as Charlotte Jay, New York, Harper, 1957.
> *The Man Who Walked Away.* London, Collins, 1958; as *The Stepfather*, New York, Harper, 1958.
> *Arms for Adonis.* London, Collins, 1960; New York, Harper, 1961.
> *A Hank of Hair.* London, Heinemann, and New York, Harper, 1964.
> *The Voice of the Crab* (as Geraldine Halls). London, Constable, and New York, Harper, 1974.

OTHER PUBLICATIONS

Novels as Geraldine Halls

> *The Silk Project.* London, Heinemann, 1956.
> *The Cats of Benares.* London, Heinemann, and New York, Harper, 1967.

The Cobra Kite. London, Constable, 1971.
The Last Summer of the Men Shortage. London, Constable, 1976.
The Felling of Thawle. London, Constable, 1979.

Charlotte Jay comments:
 I began writing mystery stories largely because of my delight in the novels of Wilkie Collins and Le Fanu and the horror stories of Poe. I read these books with terror and fascination when I was quite young and their influence can be seen in several of my early novels. When my first books were published most of the crime stories at that time were written by skilled writers of Crime and Detection, usually with a well-born ex-Oxford or Cambridge amateur detective as the central character, appearing, in the manner of the Scarlet Pimpernel, something of a fool, but omniscient and strides ahead of the reader. In America the same fashion prevailed along with crime stories following in the tradition of Dashiell Hammett and Raymond Chandler. I knew I could not compete with the excellent exponents of these various trends. Many had had direction experience of police procedure which I did not feel competent of learning anything much about. And indeed I felt no interest in doing so. I set out to frighten and mystify my readers by asking them to identify themselves with a character battling for survival in a lonely, claustrophobic situation. My publishers on several occasions demanded that, in the name of logicality, my threatened character should call the Police. I always contested their suggestions and sometimes rewrote whole chapters to accommodate my conviction that my characters must stumble on alone and unaided through their private nightmares.
 Several of my books have their genesis in dreams. The earliest of these books, *Beat Not the Bones*, *The Fugitive Eye*, and *The Man Who Walked Away*, suffer from the usual faults of immaturity. The often slipshod writing and lack of technical skill now embarrass me, but I feel they have a freshness and give off an aura of mystery and fear which carry them over their deficiencies. *The Fugitive Eye* is constructed around one of the best ideas I have ever had and I sometimes regret that I did not come to it later in my writing life when I would have been able to deal with it more capably. The last of my novels in this genre, *A Hank of Hair*, is, I feel, the most artistically successful and the one with which I am most pleased.
 The Yellow Turban and *Arms for Adonis* do not fall comfortably into the category of the mystery story and neither has a particularly well-made plot. I wrote them largely to express the interest and fascination I felt for Pakistan and Lebanon, two countries in which I lived for three years. In both books I allowed myself the luxury of digressions. The plots wander off into background descriptions and the action is held up for minor characters who have little to do with the story. In fact the plots struck me as being a nuisance and I often became exasperated with them. Gothic horror somehow burns away in bright sunshine, and I don't think that either book generates much feeling of suspense or fear. Although *The Yellow Turban* has a grim ending and *Arms for Adonis* is concerned with a grim political situation, they are both happy books, their gaiety and vitality probably deriving from the ease with which I wrote them and the pleasure they gave me.

                                   *   *   *

 In the early 1950's there was a unique and powerful experience in mystery/suspense writing engendered by a new writer who signed herself Charlotte Jay. Miss Jay was an Australian girl who had worked in the most primitive parts of the island of Papua New Guinea. From her experiences, and with a writer's inspiration, she composed the story *Beat Not the Bones*. It was received with superlatives by critics; Charlotte Armstrong wrote that the book "works you up to the revelation of a horrible secret, and the secret turns out to be the horrible surprise you hoped it would." Constant readers of mysteries are aware that fewer than one in a thousand books live up to the promise of their threats.
 For her next novel Miss Jay wrote of a superb suspense chase across the English countryside. She lived for a time in Pakistan whence came *The Yellow Turban*. From her

years in Lebanon came *Arms for Adonis*, published in 1960 and even more potent today with its Arab, Syrian, Lebanese, and English characters interwoven in mid-Eastern intrigue. Miss Jay returned to Papua New Guinea for the setting of *The Voice of the Crab*. It was another of her probing ethnological studies of the conflict of the stone age and the 20th century.

If she were not so strongly identified as one of the most important writers of far-off places and their mysterious qualities, Charlotte Jay might be more well known as one of the classic writers of the horror story. Certainly *A Hank of Hair* is one of the small number of horror books that contain scenes to set the reader screaming.

Charlotte Jay is a gifted writer; one wishes that her output were larger.

—Dorothy B. Hughes

JEFFREY, William.   See **PRONZINI, Bill.**

JEFFREYS, J. G.   See **STURROCK, Jeremy.**

JEFFRIES, Roderic.   Also writes as Peter Alding; Jeffrey Ashford; Hastings Draper; Roderic Graeme; Graham Hastings.   British.   Born in London, 21 October 1926; son of Graham Montague Jeffries, i.e. Bruce Graeme, *q.v.* Educated at Harrow View Preparatory School; University of Southampton School of Navigation, 1942–43; Gray's Inn, London: called to the Bar, 1952. Married Rosemary Powys Woodhouse in 1958; one daughter and one son. Served in the Merchant Navy, 1943–49, rising to the rank of 3rd Officer in the New Zealand Shipping Company and the Union Castle Shipping Company; practised law, 1953–54. Agent: (Roderic Jeffries) William Collins Ltd., 14 St. James's Place, London SW1A 1PS; (Jeffrey Ashford and Peter Alding) John Long Ltd., 3 Fitzroy Square, London WC1P 6JD, England. Address: Ca Na Paiaia, Pollensa, Mallorca, Spain.

CRIME PUBLICATIONS

Novels (series character: Enrique Alvarez)

> *Twice Checked* (as Graham Hastings).   London, Hale, 1959.
> *Deadly Game* (as Graham Hastings).   London, Hale, 1961.
> *Evidence of the Accused.*   London, Collins, 1961; New York, British Book Centre, 1963.
> *Exhibit No. Thirteen.*   London, Collins, 1962.

The Benefits of Death.   London, Collins, 1963; New York, Dodd Mead, 1964.
An Embarrassing Death.   London, Collins, 1964; New York, Dodd Mead, 1965.
Dead Against the Lawyers.   London, Collins, 1965; New York, Dodd Mead, 1966.
Death in the Coverts.   London, Collins, 1966.
A Deadly Marriage.   London, Collins, 1967.
A Traitor's Crime.   London, Collins, 1968.
Dead Man's Bluff.   London, Collins, 1970.
Mistakenly in Mallorca (Alvarez).   London, Collins, 1974.
Two-Faced Death (Alvarez).   London, Collins, 1976.
Troubled Deaths (Alvarez).   London, Collins, 1977; New York, St. Martin's Press, 1978.
Murder Begets Murder (Alvarez).   London, Collins, and New York, St. Martin's Press, 1979.

Novels as Roderic Graeme (series character: Blackshirt in all books)

Concerning Blackshirt.   London, Hutchinson, 1952.
Blackshirt Wins the Trick.   London, Hutchinson, 1953.
Blackshirt Passes By.   London, Hutchinson, 1953.
Salute to Blackshirt.   London, Hutchinson, 1954.
The Amazing Mr. Blackshirt.   London, Hutchinson, 1955.
Blackshirt Meets the Lady.   London, Hutchinson, 1956.
Paging Blackshirt.   London, Long, 1957.
Blackshirt Helps Himself.   London, Long, 1958.
Double for Blackshirt.   London, Long, 1958.
Blackshirt Sets the Pace.   London, Long, 1959.
Blackshirt Sees It Through.   London, Long, 1960.
Blackshirt Finds Trouble.   London, Long, 1961.
Blackshirt Takes the Trail.   London, Long, 1962.
Blackshirt on the Spot.   London, Long, 1963.
Call for Blackshirt.   London, Long, 1963.
Blackshirt Saves the Day.   London, Long, 1964.
Danger for Blackshirt.   London, Long, 1965.
Blackshirt at Large.   London, Long, 1966.
Blackshirt in Peril.   London, Long, 1967.
Blackshirt Stirs Things Up.   London, Long, 1969.

Novels as Jeffrey Ashford (series character: Detective Inspector Don Kerry)

Counsel for the Defence.   London, Long, 1960; New York, Harper, 1961.
Investigations Are Proceeding (Kerry).   London, Long, 1961; as *The D.I.*, New York, Harper, 1962.
The Burden of Proof.   London, Long, and New York, Harper, 1962.
Will Anyone Who Saw the Accident....   London, Long, 1963; New York, Harper, 1964; as *Hit and Run*, London, Arrow, 1966.
Enquiries Are Continuing (Kerry).   London, Long, 1964; as *The Superindent's Room*, New York, Harper, 1965.
The Hands of Innocence.   London, Long, 1965; New York, Walker, 1966.
Consider the Evidence.   London, Long, and New York, Walker, 1966.
Forget What You Saw.   London, Long, and New York, Walker, 1967.
Prisoner at the Bar.   London, Long and New York, Walker, 1969.
To Protect the Guilty.   London, Long and New York, Walker, 1970.
Bent Copper.   London, Long, and New York, Walker, 1971.
A Man Will Be Kidnapped Tomorrow.   London, Long, and New York, Walker, 1972.
The Double Run.   London, Long, and New York, Walker, 1973.

The Colour of Violence. London, Long, and New York, Walker, 1974.
Three Layers of Guilt. London, Long, 1975; New York, Walker, 1976.
Slow Down the World. London, Long, and New York, Walker, 1976.
Hostage to Death. London, Long and New York, Walker, 1977.
The Anger of Fear. London, Long, and New York, Walker, 1978.

Novels as Peter Alding (series characters: Constable Kerr and Inspector Fusil in all books)

The C.I.D. Room. London, Long, 1967; as *All Leads Negative*, New York, Harper, 1967.
Circle of Danger. London, Long, 1968.
Murder among Thieves. London, Long, 1969; New York, McCall, 1970.
Guilt Without Proof. London, Long, 1970.
Despite the Evidence. London, Long, 1971; New York, Saturday Review Press, 1972.
Call Back to Crime. London, Long, 1972.
Field of Fire. London, Long, 1973.
The Murder Line. London, Long, 1974.
Six Days to Death. London, Long, 1975.
Murder Is Suspected. London, Long, and New York, Walker, 1977.
Ransom Town. London, Long, and New York, Walker, 1979.

OTHER PUBLICATIONS

Novels as Hastings Draper

Wiggery Pokery. London, W. H. Allen, 1956.
Wigged and Gowned. London, W. H. Allen, 1958.
Brief Help. London, W. H. Allen, 1961.

Other (juvenile)

Brandy Ahoy! (as Roderic Graeme). London, Hutchinson, 1951.
Where's Brandy? (as Roderic Graeme). London, Hutchinson, 1953.
Brandy Goes a Cruising (as Roderic Graeme). London, Hutchinson, 1954.
Police and Detection. Leicester, Brockhampton Press, 1962; as *Against Time!*, New York, Harper, 1964.
Police Dog. Leicester, Brockhampton Press, and New York, Harper, 1965.
Police Car. Leicester, Brockhampton Press, 1967; as *Patrol Car*, New York, Harper, 1967.
Grand Prix Monaco (as Jeffrey Ashford). New York, Putnam, 1968.
River Patrol. New York, Harper, 1969.
Grand Prix Germany (as Jeffrey Ashford). New York, Putnam, 1970.
Grand Prix United States (as Jeffrey Ashford). New York, Putnam, 1971.
Police Patrol Boat. Leicester, Brockhampton Press, 1971.
Trapped. New York, Harper, 1972.
Grand Prix Britain (as Jeffrey Ashford). New York, Putnam, 1973.
Dick Knox at Le Mans (as Jeffrey Ashford). New York, Putnam, 1974.
The Riddle of the Parchment. London, Hodder and Stoughton, 1976.
The Boy Who Knew Too Much. London, Hodder and Stoughton, 1977.
Eighteen Desperate Hours. London, Hodder and Stoughton, 1979.
The Missing Man. London, Hodder and Stoughton, 1980.

Manuscript Collection: Mugar Memorial Library, Boston University.

Roderic Jeffries comments:
My earlier books were straight detective with no series character. Then in 1972 I moved to Mallorca, for health reasons, and introduced a Spanish detective, Enrique Alvarez. In these Mallorquin books I try to add to the mystery and detection a background which sketches in an island people who have known poverty and who are now adapting to a sudden prosperity brought about by tourism.

*   *   *

Roderic Jeffries, a prolific British writer with over 60 mystery stories to his credit, finds that like his character, author George Armitage in *The Colour of Violence*, he, too, must employ pseudonyms if his publisher is to allow him to continue his habit of publishing two or more books a year. As Roderic Graeme Jeffries continued the series about Blackshirt begun by his father, Bruce Graeme, adding nearly another two dozen stories. In addition, he employed his own name and the names Peter Alding, Jeffrey Ashford, and Graham Hastings for his various books, giving to each author's works a distinctive plot and character.

Roderic Jeffries and Jeffrey Ashford each wrote almost a book a year between 1961 and 1972. Jeffries spins murder tales that hinge upon clever courtroom antics and often require the accused to undertake his own defense in a last-ditch effort to win acquittal. *Evidence of the Accused, An Embarrassing Death*, and *Dead Against the Lawyers* are typical of this mode. In *Evidence of the Accused*, skilfully narrated in the first person, two men, a husband and a lover, are tried consecutively for the murder of a wealthy socialite. Each confesses to the crime when the other is being tried. The ending is a tour de force which produces the true murderer and leaves him free, outside the reaches of the law. This, surely, is Jeffries's most ingenious tale. Like Agatha Christie's *Witness for the Prosecution, Evidence of the Accused* has you guessing right to the end, and leaves you startled by the amorality of the book. In *An Embarrassing Death* circumstantial evidence points to Bill Stemple, an executive, as the murderer of a social-climbing stenographer who has been earning money on the side by posing for pornographic pictures. Stemple is tried and found guilty, but his knowledge of the stenographer's prudery, the envy and hatred of a homely female employee, and the jealousy of the stenographer's impecunious boyfriend are turned by his lawyer to his advantage and a new trial is ordered in which he is advised to undertake his own defense. He extracts an incriminating admission from the boyfriend and his lawyer steps in to win his acquittal. In *Dead Against the Lawyers* Jeffries gives his formulaic plot a novel twist; the hero, though acquitted of murder, returns to his young, weak, opportunistic wife, a captive of her sexual lures.

As Ashford, Jeffries writes suspense tales in which ordinary, likable people are placed at the center of an action over which they have little control. They find they must depend upon cunning and a survival instinct they never knew they possessed. Generally, a member of the British CID combining tedious discipline with savvy solves the mystery and arrests the criminal. It is always the psychology of the criminal and the detective that interests Ashford, and his plots, like Andrew Garve's, show considerable fascination with police procedures. Coshings occur in almost every book and usually the assaults upon women are practiced by sadists and homosexuals who delight in torturing women in unmentionable ways.

Investigations Are Proceeding is typical of Ashford's early books, but over the years Ashford grows increasingly curious about the psychology of crime and how it affects the criminal and the victim. What forces turn a law-abiding citizen into a criminal, or a political idealist into a psychopath become his concerns. *Investigations Are Proceeding* concluded with order restored. Later books end on a grimmer note. In *A Man Will Be Kidnapped Tomorrow*, the hostage is ultimately freed, but not before she has undergone acts of sadistic perversion that cannot be forgotten. In *The Double Run* the protagonist, a successful man who is unexpectedly fired, becomes indebted to dope smugglers, and is subtly blackmailed by both the criminals and the police. In order to return to the world of normality, he has to defy both the law of the police and of the criminal. In *Three Layers of Guilt* an innocent man is the unknowing pawn in a plot to defraud an insurance company. He, too, has to employ extra-legal and violent means before he can be reabsorbed into the fabric of society. In *Hostage to Death* another law-abiding citizen turns criminal, then has to battle the law and the criminals to extricate himself. Most of the books written by Ashford mix the same ingredients: a law-abiding citizen compelled by circumstance to criminal actions; a heist of some sort designed by a gang of ex-convicts who believe that a big snatch will give them loot, and, more importantly, influence and power in the world of crime; and a doggedly determined police force with an inspector who uses his intelligence and knowledge of people to ferret out the bizarre elements of the crime and rightly fathom the motives of the criminal. Usually the detective is caught between the illegal code of the criminal and the dispassionate code of law, both of which conspire against the individual and justice.

Jeffries's writings under the pseudonym of Peter Alding have much in common with those of Ashford, but these are series books, all treating Constable Kerr and Inspector Fusil in the English sea-town of Fortrow. Kerr is a young, likable, lusty detective, engaged to a proper young woman. Fusil, Kerr's superior, works long hours, is hard to please, despises criminals (perhaps because he knows too well he could be one himself), and is mothered by a protective wife. Together, Kerr and Fusil work on cases where the evidence is misleading, the public unreliable as witnesses, and the criminals often brilliant in their cunning. Kerr and Fusil are generally hamstrung by the conflicting demands of their superior who wants cases solved but no laws broken and little of his budget spent. They work defiantly, pursuing all clues, even the faintest, and tracing the evidence until they catch their prey. In *Despite the Evidence* they are pitted against the wit of a wealthy club-owner with a past record who is in the midst of planning a 2.5 million dollar jewel theft. In *Murder among Thieves* Kerr and Fusil resist the obvious explanation of the heist of a pay-truck and what appears to be the murder of two of the security guards, and finally identify the master thief who has been murdering his own co-conspirators. *Guilt Without Proof* and *The C.I.D. Room* treat a similar theme with the same cast. Alding spins a good tale, recounts the myriad details the police must put in order if they are to find the criminal, fleshes out his characters, and offers good descriptions of the seaside locale.

Jeffries in all his guises can be depended upon to tell a good tale. Nearly always the detectives or the accused must tamper with evidence if they are to convict the guilty or avoid conviction themselves; often law is inadequate to prove right and violence or trickery is used to effect a return to order; and always greed and a hunger for power motivate the criminals.

—Carol Simpson Stern

JEPSON, Selwyn. British. Born in 1899; son of the writer Edgar Jepson. Educated at St. Paul's School, London; the Sorbonne, Paris. Served in World War I, and in Military Intelligence and the Special Operations Executive during World War II: Major. Address: The Far House, Liss, Hampshire, England.

CRIME PUBLICATIONS

Novels (series characters: Eve Gill; Ian MacArthur)

The Qualified Adventurer (MacArthur). London, Hutchinson, and New York, Harcourt Brace, 1922; as *Manchu Jade*, London, Mellifont Press, 1935.
Puppets of Fate. London, Hutchinson, 1922.
That Fellow MacArthur. London, Hutchinson, 1923.
The King's Red-Haired Girl. London, Hutchinson, 1923.
Golden-Eyes. London, Harrap, 1924; as *The Sutton Papers*, New York, Dial Press, 1924.
Rogues and Diamonds. London, Harrap, and New York, Dial Press, 1925.
Snaggletooth. London, Harrap, 1926.
The Death Gong. London, Harrap, and New York, Watt, 1927.
Love – and Helen. London, Harrap, and New York, Watt, 1928.
Tiger Dawn. London, Hodder and Stoughton, 1929.
I Met Murder. London, Hodder and Stoughton, and New York, Harper, 1930.
The Floating Admiral, with others. London, Hodder and Stoughton, 1931; New York, Doubleday, 1932.
Rabbit's Paw. London, Hodder and Stoughton, 1932; as *The Mystery of the Rabbit's Paw*, New York, Harper, 1932.
Love in Peril. London, Mellifont Press, 1934.
The Wise Fool. London, Mellifont Press, 1934.
Keep Murder Quiet. London, Joseph, 1940; New York, Doubleday, 1941.
Man Running (Gill). London, Macdonald, 1948; as *Outrun the Constable*, New York, Doubleday, 1948; as *Killer by Proxy*, New York, Bantam, 1950.
Riviera Love Story. London, Mellifont Press, 1948.
Tempering Steel. London, Mellifont Press, 1949.
The Golden Dart (Gill). London, Macdonald, and New York, Doubleday, 1949.
The Hungry Spider (Gill). New York, Doubleday, 1950; London, Macdonald, 1951.
Man Dead. London, Collins, and New York, Doubleday, 1951.
The Black Italian (Gill). London, Collins, and New York, Doubleday, 1954.
The Assassin. London, Collins, and Philadelphia, Lippincott, 1956.
A Noise in the Night. London, Hart Davis, and Philadelphia, Lippincott, 1957.
The Laughing Fish (Gill). London, Hart Davis, 1960; as *Verdict in Question*, New York, Doubleday, 1960.
Fear in the Wind (Gill). London, W. H. Allen, 1964.
The Third Possibility. London, W. H. Allen, 1965.
The Angry Millionaire. New York, Harper, 1968; London, Macmillan, 1969.
Letter to a Dead Girl. London, Macmillan, 1971.

Short Stories

Heads and Tails, with Michael Joseph. London, Jarrolds, 1933.

Uncollected Short Stories

"By the Sword," in *A Century of Detective Stories*, edited by G. K. Chesterton. London, Hutchinson, 1935.
"The Tea-Leaf," with Robert Eustace, in *Tales of Detection*. London, Dent, 1936.
"The Case of the Absconding Financier," in *Creeps, Crimes, and Thrills*. London, Samuel, 1936.
"Nor the Jury," in *Ellery Queen's Mystery Magazine* (New York), February 1947.
"Letter of the Law," in *Ellery Queen's Mystery Magazine* (New York), July 1952.

OTHER PUBLICATIONS

Plays

Screenplays: *Going Gay* (*Kiss Me Goodbye*), with John Marks and K. R. G. Browne, 1933; *For Love of You*, 1933; *Money Mad*, 1934; *The Love Test*, with Jack Celestin, 1935; *The Riverside Murder*, with Leslie Landau, 1935; *Dark World*, with Leslie Landau, 1935; *Wedding Group* (*Wrath of Jealousy*), with Hugh Brooke, 1936; *The Scarab Murder Case*, 1936; *Toilers of the Sea*, 1936; *Well Done, Henry*, with Wilfred Noy and A. Barr-Smith, 1937; *Sailing Along*, with Lesser Samuels and Sonnie Hale, 1938.

Radio Plays: *The Hungry Spider* (serial), 1958; *The Bath That Sang*, 1958; *Friend of the Man Smith*, 1958; *The Commodore's Ruby*, 1958; *Tears for the Bride*, 1959; *A Noise in the Night*, 1959; *Art for Art's Sake*, 1959; *Small Brother*, 1960; *Uncle Murderer*, 1960; *Call It Greymail*, 1963; *The Golden Dart*, 1968.

Television Plays: *Scheherazade*, with Irving Rubine, 1956; *The Face of the Law*, with Lance Sieveking, 1957.

Theatrical Activities:

Director: **Film** – *Toilers of the Sea*, with Ted Fox, 1936.

Selwyn Jepson comments:
I have never pretended to write anything more serious than fairy stories for grownups.

*   *   *

Selwyn Jepson had a long career of writing thrillers – most of which feature a chase or quest of some sort. The early and uncharacteristic fairy tale for adults, *The Death Gong*, tells of Sir John Perrin's search for his beloved who has been kidnapped from Italy and is on a ship bound for Tunis. His American millionaire friend Carfew Northcote, a collector of antiquities, has triggered this situation because he urgently seeks the ancient gong whose vibrations are powerful enough to kill.

Jepson's most impressive performance, *Keep Murder Quiet*, a variation of the *Hamlet* story, has often been compared to Philip MacDonald's 1938 book, *The Nursemaid Who Disappeared*, which it resembles in technique. It tells the story of Roger Spain who swears vengence on the man who brutally murdered his father, but has next to nothing to help him identify and locate the man whom he would destroy.

Jepson's series character, the attractive Eve Gill, was featured in six thrillers written between 1948 and 1964. Although she narrates her own peripatetic adventures, her mode of story-telling is never overly-feminine, and the constant physical movement and suspenseful situations have a strong appeal to all readers, men or women. Most of Eve's problems are caused by her father Commodore Rupert Gill's constant desire to smuggle goods – usually drinkable – into England in spite of his confinement to a wheelchair. The first Eve Gill title is indicative of the plots of the series: *Man Running*, changed to *Outrun the Constable* in America.

—Charles Shibuk

JESSE, F(ryniwyd) Tennyson. British. Born in 1889. Studied painting with Stanhope Forbes in Newlyn, Cornwall. Married Harold Marsh Harwood in 1918. Journalist from age 20: reporter for the *Times* and *Daily Mail*, and reviewer for the *Times Literary Supplement* and the *English Review*, all London; staff member, *Metropolitan Magazine*, New York, 1914; War Correspondent (unaccredited), 1914–18; during World War I worked for the Ministry of Information and as a French Red Cross visitor to frontline hsopitals. Fellow, Royal Society of Literature. *Died 6 August 1958.*

CRIME PUBLICATIONS

Novels

> *The Man Who Stayed at Home* (as Beamish Tinker). London, Mills and Boon, 1915.
> *A Pin to See the Peepshow.* London, Heinemann, and New York, Doubleday, 1934.
> *Double Death*, with others. London, Gollancz, 1939.

Short Stories

> *The Solange Stories.* London, Heinemann, and New York, Macmillan, 1931.

Uncollected Short Stories

> "Last Times," in *Many Mysteries*, edited by E. Phillips Oppenheim. London, Rich and
>   Cowan, 1933.
> "Treasure Trove," in *My Best Thriller.* London, Faber, 1933.
> "The Mask," in *And the Darkness Falls*, edited by Boris Karloff. Cleveland, World,
>   1946.
> "In Death They Were Divided," in *Ellery Queen's Mystery Magazine* (New York),
>   August 1948.
> "The Railway Carriage," in *Fantasy and Science Fiction* (New York), February 1951.
> "Lord of the Moment," in *Ellery Queen's Mystery Magazine* (New York), February
>   1951.

OTHER PUBLICATIONS

Novels

> *The Milky Way.* London, Heinemann, 1913; New York, Doran, 1914.
> *Secret Bread.* London, Heinemann, and New York, Doran, 1917.
> *The White Riband; or, A Young Female's Folly.* London, Heinemann, 1921; New
>   York, Doran, 1922.
> *Tom Fool.* London, Heinemann, and New York, Knopf, 1926.
> *Moonraker; or, The Female Pirate and Her Friends.* London, Heinemann, and New
>   York, Knopf, 1927.
> *The Lacquer Lady.* London, Heinemann, 1929; New York, Macmillan, 1930.
> *Act of God.* London, Heinemann, and New York, Greystone Press, 1937.
> *The Alabaster Cup.* London, Evans, 1950.
> *The Dragon in the Heart.* London, Constable, 1956.

Short Stories

> *Beggars on Horseback.* London, Heinemann, and New York, Doran, 1915.
> *Many Latitudes.* London, Heinemann, and New York, Knopf, 1928.

Plays

The Mask, with H. M. Harwood, adaptation of a story by Jesse (as *The Black Mask*, produced New York, 1913; as *The Mask*, produced London, 1915). Published in *Three One-Act Plays*, by Harwood, London, Benn, 1926.
Billeted, with H. M. Harwood (as *The Lonely Soldiers*, produced Pittsburgh, 1917; as *Billeted*, produced New York and London, 1917). London, French, 1920.
The Hotel Mouse, with H. M. Harwood, adaptation of a play by Paul Armont and Marcel Gerbidon (produced London, 1921).
Quarantine (produced Brighton and London, 1922; New York, 1924).
The Pelican, with H. M. Harwood (produced London, 1924; New York, 1925). London Benn, 1926.
Anyhouse (produced London, 1925). London, Heinemann, 1925.
How to Be Healthy Though Married, with H. M. Harwood (produced London, 1930). London, Heinemann, 1930.
Birdcage, with Harold Dearden (produced London, 1950).
A Pin to See the Peepshow, with H. M. Harwood, adaptation of the novel by Jesse (produced London, 1951; New York, 1953).

Screenplay: *San Demetrio – London*, with Robert Hamer and Charles Frend, 1943.

Verse

The Happy Bride. London, Heinemann, and New York, Doran, 1920.
The Compass and Other Poems. London, Hodge, 1951.

Other

The Sword of Deborah: First-Hand Impressions of the British Women's Army in France. London, Heinemann, and New York, Doran, 1919.
Murder and Its Motives. London, Heinemann, and New York, Knopf, 1924; revised edition, London, Pan 1958.
Sabi Pas; or, I Don't Know. London, Heinemann, 1935.
The London Front: Letters Written to America, August 1939–July 1940, with H. M. Harwood. London, Constable, 1940; New York, Doubleday, 1941.
While London Burns: Letters Written to America, July 1940–June 1941, with H. M. Harwood. London, Constable, 1942.
The Saga of San Demetrio. London, HMSO, and New York, Knopf, 1942.
The Story of Burma. London, Macmillan, 1946.
Comments on Cain (on murder trials). London, Heinemann, 1948.

Editor, *The Trial of Madeleine Smith.* London, Hodge, 1927.
Editor, *The Trial of Samuel Henry Dougal.* London, Hodge, 1928.
Editor, *The Baffle Book*, by Lassiter Wren and Randle Mac Kay. London, Heinemann, 1930.
Editor, *The Trial of Sidney Harry Fox.* London, Hodge, 1934.
Editor, *The Trial of Alma Victoria Rattenbury and George Percy Stoner.* London, Hodge, 1947.
Editor, *The Trial of Thomas John Ley and Lawrence John Smith.* London, Hodge, 1947.
Editor, *The Trial of Timothy John Evans and John Reginald Halliday Christie.* London, Hodge, 1957.

Translator, *The City Curious*, by Jean de Bosschère. London, Heinemann, and New York, Dodd Mead, 1920.

*   *   *

Although one of Sinclair Lewis's characters admired F. Tennyson Jesse's play *The Black Mask* ("Glorious ending, where this woman looks at the man with his face all blown away, and she just gives one horrible scream"), Jesse has survived best as the author of the realistic novel *A Pin to See the Peepshow*.

Closely based on the 1922 Bywaters–Thompson case, this long narrative describes the life and death of Julia Almond, an Emma Bovary of the First World War, of Herbert Starling, her nagging older husband, and of Leonard Carr, her much younger lover, who unexpectedly attacks and kills Starling. Julia is charged with inciting him to murder, and both are executed. Jesse devoted many pages to the trial of Julia and Leonard; in her account of the trial and in her interpretation of Julia's character, she followed the Bywaters–Thompson volume edited by Filson Young in the "Notable British Trials" series, several volumes of which Jesse herself edited. Like Edith Thompson, Julia is hanged, partly because of bad luck in her defense and her judge, but chiefly because she wrote her lover many letters describing her imaginary attempts to poison her husband, fictive letters which were intended to assure him of her devotion even unto murder and which were part of Julia's continuous secret reverie. She murders in dreams and wakes to find it taken as true.

Jesse's novel begins when Julia is a school-girl, vital, vivid, already living in imagination. The author fills in much detail, physical, social, and psychological: the background of the war and its new freedoms; the early 1920's; Julia's dull, intrusive family; her first physical attraction, to Alfie, who dies in France; her satisfying, competent work for a superior dress shop; her heavy husband, demanding his "rights" in her bedroom with Chinese-patterned chintzes; her pleasure in the theatre; her brief episodes of utter delight with Leonard when flesh and fantasy unite; her sordid abortion of Herbert's child; Leonard's gift of an Italian officer's cape, which Julia's mother sells to "the waxwork people" for fifty pounds. For the murder itself Jesse drew heavily on testimony at the trial, and, like Young, she pointed out that had Edith/Julia belonged to a class in which divorce was easily affordable and socially acceptable, she would not have been destroyed.

Jesse's style is sometimes rather heavy and her ironies rather too emphatic, as when the prison doctor thinks that Julia has "evaded the womb's responsibilities, while partaking of its pleasures" and that nature has had its "last ironic revenge in the body of the man who had killed for what he had called love, making a final gesture, lewd as a sneer." Yet the description of Julia's consciousness of her dwindling life as she waits for execution and of the prison routine which delivers her, collapsed and drugged, through the door to the gallows, produces in the reader a cold realization of the helplessness of mortality and is far more effective than its sentimental prototype, "The Ballad of Reading Gaol."

—Jane W. Stedman

JOBSON, Hamilton. British. Born in London, 3 April 1914. Educated at Burlington College, London, 1925–31. Served in the Royal Air Force, 1943–45. Married Mabel Eileen Boniface in 1939; one daughter. Commercial artist for newspapers, London, 1931–34; ran a commercial library, London, 1934–36; insurance agent, 1936–37; Member of the Southend-on-Sea County Borough Police Force, Essex, 1938–68, rising to the rank of Divisional Inspector: nine commendations for special arrests. Agent: A. M. Heath, 40–42 William IV

Street, London WC2N 4DD. Address: 43 Crosby Road, Westcliff-on-Sea, Essex SS0 8LF, England.

CRIME PUBLICATIONS

Novels (series character: Inspector Anders in all books)

Therefore I Killed Him.   London, Long, 1968.
Smile and Be a Villain.   London, Long, 1969; New York, Abelard Schuman, 1971.
Naked to My Enemy.   London, Long, 1970.
The Silent Cry.   London, Long, 1970.
The House with Blind Eyes.   London, Long, 1971.
The Shadow That Caught Fire.   London, Long, 1972; New York, Scribner, 1976.
The Sand Pit.   London, Long, 1972.
Contract with a Killer.   London, Long, 1974.
The Evidence You Will Hear.   London, Collins, and New York, Scribner, 1975.
Waiting for Thursday.   London, Collins, 1977; New York, St. Martin's Press, 1978.
Judge Me Tomorrow.   London, Collins, 1978.
To Die a Little.   London, Collins, 1978; New York, St. Martin's Press, 1979.
Exit to Violence.   London, Collins, 1979.

Hamilton Jobson comments:

I am, I suppose, motived by an egocentric desire to create with the abilities at my disposal, especially as the end product may give pleasure to others and provide money for me. I do become absorbed in the characters of a story I am writing, however, sharing their vicissitudes and triumphs, if any, so in a sense the writing becomes compulsive. With the main theme in mind I allow my stories to evolve through the nature of my characters (with an occasional nudge from me). I do not like contrived situations. I feel that human nature has so many facets that relationships (which is what nearly all novels are about) have never-ending permutations.

Having been a police officer for 30 years, I have naturally acquired a fairly wide experience of human beings and the situations in which they become involved. This has helped. I do need encouragement. I am inclined at times to be over-critical of my own work. Each book is written and typed four times.

*   *   *

Hamilton Jobson is a real story-teller whose background is varied enough to supply the depth of experiences necessary for his themes to be both credible, and suspenseful. He has worked as a commercial artist, a commercial librarian, and an insurance agent, and for 30 years as a policeman, retiring as Divisional Patrol Inspector.

His stories are often based on human dilemmas and owe much to the credibility and strength of his characters. His series policeman is Inspector Anders. An efficient but kindly policeman, he understands the moral dilemmas facing the average citizen, but when confronted with extreme pressures often acts without real thought as to the consequences. Although Anders is invariably not the central character, he still somehow manages to make his presence felt; his appearance may be rather towards the end of the book than the beginning. Jobson's plots are always convincing, and he has the knack of obtaining the sympathy of the reader without becoming sentimental. Especially recommended as good examples of this author's work are *Smile and Be a Villain, The Shadow That Caught Fire*, and *The Evidence You Will Hear.*

—Donald C. Ireland

JOHNSON, E(mil) Richard.   American.   Born in 1937. Earned high school equivalency diploma in the Army; studied by correspondence with Minneapolis Writers Workshop. Served in the United States Army Intelligence: Sergeant. Worked in logging, as forester with the United States Department of Agriculture, ranch hand, well-driller. At present an inmate in Stillwater, Minnesota, State Prison, serving a third sentence. Recipient: Mystery Writers of America Edgar Allan Poe Award 1968.

CRIME PUBLICATIONS

Novels

> *Silver Street.*   New York, Harper, 1968; as *The Silver Street Killer*, London, Hale, 1969.
> *The Inside Man.*   New York, Harper, 1969; London, Macmillan, 1970.
> *Mongo's Back in Town.*   New York, Harper, 1969; London, Macmillan, 1970.
> *Cage Five Is Going to Break.*   New York, Harper, 1970; London, Macmillan, 1971.
> *The God Keepers.*   New York, Harper, 1970; London, Macmillan, 1971.
> *Case Load – Maximum.*   New York, Harper, 1971.
> *The Judas.*   New York, Harper, 1971.
> *The Cardinalli Contract.*   New York, Pyramid, 1975.

Manuscript Collection: Mugar Memorial Library, Boston University.

*   *   *

The publication of E. Richard Johnson's *Silver Street* in 1968 heralded the addition of a major new talent to the ranks of the established crime novelists. In this and the seven novels which followed, Johnson, writing from his cell in Minnesota's Stillwater State Prison, presented his uncompromising insider's view of the dark underbelly of American life – the neon-spangled world of crime, "where cruelty of man to man was a matter of fact." Urban cesspools of depravity with names like The Strip and Pimp's Row "are a cop's nightmare, a festering gash on the city's face that stinks of evil when you walk it on dark nights" and "you know the evil is real, and the hate is there."

In Johnson's urban nightmare two basic themes provide the connecting link. First, everyone is driven by compulsive needs, desires, and social pressures into ways of life, character, and behavior from which there is no escape. All are trapped – the winos, pimps, and whores, the narcotics suppliers, pushers, and addicts, the gangsters, hit-men, and killers, even the policemen, good or bad, honest or dishonest, compassionate or brutal – all alike must function according to the dictates of their own immutable natures. They have no choice. Second, everyone betrays or is betrayed by his own or others' needs. Johnson's best two novels – *Silver Street* and *Case Load – Maximum* – demonstrate both these themes superlatively. In the former, the policeman-hero discovers that the woman he loves is a prostitute, his experience thus paralleling that of the psychopathic killer of pimps he has been assigned to apprehend and forcing him to face the seeds of the killer's madness – their common bond, as it were – within himself. In *Case Load – Maximum* – a novel which shows the impossibility of any genuine relationship or communication between the truly criminal and the truly decent – an idealistic young parole officer trusts one of his charges to such a degree that he almost loses his job, but, though he learns that his faith was misplaced, he nevertheless overcomes his disillusionment by hanging on to his idealism. E. Richard Johnson, working in the tradition of the hard-boiled genre, but adding his own unique insights to it, is undoubtedly one of the best talents to appear during the 1960's and 1970's.

—Kenneth D. Alley

JORDAN, Robert Furneaux.   See PLAYER, Robert.

KANE, Frank.   Also wrote as Frank Boyd.   American.   Born in Brooklyn, New York, 19 July 1912. Educated at City College of New York, B.S.S.; night law student, St. John's University, Jamaica, New York, 1939–41. Married Ann Herlehy in 1939; three children. Columnist, New York *Press*, 1935–37; Editor-in-Chief, Trade Newspapers Corporation, New York, 1937–40; Associate Editor, New York *Journal of Commerce*, 1940–42; Public Relations Director, Conference of Alcoholic Beverage Industries, 1942–46; after 1946 freelance writer, radio and television producer, and President, Frank Kane Corporation, National Liquor Review Company, Frank Kane Associates, and Report to Writers Company. *Died 29 November 1968.*

CRIME PUBLICATIONS

Novels (series character: Johnny Liddell)

About Face (Liddell).   New York, Curl, 1947; as *Death About Face*, Kingston, New York, Quin, 1948; as *The Fatal Foursome*, New York, Dell, 1958.
Green Light for Death (Liddell).   New York, Washburn, 1949; London, Mayflower, 1966.
Slay Ride (Liddell).   New York, Washburn, 1950.
Bullet Proof (Liddell).   New York, Washburn, 1951; London, Mayflower, 1969.
Dead Weight (Liddell).   New York, Washburn, 1951.
Bare Trap (Liddell).   New York, Washburn, 1952.
Poisons Unknown (Liddell).   New York, Washburn, 1953.
Grave Danger (Liddell).   New York, Washburn, 1954.
Red Hot Ice (Liddell).   New York, Washburn, 1955; London, Boardman, 1956.
Key Witness.   New York, Dell, 1956.
A Real Gone Guy (Liddell).   New York, Rinehart, 1956; London, Boardman, 1957.
Liz.   Beacon, New York, Beacon Signal, 1958.
Syndicate Girl.   New York, Dell, 1958.
Trigger Mortis (Liddell).   New York, Rinehart, 1958.
Juke Box King.   New York, Dell, 1959.
The Line-Up (novelization of tv play).   New York, Dell, 1959; London, Consul, 1960.
Johnny Staccato (novelization of tv play; as Frank Boyd).   New York, Fawcett, 1960; London, Consul, 1964.
A Short Bier (Liddell).   New York, Dell, 1960; London, Mayflower, 1964.
Time to Prey (Liddell).   New York, Dell, 1960; London, Mayflower, 1964.
Due or Die (Liddell).   New York, Dell, 1961; London, Mayflower, 1963.
The Mourning After (Liddell).   New York, Dell, 1961.
The Conspirators.   New York, Dell, 1962.
Crime of Their Life (Liddell).   New York, Dell, 1962; London, Mayflower, 1964.
Dead Rite (Liddell).   New York, Dell, 1962; London, Mayflower, 1968.
Ring-a-Ding-Ding (Liddell).   New York, Dell, 1963; London, Mayflower, 1964.
Johnny Come Lately (Liddell).   New York, Dell, 1963; London, Mayflower, 1964.
Hearse Class Male (Liddell).   New York, Dell, 1963; London, Mayflower, 1969.
Barely Seen (Liddell).   New York, Dell, and London, Mayflower, 1964.
Final Curtain (Liddell).   New York, Dell, and London, Mayflower, 1964.

Fatal Undertaking (Liddell).   New York, Dell, 1964; London, Mayflower, 1965.
The Guilt-Edged Frame (Liddell).   New York, Dell, 1964.
Esprit de Corpse (Liddell).   New York, Dell, 1965.
Two to Tangle (Liddell).   New York, Dell, 1965.
Maid in Paris (Liddell).   New York, Dell, 1966.
Margin for Terror (Liddell).   New York, Dell, 1967.

Short Stories

Johnny Liddell's Morgue.   New York, Dell, 1956; London, Consul, 1958.
Stacked Deck.   New York, Dell, 1961; London, Mayflower, 1964.

Uncollected Short Story

"With Frame to Match," in *Come Seven, Come Death*, edited by Henry
Morrison.   New York, Pocket Books, 1965.

OTHER PUBLICATIONS

Novels

The Living End.   New York, Dell, 1957.
The Flesh Peddlers (as Frank Boyd).   Derby, Connecticut, Monarch, 1959.

Plays

Radio Plays: *The Shadow, The Fat Man, Gangbusters, Claims Agent*, and *Lawless
Twenties* series.

Television Plays: *Mike Hammer, S.A. 7*, and *The Investigators* series.

Other

Anatomy of the Whiskey Business.   Manhasset, New York, Lake House Press, 1965.
Travel Is for the Birds.   Manhasset, New York, Lake House Press, 1966.
Lewis S. Rosenstiel: Industry Statesman.   Manhasset, New York, Lake House Press, 2
vols., 1966.

*   *   *

Frank Kane's most popular work was his Johnny Liddell private eye series. Liddell first
appeared in the pulps (primarily *Crack Detective*) in 1944. During this time Kane was also
working as a script writer for such radio suspense shows as *The Shadow, The Fat Man* and
Gangbusters. The first Liddell novel was also Kane's first novel, *Above Face*. By the time of
Kane's death, the 29 books in the series had sold over five million copies. Kane never claimed
to be anything but a pulp writer, and his limitations and the high speed at which he wrote are
evident in much of his work. He often plagiarized himself, recycling entire scenes and
descriptive passages from his previous books and stories. There were little detection and
generally far too much killing in the Liddell novels. Yet the writing was always lean and
powerful, almost cinematic (during the early 1960's Kane wrote scripts for the *Mike Hammer*
tv show, among others), and the books are classic examples of the hard-boiled private eye
formula, stripped bare of any frills.

In the early books of the series Liddell is an operative for the Acme Detective Agency,
working out of New York. By the time of *Dead Weight*, however, he has branched out on his
own with an office in Manhattan and a sexy red-haired secretary named Pinky. Though Kane

rarely deviated from the basic ingredients of the private eye formula, the books were often distinguished by a gritty, authentic portrayal of New York cops and their methods. Kane's brother was a New York policeman, credited as technical advisor on the series. Kane never again matched the pace and raw storytelling drive that he achieved in *Bullet Proof*, probably the best of the Liddell books. His backgrounds were always well researched and vividly realistic, as evidenced by his colorful depiction of New York's Chinatown in *Dead Weight*. *Fatal Undertaking*, a fine late entry in the series, scores high points for both characterization and a tightly woven plot concerning dirty tricks in UN diplomatic circles.

In addition to the Liddell novels Kane produced a number of non-series suspense paperbacks. The best of these is *Key Witness*, a tersely written story about white precinct cops in Harlem dealing with a teenage gang murder. A claustrophobic air of fear and urban frustration permeates the book, and it is this that lifts *Key Witness* several notches above the better-known Liddell tales.

—Stephen Mertz

KANE, Henry. Also writes as Anthony McCall.   American.   Born in New York City in 1918. Attorney, then self-employed writer.

CRIME PUBLICATIONS

Novels (series characters: Peter Chambers; Inspector McGregor; Marla Trent)

> *A Halo for Nobody* (Chambers).   New York, Simon and Schuster, 1947; London, Boardman, 1950; as *Martinis and Murder*, New York, Avon, 1956.
> *Armchair in Hell* (Chambers).   New York, Simon and Schuster, 1948; London, Boardman, 1949.
> *Hang by Your Neck* (Chambers).   New York, Simon and Schuster, 1949; London, Boardman, 1950.
> *Edge of Panic*.   New York, Simon and Schuster, 1950; London, Boardman, 1951.
> *A Corpse for Christmas* (Chambers).   Philadelphia, Lippincott, 1951; London, Boardman, 1952; as *Homicide at Yuletide*, New York, New American Library, 1966.
> *Until You Are Dead* (Chambers).   New York, Simon and Schuster, 1951; London, Boardman, 1952.
> *Laughter Came Screaming*.   London, Boardman, 1953; New York, Avon, 1954; as *Mask for Murder*, New York, Avon, 1957.
> *My Business Is Murder* (Chambers; novelets).   New York, Avon, 1954.
> *Trilogy in Jeopardy* (Chambers; novelets).   London, Boardman, 1955.
> *Trinity in Violence* (Chambers; novelets).   New York, Avon, 1955; (different contents) London, Boardman, 1954.
> *Too French and Too Deadly* (Chambers).   New York, Avon, 1955; as *The Narrowing Lust*, London, Boardman, 1956.
> *Who Killed Sweet Sue?* (Chambers).   New York, Avon, 1956; as *Sweet Charlie*, London, Boardman, 1957.
> *The Deadly Finger*.   New York, Popular Library, 1957; as *The Finger*, London, Boardman, 1957.
> *Death on the Double* (Chambers; novelets).   New York, Avon, 1957; London, Boardman, 1958.

Death for Sale.   New York, Dell, 1957; as *Sleep Without Dreams*, London, Boardman, 1958; New York, Lancer, 1970.

Fistful of Death (Chambers).   New York, Avon, 1958; as *The Dangling Man*, London, Boardman, 1959.

Death Is the Last Lover (Chambers).   New York, Avon, 1959; as *Nirvana Can Also Mean Death*, London, Boardman, 1959.

The Deadly Doll.   Rockville Centre, New York, Zenith, 1959.

The Private Eyeful (Trent).   New York, Pyramid, 1959; London, Boardman, 1960.

Peter Gunn (novelization of tv play).   New York, Dell, 1960.

Run for Doom.   London, Boardman, 1960; New York, New American Library, 1962.

The Crumpled Cup.   London, Boardman, 1961; New York, New American Library, 1963.

Death of a Flack (Chambers).   New York, New American Library, and London, Boardman, 1961.

My Darlin' Evangeline.   New York, Dell, 1961; as *Perfect Crime*, London, Boardman, 1961; New York, Belmont, 1967.

Dead in Bed (Chambers).   New York, Lancer, 1961; London, Boardman, 1963.

Death of a Hooker (Chambers).   London, Boardman, 1961; New York, Avon, 1963.

Kisses of Death (Chambers; Trent).   New York, Belmont, 1962; as *Killer's Kiss*, London, Boardman, 1962.

Death of a Dastard (Chambers).   London, Boardman, 1962; New York, New American Library, 1963.

Never Give a Millionaire an Even Break (Chambers).   New York, Lancer, 1963; as *Murder for the Millions*, London, Boardman, 1964.

Nobody Loves a Loser (Chambers).   New York, Belmont, 1963; London, Boardman, 1964; as *Who Dies There?*, New York, Lancer, 1969.

Snatch an Eye (Chambers).   London, Boardman, 1963; New York, Permabooks, 1964.

Two Must Die.   New York, Tower, 1963.

Dirty Gertie.   London, Boardman, 1963; New York, Belmont, 1965; as *To Die or Not To Die*, New York, Belmont, 1964.

Frenzy of Evil.   London, Boardman, 1963; New York, Dell, 1966.

The Midnight Man (McGregor).   New York, Macmillan, 1965; as *Other Sins Only Speak*, London, Boardman, 1965.

Prey by Dawn.   London, Boardman, 1965.

Conceal and Disguise (McGregor).   New York, Macmillan, and London, Boardman, 1966.

The Devil to Pay (Chambers).   London, Boardman, 1966; as *Unholy Trio*, New York, Pocket Books, 1967; as *Better Wed Than Dead*, New York, Lancer, 1970.

Operation Delta (as Anthony McCall).   New York, Trident Press, 1966; London, Joseph, 1967.

Holocaust (as Anthony McCall).   New York, Trident Press, 1967.

Laughter in the Alehouse (McGregor).   New York, Macmillan, 1968; London, Penguin, 1978.

Don't Call Me Madame (Chambers).   New York, Lancer, 1969.

The Schack Job (Chambers).   New York, Lancer, 1969.

The Bomb Job (Chambers).   New York, Lancer, 1970.

Don't Go Away Dead (Chambers).   New York, Lancer, 1970.

Kiss! Kiss! Kill! Kill! (Chambers; novelets).   New York, Lancer, 1970.

The Glow Job (Chambers).   New York, Lancer, 1971.

The Moonlighter.   New York, Geis, 1971; London, Hale, 1972.

The Tail Job (Chambers).   New York, Lancer, 1971.

Come Kill with Me (Chambers).   New York, Lancer, 1972.

The Escort Job (Chambers).   New York, Lancer, 1972.

Kill for the Millions (Chambers).   New York, Lancer, 1972.

Decision.   New York, Dial Press, 1973.

A Kind of Rape. New York, Atheneum, 1974.
The Violator. New York, Warner, 1974.
The Avenger. New York, Atheneum, 1975.
Lust of Power. New York, Atheneum, 1975.
The Tripoli Documents. New York, Simon and Schuster, 1976.

Short Stories

Report for a Corpse. New York, Simon and Schuster, 1948; London, Boardman,
   1950; as *Murder of the Park Avenue Playgirl*, New York, Avon, 1957.
The Case of the Murdered Madame. New York, Avon, 1955; as *Triple Terror*,
   London, Boardman, 1958.
The Name Is Chambers. New York, Pyramid, 1957.

Uncollected Short Stories

"Sweet Charlie," in *Dames, Danger, and Death*, edited by Leo Margulies. New York,
   Pyramid, 1960.
"The Memory Guy," in *Come Seven, Come Death*, edited by Henry Morrison. New
   York, Pocket Books, 1965.

OTHER PUBLICATIONS

Novel

The Virility Factor. New York, McKay, 1971.

Other

How to Write a Song. New York, Macmillan, 1962.

Manuscript Collection: Mugar Memorial Library, Boston University.

                          *   *   *

Henry Kane's career is rather typical of that of the post-pulp era hard-boiled writer. Most
of his works have appeared in paperback only, and he has attempted to follow changing
trends in the paperback market, producing – in addition to the long-running series of Peter
Chambers private eye novels – "suspense" novels of the man-on-the-run variety (*Edge of
Panic*), television novelizations (*Peter Gunn*), and hardcore sex novels (the "X-Rated"
Chambers series, beginning in 1969). Most recently, he has turned to would-be "blockbuster"
books like *The Tripoli Documents*, a thriller involving Israeli spies and Arab assassins.
   It is the Peter Chambers private eye (Kane prefers "private Richard") series which has been
Kane's mainstay, and it contains his best work. Chambers relates his cases in the usual first-
person fashion, but though the tough-guy attitudes, generous supply of sexy women, and
sleazy-decadent milieu (New York rather than Los Angeles, for a change) are typical hard-
boiled stuff, the prose style is not. Kane writes in a distinctively eccentric prose; his characters
tend to speak in a strangely stilted circumlocutionary fashion ("And what please, in hell, does
she want?"); he delights in elaborately wacky descriptive passages ("with mammary
proportions of such prodigious insouciance as to have Brigette look warily to her breastworks
..."). Chambers is a thoroughly likeable private eye, with a tendency to indulge in much wry
self-deprecation, rendered in this florid "Kanese." As might be expected in so lengthy a series,
the quality and variety of the plotting are variable, but at his best, Kane is a first-rate plotter,

877

capable of constructing sensible, logical mysteries. It is Kane's unique approach to the hard-boiled writing style, however, that sets the Chambers series apart from the ordinary.

—Art Scott

KAVANAGH, Paul. See **BLOCK, Lawrence.**

KEATING, H(enry) R(eymond) F(itzwalter). British. Born in St. Leonards-on-Sea, Sussex, 31 October 1926. Educated at Merchant Taylors' School, London, 1940–44; Trinity College, Dublin (Vice-Chancellor's Prose Prize), 1948–52, B.A. 1952. Served in the British Army, 1945–48. Married Sheila Mary Mitchell in 1953; three sons and one daughter. Sub-Editor, *Wiltshire Herald*, Swindon, 1953–56; *Daily Telegraph*, London, 1956–58; and *Times*, London, 1958–60. Since 1967, crime books reviewer, *Times*. Chairman, Crime Writers Association, 1970–71. Recipient: Crime Writers Association Golden Dagger, 1964; Mystery Writers of America Edgar Allan Poe Award, 1965; *Ellery Queen's Mystery Magazine* prize, for short story, 1970. Agent: A. D. Peters and Company, 10 Buckingham Street, London WC2N 6BU. Address: 35 Northumberland Place, London W2 5AS, England.

Crime Publications

Novels (series character: Inspector Ganesh Ghote)

Death and the Visiting Firemen. London, Gollancz, 1959; New York, Doubleday, 1973.
Zen There Was Murder. London, Gollancz, 1960.
A Rush on the Ultimate. London, Gollancz, 1961.
The Dog It Was That Died. London, Gollancz, 1962.
Death of a Fat God. London, Collins, 1963; New York, Dutton, 1966.
The Perfect Murder (Ghote). London, Collins, 1964; New York, Dutton, 1965.
Is Skin-Deep, Is Fatal. London, Collins, and New York, Dutton, 1965.
Inspector Ghote's Good Crusade. London, Collins, and New York, Dutton, 1966.
Inspector Ghote Caught in Meshes. London, Collins, 1967; New York, Dutton, 1968.
Inspector Ghote Hunts the Peacock. London, Collins, and New York, Dutton, 1968.
Inspector Ghote Plays a Joker. London, Collins, and New York, Dutton, 1969.
Inspector Ghote Breaks an Egg. London, Collins, 1970; New York, Doubleday, 1971.
Inspector Ghote Goes by Train. London, Collins, 1971; New York, Doubleday, 1972.
Inspector Ghote Trusts the Heart. London, Collins, 1972; New York, Doubleday, 1973.
Bats Fly Up for Inspector Ghote. London, Collins, and New York, Doubleday, 1974.
A Remarkable Case of Burglary. London, Collins, 1975; New York, Doubleday, 1976.
Filmi, Filmi, Inspector Ghote. London, Collins, 1976; New York, Doubleday, 1977.
Inspector Ghote Draws a Line. London, Collins, and New York, Doubleday, 1979.

Uncollected Short Stories

"The Justice Boy," in *Ellery Queen's Mystery Parade*.   New York, New American Library, 1968.
"Inspector Ghote and the Test Match," in *Ellery Queen's Mystery Magazine* (New York), October 1969.
"An Upright Woman," in *Winter's Crimes 2*, edited by George Hardinge.   London, Macmillan, 1970.
"The Old Shell Collector," in *Ellery Queen's Headliners*.   Cleveland, World, 1971; London, Gollancz, 1972.
"The Old Haddock," in *Ellery Queen's Mystery Magazine* (New York), June 1971.
"Inspector Ghote and the Miracle," in *Ellery Queen's Mystery Magazine* (New York), January 1972.
"A Little Rain in a Few Places," in *Ellery Queen's Mystery Magazine* (New York), September 1972.
"Memorial to Speke," in *Ellery Queen's Mystery Magazine* (New York), November 1972.
"Inspector Ghote and the Hooked Fisherman," in *Ellery Queen's Mystery Magazine* (New York), January 1973.
"The Butler Did It," in *Ellery Queen's Mystery Magazine* (New York), May 1973.
"Torture Chamber," in *Ellery Queen's Mystery Magazine* (New York), September 1974.
"The Five Senses of Mrs. Craggs," in *Ellery Queen's Murdercade*.   New York, Random House, 1975.
"Inspector Ghote and the Noted British Author," in *Winter's Crimes 7*, edited by George Hardinge.   London, Macmillan, 1975.
"Liar, Liar, Pants on Fire," in *Ellery Queen's Mystery Magazine* (New York), April 1976.
"Mrs. Craggs and the Lords Spiritual and Temporal," in *John Creasey's Crime Collection*, edited by Herbert Harris.   London, Gollancz, 1978.
"Mrs. Cragg's Sixth Sense," in *Ellery Queen's Mystery Magazine* (New York), September 1978.
"The Adventure of the Suffering Ruler," in *Blackwood's* (Edinburgh), May 1979.
"Gup," in *Verdict of Thirteen*, edited by Julian Symons.   London, Faber, and New York, Harper, 1979.

OTHER PUBLICATIONS

Novels

The Strong Man.   London, Heinemann, 1971.
The Underside.   London, Macmillan, 1974.
A Long Walk to Wimbledon.   London, Macmillan, 1978.

Plays

Radio Plays: *The Dog It Was That Died*, from his own novel, 1971; *The Affair at No. 35*, 1972; *Inspector Ghote and the All-Bad Man*, 1972; *Inspector Ghote Makes a Journey*, 1973; *Inspector Ghote and the River Man*, 1974.

Other

Understanding Pierre Teilhard de Chardin: A Guide to "The Phenomenon of Man," with Maurice Keating.   London, Lutterworth Press, 1969.
Murder Must Appetize (on detective stories of the 1930's).   London, Lemon Tree Press, 1975.

"I.N.I.T.I.A.L.S.," in *Murder Ink: The Mystery Reader's Companion*, edited by Dilys Winn.   New York, Workman, 1977.

"New Patents Pending," in *Crime Writers*, edited by H. R. F. Keating.   London, BBC Publications, 1978.

Sherlock Holmes: The Man and His World.   London, Thames and Hudson, and New York, Scribner, 1979.

Editor, *Blood on My Mind.*   London, Macmillan, 1972.

Editor, *Agatha Christie: First Lady of Crime.*   London, Weidenfeld and Nicolson, and New York, Holt Rinehart, 1977.

Editor, *Crime Writers: Reflections on Crime Fiction.*   London, BBC Publications, 1978.

H. R. F. Keating comments:

Most of my crime novels are set in India and feature Inspector Ghote (pronounced Go-tay) of the Bombay CID, though Ghote has had one trip to London and I hope that one day he will visit the States. While the books do provide a reasonably accurate picture of today's India – a picture conditioned, I admit, by the fact that for the first ten years I wrote about Ghote I had not actually visited his country – I like to think they chiefly put a recognizable human being into broad general situations likely to happen to any one of us. Ghote has had to decide how far he should try to be perfect, just where his loyalties should lie, etc. And while this is my main driving-force in writing the books, I like to think too that they conform well to the canons of crime-writing, with a good mystery to solve where they promise one or with a high ration of suspense where this is what's on the menu.

*   *   *

Following a full-time career as a journalist, H. R. F. Keating became a full-fledged mystery novelist, with the Inspector Ghote detective series as his mainstay. His first novel of that series, *The Perfect Murder*, won awards from the Crime Writers Association and the Mystery Writers of America, introduced a new and distinctive international detective, and established, with the subsequent installments, Keating's reputation as a detective novelist with a difference.

Bombay Crime Branch Inspector Ganesh Ghote and the books in which he appears give a new twist to the detective novel and also to the English novel set in India. Keating has a lively interest in the diverse layers of Indian culture – caste, class, racial, religious, and regional – and his vivid panoply of the sights, sounds, tastes, and smells of India creates good local color as well as good mystery, suspenseful and action-packed. Ghote has been called "one of the few classical creations" among detective-heroes, and his adventures are cited as an acute and sympathetic picture of India, Indians, and foreigners-in-India. Keating has been commended for his special flair for conveying speech levels and styles, native terms and usages, and the cadences and syntax of Indian English, which give the Ghote books a tongue-in-cheek yet at the same time admiring view of the Indian character and voice.

With its unusual foreign setting and its uncommon detective, Keating's work is a striking example of literature (not, of course, confined to mysteries) in the tradition of E. M. Forster and Graham Greene. Works of this type are rooted in the cultural drama which has been so dominant in the current century: the meeting of subcultures within a larger national culture, as well as in the international confluence of a great diversity of national groups, races, religions, languages, and histories.

In *Inspector Ghote Goes by Train* the rich landscape of the subcontinent flashes past as the Inspector travels from Bombay on the "Calcutta Mail" to retrieve a prisoner waiting in Calcutta and finds himself in the company of a guru, two American hippies, a Bengali, and a Madrasi: this episode belongs to that subgenre of crime stories set within the special world of the passenger train. In *Inspector Ghote Hunts the Peacock* Ghote journeys to London to deliver a paper at an international conference on drug smuggling and becomes entangled in a missing persons quest; here his cross-cultural preconceptions – many of them illusions – are sorely tested as he is confronted with a modern London which refuses to conform to his nostalgic and literary notions of English life. *Inspector Ghote Trusts the Heart*, set in Bombay, explores the conflict of Ghote's own humanitarianism with the overwhelming realities of class, money, caste, and public opinion when he investigates the kidnapping of a poor man's son mistaken for that of a wealthy industrialist. In *Inspector Ghote Caught in Meshes* the killing of an American physicist on tour in India, presumably by highway robbers, reveals a more serious crime involving espionage and the Indian national image. The more recent *Filmi, Filmi, Inspector Ghote* concerns intrigue and murder in the "Bollywood" film world and on the set of the Indian version of *Macbeth*.

Throughout these adventures, the persona of Inspector Ghote is a very human web of contradiction and counterpoint: shrewd and knowing, yet self-effacing and bumbling; pompous and prim, yet sensitive and self-deprecating; determined and tenacious, yet full of self-doubts and anxious yearnings; lonely yet uxorious; maladroit yet charming; a mignon of the law, but often sentimental and at all times humane. Critics such as Anthony Boucher and Newgate Callendar have called Keating's creation "a genuine addition to the ranks of fictional detectives" and "one of the great characters of the contemporary mystery novel."

—Margaret J. King

KEELER, Harry Stephen. American. Born in Chicago, Illinois, 3 November 1890. Educated at Armour Institute (now Illinois Institute of Technology), degree in electrical engineering 1912. Married 1) Hazel Goodwin in 1919 (died, 1960); 2) Thelma Rinoldo in 1963. Electrician in steel mill; Editor, *10-Story Book* magazine, 1919–40. *Died 22 January 1967.*

CRIME PUBLICATIONS

Novels (series characters: Angus MacWhorter; Tuddleton Trotter)

> *The Voice of the Seven Sparrows.* London, Hutchinson, 1924; New York, Dutton, 1928.
> *Find the Clock.* London, Hutchinson, 1925; New York, Dutton, 1927.
> *The Spectacles of Mr. Cagliostro.* London, Hutchinson, 1926; New York, Dutton, 1929; as *The Blue Spectacles*, London, Ward Lock, 1931.
> *Sing Sing Nights.* London, Hutchinson, 1927; New York, Dutton, 1928.
> *The Amazing Web.* London, Ward Lock, 1929; New York, Dutton, 1930.
> *The Fourth King.* London, Ward Lock, 1929; New York, Dutton, 1930.
> *Thieves' Nights.* New York, Dutton, 1929; London, Ward Lock, 1930.
> *The Green Jade Hand.* New York, Dutton, and London, Ward Lock, 1930.
> *The Riddle of the Yellow Zuri.* New York, Dutton, 1930; as *The Tiger Snake*, London, Ward Lock, 1931.
> *The Matilda Hunter Murder* (Trotter). New York, Dutton, 1931; as *The Black Satchel*, London, Ward Lock, 1931.
> *The Box from Japan.* New York, Dutton, 1932; London, Ward Lock, 1933.
> *Behind That Mask.* London, Ward Lock, 1933; expanded edition, New York, Dutton, 1938.

The Face of the Man from Saturn. New York, Dutton, 1933; as *The Crilly Court Mystery*, London, Ward Lock, 1933.

The Washington Square Enigma. New York, Dutton, 1933; as *Under Twelve Stars*, London, Ward Lock, 1933.

The Mystery of the Fiddling Cracksman. New York, Dutton, and London, Ward Lock, 1934.

The Riddle of the Traveling Skull. New York, Dutton, and London, Ward Lock, 1934.

Ten Hours. London, Ward Lock, 1934; expanded edition, New York, Dutton, 1937.

The Five Silver Buddhas. New York, Dutton, and London, Ward Lock, 1935.

The Skull of the Waltzing Clown. New York, Dutton, 1935.

The Marceau Case. New York, Dutton, and London, Ward Lock, 1936.

X. Jones of Scotland Yard. New York, Dutton, 1936; as *X. Jones*, London, Ward Lock, 1936.

The Defrauded Yeggman. New York, Dutton, 1937.

The Mysterious Mr. I. London, Ward Lock, 1937; expanded edition, New York, Dutton, 1938.

The Wonderful Scheme of Mr. Christopher Thorne. New York, Dutton, 1937; as *The Wonderful Scheme*, London, Ward Lock, 1937.

Finger! Finger! New York, Dutton, 1938.

When Thief Meets Thief. London, Ward Lock, 1938.

Cheung, Detective. London, Ward Lock, 1938; as *Y. Cheung, Business Detective*, New York, Dutton, 1939.

The Chameleon. New York, Dutton, 1939.

The Man with the Magic Eardrums. New York, Dutton, 1939; as *The Magic Eardrums*, London, Ward Lock, 1939.

Find Actor Hart. London, Ward Lock, 1939; as *The Portrait of Jirjohn Cobb*, New York, Dutton, 1940.

Cleopatra's Tears. New York, Dutton, and London, Ward Lock, 1940.

The Man with the Crimson Box. New York, Dutton, 1940; as *The Crimson Box*, London, Ward Lock, 1940.

The Man with the Wooden Spectacles. New York, Dutton, 1941; as *The Wooden Spectacles*, London, Ward Lock, 1941.

The Peacock Fan. New York, Dutton, 1941; London, Ward Lock, 1942.

The Sharkskin Book. New York, Dutton, 1941; as *By Third Degree*, London, Ward Lock, 1948.

The Vanishing Gold Truck (MacWhorter). New York, Dutton, 1941; London, Ward Lock, 1942.

The Lavender Gripsack. London. Ward Lock, 1941; New York, Phoenix Press, 1944.

The Book with the Orange Leaves. New York, Dutton, 1942; London, Ward Lock, 1943.

The Bottle with the Green Wax Seal. New York, Dutton, 1942.

The Case of the Two Strange Ladies. New York, Phoenix Press, 1943; London, Ward Lock, 1945.

The Search for X-Y-Z. London, Ward Lock, 1943; as *The Case of the Ivory Arrow*, New York, Phoenix Press, 1945.

The Case of the 16 Beans. New York, Phoenix Press, 1944; London, Ward Lock, 1945.

The Iron Ring. London, Ward Lock, 1944; as *The Case of the Mysterious Moll*, New York, Phoenix Press, 1945.

The Case of the Canny Killer. New York, Phoenix Press, 1946; as *Murder in the Mills*, London, Ward Lock, 1946.

The Monocled Monster. London, Ward Lock, 1947.

The Case of the Barking Clock (Trotter), with Hazel Goodwin. New York, Phoenix Press, 1947; London, Ward Lock, 1951.

The Case of the Jeweled Ragpicker (MacWhorter). New York, Phoenix Press, 1948; as *The Ace of Spades Murder*, London, Ward Lock, 1948.

The Case of the Transposed Legs, with Hazel Goodwin. New York, Phoenix Press, 1948; London, Ward Lock, 1951.
The Murdered Mathematician. London, Ward Lock, 1949.
The Strange Will, with Hazel Goodwin. London, Ward Lock, 1949.
The Steeltown Strangler. London, Ward Lock, 1950.
The Murder of London Lew. London, Ward Lock, 1952.
Stand By – London Calling (MacWhorter), with Hazel Goodwin. London, Ward Lock, 1953.

Uncollected Short Stories

"John Jones' Dollar," in *Strange Ports of Call*, edited by August Derleth. New York, Pelligrini and Cudahy, 1948.
"The Hand of God," in *20 Great Tales of Murder*, edited by Helen McCloy and Brett Halliday. New York, Random House, 1951; London, Hammond, 1952.
"Victim No. 5," in *Maiden Murders*, edited by John Dickson Carr. New York, Harper, 1952.

Bibliography: in *The Bibliography of Crime Fiction, 1749–1975* by Allen J. Hubin, San Diego, University of California Extension, 1979.

*   *   *

Harry Stephen Keeler's more than 70 novels form a self-contained universe of monstrously complicated intrigues, blending elements of farce, Grand Guignol, and radical social criticism while also serving as a labyrinth in which he hid himself. He was the inventor of the "webwork novel," in which literally hundreds of bizarre events explode like cigars in the white-knight hero's face but ultimately prove to be mathematically interrelated, with every absurd incident making blissfully perfect sense within Keeler's zany frame of reference. His favorite devices for tying story elements together were the loony law, the nutty religious tenet, the wacky will, the crackpot contract, and – commonest of all – the interlocking network of backbreaking coincidence. He loved to have his characters converse in outrageous ethnic dialects and to toss them into quasi-science-fictional situations. He loved to attack the social evils he saw: racism, police brutality, the military, corrupt politicians, capital punishment, the maltreatment of the mentally ill, all the dark underside of an America where "Money was Emperor, and Might was Right." And most of all he loved cats, even dedicating some novels to favorite felines.

Keeler grew up among thespians of Victorian melodrama in his widowed mother's theatrical boardinghouse. Between 1914 and 1924 he published dozens of magazine serials and novelettes, then switched to novels, many expanded from earlier magazine tales. His first books, like *The Spectacles of Mr. Cagliostro* and *Thieves' Nights*, are usually set in his beloved Chicago, constructed on the Arabian Nights model and packed with grotesque characters and events, coincidence, bitter social comment, and Victorian dialogue. In the early 1930's he wrote some of the longest mystery novels of all time, like *The Box from Japan* with its 765 closely printed pages, and some of the shortest and swiftest, like *The Washington Square Enigma*. By the mid-1930's his books had become longer, wilder, wackier, and less constrained by conventional discipline than ever, including several multi-volume meganovels like *The Mysterious Mr. I* and its sequel *The Chameleon*. During the 1940's and 1950's he alternated between single titles, of standard length and brain-boggling contents, and several series of novels dealing respectively with the adventures of a book, a circus, a house, an industrial plant, and a skull. But the wilder Keeler's flights of fancy became, the fewer readers flew with him. After 1953 his books appeared only in Spanish or Portuguese translations, if at all. Nevertheless he continued to turn out novels as well as a weekly mimeographed newsletter full of theosophical and literary and cat lore. He died in 1967, leaving a dozen books unfinished, confident that one day he would be read again.

Certainly he should be. For close to half a century he spun an alternate universe totally and uniquely his own from its metaphysical underpinnings to the speech and costumes of its inhabitants. Committed humanist-radical and exuberant clown, he was the true original of Kesey's R. P. MacMurphy and Vonnegut's Kilgore Trout, the sublime nutty genius of the mystery genre, who deserves to be remembered as long as boundless creativity is cherished.

—Francis M. Nevins, Jr.

KEENE, Day.   American.   Married.   Wrote radio soap operas in 1930's and 1940's. Lived in Chicago, Florida, and California. *Died c. 1969.*

CRIME PUBLICATIONS

Novels

> *This Is Murder, Mr. Herbert, and Other Stories* (novelets).   New York, Avon, 1948.
> *Framed in Guilt.*   New York, Mill, 1949; as *Evidence Most Blind*, London, Hennel Locke, 1950.
> *Farewell to Passion.*   New York, Hanro, 1951; as *The Passion Murders*, New York, Avon, 1955.
> *My Flesh Is Sweet.*   New York, Lion, 1951.
> *Love Me and Die.*   New York, Phantom, 1951.
> *To Kiss or Kill.*   New York, Fawcett, 1951; London, Fawcett, 1953.
> *Hunt the Killer.*   New York, Phantom, 1952.
> *About Doctor Ferrel.*   New York, Fawcett, 1952; London, Fawcett, 1958.
> *Home Is the Sailor.*   New York, Fawcett, 1952.
> *If the Coffin Fits.*   Hasbrouck Heights, New Jersey, Graphic, 1952.
> *Naked Fury.*   New York, Phantom, 1952.
> *Wake Up to Murder.*   New York, Phantom, 1952.
> *Mrs. Homicide.*   New York, Ace, 1953.
> *Strange Witness.*   Hasbrouck Heights, New Jersey, Graphic, 1953.
> *The Big Kiss-Off.*   Hasbrouck Heights, New Jersey, Graphic, 1954.
> *Death House Doll.*   New York, Ace, 1954.
> *Homicidal Lady.*   Hasbrouck Heights, New Jersey, Graphic, 1954.
> *Joy House.*   New York, Lion, 1954; London, Consul, 1964.
> *Notorious.*   New York, Fawcett, 1954; London, Fawcett, 1956.
> *Sleep with the Devil.*   New York, Lion, 1954.
> *There Was a Crooked Man.*   New York, Fawcett, 1954; London, Fawcett, 1955.
> *Who Has Wilma Lathrop?*   New York, Fawcett, 1955; London, Jenkins, 1966.
> *The Dangling Carrot.*   New York, Ace, 1955.
> *Murder on the Side.*   New York and London, Fawcett, 1956.
> *Bring Him Back Dead.*   New York, Fawcett, 1956.
> *Flight by Night.*   New York, Ace, 1956; London, Red Seal, 1960.
> *It's a Sin to Kill.*   New York, Avon, 1958.
> *Passage to Samoa.*   New York, Fawcett, 1958; London, Fawcett, 1960.
> *Dead Dolls Don't Talk.*   New York, Fawcett, 1959; London, Muller, 1963.
> *Dead in Bed.*   New York, Pyramid, 1959.
> *Moran's Woman.*   Rockville Centre, New York, Zenith, 1959.

So Dead My Lovely. New York, Pyramid, 1959.
Take a Step to Murder. New York, Fawcett, 1959; London, Muller, 1960.
Too Black for Heaven. Rockville Centre, New York, Zenith, 1959.
Too Hot to Hold. New York, Fawcett, 1959; London, Muller, 1960.
The Brimstone Bed. New York, Avon, 1960.
Payola. New York, Pyramid, 1960.
Seed of Doubt. New York, Simon and Schuster, 1961; London, W. H. Allen, 1962.
Bye, Baby Bunting. New York, Holt Rinehart, and London, W. H. Allen, 1963.
Carnival of Death. New York, Macfadden, 1965.

Uncollected Short Stories

"The Stars Say Die," in *Detective Tales* (New York), November 1941.
"The Corpse That Ran Away," in *Dime Mystery* (New York), March 1942.
"Murder Is My Sponsor," in *Detective Tales* (New York), April 1942.
"A Slight Mistake in Corpses," in *Detective Tales* (New York), May 1942.
" 'Til the Day You Die," in *Ten Detective Aces* (New York), June 1942.
"The Mystery of Tarpon Key," in *Detective Tales* (New York), August 1942.
"Blaze of Glory," in *Detective Tales* (New York), November 1942.
"Hearse of Another Color," in *Dime Mystery* (New York), November 1942.
"He Who Dies Last, Dies Hardest," in *Detective Tales* (New York), May 1943.
"The Female Is More Deadly," in *Dime Detective* (New York), December 1943.
"Corpses Come in Pairs," in *Detective Tales* (New York), April 1944.
"Brother, Can You Spare a Grave?" in *Dime Mystery* (New York), July 1944.
"Make Mine Murder," in *New Detective* (New York), September 1944.
"Murder on My Mind," in *Detective Tales* (New York), July 1945.
"A Corpse Walks in Brooklyn," in *Detective Tales* (New York), October 1945.
"As Deep as the Grave," in *Detective Tales* (New York), January 1946.
"Claws of the Hell-Cat," in *Dime Mystery* (New York), January 1946.
"Doc Egg's Graveyard Reunion," in *Dime Mystery* (New York), February 1946.
"Little Miss Murder," in *Detective Tales* (New York), November 1946.
"The Case of the Sobbing Girl," in *Best Detective Stories of the Year 1946*, edited by
    David Coxe Cooke. New York, Dutton, 1946.
"So Dead the Rogue," in *New Detective* (New York), January 1947.
"Married to Murder," in *Dime Mystery* (New York), January 1947.
"No Grave Could Hold Him," in *Dime Mystery* (New York), February 1948.
"Marry the Sixth for Murder," in *Detective Tales* (New York), May 1948.
"Some Die Easy," in *New Detective* (New York), May 1948.
"Knock Twice for Murder," in *Detective Tales* (New York), June 1949.
"Wait for the Dead Man's Tide," in *Dime Mystery* (New York), August 1949.
"Murder – Do Not Disturb," in *New Detective* (New York), March 1950.
"Old Homicide Week," in *Detective Tales* (New York), April 1950.
"The Bloody Tide," in *Dime Detective* (New York), June 1950.
"Remember the Night," in *Best Detective Stories of the Year 1950*, edited by David Coxe
    Cooke. New York, Dutton, 1950.
"Murder Stop," in *Famous Detective* (Dunellen, New Jersey), November 1950.
"Blonde and Bad," in *Smashing Detective* (New York), March 1951.
"The Passing of Johnny Maguire," in *15 Story Detective* (New York), May 1951.
"Mighty Like a Rogue," in *As Tough As They Come*, edited by Will Oursler. New
    York, Doubleday, 1951.
"How Deep My Grave?" in *Famous Detective* (Dunellen, New Jersey), November 1952.
"A Great Whirring of Wings," in *Maiden Murders*, edited by John Dickson Carr. New
    York, Harper, 1952.
"Homicide House," in *Crook's Tour*, edited by Bruno Fischer. New York, Dodd
    Mead, 1953.

"A Better Mantrap," in *Dangerous Dames*, edited by Brett Halliday. New York, Dell, 1955.

OTHER PUBLICATIONS

Novels

His Father's Wife. New York, Pyramid, 1954.
Miami 59. New York, Dell, 1959; London, Mayflower, 1966.
Chautauqua, with Dwight Vincent. New York, Putnam, 1960; London, W. H. Allen, 1963.
World Without Women, with Leonard Pruyn. New York, Fawcett, 1960.
Chicago 11. New York, Dell, 1966.
Southern Daughter. New York, Macfadden, 1967.
Live Again, Love Again. New York, New American Library, 1970.
Wild Girl. New York, Macfadden, 1970.

*   *   *

During his long career, Day Keene was one of the most popular, readable, and prolific of the writers who specialized first in pulp fiction and then in the paperback original. In the 1940's his name appeared with amazing regularity on the covers and contents pages of such top crime pulps as *Black Mask*, *Dime Detective*, and *Detective Tales*. When the pulp market collapsed in the early 1950's, Keene found a ready home for his work in the burgeoning paperback field. He wrote dozens of original novels for Fawcett Gold Medal, Graphic, Ace, and others; noteworthy are *Home Is the Sailor* and *Murder on the Side*. Probably his best crime novel, however, is his first – a hardcover entitled *Framed in Guilt*; it is a nicely plotted story of blackmail, treachery, and murder involving a Hollywood screenwriter. Keene abandoned the paperback novel in the late 1950's to do more ambitious (but less crime-oriented) fiction. Keene's primary virtue as a writer was a strong sense of pace and narrative drive: he knew how to tell a story that gripped the reader immediately and held him to the end. If the quality of some of his early work suffers from the speed with which it was written, it is nonetheless entertaining and thoroughly professional.

—Bill Pronzini

KELLAND, Clarence Budington. American. Born in Portland, Michigan, 11 July 1881. Educated in public and private schools in Detroit; Detroit College of Law, LL.B. 1902. Married Betty Caroline Smith in 1907. Editor, *The Law Student's Helper* magazine, 1893; Reporter and Police Editor, Detroit *News*, 1903–07; Editor, *American Boy*, 1907–15; Lecturer on juvenile literature, University of Michigan, Ann Arbor, 1913–15; Director of Overseas Publicity, YMCA, 1918; Executive and Publicity Director, Republican National Committee from 1942; regular contributor to the *Saturday Evening Post*. Died 18 February 1964.

CRIME PUBLICATIONS

Novels

Conflict.   New York, Harper, 1922; London, Hodder and Stoughton, 1928.
Contraband.   New York, Harper, 1923; London, Hodder and Stoughton, 1928.
The Cat's Paw.   New York, Harper, 1934.
Double Treasure.   New York, Harper, 1946; London, Macdonald, 1949.
Murder for a Million.   Kingswood, Surrey, World's Work, 1947.
Stolen Goods.   New York, Harper, 1950; London, Museum Press, 1951.
The Great Mail Robbery.   New York, Harper, 1951; London, Museum Press, 1954.
No Escape.   London, Museum Press, 1951.
The Key Man.   New York, Harper, 1952; London, Hale, 1954.
Dangerous Angel.   New York, Harper, 1953; London, Hale, 1955.
Murder Makes an Entrance.   New York, Harper, 1955; London, Hale, 1956.
The Sinister Strangers.   Roslyn, New York, Detective Book Club, 1955.
The Case of the Nameless Corpse.   New York, Harper, 1956; London, Hale, 1958.
Death Keeps a Secret.   New York, Harper, 1956; London, Hale, 1957.
The Lady and the Giant.   New York, Dodd Mead, 1959; London, Hale, 1960.
Where There's Smoke.   New York, Harper, 1959; London, Hale, 1960.
Counterfeit Gentleman.   New York, Dodd Mead, 1960; London, Hale, 1961.
The Monitor Affair.   New York, Dodd Mead, 1960; London, Hale, 1961.
Mark of Treachery.   New York, Dodd Mead, 1961.
The Artless Heiress.   New York, Dodd Mead, 1962.
Party Man.   New York, Dodd Mead, 1962.

Uncollected Short Story

"An Ounce of Curiosity," in *The Best American Mystery Stories of the Year, Volume Two*, edited by Carolyn Wells.   New York, Day, 1932.

OTHER PUBLICATIONS

Novels

Thirty Pieces of Silver.   New York, Harper, 1913.
The Hidden Spring.   New York, Harper, 1916.
Sudden Jim.   New York, Harper, 1917.
The Source.   New York, Harper, 1918.
The Little Moment of Happiness.   New York, Harper, 1919.
The Highflyers.   New York, Harper, 1919.
Efficiency Edgar.   New York, Harper, 1920.
Youth Challenges.   New York, Harper, 1920.
Scattergood Baines.   New York, Harper, 1921.
The Steadfast Heart.   New York, Harper, 1924; London, Hodder and Stoughton, 1928.
Miracle.   New York, Harper, and London, Hodder and Stoughton, 1925.
Rhoda Fair.   New York, Harper, 1926; London, Hodder and Stoughton, 1928.
Dance Magic.   New York, Harper, 1927.
Jahala.   London, Hodder and Stoughton, 1927.
Knuckles.   New York, Harper, and London, Hodder and Stoughton, 1928.
Dynasty.   New York, Harper, 1929.
Mr. Bundy.   London, Hodder and Stoughton, 1929.
Hard Money.   New York, Harper, 1930; London, Consul, 1956.
Gold.   New York, Harper, 1931.
Speak Easily.   New York, Harper, 1932; London, Barker, 1937.

The Great Crooner. New York, Harper, 1933; London, Barker, 1939.
Tombstone. New York, Harper, 1933; London, Hale, 1955.
The Jealous House. New York, Harper, 1934.
Dreamland. New York, Harper, 1935; London, Barker, 1938.
Roxana. New York, Harper, 1936.
Spotlight. New York, Harper, and London, Barker, 1937.
Mr. Deeds Goes to Town. London, Barker, 1937.
Star Rising. New York, Harper, 1938.
Arizona. New York, Harper, 1939; London, Corgi, 1953.
Skin Deep. New York, Harper, 1939.
Valley of the Sun. New York, Harper, 1940; as *Desert Law*, New York, Bantam, 1949; London, Corgi, 1954.
House of Cards. London, Hodder and Stoughton, 1941.
Silver Spoon. New York, Harper, 1941.
Sugarfoot. New York, Harper, 1942; London, Corgi, 1953.
Archibald the Great. New York, Harper, 1943; Kingswood, Surrey, World's Work, 1950.
Heart on Her Sleeve. New York, Harper, 1943; Kingswood, Surrey, World's Work, 1951.
Alias Jane Smith. New York, Harper, 1944.
Land of the Torreones. New York, Harper, 1946; London, Nimmo, 1947.
Merchant of Valor. New York, Harper, 1947.
This Is My Son. New York, Harper, 1948; London, Museum Press, 1950.
West of the Law. New York, Harper, 1958; London, Hale, 1959.

Short Stories

Scattergood Returns. New York, Harper, 1940.
Scattergood Baines Pulls the Strings. New York, Harper, 1941.

Play

The Comic Jest (produced San Francisco, 1949). San Francisco, Bohemian Club, 1949.

Other

Quizzer No. 20, Being Questions and Answers on Insurance. Detroit, Sprague, 1911.
Mark Tidd: His Adventures and Strategies [in the Backwoods, in Business, Tidd's Citadel, Editor, Manufacturer, in Italy, in Egypt, in Sicily] (juvenile). New York, Harper, 9 vols., 1913–28.
Into His Own: The Story of an Airedale (juvenile). Philadelphia, McKay, 1915.
Catty Atkins [Riverman, Sailorman, Financier, Bandmaster] (juvenile). New York, Harper, 5 vols., 1920–24.

Editor, *The American Boys' Workshop.* Philadelphia, McKay, 1914.

*   *   *

Although Clarence Budington Kelland published more than 20 books classified as detective or mystery fiction from the 1920's to the 1960's, his unorthodox writing style defies classification. Even though the plots contain elements of criminal activity and perhaps a murder or two, there is very little real detection involved in solving the crimes, only a trifling amount of suspense, and an even smaller amount of mystery. However, this does not necessarily mean that Kelland's stories (frequently published in *The Saturday Evening Post*) and novels are not entertaining. They are, in fact, amusing, witty, and quite tolerable when taken in small doses.

Kelland's major fault tends to be an overstudied and too detailed presentation of the technical background material of his novels. However he does manage to use with surprising success severely stereotyped characters with outlandish names such as Miss Columbine Pepper Drugget who appears in *The Artless Heiress*, a very amusing story that lacks the boring technical date. *Death Keeps a Secret* involves a stuffy electrical scientist, Thomas Alva Edison Gimp, who, while working on a missile base, is entrapped by a childhood tormentor, blackmailed into stealing the "electronic brain," kidnapped, and forced to apply the principles of "time lag" to save himself from certain death. Skipping the tedious technical passages, the reader might find this spy spoof lightly entertaining. *The Great Mail Robbery* gives a detailed analysis of the postal system in New York, and *The Key Man* involves a television studio.

—Mary Ann Grochowski

KELLY, Mary (Theresa, née Coolican). British. Born in London, 28 December 1927. Educated at the University of Edinburgh, M.A. 1951. Married Denis Charles Kelly in 1950. Teacher in a private school and in Surrey County Council schools, 1952–54. Recipient: Crime Writers Association prize, 1961. Agent: Curtis Brown Ltd., 1 Craven Hill, London W2 3EP, England.

CRIME PUBLICATIONS

Novels (series characters: Nicholson; Inspector Nightingale)

A Cold Coming (Nightingale). London, Secker and Warburg, 1956; New York, Walker, 1968.
Dead Man's Riddle (Nightingale). London, Secker and Warburg, 1957; New York, Walker, 1967.
The Christmas Egg (Nightingale). London, Secker and Warburg, 1958; New York, Holt Rinehart, 1966.
The Spoilt Kill (Nicholson). London, Joseph, 1961; New York, Walker, 1968.
Due to a Death (Nicholson). London, Joseph, 1962; as The Dead of Summer, New York, Mill, 1963.
March to the Gallows. London, Joseph, 1964; New York, Holt Rinehart, 1965.
Dead Corse. London, Joseph, 1966; New York, Holt Rinehart, 1967.
Write on Both Sides of the Paper. London, Joseph, 1969; Elmsford, New York, London House and Maxwell, 1970.
The Twenty-Fifth Hour. London, Macmillan, 1971; New York, Walker, 1972.
That Girl in the Alley. London, Macmillan, and New York, Walker, 1974.

Uncollected Short Stories

"A Bit Out of Place," in *Winter's Crimes 1*, edited by George Hardinge. London, Macmillan, 1969.

"Life the Shadow of Death," in *Winter's Crimes 8*, edited by Hilary Watson.   London, Macmillan, 1976.

Manuscript Collection: Mugar Memorial Library, Boston University.

*   *   *

One of the best contemporary British crime writers, *but*: such must be the verdict on Mary Kelly. The "but" has two aspects, perhaps linked. She is too apt, as are some other fine writers, to skimp on the basic plot. And, more serious, she brings herself to write less and less frequently. That being said, however, there is enormous pleasure to be got from her books.

The essential quality of her art is perhaps obscured by the manner in which she began. It plainly occurred to her when she first thought of writing a crime story that the important element of "background" in the late classical whodunit (the advertising agency or the bellringing lore of Dorothy L. Sayers) could be given a more up-to-date treatment. So she found various industrial settings, papermaking, steel making, pottery manufacture, that were at least as interesting as the fields conventionally adopted by detective-story writers and which for the alert reader had extra interest as descriptions of neglected aspects of modern society.

It was a device which had its own success, but eventually Mary Kelly understandably tired of it, and in subsequent books the true nature of what she was able to do was revealed. This is the giving of pure pleasure, the taking of readers out of themselves and deeply into another world. To achieve it she patently experiences the process herself. Her writing is moment by moment intense, and is successful as such. Whatever she has to describe, whether scene or action (or sexual relations, in the description of which – a difficult task – she is particularly good), she does so in a way that puts the reader there. Unusually for crime novels, therefore, what propels the reader through the pages is not the tug of "who done it" nor the excitements of men with guns coming in through doors, but the sheer excellence of the writing.

Take a book like *The Twenty-Fifth Hour*. It tells of an Englishwoman holidaying in Normandy with a small barely illegal task to perform on the side. A story so mild as hardly to exist. The woman does later become involved in a plot concerned with an extreme Rightist organisation, but again this is pretty conventional and even tame. Yet one reads almost as eagerly as if the story had been put together by Alistair MacLean and the plot devised by Ira Levin because from her very first sentence Mary Kelly observes so meticulously, describes so exactly and economically. Hers is a never-blinking eye.

This exactness brings with it, of course, another valuable constituent for any work of fiction: a respect for human beings as they are, as individuals not figures from a mould. It is something that Mary Kelly herself, in the person of one of her characters, has called "human incorrigibility." And it marks out the best books from the merely good. A crime book can reach the status of "good" on sheer plot, on sheer storytelling, on sheer ingenuity, on sheer suspense. But to go higher real human beings are needed in its pages. They are there in plenty in Mary Kelly's work.

But. And the "but" must be re-emphasised, alas. But a novel that is all acute description, and especially a crime novel that is largely such, must be accounted to some extent a failure. A dimension of the novel is story, and a dimension of the crime novel is plot. Mary Kelly's books, even at their most perverse (*That Girl in the Alley*), do not totally lack either of these two dimensions, but they do get dangerously thin.

—H. R. F. Keating

KEMELMAN, Harry. American. Born in Boston, Massachusetts, 24 November 1908. Educated at Boston Latin School, 1920–26; Boston University, A.B. 1930; Harvard University, Cambridge, Massachusetts, M.A. 1931, further study 1932–33. Teacher in Boston high schools, 1935–41, and Monter Hall School, Cambridge, 1936–40; Northeastern University Evening Division, 1938–41; Chief Wage Administrator, United States Army Transportation Corps, Boston, 1942–46; Chief Job Analyst and Wage Administrator, War Assets Administration, New England Division, 1948–49; free-lance writer and private businessman, 1949–63; Assistant Professor of English, Franklin Technical Institute, Boston, 1963. Recipient: Mystery Writers of America Edgar Allan Poe Award, 1964. Agent: Scott Meredith Literary Agency Inc., 580 Fifth Avenue, New York, New York 10036, U.S.A.

CRIME PUBLICATIONS

Novels (series character: Rabbi David Small in all books)

> *Friday the Rabbi Slept Late.* New York, Crown, 1964; London, Hutchinson, 1965.
> *Saturday the Rabbi Went Hungry.* New York, Crown, 1966; London, Hutchinson, 1967.
> *Sunday the Rabbi Stayed Home.* New York, Putnam, and London, Hutchinson, 1969.
> *Monday the Rabbi Took Off.* New York, Putnam, and London, Hutchinson, 1972.
> *Tuesday the Rabbi Saw Red.* New York, Fields, and London, Hutchinson, 1974.
> *Wednesday the Rabbi Got Wet.* New York, Morrow, and London, Hutchinson, 1976.
> *Thursday the Rabbi Walked Out.* New York, Morrow, 1978; London, Hutchinson, 1979.

Short Stories

> *The Nine Mile Walk.* New York, Putnam, 1967; London, Hutchinson, 1968.

Uncollected Short Stories

> "The Man with Two Watches," in *Anthology 1968*, edited by Ellery Queen. New York, Davis, 1967.
> "A Winter's Tale," in *Anthology 1971*, edited by Ellery Queen. New York, Davis, 1970.

*   *   *

Harry Kemelman's "rabbi books" series has drawn critical praise and a wide following as a staple of the mystery-detective trade since 1964, with the appearance of the Edgar-winning *Friday the Rabbi Slept Late.* In the course of these self-contained but sequential narratives named after the days of the week, Kemelman's Rabbi David Small is involved in various intrigues in his role as head of a small Jewish community in Barnard's Crossing, Massachusetts.

In *Friday the Rabbi Slept Late*, he solves the murder of a young girl whose body is found in the temple parking lot; in *Saturday the Rabbi Went Hungry* he shows that Jewish scientist Abe Hirsch's apparent suicide was really a murder. *Sunday the Rabbi Stayed Home* finds him absorbed in youth culture problems; *Monday the Rabbi Took Off* has him on sabbatical in Israel involved in an incident touched by Arab terrorism. *Tuesday the Rabbi Saw Red* takes place at a small liberal-arts college where the rabbi teaches a course in Jewish philosophy, and solves a colleague's murder; *Wednesday the Rabbi Got Wet* concerns a pharmacy, mixed-up prescriptions, and the murder of a pillar of the temple. *Thursday the Rabbi Walked Out* poses the case of the town's old-style eccentric millionaire, a self-proclaimed anti-Semite, found murdered with too many suspects to sift.

Kemelman is in a class by himself in blending two unassociated literary forms: the sociological treatise and the mystery-thriller. In doing so, he attains a sparkling and provocative compound of fact and fabrication. He has also succeeded in bringing together two topics of lively current interest: the life of ethnic groups, in their traditions, language, and religion, and their assimilation into American life, together with the texture of small-town life. Kemelman's initial purpose was "to explain – via a fictional setting – the Jewish religion." Critic Anthony Boucher declares the novels to be "a primer to instruct the gentiles."

As a vital agent in his elaboration on the formulas of the detective tale, Kemelman has introduced a most unlikely hero – a rabbi-detective, unassuming, soft-spoken, complete with spectacles and rabbinical stoop. Rabbi Small, quick to become the most famous rabbi in all fiction, established himself as the unofficial Jewish arbiter with a notably minority and alienated point of view on American life for expounding on ethics, social relations, and the cultural scene in general. While the rabbi's links to G. K. Chesterton's priest-detective Father Brown are obvious, Rabbi Small's direct origins lie in a previous Kemelman creation, Professor Nicky Welt, Snowdown Professor of English Language and Literature, first featured in a sequence of short stories commissioned by *Ellery Queen's Mystery Magazine*. These stories fit the classic proportions of the armchair-intellectual mystery story in the style of the 1920's at its purest – no tricks, pure logic, all intelligence, induction, deduction, and adduction. Many of Welt's cases, like those of Mycroft, Holmes and Nero Wolfe, are quite literally solved over the conventional three pipes from the depths of an overstuffed armchair. The more characteristically American hard-boiled detective, in contrast, has an energetic role as a member of the crime's cast of characters. While this last position is also that of Small, his involvement in the solution is always primarily an intellectual and introspective affair. In this way, Kemelman weaves together two separate strands of style.

—Margaret J. King

KENDRICK, Baynard H(ardwick).   Also wrote as Richard Hayward.   American.   Born in Philadelphia, Pennsylvania, 8 April 1894. Educated at Tome School, Port Deposit, Maryland; Episcopal Academy, Philadelphia, graduated 1912. Served with the Canadian Infantry in England, France, and Salonica, 1914–18: Sergeant; instructor for blind veterans in World War II. Married 1) Edythe Stevens in 1919 (died), two daughters and one son; 2) Jean Morris in 1971. Secretary, Selden Cypress Door Company, Patalka, Florida, 1919–27; President, Trades Publishing Company, Philadelphia, 1928; General Manager, Peter Clark Inc., New York, 1929, and Bing and Bing's Hotels, New York, 1930–32. Free-lance writer after 1932. Member, Editorial Board, *Florida Historical Quarterly* and Director, Florida Historical Society; Columnist, "Florida's Fabulous Past," Tampa *Sunday Tribune*, 1961–64. First President, Mystery Writers of America, 1945. Recipient: Screen Writers Guild Robert Meltzer Award, 1951; Mystery Writers of America Grand Master Award, 1967. *Died 22 March 1977.*

CRIME PUBLICATIONS

Novels (series characters: Captain Duncan Maclain; Miles Standish Rice)

  Blood on Lake Louisa.   New York, Greenberg, 1934; London, Methuen, 1937.
  The Iron Spiders (Rice).   New York, Greenberg, 1936; London, Methuen, 1938.

The Eleven of Diamonds (Rice). New York, Greenberg, 1936; London, Methuen, 1937.

The Last Express (Maclain). New York, Doubleday, 1937; London, Methuen, 1938.

The Whistling Hangman (Maclain). New York, Doubleday, 1937; London, Hale, 1959.

Death Beyond the Go-Thru (Rice). New York, Doubleday, 1938.

The Odor of Violets (Maclain). Boston, Little Brown, and London, Methuen, 1941; as *Eyes in the Night*, New York, Grosset and Dunlap, 1942.

Blind Man's Bluff (Maclain). Boston, Little Brown, 1943; London, Methuen, 1944.

Out of Control (Maclain). New York, Morrow, 1945; London, Methuen, 1947.

Death Knell (Maclain). New York, Morrow, 1945; London, Methuen, 1946.

Make Mine Maclain (omnibus). New York, Morrow, 1947.

The Tunnel. New York, Scribner, 1949.

The Murderer Who Wanted More (Maclain). New York, Dell, 1951.

You Die Today (Maclain). New York, Morrow, 1952; London, Hale, 1958.

Trapped (as Richard Hayward). New York, Fawcett, 1952.

Blind Allies (Maclain). New York, Morrow, 1954.

The Soft Arms of Death (as Richard Hayward). New York and London, Fawcett, 1955.

Reservations for Death (Maclain). New York, Morrow, 1957; London, Hale, 1958.

Clear and Present Danger (Maclain). New York, Doubleday, 1958; London, Hale, 1959.

Hot Red Money. New York, Dodd Mead, 1959; London, Hale, 1962.

The Aluminum Turtle (Maclain). New York, Dodd Mead, 1960; as *The Spear Gun Murders*, London, Hale, 1961.

Frankincense and Murder (Maclain). New York, Dodd Mead, 1961; London, Hale, 1962.

Flight from a Firing Wall. New York, Simon and Schuster, 1966; London, Hale, 1968.

Uncollected Short Stories

"The Eye," in *Ellery Queen's Mystery Magazine* (New York), November 1945.

"Death at the Porthole," in *Murder Cavalcade*, edited by Ken Crossen. New York, Duell, 1946; London, Hammond, 1953.

"The Case of the Stuttering Sextant," in *Ellery Queen's Mystery Magazine* (New York), March 1947.

"Room for Murder," in *American Magazine* (Springfield, Ohio), September 1951.

"The Cloth-of-Gold Murders," in *American Magazine* (Springfield, Ohio), February 1956.

"Headless Angel," in *The Saint* (New York), December 1957.

"Whipsaw," in *The Saint* (New York), November 1959.

"Silent Night," in *Three Times Three*, edited by Howard Haycraft and John Beecroft. New York, Doubleday, 1964.

"5 − 4 = Murderer," in *Anthology 1965*, edited by Ellery Queen. New York, Davis, 1964.

"Murder Made in Moscow," in *The Award Espionage Reader*, edited by Hans Stefan Santesson. New York, Award, 1965.

"Mary − Mary −," in *Murder in Mind*, edited by Lawrence Treat. New York, Dutton, 1967.

OTHER PUBLICATIONS

Novels

Lights Out. New York, Morrow, 1945; London, W. H. Allen, 1948.

The Flames of Times. New York, Scribner, 1948.

Other

They Never Talk Back, with Henry Trefflick. New York, Appleton Century Crofts, 1954.
Florida Trails to Turnpikes. Gainesville, University of Florida Press, 1964.
Orlando: A Century Plus. Orlando, Florida, Sentinel Star, 1976.

*   *   *

Much of Baynard H. Kendrick's early work in the mid-1930's is only average. The exception is *The Iron Spiders*, set in Florida (where Kendrick worked from 1927) and detailing the search for a murderer who leaves spiders at the scenes of his crimes. It is one of the better and more suspenseful series murder novels; the murder is investigated by a tall deputy sheriff who frequently proclaims, "I'm Miles Standish Rice – the Hungry!" With the advent of the series character Captain Duncan Maclain, Kendrick took a giant step forward. His writing skills improved dramatically. He was able to create puzzles (often bizarre and worthy of Queen or Carr) and plots that rank with the best work of his contemporaries. The first six Maclain books are outstanding, though they have not received the critical acclaim they deserve.

Captain Maclain is blind due to an injury received in World War I, and must depend on his other senses, his friends, and his seeing-eye dogs to solve crimes. Kendrick did much research on the subject, and worked extensively with blind people. He was considered an authority on the subject, and his non-mystery *Lights Out* is an authoritative fictional work on a blind veteran's adjustment to his handicap. Maclain's first case, *The Last Express*, starts with a nightclub murder and ends with a tense subway pursuit. The last major Maclain novel, *Out of Control*, eschews detection for suspense and thrills as Maclain pursues a deranged murderess across the mountain region of Tennessee. Subsequent work declined, but the subplot of *Reservations for Death* – an airplane menaced by a bomb while in midflight – is timely today.

—Charles Shibuk

KENNEDY, Milward. Pseudonym for Milward Rodon Kennedy Burge; also wrote as Evelyn Elder; Robert Milward Kennedy. British. Born 21 June 1894. Educated at Winchester College; New College, Oxford. Served in the Military Intelligence Directorate of the War Office during World War I: Croix de Guerre; Director of the U.K. Information Office, Dominions Office, Ottawa, 1943–44. Married 1) Georgina Lee in 1921 (died, 1924); 2) Eveline Schreiber Billiat in 1926; one son. Worked for the Ministry of Finance, Cairo, 1919–20; Staff Member, Geneva Office, 1920–24, and Director of the London Office, 1924–45, International Labour Office: London Editor, *Empire Digest*, 1945–49. Crime fiction reviewer, *Sunday Times*, London, for many years. *Died 20 January 1968.*

CRIME PUBLICATIONS

Novels (series characters: Sir George Bull; Inspector Cornford)

The Bleston Mystery (as Robert Milward Kennedy), with A. Gordon MacDonnell. London, Gollancz, 1928; New York, Doubleday, 1929.
The Corpse on the Mat (Cornford). London, Gollancz, 1929; as *The Man Who Rang the Bell*, New York, Doubleday, 1929.

Corpse Guards Parade (Cornford). London, Gollancz, 1929; New York, Doubleday, 1930.

Half-Mast Murder. London, Gollancz, and New York, Doubleday, 1930.

Death in a Deck-Chair. London, Gollancz, 1930; New York, Doubleday, 1931.

Murder in Black and White (as Evelyn Elder). London, Methuen, 1931.

Death to the Rescue. London, Gollancz, 1931.

Angel in the Case (as Evelyn Elder). London, Methuen, 1932.

The Murderer of Sleep. London, Gollancz, 1932; New York, Kinsey, 1933.

The Floating Admiral, with others. London, Hodder and Stoughton 1931; New York, Doubleday, 1932.

Bull's Eye (Bull). London, Gollancz, and New York, Kinsey, 1933.

Ask a Policeman, with others. London, Barker, and New York, Morrow, 1933.

Corpse in Cold Storage (Bull). London, Gollancz, and New York, Kinsey, 1934.

Poison in the Parish. London, Gollancz, 1935.

Sic Transit Gloria. London, Gollancz, 1936; as *The Scornful Corpse*, New York, Dodd Mead, 1936.

I'll Be Judge, I'll Be Jury. London, Gollancz, 1937.

It Began in New York. London, Gollancz, 1943.

Escape to Quebec. London, Gollancz, 1946.

The Top Boot. London, Hale, 1950.

Two's Company. London, Hale, 1952.

Uncollected Short Stories

"Death in the Kitchen" and "Mr. Truefitt Detects," in *Great Short Stories of Detection, Mystery, and Horror 2*, edited by Dorothy L. Sayers. London, Gollancz, 1931; as *The Second Omnibus of Crime*, New York, Coward McCann, 1932.

"The Superfluous Murder," in *A Century of Detective Stories*. London, Hutchinson, 1935.

"End of a Judge," in *Detective Stories of Today*, edited by Raymond Postgate. London, Faber, 1940.

"The Accident," in *Evening Standard Detective Book*, 2nd series. London, Gollancz, 1951.

"The Fool," in *The Saint* (New York), January 1954.

"You've Been Warned," in *The Saint* (New York), February 1955.

"The Lost Ambassador," in *The Second Mystery Bedtime Book*, edited by John Creasey. London, Hodder and Stoughton, 1961.

OTHER PUBLICATIONS

Novel

Who Was Old Willy? London, Hutchinson, 1940.

Other

"Are Murders Meant?" and "Murderers in Fiction," in *Detective Medley*, edited by John Rhode. London, Hutchinson, 1939.

*   *   *

Milward Kennedy, better known in England than elsewhere, wrote good detective stories and wrote them in good English. He was an early member of the Detection Club and a most reliable reviewer of detective stories over many years. After 1934 he abandoned his series detectives, Sir George Bull and Inspector Cornford. He affected a light touch and even the occasional cynical solution in, for instance, *Death to the Rescue*. During the war period he wrote a quite capable thriller, *Escape to Quebec*, but it was in his earlier years that he produced his best work. *The Murderer of Sleep* is a nice puzzle with a most helpful map, a hallmark of vintage English detection. The corpses "on the mat" and "in cold storage" are well worth seeking. *Sic Transit Gloria* was written when he had become a little bored with the standard forms of the story with its rigid rules; it is certainly different and interesting. *Poison in the Parish* is well constructed and rather critical of coroners, who at that time often made their courts into miniature star-chambers. It preserves the pattern Kennedy had established of unmessy murders free from gallons of blood and noisy guns.

Milward Kennedy can be relied upon to produce a well constructed story, easily readable and with a limited number of well-delineated characters. His earlier stories are to be preferred, but in all of them lurks a light-hearted touch.

—Neville W. Wood

KENRICK, Tony. British. Born in Sydney, New South Wales, Australia, 23 August 1935. Educated at Sydney High School. Served in the Royal Australian Navy (national service). Married Joan Mary Kenrick in 1960; one daughter and one son. Advertising copywriter in Sydney, Toronto, New York, San Francisco, and London, 1953–72. Agent: Bill Berger Associates Inc., 444 East 58th Street, New York, New York 10017, U.S.A.; or Diana Avebury, 145 Park Road, London N.W.1, England. Address: 37 Godfrey Road West, Weston, Connecticut 06883, U.S.A.

CRIME PUBLICATIONS

Novels

> *The Only Good Body's a Dead One.* London, Cape, 1970; New York, Simon and
> Schuster, 1971.
> *A Tough One to Lose.* London, Joseph, and Indianapolis, Bobbs Merrill, 1972.
> *Two for the Price of One.* London, Joseph, and Indianapolis, Bobbs Merrill, 1974.
> *Stealing Lillian.* London, Joseph, and New York, McKay, 1975; as *The Kidnap Kid*,
> London, Sphere, 1976.
> *The Seven Day Soldiers.* London, Joseph, and Chicago, Regnery, 1976.
> *The Chicago Girl.* New York, Putnam, 1976; London, Joseph, 1977.
> *Two Lucky People.* London, Joseph, 1978.
> *The Nighttime Guy.* London, Granada, and New York, Morrow, 1979.
> *The 81st Site.* New York, New American Library, and London, Granada, 1980.

*   *   *

Tony Kenrick writes comedy thrillers which at their best are at least as funny as those of the acknowledged leader in the field, Donald Westlake. His crime themes are large – kidnapping, plane hi-jacking, holding New York to ransom – but the libraries are full of books with such story lines. What Kenrick does is compose alongside his criminal themes a richly comic counterpoint which adds to the reader's entertainment without detracting from the excitement. Thus in *A Tough One to Lose* he interlards a fascinating description of a plan to steal, and conceal, a 747 with a highly risible account of hard-up lawyer William

Verecker's efforts to locate the airplane. And in *Two for the Price of One* the trio of schizoid heroes who are bent on recouping from the City Fathers the cost of their wrecked jalopy trigger off by their absurd scheme a much larger and more sinister version by genuine underworld characters.

The real test of comic writing is that it should on occasion make the reader laugh out loud: Kenrick passes this test with flying colours. But such writing has its dangers too; comic invention must appear effortless. Just occasionally, as in *The Seven Day Soldiers* which shows a group of ordinary citizens getting trained to withstand an attack from The Mob, there is a sense of straining after effect. Individual sections are hilarious, but the whole doesn't quite carry conviction. This is to judge by the highest standards, but Kenrick's work deserves to be so judged, for at his best he helps to set the standards. His books are never less than interesting and when he is on top of his form he is one of the most entertaining and enthralling thriller writers around.

—Reginald Hill

KENYON, Michael. Also writes as Daniel Forbes. British. Born in Huddersfield, Yorkshire, 26 June 1931. Educated at Leighton Park School, Reading, Berkshire; Wadham College, Oxford, 1951–54, M.A. in history; Duke University, Durham, North Carolina, 1954–55. Served in the Royal Air Force, 1949–51 (national service). Married Catherine Bury in 1961; three daughters. Reporter, Bristol *Evening Post*, 1955–58; *News Chronicle*, London, 1958–60; and *Guardian*, London, 1960–64. Visiting Lecturer in Journalism, University of Illinois, Urbana, 1964–66; Visiting Lecturer in Journalism and Crime Fiction, Southampton College, Long Island University, New York, 1977–78. Since 1971, regular contributor to *Gourmet* magazine, New York. Lives in Cahors, France. Agent: Richard Scott Simon Ltd., 32 College Cross, London N1 1PR, England.

CRIME PUBLICATIONS

Novels (series character: Superintendent O'Malley)

May You Die in Ireland. London, Collins, and New York, Morrow, 1965.
The Whole Hog. London, Collins, 1967; as *The Trouble with Series Three*, New York, Morrow, 1967.
Out of Season. London, Collins, 1968.
The 100,000 Welcomes (O'Malley). London, Collins, and New York, Coward McCann, 1970.
The Shooting of Dan McGrew (O'Malley). London, Collins, 1972; New York, McKay, 1975.
A Sorry State (O'Malley). London, Collins, and New York, McKay, 1974.
Mr. Big. London, Collins, 1975; (as Daniel Forbes), New York, Coward McCann, 1975.
The Rapist. London, Collins, 1977; (as Daniel Forbes), New York, Coward McCann, 1977.
Deep Pocket. London, Collins, 1978; as *The Molehill File*, New York, Coward McCann, 1978.

Other Publications

Novel

Green Grass. London, Macmillan, 1969.

Other

Brainbox and Bull (juvenile). London, Angus and Robertson, 1976.

Michael Kenyon comments:

Asking a writer to introduce his work seems reasonable but I have this fairly desperate feeling the result will be pretentious or over-diffident, and certainly misleading. My stories are light-thrillerish rather than mysterious or puzzling. When I fell into crime writing I had read nothing in the genre and was slightly contemptuous of it, which no doubt shows, at least in the earlier books. I wanted to write not suspense fiction but "Childe Harold," and "The Night the Bed Fell" and *Lucky Jim,* and hoped to do so once a dashed-off thriller or two had brought me the time and money. Now that I have read, late in the day, a fair amount of crime fiction, I have only admiration and increasing enthusiasm for it – for the best of it – and an ambition to do as well. I like to think my more recent stories are more serious, plottier, and not necessarily duller than the earlier, jokey ones. My personal best, the really excellent crime novel, is the one about to be written, always. I have not managed it yet, but I will, I will, I will....

* * *

Michael Kenyon is a thriller writer with a genuine comic (as opposed to farcical) gift. He gives himself a head start by setting most of his books in Ireland where, to the rest of the English-speaking world, gaiety and sorrow, tragedy and mirth, have long overlapped. Where else could the investigation of rape and murder (*The Rapist*) be made funny and frightening at the same time? In this book as in several others he uses the American visitor to Ireland as the catalyst for both comedy and violence when the new world comes into confrontation with the old. Refereeing the resulting clash we find the *garda* or Irish police, most notably the sympathetic, percipient, and on occasions comically lugubrious Superintendent O'Malley. Kenyon's humour and skills of characterization and narrative are beautifully illustrated in the opening sequence of *A Sorry State* which shows O'Malley on a plane journey to the Philippines during which he demonstrates a typically Irish antidote to jet-lag. It's a richly amusing account, but the journey also provides the reader with essential background information in a single easy-to-swallow dose. To do things with easy charm has always been an Irish skill.

That Kenyon is in no way restricted to Irish settings and jokes is shown in *Mr. Big* where he goes across the sea to England and indeed to the centre of things English, Buckingham Palace. His villain/hero is plotting to rob the Queen. Here again we see displayed Kenyon's humour, ingenuity, and sense of character. Kenyon does not write on a large blockbusting scale, but within his own not inconsiderable territory he offers the discriminating reader a great deal of honest pleasure and criminal excitement.

—Reginald Hill

KERSH, Gerald. American. Born in Teddington-on-Thames, Middlesex, England, 6 August 1911; naturalized United States citizen, 1959. Educated at Regent Street Polytechnic, London. Served in the Coldstream Guards, 1940–41; transferred to special duties, 1942; Scriptwriter, Army Film Unit, 1943; Specialist in the Films Division, Ministry of Information, 1943–44; accredited to SHAEF, 1944. Married 1) Alice Thompson Rostron in 1938 (marriage dissolved, 1943); 2) Claire Alyne Pacaud in 1943 (marriage dissolved, 1955); 3) Florence Sochis in 1955. Worked as a baker, nightclub bouncer, fish and chips cook, and wrestler in the 1930's; Chief Feature Writer (as Piers England), 1941–45, and War Correspondent, 1943, *The People*, London; settled in the United States after World War II. Recipient: Mystery Writers of America Edgar Allan Poe Award, 1957. *Died 5 November 1968.*

CRIME PUBLICATIONS

Novels

Jews Without Jehovah. London, Wishart, 1934.
Men Are So Ardent. London, Wishart, 1935; New York, Morrow, 1936.
Night and the City. London, Joseph, 1938; New York, Simon and Schuster, 1946.
They Die with Their Boots Clean. London, Heinemann, 1941; in *Sergeant Nelson of the Guards*, 1945.
The Nine Lives of Bill Nelson. London, Heinemann, 1942; in *Sergeant Nelson of the Guards*, 1945.
The Dead Look On. London, Heinemann, and New York, Reynal, 1943.
Brain and Ten Fingers. London, Heinemann, 1943.
Faces in a Dusty Picture. London, Heinemann, 1944; New York, McGraw Hill, 1945.
An Ape, A Dog, and a Serpent. London, Heinemann, 1945.
Sergeant Nelson of the Guards. Philadelphia, Winston, 1945.
The Weak and the Strong. London, Heinemann, 1945; New York, Simon and Schuster, 1946.
Prelude to a Certain Midnight. New York, Doubleday, and London, Heinemann, 1947.
The Song of the Flea. New York, Doubleday, and London, Heinemann, 1948.
Clock Without Hands. London, Heinemann, 1949.
The Thousand Deaths of Mr. Small. New York, Doubleday, 1950; London, Heinemann, 1951.
The Great Wash. London, Heinemann, 1953; as *The Secret Masters*, New York, Ballantine, 1953.
Fowlers End. New York, Simon and Schuster, 1957; London, Heinemann, 1958.
A Long Cool Day in Hell. London, Heinemann, 1965.
The Angel and the Cuckoo. New York, New American Library, 1966; London, Heinemann, 1967.
Brock. London, Heinemann, 1969.

Short Stories

Selected Stories. London, Staples Press, 1943.
The Battle of the Singing Men. London, Everybody's Books, 1944.
The Horrible Dummy and Other Stories. London, Heinemann, 1944.
Neither Man nor Dog. London, Heinemann, 1946.
Clean, Bright, and Slightly Oiled. London, Heinemann, 1946.
Sad Road to the Sea. London, Heinemann, 1947.
The Brazen Bull. London, Heinemann, 1952.
The Brighton Monster and Others. London, Heinemann, 1953.

Guttersnipe: Little Novels.   London, Heinemann, 1954.
Men Without Bones and Other Stories.   London, Heinemann, 1955; abridged edition,
   New York, Paperback Library, 1962.
The Ugly Face of Love and Other Stories.   London, Heinemann, 1960.
The Terribly Wild Flowers: Nine Stories.   London, Heinemann, 1962.
More Than Once upon a Time.   London, Heinemann, 1964.
The Hospitality of Miss Tolliver and Other Stories.   London, Heinemann, 1965.
Nightshade and Damnations, edited by Harlan Ellison.   New York, Fawcett, 1968;
   London, Coronet, 1969.

Uncollected Short Stories

"The Ambiguities of Lo Yeing Pai," in *Ellery Queen's Mystery Magazine* (New York),
   June 1968.
"Karmesin and the Trismagistus Formula," in *Ellery Queen's Mystery Magazine* (New
   York), March 1969.
"The Pettifur Collection," in *Ellery Queen's Murder Menu.*   Cleveland, World, 1969.
"Karmesin the Fixer," in *Ellery Queen's Mystery Magazine* (New York), January 1970.
"Gambling Fever," in *Ellery Queen's Mystery Magazine* (New York), January 1971.
"Mr. Tomorrow," in *Ellery Queen's Headliners.*   Cleveland, World, 1971; London,
   Gollancz, 1972.
"Dr. Ox Will Die at Midnight," in *Best Detective Stories of the Year 1971*, edited by
   Allen J. Hubin.   New York, Dutton, 1971.
"One Case in a Million," in *Ellery Queen's Giants of Mystery.*   New York, Davis, 1971.
"The Scar," in *Ellery Queen's Magicians of Mystery.*   New York, Davis, 1976.

OTHER PUBLICATIONS

Novel

The Implacable Hunter.   London, Heinemann, 1961.

Short Stories

On an Odd Note.   New York, Ballantine, 1958.

Play

Screenplay: *Nine Men*, with Harry Watt, 1943.

Other

I Got References.   London, Joseph, 1939.
The Best of Gerald Kersh, edited by Simon Raven.   London, Heinemann, 1961.

*   *   *

Gerald Kersh writes about a man pursued by men without bones, about the Devil, about
insane, strange, unforgettable people. Kersh's flair for the bizarre makes him hard to
categorize. He's more than a mystery writer, though he's written excellent mysteries. He's
more than a suspense writer, though he's written hundreds of suspenseful short stories.
Gerald Kersh is an original.
   Perhaps Kersh's talent for the bizarre stems from his bizarre life. When he was four years
old, Kersh was declared dead of lung congestion. During the funeral, he sat up in his coffin,
very much alive. In World War II, while Kersh served as a war correspondent during the

London blitz, he was buried alive three times, and survived. Kersh was once a professional wrestler, and survived.

During his life Kersh produced 5000 magazine articles, 3000 short stories, and almost 40 books. His best-selling novel *Night and the City* was made into a movie. Unfortunately, Kersh's best novel, *Fowlers End*, has never been reprinted. It is a sprawling, Dickensian novel of London populated by Kersh's own brand of memorable characters.

But Gerald Kersh will be remembered chiefly for his brilliant short stories. "The Queen of Pig Island" is a love story of a beautiful girl without arms or legs who rules an island where a grim giant and a pair of midgets battle for her love. "What Ever Happened to Corporal Cuckoo?" tells of a soldier who's lived for hundreds of years by accidentally becoming immortal. His story of centuries of slaughter and death is both sad and chilling. The best of Gerald Kersh's short stories can be found in *Nightshade and Damnations* (with an introduction by Harlan Ellison), and in the original collections released by Ballantine as science fiction: *On an Odd Note* and *What Ever Happened to Corporal Cuckoo?*.

Finally, Gerald Kersh will be remembered as an outstanding stylist capable of producing startling images like this one: "We hang about the necks of our tomorrows like hungry harlots about the necks of penniless sailors." Kersh's work remains superb, important, and original.

—George Kelley

KEVERNE, Richard. Pseudonym for Clifford James Wheeler Hosken. British. Born in Norwich, Norfolk, 29 August 1882. Educated privately. Served in the Royal Flying Corps and the Royal Air Force during World War I: Captain. Married Emma Harris Foster in 1911. Member of the Editorial Staff, *Daily Mirror*, London, for 17 years. *Died 9 June 1950.*

Crime Publications

Novels (series character: Inspector Mace)

Carteret's Cure. London, Constable, and Boston, Houghton Mifflin, 1926.
William Cook, Antique Dealer. London, Constable, 1928; as *The Strange Case of "William" Cook*, New York, Harper, 1928.
The Havering Plot. London, Constable, 1928; New York, Harper, 1929.
The Sanfield Scandal. London, Constable, and New York, Harper, 1929.
The Man in the Red Hat. London, Constable, and New York, Harper, 1930.
The Fleet Hall Inheritance. London, Constable, and New York, Harper, 1931.
At the Blue Gates. London, Constable, and New York, Doubleday, 1932.
Menace. London, Constable, 1933.
Artifex Intervenes: Three Detective Adventures. London, Constable, 1934.
He Laughed at Murder. London, Constable, 1934; New York, Holt, 1935.
White Gas (Mace). London, Constable, 1937.
Open Verdict (Mace). London, Constable, 1940.
The Black Cripple. London, Collins, 1941.
The Lady in No. 4. London, Collins, 1944; as *Coroner's Verdict: Accident*, Philadelphia, McKay, 1945.

Novels as Clifford Hosken

The Pretender. London, Harrap, 1930.
The Shadow Syndicate. London, Harrap, and New York, Dial Press, 1930.
Missing from His Home. London, Putnam, 1932.

Short Stories

Crook Stuff. London, Constable, 1935.
More Crook Stuff. London, Constable, 1938.
Crooks and Vagabonds. London, Collins, 1941.

OTHER PUBLICATIONS

Other

Tales of Old Inns: The History, Legend, and Romance of Some of Our Older Hostelries (as
   Clifford Hosken).   London, Trust Houses, 1927; revised edition, London, Collins,
   1939, edited by Hammond Innes, 1947.

*   *   *

Richard Keverne's mysteries are generally straightforward tales, often told by overactive
and repetitive narrators. His writing is characterized by a firm, albeit stilted, style; and though
Keverne's mysteries are pleasant enough, it is difficult to imagine enduring more than one
reading of his works.

A fairly typical Keverne effort is *The Man in the Red Hat.* Though it is difficult to fault a
mystery story for lack of full characterization, the characters in this mystery have almost no
personality at all. Mark Wickham, the main character, appears to be motivated by forces
beyond both his and the narrator's understanding. Compounding the problem of an
apparently omniscient narrator's inability to comprehend and convey the simplest
motivations of the characters is the narrator's unnerving habit of explaining irrelevent
material in too great detail. The reader (certainly this reader) is told more than he needs or
wants to know. Though the plot of this book is uninspired, there are refreshing twists here
and there that help revive flagging interest. And the conclusion is workmanlike – many of the
seemingly random details suddenly cohere, most of the pieces of the puzzle fit more or less
snugly into place, all turns out well for the right characters, and the boy even gets the girl.

If you have heard of Keverne from a fan of his (and there are many), and would like to
sample his wares, I would recommend, in addition to *The Man in the Red Hat, William Cook,
Antique Dealer, Missing from His Home,* and *The Lady in No. 4.*

—Donald J. Pattow

KING, C(harles) Daly.   American.   Born in New York City in 1895. Educated at Newark
Academy, New Jersey; Yale University, New Haven, Connecticut, B.A. (Phi Beta Kappa);
Ph.D. in psychology 1946; Columbia University, New York, M.A. in psychology 1928.
Served in the United States Army Field Artillery in World War I: Lieutenant; Captain in the
reserve until 1926. Partner in a cotton and woollen business for five years; treasurer in an
advertising agency for two years; practised as a psychologist. *Died in 1963.*

CRIME PUBLICATIONS

Novels (series character: Michael Lord in all books except *Obelists at Sea*)

Obelists at Sea. London, John Heritage, 1932; New York, Knopf, 1933.
Obelists en Route. London, Collins, 1934.
Obelists Fly High. London, Collins, and New York, Smith and Haas, 1935.
Careless Corpse: A Thanatophony. London, Collins, 1937.
Arrogant Alibi. London, Collins, 1938; New York, Appleton Century, 1939.
Bermuda Burial. London, Collins, 1940; New York, W. Funk, 1941.

Short Stories

The Curious Mr. Tarrant. London, Collins, 1935; New York, Dover, 1977.

Uncollected Short Stories

"Lost Star," in *Ellery Queen's Mystery Magazine* (New York), September 1944.
"The Episode of the Sinister Invention," in *Ellery Queen's Mystery Magazine* (New York), December 1946.

OTHER PUBLICATIONS

Other

Beyond Behaviorism: The Future of Psychology (as Robert Courtney). New York, Grant, 1927.
Integrative Psychology: A Study of Unit Response, with W. M. Marston and Elizabeth H. Marston. London, Kegan Paul, and New York, Harcourt Brace, 1931.
The Psychology of Consciousness. London, Kegan Paul, and New York, Harcourt Brace, 1932.
The Oragean Vision (on A. R. Orage). New York, Business Photo Reproduction, 1951.
The States of Human Consciousness. New Hyde Park, New York, University Books, 1964.

Editor, with E. G. Sison, *An Interim Tracing of the Ancestry of Valerie Daly King.* Privately printed, 1956.

*   *   *

Almost everybody reads mystery stories, and people of many professions have attempted to write them. The psychologist C. Daly King is one of the rare members of his profession to have written in the genre. Curiously, some of his books were not published in his own country, but the best work in his limited output was almost, if not quite, enough to establish him as a master.

King as a mystery writer is almost as baffling and enigmatic as some of the plots and characters he created. There are times when he is absolutely brilliant, and writes with the verve and assurance of a master. At other times he is as pathetic and frustrating as the old club bore whose stories you've heard before and don't want to hear again. (In one novel he inserts a 15-page treatise on economic theory for no reason whatever.) Though he was not particularly gifted in conveying atmosphere, *Careless Corpse* is an exception. Here a murder occurs during a musical performance held in an almost inaccessible castle, and the smooth, fairly convention novel is not unlike the early work of Ellery Queen. *Arrogant Alibi*, with its wealth of suspects and perfect alibis, is also effectively set against the 1937 flood in Hartford,

Connecticut. *Bermuda Burial* is a romantic story set on the island where King spent much of his time and wrote his detective stories, but it is little more than a travelogue.

King's powers of characterization were particularly weak, and we never learn very much about his series detective, Michael Lord, except that he is reasonably young and a special officer attached to the staff of the Police Commissioner of New York. None of his recorded investigations occur in New York, but he manages to rise to the rank of Inspector because he is gifted with ratiocinative power that is almost the equal of Ellery Queen's. Lord's intelligent "Watson" is an integrative psychologist, Dr. L(ove) Rees Pons. King's other detective, Trevis Tarrant, appears in several stories, but we never learn much about him either. His "Watson," Jerry Phelan, narrates the stories and is somewhat better characterized.

King's major strength is his ability to create plots. At his best, he can concoct puzzles that are as baffling and bizarre as those created by Queen and Carr, with all the deviousness of Christie. His short story "The Episode of the Nail and the Requiem," for instance, is one of the most ingenious locked-room puzzles ever devised by a mystery writer. Ellery Queen himself said that *The Curious Mr. Tarrant* contained "the most imaginative detective short stories of our time." This collection was published only in England, and became very difficult to obtain, but a recent reprint might help to re-establish King's reputation.

King tries hard for originality, often successfully. In his first detective work, *Obelists at Sea*, he has four psychologists of varying persuasions, including Dr. Pons and Dr. B. Hayvier, investigate a series of crimes and try to solve them in the light of their experience. All are proven wrong – as were the six crime enthusiasts in Berkeley's *The Poisoned Chocolates Case*. (King, incidentally, uses the word obelists inconsistently in different novels.)

King's masterpiece, *Obelists Fly High*, is original in structure. It commences with an "epilogue" in which Lord gets shot, then flashes back to the body of the novel which concerns a great surgeon's race via airplane to save his prominent brother's life – even though his own life is threatened. The narrative continues and catches up to events in the "epilogue." At the end there is a "prologue" that answers all questions.

Anthony Boucher called King "one of the most original, inventive, and underrated detective writers of the golden thirties. His novels of detection are elaborate and extraordinary." King tried very hard, and nearly succeeded, but lacked the ultimate ability and rigid self-discipline to become a really great detective writer.

—Charles Shibuk

KING, Rufus (Frederick).   American.   Born in New York City, 3 January 1893. Educated at Dodsworth School; Yale University, New Haven, Connecticut. Served in the United States Army Cavalry on the Mexican border and in the Field Artillery in France during World War I: First Lieutenant; conspicuous service cross. Wireless operator in the Merchant Marine, and traveled in South America before beginning to write: created the detective Reginald De Puyster in magazine stories in the 1920's. *Died in 1966.*

CRIME PUBLICATIONS

Novels (series character: Lieutenant Valcour)

   Mystery De Luxe. New York, Doran, 1927; as *Murder De Luxe*, London, Leonard
      Parsons, 1927.
   The Fatal Kiss Mystery. New York, Doubleday, 1928.

Murder by the Clock (Valcour). New York, Doubleday, and London, Chapman and Hall, 1929.

A Woman Is Dead (Valcour). London, Chapman and Hall, 1929; as *Somewhere in This House*, New York, Doubleday, 1930; as *A Murderer in This House*, New York, Novel Selections, 1945.

Murder by Latitude (Valcour). New York, Doubleday, 1930; London, Heinemann, 1931.

Murder in the Willett Family (Valcour). New York, Doubleday, 1931.

Murder on the Yacht (Valcour). New York, Doubleday, and London, Hamish Hamilton, 1932.

Valcour Meets Murder. New York, Doubleday, 1932.

The Lesser Antilles Case. New York, Doubleday, 1934; as *Murder Challenges Valcour*, New York, Dell, 1944.

Profile of a Murder (Valcour). New York, Harcourt Brace, 1935.

The Case of the Constant God (Valcour). New York, Doubleday, 1936; London, Methuen, 1938.

Crime of Violence (Valcour). New York, Doubleday, 1937; London, Methuen, 1938.

Murder Masks Miami (Valcour). New York, Doubleday, and London, Methuen, 1939.

Holiday Homicide. New York, Doubleday, 1940; London, Methuen, 1941.

Design in Evil. New York, Doubleday, 1942.

A Variety of Weapons. New York, Doubleday, 1943.

The Case of the Dowager's Etchings. New York, Doubleday, 1944; London, Methuen, 1946; as *Never Walk Alone*, New York, Popular Library, 1951.

The Deadly Dove. New York, Doubleday, 1945.

Museum Piece No. 13. New York, Doubleday, 1946; as *Secret Beyond the Door*, New York, Triangle, 1947.

Lethal Lady. New York, Doubleday, 1947.

The Case of the Redoubled-Cross. New York, Doubleday, 1949.

Duenna to a Murder. New York, Doubleday, and London, Methuen, 1951.

Short Stories

Diagnosis: Murder. New York, Doubleday, 1941; London, Methuen, 1942.
Malice in Wonderland. New York, Doubleday, 1958.
The Steps to Murder. New York, Doubleday, 1960.
The Faces of Danger. New York, Doubleday, 1964.

Uncollected Short Stories

"A Lonely, Lovely Lady," in *The Saint* (New York), April 1965.
"The Patron Saint of the Impossible," in *Anthology 1967*, edited by Ellery Queen. New York, Davis, 1966.
"Anatomy of a Crime," in *Ellery Queen's Mystery Magazine* (New York), December 1966.

OTHER PUBLICATIONS

Novels

North Star: A Dog Story of the Canadian Northwest. New York, Watt, 1925.
Whelp of the Winds: A Dog Story. New York, Doran, and London, Cassell, 1926.

Plays

  Murder at the Vanities, with Earl Carroll, music and lyrics by John Green and others
    (produced New York, 1933).
  Invitation to a Murder (produced New York, 1934).   New York, French, 1934.
  I Want a Policeman, with Milton Lazarus (produced New York, 1936).   New York,
    Dramatists Play Service, 1937.

                              *   *   *

  Rufus King had only one series detective, Lieutenant Valcour, a French-Canadian serving
in the New York Police Department. Valcour is courteous, calm, and efficient. In several
cases, because the crime has occurred in isolated circumstances, Valcour must work without
the back-up of New York colleagues. *Murder on the Yacht* and *Murder by Latitude* take place
at sea, and the criminal has prevented radio communication; King also placed Valcour in
other remote places, including Canada. But Valcour was equally competent when the crime
was urban. His best-known case, *Murder by the Clock*, is set in New York, and provides –
typically for the period – many suspects and false trails. It has, moreover, a very nice twist at
the end, the kind that makes one sorry the story must finish.
  Touches of gentle humour are often lurking in King's novels and stories. One of his finest
in this regard is *The Case of the Dowager's Etchings*, a light trifle, with the necessary
ingredients of the War period. This is not a Valcour story, nor does he appear in any of the
short stories. The best of King's short stories are collected in *Malice in Wonderland*: these are
tightly constructed works from his late period, and often end with a malicious twist.

                                                              —Neville W. Wood

---

KIRK, Michael.   See **KNOX, Bill.**

KITCHIN, C(lifford) H(enry) B(enn).   British.   Born in Harrogate, Yorkshire, 17 October
1895. Educated at Clifton College, Bristol; Exeter College, Oxford (scholar); Lincoln's Inn,
London: called to the Bar, 1924. Served in the British Army in France, 1916–18. Lawyer and
member of the Stock Exchange, London. *Died 2 April 1967.*

CRIME PUBLICATIONS

  Novels (series character: Malcolm Warren in all books)

    Death of My Aunt.   London, Hogarth Press, 1929; New York, Harcourt Brace, 1930.
    Crime at Christmas.   London, Hogarth Press, 1934; New York, Harcourt Brace, 1935.
    Death of His Uncle.   London, Constable, 1939.
    The Cornish Fox.   London, Secker and Warburg, 1949.

OTHER PUBLICATIONS

Novels

> *Streamers Waving.* London, Hogarth Press, 1925.
> *Mr. Balcony.* London, Hogarth Press, 1927.
> *The Sensitive One.* London, Hogarth Press, 1931.
> *Olive E.* London, Constable, 1937.
> *Birthday Party.* London, Constable, 1938.
> *The Auction Sale.* London, Secker and Warburg, 1949.
> *The Secret River.* London, Secker and Warburg, 1956.
> *Ten Politt Place.* London, Secker and Warburg, 1957.
> *The Book of Life.* London, Davies, 1960; New York, Appleton Century Crofts, 1961.

Short Stories

> *Jumping Joan and Other Stories.* London, Secker and Warburg, 1954.

Verse

> *Curtains.* Oxford, Blackwell, 1919.
> *Winged Victory.* Oxford, Blackwell, 1921.

Other

> Editor, with Vera M. Brittain and Alan Porter, *Oxford Poetry 1920.* Oxford, Blackwell, 1920.

*   *   *

A lawyer and mainstream novelist, C. H. B. Kitchin turned to the detective story in 1929, and produced his most famous work, *Death of My Aunt*, but mistakenly chose to stress characterization at the expense of puzzle and plot. This novel features the detective Malcolm Warren, a young stockbroker, who is summoned by his rich aunt to her country home to give advice about possible investments. She dies under mysterious circumstances, and Warren (who is the narrator) is suspected. His only recourse is to discover the guilty party.

Death of My Aunt has gathered a small but vocal band of admirers, including Jacques Barzun and Wendell Hertig Taylor who find that "the clues, the ratiocination, and the interplay of feeling among the members of the large family are as effective as the terse, bare prose and the headlong drive of the narrative." I dissent. The narrator seems to be so concerned with his own esthetic sensibilities, and the reactions of the others, that the reader's interest and attention are too often diverted from the novel's narrative flow and crime problem.

Warren gets involved in another mysterious death in *Crime at Christmas*, and is forced to play detective once again. This book moves less rapidly than its predecessor, and is of less interest. *Death of His Uncle* is twice as long and much better than *Death of My Aunt*, although it's easily guessable. Warren is now much more concerned with investigating a crime problem than with himself. Warren's last investigation, *The Cornish Fox*, starts with anonymous letters, continues with burglary, and proceeds to murder. This is a charming and clever mystery.

Julian Symons summed up Kitchin by stating, "There is a great deal of pleasure to be obtained from the always urbane and at times elegant writing." Kitchin himself once wrote,

"A historian of the future will probably turn, not to blue books or statistics, but to detective stories if he wishes to study the manners of our age."

—Charles Shibuk

KLINGER, Henry.   American.

CRIME PUBLICATIONS

Novels (series character: Lieutenant Shomri Shomar in all books)

Wanton for Murder.   New York, Doubleday, 1961.
Murder Off Broadway.   New York, Doubleday, 1962.
Essence of Murder.   New York, Doubleday, 1963.
Lust for Murder.   New York, Trident Press, 1966.

*   *   *

Henry Klinger is a good example of a writer who has a number of good ideas but who fails to produce a really satisfactory mystery novel. His best creation is Shomri Shomar, an Israeli police lieutenant touring the United States to exchange ideas with law enforcement officials. In Klinger's novels, Shomar is working with the New York Police Department, and his unorthodox investigatory methods often infuriate his superior, Captain Griff Marble. (This idea of the near-Eastern detective visiting the west was successfully reversed in the movie *Coogan's Bluff* and the TV series *McCloud*, both of which featured lawmen from the west working in New York.) Shomar is handsome, with a neat beard, and shrewd; he also has an interesting background in the Israeli army. Unfortunately, he is too given to quoting Jewish apothegms such as the ones which head the chapters of each book.

Assisting Shomar in his cases is Joe Adano, an ambulance attendant who aspires to be an obstetrician. He plays a major role in *Wanton for Murder*, but though his occupation adds interest Klinger wisely relegates him to more minor parts in the subsequent novels. It is not that Adano's medical observations are not intriguing but that Adano fails to develop and becomes only a foil for Shomar.

The flaw in Klinger's books is that the plots fail to engage the attention. Thin and often far-fetched, they are not worthy of the engaging protagonist created by Klinger to solve them. As a result the Shomri Shomar stories seem likely to remain curiosities rather than classics.

—Bill Crider

KNOX, Bill (William Knox).   Also writes as Michael Kirk; Robert MacLeod; Noah Webster.   British.   Born in Glasgow, Lanarkshire, 20 February 1928.   Educated at local schools in Scotland.   Served in the Royal Naval Auxiliary.   Married Myra Ann McKill in

1950; two daughters and one son. Copy Boy, Glasgow *Evening Citizen*, 1944–45; Reporter, later Deputy News Editor, Glasgow *Evening News*, 1945–57; News Editor, later Scottish Editor, *Scottish Empire News*, Glasgow and London, 1957–60; News Editor, Scottish Television, Glasgow, 1960–62. Since 1962, free-lance author and broadcaster; since 1976, writer and presenter, "Crime Desk" programme, Scottish Television. Agent: Hutchinson Publishing Group Ltd., 3 Fitzroy Square, London W1P 6JD, England. Address: 55 Newtonlea Avenue, Newton Mearns, Glasgow G77 5QF, Scotland.

CRIME PUBLICATIONS

Novels (series characters: Chief Officer Webb Carrick; Detective Chief Inspector Colin Thane and Phil Moss)

Deadline for a Dream (Thane and Moss). London, Long, 1957; as *In at the Kill*, New York, Doubleday, 1961.
The Cockatoo Crime. London, Long, 1958.
Death Department (Thane and Moss). London, Long, 1959.
Leave It to the Hangman (Thane and Moss). London, Long, and New York, Doubleday, 1960.
Death Calls the Shots. London, Long, 1961.
Die for Big Betsy. London, Long, 1961.
Little Drops of Blood (Thane and Moss). London, Long, and New York, Doubleday, 1962.
Sanctuary Isle (Thane and Moss). London, Long, 1962; as *The Grey Sentinels*, New York, Doubleday, 1963.
The Man in the Bottle (Thane and Moss). London, Long, 1963; as *The Killing Game*, New York, Doubleday, 1963.
The Scavengers (Carrick). London, Long, and New York, Doubleday, 1964.
The Taste of Proof (Thane and Moss). London, Long, and New York, Doubleday, 1965.
Devilweed (Carrick). London, Long, and New York, Doubleday, 1966.
The Deep Fall (Thane and Moss). London, Long, 1966; as *The Ghost Car*, New York, Doubleday, 1966.
Blacklight (Carrick). London, Long, and New York, Doubleday, 1967.
Justice on the Rocks (Thane and Moss). London, Long, and New York, Doubleday, 1967.
The Klondyker (Carrick). London, Long, 1968; as *Figurehead*, New York, Doubleday, 1968.
The Tallyman (Thane and Moss). London, Long, and New York, Doubleday, 1969.
Blueback (Carrick). London, Long, and New York, Doubleday, 1969.
Children of the Mist (Thane and Moss). London, Long, 1970; as *Who Shot the Bull?*, New York, Doubleday, 1970.
Seafire (Carrick). London, Long, 1970; New York, Doubleday, 1971.
To Kill a Witch (Thane and Moss). London, Long, 1971; New York, Doubleday, 1972.
Stormtide (Carrick). London, Long, 1972; New York, Doubleday, 1973.
Draw Batons! (Thane and Moss). London, Long, and New York, Doubleday, 1973.
Whitewater (Carrick). London, Long, and New York, Doubleday, 1974.
Rally to Kill (Thane and Moss). London, Long, and New York, Doubleday, 1975.
Hellspout (Carrick). London, Long, and New York, Doubleday, 1976.
Pilot Error (Thane and Moss). London, Long, and New York, Doubleday, 1977.
Witchrock (Carrick). London, Long, 1977; New York, Doubleday, 1978.
Live Bait (Thane and Moss). New York, Doubleday, 1979.

Novels as Robert MacLeod (series characters: Talos Cord; Jonathan Gaunt; Andrew
    Laird; Gaunt books published as Noah Webster and Laird books as Michael Kirk
    in US)

Cave of Bats (Cord). London, Long, 1964; New York, Holt Rinehart, 1966.
Lake of Fury (Cord). London, Long, 1966; as *The Iron Sanctuary*, New York, Holt
    Rinehart, 1968.
Isle of Dragons (Cord). London, Long, 1967.
Place of Mists (Cord). London, Long, 1969; New York, McCall, 1970.
A Property in Cyprus (Gaunt). London, Long, 1970; as *Flickering Death*, New York,
    Doubleday, 1971.
Path of Ghosts (Cord). London, Long, and New York, McCall, 1971.
A Killing in Malta (Gaunt). London, Long, and New York, Doubleday, 1972.
Nest of Vultures (Cord). London, Long, 1973.
A Burial in Portugal (Gaunt). London, Long, and New York, Doubleday, 1973.
All Other Perils (Laird). London, Long, 1974; New York, Doubleday, 1975.
A Witchdance in Bavaria (Gaunt). London, Long, 1975; New York, Doubleday, 1976.
Dragonship (Laird). London, Long, 1976; New York, Doubleday, 1977.
A Pay-Off in Switzerland. London, Long, and New York, Doubleday, 1977.
Salvage Job (Laird). London, Long, 1978; New York, Doubleday, 1979.
Incident in Iceland (Gaunt). New York, Doubleday, 1979.

Short Stories

The View from Daniel Pike, with Edward Boyd. London, Hutchinson, and New York,
    St. Martin's Press, 1974.

Uncollected Short Stories

"The Frightened American," in *Crime Across the Sea*, edited by John Creasey. New
    York, Harper, 1964; London, Harrap, 1965.
"The Service Flat," in *John Creasey's Mystery Bedtime Book*, edited by Herbert
    Harris. London, Hodder and Stoughton, 1966.
"Deerglen Queen," in *Crime Without Murder*, edited by Dorothy Salisbury
    Davis. New York, Scribner, 1970.
"The Man Who Died Twice," in *John Creasey's Mystery Bedtime Book 1972*, edited by
    Herbert Harris. London, Hodder and Stoughton, 1971.

OTHER PUBLICATIONS

Novel

The Drum of Ungara. New York, Doubleday, 1963; as *Drum of Power*, London, Long,
    1964.

Plays

Radio Plays: *Leave It to the Hangman*, from his own novel, 1964; *Sanctuary Isle*, from
his own novel, 1964; *To Kill a Witch*, from his own novel, 1972; *Death of a Marquis*,
1972; *The Tallyman*, from his own novel, 1973; *Draw Batons*, from his own novel,
1974; *The Taste of Proof*, 1974; *The Service Flat*, from his own story, 1976.

Television Play: *Little Drops of Blood*, from his own novel, 1965.

Other

Life Begins at Midnight, with R. Colquhoun. London, Long, 1961.
Ecurie Ecosse: The Story of Scotland's International Racing Team, with David Murray. London, Paul, 1962.
Final Diagnosis, with John Glaister. London, Hutchinson, 1964.
Court of Murder (trials in Glasgow). London, Long, 1968.

Editor, *The Thin Blue Line: The Story of the City of Glasgow Police*, by Douglas Grant. London, Long, 1973.

Manuscript Collection: Mugar Memorial Library, Boston University.

Bill Knox comments:

I consider my main strength in writing is my training and experience as a journalist, particularly as a crime reporter in the 1950's. This has given me, with present TV involvement, a close knowledge of Scottish police and criminals. In the same way later journalism and broadcasting work called for much travel abroad (and still does), producing background material for those novels written under my pen-names Robert MacLeod, Michael Kirk, and Noah Webster.

My main writing output revolves around four series characters. In the Bill Knox books these are Glasgow policemen Colin Thane (procedural stories) and Scottish Fishery Protection Officer Webb Carrick (sea-going detection off the Scottish west coast). In the pseudonymous books these are Jonathan Gaunt, an external auditor with the Queen's and Lord Treasurer's Remembrancer in Edinburgh (overseas settings), and, most recently, Andrew Laird, a marine insurance claims investigator (again travel abroad).

*   *   *

Under his own name, Bill Knox has written one series of novels featuring Inspectors Thane and Moss of the Glasgow CID and another detailing the action-filled career of Chief Officer Webb Carrick of the Scottish Fishery Protection Service. As Robert MacLeod (Noah Webster in the U.S.) he has begun a third series about Jonathan Gaunt, agent for the Scottish Remembrancer's Office. Although flawed by the repetitious introduction of character and setting common in series novels (Knox repeats the same information in the same words in each novel of the separate series), the novels are competently written, and the settings, whether Glasgow, the Hebrides, or Malta, add interest without detracting from plot or action. Individual characters are clearly established, and appropriate contemporary events and attitudes are smoothly worked into the plots, which are usually plausible and well designed. A good sense of locale and frequent humorous touches counterbalance predictability in plotting and characterization to provide pleasant light entertainment.

The Thane-Moss novels, of which *The Taste of Proof* and *Children of the Mist* are typical, are police procedural novels in which necessary detail about CID activities is unobtrusively communicated to the reader. The two inspectors make a good team: Thane is married, impetuous, and intuitive; bachelor Moss, who suffers from chronic indigestion, is a diligent researcher. The combination of fact and flair enables them to reach successful conclusions to a variety of cases, each presented in separate novels. Concentration upon one major case in each novel allows Knox to provide thorough and realistic background for both character and events and to include pertinent comments upon changing aspects of Scottish life. In *The Taste of Proof* he fuses detailed knowledge of illicit whisky manufacture and customs and excise procedures with commentary upon the effectiveness of slum redevelopment projects. *Children of the Mist*, in which the victim is a prize Aberdeen Angus, treats Scottish nationalism and disaffected youth as well as criminal activities. Knox's fascination with the

Hebrides is evident in *Sanctuary Isle* which takes Thane and Moss to a bird sanctuary in the Firth of Lorne.

In the Webb Carrick novels, all set at sea and on remote islands in the Hebrides, Knox puts to good use his knowledge of ships, deep-sea diving, fishing, and island life. Mingling suspense with action, he follows the careers of Carrick, Chief Officer of *HMS Marlin*, his crusty captain, James Shannon, and Chief Petty Officer William "Clapper" Bell through encounters with smugglers, spies, gun-runners, saboteurs, and hostile islanders. Espionage and oceanographic research are staples in many of the novels, and Carrick's ability to find a girl in every port adds perfunctory romantic interest. Typical is *The Klondyker* in which an attempt to confirm plesiosaurus sightings, deep-water salvage operations, and a search for a lost Spanish galleon display Carrick's talents as an investigator.

Less successful are the novels written under the MacLeod pseudonym. Jonathan Gaunt, an ex-paratrooper turned financial investigator, is a lifeless figure each of whose adventures, whether in Malta or Munich, follows a similar pattern. Considerably more violent than Knox's other work, these books lack both skilful plotting and memorable characters.

—Jeanne F. Bedell

KNOX, Ronald A(rbuthnott). British. Born in Knibworth, Leicestershire, 17 February 1888; son of the Bishop of Manchester; brother of the writer E. V. Knox. Educated at Summer Fields school, Oxford, 1896–1900; Eton College (Co-Editor, *The Outsider*, 1906), 1900–06; Balliol College, Oxford (Davies Scholar; Hertford Scholar, 1907; Ireland and Craven Scholar, 1908; Chancellor's Prize for Latin Verse, 1910), B.A. 1910. Worked at the War Office in military intelligence, summer 1916, 1917–18. Ordained Deacon, 1911, and Priest, 1912, Church of England; Fellow and Lecturer, 1910–17, and Chaplain, 1912–17, Trinity College, Oxford: resigned on being converted to Roman Catholicism, 1917: ordained, 1919: taught at St. Edmund's College, Hertfordshire, 1919–26; Catholic Chaplain, Oxford University, 1926–39: retired in 1939 to translate the Bible. D.Litt.: National University of Ireland, Dublin, 1954. Honorary Fellow, Trinity College, Oxford, 1941, and Balliol College, Oxford, 1953. Fellow, Royal Society of Literature, 1950. Protonotary Apostolic, 1951; Member, Pontifical Academy, 1956. *Died 24 August 1957.*

CRIME PUBLICATIONS

Novels (series character: Miles Bredon)

> *The Viaduct Murder.* London, Methuen, 1925; New York, Simon and Schuster, 1926.
> *The Three Taps: A Detective Story Without a Moral* (Bredon). London, Methuen, and New York, Simon and Schuster, 1927.
> *The Footsteps at the Lock* (Bredon). London, Methuen, 1928.
> *The Floating Admiral,* with others. London, Hodder and Stoughton, 1931; New York, Doubleday, 1932.
> *The Body in the Silo* (Bredon). London, Hodder and Stoughton, 1934; as *Settled Out of Court*, New York, Dutton, 1934.
> *Still Dead* (Bredon). London, Hodder and Stoughton, and New York, Dutton, 1934.
> *Six Against the Yard,* with others. London, Selwyn and Blount, 1936; as *Six Against Scotland Yard*, New York, Doubleday, 1936.
> *Double Cross Purposes* (Bredon). London, Hodder and Stoughton, 1937.

Uncollected Short Story

"Solved by Inspection," in *My Best Detective Story*.   London, Faber, 1931.

OTHER PUBLICATIONS

Novels

Memories of the Future, Being Memories of the Years 1915–72, Written in 1988 by Opal, Lady Porstock.   London, Methuen, and New York, Doran, 1923.
Sanctions: A Frivolity.   London, Methuen, 1924.
Other Eyes Than Ours.   London, Methuen, 1926.

Plays

Londinium Defensum (in Latin).   Ware, Hertfordshire, Edmundian, 1925.
Thesauropolemopompus (in Latin), with Albert B. Purdie.   Ware, Hertfordshire, Edmundian, 1925.

Verse

Signa Severa.   Privately printed, 1906.
Remigium Alarum.   Oxford, Blackwell, 1910.
Absolute and Abitofhel.   London, Society of SS. Peter and Paul, 1915.
Q. Horati Carminum Liber Quintus, with others.   Oxford, Blackwell, 1920.
In Three Tongues, edited by Laurence Eyres.   London, Chapman and Hall, 1959.

Other

Juxta Salices.   Privately printed, 1910.
A Still More Sporting Adventure!, with Charles R. L. Fletcher.   Oxford, Blackwell, 1911.
Naboth's Vineyard in Pawn (sermons).   London, Society of SS. Peter and Paul, 1913.
Some Loose Stones, Being a Consideration of Certain Tendencies in Modern Theology.   London and New York, Longman, 1913.
The Church in Bondage (sermons).   London, Society of SS. Peter and Paul, 1914.
An Hour at the Front (prayers).   London, Society of SS. Peter and Paul, 1914; abridgement as *Ten Minutes at the Front*, 1916.
Reunion All Round; or, Jael's Hammer Laid Aside.   London, Society of SS. Peter and Paul, 1914.
Bread or Stone: Four Conferences on Impetrative Prayer.   London, Society of SS. Peter and Paul, 1915.
An Apologia.   Privately printed, 1917.
The Essentials of Spritual Unity.   London, Catholic Truth Society, 1918.
A Spiritual Aeneid.   London and New York, Longman, 1918.
Meditations on the Psalms.   London, Longman, 1919.
Patrick Shaw-Stewart.   London, Collins, 1920.
A Book of Acrostics.   London, Methuen, 1924.
An Open-Air Pulpit.   London, Constable, 1926.
The Belief of Catholics.   London, Benn, and New York, Harper, 1927.
Anglican Cobwebs (sermons).   London, Sheed and Ward, 1928.
Essays in Satire.   London, Sheed and Ward, 1928; New York, Dutton, 1930.
Miracles.   New York, Paulist Press, 1928.
The Mystery of the Kingdom and Other Sermons.   London, Sheed and Ward, 1928.
The Rich Young Man: A Fantasy.   London, Sheed and Ward, 1928.

The Church on Earth.   London, Burns Oates, and New York, Macmillan, 1929.
On Getting There.   London, Methuen, 1929.
Caliban in Grub Street.   London, Sheed and Ward, and New York, Dutton, 1930.
Broadcast Minds.   London, Sheed and Ward, 1932; New York, Sheed and Ward, 1933.
Difficulties, Being a Correspondence about the Catholic Religion Between Ronald Knox and Arnold Lunn.   London, Eyre and Spottiswoode, 1932; revised edition, 1952.
Barchester Pilgrimage.   London, Sheed and Ward, 1935; New York, Sheed and Ward, 1936.
Heaven and Charing Cross: Sermons on the Holy Eucharist.   London, Burns Oates, 1935; New York, Dutton, 1936.
Let Dons Delight, Being Variations on a Theme in an Oxford Common-Room.   London and New York, Sheed and Ward, 1939.
Captive Flames: A Collection of Panegyrics.   London, Burns Oates, 1940; New York, Spritual Book Associates, 1941.
Nazi and Nazarene.   London, Macmillan, 1940.
In Soft Garments: A Collection of Oxford Conferences.   London, Burns Oates, and New York, Sheed and Ward, 1942.
I Believe: The Religion of the Apostles' Creed.   Reading, The Tablet, 1944.
God and the Atom.   London and New York, Sheed and Ward, 1945.
A Retreat for Priests.   London and New York, Sheed and Ward, 1946.
The Mass in Slow Motion (sermons).   London and New York, Sheed and Ward, 1948.
The Creed in Slow Motion (sermons).   London and New York, Sheed and Ward, 1949.
A Selection from the Occasional Sermons, edited by Evelyn Waugh.   London, Dropmore Press, 1949.
The Trials of a Translator.   New York, Sheed and Ward, and London, Burns Oates, 1949.
Enthusiasm: A Chapter in the History of Religion, with Special Reference to the XVII and XVIII Centuries.   Oxford, Clarendon Press, and New York, Oxford University Press, 1950.
The Gospel in Slow Motion (sermons).   London and New York, Sheed and Ward, 1950.
St. Paul's Gospel.   London, Catholic Truth Society, 1950; New York, Sheed and Ward, 1951.
Stimuli (sermons).   London and New York, Sheed and Ward, 1951.
The Hidden Stream: A Further Collection of Oxford Conferences.   London, Burns Oates, 1952; New York, Sheed and Ward, 1953.
A New Testament Commentary for English Readers.   New York, Sheed and Ward, 3 vols., 1952–56; London, Burns Oates, 3 vols., 1953–56.
Off the Record.   London, Sheed and Ward, 1953; New York, Sheed and Ward, 1954.
A Retreat for Lay People.   London and New York, Sheed and Ward, 1955.
The Window in the Wall and Other Sermons on the Holy Eucharist.   London, Burns Oates, and New York, Sheed and Ward, 1956.
Bridegroom and Bride.   London and New York, Sheed and Ward, 1957.
On English Translation (lecture).   Oxford, Clarendon Press, 1957.
Literary Distractions.   London and New York, Sheed and Ward, 1958.
The Priestly Life: A Retreat.   New York, Sheed and Ward, 1958; London, Sheed and Ward, 1959.
Lightning Meditations.   New York and London, Sheed and Ward, 1959.
Proving God: A New Apologetic.   London, The Month, 1959.
Retreat for Beginners.   New York, Sheed and Ward, 1960; as *Retreat in Slow Motion,* London, Sheed and Ward, 1961.
Occasional Sermons, The Pastoral Sermons, University and Anglican Sermons, edited by Philip Caraman.   London, Burns Oates, 3 vols., 1960–63; New York, Sheed and Ward, 3 vols., 1960–64.
The Layman and His Conscience: A Retreat.   New York, Sheed and Ward, 1961; London, Sheed and Ward, 1962.

Editor and translator, *The Miracles of King Henry VI.* Cambridge, University Press, 1923.

Editor and translator, *Virgil: Aeneid, Books vii to ix.* Oxford, Clarendon Press, 1924.

Editor, with Henry Harrington, *The Best Detective Stories of the Year 1928.* London, Faber, 1929; as *The Best English Detective Stories of 1928*, New York, Liveright, 1929.

Editor, with Henry Harrington, *The Best Detective Stories of the Year 1929.* London, Faber, 1930; as *The Best English Detective Stories of the Year*, New York, Liveright, 1930.

Editor, *The Holy Bible: An Abridgement and Rearrangement.* London and New York, Sheed and Ward, 1936.

Editor and translator, with others, *Manual of Prayers.* London, Burns Oates, 1942.

Editor, *Father Brown: Selected Stories*, by G. K. Chesterton. London, Oxford University Press, 1955.

Translator, *(Selected Poems)* (translated into Theocritan hexameters), by Robert Browning. Privately printed, 1908.

Translator, *The Holy Gospel of Jesus Christ According to Matthew.* Privately printed, 1941.

Translator, *The New Testament of Our Lord and Saviour Jesus Christ.* London, Burns Oates, and New York, Sheed and Ward, 1944.

Translator, *The Epistles and Gospels for Sundays and Holidays.* London, Burns Oates, and New York, Sheed and Ward, 1946.

Translator, *The Book of Psalms in Latin and English, with the Canticles Used in the Divine Office*, edited by H. Richards. London, Burns Oates, 1947; New York, Sheed and Ward, 1948.

Translator, *The Old Testament.* New York, Sheed and Ward, 2 vols., 1948–50; London, Burns Oates, 2 vols., 1949.

Translator, with J. O'Connell and H. P. R. Finberg, *The Missal in Latin and English.* London, Burns Oates, 1949; Westminster, Maryland, Newman Press, 1958.

Translator, *Encyclical Letter – Humani Genesis – of His Holiness Pius XII.* London, Catholic Truth Society, 1950.

Translator, *Holy Week: The Text of the Holy Week Offices.* London, Burns Oates, and New York, Sheed and Ward, 1951.

Translator, *The Holy Bible* (complete version). London, Burns Oates, 1955; New York, Sheed and Ward, 1956.

Translator, *Autobiography of a Saint: Thérèse of Lisieux.* London, Harvill Press, and New York, Kenedy, 1958.

Translator, with M. Oakley, *The Imitation of Christ*, by Thomas à Kempis. London, Burns Oates, 1959; New York, Sheed and Ward, 1960.

*   *   *

Father Ronald Knox was one of the first practitioners of Sherlockian scholarship; his "Studies in the Literature of Sherlock Holmes" first appeared in the *Blue Book 1912* and was reprinted in his *Essays in Satire* (1928). Conan Doyle, in a long letter to the author, expressed himself amused by the studies, and also amazed that "anyone should spend such pains on such material."

In a lecture on detective stories, Knox characterized them as "a highly specialized art-form which deserves, as such, its own literature," and differentiated them from thrillers in that "the action takes place before the story begins." His most notable contribution to the genre, however, is a Decalogue for detective-story writers reproduced in his introduction to *The Best Detective Stories of the Year 1928*. His ten commandments forbid the use of supernatural agencies, poisons unknown to science, Chinamen, fortuitous accidents, unaccountable intuitions, unidentified clues, and identical twins, and place strict limits on secret rooms and passages and the choice of the criminal (who must be "someone mentioned in the early part of the story" – but not the detective). Knox was a prominent member of the Detection Club presided over by his friend G. K. Chesterton.

A comparison of the two Catholic detective-story authors is instructive. Chesterton entered the Church in 1922 in search, he said, of greater freedom in an age of doubt. His genius overflowed every literary form he essayed; into his Father Brown stories he packed an entire philosophy of life, and the dumpy priest holding the rolled umbrella blinks out at us almost tangibly from the printed page. Knox was an Anglican priest seeking authority and discipline when, to the dismay of his father, the low-church Bishop of Manchester, he embraced the Roman faith in 1917. Though his works range widely from poetry to sermons, from acrostics to an able translation of the Bible, each of them keeps within traditional bounds. In particular, his six detective novels, considering his deep knowledge of the field, are disappointing, and his detective Miles Bredon is a faceless nonentity.

The Viaduct Murder was written towards the end of the author's seven-year stint as a master at St. Edmund's preparatory school and seminary in Hertfordshire. The body of the local atheist is found on a golf course below a railway viaduct. The amateur sleuths are the local parson and his three garrulous friends. Robert Speaight in his *Ronald Knox the Writer* (1966) defends the story as "an amiable skit on the Higher Criticism, on the mentality which insists on rejecting *a priori* any explanation which seems likely to be true." But most readers, though they praise the writing, damn the plot, with its unlikely clues, secret passages, and stupid criminal.

By the time he wrote *The Three Taps*, Knox was installed as Chaplain to Oxford's Catholic undergraduates. In his study in the ramshackle Old Palace he would type his various books between eight-o'clock Mass and lunch, after which his time was seldom his own. Bredon now makes his appearance; he resembles his creator only in smoking a pipe and playing Patience as an aid to thought (Knox favoured a difficult form of Canfield that "comes out" only once in a thousand games). Miles and his wife, the convent-bred Angela, chatter agreeably and quite unmemorably. "To be frank," writes Speaight, "Bredon is a bore." He is employed by the Indescribable Insurance Company, which will insure almost anyone against almost anything. In his first recorded case the detective investigates the death, by gas poisoning, of a manufacturer in a country pub. The taps of the title are the valves controlling the flow of gas, the chief question being whether they were open or shut. One critic complained of the novel that "its pointlessness and incoherence are almost startling." The best that can be said of it is that one or two minor characters are well done: Mr. Pulteney, an old schoolmaster on a fishing holiday, and an Anglican priest in the Catholic bishop's household, "unfrocked by his own conscience."

The Footsteps at the Lock concerns an empty canoe on the Thames near Oxford. The mystery of the missing occupant is probed in lackadaisical fashion. "You know that Bredon will read the riddle," writes Speaight, "but you do not feel it."

Undoubtedly the best of Knox's mysteries is *The Body in the Silo* (*Settled Out of Court*). Particularly in its concluding scenes, in which the devilry of the murderer is revealed, does the story, set on the beautiful banks of the Wye, attain some of the glow of a fairly good Christie novel.

Still Dead is a Scottish mystery set in a part of the Highlands familiar to the author through his visits to Lady Lovat's home at Beaufort Castle near Inverness. Colin Reiver, driving his new sports car, runs over a little boy and is sent away until local feeling subsides. His dead body is seen early one morning near the family home; a few minutes later it is gone, only to reappear at exactly the same place 48 hours later. The clues are presented fairly, but Knox's style hardly makes for an exciting story. *Double Cross Purposes* begins with a fine description of the Highland countryside, but the mystery is implausible. The Indescribable insures a treasure-hunter against the risk of his shady partner absconding with their find, if any, and Bredon goes up to Scotland to watch the pair. Mr. Pulteney makes a welcome reappearance, but generally the book is a final disappointment. During a cruise, young Lady Acton cast her copy of the book into the Mediterranean, along with her lipstick, of which Father Knox had expressed disapproval. We applaud her judgment.

—Norman Donaldson

KURNITZ, Harry. See **PAGE, Marco.**

KYD, Thomas. Pseudonym for Alfred B(ennett) Harbage. American. Born in Philadelphia, Pennsylvania, 18 July 1901. Educated at the University of Pennsylvania, Philadelphia, A.B. 1924; A.M. 1926; Ph.D. 1929. Married Eliza Price Finnesey in 1926; two daughters and two sons. Member of the Department from 1924, and Professor, 1942–47, University of Pennsylvania; Professor of English and Comparative Literature, Columbia University, New York, 1947–52; Professor of English, 1952–60, and Cabot Professor, 1960–70, then Professor Emeritus, Harvard University, Cambridge, Massachusetts. Alexander Lecturer, Toronto University, 1954–55. Trustee, American Shakespeare Festival, Stratford, Connecticut; Member of the Editorial Board, *Studies in English Literature, Studies in Renanissance Drama, Shakespeare Studies, Shakespeare Quarterly.* General Editor, Pelican Shakespeare series. Recipient: Guggenheim Fellowship, 1952, 1965; Modern Language Association Macmillan Book Award. M.A.: Harvard University, 1952; D.Litt.: University of Pennsylvania, 1954. *Died 2 May 1976.*

CRIME PUBLICATIONS

Novels (series character: Sam Phelan)

> *Blood Is a Beggar* (Phelan).   Philadelphia, Lippincott, 1946; London, Hammond, 1949.
> *Blood of Vintage* (Phelan).   Philadelphia, Lippincott, 1947; London, Hammond, 1950.
> *Blood on the Bosom Devine* (Phelan).   Philadelphia, Lippincott, 1948.
> *Cover His Face.*   Philadelphia, Lippincott, 1949.

Uncollected Short Stories

> "High Court," in *Ellery Queen's Awards, 8th Series.*   Boston, Little Brown, 1953; London, Gollancz, 1955.
> "The Letter," in *Ellery Queen's Mystery Magazine* (New York), February 1956.
> "Cottage for August," in *Ellery Queen's Awards, 12th Series.*   New York, Simon and Schuster, 1957; London, Collins, 1959.

OTHER PUBLICATIONS as Alfred B. Harbage

Other

> *Thomas Killigrew: Cavalier Dramatist.* Philadelphia, University of Pennsylvania Press, and London, Oxford University Press, 1930.
> *Sir William Davenant, Poet-Venturer.* Philadelphia, University of Pennsylvania Press, and London, Oxford University Press, 1935.
> *Cavalier Drama.* New York, Modern Language Association, and London, Oxford University Press, 1936.
> *Annals of English Drama, 975–1700.* Philadelphia, University of Pennsylvania Press, 1940.
> *Shakespeare's Audience.* New York, Columbia University Press, 1941.
> *As They Liked It: An Essay on Shakespeare and Morality.* New York, Macmillan, 1947.
> *Shakespeare and the Rival Traditions.* New York, Macmillan, 1952.
> *Theater for Shakespeare.* Toronto, University of Toronto Press, 1955.
> *William Shakespeare: A Reader's Guide.* New York, Farrar Straus, 1963.
> *Conceptions of Shakespeare.* Cambridge, Massachusetts, Harvard University Press, 1966.
> *Shakespeare Without Words and Other Essays.* Cambridge, Massachusetts, Harvard University Press, 1972.

> Editor, *The Tempest*, by Shakespeare. New York, Crofts, 1946.
> Editor, *As You Like It*, by Shakespeare. New York, Crofts, 1948.
> Editor, *The Tragedy of Macbeth*, by Shakespeare. London, Penguin, 1956.
> Editor, *The Tragedy of King Lear*, by Shakespeare. London, Penguin, 1958.
> Editor, with Douglas Bush, *Shakespeare's Sonnets.* London, Penguin, 1961.
> Editor, *Love's Labour's Lost*, by Shakespeare. London, Penguin, 1963.
> Editor, *Shakespeare: The Tragedies: A Collection of Critical Essays.* Englewood Cliffs, New Jersey, Prentice Hall, 1964.
> Editor, with Richard Wilbur, *Poems*, by Shakespeare. London, Penguin, 1965.
> Editor, *Henry V*, by Shakespeare. London, Penguin, 1965.

*   *   *

Alfred B. Harbage was an eminent Shakespearean scholar. Under the name of Thomas Kyd, which is both a donnish disclaimer and a generic pioneer's self-assertion, he wrote in the last four years of the 1940's four rather bloody murder mysteries which combine in a unique way the essence of the hard-boiled school with a tone of academic persiflage. The first and best of the four, *Blood Is a Beggar*, is actually set in the university, dramatically setting the two styles, in the police and the dons, side by side. The last, and the least successful, *Cover His Face*, moves away from the Philadelphia of the first three to rural England, where an incredibly bumbling academic hot on Dr. Johnson's trail stumbles into a murder. In this novel Harbage is plainly the farceur, a trifle sophomoric in his depiction of academic ineptitude. Barzun and Taylor's description of the novel as a "Crispinesque entertainment" is accurate, and may be read as either invitation or admonition.

The first three novels, however, create and enlarge upon a police world, a comic chain-of-being of law officers: J. Roth Newbold, the artistocratic district attorney, college graduate, all tidy pinstripes and gold-rimmed pince-nez, is in fairly constant conflict with both Chief of Police Cleveland Jones, a literate man who has walked a beat, and the Chief's most able subordinate, the principal detective in these novels, Sam Phelan, former boxer, more thick-headed in the third than the first novel, yet practical, adaptable, and, under the hand of the Chief, not averse to some literary reading; he also plays chess.

The three novels are formulaic: the murder is committed in the first chapter (though in the third novel it comes in chapter two). The police are called in, a little self-enclosed world is scrutinized by a somewhat mystified but never overawed Phelan – the university, the landed gentry, the burlesque theatre. Phelan arrives at the wrong conclusion; then, with some help from his associates, especially the Chief, the right conclusion. He places himself at risk to flush the murderer out of hiding. Each novel ends with an attempt by the Chief to pair the unmarried Phelan with a heroine who is unsuitable to him for various reasons – the English departmental secretary (she is the murderess), the mainline aristocrat (she is too little of the earth), the striptease artiste (she is too much of the earth).

What sets Thomas Kyd off from the Inneses and the Crispins is not so much his treatment (in the first novel) of the university as a real place; Amanda Cross and, in *Deadly Meeting*, Robert Bernard would subsequently do as well or better. What stands out is his skilful depiction of the interplay between educated and cultivated people on the one hand, and practical self-educated detectives on the other. But *inter*play: the D.A. is not as cultivated as he thinks he is, and Phelan is not as much the boor as he seems to be. Harbage's particular role, as a pioneer of the realistic crime novel of academe, was to bridge the gap between the snobbish Newbolds and the philistine Phelans. Though the second and third novels, representing a diminution of quality, show him moving further from the university, he remains the hard-boiled academic, his professorial tone addressed to both gallery and groundlings, writing the detective novel as they *both* liked it.

—Barrie Hayne

KYLE, Sefton.   See **VICKERS, Roy C.**

LA BERN, Arthur (Joseph).   British.   Born in London, 28 February 1909. Educated at the Sorbonne, Paris. Journalist: crime reporter, feature writer, and war correspondent for the *Daily Mirror, Evening Standard,* and *Daily Mail,* all London. Address: Killingan Beg, Churchtown, Lezayre, Isle of Man, United Kingdom.

CRIME PUBLICATIONS

Novels

  It Always Rains on Sunday.   London, Nicholson and Watson, 1945.
  Night Darkens the Street.   London, Nicholson and Watson, 1947.
  Paper Orchid.   London, Marlowe, 1948.
  Pennygreen Street.   London, Jarrolds, 1950.
  The Big Money-Box.   London, Kimber, 1960.
  Brighton Belle.   London, W. H. Allen, 1963.
  Goodbye Piccadilly, Farewell Leicester Square.   London, W. H. Allen, 1966; New
    York, Stein and Day, 1967; as *Frenzy,* London, White Lion, 1971.

A Nice Class of People.   London, W. H. Allen, 1969.
Nightmare.   London, W. H. Allen, 1975.

Uncollected Short Story

"Sentimental Beat," in *The Saint* (New York), December 1954.

OTHER PUBLICATIONS

Novels

It Was Christmas Every Day.   London, Jarrolds, 1952.
It Will Be Warmer When It Snows.   London, W. H. Allen, 1966.
Hallelujah!   London, W. H. Allen, 1973.
The Last Cruise.   London, W. H. Allen, 1977.

Plays

Screenplays: *Freedom to Die*, 1962; *Time to Remember*, 1962; *Dead Man's Evidence*, with Gordon Wellesley, 1962; *Incident at Midnight*, 1963; *Accidental Death*, 1963; *The Verdict*, 1964.

Other

The Life and Death of a Lady-Killer (biography of George Joseph Smith). London, Frewin, 1967.
Haigh: The Mind of a Murderer.   London, W. H. Allen, 1973.

Arthur La Bern comments:
  I really don't think any novelist can make a detached statement on his own fiction. I think I am a writer of general fiction rather than a specialist in the detective genre. Most of my novels have a crime element, but the detectives, except in *The Big Money-Box*, rarely emerge as main characters.

                            *   *   *

  Surprisingly, Arthur La Bern's detective fiction, so well known in Britain, is difficult to acquire in the United States and unfamiliar. Only *Goodbye Piccadilly, Farewell Leicester Square* (reprinted as *Frenzy* and made into a film by Alfred Hitchcock) has had an American audience. His best seller *It Always Rains on Sunday*, which was made into a highly popular movie, remains unpublished in the United States. Perhaps it is that La Bern's fiction is too British, but not in the manner that Americans like. His is not the England of barristers and solicitors, nor of Scotland Yard with its inimitable cast, or of the British gentry. His is the England of London, of Piccadilly Circus or Coronet Grove, not of Curzon Street, Bloomsbury, or Fleet Street. Drab days, vulgar, dreary people struggling to make ends meet and to find a spark of gaiety in an otherwise shabby life, kip houses, pubs, and stinking tenements, and unexpected endings which profoundly disturb our sense of how things ought to be, and how detective fiction should close, are the hallmarks of his works.
  It Always Rains on Sunday opens describing a dreary, wet London day and a view of Coronet Grove. Rose Sandigate, once the lover of Tommy Swann, a petty crook, now lives with two step-daughters and a dependable, adoring, but colorless husband. A domestic spat between Rose and her stepdaughter, Vi, grows out of hand and Vi, with an innocent face and a floozy's dress, storms out of the house as Rose rages at her husband, demanding that he make his daughters toe the line. Rose has put her affair with the flashy Tommy behind her,

but when he turns up at her door on this particularly trying day, reporting that he has escaped from jail and is on the run, she is hard-pressed to know which loyalties to honor. La Bern arranges the happenings of the day chronologically, depicting the happenings of a number of the households in the Coronet Grove area. His tale starts lazily enough, giving us a panoramic view of the characters who will figure in the events of the day, showing each going about his business from the time he or she wakes until the time when events begin to catch up with each of them, and unite them in unanticipated ways. La Bern's narrative technique seems to imitate James Joyce's in "the Wandering Rocks" episode of *Ulysses*, and it achieves the same effect of diminishing the importance of the human will in shaping events. The characters are caught, in time, in place, and they can only muddle about, trying to make sense of themselves, but ill-equipped to shape either themselves or events. Fothergill, a CID cop, and Slopey Collins, a newspaper man (he reappears in other of La Bern books), arrive simultaneously at Rose's door only moments after Tommy's clumsy flight. Their combined wits bring about the capture of Swann and the arrest of several petty criminals whose theft of roller skates has been mishandled. But La Bern is not an author who believes in society's power to protect itself or its ability to make the law serve justice; nor is he a writer with much faith in human wit or will. His characters are ineffectual. They may be passionately or stubbornly committed to their own sense of who they are and what they deserve, but this commitment does not serve them well. They react rather than act; they are tenacious, but they fail. La Bern refuses to end this tale bestowing plaudits upon the detective in the manner of Arthur Conan Doyle, or, like John D. MacDonald, celebrating the cunning and peculiar breed of morality of a Travis Magee. La Bern's people bungle. When darkness falls on the Sunday of this story, Rose has committed suicide, Tommy is sentenced to hang for a murder he did not commit, Vi is outsmarted and robbed of the illegally acquired booty she holds for her lover, and her lover, Whitey, confesses to his role in a theft to prevent Fothergill from fingering him for the violent murder of Beasley, a fence. The cop and the newspaper man have done a good day's work; criminals have been caught, confessions forced, certain crimes stopped, but the criminals are facing the wrong sentences, and the capturing of them did not avert further wrongdoing, but precipitated it. Lives have been altered by the events of the day; a man has lost his wife and seen glimpses of her inner life he knew nothing about; a brash ne'er-do-well will hang because he took a few bucks off a dead man during his escape; and a sassy, nubile girl who sought a swanky hotel and glitzy musicians to turn her head lies in a flophouse, knowing that no one is coming back to court and care for her. The last scene is of Vi's father in the morgue blankly identifying the corpse of his wife.

Night Darkens the Street continues La Bern's interest in cheap, overly ambitious young girls whose stubborn independence throws them and those they come in contact with into events beyond their control. Gwen Rawlings flees her house and her father's beatings and takes a job as a hat-check girl in a London club. There she mingles with unsavory types and is framed by a scorned employee for a crime she did not commit. Sentenced to a remand home, separated from the only man who made her feel worthwhile, Gwen changes. Whatever conscience she once had is numbed by what has happened to her. Her dreams thwarted, the only love she knew denied her, when she escapes from the home it is into the hands of two men who have wantonly murdered a lorry-driver who, earlier, had picked Gwen up. Gwen is named as one of his murderers and with her criminal past and her reputation in West End as "Champagne Gwen," the trial at Old Bailey ends with her conviction. The trial brings Gwen the stardom she had always longed for, the role that had taken her away from her father's home to a life she knew nothing about. When her mother comes to visit the wretched girl in the jail, Gwen is incapable of seeing her. For her, everything always came too late.

Goodbye Piccadilly, Farewell Leicester Square is the best of La Bern's writings. The protagonist, Dick Blamey, an ex-Squadron leader who once won an award for distinguished service, has fallen on hard times. Shortly after he has called upon his ex-wife at her matrimonial agency to borrow money and has been overheard to have been arguing with her, his ex-wife is found murdered, the victim of a sex maniac, and her office mate's testimony points to Blamey. The plot is brilliantly contrived as Blamey, convinced that he must flee the law until he is able to clear his name, tries both to determine the identity of the killer and to avoid arrest himself. During this period, he becomes involved with another woman, who, too, is brutally murdered. He is caught, tried for the second murder, and found guilty. But it is the concluding chapters of the book that are the most extraordinary. Accustomed to sudden reversals at the close of detective fiction, the reader expects Blamey miraculously to save himself, or at least discover the identity of the true killer. La Bern has drawn Blamey sympathetically, and we badly want him to succeed. The end is shocking and bitter, a tour de force that totally upsets the reader's assumptions.

La Bern's plots are gripping, his characters real, and his sense of the helplessness of humans profoundly disturbing. In his chosen genre, he is a master.

—Carol Simpson Stern

LACY, Ed. Pseudonym for Len Zinberg (Leonard S. Zinberg); also wrote as Steve April. American. Born in New York City in 1911. Married; one child. Magazine writer; Correspondent for *Yank* during World War II. Recipient: Twentieth Century-Fox Literary Fellowship; Mystery Writers of America Edgar Allan Poe Award, 1958. *Died 7 January 1968.*

CRIME PUBLICATIONS

Novels (series characters: Lee Hayes; Toussaint Moore; Dave Wintino)

The Woman Aroused. New York, Avon, 1951; London, Hale, 1969.
Sin in Their Blood. New York, Eton, 1952; as *Death in Passing,* London, Boardman, 1959.
Strip for Violence. New York, Eton, 1953.
Enter Without Desire. New York, Avon, 1954.
Go for the Body. New York, Avon, 1954; London, Boardman, 1959.
The Best That Ever Did It. New York, Harper, 1955; London, Hutchinson, 1957; as *Visa to Death,* New York, Permabooks, 1956.
The Men from the Boys. New York, Harper, 1956; London, Boardman, 1960.
Lead with Your Left (Wintino). New York, Harper, and London, Boardman, 1957.
Room to Swing (Moore). New York, Harper, 1957; London, Boardman, 1958.
Breathe No More, My Lady. New York, Avon, 1958.
Devil for the Witch. London, Boardman, 1958.
Be Careful How You Live. New York, Harper, and London, Boardman, 1958; as *Dead End,* New York, Pyramid, 1960.
Shakedown for Murder. New York, Avon, 1958.
Blonde Bait. Rockville Centre, New York, Zenith, 1959.
The Big Fix. New York, Pyramid, 1960; London, Boardman, 1961.
A Deadly Affair. New York, Hillman, 1960.
Bugged for Murder. New York, Avon, 1961.
The Freeloaders. New York, Berkley, 1961; London, Boardman, 1962.
South Pacific Affair. New York, Belmont, 1961.
The Sex Castle. New York, Paperback Library, 1963; London, Digit, 1965; as *Shoot It Again,* New York, Paperback Library, 1969.
Two Hot to Handle. New York, Paperback Library, 1963; London, Digit, 1966.
Moment of Untruth (Moore). New York, Lancer, 1964; London, Boardman, 1965.

Sleep in Thunder.   New York, Grosset and Dunlap, 1964.
Pity the Honest.   London, Boardman, 1964; New York, Macfadden, 1965.
Harlem Underground (Hayes).   New York, Pyramid, 1965.
Double Trouble (Wintino).   London, Boardman, 1965; New York, Lancer, 1967.
The Hotel Dwellers.   New York, Harper, 1966; London, Hale, 1968.
In Black and Whitey (Hayes).   New York, Lancer, 1967.
The Napalm Bugle.   New York, Pyramid, 1968.
The Big Bust.   New York, Pyramid, 1969; London, New English Library, 1970.

Uncollected Short Stories

"The Real Sugar," in *Ellery Queen's Mystery Magazine* (New York), November 1957.
"I Did It for − Me," in *The Saint* (New York), September 1962.
"The Frozen Custard Caper," in *Ellery Queen's Mystery Magazine* (New York), January
    1963.
"The Devil You Know," in *The Saint* (New York), April 1963.
"Stickler for Details," in *A Pride of Felons*, edited by The Gordons.   New York,
    Macmillan, 1963.
"The Square Root of Death," in *The Saint* (New York), October 1964.
"The Juicy Mango Caper," in *Ellery Queen's Mystery Magazine* (New York), February
    1966.
"Sic Transit ...," in *The Saint* (New York), March 1966.
"Break in the Routine," in *Ellery Queen's Mystery Magazine* (New York), June 1966.
"The Eunuch," in *The Saint* (New York), August 1966.
"More Than One Way to Skin a Cat," in *Ellery Queen's Mystery Magazine* (New York),
    July 1968.

OTHER PUBLICATIONS as Len Zinberg

Novels

Walk Hard − Talk Loud.   Indianapolis, Bobbs Merrill, 1940.
What D'ya Know for Sure.   New York, Doubleday, 1947; as *Strange Desires*, New
    York, Avon, 1948.
Hold with the Hares.   New York, Doubleday, 1948.
Route 13 (as Steve April).   New York, Funk and Wagnalls, 1954.

Manuscript Collection: Mugar Memorial Library, Boston University.

*   *   *

Before the civil rights movement made it fashionable, Ed Lacy made blacks a part of
mystery fiction. Though himself a white man, Lacy had many friends in communities such as
Harlem, and he wrote with considerable understanding about blacks. Two of his books are
about Toussaint Moore, a black postal worker turned private detective. A sensitive man,
Moore is torn between the security of his government job and the chance of greater riches in
detective work which, though it repels him, he is good at. The first Moore book, *Room to
Swing*, won an Edgar. The second, *Moment of Untruth*, in addition to being a good mystery
with a bullfighting background tells much about tourism in Mexico from the viewpoint of a
black.

Lacy also created a black police detective, Lee Hayes, who, like Moore, is conscious of his
color but does not practice reverse discrimination. He is featured in *Harlem Underground* and
In Black and Whitey, both dealing with urban violence.

When the race of Lacy's detectives was not distinctive, their stature was. Barney Harris,
the private detective in *The Best That Ever Did It*, weighs 248 pounds. Hal Darling, the

private detective in *Strip for Violence*, is only 5' 1" tall but a judo expert and a former flyweight boxer; Lee Hayes had also been a fighter.

Lacy's interest in boxing was a long-standing one. His non-mystery novel *Walk Hard – Talk Loud* is about boxing and became a Broadway play. Boxers are important in his mystery short stories such as "The Real Sugar," with a welterweight who constantly overeats yet never has trouble meeting the weight limit, and "The Juicy Mango Caper," about a West Indian robbery planned by Big Gabe, a former heavyweight boxer. The dialogue is excellent, reflecting Lacy's ear for Caribbean speech. Under the pseudonym Steve April he also wrote of extravagantly planned crimes, one of which, "The Greatest Snatch in History" (1967), is about a plot to kidnap the President of the United States.

Most of Lacy's novels sold only to the paperback original market and give evidence of having been rushed in their writing. Yet they were certainly better and more subtle than the titles under which they were published – *The Woman Aroused, Sin in Their Blood, Strip for Violence, The Sex Castle*, and *The Big Bust*. Lacy's work was entertaining and remarkably consistent, and it frequently carried a great deal of meaning. He died before a new race consciousness might have found him the very large audience he deserved.

—Marvin Lachman

LANGE, John. See **CRICHTON, Michael.**

LATHEN, Emma. Pseudonym for Mary J. Latis and Martha Hennissart; also write as R. B. Dominic. The authors met as graduate students at Harvard University, Cambridge, Massachusetts. Latis is an attorney, Hennissart an economic analyst. Recipients: Crime Writers Association Silver Dagger, 1967.

CRIME PUBLICATIONS

Novels (series character: John Putnam Thatcher in all books)

Banking on Death. New York, Macmillan, 1961; London, Gollancz, 1962.
A Place for Murder. New York, Macmillan, and London, Gollancz, 1963.
Accounting for Murder. New York, Macmillan, 1964; London, Gollancz, 1965.
Death Shall Overcome. New York, Macmillan, 1966; London, Gollancz, 1967.
Murder Makes the Wheels Go Round. New York, Macmillan, and London, Gollancz, 1966.
Murder Against the Grain. New York, Macmillan, and London, Gollancz, 1967.
A Stitch in Time. New York, Macmillan, and London, Gollancz, 1968.
Come to Dust. New York, Simon and Schuster, 1968; London, Gollancz, 1969.
When in Greece. New York, Simon and Schuster, and London, Gollancz, 1969.
Murder to Go. New York, Simon and Schuster, 1969; London, Gollancz, 1970.
Pick Up Sticks. New York, Simon and Schuster, 1970; London, Gollancz, 1971.

Ashes to Ashes. New York, Simon and Schuster, and London, Gollancz, 1971.
The Longer the Thread. New York, Simon and Schuster, 1971; London, Gollancz, 1972.
Murder Without Icing. New York, Simon and Schuster, 1972; London, Gollancz, 1973.
Sweet and Low. New York, Simon and Schuster, and London, Gollancz, 1974.
By Hook or by Crook. New York, Simon and Schuster, and London, Gollancz, 1975.
Double, Double, Oil and Trouble. New York, Simon and Schuster, 1978; London, Gollancz, 1979.

Novels as R. B. Dominic (series character: Ben Safford in all books)

Murder Sunny Side Up. New York and London, Abelard Schuman, 1968.
Murder in High Place. London, Macmillan, 1969; New York, Doubleday, 1970.
There Is No Justice. New York, Doubleday, 1971; as *Murder Out of Court,* London, Macmillan, 1971.
Epitaph for a Lobbyist. New York, Doubleday, and London, Macmillan, 1974.
Murder Out of Commission. New York, Doubleday, and London, Macmillan, 1976.

*   *   *

Writing as Emma Lathen and R. B. Dominic, Martha Hennissart and Mary J. Latis have created two series of novels. Each group is well done; each has attracted many fans, but the Lathen books, featuring the Wall Street banker John Putnam Thatcher as amateur detective, were established earlier and are the better known.

The writing team's great skill at characterization is evident in almost every portrayal, ranging from the ever-present Thatcher and his Sloan Guaranty Trust colleagues through the major characters in the individual books to brief, vivid portraits of minor characters. The effect is both charming and brilliant, for the memorable characters rivet the reader's interest and simplify what could have proved an almost impossible task.

Each of the Thatcher books hinges upon some facet of the financial world. The authors must make each business deal quickly and readily clear to the readers, most of whom lack detailed knowledge of finance. The range of businesses examined is generous: chicanery at the National Calculating Company (*Accounting for Murder*), trickery during a Russian wheat deal (*Murder Against the Grain*), and duplicity in the garment industry (*The Longer the Thread*), for instance. Lathen makes the business manipulations palatable and apprehendable in two ways. First, Thatcher and his colleagues lay the situation out in simple, direct terms during staff huddles at the Sloan. Secondly, the books' other sharply drawn characters are themselves fascinated by the deals. They too discuss them freely and informatively, and their grasp is passed along to the reader who can be counted on to be patient because of his interest in the characters. *By Hook or by Crook* is an excellent example of this method. This device also ensures that the novels fall into the closed-circle-of suspects school which not only demands full characterization but also limits the field of inquiry to areas where the banker's special knowledge and habits of mind, honed by long service to the Sloan, give him an advantage over the investigating police. No animosity ensues, however, and Thatcher often works closely with professional detectives.

The authors avoid overexposure for Thatcher by releasing details of his life only bit by bit. This practice is acceptable because he is a reserved, distinguished widower whose chief interest in life is his work at the Sloan. Thatcher is human enough to be intriguing, private enough not to be overwhelming. Humanizing touches are carefully provided. While some are fairly commonplace – gifts must be purchased for grandchildren, obligatory family dinners must be endured – others are surprising – the urbane Thatcher is also a long distance hiker, and in *Pick Up Sticks* he is happily tackling the Appalachian Trail when murder interrupts. The ultimate result of these devices is that Thatcher joins the ranks of amateur sleuths whose expertise, whose well developed powers of observation, and whose entrée into special interest groups serve their powers of deduction. Wall Street may not be one of the mean streets, but Thatcher is wordly and pragmatic enough to realize that avarice and murder occur on boulevards and in mansions as well as in less privileged neighborhoods.

Traditionally, the banker is seconded by one of his fellow officers at the Sloan, most frequently by an unlikely but useful companion at detection, the elderly Everett Gabler who is given to peculiar, soothing diets. Fussy and particular, Gabler is also human, for when he helps unravel a case involving dog shows and kennel owners (*A Place for Murder*) he is captivated by a Welsh terrier and is as precise in describing bloodlines as he is in handling accounts.

The Lathen team's understanding of human nature is never more apparent than when they delineate the non-continuing characters who form the cores of the novels. In *Murder to Go*, Iris Young's intense jealousy of the superior ability and position of her husband's partner triggers a subplot creating much of the novel's interest. Iris's ambition is credible and honestly portrayed, and she is one of many characters who help the reader to understand the thrill of financial acumen and success. Careful attention is also given to the motivations of the killers. The writers never excuse misdeeds, but do ensure that the rationale for criminal behavior is clearly drawn. Thus, heroes and villains alike contribute to the realism of this series.

The authors consistently use humor to underscore their penetrating glimpses of human nature. At times the humor is gently rueful, as when the team examines the generation gap (a social phenomenon appearing in several books) in *Pick Up Sticks*, where grown children are satirized for trying to parent their own parents. The humor is generally ironic, and in the hands of these writers irony is a pointed and point-making tool.

The Dominic series, featuring the Ohio Congressman Ben Safford and a continuing cast of his legislative colleagues, naturally takes Washington as its locale and government as its source of mystery and murder, and the plots are organized as in the Lathen series. Again, the portraits of non-continuing personalities are remarkably vivid, for instance, Pauline Ives, a successful capital attorney and the neatly contrasted Neva Torrance, a beautiful social climber, in *There Is No Justice*. Safford's trips to his constituency offer other settings for mayhem (*Murder Out of Commission*) and introduce his sister and political adviser, Janet. The perennially rumpled Safford is astute though unassuming and shrewd though comfortable, like Thatcher only in his ability to apply special knowledge to amateur detection.

Both series incorporate serious social commentary, usually informed by irony. *Epitaph for a Lobbyist* treats political bribery, and *A Stitch in Time* finds Thatcher unmasking physicians who prescribe and dispense expensive drugs under their own labels. Occasionally, as in *Death Shall Overcome*, the seriousness of the subject, here racial bigotry, produces straight criticism rather than ironic treatment, though the resulting characterizations are weaker than usual.

Generally speaking, however, the books are very well crafted, and the devices brilliantly handled. In many ways, Thatcher and Safford symbolize staid members of American culture who, despite their own restraint and law-abiding natures, cannot help being touched by either less admirable citizens or the central social questions of the day, and the novels prove that social comment, humor, clever detection, and splendid plotting can go happily hand in hand.

—Jane S. Bakerman

LATIMER, Jonathan (Wyatt). Also writes as Peter Coffin. American. Born in Chicago, Illinois, 23 October 1906. Educated at Mesa Ranch School, Arizona, 1922–25; Knox College, Galesburg, Illinois, A.B. 1929. Served in the United States Navy, 1942–45.

Married 1) Ellen Baxter Peabody in 1937, one daughter and two sons; 2) Jo Ann Hanzlik in 1954. Journalist: reporter, *Herald-Examiner* (later Chicago *Tribune*), 1930–33; screenwriter after 1940. Address: 1532 Copade Oro Drive, La Jolla, California 92037, U.S.A.

CRIME PUBLICATIONS

Novels (series character: Bill Crane)

Murder in the Madhouse (Crane). New York, Doubleday, and London, Hurst and Blackett, 1935.
Headed for a Hearse (Crane). New York, Doubleday, 1935; London, Methuen, 1936.
The Lady in the Morgue (Crane). New York, Doubleday, 1936; London, Methuen, 1937.
The Search for My Great Uncle's Head (as Peter Coffin). New York, Doubleday, 1937.
The Dead Don't Care (Crane). New York, Doubleday, and London, Methuen, 1938.
Red Gardenias (Crane). New York, Doubleday, and London, Methuen, 1939; as *Some Dames Are Deadly*, New York, Spivak, 1955.
Solomon's Vineyard. London, Methuen, 1941; as *The Fifth Grave*, New York, Popular Library, 1950.
Sinners and Shrouds. New York, Simon and Schuster, 1955; London, Methuen, 1956.
Black Is the Fashion for Dying. New York, Random House, 1959; as *The Mink-Lined Coffin*, London, Methuen, 1960.

OTHER PUBLICATIONS

Novel

Dark Memory. New York, Doubleday, and London, Methuen, 1940.

Plays

Screenplays: *The Lone Wolf Spy Hunt*, 1939; *Phantom Raiders*, with William R. Lipman, 1940; *Topper Returns*, with Gordon Douglas and Paul Gerard Smith, 1941; *A Night in New Orleans*, 1941; *The Glass Key*, 1942; *They Won't Believe Me*, with Gordon McDonell, 1946; *Nocturne*, with Frank Fenton and Rowland Brown, 1946; *The Big Clock*, with Harold Goldman, 1947; *Sealed Verdict*, 1948; *Beyond Glory*, with Charles Marquis Warren and William Wister Haines, 1948; *The Night Has a Thousand Eyes*, with Barré Lyndon, 1948; *Alias Nick Beal*, with Mindret Lord, 1949; *Copper Canyon*, with Richard English, 1950; *The Redhead and the Cowboy*, with Liam O'Brien and Charles Marquis Warren, 1951; *Submarine Command*, 1951; *Botany Bay*, 1953; *Plunder of the Sun*, 1953; *Back from Eternity*, with Richard Carroll, 1956; *The Unholy Wife*, with William Durkee, 1957; *The Whole Truth*, 1958.

Television Plays: *Perry Mason* series, 1960–65.

*   *   *

At the start of the 1934 novel *Murder in the Madhouse*, one William Crane is committed to an asylum for the mentally disturbed. Some three murders and 250 pages later the reader is informed that William Crane is a private detective. The more astute and prescient among the book's original readers might well have concluded that they had been present at the debut of one of the most memorable and original detective series in modern mystery fiction. Jonathan Latimer's Bill Crane series represents the very best of the "screwball comedy" school of 1930's mystery fiction. Dashiell Hammett's *The Thin Man* (also published in 1934) is considered the archetype of the school, but Latimer's Crane mysteries, particularly *The Lady in the Morgue*, may well be considered the apotheosis. In addition, they clearly foreshadowed the tongue-in-cheek hard-boiled romps of the 1950's and 1960's: Richard S. Prather's Shell Scott series is a good example.

Some blurb writers have described Bill Crane as an "alcoholic private detective"; technically correct perhaps, but, in truth, Crane's consumption of booze is no more prodigious than that of most detectives of the hard-boiled fraternity. Crane differs from his brethren in that the stuff goes to his head; consequently, he does most of his detecting, if one can call it that, in a giddy, stuporous fog. Much the rest of the time he's hung over, in varying degrees of severity. The liquor doesn't impair his deductive abilities, nor his talent for cracking wise; but it does slow his motor reflexes – Crane is not the most reliable private eye to have handy in a brawl.

The third Crane novel, *The Lady in the Morgue*, is a genuine mystery classic. Latimer moves Crane and his drinking buddies, Doc Williams and Tom O'Malley, through a bizarre series of events at breakneck pace, beginning with a corpsenapping and ending with Crane under a sheet on a morgue slab. In between there are murders and shooting scrapes, a riot in a taxi dance hall, a midnight grave-robbing expedition, plenty of boozing, and the snappiest, wittiest dialogue to be found anywhere. *The Lady in the Morgue* is grotesque and hilarious at the same time, a masterpiece of black comedy. The murder mystery proper is slight, Crane's approach to "detection" might outrage purists, and the final unmasking is unsurprising; but the trip is so wonderfully entertaining that one can readily forgive Latimer's failure to attend to Holmesian rigor.

The final Crane novel, *Red Gardenias*, is rather more sedate, but no less entertaining. Crane is teamed with Ann Fortune, the daughter of his agency's boss, and they pose as husband and wife in an undercover investigation. Their witty exchanges are very much in the manner of Nick and Nora Charles; and one is moved to speculate that, had Hammett chosen to chronicle the cases of bachelor detective Nick Charles, they might closely resemble the investigations of Bill Crane.

Latimer moved to Hollywood shortly before the war to become a screenwriter; most noteworthy is his fine script for Hammett's *The Glass Key*. The Crane series was terminated, and Latimer did not return to the mystery novel until 1955. The two postwar novels, while excellent, lack the bawdy humor and extraordinary vigor of the Crane books. In *Sinners and Shrouds*, Latimer tackles the familiar theme of the man who wakes up to find a corpse (young, female, nude) in his room. *Black Is the Fashion for Dying* involves the murder of an unpleasant Hollywood prima donna, and Latimer makes good use of his movie studio experiences.

—Art Scott

LAWRENCE, Hilda (Hildegarde Lawrence, née Kronmiller). American. Born in Baltimore, Maryland, c. 1906. Educated at Columbia School, Rochester, New York. Married Reginald Lawrence in 1924 (divorced). Worked as reader to the blind; in clippings department of Macmillan, publishers, New York; staff member, *Publishers Weekly*; radio writer.

CRIME PUBLICATIONS

Novels (series character: Mark East)

Blood upon the Snow (East).   New York, Simon and Schuster, 1944; London, Chapman
   and Hall, 1946.
A Time to Die (East).   New York, Simon and Schuster, 1945; London, Chapman and
   Hall, 1947.
The Pavilion.   New York, Simon and Schuster, 1946; London, Chapman and Hall,
   1948.
Death of a Doll (East).   New York, Simon and Schuster, 1947; London, Chapman and
   Hall, 1948.
Duet of Death (two novelets).   New York, Simon and Schuster, and London, Chapman
   and Hall, 1949; published separately as *Death Has Four Hands* and *The Bleeding
   House*, New York, Spivak, 2 vols., 1950.

Uncollected Short Story

   "A Roof in Manhattan," in *For Love or Money*, edited by Dorothy Gardiner.   New
   York, Doubleday, 1957; London, Macdonald, 1959.

*   *   *

Hilda Lawrence once explained that, as an addict of mystery fiction, she took to writing it
herself because she couldn't find enough satisfactory titles to feed her habit. In the
mid-1940's, after a varied career (grading papers at Johns Hopkins, working at *Publishers
Weekly*, churning out radio scripts for *The Rudy Vallee Show*), she settled down to producing
a first novel that was immediately accepted for Simon and Schuster's "Inner Sanctum"
imprint. This was *Blood upon the Snow* and it introduced the cast of characters which was to
appear in her three most important books.
   She once said to an interviewer that "everything you see can be turned into something and
almost everything that happens can be used." Such a dictum is appropriate for guiding us to
what it is that sets Lawrence's books apart from the other naturalistic *romans noirs* of that
decade. For with the characters of Mark East, Beulah Pond, and Bessy Petty, she sets up a
cooperative contrast between the ways men and women perceive normality: a complete
picture is not available without both points of view.
   The facts that East is a private investigator from Manhattan – hardly a typical male – and
that Miss Beulah and Miss Bessy, as they are known locally in their New England village, are
two spinsters, one slightly scatty – also untypical of their sex – set up the opposing viewpoints
quite neatly; in addition to the sexual one, there are also insider/outsider, urban/rural,
ingenuous/disingenuous dichotomies which contribute to the sleuthing successes of this
bizarre *ménage à trois*. It is to East's credit that, within a few hours of his having set foot in
Crestwood, uncertain of the case he has been called upon to handle, he recognizes the naive
genius of the "two old maids up the lane" when it comes to observation.
   The notion that curious elderly women make excellent Sherlocks (or Watsons) is a time-
honored one in the genre, beginning in the late nineteenth century with Anna Katharine
Green's Miss Amelia Butterworth and reaching its apotheosis with Christie's Miss Jane
Marple. However, in her use of it, Lawrence takes the interesting chance of combining this
softer tradition with the hard-boiled.
   Lawrence's masterpiece is *Death of a Doll*. For its claustrophobic, inexorable quality, it
would be difficult to find an equal. Set in a New York boarding house for women only, it
deals with a young woman whose friends are her enemies. Miss Beulah and Miss Bessy have
journeyed down to the big city at the invitation of a rich young matron whom the reader had
met in Crestwood in *A Time to Die*. They plan to go out on the town with Mark East and find
they have a mystery to offer him when it turns out that their hostess's favorite sales clerk

inexplicably committed suicide on the day of moving into the ironically named Hope House, a Home for Girls. Hanging out at Hope House, the two women again become the insiders and, aided and abetted by East, they solve the crime. One unusual touch, but not an unlikely one given the dormitory atmosphere of the novel, is the covert lesbian relationship between the murderer and her benefactor.

Lawrence's plotting is far from flawless but her eye for setting and character make up for it. Her other three books are less appealing, being a trio of suspense melodramas which each resemble a cross between Mary Roberts Rinehart and Margaret Millar. Yet Lawrence has been praised by Boucher and Haycraft, and her reputation is guaranteed, particularly because of the haunting resonances of *Death of a Doll*.

—Michele Slung

LEASOR, (Thomas) James. British. Born in Erith, Kent, 20 December 1923. Educated at City of London School, 1935–40; Oriel College, Oxford (Editor, *Isis*), 1946–48, B.A. (honours) in English 1948, M.A. 1952. Served in the Royal Berkshire Regiment, in Burma, India, and Malaya, 1942–46: Captain. Married Joan M. Bevan in 1951; three sons. Reporter, *Kentish Times*, Sidcup, 1941–42; reporter, columnist (as William Hickey), feature writer, and foreign correspondent, London *Daily Express*, 1948–55; Editorial Advisor and Consultant, George Newnes and C. Arthur Pearson Ltd., London, 1955–69; Director, Elm Tree Books Ltd., London, 1970–73. Member of Lloyds of London. Since 1959, Director, Pagoda Films Ltd.; since 1964, Director, Jason Love Ltd. Member of the Order of St. John of Jerusalem; Fellow, Royal Society of Arts. Agent: William Heinemann Ltd., 15–16 Queen Street, London W1X 8BE. Address: Swallowcliffe Manor, Salisbury, Wiltshire, England.

CRIME PUBLICATIONS

Novels (series characters: Dr. Jason Love; the owner of Aristo Autos)

> *Passport to Oblivion* (Love). London, Heinemann, 1964; Philadelphia, Lippincott, 1965; as *Where the Spies Are*, London, Pan, 1965.
> *Passport to Peril* (Love). London, Heinemann, 1966; as *Spylight*, Philadelphia, Lippincott, 1966.
> *Passport in Suspense* (Love). London, Heinemann, 1967; as *The Yang Meridian*, New York, Putnam, 1968.
> *Passport for a Pilgrim* (Love). London, Heinemann, 1968; New York, Doubleday, 1969.
> *The Don't Make Them Like That Any More* (Aristo). London, Heinemann, 1969; New York, Doubleday, 1970.
> *Never Had a Spanner on Her* (Aristo). London, Heinemann, 1970.
> *Love-All.* London, Heinemann, 1971.
> *Host of Extras* (Love). London, Heinemann, 1973.
> *The Chinese Widow.* London, Heinemann, 1975.

Short Stories

> *A Week of Love, Being Seven Adventures of Jason Love.* London, Heinemann, 1969.

OTHER PUBLICATIONS

Novels

>   *Not Such a Bad Day.*   Leicester, Blackfriars Press, 1946.
>   *The Strong Delusion.*   London, Harrap, 1960.
>   *NTR: Nothing to Report.*   London, Laurie, 1955.
>   *Follow the Drum.*   London, Heinemann, and New York, Morrow, 1972.
>   *Mandarin-Gold.*   London, Heinemann, 1973; New York, Morrow, 1974.
>   *Jade Gate.*   London, Heinemann, 1976.

Plays

>   *Look Where I'm At!*, music by Jordan Ramin, lyrics by Frank H. Stanton and Murray
>   Semos, adaptation of the novel *Rain in the Doorway* by Thorne Smith (produced New
>   York, 1971).

Screenplay: *Where the Spies Are*, with Wolf Mankowitz and Val Guest, 1965.

Television Series: *The Michaels in Africa.*

Other.

>   *The Monday Story.*   London, Oxford University Press, 1951.
>   *Author by Profession.*   London, Cleaver Hume Press, 1952.
>   *Wheels of Fortune: A Brief Account of the Life and Times of William Morris, Viscount
>   Nuffield.*   London, Lane, 1954.
>   *The Sergeant Major: A Biography of R.S.M. Ronald Brittain, M.B.E., Coldstream
>   Guards.*   London, Harrap, 1955.
>   *The Red Fort: An Account of the Siege of Delhi in 1857.*   London, Laurie, 1956; New
>   York, Reynal, 1957; as *Mutiny at the Red Fort*, London, Corgi, 1959.
>   *The One That Got Away*, with Kendal Burt.   London, Joseph, 1956; New York,
>   Random House, 1957.
>   *The Millionth Chance: The Story of the R. 101.*   London, Hamish Hamilton, and New
>   York, Reynal, 1957.
>   *War at the Top* (based on the experiences of General Sir Leslie Hollis).   London,
>   Joseph, 1959; as *The Clock with Four Hands*, New York, Reynal, 1959.
>   *Conspiracy of Silence*, with Peter Eton.   London, Angus and Robertson, 1960; as *Wall
>   of Silence*, Indianapolis, Bobbs Merrill, 1960.
>   *The Plague and the Fire.*   New York, McGraw Hill, 1961; London, Allen and Unwin,
>   1962.
>   *Rudolf Hess, The Uninvited Envoy.*   London, Allen and Unwin, 1962; as *The Uninvited
>   Envoy*, New York, McGraw Hill, 1962.
>   *Singapore: The Battle That Changed the World.*   London, Hodder and Stoughton, and
>   New York, Doubleday, 1968.
>   *Green Beach* (on the Dieppe raid).   London, Heinemann, and New York, Morrow,
>   1975.
>   *Boarding Party.*   London, Heinemann, and Boston, Houghton Mifflin, 1978.

James Leasor comments:
I grew up a John Buchan enthusiast, and although I started my writing career with
non-fiction books, I always intended to write thrillers. After several false starts and 14
rewrites I sold my first, *Passport to Oblivion*, in 1964.
When I left school I became a medical student but abandoned my intention of qualifying as

a doctor to join the army in the Second World War. My elder sister qualified, however, and for many years practised in Somerset. Since I knew the background there well, I made my character, Jason Love, a Somerset physician. The name Jason is an anagram of my own Christian name, James, my wife's, Joan, and my eldest son's, Jeremy; my middle son, Andrew, provides the *a* and my youngest son, Stuart, the *s*. The surname Love was chosen because it appears continually in newspaper headlines, and I felt it might have some subliminal advertising value.

All my thrillers are based on fact and before I write them I visit the countries and places where I intend to set the action so that I can research the backgrounds thoroughly. I have long been attracted by the American Cord car and own one of the few open Cords in Britain — so I gave my fictitious character this car to drive.

I write these stories because I enjoy writing them.

*   *   *

James Leasor entered the spy novel derby at the crest of the James Bond wave with *Passport to Oblivion*. That the book was a success, and gave rise to six sequels and a short story collection, lasting well into the 1970's (long after many neo-Bonds had sunk without trace), is tribute to Leasor's considerable skill as a thriller writer, and to the appeal of his creation, Dr. Jason Love.

Love is a British country doctor, drawn into the espionage game by the appeals of Douglas MacGillivray, a comrade in Burma during the war, now highly placed in British intelligence. Their man in Teheran has been murdered, other agents are not available, their cover blown, Love is going to a malaria conference in Teheran anyway; would he help out? Love reluctantly agrees, and rapidly finds himself drawn into a net of violence, intrigue, and general nastiness far beyond his expectations. His only ostensible qualification for secret agent work is a modest skill at judo, but he taps reserves of courage and cleverness that are the equal of those of any "professional" spy one would care to name.

The Love novels represent an expert synthesis of the elements that made the Bond novels so popular: a dashing hero (though Love differs from Bond in important respects); glamorous, exotic locales (Pakistan in *Passport to Peril*, the Bahamas in *Passport in Suspense*); a good deal of sex, some of it kinky (but none of it preposterous); death and violence of considerable variety and ingenuity. The tales move along at a fast clip; plot complications are well delineated and credible. Most important, Leasor's books have that quality — so vital to the success of any spy novel — of being able subliminally to place the imaginative reader in the hero's role.

As James Bond was in some respects a romantic projection of Ian Fleming's personality, so too is Love a fantasy alter-ego of Leasor, which in large part accounts for the novels' ability to make the magic of the vicarious experience work for the reader. Leasor and Love share the same initials, and they share as well a passion for classic automobiles. Love's attachment to his supercharged Cord roadster is frequently and lovingly detailed (Leasor's own Cord was used in the film version of his first book). Much classic car lore is scattered throughout the Love adventures, and serves the same purpose as did Bond's fixation with fine liquor and clothes. Leasor is a world traveler, and his skill at depicting locale is of the first rank in the spy genre. Love differs from Bond in that he is a more human — and humane — character. He is very much more believable, and the tales are as well. Gadgetry is not overdone, and there are no Blofeldesque supervillains lurking about. Thus, Leasor has managed to find, and explore with an admirably literate style, a middle ground between the fantasy heroics of Bond (and his host of even more comic-bookish imitators) and the cynical realism of le Carré and Deighton.

Most recently Leasor has apparently abandoned the spy novel and turned to historical romance (the sort of thing that publisher's blurb writers call a "surging novel of passion") in such books as *Follow the Drum* and *Mandarin-Gold*.

—Art Scott

le CARRÉ, John. Pseudonym for David John Moore Cornwell. British. Born in Poole, Dorset, 19 October 1931. Educated at Sherborne School, Dorset; St. Andrew's Preparatory School; Berne University, Switzerland, 1948–49; Lincoln College, Oxford, B.A. (honours) in modern languages 1956. Married 1) Alison Ann Veronica Sharp in 1954 (divorced, 1971), three sons; 2) Valerie Jane Eustace in 1972, one son. Tutor at Eton College, 1956–58; Member of the British Foreign Service, 1959–64: Second Secretary, Bonn Embassy, 1961–64; Consul, Hamburg, 1963–64. Recipient: British Crime Novel Award, 1963; Maugham Award, 1964; Mystery Writers of America Edgar Alan Poe Award, 1965; Crime Writers Association Gold Dagger, 1978; Black Memorial Award, 1978. Agent: John Farquharson Ltd., 8 Bell Yard, London WC2A 2JU, England.

CRIME PUBLICATIONS

Novels (series character: George Smiley)

Call for the Dead (Smiley). London, Gollancz, 1961; New York, Walker, 1962; as *The Deadly Affair*, London, Penguin, 1966.
A Murder of Quality (Smiley). London, Gollancz, 1962; New York, Walker, 1963.
The Spy Who Came In from the Cold (Smiley). London, Gollancz, 1963; New York, Coward McCann, 1964.
The Looking-Glass War. London, Heinemann, and New York, Coward McCann, 1965.
A Small Town in Germany. London, Heinemann, and New York, Coward McCann, 1968.
Tinker, Tailor, Soldier, Spy (Smiley). London, Hodder and Stoughton, and New York, Knopf, 1974.
The Honourable Schoolboy (Smiley). London, Hodder and Stoughton, and New York, Knopf, 1977.
Smiley's People. London, Hodder and Stoughton, 1980.

Uncollected Short Stories

"Dare I Weep, Dare I Mourn," in *Saturday Evening Post* (Philadelphia), 28 January 1967.
"What Ritual Is Being Observed Tonight?," in *Saturday Evening Post* (Philadelphia), 2 November 1968.

OTHER PUBLICATIONS

Novel

The Naive and Sentimental Lover. London, Hodder and Stoughton, 1971; New York, Knopf, 1972.

*   *   *

In the tradition of Conrad, Maugham, and Greene, John le Carré's realist spy novel is a form which represents a genuine modern version of tragedy: the spy's entrapment, through his own rationality, by the "fate" of our time – bureaucratism. The international imperialist structure framing the spy's search sends real shivers down our moral spines. That it does so in a genre which is supposed to be entertaining is no more paradoxical than for the Greeks to have experienced terror and pity at such popular spectacles as *Antigone*. For in le Carré's action, in his quintessential plot, lies the same conflict between individual man at his best – most intelligent, most "mistaken" – and collective man at his worst – most rationally organized in awesomely complex governmental "apparats." When Smiley, le Carré's good spy, eventually assumes Control's position in the British Secret Service, he articulates a perpetual dilemma: "To be inhuman in defence of our humanity ... harsh in defence of compassion ... single-minded in defence of our disparity" (*The Honourable Schoolboy*). What, finally, is the difference between Control and Creon?

Le Carré's first spy novel, *Call for the Dead*, for all its modesty in plot and character, remains one of his three or four best. Not only does he introduce his hero, Smiley; he also outlines his favorite crisis in pitting this master spy-detective against a former friend and wartime pupil-associate, the German-Jewish Communist intelligence chief, Dieter Frey. Both men have integrity and each must try to kill the other out of allegiance to a different ideology; both old Nazi-fighters, the German Jew's Communism is as understandable as the Englishman's vague liberalism. The world has changed on them, however, making the "Red" an idealist of purist impulse and romantic Machiavellianism, the "White" a self-doubting hero of contradictory yearnings, to resign or not to resign from the crummy game.

Although Smiley is the hero of le Carré's next novel, *A Murder of Quality*, this time he acts simply as detective, in a straight apolitical murder. Curiously, there is more and better detection in *Call for the Dead* – evidence that the "purer" form of British crime-mystery may have no premium on ratiocinative possibilities.

The Spy Who Came In from the Cold is still le Carré's cleanest job: compact in structure; deftly deceptive in the unfolding of its triple-cross; and painfully human in the characterizations of two victims of "our" side's necessary but evil mission, Fiedler and Liz – the first a sincere Jewish Marxist who is second-in-command of the East German Abteilung, the latter the innocent mistress of Leamas, the British agent.

With *The Looking-Glass War* and *A Small Town in Germany*, le Carré abandons Smiley temporarily. The first is a lean sketch of lower-echelon spy psychology, while *A Small Town in Germany* demonstrates what some critics aver is an impossibility: the successful fusion of spy action with rich, "novelistic" detail in characterization. It is also the most bitter of le Carré's treatments of post-war politics, for it shows a morally bankrupt Whitehall arranging a "Chamberlain" pact in Bonn with resurgent Nazis.

Tinker, Tailor, Soldier, Spy is a major example of what appears to be le Carré's tragic irony: clear-headed rationality is a self-sufficient value, remaining weirdly intact in a context of utter moral-political ambiguity. This is not mere professionalism, but a perversely attractive definition of man as "he who may do little good, and much unintended evil, but at least thinks things through to their logical end." Such a credo finds its analog in le Carré's sure plotting, which always celebrates reason.

Unlike *The Honourable Schoolboy*, *Tinker, Tailor* concentrates on the plight of human intelligence and avoids getting sidetracked by local color and exotic pseudo-complexities. Hopefully, le Carré still knows Smiley is his key, both to the creation of problems and to their solution. In *Tinker, Tailor*, he begins to turn this key even more adeptly than before. Smiley is the last and truest lover of the Empire, which, in a wry personification, becomes Lady Ann, the promiscuous wife Smiley forever ponders and, in despairing hope, always returns to at the end of each case. Not only Smiley, but the spy genre itself – all detective fiction, for that matter – represents the bedraggled survival of Victorian values. His loyalty to what and who betrays him may make him the exemplar in le Carré's world, but his fussy scrupulousness and worried beneficence always suggest the "white man's burden." Le Carré's earlier rejection of Smiley's "liberalism," at the conclusion to *The Spy Who Came In from the Cold*, however, becomes only an ambivalent half-rejection in *Tinker, Tailor*. For here the last good Englishman admits to the "mole" he has trapped that he agrees with a confession of political judgments he must officially regard as treasonous. But he then draws the line at the imperative to act in behalf of those judgments, a refusal made out of loyalty to loyalty, to human nature rather than historical dialectic.

Smiley's virtue thus commendably overrides his capacity for ideology – but at the cost of sterility. His successful Cold-War case record is a record of clean-ups, past-oriented, with little positive effect (clearer still in *The Honourable Schoolboy*) on either the future workings or professional honor of the Circus. In *Tinker, Tailor*, he is haunted by his Moriarty, the

Soviet Karla, largely because Karla's ruthlessness has the enviable justification of the East's viable power, a "rising" out of Russia's suffering during the tragic war that also exhausted the British Empire. Although a fanatic to Smiley, Karla is, when the two meet in a Delhi jail, also a man who has survived private loss (despite his own wishes) and who acts out of fidelity to the revolution even when threatened by its, and his own apparat's, intention to sacrifice him. Smiley and Karla are the same man, one out of his time, the other in (like Frey and Fiedler, earlier). Both men together, and only when in conjunction, make heroic sense to le Carré, whose task in future narratives will be to explore the Conradian possibilities of this humanly political Janus.

—John Snyder

LEE, Austin.   See **AUSTWICK, John.**

LEE, Manfred B.   See **QUEEN, Ellery.**

LEJEUNE, Anthony.   Pseudonym for Edward Anthony Thompson.   British.   Born in London, 7 August 1928. Educated at Merchant Taylors' School, London; Balliol College, Oxford, 1949–53. Served in the Royal Navy, 1947–49. Deputy Editor, 1955–57, and Editor, 1957–58, *Time and Tide*, London; Special Writer, *Daily Express*, London, 1958–61, and *Sunday Times*, London, 1961–63. Regular contributor to the *Daily Telegraph*, London. Former Editorial Director, Tom Stacey Ltd., publishers, London. Address: Lane End, Hillside Road, Pinner Hill, Middlesex, England.

CRIME PUBLICATIONS

Novels (series character: Adam Gifford)

> *Crowded and Dangerous.*   London, Macdonald, 1959.
> *Mr. Diabolo.*   London, Macdonald, 1960.
> *News of Murder* (Gifford).   London, Macdonald, 1961.
> *Duel in the Shadows* (Gifford).   London, Macdonald, 1962.
> *Glint of Spears.*   London, Macdonald, 1963.
> *The Dark Trade* (Gifford).   London, Macdonald, 1965; as *Death of a Pornographer*, London, Lancer, 1967.

Uncollected Short Story

"The Interrupted Journey of James Fairbrother," in *Winter's Crimes 6*, edited by George
   Hardinge.   London, Macmillan, 1974.

OTHER PUBLICATIONS

Play

   Television Play: *Vicky's First Ball*, with Caroline Alice Lejeune.

Other

   Freedom and the Politicians.   London, Joseph, 1964.
   Enoch Powell's "Income Tax at 4s. 3d. in the £."   London, Stacey, 1970.
   The Gentlemen's Clubs of London.   London, Macdonald and Jane's, and New York,
      Mayflower, 1979.

   Editor, *Time and Tide Anthology.*   London, Deutsch, 1956.
   Editor, *The Case for South West Africa.*   London, Stacey, 1971.
   Editor, *Drink and Ink 1919–1977*, by Dennis Wheatley.   London, Hutchinson, 1979.

*   *   *

   Anthony Lejeune is an able but undistinguished writer of suspense fiction one of whose
books, *Glint of Spears*, deserves accolades.
   Several of his books spin tales around Adam Gifford, a crime reporter for a London
newspaper who also answers to the call of Arthur Blaise, a highranking official in the British
War Office. A bright, eager young woman generally figures in the story, engaging Adam's
attentions and complicating the plot. In *News of Murder* two murders lead Gifford to a ring of
international drug smugglers; in *The Dark Trade* Gifford's work on a feature article on
industrial espionage involves him in the investigation of the murder of a pornographer,
which in turn reveals a complicated Russian plot to use blackmail to compel the wealthy
owner of an industrial plant to sell atomic secrets to the Russians. Typically, the books
contain a scene where Gifford and his female companion are set upon by a gang of thugs. The
woman companion is generally depicted as a spirited lady, meant to be Gifford's match, but
doomed predictably to be rejected by him when he recognizes that his true mistress is no
woman but his job. She invariably commits some foolish act out of the finest motives, and
Gifford is left to contrive elaborate plans to guarantee her safety.
   Arthur Blaise, a hush-hush figure in Whitehall whose business it is to protect Britain's
security, is usually introduced early in the story and left to lurk behind the scenes
manipulating the action.
   The plot in all these books is quite predictable. Gifford and Blaise are fleshed out by their
author but the other characters are mere stereotypes. A journalistic description of the
network of crime that governs the story is included in every book, be it drug-abuse,
pornography, or industrial espionage. A scene or two in the newspaper office, an urgent cable
calling for a rush of "the fullest colorfullest story," and Gifford's fingers tripping over his
typewriter keys, producing fresh copy, are all part of the ordinary fare in Lejeune's fiction.
Only in *Glint of Spears* does Lejeune offer an interesting departure from his too-formulaic
suspense books.
   Glint of Spears finds its literary ancestors in Joseph Conrad's *Heart of Darkness* and in
some of Alan Paton's books about Africa, but it succeeds because it finds an action and setting
that are real and frightful. Set in post-independence Congo, it charts, hour by hour and day
by day, Andrew Marsden's journey into the Congo where he attempts to locate and rescue
Paul Buckley, a missionary whose station has been destroyed. Most of the tale recounts the

terrifying journey of Buckley and a small tightly-knit tribe of Africans led by Lobendola to escape from almost certain death at the hands of the Bakona who are murdering any white men or friends of white men they overtake. In a tautly told first-person narrative, Marsden describes the jungle; the stealthy march towards Marieville where help is; the furtive attempts to avoid an encounter with Johnny Mtala, a Bakona "king" who once was the follower of Buckley, but now leads cannibalistic Africans; and, finally, the battle between the two groups which culminates in a duel between Buckley and Mtala which is to settle the fates of the two peoples. In this book, Lejeune's journalistic flair for naturalistic detail and his skill as a story-teller have found a fit subject. The tale is gripping; the landscape, hot, wooded, fly-infested; the people cunning and desperate; and the solution problematic, befitting the precarious nature of the Congo's independence.

—Carol Simpson Stern

LEMARCHAND, Elizabeth (Wharton).   British.   Born in Barnstaple, Devon, 27 October 1906. Educated at the Ursuline Convent, Bideford, Devon, 1918–26; University of Exeter, 1926–29, London External B.A. (honours) 1927, M.A. (London) 1929; Geneva School of International Studies (scholar), 1929. Assistant Mistress, Clifton High School, Bristol, 1929–35, and Sutton High School, 1935–40; Deputy Headmistress, Godolphin School, Salisbury, 1940–60; Headmistress, Lowther College, Abergele, Wales, 1960–61. Agent: Bolt and Watson Ltd., 8–12 Old Queen Street, Storey's Gate, London SW1P 9HP. Address: 36-A The Strand, Topsham, Exeter, Devon EX3 0AY, England.

CRIME PUBLICATIONS

Novels (series character: Detective Superintendent Tom Pollard in all books)

Death of an Old Girl.   London, Hart Davis, 1967; New York, Award, 1970.
The Affacombe Affair.   London, Hart Davis, 1968.
Alibi for a Corpse.   London, Hart Davis, 1969.
Death on Doomsday.   London, Hart Davis, 1971; New York, Walker, 1975.
Cyanide with Compliments.   London, MacGibbon and Kee, 1972; New York, Walker, 1973.
Let or Hindrance.   London, Hart Davis MacGibbon, 1973; as *No Vacation from Murder*, New York, Walker, 1974.
Buried in the Past.   London, Hart Davis MacGibbon, 1974; New York, Walker, 1975.
Step in the Dark.   London, Hart Davis MacGibbon, 1976; New York, Walker, 1977.
Unhappy Returns.   London, Hart Davis MacGibbon, 1977; New York, Walker, 1978.
Suddenly While Gardening.   London, Hart Davis MacGibbon, 1978; New York, Walker, 1979.

Uncollected Short Stories

"The Beckoning Beeches," in *John Creasey's Mystery Bedside Book 1969*, edited by Herbert Harris.   London, Hodder and Stoughton, 1968.
"The Stone of Witness," in *John Creasey's Mystery Bedside Book 1970*, edited by Herbert Harris.   London, Hodder and Stoughton, 1969.

"Time to Be Going," in *More Tales of Unease*, edited by John Burke. London, Pan, 1969.

"Black Bartholomew," in *John Creasey's Mystery Bedside Book 1974*, edited by Herbert Harris. London, Hodder and Stoughton, 1973.

"The Comeback," in *John Creasey's Mystery Bedside Book 1976*, edited by Herbert Harris. London, Hodder and Stoughton, 1975.

Elizabeth Lemarchand comments:

I had to retire early because of a serious illness and began to write as a hobby in convalescence. After a modest success with short stories I felt I wanted more elbow room and decided to try my hand at a detective novel. I had always enjoyed detective fiction and it seemed the obvious choice for a late starter. It is, after all, basically the application of a formula, and one is free to concentrate on interesting settings and characterisation. I use only settings of which I have some personal knowledge, and I take a lot of trouble over them. My books are not thrillers (which are sexy and deal with sensational and violent crime), but novels with a "detective" theme of the sort normally described as "classical." Old hat, some would say, but there are still a surprising number of old hatters around.

*   *   *

For more than a decade Elizabeth Lemarchand has been writing detective stories of the classic English variety. Fans of the Golden Age writers such as Christie, Sayers, and Allingham have, if they have not yet encountered Lemarchand's works, a happy surprise in store. She employs such nostalgic niceties as timetables, floor-plans, maps, and casts of characters, and has created a pair of detectives, Scotland Yard officers Tom Pollard and Gregory Toye, who appear in each tale and advance in rank as new books succeed each other in the series. This is not to say that her books are period pieces – they are not; they are worthy new entries in the lists of genteel crime fiction and polite problem solving.

Pollard and Toye have no idiosyncrasies of the type that distinguish Nero Wolfe or Lord Peter Wimsey; they are simply thoroughly nice fellows who work well together, who apply considerable ingenuity to solving the crimes that are assigned to them, and who relentlessly pursue the evidence that allows them to eliminate fallacious conclusions. Both are family men, and Toye is shown to be a bit sentimental when he deals with attractive young women. Pollard and his wife Jane, a red-haired artist, are the parents of twins, whose birth is awaited in *The Affacombe Affair*. Subsequent books offer glimpses of the children as they grow, and when they start to school Jane takes a job in an art college. Cat hair on clothing is important evidence in *Step in the Dark*, and the cat in question, rejected by its original owners, is adopted by the Pollard family, despite the fact that it tripped Pollard on a staircase, causing him to break a leg.

The author's interest in English history and archaeology is used to good advantage. While not central to the plots, as they would be in the works of Anthony Price, history and archaeology provide interest in the settings and structure of her tales: Bronze Age barrows are part of the scenery, and quaint customs dating back to Saxon times make vivid background material. Olivia Strode, an engaging older woman who appears in *The Affacombe Affair* and again in *Cyanide with Compliments*, is writing a parish history and brings in many fascinating details as well as vital information which her curiosity leads her to uncover. A medievalist seeking to debunk the charters of his home town and thereby make a mockery of its millenary celebration, as well as a twentieth-century corpse unearthed in an excavated Roman villa, figure in *Buried in the Past*. Lemarchand is skilful at portraying the daily life of small communities – whether village, school, or vacation colony. Her characters, even minor ones who are quickly sketched, are lifelike and invite the reader's sympathy; in short, they are people one enjoys reading about whose motivations and reactions are plausible.

A retired headmistress, the author chooses school settings more than once – so that the Commissioner remarks to Pollard in one book that if he keeps on handling school cases he'll wind up teaching. Other settings include a stately home, a private literary and scientific society's headquarters, a cruise ship, and a house on a lonely moor. To take such conventional settings and bring them to life with fresh and entertaining stories is no small accomplishment. The crimes – blackmail, arson, theft, all leading to murder – are also conventional, but the inventive past histories of the characters and the clever twists of the plots are absorbing.

If the fictional England of Elizabeth Lemarchand does not really exist, it is a pleasant and comfortable place to escape to in imagination. Its inhabitants, even those who commit murder, are literate and civilized, and crimes which evoke outrage in the abstract never impinge offensively upon one's sensibilities. Charming vignettes, warmth, wit, and solid detection mark these tasteful tales of violence.

—Mary Helen Becker

LE QUEUX, William (Tufnell). British. Born in London, 2 July 1864. Educated privately in London and at Pegli, Italy; studied art in Paris. Foreign Editor, London *Globe*, 1891–93; from 1893 free-lance journalist and travel writer; Balkan Correspondent, *Daily Mail*, London, during Balkan War, 1912–13; served as Consul to the Republic of San Marino. Popularly supposed to have been a spy. Lived in Switzerland in later life. *Died 13 October 1927.*

CRIME PUBLICATIONS

Novels

Guilty Bonds. London, Routledge, 1891; New York, Fenno, 1895.
The Temptress. London, Tower, and New York, Stokes, 1895.
Zoraida: A Romance of the Harem and the Great Sahara. London, Tower, and New York, Stokes, 1895.
Devil's Dice. London, White, 1896; Chicago, Rand McNally, 1897.
Whoso Findeth a Wife. London, White, 1897; Chicago, Rand McNally, 1898.
A Madonna of the Music Halls. London, White, 1897; as *A Secret Sin*, London, Gardner, 1913.
The Eye of Ishtar. London, White, and New York, Stokes, 1897.
If Sinners Entice Thee. London, White, 1898; New York, Dillingham, 1899.
The Great White Queen. London, White, 1898.
Scribes and Pharisees. London, White, and New York, Dodd Mead, 1898.
The Veiled Man. London, White, 1899.
The Bond of Black. London, White, and New York, Dillingham, 1899.
Wiles of the Wicked. London, Bell, 1899.
The Day of Temptation. London, White, and New York, Dillingham, 1899.
England's Peril. London, White, 1899.
An Eye for an Eye. London, White, 1900.
In White Raiment. London, White, 1900.
Of Royal Blood. London, Hutchinson, 1900.
The Gamblers. London, Hutchinson, 1901.
The Sign of the Seven Sins. Philadelphia, Lippincott, 1901.

Her Majesty's Minister. London, Hodder and Stoughton, and New York, Dodd Mead, 1901.
The Court of Honour. London, White, 1901.
The Under-Secretary. London, Hutchinson, 1902.
The Unnamed. London, Hodder and Stoughton, 1902.
The Tickencote Treasure. London, Newnes, 1903.
The Three Glass Eyes. London, Treherne, 1903.
The Seven Secrets. London, Hutchinson, 1903.
The Idol of the Town. London, White, 1903.
As We Forgave Them. London, White, 1904.
The Closed Book. London, Methuen, and New York, Smart Set, 1904.
The Hunchback of Westminster. London, Methuen, 1904.
The Man from Downing Street. London, Hurst and Blackett, 1904.
The Red Hat. London, Daily Mail, 1904.
The Sign of the Stranger. London, White, 1904.
The Valley of the Shadow. London, Methuen, 1905.
Who Giveth This Woman? London, Hodder and Stoughton, 1905.
The Spider's Eye. London, Cassell, 1905.
Sins of the City. London, White, 1905.
The Mask. London, Long, 1905.
Behind the Throne. London, Methuen, 1905.
The Czar's Spy. London, Hodder and Stoughton, and New York, Smart Set, 1905.
The Great Court Scandal. London, White, 1906.
The House of the Wicked. London, Hurst and Blackett, 1906.
The Mysterious Mr. Miller. London, Hodder and Stoughton, 1906.
The Mystery of a Motor-Car. London, Hodder and Stoughton, 1906.
Whatsoever a Man Soweth. London, White, 1906.
The Woman at Kensington. London, Cassell, 1906.
The Secret of the Square. London, White, 1907.
The Great Plot. London, Hodder and Stoughton, 1907.
Whosoever Loveth. London, Hutchinson, 1907.
The Crooked Way. London, Methuen, 1908.
The Looker-On. London, White, 1908.
The Pauper of Park Lane. London, Cassell, and New York, Cupples and Leon, 1908.
Stolen Sweets. London, Nash, 1908.
The Woman in the Way. London, Nash, 1908.
The Red Room. London, Cassell, 1909; Boston, Little Brown, 1911.
The House of Whispers. London, Nash, 1909; New York, Brentano's, 1910.
Fatal Thirteen. London, Stanley Paul, 1909.
The Great God Gold. Boston, Badger, 1910.
Lying Lips. London, Stanley Paul, 1910.
The Unknown Tomorrow. London, White, 1910.
Hushed Up! London, Nash, 1911.
The Money-Spider. London, Cassell, and Boston, Badger, 1911.
The Death-Doctor. London, Hurst and Blackett, 1912.
Fatal Fingers. London, Cassell, 1912.
The Mystery of Nine. London, Nash, 1912.
Without Trace. London, Nash, 1912.
The Price of Power, Being Chapters from the Secret History of the Imperial Court of Russia. London, Hurst and Blackett, 1913.
The Room of Secrets. London, Ward Lock, 1913.
The Lost Million. London, Nash, 1913.
The White Lie. London, Ward Lock, 1914.
Sons of Satan. London, White, 1914.
The Hand of Allah. London, Cassell, 1914; as *The Riddle of the Ring*, London, Federation Press, 1927.

Her Royal Highness. London, Hodder and Stoughton, 1914.
The Maker of Secrets. London, Ward Lock, 1914.
The Four Faces. London, Stanley Paul, and New York, Bretano's, 1914.
The Double Shadow. London, Hodder and Stoughton, 1915.
At the Sign of the Sword. London, Jack, and New York, Scully and Kleinteich, 1915.
The Mysterious Three. London, Ward Lock, 1915.
The Mystery of the Green Ray. London, Hodder and Stoughton, 1915; as *The Green Ray*, London, Mellifont Press, 1944.
The Sign of Silence. London, Ward Lock, 1915.
The White Glove. London, Nash, 1915.
The Zeppelin Destroyer. London, Hodder and Stoughton, 1916.
Number 70, Berlin. London, Hodder and Stoughton, 1916.
The Place of Dragons. London, Ward Lock, 1916.
The Spy Hunter. London, Pearson, 1916.
The Man about Town. London, Long, 1916.
Annette of the Argonne. London, Hurst and Blackett, 1916.
The Broken Thread. London, Ward Lock, 1916.
Behind the German Lines. London, London Mail, 1917.
The Breath of Suspicion. London, Long, 1917.
The Devil's Carnival. London, Hurst and Blackett, 1917.
No Greater Love. London, Ward Lock, 1917.
Two in a Tangle. London, Hodder and Stoughton, 1917.
Rasputin, The Rascal Monk. London, Hurst and Blackett, 1917.
The Yellow Ribbon. London, Hodder and Stoughton, 1918.
The Secret Life of the Ex-Tsaritza. London, Odhams Press, 1918.
The Sister Disciple. London, Hurst and Blackett, 1918.
The Stolen Statesman. London, Skeffington, 1918.
The Little Blue Goddess. London, Ward Lock, 1918.
The Minister of Evil: The Secret History of Rasputin's Betrayal of Russia. London, Cassell, 1918.
Bolo, The Super-Spy. London, Odhams Press, 1918.
The Catspaw. London, Lloyd's, 1918.
Cipher Six. London, Hodder and Stoughton, 1919.
The Doctor of Pimlico. London, Cassell, 1919; New York, Macaulay, 1920.
The Forbidden Word. London, Odhams Press, 1919.
The King's Incognito. London, Odhams Press, 1919.
The Lure of Love. London, Ward Lock, 1919.
Rasputinism in London. London, Cassell, 1919.
The Secret Shame of the Kaiser. London, Hurst and Blackett, 1919.
Secrets of the White Tsar. London, Odhams Press, 1919.
The Heart of a Princess. London, Ward Lock, 1920.
The Intriguers. London, Hodder and Stoughton, 1920; New York, Macaulay, 1921.
No. 7, Saville Square. London, Ward Lock, 1920.
The Red Widow; or, The Death-Dealers of London. London, Cassell, 1920.
The Terror of the Air. London, Lloyd's, 1920.
Whither Thou Goest. London, Lloyd's, 1920.
This House to Let. London, Hodder and Stoughton, 1921.
The Lady-in-Waiting. London, Ward Lock, 1921.
The Open Verdict. London, Hodder and Stoughton, 1921.
The Power of the Borgias: The Story of the Great Film. London, Odhams Press, 1921.
Mademoiselle of Monte Carlo. London, Cassell, and New York, Macaulay, 1921.
The Fifth Finger. London, Stanley Paul, and New York, Moffat, 1921.
The Golden Face. London, Cassell, and New York, Macaulay, 1922.
The Stretton Street Affair. New York, Macaulay, 1922; London, Cassell, 1924.
Three Knots. London, Ward Lock, 1922.

The Voice from the Void.   London, Cassell, 1922; New York, Macaulay, 1923.
The Young Archduchess.   London, Ward Lock, and New York, Moffat, 1922.
Where the Desert Ends.   London, Cassell, 1923.
The Bronze Face.   London, Ward Lock, 1923; as *Behind the Bronze Door*, New York, Macaulay, 1923.
The Crystal Claw.   London, Hodder and Stoughton, and New York, Macaulay, 1924.
Fine Feathers.   London, Stanley Paul, 1924.
A Woman's Debt.   London, Ward Lock, 1924.
The Valrose Mystery.   London, Ward Lock, 1925.
The Marked Man.   London, Ward Lock, 1925.
The Blue Bungalow.   London, Hurst and Blackett, 1925.
The Broadcast Mystery.   London, Holden, 1925.
The Fatal Face.   London, Hurst and Blackett, 1926.
Hidden Hands.   London, Hodder and Stoughton, 1926; as *The Dangerous Game*, New York, Macaulay, 1926.
The Letter E.   London, Cassell, 1926; as *The Tattoo Mystery*, New York, Macaulay, 1927.
The Mystery of Mademoiselle.   London, Hodder and Stoughton, 1926.
The Scarlet Sign.   London, Ward Lock, 1926.
The Black Owl.   London, Ward Lock, 1926.
The Office Secret.   London, Ward Lock, 1927.
The House of Evil.   London, Ward Lock, 1927.
The Lawless Hand.   London, Hurst and Blackett, 1927; New York, Macaulay, 1928.
Blackmailed.   London, Nash and Grayson, 1927.
The Chameleon.   London, Hodder and Stoughton, 1927; as *Poison Shadows*, New York, Macaulay, 1927.
Concerning This Woman.   London, Newnes, 1928.
The Rat Trap.   London, Ward Lock, 1928; New York, Macaulay, 1930.
The Secret Formula.   London, Ward Lock, 1928.
The Sting.   London, Hodder and Stoughton, and New York, Macaulay, 1928.
Twice Tried.   London, Hurst and Blackett, 1928.
The Amazing Count.   London, Ward Lock, 1929.
The Crinkled Crown.   London, Ward Lock, and New York, Macaulay, 1929.
The Golden Three.   London, Ward Lock, 1930; New York, Fiction House, 1931.

Short Stories

Strange Tales of a Nihilist.   London, Ward Lock, and New York, Cassell, 1892; as *A Secret Service*, Ward Lock, 1896.
Stolen Souls.   London, Tower, and New York, Stokes, 1895.
Secrets of Monte Carlo.   London, White, 1899; New York, Dillingham, 1900.
Secrets of the Foreign Office.   London, Hutchinson, 1903.
Confessions of a Ladies' Man, Being the Adventures of Cuthbert Croom, of His Majesty's Diplomatic Service.   London, Hutchinson, 1905.
The Count's Chauffeur.   London, Nash, 1907.
The Lady in the Car, in Which the Amours of a Mysterious Motorist Are Related.   London, Nash, and Philadelphia, Lippincott, 1908.
Spies of the Kaiser: Plotting the Downfall of England.   London, Hurst and Blackett, 1909.
Revelations of the Secret Service.   London, White, 1911.
The Indiscretions of a Lady's Maid.   London, Nash, 1911.
Mysteries.   London, Ward Lock, 1913.
The German Spy.   London, Newnes, 1914.
"Cinders" of Harley Street.   London, Ward Lock, 1916.
The Bomb-Makers.   London, Jarrolds, 1917.

Beryl of the Biplane. London, Pearson, 1917.
Hushed Up at German Headquarters. London, London Mail, 1917.
The Rainbow Mystery: Chronicles of a Colour-Criminologist. London, Hodder and
  Stoughton, 1917.
The Scandal-Monger. London, Ward Lock, 1917.
The Secrets of Potsdam. London, Daily Mail, 1917.
More Secrets of Potsdam. London, London Mail, 1917.
Further Secrets of Potsdam. London, London Mail, 1917.
Donovan of Whitehall. London, Pearson, 1917.
Sant of the Secret Service. London, Odhams Press, 1918.
The Hotel X. London, Ward Lock, 1919.
Mysteries of the Great City. London, Hodder and Stoughton, 1919.
In Secret. London, Odhams Press, 1920.
The Secret Telephone. New York, McCann, 1920; London, Jarrolds, 1921.
Society Intrigues I Have Known. London, Odhams Press, 1920.
The Luck of the Secret Service. London, Pearson, 1921.
The Elusive Four: The Exciting Exploits of Four Thieves. London, Cassell, 1921.
Tracked by Wireless. London, Stanley Paul, and New York, Moffat, 1922.
The Gay Triangle: The Romance of the First Air Adventurers. London, Jarrolds, 1922.
*Bleke, The Butler, Being the Exciting Adventures of Robert Bleke During Certain Years of
  His Service in Various Families.* London, Jarrolds, 1923.
*The Crimes Club: A Record of Secret Investigations into Some Amazing Crimes, Mostly
  Withheld from the Public.* London, Nash and Grayson, 1927.
The Peril of Helen Marklove and Other Stories. London, Jarrolds, 1928.
The Factotum and Other Stories. London, Ward Lock, 1931.

Uncollected Short Story

"The Secret of the Fox Hunter," in *The Rivals of Sherlock Holmes*, edited by Hugh
  Greene. London, Bodley Head, 1970.

OTHER PUBLICATIONS

Novel

Treasure of Israel. London, Nash, 1910.

Play

The Proof (produced Birmingham, 1924; as *Vendetta*, produced London, 1924).

Other

The Great War in England in 1897. London, Tower, 1894.
The Invasion of 1910, with a Full Account of the Siege of London. London, Nash, 1906.
An Observer in the Near East. London, Nash, 1907; as *The Near East*, New York,
  Doubleday, 1907.
The Balkan Trouble; or, An Observer in the Near East. London, Nash, 1912.
The War of the Nations, vol. 1. London, Newnes, 1914.
German Atrocities: A Record of Shameless Deeds. London, Newnes, 1914.
German Spies in England: An Exposure. London, Stanley Paul, 1915.
Britain's Deadly Peril: Are We Told the Truth? London, Stanley Paul, 1915.
The Devil's Spawn: How Italy Will Defeat Them. London, Stanley Paul, 1915.
The Way to Win. London, Simpkin Marshall, 1916.
Love Intrigues of the Kaiser's Sons. London, Long, and New York, Lane, 1918.

Landru: His Secret Love Affairs. London, Stanley Paul, 1922.
Things I Know about Kings, Celebrities, and Crooks. London, Nash and Grayson, 1923.
Engelberg: The Crown Jewel of the Alps. London, Swiss Observer, 1927.
Interlaken: The Alpine Wonderland: A Novelist's Jottings. Interlaken, Official Information Bureau, n.d.

Translator, *Of the "Polar Star" in the Arctic Sea*, by Luigi Amedeo. London, Hutchinson, 1903.

*   *   *

Artist, journalist, novelist, William Le Queux was one of the earliest spy fiction writers and set the pattern for this genre for nearly a quarter century. Of his hundred-odd books which deal primarily with political intrigue, about half are about spies. His first novel, *Guilty Bonds*, dramatizes the revolutionary movement in Czarist Russia and was banned in that country. Le Queux gathered much of his background material during his foreign editorship of the *Globe* newspaper (1891–93) from which he resigned in order to devote his time to writing books. Le Queux had a lively imagination and it is difficult to separate his factual from his fictional works. He often extravagantly embellished situations and presented fiction as fact; he is a perplexing author to assess. He seems to have been involved in the British Secret Service both before and after the First World War and claimed in one of his books to have had an "intimate knowledge of the secret service of continental powers."

His early novels warned of the unpreparedness of Britain to face a European invasion, and while they lacked literary quality, the stories made potent propaganda because of their topicality and sensationalism.

In *The Great War in England in 1897*, a work of non-fiction, Le Queux dramatized a Russo-Franco plot for the invasion of England. Anti-Jewish pogroms in Russia served as a background for *A Secret Service*. Many of his spy novels emphasized the German threat to Britain. His first anti-German book was *The Invasion of 1910* and this was followed by a novel, *The Mystery of the Motor-Car*. In this story a country doctor who is called upon to treat the victim of an auto accident finds himself involved in a German plot. It is one of the best examples of Le Queux's detection-intrigue novels; though a stiff, period piece, it maintains a sense of suspense throughout.

Le Queux collaborated with British Field Marshal Lord Roberts in *The Great War* which accurately foretold the 1914–18 holocaust, and in *Spies of the Kaiser* warned that Britain was "in grave danger of invasion by Germany at a date not far distant," and that thousands of German agents were present in England. He continued this theme in *Number 70 Berlin*, *The Mystery of the Green Ray*, and *The Unbound Book*. A post-war novel, *Cipher Six*, supposedly was based on "actual events which occurred in the West End of London during the peace negotiations in the Autumn of 1918" during which time he was said to have been "engaged in assisting the police to unravel one of the most extraordinary mysteries of the past decade."

Le Queux had a sense of melodrama and was aware of the virtues of self-publicity. He said during the Great War that he habitually carried a revolver on his person since his life was in constant danger from "enemies of the State." He continued writing and lecturing on spies and spying and retired to Switzerland; many of his later books (e.g., *Hidden Hands*) had a Swiss background. The dust-jacket of *Hidden Hands* provides a vivid description of the flavor of these later spy stories: "Seton Darville, elderly novelist and secret service agent, can make love 'for business reasons' with excellent and thrillingly successful results. But between him and Edris Temperley it is a different matter altogether. She loves him – but she is young and so is Carl Weiss, ex-spy, and Darville is not. He nearly loses her, and she nearly loses both him and her unworthy Swiss lover, but comes to her senses in the nick of time."

—Daniel P. King

LESSER, Milton. See **MARLOWE, Stephen.**

LEVIN, Ira. American. Born in New York City, 27 August 1929. Educated at Drake University, Des Moines, Iowa, 1946–48; New York University, 1948–50, A.B. 1950. Served in the United States Army Signal Corps, 1953–55. Married Gabrielle Aronsohn in 1960 (divorced, 1968); three children. Recipient: Mystery Writers of America Edgar Allan Poe Award, 1954. Agent: Harold Ober Associates, 40 East 49th Street, New York, New York 10017, U.S.A.

CRIME PUBLICATIONS

Novels

> *A Kiss Before Dying.* New York, Simon and Schuster, 1953; London, Joseph, 1954.
> *Rosemary's Baby.* New York, Random House, and London, Joseph, 1967.
> *The Stepford Wives.* New York, Random House, and London, Joseph, 1972.
> *The Boys from Brazil.* New York, Random House, and London, Joseph, 1976.

OTHER PUBLICATIONS

Novel

> *This Perfect Day.* New York, Random House, and London, Joseph, 1970.

Plays

> *No Time for Sergeants,* adaptation of the novel by Mac Hyman (produced New York, 1955; London, 1956). New York, Random House, 1956.
> *Interlock* (produced New York, 1958). New York, Dramatists Play Service, 1958.
> *Critic's Choice* (produced New York, 1960; London, 1961). New York, Random House, 1961; London, Evans, 1963.
> *General Seeger* (produced New York, 1962). New York, Dramatists Play Service, 1962.
> *Drat! The Cat!,* music by Milton Schafer (produced New York, 1965).
> *Dr. Cook's Garden* (produced New York, 1967). New York, Dramatists Play Service, 1968.
> *Veronica's Room* (produced New York, 1973). New York, Random House, 1974; London, Joseph, 1975.
> *Deathtrap* (produced New York, 1978; London, 1979).
> *Break a Leg* (produced New York, 1979).

*   *   *

Ira Levin's masterpiece, and the only one of his five novels without at least a touch of fantasy, is *A Kiss Before Dying.* The beauty of this book is that it is really three books in one, each of which could almost represent a separate sub-genre of the mystery novel. Part One is told from the viewpoint of the murderer, and is something of a modern variation on *An American Tragedy.* The young man, attempting to marry into a wealthy family, is thwarted when his girl becomes pregnant and refuses to have an abortion. Knowing this will lose him her family's fortune, he kills her in a highly ingenious manner which the reader follows each step of the way. Her death is ruled a suicide.

It is not until Part Two of the novel that the reader realizes he does not know the identity of the killer. The viewpoint shifts to the dead girl's sister and the genre shifts to the detective story. The sister establishes that the apparent suicide was really murder and tracks down the killer. Unfortunately her deductions are wrong and she becomes the second victim. In Part Three, which has now become a game of wits between the two sides, a third sister and her boyfriend bring the killer to a sort of justice.

Following the clever intricacies of *A Kiss Before Dying*, Levin waited 14 years before publishing his second novel, *Rosemary's Baby*. The best-known of his works, it launched a revival of the contemporary occult-horror story in books and films. There are strong elements of mystery in the plot development of *Rosemary's Baby*, as there are in the science-fiction novel *This Perfect Day* and the contemporary fantasy *The Stepford Wives*. In each there is a problem to be solved, and there are murders along the way. *The Boys from Brazil* is an excellent contemporary neo-Nazi tale with only a single plot element – cloning – to shift it toward fantasy. In all other respects it is a suspense-intrigue story of the highest order.

Levin has written no short stories, but notice must be taken of his plays. He is a playwright by preference, and one of the few successful ones working in the mystery field. After establishing himself on Broadway with an adaptation of the non-criminous hit *No Time for Sergeants*, he wrote a trio of interesting but unsuccessful plays – a psychological melodrama, *Interlock*, a musical about a thief, *Drat! The Cat!*, and a murder melodrama, *Dr. Cook's Garden*.

Until 1973 Levin seemed to have had better success with a number of straight plays, but in that year *Veronica's Room* turned the tide and enjoyed a mild success as a mystery chiller. In 1978 Levin's long years of trying for a mystery hit on Broadway finally paid off with the success of *Deathtrap*, the best of his plays and a mystery comedy that manages even more plot twists than Anthony Shaffer's *Sleuth*.

—Edward D. Hoch

LEWIN, Michael Z. American. Born in Springfield, Massachusetts, 21 July 1942. Educated at North Central High School, Indianapolis, graduated 1960; Harvard University, Cambridge, Massachusetts (National Merit Scholar), A.B. 1964; Churchill College, Cambridge, 1964–65; University of Bridgeport, Connecticut. Married Marianne Ruth Grewe in 1965; one daughter and one son. Physics Teacher, Central High School, Bridgeport, Connecticut, 1966–68; Science Teacher, George Washington High School, New York, 1968–69. Moved to Britain in 1971. Since 1972, baseball columnist for *Somerset Standard*, Frome; has also written sketches and lyrics for revues. Agent: Wallace and Shiel Agency, 118 East 61st Street, New York, New York 10021, U.S.A.; or, Anthony Shiel Associates Ltd., 2/3 Morwell Street, London WC1B 3AR, England. Address: 5 Welshmill Road, Frome, Somerset BA11 2LA, England.

CRIME PUBLICATIONS

Novels (series character: Albert Samson in all books except *The Next Man*)

   Ask the Right Question.   New York, Putnam, 1971; London, Hamish Hamilton, 1972.

The Way We Die Now. New York, Putnam, and London, Hamish Hamilton, 1973.
The Enemies Within. New York, Knopf, and London, Hamish Hamilton, 1974.
The Next Man (novelization). New York, Warner, 1976.
Night Cover. New York, Knopf, and London, Hamish Hamilton, 1976.
The Silent Salesman. New York, Knopf, and London, Hamish Hamilton, 1978.

Uncollected Short Story

"The Loss Factor," in *Penthouse* (London), Spring 1975.

OTHER PUBLICATIONS

Plays

Radio Plays (from his own fiction): *The Way We Die Now,* 1974; *The Loss Factor,* 1975; *The Enemies Within,* 1976.

Other

How to Beat College Tests: A Practical Guide to Ease the Burden of Useless Courses. New York, Dial Press, 1970.
"Soft-Boiled But Still an Egg" (on Albert Samson), in *Murder Ink: The Mystery Reader's Companion*, edited by Dilys Winn. New York, Workman, 1977.

Michael Z. Lewin comments:
My detective novels, which form the core of my work to date, are all set in Indianapolis, Indiana, where I grew up. Four of the five are first-person stories about Albert Samson, a private detective. The other novel, *Night Cover*, centers on a policeman in Indianapolis, but Albert Samson appears as a lesser character, and is seen, for a change, not through his own eyes.

Samson, in many ways, follows the most traditional of private eye formats: he works alone, he's not well of, he suffers from virtues. But in other ways he differs. He doesn't, for instance, knock people around and shoot them very often. Which, with a relatively introspective style, probably makes him a little more contemporary than his generic progenitors. Not better, mind ... but I hope that a few more decades of work will get me within hailing distance of some of the people I admire. A sort of cross between Hammett and Jane Austen, say, with a little leaping from rooftop to rooftop.... Maybe some day.

*   *   *

Four of Michael Z. Lewin's novels feature Indianapolis private detective Albert Samson, who is the latest and most unlikely development of the hard-boiled detective. He combines the best moral qualities of the Continental Op and Lew Archer with a machismo quotient near zero. He is a serious man who works very hard to project a façade of inconsequentiality, even silliness. Samson's favorite object for his adolescent humor is himself, and his ego can be seriously deflated by losing a basketball duel to a ten-year-old. But his curiosity is piqued only by attempts to buy him off, and he has a convincing, because underplayed, concern for some of the people he deals with: those who show courage, or strength, or the capacity to love with a modicum of wisdom.

Samson's cases reflect the deceptive simplicity of his personality. They tend to start with the apparently banal and end by exposing some of the most plausibly ugly crimes in recent fiction. In *Ask the Right Question* and *The Enemies Within*, Samson traces the history of two families with secrets to hide. Lewin has learned something about the slow unfolding of horrors from Ross Macdonald; he uses them less lavishly, and just as effectively. In *The Way*

We Die Now, a Vietnam veteran whose life has been almost ruined by his country's mistakes falls into the hands of market-oriented businessmen. And in *The Silent Salesman*, American gullibility about the sacrosanct FBI produces the sweetest cover a dope ring could hope for.

—Carol Cleveland

LEWIS, (John) Roy(ston).   British.   Born in Rhondda, Glamorganshire, 17 January 1933. Educated at Pentre Grammar School, 1944–51; University of Bristol, 1951–54, LL.B. 1954; University of Exeter, 1956–57, Dip.Ed. 1957; Inner Temple, London: called to the Bar, 1965; University of Durham, 1976–78, M.A. 1978. Served in the Royal Artillery, 1954–56. Married Gwendoline Hutchings in 1955; one son and two daughters. Teacher, Okehampton Secondary School, Devon, 1957–59; Lecturer, Cannock Chase Secondary School, Staffordshire, 1959–61, Cornwall Technical College, Redruth, 1961–63, and Plymouth College of Technology, Devon, 1963–67; Inspector of Schools, Newcastle on Tyne, 1967–75. Since 1975, Deputy Principal, New College, Durham. Since 1974, Managing Director, Felton Press, educational publishers, Newcastle on Tyne. Associate, Chartered Institute of Secretaries and Administrators, 1962. Address: 207 Western Way, Darras Way, Ponteland, Newcastle on Tyne, Northumberland, England.

Crime Publications

Novels (series character: Inspector Crow)

A Lover Too Many (Crow).   London, Collins, 1969; Cleveland, World, 1971.
A Wolf by the Ears.   London, Collins, 1970; Cleveland, World, 1972.
Error of Judgment (Crow).   London, Collins, 1971.
The Fenokee Project.   London, Collins, 1971.
A Fool for a Client.   London, Collins, 1972.
The Secret Singing (Crow).   London, Collins, 1972.
Blood Money (Crow).   London, Collins, 1973.
Of Singular Purpose.   London, Collins, 1973.
A Question of Degree (Crow).   London, Collins, 1974.
Double Take.   London, Collins, 1975.
A Part of Virtue (Crow).   London, Collins, 1975.
Witness My Death.   London, Collins, 1976.
A Distant Banner.   London, Collins, 1976.
Nothing but Foxes (Crow).   London, Collins, 1977; New York, St. Martin's Press, 1979.
An Uncertain Sound.   London, Collins, 1978.
An Inevitable Fatality.   London, Collins, 1978.

Other Publications

Other as J. R. Lewis

Cases for Discussion.   Oxford, Pergamon Press, 1965.
Law of the Retailer: An Outline for Students and Business Men.   London, Allman, 1964; as *Law for the Retailer*, 1974.

An Introduction to Business Law. London, Allman, 1965.

Law in Action. London, Allman, 1965.

Questions and Answers on Civil Procedure. London, Sweet and Maxwell, 1966.

Building Law. London, Allman, 1966.

Democracy: The Theory and the Practice. London, Allman, 1966.

Managing Within the Law. London, Allman, 1967.

Principles of Registered Land Conveyancing, with John A. Holland. London, Butterworth, 1967.

Company Law. London, Allman, 1967.

Revision Notes for Ordinary Level British Constitution. London, Allman, 1967.

Civil and Criminal Procedure. London, Sweet and Maxwell, 1968.

Landlord and Tenant. London, Sweet and Maxwell, 1968.

Outlines of Equity. London, Butterworth, 1968.

Mercantile and Commercial Law, with Anne Redish. London, Heinemann, 1969.

The Company Executive and the Law (as David Springfield). London, Heinemann, 1970.

Law for the Construction Industry. London, Macmillan, 1976.

Administrative Law for the Construction Industry. London, Macmillan, 1976.

The Teaching of Public Administration in Further and Higher Education. London, Joint Universities Council, 1979.

Roy Lewis comments:

My detective fiction began with an attempt to use my legal knowledge in a crime/fictional setting and most of my books continue to have a certain legal flavour. To some extent the development of a central detective character (John Crow) has emerged, but more recently I have placed greater emphasis upon background and location. Thus one novel (*Of Singular Purpose*) is set on an actual farm location in Scotland; several novels have been located in the area where I was born and lived until I was 18 – South Wales; and more recently I have been using locations in the north east of England, where I have been living since 1967. In one book (*Error of Judgment*) I made use of my experience as an Inspector of Schools, and in *Double Take* and *An Inevitable Fatality* I have drawn upon my knowledge of the business world. I would hope my books are read for the reality of their settings, their use of legal and business backgrounds, and their development of the characters involved.

*   *   *

With Inspector Crow Roy Lewis has created a likeable, laconic protagonist, useful if not particularly original. The author seems to employ Crow for his more traditional, if never quite conventional, novels (e.g., *Nothing but Foxes*); in the Crow-less novels, Lewis displays a bolder range, both geographically and emotionally. Some of the best works are set in Wales, like *Witness My Death*, notable for the deeply felt descriptions of landscape and the cogent characterization of the remote valley folk. Even more impressive is *A Distant Banner*, again with a Welsh locale; here the actual murder and its solution are far less important than the people themselves, sympathetically and incisively portrayed. Lewis's strongest virtues are his grasp of character – his people are seldom eccentric, but lively, unexpected, even quirkish – and his unfailing sense of place, of atmosphere, whether he is writing about a Welsh building site (*A Distant Banner*), the legal world (*A Fool for a Client*), or the well-to-do bourgeoisie of Durham (*An Uncertain Sound*).

—William Weaver

LININGTON, (Barbara) Elizabeth. Also writes as Anne Blaisdell; Lesley Egan; Egan O'Neill; Dell Shannon. American. Born in Aurora, Illinois, 11 March 1921. Educated in public schools in Aurora and Hollywood, California; graduated from Herbert Hoover High School; attended Glendale College, California. Self-employed writer. Agent: Barthold Fles, 507 Fifth Avenue, New York, New York 10017. Address: 3284 South View Avenue, Arroyo Grande, California 93420, U.S.A.

CRIME PUBLICATIONS

Novels (series character: Sergeant Ivor Maddox in all books except *Nightmare*; published as Anne Blaisdell in UK)

Nightmare (as Anne Blaisdell).   New York, Harper, 1961; London, Gollancz, 1962.
Greenmask! New York, Harper, 1964; London, Gollancz, 1965.
No Evil Angel. New York, Harper, 1964; London, Gollancz, 1965.
Date with Death. New York, Harper, and London, Gollancz, 1966.
Something Wrong. New York, Harper, 1967; London, Gollancz, 1968.
Policeman's Lot. New York, Harper, 1968; London, Gollancz, 1969.
Practice to Deceive. New York, Harper, and London, Gollancz, 1971.
Crime by Chance. Philadelphia, Lippincott, 1973; London, Gollancz, 1974.
Perchance of Death. New York, Doubleday, 1977.
No Villain Need Be. New York, Doubleday, 1979.

Novels as Dell Shannon (series character: Lieutenant/Detective Luis Mendoza in all books)

Case Pending. New York, Harper, and London, Gollancz, 1960.
The Ace of Spades. New York, Morrow, 1961; London, Oldbourne, 1963.
Extra Kill. New York, Morrow, and London, Oldbourne, 1962.
Knave of Hearts. New York, Morrow, 1962; London, Oldbourne, 1963.
Death of a Busybody. New York, Morrow, and London, Oldbourne, 1963.
Double Bluff. New York, Morrow, 1963; London, Oldbourne, 1964.
Mark of Murder. New York, Morrow, 1964; London, Gollancz, 1965.
Root of All Evil. New York, Morrow, 1964; London, Gollancz, 1966.
The Death-Bringers. New York, Morrow, 1965; London, Gollancz, 1966.
Death by Inches. New York, Morrow, 1965; London, Gollancz, 1967.
Coffin Corner. New York, Morrow, 1966; London, Gollancz, 1967.
With a Vengeance. New York, Morrow, 1966; London, Gollancz, 1968.
Chance to Kill. New York, Morrow, 1967; London, Gollancz, 1968.
Rain with Violence. New York, Morrow, 1967; London, Gollancz, 1969.
Kill with Kindness. New York, Morrow, 1968; London, Gollancz, 1969.
Schooled to Kill. New York, Morrow, 1969; London, Gollancz, 1970.
Crime on Their Hands. New York, Morrow, 1969; London, Gollancz, 1970.
Unexpected Death. New York, Morrow, 1970; London, Gollancz, 1971.
Whim to Kill. New York, Morrow, and London, Gollancz, 1971.
The Ringer. New York, Morrow, 1971; London, Gollancz, 1972.
Murder with Love. New York, Morrow, and London, Gollancz, 1972.
With Intent to Kill. New York, Morrow, 1972; London, Gollancz, 1973.
No Holiday for Crime. New York, Morrow, 1973; London, Gollancz, 1974.
Spring of Violence. New York, Morrow, 1973; London, Gollancz, 1974.
Crime File. New York, Morrow, 1974; London, Gollancz, 1975.
Deuces Wild. New York, Morrow, and London, Gollancz, 1975.
Streets of Death. New York, Morrow, 1976; London, Gollancz, 1977.
Appearances of Death. New York, Morrow, 1977; London, Gollancz, 1978.
Cold Trail. New York, Morrow, 1978; London, Gollancz, 1979.

Felony at Random. New York, Morrow, and London, Gollancz, 1979.

Novels as Lesley Egan (series characters: Jesse Falkenstein and Vic Varallo in all books)

A Case for Appeal. New York, Harper, and London, Gollancz, 1961.
Against the Evidence. New York, Harper, 1962; London, Gollancz, 1963.
The Borrowed Alibi. New York, Harper, and London, Gollancz, 1962.
Run to Evil. New York, Harper, and London, Gollancz, 1963.
My Name Is Death. New York, Harper, and London, Gollancz, 1965.
Detective's Due. New York, Harper, 1965; London, Gollancz, 1966.
Some Avenger, Rise! New York, Harper, 1966; London, Gollancz, 1967.
The Nameless Ones. New York, Harper, 1967; London, Gollancz, 1968.
A Serious Investigation. New York, Harper, 1968; London, Gollancz, 1969.
The Wine of Violence. New York, Harper, 1969; London, Gollancz, 1970.
In the Death of a Man. New York, Harper, and London, Gollancz, 1970.
Malicious Mischief. New York, Harper, 1971; London, Gollancz, 1972.
Paper Chase. New York, Harper, 1972; London, Gollancz, 1973.
Scenes of Crime. New York, Doubleday, 1976.
The Blind Search. New York, Doubleday, 1977.
A Dream Apart. New York, Doubleday, 1978.
Look Back on Death. New York, Doubleday, 1978.
The Hunters and the Hunted. New York, Doubleday, 1979.

Uncollected Short Stories

"Flash Attachment," in *Tales for a Rainy Night*, edited by David Alexander. New York, Holt Rinehart, 1961; London, Dobson, 1967.
"The Practical Joke," in *Tales of Unease*, edited by John Burke. London, Pan, 1966; New York, Doubleday, 1969.

OTHER PUBLICATIONS

Novels

The Proud Man. New York, Viking Press, 1955.
The Long Watch. New York, Viking Press, 1956.
Monsieur Janvier. New York, Doubleday, 1957.
The Anglophile (as Egan O'Neill). New York, Messner, 1957; as *The Pretender*, London, W. H. Allen, 1957.
The Kingbreaker. New York, Doubleday, 1958.

Other

Forging an Empire: Elizabeth I (juvenile). Chicago, Kingston House, 1961.
Come to Think of It. Boston, Western Islands, 1965.

Manuscript Collection: Mugar Memorial Library, Boston University.

Elizabeth Linington comments:
    I don't know what to say about the crime fiction, which seems to be very popular, except that three of the series are police procedural stories and I do try to keep them authentic as far as police techniques are concerned. The various cases wandering through these books are not of primary interest to the reader – many are the usual sordid, monotonous cases any Robbery-Homicide office deals with; readers get interested in the men and their families, their

pets, homes, and so on. Since the Mendoza series has been going, several of the men have had romances, married, started families, and it seems to be this interest with the police officers' private lives which constitutes the interest on the part of the readers. I do, however, frequently use real crime cases in all these series and try to keep the cases interesting too.

*   *   *

Elizabeth Linington has written books of several types: historical novels, gothic/romantic/ suspense novels, and detective fiction. *The Proud Man*, her first novel, is set in 16th-century Ireland, where Shane O'Neill, Prince of Ulster, almost succeeds in overthrowing English rule and making himself king of a united Ireland. The second historical novel, *The Long Watch*, appeared the following year. It is set in New York during the American Revolution; the hero, an orphan of 16, runs away from Virginia to begin a new life in New York working as clerk to the editor of the New York *Courier*. *Monsieur Janvier* is set in 18th-century Scotland, Paris, and London, and *The Kingbreaker* deals with Revolution and Civil War in England at the middle of the 17th century. It stars a young Welsh gentleman, Ivor ap-Maddox, who is loyal to the king and who acts as a spy in the household of Oliver Cromwell. Linington has also written one gothic/romantic/suspense novel, *Nightmare*, about an American girl whose holiday ramble leads her into the clutches of a female religious fanatic.

In 1960 Linington, as Dell Shannon, began one of her three series of police stories. *Case Pending* introduced a lieutenant of Mexican heritage named Luis Mendoza, a bookish, scholarly, gentlemanly policeman who inherited a lot of money and began collecting expensive sports cars and exotic cats. He drives a Ferrari, an Aston Martin, and a Facel Vega; at home are several Siamese, Burmese, and Abyssinian cats, the eldest of which loves rye whisky and is named El Señor. Mendoza's first appearance drew warm reviews. Then came *Ace of Spades*, and it was becoming obvious that it was the fascination of Mendoza that readers were responding to rather than the book as a whole. The Dell Shannon books continue to attract praise, particularly in the accuracy of police procedure, and because they treat the theme of the stupidity of violence and support the idea of using reason to solve crimes.

In 1961 Linington began a second detective series, this time as Lesley Egan. This series stars Detective Vic Varallo, and is also set in the Los Angeles metropolitan area, this time in the suburb of Glendale. Also starring are Jesse Falkenstein, a Jewish lawyer, and his wife Nell, and readers seem to like the dramatization of the relationship between Falkenstein and his wife, and the domestic complications of Varallo. One of the best books in this series is *Some Avenger, Rise!* where Falkenstein takes time from his law practice to rescue his friend, Sergeant Andy Clock of the LAPD, from the serious accusation of accepting a bribe. With a recent book in this series, *A Dream Apart*, Linington is being compared positively by readers to John Creasey for her solid, diligent accounts of professional police work, with several cases to each book. In her case, however, she has just a touch too much "suburban domesticity" behind her policeman, and some reviewers point out that, in contrast to, say, the McBain 87th precinct novels, the Egan police procedural novels force characterization onto a conceived plot.

Linington began yet a third series of detective stories, under her own name, with *Greenmask!* This series features Sergeant Ivor Maddox of the Hollywood Police Department, with Detectives D'Arcy and Rodriguez and policewoman Sue Carstairs. *Greenmask!* has been highly praised as "a mystery reader's mystery novel." In the story the Hollywood police use tips from old crime novels of the 1920's to solve a series of contemporary murders.

All three of Linington's detective series continue, in the 1970's, to draw generally high praise, and she is becoming known as "Queen of the Procedurals."

—Elizabeth F. Duke

LITTLE, Constance and Gwyneth. Also wrote as Conyth Little.

CRIME PUBLICATIONS

Novels (published as Conyth Little in UK)

The Grey Mist Murders. New York, Doubleday, 1938.
The Black-Headed Pins. New York, Doubleday, 1938; London, Davies, 1939.
The Black Gloves. New York, Doubleday, 1939; London, Collins, 1940.
Black Corridors. New York, Doubleday, 1940; London, Collins, 1941.
The Black Paw. New York, Doubleday, and London, Collins, 1941.
The Black Shrouds. New York, Doubleday, 1941; London, Collins, 1942.
The Black Thumb. New York, Doubleday, 1942; London, Collins, 1943.
The Black Rustle. New York, Doubleday, 1943; as The Black Lady, London, Collins, 1944.
The Black Honeymoon. New York, Doubleday, and London, Collins, 1944.
Great Black Kanba. New York, Doubleday, 1944; as The Black Express, London, Collins, 1945.
The Black Eye. New York, Doubleday, 1945; London, Collins, 1946.
The Black Stocking. New York, Doubleday, 1946; London, Collins, 1947.
The Black Goatee. New York, Doubleday, and London, Collins, 1947.
The Black Coat. New York, Doubleday, 1948; London, Collins, 1949.
The Black Piano. New York, Doubleday, and London, Collins, 1948.
The Black House. New York, Doubleday, and London, Collins, 1950.
The Black Smith. New York, Doubleday, 1950; London, Collins, 1951.
The Blackout. New York, Doubleday, 1951; London, Collins, 1952.
The Black Dream. New York, Doubleday, 1952; London, Collins, 1953.
The Black Curl. New York, Doubleday, 1953.
The Black Iris. New York, Doubleday, and London, Collins, 1953.

*   *   *

Constance and Gwyneth Little, together Conyth Little, have been severely criticized by Barzun and Taylor in *A Catalogue of Crime* for being "among the first to show how to destroy rationality by a judicious application of nerve irritants as in *The Black Dream* about a boarding house murder." This criticism seems somewhat harsh to the many Little fans and collectors who search in vain for the missing volumes for their library. True, the characters in *The Black Dream* are shallow, the plot not as intricate as a veteran mystery fan would demand, and the ending far from satisfactory, particularly in revealing the motive for the murder, but a few tense, suspense-filled moments and some amusing repartee among the extremely diversified characters make the novel fairly good light reading.

Intriguingly, all of the Little novels, except their first, *The Grey Mist Murders*, contain the word "black" in the title. One of the most interesting is *Great Black Kanba*, set in the wilderness of Australia and involving an exciting and dangerous cross-continental train excursion. The unique combination of a beautiful young actress suffering from amnesia, the Australian mounted police, a pet lizard, and a ruthless murderer who has a penchant for slitting throats, engages the reader in a suspenseful tale fashioned in a lighthearted and witty style.

—Mary Ann Grochowski

LITVINOV, Ivy (née Low).   British.   Married the Soviet diplomat Maxim Litvinov in 1916 (died, 1951); one son and one daughter. *Died in 1977.*

CRIME PUBLICATIONS

Novel

   His Master's Voice (as Ivy Low).   London, Heinemann, 1930; as *Moscow Mystery*, New York, Coward McCann, 1943; revised edition, London, Gollancz, 1973.

OTHER PUBLICATIONS

Novels

   Growing Pains.   London, Heinemann, and New York, Doran, 1913.
   The Questing Beast.   London, Secker, 1914.

Short Stories

   She Knew She Was Right.   London, Gollancz, 1971.

Other

   Editor, *The Bolshevik Revolution*, by Maxim Litvinov.   London, British Socialist Party, 1919.

   Translator, *Bolshevism for Beginners: A Handbook for New Members of the Communist Party and for Self-Education*, by P. M. Kerzhentzev.   Moscow, Centrizdat, 1931.
   Translator, *Mourzouk*, by V. Bianchi.   London, Allen and Unwin, 1937.
   Translator, *Forest News*, by V. Bianchi.   London, Allen and Unwin, 1938.
   Translator, *The Adventures of Masha*, by Sergei Rosanov.   New York, Stokes, 1938.
   Translator, *The Russian Impact on Art*, by M. V. Alpatov.   New York, Philosophical Library, 1950.
   Translator, *The Road to Life*, by A. S. Makarenko.   London, Collett, 3 vols., 1952.
   Translator, with Tatiana Litvinov, *The Tales of Ivan Belkin*, by Pushkin.   Moscow, Foreign Languages Publishing House, 1954.
   Translator, with Tatiana Litvinov, *Dubrovsky*, by Pushkin.   Moscow, Foreign Languages Publishing House, 1955.
   Translator, with Tatiana Litvinov, *Three Short Novels: Asya, First Love, Spring Torrents*, by Turgenev.   Moscow, Foreign Languages Publishing House, 1955.
   Translator, *The Queen of Spades*, by Pushkin.   Moscow, Foreign Languages Publishing House, 1956.
   Translator, *My Uncle's Death*, by Dostoevsky.   London, Sidgwick and Jackson, 1958.
   Translator, *Literary Portraits*, by Gorky.   Moscow, Foreign Languages Publishing House, 1959.
   Translator, *One Thousand Souls*, by Alexei Pisemsky.   New York, Grove Press, and London, John Calder, 1959.
   Translator, *The Simpleton*, by Alexei Pisemsky.   Moscow, Foreign Languages Publishing House, 1960.
   Translator, with Julius Katzer, *On Literature: Selected Articles*, by Gorky.   Moscow, Foreign Languages Publishing House, 1960.
   Translator, with Tatiana Litvinov, *The Captain's Daughter*, by Pushkin.   Moscow, Progress Publishers, 1965.

Translator, with Tatiana Litvinov, *Ordeal: A Trilogy*, by Alexis Tolstoy. Moscow, Progress Publishers, 3 vols., 1967.

Translator, with Tatiana Litvinov, *The Fisherman's Son*, by Vilis Lacis. Moscow, Progress Publishers, 1968.

Translator, *The Sun's Storehouse*, by Mikhail M. Prishvin. Moscow, Progress Publishers, 1975.

*   *   *

Ivy Litvinov, an English girl married to the man who turned out to be People's Commissar for Foreign Affairs in Moscow and later Russian Ambassador inWashington, wrote only one detective novel. But it is a distinguished one, and interesting both in its own right and for the way it came into the world. *His Master's Voice* has been published three times, first in 1930 in Britain under the author's maiden name of Ivy Low ("Readers of detective fiction prefer an English author," her publishers pronounced), next in America in 1943 (when Russia and the U.S. were united against a common enemy) and again in Britain in 1973 in a revised edition. Besides this book Ivy Litvinov wrote two early novels and a volume of short stories.

The crime story may be unique among the genre for having been born as the result of hypnosis. In Moscow in 1924 the young English wife and mother longed to write a third novel but found herself unable to do so. In the apartment block where she lived there came on a visit a distinguished German professor there to investigate the brain of the recently-dead Lenin. He was also a hypnotist and eventually agreed to use his skill on Ivy Litvinov. He told her that as soon as his visit was over she should sit at her husband's desk each morning after he had left for work and she would write a novel. It so happened that when the professor left she had been reading a detective story "for the first time since I shivered over Sherlock Holmes at boarding school." So what she wrote was a detective story in her turn.

But it is a detective story with a difference. It is set in the Soviet Union in the year 1926. The detective is a nice, rather ordinary, middle-aged District Procurator, to whose chagrin the solution of his mystery is first proposed by an interfering officer of the Ogpu, grandfather of the KGB, a man of diamond-glittering charm, too apt to see Whites under the bed and slightly frightening to the hero. The whole book, too, is delightfully warm-hearted and rooted in human behaviour the same from Kansas to Katmandu.

—H. R. F. Keating

LOCKRIDGE, Richard and Frances. Americans. **LOCKRIDGE, Richard (Orson):** Born in St. Joseph, Missouri, 25 September 1898. Educated at Kansas City Junior College; University of Missouri, Columbia. Served in the United States Navy, 1918. Married 1) Frances Davis in 1922 (died, 1963); 2) Hildegarde Dolson, *q.v.*, in 1965. Reporter, Kansas City *Kansan*, 1921–22, and Kansas City *Star*, 1922; Reporter, 1922–28, and Drama Critic, 1928 to the 1940's, New York *Sun*; also associated with *The New Yorker*. Address: 206 Hillside Court, Tryon, North Carolina 28782, U.S.A. **LOCKRIDGE, Frances (Louise, née Davis):** Born in Kansas City, Missouri, 10 January 1896. Educated in public schools in Kansas City; University of Kansas, Lawrence and extension courses. Married Richard Lockridge in 1922. Reporter and Music Critic, Kansas City *Post*, 1918–22; Assistant Secretary to adoption and placement committee, State Charities Aid Association, 1922–42. *Died 17 February 1963*. The Lockridges: Co-Presidents, Mystery Writers of America, 1960. Recipient: Mystery Writers of America Edgar Allan Poe Award, for radio play, 1945, Special Award, 1962.

Crime Publications

Novels as Frances and Richard Lockridge (series characters: Paul Lane; Mr. and Mrs. North with Bill Wiegand; Nathan Shapiro; Bernard Simmons)

The Norths Meet Murder. New York, Stokes, and London, Joseph, 1940.
Murder Out of Turn (Norths). New York, Stokes, and London, Joseph, 1941.
A Pinch of Poison (Norths). New York, Stokes, 1941; London, Joseph, 1948.
Death on the Aisle (Norths). Philadelphia, Lippincott, 1942; London, Hutchinson, 1948.
Hanged for a Sheep (Norths). Philadelphia, Lippincott, 1942; London, Hutchinson, 1944.
Death Takes a Bow (Norths). Philadelphia, Lippincott, 1943; London, Hutchinson, 1945.
Killing the Goose (Norths). Philadelphia, Lippincott, 1944; London, Hutchinson, 1947.
Payoff for the Banker (Norths). Philadelphia, Lippincott, 1945; London, Hutchinson, 1948.
Death of a Tall Man (Norths). Philadelphia, Lippincott, 1946; London, Hutchinson, 1949.
Murder Within Murder (Norths). Philadelphia, Lippincott, 1946; London, Hutchinson, 1949.
Untidy Murder (Norths). Philadelphia, Lippincott, 1947.
Murder Is Served (Norths). Philadelphia, Lippincott, 1948; London, Hutchinson, 1950.
The Dishonest Murder (Norths). Philadelphia, Lippincott, 1949; London, Hutchinson, 1951.
Murder in a Hurry (Norths). Philadelphia, Lippincott, 1950; London, Hutchinson, 1952.
Murder Comes First (Norths). Philadelphia, Lippincott, 1951.
Dead as a Dinosaur (Norths). Philadelphia, Lippincott, 1952; London, Hutchinson, 1956.
Death Has a Small Voice (Norths). Philadelphia, Lippincott, 1953; London, Hutchinson, 1954.
Curtain for a Jester (Norths). Philadelphia, Lippincott, 1953.
A Key to Death (Norths). Philadelphia, Lippincott, 1954.
Death of an Angel. Philadelphia, Lippincott, 1955; London, Hutchinson, 1957; as *Mr. and Mrs. North and the Poisoned Playboy*, New York, Avon, 1957.
Murder! Murder! Murder! (omnibus). Philadelphia, Lippincott, 1956.
The Faceless Adversary (Shapiro). Philadelphia, Lippincott, 1956; as *Case of the Murdered Redhead*, New York, Avon, 1957.
Voyage into Violence (Norths). Philadelphia, Lippincott, 1956; London, Hutchinson, 1959.
The Tangled Cord (Wiegand). Philadelphia, Lippincott, 1957; London, Hutchinson, 1959.
Catch as Catch Can. Philadelphia, Lippincott, 1958; London, Long, 1960.
The Long Skeleton (Norths). Philadelphia, Lippincott, 1958; London, Hutchinson, 1960.
The Innocent House. Philadelphia, Lippincott, 1959; London, Long, 1961.
Murder and Blueberry Pie (Shapiro). Philadelphia, Lippincott, 1959; as *Call It Coincidence*, London, Long, 1962.
Murder Is Suggested (Norths). Philadelphia, Lippincott, 1959; London, Hutchinson, 1961.
The Golden Man. Philadelphia, Lippincott, 1960; London, Hutchinson, 1961.
The Judge Is Reversed (Norths). Philadelphia, Lippincott, 1960; London, Hutchinson, 1961.

The Drill Is Death (Shapiro).   Philadelphia, Lippincott, 1961; London, Long, 1963.
Murder Has Its Points (Norths).   Philadelphia, Lippincott, 1961; London, Hutchinson, 1962.
And Left for Dead (Simmons).   Philadelphia, Lippincott, and London, Hutchinson, 1962.
Night of Shadows (Lane).   Philadelphia, Lippincott, 1962; London, Long, 1964.
The Ticking Clock.   Philadelphia, Lippincott, 1962; London, Hutchinson, 1964.
Murder by the Book (Norths).   Philadelphia, Lippincott, 1963; London, Hutchinson, 1964.
The Devious Ones (Simmons).   Philadelphia, Lippincott, 1964; as *Four Hours to Fear*, London, Long, 1965.
Quest for the Bogeyman (Lane).   Philadelphia, Lippincott, 1964; London, Hutchinson, 1965.

Novels as Richard and Frances Lockridge (series character: Captain/Inspector Merton Heimrich in all books)

Think of Death.   Philadelphia, Lippincott, 1947.
I Want to Go Home.   Philadelphia, Lippincott, 1948.
Spin Your Web, Lady!   Philadelphia, Lippincott, 1949; London, Hutchinson, 1952.
Foggy, Foggy Death.   Philadelphia, Lippincott, 1950; London, Hutchinson, 1953.
A Client Is Cancelled.   Philadelphia, Lippincott, 1951; London, Hutchinson, 1955.
Death by Association.   Philadelphia, Lippincott, 1952; London, Hutchinson, 1957; as *Trial by Terror*, New York, Spivak, 1954.
Stand Up and Die.   Philadelphia, Lippincott, 1953; London, Hutchinson, 1955.
Death and the Gentle Bull.   Philadelphia, Lippincott, 1954; London, Hutchinson, 1956; as *Killer in the Straw*, New York, Spivak, 1955.
Burnt Offering.   Philadelphia, Lippincott, 1955; London, Hutchinson, 1957.
Let Dead Enough Alone.   Philadelphia, Lippincott, 1956; London, Hutchinson, 1958.
Practice to Deceive.   Philadelphia, Lippincott, 1955; London, Hutchinson, 1959.
Accent on Murder.   Philadelphia, Lippincott, 1958; London, Long, 1960.
Show Red for Danger.   Philadelphia, Lippincott, 1960; London, Long, 1961.
With One Stone.   Philadelphia, Lippincott, 1961; as *No Dignity in Death*, London, Long, 1962.
First Come, First Kill.   Philadelphia, Lippincott, 1962; London, Long, 1963.
The Distant Clue.   Philadelphia, Lippincott, 1963; London, Long, 1964.

Novels as Richard Lockridge (series characters: Captain/Inspector Merton Heimrich; Nathan Shapiro; Bernard Simmons)

Death in the Mind, with G. H. Estabrooks.   New York, Dutton, 1945.
A Matter of Taste.   Philadelphia, Lippincott, 1949; London, Hutchinson, 1951.
Murder Can't Wait (Heimrich; Shapiro).   Philadelphia, Lippincott, 1964; London, Long, 1965.
Squire of Death (Simmons).   Philadelphia, Lippincott, 1965; London, Long, 1966.
Murder Roundabout (Heimrich).   Philadelphia, Lippincott, 1966; London, Long, 1967.
Murder for Art's Sake (Shapiro).   Philadelphia, Lippincott, 1967; London, Long, 1968.
With Option to Die (Heimrich).   Philadelphia, Lippincott, 1967; London, Long, 1968.
Murder in False-Face.   Philadelphia, Lippincott, 1968; London, Hutchinson, 1969.
A Plate of Red Herrings (Simmons).   Philadelphia, Lippincott, 1968; London, Long, 1969.
Die Laughing (Shapiro).   Philadelphia, Lippincott, 1969; London, Long, 1970.
A Risky Way to Kill (Heimrich).   Philadelphia, Lippincott, 1969; London, Long, 1970.
Troubled Journey.   Philadelphia, Lippincott, 1970; London, Hutchinson, 1971.
Twice Retired (Simmons).   Philadelphia, Lippincott, 1970; London, Long, 1971.

Inspector's Holiday (Heimrich).   Philadelphia, Lippincott, 1971; London, Long, 1972.
Preach No More (Shapiro).   Philadelphia, Lippincott, 1971; London, Long, 1972.
Death in a Sunny Place.   Philadelphia, Lippincott, 1972; London, Long, 1973.
Something up a Sleeve (Simmons).   Philadelphia, Lippincott, 1972; London, Long, 1973.
Write Murder Down (Shapiro).   Philadelphia, Lippincott, 1972; London, Long, 1974.
Not I, Said the Sparrow (Heimrich).   Philadelphia, Lippincott, 1973; London, Long, 1974.
Death on the Hour (Simmons).   Philadelphia, Lippincott, 1974; London, Long, 1975.
Or Was He Pushed? (Shapiro).   Philadelphia, Lippincott, 1975; London, Long, 1976.
Dead Run (Heimrich).   Philadelphia, Lippincott, 1976; London, Long, 1977.
A Streak of Light.   Philadelphia, Lippincott, 1976; London, Long, 1978.
The Tenth Life.   Philadelphia, Lippincott, 1977; London, Long, 1979.

Uncollected Short Stories

"Nice Judge Trowbridge," in *Short Stories from the New Yorker.*   New York, Simon and Schuster, 1940.
"Death on a Foggy Morning," in *"This Week's" Stories of Mystery and Suspense*, edited by Stewart Beach.   New York, Random House, 1957.
"All Men Make Mistakes," in *Ellery Queen's 14th Annual.*   New York, Random House, 1959; London, Gollancz, 1961.
"Cat of Dreams," in *Ellery Queen's Mystery Magazine* (New York), May 1960.
"Captain Heimrich Stumbles," in *Ellery Queen's 15th Mystery Annual.*   New York, Random House, 1960; London, Gollancz, 1961.
"Pattern for Murder," in *Anthology 1961*, edited by Ellery Queen.   New York, Davis, 1960.
"The Accusing Smoke," in *Ellery Queen's Mystery Magazine* (New York), August 1961.
"The Scent of Murder," in *Ellery Queen's 16th Mystery Annual.*   New York, Random House, 1961.
"Nobody Can Ask That," in *Anthology 1962*, edited by Ellery Queen.   New York, Davis, 1961.
"The Searching Cats," in *Anthology 1965*, edited by Ellery Queen.   New York, Davis, 1964.
"Dead Boys Don't Remember," in *Anthology 1966 Mid-Year*, edited by Ellery Queen.   New York, Davis, 1966.
"Flair for Murder," in *Ellery Queen's Crime Carousel.*   New York, New American Library, 1966.
"A Winter's Tale," in *Anthology 1967 Mid-Year*, edited by Ellery Queen.   New York, Davis, 1967.
"If They Give Him Time," in *Anthology 1970 Mid-Year*, edited by Ellery Queen.   New York, Davis, 1970.

OTHER PUBLICATIONS

Novels by Richard Lockridge

Mr. and Mrs. North.   New York, Stokes, 1936; London, Joseph, 1937.
The Empty Day.   Philadelphia, Lippincott, 1965.
Encounter in Key West.   Philadelphia, Lippincott, 1966.

Play

Radio Play: *Mr. and Mrs. North*, 1945.

Other

How to Adopt a Child, by Frances Lockridge.   New York, New York Children, 1928;
  revised edition, as *Adopting a Child*, New York, Greenberg, 1948.
Darling of Misfortune: Edwin Booth, by Richard Lockridge.   New York, Century, 1932.
Cats and People.   Philadelphia, Lippincott, 1950.
The Proud Cat (juvenile).   Philadelphia, Lippincott, 1951.
The Lucky Cat (juvenile).   Philadelphia, Lippincott, 1953.
The Nameless Cat (juvenile).   Philadelphia, Lippincott, 1954.
The Cat Who Rode Cows (juvenile).   Philadelphia, Lippincott, 1955.
One Lady, Two Cats (juvenile), by Richard Lockridge.   Philadelphia, Lippincott, 1967.

Editors, *Crime for Two*.   Philadelphia, Lippincott, 1955; London, Macdonald, 1957.

*   *   *

Richard Lockridge, with Frances until her death, and alone since then, is among the most prolific of mystery writers. Beginning in the 1940's, the Lockridges produced mystery after mystery with gratifying regularity, quickly establishing themselves with their books; movies and TV series based on their books spread their fame even beyond their considerable reading public. This popularity is well deserved, though as devisers of mystery plots they have never been in the front rank. Their strength lies in the characters they created, in their descriptive ability, in their remarkable capacity for evoking a mood in a few words and depicting an aura in a couple of sentences, and, to a lesser degree, in their deft handling of witty, amusing dialogue.

Nearly all of the Lockridge novels can be considered as part of an extended series involving quite a number of interconnected sub-series, the principal characters of which often pop up in each other's novels. Indeed, the Lockridges have created an entire world of characters, centered about New York and the surrounding countryside; they handle metropolitan crime and its bucolic cousin with equal aplomb. In the city, the hamlet, or on the farm, the Lockridges are equally at home.

Mr. and Mrs. North – Jerry and Pam – were their first series characters, created in the early 1940's, and in the early days of their writing career the Lockridges confined their writing to the North series (which also included Bill Wiegand and Sergeant Mullins of the New York Police Department). Though the best known of the Lockridge series, the North novels possess characteristics which have put off a number of readers. Pam's intuition is often, perhaps even usually, a bit extreme, the North cats are overly obtrusive, and the practice of ending each novel with a terror-filled chase in which the mysterious murderer is in hot pursuit of Mrs. North soon becomes tiresome. Nevertheless, the novels have a certain charm about them and, taken in moderation, are capable of producing a pleasant glow of well-being in the reader.

Less well known, though of much higher quality in terms of plotting and characterization, is the series centered on Merton Heimrich of the New York State Police. When the Lockridges first began this series, several years after the North series had become well established, Heimrich was single, and the only other regular character in the series was his good friend and colleague, Charlie Forniss. Heimrich's character developed rapidly, and as the series progressed the Putnam County hamlet of The Corners became pleasantly familiar to the reader, especially the Old Stone Inn, featured in a number of the novels. Heimrich eventually marries a young widow, Susan Faye, who has a young son. The Lockridges' treatment of their loving marriage is warming without being cloying, and watching the young boy Michael grow up from novel to novel is just one of the many pleasant features of the series. Though not without humor, the Heimrich series is much more serious than the flighty North novels, and its characters, being better developed, are more human, likeable and believable than the North bunch.

There is also the series featuring Nathan Shapiro, a Jewish cop who usually works in homicide under Bill Wiegand – an example of the overlapping of series characters typical of the Lockridge works. In *Murder Can't Wait*, another combination, Shapiro and Heimrich, teams up to solve the murder of the sportsman Stuart Fleming, who is killed just as he is about to blow the whistle on crooked gambling in collegiate sports. Shapiro harbors considerable doubts about his competence as a policeman. Since he is in fact highly competent, this self-doubt is an endearing foible, as is Heimrich's similarly mistaken belief that he moves like a hippopotamus.

Another Lockridge series features assistant New York City D.A. Bernie Simmons, and one of the most appealing of the recurring characters is retired professor Walter Brinkley, late of Dyckman University (who has an equally likeable black majordomo named Harry Washington), who appears from time to time in the various series without having an extended series of his own.

The Lockridge regulars are all people one would like to know, and getting to know them through the numerous novels is much like acquiring real friends. The Lockridges were never ones to duck social and political issues, and having their characters encounter and react to prejudice, intolerance, and demagogy lends real substance to their books, increasing their vitality and believability.

—Guy M. Townsend

LOFTS, Norah (née Robinson).   Also writes as Juliet Astley; Peter Curtis.   British.   Born in Shipdham, Norfolk, 27 August 1904. Educated at West Suffolk County School; Norwich Training College, teaching diploma 1925. Married 1) Geoffrey Lofts in 1931 (died, 1948), one son; 2) Robert Jorisch in 1949. Taught English and history at Guildhall Feoffment Girl's School, 1925–36. Recipient: Georgette Heyer Prize, for historical novel, 1978. Agent: Curtis Brown Ltd., 575 Madison Avenue, New York, New York 10022, U.S.A. Address: Northgate House, Bury St. Edmunds, Suffolk, England.

CRIME PUBLICATIONS

Novels

> *Michael and All the Angels.*   London, Joseph, 1943; as *The Golden Fleece*, New York, Knopf, 1944.
> *Charlotte.*   London, Hodder and Stoughton, 1972; as *Out of the Dark*, New York, Doubleday, 1972.
> *Checkmate.*   London, Corgi, 1975; New York, Fawcett, 1978.

Novels as Peter Curtis

> *Dead March in Three Keys.*   London, Davies, 1940; as *No Question of Murder*, New York, Doubleday, 1959; as *The Bride of Moat House*, New York, Dell, 1969.
> *You're Best Alone.*   London, Macdonald, 1943.
> *Lady Living Alone.*   London, Macdonald, 1945.
> *The Devil's Own.*   London, Macdonald, and New York, Doubleday, 1960; as *The Witches*, London, Pan, 1966; as *The Little Wax Doll*, London, Hodder and Stoughton, and New York, Doubleday, 1970.

OTHER PUBLICATIONS

Novels

Here Was a Man: A Romantic History of Sir Walter Raleigh.   London, Methuen, and New York, Knopf, 1936.
White Hell of Pity.   London, Methuen, and New York, Knopf, 1937.
Requiem for Idols.   London, Methuen, and New York, Knopf, 1938.
Out of This Nettle.   London, Gollancz, 1938; as *Colin Lowrie*, New York, Knopf, 1939.
Blossom Like the Rose.   London, Gollancz, and New York, Knopf, 1939.
Hester Roon.   London, Davies, and New York, Knopf, 1940.
The Road to Revelation.   London, Davies, 1941.
The Brittle Glass.   London, Joseph, 1942; New York, Knopf, 1943.
Jassy.   London, Joseph, and New York, Knopf, 1944.
To See a Fine Lady.   London, Joseph, and New York, Knopf, 1946.
Silver Nutmeg.   London, Joseph, and New York, Doubleday, 1947.
A Calf for Venus.   London, Joseph, and New York, Doubleday, 1949; as *Letty*, New York, Pyramid, 1968.
Esther.   New York, Macmillan, 1950; London, Joseph, 1951.
The Lute Player.   London, Joseph, and New York, Doubleday, 1951.
Bless This House.   London, Joseph, and New York, Doubleday, 1954.
Winter Harvest.   New York, Doubleday, 1955.
Queen in Waiting.   London, Joseph, 1955; as *Eleanor the Queen*, New York, Doubleday, 1955; as *Queen in Waiting*, Doubleday, 1958.
Afternoon of an Autocrat.   London, Joseph, and New York, Doubleday, 1956; as *The Devil in Clevely*, Leeds, Morley Barker, 1968.
Scent of Cloves.   New York, Doubleday, 1957; London, Hutchinson, 1958.
The Town House.   London, Hutchinson, and New York, Doubleday, 1959.
The House at Old Vine.   London, Hutchinson, and New York, Doubleday, 1961.
The House at Sunset.   New York, Doubleday, 1962; London, Hutchinson, 1963.
The Concubine: A Novel Based upon the Life of Anne Boleyn.   New York, Doubleday, 1963; London, Hutchinson, 1964; as *Concubine*, London, Arrow, 1965.
How Far to Bethlehem?   London, Hutchinson, and New York, Doubleday, 1965.
The Lost Ones.   London, Hutchinson, 1969; as *The Lost Queen*, New York, Doubleday, 1969; London, Corgi, 1970.
Madselin.   London, Corgi, 1969.
The King's Pleasure.   New York, Doubleday, 1969; London, Hodder and Stoughton, 1970.
Lovers All Untrue.   London, Hodder and Stoughton, and New York, Doubleday, 1970.
A Rose for Virtue.   London, Hodder and Stoughton, and New York, Doubleday, 1971.
Nethergate.   London, Hodder and Stoughton, and New York, Doubleday, 1973.
Crown of Aloes.   London, Hodder and Stoughton, and New York, Doubleday, 1974.
Knight's Acre.   London, Hodder and Stoughton, and New York, Doubleday, 1975.
The Homecoming.   London, Hodder and Stoughton, 1975; New York, Doubleday, 1976.
The Fall of Midas (as Juliet Astley).   New York, Coward McCann, 1975; London, Joseph, 1976.
The Lonely Furrow.   London, Hodder and Stoughton, 1976; New York, Doubleday, 1977.
Gad's Hall.   London, Hodder and Stoughton, 1977; New York, Doubleday, 1978.
Copsi Castle (as Juliet Astley).   London, Joseph, and New York, Coward McCann, 1978.
Haunted House, London, Hodder and Stoughton, 1978; as *The Haunting of Gad's Hall*, New York, Doubleday, 1979.
The Day of the Butterfly.   London, Bodley Head, 1979; New York, Doubleday, 1980.

Short Stories

I Met a Gypsy. London, Methuen, and New York, Knopf, 1935.
Heaven in Your Hand and Other Stories. New York, Doubleday, 1958; London, Joseph, 1959.
Is Anybody There? London, Corgi, 1974; as *Hauntings: Is Anybody There?*, New York, Doubleday, 1975.

Other

Women in the Old Testament: Twenty Psychological Portraits. London, Sampson Low, and New York, Macmillan, 1949.
Eternal France: A History of France 1789–1944, with Margery Weiner. New York, Doubleday, 1968; London, Hodder and Stoughton, 1969.
The Story of Maude Reed (juvenile). London, Transworld, 1971; as *The Maude Reed Tale*, New York, Nelson, 1972.
Rupert Hatton's Story (juvenile). London, Carousel Books, 1972.
Domestic Life in England. London, Weidenfeld and Nicolson, and New York, Doubleday, 1976.
Queens of Britain. London, Hodder and Stoughton, 1977; as *The Queens of England*, New York, Doubleday, 1977.
Emma Hamilton. London, Joseph, and New York, Coward McCann, 1978.
Anne Boleyn. New York, Coward McCann, 1979.

Norah Lofts comments:
What comment can I make about my crime novels? I can tell you how they started. One day somebody was describing a practical joke and said, "If anybody did that to me I should die!" As most things do with me, that started a story: death by fright. Perfect. No clues at all. So I wrote it between two more demanding historical books, and a Chief Constable read it in order to answer one question: What could the police do? He said, "Nothing!" Well, that was in 1939 when neither in a book nor in a film was anybody allowed to get away with murder, so I had to rewrite it, scattering a few psychological clues.

*   *   *

Norah Lofts has had a successful career as a popular writer of historical romances and crime fiction, a career similar to that of Georgette Heyer. Her writings reflect her early academic interests in history and literature; a good portion of her work as Norah Lofts including such famous books as *Jassy*, belongs to the genre of historical romance. She has also written novels dealing with various aspects of the supernatural. One of her best known works is *Is Anybody There?* (in the U.S. as *Hauntings*), a series of short stories dealing with haunted houses and in many cases ESP. In the preface to the collection, Lofts explains the rationale of the stories as an exploration of her theory that "places make an impression on people, and that people, in certain circumstances, can leave an impression on places."
Under the pseudonym of Peter Curtis, a name probably inspired by her agent, Curtis Brown, she has written novels specifically associated with crime. A particularly intriguing one is *Dead March in Three Keys*. In this novel, Lofts used a striking family resemblance to bring about a murder and a favorable switch of identity. Much of the novel's appeal rests in her delineation of the psychological portrait of the murderer, Richard Curwen. A carefully constructed plot underscores the horror of Curwen's motives and emphasizes what for him are very rational and plausible reasons for his actions. In *Emma Plume* Lofts creates one of the character types familiar from her historical romances – the jealous, ever-watchful nanny – and makes her the key person in the unravelling of the murder plot.
Checkmate, one of Lofts's most contemporary novels in situation, time, and location, tells

the story of a father's revenge when his daughter is attacked. Lofts creates a systematic approach to Tom Penfold's revenge – made even more ghastly because he is an invalid. Lofts develops a gripping portrait of various levels of fear: Jenny's fear of her father; Ann's fear of throwing her husband off-balance; Terry Upworth's fear for his life; and Tom Penfold's fear that justice will beat him to his revenge. Lofts portrays graphic physical violence – a rare occurrence in her work in which, though murder may be committed, it is not customarily described in such vivid detail.

—Katherine M. Restaino

LONGRIGG, Roger. See **DRUMMOND, Ivor.**

LORAC, E. C. R. See **CARNAC, Carol.**

LORAINE, Philip. Pseudonym for Robin Estridge. British. Served in the Royal Navy. Has worked as a journalist in London and a dishwasher in Paris. Lives in France and California. Address: c/o William Collins Sons and Company Ltd., 14 St. James's Place, London SW1A 1PS, England.

CRIME PUBLICATIONS

Novels

> *White Lie the Dead.* London, Hodder and Stoughton, 1950; as *And to My Beloved Husband –*, New York, Mill, 1950.
> *Exit with Intent: The Story of a Missing Comedian.* London, Hodder and Stoughton, 1950.
> *The Break in the Circle.* London, Hodder and Stoughton, and New York, Mill, 1951; as *Outside the Law*, New York, Pocket Books, 1953.
> *The Dublin Nightmare.* London, Hodder and Stoughton, 1952; as *Nightmare in Dublin*, New York, Mill, 1952.
> *The Angel of Death.* London, Hodder and Stoughton, and New York, Mill, 1961.
> *Day of the Arrow.* London, Collins, and New York, Mill, 1964; as *The Eye of the Devil*, London, Fontana, 1966; as *13*, London, Lancer, 1966.
> *W.I.L. One to Curtis.* London, Collins, and New York, Random House, 1967.
> *The Dead Men of Sestos.* London, Collins, and New York, Random House, 1968.

A Mafia Kiss.   London, Collins, and New York, Random House, 1969.
Photographs Have Been Sent to Your Wife.   London, Collins, and New York, Random House, 1971.
Voices in an Empty Room.   London, Collins, 1973; New York, Random House, 1974.
Ask the Rattlesnake.   London, Collins, 1975; as *Wrong Man in the Mirror*, New York, Random House, 1975.

OTHER PUBLICATIONS as Robin Estridge

Novels

The Future Is Tomorrow.   London, Davies, 1947.
The Publican's Wife.   London, Davies, 1948.
Meeting on the Shore.   London, Davies, 1949.
Return of a Hero.   London, Davies, 1950; as *Sword Without Scabbard*, New York, Morrow, 1950.
The Olive Tree.   London, Davies, and New York, Morrow, 1953.
A Cuckoo's Child.   London, Davies, 1969.

Plays

Screenplays: *House of Darkness*, with John Gilling, 1948; *A Day to Remember*, 1953; *The Young Lovers (Chance Meeting)*, with George Tabori, 1954; *Simba*, with John Baines, 1955; *Above Us the Waves*, 1955; *Checkpoint*, 1956; *Campbell's Kingdom*, with Hammond Innes, 1957; *Dangerous Exile*, 1957; *North West Frontier (Flame over India)*, 1959; *No Kidding (Beware of Children)*, with Norman Hudis, 1960; *Escape from Zahrain*, 1962; *Drums of Africa*, with Arthur Hoerl, 1963; *Eye of the Devil*, with Denis Murphy, 1966; *The Boy Cried Murder*, 1966.

*   *   *

Philip Loraine is a pseudonym used by Robin Estridge for his above-average thrillers. His straight novels and film scripts have probably restricted the number of thrillers he has written, but he has maintained a high quality.

His background as both sailor and a journalist has been used to good advantage in the world-wide settings and backgrounds of his novels. His plotting is invariably intricate and full of atmosphere. A good example is *A Mafia Kiss.* Loraine obviously knows Sicily well, and the thought of a young man justifiably taking on the power of the Mafia has a strong appeal. The gangsterism and violence are conveyed readably, and the tenseness in the series of climaxes gives the book a strong pace.

Break in the Circle and *Day of the Arrow* can also be thoroughly recommended, and his trip into the supernatural – in *Voices in an Empty Room* – was highly effective, and praised by the past master Edmund Crispin.

—Donald C. Ireland

LOVELL, Marc.   See McSHANE, Mark.

LOVESEY, Peter. Also writes as Peter Lear. British. Born in Whitton, Middlesex, 10 September 1936. Educated at Hampton Grammar School, 1947–55; University of Reading, Berkshire, 1955–58, B.A. (honours) in English 1958. Served as an Education Officer in the Royal Air Force, 1958–61. Married Jacqueline Ruth Lewis in 1959; one daughter and one son. Lecturer in English, Thurrock Technical College, Essex, 1961–69; Head of General Education Department, Hammersmith College for Further Education, London, 1969–75. Recipient: Crime Writers Association Silver Dagger, 1979. Agent: John Farquharson Ltd., 8 Bell Yard, London WC2A 2JU, England.

CRIME PUBLICATIONS

Novels (series characters: Sergeant Cribb and Constable Thackeray in all books)

> *Wobble to Death.* London, Macmillan, and New York, Dodd Mead, 1970.
> *The Detective Wore Silk Drawers.* London, Macmillan, and New York, Dodd Mead, 1971.
> *Abracadaver.* London, Macmillan, and New York, Dodd Mead, 1972.
> *Mad Hatter's Holiday: A Novel of Murder in Victorian Brighton.* London, Macmillan, and New York, Dodd Mead, 1973.
> *Invitation to a Dynamite Party.* London, Macmillan, 1974; as *The Tick of Death*, New York, Dodd Mead, 1974.
> *A Case of Spirits.* London, Macmillan, and New York, Dodd Mead, 1975.
> *Swing, Swing Together.* London, Macmillan, and New York, Dodd Mead, 1976.
> *Waxwork.* London, Macmillan, and New York, Pantheon, 1978.

Uncollected Short Stories

> "The Bathroom," in *Winter's Crimes 5*, edited by Virginia Whitaker. London, Macmillan, 1973.
> "The Locked Room," in *Winter's Crimes 10*, edited by Hilary Watson. London, Macmillan, 1978.

OTHER PUBLICATIONS

Novel

> *Goldengirl* (as Peter Lear). London, Cassell, 1977; New York, Doubleday, 1978.

Other

> *The Kings of Distance: A Study of Five Great Runners.* London, Eyre and Spottiswoode, 1968.
> *The Guide to British Track and Field Literature 1275–1968*, with Tom MacNab. London, Athletics Arena, 1969.
> "The Historian: Once upon a Crime," in *Murder Ink: The Mystery Reader's Companion*, edited by Dilys Winn. New York, Workman, 1977.
> *The Official Centenary History of the Amateur Athletic Association.* London, Guinness Superlatives, 1979.

Peter Lovesey comments:

Wobble to Death, my first crime novel, was written for a competition and drew on my amusement at a curious endurance race held in Victorian London in 1879. I have since written seven other novels featuring Sergeant Cribb, who joined Scotland Yard's C.I.D. when it was formed. Each uses a theme or setting representative of Victorian life: prize-fighting, the music hall, the seaside, Irish dynamiting of public buildings, spiritualism, the river, the waxwork show. Cribb is shrewd rather than inspired, a detective who works with the limited resources of Scotland Yard in the 1880's and is hindered almost as much by his superiors as by the malefactors he pursues. The books have been described as pastiche, but I prefer to think of them as Victorian police procedural novels.

*   *   *

Of the modern writers of "historical" detective fiction, the most popular – certainly the most consistent – must be Peter Lovesey. His first novel, *Wobble to Death*, introduced the characters of Sergeant Cribb and Constable Thackeray and was greeted with enthusiasm by reviewers who regarded it as something entirely new. Since that time, the Victorian gimmick has worn a bit thin, although Lovesey easily recreates an earlier style of narration. Likewise, his grasp of historical details is always firm, and his plots are usually ingenious. The author has explained the fascination of the historical mystery as follows: "it provides an escape from modern life. But we are not at the mercy of a science-fiction writer's fantasizing. The world we enter is real and under control." This description strikes at the heart of the problem, for one feels that what is missing from some of the Lovesey books, in spite of their admirable accumulation of detail, is a spark of life or fantasy. Compensating for this lack, however, is the undercurrent of humour running through the books. They are not in any sense pastiches, but the author is wise enough to maintain a lightness of tone.

It is no mean feat to invent a pair of series detectives who hold the reader's interest through eight novels. The deliberateness of Lovesey's effort is awe-inspiring; it allows him to put his creative energies into the development of amusingly original plots, and into the amassing of the historical detail which fleshes out his narrative. The two detectives move from one unique setting to another; part of our own delight stems from their amazed reactions to the settings in which they find themselves. From the first novel, in which they are called on to investigate the poisoning of a walker in a marathon foot-race or "wobble," the detectives, in the course of their investigations, discover curious facts about various Victorian institutions and customs: the popular theatre (*Abracadaver*), the seaside resort (*Mad Hatter's Holiday*), Irish nationalists (*Invitation to a Dynamite Party*), or the world of art collectors (*A Case of Spirits*). Throughout the adventures, Cribb and Thackeray are treated with suspicion by the "genteel" people whom they must investigate. The impact of the Victorian class system is strongly felt, not only in the relations between the detectives and their suspects, but in the treatment of them by their immediate superior, Inspector Jowett (speaking in *A Case of Spirits*): " 'Sergeant Cribb and Constable Thackeray are two of the most experienced detectives in Scotland Yard,' said Jowett. It should have been a splendid affirmation of confidence. The pity was that Jowett's emphasis made it sound like an admission that the Force had problems over recruitment." Typically, Jowett is more a hindrance than a help to his men in the field, and they are frequently called upon to produce results at short notice.

Although the plots are generally intricate and convincing, the real interest in the Lovesey books is the fascinating tidbits of Victoriana which they contain. Fortunately, these are never presented in a self-conscious or "donnish" fashion; when historical notes are presented they are always relevant and judiciously placed. Lovesey is skillful, too, in his use of quotations, so that the books are free from the affectations of much fiction based upon historical fact. If the novels communicate an overall impression of restraint, it is, perhaps, that of their period – or, at any rate, of what we modern readers imagine the period to be. Though they move in the world of crime, detectives Cribb and Thackeray exude a kind of innocence which has little to do with the "mean streets" of any time or place.

—Joanne Harack Hayne

LOWNDES, Marie (Adelaide) Belloc. Also wrote as Philip Curtin. British. Born in 1868; sister of the writer Hilaire Belloc. Married the writer Frederic Sawrey Lowndes (died, 1940); one son and two daughters. *Died 14 November 1947.*

CRIME PUBLICATIONS

Novels

The Heart of Penelope. London, Heinemann, 1904; New York, Dutton, 1915.
Barbara Rebell. London, Heinemann, 1905; New York, Dodge, 1907.
The Pulse of Life. London, Heinemann, 1908; New York, Dodd Mead, 1909.
The Uttermost Farthing. London, Heinemann, 1908; New York, Kennerley, 1909.
When No Man Pursueth. London, Heinemann, 1910; New York, Kennerley, 1911.
Jane Oglander. London, Heinemann, and New York, Scribner, 1911.
The Chink in the Armour. London, Methuen, and New York, Scribner, 1912; as *The House of Peril*, London, Readers Library, 1935.
Mary Pechell. London, Methuen, and New York, Scribner, 1912.
The Lodger. London, Methuen, and New York, Scribner, 1913.
The End of Her Honeymoon. New York, Scribner, 1913; London, Methuen, 1914.
Good Old Anna. London, Hutchinson, 1915; New York, Doran, 1916.
The Red Cross Barge. London, Smith Elder, 1916; New York, Doran, 1918.
Lilla: A Part of Her Life. London, Hutchinson, 1916; New York, Doran, 1917.
Love and Hatred. London, Chapman and Hall, and New York, Doran, 1917.
Out of the War? London, Chapman and Hall, 1918; as *Gentleman Anonymous*, London, Philip Allan, 1934.
From the Vasty Deep. London, Hutchinson, 1920; as *From Out the Vasty Deep*, New York, Doran, 1921.
The Lonely House. London, Hutchinson, and New York, Doran, 1920.
What Timmy Did. London, Hutchinson, 1921; New York, Doran, 1922.
The Terriford Mystery. London, Hutchinson, and New York, Doubleday, 1924.
What Really Happened. London, Hutchinson, and New York, Doubleday, 1926.
The Story of Ivy. London, Heinemann, 1927; New York, Doubleday, 1928.
Thou Shalt Not Kill. London, Hutchinson, 1927.
Cressida: No Mystery. London, Heinemann, 1928; New York, Knopf, 1930.
Duchess Laura: Certain Days of Her Life. London, Ward Lock, 1929; as *The Duchess Intervenes*, New York, Putnam, 1933.
Love's Revenge. London, Readers Library, 1929.
One of Those Ways. London, Heinemann, and New York, Knopf, 1929.
Letty Lynton. London, Heinemann, and New York, Cape and Smith, 1931.
Vanderlyn's Adventure. New York, Cape and Smith, 1931; as *The House by the Sea*, London, Heinemann, 1937.
Jenny Newstead. London, Heinemann, and New York, Putnam, 1932.
Love Is a Flame. London, Benn, 1932.
The Reason Why. London, Benn, 1932.
Duchess Laura: Further Days from Her Life. New York, Longman, 1933.
Another Man's Wife. London, Heinemann, and New York, Longman, 1934.
The Chianti Flask. New York, Longman, 1934; London, Heinemann, 1935.
Who Rides on a Tiger. New York, Longman, 1935; London, Heinemann, 1936.
And Call It Accident. New York, Longman, 1936; London, Hutchinson, 1939.
The Second Key. New York, Longman, 1936; as *The Injured Lover*, London, Hutchinson, 1939.
The Marriage-Broker. London, Heinemann, 1937; as *The Fortune of Bridget Malone*, New York, Longman, 1937.
Motive. London, Hutchinson, 1938; as *Why It Happened*, New York, Longman, 1938.

Lizzie Borden: A Study in Conjecture. New York, Longman, 1939; London, Hutchinson, 1940.
Reckless Angel. New York, Longman, 1939.
The Christine Diamond. London, Hutchinson, and New York, Longman, 1940.
Before the Storm. New York, Longman, 1941.
She Dwelt with Beauty. London, Macmillan, 1949.

Short Stories

Studies in Wives. London, Heinemann, 1909; New York, Kennerley, 1910.
Studies in Love and Terror. London, Methuen, and New York, Scribner, 1913.
Why They Married. London, Heinemann, 1923.
Bread of Deceit. London, Hutchinson, 1925; as *Afterwards*, New York, Doubleday, 1925.
Some Men and Woman. London, Hutchinson, 1925; New York, Doubleday, 1928.
What of the Night? New York, Dodd Mead, 1943.
A Labour of Hercules. London, Todd, 1943.

Other Publications

Plays

The Lonely House, with Charles Randolph, adaptation of the novel by Lowndes (produced Eastbourne, Sussex, 1924).
The Key: A Love Drama (as *The Second Key,* produced London, 1935). London, Benn, 1930.
With All John's Love. London, Benn, 1930.
Why Be Lonely?, with F. S. A. Lowndes. London, Benn, 1931.
What Really Happened, adaptation of her own novel (produced London, 1936). London, Benn, 1932.
Her Last Adventure (produced London, 1936).
The Empress Eugenie. New York, Longman, 1938.

Other

H.R.H. the Prince of Wales: An Account of His Career (published anonymously). London, Richards, and New York, Appleton, 1898; revised edition, as *His Most Gracious Majesty King Edward VII,* as Mrs. Belloc Lowndes, Richards, 1901.
The Philosophy of the Marquise (sketches and dialogues). London, Richards, 1899.
T.R.H. the Prince and Princess of Wales (published anonymously). London, Newnes, 1902.
Noted Murder Mysteries (as Philip Curtin). London, Simpkin Marshall, 1914.
Told in Gallant Deeds: A Child's History of the War. London, Nisbet, 1914.
"I, Too, Have Lived in Arcadia": A Record of Love and of Childhood. London, Macmillan, 1941; New York, Dodd Mead, 1942.
Where Love and Friendship Dwelt (autobiography). London, Macmillan, and New York, Dodd Mead, 1943.
The Merry Wives of Westminster (autobiography). London, Macmillan, 1946.
A Passing World (autobiography). London, Macmillan, 1948.
The Young Hilaire Belloc. London, P. J. Kennedy, 1956.

Editor and Translator, with M. Shedlock, *Edmund and Jules de Goncourt, with Letters and Leaves from Their Journals.* London, Heinemann, and New York, Dodd Mead, 2 vols., 1895.

*   *   *

Marie Belloc Lowndes, descendant of Joseph Priestley, protégée of Robert Browning, and sister of Hilaire Belloc, drew on her knowledge of courts and lawyers, of recent crime cases, and of human psychology based on personal observation of such diverse friends as Oscar Wilde, Prime Minister Asquith, and Henry James, to produce a series of carefully plotted crime and suspense novels and short stories. These significant contributions to the genre share a sensitive understanding of women's problems, a modern sensibility, a concern with the psychology of crime, especially motive. They focus on ordinary persons involved in sudden violence, people "enmeshed in a web of tragic circumstances" involving jealousy, greed, sudden love or sexual entanglements, and failure to communicate. They explore questions of loyalty, particularly in January/May or childless marriages, between engaged couples, or in doctor/patient, lawyer/client, servant/master relationships.

Lizzie Borden explores the way passionate love causes an intelligent, quiet girl to commit a double murder. This theme of transformation runs throughout Marie Lowndes's novels: "this was an Agatha Cheale she did not know – a violent, unrestrained human being." Part of the horror of her books comes from this stripping away the façade of seemingly respectable women to show how greed or passion could lead them to murder, particularly by poisoning (*Letty Lynton, The Story of Ivy, The Chianti Flask, Motive, The Chink in the Armour*). The most sympathetic of these women are victims of ruined finances, domineering parents, and marriage laws whereby a sensitive woman becomes the slave of a cruel, cantankerous older husband who abuses her; the least sympathetic are totally amoral bits of fluff who seize the main chance to improve their position and who abuse the love and affection of trusting males. Often the openly suspect prove basically sound, and the solidly respectable prove capable of murder or deception. "Strange," "unnatural," "cold," "beastly," "amazing," "extraordinary," and "very clever" resound in her novels. Dreams are portentous, fortune-tellers accurate, and presentiments confirmed. Her characters turn unnaturally pale in true Victorian style, "as does a white camelia seen in a dim light." There are secret trysts, eavesdroppers, anonymous letters, and plenty of arsenic available in common household products. Often the evidence is as trivial as a missing chianti bottle, a bowl of strawberries, a passing motorist, a chance conversation. Gold-diggers dupe innocents, and the "Goddess of play attracts reptiles." Lowndes's one recurring character is a defence lawyer, Sir Joseph Molloy, "the murderer's savior," a wily, competent lawyer with a deep understanding of human nature.

Her novels reproduce court scenes effectively, realistically, and accurately. *The Chianti Flask, Motive, The Terriford Mystery, Lizzie Borden,* and *Letty Lynton* all involve lengthy inquests or trials, the latter two factual and critical résumés of actual court scenes. All depict yellow journalism, prejudging and curious crowds anxious for horror and scandal, and innocents tainted by contact with murderer or victim. *The Terriford Mystery* is typical in its cynical treatment of law and justice; a scandalmongering press, gossiping villagers, a rich, womanizing lawyer, and unimaginative police condemn an innocent man. The experienced and the amateur detectives are ineffective, and only an accidental meeting with a dying man prevents a miscarriage of justice.

Unexpected but reasonable reversals like that in *The Terriford Mystery* make Lowndes's plots continually fascinating. In *Letty Lynton*, the young, amoral murderess escapes one legal trap only to be enmeshed in a more terrifying one. In *The Chink in the Armour* and *One of Those Ways* the reversal derives from the point of view of naive, unsuspecting victims in gambling and murder conspiracies. *The End of Her Honeymoon* contrasts apparent police concern with their real willingness to cover up a plague death. In *The Lodger*, Marie Lowndes's finest work, highly praised by critics and readers (including Gertrude Stein and Ernest Hemingway), a servant couple discover that their lodger is a Jack-the-Ripper-type mass murderer, but are loath to turn him in because of self-interest and self-protection, loyalty to upper-class "gentlefolk," and "decent" values shared by murderers and landlords. The novel is a masterful analysis of inertia caused by divided loyalties; the horror, like that of all Marie Lowndes's best work, is psychological and familiar, never theatrical or stylized.

—Virginia Macdonald

LUDLUM, Robert. Also writes as Jonathan Ryder; Michael Shepherd. American. Born in New York City, 25 May 1927. Educated at Rectory School, Pomfret, Connecticut; Kent School, Connecticut; Cheshire Academy, Connecticut; Wesleyan University, Middletown, Connecticut, B.A. 1951. Served in the United States Marine Corps, 1945–47. Married Mary Ryducha in 1951; two sons and one daughter. Stage and television actor from 1952; Producer, North Jersey Playhouse, Fort Lee, 1957–60, and Playhouse-on-the-Mall, Paramus, New Jersey, 1960–69. Since 1969, free-lance writer. Agent: Henry Morrison Inc., 50 West 10th Street, New York, New York 10011, U.S.A.

CRIME PUBLICATIONS

Novels

> The Scarlatti Inheritance. Cleveland, World, and London, Hart Davis, 1971.
> The Osterman Weekend. Cleveland, World, and London, Hart Davis, 1972.
> The Matlock Paper. New York, Dial Press, and London, Hart Davis MacGibbon, 1973.
> Trevayne (as Jonathan Ryder). New York, Delacorte Press, 1973; London, Weidenfeld and Nicolson, 1974.
> The Cry of the Halidon (as Jonathan Ryder). New York, Delacorte Press, and London, Weidenfeld and Nicolson, 1974.
> The Rhinemann Exchange. New York, Dial Press, 1974; London, Hart Davis MacGibbon, 1975.
> The Road to Gandolfo (as Michael Shepherd). New York, Dial Press, 1975; London, Hart Davis MacGibbon, 1976.
> The Gemini Contenders. New York, Dial Press, and London, Hart Davis MacGibbon, 1976.
> The Chancellor Manuscript. New York, Dial Press, 1977; London, Hart Davis MacGibbon, 1977.
> The Matarese Circle. New York, David Marek, and London, Granada, 1979.

Theatrical Activities:

Actor: **Plays** – Sterling Brown in *Junior Miss* by Jerome Chodorov and Joseph Fields, New York, 1941, and Haskell Cummings on tour, 1943–44; in stock, Canton Show Shop, Connecticut, summer 1952; Soldier in *The Strong Are Lonely* by Fritz Hochwalder, New York, 1952; in stock, Ivorytown Playhouse, Connecticut, summer 1953; Third Messenger in *Richard III*, New York, 1953; Spartacus, in *The Gladiator*, New York, 1954; in stock, Cragsmoor Playhouse, New York, summer 1954; Policeman and, later, Cashel Byron in *The Admirable Bashville* by G. B. Shaw, New York, 1956; D'Estivel in *Saint Joan* by G. B. Shaw, New York, 1956; in stock, Olney Theatre, Maryland, summer 1957. **Television** – in

Treasury Men in Action, 1952, and on *Studio One*, *Kraft Television Theatre*, *Omnibus*, *Danger*, *Suspense*, and *Robert Montgomery Presents*.

*   *   *

Robert Ludlum is a writer with a deep knowledge of 20th-century history, a superb sense of current political trends, and a vivid, informed imagination: a first-rate practitioner of the fiction of political and personal intrigue. His thrillers threaten by their closeness to historical and contemporary fact. Ludlum's awareness of his alarming plausibility comes through in *The Chancellor Manuscript*, in which a writer of speculative but well-informed political thrillers fights for his right to name names and events (that J. Edgar Hoover was assassinated, for instance). The factual power structures in Ludlum's tales of domestic and international espionage are hardly less interesting than the fictional power complexes, such as Inver Brass (in *The Chancellor Manuscript*), a secret six-man watchdog group representing banking, diplomacy, learning, etc., which keeps an eye on American and liberal interests. It is Inver Brass which obtains and destroys Hoover's files containing all the personal data needed for the unscrupulous to blackmail people in high places. For Ludlum, the national/international disaster is just around the corner, and Inver Brass, illegal though its existence and methods may be, is all that prevents major scandals, the breakdown of democratic institutions, and the holocaust.

If Inver Brass is an interesting agent of prevention, Ludlum's agents of detection are no less interesting. To find some missing Hoover files Inver Brass decides to hire a failed graduate student turned successful novelist, a man with a flair for truth unrestricted by fact or the lack of it, a man "who approaches a concept, finds a basic situation and extracts *selected* facts and rearranges them to suit the reality as he perceives it. He is not bound by cause and effect; he creates it" – and thereby detects. *The Matlock Paper* has a similarly effective amateur detective, a Professor of English at a New England university, a man with enough flaws in his past and enough social mobility in his present to understand and penetrate where the professional cannot.

As *The Osterman Weekend* and *The Gemini Contenders* demonstrate, the range of crimes and mentalities that interests Ludlum is not bounded by the US, politics, and neo-politics. Though *The Osterman Weekend* boasts a CIA chief who turns out to be a double agent, the main focus is on the behavior of four couples, great friends, each of whom is led to suspect that the others are international terrorists. How their informed minds and bodies react under the strain of a weekend together is what fascinates. But Ludlum's tour de force is *The Gemini Contenders*, an epic thriller spanning 1939 to the present, Europe and America. In December 1939, a train arrives in Italy with a cargo too extraordinary to destroy or reveal – documents from a Greek monastery, supposedly written by St. Peter and saying that Jesus of Nazareth was never crucified and was not resurrected: a substitute died on Calvary. It is the search for the repository of these documents which had been known only to the devout Vittorio Fontini Cristi, a liberal Italian killed by the Nazis, which makes madmen and criminals of Vatican officials, Greek monks, and Fontini Cristi's grandchildren.

—Ann Massa

LUSTGARTEN, Edgar (Marcus). Born in Manchester, Lancashire, 3 May 1907. Educated at Manchester Grammar School; St. John's College, Oxford (President, Oxford Union, 1930), B.A. 1930. Married Joyce Goldstone in 1932 (died, 1972). Practising Barrister, 1930–40; Counter-Propaganda Broadcaster, 1940–45, and Staff Producer,

1945–48, BBC Radio, London; Organiser, "In the News" program, 1950–54, and Narrator, "Focus" program, 1965–68, BBC Television, London; Organiser, "Free Speech" program, 1955–61, and Chairman, "Fair Play" program, 1962–65, Associated Television, London. From 1952 presenter of several series of "Famous Trials," BBC Radio and TV. *Died 15 December 1978.*

CRIME PUBLICATIONS

Novels

> *A Case to Answer.*   London, Eyre and Spottiswoode, 1947; as *One More Unfortunate*, New York, Scribner, 1947.
> *Blondie Iscariot.*   New York, Scribner, 1948; London, Museum Press, 1949.
> *Game for Three Losers.*   London, Museum Press, and New York, Scribner, 1952.
> *Turn the Light Out as You Go.*   London, Elek, 1978.

Uncollected Short Story

> "Forbidden Fruit," in *Ellery Queen's Mystery Magazine* (New York), January 1963.

OTHER PUBLICATIONS

Novel

> *I'll Never Leave You.*   London, Hart Davis, 1971.

Plays

> Screenplay: *The Man Who Wouldn't Talk*, 1958.

> Radio Plays: *In the Shade of the Crabapple Tree*, 1966; *The Burden Mystery Case*, 1966; *Trial of John White Webster*, 1967; *Murder at the Follies*, 1967; *The Traitors* series, 1970.

Other

> *Verdict in Dispute.*   London, Wingate, 1949; New York, Scribner, 1950.
> *Defender's Triumph.*   London, Wingate, and New York, Scribner, 1951.
> *Prisoner at the Bar: The Famous B.B.C. Series.*   London, Deutsch, 1952.
> *The Woman in the Case.*   London, Deutsch, and New York, Scribner, 1955.
> *The Murder and the Trial*, edited by Anthony Boucher.   New York, Scribner, 1958; London, Odhams Press, 1960.
> *The Judges and the Judged.*   London, Odhams Press, 1961.
> *The Business of Murder.*   London, Harrap, and New York, Scribner, 1968.
> *The Chalk Pit Murder.*   London, Hart Davis MacGibbon, 1974.
> *A Century of Murderers.*   London, Eyre Methuen, 1975.
> *The Illustrated Story of Crime.*   London, Weidenfeld and Nicolson, and Chicago, Follett, 1976.

Theatrical Activities:

> Actor (Narrator): **Films** – *The Drayton Case*, 1953; *The Missing Man*, 1953; *The Candlelight Murder*, 1953; *The Blazing Caravan*, 1954; *The Dark Stairway*, 1954; *Late Night Final*, 1954; *The Strange Case of Blondie*, 1954; *The Silent Witness*, 1954; *Passenger*

to Tokyo, 1954; *Night Plane to Amsterdam*, 1955; *Murder Anonymous*, 1955; *Wall of Death*, 1956; *The Case of the River Morgue*, 1956; *Destination Death*, 1956; *Person Unknown*, 1956; *The Lonely House*, 1957; *Bullet from the Past*, 1957; *Inside Information*, 1957; *The Case of the Smiling Widow*, 1957; *The Mail Van Murder*, 1957; *The Tyburn Case*, 1957; *The White Cliffs Mystery*, 1957; *Night Crossing*, 1957; *Print of Death*, 1958; *Crime of Honour*, 1958; *The Crossroad Gallows*, 1958; *The Unseeing Eye*, 1959; *The Ghost Train Murder*, 1959; *The Dover Road Mystery*, 1960; *The Last Train*, 1960; *Evidence in Concrete*, 1960; *The Silent Weapon*, 1961; *The Grand Junction Case*, 1961; *The Never Never Murder*, 1961; *Wings of Death*, 1961; *The Square Mile Murder*, 1961; *The Guilty Party*, 1962; *A Woman's Privilege*, 1962; *Moment of Decision*, 1962; *The Undesirable Neighbour*, 1963; *The Invisible Asset*, 1963; *Company of Fools*, 1966; *The Haunted Man*, 1966; *Infamous Conduct*, 1966; *Payment in Kind*, 1967.

*   *   *

A British lawyer, criminologist, and novelist, Edgar Lustgarten began his writing career in the early 1930's while he was practicing law. As a busy advocate, he had little time for any major writing, but limited himself to short radio plays, feature articles, and pseudonymous song lyrics. He worked in radio and television for many years and is especially remembered for the famous series, *Prisoner at the Bar*. In his novels he demonstrated an ability to tell a good story and a sympathetic interest in the human condition.

His first novel, *A Case to Answer*, is a masterfully written narrative of the trial of a young man for the murder of a Soho prostitute. Lustgarten realistically portrays lawyers, witnesses, and judges while maintaining suspense to the end. Its realism contrasts with most legal mysteries, American and English, and its powerful climax suggests not only that the verdict is unfair but that the British system of justice is far from perfect. *Blondie Iscariot*, in contrast, is his worst book – a sordid and shoddy melodrama lacking the sensitivity and promise of his earlier tale. *Game for Three Losers* deals with an elaborate plot of blackmail involving a highly regarded member of parliament with bright prospects for a successful political career. Again Lustgarten indicts a legal system that fails to protect the innocent, and, worse, punishes them along with the guilty.

Lustgarten admitted a livelong interest in crime; in his introduction to *The Illustrated Story of Crime*, he wrote: "crime is composed mostly of the vices and the passions; seldom mixed with reason, with virtue hardly ever. Nevertheless it forms a massive part of human nature, and can no more be ignored in a review of our own species than can disease, injury, war, pestilence or death." Lustgarten emphasized that he did not write "detective stories"; his stories of crime – both factual and fictional – are perceptive and illuminating essays into the tragicomedy of crime and the failure of the legal system. He was a profound and talented writer whose best works reflect his incisive wit and probing criticism of the law.

—Daniel P. King

LUTZ, John (Thomas). American. Born in Dallas, Texas, 11 September 1939. Educated at Meramec Community College, St. Louis. Married Barbara Jean Bradley in 1958; two daughters and one son. Worked as construction worker; theater usher; warehouseman; truck driver; switchboard operator, St. Louis Metropolitan Police. Since 1975, self-employed writer. Agent: Richard Curtis, 156 East 52nd Street, New York, New York 10022. Address: 880 Providence Avenue, Webster Groves, Missouri 63119, U.S.A.

CRIME PUBLICATIONS

Novels

> *The Truth of the Matter.* New York, Pocket Books, 1971.
> *Buyer Beware.* New York, Putnam, 1976; London, Hale, 1977.
> *Bonegrinder.* New York, Putnam, 1977; London, Hale, 1978.
> *Lazarus Man.* New York, Morrow, 1979.

Uncollected Short Stories

> "Quid Pro Quo," in *Ellery Queen's Mystery Magazine* (New York), August 1967.
> "Big Game," in *Signature* (New York), August 1967.
> "The Wounded Tiger," in *Signature* (New York), November 1967.
> "Dead, You Know," in *Alfred Hitchcock's Mystery Magazine* (North Palm Beach, Florida), January 1968.
> "Death on the Silver Screen," in *Mike Shayne Mystery Magazine* (New York), April 1968.
> "The Creator of Spud Moran," in *Alfred Hitchcock's Mystery Magazine* (North Palm Beach, Florida), July 1968.
> "No Small Problem," in *Alfred Hitchcock's Mystery Magazine* (North Palm Beach, Florida), September 1968.
> "Abridged," in *Mike Shayne Mystery Magazine* (New York), October 1968.
> "King of the Kennel," in *Mike Shayne Mystery Magazine* (New York), November 1968.
> "The Weapon," in *Alfred Hitchcock's Mystery Magazine* (North Palm Beach, Florida), May 1969.
> "Hand of Fate," in *Alfred Hitchcock's Mystery Magazine* (North Palm Beach, Florida), July 1969.
> "Thieves' Manor," in *Alfred Hitchcock's Coffin Corner.* New York, Dell, 1969.
> "Two by Two," in *Alfred Hitchcock's Mystery Magazine* (North Palm Beach, Florida), November 1970.
> "The Explosives Expert," in *Alfred Hitchcock's Rolling Gravestones.* New York, Dell, 1971.
> "Garden of Dreams," in *Alfred Hitchcock's Mystery Magazine* (North Palm Beach, Florida), June 1971.
> "Prospectus on Death," in *Alfred Hitchcock's Mystery Magazine* (North Palm Beach, Florida), July 1971.
> "Fair Shake," in *Alfred Hitchcock's This One Will Kill You.* New York, Dell, 1971.
> "Murder Malignant," in *Alfred Hitchcock's Mystery Magazine* (North Palm Beach, Florida), August 1971.
> "Theft Is My Profession," in *Alfred Hitchcock's Mystery Magazine* (North Palm Beach, Florida), September 1971.
> "Case of the Dead Gossip" (as Tom Collins), in *TV Fact*, 26 September – 17 October 1971.
> "One Way," in *Alfred Hitchcock's I Am Curious Bloody.* New York, Dell, 1971.
> "Friendly Hal," in *Alfred Hitchcock's Mystery Magazine* (North Palm Beach, Florida), November 1971.
> "In Memory of...," in *Alfred Hitchcock's Mystery Magazine* (North Palm Beach, Florida), January 1972.
> "The Real Shape of the Coast," in *Ellery Queen's Mystery Bag.* Cleveland, World, 1972.
> "The Very Best," in *Alfred Hitchcock's Mystery Magazine* (North Palm Beach, Florida), March 1972.
> "Within the Law," in *Alfred Hitchcock's Mystery Magazine* (North Palm Beach, Florida), April 1972.

"Obedience School," in *Alfred Hitchcock's Happy Deathday!* New York, Dell, 1972.

"Living All Alone," in *Alfred Hitchcock's Mystery Magazine* (North Palm Beach, Florida), May 1972.

"Fractions," in *Alfred Hitchcock's Mystery Magazine* (North Palm Beach, Florida), June 1972.

"The Insomniacs Club," in *Ellery Queen's Anthology, Fall–Winter.* New York, Davis, 1972.

"A Killer Foiled," in *Mike Shayne Mystery Magazine* (Los Angeles), November 1972.

"Autumn Madness," in *Ellery Queen's Mystery Magazine* (New York), November 1972.

"So Young, So Fair, So Dead," in *Mike Shayne Mystery Magazine* (Los Angeles), March 1973.

"Shadows Everywhere," in *Alfred Hitchcock's Mystery Magazine* (North Palm Beach, Florida), June 1973.

"Objective Mirror," in *Alfred Hitchcock's Mystery Magazine* (North Palm Beach, Florida), July 1973.

"A Rare Bird," in *Alfred Hitchcock's Let It All Bleed Out.* New York, Dell, 1973.

"King of the World," in *Alfred Hitchcock's Mystery Magazine* (North Palm Beach, Florida), August 1973.

"The Basement Room," in *Mike Shayne Mystery Magazine* (Los Angeles), October 1973.

"The Lemon Drink Queen," in *Alfred Hitchcock's Mystery Magazine* (North Palm Beach, Florida), February 1974.

"Figure in Flight," in *Charlie Chan Mystery Magazine* (New York), February 1974.

"Dead Man," in *Alfred Hitchcock's Mystery Magazine* (North Palm Beach, Florida), March 1974.

"Green Death," in *Alfred Hitchcock's Mystery Magazine* (North Palm Beach, Florida), March 1974.

"A Private, Restful Place," in *Mike Shayne Mystery Magazine* (Los Angeles), May 1974.

"A Verdict of Death," in *Charlie Chan Mystery Magazine* (New York), May 1974.

"Day Shift," in *Mike Shayne Mystery Magazine* (Los Angeles), June 1974.

"The Butcher, The Baker," in *Alfred Hitchcock's Mystery Magazine* (North Palm Beach, Florida), July 1974.

"All of a Sudden," in *Alfred Hitchcock's Mystery Magazine* (North Palm Beach, Florida), August 1974.

"The Midnight Train," in *Alfred Hitchcock's Coffin Break.* New York, Dell, 1974.

"A Handgun for Protection," in *Mike Shayne Mystery Magazine* (Los Angeles, September 1974.

"Doom Signal," in *Alfred Hitchcock's Behind the Death Ball.* New York, Dell, 1974.

"Arm of the Law," in *Alfred Hitchcock's Mystery Magazine* (North Palm Beach, Florida), October 1974.

"The Other Side of Reason," in *Mike Shayne Mystery Magazine* (Los Angeles), December 1974.

"The Final Reel," in *Alfred Hitchcock's Bleeding Hearts.* New York, Dell, 1974.

"Rest Assured," in *Mike Shayne Mystery Magazine* (Los Angeles), February 1975.

"It Could Happen to You," in *Alfred Hitchcock's Mystery Magazine* (North Palm Beach, Florida), March 1975.

"Going, Going," in *Executioner* (Los Angeles), April 1975.

"Moon Children" in *87th Precinct* (New York), May 1975.

"The Ledge Walker," in *Executioner* (Los Angeles), June 1975.

"Next to the Woman from Des Moines" (as Paul Shepparton), in *Executioner* (Los Angeles), June 1975.

"The Organization Man" (as Elwin Strange), in *Executioner* (Los Angeles), June 1975.

"Room 33" (as Van McCloud), in *Executioner* (Los Angeles), June 1975.

"Day of Evil" (as John Bennett), in *Executioner* (Los Angeles), June 1975.

"You and the Music," in *Alfred Hitchcock's Mystery Magazine* (North Palm Beach, Florida), June 1975.

"Lease on Life," in *87th Precinct* (New York), June 1975.

"Personalized Copy" (as Elwin Strange), in *87th Precinct* (New York), June 1975.

"The Shooting of Curly Dan" in *Ellery Queen's Murdercade.* New York, Random House, 1975; London, Gollancz, 1976.

"The Clarion Call," in *Mike Shayne Mystery Magazine* (Los Angeles), July 1975.

"His Honor the Mayor," in *Executioner* (Los Angeles), August 1975.

"Life Sentence," in *87th Precinct* (New York), August 1975.

"Men with Motives," in *87th Precinct* (New York), August 1975.

"Understanding Electricity," in *Alfred Hitchcock's Mystery Magazine* (North Palm Beach, Florida), September 1975.

"Wonder World," in *Alfred Hitchcock's Mystery Magazine* (New York), January 1976.

"Not Just a Number," in *Mike Shayne Mystery Magazine* (Los Angeles), July 1976

"Not a Home," in *Alfred Hitchcock's Mystery Magazine* (New York), September 1976.

"Mail Order," in *Best Detective Stories of the Year 1976*, edited by Edward D. Hoch. New York, Dutton, 1976.

"The Crooked Picture," in *Tricks and Treats*, edited by Joe Gores and Bill Pronzini. New York, Doubleday, 1976; as *Mystery Writers Choice*, London, Gollancz, 1977.

"One Man's Manual," in *Alfred Hitchcock's Mystery Magazine* (New York), March 1977.

"Missing Personnel," in *Alfred Hitchcock's Mystery Magazine* (New York), June 1977.

"Pure Rotten," in *Mike Shayne Mystery Magazine* (Los Angeles), August 1977.

"Explosive Cargo," in *Alfred Hitchcock's Mystery Magazine* (New York), October 1977.

"Something for the Dark," in *Alfred Hitchcock's Mystery Magazine* (New York), November 1977.

"Death by the Numbers," in *Mike Shayne Mystery Magazine* (Los Angeles), November–December 1977.

"Something Like Murder," in *Ellery Queen's Mystery Magazine* (New York), January 1978.

"The Man in the Morgue," in *Alfred Hitchcock's Mystery Magazine* (New York), February 1978.

"Where Is, As Is," in *Alfred Hitchcock's Mystery Magazine* (New York), April 1978.

"In by the Tenth," in *Ellery Queen's Mystery Magazine* (New York), May 1978.

"The Day of the Picnic," in *Alfred Hitchcock's Murder-Go-Round.* New York, Dell, 1978.

"Marked Down," in *Alfred Hitchcock's Mystery Magazine* (New York), July 1978.

"Games for Adults," in *Alfred Hitchcock's Tales to Scare You Stiff*, edited by Eleanor Sullivan. New York, Davis, 1978.

"Have You Ever Seen This Woman?," in *Alfred Hitchcock's Anthology, Spring–Summer.* New York, Davis, 1978.

"The Other Runner," in *Ellery Queen's Mystery Magazine* (New York), October 1978.

"Close Calls," in *Alfred Hitchcock's Mystery Magazine* (New York), November 1978.

"Booth 13," in *Dark Sins, Dark Dreams*, edited by Bill Pronzini and Barry N. Malzberg. New York, Doubleday, 1978.

"Cheeseburger" (as John Barry Williams) with Barry N. Malzberg and Bill Pronzini, in *Alfred Hitchcock's Mystery Magazine* (New York), October 1978.

"Past Perfect," in *Alfred Hitchcock's Mystery Magazine* (New York), December 1978.

"Dangerous Game," in *Alfred Hitchcock's Mystery Magazine* (New York), February 1979.

"The Music from Downstairs," in *Alfred Hitchcock's Mystery Magazine* (New York), March 1979.

"Discount Fare," in *Alfred Hitchcock's Mystery Magazine* (New York), April 1979.

"Where Is Harry Beal?," in *Alfred Hitchcock's Mystery Magazine* (New York), August 1979.

OTHER PUBLICATIONS

Other

> "Setting for Suspense," in *The Writer* (Boston), July 1974.
> "Using Technology in Mysteries," in *The Writer* (Boston), July 1978.

John Lutz comments:
I hope above all that those reading my work will be compelled to continue reading. Then, if they derive nothing else from what I've written, they will have been entertained. "Entertainment" by my definition can be anything from the diversion of twiddling one's thumbs to the profound illumination of being reached by a classic work of art. I strive for craftsmanship which I hope will occasionally rise to the level of that flash of revelation which many people consider to be art. Mark Twain said, "The difference between the adequate word and the precise word is the difference between the lightning bug and the lightning." Who wants to be a lightning bug?

*   *   *

John Lutz's hundred-odd short stories (the majority in *Alfred Hitchcock's Mystery Magazine*) rarely deal with series characters and vary widely in quality and content, but much of his finest work, like "Mail Order" and "Understanding Electricity," is marked by a strong anti-business viewpoint and a bizarre imagination, as if Kafka were collaborating with Ralph Nader. A typical Lutz story might concern a lunatic trying to solve a murder in an asylum, the last hours of a tycoon accidentally locked into his walk-in vault by a watchdog, a man who claims he's being hounded by midgets, or a company that manipulates its clients' unwanted spouses into committing adultery. Many Lutz protagonists are husbands seeking to dispose of their wives.

Of his novels, *The Truth of the Matter* is a psychological chase story ranging across the Midwest, *Buyer Beware* pits a cowardly private eye against an organization of criminal businessmen, and *Bonegrinder* is a tale of mounting tensions in an Ozark village beset by a marauding Bigfoot-like monster. Like his short stories, Lutz's novels lack series characters and are united only by certain recurring themes and a high level of literary skill.

—Francis M. Nevins, Jr.

LYALL, Gavin (Tudor).   British.   Born in Birmingham, Warwickshire, 9 May 1932. Educated at King Edward VI School, Birmingham, 1943–51; Pembroke College, Cambridge, 1953–56, B.A. (honours) in English 1956. Served as a Pilot Officer in the Royal Air Force, 1951–53. Married the writer Katharine Whitehorn in 1958; two sons. Reporter, *Picture Post*, London, 1956–57; Film Director, BBC Television, London, 1958–59; Reporter and Air Correspondent, *Sunday Times*, London, 1959–62. Chairman, Crime Writers Association, 1966–67. Recipient: Crime Writers Association Silver Dagger, 1964, 1965. Agent: A. D. Peters and Company Ltd., 10 Buckingham Street, London WC2N 6BU. Address: 14 Provost Road, London NW3 4ST, England.

CRIME PUBLICATIONS

Novels

> *The Wrong Side of the Sky.*   London, Hodder and Stoughton, and New York, Scribner, 1961.
> *The Most Dangerous Game.*   New York, Scribner, 1963; London, Hodder and Stoughton, 1964.
> *Midnight Plus One.*   London, Hodder and Stoughton, and New York, Scribner, 1965.
> *Shooting Script.*   London, Hodder and Stoughton, and New York, Scribner, 1966.
> *Venus with Pistol.*   London, Hodder and Stoughton, and New York, Scribner, 1969.
> *Blame the Dead.*   London, Hodder and Stoughton, 1972; New York, Viking Press, 1973.
> *Judas Country.*   London, Hodder and Stoughton, and New York, Viking Press, 1975.

OTHER PUBLICATIONS

Play

> Screenplay: *Moon Zero Two*, with others, 1969.

Other

> *Operation Warboard* (rules for war games), with Bernard Lyall.   London, A. and C. Black, and New York, McKay, 1976.

> Editor, *The War in the Air 1939–1945: An Anthology of Personal Experiences.* London, Hutchinson, 1968; New York, Morrow, 1969.

Gavin Lyall comments:

I see my work as belonging to a fairly classical British thriller/adventure writing tradition that antedated the detective story – though like most British thriller writers who first published in the 1950's and 1960's I was heavily influenced by Hammett and Chandler. I seem to go in for heroes who have to take positive decisions – even perhaps moral ones – which change the course of the story. You might attribute this to a Quaker upbringing with its emphasis on responsibility for one's own actions. You might even say that I became a thriller writer because I wasn't allowed to play with toy guns as a boy; now I can play with as many real ones as I want – vicariously – in print. I think I write better scenes than I do plots, although this isn't uncommon in the thriller/adventure world. Still, I'd like to get my basic plots simpler and stronger. My journalistic background obviously helps my research, and the knowledge that I have done a fair amount of research gives me confidence – and really that's the most important thing for a grown man sitting down to play bang-bang-you're-dead on a typewriter every weekday morning. I am coming sadly to the conclusion that there are as many different ways of writing a book as there are books written, the sole common denominator being the need to sit down behind a typewriter and do some work. Unless you can justify writing something else, like this.

*   *   *

The Buchan tradition of thriller writing involves taking dissimilar characters and unlikely situations and then linking them together in a convincing manner. Gavin Lyall's literate novels appear to be firmly within this tradition. He can make the improbable appear not only believable, but inevitable.

There are no recurring characters in his novels, but his heroes bear a strong resemblance to one another. They walk a shadowy path between both sides of the law and often need to make moral decisions to attain their objectives. His best stories tell of clear-cut desperate situations in which his hero has to reach a goal while the reader decides who can be trusted among the other characters. The relationships between characters are often as important to the story as the plot itself. Lyall works with traditions, not clichés. His first-person viewpoint allows humor to lighten the grim path of high adventure. His heroes may adopt the flip Chandler style, but they don't overdo it. Like their creator they have a knowledge of guns and many of them are pilots. The research behind each novel is integrated into the plot and not set out as undigested fact.

In *The Wrong Side of the Sky*, Jack Clay is flying cargoes from Athens to the Libyan desert to Tripoli when he meets a wartime buddy, his sometime girl friend, the Nawab of Tungabhadra, and several million in stolen jewels. Integral to plot and to its moral decisions is the friendship between Clay and Ken Kitson who fly opposite sides of the sky. Northern Finland is the setting for *The Most Dangerous Game* in which free-lance pilot Bill Cary meets an American hunter and learns for himself what it feels like to be tracked for murder. High marks have to be given *Midnight Plus One* with its race against time by Lewis Cane to deliver a millionaire to Liechtenstein. The journey by Rolls-Royce is a slice of Dornford Yates, but the grim duel between gunmen is authentic Lyall. Keith Carr flies a camera plane for a film company on location in the Caribbean in *Shooting Script*. Murder tears the fabric of the world Lyall weaves, and there is some insight into the risk of running someone else's war like a Hollywood western. Art smuggling is the situation in *Venus with Pistol* as Bert Kemp leaves his antique gun shop in London to play the professional among amateurs who want to build an art collection the fast way. In *Blame the Dead*, bodyguard James Card, searching for the killer of a man he just met, follows a vengeance trail from Arras to Norway, and in *Judas Country*, the pilot Roy Case becomes involved in smuggling, blackmail, espionage, and murder in the Middle East.

Though the plots of these books build slowly, by the time the first bullet thuds home the reader knows the characters well enough to recognize them and, more importantly, to care about their fate on the downward plunge.

—J. Randolph Cox

LYNDS, Dennis. See **COLLINS, Michael.**

MacDONALD, John D(ann). American. Born in Sharon, Pennsylvania, 24 July 1916. Educated at the University of Pennsylvania, Philadelphia, 1934–35; Syracuse University, New York, B.S. 1938; Harvard University, Cambridge, Massachusetts, M.B.A. 1939. Served with the United States Army, Office of Strategic Services, 1940–46: Lieutenant Colonel. Married Dorothy Mary Prentiss in 1937; one son. Writer in several genres and under a number of pseudonyms for the pulps and other magazines. President, Mystery Writers of America, 1962. Recipient: Benjamin Franklin Award, for short story, 1955; Grand Prix de Littérature Policière, 1964; Mystery Writers of America Grand Master Award, 1972. Agent:

Littauer and Wilkinson, 500 Fifth Avenue, New York, New York 10036. Address: 1430 Point Crisp Road, Sarasota, Florida, U.S.A.

CRIME PUBLICATIONS

Novels (series character: Travis McGee)

The Brass Cupcake.   New York, Fawcett, 1950; London, Muller, 1955.
Judge Me Not.   New York, Fawcett, 1951; London, Muller, 1964.
Murder for the Bride.   New York, Fawcett, 1951; London, Fawcett, 1954.
Weep for Me.   New York, Fawcett, 1951; London, Muller, 1964.
The Damned.   New York, Fawcett, 1952; London, Muller, 1964.
Dead Low Tide.   New York, Fawcett, 1953; London, Fawcett, 1955.
The Neon Jungle.   New York, Fawcett, 1953; London, Fawcett, 1954.
All These Condemned.   New York, Fawcett, 1954.
Area of Suspicion.   New York, Dell, 1954; London, Hale, 1956; revised edition, New York, Fawcett, 1961.
A Bullet for Cinderella.   New York, Dell, 1955; London, Hale, 1960; as *On the Make*, New York, Dell, 1960.
Cry Hard, Cry Fast.   New York, Popular Library, 1955; London, Hale, 1969.
April Evil.   New York, Dell, 1956; London, Hale, 1957.
Border Town Girl (novelets).   New York, Popular Library, 1956; as *Five Star Fugitive*, London, Hale, 1970.
Murder in the Wind.   New York, Dell, 1956; as *Hurricane*, London, Hale, 1957.
You Live Once.   New York, Popular Library, 1956; London, Hale, 1976; as *You Kill Me*, New York, Fawcett, 1961.
Death Trap.   New York, Dell, 1957; London, Hale, 1958.
The Empty Trap.   New York, Popular Library, 1957.
The Price of Murder.   New York, Dell, 1957; London, Hale, 1958.
A Man of Affairs.   New York, Dell, 1957; London, Hale, 1959.
Clemmie.   New York, Fawcett, 1958.
The Executioners.   New York, Simon and Schuster, 1958; London, Hale, 1959; as *Cape Fear*, New York, Fawcett, 1962.
Soft Touch.   New York, Dell, 1958; London, Hale, 1960; as *Man-Trap*, London, Pan, 1961.
The Deceivers.   New York, Fawcett, 1958; London, Hale, 1968.
The Beach Girls.   New York, Fawcett, 1959; London, Muller, 1964.
The Crossroads.   New York, Simon and Schuster, 1959; London, Hale, 1961.
Deadly Welcome.   New York, Dell, 1959; London, Hale, 1961.
The End of the Night.   New York, Simon and Schuster, 1960; London, Hale, 1964.
The Only Girl in the Game.   New York, Fawcett, 1960; London, Hale, 1962.
Slam the Big Door.   New York, Fawcett, 1960; London, Hale, 1961.
One Monday We Killed Them All.   New York, Fawcett, 1961; London, Hale, 1963.
Where Is Janice Gantry?   New York, Fawcett, 1961; London, Hale, 1963.
A Flash of Green.   New York, Simon and Schuster, 1962; London, Hale, 1971.
The Girl, The Gold Watch, and Everything.   New York, Fawcett, 1962; London, Hodder and Stoughton, 1968.
A Key to the Suite.   New York, Fawcett, 1962; London, Hale, 1968.
The Drowner.   New York, Fawcett, 1963; London, Hale, 1964.
On the Run.   New York, Fawcett, 1963; London, Hale, 1965.
The Deep Blue Goodby (McGee).   New York, Fawcett, 1964; London, Hale, 1965.
Nightmare in Pink (McGee).   New York, Fawcett, 1964; London, Hale, 1966.
A Purple Place for Dying (McGee).   New York, Fawcett, 1964; London, Hale, 1966.
The Quick Red Fox (McGee).   New York, Fawcett, 1964; London, Hale, 1966.

A Deadly Shade of Gold (McGee).   New York, Fawcett, 1965; London, Hale, 1967.
Bright Orange for the Shroud (McGee).   New York, Fawcett, 1965; London, Hale, 1967.
Darker Than Amber (McGee).   New York, Fawcett, 1966; London, Hale, 1968.
One Fearful Yellow Eye (McGee).   New York, Fawcett, 1966; London, Hale, 1968.
The Last One Left.   New York, Doubleday, 1967; London, Hale, 1968.
Three for McGee (omnibus).   New York, Doubleday, 1967.
Pale Gray for Guilt (McGee).   New York, Fawcett, 1968; London, Hale, 1969.
The Girl in the Plain Brown Wrapper (McGee).   New York, Fawcett, 1968; London, Hale, 1969.
Dress Her in Indigo (McGee).   New York, Fawcett, 1969; London, Hale, 1971.
The Long Lavender Look (McGee).   New York, Fawcett, and London, Fawcett, 1970.
A Tan and Sandy Silence (McGee).   New York, Fawcett, 1972; London, Hale, 1973.
The Scarlet Ruse (McGee).   New York, Fawcett, 1973; London, Hale, 1975.
The Turquoise Lament (McGee).   Philadelphia, Lippincott, 1973; London, Hale, 1975.
McGee (omnibus).   London, Hale, 1975.
The Dreadful Lemon Sky (McGee).   Philadelphia, Lippincott, 1975; London, Hale, 1976.
The Empty Copper Sea (McGee).   Philadelphia, Lippincott, 1978.
The Green Ripper (McGee).   Philadelphia, Lippincott, 1979.

Short Stories

End of the Tiger and Other Stories.   New York, Fawcett, 1966; London, Hale, 1967.
Seven.   New York, Fawcett, 1971.

Uncollected Short Stories

"Double Hannenframmis," in *Just My Luck.*   Chicago, Playboy Press, 1976.
"He Was Always a Nice Boy," in *Ellery Queen's Giants of Mystery.*   New York, Davis, 1976.
"Wedding Present," in *Antaeus* (New York), Spring–Summer 1977.

OTHER PUBLICATIONS

Novels

Wine of the Dreamers.   New York, Greenberg, 1951; as *Planet of the Dreamers*, New York, Pocket Books, 1953; London, Hale, 1954.
Ballroom of the Skies.   New York, Greenberg, 1952.
Cancel All Our Vows.   New York, Appleton Century Crofts, 1953; London, Hale, 1955.
Contrary Pleasure.   New York, Appleton Century Crofts, 1954; London, Hale, 1955.
Please Write for Details.   New York, Simon and Schuster, 1959.
I Could Go On Singing (novelization of screenplay).   New York, Fawcett, 1963; London, Hale, 1964.
Condominium.   Philadelphia, Lippincott, and London, Hale, 1977.

Other

The House Guests.   New York, Doubleday, 1965; London, Hale, 1966.
No Deadly Drug.   New York, Doubleday, 1968.

Editor, *The Lethal Sex.*   New York, Dell, 1959; London, Collins, 1962.

Manuscript Collection: University of Florida Library, Gainesville.

*   *   *

John D. MacDonald has written more than 60 novels published as paperback originals. Like the recent *Condominium*, which was published in hard cover, many of the paperback originals deal with contemporary issues and corporate swindles, focus on corporations grabbing land in Florida or the network of violence and pay-off operating hotels and gambling casinos. Other novels concentrate on the corruptions of local politics or, like *Cancel All Our Vows*, on the fragility and irresponsibility of suburban marriages. MacDonald is, however, probably (apart, perhaps from *Condominium*) best known for the series of novels, all with colors in the title, told through the persona of Travis McGee. Some of the non-McGee novels, like *The Only Girl in the Game*, about a rebellious and warm-hearted girl blackmailed into working for a criminal syndicate operating a Las Vegas hotel, finally killed, and then avenged by an old apparent hayseed millionaire from Texas and a young efficient hotel manager, are too full of stereotypes, outraged innocence, banal writing, and protests against a "system" so remote in origin that even the most violent of the criminals seem strangely victimized and sympathetic. The figure of McGee, however, is sufficiently attractive and complex to hold together both pointed commentary on contemporary America and a sense of vital experience. Handsome, strong, a former minor professional football player, six feet four, and omni-competent, McGee lives independently on his secure and comfortable boat, the "Busted Flush," moored in Bahia Mar in Fort Lauderdale, and earns the funds to sustain his "retirement" through what he frequently describes as "salvage operations." Typically, he is drawn into a situation through some obligation from his past, learning that the wife or the daughter or the sister of some old close friend is being destroyed by one of the various corrupt forces. McGee pursues these legacies with fervor, with total involvement, relying on his strength, his intelligence, and, sometimes, his contacts with people in positions of authority around the world who owe him favors. McGee's "salvage" is emotional as well as protective and financial, for he frequently restores his legacies by taking them, alone, for long cruises in his boat to little-known islands off the Florida Coast or in the Caribbean. He is the skillful contemporary knight-errant, as well as the therapist building strong individual virtues to survive the corporate corruptions of the modern world.

McGee's attitude is frankly moralistic, and the novels are full of inserted essays. The ecological dangers of industrial pollution, forwarded by corporations with an interest only in making money, are frequently both the subject of essays and the theme of the novels. And MacDonald does not hesitate to add the specific names of the big companies he holds most responsible. Dedicated to order, care, and cleanliness on his own boat (a sloppy or ill-kept boat indicates an emotionally irresponsible owner), McGee objects to commercial packaging, the "locust population" of large cities, and "manufactured air." Although the good and responsible characters may resort to air-conditioning in the humid Florida summers, they always do so apologetically. In all the novels, McGee forcefully and effectively satirizes the drug culture, all forms of conspicuous consumption, hunting and hand-guns, sex without emotion, and attempts to alter human consciousness. In the novels of the 1960's like *One Fearful Yellow Eye*, the corruptions of the modern world are more likely to be attributed to social and external causes, to the racist southern culture or to a Nazi past; in the novels of the 1970's the origin of corruption is more likely to be seen in individual psychological terms or in a generalized sense of human greed. Sometimes McGee enjoys particular forms of corruption. In *Pale Gray for Guilt* McGee and his friend Meyer (a brilliant, hairy, chess-playing retired economist who is McGee's sidekick in many of the novels) cleverly float a large and false stock issue which enables them, simultaneously, to secure a considerable sum for themselves, to help, lavishly, the widow of their murdered friend, and to trap the corporate criminals. The novels are knowledgeable and interesting about process, about the way the stock market works or complicated machinery functions, or how to escape the ocean's undertow or to arrange for elegant call girls in a large city. McGee is far from a primitive moralist, far from the tone of simple outraged innocence that mars some of the other novels. He is knowledgeable about travel, food and drink, women, and literature. He can quote, appropriately, Rilke as well as Sinclair Lewis.

Supreme sexual stud that he is on the surface, McGee nevertheless has a code of sexual behavior carefully worked out. He hates some of his past casual promiscuity, frequently makes fun of Hemingway's false machismo, as he makes fun of George Patton's brutality. McGee will never touch a friend's woman, no matter how closely he helps her. On the therapeutic cruises, he often waits weeks or months, until the woman is healthy, active, and able to talk out her recent trauma, before he makes love to her. McGee's sexuality is a relationship, an appreciation of women, a respect for old-fashioned "sexual mystery," a humane and restorative force, not a simple and mechanical exercise. Even in the non-McGee novels, MacDonald insists on the humanizing effect of honest sexuality: in *A Flash of Green*, for example, the ambivalent and detached newspaper reporter, the central character, goes along with a crooked corporate land grab until one episode with a large, casual, yet totally honest young girl turns him into dedicated opposition, no matter how futile or "quixotic," to the destructive scam. The character of Travis McGee also humanizes the stereotyped figure of the hard-boiled detective in ways other than sexual, for he calls the human brain a "random computer," talks of pieces that do not fit the puzzle at all, and satirizes those fables in which the detective displays extraordinary feats of either deduction or physical bravery.

The world around McGee is violent as well as corrupt, full of evil. McGee confronts the evil with skill, knowledge, and integrity, MacDonald creating him with a terse, biting, yet sometimes metaphorical, sensitive, and humorous prose (a dishonest middle-aged lawyer calls the boat, on which he tries to swing with the younger generation, the "Strawberry Tort"). In some of the earlier novels of the series, McGee is the defender of past American values, loyal to war buddies, seeing the corporation as alien, the criminal as escaped Nazi or racist. In more recent novels, the sense of evil is more complicated, and some of it more likely to be internalized. In novels like *A Tan and Sandy Silence* and *The Turquoise Lament*, McGee recognizes that he himself has the capacity to kill unjustifiably, experiences greed and indifference to others. Although he still delivers maxims like "Integrity is not a conditional word," survival becomes more and more difficult as McGee becomes more self-questioning and complex, even more vulnerable. The latter novel ends with a significant switch in the conventional plot. In most of the other novels, after the restorative cruise, McGee sends the girl away, preserving his final sexual independence (although, in one earlier novel, *Pale Gray for Guilt*, the girl had left McGee, but only because she was dying of a rare disease and wanted to do it bravely). In *The Turquoise Lament*, however, after having seen McGee's vulnerability on the cruise, the girl, a legacy from her now dead father and rescued by McGee from a diabolically insane husband, realizes that gratitude, allegiance to the past, and strong attraction are not the same as love and decides to leave McGee for someone else. McGee can "salvage" himself, too.

—James Gindin

MACDONALD, John Ross. See **MACDONALD, Ross.**

MacDONALD, Philip. Also writes as Oliver Fleming; Anthony Lawless; Martin Porlock. British. Born in 1899; grandson of the writer George MacDonald. Served in a cavalry regiment in Mesopotamia during World War I. Married to the writer F. Ruth Howard. After World War I, trained horses for the army, and was a show jumper; moved to Hollywood in 1931 and worked as a scriptwriter and Great Dane breeder. Recipient: Mystery Writers of America Edgar Allan Poe Award, 1953, 1956.

CRIME PUBLICATIONS

Novels (series character: Colonel Anthony Ruthven Gethryn)

Ambrotox and Limping Dick (as Oliver Fleming), with Ronald MacDonald. London, Ward Lock, 1920.
The Spandau Quid (as Oliver Fleming), with Ronald MacDonald. London, Palmer, 1923.
The Rasp (Gethryn). London, Collins, 1924; New York, Dial Press, 1925.
The White Crow (Gethryn). New York, Dial Press, 1928; London, Collins, 1929.
The Link (Gethryn). London, Collins, and New York, Doubleday, 1930.
The Noose (Gethryn). London, Collins, and New York, Dial Press, 1930.
Rynox. London, Collins, 1930; as *The Rynox Murder Mystery*, New York, Doubleday, 1931; as *The Rynox Mystery*, Collins, 1933.
The Choice (Gethryn). London, Collins, 1931; as *The Polferry Riddle*, New York, Doubleday, 1931; as *The Polferry Mystery*, Collins, 1932.
Harbour (as Anthony Lawless). London, Collins, and New York, Doubleday, 1931.
Persons Unknown (Gethryn). New York, Doubleday, 1931; as *The Maze*, London, Collins, 1932.
Murder Gone Mad. London, Collins, and New York, Doubleday, 1931.
The Wraith (Gethryn). London, Collins, and New York, Doubleday, 1931.
The Crime Conductor (Gethryn). New York, Doubleday, 1931; London, Collins, 1932.
Rope to Spare (Gethryn). London, Collins, and New York, Doubleday, 1932.
Death on My Left. London, Collins, and New York, Doubleday, 1933.
R.I.P. London, Collins, 1933; as *Menace*, New York, Doubleday, 1933.
The Nursemaid Who Disappeared (Gethryn). London, Collins, 1938; as *Warrant for X*, New York, Doubleday, 1938.
The Dark Wheel, with A. Boyd Correll. London, Collins, and New York, Morrow, 1948; as *Sweet and Deadly*, Rockville Centre, New York, Zenith, 1959.
Guest in the House. New York, Doubleday, 1955; London, Jenkins, 1956; as *No Time for Terror*, New York, Spivak, 1956.
The List of Adrian Messenger (Gethryn). New York, Doubleday, 1959; London, Jenkins, 1960.

Novels as Martin Porlock

Mystery at Friar's Pardon. London, Collins, 1931; New York, Doubleday, 1932.
Mystery in Kensington Gore. London, Collins, 1932; as *Escape*, New York, Doubleday, 1932.
X v. Rex. London, Collins, 1933; as *Mystery of the Dead Police*, New York, Doubleday, 1933; as *The Mystery of Mr. X*, London, Literary Press, 1934.

Short Stories

Something to Hide. New York, Doubleday, 1952; as *Fingers of Fear and Other Stories*, London, Collins, 1953.

The Man Out of the Rain and Other Stories. New York, Doubleday, 1955; London, Jenkins, 1957.
Death and Chicanery. New York, Doubleday, 1962; London, Jenkins, 1963.

Uncollected Short Story

"The Star of Starz," in *Ellery Queen's Murdercade.* New York, Random House, 1975.

OTHER PUBLICATIONS

Novels

Queen's Mate. London, Collins, 1926; New York, Dial Press, 1927.
Patrol. London, Collins, and New York, Harper, 1927; as *The Last Patrol*, London, Novel Library, 1934.
Likeness of Exe. London, Collins, 1929.
Moonfisher. London, Gollancz, 1931; (as Anthony Lawless), New York, Doubleday, 1932.

Plays

Rebecca, with others, in *Twenty Best Film Plays*, edited by John Gassner and Dudley Nichols. New York, Crown, 1943.

Screenplays: *The Star Reporter*, with Ralph Smart, 1931; *Hotel Splendide*, with Ralph Smart, 1932; *C.O.D.*, with Ralph Smart, 1932; *The Last Outpost*, 1935; *The Mystery Woman*, 1935; *Yours for the Asking*, with others, 1936; *Ourselves (River of Unrest)*, with others, 1936; *The Princess Comes Across*, with others, 1936; *The Mysterious Mr. Moto*, with Norman Foster, 1938; *Mr. Moto's Last Warning*, with Norman Foster, 1938; *Mr. Moto Takes a Vacation*, with Norman Foster, 1938; *Blind Alley*, with Michael Blankfort and Albert Duffy, 1939; *Rebecca*, with others, 1940; *Whispering Ghosts*, with Lou Breslow, 1942; *Street of Chance*, with Garrett Fort, 1942; *Sahara*, with others, 1943; *Action in Arabia*, with Herbert Biberman, 1944; *The Body Snatcher*, with Carlos Keith, 1945; *Strangers in the Night*, with Bryant Ford and Paul Gangelin, 1945; *Dangerous Intruder*, with Martin Goldsmith and F. Ruth Howard, 1945; *Love from a Stranger*, 1947; *The Dark Past*, with others, 1949; *The Man Who Cheated Himself*, with Seton I. Miller, 1951; *Mask of the Avenger*, with others, 1951; *Circle of Danger*, 1951; *Ring of Fear*, with Paul Fix and James Edward Grant, 1954; *Tobor the Great*, with Richard Goldstone and Carl Dudley, 1954.

Radio Play: *Glitter*, 1978.

Television Play: *Thin Ice (Five Fingers* series), 1959–60.

*   *   *

The works of Philip MacDonald appear to have fallen into obscurity to some extent, which is a great pity. He could demonstrate with ease the classic features of detective fiction, sometimes adding touches of the macabre, while on other occasions injecting passages little short of farce. His writing had a typically English flavour, although he moved to the United States comparatively early in his life and embarked on a script-writing career in Hollywood.

His first detective novel, *The Rasp*, introduced a series character who was to become an important part of the genre's Golden Age – Colonel Anthony Ruthven Gethryn, very much the attractive and stiff-upper-lipped hero but one who, for a change, does not resort to violence or unnecessary dramatics. *The Rasp* uses the well-worn theme of an eminent body in the study of a country residence, but MacDonald handled this situation rather better than most. By a process of logical deduction, carried out while he was acting as father-confessor to more than one lady in distress, Gethryn arrives at the solution to a seemingly impossible problem. MacDonald adds his own special touches of humour, with here and there a dash of the bizarre. Unlike many of his contemporaries, he was skilled at characterisation; very few of his characters are merely pasteboard puppets. Each of these points, plus his innate desire to play fair with the reader in the revelation of clues, was to set the tone for a long series of Gethryn novels.

Two other excellent early books are *The Link*, a Gethryn mystery set in a country village with a veterinary surgeon as the principal character, and undoubtedly one of the most ingeniously contrived crimes in detective fiction; and *Rynox*, recounting the fate of a large sum of money delivered to an insurance company, in which the author takes the reader into his confidence to an even greater degree than usual. On this latter point, MacDonald made his views clear before writing *Persons Unknown*, stating that he proposed "a due and proper unfolding to the reader of the tale and of the relevant pieces, however small, of the puzzle ... the ideal detective story is a sort of competition between author and reader." His techniques are more clearly to be seen in *The Noose*, highly praised by Arnold Bennett for its startling yet convincing revelation of the criminal's identity; suspense is guaranteed by the fact that Gethryn has to prove the innocence of a condemned man, with just five days in hand before the execution.

It is virtually impossible, with an author of MacDonald's quality, to label his most outstanding books. There are three, however, which will always epitomise his art. *Murder Gone Mad* is a tour de force, selected by John Dickson Carr as one of the ten best detective novels, with MacDonald's penchant for the macabre in full flight as an unknown person carries out a daring series of killings and gives the police prior warning of each. Detective novels with too many murders are likely to become monotonous and lose the reader's interest by their very artificiality, but MacDonald showed that he could pull it off without making this sacrifice. What is more, he repeated the exercise in an even better book – *X v. Rex*, originally published under the pseudonym Martin Porlock – this time with the maniac murdering police officers in series. The third of MacDonald's key contributions, and considered by many critics to be his best, was *The Nursemaid Who Disappeared*. This Gethryn novel begins with a conversation overheard by a young American in a London teashop and evolves into one of Gethryn's most enthralling cases. This book features a considerable amount of action, as well as a prime example of MacDonald's delight in hingeing his plots upon small clues; it is also probably the best instance in the field of the positively wraith-like criminal.

MacDonald's literary output thinned in the 1940's and 1950's presumably as his film work increased, but his late period produced some excellent short stories and at least one interesting novel. The latter, *The List of Adrian Messenger*, saw the return of Anthony Gethryn in a very strange and elaborate plot concerning a list of people who appear to have died accidentally. Gethryn is somewhat superfluous, but it is a lively thriller with that touch of sensationalism with which MacDonald's experience in the movies seems to have endowed his last novels. This influence is also noticeable in his short stories, but is to their benefit. Two volumes in particular, *The Man Out of the Rain* and *Something to Hide*, contain clear evidence of MacDonald's abilities in the short form. Some feature Gethryn, others introduce the prophetic Dr. Alcazar, but most are gems of the situation crime story. In these, MacDonald's well-established talent for suspense, twist climaxes, and the combination of farce with horror is seen again. Towering over these attributes, however, is an almost Hitchcockian facility for squeezing something completely terrifying out of a situation which is otherwise normal; the commonplace instantly becomes the bizarre.

MacDonald was given to experimentation; he was very much a part of mainstream detective fiction in the 1920's and 1930's yet rebelled against those devices that made classic detective fiction frankly boring. Anthony Boucher, whose opinion cannot be gainsaid, wrote: "MacDonald is at once a craftsman of writing, whose prose, characterisation and evocation of mood (comic or terrible) might be envied by the most serious literary practitioner, and a craftsman of plot technique, whose construction and misdirection should delight (and startle)

Carr or Christie." Although Boucher was referring specifically to the short stories, the comment may be appropriately applied to MacDonald's entire output.

—Melvyn Barnes

MACDONALD, Ross. Pseudonym for Kenneth Millar; also wrote as John Macdonald; John Ross Macdonald. American. Born in Los Gatos, California, 13 December 1915. Educated at the University of Western Ontario, London, 1933–38, B.A. 1938; University of Toronto, 1938–39; University of Michigan, Ann Arbor, 1941–44, 1948–49 (Graduate Fellow, 1941–42; Rackham Fellow, 1942–43), M.A. 1942, Ph.D. 1951. Served in the United States Naval Reserve, 1944–46: Lieutenant Junior Grade. Married Margaret Sturm, i.e. Margaret Millar, *q.v.*, in 1938; one child, now deceased. Teacher of English and History, Kitchener–Waterloo Collegiate Institute, Ontario, 1939–41; Teaching Fellow, University of Michigan, 1942–44, 1948–49; book reviewer, San Francisco *Chronicle*, 1957–60. Member, Board of Directors, 1960–61, 1964–65, and President, Mystery Writers of America. Recipient: Crime Writers Association Silver Dagger, 1965; University of Michigan Outstanding Achievement Award, 1972; Mystery Writers of America Grand Master Award, 1973; Popular Culture Association Award of Excellence, 1973. Address: 4420 Via Esperanza, Santa Barbara, California 93110, U.S.A.

CRIME PUBLICATIONS

Novels (series character: Lew Archer in all books except *The Ferguson Affair* and *The Wycherly Woman*)

The Moving Target (as John Macdonald). New York, Knopf, 1949; London, Cassell, 1951; as *Harper*, New York, Pocket Books, 1966.
The Barbarous Coast. New York, Knopf, 1956; London, Cassell, 1957.
The Doomsters. New York, Knopf, and London, Cassell, 1958.
The Galton Case. New York, Knopf, 1959; London, Cassell, 1960.
The Ferguson Affair. New York, Knopf, 1960; London, Collins, 1961.
The Wycherly Woman. New York, Knopf, 1961; London, Collins, 1962.
The Zebra-Striped Hearse. New York, Knopf, 1962; London, Collins, 1963.
The Chill. New York, Knopf, and London, Collins, 1964.
The Far Side of the Dollar. New York, Knopf, and London, Collins, 1965.
Black Money. New York, Knopf, and London, Collins, 1966.
The Instant Enemy. New York, Knopf, and London, Collins, 1968.
The Goodbye Look. New York, Knopf, and London, Collins, 1969.
The Underground Man. New York, Knopf, and London, Collins, 1971.
Sleeping Beauty. New York, Knopf, and London, Collins, 1973.
The Blue Hammer. New York, Knopf, and London, Collins, 1976.

Novels as Kenneth Millar (series character: Chet Gordon)

The Dark Tunnel (Gordon). New York, Dodd Mead, 1944; as *I Die Slowly*, London, Lion, 1955.
Trouble Follows Me (Gordon). New York, Dodd Mead, 1946; as *Night Train*, London, Lion, 1955.

Blue City.   New York, Knopf, 1947; London, Cassell, 1949.
The Three Roads.   New York, Knopf, 1948; London, Cassell, 1950.

Novels as John Ross Macdonald (series character: Lew Archer in all books except *Meet Me at the Morgue*)

The Drowning Pool.   New York, Knopf, 1950; London, Cassell, 1952.
The Way Some People Die.   New York, Knopf, 1951; London, Cassell, 1953.
The Ivory Grin.   New York, Knopf, 1952; London, Cassell, 1953; as *Marked for Murder*, New York, Pocket Books, 1953.
Meet Me at the Morgue.   New York, Knopf, 1953; as *Experience with Evil*, London, Cassell, 1954.
Find a Victim.   New York, Knopf, 1954; London, Cassell, 1955.

Short Stories

The Name Is Archer (as John Ross Macdonald).   New York, Bantam, 1955.
Lew Archer, Private Investigator.   Yonkers, New York, Mysterious Press, 1977.

OTHER PUBLICATIONS

Other

On Crime Writing.   Santa Barbara, California, Capra Press, 1973.
"Down These Streets a Mean Man Must Go," in *Antaeus* (New York), Spring–Summer, 1977.

Editor, *Great Stories of Suspense.*   New York, Knopf, 1974.

Bibliography: *Kenneth Millar/Ross Macdonald: A Checklist* by Matthew J. Bruccoli, Detroit, Gale, 1971.

Manuscript Collection: University of California Library, Irvine.

*   *   *

Ross Macdonald ranks among the finest detective novelists writing today. His Lew Archer series is a monumental contribution to detective literature. The sustained excellence of his work over 35 years and the innovations he has brought to the genre have led to various honors, and the rare distinction of being represented both on the best-seller lists and in college literature courses. This brief assessment will not attempt to survey the scope of his work or identify his best novels, but will simply suggest some of the tendencies his fiction has shown.

Some of the patterns in Macdonald's early work can be found in his third novel, *Blue City*. The texture of the world in this novel is reminiscent of Dashiell Hammett's fiction, though its sensibility and imagery show the influence of Raymond Chandler as well. The central figure is an angry young man who returns to his home town after cutting himself adrift five years earlier and serving a hitch in the army. John Weather arrives through the kindness of a trucker, stops at a tavern for a beer, and finds himself a stranger defending an old derelict from two thugs who had lingered on after having been brought in as strike-breakers. When Weather discovers that his father had been the victim of an unsolved murder after marrying a much younger woman, he battles his way toward the solution of the crime and comes to understand his father's contribution to the general corruption of the town. Weather is familiar with Veblen, Marx, Engels, and other social critics. The early part of the novel would appear to be headed toward direct social criticism, as it contrasts Sanford, who owns most of the town, with Kaufman, a radical thinker whose meagre income derives from a secondhand store. But the story shifts to Weather's young stepmother and the mobster who is found to have manipulated her and killed Weather's father. The mixture of Hammett's harsh world of political corruption and Chandler's sensual decadence are both apparent here.

Nearly two decades later Macdonald would compare *Blue City* to the last scene of Chandler's *The Long Goodbye*: "this scene was written by a man of tender and romantic sensibility who had been injured. Chandler used Marlowe to shield himself while half-expressing his sensibility and its private hurts." Macdonald sees this tendency in his own work prior to *The Doomsters*, which he feels marks "a fairly clean break with the Chandler tradition." In the decades following *Blue City*, Macdonald's angry young man appears often, but he finds himself in more trouble than he alone can handle. The implicit class struggle is gradually blunted in favor of a psychological view of crime where the "mentally sick people and the criminal" belong to "the same group," so that criticism of the social structure operates on the acausal level of metaphor. The leaking offshore oil platform in *Sleeping Beauty* that protrudes "like the metal handle of a dagger that had stabbed the world and made it spill black blood," has a "psychological connection" to other crimes, but no direct connection to corporate practices or the ambivalent ideals embodied in modern technology. Although Macdonald is clearly concerned about these matters, his emphasis on familial and psychological history leading to crime in effect moves his fiction back toward the class assumptions of British detective fiction that Hammett and Chandler had rejected.

With *The Doomsters* the moral center of the novels moves out of the detective into those with whom he comes in contact, so that the detective has become a kind of psychologist who prompts people to reveal their interpretations of events and, ultimately, the illusions surrounding them. One of the characters in this novel is actually a psychologist and it is not surprising that all the characters tend to talk too much. It is not until *The Galton Case*, about which Macdonald has written candidly and affectionately, that the implications of his aesthetic perspective begin to become clear. In it Archer bests the angry young man convincingly, and the novel as a whole is better balanced than the earlier works. What Macdonald had discovered was his own contribution to the genre. His detective would become more clearly "the mind of the novel, ... a consciousness in which the meanings of other lives emerge." As other lives become the substance of this consciousness, their various forms of brokenness and partial fulfillment yield in the conclusion a final understanding that reverberates back through the work.

Macdonald's sensitivity to people who are caught in the conflicts of social change is apparent throughout his fiction. Husbands and wives fail to learn to work together and their children run away from them or are torn asunder by the dissension. Young women and men break the patterns of their lives to circle warily and uncomprehendingly around the secret tragedies of their elders. Throughout Macdonald's fiction people live illusions in order to conceal from themselves and others their own inadequacies and carry with them petty grievances that they have steadfastly refused to place in perspective. Archer is often spectator to arguments that have been worn down through repetition, but which are repeated once more for a new audience. The guilt that emerges in the novels is rarely traced to one person, but usually involves the full or partial commitments of several people at one stage or another. In many of the novels the identities of characters are interchanged, unexpected parenthood is revealed, or new identities have been assumed.

The plots resulting from these complexities are intricate, the dialogue is a studied vernacular, and the imagery is "intended to have deep psychological and social meanings." Macdonald places his reader between the innocence of the very young and murder, his objective correlative of guilt, so that Lew Archer is intended finally as a window into ourselves. The process of demystification that occurs as Archer conducts his investigations creates resonances within the reader that urge him toward self-recognition. The critical questions that Macdonald had early posed had been how he could achieve a greater truth and a higher art. A reading of his fiction will leave little doubt that he has achieved both.

—Larry N. Landrum

MacHARG, William.   See BALMER, Edwin.

MacINNES, Helen (Clark).   American.   Born in Glasgow, Scotland, 7 October 1907; emigrated to the United States in 1937; naturalized, 1951. Educated at Hermitage School, Helensburgh; High School for Girls, Glasgow; Glasgow University, M.A. 1928; University College, London, Diploma in Librarianship 1931. Married the writer Gilbert Highet in 1932 (died, 1978); one son. Special Cataloguer, Ferguson Collection, University of Glasgow, 1928–29; employed by the Dunbartonshire Education Authority to select books for county libraries, 1929–30; acted with the Oxford University Dramatic Society and with the Oxford Experimental Theatre, 1934–37. Recipient: Columba Prize in Literature, Iona College, New Rochelle, New York, 1966. Address: 15 Jeffreys Lane, East Hampton, Long Island, New York 11937, U.S.A.

CRIME PUBLICATIONS

Novels

>   *Above Suspicion.*   Boston, Little Brown, and London, Harrap, 1941.
>   *Assignment in Brittany.*   Boston, Little Brown, and London, Harrap, 1942.
>   *While Still We Live.*   Boston, Little Brown, 1944; as *The Unconquerable*, London, Harrap, 1944.
>   *Horizon.*   London, Harrap, 1945; Boston, Little Brown, 1946.
>   *Neither Five Nor Three.*   New York, Harcourt Brace, and London, Collins, 1951.
>   *I and My True Love.*   New York, Harcourt Brace, and London, Collins, 1953.
>   *Pray for a Brave Heart.*   New York, Harcourt Brace, and London, Collins, 1955.
>   *North from Rome.*   New York, Harcourt Brace, and London, Collins, 1958.
>   *Decision at Delphi.*   New York, Harcourt Brace, and London, Collins, 1961.
>   *The Venetian Affair.*   New York, Harcourt Brace, 1963; London, Collins, 1964.
>   *The Double Image.*   New York, Harcourt Brace, and London, Collins, 1966.
>   *The Salzburg Connection.*   New York, Harcourt Brace, 1968; London, Collins, 1969.
>   *Message from Málaga.*   New York, Harcourt Brace, and London, Collins, 1971.
>   *Snare of the Hunter.*   New York, Harcourt Brace, and London, Collins, 1974.
>   *Agent in Place.*   New York, Harcourt Brace, and London, Collins, 1976.
>   *Prelude to Terror.*   New York, Harcourt Brace, and London, Collins, 1978.

OTHER PUBLICATIONS

Novels

>   *Friends and Lovers.*   Boston, Little Brown, 1947; London, Harrap, 1948.
>   *Rest and Be Thankful.*   Boston, Little Brown, and London, Harrap, 1949.

Play

>   *Home Is the Hunter.*   New York, Harcourt Brace, 1964.

Other

> Translator, with Gilbert Highet, *Sexual Life in Ancient Rome*, by Otto Kiefer.   London,
> Routledge, 1934; New York, Dutton, 1935.
> Translator, with Gilbert Highet, *Friedrich Engels: A Biography*, by Gustav
> Mayer.   London, Chapman and Hall, 1936.

Manuscript Collection: Princeton University Library, New Jersey.

*   *   *

The appearance of a Helen MacInnes novel is often the appearance of a best seller which may become a movie (*Above Suspicion* and *Assignment in Brittany*) or a Book-of-the-Month Club Selection (*Prelude to Terror*). Early academic training gave MacInnes skill and patience for research; extensive travel has provided convincing backgrounds for settings that range from Switzerland to Granada, from Paris to East Hampton, from Venice to Vienna. If reviews in the *Times Literary Supplement* charge that "Miss MacInnes is not interested in achieving even a semblance of authenticity in her novels," reviews in the New York *Times* cite the carefully researched locales as part of the attraction of her books.

In a 1965 interview MacInnes said of her work: "Underlying everything is the fact that I'm interested in international politics, in analyzing news, to read newspapers both on and between the lines, to deduct and add, to utilize memory." Her adventure-suspense novels reflect this persistent concern about contemporary affairs. Plots center on World War II – *Above Suspicion, Assignment in Brittany, While Still We Live*, and *Horizon*; adventures involve World War II secrets, still explosive after the war – *Pray for a Brave Heart* and *The Salzburg Connection*; and political intrigues focus on Communist threats to the West – *I and My True Love, Neither Five Nor Three, North from Rome, Decision at Delphi, The Venetian Affair, Message from Málaga, Snare of the Hunter, Agent in Place*, and *Prelude to Terror*. Her two non-suspense novels, *Rest and Be Thankful* and *Friends and Lovers*, were not especially successful and she abandoned this vein when, as she said, "I realized that our international world had gone terribly wrong again."

Her most recent novels are typical of her skill and appeal. *Snare of the Hunter* plunges an amateur agent (music critic David Mennery) into the dangerous rescue of Irina Kusak from Czechoslovakia to the West. Further plot complications involve danger to Irina's famous father (a writer who has escaped from behind the Iron Curtain and whose explosives notebooks the daughter carries); threats from Irina's ex-husband, Jiri Kradek, a Communist official; and a romance between David and Irina rekindled after 16 years. Narrow escapes, violent deaths, exciting chases, and betrayals combine to make the danger and potential destruction hair raising.

Agent in Place involves double and triple agents, a secret NATO memorandum, and occasional heavy-handed propaganda. Published before newspaper reporters' confidential sources were seriously threatened, this novel centers on an amateur, Tom Kelso (whose brother gave Part I of the memorandum to a New York *Times* reporter), and a professional, Tony Lawton. Enemy agents are a bit too sinister; Tom and Dorothea Kelso act too bravely; Chuck Kelso dies for being too idealistic. Coded messages, frequent disguises, minute plans for meetings and escapes abound; in short, familiar characteristics of a MacInnes novel to please her faithful readers. In *Prelude to Terror*, Colin Grant, a New York art expert, arrives in Vienna to bid at auction for a Ruysdael painting on behalf of wealthy industrialist-collector. Predictably, MacInnes's amateur is embroiled in the frightening world of conspiracy, murder, kidnapping, and international intrigue; and he must himself perform a bit of derring-do.

Ralph Harper in *The World of the Thriller* points out that suspense writers like Graham Greene and John le Carré are "able to force the reader into self-examination and self-judgment." MacInnes's novels fail to reach such a philosophical level: characters are good or bad; poetic justice often comes neatly; readers are entertained, not tested. Nevertheless, to the pro-Western lover of adventure and suspense, Helen MacInnes deserves the epithets her critics have bestowed: "Reigning queen of suspense" and "Master teller of spy stories."

—Elizabeth Evans

MacKENZIE, Donald. Canadian. Born in Toronto, Ontario, 11 August 1918. Educated at schools in England, Canada, and Switzerland. Describes his life's stages as: full-time playboy, 1938–41; professional thief, 1930–48; since 1948 self-employed author. Agent: Russell and Volkening Inc. 551 Fifth Avenue, New York, New York, 10017, U.S.A.

CRIME PUBLICATIONS

Novels (series characters: Harry Chalice and Crying Eddie; John Raven)

Nowhere to Go. London, Elek, 1956; as *Manhunt*, Boston, Houghton Mifflin, 1957.
The Juryman. London, Elek, 1957; Boston, Houghton Mifflin, 1958.
Scent of Danger. London, Collins, and Boston, Houghton Mifflin, 1958; as *Moment of Danger*, London, Pan, 1959.
Dangerous Silence. London, Collins, and Boston, Houghton Mifflin, 1960.
Knife Edge. Boston, Houghton Mifflin, 1961; London, Pan, 1962.
The Genial Stranger. London, Collins, and Boston, Houghton Mifflin, 1962.
Double Exposure. London, Collins, and Boston, Houghton Mifflin, 1963; as *I Spy*, New York, Avon, 1964.
Cool Sleeps Balaban. London, Collins, and Boston, Houghton Mifflin, 1964.
The Lonely Side of the River. London, Hodder and Stoughton, and Boston, Houghton Mifflin, 1965.
Salute from a Dead Man (Chalice and Eddie). London, Hodder and Stoughton, and Boston, Houghton Mifflin, 1966.
Death Is a Friend (Chalice and Eddie). London, Hodder and Stoughton, and Boston, Houghton Mifflin, 1967.
Three Minus Two. London, Hodder and Stoughton, 1968; as *The Quiet Killer*, Boston, Houghton Mifflin, 1968.
Dead Straight. London, Hodder and Stoughton, and Boston, Houghton Mifflin, 1969.
Night Boat from Puerto Vedra. London, Hodder and Stoughton, and Boston, Houghton Mifflin, 1970.
The Kyle Contract. Boston, Houghton Mifflin, 1970; London, Hodder and Stoughton, 1971.
Sleep Is for the Rich (Chalice and Eddie). London, Macmillan, and Boston, Houghton Mifflin, 1971; as *The Chalice Caper*, London, Mayflower, 1974.
Postscript to a Dead Letter. London, Macmillan, and Boston, Houghton Mifflin, 1973.
Zaleski's Percentage. London, Macmillan, and Boston, Houghton Mifflin, 1974.
The Spreewald Collection. London, Macmillan, and Boston, Houghton Mifflin, 1975.
Raven in Flight. Boston, Houghton Mifflin, 1976.
Raven and the Ratcatcher. Boston, Houghton Mifflin, 1977.
Raven and the Kamikaze. Boston, Houghton Mifflin, 1977.
Raven Settles a Score. Boston, Houghton Mifflin, 1978; London, Macmillan, 1979.
Raven after Dark. Boston, Houghton Mifflin, 1979.

OTHER PUBLICATIONS

Other

> *Occupation: Thief* (autobiography). Indianapolis, Bobbs Merrill, 1955; as *Fugitives*,
> London, Elek, 1955.
> *Gentleman at Crime* (autobiography). London, Elek, 1956.

Manuscript Collection: Mugar Memorial Library, Boston University.

*   *   *

As a former burglar, prison inmate, and European traveler, Donald MacKenzie is in an appropriate position to write crime novels. His early work reflects those periods of his life with a bitterness and realism that make the horrors of prison believable, but with the touch of a super-hero and adventure needed to make enjoyable suspense fiction. MacKenzie's work is essentially in the thriller-adventure field, encompassing almost no detection or surprise endings unmasking the villain. Many of the early books are concerned with a small-time burglar who has already served one or two prison terms and is trapped in a situation where he must save himself from returning to prison or death. Murders do occur but are only by-products of the main action. MacKenzie relates many of the details of prison life and the court procedures that take away one's freedom. His characters are desperate men who are driven by circumstances to violence. Often those heroes are portrayed as victims who have little choice in their actions. They are the pawns of society or other, more vicious criminals.

A typical MacKenzie thief is Canadian, bears a Scottish name and is currently down in his luck, but comes from a well-to-do family who now wants nothing to do with him. The bitterness of these men's lives has faded in the later novels, and recent books feature John Raven – a police inspector in two books and then a fiercely independent knight errant battling the windmills of society. Raven is similar to the Canadians in his aloofness, upper-class background, and sense of being out of step. They are all set apart from the world by their very being and holding to ideals and honor. The Raven books also use Europe as background; they are either set in Spain or use continental characters. Raven himself is a loner who uses illegal and unorthodox procedures in his police work and later must use them to prevent being framed for crimes he did not commit.

Two books are notable for their break from many of MacKenzie's traditions. *Salute from a Dead Man* uses a spy-thriller situation. The hero, Duncan, is coerced into helping the police catch an espionage agent whose life is virtually destroyed in a battle which he doesn't understand and has no control over. *The Kyle Contract* is set in California. The main character is framed and sent to jail where he meets a Canadian. Honor and trust among thieves are stressed, but only the Canadian lives up to the ideal. Setting and resolution are the unique elements.

Stylistically MacKenzie is always consistent. He uses character names as chapter headings to sharpen the focus. Danger and suspense are paramount over puzzle. The hero fights to help someone else (often a close friend who is betraying him or a woman in danger); a chase scene climaxes the book; and while there is a quick resolution to the plot, other questions remain. MacKenzie has a pat formula for quality suspense.

—Fred Dueren

MacLEAN, Alistair (Stuart). Also writes as Ian Stuart. Swiss. Born in Glasgow, Lanarkshire, Scotland, in 1922. Educated at Glasgow University. Served in the Royal Navy during World War II. Married Marcelle Georgeus in 1972 (second marriage). Taught English and history in a secondary school, Rutherglen, Glasgow, after World War II. Address: c/o William Collins Sons and Company Ltd., 14 St. James's Place, London SW1A 1PS, England.

CRIME PUBLICATIONS

Novels

H.M.S. Ulysses. London, Collins, 1955; New York, Doubleday, 1956.
The Guns of Navarone. London, Collins, and New York, Doubleday, 1957.
South by Java Head. London, Collins, and New York, Doubleday, 1958.
The Last Frontier. London, Collins, 1959; as *The Secret Ways*, New York, Doubleday, 1959.
Night Without End. London, Collins, and New York, Doubleday, 1960.
Fear Is the Key. London, Collins, and New York, Doubleday, 1961.
The Golden Rendezvous. London, Collins, and New York, Doubleday, 1962.
Ice Station Zebra. London, Collins, and New York, Doubleday, 1963.
When Eight Bells Toll. London, Collins, and New York, Doubleday, 1966.
Where Eagles Dare. London, Collins, and New York, Doubleday, 1967.
Force 10 from Navarone. London, Collins, and New York, Doubleday, 1968.
Puppet on a Chain. London, Collins, and New York, Doubleday, 1969.
Caravan to Vaccarès. London, Collins, and New York, Doubleday, 1970.
Bear Island. London, Collins, and New York, Doubleday, 1971.
The Way to Dusty Death. London, Collins, and New York, Doubleday, 1973.
Breakheart Pass. London, Collins, and New York, Doubleday, 1974.
Circus. London, Collins, and New York, Doubleday, 1975.
The Golden Gate. London, Collins, and New York, Doubleday, 1976.
Seawitch. London, Collins, and New York, Doubleday, 1977.
Goodbye California. London, Collins, 1977; New York, Doubleday, 1978.

Novels as Ian Stuart

The Snow on the Ben. London, Ward Lock, 1961.
The Dark Crusader. London, Collins, 1961; as *The Black Shrike*, New York, Scribner, 1961.
The Satan Bug. London, Collins, and New York, Scribner, 1962.
Death from Disclosure. London, Hale, 1976.
Flood Tide. London, Hale, 1977.
Sand Trap. London, Hale, 1977.
Fatal Switch. London, Hale, 1978.
A Weekend to Kill. London, Hale, 1978.

OTHER PUBLICATIONS

Plays

Screenplays: *Where Eagles Dare*, 1968; *Puppet on a Chain*, with Don Sharp and Paul Wheeler, 1970.

Other

All about Lawrence of Arabia (juvenile).   London, W. H. Allen, 1962; as *Lawrence of Arabia*, New York, Random House, 1962.
Captain Cook.   London, Collins, and New York, Doubleday, 1972.

*   *   *

In Alistair MacLean's action-packed adventure stories the hero is plunged into danger in the opening chapter and moves rapidly from crisis to crisis until the final wrap-up. Several books contain mystery. In these books, at the final climactic moments, killers are unmasked, motives are revealed, or major characters switch loyalty. In other books the suspense comes not from who did it or why, but from how – how will the hero stave off catastrophe? In *The Golden Gate* and *Seawitch* the reader knows immediately who the villains are and what they are trying to accomplish. In *Breakheart Pass* mysterious murders are explained at mid-book because the mystery is only incidental to the question of how the hero will get the train through.

MacLean's heroes are men of incredible endurance. Some modestly claim to be human (Carpenter in *Ice Station Zebra*); some immodestly announce that they are infallible (Harlow in *The Way to Dusty Death*). But all have unlimited reserves of energy and quick enough reflexes to foil the strongest villains. Sometimes the heroes possess uncanny skill that is crucial in the contexts of the stories. Mitchell's cat-like night vision in *Seawitch*, Andrea's unusual strength in *The Guns of Navarone* and *Force 10 from Navarone*, and Bruno's excellent high wire walking in *Circus* are all essential to the happy endings. In addition to being shrewd psychologists and karate experts, the heroes are equipped with photographic memories and are witty and charming. In spite of these outstanding traits, however, the heroes are not superhuman. MacLean leads them through wins and losses, pain and pleasure, by unexpected twists of the plot and shifts in the tempo.

An offensive note in some novels is a moralistic dialogue on the need for violence. Later novels use a set conversation in which the hero defends his killing to the heroine with words such as, "All I do is exterminate vermin. To me, all crooks, armed or not, are vermin" (*Seawitch*). In the good guy-bad guy world of breakneck adventure, such conversations slow down the action as well as force the reader to see the hero as a murderer and the heroine as a fool.

In many books the real stars are the elements. MacLean uses locations and machinery very effectively. In his several novels set north of the Arctic Circle, he makes the noise, the stinging wind-blown ice particles, and the frigid sea real and terrifying. In the many ship stories, the perils relating directly to the ship have a metallic clang of reality. MacLean also uses cable cars, trains, and helicopters for great cling-to, dangle-from, and fight-atop scenes. Another zestful ingredient of MacLean's stories is that the characters play for such big stakes. The President of the United States and two Arab leaders are taken hostage in the middle of the Golden Gate Bridge for a half-billion-dollar ransom. A master criminal plots to rob all the banks in London in one night in *The Satan Bug*. In *Goodbye California* the hostage is – California.

Each MacLean novel delivers adventure that is fast and physical. Through war, crime, and espionage plots MacLean uses vivid descriptions of technology, environment, and emotions which involve the reader quickly and totally.

—Neysa Chouteau and Martha Alderson

MacLEOD, Robert. See **KNOX, Bill.**

MacNEIL, Duncan. See **McCUTCHAN, Philip.**

MacNEIL, Neil. See **BALLARD, Willis Todhunter.**

MALING, Arthur (Gordon). American. Born in Chicago, Illinois, 11 June 1923. Educated at the Francis W. Parker School, Chicago, graduated 1940; Harvard University, Cambridge, Massachusetts (Bliss Prize, 1941), B.A. (cum laude) 1944. Served in the United States Navy, 1944–45: Ensign. Married Beatrice Goldberg in 1949 (divorced, 1958); one son and one daughter. Reporter, San Diego *Journal*, California, 1945–46; Executive, Maling Brothers Inc., retail shoe chain, Chicago, 1946–72. Address: 111 East Chestnut Street, Chicago, Illinois 60611, U.S.A.

Crime Publications

Novels (series character: Brock Potter)

> *Decoy.* New York, Harper, 1969; London, Joseph, 1971.
> *Go-Between.* New York, Harper, 1970; as *Lambert's Son*, London, Joseph, 1972.
> *Loophole.* New York, Harper, 1971.
> *The Snowman.* New York, Harper, 1973.
> *Dingdong.* New York, Harper, 1974.
> *Bent Man.* New York, Harper, 1975; London, Prior, 1976.
> *Ripoff* (Potter). New York, Harper, 1976; London, Hale, 1977.
> *Schroeder's Game* (Potter). New York, Harper, and London, Gollancz, 1977.
> *Lucky Devil* (Potter). New York, Harper, 1978; London, Gollancz, 1979.
> *The Rheingold Route.* New York, Harper, and London, Gollancz, 1979.
> *The Koberg Link* (Potter). New York, Harper, 1979.

Other Publications

Other

> Editor, *When Last Seen.* New York, Harper, 1977.
> Editor, *Mystery Writers' Choice.* London, Gollancz, 1978.

Manuscript Collection: Mugar Memorial Library, Boston University.

*   *   *

With his first book, *Decoy*, Arthur Maling established himself as an author of the crime novel as opposed to the novel of detection. He concentrates on an average man, usually defeated or down-in-his-luck, who is drawn into a situation that takes him outside the bounds of the law. Maling is similar to Ambler in that he shows a common man fighting stronger evil forces without intentionally meaning to get involved. Unlike the motives in Ambler's books, the motives behind Maling's crimes are greed and money, not duty or state secrets. In *Decoy* and *Go-Between* the narrator-hero is nameless; characteristically, he is based in Chicago, but the problem may take him anywhere in the USA or to Mexico or Switzerland. One other common theme, delineated most forcefully in *The Snowman*, is the unique relationship of a father and his son. Frequently protection of a son is the motivating force in the hero's life; the son is the reason to endure the beating that Maling's hero is sure to get before the end of any book.

Maling's books are all first-person narratives, with the narrators well-characterized. We're privy to their thoughts, actions, prejudices, and we experience the problems of their everyday lives, complicated by the immediate problem or danger. Most of the other characters are less well developed. One notable exception to that is Dingdong – the violent amoral thug of the novel that bears his name. The terror of his meaningless, unmindful willingness to inflict pain becomes agonizingly real.

In recent books Maling has broken slightly with his pattern by introducing a series hero, Brock Potter, a research analyst for a Wall Street brokerage firm. Potter is more attuned to the affluent life that the other heroes saw only from the outside; but he is still a loner, unsure of close emotional relationships. His interest in the problems posed in each book begins as business, making him more of a private investigator than Maling's amateurs. In all the books the story line is brisk and direct and provides a white knight, easily identifiable, who overcomes the evil, disruptive forces of the world.

—Fred Dueren

MALLOCH, Peter. See **DUNCAN, W. Murdoch.**

MANN, Jessica. British. Born in London. Educated at St. Paul's Girls' School, London; Newnham College, Cambridge, B.A. in archaeology and Anglo-Saxon, M.A.; University of Leicester, LL.B. Married to Charles Thomas; two sons and two daughters. Agent: Sheila Watson, Bolt and Watson Ltd., 8–12 Old Queen Street, Storey's Gate, London SW1H 9HP. Address: Lambessow, St. Clement, Truro, Cornwall, England.

CRIME PUBLICATIONS

Novels

A Charitable End. London, Collins, and New York, McKay, 1971.
Mrs. Knox's Profession. London, Macmillan, and New York, McKay, 1972.
The Only Security. London, Macmillan, 1973; as *Troublecross*, New York, McKay, 1973.
The Sticking Place. London, Macmillan, and New York, McKay, 1974.
Captive Audience. London, Macmillan, and New York, McKay, 1975.
The Eighth Deadly Sin. London, Macmillan, 1976.
The Sting of Death. London, Macmillan, 1978.

Jessica Mann comments:
Like most novelists, I try to write the kind of book which I enjoy reading; I have always spent more time than I should reading crime novels. I am interested in what happens to people confronting unusual predicaments. I write books, and prefer other authors' books, which concentrate on people, places, and puzzles in that order. The process of detection, unless the detective is interesting himself or herself, is of less concern to me. I would prefer to be regarded, not as a mystery writer, but as a novelist whose characters get involved in crime, and whose responses arise from their personalities.

* * *

Literacy, a vivid sense of locale, and a feeling that sinister things happen with alarming frequency behind ordinary closed doors – these qualities characterize Jessica Mann's slim, ironic novels. There is little external violence. Much more violence exists – inferentially, implicitly – inside the heads of Mann's characters than in the outside events which enmesh them. With quiet understatement the author conveys a pervasive sense of menace. It seeps from the characters and gradually permeates the stories, giving to small details and observations an aura of uncertainty and uneasy ambiguity. The reader is not sure: are the Jewish wife's suspicions in *The Sticking Place* grounded in fact, or are they merely aspects of insecurity from her own past? Is the invalid journalist's growing rage in *Captive Audience* only the result of his immobility, or is it caused by something he has seen?

Whether they be the tweedy conventional ladies of an Edinburgh do-good group (*A Charitable End*), the Leicester housewife compensating for grey humdrumness by acting out her more colorful fantasies (*Mrs. Knox's Profession*), or the bright, observant archaeologist coping with the in-group bickering of a Cornish university community (*The Only Security* and *Captive Audience*) – the protagonists' routines as well as their self-images are suddenly warped and jarred by something that happens. The disturbance can be anonymous letters, or student unrest, or even murder. The author is as interested in her characters' reactions to such events as in the events themselves. Detection can prove as unsettling as what is being detected. What takes place at the edges of an unusual occurrence is often more interesting or perplexing than the actual happening.

Mann's endings are quick, explosive and wry, but not quirky. They cap the plot with that most astonishing of qualities – logic.

—Ellen Bleiler

MANTON, Peter. See **CREASEY, John.**

MARLOWE, Dan J(ames). American. Born in Lowell, Massachusetts, 10 July 1914. Attended Bentley School of Accounting and Finance. Worked in accounting, insurance, and public relations until 1957. Self-employed writer. Served on City Council and as Mayor pro tem of Harbor Beach, Michigan. Writes weekly column for Michigan newspapers and reviews for the Detroit *Free Press*. Address: 123 North 1st Street, Harbor Beach, Michigan 48441, U.S.A.

CRIME PUBLICATIONS

Novels (series characters: Earl Drake; Johnny Killain)

Doorway to Death (Killain). New York, Avon, and London, Digit, 1959.
Killer with a Key (Killain). New York, Avon, 1959.
Doom Service (Killain). New York, Avon, 1960.
The Fatal Frails (Killain). New York, Avon, 1960.
Shake a Crooked Town (Killain). New York, Avon, 1961.
Backfire. New York, Berkley, 1961.
The Name of the Game Is Death (Drake). New York, Fawcett, 1962; London, Muller, 1963; as *Operation Overkill*, London, Hodder and Stoughton, 1973.
Strongarm. New York, Fawcett, 1963.
Never Live Twice. New York, Fawcett, 1964.
Death Deep Down. New York, Fawcett, 1965.
Four for the Money. New York, Fawcett, 1966.
The Vengeance Man. New York, Fawcett, 1966.
The Raven Is a Blood Red Bird, with William Odell. New York, Fawcett, 1967.
Route of the Red Gold. New York, Fawcett, 1967.
One Endless Hour (Drake). New York, Fawcett, 1969; London, Gold Lion, 1973; as *Operation Endless Hour*, London, Hodder and Stoughton, 1975.
Operation Fireball (Drake). New York, Fawcett, 1969; London, Hodder and Stoughton, 1972.
Flashpoint (Drake). New York, Fawcett, 1970; as *Operation Flashpoint*, New York, Fawcett, and London, Hodder and Stoughton, 1972.
Operation Breakthrough (Drake). New York, Fawcett, 1971; London, Hodder and Stoughton, 1972.
Operation Drumfire (Drake). New York, Fawcett, and London, Hodder and Stoughton, 1972.
Operation Checkmate (Drake). New York, Fawcett, 1972; London, Hodder and Stoughton, 1973.
Operation Stranglehold (Drake). New York, Fawcett, 1973; London, Hodder and Stoughton, 1974.
Operation Whiplash (Drake). New York, Fawcett, 1973; London, Hodder and Stoughton, 1974.
Operation Hammerlock (Drake). New York, Fawcett, 1974; London, Hodder and Stoughton, 1975.
Operation Deathmaker (Drake). New York, Fawcett, 1975; London, Hodder and Stoughton, 1977.

Uncollected Short Stories

"The Short and Simple Annals," in *Best Detective Stories of the Year*, edited by Anthony Boucher. New York, Dutton, 1965.

"The Donor," in *Tricks and Treats*, edited by Joe Gores and Bill Pronzini. New York, Doubleday, 1976; as *Mystery Writers Choice*, London, Gollancz, 1977.

"All the Way Home," in *When Last Seen*, edited by Arthur Maling. New York, Harper, 1977.

"The Man in Charge," in *Ellery Queen's Mystery Magazine* (New York), November 1977.

"Don't Lose Your Cool," in *Alfred Hitchcock's Tales to Scare You Stiff*, edited by Eleanor Sullivan. New York, Davis, 1978.

*   *   *

Dan J. Marlowe's masterpiece is *The Name of the Game Is Death*, the first of the Earl Drake series. It's a chilling story of how Drake becomes a professional thief, pulling off well-executed robberies and capers. Along with Marlowe's expertise, his humanity is evident in his best-drawn, toughest characters, Johnny Killain and Earl Drake. Marlowe's first five books feature Killain, a semi-detective who is violent with mild flashes of sensitivity. The Earl Drake books, especially *The Name of the Game Is Death*, display an intelligent, sensitive character who turns to crime because of the brutality of middle-class life. Although Marlowe's editors at Fawcett eventually sanitized Drake by changing him from a professional thief to a secret agent, the theme of justice and retribution for wrongs pervades most of the Drake books.

But the post-1962 books Marlowe wrote improved for several reasons. Chief among them is Marlowe's relationship with Al Nussbaum, a bank robber whom Marlowe had helped get paroled. Nussbaum shared his intimate knowledge about weapons, ballistics, locks, safes, vaults, and alarm systems with Marlowe; that detail lent realism to Marlowe's books, so much so Marlowe found himself leaving out one important detail of a process so he wouldn't be accused of writing caper manuals for professional thieves. Two of Marlowe's best novels, *One Endless Hour* and *Four for the Money*, benefited directed from Nussbaum's information. Two other books explore Marlowe's major theme of justice and retribution: *Never Live Twice*, with an ingenious amnesia plot, and *The Vengeance Man*, a powerful thriller with a shattering conclusion.

—George Kelley

MARLOWE, Derek. British. Born in London, 21 May 1938. Educated at Cardinal Vaughan School, London, 1949–57; University of London, 1957–60. Married Sukie Phipps in 1968; two daughters and three sons. Recipient: Writers Guild Award, 1972, and Emmy Award, 1972, both for television writing. Agent: Tim Corrie, Fraser and Dunlop Scripts Ltd., 91 Regent Street, London W1R 8RU, England.

CRIME PUBLICATIONS

Novels

A Dandy in Aspic. London, Gollancz, and New York, Putnam, 1966.
The Memoirs of Venus Lackey. London, Cape, and New York, Viking Press, 1968.
Echoes of Celandine. London, Cape, and New York, Viking Press, 1970; as *The Disappearance*, London, Penguin, 1977.
Somebody's Sister. New York, Viking Press, and London, Cape, 1974.
Nightshade. London, Weidenfeld and Nicolson, 1975; New York, Viking Press, 1976.

OTHER PUBLICATIONS

Novels

A Single Summer with L.B.: The Summer of 1816. London, Cape, 1969; as *A Single Summer with Lord B.*, New York, Viking Press, 1970.
Do You Remember England? London, Cape, and New York, Viking Press, 1972.
The Rich Boy from Chicago. London, Weidenfeld and Nicolson, 1980.

Plays

The Seven Who Were Hanged, adaptation of a novel by Andreyev (produced Edinburgh, 1961; as *The Scarecrow*, produced London, 1964).
The Lower Depths, adaptation of a translation by Moura Budberg of a play by Gorki (produced London, 1962).
How Disaster Struck the Harvest (produced London, 1964).
How I Assumed the Role of a Popular Dandy for Purposes of Seduction and Other Base Matters (produced London, 1965).

Screenplays: *A Dandy in Aspic*, 1968; *A Single Summer*, 1979; *The Knight*, 1979.

Television Films: *Requiem for Modigliani*, 1970; *The Search for the Nile* series, 1971; *The Knight* series, 1978; *Nancy Astor*, 1979.

Derek Marlowe comments:
I have written to date (1978) eight novels, only four of which could be considered thrillers. There is no premeditated purpose to this on my part: I do not choose in advance to write an "entertainment" as opposed to a "novel." Locations influence me very much and usually provoke the story – Berlin for *A Dandy in Aspic*, Haiti for *Nightshade* and, more especially, San Francisco for *Somebody's Sister* which is probably the purest detective story of them all.
I like to intrigue the reader; perhaps this may happen more in a romantic novel (*A Single Summer with L. B.*) than in a straight thriller. I have no answers to *why* I write the particular book at the particular time except that my own state of mind (very mercurial) dictates it. I am Ford Madox Ford wanting to be Chandler or Woolrich, and vice versa.

*   *   *

Derek Marlowe has published a number of mysteries, each using a rather different formula in an interesting but not wholly satisfactory way. His first novel, *A Dandy in Aspic*, is a spy novel somewhat in the manner of John le Carré and based on the excellent, intriguing notion that a double agent is assigned to kill himself. As with Marlowe's other work the result is highly literate (and literary), stylistically most elegant, and with a well-researched, totally credible background (in this case, Berlin). Like le Carré and unlike, say, Ian Fleming,

Marlowe depicts the world of espionage as infinitely cold, grey, and maze-like. His range of literary and cultural reference suggests that there is an abiding world of beauty which espionage and all it stands for attempts to negate. The central character, Eberlin, feels that he is "merely marking time" until death, and the world of this novel might easily evoke Eliot's "I had not thought death had undone so many." Despite some moments of pretentiousness the novel is an impressive debut, not least in the adroitness with which Marlowe keeps the reader, along with Eberlin, guessing.

Echoes of Celandine is something of a let-down. Again, the basic idea – that a professional assassin, trying to find his estranged wife, should end by killing her when he believes he is fulfilling an assignment – is reasonably original, but here Marlowe's ability to enmesh the reader in the hero's bewilderment and growing fear is countered by an arch first-person narrator and an intrusive Grail Quest motif (the hero is called Jay Mallory and, like Gatsby, searches for the Grail in the figure of a lost love), coupled with an uneasy use of the isolated locale and remote mastermind figure.

When one reads through Marlowe's books one after the other it seems as though he is never quite sure whether or not he is writing pastiche (albeit serious pastiche). If the first novel owes much to le Carré and *Echoes of Celandine* reminds the reader of Graham Greene, then *Somebody's Sister* undoubtedly represents a move to the world of Hammett and Chandler. Its hero, Walter Brackett, is a middle-aged, unsuccessful British-born private eye who entered the profession with dreams of being like Spade and Marlowe only to discover that he "hadn't just stepped out of the pages of *Dime Detective*. That was simply what [he was] worth." Marlowe rarely puts a foot wrong in depicting the American scene, characters, and dialogue, but Brackett remains a rather shadowy figure and the plot is so mystifying that the world outside the hero, though accurately rendered, is insubstantial. The novel is not, as one reviewer suggested, "a valentine to a romantic legend" so much as a rather shaky tangent to that legend. The mean streets are not mean enough.

Nightshade takes place mostly in a Haiti seen as a nightmarish testing-ground for the inadequate married couple, Edward and Amy Lytton, who are on holiday there. Part psychological novel, part occult thriller, *Nightshade*, as the title suggests, uses an exotic island as a vision of what happens when civilised man steps outside the controls of civilisation and finds himself face to face with his deepest fears and desires. The novel is often gripping but is flawed by having an unnamed narrator whose intrusions into the novel are fussy and pretentious: "within hours Daniel Azevedo had stepped from the periphery and entered their lives, both Edward's and Amy's, and from that moment the tragedy – for that surely was what it was – took hold of them all. One by one."

Derek Marlowe's talent has now declared itself beyond doubt. Yet since he has written in several thriller formulae, as well as in the genres of romance and historical novel, a doubt remains as to whether he has yet made any of these modes truly his own.

—John S. Whitley

MARLOWE, Hugh. Pseudonym for Henry Patterson; also writes as Martin Fallon; James Graham; Jack Higgins. British. Born in Newcastle on Tyne, 27 July 1929. Educated at Leeds Training College for Teachers, Cert. Ed. 1958; University of London, B.Sc. 1961. Served in the Royal Horse Guards, British Army, 1947–49. Married Amy Margaret Hewitt in 1958; three daughters and one son. Worked in commercial and civil service posts, 1950–55; History Teacher, Allerton Grange Comprehensive School, Leeds, 1958–64; Lecturer in Liberal Studies, Leeds College of Commerce, 1964–68; Senior Lecturer in Education, James Graham College, New Farnley, Yorkshire, 1968–70; Tutor, Leeds University, 1971–73.

Fellow, Royal Society of Arts. Agent: David Higham Associates Ltd., 5–8 Lower John Street, London W1R 4HA, England.

CRIME PUBLICATIONS

Novels

Seven Pillars to Hell.   London and New York, Abelard Schuman, 1963.
Passage by Night.   London and New York, Abelard Schuman, 1964.
A Candle for the Dead.   London and New York, Abelard Schuman, 1966; as *The Violent Enemy*, London, Hodder and Stoughton, 1969.

Novels as Harry Paterson (series character: Nick Miller; published as Jack Higgins in US)

Sad Wind from the Sea.   London, Long, 1959.
Cry of the Hunter.   London, Long, 1960.
The Thousand Faces of Night.   London, Long, 1961.
Comes the Dark Stranger.   London, Long, 1962.
Hell Is Too Crowded.   London, Long, 1962; New York, Fawcett, 1976.
Pay the Devil.   London, Barrie and Rockliff, 1963.
The Dark Side of the Island.   London, Long, 1963; New York, Fawcett, 1977.
A Phoenix in the Blood.   London, Barrie and Rockliff, 1964.
Thunder at Noon.   London, Long, 1964.
Wrath of the Lion.   London, Long, 1964; New York, Fawcett, 1977.
The Graveyard Shift (Miller).   London, Long, 1965.
The Iron Tiger.   London, Long, 1966; New York, Fawcett, 1974.
Brought in Dead (Miller).   London, Long, 1967.
Hell Is Always Today.   London, Long, 1968; New York, Fawcett, 1979.
Toll for the Brave.   London, Long, 1971; New York, Fawcett, 1976.
The Valhalla Exchange.   New York, Stein and Day, 1976; London, Hutchinson, 1977.
To Catch a King.   New York, Stein and Day, and London, Hutchinson, 1979.

Novels as Martin Fallon (series character: Paul Chavasse in all books; published as Jack Higgins in US)

The Testament of Caspar Schultz.   London and New York, Abelard Schuman, 1962.
Year of the Tiger.   London and New York, Abelard Schuman, 1963.
The Keys of Hell.   London and New York, Abelard Schuman, 1965.
Midnight Never Comes.   London, Long, 1966; New York, Fawcett, 1975.
Dark Side of the Street.   London, Long, 1967; New York, Fawcett, 1974.
A Fine Night for Dying.   London, Long, 1969; London, Hutchinson, 1977.

Novels as Jack Higgins

East of Desolation.   London, Hodder and Stoughton, 1968; New York, Doubleday, 1969.
In the Hour Before Midnight.   London, Hodder and Stoughton, 1969; as *The Sicilian Heritage*, New York, Lancer, 1970.
Night Judgment at Sinos.   London, Hodder and Stoughton, 1970; New York, Doubleday, 1971.
The Last Place God Made.   London, Collins, 1971; New York, Holt Rinehart, 1972.
The Savage Day.   London, Collins, and New York, Holt Rinehart, 1972.
A Prayer for the Dying.   London, Collins, 1973; New York, Holt Rinehart, 1974.
The Eagle Has Landed.   London, Collins, and New York, Holt Rinehart, 1975.

Storm Warning.   London, Collins, and New York, Holt Rinehart, 1976.
Day of Judgement.   London, Collins, 1978; New York, Holt Rinehart, 1979.
The Cretan Lover.   London, Collins, and New York, Holt Rinehart, 1980.

Novels as James Graham

A Game for Heroes.   London, Macmillan, and New York, Doubleday, 1970.
The Wrath of God.   London, Macmillan, and New York, Doubleday, 1971.
The Khufra Run.   London, Macmillan, 1972; New York, Doubleday, 1973.
Bloody Passage.   London, Macmillan, 1974; as *The Run to Morning*, New York, Stein
and Day, 1974.

*   *   *

Prior to 1975 Henry Patterson had published prolifically under several pseudonyms for nearly two decades, enjoying modest success with his stories of adventure and intrigue; then, as Jack Higgins, he wrote *The Eagle Has Landed*, a suspenseful World War II account of a German plot to kidnap Churchill and a book which became a best-seller. The next Higgins entry, *Storm Warning*, had Germans for its heroes, World War II for its setting, and the raging North Atlantic for its enemy. After two such successes, many earlier Patterson efforts have been reprinted as by Jack Higgins, and the other pseudonyms have been dropped.

Like most successful writers of popular fiction, Patterson writes highly formulaic literature, with fast-paced plots, adventuring heroes, beautiful women, alien and often sadistic villains, and exotic settings. The heroes are typically Renaissance men: adventurous and bold soldiers-of-fortune or superspies, often war veterans, skilled in handling airplanes or boats; at the same time they are intellectuals, men with doctorates in modern languages (Paul Chavasse, the superspy series hero who is multi-lingual) or in music (Matt Brady in *Hell Is Too Crowded*), capable of quoting Wordsworth or Shakespeare amid violent surroundings; and too, they are romantics, chivalric heroes protecting and trusting (naively and dangerously, sometimes) all womanhood.

Patterson's women are commonly innocents or seeming-innocents; nuns are stock characters, either as heroines or as secondary characters. Beautiful Sister Claire of *The Khufra Run* uses her innocent charms to encourage the Australian hero, Jack Nelson, and his American companion, a heroin addict, to help her recover a religious relic in the Algerian swamps. Another innocent, a beautiful blind girl, niece and ward to a priest, is the apparent target for the Irish revolutionary Martin Fallon in *A Prayer for the Dying*. ("Martin Fallon" is both the hero of this book and a Patterson pseudonym of the 1960's.) The romantic heroines sometimes die at the story's end – especially if they are innocents; some turn out to be surprise traitors, as in *The Keys of Hell* and *The Khufra Run*; and occasionally hero and heroine share a "happily ever after" conclusion, as do Anne Dunning and Matt Brady in *Hell Is Too Crowded*.

The fast-paced stories do have a few of the weaknesses common to some popular fiction: Patterson relies heavily on clichés, and one of his apparent favorites, "dying fall," appears as phrase, sentence, or chapter title in many books and with great regularity; he tends, too, to shift whole conversations verbatim from book to book – compare, for example, the Chavasse-Youngblood (*Dark Side of the Street*) and Brady-Evans (*Hell Is Too Crowded*) conversations in prison after each hero has a lady visitor. One might also quarrel with Patterson's occasional introduction of more controversial and substantive topics – rehabilitation and prison life in *Dark Side of the Street* or primitive civilization confronted by modern technology in *The Last Place God Made*, for example – hinting at serious examination but providing only superficial treatment.

But these are quibbles. Patterson (as Hugh Marlowe, especially) has provided a few standard mysteries, and more importantly, many tales of intrigue and suspense, tales in which bold hero and attractive heroine, mysterious and violent villain, exotic and varied setting, and fast-paced plot come together to create popular suspense and adventure fiction.

—Elmer Pry

MARLOWE, Stephen. Pseudonym for Milton Lesser; also writes as Andrew Frazer; Jason Ridgway; C. H. Thames. American. Born in New York City, 7 August 1928. Educated at the College of William and Mary, Williamsburg, Virginia, B.A. 1949. Served in the United States Army, 1952–54. Married Ann Humbert (second wife); two children. Self-employed writer. Writer-in-residence, College of William and Mary; Member of the Board of Directors, Mystery Writers of America. Agent: Scott Meredith Literary Agency Inc., 580 Fifth Avenue, New York, New York 10036, U.S.A.

Crime Publications

Novels (series character: Chester Drum)

 Catch the Brass Ring. New York, Ace, 1954.
 Turn Left for Murder. New York, Ace, 1955.
 Model for Murder. Hasbrouck Heights, New Jersey, Graphic, 1955.
 The Second Longest Night (Drum). New York, Fawcett, 1955; London, Fawcett, 1958.
 Dead on Arrival. New York, Ace, 1956.
 Mecca for Murder (Drum). New York, Fawcett, 1956; London, Fawcett, 1957.
 Violence Is Golden (as C. H. Thames). New York, Bouregy, 1956.
 Killers Are My Meat (Drum). New York, Fawcett, 1957; London, Fawcett, 1958.
 Murder Is My Dish (Drum). New York, Fawcett, 1957.
 Trouble Is My Name (Drum). New York, Fawcett, 1957; London, Fawcett, 1958.
 Violence Is My Business (Drum). New York, Fawcett, 1958; London, Fawcett, 1959.
 Terror Is My Trade (Drum). New York, Fawcett, 1958; London, Muller, 1960
 Blonde Bait. New York, Avon, 1959.
 Double in Trouble (Drum), with Richard S. Prather. New York, Fawcett, 1959.
 Find Eileen Hardin – Alive! (as Andrew Frazer). New York, Avon, 1959.
 Passport to Peril. New York, Fawcett, 1959.
 Homicide Is My Game (Drum). New York, Fawcett, 1959; London, Muller, 1960.
 Danger Is My Line (Drum). New York, Fawcett, 1960; London, Muller, 1961.
 Death Is My Comrade (Drum). New York, Fawcett, 1960; London, Muller, 1961.
 The Fall of Marty Moon (as Andrew Frazer). New York, Avon, 1960.
 Peril Is My Pay (Drum). New York, Fawcett, 1960; London, Muller, 1961.
 Manhunt Is My Mission (Drum). New York, Fawcett, 1961; London, Muller, 1962.
 Jeopardy Is My Job (Drum). New York, Fawcett, 1962; London, Muller, 1963.
 Blood of My Brother (as C. H. Thames). New York, Permabooks, 1963.
 Francesca (Drum). New York, Fawcett, and London, Muller, 1963.
 Drum Beat – Berlin. New York, Fawcett, 1964.
 Drum Beat – Dominique. New York, Fawcett, 1965.
 Drum Beat – Madrid. New York, Fawcett, 1966.
 The Search for Bruno Heidler. New York, Macmillan, 1966; London, Boardman,
  1967.
 Drum Beat – Erica. New York, Fawcett, 1967.

Come Over, Red Rover. New York, Macmillan, 1968.
Drum Beat – Marianne. New York, Fawcett, 1968.
The Summit. New York, Geis, 1970.
The Man with No Shadow. Englewood Cliffs, New Jersey, Prentice Hall, and London,
    W. H. Allen, 1974.
The Cawthorn Journals. Englewood Cliffs, New Jersey, Prentice Hall, 1975; London,
    W. H. Allen, 1976; as *Too Many Chiefs*, London, New English Library, 1977.
Translation. Englewood Cliffs, New Jersey, Prentice Hall, 1976.

Novels as Jason Ridgway (series character: Brian Guy)

West Side Jungle. New York, New American Library, 1958.
Adam's Fall (Guy). New York, Permabooks, 1960.
People in Glass Houses (Guy). New York, Permabooks, 1961.
Hardly a Man Is Now Alive (Guy). New York, Permabooks, 1962.
The Treasure of the Cosa Nostra (Guy). New York, Pocket Books, 1966.

Uncollected Short Stories

"The Shill," in *A Choice of Murders*, edited by Dorothy Salisbury Davis. New York,
    Scribner, 1958; London, MacDonald, 1960.
"Drum Beat," in *Best Detective Stories of the Year*, edited by Brett Halliday. New
    York, Dutton, 1962.
"Wanted, Dead or Alive," in *Best Detective Stories of the Year*, edited by Anthony
    Boucher. New York, Dutton, 1964.
"Baby Sitter," in *Come Seven, Come Death*, edited by Henry Morrison. New York,
    Pocket Books, 1965.

OTHER PUBLICATIONS as Milton Lesser

Novels

Earthbound. Philadelphia, Winston, 1952; London, Hutchinson, 1955.
The Star Seekers. Philadelphia, Winston, 1953.
Stadium Beyond the Stars. Philadelphia, Winston, 1960.
The Shining (as Stephen Marlowe). New York, Trident Press, 1963.
Secret of the Black Planet. New York, Belmont, 1965.

Other

Spacemen Go Home (juvenile). New York, Holt Rinehart, 1961.
Lost Worlds and the Men Who Found Them (juvenile). Racine, Wisconsin, Whitman,
    1962.
Walt Disney's Strange Animals of Australia (juvenile). Racine, Wisconsin, Whitman,
    1963.

Editor, *Looking Forward: An Anthology of Science Fiction.* New York, Beechhurst
    Press, 1953; London, Cassell, 1955.

*   *   *

Stephen Marlowe was already an established science fiction writer under his real name,
Milton Lesser, when he began publishing his paperback original mystery novels in the
mid-1950's. He has also published mysteries under three other pseudonyms, Andrew Frazer

(including the very successful *The Fall of Marty Moon*), Jason Ridgway (a short series about Brian Guy), and C. H. Thames (two of his weaker novels).

Most of the books published by Marlowe are Chester Drum private eye titles. The Marlowe name is an obvious homage to Raymond Chandler, but Drum, at least in his early adventures, was more of a Spillane-type hero. Like Mike Hammer's, Drum's jobs were often as much espionage/counterespionage as they were sleuthing. The carefully established Drum background, including valuable service as an FBI fieldman which yielded invaluable connections in high places, and the location of his office in Washington, D.C., made his frequent involvement in intelligence affairs all the more convincing. His adventures were paced a bit slower than the models Spillane provided and had less spectacular comeuppances for the villains, but they remain among the best of the many imitations of Spillane that appeared in the 1950's. On occasion, as in *Death Is My Comrade*, Marlowe outdid his mentor in his audacious demands for "suspension of disbelief." That book began with a rather conventional murder and an assault on the hero, then moved rapidly through an outlandish CIA plot to spirit a would-be defector out of Russia by exchanging his fabulously successful industrialist brother for him, encounters with impressive Russian security officers who had penetrated Drum's cover before his arrival in Moscow, an escape overland to Finland, and the kidnapping of the female villain by Russian gypsies.

Most of the early books had patterned titles, resembling *Murder Is My Dish* and *Trouble Is My Name*, which were two of the best. Especially in the last five Drum books (the "Drum Beat" series) and in *Francesca*, Marlowe managed a very mature series of international detective adventures combining the exotic locales and furious action more typically seen in the most adventurous spy fiction (yet rarely involving espionage) with quite satisfactory detective puzzles of the hard-boiled variety. The earlier tour de force collaboration with Richard S. Prather, *Double in Trouble*, had Drum and Prather's usually more light-hearted detective hero Shell Scott working at very interesting cross-purposes.

Marlowe's more recent books, almost all involving espionage, are much more interesting than those which preceded the Drum series. *The Search for Bruno Heidler*, about the tracing of a still dangerous war criminal, *The Summit*, with international intrigue at the highest levels, and *Come Over, Red Rover* are all highly recommended. Among the early non-series books, those involving espionage now seem badly dated, as do early Drum novels with similar content. However, two tough early mysteries, *Model for Murder* and *Catch the Brass Ring*, though not the equals of much of Marlowe's most recent work, remain brilliant early pieces.

—Jeff Banks

MARQUAND, John P(hillips). American. Born in Wilmington, Delaware, 10 November 1893. Educated at Newburyport High School, Massachusetts; Harvard University, Cambridge, Massachusetts, 1912–15, A.B. 1915. Served with the Massachusetts National Guard in the Mexican Border Service, 1916; student, Camp Plattsburg, 1917; commissioned 1st Lieutenant in the Field Artillery, and served with the 4th Brigade in France, 1917–18; Special Consultant to the Secretary of War, Washington, D.C., 1944–45; War Correspondent for the United States Navy, 1945. Married 1) Christina Davenport Sedgwick in 1922 (divorced, 1935), one son and one daughter; 2) Adelaide Hooker in 1937 (divorced, 1958), two sons and one daughter. Assistant Magazine Editor, Boston *Transcript*, 1915–17; with the Sunday Magazine Department, New York *Tribune*, 1919–20; advertising copywriter, J. Walter Thompson Company, New York, 1920–21. Member, Board of Overseers, Harvard University; Member, Editorial Board, Book-of-the-Month Club, New

York, Recipient: Pulitzer Prize, 1938; Sarah Josepha Hale Award, 1957. Litt. D.: University of Maine, Orono, 1941; University of Rochester, New York, 1944; Yale University, New Haven, Connecticut, 1950; D.H.L.: Bates College, Lewiston, Maine, 1954. Member, National Institute of Arts and Letters. *Died 16 July 1960.*

CRIME PUBLICATIONS

Novels (series character: Mr. Moto)

> *Ming Yellow.* Boston, Little Brown, and London, Lovat Dickson, 1935.
> *No Hero.* Boston, Little Brown, 1935; as *Mr. Moto Takes a Hand*, London, Hale, 1940; as *Your Turn, Mr. Moto*, New York, Berkley, 1963.
> *Thank You, Mr. Moto.* Boston, Little Brown, 1936; London, Jenkins, 1937.
> *Think Fast, Mr. Moto.* Boston, Little Brown, 1937; London, Hale, 1938.
> *Mr. Moto Is So Sorry.* Boston, Little Brown, 1938; London, Hale, 1939.
> *Don't Ask Questions.* London, Hale, 1941.
> *Last Laugh, Mr. Moto.* Boston, Little Brown, 1942; London, Hale, 1943.
> *It's Loaded, Mr. Bauer.* London, Hale, 1949.
> *Stopover: Tokyo.* Boston, Little Brown, and London, Collins, 1957; as *The Last of Mr. Moto*, New York, Berkley, 1963; as *Right You Are, Mr. Moto*, New York, Popular Library, 1977.

OTHER PUBLICATIONS

Novels

> *The Unspeakable Gentleman.* New York, Scribner, and London, Hodder and Stoughton, 1922.
> *The Black Cargo.* New York, Scribner, and London, Hodder and Stoughton, 1925.
> *Do Tell Me, Doctor Johnson.* Privately printed, 1928.
> *Warning Hill.* Boston, Little Brown, 1930.
> *Haven's End.* Boston, Little Brown, 1933; London, Hale, 1938.
> *The Late George Apley: A Novel in the Form of a Memoir.* Boston, Little Brown, and London, Hale, 1937.
> *Wickford Point.* Boston, Little Brown, and London, Hale, 1939.
> *H.M. Pulham, Esquire.* Boston, Little Brown, and London, Hale, 1942.
> *So Little Time.* Boston, Little Brown, 1943; London, Hale, 1944.
> *Repent in Haste.* Boston, Little Brown, 1945; London, Hale, 1949.
> *B.F.'s Daughter.* Boston, Little Brown, 1946; as *Polly Fulton*, London, Hale, 1947.
> *Point of No Return.* Boston, Little Brown, and London, Hale, 1949.
> *Melville Goodwin, USA.* Boston, Little Brown, 1951; London, Hale, 1952.
> *Sincerely, Willis Wayde.* Boston, Little Brown, and London, Hale, 1955.
> *Women and Thomas Harrow.* Boston, Little Brown, 1958; London, Collins, 1959.

Short Stories

> *Four of a Kind.* New York, Scribner, 1923.
> *Sun, Sea, and Sand.* New York, Dell, 1950.
> *Life at Happy Knoll.* Boston, Little Brown, 1957; London, Collins, 1958.

Play

> *The Late George Apley*, with George S. Kaufman, adaptation of the novel by Marquand (produced New York, 1944). New York, Dramatists Play Service, 1946.

Other

Prince and Boatswain: Sea Tales from the Recollections of Rear-Admiral Charles E. Clark, with James Morris Morgan. Greenfield, Massachusetts, E. A. Hall, 1915.
Lord Timothy Dexter of Newburyport, Mass. New York, Minton Balch, and London, Unwin, 1926.
Federalist Newburyport; or, Can Historical Fiction Remove a Fly from Amber? New York, Newcomer Society, 1952.
Thirty Years (miscellany). Boston, Little Brown, 1954; London, Hale, 1955.
Timothy Dexter Revisited. Boston, Little Brown, 1960.

Bibliography: "A John P. Marquand Checklist Based on Bibliography of William White," in *The Late John Marquand: A Biography* by Stephen Birmingham, Philadelphia, Lippincott, 1972.

*   *   *

The Pulitzer Prize-winning author John P. Marquand won critical acclaim for his fictional analyses of men, manners, and money in a conservative New England setting. Marquand was less proud of his popular mystery fiction. In a 1959 interview, he said of his slight but sinister Japanese secret agent, "Mr. Moto was my literary disgrace. I wrote about him to get shoes for the baby. I can't say why people still remember him." Today's readers disagree. They still find Marquand's six Mr. Moto novels memorable.

Mr. Moto first appeared, fully developed, in *No Hero*. A Japanese aristocrat of many talents and devious ways, university-educated Mr. Moto speaks an impressive number of languages. He can navigate, wait on tables, mix drinks, and act as a competent valet and careful chauffeur. Short, slim, gold-toothed Mr. Moto is agile, an acute judge of character, and an excellent shot proud to risk his life for his Emperor. Although he is a formidable enemy, strong on liquidation, he respects courage, loyalty, patriotism, and professionalism in other agents he meets. His appearance is always impeccable; his English is always flawless, although very Japanese.

The Mr. Moto novels fall into a memorably workable formula. They are set in an exotic foreign locale, and their hero is always a weak, untried, sometimes rather disreputable young American who meets and falls in love with an attractive girl involved directly or indirectly in international espionage. In the course of their adventures this couple will encounter Mr. Moto, sometimes as adversary, sometimes as ally, sometimes as both. After much intrigue and some violence, the American hero will resolve the conflict and end the intrigue, winning both the girl's heart and Mr. Moto's commendation.

In *No Hero*, Casey Lee, a down-and-out flier in Tokyo, is sent to Singapore by a beautiful Russian to search for a secret aviation fuel formula. Lee destroys the formula to prevent it from falling into the hands of America's enemies. In Peking, Tom Nelson, the expatriate hero of *Thank You, Mr. Moto*, blunders into a plot to steal priceless Chinese scroll paintings and to create an anti-American incident. With the help of Mr. Moto and a pretty buyer for an American museum, the rebels are liquidated and the paintings rescued. In *Think Fast, Mr. Moto*, William Hitchings, a member of a prominent Singapore banking firm, travels to Honolulu to close a disreputable gambling house. He finds that the house's profits are funding Chinese rebels, but that its owner is young and beautiful. With Mr. Moto's help he ends the scandal and marries the girl. As Calvin Gates (*Mr. Moto Is So Sorry*) drifts toward an archeological dig in North China, he meets a pretty young archeologist, her sinister Russian guide, and Mr. Moto. A coded cigarette case resolves the Russian-Japanese struggle for power in Mongolia and Calvin's personal problems. *Last Laugh, Mr. Moto* pits Bob Bolles, a hard-drinking ex-Navy pilot, against a Nazi, a lovely Vichy French agent, and Mr. Moto in a search for a secret American aviation device lost on an obscure Caribbean island. *Stopover: Tokyo*, Marquand's most successful mystery, is a sensitive depiction of Jack Rhyce and Ruth Bogart, two American agents who must live out their cover roles as do-gooders in a suspicious Tokyo organization which masks a Soviet plot against the United States. Mr. Moto is able to prevent the international incident, but only at the cost of Ruth's life. In this last novel Marquand brilliantly describes the constant tension, danger, and responsibility a professional secret agent must endure on a mission.

Most memorably, the Mr. Moto novels evoke the atmosphere and mystery of far-off places. Marquand loved travel; he visited Europe, Africa, the Middle East, the Amazon Valley, the Caribbean, Japan, and China. The Mr. Moto novels always use detail to suggest the spectacular and the mundane; to develop a feeling for time, place and custom; to create the beautiful and alien world in which Mr. Moto lives, lurks, and operates.

—Katherine Staples

MARRIC, J. J. See **CREASEY, John.**

MARSH, (Edith) Ngaio. New Zealander. Born in Christchurch, 23 April 1899. Educated at St. Margaret's College, Christchurch, 1910–14; Canterbury University College School of Art, Christchurch, 1915–20. Actress in Australia and New Zealand, 1920–23; Theatrical Producer, New Zealand, 1923–27; Interior Decorator, in partnership with Mrs. Tahu Rhodes, London, 1928–32. Served in a New Zealand Red Cross transport unit during World War II. Producer for D. D. O'Connor Theatre Management, New Zealand, 1944–52. Honorary Lecturer in Drama, Canterbury University, 1948. Ngaio Marsh Theatre founded at Canterbury University, 1962. Recipient: Mystery Writers of America Grand Master Award, 1977. D.Litt.: Canterbury University, 1963. Fellow, Royal Society of Arts. O.B.E. (Officer, Order of the British Empire), 1948; D.B.E. (Dame Commander, Order of the British Empire), 1966. Agent: Hughes Massie Ltd., 69 Great Russell Street, London WC1B 3DH, England. Address: 37 Valley Road, Cashmere, Christchurch 2, New Zealand.

CRIME PUBLICATIONS

Novels (series character: Inspector/Superintendent Roderick Alleyn in all books)

A Man Lay Dead. London, Bles, 1934; New York, Sheridan, 1942.
Enter a Murderer. London, Bles, 1935; New York, Pocket Books, 1941.
The Nursing-Home Murder, with Henry Jellett. London, Bles, 1935; New York, Sheridan, 1941.
Death in Ecstasy. London, Bles, 1936; New York, Sheridan, 1941.
Vintage Murder. London, Bles, 1937; New York, Sheridan, 1940.
Artists in Crime. London, Bles, and New York, Furman, 1938.
Death in a White Tie. London, Bles, and New York, Furman, 1938.
Overture to Death. London, Collins, and New York, Furman, 1939.
Death at the Bar. London, Collins, and Boston, Little Brown, 1940.

Death of a Peer.   Boston, Little Brown, 1940; as *Surfeit of Lampreys*, London, Collins, 1941.
Death and the Dancing Footman.   Boston, Little Brown, 1941; London, Collins, 1942.
Colour Scheme.   London, Collins, and Boston, Little Brown, 1943.
Died in the Wool.   London, Collins, and Boston, Little Brown, 1945.
Final Curtain.   London, Collins, and Boston, Little Brown, 1947.
Swing, Brother, Swing.   London, Collins, 1949; as *A Wreath for Rivera*, Boston, Little Brown, 1949.
Opening Night.   London, Collins, 1951; as *Night at the Vulcan*, Boston, Little Brown, 1951.
Spinsters in Jeopardy.   Boston, Little Brown, 1953; London, Collins, 1954; as *The Bride of Death*, New York, Spivak, 1955.
Scales of Justice.   London, Collins, and Boston, Little Brown, 1955.
Death of a Fool.   Boston, Little Brown, 1956; as *Off with His Head*, London, Collins, 1957.
Singing in the Shrouds.   Boston, Little Brown, 1958; London, Collins, 1959.
False Scent.   Boston, Little Brown, and London, Collins, 1960.
Hand in Glove.   Boston, Little Brown, and London, Collins, 1962.
Dead Water.   Boston, Little Brown, 1963; London, Collins, 1964.
Killer Dolphin.   Boston, Little Brown, 1966; as *Death at the Dolphin*, London, Collins, 1967.
Clutch of Constables.   London, Collins, 1968; Boston, Little Brown, 1969.
When in Rome.   London, Collins, 1970; Boston, Little Brown, 1971.
Tied Up in Tinsel.   London, Collins, and Boston, Little Brown, 1972.
Black as He's Painted.   London, Collins, and Boston, Little Brown, 1975.
Last Ditch.   Boston, Little Brown, and London, Collins, 1977.
Grave Mistake.   Boston, Little Brown, and London, Collins, 1978.

Uncollected Short Stories

"I Can Find My Way Out," in *Queen's Awards 1946*, edited by Ellery Queen.   Boston, Little Brown, and London, Gollancz, 1946.
"Death on the Air," in *Anthology 1969*, edited by Ellery Queen.   New York, Davis, 1968.
"Chapter and Verse," in *Ellery Queen's Murdercade*.   New York, Random House, 1975.
"A Fool about Money," in *Ellery Queen's Crime Wave.*   New York, Putnam, 1976.

OTHER PUBLICATIONS

Plays

False Scent, adaptation of her own novel (produced Worthing, Sussex, 1961).
The Christmas Tree (juvenile).   London, S.P.C.K., 1962.
A Unicorn for Christmas, music by David Farquhar (produced Sydney, 1965).
Murder Sails at Midnight (produced Bournemouth, Hampshire, 1972).

Television Play: *Evil Liver* (*Crown Court* series), 1975.

Other

New Zealand, with Randal Matthew Burdon.   London, Collins, 1942.
A Play Toward: A Note on Play Production.   Christchurch, Caxton Press, 1946.
Perspectives: The New Zealander and the Visual Arts.   Auckland, Auckland Gallery Associates, 1960.

New Zealand. New York, Macmillan, 1964; London, Collier Macmillan, 1965.
Black and Honeydew: An Autobiography. Boston, Little Brown, 1965; London, Collins, 1966.

Manuscript Collections: Mugar Memorial Library, Boston University; Alexander Turnbull Library, Wellington.

Theatrical Activities:

Director: **Play** – *Six Characters in Search of an Author* by Pirandello, London, 1950.

*   *   *

There are three aspects of Ngaio Marsh's work which stand out: the theatrical flavour, her detective, and the characterisations. It is probably because of these three that her detective fiction has been so popular for so long.

Ngaio Marsh has won many honours for her work in the theatre. Almost every one of her novels contains some reference to one of Shakespeare's plays, and in *Killer Dolphin* we even have a recreation of Shakespeare's life on the stage. Some of the stories are set in the theatre: *Enter a Murderer, Opening Night, Vintage Murder, Death at the Dolphin.* These stories underline her great knowledge of the theatre and manage to give a little of the atmosphere of actors and their tensions and jealousies. *Colour Scheme* is not set in the theatre, but here we have a successful actor writing his memoirs.

Most of her stories are conceived through the eyes of the dramatist, which may be why several of her novels have been made into stage or television plays. The settings display a great deal of visual detail, the sort of thing vital for a good backdrop. She creates an atmosphere that provides an arena in which the protagonists can do their battle. In *Died in the Wool* the setting is that of a New Zealand high country sheep station – a vast panorama of high snow-capped mountains in the distance, a very large, flat valley floor, and the cold at night. This reminds the reader constantly of the isolation necessary to the story – the telephone exchange that closes down at midnight, the service car that calls now and then at the gate a few miles from the homestead, the distance to the mountain pass and other human beings. Within this setting the scenery changes only a few times from the living room to the study to the wool shed to Alleyn's bedroom and obviously was conceived in terms of stage-set economy. All necessary information is supplied by what the characters say about each other. The unity of time is also observed: Alleyn solves the murder in just over 24 hours. Many murders take Alleyn even less time to solve. Sometimes Alleyn's presence is required for a longer time because of internal developments or the time it takes the murderer to make his next step.

As one reads Ngaio Marsh's books one cannot help becoming very interested in Alleyn. She chose for her character's surname that of the Elizabethan actor Edward Alleyn who founded Dulwich College in London to which her father had gone. Chief Detective Inspector Roderick Alleyn first appeared in chapter four of *A Man Lay Dead.* Angela North, frequent companion and later wife of Nigel Bathgate, a journalist and friend of Alleyn's, describes him thus:

> Alleyn did not resemble a plain-clothes policeman she felt sure, nor was he in the romantic manner – white faced and gimlet eyed. He looked like one of her Uncle Hubert's friends, the sort that they knew would "do" for houseparties. He was very tall and lean, his hair was dark, and his eyes grey, with corners that turned down. They looked as if they would smile easily, but his mouth didn't.

Alleyn is 6'2" tall, had originally trained as diplomat, and is now on his first murder case. He has Det. Sgt. Bailey, the fingerprint expert, already in tow, and by the end of the book has acquired the Russian Vassili as manservant, and the friendship of Bathgate. In later books we follow his career and his marriage to Agatha Troy. Other recurring characters and cross references give a certain cohesion to the novels.

If one of the faults of Ngaio Marsh's novels is that all too often Alleyn's friends and relatives are involved or present at the scene – then these coincidences very quickly disappear behind the wonderful characters. The antics of the Lamprey family in *Death of a Peer* almost overshadow the detective aspect of the novel – something that happens again in *Final Curtain* with the most entertaining Ancreds, in *Tied Up in Tinsel* with the Christmas Party and the "rehabilitated murderers," and in *Colour Scheme* with the Claire family.

Perhaps there is more of the serious novelist in Ngaio Marsh than in most detective fiction writers. The little bits of romance in her books are very enjoyable; so also are her very polished prose and her plot construction. In *Died in the Wool* (as also in many others) she manages the local idiom magnificently: characters can be recognised by their dialect (the Cuddys in *Singing in the Shrouds*). The murder in this well-structured book had occurred over a year before Alleyn appears. He gains a picture of the victim from the ideas the others have of her, and this "reported personality" then gives him the key to the mystery. In *Clutch of Constables* we have two strands of narrative: one with Troy as the viewer and character involved in the action, and the other with Alleyn lecturing in retrospect to his students from information received in Troy's letters while he was in the U.S. The two narratives run simultaneously and combine into one from the point of Alleyn's appearance on the scene in Troy's narrative near the end of the book. This is a very cleverly conceived plot.

Ngaio Marsh says herself that even though she has written some 30 detective novels, is a member of the Detection Club, and has received the Grand Master Award of the Mystery Writers of America, her main interest is the theatre. Fortunately this did not seem to prevent her from writing her books. She plays no tricks on the readers (only in her first novel did Alleyn have extra information the reader could not possibly have) and states all the evidence. But since all the characters present usually have some motive and also the opportunity to murder, it is not easy to predict "whodunit."

Some of her books, namely *Death in Ecstasy, Scales of Justice* and *When in Rome*, are not as good as her others because of weaknesses in the plot – too involved, the motive not convincing, or the story rather far-fetched – but that does not detract from her overall achievement. Her methods of murder are often gruesome: a knock on the head with suffocation in a wool press or a broken neck from a fall out of a window; a meat skewer through the eye into the brain; head crushed by a falling magnum bottle of champagne; head crushed by a falling drain pipe; a push into a boiling mud pool; a spear pinning the victim to the ground.

It is the plot structure, the characterisation, and the quality of her prose that give Ngaio Marsh's books their unique flavour and that have made Roderick Alleyn a household word with the fans of detective fiction.

—Manfred A. Bertram

MARSHALL, Lovat. See **DUNCAN, W. Murdoch.**

MARSHALL, Raymond. See **CHASE, James Hadley.**

MARSTEN, Richard. See **McBAIN, Ed.**

MASON, A(lfred) E(dward) W(oodley). British. Born in Camberwell, London, 7 May 1865. Educated at Dulwich College, London, 1878–84; Trinity College, Oxford (exhibitioner in classics, 1887), 1884–87, degrees in classics 1886, 1888. Served in the Royal Marine Light Infantry in World War I, and involved in Naval Intelligence Division secret service missions in Spain, Morocco, and Mexico. Actor, in provincial touring companies, 1888–94 (appeared in first performance of *Arms and the Man*, 1894); Liberal Member of Parliament for Coventry, 1906–10. Honorary Fellow, Trinity College, 1943. *Died 22 November 1948.*

CRIME PUBLICATIONS

Novels (series character: Inspector Hanaud)

The Watchers. Bristol, Arrowsmith, and New York, Stokes, 1899.
Running Water. London, Hodder and Stoughton, and New York, Century, 1907.
At the Villa Rose (Hanaud). London, Hodder and Stoughton, and New York, Scribner, 1910.
The Witness for the Defence. London, Hodder and Stoughton, 1913; New York, Scribner, 1914.
The Summons. London, Hodder and Stoughton, and New York, Doran, 1920.
The Winding Stair. London, Hodder and Stoughton, and New York, Doran, 1923.
The House of the Arrow (Hanaud). London, Hodder and Stoughton, and New York, Doran, 1924.
No Other Tiger. London, Hodder and Stoughton, and New York, Doran, 1927.
The Prisoner in the Opal (Hanaud). London, Hodder and Stoughton, and New York, Doubleday, 1928.
The Sapphire. London, Hodder and Stoughton, and New York, Doubleday, 1933.
They Wouldn't Be Chessmen (Hanaud). London, Hodder and Stoughton, and New York, Doubleday, 1935.
The House in Lordship Lane (Hanaud). London, Hodder and Stoughton, and New York, Dodd Mead, 1946.

Short Stories

Ensign Knightley and Other Stories. London, Constable, and New York, Stokes, 1901.
The Clock. New York, Paget, 1910.
The Four Corners of the World. London, Hodder and Stoughton, and New York, Scribner, 1917.
Dilemmas. London, Hodder and Stoughton, 1934; New York, Doubleday, 1935.

The Secret Fear.   New York, Doubleday, 1940.

Uncollected Short Stories

"The Vicar's Conversion," in *Strand* (London), December 1900.
"The Trouble at Beaulieu," in *Lippincott's* (Philadelphia), 19 January 1901.
"The Schoolmaster and Felicia," in *Punch's Holiday Book*, edited by E. T. Reed.   London, Punch Office, 1901.
"The Picture in the Bath," in *Illustrated London News*, Christmas, 1901.
"The Man from Socotra," in *Illustrated London News*, 22 November 1902.
"The Guide," in *Daily Mail* (London), 1904.
"Dimoussi and the Pistol," in *London Magazine*, September 1905.
"The Silver Flask," in *Metropolitan Magazine* (New York), July 1907.
"Making Good," in *Cornhill* (London), January 1910.
"The Silver Ship," in *Metropolitan Magazine* (New York), January 1917.
"The Ear," in *Strand* (London), June 1937.
"The Conjuror," in *The Queen's Book of the Red Cross*.   London, Hodder and Stoughton, 1939.
"The Watch," in *Homes and Gardens* (London), June 1945.
"Not in the Log," in *Strand* (London), May 1948.
"The Ginger King," in *Great Stories of Detection*, edited by R. C. Bull.   London, Barker, 1960.

OTHER PUBLICATIONS

Novels

A Romance of Wastdale.   London, Mathews, and New York, Stokes, 1895.
The Courtship of Morrice Buckler.   London, Macmillan, 1896; New York, Macmillan, 1903.
Lawrence Clavering.   London, Innes, and New York, Dodd Mead, 1897.
The Philanderers.   London and New York, Macmillan, 1897.
Miranda of the Balcony.   London and New York, Macmillan, 1899.
Parson Kelly.   London and New York, Longman, 1900.
Clementina.   London, Methuen, and New York, Stokes, 1901.
The Four Feathers.   London, Smith Elder, and New York, Macmillan, 1902.
The Truants.   London, Smith Elder, and New York, Harper, 1904.
The Broken Road.   London, Smith Elder, and New York, Scribner, 1907.
The Turnstile.   London, Hodder and Stoughton, and New York, Scribner, 1912.
The Dean's Elbow.   London, Hodder and Stoughton, 1930; New York, Doubleday, 1931.
The Three Gentlemen.   London, Hodder and Stoughton, and New York, Doubleday, 1932.
Fire over England.   London, Hodder and Stoughton, and New York, Doubleday, 1936.
The Drum.   London, Hodder and Stoughton, and New York, Doubleday, 1937.
Königsmark.   London, Hodder and Stoughton, 1938; New York, Doubleday, 1939.
Musk and Amber.   London, Hodder and Stoughton, and New York, Doubleday, 1942.

Short Stories

Making Good.   New York, Paget, 1910.
The Episode of the Thermometer.   New York, Paget, 1918.

Plays

Blanche de Malètroit, adaptation of the story "The Sire de Malètroit's Door" by Robert
  Louis Stevenson (produced London, 1894).   London, Capper and Newton, 1894.
The Courtship of Morrice Buckler, with Isabel Bateman, adaptation of the novel by
  Mason (produced London, 1897).
Marjory Strode (produced London, 1908).
Colonel Smith (produced London, 1909).   London, privately printed, 1909; revised
  version, as Green Stockings (produced New York, 1911), New York and London,
  French, 1914.
The Princess Clementina, with George Pleydell Bancroft, adaptation of the novel
  Clementina by Mason (produced Cardiff and London, 1910).
The Witness for the Defence, adaptation of his own novel (produced London and New
  York, 1911).   Privately printed, 1911.
Open Windows (produced London, 1913).
At the Villa Rose, adaptation of his own novel (produced London, 1920).   London,
  Hodder and Stoughton, 1928.
Running Water (produced London, 1922).
The House of the Arrow, adaptation of his own novel (produced London, 1928).
No Other Tiger, adaptation of his own novel (produced Leicester and London, 1928).
A Present from Margate, with Ian Hay (produced London, 1933).   London, French,
  1934.

Other

The Royal Exchange.   London, Royal Exchange, 1920.
"Detective Novels," in Nation and Athenaeum (London), 7 February 1925.
Sir George Alexander and the St. James' Theatre.   London, Macmillan, 1935.
The Life of Francis Drake.   London, Hodder and Stoughton, 1941; New York,
  Doubleday, 1942.

*   *   *

An accomplished novelist, A. E. W. Mason wrote several mystery novels in which he tried
to "combine the crime story which produces a shiver with the detective story which aims at a
surprise." His detective, M. Hanaud of the French Sûreté, is a literary descendent of Lecoq – a
stout, broad-shouldered bourgeois with a gift of humor. Although conscious of his
reputation, Hanaud has no illusions as to his own infallibility; he describes detectives as
"servants of chance." Their skill, he says, is "to seize quickly the hem of her skirt when it
flashes for the fraction of a second" before their eyes.
  The first Hanaud novel was At the Villa Rose which brought a needed freshness to the
detective story of its period. Hanaud and his very distinctive Watson, the wine-loving
bachelor Ricardo, work to defend the reputation of a young Englishwoman accused of
murder when her wealthy companion is found dead and robbed. The reader, following
Hanaud's adroitness and inventiveness, engages in the interesting process of putting two and
two together. The puzzle is quickly solved when Mason begins to throw light upon it and the
story loses its hold before the concluding chapter.
  Mason's second Hanaud novel came fourteen years later. The House of the Arrow is
regarded as almost perfect in its conception and plot. Mason shows his immense skill in
narrative and characterization; all of the attributes of a first-rate novel are there: compelling
atmosphere, remarkable conception of character, devastating sense of evil, and magnificent
satire. The story concerns the murder of the widow of a wealthy English art connoisseur in
the old provincial town of Dijon. Her niece, Betty Harlowe, is the center of suspicion since it
is she who is to inherit the estate. The local police, plagued by a score of anonymous letters,

enlist the aid of the great Parisian detective. The reader is kept guessing until the final chapter in this tense and sinister tale.

Hanaud and Ricardo return in *The Prisoner in the Opal*, the title referring to Ricardo's view of the world "as a vast opal inside which I stood." Devil-worship and the celebration of a Black Mass play a prominent role in this morbid story set in the Bordeaux region of France. Devil-worship is not the usual concern of the police, but when a murder is involved, it becomes Hanaud's duty to investigate. Ricardo is in a constant state of mystification since he is not taken completely into Hanaud's confidence.

They Wouldn't Be Chessmen is set in Trouville and involves murder, theft, a tidal wave, and a confusion of personalities and motives. Mason's last Hanaud novel, *The House in Lordship Lane*, is set in Brittany. Written when Mason was over 80, it suffers from period faults, although it is certainly readable.

Mason was a prolific writer who was at his best in the historical novel. His cloak and dagger stories paralleled his own exploits as the civilian head of British Naval Intelligence during the First World War. His substantial earnings from his books enabled him to travel widely which he did with a schoolboy zest for adventure and with an eye for local color. In the mystery genre, he made ample use of the psychological element – and in doing so, was in advance of his time.

—Daniel P. King

MASON, F(rancis) Van Wyck. Also wrote as Geoffrey Coffin (with H. Brawner); Frank W. Mason; Ward Weaver. American. Born in Boston, Massachusetts, 11 November 1901. Educated at Berkshire School, 1919–20; Harvard University, Cambridge, Massachusetts, B.S. 1924. Served in the Allied Expeditionary Forces in France, 1918–19: Second Lieutenant; New York National Guard Cavalry, 1924–29: Sergeant; Maryland National Guard Field Artillery, 1930–33: First Lieutenant; General Staff Corps Officer and Chief Historian, Civil and Military Government Section, 1942–45; Supreme Headquarters, Allied Expeditionary Force, 1943–45: Colonel; Medaille de Sauvetage, Croix de Guerre with two palms, French Legion of Honor. Married 1) Dorothy Louise Macready in 1927 (died, 1958); two children; 2) Jeanne-Louise Hand in 1958. Importer and after 1928 self-employed writer. Lived in Bermuda, 1956–78. Recipient: Valley Forge Foundation Medal, 1953; Society of Colonial Wars Citation of Honour, 1960. *Died 29 August 1978.*

CRIME PUBLICATIONS

Novels (series character: Hugh North in all Mason books except *Spider House*; Inspector Scott Stuart)

> *Seeds of Murder.* New York, Doubleday, 1930; London, Eldon Press, 1937.
> *The Vesper Service Murders.* New York, Doubleday, 1931; London, Eldon Press, 1935.
> *The Fort Terror Murders.* New York, Doubleday, 1931; London, Eldon Press, 1936.
> *The Yellow Arrow Murders.* New York, Doubleday, 1932; London, Eldon Press, 1935.
> *The Branded Spy Murders.* New York, Doubleday, 1932; London, Eldon Press, 1936.
> *Spider House.* New York, Mystery League, 1932; London, Hale, 1959.

The Shanghai Bund Murders. New York, Doubleday, 1933; London, Eldon Press, 1934; revised edition, as *The China Sea Murders*, New York, Pocket Books, 1959.
The Sulu Sea Murders. New York, Doubleday, 1933; London, Eldon Press, 1936.
Oriental Division G-2 (omnibus). New York, Reynal, n.d.
The Budapest Parade Murders. New York, Doubleday, and London, Eldon Press, 1935.
Murder in the Senate (Stuart; as Geoffrey Coffin, with H. Brawner). New York, Dodge, 1935; London, Hurst and Blackett, 1936.
The Washington Legation Murders. New York, Doubleday, 1935; London, Eldon Press, 1937.
The Forgotten Fleet Mystery (Stuart; as Geoffrey Coffin, with H. Brawner). New York, Dodge, 1936; London, Jarrolds, 1943.
The Seven Seas Murders (novelets). New York, Doubleday, 1936; London, Eldon Press, 1937.
The Castle Island Case. New York, Reynal, 1937; London, Jarrolds, 1938; revised edition, as *The Multi-Million Dollar Murders*, New York, Pocket Books, 1960.
The Hongkong Airbase Murders. New York, Doubleday, 1937; London, Jarrolds, 1940.
The Cairo Garter Murders. New York, Doubleday, and London, Jarrolds, 1938.
The Singapore Exile Murders. New York, Doubleday, and London, Jarrolds, 1939.
The Bucharest Ballerina Murders. New York, Stokes, 1940; London, Jarrolds, 1941.
Military Intelligence − 8 (omnibus). New York, Stokes, 1941.
The Rio Casino Intrigue. New York, Reynal, 1941; London, Jarrolds, 1942.
The Man from G-2 (omnibus). New York, Reynal, n.d.
Saigon Singer. New York, Doubleday, 1946; London, Barker, 1948.
Dardanelles Derelict. New York, Doubleday, 1949; London, Barker, 1950.
Himalayan Assignment. New York, Doubleday, 1952; London, Hale, 1953.
Two Tickets to Tangier. New York, Doubleday, 1955; London, Hale, 1956.
The Gracious Lily Affair. New York, Doubleday, 1957; London, Hale, 1958.
Secret Mission to Bangkok. New York, Doubleday, 1960; London, Hale, 1961.
Trouble in Burma. New York, Doubleday, 1962; London, Hale, 1963.
Zanzibar Intrigue. New York, Doubleday, 1963; London, Hale, 1964.
Maracaibo Mission. New York, Doubleday, 1965; London, Hale, 1966.
The Deadly Orbit Mission. New York, Doubleday, and London, Hale, 1968.

Uncollected Short Stories

"The Port of Peril," in *The Saint* (New York), August 1955.
"The Plum-Colored Corpse," in *The Saint* (New York), September 1956.

OTHER PUBLICATIONS

Novels

Captain Nemesis. New York, Putnam, 1931; London, Hale, 1959.
Three Harbours. Philadelphia, Lippincott, 1938; London, Jarrolds, 1939.
Stars on the Sea. Philadelphia, Lippincott, and London, Jarrolds, 1940.
Hang My Wreath (as Ward Weaver). New York, Funk and Wagnalls, 1941; London, Jarrolds, 1942.
Rivers of Glory. Philadelphia, Lippincott, 1942; London, Jarrolds, 1944.
End of Track (as Ward Weaver). New York, Reynal, 1943.
Eagle in the Sky. Philadelphia, Lippincott, 1948; London, Jarrolds, 1949.
Cutlass Empire. New York, Doubleday, 1949; London, Jarrolds, 1950.
Valley Forge: 24 December 1777. New York, Doubleday, 1950.
Proud New Flags. Philadelphia, Lippincott, 1951; London, Jarrolds, 1952.

Golden Admiral: A Novel of Sir Francis Drake and the Armada. New York, Doubleday, 1953; London, Jarrolds, 1954.
Wild Drum Beat. New York, Pocket Books, 1953.
The Barbarians. New York, Pocket Books, 1954; London, Hale, 1956.
Blue Hurricane. Philadelphia, Lippincott, 1954; London, Jarrolds, 1955.
Silver Leopard. New York, Doubleday, 1955; London, Jarrolds, 1956.
Captain Judas. New York, Pocket Books, 1955; London, Hale, 1957.
Our Valiant Few. Boston, Little Brown, 1956; as *To Whom Be Glory*, London, Jarrolds, 1957.
Lysander. New York, Pocket Books, 1956; London, Hale, 1958.
The Young Titan. New York, Doubleday, 1959; London, Hutchinson, 1960.
Return of the Eagles. New York, Pocket Books, 1959.
Manila Galleon. Boston, Little Brown, and London, Hutchinson, 1961.
The Sea 'venture. New York, Doubleday, 1961; London, Hutchinson, 1962.
Rascals' Heaven. New York, Doubleday, and London, Hutchinson, 1965.
Wild Horizon. Boston, Little Brown, 1966.
Harpoons in Eden. New York, Doubleday, 1969.
Brimstone Club. Boston, Little Brown, 1971.
Roads to Liberty. Boston, Little Brown, 1972.

Novels as Frank W. Mason

Q-Boat. Philadelphia, Lippincott, 1943.
Pilots, Man Your Planes! Philadelphia, Lippincott, 1944.
Flight into Danger. Philadelphia, Lippincott, 1946.

Other

The Winter at Valley Forge (juvenile). New York, Random House, 1953; as *Washington at Valley Forge*, Eau Claire, Wisconsin, E. M. Hale, 1953.
The Battle of Lake Erie (juvenile). Boston, Houghton Mifflin, 1960.
The Battle for New Orleans (juvenile). Boston, Houghton Mifflin, 1962.
The Battle for Quebec (juvenile). Boston, Houghton Mifflin, 1965.
The Maryland Colony (juvenile). New York, Macmillan, 1969.

Editor, *The Fighting American.* New York, Reynal, 1943; London, Jarrolds, 1945.
Editor, *American Men at Arms.* Boston, Little Brown, 1964.

*　　*　　*

While Van Wyck Mason wrote a few mysteries without a series hero it is for the 26 books about Army Intelligence officer Hugh North that he will be remembered.

Some critics have classed Mason's stories in the Oppenheim tradition of international intrigue. The early North novels are fairly straightforward detection, the first two narrated, in the Watson tradition, by a Dr. Walter Allan. Mason apparently felt hampered by this format and dropped the character in *The Fort Terror Murders*. North investigates these early cases mostly because he happens to be on the scene and not because he is a member of Army Intelligence. In *The Vesper Service Murders* his only logical excuse for supervising the investigation comes when another army officer is murdered. These early novels may be called unsophisticated melodrama. They are delightfully dated by a few over-written passages of suspense, a heritage of Mason's pulp training. By the fourth novel, *The Yellow Arrow Murders*, with North assigned by G-2 to get the secret of the Doelger torpedo and solve the murder of a Navy Intelligence agent, the series becomes *sophisticated* melodrama.

Stripped to their essential detective structure, the novels involve a problem for North to solve which includes a series of murders and a puzzle to unravel. This may be a message to be deciphered, the true meaning of a word or phrase, or the location of a treasure, all of which become keys to the larger mystery. The vivid background based on careful research and Mason's own travels is part of the appeal of the stories.

Hugh North is an older version of his creator, according to dust jacket blurbs and the brief biographical sketch in some of the early novels. A Captain in the first dozen novels, he was promoted to Major in *The Singapore Exile Murders* because his mission demanded a higher rank. North, himself, would have been happy to remain a Captain. He became a Colonel in *Himalayan Assignment* and retained that rank for the remainder of his adventures. He is tall, bronzed, with high cheek-bones suggesting a possible American Indian ancestry and a neatly trimmed mustache, and only the patch of gray hair above his ears shows his age. The long career of Hugh North takes him to Cuba, the Middle East, the Balkans, Africa, and most often to the Orient. In the novels may be found a popular capsule history of the changing pattern of U.S. foreign affairs. From Long Island (*Seeds of Murder*) to Tangier (*The Deadly Orbit Mission*), munitions in Budapest, trouble in Palestine, coming to the rescue of the CIA, Mason keeps his man from G-2 in topical and typical hot water. His own development as a writer may be charted in the North books: from pulp thrillers to smooth, professional entertainment.

—J. Randolph Cox

MASTERSON, Whit. See **MILLER, Wade.**

MASUR, Harold Q. American. Born 29 January 1909. Educated at Bordentown Military Institute, 1926–28; New York University, B.A. 1932; New York University School of Law, J.D. 1934. Served in the United States Air Force. Engaged in the private practice of law, 1935–42; began writing for pulp magazines in 1940's; has taught detective story writing at New York University, the Cape Cod Writers' Conference, and Iona College Writers' Conference. Past President and currently General Counsel, Mystery Writers of America. Recipient: Mutual Broadcasting System Story Teller's Award. Address: 520 East 20th Street, New York, New York 10009, U.S.A.

CRIME PUBLICATIONS

Novels (series character: Scott Jordan in all books except *You Can't Live Forever* and *The Attorney*)

Bury Me Deep. New York, Simon and Schuster, 1947; London, Boardman, 1948.
Suddenly a Corpse. New York, Simon and Schuster, 1949; London, Boardman, 1950.
You Can't Live Forever. New York, Simon and Schuster, 1950; London, Boardman, 1951.
So Rich, So Lovely, and So Dead. New York, Simon and Schuster, 1952; London, Boardman, 1953.

The Big Money.   New York, Simon and Schuster, 1954; London, Boardman, 1955.
Tall, Dark, and Deadly.   New York, Simon and Schuster, 1956; London, Boardman, 1957.
The Last Gamble.   New York, Simon and Schuster, 1958; as *The Last Breath*, London, Boardman, 1958; as *Murder on Broadway*, New York, Dell, 1959.
Send Another Hearse.   New York, Simon and Schuster, and London, Boardman, 1960.
Make a Killing.   New York, Random House, and London, Boardman, 1964.
The Legacy Lenders.   New York, Random House, and London, Boardman, 1967.
The Attorney.   New York, Random House, 1973; London, Souvenir Press, 1974.

Short Stories

The Name Is Jordan.   New York, Pyramid, 1962.

Uncollected Short Stories

"The Corpse Maker," in *Come Seven, Come Death*, edited by Henry Morrison.   New York, Pocket Books, 1965.
"Murder Matinee," in *Alfred Hitchcock Presents: A Month of Mystery.*   New York, Random House, 1969; London, Reinhardt, 1970.
"The Silent Butler," in *Alfred Hitchcock Presents: Stories to Stay Awake By.*   New York, Random House, 1971.
"Squealer's Reward," in *Killers of the Mind*, edited by Lucy Freeman.   New York, Random House, 1974.
"The Graft Is Green," in *Alfred Hitchcock Presents: Stories to Be Read with the Door Locked.*   New York, Random House, 1975.
"The $1,000,000 Disappearing Act," in *Ellery Queen's Crime Wave.*   New York, Putnam, and London, Gollancz, 1976.
"Framed for Murder," in *Ellery Queen's Mystery Magazine* (New York), June 1976.
"Murder Never Solves Anything," in *Ellery Queen's Mystery Magazine* (New York), August 1976.
"Dead Game," in *Alfred Hitchcock Presents: Stories That Go Bump in the Night.*   New York, Random House, 1977.
"One Thing Leads to Another," in *Ellery Queen's Mystery Magazine* (New York), April 1978.
"Lawyer's Holiday," in *Ellery Queen's Napoleons of Mystery.*   New York, Davis, 1978.
"Trial and Terror," in *Ellery Queen's Mystery Magazine* (New York), May 1979.

OTHER PUBLICATIONS

Other

Editor, *Dolls Are Murder.*   New York, Lion, 1957.
Editor, *Murder Most Foul.*   New York, Walker, 1971.

Ghostwriter: *The Metropolitan Opera Murders* by Helen Traubel, New York, Simon and Schuster, 1951.

Harold Q. Masur comments:
    The series character, Scott Jordan, a New York attorney, was first conceived to fall somewhere between Perry Mason and Archie Goodwin. It was the author's hope to invent plots as ingenious as Gardner's, featuring a protagonist with the dash and insouciance of Rex Stout's Archie. With one additional ingredient: instead of being approached for help by prospective clients, Jordan would himself be personally involved in each case. And the

reader, hopefully identifying with the hero, would thus be drawn into the simmering kettle, intensifying interest and suspense.

*   *   *

Because Harold Q. Masur is a lawyer, writing about lawyer-detective Scott Jordan, comparisons with Erle Stanley Gardner's Perry Mason are perhaps inevitable. There are more points of difference than similarity, however. The Jordan tales generally eschew the elaborately staged courtroom scenes, replete with legalistic fireworks, that are the hallmark of the Perry Mason series. Masur, rather, draws on his legal background to provide plot springboards which turn on some interesting aspect of law which Jordan encounters in his practice. The legal problem generally gives rise to the murder problem (in the Mason novels the murder usually *is* the legal problem). Jordan functions more as a conventional private detective, active away from the office and courtroom, and things are usually wrapped up before the legal proceedings are too far along. The Jordan books are tightly plotted, well clued and frequently surprising in denouement, but they are not the elaborate (and frequently far-fetched) Chinese puzzle box affairs that Gardner was so adept at devising.

Jordan, who narrates his cases in the first person, is a relaxed, non-cynical sort of character, who often seems both distressed and bemused to find himself at the center of a web of greedy scheming and murder. Despite his low-key personality, though, Jordan is capable of fast action and quick thinking. He has a good working relationship with his police contact, homicide detective John Nola, though they are occasionally at odds when Jordan is forced to indulge in a bit of thin ice skating of the Mason variety. Jordan also relates well to the attractive women inevitably involved in his cases, in a not overly wolfish manner. The Jordan novels are compact and fast-paced, the dialogue is crisp and convincing, the supporting characters are free of the taint of cardboard. Murder motives are well-developed and credible.

In *The Legacy Lenders* Jordan investigates a case involving a firm which lends money to prospective heirs on their "expectations." The point at issue: do the lenders hurry things along a bit? *Make a Killing* finds Jordan in the midst of an involved proxy fight for control of a movie studio. In *Tall, Dark, and Deadly* Jordan's career is at stake as he is accused of having faked evidence in a divorce case. *Send Another Hearse* concerns embezzlement at a literary agency and police corruption. This novel is particularly noteworthy for a shock plot twist seldom seen in series books – the murder of one of the continuing supporting characters.

Masur has also written a number of short stories involving Jordan for the mystery magazines. His skill at maintaining a fast pace and tight plot serve him well in the short form. Ten of these tales were collected in the paperback anthology, *The Name Is Jordan*.

—Art Scott

MATHER, Berkely.   Pseudonym for John Evan Weston Davies.   British.   Soldier in the British Army for 30 years: Lieutenant Colonel. Chairman, Crime Writers Association, 1966. Recipient: Crime Writers Association Award, for television plays, 1962. Agent: Curtis Brown Ltd., 1 Craven Hill, London W2 3EP, England.

CRIME PUBLICATIONS

Novels (series character: Peter Feltham)

The Achilles Affair (Feltham).   London, Collins, and New York, Scribner, 1959.
The Pass Beyond Kashmir.   London, Collins, and New York, Scribner, 1960.
The Road and the Star.   London, Collins, and New York, Scribner, 1965.
The Gold of Malabar.   London, Collins, and New York, Scribner, 1967.
The Springers.   London, Collins, 1968; as *A Spy for a Spy*, New York, Scribner, 1968.
The Break in the Line.   London, Collins, 1970; as *The Break*, New York, Scribner, 1970.
The Terminators.   London, Collins, and New York, Scribner, 1971.
Snowline.   London, Collins, and New York, Scribner, 1973.
The White Dacoit.   London, Collins, 1974.
With Extreme Prejudice (Feltham).   London, Collins, 1975; New York, Scribner, 1976.
The Memsahib.   London, Collins, and New York, Scribner, 1977.
The Pagoda Tree.   London, Collins, 1979.

Short Stories

Geth Straker and Other Stories (from television series).   London, Collins, 1962.

Uncollected Short Stories

"Cri de Coeur," in *Ellery Queen's Mystery Magazine* (New York), August 1961.
"The Fish of My Uncle's Cat," in *Ellery Queen's Mystery Magazine* (New York), November 1961.
"The Diamond Watch," in *Saturday Evening Post* (Philadelphia), 8 April 1967.
"Blood Feud," in *John Creasey's Mystery Bedside Book*, edited by Herbert Harris.   London, Hodder and Stoughton, 1967.
"The Man in the Well," in *The Playboy Book of Crime and Suspense.*   Chicago, Playboy Press, 1968.
"Ma Tante Always Done Her Best," in *Ellery Queen's Mystery Magazine* (New York), December 1968.
"Moon of the Cat," in *John Creasey's Mystery Bedside Book 1969*, edited by Herbert Harris.   London, Hodder and Stoughton, 1968.
"Apprentice to Danger," in *John Creasey's Mystery Bedside Book 1970*, edited by Herbert Harris.   London, Hodder and Stoughton, 1969.
"Contraband," in *John Creasey's Mystery Bedside Book 1971*, edited by Herbert Harris.   London, Hodder and Stoughton, 1970.
"For Want of a Nail," in *Ellery Queen's Grand Slam.*   Cleveland, World, 1970.
"The Rajah's Emeralds," in *Ellery Queen's Mystery Magazine* (New York), April 1971.
"Treasure Trove," in *Ellery Queen's Mystery Magazine* (New York), July 1971.
"There's a Moral in It Somewhere," in *John Creasey's Mystery Bedside Book 1972*, edited by Herbert Harris.   London, Hodder and Stoughton, 1971.
"No Questions Asked," in *Ellery Queen's Mystery Magazine* (New York), April 1972.
"Bed and Breakfast," in *John Creasey's Mystery Bedside Book 1974*, edited by Herbert Harris.   London, Hodder and Stoughton, 1973.
"Terror Ride," in *Ellery Queen's Aces of Mystery.*   New York, Davis, 1975.
"The Big Bite," in *Ellery Queen's Giants of Mystery.*   New York, Davis, 1976.

OTHER PUBLICATIONS

Novel

   Genghis Khan (novelization of screenplay).   London, Collins, and New York, Dell, 1965.

Plays

   Screenplays: *Information Received*, with Paul Ryder, 1961; *Dr. No*, with Richard Maibaum and Johanna Harwood, 1962; *The Long Ships*, with Beverley Cross, 1964; *Genghis Khan*, with Beverley Cross and Clarke Reynolds, 1965.

   Radio Plays: *The Sand Leopard* series, 1961; *You Can't Win* series, 1961; *The Consolation Prize*, 1961; *Apprentice to Danger*, 1962; *A Necklace for the Warriors*, 1963; *Touch of an Angel*, 1963; *Letter from a Lady*, 1964; *The Maresciallo*, with Victor Francis, 1964; *The Blue Ox*, 1965; *The Bounce Back*, 1967; *The Hard Buy*, 1968; *Tales from the Poona Club*, 1970.

   Television Plays: *Mid Level*; *Bamboo Bars*; *Old Man of the Air*; *Tales from Soho* series, 1958; *As I Was Saying* series, 1958; *I Spy* (USA); *Charlesworth* series (53 episodes), 1959–64; *Needle Point*, 1962; *To Bury Caesar*, 1963 (USA).

Other

   "Establishing a Cover," in *Murder Ink: The Mystery Reader's Companion*, edited by Dilys Winn.   New York, Workman, 1977.

Berkely Mather comments:
   I admire professionalism. I was a professional soldier – and amateur writer – for 30 years. I found I preferred writing, so I stopped being a soldier and became – horrible term – a professional author, crowding into some 12 years that which I would no doubt have done much better had I taken longer.

                              *   *   *

   Berkely Mather's thrillers have the two main ingredients necessary for success, something old that works and something new that works. The old is the well-tried and well-loved agent/boss relationship in which a ruthless unfeeling spy-master manipulates a reluctant agent. This reluctance may be caused by either private emotion or public distaste, and Mather manages both, offering those who read his books in sequence the intriguing spectacle of one hero, the pleasant, reliable, concerned James Wainwright, being superseded by another, the cynical aggressive Idwal Rees. All they have in common is being in the hands of the same ruthless master, the ghastly Gaffer.
   The new in Mather's books is the setting, basically India with forays into various neighbouring territories. For the most part it is modern India that Mather shows us, still with its centuries-old problems and some – like the hippie influx of the 1960's – not so old. All the background, from the teeming streets of Bombay and Calcutta to the vast empty mountain wilderness of the North, is portrayed with tremendous realism of colour and detail. In settings as beautifully realized as these, fast-moving action-packed tales of espionage and drug smuggling cannot but grip. His characters live too, whether they are the European incomers or the vast variety of ethnic types to be found in the subcontinent. But it is the settings that lift the books out of the ordinary, and their timelessness permits the thriller aficionado to move

with ease from the modern world to that of Mather's historical novel, *The Road and the Star*, or to the 1920's in *The White Dacoit*, possibly his most substantial work so far.

—Reginald Hill

MAUGHAM, Robin (Robert Cecil Romer Maugham; became 2nd Viscount Maugham of Hartfield, 1958); nephew of the writer Somerset Maugham. British. Born in London, 17 May 1916. Educated at Eton College; Trinity Hall, Cambridge, B.A. Served in the British Army, 1939–44; served in the Inns of Court Regiment, 1939; commissioned Fourth County of London Regiment, 1940; served in the Western Desert, 1941–42 (wounded; mentioned in despatches), and in the Middle East Intelligence Centre, 1943. Barrister, Lincoln's Inn, London, until 1939. Lives in Brighton. Address: c/o W. H. Allen, 44 Hill Street, London W1X 8LB, England.

CRIME PUBLICATIONS

Novels

> *Line on Ginger.* London, Chapman and Hall, 1949; New York, Harcourt Brace, 1950; as *The Intruder*, London, New English Library, 1968.
> *The Man with Two Shadows.* London, Longman, 1958; New York, Harper, 1959.
> *November Reef: A Novel of the South Seas.* London, Longman, 1962.
> *The Link: A Victorian Mystery.* London, Heinemann, and New York, McGraw Hill, 1969.
> *The Barrier.* London, W. H. Allen, 1973; New York, McGraw Hill, 1974.
> *Knock on Teak.* London, W. H. Allen, 1976.

Short Stories

> *The 1946 MS.* London, War Facts Press, 1943.
> *Testament: Cairo 1898.* London, Michael deHartington, 1972.

OTHER PUBLICATIONS

Novels

> *The Servant.* London, Falcon Press, 1948; New York, Harcourt Brace, 1949.
> *The Rough and the Smooth.* London, Chapman and Hall, and New York, Harcourt Brace, 1951.
> *Behind the Mirror.* London, Longman, and New York, Harcourt Brace, 1955.
> *The Green Shade.* London, Heinemann, and New York, New American Library, 1966.
> *The Wrong People* (as David Griffin). New York, Paperback Library, 1967; revised edition, as Robin Maugham, London, Heinemann, 1970; New York, McGraw Hill, 1971.
> *The Second Window.* London, Heinemann, and New York, McGraw Hill, 1968.
> *The Last Encounter.* London, W. H. Allen, 1972; New York, McGraw Hill, 1973.
> *The Sign.* London, W. H. Allen, and New York, McGraw Hill, 1974.

The Dividing Line. London, W. H. Allen, 1979.

Short Stories

The Black Tent and Other Stories. London, W. H. Allen, 1973.
Lovers in Exile. London, W. H. Allen, 1977.

Plays

He Must Return (produced London, 1944).
The Rising Heifer (produced Dallas, 1952; High Wycombe, Buckinghamshire, 1955).
The Leopard (produced Worthing, Sussex, 1956).
Mister Lear (produced Worthing, Sussex, 1956). London, English Theatre Guild, 1963.
The Last Hero (produced London, 1957).
A Lonesome Road, with Philip King (produced London, 1957). London, French, 1959.
Odd Man In, adaptation of a play by Claude Magnier (produced London, 1957). London, French, 1958.
The Servant (produced Worthing, Sussex, 1958; New York, 1974). London, French, n.d.
The Hermit, with Philip King (produced Harrogate, Yorkshire, 1959).
It's in the Bag, adaptation of a play by Claude Magnier (produced Brighton, 1959; London, 1960).
The Claimant (produced Worthing, Sussex, 1962; London, 1964).
Azouk, with Willis Hall, adaptation of a play by Alexandre Rivemale (produced Newcastle upon Tyne, 1962).
Winter in Ischia (produced Worthing, Sussex, 1964).
Enemy! (produced Guildford, Surrey, and London, 1969; New York, 1978). London, French, 1971.

Screenplays: *The Intruder*, with John Hunter and Anthony Squire, 1953; *The Black Tent*, with Bryan Forbes, 1956; *The Man with Two Shadows*, 1960; *November Reef*, 1962; *The Carrier*, 1969; *Willie*, 1969; *The Barrier*, 1972.

Television Play: *Wise Virgins of Hove*, 1960.

Other

Come to Dust. London, Chapman and Hall, 1945.
Approach to Palestine. London, Falcon Press, 1947.
Nomad. London, Chapman and Hall, 1947; New York, Viking Press, 1948.
North African Notebook. London, Chapman and Hall, 1948; New York, Harcourt Brace, 1949.
Journey to Siwa. London, Chapman and Hall, 1950; New York, Harcourt Brace, 1951.
The Slaves of Timbuktu. London, Longman, and New York, Harper, 1961.
The Joyita Mystery. London, Parrish, 1962.
Somerset and All the Maughams. London, Heinemann-Longman, and New York, New American Library, 1966.
Escape from the Shadows: Robin Maugham, His Autobiography. London, Hodder and Stoughton, 1972; New York, McGraw Hill, 1973.
Search for Nirvana. London, W. H. Allen, 1975.
Conversations with Willie: Recollections of W. Somerset Maugham. London, W. H. Allen, and New York, Simon and Schuster, 1978.

Editor, *The Convoy File: Stories, Articles, Poems from the Forces, Factories, Mines and Fields.* London, Collins, 1945.

*   *   *

Though most of Robin Maugham's novels use the format of conventional thrillers, often with exotic locales and sometimes with historical settings, his focusing on the unconventional erotic adventures of his characters weakens his plots. This blurring flaws even his first novels, still set in England: *The Servant* depicts a devious manservant's gradual domination of his young master; *Line on Ginger* traces a barrister's attempted rescue of a former war comrade from a life of crime. Both books, however, partially sacrifice the thriller plot to examine the protagonists' dissatisfaction with the status quo and desire to explore other social levels. Despite its suggestions of political and social idealism, this desire implies an unacknowledged homosexual impulse, a theme left implicit until the later novels. Though both books work reasonably well as erotic thrillers, their blurred focus foreshadows more serious problems in Maugham's work.

The Rough and the Smooth inaugurates the archetypal Maugham situation in which a middle-aged man pursues a much younger person, a nineteen-year-old girl in this novel, increasingly younger girls and boys in later books. Since Maugham inevitably depicts these ageing pursuers as grossly unattractive, they must plan ingenious, often sinister, schemes to capture their quarries. Whether motivated by lust or a perverse pedagogical drive, these protagonists, like the malefactors in conventional thrillers, inevitably fail. Such anguished characters often flee to Africa or Asia to escape sexual scandal (Hartleigh in *Behind the Mirror*), or choose them as tolerant backdrops for sexual unorthodoxy (Dr. Stacy in *November Reef*). Despite constantly mentioning foreign words and customs, Maugham gives an insufficient sense of the alien culture, but still allows this material to impede the movement of his plots. Thus, *The Barrier* succeeds neither as thriller nor as picture of Victorian repression confronting the romantic East. *The Last Encounter*, disconcertingly shifting from General Gordon's military and political struggles at Khartoum to his "perpetual struggle against the evils of the flesh," reinforces his understandable perplexity: "Why do I write such strange nonsense in these journals of mine?"

Additional problems are Maugham's inadequate technique and his unsuccessful attempts at psychological or philosophical depth. He often translates sexual activity to violent sea metaphors: "the waves of passion hissed and swirled around him..." (*The Wrong People*). Such over-ripeness threatens the thriller content and negates serious sexual analysis. Frequent flash-backs destroy needed surprise and permit summarized narrative rather than dramatized incident. Formulaic beginnings would be acceptable if the books sustained the note of melodramatic intensity: "I have a full bottle of whiskey and at least five hours before they come for me. I will write down the facts as best I can. That is my only hope" (*The Man with Two Shadows*, and a variant of the opening of *The 1946 MS*). But the books unfortunately try to mix melodrama with serious content. Maugham uses multiple narrators in *The Sign*, the story of Joseph of Arimithea's sexual and political responses to a possible messiah in A.D. 20, and in *The Link*, a Victorian mystery about the claimant to an aristocratic title. But in both books the narrators sound alike and weaken both the suspense and erotic density. *November Reef* begins as a straight South Sea thriller about a utopian colony led by an unbalanced idealist, but the book seems to lose interest in the plotting and offers few compensating insights into character or idea.

Yet, despite these weaknesses, Maugham, with unwavering persistence, presented sexual unorthodoxy in popular thrillers at a time when such material rarely found a large audience. The most hopeful sign in Maugham's prolific career is that for the first time he reveals his awareness of the pitfalls of the genre in *Knock on Teak*, an amusing parody of the clichés of international thrillers and cross-cultural conflicts.

—Burton Kendle

MAUGHAM, W(illiam) Somerset.   British.   Born in Paris, 25 January 1874, of English parents. Educated at King's School, Canterbury, Kent, 1887–91; University of Heidelberg, 1891–92; studied medicine at St. Thomas's Hospital, London, 1892–97; interned in Lambeth, London; qualified as a surgeon, L.R.C.P., M.R.C.S., 1897, but never practised. Served with the Red Cross Ambulance Unit, later with the British Intelligence Corps, in World War I. Married Syrie Barnardo Wellcome in 1915 (divorced, 1927); one daughter. Writer from 1896; lived abroad, mainly in Paris, 1897–1907; travelled widely during the 1920's, in the South Seas, Malaya, and China; lived at Cap Ferrat in the south of France from 1928; lived in the United States during World War II; instituted annual prize for promising young British writer, 1947. D.Litt.: Oxford University; University of Toulouse. Fellow, and Companion of Literature, 1961, Royal Society of Literature. Commander, Legion of Honour; Honorary Senator, University of Heidelberg; Honorary Fellow, Library of Congress, Washington, D.C.; Honorary Member, American Academy of Arts and Letters. Companion of Honour, 1954. *Died 16 December 1965.*

Crime Publications

Short Stories

> *The Casuarina Tree.*   London, Heinemann, and New York, Doran, 1926; as *The Letter: Stories of Crime,* London, Collins, 1930.
> *Ashenden; or, The British Agent.*   London, Heinemann, and New York, Doubleday, 1928.
> *Ah King: Six Stories.*   London, Heinemann, and New York, Doubleday, 1933.

Other Publications

Novels

> *Liza of Lambeth.*   London, Unwin, 1897; New York, Doran, 1921.
> *The Making of a Saint.*   Boston, Page, and London, Unwin, 1898.
> *The Hero.*   London, Hutchinson, 1901.
> *Mrs. Craddock.*   London, Heinemann, 1902; New York, Doran, 1920.
> *The Merry-Go-Round.*   London, Heinemann, 1904.
> *The Bishop's Apron: A Study in the Origins of a Great Family.*   London, Chapman and Hall, 1906.
> *The Explorer.*   London, Heinemann, 1907; New York, Baker and Taylor, 1909.
> *The Magician.*   London, Heinemann, 1908; New York, Duffield, 1909; with *A Fragment of Autobiography,* Heinemann, 1956; New York, Doubleday, 1957.
> *Of Human Bondage.*   New York, Doran, and London, Heinemann, 1915.
> *The Moon and Sixpence.*   London, Heinemann, and New York, Doran, 1919.
> *The Painted Veil.*   New York, Doran, and London, Heinemann, 1925.
> *Cakes and Ale; or, The Skeleton in the Cupboard.*   London, Heinemann, and New York, Doubleday, 1930.
> *The Book-Bag.*   Florence, G. Orioli, 1932.
> *The Narrow Corner.*   London, Heinemann, and New York, Doubleday, 1932.
> *Theatre.*   New York, Doubleday, and London, Heinemann, 1937.
> *Christmas Holiday.*   London, Heinemann, and New York, Doubleday, 1939.
> *Up at the Villa.*   New York, Doubleday, and London, Heinemann, 1941.
> *The Hour Before the Dawn.*   New York, Doubleday, 1942.
> *The Razor's Edge.*   New York, Doubleday, and London, Heinemann, 1944.
> *Then and Now.*   London, Heinemann, and New York, Doubleday, 1946.
> *Catalina: A Romance.*   London, Heinemann, 1948; New York, Doubleday, 1949.

Short Stories

Orientations.   London, Unwin, 1899.
The Trembling of the Leaf: Little Stories of the South Sea Islands.   New York, Doran,
   and London, Heinemann, 1921; as *Sadie Thompson and Other Stories of the South
   Seas*, London, Readers Library, 1928; as *Rain and Other Stories*, Readers Library,
   1933.
Six Stories Written in the First Person Singular.   New York, Doubleday, and London,
   Heinemann, 1931.
The Judgement Seat.   London, Centaur Press, 1934.
East and West: Collected Short Stories.   New York, Doubleday, 1934; as *Altogether*,
   London, Heinemann, 1934.
Cosmopolitans.   New York, Doubleday, 1936; as *Cosmopolitans: Very Short Stories*,
   London, Heinemann, 1936.
The Favorite Short Stories of W. Somerset Maugham.   New York, Doubleday, 1937.
The Mixture as Before.   London, Heinemann, and New York, Doubleday, 1940.
The Unconquered.   New York, House of Books, 1944.
Creatures of Circumstance.   London, Heinemann, and New York, Doubleday, 1947.
East of Suez: Great Stories of the Tropics.   New York, Avon, 1948.
Here and There: Short Stories.   London, Heinemann, 1948.
Complete Short Stories.   London, Heinemann, 3 vols., 1951.
The World Over: Stories of Manifold Places and People.   New York, Doubleday, 1952.
The Best Short Stories, edited by John Beecroft.   New York, Modern Library, 1957.
A Maugham Twelve: Stories, edited by Angus Wilson.   London, Heinemann, 1966;
   with *Cakes and Ale*, New York, Doubleday, 1967.
Malaysian Stories, edited by Anthony Burgess.   Singapore, Heinemann, 1969.
Seventeen Lost Stories, edited by Craig V. Showalter.   New York, Doubleday, 1969.

Plays

Marriages Are Made in Heaven (as *Schiffbrüchig*, produced Berlin, 1902).   Published in
   The Venture Annual, edited by Maugham and Laurence Housman, London, Baillie,
   1903.
A Man of Honour (produced London, 1903).   London, Chapman and Hall, 1903;
   Chicago, Dramatic Publishing Company, 1912.
Mademoiselle Zampa (produced London, 1904).
Lady Frederick (produced London, 1907).   London, Heinemann, 1911; Chicago,
   Dramatic Publishing Company, 1912.
Jack Straw (produced London, 1908).   London, Heinemann, 1911; Chicago, Dramatic
   Publishing Company, 1912.
Mrs. Dot (produced London, 1908).   London, Heinemann, and Chicago, Dramatic
   Publishing Company, 1912.
The Explorer: A Melodrama (produced London, 1908).   London, Heinemann, and
   Chicago, Dramatic Publishing Company, 1912.
Penelope (produced London, 1909).   London, Heinemann, and Chicago, Dramatic
   Publishing Company, 1912.
The Noble Spaniard, adaptation of a work by Ernest Grenet-Dancourt (produced
   London, 1909).   London, Evans, 1953.
Smith (produced London, 1909).   London, Heinemann, and Chicago, Dramatic
   Publishing Company, 1913.
The Tenth Man: A Tragic Comedy (produced London, 1910).   London, Heinemann,
   and Chicago, Dramatic Publishing Company, 1913.
Landed Gentry (as *Grace*, produced London, 1910).   London, Heinemann, and
   Chicago, Dramatic Publishing Company, 1913.
Loaves and Fishes (produced London, 1911).   London, Heinemann, 1924.

A Trip to Brighton, adaptation of a play by Abel Tarride (produced London, 1911).
The Perfect Gentleman, adaptation of a play by Molière (produced London, 1913). Published in *Theatre Arts* (New York), November 1955.
The Land of Promise (produced New Haven, Connecticut, 1913; London, 1914). London, Bickers, 1913.
The Unattainable (as *Caroline*, produced London, 1916). London, Heinemann, 1923; included in *Six Comedies*, 1937.
Our Betters (produced New York, 1917; London, 1923). London, Heinemann, 1923; New York, Doran, 1924.
Love in a Cottage (produced London, 1918).
Caesar's Wife (produced London, 1919). London, Heinemann, 1922; New York, Doran, 1923.
Home and Beauty (produced Atlantic City, New Jersey, and London, 1919; as *Too Many Husbands*, produced New York, 1919). London, Heinemann, 1923; included in *Six Comedies*, 1937.
The Unknown (produced London, 1920). London, Heinemann, and New York, Doran, 1920.
The Circle (produced London, 1921). London, Heinemann, and New York, Doran, 1921.
East of Suez (produced London, 1922). London, Heinemann, and New York, Doran, 1922.
The Camel's Back (produced Worcester, Massachusetts, 1923; London, 1924).
The Constant Wife (produced New York, 1926; London, 1927). New York, Doran, and London, Heinemann, 1927.
The Letter, adaptation of his own story (produced London, 1927). London, Heinemann, and New York, Doran, 1927.
The Sacred Flame (produced New York, 1928; London, 1929). New York, Doubleday, and London, Heinemann, 1928.
The Bread-Winner (produced London, 1930. London, Heinemann, 1930; New York, Doubleday, 1931.
Dramatic Works. London, Heinemann, 6 vols., 1931–34; as *Collected Plays*, 3 vols., 1952.
For Services Rendered (produced London, 1932). London, Heinemann, 1932; New York, Doubleday, 1933.
The Mask and the Face, adaptation of a play by Luigi Chiarelli (produced Boston, 1933).
Sheppey (produced London, 1933). London, Heinemann, 1933; Boston, Baker, 1949.
Six Comedies. New York, Garden City Publishing Company, 1937.
Trio: Stories and Screen Adaptations, with R. C. Sherriff and Noel Langley. London, Heinemann, and New York, Doubleday, 1950.

Screenplay: *The Verger* (in *Trio*), 1950.

Other

The Land of the Blessed Virgin: Sketches and Impressions of Andalusia. London, Heinemann, 1905; New York, Knopf, 1920.
On a Chinese Screen. New York, Doran, and London, Heinemann, 1922.
The Gentleman in the Parlour: A Record of a Journey from Rangoon to Haiphong. London, Heinemann, and New York, Doubleday, 1930.
The Non-Dramatic Works. London, Heinemann, 28 vols., 1934–69.
Don Fernando; or, Variations on Some Spanish Themes. London, Heinemann, and New York, Doubleday, 1935.
My South Sea Island. Chicago, privately printed, 1936.
The Summing Up. London, Heinemann, and New York, Doubleday, 1938.
Books and You. London, Heinemann, and New York, Doubleday, 1940.

France at War.   London, Heinemann, and New York, Doubleday, 1940.

Strictly Personal.   New York, Doubleday, 1941; London, Heinemann, 1942.

The Somerset Maugham Sampler, edited by Jerome Weidman.   New York, Garden City Publishing Company, 1943; as *The Somerset Maugham Pocket Book*, New York, Pocket Books, 1944.

Of Human Bondage, with a Digression on the Art of Fiction (address).   Washington, D.C., Library of Congress, 1946.

Great Novelists and Their Novels: Essays on the Ten Greatest Novels of the World and the Men and Women Who Wrote Them.   Philadelphia, Winston, 1948; revised edition, as *Ten Novels and Their Authors*, London, Heinemann, 1954; as *The Art of Fiction*, New York, Doubleday, 1955.

A Writer's Notebook.   London, Heinemann, and New York, Doubleday, 1949.

A Maugham Reader, edited by Glenway Wescott.   New York, Doubleday, 1950.

The Writer's Point of View (lecture).   London, Cambridge University Press, 1951; Folcroft, Pennsylvania, Folcroft Editions, 1973.

The Vagrant Mood: Six Essays.   London, Heinemann, 1952; New York, Doubleday, 1953.

Mr. Maugham Himself, edited by John Beecroft.   New York, Doubleday, 1954.

The Partial View (includes *The Summing Up* and *A Writer's Notebook*).   London, Heinemann, 1954.

Points of View.   London, Heinemann, 1958; as *Points of View: Five Essays*, New York, Doubleday, 1959.

Purely for My Pleasure.   London, Heinemann, and New York, Doubleday, 1962.

Selected Prefaces and Introductions.   New York, Doubleday, 1963; London, Heinemann, 1964.

Wit and Wisdom, edited by Cecil Hewetson.   London, Duckworth, 1966.

Essays on Literature.   New York, New American Library, and London, New English Library, 1967.

Editor, with Laurence Housman, *The Venture Annual of Art and Literature.*   London, Baillie, 1903.

Editor, with Laurence Housman, *The Venture Annual of Art and Literature 1905.*   London, Simpkin Marshall, 1904.

Editor, *The Truth at Last*, by Charles Hawtrey.   London, Butterworth, 1924.

Editor, *The Travellers' Library.*   New York, Doubleday, 1933; as *Fifty Modern English Writers*, New York, Doubleday, 1933.

Editor, *Tellers of Tales: 100 Short Stories from the United States, England, France, Russia, and Germany.*   New York, Doubleday, 1939; as *The Greatest Stories of All Times*, New York, Garden City Publishing Company, 1943.

Editor, *A Choice of Kipling's Prose.*   London, Macmillan, 1952; as *Maugham's Choice of Kipling's Best*, New York, Doubleday, 1953.

Bibliography: *A Bibliography of the Works of Maugham* by Raymond Toole Scott, London, Nicholas Vane, 1956; revised edition, London, Kaye and Ward, 1973.

*   *   *

Secure in its niche in literary history, *Ashenden* is accepted as the prototype of realistic spy fiction and, after the manner of treatment of such venerable works, quoted and deferred to, but not read. This is unfortunate. Though W. Somerset Maugham's only significant contribution to mystery fiction consists of this one work, it is sufficiently innovative and good – comparing favorably with his best fiction – to deserve the place accorded it. Maugham's comments in the preface on his experience in the Intelligence Corps establish both tone and authorial intent: "The work of an agent ... is on the whole extremely monotonous. A lot of it is uncommonly useless.... In 1917 I went to Russia. I was sent to prevent the Bolshevik

Revolution and to keep Russia in the war. The reader will know that my efforts did not meet with success."

Growing out of such experiences, *Ashenden* was unlikely to become either a paean to the glories of Britain or a description of the glamorous life of a spy. A cross between a collection of stories and a novel, narrated in a cool, often epigrammatic style, the work describes the rather minor role played in a series of encounters and catastrophes by the writer Ashenden (no other name is ever given), who has been recruited to the spying trade in the quiet and unexpected circumstances typical of the developed tradition of such fiction. Ashenden has been described as a kind of litmus paper, registering but not participating in the events of the work in which he appears. This is only partly true. What is true is that the central figure is never allowed to take himself with the seriousness characteristic of so many of his contemporaries and that he is not cast in the mold of "The Great Detective." His greatest joy is a hot bath, his worst fear missing a train, and his view of firearms that they are "apt to go off at the wrong time and make a noise." His hired-assassin acquaintance, the Hairless Mexican, advises him never to play cards with strangers. He takes his Russian lover to Paris on a pre-marriage honeymoon, to avoid embarrassing her husband, only to give her up after concluding that not to do so would mean eating scrambled eggs every morning for the rest of his life.

The effects of love on spies and diplomats is a unifying theme in the series of incidents which make up the work. As a powerful, irrational, and even transfiguring force, it diverts from their apparently destined paths – or dooms – a number of figures. Neither the French peasant woman, nor the Hairless Mexican, nor the fanatic Indian rebel, Chandra Lal, nor the British traitor, nor his German wife is immune. Love tempts the brilliant young diplomat, Byring, and a famous courtesan into a marriage which will end both their promising careers. Even the British Ambassador finds his present success negated by the memory of a lost love. Implicit in the final chapter are assessments of both love and spying. Ashenden's own experience suggests that the destructive forces of love can only be countered by an ironic view which precludes such abandonment of normal reason as commonly accompanies that emotion. As for the turbulent world of the spy, effectively represented by Russia in 1917, death in it is something absurd and rude, as dreadful as hitting a child, almost farce – nothing approaching high tragedy.

In *Ashenden* there is little profound but nothing foolish. If the work does not entirely anticipate the atmosphere of the "cold war," it achieves an effect of thoroughgoing practicality in its presentation of the work of a spy.

—Nancy Ellen Talburt

MAYO, James, See **COULTER, Stephen.**

McBAIN, Ed. Pseudonym for Evan Hunter; also writes as Curt Cannon; Hunt Collins; Ezra Hannon; Richard Marsten. American. Born in New York City, 15 October 1926. Educated at Cooper Union, New York, 1943–44; Hunter College, New York, B.A. 1950 (Phi Beta Kappa). Served in the United States Navy, 1944–46. Married 1) Anita Melnick in 1949 (divorced), three children; 2) Mary Vann Finley in 1973, one step-daughter. Recipient: Mystery Writers of America Edgar Allan Poe Award, 1957. Agent: Owen Laster, William Morris Agency, 1350 Avenue of the Americas, New York, New York 10019. Address: 179 Perry Avenue, Norwalk, Connecticut 06850, U.S.A.

CRIME PUBLICATIONS

Novels (series characters: Officers of the 87th Precinct)

Cut Me In (as Hunt Collins). New York, Abelard Schuman, 1954; London, Boardman, 1960; as *The Proposition*, New York, Pyramid, 1955.

Cop Hater (87th Precinct). New York, Simon and Schuster, 1956; London, Boardman, 1958.

The Mugger (87th Precinct). New York, Simon and Schuster, 1956; London, Boardman, 1959.

The Pusher (87th Precinct). New York, Simon and Schuster, 1956; London, Boardman, 1959.

The Con Man (87th Precinct). New York, Simon and Schuster, 1957; London, Boardman, 1960.

Killer's Choice (87th Precinct). New York, Simon and Schuster, 1958; London, Boardman, 1960.

Killer's Payoff (87th Precinct). New York, Simon and Schuster, 1958; London, Boardman, 1960.

April Robin Murders, with Craig Rice (completed by McBain). New York, Random House, 1958; London, Hammond, 1959.

Lady Killer (87th Precinct). New York, Simon and Schuster, 1958; London, Boardman, 1961.

I'm Cannon — For Hire (as Curt Cannon). New York, Fawcett, 1958; London, Fawcett, 1959.

Killer's Wedge (87th Precinct). New York, Simon and Schuster, 1959; London, Boardman, 1961.

'Til Death (87th Precinct). New York, Simon and Schuster, 1959; London, Boardman, 1961.

King's Ransom (87th Precinct). New York, Simon and Schuster, 1959; London, Boardman, 1961.

Give the Boys a Great Big Hand (87th Precinct). New York, Simon and Schuster, 1960; London, Boardman, 1962.

The Heckler (87th Precinct). New York, Simon and Schuster, 1960; London, Boardman, 1962.

See Them Die (87th Precinct). New York, Simon and Schuster, 1960; London, Boardman, 1963.

Lady, Lady, I Did It! (87th Precinct). New York, Simon and Schuster, 1961; London, Boardman, 1963.

Like Love (87th Precinct). New York, Simon and Schuster, 1962; London, Boardman, 1964.

Ten Plus One (87th Precinct). New York, Simon and Schuster, 1963; London, Hamish Hamilton, 1964.

Ax (87th Precinct). New York, Simon and Schuster, and London, Hamish Hamilton, 1964.

The Sentries. New York, Simon and Schuster, and London, Hamish Hamilton, 1965.

He Who Hesitates (87th Precinct). New York, Delacorte Press, and London, Hamish Hamilton, 1965.

Doll (87th Precinct). New York, Delacorte Press, 1965; London, Hamish Hamilton, 1966.

Eighty Million Eyes (87th Precinct). New York, Delacorte Press, and London, Hamish Hamilton, 1966.

Fuzz (87th Precinct). New York, Doubleday, and London, Hamish Hamilton, 1968.

Shotgun (87th Precinct). New York, Doubleday, and London, Hamish Hamilton, 1969.

Jigsaw (87th Precinct). New York, Doubleday, and London, Hamish Hamilton, 1970.

Hail, Hail, The Gang's All Here! (87th Precinct). New York, Doubleday, and London, Hamish Hamilton, 1971.

Sadie When She Died (87th Precinct). New York, Doubleday, and London, Hamish Hamilton, 1972.

Let's Hear It for the Deaf Man (87th Precinct). New York, Doubleday, and London, Hamish Hamilton, 1973.

Hail to the Chief (87th Precinct). New York, Random House, and London, Hamish Hamilton, 1973.

Bread (87th Precinct). New York, Random House, and London, Hamish Hamilton, 1974.

Where There's Smoke. New York, Random House, and London, Hamish Hamilton, 1975.

Blood Relatives (87th Precinct). New York, Random House, 1975; London, Hamish Hamilton, 1976.

Doors (as Ezra Hannon). New York, Stein and Day, 1975; London, Macmillan, 1976.

Guns. New York, Random House, and London, Hamish Hamilton, 1976.

So Long as You Both Shall Live (87th Precinct). New York, Random House, and London, Hamish Hamilton, 1976.

Long Time No See (87th Precinct). New York, Random House, and London, Hamish Hamilton, 1977.

Goldilocks. New York, Arbor House, and London, Hamish Hamilton, 1978.

Calypso (87th Precinct). New York, Viking Press, and London, Hamish Hamilton, 1979.

Ghosts. London, Hamish Hamilton, 1980.

Novels as Evan Hunter

The Big Fix. N.p., Falcon, 1952; as *So Nude, So Dead* (as Richard Marsten), New York, Fawcett, 1956.

Don't Crowd Me. New York, Popular Library, 1953; London, Consul, 1960; as *The Paradise Party*, London, New English Library, 1968.

The Blackboard Jungle. New York, Simon and Schuster, 1954; London, Constable, 1955.

A Matter of Conviction. New York, Simon and Schuster, and London, Constable, 1959; as *The Young Savages*, New York, Pocket Books, 1966.

A Horse's Head. New York, Delacorte Press, 1967; London, Constable, 1968.

Nobody Knew You Were There. New York, Doubleday, and London, Constable, 1971.

Every Little Crook and Nanny. New York, Doubleday, and London, Constable, 1972.

Come Winter. New York, Doubleday, 1973.

Novels as Richard Marsten

Runaway Black. New York, Fawcett, 1954; London, Red Seal, 1957.

Murder in the Navy. New York, Fawcett, 1955; as *Death of a Nurse* (as Ed McBain), New York, Pocket Books, 1968; London, Hodder and Stoughton, 1972.

The Spiked Heel. New York, Holt, 1956; London, Constable, 1957.

Vanishing Ladies. New York, Permabooks, 1957; London, Boardman, 1961.

Even the Wicked. New York, Permabooks, 1958; London, Severn House, 1979.

Big Man. New York, Pocket Books, 1959.

Short Stories as Evan Hunter

The Jungle Kids.   New York, Pocket Books, 1956; augmented edition, as *The Last Spin and Other Stories*, London, Constable, 1960.
I Like 'em Tough (as Curt Cannon).   New York, Fawcett, 1958.
The Empty Hours (87th Precinct; as Ed McBain).   New York, Simon and Schuster, 1962; London, Boardman, 1963.
Happy New Year, Herbie, and Other Stories.   New York, Simon and Schuster, 1963; London, Constable, 1965.

Uncollected Short Stories as Evan Hunter

"Ticket to Death" and "Chinese Puzzle" (as Richard Marsten), in *Best Detective Stories of the Year 1955*, edited by David Coxe Cooke.   New York, Dutton, 1955.
"A Very Small Homicide," in *The Saint* (New York), July 1959.
"Classification: Dead" (as Richard Marsten), in *Dames, Danger, and Death*, edited by Leo Margulies.   New York, Pyramid, 1960.
"Easy Money," in *Ellery Queen's Mystery Magazine* (New York), September 1960.
"Nightshade" (as Ed McBain), in *Ellery Queen's Mystery Magazine* (New York), August 1970.
"Someone at the Door," in *Ellery Queen's Mystery Magazine* (New York), October 1971.
"Eighty Million Eyes" (as Ed McBain), in *Ellery Queen's Giants of Mystery*.   New York, Davis, 1976.
"What Happened to Annie Barnes?," in *Ellery Queen's Mystery Magazine* (New York), June 1976.

OTHER PUBLICATIONS

Novels as Evan Hunter

Tomorrow and Tomorrow (as Hunt Collins).   New York, Pyramid, 1955; as *Tomorrow's World*, New York, Avalon, 1956.
Second Ending.   New York, Simon and Schuster, and London, Constable, 1956.
Strangers When We Meet.   New York, Simon and Schuster, and London, Constable, 1958.
Mothers and Daughters.   New York, Simon and Schuster, and London, Constable, 1961.
Buddwing.   New York, Simon and Schuster, and London, Constable, 1964.
The Paper Dragon.   New York, Delacorte Press, 1966; London, Constable, 1967.
Last Summer.   New York, Doubleday, 1968; London, Constable, 1969.
Sons.   New York, Doubleday, 1969; London, Constable, 1970.
Streets of Gold.   New York, Harper, 1974; London, Macmillan, 1975.
The Chisholms: A Novel of the Journey West.   New York, Harper, and London, Hamish Hamilton, 1976.
Walk Proud.   New York, Bantam, 1979.

Short Stories

The Beheading and Other Stories.   London, Constable, 1971.
The Easter Man: A Play and Six Stories.   New York, Doubleday, 1972.
Seven.   London, Constable, 1972.

Plays

The Easter Man (produced Birmingham and London, 1964; as A Race of Hairy Men, produced New York, 1965). Included in The Easter Man: A Play and Six Stories, 1972.
The Conjuror (produced Ann Arbor, Michigan, 1969).
Stalemate (produced New York, 1975).

Screenplays: Strangers When We Meet, 1960; The Birds, 1962; Walk Proud, 1979.

Other (juvenile)

Find the Feathered Serpent. Philadelphia, Winston, 1952.
Rocket to Luna (as Richard Marsten). Philadelphia, Winston, 1953; London, Hutchinson, 1954.
Danger: Dinosaurs (as Richard Marsten). Philadelphia, Winston, 1953.
The Remarkable Harry. London, Abelard Schuman, 1961.
The Wonderful Button. New York, Abelard Schuman, 1961; London, Abelard Schuman, 1962.
Me and Mr. Stenner. Philadelphia, Lippincott, 1976; London, Hamish Hamilton, 1977.

Manuscript Collection: Mugar Memorial Library, Boston University.

*   *   *

Evan Hunter has written an imposing body of popular fiction under his own name, but crime readers know him best as Ed McBain, author of the 87th Precinct stories, the longest, the most varied, and by all odds the most popular police procedural series in the world. According to the disclaimer page at the front of each volume, the 87th Precinct is located in an "imaginary city," but most readers will quickly realise that the setting is New York with names of areas and localities changed. The "city," for example, is composed of five boroughs: Isola (Manhattan), where the 87th is located, Riverhead (the Bronx), Majesta (Queens), Calm's Point (Brooklyn), and Bethtown (Staten Island). The reader may be puzzled by the fact that the two big rivers, the Harb and the Dix (the Hudson and East rivers) flow in a westerly direction although the city is located on the east coast, until he realizes that the city is New York rolled over on its side, so that north becomes east, east becomes south, and so on around the compass. The 87th Precinct is particularly well situated for the commission of upper-, middle-, and lower-class crimes. Within its borders are located at least one swanky downtown high-rise residential district, an affluent suburb, several large middle-income areas, blocks upon blocks of festering slums, a large university, and even a convenient number of old gothic mansions.

Ed McBain's stories fit the police procedural pattern better than most series because the work of crime detection is carried on by groups of detectives working in teams. If there is is a "hero" it would be Steve Carella, who is featured in most of the stories, but Carella usually shares the stage with some of the other regulars. There are Lieutenant Peter Byrnes, the competent and respected chief of the detective squad; Meyer Meyer, who learned patience as a Jew growing up in a gentile neighborhood; Bert Kling, who learns both police work and life as a result of mistakes and sorrows; Cotton Hawes, the son of a Protestant minister, who has an almost incredible attraction for women; and a number of other regulars. Generally, the main characters change and mature as the series proceeds. Steve Carella, always a conscientious cop who gives everything he has to his profession, develops a growing empathy with all kinds of people as a result of his happy marriage and the mutual affection between himself and his children. Meyer Meyer, who has not seen the inside of a synagogue in 20 years, faces an identity crisis in the novelette "J" that forces him to question the position of a Jew in modern America. Bert Kling, appearing as a green rookie patrolman at the beginning of the series, matures somewhat with experience, is shattered by the murder of his first fiancée, recovers and lives through two more successive engagements. Some of the characters remain static, however: Andy Parker continues to be a sadist; Arthur Brown, the only black cop on the squad, remains impatient; Dick Genero, surely the stupidest cop in fiction, never learns anything.

Most series writers, once they have hit upon a successful formula, use it over and over until it wears out, but Ed McBain likes to experiment with new patterns. In *Killer's Wedge* he keeps two apparently disparate plots going side by side, one a grisly naturalistic cliff-hanger in which a disturbed woman threatens to blow up the 87th squad with a bottle of nitroglycerine, and the other an old-fashioned locked-room story, the two strands neatly unified by the thematic image stated in the title. *He Who Hesitates* is an experiment in point of view, the story of a "perfect crime" seen entirely through the eyes of the murderer, with the police as only minor figures on the stage. In *Hail, Hail, The Gang's All Here!* McBain manages fourteen distinct story-lines and a cast of characters almost as big as the whole precinct. *Fuzz* is a farce in which the police seem incapable of doing anything right.

The one experimental failure in the series is *Hail to the Chief*, obviously designed as political satire but failing as crime fiction because the Nixon parallel, too labored and too obvious, serves only to obstruct the movement of the narrative. On the other hand, McBain has succeeded with one device never before attempted in the police procedural, the introduction of a series villain. The Deaf Man, who escapes capture at the end of *The Heckler*, re-appears in *Fuzz* and *Let's Hear It for the Deaf Man*, and appears to be indestructible. Each of his episodes involves some fantastic caper which the police manage to foil, but the Deaf Man is always left alive with the prospect of a future re-entry.

Ed McBain is a master of irony, never subtle but always appropriate. It is most obvious in the case of Roger Broome in *He Who Hesitates*: having murdered a young woman and successfully disposed of her body, he never comes under the suspicion of the police, but in a later story gets drunk and makes a public confession of his crime. The irony is also heavy in the promotion of Patrolman Genero, who quite by accident blunders upon a pair of hoodlums and manages to capture them, and in the next story has been promoted to detective third grade for "cracking" the case. The ironic tone is strong in "J," where there is an anti-semitic theme growing out of the murder of a rabbi: the date of the crime is the second day of the Passover *seder* and Easter eve, but it is also April Fool.

The comic spirit is seldom absent from the 87th Precinct stories and has contributed to their success. This spirit makes itself felt in the heavy ironies like those just described, and it is also kept alive in such bizarre characters as Monoghan and Monroe, the almost indistinguishable Tweedledum and Tweedledee of Homicide, who usually make a perfunctory appearance at the scene of a crime, tell a few ribald jokes, suggest a few ways of sweeping the dirt under the rug, and then disappear to more comfortable quarters. There is, of course, an abundance of pathos and even tragedy in the stories, but the comic spirit serves as a leaven and gives the series a balanced tone that is unique in crime fiction.

—George N. Dove

McCARRY, Charles. American. Born in 1929. Journalist and speech writer for the White House; staff member, Central Intelligence Administration, 1957–c. 67.

CRIME PUBLICATIONS

Novels (series character: Paul Christopher in all books except *The Better Angels*)

The Miernik Dossier. New York, Saturday Review Press, 1973; London, Hutchinson, 1974.
The Tears of Autumn. New York, Saturday Review Press, and London, Hutchinson, 1975.
The Secret Lovers. New York, Dutton, and London, Hutchinson, 1977.
The Better Angels. New York, Dutton, and London, Hutchinson, 1979.

OTHER PUBLICATIONS

Other

Citizen Nader. New York, Saturday Review Press, 1972.
Double Eagle, with others. Boston, Little Brown, 1979.

*   *   *

One of the newer generation of thriller writers, Charles McCarry has displayed sensitive writing, versatile plotting and characterization, and masterful attention to detail and background. *The Tears of Autumn* is one of the best of the post-Kennedy assassination thrillers, a sub-genre that has flourished since the event and remains an important index to the cultural paranoia of the country and the time. McCarry has written two spy novels, *The Miernik Dossier* and *The Secret Lovers*, which promise a glowing future in the field.

The major figure of both novels is Paul Christopher, an American agent working in Europe; Christopher is a poet of sorts, a fact which may seem a bit too corny to be true but at least establishes a certain sensitivity in his character. The novels display an almost Jamesian awareness of their European locale, the special authenticity of a loving expatriate writing of an adopted foreign land. *The Secret Lovers*, in a somewhat overripe way, is in fact a rather Jamesian spy novel, detailing the satisfyingly complicated search for a traitor while also examining some rather complicated personal relationships. The most closely examined is the one between Paul Christopher and his wife; it is fascinating and beautifully drawn for about half the book, but then begins to cloy as it detracts from the other relationships it is supposed to parallel. Otherwise, the novel is a fine job, complex, absorbing, elegantly written.

The Miernik Dossier, on the other hand, is something of a masterpiece, a novel of espionage that succeeds at every ambitious level the author attempts and reverberates with possibility. The narrative is carried solely by documents – the reports of various agents, their debriefings, letters, bugged telephone conversations, comments, diaries – and concerns a group of disparate people, all of whom are in one way or another involved in espionage. They travel with a gigantic African prince from Switzerland to his country, reporting on his activity, the work of an apparent revolutionary group, and the person of one Tadeusz Miernik, who may or may not be a spy. The characters are all wonderfully believable, the suspense is beautifully handled, and the question of Miernik's guilt remains a puzzle even to the end, when his death appears to transfigure him in an immolation that is as moving as it is utterly credible. *The Miernik Dossier* is indeed a dossier, but demonstrates an artfulness and meaning that its documentary authenticity suggests without belaboring; it is truly a remarkable book, one of the finest novels of espionage to appear in recent years. If McCarry continues to write as well in the future, he may turn out to be the American John le Carré; there is no higher praise a spy novelist can earn.

—George Grella

McCLOY, Helen (Worrell Clarkson). Also writes as Helen Clarkson. American. Born in New York City, 6 June 1904. Educated at Brooklyn Friends School, 1908–19; the Sorbonne, Paris, 1923–24. Married Davis Dresser, i.e., Brett Halliday, *q.v.*, in 1946 (divorced, 1961), one daughter. Lived abroad, 1923–32: Staff Correspondent, Universal Service (Hearst), Paris, 1927–32; Paris art critic for *International Studio*, 1930–31, and London art critic for *New York Times*, 1930–32; free-lance contributor to London *Morning Post* and *Parnassus*; Co-Founder, with Davis Dresser, Torquil Publishing Company, and Halliday and McCloy Literary Agency, 1953–64; co-author of review column for Connecticut newspapers in 1950's and 1960's. Past President, Mystery Writers of America. Recipient: Mystery Writers of America Edgar Allan Poe Award, for criticism, 1953. Lives in Boston. Agent: Robert P. Mills Ltd., 156 East 52nd Street, New York, New York 10022, U.S.A.

CRIME PUBLICATIONS

Novels (series character: Dr. Basil Willing)

Dance of Death (Willing). New York, Morrow, 1938; as *Design for Dying*, London, Heinemann, 1938.
The Man in the Moonlight (Willing). New York, Morrow, and London, Hamish Hamilton, 1940.
The Deadly Truth (Willing). New York, Morrow, 1941; London, Hamish Hamilton, 1942.
Who's Calling (Willing). New York, Morrow, 1942; London, Nicholson and Watson, 1948.
Cue for Murder (Willing). New York, Morrow, 1942.
Do Not Disturb. New York, Morrow, 1943.
The Goblin Market (Willing). New York, Morrow, 1943; London, Hale, 1951.
Panic. New York, Morrow, 1944; London, Gollancz, 1972.
The One That Got Away (Willing). New York, Morrow, 1945; London, Gollancz, 1954.
She Walks Alone. New York, Random House, 1948; London, Coker, 1950; as *Wish You Were Dead*, New York, Spivak, 1958.
Through a Glass, Darkly (Willing). New York, Random House, 1950; London, Gollancz, 1951.
Better Off Dead. New York, Dell, 1951.
Alias Basil Willing. New York, Random House, and London, Gollancz, 1951.
Unfinished Crime. New York, Random House, 1954; as *He Never Came Back*, London, Gollancz, 1954.
The Long Body (Willing). New York, Random House, 1955; London, Gollancz, 1956.
Two-Thirds of a Ghost (Willing). New York, Random House, 1956; London, Gollancz, 1957.
The Slayer and the Slain. New York, Random House, 1957; London, Gollancz, 1958.
Before I Die. New York, Torquil, and London, Gollancz, 1963.
The Futher Side of Fear. New York, Dodd Mead, and London, Gollancz, 1967.
Mr. Splitfoot (Willing). New York, Dodd Mead, 1968; London, Gollancz, 1969.
A Question of Time. New York, Dodd Mead, and London, Gollancz, 1971.
A Change of Heart. New York, Dodd Mead, and London, Gollancz, 1973.
The Sleepwalker. New York, Dodd Mead, and London, Gollancz, 1974.
Minotaur Country. New York, Dodd Mead, and London, Gollancz, 1975.
The Changeling Conspiracy. New York, Dodd Mead, 1976; as *Cruel as the Grave*, London, Gollancz, 1977.
The Imposter. New York, Dodd Mead, 1977; London, Gollancz, 1978.
The Smoking Mirror. New York, Dodd Mead, and London, Gollancz, 1979.

Short Stories

The Singing Diamonds and Other Stories. New York, Dodd Mead, 1965; as *Surprise,
Surprise*, London, Gollancz, 1965.

Uncollected Short Stories

"A Case of Innocent Eavesdropping," in *Ellery Queen's Mystery Magazine* (New York),
March 1978.
"Murphy's Law," in *Ellery Queen's Mystery Magazine* (New York), May 1979.
"That Bug That's Going Around," in *Ellery Queen's Mystery Magazine* (New York),
August 1979.

OTHER PUBLICATIONS

Novel

The Last Day (as Helen Clarkson). New York, Torquil. 1959.

Other

Editor, with Brett Halliday, *20 Great Tales of Murder.* New York, Random House,
1951; London, Hammond, 1952.

Manuscript Collection: Mugar Memorial Library, Boston University.

Helen McCloy comments:
Self-criticism is as difficult an art as autobiography, both being forms of fiction. How can
any writer be detached enough to see himself or his work objectively? I cannot say what I
have done. I can only say what I have tried to do.
I began in 1938 trying to write the classic detective story with a detective who appears in
each book, a startling or puzzling beginning followed by twists and turns in the plot,
including hidden clues to the murderer, and a surprise ending in which those clues are shown
to lead rationally to one guilty person.
It is a form as rigid as the sonnet or the haiku, and novels of killing, torture, and sex in
which crime and detection are incidental have nothing to do with it. The true detective story
is fun to write and fun to read. Perhaps that is why a society still unconsciously puritanical in
some things frowns upon it. "A good read" is a critic's term of reproach. Readers are not
supposed to get pleasure out of reading. It is supposed to be a painful duty and therefore an
act of virtue. To this day some people state with unmistakable pride that they read only a
curiously negative form of literature known as "non-fiction." The pride seems to stem from
the fact that so much non-fiction is so inexorably tedious that only an heroic reader can
struggle through it. When the novel itself first developed it was scorned for the same reason.
It gave pleasure and who wants pleasure?
I hope that my own detective, Dr. Basil Willing, gave pleasure to the readers of the books
and stories in which he appeared. I liked him myself. He was, I believe, the first American
psychiatrist detective and I am pretty sure he was the first psychiatrist detective to use
psychiatry in detecting clues as well as in analyzing the criminal mind. He came from
Baltimore, but he had a Russian mother. This made it plausible for him to be a fluent linguist,
who could study psychiatry in Paris and Vienna after beginning at Johns Hopkins.
When we first meet him in *Dance of Death*, he is a forensic psychiatric assistant to the
District Attorney of New York County, and he lives on Murray Hill, where there were still
more brownstones than skyscrapers in 1938. Two books, *The Goblin Market* and *The One
That Got Away*, tell us a good deal about his war career in Naval Intelligence, but the war

haunts all the early books. When they are re-issued, references to the war are sometimes deleted. I now think this was a mistake. Those war references have real historical interest today. In the tenth book, *Through a Glass, Darkly*, Willing marries an Austrian refugee, Gisela von Hohenems, who first appeared in *The Man in the Moonlight*. In later short stories we find him a widower, removed to Boston, writing books and lecturing at Harvard, with a daughter named Gisela after her mother.

Anyone reading my books in series will notice that they get further and further away from the classic detective story pattern as they go along. Apparently I was responding to a trend which came after the war demanding more suspense and less detection. I think that was another mistake, one I hope to rectify in future. I have a feeling that we are now on the verge of a return to the classic detective story. The only thing about fashion that is certain is that it will change. These changes are brought about periodically in all the arts by satiety. When any school of writing or painting or music is run into the ground, the public turns to something new which is usually something old in disguise.

Mystery writers are often asked why the detective story is popular. Could this popularity come from the fact that the detective story is one of the few surviving forms of story-telling? Love of the story is older than any folk-lore we know, as old as human language itself. In the 19th century someone said that a picture must never tell a story. In the 20th century a great many writers seem to believe that a story should never tell a story, so the readers turn to the painful prestige of non-fiction or the detective story.

*   *   *

Helen McCloy's 40-year career as a writer, critic, and editor of mystery stories has enabled her to produce an imposing body of work, impressive in its quality as well as its quantity. Her cosmopolitan schooling in the United States and France and her work as a newspaper correspondent in Paris have furnished her with a rich background, often featured in her fiction. McCloy's versatility is manifest in the structure, setting, and theme of her works. She has employed both the classic plot of detection as well as the more loosely structured psychological thriller. For her settings she writes convincingly about New York City, Boston, rural New England, Scotland, Latin America, and, in at least one short story, China. That she frequently ties her stories to some document of literary or historical interest is evidence of her wide reading.

Dr. Basil Willing is the detective she uses most often in her early novels, which, like those of Ellery Queen, are most dependably modeled on the classic pattern. In his development over the years he bears a particularly strong resemblance to Ngaio Marsh's Roderick Alleyn: through the course of the novels he meets, marries, and is widowed by the exotic Gisela von Hohenems. Also like many fictional detectives during World War II, Willing saw military service. However, Willing is not merely a pale copy of earlier detectives. As McCloy points out, he is unusual in that he is the first American psychiatrist detective and the first to use psychiatry in discovering clues, as well as in understanding the criminal personality. Dr. Willing appears in 12 of McCloy's novels, and in several short stories.

Novels that do not have the benefit of Willing's expertise tend to be psychological thrillers which focus on an innocent relative of the criminal suspect. An example of this sort of plot is *A Change of Heart*, in which the protagonist's father suffers from the fear that he has accidentally murdered a man. Similarly, *Before I Die* is told from the point of view of a wronged wife, who eventually manages to clear her husband from the suspicion of the murder of the wronged husband. McCloy is as adept at writing the psychological thriller as she is the standard "whodunit," although she has indicated a personal preference for the earlier form.

One of the most impressive characteristics of McCloy's work is her use of literary sources both as a thematic and structural device. Thus the title of *The Goblin Market* is a borrowing from Christina Rossetti and *The Long Body* refers to a philosophical concept in the Upanishads. *Cue for Murder* is a celebrated early novel not only because it captures the flavor of war-time New York so well, but also because it revolves around a revival of Sardou's

Fédora. Two-Thirds of a Ghost, her spoof on publishing practices, contains several comments on the current literary scene and compares serious literature to popular writing. For example, one of the professional critics in the novel concludes a brief discourse on literary fashion with "Today a plot is indecent anywhere outside a mystery, the last refuge of the conservative writer."

In good Holmesian tradition, McCloy has her detectives solve problems by keen observation and application of arcane scientific truths. The use of poisons, the unravelling of codes, optical illusions of various sorts, and other physiological and psychological clues are typical ploys. For instance, in "A Case of Innocent Eavesdropping" the crime is solved through Willing's ability to test eye dominance.

Running counter to traditional practice, McCloy also includes in her mysteries such non-scientific phenomena as flying saucers, poltergeists, and pre-vision. Both the short story and novel entitled *Through a Glass, Darkly* deal skillfully with the *doppelgänger*, an element of plot that flies in the face of Ronald Knox's prohibition against doubles in his ten commandments for the detective story writer.

Surprisingly and regrettably, critics have tended to neglect Helen McCloy's work, perhaps because it sometimes is unfashionably solemn. Yet the variety and the urbane erudition demonstrated in her short stories and novels make them an undisputed and valuable contribution to American detective fiction.

—Nancy C. Joyner

McCLURE, James (Howe). British. Born in Johannesburg, South Africa, 9 October 1939. Educated at Scottsville School, 1947–51, Cowan House, 1952–54, and Maritzburg College, 1955–58, all in Pietermaritzburg, Natal. Married Lorelee Ellis in 1962; two sons and one daughter. Commercial photographer, 1958–59; taught English and art at Cowan House, 1959–63; Reporter, *Natal Witness*, 1963–64, *Natal Mercury*, 1964–65, and *Daily News*, 1965, all Pietermaritzburg; Sub-Editor, *Daily Mail*, Edinburgh, 1965–66, and *Oxford Mail* and *Oxford Times*, 1966–73; Deputy Editor, Oxford Times Group, 1973–74. Since 1975, Managing Director, Sabensa Gakulu Ltd., Oxford. Recipient: Crime Writers Association Gold Dagger, 1971, and Silver Dagger, 1976. Agent: A. D. Peters and Company Ltd., 10 Buckingham Street, London WC2N 6BU. Address: Sabensa Gakulu Ltd., 14 York Road, Headington, Oxford OX3 8NW, England.

CRIME PUBLICATIONS

Novels (series characters: Lieutenant Kramer and Sergeant Zondi in all books except *Four and Twenty Virgins* and *Rogue Eagle*)

The Steam Pig. London, Gollancz, 1971; New York, Harper, 1972.
The Caterpillar Cop. London, Gollancz, 1972; New York, Harper, 1973.
Four and Twenty Virgins. London, Gollancz, 1973.
The Gooseberry Fool. London, Gollancz, and New York, Harper, 1974.
Snake. London, Gollancz, 1975; New York, Harper, 1976.
Rogue Eagle. London, Macmillan, and New York, Harper, 1976.
The Sunday Hangman. London, Macmillan, and New York, Harper, 1977.

Uncollected Short Stories

"Scandal at Sandkop," in *Winter's Crimes 7*, edited by George Hardinge. London, Macmillan, 1975.
"Daddy's Turn," in *Winter's Crimes 9*, edited by George Hardinge. London, Macmillan, 1977.

OTHER PUBLICATIONS

Other

Killers. London, Fontana, 1976.
"Book One: To Be Continued" and "Corella of the 87th," in *Murder Ink: The Mystery Reader's Companion*, edited by Dilys Winn. New York, Workman, 1977.

*   *   *

James McClure is no doubt one of the most interesting crime writers to have appeared during the last decade. There are many reasons for this judgment.

McClure's novels are set in South Africa, mostly in the town of Trekkersburg, which seems to be a fairly accurate picture of Pietermaritzburg, where the author lived for many years. The most astonishing fact concerning these crime novels, which feature the police team of Lieutenant Kramer and his Zulu assistant Sergeant Zondi, is that McClure succeeds in making them into very acrimonious and unveiled reports on the current South African system without raising his voice and above all without being demagogic. The facts he reveals about the racial situation are sufficient to get his readers to think and to draw their own conclusions. In my opinion McClure's novels become as important in this respect as the works of Alan Paton, Nadine Gordimer, and André Brink. McClure's choice of genre was a very conscious one. He felt that while young people may read books and essays critical of the South African regime, older people were not likely to be as interested. By writing detective fiction, a favourite reading for many elderly people, McClure thought he could influence that generation.

In an interview McClure told me that he had taken a great interest in the 87th Precinct novels by Ed McBain. In a way his own books belong to the procedural school, for in a very convincing, realistic way they show the hard work done by the police force. This is especially true of *The Sunday Hangman*, one of his best novels. John D. MacDonald is also among his favourites in the genre. Although he isn't fond of the puzzle stories of the Golden Thirties, his plots are very cleverly constructed, particularly that of *The Caterpillar Cop*. Among McClure's works outside the Kramer-Zondi cycle the most ambitious is *Rogue Eagle*, a thriller set in the present-day Lesotho. This is one of the best political thrillers for a long time, and in some ways is even better than the Kramer-Zondi novels which run the risk of being somewhat alike.

—Jan Broberg

McCOY, Horace. American. Born in Pegram, Tennessee, 14 April 1897. Educated in schools in Nashville. Served in the United States Army Air Corps during World War I. Sports Editor, Dallas *Journal* 1919–30; co-founder of Dallas Little Theatre; scriptwriter in Hollywood after 1931. *Died in 1959.*

CRIME PUBLICATIONS

Novels

> *They Shoot Horses, Don't They?* New York, Simon and Schuster, and London, Barker, 1935.
> *No Pockets in a Shroud.* London, Barker, 1937; New York, New American Library, 1948.
> *I Should Have Stayed Home.* New York, Knopf, and London, Barker, 1938.
> *Kiss Tomorrow Goodbye.* New York, Random House, 1948; London, Barker, 1949.
> *Scalpel.* New York, Appleton Century Crofts, 1952; London, Barker, 1953.
> *Corruption City.* New York, Dell, 1959; London, Consul, 1961.

Uncollected Short Story

> "Girl in the Grave," in *Half-a-Hundred: Tales by Great American Writers*, edited by Charles Grayson. New York, Garden City Publishing Company, 1945.

OTHER PUBLICATIONS

Plays

> *I Should Have Stayed Home* (screenplay), edited by Bruce S. Kupelnick. New York, Garland, 1978.

Screenplays: *Postal Inspector*, with Robert Presnell, Sr., 1936; *The Trail of the Lonesome Pine*, with Grover Jones and Harvey Thew, 1936; *Parole!*, with others, 1936; *Dangerous to Know*, with William R. Lipman, 1938; *Hunted Men*, with William R. Lipman, 1938; *King of the Newsboys*, with others, 1938; *Persons in Hiding*, with William R. Lipman, 1939; *Parole Fixer*, with William R. Lipman, 1939; *Television Spy*, with others, 1939; *Island of Lost Men*, with William R. Lipman, 1939; *Undercover Doctor*, with others, 1939; *Women Without Names*, with William R. Lipman, 1940; *Texas Rangers Ride Again*, with William R. Lipman, 1940; *Queen of the Mob*, with William R. Lipman, 1940; *Wild Geese Calling*, 1941; *Texas*, with Lewis Meltzer and Michael Blankfort, 1941; *Valley of the Sun*, 1942; *Gentleman Jim*, with Vincent Lawrence, 1942; *Flight for Freedom*, with others, 1943; *Appointment in Berlin*, with Michael Hogan and B. P. Fineman, 1943; *There's Something about a Soldier*, with Barry Trivers, 1943; *The Fabulous Texan*, with Lawrence Hazard and Hal Long, 1947; *Montana Belle*, with others, 1949; *The Fireball*, with Tay Garnett, 1950; *Bronco Buster*, with Lillie Hayward and Peter B. Kyne, 1952; *The Lusty Men*, with David Dortort and Claude Stanush, 1952; *The World in His Arms*, with Borden Chase, 1952; *The Turning Point*, with Warren Duff, 1953; *Bad for Each Other*, with Irving Wallace, 1954; *Dangerous Mission*, with others, 1954; *Rage at Dawn*, with Frank Gruber, 1955; *The Road to Denver*, with Allen Rivkin, 1955; *Texas Lady*, 1955.

Bibliography: in "The Life and Writings of Horace McCoy" by John Thomas Sturak, unpublished dissertation, Los Angeles, University of California, 1976.

*   *   *

Four of Horace McCoy's novels deal with violent death, but in two of them, *They Shoot Horses, Don't They?* and *I Should Have Stayed Home*, the deaths result from circumstances inherent in McCoy's grim, deterministic Southern California (which the marathon dance contest of his first novel captures with a brilliant intensity never repeated in his later work) rather than from mystery or thriller formulas. Two of his novels, *No Pockets in a Shroud* and *Kiss Tomorrow Goodbye*, however, show clearly why he is generally regarded as a leading member of the "hard-boiled" school of fiction. Both novels, like Hammett's *Red Harvest*, vividly depict the American city of the 1930's as almost totally corrupt, with violence and depravity as the casual by-products of everyday existence, and both novels have central characters who are individualistic, tough, and doomed. In the earlier novel Mike Dolan, a crusading reporter, is destroyed through a mixture of his own impetuosity and the forces of evil in his city; in the later novel, Ralph Cotter, a Dolan turned criminal psychopath, falls foul of the same two forces. At his best McCoy has a vigorous style, a keen ear for dialogue, and a robust sense of the dark underside of the American dream. These virtues are, however, sometimes vitiated by inconsistency of characterisation deriving from repetitive and hurried plotting and a penchant for including "topical" material, such as the fascist group in *No Pockets in a Shroud* or the Oedipal complexities of Cotter's memory in *Kiss Tomorrow Goodbye*, with too little attempt to relate these aspects either to the requirements of the plot or to a coherent social/psychological view of man.

—John S. Whitley

McCUTCHAN, (Donald) Philip. Also writes as Robert Conington Galway; Duncan MacNeil; T. I. G. Wigg. British. Born in Cambridge, 13 October 1920. Educated at St. Helen's College, Southsea, Hampshire, 1926–34; studied for H.M. Forces entry examination, 1934–38; Royal Military College, Sandhurst, 1938. Served in the Royal Naval Volunteer Reserve, 1939–46: Lieutenant. Married Elizabeth May Ryan in 1951; one son and one daughter. Assistant Purser, Orient Steam Navigation Company, London, 1946–49; Accounts Assistant, Anglo-Iranian Oil Company, London, 1949–52; taught in preparatory schools, 1952–54; ran a teashop, 1953–60. Full-time writer since 1960. Chairman, Crime Writers Association, 1965–66. Address: c/o Barclays Bank Ltd., 90 Osborne Road, Southsea, Hampshire PO5 3LW, England.

CRIME PUBLICATIONS

Novels (series characters: Lieutenant St. Vincent Halfhyde; Detective Chief Superintendent Simon Shard; Commander Edmonde Shaw)

Whistle and I'll Come. London, Harrap, 1957.
The Kid. London, Harrap, 1958.
Storm South. London, Harrap, 1959.
Gibraltar Road (Shaw). London, Harrap, 1960; New York, Berkley, 1965.
Redcap (Shaw). London, Harrap, 1961; New York, Berkley, 1965.

Hopkinson and the Devil of Hate. London, Harrap, 1961.
Bluebolt One (Shaw). London, Harrap, 1962; New York, Berkley, 1965.
Leave the Dead Behind Us. London, Harrap, 1962.
Marley's Empire. London, Harrap, 1963.
The Man from Moscow (Shaw). London, Harrap, 1963; New York, Day, 1965.
Warmaster (Shaw). London, Harrap, 1963; New York, Day, 1964.
Moscow Coach (Shaw). London, Harrap, 1964; New York, Day, 1966.
Bowering's Breakwater. London, Harrap, 1964.
Sladd's Evil. London, Harrap, 1965; New York, Day, 1967.
A Time for Survival. London, Harrap, 1966.
The Dead Line (Shaw). London, Harrap, and New York, Berkley, 1966.
Skyprobe (Shaw). London, Harrap, 1966; New York, Day, 1967.
Poulter's Passage. London, Harrap, 1967.
The Day of the Coastwatch. London, Harrap, 1968.
The Screaming Dead Balloons (Shaw). London, Harrap, and New York, Day, 1968.
The Bright Red Businessmen (Shaw). London, Harrap, and New York, Day, 1969.
The All-Purpose Bodies (Shaw). London, Harrap, 1969; New York, Day, 1970.
Hartinger's Mouse (Shaw). London, Harrap, 1970.
Man, Let's Go On. London, Harrap, 1970.
Half a Bag of Stringer. London, Harrap, 1970.
This Drakotny (Shaw). London, Harrap, 1971.
The German Helmet. London, Harrap, 1972.
The Oil Bastards. London, Harrap, 1972.
Pull My String. London, Harrap, 1973.
Coach North. London, Harrap, 1974; New York, Walker, 1975.
Beware, Beware the Bight of Benin (Halfhyde). London, Barker, 1974; as *Beware the Bight of Benin*, New York, St. Martin's Press, 1975; London, Futura, 1976.
Call for Simon Shard. London, Harrap, 1974.
A Very Big Bang (Shard). London, Hodder and Stoughton, 1975.
Halfhyde's Island. London, Weidenfeld and Nicolson, 1975; New York, St. Martin's Press, 1976.
Blood Run East (Shard). London, Hodder and Stoughton, 1976.
The Guns of Arrest (Halfhyde). London, Weidenfeld and Nicolson, and New York, St. Martin's Press, 1976.
The Eros Affair (Shard). London, Hodder and Stoughton, 1977.
Halfhyde to the Narrows. London, Weidenfeld and Nicolson, and New York, St. Martin's Press, 1977.
Blackmail North (Shard). London, Hodder and Stoughton, 1978.
Halfhyde for the Queen. London, Weidenfeld and Nicolson, and New York, St. Martin's Press, 1978.
Sunstrike (Shaw). London, Hodder and Stoughton, 1979.
Halfhyde Ordered South. London, Weidenfeld and Nicolson, 1979.

Novels as T. I. G. Wigg

A Job with the Boys. London, Dobson, 1958.
For the Sons of Gentlemen. London, Dobson, 1960.
A Rum for the Captain. London, Dobson, 1961.

Novels as Robert Conington Galway (series character: James Packard in all books)

Assignment New York. London, Hale, 1963.
Assignment London. London, Hale, 1963.
Assignment Andalusia. London, Hale, 1965.
Assignment Malta. London, Hale, 1966.

Assignment Gaolbreak. London, Hale, 1968.
Assignment Argentina. London, Hale, 1969.
Assignment Fenland. London, Hale, 1969.
Assignment Seabed. London, Hale, 1969.
Assignment Sydney. London, Hale, 1970.
Assignment Death Squad. London, Hale, 1970.
The Negative Man. London, Hale, 1971.

Novels as Duncan MacNeil (series character: Captain James Ogilvie in all books)

Drums along the Khyber. London, Hodder and Stoughton, 1969; New York, St. Martin's Press, 1973.
Lieutenant of the Line. London, Hodder and Stoughton, 1970; New York, St. Martin's Press, 1973.
Sadhu on the Mountain Peak. London, Hodder and Stoughton, 1971; New York, St. Martin's Press, 1974.
The Gates of Kunarja. London, Hodder and Stoughton, 1972; New York, St. Martin's Press, 1974.
The Red Daniel. London, Hodder and Stoughton, 1973; New York, St. Martin's Press, 1974.
Subaltern's Choice. London, Hodder and Stoughton, and New York, St. Martin's Press, 1974.
By Command of the Viceroy. London, Hodder and Stoughton, and New York, St. Martin's Press, 1975.
The Mullah from Kashmir. London, Hodder and Stoughton, 1976; New York, St. Martin's Press, 1977.
Wolf in the Fold. London, Hodder and Stoughton, and New York, St. Martin's Press, 1977.
Charge of Cowardice. London, Hodder and Stoughton, and New York, St. Martin's Press, 1978.
The Restless Frontier. London, Hodder and Stoughton, 1979.

OTHER PUBLICATIONS

Plays

Radio Plays and Features: *The Proper Service Manner*, 1954; *Unlawful Occasions*, 1954; *First Command*, 1954; *The Feast of Lanterns*, 1955; *Thirty-Four for Tea*, 1955; *A Run Ashore*, 1956; *Flash Point*, 1956; *The Great Siege*, 1956; *In Partnership*, 1958; *O'Flynn of UB1* (for children), 1963.

Other

On Course for Danger (juvenile). London, Macmillan, and New York, St. Martin's Press, 1959.
Tall Ships: The Golden Age of Sail. London, Weidenfeld and Nicolson, and New York, Crown, 1976.
Great Yachts. London, Weidenfeld and Nicolson, and New York, Crown, 1979.

Philip McCutchan comments:
My main work falls into four, or perhaps I should say five, groups: "individual" novels using different characters each time; a series featuring Commander Shaw, initially of Naval Intelligence but later of the semi-official organization known as 6D2; another series featuring Detective Chief Superintendent Simon Shard, seconded to the Foreign Office from Scotland

Yard; and yet another series set in the Royal Navy of the 1890's, when steam had not long replaced sail, featuring Lieutenant St. Vincent Halfhyde, R.N., descendant of a gunner's mate who had fought at Trafalgar under Lord Nelson. In addition, under the pseudonym Duncan MacNeil, I write a series of military novels, set on the North-West Frontier of India in the 1890's and featuring Captain James Ogilvie of the 114th Highlanders, The Queen's Own Royal Strathspeys. I have a consuming interest in the 1890's as may perhaps be judged, but also very much enjoy writing the kind of book in which Shaw and Simon Shard appear. As to the "individual" books, I find that I have been taken over by my series characters to such an extent that I find no time in which to write anything else these days – and, in any case, I have grown fond of all my series characters and can't wait to get back to the next one as I finish (regretfully) the one before!

*   *   *

Philip McCutchan's early novels were primarily concerned with the sea, where his experience in the Royal Navy and the Merchant Navy provided authentic detail for the background of his stories. Sea thrillers in themselves are not the easiest of subjects and, without a series character, very much rely upon the author's story-telling to remain convincing. McCutchan's characterisation is excellent and he can sustain suspense until the last page. *Hopkinson and the Devil of Hate* and *Storm South* are good examples of this type of novel. It is not unnatural that his first series character should have a naval background. Commander Esmonde Shaw works for one of the branches of the Ministry of Defence – 6D2. All his assignments are invariably politically sensitive and, in consequence, the pace is fast and the plots inventive.

Latterly McCutchan has moved away from the sea and one has a feeling that this could well have happened before to the advantage of both McCutchan and his readers. *Coach North*, the story of a coach hijack, is a first rate thriller. Also in 1974 he introduced a new series character called Simon Shard, a particularly engaging detective. He is both ruthless and efficient, backed up by plots that are well worked out as well as being entertaining. *A Very Big Bang* is Shard at his best.

—Donald C. Ireland

MCDONALD, Gregory. American. Born in Shrewsbury, Massachusetts, 15 February 1937. Educated at Chauncy Hall School; Harvard University, Cambridge, Massachusetts, B.A. 1958. Married Susan Aiken in 1963; two sons. Journalist: Arts and Humanities Editor and Critic-at-Large, Boston *Globe*, 1966–73. Self-employed writer. Recipient: U.P.I. award, for journalism; Mystery Writers of America Edgar Allan Poe Award, 1975, 1977. Agent: William Morris Agency, 1350 Avenue of the Americas, New York, New York 10019. Address: P.O. Box 193, Lincoln, Massachusetts 01773, U.S.A.

CRIME PUBLICATIONS

Novels (series character: Irwin "Fletch" Fletcher)

> *Fletch.* Indianapolis, Bobbs Merrill, 1974; London, Gollancz, 1976.
> *Confess, Fletch.* New York, Avon, 1976; London, Gollancz, 1977.
> *Flynn.* New York, Avon, 1977; London, Gollancz, 1978.

Fletch's Fortune.   New York, Avon, and, London, Gollancz, 1978.
Fletch Forever.   New York, Doubleday, 1978.

OTHER PUBLICATIONS

Novels

Running Scared.   New York, Obolensky, 1964; London, Gollancz, 1977.
Love among the Mashed Potatoes.   New York, Dutton, 1978.

Manuscript Collection: Mugar Memorial Library, Boston University.

*   *   *

Gregory Mcdonald burst upon the mystery field with Edgar Awards for his first two books, *Fletch* and *Confess, Fletch,* and a nomination for his third, *Flynn.* He writes fast-moving, well-plotted stories featuring humorous, likeable characters and sparkling, witty dialogue.

Fletch introduces his principal series character, Irwin Maurice Fletcher, known as Fletch, a top investigative reporter. While working undercover at a beach to expose a drug ring Fletch is offered fifty thousand dollars by a dying millionaire to kill him, ostensibly so the man's wife will benefit from a huge insurance policy. Fletch is skeptical, and, through the use of some very felicitous (and amusing) lying, is able to solve both cases. Much of the book, like the ones that have followed it, is written in dialogue, at which Mcdonald is expert.

After *Fletch's* success in paperback, Mcdonald decided to publish his subsequent books as paperback originals. In *Confess, Fletch* Fletch, in Boston to search for some stolen paintings, finds a naked female corpse in his borrowed apartment. He comes up against a formidable (but engaging) opponent in Inspector Francis Xavier Flynn, who was popular enough to warrant a book of his own, *Flynn,* where he investigates the explosion of an airliner shortly after takeoff. *Fletch's Fortune* has Fletch blackmailed by the CIA into bugging a convention of journalists. Mcdonald is one of the real discoveries of the seventies.

—Jeffrey Meyerson

McGERR, Patricia. American. Born in Falls City, Nebraska, 26 December 1917. Educated at Trinity College, Washington, D.C., 1933–34; University of Nebraska, Lincoln, B.A. 1936; Columbia University, New York, M.S. in journalism 1937. Director of Public Relations, American Road Builders Association, Washington, D.C., 1937–43; Assistant Editor, *Construction Methods* magazine, New York, 1943–48. Self-employed writer. Recipient: Catholic Press Association prize, 1950; Grand Prix de Littérature Policière, 1952; *Ellery Queen's Mystery Magazine* prize, 1967. Agent: Curtis Brown Ltd., 575 Madison Avenue, New York, New York 10022. Address: 5415 Connecticut Avenue N.W., Washington, D.C. 20015, U.S.A.

Crime Publications

Novels (series character: Selena Mead)

> *Pick Your Victim.* New York, Doubleday, 1946; London, Collins, 1947.
> *The Seven Deadly Sisters.* New York, Doubleday, 1947; London, Collins, 1948.
> *Catch Me If You Can.* New York, Doubleday, 1948; London, Collins, 1949.
> *Save the Witness.* New York, Doubleday, 1949; London, Collins, 1950.
> *... Follow, As the Night....* New York, Doubleday, 1950; as *Your Loving Victim*, London, Collins, 1951.
> *Death in a Million Living Rooms.* New York, Doubleday, 1951; as *Die Laughing*, London, Collins, 1952.
> *Fatal in My Fashion.* New York, Doubleday, 1954; London, Collins, 1955.
> *Is There a Traitor in the House?* (Mead). New York, Doubleday, 1964; London, Collins, 1965.
> *Murder Is Absurd.* New York, Doubleday, and London, Gollancz, 1967.
> *Stranger with My Face.* Washington, Luce, 1968; London, Hale, 1970.
> *For Richer, For Poorer, Till Death.* Washington, Luce, 1969; London, Hale, 1971.
> *Legacy of Danger* (Mead). Washington, Luce, 1970.
> *Daughter of Darkness.* New York, Popular Library, 1974.
> *Dangerous Landing.* New York, Dell, 1975.

Uncollected Short Stories

> "Murder to the Twist," in *Ellery Queen's Mystery Magazine* (New York), October 1962.
> "The Washington, D.C. Murders," in *Ellery Queen's Mystery Magazine* (New York), September 1963.
> "Justice Has a High Price," in *Ellery Queen's Mystery Mix.* New York, Random House, 1963; London, Gollancz, 1964.
> "The King Will Die Tonight," in *This Week* (New York), 27 October 1963.
> "Question, Mr. President," in *This Week* (New York), 8 December 1963.
> "Grand Prize for Selena," in *This Week* (New York), 23 February 1964.
> "Holiday for a Lady Spy," in *This Week* (New York), 5 April 1964.
> "Latin Lesson," in *This Week* (New York), 21 June 1964.
> "Easy Conquest," in *This Week* (New York), 5 July 1964.
> "Secret of Carthage," in *This Week* (New York), 27 September 1964.
> "Murder in Red," in *This Week* (New York), 4 October 1964.
> "Fox Hunt for Selena," in *This Week* (New York), 12 December 1964.
> "Fellow Traveler," in *This Week* (New York), 14 March 1965.
> "Ballad for a Spy," in *This Week* (New York), 18 April 1965.
> "Truth or Consequences," in *This Week* (New York), 27 June 1965.
> "Selena's Black Sheep," in *This Week* (New York), 15 August 1965.
> "Good Loser," in *This Week* (New York), 5 September 1965.
> "Prophet Without Honor," in *This Week* (New York), 17 October 1965.
> "Legacy of Danger," in *Alfred Hitchcock Presents: Sinister Spies.* New York, Random House, 1966; London, Reinhardt, 1967.
> "A Time to Die," in *This Week* (New York), 16 January 1966.
> "Palace Spy," in *This Week* (New York), 6 March 1966.
> "Silent Night, Frantic Night," in *This Week* (New York), 25 December 1966.
> "Ladies with a Past" and "Selena in Atlantic City," in *Spies and More Spies*, edited by Robert Arthur. New York, Random House, 1967.
> "Match Point in Berlin," in *Ellery Queen's Murder Menu.* Cleveland, World, and London, Gollancz, 1969.
> "Selena Robs the White House," in *Murder Most Foul*, edited by Harold Q. Masur. New York, Walker, 1971.

"Campaign Fever," in *Alfred Hitchcock Presents: Stories to Stay Awake By.* New York, Random House, 1971.

"This One's a Beauty," in *Ellery Queen's Mystery Bag.* Cleveland, World, 1972; London, Gollancz, 1973.

"The Last Check," in *Ellery Queen's Mystery Magazine* (New York), March 1972.

"Winner Takes All," in *Ellery Queen's Crookbook.* New York, Random House, and London, Gollancz, 1974.

"View by Moonlight," in *Alfred Hitchcock Presents: Stories to Be Read with the Door Locked.* New York, Random House, 1975.

"Hide and Seek, Russian Style," in *Ellery Queen's Mystery Magazine* (New York), April 1976.

"Nothing But the Truth," in *Ellery Queen's Masks of Mystery.* New York, Davis, 1978.

"In the Clear," in *Ellery Queen's Mystery Magazine* (New York), April 1978.

"The Writing on the Wall," in *Ellery Queen's Mystery Magazine* (New York), August 1978.

"A Choice of Murders," in *Ellery Queen's Napoleons of Mystery.* New York, Davis, 1978.

"The Day of the Bookmobile," in *Ellery Queen's Mystery Magazine* (New York), January 1979.

"Chain of Terror," in *Ellery Queen's Mystery Magazine* (New York), October 1979.

OTHER PUBLICATIONS

Novels

The Missing Years. New York, Doubleday, 1953; London, W. H. Allen, 1954.
Martha, Martha. New York, Kenedy, 1960; London, Hodder and Stoughton, 1961.
My Brothers, Remember Monica. New York, Kenedy, 1964.

Manuscript Collections: Institute of Popular Culture, Bowling Green University, Ohio; (non-mystery) Trinity College, Washington, D.C.

Patricia McGerr comments:

I was first inspired to write a mystery novel by the announcement of a contest (which I didn't win). From my reading I knew that a classic mystery included a murderer, a victim, and several suspects. So I began by assembling the cast of characters. But when I began to assign roles, it was obvious that only one of them could commit murder, whereas any of the other ten might be his victim. So, reversing the formula, I named the murderer on page one and centered the mystery around the identity of the victim. In my next book I carried that idea a little farther by asking the reader to discover both murderer and victim and then, in the third, presented a murderer whose problem was to pierce the disguise of the detective. A witness to the crime was the unknown element in the fourth book and in the fifth, having exhausted the possibilities, I returned to the design of my first crime with the question mark again beside the name of the corpse. Since then I've been writing more conventional mysteries, but in all of them I've tried to make the development of character as interesting as the puzzle.

*   *   *

Patricia McGerr is perhaps best known for her creative genius and technical skill in producing what Barzun and Taylor have aptly called the "*whodunin?*" wherein the victim of the crime, rather than the culprit, is unknown. Her forte, indeed, her major contribution to the genre, is the mystery with this completely new twist. In her first and most widely acclaimed tour de force, *Pick Your Victim*, a group of Marines in the Aleutians passes the time by attempting to solve a murder committed in Washington, D.C., at the supposedly philanthropic organization SUDS (Society for the Uplift of Domestic Service). A torn clipping from a hometown newspaper informs them of the murderer's name and confession, but a missing segment prompts them to initiate their far-off investigation into the identity of the corpse, which could have been any of some ten persons.

Another large cast is assembled in Patricia McGerr's second work, *The Seven Deadly Sisters*, in which Sally Bowen discovers through a letter that one of her seven aunts has murdered her husband. In many respects superior to its predecessor, this novel entails the unmasking of victim and culprit alike. The very nature of these early puzzlers demands close character studies, a skill at which Miss McGerr excels – indeed, she is at her very best with a large and assorted cast of characters, all of whom she manages to define and individualize with the utmost ease and care. Pacing, however, is consequently much slower than in her later works in which she reverts to the more conventional "whodunit" such as *Fatal in My Fashion* where murder visits the world of *haute couture* in Paris. If some of the characters in her later works appear somewhat less than believable, the high degree of originality in plotting in each case easily permits suspension of any disbelief. *Death in a Million Living Rooms* with its television setting, and *Murder Is Absurd* with its theatrical background are both especially well executed, as are ... *Follow, As the Night* ..., *Stranger with My Face*, and *For Richer, For Poorer, Till Death*.

There is little or no use of the customary detective or police investigator in Patricia McGerr's works, which are primarily novels of suspense and intrigue, often displaying a rich vein of humor. But McGerr has also created one memorable series character in Selena Mead – a Washington, D.C., socialite, magazine writer, and counter-espionage agent with a top-secret security branch known as Section Q. Ex-widow Selena is now remarried to her immediate superior, Hugh Pierce. Her first published appearance was in *This Week* magazine in October, 1963, which described the knifing death of her first agent-husband, Simon Mead. Since then Selena Mead has appeared in some twenty-five short stories, two novelets, and two novels, *Is There a Traitor in the House?* and *Legacy of Danger*, the later of which incorporates several short story exploits.

—James R. McCahery

McGIRR, Edmund. Pseudonym for Kenneth Giles; also writes as Charles Drummond. British. Born in 1922. *Died in 1972.*

Crime Publications

Novels (series character: Piron)

> *The Funeral Was in Spain* (Piron). London, Gollancz, 1966.
> *The Hearse with Horses* (Piron). London, Gollancz, 1967.
> *Here Lies My Wife.* London, Gollancz, 1967.
> *The Lead-Lined Coffin.* London, Gollancz, 1968.
> *An Entry of Death* (Piron). London, Gollancz, and New York, Walker, 1969.
> *Death Pays the Wages.* London, Gollancz, 1970.
> *No Better Fiend* (Piron). London, Gollancz, and New York, Walker, 1971.
> *Bardel's Murder* (Piron). London, Gollancz, 1973; New York, Walker, 1974.

A Murderous Journey (Piron).   London, Gollancz, 1974; New York, Walker, 1975.

Novels as Kenneth Giles (series character: Inspector Harry James)

Some Beasts No More (James).   London, Gollancz, 1965; New York, Walker, 1968.
A Provenance of Death (James).   London, Gollancz, 1966; New York, Simon and
   Schuster, 1967; as *A Picture of Death*, St. Albans, Hertfordshire, Granada, 1970.
The Big Greed.   London, Gollancz, 1966.
Death and Mr. Prettyman (James).   London, Gollancz, 1967; New York, Walker, 1969.
Death in Diamonds (James).   London, Gollancz, 1967; New York, Simon and Schuster,
   1968.
Death among the Stars (James).   London, Gollancz, and New York, Walker, 1968.
Death Cracks a Bottle (James).   London, Gollancz, 1969; New York, Walker, 1970.
Death in the Church.   London, Gollancz, 1970.
Murder Pluperfect (James).   London, Gollancz, and New York, Walker, 1970.
A File on Death (James).   London, Gollancz, and New York, Walker, 1973.

Novels as Charles Drummond (series character: Sergeant Reed in all books)

Death at the Furlong Post.   London, Gollancz, 1967; New York, Walker, 1968.
Death and the Leaping Ladies.   London, Gollancz, 1968; New York, Walker, 1969.
The Odds on Death.   London, Gollancz, 1969; New York, Walker, 1970.
Stab in the Back.   London, Gollancz, and New York, Walker, 1970.
A Death at the Bar.   London, Gollancz, 1972; New York, Walker, 1973.

*   *   *

Kenneth Giles, writing under his own name and the pseudonyms Edmund McGirr and
Charles Drummond, wrote some two dozen mysteries between 1965 and his death in 1972.
The series by Giles introduced a bright young Sergeant, Harry James of Scotland Yard, who
rises through the ranks and takes on a wife and children as the series progresses.
Drummond's protagonist is Sergeant Reed of Scotland Yard, a brilliant but bibulous man
whose name has been removed from the Recommended for Inspectorship list as a result of
two charges brought against him, one for violence, the other for accepting the favors of a
prostitute, neither of which was proven, but both of which contributed to the decision to use
Reed for odd jobs in the Department. McGirr's series features a New York-based Detective
Agency run by the Old Man and employing a private investigator, Piron. Some of the books
in this last series are set in New York, but most return to England, a more familiar landscape
for Giles, where Piron handles work for both the American Embassy and the British
government. All the mysteries introduce a lively cast of eccentrics, pub-crawlers, petty
crooks, and garrulous landladies, and all display ingenious plots.
   In *Some Beasts No More*, Giles's first mystery, Superintendent Hawker, presiding over the
statistics kept in the government files, given to racy speech and surprisingly right hunches,
and wizened to the foibles and ambitions of the members of the Yard, assigns young
Detective-Sergeant Harry James to investigate a murder. The murder has caught Hawker's
attention because it involves a woman who is the only link between four murderers who
have themselves been murdered. Elizabeth Holland, also known as Rhonda Gentry, is a
beautiful redhead, with a full figure and an intelligent face, and she excites more than the
detective in Harry James. James, a bright young man with a knowledge of accountancy and
experience in investigative work, is eager for advancement and a comfortable niche in life.
Typical of Giles's story-telling strategy, this story unwinds as James pounds the pavements
and frequents pubs and hotels, questioning the local people and following their leads. The
characters he encounters are also representative. There are a landlady who was a music-hall
star, a distinguished ex-commando, and a member of the British peerage. Giles's gift for
dialect and love of convoluted sentences amply sprinkled with British colloquialisms are also

evident. Only Giles's fixation with food is missing from this work. It is not until the third mystery, *A Provenance of Death*, that Giles creates Sergeant Honeybody, and revels in baroque extravagances while describing the eating habits of James, Elizabeth Holland, who has now become James's fiancée, and Honeybody.

The other books in the series take a more mature James, assisted by Elizabeth and Honeybody, who daily grows more satisfied with pubs and more discontented with his dour Scots wife, through even bloodier murders. Each murder solved advances James through the ranks until he is finally promoted to Chief Inspector. Whether Giles is depicting the world of diamond or art smugglers, or the world of solicitors, wine importers, or newspaper men, he always knows the world he describes and describes it with an accuracy and a sense of its unique flavor. His literary tastes are always evident in his books: his love for the 18th century is particularly clear. His stories are always fair: their endings, like Agatha Christie's, can generally be guessed by a reader who is wary of jumping at his false clues and accustomed to his sudden denouements. And his flair for extravagant characters and culinary arts gives his detective stories a texture more commonly found in a good novel.

The range of plots of the James series is repeated in the two series by Drummond and McGirr. International art smuggling, faking antique silver and banknotes, diamond smuggling, and fixed horse-racing run through a number of the books in the Drummond series, and are incidental to the plot in a number of McGirr's mysteries. Plots that hinge upon mistaken identity and impostors are common to all the books. What distinguishes the books of Giles is the character of the protagonist. Otherwise, the plot, the method of investigation, the sets, and the other characters are much the same.

Drummond's Sergeant Reed, unlike Inspector Harry James, often finds himself suspected of an involvement in the crimes he investigates. In *The Odds on Death*, Reed has the reputation among the racing underworld of being a "bad copper," but he matches his wits against those of the Marquis of Sous-Jouarre, the mastermind of a ring of international criminals, and solves the mystery of the death of a small, failed jockey, breaks the ring of international swindlers in London, and quietly sets a snare for the Marquis when the Yard itself had determined that the man, although criminal, is untouchable. In *A Death at the Bar*, Harry Alwyn, the crooked owner of a bar, is found with his head bashed in by a bottle (reminiscent of the murder committed in Giles's *Death Cracks a Bottle*) and Reed's cunning leads him to the murderer and the loot. He does not arrest the killer who had killed in self-defense, but had not admitted his role in the crime because he saw a quick way to seize the loot. Rather, Reed walks away, saying "arresting you would get me no promotion, just a lot of blooming paper-work," and warning the barman not to touch the money and to get himself a good lawyer. This stance is typical of the bright but disappointed Sergeant whose own code of law and justice is the one he satisfies.

The mysteries written under the name McGirr are of a piece with Giles's other writings: the English peerage, quaint and esoteric encyclopaedists, racketeers, and drug-traffickers are still the people of his plots; he still captures the colloquial speech patterns of his crooks and landladies, and he still describes his landscapes with an eye for detail. Only now his protagonist is a private eye who often serves the government, but only in cases which for reasons of decorum or policy the government is loath to touch. And Piron has his own sleuths and his own style of investigation. Like Reed and Honeybody, he is quick to cheat on his expenses and pocket at little cash. Like Reed, he often uses his own cunning and violence to trap the criminal, and he is likely to step outside the law in these endeavors. *A Murderous Journey* is probably the best book in this series, with the most ingenious plot and the most exciting and unexpected denouement.

Giles, writing under any name, is a skilled stylist and a writer gifted with an uncanny sense of the eccentric. His mysteries tease and entertain.

—Carol Simpson Stern

McGIVERN, William P(eter).   Also writes as Bill Peters.   American.   Born in Chicago, Illinois, 6 December 1927. Educated at the University of Birmingham, 1945–46. Served in the United States Army, 1943–46: Line Sergeant; Soldiers Medal, 1944. Married the writer Maureen Daly in 1948; two children. Reporter and reviewer, Philadelphia *Evening Bulletin*, 1949–51. Self-employed writer. Recipient: Mystery Writers of America Edgar Allan Poe Award, 1952. Agent: Marvin Moss, 9229 Sunset Boulevard, Los Angeles, California 90069. Address: 73–305 Ironwood Drive, Palm Desert, California, U.S.A.

CRIME PUBLICATIONS

Novels

> *But Death Runs Faster.*   New York, Dodd Mead, 1948; London, Boardman, 1949; as
>   *The Whispering Corpse,* New York, Pocket Books, 1950.
> *Heaven Ran Last.*   New York, Dodd Mead, 1949; London, Digit, 1958.
> *Very Cold for May.*   New York, Dodd Mead, 1950.
> *Shield for Murder.*   New York, Dodd Mead, 1951.
> *Blondes Die Young* (as Bill Peters).   New York, Dodd Mead, 1952; London, Foulsham,
>   1956.
> *The Crooked Frame.*   New York, Dodd Mead, 1952.
> *The Big Heat.*   New York, Dodd Mead, and London, Hamish Hamilton, 1953.
> *Margin of Terror.*   New York, Dodd Mead, 1953; London, Collins, 1955.
> *Rogue Cop.*   New York, Dodd Mead, 1954; London, Collins, 1955.
> *The Darkest Hour.*   New York, Dodd Mead, 1955; London, Collins, 1956; as
>   *Waterfront Cop,* New York, Pocket Books, 1956.
> *The Seven File.*   New York, Dodd Mead, 1956; London, Collins, 1957; as *Chicago-7*,
>   London, Sphere, 1970.
> *Night Extra.*   New York, Dodd Mead, 1957; London, Collins, 1958.
> *Odds Against Tomorrow.*   New York, Dodd Mead, 1957; London, Collins, 1958.
> *Savage Streets.*   New York, Dodd Mead, 1959; London, Collins, 1960.
> *Seven Lies South.*   New York, Dodd Mead, 1960; London, Collins, 1961.
> *The Road to the Snail.*   New York, Dodd Mead, 1961.
> *A Pride of Place.*   New York, Dodd Mead, 1962.
> *Police Special* (omnibus).   New York, Dodd Mead, 1962.
> *A Choice of Assassins.*   New York, Dodd Mead, 1963; London, Collins, 1964.
> *The Caper of the Golden Bulls.*   New York, Dodd Mead, 1966; London, Collins, 1967.
> *Lie Down, I Want to Talk to You.*   New York, Dodd Mead, 1967; London, Collins,
>   1968.
> *Caprifoil.*   New York, Dodd Mead, 1972; London, Collins, 1973.
> *Reprisal.*   New York, Dodd Mead, 1973; London, Collins, 1974.
> *Night of the Juggler.*   New York, Putnam, and London, Collins, 1975.

Short Stories

> *Killer on the Turnpike.*   New York, Pocket Books, 1961.

Uncollected Short Story

> "Graveyard Shift," in *Alfred Hitchcock's Tales to Scare You Stiff*, edited by Eleanor
>   Sullivan.   New York, Davis, 1978.

OTHER PUBLICATIONS

Novel

Soldiers of '44.   New York, Arbor House, and London, Collins, 1979.

Plays

Screenplays: *I Saw What You Did*, 1965; *Chicago 7*, 1968; *Lie Down I Want to Talk to You*, 1968; *The Wrecking Crew*, 1969; *Caprifoil*, 1973; *Brannigan*, 1975; *Night of the Juggler*, 1975.

Television Plays: *San Francisco International Airport* series, 1970; *The Young Lawyers* series, 1970; *Banyon* series, 1972; *Kojak* series, 1973–77.

Other

Mention My Name in Mombasa: The Unscheduled Adventures of an American Family Abroad, with Maureen Daly.   New York, Dodd Mead, 1958.

Manuscript Collection: Mugar Memorial Library, Boston University.

*   *   *

William P. McGivern has written over 20 novels covering the gamut of crime – homicide detection, espionage, political corruption, the world of the psychopath, the crooked cop. A number of his novels deal with the metaphor of the jungle – the jungle of crime. In some cases the "good guy" battles the forces of spreading crime and corruption in the big city. Dave Bannion, the detective who refuses to compromise, a big man physically and morally ("always the out-sized one, in high school and college, even on football teams"), feels the big heat of racketeers and corrupt politicians and law enforcers. They, in turn, feel the pressure of the big heat he creates as he seeks the reasons behind the suicide of a colleague, Tom Deery, and the men responsible for the death of his own wife, Kate. Bannion, a man of the streets, has an intellectual fervor unmatched by his colleagues; he reads St. John's *Ascent of Mount Carmel* as a means of self-restoration. But books are abandoned when he sets out on his personal revenge – reflection could distort his mission. St. John does enter Bannion's meditations again until the close of *The Big Heat* – "My house being now at rest –."

Throughout *The Big Heat*, Dave Bannion stalks through the jungle of crime – city streets, bars, highways, hotel rooms. He does not rest until his work is done. The intense pressure, the constant tracking of suspects, the delaying tactics to avoid being caught in a trap, reappear in *Rogue Cop* where McGivern unfolds a classic story of two brothers – one an honest cop; the other, a sergeant on the take, a man who has given up the principles of two fathers – one, his own, now deceased father, a former policeman; the other, God the Father. Sgt. Mike Carmody has allowed himself to succumb to the good life afforded him by racketeers. He falls into the trap of trying to save himself and his brother; he loses his brother, but regains himself and ultimately returns to the memory of his father and the forgiveness of God the Father.

The snare of entrapment moves to a smaller town in *Odds Against Tomorrow* where two men involved in a bank job operate in a jungle of fear. Earl Slater, a white ex-con, highly prejudiced, has as his partner a black, John Ingram. Slater fears betrayal by blacks; Ingram fears because he is black. The distrust and fears of the two men are the real focus of *Odds Against Tomorrow*; survival depends on physical strength and mental capacity. Ingram is dehumanized and treated as an animal by Slater; ironically, Ingram's own fear of betrayal prevents him from betraying Slater. The characterizations are savage portrayals of two beasts in a Pennsylvania jungle of rural life.

The jungle metaphor is most precisely drawn in *Night of the Juggler*, an engrossing study of a psychopathic killer, Gus Soltik, a demented inhabitant of the South Bronx who cannot read or write but who instinctively knows when the anniversary of his mother's death arrives. As the anniversary nears, Gus prepares for his commemoration of his mother. For the fifth time he is about to kill a young girl. The fifth anniversary brings him to Central Park where he will encounter the stalking techniques of the professional law officers Max Prima and Gypsy Tonnelli and a retired military man, Luther Boyd. The map of the jungle-battlefield, Central Park, precedes McGivern's text, and the reader is drawn into a number of arenas simultaneously – the park as the battleground, the instinctive and animal-like reactions of Gus Soltik (an appropriately transparent name), and the strategic thought-processes of the other principals, the searchers.

The characters in all of McGivern's novels are developed precisely. The reader participates in the twistings of the psychopathic mind in *Night of the Juggler* and *A Choice of Assassins* where a man agrees to kill for the price of a drink. The tightrope mentality of McGivern's rogue cops is not merely understood, but actually experienced by the reader. McGivern is not given to excesses in characterization or action. Consequently, his work does not lend itself to stereotypes. A good example of his work is *Killer on the Turnpike*, a collection of short stories which includes the title story, about a psychopath; "Without a Prayer," a variant of the priest-police conflict over a hoodlum; "Old Willie," a city news reporter who becomes involved with mobsters; "The Record of M. Duval," a tale of a man who tries to get away with his wife's murder; and "Missing in Berlin," a precursor of McGivern's work in the espionage story, later realized in his novel, *Caprifoil*.

—Katherine M. Restaino

McGUIRE, (Dominic) Paul. Australian. Born in South Australia, 3 April 1903. Educated at the Christian Brothers' College, Adelaide; University of Adelaide (Tinline Scholar in Australian History). Served in the Royal Australian Naval Volunteer Reserve, 1939–45. Married Frances Margaret Cheadle in 1927. Lecturer, Workers' Educational Association, and University Extension of the University of Adelaide for several years; lectured in the United States, 1936–40, 1946; Diplomat: Australian Delegate, United Nations Assembly, New York, 1953; Australian Minister to Italy, 1954–58, and Ambassador to Italy, 1958–59; Envoy Extraordinary to the Holy See at Coronation of Pope John XXIII, 1958. C.B.E. (Commander, Order of the British Empire), 1951. Knight Grand Cross, Order of St. Sylvester, 1959. Commendatore, Order of Merit, Italy, 1967. Address: 136 Mills Terrace, North Adelaide, South Australia 5006, Australia.

CRIME PUBLICATIONS

Novels (series characters: Chief Inspector Cummings; Inspector/Superintendent Fillinger)

    Murder in Bostall (Cummings).   London, Skeffinton, 1931; as *The Black Rose Murder*, New York, Brentano's, 1932.
    Three Dead Men (Cummings).   London, Skeffington, 1931; New York, Brentano's, 1932.
    The Tower Mystery (Fillinger).   London, Skeffington, 1932; as *Death Tolls the Bell*, New York, Coward McCann, 1933.
    Murder by the Law (Fillinger).   London, Skeffington, 1932.

Death Fugue (Fillinger).   London, Skeffington, 1933.

There Sits Death (Fillinger).   London, Skeffington, 1933.

Daylight Murder (Cummings; Fillinger).   London, Skeffington, 1934; as *Murder at High Noon*, New York, Doubleday, 1935.

Murder in Haste (Cummings; Fillinger).   London, Skeffington, 1934.

7.30 Victoria (Cummings).   London, Skeffington, 1935.

Born to Be Hanged.   London, Skeffington, 1935.

Prologue to the Gallows.   London, Skeffington, 1936.

Threepence to Marble Arch.   London, Skeffington, 1936.

Cry Aloud for Murder.   London, Heinemann, 1937.

W.1.   London, Heinemann, 1937.

Burial Service.   London, Heinemann, 1938; as *A Funeral in Eden*, New York, Morrow, 1938.

The Spanish Steps.   London, Heinemann, 1940; as *Enter Three Witches*, New York, Morrow, 1940.

OTHER PUBLICATIONS

Verse

The Two Men and Other Poems.   Adelaide, Preece, 1932.

Other

The Poetry of Gerard Manley Hopkins: A Lecture.   Adelaide, Preece, 1934.

Australian Journey.   London, Heinemann, 1939; revised edition, 1947; as *Australia: Her Heritage, Her Future*, New York, Stokes, 1939.

Westward the Course: The New World of Oceania.   London, Oxford University Press, and New York, Morrow, 1942.

The Price of Admiralty, with Frances Margaret McGuire.   Melbourne, Oxford University Press, 1944.

The Three Corners of the World: An Essay in the Interpretation of Modern Politics.   London, Heinemann, 1948; as *Experiment in World Order*, New York, Morrow, 1948.

The Australian Theatre, with Betty Arnott and Frances Margaret McGuire.   London, Oxford University Press, 1948.

There's Freedom for the Brave: An Approach to World Order.   London, Heinemann, and New York, Morrow, 1949.

Inns of Australia.   Melbourne, Heinemann, 1952; London, Heinemann, 1953.

Editor, with John Fitzsimons, *Restoring All Things: A Guide to Catholic Action.*   New York, Sheed and Ward, 1938; London, Sheed and Ward, 1939.

*   *   *

Although born in Australia, Paul McGuire, unlike S. H. Courtier or the transplanted Englishman Arthur W. Upfield, never chose to set his mystery novels there. Much of McGuire's early work is of interest, though not for its detection which is often weak. Some of his later work is classic.

Murder in Bostall introduces Inspector Cummings and Sergeant Wittler who reappear (with promotions) in later books. Their problem is to solve the murder of Edward Steyne who works for his uncle's detective agency in London. The uncle, Jacob Modstone, gives what help he can to the police, but launches out on an investigation of his own which hinders them. Modstone eventually joins forces with the police, and together they bring the case to a satisfactory conclusion – but not through fair-play detection! This novel is not only notable for its sympathetic treatment of a Jew – uncommon in British mystery fiction of the period – but it also presents the only Jewish detective to function during the Golden Age.

A murder victim is found on the beach in *Murder by the Law*; the blunt instrument in this case is a cannon ball. McGuire's most widely-used series detective, Superintendent Fillinger, a huge man who easily outweighs Nero Wolfe, is introduced. *There Sits Death* is about a murderer who slashes jugulars, and is one of the best of the early McGuire novels. *7.30 Victoria* is more of a thriller than a detective story, and does not quite come off, but its attractive blend of plot, humor, and appealing characters manages to linger in the mind.

McGuire's reputation is assured by *Burial Service* – an absolute masterpiece by any standard. *Burial Service* takes place on the out-of-the-way and idyllic island of Kaitai whose serenity is abruptly shattered when an unpopular and worrisome stranger is found lying dead on the beach with a fractured skull. A tempest of suspicion reveals the hitherto shrouded pasts of many of the inhabitants, and fear and unhappiness reign supreme until the murderer can be found. The many excellences of plot, character, atmosphere, setting, wit, and detection are exceeded only by McGuire's brilliant use of dialogue that tells much about the characters and their relationships, sets the tone of the story, and gives the reader a great deal of exposition in an enjoyable manner.

McGuire's last novel, *The Spanish Steps*, received rave reviews and is considered by many to be the equal of *Burial Service*. It is written with distinction but, except for a chase scene in and about an Italian estate, absolutely nothing happens until one of the characters is murdered almost at the end of the novel. The hero is another newspaper man, and detection is minimal. Unfortunately, nothing, to my mind, can compensate for the static qualities of this novel.

—Charles Shibuk

McMAHON, Pat.   See **HOCH, Edward D.**

McMULLEN, Mary.   American.   Born in Yonkers, New York, in 1920; daughter of Helen Reilly, *q.v.*, and the artist Paul Reilly; sister of Ursula Curtis, *q.v.* Studied art, and worked in fashion design and advertising. Recipient: Mystery Writers of America Edgar Allan Poe Award, 1952. Address: c/o Doubleday & Company Inc., 245 Park Avenue, New York, New York 10017, U.S.A.

<small>CRIME PUBLICATIONS</small>

Novels

>   *Stranglehold.*   New York, Harper, 1951; as *Death of Miss X*, London, Collins, 1952.
>   *The Doom Campaign.*   New York, Doubleday, 1974; London, Hale, 1976.
>   *A Country Kind of Death.*   New York, Doubleday, 1975; London, Hale, 1977.
>   *The Pimlico Plot.*   New York, Doubleday, 1975; London, Hale, 1977.

Funny, Jonas, You Don't Look Dead. New York, Doubleday, 1976; London, Hale, 1978.
A Dangerous Funeral. New York, Doubleday, 1977; London, Hale, 1978.
Death by Bequest. New York, Doubleday, 1977; London, Hale, 1979.
Prudence Be Damned. New York, Doubleday, 1978; London, Hale, 1979.
The Man with Fifty Complaints. New York, Doubleday, 1978.
Welcome to the Grave. New York, Doubleday, 1979.
But Nellie Was So Nice. New York, Doubleday, 1979.

Uncollected Short Story

"Her Heart's Home," in *Ellery Queen's Mystery Magazine* (New York), May 1977.

*   *   *

Mary McMullen's novels feature fairly small casts of characters, and several are suspense rather than detective stories. The author pays close attention to characters' preferences in clothing, food, and drink; these evidences of taste, along with the literate, rather brittle dialogue, serve as characterization. Weather imagery is important to the mood, and detailed comments about the settings, both in the United States and abroad, lend realism to fairly sensational plots.

McMullen's heroines are stunningly lovely, strong beneath a gentle surface; often they are successful career women. These protagonists engage in intense love affairs, and the heroes, whether suitor or husband, are tall, attractive, and expert at their professions. Some villains, like Desmond Byrne of *The Pimlico Plot*, are addicted to danger; others, like Bernard Caldwell, *Death by Bequest*, are simply greedy.

Stranglehold employs the convention of the murdered stranger and is set against the office politics of a New York advertising firm. Some interesting insights into the roles of women in advertising in the 1950's as well as the characterization of the heroine, Eve Fitzsimmons, strengthen the book. In *Prudence Be Damned*, perhaps McMullen's best novel, Madeline Devore is kidnapped and held for ransom by her son and his current girl. The motivations and emotions of these unlikely abductors, of their victim, and of the other family members are particularly well delineated.

Mary McMullen's novels, swift-moving and tightly knit, are intriguing contributions to the genre.

—Jane S. Bakerman

McNEILE, H. C. See **SAPPER.**

McSHANE, Mark. Also writes as Marc Lovell. British. Born in Sydney, Australia, 28 November 1929. Educated in Blackpool, Lancashire, 1935–45. Married Pamela Rosemary Armstrong in 1963; one daughter and three sons (one deceased). Agent: Oliver Swan, 280

Madison Avenue, New York, New York 10016, U.S.A.; or, Diana Avebury, 145 Park Road, London N.W.1, England. Address: Can Tumi, La Cabaneta, Mallorca, Spain.

CRIME PUBLICATIONS

Novels (series characters: Myra Savage; ex-Detective Sergeant Norman Pink)

> *The Straight and the Crooked.* London, Long, 1960.
> *Séance on a Wet Afternoon* (Savage). London, Cassell, 1961; as *Séance*, New York, Doubleday, 1962.
> *The Passing of Evil.* London, Cassell, 1961.
> *Untimely Ripped.* London, Cassell, 1962; New York, Doubleday, 1963.
> *The Girl Nobody Knows* (Pink). New York, Doubleday, 1965; London, Hale, 1966.
> *Night's Evil* (Pink). New York, Doubleday, and London, Hale, 1966.
> *The Crimson Madness of Little Doom.* New York, Doubleday, 1966; London, Hale, 1967.
> *The Way to Nowhere* (Pink). London, Hale, 1967.
> *Ill Met by a Fish Shop on George Street.* New York, Doubleday, 1968; London, Hodder and Stoughton, 1969.
> *The Singular Case of the Multiple Dead.* New York, Putnam, 1969; London, Hodder and Stoughton, 1970.
> *The Man Who Left Well Enough.* New York, McCall, 1971.
> *Séance for Two* (Savage). New York, Doubleday, 1972; London, Hale, 1974.
> *The Othello Complex.* Paris, Gallimard, 1974.
> *The Headless Snowman.* Paris, Gallimard, 1974.
> *Lashed But Not Leashed.* New York, Doubleday, 1976; London, Hale, 1978.
> *Lifetime.* New York, Manor Books, 1977.
> *The Hostage Game.* New York, Zebra Books, 1979.

Novels as Marc Lovell (series character: Jason Galt)

> *The Ghost of Megan.* New York, Doubleday, 1968; as *Memory of Megan*, New York, Ace, 1970.
> *The Imitation Thieves.* New York, Doubleday, 1971.
> *A Presence in the House.* New York, Doubleday, 1972.
> *An Enquiry into the Existence of Vampires.* New York, Doubleday, 1974; as *Vampires in the Shadows*, London, Hale, 1976.
> *Dreamers in a Haunted House.* New York, Doubleday, 1975; London, Hale, 1976.
> *The Blind Hypnotist* (Galt). New York, Doubleday, 1976.
> *The Second Vanetti Affair* (Galt). New York, Doubleday, 1977.
> *The Guardian Spectre.* New York, Manor Books, 1977.
> *Fog Sinister.* New York, Manor Books, 1977.
> *A Voice from the Living.* New York, Doubleday, 1978.
> *And They Say You Can't Buy Happiness.* London, Hale, 1979.
> *Hand over Mind.* New York, Doubleday, 1979.

Manuscript Collection: Mugar Memorial Library, Boston University.

Mark McShane comments:

In my teens I read Gerald Kersh's *Prelude to a Certain Midnight*. To me it was a minor revelation. Up until then my reading in crime-suspense-mystery had been in the category in which all turns out well in the end, and the relationship to reality is a tenth cousin forcibly removed. So I'd been little interested in this field, except as a time-passer. When I started writing, over ten years later, it was that book's influence that made me do what, in most of my work, I'm still doing: trying to see how far I can take the crime novel away from the cardboard goodies-baddies scene and into a third world not straight, not bent; at the same time pressing whenever possible my brief that the so-called occult is as real and natural as memory; being a didactic nuisance on the values of liberalism; never writing the same book twice; earning a living.

*   *   *

Given his obsession with man's variability and quirkiness, it is not surprising that Mark McShane has written odd crime novels, each one quite different. The strangeness and singularity of his works are evident in his choice of titles such as *The Crimson Madness of Little Doom* and *Lashed But Not Leashed*. They are evident as well in his plots, which range from a medium seeking to establish her spiritualistic powers by predicting a kidnapping that will be done by her husband and herself (*Séance on a Wet Afternoon*) to an ex-policeman trying to identify a nine-year-old girl accidentally killed in a train wreck (*The Girl Nobody Knows*) to a group of artistically misinclined social misfits planning to assassinate the Chancellor of the Exchequer for imposing a one-penny tax on theater seats (*The Singular Case of the Multiple Dead*). McShane's writing is also remarkable in its range; he has produced suspense novels tinged with the supernatural (*Séance on a Wet Afternoon* and *Séance for Two*), straight crime novels that are a little bent (*The Girl Nobody Knows* and *Night's Evil*), psychological crime novels that are bent almost to the breaking point (*Ill Met by a Fish Shop on George Street* and *Lashed But Not Leashed*), and bizarre, intriguing mixtures of the whodunit and the crime novel that additionally combine tragedy and comedy (*The Singular Case of the Multiple Dead* and *The Crimson Madness of Little Doom*).

McShane's penchant for the offbeat, when used effectively, has enabled him to invent plots that are fascinating because the oddity of his characters makes their behavior and its outcome nearly unpredictable. It has also led him to explore seldom observed corners of the mind and hence discover new angles of vision (it should be noted that he likes punning). In addition, it has inspired him to enrich the mystery genre with both mordant and extravagant humor. Used irresponsibly, however, this penchant has resulted in the lifeless grotesques, Krafft-Ebing kinkiness, and superabundance of Inspector Clouseau-esque pratfalls of *The Man Who Left Well Enough* (McShane didn't) and the disheartening mixture of plot ingenuity and soft-core pornography of *Lifetime*.

Throughout his work, McShane has emphasized man's vulnerability to chance, the role of circumstance in creating criminals, the nuttiness of the seemingly normal, and the dangers of excessive idealism. Again and again, he has shown the madness behind too strong a drive for psychological, social, political, or moral purity. In *The Man Who Left Well Enough*, for example, he focuses on the Hitler-like founder of a bricklayer's society who inspires his followers to kill some plasterers for scoffing at the purity of bricklaying. Similarly, in *The Crimson Madness of Little Doom*, he depicts a woman who wrote poison pen letters to people who failed to meet her standard of sexual purity. In *Untimely Ripped*, he shows just how thin the line between a passion for morality and madness is when he portrays a policeman who is an insane killer and a lunatic who discovers this through detective work. McShane's philosophy seems to be: human beings are screwed-up enough as they are; tamper with them and they become worse. He also notes that a man's own hatred can hurt him more than anyone else's can.

—Steven Carter

MEADE, L. T. (Elizabeth Thomasina Meade). Irish. Born in Bandon, County Cork, in 1854. Married Alfred Toulmin Smith in 1879; one son and two daughters. Worked in the British Museum, London; Editor, with A. A. Leith, *Atalanta* girls' magazine for six years. *Died 26 October 1914.*

CRIME PUBLICATIONS

Novels

This Troublesome World, with Clifford Halifax. London, Chatto and Windus, 1893.
The Voice of the Charmer. London, Chatto and Windus, 3 vols., 1895.
Dr. Rumsey's Patient: A Very Strange Story, with Clifford Halifax. London, Chatto and Windus, 1896.
A Son of Ishmael. London, White, and New York, New Amsterdam Book Company, 1896.
On the Brink of a Chasm. London, Chatto and Windus, and New York, Buckles, 1899.
The Secret of the Dead. London, White, 1901.
Confessions of a Court Milner. London, Long, 1902.
A Double Revenge. London, Digby Long, 1902.
The Lost Square, with Robert Eustace. London, Ward Lock, 1902.
From the Hand of the Hunter. London, Long, 1906.
The Golden Shadow. London, Ward Lock, 1906.
The Chateau of Mystery. London, Everett, 1907.
The Necklace of Parmona. London, Ward Lock, 1909.
Twenty-Four Hours. London, White, 1911.
The House of the Black Magic. London, White, 1912.

Short Stories

Stories from the Diary of a Doctor, with Clifford Halifax. London, Newnes, 1894; Philadelphia, Lippincott, 1895; *Second Series*, London, Bliss, 1896.
Under the Dragon Throne, with Robert Kennaway Douglas. London, Wells Gardner, 1897.
A Master of Mysteries, with Robert Eustace. London, Ward Lock, 1898.
The Gold Star Line, with Robert Eustace. London, Ward Lock, 1899; New York, New Amsterdam Book Company, n.d.
The Brotherhood of the Seven Kings, with Robert Eustace. London, Ward Lock, 1899.
Where the Shoe Pinches, with Clifford Halifax. London, Chambers, 1900.
The Sanctuary Club, with Robert Eustace. London, Ward Lock, 1900.
A Race with the Sun, with Clifford Halifax. London, Ward Lock, 1901.
The Sorceress of the Strand, with Robert Eustace. London, Ward Lock, 1903.
Silenced. London, Ward Lock, 1904.
The Oracle of Maddox Street. London, Ward Lock, 1904.
Micah Faraday, Adventurer. London, Ward Lock, 1910.

Uncollected Short Story

"The Face in the Dark," with Robert Eustace, in *Great Short Stories of Detection, Mystery, and Horror*, vol. 1, edited by Dorothy L. Sayers. London, Gollancz, 1928; as *The Omnibus of Crime*, New York, Payson and Clarke, 1929.

OTHER PUBLICATIONS

Novels

Lotty's Last Home. London, Shaw, 1875.
David's Little Lad. London, Shaw, 1877; New York, Harper, 1878.
A Knight of Today. London, Shaw, 1877.
Scamp and I: A Story of City By-Ways. London, Shaw, 1877; New York, Carter, 1878.
Bel Marjory. London, Shaw, 1878.
The Children's Kingdom. London, Shaw, 1878; New York, Burt, n.d.
Your Brother and Mine: A Cry from the Great City. London, Shaw, 1878.
Dot and Her Treasures. London, Shaw, 1879.
Water Gipsies: A Story of Canal Life in England. New York, Carter, 1879; London, Shaw, 1883.
Andrew Harvey's Wife. London, Isbister, 1880.
A Dweller in Tents. London, Isbister, 1880.
Mou-Setsé: A Negro Hero. London, Isbister, 1880.
The Floating Light of Ringfinnan, and Guardian Angels. Edinburgh, Macniven and Wallace, 1880.
Mother Herring's Chicken. London, Isbister, and New York, Carter, 1881.
A London Baby: The Story of King Roy. London, Nisbet, 1882.
The Children's Pilgrimage. London, Nisbet, 1883.
How It All Came Round. London, Hodder and Stoughton, and New York, Lovell, 1883.
The Autocrat of the Nursery. London, Hodder and Stoughton, 1884; New York, Armstrong, 1886.
A Band of Three. London, Isbister, 1884; New York, Seaside Library, n.d.
Scarlet Anemones. London, Hodder and Stoughton, 1884.
The Two Sisters. London, Hodder and Stoughton, 1884.
The Angel of Love. London, Hodder and Stoughton, 1885; Boston, Earle, 1887.
A Little Silver Trumpet. London, Hodder and Stoughton, 1885.
A World of Girls: The Story of a School. London, Cassell, 1886; New York, Mershon, n.d.
Daddy's Boy. London, Hatchards, 1887; New York, White and Allen, 1889.
The O'Donnell's of Inchfawn. London, Hatchards, and New York, Harper, 1887.
The Palace Beautiful. London, Cassell, 1887; New York, Grosset and Dunlap, n.d.
Sweet Nancy. London, Partridge, 1887.
Deb and the Duchess. London, Hatchards, 1888; New York, White and Allen, 1889.
Nobody's Neighbours. London, Isbister, 1888.
A Farthingful. London, Chambers, 1889.
The Golden Lady. London, Chambers, 1889; New York, Whittaker, n.d.
The Lady of the Forest. London, Partridge, and New York, Warne, 1889.
The Little Princess of Tower Hill. London, Partridge, 1889.
Polly, A New-Fashioned Girl. London, Cassell, 1889; New York, Hurst, n.d.
Poor Miss Carolina. London, Chambers, 1889.
The Beresford Prize. London, Longman, 1890.
Dickory Dock. London, Chambers, 1890.
Engaged to Be Married. London, Simpkin Marshall, 1890.
Frances Kane's Fortune. London, Warne, and New York, Lovell, 1890.
Heart of Gold. London, Warne, and New York, United States Book Company, 1890.
Just a Love Story. London, Blackett, 1890.
Marigold. London, Partridge, 1890.
The Honourable Miss. New York, United States Book Company, 1890; London, Methuen, 2 vols. 1891.

A Girl of the People. London, Methuen, and New York, Lovell, 1890.

Hepsy Gipsy. London, Methuen, 1891.

A Life for a Love. New York, United States Book Company, 1891; London, Digby Long, 1894.

The Children of Wilton Chase. London, Chambers, and New York, Cassell, 1891.

A Sweet Girl-Graduate. London, Cassell, 1891; New York, Allison, n.d.

Bashful Fifteen. London and New York, Cassell, 1892.

Four on an Island. London, Chambers, and New York, Cassell, 1892.

Jill, A Flower Girl. New York, United States Book Company, 1892; London, Isbister, 1893.

The Medicine Lady. London and New York, Cassell, 3 vols., 1892.

Out of the Fashion. London, Methuen, and New York, Cassell, 1892.

A Ring of Rubies. London, Innes, and New York, Cassell, 1892.

Beyond the Blue Mountains. London, Cassell, 1893.

A Young Mutineer. London, Wells Gardner, and New York, Hurst, 1893.

This Troublesome World. New York, Macmillan, 1893.

Betty, A School Girl. London, Chambers, 1894; New York, Cassell, n.d.

In an Iron Grip. London, Chatto and Windus, 2 vols., 1894.

Red Rose and Tiger Lily. London and New York, Cassell, 1894.

A Soldier of Fortune. London, Chatto and Windus, 3 vols., 1894; New York, Fenno, 1 vol., 1894.

Girls, New and Old. London, Chambers, and New York, Cassell, 1895.

A Princess of the Gutter. London, Wells Gardner, 1895; New York, Putnam, 1896.

Catalina, Art Student. London, Chambers, 1896; Philadelphia, Lippincott, 1897.

A Girl in Ten Thousand. Edinburgh, Oliphant, 1896; New York, Whittaker, 1897.

Good Luck. London, Nisbet, 1896; New York, Grosset and Dunlap, n.d.

A Little Mother to the Others. London, White, 1896.

Merry Girls of England. London, Cassell, 1896; Boston, Bradley, 1897.

Playmates. London, Chambers, 1896.

The White Tzar. London, Marshall Russell, 1896.

The House of Surprises. London, Longman, 1896.

Bad Little Hannah. London, White, 1897; New York, Mershon, n.d.

A Handful of Silver. Edinburgh, Oliphant, 1897; New York, Dutton, 1898.

The Way of a Woman. London, White, 1897.

Wild Kitty. London, Chambers, 1897; New York, Burt, n.d.

Cave Perilous. London, Religious Tract Society, 1898.

A Bunch of Cherries. London, Nister, and New York, Dutton, 1898.

The Cleverest Woman in England. London, Nisbet, 1898; Boston, Bradley, 1899.

The Girls of St. Wode's. London, Chambers, 1898; New York, Mershon, n.d.

Mary Gifford, M.B. London, Wells Gardner, 1898.

The Rebellion of Lil Carrington. London, Cassell, 1898.

The Siren. London, White, 1898.

Adventuress. London, Chatto and Windus, 1899.

All Sorts. London, Nisbet, 1899.

The Temptation of Olive Latimer. New York, Mershon, 1899; London, Hutchinson, 1900.

The Desire of Man: An Impossibility. London, Digby Long, 1899.

Light o' the Morning: The Story of an Irish Girl. London, Chambers, 1899; New York, Dutton, n.d.

The Odds and the Evens. London, Chambers, 1899; New York, Burt, n.d.

Wages. London, Nisbet, 1900.

A Plucky Girl. Philadelphia, Jacobs, 1900.

The Beauforts. London, Griffith and Farran, 1900.

A Brave Poor Thing. London, Isbister, 1900.

Daddy's Girl. London, Newnes, 1900; Philadelphia, Lippincott, 1901.

Miss Nonentity. London, Chambers, 1900; New York, Grosset and Dunlap, n.d.

Seven Maids. London, Chambers, 1900.

A Sister of the Red Cross: A Tale of the South African War. London, Nelson, 1900.

The Time of Roses. London, Nister, 1900; New York, Hurst, n.d.

Wheels of Iron. London, Nisbet, 1901.

The Blue Diamond. London, Chatto and Windus, 1901.

Cosey Corner; or, How They Kept a Farm. London, Chambers, 1901.

Girls of the True Blue. London, Chambers, and New York, Dutton, 1901.

The New Mrs. Lascelles. London, Clarke, 1901.

A Stumble by the Way. London, Chatto and Windus, 1901.

A Very Naughty Girl. London, Chambers, 1901; New York, Hurst, n.d.

Drift. London, Methuen, 1902.

Girls of the Forest. London, Chambers, 1902; New York, Dutton, n.d.

Margaret. London, White, 1902.

The Pursuit of Penelope. London, Digby, 1902.

Queen Rose. London, Chambers, 1902.

The Rebel of the School. London, Chambers, 1902; New York, Burt, n.d.

The Squire's Little Girl. London, Chambers, 1902.

Through Peril for a Wife. London, Digby, 1902.

The Witch Maid. London, Nisbet, 1903.

The Burden of Her Youth. London, Long, 1903.

By Mutual Consent. London, Digby Long, 1903.

A Gay Charmer. London, Chambers, 1903.

The Manor School. London, Chambers, and New York, Mershon, 1903.

Peter the Pilgrim. London, Chambers, 1903.

Resurgam. London, Methuen, 1903.

Rosebury. London, Chatto and Windus, 1903.

That Brilliant Peggy. London, Hodder and Stoughton, 1903.

A Maid of Mystery. London, White, 1904.

The Adventures of Miranda. London, Long, 1904.

At the Back of the World. London, Hurst and Blackett, 1904.

Castle Poverty. London, Nisbet, 1904.

The Girls of Mrs. Pritchard's School. London, Chambers, 1904; New York, Burt, n.d.

Love Triumphant. London, T. Fisher Unwin, 1904.

A Madcap. London, Cassell, and New York, Mershon, 1904.

A Modern Tomboy. London, Chambers, 1904; New York, Dutton, n.d.

Nurse Charlotte. London, Long, 1904.

Petronella, and The Coming of Polly. London, Chambers, 1904.

Wilful Cousin Kate. London, Chambers, 1905.

Bess of Delaney's. London, Digby Long, 1905.

A Bevy of Girls. London, Chambers, and New York, Still, 1905.

Dumps: A Plain Girl. London, Chambers, and New York, Dutton, 1905.

His Mascot. London, Long, 1905.

Little Wife Hester. London, Long, 1905.

Loveday: The Story of an Heiress. London, Hodder and Stoughton, 1905.

Old Readymoney's Daughter. London, Partridge, 1905.

The Other Woman. London, Walter Scott Publishing Company, 1905.

Virginia. London, Digby, 1905.

The Colonel and the Boy. London, Hodder and Stoughton, 1906.

The Face of Juliet. London, Long, 1906.

The Girl and Her Fortune. London, Hodder and Stoughton, 1906.

The Heart of Helen. London, Long, 1906.

The Hill-Top Girl. London, Chambers, 1906; New York, Burt, n.d.

The Home of Sweet Content. London, White, 1906.

In the Flower of Her Youth. London, Nisbet, 1906.

The Maid with the Goggles. London, Digby, 1906.
Sue. London, Chambers, 1906.
Turquoise and Ruby. London, Chambers, and New York, Chatterton Peck, 1906.
Victory. London, Methuen, 1906.
The Colonel's Conquest. Philadelphia, Jacobs, 1907.
The Curse of the Feverals. London, Long, 1907.
A Girl from America. London, Chambers, 1907.
The Home of Silence. London, Sisley's, 1907.
Kindred Spirits. London, Long, 1907.
The Lady of Delight. London, Hodder and Stoughton, 1907.
Little Josephine. London, Long, 1907.
The Little School-Mothers. London, Cassell, and Philadelphia, McKay, 1907.
The Love of Susan Cardigan. London, Digby Long, 1907.
The Red Cap of Liberty. London, Nisbet, 1907.
The Red Ruth. London, Laurie, 1907.
The Scamp Family. London, Chambers, 1907; New York, Burt, n.d.
Three Girls from School. London, Chambers, 1907; New York, Burt, n.d.
The Aim of Her Life. London, Long, 1908.
Betty of the Rectory. London, Cassell, 1908; New York, Grosset and Dunlap, n.d.
The Court-Harman Girls. London, Chambers, 1908.
The Courtship of Sybil. London, Long, 1908.
Hetty Beresford. London, Hodder and Stoughton, 1908.
Sarah's Mother. London, Hodder and Stoughton, 1908.
The School Favourite. London, Chambers, 1908.
The School Queens. London, Chambers, 1908; New York, New York Book Company, 1910.
Wild Heather. London, Cassell, 1909.
Oceana's Girlhood. New York, Hurst, 1909.
Aylwyn's Friends. London, Chambers, 1909.
Betty Vivian: A Story of Haddo Court School. London, Chambers, 1909.
Blue of the Sea. London, Nisbet, 1909.
Brother or Husband. London, White, 1909.
The Fountain of Beauty. London, Long, 1909.
I Will Sing a New Song. London, Hodder and Stoughton, 1909.
The Princess of the Revels. London, Chambers, 1909; New York, New York Book Company, 1910.
The Stormy Petrel. London, Hurst and Blackett, 1909.
The A.B.C. Girl. London, White, 1910.
Belinda Treherne. London, Long, 1910.
A Girl of Today. London, Long, 1910.
Lady Anne. London, Nisbet, 1910.
Miss Gwendoline. London, Long, 1910.
Nance Kennedy. London, Partridge, 1910.
Pretty-Girl and the Others. London, Chambers, 1910.
Rose Regina. London, Chambers, 1910.
A Wild Irish Girl. London, Chambers, and New York, Hurst, 1910.
A Bunch of Cousins, and The Barn "Boys." London, Chambers, 1911.
Desborough's Wife. London, Digby Long, 1911.
The Doctor's Children. London, Chambers, and Philadelphia, Lippincott, 1911.
For Dear Dad. London, Chambers, 1911.
The Girl from Spain. London, Digby Long, 1911.
The Girls of Merton College. New York, Hurst, 1911.
Mother and Son. London, Ward Lock, 1911.
Ruffles. London, Stanley Paul, 1911.
The Soul of Margaret Rand. London, Ward Lock, 1911.

Daddy's Girl and Consuelo's Quest of Happiness. New York, New York Book
  Company, 1911.
Corporal Violet. London, Hodder and Stoughton, 1912.
A Girl of the People. London, Everett, 1912.
Kitty O'Donovan. London, Chambers, and New York, Hurst, 1912.
Lord and Lady Kitty. London, White, 1912.
Love's Cross Roads. London, Stanley Paul, 1912.
Peggy from Kerry. London, Chambers, and New York, Hurst, 1912.
The Chesterton Girl Graduates. New York, Hurst, 1913.
The Girls of Abinger Close. London, Chambers, 1913.
The Girls of King's Royal. New York, Hurst, 1913.
The Passion of Kathleen Duveen. London, Stanley Paul, 1913.
A Band of Mirth. London, Chambers, 1914.
Col. Tracy's Wife. London, Aldine, 1914.
Elizabeth's Prisoner. London, Stanley Paul, 1914.
A Girl of High Adventure. London, Chambers, 1914.
Her Happy Face. London, Ward Lock, 1914.
The Queen of Joy. London, Chambers, and New York, Hurst, 1914.
The Wooing of Monica. London, Long, 1914.
The Darling of the School. London, Chambers, 1915.
The Daughter of a Soldier: A Colleen of South Ireland. New York, Hurst, 1915.
Greater Than Gold. London, Ward Lock, 1915.
Jill the Irresistible. New York, Hurst, 1915.
Hollyhock. London, Chambers, 1916.
Madge Mostyn's Nieces. London, Chambers, 1916.
The Maid Indomitable. London, Ward Lock, 1916.
Mother Mary. London, Chambers, 1916.
Daughters of Today. London, Hodder and Stoughton, 1916.
Better Than Riches. London, Chambers, 1917.
The Fairy Godmother. London, Chambers, 1917.
Miss Patricia. London, Long, 1925.
Roses and Thorns. London, Long, 1928.
In Time of Roses. New York, Grosset and Dunlap, n.d.

Short Stories

Water Lilies and Other Tales. London, Shaw, 1878.
Hermie's Rose-Buds and Other Stories. London, Hodder and Stoughton, 1883.
Little Mary and Other Stories. London, Chambers, 1891.
The Least of These and Other Stories. Cincinnati, Cranston and Curts, 1895.
The Princess Who Gave Away All, and The Naughty One of the Family. London, Nister,
  1902.
The Lady Cake-Maker. London, Hodder and Stoughton, 1904.
A Lovely Fiend and Other Stories. London, Digby, 1908.

Play

The Brotherhood of the Seven Kings, with Robert Eustace and Max Elgin, adaptation of
  the story by Meade and Eustace (produced South Shields, County Durham, 1900).

Other

A Public School Boy (on H. S. Wristbridge).   London, Nisbet, 1899.
Stories from the Old, Old Bible.   London, Newnes, 1903.

*   *   *

L. T. Meade probably wrote more girls' books than any other author of her day, yet today she is remembered almost solely for her mystery story-chains: *Stories from the Diary of a Doctor*, *A Master of Mysteries*, *The Brotherhood of the Seven Kings*, *The Gold Star Line*, *The Sanctuary Club*, *A Race with the Sun*, and *The Sorceress of the Strand*.

First published as instalments in *The Strand Magazine* and other periodicals, these were usually mystery-adventure stories told in the first person, often based upon some (slightly fantastic) scientific or medical snippet. It is assumed that Meade's collaborators provided such ideas and that she did the actual writing. Unifying factors within each chain could include criminal secret societies, femmes fatales, female masterminds of crime, and similar elements. Meade's fiction often embodied a strange dichotomy between sensational subject matter and a very stuffy *Weltanschauung*.

Meade wrote many other works dealing with crime and mystery, but her exact bibliography is not clear. Her books are now exceedingly rare, and sometimes misleading in title. In the opinion of this reviewer, her best work is not among the famous titles listed above, but is the series, written with Robert Eustace, about Miss Cusack, a female detective.

—E. F. Bleiler

MEGGS, Brown (Moore).   American.   Born in Los Angeles, California, 20 October 1930. Educated at St. Luke's School, New Canaan, Connecticut; California Institute of Technology, Pasadena; Harvard University, Cambridge, Massachusetts. Served in the United States Army Counter-Intelligence, 1953–54. Married Nancy Bates Meachen in 1954; one son. Joined Capitol Records, Hollywood, in 1958: merchandising assistant, later Executive Vice-President, Chief Operating Officer, and member of the Board of Directors; resigned 1976. Agent: Ned Brown, 407 North Maple Drive, Beverly Hills, California 90210. Address: 1450 El Mirador Drive, Pasadena, California 91103, U.S.A.

CRIME PUBLICATIONS

Novels

Saturday Games.   New York, Random House, 1974; London, Collins, 1975.
The Matter of Paradise.   New York, Random House, 1975; London, Collins, 1976.

OTHER PUBLICATIONS

Other

Aria. New York, Atheneum, and London, Hamish Hamilton, 1978.

Brown Meggs comments:
 I am interested in the "mystery" or "detective" or "crime" novel as a means to treating contemporary themes in an entertaining way. My own favorite writers in this field are Graham Greene, Nicolas Freeling, and Georges Simenon.

*   *   *

Connoisseurs of the mystery will not soon forget when the name of Brown Meggs first came to notice. *Saturday Games*, published in 1974, was exceptional for the quirks of its story, the quicksilver of its construction, its distillation of the very essence of a quiet, upper-stratum residential community and its hidden decadence. Somehow all parts meshed and created a bright, hard, and brilliantly faceted gem. *Saturday Games* received an Edgar scroll, and, in the opinion of many critics, it missed the top award only because its Saturnalian excesses were offensive to many readers. Yet in the 1970's, when excess in sexual and even pornographic material became a mystery cliché, such scenes in the Meggs novel were not quick insertions for exploitation purposes. They were written as an intrinsic part of the basic design. They uncovered what roiled beneath the social, cultural, and economic life of that conservative dowager of Southern California, Pasadena.
 After the bravura performance of *Saturday Games*, readers quite naturally wondered, what next? They need not have been anxious. In his second novel, Meggs did not repeat himself, nor did he exploit the shock technique with which he had made his debut. What he did was surprising. *The Matter of Paradise* was a sensitive study of the 25th reunion of the boys of a graduating class of a small, exclusive New England preparatory school. The narrator, a music critic, attends the gathering because he is curious about a succession of recent deaths among the classmates, and the story as constructed and developed corroborated the major talent of the author.
 After the critical and popular acclaim for his first two mysteries, Meggs wrote a book about opera stars and the recording of *Otello*, *Aria*. It is probable that he has not departed mystery forever. He is too good. He could, if he chose, become one of the most important writers in the genre.

—Dorothy B. Hughes

MELVILLE, Jennie.   See BUTLER, Gwendoline.

MERTZ, Barbara G. See PETERS, Elizabeth.

MEYER, Nicholas. American. Born in New York City, 24 December 1945. Educated at Fieldston High School, Riverdale, New York; University of Iowa, Iowa City, B.A. 1968. Associate Publicist, Paramount Pictures, New York, 1968–70; Story Editor, Warner Brothers, New York, 1970–71. Recipient: Crime Writers Association Golden Dagger. Address: c/o Pollock Rigrod and Bloom, 9255 Sunset Boulevard, Los Angeles, California 90069, U.S.A.

CRIME PUBLICATIONS

Novels

>   *Target Practice.* New York, Harcourt Brace, 1974; London, Hodder and Stoughton, 1975.
>   *The Seven-Per-Cent Solution, Being a Reprint from the Reminiscences of John H. Watson, M.D.* New York, Dutton, 1974; London, Hodder and Stoughton, 1975.
>   *The West End Horror: A Posthumous Memoir of John H. Watson, M.D.* New York, Dutton, and London, Hodder and Stoughton 1976.
>   *Black Orchid*, with Barry J. Kaplan. New York, Dial Press, 1977.

OTHER PUBLICATIONS

Plays

>   Screenplays: *The Seven-Per-Cent Solution*, 1976; *Time after Time*, 1979.

>   Television Plays: *Judge Dee*, 1974; *The Night That Panicked America*, 1975.

Nicholas Meyer comments:
  I try my best to be a story-teller. I do not originate material (as a rule); I stumble onto something that interests me and try to build on it. In this practice I do not know that I differ greatly from other writers of fiction. As to what interests me, I suppose my range is catholic. I read where my nose takes me, not really looking for anything in particular, comic or tragic will do. I am entertained by stories and trust that others may be as well; by entertained, I am not implying superficial or mindless recreation. Good entertainment is supposed to move the reader or audience. *King Lear* is the best entertainment I have ever seen. Sensation in story-telling is all well and good, but shock does not move. It stuns and is not a substitute for the tales that make us laugh or cry. I am not afraid of making demands on an audience. I like to challenge audiences to keep up. By this I do not mean the puerile process of guessing "whodunit." My meaning encompasses rather larger questions and social or moral issues.

*   *   *

  Michael Harrison, the noted Sherlock Holmes authority, has commented that Nicholas Meyer "is the brilliant young author of the most successful Sherlockian book of recent years, *The Seven-Per-Cent Solution*"; and in fact not since 1944, when three Sherlockian books were published, has there been generated such an interest in Sherlockiana, and Meyer must be given the credit.

Obviously, there have been a few Sherlockian pastiches published since *The Seven-Per-Cent Solution* and Meyer's sequel, *The West End Horror*, but none has matched the ingenious talent displayed by the young writer from New York. As Harrison further noted, Meyer is a newcomer to the Sherlockian scene, and "it is precisely this quality which enables him to see certain trends in Sherlockian scholarship with a fresh and discerning eye."

Although Meyer received his fair share of criticism from many of the purists, due to the nature of Sherlock Holmes' infatuation with cocaine, Meyer obviously admires Sir Arthur Conan Doyle: "The man didn't know how to write a boring sentence." Meyer further notes that "it is in fact a tribute to Doyle's magnetism and the narcotic appeal of the Sherlock Holmes stories that even today ... readers both new and old to the Holmes Canon come upon them with an enormous sense of relief [that] Holmes did not die." Meyer has contributed significantly to this premise, and, because of him (and some others), Sherlock Holmes continues to live.

—Larry L. French

MEYNELL, Laurence (Walter). Also writes as Valerie Baxter; Robert Eton; Geoffrey Ludlow; A. Stephen Tring. British. Born in Wolverhampton, Staffordshire, 9 August 1899. Educated at St. Edmund's College, Ware, Hertfordshire. Served in the Honourable Artillery Company during World War I; Royal Air Force, 1939–45: mentioned in despatches. Married 1) Shirley Ruth Darbyshire in 1932 (died, 1955), one daughter; 2) Joan Belfrage in 1956. Articled pupil in a land agency in the 1920's; worked as a schoolteacher and an estate agent. General Editor, Men of the Counties series, Bodley Head, publishers, London, 1955–57; Literary Editor, *Time and Tide*, London, 1958–60. Address: 9 Clifton Terrace, Brighton, Sussex BN1 3HA, England.

CRIME PUBLICATIONS

Novels (series characters: George Stanhope Berkley; Hooky Hefferman)

Bluefeather (Berkley). London, Harrap, and New York, Appleton, 1928.
Death's Eye. London, Harrap, 1929; as *The Shadow and the Stone*, New York, Appleton, 1929.
Camouflage. London, Harrap, 1930; as *Mystery at Newton Ferry*, Philadelphia, Lippincott, 1930.
Asking for Trouble. London, Ward Lock, 1931.
Consummate Rose. London, Hutchinson, 1931.
Storm Against the Wall. London, Hutchinson, and Philadelphia, Lippincott, 1931.
The House on the Cliff. London, Hutchinson, and Philadelphia, Lippincott, 1932.
Paid in Full. London, Harrap, 1933; as *So Many Doors*, Philadelphia, Lippincott, 1933.
Watch the Wall. London, Harrap, 1933; as *Gentlemen Go By*, Philadelphia, Lippincott, 1934.
Odds on Bluefeather (Berkley). London, Harrap, 1934; Philadelphia, Lippincott, 1935.
Third Time Unlucky! London, Harrap, 1935.
On the Night of the 18th.... London, Nicholson and Watson, and New York, Harper, 1936.

The Door in the Wall. London, Nicholson and Watson, and New York, Harper, 1937.
The House in the Hills. London, Nicholson and Watson, 1937; New York, Harper, 1938.
The Dandy. London, Nicholson and Watson, 1938.
The Hut. London, Nicholson and Watson, 1938.
His Aunt Came Late. London, Nicholson and Watson, 1939.
And Be a Villain. London, Nicholson and Watson, 1939.
The Creaking Chair. London, Collins, 1941.
The Dark Square. London, Collins, 1941.
Strange Landing. London, Collins, 1946.
The Evil Hour. London, Collins, 1947.
The Bright Face of Danger. London, Collins, 1948.
The Echo in the Cave. London, Collins, 1949.
The Lady on Platform One. London, Collins, 1950.
Party of Eight. London, Collins, 1950.
The Man No One Knew. London, Collins, 1951.
The Frightened Man (Hefferman). London, Collins, 1952.
Danger round the Corner (Hefferman). London, Collins, 1952.
Too Clever by Half (Hefferman). London, Collins, 1953.
Give Me the Knife. London, Collins, 1954.
Where Is She Now? London, Collins, 1955.
Saturday Out. London, Collins, 1956; New York, Walker, 1962.
The Breaking Point. London, Collins, 1957.
One Step from Murder. London, Collins, 1958.
The Abandoned Doll. London, Collins, 1960.
The House in Marsh Road. London, Collins, 1960.
The Pit in the Garden. London, Collins, 1961.
Virgin Luck. London, Collins, 1963; New York, Simon and Schuster, 1964.
Sleep of the Unjust. London, Collins, 1963.
More Deadly Than the Male. London, Collins, 1964.
Double Fault. London, Collins, 1965.
Die by the Book. London, Collins, 1966.
The Mauve Front Door. London, Collins, 1967.
Death of a Philanderer. London, Collins, 1968; New York, Doubleday, 1969.
Of Malicious Intent. London, Collins, 1969.
The Shelter. London, Hale, 1970.
The Curious Crime of Miss Julia Blossom. London, Macmillan, 1970.
The End of the Long Hot Summer. London, Hale, 1972.
Death by Arrangement. London, Macmillan, and New York, McKay, 1972.
A Little Matter of Arson. London, Macmillan, 1972.
A View from the Terrace. London, Hale, 1972.
The Fatal Flaw. London, Macmillan, 1973; New York, Stein and Day, 1978.
The Thirteen Trumpeters (Hefferman). London, Macmillan, 1973; New York, Stein and Day, 1978.
The Fortunate Miss East. London, Hale, 1973.
The Woman in Number Five. London, Hale, 1974; as *Burlington Square*, New York, Coward McCann, 1975.
The Fairly Innocent Little Man (Hefferman). London, Macmillan, 1974; New York, Stein and Day, 1977.
The Footpath. London, Hale, 1975.
Don't Stop for Hooky Hefferman. London, Macmillan, 1975; New York, Stein and Day, 1977.
Hooky and the Crock of Gold. London, Macmillan, 1975.
The Lost Half Hour. London, Macmillan, 1976; New York, Stein and Day, 1977.
The Vision Splendid. London, Hale, 1976.

The Folly of Henrietta Dale. London, Hale, 1976.
The Little Kingdom. London, Hale, 1977.
Folly to Be Wise. London, Hale, 1977.
Hooky Gets the Wooden Spoon. London, Macmillan, and New York, Stein and Day, 1977.
Papersnake (Hefferman). London, Macmillan, 1978.
The Dangerous Year. London, Hale, 1978.
The Sisters. London, Hale, 1979.
Hooky and the Villainous Chauffeur. London, Macmillan, 1979.

Uncollected Short Stories

"38," in *My Best Spy Story.* London, Faber, 1938.
"The Cleverest Clue," in *My Best Mystery Story.* London, Faber, 1939.
"Death in My Dreams," in *The Saint* (New York), December 1964.
"Advice to the Cobbler," in *Winter's Crimes 2*, edited by George Hardinge. London, Macmillan, 1970.

Other Publications

Novels

Mockbeggar. London, Harrap, 1924; New York, Appleton, 1925.
Lois. London, Harrap, and New York, Appleton, 1927.
Inside Out! or, Mad as a Hatter (as Geoffrey Ludlow). London, Harrap, 1934.
Women Had to Do It! (as Geoffrey Ludlow). London, Nicholson and Watson, 1936.
The Sun Will Shine. London, Transworld, 1956.
Moon over Ebury Square. London, Hale, 1962.
The Imperfect Aunt. London, Hale, 1966.
Week-end in the Scampi Belt. London, Hale, 1967.

Novels as Robert Eton

The Pattern. London, Harrap, 1934.
The Dividing Air. London, Harrap, 1935.
The Bus Leaves for the Village. London, Nicholson and Watson, 1936.
Not in Our Stars. London, Nicholson and Watson, 1937.
The Journey. London, Nicholson, and Watson, 1938.
Palace Pier. London, Nicholson and Watson, 1938.
The Legacy. London, Nicholson and Watson, 1939.
The Faithful Years. London, Nicholson and Watson, 1939.
The Corner of Paradise Place. London, Nicholson and Watson, 1940.
St. Lynn's Advertiser. London, Nicholson and Watson, 1947.
The Dragon at the Gate. London, Nicholson and Watson, 1949.

Play

Screenplay: *The Umbrella*, with H. Fowler Mear, 1933.

Verse

The Ballad of Pen Fields, with a Plan of the Battlefield.   Privately printed, 1927.

Other (juvenile)

Bedfordshire (for adults).   London, Hale, 1950.
Famous Cricket Grounds (for adults).   London, Phoenix House, 1951.
"Plum" Warner (for adults).   London, Phoenix House, 1951.
Smoky Joe.   London, Lane, 1952.
Builder and Dreamer: A Life of Isambard Kingdom Brunel.   London, Lane, 1952;
    revised edition, as *Isambard Kingdom Brunel*, London, Newnes, 1955.
Exmoor (for adults).   London, Hale, 1953.
Smoky Joe in Trouble.   London, Lane, 1953.
Policeman in the Family.   London, Oxford University Press, 1953.
Rolls, Man of Speed: A Life of Charles Stewart Rolls.   London, Lane, 1953; revised
    edition, as *The Hon. C. S. Rolls*, London, Newnes, 1955.
Under the Hollies.   London, Oxford University Press, 1954.
Bridge under the Water.   London, Phoenix House, 1954; New York, Roy, 1957.
Great Men of Staffordshire.   London, Lane, 1955.
The First Men to Fly: A Short History of Wilbur and Orville Wright.   London, Laurie,
    1955.
Animal Doctor.   London, Oxford University Press, 1956.
Smoky Joe Goes to School.   London, Lane, 1956.
James Brindley: The Pioneer of Canals.   London, Laurie, 1956.
Our Patron Saints.   London, Acorn Press, 1957.
Thomas Telford: The Life Story of a Great Engineer.   London, Lane, 1957.
Sonia Back Stage.   London, Chatto and Windus, 1957.

Farm Animals.   London, Edmund Ward, 1958.
The Young Architect.   London, Oxford University Press, 1958.
District Nurse Carter.   London, Chatto and Windus, 1958.
Nurse Ross Takes Over.   London, Hamish Hamilton, 1958.
The Hunted King.   London, Bodley Head, 1959.
Nurse Ross Shows the Way.   London, Hamish Hamilton, 1959.
Monica Anson, Travel Agent.   London, Chatto and Windus, 1959.
Nurse Ross Saves the Day.   London, Hamish Hamilton, 1960.
Bandaberry.   London, Bodley Head, 1960.
Nurse Ross and the Doctor.   London, Hamish Hamilton, 1962.
The Dancers in the Reeds.   London, Hamish Hamilton, 1963.
Good Luck, Nurse Ross.   London, Hamish Hamilton, 1963.
*Airmen on the Run: True Stories of Evasion and Escape by British Airmen of World War
    II.*   London, Odhams Press, 1963.
Scoop.   London, Hamish Hamilton, 1964.
The Empty Saddle.   London, Hamish Hamilton, 1965.
Break for Summer.   London, Hamish Hamilton, 1965.
Shadow in the Sun.   London, Hamish Hamilton, 1966.
The Suspect Scientist.   London, Hamish Hamilton, 1966.
The Man in the Hut.   London, Kaye and Ward, 1967.
Peter and the Picture Thief.   London, Kaye and Ward, 1969.
The Beginning of Words: How English Grew, with Colin Pickles.   London, Blond,
    1970; New York, Putnam, 1971.
Jimmy and the Election.   London, Kaye and Ward, 1970.
Tony Trotter and the Kitten.   London, Kaye and Ward, 1971.
The Great Cup Tie.   London, Kaye and Ward, 1974.

Other as A. Stephen Tring (juvenile)

The Old Gang. London, Oxford University Press, 1947.
Penny Dreadful. London, Oxford University Press, 1949.
The Cave by the Sea. London, Oxford University Press, 1950.
Barry's Exciting Year [*Gets His Wish, Great Day*]. London, Oxford University Press, 3
   vols., 1951–54.
Young Master Carver: A Boy in the Reign of Edward III. London, Phoenix House,
   1952; New York, Roy, 1957.
Penny Triumphant [*Penitent, Puzzled, Dramatic, in Italy, and the Pageant, Says Good-
   bye*]. London, Oxford University Press, 7 vols., 1953–61.
The Kite Man. Oxford, Blackwell, 1955.
Frankie and the Green Umbrella. London, Hamish Hamilton, 1957.
Pictures for Sale. London, Hamish Hamilton, 1958.
Peter's Busy Day. London, Hamish Hamilton, 1959.
Ted's Lucky Ball. London, Hamish Hamilton, 1961.
The Man with the Sack. London, Hamish Hamilton, 1963.
Chad. London, Hamish Hamilton, 1966.

Other as Valerie Baxter (juvenile)

Jane: Young Author. London, Lane, 1954.
Elizabeth: Young Policewoman. London, Lane, 1955.
Shirley: Young Bookseller. London, Lane, 1956.
Hester: Ship's Officer. London, Lane, 1957.

Manuscript Collection: Mugar Memorial Library, Boston University.

*   *   *

Laurence Meynell, a prolific writer in many fields of fiction and non-fiction, may be said to
have emerged properly as a crime writer only late in his career with *A View from the Terrace*
(1972). In the years since he has produced a regular flow of books which may be divided into
two distinct sorts. There are the books that have no running hero but generally have some
somewhat outré circumstance as their mainspring, and there is the series of charming and
salty books that feature "Hooky" Hefferman, a character so well conceived that he lifts the
works in which he appears into a class of their own.

It is in these books that the typical Meynell tone of voice, which shows intermittently
elsewhere when it is appropriate, comes into its own. Hooky is a man of the bars, and the
Meynell voice is a voice heard in bars. But it must be understood what "a man of the bars" is.
He is not a bar-fly, someone who can scarcely leave a bar, who cadges drinks and company.
He is not, by a long chalk, a drunk. Though he likes drink and is somewhat of a connoisseur
of it – Hooky usually drinks a Pimm's No. 1 himself – it is not for the drink alone that he
finds bars attractive. It is for the conversation, that special brand of conversation confined to
bars. Conversation in clubs and commonrooms may sometimes be as worldly and sometimes
more witty, but bar conversation is unique.

So Hooky is most at home in the right sort of bar, and Meynell's characteristic voice is
much the voice of bar talk, salty, man-of-the-world, sexy but not dirty, tolerant, with its
standards. As to the time that Hooky does not spend in bars, he makes a living, rather a
precarious one, as a classy private inquiry agent, having worked once on the edges of
journalism. He is often to be found in attractive young ladies' beds (or they may be found in
his), but woman plainly take only second place in his life. He is sometimes to be found,
unwilling and willing, in the flat in sedate Hove, Sussex, where lives his aunt, the formidable,
the rich, the Hon. Mrs. Theresa Page-Foley, one of the aunts of literature. Quite often it is this
dragon lady who somehow sets Hooky off on some adventure. These are neatly worked out

(they might almost be good stage comedies) and show the Hooky virtues – amiability, forcefulness when necessary, and a sort of direct cunning – at their best.

The books outside the Hooky canon are rather more variable. Depending as they generally do on a curious situation or an intriguing set of circumstances, they are apt to be either better or worse according to the effectiveness of their initial premise. Sometimes they will contain, rather unexpectedly, a passage or a character written at a more serious level than the rest of the book. The portrait of a headmistress in *Death of a Philanderer*, an otherwise jaunty whodunit set in a girls' school, is a case in point.

—H. R. F. Keating

MICHAELS, Barbara.   See PETERS, Elizabeth.

MILLAR, Kenneth.   See MACDONALD, Ross.

MILLAR, Margaret (Ellis, née Sturm).   American.   Born in Kitchener, Ontario, Canada, 5 February 1915. Educated at Kitchener Collegiate Institute, 1929–33; University of Toronto, 1933–36. Married Kenneth Millar, i.e., Ross Macdonald, *q.v.*, in 1938; one child, now deceased. Screen Writer, Warner Brothers, Hollywood, 1945–46. President, Mystery Writers of America, 1957–58. Recipient: Mystery Writers of America Edgar Allan Poe Award, 1956; Los Angeles *Times* Woman of the Year Award, 1965. Agent: Harold Ober Associates Inc., 40 East 49th Street, New York, New York 10017. Address: 4420 Via Esperanza, Santa Barbara, California 93105, U.S.A.

CRIME PUBLICATIONS

Novels (series characters: Dr. Paul Prye; Inspector Sands)

> *The Invisible Worm* (Prye).   New York, Doubleday, 1941; London, Long, 1943.
> *The Weak-Eyed Bat* (Prye).   New York, Doubleday, 1942.
> *The Devil Loves Me* (Prye).   New York, Doubleday, 1942.
> *Wall of Eyes* (Sands).   New York, Random House, 1943; London, Lancer, 1966.
> *Fire Will Freeze.*   New York, Random House, 1944.
> *The Iron Gates* (Sands).   New York, Random House, 1945; as *Taste of Fears*, London, Hale, 1950.
> *Do Evil in Return.*   New York, Random House, 1950; London, Museum Press, 1952.

Rose's Last Summer. New York, Random House, 1952; London, Museum Press, 1954; as *The Lively Corpse*, New York, Dell, n.d.
Vanish in an Instant. New York, Random House, 1952; London, Museum Press, 1953.
Beast in View. New York, Random House, and London, Gollancz, 1955.
An Air That Kills. New York, Random House, 1957; as *The Soft Talkers*, London, Gollancz, 1957.
The Listening Walls. New York, Random House, and London, Gollancz, 1959.
A Stranger in My Grave. New York, Random House, and London, Gollancz, 1960.
How Like an Angel. New York, Random House, and London, Gollancz, 1962.
The Fiend. New York, Random House, and London, Gollancz, 1964.
Beyond This Point Are Monsters. New York, Random House, 1970; London, Gollancz, 1971.
Ask for Me Tomorrow. New York, Random House, 1976; London, Gollancz, 1977.
The Murder of Miranda. New York, Random House, 1979.

Uncollected Short Stories

"The Couple Next Door," in *Ellery Queen's Awards: Ninth Series.* Boston, Little Brown, 1954; London, Collins, 1956.
"The People Across the Canyon," in *Ellery Queen's Mystery Magazine* (New York), October 1962.
"McGowney's Miracle," in *Every Crime in the Book.* New York, Putnam, 1975.

OTHER PUBLICATIONS

Novels

Experiment in Springtime. New York, Random House, 1947.
It's All in the Family. New York, Random House, 1948.
The Cannibal Heart. New York, Random House, 1949; London, Hamish Hamilton, 1950.
Wives and Lovers. New York, Random House, 1954.

Other

The Birds and Beasts Were There (autobiography). New York, Random House, 1968.

*   *   *

Following three humorous mystery novels about a somewhat whimsical psychiatrist detective named Paul Prye, Margaret Millar decided to put psychiatry to more serious uses. The result was *Wall of Eyes*, the first of two novels about Inspector Sands of the Toronto Police Department. *Wall of Eyes* was not an immediate success, however, and it wasn't until the second Inspector Sands novel, *The Iron Gates*, that she began to attract the critical acclaim she deserved. The bizarre plot elements – a severed finger, an escape from a mental hospital – combined with a solid psychological puzzle that kept the reader guessing till the end. In America the volume was chosen to launch a new mystery book club, which then went on to resurrect *Wall of Eyes* for its members. Sadly, these are the only two novels about lonely Inspector Sands, though the reader is pleased to encounter him retired to California in a single short story "The Couple Next Door."

After writing three non-criminous novels, Margaret Millar returned to the mystery with *Do Evil in Return* and the lighter-hearted *Rose's Last Summer*. *Vanish in an Instant*, set in a Michigan college town during a murderous winter, paved the way for Mrs. Millar's best novel up to that time, *Beast in View*. Unfortunately, the shock of this book's central plot device has been weakened by repeated use in later books by other authors, but rarely has it been done as effectively as here. *Beast in View* was the beginning of a string of exceptional mystery novels. *An Air That Kills* offered a bit of satire along with the mystery, and the next three novels offered something even more special. They are, in a special sense, the peak of the mystery writer's art in that each of them withholds the key element of its solution until the very end of the book.

The first of this special trio was *The Listening Walls*, about an overheard conversation, murder, and a tangled web of trickery that leads to Mexico. The twist, or double twist, is saved until the book's very last words. *A Stranger in My Grave* introduces Steve Pinata, the first private investigator to appear in Mrs. Millar's novels. Just as the success of her early novels helped launch her husband, Kenneth Millar (Ross Macdonald), on his career as a mystery writer, there is some evidence in *A Stranger in My Grave* and her following novel that she has been influenced by the California tradition of sleuths like Lew Archer. The plot concerns a young woman who dreams she sees her own grave. One day while awake she actually does see it. Like the best of Ross Macdonald's novels the solution lies in the past, in tangled family relationships that are not made completely clear until the last two words of the novel.

The third of this group, and Margaret Millar's finest novel, is *How Like an Angel*. Joe Quinn, formerly a Reno casino cop, comes in contact with a California religious cult called the True Believers. Sister Blessing persuades him to investigate the disappearance and possible death of a man named Patrick O'Gorman. Again there is crime in the past, and tangled relationships. But best of all there is a moving and very real portrait of this strange religious community.

Since the mid-1960's, Millar's novels have become less frequent. Their quality has remained high, however. *The Fiend* deals with a possible mental case who may or may not be guilty of child abuse. *Beyond This Point Are Monsters*, set in the San Diego area, offers a moving portrait of Chicanos in the region. And *Ask for Me Tomorrow* follows a young lawyer to Mexico on the trail of a wealthy woman's missing first husband. After scenes in Baja California and a Mexican prison, with murder along the way, the lawyer Tom Aragon reaches the end of his quest – and uncovers a surprising trick of identity worthy of Millar's best novels.

Margaret Millar has produced only a handful of short stories. In addition to the Inspector Sands story mentioned above there is a suspense tale entitled "The People Across the Canyon." And there is a little gem of a story called "McGowney's Miracle," about an undertaker's strange new wife.

Best of all in the novels of Margaret Millar has been her ability to conjure up what Julian Symons rightly describes as "an atmosphere of uneasiness." Things are never quite right in the worlds she so vividly portrays, and we keep reading to find out why.

—Edward D. Hoch

MILLER, Wade. Pseudonym for Robert Wade and Bill Miller; also wrote as Will Daemer; Whit Masterson; Dale Wilmer. **MILLER, Bill:** Born in Garrett, Indiana, in 1920. Educated at Woodrow Wilson Junior High School, San Diego; San Diego State College. Served in the United States Air Force in the Pacific during World War II: Sergeant. Married; one daughter and one son. *Died 21 August 1961.* **WADE, Robert:** Born in San Diego, California, in 1920. Educated at Woodrow Wilson Junior High School, San Diego; San Diego State College. Served in the United States Air Force in Europe during World War II: Sergeant. Married; two daughters and two sons. Wade and Miller began their collaboration while still in school; they edited the East San Diego *Press*, and also wrote radio plays.

CRIME PUBLICATIONS

Novels (series character: Max Thursday)

Deadly Weapon. New York, Farrar Straus, 1946; London, Sampson Low, 1947.
Guilty Bystander (Thursday). New York, Farrar Straus, 1947; London, Sampson Low, 1948.
Pop Goes the Queen (as Bob Wade and Bill Miller). New York, Farrar Straus, 1947; as *Murder − Queen High*, London, W. H. Allen, 1958.
Fatal Step (Thursday). New York, Farrar Straus, 1948; London, Sampson Low, 1949.
Uneasy Street (Thursday). New York, Farrar Straus, 1948; London, Sampson Low, 1949.
Devil on Two Sticks. New York, Farrar Straus, 1949; as *Killer's Choice*, New York, New American Library, 1950.
Calamity Fair (Thursday). New York, Farrar Straus, 1950.
Devil May Care. New York, Fawcett, 1950; London, Fawcett, 1957.
Murder Charge (Thursday). New York, Farrar Straus, 1950.
Stolen Woman. New York, Fawcett, 1950; London, Fawcett, 1958.
The Case of the Lonely Lovers (as Will Daemer). New York, Farrell, 1951.
The Killer. New York, Fawcett, 1951; London, Fawcett, 1957.
Shoot to Kill (Thursday). New York, Farrar Straus, 1951; London, W. H. Allen, 1953.
The Tiger's Wife. New York, Fawcett, 1951; London, Red Seal, 1958.
Branded Woman. New York, Fawcett, 1952; London, Fawcett, 1954.
The Big Guy. New York, Fawcett, 1953; London, Red Seal, 1958.
South of the Sun. New York, Fawcett, and London, Red Seal, 1953.
Mad Baxter. New York, Fawcett, 1955; London, Fawcett, 1956.
Kiss Her Goodbye. New York, Lion, 1956; London, W. H. Allen, 1957.
Kitten with a Whip. New York, Fawcett, 1959; London, Muller, 1960.
Sinner Take All. New York, Fawcett, 1960; London, Muller, 1961.
Nightmare Cruise. New York, Ace, 1961; as *The Sargasso People*, London, W. H. Allen, 1961.
The Girl from Midnight. New York, Fawcett, 1962.

Novels as Dale Wilmer

Memo for Murder. Hasbrouck Heights, New Jersey, Graphic, 1951.
Dead Fall. New York, Bouregy, 1954.
Jungle Heat. New York, Pyramid, 1954; London, Panther, 1962.

Novels as Whit Masterson (continued by Robert Wade alone after 1961)

All Though the Night. New York, Dodd Mead, 1955; London, W. H. Allen, 1956; as *A Cry in the Night*, New York, Bantam, 1956.
Dead, She Was Beautiful. New York, Dodd Mead, and London, W. H. Allen, 1955.
Badge of Evil. New York, Dodd Mead, and London, W. H. Allen, 1956; as *Touch of Evil*, New York, Bantam, 1958.
A Shadow in the Wild. New York, Dodd Mead, and London, W. H. Allen, 1957.
The Dark Fantastic. New York, Dodd Mead, 1959; London, W. H. Allen, 1960.
A Hammer in His Hand. New York, Dodd Mead, and London, W. H. Allen, 1960.
Evil Come, Evil Go. New York, Dodd Mead, and London, W. H. Allen, 1961.
Man on a Nylon String. New York, Dodd Mead, and London, W. H. Allen, 1963.

711 — Officer Needs Help. New York, Dodd Mead, 1965; as *Killer with a Badge*,
    London, W. H. Allen, 1966; as *Warning Shot*, New York, Popular Library, 1967.
Play Like You're Dead. New York, Dodd Mead, 1967; London, Hale, 1969.
The Last One Kills. New York, Dodd Mead, 1969; London, Hale, 1972.
The Death of Me Yet. New York, Dodd Mead, 1970; London, Hale, 1972.
The Gravy Train. New York, Dodd Mead, 1971; London, Hale, 1972; as *The Great*
    Train HiJack, New York, Pinnacle, 1976.
Why She Cries, I Do Not Know. New York, Dodd Mead, 1972; London, Hale, 1974.
The Undertaker Wind. New York, Dodd Mead, 1973; London, Hale, 1974.
The Man With Two Clocks. New York, Dodd Mead, 1974; London, Hale, 1975.
Hunter of the Blood. New York, Dodd Mead, 1977; London, Hale, 1978.
The Slow Gallows. New York, Dodd Mead, 1979.

Novels as Robert Wade

The Stroke of Seven. New York, Morrow, 1965; London, Heinemann, 1966.
Knave of Eagles. New York, Random House, 1969; London, Hale, 1970.

Uncollected Short Stories

"Invitation to an Accident," in *Ellery Queen's Awards, 10th Series.* Boston, Little
    Brown, 1955; London, Collins, 1957.
"A Bad Time of Day," in *Ellery Queen's Awards, 11th Series.* New York, Simon and
    Schuster, 1956; London, Collins, 1958.
"We Were Picked as the Odd Ones," in *The Saint* (New York), July 1960.
"The Memorial Hour," in *Ellery Queen's 15th Annual.* New York, Random House,
    1960; London, Gollancz, 1961.
"The Morning After," in *The Playboy Book of Crime and Suspense.* Chicago, Playboy
    Press, 1966.

Uncollected Short Stories as Whit Masterson

"The Women in His Life," in *Ellery Queen's 13th Annual.* New York, Random House,
    1958; London, Collins, 1960.
"Dark Fantastic," in *Cosmopolitan* (New York), February 1959.
"Suddenly It's Midnight," in *Anthology 1970 Mid-Year*, edited by Ellery Queen. New
    York, Davis, 1970.

*   *   *

In an era when the private-eye novels of Hammett, Chandler, and Macdonald are the
subject of serious literary discussion it's odd that virtually no attention is given to the early
works of Wade Miller. Certainly Miller's private eye, Max Thursday, is not in the same class
as Spadè, Marlowe, and Archer, but he is still someone worth knowing, and his six cases,
written during a five-year period (1947–1951), are still a pleasure to read.

Even before he created Thursday, Wade Miller wrote an excellent first novel, *Deadly
Weapon*. The private eye here is named Walter James, and the novel opens with a murder at
a San Diego burlesque house. Also prominent in the proceedings is Lieutenant Austin Clapp
of the San Diego police. There is something of the pace and violence of Hammett here,
together with an ending unique in the private-eye genre. Though praised at the time of its
publication, the book is too little known today.

Miller's next novel, *Guilty Bystander*, introduced the San Diego private detective Max
Thursday and brought back Lieutenant Austin Clapp as well. Clapp figures in all of the
Thursday novels, occasionally serving as a commentator on violence and the human
condition. Thursday's career begins as a house detective in a cheap hotel. He is divorced and

drinking too much. He is drawn into a case when his child is kidnapped. The solving of it rehabilitates him and he becomes a successful private eye – though one with a hair-trigger temper that often flares into violence. The first few books end in a burst of violence, until finally he becomes reluctant to carry a gun.

During the late 1940's Miller produced two other fine novels. *Pop Goes the Queen* was published originally as by Bob Wade and Bill Miller, apparently because its amusing plot, involving a young couple in the California desert, was far from the grim realism of the Wade Miller books, but it has a solid mystery plot with a spectacular ending. *Devil on Two Sticks* also offered something new. The "detective" is a member of a criminal gang, chosen by the boss to discover and kill a police informer in their midst. The complete reversal of the usual detective story works quite well; the novel deserves rediscovery.

Shoot to Kill was, unfortunately, the last Wade Miller novel to appear in hard covers. That byline was used during the 1950's on a string of paperback originals like *Kitten with a Whip*, while the authors turned their attention to a new hardcover pseudonym, Whit Masterson. The best of these were probably *All Through the Night*, about a kidnapping; *Badge of Evil*, the basis for the memorable Orson Welles film *Touch of Evil*; and *A Hammer in His Hand*, with a policewoman protagonist.

The authors also wrote three books as Dale Wilmer; the best of these was *Dead Fall*, about murder and espionage in a California aircraft plant.

—Edward D. Hoch

MILNE, A(lan) A(lexander). British. Born in London, 18 January 1882. Educated at Westminster School, London (Queen's Scholar), 1893–1900; Trinity College, Cambridge (Editor, *Granta*, 1902), 1900–03, B.A. in mathematics 1903. Served in the Royal Warwickshire Regiment, 1914–18. Married Dorothy de Sélincourt in 1913; one son, the writer Christopher Robin Milne. Free-lance journalist, 1903–06; Assistant Editor, *Punch*, London, 1906–14. *Died 31 January 1956.*

CRIME PUBLICATIONS

Novels

    The Red House Mystery. London, Methuen, and New York, Dutton, 1922.
    Four Days' Wonder. London, Methuen, and New York, Dutton, 1933.

Short Stories   •

    A Table near the Band and Other Stories. London, Methuen, and New York, Dutton, 1950.

Uncollected Short Stories

    "A Savage Game" and "Bread upon the Waters," in *The Evening Standard Detective Book.* London, Gollancz, 1950.
    "It Was a Long Time Ago," in *Ellery Queen's Mystery Magazine* (New York), July 1950.
    "It Could Have Happened That Way," in *Ellery Queen's Mystery Magazine* (New York), May 1951.

"Nearly Perfect," in *Best Detective Stories of the Year 1951*, edited by David Coxe Cooke.   New York, Dutton, 1951.
"A Perfectly Ordinary Case of Blackmail," in *Ellery Queen's Mystery Magazine* (New York), November 1952.

OTHER PUBLICATIONS

Novels

Mr. Pim.   London, Hodder and Stoughton, 1921; New York, Doran, 1922; as *Mr. Pim Passes By*, London, Methuen, 1929.
Two People.   London, Methuen, and New York, Dutton, 1933.
One Year's Time.   London, Methuen, 1942.
Chloe Marr.   London, Methuen, and New York, Dutton, 1946.

Short Stories

The Secret and Other Stories.   London, Methuen, and New York, Fountain Press, 1929.
Birthday Party and Other Stories.   New York, Dutton, 1948; London, Methuen, 1949.

Plays

Wurzel-Flummery (produced London, 1917).   London and New York, French, 1921; revised version, in *First Plays*, 1919.
Belinda: An April Folly (produced London and New York, 1918).   Included in *First Plays*, 1919.
The Boy Comes Home (produced London, 1918).   Included in *First Plays*, 1919.
Make-Believe (for children), music by George Dorlay, lyrics by C. E. Burton (produced London, 1918).   Included in *Second Plays*, 1921.
First Plays (includes *Wurzel-Flummery*, *The Lucky One*, *The Boy Comes Home*, *Belinda*, *The Red Feathers*).   London, Chatto and Windus, and New York, Knopf, 1919.
The Red Feathers (produced Leeds, 1920; London, 1921).   Included in *First Plays*, 1919.
The Lucky One (produced New York, 1922; Cambridge, 1923; London, 1924).   Included in *First Plays*, 1919.
The Camberley Triangle (produced London, 1919).   Included in *Second Plays*, 1921.
Mr. Pim Passes By (produced Manchester, 1919; London, 1920; New York, 1921).   Included in *Second Plays*, 1921.
The Romantic Age (produced London, 1920; New York, 1922).   Included in *Second Plays*, 1921.
The Stepmother (produced London, 1920).   Included in *Second Plays*, 1921.
Second Plays (includes *Make-Believe*, *Mr. Pim Passes By*, *The Camberley Triangle*, *The Romantic Age*, *The Stepmother*).   London, Chatto and Windus, 1921; New York, Knopf, 1922.
The Great Broxopp: Four Chapters in Her Life (produced New York, 1921; London, 1923).   Included in *Three Plays*, 1922.
The Truth about Blayds (produced London, 1921; New York, 1922).   Included in *Three Plays*, 1922.
The Dover Road (produced New York, 1921; London, 1922).   Included in *Three Plays*, 1922.
Three Plays (includes *The Dover Road*, *The Truth about Blayds*, *The Great Broxopp*).   New York, Putnam, 1922; London, Chatto and Windus, 1923.
Berlud, Unlimited (produced London and New York, 1922).

Success (produced London, 1923; as *Give Me Yesterday*, produced New York,
    1931). London, Chatto and Windus, 1923; New York, French, 1924.
The Artist: A Duologue. London and New York, French, 1923.
The Man in the Bowler Hat: A Terribly Exciting Affair (for children; produced New
    York, 1924; London, 1925). London and New York, French, 1923.
To Have the Honour (produced London, 1924; as *To Meet the Prince*, produced New
    York, 1929). London and New York, French, 1925.
Ariadne; or, Business First (produced New York and London, 1925). London and
    New York, French, 1925.
Portrait of a Gentleman in Slippers: A Fairy Tale (produced Liverpool, 1926; London,
    1927). London and New York, French, 1926.
Four Plays (includes *To Have the Honour, Ariadne, Portrait of a Gentleman in Slippers,
    Success*). London, Chatto and Windus, 1926.
Miss Marlow at Play (produced London, 1927; New York, 1940). London and New
    York, French, 1936.
The Ivory Door: A Legend (produced New York, 1927; London, 1929). New York,
    Putnam, 1928; London, Chatto and Windus, 1929.
The Princess and the Woodcutter, in *Eight Modern Plays for Juniors*, edited by John
    Hampden. London, Nelson, 1927.
Let's All Talk about Gerald (produced London, 1928).
Gentleman Unknown (produced London, 1928).
The Fourth Wall: A Detective Story (produced London, 1928; as *The Perfect Alibi*,
    produced New York, 1928). New York, French, 1929; London, French, 1930.
Michael and Mary (produced New York, 1929; London, 1930). London, Chatto and
    Windus, 1930; New York, French, 1932.
Toad of Toad Hall (for children), music by H. Fraser-Simson, adaptation of the story *The
    Wind in the Willows* by Kenneth Grahame (produced Liverpool, 1929; London,
    1930). London, Methuen, and New York, Scribner, 1929.
They Don't Mean Any Harm (produced New York, 1932).
Four Plays (includes *Michael and Mary, To Meet the Prince, The Perfect Alibi, Portrait of
    a Gentleman in Slippers*). New York, Putnam, 1932.
Other People's Lives (produced London, 1933). London and New York, French, 1935.
More Plays (includes *The Ivory Door, The Fourth Wall, Other People's Lives*). London,
    Chatto and Windus, 1935.
Miss Elizabeth Bennet, adaptation of the novel *Pride and Prejudice* by Jane Austen
    (produced London, 1938). London, Chatto and Windus, 1936.
Sarah Simple (produced London, 1937; New York, 1940). London, French, 1939.
The Ugly Duckling (for children). London, French, 1941.
Before the Flood. London and New York, French, 1951.

Verse

When We Were Very Young (juvenile). London, Methuen, and New York, Dutton,
    1924.
For the Luncheon Interval: Cricket and Other Verses. London, Methuen, and New
    York, Dutton, 1925.
Now We Are Six (juvenile). London, Methuen, and New York, Dutton, 1927.
Behind the Lines. London, Methuen, and New York, Dutton, 1940.
Sneezles and Other Selections (juvenile). New York, Dutton, 1947.
The Norman Church. London, Methuen, 1948.

Other

Lovers in London. London, Alston Rivers, 1905.
The Day's Play (*Punch* sketches). London, Methuen, 1910; New York, Dutton, 1925.
The Holiday Round (*Punch* sketches). London, Methuen, 1912; New York, Dutton, 1925.
Once a Week (*Punch* sketches). London, Methuen, 1914; New York, Dutton, 1925.
Happy Days (*Punch* sketches). New York, Doran, 1915.
Once on a Time (juvenile). London, Hodder and Stoughton, 1917; New York, Putnam, 1922.
Not That It Matters. London, Methuen, 1919; New York, Dutton, 1920.
If I May. London, Methuen, 1920; New York, Dutton, 1921.
The Sunny Side. London, Methuen, 1921; New York, Dutton, 1922.
A Gallery of Children (juvenile). London, Stanley Paul, and Philadelphia, McKay, 1925.
Winnie-the-Pooh (juvenile). London, Methuen, and New York, Dutton, 1926.
(Selected Works). London, Library Press, 7 vols., 1926.
The Ascent of Man. London, Benn, 1928.
The House at Pooh Corner (juvenile). London, Methuen, and New York, Dutton, 1928.
By Way of Introduction. London, Methuen, and New York, Dutton, 1929.
Those Were the Days: The Day's Play, The Holiday Round, Once a Week, The Sunny Side. London, Methuen, and New York, Dutton, 1929.
When I Was Very Young (autobiography). London, Methuen, and New York, Fountain Press, 1930.
The Very Young Calendar 1930 (juvenile). New York, Dutton, 1930.
A. A. Milne (selections). London, Methuen, 1933.
Peace with Honour: An Enquiry into the War Convention. London, Methuen, and New York, Dutton, 1934; revised edition, Methuen and Dutton, 1935.
It's Too Late Now: The Autobiography of a Writer. London, Methuen, 1939; as *Autobiography*, New York, Dutton, 1939.
War with Honour. London, Macmillan, 1940.
War Aims Unlimited. London, Methuen, 1941.
Going Abroad? London, Council for Education in World Citizenship, 1947.
Books for Children: A Reader's Guide. London, Cambridge University Press, 1948.
Year In, Year Out. London, Methuen, and New York, Dutton, 1952.
On Lewis Carroll. Lexington, Helm Press, 1964.
Prince Rabbit, and The Princess Who Could Not Laugh (juvenile). London, Edmund Ward, and New York, Dutton, 1966.

*   *   *

A. A. Milne's single true-detective novel, *The Red House*, has been justly praised, as well as overpraised. It is not "one of the three best mystery stories of all time," but it is, nearly 60 years after it was written, readable, genuinely puzzling, and, within the limits of its sensibility, charming. Raymond Chandler's comments about the credibility of the police procedure in the novel are certainly accurate, but the same criticisms could be levelled at any number of detective and suspense novels, some of which have a tone of pompous and spurious "knowingness" happily foreign to Milne. The hero of *The Red House* also talks as though he had inside knowledge, but only of the conventions of Holmesian detective fiction.

One of the pleasures of the novel is Antony Gillingham's sorting out of the Holmes-Watson relationship with his friend Bill Beverly. Tony generously gives Bill full warning of the masochistic aspects of the role, even as he asks him to play it. Later, he cheerfully admits his mistakes as he discovers them. The effect is tonic. Milne shows the same comradely regard for the reader, directing his attention from the outset to the real murderer, pointing out the suspicious oddities in his behavior at every turn. At the same time, he is, of course, misdirecting the reader's attention from the crucial problem with a fine display of Tony's theoretical imagination. *The Red House* remains an excellent example of the classic English detective novel.

—Carol Cleveland

MITCHELL, Gladys (Maude Winifred). Also writes as Stephen Hockaby; Malcolm Torrie. British. Born in Cowley, Oxfordshire, 19 April 1901. Educated at the Green School, Isleworth, Middlesex; Goldsmiths' College, University of London, 1919–21; University College, London, external diploma in history 1926. Taught English and history at St. Paul's School, Brentford, Middlesex, 1921–25, St. Ann's Senior Girls' School, Ealing, London, 1925–39, Senior Girls' School, Brentford, 1941–50, and Matthew Arnold School, Staines, Middlesex, 1953–61. Recipient: Crime Writers Association Silver Dagger, 1976. Agent: Curtis Brown Ltd., 1 Craven Hill, London W2 3EP. Address: 1 Cecil Close, Corfe Mullen, Dorset BH21 3PW, England.

CRIME PUBLICATIONS

Novels (series character: Mrs. Beatrice Lestrange Bradley in all books)

Speedy Death. London, Gollancz, and New York, Dial Press, 1929.
The Mystery of a Butcher's Shop. London, Gollancz, 1929; New York, Dial Press, 1930.
The Longer Bodies. London, Gollancz, 1930.
The Saltmarsh Murders. London, Gollancz, 1932; Philadelphia, Macrae Smith, 1933.
Ask a Policeman, with others. London, Barker, and New York, Morrow, 1933.
Death at the Opera. London, Grayson, 1934; as *Death in the Wet*, Philadelphia, Macrae Smith, 1934.
The Devil at Saxon Wall. London, Grayson, 1935.
Dead Men's Morris. London, Joseph, 1936.
Come Away, Death. London, Joseph, 1937.
St. Peter's Finger. London, Joseph, 1938.
Printer's Error. London, Joseph, 1939.
Brazen Tongue. London, Joseph, 1940.
Hangman's Curfew. London, Joseph, 1941.
When Last I Died. London, Joseph, 1941; New York, Knopf, 1942.
Laurels Are Poison. London, Joseph, 1942.
The Worsted Viper. London, Joseph, 1943.
Sunset over Soho. London, Joseph, 1943.
My Father Sleeps. London, Joseph, 1944.
The Rising of the Moon. London, Joseph, 1945.
Here Comes a Chopper. London, Joseph, 1946.
Death and the Maiden. London, Joseph, 1947.
The Dancing Druids. London, Joseph, 1948.
Tom Brown's Body. London, Joseph, 1949.
Groaning Spinney. London, Joseph, 1950.
The Devil's Elbow. London, Joseph, 1951.

The Echoing Strangers. London, Joseph, 1952.
Merlin's Furlong. London, Joseph, 1953.
Faintley Speaking. London, Joseph, 1954.
Watson's Choice. London, Joseph, 1955; New York, McKay, 1976.
Twelve Horses and the Hangman's Noose. London, Joseph, 1956.
The Twenty-Third Man. London, Joseph, 1957.
Spotted Hemlock. London, Joseph, 1958.
The Man Who Grew Tomatoes. London, Joseph, and New York, British Book Centre, 1959.
Say It with Flowers. London, Joseph, 1960.
The Nodding Canaries. London, Joseph, 1961.
My Bones Will Keep. London, Joseph, and New York, British Book Centre, 1962.
Adders on the Heath. London, Joseph, and New York, British Book Centre, 1963.
Death of a Delft Blue. London, Joseph, 1964; New York, British Book Centre, 1965.
Pageant of Murder. London, Joseph, and New York, British Book Centre, 1965.
The Croaking Raven. London, Joseph, 1966.
Skeleton Island. London, Joseph, 1967.
Three Quick and Five Dead. London, Joseph, 1968.
Dance to Your Daddy. London, Joseph, 1969.
Gory Dew. London, Joseph, 1970.
Lament for Leto. London, Joseph, 1971.
A Hearse on May-Day. London, Joseph, 1972.
The Murder of Busy Lizzie. London, Joseph, 1973.
A Javelin for Jonah. London, Joseph, 1974.
Winking at the Brim. London, Joseph, 1974; New York, McKay, 1977.
Convent on Styx. London, Joseph, 1975.
Late, Late in the Evening. London, Joseph, 1976.
Noonday and Night. London, Joseph, 1977.
Fault in the Structure. London, Joseph, 1977.
Wraiths and Changelings. London, Joseph, 1978.
Mingled with Venom. London, Joseph, 1978.
Nest of Vipers. London, Joseph, 1979.
The Mudflats of the Dead. London, Joseph, 1979.

Novels as Malcolm Torrie (series character: Timothy Herring in all books)

Heavy as Lead. London, Joseph, 1966.
Late and Cold. London, Joseph, 1967.
Your Secret Friend. London, Joseph, 1968.
Churchyard Salad. London, Joseph, 1969.
Shades of Darkness. London, Joseph, 1970.
Bismarck Herrings. London, Joseph, 1971.

Uncollected Short Stories

"The Case of the 100 Cats," in *Fifty Famous Detectives of Fiction.* London, Odhams Press, 1938.
"Daisy Bell," in *Detective Stories of Today,* edited by Raymond Postgate. London, Faber, 1940.
"Stranger's Hall" and "A Light on Murder," in *The Evening Standard Detective Book.* London, Gollancz, 1951.
"The Jar of Ginger" and "Manor Park," in *The Evening Standard Detective Book,* 2nd series. London, Gollancz, 1951.

OTHER PUBLICATIONS

Novels as Stephen Hockaby

Marsh Hay. London, Grayson, 1933.
Seven Stars and Orion. London, Grayson, 1934.
Gabriel's Hold. London, Grayson, 1935.
Shallow Brown. London, Joseph, 1936.
Grand Master. London, Joseph, 1939.

Other

Outlaws of the Border (juvenile). London, Pitman, 1936.
The Three Fingerprints (juvenile). London, Heinemann, 1940.
Holiday River (juvenile). London, Evans, 1948.
The Seven Stones Mystery (juvenile). London, Evans, 1949.
The Malory Secret (juvenile). London, Evans, 1950.
Pam at Storne Castle (juvenile). London, Evans, 1951.
Caravan Creek. London, Blackie, 1954.
On Your Marks (juvenile). London, Heinemann, 1954; revised edition, London, Parrish, 1964.
The Light-Blue Hills (juvenile). London, Bodley Head, 1959.
"Why Do People Read Detective Stories?," in *Murder Ink: The Mystery Reader's Companion,* edited by Dilys Winn. New York, Workman, 1977.

*   *   *

There is no doubt that Gladys Mitchell is a special taste and that, even among her admirers, a careful reading of her large *oeuvre* will reinforce affectionately held ambivalences. She has been little published in the United States since the beginning of her career. Yet to mystery readers in England who have followed the classic school she is practically an institution. What is more, from her "retirement" (after many years as a schoolteacher and games-mistress) in a tiny village in Dorset, this *grande dame* of the genre still produces a book a year. It is worth remembering, too, that Mitchell was an early member of the justly famous Detection Club, whose active participants included such luminaries as Chesterton, Sayers, and Christie.

With the release of *Speedy Death* in 1929, Mitchell unleashed upon the proverbially unsuspecting public that repellently delightful, now immortal, sleuth, Beatrice Adela Lestrange Bradley. It can be said that Mrs. Bradley, later Dame Beatrice, makes in *Speedy Death* a debut which no other detective of such longevity can match. To wit, she *commits* the novel's second murder, is put on trial for it, is pronounced not guilty by a jury, and then blithely admits her culpability to her defense lawyer (who just happens to be her son by her first marriage). And, on top of all this, the reader has to swallow the fact that the first corpse is a well-known, virile explorer who, when found drowned and naked in the bath, turns out to be a woman!

To put it mildly, eccentric goings-on are Mitchell's hallmark. And although some critics have felt that her plots suffered from too much attention paid to witchcraft, the supernatural, and folklore esoterica, this proclivity is what gives her work a consistent flavor, fine for those who like it and to be avoided by those who don't.

A secondary consideration, meshing with the above tendencies, is Mitchell's special feeling for the mystical nature of things British. Barrows and earthworks and Arthurian relics, morris dancing and may-day rituals: all of these are carefully and intricately dealt into the stories, illustrating Mitchell's lifelong fascination with the antiquities of the British Isles and their accompanying superstitions. The "green man" of legend figures in one book, and,

Mitchell being an unregenerate believer in the Loch Ness monster, a cousin of "Nessie" surfaces to wink a wet eye at Mrs. Bradley's niece in another.

Mrs. Bradley, it seems likely, is a partial stand-in for her creator, for their interests are identical. However, the former is already of an advanced age when first we meet her, in *Speedy Death*, and remains pretty much the same in the years and titles thereafter. Her official profession is that of psychologist, and she runs a clinic and is also a consultant to the Home Office. She is the author of *A Small Handbook of Psychoanalysis*, and her detecting methods combine hocus-pocus and Freud, seasoned with sarcasm and the patience of a predator toying with its intended victim. Those familiar with the many books featuring Mrs. Bradley are aware that her physical appearance is singular, for she is said to look like a sinister pterodactyl with a Cheshire Cat smile. Yet, though she is shrivelled and crone-like, she has a wonderful, treacle-smooth speaking voice, and, in the manner of the best village witches, she is mesmerizing to, and adored by, children and animals.

In addition to writing the Bradley adventures, Mitchell has also written under two pseudonyms, Stephen Hockaby and Malcolm Torrie. There seems to be no particular reason why these are masculine, although the Torrie books have a hero (eventually joined by a wife), Timothy Herring, who runs a society for the Preservation of Buildings of Historic Interest. It is really not possible to single out Mitchell's most important book or her greatest achievement; at different times *The Rising of the Moon*, *Sunset over Soho*, *The Saltmarsh Murders*, and *Watson's Choice* have been highly acclaimed. A survivor of the Golden Age, Mitchell is significant, most of all, because she is *sui generis*.

—Michele Slung

MOFFAT, Gwen. British. Born in Brighton, Sussex, 3 July 1924. Educated at Hove County Grammar School, Sussex. Served in the Auxiliary Territorial Service, 1943–47. Married 1) Gordon Moffat in 1948; one daughter; 2) John Lees in 1956. Has worked as a mountain guide; frequent broadcaster and contributor to newspapers on mountain climbing, travel, camping, and related subjects. Recipient: Welsh Arts Council bursary, 1973. Agent: Mark Hamilton, A. M. Heath and Company Ltd., 40–42 William IV Street, London WC2N 4DD, England. Address: Cefn y Waun, Waunfawr, Caernarvon, Gwynedd, Wales.

CRIME PUBLICATIONS

Novels (series character: Melinda Pink in all books except *Deviant Death* and *The Corpse Road*)

Lady with a Cool Eye. London, Gollancz, 1973.
Deviant Death. London, Gollancz, 1973.
The Corpse Road. London, Gollancz, 1974.
Miss Pink at the Edge of the World. London, Gollancz, and New York, Scribner, 1975.
Over the Sea to Death. London, Gollancz, and New York, Scribner, 1976.
A Short Time to Live. London, Gollancz, 1976.
Persons Unknown. London, Gollancz, 1978.

OTHER PUBLICATIONS

Novel

   Hard Option. London, Gollancz, 1975.

Other

   Space below My Feet (autobiography). London, Hodder and Stoughton, and New
     York, Houghton Mifflin, 1961.
   Two Star Red: A Book about R.A.F. Mountain Rescue. London, Hodder and
     Stoughton, 1964.
   On My Home Ground (on climbing). London, Hodder and Stoughton, 1968.
   Survival Count (on conservation). London, Gollancz, 1972.

Gwen Moffat comments:
   My books are set in areas with which I'm familiar, usually because I've lived there: wild,
beautiful, slightly off-centre places. If I do use a famous beauty spot, the action takes place in
the off-season, as in *A Short Time to Live*: a Lakeland dale in November. Background is
carefully researched: a day in a quarry for *Deviant Death*; swimming into wet sea caverns for
Persons Unknown; burning bones and human teeth on the study fire to determine the rate of
calcification for *The Corpse Road*.
   I exploit my own interests and these are legion. Wildlife, good food and wine, cats.
Organic living, prehistory, and the supernatural – these provide background; but juvenile
delinquents, the permissive society and its backlash – these are the stuff from which plots
proliferate. The curiosity of it is that if you set the basic problems of violence, greed, joyless
sex, in a wilderness area, they are no longer merely problems over-exposed by the media;
they revert to their context, and they spawn moral anarchy.
   I juxtapose human cosiness with elemental violence. Initially there is an ambiance where
people have learned to live with Nature, however untamed; perhaps some of them preserving
only a fragile balance but managing to maintain it somehow. Then an event occurs, a visitor
arrives; the cosiness cracks and the horror oozes out. First menace, then fear, then,
inevitably, murder.
   Miss Pink, who appears in five of the novels, is a middle-aged J.P. with incipient arthritis
and a weight problem – but Miss Pink is not cosy. That is only the mask, a mask also worn by
Chief Inspector Page in *The Corpse Road*; he is a similar character: wise, dependable, cool.
Both are compassionate, both ruthless, yet neither is inconsistent. Pink and Page know where
they're going and, although they are open-minded (no investigator is worth his salt unless
fascinated by new experiences), their reactions are consistent with their principles.
Compassion is there for people who make mistakes, for the repentant; but where evil
appears, in the true villain, the sadist, the malicious, it is dealt with like the diseased runt of
the litter, and implacably. Miss Pink is human, with a sense of humour, but she is no joke.
There are times when she threatens to awe me.

*   *   *

   Miss Pink is a mountain climber. Miss Moffat is a mountain climber. Both are
professionals. In fact, Gwen Moffat was the first woman to become a rock-climbing guide,
and was for 20 years a member of rescue teams in British mountains and in the Swiss Alps.
She has given her leading character, Miss Melinda Pink, J.P., the same proficiency. Both
ladies are also successful novelists.
   Although Gwen Moffat had written two previous mystery novels, it was with the
estimable Miss Pink that she made her second debut in 1975, one which has given her a
special place in the hearts of mystery readers. Moffat's home is near Caernarvon in North

Wales. However, she has not yet sent Miss Pink up to the Snowdonian crests. Both *Miss Pink at the Edge of the World* and *Over the Sea to Death* take place in Scotland. For background alone, these two books are outstanding. Moffat has the gift of bringing to the reader the veritable spirit of the mountains and hamlets off the beaten track in Britain. Her descriptions offer vivid reminders to those who know the terrain and exciting introductions to those unfamiliar with it. In both books the conversation is good, the puzzles enterprising. There should be many more climbs to come.

—Dorothy B. Hughes

MONIG, Christopher.   See **CROSSEN, Ken.**

MORICE, Anne.   Pseudonym for Felicity Shaw. British. Born in Kent in 1918. Educated privately and at Francis Holland School, London, and in Paris and Munich. Married Alexander Shaw in 1939; two daughters. Address: 41 Hambleden Village, Henley-on-Thames, Oxfordshire, England.

CRIME PUBLICATIONS

Novels (series character: Tessa Crichton Price in all books)

Death in the Grand Manor.   London, Macmillan, 1970.
Murder in Married Life.   London, Macmillan, 1971.
Death of a Gay Dog.   London, Macmillan, 1971.
Murder on French Leave.   London, Macmillan, 1972.
Death and the Dutiful Daughter.   London, Macmillan, 1973; New York, St. Martin's Press, 1974.
Death of a Heavenly Twin.   London, Macmillan, and New York, St. Martin's Press, 1974.
Killing with Kindness.   London, Macmillan, 1974; New York, St. Martin's Press, 1975.
Nursery Tea and Poison.   London, Macmillan, and New York, St. Martin's Press, 1975.
Death of a Wedding Guest.   London, Macmillan, and New York, St. Martin's Press, 1976.
Murder in Mimicry.   London, Macmillan, and New York, St. Martin's Press, 1977.
Scared to Death.   London, Macmillan, 1977; New York, St. Martin's Press, 1978.
Murder by Proxy.   London, Macmillan, and New York, St. Martin's Press, 1978.
Murder in Outline.   London, Macmillan, 1979.

OTHER PUBLICATIONS

Novels as Felicity Shaw

The Happy Exiles.   London, Hamish Hamilton, and New York, Harper, 1956.
Sun Trap.   London, Blond, 1958.

Play

Dummy Run (produced Henley-on-Thames, Oxfordshire, 1977).

Manuscript Collection: Mugar Memorial Library, Boston University.

Anne Morice comments:
Since numerous members of my family (including my father, sister, two daughters, and three nephews) are or were closely connected with the theatre and cinema, in one capacity of another, and I married a film director, this was the background I was most familiar with, and so created Tessa Crichton for the foreground. She has so far appeared in every book.

*   *   *

The considerable charm of Anne Morice's mystery novels comes from the character of their heroine, Tessa Crichton Price, and the relaxed authority of the prose in which she narrates her adventures. Morice can be compared with America's Emma Lathen team for her lightness of touch, acute observation of manners and understanding of psychology, and her constant flow of wit, if wit so dry can be said to flow. Tessa is an actress, currently in her twenties, around whom murders keep happening. Her sharp eyes, keen mind, and unobtrusive nosiness inevitably lead her to the murderer. Her husband, Robin Price, is a self-effacing policeman who amiably plays several supporting roles: he serves as sounding board for Tessa's preliminary theories, and is available to rescue her from the occasional murderer at bay.

The form of the novels is straight from the tradition of Christie and Marsh. A cast of characters is introduced and placed in a situation that simmers with incipient violence. The exposition is sometimes so leisurely that murder is not committed until halfway through the book, but the characters are so lively and Tessa's commentary so entertaining that the pace is not noticeably slowed. In the classic detective tradition, all the necessary clues are faithfully laid out, attention is masterfully misdirected from them, and Tessa explains all in a final conversation, often with Robin and her cousin Toby Crichton, a reclusive and crotchety playwright. Although the form is classic, the flavor of the social world that Morice explores is much sharper than Christie's or Marsh's. Ordinary society as Tessa describes it consists of a thin film of civility floating on a thick stew of folly, passion, vice, and warped development.

In fact, some of her most arresting characters are those whose perfect manners hide a considerable brutality. The villain in *Killing with Kindness* is renowned for his thoughtfulness – a verray parfit gentil knight. What piques Tessa's curiosity is the fact that his wife seems to be an alcoholic wreck. In *Murder in Married Life*, the portrait of "Sandy" Sanderson apparently begins as a gentle exercise in social comedy: the denouement reveals an ungentle exercise in fraud, and puts Tessa in convincing peril. It is one of few such episodes in Morice's work, whose major deficiency is a scarcity of directly reported action. Everything in the novels is filtered through Tessa's consciousness, and to some tastes there will be too much clever talk in these books.

The highly individual texture of Morice's work comes from the contrast between the dry urbanity of Tessa's mind and the messy realism of the social world she observes. An extremely high percentage of the characters are convincing, and not all of them are as nasty as her villains. A three-year-old protégé and a charming adolescent in *Death of a Wedding*

Guest, an American friend in *Murder in Mimicry*, and an African exchange student in *Death of a Heavenly Twin* are all free-standing figures, no matter how brief their appearances. The most dependable relief from the depressing social realism in these books is the continuing characterization of Tessa herself. Despite her premature skepticism about human motives, she retains a measure of youthful enthusiasm. And when her tendency to self-dramatization gets out of hand and is briskly deflated by her husband or cousin, she usually responds by seeing the joke.

If tact and clear sight are the marks of Morice's handling of characterization, tight economy is the chief virtue of her plots. She never drops an obvious clue and never belabors a clue's significance. Morice provides a high quality of entertainment for adults: a realistic imitation of the social world and vigorous exercise for any reader's wits.

—Carol Cleveland

MORLAND, Nigel. Also writes as Mary Dane; John Donavan; Norman Forrest; Roger Garnett; Vincent McCall; Neal Shepherd. British. Born in London, 24 June 1905. Educated privately. Married 1) Peggy Barwell (divorced); 2) Pamela Hunnex (divorced); 3) Jill Harvey (divorced); one daughter and two sons. Since the age of 14 has had numerous jobs in journalism and publishing in England and the East: Editor, *Shanghai Sports*, *Doctor*, *Edgar Wallace Mystery Magazine*; on editorial staff of *Shanghai Mercury*, *China Press*, *Covers*, *Fiction Monthly*, *Movie Day*, New York *Post*, Hearst newspapers, Odhams Press, London, Lettercraft Publishers and Covers Ltd., both in China, Nicholson and Watson Ltd., London, Street and Massey Ltd; Proprietor, The Book Guild and Mystery Book Club. Founding Editor, *The Criminologist*, since 1966, *Forensic and Medico-Legal Photography*, since 1972, and *The International Journal of Forensic Dentistry* and *Current Crime*, both since 1973. Co-Founder, Crime Writers Association, 1953. Address: The Press Club, 76 Shoe Lane, London E.C.4, England.

CRIME PUBLICATIONS

Novels (series characters: John Finnegan; Detective Inspector Rory Luccan; Steven Malone; Chief Inspector Andy McMurdo; Mrs. Palmyra Pym)

The Phantom Gunman (Pym).   London, Cassell, 1935.
The Moon Murders (Pym).   London, Cassell, 1935.
The Street of the Leopard (Pym).   London, Cassell, 1936.
The Clue of the Bricklayer's Aunt (Pym).   London, Cassell, 1936; New York, Farrar and Rinehart, 1937.
Death Took a Publisher (Finnegan; as Norman Forrest).   London, Harrap, 1936; New York, Curl, 1938.
Death Took a Greek God (Finnegan; as Norman Forrest).   London, Harrap, 1937; New York, Curl, 1938.
The Clue in the Mirror (Pym).   London, Cassell, 1937; New York, Farrar and Rinehart, 1938.
The Case Without a Clue (Pym).   London, Cassell, and New York, Farrar and Rinehart, 1938.
Death Traps the Killer (as Mary Dane).   London, Wright and Brown, 1938.

A Rope for the Hanging (Pym). London, Cassell, 1938; New York, Farrar and Rinehart, 1939.
A Knife for the Killer (Pym). London, Cassell, 1939; as *Murder at Radio City*, New York, Farrar and Rinehart, 1939.
A Gun for a God (Pym). London, Cassell, 1940; as *Murder in Wardour Street*, New York, Farrar and Rinehart, 1940.
The Clue of the Careless Hangman (Pym). London, Cassell, 1940; as *The Careless Hangman*, New York, Farrar Rinehart, 1941.
Dumb Alibi. New York, MB Books, 1941.
The Corpse on the Flying Trapeze (Pym). London, Cassell, and New York, Farrar and Rinehart, 1941.
A Coffin for the Body (Pym). London, Cassell, 1943.
Death Spoke Sweetly. London, Wright and Brown, 1946.
Murder Runs Wild. London, Halle, 1946.
Strangely She Died (Malone). London, Jenkins, 1946.
Smash and Grab (as Vincent McCall). London, Arrow, 1946.
Dressed to Kill (Pym). London, Cassell, 1947.
The Hatchet Murders. London, Arrow, 1947.
Dusky Death. London, Wright and Brown, 1948.
She Didn't Like Dying (McMurdo). London, Sampson Low, 1948.
Fish Are So Trusting. London, Century Press, 1948.
No Coupons for a Shroud (McMurdo). London, Sampson Low, 1949.
Two Dead Charwomen (McMurdo). London, Sampson Low, 1949.
Death Takes an Editor (Malone). London, Aldus, 1949.
The Corpse Was No Lady (McMurdo). London, Sampson Low, 1950.
Blood on the Stars (McMurdo). London, Sampson Low, 1951.
Death When She Wakes (Luccan). London, Evans, 1951.
He Hanged His Mother on Monday (McMurdo). London, Sampson Low, 1951.
The Lady Had a Gun (Pym). London, Cassell, 1951.
Call Him Early for the Murder (Pym). London, Cassell, 1952.
A Girl Died Singing (Luccan). London, Evans, 1952.
The Moon Was Made for Murder (McMurdo). London, Sampson Low, 1953.
Sing a Song of Cyanide (Pym). London, Cassell, 1953.
Death for Sale (McMurdo). London, Hale, 1957.
Look in Any Doorway (Pym). London, Cassell, 1957.
A Bullet for Midas (Pym). London, Cassell, 1958.
Death and the Golden Boy (Pym). London, Cassell, 1958.
Death to the Ladies (McMurdo). London, Hale, 1959.
The Concrete Maze (Pym). London, Cassell, 1960.
So Quiet a Death (Pym). London, Cassell, 1960.
The Dear, Dead Girls (Pym). London, Cassell, 1961.

Novels as John Donavan (series character: Sergeant Johnny Lamb in all books except *The Dead Have No Friends*)

The Case of the Rusted Room. London, Hale, and New York, Curl, 1937.
The Case of the Beckoning Dead. London, Hale, and New York, Curl, 1938.
The Case of the Talking Dust. London, Hale, 1938; New York, Arcadia House, 1941.
The Case of the Coloured Wind. London, Hodder and Stoughton, 1939; as *The Case of the Violet Smoke*, New York, Arcadia House, 1940.
The Case of the Plastic Man. London, Hodder and Stoughton, 1940; as *The Case of the Plastic Mask*, New York, Arcadia House, 1941.
The Dead Have No Friends. London, Home and Van Thal, 1952.

Novels as Roger Garnett (series characters: Chief Inspector Jonathan Black; R. I. Perkins)

Death in Piccadilly (Black). London, Wright and Brown, 1937.
Starr Bedford Dies (Perkins). London, Wright and Brown, 1937.
The Killing of Paris Norton (Perkins). London, Wright and Brown, 1938.
The Croaker (Black). London, Wright and Brown, 1938.
Danger – Death at Work (Black). London, Wright and Brown, 1939.
A Man Died Talking (Black). London, Wright and Brown, 1943.

Novels as Neal Shepherd (series character: Chief Inspector Michael "Napper" Tandy in all books)

Death Flies Low. London, Constable, 1938.
Death Walks Softly. London, Constable, 1938.
Death Rides Swiftly. London, Constable, 1939.
Exit to Music: A Problem in Detection. London, Constable, 1940.

Short Stories

Death Takes a Star. London, Todd, 1943.
The Sooper's Cases. London, Todd, 1943.
The Laboratory Murder and Other Stories. London, Vallancey Press, 1944.
Corpse in the Circus. London, Vallancey Press, 1945.
Eleven Thrilling Mysteries (as Vincent McCall). London, Arrow, 1945.
The Corpse in the Circus and Other Stories. London, Vallancey Press, 1946.
The Big Killing. Hounslow, Middlesex, Foster, 1946.
Mrs. Pym of Scotland Yard. London, Hodgson, 1946.
How Many Coupons for a Shroud? London, Morgan Laird, 1946.
26 Three Minute Thrillers: A Collection of Ingenious Puzzle Yarns. London, Arrow, 1947.
Eve Finds the Killer (as Roger Garnett). London, Arrow, 1947.
The Case of the Innocent Wife. London, Arrow, 1947.
Exit to Music and Other Stories. London, Bonde, 1947; abridged edition, as *Death's Sweet Music*, London, Century Press, 1947.
Mrs. Pym and Other Stories. Henley-on-Thames, Oxfordshire, Aidan Ellis, 1976.

OTHER PUBLICATIONS

Short Story

"Mary!" A Story of the Magdalene, with Peggy Barwell. Paris, Felix Barbier, 1932.

Plays

The Goofus Man: A Fantasy for Children. London, Eric Partridge, 1930.
Dawn Was Theirs, with Peggy Barwell. Paris, Felix Barbier, 1931.

Screenplay: *Mrs. Pym of Scotland Yard*, with Fred Elles and Peggy Barwell, 1939.

Verse

Cachexia: A Collection of Prose Poems, with Peggy Barwell. Paris, Felix Barbier, 1930; revised edition, 1931.
Abrakadabra! Verse for Modern Children, with Peggy Barwell. Paris, Felix Barbier, 1932.

Other

People We Have Never Met: A Book of Superficial Cameos, with Peggy Barwell.   Paris,
    Felix Barbier, 1931.
Finger Prints: An Introduction to Scientific Criminology.   London, Street and Massey,
    1936.
How to Write Detective Novels.   London, Allen and Unwin, 1936.
The Conquest of Crime.   London, Cassell, 1937.
Crime Against Children: An Aspect of Sexual Criminology.   London, Cassell, 1939.
An Outline of Scientific Criminology.   London, Cassell, and New York, Philosophical
    Library, 1950; revised edition, Cassell, 1971.
Hangman's Clutch.   London, Laurie, 1954.
Background to Murder.   London, Laurie, 1955.
This Friendless Lady.   London, Muller, 1957.
That Nice Miss Smith.   London, Muller, 1958.
Science in Crime Detection.   London, Hale, 1958; New York, Emerson, 1960.
An Outline of Sexual Criminology.   Oxford, Tallis, 1966; New York, Hart, 1967.
Pattern of Murder.   London, Elek, 1966.
An International Pattern of Murder.   Hornchurch, Essex, Ian Henry, 1977.
Who's Who in Crime Fiction.   London, Elm Tree Books, 1980.

Editor, *Papers from the "Criminologist."*   London, Wolfe, 1971; New York, Library
    Press, 1972.
Editor, *Victorian Crime Stories.*   Hornchurch, Essex, Ian Henry, 1978.

Nigel Morland comments:
  Between 1927 and 1934, Nigel Morland was a hard-working pulp-writer for U.S. and
U.K. publishers, turning out a steady average of 30,000 to 50,000 words a week which he
(unwisely!) sold outright under pseudonyms for cash; this includes several non-fiction
popular volumes and several ghosted works for top screen and notoriety names. Morland
kept few records, and such material or notes he had on his work were destroyed during the
London Blitz. Dozens of these crude pulps Morland has completely forgotten, but he does
recall that his first hard-back was *The Sibilant Whisper* published in Shanghai in 1923,
followed by several more locally published works before he returned to England, plus many
short stories. His second book, he recalls, was a study of English people for a Chinese
publisher translated directly into Chinese and never issued in English.

                              *   *   *

  Nigel Morland was at one time secretary to Edgar Wallace, and on Wallace's death, the
mantle of the old master seems to have fallen upon his shoulders. A founder of the Crime
Writers Association in 1953 (along with John Creasey), Morland has written a great many
books on crime, most of them detective novels. He gave up fiction in 1965, saying that
writing it bored him to tears. Since then he has kept busy editing *The Criminologist* (a journal
surveying forensic science, criminology, police, and the law) and *Current Crime* (a review of
new crime fiction) and turning out non-fiction books on all aspects of crime.
  Mrs. Palmyra Pym is Morland's best-known character. She is an employee of the British
War Department, but has been assigned to Scotland Yard for "special investigations."
Straight from the hard-bitten school of detectives, Mrs. Pym is determined and resourceful
and once she begins investigating, there is no stopping her. She is a terror to evil-doers and
unconventional in the eyes of her superiors. She often packs a gun, but usually relies on her
fists in tight situations. She is oblivious to regulations and traditions of the Yard and is
permitted a freer hand than are her male colleagues. When Mrs. Pym made her appearance
in 1935, she was considered too rough and unconventional for a British detective; her clothes

were jaunty and eccentric and her language perhaps a bit too blunt. She was brave, skillful, outrageous – an awesome sight when she went into battle. As the years wore on, she became something of a bore, but her clothes changed for the better and her manners became more agreeable. She continued, however, to use her third degree methods and interpreted Scotland Yard regulations to suit herself. The stories themselves are often fantastic and unashamedly in imitation of Edgar Wallace.

The Clue of the Bricklayer's Aunt opens with the strange behavior of a bedridden paralytic – the bricklayer's aunt – whose wild dancing and throwing of furniture about attract the attention of the neighbors. Mrs. Pym finds the connection between this curious behavior and the robberies and murders that follow. The next Pym book, *The Clue in the Mirror*, finds her uncovering a long and involved trail of crime which leads her from a warehouse in Wapping to respectable financial circles. *The Case Without a Clue* deals with Mrs. Pym's efforts to discover why the galley proof of a suppressed book was stolen from a publisher's safe and why a murder followed. The plot is well-conceived, but Mrs. Pym is now engagingly proper – and boring. *A Rope for the Hanging* concerns a street brawl in which a drunken laborer is killed – at first a seemingly common case in which a deputy assistant commissioner of Scotland Yard would scarcely be interested. But once Mrs. Pym begins investigating, the mystery is penetratingly illuminated. Mrs. Pym uses her unconventional third degree methods in *A Knife for the Killer* to solve the mystery of a parachutist who alights on the "Rockefeller Building" and is found by police to be dying of a gunshot wound. *The Corpse on the Flying Trapeze* has her investigating how and why an acrobat was beheaded while swinging from a trapeze in full view of a crowded theatre. The bloody beginning is only a prelude to more murders later on – all seemingly without a motive until Mrs. Pym comes on the scene. The Mrs. Pym stories continued through the 1940's and the plots grew better as the lady's eccentricities became less pronounced.

Morland wrote under several pseudonyms: Mary Dane, John Donavan, Norman Forrest, Roger Garnett, and Neal Shepherd. The best, I think, were the books as Shepherd; *Death Walks Softly* is representative of his style at its best. It is a tale of industrial spying and is characteristic of the Shepherd novels with its brisk writing and clever detection.

—Daniel P. King

MORRISON, Arthur. British. Born in Poplar, London, 1 November 1863. Married Elizabeth Adelaide Thatcher in 1892; one son. Clerk at the People's Palace, London, 1886–90, and sub-editor, *Palace Journal*, 1889–90; free-lance journalist, 1890–1913; collector of Chinese and Japanese paintings which were acquired by the British Museum in 1913; Chief Inspector of the Special Constabulary of Epping Forest, Essex, during World War I. Fellow, 1924, and Member of the Council, 1935, Royal Society of Literature. *Died 4 December 1945.*

CRIME PUBLICATIONS

Novels

    The Hole in the Wall. London, Methuen, and New York, McClure Phillips, 1902.
    The Red Triangle, Being Some Further Chronicles of Martin Hewitt, Investigator. London, Nash, and Boston, Page, 1903.

Short Stories (series character: Martin Hewitt)

> *Martin Hewitt, Investigator.*   London, Ward Lock, and New York, Harper, 1894.
> *Chronicles of Martin Hewitt.*   London, Ward Lock, 1895; New York, Appleton, 1896.
> *Adventures of Martin Hewitt.*   London, Ward Lock, 1896.
> *The Dorrington Deed-Box.*   London, Ward Lock, 1897.
> *The Green Eye of Goona: Stories of a Case of Tokay.*   London, Nash, 1904; as *The Green Diamond*, Boston, Page, 1904.

OTHER PUBLICATIONS

Novels

> *A Child of the Jago.*   London, Methuen, and Chicago, Stone, 1896.
> *To London Town.*   London, Methuen, and Chicago, Stone, 1899.
> *Cunning Murrell.*   London, Methuen, and New York, Doubleday, 1900.

Short Stories

> *The Shadows Around Us: Authentic Tales of the Supernatural.*   London, Simpkin Marshall, 1891.
> *Tales of Mean Streets.*   London, Methuen, 1894; Boston, Roberts, 1895.
> *Zig-Zags at the Zoo.*   London, Newnes, 1895.
> *Divers Vanities.*   London, Methuen, 1905.
> *Green Ginger.*   London, Hutchinson, and New York, Stokes, 1909.
> *(Stories).*   London, Harrap, 1929.
> *Fiddle O'Dreams.*   London, Hutchinson, 1933.

Plays

> *That Brute Simmons*, with Herbert C. Sargent, adaptation of the story by Morrison (produced London, 1904).   London, French, 1904.
> *The Dumb-Cake*, with Richard Pryce, adaptation of a story by Morrison (produced London, 1907).   London, French, 1907.
> *A Stroke of Business*, with Horace Newte (produced London, 1907).

Other

> *The Painters of Japan.*   London, Jack, 2 vols., and New York, Stoke, 2 vols., 1911.

*   *   *

Arthur Morrison was highly regarded by his contemporaries as one of the pioneers of the New Realism. His collection *Tales of Mean Streets* and his novel *A Child of the Jago* set the pattern for a new hard, factual, unsentimental recording of life and crime in the slums of London. It came, therefore, as an unwelcome surprise when the Martin Hewitt stories began to appear in *The Strand Magazine.* They were skilled commercial work, but without the power of Morrison's serious fiction.

The Martin Hewitt stories adhere closely to the pattern of the Sherlock Holmes stories – consultation, investigation, strange circumstances, and a resolution which clears away difficulties. Hewitt is himself patterned after Holmes, with certain superficial distinctions to conceal the likeness. The stories, however, are ingenious in concept, well-written, and entertaining. If they lack the idiosyncratic snap of Doyle's work, they are smoother and more relaxed. Altogether there are 18 short stories about Hewitt. The first series of six stories appeared in *The Strand Magazine*, while the second and third appeared in *The Windsor*

Magazine. An episodic novel, *The Red Triangle*, also centers upon Hewitt, but it is more sensational than the short stories. It deals with a West Indian master criminal who uses hypnosis to control his henchmen. While *The Red Triangle* is not to be taken seriously, the other Hewitt stories still remain second only to Doyle's work in the period 1890–1905.

Morrison wrote two other books in the same commercial vein as the Martin Hewitt stories. *The Dorrington Deed-Box* describes the adventures of a criminal who occasionally performs feats of detection when it is to his own interest. The last adventure in the book is noteworthy as Morrison's sole attempt to link slum naturalism with the commercially patterned detective story. *The Green Eye of Goona*, on the other hand, is a light detective fantasy about a gem which is smuggled out of India in a magnum of wine, and the various attempts to gain possession of it. The novel is successful in combining topical humor and mystery. There are also occasional short stories with minor elements of crime in *Divers Vanities* and *Green Ginger*, but these are not significant.

Although few details are available about Morrison's early life, since he was an extremely reticent man, it is known that he grew up in the slums of East London, and that a childhood amid poverty, squalor, and crime left a heavy mark on him. Much of his fiction seems to have been written (probably unconsciously) to break the hold which this past held on him. Indeed, the single theme of his serious fiction is Escape. In his later life, too, Morrison experienced the underworld in his search for material for *A Child of the Jago*. As a result of this background Morrison was the only significant author of his day who had both the literary genius and the personal experience to broaden the scope of the detective story, or, as it has been put, to take the detective story out of 221B Baker Street. Unfortunately, Morrison wrote only a single work in this direction. This was *The Hole in the Wall*, which in the opinion of most critics is Morrison's finest work. Told from several points of view, it is the story of a boy who lives with his grandfather in a disreputable water-front pub and becomes embroiled in theft and murder. It is brilliantly imagined and vividly told.

—E. F. Bleiler

MORTON, Anthony.   See **CREASEY, John.**

MOYES, Patricia.   British.   Born in Bray, County Wicklow, Ireland, 19 January 1923. Educated at Overstone School, Northampton, 1934–39, Cambridge School Certificate 1939. Served in the radar section of the Women's Auxiliary Air Force, 1940–45: Flight Officer. Married 1) John Moyes in 1951 (divorced, 1959); 2) John S. Haszard in 1962. Company Secretary, Peter Ustinov Productions Ltd., London, 1945–53; Assistant Editor, *Vogue*, London, 1953–58. Lived in Switzerland, 1958–62, Holland, 1962–72, and Washington, D.C., 1972–77. Recipient: Mystery Writers of America Edgar Allan Poe Award, 1971. Agent: Curtis Brown Ltd., 1 Craven Hill, London W2 3EP, England. Address: P.O. Box 1, Virgin Gorda, British Virgin Islands, West Indies.

Novels (series characters: Henry and Emmy Tibbett in all books)

Dead Men Don't Ski.   London, Collins, 1959; New York, Rinehart, 1960.
The Sunken Sailor.   London, Collins, 1961; as *Down among the Dead Men*, New York, Holt Rinehart, 1961.
Death on the Agenda.   London, Collins, and New York, Holt Rinehart, 1962.
Murder à la Mode.   London, Collins, and New York, Holt Rinehart, 1963.
Falling Star.   London, Collins, and New York, Holt Rinehart, 1964.
Johnny under Ground.   London, Collins, 1965; New York, Holt Rinehart, 1966.
Murder Fantastical.   London, Collins, and New York, Holt Rinehart, 1967.
Death and the Dutch Uncle.   London, Collins, and New York, Holt Rinehart, 1968.
Who Saw Her Die?   London, Collins, 1970; as *Many Deadly Returns*, New York, Holt Rinehart, 1970.
Season of Snows and Sins.   London, Collins, and New York, Holt Rinehart, 1971.
The Curious Affair of the Third Dog.   London, Collins, and New York, Holt Rinehart, 1973.
Black Widower.   London, Collins, and New York, Holt Rinehart, 1975.
To Kill a Coconut.   London, Collins, 1977; as *The Coconut Killings*, New York, Holt Rinehart, 1977.
Who Is Simon Warwick?   London, Collins, 1978; New York, Holt Rinehart, 1979.

Uncollected Short Stories

"The Representative," "The Revenge," "The Judgment of Solomon," "A Question of Timing," "A Dream of a Girl," and "Fairy God-Daughter," in *Evening News* (London), 1961.
"The Holly Wreath," in *Women's Mirror* (London), 1965.

Plays

Time Remembered, adaptation of a play by Jean Anouilh (broadcast, 1954; produced London, 1954; New York, 1957).   London, Methuen, 1955.

Screenplay: *School for Scoundrels*, with Peter Ustinov and Hal E. Chester, 1960.

Radio Play: *Time Remembered*, 1954.

Other

Helter-Skelter (juvenile).   New York, Holt Rinehart, 1968; London, Macdonald, 1969.
"Making a Mystery," in *Techniques of Novel Writing*.   Boston, The Writer, 1973.
After All, They're Only Cats.   New York, Curtis, 1973.
"The Joys of Inexperience," in *The Writer* (Boston), 1973.
"Mysteries Within Mysteries," in *The Writer* (Boston), 1975.
How to Talk to Your Cat.   London, Barker, and New York, Holt Rinehart, 1978.

Patricia Moyes comments:
Really, all I can say about my work is that I try to write the sort of books that I enjoy reading – that is, I write for my own pleasure and never try to appeal to a particular market. My preference is for mystery stories that are well-plotted (and never cheat the reader), that are

ingenious and amusing rather than vicious, and that are placed in a setting which the author clearly knows well, and peopled with characters who are more than dummies to be pushed around by the exigencies of the plot. I know that this sets a high standard, and I can't honestly pretend that I always achieve it − but I do try.

Apart from *Helter-Skelter* (written for teenagers), all my mystery stories feature Henry and Emmy Tibbett, and it has been one of my amusements over the years to round out their lives: Emmy's sister Jane, brother-in-law Bill, and niece Veronica feature in several books; we know where the Tibbetts live, what they like to eat and drink, what their hobbies are, and so on. I am delighted to know that there are readers who can document the Tibbetts almost as thoroughly as I can talk about Lady Constance Keeble (née Threepwood), now Lady Constance Schoonmaker of New York City (I need hardly add that the late and great P. G. Wodehouse is my favourite author). Talking of Wodehouse, I do not feel that what Noël Coward called "a talent to amuse" is something to be despised. Frankly, I would sooner divert people than put their souls through an emotional meat-grinder, and I have long ago stopped apologizing for not being a "serious" writer.

*   *   *

The advent of World War Two appears, to many historians of the genre, to mark the exodus of the great Golden Age of the formal detective story. There is much evidence to justify this viewpoint. Several major authors such as Biggers, Freeman, and Van Dine died. Others, including Abbot, Berkeley, Hammett, and Sayers, abandoned the form for different pursuits. A few writers tried to extend the range of the detective story into that of the mainstream novel − often with disastrous results. An appreciable group concentrated on characterization and psychology to the detriment of puzzle and plot. Others emphasized action or suspense. Some eschewed ratiocination in favor of the crime novel. Prominent authors including Hull, Upfield, and Wade produced little or no work during the wartime years. Finally, the skills of too many writers simply fell into decline during this period. Yet a fair number of authors, including a handful of exceptionally talented newcomers, have stubbornly persisted in mining the vein of classic detection; one of the brightest of these luminaries is Patricia Moyes.

This author retains the Golden Age skill of evolving unusually well-constructed plots and puzzles. Her settings, based on travel and personal observation, are vivid, but never obtrusive. Her people, even the minor ones, are characterized with more skill and depth than are commonly found in Golden Age narratives. Almost all her novels are attractive and charming. Her series character, Henry Tibbett, is a slight and unmemorable person − a perfectly ordinary human being. He starts as a Chief Inspector at Scotland Yard, and eventually achieves the rank of Detective Chief Superintendent. His wife Emmy is frequently involved in his investigations, and is usually described as "nice" by most critics. Obviously a model of her sex.

Dead Men Don't Ski, a notable first novel, is set in the Italian Tirol, and starts with the discovery of a corpse in a ski lift. An excellent follow-up novel, *The Sunken Sailor*, concerns an investigation into the year-old death of a yachtsman. Sailing, another Moyes enthusiasm, is well integrated into the fabric of this novel. *Death on the Agenda* has Tibbett in his official capacity attending an international conference on narcotics in Geneva. Somehow, the customary Moyes magic seems to be missing in this minor effort, but a strong recovery is evident in *Murder à la Mode*. Set in the editorial offices of a fashion magazine, and concerned with the murder of an employee, this novel received rave reviews − especially from Anthony Boucher who was reminded of the golden days when Allingham, Blake, and Marsh were reshaping the detective novel.

Miss Moyes's most impressive achievement is *Falling Star* whose victim dies while acting in a film production. The author's work as a secretary to Peter Ustinov, as well as her work as a screenwriter, provided insight into the film-making process, and ensured an authentic background. *Falling Star* has a lighter, more easily flowing narrative style, and seems to be the beginning of Moyes's tendency to stress characterization over plot and puzzle. The usual third-person narration is here changed to the viewpoint of one of the film executives. *Johnny under Ground* details a murder problem with its roots in Emmy's wartime past while she was serving (as Moyes herself did) in the WAAFS; it is not a major effort, but is interesting for its biographical details about Emmy. More conventional is *Murder Fantastical* with two murders, a little espionage, and an eccentric – to put it mildly – family living in the English countryside.

Death and the Dutch Uncle starts with the murder of a minor crook in a dreary London pub, escalates into a problem between two newly-created African nations, and evolves into a situation where Tibbett is forced to play nurse-maid to a short-tempered Dutch diplomat in his native land. A birthday party for an eccentric old lady ends with her demise in *Who Saw Her Die?* Tibbett suspects foul play, but the medical authorities say natural causes. This is an engaging combination of the weekend house party and the perfect crime, and is one of Moyes's most successful books. Even better is *Season of Snows and Sins* which starts with an unfaithful husband's murder by his pregnant wife, and continues with enough ramifications to threaten the security of the French government. This novel is set in a Swiss skiing resort, and is narrated by Emmy and two other women. *The Curious Affair of the Third Dog* includes exciting greyhound racing, a missing hound, and the inevitable murder problem. *Black Widower*, a minor effort, is set in Washington and the Caribbean republic of Tampica – whose ambassador's wife has been murdered. The authorities summon Tibbett from Scotland Yard, and hope that his investigation will be discreet and effective. *To Kill a Coconut* is about the murder of an American senator while he is visiting the British Seaward Islands. This book is not a major effort, but it has been unfairly maligned by many critics; it contains all the virtues (including detection) one can always expect from a story by Moyes.

—Charles Shibuk

MUIR, Dexter. See **GRIBBLE, Leonard.**

MURRAY, Max. Born in Australia in 1901. *Died in 1956.*

CRIME PUBLICATIONS

Novels

    The Voice of the Corpse. New York, Farrar Straus, 1947; London, Joseph, 1948.
    The King and the Corpse. New York, Farrar Straus, 1948; London, Joseph, 1949.
    The Queen and the Corpse. New York, Farrar Straus, 1949; as *No Duty on a Corpse*, London, Joseph, 1950.
    The Neat Little Corpse. New York, Farrar Straus, 1950; London, Joseph, 1951.
    Good Luck to the Corpse. New York, Farrar Straus, 1951; London, Joseph, 1953.
    The Right Honorable Corpse. New York, Farrar Straus, 1951; London, Joseph, 1952.
    The Doctor and the Corpse. New York, Farrar Straus, 1952; London, Joseph, 1953.

The Sunshine Corpse. London, Joseph, 1954.
Royal Bed for a Corpse. London, Joseph, and New York, Washburn, 1955.
Breakfast with a Corpse. London, Joseph, 1956; as *A Corpse for Breakfast*, New York, Washburn, 1957.
Twilight at Dawn. London, Joseph, 1957.
Wait for a Corpse. London, Joseph, and New York, Washburn, 1957.

OTHER PUBLICATIONS

Play

The Admiral's Chair (produced London, 1931).

Other

The World's Back Doors. London, Cape, 1927; New York, Cape and Smith, 1929.
Long Way to London. London, Cape, 1931.

*   *   *

Max Murray produced twelve "corpse" books in his ten-year literary career. The settings of his books range from the quiet, ordinary New England village in *The Voice of the Corpse* to the Riviera in *Breakfast with a Corpse*. Within these settings, Murray advances several theories of the criminal mind; one of the most prominent is that of the benevolent murderer. He questions society's role in inflicting punishment and often leaves justice in the hands of fate.

Murray's perception of crime as benevolently motivated is evident in his very first book: in *The Voice of the Corpse* Angela Mason Pewsey is murdered by the kind-hearted vicar because she has been blackmailing his parishioners. In *The Doctor and the Corpse* Mrs. Walters kills her lover because he, like Angela, has been gathering incriminating evidence against those around him.

The stories Murray builds around his benevolent murderers depict the living, not the "corpse," as the victim. When the dead person is alive, he hounds the community; when he is murdered, the murderer suffers personal guilt but not exile from that community. In many of Murray's books, the murderer finds security in the community, where his crime is silently condoned because of the evil nature of the murdered person. To avoid punishing the criminal, the community dissociates itself from the incident. But the murderer eventually suffers. The vicar slips off a cliff and Mrs. Walters dies of a heart attack after the truth is learned. In each case, the townspeople who know the truth withhold the identity of the murderers after their death.

Murray's portrayal of human existence grows more cynical as his career progresses. The sleuth becomes less innocent and the murderer less heroic. In *The Voice of the Corpse*, Prentice, the slow-witted sleuth, sympathizes with the murderer. Michael West, in *The Doctor and the Corpse*, is also forgiving, but more aware of the weaknesses in human nature. The pianist/secret agent in *The Right Honorable Corpse* goes out of his way to make everyone hate him for his cynical but perceptive outlook on life. Finally, the sleuth in *Breakfast with a Corpse* is even more discerning regarding human actions; and the murderer, unlike his predecessors, lacks dignity in death – he commits suicide. Murray at this stage has accepted that man is trapped. Either he allows himself to be victimized, or he takes action – but if he takes action, he must be punished.

Murray's mystery novels reveal considerable versatility of prose, a smooth though sometimes too slow plot, and some vivid characterizations. Too often, however, the murderer's motives, though benevolent, seem contrived and the mechanics of the murder appear clumsy.

—Donna Rose Casella Kern

NEBEL, (Louis) Frederick.   American.

CRIME PUBLICATIONS

Novels

Sleepers East.   Boston, Little Brown, 1933; London, Gollancz, 1934.
Fifty Roads to Town.   Boston, Little Brown, and London, Cape, 1936.

Short Stories

Six Deadly Dames.   New York, Avon, 1950.

Uncollected Short Stories

"Mask of Murder," in *Saturday Evening Post* (Philadelphia), 8 October 1955.
"Chance Is Sometimes an Enemy," in *Ellery Queen's Mystery Magazine* (New York), April 1956.
"Try It My Way," in *Ellery Queen's Awards, 11th Series.*   New York, Simon and Schuster, 1956; London, Collins, 1958.
"You Can Take So Much," in *Ellery Queen's Mystery Magazine* (New York), October 1956.
"The Man Who Knew," in *Ellery Queen's Mystery Magazine* (New York), December 1956.
"That's Just Too Bad," in *Ellery Queen's Mystery Magazine* (New York), May 1957.
"No Kid Stuff," in *Ellery Queen's Mystery Magazine* (New York), April 1958.
"Wanted: An Accomplice," in *Ellery Queen's Mystery Magazine* (New York), July 1958.
"Pity the Poor Underdog," in *Ellery Queen's Mystery Magazine* (New York), August 1958.
"The Fifth Question," in *Ellery Queen's Mystery Magazine* (New York), January 1959.
"Killer at Large," in *Ellery Queen's Mystery Magazine* (New York), September 1961.
"Needle in a Haystack," in *Ellery Queen's Mystery Magazine* (New York), August 1962.
"Reprieve at Eleven" and "Ghost of a Chance," in *The Saint* (New York), April 1956.
"Winter Kill," in *The Hardboiled Dicks,* edited by Ron Goulart.   Los Angeles, Sherbourne Press, 1965; London, Boardman, 1967.
"Take It and Like It," in *The Hard-Boiled Detective: Stories from Black Mask Magazine (1920–1951),* edited by Herbert Ruhm.   New York, Vintage, 1977.

OTHER PUBLICATIONS

Novel

But Not the End.   Boston, Little Brown, 1934.

Manuscript Collection: University of Oregon Library, Eugene.

* * *

The hard-boiled detective is an improbable creation. He is a Galahadian hero in an unglamorous profession who is bound by a moral code that embraces a sense of duty and a streak of sentimentality. He is often a wise-cracking humorist and always violent. But above all, he must be tough, for he exists in a hard world and must be equal to that world and the worst of its inhabitants. The challenge of the hard-boiled detective story is to create a believable character out of these traits who will not conflict with the realistic milieu. The best of the hard-boiled writers temper toughness with humor, but this is difficult to manage and, as there exists little room for improvement in the story type, the genre has become particularly vulnerable to excess and parody, as the writings of Mickey Spillane and Richard S. Prather show.

One of the few writers to portray the tough detective realistically was Frederick Nebel, who wrote for *Black Mask* and its early rival, *Dime Detective*, for most of his short career. For these two magazines, Nebel created several characters, Ben "tough dick" Donohue, Cardigan of the Cosmos Detective Agency, and the team of of Homicide Captain Steve MacBride and *Free Press* reporter Kennedy. Nebel's characters are genuinely hard-boiled, and his stories realistic. He employs a wry, wise-cracking kind of humor that is acceptable within the contexts of his stories. In the MacBride and Kennedy stories, the humor borders on burlesque when Kennedy's whimsical presence dominates (as it does in "Take It and Like It"), but Nebel never loses his control over the mood.

Nebel's stories are set in the grim world of Depression America in which survival is the guiding imperative. This is a world of greed, political corruption, and inter-familial violence, and his detectives, as a result, are insular, pragmatic men who live by stern moral codes. They are survivors who pride themselves on their toughness and their ability to "take it," i.e. to endure the repercussions when their morality brings them into conflict with a corrupt society, as Ben Donohue demonstrates in "He Could Take It."

To Donohue, Cardigan, and MacBride, duty is an everyday affair. When they are compelled to step beyond the limits of duty, as most hard-boiled detectives are, they are never motivated by sentiment, but rather by pride or responsibility. Ben Donohue is Nebel's quintessential hard-boiled character. He is as tough as tendon in "Pearls Are Tears" when he guns down a cop-killer, not for his crime – Donohue believes that the cop "deserved it" – but to protect himself and his client from complicity in a blackmail cover-up. He endures a savage beating in "He Could Take It" rather than relinquish the evidence that will convict his attackers, only because he wants them to pay for the beating.

Captain Steve MacBride is equally hard, though his hardness is offset by his foil, Kennedy. He feels fear in "Take It and Like It" when it appears that Kennedy is a murderer. In "Some Die Young," his hunt for the killer of a young girl takes on added meaning by his comparison of the dead girl to his own daughter. Though he is a less insular person that Donohue, it is pride, not sentiment, that governs his actions. He goes beyond duty in "Doors in the Dark" to prove that his close friend was murdered, though the evidence indicates suicide, because his pride won't allow him to be wrong. Similarly, Donohue refuses to let the daughter of a notorious vice queen follow in her mother's footsteps in "The Red Web" because he was hired to prevent that and as he tells her, "I hate like hell to lose. I'm the world's sorest loser."

Such attitudes are understandable in the contexts. Toughness is a strategy for survival and, as Nebel seems to indicate in *Sleepers East*, perhaps the only way to survive.

—Will Murray

NEVILLE, Margot. Pseudonym for Margot Goyder and Anne Neville Goyder Joske. Australians. **GOYDER, Margot:** Born in Melbourne in 1903. **JOSKE, Anne Neville, née Goyder:** Born in Melbourne in 1893.

CRIME PUBLICATIONS

Novels (series character: Inspector Grogan in all books except *Come, Thick Night* and *The Hateful Voyage*).

Lena Hates Men. New York, Arcadia House, 1943; as *Murder in Rockwater*, London, Bles, 1944.
Murder and Gardenias. London, Bles, 1946.
Murder in a Blue Moon. London, Bles, 1948; New York, Doubleday, 1949.
Murder of a Nymph. London, Bles, 1949; New York, Doubleday, 1950.
Come, Thick Night. London, Bles, 1951; as *Divining Rod for Murder*, New York, Doubleday, 1952.
Murder Before Marriage. London, Bles, and New York, Doubleday, 1951.
The Seagull Said Murder. London, Bles, 1952.
Murder of the Well-Beloved. London, Bles, and New York, Doubleday, 1953.
Murder and Poor Jenny. London, Bles, 1954.
The Hateful Voyage. London, Bles, 1956.
Murder of Olympia. London, Bles, 1956.
Murder to Welcome Her. London, Bles, 1957.
The Flame of Murder. London, Bles, 1958.
Sweet Night for Murder. London, Bles, 1959.
Confession of Murder. London, Bles, 1960.
Murder Beyond the Pale. London, Bles, 1961.
Drop Dead. London, Bles, 1962.
Come See Me Die. London, Bles, 1963.
My Bad Boy. London, Bles, 1964.
Ladies in the Dark. London, Bles, 1965.
Head on the Sill. London, Bles, 1966.

OTHER PUBLICATIONS

Novels

Marietta Is Stolen. London, Parsons, 1922.
This Can't Be I. London, Parsons, 1923.
Safety First. London, Hodder and Stoughton, and Boston, Houghton Mifflin, 1924.
Kiss Proof. London, Chapman and Hall, 1928; New York, McBride, 1929.
Giving the Bride Away. London, Chapman and Hall, and New York, McBride, 1930.

Plays

Once a Husband, with Brett Hay (produced London, 1932).
Heroes Don't Care (produced London, 1936). London, French, 1936.
Giving the Bride Away, with Gerald Kirby (produced London, 1939).

*   *   *

The two Australian women who wrote under the pseudonym of Margot Neville began their successful collaboration in crime fiction in the 1940's and wrote prolifically for 20 years. Success came with their first books, *Lena Hates Men* and *Murder and Gardenias*. Most of their books are distinguishable by the fact that the word "murder" occurs in the title. Many of these murder stories have an Australian background, generally with a sophisticated Sydney setting, and feature a highly skilled detective named Grogan, who tracks down the killers with all the finesse associated with the best Scotland Yard practitioners.

—Herbert Harris

NEVINS, Francis M(ichael), Jr. American. Born in Bayonne, New Jersey, 6 January 1943. Educated at St. Peter's College, Jersey City, A.B. (magna cum laude) 1964; New York University School of Law, J.D. (cum Laude) 1967, admitted to New Jersey Bar, 1967. Served in the United States Army Reserve: Instructor, Fort Sill, Oklahoma, 1968–69: Captain. Assistant to Editor-in-Chief, Clark Boardman Co., Law Publishers, New York City, 1967; Adjunct Instructor, St. Peter's College, 1967; Staff Attorney, Middlesex County Legal Services Corp., New Brunswick, New Jersey, 1970–71. Assistant Professor, 1971–75, Associate Professor, 1975–78, and since 1978 Professor, St. Louis University School of Law, Missouri. Recipient: Mystery Writers of America Edgar Allan Poe Award, for criticism, 1975. Agent: Oliver Swan, Collier Associates, 280 Madison Avenue, New York, New York 10016. Address: 7045 Cornell, University City, Missouri 63130, U.S.A.

CRIME PUBLICATIONS

Novels (series character: Loren Mensing in both books)

Publish and Perish. New York, Putnam, 1975; London, Hale, 1977.
Corrupt and Ensnare. New York, Putnam, 1978; London, Hale, 1979.

Uncollected Short Stories

"After the Twelfth Chapter," in *Ellery Queen's Mystery Magazine* (New York), September 1972.
"Murder of a Male Chauvinist," in *Ellery Queen's Mystery Magazine* (New York), May 1973.
"Leap Day," in *Ellery Queen's Mystery Magazine* (New York), July 1973.
"Six Thousand Little Bonapartes," in *Ellery Queen's Mystery Magazine* (New York), December 1973.
"The Possibility of Termites," in *Ellery Queen's Mystery Magazine* (New York), May 1974.
"Open Letter to Survivors," in *Ellery Queen's Crookbook.* New York, Random House, and London, Gollancz, 1974.
"The Ironclad Alibi," in *Ellery Queen's Mystery Magazine* (New York), November 1974.
"An Ear for the Language," in *Alfred Hitchcock's Mystery Magazine* (North Palm Beach, Florida), March 1975.
"Because the Constable Blundered," in *Best Detective Stories of the Year 1974*, edited by Allen J. Hubin. New York, Dutton, 1975.
"The Benteen Millions," in *Ellery Queen's Mystery Magazine* (New York), May 1975.
"The Kumquat Affair," in *Ellery Queen's Mystery Magazine* (New York), October 1975.
"Funeral Music," in *Ellery Queen's Mystery Magazine* (New York), February 1976.

"The Matchwit Club," in *Ellery Queen's Mystery Magazine* (New York), July 1976.

"Superscam," in *Alfred Hitchcock's Anthology 2*.   New York, Davis, 1977.

"A Picture in the Mind," in *Alfred Hitchcock's Mystery Magazine* (New York), February 1977.

"The Dogsbody Case," in *Ellery Queen's Mystery Magazine* (New York), February 1977.

"To Catch a Con Man," in *Ellery Queen's Mystery Magazine* (New York), October 1977.

"Fair Game," in *Cop Cade*, edited by John Ball.   New York, Doubleday, 1978.

"Doomchild," in *Alfred Hitchcock's Mystery Magazine* (New York), September 1978.

"Evensong," in *Ellery Queen's Mystery Magazine* (New York), March 1979.

"Black Spider," in *Ellery Queen's Mystery Magazine* (New York), August 1979.

"The Scrabble Clue," in *Ellery Queen's Anthology 37*.   New York, Davis, 1979.

"Film Flam," in *Best Detective Stories of the Year*, edited by Edward D. Hoch.   New York, Dutton, 1979.

OTHER PUBLICATIONS

Other

Detectionary, with others.   New York, Hammermill Paper, 1971; revised edition, New York, Overlook Press, 1977.

Royal Bloodline: Ellery Queen, Author and Detective.   Bowling Green, Ohio, Popular Press, 1974.

"The Law of the Mystery Writer v. the Law of the Courts," in *Popular Culture Scholar* (Frostburg, Maryland), 1976.

"The Marquis of Unremembered Manhunters," in *Xenophile* (St. Louis), 1976.

"Name Games: Mystery Writers and Their Pseudonyms," in *The Mystery Story*, edited by John Ball.   San Diego, University of California Extension, 1976.

"The World of Milton Propper," in *Armchair Detective* (Del Mar, California), July 1977.

"Murder Like Crazy: Harry Stephen Keeler," in *New Republic* (Washington, D.C.), 30 July 1977.

"Private Eye in an Evil Time: Mark Sadler's Paul Shaw," in *Xenophile* (St. Louis), March–April 1978.

"Murder at Noon: Michael Avallone," in *New Republic* (Washington, D.C.), 22 July 1978.

"The Sound of Suspense: John Dickson Carr as a Radio Writer," in *Armchair Detective* (Del Mar, California), October 1978.

Editor, *The Mystery Writer's Art*.   Bowling Green, Ohio, Popular Press, 1971.

Editor, *Nightwebs: A Collection of Stories by Cornell Woolrich*.   New York, Harper, 1971; London, Gollancz, 1973.

Co-Editor, *Multiplying Villainies: Selected Mystery Criticism of Anthony Boucher.*   Privately printed, 1973.

Francis M. Nevins, Jr. comments:

My concept of the ideal mystery novel is one that combines Erle Stanley Gardner's crackling pace and legal ingenuity, Ellery Queen's labyrinthine plot structure and deductive fair play, and Cornell Woolrich's feel for suspense and the anguish of living and compellingly visual style. If I ever come close to writing that ideal book, most of the credit will go to those three masters.

*   *   *

Even a cursory glance at the writings of Francis M. Nevins, Jr. reveals his depth and range of interest in the mystery crime field. The completion of *The Mystery Writer's Art*, *Nightwebs*, and *Royal Blood Line* are testaments to his scholarly commitment to the non-fictional areas of the field. With the publication of his first two stories, "Open Letter to Survivors" and "After the Twelfth Chapter," Nevins demonstrated an equal range and skill in the area of mystery fiction. The first story is a pastiche of the traditional and the unusual in detective fiction, a blend of old and new that becomes a Nevins trademark. The second story introduces a Professor of Law detective, Loren Mensing, who becomes the central Nevins character in six other stories and two novels.

A critical assessment of Nevins's work shows him to be a consummate storyteller. Whether working in short fiction, with all of its restrictions and demand for economy and telling detail, or in the novel, with its demands for complex plot structure and sustained character development, he consistently produces entertaining and skilful work. His major fictional detectives, Loren Mensing and Milo Turner, are deftly drawn, complex characters who capture a reader's imagination and challenge his intellect.

Though there is no Nevins "formula," there is a Nevins intention. In most of his works, short or long, Nevins attempts to balance four elements: clues and deductions, visual and suspenseful elements, legal gimmicks, and human relationships. In his best works, and particularly in his two novels, Nevins strives for a synthesis of the best of Doyle, Gardner, Woolrich, and Queen. *Publish and Perish* is notable for its complex denouement, with its ironic reversals and red-herring endings. *Corrupt and Ensnare* combines an interesting story with strong character development.

In short, a reader can expect intelligent and skilful plotting, good drama, and quality writing in the fictional world of Francis Nevins. His mind is agile, his pen sure – a combination that provides many pleasurable hours of good reading.

—George J. Thompson

NEWMAN, Bernard. Also wrote as Don Betteridge. British. Born in Ibstock, Leicestershire, 8 May 1897. Educated at Bosworth School. Served in the British Expeditionary Forces in France, 1915–19; Staff Lecturer, Ministry of Information, 1940–45. Married 1) Marjorie Edith Donald in 1928; three daughters; 2) Helen Johnston in 1966. Joined the Civil Service in 1920; lectured for the Ministry of Information and the Department of Army Education in the 1940's and 1950's. Fellow, Royal Society of Arts. Chevalier, Legion of Honour. *Died 19 February 1968.*

CRIME PUBLICATIONS

Novels (series character: Papa Pontivy)

> *Death of a Harlot.* London, Laurie, 1934; New York, Godwin, 1935.
> *Secret Servant.* London, Gollancz, 1935; New York, Curl, 1936.
> *Germany Spy.* London, Gollancz, and New York, Curl, 1936.
> *Lady Doctor – Woman Spy.* London, Hutchinson, 1937.
> *Death under Gibraltar.* London, Gollancz, 1938.
> *Death to the Spy* (Pontivy). London, Gollancz, 1939.
> *The Mussolini Murder Plot.* London, Hutchinson, and New York, Curl, 1939.
> *Maginot Line Murder.* London, Gollancz, 1939; as *Papa Pontivy and the Maginot Murder*, New York, Holt, 1940.

Siegfried Spy. London, Gollancz, 1940.
Secret Weapon. London, Gollancz, 1941.
Death to the Fifth Column (Pontivy). London, Gollancz, 1941.
Black Market (Pontivy). London, Gollancz, 1942.
Second Front – First Spy (Pontivy). London, Gollancz, 1944.
The Spy in the Brown Derby. London, Gollancz, 1945.
Dead Man Murder. London, Gollancz, 1946.
Moscow Murder (Pontivy). London, Gollancz, 1948.
Shoot! London, Gollancz, 1949.
Cup Final Murder. London, Gollancz, 1950.
Centre Court Murder. London, Gollancz, 1951.
Death at Lord's. London, Gollancz, 1952.
The Wishful Think. London, Hale, 1954.
The Double Menace (Pontivy). London, Hale, 1955; New York, Viking Press, 1956.
Operation Barbarossa (Pontivy). London, Hale, 1956.
The Otan Plot (Pontivy). London, Hale, 1957.
Taken at the Flood. London, Hale, 1958.
Silver Greyhound. London, Hale, 1960.
This Is Your Life (Pontivy). London, Hale, 1963.
The Travelling Executioners. London, Hale, 1964.
The Spy at Number 10 (Pontivy). London, Hale, 1965.
Evil Phoenix. London, Hale, 1966.
The Dangerous Age. London, Hale, 1967.
Draw the Dragon's Teeth. London, Hale, 1967.
The Jail-Breakers. London, Hale, 1968.

Novels as Don Betteridge

Scotland Yard Alibi. London, Gollancz, 1938.
Cast Iron Alibi. London, Jenkins, 1939.
Balkan Spy. London, Jenkins, 1942.
The Escape of General Gerard. London, Jenkins, 1943.
Dictator's Destiny. London, Jenkins, 1945.
The Potsdam Murder Plot. London, Jenkins, 1947.
Spies Left! London, Hale, 1950.
Not Single Spies. London, Hale, 1951.
Spy – Counter Spy. London, Hale, 1953.
The Case of the Berlin Spy. London, Hale, 1954.
The Gibraltar Conspiracy. London, Hale, 1955.
The Spies of Peenemünde. London, Hale, 1958.
Contact Man. London, Hale, 1960.
The Package Holiday Spy Case. London, Hale, 1962.

Short Stories

Spy Catchers. London, Gollancz, 1945.

Uncollected Short Stories

"Death at the Wicket," in *Butcher's Dozen.* London, Heinemann, 1956.
"Element of Doubt," in *John Creasey's Mystery Bedside Book 1969*, edited by Herbert
    Harris. London, Hodder and Stoughton, 1968.

OTHER PUBLICATIONS

Novels

> *The Cavalry Went Through.* London, Gollancz, 1930; as *The Cavalry Goes Through,*
> New York, Holt, 1930.
> *Hosanna!* London, Archer, 1933.
> *Death in the Valley: A Tale Based on the Origin of the Oberammergau Passion
> Play.* London, Archer, 1934.
> *The Flying Saucer.* London, Gollancz, 1948; New York, Macmillan, 1950.
> *Flowers for the Living,* with Guy Bolton. London, Jenkins, 1958.

Plays

> *One Silk Stocking.* London, Reynolds, 1926.
> *Burlesque Orations and Comedy Lectures.* London, McGlennon, 1929.
> *Cross-Talk Arguments.* London, McGlennon, 1929.
> *The Dunmow Flitch: A Humorous Mock Trial.* London, McGlennon, 1929.
> *Humorous Monologues for Ladies.* London, McGlennon, 1929.
> *Humorous Monologues on Sport.* London, McGlennon, 1929.
> *The Phantom Voice.* London, McGlennon, 1929.
> *The Second Book of Monologues, Humorous and Dramatic.* London, McGlennon,
> 1929.
> *Back-Chat for Cross-Talk Comedians,* with Charles Hickman. London, McGlennon,
> 1929.
> *Appearances and Deceptions: A Comedy Sketch.* London, McGlennon, 1930; with
> *Musical Interruptions,* McGlennon, 1930.
> *Cupid's Agent.* London, McGlennon, 1930.
> *Farcical Sketches for Male Characters.* London, McGlennon, 1930.
> *Half-Hour Comedies.* London, McGlennon, 1930.
> *Model Artists.* London, McGlennon, 1930.
> *No Followers Allowed.* London, McGlennon, 1930.
> *Poets Made to Order.* London, McGlennon, 1930.

Other

> *How to Run an Amateur Concert Party.* London, Reynolds, 1925.
> *Character Monologues and How to Perform Them.* London, Pearson, 1926.
> *Round about Andorra.* London, Allen and Unwin, and Boston, Houghton Mifflin,
> 1928.
> *Mock Trials and How to Run Them.* London, McGlennon, 1929.
> *Modern Parody Monologues and How to Recite Them.* London, McGlennon, 1929.
> *Armoured Doves: A Peace Book.* London, Jarrolds, 1931.
> *In the Trail of the Three Musketeers.* London, Jenkins, 1934.
> *Pedalling Poland.* London, Jenkins, 1935.
> *Spy.* London, Gollancz, and New York, Appleton Century, 1935.
> *The Blue Danube.* London, Jenkins, 1935.
> *Tunnellers: The Story of the Tunnelling Companies,* with W. G. Grieve. London,
> Jenkins, 1936.
> *Albanian Back-Door.* London, Jenkins, 1936.
> *Cycling in France – Northern.* London, Jenkins, 1936.
> *I Saw Spain.* London, Jenkins, 1937.
> *Albanian Journey.* London, Pitman, 1938.
> *Danger Spots of Europe.* London, Hale, 1938; revised edition, 1939.
> *Ride to Russia.* London, Jenkins, 1938.

Baltic Roundabout. London, Jenkins, 1939; revised edition, 1940.

Secrets of German Espionage. London, Hale, 1940; as *German Secret Service at Work*, New York, McBride, 1940.

The Story of Poland. London, Hutchinson, 1940.

Savoy! Corsica! Tunis! Mussolini's Dream Lands. London, Jenkins, 1940.

One Man's Year. London, Gollancz, 1941.

The New Europe. London, Hale, 1942; New York, Macmillan, 1943.

American Journey. London, Hale, 1943.

The People of Poland. Birkenhead, Cheshire, Polish Publications Committee, 1943.

The Face of Poland. Birkenhead, Cheshire, Polish Publications Committee, 1944.

Balkan Background. London, Hale, 1944; New York, Macmillan, 1945.

British Journey. London, Hale, 1945.

Russia's Neighbour – The New Poland. London, Gollancz, 1946.

Middle Eastern Journey. London, Gollancz, 1947.

The Red Spider Web: The Story of Russian Spying in Canada. London, Latimer House, 1947.

News from the East. London, Gollancz, 1948.

The Captured Archives: The Story of the Nazi-Soviet Documents. London, Latimer House, 1948.

Mediterranean Background. London, Hale, 1949.

The Lazy House. London, Jenkins, 1949.

Come Adventuring with Me. London, Latimer House, 1949.

The Sisters Alsace-Lorraine. London, Jenkins, 1950.

Epics of Espionage. London, Laurie, and New York, Philosophical Library, 1950.

Turkish Cross-Roads. London, Hale, 1951; New York, Philosophical Library, 1952.

Oberammergau Journey. London, Jenkins, 1952.

They Saved London. London, Warner, 1952.

Soviet Atomic Spies. London, Hale, 1952.

Both Sides of the Pyrenees. London, Jenkins, 1952.

Tito's Yugoslavia. London, Hale, 1952.

Morocco Today. London, Hale, 1953.

Ride to Rome. London, Jenkins, 1953.

Yours for Action. London, Jenkins, 1953.

Report on Indo-China. London, Hale, 1953; New York, Praeger, 1954.

Berlin and Back. London, Jenkins, 1954.

The Sosnowski Affair: Inquest on a Spy. London, Laurie, 1954.

North African Journey. London, Hale, 1955.

Still Flows the Danube. London, Jenkins, 1955.

Inquest on Mata Hari. London, Hale, 1956.

Real Life Spies. London, Hutchinson, 1956.

The Three Germanies. London, Hale, 1957.

Spain on a Shoestring. London, Jenkins, 1957.

One Hundred Years of Good Company. Lincoln, Ruston and Hornsby, 1957.

Unknown Germany. London, Jenkins, 1958; New York, McBride, 1959.

Portrait of Poland. London, Hale, 1959.

Danger Spots of the World. London, Hale, 1959.

Visa to Russia. London, Jenkins, 1959.

Speaking from Memory (autobiography). London, Jenkins, 1960.

Unknown Yugoslavia. London, Jenkins, 1960.

Bulgarian Background. London, Hale, 1961.

Far Eastern Journey: Across India and Pakistan to Formosa. London, Jenkins, 1961.

Let's Look at Germany. London, Museum Press, and New York, Pitnam, 1961.

The Blue Ants: The First Authentic Account of the Russian-Chinese War of 1970. London, Hale, 1962.

The World of Espionage. London, Souvenir Press, 1962; New York, British Book
  Centre, 1963.
Mr. Kennedy's America. London, Jenkins, 1962.
Unknown France. London, Jenkins, 1963.
Round the World in Seventy Days. London, Jenkins, 1964.
Behind the Berlin Wall. London, Hale, 1964.
Spies in Britain. London, Hale, 1964.
Background to Viet-Nam. London, Hale, 1965; New York, Roy, 1966.
Let's Visit France (juvenile). London, Burke, 1965; New York, Roy, 1967.
South African Journey. London, Jenkins, 1965.
Let's Visit Malaysia and Her Neighbours (juvenile). London, Burke, 1965.
Spain Revisited. London, Jenkins, 1966.
Let's Visit Vietnam (juvenile). London, Burke, 1967.
To Russia and Back. London, Jenkins, 1967.
Let's Visit South Africa (juvenile). London, Burke, 1967; New York, Day, 1968.
The Bosworth Story. London, Jenkins, 1967.
Portrait of the Shires. London, Hale, 1968.
Turkey and the Turks. London, Jenkins, 1968.
The New Poland. London, Hale, 1968.
Spy and Counter-Spy: Bernard Newman's Story of the British Secret Service, edited by I.
  O. Evans. London, Hale, 1970.

Editor, with I. O. Evans, *Anthology of Armageddon.* London, Archer, 1935.
Editor, *Presenting People Living Dangerously.* London, Hamlyn, 1961.

*   *   *

Bernard Newman, throughout a long and prolific career, wrote a great many novels, many
under the pseudonym of Don Betteridge. Most were spy thrillers linked to current events,
adventure stories with a taste of detection but no crime, or murder mysteries.

The spy thrillers of the 1930's and 1940's are set in wartime; those of the 1950's and
1960's are cast against a backdrop of international events and civil strife. Much of the
historical detail in these novels is accurate, but Newman's perception of espionage is highly
romanticized. Characters like Henry and Pontivy, from *Black Market, Second Front − First
Spy, The Spy in the Brown Derby*, and *Death of the Fifth Column*, perceive themselves as the
vital cogs in the German Secret Service in Britain. *German Spy*, a fictionalized account of the
life of the German spy Grein, is filled with intrigue and acts of courage. Grein is Newman's
folk hero, an example for all his subsequent heroes of the political and moral supremacy of a
nation's spy.

The 1950's marked the beginning of Newman's murder mysteries. The adventure and
suspense evident in the war novels emerges in mystery stories like *Centre Court Murder* and
Cup Final Murder. The latter book chronicles Nicholas Prince's relentless search for a
murderer. Prince excels in police work but his resistance to corruption has kept him from
securing a position in the field. Prince's investigation is admirably detailed and Newman's
characterizations are impeccable. The investigation unearths, not surprisingly, some political
intrigue.

A study of Newman's works reveals a fine line between what he considers truth and what
he considers fiction. Life for Newman is adventure. His spy thrillers and murder mysteries,
though based on fact, reveal a bent for the romantic. Even his travel/adventure accounts and
history books share this quality. Newman's perception of the suspense genre is perhaps best
illustrated in his analysis of the book by Grein that led him to write *German Spy*. Grein, he
says, "would scarcely be human if he did not romanticize a little."

—Donna Rose Casella Kern

1113

NICHOLS, (John) Beverley. British. Born in Bristol. 9 September 1898. Educated at Marlborough College; Balliol College, Oxford (Editor, *Isis*; Founding Editor, *The Oxford Outlook*; President, Oxford Union), B.A. Drama Critic, *The Weekly Dispatch*, 1926; Editor, *The American Sketch*, New York, 1928–29. Address: Sudbrook Cottage, Ham Common, Surrey, England.

CRIME PUBLICATIONS

Novels (series character: Horatio Green in all books)

No Man's Street. London, Hutchinson, and New York, Dutton, 1954.
The Moonflower. London, Hutchinson, 1955; as *The Moonflower Murder*, New York, Dutton, 1955.
Death to Slow Music. London, Hutchinson, and New York, Dutton, 1956.
The Rich Die Hard. London, Hutchinson, 1957; New York, Dutton, 1958.
Murder by Request. London, Hutchinson, and New York, Dutton, 1960.

OTHER PUBLICATIONS

Novels

Prelude. London, Chatto and Windus, 1920.
Patchwork. London, Chatto and Windus, 1921; New York, Holt, 1922.
Self. London, Chatto and Windus, 1922.
Crazy Pavements. London, Cape, and New York, Doran, 1927.
Evensong. London, Cape, and New York, Doubleday, 1932.
Revue. London, Cape, and New York, Doubleday, 1939.
Laughter on the Stairs. London, Cape, 1953; New York, Dutton, 1954.
Sunlight on the Lawn. London, Cape, and New York, Dutton, 1956.

Short Stories

Men Do Not Weep. London, Cape, 1941; New York, Harcourt Brace, 1942.

Plays

Picnic (revue; composer only) (produced London, 1927).
Many Happy Returns (revue; composer only), by Herbert Farjeon (produced London, 1928).
The Stag (produced London, 1929). Included in *Failures*, 1933.
Cochran's 1930 Revue, music by Nichols and Vivian Ellis (produced London, 1930).
Avalanche (produced Edinburgh, 1931; London, 1932). Included in *Failures*, 1933.
Evensong, with Edward Knoblock, adaptation of the novel by Nichols (produced London, 1932; New York, 1933). London and New York, French, 1933.
When the Crash Comes (produced Birmingham, 1933). Included in *Failures*, 1933.
Failures: Three Plays (includes *The Stag, Avalanche, When the Crash Comes*). London, Cape, and New York, Peter Smith, 1933.
Mesmer (produced London, 1938). London, Cape, 1935.
Floodlight, music by Nichols (revue; produced London, 1937).
Shadow of the Vine (produced London, 1954). London, Cape, 1949.
La Plume de Ma Tante (produced Bromley, Kent, 1953).

Other Plays: *Song on the Wind* (operetta), 1948; *Lady's Guide*, 1950.

Screenplay: *Nine till Six*, with Alma Reveille and John Paddy Carstairs, 1932.

Radio Play: *You Bet Your Life*, with Rupert Croft-Cooke, 1938.

Other

25, Being a Young Man's Candid Recollections of His Elders and Betters. London,
   Cape, and New York, Doran, 1926.
*Are They the Same at Home? Being a Series of Bouquets Diffidently
   Distributed.* London, Cape, and New York, Doran, 1927.
The Star-Spangled Manner. London, Cape, and New York, Doubleday, 1928.
Women and Children Last. London, Cape, and New York, Doubleday, 1931.
Down the Garden Path. London, Cape, and New York, Doubleday, 1932.
For Adults Only. London, Cape, 1932; New York, Doubleday, 1933.
In the Next War I Shall Be a Conscientious Objector. London, Friends' Peace
   Committee, 1932.
Cry Havoc! London, Cape, and New York, Doubleday, 1933.
Puck at Brighton: The Official Handbook of the Corporation of Brighton. Brighton,
   Corporation of Brighton, 1933.
A Thatched Roof. London, Cape, and New York, Doubleday, 1933.
The Valet as Historian. London, Forsyth, 1934.
A Village in a Valley. London, Cape, and New York, Doubleday, 1934.
How Does Your Garden Grow? (broadcast talks), with others. London, Allen and
   Unwin, and New York, Doubleday, 1935.
The Fool Hath Said. London, Cape, and New York, Doubleday, 1936.
No Place Like Home (travel). London, Cape, and New York, Doubleday, 1936.
News of England; or, A Country Without a Hero. London, Cape, and New York,
   Doubleday, 1938.
Green Grows the City: The Story of a London Garden. London, Cape, and New York,
   Harcourt Brace, 1939.
Verdict on India. London, Cape, and New York, Harcourt Brace, 1944.
The Tree That Sat Down (juvenile). London, Cape, 1945.
The Stream That Stood Still (juvenile). London, Cape, 1948.
All I Could Never Be: Some Recollections. London, Cape, 1949; New York, Dutton,
   1952.
Yours Sincerely (*Woman's Own* articles), with Monica Dickens. London, Newnes,
   1949.
The Mountain of Magic (juvenile). London, Cape, 1950.
Uncle Samson (on America). London, Evans, 1950.
Merry Hall. London, Cape, 1951; New York, Dutton, 1953.
A Pilgrim's Progress. London, Cape, 1952.
The Queen's Coronation Day: The Pictorial Record of the Great Occasion. London,
   Pitkin, 1953.
Cat Book. London, Nelson, 1955.
The Sweet and Twenties. London, Weidenfeld and Nicolson, 1958.
The Tree That Sat Down, and The Stream That Stood Still (abridged editions). London,
   Cape, 1960; New York, St. Martin's Press, 1966.
Cats' ABC. London, Cape, and New York, Dutton, 1960.
Cats' XYZ. London, Cape, and New York, Dutton, 1961.
Garden Open Today. London, Cape, and New York, Dutton, 1963.
Forty Favourite Flowers. London, Studio Vista, 1964; New York, St. Martin's Press,
   1965.
Powers That Be. London, Cape, and New York, St. Martin's Press, 1966.
A Case of Human Bondage (on Somerset Maugham). London, Secker and Warburg,
   and New York, Award Books, 1966.

The Art of Flower Arrangement. London, Collins, and New York, Viking Press, 1967.
Garden Open Tomorrow. London, Heinemann, 1968; New York, Dodd Mead, 1969.
The Sun in My Eyes: or, How Not to Go Around the World. London, Heinemann, 1969.
The Wickedest Witch in the World (juvenile). London, W. H. Allen, 1971.
Father Figure. London, Heinemann, and New York, Simon and Schuster, 1972.
Down the Kitchen Sink (autobiography). London, W. H. Allen, 1974.
Cats' A–Z (includes *Cats' ABC* and *Cats' XYZ*). London, W. H. Allen, 1977.
The Unforgiving Minute: Some Confessions from Childhood to the Outbreak of the Second World War. London, W. H. Allen, 1978.

Editor, *A Book of Old Ballads.* London, Hutchinson, and New York, Loring and Mussey, 1934.

Manuscript Collection: Humanities Research Center, University of Texas, Austin.

*   *   *

Beverley Nichols had been a successful writer for 30 years when his first detective novel was published in 1954. Four more appeared in the next few years, before he abandoned the form, discouraged by hostile criticism. It is hard to see why the books were ill-received, since they were accomplished and alluring mysteries in the classic mode, intricate, ingenious, shapely, and continually absorbing: alibis seem impregnable, suspicion spreads impartially, red herrings proliferate, and the great detective sums up at the end. They are remarkably elegant novels, meticulously contrived and controlled, and stylishly written, with a relative austerity unexpected in a writer so avowedly romantic.

No Man's Street features an opulent retired diva and an eminent conductor in a search for a unique record that has strangely disappeared. The victim is a blackmailing music critic, hated by his lesbian sister and her alcoholic lover. The anonymity of the street where he lives is a key feature of the case. *The Moonflower* is a more exotic confection of greater complexity. What seems a simple case of an old woman murdered for her jewels by an escaped convict ramifies enticingly into a much richer pattern. The flower plays an essential role, blooming too soon and beginning to die even as it reaches perfection. *Death to Slow Music* is a rather sinister story set by the sea and revolving round a star actor in the throes of rehearsal for his new musical show. His unstable accompanist is accused of murder but himself becomes a murder victim. The narrative combines a febrile theatrical gaiety with a darker, more menacing quality. *The Rich Die Hard* centres on a Queen Anne mansion and the great private art collection housed in it. The action links the murder of a tycoon's mistress with the destruction of a great painting and a savage bonfire of schoolboy relics. *Murder by Request* is a mischievous coda to the other novels, set at a health farm called Harmony Hall, and deploying to ironic effect the improbable trappings of a traditional detective story: not for nothing is the first victim an ardent reader of mystery fiction.

The investigator throughout is Horatio Green, a famous detective, now retired but unable to resist a mystery. He is a plump, mild little man known to the Yard as the Human Bloodhound, from an exceptional "olfactory sense" that enables him to determine ethnic origin from body odour. He conducts himself in the time-honoured manner of the great fictional detectives, uttering "cryptic remarks," indulging in "unaccountable behaviour," blinking furiously at moments of "cerebral activity," and outstripping the police with prodigies of perception and deduction. His insights are invariably subtle, deriving from "scraps of dialogue – shadows on faces – fleeting gestures": a murdered woman's expression seems inappropriate to the way she died; a bust described by a blind man points to a daring musical fraud; a strident record played by a woman of refined taste suggests a guilty secret. There is much to enjoy in Green's career.

—B. A. Pike

NICOLE, Christopher. See **YORK, Andrew.**

NIELSEN, Helen (Berniece). American. Born in Roseville, Illinois, 23 October 1918. Educated at Kelvyn Park High School, Chicago; Chicago Art Institute; United States Defense Engineering Program, rated Aero-Layout Engineer, 1942. Free-lance Commercial Artist, Chicago, 1938–42; Draftsman and Loftsman, Aero-Engineering, Los Angeles, 1942–46; Apartment House Owner and Manager, 1942–78. Agent: Ann Elmo Agency Inc., 60 East 42nd Street, New York, New York 10017. Address: 2622 Victoria Drive, Laguna Beach, California 92651, U.S.A.

CRIME PUBLICATIONS

Novels (series character: Simon Drake)

The Kind Man. New York, Washburn, and London, Gollancz, 1951.
Gold Coast Nocturne (Drake). New York, Washburn, 1951; as *Murder by Proxy*, London, Gollancz, 1952; as *Dead on the Level*, New York, Dell, 1954.
Obit Delayed. New York, Washburn, 1952; London, Gollancz, 1953.
Detour. New York, Washburn, 1953; as *Detour to Death*, New York, Dell, 1955.
The Woman on the Roof. New York, Washburn, 1954; London, Gollancz, 1955.
Stranger in the Dark. New York, Washburn, 1955; London, Gollancz, 1956.
The Crime Is Murder. New York, Morrow, 1956; London, Gollancz, 1957.
Borrow the Night. New York, Morrow, and London, Gollancz, 1957; as *Seven Days Before Dying*, New York, Dell, 1958.
The Fifth Caller. New York, Morrow, and London, Gollancz, 1959.
False Witness. New York, Ballantine, 1959.
Sing Me a Murder. New York, Morrow, 1960; London, Gollancz, 1961.
Verdict Suspended. New York, Morrow, 1964; London, Gollancz, 1965.
After Midnight (Drake). New York, Morrow, 1966; London, Gollancz, 1967.
A Killer in the Street. New York, Morrow, and London, Gollancz, 1967.
Darkest Hour (Drake). New York, Morrow, and London, Gollancz, 1969.
Shot on Location. New York, Morrow, and London, Gollancz, 1971.
The Severed Key (Drake). London, Gollancz, 1973.
The Brink of Murder (Drake). London, Gollancz, 1976.

Short Stories

Woman Missing and Other Stories. New York, Ace, 1961.

Uncollected Short Stories

"The Hopeless Case," in *Ellery Queen's Mystery Magazine* (New York), June 1962.
"Witness for the Defense," in *Ellery Queen's Mystery Magazine* (New York), September 1963.
"Death Scene," in *Ellery Queen's Double Dozen.* New York, Random House, 1964.
"The Breaking Point," in *Ellery Queen's Mystery Magazine* (New York), August 1965.
"The Chicken Feed Mice," in *Ellery Queen's Mystery Magazine* (New York), December 1966.

"Cop's Day Off," in *Ellery Queen's Anthology, 1969.*   New York, Davis, 1968.
"No Legal Evidence," in *Ellery Queen's Mystery Magazine* (New York), March 1969.
"The Man Is Dangerous," in *Ellery Queen's Anthology, 1970.*   New York, Davis, 1969.
"The Perfect Servant," in *Ellery Queen's Mystery Bag.*   Cleveland, World, 1972.

OTHER PUBLICATIONS

Plays

Television Plays: *Alfred Hitchcock Presents, Perry Mason, Markham, Alcoa Theatre, 87th Precinct, Four Star Theatre,* and *Checkmate* series.

Manuscript Collection: Mugar Memorial Library, Boston University.

Helen Nielsen comments:
I am old-fashioned enough to believe that characters still make a story, and that every story, especially a mystery, must have a beginning, a middle and an ending. Although the trend today is for more violence, the mystery is still the most demanding form of fiction. No matter how deep the gore flows or how high the bodies are stacked, there must be logic in each crime and no loose ends dangling after the last page. A critic's comment: "plays fair" is the disciplined mystery writer's reward.

*   *   *

Born in Illinois, Helen Nielsen moved to Southern California in her youth and seems to have adopted this state for her stories almost completely. It is seldom that she sets her fictional foot outside the state, and it is almost a shock when she places the first part of *A Killer in the Street* in New York City. On a rainy night in Manhattan, Kyle Walker is unfortunate enough to witness the strangling of the garage attendant in his apartment house garage. He stands there appalled looking at the boy who is bound and gagged. "His face was a flash of white terror – his mouth opened in a scream that never reached sound" producing the anxiety and tension of a lightning flash that does not give forth thunder. For one horrible moment, Walker is seen standing mutely there, and he knows he must abandon his present life and flee to other parts of the country. Helen Nielsen chooses to send Walker and his wife to California.

Southern California must be a paradise upon earth for a mystery writer, with its strange people, weird situations, and peculiar professions and living habits, although Nielsen persists in stressing the winter rains and the thick, damp fogs. In *The Fifth Caller* a doctor is found dead in her home/office. Dr. Whitehall, who lived a strange and muddled life, specialised in mental problems, though equipped with only a mail-order degree and a second one from the metaphysical college founded by herself. Her assistant, a Hungarian refugee, is qualified as a doctor in her own country and naturally cannot help disapproving of Dr. Whitehall's activities. She falls under suspicion, especially after her attempted suicide on a Santa Monica beach; much of the novel is set in her hospital room as she recovers from the wrist slashing.

Most of the mysteries feature water, lakes, sea, or rain. It seems as if Nielsen is not anxious to encourage others to join her in the state of her choice. She does defect once or twice. *Detour* is set in a small desert community where Danny Ross, an outsider, is accused of the local doctor's murder. In that isolated and unfriendly place he is not allowed to speak in his own defence, but fortunately a local person takes an interest in him and finds the real killer. In *The Crime Is Murder*, the water is Lake Michigan, and the murder is set at the annual festival celebrating a local celebrity. As it is a small community "quite devoid of distinction" they gladly grab any person who fills the description of an artist of any kind.

Even Southern California has its scenic failures, such as Enchanto-by-the-Sea, a place meant to be a successful resort but which failed to meet the town planners' expectations.

Enchanto is by-passed by both the tourists and the characters in *Darkest Hour* as they shoot up and down the coast highway; most of them are has-been actors, including one of the victims, and the lawyer, Simon Drake, provides a home for one ex-actress who is the hostess/housekeeper. *Sing Me a Murder* is another show business story full of the rootless, rich but dispossessed. The husband of a famous singer, killed in a Canyon fire, becomes involved in the murder of her look-alike who is a waitress. A man has been arrested for this murder, but Ty Leander feels sure that he did not do it as he seems to sense a message from his dead wife each time he thinks about the case. He is able to drown some of his grief as he rushes around searching for witnesses, looking for clues until he triumphs with the help of the police.

Nielsen also deals with the lower edges of society, as in *The Woman on the Roof*. Wilma Rathjen, in spite of a rich and successful brother, is not a success, and has done time in a mental asylum. She is working at a bakery and, like many of the handicapped, she is anxious and conscientious. This leads her into becoming involved in finding a murderer in her bungalow court, owned by her brother. The excitement and tension seem to improve her rather than produce a slide back into mental ill-health as might have been expected.

These mysteries often feature the more exciting professions. As well as show business, there are a threatened Judge in *Borrow the Night* and a reporter in *Obit Delayed*; normal enough jobs indeed, but always managing to be a trifle strange in Southern California. There seems to be more rain than usual in the weather forecasts, and an unnatural amount of fog, pure, dripping, and yellow, and not the more expected smog. Helen Nielsen is good for the mystery reader but perhaps tourists should look elsewhere for guidance.

—Mary Groff

NILE, Dorothea.   See **AVALLONE, Michael.**

NOLAN, William F(rancis).   American.   Born in Kansas City, Missouri, 6 March 1928. Educated at Kansas City Art Institute, 1946–47; San Diego State College, California, 1947–48; Los Angeles City College, 1953. Married Marilyn Seal in 1970. Commercial artist, credit clerk, and aircraft worker; Contributing Editor, *Chase*; Managing Editor, *GAMMA*; West Coast Editor, *Auto*; Associate Editor, *Motor Sport Illustrated*; Reviewer, Los Angeles *Times*. Since 1956, free-lance writer. Founder, with Jack Kaplan, Dashiell Hammett Society of San Francisco, 1977. Recipient: Academy of Science Fiction and Fantasy Award, for fiction, and film, 1976. Honorary Doctorate: American River College, Sacramento, California. Address: 22720 Cavalier Street, Woodland Hills, California 91364, U.S.A.

<small>CRIME PUBLICATIONS</small>

Novels (series character: Bart Challis)

> *Death Is for Losers* (Challis).   Los Angeles, Sherbourne Press, 1968.
> *The White Cad Cross-Up* (Challis).   Los Angeles, Sherbourne Press, 1969.

Logan's Run, with G. C. Johnson.   New York, Dial Press, 1967; London, Gollancz, 1968.
Space for Hire.   New York, Lancer, 1971.
Logan's World.   New York, Bantam, 1977; London, Corgi, 1978.

Short Stories

Impact-20.   New York, Paperback Library, 1963; London, Corgi, 1966.

Uncollected Short Stories

"Dark Encounter," in *Murder Most Foul*, edited by Harold Q. Masur.   New York, Walker, 1971.
"Down the Long Night," in *Men and Malice*, edited by Dean Dickensheet.   New York, Doubleday, 1973.
"Coincidence," in *The Berserkers*, edited by Roger Elwood.   New York, Trident, 1973.
"The Strange Case of Mr. Pruyn," in *Alfred Hitchcock Presents: Stories to Be Read with the Lights On.*   New York, Random House, 1973.
"Violation," in *Tricks and Treats*, edited by Joe Gores and Bill Pronzini.   New York, Doubleday, 1976; as *Mystery Writers Choice*, London, Gollancz, 1977.
"Saturday's Shadows," in *Shadows 2*, edited by Charles Grant.   New York, Doubleday, 1979.

OTHER PUBLICATIONS

Short Stories

Alien Horizons.   New York, Pocket Books, 1974.
Wonderworlds.   London, Gollancz, 1977.

Other

Adventure on Wheels: The Autobiography of a Road Racing Champion, with John Fitch.   New York, Putnam, 1959.
Barney Oldfield.   New York, Putnam, 1961.
Phil Hill, Yankee Champion.   New York, Putnam, 1962.
Men of Thunder: Fabled Daredevils of Motor Sport.   New York, Putnam, 1964.
Sinners and Supermen.   North Hollywood, All Star, 1965.
John Huston, King Rebel.   Los Angeles, Sherbourne Press, 1965.
Dashiell Hammett: A Casebook.   Santa Barbara, California, McNally and Loftin, 1969.
Steve McQueen: Star on Wheels.   New York, Putnam, 1972.
Carnival of Speed.   New York, Putnam, 1973.
Hemingway: Last Days of the Lion.   Santa Barbara, California, Capra Press, 1974.
The Ray Bradbury Companion.   Detroit, Gale, 1975.

Editor, with Charles Beaumont, *Omnibus of Speed.*   New York, Putnam, 1958; London, Paul, 1961.
Editor, with Charles Beaumont, *When Engines Roar.*   New York, Bantam, 1964.
Editor, *Man Against Tomorrow.*   New York, Avon, 1965.
Editor, *The Pseudo People: Androids in Science Fiction.*   Los Angeles, Sherbourne Press, 1965; as *Almost Human*, London, Souvenir Press, 1966.
Editor, *3 to the Highest Power.*   New York, Avon, 1968; London, Corgi, 1971.
Editor, *A Wilderness of Stars.*   Los Angeles, Sherbourne Press, 1969; London, Gollancz, 1970.
Editor, *A Sea of Space.*   New York, Bantam, 1970.

Editor, *The Future Is Now*.   Los Angeles, Sherbourne Press, 1970.
Editor, *The Human Equation*.   Los Angeles, Sherbourne Press, 1971; London, Springwood, 1979.
Editor, *The Edge of Forever*.   Los Angeles, Sherbourne Press, 1971.

Plays

Screenplays: *The Legend of Machine-Gun Kelly*, 1973; *Logan's Run*, 1976; *Burnt Offerings*, 1976.

Television plays: *The Joy of Living*, 1971; *The Norliss Tapes*, 1973; *Melvin Purvis, G-Man*, 1974; *The Turn of the Screw*, 1974; *The Kansas City Massacre*, 1975; *Sky Heist*, 1975; *Trilogy of Terror*, 1975; *Logan's Run* series, 1977.

Bibliography: *William F. Nolan: A Checklist* by Charles E. Yenter, Tacoma, Washington, Charles E. Yenter, 1974.

William F. Nolan comments:
Communication is the key to all good writing in *any* field – and I attempt to communicate as directly as possible with my readers by utilizing a clear, swift, uncluttered narrative style in *all* my work, mystery, science fiction, biographical profiles, reviews, articles, and essays. I enjoy the challenge of variety in my career – which is why I work in so many fields, including television and motion pictures. That way I stay fresh, stay excited and involved. As a writer, I am never bored, and try never to bore my readers.
My best-known novels, *Logan's Run* and *Logan's World*, are both basically science-fiction books – *but* they also may be considered "future crime" novels, since their "hero," Logan, is a policeman whose job it is to hunt down runners who defy the laws of this future state. In my novels the police are known as "Sandmen." Thus, both Logan books fall into the SF/Crime-Suspense genre.

*   *   *

Crime-suspense and science fiction are deftly and delightfully fused in William F. Nolan's wacky extravaganza, *Space for Hire* which begins when hard-boiled private eye "Sam Space," from Mars, is hired by a beautiful three-headed female from Venus. Robotics, time-travel, multiple universes and all nine planets in our solar system figure into the frantic action of this unique, award-winning mystery/SF novel.
More conventionally, Nolan is also the creator of the Los Angeles detective Bart Challis. *Death Is for Losers* and *The White Cad Cross-Up* are set against a surreal, gaudily modern Southern California background, abrim with bullets and blondes. The Nolan style is bright, fast, compulsively readable, often laced with sharp poetic imagery. The best of Nolan's short crime fiction surfaced in book form in his collection *Impact-20*. Nolan has also written for films and television, often within the crime genre, as in *Melvin Purvis, G-Man* and *Sky Heist*.
William F. Nolan is a popular writer in the best sense of the term, a precise craftsman who always manages to reveal depth beneath the smooth commercial surface of his work. He is a potent entertainer.

—Ray Russell

NOONE, Edwina. See **AVALLONE, Michael.**

NORMAN, James (James Norman Schmidt). American. Born in Chicago, Illinois, 10 January 1912. Educated at Loyola University, Chicago; Ecole des Beaux Arts, Paris, Certificat; University of the Americas, Mexico, A.B. 1953; Universidad de Guanajuato, Instituto de Allende, M.A. 1967. Served in the United States Army, 8th Information and Historical Service during World War II. Married Margaret Fox in 1962; one daughter and one son. Journalist, Chicago *Tribune*, Paris, 1932–33, and United Press, Chicago, 1935–36; Newscaster, Station EAQ, Madrid, 1938–39; Sports Editor, Chicago *Record*, 1939–40; Editor, *Compton's Encyclopedia*, Chicago, 1941–42; Free-Lance writer, 1946–65; Lecturer, Academia Hispanoamericana, Mexico, 1957–65. Lecturer, 1965–68, and since 1968, Professor, Ohio University, Athens. Recipient: La Pluma de Plata from Mexican government, 1977, 1978. Honorary Member, Phi Beta Kappa. Agent: Paul R. Reynolds Inc., 12 East 41st Street, New York, New York, 10017 Address: 18 Second Street, Athens, Ohio 45701, U.S.A.

CRIME PUBLICATIONS

Novels (series character: Gimiendo Hernandez Quinto)

Murder, Chop Chop (Quinto). New York, Morrow, 1942; London, Joseph, 1943.
An Inch of Time (Quinto). New York, Morrow, 1944; London, Joseph, 1945.
The Nightwalkers (Quinto). Chicago, Ziff Davis, 1947; London, Joseph, 1948.
Valley of Lotus House. London, Davies, 1956.

OTHER PUBLICATIONS

Novels

A Little North of Everywhere. New York, Pellegrini and Cudahy, 1951.
Cimmaron Trace. New York, Dell, and London, Collins, 1956.
Juniper and the General. New York, Morrow, and London, Joseph, 1957.
The Fell of Dark. Philadelphia, Lippincott, and London, Joseph, 1960.
The Obsidian Mirror. Pomeroy, Ohio, Carpenter, 1977.

Plays

Juniper and the Pagans, with John Patrick (produced Boston, 1959).

Radio Plays: *Studio One* series.

Television Plays: *Herald Theatre* and *Loretta Young Show* series.

Other

Handbook to the Christian Liturgy. London, SPCK, and New York, Macmillan, 1944.
In Mexico: Where to Look, How to Buy Mexican Popular Arts and Crafts. New York, Morrow, 1959; revised edition, as *A Shopper's Guide to Mexico*, New York, Doubleday, 1966.

Terry's Guide to Mexico, revised edition. New York, Doubleday, 1962; revised edition, 1972.

Mexican Hill Town, photographs by Allan W. Kahn. Santa Monica, California, Fisher Edwards, 1963.

The Navy That Crossed Mountains (juvenile). New York, Putnam, 1964.

The Forgotten Empire (juvenile). New York, Putnam, 1965.

The Strange World of Reptiles (juvenile). New York, Putnam, 1966.

The Riddle of the Incas: The Story of Hiram Bingham and Machu Picchu (juvenile). New York, Hawthorn, 1968.

The Young Generals (juvenile). New York, Putnam, 1968.

Charro: Mexican Horseman (juvenile). New York, Putnam, 1970.

Kearny Rode West (juvenile). New York, Putnam, 1971.

Ancestral Voices. New York, Four Winds, 1977.

*   *   *

James Norman's three "true" mysteries – *Murder, Chop Chop*, *The Nightwalkers*, and *An Inch of Time* – are set in China during the Japanese invasion and World War II. As mystery-adventure stories, Norman's works bow to established formulas: there are the obligatory confused love interests, the murders complete with eccentric sleuth and predictable solution, the webs of treasonous and murderous dealings in drugs and money, and an emphasis more on venturesome discovery than ratiocination (though *Murder, Chop Chop*, the best of the three, has its twists). Still these novels have an appeal absent from the British puzzle mysteries as well as from the American rough-and-tumble assortment, the appeal arising from the novels' unlikely Sherlock, Gimiendo Hernandez Quinto, and from an exotic awareness of civilizations older than mere Western reason.

Quinto is a gigantic Mexican whose fame stems from his being both a cousin of Pancho Villa and a leader of Chinese republican guerilla forces. An intriguing blend of barbarism and super-subtlety, Quinto discounts the value of human life in war but refuses to let unauthorized murder stalk his camp. Cumbersome and uncouth, Quinto is yet sensitive enough to be assimilated into the highly formal Chinese culture and to insinuate himself into the psyches of his colleagues and suspects. Quinto's Watson is a lovely Eurasian named "Mountain of Virtue" whose virtues range from intuitive deduction to seductive persuasion. For all her delicate air of innocence, Virtue is a ruthless operator and a puzzle even to Quinto. Virtue's enigmatic air is also the atmosphere of Norman's China in small. Norman is fond of noting Chinese inscrutability and the Chinese method of suggestion rather than statement. The uncertainty that permeates the process of investigation and lingers after the problem is "solved" suggests that the real mystery is partly China and partly the inevitable elusiveness of human truth.

This genius for unfocussed reality appears also in a later novel, *The Obsidian Mirror*. Set in Mexico, and only superficially a murder mystery, *The Obsidian Mirror* reiterates more strongly what the earlier books suggest – that the ultimate, ongoing, and only worthy mystery is the beauty and terror of the race's past.

—Joan Y. Worley

NORTH, Gil. Pseudonym for Geoffrey Horne. British. Born in Skipton, Yorkshire, 12 July 1916. Educated at Ermysted's Grammar School, Skipton, 1925–35; Christ's College, Cambridge (exhibitioner; scholar), 1935–38, 1951–52, B.A. (honours) 1938, M.A. 1942, diploma in social anthropology 1952. Married Betty Duthie in 1949; one son and one daughter. Administrative Officer, Colonial Service, South-East Nigeria and Cameroons, 1938–55. Address: North Bank, 1 Raikes Avenue, Skipton, North Yorkshire BD23 1LP, England.

CRIME PUBLICATIONS

Novels (series character: Sergeant Caleb Cluff)

> *Sergeant Cluff Stands Firm.* London, Chapman and Hall, 1960.
> *The Methods of Sergeant Cluff.* London, Chapman and Hall, 1961.
> *Sergeant Cluff Goes Fishing.* London, Chapman and Hall, 1962.
> *More Deaths for Sergeant Cluff.* London, Chapman and Hall, 1963.
> *Sergeant Cluff and the Madmen* (includes *The Blindness of Sergeant Cluff* and *Sergeant Cluff Laughs Last*). London, Chapman and Hall, 1964.
> *Sergeant Cluff and the Price of Pity.* London, Chapman and Hall, 1965.
> *The Confounding of Sergeant Cluff.* London, Chapman and Hall, 1966.
> *Sergeant Cluff and the Day of Reckoning.* London, Chapman and Hall, 1967.
> *The Procrastination of Sergeant Cluff.* London, Eyre and Spottiswoode, 1969.
> *No Choice for Sergeant Cluff.* London, Eyre and Spottiswoode, 1971.
> *Sergeant Cluff Rings True.* London, Eyre Methuen, 1972.
> *A Corpse for Kofi Katt.* London, Hale, 1978.

OTHER PUBLICATIONS

Novels as Geoffrey Horne

> *Winter.* London, Hutchinson, 1957.
> *Land of No Escape.* London, Hutchinson, 1958.
> *Quest for Gold* (juvenile). London, Hutchinson, 1959.
> *The Man Who Was Chief.* London, Chapman and Hall, 1960.
> *The Portuguese Diamonds.* London, Chapman and Hall, 1961.

Plays

> Television Plays: *Cluff* series (20 episodes), 1964.

*   *   *

Gil North's books are of no outstanding merit in terms of plot or literary quality, and not complex as detective stories, but similar remarks could be levelled at the Maigret novels of Simenon, who is widely regarded as the world's foremost crime novelist. Intentionally or otherwise, North has succeeded in presenting Sergeant Caleb Cluff as a sort of Yorkshire version of Maigret. Throughout the small town of Gunnarshaw and the surrounding area this obstinate but likeable countryman is known and respected by young and old, including the tearaways and those with something to hide. His love of the fells is matched by love of his fellow men, and Cluff exudes compassion rather than sentimentality. There is no clear dividing line between his private and official life, and in the latter capacity Cluff is motivated to right wrongs rather than to seek retribution.

One recalls Cluff's love/hate relationship with his housekeeper, Annie Croft, the constant companionship of dog Clive, the gruff Yorkshire dialect which has proved almost incomprehensible to American critics, and the author's profound approach to such themes as the clash between parents and children (*No Choice for Sergeant Cluff*) or the mental state of men long past their prime (*Sergeant Cluff and the Madmen*). Cluff's methods are unorthodox and even lethargic at times. Often it is a case of waiting and watching the world go by, with the occasional noncommittal nod in the suspect's direction, and there is an over-riding assumption that the murderer (particularly in a domestic situation) will eventually bare his soul.

—Melvyn Barnes

O'CONNOR, Richard.   See **WAYLAND, Patrick**.

O'DONNELL, Lillian.   American. Born in Trieste, Italy, in 1926. Educated at the American Academy of Dramatic Arts, New York. Married J. Leonard O'Donnell in 1954. Actress in Broadway and television productions, and Stage Manager and Director, Schubert Organization, New York, 1944–54. Agent: Roberta Vient, Kohler-Levy Agency, Sunset Boulevard, Hollywood, California. Address: 22 East 65th Street, New York, New York 10021, U.S.A.

CRIME PUBLICATIONS

Novels (series characters: Mici Anhalt; Norah Mulcahaney)

> *Death on the Grass.*   New York, Arcadia House, 1960.
> *Death Blanks the Screen.*   New York, Arcadia House, 1961.
> *Death Schuss.*   New York and London, Abelard Schuman, 1963.
> *Murder under the Sun.*   New York and London, Abelard Schuman, 1964.
> *Death of a Player.*   New York and London, Abelard Schuman, 1964.
> *Babes in the Woods.*   New York and London, Abelard Schuman, 1965.
> *The Sleeping Beauty Murders.*   New York and London, Abelard Schuman, 1967.
> *The Face of the Crime.*   New York and London, Abelard Schuman, 1968.
> *The Phone Calls* (Mulcahaney).   New York, Putnam, and London, Hodder and Stoughton, 1972.
> *Don't Wear Your Wedding Ring* (Mulcahaney).   New York, Putnam, 1973; London, Barker, 1974.
> *Dial 577 R-A-P-E* (Mulcahaney).   New York, Putnam, and London, Barker, 1974.
> *The Baby Merchants* (Mulcahaney).   New York, Putnam, 1975; London, Bantam, 1976.
> *Leisure Dying* (Mulcahaney).   New York, Putnam, 1976.
> *Aftershock* (Anhalt).   New York, Putnam, 1977; London, Hale, 1979.
> *No Business Being a Cop* (Mulcahaney).   New York, Putnam, 1979.
> *Falling Star* (Anhalt).   New York, Putnam, 1979.

OTHER PUBLICATIONS

Novels

The Tachi Tree. New York and London, Abelard Schuman, 1968.
Dive into Darkness. New York, Abelard Schuman, 1971; London, Abelard Schuman, 1972.

Other

"Rules and Routines of the Police Procedural," in *The Writer* (Boston), February 1978.
"Fact or Fiction," in *Murderess Ink*, edited by Dilys Winn. New York, Workman, 1979.

Manuscript Collection: Mugar Memorial Library, Boston University.

*   *   *

The mystery suspense novels of Lillian O'Donnell can be divided into two distinct categories; the second, her more recent work, is unquestionably the more interesting. O'Donnell's first mystery novels primarily featured suspense; the amateur detecting is subordinated to considerable anxiety by the characters about their safety, the unlikely death of one of their number, and the lack of motive or serious clue to solve the mystery. The confusion which surrounds the cases is never really penetrated by the detectives, and police seldom appear with recognizable success. Generally the detective turns up a great deal of indiscriminate evidence which is not put in place during the denouement or, frequently, withholds important clues from the reader. In either case, simultaneous detection by the reader is forestalled.

The half-dozen police procedural novels featuring Norah Mulcahaney involve insights into not only professional and technical aspects of detection but also the private lives of Mulcahaney and her family. The novels do not resemble the best-known police procedural novels. Unlike the Gideon series of J. J. Marric, the novels' investigations center around a single case, with other apparently unrelated crimes eventually discovered to be sub-plots of the major investigation; unlike the procedural novels of Ed McBain's 87th precinct, O'Donnell's New York-based detective novels focus on the relationship between Norah's professional and private lives. They are a combination of the efficient and team-oriented police novel and the traditional domestic mystery with its emphasis on personal relationships.

In the course of the novels, which begin the year after her graduation from the police academy, Norah Mulcahaney is promoted, marries, and adopts a child; her extended family of Irish politico father and domineering Italian mother-in-law becomes involved in the solution of crimes. The novels have a predictable tendency to over-do the blending of stories: several of the investigations are necessary because Pat Mulcahaney, interfering in his daughter's private life, involves her. In other cases, her assumptions about professional rivalry that her husband, Lieutenant (formerly Detective) Joe Capretto, might feel lead to her unwise and dangerous independent investigation. Even her unsuccessful attempts to become pregnant involve the entire family in a bizarre series of Mafia vendettas, some 15 years old. However, the independent spirit and personal appeal of Norah Mulcahaney Capretto are evident throughout the novels. Her tendency to conceal her concerns gives the reader a unique insight into a believable professional's concern for the successful integration of all the aspects of her personality. The supporting cast of family, though the Italian mother-in-law and Irish father are not deeply characterized, provides a good foil for her introspection.

Compared with other novels about policewomen (the newest trend of the 1970's) these novels are clearly the most competently plotted and written, the most interestingly executed. The technical demands of police work are neither over emphasized nor overlooked; the development of series characters is consistent and progressive; the interplay between a demanding professional life and a desired private one is realistically presented. It is certainly here that Lillian O'Donnell has made a unique contribution to the genre.

—Kathleen G. Klein

O'DONNELL, Peter. British. Born in London, 11 April 1920. Educated at Catford Central School, London. Served in the Royal Corps Signals, 1938–46. Married Constance Doris Green in 1940; two daughters. Author of strip cartoons: *Garth*, 1953–66, *Tug Transom*, 1954–66, *Romeo Brown*, 1956–62, and since 1963, *Modesty Blaise*. Lives in Kent. Address: 47 Fleet Street, London EC4Y 1BJ, England.

CRIME PUBLICATIONS

Novels (series character: Modesty Blaise in all books)

Modesty Blaise. London, Souvenir Press, and New York, Doubleday, 1965.
Sabre-Tooth. London, Souvenir Press, and New York, Doubleday, 1966.
I, Lucifer. London, Souvenir Press, and New York, Doubleday, 1967.
A Taste for Death. London, Souvenir Press, and New York, Doubleday, 1969.
The Impossible Virgin. London, Souvenir Press, and New York, Doubleday, 1971.
The Silver Mistress. London, Souvenir Press, 1973.
Last Day in Limbo. London, Souvenir Press, 1976.
Dragon's Claw. London, Souvenir Press, 1978.

Short Stories

Pieces of Modesty. London, Pan, 1972.

OTHER PUBLICATIONS

Plays

Murder Most Logical (produced Windsor, 1974).

Screenplays: *Modesty Blaise*, with Stanley Dubens and Evan Jones, 1966; *The Vengeance of She*, 1968.

Television Play: *Take a Pair of Private Eyes* serial, 1966.

Other

"Becoming Modesty," in *Murder Ink: The Mystery Reader's Companion*, edited by Dilys Winn. New York, Workman, 1977.

*   *   *

Few writers can claim creation of a mythic character that seems to have a life of its own. In the gigantic mystery-suspense field, perhaps a dozen have achieved it. Peter O'Donnell, a very prolific writer, did it with hardly more than a half-dozen books in the Modesty Blaise series.

That Modesty began as a comic strip heroine should neither be overlooked nor frowned upon. After all, Dick Tracy is even more successful. But it is the books by which she is best, if not most widely, known. These began as fictionalizations of scripts from the comic strip; it is possible that all of them are such fictionalizations, but they serve more than satisfactorily as novels and short stories in their own right.

Modesty may have been conceived as a "female James Bond" (another of the mythic dozen), but she is 007's superior in many ways. For breakneck action and economy of wording, though the novels are quite long, O'Donnell has no peer. This is largely ascribable to his comic scripting, a field in which both characteristics are essential. Yet, it would be grossest error to dismiss the series as being *merely* plot. Modesty and other continuing characters have become as much old and dear friends to O'Donnell's avid readers as Holmes and Watson are to Doyle's.

Modesty stands lovely head and shoulders above other sexy heroines. The greatest difficulty to becoming one of her fans is that old devil "suspension of disbelief," for reducing either her frankly outlandish background or the details of any single adventure to even a very detailed summary results in the incredible. Such a character could no more exist in the real world, or do the things described, than could a Holmes, a Bond, or a Tarzan.

—Jeff Banks

OFFORD, Lenore Glen. American. Born in Spokane, Washington, 24 October 1905. Educated at Mills College, Oakland, California, B.A. 1925. Married Harold R. Offord in 1929; one daughter. Since 1950, Mystery Book Critic, San Francisco *Chronicle*. Address: 641 Euclid Avenue, Berkeley, California 94708, U.S.A.

CRIME PUBLICATIONS

Novels (series characters: Bill and Coco Hastings; Todd McKinnon)

> *Murder on Russian Hill* (Hastings). Philadelphia, Macrae Smith, 1938; as *Murder Before Breakfast*, London, Jarrolds, 1938.
> *The 9 Dark Hours.* New York, Duell, and London, Eldon Press, 1941.
> *Clues to Burn* (Hastings). New York, Duell, 1942; London, Grayson, 1943.
> *Skeleton Key* (McKinnon). New York, Duell, 1943; London, Eldon Press, 1944.
> *The Glass Mask* (McKinnon). New York, Duell, 1944; London, Jarrolds, 1946.
> *... My True Love Lies.* New York, Duell, 1947; as *And Turned to Clay*, London, Jarrolds, 1950.
> *The Smiling Tiger* (McKinnon). New York, Duell, 1949; London, Jarrolds, 1951.
> *The Marble Forest* (as Theo Durrant, with others). New York, Knopf, 1951; as *The Big Fear*, New York, Popular Library, 1953.
> *Walking Shadow* (McKinnon). New York, Simon and Schuster, 1959; London, Ward Lock, 1961.

OTHER PUBLICATIONS

Novels

Cloth of Silver.   Philadelphia, Macrae Smith, 1939.
Angels Unaware.   Philadelphia, Macrae Smith, 1940.
Distinguished Visitors.   London, Eldon Press, 1942.
The Girl in the Belfry, with Joseph Henry Jackson.   New York, Fawcett, 1957.

Other

Enchanted August (juvenile).   Indianapolis, Bobbs Merrill, 1956.

Manuscript Collections: Bancroft Library, University of California, Berkeley; University of Oregon Library, Eugene.

*   *   *

Appearing late in the classical age of detection, Lenore Glen Offord's handful of mysteries concentrated on romantic entanglements of the heroines and the unpleasant realities of a murder investigation. Suspicion among friends is frequently referred to in *Clues to Burn* and *... My True Love Lies.* The fluctuations of love affairs, however, are as important to the heroines, Georgine Wyeth, Noel Bruce, and, later, Georgine's daughter Barbie, as the uncovering of the criminal.

Primarily focussing on the women, Offord blends the everyday chores of cooking, housekeeping, and worrying about raising children with the more sinister elements. The result is a burying of clues among apparently immaterial events. *Walking Shadow* particularly concentrates so much on the work of producing a Shakespeare festival that the mystery takes a secondary position. What is lost in tautness and suspense is compensated for by believability, likeable characters, and the appearance of San Francisco and the northwest coast area as an alluring locale.

Todd McKinnon's work as a detective in *Skeleton Key*, *Walking Shadow*, and *The Smiling Tiger* is representative of Offord's books. The villain has the upper hand through most of the book but is trapped in the chase or flurry of excitement at the end. Until that time, Todd has been merely an observer. Finally, a short explanation tells who did what and why, but the steps of deduction and how the detective knew the answer are missing. Although she broke no new ground, Offord produced high quality examples of the 1940's and 1950's mystery.

—Fred Dueren

O'HARA, Kevin.   See **CUMBERLAND, Marten**.

OLSEN, D. B. Pseudonym for (Julia Clara Catherine) Dolores (Birk Olsen) Hitchens; also wrote as Dolan Birkley; Noel Burke. American. Born in 1907. *Died in 1973.*

CRIME PUBLICATIONS

Novels (series characters: Lieutenant Stephen Mayhew; Rachel and Jennifer Murdock; Professor A. Pennyfeather)

The Clue in the Clay (Mayhew). New York, Phoenix Press, 1938.
The Cat Saw Murder (Murdock: Mayhew). New York, Doubleday, 1939; London, Heinemann, 1940.
Death Cuts a Silhouette. New York, Doubleday, 1939.
The Ticking Heart (Mayhew). New York, Doubleday, 1940.
The Blue Geranium (as Dolan Birkley). New York, Simon and Schuster, 1941.
The Alarm of the Black Cat (Murdock). New York, Doubleday, 1942.
The Shivering Bough (as Noel Burke). New York, Dutton, 1942.
Cat's Claw (Murdock; Mayhew). New York, Doubleday, 1943.
Catspaw for Murder (Murdock; Mayhew). New York, Doubleday, 1943.
The Cat Wears a Noose (Murdock; Mayhew). New York, Doubleday, 1944.
Bring the Bride a Shroud (Pennyfeather). New York, Doubleday, and London, Aldor, 1945.
Cats Don't Smile (Murdock). New York, Doubleday, 1945; London, Aldor, 1948.
Cats Don't Need Coffins (Murdock; Mayhew). New York, Doubleday, and London, Aldor, 1946.
Gallows for the Groom (Pennyfeather). New York, Doubleday, 1947.
Widows Ought to Weep. New York, Ziff Davis, 1947.
Cats Have Tall Shadows (Murdock). New York, Ziff Davis, 1948.
Devious Design (Pennyfeather). New York, Doubleday, 1948.
The Cat Wears a Mask (Murdock). New York, Doubleday, 1949.
Death Wears Cat's Eyes (Murdock). New York, Doubleday, 1950.
Something about Midnight (Pennyfeather). New York, Doubleday, 1950.
The Cat and Capricorn (Murdock). New York, Doubleday, 1951.
Love Me in Death (Pennyfeather). New York, Doubleday, 1951.
Enrollment Cancelled (Pennyfeather). New York, Doubleday, 1952; as *Dead Babes in the Wood*, New York, Dell, 1954.
The Cat Walk (Murdock). New York, Doubleday, 1953.
Death Walks on Cat Feet (Murdock). New York, Doubleday, 1956.
Night of the Bowstring. London, Hale, 1963.
The Unloved (as Dolan Birkley). New York, Doubleday, 1965; London, Hale, 1967.

Novels as Dolores Hitchens (series character: Jim Sader)

Stairway to an Empty Room. New York, Doubleday, 1951.
Nets to Catch the Wind. New York, Doubleday, 1952; as *Widows Won't Wait*, New York, Dell, 1954.
Terror Lurks in Darkness. New York, Doubleday, 1953.
Beat Back the Tide. New York, Doubleday, 1954; London, Macdonald, 1955; as *The Fatal Flirt*, New York, Spivak, 1956.
Sleep with Strangers (Sader). New York, Doubleday, 1955; London, Macdonald, 1956.
Fools' Gold. New York, Doubleday, and London, Boardman, 1958.
The Watcher. New York, Doubleday, and London, Boardman, 1959.
Sleep with Slander (Sader). New York, Doubleday, 1960; London, Boardman, 1961.
Footsteps in the Night. New York, Doubleday, and London, Boardman, 1961.

The Abductor.   New York, Simon and Schuster, and London, Boardman, 1962.
The Bank with the Bamboo Door.   New York, Simon and Schuster, and London, Boardman, 1965.
The Man Who Cried All the Way Home.   New York, Simon and Schuster, 1966; London, Hale, 1967.
Postscript to Nightmare.   New York, Putnam, 1967; as *Cabin of Fear*, London, Joseph, 1968.
A Collection of Strangers.   New York, Putnam, 1969; London, Macdonald, 1971.
The Baxter Letters.   New York, Putnam, 1971; London, Hale, 1973.
In a House Unknown.   New York, Doubleday, 1973; London, Hale, 1974.

Novels by Bert Hitchens and Dolores Hitchens (series characters: Collins and McKechnie; John Farrel)

F.O.B. Murder (Collins and McKechnie).   New York, Doubleday, 1955; London, Boardman, 1957.
One-Way Ticket.   New York, Doubleday, 1956; London, Boardman, 1958.
End of the Line (Farrel).   New York, Doubleday, and London, Boardman, 1957.
The Man Who Followed Women (Collins and McKechnie).   New York, Doubleday, 1959; London, Boardman, 1960.
The Grudge (Farrel).   New York, Doubleday, 1963; London, Boardman, 1964.

Uncollected Short Stories

"The Fuzzy Things," in *Four and Twenty Bloodhounds*, edited by Anthony Boucher.   New York, Simon and Schuster, 1950; London, Hammond, 1951.
"The Absent Hat Pin," in *20 Great Tales of Murder*, edited by Helen McCloy and Brett Halliday.   New York, Random House, 1951; London, Hammond, 1952.

OTHER PUBLICATIONS as Dolores Hitchens

Plays

A Cookie for Henry.   New York, French, 1941.
To Tommy with Love.   New York, French, 1941.

Manuscript Collection: Mugar Memorial Library, Boston University.

*   *   *

D. B. Olsen wrote a standardized formula novel that followed the rules of mystery fiction for the 1940's, usually light and breezy, lots of characters to spread suspicion among, and a touch of humor to keep out the brutality of murder. Toward the end of her career in the mid-1950's she used more serious themes and allowed reality to creep in, but enjoyment and diversion remained the prime objective. Most of the allure of her highly popular books lies in the characters of her two series detectives, Rachel Murdock and Professor A. Pennyfeather.

Elderly spinsters, Rachel and Jennifer Murdock achieve their interest and humor through contrast. Jennifer, two years older, is the thin, rigid, conventional epitome of an old lady: a battleax incarnate. Rachel (always accompanied by Samantha, her coal-black cat), conscientiously refusing to conform to expectations, belies her slim, tiny figure, snow white hair, and cheery blue eyes, and is determined to experience any excitement she can: whether it is a surreptitious drink, an afternoon at the movies, or meddling in a murder. Jennifer vociferously objects to Rachel's antics but is always there, once even witnessing a murder in *The Cat Wears a Noose*, and then admitting she found a night in jail interesting. Jennifer adds humor and a few diversions, but Rachel is the detective. An inquisitive nature and a tendency to stir things up account for much of her investigation. She watches for the nuances of character or emotion (things that friendly rival Lieutenant Stephen Mayhew would never catch) in order to arrive at her intuitive solution. Clues or oddities that she had noted along the way are used to support her conclusions, but the killer often gives himself away at some trap she had either set up or been caught in herself.

Professor Pennyfeather is similar in his methods but uses the logic and methods derived from a classical education to impart respectability to his detection. While Rachel gets involved in a case through chance or nosiness, Pennyfeather is asked by a friend or relative to help them out of trouble. His first cases, *Bring the Bride a Shroud*, *Gallows for the Groom*, and *Devious Design*, occur away from the college environment, often in the southwest desert that Olsen also used for *The Cat Wears a Mask* and *The Cat and Capricorn*. Later books, *Love Me in Death* and *Enrollment Cancelled*, are set on the Clarendon campus and involve more than vague hints at the passions behind murder. Both use sex as underlying problems of the characters. *Enrollment Cancelled* includes a suspect who is almost banished from the college because he has a shoe fetish. Although the handling of these elements is bland by today's standards, it was rather surprising in the 1950's.

The Clue in the Clay and *The Ticking Heart* are first efforts involving Mayhew only. With *The Cat Saw Murder* Olsen developed Rachel and Jennifer to establish the pattern for almost all the rest of her work. One exception was *Widows Ought to Weep*, featuring Mr. Puckett as the detective. This book relies on mood and atmosphere more than most of Olsen's work and builds suspense by involving characters in dangerous situations, then shifting the scene. Both *Widows Ought to Weep* and *The Cat Wears a Noose* use monsters or werewolves to induce an artificial chill, but human monsters are the only real danger in all Olsen's enjoyable output.

—Fred Dueren

OPPENHEIM, E(dward) Phillips. Also wrote as Anthony Partridge. British. Born in London, 22 October 1866. Educated at Wyggeston Grammar School, Leicester. Served in the Ministry of Information during World War I. Married Elsie Clara Hopkins in 1892; one daughter. Worked in his father's leather business in Leicester to age 40; lived in Norfolk until 1922, then in France and Guernsey. *Died 3 February 1946.*

CRIME PUBLICATIONS

Novels

The Peer and the Woman. New York, Taylor, 1892; London, Ward Lock, 1895.
A Monk of Cruta. London, Ward Lock, and New York, Neely, 1894.
A Daughter of the Marionis. London, Ward and Downey, 1895; as *To Win the Love He Sought*, New York, Collier, 1915.
False Evidence. London, Ward Lock, 1896; New York, Ward Lock 1897.
The Postmaster of Market Deignton. London, Routledge, 1896(?).
A Modern Prometheus. London, Unwin, 1896; New York, Neely, 1897.
The Mystery of Mr. Bernard Brown. London, Bentley, 1896; Boston, Little Brown, 1910; as *The New Tenant*, New York, Collier, 1912; as *His Father's Crime*, New York, Street and Smith, 1929.
The Wooing of Fortune. London, Ward and Downey, 1896.

The World's Great Snare.   London, Ward and Downey, and Philadelphia, Lippincott, 1896.

The Amazing Judgment.   London, Downey, 1897.

As a Man Lives.   London, Ward Lock 1898; Boston, Little Brown, 1908; as *The Yellow House*, New York, Doscher, 1908.

A Daughter of Astrea.   Bristol, Arrowsmith, 1898; New York, Doscher, 1909.

Mysterious Mr. Sabin.   London, Ward Lock, 1898; Boston, Little Brown, 1905.

The Man and His Kingdom.   London, Ward Lock, and Philadelphia, Lippincott, 1899.

Mr. Marx's Secret.   London, Simpkin Marshall, 1899; New York, Street and Smith, 1899(?).

A Millionaire of Yesterday.   London, Ward Lock, and Philadelphia, Lippincott, 1900.

Master of Men.   London, Methuen, 1901; as *Enoch Strone*, New York, Dillingham, 1902.

The Survivor.   London, Ward Lock, and New York, Brentano's, 1901.

The Traitors.   London, Ward Lock, 1902; New York, Dodd Mead, 1903.

The Great Awakening.   London, Ward Lock, 1902; as *A Sleeping Memory*, New York, Dillingham, 1902.

A Prince of Sinners.   London, Ward Lock, and Boston, Little Brown, 1903.

The Yellow Crayon.   London, Ward Lock, and New York, Dodd Mead, 1903.

The Master Mummer.   Boston, Little Brown, 1904; London, Ward Lock, 1905.

The Betrayal.   London, Ward Lock, and New York, Dodd Mead, 1904.

Anna the Adventuress.   London, Ward Lock, and Boston, Little Brown, 1904.

A Maker of History.   London, Ward Lock, and Boston, Little Brown, 1905.

Mr. Wingrave, Millionaire.   London, Ward Lock, 1906; as *The Malefactor*, Boston, Little Brown, 1906.

A Lost Leader.   London, Ward Lock, and Boston, Little Brown, 1906.

The Vindicator.   Boston, Little Brown, 1907.

The Missioner.   Boston, Little Brown, 1907; London, Ward Lock, 1908.

The Secret.   London, Ward Lock, 1907; as *The Great Secret*, Boston, Little Brown, 1907.

Conspirators.   London, Ward Lock, 1907; as *The Avenger*, Boston, Little Brown, 1908.

Berenice.   Boston, Little Brown, 1907; London, Ward Lock, 1910.

Jeanne of the Marshes.   Boston, Little Brown, 1908; London, Ward Lock, 1909.

The Governors.   London, Ward Lock, 1908; Boston, Little Brown, 1909.

The Moving Finger.   Boston, Little Brown, 1910; as *The Falling Star*, London, Hodder and Stoughton, 1911.

The Illustrious Prince.   London, Hodder and Stoughton, and Boston, Little Brown, 1910.

The Missing Delora.   London, Methuen, 1910; as *The Lost Ambassador*, Boston, Little Brown, 1910.

Havoc.   Boston, Little Brown, 1911; London, Hodder and Stoughton, 1912.

The Tempting of Tavernake.   Boston, Little Brown, 1911; as *The Temptation of Tavernake*, London, Hodder and Stoughton, 1913.

The Lighted Way.   London, Hodder and Stoughton, and Boston, Little Brown, 1912.

The Mischief-Maker.   Boston, Little Brown, 1912; London, Hodder and Stoughton, 1913.

The Double Life of Mr. Alfred Burton.   Boston, Little Brown, 1913; London, Methuen, 1914.

The Way of These Women.   Boston, Little Brown, 1913; London, Methuen, 1914.

A People's Man.   Boston, Little Brown, 1914; London, Methuen, 1915.

The Vanished Messenger.   Boston, Little Brown, 1914; London, Methuen, 1916.

The Black Box (novelization of screenplay).   New York, Grosset and Dunlap, 1915; London, Hodder and Stoughton, 1917.

The Double Traitor.   Boston, Little Brown, 1915; London, Hodder and Stoughton, 1918.

Mr. Grex of Monte Carlo. London, Methuen, and Boston, Little Brown, 1915.

The Kingdom of the Blind. Boston, Little Brown, 1916; London, Hodder and Stoughton, 1917.

The Hillman. London, Methuen, and Boston, Little Brown, 1917.

The Cinema Murder. Boston, Little Brown, 1917; as *The Other Romilly*, London, Hodder and Stoughton, 1918.

The Zeppelin's Passenger. Boston, Little Brown, 1918; as *Mr. Lessingham Goes Home*, London, Hodder and Stoughton, 1919.

The Pawns Count. London, Hodder and Stoughton, and Boston, Little Brown, 1918.

The Curious Quest. Boston, Little Brown, 1919; as *The Amazing Quest of Mr. Ernest Bliss*, London, Hodder and Stoughton, 1922.

The Strange Case of Mr. Jocelyn Thew. London, Hodder and Stoughton, 1919; as *The Box with Broken Seals*, Boston, Little Brown, 1919.

The Wicked Marquis. London, Hodder and Stoughton, and Boston, Little Brown, 1919.

The Devil's Paw. Boston, Little Brown, 1920; London, Hodder and Stoughton, 1921.

The Great Impersonation. London, Hodder and Stoughton, and Boston, Little Brown, 1920.

Jacob's Ladder. London, Hodder and Stoughton, and Boston, Little Brown, 1921.

Nobody's Man. Boston, Little Brown, 1921; London, Hodder and Stoughton, 1922.

The Profiteers. London, Hodder and Stoughton, and Boston, Little Brown, 1921.

The Evil Shepherd. Boston, Little Brown, 1922; London, Hodder and Stoughton, 1923.

The Great Prince Shan. London, Hodder and Stoughton, and Boston, Little Brown, 1922.

The Mystery Road. Boston, Little Brown, 1923; London, Hodder and Stoughton, 1924.

The Inevitable Millionaires. London, Hodder and Stoughton, 1923; Boston, Little Brown, 1925.

The Passionate Quest. London, Hodder and Stoughton, and Boston, Little Brown, 1924.

The Wrath to Come. Boston, Little Brown, 1924; London, Hodder and Stoughton, 1925.

Gabriel Samara. London, Hodder and Stoughton 1925; as *Gabriel Samara, Peacemaker*, Boston, Little Brown, 1925.

Stolen Idols. London, Hodder and Stoughton, and Boston, Little Brown, 1925.

The Interloper. Boston, Little Brown, 1926; as *The Ex-Duke*, London, Hodder and Stoughton, 1927.

The Golden Beast. London, Hodder and Stoughton, and Boston, Little Brown, 1926.

Harvey Garrard's Crime. Boston, Little Brown, 1926; London, Hodder and Stoughton, 1927.

Prodigals of Monte Carlo. London, Hodder and Stoughton, and Boston, Little Brown, 1926.

Miss Brown of X.Y.O. London, Hodder and Stoughton, and Boston, Little Brown, 1927.

The Fortunate Wayfarer. London, Hodder and Stoughton, and Boston, Little Brown, 1928.

Matorni's Vineyard. Boston, Little Brown, 1928; London, Hodder and Stoughton, 1929.

The Light Beyond. London, Hodder and Stoughton, and Boston, Little Brown, 1928.

Blackman's Wood. London, Readers Library, 1929.

The Glenlitten Murder. London, Hodder and Stoughton, and Boston, Little Brown, 1929.

The Treasure House of Martin Hews. London, Hodder and Stoughton, and Boston, Little Brown, 1929.

The Lion and the Lamb. London, Hodder and Stoughton, and Boston, Little Brown, 1930.

The Million Pound Deposit. London, Hodder and Stoughton, and Boston, Little Brown, 1930.

Up the Ladder of Gold. London, Hodder and Stoughton, and Boston, Little Brown, 1931.

Simple Peter Cradd. London, Hodder and Stoughton, and Boston, Little Brown, 1931.

Moran Chambers Smiled. London, Hodder and Stoughton, 1932; as *The Man from Sing Sing*, Boston, Little Brown, 1932.

The Ostrekoff Jewels. London, Hodder and Stoughton, and Boston, Little Brown, 1932.

Jeremiah and the Princess. London, Hodder and Stoughton, and Boston, Little Brown, 1933.

Murder at Monte Carlo. London, Hodder and Stoughton, and Boston, Little Brown, 1933.

The Strange Boarders of Palace Crescent. Boston, Little Brown, 1934; London, Hodder and Stoughton, 1935.

The Bank Manager. London, Hodder and Stoughton, 1934; as *The Man Without Nerves*, Boston, Little Brown, 1934.

The Gallows of Chance. London, Hodder and Stoughton, and Boston, Little Brown, 1934.

The Battle of Basinghall Street. London, Hodder and Stoughton, and Boston, Little Brown, 1935.

The Spy Paramount. London, Hodder and Stoughton, and Boston, Little Brown, 1935.

The Bird of Paradise. London, Hodder and Stoughton, 1936; as *Floating Peril*, Boston, Little Brown, 1936.

Judy of Bunter's Buildings. London, Hodder and Stoughton, 1936; as *The Magnificent Hoax*, Boston, Little Brown, 1936.

The Dumb Gods Speak. London, Hodder and Stoughton, and Boston, Little Brown, 1937.

Envoy Extraordinary. London, Hodder and Stoughton, and Boston, Little Brown, 1937.

The Mayor on Horseback. Boston, Little Brown, 1937.

The Colossus of Arcadia. London, Hodder and Stoughton, and Boston, Little Brown, 1938.

The Spymaster. London, Hodder and Stoughton, and Boston, Little Brown, 1938.

Exit a Dictator. London, Hodder and Stoughton, and Boston, Little Brown, 1939.

Sir Adam Disappeared. London, Hodder and Stoughton, and Boston, Little Brown, 1939.

The Strangers' Gate. Boston, Little Brown, 1939; London, Hodder and Stoughton, 1940.

The Grassleyes Mystery. London, Hodder and Stoughton, and Boston, Little Brown, 1940.

Last Train Out. Boston, Little Brown, 1940; London, Hodder and Stoughton, 1941.

The Shy Plutocrat. London, Hodder and Stoughton, and Boston, Little Brown, 1941.

The Man Who Changed His Plea. London, Hodder and Stoughton, and Boston, Little Brown, 1942.

Mr. Mirakel. London, Hodder and Stoughton, and Boston, Little Brown, 1943.

Novels as Anthony Partridge

The Ghosts of Society. London, Hodder and Stoughton, 1908; as *The Distributors*, New York, McClure, 1908.

The Kingdom of Earth. London, Mills and Boon, and Boston, Little Brown, 1909; as *The Black Watcher*, as E. Phillips Oppenheim, London, Hodder and Stoughton, 1912.

Passers-By. Boston, Little Brown, 1910; London, Ward Lock, 1911.

The Golden Web. Boston, Little Brown, 1910; as *The Plunderers*, as E. Phillips Oppenheim, London, Hodder and Stoughton, 1916.

The Court of St. Simon. Boston, Little Brown, 1912; as *Seeing Life*, as E. Phillips Oppenheim, London, Lloyds, 1919.

Short Stories (series character: Peter Ruff)

The Long Arm of Mannister. Boston, Little Brown, 1908; as *The Long Arm*, London, Ward Lock, 1909.

The Double Four. London, Cassell, 1911; as *Peter Ruff and the Double Four*, Boston, Little Brown, 1912.

Peter Ruff. London, Hodder and Stoughton, 1912.

Those Other Days. London, Ward Lock, 1912; Boston, Little Brown, 1913.

For the Queen. London, Ward Lock, 1912; Boston, Little Brown, 1913.

Mr. Laxworthy's Adventures. London, Cassell, 1913.

The Amazing Partnership. London, Cassell, 1914; included in *Shudders and Thrills*, 1932.

The Game of Liberty. London, Cassell, 1915; as *The Amiable Charlatan*, Boston, Little Brown, 1916.

Mysteries of the Riviera. London, Cassell, 1916.

Ambrose Lavendale, Diplomat. London, Hodder and Stoughton, 1920.

Aaron Rod, Diviner. London, Hodder and Stoughton, 1920; Boston, Little Brown, 1927.

The Honorable Algernon Knox, Detective. London, Hodder and Stoughton, 1920.

Michael's Evil Deeds. Boston, Little Brown, 1923; London, Hodder and Stoughton, 1924.

The Seven Conundrums. Boston, Little Brown, 1923; London, Hodder and Stoughton, 1924.

The Terrible Hobby of Sir Joseph Londe, Bt. London, Hodder and Stoughton, 1924; Boston, Little Brown, 1927.

The Adventures of Mr. Joseph P. Cray. London, Hodder and Stoughton, 1925; Boston, Little Brown, 1927.

The Little Gentleman from Okehampstead. London, Hodder and Stoughton, 1926.

The Channay Syndicate. London, Hodder and Stoughton, and Boston, Little Brown, 1927.

Madame. London, Hodder and Stoughton, 1927; as *Madame and Her Twelve Virgins*, Boston, Little Brown, 1927.

Mr. Billingham, The Marquis and Madelon. London, Hodder and Stoughton, 1927; Boston, Little Brown, 1929.

Nicholas Goade, Detective. London, Hodder and Stoughton, 1927; Boston, Little Brown, 1929.

Chronicles of Melhampton. London, Hodder and Stoughton, 1928.

The Exploits of Pudgy Pete & Co. London, Hodder and Stoughton, 1928.

The Human Chase. London, Hodder and Stoughton, 1929; included in *Shudders and Thrills*, 1932.

Jennerton & Co. London, Hodder and Stoughton, 1929; included in *Clowns and Criminals*, 1931.

What Happened to Forester. London, Hodder and Stoughton, 1929; Boston, Little Brown, 1930.

Slane's Long Shots. London, Hodder and Stoughton, and Boston, Little Brown, 1930.

Sinners Beware. London, Hodder and Stoughton, 1931; Boston, Little Brown, 1932.

Inspector Dickins Retires. London, Hodder and Stoughton, 1931; as *Gangster's Glory*, Boston, Little Brown, 1931.

Clowns and Criminals (omnibus). Boston, Little Brown, 1931.

Shudders and Thrills (omnibus). Boston, Little Brown, 1932.

Crooks in the Sunshine.   London, Hodder and Stoughton, 1932; Boston, Little Brown, 1933.

The Ex-Detective.   London, Hodder and Stoughton, and Boston, Little Brown, 1933.

General Besserley's Puzzle Box.   London, Hodder and Stoughton, and Boston, Little Brown, 1935.

Advice Limited.   London, Hodder and Stoughton, 1935; Boston, Little Brown, 1936.

Ask Miss Mott.   London, Hodder and Stoughton, 1936; Boston, Little Brown, 1937.

Curious Happenings to the Rooke Legatees.   London, Hodder and Stoughton, 1937; Boston, Little Brown, 1938.

And Still I Cheat the Gallows: A Series of Stories.   London, Hodder and Stoughton, 1938.

A Pulpit in the Grill Room.   London, Hodder and Stoughton, 1938; Boston, Little Brown, 1939.

General Besserley's Second Puzzle Box.   London, Hodder and Stoughton, 1939; Boston, Little Brown, 1940.

The Milan Grill Room: Further Adventures of Louis, the Manager, and Major Lyson, the Raconteur.   London, Hodder and Stoughton, 1940; Boston, Little Brown, 1941.

The Great Bear.   London, Todd, 1943.

The Man Who Thought He Was a Pauper.   London, Todd, 1943.

The Hour of Reckoning, and The Mayor of Ballydaghan.   London, Todd, 1944.

OTHER PUBLICATIONS

Plays

The Money-Spider (produced London, 1908).

The King's Cup, with H. D. Bradley (produced London, 1909).   London, French, 1913.

The Gilded Key (produced Blackpool, Lancashire, 1910; London, 1911).

The Eclipse, with Fred Thompson, music by H. Darewski and M. Gideon (produced London, 1919).

Other

My Books and Myself.   Boston, Little Brown, 1922.

The Quest for Winter Sunshine.   London, Methuen, 1926; Boston, Little Brown, 1927.

The Pool of Memory: Memoirs.   London, Hodder and Stoughton, 1941; Boston, Little Brown, 1942.

Editor, *Many Mysteries.*   London, Rich and Cowan, 1933.

*   *   *

"The Prince of Storytellers" deserves his title. E. Phillips Oppenheim, who by his own account began each new novel with only a sense of "the first chapter, and an inkling of something to follow," spun 150 novels out of one of the most fertile imaginations ever to apply itself to the thriller; and less than a tenth of that number can be written off as dull reading.

Oppenheim made an immense amount of money from his writing, and lived the opulent life of so many of his heroes (though he never gave them the kind of sultanic existence he seems to have had himself). He lived much of his life on the Riviera, where many of his fictions are set. When the setting is London, it is the West End, around the Savoy and Milan Hotels; the mean streets do not often appear.

Oppenheim's novels include the Graustarkian mode (*Jeremiah and the Princess, The Stranger's Gate*), but most are set in the present. Typically there are killings, often by villains of exotic race; the hero is often outwardly one who lives idly for pleasure, but is in fact working to save his country; there is usually a love interest; and Oppenheim has as much sense as Alfred Hitchcock of how terror may impinge upon the commonplace. A representative novel is *Miss Brown of X.Y.O.*: Miss Brown, a secretary, bored with "the starvation of her simple life," sits to rest (with her typewriter) on the steps of a London mansion. She is summoned within to take the dying dictation of a famous explorer who is actually a secret agent – his deposition in the hands of the enemy, the Bolshevists, would cause "an instant European war." Miss Brown is badgered, threatened, attacked by those seeking the document, but she stands firm, and works with the agent, who has not died but gone under cover, to save England. The novel fades out on their first kiss.

Oppenheim did write a number of mystery novels (*The Cinema Murders, The Grassleyes Mystery*), as well as a number of detective stories, with a variety of detectives. In *Curious Happenings to the Rooke Legatees*, five beneficiaries to a will join forces to detect the murderer of the testator. But Oppenheim's talent for plotting is primarily a talent for building suspense rather than for unravelling a mysterious chain of events, at least at great length; his best detective stories are short stories. *Advice Limited* traces eleven adventures of Clara, Baroness Linz and her secret service agency. The title character of *Nicholas Goade, Detective* is a traveller, with dog, motoring through rural Devon. *General Besserley's Puzzle Box* (and its sequel) introduces the retired secret service official from Washington, now a very popular member of Monaco society, where he is innocuously providing financial advice at the tables, but actually solving crimes. Another detective is Sir Jasper Slane, gentleman and amateur, who solves crimes the police cannot, in *Slane's Long Shots* (though in one of the best of these stories it is the police who are triumphant). Perhaps Oppenheim's most interesting detective is Louis, the *Maître d'* of the Milan Hotel, crippled in the war, who solves crimes from his table in the grill room in collaboration with his friend Lyson, a retired Army officer now a journalist (*A Pulpit in the Grill Room* and *Milan Grill Room*). The common denominator of these detectives is their outward innocence or ineptitude: the Zorro figure is very nearly ubiquitous in Oppenheim's fiction.

The genre Oppenheim made his own (for even about his detective stories there is frequently the whiff of the secret service) is the novel of international intrigue, again with the apparent milksop or ne'er-do-well as hero. While Oppenheim always had the greatest respect for the aristocratic classes, especially the English, many of his supermen act on behalf of the little men; it is a case of *noblesse oblige*. In *The Profiteers* an American millionaire, to lower the exorbitant price of wheat, breaks the power of the controlling business syndicate by kidnapping and starving its principals. In *Prodigals of Monte Carlo* a wealthy baronet, told by his doctor that he is shortly to die, provides a holiday on the Riviera for a young woman and her chosen companion. In *Up the Ladder of Gold*, the most remarkable of these fantasies of the great power of money, "the richest man in the world" buys up most of the world's gold bullion and bribes the great powers, through a legal trustee device, not to go to war for 40 years. While the ending of *Up the Ladder of Gold* is unusually pessimistic for Oppenheim, the novel embodies his favorite theme of world domination for good purpose, especially pacifism, his admiration for the superman of wealth, and his fascination with the game of world politics played as on a chess board. These themes and concerns appear in various forms from *Mysterious Mr. Sabin* (1898) to his last novel, *Mr. Mirakel* (1943), where the character of the title transports a group of people from a world torn by war, and eventually by earthquake ("the revolt of Nature against mankind") to his own private Shangri-La, where they pair off and project the future of the race.

Some of Oppenheim's best books, however, find not supermen controlling international events, but ordinary diplomats and aristocrats caught up in them before they control them. An early novel, *A Maker of History*, sets the tone: an English youth witnesses a meeting between the Kaiser and the Czar and comes away with a sheet of the secret treaty in which they have agreed to launch war against England. In *The Double Traitor*, on the eve of the Great War a young diplomat gets possession of a list of German spies in England; he plays a good part in England's preparedness when the war comes. *The Kingdom of the Blind*, in which a prominent member of English society is shown to be a German spy, is to be set against the best of this group, and probably Oppenheim's best and most famous novel, *The*

Great Impersonation. Here an English aristocrat, fallen down the human scale through drink and dissipation, thwarts the attempt of a German, his physical double, to replace him, and so introduce a Trojan horse into the very citadel of the British ruling class. This is one of the few novels of Oppenheim's which depends upon surprise, and the secret is well kept to the end.

A final group of Oppenheim's novels are not content with playing the game of world politics – they project it into the future. *The Great Prince Shan* (1922) is set in 1934; *The Wrath to Come* (1924) in 1950; and *The Dumb Gods Speak* (1937) in 1947. Germany, Russia, and Japan are the usual antagonists of England and the United States, and the happy ending of *The Dumb Gods Speak* is signalled with the restoration of the Czarist regime, now benevolent and democratically based.

No one will contest the readability of Oppenheim's novels, which Grant Overton long ago attributed to the author's own infectious enthusiasm for his story. Oppenheim's novels are written without Buchan's subtlety of intellect, but not without his moral concern; they are free – except for some reserve towards Oriental villains – of Sapper's exclusive Anglo-Saxonism. As a *New York Times* reviewer sniffed in 1927, Oppenheim "has long been accustomed to analyze with a butcher knife and depict with a fence rail." But for readers looking for diversion with a shudder or a thrill one can still repeat Will Cuppy's 1934 axiom: "When in doubt, grab an Oppenheim."

—Barrie Hayne

ORCZY, Baroness (Emma Madgalena Rosalia Maria Josefa Barbara Orczy). British. Born in Tarna-Ors, Hungary, 23 September 1865. Educated in Brussels and Paris; West London School of Art; Heatherley School of Art, London. Married Montagu Barstow in 1894 (died, 1943); one son. Artist: exhibited work at the Royal Academy, London. *Died 12 November 1947.*

CRIME PUBLICATIONS

Short Stories (series character: Bill Owen, the Old Man in the Corner)

The Case of Miss Elliott. London, Unwin, 1905.
The Old Man in the Corner. London, Greening, 1909; as *The Man in the Corner*, New York, Dodd Mead, 1909.
Lady Molly of Scotland Yard. London, Cassell, 1910; New York, Arno, 1976.
The Man in Grey, Being Episodes of the Chouan Conspiracies in Normandy During the First Empire. London, Cassell, and New York, Doran, 1918.
Castles in the Air. London, Cassell, 1921; New York, Doran, 1922.
The Old Man in the Corner Unravels the Mystery of the Khaki Tunic. New York, Doran, 1923.
The Old Man in the Corner Unravels the Mystery of the Pearl Necklace, and The Tragedy in Bishop's Road. New York, Doran, 1924.
The Old Man in the Corner Unravels the Mystery of the Russian Prince and of Dog's Tooth Cliff. New York, Doran, 1924.
The Old Man in the Corner Unravels the Mystery of the White Carnation, and The Montmartre Hat. New York, Doran, 1925.
The Old Man in the Corner Unravels the Mystery of the Fulton Gardens Mystery, and The Moorland Tragedy. New York, Doran, 1925.
The Miser of Maida Vale. New York, Doran, 1925.

Unravelled Knots. London, Hutchinson, 1925; New York, Doran, 1926.
Skin o' My Tooth. London, Hodder and Stoughton, and New York, Doubleday, 1928.

OTHER PUBLICATIONS

Novels

The Emperor's Candlesticks. London, Pearson, 1899; New York, Doscher, 1908.
The Scarlet Pimpernel. London, Greening, and New York, Putnam, 1905.
By the Gods Beloved. London, Greening, 1905; as *Beloved of the Gods*, New York, Knickerbocker Press, 1905; as *The Gates of Kamt*, New York, Dodd Mead, 1907.
A Son of the People. London, Greening, and New York, Putnam, 1906.
I Will Repay. London, Greening, and Philadelphia, Lippincott, 1906.
In Mary's Reign. New York, Cupples and Leon, 1907.
The Tangled Skein. London, Greening, 1907.
Beau Brocade. Philadelphia, Lippincott, 1907; London, Greening, 1908.
The Elusive Pimpernel. London, Hutchinson, and New York, Dodd Mead, 1908.
The Nest of the Sparrowhawk. London, Greening, and New York, Stokes, 1909.
Petticoat Government. London, Hutchinson, 1910; as *Petticoat Rule*, New York, Hodder and Stoughton, 1910.
A True Woman. London, Hutchinson, 1911; as *The Heart of a Woman*, New York, Doran, 1911.
Meadowsweet. London, Hutchinson, and New York, Doran, 1912.
Fire in the Stubble. London, Methuen, 1912; as *The Noble Rogue*, New York, Doran, 1912.
Eldorado: A Story of the Scarlet Pimpernel. London, Hodder and Stoughton, and New York, Doran, 1913.
Unto Caesar. London, Hodder and Stoughton, and New York, Doran, 1914.
The Laughing Cavalier. London, Hodder and Stoughton, and New York, Doran, 1914.
A Bride of the Plains. London, Hutchinson, and New York, Doran, 1915.
The Bronze Eagle. London, Hodder and Stoughton, and New York, Doran, 1915.
Leatherface: A Tale of Old Flanders. London, Hodder and Stoughton, and New York, Doran, 1916.
A Sheaf of Bluebells. London, Hutchinson, and New York, Doran, 1917.
Lord Tony's Wife: An Adventure of the Scarlet Pimpernel. London, Hodder and Stoughton, and New York, Doran, 1917.
Flower o' the Lily. London, Hodder and Stoughton, 1918; New York, Doran, 1919.
The League of the Scarlet Pimpernel. London, Cassell, and New York, Doran, 1919.
His Majesty's Well-Beloved. London, Hodder and Stoughton, and New York, Doran, 1919.
The First Sir Percy: An Adventure of the Laughing Cavalier. London, Hodder and Stoughton, 1920; New York, Doran, 1921.
Nicolette. London, Hodder and Stoughton, and New York, Doran, 1922.
The Triumph of the Scarlet Pimpernel. London, Hodder and Stoughton, and New York, Doran, 1922.
The Honourable Jim. London, Hodder and Stoughton, and New York, Doran, 1924.
Pimpernel and Rosemary. London, Cassell, 1924; New York, Doran, 1925.
The Celestial City. London, Hodder and Stoughton, and New York, Doran, 1926.
Sir Percy Hits Back: An Adventure of the Scarlet Pimpernel. London, Hodder and Stoughton, and New York, Doran, 1927.
Blue Eyes and Grey. London, Hodder and Stoughton, 1928; New York, Doubleday, 1929.
Marivosa. London, Cassell, 1930; New York, Doubleday, 1931.
A Child of the Revolution. London, Cassell, and New York, Doubleday, 1932.

A Joyous Adventure.   London, Hodder and Stoughton, and New York, Doubleday, 1932.
The Way of the Scarlet Pimpernel.   London, Hodder and Stoughton, 1933; New York, Putnam, 1934.
A Spy of Napoleon.   London, Hodder and Stoughton, and New York, Putnam, 1934.
The Uncrowned King.   London, Hodder and Stoughton, and New York, Putnam, 1935.
Sir Percy Leads the Band.   London, Hodder and Stoughton, 1936.
The Divine Folly.   London, Hodder and Stoughton, 1937.
No Greater Love.   London, Hodder and Stoughton, 1938.
Mam'zelle Guillotine: An Adventure of the Scarlet Pimpernel.   London, Hodder and Stoughton, 1940.
Pride of Race.   London, Hodder and Stoughton, 1942.
Will-o'-the-Wisp.   London, Hutchinson, 1947.

Short Stories

The Traitor.   New York, Paget, 1912.
Two Good Patriots.   New York, Paget, 1912.
The Old Scarecrow.   New York, Paget, 1916.
A Question of Temptation.   New York, Doran, 1925.
Adventures of the Scarlet Pimpernel.   London, Hutchinson, and New York, Doubleday, 1929.
In the Rue Monge.   New York, Doubleday, 1931.

Plays

The Scarlet Pimpernel, with Montagu Barstow (produced Nottingham, 1903; London, 1905; New York, 1910).
The Sin of William Jackson, with Montagu Barstow (produced London, 1906).
Beau Brocade, with Montagu Barstow, adaptation of the novel by Orczy (produced Eastbourne, Sussex, and London, 1908).
The Duke's Wager (produced Manchester, 1911).
The Legion of Honour, adaptation of her novel *A Sheaf of Bluebells* (produced Bradford, 1918; London, 1921).
Leatherface, with Caryl Fiennes, adaptation of the novel by Orczy (produced Portsmouth and London, 1922).

Other

Les Beaux et les Dandys des Grands Siècles en Angleterre.   Monaco, Société des Conférences, 1924.
The Scarlet Pimpernel Looks at the World (essays).   London, John Heritage, 1933.
The Turbulent Duchess: H.R.H. Madame le Duchesse de Berri.   London, Hodder and Stoughton, 1935; New York, Putnam, 1936.
Links in the Chain of Life (autobiography).   London, Hutchinson, 1947.

Editor and Translator, with Montagu Barstow, *Old Hungarian Fairy Tales.*   London, Dean, and Philadelphia, Wolf, 1895.
Editor and Translator, *The Enchanted Cat* (fairy tales).   London, Dean, 1895.
Editor and Translator, *Fairyland's Beauty (The Suitors of Princess Fire-fly).*   London, Dean, 1895.

Editor and Translator, *Uletka and the White Lizard* (fairy tales).   London, Dean, 1895.

*   *   *

When Baroness Orczy was a struggling young author in London, before the success of *The Scarlet Pimpernel* in play and novel form, the editor of the Pearson magazines suggested that she profit from the popularity of Sherlock Holmes by writing a series of detective stories. The result was the Old Man in the Corner, one of the great figures in the early detective story. The Old Man (Bill Owen) sits in a cheap restaurant frequented by journalists and plays with a bit of string, which he ties into elaborate knots as he talks. Addressing himself to Polly Burton, a young newspaperwoman with whom he has struck up a slight acquaintance, he focuses upon crimes mentioned in the newspapers. He summarizes the circumstances, describes the personalities, and then sneeringly provides the correct solution, which has evaded the police.

Thirty-eight stories are devoted to the Old Man and Polly Burton. The first three series of stories appeared in *The Royal Magazine* between 1901 and 1904. The third series was published in book form as *The Case of Miss Elliott*, while the first and second were combined into *The Old Man in the Corner*. A fourth series, *Unravelled Knots*, was an unsuccessful attempt to capture the mood of the earlier stories. Typologically the stories are quite important. They are the first significant modern stories about an armchair detective, and structurally they take an extreme position: the explanation-denouement has been enlarged to such an extent that it swallows the antecedents, the crime, and the investigation, which are presented only in retrospective summary.

Four other books of short stories are much less significant. In *Lady Molly of Scotland Yard* a female detective solves 12 cases, some of which are true detective stories and some mystery adventures. Narrated by a female assistant, they are mildly feminist in attitude, but overwritten and sentimental. An unusual formal feature is that the narrator offers a précis of the crime before the entrance of the detective. *Skin o' My Tooth* contains 12 stories about Patrick Mulligan, an Irish lawyer practicing in England. His cases resemble those of Lady Molly de Mazareen, but are superior in execution. Two minor collections, *The Man in Grey* and *Castles in the Air*, combine historical adventure with elements of crime and mystery. *The Man in Grey* chronicles the triumph of the Napoleonic secret agent Fernand against members of the Chouans in 1809, while *Castles in the Air* contains seven cases of M. Hector Ratichon, a highly unscrupulous "volunteer police agent" in the Paris of 1813. They both reflect the attitudes of *The Scarlet Pimpernel*.

—E. F. Bleiler

ORMEROD, Roger.   British.   Born in Wolverhampton, Staffordshire. Married. Has worked as a county court officer, an executive officer in the Department of Social Security, and a postman. Currently works as a shop loader in an engineering factory. Lives in Wolverhampton. Address: c/o Robert Hale Ltd., 45–47 Clerkenwell Green, London EC1R 0HT, England.

CRIME PUBLICATIONS

Novels

Time to Kill.   London, Hale, 1974.

The Silence of the Night.   London, Hale, 1974.
Full Fury.   London, Hale, 1975.
A Spoonful of Luger.   London, Hale, 1975.
Sealed with a Loving Kill.   London, Hale, 1976.
The Colour of Fear.   London, Hale, 1976.
A Glimpse of Death.   London, Hale, 1976.
Too Late for the Funeral.   London, Hale, 1977.
This Murder Come to Mind.   London, Hale, 1977.
A Dip into Murder.   London, Hale, 1978.
The Weight of Evidence.   London, Hale, 1978.
The Bright Face of Danger.   London, Hale, 1979.
The Amnesia Hearse.   London, Hale, 1979.
Cart Before the Hearse.   London, Hale, 1979.

OTHER PUBLICATIONS

Plays

Television Plays: *I'll Go along with That*, 1971; *All Too Tidy*, 1973.

*   *   *

Roger Ormerod specialises in the traditional detective novel, liberally sprinkled with clues and red herrings, and aims to surprise the reader at the finish, although his stories normally have rather more action than the purely classical type. *This Murder Come to Mind* is the only one of his novels that can truthfully be called a thriller. He uses the same two private detectives in all the rest of his novels, sometimes singly, sometimes together, with first-person narration. In *A Dip into Murder* he tells the story from the point of view of the wife of one of his main detectives, as it had to be a story told by a woman. He uses his professional experience as Social Security Inspector, and his work in a factory, to give authenticity to his books.

—Herbert Harris

OURSLER, Fulton.   See **ABBOT, Anthony**.

PACKARD, Frank L(ucius).   Canadian.   Born in Montreal of American parents, 2 February 1877. Educated at McGill University, Montreal, B.Sc. 1897; L'Institut Montefiore, Université de Liège, Belgium, 1897–98. Married Marguerite Pearl Macintyre in 1910; one daughter and three sons. Civil engineer from 1898; worked in Canadian Pacific Railroad shops and as an engraver in the United States. *Died 17 February 1942.*

CRIME PUBLICATIONS

Novels (series character: Jimmie Dale)

The Miracle Man. New York, Doran, and London, Hodder and Stoughton, 1914.
The Adventures of Jimmie Dale. New York, Doran, 1917; London, Cassell, 1918.
The Sin That Was His. New York, Doran, 1917; London, Hodder and Stoughton, 1926.
The Further Adventures of Jimmie Dale. London, Hodder and Stoughton, 1917; New York, Doran, 1919.
The Wire Devils. New York, Doran, 1918.
From Now On. New York, Doran, 1919.
The White Moll. New York, Doran, and London, Hodder and Stoughton, 1920.
Pawned. New York, Doran, and London, Hodder and Stoughton, 1921.
Doors of the Night. New York, Doran, and London, Hodder and Stoughton, 1922.
Jimmie Dale and the Phantom Clue. New York, Doran, 1922; London, Hodder and Stoughton, 1923.
The Four Stragglers. New York, Doran, and London, Hodder and Stoughton, 1923.
The Locked Book. New York, Doran, and London, Hodder and Stoughton, 1924.
Broken Waters. New York, Doran, 1925; London, Hodder and Stoughton, 1927.
The Red Ledger. New York, Doran, and London, Hodder and Stoughton, 1926.
The Devil's Mantle. New York, Doran, 1927; London, Hodder and Stoughton, 1928.
Two Stolen Idols. New York, Doran, 1927; as *The Slave Junk*, London, Hodder and Stoughton, 1927.
Tiger Claws. New York, Doubleday, 1928; London, Hodder and Stoughton, 1929.
The Big Shot. New York, Doubleday, and London, Hodder and Stoughton, 1929.
Jimmie Dale and the Blue Envelope Murder. New York, Doubleday, and London, Hodder and Stoughton, 1930.
The Gold Skull Murders. New York, Doubleday, and London, Hodder and Stoughton, 1931.
The Hidden Door. New York, Doubleday, and London, Hodder and Stoughton, 1933.
The Purple Ball. New York, Doubleday, 1933; London, Hodder and Stoughton, 1934.
Jimmie Dale and the Missing Hour. New York, Doubleday, and London, Hodder and Stoughton, 1935.
The Dragon's Jaws. New York, Doubleday, and London, Hodder and Stoughton, 1937.

Short Stories

Shanghai Jim. New York, Doubleday, and London, Hodder and Stoughton, 1928.
More Knaves Than One. New York, Doubleday, and London, Hodder and Stoughton, 1938.

OTHER PUBLICATIONS

Novels

Greater Love Hath No Man. New York, Doran, and London, Hodder and Stoughton, 1913.
The Beloved Traitor. New York, Doran, 1915; London, Hodder and Stoughton, 1916.

Short Stories

On the Iron at Big Cloud. New York, Crowell, 1911.
The Night Operator. New York, Doran, 1919.

Running Special.   New York, Doran, 1925; London, Hodder and Stoughton, 1926.

*   *   *

Frank L. Packard's crime novels are romances, set in New York's pre-organized crime underworld, that concern the moral dilemmas of those who come into contact with the criminal element. Products of a less egalitarian time, they are predicated upon the gap between the poor and potentially criminal and the upper level of society. Packard's protagonists, like the self-appointed benefactor of the down-trodden, Rhoda Gray (*The White Moll*), are people of the "better class" who are forced to operate within the underworld and to adopt its rules and, as a result, become the victims of a moral erosion that will inevitably result in their assimilation into criminal society.

This problem is central to Packard's novels about Jimmie Dale, the wealthy dilettante clubman who cracks safes by night as the Gray Seal. Jimmie Dale is a modern Robin Hood who preys on other criminals in the tradition of E. W. Hornung's Raffles and Leslie Charteris's Simon Templar. Jimmie Dale is not averse to stealing from thieves, or to being hunted by the police and the underworld, but he is horrified when he becomes involved with murder, or when he is blackmailed into committing criminal acts by a woman who may be a criminal herself. Unlike some of his more hardened counterparts, Jimmie Dale does not easily move through the sordid world of crime, and his deepest fear is not of death, but of bringing disgrace to his name and position in society.

—Will Murray

PAGE, Emma.   Pseudonym for Honoria Tirbutt.   British.   Born in West Hartlepool, County Durham. Educated at St. Anne's College, Oxford, M.A. Lives in Worcestershire. Address: c/o Robert Hale Ltd., 45–47 Clerkenwell Green, London EC1R 0HT, England.

CRIME PUBLICATIONS

Novels

> *In Loving Memory.*   London, Collins, 1970.
> *Family and Friends.*   London, Collins, 1972.
> *A Fortnight by the Sea.*   London, Collins, 1973; as *Add a Pinch of Cyanide*, New York, Walker, 1973.
> *Element of Chance.*   London, Collins, 1975.

OTHER PUBLICATIONS

Plays as Honoria Tirbutt

> Radio Plays: *The Seeker*, 1964; *Years of Discretion*, 1964; *You're Only Middleaged Once*, 1964; *Prince of Life*, 1965; *Face among the Shadows*, 1966; *Spring Comes Once*, 1966.

*   *   *

Emma Page writes the kind of detective novel that derives its popularity as much from its easy readability as from its clever plotting and skilfully drawn characters. Her settings are invariably small-town and her personalities the sort that most of us feel we know. Without elaborate description her people come to life and are eminently believable. Her plotting is good, never appearing contrived and she generally keeps her reader guessing to the end.

The review of her first full-length novel in the *Times Literary Supplement* compared her to Agatha Christie in "her classic days." This book was *In Loving Memory* and concerned a rich old man in poor health, who met his end by consuming a fatal combination of tablets and alcohol. Several members of his family and household had reason to believe they would benefit from his death, so that there was no shortage of motives for the murder. The plot was indeed the type that Agatha Christie used but the resemblance to Christie is perhaps even more marked in the style of the narrative. Page, like Christie, is a natural story teller, and keeps her reader's interest throughout the book. Her three subsequent novels have been in the same vein. She appears to confine herself to the sort of settings and people of which she has personal knowledge, and this no doubt gives her stories their real life quality. Taking the comparison with Christie a little further it might be said that while she does not match Christie's skill in the plotting line, her characters have more depth and are better drawn. Emma Page is certainly a writer one can always rely upon for "a good read."

—Alison Susan Adey

PAGE, Marco. Pseudonym for Harry Kurnitz. American. Born in Philadelphia, Pennsylvania, 5 January 1909. Educated in public schools; the University of Pennsylvania, Philadelphia. Book and music reviewer for the Philadelphia *Record*; screen writer for Metro-Goldwyn-Mayer after 1938. *Died 18 March 1968.*

CRIME PUBLICATIONS

Novels

> *Fast Company.* New York, Dodd Mead, and London, Heinemann, 1938.
> *The Shadowy Third.* New York, Dodd Mead, 1946; as *Suspects All*, London, Cherry Tree, 1948.
> *Reclining Figure.* New York, Random House, and London, Eyre and Spottiswoode, 1952.
> *Invasion of Privacy* (as Harry Kurnitz). New York, Random House, 1955; London, Eyre and Spottiswoode, 1956.

OTHER PUBLICATIONS as Harry Kurnitz

Plays

> *Reclining Figure*, adaptation of his own novel (produced New York, 1954). New York, Dramatists Play Service, 1955.
> *Once More, with Feeling* (produced New York, 1958; London, 1959). New York, Random House, 1959.
> *A Shot in the Dark*, adaptation of a play by Marcel Achard (produced New York, 1961; London, 1963). New York, Random House, 1962.
> *The Girl Who Came to Supper*, music and lyrics by Noël Coward, adaptation of the play *The Sleeping Prince* by Terence Rattigan (produced New York, 1963).

Screenplays: *Fast Company* (as Marco Page), with Harold Tarshis, 1938; *Fast and Furious*, 1939; *Fast and Loose*, 1939; *I Love You Again*, with Charles Lederer and George Oppenheimer, 1940; *Shadow of the Thin Man*, with Irvine Brecher, 1941; *Ship Ahoy*, with others, 1942; *They Got Me Covered*, with others, 1942; *Pacific Rendezvous*, with P. J. Wolfson and George Oppenheimer, 1942; *The Heavenly Body*, with others, 1943; *See Here, Private Hargrove*, 1944; *The Thin Man Goes Home*, with Robert Riskin and Dwight Taylor, 1945; *What Next, Private Hargrove*, 1945; *The Web*, with William Bowers and Bertram Millhauser, 1947; *Something in the Wind*, with others, 1947; *A Kiss in the Dark*, with Everett Freeman and Devery Freeman, 1948; *One Touch of Venus*, with Frank Tashlin, 1948; *The Adventures of Don Juan*, with George Oppenheimer and Herbert Dalmas, 1949; *My Dream Is Yours*, with others, 1949; *The Inspector General*, with Philip Rapp, 1949; *Pretty Baby*, with others, 1950; *Of Men and Music*, with others, 1951; *Tonight We Sing*, with George Oppenheimer, 1953; *Melba*, 1953; *The Man Between*, with Walter Ebert, 1953; *Land of the Pharaohs*, with William Faulkner and Harold Jack Bloom, 1955; *The Happy Road*, with Arthur Julian and Joseph Morhain, 1957; *Witness for the Prosecution*, with Billy Wilder and Larry Marcus, 1957; *The Love Lottery*, with Monja Danischewsky, 1957; *Once More, with Feeling*, 1960; *Surprise Package*, 1960; *Hatari!*, with Leigh Brackett, 1962; *Goodbye Charlie*, 1964; *How to Steal a Million*, 1966.

*   *   *

The delight of the regrettably few Marco Page novels lies in Page's remarkably adroit use of sprightly and highly amusing dialogue and in his selection of gripping situations around which to construct his stories.

His first mystery, *Fast Company*, involves bookman Joel Glass in a search for some rare books whose disappearance eventually leads to murder. In *The Shadowy Third* lawyer David Calder scrambles after a Stradivarius violin whose theft has similar consequences. Page really hit his stride in *Reclining Figure*, in which a New York art dealer, Ellis Blaise, journeys to California to investigate possible forgeries in a fabulously valuable collection of modern art. Murder, of course, ensues, and the reader is treated to a brief but fascinating glimpse into the world of art forgery in addition to a fast-paced, tightly knit detective tale whose dialogue positively sparkles. Running a very close second to *Reclining Figure* is *Invasion of Privacy* which involves the efforts of Mike Zorn, New York representative of Hollywood's Continental Films, to extricate himself and his company from the consequences arising from the fact that the events portrayed in a just completed movie about an unsolved murder turn out to be a real rather than fictional.

Page wrote entertainingly about interesting subjects. He had more than a smidgen of knowledge about rare books, violins, and paintings, and about the workings of the Hollywood film industry, and he used his knowledge to construct convincing backdrops for his novels.

—Guy M. Townsend

PALMER, John Leslie.   See **BEEDING, Francis.**

PALMER, (Charles) Stuart. Also wrote as Jay Stewart. American. Born in Baraboo, Wisconsin, 21 June 1905. Educated at the Chicago Art Institute, 1922–24; University of Wisconsin, Madison, 1924–26; University of California, Los Angeles, 1961. Served in the United States Army as liaison chief for official Army film making, 1943–48; Major. Married 1) Melina Racioppi in 1928 (divorced, 1937); 2) Margaret Greppin in 1939 (divorced, 1945), one daughter and one son; 3) Ann Higgins in 1947 (divorced, 1950), one son; 4) Winifred Graham in 1952 (divorced, 1963); 5) Jennifer Elaine Venala in 1966. Screenwriter from 1932. President, Mystery Writers of America, 1954–55. *Died 4 February 1968.*

CRIME PUBLICATIONS

Novels (series characters: Howie Rook; Hildegarde Withers)

Ace of Jades. New York, Mohawk Press, 1931.
The Penguin Pool Murder (Withers). New York, Brentano's, 1931; London, Long, 1932.
Murder on Wheels (Withers). New York, Brentano's, and London, Long, 1932.
Murder on the Blackboard (Withers). New York, Brentano's, 1932; London, Eldon Press, 1934.
The Puzzle of the Pepper Tree (Withers). New York, Doubleday, 1933; London, Jarrolds, 1934.
The Puzzle of the Silver Persian (Withers). New York, Doubleday, 1934; London, Collins, 1935.
The Puzzle of the Red Stallion (Withers). New York, Doubleday, 1936; as *The Puzzle of the Briar Pipe*, London, Collins, 1936.
Omit Flowers. New York, Doubleday, 1937; as *No Flowers by Request*, London, Collins, 1937.
The Puzzle of the Blue Banderilla (Withers). New York, Doubleday, and London, Collins, 1937.
The Puzzle of the Happy Hooligan (Withers). New York, Doubleday, and London, Collins, 1941.
Miss Withers Regrets. New York, Doubleday, 1947; London, Collins, 1948.
Four Lost Ladies (Withers). New York, Mill, 1949; London, Collins, 1950.
Before It's Too Late (as Jay Stewart). New York, Mill, 1950.
The Green Ace (Withers). New York, Mill, 1950; as *At One Fell Swoop*, London, Collins, 1951.
Nipped in the Bud (Withers). New York, Mill, 1951; London, Collins, 1952; as *Trap for a Redhead*, New York, Spivak, 1955.
Cold Poison (Withers). New York, Mill, 1954; as *Exit Laughing*, London, Collins, 1954.
Unhappy Hooligan (Rook). New York, Harper, 1956; as *Death in Grease Paint*, London, Collins, 1956.
Rook Takes Knight. New York, Random House, 1968.
Hildegarde Withers Makes the Scene, with Fletcher Flora. New York, Random House, 1969.

Short Stories

The Riddles of Hildegarde Withers, edited by Ellery Queen. New York, Spivak, 1947.
The Monkey Murder and Other Hildegarde Withers Stories, edited by Ellery Queen. New York, Spivak, 1950.
People vs. Withers and Malone, with Craig Rice. New York, Simon and Schuster, 1963.

The Adventures of the Marked Man and One Other.   Boulder, Colorado, Aspen Press, 1973.

OTHER PUBLICATIONS

Plays

Screenplays: *Yellowstone*, with others, 1936; *Hollywood Stadium Mystery*, with Dorrell and Stuart McGowan, 1938; *Bulldog Drummond's Peril*, 1938; *Arrest Bulldog Drummond*, 1939; *Bulldog Drummond's Bride*, with Weston Garnett, 1939; *Death of a Champion*, with Cortland Fitzsimmons, 1939; *Seventeen*, with Agnes Christine Johnston, 1940; *Emergency Squad*, with others, 1940; *Opened by Mistake*, with others, 1940; *Who Killed Aunt Maggie?*, with Frank Gill, Jr. and Hal Fimberg, 1940; *Secrets of the Lone Wolf*, 1941; *The Smiling Ghost*, with Kenneth Gamet, 1941; *Pardon My Stripes*, with others, 1942; *X Marks the Spot*, with others, 1942; *Half Way to Shanghai*, 1942; *Home in Wyoming*, with Robert Tasker and M. Coates Webster, 1942; *The Falcon's Brother*, with Craig Rice, 1942; *Murder in Times Square*, with Paul Gangelin, 1943; *Petticoat Larceny*, with Jack Townley, 1943; *The Falcon Strikes Back*, with Edward Dein and Gerald Geraghty, 1943; *Step by Step*, with George Callahan, 1946; *Mrs. O'Malley and Mr. Malone*, with Craig Rice and William Bowers, 1951.

Other

"Some of My Best Friends," in *Ellery Queen's Mystery Magazine* (New York), June 1950.
"Profile of a Bloodhound," in *The Saint* (New York), October 1964.

*   *   *

Stuart Palmer made his debut as a mystery novelist with *Ace of Jades* in 1931, but it was his next book, *The Penguin Pool Murder*, that established his reputation and provided him with a series character to whom he would be closely wedded thereafter. His creation was Hildegarde Withers, a snoopy old maid sleuth extraordinaire. Withers's personality is quite unlike that of the most famous spinster detective, Agatha Christie's quiet, unassuming Miss Marple. Withers is a schoolteacher, of the sharp-tongued, knuckle-rapping variety, with a take-charge attitude and a tendency to treat suspects and police alike as if they were little boys caught cheating in class. She is lean and horsefaced, and given to wearing ghastly hats. It is perhaps unnecessary to note that beneath the formidable exterior there is a great deal of kindness and sentimentality. She is clearly a caricature, uncomfortably broad at times; but she is difficult to dislike, even if Palmer himself was wont to refer to her as "that meddlesome old battleaxe."

In *The Penguin Pool Murder*, Withers is escorting her class on a tour of an aquarium when she discovers a body amongst the penguins. Her curiosity, and her impatience with stupidity (which she finds the police exhibiting), lead her to see to the solution of the mystery. In this and later investigations her perennial foil (and an excellent one) is New York homicide Inspector Oscar Piper, a harried, cigar-chomping vulgarian – very much the opposite in character to the abstemious schoolteacher.

Though the chief appeal of the Withers novels is the character of "Hildy," and the interplay between her and Piper, Palmer can be credited with an ear for bright and clever dialogue, and he was a fine crafter of puzzle plots. The major weakness of the books is the slight characterization given to the supporting players. The Withers novels were transferred to the screen in a series of six films. Palmer moved to Hollywood to work as a screenwriter, and Withers moved to Los Angeles along with him. Perhaps the best of the later Withers novels is *Cold Poison*, in which Palmer makes an excellent use of background, setting the mystery in a Hollywood animation studio.

Ellery Queen was a great fan of Withers, and Palmer produced a number of short stories for *Ellery Queen's Mystery Magazine*. These were collected in *The Riddles of Hildegarde Withers* and *The Monkey Murder*. Palmer's skill at puzzle plot construction was put to good use in the short form. Withers also appeared in another unique series of short stories, in which she was teamed with Craig Rice's character John J. Malone. This represents one of the very few collaborative pairings of detective characters. Palmer wrote the stories and Rice provided plot springboards and bits of dialogue. Withers and Malone proved a natural yin-yang pairing – boozy, skirt-chasing lawyer versus prim spinster – and the tales are great fun. The stories were collected in *People vs. Withers and Malone*.

Late in his career, Palmer introduced another appealing series character, Howie Rook, a middle-aged, overweight ex-newsman with a streak of misogyny. The first of the two Rook novels, *Unhappy Hooligan*, takes place in a circus setting, Palmer drawing on his own experience as a clown for Ringling Brothers. The light approach to murderous doings that marked the Withers books is also much in evidence in the Rook novels.

—Art Scott

PARGETER, Edith.   See PETERS, Ellis.

PARKER, Robert B(rown).   American.   Born in Springfield, Massachusetts, 17 September 1932. Educated at Colby College, Waterville, Maine, B.A. 1954; Boston University, M.A. 1957, Ph.D. 1971. Served in the United States Army, 1954–56. Married Joan Hall in 1956; two sons. Technical Writers and Group Leader, Raytheon Company, 1957–59; Copy Writer and Editor, Prudential Insurance Company, Boston, 1959–62; Partner, Parker Farman Company, advertising, Boston, 1960–62; Teaching Fellow and Lecturer, Boston University, 1962–64; Instructor, Massachusetts State College, Lowell, 1964–66; Lecturer, Suffolk University, Boston, 1965–66; Instructor, Massachusetts State College, Bridgewater, 1964–68; Assistant Professor, 1968–74, Associate Professor, 1974–77, and Professor, 1977–79, Northeastern University, Boston. Recipient: Mystery Writers of America Edgar Allan Poe Award, 1976. Lives in Massachusetts. Agent: Brann-Hartnett Agency, 14 Sutton Place South, New York, New York 10022, U.S.A.

CRIME PUBLICATIONS

Novels (series character: Spenser in all books)

The Godwulf Manuscript.   Boston, Houghton Mifflin, 1973; London, Deutsch, 1974.
God Save the Child.   Boston, Houghton Mifflin, 1974; London, Deutsch, 1975.
Mortal Stakes.   Boston, Houghton Mifflin, 1975; London, Deutsch, 1976.
Promised Land.   Boston, Houghton Mifflin, 1976; London, Deutsch, 1977.
The Judas Goat.   Boston, Houghton, Mifflin, 1978; London, Deutsch, 1979.

OTHER PUBLICATIONS

Novel

Wilderness.   New York, Delacorte Press, 1979.

Other

Sports Illustrated Training with Weights.   Philadelphia, Lippincott, 1974.
"Marlowe's Moral Code," in *Popular Culture Scholar* (Frostburg, Maryland), 1976.
"Marxism and the Mystery," in *Murder Ink: The Mystery Reader's Companion*, edited
   by Dilys Winn.   New York, Workman, 1977.
Three Weeks in Spring, with Joan H. Parker.   Boston, Houghton Mifflin, and London,
   Deutsch, 1978.

Editor, *The Personal Response to Literature.*   Boston, Houghton Mifflin, 1971.
Editor, *Order and Diversity.*   New York, Wiley, 1973.

Manuscript Collection: Colby College, Waterville, Maine.

*   *   *

Long-time student and critic of the American private-eye tradition, Robert B. Parker has
himself created an indigenously American series. Blending much of the best of the hard-
boiled tradition – the stark realism of Dashiell Hammett, the adroit, quick-witted dialogue of
Raymond Chandler, and the moral and social ambience of Ross Macdonald (the three writers
on whom he wrote his Ph.D. dissertation) – his books also develop an engaging and unique
character, the Boston-based detective Spenser. Parker is an inventive craftsman whose plots
are skilfully designed to involve Spenser in a series of meaningful and probable incidents
which test him as a detective.
    In the first novel, *The Godwulf Manuscript*, Spenser is hired by a local university to locate a
missing fourteenth-century illuminated manuscript stolen from the library. As the case
deepens into one involving two murders, drugs, adultery, and extortion, the heart of the
novel becomes Spenser's attempt to prove a young girl innocent of murder, a crime he
believes is tied in with the stolen manuscript. In *God Save the Child* Spenser is hired to locate
a missing boy, and eventually uncovers bizzare extortion attempts, murder, and a sex-drug
ring. In *Mortal Stakes* Spenser is hired by the Red Sox organization to determine if star
pitcher Marty Rabb is involved with gamblers. Spenser discovers that he is, but chooses to
help the Rabb family free themselves from blackmail and save Rabb's career. In *Promised
Land* Spenser again searches for a missing person, this time a runaway wife of a builder of
leisure communities. The wife has become involved in a robbery and murder, and the
husband, who has misappropriated public funds, is in debt to a vicious loan shark. Spenser
arranges an entrapment scheme which ensnares both the wife's revolutionary confederates
and the gangster shylock, thus freeing the couple.
    In *The Judas Goat* Spenser is hired by a millionaire industrialist to hunt down the nine
terrorists who killed his wife and daughter in London and put him in a wheelchair with only
vengeance to sustain him. This is the first novel not set in or around Boston, and the first time
that Spenser employs someone to assist him – Hawk, the enforcer figure in *Promised Land*,
and long-time professional acquaintance. They travel from London to Copenhagen to
Amsterdam to Montreal as they capture or kill the terrorists. They also take on the added
mission of capturing the leader of racist group, Liberty, a decision which again leads Spenser
beyond his original job and results in the best of the many fine confrontation scenes in
Parker's novels.
    Parker's plots, consistently demonstrating that people are more important than money or
the finer points of law, require that the center of each novel be Spenser committing himself to

wrestle with the social and moral implications of his cases. Progressively Spenser grows as a character. In *Godwulf*, he is essentially one dimensional, possessing a worthy motive for action and an engaging independence of spirit. Even in *God Save the Child* he remains a surface character, despite deep commitment to his work and his compassion for the lost and alienated boy. Parker seems to use these two novels to establish his idiosyncratic Spenser with a passion for cooking and good food, jogging and weight-lifting, and an almost medieval sense of honor.

The character is more fully realized in *Mortal Stakes*, not only because Parker chooses to articulate his code more elaborately but because the plot tests the code against harsh realities. Marty Rabb, whose "jock ethic" depends on the rules of the game, discovers that because of his wife's past he must violate the rules or endanger his family. In trying to help Rabb, Spenser discovers that one strand of his own code – never to allow innocents to be victimized – conflicts with another – never to kill except involuntarily. Like Rabb before him, Spenser must choose. His choice is probable and moral, but it leaves him feeling "diminished," with a sense of his own mortality.

In *Promised Land* Parker amplifies the character of Spenser by making Susan Silverman, his girl friend from past novels, a more intimate part of his life and by deepening his relationship with Hawk. At one point, while defining himself to Susan, Spenser says he is a "gut person" who thinks in images and patterns. He does what *feels* right, his morality considers wholes rather than parts, particulars rather than abstractions, so throughout the novel, Spenser habitually trusts his instincts: he refuses to tell his client where his wife is; he refuses to abandon the Shepards to the shylock; and he chooses to warn Hawk of the impending police dragnet at the end. In short, Parker's provision of an almost Thoreau-like independence and moral compassion to Spenser rounds out the characterization. *The Judas Goat* works similarly through the portrayal of Spencer's growing friendship with Hawk. They are depicted as brotherly alter egos – both are tough, independent, and thoroughly professional. His decision to free the ninth terrorist because he has used her as his judas goat and "she has become one of us" illustrates his penchant for fine moral distinctions and independence of judgment.

A detective, like all literary characters, is defined by how he chooses to operate in the world in which he finds himself. In the violent and unpredictable world of Parker's novels, Spenser manages to retain his humor, his compassionate moral sensitivity, and a philosophical ethic that guides his behavior. A key to his, and perhaps Parker's, perspective is the title of the book he reads in the fifth novel. The book is Richard Slotkin's *Regeneration Through Violence*. In light of this it is interesting that in *Godwulf*, Spenser sees dignity and love reflected in Mrs. Hayden's fight to the death with a gangster; in *God Save the Child*, the climactic fight scene with Vic Harroway is the occasion of renewed dignity; in *Mortal Stakes* Linda Rabb earns Spenser's admiration when she braves the violence of public opinion; in *Promised Land* Spenser described violence as "one of those places that you can be honorable" because it is not easy; and, finally, in *The Judas Goat* the climactic fight scene is treated as a "cleansing action" that follows the nightmare of the hunt. In each novel violence shatters abstractions and illusions, forcing characters to reach deep within themselves to discover what really matters.

Parker can tell a good story and make it significant. Spenser captures our imagination. The hard-boiled detective novel has found its modern voice.

—George J. Thompson

———

PARTRIDGE, Anthony. See **OPPENHEIM, E. Phillips.**

———

PATRICK, Q.   See **QUENTIN, Patrick.**

PATTERSON, Henry.   See **MARLOWE, Hugh.**

PAUL, Elliot (Harold).   Also wrote as Brett Rutledge.   American.   Born in Malden, Massachusetts, 11 February 1891. Educated at Malden High School; University of Maine, Orono, 1908–09. Served in 317th Field Signal Battalion in World War I; Sergeant. Had one son by first marriage, then married 2) Flora Thompson Brown in 1935; 3) Barbara Mayock in 1945; 4) Nancy Dolan. Surveyor and timekeeper on irrigation project in Idaho and Wyoming, 1909; worked on Boston newspapers to 1914; Secretary, Massachusetts Soldiers' and Sailors' Commission, 1919–21; worked in Paris after the war for Associated Press, Chicago *Tribune*, 1925–26, and as literary editor on Paris edition of New York *Herald*, 1930. Founder, with Eugène Jolas, *Transition*, Paris 1927–28; lived in Santa Eulalia, Ibiza, in the 1930's. *Died 7 April 1958.*

CRIME PUBLICATIONS

Novels (series character: Homer Evans in all Paul books)

    The Mysterious Mickey Finn; or, Murder at the Café du Dôme.   New York, Modern Age, 1939; London, Penguin, 1952.
    Hugger-Mugger in the Louvre.   New York, Random House, 1940; London, Nicholson and Watson, 1949.
    The Death of Lord Haw Haw (as Brett Rutledge).   New York, Random House, 1940; London, Laurie, 1941.
    Fracas in the Foothills.   New York, Random House, 1940.
    Mayhem in B-Flat.   New York, Random House, 1940; London, Corgi, 1951.
    I'll Hate Myself in the Morning, and Summer in December.   New York, Random House, 1945; London, Nicholson and Watson, 1949.
    Murder on the Left Bank.   New York, Random House, and London, Corgi, 1951.
    The Black Gardenia.   New York, Random House, 1952.
    Waylaid in Boston.   New York, Random House, 1953.
    The Black and the Red.   New York, Random House, 1956.

OTHER PUBLICATIONS

Novels

    Indelible.   Boston, Houghton Mifflin, 1922; London, Jarrolds, 1924.
    Impromptu.   New York, Knopf, 1923.
    Imperturbe.   New York, Knopf, 1924.
    Low Run Ride and Lava Rock.   New York, Liveright, 1929.

The Governor of Massachusetts. New York, Liveright, 1930.
The Amazon. New York, Liveright, 1930.
Concert Pitch. New York, Random House, 1938.
The Stars and Stripes Forever. New York, Random House, 1939.
With a Hays Nonny Nonny. New York, Random House, 1942.
Understanding the French. London, Muller, 1954; New York, Random House, 1955.
That Crazy American Music. Indianapolis, Bobbs Merrill, 1957; as *That Crazy Music,* London, Muller, 1957.

Plays

Screenplays: *A Woman's Face,* with Donald Ogden Stewart, 1941; *Our Russian Front,* 1942; *Rhapsody in Blue,* with Howard Koch and Sonya Levien, 1945; *It's a Pleasure,* with Lynn Starling, 1945; *London Town* (*My Heart Goes Crazy*), with Sig Herzig and Wesley Ruggles, 1946; *New Orleans,* with Dick Irving Hyland and Herbert J. Biberman, 1947.

Other

The Life and Death of a Spanish Town. New York, Random House, and London, Davies, 1937.
All the Brave, with Jay Allen. New York, Modern Age, 1939.
Intoxication Made Easy. New York, Modern Age, 1940.
The Last Time I Saw Paris. New York, Random House, 1942; as *A Narrow Street,* London, Cresset Press, 1942.
Paris, photographs by Fritz Henle. Chicago, Ziff Davis, 1947.
Linden on the Saugus Branch. New York, Random House, 1947; London, Cresset Press, 1948.
A Ghost Town on the Yellowstone. New York, Random House, 1948; London, Cresset Press, 1949.
My Old Kentucky Home. New York, Random House, 1949; London, Cresset Press, 1950.
Springtime in Paris. New York, Random House, 1950; London, Cresset Press, 1951.
Desperate Scenery. New York, Random House, 1954; London, Cresset Press, 1955.
Flim Flam. London, Muller, 1956.

* * *

Elliot Paul, author, bon vivant, and boogie woogie pianist, cut his writing teeth as a newspaperman in Boston. His reflections on that city, and its Watch and Ward Society, have appeared in his later works. It is possible that Boston may never fully recover. Paul first came to wide notice with two non-crime books, *The Life and Death of a Spanish Town* and *The Last Time I Saw Paris,* an excellent account of pre-World War II Paris, deeply personal in nature, that quickly achieved something close to classic stature.

Like many another, Paul read the Philo Vance stories of S. S. Van Dine and found Vance himself an insufferable snob. His response to this was to parody Vance with his own creation, Homer Evans. An American living by choice in Paris, Evans outdoes Vance in almost every department: he speaks more languages, is capable of even more languid conduct, and is surrounded by a world of wild characters that would confound the Marx brothers. This ménage first appeared in *The Mysterious Mickey Finn* in 1939; perhaps mercifully Van Dine died the same year. Much to Paul's surprise, his cutting satire was taken seriously as a mystery story and there was a loud demand for more, particularly since the book's deft humor was enormously entertaining. The following year Paul obliged with *Hugger-Mugger in the Louvre* in which even more people met with fascinating, if violent, deaths. A fit companion and mate for Evans is his girlfriend, Miriam Leonard, a sharpshooting cowgirl from the American West who is in Paris to study the harpsichord. On one occasion when Homer failed to catch the eye of a gendarme on the far corner of a wide boulevard, Miriam drew, fired, and gently rang the bell on the officer's bicycle.

When Paris fell, Homer and Miriam returned to their homeland bringing with them many of their Parisian friends, including the Medical Examiner, Dr. Hyacinthe Toudoux. In the lower Yellowstone Valley of Montana, Miriam, at least, is fully at home and introduces Dr. Toudoux to his professional colleague, the Blackfoot medicine man, Trout-tail III. In addition to the two doctors, there are the Blackfoot Chief, Shot-on-Both-Sides, and the unforgettable Moritz, the Thinking Dog, whose mental powers are revealed as *Fracas in the Foothills* runs its mad course.

In all there are nine volumes in the Homer Evans canon, most of them filled with wild action and funny enough to make most readers laugh aloud in an empty room. In the whole field of mystery literature Paul is probably unique in his ability to blend far-out humor, satire, and the traditional detective story into a homogeneous whole. The author's knowledge of both classic and popular music adds spice, and few Bostonians will be able to read *Waylaid in Boston* unmoved. Some critics have maintained that a detective story once read can never be as entertaining again. Elliot Paul has proved otherwise.

—John Ball

PEMBERTON, Max. British. Born in Birmingham, Warwickshire, 19 June 1863. Educated at the Merchant Taylors' School, London; Caius College, Cambridge, M.A. Editor, *Chums* magazine, London, 1892–93, and *Cassell's Magazine*, London, 1894–1906; also edited *Tit-bits*, London; Director, Northcliffe Newspapers, from 1920. A Founder, London School of Journalism, 1920. Knighted, 1928. *Died 22 February 1950.*

CRIME PUBLICATIONS

Novels (series character: Captain Black)

The Diary of a Scoundrel. London, Ward and Downey, 1891.
The Iron Pirate (Black). London, Cassell, 1893; Chicago, Rand McNally, 1896.
A Gentleman's Gentleman. London, Innes, and New York, Harper, 1896.
The Phantom Army. London, Pearson, and New York, Appleton, 1898.
The Giant's Gate. London, Cassell, and New York, Stokes, 1901.
The Diamond Ship. London, Cassell, and New York, Appleton, 1907.
Wheels of Anarchy. London, Cassell, 1908.
The Man Who Drove the Car. London, Nash, 1910.
The Mystery of the Green Heart. London, Methuen, and New York, Dodd Mead, 1910.
Captain Black: A Sequel to The Iron Pirate. London, Cassell, and New York, Doran, 1911.
White Motley. New York, Sturgis and Walton, 1911; London, Cassell, 1913.
Two Women. London, Methuen, 1914.
Behind the Curtain. London, Nash, 1916.
A Bagman in Jewels. London, Skeffington, 1919.
John Dighton, Mystery Millionaire. London, Cassell, 1923.

Short Stories

Jewel Mysteries I Have Known. London, Ward Lock, 1894; as *Jewel Mysteries from a Dealer's Note Book,* New York, Fenno, 1904.
Dolores and Some Others. London, Mills and Boon, 1931.

Uncollected Short Stories

"The Double Life of Edith Thompson," in *Famous Crime Mysteries and Romances,* edited by Max Pemberton. London, Newnes, 1924.
"The Spirit of Black Hawk," in *My Best Thriller.* London, Faber, 1933.

OTHER PUBLICATIONS

Novels

The Sea Wolves. London, Cassell, and New York, Harper, 1894.
The Impregnable City. London, Cassell, and New York, Dodd Mead, 1895.
The Little Huguenot. London, Cassell, and New York, Dodd Mead, 1895.
A Puritan's Wife. London, Cassell, and New York, Dodd Mead, 1896.
Christine of the Hills. London, Innes, and New York, Dodd Mead, 1897.
Kronstadt. London, Cassell, and New York, Appleton, 1898; as *A Woman of Kronstadt,* Leipzig, Tauchintz, 1898.
The Garden of Swords. London, Cassell, and New York, Dodd Mead, 1899.
Feó. London, Hodder and Stoughton, and New York, Dodd Mead, 1900.
Love the Harvester. New York, Dodd Mead, 1900; London, Methuen, 1908.
The Footsteps of a Throne. London, Methuen, and New York, Dodd Mead, 1900.
Pro Patria. London, Ward Lock, and New York, Dodd Mead, 1901.
I Crown Thee King. London, Methuen, 1902.
The House under the Sea. London, Newnes, and New York, Appleton, 1902.
The Gold Wolf. London, Ward Lock, and New York, Dodd Mead, 1903.
Doctor Xavier. London, Hodder and Stoughton, and New York, Appleton, 1903.
Red Morn. London, Cassell, 1904.
Beatrice of Venice. London, Hodder and Stoughton, and New York, Dodd Mead, 1904.
A Daughter of the States. New York, Dodd Mead, 1904.
Mid the Thick Arrows. London, Hodder and Stoughton, 1905.
The Hundred Days. London, Cassell, and New York, Appleton, 1905.
The Lady Evelyn. London, Hodder and Stoughton, and New York, Authors and Newspapers Association, 1906.
My Sword for Lafayette. London, Hodder and Stoughton, and New York, Dodd Mead, 1906.
The Lodestar. London, Ward Lock, and New York, Authors and Newspapers Association, 1907; as *Aladdin of London; or, Lodestar,* New York, Empire Book Company, 1907.
The Shadow on the Sea. Cleveland, Westbrook, 1907.
Sir Richard Escombe. London, Cassell, and New York, Harper, 1908.
The Adventures of Captain Jack. London, Mills and Boon, 1909.
The Show Girl. London, Cassell, and Philadelphia, Winston, 1909.
The Fortunate Prisoner. London, Hodder and Stoughton, and New York, Dillingham, 1909.
White Walls. London, Ward Lock, 1910.
The Girl with the Red Hair. London, Cassell, 1910.
War and the Woman. London, Cassell, 1912; as *Swords Reluctant,* New York, Dillingham, 1912.

The House of Fortune.   London, Nash, 1912.
The Virgin Fortress.   London, Cassell, 1912.
Millionaire's Island.   London, Cassell, 1913.
Leila and Her Lover.   London, Ward Lock, 1913.
The Great White Army.   London, Cassell, 1915.
The Man of Silver Mount.   London, Cassell, 1918.
Prince of the Palais Royal.   London, Cassell, 1921.
Paulina.   London, Cassell, 1922.
The Mad King Dies.   London, Cassell, 1928.

Short Stories

Queen of the Jesters.   London, Pearson, and New York, Dodd Mead, 1897.
Signors of the Night.   London, Pearson, and New York, Dodd Mead, 1899.
The Summer Book.   London, Mills and Boon, 1911.
Her Wedding Night: A Story from the German Lines, and Other Stories.   London, Jenkins, 1918.
A Woman Who Knew.   London, Hutchinson, 1921.
Lucienne, with Isabelle, and Horizon of God.   London, Mills and Boon, 1925.
Night Lights and Others.   London, Mills and Boon, 1929.

Plays

Gems of The Brazilian, with Edgar Smith, music by Francis Chassaigne (produced New York).   New York, Pond, 1890.
The Huguenot Lover, with James McArthur (produced London, 1901).
The Finishing School (produced London, 1904).
The Prima Donna.   London, French, 1906.
Lights Out!   London, French, 1906.
The House of Nightingales.   London, French, 1907.
A Woman of Kronstadt, with George Fleming, adaptation of the novel *Kronstadt* by Pemberton (produced London, 1908).
The Lady of the Pageant, with C. W. Hogg (produced Eastbourne, 1908).
The Grey Room, with Eille Norwood (produced York, 1911).   London, French, 1912.
Diane's Diamonds (produced London, 1912).
Garrick (produced London, 1913).
The Bells of St. Valoir (produced London, 1914).
The Haunted Husband (produced London, 1915).
Vivien, with Arthur Wimperis, music by H. Talbot and H. Finch (produced Birmingham, 1915; as *My Lady Frayle*, produced London, 1916).
Oh Caesar!, with Alexander M. Thompson (produced Edinburgh, 1916).
Oh! Don't, Dolly!, with Eustace Ponsonby, music by G. Dorlay (produced Folkestone, Kent, and London, 1919).

Other

The Amateur Motorist.   London, Hutchinson, 1907; Chicago, McClurg, 1908.
Lord Northcliffe: A Memoir.   London, Hodder and Stoughton, and New York, Doran, 1922.
The Red Lion Inn, Henley-on-Thames.   London, True Temperance Association, 1931.
The White Horse at Shere.   London, True Temperance Association, 1932.
The Life of Sir Henry Royce.   London, Selwyn and Blount, 1934.
Sixty Years Ago and After.   London, Hutchinson, 1936.

Editor, *Pelman Pie.*   London, Hodder and Stoughton, 1919.

Editor, *Famous Crime Mysteries and Romances.* London, Newnes, 1924.
Editor, *Tit-bits Jubilee Book.* London, Newnes, 1931.

*   *   *

Max Pemberton, though he wrote many books, was not a prolific crime writer. His most memorable book in the genre was conceived during his period as the first editor of the juvenile publication *Chums.* This book was *The Iron Pirate,* serialised in *Chums* and published as a novel in 1893. Strangely enough, it was not until 1911 that its sequel, *Captain Black,* appeared. After his stint on *Chums,* Pemberton's work took on a more mature style though even so it was still suitable for a *Chums* readership. Even today his style does not appear cramped, and it is certainly more enjoyable to read than that of many of his contemporaries.

A Gentleman's Gentleman with its interesting pair of rogues, one a gentleman, the other his valet and aide, predates Raffles and Bunny by three years. Of his other books in the genre, the best are *Jewel Mysteries I Have Known, The Diary of a Scoundrel, The Mystery of the Green Heart,* and *John Dighton, Mystery Millionaire.* Each of these is written with care and attention and shows the hand of a writer a little above normal standards.

—Derek Adley and W. O. G. Lofts

PENDLETON, Don(ald Eugene). Also writes as Dan Britain; Stephan Gregory. American. Born in Little Rock, Arkansas, 12 December 1927. Served in the United States Navy, 1942–47, 1952–54: Naval Commendation Medal, Iwo Jima, 1945. Married Marjorie Williamson in 1946; two daughters and four sons. Telegrapher, Southern Pacific Railroad, San Francisco, 1948–55; Air Traffic Control Specialist, Federal Aviation Administration, Western Region, 1957–61; Engineering Supervisor, Martin Company, Denver, 1961–64; Engineering Administrator, General Electric, NASA-Mississippi Test Facility, 1964–66, and Lockheed Corporation, Marietta, Georgia, 1966–67: Participated in the Titan II project, NASA Moonshot, and United States Air Force C-5 Galaxy program. Senior Editor and Columnist, *Orion* magazine, 1967–70. Agent: Scott Meredith Literary Agency Inc., 845 Third Avenue, New York, New York 10022. Address: 4595 North Maple Grove Road, Bloomington, Indiana 47401, U.S.A.

CRIME PUBLICATIONS

Novels (series character: Mack Bolan, The Executioner in all books)

War Against the Mafia. New York, Pinnacle, 1969; London, Sphere, 1973.
Death Squad. New York, Pinnacle, 1969; London, Sphere, 1973.
Battle Mask. New York, Pinnacle, 1970; London, Sphere, 1973.
Miami Massacre. New York, Pinnacle, 1970; London, Corgi, 1973.
Continental Contract. New York, Pinnacle, 1971; London, Sphere, 1973.
Assault on Soho. New York, Pinnacle, 1971; London, Corgi, 1973.
Nightmare in New York. New York, Pinnacle, 1971; London, Corgi, 1973.
Chicago Wipe-Out. New York, Pinnacle, 1971; London, Corgi, 1973.
Vegas Vendetta. New York, Pinnacle, 1971; London, Corgi, 1973.
Caribbean Kill. New York, Pinnacle, 1972; London, Corgi, 1973.

California Hit. New York, Pinnacle, 1972; London, Corgi, 1974.
Boston Blitz. New York, Pinnacle, 1972; London, Corgi, 1974.
Washington IOU. New York, Pinnacle, 1972; London, Corgi, 1974.
San Diego Siege. New York, Pinnacle, 1972; London, Corgi, 1974.
Panic in Philly. New York, Pinnacle, 1973; London, Corgi, 1975.
Jersey Guns. New York, Pinnacle, 1974; London, Corgi, 1975.
Texas Storm. New York, Pinnacle, 1974; London, Corgi, 1975.
Detroit Deathwatch. New York, Pinnacle, 1974; London, Corgi, 1976.
New Orleans Knockout. New York, Pinnacle, 1974; London, Corgi, 1976.
Firebase Seattle. New York, Pinnacle, 1975; London, Corgi, 1976.
Hawaiian Hellground. New York, Pinnacle, 1975; London, Corgi, 1976.
Canadian Crisis. New York, Pinnacle, 1975; London, Corgi, 1977.
St. Louis Showdown. New York, Pinnacle, 1975; London, Corgi, 1977.
Colorado Kill-Zone. New York, Pinnacle, 1976; London, Corgi, 1977.
Acapulco Rampage. New York, Pinnacle, 1976; London, Corgi, 1977.

Dixie Convoy. New York, Pinnacle, 1976; London, Corgi, 1978.
Savage Fire. New York, Pinnacle, 1977; London, Corgi, 1978.
Command Strike. New York, Pinnacle, 1977; London, Corgi, 1978.
Cleveland Pipeline. Los Angeles, Pinnacle, 1977; London, Corgi, 1978.
Arizona Ambush. Los Angeles, Pinnacle, 1977; London, Corgi, 1979.
Tennessee Smash. Los Angeles, Pinnacle, 1978; London, Corgi, 1979.
Monday's Mob. Los Angeles, Pinnacle, 1978; London, Corgi, 1979.
Terrible Tuesday. Los Angeles, Pinnacle, 1979; London, Corgi, 1980.
Wednesday's Wrath. Los Angeles, Pinnacle, 1979; London, Corgi, 1980.
Thermal Thursday. Los Angeles, Pinnacle, 1979; London, Corgi, 1980.
Friday's Feast. Los Angeles, Pinnacle, 1979; London, Corgi, 1980.

Novels as Stephan Gregory (series character: Stewart Mann in all books except *Frame Up*)

Frame Up. Fresno, California, Vega, 1960.
The Insatiables. New York, Pinnacle, 1967.
The Sex Goddess. New York, Pinnacle, 1967.
Madame Murder. Las Vegas, Neva, 1967.
The Sexy Saints. San Diego, PEC, 1967.
The Hot One. San Diego, PEC, 1967.

Uncollected Short Story

"Willing to Kill," in *The Great American Detective*, edited by William Kittredge and
   Steven M. Krauzer. New York, New American Library, 1978.

OTHER PUBLICATIONS

Novels

All the Trimmings (as Stephan Gregory). New York, Tower, 1966.
The Huntress (as Stephan Gregory). New York, Pinnacle, 1966.
Color Her Adultress (as Stephan Gregory). North Hollywood, Brandon, 1967.
All Lovers Accepted (as Stephan Gregory). San Diego, Greenleaf, 1968.
Revolt. New York, Pinnacle, 1968; revised edition, as *Civil War II*, New York,
   Pinnacle, 1971.
The Olympians. San Diego, Greenleaf, 1969.
Cataclysm. New York, Pinnacle, 1969.
The Guns of Terra 10. New York, Pinnacle, 1970.

1989: Population Doomsday.   New York, Pinnacle, 1970.
The Godmakers (as Dan Britain).   New York, Pinnacle, 1970.

Short Stories

All Heart.   Lakemont, Georgia, Orion, 1968.
The Day God Appeared.   Lakemont, Georgia, Orion, 1968.

Play

Screenplay: *The Executioner*, 1980.

Verse

The Search.   Lakemont, Georgia, CSA Press, 1967.
The Place.   Lakemont, Georgia, CSA Press, 1967.

Other as Stephan Gregory

How to Achieve Sexual Ecstasy.   Los Angeles, Sherbourne Press, 1968; London,
   Running Man Press, 1969.
The Sexually Insatiable Female.   Los Angeles, Sherbourne Press, 1968.
Hypnosis and the Sexual Life.   San Diego, Greenleaf, 1968.
Religion and the Sexual Life.   San Diego, Greenleaf, 1968.
Society and the Sexual Life.   San Diego, Greenleaf, 1968.
Sex and the Supernatural.   San Diego, Greenleaf, 1968.
ESP and the Sex Mystique.   San Diego, Greenleaf, 1968.
Dialogues on Human Sexuality.   San Diego, Greenleaf, 1968.
Secret Sex Desires.   San Diego, Greenleaf, 1968.
The Sexuality Gap.   San Diego, Greenleaf, 1968.
Hypnosis and the Free Female.   San Diego, Greenleaf, 1969.

Other as Don Pendleton

The Truth about Sex.   San Diego, Greenleaf, 1969.
The Executioner's War Book.   New York, Pinnacle, 1977.

Manuscript Collection: Lilly Library, Indiana University, Bloomington.

Don Pendleton comments:
   I am a "mystery writer" only by the broadest of definitions – and only, I fear, because
there is no more acceptable genre of fiction under which my Executioner novels may travel.
By the same sense and reasoning, I am a "romance writer" (*The Huntress*, etc.), a "SciFi
writer" (*The Godmakers*, etc.), a "sex writer" (*The Truth About Sex*, etc.), a "metaphysical
writer" (CSA Press and Orion Magazine), and a "futurist" (*Cataclysm*, etc.). Put all that
together and what you have is a guy with no formal training as a writer, working entirely at
the gut level within no particular genre, who blindly struck it lucky and thereafter found
himself being shaped by forces beyond his direction and control. And although the
Executioner series is far and away my most "significant" contribution to world literature, I
still do not perceive myself as "belonging" to any particular literary niche. I am simply a

storyteller, an entertainer who hopes to enthrall with visions of the reader's own incipient greatness. But go ahead: call me a mystery writer; I am proud to wear the label.

*   *   *

The detective in popular literature has manifested himself in a diversity of incarnations as the mystery genre has changed and evolved. Largely, the changes which the field has witnessed have been those of innovation and variation, not creation. The nature of the mystery story itself has not been altered significantly since Poe, though the fiction detective, always a product of his time, has changed in response to sociological and cultural trends. Don Pendleton, through his series of novels about Mack Bolan, the self-styled Executioner, is a recent innovator whose work has had an impact on the genre. Just as, decades earlier, Carroll John Daly inadvertently created the hard-boiled detective when he transformed the American cowboy into the modern private eye, Don Pendleton has transplanted the combat soldier into the urban jungle and thereby initiated a splinter movement within the mystery field.

The Executioner books typify a sub-genre of novels of violence which derive from the mystery story, but which repudiate the mystery's *raison d'être*, the very element of mystery itself. They are allied with the suspense story, but appear to owe an equal debt to the war novel. Trace elements of the hard-boiled style also can be found (Pendleton, prior to his creation of the Executioner, wrote tongue-in-cheek private eye novels under the pseudonym Stephan Gregory), but the sentimentalism of the hard-boiled school is replaced by macho philosophy ("Live large and stay hard") and the writing cobbles together underworld slang, ("The guy had *hitman* written all over him") military jargon ("My recon is complete and target identification positive"), and purple prose ("The hellfire trail had only just begun").

Traditionally, the detective in fiction has concerned himself with unraveling mysteries and unmasking the guilty in order to bring the latter to justice (of whatever kind). His motivations vary from the professional to the idealistic, not excluding the vengeful. Mack Bolan is not a detective, however; he is a trained combat veteran engaged in a crusade against organized crime as symbolized by the Mafia. Accordingly, he applies the skills and tactics of the jungle soldier in lieu of the detective's tools. These include reconnaissance, infiltration, psychological warfare, mechanized assault, and assassination. Detection and deduction are eschewed in favor of intelligence gathering and, less convincingly, "jungle instinct." Where the familiar circumstances of kidnapping (*Boston Blitz*) and murder (*Nightmare in New York*) do appear, they exist only as justifications for specific battles in an ongoing city-by-city campaign of extermination.

Central to the Executioner canon is the theme of the lone man of vengeance committed to a struggle against an overpoweringly corrupt economic and political machine. Mack Bolan is the Everyman of the 1970's, relying on the technology of violence and destruction, who plays the multiple roles of rescuer (*Boston Blitz*), Robin Hood (*Vegas Vendetta*), counter-revolutionary (*Washington IOU*), and assassin (*Command Strike*).

Implicit in the character is a philosophy, ostensibly one of good versus evil and the affirmation of life, but which, under scrutiny, reveals itself to be confused and contradictory. Mack Bolan believes in the sanctity of life, yet engages in wholesale slaughter. An anarchist who is pledged to preserve society, he refuses official sanction because he is unable to reconcile the necessity of his crusade with its illegality. This dilemma is an extension of the moral confusion over Vietnam (as is Mack Bolan's war of attrition) in which the common man is ground between the rocks of evident neccessity and obvious immorality. Here, perhaps, lies the key to the success of Pendleton's creation.

—Will Murray

PENDOWER, Jacques.   See **JACOBS, T. C. H.**

PENTECOST, Hugh.   Pseudonym for Judson (Pentecost) Philips.   American.   Born in Northfield, Massachusetts, 10 August 1903. Educated in London; Mohegan Lake Military Academy; Columbia University, New York, A.B. 1925. Married Norma Burton in 1951; one son; one daughter and two sons by a former marriage. Sports Report for New York *Tribune* while in high school; contributor to pulps and slicks in 1940's and 1950's. Co-Owner and Editor, Harlem Valley *Times*, 1949–56; Founder and Producer, Sharon Playhouse, Connecticut, 1950–77; political columnist and book reviewer, Lakeville *Journal*; radio talk show host, WTOR, Terrington, Connecticut. Past President, Mystery Writers of America. Recipient: Mystery Writers of America Grand Master Award, 1973. Agent: Brandt and Brandt, 101 Park Avenue, New York, New York 10017. Address: Emmons Lane, Canaan, Connecticut 06018, U.S.A.

CRIME PUBLICATIONS

Novels (series characters: Luke Bradley; Pierre Chambrun; John Jericho; Lieutenant Pascal; Julian Quist; Grant Simon; Dr. John Smith)

Cancelled in Red (Bradley).   New York, Dodd Mead, and London, Heinemann, 1939.
The 24th Horse (Bradley).   New York, Dodd Mead, 1940; London, Hale, 1951.
I'll Sing at Your Funeral (Bradley).   New York, Dodd Mead, 1942; London, Hale, 1945.
The Brass Chills (Bradley).   New York, Dodd Mead, 1943; London, Hale, 1944.
Cat and Mouse.   New York, Royce, 1945.
The Dead Man's Tale.   New York, Royce, 1945.
Memory of Murder (3 novelets; Smith).   New York, Ziff Davis, 1947.
Where the Snow Was Red (Smith).   New York, Dodd Mead, 1949; London, Hale, 1951.
Shadow of Madness (Smith).   New York, Dodd Mead, 1950.
Chinese Nightmare.   New York, Dell, 1951.
Lieutenant Pascal's Tastes in Homicide.   New York, Dodd Mead, 1954; London, Boardman, 1955.
The Assassins.   New York, Dodd Mead, 1955.
The Obituary Club (Simon).   New York, Dodd Mead, 1958; London, Boardman, 1959.
The Lonely Target (Simon).   New York, Dodd Mead, 1959; London, Boardman, 1960.
The Kingdom of Death.   New York, Dodd Mead, 1960; London, Boardman, 1961.
The Deadly Friend.   New York, Dodd Mead, 1961; London, Boardman, 1962.
Choice of Violence.   New York, Dodd Mead, 1961; London, Boardman, 1962.
The Cannibal Who Overate (Chambrun).   New York, Dodd Mead, 1962; London, Boardman, 1963.
The Tarnished Angel.   New York, Dodd Mead, and London, Boardman, 1963.
Only the Rich Die Young (Pascal).   New York, Dodd Mead, and London, Boardman, 1964.
The Shape of Fear (Chambrun).   New York, Dodd Mead, and London, Boardman, 1964.
Sniper (Jericho).   New York, Dodd Mead, 1965; London, Boardman, 1966.

The Evil That Men Do (Chambrun).   New York, Dodd Mead, and London, Boardman, 1966.
Hide Her from Every Eye (Jericho).   New York, Dodd Mead, and London, Boardman, 1966.
The Creeping Hours (Jericho).   New York, Dodd Mead, 1966; London, Boardman, 1967.
Dead Woman of the Year (Jericho).   New York, Dodd Mead, 1967; London, Macdonald, 1968.
The Golden Trap (Chambrun).   New York, Dodd Mead, 1967; London, Macdonald, 1968.
The Gilded Nightmare (Chambrun).   New York, Dodd Mead, 1968; London, Gollancz, 1969.
Girl Watcher's Funeral (Chambrun).   New York, Dodd Mead, 1969; London, Gollancz, 1970.
The Girl with Six Fingers (Jericho).   New York, Dodd Mead, 1969; London, Gollancz, 1970.
A Plague of Violence (Jericho).   New York, Dodd Mead, 1970; London, Hale, 1972.
The Deadly Joke (Chambrun).   New York, Dodd Mead, 1971; London, Hale, 1972.
Don't Drop Dead Tomorrow (Quist).   New York, Dodd Mead, 1971; London, Hale, 1973.
The Champagne Killer (Quist).   New York, Dodd Mead, 1972; London, Hale, 1974.
Birthday, Deathday (Chambrun).   New York, Dodd Mead, 1972; London, Hale, 1975.
The Beautiful Dead (Quist).   New York, Dodd Mead, 1973; London, Hale, 1975.
Walking Dead Man (Chambrun).   New York, Dodd Mead, 1973; London, Hale, 1975.
Bargain with Death (Chambrun).   New York, Dodd Mead, 1974; London, Hale, 1976.
The Judas Freak (Quist).   New York, Dodd Mead, 1974; London, Hale, 1976.
Time of Terror (Chambrun).   New York, Dodd Mead, 1975.
Honeymoon with Death (Quist).   New York, Dodd Mead, 1975; London, Hale, 1976.
Backlash.   New York, Dodd Mead, 1976.
Die after Dark.   New York, Dodd Mead, 1976; London, Hale, 1977.
The Fourteen Dilemma.   New York, Dodd Mead, 1976; London, Hale, 1977.
Five Roads to Death.   New York, Dodd Mead, 1977.
The Day the Children Vanished.   London, Hale, 1977.
The Steel Palace (Quist).   New York, Dodd Mead, 1977; London, Hale, 1978.
Murder as Usual.   New York, Dodd Mead, 1977; London, Hale, 1978.
Death after Breakfast (Chambrun).   New York, Dodd Mead, 1978; London, Hale, 1979.
Deadly Trap (Quist).   New York, Dodd Mead, 1978; London, Hale, 1979.
Random Killer (Chambrun).   New York, Dodd Mead, 1979.
The Homicidal Horse (Quist).   New York, Dodd Mead, 1979.

Novels as Judson Philips (series characters: Coyle and Donovan; Peter Styles; Carole Trevor and Max Blythe)

Red War, with Thomas M. Johnson.   New York, Doubleday, 1936.
The Death Syndicate (Trevor and Blythe).   New York, Washburn, 1938; London, Hurst and Blackett, 1939.
Death Delivers a Postcard (Trevor and Blythe).   New York, Washburn, 1939; London, Hurst and Blackett, 1940.
Murder in Marble.   New York, Dodd Mead, 1940; London, Hale, 1950.
Odds on the Hot Seat (Coyle and Donovan).   New York, Dodd Mead, 1941; London, Hale, 1946.
The Fourteenth Trump (Coyle and Donovan).   New York, Dodd Mead, 1942; London, Hale, 1951.
Killer on the Catwalk.   New York, Dodd Mead, 1959; London, Gollancz, 1960.

Whisper Town.   New York, Dodd Mead, 1960; London, Gollancz, 1961.
Murder Clear, Track Fast.   New York, Dodd Mead, 1961; London, Gollancz, 1962.
A Dead Ending.   New York, Dodd Mead, 1962; London, Gollancz, 1963.
The Dead Can't Love.   New York, Dodd Mead, and London, Gollancz, 1963.
The Laughter Trap (Styles).   New York, Dodd Mead, 1964; London, Gollancz, 1965.
The Black Glass City (Styles).   New York, Dodd Mead, and London, Gollancz, 1965.
The Twisted People (Styles).   New York, Dodd Mead, and London, Gollancz, 1965.
The Wings of Madness (Styles).   New York, Dodd Mead, 1966; London, Gollancz, 1967.
Thursday's Folly (Styles).   New York, Dodd Mead, 1967; London, Gollancz, 1968.
Hot Summer Killing (Styles).   New York, Dodd Mead, 1968; London, Gollancz, 1969.
Nightmare at Dawn (Styles).   New York, Dodd Mead, 1970; London, Gollancz, 1971.
Escape a Killer (Styles).   New York, Dodd Mead, 1971; London, Gollancz, 1972.
The Vanishing Senator (Styles).   New York, Dodd Mead, 1972; London, Gollancz, 1973.
The Larkspur Conspiracy (Styles).   New York, Dodd Mead, 1973; London, Gollancz, 1974.
The Power Killers (Styles).   New York, Dodd Mead, 1974; London, Gollancz, 1975.
Walk a Crooked Mile (Styles).   New York, Dodd Mead, 1975; London, Gollancz, 1976.
A Murder Arranged (Styles).   New York, Dodd Mead, 1978; London, Gollancz, 1979.
Why Murder (Styles).   New York, Dodd Mead, 1979.

Short Stories

Secret Corridors.   New York, Century, 1945.
Death Wears a Copper Necktie and Other Stories.   London, Edwards, 1946.
Around Dark Corners.   New York, Dodd Mead, 1970.

Uncollected Short Stories

"Pierre Chambrun and the Last Fling," in *Ellery Queen's Mystery Magazine* (New York), September 1971.
"Jericho and the Dead Clue," in *Ellery Queen's Mystery Magazine* (New York), December 1971.
"Pierre Chambrun Defends Himself," in *Ellery Queen's Mystery Magazine* (New York), November 1972.
"Jericho and the Two Ways to Die," in *Ellery Queen's Crookbook.*   New York, Random House, 1974.
"Blood-Red in the Morning," in *Ellery Queen's Masters of Mystery.*   New York, Davis, 1975.
"The Dark Plan," in *Ellery Queen's Mystery Magazine* (New York), February 1976.
"The Dark Gambit," in *Ellery Queen's Mystery Magazine* (New York), March 1976.
"The Dark Encounter," in *Ellery Queen's Mystery Magazine* (New York), April 1976.
"The Dark Maneuver," in *Ellery Queen's Mystery Magazine* (New York), August 1976.
"Jericho on Campus," in *Ellery Queen's Mystery Magazine* (New York), October 1976.
"The Dark Intuition," in *Ellery Queen's Mystery Magazine* (New York), December 1976.
"Chambrun and the Matter of Inches," in *Ellery Queen's Mystery Magazine* (New York), February 1977.
"The Show Must Go On," in *Ellery Queen's Mystery Magazine* (New York), July 1977.
"The Dark Gamble: End of the Trail," in *Ellery Queen's Mystery Magazine* (New York), October 1977.
"Jericho and the Unknown Lover," in *Ellery Queen's Searches and Seizures.*   New York, Davis, 1977.

"Chambrun Plays It Cool," in *Ellery Queen's Who's Who of Whodunits*.   New York, Davis, 1977.
"Jericho Plays It Cool," in *Ellery Queen's Who's Who of Whodunits*.   New York, Davis, 1977.
"The Birthday Killer," in *Ellery Queen's Mystery Magazine* (New York), July 1978.
"Chambrun Corrects an Imperfection," in *Ellery Queen's Mystery Magazine* (New York), October 1978.
"Jericho and the Deadly Errand," in *Ellery Queen's Masters of Mystery*.   New York, Davis, 1978.
"Jericho and the Million-to-One Clue," in *Ellery Queen's Mystery Magazine* (New York), February 1979.
"The Man Who Stirred Champagne," in *Ellery Queen's Mystery Magazine* (New York), September 1979.

OTHER PUBLICATIONS

Plays

Lonely Boy (produced Sharon, Connecticut, 1954).
The Lame Duck Party (produced Sharon, Connecticut, 1977).

Radio Plays: *Suspense*; *Father Brown*; *The Whisper Men*.

Television Plays: *The Web*; *The Ray Milland Show*; *Studio One*; *Hallmark Hall of Fame*.

Other

Hold 'em Girls: The Intelligent Woman's Guide to Men and Football, with Robert W. Wood, Jr.   New York, Putnam, 1936.
"The Short Story," in *How I Write*, with Robert Hayden and Lawson Carter.   New York, Harcourt Brace, 1972.

Editor, *Cream of the Crime*.   New York, Dodd Mead, 1961.

Judson P. Philips comments:
I suppose, after you have written more than a hundred mystery and suspense novels and hundreds of short stories, the most frequently asked question is, "Where do you get your plots?" It has been said that there are only 36 dramatic situations, only about half of which are not too raunchy to use. Those usable situations have been used by me and hundreds of other writers over and over again. The only variation any writer has is the people he writes about. There are endless variations in people. I once used to claim a deduction on my income tax for "saloon talk," explaining in a note that people were the source of my income and that I had to go where they were and listen to them. The IRS approved but insisted that I call it "research." The name of the game is people, and they are endlessly rewarding, never uninteresting, and where everything begins and ends.

*   *   *

"Professional" is the word most often applied to Judson Philips, whether he writes under his own name or his better-known pseudonym, Hugh Pentecost. Critics, using that adjective, refer to the length of his writing career and the volume of words he has produced, with surprisingly good quality. Philips's own definition of a "professional writer" showed he had few illusions; he felt he had reached that status when "I actually paid the rent and fed myself on the product of my typewriter."

His career began when still a senior at Columbia University. By 1936 Philips had turned to books and began to create the large number of series detectives that are his hallmark. His early series detectives, compared with his later creations, tended to be bland. Luke Bradley is a soft-spoken Inspector of the New York City Police. In physical appearance psychiatrist-detective John Smith is as difficult to remember as his name. Lt. Pascal is a casual, good-natured policeman who is not above an apology to a suspect if that will make his interrogation easier.

Recent detectives tend to be more easily remembered. Pentecost has written of George Crowder in the novel *Choice of Violence* and in ten short stories, nine of which were collected in *Around Dark Corners*. One of these, "My Dear Uncle Sherlock," emphasizes the relationship between 12-year-old Joey Trimble and his uncle George, who was once a County Prosecutor with a brilliant political future. He gave it all up and went into seclusion when it was shown that a man he had sent to the electric chair had been innocent. However, he is not too far removed from society to be unwilling to provide counsel and friendship for his nephew and the solution to local murders. If Hugh Pentecost's next series detective, Pierre Chambrun, who first appeared in the intriguingly titled *The Cannibal Who Overate*, is not physically distinctive, his milieu certainly is. Resident-manager of New York's luxury Hotel Beaumont, he functions as "Mayor" of his own small city, meanwhile infecting his staff with what one character calls "Chambrun's Disease, a passion for the smooth running of the hotel." When crime threatens to disturb his hotel's calm and reputation, Chambrun steps in as detective, using his organizing ability, intelligence, and the experience he gained as an agent in his native France's World War II underground. *Newsday*'s columnist Peter Styles is a crusader with a reason for his vendetta against criminals. In *The Laughter Trap*, first in a series of slickly written novels, he loses one leg in an automobile accident arranged by some gangsters he had exposed. The giant (6'6'', 240 pound) painter, John Jericho, is a crusader whose stature, flaming red beard, and Viking-like appearance make him stand out. The Jericho series is marred by simple plotting and simpler, intrusive moralizing. Jericho's involvement in crimes is more difficult to believe than in most series because with disturbing frequency he comes upon a crime while driving or when one of his ex-lovers has called to ask his help. Julian Quist, whose first appearance was in *Don't Drop Dead Tomorrow*, is a very "mod" public relations man. Jason Dark has been hero of a series of short stories, which began in 1976, telling of the battle of a middle-aged detective against Quadrant International, a multi-national corporation responsible for a large portion of the world's crime. When Dark refuses to stop investigating them, their agents beat him brutally, causing the amputation of one hand.

When a writer produces as much fiction as Pentecost, subject matter becomes difficult to come by. Increasingly, he has gone to current events. In the early 1960's he published stories about crime on New York's waterfronts. The Chambrun series frequently has involved crime on an international scale with the UN, terrorism, and spying involved. A 1965 short story, "Jericho and the Silent Witnesses," was clearly derivative of the Kitty Genovese case in Queens in which a young woman was murdered while 38 witnesses did nothing. A 1966 story, "Jericho and the à Go-Go Clue," seems as dated now as a story about the hoop skirt. In *Hot Summer Killing*, a Peter Styles novel, letters from an alleged black militant group promises destruction of Grand Central Terminal at rush hour if its demands are not met. In a bizarre event, newspaper headlines *followed* a Pentecost novelet in July 1976. A busload of children in California disappeared, and while police searched, a reader called the FBI to point out the similarity to his "The Day the Children Vanished" (1958). The children and their kidnappers were discovered, and there was no evidence that the plot had been actually based on the story. However, a paperback publisher did capitalize on the publicity by having Pentecost expand his work into a novel.

Philips is often at his best in stories about children. In addition to those already described, "Lonely Boy," "The Lame Duck House Party," and "A Kind of Murder," all stories about boys' schools, are outstanding, giving evidence of greater subtlety than most of his work.

Even *Sniper*, the first Jericho novel, about the murder of the headmaster of a New England prep school, is generally regarded as the best in that series. In much of his work he gives evidence of careful research to provide authenticity and unusual backgrounds – e.g., *Cancelled in Red* about stamp collecting, *The 24th Horse* about a horse show at Madison Square Garden, and *The Brass Chills* about a New England submarine base.

A variety of New England settings appear in his short stories. Seldom, if ever, has the professionalism of Philips-Pentecost been as evident as in "In the Middle of Nowhere," a Crowder story. Suspense is derived as much from an impending hurricane as from the search for a murderer in this story of the rural Connecticut scene which the author describes so well.

—Marvin Lachman

PEROWNE, **Barry.** Pseudonym for Philip Atkey; also wrote as Pat Merriman. British. Born in Redlynch, Wiltshire, 25 June 1908. Educated at Central School, Oxford. Served in the Wiltshire Regiment of the British Army, 1940–43, and the Intelligence Corps, 1943–45; mentioned in despatches. Married Marjorie Florence Atkey in 1932 (divorced, 1946); one daughter. Worked for a manufacturer of carnival equipment, and as a secretary to Bertram Atkey, 1922–25; Assistant Editor, George Newnes Ltd., publishers, London, 1925–27. Agent: Michael Horniman, A. P. Watt and Son Ltd., 26–28 Bedford Row, London WC1R 4HL, England.

CRIME PUBLICATIONS

Novels (series character: A. J. Raffles)

Arrest These Men! London, Cassell, 1932.
Enemy of Women. London, Cassell, 1934.
Ladies in Retreat. London, Cassell, 1935.
She Married Raffles. London, Cassell, 1936.
Raffles' Crime in Gibraltar. London, Amalgamated Press, 1937; as *They Hang Them in Gibraltar*, New York, Curl, 1939.
Raffles vs. Sexton Blake. London, Amalgamated Press, 1937.
Ask No Mercy. London, Cassell, 1937.
I'm No Murderer. London, Cassell, 1938; New York, Curl, 1939.
The Girl on Zero. London, Cassell, 1939.
The A. R. P. Mystery (Raffles). London, Amalgamated Press, 1939.
The Whispering Cracksman. London, Cassell, 1940; as *Ten Words of Poison*, New York, Arcadia House, 1941.
Blonde Without Escort. London, Cassell, 1940.
Raffles and the Key Man. Philadelphia, Lippincott, 1940.
Gibraltar Prisoner. London, Cassell, 1942; as *All Exits Blocked*, New York, Arcadia House, 1942.
The Tilted Moon. London, Cassell, 1949; as *Rogues' Island*, New York, Mill, 1950.
A Singular Conspiracy. Indianapolis, Bobbs Merrill, 1974.

Novels as Philip Atkey

Blue Water Murder. London, Cassell, 1935.
Heirs of Merlin. London, Cassell, 1945.

Juniper Rock. London, Cassell, 1953.

Short Stories (series character: A. J. Raffles)

Raffles after Dark. London, Cassell, 1933; revised edition, as *The Return of Raffles,*
  New York, Day, 1933.
Raffles in Pursuit. London, Cassell, 1934.
Raffles under Sentence. London, Cassell, 1936.
Raffles Revisited. New York, Harper, 1974; London, Hamish Hamilton, 1975.
Raffles of the Albany. London, Hamish Hamilton, and New York, St. Martin's Press,
  1976.
Raffles of the M.C.C. New York, St. Martin's Press, and London, Macmillan, 1979.

OTHER PUBLICATIONS

Novel

Night Call (as Pat Merriman). London, Hutchinson, 1939.

Plays

Screenplay: *Walk a Crooked Path,* 1970.

Radio Plays: *Rescue from the Rock,* 1970; *Edgar and Charles,* 1970.

*   *   *

Although Barry Perowne has written other mystery novels, his reputation as a crime
writer will probably be based ultimately on his revival, in a series of magazine stories and
novels, of the character of Raffles, the celebrated turn-of-the-century Gentleman Crook. The
original Raffles, as created by E. W. Hornung in *The Amateur Cracksman,* 1899, is a
gentleman and sportsman (a champion cricketer – "the finest slow bowler of his decade")
who is also an expert burglar, a second calling which he takes to with all the ardor of the
sportsman and the passion of the artist. In fact, in talking of the perfectly executed burglary,
Hornung's Raffles evokes (and actually alludes to) the fin-de-siècle concern with art for art's
sake. But he also steals in order to keep himself and his cohort Bunny Manders in elegant
style at London's Albany and the various gentlemen's clubs which they frequent.
   Perowne's Raffles is a changed man. While the ardor of the sportsman remains, it is
tempered significantly by the addition of socially redeeming features: he still steals, but never
simply for gain or thrills; his thefts are now motivated by desire to aid others. An aristocratic
family fallen on hard times, a damsel in distress, an old friend unjustly menaced – in these
cases and many like them, Raffles and Bunny put their criminal skills to work for a higher
purpose. Perowne has laundered his Raffles, made him more socially acceptable (and
sentimentally romantic) than his morally ambiguous predecessor. But if Perowne's Raffles
has something less of the fascination of the pure criminal, this deficiency is made up for in
stories that are exciting, exotic, and frequently more richly evocative of the gaslit era of the
1890's than Hornung's originals.

—Frank Occhiogrosso

PERRY, Ritchie (John Allen). Also writes as John Allen. British. Born in King's Lynn, Norfolk, 7 January 1942. Educated at King Edward VII School, King's Lynn; St. John's College, Oxford, B.A. (honours) in history 1964. Married Lynn Perry in 1976; two daughters. Trainee Manager, Bank of London and South America, Brazil, 1964–66; Teacher, Docking, Norfolk, 1966, King's Lynn, 1967, Nottingham, 1967, and Ingoldisthorpe, Norfolk, 1967–74. Since 1975, Teacher for the Bedfordshire County Council, Luton. Agent: A. D. Peters and Company Ltd., 10 Buckingham Street, London WC2N 6BU. Address: 4 The Close, Limbury, Luton, Bedfordshire, England.

CRIME PUBLICATIONS

Novels (series character: Philis in all books)

> *The Fall Guy.* London, Collins, and Boston, Houghton Mifflin, 1972.
> *Nowhere Man.* London, Collins, 1973; as *A Hard Man to Kill*, Boston, Houghton Mifflin, 1973.
> *Ticket to Ride.* London, Collins, 1973; Boston, Houghton Mifflin, 1974.
> *Holiday with a Vengeance.* London, Collins, 1974; Boston, Houghton Mifflin, 1975.
> *Your Money and Your Wife.* London, Collins, 1975; Boston, Houghton Mifflin, 1976.
> *One Good Death Deserves Another.* London, Collins, 1976; Boston, Houghton Mifflin, 1977.
> *Dead End.* London, Collins, 1977.
> *Dutch Courage.* London, Collins, 1978.
> *Bishop's Pawn.* London, Collins, and New York, Pantheon, 1979.

Novels as John Allen

> *Copacabana Stud.* London, Hale, 1977.
> *Up Tight.* London, Hale, 1979.

OTHER PUBLICATIONS

Other

> *Brazil: The Land and Its People.* London, Macdonald, 1977.

Manuscript Collection: Mugar Memorial Library, Boston University.

Ritchie Perry comments:
There was never any stage in my childhood or adolescence when my ambition was to become an author. None of my teachers ever said, "Young Perry has the fires of creative genius burning inside him." To the best of my knowledge nobody has said it since. As with most things in my life, I drifted into writing. The local library could no longer provide me with the dozen or so books I needed each week and it occurred to me that I ought to be able to produce fiction of my own. As such my books are self-indulgences, designed as much to entertain me as any potential readers. A shocking admission, but there it is. If I knew how one of my books was going to finish before I started work on it, the book would never be typed out. It would bore me as much as it would to read a work by another author when I knew how the story was going to end. I suspect this may be one of the strengths of my stories – it must be very difficult for a reader to guess how a book will finish when the author isn't sure himself.

*   *   *

Ritchie Perry is one of the better writers of adventure thrillers, and the semi-political background adds rather than detracts from his books. The central character in all his novels is Philis, who works for Pawson in SR 2, a somewhat nebulous Government Department. The characterisation of Philis and Pawson is sound and is accompanied by a wry humour which tends to give the reader a sympathetic view of both men. Although the books are not short of violence, it is never violence for its own sake. Perry can tell a good story and his backgrounds, be they in Europe or South America, are obviously well researched. His villains usually have traits which make them very believable, if not likable, and the cynical approach of the writer rather adds than detracts from his characterisation of them.

There are no detective "knots" for the reader to unravel but the gradually mounting tension puts the books into the "hard to put down" class. Although there is plenty of suspense and violence, explicit sex is lacking, for which many readers will be thankful. There is no shortage of amorous female characters but even the "near love scenes" are dealt with in a wry and humorous way. Perry's best books so far are *Nowhere Man* and *Ticket to Ride*.

—Donald C. Ireland

PETERS, Elizabeth. Pseudonym for Barbara (Louise) G(ross) Mertz; also writes as Barbara Michaels. American. Born in Canton, Illinois, 29 September 1927. Educated at the University of Chicago Oriental Institute, Ph.D. 1952. Divorced; one daughter and one son. Address: c/o Dodd Mead and Co., 79 Madison Avenue, New York, New York 10016, U.S.A.

CRIME PUBLICATIONS

Novels (series characters: Vicky Bliss; Jacqueline Kirby)

The Jackal's Head. New York, Meredith, 1968; London, Jenkins, 1969.
The Camelot Caper. New York, Meredith, 1969; London, Cassell, 1976.
The Dead Sea Cipher. New York, Dodd Mead, 1970; London, Cassell, 1975.
The Night of Four Hundred Rabbits. New York, Dodd Mead, 1971; as *Shadows in the Moonlight*, London, Hodder and Stoughton, 1975.
The Seventh Sinner (Kirby). New York, Dodd Mead, 1972; London, Hodder and Stoughton, 1975.
Borrower of the Night (Bliss). New York, Dodd Mead, 1973; London, Cassell, 1974.
The Murders of Richard III (Kirby). New York, Dodd Mead, 1974.
Crocodile on the Sandbank. New York, Dodd Mead, 1975; London, Cassell, 1976.
Legend in Green Velvet. New York, Dodd Mead, 1976; London, Cassell, 1977.
Devil-May-Care. New York, Dodd Mead, 1977; London, Cassell, 1978.
Street of the Five Moons (Bliss). New York, Dodd Mead, 1978.
Summer of the Dragon. New York, Dodd Mead, 1979.

Novels as Barbara Michaels

The Master of Blacktower. New York, Appleton Century Crofts, 1966; London, Jenkins, 1967.
Sons of the Wolf. New York, Meredith, 1967; London, Jenkins, 1968.
Ammie, Come Home. New York, Meredith, 1968; London, Jenkins, 1969.

Prince of Darkness. New York, Meredith, 1969; London, Hodder and Stoughton, 1971.

The Dark on the Other Side. New York, Dodd Mead, 1970; London, Souvenir Press, 1973.

The Crying Child. New York, Dodd Mead, and London, Souvenir Press, 1973.

Greygallows. New York, Dodd Mead, 1972; London, Souvenir Press, 1974.

Witch. New York, Dodd Mead, 1973; London, Souvenir Press, 1975.

House of Many Shadows. New York, Dodd Mead, 1974; London, Souvenir Press, 1976.

The Sea King's Daughter. New York, Dodd Mead, 1975; London, Souvenir Press, 1977.

Patriot's Dream. New York, Dodd Mead, and London, Souvenir Press, 1976.

Wings of the Falcon. New York, Dodd Mead, 1977.

Wait for What Will Come. New York, Dodd Mead, 1978.

The Walker in Shadows. New York, Dodd Mead, 1979.

OTHER PUBLICATIONS

Other as Barbara G. Mertz.

Temples, Tombs, and Hieroglyphs: The Story of Egyptology. New York, Coward McCann, and, London, Gollancz, 1964; revised edition, New York, Dodd Mead, 1978.

Red Land, Black Land: The World of the Ancient Egyptians. New York, Coward McCann, 1966; London, Hodder and Stoughton, 1967; revised edition, New York, Dodd Mead, 1978.

Two Thousand Years in Rome, with Richard Mertz. New York, Coward McCann, 1968; London, Dent, 1969.

Manuscript Collection: Mugar Memorial Library, Boston University.

Elizabeth Peters comments:

Under my own name, I write popular non-fiction on Egyptology. Under two pseudonyms I write what are (in the United States) usually referred to as "gothics." I prefer the term "romantic suspense stories." "Barbara Michaels" concentrates on historical suspense and on novels with a supernatural atmosphere; "Elizabeth Peters" prefers modern settings, often with archaeological backgrounds, and she is much more frivolous in her approach than is Michaels – in fact, she is sometimes rather giddy. Having been trained in historical research I try to make my books as accurate as possible, and I believe that precise, accurate detail is necessary in order to create an impression of authenticity.

*   *   *

Elizabeth Peters is the detective pseudonym of the split literary personality of Barbara Mertz. As Barbara Michaels, she has published a number of gothic romances. In the Peters novels, some elements of the gothic are retained in what are primarily detective/suspense novels. The heroine is active and endangered; a small group of attractive men competes for the heroine's attention or her hand; and in about half the novels someone wins it. One of the pleasures of these entertainments is the readiness with which Peters turns gothic conventions upside down. In *The Night of Four Hundred Rabbits*, the darkly handsome, ruthlessly suave character who should metamorphose into the hero is revealed as a thorough villain. The stand-by suitor, an American boy-next-door, is corrupted by drugs into the villain's dupe, and the character introduced as a drunken lecher turns out to be the brave, if not brilliant, hero. *Borrower of the Night* and *Street of the Five Moons* have for their heroine a Ph.D. in history who is nearly six feet tall, and chary of marriage on principle. At the end of the first novel, true to her code, she refused two suitors, planning instead on being courted by both for an indefinite period. At the end of the second novel, she has added a jewel thief to her retinue. The heroine of both *The Seventh Sinner* and *The Murders of Richard III* is a middle-aged librarian and scholar with two grown children, an overstuffed handbag, and a steel trap mind.

Mertz has written under her own name on Egyptology. Not surprisingly, each of the Peters novels works in some scholarly notes on the more flamboyant aspects of the country in which it is set. *The Jackal's Head* provides a convincing account of the imagined discovery of Nefertiti's tomb, and *Crocodile on the Sandbank* gives a glimpse of the state of Egyptology in the 19th century. The vexed question of Richard III's guilt gets a lucid summary in *The Murders of Richard III*. *Legend in Green Velvet* interweaves the history of the Highlands and Bonnie Prince Charlie with a running argument between the hero and heroine on the virtue of the romantic temperament. And *The Dead Sea Cipher* imagines the discovery of a contemporary life of Christ and Mary, and then suggests a highly plausible fate for those invaluable documents.

Peters writes in a semi-pastoral world, in which reality intrudes, but never too much. A number of her villains come from the academic world, one driven mad by its insatiable demand for original brilliance, and several driven to crime by academic poverty. Her heroines see the realities of peasant life in the Near East, but they move mostly through the sunlight of their own good humor, common sense, and intelligence. At the top of her form, Peters can provide light entertainment that is as highly polished as it is full of fun. In *Crocodile on the Sandbank* Peters uses almost every cliché character and plot twist of Victorian fiction, and in perfect consciousness of the age of these skeletons gives them new comic flesh. The archeologist hero glooms like Rochester until he is subdued by the heroine, a sort of Dorothea Brooke in hiking boots. Here, as in all the Peters books, the action is fast and the dialogue is crisp.

—Carol Cleveland

PETERS, Ellis. Pseudonym for Edith Mary Pargeter. British. Born in Horsehay, Shropshire, 28 September 1913. Educated at Dawley Church of England Elementary School, Shropshire; Coalbrookdale High School for Girls, Oxford School Certificate. Served in the Women's Royal Navy Service, 1940–45: British Empire Medal, 1944. Worked as a chemist's assistant, Dawley, 1933–40. Recipient: Mystery Writers of America Edgar Allan Poe Award, 1963; Czechoslovak Society for International Relations Gold Medal, 1968. Fellow, International Institute of Arts and Letters, 1961. Agent: Deborah Owen, 78 Narrow Street, London E14 8BP. Address: Parkville, Park Lane, Madeley, Telford, Shropshire TF7 5HE, England.

CRIME PUBLICATIONS

Novels (series characters: Brother Cadfael; members of the Felse family – Inspector George Felse, Bunty Felse, Dominic Felse)

   Fallen into the Pit (Felse; as Edith Pargeter). London, Heinemann, 1951.
   Death Mask. London, Collins, 1959; New York, Doubleday, 1960.

The Will and the Deed (Felse).   London, Collins, 1960; as *Where There's a Will*, New
   York, Doubleday, 1960; as *The Will and the Deed*, New York, Avon, 1966.
Death and the Joyful Woman (Felse).   London, Collins, 1961; New York, Doubleday,
   1962.
Funeral of Figaro.   London, Collins, 1962; New York, Morrow, 1964.
Flight of a Witch (Felse).   London, Collins, 1964.
A Nice Derangement of Epitaphs (Felse).   London, Collins, 1965; as *Who Lies Here?*,
   New York, Morrow, 1965.
The Piper on the Mountain (Felse).   London, Collins, and New York, Morrow, 1966.
Black Is the Colour of My True-Love's Heart (Felse).   London, Collins, and New York,
   Doubleday, 1967.
The Grass-Widow's Tale (Felse).   London, Collins, and New York, Doubleday, 1968.
The House of Green Turf (Felse).   London, Collins, and New York, Morrow, 1969.
Mourning Raga (Felse).   London, Macmillan, 1969; New York, Morrow, 1970.
The Knocker on Death's Door (Felse).   London, Macmillan, 1970; New York, Morrow,
   1971.
Death to the Landlords! (Felse).   London, Macmillan, and New York, Morrow, 1972.
City of Gold and Shadows (Felse).   London, Macmillan, 1973; New York, Morrow,
   1974.
The Horn of Roland.   London, Macmillan, and New York, Morrow, 1974.
Never Pick Up Hitch-Hikers!   London, Macmillan, and New York, Morrow, 1976.
A Morbid Taste for Bones: A Mediaeval Whodunnit (Cadfael).   London, Macmillan,
   1977; New York, Morrow, 1978.
Rainbow's End (Felse).   London, Macmillan, 1978; New York, Morrow, 1979.
One Corpse Too Many (Cadfael).   London, Macmillan, 1979.

Short Stories

The Assize of the Dying (as Edith Pargeter).   London, Heinemann, and New York,
   Doubleday, 1958.

Uncollected Short Stories

"The Chestnut Calf," in *This Week* (New York), December 1963.
"With Regrets," in *This Week* (New York), May 1965.
"Golden Girl," in *Alfred Hitchcock Presents: Stories Not for the Nervous.*   New York,
   Random House, 1965.
"Villa for Sale," in *This Week* (New York), December 1965.
"A Grain of Mustard Seed," in *This Week* (New York), January 1966.
"Guide to Doom," in *Alfred Hitchcock Presents: Stories That Scared Even Me.*   New
   York, Random House, 1967.
"Maiden Garland," in *Winter's Crimes 1*, edited by George Hardinge.   London,
   Macmillan, 1969.
"The Trinity Cat," in *Winter's Crimes 8*, edited by Hilary Watson.   London,
   Macmillan, 1976.

OTHER PUBLICATIONS as Edith Pargeter

Novels

Hortensius, Friend of Nero.   London, Lovat Dickson, 1936; New York, Greystone
   Press, 1937.
Iron-Bound.   London, Lovat Dickson, 1936.
The City Lies Foursquare.   London, Heinemann, and New York, Reynal, 1939.

Ordinary People. London, Heinemann, 1941; as *People of My Own*, New York, Reynal, 1942.
She Goes to War. London, Heinemann, 1942.
The Eighth Champion of Christendom. London, Heinemann, 1945.
Reluctant Odyssey. London, Heinemann, 1946.
Warfare Accomplished. London, Heinemann, 1947.
The Fair Young Phoenix. London, Heinemann, 1948.
By Firelight. London, Heinemann, 1948; as *By This Strange Fire*, New York, Reynal, 1948.
Lost Children. London, Heinemann, 1951.
Holiday with Violence. London, Heinemann, 1952.
This Rough Magic. London, Heinemann, 1953.
Most Loving Mere Folly. London, Heinemann, 1953.
The Soldier at the Door. London, Heinemann, 1954.
A Means of Grace. London, Heinemann, 1956.
The Heaven Tree. London, Heinemann, and New York, Doubleday, 1960.
The Green Branch. London, Heinemann, 1962.
The Scarlet Seed. London, Heinemann, 1963.
A Bloody Field by Shrewsbury. London, Macmillan, 1972; New York, Viking Press, 1973.
Sunrise in the West. London, Macmillan, 1974.
Dragon at Noonday Sun. London, Macmillan, 1975.
Hounds of Sunset. London, Macmillan, 1976.
Afterglow and Nightfall. London, Macmillan, 1977.
The Marriage of Meggotta. London, Macmillan, and New York, Viking Press, 1979.

Short Stories

The Lily Hand and Other Stories. London, Macmillan, 1965.

Plays

Radio Plays: *Mourning Raga* (as Ellis Peters), from her own novel, 1971; *The Heaven Tree*, 1975.

Other

The Coast of Bohemia. London, Heinemann, 1950.
"The Thriller Is a Novel," in *Techniques of Novel-Writing*, edited by A. S. Burack. Boston, The Writer, 1973.

Translator, *Tales of the Little Quarter: Stories*, by Jan Neruda. London, Heinemann, 1957; New York, Greenwood Press, 1976.
Translator, *The Sorrowful and Heroic Life of John Amos Comenius*, by Frantisek Kosík. Prague, State Educational Publishing House, 1958.
Translator, *A Handful of Linden Leaves: An Anthology of Czech Poetry*. Prague, Artia, 1958.
Translator, *Don Juan*, by Josef Toman. London, Heinemann, and New York, Knopf, 1958.
Translator, *The Abortionists*, by Valja Stýblová. London, Secker and Warburg, 1961.
Translator, *Granny*, by Bozena Nemcová. Prague, Artia, 1962; New York, Greenwood Press, 1976.
Translator, with others, *The Linden Tree* (anthology). Prague, Artia, 1962.
Translator, *The Terezín Requiem*, by Josef Bor. London, Heinemann, and New York, Knopf, 1963.

Translator, *Legends of Old Bohemia*, by Alois Jirásek.   London, Hamlyn, 1963.
Translator, *May*, by Karel Hynek Mácha.   Prague, Artia, 1965.
Translator, *The End of the Old Times*, by Vladislav Vancura.   Prague, Artia, 1965.
Translator, *A Close Watch on the Trains*, by Bohumil Hrabal.   London, Cape, 1968.
Translator, *Report on My Husband*, by Josefa Slánská.   London, Hutchinson, 1969.
Translator, *A Ship Named Hope*, by Ivan Klíma.   London, Gollancz, 1970.
Translator, *Mozart in Prague*, by Jaroslav Seifert.   Prague, Orbis, 1970.

Ellis Peters comments:
I came to the field of the mystery after half a lifetime of novel-writing, and accepted the need to separate it from my previous work only because I discovered, having in the case of one book approached the detective story almost inadvertently, that though I refuse to categorise my books and like doing something different every time, the reading public likes to know just what to expect from an author, and resent being disconcerted. It's not, they said, a bit like your other books! In fact it was not very different, except that it included the act of murder; but I acknowledged, reluctantly, that a pseudonym might after all be more, not less, honest, and that those who wanted only one side of me had a right to some guidance as to where to find it. Naturally I have been influenced myself by the separation, and the categories have crystallised more and more since I began using two names.

But for me the thriller *is a novel*. My attitude to it is summed up in the article I wrote for *The Writer*. The pure puzzle, with a cast of characters kept deliberately two-dimensional and all equally expendable at the end, has no attraction for me. But the paradoxical puzzle, the impossible struggle to create a cast of genuine, rounded, knowable characters caught in conditions of stress, to let the readers know everything about them, feel with them, like or dislike them, and still to try to preserve to the end the secret of which of these is a murderer – this is the attraction for me. The better a novel you write, the more you deploy characters realised and developed and consistently true to themselves, the more difficult you have made your own task of keeping the secret to the end. No use offering your readers as murderer a man they have got to know like their own kin, and whom, by that time, they know to be quite incapable of committing that particular crime, in those circumstances, and for that motive. They will rise up in wrath and give you the lie. But if just once you can provide them with a solution which is both startling and yet right and inevitable, the satisfaction is enormous. Does it ever happen? Now and again it may.

Apart from treating my characters with the same respect as in any other form of novel, I have one sacred rule about the thriller. It is, it ought to be, it must be, a morality. If it strays from the side of the angels, provokes total despair, wilfully destroys – without pressing need in the plot – the innocent and the good, takes pleasure in evil, that is unforgivable sin. I use the word deliberately and gravely.

It is probably true that I am not very good at villains. The good interest me so much more.

*   *   *

An English Scheherazade, Ellis Peters presents not Arabian nights, but British, Austrian, Indian, and Czechoslovakian nights – without genies. Realistic and vivid settings, integral to suspenseful plots often based on the past, richly molded characters, and a superb atmosphere are magic enough. She introduced the Felse family in *Fallen into the Pit* in which 13-year-old Dominic discovers the corpse of his father's first murder case and gets involved. Her Edgar-winning *Death and the Joyful Woman* continues favorite subjects begun in her first mystery novel: music and adolescents. The professional detective is again CID Detective Sgt. George Felse of Comerford, and once more Dominic is the apt amateur. Dominic is engaging and believable in his attraction toward an heiress suspect and in his sleuthing. Going to music lessons gives him his first look at the heiress and later provides him with the excuse to trap the murderer of a beer baron. There is no formula in the Felse series. Dominic is on the fringes of action with his father in *Flight of a Witch*, and at eighteen vacations with his parents on the Cornish coast for *A Nice Derangement of Epitaphs*.

While studying at Oxford Dominic travels with three companions to Czechoslovakia (*The Piper on the Mountain*); he meets Tossa Barber who thereafter is close to the Felses. Dominic brings her home (*Black Is the Colour of My True-Love's Heart*) and travels with her to New Delhi (*Mourning Raga*). After graduation, Dominic works for the Swami's mission there (*Death to the Landlords!*). George Felse rises to Detective Chief Inspector and has other cases close to home: *Black Is the Colour*, *The Knocker on Death's Door*, *City of Gold and Shadows*, and one, *The House of Green Turf*, in Austria, where he takes his wife, Bunty. Bernarda Elliot (Bunty), a concert contralto before she chose marriage, proves as fearless a detective as the men in her family in her own case, *The Grass-Widow's Tale*. Characters are frequently musicians, and there is timely infiltration of music in Felse cases, e.g., the whistled notes of an Indian raga are a music clue in *Mourning Raga*. Music worlds are directly involved in non-Felse novels: *The Will and the Deed*, *Funeral of Figaro*, and *The Horn of Roland*.

If Dominic Felse is a dramatization of youth maturing in a loving home, other adolescents illustrate more trying contemporary situations: one-parent homes (death or divorce), unrest, and independence. None is mawkish or grossly stereotyped.

Ellis Peters is frequently compared to Mary Stewart, but there are differences: except for *Death Mask*, she has no narrator character, and she has no Gothic heroine. Peters's chase, escape, or confrontation action scenes are well developed, sometimes melodramatic, sometimes as body-punishing as in hard-boiled thrillers, but always intriguing elements of the plot and setting. What of the hitch-hiker in *Never Pick Up Hitch-Hikers*? Clean-cut Willie Banks, twenty, might join the police, but is this novel presented tongue-in-cheek? With "designed concealment" and suspense, Ellis Peters is a master storyteller.

—Jane Gottschalk

PETERS, Ludovic. Pseudonym for Peter Ludwig Brent. British. Born in Beuthen, Germany, 26 July 1931. Educated at a secondary school in England. Has worked as a cleaner, editor, film extra, porter, post office sorter, teacher, doorman, and dishwasher. Agent: Jonathan Clowes Ltd., 19 Jeffrey's Place, London NW1 9PP, England.

CRIME PUBLICATIONS

Novels (series character: Ian Firth)

>*Cry Vengeance.* London, and New York, Abelard Schuman, 1961.
>*A Snatch of Music* (Firth). London and New York, Abelard Schuman, 1962.
>*Tarakian* (Firth). London and New York, Abelard Schuman, 1963.
>*Two Sets to Murder* (Firth). London, Hodder and Stoughton, 1963; New York, Coward McCann, 1964.
>*Out by the River* (Firth). London, Hodder and Stoughton, 1964; New York, Walker, 1965.
>*Two after Malic* (Firth). London, Hodder and Stoughton, 1965; New York, Walker, 1966.
>*Riot '71* (Firth). London, Hodder and Stoughton, and New York, Walker, 1967.
>*Double-Take.* London, Hodder and Stoughton, 1968.
>*Fall of Terror.* London, Hodder and Stoughton, 1968.

The Killing Game.   London, Hodder and Stoughton, 1969.
No Way Back from Prague (as Peter Brent).   London, Hodder and Stoughton, 1970.

OTHER PUBLICATIONS as Peter Brent

Novels

Exit.   London, Faber, 1962.
A Kind of Wild Justice.   London, Bodley Head, 1964.

Plays

Chance of Heaven (produced London, 1955).

Screenplay: *Makarios: The Long Journey*, 1977.

Television Play: *Elimination Round*, 1969.

Other

Enzo Sereni: A Hero of Our Time, with Clara Urquhart.   London, Hale, 1967.
The Edwardians.   London, BBC Publications, 1972.
Godmen of India.   London, Allen Lane, and New York, Quadrangle Books, 1972.
Captain Scott and the Antarctic Tragedy.   London, Weidenfeld and Nicolson, and New York, Saturday Review Press, 1974.
Lord Byron.   London, Weidenfeld and Nicolson, 1974.
T. E. Lawrence.   London, Weidenfeld and Nicolson, and New York, Putnam, 1975.
The Viking Saga.   London, Weidenfeld and Nicolson, and New York, Putnam, 1975.
The Mongol Empire.   London, Weidenfeld and Nicolson, 1976; as *Genghis Khan*, New York, McGraw Hill, 1976.
Black Nile: Mungo Park and the Quest for the Niger.   London, Gordon and Cremonesi, 1977.
Far Arabia: Explorers of the Myth.   London, Weidenfeld and Nicolson, 1977.
Charles Darwin: He Who Understand Baboon.   London, Heinemann, and Philadelphia, Lippincott, 1980.

Editor, *Young Commonwealth Poets '65.*   London, Heinemann, 1965.

*   *   *

Working in the specialized area of the spy/intrigue field, Ludovic Peters has zeroed in on the theme of fascism. His first work, *Cry Vengence*, introduced the theme of an English "agent" who single-handedly controls an erupting Balkan situation and saves the world from a Doomsday war. Colonel Rhys was dropped after that first book to be replaced by Ian Firth and his associates, John Smith and Godwin Stamberger. The culmination of these outbreaks of right-wing extremism came in *Riot '71*, depicting racial-economic tension and the resulting plot to topple the English throne.

Peters's works are essentially thrillers, concentrating on action, violence, a little sex, and exotic or eastern settings. Often, as in *Tarakian* or *Out by the River*, the country involved is an unnamed communist one, with buffoons for leaders. Others, as *A Snatch of Music* and *Two Sets to Murder*, use the international glitter of Capri, the Riviera, and San Francisco. Peters succeeds in the use the background but not in capturing the feeling or charm of the setting. Likewise his characters are rather flat and ordinary. Firth, Smith, and Stamberger become real through reappearance, but being repeatedly cast as saviors diminishes their believability.

One of the important exceptions to the bulk of Peter's work is *Two Sets to Murder*. It doesn't involve political intrigue but a blackmail scheme to force well-known sports figures into a drug-smuggling operation. It also gives Firth a rare opportunity to develop his detecting abilities (he is, after all, a private eye with all those connotations of sex and blood). Most of the plot, however, is still revealed by the midpoint of the book and the last half is a build-up of the finale. There is also the usual nick-of-time resolution. One other apparent exception, *Out by the River*, is notable for the humor and parody of intrigue in the beginning pages before reverting to seriousness.

—Fred Dueren

PETRIE, Rhona. Pseudonym for Eileen Marie Duell Buchanan. British. Born in Hastings, Sussex, in 1922. Educated at the University of London, B.A. (honours) 1944; Associateship of King's College 1944. Has worked as an interpreter, translator, teacher, and secretary. Lives in Gerrards Cross, Buckinghamshire. Agent: Jackie Baldick, London Management, 235 Regent Street, London W1A 2JT, England; or, Elaine Markson Literary Agency, 44 Greenwich Avenue, New York, New York 10011, U.S.A.

CRIME PUBLICATIONS

Novels (series characters; Inspector Marcus MacLurg; Dr. Nassim Pride)

> *Death in Deakins Wood* (MacLurg).   London, Gollancz, 1963; New York, Dodd Mead, 1964.
> *Murder by Precedent* (MacLurg).   London, Gollancz, 1964.
> *Running Deep* (MacLurg).   London, Gollancz, 1965.
> *Dead Loss.*   London, Gollancz, 1966.
> *Foreign Bodies* (Pride).   London, Gollancz, 1967.
> *MacLurg Goes West.*   London, Gollancz, 1968.
> *Despatch of a Dove* (Pride).   London, Gollancz, 1969.
> *Thorne in the Flesh.*   London, Gollancz, 1971.

Short Stories

> *Come Hell and High Water: Eleven Short Stories.*   London, Gollancz, 1970.

OTHER PUBLICATIONS as Marie Buchanan

Novels

> *Greenshards.*   London, Gollancz, 1972; as *Anima*, New York, St. Martin's Press, 1972.
> *An Unofficial Death.*   London, Hodder and Stoughton, and New York, St. Martin's Press, 1973.

The Dark Backward.   New York, Coward McCann, 1975.
Morgana.   New York, Doubleday, 1977.

*   *   *

Rhona Petrie has established herself as a detective-story writer of well-above-average literary skill and distinction. Making a late start in 1963, she quickly gained a foothold in crime-writing with a series of detective novels in the "whodunit" tradition and featuring a detective named MacLurg. But it was for *Foreign Bodies* that she won the warmest critical acclaim. This introduced her scientific sleuth Dr. Nassim Pride, who was to feature in the excellent *Despatch of a Dove* as well. Nassim Pride was a real creation, a diminutive and urbane Anglo-Sudanese scientist with a profound love of all things British.

She has also published some novels as Marie Buchanan. These are concerned with strange manifestations of the human mind, extra-sensory perception, unnatural extensions of human faculties, psychic warfare, travelling in the subconscious, and new psychological dimensions. Many consider that she writes more powerfully as Marie Buchanan than as Rhona Petrie.

—Herbert Harris

PHILIPS, Judson.   See **PENTECOST, Hugh.**

PHILLIPS, James Atlee.   See **ATLEE, Philip.**

PHILLPOTTS, Eden.   Also wrote as Harrington Hext.   British.   Born in Mount Aboo, India, 4 November 1862. Educated at Mannamead School, now Plymouth College. Married 1) Emily Topham in 1892 (died, 1928); one son and one daughter; 2) Lucy Robina Webb in 1929. Clerk, Sun Fire Office, London, 1880–90; Assistant Editor, *Black and White*, London, for several years in the 1890's. Regular contributor to *The Idler*, London. Lived in Devon from 1898. *Died 29 December 1960.*

CRIME PUBLICATIONS

Novels (series characters: Avis Bryden; John Ringrose)

The End of a Life.   Bristol, Arrowsmith, 1891.
A Tiger's Cub.   Bristol, Arrowsmith, 1892.

A Deal with the Devil. London, Bliss, 1895; New York, Warne, 1901.

The Farm of the Dagger. London, Newnes, and New York, Dodd Mead, 1904.

The Secret Woman. London, Methuen, and New York, Macmillan, 1905.

Doubloons, with Arnold Bennett. New York, McClure, 1906; as *The Sinews of War,* London, Laurie, 1906.

The Unlucky Number. London, Newnes, 1906.

The Statue, with Arnold Bennett. London, Cassell, and New York, Moffat Yard, 1908.

The Beacon. London, Unwin, and New York, Lane, 1911.

The Three Knaves. London, Macmillan, 1912.

The Master of Merripit. London, Ward Lock, 1914.

Faith Tresilion. New York, Macmillan, 1914; London, Ward Lock, 1916.

Miser's Money. London, Heinemann, and New York, Macmillan, 1920.

The Bronze Venus. London, Richards, 1921.

The Grey Room. New York, Macmillan, and London, Hurst and Blackett, 1921.

The Red Redmaynes. New York, Macmillan, 1922; London, Hutchinson, 1923.

A Voice from the Dark (Ringrose). London, Hutchinson, and New York, Macmillan, 1925.

The Marylebone Miser (Ringrose). London, Hutchinson, 1926; as *Jig-Saw,* New York, Macmillan, 1926.

The Jury. London, Hutchinson, and New York, Macmillan, 1927.

The Ring Fence. London, Hutchinson, and New York, Macmillan, 1928.

"Found Drowned." London, Hutchinson, and New York, Macmillan, 1931.

A Clue from the Stars. London, Hutchinson, and New York, Macmillan, 1932.

Bred in the Bone (Bryden). London, Hutchinson, 1932; New York, Macmillan, 1933.

The Captain's Curio. London, Hutchinson, and New York, Macmillan, 1933.

Mr. Digweed and Mr. Lumb. London, Hutchinson, 1933; New York, Macmillan, 1934.

A Shadow Passes (Bryden). London, Hutchinson, 1933; New York, Macmillan, 1934.

Witch's Cauldron (Bryden). London, Hutchinson, and New York, Macmillan, 1933.

Minions of the Moon. London, Hutchinson, 1934; New York, Macmillan, 1935.

The Wife of Elias. London, Hutchinson, 1935; New York, Dutton, 1937.

Physician, Heal Thyself. London, Hutchinson, 1935; as *The Anniversary Murder,* New York, Dutton, 1936.

The Book of Avis (omnibus). London, Hutchinson, 1936.

A Close Call. London, Hutchinson, and New York, Macmillan, 1936.

Lycanthrope: The Mystery of Sir William Wolf. London, Butterworth, 1937; New York, Macmillan, 1938.

Portrait of a Scoundrel. London, Murray, and New York, Macmillan, 1938.

Monkshood. London, Methuen, and New York, Macmillan, 1939.

Awake Deborah! London, Methuen, 1940; New York, Macmillan, 1941.

A Deed Without a Name. London, Hutchinson, 1941; New York, Macmillan, 1942.

Ghostwater. London, Methuen, and New York, Macmillan, 1941.

Flower of the Gods. London, Hutchinson, 1942; New York, Macmillan, 1943.

They Were Seven. London, Hutchinson, 1944; New York, Macmillan, 1945.

The Changeling. London, Hutchinson, 1944.

There Was an Old Woman. London, Hutchinson, 1947.

Address Unknown. London, Hutchinson, 1949.

Dilemma. London, Hutchinson, 1949.

George and Georgina. London, Hutchinson, 1952.

The Hidden Hand. London, Hutchinson, 1952.

There Was an Old Man. London, Hutchinson, 1959.

Novels as Harrington Hext

Number 87. London, Butterworth, and New York, Macmillan, 1922.

The Thing at Their Heels.   London, Butterworth, and New York, Macmillan, 1923.
Who Killed Diana?   London, Butterworth, 1924; as *Who Killed Cock Robin?*, New York, Macmillan, 1924.
The Monster.   New York, Macmillan, 1925.

Short Stories

My Adventure in the Flying Scotsman: A Romance of London and North-Western Railway Shares.   London, Hogg, 1888; edited by Tom Schatz, Boulder, Colorado, Aspen Press, 1975.
The Transit of the Red Dragon and Other Tales.   Bristol, Arrowsmith, 1903.
The Unlucky Number.   London, Newnes, 1906.
Tales of the Tenements.   London, Murray, and New York, Lane, 1910.
The Judge's Chair.   London, Murray, 1914.
Black, White, and Brindled.   London, Richards, and New York, Macmillan, 1923.
Peacock House and Other Mysteries.   London, Hutchinson, 1926; New York, Macmillan, 1927; selection, as *The End of Count Rollo and Other Stories*, London, Todd, 1946.
It Happened Like That.   London, Hutchinson, and New York, Macmillan, 1928.
Once Upon a Time.   London, Hutchinson, 1936.

OTHER PUBLICATIONS

Novels

Folly and Fresh Air.   London, Trischler, 1891; New York, Harper, 1892; revised edition, London, Hurst and Blackett, 1899.
Some Every-Day Folks.   London, Osgood, 3 vols., 1894; New York, Harper, 1895.
Lying Prophets.   London, Innes, and New York, Stokes, 1896.
Children of the Mist.   London, Innes, 1898; New York, Putnam, 1899.
The Complete Human Boy.   London, Hutchinson, 1930.
   The Human Boy.   London, Methuen, 1899; New York, Harper, 1900.
   The Human Boy Again.   London, Chapman and Hall, 1908.
   From the Angle of Seventeen.   London, Murray, 1912; Boston, Little Brown, 1914.
   The Human Boy and the War.   London, Methuen, and New York, Macmillan, 1916.
   The Human Boy's Diary.   London, Heinemann, and New York, Macmillan, 1924.
Sons of Morning.   London, Methuen, and New York, Putnam, 1900.
The Good Red Earth.   Bristol, Arrowsmith, and New York, Doubleday, 1901; as *Johnny Fortnight*, Arrowsmith, 1904; revised edition, Arrowsmith, 1920.
The River.   London, Methuen, and New York, Stokes, 1902.
The Golden Fetich.   London, Harper, and New York, Dodd Mead, 1903.
The American Prisoner.   New York, Macmillan, 1903; London, Methuen, 1904.
The Farm of the Dagger.   London, Newnes, and New York, Dodd Mead, 1904.
The Portreeve.   London, Methuen, and New York, Macmillan, 1906.
The Poacher's Wife.   London, Methuen, 1906; as *Daniel Sweetland*, New York, Authors and Newspapers Association, 1906.
The Virgin in Judgment.   New York, Reynolds, 1907; London, Cassell, 1908; abridged edition, as *A Fight to the Finish*, Cassell, 1911.
The Whirlwind.   London, Chapman and Hall, and New York, McClure, 1907.
The Mother.   London, Ward Lock, 1908; as *The Mother of the Man*, New York, Dodd Mead, 1908.
The Three Brothers.   London, Hutchinson, and New York, Macmillan, 1909.
The Haven.   London, Murray, and New York, Lane, 1909.
The Thief of Virtue.   London, Murray, and New York, Lane, 1910.

The Flint Heart: A Fairy Story.   London, Smith Elder, and New York, Dutton, 1910; revised edition, London, Chapman and Dodd, 1922.
Demeter's Daughter.   London, Methuen, and New York, Lane, 1911.
The Beacon.   London, Unwin, and New York, Lane, 1911.
The Forest on the Hill.   London, Murray, and New York, Lane, 1912.
The Lovers: A Romance.   London, Ward Lock, and Chicago, Rand McNally, 1912.
Widecombe Fair.   London, Murray, and Boston, Little Brown, 1913.
The Joy of Youth: A Comedy.   London, Chapman and Hall, and Boston, Little Brown, 1913.
Brunel's Tower.   London, Heinemann, and New York, Macmillan, 1915.
Old Delabole.   London, Heinemann, and New York, Macmillan, 1915.
The Green Alleys.   London, Heinemann, and New York, Macmillan, 1916.
The Girl and the Faun.   London, Palmer and Hayward, 1916; Philadelphia, Lippincott, 1917.
The Nursery (Banks of Colne).   London, Heinemann, 1917; as *The Banks of Colne*, New York, Macmillan, 1917.
The Chronicles of St. Tid.   London, Skeffington, 1917; New York, Macmillan, 1918.
The Spinners.   London, Heinemann, and New York, Macmillan, 1918.
Storm in a Teacup.   London, Heinemann, and New York, Macmillan, 1919.
Evander.   London, Richards, and New York, Macmillan, 1919.
Orphan Dinah.   London, Heinemann, 1920; New York, Macmillan, 1921.
Eudocia.   London, Heinemann, and New York, Macmillan, 1921.
Pan and the Twins.   London, Richards, and New York, Macmillan, 1922.
Children of Men.   London, Heinemann, and New York, Macmillan, 1923.
The Lavender Dragon.   London, Richards, and New York, Macmillan, 1923.
Cheat-the-Boys.   London, Heinemann, and New York, Macmillan, 1924.
Redcliff.   London, Hutchinson, and New York, Macmillan, 1924.
The Treasures of Typhon.   London, Richards, 1924; New York, Macmillan, 1925.
George Westover.   London, Hutchinson, 1925; New York, Macmillan, 1926.
Circé's Island, and The Girl and the Faun.   London, Richards, and New York, Macmillan, 1926.
The Miniature.   London, Watts, 1926; New York, Macmillan, 1927.
A Cornish Droll.   London, Hutchinson, 1926; New York, Macmillan, 1928.
Arachne.   London, Faber and Gwyer, 1927; New York, Macmillan, 1928.
Dartmoor Novels (Widecombe Edition: includes stories).   New York, Macmillan, 20 vols., 1927–28.
Tryphena.   London, Hutchinson, and New York, Macmillan, 1929.
The Apes.   London, Faber, and New York, Macmillan, 1929.
The Three Maidens.   London, Hutchinson, and New York, Smith, 1930.
Alcyone: A Fairy Story.   London, Benn, 1930.
Stormbury.   London, Hutchinson, 1931; New York, Macmillan, 1932.
The Broom Squires.   London, Benn, and New York, Macmillan, 1932.
Nancy Owlett.   London, Tuck, and New York, Macmillan, 1933.
The Oldest Inhabitant: A Comedy.   London, Hutchinson, and New York, Macmillan, 1934.
Portrait of a Gentleman.   London, Hutchinson, 1934.
Ned of the Caribbees.   London, Hutchinson, 1935.
The Owl of Athene.   London, Hutchinson, 1936.
Wood-Nymph.   London, Hutchinson, 1936; New York, Dutton, 1937.
Farce in Three Acts.   London, Hutchinson, 1937.
Dark Horses.   London, Murray, 1938.
Saurus.   London, Murray, 1938.
Tabletop.   London, Macmillan, 1939.
Thorn in Her Flesh.   London, Murray, 1939.
Chorus of Clowns.   London, Methuen, 1940.

Goldcross. London, Methuen, 1940.
Pilgrims of the Night. London, Hutchinson, 1942.
A Museum Piece. London, Hutchinson, 1943.
The Drums of Dombali. London, Hutchinson, 1945.
Quartet. London, Hutchinson, 1946.
Fall of the House of Heron. London, Hutchinson, 1948.
The Waters of Walla. London, Hutchinson, 1950.
Through a Glass Darkly. London, Hutchinson, 1951.
His Brother's Keeper. London, Hutchinson, 1953.
The Widow Garland. London, Hutchinson, 1955.
Connie Woodland. London, Hutchinson, 1956.
Giglet Market. London, Methuen, 1957.

Short Stories

Summer Clouds and Other Stories. London, Tuck, 1893.
Down Dartmoor Way. London, Osgood McIlvaine, 1895.
Loup-Garou! London, Sands, 1899.
The Striking Hours. London, Methuen, and New York, Stokes, 1901.
Fancy Free. London, Methuen, 1901.
Knock at a Venture. London, Methuen, and New York, Macmillan, 1905.
The Folk Afield. London, Methuen, and New York, Putnam, 1907.
The Fun of the Fair. London, Murray, 1909.
The Old Time Before Them. London, Murray, 1913; revised edition, as *Told at The Plume*, London, Hurst and Blackett, 1921.
Up Hill, Down Dale. London, Hutchinson, and New York, Macmillan, 1925.
The Torch and Other Tales. London, Hutchinson, and New York, Macmillan, 1929.
(Selected Stories). London, Harrap, 1929.
Cherry Gambol and Other Stories. London, Hutchinson, 1930.
They Could Do No Other. London, Hutchinson, and New York, Macmillan, 1933.
The King of Kanga, and The Alliance. London, Todd, 1943.

Plays

The Policeman, with Walter Helmore (produced London, 1887).
A Platonic Attachment (produced London, 1889).
A Breezy Morning (produced Leeds and London, 1891). London, French, 1895.
Allendale, with G. B. Burgin (produced London, 1893).
The Prude's Progress, with Jerome K. Jerome (produced Cambridge and London, 1895). London, Chatto and Windus, 1895; revised edition, London, French, 1900.
The MacHaggis, with Jerome K. Jerome (produced Peterborough and London, 1897).
A Golden Wedding, with Charles Groves (produced London, 1898). London, French, 1899.
For Love of Prim (produced London, 1899).
A Pair of Knickerbockers (produced London, 1899). London and New York, French, 1900.
The Secret Woman, adaptation of his own novel (produced London, 1912). London, Duckworth, 1912; New York, Brentano's, 1914; revised version, Duckworth, 1935.
Curtain Raisers (includes *The Point of View, Hiatus, The Carrier-Pigeon*). London, Duckworth, 1912; New York, Brentano's, 1914.
The Carrier-Pigeon (produced Glasgow, 1913). Included in *Curtain Raisers*, 1912.
Hiatus (produced Manchester and London, 1913). Included in *Curtain Raisers*, 1912.
The Point of View (produced London, 1913). Included in *Curtain Raisers*, 1912.
The Shadow (produced Manchester and London, 1913; New York, 1922). London, Duckworth, 1913; New York, Brentano's, 1914.

The Mother, adaptation of his own novel (produced Liverpool, 1913; London, 1926). London, Duckworth, 1913; New York, Brentano's, 1914.

The Angel in the House, with Basil Macdonald Hastings (produced London and New York, 1915). London and New York, French, 1915.

Bed Rock, with Basil Macdonald Hastings (produced Manchester, 1916; London, 1924). London, The Stage, 1924.

The Farmer's Wife (produced Birmingham, 1916; London and New York, 1924). London, Duckworth, and New York, Brentano's, 1916.

St. George and the Dragons (produced Birmingham, 1918; London, 1919). London, Duckworth, 1919; as *The Bishop's Night Out*, Boston, Baker, 1929.

The Market-Money (produced Liverpool, 1929). London, Gowans and Gray, and Boston, Phillips, 1923.

Devonshire Cream (produced Birmingham, 1924; London, 1926). London, Duckworth, and New York, Macmillan, 1925.

A Comedy Royal, adaptation of his novel *Eudocia*. London, Laurie, 1925; revised version, London, Duckworth, 1932.

Jane's Legacy: A Folk Play (produced Birmingham, 1925; London, 1930). London, Duckworth, 1931.

The Blue Comet (produced Birmingham, 1926; London, 1927). London, Duckworth, 1927.

Yellow Sands, with Adelaide Eden Phillpotts (produced London, 1926; New York, 1927). London, Duckworth, 1926; New York, French, 1927.

The Purple Bedroom (produced London, 1926). Included in *Three Short Plays*, 1928.

Devonshire Plays (includes *The Farmer's Wife*, *Devonshire Cream*, *Yellow Sands*). London, Duckworth, 1927.

Something to Talk About (produced London, 1927). Included in *Three Short Plays*, 1928.

Three Short Plays (includes *The Market-Money*, *Something to Talk About*, *The Purple Bedroom*). London, Duckworth, 1928.

My Lady's Mill, with Adelaide Eden Phillpotts (produced London, 1928).

The Runaways (produced Birmingham and London, 1928). London, Duckworth, 1928.

Buy a Broom. London, Duckworth, 1929.

Bert. London, French, 1932.

The Good Old Days, with Adelaide Eden Phillpotts (produced London, 1935). London, Duckworth, and New York, French, 1932.

A Cup of Happiness (produced London, 1932). London, Duckworth, 1933.

At the 'Bus Stop: A Duologue for Two Women. London, French, 1943.

The Orange Orchard, with Nancy Price, adaptation of the novel *The Waters of Walla* by Phillpotts (broadcast, 1949; produced London, 1950). London, French, 1951.

Radio Plays: *Old Bannerman*, 1938; *Witch's Cauldron*, from his novel, 1940; *The Tiger's Tail*, 1941; *The Gentle Hangman*, 1942; *Honest to Goodness Noah*, 1943; *The Poetical Gentleman*, 1944; *Brownberry*, 1944; *Hey-Diddle-Diddle*, 1946; *On the Night of the Fair*, 1947; *The Master Plumber*, 1947; *Hunter's Moon*, 1948; *The Orange Orchard*, 1949; *On Parole*, 1951; *Kitty Brown of Bristol*, 1953; *Quoth the Raven*, 1953; *The Laughing Widow*, 1954; *Aunt Betsey's Birthday*, 1955; *The Outward Show*, 1958; *The Red Dragon*, 1959; *Between the Deep Sea and the Devil*, 1960.

Verse

Up-Along and Down-Along. London, Methuen, 1905.

Wild Fruit. London, Lane, 1911.

The Iscariot. London, Murray, and New York, Lane, 1912.

Delight. London, Palmer and Hayward, 1916.

Plain Song 1914–1916. London, Heinemann, and New York, Macmillan, 1917.
As the Wind Blows. London, Elkin Mathews, and New York, Macmillan, 1920.
A Dish of Apples. London, Hodder and Stoughton, 1921.
Pixies' Plot. London, Richards, 1922.
Cherry-Stones. London, Richards, 1923; New York, Macmillan, 1924.
A Harvesting. London, Richards, 1924.
Brother Man. London, Richards, 1926.
(Selected Poems). London, Benn, 1926.
Brother Beast. London, Martin Secker, 1928.
Goodwill. London, Watts, 1928.
For Remembrance. Privately printed, 1929.
A Hundred Sonnets. London, Benn, 1929.
A Hundred Lyrics. London, Benn, and New York, Smith, 1930.
Becoming. London, Benn, 1932.
Song of a Sailor Man: Narrative Poem. London, Benn, 1933; New York, Macmillan, 1934.
Sonnets from Nature. London, Watts, 1935.
A Dartmoor Village. London, Watts, 1937.
Miniatures. London, Watts, 1942.
The Enchanted Wood. London, Watts, 1948.

Other

In Sugar-Cane Land (on the West Indies). New York, McClure, 1893.
My Laughing Philosopher (essays). London, Innes, 1896.
Little Silver Chronicles. Philadelphia, Biddle, 1900.
My Devon Year. London, Methuen, and New York, Macmillan, 1903.
My Garden. London, Country Life, and New York, Scribner, 1906.
The Mound by the Way. Philadelphia, Biddle, 1908.
Dance of the Months (sketches and verse). London, Gowans and Gray, 1911.
My Shrubs. London and New York, Lane, 1915.
The Eden Phillpotts Calendar, edited by H. Cecil Palmer. London, Palmer and Hayward, 1915.
A Shadow Passes (sketches and verse). London, Palmer and Hayward, 1918; New York, Macmillan, 1919.
One Hundred Pictures from Eden Phillpotts, edited by L. H. Brewitt. London, Methuen, 1919.
A West Country Pilgrimage (essays and verse). London, Parsons, and New York, Macmillan, 1920.
Thoughts in Prose and Verse. London, Watts, 1924.
A West Country Sketch Book. London, Hutchinson, 1928.
Essays in Little. London, Hutchinson, 1931.
A Year with Bisshe-Bantam (on rural life). London, Blackie, 1934.
The White Camel (juvenile). London, Country Life, 1936; New York, Dutton, 1938.
Golden Island (juvenile). London, Everett, 1938.
A Mixed Grill (essays). London, Watts, 1940.
From the Angle of 88 (autobiography). London, Hutchinson, 1951.
One Thing and Another. London, Hutchinson, 1954.

Bibliography: *Eden Phillpotts: A Bibliography of First Editions* by Percival Hinton, Birmingham, George Worthington, 1931.

*   *   *

In the course of his long productive life Eden Phillpotts wrote over one hundred novels, among them several mysteries. His weak points are his conventional characters, including his detectives, and his penchant for leisurely elaboration which could uncharitably be called padding; his strong points are his evocation of milieu and his ingenious situations. Phillpotts's gallery of characters is wide, but they are often stereotyped and romanticized, bluff honest countrymen and shrewd doctors and coroners abounding. His detectives fall into two classes, both conventional: the young and earnest who are apt to be misled by their feelings, and the old and cynical who solve the mysteries. John Ringrose, retired from Scotland Yard, is the very model of the latter type, penetrating, analytical, undeterred in his quest, as is Peter Ganns, the great American sleuth, whose slang (in Phillpotts's version) makes him a caricature until his creator forgets it while Ganns pursues the criminals. Other characters are similarly one-sided although in extenuation it may be said that Phillpotts does create a number of interesting eccentrics.

His tendency to pad out his stories is less forgivable. He seizes every opportunity pursue the red herring of digression, reciting at length for the coroner's jury every detail of a case we have just been through, recounting in complete detail an interminable debate between a fanatic clergyman and a materialist detective concerning supernaturalism, dragging the story out over years with other events only tenuously related to the case. The result of this habit is, for the reader, simple boredom.

Because his stories often take off in these directions from some aspect of the milieu, one suspects that Phillpotts wrote mysteries only as an adjunct to his basic interest in his region, southwest England. Most of his novels are about Devon and Cornwall, done with the loving attention to detail of the regionalist, from topography to local attitudes and customs. These features of the mysteries are admittedly interesting for their own sake but they do get in the way of the tale itself. This tendency is true even of the stories where we are whisked off to the Italian lakes, of which Phillpotts was clearly very fond, and which he describes in rich evocative passages.

It is nevertheless true that he did contribute to the detective mystery some notably original situations, though they often are so bizarre as to call for indulgent willingness to suspend disbelief on the reader's part. *The Marylebone Miser*, for instance, is the locked-room case with a vengeance, the room lined with steel, the door double-bolted from the inside, and so on. Phillpotts solves the puzzle by having the old miser who lived in the room killed by a dagger suspended from the single light bulb the miser permitted himself, so that his meanness is partly the cause of his demise. And the murderer, a fine young chap, gets away scot-free. *The Grey Room* is intriguing mostly because the famous detective, Peter Hardcastle, called in to solve the problem of mysterious deaths in the room, becomes himself a victim – rather a disappointment after the build-up he has had. The dead turn out to be, of all things, victims of the Borgia's, for the bed is one of their infernal devices (still functioning after 400 years) which emits poisonous fumes when warmed by a body.

Stories like *A Voice from the Dark* and *The Red Redmaynes*, while unusual, are more credible. In *The Red Redmaynes* the plot turns on an initial deception, in which the murderer is thought to be murdered and his victim to be the murderer, whose role he plays by being seen in disguise from time to time. Many complications and another effective disguise elaborate the story which is eventually solved by Peter Ganns, who has seen through the whole thing, a younger detective having been bamboozled by the murderer's beautiful wife. *A Voice from the Dark* has John Ringrose tracking down a crime already a year old, when a sickly child was frightened to death for his inheritance. Ringrose figures out the perpetrator and the method; the rest of the story concerns his efforts to catch Lord Brooke for the murder both of his brother and the nephew. The twists of the plot are intriguing, especially the climax when Ringrose lays a trap for Brooke high on a mountain near Lake Lugano. Other original tales, though these are marred by padding, are *A Clue from the Stars* in which the weapon is a dangerous bull, and *Monkshood* in which a chef whose unfaithful wife tried to poison him with monkshood, instead poisons her and her lover with such patience and skillful role-playing that he is never even suspected until his own later suicide, which looks like murder. Dr. Thorne, amateur detective, explains the mystery by reconstruction long after the fact, in a lengthy account delivered to the murderer's foster father, another bizarre twist.

Phillpotts's mysteries, plodding, drawn-out, and conventional in characterization, are principally of historical interest. But a few of them, like *A Voice from the Dark*, *Monkshood*, and particularly *The Red Redmaynes*, can still hold the reader's attention.

—Richard C. Carpenter

PIKE, Robert L.   See **FISH, Robert L.**

PILGRIM, David.   See **BEEDING, Francis.**

PIPER, Evelyn.   Pseudonym for Merriam Modell.   American.   Born in New York City in 1908. Educated at Cornell University, Ithaca, New York, B.A. Worked as model, salesclerk, magazine editor.

CRIME PUBLICATIONS

Novels

    The Innocent.   New York, Simon and Schuster, 1949; London, Boardman, 1951.
    The Motive.   New York, Simon and Schuster, 1950; London, Boardman, 1951; as *Death of a Nymph*, New York, Spivak, 1951.
    The Plot.   New York, Simon and Schuster, 1951; London, Boardman, 1952.
    The Lady and Her Doctor.   New York, Doubleday, 1956.
    Bunny Lake Is Missing.   New York, Harper, 1957; London, Secker and Warburg, 1958.
    Hanno's Doll.   New York, Atheneum, 1961; London, Secker and Warburg, 1962.
    The Naked Murderer.   New York, Atheneum, 1962.
    The Nanny.   New York, Atheneum, 1964; London, Secker and Warburg, 1965.
    The Stand-In.   New York, McKay, 1970.

OTHER PUBLICATIONS

Novels as Merriam Modell

    The Sound of Years.   New York, Simon and Schuster, 1946; London, Cassell, 1947.
    My Sister, My Bride.   New York, Simon and Schuster, 1948; London, Cassell, 1949.

Manuscript Collection: Mugar Memorial Library, Boston University.

*   *   *

The Nanny and *Bunny Lake Is Missing* are the two novels, each a minor classic, that represent the thrust and focus of all Evelyn Piper's work. Specializing in suspense and development of character, from her first book, *The Innocent*, Piper has presented in each later work the theme of evil revealed in the destructiveness of possessive or overbearing love.

The stories start with someone who is blindly devoted to spouse or child. The object of that love (Charles in *The Innocent*, or Puppchen in *Hanno's Doll*) is a self-centered person whose amoral selfishness is apparent to everyone else, if not to the naive protagonist who gradually sees the truth and enters a desperate struggle to survive.

Piper is one of the few writers who effectively uses children in her suspense novels. Together with a mild domestic scene children are integrated into all her plots. *The Nanny*, for example, contrasts a child, a teenager, and an old woman. Each expresses an evil – the old woman acts out of self-justification, the teenager out of irresponsible mischievousness, and the child out of fear and ignorance. Piper depicts every shade and nuance, every effect and horrifying result of smothering overindulgent love. The effects of that grasping, protectively vicious love are, then, reflected in a small baby and the man who competes with that baby for attention.

Two of Piper's books are notable for departures from her usual pattern. *The Naked Murderer*, billed as her first "whodunit" rather than a suspense thriller, uses traditional detective elements to produce a form of a mystery, but the effect of the twist ending is spoiled by the reader's feeling of being tricked. In *The Stand-In* Piper leaves New York and uses a well-done English setting, and characters who are anything but domestic. The plot involves the cast of a film crew on location; a more selfish profession has seldom been portrayed. A bitterly ironic ending rounds out the frustrations of all the major characters.

Piper's strong suspense and analysis of psychology in familiar situations produce a series of books that are fascinating despite their reworking of the same basic material.

—Fred Dueren

PLAYER, Robert. Pseudonym for Robert Furneaux Jordan. British. Born in Birmingham, Warwickshire, 10 April 1905. Educated at King Edward VII School, Birmingham; Birmingham School of Art; Architectural Association School, London, Dip.A.A. 1928: Associate, Royal Institute of British Architects, 1928. Married Eira Furneaux Jordan in 1965. In private practice as architect, 1928–61; Lecturer, 1934–63, and Principal, 1948–51, Architectural Association School; Hoffman Wood Professor of Architecture, University of Leeds, 1961–62; Visiting Professor, Syracuse University, New York. Frequent broadcaster and lecturer; Architectural Correspondent, *Observer*, London, 1951–61. Fellow, Royal Institute of British Architects. *Died 14 May 1978.*

CRIME PUBLICATIONS

Novels

The Ingenious Mr. Stone; or, The Documents in the Langdon-Miles Case. London, Gollancz, 1945; New York, Rinehart, 1946.

The Homicidal Colonel. London, Gollancz, 1970.
Oh! Where Are Bloody Mary's Earrings? London, Gollancz, 1972; New York, Harper, 1973.
Let's Talk of Graves, of Worms, and Epitaphs. London, Gollancz, 1975.
The Month of the Mangled Models. London, Gollancz, 1977.

OTHER PUBLICATIONS as Robert Furneaux Jordan

Other

The Charm of the Timber House. London, Nicholson and Watson, 1936.
A Picture History of the English House. London, Hulton, 1959; New York, Macmillan, 1960.
The Medieval Vision of William Morris (lecture). London, William Morris Society, 1960.
Lectures on Modern Architecture. London, Royal Institute of British Architects, 1961.
European Architecture in Colour. London, Thames and Hudson, 1961; as *The World of Great Architecture*, New York, Viking Press, 1961.
Victorian Architecture. London, Penguin, 1966.
A Concise History of Western Architecture. London, Thames and Hudson, 1969; New York, Harcourt Brace, 1970.
Le Corbusier. New York, Lawrence Hill, 1972.

*   *   *

In all of his mysteries, Robert Player never hesitates to trample on sacred cows. He is never conventional in his treatment of death and does not use a series detective; usually his characters tell their own stories. Ambition's deadly effect upon a religious career is the subject of *Let's Talk of Graves, of Worms, and Epitaphs* when a Protestant clergyman becomes a Catholic as soon as his wife conveniently dies. He leaves for Rome, not hesitating to abandon his young children without a thought. Although welcomed joyously into the Church, he leaves behind him some carping and suspicious minds concerning his wife's death. The "right sort of school" is considered in *The Ingenious Mr. Stone* with amusement and not too much restraint. The death of the headmistress of strychnine poisoning, while giving a lecture in London, surely cannot do too much to persuade prospective parents of the general excellence of this establishment. Even the Royal Family does not escape Mr. Player's tender attentions. *Oh! Where Are Bloody Mary's Earrings?* examines the adventures of Mary Tudor's gift from her unwilling husband, Philip of Spain. These earrings were to have been destined to become sacred relics if or when Mary became pregnant. They disappeared to become, perhaps, set into a tiara designed by Prince Albert for Victoria and always eyed hopefully by young Prince Bertie, forever in need of cash and jewelry. Even the most devoted Royalists can hardly fail to be amused by the descriptions of life at the Royal residences that were stifling, dull, and unwholesome.

The results of Player's mysteries are never predictable as he writes of a world that is often slightly out of focus.

—Mary Groff

POPKIN, Zelda (née Feinberg). American. Born in Brooklyn, New York, 5 July 1898. Educated at Wilkes-Barre High School, Pennsylvania, graduated 1914; Columbia University, New York, 1916–18; New York University Law School, 1945. Married Louis Popkin in 1919 (died, 1943); two sons. Reporter, Wilkes-Barre *Times-Leader*, 1914–16; Partner, with Louis Popkin, Public Relations Bureau, New York, 1918–43; worked with the American Red Cross in Europe, 1945–46; lectured extensively in the United States and Canada, 1946–69; temporary public relations assignments in the United States and Canada. Agent: Roberta Pryor, International Creative Management, 40 West 57th Street, New York, New York 10019. Address: 272 First Avenue, New York, New York 10009, U.S.A.

CRIME PUBLICATIONS

Novels (series character: Mary Carner in all books except *So Much Blood* and *A Death of Innocence*)

Death Wears a White Gardenia. Philadelphia, Lippincott, 1938; London, Hutchinson, 1939.
Time Off for Murder. Philadelphia, Lippincott, and London, Hutchinson, 1940.
Murder in the Mist. Philadelphia, Lippincott, 1940; London, Hutchinson, 1941.
Dead Man's Gift. Philadelphia, Lippincott, 1941; London, Hutchinson, 1948.
No Crime for a Lady. Philadelphia, Lippincott, 1942.
So Much Blood. Philadelphia, Lippincott, 1944; London, Hutchinson, 1946.
A Death of Innocence. Philadelphia, Lippincott, 1971; London, W. H. Allen, 1972.

OTHER PUBLICATIONS

Novels

The Journey Home. Philadelphia, Lippincott, 1945.
Small Victory. Philadelphia, Lippincott, 1947.
Walk Through the Valley. Philadelphia, Lippincott, 1949.
Quiet Street. Philadelphia, Lippincott, 1951.
Herman Had Two Daughters. Philadelphia, Lippincott, 1968; London, W. H. Allen, 1973.
Dear Once. Philadelphia, Lippincott, 1975; London, W. H. Allen, 1976.

Other

Open Every Door (autobiography). New York, Dutton, 1956.

Zelda Popkin comments:
I look back with satisfaction to my long-ago years of mystery-story writing for they were my apprenticeship for the serious novel. I learned to build a plot, i.e., to move my characters purposefully from here to there and to sustain a pace that holds the reader's attention.

*　　*　　*

Zelda Popkin has written seven mysteries, most of them featuring Mary Carner, a department store detective. There is little merit in the first few novels, but the writing improves, and the last one, especially, is worthwhile. *No Crime for a Lady* is loosely based (like Cain's *Double Indemnity*) on the 1927 Snyder-Gray case. Popkin reverses the sex of the victim and enhances the meaning of a crime of passion by setting it amidst political corruption. *The Journey Home* is a bright World War II novel, and she did several chronicles of Jewish-American family life with strong universal appeal. Her work up to 1971 may be seen as a prelude to her best novel, *A Death of Innocence*. A serious treatment of crime in the context of the American family, it dramatizes the trial of a young girl for the killing of an elderly woman. The author used her detective writing skills to have the girl's mother probe the guilt or innocence of her daughter herself, coming to terms with moral values and responsibility. The author's view of crime might be summed up in this passage from *No Crime for a Lady*: "You find yourself floundering in a mess of lies. A cesspool.... You never know what'll crawl out next." In *Dead Man's Gift*, she says: "Mary Carner caught thieves ... because she didn't look as if she could, and because her senses were sharp, with a keen, co-ordinating brain behind them, and her courage was high." There is an overall scornful attitude toward mankind that sometimes spurns idealism, but a fine mind is at work, a writer continually improving. Like her heroines, there is moral purpose in Zelda Popkin's novels – a challenge to philosophy, an antidote to incompetence, and a convenant with the future.

—Newton Baird

PORLOCK, Martin.   See MacDONALD, Philip.

PORTER, Joyce.   British.   Born in Marple, Cheshire, 28 March 1924. Educated at the High School for Girls, Macclesfield, Cheshire, 1935–42; King's College, London, 1942–45, B.A. (honours) 1945. Served in the Women's Royal Air Force, 1949–63: Flight Officer. Agent: Curtis Brown Ltd., 1 Craven Hill, London W2 3EP. Address: 68 Sand Street, Longbridge Deverill, near Warminster, Wiltshire, England.

CRIME PUBLICATIONS

Novels (series characters: Inspector Wilfred Dover; Edmund Brown; Constance Ethel Morrison-Burke)

Dover One.   London, Cape, and New York, Scribner, 1964.
Dover Two.   London, Cape, and New York, Scribner, 1965.
Dover Three.   London, Cape, 1965; New York, Scribner, 1966.
Sour Cream with Everything (Brown).   London, Cape, and New York, Scribner, 1966.
Dover and the Unkindest Cut of All.   London, Cape, and New York, Scribner, 1967.
The Chinks in the Curtain (Brown).   London, Cape, 1967; New York, Scribner, 1968.
Dover Goes to Pott.   London, Cape, and New York, Scribner, 1968.
Neither a Candle nor a Pitchfork (Brown).   London, Weidenfeld and Nicolson, 1969; New York, McCall, 1970.
Rather a Common Sort of Crime (Morrison-Burke).   London, Weidenfeld and Nicolson, and New York, McCall, 1970.
Dover Strikes Again.   London, Weidenfeld and Nicolson, 1970; New York, McKay, 1973.

Only with a Bargepole (Brown).   London, Weidenfeld and Nicolson, 1971; New York, McKay, 1974.

A Meddler and Her Murder (Morrison-Burke).   London, Weidenfeld and Nicolson, 1972; New York, McKay, 1973.

It's Murder with Dover.   London, Weidenfeld and Nicolson, and New York, McKay, 1973.

The Package Included Murder (Morrison-Burke).   London, Weidenfeld and Nicolson, 1975; Indianapolis, Bobbs Merrill, 1976.

Dover and the Claret Tappers.   London, Weidenfeld and Nicolson, 1977.

Who the Heck Is Sylvia (Morrison-Burke).   London, Weidenfeld and Nicolson, 1977.

Dead Easy for Dover.   London, Weidenfeld and Nicolson, 1978; New York, St. Martin's Press, 1979.

The Cart Before the Crime (Morrison-Burke).   London, Weidenfeld and Nicolson, 1979.

Uncollected Short Stories

"Dover and the Sense of Justice," in *Ellery Queen's Mystery Magazine* (New York), 1968.

"Dover Pulls a Rabbit," in *Ellery Queen's Mystery Magazine* (New York), February 1969.

"Dover Fails to Make His Mark," in *Ellery Queen's Mystery Magazine* (New York), 1970.

"A Terrible Drag for Dover," in *Ellery Queen's Mystery Magazine* (New York), 1971.

"Dover and the Dark Lady," in *Ellery Queen's Mystery Magazine* (New York), May 1972.

"Dover Tangles with High Finance," in *Ellery Queen's Masters of Mystery.*   New York, Davis, 1975.

"Dover Does Some Spadework," in *Best Detective Stories of the Year 1977*, edited by Edward D. Hoch.   New York, Dutton, 1977.

"When Dover Got Knotted," in *Ellery Queen's Mystery Magazine* (New York), 1977.

"Dover Goes to School," in *Ellery Queen's Mystery Magazine* (New York), February 1978.

"Dover Doesn't Dilly-Dally," in *Alfred Hitchcock's Mystery Magazine* (New York), 1978.

"A Gross Miscarriage of Justice," in *Alfred Hitchcock's Mystery Magazine* (New York), July 1978.

"Dover Without Perks," in *Ellery Queen's Mystery Magazine* (New York), November 1978.

OTHER PUBLICATIONS

Other

"The Solitary Life of the Writer," in *Murder Ink: The Mystery Reader's Companion*, edited by Dilys Winn.   New York, Workman, 1977.

Joyce Porter comments:
I try to write books that will while away a couple of hours for the reader – and make as much money as possible for me!

*   *   *

Though occasionally outrageous in their exaggeration, Joyce Porter's comic variants of the international thriller with secret agent Eddie Brown, the police procedural novel with Detective-Inspector Dover, and the amateur-cum-private-eye novel with the Honourable Constance Ethel Morrison-Burke (the Hon-Con) ultimately play fair by observing the conventions of the three genres. The books delight in reducing human behavior to its lowest common denominator and then shocking the reader by descending further: anonymous letters in *Dover Three* hint at everything from "algolagnia to zoophilism." Unfortunately such exotic delights occur infrequently, and the reader must settle for quotidian activities like incest, lesbianism, and cannibalism. Typically, cold and rainy weather and muddy terrain worsen already unattractive tempers and appearances. Porter characters, driven by greed and malice, only rarely achieve the scientific detachment of the old man in *Dover Three* who coolly watches dangerous lorries threaten pedestrians on a lethal road.

The Eddie Brown books explore dangerous foreign locales, where the threat is as much his own ineptness and sex with unattractive females as the KGB: in *Neither a Candle nor a Pitchfork* a lesbian Russian official tries to seduce Eddie while he is in female disguise. Eddie's climactic attack on a prison which would be the high point of a conventional thriller is subsidiary to jokes about miscegenation. Russian officialdom is so corrupt and murderous, the Russian masses so bestial, especially the lethal children frequent in Porter, that Russia seems interchangeable with England.

Unlike the bland Eddie Brown, the Hon-Con and Dover, obese embarrassment to New Scotland Yard, are authentic grotesques who provide most of the humor in their books. Porter is ambivalent about Dover's intelligence, since he does, after all, solve the crimes the novels catalogue: "The fact that his career as a detective had endured, and even flourished in a mild way, was almost entirely due to the fact that most criminals, incredible as it may seem, were even more inept and stupid" (*Dover One*). Dover's forays into remote and inhospitable villages to aid the local police focus primarily on his quest for animal comfort (Porter dwells lovingly on his unhygienic habits and digestive malfunctions) and only secondarily on crime. Personal pique overrides professionalism: in *Dover Three* he delays solving a case until a hated sister-in-law ends her visit to his home; then, rushing to wind up affairs, he allows everyone to believe an aggressive woman he dislikes guilty. When the real murderer commits suicide after confessing to Dover, he is too lazy or malicious to set the record straight (in a world where criminal is as nasty as victim, justice seems irrelevant). *Dover and the Unkindest Cut of All*, the only Porter novel which carries her view of humanity to its bizarre conclusion, plays with the comic horror of castration and leaves the guilty both unpunished and unrepentant. Like stereotyped rape victims, the mutilated roués who survive punishment at the hands of a civic-minded ladies group choose suicide or silence. As in the entire series, Dover's skirmishes with his elegant assistant Sgt. MacGregor, whom he almost sacrifices to these ladies, help define the solid police procedures supporting the grotesque façade of the novel.

The Hon-Con, a gentlewoman of independent means, turns to detection because vigorous calisthenics fail to satisfy her tremendous energy: "she went at everything like a bull at a gate" (*Rather a Common Sort of Crime*). Though protective of young girls, Con is "always the perfect gentleman" (*The Package Included Murder*) and remains true to her long-suffering companion, Miss Jones, and presumably innocent about elementary sexual facts and the unconventional behavior of other characters, like Mr. Welks, who supplies beauty advice. With characteristic equivocation Porter defines Con as not "as big a fool as many people thought her"; but her tactlessness and police shortsightedness undermine her accomplishments and leave her frustrated enough to contemplate founding "the first ever Ladies' Rugby Football Club in the World" (*A Meddler and Her Murder*). In all three genres, despite inconsistencies about the wisdom of her protagonists, Porter balances her talent for straightforward thrillers with her delight in spoofing the forms.

—Burton Kendle

POST, Melville Davisson. American. Born in Romines Mills, West Virginia, 19 April 1869. Educated at Buckhannon Academy, West Virginia, graduated 1885; West Virginia University, Morgantown, A.B. 1891, LL.B. 1892. Married Ann Bloomfield Gamble in 1903 (died, 1919); one son. Practiced criminal and corporate law in Wheeling for eleven years, traveled extensively, and settled near Clarksburg, West Virginia in 1914. Presidential Elector-at-large, Democratic Party, Secretary, Electoral College, 1892; Chairman, West Virginia Democratic Congressional Committee, 1898; Member, Advisory Committee of the National Economic League, 1914–15; headed group of writers supporting John W. Davis, Democratic candidate for President, 1924. *Died 23 June 1930.*

CRIME PUBLICATIONS

Short Stories (series characters: Uncle Abner; Randolph Mason)

The Strange Schemes of Randolph Mason. New York, Putnam, 1896.
The Man of Last Resort; or, The Clients of Randolph Mason. New York, Putnam, 1897.
The Corrector of Destinies (Mason). New York, Clode, 1908.
The Nameless Thing. New York, Appleton, 1912.
Uncle Abner, Master of Mysteries. New York, Appleton, 1918; London, Stacey, 1972.
The Mystery at the Blue Villa. New York, Appleton, 1919.
The Sleuth of St. James's Square. New York, Appleton, 1920.
Monsieur Jonquelle, Prefect of Police of Paris. New York, Appleton, 1923.
Walker of the Secret Service. New York, Appleton, 1924.
The Bradmoor Murder. New York, Sears, 1929; as *The Garden in Asia*, London, Brentano's, 1929.
The Silent Witness. New York, Farrar and Rinehart, 1930.
The Methods of Uncle Abner. Boulder, Colorado, Aspen Press, 1974.
The Complete Uncle Abner. San Diego, University of California Extension, 1977.

Uncollected Short Stories

"The Ventures of Mr. Clayvarden," in *Law Student's Helper* (Detroit), February 1898.
"The Plan of Malcolm Van Staak," in *Law Student's Helper* (Detroit), April 1898.
"The Marriage Contract," in *Pearson's Magazine* (New York), June 1908.
"The Unknown Disciple," in *Pictorial Review* (New York), December 1920.
"The Laughing Woman," in *Red Book* (Chicago), February 1923.
"The Miracle," in *Pictorial Review* (New York), December 1924.
"The Devil's Track," in *Country Gentleman* (Philadelphia), July 1927.
"The Mystery at the Mill," in *American Magazine* (Springfield, Ohio), August 1929.

OTHER PUBLICATIONS

Novels

Dwellers in the Hills. New York, Putnam, 1901.
The Gilded Chair. New York, Appleton, 1910.
The Mountain School-Teacher. New York, Appleton, 1922.
The Revolt of the Birds. New York, Appleton, 1927.

Other

"Mysteries of the Law ..." (7 articles), in *Saturday Evening Post* (Philadelphia), 14 May–27 August 1910.

"Extraordinary Cases ..." (6 articles), in *Saturday Evening Post* (Philadelphia), 23
   September 1911–20 April 1912.
"The Blight," in *Saturday Evening Post* (Philadelphia), 20 December 1914.
"The Mystery Story," in *Saturday Evening Post* (Philadelphia), 27 February 1915.
"The Invisible Army," in *Saturday Evening Post* (Philadelphia), 10 April 1915.
"Secret Ciphers," in *Saturday Evening Post* (Philadelphia), 8 May 1915.
"Spy Methods in Europe," in *Saturday Evening Post* (Philadelphia), 15 May 1915.
"The Great Terror," in *Saturday Evening Post* (Philadelphia), 12 June 1915.
"Nick Carter, Realist," in *Saturday Evening Post* (Philadelphia), 3 March 1917.
"Spy Stories," in *Saturday Evening Post* (Philadelphia), 10 March 1917.
The Man Hunters.   New York, Sears, 1926; London, Hutchinson, 1927.

Bibliography: in *Melville Davisson Post, Man of Many Mysteries*, by Charles A. Norton, Bowling Green, Ohio, Popular Press, 1973; in *The Complete Uncle Abner* by Allen J. Hubin, San Diego, University of California Extension, 1977.

*   *   *

The lawyer Melville Davisson Post became involved early in his career in judicial reform and local politics and, for a brief period in the mid-1920's, in a national political campaign. But his greatest achievements were as an author, particularly as a short story writer.

After publishing two books of crime stories in 1896 and 1897, Post wrote almost exclusively for popular, wide-circulation magazines. His commercial success was unparalleled in his time. His forte was plotting and his stories invariably were constructed so as to capture and hold the reader's interest. While many of his tales reveal carelessness in style and details, their entertainment value was high.

Post's first book of crime stories was *The Strange Schemes of Randolph Mason* whose protagonist – like Post himself – was a lawyer. Randolph Mason, however, was a strikingly new type of character: he was a skilled, unscrupulous lawyer who used his knowledge of the law to defeat the ends of justice. Mason assisted criminals by cynically employing his familiarity with legal loop-holes. To complaints that these concepts might abet actual criminals, Post replied, in the preface to a second collection of Mason stories, *The Man of Last Resort*, that "nothing but good could come of exposing the law's defects." Some of Post stories, in fact, did bring about changes in the criminal law codes. However, in the third and final book in the Mason series, *The Corrector of Destinies*, Post had his lawyer modify his attitude and decide to practice thereafter in the interests of the written law.

Post published several valuable articles on the theory of detective story plotting and structure. Brief excerpts from Post's own subsequent reworking of these pieces indicate the significant rethinking he was giving to the concept of the detective story. "The developing of the mystery and the developing toward its solution," Post proposed, "would go forward side by side; and when all the details of the mystery were uncovered, the solution also would be uncovered and the end of the story arrived at.... This new formula, as will at once be seen, very markedly increases the rapidity of action in a story, holds the reader's interest throughout, and eliminates any impression of moving at any time over ground previously covered."

In the celebrated Uncle Abner tales one perceives a powerful sense of place – of the wild hills and lawless Virginia backlands where crimes against God and man were conceived and carried out and where God's and man's avenger could be impersonated only by the Old Testament moral grandeur of a man like Abner. If Post's early stories were novel in the protagonist's approach to the practice of law and the use (or misuse) of technical legal knowledge, his later stories, of which the Uncle Abner series is the best illustration, are striking (and intrinsically better) in their deliberate and effective blend (within the prescription of the detective tale itself) of character and place – dignity of character and dignity of place.

—Donald A. Yates

POSTGATE, Raymond (William). British. Born in Cambridge, 6 November 1896; brother of Margaret Postgate, i.e., Margaret Cole, *q.v.* Educated at Perse School, Cambridge; Liverpool College; St. John's College, Oxford. Married Daisy Lansbury in 1918; two sons. Journalist and writer from 1918: Sub-Editor, *Daily Herald*; Assistant Editor, *Lansbury's Weekly*; Departmental Editor, *Encyclopaedia Britannica*, 14th edition, 1927–28; European Representative for Alfred A. Knopf, publishers, 1929–49; Editor, *Tribune*, 1940–42; worked at the Board of Trade and Ministry of Supply, 1942–48. Founder, Good Food Club, 1950. Fellow, Trinity College, Cambridge. *Died 29 March 1971.*

CRIME PUBLICATIONS

Novels

    Verdict of Twelve. London, Collins, and New York, Doubleday, 1940.
    Somebody at the Door. London, Joseph, and New York, Knopf, 1943.
    The Ledger Is Kept. London, Joseph, 1953.

Uncollected Short Story

    "The Respectable Mr. Thompson," in *Murder Plain and Fanciful*, edited by James Sandoe. New York, Sheridan House, 1948.

OTHER PUBLICATIONS

Novel

    No Epitaph. London, Hamish Hamilton, 1932; as *Felix and Anne*, New York, Vanguard Press, 1933.

Other

    The International (Socialist Bureau) During the War. London, The Herald, 1918.
    Doubts Concerning a League of Nations. London, The Herald, 1919.
    The Bolshevik Theory. London, Richards, and New York, Dodd Mead, 1920.
    The Workers' International. London, Swarthmore Press, and New York, Harcourt Brace, 1920.
    Chartism and the "Trades Union." London, Labour Research Department, 1922.
    Out of the Past: Some Revolutionary Sketches. London, Labour Publishing Company, 1922; Boston, Houghton Mifflin, 1923.
    Revolutionary Biographies. Madras, Arka, 1922.
    The Builders' History. London, Labour Publishing Company, 1923.
    A Short History of the British Workers. London, Plebs League, 1926.
    A Workers' History of the Great Strike. London, Plebs League, 1927.
    That Devil Wilkes. New York, Vanguard Press, 1929; London, Constable, 1930; revised edition, London, Dobson, 1956.
    Robert Emmet. London, Secker and Warburg, 1931; as *Dear Robert Emmet*, New York, Vanguard Press, 1932.
    Karl Marx. London, Hamish Hamilton, 1933.
    How to Make a Revolution. London, Hogarth Press, and New York, Vanguard Press, 1934.
    What to Do with the B.B.C. London, Hogarth Press, 1935.
    A Pocket History of the British Workers to 1919. London, Fact, 1937.

Those Foreigners: The English People's Opinions on Foreign Affairs as Reflected in Their
   Newspapers since Waterloo, with Aylmer Vallance.   London, Harrap, 1937; as
   England Goes to Press, Indianapolis, Bobbs Merrill, 1937.
The Common People 1746–1938, with G. D. H. Cole.   London, Methuen, 1938; revised
   edition, 1946; as *The British Common People*, New York, Knopf, 1939; revised
   edition, as *The British People*, Knopf, 1947.
Let's Talk It Over: An Argument about Socialism.   London, Fabian Society, 1942.
The Plain Man's Guide to Wine.   London, Joseph, 1951; revised edition, 1957, 1965;
   New York, Taplinger, 1960.
The Life of George Lansbury.   London, Longman, 1951.
An Alphabet of Choosing and Serving Wine.   London, Jenkins, 1955.
Story of a Year, 1848.   London, Cape, 1955; New York, Oxford University Press,
   1956.
The Home Wine Cellar.   London, Jenkins, 1960.
Every Man Is God.   London, Joseph, 1959; New York, Simon and Schuster, 1960.
Story of a Year, 1798.   London, Longman, and New York, Harcourt Brace, 1969.
Portuguese Wine.   London, Dent, 1969.

Editor, *Revolution from 1789–1906: Documents.*   London, Richards, 1920; Boston,
   Houghton Mifflin, 1921.
Editor and Translator, *Pervigilium Venus: The Eve of Venus.*   London, Richards, and
   Boston, Houghton Mifflin, 1924.
Editor, *Murder, Piracy and Treason: A Selection of Notable English Trials.*   London,
   Cape, and Boston, Houghton Mifflin, 1925.
Editor, *The Conversations of Dr. Johnson*, by James Boswell.   London, Knopf, and New
   York, Vanguard Press, 1930.
Editor, *Detective Stories of Today.*   London, Faber, 1940.
Editor, *"By Me …": A Report upon the Apparent Discovery of Some Working Notes by
   William Shakespeare*, by Moray MacLaren.   London, Redington, 1949.
Editor, *The Outline of History*, by H. G. Wells.   New York, Garden City Publishing
   Company, 1949; London, Cassell, 1956
Editor, *The Good Food Guide 1951–52.*   London, Cassell, 1951 (and later editions).

Translator, *Mitsou*, by Colette.   London, Secker and Warburg, 1951.

                              *   *   *

   Raymond Postgate, the noted social historian and close associate of the socialist leader
George Lansbury, prefaced his best-known crime novel, *Verdict of Twelve*, with Marx's
statement that man's social existence determines his consciousness. It could serve equally
well to introduce *Somebody at the Door* or *The Ledger Is Kept*. Although all three novels are
solidly plotted with sufficient detection to engage a reader of traditional detective fiction,
Postgate's real concern is not with revealing the identity of the murderer but with analyzing
the circumstances which shaped murderer, victim, or jury member and made their decisions
and actions seemingly inevitable. While stressing the importance of early social and
economic environment upon the development of personality and values, he understands that
character formation is a dynamic process and that new experiences may modify or challenge
existing attitudes. Although deterministic, Postgate's view of character does not negate
individuality; rather, it enhances it. His novels are filled with fully realized, recognizable
human beings who come alive as do few characters in detective fiction.
   The technique used in the memorable *Verdict of Twelve* is typical of Postgate's approach to
the detective novel. He gives detailed biographies of six of the 12 jurors who must decide
whether a middle-aged woman has murdered her nephew. Each juror brings to his task a set
of personal attitudes and problems which prevent his considering the evidence objectively;
each responds emotionally rather than rationally to the crime. Because the reader

understands the jurors, he is able to anticipate their reactions. Postgate's real skill, however, lies in his ability to show how these seemingly predictable reactions are modified or changed once discussion of the case begins, and subtle interplay of class distinctions and personality gradually causes the weaker jurors to side with the majority. The jury deliberations form the core of the novel, but they are buttressed by careful delineation of both accused and victim. Postgate also makes superb use of literary allusion and offers as neatly handled a twist ending as one could wish for.

A similar technique is less successful in *Somebody at the Door* because of diffusion of emphasis and a number of unconvincing suspects, but the novel does offer well-developed motivation in its central characters and an unusual method of murder. Sensitive to the nuances of romantic love, Postgate depicts an intense love affair between a woman approaching 40 and a man many years younger which gives substance and interest to a novel lacking structural coherence.

In *The Ledger Is Kept*, Postgate achieved what many detective novelists have dreamed of doing: he wrote a detective story which is also a first-rate realistic novel. Concentrating upon the life of the victim, Henry Proctor, he shows that the interaction of circumstance and character made Proctor's murder inevitable. Proctor is the child of an unsuccessful shoemaker and is brought up in an obscure and puritanical religious sect; his academic brilliance takes him to Oxford where he learns to appreciate the richness and variety of life but must also grapple with the conflict between his desire for social acceptance and the opposed values of his early training. Profoundly lonely in late middle age, he makes one last attempt at happiness through an affair with his teenaged housemaid. This brief and poignant love leads to his death. In this novel Postgate brings reality to the never-never land of detective fiction. Understanding of and respect for people of different educational, social, and intellectual levels, coupled with sure technical skill, have produced a detective novel which transcends the limitations of the genre.

—Jeanne F. Bedell

POTTS, Jean. American. Born in St. Paul, Nebraska, 17 November 1910. Educated at Nebraska Wesleyan University, Lincoln. Journalist in Nebraska; then free-lance writer in New York. Recipient: Mystery Writers of America Edgar Allan Poe Award, 1954. Agent: McIntosh and Otis Inc., 475 Fifth Avenue, New York, New York 10017. Address: 53 Irving Place, Apartment 6D, New York, New York 10003, U.S.A.

CRIME PUBLICATIONS

Novels

Go, Lovely Rose. New York, Scribner, 1954; London, Gollancz, 1955.
Death of a Stray Cat. New York, Scribner, and London, Gollancz, 1955.
The Diehard. New York, Scribner, and London, Gollancz, 1956.
The Man with the Cane. New York, Scribner, 1957; London, Gollancz, 1958.
Lightning Strikes Twice. New York, Scribner, 1958; as *Blood Will Tell*, London, Gollancz, 1959.
Home Is the Prisoner. New York, Scribner, and London, Gollancz, 1960.
The Evil Wish. New York, Scribner, and London, Gollancz, 1962.
The Only Good Secretary. New York, Scribner, 1965; London, Gollancz, 1966.

The Footsteps on the Stairs. New York, Scribner, 1966; London, Gollancz, 1967.
The Trash Stealer. New York, Scribner, and London, Gollancz, 1968.
The Little Lie. New York, Scribner, 1968; London, Gollancz, 1969.
An Affair of the Heart. New York, Scribner, and London, Gollancz, 1970.
The Troublemaker. New York, Scribner, 1972; London, Gollancz, 1973.
My Brother's Killer. New York, Scribner, 1975; London, Gollancz, 1976.

Uncollected Short Stories

"The Withered Heart," in *Cream of the Crime.* New York, Holt Rinehart, 1962;
London, Harrap, 1964.
"The Inner Voices," in *Ellery Queen's All-Star Lineup.* New York, New American
Library, 1967; London, Gollancz, 1968.
"Murderer No. 2," in *Alfred Hitchcock's Tales to Keep You Spellbound*, edited by
Eleanor Sullivan. New York, Davis, 1976.

OTHER PUBLICATIONS

Novel

Someone to Remember. Philadelphia, Westminster Press, 1943.

*   *   *

The mystery novel faced a period of change in the late 1940's and early 1950's. In a new
push for realism, old masters (like Margery Allingham) and newcomers alike developed a
"police procedural" approach. Others employed a more believable brand of private eye. Jean
Potts took a more unusual approach. In her novels, realism stems, not from the professional
sleuth or his investigation, but from the realistic portrayal of a small, inter-related group of
people (i.e., the "suspects") confronted with unnatural death.

Potts's career began auspiciously with *Go, Lovely Rose*, which won an Edgar in 1954.
More than most of her subsequent novels, it closely resembles a classic whodunit. There are
official sleuths: Sheriff Jeffreys and Mr. Pigeon. But they can only get at part of the truth. The
murder is finally solved by those most intimately involved – a cross-purpose collection of the
major suspects. After her first mystery, Potts seldom bothered portraying police characters at
all. Their part of the action occurs off-stage and is extraneous to the real process of tragic
discovery for the central characters. Potts's style of domestic investigation is intense, if
unorthodox. And since the law is unimportant, there is no stockpiling of evidence with a trial
in view. Instead, a fortuitous bit of circumstantial evidence is often presented to the culprit by
other suspects. A confession is often followed by suicide or mental collapse. All this is
witnessed by the murderer's peers – as collective nemesis and mourner.

In addition to a healthy disrespect for legal procedures, Potts's novels also show a marked
tendency to stray (much to the distaste of purist-critics) from the plot formulas of the
traditional mystery. Her third novel, *The Diehard*, is the story of a small-town tyrant ego-
muscling his way to an early grave. But as the tyrant dies at the end, and not at the beginning,
of the novel, the question is not whodunit, but who (of the many candidates) *will* do it. The
story is nicely suspenseful (complete with surprise ending) and almost allegorical. Love, we
are shown, can be even more lethal than hatred. Potts continued to write mystery parables.
The Evil Wish teaches that the intent to murder can be as morally destructive as the act. And
The Little Lie is an extremely macabre illustration of the old adage: "What a tangled web we
weave...."

Suspense or whodunit, the most important aspect of Potts's novels is character. The
mystery plot, whatever its form, is but a means to that end. There are few absolute good guys
or villains here. Characters are generally both unlovable and unhateable. They only evoke, in
the reader, and repeatedly in one another, a sense of helpless pity. All are painfully human,

and recognizable without being stereotypical. Take, for example, the passive antagonist – a character Potts carefully observes in such books as *Death of a Stray Cat* and *The Troublemaker*. These are born victims (both, not surprisingly, women) who unconsciously incite violence in others. Potts adds new, honest meaning to the old sexist concept of the girl "who asked for it." This is one author who doesn't trade in happily-ever-afters. Her characters, even the most blameless, cannot go unscathed by the violence around them. They carry their share of guilt and anguish. And it is a clear case of the survival of the fittest. Only those characters with sufficient mental and emotional strength will "survive." The murder (or death) and its investigation represent a crisis point for all involved. For some, like Martin Shipley in *The Footsteps on the Stairs*, the crisis provides the impetus to re-commit themselves to life. But these are the lucky few.

Jean Potts does not, perhaps, write the most cheerful of mystery novels. But her exploration of the effects of violence on life-like characters is no mean accomplishment. Her steady eye, quiet wit, and unfailing compassion make her an important contributor to the modern mystery novel.

—Kathleen L. Maio

POWELL, James. Canadian. Born in Toronto, 12 June 1932. Educated at St. Michael's College, University of Toronto, B.A. 1955; University of Paris, 1955–56. Teacher in France; journalist; editor of antiques newspaper, Pennsylvania. Agent: Scott Meredith Literary Agency Inc., 845 Third Avenue, New York, New York 10022. Address: Box 142, Marietta, Pennsylvania 17547, U.S.A.

CRIME PUBLICATIONS

Short Stories

"Have You Heard the Latest," in *Caper* (New York), April 1967.
"The Friends of Hector Jouvet," in *Ellery Queen's All-Star Lineup.* New York, New American Library, 1967; London, Gollancz, 1968.
"The Stollmeyer Sonnets," in *Best Detective Stories of the Year*, edited by Anthony Boucher. New York, Dutton, 1967.
"The Daring Daylight Melon Robbery," in *Ellery Queen's Mystery Magazine* (New York), October 1968.
"The Great Paleontological Murder Mystery," in *Ellery Queen's Mystery Magazine* (New York), November 1968.
"The Beddoes Scheme," in *Best Detective Stories of the Year*, edited by Anthony Boucher. New York, Dutton, 1968.
"Maze in the Elevator," in *Ellery Queen's Murder Menu.* Cleveland, World, and London, Gollancz, 1969.
"The Altdorf Syndrome," in *Ellery Queen's Grand Slam.* Cleveland, World, 1970; London, Gollancz, 1971.
"Kleber on Murder in 30 Volumes," in *Best Detective Stories of the Year*, edited by Allen J. Hubin. New York, Dutton, 1970.
"The Plot Against Santa Claus," in *Ellery Queen's Mystery Magazine* (New York), January 1971.

"Three Men in a Tub," in *Ellery Queen's Mystery Magazine* (New York), September 1971.

"Coins in the Frascati Fountain," in *Best Detective Stories of the Year*, edited by Allen J. Hubin.   New York, Dutton, 1971.

"Trophy Day at the Chateau Gai," in *Ellery Queen's Mystery Magazine* (New York), February 1972.

"The Mandalasian Garotte," in *Ellery Queen's Mystery Magazine* (New York), July 1972.

"Ganelon and the Master Thief," in *Ellery Queen's Mystery Magazine* (New York), October 1972.

"The Gobineau Necklace," in *Ellery Queen's Mystery Bag.*   Cleveland, World, 1972; London, Gollancz, 1973.

"The Ascent of the Grimselhorn," in *Ellery Queen's Mystery Magazine* (New York), April 1973.

"The Pomeranian's Whereabouts," in *Ellery Queen's Mystery Magazine* (New York), January 1973.

"The Bee on the Finger," in *Playboy* (Chicago), September 1973.

"The Theft of the Fabulous Hen" in *Ellery Queen's Mystery Magazine* (New York), November 1973.

"The Oubliette Cipher," in *Ellery Queen's Mystery Magazine* (New York), November 1974.

"A Murder Coming," in *Best Detective Stories of the Year 1974*, edited by Allen J. Hubin.   New York, Dutton, 1974.

"The Eye of Shafti," in *Every Crime in the Book*, edited by Robert L. Fish.   New York, Putnam, 1975.

"Bianca and the Seven Sleuths," in *Ellery Queen's Searches and Seizures.*   New York, Davis, 1977.

James Powell comments:

Since it may not come round again I mustn't let pass this chance to offer a few words of introduction to my modest body of work. I see myself as a writer of humorous fiction who is attracted to the mystery story. I don't find this strange. Both the funny story and the mystery travel down a strongly plotted road all the while preparing the reader for the punch line, the unexpected ending which he must instantly understand was the only ending there ever could have been.

Where they fall into groups my stories are currently of three kinds: those that relate the adventures of Acting Sergeant Maynard Bullock of the Royal Canadian Mounted Police, an earnest bungler of whom I am unashamedly fond; those fantasies of mystery and detection told in nursery story or fairy tale settings; and stories about the Riviera principality of San Sebastiano. Among these can be found the cases of the Ambrose Ganelons, four generations of detectives with the same name whose activities span 125 years. Having fashioned a history for San Sebastiano worthy of any country in Europe, laid down its ample boulevards, set its buildings in place, and originated its many quaint customs I find myself replying sharply to those who suggest it is only Monaco under another name. In fact the truth is quite the other way around.

*   *   *

It is difficult to explain why the talents of James Powell have largely gone unappreciated and his stories uncollected and seldom anthologized. The S. J. Perelman of the mystery story, he specializes in outrageous, hilarious satires, dealing with international crime and surprise endings.

In "The Eye of Shafti" Powell dares to do a story about the theft of a jewel from an Asian temple. He includes a hilarious scene of temple priests pursuing the thief along the Street of

Flowering Garbage. "The Beddoes Scheme" is a story about an incredible alternative to the atom bomb as a means of ending World War II. Many Powell stories are set in the fictional Riviera state of San Sebastiano. Stories such as "Coins in the Frascati Fountain," the longest and best of these, recount the adventures of Inspector Flanel, the Ambrose Ganelon Detective Agency, Warden Alfred Panache, and others. Another Powell series features the dim-witted Acting Sergeant Maynard Bullock of the Canadian mounties. In his first story, "The Stollmeyer Sonnets," Bullock explains, "for the last couple of years I've been guarding the flowerbeds in front of the Parliament Buildings in Ottawa.... It's exciting work in its own way. You never hear the bee that has your name on it." In "The Mandalasian Garotte" he parachutes into the jungles of Asia and ends up claiming territory in the name of Canada. Powell has even written a series of mysteries based on fairy tales, including "The Plot Against Santa Claus," "Three Men in a Tub," "The Theft of the Fabulous Hen," and "Bianca and the Seven Sleuths," a Snow White take-off. One of his rare "serious" stories is "Maze in the Elevator," about two men trapped in an elevator. It is the kind of terror-filled urban situation most city dwellers dread – but told with a typically unusual, unguessable Powell finish.

—Marvin Lachman

PRATHER, Richard S(cott). Also writes as David Knight; Douglas Ring. American. Born in Santa Ana, California, 9 September 1921. Educated at Riverside Junior College, California, 1940–41. Served as a fireman, oiler, and engineer in the United States Merchant Marine, 1942–45. Married Tina Hager in 1945. Civil Service clerk, March Air Force Base, Riverside, 1945–49. Since 1949, self-employed writer and avocado farmer. Twice Member of the Board of Directors, Mystery Writers of America. Address: 2373 Wilt Road, Fallbrook, California 92028, U.S.A.

Crime Publications

Novels (series character: Shell Scott)

> *Case of the Vanishing Beauty* (Scott). New York, Fawcett, 1950; London, Fawcett, 1957.
> *Bodies in Bedlam* (Scott). New York, Fawcett, 1951; London, Fawcett, 1957.
> *Everybody Had a Gun* (Scott). New York, Fawcett, 1951; London, Muller, 1953.
> *Find This Woman* (Scott). New York, Fawcett, 1951; London, Fawcett, 1957.
> *Way of a Wanton* (Scott). New York, Fawcett, 1952; London, Fawcett, 1958.
> *Pattern for Murder* (as David Knight). Hasbrouck Heights, New Jersey, Graphic, 1952; as *The Scrambled Yeggs*, New York, Fawcett, 1958; London, Muller, 1961.
> *Lie Down, Killer.* New York, Lion, 1952; London, Fawcett, 1958.
> *Dagger of Flesh.* New York, Falcon, 1952.
> *Darling, It's Death* (Scott). New York, Fawcett, 1952; London, Fawcett, 1957.
> *The Peddler* (as Douglas Ring). New York, Lion, 1952; London, Muller, 1963.
> *Ride a High Horse* (Scott). New York, Fawcett, 1953; as *Too Many Crooks*, New York, Fawcett, 1956; London, Fawcett, 1957.
> *Always Leave 'em Dying* (Scott). New York, Fawcett, 1954; London, Fawcett, 1957.
> *Pattern for Panic.* New York, Abelard Schuman, 1954; revised edition (Scott), New York, Fawcett, 1961; London, Muller, 1962.
> *Strip for Murder* (Scott). New York, Fawcett, 1955; London, Fawcett, 1957.

Dragnet: Case No. 561 (Scott).   New York, Pocket Books, 1956; London, Consul, 1957.
The Wailing Frail (Scott).   New York, Fawcett, 1956; London, Fawcett, 1957.
Three's a Shroud (3 novelets; Scott).   New York, Fawcett, 1957; London, Gold Lion, 1973.
Slab Happy (Scott).   New York, Fawcett, 1958.
Take a Murder, Darling (Scott).   New York, Fawcett, 1958; London, Muller, 1961.
Over Her Dear Body (Scott).   New York, Fawcett, 1959; London, Panther, 1960.
Double in Trouble (Scott), with Stephen Marlowe.   New York, Fawcett, 1959.
Dance with the Dead (Scott).   New York, Fawcett, 1960; London, Muller, 1962.
Dig That Crazy Grave (Scott).   New York, Fawcett, 1961; London, Muller, 1962.
Kill the Clown (Scott).   New York, Fawcett, 1962; London, Muller, 1963.
Dead Heat (Scott).   New York, Pocket Books, 1963.
Joker in the Deck (Scott).   New York, Fawcett, 1964; London, Muller, 1965.
The Cockeyed Corpse (Scott).   New York, Fawcett, 1964.
The Trojan Hearse (Scott).   New York, Pocket Books, 1964; London, New English Library, 1967.
Kill Him Twice (Scott).   New York, Pocket Books, 1965.
Dead Man's Walk (Scott).   New York, Pocket Books, 1965; London, New English Library, 1968.
The Meandering Corpse (Scott).   New York, Trident Press, 1965; London, New English Library, 1967.
The Kubla Khan Caper (Scott).   New York, Trident Press, 1966.
Gat Heat (Scott).   New York, Trident Press, 1967; London, New English Library, 1968.
The Cheim Manuscript (Scott).   New York, Pocket Books, 1969.
Kill Me Tomorrow (Scott).   New York, Pocket Books, 1969.
Shell Scott's Murder Mix (omnibus).   New York, Trident Press, 1970.
Dead-Bang (Scott).   New York, Pocket Books, 1971.
The Sweet Ride (Scott).   New York, Pocket Books, 1972.
The Sure Thing (Scott).   New York, Pocket Books, 1975.

Short Stories

Have Gat – Will Travel.   New York, Fawcett, 1957; London, Fawcett, 1958.
Shell Scott's Seven Slaughters.   New York, Fawcett, 1961; London, Muller, 1962.
The Shell Scott Sampler.   New York, Pocket Books, 1969.

OTHER PUBLICATIONS

Other

Editor, *The Comfortable Coffin: A Gold Medal Anthology.*   New York, Fawcett, 1960.

*   *   *

A critical reader of Richard S. Prather's Shell Scott fiction will notice the uneven plots and dialogue, wordy exposition, mixed similes, sexual hyperbole, off-color puns and one-liners, yet he will also notice the comic vitality that has carried Prather's fiction through more than two decades. The detective, Shell Scott, a seamy wisecracking ex-Marine with short-cropped white hair, inverted V eyebrows and an eye for women, works out of Hollywood and drives at various times a battered or flashy Cadillac. At times he seems not very bright, but he knows this and is courageous, and his instincts are passably honorable. This comic storm-trooper of a detective was spawned in the wake of World War II in the midst of the Cold War. In *Pattern for Panic*, set in Mexico, he is found in the center of the hysterical violence and pornography that characterized the Communist Menace in adventure fiction of the 1950's, but the breezy spirit found in most of Prather's stories soon strayed from such seriousness. In *Dead-Bang* the conflict is between a fundamentalist religious leader and the inventor of a euphoria-inducing concoction, the crises are simple kidnapping and murder, and Shell Scott aligns himself with the angels – or so he feels.

The early novels, of which *Ride a High Horse* is typical, demonstrate a craftsmanship that many of his subsequent novels lack. In the later novels Prather often resorts to crude stereotypes, as in *The Cheim Manuscript*, where Putrid Stanley's damaged face suggests a permanent reaction to foul odors and his fellow hood Burper McGee has a gas problem that causes him to belch continually. When Burper tries to ambush Scott his rumbling stomach gets him shot. Throughout the novels the women are so young and beautiful that Scott's disappointment at meeting a plain one becomes a running joke. Sexual scenes and bathroom jokes tend to shade the fiction into soft pornography, but they are a part of the formula that Prather mined for the commercial market. If Prather's fiction tends toward self-parody and gross exaggeration of its form, it is also an accurate index of the changing tastes of the original paperback market in fast-paced adventure fiction. In many ways the fiction is similar to the dime-novel, with large doses of contemporary frankness. Prather is capable of creating striking imagery in the hard-boiled tradition, as when Scott is beaten up in an alley and regains consciousness: "I pulled myself over toward the wall and my hand sank into something squishy on the asphalt, and for one horrible moment I thought it was part of me." But, in typical Prather fashion, Scott discovers that his attackers had only turned a garbage can over on him. It is this tendency to cultivate, then mock the grotesque that separates Prather's work from the less successful writers in the newsstand trade.

—Larry N. Landrum

PREEDY, George. See **SHEARING, Joseph.**

PRICE, Anthony. British. Born in Hertfordshire, 16 August 1928. Educated at the King's School, Canterbury, 1941–47; Merton College, Oxford (exhibitioner), 1949–52, B.A. (honours) in history 1952, M.A. Served in the British Army (national service), 1947–49: (Temporary) Captain. Married Ann Stone in 1953; two sons and one daughter. Has worked for the Westminster Press since 1952; since 1972, Editor, *Oxford Times*. Recipient: Crime Writers Association Silver Dagger, 1971, and Gold Dagger, 1975; Swedish Academy of Detection Award, 1979. Agent: Hilary Rubinstein, A. P. Watt and Son, 26–28 Bedford Row, London WC1R 4HL. Address: Wayside Cottage, Horton-cum-Studley, Oxford, England.

CRIME PUBLICATIONS

Novels (series character: Dr. David Audley in all books)

The Labyrinth Makers. London, Gollancz, 1970; New York, Doubleday, 1971.

The Alamut Ambush. London, Gollancz, 1971; New York, Doubleday, 1972.
Colonel Butler's Wolf. London, Gollancz, 1972; New York, Doubleday, 1973.
October Men. London, Gollancz, 1973; New York, Doubleday, 1974.
Other Paths to Glory. London, Gollancz, 1974; New York, Doubleday, 1975.
Our Man in Camelot. London, Gollancz, 1975; New York, Doubleday, 1976.
War Game. London, Gollancz, 1976; New York, Doubleday, 1977.
The '44 Vintage. London, Gollancz, and New York, Doubleday, 1978.
Tomorrow's Ghost. London, Gollancz, and New York, Doubleday, 1979.

Uncollected Short Story

"A Green Boy," in *Winter's Crimes 5*, edited by Virginia Whitaker. London, Macmillan, 1973.

Anthony Price comments:
I started out with the aim of combining elements of the spy thriller with the detective mystery, through a group of characters who would appear and reappear in the series, taking it in turns to play the lead (though one character, David Audley, would have a linking role in all the stories). In addition – very obviously – the setting or background of each story reflects whatever piece of private research (or hobby) I am engaged in at the time – Roman history (*Colonel Butler's Wolf*), the 1914–18 war (*Other Paths to Glory*) and so on. It has been said (by one kind critic) that my obsession is with loyalty. That's fine – and I would hope to add all William Faulkner's "truths of the heart" to that. I take the (old-fashioned?) view, also, that "Our Side," with all its warts and all the character defects of my heroes and heroines, is Good, and "Their Side," whatever virtues they may have, is Bad. Of course, things are never quite as simple as that in practice. But that, for me, is where it all begins and ends.

*   *   *

Anthony Price is a spy writer of the third generation among the moderns. There were at the start Fleming and James Bond, simplicity with snobbery. Then in reaction we got Deighton and le Carré, complication with humanity. So what was an intelligent person, himself an aware critic of the crime novel, to do when in these footsteps he wanted to write espionage fiction? A first, and almost inescapable, step was to invent stories that were even more complicated. But simply to outdo the masters of the treble cross would not have produced a satisfying book, and would even have been self-defeating. A reader, however hopeful of being dazed and dazzled, can take only so much. Indeed, occasionally one feels that Price with his subsequent books has to some extent gone too far.

However, his contribution to spy fiction, and the reason, I think, for his success in it, has been that he has used the sub-genre, the typical story of bluff and counter-bluff, to do something else as well as give us our familiar delightful complications. Thus in his first book, *The Labyrinth Makers* (telling title), he used a typical spy story – there is a mysterious container lost since 1945 somewhere in Britain and Moscow wants to get hold of it come what may – in order to explore a certain sort of person, a person of whom there were at the start of the 1970's in Britain a good many about, the liberal intellectual faced with some concrete and brutal facts.

In other books Price has, while still keeping to the broad formula of espionage fiction, explored other subjects. *Colonel Butler's Wolf* (Butler, together with the cool donnish David Audley, is one of Price's running heroes), for instance, was about the personality of the soldier. In it one of Price's long-standing preoccupations, military history, also played its part. Ingeniously (and Price is nothing if not diabolically ingenious, both as technician of fiction and spinner of spy plots) he set this espionage adventure in the country round Hadrian's Wall, the long line of defences that once separated civilised Roman Britain from the savage hordes to the north, and thus was able to reflect on the military life right back to those long-

1205

ago days. In the equally ingenious *Other Paths to Glory* he contrived a present-day spy plot which closely depended on details of the Battle of the Somme in the 1914–18 War, and so was able to write about the particular ethos of those fighting days. Archaeology is another of his interests, and *Our Man in Camelot* cleverly combines theorising about ancient Britain with a monster KGB plot.

One other thing remains to be said about Price's art: he uses his considerable intelligence to make sharp incidental sociological points (save that he spares us the sociologist's jargon), points about the Britain he knows at the time of writing. As a guide to the thoughts and interests of what might broadly be called Establishment Britain from 1970 onwards he will be of more than a little use to the historian of ideas and the historian of manners.

—H. R. F. Keating

PRIESTLEY, J(ohn) B(oynton). British. Born in Bradford, Yorkshire, 13 September 1894. Educated in Bradford schools, and at Trinity Hall, Cambridge, M.A. Served with the Duke of Wellington's and Devon Regiments, 1914–19. Married 1) Patricia Tempest (died, 1925), two daughters; 2) Mary Wyndham Lewis (divorced, 1952), two daughters and one son; 3) the writer Jacquetta Hawkes in 1953. Director, Mask Theatre, London, 1938–39; radio lecturer on BBC programme "Postscripts" during World War II; regular contributor, *New Statesman*, London. President, P.E.N., London, 1936–37; United Kingdom Delegate, and Chairman, UNESCO International Theatre Conference, Paris, 1947, and Prague, 1948; Chairman, British Theatre Conference, 1948; President, International Theatre Institute, 1949; Member, National Theatre Board, London, 1966–67. Recipient: Black Memorial Prize, 1930; Ellen Terry Award, 1948. LL.D.: University of St. Andrews; D.Litt.: University of Birmingham; University of Bradford. Honorary Freeman, City of Bradford, 1973; Order of Merit, 1977; Honorary Student, Trinity Hall, Cambridge, 1978. Address: Kissing Tree House, Alveston, Stratford upon Avon, Warwickshire, England.

CRIME PUBLICATIONS

Novels

> *Benighted.* London, Heinemann, 1927; as *The Old Dark House*, New York, Harper, 1928.
> *I'll Tell You Everything*, with Gerald Bullett. New York, Macmillan, 1932; London, Heinemann, 1933.
> *The Doomsday Men.* London, Heinemann, and New York, Harper, 1938.
> *Black-Out in Gretley: A Story of – and for – Wartime.* London, Heinemann, and New York, Harper, 1942.
> *Saturn over the Water: An Account of His Adventures in London, South America and Australia by Tim Bedford, Painter; Edited, with Some Preliminary and Concluding Remarks, by Henry Sulgrave and Here Presented to the Reading Public.* London, Heinemann, and New York, Doubleday, 1961.
> *The Shapes of Sleep: A Topical Tale.* London, Heinemann, and New York, Doubleday, 1962.
> *Salt Is Leaving.* London, Pan, 1966; New York, Harper, 1975.

OTHER PUBLICATIONS

Novels

Adam in Moonshine. London, Heinemann, and New York, Harper, 1927.
Farthing Hall, with Hugh Walpole. London, Macmillan, and New York, Doubleday, 1929.
The Good Companions. London, Heinemann, and New York, Harper, 1929.
Angel Pavement. London, Heinemann, and New York, Harper, 1930.
Faraway. London, Heinemann, and New York, Harper, 1932.
Wonder Hero. London, Heinemann, and New York, Harper, 1933.
They Walk in the City: The Lovers in the Stone Forest. London, Heinemann, and New York, Harper, 1936.
Let the People Sing. London, Heinemann, 1939; New York, Harper, 1940.
Daylight on Saturday: A Novel about an Aircraft Factory. London, Heinemann, and New York, Harper, 1943.
Three Men in New Suits. London, Heinemann, and New York, Harper, 1945.
Bright Day. London, Heinemann, and New York, Harper, 1946.
Jenny Villiers: A Story of the Theatre. London, Heinemann, and New York, Harper, 1947.
Festival at Farbridge. London, Heinemann, 1951; as *Festival*, New York, Harper, 1951.
The Magicians. London, Heinemann, and New York, Harper, 1954.
Low Notes on a High Level: A Frolic. London, Heinemann, and New York, Harper, 1954.
The Thirty-First of June: A Tale of True Love, Enterprise and Progress in the Arthurian and ad-Atomic Ages. London, Heinemann, 1961; New York, Doubleday, 1962.
Sir Michael and Sir George: A Tale of COSMA and DISCUS and the New Elizabethans. London, Heinemann, 1964; Boston, Little Brown, 1965(?).
Lost Empires, Being Sir Richard Herncastle's Account of His Life on the Variety Stage from November 1913 to August 1914, Together with a Prologue and Epilogue. London, Heinemann, and Boston, Little Brown, 1965.
It's an Old Country. London, Heinemann, and Boston, Little Brown, 1967.
The Image Men: Out of Town, and London End. London, Heinemann, 2 vols., 1968; Boston, Little Brown, 1969.
Found, Lost, Found; or, The English Way of Life. London, Heinemann, 1976; New York, Stein and Day, 1977.

Short Stories

The Town Major of Miraucourt. London, Heinemann, 1930.
Albert Goes Through. London, Heinemann, and New York, Harper, 1933.
Going Up: Stories and Sketches. London, Pan, 1950.
The Other Place and Other Stories of the Same Sort. London, Heinemann, and New York, Harper, 1953.
The Carfitt Crisis and Two Other Stories. London, Heinemann, 1975; New York, Stein and Day, 1976.

Plays

The Good Companions, with Edward Knoblock, adaptation of the novel by J. B. Priestley (produced London and New York, 1931). London and New York, French, 1935.
Dangerous Corner (produced London and New York, 1932). London, Heinemann, and New York, French, 1932.

The Roundabout (produced Liverpool, London, and New York, 1932). London, Heinemann, and New York, French, 1933.

Laburnum Grove: An Immoral Comedy (produced London, 1933; New York, 1935). London, Heinemann, 1934; New York, French, 1935.

Eden End (produced London, 1934; New York, 1935). London, Heinemann, 1934; in *Three Plays and a Preface*, 1935.

Cornelius: A Business Affair in Three Transactions (produced Birmingham and London, 1935). London, Heinemann, 1935; New York, French, 1936.

Duet in Floodlight (produced Liverpool and London, 1935). London, Heinemann, 1935.

Three Plays and a Preface (includes *Dangerous Corner*, *Eden End*, *Cornelius*). New York, Harper, 1935.

Bees on the Boat Deck: A Farcical Tragedy (produced London, 1936). London, Heinemann, and Boston, Baker, 1936.

Spring Tide (as Peter Goldsmith), with George Billam (produced London, 1936). London, Heinemann, and New York, French, 1936.

The Bad Samaritan (produced Liverpool, 1937).

Time and the Conways (produced London, 1937; New York, 1938). London, Heinemann, 1937; New York, Harper, 1938.

I Have Been Here Before (produced London, 1937; New York, 1938). London, Heinemann, 1937; New York, Harper, 1938.

Two Time Plays (includes *Time and The Conways* and *I Have Been Here Before*). London, Heinemann, 1937.

I'm a Stranger Here (produced Bradford, 1937).

People at Sea (produced London, 1937). London, Heinemann, and New York, French, 1937.

Mystery at Greenfingers: A Comedy of Detection (produced London, 1938). London, French, 1937; New York, French, 1938.

When We Are Married: A Yorkshire Farcical Comedy (produced London, 1938; New York, 1939). London, Heinemann, 1938; New York, French, 1940.

Music at Night (produced Malvern, Worcestershire, 1938; London, 1939). Included in *Three Plays*, 1943; in *Plays I*, 1948.

Johnson over Jordan (produced London, 1939). Published as *Johnson over Jordan: The Play, and All about It (An Essay)*, London, Heinemann, and New York, Harper, 1939.

The Long Mirror (produced Oxford, 1940; London, 1945). Included in *Three Plays*, 1943; in *Four Plays*, 1944.

Good Night Children: A Comedy of Broadcasting (produced London, 1942). Included in *Three Comedies*, 1945; in *Plays II*, 1949.

Desert Highway (produced Bristol, 1943; London, 1944). London, French, 1944; in *Four Plays*, 1944.

They Came to a City (produced London, 1943). Included in *Three Plays*, 1943; in *Four Plays*, 1944.

Three Plays (includes *Music at Night*, *The Long Mirror*, *They Came to a City*). London, Heinemann, 1943.

How Are They at Home? A Topical Comedy (produced London, 1944). Included in *Three Comedies*, 1945; in *Plays II*, 1949.

The Golden Fleece (as *The Bull Market*, produced Bradford, 1944). Included in *Three Comedies*, 1945.

Four Plays (includes *Music at Night*, *The Long Mirror*, *They Came to a City*, *Desert Highway*). New York, Harper, 1944; London, Heinemann, 1945.

Three Comedies (includes *Good Night Children*, *The Golden Fleece*, *How Are They at Home?*). London, Heinemann, 1945.

An Inspector Calls (produced Moscow, 1945; London, 1946; New York, 1947). London, Heinemann, 1947; New York, Dramatists Play Service, 1948(?).

Jenny Villiers (produced Bristol, 1946).

The Rose and Crown (televised, 1946).   London, French, 1947.

Ever Since Paradise: An Entertainment, Chiefly Referring to Love and Marriage (also
   director: produced on tour, 1946; London, 1947).   London and New York, French,
   1949.

Three Time Plays (includes *Dangerous Corner, Time and the Conways, I Have Been Here
   Before*).   London, Pan, 1947.

The Linden Tree (produced Sheffield and London, 1947; New York, 1948).   London,
   Heinemann, and New York, French, 1948.

The Plays of J. B. Priestley:

   I. *Dangerous Corner, I Have Been Here Before, Johnson over Jordan, Music at Night,
      The Linden Tree, Eden End, Time and the Conways*.   London, Heinemann, 1948;
      as *Seven Plays*, New York, Harper, 1950.

   II. *Laburnum Grove, Bees on the Boat Deck, When We Are Married, Good Night
      Children, The Good Companions, How Are They at Home?, Ever Since Paradise*.
      London, Heinemann, 1949; New York, Harper, 1951.

   III. *Cornelius, People at Sea, They Came to a City, Desert Highway, An Inspector
      Calls, Home Is Tomorrow, Summer Day's Dream*.   London, Heinemann, 1950;
      New York, Harper, 1952.

Home Is Tomorrow (produced Bradford and London, 1948).   London, Heinemann,
   1949; in *Plays III*, 1950.

The High Toby: A Play for the Toy Theatre (produced London, 1954).   London,
   Penguin-Pollock, 1948.

Summer Day's Dream (produced Bradford and London, 1949).   Included in *Plays III*,
   1950.

The Olympians, music by Arthur Bliss (produced London, 1949).   London, Novello,
   1949.

Bright Shadow: A Play of Detection (produced Oldham and London, 1950).   London,
   French, 1950.

Treasure on Pelican (as *Treasure on Pelican Island*, televised, 1951; as *Treasure on
   Pelican*, produced Cardiff and London, 1952).   London, Evans, 1953.

Dragon's Mouth: A Dramatic Quartet, with Jacquetta Hawkes (also director: produced
   Malvern and London, 1952; New York, 1955).   London, Heinemann and New
   York, Harper, 1952.

Private Rooms: A One-Act Comedy in the Viennese Style.   London, French, 1953.

Mother's Day.   London, French, 1953.

Try It Again (produced London, 1965).   London, French, 1953.

A Glass of Bitter.   London, French, 1954.

The White Countess, with Jacquetta Hawkes (produced Dublin and London, 1954).

The Scandalous Affair of Mr. Kettle and Mrs. Moon (produced Folkestone and London,
   1955).   London, French, 1956.

These Our Actors (produced Glasgow, 1956).

Take the Fool Away (produced Vienna, 1956; Nottingham, 1959).

The Glass Cage (produced Toronto and London, 1957).   London, French, 1958.

The Thirty-First of June (produced Toronto and London, 1957).

The Pavilion of Masks (produced Bristol, 1963).   London, French, 1958.

A Severed Head, with Iris Murdoch, adaptation of the novel by Murdoch (produced
   Bristol and London, 1963; New York, 1964).   London, Chatto and Windus, 1964.

Screenplays: *Sing As We Go*, with Gordon Wellesley, 1934; *We Live in Two Worlds*,
1937; *Jamaica Inn*, with Sidney Gilliat and Joan Harrison, 1939; *Britain at Bay*, 1940;
Our Russian Allies, 1941; *The Foreman Went to France (Somewhere in France)*, with
others, 1942; *Last Holiday*, 1950.

Radio Plays: *The Return of Jess Oakroyd*, 1941; *The Golden Entry*, 1955; *End Game at
the Dolphin*, 1956; *An Arabian Night in Park Lane*, 1965.

Television Plays: *The Rose and Crown*, 1946; *Treasure on Pelican Island*, 1951; *The Stone Face*, 1957; *The Rack*, 1958; *Doomsday for Dyson*, 1958; *The Fortrose Incident*, 1959; *Level Seven*, 1966; *The Lost Peace* series, 1966; *Anyone for Tennis*, 1968; *Linda at Pulteneys*, 1969.

Verse

The Chapman of Rhymes (juvenilia).   London, Alexander Moring, 1918.

Other

Brief Diversions, Being Tales, Travesties and Epigrams.   Cambridge, Bowes and Bowes, 1922.
Papers from Lilliput.   Cambridge, Bowes and Bowes, 1922.
I for One.   London, Lane, 1923; New York, Dodd Mead, 1924.
Figures in Modern Literature.   London, Lane, and New York, Dodd Mead, 1924.
Fools and Philosophers: A Gallery of Comic Figures from English Literature.   London, Lane, 1925; as *The English Comic Characters*, New York, Dodd Mead, 1925.
George Meredith.   London, Macmillan, and New York, Macmillan, 1926.
Talking: An Essay.   London, Jarrolds, and New York, Harper, 1926.
(Essays).   London, Harrap, 1926.
Open House: A Book of Essays.   London, Heinemann, and New York, Harper, 1927.
Thomas Love Peacock.   London, Macmillan, and New York, Macmillan, 1927.
The English Novel.   London, Benn, 1927; revised edition, London, Nelson, 1935; Folcroft, Pennsylvania, Folcroft Editions, 1974.
Too Many People and Other Reflections.   New York and London, Harper, 1928.
Apes and Angels: A Book of Essays.   London, Methuen, 1928.
The Balconinny and Other Essays.   London, Methuen, 1929; as *The Balconinny*, New York, Harper, 1930.
English Humour.   London and New York, Longman, 1929.
Self-Selected Essays.   London, Heinemann, and New York, Harper, 1932.
Four-in-Hand (miscellany).   London, Heinemann, 1934.
English Journey: Being a Rambling But Truthful Account of What One Man Saw and Heard and Felt and Thought During a Journey Through England During the Autumn of the Year 1933.   London, Heinemann-Gollancz, and New York, Harper, 1934.
Midnight on the Desert: A Chapter of Autobiography.   London, Heinemann, 1937; as *Midnight on the Desert: Being an Excursion into Autobiography During a Winter in America, 1935–36*, New York, Harper, 1937.
Rain upon Godshill: A Further Chapter of Autobiography.   London, Heinemann, and New York, Harper, 1939.
Britain Speaks (radio talks).   New York, Harper, 1940.
Postscripts (radio talks).   London, Heinemann, 1940.
Out of the People.   London, Collins-Heinemann, and New York, Harper, 1941.
Britain at War.   New York, Harper, 1942.
British Women Go to War.   London, Collins, 1943.
Here Are Your Answers.   London, Socialist Book Centre, 1944.
Letter to a Returning Serviceman.   London, Home and Van Thal, 1945.
The Secret Dream: An Essay on Britain, America and Russia.   London, Turnstile Press, 1946.
Russian Journey.   London, Writers Group of the Society for Cultural Relations with the USSR, 1946.
The New Citizen (address).   London, Committee for Education in World Citizenship, 1946.
Theatre Outlook.   London, Nicholson and Watson, 1947.

The Arts under Socialism: Being a Lecture Given to the Fabian Society, With a Postscript on What the Government Should Do for the Arts Here and Now. London, Turnstile Press, 1947.

Delight. London, Heinemann, and New York, Harper, 1949.

A Priestley Companion: A Selection from the Writings of J. B. Priestley. London, Penguin-Heinemann, 1951.

Journey down a Rainbow, with Jacquetta Hawkes (travel). London, Cresset Press-Heinemann, and New York, Harper, 1955.

All about Ourselves and Other Essays, edited by Eric Gillett. London, Heinemann, 1956.

The Writer in a Changing Society (lecture). Aldington, Kent, Hand and Flower Press, 1956.

Thoughts in the Wilderness (essays). London, Heinemann, and New York, Harper, 1957.

The Art of the Dramatist: A Lecture Together with Appendices and Discursive Notes. London, Heinemann, 1957; Boston, The Writer, 1958.

Topside; or, The Future of England: A Dialogue. London, Heinemann, 1958.

The Story of Theatre (juvenile). London, Rathbone, 1959; as *The Wonderful World of the Theatre*, New York, Doubleday, 1959; London, Macdonald, 1969.

Literature and Western Man. London, Heinemann, and New York, Harper, 1960.

William Hazlitt. London, Longman, 1960.

Charles Dickens: A Pictorial Biography. London, Thames and Hudson, 1961; New York, Viking Press, 1962; as *Charles Dickens and His World*, Thames and Hudson, 1969; New York, Scribner, 1978.

Margin Released: A Writer's Reminiscences and Reflections. London, Heinemann, 1962; New York, Harper, 1963.

Man and Time. London, Aldus Books, and New York, Doubleday, 1964.

The Moments and Other Pieces. London, Heinemann, 1966.

The World of J. B. Priestley, edited by Donald G. MacRae. London, Heinemann, 1967.

All England Listened: J. B. Priestley's Wartime Broadcasts. New York, Chilmark Press, 1968.

Essays of Five Decades, edited by Susan Cooper. Boston, Little Brown, 1968; London, Heinemann, 1969.

Trumpets over the Sea: Being a Rambling and Egotistical Account of the London Symphony Orchestra's Engagement at Daytona Beach, Florida, in July–August 1967. London, Heinemann, 1968.

The Prince of Pleasure and His Regency, 1811–1820. London, Heinemann, and New York, Harper, 1969.

The Edwardians. London, Heinemann, and New York, Harper, 1970.

Snoggle (juvenile). London, Heinemann, 1971; New York, Harcourt Brace, 1972.

Victoria's Heyday. London, Heinemann, and New York, Harcourt Brace, 1972.

Over the Long High Wall: Some Reflections and Speculations on Life, Death and Time. London, Heinemann, 1972.

The English. London, Heinemann, and New York, Viking Press, 1973.

Outcries and Asides. London, Heinemann, 1974.

A Visit to New Zealand. London, Heinemann, 1974.

Particular Pleasures, Being a Personal Record of Some Varied Arts and Many Different Artists. London, Heinemann, and New York, Stein and Day, 1975.

The Happy Dream (biography). Andoversford, Gloucestershire, Whittington Press, 1976.

Instead of Trees: A Final Chapter of Autobiography. London, Heinemann, and New York, Stein and Day, 1977.

Editor, *Essayists Past and Present: A Selection of English Essays.* London, Jenkins, and New York, Dial Press, 1925.

Editor, *Tom Moore's Diary: A Selection.*   London, Cambridge University Press, 1925.
Editor, *The Book of Bodley Head Verse.*   London, Lane, and New York, Dodd Mead, 1926.
Editor, *The Female Spectator: Selections from Mrs. Eliza Haywood's Periodical, 1744-1746.*   London, Lane, 1929.
Editor, *Our Nation's Heritage.*   London, Dent, 1939.
Editor, *Scenes of London Life, From Sketches by Boz by Charles Dickens.*   London, Pan, 1947.
Editor, *The Best of Leacock.*   Toronto, McClelland and Stewart, 1957; as *The Bodley Head Leacock,* London, Bodley Head, 1957.
Editor, with O. B. Davis, *Four English Novels.*   New York, Harcourt Brace, 1960.
Editor, with O. B. Davis, *Four English Biographies.*   New York, Harcourt Brace, 1961.
Editor, *Adventures in English Literature.*   New York, Harcourt Brace, 1963.
Editor, *An Everyman Anthology.*   London, Dent, 1966.

Theatrical Activities:

Director: **Plays** – *Ever Since Paradise,* tour, 1946, and London, 1947; *Dragon's Mouth,* London, 1952.

*   *   *

An enormously prolific and versatile writer, J. B. Priestley has generously contributed also to the crime genre. In a wider sense this contribution embraces such divergent novels as *Adam in Moonshine* (his very first), *Benighted,* and *The Magicians,* stories like "The Grey Ones" (in eeriness akin to Dahl) and "The Carfitt Crisis" as well as *I'll Tell You Everything,* a hilarious early cloak-and-dagger yarn written with Gerald Bullett; in drama mainly *Mystery at Greenfingers,* a delightfully clever pastiche of the detective play, and also *Home Is Tomorrow* and *Treasure on Pelican.* There are no sharp dividing lines in Priestley's work. His late, quite differently angled novel *It's an Old Country* contains one of his satirical portraits of "private investigators," first-rate failures to a man. And *An Inspector Calls,* his most lasting international success in drama, uses the guise of the detective play for an excruciating analysis of pre-1914 industrialism. The characters on stage and in the audience take long to realise that Goole (an elder and more solid cousin of The Unidentified Guest in Eliot's *The Cocktail Party*) is no policeman. No one knows what he is, but it does not matter. He has done his job.

In a narrower sense, there are five long prose works one can call crime novels. They have no surface links; each is essentially an unrepeated experiment. They do share certain characteristics, however. Their central figures are not "professionals," but professional men. No longer young, they are good (and discerning) livers and good at their profession which they temporarily abandon to investigate the mystery circumstances fling at them. There is a lot of humour and an "open" plot as opposed to the "closed-group-in-an-inaccessible-spot" (employed in *Benighted, Mystery at Greenfingers, Treasure on Pelican*). The ending is successful – crimes are elucidated or disasters averted, though the general outlook may remain bleak – and happy: no sequel being envisaged, the (strong) love interest can safely lead to marriage. These novels are remote from the intellectual puzzle and the story of massive, non-committal violence; their romantic albeit sober endings separate them also from the desolate alienation depicted in much recent British crime fiction (Deighton, Garve, le Carré, Symons). There are formal and conceptual links with Priestley's other writings, and the realism is coloured (though not impaired) by the strong commitment to human values of this ardent social critic, cultural historian, and philosopher.

Two are "global crime" stories. In *The Doomsday Men* pseudo-religious indoctrination (compare Hammett's *Dain Curse*) and advanced technology (compare Fleming's *You Only Live Twice*) are used by a despairing maniac for the (attempted) annihilation of all life on earth. This book, though set in the States, can nevertheless be seen as a shrewd (and thrilling) analysis of the Hitlerian death-drive. And in *Saturn over the Water* (structurally related to *Lost Empires*, thematically to *The Magicians*) an international set of powerful men conspire to drive mankind over the edge to self-destruction. *The Shapes of Sleep* is (like le Carré's *A Small Town in Germany*) a more thoughtful than violent cold war spy thriller concerning a psychological discovery equally useful for subliminal sales promotion, political propaganda, and enemy disorientation. It also (like Watson's *Hopjoy Was Here*) debunks our world of secret services. *Black-Out in Gretley* is a gripping counter-espionage story, authentically embedded in the life of a northern industrial city. One of Priestley's many contributions to the War Effort (and related to *Daylight on Saturday*) it compares favourably to corresponding works by Allingham, Blake, Christie, and Michael Innes. *Salt Is Leaving* (its title character gave something to Tuby and Saltana in *The Image Men*) is exactly what the publishers say on the cover: "a pungent novel of crime and detection." It is also a cheerfully biased, but uncomfortably close portrait of British society in the 1960's.

Viewed overall, Priestley is an exponent of the modern trend to dissolve the neatly isolated literature of crime in the more ambiguous, wider literature with a crime angle. Viewed as an occasional guest among "professional" crime writers, he has created five books with an unusual edge; all creditable, two outstanding. Not surprisingly, written as they are by so experienced a dramatist, all five novels would very easily make remarkable films.

—H. M. Klein

PRIOR, Allan. British. Born in Newcastle on Tyne, Northumberland. Educated at South Shore School, Blackpool, Lancashire. Served in the Royal Air Force, 1942–46. Married Edith Playford in 1944; one son and one daughter. Recipient: Crime Writers Association Award, 1962, 1964; Writers Guild of Great Britain Award, 1962, 1965; Grand Prix de Littérature Policière, 1963; British Academy Award, 1974. Address: Summerhill, Waverley Road, St. Albans, Hertfordshire, England.

CRIME PUBLICATIONS

Novels

> *One Away.* London, Eyre and Spottiswoode, 1961.
> *Z Cars Again* (novelization of tv series). London, Trust Books, 1963.
> *The Interrogators.* London, Cassell, and New York, Simon and Schuster, 1965.
> *The Operators.* London, Cassell, 1966; New York, Simon and Schuster, 1967.

OTHER PUBLICATIONS

Novels

> *A Flame in the Air.* London, Joseph, 1951.
> *The Joy Ride.* London, Joseph, 1952.
> *The One-Eyed Monster: A Novel about Television.* London, Bodley Head, 1958.
> *The Loving Cup.* London, Cassell, 1968; New York, Simon and Schuster, 1969.
> *The Contract.* London, Cassell, 1970; New York, Simon and Schuster, 1971.
> *Paradiso.* London, Cassell, 1972; New York, Simon and Schuster, 1973.
> *Affair.* London, Cassell, and New York, Simon and Schuster, 1976.

Never Been Kissed in the Same Place Twice. London, Cassell, 1978; New York, Harper, 1979.

Plays

Screenplays: *All Coppers Are ...*, 1971; *One Away*, 1974.

Radio Plays: *The Prawn King*, 1951; *A Personal Affair*, 1952; *A Flame in the Air*, 1953; *Memo to Mr. Alexander*, 1953; *Worker in the Dawn*, 1953; *Missing from His Home*, 1953; *Power of the Press* (2 series), 1953–55; *The Running Man*, 1955; *Slack Water*, from a work by K. H. Thomas, 1955; *The Gorgio Girl*, 1956; *United Wives*, 1957; *Neighbours*, 1957; *Blind Orchid*, 1957; *The Gift Giver*, 1959; *A Young Affair*, 1959; *Family Business*, 1961; *The Girl Richards*, 1961; *Crack-Up*, 1964; *The Joy Ride*, 1966; *Paradiso*, 1975; *The One-Eyed Monster*, 1976; *Aaros in Winter*, 1977; *The Chief*, 1977; *Pity the Poor Potters*, 1979.

Television Plays: *The Common Man*, 1956; *Bed, Board, and Romance*, from a play by Harry Jackson, 1957; *Starr and Company* (serial), 1958; *A Young Affair*, 1958; *Man at the Door* (serial), 1960; *Yorky* (serial), with Bill Naughton, 1960, 2nd series, 1961; *Town Vet* (documentary), 1961; *Magnolia Street*, from the novel by Louis Golding, 1961; *Deadline Midnight* series (3 episodes), 1961; *Top Secret* series (1 episode), 1962; *Z Cars* series (86 episodes), 1962–78; *Moonstrike* series (8 episodes), 1963; *Sergeant Cork* series (4 episodes), 1964–66; *The Case of Oscar Brodski*, and *Thorndyke* (serial), both from works by R. Austin Freeman; *Undercurrent*, from a work by Keith Watson, 1964; *They'll Throw It at You*, 1964; *The Girl in the Picture*, 1964; *I've Got a System*, 1965; *The Welcome*, 1965; *Four of Hearts*, 1965; *Knock on Any Door*, 1965; *Dr. Finlay's Casebook* series (2 episodes), 1965; *Old Mrs. Jones*, from a work by Mrs. J. H. Liddell, 1965 (USA), as *The Beckoning Window*, 1966; *Softly, Softly* series (37 episodes), 1966–76; *The Gold Robbers* series (1 episode), 1969; *Parkin's Patch* series (3 episodes), 1969; *The Borderers* series (1 episode), 1969; *Trespassers*, 1969; *Two-Way Traffic*, 1969; *Ryan International* series (1 episode), 1970; *The Ten Commandments*, 1971; *The Onedin Line* series (4 episodes), 1972–77; *Marked Personal*, 1973; *Hawkeye the Pathfinder* (serial), with Alistair Bell, 1973; *Barlow at Large* series, and later series (7 episodes), 1973–75; *The Brave One*, 1973; *Crown Court* series (1 episode), 1974; *The Carnforth Practice* series (1 episode), 1974; *Sutherland's Law* series (1 episode), 1974; *One Pair of Eyes* (documentary), 1974; *Warship* series (3 episodes), 1974; *The Sweeney* series (2 episodes), 1975; *Ben Hall* series (1 episode), 1975; *The Expert* series (2 episodes), 1976; *General Hospital* series (2 episodes), 1976–79; *Blake's Seven* series (3 episodes), 1979.

Manuscript Collection: Mugar Memorial Library, Boston University.

Allan Prior comments:

I have written only three original novels that can be considered "crime" books. On the other hand, I have written 150 hours of crime fiction on British television, in *Z Cars*, *Softly, Softly*, and *The Sweeney*. I write "police" novels rarely and have done only two: *The Interrogators* and *The Operators*. Julian Symons was kind enough to call me (in a broadcast) "the best police procedural writer we have." My defence rests!

*   *   *

Allan Prior is one of those accomplished British professional writers who always seem less sensational but more polished than their American counterparts. Among other achievements in crime writing he was responsible for the popular British television police procedural series

Z Cars and its follow-up, *Softly, Softly*. He has written a number of genre novels, including some interesting work in the mystery and detective area.

The Operators is a very fine big caper novel, with a nicely assorted cast of characters and a well-planned airport heist at its center; in addition, it has an extremely successful and realistic atmosphere, whether in its scenes of prison and the life of an English criminal, or in its picture of the actual work that goes on daily around a great airport. It also has a strong and pungent flavor of the English criminal classes, with their sense of hatred for the system they inhabit, one of the few novels that suggests the importance of class in English crime, where the fiction of gentlemanly or even comic criminals has been the rule.

His best novel may be *The Interrogators*, which could also be the best British police procedural novel ever written. The novel does everything that this sort of work should do but usually doesn't: instead of presenting the professional policemen as sturdy, hearts-of-oak yeomen in the great sentimental tradition of English fiction, it shows them as hard, tough, often corrupt men who are necessarily of the working classes (the titled Oxonian policeman is one of the most offensive inventions of detective fiction) and effectively representative of their society. Following the investigation of the rape and murder of a child – always the most reprehensible crime in English fiction – we see into the lives of Jack Eaves, a young detective, and his hard-bitten superior, Savage. In the process we witness the life of a smoky, gritty, industrial city, the gray misery of working-class life, the immense patience and discipline of police routine, the development of those qualities that go into the creation of a good policeman. The novel presents a detailed and absolutely credible picture of the society in which such a crime can take place and the effect such an event can have on the lives of the investigators. It becomes, besides a remarkable delineation of its locale and subject, a kind of horribly ironic *Bildungsroman*: Jack Eaves finds the murderer and demonstrates the combination of effort, thought, and intuition that makes up the good detective, but in the process he loses something of himself, whatever innocence he still possessed. He discovers, in fact, that to be a good cop can mean abandoning something of his own humanity; the powerful ending of the book precisely suggests the terrible ambiguity of his victory. With the talents he displays in this fiercely honest book, Prior could very well be the best writer of police novels in England; it seems that his own facility and versatility, which cause him to write so much for television, prevent this from occurring, a decided loss for crime fiction.

—George Grella

PROCTER, Maurice. British. Born in Nelson, Lancashire, 4 February 1906. Educated at Nelson Grammar School. Served in the British Army, 1921–26. Married Winifred Blakey in 1933; one son. Constable, Halifax Borough Police, Yorkshire, 1927–46. *Died in 1973*.

CRIME PUBLICATIONS

Novels (series characters: Detective Superintendent Philip Hunter; Detective Chief Inspector Harry Martineau)

> *No Proud Chivalry.* London, Longman, 1947.
> *Each Man's Destiny.* London, Longman, 1947.
> *The End of the Street.* London, Longman, 1949.
> *The Chief Inspector's Statement* (Hunter). London, Hutchinson, 1951; as *The Pennycross Murders*, New York, Harper, 1953.

Hurry the Darkness. New York, Harper, 1951; London, Hutchinson, 1952.

Rich Is the Treasure. London, Hutchinson, 1952.

Hell Is a City (Martineau). London, Hutchinson, 1954; as *Somewhere in This City*, New York, Harper, 1954; as *Murder Somewhere in This City*, New York, Avon, 1956.

The Pub Crawler. London, Hutchinson, 1956; New York, Harper, 1957.

I Will Speak Daggers (Hunter). London, Hutchinson, 1956; as *The Ripper*, New York, Harper, 1956; as *The Ripper Murders*, New York, Avon, 1957.

The Midnight Plumber (Martineau). London, Hutchinson, 1957; New York, Harper, 1958.

Three at the Angel. London, Hutchinson, and New York, Harper, 1958.

Man in Ambush (Martineau). London, Hutchinson, 1958; New York, Harper, 1959.

Killer at Large (Martineau). London, Hutchinson, and New York, Harper, 1959.

Devil's Due (Martineau). London, Hutchinson, and New York, Harper, 1960.

The Spearhead Death. London, Hutchinson, 1960.

The Devil Was Handsome (Martineau). London, Hutchinson, and New York, Harper, 1961.

Devil in Moonlight. London, Hutchinson, 1962.

A Body to Spare (Martineau). London, Hutchinson, and New York, Harper, 1962.

Moonlight Flitting (Martineau). London, Hutchinson, 1963; as *The Graveyard Rolls*, New York, Harper, 1964.

Two Men in Twenty (Martineau). London, Hutchinson, and New York, Harper, 1964.

Death Has a Shadow (Martineau). London, Hutchinson, 1965; as *Homicide Blonde*, New York, Harper, 1965.

His Weight in Gold (Martineau). London, Hutchinson, and New York, Harper, 1966.

Rogue Running (Martineau). London, Hutchinson, and New York, Harper, 1967.

Exercise Hoodwink (Martineau). London, Hutchinson, and New York, Harper, 1967.

Hideaway (Martineau). London, Hutchinson, and New York, Harper, 1968.

The Top Dog. London, Hutchinson, 1969.

Uncollected Short Stories

"Fox in the Pennine Hills," in *Crook's Tour*, edited by Bruno Fischer. New York, Dodd Mead, 1953; London, Macdonald, 1954.

"No Place for Magic," in *Butcher, Baker, Murder-Maker*, edited by George Harmon Cox. New York, Knopf, 1954.

"West Riding to Maryland," in *Tales for a Rainy Night*, edited by David Alexander. New York, Holt Rinehart, 1961.

"The Policeman and the Lamp," in *Ellery Queen's Mystery Magazine* (New York), July 1961.

"Diamonds for the Million," in *The Fourth Mystery Bedside Book*, edited by John Creasey. London, Hodder and Stoughton, 1963.

"The Million Dollar Mystery," in *Anthology 1968 Mid-Year*, edited by Ellery Queen. New York, Davis, 1968.

Manuscript Collection: Mugar Memorial Library, Boston University.

*   *   *

Maurice Procter is a transitional figure in the history of detective fiction. His main series character, Detective Chief Inspector Harry Martineau, has some of the qualities of the Great Policeman tradition represented by Ngaio Marsh's Inspector Alleyn and Josephine Tey's Inspector Grant, but he also belongs in the mode of the police procedural story, along with John Creasey's George Gideon. Some of this mixture in Martineau is undoubtedly the result of his chronological position in the development of the police procedural novel. The first story in which he appears, *Hell Is a City*, was published in February 1955, thus preceding the "pure" procedural series of Creasey by a few months and that of Ed McBain by a year.

In his first appearance Martineau shows several traits of the Gentleman Policeman. He loves to play the piano, and when a prostitute turns and flees after recognizing him he regrets "the social handicaps of being a prominent copper. The leper of the law." His reputation is already established as "the great Inspector Martineau." In later stories, however, Martineau comes to bear an increasing resemblance to George Gideon, particularly in his tendency to doubt his own abilities and motives; having killed a criminal in the process of capture, Martineau tells himself that he had been able to control his hatred right up until the last moment and then had given way to it. He shares another quality of Gideon, the ability to recognize promise in a young officer and to build up a loyal following among such bright young men by using their talents and rewarding their good work with promotions.

Procter's other series protagonist, Detective Superintendent Philip Hunter, is as abrasive as Martineau is smooth. He badgers witnesses and suspects unmercifully, and he is harsh toward his subordinates, blaming them severely when they make a mistake, bawling them out in public and then telling them they needn't shout.

The police methods in Procter's stories are based somewhat less on modern forensic science than on common sense and an understanding of human nature. Martineau, for example, knows how to put pressure on an underworld type to force him to turn informer. Hunter passes on gossip from one suspect to another to set them at odds with each other and start them talking. There is some use of the police lab, but most of the results are obtained by careful investigation and painstaking questioning. The settings of the Procter stories are several imaginary cities in the North of England. In the Martineau series it is "Granchester," which might be Manchester or Liverpool, called the "Metropolis of the North," with a well-staffed police department that can do anything Scotland Yard can do. "Yoreborough" (York), the scene of the Philip Hunter stories, is a somewhat smaller town, having practically no industry but, like "Granchester," boasting a highly efficient CID.

—George N. Dove

PRONZINI, Bill. Also writes as Jack Foxx; William Jeffrey; Alex Saxon. American. Born in Petaluma, California, 13 April 1943. Attended a junior college for 2 years. Married 1) Laura Patricia Adolphson in 1965 (divorced, 1966); 2) Brunhilde Schier in 1972. Has worked as newsstand clerk, sports reporter, warehouseman, typist, salesman, civilian guard with U.S. Marshall's office. Since 1969, self-employed writer. Traveled extensively in Europe; lived in Majorca and West Germany, 1970–73. Member of the Board of Directors, Mystery Writers of America. Agent: Clyde Taylor, 34 Perry Street, New York, New York 10014. Address: P.O. Box 27368, San Francisco, California 94127, U.S.A.

CRIME PUBLICATIONS

Novels (series character: a nameless private eye)

The Stalker.   New York, Random House, 1971; London, Hale, 1974.
The Snatch (private eye).   New York, Random House, 1971; London, Hale, 1974.
Panic!   New York, Random House, 1972; London, Hale, 1974.
A Run in Diamonds (as Alex Saxon).   New York, Pocket Books, 1973.

The Vanished (private eye).   New York, Random House, 1973; London, Hale, 1974.
Undercurrent (private eye).   New York, Random House, 1973; London, Hale, 1975.
Snowbound.   New York, Putnam, 1974; London, Weidenfeld and Nicolson, 1975.
Games.   New York, Putnam, 1976; Feltham, Middlesex, Hamlyn Books, 1978.
The Running of Beasts, with Barry N. Malzberg.   New York, Putnam, 1976.
Blowback (private eye).   New York, Random House, 1977; London, Hale, 1978.
Acts of Mercy, with Barry N. Malzberg.   New York, Putnam, 1977.
Twospot (private eye), with Collin Wilcox.   New York, Putnam, 1978.
Night Screams, with Barry N. Malzberg.   Chicago, Playboy Press, 1979.

Novels as Jack Foxx (series character: Dan Connell)

The Jade Figurine (Connell).   Indianapolis, Bobbs Merrill, 1972.
Dead Run (Connell).   Indianapolis, Bobbs Merrill, 1975.
Freebooty.   Indianapolis, Bobbs Merrill, 1976.
Wildfire.   Indianapolis, Bobbs Merrill, 1978.

Uncollected Short Stories

"You Don't Know What It's Like," in *Shell Scott Mystery Magazine* (New York), November 1966.
"Night Freight," in *Mike Shayne Mystery Magazine* (New York), May 1967.
"A Man Called Vinelli," in *Man from U.N.C.L.E.* (New York), May 1967.
"The Long Knives Wait," in *Mike Shayne Mystery Magazine* (New York), September 1967.
"The Pillars of Salt Affair" (as Robert Hart Davis), in *Man from U.N.C.L.E.* (New York), December 1967.
"The Swabbie and the Sexpot," in *Body Shop*, December 1967.
"Opportunity," in *Alfred Hitchcock's Mystery Magazine* (North Palm Beach, Florida), December 1967.
"The Ethical Eye," in *Alfred Hitchcock's Mystery Magazine* (North Palm Beach, Florida), February 1968.
"A Quiet Night," in *Alfred Hitchcock's Mystery Magazine* (North Palm Beach, Florida), March 1968.
"Who's Afraid of Sherlock Holmes?," in *Mike Shayne Mystery Magazine* (New York), April 1968.
"The Bomb Expert," in *Mike Shayne Mystery Magazine* (New York), May 1968.
"Words Do Not a Book Make," in *Alfred Hitchcock's Mystery Magazine* (North Palm Beach, Florida), May 1968.
"The Perfect Crime," in *Mike Shayne Mystery Magazine* (New York), July 1968.
"You Can't Fight City Hall, Pete," in *Alfred Hitchcock's Mystery Magazine* (North Palm Beach, Florida), July 1968.
"The Accident," in *Mike Shayne Mystery Magazine* (New York), September 1968.
"Waiting, Waiting," in *Alfred Hitchcock's Mystery Magazine* (North Palm Beach, Florida), November 1968.
"Don't Spend It All in One Place," in *Alfred Hitchcock's Mystery Magazine* (North Palm Beach, Florida), December 1968.
"The Running Man," in *Alfred Hitchcock Presents: Murders I Fell In Love with.*   New York, Dell, 1969.
"A Lot on His Mind," in *Crimes and Misfortunes.*   New York, Random House, 1969.
"Retirement," in *Mike Shayne Mystery Magazine* (New York), April 1969.
"Escape" (as Jack Foxx), in *Mike Shayne Mystery Magazine* (New York), May 1969.
"Method of Operation" (as Jack Foxx), in *Alfred Hitchcock's Mystery Magazine* (North Palm Beach, Florida), June 1969.

"You Can Never Really Know," in *Mike Shayne Mystery Magazine* (New York), September 1969.

"The Almost Perfect Hiding Place," in *Mike Shayne Mystery Magazine* (New York), October 1969.

"A Nice Place to Visit, But ...," in *Mike Shayne Mystery Magazine* (New York), November 1969.

"The Crank," in *Mike Shayne Mystery Magazine* (New York), January 1970.

"The Snatch," in *Best Detective Stories of the Year 1970*, edited by Allen J. Hubin. New York, Dutton, 1970.

"The Way the World Spins," in *Alfred Hitchcock's Mystery Magazine* (North Palm Beach, Florida), May 1970.

"There's One Born Every Minute," in *Mike Shayne Mystery Magazine* (New York), July 1970.

"A Dip in the Poole," in *Alfred Hitchcock's Mystery Magazine* (North Palm Beach, Florida), August 1970.

"The $50,000 Bosom," in *Adventure* (Glendale, California), December 1970.

"Beautiful Smuggler," in *Argosy* (New York), December 1970.

"The Jade Figurine," in *Alfred Hitchcock's Mystery Magazine* (North Palm Beach, Florida), January 1971.

"Cain's Mark," in *Best Detective Stories of the Year 1971*, edited by Allen J. Hubin. New York, Dutton, 1971.

"Perfect Timing," in *Alfred Hitchcock's Mystery Magazine* (North Palm Beach, Florida), February 1971.

"Ice and Snow," in *Mike Shayne Mystery Magazine* (Los Angeles) March 1971.

"Muggers' Moon," in *Alfred Hitchcock's Mystery Magazine* (North Palm Beach, Florida), April 1971.

"The Imperfect Crime," in *Alfred Hitchcock's Mystery Magazine* (North Palm Beach, Florida), July 1971.

"I Know a Way," in *Mike Shayne Mystery Magazine* (Los Angeles), September 1971.

"Skeletons Go Forth," in *Alfred Hitchcock's Mystery Magazine* (North Palm Beach, Florida), October 1971.

"The Killing," in *Alfred Hitchcock's Mystery Magazine* (North Palm Beach, Florida), December 1971.

"Decision," in *Dear Dead Days*, edited by Edward D. Hoch. New York, Walker, 1972; London, Gollancz, 1974.

"The Assignment," in *Alfred Hitchcock's Mystery Magazine* (North Palm Beach, Florida), February 1972.

"Danger: Michael Shayne at Work!" (as Brett Halliday), with Jeff Wallmann, in *Mike Shayne Mystery Magazine* (Los Angeles), April 1972.

"The Amateur Touch," in *Alfred Hitchcock's Mystery Magazine* (North Palm Beach, Florida), July 1972.

"All the Same," in *Alfred Hitchcock's Mystery Magazine* (North Palm Beach, Florida), September 1972.

"Blowback," in *Argosy* (New York), September 1972.

"Majorcan Assignment," in *Mike Shayne Mystery Magazine* (Los Angeles), October 1972.

"The Web," in *Alfred Hitchcock's Mystery Magazine* (North Palm Beach, Florida), January 1973.

"It's a Lousy World," in *Alfred Hitchcock Presents: Stories to Be Read with the Lights On*. New York, Random House, 1973.

"Death of a Nobody," in *Mirror, Mirror, Fatal Mirror*, edited by Hans Stefan Santesson. New York, Doubleday, 1973.

"Sacrifice," in *Alfred Hitchcock's Mystery Magazine* (North Palm Beach, Florida), February 1973.

"The Follower," in *Alfred Hitchcock's Mystery Magazine* (North Palm Beach, Florida), March 1973.

"The Scales of Justice," in *Alfred Hitchcock's Mystery Magazine* (North Palm Beach, Florida), July 1973.

"The Methodical Cop," in *Mike Shayne Mystery Magazine* (Los Angeles), July 1973.

"Buttermilk," in *Killers of the Mind*, edited by Lucy Freeman. New York, Random House, 1974.

"The Riverboat Gold Robbery," in *Alfred Hitchcock's Mystery Magazine* (North Palm Beach, Florida), March 1974.

"Memento Mori," in *Alfred Hitchcock's Mystery Magazine* (North Palm Beach, Florida), April 1974.

"It's Not a Coffin," in *Mike Shayne Mystery Magazine* (Los Angeles), June 1974.

"Here Lies Another Blackmailer ...," in *Alfred Hitchcock's Mystery Magazine* (North Palm Beach, Florida), June 1974.

"A Matter of Life and Death," with Barry N. Malzberg, in *Mike Shayne Mystery Magazine* (Los Angeles), July 1974.

"The Pawns of Death" (as Robert Hart Davis), with Jeff Wallmann, in *Charlie Chan Mystery Magazine* (New York), August 1974.

"Unchained," in *Alfred Hitchcock's Mystery Magazine* (North Palm Beach, Florida), August 1974.

"Dog Story," with Michael Kurland, in *Mike Shayne Mystery Magazine* (Los Angeles), October 1974.

"Up to Snuff," in *Alfred Hitchcock's Mystery Magazine* (North Palm Beach, Florida), October 1974.

"Proof of Guilt," in *Ellery Queen's Murdercade*. New York, Random House, 1975.

"The Storm Tunnel," in *Mike Shayne Mystery Magazine* (Los Angeles), April 1975.

"For Love," in *Alfred Hitchcock's Mystery Magazine* (North Palm Beach, Florida), April 1975.

"Free-Lance Operation," in *Alfred Hitchcock's Mystery Magazine* (North Palm Beach, Florida), May 1975.

"Once a Thief," with Jeff Wallmann, in *Ellery Queen's Mystery Magazine* (New York), August 1975.

"Quicker Than the Eye," with Michael Kurland, in *Alfred Hitchcock's Mystery Magazine* (North Palm Beach, Florida), September 1975.

"I Ought to Kill You," with Barry N. Malzberg, in *Every Crime in the Book*, edited by Robert L. Fish. New York, Putnam, 1975.

"The Pattern," in *Alfred Hitchcock Presents: Stories to Be Read with the Door Locked*. New York, Random House, 1975.

"Private Eye Blues," in *Best Detective Stories of the Year 1976*, edited by Edward D. Hoch. New York, Dutton, 1976.

"Multiples," with Barry N. Malzberg, in *Tricks and Treats*, edited by Joe Gores and Bill Pronzini. New York, Doubleday, 1976.

"A Cold Day in November," in *Tales to Keep You Spellbound*, edited by Eleanor Sullivan. New York, Dial Press, 1976.

"Vanishing Act," with Michael Kurland, in *Alfred Hitchcock's Mystery Magazine* (New York), January 1976.

"If You Play with Fire ...," in *Mike Shayne Mystery Magazine* (Los Angeles), February 1976.

"Problems Solved," with Barry N. Malzberg, in *Ellery Queen's Mystery Magazine* (New York), June 1976.

"A Matter of Survival," with Barry N. Malzberg, in *Alfred Hitchcock's Mystery Magazine* (New York), December 1976.

"Sweet Fever," in *Best Detective Stories of the Year 1977*, edited by Edward D. Hoch. New York, Dutton, 1977.

"Putting the Pieces Back," in *When Last Seen*, edited by Arthur Maling. New York, Harper, 1977.

"What Kind of Person Are You?," with Barry N. Malzberg, in *Alfred Hitchcock's Mystery Magazine* (New York), April 1977.

"The Last Plagiarism," with Barry N. Malzberg, in *Alfred Hitchcock's Mystery Magazine* (New York), May 1977.

"The Dark Side," in *Mike Shayne Mystery Magazine* (Los Angeles), May 1977.

"Night Rider," with Barry N. Malzberg, in *Alfred Hitchcock's Mystery Magazine* (New York), June 1977.

"The Man Who Collected *The Shadow*," in *Dark Sins, Dark Dreams: Crime in Science Fiction*, edited by Barry N. Malzberg and Bill Pronzini. New York, Doubleday, 1978.

"The Arrowmont Prison Riddle," in *Alfred Hitchcock's Tales to Take Your Breath Away*, edited by Eleanor Sullivan. New York, Dial Press, 1978.

"Deathlove," in *Shadows*, edited by Charles L. Grant. New York, Doubleday, 1978.

"Smuggler's Island," in *Best Detective Stories of the Year 1978*, edited by Edward D. Hoch. New York, Dutton, 1978.

"The Half-Invisible Man," with Jeff Wallmann, in *Cop Cade*, edited by John Ball. New York, Doubleday, 1978.

"I Don't Understand It," in *Alfred Hitchcock's Tales to Scare You Stiff*, edited by Eleanor Sullivan. New York, Dial Press, 1978.

"A Cold Foggy Day," in *Ellery Queen's Mystery Magazine* (New York), April 1978.

"Birds of a Feather," with Barry N. Malzberg, in *Alfred Hitchcock's Mystery Magazine* (New York), April 1978.

"Bank Job," in *Ellery Queen's Mystery Magazine* (New York), August 1978.

"Cheeseburger" (as John Barry Williams), with Barry N. Malzberg and John Lutz, in *Alfred Hitchcock's Mystery Magazine* (New York), October 1978.

"Caught in the Act," in *Ellery Queen's Mystery Magazine* (New York), December 1978.

"Under the Skin," in *Ellery Queen's Scenes of the Crime*. New York, Dial Press, 1979.

"Clocks," with Barry N. Malzberg, in *Shadows 2*, edited by Charles L. Grant. New York, Doubleday, 1979.

"Peekaboo," in *Nightmares*, edited by Charles L. Grant. Chicago, Playboy Press, 1979.

"Strangers in the Fog," in *Best Detective Stories of the Year 1979*, edited by Edward D. Hoch. New York, Dutton, 1979.

"The Same Old Grind," in *Alfred Hitchcock Presents: The Master's Choice*. New York, Random House, 1979.

"His Name Was Legion," in *Mike Shayne Mystery Magazine* (Los Angeles), January 1979.

"Murder Is My Business," with Barry N. Malzberg, in *Mike Shayne Mystery Magazine* (Los Angeles), January 1979.

"The Private Eye Who Collected Pulps," in *Ellery Queen's Mystery Magazine* (New York), February 1979.

"Final Exam," with Barry N. Malzberg, in *Alfred Hitchcock's Mystery Magazine* (New York), February 1979.

"Rebound," with Barry N. Malzberg, in *Ellery Queen's Mystery Magazine* (New York), April 1979.

"Thin Air," in *Alfred Hitchcock's Mystery Magazine* (New York), May 1979.

"Million-to-One Shot," with Barry N. Malzberg, in *Ellery Queen's Mystery Magazine* (New York), July 1979.

"Black Wind," in *Ellery Queen's Mystery Magazine* (New York), September 1979.

"A Nice Easy Job," in *Ellery Queen's Mystery Magazine* (New York), November 1979.

Uncollected Short Stories as Jack Foxx

"Escape," in *Mike Shayne Mystery Magazine* (New York), May 1969.

"Method of Operation," in *Alfred Hitchcock's Mystery Magazine* (North Palm Beach, Florida), June 1969.

"Little Old Ladies Can Be Dangerous," in *Mike Shayne Mystery Magazine* (New York), September 1969.

"The Clincher," in *Alfred Hitchcock's Mystery Magazine* (North Palm Beach, Florida), December 1969.

"The Right Move," in *Alfred Hitchcock's Mystery Magazine* (North Palm Beach, Florida), March 1970.

"You're Safe Here," in *Mike Shayne Mystery Magazine* (Los Angeles), April 1970.

"One of Those Days," in *Alfred Hitchcock's Mystery Magazine* (North Palm Beach, Florida), October 1970.

"Roadblock," in *Alfred Hitchcock's Mystery Magazine* (North Palm Beach, Florida), May 1971.

"The Duel," in *Mike Shayne Mystery Magazine* (Los Angeles), April 1972.

"Suicide Note," in *Alfred Hitchcock's Mystery Magazine* (North Palm Beach, Florida), May 1972.

"Incident in Three Crossings," in *Charlie Chan Mystery Magazine* (New York), May 1974.

"Your Choice," in *Mike Shayne Mystery Magazine* (Los Angeles), April 1976.

Uncollected Short Stories as William Jeffrey

"Fire Hazard," in *Alfred Hitchcock's Mystery Magazine* (North Palm Beach, Florida), April 1970.

"The Day of the Moon," in *Alfred Hitchcock's Mystery Magazine* (North Palm Beach, Florida), June 1970.

"Monday Is the Dullest Night of the Week," in *Mike Shayne Mystery Magazine* (Los Angeles), July 1970.

"Retribution," in *Mike Shayne Mystery Magazine* (Los Angeles), August 1970.

"The Facsimile Shop," in *Ellery Queen's Mystery Magazine* (New York), September 1970.

"Murder Is No Man's Friend," in *Mike Shayne Mystery Magazine* (Los Angeles), November 1970.

"The Ten Million Dollar Hijack," in *Alfred Hitchcock's Mystery Magazine* (North Palm Beach, Florida), January 1972.

"A Run of Bad Luck," in *Alfred Hitchcock's Mystery Magazine* (North Palm Beach, Florida), March 1972.

"The Island," in *Alfred Hitchcock's Mystery Magazine* (North Palm Beach, Florida), August 1972.

"Shell Game," in *Best Detective Stories of the Year 1973*, edited by Allen J. Hubin. New York, Dutton, 1973.

"I Want a Lawyer," in *Mike Shayne Mystery Magazine* (Los Angeles), March 1973.

"A Slight Case of Suspicion," in *Alfred Hitchcock's Mystery Magazine* (North Palm Beach, Florida), September 1973.

"A Case for Quiet," in *Alfred Hitchcock Presents: Stories to Be Read with the Door Locked*. New York, Random House, 1975.

"O'Flaherty's Wake," in *Mike Shayne Mystery Magazine* (Los Angeles), September 1975.

Other

"The Mystery Career of Evan Hunter," in *Armchair Detective* (White Bear Lake, Minnesota), April 1972.

"The Sage of the Phoenix that Probably Should Never Have Arisen," in *Armchair Detective* (Del Mar, California), April 1977.

"Writing the Mystery Short-Short," in *The Writer* (Boston), December 1977.

"The Elements of Suspense," in *Writing Suspense and Mystery Fiction*, edited by A. S. Burack. Boston, The Writer, 1977.

Editor, with Joe Gores, *Tricks and Treats*. New York, Doubleday, 1976; as *Mystery Writers Choice*, London, Gollancz, 1977.
Editor, *Midnight Specials*. Indianapolis, Bobbs Merrill, 1977; London, Souvenir Press 1978.
Editor, with Barry N. Malzberg, *Dark Sins, Dark Dreams*. New York, Doubleday, 1978.
Editor, *Werewolf*. New York, Arbor House, 1979.

Manuscript Collection: Mugar Memorial Library, Boston University.

*   *   *

Some mystery writers start big, with an instant classic they are never able to surpass. Others, like Bill Pronzini, seem to improve from book to book, building a solid professional foundation. In Pronzini's early novels and short stories the influence of the pulp magazines he and one of his detective protagonists collected seems especially noticeable. Certainly his nameless private eye operating out of San Francisco owes something to Hammett's Continental Op. though his personality is more reminiscent of Thomas B. Dewey's "Mac."

The first of more than a dozen Pronzini novels published to date was *The Stalker*. It deals with six ex-servicemen who had successfully teamed up to rob an armored car years before. Now, as someone begins tracking them down and killing them one by one, terror increases for the survivors. It is a classic situation, bringing to mind books like *The League of Frightened Men* or *The Bride Wore Black*, and Pronzini does well by it. One only regrets that the half-anticipated double-twist ending fails to materialize.

The Snatch, the first of Pronzini's "nameless" private eye series, was expanded from a 1969 short story. It works much better than this sort of expansion usually does, and the story of kidnapping and murder reads well in either version. The unnamed private eye returns in *The Vanished, Undercurrent*, and *Blowback*, even surviving the author's attempt to kill him off at the end of the short story "Private Eye Blues." Pronzini's other published novels fall more into the category of suspense novels, generally built around a menace at some inaccessible location. *Panic!* has the hero and a girl fleeing across the southwest desert pursued by killers. *Snowbound*, the most successful of Pronzini's solo novels, has three robbers planning to loot an entire snowbound village in the Sierra Nevadas. *Games* follows a wealthy U.S. Senator to a remote Maine island for a terror-filled weekend. The suspense mounts throughout, though the final surprise can be foreseen by clever readers.

Pronzini has also published novels under the names of Jack Foxx and Alex Saxon, usually mystery-adventure tales with exotic foreign settings. Even with the publication of two or more novels a year he has remained a regular contributor of short stories to the mystery magazines. In addition to those mentioned above, notable short tales include "Cain's Mark," "Sweet Fever," and "Smuggler's Island."

A striking aspect of Pronzini's writing is his unmatched collaborative ability. There have been many successful collaborations in the mystery field, but probably no other writer has done it so successfully with so many partners. He has written short stories with Jeff Wallmann, Michael Kurland, and John Lutz, the novel *Twospot* with Collin Wilcox, and both stories and novels with Barry N. Malzberg. The first of the Malzberg collaborations produced Pronzini's best and most striking novel, *The Running of Beasts*, with its viewpoint shifting among four men in an upstate New York town. One of the men is unaware that in another personality he is a Ripper-type killer terrorizing the region. The neat trick of limiting the mystery to only four suspects and still surprising the reader with a final twist is deftly and admirably performed by Pronzini and Malzberg. A second collaboration, *Acts of Mercy*, carried the same feeling of impending doom, and its gimmick of a split personality in the White House is an intriguing one, but it is less successful than *Beasts*.

—Edward D. Hoch

PROPPER, Milton (Morris).   American.   Born in Philadelphia, Pennsylvania, in 1906. Educated at Nazreth Hall Military Academy, Pennsylvania; University of Pennsylvania, Philadelphia (Associate Editor, *Law Review*), B.A. 1926, Ll.B. 1929; called to the Bar, 1929. Book and theatre critic for Philadelphia *Public Ledger* while an undergraduate; employed by the Social Security Administration in Philadelphia and Atlanta, Georgia; lived in Philadelphia after1944. *Died (suicide) in 1962.*

CRIME PUBLICATIONS

Novels (series character: Tommy Rankin in all books)

> *The Strange Disappearance of Mary Young.*   New York, Harper, 1929; London, Harrap, 1932.
> *The Ticker-Tape Murder.*   New York, Harper, 1930; London, Faber, 1932.
> *The Boudoir Murder.*   New York, P. F. Collier, 1930; as *And Then Silence*, London, Faber, 1932.
> *The Student Fraternity Murder.*   Indianapolis, Bobbs Merrill, 1932; as *Murder of an Initiate*, London, Faber, 1933.
> *The Divorce Court Murder.*   New York, Harper, and London, Faber, 1934.
> *The Family Burial Murders.*   New York, Harper, 1934; London, Harrap, 1935.
> *The Election Booth Murder.*   New York, Harper, 1935; as *Murder at the Polls*, London, Harrap, 1937.
> *One Murdered, Two Dead.*   New York, Harper, 1936; London, Harrap, 1937.
> *The Great Insurance Murders.*   New York, Harper, 1937; London, Harrap, 1938.
> *The Case of the Cheating Bride.*   New York, Harper, 1938; London, Harrap, 1939.
> *Hide the Body!*   New York, Harper, 1939; London, Harrap, 1940.
> *The Station Wagon Murder.*   New York, Harper, 1940.
> *The Handwriting on the Wall.*   New York, Harper, 1941; as *You Can't Gag the Dead*, London, Jenkins, 1949.
> *The Blood Transfusion Murders.*   New York, Harper, 1943; as *Murders in Sequence*, London, Jenkins, 1947.

*   *   *

Milton Propper passed the Pennsylvania Bar exam in 1929, but he sold his first detective novel the same year and chose writing rather than law as his career. His 14 mysteries are set in Philadelphia and its suburbs and are solved by young Tommy Rankin, homicide specialist on that city's police force. Propper writes hopelessly dull prose, peoples his books with nonentities, flaunts his belief that the police and the powerful are above the law, and refuses to play fair with the reader. Yet paradoxically his best books, like *The Family Burial Murders* and *The Great Insurance Murders*, hold some of the intellectual excitement of early Ellery Queen.

Propper generally begins with the discovery of a body in bizarre circumstances (on an amusement park's scenic rail-way, during a college fraternity initiation, in a voting booth) and then scatters suspicion among several characters with much to hide, all the while juggling clues and counterplots with dazzling nimbleness. His gifted detectives can make startlingly accurate deductions from a glance at a person's face, and casually commit burglary and other crimes while searching for evidence. His novels often involve varied forms of mass transportation and complex legal questions over the succession to a large estate. Near the end of his books, having established the innocence of all known suspects, Rankin invariably puts together some as yet unexplained pieces of the puzzle, concludes that the murderer was an avenger from the past who infiltrated the victim's milieu in disguise, and launches a breakneck chase to collar the killer before he or she escapes. Such is the Propper pattern, and despite their predictability and stylistic dullness his novels still interest aficionados. Unlike his books, Propper's life was wretched and messy. He alienated his family, lived in squalor, was picked up for homosexual activities by the police whose crimes he glorified, eventually lost all markets for his writing and, in 1962, killed himself.

—Francis M. Nevins, Jr.

QUEEN, Ellery. Pseudonym for the cousins Frederic Dannay and Manfred B. Lee; also wrote as Barnaby Ross. Americans. **DANNAY, Frederic:** Born Daniel Nathan in Brooklyn, New York, 20 October 1905; grew up in Elmira, New York. Educated at Boys' High School, Brooklyn. Married 1) Mary Beck in 1926 (died), two sons; 2) Hilda Wisenthal in 1947 (died, 1972), one son; 3) Rose Koppel in 1976. Writer and art director for a New York advertising agency prior to 1931; full-time writer, with Lee, 1931–71, and on his own from 1971. Visiting Professor, University of Texas, Austin, 1958–59. Lives in Larchmont, New York. **LEE, Manfred B(ennington):** Born Manford Lepofsky in Brooklyn, New York, 11 January 1905. Educated at Boys' High School, Brooklyn; New York University. Married the actress Kaye Brinker (second wife), in 1942; four daughters and four sons. Publicity writer in New York for film companies prior to 1931; full-time writer, with Danny, 1931 until his death. Justice of the Peace, Roxbury, Connecticut, 1957–58. *Died 3 April 1971.* Dannay and Lee were under contract to film companies in the 1930's; they edited *Mystery League* magazine, 1933–34, and *Ellery Queen's Mystery Magazine,* from 1941 (Dannay the active editor); they wrote the *Adventures of Ellery Queen* radio series, 1939–48. Co-Founders and Co-Presidents, Mystery Writers of America. Recipient: Mystery Writers of America Edgar Allan Poe Award, for radio play, 1945, for story, 1947, 1949, special award, 1951, 1968, and Grand Master Award, 1960.

CRIME PUBLICATIONS

Novels (series characters: Ellery Queen and Inspector Richard Queen in all books except *The Glass Village* and *Cop Out*)

The Roman Hat Mystery. New York, Stokes, and London, Gollancz, 1929.
The French Powder Mystery. New York, Stokes, and London, Gollancz, 1930.
The Dutch Shoe Mystery. New York, Stokes, and London, Gollancz, 1931.
The Greek Coffin Mystery. New York, Stokes, and London, Gollancz, 1932.
The Egyptian Cross Mystery. New York, Stokes, 1932; London, Gollancz, 1933.
The American Gun Mystery. New York, Stokes, and London, Gollancz, 1933; as *Death at the Rodeo,* New York, Spivak, 1951.
The Siamese Twin Mystery. New York, Stokes, 1933; London, Gollancz, 1934.
The Chinese Orange Mystery. New York, Stokes, and London, Gollancz, 1934.
The Spanish Cape Mystery. New York, Stokes, and London, Gollancz, 1935.
Halfway House. New York, Stokes, and London, Gollancz, 1936.
The Door Between. New York, Stokes, and London, Gollancz, 1937.
The Devil to Pay. New York, Stokes, and London, Gollancz, 1938.
Ellery Queen's Big Book (omnibus). New York, Grosset and Dunlap, 1938.
The Four of Hearts. New York, Stokes, 1938; London, Gollancz, 1939.
The Dragon's Teeth. New York, Stokes and London, Gollancz, 1939; as *The Virgin Heiress,* New York, Pocket Books, 1954.
Calamity Town. Boston, Little Brown, and London, Gollancz, 1942.

There Was an Old Woman. Boston, Little Brown, 1943; London, Gollancz, 1944; as *The Quick and the Dead*, New York, Pocket Books, 1956.
Ellery Queen's Mystery Parade (omnibus). Cleveland, World, 1944.
The Murderer Is a Fox. Boston, Little Brown, and London, Gollancz, 1945.
Ten Days' Wonder. Boston, Little Brown, and London, Gollancz, 1948.
Cat of Many Tails. Boston, Little Brown, and London, Gollancz, 1949.
Double, Double. Boston, Little Brown, and London, Gollancz, 1950; as *The Case of the Seven Murders*, New York, Pocket Books, 1958.
The Origin of Evil. Boston, Little Brown, and London, Gollancz, 1951.
The King Is Dead. Boston, Little Brown, and London, Gollancz, 1952.
The Scarlet Letters. Boston, Little Brown, and London, Gollancz, 1953.
The Glass Village. Boston, Little Brown, and London, Gollancz, 1954.
Inspector Queen's Own Case. New York, Simon and Schuster, and London, Gollancz, 1956.
The Wrightsville Murders (omnibus). Boston, Little Brown, 1956.
The Hollywood Murders (omnibus). Philadelphia, Lippincott, 1957.
The Finishing Stroke. New York, Simon and Schuster, and London, Gollancz, 1958.
The New York Murders (omnibus). Boston, Little Brown, 1958.
The Bizarre Murders (omnibus). Philadelphia, Lippincott, 1962.
The Player on the Other Side. New York, Random House, and London, Gollancz, 1963.
And on the Eighth Day. New York, Random House, and London, Gollancz, 1964.
The Fourth Side of the Triangle. New York, Random House, and London, Gollancz, 1965.
A Study in Terror (novelization of screenplay). New York, Lancer, 1966; as *Sherlock Holmes Versus Jack the Ripper*, London, Gollancz, 1967.
Face to Face. New York, New American Library, and London, Gollancz, 1967.
The House of Brass. New York, New American Library, and London, Gollancz, 1968.
Cop Out. Cleveland, World, and London, Gollancz, 1969.
The Last Woman in His Life. Cleveland, World, and London, Gollancz, 1970.
A Fine and Private Place. Cleveland, World, and London, Gollancz, 1971.

Novels as Barnaby Ross (series character: Drury Lane in all books)

The Tragedy of X. New York, Viking Press, and London, Cassell, 1932.
The Tragedy of Y. New York, Viking Press, and London, Cassell, 1932.
The Tragedy of Z. New York, Viking Press, and London, Cassell, 1933.
Drury Lane's Last Case. New York, Viking Press, and London, Cassell, 1933.
The XYZ Murders (omnibus). Philadelphia, Lippincott, 1961.

Short Stories

The Adventures of Ellery Queen. New York, Stokes, 1934; London, Gollancz, 1935.
The New Adventures of Ellery Queen. New York, Stokes, and London, Gollancz, 1940; with varied contents as *More Adventures of Ellery Queen*, New York, Spivak, 1940.
The Case Book of Ellery Queen. New York, Spivak, 1945.
The Case Book of Ellery Queen (omnibus). London, Gollancz, 1949.
Calendar of Crime. Boston, Little Brown, and London, Gollancz, 1952.
QBI: Queen's Bureau of Investigation. Boston, Little Brown, 1954; London, Gollancz, 1955.
Queens Full. New York, Random House, 1965; London, Gollancz, 1966.
QED: Queen's Experiments in Detection. New York, New American Library, 1968; London, Gollancz, 1969.

Uncollected Short Stories

"Terror Town," in *Best Detective Stories of the Year*, edited by David Coxe Cooke. New York, Dutton, 1957.

"Wedding Anniversary," in *Ellery Queen's Mystery Magazine* (New York), September 1967.

"Uncle from Australia," in *Ellery Queen's Mystery Magazine* (New York), November 1967.

"The Three Students," in *Playboy* (Chicago), March 1971.

"The Odd Man," in *Playboy* (Chicago), June 1971.

"The Honest Swindler," in *Saturday Evening Post* (Philadelphia), Summer 1971.

OTHER PUBLICATIONS

Novel

The Golden Summer (as Daniel Nathan; by Dannay).   Boston, Little Brown, 1953.

Plays

Danger, Men Working, with Lowell Brentano (produced Baltimore and Philadelphia, c. 1936).

"The Adventure of the Frightened Star," in *Ellery Queen's Mystery Magazine* (New York), Spring 1942.

"The Adventure of the Meanest Man in the World," in *Ellery Queen's Mystery Magazine* (New York), July 1942.

"The Adventure of the Good Samaritan," in *Ellery Queen's Mystery Magazine* (New York), November 1942.

"The Adventure of the Mark of Cain," in *The Pocket Mystery Reader*, edited by Lee Wright. New York, Pocket Books, 1942.

"The Adventure of the Fire Bug," in *Ellery Queen's Mystery Magazine* (New York), March 1943.

"The Adventure of the Man Who Could Double the Size of Diamonds," in *Ellery Queen's Mystery Magazine* (New York), May 1943.

"The Adventure of the Blind Bullet," in *Ellery Queen's Mystery Magazine* (New York), September 1943.

"The Adventure of the One-Legged Man," in *Ellery Queen's Mystery Magazine* (New York), November 1943.

"The Adventure of the Wounded Lieutenant," in *Ellery Queen's Mystery Magazine* (New York), July 1944.

"The Disappearance of Mr. James Phillimore," in *The Misadventures of Sherlock Holmes*, edited by Ellery Queen. Boston, Little Brown, 1944.

"Ellery Queen, Swindler," in *Rogues' Gallery: The Great Criminals of Modern Fiction*, edited by Ellery Queen. Boston, Little Brown, 1945; London, Faber, 1947.

"The Double Triangle" and "The Invisible Clock," in *The Case Book of Ellery Queen*. New York, Spivak, 1945.

"The Invisible Clue," in *Adventures in Radio*, edited by Margaret Cuthbert. New York, Howell Soskin, 1945.

"The Adventure of the Murdered Ship," in *The Saint's Choice, Volume 7: Radio Thrillers*, edited by Leslie Charteris. Hollywood, Saint Enterprises, 1946.

"The Adventure of the Curious Thefts," in *Story Digest*, September 1946.

"The Adventure of the Mouse's Blood," in *Fireside Mystery Book*, edited by Frank Owen. New York, Lantern Press, 1947.

"The Adventure of the Last Man Club" and "The Adventure of the Murdered Millionaire," in *The Last Man Club*. New York, Pyramid, 1968.

Radio Plays: most scripts for *The Adventures of Ellery Queen*, 1939–48.

Other

The Detective Short Story: A Bibliography. Boston, Little Brown, 1942.
Queen's Quorum: A History of the Detective-Crime Short Story as Revealed by the 106 Most Important Books Published in This Field Since 1845. Boston, Little Brown, 1951; London, Gollancz, 1953; revised edition, New York, Biblo and Tannen, 1969.
In the Queen's Parlor, and Other Leaves from the Editors' Notebook. New York, Simon and Schuster, and London, Gollancz, 1957.
Ellery Queen's International Case Book (true crime). New York, Dell, 1964.
The Woman in the Case (true crime). New York, Bantam, 1966; as *Deadlier Than the Male*, London, Corgi, 1967.

Editor, *Challenge to the Reader.* New York, Stokes, 1938.
Editor, *101 Years' Entertainment: The Great Detective Stories, 1841–1941.* Boston, Little Brown, 1941; revised edition, New York, Modern Library, 1946.
Editor, *Sporting Blood: The Great Sports Detective Stories.* Boston, Little Brown, 1942; as *Sporting Detective Stories*, London, Faber, 1946.
Editor, *The Female of the Species: The Great Women Detectives and Criminals.* Boston, Little Brown, 1943; as *Ladies in Crime: A Collection of Detective Stories by English and American Writers*, London, Faber, 1947.
Editor, *The Misadventures of Sherlock Holmes.* Boston, Little Brown, 1944.
Editor, *Best Stories from Ellery Queen's Mystery Magazine.* Roslyn, New York, Detective Book Club, 1944.
Editor, *The Adventures of Sam Spade and Other Stories*, by Dashiell Hammett. New York, Spivak, 1944; as *They Can Only Hang You Once*, New York, Spivak, 1949; reprinted in part as *A Man Called Spade*, New York, Dell, 1945.
Editor, *Rogues' Gallery: The Great Criminals of Modern Fiction.* Boston, Little Brown, 1945; London, Faber, 1947.
Editor, *The Continental Op*, by Dashiell Hammett. New York, Spivak, 1945.
Editor, *The Return of the Continental Op*, by Dashiell Hammett. New York, Spivak, 1945.
Editor, *To the Queen's Taste: The First Supplement to 101 Years' Entertainment, Consisting of the Best Stories Published in the First Five Years of Ellery Queen's Mystery Magazine.* Boston, Little Brown, 1946; London, Faber, 1949.
Editor, *Hammett Homicides*, by Dashiell Hammett. New York, Spivak, 1946.
Editor, *The Queen's Awards* (from *Ellery Queen's Mystery Magazine*). Boston, Little Brown, 10 vols, 1946–55, New York, Simon and Schuster, 2 vols., 1956–57; London, Gollancz, 8 vols., 1948–55, London, Collins, 4 vols., 1956–59; continued as *Mystery Annuals*, New York, Random House, 4 vols., 1958–61; Collins, 2 vols., 1960–61, Gollancz, 2 vols., 1961–62; then continued as anthologies:
To Be Read Before Midnight. New York, Random House, 1962; London, Gollancz, 1963.
Mystery Mix. New York, Random House, 1963; London, Gollancz, 1964.
Double Dozen. New York, Random House, 1964; London, Gollancz, 1965.
20th Anniversary Annual. New York, Random House, 1965; London, Gollancz, 1966.
Crime Carousel. New York, New American Library, 1966; London, Gollancz, 1967.
All-Star Lineup. New York, New American Library, 1966; London, Gollancz, 1968.
Mystery Parade. New York, New American Library, 1968; London, Gollancz, 1969.
Murder Menu. Cleveland, World, and London, Gollancz, 1969.

Grand Slam. Cleveland, World, 1970; London, Gollancz, 1971.
Headliners. Cleveland, World, 1971; London, Gollancz, 1972.
Mystery Bag. Cleveland, World, 1972; London, Gollancz, 1973.
Crookbook. New York, Random House, and London, Gollancz, 1974.
Murdercade. New York, Random House, 1975; London, Gollancz, 1976.
Crime Wave. New York, Putnam, and London, Gollancz, 1976.
Searches and Seizures. New York, Davis, 1977.
A Multitude of Sins. New York, Davis, 1978.
Editor, *Murder by Experts.* New York, Ziff Davis, 1947; London, Sampson Low, 1950.
Editor, *Dead Yellow Women*, by Dashiell Hammett. New York, Spivak, 1947.
Editor, *The Riddles of Hildegarde Withers*, by Stuart Palmer. New York, Spivak, 1947.
Editor, *Dr. Fell, Detective, and Other Stories*, by John Dickson Carr. New York, Spivak, 1947.
Editor, *The Department of Dead Ends*, by Roy Vickers. New York, Spivak, 1947.
Editor, *The Case Book of Mr. Campion*, by Margery Allingham. New York, Spivak, 1947.
Editor, *20th Century Detective Stories.* Cleveland, World, 1948; revised edition, New York, Popular Library, 1964.
Editor, *Nightmare Town*, by Dashiell Hammett. New York, Spivak, 1948.
Editor, *Cops and Robbers*, by O. Henry. New York, Spivak, 1948.
Editor, *The Literature of Crime: Stories by World-Famous Authors.* Boston, Little Brown, 1950; London, Cassell, 1952; as *Ellery Queen's Book of Mystery Stories*, London, Pan, 1957.
Editor, *The Creeping Siamese*, by Dashiell Hammett. New York, Spivak, 1950.
Editor, *The Monkey Murder and Other Hildegarde Withers Stories*, by Stuart Palmer. New York, Spivak, 1950.
Editor, *Woman in the Dark*, by Dashiell Hammett. New York, Spivak, 1952.
Editor, *Ellery Queen's 1960 Anthology.* New York, Davis, 13 vols., 1959–71: later accompanied by *Mid-Year Editions*, 8 vols., 1963–70: continued as *Spring–Summer* and *Fall–Winter* editions, 6 vols., 1971–73; then continued as anthologies:
Christmas Hamper. New York, Davis, 1974; London, Gollancz, 1975.
Aces of Mystery. New York, Davis, 1975.
Masters of Mystery. New York, Davis, 1975; London, Gollancz, 1977.
Giants of Mystery. New York, Davis, 1976; London, Gollancz, 1977.
Magicians of Mystery. New York, Davis, 1976; London, Gollancz, 1978.
Champions of Mystery. New York, Davis, 1977; London, Gollancz, 1979.
Faces of Mystery. New York, Davis, 1977; London, Gollancz, 1978.
Who's Who of Whodunits. New York, Davis, 1977.
Masks of Mystery. New York, Davis, 1977.
Napoleons of Mystery. New York, Davis, 1978.
The Supersleuths. New York, Davis, 1978.
Wings of Mystery. New York, Davis, 1979.
Scenes of the Crime. New York, Davis, 1979.
Editor, *A Man Named Thin and Other Stories*, by Dashiell Hammett. New York, Spivak, 1962.
Editor, *12.* New York, Dell, 1964.
Editor, *Lethal Black Book.* New York, Dell, 1965.
Editor, *Poetic Justice: 23 Stories of Crime, Mystery and Detection by World-Famous Poets from Geoffrey Chaucer to Dylan Thomas.* New York, New American Library, 1967.
Editor, *The Case of the Murderer's Bride and Other Stories*, by Erle Stanley Gardner. New York, Davis, 1969.
Editor, *Minimysteries: 70 Short-Short Stories of Crime, Mystery and Detection.* Cleveland, World, 1969.

Editor, *Murder – In Spades!* New York, Pyramid, 1969.
Editor, *Shoot the Works!* New York, Pyramid, 1969.
Editor, *Mystery Jackpot.* New York, Pyramid, 1970.
Editor, *P as in Police*, by Lawrence Treat. New York, Davis, 1970.
Editor, *The Golden 13: 13 First Prize Winners from Ellery Queen's Mystery Magazine.* Cleveland, World, 1971; London, Gollancz, 1972.
Editor, *The Spy and the Thief*, by Edward D. Hoch. New York, Davis, 1971.
Editor, *Ellery Queen's Best Bets.* New York, Pyramid, 1972.
Editor, *Amateur in Violence*, by Michael Gilbert. New York, Davis, 1973.
Editor, *Kindly Dig Your Grave and Other Stories*, by Stanley Ellin. New York, Davis, 1975.
Editor, *How to Trap a Crook and 12 Other Mysteries*, by Julian Symons. New York, Davis, 1977.
Editor, *Japanese Golden Dozen: The Detective Story World in Japan.* Rutland, Vermont, Charles Tuttle, 1978.

Bibliography: in *Royal Bloodline: Ellery Queen, Author and Detective* by Francis M. Nevins, Jr., Bowling Green, Ohio, Popular Press, 1974.

Manuscript Collection: Humanities Research Center, University of Texas, Austin.

*   *   *

Ellery Queen is both the pseudonym and the detective creation of two Brooklyn-born first cousins, Frederic Dannay and Manfred B. Lee. At the time they created Ellery Dannay was a copywriter and art director for a Manhattan advertising agency and Lee a publicity writer for the New York office of a film studio. The announcement of a $7500 prize contest for a detective novel catalyzed the cousins into literary action in 1928, and Ellery's first adventure was published the following year. Dannay's experience in advertising may have inspired the innovation of using the same name for the cousins' deductive protagonist and for their own joint byline – a device that, along with the excellence of the books themselves, turned Ellery Queen into a household name and his creators into wealthy men.

In the late 1920's the dominant figure in American detective fiction was S. S. Van Dine (Willard Huntington Wright), an erudite art critic whose novels about the impossibly intellectual aesthete-sleuth Philo Vance were consistent best-sellers of the time. The early Ellery Queen novels, with their patterned titles and their scholarly dilettante detective forever dropping classical quotations, were heavily influenced by Van Dine, though superior in plotting, characterization, and style. Ellery is a professional mystery writer and amateur sleuth who assists his father, Inspector Richard Queen, whenever a murder puzzle becomes too complex for ordinary police methods. His first-period cases, from *The Roman Hat Mystery* (1929) through *The Spanish Cape Mystery* (1935), are richly plotted specimens of the Golden Age deductive puzzle at its zenith, full of bizarre circumstances, conflicting testimony, enigmatic clues, alternative solutions, fireworks displays of virtuoso reasoning and a constant crackle of intellectual excitement. All the facts are presented, trickily but fairly, and the reader is formally challenged to solve the puzzle ahead of Ellery. Most of Queen's distinctive story motifs – the negative clue, the dying message, the murderer as Iagoesque manipulator, the patterned series of clues deliberately left at scenes of crimes, the false answer followed by the true and devastating solution – originated in these early novels. Perhaps the best works of the first period are *The Greek Coffin Mystery* and *The Egyptian Cross Mystery*, which both appeared in 1932, the same year in which, under the second pseudonym of Barnaby Ross, Dannay and Lee published the first and best two novels in the tetralogy dealing with actor-detective Drury Lane: *The Tragedy of X* and *The Tragedy of Y*.

By 1936 the Van Dine touches had left Queen's work and been replaced by the influence of the slick-paper magazines and the movies, to both of which the cousins had begun to sell. In second-period Queen the patterned titles vanish and Ellery gradually becomes less priggish and more human. In several stories of the period he is seen working as a Hollywood screenwriter, reflecting the cousins' brief stints at Columbia, Paramount, and M-G-M. Most of Queen's work in the late Thirties is thinly plotted, overburdened with "love interest" and too obviously written with film sales in mind, but the best book of the period, *The Four of Hearts* (1938), is an excellent detective story as well as a many-faceted evocation of Hollywood in its peak years.

At the start of the new decade most of the cousins' energies went into writing a script a week for the long-running *Adventures of Ellery Queen* radio series and accumulating a vast library of detective short stories. Out of this collection came Queen's *101 Years' Entertainment*, the foremost anthology of the genre, and *Ellery Queen's Mystery Magazine*, which throughout its life from 1941 till today has been edited solely by Fred Dannay. In 1942 the cousins returned to fiction with the superbly written and characterized *Calamity Town*, a semi-naturalistic detective novel in which Ellery solves a murder in the "typical small town" of Wrightsville, U.S.A. Their third and richest period as mystery writers lasted sixteen years and embraced twelve novels, two short story collections and Dannay's autobiographical novel *The Golden Summer* (1953), published as by Daniel Nathan. In third-period Queen the complex deductive puzzle is fused with in-depth character studies, magnificently detailed evocations of place and mood, occasional ventures into a topsy-turvy Alice in Wonderland otherworld reflecting Dannay's interest in Lewis Carroll, and explorations into historical, psychiatric and religious dimensions. The best novels of this period are *Calamity Town* itself; *Ten Days' Wonder* (1948) with its phantasmagoria of biblical symbolism; *Cat of Many Tails* (1949) with its unforgettable images of New York City menaced by a heat wave, a mad strangler of what seem to be randomly chosen victims, and the threat of World War III; and *The Origin of Evil* (1951), in which Darwinian motifs underlie the clues and deductions. Finally, in *The Finishing Stroke* (1958) the cousins nostalgically recreated Ellery's young manhood in 1929, just after the publication of "his" first detective novel, *The Roman Hat Mystery*.

"In my end is my beginning," says Eliot; and the cousins apparently meant to retire as active writers after *The Finishing Stroke*. Five years later, however, they launched a fourth and final group of Ellery Queen novels, from *The Player on the Other Side* (1963), the best book of the period, to *A Fine and Private Place* (1971), published almost simultaneously with Manfred Lee's death of a heart attack. The novels and short stories of period four retreat from all semblance of naturalistic plausibility and rely on what Dannay has called "fun and games" – heavily stylized plots and characterizations and the repetition of dozens of motifs from the earlier periods.

No new novels have appeared since Lee's death and none are likely in the future, although Dannay remains active and perceptive as ever in his capacity as editor of *EQMM*. But the reputation of Ellery Queen, author and detective, has long been assured. Of all America's mystery writers Queen is the supreme practitioner of that noble but now dying genre, the classic formal detective story.

—Francis M. Nevins, Jr.

QUEEN, Ellery.   See **VANCE, John Holbrook.**

QUENTIN, Patrick. Pseudonym for Hugh (Callingham) Wheeler; collaborated with Richard Wilson Webb to 1952; also wrote as Q. Patrick and Jonathan Stagge, both with Webb. American. Born in London, England, 19 March 1912; naturalized American citizen, 1942. Educated at Clayesmore School, Iwerne Minster, Dorset; University of London, B.A. in English 1932. Served in the United States Army Medical Corps during World War II. Recipient: Mystery Writers of America Edgar Allan Poe Award, 1962; Tony Award, for drama, 1973, 1979; New York Drama Critics Circle Award, 1973, 1976; Drama Desk Award, 1973. Address: Twin Hills Farm, Monterey, Massachusetts 01245, U.S.A.

CRIME PUBLICATIONS

Novels (series characters: Peter Duluth; Lieutenant Timothy Trant)

A Puzzle for Fools (Duluth). New York, Simon and Schuster, and London, Gollancz, 1936.
Puzzle for Players (Duluth). New York, Simon and Schuster, 1938; London, Gollancz, 1939.
Puzzle for Puppets (Duluth). New York, Simon and Schuster, and London, Gollancz, 1944.
Puzzle for Wantons (Duluth). New York, Simon and Schuster, 1945; London, Gollancz, 1946; as Slay the Loose Ladies, New York, Pocket Books, 1948.
Puzzle for Fiends (Duluth). New York, Simon and Schuster, 1946; London, Gollancz, 1947; as Love Is a Deadly Weapon, New York, Pocket Books, 1949.
Puzzle for Pilgrims (Duluth). New York, Simon and Schuster, 1947; London, Gollancz, 1948; as The Fate of the Immodest Blonde, New York, Pocket Books, 1950.
Run to Death (Duluth). New York, Simon and Schuster, and London, Gollancz, 1948.
The Follower. New York, Simon and Schuster, and London, Gollancz, 1950.
Black Widow (Duluth). New York, Simon and Schuster, 1952; as Fatal Woman, London, Gollancz, 1953.
My Son, The Murderer (Trant). New York, Simon and Schuster, 1954; as The Wife of Ronald Sheldon, London, Gollancz, 1954.
The Man with Two Wives (Trant). New York, Simon and Schuster, and London, Gollancz, 1955.
The Man in the Net. New York, Simon and Schuster, and London, Gollancz, 1956.
Suspicious Circumstances. New York, Simon and Schuster, and London, Gollancz, 1957.
Shadow of Guilt (Trant). New York, Random House, and London, Gollancz, 1959.
The Green-Eyed Monster. New York, Random House, and London, Gollancz, 1960.
Family Skeletons (Trant). New York, Random House, and London, Gollancz, 1965.

Novels as Q. Patrick (series character: Lieutenant Timothy Trant)

Death Goes to School. New York, Smith and Haas, and London, Cassell, 1936.
Death for Dear Clara (Trant). New York, Simon and Schuster, and London, Cassell, 1937.
The File on Fenton and Farr. New York, Morrow, 1937; London, Jarrolds, 1938.
The File on Claudia Cragge. New York, Morrow, and London, Jarrolds, 1938.
Death and the Maiden (Trant). New York, Simon and Schuster, and London, Cassell, 1939.
Return to the Scene. New York, Simon and Schuster, 1941; as Death in Bermuda, London, Cassell, 1941.
Danger Next Door. New York, Simon and Schuster, 1950; London, Cassell, 1951.

Novels as Jonathan Stagge (series character: Dr. Hugh Westlake in all books)

Murder Gone to Earth.   London, Joseph, 1936; as *The Dogs Do Bark*, New York, Doubleday, 1937.
Murder or Mercy.   London, Joseph, 1937; as *Murder by Prescription*, New York, Doubleday, 1938.
The Stars Spell Death.   New York, Doubleday, 1939; as *Murder in the Stars*, London, Joseph, 1940.
Turn of the Table.   New York, Doubleday, 1940; as *Funeral for Five*, London, Joseph, 1940.
The Yellow Taxi.   New York, Doubleday, 1942; as *Call a Hearse*, London, Joseph, 1942.
The Scarlet Circle.   New York, Doubleday, 1943; as *Light from a Lantern*, London, Joseph, 1943.
Death My Darling Daughters.   New York, Doubleday, 1945; London, Joseph, 1946.
Death's Old Sweet Song.   New York, Doubleday, 1946; London, Joseph, 1947.
The Three Fears.   New York, Doubleday, and London, Joseph, 1949.

Short Stories

The Ordeal of Mrs. Snow and Other Stories.   London, Gollancz, 1961; New York, Random House, 1962.

Uncollected Short Stories as Q. Patrick

"Murder on New Year's Eve," in *American Magazine* (Springfield, Ohio), October 1937.
"Witness for the Prosecution," in *Ellery Queen's Mystery Magazine* (New York), July 1946.
"The Plaster Cat," in *Mystery Book* (New York), July 1946.
"White Carnations," in *Best Detective Stories of the Year 1946*, edited by David Coxe Cooke.   New York, Dutton, 1946.
"This Way Out," in *Mystery Book* (New York), March 1947.
"Little Boy Lost," in *Ellery Queen's Mystery Magazine* (New York), October 1947.
"The Corpse in the Closet," in *Ellery Queen's Mystery Magazine* (New York), January 1948.
"Farewell Performance," in *Ellery Queen's Mystery Magazine* (New York), September 1948.
"The Jack of Diamonds," in *Ellery Queen's Mystery Magazine* (New York), February 1949.
"Thou Lord Seest Me," in *Ellery Queen's Mystery Magazine* (New York), July 1949.
"Murder in One Scene," in *Best Detective Stories of the Year 1949*, edited by David Coxe Cooke.   New York, Dutton, 1949.
"This Will Kill You," in *Ellery Queen's Mystery Magazine* (New York), November 1950.
"Girl Overboard," in *Four and Twenty Bloodhounds*, edited by Anthony Boucher.   New York, Simon and Schuster, 1950; London, Hammond, 1951.
"Another Man's Poison," in *Ellery Queen's Mystery Magazine* (New York), January 1951.
"Who Killed the Mermaid?" in *Ellery Queen's Mystery Magazine* (New York), February 1951.
"Town Blonde, Country Blonde," in *Ellery Queen's Mystery Magazine* (New York), August 1951.
"All the Way to the Moon," in *Ellery Queen's Awards, 6th Series.*   Boston, Little Brown, and London, Gollancz, 1951.

"This Looks Like Murder," in *Ellery Queen's Mystery Magazine* (New York), March 1952.
"The Pigeon Woman," in *Ellery Queen's Mystery Magazine* (New York), July 1952.
"Death on the Riviera," in *Ellery Queen's Mystery Magazine* (New York), September 1952.
"Death on Saturday Night," in *Ellery Queen's Mystery Magazine* (New York), January 1953.
"Woman of Ice," in *Ellery Queen's Mystery Magazine* (New York), February 1953.
"The Hated Woman," in *The Saint* (New York), August 1953.
"The Red Balloon," in *Weird Tales* (Chicago), November 1953.
"The Glamorous Opening," in *Ellery Queen's Mystery Magazine* (New York), January 1954.
"Death and Canasta," in *Ellery Queen's Mystery Magazine* (New York), April 1954.
"The Predestined," in *Weird Tales* (Chicago), May 1954.
"Death Before Breakfast," in *Crime for Two*, edited by Frances and Richard Lockridge.   Philadelphia, Lippincott, 1955; London, Macdonald, 1957.
"On the Day of the Rose Show," in *Ellery Queen's Mystery Magazine* (New York), March 1956.
"Going, Going, Gone!" in *Ellery Queen's Mystery Magazine* (New York), October 1956.
"Murder in the Alps," in *"This Week's" Stories of Mystery and Suspense*, edited by Stewart Beach.   New York, Random House, 1957.
"Lioness vs. Panther," in *Ellery Queen's Mystery Magazine* (New York), July 1958.

OTHER PUBLICATIONS as Hugh Wheeler

Novel

The Crippled Muse.   London, Hart Davis, 1951; New York, Rinehart, 1952.

Plays

Big Fish, Little Fish (produced New York, 1961; London, 1962).   New York, Random House, and London, Hart Davis, 1961.
Look! We've Come Through! (produced New York, 1961).   New York, Dramatists Play Service, 1963.
Rich Little Rich Girl, adaptation of a play by Miguel Mihura and Alvaro deLaiglesia (produced Philadelphia, 1964).
We Have Always Lived in the Castle, adaptation of the novel by Shirley Jackson (produced New York, 1966).   New York, Dramatists Play Service, 1967.
A Little Night Music, music and lyrics by Stephen Sondheim, adaptation of a film by Ingmar Bergman (produced New York, 1973; London, 1975).
Irene, with Joseph Stein, adaptation by Harry Rigby, music by Harry Tierney, lyrics by Joseph McCarthy, adaptation of the play by James Montgomery (produced New York, 1973; London, 1976).
Candide, music by Leonard Bernstein, lyrics by Richard Wilbur, adaptation of the novel by Voltaire (produced New York, 1973).
Pacific Overtures, with John Weidmann, music and lyrics by Stephen Sondheim (produced New York, 1976).
Truckload, music by Louis St. Louis, lyrics by Wes Harris (produced New York, 1975).
Sweeney Todd, The Demon Barber of Fleet Street, music and lyrics by Stephen Sondheim, adaptation of the play by C. G. Bond (produced New York, 1979).   New York, Dodd Mead, 1979.

Screenplays: *Five Miles to Midnight*, with Peter Viertel, 1962; *Something for Everyone*, 1969; *Cabaret*, 1972; *Travels with My Aunt*, with Jay Presson Allen, 1973.

Other

"Who'd Do It?," in *Chimera* (Princeton, New Jersey), Summer 1947.
The Girl on the Gallows (as Q. Patrick). New York, Fawcett, 1954.

*   *   *

With the publication in 1936 of the first of Simon and Schuster's "Inner Sanctum" mysteries, *A Puzzle for Fools*, mystery readers were presented with a new byline, Patrick Quentin, and a new detective, Peter Duluth. Both made an immediate impression on readers and critics alike, and the new mystery series was off to a flying start. When Q. Patrick's *Death for Dear Clara* was published in the same series a year later, the publishers took the unusual step of devoting the book's endpapers to a revelation that the already familiar Q. Patrick and the newly introduced Patrick Quentin were both pseudonyms for the same pair of Harvard-educated Englishmen. This was true enough as far as it went, but it was far from being the whole story.

The byline Q. Patrick was first used on *Cottage Sinister*, a well-crafted novel about a series of poisonings in a small English village. At this time, the byline hid the collaboration of two English writers, Richard Wilson Webb and Martha Mott Kelley. The second Q. Patrick novel, by the same pair, was less successful: *Murder at the Women's City Club* was nominally set in a small city near Philadelphia, but neither the setting nor the characters were convincingly American. With *S.S. Murder* Webb acquired a different collaborator, Mary Louise Aswell, while *Murder at Cambridge* was by Webb alone. A second collaboration with Mary Aswell, *The Grindle Nightmare*, a brooding study of sadism and child-murder, brought the first phase of the Q. Patrick career to a close.

Death Goes to School inaugurated a highly successful collaboration between Webb and Hugh Wheeler. All subsequent Q. Patrick stories were by this team. *Death for Dear Clara* introduced the New York police detective Lieutenant Timothy Trant, Princeton-educated and sartorially elegant, in whom "the impulsive human being and the shrewd detective always worked in harness." Trant also appeared in *Death and the Maiden*, perhaps the most memorable of his cases, and in a series of short stories. After *Return to the Scene*, set in Bermuda, the Q. Patrick byline appeared only on short stories during the 1940's. A final Q. Patrick novel, *Danger Next Door*, appeared in 1950. The last Q. Patrick book of all, however, was nonfiction: *The Girl on the Gallows*, a study of the Edith Thompson murder case.

Returning to 1936: the second Webb-Wheeler collaboration, after *Death Goes to School*, was a different type of mystery novel from those with which the Q. Patrick name had become associated. The publishers suggested that a new byline should be used, and so Patrick Quentin was born. *A Puzzle for Fools* takes place in a posh sanitarium ("just an expensive nuthouse for people ... who had lost control") where Peter Duluth, once a successful Broadway producer, is drying out after a couple of alcoholic years. When murder strikes among the patients, Duluth finds himself cast as detective, unraveling clues while battling post-alcoholic jitters. In *Puzzle for Players* Peter and his future wife, Iris, whom he had met in the sanitarium, are involved with a Broadway play being staged in an apparently jinxed theater. Peter and Iris go on to encounter crime in seven more novels and several shorter works. A distinguishing feature of the series is that Peter and Iris are not present merely to investigate murder among strangers; they are always the central characters in the books, and the plots revolve around crucial events in their own lives. For example, *Puzzle for Pilgrims* and *Run to Death* are concerned with the break-up and eventual repair of the Duluths' marriage, intermixed with intrigue and sudden death in Mexico.

In 1952, Richard Wilson Webb left the writing partnership, and subsequent Patrick Quentin novels were written by Hugh Wheeler alone. The first of these solo productions marked the final appearance of Peter and Iris Duluth, who serve as subsidiary characters along with Trant. The central figure in *My Son, The Murderer* is Peter's brother, Jake Duluth, with his unshakeable faith in the innocence of his son when he is accused of murder. Spurred by this faith, Peter and Trant together unmask the killer. Trant appears as the detective in three subsequent novels, *The Man with Two Wives*, *Shadow of Guilt* and *Family Skeletons*. After the latter book, Wheeler abandoned detective fiction and devoted himself most successfully to plays and film scripts.

Returning once more to that watershed year of 1936: two pen-names were not enough to cover the output of the Webb-Wheeler collaboration, so they adopted a third identity, Jonathan Stagge. Between 1936 and 1949, nine novels appeared under the Stagge byline, all featuring Dr. Hugh Westlake, general practitioner in a small country town in Pennsylvania. With remarkable frequency Westlake and his precocious daughter, Dawn, become involved with impersonations, mysterious deaths, and secrets out of the past.

In addition to the novels, Q. Patrick and Patrick Quentin were noted for their short stories. A collection of these shorter works, *The Ordeal of Mrs. Snow and Other Stories*, contains several stories that have established themselves as classics, notably "A Boy's Will," "Mother, May I Go Out to Swim?," and "Love Comes to Miss Lucy."

Anthony Boucher, in the *New York Times*, said, "Patrick Quentin is one of the truly great plotters in the field of suspense," and British critic Francis Iles (Anthony Berkeley) said, "To me he's the Number One of American crime novelists." All of the Q. Patrick/Patrick Quentin/Jonathan Stagge novels are characterized by intricate plots, cleverly planted clues, and endings which legitimately surprise the reader.

—R. E. Briney

RADFORD, E. and M. A. British. **RADFORD, E(dwin Isaac):** Born in West Bromwich, Staffordshire, in 1891. Educated at Sherborne School, Dorset; Cambridge University, M.A. Married Mona Augusta Mangan. Journalist for 45 years: Acting Editor, Bradford *Evening Argus*; Production Editor, Leicester *Mail*; Chief Sub-Editor and Deputy Editor, Nottingham *Evening News*; Dramatic and Music Critic, Nottingham *Daily Express*; Art Editor-in-Chief and Columnist, *Daily Mirror*, London. Member, Royal Society of Arts. **RADFORD, Mona Augusta, née Mangan:** Married Edwin Isaac Radford.

CRIME PUBLICATIONS

Novels (series character: Doctor Manson)

Murder Jigsaw (Manson).   London, Melrose, 1944.
Inspector Manson's Success.   London, Melrose, 1944.
Crime Pays No Dividends (Manson).   London, Melrose, 1945.
Murder Isn't Cricket (Manson).   London, Melrose, 1946.
It's Murder to Live (Manson).   London, Melrose, 1947.
Who Killed Dick Whittington? (Manson).   London, Melrose, 1947.
John Kyleing Died (Manson).   London, Melrose, 1949.
The Heel of Achilles (Manson).   London, Melrose, 1950.
Look in at Murder (Manson).   London, Long, 1956.
Death on the Broads (Manson).   London, Long, 1957.
The Six Men.   London, Hale, 1958.
Married to Murder.   London, Hale, 1959.
Death of a Frightened Editor (Manson).   London, Hale, 1959.
Death at the Château Noir (Manson).   London, Hale, 1960.
Murder on My Conscience (Manson).   London, Hale, 1960.

Death's Inheritance (Manson).   London, Hale, 1961.
Death and the Professor.   London, Hale, 1961.
Death Takes the Wheel (Manson).   London, Hale, 1962.
From Information Received (Manson).   London, Hale, 1962.
Murder of Three Ghosts (Manson).   London, Hale, 1963.
A Cosy Little Murder (Manson).   London, Hale, 1963.
The Hungry Killer (Manson).   London, Hale, 1964.
Mask of Murder (Manson).   London, Hale, 1965.
Murder Magnified (Manson).   London, Hale, 1965.
Death of a "Gentleman" (Manson).   London, Hale, 1966.
Jones's Little Murders (Manson).   London, Hale, 1967.
The Middlefold Murders (Manson).   London, Hale, 1967.
No Reason for Murder (Manson).   London, Hale, 1967.
The Safety First Murders (Manson).   London, Hale, 1968.
Trunk Call to Murder (Manson).   London, Hale, 1968.
Death of an Ancient Saxon (Manson).   London, Hale, 1969.
Death of a Peculiar Rabbit (Manson).   London, Hale, 1969.
Two Ways to Murder (Manson).   London, Hale, 1969.
Murder Speaks (Manson).   London, Hale, 1970.
Murder Is Red Ruby.   London, Hale, 1970.
The Greedy Killers (Manson).   London, Hale, 1971.
Dead Water (Manson).   London, Hale, 1971.
Death Has Two Faces.   London, Hale, 1972.

OTHER PUBLICATIONS

Play

Screenplay: *The Six Men*, with others, 1951.

Other

Crowther's Encyclopaedia of Phrases and Origins (by E. Radford).   London, Crowther, 1945; as *Unusual Words and How They Came About*, New York, Philosophical Library, 1946.
Encyclopaedia of Superstitions.   London, Rider, 1948; New York, Philosophical Library, 1949.

*   *   *

E. and M. A. Radford were, throughout their long lives (working into their eighties), among the durable husband-and-wife crime-writing teams, comparable with G. D. H. and Margaret Cole in the UK and Richard and Frances Lockridge in the USA. They turned out numerous workmanlike crime novels over many years, besides compiling reference-works on such subjects as superstitions and word usage and origins.

But it will be for their brisk, fast-paced thrillers, and the creation of two CID characters, Inspector Manson and Inspector Holroyd, that they will be remembered. For one of their best books, Edwin drew upon his years as newspaper reporter and editor. This was *Death of a Frightened Editor*, in which a scurrilous gossip-columnist is poisoned by strychnine on a London-to-Brighton train. Some of their stories take place on the Riviera, and *Death on the Broads*, one of their finest cases, was placed on the Norfolk Broads.

—Herbert Harris

RAE, Hugh C(rawford). Also writes as Robert Crawford; R. B. Houston; Stuart Stern. Scottish. Born in Glasgow, Lanarkshire, 22 November 1935. Educated at Knightswood School, Glasgow, 1940–51. Served in the Royal Air Force (national service), 1953–54. Married Elizabeth McMillan Dunn in 1960; one daughter. Bookseller, John Smith and Son, Glasgow, 1954–64. President, Scottish Association of Writers, 1974–78. Since 1975, Member, Scottish Arts Council. Agent: Fraser and Dunlop Scripts Ltd., 91 Regent Street, London W1R 8RU, England. Address: Drumore Farm, Balfron Station, Stirlingshire, Scotland.

CRIME PUBLICATIONS

Novels

> *Skinner.* London, Blond, and New York, Viking Press, 1965.
> *Night Pillow.* London, Blond, and New York, Viking Press, 1967.
> *A Few Small Bones.* London, Blond, 1968; as *The House at Balnesmoor*, New York, Coward McCann, 1969.
> *The Interview.* London, Blond, and New York, Coward McCann, 1969.
> *The Saturday Epic.* London, Blond, and New York, Coward McCann, 1970.
> *The Marksman.* London, Constable, and New York, Coward McCann, 1971.
> *The Shooting Gallery.* London, Constable, and New York, Coward McCann, 1972.
> *Two for the Grave* (as R. B. Houston). London, Hale, 1972.
> *The Rock Harvest.* London, Constable, 1973.
> *The Rookery.* London, Constable, 1974; New York, St. Martin's Press, 1975.
> *The Minotaur Factor* (as Stuart Stern). London, Futura, 1977; Chicago, Playboy Press, 1978.
> *The Poison Tree* (as Stuart Stern). London, Futura, and Chicago, Playboy Press, 1978.
> *Sullivan.* London, Constable, and Chicago, Playboy Press, 1978.
> *The Haunting at Waverley Falls.* London, Constable, 1980.

Novels as Robert Crawford

> *The Shroud Society.* London, Constable, and New York, Putnam, 1969.
> *Cockleburr.* London, Constable, 1969; New York, Putnam, 1970; as *Pay as You Die*, New York, Berkley, 1971.
> *Kiss the Boss Goodbye.* London, Constable, 1970; New York, Putnam, 1971.
> *The Badger's Daughter.* London, Constable, 1971.
> *Whip Hand.* London, Constable, 1972.

OTHER PUBLICATIONS

Novels

> *Harkfast: The Making of a King.* London, Constable, and New York, St. Martin's Press, 1976.
> *The Travelling Soul.* New York, Avon, 1978.

Plays

> *The Freezer* (broadcast, 1972; produced Leicester, 1973).

> Radio Play: *The Freezer*, 1972.

> Television Plays: *The Dear Ones*, 1966; *Swallowtale*, 1969.

Other

Editor, with Philip Ziegler and James Allen Fort, *Scottish Short Stories 1977*.   London,
Collins, 1977.
Editor, *Scottish Short Stories 1978*.   London, Collins, 1978.

Hugh C. Rae comments:
There can be little enough to say about a person who has spent most of his life at a
typewriter. Originally I made a technical and subjective differentiation between my "crime
novels" and my "thrillers," publishing the latter titles under the name Robert Crawford. It
was my belief that it might be possible, in Britain, to deliver material of some import – in
terms of theme and statement – within the confines of the criminal *roman*, and my studies of
the criminal and his victims in the early Rae novels are in effect studies of fragments of the
Scottish environment and personality examined through the medium of the police
investigation. A common enough technique but not one that goes down well either with
serious critics, or with the reading public.
The lightweight guns'n'gals thrillers under the Crawford name were economically
necessary if I were to remain a fulltime writer. A branching out into "historical crime" with
The Rookery, together with more experimental work in *The Interview* and *The Rock Harvest*,
led eventually to a broadening of the base, the "view of the fictional field," and to more
complex medical/scientific thrillers (written with the direct help of a London doctor) under
the name Stuart Stern. Most recently I have developed a keen interest in the "mythology" of
international espionage and crime: a transatlantic approach, rather than a provincial one.
Sullivan is an example.
My "technique," if it can be so called, is based on the synthesis of popularly available
attitudes which I endeavour, to some degree or another, to turn around by using a
supercharged and compacted language structure, a heightening of reality that creates a serio-
comic irony between "Mass Image" and authentic historical fact, between popularly
disseminated "fictions" and how-it-is. At root, I'm interested in language and, through
language, in character. Plot, per se, kind of follows on like a wooden duck on a string, though
I am generally – now – inventive enough to bridge the credibility gap.

*   *   *

Carefully utilizing the settings of suburban and slum Glasgow, of the Hebrides, of Belfast,
and of the Scottish countryside, Hugh C. Rae creates a color and an atmosphere which are
authentic. His use of the vernacular and the snarling gutter language reinforces this
authenticity in novels variously categorized as thrillers or novels of psychological suspense.
With his very first novel, *Skinner*, Rae began to investigate the mind and manners of those
living on the seamier side of life. His pathological killer at large in a quiet Scottish community
is a portrait of an animal possessed. In *The Marksman* we find a sensitive exploration of
character as an underworld figure seeks revenge on the killer of his illegitimate son. Many of
Rae's characters are perceptively well-rounded, and the novels' actions grow out of these
characters. Although there may be unpleasant characters and violent plots, the complexity of
both makes for intelligent and convincing explorations of criminal types.
Rae's plots begin with an immediate impact and grow organically. He maintains strict
control, provides tension throughout and often shattering conclusions. In *A Few Small Bones*,
a tale of dogged police investigation, each character is believably suspect.
Authentic language and locales, well-rounded characters, in-depth portrayals, tight
plotting, and satisfying conclusions make Hugh C. Rae a writer whose novels should be
better known.

—Frank Denton

1239

RAFFERTY, S. S. Pseudonym for John J. Hurley; also writes as Duffy Carpenter. American. Born in New Haven, Connecticut, 4 August 1930. Educated in public schools in New Haven; Columbia University, New York; University of Bridgeport, Connecticut. Served in the United States Marine Corps. Married Catherine Tinker; has one son and one daughter. Reporter, Bridgeport *Post Telegram*, 1955–57; Senior Vice-President, Rozene Advertising, Connecticut, 1957–61; Vice-President, Gaynor and Ducas Advertising, New York, 1961–70. Address: 231 East 76th Street, New York, New York 10021, U.S.A.

CRIME PUBLICATIONS

Short Stories

    Fatal Flourishes. New York, Avon, 1979.

Uncollected Short Stories

    "Murder by Scalping," in *Ellery Queen's Mystery Magazine* (New York), July 1973.
    "Hang In, Chick!," in *Ellery Queen's Mystery Magazine* (New York), January 1974.
    "Call 'em, Chick!," in *Ellery Queen's Mystery Magazine* (New York), April 1974.
    "Show 'em, Chick!," in *Ellery Queen's Mystery Magazine* (New York), September 1974.
    "Captain Cork's Second Case," in *Ellery Queen's Mystery Magazine* (New York), November 1974.
    "Press On, Chick!," in *Ellery Queen's Mystery Magazine* (New York), February 1975.
    "The Death Desk," in *Alfred Hitchcock's Mystery Magazine* (North Palm Beach, Florida), March 1975.
    "Live and Let Live, Chick!," in *Ellery Queen's Mystery Magazine* (New York), May 1975.
    "Play It Cool, Chick!," in *Ellery Queen's Mystery Magazine* (New York), July 1975.
    "The Greatest Crook in Christendom," in *Alfred Hitchcock's Mystery Magazine* (North Palm Beach, Florida), August 1975.
    "Daley's Doubles," in *Alfred Hitchcock's Mystery Magazine* (North Palm Beach, Florida), December 1975.
    "Deal 'em, Chick!," in *Ellery Queen's Mystery Magazine* (New York), January 1976.
    "Keep 'em Laughing, Chick!," in *Ellery Queen's Mystery Magazine* (New York), March 1976.
    "Here Comes Mr. Pritchard," in *Alfred Hitchcock's Mystery Magazine* (New York), May 1976.
    "Right On, Chick!," in *Ellery Queen's Crime Wave.* New York, Putnam, and London, Gollancz, 1976.
    "Buzz 'em, Chick!," in *Ellery Queen's Mystery Magazine* (New York), June 1976.
    "Things That Go Bump and Grind in the Night," in *Alfred Hitchcock's Mystery Magazine* (New York), September 1976.
    "Morte D'Arthur," in *Alfred Hitchcock's Mystery Magazine* (New York), October 1976.
    "A Vision of Death," in *Mystery Monthly* (New York), December 1976.
    "Electryon Slept," in *Alfred Hitchcock's Mystery Magazine* (New York), June 1977.
    "Curtain Going Up, Chick!," in *Ellery Queen's Mystery Magazine* (New York), June 1977.
    "Mr. Morby's Murder Method," in *Alfred Hitchcock's Mystery Magazine* (New York), July 1977.
    "Murder in Small Claims Court," in *Alfred Hitchcock's Mystery Magazine* (New York), December 1977.
    "No Visible Means," in *Ellery Queen's Mystery Magazine* (New York), December 1977.
    "The House on 13th Street," in *Alfred Hitchcock's Mystery Magazine* (New York), January 1978.

"Ladies of the Evening," in *Alfred Hitchcock's Mystery Magazine* (New York), March 1978.
"Money Talks, Chick!," in *Ellery Queen's Mystery Magazine* (New York), June 1979.
"Going, Going, Gone," in *Alfred Hitchcock's Mystery Magazine* (New York), July 1979.
"The Hawk Shops for Justice," in *Alfred Hitchcock's Mystery Magazine* (New York), September 1979.

Uncollected Short Stories as Duffy Carpenter

"The Last Cigar," in *Ellery Queen's Mystery Magazine* (New York), July 1976.
"Last of the Big Time Spenders," in *Alfred Hitchcock's Mystery Magazine* (New York), November 1976.
"The First Moon Tourist," in *Alfred Hitchcock's Mystery Magazine* (New York), December 1976.

*　　*　　*

S. S. Rafferty is one of many excellent short story writers discovered through the Department of First Stories in *Ellery Queen's Mystery Magazine*. His career was launched with "Murder by Scalping," a memorable debut that introduced Colonial sleuth Captain Cork investigating an impossible crime that seems to be the work of an invisible Indian.

The Captain Cork series has probably been Rafferty's most successful, combining an unusual period detective with solid deductive plots often involving little-known historical oddities. A timely inspiration led the author to produce thirteen new Captain Cook stories during the American Bicentennial celebration – one set in each of the thirteen original Colonies. Notable in this group are the "The New Jersey Flying Machine" and "The Georgia Resurrection" in *Fatal Flourishes*.

A second long-running series from S. S. Rafferty features Chick Kelly, a nightclub comic who speaks in show business slang. His cases involve the contemporary New York scene. The action is fast and funny, and the plots are often ingenious. First of the series was "Hang In, Chick!" The best to date have probably been "Right On, Chick!" and "Buzz 'em, Chick!" Notable among Rafferty's non-series stories is "The Death Desk."

—Edward D. Hoch

RANDOLPH, Marion. Pseudonym for Marie (Freid) Rodell. American. Born in 1912. Educated at Vassar College, Poughkeepsie, New York. Head of Mystery Department and Associate Editor, Duell Sloan and Pearce, New York, 1939–48; after 1948, literary agent in firm that became Marie Rodell–Frances Collins Literary Agency. Director, Rachel Carson Trust for Living Environment. *Died 9 November 1975.*

Crime Publications

Novels

Breathe No More. New York, Holt, and London, Heinemann, 1940.
This'll Kill You. New York, Holt, 1940; London, Museum Press, 1944.
Grim Grow the Lilacs. New York, Holt, 1941; London, Museum Press, 1943.

Uncollected Short Story

"Tell Me the Time," in *Ellery Queen's Mystery Magazine* (New York), December 1949.

OTHER PUBLICATIONS

Other

Mystery Fiction: Theory and Technique (as Marie Rodell).   New York, Duell, 1943; revised edition, New York, Hermitage House, 1952; London, Hammond, 1954.

*   *   *

Marie Rodell, in *Mystery Fiction: Theory and Technique*, insisted upon structural and procedural rigour and approached the writing of mystery fiction as a project that requires discipline and meticulous attention to detail. The first edition of this sensible guide appeared two years after the publication of the third – and final – of Marion Randolph's mystery novels and it is apparent that Mrs. Rodell based her handbook both on her wide reading in the field and on her experience as an editor and as the pseudonymous Randolph.

Although *Breathe No More* and *This'll Kill You* may be viewed as exercises leading toward the formal ease that Randolph achieves in *Grim Grow the Lilacs*, they are both competent and readable fictions. *Breathe No More* and *Grim Grow the Lilacs* are country house weekend party murder mysteries, while *This'll Kill You*, with its ironical, humorous title, appears to be an uncharacteristic police procedural novel, outfitted with dumb but persistent gumshoes and wise-cracking period characters. It is also the only Randolph novel in which the crime is solved by a police official rather than by a gifted amateur, although the young assistant to the chief who solves the mystery uses unorthodox methods that are a potential threat to the procedural resolution.

It is, however, *Breathe No More* and *Grim Grow the Lilacs* – which must have been conceived as complementary novels – that are the more structurally satisfying and which best reveal Randolph's skill at setting, plotting, and character. In both novels, the victim is unpleasant enough to provoke a number of potential murderers and before the exposure of the real criminal, an innocent man is accused and jailed and even – in *Grim Grow the Lilacs* – sentenced to death. Yet one of Marie Rodell's dicta is that the author must play fair with the reader, and although the novels are intricately plotted and the reader's suspicions cannily misdirected it is possible for the reader to arrive at the solution at least a few sentences in advance of the police representatives who listen patiently to the amateur's reconstruction of the crime.

In *Breathe No More* the victim is a self-styled modern descendent of Napoleon Bonaparte who rules his household and his guests with a hand as firm as that of his dictatorial namesake; it is this sense of unbearable, oppressive relationships and situations that is most characteristic of Randolph, even in the apparently atypical *This'll Kill You*. This novel, if one excludes the proto-procedural trappings and awkward humor, reveals the same interest in closely entwined family relationships – and their histories – that marks *Breathe No More*. Both these novels are third-person narratives, although the point-of-view in *Breathe No More* is clearly established as that of an editor and writer of mystery stories who would seem to be a masculine counterpart of Rodell.

Ultimately, however, it is *Grim Grow the Lilacs* which is the most attractive and most personal of the trio, in large part because of its first-person narrator, a middle-aged woman of taste and intelligence. She also shares in common with the characters in *Breathe No More* an interest in art and flowers. In *Breathe No More* the country setting which would seem to call for banks of flowers is notable for their absence – an absence that is finally significantly linked to the solution of the murder – while in *Grim Grow the Lilacs* the flowers of the title give their name to the murder victim. Their color dominates the pages of this novel and, in writing of a small colony of artists and hangers-on, Randolph shows herself to be perceptive about the way artists work and feel; her use of color resembles that of a painter who carefully applies pigment for significant effect.

It is probably not helpful to speculate on why a writer as accomplished as Rodell wrote only three novels. But she must have taken particular satisfaction in the fluency of her last novel, and it is a swan song of uncommon grace.

—Walter Albert

RANSOME, Stephen. See **DAVIS, Frederick C.**

RATHBONE, Julian. British. Born in London, 10 February 1935. Educated at Clayesmore School, Iwerne Minster, Dorset, 1948–53; Magdalene College, Cambridge, B.A. (honours) in English 1958. Teacher of English in Turkey and England 1959–73. Since 1973, full-time writer. Agent: C. & J. Wolfers, 3 Regent Square, London WC1H 8HZ. Address: Decoy Pond Farm, Beaulieu Road, Brockenhurst SO4 7YQ, England.

CRIME PUBLICATIONS

Novels (series character: Nur Bey)

Diamonds Bid (Bey). London, Joseph, 1966; New York, Walker, 1967.
Hand Out (Bey). London, Joseph, and New York, Walker, 1968.
With My Knives I Know I'm Good. London, Joseph, 1969; New York, Putnam, 1970.
Trip Trap (Bey). London, Joseph, and New York, St. Martin's Press, 1972.
Kill Cure. London, Joseph, and New York, St. Martin's Press, 1975.
Bloody Marvellous. London, Joseph, 1975; New York, St. Martin's Press, 1976.
Carnival! London, Joseph, and New York, St. Martin's Press, 1976.
A Raving Monarchist. London, Joseph, and New York, St. Martin's Press, 1978.
The Euro-Killers. London, Joseph, 1979.

OTHER PUBLICATIONS

Novels

King Fisher Lives. London, Joseph, and New York, St. Martin's Press, 1976.
The Princess, A Nun, with Hugh Ross Williamson. London, Joseph, 1978.
Joseph. London, Joseph, 1979.

Julian Rathbone comments:

My "detective" fiction has had very little detection in it and really not much mystery. The appeal has lain I think in suspense, very often the sort of ironical suspense arising from situations where the reader knows more than the characters, from realistic characterization allowing the interplay of real emotions, and from vivid descriptions of more or less exotic locales. For the last few years I have been trying to move out of the thriller "genre" into something more completely novelistic – the first successful attempt in this line was *King Fisher Lives*, which was highly praised in the press as a "philosophical thriller" and which was short-listed for the Booker Prize in 1976. For the last four years I have been working on the long novel called *Joseph*, set in Spain during the Peninsular War (1808–13).

*   *   *

Julain Rathbone writes a good suspense story. His plots are well thought-out, his characters strong and well-defined, his heroes unusual in being for the most part unheroic. But what sets Julian Rathbone apart from all other writers in this genre is his ability to describe his background scenes so vividly that you can not only see them but smell and hear them also.

His first five books are set in Turkey, a country he came to know well in the early 1960's while a teacher in Ankara. *Diamonds Bid* is an exciting yarn concerning Jonathan Smollet who is arrested for driving too fast on the wrong side of the road. While he is being detained he sees a large sum of money being passed surreptitiously; he has too much of a hangover to give it a second thought, but the men involved cannot be sure he will not talk and he is coerced into an assassination plot. Smollet is neither an attractive nor a moral man, but this book introduces Colonel Nur Arslan, the totally incorruptible policeman, and his senior colleague, Deputy Director Alp Vural. We would like to see more of these two convincing characters. Nur Bey is a tall, thin, handsome man, though years of overwork have left their mark. The gravelly-voiced Alp Bey is older, overweight, and flabby, and has a reputation as a fixer.

In *Hand Out* the British spy, Adrian Hand, slips across the border into Russia and films a strange installation concealed in the mountains, but the gossip of the expatriates in Ankara betrays him. Hunted by both Russians and Turks he frantically ricochets across Turkey in an attempt to get the film to the British. Badly injured, he manages to reach safety with friends on the Mediterranean coast, only to be quietly relieved of the film. Rathbone's excellent *With My Knives I Know I'm Good* is told by the expert knife-thrower Aziz Milyutin, a member of a Russian group of entertainers, who defects to Lebanon. His desire to avenge the murder of his twin brother and acquire enough money to buy land in Turkey leads him into wild and hair-raising adventures with some very strange characters. *Trip Trap*, set in the Turkish port of Izmir, brings back Nur Bey. Edward Amberley is a naive English tractor salesman who is gulled by a beautiful but corrupt woman into the drug traffic; the story is complicated by the fact that the father of Nur Bey is peripherally implicated. The final book in the Turkish series is terrifying and fast-paced, *Kill Cure*. Claire Mundham joins a group called Christian Help to Asian Peoples which she believes is taking antibiotics to Bangladesh. But among the vials are some containing a virulent botulin, a few drops of which can wipe out a city and which must not be allowed to get into revolutionary hands.

Rathbone switches the scene to Spain for his next four books, and he proves again his talent to evoke in depth all aspects of a country. In *Bloody Marvellous* Mark Elmer, a bored young man, is persuaded to pose as a tourist in order to smuggle 30 kilos of hashish back to Britain. He tries the dangerous game of double-cross, only to find himself double-crossed in turn. Mark crashes his van while engrossed by the spectacle of azure-winged magpies. The hero of *Carnival!* is scriptwriter Colin Shedfield; like Elmer he is a bird-watcher. The story, set on the Spanish-Portuguese border, concerns a four-man television crew which films the brutal murder of an old Civil War veteran. The struggle to obtain the negative occurs in the streets of the little town of Ciudad Rodrigo, seething with bull-fighting enthusiasts. (The sex-ridden *King Fisher Lives* is in startling contrast to Rathbone's previous books, but readers will find themselves totally absorbed by this horrifying adventure of an American hippie's search for a way to live apart from what he believes to be totally corrupt society. This is a bold, clever book which well deserved its place on the Booker Prize short-list.)

In *A Raving Monarchist* Archie Connaught, unaware that his friend Maurice is being blackmailed, cannot understand his involvement with Paco Blas. This desperate character is a deadly threat to someone in Spain, but given the complicated political situation in that country, whose side is he on and whom does he plan to kill? This novel, rich in architectural description, is climaxed when the vertiginous Maurice scales Santiago Cathedral in a desperate attempt to thwart Paco's assassination plot.

—Betty Donaldson

RATTRAY, Simon. See **TREVOR, Elleston.**

RAWSON, Clayton. Also wrote as The Great Merlini; Stuart Towne. American. Born in Elyria, Ohio, 15 August 1906. Educated at Ohio State University, Columbus, B.A. 1929; Chicago Art Institute. Married Catherine Stone in 1929; two daughters and two sons. Associate Editor, *True Detective*, Editor, *Master Detective*, New York, 1942–46; Mystery Editor, Ziff Davis, Chicago, 1946–47; Director, Unicorn Mystery Book Club, 1948–52, and Art Director, Unicorn Books, New York, 1952–59; Editor, Inner Sanctum Mystery series, Simon and Schuster, New York, 1959–62; Managing Editor, *Ellery Queen's Mystery Magazine*, New York, 1963–70. Member, Society of American Magicians. *Died 1 March 1971.*

CRIME PUBLICATIONS

Novels (series character: The Great Merlini in all Rawson books)

Death from a Top Hat. New York, Putnam, and London, Collins, 1938.
The Footprints on the Ceiling. New York, Putnam, and London, Collins, 1939.
The Headless Lady. New York, Putnam, and London, Collins, 1940.
Death Out of Thin Air (2 novelets; as Stuart Towne). New York, Coward McCann, 1941; London, Cassell, 1947.
No Coffin for the Corpse. Boston, Little Brown, 1942; London, Stacey, 1972.

Short Stories

The Great Merlini: The Complete Stories of the Magician Detective. Boston, Gregg Press, 1979.

OTHER PUBLICATIONS

Other

Scarne on Dice, with John Scarne. New York, Stackpole, 1945.

Al Baker's Pet Secrets.   New York, Starke, 1951.
How to Entertain Children with Magic You Can Do (as The Great Merlini).   New York,
   Simon and Schuster, 1962; London, Faber, 1964.
The Golden Book of Magic (juvenile; as The Great Merlini).   New York, Golden Press,
   1964.

*   *   *

Magic and mystery were intimately intertwined in the unique career of Clayton Rawson. After a stint as art director of several prominent business firms in the mid-1930's, he wrote his own professional stage identity as a magician called The Great Merlini into four mystery novels. In the first of these, *Death from a Top Hat*, the detective character named Merlini solves a series of New York City murders that occur in surroundings where magicians proliferate, bookish references to the occult accumulate on every hand, and the detective novel form itself is gently mocked. Rawson also wrote some pulp novelettes about another magician-sleuth called Don Diavolo, two of which were collected in *Death Out of Thin Air* and published under the pseudonym of Stuart Towne. As the real-life Merlini, Rawson created and marketed some 50 original tricks and wrote two books on magic.

Rawson's novels and stories are characteristically keyed to "impossible" situations, in the grand tradition of John Dickson Carr. In fact, the two writers carried out a series of challenges in the pages of the Queen magazine – with one proposing an "impossible" circumstance and the other inventing a solution and explanation. Characterization and setting were not usually well-developed in Rawson's work; the plot was always pre-eminent. In this sense, he belongs to a fondly remembered period of the past. He was not an innovator, but rather a clever and quick-witted cultivator of the genre to which he devoted his career.

—Donald A. Yates

REED, Eliot.   See **AMBLER, Eric.**

REED, Ishmael.   Afro-American.   Born in Chattanooga, Tennessee, 22 February 1938. Educated at the University of Buffalo, New York, 1956–60. Married to Carla Blank-Reed; one daughter by a previous marriage. Co-Founder of the *East Village Other*, New York, and *Advance*, Newark, New Jersey, 1965. Since 1971, Chairman and President of Yardbird Publishing Company; since 1973, Director, Reed Cannon and Johnson Communications. Guest lecturer, University of California, Berkeley, 1968, 1969, 1974, 1976; Lecturer, University of Washington, Seattle, 1969–70; Senior Lecturer, University of California, Berkeley; Visiting Professor, Yale University, New Haven, Connecticut, Fall 1979. Recipient: National Endowment for the Arts Grant, 1974; Rosenthal Foundation Award, 1975; Guggenheim Fellowship, 1975. Address: 8646 Terrace Drive, El Cerrito, California 94530, U.S.A.

CRIME PUBLICATIONS

Novels (series character: PaPa LaBas in both books)

Mumbo Jumbo. New York, Doubleday, 1972.
The Last Days of Louisiana Red. New York, Random House, 1974.

OTHER PUBLICATIONS

Novels

The Free-Lance Pallbearers. New York, Doubleday, 1967; London, MacGibbon and
Kee, 1968.
Yellow/Back Radio Broke-Down. New York, Doubleday, 1969; London, Allison and
Busby, 1971.
Flight to Canada. New York, Random House, 1976.

Verse

Catechism of d neoamerican hoodoo church. London, Paul Breman, 1970.
Conjure: Selected Poems, 1963–70. Amherst, University of Massachusetts Press,
1972.
Chattanooga: Poems. New York, Random House, 1973.
Secretary to the Spirits. New York, Nok, 1977.

Other

The Rise, Fall, and ...? of Adam Clayton Powell (as Emmett Coleman, with
others). New York, Bee-Line Books, 1967.
Shrovetide in Old New Orleans (essays). New York, Doubleday, 1978.

Editor, *19 Necromancers from Now.* New York, Doubleday, 1970.
Editor, *Yardbird Reader.* Berkeley, California, Yardbird, 1972 (annual).
Editor, *Calafia: The California Poetry.* Berkeley, California, Yardbird, 1979.

Bibliography: "Mapping Out the Gumbo Works: An Ishmael Reed Bibliography" by Joe
Weixlmann, Robert Fikes, Jr., and Ishmael Reed, in *Black American Literature Forum* (Terre
Haute, Indiana), Spring 1978.

*   *   *

In Julian Symons's classic, *Bloody Murder*, he discusses the detective story as "The Folk-
Myth of the Twentieth Century," with the detective as the "sacred witch doctor who is able to
smell out the evil that is corrupting society, and pursue it through what may be a variety of
disguises to its source." This insight fits startlingly the unique, dizzying myths created in the
historical detective stories of Ishmael Reed, one of the few black writers who has attempted
the genre.
    The plots of Reed's two detective novels, *Mumbo Jumbo* and *The Last Days of Louisiana
Red*, almost defy summary. Reed's experimental style further complicates matters,
employing daring metaphors, anachronisms, allusions to jazz and popular media, flat
characters, street talk, academic jargon, and wild exaggeration that somehow contains the
sting of truth. There are, however, a mystery to unravel, murders to solve, and a detective,
the hoo-doo priest PaPa LaBas, to solve them. But Reed is primarily a satirist and a parodist,
bending the detective-story form to suit his view of the writer as "a witch doctor who frees
his fellow victims from the psychic attack launched by demons of the inner and outer world."

In *Mumbo Jumbo*, the setting is America in the 1920's, the problem is official panic over the dance-craze and wild misbehavior of the Flapper era, and Reed-LaBas's solution lies in exposure of the true history of American race relations. The dance-craze is traced to New Orleans and then to Haiti, prompting President Wilson to dispatch the Marines to that center of Voo-Doo. But "Jes Grew," the dance-virus, and the Establishment response to it, are manifestations of an age-old struggle between instinct and reason, between spontaneity and order, between Middle Eastern African-Egyptian religion and Western Christianity-and-science. The historical texts of Osiris's dances still exist; if located, some fear that they will liberate not only blacks but will inundate the white world in a "black tide of mud." Hinckle Von Vampton (Carl Van Vechten) is a medieval knight templar who has survived a thousand years and wants the secret book in order to gain power. He is opposed by PaPa LaBas, conjure man and black detective, who would employ the Osiris Texts righteously. The texts, which were divided and distributed among 14 persons to protect them over the centuries, are being hunted down and re-assembled. The paper chase involves a gallery of grotesque characters – Biff Musclewhite, Black Herman, Chester Gould, Presidents Wilson and Harding, the Wallflower Order, etc. – and drives erratically towards a surprise finish.

The Last Days of Louisiana Red does not reach back to pre-history, but, like all of Reed's novels, it develops a symbolic conflict between abstract historical forces that represent good and evil, in other words, myth. Evil this time masquerades as Louisiana Red, a hot sauce or poisonous soul food of hatred and violence; good is embodied in Gumbo, representing the healthy, nurturing black tradition ("mumbo jumbo," "jes grew," and "hoo doo" in the previous work). Ed Yellings, the enterprising black capitalist of the Solid Gumbo Works, has been murdered, presumably by agents of the rival Louisiana Red company. The trail leads PaPa LaBas to Street Yellings, a militant loudmouth and son of Ed (read Oedipus), and to Ed's daughter, Minnie the Moocher (who is a dead ringer for Antigone and also Angela Davis). PaPa LaBas, now in his "young seventies," threads his way among the whining Moochers; the modernist Rev. Rookie, with his psychedelic music and mojo jumpsuit; Big Sally, a Ph.D with "a top job in the 1960's version of the Freedmen's Bureau"; Cinnamon Easterhood, lickspittle "hi-yellow editor of the Moocher Monthly"; and Maxwell Kasavubu, a white scholar who obsessively dreams he is Mary Dalton being raped by Bigger Thomas of Richard Wright's *Native Son*. LaBas's "million-year old olmec face" fits his sleuthing methods: he consults with a baboon, receives messengers from the other world, and attends "readings." He shuns guns.

Reed's fragmented, free-swinging style violates every rule of the traditional novel as well as of the detective story. His purposes are political; his subject is revised, legendized history; his technique is innovative and experimental; his tone is impudent and hilarious; and his narrative is, loosely, a detective story.

—Frank Campenni

REEVE, Arthur B(enjamin). American. Born in Patchogue, Long Island, New York, 15 October 1880. Educated in public schools in Brooklyn, New York; Princeton University, New Jersey, A.B. 1903 (Phi Beta Kappa); New York Law School. Married Margaret Allen Wilson in 1906; one daughter and two sons. Journalist: Assistant Editor, *Public Opinion*, 1906; staff member, *Survey*, 1907; Editor of annual *Our Own Times*, 1906–10. Invited to help establish detection laboratory in World War I. *Died 9 August 1936.*

CRIME PUBLICATIONS

Novels (series character: Professor Craig Kennedy)

Guy Garrick. New York, Hearst's International Library, 1914; London, Hodder and Stoughton, 1916.
The Gold of the Gods (Kennedy). New York, Hearst's International Library, 1915; London, Hodder and Stoughton, 1916.
The Exploits of Elaine (Kennedy; novelization of screenplay). New York, Hearst's International Library, and London, Hodder and Stoughton, 1915.
The Romance of Elaine (Kennedy; novelization of screenplay). New York, Hearst's International Library, and London, Hodder and Stoughton, 1916.
The Triumph of Elaine (Kennedy; novelization of screenplay). London, Hodder and Stoughton, 1916.
The Ear in the Wall (Kennedy). New York, Hearst's International Library, 1916; London, Hodder and Stoughton, 1917.
The Adventuress (Kennedy). New York, Harper, 1917; London, Collins, 1918.
The Master Mystery (novelization of screenplay), with John W. Grey. New York, Grosset and Dunlap, 1919.
The Soul Scar (Kennedy). New York, Harper, 1919.
The Film Mystery (Kennedy). New York, Harper, 1921; London, Hodder and Stoughton, 1922.
Atavar (Kennedy). New York, Harper, 1924.
The Radio Detective (Kennedy; novelization of screenplay). New York, Grosset and Dunlap, 1926.
Pandora (Kennedy). New York, Harper, 1926.
The Kidnap Club (Kennedy). New York, Macaulay, 1932.
The Clutching Hand (Kennedy). Chicago, Reilly and Lee, 1934.
Enter Craig Kennedy (novelets; adapted by Ashley Locke). New York, Macaulay, 1935.
Tarzan the Mighty (novelization of screenplay). Kansas City, Missouri, Vernell Coriell, 1974.

Short Stories

The Silent Bullet: Adventures of Craig Kennedy, Scientific Detective. New York, Dodd Mead, 1912; as *The Black Hand*, London, Nash, 1912.
The Poisoned Pen. New York, Dodd Mead, 1913; London, Hodder and Stoughton, 1916.
Constance Dunlap, Woman Detective. New York, Harper, 1913; London, Hodder and Stoughton, 1916.
The Dream Doctor. New York, Hearst's International Library, 1914; London, Hodder and Stoughton, 1916.
The War Terror. New York, Hearst's International Library, 1915; as *Craig Kennedy, Detective*, London, Simpkin Marshall, 1916.
The Social Gangster. New York, Hearst's International Library, 1916; as *The Diamond Queen*, London, Hodder and Stoughton, 1917.
The Treasure Train. New York, Harper, 1917; London, Collins, 1920.
The Panama Plot. New York, Harper, 1918; London, Collins, 1920.
Craig Kennedy Listens In. New York, Harper, 1923; London, Hodder and Stoughton, 1924.
The Fourteen Points: Tales of Craig Kennedy, Master of Mystery. New York, Harper, 1925.
Craig Kennedy on the Farm. New York, Harper, 1925.
The Boy Scouts' Craig Kennedy. New York, Harper, 1925.

Uncollected Short Stories

"Kennedy Gets the Dope," in *Detective Story* (New York), 28 July 1928.
"Craig Kennedy and the Model," in *Detective Story* (New York), 11 August 1928.
"Craig Kennedy and the Ghost," in *Detective Story* (New York), 25 August 1928.
"Craig Kennedy Splits Hairs," in *Detective Story* (New York), 27 October 1928.
"Blood Will Pay," in *Detective Fiction Weekly* (New York), 22 September 1928.
"Radiant Doom," in *Detective Fiction Weekly* (New York), 6 October 1928.
"Craig Kennedy's Christmas Case," in *Detective Fiction Weekly* (New York), 22 December 1928.
"The Mystery Ray," in *Detective Fiction Weekly* (New York), 23 February–9 March 1929.
"The Beauty Wrecker," in *Detective Fiction Weekly* (New York), 16 March 1929.
"Poisoned Music," in *Detective Fiction Weekly* (New York), 31 August 1929.
"The Crime Student," in *Detective Fiction Weekly* (New York), 7 September 1929.
"The Mystery of the Bulawayo Diamond," in *Scientific Detective*, January 1930.
"The Junior League Murder," in *Complete Detective Novel Magazine* (New York), June 1932.
"Murder in the Tourist Camp," in *Complete Detective Novel Magazine* (New York), December 1932.
"The Golden Grave," in *Dime Detective* (New York), 1 October 1933.
"Doped," in *World Manhunters*, February 1934.
"The Royal Racket," in *Complete Detective Novel Magazine* (New York), January–February 1935.
"The Death Cry," in *Weird Tales* (Chicago), May 1935.

OTHER PUBLICATIONS

Plays

Screenplays (serials): *The Exploits of Elaine*, with Charles William Goddard, 1914; *The New Exploits of Elaine*, 1915; *The Romance of Elaine*, 1915; *The Hidden Hand*, with Charles A. Logue, 1917; *The House of Hate*, with Charles A. Logue, 1918; *The Master Mystery*, with Charles A. Logue, 1919; *The Carter Case*, with John W. Grey, 1919; *The Tiger's Trail*, with Charles A. Logue, 1919; *One Million Dollars Reward*, with John W. Grey, 1920; *The Mystery Mind*, with John W. Grey, 1920; *The Radio Detective*, 1926; *The Clutching Hand*, 1926; *The Return of the Riddle Rider*, 1927; (features): *The Grim Game*, with John W. Grey, 1919; *Terror Island*, with John W. Grey, 1920; *Unmasked*, with others, 1929.

Other

The Golden Age of Crime.   New York, Mohawk Press, 1931.

Editor, *The Best Ghost Stories.*   New York, Modern Library, 1930.

Bibliography: "Arthur B. Reeve and the American Sherlock Holmes" by John Harwood in *Armchair Detective* (Del Mar, California), October 1977; "A Chronological Bibliography of the Books of Arthur B. Reeve" by J. Randolph Cox in *Armchair Detective* (Del Mar, California), January 1978.

*   *   *

Arthur B. Reeve's creation, Professor Craig Kennedy, was sometimes referred to as "the American Sherlock Holmes." Like Holmes, Kennedy had his own Watson in the person of

Walter Jameson, a newspaper reporter, who roomed with Kennedy and accompanied him on most of his cases.

A typical story started with a client arriving at the rooms of the two friends or at Kennedy's laboratory (he taught chemistry at Columbia University in New York). Many of Kennedy's cases ended with the gathering of all the persons concerned with the crime in the detective's laboratory. He would explain how a new scientific device worked and how it pointed to the identity of the criminal. Then he would expose the wrongdoer in much the same fashion as Nero Wolfe did many years later. Usually he acted as a private detective, but often he was brought into a case by the New York Police Department or one of the Federal Government's investigative organizations like the Secret Service. The high point of each mystery occurred when a new scientific device, adapted by Kennedy to crime investigation, revealed the identity of the criminal. Many much-used instruments of today first appeared in the works of Reeve when he showed Kennedy using the dictaphone, X-ray, blood sampling, handwriting or typing identification, and early versions of the lie detector.

Long before the FBI came into existence, Kennedy had files of tire tracks, types of paper, inks, and other materials. He also believed that in the future public places would use hidden cameras as deterrents to crime, much like the closed-circuit TV cameras of today's banks. Some people think these early stories led to the scientific investigation of crime by police laboratories in later years. During World War I Reeve was asked by the federal government to create a scientific crime lab for use against spies and saboteurs. This laboratory was supposed to have been the finest known in any nation up to that time.

Although the Craig Kennedy books aren't very popular today, they did have a huge following from 1912 into the 1920's. At one time during that period Reeve was the best-selling American mystery author in England. By 1914 the Craig Kennedy stories became so popular that Reeve was asked to adapt stories of his famous sleuth for film. *The Exploits of Elaine*, featuring Pearl White, was so popular that two sequels were produced. He went on to write 16 movies in all, serials and features, about Kennedy and other characters. Several of the screenplays were later turned into book form.

Reeve was essentially a short story writer and many of his books were collections of short stories. Each novel was actually a series of interconnected short stories. At the end of each episode, instead of revealing the identity of the criminal, Kennedy showed how the villain committed the crime or the detective found a clue that led him further along the trail to the solution. Reeve is an almost forgotten author today and if he is read at all it is from a sense of nostalgia in an effort to bring back memories of the days when the American Sherlock Holmes was at the height of his popularity.

—John Harwood

REILLY, Helen (née Kieran). Also wrote as Kieran Abbey. American. Born in New York City in 1891. Married the artist Paul Reilly (died, 1944); four daughters, including Ursula Curtiss and Mary McMullen, *qq.v.* Lived in Westport, Connecticut, New York City, 1944–60, and New Mexico after 1960. President, Mystery Writers of America, 1953. *Died 11 January 1962.*

CRIME PUBLICATIONS

Novels (series character: Inspector Christopher McKee)

The Thirty-First Bullfinch. New York, Doubleday, 1930.
The Diamond Feather (McKee). New York, Doubleday, 1930.
Man with the Painted Head. New York, Farrar and Rinehart, 1931.
Murder in the Mews (McKee). New York, Doubleday, 1931.
The Doll's Trunk Murder. New York, Farrar and Rinehart, 1932; London, Hutchinson, 1933.
The Line-Up (McKee). New York, Doubleday, 1934; London, Cassell, 1935.
McKee of Centre Street. New York, Doubleday, 1934.
Mr. Smith's Hat (McKee). New York, Doubleday, and London, Cassell, 1936.
Dead Man Control (McKee). New York, Doubleday, 1936; London, Heinemann, 1937.
File on Rufus Ray. New York, Morrow, and London, Jarrolds, 1937.
All Concerned Notified (McKee). New York, Doubleday, and London, Heinemann, 1939.
Dead for a Ducat (McKee). New York, Doubleday, and London, Heinemann, 1939.
The Dead Can Tell (McKee). New York, Random House, 1940.
Death Demands an Audience (McKee). New York, Doubleday, 1940.
Murder in Shinbone Alley (McKee). New York, Doubleday, 1940.
Mourned on Sunday (McKee). New York, Random House, 1941.
Three Women in Black (McKee). New York, Random House, 1941.
Name Your Poison (McKee). New York, Random House, 1942.
The Opening Door (McKee). New York, Random House, 1944.
Murder on Angler's Island (McKee). New York, Random House, 1945; London, Hammond, 1948.
The Silver Leopard (McKee). New York, Random House, 1946; London, Hammond, 1949.
The Farmhouse (McKee). New York, Random House, 1947; London, Hammond, 1950.
Staircase 4 (McKee). New York, Random House, 1949; London, Hammond, 1950.
Murder at Arroways (McKee). New York, Random House, 1950; London, Museum Press, 1952.
Lament for the Bride (McKee). New York, Random House, 1951; London, Museum Press, 1954.
The Double Man (McKee). New York, Random House, 1952; London, Museum Press, 1954.
The Velvet Hand (McKee). New York, Random House, 1953; London, Museum Press, 1955.
Tell Her It's Murder (McKee). New York, Random House, 1954; London, Museum Press, 1955.
Compartment K (McKee). New York, Random House, 1955; as *Murder Rides the Express*, London, Hale, 1956.
The Canvas Dagger (McKee). New York, Random House, 1956; London, Hale, 1957.
Ding, Dong, Bell (McKee). New York, Random House, 1958; London, Hale, 1959.
Not Me, Inspector (McKee). New York, Random House, 1959; London, Hale, 1960.
Follow Me (McKee). New York, Random House, 1960; London, Hale, 1961.
Certain Sleep (McKee). New York, Random House, 1961; London, Hale, 1962.
The Day She Died (McKee). New York, Random House, 1962; London, Hale, 1963.

Novels as Kieran Abbey

Run with the Hare. New York, Scribner, 1941.

And Let the Coffin Pass. New York, Scribner, 1942.
Beyond the Dark. New York, Scribner, 1944.

Uncollected Short Story

"The Phonograph Murder," in *Anthology 1965*, edited by Ellery Queen.   New York, Davis, 1964.

*   *   *

In her famous detective series featuring Inspector Christopher McKee, Helen Reilly's most effective devices are point of view and characterization. The reader often shares McKee's viewpoint, searching with him to identify key clues; at other times, Reilly alternates the point of view between McKee and another sympathetic character. On other occasions, she indulges in a more Holmesian technique, and the Inspector keeps his own counsel until the dramatic disclosure scene. All these variations are deftly handled, and, combined with Reilly's ability to characterize swiftly and vividly, often using physical traits as symbols for personality, they produce brisk, readable, exciting fiction.

McKee, the Scotsman of the "short, thick eyelashes," well-worn tweeds, brown eyes, and lined face, is the head of the Manhattan Homicide Squad. It is instinct that focuses McKee's attention on key clues, hunches which often taunt him about an important observation hovering just outside his grasp, and hard perceptive detective work which brings him to his accurate and often amazing conclusions. Another of his tools is his keen ability to understand people; he trusts his judgments about suspects and is clear-headed in his evaluations. While he has an eye for a pretty woman, he finds beauty alone an empty trait and saves his sympathy for women whose physical charm is enhanced by vitality and intelligence. The Inspector is aided by a well-conceived and neatly developed cast of continuing characters: District Attorney Dwyer, stubborn and ambitious; Peirson, a good witness and an able officer; Dr. Fernandez, assistant medical examiner, in discussions with whom McKee tests his theories; and Lucy Sturm, nurse and undercover agent. One of Reilly's best strokes is Todhunter – unobtrusive, seemingly innocuous, but a clever detective – who is featured prominently in *Compartment K* while McKee detects long-distance.

Female characters are important throughout Reilly's work. Her portraits of older women are intriguing, for she frequently involves them in late romances, and they are generally attractive people of stamina and perception. The central characters are usually young women of sensitive consciences and high honor who feel bound to keep even impulsive or unwise promises. They tend to be independent and self-supporting and often know things, sometimes by chance, that place them in jeopardy either as chief suspects or crucial witnesses. Their tangled love affairs provide subplots; their well-meant allegiance to the wrong men and their struggle to subdue growing passion for other attractive males are made believable and interesting. Most of these suitors are suspects, and some are shrouded in mystery. The ill-chosen fiancés are handsome but weak; the true matches are strong and attractive but brusque; all conceal essential facts as well as their motives. All these factors lend a touch of the gothic to the novels.

Though the books stress tough, grim, realistic police procedure (some of which would no longer be acceptable methodology), they do not feature the mean streets, but rather focus upon closed circles of upper-class suspects, members of wealthy, extended families. The complex family relationships, the money, and often the false identities of some members are motives for duplicity and crime as well as for protectiveness and affection. Both sets of motives lend complication to the well-made plots whose melodramatic incidents are balanced by the even tone of the writing.

Reilly also wrote good, non-series mysteries such as the early *The Thirty-First Bullfinch*, which demonstrates that a local sheriff can be clever though unassuming. All told, her work makes a major contribution to the genre and reveals an able writer with an excellent grasp of police methods.

—Jane S. Bakerman

RENDELL, Ruth. British. Born in London, 17 February 1930. Educated at Loughton High School, Essex. Married Donald Rendell in 1950 (divorced); remarried in 1977; one son. Reporter and Sub-Editor, Express and Independent Newspapers, West Essex, 1948–52. Recipient: Mystery Writers of America Edgar Allan Poe Award, for short story, 1975; Crime Writers Association Gold Dagger, 1977. Address: 3 Shepherds Close, London N.6, England.

CRIME PUBLICATIONS

Novels (series character: Detective Chief Inspector Reginald Wexford)

> *From Doon with Death* (Wexford). London, Hutchinson, 1964; New York, Doubleday, 1965.
> *To Fear a Painted Devil.* London, Long, and New York, Doubleday, 1965.
> *Vanity Dies Hard.* London, Long, 1965; as *In Sickness and in Health*, New York, Doubleday, 1966; as *Vanity Dies Hard*, New York, Beagle, 1970.
> *A New Lease of Death* (Wexford). London, Long, and New York, Doubleday, 1967; as *Sins of the Fathers*, New York, Ballantine, 1970.
> *Wolf to the Slaughter* (Wexford). London, Long, 1967; New York, Doubleday, 1968.
> *The Secret House of Death.* London, Long, 1968; New York, Doubleday, 1969.
> *The Best Man to Die* (Wexford). London, Long, 1969; New York, Doubleday, 1970.
> *A Guilty Thing Surprised* (Wexford). London, Hutchinson, and New York, Doubleday, 1970.
> *No More Dying Then* (Wexford). London, Hutchinson, 1971; New York, Doubleday, 1972.
> *One Across, Two Down.* London, Hutchinson, and New York, Doubleday, 1971.
> *Murder Being Done Once* (Wexford). London, Hutchinson, and New York, Doubleday, 1972.
> *Some Lie and Some Die* (Wexford). London, Hutchinson, and New York, Doubleday, 1973.
> *The Face of Trespass.* London, Hutchinson, and New York, Doubleday, 1974.
> *Shake Hands for Ever* (Wexford). London, Hutchinson, and New York, Doubleday, 1975.
> *A Demon in My View.* London, Hutchinson, 1976; New York, Doubleday, 1977.
> *A Judgement in Stone.* London, Hutchinson, 1977; New York, Doubleday, 1978.
> *A Sleeping Life* (Wexford). London, Hutchinson, and New York, Doubleday, 1978.
> *Make Death Love Me* (Wexford). London, Hutchinson, and New York, Doubleday, 1979.

Short Stories

> *The Fallen Curtain and Other Stories.* London, Hutchinson, and New York, Doubleday, 1976.

Means of Evil and Other Stories.   London, Hutchinson, 1979.

OTHER PUBLICATIONS

Play

Radio Play: *A Drop Too Much*, from her own story, 1976.

*   *   *

Ruth Rendell has said that her chief interest as a writer is the creation of character. This preoccupation (along with her sharply defined settings and her penetrating social criticism) is a prime factor in the high quality of her novels and short stories. Rendell's canon divides into two general categories: the Kingsmarkhan series, featuring Inspector Wexford, and intriguing works which are independent units and do not include continuing characters.

Detective Chief Inspector Reginald Wexford is a central character who is complex enough to remain fascinating through a long series of appearances. Perceptions are presented through his vision; the world is weighed according to his values, and the reader finds those perceptions and values healthy and decent. Wexford is never "used-up," however, because he continues to grow and change, and, importantly, because he is surrounded by an interesting corps of family, friends, and associates who also develop and who are featured in important subplots in the novels. These subplots, always well wrought, command a good deal of the reader's attention.

Wexford is no romantic hero, even though in *Shake Hands for Ever* an attractive widow sets out to seduce him. A man of late middle age, the Inspector is comfortably married and the father of two grown daughters. One of his chief characteristics is tolerance; Wexford can always make a leap of imagination and perceive the stress and tension which motivate the criminal. A great reader, he is always ready with an appropriate quotation, these comments often serving the symbolic structure of the novels. Wexford's tolerance also manifests itself in his response to young people – he is quick to understand the children of his subordinate, Mike Burden, for example, and his grasp of the standards and values of the rock generation is a key to his success in *Some Lie and Some Die*. This sensitivity is, however, at odds with his appearance – gray, wrinkled, with small eyes and "three-cornered ears," and he's bulky, even when adhering to the diet prescribed for his hypertension. Capable but not infallible, determined but vulnerable, Wexford is a realistic, effective character.

The members of the Wexford family are among the subordinate characters who lend interest to the series. In *A Sleeping Life*, his daughter Sylvia's altered sense of herself and of her life as wife and mother allows Rendell to examine some facets of the women's movement. Sheila, whose developing career as a successful actress is traced throughout the series, is close to her father, and they communicate well. This healthy companionship is contrasted with the damaging parent-child relationship of the Fanshawes in *The Best Man to Die*. Less vivid than her daughters, Dora Wexford figures mainly as the supportive spouse who provides a haven from the ugliness of murder investigation, but in the story "Inspector Wexford on Holiday" she emerges a bit more forcefully and provides a necessary clue to the mystery.

The life of Michael Burden, Wexford's aide, also unfolds to lend interest and depth. Strait-laced and unyielding, the widowed Burden is nevertheless a passionate man who adored his wife and is determined to be a model father to their two children. In *No More Dying Then*, Rendell explores Burden's obsessive grief and his terrible loneliness. The book's subplot revolves around Mike's surprising but realistic affair with Gemma Lawrence, the mother of a kidnapped child. As both cope with almost unbearable grief, they find comfort in one another, and their story enhances the book enormously.

Rendell's remarkable skill at characterization is also important to the success of her nonseries works. In *A Demon in My View*, she examines the lives of a group of London neighbors. Two tenants of the same building, Anthony Johnson and Arthur Johnson, who share a name but are not related, figure centrally in the novel's two important plots. As is known from the beginning, Arthur is a psychotic personality who sublimates his drive to murder women by periodically "strangling" a show window dummy. Anthony, working on his doctoral thesis in criminal psychology, is deeply involved with a married woman, and the affair has reached a crisis. As each man struggles with his demon – his preoccupation with self, his sexuality, his ability or inability to function in the real world – two characterizations emerge in brilliantly crafted detail, and it is the fascination with character rather than with the chase which carries the suspense, a pattern common to Rendell's non-series books.

The plot of *The Face of Trespass* examines the disintegration of an impoverished young author, Graham Lanceton, who struggles with an illicit love affair, his estranged mother's terminal illness, and a massive writer's block. Graham's inner nightmare is splendidly symbolized by the setting, Epping Forest, a near-wilderness on the edge of London. Able to compromise almost any principle, Graham clings to the last shreds of his self-respect by refusing to implement his mistress's plan to murder her wealthy husband, only to find himself accused of that crime. Rendell balances the suspense of the murder mystery against the suspense of Graham's crimes against himself with remarkable skill; the book is one of her most effective blends of character study and crime novel.

Rendell's attention to characterization, then, is crucial to the success of all her books. In the Wexford series, where the chief focus is on solving a crime, characterization adds depth, breadth, subplot. In the non-series works, the central focus is on character, the crimes being a means of exploring that character. The author is in good command of both methods; in a Rendell mystery, the emphasis falls as much upon the "who" as on the "done it"!

—Jane S. Bakerman

RHODE, John. Pseudonym for Cecil John Charles Street; also wrote as Miles Burton. British. Born in 1884. Career Army Officer: Major; Military Cross. O.B.E. (Officer, Order of the British Empire). *Died in January 1965.*

CRIME PUBLICATIONS

Novels (series character: Dr. Lancelot Priestley)

> *A.S.F.: The Story of a Great Conspiracy.* London, Bles, 1924; as *The White Menace*, New York, McBride, 1926.
> *The Double Florin.* London, Bles, 1924.
> *The Alarm.* London, Bles, 1925.
> *The Paddington Mystery* (Priestley). London, Bles, 1925.
> *Dr. Priestley's Quest.* London, Bles, 1926.
> *The Ellerby Case* (Priestley). London, Bles, 1926; New York, Dodd Mead, 1927.
> *Mademoiselle from Armentières.* London, Bles, 1927.
> *The Murders in Praed Street* (Priestley). London, Bles, and New York, Dodd Mead, 1928.
> *Tragedy at the Unicorn* (Priestley). London, Bles, and New York, Dodd Mead, 1928.
> *The House on Tollard Ridge* (Priestley). London, Bles, and New York, Dodd Mead, 1929.
> *The Davidson Case* (Priestley). London, Bles, 1929; as *Murder at Bratton Grange*, New York, Dodd Mead, 1929.

Peril at Cranbury Hall (Priestley). London, Bles, and New York, Dodd Mead, 1930.

Pinehurst. London, Bles, 1930; as *Dr. Priestley Investigates*, New York, Dodd Mead, 1930.

The Hanging Woman (Priestley). London, Collins, and New York, Dodd Mead, 1931.

The Floating Admiral, with others. London, Hodder and Stoughton, 1931; New York, Doubleday, 1932.

Tragedy on the Line (Priestley). London, Collins, and New York, Dodd Mead, 1931.

Mystery at Greycombe Farm (Priestley). London, Collins, 1932; as *The Fire at Greycombe Farm*, New York, Dodd Mead, 1932.

Dead Men at the Folly (Priestley). London, Collins, and New York, Dodd Mead, 1932.

The Claverton Mystery (Priestley). London, Collins, 1933; as *The Claverton Affair*, New York, Dodd Mead, 1933.

The Motor Rally Mystery. London, Collins, 1933; as *Dr. Priestley Lays a Trap*, New York, Dodd Mead, 1933.

Ask a Policeman, with others. London, Barker, and New York, Morrow, 1933.

The Venner Crime (Priestley). London, Odhams Press, 1933; New York, Dodd Mead, 1934.

Poison for One (Priestley). London, Collins, and New York, Dodd Mead, 1934.

The Robthorne Mystery (Priestley). London, Collins, and New York, Dodd Mead, 1934.

Shot at Dawn (Preistley). London, Collins, 1934; New York, Dodd Mead, 1935.

The Corpse in the Car (Priestley). London, Collins, and New York, Dodd Mead, 1935.

Hendon's First Case (Priestley). London, Collins, and New York, Dodd Mead, 1935.

Mystery at Olympia (Priestley). London, Collins, 1935; as *Murder at the Motor Show*, New York, Dodd Mead, 1936.

Death at Breakfast (Priestley). London, Collins, and New York, Dodd Mead, 1936.

In Face of the Verdict (Priestley). London, Collins, 1936; as *In the Face of the Verdict*, New York, Dodd Mead, 1940.

Death in the Hop Fields (Priestley). London, Collins, 1937; as *The Harvest Murder*, New York, Dodd Mead, 1937.

Death on the Board (Priestley). London, Collins, 1937; as *Death Sits on the Board*, New York, Dodd Mead, 1937.

Proceed with Caution (Priestley). London, Collins, 1937; as *Body Unidentified*, New York, Dodd Mead, 1938.

The Bloody Tower (Priestley). London, Collins, 1938; as *The Tower of Evil*, New York, Dodd Mead, 1938.

Invisible Weapons (Priestley). London, Collins, and New York, Dodd Mead, 1938.

Death on Sunday (Priestley). London, Collins, 1939; as *The Elm Tree Murder*, New York, Dodd Mead, 1939.

Death Pays a Dividend (Priestley). London, Collins, and New York, Dodd Mead, 1939.

Drop to His Death, with Carter Dickson. London, Heinemann, 1939; as *Fatal Descent*, New York, Dodd Mead, 1939.

Death on the Boat-Train (Priestley). London, Collins, and New York, Dodd Mead, 1940.

Murder at Lilac Cottage (Priestley). London, Collins, and New York, Dodd Mead, 1940.

Death at the Helm (Priestley). London, Collins, and New York, Dodd Mead, 1941.

They Watched by Night (Priestley). London, Collins, 1941; as *Signal for Death*, New York, Dodd Mead, 1941.

The Fourth Bomb (Priestley). London, Collins, and New York, Dodd Mead, 1942.

Night Exercise. London, Collins, 1942; as *Dead of the Night*, New York, Dodd Mead, 1942.

Dead on the Track (Priestley). London, Collins, and New York, Dodd Mead, 1943.

Men Die at Cyprus Lodge (Priestley). London, Collins, 1943; New York, Dodd Mead, 1944.

Death Invades the Meeting (Priestley).   London, Collins, and New York, Dodd Mead, 1944.

The Bricklayer's Arms (Priestley).   London, Collins, 1945; as *Shadow of a Crime*, New York, Dodd Mead, 1945.

Death in Harley Street (Priestley).   London, Bles, and New York, Dodd Mead, 1946.

The Lake House (Priestley).   London, Bles, 1946; as *The Secret of the Lake House*, New York, Dodd Mead, 1946.

Death of an Author (Priestley).   London, Bles, 1947; New York, Dodd Mead, 1948.

Nothing But the Truth (Priestley).   London, Bles, 1947; as *Experiment in Crime*, New York, Dodd Mead, 1947.

The Paper Bag (Priestley).   London, Bles, 1948; as *The Links in the Chain*, New York, Dodd Mead, 1948.

The Telephone Call (Priestley).   London, Bles, 1948; as *Shadow of an Alibi*, New York, Dodd Mead, 1949.

Blackthorn House (Priestley).   London, Bles, and New York, Dodd Mead, 1949.

Up the Garden Path (Priestley).   London, Bles, 1949; as *The Fatal Garden*, New York, Dodd Mead, 1949.

Family Affairs (Priestley).   London, Bles, 1950; as *The Last Suspect*, New York, Dodd Mead, 1951.

The Two Graphs (Priestley).   London, Bles, 1950; as *Double Identities*, New York, Dodd Mead, 1950.

The Secret Meeting (Priestley).   London, Bles, 1951; New York, Dodd Mead, 1952.

Dr. Goodwood's Locum (Priestley).   London, Bles, 1951; as *The Affair of the Substitute Doctor*, New York, Dodd Mead, 1951.

Death in Wellington Road (Priestley).   London, Bles, and New York, Dodd Mead, 1952.

Death at the Dance (Priestley).   London, Bles, 1952; New York, Dodd Mead, 1953.

By Registered Post (Priestley).   London, Bles, 1953; as *The Mysterious Suspect*, New York, Dodd Mead, 1953.

Death at the Inn (Priestley).   London, Bles, 1953; as *The Case of the Forty Thieves*, New York, Dodd Mead, 1954.

Death on the Lawn (Priestley).   London, Bles, 1954; New York, Dodd Mead, 1955.

The Dovebury Murders (Priestley).   London, Bles, and New York, Dodd Mead, 1954.

Death of a Godmother (Priestley).   London, Bles, 1955; as *Delayed Payment*, New York, Dodd Mead, 1956.

The Domestic Agency (Priestley).   London, Bles, 1955; as *Grave Matters*, New York, Dodd Mead, 1955.

An Artist Dies (Priestley).   London, Bles, 1956; as *Death of an Artist*, New York, Dodd Mead, 1956.

Open Verdict (Priestley).   London, Bles, 1956; New York, Dodd Mead, 1957.

Death of a Bridegroom (Priestley).   London, Bles, 1957; New York, Dodd Mead, 1958.

Robbery with Violence (Priestley).   London, Bles, and New York, Dodd Mead, 1957.

Death Takes a Partner (Priestley).   London, Bles, 1958; New York, Dodd Mead, 1959.

Murder at Derivale (Priestley).   London, Bles, and New York, Dodd Mead, 1958.

Licensed for Murder (Priestley).   London, Bles, 1958; New York, Dodd Mead, 1959.

Three Cousins Die (Priestley).   London, Bles, 1959; New York, Dodd Mead, 1960.

The Fatal Pool (Priestley).   London, Bles, 1960; New York, Dodd Mead, 1961.

Twice Dead (Priestley).   London, Bles, and New York, Dodd Mead, 1960.

The Vanishing Diary (Priestley).   London, Bles, and New York, Dodd Mead, 1961.

Novels as Miles Burton (series characters: Inspector Arnold and Desmond Merrion in all books except *The Hardway Diamonds Mystery* and *Murder at the Moorings*)

The Hardway Diamonds Mystery.   London, Collins, and New York, Mystery League, 1930.

The Secret of High Eldersham. London, Collins, 1930; New York, Mystery League, 1931; as *The Mystery of High Eldersham*, Collins, 1933.

The Menace on the Downs. London, Collins, 1931.

The Three Crimes. London, Collins, 1931.

Murder at the Moorings. London, Collins, 1932; New York, Sears, 1934.

Death of Mr. Gantley. London, Collins, 1932.

Death at the Cross-Roads. London, Collins, 1933.

Fate at the Fair. London, Collins, 1933.

Tragedy at the Thirteenth Hole. London, Collins, 1933.

The Charabanc Mystery. London, Collins, 1934.

To Catch a Thief. London, Collins, 1934.

The Devereux Court Mystery. London, Collins, 1935.

The Milk-Churn Murders. London, Collins, 1935; as *The Clue of the Silver Brush*, New York, Doubleday, 1936.

Death in the Tunnel. London, Collins, 1936; as *Dark Is the Tunnel*, New York, Doubleday, 1936.

Murder of a Chemist. London, Collins, 1936.

Where Is Barbara Prentice? London, Collins, 1936; as *The Clue of the Silver Cellar*, New York, Doubleday, 1937.

Death at the Club. London, Collins, 1937; as *The Clue of the Fourteen Keys*, New York, Doubelday, 1937.

Murder in Crown Passage. London, Collins, 1937; as *The Man with the Tattooed Face*, New York, Doubleday, 1937.

Death at Low Tide. London, Collins, 1938.

The Platinum Cat. London, Collins, and New York, Doubleday, 1938.

Death Leaves No Card. London, Collins, 1939.

Mr. Babbacombe Dies. London, Collins, 1939.

Death Takes a Flat. London, Collins, 1940; as *Vacancy with Corpse*, New York, Doubleday, 1941.

Mr. Westerby Missing. London, Collins, and New York, Doubleday, 1940.

Murder in the Coalhole. London, Collins, 1940; as *Written in Dust*, New York, Doubleday, 1940.

Death of Two Brothers. London, Collins, 1941.

Up the Garden Path. London, Collins, 1941; as *Death Visits Downspring*, New York, Doubleday, 1941.

This Undesirable Residence. London, Collins, 1942; as *Death at Ash House*, New York, Doubleday, 1942.

Murder, M.D. London, Collins, 1943; as *Who Killed the Doctor?*, New York, Doubleday, 1943.

Dead Stop. London, Collins, 1943.

Four-Ply Yarn. London, Collins, 1944; as *The Shadow on the Cliff*, New York, Doubleday, 1944.

The Three Corpse Trick. London, Collins, 1944.

Not a Leg to Stand On. London, Collins, and New York, Doubleday, 1945.

Early Morning Murder. London, Collins, 1945; as *Accidents Do Happen*, New York, Doubleday, 1946.

The Cat Jumps. London, Collins, 1946.

Situation Vacant. London, Collins, 1946.

Heir to Lucifer. London, Collins, 1947.

A Will in the Way. London, Collins, and New York, Doubleday, 1947.

Death in Shallow Water. London, Collins, 1948.

Devil's Reckoning. London, Collins, 1948; New York, Doubleday, 1949.

Death Takes the Living. London, Collins, 1949; as *The Disappearing Parson*, New York, Doubleday, 1949.

Look Alive. London, Collins, 1949; New York, Doubleday, 1950.

Ground for Suspicion. London, Collins, 1950.
A Village Afraid. London, Collins, 1950.
Murder Out of School. London, Collins, 1951.
Beware Your Neighbour. London, Collins, 1951.
Murder on Duty. London, Collins, 1952.
Heir to Murder. London, Collins, 1953.
Something to Hide. London, Collins, 1953.
Murder in Absence. London, Collins, 1954.
Unwanted Corpse. London, Collins, 1954.
Murder Unrecognized. London, Collins, 1955.
A Crime in Time. London, Collins, 1955.
Death in a Duffle Coat. London, Collins, 1956.
Found Drowned. London, Collins, 1956.
The Chinese Puzzle. London, Collins, 1957.
The Moth-Watch Murder. London, Collins, 1957.
Death Takes a Detour. London, Collins, 1958.
Bones in the Brickfield. London, Collins, 1958.
Return from the Dead. London, Collins, 1959.
A Smell of Smoke. London, Collins, 1959.
Legacy of Death. London, Collins, 1960.
Death Paints a Picture. London, Collins, 1960.

Uncollected Short Stories

"The Elusive Bullet," in *Great Short Stories of Detection, Mystery, and Horror 2*, edited
  by Dorothy L. Sayers.   London, Gollancz, 1931; as *The Second Omnibus of Crime*,
  New York, Coward McCann, 1932.
"The Vanishing Diamond," in *The Great Book of Thrillers*, edited by H. Douglas
  Thomson.   London, Odhams Press, 1933.
"The Purple Line," in *The Evening Standard Detective Book*.   London, Gollancz, 1950.

OTHER PUBLICATIONS as C. J. C. Street

Novel

The Worldly Hope (as F.O.O.).   London, Nash, 1917.

Other

With the Guns (as F.O.O.).   London, Nash, 1916.
The Making of a Gunner (as F.O.O.).   London, Nash, 1916.
The Administration of Ireland (as I.O.).   London, Philip Allan, 1921.
Ireland in 1921. London, Philip Allan, 1922.
Rhineland and Ruhr. London, Couldrey, 1923.
Hungary and Democracy. London, Unwin, 1923.
The Treachery of France. London, Philip Allan, 1924.
East of Prague. London, Bles, 1924.
A Hundred Years of Printing 1795–1895. Frome, Somerset, Butler and Tanner, 1927.
Lord Reading. London, Bles, and New York, Stokes, 1928.
Slovakia Past and Present. London, King, 1928.
The Case of Constance Kent. London, Bles, and New York, Scribner, 1928.
President Masaryk. London, Bles, 1930; as *Thomas Masaryk of Czechoslovakia*, New
  York, Dodd Mead, 1930.

Editor, *Detective Medley*.   London, Hutchinson, 1939; shortened version, as *Line-up: A Collection of Crime Stories by Famous Mystery Writers*, New York, Dodd Mead, 1940; as *The Avon Book of Modern Crime Stories*, New York, Avon, 1942.

Translator, *Vauban, Builder of Fortresses*, by Daniel Halévy.   London, Bles, 1924.
Translator, *French Headquarters 1915–1918*, by Jean de Pierrefeu.   London, Bles, 1924.
Translator, *Captain Cook, Navigator and Discoverer*, by Maurice Thiéry.   New York, McBride, 1930.

*   *   *

John Rhode's novels are of considerable technical competence. The first, *A.S.F.*, was a thriller concerning the cocaine traffic in England. It would be pretentious to suggest that it had any positive social purpose, although it dealt with a genuine problem. At the time, it must have given little promise of the author's successful career to come as a writer of pure detection, and still less of his imminent introduction of a series character of great importance in the field, Dr. Lancelot Priestley.

Priestley was in complete contrast to the urbane young men-about-town then so popular in detective fiction. He had some of the characteristics of Freeman's Dr. Thorndyke and of Professor Van Dusen, "The Thinking Machine" of Jacques Futrelle. An academic, in his later years, with little apparent sense of humour, doing much of his detecting through various intermediaries, Priestley passes a comfortable existence in scientific research and in the application of his brilliantly logical mind to criminal problems. He does so with the scientist's lack of passion or emotional involvement, and with neither flair nor liking for the intuitional approach, propounding his solutions in after-dinner conversation with his friends, who gather round him as if in adoration of the Supreme Being. It would be an understatement, therefore, to describe Priestley as a larger-than-life character; he is, however, extremely well drawn by Rhode, whose ability in characterisation was normally limited indeed.

In *The Paddington Mystery* Priestley clears the name of Harold Merefield, who in later books is the Doctor's secretary and son-in-law. Although not recognised as among Rhode's best mysteries, it sets the scene for the series by presenting the biographical background of the regular characters. Of the long series of Priestley novels which followed, it is difficult to single out those of special merit; Rhode was a reliable writer, working to something of a pattern, and in such a case it is always easier to identify the few books which were disappointing or below standard. There are, nevertheless, some with special features that stand out from such a large and uniform output. *The Murders in Praed Street* is not only a good example of early Priestley before he became tied to his armchair in cerebral splendour, but also shows that the multi-murder story does not have to be monotonous and artificial. *The House on Tollard Ridge*, concerning the death of a rich eccentric, is perhaps the best technologically, has a good line of suspense, and (for Rhode) some surprisingly credible romantic interest.

Rhode was supreme in devising unusual methods of murder; one of the most unusual occurs in *The Claverton Mystery*, which also has spiritualism for good measure. He was excellent, too, when presenting murder against a transport or technical background, as in *The Motor Rally Mystery*, *Mystery at Olympia*, and *Death on the Boat Train*. *Hendon's First Case* is not only a first-class story, but introduced Inspector Jimmy Waghorn, who was to become Priestley's leg-man. One should not forget, also, that Rhode applied his own powers of reasoning most skilfully to the Julia Wallace murder in *The Telephone Call*, which was a fictionalised but impressive account, and further evidence of his analytical expertise is to be found in his non-fiction volume *The Case of Constance Kent*.

Street's novels under the Miles Burton pseudonym have not received the praise afforded to his work as John Rhode, although they are equally ingenious and carefully plotted. Perhaps Rhode had the advantage because of the presence of Dr. Priestley, a formidable force. Burton had his own series characters, Desmond Merrion and Inspector Arnold, but they never achieved the popularity of Priestley and his retinue. Merrion, regularly called upon to assist the police, does not possess the omnipotence of Priestley; Inspector Arnold, with whom Merrion enjoys a sometimes prickly relationship, is more than equal to the occasion in many of their joint cases. Merrion is a more imaginative and intuitive character than the scientific Priestley, and his manner permits the introduction of some lighter moments than one finds in the Priestley books. Although there is in the Burton books greater depth of characterisation, under neither name did Street permit this to interfere with the development of the plot; the story is everything, the solution of the mystery paramount. The majority of Burton's novels fall within one of two categories. There are those set in the countryside or at the seaside, with murder of the domestic variety or associated with other crimes such as smuggling. Good examples are *The Secret of High Eldersham*, with witchcraft as the central theme; *The Chinese Puzzle*, with some unusual occurrences in an English port; and *Legacy of Death*, with its well-drawn setting of a convalescent home. In the second category are novels depicting Merrion's wartime adventures in counter-espionage. *Death Visits Downspring* and *Four-Ply Yarn* are both enthralling and have more activity than most of Burton's stories. It is difficult with Burton, as with Rhode, to name his best books. High on the list, however, are *Death in the Tunnel*, one of the best railway detective novels, and *Death Leaves No Card*, a nicely contrived solo case for Inspector Arnold.

The works of Rhode and Burton deserve to be remembered as good examples of the workmanlike and traditional type of detective fiction always so popular. Although unnecessarily pedantic at times, they gave readers what they wanted and what they expected. Some may now appear dated, particularly when an enlightened modern readership considers Priestley's pseudo-scientific utterances. Nevertheless, the inventiveness and direct style of Rhode/Burton have earned the lingering affection of many readers on both sides of the Atlantic.

—Melvyn Barnes

RICE, Craig. Pseudonym for Georgiana Ann Randolph; also wrote as Daphne Sanders; Michael Venning. American. Born in Chicago, Illinois, 5 June 1908. Educated privately. Marriages include: Lawrence Lipton in 1939 (divorced, 1948); H. W. DeMott, Jr.; two daughters and one son. Journalist, 1925–30; radio writer and producer, 1931–38; free-lance writer from 1938. *Died 28 August 1957.*

CRIME PUBLICATIONS

Novels (series characters: John J. Malone and the Justuses; Bingo Riggs and Handsome Kusak)

8 Faces at 3 (Malone and Justuses). New York, Simon and Schuster, and London, Eyre and Spottiswoode, 1939; as *Death at Three*, London, Cherry Tree, 1941.
The Corpse Steps Out (Malone and Justuses). New York, Simon and Schuster, and London, Eyre and Spottiswoode, 1940.
The Wrong Murder. New York, Simon and Schuster, 1940; London, Eyre and Spottiswoode, 1942.
The Right Murder (Malone and Justuses). New York, Simon and Schuster, 1941; London, Eyre and Spottiswoode, 1948.
Trial by Fury (Malone and Justuses). New York, Simon and Schuster, 1941; London, Hammond, 1950.

The Big Midget Murders (Malone and Justuses).   New York, Simon and Schuster, 1942.

The Sunday Pigeon Murders (Riggs and Kusak).   New York, Simon and Schuster, 1942; London, Nicholson and Watson, 1948.

Telefair.   Indianapolis, Bobbs Merrill, 1942; as *Yesterday's Murder*, New York, Popular Library, 1950.

Having Wonderful Crime (Malone and Justuses).   New York, Simon and Schuster, 1943; London, Nicholson and Watson, 1944.

To Catch a Thief (as Daphne Sanders).   New York, Dial Press, 1943.

The Thursday Turkey Murders (Riggs and Kusak).   New York, Simon and Schuster, 1943; London, Nicholson and Watson, 1946.

Home Sweet Homicide.   New York, Simon and Schuster, 1944.

The Lucky Stiff (Malone and Justuses).   New York, Simon and Schuster, 1945.

The Fourth Postman (Malone and Justuses).   New York, Simon and Schuster, 1948; London, Hammond, 1951.

Innocent Bystander.   New York, Simon and Schuster, 1949; London, Hammond, 1958.

Knocked for a Loop (Malone and Justuses).   New York, Simon and Schuster, 1957; as *The Double Frame*, London, Hammond, 1958.

My Kingdom for a Hearse (Malone and Justuses).   New York, Simon and Schuster, 1957; London, Hammond, 1959.

The April Robin Murders (Riggs and Kusak), completed by Ed McBain.   New York, Random House, 1958; London, Hammond, 1959.

But the Doctor Died (Malone and Justuses).   New York, Lancer, 1967.

Novels as Michael Venning (series character: Melville Fairr in all books)

The Man Who Slept All Day.   New York, Coward McCann, 1942.

Murder Through the Looking Glass.   New York, Coward McCann, 1943; London, Nicholson and Watson, 1947.

Jethro Hammer.   New York, Coward McCann, 1944; London, Nicholson and Watson, 1947.

Short Stories

The Name Is Malone.   New York, Pyramid, 1958; London, Hammond, 1960.

People vs. Withers and Malone, with Stuart Palmer.   New York, Simon and Schuster, 1963.

Uncollected Short Stories

"The Case of the Common Cold," in *The Saint* (New York), March 1964.

"The Man Who Swallowed a Horse," in *Anthology 1966*, edited by Ellery Queen.   New York, Davis, 1965.

Other Publications

Plays

Screenplays: *The Falcon's Brother*, with Stuart Palmer, 1942; *The Falcon in Danger*, with Fred Niblo, Jr., 1943; *Mrs. O'Malley and Mr. Malone*, with William Bowers and Stuart Palmer, 1951.

Radio play: *Miracle at Midnight.*

Other

45 Murderers: A Collection of True Crime Stories. New York, Simon and Schuster, 1952.

Editor, Los Angeles Murders. New York, Dell, 1947.

Ghostwriter: The G-String Murders by Gypsy Rose Lee, New York, Simon and Schuster, 1941, as The Strip-Tease Murders, London, Lane, 1943; Mother Finds a Body by Gypsy Rose Lee, New York, Simon and Schuster, 1942, London, Lane, 1944; (with Cleve Cartmill) Crime on My Hands by George Sanders, New York, Simon and Schuster, 1944.

*   *   *

It is difficult to assess Craig Rice properly. Her complete canon has yet to be established. There are many short stories and novelettes from the 1950's which have never been collected and there are rumors about the authenticity of some of the later texts. She served as ghost writer for Gypsy Rose Lee and George Sanders, but there have been suggestions that she herself had substitute ghosts part of the time. Her readers, of course, never cared about such fine points: they just enjoyed the stories.

Few critics have ever tried to explain the reasons for her popularity. If she can't be considered the first writer of humorous hard-boiled detective fiction, she can certainly be considered among the most successful. While not all of her work is intended to be enjoyed for its combination of mayhem and mirth, the majority of it is lighthearted: "screwball comedy" – part wisecrack and part comedy of situation. Her own brand of comedy can hardly be mistaken for that of anyone else; it is Damon Runyon without the idiomatic English, Thorne Smith without the fantasy. It is a difficult style to sustain and is perhaps best appreciated in small doses. Her introspective stories (such as those she wrote as Michael Venning) indicate a sensitivity sometimes lacking in her usual gangland romances.

Her most famous character is Chicago lawyer John J. Malone. He is no Perry Mason or Mr. Tutt except in his success in the courtroom, a setting we are never shown. It is said that his manner before a jury is "not so much technical as pyrotechnical" (Trial by Fury). Short and pudgy, with a red face and hair always in need of combing, Malone wears a suit with a perpetual slept-in look, his shirt front and vest covered with cigar ashes. His favourite drink is rye, but he also enjoys gin with a beer chaser. In a running parody of the standard hard-boiled detective cliché, he keeps his liquor in various drawers of his filing cabinet under labels like "Confidential," "Unanswered Correspondence," or "Emergency." Also like many of his hard-boiled colleagues in crime, Malone enjoys the company of beautiful women. It is rumored that someone named Louise meant something in his life once. Malone's compelling interest in life, however, is justice. He will reveal the guilty party in a story, then turn and offer to defend that person in the coming trial. His motto is "I've never lost a client yet." In an early novel, The Wrong Murder, he says: "I'm not an officer of the law ... my profession has always put me on the other side of the fence. I've never served the cause of justice ... but rather the cause of injustice."

A stock company of interesting secondary characters and the repetition of familiar scenes in a well-defined milieu help make the stories a real saga and not merely a series of episodes. The early novels are linked by events that carry over from book to book like variations on a theme. Jake and Helene Justus are central characters, along with Malone, in several novels. They are in the tradition of the husband and wife who stumble into problems that they can't solve entirely on their own. Jake, a press agent, does not have the steadiest job in town. His marriage to a beautiful blond heiress creates tension that provides a number of interesting story situations. Craig Rice gave this trio equal parts of ineptitude, wit, and the ability to absorb liquor. That balance, plus some truly imaginative plot ideas, were enough to assure her of a large and devoted following. Other regulars in the series include Daniel von

Flanagan, captain of homicide, who tries to play down his role as an Irish cop by adding the "von" to his name. He dreams of escaping Malone and the Justuses to a retirement raising mink or pecans in Georgia or running a weekly newspaper. Max Hook, the head of Chicago's gambling syndicate, is less trouble than the terrible trio. Many of the stories begin in Joe the Angel's City Hall Bar, run by Joe diAngelo, whose cousin, Rico, the undertaker, sometimes calls on Malone for help.

The basic format of a Craig Rice novel involves a statement of the problem in an imaginative opening scene told from the point of view of the victim, chief suspect, or even the murderer. The scene then shifts to introduce von Flanagan, the Justuses, or Malone. Complications accumulate until the solution is found. Whether the characters or the problems are more appealing will depend on the individual reader. The victim is found in a room where the clocks have all stopped at three; a murder on a crowded street corner goes unnoticed; the murder victim's clothes all vanish on the way to the morgue; a reprieved murderess plans to haunt the people who sent her to jail. Her trilogy about street photographers Bingo Riggs and Handsome Kusak is in the comic tradition of the detective in spite of himself. *Home Sweet Homicide*, often ranked with *Trial by Fury* among her best novels, is the slightly autobiographical story of a mystery writer whose three children solve the murder of their next-door neighbor.

Those with a taste for strict realism in crime fiction may find fault with Rice's romantic version of Chicago's gangland, but the tone of some of her short stories and true crime articles could serve as a corrective. The warmth and humanity in her writing were matched by a sense of form and discipline all her own. She never forgot that the primary purpose of the detective story was entertainment.

—J. Randolph Cox

RICHARDS, Clay. See **CROSSEN, Ken**.

RIDGWAY, Jason. See **MARLOWE, Stephen**.

RINEHART, Mary Roberts. American. Born in Pittsburgh, Pennsylvania, in 1876. Educated in elementary and high schools in Pittsburgh; Pittsburgh Training School for nurses, graduated 1896. Married Dr. Stanley Marshall Rinehart in 1896 (died, 1932); three sons. Full-time writer from 1903. Correspondent for *Saturday Evening Post* in World War I; reported Presidential nominating conventions. Lived in Pittsburgh until 1920, in Washington, D.C., 1920–32, and in New York City from 1932. Recipient: Mystery Writers of America Special Award, 1953. Litt.D.: George Washington University, Washington, D.C., 1923. *Died 22 September 1958.*

Novels (series character: Nurse Hilda Adams, "Miss Pinkerton")

The Circular Staircase. Indianapolis, Bobbs Merrill, 1908; London, Cassell, 1909.
The Man in Lower Ten. Indianapolis, Bobbs Merrill, and London, Cassell, 1909.
The Window at the White Cat. Indianapolis, Bobbs Merrill, 1910; London, Nash, 1911.
Where There's a Will. Indianapolis, Bobbs Merrill, 1912.
The Case of Jennie Brice. Indianapolis, Bobbs Merrill, 1913; London, Hodder and Stoughton, 1919.
The After House. Boston, Houghton Mifflin, 1914; London, Simpkin Marshall, 1915.
The Street of Seven Stars. Boston, Houghton Mifflin, 1914; London, Cassell, 1915.
K. Boston, Houghton Mifflin, and London, Smith Elder, 1915.
The Amazing Interlude. New York, Doran, and London, Murray, 1918.
Dangerous Days. New York, Doran, and London, Hodder and Stoughton, 1919.
Sight Unseen, and The Confession. New York, Doran, and London, Hodder and Stoughton, 1921.
The Breaking Point. New York, Doran, and London, Hodder and Stoughton, 1922.
The Red Lamp. New York, Doran, 1925; as *The Mystery Lamp*, London, Hodder and Stoughton, 1925.
The Bat (novelization of play), with Avery Hopwood. New York, Doran, and London, Cassell, 1926.
Lost Ecstacy. New York, Doran, and London, Hodder and Stoughton, 1927; as *I Take This Woman*, New York, Grosset and Dunlap, 1927.
Two Flights Up. New York, Doubleday, and London, Hodder and Stoughton, 1928.
This Strange Adventure. New York, Doubleday, and London, Hodder and Stoughton, 1929.
The Door. New York, Farrar and Rinehart, and London, Hodder and Stoughton, 1930.
Miss Pinkerton. New York, Farrar and Rinehart, 1932; as *The Double Alibi*, London, Cassell, 1932.
Mary Roberts Rinehart's Crime Book (Adams; novelets). New York, Farrar and Rinehart, 1933; London, Cassell, 1958.
The Album. New York, Farrar and Rinehart, and London, Cassell, 1933.
The State Versus Elinor Norton. New York, Farrar and Rinehart, 1934; as *The Case of Elinor Norton*, London, Cassell, 1934.
The Wall. New York, Farrar and Rinehart, and London, Cassell, 1938.
The Great Mistake. New York, Farrar and Rinehart, 1940; London, Cassell, 1941.
Haunted Lady (Adams). New York, Farrar and Rinehart, and London, Cassell, 1942.
The Yellow Room. New York, Farrar and Rinehart, 1945; London, Cassell, 1949.
The Curve of the Catenary. New York, Royce, 1945.
Episode of the Wandering Knife: Three Mystery Tales. New York, Rinehart, 1950; as *The Wandering Knife*, London, Cassell, 1952.
The Swimming Pool. New York, Rinehart, 1952; as *The Pool*, London, Cassell, 1952.

Short Stories

The Amazing Adventures of Letitia Carberry. Indianapolis, Bobbs Merrill, 1911; London, Hodder and Stoughton, 1919.
Alibi for Isabel and Other Stories. New York, Farrar and Rinehart, 1944; London, Cassell, 1946.

The Frightened Wife and Other Murder Stories. New York, Rinehart, 1953; London, Cassell, 1954.

Uncollected Short Stories

"The Dog in the Orchard," in *The Second Mystery Book.* New York, Farrar Straus, 1940.

"The Treasure Hunt," in *101 Years' Entertainment*, edited by Ellery Queen. Boston, Little Brown, 1941.

"The Splinter," in *Ellery Queen's Awards, 10th Series.* Boston, Little Brown, and London, Collins, 1955.

"Case Is Closed," in *"This Week's" Stories of Mystery and Suspense*, edited by Stewart Beach. New York, Random House, 1957.

"Four A.M.," in *Anthology 1962*, edited by Ellery Queen. New York, Davis, 1961.

OTHER PUBLICATIONS

Novels

When a Man Marries. Indianapolis, Bobbs Merrill, 1909; London, Hodder and Stoughton, 1920.

Bab, A Sub-Deb. New York, Doran, 1917; London, Hodder and Stoughton, 1920.

Long Live the King! Boston, Houghton Mifflin, and London, Murray, 1917.

Twenty-Three and a Half Hours' Leave. New York, Doran, 1918.

A Poor Wise Man. New York, Doran, and London, Hodder and Stoughton, 1920.

The Out Trail. New York, Doran, 1923.

Mr. Cohen Takes a Walk. New York, Farrar and Rinehart, 1934.

The Doctor. New York, Farrar and Rinehart, and London, Cassell, 1936.

A Light in the Window. New York, Rinehart, and London, Cassell, 1948.

Short Stories

Tish. Boston, Houghton Mifflin, 1916; London, Hodder and Stoughton, 1917.

Love Stories. New York, Doran, 1920.

The Truce of God. New York, Doran, 1920.

Affinities and Other Stories. New York, Doran, and London, Hodder and Stoughton, 1920.

More Tish. New York, Doran, and London, Hodder and Stoughton, 1921.

Temperamental People. New York, Doran, and London, Hodder and Stoughton, 1924.

Tish Plays the Game. New York, Doran, 1926; London, Hodder and Stoughton, 1927.

Nomad's Land. New York, Doran, 1926.

The Romantics. New York, Farrar and Rinehart, 1929; London, Hodder and Stoughton, 1930.

Married People. New York, Farrar and Rinehart, and London, Cassell, 1937.

Tish Marches On. New York, Farrar and Rinehart, 1937; London, Cassell, 1938.

Familiar Faces: Stories of People You Know. New York, Farrar and Rinehart, 1941; London, Cassell, 1943.

The Best of Tish. New York, Rinehart, 1955; London, Cassell, 1956.

Plays

Seven Days, with Avery Hopwood (produced Trenton and New York, 1909; Harrogate, 1913; London, 1915). New York, French, 1931.

Cheer Up (produced New York, 1912).

Spanish Love, with Avery Hopwood (produced New York, 1920).

The Bat, with Avery Hopwood, adaptation of the novel *The Circular Staircase* by
  Rinehart (produced New York, 1920; London, 1921). New York, French, 1931.
The Breaking Point (produced New York, 1923).

Screenplay: *Aflame in the Sky*, with Ewart Anderson, 1927.

Other

Kings, Queens, and Pawns: An American Woman at the Front. New York, Doran,
  1915.
Through Glacier Park: Seeing America First with Howard Eaton. Boston, Houghton
  Mifflin, 1916.
The Altar of Freedom. Boston, Houghton Mifflin, 1917.
*Tenting Tonight: A Chronicle of Sport and Adventure in Glacier Park and the Cascade
  Mountains.* Boston, Houghton Mifflin, 1918.
Isn't That Just Like a Man! New York, Doran, 1920.
My Story (autobiography). New York, Farrar and Rinehart, 1931; London, Cassell,
  1932; revised edition, New York, Rinehart, 1948.
Writing Is Work. Boston, The Writer, 1939.

Manuscript Collection: University of Pittsburgh Library.

*   *   *

Although she has recently come to be regarded, somewhat condescendingly, as a
"woman's writer," Mary Roberts Rinehart was once the highest paid author in America, and
the best of her works continues to entertain men and women alike. Although she wrote
romances, adventure stories, and humorous sketches – of which the best-known are probably
the "Tish" stories, chronicling the adventures of Miss Laetitia Carberry – Rinehart is best
known for inventing what has come to be called the "Had-I-But-Known" device, which has
since been employed, with much less success, by myriads of mystery and gothic romance
novelists.
  Given the prevalence of the "Had-I-But-Known" school in subsequent years, it is easy to
deprecate the originality of the invention. Rinehart is the spiritual descendant of Anna
Katharine Green, but she differs from her predecessor in several important respects. First,
Rinehart owes relatively little to the conventions of European detective fiction that influenced
Green. Her novels tend to be mysteries or mystery/romances rather than novels of pure
detection. Consequently, attention to forensic details, for example, is slight, since the object of
the narrative is to arouse in the reader the same spine-chilling terror experienced by the
central character. Similarly, the professional detective figures only sketchily in the typical
Rinehart novel. The only continuing detective heroine is Nurse Hilda Adams, nicknamed
"Miss Pinkerton" by Inspector Patton, for whom she does unofficial investigative duty.
Implicit in what Julian Symons has called "The Rinehart Formula" is the complete emotional
identification of the reader with the central character – usually the narrator – and no objective
deduction or "professional" business is allowed to detract from that identification.
  The now famous "Had-I-But-Known" device was probably invented in response to the
requirements of serial publication. Given the necessity of maintaining a state of cozy terror
between installments, it was appropriate for the narrator to remark at least once in each
chapter, "If only we had left before it was too late!" or "Had I known then what I know
now, I might have prevented the tragedy." The device raises our expectation of terrors to
come, at the same time that it reassures us of the omniscience of the narrator, who, given a
suitable number of chapters, will eventually explain all. Although this device is annoyingly
redundant in a series of full-length novels, it was quite successful when occurring in serial
installments. Logically, the reader might contend that foreknowledge on the part of the
narrator would have changed nothing; however, one is rarely compelled to employ logic in a

narrative which emphasizes forward action and suspense rather than deduction or ratiocination.

Another characteristic of "The Rinehart Formula," one which was subsequently exploited by such writers as Mignon G. Eberhart, is the predominance of romantic complications amidst murder and mayhem. Such love interest usually takes second place to the mystery, but it is inevitably present. When the narrator is a confirmed spinster, as in *The Circular Staircase*, the love interest is provided by a young niece and nephew. Nurse Hilda Adams is the object of admiration of Inspector Patton. In *The Man in Lower Ten*, the narrator himself becomes enamored of Miss Alison West, one of the suspects. These romantic interests, which tend to detract from the puzzles, also serve to soften the brutality of multiple murders, which are generally of a violent nature not usually associated with "women's novels." The lovers serve as symbols of normality amidst the extraordinary and sensational situations into which the principal characters are accidentally thrust.

The status quo which Rinehart's novels support is, as Julian Symons has pointed out, essentially agrarian rather than urban. Although some of her stories take place in town, or in New York City, their mood is that of an enclosed world – essentially the country house where pressures from the outside world of business or politics are rarely felt. Characters are classified as doctor, or lawyer, or chauffeur, or governess; but they are rarely shown at work. Nurse Adams, who is invariably hired by an unsuspecting family to nurse a sick relative or tend the children, when in fact she is on a "case" for Inspector Patton, has a great deal of time in which to investigate mysterious noises in the cellar or stealthy footsteps upon the back staircase; and when "Miss Pinkerton" is following the trail of a suspect, her patient never seems to miss her. In spite of the occurrence of innumerable criminal events, reporters never seem to obtrude into the closed world of the Rinehart story; and the official police are oblivious of attempts by the various characters to obstruct justice, so grateful are they for the help which the plucky narrators provide in the end. As in the classic detective story, legality is unimportant, so long as the cause of common-sense rough justice is served. In "Locked Doors," we are expected to believe that a potential outbreak of bubonic plague has been averted simply because Inspector Patton, with the aid of Nurse Adams, has solved the mystery of a locked basement laboratory which once contained infected rats (some of the rats are still missing, but Inspector Patton thinks that they have probably died without passing on the disease). Our sympathy is never diverted to the helpless victims of crime; it remains with the unofficial investigator, who must endure confusion after confusion, terror after terror, but whose common-sense and determination to unravel the mystery are ultimately rewarded.

The Circular Staircase reveals all the characteristics of the Rinehart formula at its best. The story captured the imagination of a wide public, and enshrined the formula in the public imagination. A middle-aged spinster, Rachel Innes, rents a summer house in the country with her niece and nephew, little dreaming that the house hides a guilty secret. Evidence that the house is "haunted" catapults Miss Innes into a series of eerie experiences which culminate in her being locked in a secret room with a multiple murderer: "There was someone else in the darkness, someone who breathed hard and was so close I could have touched him by the hand." Eventually, the "ghost" is revealed to be an embezzler, but only after five murders have been committed – "five lives were sacrificed in the course of this grim conspiracy." Repetitions of the original murder result largely from the reluctance of all the innocent parties to confide in the police. Nevertheless, the novel ends with the promise of two marriages; and Miss Innes, ruminating on the grisly events of the past, observes, "To be perfectly frank, I never really lived until that summer." We must conclude that, "had she but known" what was in store for her, she would have behaved in exactly the same way. Sensation is obviously its own reward. *The Circular Staircase* remains a success, in spite of the passage of time.

At their best, the works of Mary Roberts Rinehart are barely disguised adventure stories for adults, providing an opportunity for the reader to become, briefly, an accidental private eye. The effect is not unlike that which might be produced were Watson to solve cases without the direction of Holmes; hardly satisfying from a deductive point of view, but thoroughly justified from a sentimental one. In the later Rinehart novels *(The Album, The*

Great Mistake, The Yellow Room), the reader's credulity is strained by a succession of increasingly implausible situations and bizarre motivations, as well as by the limitations of the self-enclosed worlds which are presented. Her early works, however, support Howard Haycraft's designation of Rinehart as America's "unquestioned dean of crime writing by and for women."

—Joanne Harack Hayne

RIPLEY, Jack. See **WAINWRIGHT, John.**

RITCHIE, Jack (John George Reitci). American. Born 26 February 1922. Educated at Milwaukee State Teachers College, Wisconsin, 2 years. Served in the United States Army during World War II. Divorced; two daughters and two sons. Agent: Larry Sternig, 742 Robertson Street, Milwaukee, Wisconsin 53213. Address: 100 Spry Street, Apartment 25, Ft. Atkinson, Wisconsin 53538, U.S.A.

CRIME PUBLICATIONS

Short Stories

A New Leaf and Other Stories. New York, Dell, 1971.

Uncollected Short Stories

"Shatter Proof," in *Best Detective Stories of the Year 1961*, edited by Brett Halliday. New York, Dutton, 1961.
"Plan Nineteen," in *Crimes and Misfortunes*, edited by J. Francis McComas. New York, Random House, 1970.
"By Child Undone," in *Best Detective Stories of the Year*, edited by Anthony Boucher. New York, Dutton, 1968.
"For All the Rude People," in *Best of the Best Detective Stories*, edited by Allen J. Hubin. New York, Dutton, 1971.
"Take Another Look," in *Best Detective Stories of the Year 1972*, edited by Allen J. Hubin. New York, Dutton, 1972.
"Bedlam at the Budgie," in *Alfred Hitchcock's Mystery Magazine* (North Palm Beach, Florida), May 1975.
"The Magnum," in *Alfred Hitchcock Presents: Stories to Be Read with the Door Locked.* New York, Random House, 1975.
"When the Sheriff Walked," in *Best Detective Stories of the Year 1975*, edited by Allen J. Hubin. New York, Dutton, 1975.
"The Deveraux Monster," in *Tricks and Treats*, edited by Joe Gores and Bill Pronzini. New York, Doubleday, 1976.

"The Many-Flavored Crime," in *Best Detective Stories of the Year 1976*, edited by Edward D. Hoch. New York, Dutton, 1976.

"Beauty Is as Beauty Does," in *Ellery Queen's Mystery Magazine* (New York), June 1976.

"Nobody Tells Me Anything," in *Ellery Queen's Mystery Magazine* (New York), October 1976.

"An Odd Pair of Socks," in *Alfred Hitchcock's Mystery Magazine* (New York), May 1977.

"The Operator," in *Alfred Hitchcock Presents: Stories That Go Bump in the Night*. New York, Random House, 1977.

"The Seed Caper," in *Ellery Queen's Mystery Magazine* (New York), August 1977.

"The Canvas Caper," in *Alfred Hitchcock's Mystery Magazine* (New York), August 1977.

"Kid Cardula," in *Alfred Hitchcock's Tales to Take Your Breath Away*, edited by Eleanor Sullivan. New York, Davis, 1977.

"Variations on a Scheme," in *Alfred Hitchcock's Mystery Magazine* (New York), September 1977.

"The Willinger Predicament," in *Ellery Queen's Mystery Magazine* (New York), October 1977.

"Next in Line," in *Best Detective Stories of the Year 1977*, edited by Edward D. Hoch. New York, Dutton, 1977.

"Hung Jury," in *Best Detective Stories of the Year 1978*, edited by Edward D. Hoch. New York, Dutton, 1978.

"The School Bus Caper," in *Ellery Queen's Mystery Magazine* (New York), March 1978.

"The Scent of Camellias," in *Alfred Hitchcock's Mystery Magazine* (New York), March 1978.

"Cardula and the Kleptomaniac," in *Alfred Hitchcock's Mystery Magazine* (New York), April 1978.

"No Wider Than a Nickel," in *Ellery Queen's Mystery Magazine* (New York), October 1978.

"The Green Heart," in *Alfred Hitchcock's Tales to Scare You Stiff*, edited by Eleanor Sullivan. New York, Davis, 1978.

"Cardula's Revenge," in *Alfred Hitchcock's Mystery Magazine* (New York), November 1978.

"The Hanging Tree," in *Alfred Hitchcock's Mystery Magazine* (New York), January 1979.

"The Midnight Strangler," in *Elllery Queen's Mystery Magazine* (New York), January 1979.

"The 23 Brown Paper Bags," in *Ellery Queen's Mystery Magazine* (New York), May 1979.

"Some Days Are Like That," in *Ellery Queen's Mystery Magazine* (New York), June 1979.

"You Could Get Killed," in *Alfred Hitchcock's Mystery Magazine* (New York), June 1979.

"The Gourmet Kidnapper," in *Ellery Queen's Mystery Magazine* (New York), September 1979.

*   *   *

One hallmark of a mystery short story writer's success is the frequency with which his stories are reprinted in anthologies, especially in annual volumes like *Best Detective Stories of the Year*. By this standard Jack Ritchie has no equal. He has appeared in *Best Detective Stories* seventeen times since 1961, under four different editors, and he has also been reprinted in virtually all the hardcover Alfred Hitchcock anthologies. Ritchie has never published a novel, and only one collection of his short stories has appeared, *A New Leaf and Other Stories*.

Though he began publishing in 1953, his best work has been the stories published during the 1960's and 1970's. One is tempted to generalize and say that the offbeat humor which is now Ritchie's trademark has become more pronounced in the 1970's, though certainly an early story like "The Deveraux Monster" (1962) is tongue-in-cheek, to say the least.

Others from the early 1960's are in a more serious vein. "Shatter Proof" (1961) presents a man's confrontation with a hired killer sent by his wife. "For All the Rude People" (1961) has some humor but is mainly an angry tale of a man with only four months to live who sets out to murder those who have been rude to him. "The Operator" (1963) is about an undercover cop on the trail of a stolen car ring, and reveals something of Ritchie's debt to the best of the old medium-tough pulp writing.

But mainly Ritchie's world is a topsy-turvy creation full of bumbling detectives who occasionally stumble upon the right solution by accident, or who fail because no one told them some key fact everyone else knew. It is a world of bathtubs full of jello ("The Many-Flavored Crime"), or bungled prison breaks ("Plan Nineteen"), or the theft of flower seeds ("The Seed Caper"). It is even a world where, occasionally, the butler did it.

In recent years Ritchie's stories have dealt more with detection, though here too his detectives are anything but orthodox. One series features Cardula, a vampire private eye. And a story aptly titled "By Child Undone" features a ten-year-old child who spots the single factor linking a series of baffling murders. Another series murder is solved by a Double-Crostics expert ("Hung Jury"). By its very nature the whimsey of Ritchie's plots works best in the short story length. "Next in Line" is a rare novelet where the humor – about the heirs to a large estate – is sustained for some 8500 words, helped by the author's usual deft characterizations.

—Edward D. Hoch

ROBERTS, James Hall.   Pseudonym for Robert L(ipscomb) Duncan.   American.   Born in 1927.

CRIME PUBLICATIONS

Novels

>   *The Q Document.*   New York, Morrow, 1964; London, Cape, 1965.
>   *The Burning Sky.*   New York, Morrow, 1966.
>   *The February Plan.*   New York, Morrow, and London, Deutsch, 1967.

Novels as Robert L. Duncan

>   *The Day the Sun Fell.*   New York, Morrow, 1970.
>   *The Dragons at the Gate.*   New York, Morrow, 1975; London, Joseph, 1976.
>   *Temple Dogs.*   New York, Morrow, 1977; London, Joseph, 1978.
>   *Fire Storm.*   New York, Morrow, 1978; London, Joseph, 1979.

*   *   *

In three very interesting novels, two of which (*The Q Document* and *The Burning Sky*) approach genuine excellence, James Hall Roberts demonstrates the generally neglected potentiality of the thriller to offer both factual and spiritual instruction. Roberts combines the thriller's necessary plot device of the search for a solution to a mystery or a problem with other sorts of quests – the quest for knowledge and the quest for faith. In the process his novels display a fascinating erudition and grapple convincingly with the problem of religious belief. In *The Q Document, The February Plan,* and *The Burning Sky* his three protagonists are linked by the modernity of their malaise, a hardening of the heart, a withdrawal and detachment of the self from its humanity in reaction to some personal difficulty or catastrophe. Encountering a puzzle, the men also encounter themselves; their search for particular facts becomes the discovery of general truths. The two most important books present their puzzles as intimately connected with belief – in *The Q Document* a scholar has to authenticate some ostensibly ancient documents, one of which may even be written by Jesus; in *The Burning Sky* an archaeologist and a priest, for different reasons, investigate the survival of an ancient American Indian culture. The protagonists not only discover the solutions to their mysteries but also their own connections with humanity. Their awakening derives from an objective search for truth but leads to an intensely personal recognition of faith, redeeming them from solitude and apostasy.

Aside from the intrinsic appeal of Roberts's theme of faith, one of the most remarkable qualities of his two best novels is their coherent and learned use of specialized scholarly disciplines – archaeology and anthropology in *The Burning Sky* and Biblical linguistics and scholarship in *The Q Document*; the clear and functional exposition of abstruse and utterly absorbing kinds of knowledge is little short of brilliant. It has been some time since the novel of suspense was prized as a vehicle of information; Roberts's books revive that aspect of the form, carrying it considerably further than the usual instruction in technical details. He explores more than just essential factual background, but demonstrates real learning and real love of learning. The moral dimension of his books enhances their instructional value – there is no reason why the novel of suspense cannot, like other kinds of literature, provide spiritual edification.

Roberts's novels are not simply fact-filled religious tracts, however; they are interesting and absorbing suspense narratives, as entertaining as any reader could wish. Although he may lack their stylistic brilliance, he can obviously be compared with Chesterton and Greene, which is high praise indeed; like them, he perceives that the most difficult and fundamental of all mysteries is the central mystery of faith, the Mystery. James Hall Roberts may some day be considered the American Graham Greene, which would place him among the highest ranks of writers of thrillers, students of belief, or novelists of any persuasion.

—George Grella

ROBESON, Kenneth. See **DENT, Lester; GOULART, Ron.**

RODELL, Marie. See **RANDOLPH, Marion.**

ROFFMAN, Jan. See **SUMMERTON, Margaret.**

ROGERS, Joel Townsley. American. Born in Sedalia, Missouri, 22 November 1896.
Educated at Harvard University, Cambridge, Massachusetts, B.A. 1917 (Chairman of the
Editorial Board, Harvard *Crimson*). Served in the United States Naval Air Force, 1917–19.
Married Winifred Whitehouse. Worked in public relations and as editor of *Book Chat* for
Brentano's; employed by Century Publishing Company.

<small>CRIME PUBLICATIONS</small>

Novels

> *Once in a Red Moon.* New York, Brentano's, 1923.
> *The Red Right Hand.* New York, Simon and Schuster, 1945.
> *Lady with the Dice.* Kingston, New York, Quin, 1946.
> *The Stopped Clock.* New York, Simon and Schuster, 1958; as *Never Leave My Bed*,
>   Beacon, New York, Beacon Signal, 1960.

Uncollected Short Story

> "The Murderer," in *Best Detective Stories of the Year 1947*, edited by David Coxe
> Cooke. New York, Dutton, 1947.

*   *   *

Joel Townsley Rogers, best known as the author of the classic mystery novel *The Red
Right Hand*, was a free-lance fiction writer for pulp and slick magazines for more than forty
years. In addition to his periodical fiction, Rogers has published four book-length works,
including *Once in a Red Moon*, described by him as "a hocus-pocus, semi-mystery novel";
Lady with the Dice, expanded from the 1938 pulp story "A Date with Lachesis"; and *The
Stopped Clock*.

Rogers's best book is *The Red Right Hand*, the story of a young doctor, apparently
implicated in a series of maniacal murders, who attempts to discover the identity of the real
killer by painstakingly reviewing the details of the case while his own death is being planned.
The nightmare setting of the story, its hallucinatory incidents, and its breathless prose all lend
a kind of mythic grandeur to the events and help make the book one of the most distinguished
in its genre.

—Elliot L. Gilbert

ROHMER, Sax. Pseudonym for Arthur Henry Sarsfield Ward; adopted name Sarsfield at
the age of 18; later used Sax Rohmer even in personal life; also wrote as Michael

Furey. British. Born in Birmingham, Warwickshire, 15 February 1883. Married Rose Elizabeth Knox in 1909. Journalist: covered the underworld in London's Limehouse; wrote songs and sketches for entertainers. Later lived in New York City. *Died 1 June 1959.*

CRIME PUBLICATIONS

Novels (series characters: Fu Manchu; Paul Harley; Daniel "Red" Kerry; Gaston Max; Sūmurū)

The Mystery of Dr. Fu-Manchu. London, Methuen, 1913; as *The Insidious Dr. Fu-Manchu,* New York, McBride, 1913.
The Sins of Séverac Bablon. London, Cassell, 1914; New York, Bookfinger, 1967.
The Yellow Claw (Max). London, Methuen, and New York, McBride, 1915.
The Devil Doctor. London, Methuen, 1916; as *The Return of Dr. Fu-Manchu,* New York, McBride, 1916.
The Si-Fan Mysteries. London, Methuen, 1917; as *The Hand of Fu-Manchu,* New York, McBride, 1917.
Brood of the Witch Queen. London, Pearson, 1918; New York, Doubleday, 1924.
The Quest of the Sacred Slipper. London, Pearson, and New York, Doubleday, 1919.
Dope (Kerry). London, Cassell, and New York, McBride, 1919.
The Golden Scorpion (Fu Manchu; Max). London, Methuen, 1919; New York, McBride, 1920.
The Green Eyes of Bâst. London, Cassell, and New York, McBride, 1920.
Bat-Wing (Harley). London, Cassell, and New York, Doubleday, 1921.
Fire-Tongue (Harley). London, Cassell, 1921; New York, Doubleday, 1922.
Grey Face. London, Cassell, and New York, Doubleday, 1924.
Yellow Shadows (Kerry). London, Cassell, 1925; New York, Doubleday, 1926.
Moon of Madness. New York, Doubleday, and London, Cassell, 1927.
She Who Sleeps. New York, Doubleday, and London, Cassell, 1928.
The Emperor of America. New York, Doubleday, and London, Cassell, 1929.
The Day the World Ended (Max). New York, Doubleday, and London, Cassell, 1930.
Daughter of Fu Manchu. New York, Doubleday, and London, Cassell, 1931.
Yu'an Hee See Laughs. New York, Doubleday, and London, Cassell, 1932.
The Mask of Fu Manchu. New York, Doubleday, 1932; London, Cassell, 1933.
Fu Manchu's Bride. New York, Doubleday, 1933; as *The Bride of Fu Manchu,* London, Cassell, 1933.
The Trail of Fu Manchu. New York, Doubleday, and London, Cassell, 1934.
The Bat Flies Low. New York, Doubleday, and London, Cassell, 1935.
President Fu Manchu. New York, Doubleday, and London, Cassell, 1936.
White Velvet. New York, Doubleday, and London, Cassell, 1936.
The Drums of Fu Manchu. New York, Doubleday, and London, Cassell, 1939.
The Island of Fu Manchu. New York, Doubleday, and London, Cassell, 1941.
Seven Sins (Max). New York, McBride, 1943; London, Cassell, 1944.
Egyptian Nights. London, Hale, 1944; as *Bimbâshi Barûk of Egypt* (short stories version), New York, McBride, 1944.
Shadow of Fu Manchu. New York, Doubleday, 1948; London, Jenkins, 1949.
Hangover House. New York, Random House, 1949; London, Jenkins, 1950.
Nude in Mink. New York, Fawcett, 1950; as *Sins of Sūmurū,* London, Jenkins, 1950.
Wulfheim (as Michael Furey). London, Jarrolds, 1950.
Sūmurū. New York, Fawcett, 1951; as *Slaves of Sūmurū,* London, Jenkins, 1952.
The Fire Goddess (Sūmurū). New York, Fawcett, 1952; as *Virgin in Flames,* London, Jenkins, 1953.
The Moon Is Red. London, Jenkins, 1954.

Return of Sūmurū. New York, Fawcett, 1954; as *Sand and Satin*, London, Jenkins, 1955.

Sinister Madonna (Sūmurū). London, Jenkins, and New York, Fawcett, 1956.

Re-Enter Fu Manchu. New York, Fawcett, 1957; as *Re-Enter Dr. Fu Manchu*, London, Jenkins, 1957.

Emperor Fu Manchu. London, Jenkins, and New York, Fawcett, 1959.

Short Stories

The Exploits of Captain O'Hagan. London, Jarrolds, 1916; New York, Bookfinger, 1968.

Tales of Secret Egypt. London, Methuen, 1918; New York, McBride, 1919.

The Dream-Detective. London, Jarrolds, 1920; New York, Doubleday, 1925.

The Haunting of Low Fennel. London, Pearson, 1920.

Tales of Chinatown. London, Cassell, and New York, Doubleday, 1922.

Tales of East and West. London, Cassell, 1932; with different contents, New York, Doubleday, 1933.

Salute to Bazarada and Other Stories. London, Cassell, 1939; New York, Bookfinger, 1971.

The Secret of Holm Peel and Other Strange Stories. New York, Ace, 1970.

The Wrath of Fu Manchu and Other Stories. London, Stacey, 1973; New York, Daw, 1976.

Uncollected Short Stories

"The Oversized Trunk," in *This Week* (New York), 22 October 1944.

"The Stolen Peach Stone," in *This Week* (New York), 19 November 1944.

"Serpent Wind," in *Murder for the Millions*, edited by Frank Owen. New York, Fell, 1946.

"The Secret of the Ruins," in *Fourth Mystery Companion*, edited by Abraham Louis Furman. New York, Lantern Press, 1946.

"The Picture of Innocence," in *This Week* (New York), 9 May 1948.

"The Mysterious Harem," in *This Week* (New York), 26 September 1948.

"Seventeen Lotus Blossoms," in *National Home Weekly* (Winnipeg), March 1949.

"Jamaican Rose," in *To-day Magazine* (Philadelphia), 4 December 1949.

"Cease Play at Eleven," in *To-day Magazine* (Philadelphia), 22 January 1950.

"A Broken Blade," in *Blue Book* (Chicago), November 1950.

"X.Y.Z. Calls," in *Blue Book* (Chicago), January 1951.

"One Brother Was Evil," in *This Week* (New York), 29 April 1951.

"Kiss of the Scorpion," in *Blue Book* (Chicago), June 1951.

"Flee from Danger," in *This Week* (New York), 16 September 1951.

"Narky," in *Ellery Queen's Mystery Magazine* (New York), February 1952.

"The Bride's Dungeon," in *This Week* (New York), 7 November 1954.

"The Case of the Missing Heirloom," in *This Week* (New York), 22 April 1956.

"The Fugitive Celebrity," in *This Week* (New York), 22 April 1956.

"The Mystery of the Vanishing Treasure," in *"This Week's" Stories of Mystery and Suspense*, edited by Stewart Beach. New York, Random House, 1957.

"Deadly Blonde of Dartmoor," in *This Week* (New York), 19 October 1958.

"Death Is My Hostess," in *Spy in the Shadows*, edited by Marvin Allen Karp. New York, Popular Library, 1965.

"The Green Scarab," in *Edgar Wallace Mystery Magazine* (London), June 1966.

"The Night of the Jackal," in *Edgar Wallace Mystery Magazine* (London), November 1966.

OTHER PUBLICATIONS

Novel

   The Orchard of Tears.   London, Methuen, 1918; New York, Bookfinger, 1970.

Plays

   Round in 50, with Julian and Lauri Wylie, music by H. Finck and J. Tate (produced
      Cardiff and London, 1922).
   The Eye of Siva (produced London, 1923).
   Secret Egypt (produced London, 1928).
   The Nightingale, with Michael Martin-Harvey, music by Kennedy Russell (produced
      London, 1947).

Other

   Pause! (published anonymously).   London, Greening, 1910.
   The Romance of Sorcery.   London, Methuen, 1914; New York, Dutton, 1915.

   Ghostwriter: *Little Tich: A Book of Travels and Wanderings*, by Harry Relph, London,
      Greening, 1911.

Bibliography: "Chronological Bibliography of the Books of Sax Rohmer," in *Master of
Villainy* by Cay Van Ash and Elizabeth Sax Rohmer, edited by R. E. Briney, Bowling Green,
Ohio, Popular Press, 1972; *Sax Rohmer: A Bibliography* by B. M. Day, Denver, New York,
Science Fact and Fantasy, 1963.

                              *   *   *

   Nowadays the credit (or more often blame) for the "Yellow Peril" school of mystery
thriller is placed firmly upon the shoulders of Sax Rohmer. Certainly Rohmer did not invent
the concept, which was a staple of sensational journalism before the end of the 19th century.
What he did was to find just the right variations on the theme, the proper ingredients for
widespread popular success. First of all, Rohmer provided an assortment of vividly described
and exotically appointed settings for his stories: perfumed apartments, strewn with cushions,
furnished with carved teakwood tables and lacquer cabinets, and lit by brass lamps of strange
design. Against such backgrounds the villains' whispered threats and the confidences of
imperiled heroines seemed not at all out of place. These splashes of color alternated with set-
pieces of the familiar-made-mysterious: fog-shrouded London streets, isolated manor houses,
boats plying the darkened Thames. Next, Rohmer divorced the "Yellow Peril" story from the
military context which most earlier writers had used. (M. P. Shiel's *The Yellow Danger* of
1898 is typical.) Rather than an invading army from the East, the reader was invited to
shudder at a more personal menace: a paralyzing drug, a deadly insect searching out its prey,
a Dacoit with his weird cry and strangler's kerchief. And finally, Rohmer had the talent and
good fortune to create a near-mythic figure who embodied all the fancied villainy of the East
combined with all the science of the West: "imagine a person, tall, lean and feline, high-
shouldered, with a brow like Shakespeare and a face like Satan, a close-shaven skull, and
long, magnetic eyes of the true cat-green.... Imagine that awful being, and you have a mental
picture of Dr. Fu-Manchu, the yellow peril incarnate in one man."
   Fu Manchu was introduced in the story "The Zayat Kiss" in the October 1912 issue of the
British magazine *The Story-Teller*. This was the first of a series of ten adventures, gathered in
book form as an episodic "novel," *The Mystery of Dr. Fu-Manchu.* During the next four
years, two further series were published, each duly appearing in both magazine and book
form. Although they were written and published during Britain's involvement in World War

I, Rohmer allowed no hint of the war to intrude in the stories, which seem to take place in a sort of permanent 1912. At the end of the third book, *The Si-Fan Mysteries*, Fu Manchu was apparently killed, and readers may justifiably have thought they had seen the last of him. Rohmer probably intended this to be the case, since it was nine years before he planned another Fu Manchu adventure, and four years after that before it appeared in print: *Daughter of Fu Manchu*. With this novel, the series entered "real time" again, and subsequent volumes in the 1930's reflected, as in a distorting mirror, the political developments of the times. In *President Fu Manchu*, Fu Manchu was the power behind a U.S. presidential candidate, and disguised versions of Father Coughlin and Huey Long took part in the action. In *The Drums of Fu Manchu*, Fu Manchu fought Fascism, and disposed of a European dictator bearing the transparent pseudonym "Rudolph Adlon." After attempting to gain control of the Panama Canal in *The Island of Fu Manchu*, Rohmer's villain slumbered during World War II, only to return as an anti-Communist crusader in *Shadow of Fu Manchu*. In his final appearance, *Emperor Fu Manchu*, Fu Manchu was still plotting against "these unclean creatures [who] retain their hold upon China, my China."

In the early Fu Manchu stories, the thrills were intermixed with the casual xenophobia of the times, but Fu Manchu himself was always depicted as a man of impeccable integrity, an aristocrat, consistently more clever and resourceful than his opponents. His periodic defeats were caused by unforeseen accidents or, more often, by reliance on untrustworthy agents (usually women who had fallen in love with the hero/narrator). As the series progressed, Fu Manchu became less specifically Oriental and more of a generalized super-criminal. The peak of Fu Manchu's (and Sax Rohmer's) popularity was in the 1930's, when an enormous audience impatiently awaited each new serial. The books have seldom been out of print since their initial publication, and are still finding an audience today.

At the beginning of his writing career, there was no hint that Rohmer's greatest success would come from stories about a Chinese super-criminal. His main interest at that time (and indeed throughout much of his life) was the Near East, especially ancient Egypt. His first fiction sale, published while Rohmer was only 20 years old, was "The Mysterious Mummy" (*Pearson's Weekly*, 1903), a clever and amusing crime story about the theft of an Egyptian artifact from a London museum. During 1913 and 1914 he produced many stories and serials which would not see book publication for several years. The earliest of these were the stories about the psychic detective Moris Klaw (*The Dream-Detective*) who solved a series of bizarre crimes by his method of "odic photography." Klaw's cases included locked-room mysteries as well as hauntings and other supernatural manifestations. *The Quest of the Sacred Slipper*, the story of Hassan of Aleppo's attempts to recover a slipper of Mohammed which had been stolen from Mecca and taken to England, is also from this productive period. The serial version of *Brood of the Witch-Queen* appeared in 1914. This story of the survival of ancient Egyptian sorcery in the modern world is widely regarded as Rohmer's best book.

In 1915 Rohmer's detective character Gaston Max first appeared in *The Yellow Claw*. This was an "Oriental menace" story in the Fu Manchu vein, as was its successor *The Golden Scorpion*, in which Fu Manchu made a brief, anonymous appearance. Max next appeared in *The Day the World Ended* to battle a baroque scientific super-criminal called Anubis in Germany's Black Forest, and returned to combat Axis agents in wartime London in *Seven Sins*. Another of Rohmer's principal detectives is Paul Harley, who appeared in the novels *Bat-Wing* and *Fire-Tongue*, the stage play *The Eye of Siva*, and eleven shorter works published between 1920 and 1939. Chief Inspector Daniel "Red" Kerry appeared in *Dope*, *Yellow Shadows*, and in a few short stories.

In *Yu'an Hee See Laughs* Rohmer introduced an Oriental smuggler and white slaver with all of Fu Manchu's villainy but none of his imagination or nobility. The character did not prove popular, and was not used again. *White Velvet*, based on a film treatment intended as a vehicle for Marlene Dietrich, is a story of drug smuggling in the Mediterranean. *Egyptian Nights* is a collection of crime and espionage stories set in England and the Near East. *Hangover House* is a traditional "isolated house party" murder mystery, based on an unproduced play. *The Moon Is Red* is a bizarre murder mystery set in Florida, and is one of the best of Rohmer's later novels.

The series of five novels about Sūmurū revived the Fu Manchu formula, but featured a carefully de-ethnicized female villain. The stories were popular in their U.S. paperback editions, but Rohmer did not think much of them. The series was dropped when Fu Manchu himself was revived in 1957, and Rohmer brought his writing career to a close by returning full-circle to the source of his greatest fame.

—R. E. Briney

ROLLS, Anthony. See **VULLIAMY, C. E.**

RONNS, Edward. See **AARONS, Edward S.**

ROOS, Kelley. Joint pseudonym for Audrey Roos (née Kelley) and William Roos; William Roos also writes as William Rand. Americans. Audrey Roos born in 1912, William Roos in 1911. Recipient: Mystery Writers of America Edgar Allan Poe Award, for television play, 1961.

CRIME PUBLICATIONS

Novels (series characters: Jeff and Haila Troy)

> *Made Up to Kill* (Troy). New York, Dodd Mead, 1940; as *Made Up for Murder*, London, Jarrolds, 1941.
> *If the Shroud Fits* (Troy). New York, Dodd Mead, 1941; as *Dangerous Blondes*, New York, Spivak, 1951.
> *The Frightened Stiff* (Troy). New York, Dodd Mead, 1942; London, Hale, 1951.
> *Sailor, Take Warning!* (Troy). New York, Dodd Mead, 1944; London, Hale, 1952.
> *There Was a Crooked Man* (Troy). New York, Dodd Mead, 1945; London, Hale, 1953.
> *Ghost of a Chance* (Troy). New York, Wyn, 1947.
> *Murder in Any Language* (Troy). New York, Wyn, 1948.
> *Triple Threat* (Troy; novelets). New York, Wyn, 1949.
> *Beauty Marks the Spot* (Troy). New York, Dell, 1951.
> *The Blonde Died Dancing.* New York, Dodd Mead, 1956; as *She Died Dancing*, London, Eyre and Spottiswoode, 1957.

Requieum for a Blonde. New York, Dodd Mead, 1958; as *Murder Noon and Night*,
   London, Eyre and Spottiswoode, 1959.
Scent of Mystery (novelization of screenplay). New York, Dell, 1959.
Grave Danger. New York, Dodd Mead, 1965; London, Eyre and Spottiswoode, 1966.
Necessary Evil. New York, Dodd Mead, and London, Eyre and Spottiswoode, 1965.
A Few Days in Madrid (as Audrey and William Roos). New York, Scribner, 1965;
   London, Deutsch, 1966.
Cry in the Night. New York, Dodd Mead, 1966.
One False Move (Troy). New York, Dodd Mead, 1966.
Who Saw Maggie Brown? New York, Dodd Mead, 1967.
To Save His Life. New York, Dodd Mead, 1968; London, Cassell, 1969.
Suddenly One Night. New York, Dodd Mead, 1970.
What Did Hattie See? New York, Dodd Mead, and London, Cassell, 1970.
Bad Trip. New York, Dodd Mead, 1971.

Uncollected Short Stories

"Two over Par," in *Four and Twenty Bloodhounds*, edited by Anthony Boucher, New
   York, Simon and Schuster, 1950; London, Hammond, 1951.
"Scream in the Night," in *American Magazine* (Springfield, Ohio), April 1953.
"One Victim Too Many," in *American Magazine* (Springfield, Ohio), September 1953.
"Case of the Hanging Gardens," in *American Magazine* (Springfield, Ohio), July 1954.
"Murder Underground," in *Ellery Queen's Mystery Magazine* (New York), June 1966.
"The 'Watch Out!' Girls," in *Ellery Queen's Mystery Magazine* (New York), August
   1968.
"Murder in the Antique Car Museum," in *Anthology 1971*, edited by Ellery
   Queen. New York, Davis, 1970.

OTHER PUBLICATIONS by William Roos

Novel

The Hornet's Longboat. Boston, Houghton Mifflin, 1940.

Plays

Triple Play (produced Milford, Connecticut, 1937).
January Thaw (produced New York, 1946). Chicago, Dramatic Publishing Company,
   1946.
Boy Wanted. New York, French, 1947.
Ellery Queen's The Four of Hearts Mystery (as William Rand). Chicago, Dramatic
   Publishing Company, 1948.
Belles on Their Toes. Chicago, Dramatic Publishing Company, 1952.
Speaking of Murder, with Audrey Roos. New York, Random House, 1957; London,
   French, 1959.

Television Play: *The Case of the Burning Court*, 1960.

Manuscript Collection: Mugar Memorial Library, Boston University.

*   *   *

Writing from 1940 to 1971, Kelley Roos is notable as an example of the changes in
emphasis in mystery novels of that period. The first Jeff and Haila Troy books were typical of
the light, breezy style practiced by Craig Rice, the Lockridges, Leslie Ford, and Stuart Palmer.

Wit, sophistication, non-violent narration, and heroines in last-chapter-distress were hallmarks of the husband/wife detective teams. Roos let the Troys break no new ground in their eight early cases but used puzzle elements and likeable characters to entertain his audience. Throughout his career, Roos wrote for those who read for enjoyment, rather than aiming for the analytic or adventuresome reader.

Made Up to Kill began Roos's use of theatrical settings – a background to be repeated into the 1970's with *What Did Hattie See?* and the novelette "Death of a Trooper." Jeff was the "detective," often hampering as well as helping the police, but Haila would spot an essential clue that would lead her to the killer one step ahead of Jeff. For the most part, Jeff and Haila were the only ones fully characterized (and we see Jeff through Haila's eyes) so there is little sympathy for the killer or the victim. In addition to the Troys' romance there were usually other young lovers torn by suspicion and a need to hide something. Lieutenant George Hankins maintained a friendly rivalry with Jeff – both ridiculing his amateur status, yet willing to accept an outsider's perspective. From *Murder in Any Language* in 1948 to *The Blonde Died Dancing* in 1956 there is a void. When it was filled it was the first step in Roos's conversion to modern suspense novels. *The Blonde Died Dancing* was not about the Troys but about another young New York couple, making a small but significant break from the series formula. Connie and Steve Barton are very similar to the Troys, however, and their mystery is very reminiscent of *Murder in Any Language*. A few years later Roos produced *Scent of Mystery*, the milestone in the evolution of his work from mysteries to intrigue/suspense. Roos took the plot elements of *Ghost of a Chance*, set it in Spain and replaced Jeff and Haila with another couple. The love interest and concentration on exotic locales superseded the priority of puzzle. These new emphases were continued in later works as the general trend to crime/suspense books became stronger. By the time of *Cry in the Night* and *Grave Danger* the culprit is known early on.

One False Move is a throwback to earlier work, bringing Jeff and Haila up to date (without aging them). Yet it is still a blend of old and new. There are the familiar elements of a theater background, naive lovers trying to hide a problem, and Haila's witty understatement and catty jealousy. But it's modern in that the scene is moved out of New York to a small Texas town and Jeff and Haila have been recently divorced (they are reconciled at the end).

Roos's last books reveal the final transition to a modern romance/suspense/intrigue formula. Although Jeff seldom explained his logic or deductions, he gave an impression of detection by relating full details of the criminal's actions. These last books often take the reader inside the killer's mind, with no pretense of puzzle or "whodunit." In all cases Roos provided a substantial plot, good characters, and relief from the anxieties of a commonplace world.

—Fred Dueren

ROSS, Angus. Pseudonym for Kenneth Giggal. British. Born in Dewsbury, Yorkshire, 19 March 1927. Educated at grammar school. Served in the Fleet Air Arm of the Royal Navy, 1944–52. Married Alice Drummond in 1947; one daughter. Sales Manager, D. C. Thomson, publishers, Dundee and London, 1952–71. Lives in Yorkshire. Address: c/o Hutchinson Publishing Group Ltd., 3 Fitzroy Square, London W1P 6JD, England.

CRIME PUBLICATIONS

Novels (series character: Marcus Aurelius Farrow in all books)

The Manchester Thing.   London, Long, 1970.
The Huddersfield Job.   London, Long, 1971.
The London Assignment.   London, Long, 1972.
The Dunfermline Affair.   London, Long, 1973.
The Bradford Business.   London, Long, 1974.
The Amsterdam Diversion.   London, Long, 1974.
The Leeds Fiasco.   London, Long, 1975.
The Edinburgh Exercise.   London, Long, 1975.
The Ampurias Exchange.   London, Long, 1976; New York, Walker, 1977.
The Aberdeen Conundrum.   London, Long, 1977.
The Burgos Contract.   London, Long, 1978; New York, Walker, 1979.
The Congleton Lark.   London, Long, 1979.
The Hamburg Switch.   London, Long, 1980.

OTHER PUBLICATIONS

Plays

Dear Elsie (produced Wakefield, Yorkshire, 1977).

Television Play: *Runaround*, 1977.

Bibliography: by Iwan Hedman-Morelius, in *DAST* (Strängnäs, Sweden), August 1977.

Angus Ross comments:
My 12 years in Fleet Street taught me that acts of espionage do not happen only in cities like Bonn and Washington and London. Espionage happens everywhere, and often in the most unlikely places. It is also true to say that people engaged in espionage work are by no means always young and attractive and possessed of super powers. So it was, with these facts firmly in mind, that I set out in 1970 to write a series of espionage novels that would portray the whole business in a simple, down-to-earth manner. Every novel in the series has an absolutely authentic setting, and the espionage targets actually do exist. I do a great deal of research – although I might use only a fraction of it in the final draft of the book – and, so far, have set the action only in towns or cities I really do know well. Asked once by an interviewer why it was that so many people in so many countries were willing to go on buying books set in largely unheard-of British towns, I had to say I did not know. It might of course be that most people are interested in other people, rather than in abstract political principles. I hope it is because I write about real, fallible people caught up in situations which are sufficiently interesting in themselves as to preclude any necessity of flights into fantasy.
  The series is written around a central character, Marcus Aurelius (Mark) Farrow. He does, however, have a senior partner, Charles McGowan, and McGowan often features quite largely. Farrow is quite definitely a reluctant hero. He was drawn into the business almost inadvertently (see *The Manchester Thing*) and is frequently seen to be trying to get out of it. Basically, he is a decent, humane man, and he does not have the mental stomach for some of the harsher contingencies forced upon him in the course of his Section duties. He is a political cynic, and bitterly resents the manipulation by faceless bureaucrats of ordinary people's lives. Most, though not all, of Farrow's attitudes represent my own. We are the same age, have much the same background, and like the same sort of things. This is a device to assist in the writing; it obviates the need to keep elaborate biographical notes. Farrow is not married, but although he is not a celibate man, his sexual encounters never take place within the context of

the novels themselves. This, however, is largely because the term of action in any one book rarely exceeds five days. He simply doesn't have the time.

Charlie McGowan is a different man. He is totally bereft of compassion and completely pitiless in his pursuit of those who would do his country harm. He is cold and clever and calculating, and his life is dedicated utterly and unconditionally to the Service. Thus he is often infuriated by Farrow's respect for the human dignities and by Farrow's insistence that, sometimes, people are more important than principles. Theirs is a curious ambivalent association, but each has much unspoken respect for the other and they do in fact work exceptionally well as a team.

*   *   *

Angus Ross has written some dozen novels, all political/spy thrillers. The central characters are agent Mark Farrow and his over-lord, Charlie McGowan. Ross is a powerful writer who relies not upon sex and violence to substantiate his characters, but uses authentic backgrounds and laconic humour instead. This humour, and an insight into human relationships, are the backbone of the novels. Violence does occur around the cynical Farrow, though, and his toughness is all it should be for a leading member of the Security Forces. Pace is all important in these novels, and the dialogue invariably matches the action. The perennial battles of will between Farrow and McGowan are predictable but interesting. One knows what the outcome will be, but the barbed interchanges between them are enjoyable nonetheless.

Ross is not a genius at creating plots, but each of his books has a twist which makes the last chapters interesting. The backgrounds (European and North England) are varied and well-researched.

One wonders how many more novels in this vein Mr. Ross can write without becoming predictable. I suspect quite a few more, as his approach is original and his characterisations strong enough to avoid the "same as before" tag. I recommend *The Manchester Thing* and *The Dunfermline Affair* as good examples of this writer's craft.

—Donald C. Ireland

ROSS, Barnaby.   See **QUEEN, Ellery.**

ROSS, Jonathan.   Pseudonym for John Rossiter.   British.   Born in Staverton, Devon, 2 March 1916. Educated at military schools in Woolwich, London, and in Bulford, Devon; Police College, Bramshill, Hampshire, 1949, 1959. Served in the Royal Air Force, 1943–45: Flight Lieutenant. Married Joan Gaisford in 1942; one daughter. Detective Chief Superintendent, Wiltshire Constabulary, 1939–69. Columnist, *Wiltshire Courier*, Swindon, 1963–64. Lived in Spain, 1969–76. Agent: Murray Pollinger, 4 Garrick Street, London WC2E 9BH. Address: 2 Church Close, Orcheston, near Salisbury, Wiltshire SP3 4RP, England.

CRIME PUBLICATIONS

Novels (series character: Inspector/Detective Superintendent George Rogers in all books)

The Blood Running Cold. London, Cassell, 1968.
Diminished by Death. London, Cassell, 1968.
Dead at First Hand. London, Cassell, 1969.
The Deadest Thing You Ever Saw. London, Cassell, 1969; New York, McCall, 1970.
Here Lies Nancy Frail. London, Constable, and New York, Saturday Review Press, 1972.
The Burning of Billy Toober. London, Constable, 1974; New York, Walker, 1976.
I Know What It's Like to Die. London, Constable, 1976; New York, Walker, 1978.
A Rattling of Old Bones. London, Constable, 1979.

Novels as John Rossiter (series character: Roger Tallis)

The Murder Makers (Tallis). London, Cassell, 1970; New York, Walker, 1977.
The Deadly Green (Tallis). London, Cassell, 1970; New York, Walker, 1971.
The Victims. London, Cassell, 1971.
A Rope for General Dietz (Tallis). London, Constable, and New York, Walker, 1972.
The Manipulators. London, Cassell, 1973; New York, Simon and Schuster, 1974.
The Villains. London, Cassell, 1974; New York, Walker, 1976.
The Golden Virgin (Tallis). London, Constable, 1975; as *The Deadly Gold*, New York, Walker, 1975.

Uncollected Short Story

"Yes, Sir: No, Sir," in *John Creasey's Crime Collection 1978*, edited by Herbert Harris. London, Gollancz, 1978.

OTHER PUBLICATIONS as John Rossiter

Novel

The Man Who Came Back. London, Hamish Hamilton, 1978; Boston, Houghton Mifflin, 1979.

Jonathan Ross comments:
Having been a policeman for 30 years, I intend that my novels should depict police work as it is, with a policeman's attitude towards crime and the criminal, toward the processes of law and justice (not always synonymous) and the mechanics of detection. Where there are warts, I have shown them. Where law and justice fail the police and society, I have shown it. I have shown policemen as men who sweat, who get tired and disillusioned, who are not necessarily good husbands and lovers, and who do, in fact, come from the same mould as the rest of *Homo sapiens*.

*   *   *

Jonathan Ross is one of Britain's leading writers of the police procedural novel. The books published under his own name feature Detective Superintendent George Rogers; as John Rossiter, he writes adventure thrillers featuring Roger Tallis.
The early Rossiter novels I find extremely difficult to put down. The main character, Tallis, has a police background, and is as credible as the situations in which he finds himself. Tallis, a British agent, is never portrayed as superman, except perhaps in his ability to attract

women. The stories involve more detection than usual in this type of novel and the interest is kept going until the last page. *The Murder Makers* and *The Deadly Green* are especially good.

There are certain similarities between Tallis and Rogers, though the latter is a more well-rounded character. In the Ross books characterisation is backed up by a real knowledge of police procedure (to be expected of an ex-Detective Chief Superintendent). Perhaps the most interesting feature of these books is their atmosphere. *The Blood Running Cold* and *The Deadest Thing You Ever Saw* are particularly good examples of Ross's writing. One can only hope that Ross might be tempted to increase his output to rather more than one novel a year – not too hard a task for a born storyteller.

—Donald C. Ireland

ROSSITER, John. See **ROSS, Jonathan.**

ROTH, Holly. Also wrote as K. G. Ballard; P. J. Merrill. American. Born in Chicago, Illinois, in 1916; grew up in Brooklyn and London. Married Josef Franta. Worked as model, then held editorial jobs with *Cosmopolitan*, Dell Books, *Seventeen, American Journal of Surgery*, and New York *Post*. Formerly Secretary, Mystery Writers of America. *Died in 1964*.

CRIME PUBLICATIONS

Novels (series character: Inspector Medford)

> *The Content Assignment.* New York, Simon and Schuster, and London, Hamish Hamilton, 1954; as *The Shocking Secret*, New York, Dell, 1955.
> *The Mask of Glass.* New York, Vanguard Press, 1954; London, Hamish Hamilton, 1955.
> *The Sleeper.* New York, Simon and Schuster, and London, Hamish Hamilton, 1955.
> *The Crimson in the Purple.* New York, Simon and Schuster, 1956; London, Hamish Hamilton, 1957.
> *Shadow of a Lady* (Medford). New York, Simon and Schuster, and London, Hamish Hamilton, 1957.
> *The Slender Thread* (as P. J. Merrill). New York, Harcourt Brace, 1959; London, Macdonald, 1960.
> *The Van Dreisen Affair.* New York, Random House, and London, Hamish Hamilton, 1960.
> *Operation Doctors* (Medford). London, Hamish Hamilton, 1962; as *Too Many Doctors*, New York, Random House, 1963.
> *Button, Button.* New York, Harcourt Brace, 1966; London, Hamish Hamilton, 1967.

Novels as K. G. Ballard

The Coast of Fear. New York, Doubleday, 1957; as *Five Roads to S'Agaro*, London, Boardman, 1958.
Bar Sinister. New York, Doubleday, 1960; London, Boardman, 1961.
Trial by Desire. London, Boardman, 1960.
Gauge of Deception. New York, Doubleday, 1963; London, Boardman, 1964.

Uncollected Short Stories

"They Didn't Deserve Her Death," in *Ellery Queen's Mystery Magazine* (New York), October 1958.
"The Six Mistakes," in *Ellery Queen's Mystery Magazine* (New York), June 1960.
"As with a Piece of Quartz," in *Ellery Queen's Mystery Magazine* (New York), April 1963.
"A Sense of Dynasty," in *Ellery Queen's Double Dozen.* New York, Random House, 1964; London, Gollancz, 1965.
"The Loves in George's Life," in *Ellery Queen's Mystery Magazine* (New York), February 1964.
"The Spy Who Was So Obvious," in *Ellery Queen's Twentieth Anniversary Annual.* New York, Random House, and London, Gollancz, 1965.
"Who Walks Behind?" in *Ellery Queen's Crime Carousel.* New York, New American Library, 1966; London, Gollancz, 1967.
"The Game's the Thing," in *Ellery Queen's All-Star Lineup.* New York, New American Library, 1967; London, Gollancz, 1968.
"The Girl Who Saw Too Much," in *Ellery Queen's Giants of Mystery.* New York, Davis, 1976; London, Gollancz, 1977.

*   *   *

Chicago-born Holly Roth deserted a modeling career to become a writer, first for newspapers and magazines, then as a successful author of mystery and espionage novels. Writing under the names of K. G. Ballard and P. J. Merrill as well as her own, she wrote 14 books in the 12 years of her short career as a mystery author.

One of Roth's earliest books, *The Content Assignment*, was also one of her most popular. Hailed by Barzun and Taylor in *A Catalogue of Crime* as "an excellent spy and counterspy story," *The Content Assignment* is based on the romantic premise of "love at first sight." When John Terrant, a 32-year-old English newspaper reporter assigned to Berlin, meets a female CIA agent, Ellen Content, one autumn evening in 1948, it is not only the start of a romance, but the beginning of a dangerous and fatal mission. The division of Berlin has placed The Russian Inn, a famous restaurant, in Communist territory although its proprietors are not Communists. A vital message concerning Russian warfare plans is overheard by the proprietor and Ellen Content is assigned to escort him and his family to safety. Unfortunately Ellen disappears while en route to New York, and is presumed dead. John Terrant, never ceasing in his efforts to locate Ellen, happens to read two years later that a dancer named Ellen Content is leaving London to tour the U.S. Knowing that the proprietor's daughter, Natasha, was an exotic dancer, Terrant persuades his editor to assign him to follow the dancer to New York in the hope of finding the real Ellen. His brash blundering methods prove an inadvertent aid to the CIA. A witty, entertaining, descriptive style make this an appealing tale, even though the hinges of the plot sometimes creak.

Written when the fear of insidious communist infiltration of the government was running high, *The Mask of Glass* is a chilling story of a plot to take over the United States by a well-organized and powerful Communist group. Well-respected and prominent citizens such as a United States Senator, the head of the Philadelphia branch of the FBI, and the head of the CIA are blackmailed into performing small tasks for the opposition, and are eventually replaced by well-rehearsed Communist look-alikes who have undergone plastic and dental surgery. When young James Kennemore, an inexperienced and brash private in the CIA, blunders into this desperate operation, he is practically blown to bits by what he thinks are members of his own organization. Rescued by a physician friend, he tries to fit together the pieces of his shattered body and the tatters of his reality. Good dialogue, fast-moving action-packed scenes, vivid description, and effective use of the flash-back are Roth's successful stylistic tools. *The Crimson in the Purple* takes on a Gothic character with a creepy mansion setting, hints of ghostly menace, and a playwright who is also a licensed private detective, all providing romance and drama to a haunting tale of blackmail and fraud combined with murder.

Roth's only series character, Inspector Medford, appears first in *Shadow of a Lady*, a very well-written tale with a tight plausible plot, and interesting character studies. In *Operation Doctors* the combination of an amnesia case, a ship at sea, and murdered physicians provides an engaging challenge for the shrewd deduction of Inspector Medford.

—Mary Ann Grochowski

ROYCE, Kenneth. Pseudonym for Kenneth Royce Gandley; also writes as Oliver Jacks. British. Born in Croydon, Surrey, 11 December 1920. Served in the London Irish Rifles, Royal Ulster Rifles, 1st Northern Rhodesia Regiment, and King's African Rifles, 1939–46: Captain. Married Stella Amy Parker in 1946. Founder and Managing Director, Business and Holiday Travel Ltd., London, 1948–72. Agent: David Higham Associates Ltd., 5–8 Lower John Street, London W1R 4HA, England; or, Harold Ober Associates Inc., 40 East 49th Street, New York, New York 10017, U.S.A. Address: 3 Abbotts Close, Abbotts Ann, Andover, Hampshire, England.

CRIME PUBLICATIONS

Novels (series character: Spider Scott)

> *My Turn to Die.* London, Barker, 1958.
> *The Soft-Footed Moor.* London, Barker, 1959.
> *The Long Corridor.* London, Cassell, 1960.
> *No Paradise.* London, Cassell, 1961.
> *The Night Seekers.* London, Cassell, 1962.
> *The Angry Island.* London, Cassell, 1963.
> *The Day the Wind Dropped.* London, Cassell, 1964.
> *Bones in the Sand.* London, Cassell, 1967.
> *A Peck of Salt.* London, Cassell, 1968.
> *A Single to Hong Kong.* London, Hodder and Stoughton, 1969.
> *The XYY Man* (Scott). London, Hodder and Stoughton, and New York, McKay, 1970.
> *The Concrete Boot* (Scott). London, Hodder and Stoughton, and New York, McKay, 1971.
> *The Miniatures Frame* (Scott). London, Hodder and Stoughton, and New York, Simon and Schuster, 1972.
> *Spider Underground.* London, Hodder and Stoughton, 1973; as *The Masterpiece Affair*, New York, Simon and Schuster, 1973.
> *Trap Spider.* London, Hodder and Stoughton, 1974.

The Woodcutter Operation. London, Hodder and Stoughton, and New York, Simon and Schuster, 1975.
Bustillo. London, Hodder and Stoughton, and New York, Coward McCann, 1976.
The Satan Touch. London, Hodder and Stoughton, 1978.
The Third Arm. London, Hodder and Stoughton, and New York, McGraw Hill, 1980.

Novels as Oliver Jacks

Man on a Short Leash. London, Hodder and Stoughton, and New York, Stein and Day, 1974.
Assassination Day. London, Hodder and Stoughton, and New York, Stein and Day, 1976.
Autumn Heroes. London, Hodder and Stoughton, 1977; New York, St. Martin's Press, 1978.
Implant. London, Collins, 1980.

Kenneth Royce comments:
I always think the book I am writing is going to be my best, but as soon as I'm finished I am left in doubt. I put a great deal into each book and believe that revision plays the biggest part in success. I also believe in visiting those places I write about. I simply go on hoping to be better and go on believing that I am. Writing full time is a great help: the time is there, and acts as a spur. I find it difficult to understand how some writers can publicly criticise others. Having said that I will add that I have no personal beef about reviewers – overall they have been quite kind to me. I am involved in my own fiction; involved to a point where I firmly believe that it can happen. Here and there in my experience it *has* happened. As I go on the themes seem to become more complex but never, I hope, too much so. With complexity come more sophisticated plots and presentation. I find structure comes instinctively. I never plan beyond a broad outline: only in this way can a sense of realism obviate manifest contrivance. In my view writing is a profession from which the only retirement is death. To put down the pen finally is to acknowledge that the brain has ceased to function.

*   *   *

Kenneth Royce has been writing novels since 1958 although it is only lately that he has received popular general acclaim, and this through his character Spider Scott. Most serious readers of adventure thrillers, however, would find his earlier novels, e.g., *No Paradise* and *A Peck of Salt*, almost classics of their kind. Royce is a writer with depth and *intricacy* of plot. His locations range from Bangkok to Tangier – his background as a director of a travel firm may well assist him here – but one would suspect that his choice of locations stems from personal experiences. Only in recent years have his settings been concentrated in the U.K.
He is very much a craftsman in his work: his characterisation is excellent, and his stories are ingenious with plenty of adventure and atmosphere. The pace of his novels is fast, and his knack of being able to end a chapter leaving the reader anxious to begin the next is a good lesson for would-be authors, especially thriller writers. The art of going from climax to climax without artificiality is not easy; Royce achieves this laconically, and the reader finds it difficult to assess the ultimate outcome of the story until the last chapter. This especially applies to his thrillers in a non-U.K. setting. The XYY Man stories do not quite fall into this category and, although they have been popular enough to feature in a television series, I hope that he will revert to his more exotic settings. One can especially recommend of his latter books *The Concrete Boot* and *The Satan Touch.*

—Donald C. Ireland

RUELL, Patrick.   See **HILL, Reginald.**

RUSSELL, Martin (James).   British.   Born in Bromley, Kent, 25 September 1934. Educated at Bromley Grammar School, 1946–51. Served in the Royal Air Force (national service) for two years. Reporter, *Kentish Times*, Bromley, 1951–58; Reporter and Sub-Editor, *Croydon Advertiser*, Croydon, Surrey, and Beckenham, Kent, 1958–73. Agent: Authors' Alliance, 64 The Dean, Alresford, Hampshire. Address: 21 Cromarty Court, Widmore Road, Bromley, Kent, England.

CRIME PUBLICATIONS

Novels (series character: Jim Larkin)

No Through Road.   London, Collins, 1965; New York, Coward McCann, 1966.
No Return Ticket.   London, Collins, 1966.
Danger Money.   London, Collins, 1968.
Hunt to a Kill.   London, Collins, 1969.
Deadline (Larkin).   London, Collins, 1971.
Advisory Service.   London, Collins, 1971.
Concrete Evidence (Larkin).   London, Collins, 1972.
Double Hit.   London, Collins, 1973.
Crime Wave (Larkin).   London, Collins, 1974.
Phantom Holiday (Larkin).   London, Collins, 1974.
The Client.   London, Collins, 1975.
Murder by the Mile (Larkin).   London, Collins, 1975.
Double Deal.   London, Collins, 1976.
Terror Trade (as Mark Lester).   London, Hale, 1976.
Mr. T.   London, Collins, 1977; as *The Man Without a Name*, New York, Coward McCann, 1977.
Dial Death.   London, Collins, 1977.
Daylight Robbery.   London, Collins, 1978.
A Dangerous Place to Dwell.   London, Collins, 1978.
Touchdown.   London, Collins, 1979.

Martin Russell comments:
    In writing a crime novel my chief aim is to entertain, amuse, and intrigue the reader. If, in the bargain, I can baffle him until the final few pages, so much the better; if I bore anybody, I have failed. I should like to think that a few of my books also include an element of exploration into minds and motivations. Human psychology is an infinite jungle, and there is no end to the paths that can be pursued ... or the dark destinations to which they can lead. To me there is more excitement in the mental processes of a schizophrenic than in a hundred pistol shots. If a percentage of crime fiction readers feel likewise, it is at them that much of my work is directed.

*   *   *

Martin Russell's crime novels are totally unpretentious; he quite simply aims to entertain with a fast story which thrills and puzzles the reader through the revelation and solution of a crime. His characters exist only within the context of the story and are generally subordinate to events to the extent that when occasion demands, as in *The Client*, he manages to hold our interest without a single sympathetic character.

This is not to imply that his characterization is faulty but that on the whole it is content to be functional. Even when a character makes frequent appearances, as does his journalist hero Jim Larkin, he never really gets "fleshed out." His profession is the important thing, serving the useful double function of permitting the hero to get involved with crime more credibly than is usual with amateur detectives and at the same time allowing Russell to use his own considerable real-life journalistic expertise.

But it is the *stories*, the plots, complications, and surprises, which are the centre of this writer's art. He is an ingenious puzzler, adept at the creation of suspense and with a good line in action. A book like *Mr. T*, which starts with the intriguing situation of a man arriving home to find that his wife does not recognize him and claims her husband has been dead for months, shows Russell at his best. His canvas is by choice small but his rapid sketches thereon can give a disproportionate amount of pleasure.

—Reginald Hill

RUSSELL, Ray. American. Born in Chicago, Illinois, 4 September 1924. Educated at the Chicago Conservatory of Music, 1947–48; Goodman Memorial Theater, Chicago, 1949–51. Served in the United States Army Air Force, 1943–46. Married Ada Beth Stevens in 1950; one daughter and one son. Associate Editor, 1954–55, Executive Editor, 1955–60, and Contributing Editor, 1968–75, *Playboy*, Chicago. Recipient: Festival Internazionale del Film di Fantascienza Silver Globe Award, 1963; Sri Chinmoy Poetry Award, 1977. Agent: H. N. Swanson Inc., 8523 Sunset Boulevard, Los Angeles, California 90069, U.S.A.

CRIME PUBLICATIONS

Novels

    The Case Against Satan. New York, Obolensky, 1962; London, Souvenir Press, 1963.
    The Colony. Los Angeles, Sherbourne Press, 1969; London, Sphere, 1971.
    Incubus. New York, Morrow, 1976; London, Sphere, 1977.
    Princess Pamela. Boston, Houghton Mifflin, 1979.

Short Stories

    Sardonicus and Other Stories. New York, Ballantine, 1962.
    Unholy Trinity. New York, Bantam, 1967; London, Sphere, 1971.
    Prince of Darkness. London, Sphere, 1971.
    Sagittarius. Chicago, Playboy Press, 1971.
    The Devil's Mirror. London, Sphere, 1980.
    The Book of Hell. London, Sphere, 1980.

OTHER PUBLICATIONS

Plays

Screenplays: *Mr. Sardonicus*, 1961; *Zotz!*, 1962; *The Premature Burial*, with Charles Beaumont, 1962; *X – The Man with X-Ray Eyes*, with Robert Dillon, 1963; *The Horror of It All*, 1964; *Chamber of Horrors*, with Stephen Kandel, 1966.

Other

The Little Lexicon of Love.   Los Angeles, Sherbourne Press, 1966.
Holy Horatio! The Strange Life and Paradoxical Works of the Legendary Mr. Alger.   Santa Barbara, California, Capra Press, 1976.

Editor, *Playboy's Ribald Classics.*   New York, Waldorf, 1957.
Editor, *The Permanent Playboy.*   New York, Crown, 1959.

Manuscript Collection: University of Wyoming Library, Cheyenne.

Ray Russell comments:
  I consider myself, for want of a better word, a "mainstream" writer, but I can't seem to keep murder out of my work. Psychoanalysts may make of that what they will. Even my rare forays into science fiction inevitably include a murder or two. For instance, when I was a boy of nine, I wrote a group of miniature tales about a certain intrepid Captain Clark of the Space Patrol; these were really cops-and-robbers stories in outer space. My first professional sale, to *Esquire* (1953), was a murder story (which, however, they never published, so I bought it back and it eventually appeared in *Manhunt*). Most of my *Playboy* pieces (I hold the record as their most prolific contributor) are murder stories or, at the very least, examples of what the French call the *conte cruel*. Why does murder attract me so? Perhaps because I prefer to write about what Susan Sontag calls "the extreme forms of human consciousness." All of my characters stand on the brink of normality, their heels on the solid ground of the workaday world, their toes precariously gripping the edge. And so if, on the basis of the evidence, I were to be accused of being a closet mystery writer, I would have to respond, proudly and defiantly: Guilty as charged.

                              *   *   *

  Ray Russell regularly invades the mystery field. His stories have appeared in leading magazines, and his novels often display strong elements of murder mystery: *Incubus* was called "the ultimate whodunit" by one reviewer, although it wears the dark mantle of the horror story: it includes a locked-room puzzle to end all locked-room puzzles (in this case, a locked dormitory), and the identity of the multiple-murderer is skilfully concealed until the closing pages. His first novel, *The Case Against Satan*, about two priests who exorcise the Devil from a young girl, also contains a murder, thought to be an accident until the culprit is revealed near the book's end. His Gothic novellas, *Sardonicus*, *Sagittarius* and *Sanguinarius*, all deal with murder, mayhem, hidden clues, sudden reversals and surprises. Several novellas were collectively published as *Unholy Trinity*. Typifying the homicidal bent of even his more experimental work, the complex *Evil Star* (*Paris Review*, 1976) is a cunning disclosure of a murder.
  Fast action and crisp dialogue come naturally to this experienced screenwriter, but the true hallmarks of his craft are intricate plotting, irony, Nabokovian sleight-of-hand, and a dapper

style that approaches Jamesian sonority when he ventures into 19th-century idiom. These qualities add up to a virtuoso performer.

—William F. Nolan

RUTHERFORD,   Douglas. Pseudonym   for   James   Douglas   Rutherford McConnell.   British.   Born in Kilkenny, Ireland, 14 October 1915. Educated at Sedbergh School, Yorkshire; Clare College, Cambridge, 1934–37, M.A.; University of Reading, M.Phil. in education 1977. Served in the British Army Intelligence Corps in North Africa and Italy, 1940–46: mentioned in despatches. Married Margaret Laura Goodwin in 1953; one son. Language teacher and Housemaster, Eton College, 1946–73. Agent: Curtis Brown Ltd., 1 Craven Hill, London W2 3EP. Address: Hal's Croft, Monxton, Andover, Hampshire SP11 8AS, England.

CRIME PUBLICATIONS

Novels

> *Comes the Blind Fury.*   London, Faber, 1950.
> *Meet a Body.*   London, Faber, 1951.
> *Telling of Murder.*   London, Faber, 1952; as *Flight into Peril*, New York, Dodd Mead,
>   1952.
> *Grand Prix Murder.*   London, Collins, 1955.
> *The Perilous Sky.*   London, Collins, 1955.
> *The Long Echo.*   London, Collins, 1957; New York, Abelard Schuman, 1958.
> *A Shriek of Tyres.*   London, Collins, 1958; as *On the Track of Death*, New York,
>   Abelard Schuman, 1959.
> *Murder Is Incidental.*   London, Collins, 1961.
> *The Creeping Flesh.*   London, Collins, 1963; New York, Walker, 1965.
> *The Black Leather Murders.*   London, Collins, and New York, Walker, 1966.
> *Skin for Skin.*   London, Collins, and New York, Walker, 1968.
> *The Gilt-Edged Cockpit.*   London, Collins, 1969; New York, Doubleday, 1971.
> *Clear the Fast Lane.*   London, Collins, 1971; New York, Holt Rinehart, 1972.
> *The Gunshot Grand Prix.*   London, Collins, 1972.
> *Killer on the Track.*   London, Collins, 1973.
> *Kick Start.*   London, Collins, 1973; New York, Walker, 1974.
> *Rally to the Death.*   London, Collins, 1974.
> *Race Against the Sun.*   London, Collins, 1975.
> *Mystery Tour.*   London, Collins, 1975; New York, Walker, 1976.
> *Return Load.*   London, Collins, and New York, Walker, 1977.
> *Collision Course.*   London, Macmillan, 1978.

Novels with Francis Durbridge as Paul Temple (series character: Paul Temple in both
       books)

> *The Tyler Mystery.*   London, Hodder and Stoughton, 1957.
> *East of Algiers.*   London, Hodder and Stoughton, 1959.

OTHER PUBLICATIONS as James McConnell

Other

The Chequered Flag (as Douglas Rutherford).   London, Collins, 1956.
Learn Italian Quickly.   London, MacGibbon and Kee, 1960.
Learn Spanish Quickly.   London, MacGibbon and Kee, 1961; New York, Citadel
  Press, 1963.
Learn French Quickly.   London, MacGibbon and Kee, 1966.
Eton: How It Works.   London, Faber, 1967; New York, Humanities Press, 1968.
Eton Repointed: The New Structures of an Ancient Foundation.   London, Faber, 1970.

Editor (as Douglas Rutherford), *Best Motor Racing Stories.*   London, Faber, 1965.
Editor (as Douglas Rutherford), *Best Underworld Stories.*   London, Faber, 1969.
Editor, *Treasures of Eton.*   London, Chatto and Windus, 1976.

Douglas Rutherford comments:
  My novels deal more with speed and suspense than with crime. I started writing them as a
relaxation and change from my more academic life. They had to be written during the short
period of the holidays and at great speed. It was therefore suitable to write about fast vehicles
and fast-moving situations, which is why many of my stories feature racing or sports cars,
fast motorbikes, long-distance lorries, etc. Researching such subjects made a welcome change
from teaching the young.

                                      *   *   *

  Douglas Rutherford spent part of his wartime service in counter-intelligence in Europe and
his knowledge of the real life international crime scene gives the stamp of authenticity to all
of his writings. Many of his most popular novels have a Grand Prix or motor racing
background. I find the most absorbing of these are *The Long Echo* and *Meet a Body*. The
Perilous Sky deals with the world of commercial flying and is portrayed as realistically as any
of his motor racing stories. The pace of Rutherford's stories is fast, his plots are well worked
out, and his skill as a story teller keeps his reader riding on a crest of excitement and tension
right up unto the last page. His collaborations with Francis Durbridge, *East of Algiers* and
The Tyler Mystery, both feature Paul Temple and are well worth reading.

                                                                      —Donald C. Ireland

---

RYDELL, Forbes.   See **FORBES, Stanton.**

SADLER, Mark.   See **COLLINS, Michael.**

SALE, Richard (Bernard). American. Born in New York City, 17 December 1911. Educated at Washington and Lee University, Lexington, Virginia, 1930–33. Married Mary Anita Loos (second wife) in 1946; three children. Free-lance pulp magazine writer 1930–44; screen writer for Paramount, 1944, Republic, 1945–48, Twentieth Century-Fox, 1948–52, British Lion, 1953–54, United Artists, 1954, Columbia, 1956; television writer, director, and producer, Columbia Broadcasting System, 1958–59; film composer. Agent: Paul R. Reynolds Inc., 12 East 41st Street, New York, New York 10017. Address: 219 North Star Lane, Newport Beach, California, U.S.A.

CRIME PUBLICATIONS

Novels

> *Cardinal Rock.* London, Cassell, 1940.
> *Destination Unknown.* Kingswood, Surrey, World's Work, 1943; as *Death at Sea*, New York, Popular Library, 1948.
> *Lazarus No. 7.* New York, Simon and Schuster, 1942; as *Death Looks In*, London, Cassell, 1943; as *Lazarus Murder Seven*, Kingston, New York, Quin, 1943.
> *Sailor, Take Warning.* London, Wells Gardner, 1942.
> *Passing Strange.* New York, Simon and Schuster, 1942.
> *Benefit Performance.* New York, Simon and Schuster, 1946.
> *Home Is the Hangman* (novelets). New York, Popular Library, 1949.
> *Murder at Midnight* (novelets). New York, Popular Library, 1950.
> *For the President's Eyes Only.* New York, Simon and Schuster, 1971; as *The Man Who Raised Hell*, London, Cassell, 1971.

Uncollected Short Stories

> "Active Duty," in *Mystery Companion*, edited by Abraham Louis Furman. New York, Fawcett, 1943.
> "Ghosts Don't Make Noise," in *Second Mystery Companion*, edited by Abraham Louis Furman. New York, Fawcett, 1944.
> "Death Had a Pencil," in *Third Mystery Companion*, edited by Abraham Louis Furman. New York, Fawcett, 1945.
> "The Mad Brain," in *Giant Detective Annual.* New York, Best Books, 1950.
> "The Mother Goose Murders," in *The Saint* (New York), Spring 1953.
> "Three Wise Men of Babylon," in *The Saint* (New York), September 1954.
> "Death Flies High," in *The Saint* (New York), March 1955.
> "The Ghost of a Dog," in *The Saint* (New York), January 1956.
> "A Nose for News," in *The Hardboiled Dicks*, edited by Ron Goulart. Los Angeles, Sherbourne Press, 1965; London, Boardman, 1967.

OTHER PUBLICATIONS

Novels

> *Not Too Narrow, Not Too Deep.* New York, Simon and Schuster, and London, Cassell, 1936.
> *Is a Ship Burning?* London, Cassell, 1937; New York, Dodd Mead, 1938.
> *The Oscar.* New York, Simon and Schuster, 1963.

Plays

> Screenplays: *Find the Witness*, with Grace Neville and Fred Niblo, Jr., 1937; *The Dude*

Goes West, with Mary Loos, 1938; *Shadows over Shanghai*, with Joseph Hoffman, 1938; *Rendezvous with Annie*, with Mary Loos, 1946; *Calendar Girl*, with Mary Loos and Lee Loeb, 1947; *Northwest Outpost*, with others, 1947; *Driftwood*, with Mary Loos, 1947; *The Inside Story*, with others, 1948; *Campus Honeymoon*, with Jerry Gruskin and Thomas R. St. George, 1948; *The Tender Years*, with others, 1948; *Lady at Midnight*, 1948; *Mother Is a Freshman*, with Mary Loos and Raphael Blau, 1949; *Mr. Belvedere Goes to College*, with Mary Loos and Mary C. McCall, 1949; *Father Was a Fullback*, with others, 1949; *When Willie Comes Marching Home*, with Mary Loos and Sy Gomberg, 1950; *A Ticket to Tomahawk*, with Mary Loos, 1950; *I'll Get By*, with others, 1950; *Meet Me after the Show*, with others, 1951; *Let's Do It Again*, with Mary Loos, 1953; *The French Line*, with others, 1954; *Woman's World*, with others, 1954; *Suddenly*, 1954; *Gentlemen Marry Brunettes*, with Mary Loos, 1955; *Over-Exposed!*, with others, 1956; *Torpedo Run*, with William Wister Haines, 1958.

Television Plays: *Young Derringer* series.

Theatrical Activities

Director: **Films** – *A Ticket to Tomahawk*, 1950; *I'll Get By*, 1950; *Half Angel*, 1951; *Meet Me after the Show*, 1951; *Let's Make It Legal*, 1951; *My Wife's Best Friend*, 1952; *The Girl Next Door*, 1953; *Fire over Africa*, 1954; *Gentlemen Marry Brunettes*, 1955; *Abandon Ship*, 1957.

*   *   *

Richard Sale began his career in mystery writing in the early 1930's, selling stories to such pulp magazines as *Super Detective* and *Detective Fiction Weekly*. The latter publication featured Sale's reporter/detective Daffy Dill in a number of tales. Sale's first novel, *Not Too Narrow, Not Too Deep*, was not so much a mystery as an allegorical adventure about ten convicts, their escape from a French penal colony much like Devil's Island, and the enigmatic stranger who accompanies them on their journey. This tour-de-force was followed in the 1940's by several mystery novels, the most interesting being *Lazarus No. 7* and *Passing Strange*, both of which have medical themes, are narrated by doctors, and feature a number of the same characters, the most notable of whom is a police detective named Danile Webster. Both also demonstrate Sale's flair for the bizarre. *Lazarus No. 7* features a resurrectionist and Hollywood stars, writers, and producers, combined with murder and leprosy. *Passing Strange* includes a scene depicting the murder of a doctor who is shot while watching another doctor perform a Caesarean section on a famous actress. The two books contain well-drawn characters and bright dialogue as well as somewhat conventional love stories.

Sale's best book, *For the President's Eyes Only*, is a spy thriller that appeared a few years after the real vogue in such things had passed, probably the only reason it failed to become a best seller. It has more action, adventure, intrigue, and glamor than any two or three similar novels, and a fine, tough hero besides. Reading it makes one wish that Sale had devoted less of his time to writing for movies and television and more to writing books like this.

—Bill Crider

SANDERS, Lawrence. American. Born in Brooklyn, New York, in 1920. Educated at Wabash College, Crawfordsville, Indiana, B.A. 1940. Staff member, *Mechanix Illustrated*; Editor, *Science and Mechanics*. Recipient: Mystery Writers of America Edgar Allan Poe Award, 1970. Address: c/o G. P. Putnam's Sons, 200 Madison Avenue, New York, New York 10016, U.S.A.

CRIME PUBLICATIONS

Novels

> *The Anderson Tapes.* New York, Putnam, and London, W. H. Allen, 1970.
> *The First Deadly Sin.* New York, Putnam, 1973; London, W. H. Allen, 1974.
> *The Tomorrow File.* New York, Putnam, 1975; London, Hale, 1979.
> *The Tangent Objective.* New York, Putnam, 1976.
> *The Second Deadly Sin.* New York, Putnam, 1977.
> *The Marlow Chronicles.* New York, Putnam, 1977; Loughton, Essex, Piatkus, 1979.
> *The Tangent Factor.* New York, Putnam, 1978.
> *The Sixth Commandment.* New York, Putnam, and London, Granada, 1979.

OTHER PUBLICATIONS

Novels

> *The Pleasures of Helen.* New York, Putnam, 1971.
> *Love Songs.* New York, Putnam, 1972.

Other

> *Handbook of Creative Crafts*, with Richard Carol. New York, Pyramid, 1968.

> Editor, *Thus Be Loved: A Book for Lovers.* New York, Arco, 1966.

*   *   *

One of the few bestselling novelists who works squarely within the mystery and detective tradition, Lawrence Sanders is well known as a writer of "blockbuster" successes. He combines with great adroitness the necessary bestseller ingredients of sensationalism, sex, violence, distinctive characterization, and sociological observation; he packages his material within a slick and attractive wrapping of glossy style and suspenseful narrative. These comments are not meant to be patronizing: Sanders's novels may even be better than the reviewers think. He may, in fact, prove to be one of the most important and innovative recent writers of mystery and detective fiction. His most interesting novels are *The Anderson Tapes*, *The First Deadly Sin*, and *The Second Deadly Sin*. The first is one of the most technically inventive thrillers of the last decade, a big caper novel told entirely through documents, mostly the evidence of a variety of surveillance measures – wiretaps, listening devices, police reports – proving that a lot more than lyric poetry is the art of the overheard. The novel shows a powerful picture of a criminal world and a pervasively corrupt society; besides its unique narrative use of electronic eavesdropping, the book very clearly indicates, long before Watergate, the threat to individual freedom and privacy posed by the enormous amount of technical snooping in America by a remarkable array of agencies, institutions, and individuals.

Taking an important minor character from *The Anderson Tapes* – Edward X. "Iron Balls" Delaney – and employing some of that book's vision of society, Sanders crosses the police procedural novel with the crime novel in *The First Deadly Sin* and with the classic whodunit in *The Second Deadly Sin*. Delaney is a retired chief of police in the third novel, conducting semi-official investigations of some difficult cases, one a series of motiveless killings, the other the murder of a great American artist. The first novel revolves around the sin of pride, the terrible vanity of the murderer that drives him to his acts and the righteous pride of Delaney in bringing the man to his death. The second novel deals with greed, a quality that, once again, every character in the book appears to possess, thus supplying plenty of motives for the detective to pursue. Both books are distinguished by a good feel for character and a real mastery of narrative movement. Sanders possesses, in addition, one of the important philosophical qualities of any novelist – a sense not only for crime, but for sin. If he makes a series around the deadly sins with the talents he displays in his other novels, he may turn out to be one of the most important contributors to the art of the mystery in the second half of the century.

—George Grella

SAPPER. Pseudonym for Herman Cyril McNeile. British. Born in Bodmin, Cornwall, 28 September 1888. Educated at Cheltenham College, Gloucestershire; Royal Military Academy, Woolwich. Served in the Royal Engineers, 1907–19: became Captain in 1914; retired as Lieutenant Colonel: Military Cross. Married Violet Douglas in 1914; two sons. *Died 14 August 1937.*

CRIME PUBLICATIONS

Novels (series characters: Captain Hugh "Bulldog" Drummond; Ronald Standish; published as H. C. McNeile in US)

Mufti (as H.C. McNeile). London, Hodder and Stoughton, and New York, Doran, 1919.
Bull-Dog Drummond: The Adventures of a Demobilized Officer Who Found Peace Dull (as H. C. McNeile). London, Hodder and Stoughton, and New York, Doran, 1920.
The Black Gang (Drummond; as H.C. McNeile). London, Hodder and Stoughton, and New York, Doran, 1922.
Jim Maitland (as H. C. McNeile). London, Hodder and Stoughton, 1923; New York, Doran, 1924.
The Third Round (as H. C. McNeile). London, Hodder and Stoughton, 1924; as *Bulldog Drummond's Third Round*, New York, Doran, 1924.
The Final Count (Drummond). London, Hodder and Stoughton, and New York, Doran, 1926.
Jim Brent. London, Hodder and Stoughton, 1926.
The Female of the Species. London, Hodder and Stoughton, and New York, Doubleday, 1928; as *Bulldog Drummond Meets the Female of the Species*, New York, Sun Dial Press, 1943; as *Bulldog Drummond Meets a Murderess*, New York, Thriller Novel Classic, n.d.
Temple Tower (Drummond). London, Hodder and Stoughton, and New York, Doubleday, 1929.
Tiny Carteret. London, Hodder and Stoughton, and New York, Doubleday, 1930.
The Island of Terror. London, Hodder and Stoughton, 1931; as *Guardians of the Treasure*, New York, Doubleday, 1931.

The Return of Bull-Dog Drummond.   London, Hodder and Stoughton, 1932; as *Bulldog Drummond Returns*, New York, Doubleday, 1932.
Knock-Out.   London, Hodder and Stoughton, 1933; as *Bulldog Drummond Strikes Back*, New York, Doubleday, 1933.
Ronald Standish.   London, Hodder and Stoughton, 1933.
Bulldog Drummond at Bay (Standish).   London, Hodder and Stoughton, and New York, Doubleday, 1935.
Challenge (Drummond).   London, Hodder and Stoughton, and New York, Doubleday, 1937.

Short Stories (published as H. C. McNeile in US)

The Lieutenant and Others.   London, Hodder and Stoughton, 1915.
Sergeant Michael Cassidy, R.E.   London, Hodder and Stoughton, 1915; as *Michael Cassidy, Sergeant*, New York, Doran, 1916.
Men, Women, and Guns.   London, Hodder and Stoughton, and New York, Doran, 1916.
No Man's Land.   London, Hodder and Stoughton, and New York, Doran, 1917.
The Human Torch.   London, Hodder and Stoughton, and New York, Do.an, 1918.
The Man in Ratcatcher and Other Stories (as H. C. McNeile).   London, Hodder and Stoughton, and New York, Doran, 1921.
The Dinner Club.   London, Hodder and Stoughton, and New York, Doran, 1923.
Out of the Blue.   London, Hodder and Stoughton, and New York, Doran, 1925.
Word of Honour.   London, Hodder and Stoughton, and New York, Doran, 1926.
The Saving Clause.   London, Hodder and Stoughton, 1927.
The Finger of Fate.   London, Hodder and Stoughton, 1930; New York, Doubleday, 1931.
Sapper's War Stories.   London, Hodder and Stoughton, 1930.
When Carruthers Laughed.   London, Hodder and Stoughton, 1934.
51 Stories.   London, Hodder and Stoughton, 1934.
Ask for Ronald Standish.   London, Hodder and Stoughton, 1936.

OTHER PUBLICATIONS

Plays

Bulldog Drummond, with Gerald du Maurier, adaptation of the novel by Sapper (produced London and New York, 1921).   London, French, 1925.
The Way Out (produced London, 1930).
Bulldog Drummond Hits Out, with Gerard Fairlie (produced Brighton and London, 1937).

Screenplay: *Bulldog Jack* (*Alias Bulldog Drummond*), with Gerard Fairlie and J. O. C. Orton, 1935.

Other

Editor, *The Best of O. Henry: One Hundred of His Stories.*   London, Hodder and Stoughton, 1929.

*   *   *

Sapper, the creator of one of the most popular heroes of thriller fiction, is nonetheless an anomaly in the last quarter of the 20th century, for he is ineluctably locked into its second quarter. His characters talk (and he himself often writes) in that upper bourgeois language of

Saki, P. G. Wodehouse, and Noel Coward: one's friends are addressed as "old lad," "old girl," "old thing," and one's enemies are "swine," "devils," "not human" – above all, not English and not public school. For Sapper's heroes are all of "the Breed," Dagoes begin at Calais, and the life of adventure so avidly sought is constantly characterized in playing field (or boxing ring) terms. Bulldog Drummond goes his "four rounds" with Carl Peterson, and the best of the Drummond novels, *The Female of the Species*, is actually plotted upon a paper chase, with each clue leading Drummond closer to his kidnapped wife, and, it is planned, his own death. Drummond begins his career, in fact, by advertising for "diversion" – "legitimate, if possible, but crime, if of a comparatively humorous description, no objection."

The motive power of all Sapper's heroes is that like Drummond they find peace "incredibly tedious," and in an age of deepening moral incertitude they find themselves justified in fighting England's enemies – the foreigners, especially of course the filthy Boche, and, increasingly in the 1920's, Bolshevists, "butcherers of women and children whose sole fault lay in the fact that they washed." Women especially are the objects of protection for these muscular public-school boys, who approach them, moreover, with great awe. Sapper's women, both good and bad, are an adolescent boy's dream: from Drummond's wife Phyllis, or the innumerable Mollys of the lesser fiction, all white to the core, all helpful in a tight corner while remaining properly feminine, to the immortal Irma, so often Drummond's antagonist after the death of her lover Carl Peterson, and still going strong in Gerard Fairlie's sequels. Particularly suggestive is the sixth Drummond book, *Temple Tower*, which ends as it begins, the heroes' bloodthirsty adventures framed by their wives' question, on departure and return: "Now mind you're both good while we're away./Have you both been good while we've been away?" These are Tom Sawyer games, with Aunt Polly, approving-reproving, watching from the proper distance.

These boys do not prize the life of the mind: Sapper's villains are almost always highly intelligent, even artistic. It is Drummond's practical straightforwardness – his bulldog quality – which defeats their guile. There is even something essentially feminine about them, and Drummond's relationship with Peterson (and Irma) is finally more sexually charged than is his relationship with Phyllis. (More than once, he "lovingly" strangles an antagonist.) Sapper's most intellectual hero is Ronald Standish, the private detective, his cases and his methods closely patterned after Holmes's, and he redeems himself by being a first-class cricketer, who takes only cases which "amuse" him, since he is independently wealthy. On the three occasions when he works with Drummond, it is Drummond's fists rather than Standish's brains that save the day. Sapper's other important hero, Jim Maitland, carries further what is in Drummond a mere suggestion of the Scarlet Pimpernel-Zorro figure – the public fool and the private hero. He is outwardly a "toff," and wears a monocle ("Rumour has it that once some man laughed at that eyeglass").

What makes Sapper finally an embarrassment in the post-atomic world is his sense of easy solution, his simple-minded chauvinism and even "racism," and his sadism. He remains, however, a real spellbinder on the level of story, and ought to retain his audience amongst the intelligent under-16's, preferably those who do not take too seriously the ethos of the playing fields.

—Barrie Hayne

SAUNDERS, Hilary Aidan St. George.   See BEEDING, Francis.

SAYERS, Dorothy L(eigh). British. Born in Oxford, 13 July 1893. Educated at the Godolphin School, Salisbury, Wiltshire, 1909–11; Somerville College, Oxford (Gilchrist Scholar), 1912–15, B.A. (honours) in French 1915, M.A. 1920. Married Oswald Arthur Fleming in 1926 (died, 1950). Taught modern languages at Hull High School for Girls, Yorkshire, 1915–17; Reader for Blackwell, publishers, Oxford, 1917–18; assistant at the Les Roches School, France, 1919–20; copywriter for Benson's advertising agency, London, 1921–31; full-time writer and broadcaster from 1931; Editor, with Muriel St. Clare Byrne, Bridgeheads series, Methuen, London, 1941–46. Vicar's Warden, St. Thomas's, Regent Street, London, 1952–54, and St. Paul's, Covent Garden, London, from 1954. President, Modern Language Association, 1939–45, and the Detection Club, 1949–57. *Died 17 December 1957.*

CRIME PUBLICATIONS

Novels (series character: Lord Peter Wimsey in all books except *The Documents in the Case*)

> *Whose Body?* New York, Boni and Liveright, and London, Unwin, 1923.
> *Clouds of Witness.* London, Unwin, 1926; New York, Dial Press, 1927.
> *Unnatural Death.* London, Benn, 1927; as *The Dawson Pedigree*, New York, Dial Press, 1928.
> *The Unpleasantness at the Bellona Club.* London, Benn, and New York, Payson and Clarke, 1928.
> *The Documents in the Case,* with Robert Eustace. London, Benn, and New York, Brewer and Warren, 1930.
> *Strong Poison.* London, Gollancz, and New York, Brewer and Warren, 1930.
> *The Five Red Herrings.* London, Gollancz, 1931; as *Suspicious Characters*, New York, Brewer Warren and Putnam, 1931.
> *The Floating Admiral,* with others. London, Hodder and Stoughton, 1931; New York, Doubleday, 1932.
> *Have His Carcase.* London, Gollancz, and New York, Brewer Warren and Putnam, 1932.
> *Murder Must Advertise.* London, Gollancz, and New York, Harcourt Brace, 1933.
> *Ask a Policeman,* with others. London, Barker, and New York, Morrow, 1933.
> *The Nine Tailors.* London, Gollancz, and New York, Harcourt Brace, 1934.
> *Gaudy Night.* London, Gollancz, 1935; New York, Harcourt Brace, 1936.
> *Six Against the Yard,* with others. London, Selwyn and Blount, 1936; as *Six Against Scotland Yard*, New York, Doubleday, 1936.
> *Busman's Honeymoon.* London, Gollancz, and New York, Harcourt Brace, 1937.
> *Double Death: A Murder Story,* with others. London, Gollancz, 1939.

Short Stories (series character: Lord Peter Wimsey)

> *Lord Peter Views the Body.* London, Gollancz, 1928; New York, Payson and Clarke, 1929.
> *Hangman's Holiday.* London, Gollancz, and New York, Harcourt Brace, 1933.
> *In the Teeth of the Evidence and Other Stories.* London, Gollancz, 1939; New York, Harcourt Brace, 1940.
> *A Treasury of Sayers Stories.* London, Gollancz, 1958.
> *Lord Peter: A Collection of All the Lord Peter Wimsey Stories,* edited by James Sandoe. New York, Harper, 1972; augmented edition, 1972.
> *Striding Folly.* London, New English Library, 1972.

OTHER PUBLICATIONS

Plays

Behind the Screen (serial), with others (broadcast, 1930). Episode by Sayers published
in *The Listener* (London), 2 July 1930.
The Scoop (serial), with others (broadcast, 1931). Episodes by Sayers published in *The
Listener* (London), 14 January and 8 April 1931.
Busman's Honeymoon, with Muriel St. Clare Byrne (produced Birmingham and
London, 1936; Mt. Kisco, New York, 1937). London, Gollancz, 1937; New York,
Dramatists Play Service, 1939.
The Zeal of Thy House (produced Canterbury, 1937; London, 1938). London,
Gollancz, and New York, Harcourt Brace, 1937.
The Devil to Pay, Being the Famous Play of John Faustus (produced Canterbury and
London, 1939). London, Gollancz, and New York, Harcourt Brace, 1939.
He That Should Come: A Nativity Play (broadcast, 1938). London, Gollancz, 1939.
Love All (produced London, 1940).
The Man Born to Be King: A Play-Cycle on the Life of Our Lord and Saviour Jesus Christ
(broadcast, 1941–42). London, Gollancz, 1943; New York, Harper, 1949.
The Just Vengeance (produced Lichfield, 1946). London, Gollancz, 1946.
The Emperor Constantine: A Chronicle (produced Colchester, 1951). London,
Gollancz, and New York, Harper, 1951; revised version, as *Christ's Emperor* (also co-
director: produced London, 1952).

Screenplay: *The Silent Passenger*, with Basil Mason, 1935.

Radio Plays: *Behind the Screen* (serial), with others, 1930; *The Scoop* (serial), with
others, 1931; *He That Should Come*, 1938; *The Golden Cockerel*, from the story by
Pushkin, 1941; *The Man Born to Be King*, 1941–42; *Where Do We Go from Here?*, with
others, 1948.

Verse

Op. 1. Oxford, Blackwell, 1916.
Catholic Tales and Christian Songs. Oxford, Blackwell, 1918.
Lord, I Thank Thee –. Stamford, Connecticut, Overbrook Press, 1943.
The Story of Adam and Christ. London, Hamish Hamilton, 1955.

Other

Papers Relating to the Family of Wimsey. Privately printed, 1936.
An Account of Lord Mortimer Wimsey, The Hermit of the Wash. Privately printed,
1937.
The Greatest Drama Ever Staged (on Easter). London, Hodder and Stoughton, 1938.
Strong Meat. London, Hodder and Stoughton, 1939.
Begin Here: A War-Time Essay. London, Gollancz, 1940; New York, Harcourt Brace,
1941.
Creed or Chaos? (address). London, Hodder and Stoughton, 1940.
The Mysterious English. London, Macmillan, 1941.
The Mind of the Maker. London, Methuen, and New York, Harcourt Brace, 1941.
Why Work? (address). London, Methuen, 1942.
The Other Six Deadly Sins (address). London, Methuen, 1943.
Even the Parrot: Exemplary Conversations for Enlightened Children. London,
Methuen, 1944.
Unpopular Opinions. London, Gollancz, 1946; New York, Harcourt Brace, 1947.

Making Sense of the Universe (address).   London, St. Anne's Church House, 1946.
Creed or Chaos? and Other Essays in Popular Theology.   London, Methuen, 1947;
   New York, Harcourt Brace, 1949.
The Lost Tools of Learning (address).   London, Methuen, 1948.
The Days of Christ's Coming.   London, Hamish Hamilton, 1953; revised edition, 1960;
   New York, Harper, 1960.
Introductory Papers on Dante.   London, Methuen, 1954; New York, Harper, 1955.
The Story of Easter.   London, Hamish Hamilton, 1955.
The Story of Noah's Ark.   London, Hamish Hamilton, 1956.
Further Papers on Dante.   London, Methuen, and New York, Harper, 1957.
*The Poetry of Search and the Poetry of Statement, and Other Posthumous Essays on
   Literature, Religion, and Language.*   London, Gollancz, 1963.
Christian Letters to a Post-Christian World: A Selection of Essays, edited by Roderick
   Jellema.   Grand Rapids, Michigan, Eerdmans, 1969.
A Matter of Eternity: Selections from the Writings of Dorothy L. Sayers, edited by
   Rosamond Kent Sprague.   Grand Rapids, Michigan, Eerdmans, 1969; London,
   Mowbray, 1973.
Wilkie Collins: A Critical and Biographical Study, edited by E. R. Gregory.   Toledo,
   Ohio, Friends of the University of Toledo Libraries, 1977.

Editor, with Wilfred R. Childe and Thomas W. Earp, *Oxford Poetry 1917.*   Oxford,
   Blackwell, 1918.
Editor, with Thomas W. Earp and E. F. A. Geach, *Oxford Poetry 1918.*   Oxford,
   Blackwell, 1918.
Editor, with Thomas W. Earp and Siegfried Sassoon, *Oxford Poetry 1919.*   Oxford,
   Blackwell, 1919.
Editor, *Great Short Stories of Detection, Mystery, and Horror.*   London, Gollancz, 3
   vols., 1928–34; as *The Omnibus of Crime,* New York, Payson and Clarke, 1929;
   Second and *Third Omnibus,* New York, Coward McCann, 1932–35.
Editor, *Tales of Detection.*   London, Dent, 1936.

Translator, *Tristan in Brittany,* by Thomas the Troubadour.   London, Benn, and New
   York, Payson and Clarke, 1929.
Translator, *The Heart of Stone, Being the Four Canzoni of the "Pietra" Group,* by
   Dante.   Witham, Essex, J. H. Clarke, 1946.
Translator, *Hell, Purgatory, Paradise* (the last volume with Barbara Reynolds), by
   Dante.   London and Baltimore, Penguin, 3 vols., 1949–62.
Translator, *The Song of Roland.*   London, Penguin, 1957.

Bibliography: *A Bibliography of the Works of Dorothy L. Sayers* by Colleen B. Gilbert,
Hamden, Connecticut, Shoe String Press, 1978; London, Macmillan, 1979.

Manuscript Collections: Humanities Research Center, University of Texas, Austin; Marion
E. Wade Collection, Wheaton College, Illinois.

Theatrical Activities:

Director: **Play** – *Christ's Emperor* (co-director, with Graham Suter), London, 1952.

*   *   *

In a 1939 essay entitled "Other People's Great Detectives," Dorothy L. Sayers pronounced:
"Call no character great until the copyright has expired." She went on to say that a great
fictional sleuth is not the same as a great real-life detective. She did not, she explained, "mean
a man who displays unusual talent and ingenuity in his methods of detection, nor one who

enjoys conspicuous success in bringing criminals to justice." Not ingenious problem-solving, not arduous legwork, but rather "the presentation of the character" is the criterion for affixing the highest superlative to a detective-in-fiction. So she believed.

At that time, with ornery modesty, Sayers added that a few hasty enthusiasts had asserted the greatness of her creation, Lord Peter Wimsey. For herself, she said, "I am obliged to them; but I shall feel more confidence if they are still saying it in fifty years." It is now only forty years later but one doubts that another decade would make a difference in this matter. Even allowing for Wimseyphobes, there is no denying that Lord Peter is, by Sayers's own standards, great. And there is no more telling tribute to her (and Lord Peter's) success than that all of the Wimsey novels are currently in print and available. So, with her presentation of his character, she wrought an immortal of the genre. Her spectral reservations would be futile. Having introduced Wimsey in 1923 and having perceived his presence in her life as "ineluctable" as late as 1937, by 1940 she had experienced a change of heart. Preferring to pursue a course of religious writing, she closed the door on Lord Peter, leaving him forever in an arbitrary limbo of 11 novels and 21 stories.

Any regret that there are not more novels, more tales, is exceeded by the pleasure in knowing that what does exist exists. Like any special delight, perhaps the limitations of the Sayers-Wimsey canon enhance the satisfaction. Better to have Peter Wimsey stranded in time that to have him tottering through geriatric final adventures as did some of his peers in the pantheon of great detectives. He was in his prime and Sayers had been allowing him to evolve when she quit. Unlike Nero Wolfe he was not immutable; unlike Campion or Poirot he did not survive to become an anachronism. And unlike Sherlock Holmes he has not become a revenant. Authors are not immortal but characters can be. Fatalism did not inform Sayers; she simply changed her mind and in doing so left Lord Peter Wimsey intact for the ages.

When Wimsey is first seen, in *Whose Body?*, he is wearing a top hat. This is extremely appropriate to a discussion of what Wimsey's appeal stems from: style. It should not at all be an invidious comparison to say that the enduring popularity of Lord Peter Wimsey bears a notable resemblance to that of Fred Astaire. Fair, slender, well-groomed, and dapper, athletic without being brawny, graceful, dignified but able to behave with humor in bizarre situations, chivalrous, romantic: all of these traits are common to them both. Wimsey is a gentleman-scholar and a bibliophile and is depicted as having more of an eclectic intellectual curiosity than does Astaire, but, after all, Sayers had taken honours in medieval studies at Oxford and the demands of literature are different from those of film. What is more interesting is the notion of masculinity which Wimsey and Astaire alike present; they are sexless and sexy at the same time, underpoweringly sensuous, supremely attractive to women in ways that are inexplicable often to other men. Moreover, their peak periods coincided exactly; as heroes, both Wimsey and Astaire epitomize that golden era of effortless expertise and nonchalance and very high style.

And, just as Fred Astaire existed in a world peopled by distinctive personalities (Ginger Rogers, Eric Blore, Edward Everett Horton, Helen Broderick) so did Peter Wimsey: Harriet Vane, Bunter, Charles Parker, Miss Climpson, Mr. Murbles, Sir Impey Biggs, the Dowager Duchess. Though not all of these characters appear in all of the works still they are a repertory company supporting a leading man, except in such books as *Have His Carcase* or *Gaudy Night* in which Harriet Vane is far more than the love interest or the second banana. (Regarding the relationship between Peter and Harriet, it might be said that Sayers invented the latter so that she, Sayers, could consummate her, Sayers's, affair with the former. If an author desires a character she has created, is it incest? It could be argued that Wimsey's lengthy wooing period before Harriet capitulates is a result of Sayers's own unresolved feelings about "sinning" with the hero she has invented. But, this semi-facetious psychoanalyzing aside, Sayers herself does state that she first began *Strong Poison* "with the infanticidal intention of doing away with Peter; that is, of marrying him off and getting rid of him – for a lingering instinct of self-preservation.")

The perverseness of the relationship between Peter and Harriet catches the modern reader by surprise: there seems no rhyme or reason to it. But it must embrace the necessary changes in Wimsey (as Sayers explicates, in the 1937 essay "Gaudy Night," from which I've just quoted), *not* in Harriet, although it is the change in Harriet's attitude towards Peter which the reader is directed to notice rather than the metamorphosis in Peter himself. From a cliché idiot-aristocrat, charming in the manner of a Wodehouse or Saki character given to brightly delivered chatter Sayers transforms Lord Peter into a man with a past and a future; throughout this development, however, and even with added dimensions, he remains eccentric and elegant. The name Wimsey, in fact, is an inspired choice (family motto: *As my Whimsey takes me*) because it provides the right note of *esprit* between the "old" Peter and the "new" Peter.

Sayers also wrote 11 stories but no novels about Montague Egg, a commercial traveler in wines and spirits, but these are little more than pallid exercises in dropped clues and timetables. Her single non-Wimsey book of fiction, *The Documents in the Case*, is an epistolary novel about a tedious middlebrow illicit passion, and the toxological details contained therein are only slightly more interesting than the protagonists, which isn't saying much.

However, even if Dorothy L. Sayers had not bestowed Lord Peter Wimsey upon the world, she would be an important figure in the history of the genre. Her introduction and her footnotes alone to the first book of her three-volume *Great Short Stories of Detection, Mystery, and Horror* are worth many another writer's entire career. In it, writing some of the earliest serious and scholarly interpretations, pronouncements, and recommendations about mystery fiction she pays homage to her predecessors and her peers. In it, also, she refers to the detective as "the latest of the popular heroes, the true successor of Roland and Lancelot." If this was the light in which she created Lord Peter then, try as she would, she could never untie her colors from his sleeve.

—Michele Slung

SCHERF, Margaret (Louise). American. Born in Fairmont, West Virginia, 1 April 1908. Educated in public schools in New Jersey, Wyoming, and Cascade, Montana; Antioch College, Yellow Springs, Ohio, three years. Married Perry E. Beebe in 1965. Staff member, Robert M. McBride, publishers, New York, 1928–29; Camp Fire Girls national magazine, 1932–34; Wise Book Co., New York City, 1934–39; since 1939 a self-employed writer, except for a period as Secretary to the Naval Inspector, Bethlehem Steel Shipyard, Brooklyn, during World War II. Served in the House of the Montana State Legislature, 1965 session; active in Democratic Party. Agent: Lurton Blassingame, 60 East 42nd Street, New York, New York 10017. Address: 195 Lake Hills Drive, Bigfork, Montana 59911, U.S.A.

CRIME PUBLICATIONS

Novels (series characters: Emily and Henry Bryce; the Reverend Martin Buell; Grace Severance)

The Corpse Grows a Beard.   New York, Putnam, 1940; London, Partridge, 1946.
The Case of the Kippered Corpse.   New York, Putnam, 1941.
They Came to Kill.   New York, Putnam, 1942.
The Owl in the Cellar.   New York, Doubleday, 1945; London, Nimmo, 1947.
Always Murder a Friend (Bryce).   New York, Doubleday, 1948; London, Sampson Low, 1949.

Murder Makes Me Nervous. New York, Doubleday, 1948; London, Sampson Low, 1952.
Gilbert's Last Toothache (Buell). New York, Doubleday, 1949; as *For the Love of Murder*, New York, Spivak, n.d.
The Gun in Daniel Webster's Bust (Bryce). New York, Doubleday, 1949.
The Curious Custard Pie (Buell). New York, Doubleday, 1950; as *Divine and Deadly*, New York, Spivak, 1953.
The Green Plaid Pants (Bryce). New York, Doubleday, 1951; as *The Corpse with One Shoe*, Roslyn, New York, Detective Book Club, 1951.
The Elk and the Evidence (Buell). New York, Doubleday, 1952.
Dead: Senate Office Building. New York, Doubleday, 1953; as *The Case of the Hated Senator*, New York, Ace, 1954.
Glass on the Stairs (Bryce). New York, Doubleday, 1954; London, Barker, 1955.
The Cautious Overshoes (Buell). New York, Doubleday, 1956.
Judicial Body. New York, Doubleday, 1957.
Never Turn Your Back (Buell). New York, Doubleday, 1959.
The Diplomat and the Gold Piano (Bryce). New York, Doubleday, 1963; as *Death and the Diplomat*, London, Hale, 1964.
The Corpse in the Flannel Nightgown (Buell). New York, Doubleday, 1965; London, Hale, 1966.
The Banker's Bones (Severance). New York, Doubleday, 1968; London, Hale, 1969.
The Beautiful Birthday Cake (Severance). New York, Doubleday, 1971.
To Cache a Millionaire (Severance). New York, Doubleday, 1972.
If You Want a Murder Well Done. New York, Doubleday, 1974.
Don't Wake Me Up While I'm Driving. New York, Doubleday, 1977.
The Beaded Banana. New York, Doubleday, 1978; London, Hale, 1979.

Uncollected Short Story

"The Man Who Liked Roquefort," in *Ellery Queen's Mystery Magazine* (New York), March 1960.

OTHER PUBLICATIONS

Novel

Wedding Train. New York, Doubleday, 1960.

Other (juvenile)

The Mystery of the Velvet Box. New York, Watts, 1963.
The Mystery of the Empty Trunk. New York, Watts, 1964.
The Mystery of the Shaky Staircase. New York, Watts, 1965.

Manuscript Collection: University of Oregon Library, Eugene.

Margaret Scherf comments:
I began writing mysteries in the days of S. S. Van Dine, admired Agatha Christie very much, probably started reading Conan Doyle first. My idea was to write amusing books, without too much gore but with sufficient suspense to carry the reader on. Small town characters, especially Episcopalians, were my delight, although I used two New York decorators in several books. Las Vegas and Howard Hughes were the material for *To Cache a Millionaire*, and the Arizona desert with its winter visitors figured in *The Banker's Bones*.

My theory is that mysteries appeal to people because the central problem is soluble, unlike most of the problems in the real world.

*   *   *

The variety of series and non-series detectives who inhabit Margaret Scherf's mystery novels range from a Prohibition rum-runner through a retired pathologist to an increasingly overweight rural reverend. Always touched with humor, the works adhere to traditional means of detection, thoughtfully written and carefully plotted.

Set in Minot, North Dakota during Prohibition, *Don't Wake Me Up While I'm Driving* is the most exaggerated example of her unusual characters. Almost slapstick in the Laurel and Hardy vein, the plot is more concerned with whether Hal Brady will again postpone his luckless brother's wedding than with the investigation of a bank robbery in which he is accused. Scherf goes almost too far as the threads of detection are lost in local color, only to appear unexpectedly in the end. The characters are vividly drawn; even a dog, a blue chair, and Hal's car are thoroughly characterized.

With the Reverend Martin Buell, the most regular series detective, is retired pathologist Dr. Grace Severance whose wit and enjoyment are not diminished by age, only by her relatives. Her nephew Clarence is particularly officious, but in *To Cache a Millionaire*, set in Las Vegas in clear imitation of the Howard Hughes story, she outwits him and the security guards of multi-millionaire Arthur Acuff. The clever trick and bold determination with which she penetrates Acuff's hideaway capture the personality which she displays in all her investigations. Her background as a non-practising doctor and pathologist does not help with injured victims but rather in sniffling faint traces of formaldehyde or noticing similarities in skull shapes. Even so, her detecting is often intuitive.

Scherf combines typically traditional detective work with a touch of humor – usually surrounding the detective. While her novels include no startling new techniques, the characters are interesting and the plots, though somewhat predictable, are not dull.

—Kathleen G. Klein

SCOTT, R(eginald) T(homas) M(aitland). Canadian. Born in Woodstock, Ontario, 14 August 1882. Educated at the Royal Military College, Kingston, Ontario. Served in the Canadian Expeditionary Force in World War I: Major. Married Leslie Rose Asenath Grant in 1907; one son, the writer R. T. M. Scott II, who wrote "The Spider" novels often attributed to his father. Engineer for International Marine Signal Company, in India, Burma, and Ceylon, 1908–11. Later lived in New York City. Created *Secret Service Smith* radio series, 1935.

CRIME PUBLICATIONS

Novels (series character: Aurelius Smith in all books)

The Black Magician. New York, Dutton, 1925; London, Heinemann, 1926.
Ann's Crime. New York, Dutton, 1926; London, Heinemann, 1927; as *Smith of the Secret Service*, London, Amalgamated Press, 1929.
The Mad Monk. New York, Kendall, 1931; London, Rich and Cowan, 1933.
Murder Stalks the Mayor. London, Rich and Cowan, 1935; New York, Dutton, 1936.

The Agony Column Murders. New York, Dutton, 1946.
The Nameless Ones. New York, Dutton, 1947.

Short Stories

Secret Service Smith. New York, Dutton, 1923; London, Hodder and Stoughton, 1924.
Aurelius Smith – Detective. New York, Dutton, 1927; London, Heinemann, 1928.

Uncollected Short Stories

"Bombay Duck," in *The World's Best One Hundred Detective Stories*, edited by Eugene Thwing. New York, Funk and Wagnalls, 10 vols., 1929.
"The Stubborn Heiress," in *Best American Mystery Stories of the Year, Volume Two*, edited by Carolyn Wells. New York, Day, 1932.

*   *   *

R. T. M. Scott belongs to that group of mystery writers which includes S. S. Van Dine, Ellery Queen, and Edgar Wallace who began writing before the advent of the hard-boiled school and who remained impervious to its influence. As did many of these writers, Scott believed that Doyle's Sherlock Holmes stories represented the highest state to which the genre could aspire. Scott's work is therefore consciously patterned after Doyle's and almost exclusively concerns the exploits of his idiosyncratic detective Aurelius Smith.

Smith first appeared in print as a secret service agent operating in colonial India during a period in which such agents were in vogue among mystery writers. Smith's later career, which is depicted in the majority of Scott's short stories and all of his novels, is that of a dilettante New York criminologist. In both phases of his life, Smith is an appropriately Holmesian figure. He possesses a cool, rational mind whose analytical workings are not deflected by the presence of a Doctor Watson.

Scott's best work lies in his short stories. Of those tales set in India, "Mystery Mountain" and "Such Bluff as Dreams Are Made Of" hold up despite being dated. Smith's analytical skill shines in "The Crushed Pearl" and "Underground," while "Bombay Duck," perhaps Scott's best story, is a superb exercise in psychological manipulation. Scott's novels are also excellent, though the occult overtones of some, particularly *The Black Magician* and *The Nameless Ones*, may put off some readers.

—Will Murray

SCOTT, Warwick. See TREVOR, Elleston.

SEELEY, Mabel (née Hodnefield). American. Born in Herman, Minnesota, 25 March 1903. Educated at schools in Illinois, Iowa, Wisconsin, and Minnesota; University of Minnesota, St. Paul, B.A. 1926. Married Kenneth Seeley in 1926; one son. Advertising copywriter in Chicago and Minneapolis, 1926–35.

CRIME PUBLICATIONS

Novels

> *The Listening House.* New York, Doubleday, 1938; London, Collins, 1939.
> *The Crying Sisters.* New York, Doubleday, 1939; London, Collins, 1940.
> *The Whispering Cup.* New York, Doubleday, 1940; London, Collins, 1941.
> *The Chuckling Fingers.* New York, Doubleday, 1941; London, Collins, 1942.
> *Eleven Came Back.* New York, Doubleday, and London, Collins, 1943.
> *The Beckoning Door.* New York, Doubleday, and London, Collins, 1950.
> *The Whistling Shadow.* New York, Doubleday, 1954; London, Jenkins, 1958; as *The Blonde with the Deadly Past,* New York, Spivak, 1955.

Uncollected Short Stories

> "The House That Nella Lived In," in *Queen's Awards, 7th Series.* Boston, Little Brown, 1952; London, Gollancz, 1954.
> "Let Run, or Catch?" in *Ellery Queen's Mystery Magazine* (New York), December 1955.

OTHER PUBLICATIONS

Novel

> *Woman of Property.* New York, Doubleday, 1947; London, Joseph, 1948.
> *The Stranger Beside Me.* New York, Doubleday, 1951; London, Muller, 1953.

*   *   *

Mabel Seeley spent her formative years in the upper midwest. Her Norwegian ancestry and story-telling family circle influenced her development. Generous in praise of her mentors and filled with a self-confident pride in her origins, she was determined to portray the region and its people in her books. After several years writing advertising copy, much of it for department stores, she retired from a scene she claimed was too fast-paced and turned her attention to the creation of murder mysteries.

Unpretentious in regard to the "art" of writing, she meant to please the reader. She states as a premise of her mystery writing that "terror would be more terrible, horror more horrible, when visited on people the reader would feel were real, in places he would recognize as real." Her first suspense novel, *The Listening House,* was set in a squalid rooming house, presumably in St. Paul. The ladylike – though divorced – narrator establishes herself in what are surely unsuitable surroundings and becomes part of a sordid story involving white slavery, gangsters, narcotics, and a disgustingly gruesome cadaver fed upon by hungry household pets. The plot is complicated and there are numerous characters to keep track of. Despite the evil landlady, her sluttish niece, and their down-and-out clientele, the heroine finds herself a presentable suitor, and the couple may live happily ever after on their dubiously acquired if not absolutely ill-gotten gains. The tale is a strange mixture of romantic thriller, some hard-boiled features, and a naturalism a bit reminiscent of Zola – all of this in an American city in the 1930's. It is a tale that can be read with some interest today.

The Whispering Cup takes place in a small Minnesota farming community and in its grain elevator. One victim, a monstrously greedy would-be opera star who sings solos at the local church, deserves to be murdered as much as any female personage in the annals of crime fiction; the heroine, in spite of her rather cloying spunkiness, deserves to win out in the end. Local color is well done, and small-town life in the midwest is shown at its most awful. This is probably Seeley's best mystery.

In *Eleven Came Back*, the Minnesota protagonists are transported to a ranch in the Teton Mountains of Wyoming. The landscape is endowed with "some vague, formless, imminent evil." The somewhat forced "horrors" and spuriously invoked menace notwithstanding, the story is fairly good. *The Chuckling Fingers*, in which Seeley is seen at her least convinving, is an overpopulated melodrama set in Minnesota on the shore of Lake Superior, a setting where nature is unfairly blamed for the shudders of the heroine who muses about "death walking hooded in the night, relentless and remorseless and successful." The author calls *Woman of Property* and *The Stranger Beside Me* "straight" novels. Both have small department stores as settings. In these books, where there is as much suspense as in her thrillers, Seeley felt freer to develop character and background and succeeds in depicting the struggles of immigrant families and of ambitious working-class characters to attain the "American dream."

Highly acclaimed when it first appeared, *The Listening House* is the 1938 entry in Howard Haycraft's "Cornerstones" list. In the 1941 edition of his *Murder for Pleasure*, Haycraft heaps lavish praise on Seeley, relishing her "drab" and "commonplace" settings, comparing her to Alfred Hitchcock (a comparison scarcely imaginable today), and calling her the "White Hope" of the American feminine detective story. Ben Hecht's delightful parody "The Whistling Corpse" (in *The Art of the Mystery Story*, edited by Haycraft, 1946), seems a more perceptive critique. Some three decades later Jacques Barzun declared in *A Catalogue of Crime* that "HIBK [Had I But Known] may be found at its best (i.e., worst) in *The Listening House* ... or *The Chuckling Fingers*."

Mabel Seeley wrote romantic thrillers which have much in common with soap opera. In both *The Whispering Cup* and *The Beckoning Door*, for example, the heroines are in love with men married to their bitter enemies and rivals, in each case members – a step-sister, a cousin – of their own families. The Scandinavian-American characters are not made as interesting to the reader as they seem to be to the author, nor is there much detection. Seeley does not always find felicitous expression for her ideas, and her attempts to inject nameless terrors into everyday scenes detract from her narratives. Some readers will not care for these tales, others will become absorbed in a story, rapidly turn the pages as the heroine blunders through unspeakable dangers, and finally will arrive, along with the heroine, at the happy ending.

—Mary Helen Becker

SELWYN, Francis. British. Born in Brighton, Sussex, 20 August 1935. Educated at Taunton School, Somerset, 1948–54; Oxford University, 1956–60. Adult Education Organiser, 1961–65; Research Assistant, BBC, London, 1966–71. Since 1971, free-lance translator and regular contributor to *Penthouse*, London. Address: c/o André Deutsch Ltd., 105 Great Russell Street, London WC1B 3LJ, England.

CRIME PUBLICATIONS

Novels (series character: Sergeant William Verity in all books)

Cracksman on Velvet. London, Deutsch, and New York, Stein and Day, 1974; as *Sergeant Verity and the Cracksman*, London, Futura, 1975.

Sergeant Verity and the Imperial Diamond.   London, Deutsch, 1975; New York, Stein and Day, 1976.
Sergeant Verity Presents His Compliments.   London, Deutsch, and New York, Stein and Day, 1977.
Sergeant Verity and the Blood Royal.   London, Deutsch, and New York, Stein and Day, 1979.

*   *   *

Francis Selwyn is a most historically-conscientious writer, using crime fiction as a way to portray history rather than using history as an interesting background for crime. He does such an excellent job of creating suspense in both areas, that the reader is as interested in the historical as the criminal outcome.

Sergeant William Clarence Verity is the portly, plodding investigator who leads us through the underworld slums of Victorian London in *Cracksman on Velvet.* Through his prudish, moralistic remarks and opinions the bull-headed sergeant represents the outward or public face of the times. But he moves in the slime and hypocritical world that allows almost any behavior as long as the outward appearances are kept intact. Verity himself is a product of those morals and lets a gentleman villain kill himself rather than face the dishonor of public disgrace. Vigorously representing righteousness in *Sergeant Verity and the Imperial Diamond*, he faces the heathen society of mutinous India in the 1850's and comes out ahead. He is also an unacknowledged expert in the art of deduction – using details of one incident to find the objective logic behind it, and then applying that logic to another incident, thereby moving toward the solution of the crime.

Selwyn's sense of humor shouldn't be overlooked. It emerges in Verity's constant battle with higher authorities and less-perceptive co-workers. His later adventures seem a bit stretched in believability at times, but Verity's deductive mind finds escape routes and answers that few readers will anticipate. All elements from royalty to a meeting with Sergeant Cuff, from bawdy sex to a description of the abominable conditions of an insane asylum, contribute to suspenseful, educational entertainment.

—Fred Dueren

SHAFFER, Anthony.   See **ANTONY, Peter.**

SHAFFER, Peter.   See **ANTONY, Peter.**

SHANNON, Dell. See **LININGTON, Elizabeth.**

SHEARING, Joseph. Pseudonym for Gabrielle Margaret Vere Campbell; also wrote as Marjorie Bowen; George Preedy. British. Born on Hayling Island, Hampshire, 29 October 1886. Married 1) Zeffirino Emilio Costanzo in 1912 (died, 1916), one son; 2) Arthur L. Long in 1917, two sons. *Died 23 December 1952.*

CRIME PUBLICATIONS

Novels

> *Withering Fires* (as Marjorie Bowen).   London, Collins, 1931.
> *The Shadow on Mockways* (as Marjorie Bowen).   London, Collins, 1932.
> *Forget-Me-Not.*   London, Heinemann, 1932; as *Lucile Cléry*, New York, Harper, 1932; as *The Strange Case of Lucile Cléry*, Harper, 1941.
> *Album Leaf.*   London, Heinemann, 1933; as *The Spider in the Cup*, New York, Smith and Haas, 1934.
> *Moss Rose.*   London, Heinemann, 1934; New York, Smith and Haas, 1935.
> *The Golden Violet: The Story of a Lady Novelist.*   London, Heinemann, 1936; New York, Smith and Durrell, 1941.
> *Blanche Fury; or, Fury's Ape.*   London, Heinemann, and New York, Harrison Hilton, 1939.
> *Aunt Beardie.*   London, Hutchinson, and New York, Harrison Hilton, 1940.
> *Laura Sarelle.*   London, Hutchinson, 1940; as *The Crime of Laura Sarelle*, New York, Smith and Durrell, 1941.
> *The Fetch.*   London, Hutchinson, 1942; as *The Spectral Bride*, New York, Smith and Durrell, 1942.
> *Airing in a Closed Carriage.*   London, Hutchinson, and New York, Harper, 1943.
> *The Abode of Love.*   London, Hutchinson, 1945.
> *For Her to See.*   London, Hutchinson, 1947; as *So Evil My Love*, New York, Harper, 1947.
> *Mignonette.*   New York, Harper, 1948; London, Heinemann, 1949.
> *Within the Bubble.*   London, Heinemann, 1950; as *The Heiress of Frascati*, New York, Berkley, 1966.
> *To Bed at Noon.*   London, Heinemann, 1951.
> *Night's Dark Secret* (as Margaret Campbell).   New York, Signet, 1975.

Novels as George Preedy

> *The Devil Snar'd.*   London, Benn, 1932.
> *Dr. Chaos, and The Devil Snar'd.*   London, Cassell, 1933.
> *The Poisoners.*   London, Hutchinson, 1936.
> *My Tattered Loving.*   London, Jenkins, 1937; as *The King's Favourite* (as Marjorie Bowen), London, Fontana, 1971.
> *Painted Angel.*   London, Jenkins, 1938.
> *The Fair Young Widow.*   London, Jenkins, 1939.

Short Stories

Orange Blossoms. London, Heinemann, 1938.
The Bishop of Hell and Other Stories (as Marjorie Bowen).   London, Lane, 1949.

Uncollected Short Stories

"The Chinese Apple," in *Ellery Queen's Mystery Magazine* (New York), April 1949.
"The Scoured Milk," in *Ellery Queen's Mystery Magazine* (New York), August 1951.

OTHER PUBLICATIONS as Marjorie Bowen

Novels

The Viper of Milan. London, Alston Rivers, and New York, McClure Phillips, 1906.
The Glen o' Weeping. London, Alston Rivers, 1907; as *The Master of Stair*, New York, McClure Phillips, 1907.
The Sword Decides! London, Alston Rivers, and New York, McClure, 1908.
Black Magic: A Tale of the Rise and Fall of Antichrist. London, Alston Rivers, 1909.
The Leopard and the Lily. New York, Doubleday, 1909; London, Methuen, 1920.
I Will Maintain. London, Methuen, 1910; New York, Dutton, 1911; revised edition, London, Penguin, 1943.
Defender of the Faith. London, Methuen, and New York, Dutton, 1911.
God and the King. London, Methuen, 1911; New York, Dutton, 1912.
Lovers' Knots. London, Everett, 1912.
The Quest of Glory. London, Methuen, and New York, Dutton, 1912.
The Rake's Progress. London, Rider, 1912.
The Soldier from Virginia. New York, Appleton, 1912; as *Mister Washington*, London, Methuen, 1915.
The Governor of England. London, Methuen, 1913; New York, Dutton, 1914.
A Knight of Spain. London, Methuen, 1913.
The Two Carnations. London, Cassell, and New York, Reynolds, 1913.
Prince and Heretic. London, Methuen, 1914; New York, Dutton, 1915.
Because of These Things.... London, Methuen, 1915.
The Carnival of Florence. London, Methuen, and New York, Dutton, 1915.
William, By the Grace of God –. London, Methuen, 1916; New York, Dutton, 1917; abridged edition, Methuen, 1928.
The Third Estate. London, Methuen, 1917; New York, Dutton, 1918; revised edition, as *Eugénie*, London, Fontana, 1971.
The Burning Glass. London, Collins, 1918; New York, Dutton, 1919.
Kings-at-Arms. London, Methuen, 1918; New York, Dutton, 1919.
Mr. Misfortunate. London, Collins, 1919.
The Cheats. London, Collins, 1920.
The Haunted Vintage. London, Odhams Press, 1921.
Roccoco. London, Odhams Press, 1921.
The Jest. London, Odhams Press, 1922.
Affairs of Men (selections from novels). London, Cranton, 1922.
Stinging Nettles. London, Ward Lock, and Boston, Small Maynard, 1923.
The Presence and the Power. London, Ward Lock, 1924.
Five People. London, Ward Lock, 1925.
Boundless Water. London, Ward Lock, 1926.
Nell Gwyn: A Decoration. London, Hodder and Stoughton, 1926; as *Mistress Nell Gwyn*, New York, Appleton, 1926; London, Mellifont Press, 1949.

Five Winds. London, Hodder and Stoughton, 1927.
The Pagoda: Le Pagode de Chanteloup. London, Hodder and Stoughton, 1927.
The Countess Fanny. London, Hodder and Stoughton, 1928.
Renaissance Trilogy:
    The Golden Roof. London, Hodder and Stoughton, 1928.
    The Triumphant Beast. London, Lane, 1934.
    Trumpets at Rome. London, Hutchinson, 1936.
Dickon. London, Hodder and Stoughton, 1929.
The English Paragon. London, Hodder and Stoughton, 1930.
The Devil's Jig (as Robert Paye). London, Lane, 1930.
Brave Employments. London, Collins, 1931.
Dark Rosaleen. London, Collins, 1932; Boston, Houghton Mifflin, 1933.
Passion Flower. London, Collins, 1932; as *Beneath the Passion Flower* (as George
    Preedy), New York, McBride, 1932.
Idlers' Gate (as John Winch). London, Collins, and New York, Morrow, 1932.
Julia Roseingrave (as Robert Paye). London, Benn, 1933.
I Dwelt in High Places. London, Collins, 1933.
Set with Green Herbs. London, Benn, 1933.
The Stolen Bride. London, Lovat Dickson, 1933; abridged edition, London, Mellifont
    Press, 1946.
The Veil'd Delight. London, Odhams Press, 1933.
A Giant in Chains: Prelude to Revolution – France 1775–1791. London, Hutchinson.
    1938.
Trilogy:
    God and the Wedding Dress. London, Hutchinson, 1938.
    Mr. Tyler's Saints. London, Hutchinson, 1939.
    The Circle in the Water. London, Hutchinson, 1939.
Exchange Royal. London, Hutchinson, 1940.
Today Is Mine. London, Hutchinson, 1941.
The Man with the Scales. London, Hutchinson, 1954.

Novels as George Preedy

General Crack. London, Lane, and New York, Dodd Mead, 1928.
The Rocklitz. London, Lane, 1930; as *The Prince's Darling*, New York, Dodd Mead,
    1930.
Tumult in the North. London, Lane, and New York, Dodd Mead, 1931.
The Pavilion of Honour. London, Lane, 1932.
Violante: Circe and Ermine. London, Cassell, 1932.
Double Dallilay. London, Cassell, 1933; as *Queen's Caprice*, New York, King, 1934.
The Autobiography of Cornelius Blake, 1773–1810, of Ditton See,
    Cambridgeshire. London, Cassell, 1934.
Laurell'd Captains. London, Hutchinson, 1935.
Dove in the Mulberry Tree. London, Jenkins, 1939.
Primula. London, Hodder and Stoughton, 1940.
Black Man – White Maiden. London, Hodder and Stoughton, 1941.
Findernes' Flowers. London, Hodder and Stoughton, 1941.
Lyndley Waters. London, Hodder and Stoughton, 1942.
Lady in a Veil. London, Hodder and Stoughton, 1943.
The Fourth Chamber. London, Hodder and Stoughton, 1944.
Nightcap and Plume. London, Hodder and Stoughton, 1945.
No Way Home. London, Hodder and Stoughton, 1947.
The Sacked City. London, Hodder and Stoughton, 1949.
Julia Ballantyne. London, Hodder and Stoughton, 1952.

Short Stories

God's Playthings. London, Smith Elder, 1912; New York, Dutton, 1913.
Shadows of Yesterday: Stories from an Old Catalogue. London, Smith Elder, and New York, Dutton, 1916.
Curious Happenings. London, Mills and Boon, 1917.
Crimes of Old London. London, Odhams Press, 1919.
The Pleasant Husband and Other Stories. London, Hurst and Blackett, 1921.
Seeing Life! and Other Stories. London, Hurst and Blackett, 1923.
The Seven Deadly Sins. London, Hurst and Blackett, 1926.
Dark Ann and Other Stories. London, Lane, 1927.
The Georgeous Lover and Other Tales. London, Lane, 1929.
Sheep's-Head and Babylon, and Other Stories of Yesterday and Today. London, Lane, 1929.
Old Patch's Medley; or, A London Miscellany. London, Selwyn and Blount, 1930.
Bagatelle and Some Other Diversions (as George Preedy). London, Lane, 1930; New York, Dodd Mead, 1931.
Grace Latouche and the Warringtons: Some Nineteenth-Century Pieces, Mostly Victorian. London, Selwyn and Blount, 1931.
Fond Fancy and Other Stories. London, Selwyn and Blount, 1932.
The Last Bouquet: Some Twilight Tales. London, Lane, 1932.
The Knot Garden: Some Old Fancies Re-Set (as George Preedy). London, Lane, 1933.

Plays

Captain Banner (as George Preedy) (produced London, 1929). London, Lane, 1930.
A Family Comedy, 1840. London, French, 1930.
The Question. London, French, 1931.
The Rocklitz (as George Preedy) (produced London, 1931).
Rose Giralda (as George Preedy) (produced London, 1933).
Court Cards (as George Preedy) (produced London, 1934).
Royal Command (as George Preedy) (produced Wimbledon, Surrey, 1952).

Screenplay: *The Black Tulip*, 1921.

Other

Luctor et Emergo, Being an Historical Essay on the State of England at the Peace of Ryswyck. Newcastle upon Tyne, Northumberland Press, 1925.
The Netherlands Display'd; or, The Delights of the Low Countries. London, Lane, 1926; New York, Dodd Mead, 1927.
Holland, Being a General Survey of the Netherlands. London, Harrap, 1928; New York, Doubleday, 1929.
The Winged Trees (juvenile). Oxford, Blackwell, 1928.
The Story of the Temple and Its Associations. London, Griffin Press, 1928.
Sundry Great Gentlemen: Some Essays in Historical Biography. London, Lane, and New York, Dodd Mead, 1928.
William, Prince of Orange, Afterwards King of England, Being an Account of His Early Life. London, Lane, and New York, Dodd Mead, 1928.
The Lady's Prisoner (juvenile). Oxford, Blackwell, 1929.
Mademoiselle Maria Gloria (juvenile). Oxford, Blackwell, 1929.
The Third Mary Stuart, Being a Character Study with Memoirs and Letters of Queen Mary II of England 1662–1694. London, Lane, 1929.
Exits and Farewells, Being Some Account of the Last Days of Certain Historical Characters. London, Selwyn and Blount, 1930.

Mary, Queen of Scots, Daughter of Debate. London, Lane, 1934; New York, Putnam, 1935.

The Scandal of Sophie Dawes. London, Lane, 1934; New York, Appleton Century, 1935.

Patriotic Lady: A Study of Emma, Lady Hamilton, and the Neapolitan Revolution of 1799. London, Lane, 1935; New York, Appleton Century, 1936.

The Angel of Assassination: Marie-Charlotte de Corday d'Armont, Jean-Paul Marat, Jean-Adam Lux: Three Disciples of Rousseau (as Joseph Shearing). London, Heinemann, and New York, Smith and Haas, 1935.

Peter Porcupine: A Study of William Cobbett, 1762–1835. London, Longman, 1935; New York, Longman, 1936.

William Hogarth, The Cockney's Mirror. London, Methuen, and New York, Appleton Century, 1936.

Crowns and Sceptres: The Romance and Pageantry of Coronations. London, Long, 1937.

The Lady and the Arsenic: The Life and Death of a Romantic, Marie Cappelle, Madame Lafarge (as Joseph Shearing). London, Heinemann, 1937; New York, A. S. Barnes, 1944.

This Shining Woman: Mary Wollstonecraft Godwin 1759–1797 (as George Preedy). London, Collins, and New York, Appleton Century, 1937.

Wrestling Jacob: A Study of the Life of John Wesley and Some Members of His Family. London, Heinemann, 1937; abridged edition, London, Watts, 1948.

World's Wonder and Other Essays. London, Hutchinson, 1938.

The Trumpet and the Swan: An Adventure of the Civil War (juvenile). London, Pitman, 1938.

The Debate Continues, Being the Autobiography of Marjorie Bowen, by Margaret Campbell. London, Heinemann, 1939.

Ethics in Modern Art (lecture). London, Watts, 1939.

Child of Chequer'd Fortune: The Life, Loves, and Battles of Maurice de Saxe, Maréchal de France (as George Preedy). London, Jenkins, 1939.

Strangers to Freedom (juvenile). London, Dent, 1940.

The Life of John Knox (as George Preedy). London, Jenkins, 1940.

The Life of Rear-Admiral John Paul Jones, 1747–1792 (as George Preedy). London, Jenkins, 1940.

The Courtly Charlatan: The Enigmatic Comte de St. Germain (as George Preedy). London, Jenkins, 1942.

The Church and Social Progress: An Exposition of Rationalism and Reaction. London, Watts, 1945.

In the Steps of Mary, Queen of Scots. London, Rich and Cowan, 1952.

Editor, *Great Tales of Horror.* London, Lane, 1933.
Editor, *More Great Tales of Horror.* London, Lane, 1935.
Editor, *Some Famous Love Letters.* London, Jenkins, 1937.

*   *   *

Joseph Shearing's most successful novels are those which reconstruct famous nineteenth-century mysteries such as the Bravo case (*For Her to See*), the Maybrick poisoning (*Airing in a Closed Carriage*), and the murder of the Duchesse de Praslin (*Forget-Me-Not*). Sometimes Shearing follows the known historical details closely, but interprets them anew; sometimes, as her foreword to *Moss Rose* tells us, "Nothing but the bare outline and a few unimportant details have been used"; sometimes, as in *Laura Sarelle*, the setting is authentically Victorian, but the crime and characters are largely imaginary. Shearing was obviously well-read in the cases she re-created, but retained the novelist's freedom of interpretation and invention, "to try to arrive at the truth not by study of actions alone, but by the study of the characters and events that produce those actions," as she said in *Airing in a Closed Carriage*.

In *For Her to See*, for instance, Shearing used not only the outline of the unsolved 1876 Charles Bravo case (husband supposedly poisoned by wife), but its secondary characters as well: Florence Bravo's dead first husband; her lover, the famous Dr. Gully (Sir John Curle in the novel); her antagonistic mother-in-law (but not her equally antagonistic father-in-law). The fiction even absorbs and reproduces portions of the two inquests. But the focus is no longer Florence Bravo, here called Susan Rue; instead, it is Mrs. Olivia Sacret, Shearing's version of Mrs. Cox, Florence's prim companion and, in popular opinion, her accomplice. It is Mrs. Sacret who provides Susan with drink, who blackmails her, who poisons Martin Rue, and is in turn punished by the avenging mother-in-law, too late aware of Susan's innocence.

Mrs. Sacret's motivation is partly her desire for comfort, fine clothes, and domestic power; partly her distorted sense that these things are her due; and partly her strange, will-less domination by a scoundrel and murderer, for whose benefit she victimizes Susan and of whom she is herself a victim. This attraction to a psychopath even against one's better judgment also motivates Belle, the otherwise cool and self-serving heroine of *Moss Rose*, based on an 1872 murder. Indeed, victimization of some sort is a recurrent motif in Shearing's novels, along with madness and religious fanaticism. Laura Sarelle, already over-excitable, slowly succumbs to the influence of Leppard Hall, haunted by the mysterious crime of her namesake. Under the spell of "the dreams of the dead," Laura, too, poisons her brother and falsely accuses her unloved husband. Accompanied by her ghostly predecessor, she drowns herself in the Avon.

In *The Abode of Love*, Rev. Stephen Finett, called "Beloved," and his devotees await the end of the world, with grotesque interludes of mass hysteria and love feasts in a fantastically decorated mansion. Finett's elderly wife is able to lead him safely back to anonymity just as his remaining disciples prepare to crucify "Beloved" in anticipation of a resurrection.

Shearing's plots generally begin slowly (*Moss Rose* is a notable exception) with the careful establishment of a domestic status quo which will be broken either by the main character's desire to change her way of life or by some disturbing or dangerous external element, usually masculine, or by both as in *Forget-Me-Not*. Although these are not feminist novels, they often show Victorian women bored by narrow interests, incapable of self-preservation, held down by male authority, and Shearing is very successful in establishing a tone of brutal sexuality without recourse to explicit detail. Yet many of her "strong" women, although fascinating, are unsympathetic, calculating, manipulative: "Ah, it was delicious to be of such importance!" thinks the governess Lucile, feeling her power in a noble family.

Most physical violence takes place off-stage, and horror is usually reserved for the denouement, as when, for example, mad Lord Seagrove strikes Caroline Fenton dead in a re-enactment of his ancestor's crime (*The Fetch*) or when Belle lies waiting for the embrace of Pastor Morl (*Moss Rose*), only to see him methodically preparing to cut her throat.

Between the quiet beginnings which draw the reader into the story and the shock of the strong endings, the novels frequently suffer from mid-plot repetition and lack of invention. Reversals become almost mechanical, as in *The Abode of Love*, or arbitrary, as in *For Her to See*. In *Forget-Me-Not* the heroine roams the streets of Paris ostensibly to satisfy "a restless, a brutal curiosity," but really to bring in atmosphere and historicity. We are too often led along a character's one-track mind, and are reminded too often of the symbols which give some of the novels their titles, e.g., *Moss Rose* and *The Golden Violet*. Shearing also uses symbols and similes as characterization (May Tyler is persistently identified with the ephemeral mayfly) and as clues (laurel leaves from which both Lauras distill poison). The reader, however, realizes and finds their significance exhausted long before the novelist ceases to call attention to them. In fact, Shearing's plots are not exercises in detection through the discovery and analysis of recondite clues, but are, rather, wanderings deeper into peril. Even in *Aunt Beardie*, the reader will very likely have guessed the name character's secret, but Shearing is always successful in depicting a character's stupefied or willing suspension of apprehension.

Like the "Silver Fork" novelists of the 1830's and 1840's, Shearing gives pleasure by detailed description of clothing, rooms, furnishings, possessions. The setting is almost always

England, with occasional excursions to the Continent or America: *To Bed at Noon* is a version of the early 19th-century "Kentucky Tragedy." At times the author's pictures of London and Paris have a Dickensian scruffiness in the greasy backstage squalor of a music hall, the filthiness of gutters and slaughterhouses, the sordidness of mean streets. But she is adept at displaying luxurious upholstery and garments. Susan Rue, for instance, weeps in "a striped blue satin chair" and wears "a loose rose-colored boudoir gown, edged with swan's-down," which Mrs. Sacret, "in pearl-gray color shot with lilac and azure tones," despises. The hallucinatory plot of *The Fetch* begins with "a pink bonnet with long satin strings ... and two rosy-colored ostrich feathers, and a little wreath of velvet flowers inside the brim," and Laura Sarelle goes mad in yellow silk.

—Jane W. Stedman

SHEPARD, Neal.   See MORLAND, Nigel.

SHUTE, Nevil.   Pseudonym for Nevil Shute Norway.   British.   Born in Ealing, London, 17 January 1899. Educated at Dragon School, Oxford; Shrewsbury School, Shropshire; Royal Military Academy, Woolwich, London; Balliol College, Oxford, B.A. Served as a private in the Suffolk Regiment, British Army, 1918; commissioned in the Royal Naval Volunteer Reserve, 1940; Lietenant Commander; retired 1945. Married Frances Mary Heaton in 1931; two daughters. Calculator, de Havilland Aircraft Company, 1922–24; Chief Calculator, 1925, and Deputy Chief Engineer, 1928, on the construction of Rigid Airship R.100 for the Airship Guarantee Company; twice flew Atlantic in R.100, 1930; Managing Director, Yorkshire Aeroplane Club Ltd., 1927–30; Founder and Joint Managing Director, Airspeed Ltd., airplane constructors, 1931–38. After World War II lived in Australia. Fellow, Royal Aeronautical Society. *Died 12 January 1960.*

CRIME PUBLICATIONS

Novels

> *Marazan.*   London, Cassell, 1926.
> *So Disdained.*   London, Cassell, 1928; as *Mysterious Aviator*, Boston, Houghton Mifflin, 1928.
> *Lonely Road.*   London, Cassell, and New York, Morrow, 1932.
> *Ruined City.*   London, Cassell, 1938; as *Kindling*, New York, Morrow, 1938.
> *What Happened to the Corbetts.*   London, Heinemann, 1939; as *Ordeal*, New York, Morrow, 1939.
> *Landfall: A Channel Story.*   London, Heinemann, and New York, Morrow, 1940.
> *An Old Captivity.*   London, Heinemann, and New York, Morrow, 1940.
> *Pied Piper.*   New York, Morrow, 1941; London, Heinemann, 1942.
> *Pastoral.*   London, Heinemann, and New York, Morrow, 1944.

Most Secret. London, Heinemann, and New York, Morrow, 1945.
The Chequer Board. London, Heinemann, and New York, Morrow, 1947.
No Highway. London, Heinemann, and New York, Morrow, 1948.
A Town Like Alice. London, Heinemann, 1950; as *The Legacy*, New York, Morrow, 1950.
Round the Bend. London, Heinemann, and New York, Morrow, 1951.
The Far Country. London, Heinemann, and New York, Morrow, 1952.
In the Wet. London, Heinemann, and New York, Morrow, 1953.
Requiem for a Wren. London, Heinemann, 1955; as *The Breaking Wave*, New York, Morrow, 1955.
Beyond the Black Stump. London, Heinemann, and New York, Morrow, 1956.
On the Beach. London, Heinemann, and New York, Morrow, 1957.
The Rainbow and the Rose. London, Heinemann, and New York, Morrow, 1958.
Trustee from the Toolroom. London, Heinemann, and New York, Morrow, 1960.
Stephen Morris. London, Heinemann, and New York, Morrow, 1961.

OTHER PUBLICATIONS

Play

Vinland the Good (screenplay). London, Heinemann, and New York, Morrow, 1946.

Other

Slide Rule: The Autobiography of an Engineer. London, Heinemann, and New York, Morrow, 1954.

*   *   *

Nevil Shute attracted and held an extremely wide readership largely because of his ability to construct suspenseful plots. Usually he blended highly plausible, if thinly drawn, personalities into situations heavily tinctured with the engineering technology he knew by virtue of his extensive first-hand experience of the aircraft industry between the World Wars. In several of his most memorable novels (*Marazan, So Disdained, No Highway, The Rainbow and the Rose*) Shute dealt compellingly with the exciting and volatile medley of dangers and opportunities created by the advent of air travel. In others, including the very timely *What Happened to the Corbetts* and the immensely popular *On the Beach*, he described, in the manner of the predictive epic, the experiences of ordinary, decent people who had to confront, in the form of saturation bombing or all-out nuclear war, an advancing wave of technological capability which would demolish them unless it were brought quickly under rational control. In yet other of his stories (notably, *An Old Captivity, Round the Bend, In the Wet*), Shute used transportation technology as a context within which to focus attention upon the psychological states and moral and political values of sensible, sensitive persons who had to cope with the human implications of material and social "progress."

Almost never a writer of "mysteries" in any narrow definition of that term, Nevil Shute nonetheless managed to identify some of the main filaments of change in the texture of contemporaneous life and, by artful extrapolation from them, to invent scenarios whose beguilingly matter-of-fact quality evoked a sense of fascination and wonder in a large and appreciative audience.

—Donald Lammers

SILLER, Van.   Pseudonym for Hilda van Siller.   British.

CRIME PUBLICATIONS

Novels (series characters: Richard Massey; Allan Stewart)

> *Echo of a Bomb* (Massey).   New York, Doubleday, 1943; London, Jarrolds, 1944.
> *Good Night, Ladies.*   New York, Doubleday, 1943; London, Jarrolds, 1945.
> *Under a Cloud.*   New York, Doubleday, 1944; London, Jarrolds, 1946.
> *Somber Memory.*   New York, Doubleday, 1945; London, Jarrolds, 1946.
> *One Alone.*   New York, Doubleday, 1946; London, Jarrolds, 1948.
> *The Curtain Between* (Massey).   New York, Doubleday, 1947; London, Jarrolds, 1949; as *Fatal Bride*, New York, Spivak, 1948.
> *Paul's Apartment.*   New York, Doubleday, 1948; London, Hammond, 1953.
> *The Last Resort.*   Philadelphia, Lippincott, 1951; London, Hammond, 1954; as *Fatal Lover*, New York, Spivak, 1953.
> *Bermuda Murder.*   London, Hammond, 1956.
> *Murder Is My Business.*   London, Hammond, 1958.
> *The Widower.*   New York, Doubleday, 1958; London, Hammond, 1959.
> *The Road.*   London, Hammond, 1960.
> *A Complete Stranger* (Stewart).   New York, Doubleday, 1965; London, Ward Lock, 1966.
> *The Lonely Breeze.*   New York, Doubleday, 1965; as *The Murders at Hibiscus Key*, London, Hammond, 1965.
> *The Mood for Murder* (Stewart).   New York, Doubleday, 1966; London, Ward Lock, 1967.
> *The Red Geranium.*   London, Hammond, 1966.
> *The Biltmore Call* (Stewart).   London, Ward Lock, 1967.
> *Sudden Storm.*   London, Jenkins, 1968.
> *The Watchers.*   New York, Doubleday, and London, Hale, 1969.
> *Whisper of Death.*   New York, Doubleday, 1969; London, Hale, 1971.
> *It Had to Be You.*   New York, Doubleday, 1970.
> *The Old Friend.*   New York, Doubleday, 1973; as *Deception of Death*, London, Hale, 1974.
> *The Hell with Elaine.*   New York, Doubleday, 1974; London, Hale, 1975.

*   *   *

Van Siller has written quite a number of murder mysteries most with a romantic element which may appeal primarily to a feminine audience. Plotting and settings come easier to Siller than does convincing characterization.

Under a Cloud is set on a Montana dude ranch. The hero, a wounded Army captain on recuperative leave, is an amateur detective attracted by a mystery involving friends of his family. Details of the wartime atmosphere and the western scene are adequate, but the reader is never made to care very much what happens to the characters and feels tricked by the author when the killer turns out to be a psychopath. *The Last Resort*, set in Bermuda, starts out well, though slowly, with a promising situation but unfortunately founders before the end of the book. *The Watchers* has an intriguing, if not original, premise – an attempt to discredit someone by casting doubts on his sanity. Iranian oil and murder in Teheran bring in the CIA, who are still heroes in this story. *It Had to Be You*, a romantic thriller with scandal and murder among the well-to-do, shows Siller at her best. The book is marred, however, by its cardboard characters; since they have not been made to take on life, the reversals and surprises in the book seem contrived. *The Old Friend*, an almost Gothic yarn, is overloaded with horsy jargon and gratuitous details about fox hunting. *The Hell with Elaine* is typical of Siller, with deceit and murder in a soap-opera setting.

The author has improved with practice – more recent stories are certainly better than earlier ones. Some readers may enjoy Siller's mystery fiction for the illusion of murderous machinations in chic surroundings. The books reflect current fashions and topical interests much as second-rate television drama does. Middle-class morality prevails. Despite their general mediocrity, her books her fairly entertaining and may be just the proper soporific for a tedious trip by bus or plane.

—Mary Helen Becker

SIMON, Roger L(ichtenberg). American. Born in 1943. Educated at Dartmouth College, Hanover, New Hampshire, B.A.; Yale University Drama School, New Haven, Connecticut, M.F.A. Married; two sons. Self-employed writer. Recipient: Crime Writers Association John Creasey Memorial Award, 1974.

Crime Publications

Novels (series character: Moses Wine in all books)

The Big Fix. New York, Simon and Schuster, 1973; London, Deutsch, 1974.
Wild Turkey. New York, Simon and Schuster, 1975; London, Deutsch, 1976.
Peking Duck. New York, Simon and Schuster, and London, Deutsch, 1979.

Other Publications

Novels

Heir. New York, Macmillan, 1968.
The Mama Tass Manifesto. New York, Holt Rinehart, 1970.

*   *   *

In *The Mama Tass Manifesto* Roger L. Simon explored the cultural conflicts of the 1960's in the United States, adopting as his persona a young woman, a radical leftist and former student at Columbia University. Although Simon deftly and authentically catches the student rhetoric of the period, the story is all surface; his persona is glib rather than compelling. Simon's later novels *The Big Fix* and *Wild Turkey* are both examples of the so-called hard-boiled school of detective fiction. The former openly invites comparison with Raymond Chandler's first novel, *The Big Sleep.* Although highly praised, *The Big Fix* is a curious mixture of the trendy and the cliché-ridden. Definitely trendy is Simon's cynically hip, slightly spaced-out private investigator, Moses Wine. Wine, a Berkeley student radical in the turbulent 1960's, finds himself a decade later an over-thirtyish, dope-smoking divorced father of two young boys, living hand to mouth on the margin of that Southern California society, all surface glitter and spiritual vacuity, which has been the setting for so much of the best American detective fiction. But if Simon strikes something of a new note with the character of Moses Wine, other elements in the story are straight off the shelf – a Satanist cult, an aging abortionist, the usual assortment of policemen, and the smoothly menacing corporate manipulator Oscar Procari, whose conspiracy Wine manages to unravel and thwart. Even by the relaxed standards of detective fiction, Wine's case – or, rather, his having the case at all – is improbable. That someone is attempting to sabotage a Presidential primary campaign is no more improbable than yesterday's newspaper, to be sure; but that a detective resembling Moses Wine could be hired to deal with the threat taxes the reader's credulity, despite Simon's best efforts to motivate Wine's hiring though a former girlfriend.

The Mama Tass Manifesto showed that Simon needed something like the conventions of the hard-boiled detective novel to set off to best advantage his skill at rendering dialogue; but *The Big Fix* is apprentice work, not to be compared with *The Big Sleep*, behind which lay the considerable achievement of Chandler's *Black Mask* stories. It remains to be seen whether Simon can make good on the promise of *The Big Fix* – as, for example, Robert B. Parker has done in the novels that have succeeded his uneven first effort *The Godwulf Manuscript*.

—R. Gordon Kelly

SIMON, S. J.   See BRAHMS, Caryl.

SIMPSON, Helen (de Guerry).   Australian.   Born in Sydney, New South Wales, 1 December 1897. Educated at Sacred Heart Convent, Rose Bay, New South Wales; Abbotsleigh, Wahroonga, New South Wales; Oxford University. Served in the Women's Royal Naval Service during World War I. Married Denis J. Browne in 1927; one daughter. Recipient: Black Memorial Prize, 1933. *Died 14 October 1940.*

CRIME PUBLICATIONS

Novels (series character: Sir John Saumarez)

> *Enter Sir John*, with Clemence Dane.   London, Hodder and Stoughton, and New York, Cosmopolitan, 1928.
> *Printer's Devil* (Sir John), with Clemence Dane.   London, Hodder and Stoughton, 1930; as *Author Unknown*, New York, Cosmopolitan, 1930.
> *'Vantage Striker.*   London, Heinemann, 1931; as *The Prime Minister Is Dead*, New York, Doubleday, 1931.
> *Re-Enter Sir John*, with Clemence Dane.   London, Hodder and Stoughton, and New York, Farrar and Rinehart, 1932.
> *Ask a Policeman*, with others.   London, Barker, and New York, Morrow, 1933.

Uncollected Short Story

> "A Posteriori," in *Ellery Queen's Mystery Magazine* (New York), September 1954.

OTHER PUBLICATIONS

Novels

Acquittal. London, Heinemann, and New York, Knopf, 1925.
Cups, Wands, and Swords. London, Heinemann, 1927; New York, Knopf, 1928.
The Desolate House. London, Heinemann, 1929; as *Desires and Devices*, New York, Doubleday, 1930.
Boomerang. London, Heinemann, and New York, Doubleday, 1932.
The Woman on the Beast, Viewed from Three Angles. London, Heinemann, 1933.
Saraband for Dead Lovers. London, Heinemann, and New York, Doubleday, 1935.
Under Capricorn. London, Heinemann, 1937; New York, Macmillan, 1938.
Maid No More. London, Heinemann, and New York, Reynal, 1940.

Short Stories

The Baseless Fabric. London, Heinemann, and New York, Knopf, 1925.
The Female Felon. London, Dickson and Thompson, 1935.
Imaginary Biographies, with others. London, Allen and Unwin, 1936.

Plays

Truth, The Real Helena, The Witch, Masks: Lightning Sketches. Oxford, Blackwell, 1918.
Masks (produced Sydney, 1921). Included in *Truth ...*, 1918.
A Man of His Time (produced Sydney, 1923). Sydney, Angus and Robertson, 1923.
Pan in Pimlico, in *Double Demon and Other One-Act Plays*. New York, Appleton, 1924; published separately, Oxford, Blackwell, 1926.
The Cautious Lovers (produced London, 1924).
The School for Wives, adaptation of a play by Molière (produced London, 1925).
The Women's Comedy (published anonymously). London, Pelican Press, 1926.
Gooseberry Fool, with Clemence Dane (produced London, 1929).

Screenplay: *Sabotage* (*The Woman Alone*), with others, 1936.

Verse

Philosophies in Little. Sydney, Angus and Robertson, 1921.

Other

Mumbudget (juvenile). London, Heinemann, 1928; New York, Doubleday, 1929.
The Spanish Marriage (on Mary I). London, Davies, and New York, Putnam, 1933.
The Happy Housewife: A Book for the House That Is or Is to Be. London, Hodder and Stoughton, 1934.
Henry VIII. London, Davies, and New York, Appleton Century, 1934.
A Woman among Wild Men: Mary Kingsley. London, Nelson, 1938.
A Woman Looks Out (broadcasts). London, Religious Tract Society-Lutterworth Press, 1940.

Editor, with Petrie Townshend, *The Cold Table: A Book of Recipes for the Preparation of Cold Food and Drink.* London, Cape, 1935; New York, Macmillan, 1936.
Editor, *The Anatomy of Murder: Famous Crimes Critically Considered by Members of the Detection Club.* London, Lane, 1936; New York, Macmillan, 1937.

Translator, *The Waiting City: Paris 1782–1788*, by L.-S. Mercier. London, Harrap, 1933.

Translator, *Heartsease and Honesty, Being the Pastimes of the Sieur de Grammont, Steward to the Duc de Richelieu in Touraine.* London, Golden Cockerel Press, 1935.

*   *   *

The rather different literary talents of Clemence Dane and Helen Simpson combined in the late 1920's and early 1930's to produce three detective novels featuring the very histrionic actor-manager of the Sheridan Theatre, London: Sir John Saumarez, born Johnny Simmonds. Clemence Dane's long literary career was much involved with the theatre; her most famous novel, *Broome Stages*, is a *roman-fleuve* of the English stage. Helen Simpson's first novel, *Acquittal*, is a murder story; her most famous novel is the historical mystery *Under Capricorn*, made into a film by Alfred Hitchcock. Sir John, one guesses, along with his theatrical background, is more Clemence Dane's creation, the plotting of the mystery more Helen Simpson's; the romantic element in all three plots is in line with the interests of both writers.

In *Enter Sir John*, Sir John strives to clear a young actress of a murder conviction, and the novel ends with their engagement. The mystery taxes the ingenuity of neither Sir John nor the reader. In *Printer's Devil* the love interest moves out of centre stage, and Sir John himself becomes a peripheral character, an actor who has helped to bring fame to a celebrated dramatist who is now about to publish his highly scandalous memoirs – a murder follows. Here the mystery is more hidden, but its revelation pedestrian. The best of the three novels is *Re-Enter Sir John*, in which murder is committed to cover up both an old marriage and a paternity, and there are several plausible candidates for murderer. Sir John unravels the mystery with some help from his wife, the convicted-accused of the first novel, and procures a confession by the same characteristically theatrical device he used in that novel – the performance to catch the conscience of the criminal, which he owes to *Hamlet*. In *Re-Enter Sir John*, moving with the times, Sir John's performance is a cinematic one, and the more strikingly effective.

Helen Simpson wrote one detective novel on her own, the year before *Re-Enter Sir John*. The background of *'Vantage Striker* is the wider stage of world affairs, as in her historical novels, but again one centre of interest is in the love affair between the pertinacious young woman and the violent tennis champion/war veteran who seems to have been the last to visit the prime minister before his death. This is a better psychological novel than the other three, and it raises more serious questions – of the effect of the Great War upon a whole generation of English youth; of the tensions between that generation and those too young to remember the war; of the morality of the will to political power. Written in the year of the National Government and the mediocrities of MacDonald and Baldwin, it sympathetically treats a politician of transcendent abilities whose sense of his own mission is balanced against man-made laws and national security. The detective-physician allows the technical murderer to escape the exercise of the law at the end. *'Vantage Striker* is a more sophisticated, less frivolous work than the three collaborative novels.

The chief contribution of these two writers to detective fiction, however, must be the creation of Sir John, the typical actor in his lust for an audience, who decides to "seize the opportunity of fulfilling his double function, to apply the technique of his art to a problem of real life." What brings him his success is less his ratiocinative powers (even as an actor he is a showman) than his charm, his ease with people, and his persistence.

—Barrie Hayne

SIMS, George (Frederick Robert). British. Born in Hammersmith, London, 3 August 1923. Educated at the Lower School of John Lyon, Harrow, Middlesex, 1934–40. Served in the British Army, 1942–47. Married Beryl Simcock in 1943; one daughter and two sons. Junior Reporter, Press Association, London, 1940–42; worked for an antiquarian bookseller, Harrow, 1947–48. Since 1948, owner G. F. Sims (Rare Books), first in Harrow, and since 1954 in Hurst, Berkshire. Agent: A. D. Peters and Company Ltd., 10 Buckingham Street, London WC2N 6BU. Address: Peacocks, Hurst, near Reading, Berkshire, England.

CRIME PUBLICATIONS

Novels

The Terrible Door. London, Bodley Head, and New York, Horizon Press, 1964.
Sleep No More. London, Gollancz, and New York, Harcourt Brace, 1966.
The Last Best Friend. London, Gollancz, 1967; New York, Stein and Day, 1968.
The Sand Dollar. London, Gollancz, 1969.
Deadhand. London, Gollancz, 1971.
Hunters Point. London, Gollancz, 1973; New York, Penguin, 1977.
The End of the Web. London, Gollancz, and New York, Walker, 1976.
Rex Mundi. London, Gollancz, 1978.

Uncollected Short Stories

"Experimental One," in *Points* (Paris), n.d.
"The Charlie Adams Affair," in *Pick of Today's Short Stories* 7, edited by John Pudney. London, Putnam, 1956.

OTHER PUBLICATIONS

Verse

The Swallow Lovers. London, privately printed, 1942.
Poems. London, Fortune Press, 1944.
The Immanent Goddess. London, Fortune Press, 1944.
Some Cadences: Poems Written in 1945. Reading, Berkshire, privately printed, 1960.

Other

A Catalogue of Letters, Manuscript Papers and Books of Frederick Rolfe, Baron Corvo. Harrow, Middlesex, G. F. Sims, 1949.
A Catalogue of Llewelyn Powys Manuscripts. Hurst, Berkshire, G. F. Sims, n.d.

George Sims comments:
Though my books are published as "thrillers," I consider them to be "novels of suspense." I am incapable of writing a straightforward detective story because I am primarily interested in describing characters and conveying atmosphere. My books are a mixture of fact and fiction: fictional stuff builds up gradually in my mind, perhaps for a year, about something I've seen or experienced. I once read a newspaper paragraph about a famous art collection that had disappeared since the Nazi occupation of Paris, and had the urge to go there, make enquiries, and see if I could trace any of the people involved. I soon realised this would take too much time for a non-professional author and I had to drop the plan – but the idea did give me the basis for *The Last Best Friend.* I have long been an admirer of Scott Fitzgerald, and a quotation from him, "the terrible door into the past," gave me the title for my first book.

Another quotation, from *The Crack-Up*, I take as my motto: "... necessary to marry the futility of the effort with the urge to strive...." I am not foolish enough to hope ever to write a book a quarter as good as *Middlemarch*; my ambition is to write a book a quarter as good as *The Great Gatsby*.

*   *   *

Publishers' blurbs are not renowned for the strict accuracy with which they weigh up and describe their books. But a blurb writer for George Sims's British publisher once said that he never wrote "predictably, and never less predictably than here" (the book in question was *The End of the Web*), and though I might challenge the last part of that statement I must concede that its first part sums up Sims exactly. He is unpredictable, wildly unpredictable.

He is in fact an amateur writer, and that is by no means intended as a jibe. Like a good many other writers of crime stories, Sims is a part-timer. But with most of the others the amateur status either does not particularly show up at all, their books being as expert as any full-time writer's, or the amateurishness manifests itself in books that are frankly not awfully good. But Sims's books are awfully good. Yet he breaks, time and again, the rules. Often there is no harm in that, and the greatest writers have achieved some of their greatest successes in flouting the canons. But Sims breaks the rules with such splendid disregard, so wholeheartedly, that his wilfulness does, alas, often affect the quality of the whole.

Look at one example, that 1976 book to which his publisher affixed the label "unpredictable." It begins as the story, told with fine skill, of a fiftyish London antiques dealer caught up in some mysterious, half-dubious transaction while at the same time, so as to reassure himself, embarking half-willingly, half-unwillingly, on an affair with a young girl. It makes you really feel you are this man, and this man is a representative sort of human being. Until page 50. When our hero is brutally killed.

You can't do it. But an amateur does. There's something else he wants to write about (while still keeping some sort of a story going) and he damn well writes about it. And he writes damn well about it. Which is the reason that over and over again one forgives Sims.

He has all the skill of many of the considerable novelists in the mainstream. As we have seen, he depicts a character marvellously. The man in middle age is one of his specialities. There is an excellent study in *Deadhand* of a hero facing – Sims uses the expressive German word – Torschusspanik (panic that all doors seem to be shutting in your face). Love is another of his successes, often the love of an older man for a younger girl. He describes the way it envelopes a person despite his better judgment, and the simultaneous sadness and unholy joy of it. He can even do that difficult thing, almost impossible in the narrow confines of a standard crime novel, of showing us a person changing, as he does wonderfully in *The Last Best Friend*. And he can do another more minor but very tricky thing: he can describe a fight and make you know just what went on.

Yet for all his achievement he has his faults, the faults of the amateur. He loves facts, all sorts of odd, inconsequent facts (London and its curiosities is one of his great delights) and he often pleases himself entirely to get a fact or two in. So sometimes there is in the books an air of knowingness which can only put off a considerable proportion of readers. On the other hand, the facts are often nuttily interesting and the books are the more enjoyable for their being in them.

—H. R. F. Keating

SLESAR, Henry. Also writes as O. H. Leslie. American Born in Brooklyn, New York, 12 June 1927. Educated in public schools. Served in the United States Air Force, 1946–47. Married 1) Oenone Scott in 1953; 2) Jan Maakestad in 1970; 3) Manuela Jone in 1974; one daughter and one son. Advertising Executive: Vice-President and Creative Director, Robert W. Orr Inc., New York, 1949–57; Fuller and Smith and Ross, New York, 1957–60; West Wir and Bartel, New York, 1960–64. President and Creative Director, Slesar and Kanzer, New York, 1964–69, and since 1974, Slesar and Manuela. Recipient: Mystery Writers of America Edgar Allan Poe Award, for novel, 1960, for television serial, 1977; Emmy Award, 1974. Agent: Jerome S. Siegel Associates, 8733 Sunset Boulevard, Hollywood, California 90069. Address: 125 East 72nd Street, New York, New York 10021, U.S.A.

Crime Publications

Novels

> *The Gray Flannel Shroud.* New York, Random House, 1959; London, Deutsch, 1960.
> *Enter Murderers.* New York, Random House, 1960; London, Gollancz, 1961.
> *The Bridge of Lions.* New York, Macmillan, 1963; London, Gollancz, 1964.
> *The Seventh Mask* (novelization of tv play). New York, Ace, 1969.
> *The Thing at the Door.* New York, Random House, 1974; London, Hamish Hamilton, 1975.

Short Stories

> *A Bouquet of Clean Crimes and Neat Murders.* New York, Avon, 1960.
> *A Crime for Mothers and Others.* New York, Avon, 1962.

Uncollected Short Stories

> "Goodbye Charlie," in *Alfred Hitchcock's Mystery Magazine* (North Palm Beach, Florida), January 1963.
> "The Second Verdict," in *Alfred Hitchcock's Mystery Magazine* (North Palm Beach, Florida), February 1963.
> "Starring the Defense," in *Alfred Hitchcock's Mystery Magazine* (North Palm Beach, Florida), April 1963.
> "Sea of Troubles," in *Alfred Hitchcock's Mystery Magazine* (North Palm Beach, Florida), May 1963.
> "Tony's Death," in *Alfred Hitchcock's Mystery Magazine* (North Palm Beach, Florida), September 1963.
> "The Return of the Moresbys," in *Ellery Queen's Mystery Magazine* (New York), January 1964.
> "Federal Offense," in *Ellery Queen's Mystery Magazine* (New York), April 1964.
> "The Horse That Wasn't for Sale," in *Ellery Queen's Mystery Magazine* (New York), May 1964.
> "Three Miles to Marleybone," in *Alfred Hitchcock's Mystery Magazine* (North Palm Beach, Florida), September 1964.
> "The Old Ones Are Hard to Kill," in *Mike Shayne Mystery Magazine* (New York), January 1965.
> "The Ring of Truth," in *Mike Shayne Mystery Magazine* (New York), February 1965.
> "Gomber's Army," in *Alfred Hitchcock's Mystery Magazine* (North Palm Beach, Florida), April 1965.
> "One of Those Days," in *The Saint* (New York), October 1965.
> "Cop in a Rocker," in *Alfred Hitchcock's Mystery Magazine* (North Palm Beach, Florida), 1965.

"A Choice of Witnesses," in *Alfred Hitchcock's Mystery Magazine* (North Palm Beach, Florida), March 1966.
"The Cop Who Loved Flowers," in *Ellery Queen's Mystery Magazine* (New York), November 1966.
"The Diagnosis," in *Alfred Hitchcock's Mystery Magazine* (North Palm Beach, Florida), February 1967.
"The Bluff," in *Alfred Hitchcock's Mystery Magazine* (North Palm Beach, Florida), April 1967.
"The House on Damn Street," in *Alfred Hitchcock's Mystery Magazine* (North Palm Beach, Florida), 1967.
"You Can Bet on Ruby Martinson," in *Alfred Hitchcock's Mystery Magazine* (North Palm Beach, Florida), 1967.
"The Job," in *Alfred Hitchcock's Mystery Magazine* (North Palm Beach, Florida), October 1968.
"Death of the Kerry Blue," in *Alfred Hitchcock's Mystery Magazine* (North Palm Beach, Florida), November 1968.
"Don't I Know You?," in *Ellery Queen's Mystery Magazine* (New York), September 1968.
"The Loan," in *Alfred Hitchcock's Mystery Magazine* (North Palm Beach, Florida), December 1972.
"The Intruder," in *Alfred Hitchcock's Mystery Magazine* (North Palm Beach, Florida), March 1973.
"Happiness Before Death," in *Alfred Hitchcock's Mystery Magazine* (North Palm Beach, Florida), 1973.
"The Memory Expert," in *Alfred Hitchcock's Mystery Magazine* (North Palm Beach, Florida), 1973.
"The Seersucker Heart," in *Alfred Hitchcock's Mystery Magazine* (North Palm Beach, Florida), February 1974.
"The Haunted Man," in *Ellery Queen's Mystery Magazine* (New York), April 1974.
"The Poisoned Pawn," in *Alfred Hitchcock's Mystery Magazine* (North Palm Beach, Florida), June 1974.
"The Kidnappers," in *Ellery Queen's Mystery Magazine* (New York), 1974.
"Hiding Out," in *Alfred Hitchcock's Mystery Magazine* (New York), March 1976.
"Sea Change," in *Alfred Hitchcock's Tales to Scare You Stiff*, edited by Eleanor Sullivan. New York, Davis, 1978.
"The Kindest Man in the World," in *Ellery Queen's Mystery Magazine* (New York), July 1979.

OTHER PUBLICATIONS

Plays

Screenplays: *Two on a Guillotine*, with John Kneubuhl, 1965; *Murders in Rue Morgue*, with Christopher Wilding, 1970.

Radio Plays: *CBS Radio Mystery Theatre* (39 plays).

Television Plays: *The Edge of Night* series, 1968–79; 100 scripts to other shows.

*   *   *

Henry Slesar, when not creating ads at Slesar and Manuela Inc., writes fiction. Slesar's ability to delight his readers is exemplified throughout his work: in *Enter Murderers*, in which he concludes his story by littering the stage with corpses; in *The Bridge of Lions*, in which he cleverly combines foreign travel, espionage, chemical secrets, and beautiful women; and in his ingenious Janus Mystery Jigsaw Puzzle No. 1, *The Case of the Snoring Skinflint*, and No. 2, *The Case of the Shaky Showman*, a perplexing locked-room problem and a hilarious whodunit respectively, in which Slesar cunningly makes the puzzlemakers fit the pieces of the mysteries together. Moreover, Slesar has written at least 500 short stories, novelettes, and novels in magazines; several motion pictures; and many plays for radio and television.

Although it is his first novel, *The Gray Flannel Shroud* shows how Slesar typically entertains his readers: in this book Slesar combines the detective and the crime story with romance. The novel presents legitimate clues, colorless yet sympathetic suspects, and a puzzle – who killed Bob Bernstein, the friendly photographer, Anne Gander, the "voluptuous" model, and Willie Shenk, the "pretty boy" thug. However, Dave Robbins, an ad-man turned amateur sleuth, is hardly detective fiction's stock brilliant bloodhound: sidetracked from the clues by his personal involvement in the Burke Baby Foods Account, Dave ponders what would make a silver-haired, paunchy businessman commit murder, but with the help of Max Theringer, a journalistic crime reporter, Dave stumbles into the real culprit. Even though the criminal's motive becomes an executive's moral (Dave says the real crime is loving money and never earning a cent of it), and the mystery is interspersed with somewhat irrelevant scenes of seduction, *The Gray Flannel Shroud* ends satisfactorily: Dave gets the murderer, and the girl.

Similarly, *The Thing at the Door*, Slesar's last and perhaps most popular mystery, is not without the typical trappings of crime fiction: a clue, a sinister murderer, a motive, and an investigator. Slesar quickly reveals the clue to "the thing," the murderer, and the motive. Slesar's self-employed private eye, Steve Tyner, works hard to solve the conspiracy, but in Slesar's fictional method the reader is usually one step ahead of the hero. The reader thus plays an active role in the book, beginning in the opening pages when Cousin Piers compels the horror-stricken child, Gail Gunnerson, to look upon the ugly man in black, the "thing." Slesar builds his story around Piers's terrorizing Gail with two staged suicides, one bloody murder, many cruel innuendos, and too many hallucinative drugs. And he concludes his mystery with Piers forcing his 24-year-old cousin into her bedroom for her to see "the thing at her door," in effect pushing her back into a mental institution. In *The Thing at the Door* Slesar skillfully unravels a psychological drama of suspense – will Gail, the pretty heiress, remain sane? Or will the villain drive her insane?

Slesar's mystery fiction may fail to appeal to readers looking for an intellectual solution to a complex puzzle; his is not the classical formula. But his works will please those who enjoy a mixture of detection, popular psychology, gothic horror, and romance.

—Frances McConachie

SMITH, Shelley. Pseudonym for Nancy Hermione Bodington, née Courlander. British. Born in Richmond, Surrey, 12 July 1912. Educated at Cours Maintenon, Cannes, 1926; College Femina, Paris, 1928; the Sorbonne, Paris, 1929–31. Married Stephen Bodington in 1933 (divorced, 1938). Agent: McIntosh and Otis Inc., 475 Fifth Avenue, New York, New York 10017, U.S.A. Address: Old Orchard, Steyning, Sussex, England.

Novels (series character: Jacob Chaos)

Background for Murder (Chaos).   London, Swan, 1942.
Death Stalks a Lady.   London, Swan, 1945.
This Is the House.   London, Collins, 1945.
Come and Be Killed!   London, Collins, 1946; New York, Harper, 1947.
He Died of Murder! (Chaos).   London, Collins, 1947; New York, Harper, 1948.
The Woman in the Sea.   London, Collins, and New York, Harper, 1948.
Man with a Calico Face.   New York, Harper, 1950; London, Collins, 1951.
Man Alone.   London, Collins, 1952; as *The Crooked Man*, New York, Harper, 1952.
An Afternoon to Kill.   London, Collins, 1953; New York, Harper, 1954.
The Party at No. 5.   London, Collins, 1954; as *The Cellar at No. 5*, New York, Harper, 1954.
The Lord Have Mercy.   London, Hamish Hamilton, 1956; as *The Shrew Is Dead*, New York, Dell, 1959.
The Ballad of the Running Man.   London, Hamish Hamilton, 1961; New York, Harper, 1962.
A Grave Affair.   London, Hamish Hamilton, 1971; New York, Doubleday, 1973.
A Game of Consequences.   London, Macmillan, 1978.

Short Stories

Rachel Weeping: A Triptych.   London, Hamish Hamilton, and New York, Harper, 1957.

OTHER PUBLICATIONS as Nancy Bodington

Short Stories

How Many Miles to Babylon?   London and New York, Wingate, 1950.

Play

Screenplay: *Tiger Bay*, with John Hawkesworth, 1959.

Shelley Smith comments:
I began by writing whodunits but soon moved away from the formula to a type of story that was more a study of the psychology of the criminal and the situation which leads to crime. Even this sounds to me rather pretentious for what are really entertainments. I would add, for the benefit of those who have never come across my work, that I have never followed a pattern or formula and each book is quite distinct in form and story from the others. The reader who likes the same story repeated with variations (made recognisable by the same cosy protagonist) will, I fear, be disappointed with Shelley Smith. But I hope the books will satisfy those who look for something more penetrating.

*   *   *

The unattached, jobless, and friendless; these are some of the people used by Shelley Smith to populate her mysteries. Sometimes the individual is so completely alone or separated from family or friends that no one can be aware of his distress until it is far too late (*Come and Be Killed!*); and even when there is a family, it is often too far-removed or too unconcerned to provide any help. In *The Party at No. 5* a daughter's interference forces an elderly eccentric to take in a lodger that she does not want which leads to immediate and fatal troubles. In *The Ballad of the Running Man* it is the lack of social commitments, moral principles, and a sense of purpose in life that leads to insurance frauds and inevitable disaster. In *Man Alone*, Shelley Smith, like many other mystery writers, uses a true crime case. Thomas Bates has many of the qualities of George Joseph Smith and uses more-or-less the same methods.

Few of these characters, victims or murderers, are particularly attractive but all of them are interesting, perhaps in some of the cases due to their total lack of moral decay: if you are rotten how can you possibly deteriorate? The victims are sometimes so pathetic that they entirely fail to be likeable; in the Bates murders, the potential brides are so eager to run to their fates that it becomes impossible to sympathise with them. A great many of these mysteries are set at the end of World War II, when the age of the extended family was over forever and the new society of casual living conditions and transient renters started to take over many communities. The messes that the Smith characters make of their lives are nearly always entirely their own fault and the reader is able to enjoy watching them destroy themselves with a sense of excitement and enjoyment that is unencumbered by any regrets. Both the clever and the gullible are manipulated by the determined who, in their turn, are ruled either by other stronger minds or by circumstances.

Perhaps the most interesting of these novels is *An Afternoon to Kill* where the fraud is actually perpetrated upon the reader; even the most voracious mystery fan, relying on a lifetime of homicidal experiences, will fail to arrive at the true results beforehand. As in so many mystery novels, unhappy human relationships provide a greater part of the drama than does any craving for money or property. *Man with a Calico Face* and *The Lord Have Mercy* deal with situations that are repeated regularly in life; marriages that do not work, or greed for the possessions of someone else. Sometimes her characters seem to be totally detached from their guilt, not exactly amoral, but with a sense that anything is right so long as it is for their own advantage. In *Man Alone* Bates feels a tremendous sense of relief when he is cleared of causing the death of a mentally disturbed wife, without having any sense of guilt about marrying her to control her money. He feels it is most unjust when past murders are brought up against him and seems to feel that they should have been forgotten, having happened a while back.

In each of her books Shelley Smith produces a tense, interesting, and compact mystery. She well deserves the success she has achieved.

—Mary Groff

SOMERS, Paul. See GARVE, Andrew.

SPAIN, John. See ADAMS, Cleve F.

SPICER, Bart. Also writes as Jay Barbette (with Betty Coe Spicer). American. Born in Virginia in 1918. Served in the United States Army in World War II: Captain. Journalist: worked for Scripps-Howard Syndicate and as a radio news writer; after the war worked in public relations for Universal Military Training, 3 years, and World Affairs Council, 1 year.

CRIME PUBLICATIONS

Novels (series character: Carney Wilde)

The Dark Light (Wilde). New York, Dodd Mead, 1949; London, Collins, 1950.
Blues for the Prince (Wilde). New York, Dodd Mead, 1950; London, Collins, 1951.
The Golden Door (Wilde). New York, Dodd Mead, and London, Collins, 1951.
Black Sheep, Run (Wilde). New York, Dodd Mead, 1951; London, Collins, 1952.
The Long Green (Wilde). New York, Dodd Mead, 1952; as Shadow of Fear, London, Collins, 1953.
The Taming of Carney Wilde. New York, Dodd Mead, 1954; London, Hodder and Stoughton, 1955.
The Day of the Dead. New York, Dodd Mead, 1955; London, Hodder and Stoughton, 1956.
Exit, Running (Wilde). New York, Dodd Mead, 1959; London, Hodder and Stoughton, 1960.
Act of Anger. New York, Atheneum, 1962; London, Barker, 1963.
The Burned Man. New York, Atheneum, 1966; London, Hale, 1967.
Kellogg Junction. New York, Atheneum, 1969; London, Hodder and Stoughton, 1970.
The Adversary. New York, Putnam, and London, Hart Davis MacGibbon, 1974.

Novels as Jay Barbette

Final Copy. New York, Dodd Mead, 1950; London, Barker, 1952.
Dear Dead Days. New York, Dodd Mead, 1953; London, Barker, 1954; as Death's Long Shadow, New York, Bantam, 1955.
The Deadly Doll. New York, Dodd Mead, 1958; London, Long, 1959.
Look Behind You. New York, Dodd Mead, 1960; London, Long, 1961.

OTHER PUBLICATIONS

Novels

The Wild Ohio. New York, Dodd Mead, and London, Hodder and Stoughton, 1954.
The Tall Captains. New York, Dodd Mead, 1957.
Brother to the Enemy. New York, Dodd Mead, 1958; London, Hodder and Stoughton, 1959.
The Day Before Thunder. New York, Dodd Mead, 1960.
Festival. New York, Atheneum, 1970.

*   *   *

Bart Spicer has had two distinct writing careers. The first, beginning with *The Dark Light* in 1949, was as a hard-boiled series writer of great distinction. *Act of Anger*, published in 1962, marks the beginning of the second phase of his work, in which he abandoned strict genre material, and turned to writing books which, while strong in crime and suspense elements, are clearly aimed at the bestseller market rather than the specialized mystery readership.

The seven mysteries which feature Spicer's private-eye hero, Carney Wilde, neatly span the 1950's; and that period was the great decade of the series hard-boiled dick, with the paperback explosion and the Mickey Spillane phenomenon. Spicer's Wilde tales are among the very best private-eye novels of that or any decade, and it is regrettable that they have been largely ignored in the recent spate of private-eye criticism of what Michael Avallone has called the "Father, Son and Holy Ghost" school (i.e., concentration on the works of Hammett, Chandler, and Ross Macdonald to the exclusion of practically everyone else). The Wilde books are beautifully crafted. Spicer's plotting is coherent, with credible twists and surprises; his style strikes a satisfying balance between the telegraphic and the over-ripe; he writes convincing dialogue and makes imaginative use of the "hard-boiled simile." Wilde himself is an admirable, believeable hero, not the formularized caricature that can be found in too many tough-guy series of the period. Wilde's first-person narration flows smoothly, steering clear of both excessive wisecrackery and windy philosophizing. The secondary characters, continuing and otherwise, are varied and interesting (Spicer's treatment of the cops, and Wilde's relations with them, is particularly good), and the settings are fresh. Wilde is based in Philadelphia (a welcome respite from Los Angeles and New York), but travels to Arizona in *The Long Green* and down the Mississippi in *The Taming of Carney Wilde*. *Blues for the Prince*, one of the best of the series, draws on Spicer's own passion for New Orleans jazz.

During the 1950's Spicer also wrote several non-Wilde mysteries: four collaborative works with his wife, Betty Coe Spicer, under the pseudonym Jay Barbette; and *The Day of the Dead*, a fast-paced spy novel set in Mexico. Spicer's books of the 1960's and 1970's mark a clear break with the insular world of straight genre fiction, reflecting the simultaneous decline in the popularity of the private-eye novel (he made the break decisive by gracefully "retiring" Carney Wilde to marriage and a less strenuous occupation in *Exit, Running*). *Act of Anger* and *The Adversary* are both courtroom dramas, powerfully written, rich in detail and characterization. *The Burned Man* is a vigorous, complex espionage novel, unmarred by post-Bondian cliché. *Kellogg Junction* concerns the effects of a campaign to legalize gambling in a corrupt town. These novels are fundamentally different from the Wilde books in market orientation, but they are nevertheless tales of crime and suspense; and they share with the earlier work the fine prose style, sharp eye for detail and characterization, and overall high marks as fictional entertainment.

—Art Scott

SPILLANE, Mickey (Frank Morrison Spillane). American. Born in Brooklyn, New York, 9 March 1918. Attended Kansas State University, Manhattan. Served in the United States Army Air Force during World War II. Married 1) Mary Spillane c. 1944 (divorced, 1962); four children; 2) Sherri Spillane in 1965. Began selling stories in 1935; wrote for the comic books *Captain Marvel*, *Captain America*, and others; trampoline artist, Ringling Brothers Barnum and Bailey Circus; Founder, with Robert Fellows, Spillane-Fellows Productions (films). Address: 225 East 57th Street, New York, New York 10022, U.S.A.

CRIME PUBLICATIONS

Novels (series characters: Mike Hammer; Tiger Mann)

I, The Jury (Hammer). New York, Dutton, 1947; London, Barker, 1952.

My Gun Is Quick (Hammer).   New York, Dutton, 1950; London, Barker, 1951.
Vengeance Is Mine! (Hammer).   New York, Dutton, 1950; London, Barker, 1951.
The Big Kill (Hammer).   New York, Dutton, 1951; London, Barker, 1952.
The Long Wait.   New York, Dutton, 1951; London, Barker, 1953.
One Lonely Night (Hammer).   New York, Dutton, 1951; London, Barker, 1952.
Kiss Me, Deadly (Hammer).   New York, Dutton, 1952; London, Barker, 1953.
The Deep.   New York, Dutton, and London, Barker, 1961.
The Girl Hunters (Hammer).   New York, Dutton, and London, Barker, 1962.
Me, Hood! (novelets).   London, Corgi, 1963.
Day of the Guns (Mann).   New York, Dutton, 1964; London, Barker, 1965.
The Flier (novelets).   London, Corgi, 1964.
Return of the Hood (novelets).   London, Corgi, 1964.
The Snake (Hammer).   New York, Dutton, and London, Barker, 1964.
Bloody Sunrise (Mann).   New York, Dutton, and London, Barker, 1965.
The Death Dealers (Mann).   New York, Dutton, 1965; London, Barker, 1966.
Killer Mine (novelets).   London, Corgi, 1965; New York, New American Library, 1968.
The By-Pass Control (Mann).   New York, Dutton, 1966; London, Barker, 1967.
The Twisted Thing (Hammer).   New York, Dutton, and London, Barker, 1966.
The Body Lovers (Hammer).   New York, Dutton, and London, Barker, 1967.
The Delta Factor.   New York, Dutton, 1967; London, Corgi, 1969.
Me, Hood! (novelets; different book from previous title).   New York, New American Library, 1969.
The Tough Guys (novelets).   New York, New American Library, 1969.
Survival ... Zero! (Hammer).   New York, Dutton, and London, Corgi, 1970.
The Erection Set.   New York, Dutton, and London, W. H. Allen, 1972.
The Last Cop Out.   New York, Dutton, and London, W. H. Allen, 1973.

Uncollected Short Stories

"The Veiled Woman," in *Fantastic* (New York), November 1952.
"Everybody's Watching Me" (novelet), in *Manhunt* (New York), January–April 1953.
"The Girl Behind the Hedge," in *Manhunt* (New York), October 1953.
"The Pickpocket," in *Manhunt* (New York), December 1954.
"Stand Up and Die," in *Cavalier* (New York), June 1958.
"I'll Die Tomorrow," in *Cavalier* (New York), March 1960.
"Tomorrow I Die," in *Cavalier* (New York), 1960.
"The Lady Says Die," in *Bizarre* (New York), January 1966.
"The Gold Fever Tapes," in *Stag Annual* (New York), 1973.

Play

Screenplay: *The Girl Hunters*, with Roy Rowland and Robert Fellows, 1963.

Theatrical Activities:

Actor: **Films** – *Ring of Fear*, 1953; *The Girl Hunters*, 1963. **Television** – *Colombo* series, 1973.

*   *   *

Mickey Spillane was the most popular American novelist (not just mystery or detective novelist) of the 1950's. His popularity was based primarily upon the creation of Mike Hammer, courageous, loyal, patriotic, much more intelligent than critics have generally allowed, but above all else *tough*. Hammer's career as a private eye and Spillane's as a novelist began together with *I, The Jury*, the first mystery to exceed 6 million sales in the United States. For a decade or more Spillane himself, with his next six books (five of them further adventures of Hammer), provided the only serious sales competition for that first book.

The plots of the Hammer books deal, of course, with murder, almost always to cover up some other crime, or to protect the murderer from some danger. In *I, The Jury*, murder was motivated by the fear of the highly respectable murderer of exposure as a trafficker in drugs. Blackmailers killed to protect their lucrative rackets in *Vengeance Is Mine!* and *The Big Kill*. Organized crime, a prostitution ring, and the Mafia killed for protection in *My Gun Is Quick* and *Kiss Me, Deadly*. In *One Lonely Night*, Spillane's least popular and most misunderstood early work, a madman killed to protect a masquerade that he hoped would prevent his return to an institution. Hammer, in every early case, was at least eventually motivated primarily by desire for revenge. Using detection methods highlighted by rough methodology, but never entirely without cerebration, he always achieved it, dispensing a showy rough brand of poetic justice in each book's last chapter.

Spillane's first non-Hammer book was a clever mosaic of clichés – amnesia, physical doubles and deliberate masquerades, mistaken identities, and even a Chandleresque murder long misunderstood. These seven early books which preceded Spillane's first retirement, though they account for less than a third of his total output, represent two-thirds of his sales. They supplied subjects for two-thirds of the Spillane films (four about Hammer and two based on non-series books). Further, critical notice of Spillane (almost uniformly unkind) has been largely confined to them.

"Nothing succeeds like success" is a maxim that has always applied to book publishing, and the mystery field has never pretended to exemption from it. Spillane, with his ease and speed of composition, surely could have achieved an output approaching that of Gardner and Christie. When, instead, he suddenly stopped writing, a legion of facile imitators rushed to supply the market which he had created. John B. West (the Rocky Steel series), Garrity (later J. Dave Gerrity), Carter Brown (an Australian whose sales eventually came close to Spillane's), and Evan Hunter (writing as Curt Cannon) were foremost among those who emulated the Spillane style, stance, and milieu. Richard S. Prather, Stephen Marlow, John D. MacDonald and Michael Avallone first became prominent through copying Spillane, but went on to develop their own strong writing personalities. The paperback suspense novel, especially the paperback original as developed most distinctively by Fawcett and New American Library, may be fairly said to have been inspired by Spillane and his unprecedented popularity. The conservative/reactionary political bias, lack of any considerable puzzle, and dependance upon naked violence to apprehend the guilty – all typical of the form in the 1950's and 1960's – stemmed directly from his example.

A fiercely private person, Spillane has dared to retain more privacy than a less successful writer could afford. Such questions as how much writing preceded his first novel, why he chose to stop writing in the early 1950's, why he began again in the early 1960's, have several possible answers.

His second and most prolific writing period, 1961–67, added four new Hammer adventures to the original six, four novels about a new series character (Tiger Mann, surely the most unusual prominent American spy hero, intended to compete directly with James Bond), two non-series novels, and four books of shorter works published originally in Great Britain. Besides the counter-espionage emphasis in the Tiger Mann books, two of the Hammer novels (*The Girl Hunters* and *The Body Lovers*, the latter xenophobic without being anti-Communist), the non-series novel *The Delta Factor*, and a pair of short works (*The Flyer* and *Return of the Hood*) were responses of one sort or another to the Bond boom.

While the Mann books as a group are rightly regarded as Spillane's weakest effort, all feature memorable surprise ending gimmicks. The first, *Day of the Guns*, is notable for its distinct echoes of *The Long Wait* and *One Lonely Night*, and for its establishment of the series' highly unusual premise, while the last, *The By-Pass Control*, though troubled by unusual wordiness, might have served as a suitable vehicle for Hammer. The two non-spy Hammer books each have unusual qualities. *The Snake* begins precisely where *The Girl Hunters* stops and is thus more closely related to the book before it than any other Hammer story; it is also as good a Raymond Chandler counterfeit as any writer has produced. *The Twisted Thing* is a re-write of *Whom the Gods Would Destroy*, an unpublished early Hammer novel.

The second career saw other frequent repetitions. *The Deep*, which launched it, partially reworked *The Long Wait* and had interesting parallels with "The Bastard Bannerman," "The Seven Year Kill," "Me, Hood!," and "Killer Mine." *The Body Lovers* and "Kick It or Kill" have similar plots and endings. Two shorter works, and "Affair with the Dragon Lady," echo Spillane's aviation background (otherwise glimpsed briefly only in *The By-Pass Control*). "Dragon Lady" is particularly nostalgic, and displays the writer's sense of humor more fully than anything since Chapter 2 of *I, The Jury.*

Spillane's third period, 1970–73, was his least prolific, but certainly his most experimental. This began with *Survival ... Zero!* which is a thus-far final outing for Hammer in what could have been a very strong Tiger Mann counterspy adventure. Then in *The Erection Set*, which the writer publicized as an attempt to counter the immense popularity of such writers as Jacqueline Susann with "an even dirtier book than these women writers'," he experimented with occasional passages told in third-person, something he had done before under his own name only in a few short stories in *Cavalier* magazine. Finally, he produced *The Last Cop Out*, written entirely in third-person, in an apparent response to the many very popular (and ultimately imitative of Spillane's *Kiss Me, Deadly*) Mafia books by such writers as Don Pendleton.

—Jeff Banks

SPRIGG, Christopher St. John. Also wrote as Christopher Caudwell. British. Born in Putney, London, 20 October 1907. Educated at Ealing Priory School (Benedictine), London. Worked for the *Yorkshire Post* and later as editor of *British Malaya*. Formed as aeronautical publishing company and published designs in *Automobile Engineer*; Founder, *Aircraft Engineering*. Joined the Communist Party in 1935 (Poplar Branch) and the International Brigade (British Battalion) in 1936. *Killed in the battle of Jarama River, Spain, 12 February 1937.*

CRIME PUBLICATIONS

Novels (series character: Charles Venables)

Crime in Kensington. London, Eldon Press, 1933; as *Pass the Body*, New York, Dial Press, 1933.
Fatality in Fleet Street (Venables). London, Eldon Press, 1933.
The Perfect Alibi (Venables). London, Eldon Press, and New York, Doubleday, 1934.
Death of an Airman. London, Hutchinson, 1934; New York, Doubleday, 1935.
Death of a Queen (Venables). London, Nelson, 1935.
The Corpse with the Sunburnt Face. London, Nelson, and New York, Doubleday, 1935.
The Six Queer Things. London, Jenkins, and New York, Doublday, 1937.

OTHER PUBLICATIONS as Christopher Caudwell

Novel

   This My Hand.   London, Hamish Hamilton, 1936.

Verse

   Poems.   London, Lane, 1939.

Other

   The Airship: Its Design, History, Operation, and Future.   London, Sampson Low, 1931.
   Fly with Me: An Elementary Textbook on the Art of Piloting, with Henry D.
      Davis.   London, John Hamilton, 1932.
   British Airways (juvenile).   London and New York, Nelson, 1934.
   Great Flights.   London, Nelson, 1935.
   Let's Learn to Fly.   London, Nelson, 1937.
   Illusion and Reality: A Study of the Sources of History.   London, Macmillan, 1937;
      New York, International Publishers, 1947.
   Studies in a Dying Culture.   London, Lane, and New York, Dodd Mead, 1938.
   The Crisis in Physics, edited by H. Levy.   London, Lane, 1939; New York, Dodd Mead,
      1951.
   Further Studies in a Dying Culture, edited by Edgell Rickword.   London, Lane, 1949;
      New York, Dodd Mead, 1951.
   The Concept of Freedom, edited by George Thomson.   London, Lawrence and Wishart,
      1965.
   Romance and Realism: A Study in English Bourgeois Literature, edited by Samuel
      Hynes.   Princeton, New Jersey, Princeton University Press, 1970.
   The Breath of Discontent: A Study in Bourgeois Religion.   New York, Oriole Editions,
      n.d.
   Consciousness: A Study in Bourgeois Psychology.   New York, Oriole Editions, n.d.
   Liberty: A Study in Bourgeois Illusion.   New York, Oriole Editions, n.d.
   Pacificism and Violence: A Study in Bourgeois Ethics.   New York, Oriole Editions, n.d.
   Men and Nature: A Study in Bourgeois History.   New York, Oriole Editions, n.d.
   Reality: A Study in Bourgeois Philosophy.   New York, Oriole Editions, n.d.

   Editor, *Uncanny Stories.*   London, Nelson, 1936.

                              *   *   *

It is common enough for a writer to produce detective novels under a pseudonym while reserving his real name for more serious work. Christopher St. John Sprigg, however, published his seven detective novels under his own name and used the pseudonym Christopher Caudwell for his book on physics and his Marxist writings. The conjunction of detective fiction and Marxism is both surprising and suggestive, but for the most part Sprigg's detective stories are no more innovative or radical than those of left-wing contemporaries like C. Day Lewis or G. D. H. and Margaret Cole. Marxism was Sprigg's avocation; detective fiction was his way of paying the rent.

Death of an Airman is typical of the creditable but not very distinguished nature of Sprigg's work. The atmosphere is light-hearted, the characters mostly comic, and the solution suitably ingenious: a murderous stuntman falsifies the time and circumstances of his victim's death by faking an aeroplane crash. Most of these ingredients, together with Sprigg's favourite detective combination of fallible policeman and enthusiastic amateur, appear in several other novels. *Crime in Kensington* is especially notable for the deft way in which its setting, a shady private hotel, is evoked.

Less conventional elements appear in two novels. *The Corpse with the Sunburnt Face* contains a sketchy but powerful rendition of the hero's reactions when drugged. In *The Six Queer Things* the heroine is the victim of a nearly successful conspiracy to drive her insane. Sprigg's other work shows him to be well versed in Freud, Jung, and Adler, and had he lived this interest in abnormal psychological states, unusual for a detective novelist of his generation, would probably have been developed further.

—Ian Ousby

STAGGE, Jonathan. See **QUENTIN, Patrick.**

STANTON, Vance. See **AVALLONE, Michael.**

STARK, Richard. See **WESTLAKE, Donald E.**

STARRETT, (Charles) Vincent (Emerson). American. Born in Toronto, Canada, 26 October 1886. Educated in public schools in Chicago. Journalist: with Chicago *Inter-Ocean*, 1905–06, and Chicago *Daily News*, 1906–16 (war correspondent in Mexico 1914–15); Editor, *The Wave* magazine, 1921–22; taught writing at Northwestern University, Evanston, Illinois; columnist, "Books Alive," Chicago *Tribune*, 1942–74. Co-founder, with Christopher Morley, Baker Street Irregulars; President, Society of Midland Authors; President, Mystery Writers of America, 1961. Recipient: Mystery Writers of America Grand Master Award, 1957. *Died 4 January 1974.*

CRIME PUBLICATIONS

Novels (series characters: Riley Blackwood; Walter Ghost)

Murder on "B" Deck (Ghost). New York, Doubleday, 1929; Kingswood, Surrey, World's Work, 1936.
Dead Man Inside (Ghost). New York, Doubleday, 1931; Kingswood, Surrey, World's Work, 1935.
The End of Mr. Garment (Ghost). New York, Doubleday, 1932.
The Great Hotel Murder (Blackwood). New York, Doubleday, and London, Nicholson and Watson, 1935.
Midnight and Percy Jones (Blackwood). New York, Covici Friede, 1936; London, Nicholson and Watson, 1938.
The Laughing Buddha. Mount Morris, Illinois, Magna, 1937; as *Murder in Peking*, New York, Lantern Press, 1946; London, Edwards, 1947.

Short Stories

The Unique Hamlet: A Hitherto Unchronicled Adventure of Mr. Sherlock Holmes. Privately printed, 1920.
Coffins for Two. Chicago, Covici McGee, 1924.
The Blue Door. New York, Doubleday, 1930.
The Case Book of Jimmie Lavender. New York, Fawcett, 1944.
The Quick and the Dead. Sauk City, Wisconsin, Arkham House, 1965.

Uncollected Short Stories

"Fog over Hong Kong," in *Fourth Mystery Companion*, edited by Abraham Louis Furman. New York, Lantern Press, 1946.
"The Day of the Cripples," in *The Saint* (New York), October 1956.
"The Tragedy of Papa Ponsard," in *Ellery Queen's Mystery Magazine* (New York), January 1959.
"Man in Hiding," in *Ellery Queen's Mystery Magazine* (New York), December 1964.
"Crazy Like a Fox," in *Anthology 1965*, edited by Ellery Queen. New York, Davis, 1964.
"The Eleventh Juror," in *Rogues' Gallery*, edited by Walter B. Gibson. New York, Doubleday, 1969.

OTHER PUBLICATIONS

Novel

Seaports in the Moon: A Fantasia on Romantic Themes. New York, Doubleday, 1928.

Short Stories

Snow for Christmas. Privately printed, 1935.

Verse

Rhymes for Collectors. Privately printed, 1921.
Ebony Flame. Chicago, Covici McGee, 1922.
Banners in the Dawn: Sixty-Four Sonnets. Chicago, Hill, 1923.
Flames and Dust. Chicago, Covici McGee, 1924.
Fifteen More Poems. Privately printed, 1927.

Other

Autolycus in Limbo.   New York, Dutton, 1943.
Sonnets and Other Verse.   Chicago, Dierkes Press, 1949.

Arthur Machen: A Novelist of Ecstasy and Sin.   Chicago, Hill, 1918.
The Escape of Alice: A Christmas Fantasy.   Privately printed, 1919.
Ambrose Bierce.   Chicago, Hill, 1920.
A Student of Catalogues.   Privately printed, 1921.
Stephen Crane: A Bibliography.   Philadelphia, Centaur Book Shop, 1923.
Buried Caesars: Essays in Literary Appreciation.   Chicago, Covici McGee, 1923.
Ambrose Bierce: A Bibliography.   Philadelphia, Centaur Book Shop, 1929.
Penny Wise and Book Foolish.   New York, Covici Friede, 1929.
All About Mother Goose.   Privately printed, 1930.
The Private Life of Sherlock Holmes.   New York, Macmillan, 1933; London, Nicholson and Watson, 1934; revised edition, Chicago, University of Chicago Press, 1960; London, Allen and Unwin, 1961.
Persons from Porlock (essays).   Chicago, Normandie House, 1938.
Oriental Encounter: Two Essays in Bad Taste.   Chicago, Normandie House, 1938.
Books Alive.   New York, Random House, 1940.
Bookman's Holiday: The Private Satisfactions of an Incurable Collector.   New York, Random House, 1942.
Books and Bipeds.   New York, Argus, 1947.
Stephen Crane: A Bibliography, with Ames W. Williams.   Glendale, California, J. Valentine, 1948.
Best Loved Books of the Twentieth Century.   New York, Bantam, 1955.
The Great All-Star Animal League Ball Game (juvenile).   New York, Dodd Mead, 1957.
Book Column.   New York, Caxton Club, 1958.
Born in a Bookshop: Chapters from the Chicago Renascence (autobiography).   Norman, University of Oklahoma Press, 1965.
Late, Later and Possibly Last: Essays.   St. Louis, Autolycus Press, 1973.
Sincerely Tony/Faithfully Vincent: The Correspondence of Anthony Boucher and Vincent Starrett, edited by Robert W. Hahn.   Chicago, Catullus Press, 1975.

Editor, *In Praise of Stevenson.*   Chicago, Bookfellows, 1919.
Editor, *Men, Women and Boats*, by Stephen Crane.   New York, Boni and Liveright, 1921.
Editor, *The Shining Pyramids*, by Arthur Machen.   Chicago, Covici McGee, 1923.
Editor, *The Glorious Mystery*, by Arthur Machen.   Chicago, Covici McGee, 1924.
Editor, *Et Cetera: A Collector's Scrap Book.*   Chicago, Covici McGee, 1924.
Editor, *Sins of the Fathers and Other Tales*, by George Gissing.   Chicago, Pascal Covici, 1924.
Editor, *Fourteen Great Detective Stories.*   New York, Modern Library, 1928.
Editor, *Maggie, A Girl of the Streets, and Other Stories*, by Stephen Crane.   New York, Modern Library, 1933.
Editor, *A Modern Book of Wonders: Amazing Facts in a Remarkable World.*   Chicago, University of Knowledge, 1938.
Editor, with others, *221B: Studies in Sherlock Holmes.*   New York, Macmillan, 1940.
Editor, *The Mystery of Edwin Drood*, by Charles Dickens.   New York, Heritage Press, 1941.

Editor, *World's Great Spy Stories.*   Cleveland, World, 1944.
Editor, *The Moonstone*, by Wilkie Collins.   New York, Limited Editions Club, 1959.

*   *   *

Journalist, teacher, poet, scholar of detective fiction in general and Sherlock Holmes in particular, mystery writer, respected bibliophile – Vincent Starrett was among the more versatile talents to grace the world of detective fiction. His major contributions to the mystery genre are his Sherlock Holmes writings, with his remarkable *The Private Life of Sherlock Holmes* the first biographical study of a fictional detective hero. This book collects many earlier Starrett essays on Holmes, adds a few new ones, and becomes a compendium of Sherlockiana. Starrett's written contributions go beyond his Holmes scholarship: he has also written what is generally considered the best Holmes pastiche, *The Unique Hamlet*. This story, detailing Holmes's search for a missing inscribed first edition of Shakespeare's famous tragedy, is not only a masterful Sherlockian burlesque – it is also an amusing satire on both book collecting and Shakespeare scholars. Starrett also advanced Sherlockiana significantly as a founding father of the Baker Street Irregulars.

For his own mystery fiction, Starrett enjoys a reputation as a deft creator of plots, often in the Holmes tradition of the intriguing puzzle and often showing Poe's influence as well. Starrett was neither a particularly effective nor a consistent creator of characters: his best-known series detective, Chicagoan Jimmie Lavender, was named for a fair-to-good Chicago Cubs pitcher of the 1910's, and in his earliest of about 50 appearances in print, the Lavender is noteworthy chiefly for his two different colored eyes, a physical quirk which Starrett later eliminates altogether. The best of the Lavender stories were collected as the *Case Book* in 1944.

Murder on "B" Deck, his first longer mystery, was highly acclaimed critically; though it began as a Lavender book, it became in the writing process a vehicle for another series hero, the amateur sleuth Walter Ghost, who solves the murder of the exotic Countess Fogartini aboard the *Latakia* by awaiting the answers to several cablegrams; his companion Mollock, a Watson, seems simply inept – a good example both of the Holmes influence and of Starrett's comparative weakness at characterization. *The Great Hotel Murder* appeared first in serialized form, then as a novel, and finally as a film – although the movie is so unlike its source that Starrett admits (in his autobiography) that "Nobody was more surprised than the author by the revelation of the killer's identity." This story also follows the Holmes-Watson formula, as a hotel detective and a drama critic work together to solve the murder of a hotel guest.

Two other important Starrett publications are short-story collections, *The Blue Door* and *The Quick and the Dead*. The former is notable for the presence of Jimmie Lavender in two of its ten stories and for the introduction of the bibliophile and amateur sleuth G. Washington Troxell, who unfortunately appears in only a few scattered tales. This volume also includes a justly celebrated fictional rendering of the Oscar Slater case entitled "Too Many Sleuths." *The Quick and the Dead* reveals fully his debt to Poe: Poe's interest in popular pseudo-sciences is reflected in "The Elixir of Death" in which an undertaker and his assistant discover a potion which will banish death and in "The Tattooed Man" in which a doctor tries to discover ways to eliminate some rather bizarre tattoos. Also derived from Poe are the device of burial alive and the repeated insistence on the greatest of all human fears – the inexplicable failure to perceive exactly what it is that so frightens. Throughout the book, irony and clever plotting provide strength: "The Head of Cromwell" follows the adventures of Cromwell's skull, which finally becomes an "excellent tobacco jar"; in "Footsteps of Fear" a man commits the perfect murder, but is pursued by fear of discovery, so when the police arrive he conceals himself in what proves to be a self-locking trunk – the policemen depart disappointed, unable to sell their benefit tickets, and the murderer suffocates.

Starrett's reading of Chinese fiction is also noteworthy; in his 1942 essay, "Some Chinese Detective Stories," Starrett introduced many Westerners to such famous figures as Judge Dee and Magistrate Pao. As always, Starrett's critical perceptions were acute and his judgments sound.

Starrett was a bookman's bookman: in his autobiography, Starrett borrows Eugene Field's neologism to label himself a "Dofab" – a "damned old fool about books." He was a studious critic and reviewer of detective literature. And he contributed substantively to the library of mystery fiction. But his greatest achievements and his ultimate reputation rest upon his eminence as an imaginative Sherlock Holmes reader and scholar.

—Elmer Pry

STEELE, Curtis. See **DAVIS, Frederick C.**

STEIN, Aaron Marc. Also writes as George Bagby; Hampton Stone. American. Born in New York City, 15 November 1906. Educated at Ethical Culture School, New York, 1916–23; Princeton University, New Jersey, A.B. (summa cum laude) 1927 (Phi Beta Kappa). Served in the United States Army, 1943–45. Critic and Columnist, New York *Evening Post*, 1927–38; Editor, *Time*, New York City, 1938. Since 1939 free-lance writer. Past President, Mystery Writers of America. Recipient: Mystery Writers of America Grand Master Award, 1979. Agent: H. N. Swanson Inc., 8523 Sunset Boulevard, Los Angeles, California 90069. Address: 1070 Park Avenue, Apartment 4D, New York, New York 10028, U.S.A.

CRIME PUBLICATIONS

Novels (series characters: Matt Erridge; Tim Mulligan and Elsie Mae Hunt)

The Sun Is a Witness (Mulligan and Hunt). New York, Doubleday, 1940.
Up to No Good (Mulligan and Hunt). New York, Doubleday, 1941.
Only the Guilty (Mulligan and Hunt). New York, Doubleday, 1942.
The Case of the Absent-Minded Professor (Mulligan and Hunt). New York, Doubleday, 1943.
... and High Water (Mulligan and Hunt). New York, Doubleday, 1946.
We Saw Him Die (Mulligan and Hunt). New York, Doubleday, 1947.
Death Takes a Paying Guest (Mulligan and Hunt). New York, Doubleday, 1947.
The Cradle and the Grave (Mulligan and Hunt). New York, Doubleday, 1948.
The Second Burial (Mulligan and Hunt). New York, Doubleday, 1949.
Days of Misfortune (Mulligan and Hunt). New York, Doubleday, 1949.
Three – with Blood (Mulligan and Hunt). New York, Doubleday, 1950.
Frightened Amazon (Mulligan and Hunt). New York, Doubleday, 1950.
Shoot Me Dacent (Mulligan and Hunt). New York, Doubleday, 1951; London, Macdonald, 1957.
Pistols for Two (Mulligan and Hunt). New York, Doubleday, 1951.
Mask for Murder (Mulligan and Hunt). New York, Doubleday, 1952.
The Dead Thing in the Pool (Mulligan and Hunt). New York, Doubleday, 1952.

Death Meets 400 Rabbits (Mulligan and Hunt). New York, Doubleday, 1953.

Moonmilk and Murder (Mulligan and Hunt). New York, Doubleday, 1955; London, Macdonald, 1956.

Sitting Up Dead (Erridge). New York, Doubleday, 1958; London, Macdonald, 1959.

Never Need an Enemy (Erridge). New York, Doubleday, 1959; London, Boardman, 1960.

Home and Murder (Erridge). New York, Doubleday, 1962.

Blood on the Stars (Erridge). New York, Doubleday, and London, Hale, 1964.

I Fear the Greeks (Erridge). New York, Doubleday, 1966; as *Executioner's Rest*, London, Hale, 1967.

Deadly Delight (Erridge). New York, Doubleday, 1967; London, Hale, 1969.

Snare Andalucian (Erridge). New York, Doubleday, 1968; as *Faces of Death*, London, Hale, 1968.

Kill Is a Four-Letter Word (Erridge). New York, Doubleday, 1968; London, Hale, 1969.

Alp Murder (Erridge). New York, Doubleday, 1970; London, Hale, 1971.

The Finger (Erridge). New York, Doubleday, 1973; London, Hale, 1974.

Lock and Key. New York, Doubleday, 1973.

Coffin Country (Erridge). New York, Doubleday, and London, Hale, 1976.

Lend Me Your Ears (Erridge). New York, Doubleday, 1977; London, Hale, 1978.

Body Search (Erridge). New York, Doubleday, and London, Hale, 1978.

Nowhere? (Erridge). New York, Doubleday, and London, Hale, 1978.

Chill Factor (Erridge). New York, Doubleday, 1978; London, Hale, 1979.

The Rolling Heads (Erridge). New York, Doubleday, and London, Hale, 1979.

One Dip Dead (Erridge). New York, Doubleday, 1979.

The Cheating Butcher (Erridge). New York, Doubleday, 1980.

Novels as George Bagby (series character: Inspector Schmidt in all books)

Murder at the Piano. New York, Covici Friede, 1935; London, Sampson Low, 1936.

Ring Around a Murder. New York, Covici Friede, 1936.

Murder Half Baked. New York, Covici Friede, 1937; London, Cassell, 1938.

Murder on the Nose. New York, Doubleday, 1938; London, Cassell, 1939.

Bird Walking Weather. New York, Doubleday, 1939; London, Cassell, 1940.

The Corpse with the Purple Thighs. New York, Doubleday, 1939.

The Corpse Wore a Wig. New York, Doubleday, 1940, as *The Bloody Wig Murders*, n.p., Best Detective Selection, 1942.

Here Comes the Corpse. New York, Doubleday, 1941; London, Long, 1943.

Red Is for Killing. New York, Doubleday, 1941; London, Long, 1944.

Murder Calling "50". New York, Doubleday, 1942.

Dead on Arrival. New York, Doubleday, 1946.

The Original Carcase. New York, Doubleday, 1946; London, Aldor, 1947; as *A Body for the Bride*, New York, Spivak, 1954.

The Twin Killing. New York, Doubleday, 1947.

The Starting Gun. New York, Doubleday, 1948.

In Cold Blood. New York, Doubleday, 1948.

Drop Dead. New York, Doubleday, 1949.

Coffin Corner. New York, Doubleday, 1949.

Blood Will Tell. New York, Doubleday, 1950.

Death Ain't Commercial. New York, Doubleday, 1951.

Scared to Death. New York, Doubleday, 1952.

The Corpse with Sticky Fingers. New York, Doubleday, 1952.

Give the Little Corpse a Great Big Hand. New York, Doubleday, 1953; London, Macdonald, 1954; as *A Big Hand for the Corpse*, Roslyn, New York, Detective Book Club, 1953.

Dead Drunk. New York, Doubleday, 1953; London, Macdonald, 1954.
The Body in the Basket. New York, Doubleday, 1954; London, Macdonald, 1956.
A Dirty Way to Die. New York, Doubleday, 1955; London, Macdonald, 1956; as
  Shadow on the Window, Roslyn, New York, Detective Book Club, 1955.
Dead Storage. New York, Doubleday, 1956; London, Boardman, 1959.
Cop Killer. New York, Doubleday, 1956; London, Boardman, 1957.
Dead Wrong. New York, Doubleday, 1957; London, Boardman, 1958.
The Three-Time Losers. New York, Doubleday, and London, Boardman, 1958.
The Real Gone Goose. New York, Doubleday, 1959; London, Boardman, 1960.
Evil Genius. New York, Doubleday, 1961; London, Hammond, 1964.
Murder's Little Helper. New York, Doubleday, 1963; London, Hammond, 1964.
Mysteriouser and Mysteriouser. New York, Doubleday, 1965; as *Murder in
  Wonderland*, London, Hammond, 1965.
Dirty Pool. New York, Doubleday, 1966; as *Bait for Killer*, London, Hammond, 1967.
Corpse Candle. New York, Doubleday, 1967; London, Hale, 1968.
Another Day – Another Death. New York, Doubleday, and London, Hale, 1968.
Honest Reliable Corpse. New York, Doubleday, and London, Hale, 1969.
Killer Boy Was Here. New York, Doubleday, 1970; London, Hale, 1971.
Two in the Bush. New York, Doubleday, and London, Hale, 1976.
Innocent Bystander. New York, Doubleday, 1976; London, Hale, 1978.
My Dead Body. New York, Doubleday, 1976; London, Hale, 1978.
The Tough Get Going. New York, Doubleday, 1977; London, Hale, 1978.
Better Dead. New York, Doubleday, 1978; London, Hale, 1979.
Guaranteed to Fade. New York, Doubleday, 1978.
I Could Have Died. New York, Doubleday, 1979.
Mugger's Day. New York, Doubleday, 1979.

Novels as Hampton Stone (series characters: Jeremiah X. Gibson and Mac in all books)

The Corpse in the Corner Saloon. New York, Simon and Schuster, 1948.
The Girl with the Hole in Her Head. New York, Simon and Schuster, 1949; London,
  Boardman, 1958.
The Needle That Wouldn't Hold Still. New York, Simon and Schuster, 1950; London,
  Boardman, 1958.
The Murder That Wouldn't Stay Solved. New York, Simon and Schuster, 1951.
The Corpse That Refused to Stay Dead. New York, Simon and Schuster, 1952;
  London, Dobson, 1954.
The Corpse Who Had Too Many Friends. New York, Simon and Schuster, 1953;
  London, Foulsham, 1954.
The Man Who Had Too Much to Lose. New York, Simon and Schuster, and London,
  Foulsham, 1955.
The Strangler Who Couldn't Let Go. New York, Simon and Schuster, 1956; as *The
  Strangler*, London, Foulsham, 1957.
The Girl Who Kept Knocking Them Dead. New York, Simon and Schuster and
  London, Foulsham, 1957.
The Man Who Was Three Jumps Ahead. New York, Simon and Schuster, 1959;
  London, Boardman, 1960.
The Man Who Looked Death in the Eye. New York, Simon and Schuster, 1961.
The Babe with the Twistable Arm. New York, Simon and Schuster, 1962; London,
  Hale, 1964.
The Real Serendipitous Kill. New York, Simon and Schuster, 1964.
The Kid Was Last Seen Hanging Ten. New York, Simon and Schuster, 1966.
The Funniest Killer in Town. New York, Simon and Schuster, 1967.
The Corpse Was No Bargain at All. New York, Simon and Schuster, 1968; London,
  Hale, 1969.

The Swinger Who Swung by the Neck. New York, Simon and Schuster, 1970.
The Kid Who Came Home with a Corpse. New York, Simon and Schuster, 1972.

Uncollected Short Stories

"Body Snatcher" (as George Bagby), in *Manhunt* (New York), June 1955.
"Battle of Wits," in *The Saint* (New York), September 1957.
"This Was Willi's Day," in *Best Detective Stories of the Year*, edited by David Coxe
   Cooke. New York, Dutton, 1957.
"A Few Dead Birds" (as George Bagby), in *Ed McBain's Mystery Book* (New York),
   1960.
"The Mourners at the Bedside" (as Hampton Stone), in *Ed McBain's Mystery Book* (New
   York), 1961.
"Stamped and Self-Addressed," in *Ellery Queen's Mystery Magazine* (New York), April
   1979.

OTHER PUBLICATIONS

Novels

Spirals. New York, Covici Friede, 1930.
Her Body Speaks. New York, Covici Friede, 1931.
Bachelor's Wife (as George Bagby). New York, Covici Friede, 1932.

Other

"The Detective Story – How and Why," in *Princeton University Library Bulletin* (New
   Jersey), August 1974.
"Style," in *The Mystery Writer's Handbook*, edited by Lawrence Treat. Cincinnati,
   Writer's Digest, 1976.
"The Mystery Story in Cultural Perspective," in *The Mystery Story*, edited by John
   Ball. San Diego, University of California Extension, 1976.
"A Good Address," in *I, Witness*, edited by Brian Garfield. New York, Times Books,
   1978.

Manuscript Collection: Firestone Library, Princeton University, New Jersey.

Aaron Marc Stein comments:
   I began by writing radical experiments in style, stream-of-consciousness novels. They were
well received by the critics, but they reached only a small audience. Pushed by my publishers
to attempt something that might bring them and me a greater monetary return, I attempted a
popular romance and it was published under the George Bagby pseudonym. I found no
pleasure in writing it and, although its royalties were slightly better than those on the first two
books, the difference was not great enough to induce me to go on with it. At that time I found
myself developing a detective story plot. Why or how it came to me I don't know. One day it
just was there. Published under the Bagby pseudonym, it was a critical and popular success. I
found that I enjoyed writing detective stories and with them I could reach a larger audience
that had an appreciation of what I was doing. It seems to me that, with the possible exception
of science fiction, the mystery story is the only form of fiction which has more than a small,
select audience with any interest in a novelist's technique.

*   *   *

During a period of hospitalization in the 1930's, Aaron Marc Stein ran out of mystery reading material. Like fellow writers S. S. Van Dine and Margaret Millar at similar periods of illness in their lives, he became convinced that he could do as well as any author he had been reading, and in fact he has published almost 100 novels since 1932. He has created three different types of mysteries under as many names. The common element has been the success of each.

As George Bagby, Stein has written a long series of novels about Inspector Schmidt, Chief of Manhattan's Homicide Squad. The books are narrated by a "Watson" named, appropriately, George Bagby whom a publisher assigned to help Schmidt write a book on his experiences. They became friends, and Bagby continued to travel with Schmidt to gather material for additional books. Later, Bagby operated more independently but would get into trouble and have to be rescued by Schmidt. Often he is in danger because of his own senselessness, thus defying the convention that only females in mysteries act that way.

Typical is *The Body in the Basket* in which Bagby becomes involved in the murder of a man in a policeman's uniform at a Spanish hotel. He has contributed, in large measure, to his own predicament by interfering in the arrest of a teen-age thief and then not reporting a beating he receives. In his own version of Had-I-But-Known, Bagby says before acting: "I still can't explain what happened to me.... If I'd had time to think about it I'm certain I never could have carried it off." Yet, this book, one of the most highly regarded of the Bagby series, also shows many of Stein's virtues – e.g., the excellent interweaving of Spanish attitudes (ranging from the fear of Franco's political police down to dining habits) into the plot. The setting of *The Body in the Basket* is exceptional in the Bagby series, most of which are set in New York City. Even nearby New Jersey, the scene of *Corpse Candle*, is atypical, though it is here that Bagby gets in trouble, involved with hippies, before Schmidt rescues him. As Bagby, Stein has always sought characteristic New York City settings. In *The Starting Gun* and *Coffin Corner* he used the local sports scene: a track meet at Madison Square Garden and a football game at Columbia's Baker Field. *Mysteriouser and Mysteriouser* is about a corpse discovered near the Alice in Wonderland statue in Central Park. In *Innocent Bystander* there is a Times Square setting including male homosexuality and pornographic films. In one book, *A Dirty Way to Die*, he even has Schmidt as the victim of a mugging.

The series Stein writes as Hampton Stone is as lively as his Bagby books but more believable and humorous. The heroes of this series are two Manhattan Assistant District Attorneys, Jeremiah X. Gibson and his friend "Mac," narrator of the series. As Stone, Stein also keeps up with the changing scene in New York where he lives. *The Corpse in the Corner Saloon* is about Third Avenue bars. *The Murder That Wouldn't Stay Solved* is about homosexuality and Manhattan hotels. *The Man Who Looked Death in the Eye* deals with Manhattan call girls. Other books feature such diverse settings as the 42nd Street Library in *The Funniest Killer in Town* and boxing at Madison Square Garden in *The Swinger Who Swung by the Neck*. Murder occurs at a Greenwich Village "happening" in *The Real Serendipitous Kill*.

Under his own name, Stein created two series in which he made use of the extensive travelling he has always loved. In 18 books about archeologists Tim Mulligan and Elsie Mae Hunt, Stein has placed them into such locations as France in *Moonmilk and Murder* and Yucatan in *Mask for Murder*. In 1958, Stein replaced the team with engineer Matt Erridge whose occupation involves much travelling. It, too, is a lively series, marred by the hero-narrator's labored attempt to use modern argot and his habit of addressing the reader as "Charlie."

One of Stein's rare short stories, "This Was Willi's Day," is outstanding for its characterizations and a well-described Lake Lucerne setting. Unsurprisingly, Stein, who is a keen observer of his surroundings, whether in New York, or abroad, was in Switzerland when he wrote it.

—Marvin Lachman

STERN, Richard Martin. American. Born in Fresno, California, 17 March 1915. Educated at Harvard University, Cambridge, Massachusetts, 1933–36. Married Dorothy Helen Atherton in 1937; one adopted daughter. General Advertising, Hearst Corporation, 1936–37; Dehydrator Foreman, Boothe Fruit Company, Modesto, California, 1938–39; Engineer, Lockheed Aircraft, Burbank, California, 1940–45. Self-employed writer. President, Mystery Writers of America, 1971; Member, Editorial Board, *The Writer*, Boston. Recipient: Mystery Writers of America Edgar Allan Poe Award, 1958. Agent: Brandt and Brandt, 101 Park Avenue, New York, New York 10017; or, A. M. Heath & Co. Inc., 40–42 King William IV Street, London WC2N 4DD, England. Address: Route 3, Box 55, Santa Fe, New Mexico 87501, U.S.A.

CRIME PUBLICATIONS

Novels (series character: Johnny Ortiz)

The Bright Road to Fear. New York, Ballantine, 1958; London, Secker and Warburg, 1959.
Suspense: Four Short Novels. New York, Ballantine, 1959.
The Search for Tabitha Carr. New York, Scribner, and London, Secker and Warburg, 1960.
These Unlucky Deeds. New York, Scribner, 1961; as *Quidnunc County*, London, Eyre and Spottiswoode, 1961.
Cry Havoc. New York, Scribner, 1963; London, Cassell, 1964.
I Hide, We Seek. New York, Scribner, 1965; London, Deutsch, 1966.
The Kessler Legacy. New York, Scribner, 1967; London, Cassell, 1968.
Merry Go Round. New York, Scribner, 1969; London, Cassell, 1970.
Manuscript for Murder. New York, Scribner, 1970; London, Hale, 1973.
Murder in the Walls (Ortiz). New York, Scribner, 1971; London, Hale, 1973.
You Don't Need an Enemy (Ortiz). New York, Scribner, 1971; London, Hale, 1973.
Death in the Snow (Ortiz). New York, Scribner, 1973; London, Hale, 1974.

Uncollected Short Stories

"Present for Minna," in *Crime Without Murder*, edited by Dorothy Salisbury Davis. New York, Scribner, 1970.
"Will," in *Good Housekeeping* (New York), May 1976.

OTHER PUBLICATIONS

Novels

High Hazard. New York, Scribner, 1962.
Right Hand Opposite. New York, Scribner, 1964.
Brood of Eagles. Cleveland, World, 1969.
Stanfield Harvest. Cleveland, World, 1972.
The Tower. New York, McKay, and London, Secker and Warburg, 1973.
Power. New York, McKay, and London, Secker and Warburg, 1975.
The Will. New York, Doubleday, 1976.
Snowbound Six. New York, Doubleday, 1977.
Flood. New York, Doubleday, and London, Secker and Warburg, 1979.

Manuscript Collection: Mugar Memorial Library, Boston University.

*   *   *

One of the most inventive and respected writers of the American mystery is Richard Martin Stern. Before becoming identified with the novel, he was a successful magazine writer, both in short and long stories. Regularly featured in *Good Housekeeping* and *The Saturday Evening Post*, he also wrote for most of the other top-ranking fiction magazines of the time. His first novel, *The Bright Road to Fear*, won an Edgar.

Stern continued writing mystery and suspense novels throughout the 1960's. Among the foremost of his works was *Cry Havoc*, a psychological suspense story of the effect of crime on a small town. His re-creation of the town and its people was exceptional. In the 1960's he also wrote a number of suspense-oriented espionage tales, such as *I Hide, We Seek*, with its background of the Scottish Highlands. Stern has traveled widely and has resided in many of the colorful places of which he has written. His backgrounds are as important as the story lines of his plots. After moving to Santa Fe, New Mexico in the mid-1960's, he soon developed a new series against the Spanish-Indian-Anglo background, with a detective indigenous to the scene.

In the 1970's Stern temporarily abandoned the mystery story to write *The Tower*. He did not, however, abandon suspense in this story of a skyscraper whose construction was flawed through business and political short cuts. Stern has since concentrated on general fiction.

Stern's style is not influenced by fads and fancies. He writes the prose of an educated, intelligent man, who has a keen curiosity as to the whys of events, a curiosity only to be satisfied by solving the puzzles propounded.

—Dorothy B. Hughes

STEVENS, R. L.   See **HOCH, Edward D.**

STEWART, J. I. M.   See **INNES, Michael.**

STEWART, Mary (Florence Elinor, née Rainbow).   British.   Born in Sunderland, County Durham, 17 September 1916. Educated at Eden Hall, Penrith, Cumberland; Skellfield School, Ripon, Yorkshire; St. Hild's College, University of Durham, B.A. (honours) 1938, teaching diploma 1939, M.A. 1941. Served in the Royal Observer Corps during World War II. Married Sir Frederick Henry Stewart in 1945. Head of English and Classics, Abbey School, Malvern Wells, Worcestershire, 1940–41; Assistant Lecturer in English, Durham

University, 1941–45; Part-time Lecturer in English, St. Hild's Training College, Durham, and Durham University, 1948–56. Recipient: Crime Writers Association Silver Dagger, 1961; Frederick Niven Award, 1971; Scottish Arts Council Award, 1975. Fellow, Royal Society of Arts, 1968. Lives in Edinburgh. Address: c/o Hodder and Stoughton Ltd., Mill Road, Dunton Green, Sevenoaks, Kent TN13 2YA England.

CRIME PUBLICATIONS

Novels

> *Madam, Will You Talk?* London, Hodder and Stoughton, 1955; New York, Mill, 1956.
> *Wildfire at Midnight.* London, Hodder and Stoughton, and New York, Appleton Century Crofts, 1956.
> *Thunder on the Right.* London, Hodder and Stoughton, 1957; New York, Mill, 1958.
> *Nine Coaches Waiting.* London, Hodder and Stoughton, 1958; New York, Mill, 1959.
> *My Brother Michael.* London, Hodder and Stoughton, and New York, Mill, 1960.
> *The Ivy Tree.* London, Hodder and Stoughton, 1961; New York, Mill, 1962.
> *The Moon-Spinners.* London, Hodder and Stoughton, 1962; New York, Mill, 1963.
> *This Rough Magic.* London, Hodder and Stoughton, and New York, Mill, 1964.
> *Airs above the Ground.* London, Hodder and Stoughton, and New York, Mill, 1965.
> *The Gabriel Hounds.* London, Hodder and Stoughton, and New York, Mill, 1967.
> *Touch Not the Cat.* London, Hodder and Stoughton, and New York, Morrow, 1976.

OTHER PUBLICATIONS

Novels

> *The Wind off the Small Isles.* London, Hodder and Stoughton, 1968.
> *The Crystal Cave.* London, Hodder and Stoughton, and New York, Morrow, 1970.
> *The Hollow Hills.* London, Hodder and Stoughton, and New York, Morrow, 1973.
> *The Last Enchantment.* London, Hodder and Stoughton, and New York, Morrow, 1979.

Plays

> Radio Plays: *Lift from a Stranger, Call Me at Ten-Thirty, The Crime of Mr. Merry,* and *The Lord of Langdale,* 1957–58.

Other

> *The Little Broomstick* (juvenile). Leicester, Brockhampton Press, 1971; New York, Morrow, 1972.
> *Ludo and the Star Horse* (juvenile). Leicester, Brockhampton Press, 1974; New York, Morrow, 1975.

*   *   *

"No one writes the damsel-in-distress tale with greater charm or urgency," wrote Anthony Boucher, reviewing *The Ivy Tree.* The romantic suspense novel, a mystery with a love story, has seldom had attention from reviewers and critics. Mary Stewart's work, however, is a striking exception; she has earned the respect of readers and critics alike, and her novels have set a high standard for excellence in the genre because they are so literate and so intelligently developed. Stewart's craftsmanship – a year or more in the writing of each work – has won for her a wide audience that is more heterogeneous than that of many other romantic suspense writers, since she has a number of male fans in addition to the traditionally female readership for such fiction.

Although her works often resemble the modern gothic formula, they clearly transcend it. Thoroughly contemporary, her heroines innocently embark upon an adventure that quickly turns sinister. Most often, the terrifying events occur while the protagonists are cut off from safety on vacation in an exotic locale, such as Greece, Crete, the Pyrenees, or the Isle of Skye; in *Nine Coaches Waiting*, Stewart employs a modern version of the classic governess tale, and in *The Ivy Tree* and *Touch Not the Cat*, her characters return to their ancestral homes to find danger. In each book, however, the heroines are forced into solving the mystery in order to save others as well as themselves. Often, the threatened victim is an adolescent or a young child, so the heroine assumes a strongly protective or maternal role. The novels often conclude with a harrowing chase across unfamiliar terrain during which the villain is exposed and defeated.

The love story is integral to the plot, for it is only through exposing the villain and vindicating the hero that the moral order of the fictional world can be revealed. In *Nine Coaches Waiting* the man the heroine loves has an excellent motive for wishing to murder her young charge. In *Airs above the Ground* the wife has reason to distrust her husband's honesty. The unmasking of the real villain in these and the other books is necessary to allow the heroine to follow her instinct to trust the hero as well as to love him. Mary Stewart's novels, however, almost always avoid cliché.

One of her finest qualities is her extraordinary descriptive writing. Her ability to evoke a highly specific time and place, through sensuous descriptions of locale, character, and food, provides an immediacy that is often lacking in mystery fiction. Her academic background in English literature also contributes to her work, lending thematic and dramatic elements in the epigrams to her chapters and the literary allusions within the works. In addition to her works of romantic suspense, she is also the author of two children's books, two best-selling historical novels about King Arthur and Merlin, and some shorter fiction.

In an interview with Roy Newquist, published in *Counterpoint* (1964), Stewart commented upon her own work, as well as that of other writers she admires. The interview reveals her to be highly conscious of what she is doing in fiction, although she resists attempts to put a genre label on her work. She expresses a desire to entertain her audience and to write about characters who are admirable rather than perverse. Her published essays in *The Writer* reveal her concern for careful plotting and vivid description, the hallmarks of her work. That other writers of romantic suspense fiction must contend with the work and reputation of Mary Stewart is clearly shown by the number of times that her work is evoked on the paperback covers of other writers' novels. "In the tradition of Mary Stewart" imprinted on such books is a high accolade.

—Kay J. Mussell

STOKER, Bram. Irish. Born Abraham Stoker in Dublin; 8 November 1847. Educated in a private school in Dublin: Trinity College, Dublin, 1866–70, B.A. 1870; entered Middle Temple, London: called to the Bar, 1890. Married Florence Anne Lemon Balcombe in 1878; one son. Civil Servant in Dublin, 1867–77; Drama Critic, *Dublin Mail*, 1871–78; Editor, The Halfpenny Press, Dublin, 1874; settled in London: Acting Manager for Henry Irving, 1878–1905, and Manager of Irving's Lyceum chain, 1878–1902; writer from 1880. President, Philosophical Society. *Died 20 April 1912.*

CRIME PUBLICATIONS

Novels

> *Under the Sunset.*   London, Sampson Low, 1881.
> *The Snake's Pass.*   London, Sampson Low, and New York, Harper, 1890.
> *Dracula.*   London, Constable, 1897; New York, Doubleday, 1899.
> *The Mystery of the Sea.*   London, Heinemann, and New York, Doubleday, 1902.
> *The Jewel of Seven Stars.*   London, Heinemann, 1903; New York, Harper, 1904.
> *The Man.*   London, Heinemann, 1905.
> *The Lady of the Shroud.*   London, Heinemann, 1909; New York, Paperback Library, 1966.
> *The Lair of the White Worm.*   London, Rider, 1911; as *The Garden of Evil*, New York, Paperback Library, 1966.

Short Stories

> *Dracula's Guest and Other Weird Stories.*   London, Routledge, 1914; New York, Curl, 1937; as *Dracula's Curse*, New York, Tower, 1968.
> *The Bram Stoker Bedside Companion: Stories of Fantasy and Horror*, edited by Charles Osborne.   London, Gollancz, 1973; New York, Taplinger, 1979.

OTHER PUBLICATIONS

Novels

> *The Watter's Mou'.*   London, Constable, and New York, De Vinne, 1894.
> *The Shoulder of Shasta.*   London, Constable, 1895.
> *Miss Betty.*   London, Pearson, 1898.
> *Lady Athlyne.*   London, Heinemann, and New York, Reynolds, 1908.
> *Snowbound: The Record of a Theatrical Touring Party.*   London, Collier, 1908.
> *The Gates of Life.*   New York, Cupples and Leon, 1908.

Short Stories

> *Crooken Sands.*   New York, De Vinne, 1894.
> *The Man from Shorrox's.*   New York, De Vinne, 1894.

Other

> *The Duties of Clerks of Petty Sessions in Ireland.*   Privately printed, 1879.
> *A Glimpse of America* (lecture).   London, Sampson Low, 1886.
> *Personal Reminiscences of Henry Irving.*   London, Heinemann, 2 vols., and New York, Macmillan, 2 vols., 1906; revised edition, Heinemann, 1907.
> *Famous Imposters.*   London, Sidgwick and Jackson, and New York, Sturgis and Walton, 1910.

*   *   *

The mixture of fact and fantasy in Bram Stoker's *Dracula* is heady stuff. The action in Transylvania, Whitby, London, and finally in Transylvania again where the fierce ending takes place, is based on details of names and firms, of streets, of ships, of railway timetables and newspaper cuttings; and the events, though fantastic, strike home to basic fears in the reader. For this is the horror story *par excellence*, following in the track of earlier Gothic novels including those by Stoker's countrymen – Charles Robert Maturin's *Melmoth the*

Wanderer (1820), and Sheridań Le Fanu's many examples of the genre. Le Fanu's vampire play *Carmilla*, indeed, influenced Stoker's novel which conveys all the pressures of the supernatural, the symbolism of day and night, of good and evil, of Christ and the Devil. Dracula, the vampire, may owe something to the subject of John Polidori's *The Vampyre* (1819) and Thomas Presket Prest's *Varney the Vampyre* (1847) as well as to its creator's nightmare brought on by "a too generous helping of dressed crab at supper"; but the story's use of folklore and its smack of authenticity come from Stoker's solid reading in the British Museum, where he studied accounts of life in Transylvania, and, in particular, the life of Vlad Tepes, the voivode of Wallachia.

Out of these ingredients, and his own powerful imagination, he created the fiercely energetic count, whose climbing down the walls of his mysterious castle creates a *frisson* in the toughest reader. This daemonic energy is balanced, of course, by the images of the "Non-dead" in their coffins. Indeed the whole novel is balanced between pallor and blood, between sanity and madness, and the tension is kept up, except in occasional passages of verbose Victorian sentimentality. Stoker kept the story moving well, fully establishing the fate of one young woman, Lucy Westrena, in order that the dangers of the second, Mina Harkness, can be fully fathomed by the reader – and by the men who seek to free her from Dracula's domination as well as to check his diabolical career. The staking of the vampires – begun in the London churchyard – has a macabre quality about it, and this is intensified as Mina realises this may well be necessary for her salvation. And there is a slowly unfolding subplot in the madhouse with the eater of flies, also dominated by Dracula, which keeps the reader's curiosity alert. But then it would be hard to pick out the most effective touches of horror in the story, whether they be the multiplicity of wolves, bats, and rats which seethe about the buildings, the murders, the gradual growth of human teeth into fang-like shape, the enticement of children, or even the primitive blood transfusions and trepanning. The technique of using various diaries, letters, telegrams, and excerpts from newspapers provides a shifting point of view, and is effective in conveying the sense of fear and strain imposed upon the characters in their struggle with an adversary whose powers, though limited in some respects, are so effective, so unexpected, and, at first, so difficult to counter.

Leonard Wolf has pointed out that Dracula himself appears on only 62 of the original edition's 390 pages, and so we approach him through the tearful and revengeful attitudes of those who seek to resist his murderous bloodlust. The compulsive dramatic tension is kept up, however, by the underlying issues raised by this human struggle against satanic evil. Its appeal to popular imagination is great indeed and not only has it gone through many British and American editions and been widely translated, but it has given rise to many films which have developed the visual images of horror put forward so effectively in the novel itself.

—A. Norman Jeffares

STONE, Hampton. See **STEIN, Aaron Marc.**

STOUT, Rex (Todhunter). American. Born in Noblesville, Indiana, 1 December 1886. Educated at Topeka High School, Kansas; University of Kansas, Lawrence. Served in the

United States Navy as a Yeoman on President Theodore Roosevelt's yacht, 1906–08. Married 1) Fay Kennedy in 1916 (divorced, 1933); 2) Pola Hoffman in 1933; two daughters. Worked as an office boy, store clerk, bookkeeper, hotel manager, 1916–27; invented the banking system for school children; full-time writer from 1927. Founding Director, Vanguard Press, New York; Master of Ceremonies, "Speaking of Liberty," "Voice of Freedom," and "Our Secret Weapon" radio programs, 1941–43. Chairman of the Writers' War Board, 1941–46, and the World Government Writers Board, 1949–75; President, Friends of Democracy, 1941–51, Authors' Guild, 1943–45, and Society for the Prevention of World War III, 1943–46; President, 1951–55, 1962–69, and Vice-President, 1956–61, Authors League of America; Treasurer, Freedom House, 1957–75; President, Mystery Writers of America, 1958. Recipient: Mystery Writers of America Grand Master Award, 1959. *Died 27 October 1975.*

Crime Publications

Novels (series characters: Tecumseh Fox; Nero Wolfe)

Fer-de-Lance (Wolfe).   New York, Farrar and Rinehart, 1934; London, Cassell, 1935.
The President Vanishes (published anonymously).   New York, Farrar and Rinehart, 1934.
The League of Frightened Men (Wolfe).   New York, Farrar and Rinehart, and London, Cassell, 1935.
The Rubber Band (Wolfe).   New York, Farrar and Rinehart, and London, Cassell, 1936; as *To Kill Again*, New York, Curl, 1960.
The Red Box (Wolfe).   New York, Farrar and Rinehart, and London, Cassell, 1937.
The Hand in the Glove.   New York, Farrar and Rinehart, 1937; as *Crime on Her Hands*, London, Collins, 1939.
Too Many Cooks (Wolfe).   New York, Farrar and Rinehart, and London, Collins, 1938.
Some Buried Caesar (Wolfe).   New York, Farrar and Rinehart, and London, Collins, 1939; as *The Red Bull*, New York, Dell, 1945.
Mountain Cat.   New York, Farrar and Rinehart, 1939; London, Collins, 1940.
Double for Death (Fox).   New York, Farrar and Rinehart, 1939; London, Collins, 1940.
Red Threads, in *The Mystery Book*.   New York, Farrar and Rinehart, 1940; London, Collins, 1945.
Over My Dead Body (Wolfe).   New York, Farrar and Rinehart, and London, Collins, 1940.
Bad for Business (Fox), in *The Second Mystery Book*.   New York, Farrar and Rinehart, 1940; London, Collins, 1945.
Where There's a Will (Wolfe).   New York, Farrar and Rinehart, 1940; London, Collins, 1941.
The Broken Vase (Fox).   New York, Farrar and Rinehart, 1941; London, Collins, 1942.
Alphabet Hicks.   New York, Farrar and Rinehart, 1941; London, Collins, 1942; as *The Sound of Murder*, New York, Pyramid, 1965.
Black Orchids (novelets; Wolfe).   New York, Farrar and Rinehart, 1942; London, Collins, 1943.
Not Quite Dead Enough (novelets; Wolfe).   New York, Farrar and Rinehart, 1944.
The Silent Speaker (Wolfe).   New York, Viking Press, 1946; London, Collins, 1947.
Too Many Women (Wolfe).   New York, Viking Press, 1947; London, Collins, 1948.
And Be a Villain (Wolfe).   New York, Viking Press, 1948; as *More Deaths Than One*, London, Collins, 1949.

The Second Confession (Wolfe). New York, Viking Press, 1949; London, Collins, 1950.

Trouble in Triplicate (novelets; Wolfe). New York, Viking Press, and London, Collins, 1949.

Three Doors to Death (novelets; Wolfe). New York, Viking Press, and London, Collins, 1950.

In the Best Families (Wolfe). New York, Viking Press, 1950; as *Even in the Best Families*, London, Collins, 1951.

Curtains for Three (novelets; Wolfe). New York, Viking Press, 1950; London, Collins, 1951.

Murder by the Book (Wolfe). New York, Viking Press, 1951; London, Collins, 1952.

Triple Jeopardy (novelets; Wolfe). New York, Viking Press, 1951; London, Collins, 1952.

Prisoner's Base (Wolfe). New York, Viking Press, 1952; as *Out Goes She*, London, Collins, 1953.

The Golden Spiders (Wolfe). New York, Viking Press, 1953; London, Collins, 1954.

Three Men Out (novelets; Wolfe). New York, Viking Press, 1954; London, Collins, 1955.

The Black Mountain (Wolfe). New York, Viking Press, 1954; London, Collins, 1955.

Before Midnight (Wolfe). New York, Viking Press, 1955; London, Collins, 1956.

Might As Well Be Dead (Wolfe). New York, Viking Press, 1956; London, Collins, 1957.

Three Witnesses (novelets; Wolfe). New York, Viking Press, and London, Collins, 1956.

Three for the Chair (novelets; Wolfe). New York, Viking Press, 1957; London, Collins, 1958.

If Death Ever Slept (Wolfe). New York, Viking Press, 1957; London, Collins, 1958.

Champagne for One (Wolfe). New York, Viking Press, 1958; London, Collins, 1959.

And Four to Go (novelets; Wolfe). New York, Viking Press, 1958; as *Crime and Again*, London, Collins, 1959.

Plot It Yourself (Wolfe). New York, Viking Press, 1959; as *Murder in Style*, London, Collins, 1960.

Three at Wolfe's Door (novelets; Wolfe). New York, Viking Press, 1960; London, Collins, 1961.

Too Many Clients (Wolfe). New York, Viking Press, 1960; London, Collins, 1961.

The Final Deduction (Wolfe). New York, Viking Press, 1961; London, Collins, 1962.

Gambit (Wolfe). New York, Viking Press, 1962; London, Collins, 1963.

Homicide Trinity (novelets; Wolfe). New York, Viking Press, 1962; London, Collins, 1963.

The Mother Hunt (Wolfe). New York, Viking Press, 1963; London, Collins, 1964.

Trio for Blunt Instruments (novelets; Wolfe). New York, Viking Press, 1964; London, Collins, 1965.

A Right to Die (Wolfe). New York, Viking Press, 1964; London, Collins, 1965.

The Doorbell Rang (Wolfe). New York, Viking Press, 1965; London, Collins, 1966.

Death of a Doxy (Wolfe). New York, Viking Press, 1966; London, Collins, 1967.

The Father Hunt (Wolfe). New York, Viking Press, 1968; London, Collins, 1969.

Death of a Dude (Wolfe). New York, Viking Press, 1969; London, Collins, 1970.

Please Pass the Guilt (Wolfe). New York, Viking Press, 1973; London, Collins, 1974.

A Family Affair (Wolfe). New York, Viking Press, 1975; London, Collins, 1976.

Short Stories

Justice Ends at Home and Other Stories, edited by John McAleer. New York, Viking Press, 1977.

OTHER PUBLICATIONS

Novels

Her Forbidden Knight, in *All-Story Magazine* (New York), August–December 1913.
Under the Andes, in *All-Story Magazine* (New York), February 1914.
A Prize for Princes, in *All-Story Weekly* (New York), 7 March–30 May 1914.
The Great Legend, in *All-Story Weekly* (New York), 1 January–29 January 1916.
How Like a God. New York, Vanguard Press, 1929.
Seed on the Wind. New York, Vanguard Press, 1930.
Golden Remedy. New York, Vanguard Press, 1931.
Forest Fire. New York, Farrar and Rinehart, 1933.
O Careless Love! New York, Farrar and Rinehart, 1935.
Mr. Cinderella. New York, Farrar and Rinehart, 1938.

Other

The Nero Wolfe Cook Book, with others. New York, Viking Press, 1973.

Editor, *The Illustrious Dunderheads.* New York, Knopf, 1942.
Editor, with Louis Greenfield, *Rue Morgue No. 1.* New York, Creative Age Press, 1946.
Editor, *Eat, Drink, and Be Buried.* New York, Viking Press, 1956; as *For Tomorrow We Die*, London, Macdonald, 1958.

Bibliography: in *Rex Stout: A Biography* by John McAleer, Boston, Little Brown, 1977.

Manuscript Collection: University of North Carolina Libraries, Chapel Hill.

*   *   *

Rex Stout's writing covered a broad spectrum, from mainstream novels to science fiction, but the bulk of his writing was in the mystery field. Here his range was also broad, covering a number of non-series and short series novels and short stories. These items are not without merit, but neither do they stand up to comparison with Stout's greatest achievement, the Nero Wolfe series, nearly 40 each of novels and short stories which comprise the most outstanding achievement in the mystery field in the post-Holmes era.

Without doubt, 221B Baker Street is the most famous fictional address in the history of literature. For all its fame, however, the Baker Street address must yield pride of place in matters of careful and loving delineation to Nero Wolfe's Manhattan brownstone, uncertainly located somewhere on West 35th Street. There, not just one room – as is the case with the Baker Street flat – but the entire house becomes familiar as the series progresses: the chef's quarters and the billiard room in the basement; the office, front room, kitchen and dining room on the ground floor; the bedrooms on the next two floors; the plant rooms and gardener's quarters on the roof. And not just the rooms themselves, but (with the exceptions of the chef's and the gardener's quarters) their very contents and even the arrangement of those contents become familiar to the follower of the series, until he is as much at home in the brownstone as in his own abode. Of course, like the Baker Street flat, the brownstone achieves immortality not in its own right but as the home and headquarters of a remarkable man, and as the focus of many an interesting and entertaining tale. The stories are memorable for their ingenuity, their well-drawn, substantial characters, the wit and wisdom which Stout sprinkles liberally throughout, and, to a very large degree, the relationship which exists between its two principal characters.

Conan Doyle used Watson principally to shine light on Holmes. No such lop-sidedness exists in the Saga. It is the *Nero Wolfe* Saga, unquestionably; he is the eccentric genius, not

Archie. But their relationship is symbiotic – Wolfe could continue to function without Archie (as he did before their paths crossed), and Archie could make it on his own as a private detective (as, indeed, he does at one point in the Saga). But the two function most effectively together, which is part of the reason why someone of Archie's capacities would be content working for Wolfe rather than on his own. The rest of the reason goes beyond professional considerations to what may be the greatest charm of the series: Wolfe and Archie are friends. What began as an employer/employee relationship quickly developed beyond that; as each came to appreciate the other's abilities and capacities, affection – though rarely admitted – grew between them and developed at length into that very rare thing, manly love. (The suggestion that their relationship was a homosexual one rates mentioning only to be dismissed.) They are very important parts of each other's lives, and although their behavior toward each other is frequently antagonistic it does not disguise the fact that the underlying foundation of their relationship is respect and deep affection.

Wolfe is a polymath, a misogynist, and a man of great though discerning appetite. Wolfe is in his fifties; his weight hovers around a seventh of a ton, kept there by the consumption of large quantities of the best food in North America, prepared by the priceless Fritz Brenner, and by the downing of gallons of beer daily. He is also an omnivorous reader, frequently reading several books at the same time (and committing the appalling barbarity of dog-earing their pages), and he is a passionate orchid fancier, spending two hours every morning and afternoon in the rooftop plant rooms among his 10,000 plants. His various eccentricities include a reluctance to leave the house on business and an aversion, almost a phobia, to travelling in any mechanized vehicle. And he is a genius at solving problems, usually murders, when he can overcome his chronic laziness regarding matters of business.

Which is where Archie comes in. Tall, fit, handsome, and in his early thirties, Archie Goodwin does Wolfe's leg work for him, combining a respectable intelligence with considerable cunning and native wit to produce results on even some of Wolfe's more unreasonable instructions. But Archie does not merely carry out Wolfe's instructions – he frequently has to goad his employer into giving them. Whenever the bank balance drops too low, or whenever Archie thinks Wolfe has been loafing long enough, he goads and prods and generally annoys Wolfe until at last the great man gives in and undertakes – often with the worst possible grace – whatever case Archie has decided he should tackle. And while Wolfe supplies the genius which solves the case, there is no doubt that he appreciates the talents and resources of his capable, if frequently worrisome, assistant. As the narrator of the tales, Archie supplies entertaining commentary and he contributes substantially to the highly witty dialogue which is one of the hallmarks of the series.

Wolfe and Archie are joined by a host of well-drawn minor and not-so-minor regular characters. These include Inspector Cramer, whose reaction to Wolfe's involvement in murder cases ranges from mere impatience to outright rage; Saul Panzer, an innocuous-looking but supremely effective free-lance private detective; Lily Rowan, Archie's sometime girl friend, who achieved the remarkable feat of necking with Wolfe in the back seat of an automobile; and Fritz Brenner, Wolfe's majordomo and chef par excellence.

Stout had a wonderful gift for creating realistic characters and interesting his readers in their lives. Indeed, these characters and the dialogue between them really make the Nero Wolfe tales. The story plots are usually more than adequate and are sometimes very good indeed, but without these incomparable characters they would not be especially memorable. With them, the Saga is not merely memorable, it is immortal.

—Guy M. Townsend

STRAKER, J(ohn) F(oster). British. Born in Farnborough, Kent, 26 March 1904. Educated at Framlingham College, Suffolk (scholar). Served in the Buffs, British Army, 1940–45: Major. Married Margaret Brydon in 1935; one son. Senior Mathematics Master, Kingsland Grange School, Shrewsbury, Shropshire, 1927–35; Headmaster, Blackheath Preparatory School, London, 1936–39; Senior Mathematics Master, Cumnor House School, Danehill, Sussex, 1945–78. Agent: Michael Motley Ltd., 78 Gloucester Terrace, London W2 3HH. Address: Lincoln Cottage, Horsted Keynes, Sussex RH17 7AW, England.

CRIME PUBLICATIONS

Novels (series characters: Johnny Inch; Inspector Pitt)

Postman's Knock (Pitt).   London, Harrap, 1954.
Pick Up the Pieces (Pitt).   London, Harrap, 1955.
The Ginger Horse (Pitt).   London, Harrap, 1956.
A Gun to Play With.   London, Harrap, 1956.
Good-bye, Aunt Charlotte! (Pitt).   London, Harrap, 1958.
Hell Is Empty.   London, Harrap, 1958.
Death of a Good Woman (Pitt).   London, Harrap, 1961.
Murder for Missemily (Pitt).   London, Harrap, 1961.
A Coil of Rope.   London, Harrap, 1962.
Final Witness.   London, Harrap, 1963.
The Shape of Murder.   London, Harrap, 1964.
Ricochet.   London, Harrap, 1965.
Miscarriage of Murder.   London, Harrap, 1967.
Sin and Johnny Inch.   London, Harrap, 1968.
A Man Who Cannot Kill.   London, Harrap, 1969.
Tight Circle (Inch).   London, Harrap, 1970.
A Letter for Obi (Inch).   London, Harrap, 1971.
The Goat (Inch).   London, Harrap, 1972.
Arthurs' Night.   London, Hale, 1976.
Swallow Them Up.   London, Hale, 1977.
Death on a Sunday Morning.   London, Hale, 1978.
A Pity It Wasn't George.   London, Hale, 1979.

Uncollected Short Stories

"Advanced Judgment," and "Overdose of Vanity," in *Evening Standard* (London), December 1950.
"The Key," in *Evening News* (London), August 1961.

OTHER PUBLICATIONS

Novel

The Droop (as Ian Rosse).   London, New English Library, 1972.

J. F. Straker comments:
  My books have been described by one reviewer as "typically English." They are strong on character and plot, and always have an unexpected twist in the tail.
  May I, in all modesty, quote from an article on me by Bill Newton, another crime writer (Darlington *Evening Despatch*, 19 May 1973): "If a panel of experts on crime-writing was asked to list the top ten authors who consistently entertain with ingenious plots and sheer

brilliance in their detectives' investigation, one of these would have to be John Foster Straker. Without hesitation I name his book, *Postman's Knock*, as one of the top twenty detective stories ever written."

* * *

J. F. Straker's first novel, *Postman's Knock*, featured Inspector Pitt, an elderly, sympathetic policeman, who appeared in several more books. Straker then dropped Pitt, who was "cramping his style," and the next dozen or so books varied in pattern, some strong on detection, others straightforward thrillers. Sex featured in some, but only where it helped the plot.

In 1968 he invented a new central figure, Johnny Inch, a cheerful young detective attached to a special CID squad at Scotland Yard. He appeared in *Sin and Johnny Inch* and *Tight Circle*, then went "private" in *A Letter for Obi* and *The Goat*. Straker turned to straight fiction for a time, then returned to crime with *Arthurs' Night*. *A Pity It Wasn't George*, a recent book, deals more with the effect of murder on boys and staff at a preparatory school than with actual police work. The central character may come to be used in other books. Straker makes his police work authentic (he sometimes seeks the help of his local police) and his work has a documentary air. He avoids violence for the sake of violence, and usually contrives a "twist in the tail."

—Herbert Harris

STRANGE, John Stephen. Pseudonym for Dorothy Stockbridge Tillett. American. Born in 1896.

CRIME PUBLICATIONS

Novels (series characters: Barney Gantt; Lieutenant/Captain George Honegger; Van Dusen Ormsberry)

The Man Who Killed Fortescue (Ormsberry). New York, Doubleday, 1928; London, Collins, 1929.
The Clue of the Second Murder (Ormsberry). New York, Doubleday, and London, Collins, 1929.
The Strangler Fig. New York, Doubleday, 1930; London, Collins, 1931; as *Murder at World's End*, New York, Novel Selections, 1943.
Murder on the Ten-Yard Line (Ormsberry). New York, Doubleday, 1931; as *Murder Game*, London, Collins, 1931.
Black Hawthorn. New York, Doubleday, 1933; as *The Chinese Jar Mystery*, London, Collins, 1934.
For the Hangman. New York, Doubleday, 1934; London, Collins, 1935.
The Bell in the Fog (Gantt). New York, Doubleday, 1936; London, Collins, 1937.
Silent Witnesses (Gantt). New York, Doubleday, 1938; as *The Corpse and the Lady*, London, Collins, 1938.
Rope Enough (Gantt). New York, Doubleday, 1938; London, Collins, 1939; as *The Ballot Box Murders*, New York, Novel Selections, 1943.
A Picture of the Victim (Gantt). New York, Doubleday, and London, Collins, 1940.

Murder Gives a Lovely Light (Honegger).   New York, Doubleday, 1941; London, Collins, 1942.

Look Your Last (Gantt).   New York, Doubleday, 1943; London, Collins, 1944.

Make My Bed Soon (Gantt).   New York, Doubleday, and London, Collins, 1948.

All Men Are Liars (Honegger).   New York, Doubleday, 1948; as *Come to Judgment*, London, Collins, 1949.

Unquiet Grave.   New York, Doubleday, 1949; as *Uneasy Is the Grave*, London, Collins, 1950.

Reasonable Doubt.   New York, Doubleday, and London, Collins, 1951; as *The Fair and the Dead*, New York, Spivak, 1953.

Deadly Beloved (Gantt).   New York, Doubleday, and London, Collins, 1952.

Let the Dead Past –   New York, Doubleday, 1953; as *Dead End*, London, Collins, 1953.

Catch the Gold Ring.   New York, Doubleday, 1955; as *A Handful of Silver*, London, Collins, 1955.

Night of Reckoning.   New York, Doubleday, 1958; London, Collins, 1959.

Eye Witness (Honegger).   New York, Doubleday, 1961; London, Collins, 1962.

The House on 9th Street (Gantt).   New York, Doubleday, 1976.

OTHER PUBLICATIONS as Dorothy Stockbridge

Novel

Angry Dust.   New York, Doubleday, 1946.

Play

Jezebel, in *Contemporary One-Act Plays of 1921*, edited by Frank Shay.   Cincinnati, Stewart Kidd, 1922.

Verse

Paths of June.   New York, Dutton, 1920.

*   *   *

Starting with *The Man Who Killed Fortescue* in 1928, Dorothy Stockbridge Tillett, under the pseudonym of John Stephen Strange, wrote more than 20 mystery novels primarily in the classic puzzler tradition. Although not very well known today, her books were very popular from the 1930's to the 1950's. In fact, her third book, *The Strangler Fig*, was selected by William Lyon Phelps as one of the ten best detective stories published from 1928 to 1933. Her books reflect the times in which they were written. Earlier books, in the best classic puzzler style, had the murder taking place early in the book. Several suspects and much passion later, the murderer was revealed in a tense drawing-room scene. Plot lines of later books varied to include courtroom scenes, gangsters, and even a hurricane.

In *The Man Who Killed Fortescue*, Strange provides a slightly different slant to the murder by having the victim killed while riding on the top of a double-decker bus. The victim is an author and criminologist who had been working on a solution to a two-year-old unsolved murder. The two murders are definitely linked and Detective Van Dusen Ormsberry, aided by a juvenile Sherlock Holmes, Bill Adams, follows a course of deductive reasoning which involves the members of an exclusive men's club, a relatively unnecessary third murder, and a few romantic twists to a successful and not readily anticipated conclusion.

Black Hawthorn displays the same careful plotting but adds an element of superstitious suspense. A family heirloom threatens the bodily safety and the sanity of a seafaring family which, though steeped in tradition, has wealth based on the opium trade. Several plot twists take place and the inevitable third murder occurs before Detective Sergeant Potter of the New London Police is able to piece together the psychological portrait of the ruthless family murderer.

Her series character Barney Gantt, a Pulitzer Prize-winning photographer, is introduced in *The Bell in the Fog*. Barney is unlucky in love – until he meets Muriel, the *Globe*'s lonely hearts columnist – but is extremely good at unravelling complicated intrigues. He is thin, of medium height, with a sharp face dominated by an aggressive nose, very keen blue eyes, and a wide mouth. In a crowd he is indistinguishable, which is just how he likes it. Barney appears in eight novels, including the latest, *The House on 9th Street*. This is a modern novel of suspense and intrigue involving a violent revolutionary youth group and their bomb factory. Barney returns home from a tour of Africa (with insights into African revolutionaries) to find Muriel recovering from a car accident and his paper, *The Globe*, embroiled in an investigation of revolutionary activities in New England. A kidnapping, a murder, and an exciting climax polish off this fast-paced novel.

—Mary Ann Grochowski

STRIBLING, T(heodore) S(igismund). American. Born in Clifton, Tennessee, 4 March 1881. Educated in public schools in Clifton; Normal College, Florence, Alabama, graduated 1903; studied law at the University of Alabama, LL.B. 1904. Married Louella Kloss in 1930. Practice law in Florence, 1906; member of the staff of the *Taylor-Trotwood Magazine*, Nashville, 1906–07; thereafter a full-time writer; Instructor in Creative Writing, Columbia University, New York, 1936, 1940. Recipient: Pulitzer Prize, 1933. LL.D.: Oglethorpe University, Atlanta, 1936. *Died 10 July 1965.*

CRIME PUBLICATIONS

Short Stories

>   *Clues of the Caribbees, Being Certain Criminal Investigations of Henry Poggioli, Ph.D.* New York, Doubleday, 1929; London, Heinemann, 1930.
>   *Best Dr. Poggioli Detective Stories.* New York, Dover, 1975; London, Dover, 1976.

Uncollected Short Stories

>   "The Resurrection of Chin Lee," in *101 Years' Entertainment*, edited by Ellery Queen. Boston, Little Brown, 1941.
>   "The Cablegram," in *Best Stories from Ellery Queen's Mystery Magazine*. Roslyn, New York, Detective Book Club, 1944.
>   "The Mystery of the Paper Wad," in *Ellery Queen's Mystery Magazine* (New York), July 1946.
>   "The Shadow," in *20th Century Detective Stories*, edited by Ellery Queen. Cleveland, World, 1948.
>   "Judge Lynch," in *Ellery Queen's Mystery Magazine* (New York), September 1950.
>   "The Mystery of the Choir Boy," in *Ellery Queen's Mystery Magazine* (New York), January 1951.
>   "Poggioli and the Refugees," in *The Saint* (New York), June–July 1953.

"The Mystery of the Five Money Orders," in *Ellery Queen's Mystery Magazine* (New York), March 1954.
"Murder at Flowtide," in *The Saint* (New York), March 1955.
"Murder in the Hills," in *The Saint* (New York), February 1956.

OTHER PUBLICATIONS

Novels

The Cruise of the Dry Dock.   Chicago, Reilly and Britton, 1917.
Birthright.   New York, Century, 1922; London, Collins, 1925.
Fombombo.   New York, Century, and London, Nisbet, 1923.
Red Sand.   New York, Harcourt Brace, and London, Nisbet, 1924.
Teeftallow.   New York, Doubleday, and London, Nisbet, 1926.
Bright Metal.   New York, Doubleday, and London, Nisbet, 1928.
East Is East.   New York, L. Harper Allen, 1928.
Strange Moon.   New York, Doubleday, and London, Heinemann, 1929.
Backwater.   New York, Doubleday, and London, Heinemann, 1930.
The Forge.   New York, Doubleday, and London, Heinemann, 1931.
The Store.   New York, Doubleday, and London, Heinemann, 1932.
Unfinished Cathedral.   New York, Doubleday, and London, Heinemann, 1934.
The Sound Wagon.   New York, Doubleday, 1935; London, Gollancz, 1936.
These Bars of Flesh.   New York, Doubleday, 1938.

Play

Rope, with David Wallace, adaptation of the novel *Teeftallow* by Stribling (produced New York, 1928).

*   *   *

T. S. Stribling, best known for his novels of Tennessee, also wrote a number of interesting stories featuring one of detective fiction's early psychologist-criminologists, Henry Poggioli, a psychology professor at Ohio State University. Poggioli is rarely seen in pursuit of his official profession in Ohio, but seems to spend most of his time in pursuit of his unofficial occupation in the Caribbean and Latin America. He is a slightly comical character, often scared but always curious, who initially gets involved in investigation by accident, and often, subsequently, against his will. His first case comes when he is staying in a hotel in Curaçao. The proprietor of the hotel dies and Poggioli is drawn into the investigation because he is interested in the psychological makeup of the main suspect, Pompalone, an ex-dictator from Venezuela. Poggioli solves the crime – the proprietor had intended to murder Pompalone, but in a mix-up of wine bottles (the identifying cobwebs had been accidentally wiped from the poisoned bottle) drinks the poisoned wine himself. The "detective" then goes to visit Haiti, and finds that his reputation has gone before him; he is virtually forced to help the government demonstrate that Voodooism is fraudulent. Ironically, he discovers that the Voodoo leaders are using truth drugs, his own detective tool, to read minds and enslave followers.

What ultimately attracts Poggioli to detection is his strong sense of social and racial justice. He longs for races to free themselves from superstition; he can't bear to see a poor man accused where a rich one is guilty. He develops an elaborate, compassionate philosophy of crime – it is a question of environmental conditioning. He believes that a Futuristic architecture will produce increasingly original criminals, and that the bizarre murals he observes in Martinique will lead to grotesque crimes. He believes also that certain races will commit certain kinds of crime – for instance, a criminal who has carried out his crime with a slow, deliberate perfection may well be of mixed French and Negro blood, the French in him accounting for the perfectionist, the Negro for the deliberation.

Poggioli is not free from a certain pride in his skill. He competes with local policemen, and in one instance goes so far as to make a wager with an informed stranger that he and not the stranger will be able to find the perpetrators of the next six crimes committed in the French town in which they are staying. But Poggioli's enthusiasm for the theory and science of crime and for his own skill are always sharply modified when his enthusiasm brings him into contact with gruesome facts. And his sense of triumph at solving a crime worries him; he may come to relish crime because it provides the opportunity for him to demonstrate his skill. "The detection of crime is a damnable occupation," he reflects; "A man who follows it will become a monster." Poggioli remains intensely human; his perception of the perverse dangers besetting the criminologist is one of the touches with which Stribling makes his thoughtful detective such an engaging character.

—Ann Massa

STUART, Ian.   See **MacLEAN, Alistair.**

STUART, Sidney.   See **AVALLONE, Michael.**

STUBBS, Jean.   British.   Born in Denton, Lancashire, 23 October 1926. Educated at Manchester High School for Girls, 1938–44; Manchester School of Art, 1944–47. Married; one daughter and one son. Since 1966, regular reviewer, *Books and Bookmen*, London. Recipient: Tom-Gallon Trust Award, for short story, 1965. Agent: Teresa Sacco, Macmillan London Ltd., Little Essex Street, London WC2R 3LF. Address: Trewin, Nancegollan, near Helston, Cornwall TR13 0AJ, England.

CRIME PUBLICATIONS

Novels (series character: Inspector John Joseph Lintott)

My Grand Enemy.   London, Macmillan, 1967; New York, Stein and Day, 1968.
The Case of Kitty Ogilvie.   London, Macmillan, 1970; New York, Walker, 1971.
Dear Laura (Lintott).   London, Macmillan, and New York, Stein and Day, 1973.
The Painted Face (Lintott).   London, Macmillan, and New York, Stein and Day, 1974.

The Golden Crucible Lintott). London, Macmillan, and New York, Stein and Day, 1976.

Uncollected Short Stories

"Question of Honour," in *Winter's Crimes 1*, edited by George Hardinge. London, Macmillan, 1969.
"The Belvedere," in *Winter's Crimes 3*, edited by George Hardinge. London, Macmillan, 1971.

OTHER PUBLICATIONS

Novels

The Rose-Grower. London, Macmillan, 1962; New York, St. Martin's Press, 1963.
The Travellers. London, Macmillan, and New York, St. Martin's Press, 1963.
Hanrahan's Colony. London, Macmillan, 1964.
The Straw Crown. London, Macmillan, 1966.
The Passing Star. London, Macmillan, 1970; as *Eleanora Duse*, New York, Stein and Day, 1970.
An Unknown Welshman. London, Macmillan, and New York, Stein and Day, 1972.
A Timeless Place. London, Macmillan, 1978.
Kit's Hill. London, Macmillan, 1979; as *By Our Beginnings*, New York, St. Martin's Press, 1979.

Play

Television Play: *Family Christmas*, 1965.

Jean Stubbs comments:
I became fascinated by crime-writing in 1966 when I found an old book on the library shelves called *Famous Trials*. Among the trials was the case of Mary Blandy, who was hanged for poisoning her father at Henley in 1752. I felt that Mary had received poor treatment and researched the case in the British Museum, producing my first crime documentary, *My Grand Enemy*. I based this, and *The Case of Kitty Ogilvie* (another 18th-century murder), on the facts and wrote it like a novel. Later someone created the word "faction" which seemed to describe what I was trying to achieve.

I write other books and it was 1972 before I again felt I should like to try another crime documentary, and to set it in the late-Victorian era. I enjoy researching history and such research has become a necessary factor in any book I contemplate. This time the Victorians were too well documented to be reproduced, so I composed my own "classic" plot for *Dear Laura*. The success, on both sides of the Atlantic, of this Victorian thriller brought along *The Painted Face* (set in Paris, 1902) and *The Golden Crucible* (set in San Francisco, 1906), all of them featuring Inspector Lintott, an elderly detective with mutton-chop whiskers. I am now engaged on "something completely different," a quintology of novels about a Lancashire family from 1760 to the present day. But the "bones" of an early Lintott, set around 1860, are sitting on my bookshelf, waiting to be fleshed some day.

I always say I write *why-done-its* and not *who-done-its*.

*   *   *

Jean Stubbs is a welcome addition to the ranks of mystery fiction writers. *Dear Laura, The*

Painted Face, and *The Golden Crucible* have style, complexity, wondrously believable female characters, and a delightful new detective-inspector – John Joseph Lintott.

Until a few years ago, Stubbs was writing historical and romantic fiction; she is thoroughly familiar with the sociology of her chosen Victorian period and her scene setting is vivid. She makes good sense of the psychology not only of her central characters, but also of many minor ones. And she takes the reader along a splendidly winding path at the end of which she manages to create surprise. Stubbs's books could be a good introduction to detective mysteries for a devoted reader of the modern psychological novel.

For the purists who want only ingenious plotting and detection, Stubbs's artful characterization and the echoes of Victorian literature could be disturbing. She uses the Victorian period to point to the beginning of our own times. The three Lintott mysteries are linked in their pictures of emerging modern women. The heroines are women of some depth. They grapple their ways to maturity in stages that make sense to other women. While their circumstances are unusual, the characters themselves, rather like Galsworthy's, are neither larger nor more glittering than life.

Neophyte or purist, all readers will agree that Inspector Lintott of Scotland Yard, retired, is a worthy character. Far from the hard-boiled private eye of American fiction, Lintott is sturdily British. As earthy as a character from Dickens, he is a family man and a guardian of Victorian values. He is a devoted husband to good, plain Bessie and bewildered father of the defiant young feminist, Lizzie. A representative of Scotland Yard, Lintott knows all that is seamy about 19th-century London. He speaks two languages – his own middle-class English and the patois of the gutter. When he questions the members of a household, he has them trusting, cowed, shaped-up, and comforted so quickly that you want to reread to see how it happened. And, when you do, it's clear! Having created Lintott, Stubbs appears to enjoy him as much as the reader. She pushes him into unlikely settings and we watch him struggle to grow. Before he retired, Lintott had never been more than fifty miles outside of London, but he agrees to follow a case to Paris. With no French to defend himself and with his staid English eye, Lintott learns to enjoy rural France and to survive an encounter with a wily courtesan in whose boudoir he must sit, uncomfortably massive, while he accounts for every penny he has spent in Paris. But the good old inspector is no superman. His gaffes are painful. His sensitivity to ordinary people is heartwarming, but he never understands the heroine of *The Painted Face* nor his own daughter.

In *The Golden Crucible* Stubbs sends her detective to America – to San Francisco tottering on the verge of the Great Quake. Lintott's daughter has failed to adapt to what appeared to be a suitable marriage, so the American mission includes a role for her. These two travel separately and Lizzie's very modern love story runs contrapuntally to her father's exploration of a sparkling, corrupt San Francisco at the turn of the century.

A major element in Jean Stubbs's mystery novels is a concern for justice, less a legalistic matter than the workings of the gods. High prices are paid for failures in decent human interaction and love is the reward for giving and caring. Lintott says, "Justice is more than the law, sir, though the law administers justice. There are strange ways of bringing it about, and it happens in a way you couldn't have planned. It's personal, too, sir. Each man carries his own justice with him. I've done a few things in my time, I don't mind admitting, which ain't exactly the letter of the law. But they were always a form of justice." It is one of the pleasures of these books to watch the author devise a punishment that fits each crime.

Nevertheless, there are drawbacks to Stubbs's approach to mystery fiction. In *Dear Laura*, a stream of consciousness carries much of the richness of Laura's memory. Unfortunately, the device is often a nuisance to interpret – too much meditating is inappropriate for mysteries. Even more disconcerting is the author's tendency to stop at plot junctures and ruminate on her themes. Whenever this happens, something of the plot is given away. But *The Painted Face* is much more straightforward than *Dear Laura*, and *The Golden Crucible* is a fast-moving story from beginning to end.

Jean Stubbs's work is genuinely in the art of the mystery novel – stylish, atmospherically accurate, and totally engrossing. You care about her people because it is quickly apparent that she cares. Along with the fine characterization and the well-drawn settings, Stubbs constructs a first-rate suspense story. Leading you through a maze of unfolding impressions and workable clues, she lets you bump time and again into the mirror of assumption before revealing her astonishing endings.

—Carol Washburne

* * *

STURROCK, Jeremy. Pseudonym for Benjamin James Healey; also writes as J. G. Jeffreys. British. Born in Birmingham, Warwickshire, 26 June 1908. Educated at Birmingham School of Art; Birmingham University, 1923–26. Served in the Royal Air Force 1940–45. Married Muriel Rose Herd in 1951. Scenic Artist and Stage Designer, Birmingham Repertory Theatre, 1926–31; Art Designer, Decorative Crafts, Birmingham, 1935–40; Scenic Artist, Denham Film Studios, London, 1946–47; Scenic Artist and Art Director, Riverside Film Studios, London, 1947–50; Free-lance scenic artist or art director for various film companies, 1951–67. Agent: Dr. Jan Van Loewen Ltd., 81–83 Shaftesbury Avenue, London W1V 8BX. Address: 19 Granard Avenue, Putney, London SW15 6HH, England.

Crime Publications

Novels (series character: Jeremy Sturrock in all books; published as J. G. Jeffreys in US)

> *The Village of Rogues.* London, Macmillan, 1972; as *The Thieftaker*, New York, Walker, 1972.
> *A Wicked Way to Die.* London, Macmillan, and New York, Walker, 1973.
> *The Wilful Lady.* London, Macmillan, and New York, Walker, 1975.
> *A Conspiracy of Poisons.* London, Hale, and New York, Walker, 1977.

Novels as Ben Healey (series characters: Harcourt d'Espinal; Paul Hedley)

> *Waiting for a Tiger* (Hedley). London, Hale, and New York, Harper, 1965.
> *The Millstone Men* (Hedley). London, Hale, 1966.
> *Death in Three Masks* (Hedley). London, Hale, 1967; as *The Terrible Pictures*, New York, Harper, 1967.
> *Murder Without Crime* (Hedley). London, Hale, 1968.
> *The Trouble with Penelope* (Hedley). London, Hale, 1972.
> *The Vespucci Papers* (d'Espinal). London, Hale, and Philadelphia, Lippincott, 1972.
> *The Stone Baby* (d'Espinal). Philadelphia, Lippincott, 1973; London, Hale, 1974.
> *The Horstmann Inheritance* (d'Espinal). London, Hale, 1975.
> *The Blanket of the Dark* (Hedley). London, Hale, 1976.
> *The Snapdragon Murders.* London, Hale, 1978.

Other Publications

Novels as Ben Healey

> *The Red Head Herring.* London, Hale, 1969.
> *Captain Havoc.* London, Hale, 1977.
> *Havoc in the Indies.* London, Hale, 1979.

Plays as Ben Healey

Television Series: *The Black Arrow*, 1972–73.

Other as B. J. Healey

A Gardener's Guide to Plant Names.   New York, Scribner, 1972.
The Plant Hunters.   New York, Scribner, 1975.

Manuscript Collection: Mugar Memorial Library, Boston University.

Jeremy Sturrock comments:
There is very little to say about my crime fiction except that it is intended solely as light entertaining fiction with no particular message. My main interests are art, books, history, and gardening, and these are usually reflected in my work. Apart from the Sturrock series, which I hope may continue, I am tending to turn away from conventional detective fiction in favour of historical novels. Work in progress is a late Renaissance tragedy based on the life of Bianca Capello, Grand Duchess of Tuscany from 1578 to 1587.

*   *   *

Following the recent trend of setting a plot in the past, the Jeremy Sturrock books go back to the beginnings of the English police force. In a note at the beginning of *The Village of Rogues* Sturrock states that his character is based generally on a real Bow Street Runner named Townsend. Combining that with frequent references to King George III, the playwright Sheridan, and conflict with Napoleon, Sturrock succeeds in removing the reader from the modern world. The historical elements blend in smoothly, however, and do not distract from the plot or immediate action. The bawdiness and roughness just beneath the thin surface of the upper classes comes through clearly. The dislike and contempt that people felt for the Bow Street Runners doesn't come through, however – people cooperate with Sturrock and readers find him likeable.

Sturrock is the narrator of the stories, presenting himself as almost all-knowing, boastful, humorous. He associates with and is aware of all the intrigue of the gentility, but he also knows the habits and coarseness of the working man (into whose class he was born). He claims to be the creator of the Art and Science of Detection – preceding Holmes by three-quarters of a century. Sturrock does come through with some actual detection, misleading his suspects by continually asking questions that seem irrelevant or inconsequential. The solution or plot behind all the mysterious activity tends to appear suddenly. Sturrock also anticipates Holmes by his use of Magsy, a street urchin used for shadowing, eavesdropping, and other various chores. Magsy also provides a large part of the humor as a foil for Sturrock's assumed suaveness.

—Fred Dueren

SUMMERTON, Margaret.   Also writes as Jan Roffman.   British.   Born in Birmingham, Warwickshire. Educated at a convent school and schools in Derbyshire and London. Worked for a publishing house in Paris; Reporter for London *Daily Mail* in the Netherlands and

Germany during and immediately after World War II; after the war worked on several magazines in London. Address: Roff Cottage, Burgh Hill, Etchingham, Sussex, England.

CRIME PUBLICATIONS

Novels

> The Sunset Hour. London, Hodder and Stoughton, 1957.
> The Red Pavilion. London, Hodder and Stoughton, 1958.
> A Small Wilderness. London, Hodder and Stoughton, 1959.
> The Sea House. London, Hodder and Stoughton, and New York, Holt Rinehart, 1961.
> Theft in Kind. London, Hodder and Stoughton, 1962.
> Nightingale at Noon. London, Hodder and Stoughton, and New York, Dutton, 1963.
> Quin's Hide. London, Hodder and Stoughton, 1964; New York, Dutton, 1965.
> Ring of Mischief. London, Hodder and Stoughton, and New York, Dutton, 1965.
> A Memory of Darkness. London, Hodder and Stoughton, and New York, Dutton, 1967.
> The Sand Rose. London, Collins, and New York, Doubleday, 1969.
> Sweetcrab. London, Collins, and New York, Doubleday, 1971.
> The Ghost Flowers. London, Collins, and New York, Doubleday, 1973.
> The Saffron Summer. London, Collins, 1974; New York, Doubleday, 1975.
> A Dark and Secret Place. London, Collins, and New York, Doubleday, 1977.

Novels as Jan Roffman

> With Murder in Mind. New York, Doubleday, 1963.
> Likely to Die. London, Bles, 1964.
> Winter of the Fox. London, Bles, 1964; as Death of a Fox, New York, Doubleday, 1964; as Reflection of Evil, New York, Ace, 1967.
> A Penny for the Guy. London, Bles, and New York, Doubleday, 1965; as Mask of Words, New York, Ace, 1973.
> The Hanging Woman. London, Bles, 1965.
> Ashes in an Urn. New York, Doubleday, 1966.
> A Daze of Fears. New York, Doubleday, 1968.
> Grave of Green Water. London, Long, and New York, Doubleday, 1968.
> Seeds of Suspicion. London, Long, 1968.
> A Walk in the Dark. London, Long, 1969; New York, Doubleday, 1970.
> A Bad Conscience. New York, Doubleday, 1972.
> A Dying in the Night. New York, Doubleday, 1974; London, Macdonald and Jane's, 1975.
> Why Someone Had to Die. London, Macdonald and Jane's, and New York, Doubleday, 1976.
> One Wreath with Love. New York, Doubleday, 1978.

Uncollected Short Story

> "Promise from a Stranger," in Good Housekeeping (Des Moines, Iowa), January 1977.

*   *   *

Margaret Summerton has unfortunately now "phased out of writing" (to use her own expression), a disappointment for the many women readers who enjoyed her frequently eerie style of thriller. As Margaret Summerton she produced some memorable books like Theft in Kind, Ring of Mischief, and A Memory of Darkness, but many preferred her thrillers written as

Jan Roffman including such books as *The Hanging Woman* and *Grave of Green Water*. The *Hanging Woman* is an outstanding example of her style – a clever but curious story of the death of a deftly drawn young woman with a sick small boy, the solution being reached through the memory of unpleasant happenings in the past. It is a book with a characteristically feminine slant.

—Herbert Harris

STYLES, Showell.   See **CARR, Glyn.**

SYMONS, Julian (Gustave). British. Born in London, 30 May 1912. Educated in various state schools. Married Kathleen Clark in 1941; one son and one daughter (deceased). Has worked as a shorthand typist, secretary for an engineering company, and advertising copywriter. Founding Editor, *Twentieth Century Verse*, London, 1937–39; Reviewer, Manchester *Evening News*, 1947–56; Editor, Penguin Mystery Series, 1974–77. Since 1958, Reviewer for the *Sunday Times*, London. Visiting Professor, Amherst College, Massachusetts, 1975–76. Co-Founder, 1953, and Chairman, 1958–59, Crime Writers Association; Chairman, Committee of Management, Society of Authors, 1969–71. Since 1976, President, Detection Club. Recipient: Crime Writers Association Award, 1957, 1966; Mystery Writers of America Edgar Allan Poe Award, 1961, 1973; Swedish Academy of Detection Grand Master Diploma, 1977. Fellow, Royal Society of Literature, 1975. Address: 147 Ramsden Road, London SW12 8RF, England.

CRIME PUBLICATIONS

Novels (series character: Inspector Bland)

The Immaterial Murder Case (Bland). London, Gollancz, 1945; New York, Macmillan, 1957.
A Man Called Jones (Bland). London, Gollancz, 1947.
Bland Beginning. London, Gollancz, and New York, Harper, 1949.
The Thirty-First of February. London, Gollancz, and New York, Harper, 1950.
The Broken Penny. London, Gollancz, and New York, Harper, 1953.
The Narrowing Circle. London, Gollancz, and New York, Harper, 1954.
The Paper Chase. London, Collins, 1956; as *Bogue's Fortune*, New York, Harper, 1957.
The Colour of Murder. London, Collins, and New York, Harper, 1957.
The Gigantic Shadow. London, Collins, 1958; as *The Pipe Dream*, New York, Harper, 1959.
The Progress of a Crime. London, Collins, and New York, Harper, 1960.
The Killing of Francie Lake. London, Collins, 1962; as *The Plain Man*, New York, Harper, 1962.

The End of Solomon Grundy.   London, Collins, and New York, Harper, 1964.
The Belting Inheritance.   London, Collins, and New York, Harper, 1965.
The Man Who Killed Himself.   London, Collins, and New York, Harper, 1967.
The Man Whose Dreams Came True.   London, Collins, 1968; New York, Harper, 1969.
The Man Who Lost His Wife.   London, Collins, 1970; New York, Harper, 1971.
The Players and the Game.   London, Collins, and New York, Harper, 1972.
The Plot Against Roger Rider.   London, Collins, and New York, Harper, 1973.
A Three-Pipe Problem.   London, Collins, and New York, Harper, 1975.
The Blackheath Poisonings.   London, Collins, 1978; New York, Harper, 1979.

Short Stories (series character: Francis Quarles)

Murder! Murder! (Quarles).   London, Fontana, 1961.
Francis Quarles Investigates.   London, Panther, 1965.
Ellery Queen Presents Julian Symons' How To Trap a Crook and Twelve Other Mysteries.   New York, Davis, 1977.

Uncollected Short Stories

"The Post-Mortem," in *Ellery Queen's Mystery Magazine* (New York), May 1979.
"Flowers That Bloom in the Spring," in *Ellery Queen's Mystery Magazine* (New York), July 1979.
"Waiting for Mr. McGregor," in *Verdict of Thirteen*, edited by Julian Symons.   London, Faber, and New York, Harper, 1979.

OTHER PUBLICATIONS

Plays

Radio Plays: *Affection Unlimited*, 1968; *Night Rider to Dover*, 1969.

Television Plays: *I Can't Bear Violence*, 1963; *Miranda and a Salesman*, 1963; *The Witnesses*, 1964; *The Finishing Touch*, 1965; *Curtains for Sheila*, 1965; *Tigers of Subtopia*, 1968; *The Pretenders*, 1970; *Whatever's Peter Playing At*, 1974.

Verse

Confusions about X.   London, Fortune Press, 1939.
The Second Man.   London, Routledge, 1943.
A Reflection on Auden.   London, Poem-of-the-Month Club, 1973.
The Object of an Affair and Other Poems.   Edinburgh, Tragara Press, 1974.

Other

A. J. A. Symons: His Life and Speculations.   London, Eyre and Spottiswoode, 1950.
Charles Dickens.   London, Barker, and New York, Roy, 1951.
Thomas Carlyle: The Life and Ideas of a Prophet.   London, Gollancz, and New York, Oxford University Press, 1952.
Horatio Bottomley.   London, Cresset Press, 1955.
The General Strike: A Historical Portrait.   London, Cresset Press, 1957; Chester Springs, Pennsylvania, Dufour, 1963.
The 100 Best Crime Stories.   London, Sunday Times, 1959.
The Thirties: A Dream Revolved.   London, Cresset Press, 1960; Chester Springs, Pennsylvania, Dufour, 1963; revised edition, London, Faber, 1975.

A Reasonable Doubt: Some Criminal Cases Re-examined.   London, Cresset Press, 1960.
The Detective Story in Britain.   London, Longman, 1962.
Buller's Campaign.   London, Cresset Press, 1963.
England's Pride: The Story of the Gordon Relief Expedition.   London, Hamish Hamilton, 1965.
Crime and Detection: An Illustrated History from 1840.   London, Studio Vista, 1966; as *A Pictorial History of Crime*, New York, Crown, 1966.
Critical Occasions.   London, Hamish Hamilton, 1966.
Bloody Murder.   London, Faber, 1972; as *Mortal Consequences*, New York, Harper, 1972.
Between the Wars: Britain in Photographs.   London, Batsford, 1972.
Notes from Another Country.   London, London Magazine Editions, 1972.
"Dashiell Hammett: The Onlie Begetter," in *Crime Writers*, edited by H. R. F. Keating.   London, BBC Publications, 1978.
The Tell-Tale Heart: The Life and Works of Edgar Allan Poe.   London, Faber, and New York, Harper, 1978.

Editor, *An Anthology of War Poetry.*   London, Penguin, 1942.
Editor, *Selected Writings of Samuel Johnson.*   London, Grey Walls Press, 1949.
Editor, *Selected Works, Reminiscences and Letters*, by Thomas Carlyle.   London, Hart Davis, 1956; Cambridge, Massachusetts, Harvard University Press, 1957.
Editor, *Essays and Biographies*, by A. J. A. Symons.   London, Cassell, 1969.
Editor, *The Woman in White*, by Wilkie Collins.   London, Penguin, 1974.
Editor, *The Angry 30's.*   London, Eyre Methuen, 1976.
Editor, *Verdict of Thirteen: A Detection Club Anthology.*   London, Faber, and New York, Harper, 1979.

Manuscript Collection: Humanities Research Center, University of Texas, Austin.

Julian Symons comments:
  I would still go along with the statement about my intentions made in my 1966 omnibus volume, with the qualification only that a crime writer is first of all an entertainer, and that if he fails as an entertainer his books won't succeed in any other way. Otherwise, let me repeat what I said in the omnibus:

  The thing that absorbs me most in our age is the violence behind respectable faces, the civil servant planning how to kill Jews most efficiently, the judge speaking with passion about the need for capital punishment, the quiet obedient boy who kills for fun. These are extreme cases, but if you want to show the violence that lives behind the bland faces most of us present to the world, what better vehicle can you have than the crime novel?

*   *   *

  Julian Symons published his first detective novel, *The Immaterial Murder Case*, in 1945, and its appearance marked, if it did not actually cause, an important turning point in his career as a writer. During the 1930's Symons was one of the leading members of the group of younger poets who, later in the decade, moved into prominence as successors to the Auden-Spender group. He edited *Twentieth Century Verse*, the rival of Geoffrey Grigson's historic *New Verse*, he published two volumes of his own sharply rational poems, and he began to emerge before the outbreak of World War II as an astute and sensitive literary critic. Today Symons is undoubtedly best known, on the basis of a score of novels, a couple of volumes of short stories, and an erudite account of crime literature, *Bloody Murder*, as one of our leading writers of mysteries, the nearest we have to an heir of Dorothy L. Sayers and Agatha Christie.

In his memoirs of his early days, *Notes from Another Country*, Symons has told how light-heartedly he entered the field of crime fiction, writing *The Immaterial Murder Case* during the 1930's as part of an elaborate joke shared with a fellow poet and leaving it six years in a drawer before he finally submitted it for publication. And in fact, though crime stories have become materially the most profitable side of Symons's writing life, he has not allowed them to deflect him from other types of writing. He is still a practicing critic and book reviewer; he has written books on Charles Dickens and Thomas Carlyle, on Edgar Allan Poe and on his own brother A. J. A. Symons. He has also written historical studies of the 1926 General Strike, the 1930's, and the Gordon Relief Expedition, and he has dabbled in autobiography.

Yet over the years one is conscious that Symons's interest in the crime novel, which at first seemed peripheral to his ambition to become a serious writer, has steadily moved into the centre of his literary career. In other words, he has come to regard it also as a form of serious writing, of equal importance to his historical and critical writings, to his biographies and memoirs and poetry.

His detective novels, at least from *The Thirty-First of February* onwards, are strongly thematic works whose governing ideas might, as he admits, have been exemplified in other times and places more appropriately in the orthodox or "straight" novel. And certainly his way of approaching his subject has diverged markedly from that of earlier detective story writers. Usually, indeed, there is a crime to be considered, though this is not always the case; *The Thirty-First of February*, for instance, gains a great deal of its sinister force from the fact that there is no crime at all except in the mind of the detective who hounds an innocent man to his death.

In his best novels, like *The Broken Penny*, *The Narrowing Circle*, *The Colour of Murder*, *The End of Solomon Grundy*, Symons is not really concerned to create the well-made detective story which works itself out as the intellectually satisfying solution of a complex puzzle through the right manipulation of given clues. His plots are often loose rather than tight, sometimes they are disconcertingly open and obvious, and often the denouements are deliberately anti-climactic. There is more than a little irony in his attitude to such matters, and he is quite capable of leaving a little fog of mystery unresolved to annoy the meticulous reader.

What he does inject into these often disjointed variants on the classic crime-and-detection plot is the kind of content that comes from his own world view, that of a radical critic who looks on existing political and social orders with a great deal of sardonic scepticism. Symons is concerned with how the crimes he portrays reflect the decay of society, with the pretences of the world of culture, and with politics and power as corrupting elements. The world he has peculiarly made his own is that Bohemian half-world where failed writers and hack artists and the calculating hangers-on of the arts combine to create a setting in which alienation encourages the emergence of crime; this is a world where the murderer and the victim seem to attract each other, a world dominated by frauds and hollow men whose presence suggests that Symons not merely knew Wyndham Lewis, as he did in his youth, but was also influenced by him. It is a world of ambiguous guilts, where the hunted man may be objectively innocent but subjectively culpable, and where the forces of law are unpredictable as the defenders of true order. In the end, it is not for the way he solves the details of crimes that Symons's novels are interesting, but rather for the way he finds their causes in the minds of men and the shapes of societies.

—George Woodcock

TAYLOR, H. Baldwin. See WAUGH, Hillary.

TAYLOR, Phoebe Atwood. Also wrote as Alice Tilton. American. Born in Boston, Massachusetts, 18 May 1909. Educated at Barnard College (Lucille Pulitzer Scholar), New York, B.A. 1930. Married Dr. Grantly Walden Taylor. Full-time writer from 1931. Lived in Weston, Massachusetts. *Died 9 January 1976.*

CRIME PUBLICATIONS

Novels (series character: Asey Mayo in all books)

> *The Cape Cod Mystery.* Indianapolis, Bobbs Merrill, 1931.
> *Death Lights a Candle.* Indianapolis, Bobbs Merrill, 1932.
> *The Mystery of the Cape Cod Players.* New York, Norton, 1933; London, Eyre and Spottiswoode, 1934.
> *The Mystery of the Cape Cod Tavern.* New York, Norton, 1934; London, Eyre and Spottiswoode, 1935.
> *Sandbar Sinister.* New York, Norton, 1934; London, Gollancz, 1936.
> *The Tinkling Symbol.* New York, Norton, and London, Gollancz, 1935.
> *Deathblow Hill.* New York, Norton, 1935; London, Gollancz, 1936.
> *The Crimson Patch.* New York, Norton, and London, Gollancz, 1936.
> *Out of Order.* New York, Norton, 1936; London, Gollancz, 1937.
> *Figure Away.* New York, Norton, 1937; London, Collins, 1938.
> *Octagon House.* New York, Norton, 1937; London, Collins, 1938.
> *The Annulet of Gilt.* New York, Norton, 1938; London, Collins, 1939.
> *Banbury Bog.* New York, Norton, 1938; London, Collins, 1939.
> *Spring Harrowing.* New York, Norton, and London, Collins, 1939.
> *The Criminal C.O.D.* New York, Norton, and London, Collins, 1940.
> *The Deadly Sunshade.* New York, Norton, 1940; London, Collins, 1941.
> *The Perennial Boarder.* New York, Norton, 1941; London, Collins, 1942.
> *The Six Iron Spiders.* New York, Norton, 1942; London, Collins, 1943.
> *Three Plots for Asey Mayo* (novelets). New York, Norton, 1942.
> *Going, Going, Gone.* New York, Norton, 1943; London, Collins, 1944.
> *Proof of the Pudding.* New York, Norton, and London, Collins, 1945.
> *The Asey Mayo Trio* (novelets). New York, Messner, and London, Collins, 1946.
> *Punch with Care.* New York, Farrar Straus, 1946; London, Collins, 1947.
> *Diplomatic Corpse.* Boston, Little Brown, and London, Collins, 1951.

Novels as Alice Tilton (series character: Leonidas Witherall in all books)

> *Beginning with a Bash.* London, Collins, 1937; New York, Norton, 1972.
> *The Cut Direct.* New York, Norton, and London, Collins, 1938.
> *Cold Steal.* New York, Norton, 1939; London, Collins, 1940.
> *The Left Leg.* New York, Norton, 1940; London, Collins, 1941.
> *The Hollow Chest.* New York, Norton, 1941; London, Collins, 1942.
> *File for Record.* New York, Norton, 1943; London, Collins, 1944.
> *Dead Ernest.* New York, Norton, 1944; London, Collins, 1945.
> *The Iron Clew.* New York, Farrar Straus, 1947; as *The Iron Hand*, London, Collins, 1947.

Uncollected Short Story

"Swan-Boat Murders," in *Murder Cavalcade*, edited by Ken Crossen. New York, Duell, 1946; London, Hammond, 1953.

Manuscript Collection: Mugar Memorial Library, Boston University.

*   *   *

Phoebe Atwood Taylor, who also used the pseudonym Alice Tilton, produced some 30 mystery novels and a number of shorter tales, most of them written during the 1930's and 1940's. Though she was able to devise the plots and puzzles that were popular during that period, she was above all a humorist, sometimes understated and subtle, often wild and farcical, always witty and amusing. She created two major heroes, Asey Mayo and Leonidas Witherall, as well as a host of other well-drawn characters.

Asey Mayo of Wellfleet, on Cape Cod, is the quintessential Yankee. He thinks straight and talks plain, in a dialect masterfully recorded by his author. Independent, taciturn, tough, and extraordinarily clever, he embodies the traditional Yankee virtues. He went to sea as a boy and later became a mechanic and racing driver for an early automobile manufacturer. According to a newspaper article quoted in *Spring Harrowing*, "Sleuth Mayo pioneered Porter cars, made coast-to-coast tour in 1899 in two-cylindered Porter Century; drove Porter Bullet II in 1904 at Daytona Beach to beat fastest foreign racing car...." Made famous by his exploits, he is "widely roto-gravured," and called, variously, the Codfish Sherlock, the Homespun Sleuth, and Jack-of-All-Trades; made rich by his ingenuity and hard work, he nevertheless relishes the simple life, preferring his old corduroys and ancient yachting cap to his good white flannels. The "Codfish Sherlock" does not lack a Watson – the local favourite "Doc" Cummings.

Asey's logic and clear-sightedness are indispensable in solving mysteries since the local lawmen, who are usually referred to as "combing" the area or "scouring" the underbrush, are none too bright. Details of Cape Cod atmosphere are interwoven with plot and character to provide gems like "Miss Curran of the dubious beachplum Currans" (*Proof of the Pudding*); a boarding house which seeks "Old fashioned boarders ... for impossibly inconvenient house with no modern improvements whatsoever. Oil lamps, outhouse, pump. Prunes for breakfast, catch your own fish, dig your own clams!" (*Octagon House*); and Asey's views on a freshwater pond: "There's a pond up near the hollow where people do go ... though I wouldn't give two cents for it myself. Tourists wash there, and cottages without any bathtubs take a cake of soap an' dabble with the outer layers, an' any number of dogs get washed there, too" (*Figure Away*). Cranberry bogs, old shipwrecks and legends of pirates' gold, summer visitors who descend on people lucky enough to have cottages, and natives who profit from every opportunity to make money from the tourists, all appear in these tales.

The Leonidas Witherall stories, by Alice Tilton, set in mythical suburbs of Boston, present such chaotic situations that ordinary suspense is superseded by curiosity about how the author can possibly extricate her protagonists from the shambles. Leonidas, who resembles well-known likenesses of Shakespeare and thus is called Will Shakespeare – or even Bill – by his cohorts, is first seen as a retired professor who hunts books for wealthy but lazy Boston collectors, later as owner of Meredith's Academy, a private boys school of venerable, if not always decorous, tradition. Unknown to other characters in the tales, Leonidas Witherall is the author of the "blood-and-thunder" thrillers featuring the intrepid Lieutenant Haseltine, whose adventures are invariably called to mind by those characters in the midst of their own problems. Witherall, cynic and intellectual, whose speech is stilted and pompous (and funny), and who appears to be a model of the dignified solid citizen, fails to report corpses (sometimes he even moves them), covers up burglaries, lies to the police, and behaves – it must be admitted – in a most irregular way. The reader, however, can scarcely fail to sympathize with "Bill Shakespeare," prevaricator and conspirator though he occasionally is, since he unfailingly pursues ultimate truth and justice.

Just as Witherall's companions in mischief see themselves as actors in thrillers within thrillers, other characters remark upon their own perplexities in contrast to those of the unlikely denizens of "fiction." In *Going, Going, Gone*, one fellow complains: " 'I can always figure out book murders from the first page! I'm good at them!' 'It's a matter of extraneous odds an' ends,' Asey said. 'You run into more of 'em this way than you do in books. An' nobody presents you with printed descriptions. You got to figger out for yourself if the New York lawyer an' his fat sister an' his big-nosed nephew an' the antique lady an' the semi-antique man ... an' the rich Madisons is all lyin' in whole, or in part, an' if so, which part.' " Miss Taylor, in her game of mirrors, also has a Wellfleet woman comment on an outlander lady novelist: "She's mixed in with the women here in town, but I've always steered a little clear of her. I think her heartiness, like when she comes to the club, is just a put-on job. It's always been my opinion she was scratchin' up local color for one of her stories" (*Proof of the Pudding*).

The author was expert in depicting the everyday life of the times. Country auctions, local politics (including a mural containing malicious caricatures of local figures painted at government expense in a pork-barrel post office), opinion polls, lawn fetes, cake sales and other fund-raisers, old home weeks, ladies' clubs, radio soap operas, and such wartime phenomena as blackouts, wardens, codes, and gasoline rationing, form the background of these stories. Her comic vision combined with a superb eye for detail enabled her to create tales that are period pieces in the best sense, never dated, but as fresh and full of fun as when they were written. Her works are a treasure for popular culture enthusiasts and connoisseurs of American humor. Phoebe Atwood Taylor should find a new audience – even if not the masses – in each generation of crime fiction fans.

—Mary Helen Becker

TEY, Josephine. Pseudonym for Elizabeth Mackintosh; also wrote as Gordon Daviot. British. Born in Inverness, Scotland, in 1897. Educated at the Royal Academy, Inverness; Anstey Physical Training College, Birmingham. Taught physical education in various schools in the 1920's. Lived in London. *Died 13 February 1952.*

CRIME PUBLICATIONS

Novels (series character: Inspector Alan Grant)

The Man in the Queue (Grant; as Gordon Daviot). London, Methuen, and New York, Dutton, 1929; as *Killer in the Crowd*, New York, Spivak, 1954.
A Shilling for Candles: The Story of a Crime (Grant). London, Methuen, 1936; New York, Macmillan, 1954.
Miss Pym Disposes. London, Davies, 1946; New York, Macmillan, 1948.
The Franchise Affair. London, Davies, 1948; New York, Macmillan, 1949.
Brat Farrar. London, Davies, 1949; New York, Morrow, 1950; as *Come and Kill Me*, New York, Pocket Books, 1951.
To Love and Be Wise (Grant). London, Davies, 1950; New York, Macmillan, 1951.
The Daughter of Time (Grant). London, Davies, 1951; New York, Macmillan, 1952.
The Singing Sands (Grant). London, Davies, 1952; New York, Macmillan, 1953.

OTHER PUBLICATIONS as Gordon Daviot

Novels

Kif: An Unvarnished History. London, Benn, and New York, Appleton, 1929.
The Expensive Halo. London, Benn, and New York, Appleton, 1931.
The Privateer. London, Davies, and New York, Macmillan, 1952.

Plays

Richard of Bordeaux (produced London, 1932). London, Gollancz, and Boston, Little
    Brown, 1933.
The Laughing Woman (produced London, 1934). London, Gollancz, 1934.
Queen of Scots (produced London, 1934). London, Gollancz, 1934.
The Stars Bow Down (produced Malvern, Worcestershire, 1939). London, Duckworth,
    1939.
Leith Sands and Other Short Plays (includes *The Three Mrs. Madderleys, Mrs. Fry Has a
    Visitor, Remember Caesar, Rahab, The Mother of Masé, Sara, Clarion
    Call*). London, Duckworth, 1946.
The Little Dry Thorn (produced London, 1947). Included in *Plays 1*, 1953.
Valerius (produced London, 1948). Included in *Plays 1*, 1953.
The Pen of My Aunt (broadcast, 1950). Included in *Plays 2*, 1954.
Plays. London, Davies, 3 vols., 1953–54.
Dickon (produced Salisbury, 1955). Included in *Plays 1*, 1953.
The Pomp of Mr. Pomfret (broadcast, 1954). Included in *Plays 2*, 1954.
Cornelia (broadcast, 1955). Included in *Plays 2*, 1954.
Sweet Coz (produced Farnham, Surrey, 1956). Included in *Plays 3*, 1954.

Radio Plays: *Leith Sands,* 1941; *The Three Mrs. Madderleys,* 1944; *Mrs. Fry Has a
Visitor,* 1944; *Remember Caesar,* 1946; *The Pen of My Aunt,* 1950; *The Pomp of Mr.
Pomfret,* 1954; *Cornelia,* 1955.

Other

Claverhouse (biography). London, Collins, 1937.

*   *   *

Josephine Tey's novels of mystery and detection are often categorized with those of
Dorothy L. Sayers and Ngaio Marsh. While her work differs from theirs in several respects, it
undoubtedly belongs to the Golden Age of detective fiction. Her style is pure, her plots and
characters carefully wrought, and her adherence to the classical traditions dependable. Tey
wrote several non-series examples of detection and mystery in addition to her creation of the
gentleman-police officer Alan Grant, whose shoes never revealed his status as CID
investigator.

Tey's amateur detectives are each different from the other. In *Miss Pym Disposes* a former
French teacher who has casually and flippantly written a popular psychology book begins to
believe in her ability to understand the human psyche. At a girl's physical education college,
which is described with fascinating details of programs of study, sport activities, and
employment inquiries, Miss Pym undertakes the discovery of a murderer of an unpleasant
student. The investigation gives Tey great opportunity to describe an improbable gathering of
teen-aged physical education students: the independent and attractive Head Girl, "Beau"
Nash; her pleasant, intelligent, competent friend, Mary Innes; and the fiery Latin American
exchange student, far more sexually mature than her peers, who wants only to dance.

Miss Pym's faith in discovering people's guilt in crime by understanding their personalities is shared by Lawyer Robert Blair who solves *The Franchise Affair* for his client Marion Sharpe. Unfortuantely, Tey's adaptation of a true 18th-century crime is somewhat slow-paced and the tracking down of the accused seems too casually accomplished. The important developments in concluding the investigation appear later in the novel so that character study is the most significant activity: Tey draws vivid pictures of old Mrs. Sharpe and Blair's maiden Aunt Lin; even the girl Betty is clearly portrayed, her child's demure face and costume hiding a devious and self-centered core.

Deliberate detective work is minimized in Tey's only other non-Alan Grant mystery, *Brat Farrar*. A young man who closely resembles the dead son of a comfortable, horse-breeding English family, agrees to impersonate the young man, who is thought to have killed himself. The relationship between the imposter and his "family," including a young relative who begins to love him in a very unfamilial way, seems to provide the center of the story. However, the young man stumbles upon information about his new identity which could lead to murder. The difficulties of continuing the investigation and the imposture simultaneously are intertwined; the answer to one is the solution to both.

Although Alan Grant is a fairly fixed character throughout several novels, neither courting nor marrying (unlike Lord Peter Wimsey and Roderick Alleyn), he is clearly as significant a creation and as personal and human a character. His personality is defined in his first appearance in *The Man in the Queue* and while other characteristics are revealed subsequently, he is reliably predictable in his behavior. Recipient of a comfortable legacy, Grant chose to continue police work for the satisfaction he received in working out the puzzles of an investigation. He is a gentleman at the Yard (like Roderick Alleyn) and his manner and manners are intelligent and well-bred. Natty without looking like a tailor's dummy, he is more successful with the upper classes than his faithful Watson, Sergeant Williams; his unfailing courtesy makes him equally successful with the lower orders and the criminal class. His enjoyment of the sport and open spaces of the countryside is a common motif in the novels and is employed as a cure for his claustrophobia, induced by a severe injury. This "weakness," as Grant calls it in *The Singing Sands*, mortifies him; his investigations, requiring rides in closed cars, trains, and small aeroplanes, provide the motive to conquer rather than avoid this fear. When he finds a major clue to a mystery, he is suddenly able to make a return plane trip without this debilitating and demoralizing fear. This method of not concentrating on his most serious problem is also Grant's style of detection: while his chief "worries a case to death," Grant deliberately puts it from his mind when he reaches a stalemate to let his unconscious find the next move. Because of his good fortune in using this technique, he is credited by his colleagues with "flair." It should be acknowledged that Grant's flair often misleads him in his investigations; *The Man in the Queue* is the best example of perfect deduction being entirely wrong.

Grant's most famous case, in *The Daughter of Time*, is undertaken from a hospital bed as he re-examines the supposed murder by Richard III of his two nephews in the Tower of London in the 1480's. This famous crime, unchallenged in school texts and magnified by Shakespeare's successful portrayal of villainy personified, intrigues Grant who investigates contemporary sources to learn of Richard's innocence. When he and his assistant prove their case, both are shocked to discover their conclusions supported by similar claims since the 17th century; none has shaken the general public's belief. Grant's dismay and American Brent Carradine's crusade to educate are at the heart of the novel. Tey's introduction of similar episodes of belief opposing fact and her cast of characters ranged against Grant and Carradine's truth demonstrate the potency of "hearsay evidence." The intensity of Grant's search for accurate information mystifies his nurses, the porter, and sometimes even friends. Besides being a unique example of detection, the novel clearly presents the difficulty of establishing facts in the face of people's preference for what they believe to be the truth.

Because Tey writes so compelling a mystery novel, she is unquestionably one of the most significant authors in the genre. But her talent is not limited to the plotting and deducing of that form; in her detective and her characters she creates credible personalities whose individuality and relationships are realistic and complex. Beyond this, she is concerned, at the core of her work, with moral questions which go beyond the conventions of detective fiction without ever being extraneous to the carefully controlled structure and plot. The critical and popular success of her eight detective novels attests to the unmistakably fine quality of her work.

—Kathleen G. Klein

THAYER, Lee (Emma Redington Thayer, née Lee). American. Born in Troy, Pennsylvania, 5 April 1874. Educated at Cooper Union and Pratt Institute, New York City. Married Henry W. Thayer in 1909. Artist and illustrator: paintings displayed at Chicago World's Fair, 1893; produced designs for book jackets. Interior decorator, Associated Artists, New York, 1890–96; Director, Decorative Designers, New York, 1896–1932. *Died 18 November 1973.*

CRIME PUBLICATIONS

Novels (series character: Peter Clancy in all books except *Doctor S.O.S.)*

The Mystery of the Thirteenth Floor. New York, Century, 1919.
The Unlatched Door. New York, Century, 1920.
That Affair at "The Cedars." New York, Doubleday, 1921; London, Hurst and Blackett, 1924.
Q.E.D. New York, Doubleday, 1922; as *The Puzzle*, London, Hurst and Blackett, 1923.
The Sinister Mark. New York, Doubleday, and London, Hurst and Blackett, 1923.
The Key. New York, Doubleday, and London, Hurst and Blackett, 1924.
Doctor S.O.S. New York, Doubleday, and London, Hurst and Blackett, 1925.
Poison. New York, Doubleday, and London, Heinemann, 1926.
Alias Dr. Ely. New York, Doubleday, and London, Hurst and Blackett, 1927.
The Darkest Spot. New York, Sears, and London, Hurst and Blackett, 1928.
Dead Men's Shoes. New York, Sears, and London, Hurst and Blackett, 1929.
They Tell No Tales. New York, Sears, and London, Hurst and Blackett, 1930.
The Last Shot. New York, Sears, and London, Hurst and Blackett, 1931.
Set a Thief. New York, Sears, 1931; as *To Catch a Thief*, London, Hurst and Blackett, 1932.
The Glass Knife. New York, Sears, and London, Hurst and Blackett, 1932.
The Scrimshaw Millions. New York, Sears, 1932; London, Hurst and Blackett, 1933.
Counterfeit. New York, Sears, 1933; as *The Counterfeit Bill*, London, Hurst and Blackett, 1934.
Hell-Gate Tides. New York, Sears, and London, Hurst and Blackett, 1933.
The Second Bullet. New York, Sears, 1934; as *The Second Shot*, London, Hurst and Blackett, 1935.
Dead Storage. New York, Dodd Mead, 1935; as *The Death Weed*, London, Hurst and Blackett, 1935.
Sudden Death. New York, Dodd Mead, 1935; as *Red-Handed*, London, Hurst and Blackett, 1936.
Dark of the Moon. New York, Dodd Mead, 1936; as *Death in the Gorge*, London, Hurst and Blackett, 1937.

Dead End Street, No Outlet.   New York, Dodd Mead, 1936; as *Murder in the Mirror*, London, Hurst and Blackett, 1936.

Last Trump.   New York, Dodd Mead, and London, Hurst and Blackett, 1937.

A Man's Enemies.   New York, Dodd Mead, 1937; as *This Man's Doom*, London, Hurst and Blackett, 1938.

Ransom Racket.   New York, Dodd Mead, and London, Hurst and Blackett, 1938.

That Strange Sylvester Affair.   New York, Dodd Mead, 1938; London, Hurst and Blackett, 1939.

Lightning Strikes Twice.   New York, Dodd Mead, and London, Hurst and Blackett, 1939.

Stark Murder.   New York, Dodd Mead, 1939; London, Hurst and Blackett, 1940.

Guilty.   New York, Dodd Mead, 1940; London, Hurst and Blackett, 1941.

X Marks the Spot.   New York, Dodd Mead, 1940; London, Hurst and Blackett, 1941.

Hallowe'en Homicide.   New York, Dodd Mead, 1941; London, Hurst and Blackett, 1942.

Persons Unknown.   New York, Dodd Mead, 1941; London, Hurst and Blackett, 1942.

Murder Is Out.   New York, Dodd Mead, 1942; London, Hurst and Blackett, 1943.

Murder on Location.   New York, Dodd Mead, 1942; London, Hurst and Blackett, 1944.

Accessory after the Fact.   New York, Dodd Mead, 1943; London, Hurst and Blackett, 1944.

Hanging's Too Good.   New York, Dodd Mead, 1943; London, Hurst and Blackett, 1945.

A Plain Case of Murder.   New York, Dodd Mead, 1944; London, Hurst and Blackett, 1945.

Five Bullets.   New York, Dodd Mead, 1944; London, Hurst and Blackett, 1947.

Accident, Manslaughter, or Murder?   New York, Dodd Mead, 1945; London, Hurst and Blackett, 1946.

A Hair's Breadth.   New York, Dodd Mead, 1946; London, Hurst and Blackett, 1947.

The Jaws of Death.   New York, Dodd Mead, 1946; London, Hurst and Blackett, 1948.

Murder Stalks the Circle.   New York, Dodd Mead, 1947; London, Hurst and Blackett, 1949.

Out, Brief Candle!   New York, Dodd Mead, 1948; London, Hurst and Blackett, 1950.

Pig in a Poke.   New York, Dodd Mead, 1948; as *A Clue for Clancy*, London, Hurst and Blackett, 1950.

Evil Root.   New York, Dodd Mead, 1949; London, Hurst and Blackett, 1951.

Within the Vault.   New York, Dodd Mead, 1950; as *Death Within the Vault*, London, Hurst and Blackett, 1951.

Too Long Endured.   New York, Dodd Mead, 1950; London, Hurst and Blackett, 1952.

Do Not Disturb.   New York, Dodd Mead, 1951; as *Clancy's Secret Mission*, London, Hurst and Blackett, 1952.

Guilt Edged.   New York, Dodd Mead, 1951; as *Guilt-Edged Murder*, London, Hurst and Blackett, 1953.

Blood on the Knight.   New York, Dodd Mead, 1952; London, Hurst and Blackett, 1953.

The Prisoner Pleads "Not Guilty."   New York, Dodd Mead, 1953; London, Hurst and Blackett, 1954.

Dead Reckoning.   New York, Dodd Mead, 1954; as *Murder on the Pacific*, London, Hurst and Blackett, 1955.

No Holiday for Death.   New York, Dodd Mead, 1954; London, Hurst and Blackett, 1955.

Who Benefits?   New York, Dodd Mead, 1955; as *Fatal Alibi*, London, Hurst and Blackett, 1956.

Guilt Is Where You Find It.   New York, Dodd Mead, 1957; London, Long, 1958.

Still No Answer.   New York, Dodd Mead, 1958; as *Web of Hate*, London, Long, 1959.

Two Ways to Die.   New York, Dodd Mead, 1959; London, Long, 1961.

Dead on Arrival. New York, Dodd Mead, 1960; London, Long, 1962.
And One Cried Murder. New York, Dodd Mead, 1961; London, Long, 1962.
Dusty Death. New York, Dodd Mead, 1966; as *Death Walks in Shadow*, London, Long, 1966.

OTHER PUBLICATIONS

Other

Alice and the Wonderland People (stencil pictures). New York, Bungalow Book and Toy Company, 1914.
When Mother Lets Us Draw (juvenile). New York, Moffat Yard, 1916.

* * *

Perhaps the oldest-ever mystery novelist, Lee Thayer wrote her last book at the age of 92 and published some 60 novels during a career that began in 1919. Although Thayer considered herself an artist, not a writer, her prolific writing career could hardly be considered a mere hobby. Her artistic ability did prove useful, though, since she occasionally drew pictorial designs for book bindings and dust jackets, including many for her own books.

Except for *Doctor S.O.S.*, all of her mystery novels star a man-about-town private eye, Peter Clancy, and his very proper English valet, Wiggar. The atmosphere and charm of the Thayer novels depend heavily upon the relationship between Clancy and Wiggar which is curiously reminiscent of P. G. Wodehouse's team Bertie Wooster and Jeeves. Thayer's use of the master-butler relationship, however, is merely a diversion from the mystery plot, adding character and wit to the stories, whereas Wodehouse's use of Wooster and Jeeves is more a comic study of character interplay with less emphasis on plot. Although Wooster and Jeeves may, incidentally, solve a few mysteries, it is Wooster's comical bungling and Jeeves's masterful rescue of his master that are the essence of the Wodehouse novels. In contrast to Wooster, Peter Clancy is no common bungler, but a very adept private eye, aided and abetted by the extremely righteous Wiggar. Their humorous relationship, with Clancy often submitting to Wiggar's precise knowledge of correct behavior, adds richness and humor to their adventures.

Although fraught with dated devices of the "Had I But Known" school of mystery authors, Thayer's plots are nevertheless original, interesting, and credible. All of the plots contain some sort of damsel in distress, a dashing hero (usually wrongfully accused of the murder), a neurotic or at times even psychotic red herring of a character meant to mislead the reader, and, of course, the true villain, motivated by passion.

The settings vary greatly, from New England to California to Europe. Usually each book features but one murder, although other crimes ranging from bank robbery to blackmail may also take place during the course of the story. In *Within the Vault* a bank's stockholder is found murdered within the safety deposit vault only a few days after the bank had been the scene of a daring daylight robbery. Of course Clancy and Wiggar happen casually upon the scene and are invited to participate in the investigation, much to the advantage of the local police. Even though the case appears to be a simple one, since everyone entering the vault, except bank employees, had to sign a card recording the time of their entrance, Clancy, Wiggar, and Captain Michael Shannon have to work against time to prove that the most likely suspect was not the guilty party after all.

Too Long Endured and *Murder on Location*, as well as several other Thayer novels, feature actors or actresses as either victims or culprits. *Five Bullets* finds a college psychology experiment gone awry when a student is shot in a classroom by a gun supposedly filled with blanks.

Although Thayer's works are done primarily in the pre-war style, her unique characters and interesting settings make them worth sampling.

—Mary Ann Grochowski

THOMAS, Ross. Also writes as Oliver Bleeck. American. Born in Oklahoma City, Oklahoma, 19 February 1926. Educated at the University of Oklahoma, Norman, B.A. 1949. Served in the United States Army Infantry in the Philippines, 1944–46. Married Rosalie Appleton in 1974. Worked as journalist, editor, and public relations executive in the United States, Europe, and Africa. Recipient: Mystery Writers of America Edgar Allan Poe Award, 1967. Agent: Curtis Brown Ltd., 575 Madison Avenue, New York, New York 10022. Address: 28124 Pacific Coast Highway, Malibu, California 90265, U.S.A.

CRIME PUBLICATIONS

Novels (series characters: McCorkle and Padillo)

The Cold War Swap (McCorkle and Padillo). New York, Morrow, 1966; as Spy in the Vodka, London, Hodder and Stoughton, 1967.
Cast a Yellow Shadow (McCorkle and Padillo). New York, Morrow, 1967; London, Hodder and Stoughton, 1968.
The Seersucker Whipsaw. New York, Morrow, 1967; London, Hodder and Stoughton, 1968.
The Singapore Wink. New York, Morrow, and London, Hodder and Stoughton, 1969.
The Fools in Town Are on Our Side. London, Hodder and Stoughton, 1970; New York, Morrow, 1971.
The Backup Men (McCorkle and Padillo). New York, Morrow, and London, Hodder and Stoughton, 1971.
The Porkchoppers. New York, Morrow, 1972; London, Hamish Hamilton, 1974.
If You Can't Be Good. New York, Morrow, 1973; London, Hamish Hamilton, 1974.
The Money Harvest. New York, Morrow, and London, Hamish Hamilton, 1975.
Yellow-Dog Contract. New York, Morrow, 1976; London, Hamish Hamilton, 1977.
Chinaman's Chance. New York, Simon and Schuster, and London, Hamish Hamilton, 1978.
The Eighth Dwarf. New York, Simon and Schuster, and London, Hamish Hamilton, 1979.

Novels as Oliver Bleeck (series character: Philip St. Ives in all books)

The Brass Go-Between. New York, Morrow, 1969; London, Hodder and Stoughton, 1970.
Protocol for a Kidnapping. New York, Morrow, and London, Hodder and Stoughton, 1971.
The Procane Chronicle. New York, Morrow, 1972; as The Thief Who Painted Sunlight, London, Hodder and Stoughton, 1972; as St. Ives, New York, Pocket Books, 1976.
The Highbinders. New York, Morrow, and London, Hamish Hamilton, 1974.
No Questions Asked. New York, Morrow, and London, Hamish Hamilton, 1976.

OTHER PUBLICATIONS

Other

Warriors for the Poor: The Story of VISTA, with William H. Crook.   New York,
Morrow, 1969.

*   *   *

As a writer of political thrillers, Ross Thomas is America's answer to Len Deighton and
John le Carré, except that Thomas is funnier than either. He assumes what some le Carré
characters have still to learn – that no government or institution can be trusted, and that
individuals are only slightly more reliable than institutions. His impressive first novel, *The
Cold War Swap*, concerns an "amortized," or expendable, American agent, surveys
governments' "recruitment" methods for spies, and suggests how important public image has
become even in espionage. With Deighton, Thomas shares a fascination with how things
work, although his field of interest is different. In *The Porkchoppers* the reader finds out how
a union election campaign is managed, and rigged; in *The Money Harvest*, how the
commodities market works, and how it could be rigged; and in *The Seersucker Whipsaw*,
how a political campaign in an emerging African nation might be directed, and manipulated.
Before turning to the novel, Ross Thomas pursued careers in journalism and public relations,
and nothing of what he learned was lost on him.

Each Ross Thomas book runs like a well-oiled machine for entertaining readers who have
good general intelligence and strong suspicions about the motives of the people in charge of
things. As Ross Thomas, he has written a dozen books about reluctant spies and political
skulduggery. As Oliver Bleeck, he has written five books about Philip St. Ives, a professional
go-between who functions as the point of contact between people who own valuable things
and thieves who steal them – these classes overlap fairly often, of course. The formula and
major components in all these books are the same: a group of protagonists who are
knowledgeable, likeable, and for whom heroism is a last resort; a collection of secondary
characters as various and colorful as the protagonists are similar and conservative;
convincing settings; a deceptively relaxed and always literate prose style; and plots as lucid as
they are complicated. Thomas's heroes are cousins to Deighton's hero and lineal descendants
of Bret Maverick; they are so laid back as to be almost supine. A few Thomas heroes are
married, and those who are not are provided with companionship. Thomas's female
characters deserve special mention: they are either cooly or warmly intelligent, have no more
illusions than the men they work with, and take their sex like adults. Thomas never descends
to overheated "Stud prose" in describing sex. And it may or may not be a comment on Travis
McGee that one of the heroes of *Chinaman's Chance* has been suffering from a nasty case of
psychologically based impotence until he is cured by the love of a good woman.

After the horrific insights into the way things work, the adult characters, and the
beautifully paced plots, the major attraction of these books is their humor. Thomas prefers
the kind that ambushes the reader, often in the dryly bemused narrative, or in the characters'
understated dialogue. One of them, the redoubtable Park Tyler Wisdom III from Bleeck's
Protocol for a Kidnapping, has expected to be court martialled for a deed "of incredible
pusillanimity" in Vietnam. Given a Silver Star instead, he chose to laugh rather than cry.
Thomas's characters are often presented with similar dilemmas, and they always choose the
path of wisdom. And Thomas is definitely not above a quiet literary joke. In *The Eighth
Dwarf* one of the characters is a young woman whose prose and conversational styles were
formed by unrelieved exposure to a library of Victorian literature. It is not until the hero takes
her to bed that he discovers it was a complete Victorian library, and she had read everything
in the locked case too.

—Carol Cleveland

THOMSON, Basil (Home). British. Born 21 April 1861. Educated at Eton College; New College, Oxford; Inner Temple, London: called to the Bar. Married in 1889; three children. Worked in the Foreign Service: Prime Minister of Tonga in early 1890's; entered the Civil Service and became Governor of Dartmoor Prison, Devon, until 1907, and of Wormwood Scrubs Prison, London, 1907; Secretary to the Prison Commission, 1908; Assistant Commissioner, Metropolitan Police, London, 1913–19; Director of Intelligence, 1919–21. Recipient: Royal Humane Society Silver Medal. Companion, 1916, and Knight Commander of the Bath, 1919; Commander, Crown of Italy; Member, Order of the Rising Sun, Japan; Member, Order of Leopold, and of the Crown, Belgium. *Died 26 March 1939.*

CRIME PUBLICATIONS

Novels (series character: Police Constable/Superintendent Richardson)

A Court Intrigue. London, Heinemann, 1896.
Carfax Abbey. London, Methuen, 1928.
The Metal Flask. London, Methuen, 1929.
The Prince from Overseas. London, Chapman and Hall, 1930.
P.C. Richardson's First Case. London, Eldon Press, and New York, Doubleday, 1933.
The Kidnapper. London, Eldon Press, 1933.
Richardson Scores Again. London, Eldon Press, 1934; as *Richardson's Second Case*, New York, Doubleday, 1934.
Inspector Richardson, C.I.D. London, Eldon Press, 1934; as *The Case of Naomi Clynes*, New York, Doubleday, 1934.
Richardson Goes Abroad. London, Eldon Press, 1935; as *The Case of the Dead Diplomat*, New York, Doubleday, 1935.
Richardson Solves a Dartmoor Mystery. London, Eldon Press, 1935; as *The Dartmoor Enigma*, New York, Doubleday, 1936.
Death in the Bathroom (Richardson). London, Eldon Press, 1936; as *Who Killed Stella Pomeroy?*, New York, Doubleday, 1936.
Milliner's Hat Mystery (Richardson). London, Eldon Press, 1937; as *The Mystery of the French Milliner*, New York, Doubleday, 1937.
A Murder Arranged (Richardson). London, Eldon Press, 1937; as *When Thieves Fall Out*, New York, Doubleday, 1937.

Short Stories

Mr. Pepper, Investigator. London, Castle, 1925.

OTHER PUBLICATIONS

Novel

The Indiscretions of Lady Asneath. London, Innes, 1898.

Play

The Elixir (produced London, 1917).

Other

The Diversions of a Prime Minister (history of Tonga). Edinburgh, Blackwood, 1894.
South Sea Yarns. Edinburgh, Blackwood, 1894.
Savage Island: An Account of a Sojourn in Niué and Tonga. London, Murray, 1902.

The Story of Dartmoor Prison. London, Heinemann, 1907.
The Fijians: A Study of the Decay of Custom. London, Heinemann, 1908.
Queer People. London, Hodder and Stoughton, 1922; as *My Experiences at Scotland Yard*, New York, Doubelday, 1923.
The Criminal. London, Hodder and Stoughton, 1925.
The Allied Secret Service in Greece. London, Hutchinson, 1930.
The Story of Scotland Yard. London, Grayson, 1935; New York, Doubleday, 1936.
The Gold Repeater: A Detective Story for Boys. London, A. and C. Black, 1936.
The Scene Changes (autobiography). New York, Doubleday, 1937; London, Collins, 1939.

Editor, with W. A. T. Amherst, *The Discovery of the Solomon Islands by Alvaro de Mendaña in 1568.* London, Bedford Press, 2 vols., 1901.
Editor, *The Skene Papers: Memories of Sir Walter Scott*, by James Skene. London, Murray, 1909.

*   *   *

Sir Basil Thomson served as colonial administrator, diplomat, governor of Dartmoor Prison, head of the CID of Scotland Yard during World War I, and director of intelligence in the postwar years. He also wrote numerous books, including Oceanic area studies, anthropology, historical criminology, memoirs, and fiction.

Thomson drew heavily upon his prison and police experiences in preparing eight detective novels that are set in Scotland Yard. Based on the career of Richardson, who rises from a probationer to the position of Chief Constable, they combine classical concepts of crime and narrative structure with an emphasis on procedural matters. Richardson, like his fellows at the Yard, is neither a superman nor an oaf; instead he is a conscientious, intelligent craftsman who must obtain permission from superiors, clear with the legal experts, fill out forms, and most of all bear the budget in mind. In the first six novels Richardson himself acts as detective; in the last two, because of his high position, he enters simply as instructor or coordinator. The Richardson novels are well-written and imaginative, with a wealth of detail about police operations, but there is little mystery per se in them, since the obvious suspect (as in life) is usually guilty. At its best – *P.C. Richardson's First Case, Richardson Solves a Dartmoor Mystery* – Thomson's work conveys a leisurely charm that is reminiscent of R. Austin Freeman's.

Thomson's other mystery-detective fiction includes a borderline romance, *A Court Intrigue*, which mingles Graustark, crime, and a spoof; *The Kidnapper*, which abandons the realistic mode of the Richardson novels; and two minor works, *Carfax Abbey* and *The Metal Flask. Mr. Pepper, Investigator* is a collection of humorous short stories based upon a clownish American who poses as a great private detective. Pepper also appears in *The Kidnapper*. All these works are much inferior to the Richardson novels.

Criminology was also one of Thomson's interests. *The Criminal* is a social study based upon his prison experiences; *The Story of Dartmoor Prison* and *The Story of Scotland Yard* are anecdotal accounts stressing important crimes. His two volumes of memoirs say little about detective work or his writing experiences.

—E. F. Bleiler

THOMSON, June. British. Born in Kent, 24 June 1930. Educated at Chelmsford High School for Girls, Essex, 1941–49; Bedford College, University of London, 1949–52, B.A.

(honours) in English 1952. Divorced; two sons. Has taught, full-time and part-time, in schools in Stoke-on-Trent, London, and Hertfordshire. Agent: Leslie Gardner, London Management, 235 Regent Street, London W1A 2JT. Address: c/o Constable & Co. Ltd., 10 Orange Street, London WC2H 7EG, England.

CRIME PUBLICATIONS

Novels (series character: Inspector Finch in all books; in US called Inspector Rudd)

Not One of Us. New York, Harper, 1971; London, Constable, 1972.
Death Cap. London, Constable, 1973; New York, Doubleday, 1977.
The Long Revenge. London, Constable, 1974; New York, Doubleday, 1975.
Case Closed. London, Constable, and New York, Doubleday, 1977.
A Question of Identity. New York, Doubleday, 1977; London, Constable, 1978.
Deadly Relations. London, Constable, 1979; as *The Habit of Loving*, New York, Doubleday, 1979.

Uncollected Short Story

"Crossing Bridges," in *Winter's Crimes 10*, edited by Hilary Watson. London, Macmillan, 1978.

June Thomson comments:
I have always enjoyed reading detective fiction: a mystery or a puzzle has its fascination. So has the process of unravelling. Writing detective fiction gives the opportunity to examine character and relationships in a very special way – pushed to the limit so to speak, and in jeopardy. I am interested in the personality of the outsider – the person who doesn't quite fit in with his environment. I use a country setting because I know it and feel I understand the kind of relationships, close and closed, that can develop in a small community with its own special loyalties and tensions. Inspector Finch (Rudd in the US) can understand and sympathise with these loyalties and tensions, and sometimes exploit them.

* * *

The mystery world of June Thomson is frequently rather a solitary one, a world full of suspects and victims who are living in a mutual rejection pact with society. Isolated living places abound, whether the farm in *A Question of Identity* where the family has always carefully avoided any contact with the village, or the small and lonely cottage on the outskirts of village life in *Not One of Us*. Even those characters who are quite close to the crime can remain detached, as does the murdered girl's father in *Case Closed*. He prefers his own society and a tranquil life on a houseboat to the troubles of parenthood.

Inspector Finch, quiet and self-sufficient, is the series detective, although in *The Long Revenge* a Secret Service agent seeks out his own intended killer by searching amongst the vacant shacks and houses in the Suffolk Marshes. Finch occupies a house with his sister and a dog that he rescued from abandonment at the end of one of his cases. He felt that the animal would provide companionship for his sister just as he did for the solitary homosexual who was a suspect in *Not One of Us*.

Thomson seems to prefer to keep her characters away from city life when she can, locating them in the country or in hostile small towns. In *Death Cap*, she uses a country kind of poison – fungi mixed with mushrooms – the investigation being even more difficult than usual when it comes to finding out who really knew about what was eatable and what was not. In very small communities hostility is often directed towards those who oppose the village standards of morality or etiquette, and individuality is not regarded as important.

Sometimes these places are devoid of any community life and are rife with trouble-making, their placid surface notwithstanding. June Thomson digs downwards to show the rot beneath.

—Mary Groff

TIDYMAN, Ernest. American. Born in Cleveland, Ohio, 1 January 1928. Educated in public schools in Cleveland to the seventh grade. Served in the United States Army, 1945–46. Married Susan Gould in 1970; four sons, two by previous marriage. Journalist for newspapers in Cleveland, 1943–66; magazine editor, 1966–69. Since 1969, self-employed writer and film producer. Recipient: Writers Guild of America Award, Mystery Writers of America Edgar Allan Poe Award, and Academy Award, all for screenplay, 1972; National Association for the Advancement of Colored People Image Award. Agent: Fred Whitehead, International Creative Management, 8899 Beverly Boulevard, Los Angeles, California 90048, U.S.A.

CRIME PUBLICATIONS

Novels (series character: John Shaft)

> *Shaft.* New York, Macmillan, 1970; London, Joseph, 1971.
> *Shaft among the Jews.* New York, Dial Press, 1972; London, Weidenfeld and Nicolson, 1973.
> *Shaft's Big Score.* New York, Bantam, and London, Corgi, 1972.
> *Shaft Has a Ball.* New York, Bantam, and London, Corgi, 1973.
> *Goodbye, Mr. Shaft.* New York, Dial Press, 1973; London, Weidenfeld and Nicolson, 1974.
> *Shaft's Carnival of Killers.* New York, Bantam, 1974; London, Bantam, 1975.
> *Line of Duty.* Boston, Little Brown, and London, W. H. Allen, 1974.
> *The Last Shaft.* London, Weidenfeld and Nicolson, 1975.
> *Starstruck.* London, W. H. Allen, 1975.

OTHER PUBLICATIONS

Novels

> *Flower Power.* New York, Paperback Library, 1968.
> *Absolute Zero.* New York, Dial Press, 1971.
> *High Plains Drifter.* New York, Bantam, and London, Corgi, 1973.
> *Table Stakes.* Boston, Little Brown, 1979.

Plays

> Screenplays: *The French Connection,* 1971; *Shaft,* 1971; *Shaft's Big Score,* 1972; *High Plains Drifter,* 1973; *Report to the Commissioner,* 1975; *Street People,* 1976; *A Force of One,* 1979.

> Television Plays: *To Kill a Cop,* 1978; *Dummy,* 1979; *Power: An American Saga,* 1979.

Other

The Anzio Death Trap. New York, Belmont, 1968.
Dummy. Boston, Little Brown, and London, W. H. Allen, 1974.

* * *

No matter what else he writes, Ernest Tidyman will no doubt always be known as the creator of Shaft, the black detective. He was high-styled, as violent in action as any of the descendants of Mike Hammer, but as intelligent as he was tough. Shaft became an even bigger star on the screen, important as a new type of detective, a sex symbol as well as a formidable fighter for good against evil. Nevertheless, Tidyman is not a one-theme writer. Though he produced some half dozen Shaft cases, he has also written other police stories based on crimes besetting a modern city. One of these, *Line of Duty*, was a best seller. Tidyman's city is Cleveland, where he worked as a reporter for 25 years before becoming a full-time writer. His style is less reportorial than it is out of *Black Mask*; it punches, is heavy on similes, and features odd characters.

—Dorothy B. Hughes

TILTON, Alice. See **TAYLOR, Phoebe Atwood**.

TORRIE, Malcolm. See **MITCHELL, Gladys**.

TRAIN, Arthur (Cheney). American. Born in Boston, Massachusetts, 6 September 1875. Educated at Prince School, Boston; Boston Latin School; St. Paul's School, Concord, New Hampshire; Harvard University, Cambridge, Massachusetts, A.B. 1896, LL.B. 1899; admitted to the Massachusetts bar 1899. Married 1) Ethel Kissam in 1897 (died, 1923); three daughters and one son; 2) Helen C. Gerard in 1926; one son. Lawyer: worked in firm of Robinson Biddle and Ward, 1900; Assistant District Attorney for New York, 1901–08; in private practice (Train and Olney, later Perkins and Train) after 1908; Attorney General, Commonwealth of Massachusetts. Prolific story writer from 1904. President, National Institute of Arts and Letters, 1941–45. *Died 22 December 1945.*

CRIME PUBLICATIONS

Novels (series character: Ephraim Tutt)

The Confessions of Artemas Quibble. New York, Scribner, 1911.
"C.Q."; or, In the Wireless House. New York, Century, 1912.
The Hermit of Turkey Hollow (Tutt). New York, Scribner, 1921.
The Blind Goddess. New York, Scribner, 1926.
The Adventures of Ephraim Tutt. New York, Scribner, 1930.
Manhattan Murder. New York, Scribner, 1936.
Murderers' Medicine. London, Constable, 1937.
Yankee Lawyer – Autobiography of Ephraim Tutt. New York, Scribner, 1943.

Short Stories

McAllister and His Double. New York, Scribner, and London, Newnes, 1905.
Mortmain. New York, Appleton, 1907.
Tutt and Mr. Tutt. New York, Scribner, 1920.
By Advice of Counsel. New York, Scribner, 1921.
Tut, Tut! Mr. Tutt. New York, Scribner, 1923; London, Nash, 1924.
Page Mr. Tutt. New York, Scribner, 1926.
When Tutt Meets Tutt. New York, Scribner, 1927.
Tutt for Tutt. New York, Scribner, 1934.
Mr. Tutt Takes the Stand. New York, Scribner, 1936.
Mr. Tutt's Case Book (omnibus). New York, Scribner, 1936.
Old Man Tutt. New York, Scribner, 1938.
Mr. Tutt Comes Home. New York, Scribner, 1941.
Mr. Tutt Finds a Way. New York, Scribner, 1945.
Mr. Tutt at His Best, edited by Harold R. Medina. New York, Scribner, 1961.

OTHER PUBLICATIONS

Novels

The Butler's Story. New York, Scribner, and London, Laurie, 1909.
The Man Who Rocked the Earth, with Robert William Wood. New York, Doubleday, 1915.
The World and Thomas Kelly. New York, Scribner, 1917.
As It Was in the Beginning. New York, Macmillan, 1921.
His Children's Children. New York, Scribner, and London, Nash, 1923.
The Needle's Eye. New York, Scribner, 1924.
The Lost Gospel. New York, Scribner, 1925.
High Winds. New York, Scribner, and London, Nash, 1927.
Ambition. New York, Scribner, and London, Nash, 1928.
The Horns of Ramadan. New York, Scribner, 1928; London, Nash, 1929.
Illusion. New York, Scribner, and London, Nash, 1929.
Paper Profits. New York, Liveright, and London, Mathews and Marrot, 1930.
Princess Pro Tem. New York, Scribner, 1932.
No Matter Where. New York, Scribner, 1933.
Jacob's Ladder. New York, Scribner, 1935.
Tassels on Her Boots. New York, Scribner, and London, Hutchinson, 1940.
The Moon Maker, with Robert William Wood. Hamburg, New York, Krueger, 1958.

Other

The Prisoner at the Bar. New York, Scribner, 1906; London, Laurie, 1907; revised
    edition, 1908; revised edition, as *From the District Attorney's Office,* 1939.
True Stories of Crime from the District Attorney's Office. New York, Scribner, and
    London, Laurie, 1908.
Courts, Criminals, and the Camorra. New York, Scribner, and London, Chapman and
    Hall, 1912.
The Earthquake. New York, Scribner, 1918.
Courts and Criminals (selection). New York, Scribner, 1921.
On the Trail of the Bad Men. New York, Scribner, 1925.
Puritan's Progress. New York, Scribner, 1931.
The Strange Attacks on Herbert Hoover. New York, Day, 1932.
My Day in Court (autobiography). New York, Scribner, 1939.

Editor, *The Goldfish, Being the Confessions of a Successful Man.* New York, Century,
    1914.

*　　*　　*

As Assistant District Attorney for New York County, Arthur Train saw stories in the
procession of human comedies and tragedies that passed through the criminal court building.
His first book, *McAllister and His Double,* concerns a wealthy clubman whose look-alike valet
is a known felon. It also contains four stories about a young Deputy District Attorney, John
Dockbridge, who is a forerunner of Train's most famous character, Ephraim Tutt.

Though the bulk of Train's fiction deals with other characters, it is for Mr. Tutt that he is
remembered. The Lincolnesque lawyer with his frock coat, stove pipe hat, and fondness for
stogies is a vivid character. The stories all follow a formula: the statement of the problem, the
seeming impossibility of the triumph of justice over the technicalities of the law, and Mr.
Tutt's solution to the problem. They are solid Americana, and Tutt is a figure from American
folklore, the shrewd Yankee on the side of the underdog.

Most of Train's many other books do not deal with crime or the law, but with human
nature. *His Children's Children* has been compared with *The Forsyte Saga. The Prisoner at
the Bar* (non-fiction) and *The Blind Goddess* deal with the workings of the courts. *The
Confessions of Artemas Quibble* is a genial satire on the legal profession, while *Manhattan
Murder* is a vivid, if romantic, portrait of New York in the gangster era.

—J. Randolph Cox

TREAT, Lawrence. American. Born Lawrence Arthur Goldstone in New York City, 21
December 1903. Educated at Dartmouth College, Hanover, New Hampshire, B.A. 1924;
Columbia University School of Law, New York, LL.B. 1927. Married Rose Ehrenfreud in
1943. Past President, Mystery Writers of America. Recipient: Mystery Writers of America
Edgar Allan Poe Award, 1965, 1978. Agent: Robert P. Mills Ltd., 156 East 52nd Street, New
York, New York 10022. Address: RFD Box 475A, Edgartown, Massachusetts 02539, U.S.A.

CRIME PUBLICATIONS

Novels (series characters: Bill Decker; Jub Freeman; Mitch Taylor; Carl Wayward)

Run Far, Run Fast (as Lawrence A. Goldstone).   New York, Greystone Press, 1937.
B as in Banshee (Wayward).   New York, Duell, 1940; as *Wail for the Corpses*, New York, Select, 1943.
D as in Dead (Wayward).   New York, Duell, 1941.
H as in Hangman (Wayward).   New York, Duell, 1942.
O as in Omen (Wayward).   New York, Duell, 1943.
The Leather Man.   New York, Duell, 1944; London, Rich and Cowan, 1947.
V as in Victim (Taylor; Freeman).   New York, Duell, 1945; London, Rich and Cowan, 1950.
H as in Hunted (Freeman).   New York, Duell, 1946; London, Boardman, 1950.
Q as in Quicksand (Taylor; Freeman).   New York, Duell, 1947; as *Step into Quicksand*, London, Boardman, 1959.
T as in Trapped (Taylor; Freeman).   New York, Morrow, 1947.
F as in Flight (Freeman; Decker).   New York, Morrow, 1948; London, Boardman, 1949.
Over the Edge (Freeman; Decker).   New York, Morrow, 1948; London, Boardman, 1958.
Trial and Terror.   New York, Morrow, 1949; London, Boardman, 1958.
Big Shot (Taylor; Decker; Freeman).   New York, Harper, 1951; London, Boardman, 1952.
Weep for a Wanton (Taylor; Freeman).   New York, Ace, 1956; London, Boardman, 1957.
Lady, Drop Dead (Taylor; Freeman).   New York and London, Abelard Schuman, 1960.
Venus Unarmed.   New York, Doubleday, 1961.

Short Stories

P as in Police, edited by Ellery Queen.   New York, Davis, 1970.

Uncollected Short Stories

"An Accident in Hudson Heights," in *Ellery Queen's Mystery Magazine* (New York), February 1971.
"Crime at Red Spit," in *Ellery Queen's Mystery Magazine* (New York), April 1971.
"Jackpot," in *Ellery Queen's Mystery Magazine* (New York), May 1971.
"The Mushroom Fanciers," in *Ellery Queen's Mystery Magazine* (New York), July 1971.
"The Verdict," in *Best Detective Stories of the Year*, edited by Allen J. Hubin.   New York, Dutton, 1971.
"K as in Kidnapping," in *Ellery Queen's Mystery Magazine* (New York), December 1971.
"The Cautious Man," in *Murder Most Foul*, edited by Harold Q. Masur.   New York, Walker, 1971.
"Wife Trouble," in *Ellery Queen's Mystery Magazine* (New York), March 1972.
"B as in Bandit," in *Ellery Queen's Mystery Magazine* (New York), April 1972.
"The Haunted Portrait," in *Ellery Queen's Mystery Magazine* (New York), July 1972.
"G as in Garrote," in *Ellery Queen's Mystery Magazine* (New York), August 1972.
"C as in Cutthroat," in *Ellery Queen's Mystery Magazine* (New York), December 1972.
"The Motive," in *Every Crime in the Book*, edited by Robert L Fish.   New York, Putnam, 1975.
"Moment of Truth," in *Ellery Queen's Mystery Magazine* (New York), January 1976.

"P as in Poison," in *Ellery Queen's Mystery Magazine* (New York), June 1976.
"R as in Rookie," in *Ellery Queen's Magicians of Mystery.* New York, Davis, 1976.
"B as in Bludgeon," in *Ellery Queen's Crime Wave.* New York, Putnam, 1976.
"The Candle Flame," in *Best Detective Stories of the Year 1976*, edited by Edward D. Hoch. New York, Dutton, 1976.
"C as in Crooked," in *Ellery Queen's Mystery Magazine* (New York), January 1977.
"T as in Terror," in *Ellery Queen's Mystery Magazine* (New York), March 1977.
"The Killing of Wincoe Jones," in *Alfred Hitchcock's Mystery Magazine* (New York), May 1977.
"The Bottle of Wine," in *Mike Shayne Mystery Magazine* (Los Angeles), January 1978.
"The Two-Timer," in *Mike Shayne Mystery Magazine* (Los Angeles), February 1978.
"M as in Missing," in *Ellery Queen's Masters of Mystery.* New York, Davis, 1978.
"A Matter of Arson," in *Alfred Hitchcock's Mystery Magazine* (New York), April 1978.
"A Matter of Mushrooms," in *Alfred Hitchcock's Mystery Magazine* (New York), July 1978.
"Cop Goes the Weasel," in *Alfred Hitchcock's Mystery Magazine* (New York), October 1978.
"Dead Duck," in *Alfred Hitchcock's Tales to Scare You Stiff*, edited by Eleanor Sullivan. New York, Davis, 1978.
"A Matter of Morality," in *Alfred Hitchcock's Mystery Magazine* (New York), January 1979.
"A Matter of Kicks," with Richard Plotz, in *Alfred Hitchcock's Mystery Magazine* (New York), August 1979.
"To Love Thy Neighbor," in *Mike Shayne Mystery Magazine* (Los Angeles), September 1979.

OTHER PUBLICATIONS

Other

Bringing Sherlock Home (puzzle book). New York, Doubleday, 1930.
"Creating a Mystery Game," in *Murder Ink: The Mystery Reader's Companion*, edited by Dilys Winn. New York, Workman, 1977.

Editor, *Murder in Mind.* New York, Dutton, 1967.
Editor, *The Mystery Writer's Handbook.* Cincinnati, Writer's Digest, 1976.

*   *   *

Lawrence Treat is frequently called the "father" of the police procedural novel, but there are two reasons for questioning the appropriateness of the title. The first is that Treat himself disclaims any intention of creating a new form of detective fiction. The other is that the big impetus for the police procedural story came not from Treat's early books but a few years later from the radio and television show *Dragnet*, whose popularity created a climate for the beginning of successful series like Creasey's Gideon stories and McBain's 87th Precinct saga.

But whether he "invented" the procedural novel or not, Lawrence Treat set a pattern that has been rather consistently followed by writers in this sub-genre. The nine novels and numerous short stories featuring the police trio Mitch Taylor, Jub Freeman, and Bill Decker are different from the traditional detective story in that the work of crime detection is carried on not by a single masterful personality like Sherlock Holmes or Inspector Maigret but by a team of hard-working and believeable cops. Another important component of the Treat pattern is the use of such ordinary police methods as tailings, stakeouts, informants, and the principles of forensic science in the solution of crimes. It is, of course, this reliance on routines and procedures that gives the police procedural story its name. Treat not only set the narrative pattern of the procedural story but established a set of conventional situations that have been used repeatedly by writers of police fiction. There is the convention of the cop with family problems (Mitch Taylor worries about how he will support his beloved Amy), the hostile public ("People who aren't busy lying to you look at you as if you were a mechanical man"), the inter- and intra-departmental rivalries (detectives versus patrolmen, conventional cops versus the police lab), and the perennially under-staffed and over-worked squad (a policeman is never off duty). The formula has come to be as thoroughly established in the police procedural as the Poe conventions in the classic detective story and the *Black Mask* pattern in the hard-boiled school.

Treat made a particularly happy selection in his three series characters, because each of them plausibly represents an aspect of the police sub-culture. Mitch Taylor, the "veteran of an unjust world and experienced in warfare against his superiors," is the traditional flatfoot, inclined to cut corners and to gold-brick where work is involved. Mitch is not very intelligent, and sometimes worries a little because he does not read more. He is not above establishing a little "cushion" (graft on the side) for himself, and he considers himself fortunate in having a "rabbi," an influential relative who looks after his interests. Mitch's basic attitude toward his job is, Get along, Stay out of trouble, Don't stick your neck out. It is significant that Treat relegated Mitch Taylor to a minor role, and gave an increasingly important part to Jub Freeman, the new-style scientific detective. Jub's field of operation is the police lab, and he has the qualities of the dedicated scientist, including meticulous analysis, suspension of judgment until all the data have been examined, and empirical support for every statement he makes on the witness stand. Jub knows his forensic science: he can identify a brand of ink by spectrophotometric analysis that breaks a substance up into color components, and he can prove that a suspect acted in self-defense by demonstrating that her hand-marks were on the barrel of a pistol only, not on the butt or trigger. Homicide Lieutenant Bill Decker, the third character, is a competent, business-like officer who runs a tight ship, who drives his men relentlessly and has to be extra-sure of his own men because he has not much use for the rest of the department. Decker can also be warm and understanding; he supports his men, and he does not hesitate to sit down and have a drink with them – after hours, of course. He encourages them to be unorthodox, to break minor rules or cut through red tape when necessary. As a result of his leadership, morale in Homicide is the highest in the department.

As a pioneer in police procedural fiction Lawrence Treat established one important precedent: a writer of police fiction must know the real-world cops, their methods and their attitudes. The reading public will tolerate a degree of fantasy in other types of detective fiction because very few people have ever seen a consulting detective or a private investigator, but everybody knows uniformed policemen and has at least some role-expectations for plainclothesmen. Treat's police detectives, with their politicking and their eye on the promotion-lists, their fallibility and their frequent reliance on sheer luck, have apparently satisfied those expectations. If Lawrence Treat did not "invent" the police procedural novel, he certainly found an ideal medium when he began writing them. His novels before *V as in Victim* feature Carl Wayward, a devious, intuitive criminologist; the plots are conventional, the characters transparent and brittle as glass, the dialogue stiff and forced. When he turned to this world of policemen, however, Treat developed an easy natural prose and the ability to construct a narrative framework that is at once plausible and vivid.

—George N. Dove

TREE, Gregory. See BARDIN, John Franklin.

TRENCH, John (Chenevix). British. Born in Newick, Sussex, 17 October 1920. Educated at Wellington College, Berkshire, 1933–38; Royal Military Academy, Woolwich, London, 1939. Served in the Royal Signals in Africa and Europe, 1939–46. Married Ann Moore in 1944; one daughter and one son. Copywriter, 1945–56, Copy Group Head, 1956–62, and Creative Group Head, 1962–70, S. H. Benson Ltd., London. Since 1970, Creative Director, Foster Turner and Benson Ltd., London. Chairman of the Council, Buckinghamshire Archaeological Society, 1977; Parish Councillor and Churchwarden. Recipient: Advertising Creative Circle Essay Prize, 1969; World's Press News Copywriting award, 1956, 1963. Agent: Anthony Shiel Associates Ltd., 2–3 Morwell Street, London WC1B 2AR. Address: Windmill Farm, Coleshill, Amersham, Buckinghamshire, England.

CRIME PUBLICATIONS

Novels (series character: Martin Cotterell in all books except *Beyond the Atlas*)

    Docken Dead. London, Macdonald, 1953; New York, Macmillan, 1954.
    Dishonoured Bones. London, Macdonald, 1954; New York, Macmillan, 1955.
    What Rough Beast. London, Macdonald, and New York, Macmillan, 1957.
    Beyond the Atlas. London, Macdonald, and New York, Macmillan, 1963.

OTHER PUBLICATIONS

Other

    Archaeology Without a Spade. London, Newman Neame, 1960.
    History for Postmen. London, Newman Neame, 1961.
    The Bones of Britain. London, Newman Neame, 1962.

    Editor, *The Harp Book of Graces.* London, Harp Lager, 1962.

*   *   *

Each of John Trench's series detective novels bears the hallmarks of the high English tradition: incisive wit, spirited invention, intricate and various action, frequent literary allusion, powerful feeling for locality, and pungent observation of character and customs, with an especially keen eye for the eccentric. As a stylist, Trench is comparable to any of his peers: even his detractors concede that he writes well.

The civil and military confusions of *Docken Dead* generate a continuous excitement, entangling an upper-crust family with a dead major, a secret weapon, and a lost Arthurian manuscript. It is a crowded, zestful book, as invigorating as its northern landscape, and lucid and shapely for all its teeming vitality. *Dishonoured Bones* is a rather wry book unfolding a complex deception against a background of local tensions in a Dorset quarrying community. A dig reveals a recent corpse; antiques vanish from the manor; a social solecism prompts a murder. By a neat poetic justice, the quarrymen encompass the murderer's destruction. *What Rough Beast* moves beyond its predecessors to heartfelt protest against the brutal ethos of modern times. A deep, fierce book, it lives up to its Yeatsian title, effective both as mystery and as statement of faith. Its vicious teenage gang is seen in a dual light: as destroyers of the peace and as victims of a ravaged environment. All three novels feature Martin Cotterell, an erudite archaeologist with an acutely "associative" mind. Tough, lean, exuberant, inquisitive, well-connected, one-handed, and chronically untidy, he deserves a wider fame.

—B. A. Pike

TREVANIAN. Pseudonym for Rodney Whitaker. Also writes as J-L. Moran; Nicholas Seare; Benat le Cagat. American. Born in Tokyo, 12 January 1925. Holds four university degrees, including Ph.D. in Communications. Formerly Professor, University of Texas, Austin. Address: c/o Crown Publishers Inc., 419 Park Avenue South, New York, New York 10016, U.S.A.

CRIME PUBLICATIONS

Novels (series character: Jonathan Hemlock)

> *The Eiger Sanction* (Hemlock). New York, Crown, 1972; London, Heinemann, 1973.
> *The Loo Sanction* (Hemlock). New York, Crown, 1973; London, Heinemann, 1974.
> *The Main.* New York, Harcourt Brace, 1976; London, Hart Davis, 1977.
> *Shibumi.* New York, Crown, and London, Granada, 1979.

OTHER PUBLICATIONS

Other

> *The Language of Film* (as Rod Whitaker). Englewood Cliffs, New Jersey, Prentice Hall, 1970.
> *Thirteen Thirty Nine or So, Being an Apology for a Pedlar* (as Nicholas Seare). New York, Harcourt Brace, 1975.

*   *   *

Tough, unlikable, and unlikely, Trevanian's Jonathan Hemlock is a snob, art history professor, world-class mountain climber, and assassin for the CII, an American intelligence organization headed by Yurasis Dragon, an albino. Hemlock's $10,000 fee per "sanction" (counter-assassination) pays for his two passions, his home – a converted church – and his illegally purchased Impressionist paintings. Cold and self-consciously emotionless, Hemlock yet has a rigid code of friendship and love, constantly violated by others in *The Eiger Sanction.* That novel's plot involves Hemlock's attempt to discover and sanction one of three others during a climb of the Eigerwand, and the climbing scenes are particularly well-done, tense and exciting. In the second novel, the British equivalent of the CII, the Loo, blackmails Hemlock, forcing him out of a four-year retirement to sanction Maxmillian Strange, who means to auction films of governmental officials at their sexual play and thus to topple the British Empire. Hemlock here is a rather more sympathetic figure, because of his love throughout of Maggie Coyne. The grim and convolute conclusion is once again exceptionally well-done. Hemlock's acerbic snobbery, Trevanian's snide narrative asides, and his bawdy naming of characters all suggest a Bondish derivation, but Trevanian's writing is more intelligent, witty, and stylish than Fleming's.

The Main, a very fine police procedural novel, is also a moving study of Claude LaPointe, the lonely, scruffy, tough-but-not-hard police lieutenant who is The Law in the Montreal district of the novel's title. As LaPointe investigates a murder, the contrast between his older methods and ideas and those of the forces of modernism – a college-educated policeman, a "liberal" police commissioner, and a young whore – provides additional interest and tension. The revelation of the murderer's identity is somewhat improbable, but otherwise the novel is strong.

—David K. Jeffrey

TREVOR, Elleston. Also writes as Mansell Black; Trevor Burgess; T. Dudley-Smith; Roger Fitzalan; Adam Hall; Howard North; Simon Rattray; Warwick Scott; Caesar Smith. British. Born in Bromley, Kent, 17 February 1920. Educated at Yardley Court Preparatory School, Kent, 1928–32; Sevenoaks School, Kent, 1932–38. Served in the Royal Air Force, 1939–45: Flight Engineer. Married Jonquil Burgess in 1947; one son. Lived in France, 1958–73, and in the United States since 1973. Recipient: Mystery Writers of America Edgar Allan Poe Award 1965. Agent: Scott Meredith Literary Agency Inc., 845 Third Avenue, New York, New York 10022. Address: Fountain Hills, Arizona 85268, U.S.A.

CRIME PUBLICATIONS

Novels

The Immortal Error. London, Swan, 1946.
The Mystery of the Missing Book (as Trevor Burgess). London, Hutchinson, 1950.
Chorus of Echoes. London and New York, Boardman, 1950.
Redfern's Miracle. London and New York, Boardman, 1951.
Tiger Street. London, Boardman, 1951; New York, Lion, 1954.
A Blaze of Roses. London, Heinemann, and New York, Harper, 1952; as *The Fire-Raiser*, London, New English Library, 1970.
The Passion and the Pity. London, Heinemann, 1953.
The Big Pick-Up. London, Heinemann, and New York, Macmillan, 1955.
Squadron Airborne. London, Heinemann, 1955; New York, Macmillan, 1956.
The Killing Ground. London, Heinemann, 1956; New York, Macmillan, 1957.
Gale Force. London, Heinemann, 1956; New York, Macmillan, 1957.
The Pillars of Midnight. London, Heinemann, 1957; New York, Morrow, 1958.
Heat Wave (as Caesar Smith). London, Wingate, 1957; New York, Ballantine, 1958.
Dream of Death. London, Brown and Watson, 1958.
Silhouette. London, Swan, 1959.
The V.I.P. London, Heinemann, 1959; New York, Morrow, 1960.
The Billboard Madonna. London, Heinemann, 1960; New York, Morrow, 1961.
The Mind of Max Duvine. London, Swan, 1960.
The Burning Shore. London, Heinemann, 1961; as *The Pasang Run*, New York, Harper, 1962.
The Flight of the Phoenix. London, Heinemann, and New York, Harper, 1964.
The Second Chance. London, Consul, 1965.
Weave a Rope of Sand. London, Consul, 1965.
The Shoot. London, Heinemann, and New York, Doubleday, 1966.
The Freebooters. London, Heinemann, and New York, Doubleday, 1967.
A Blaze of Arms (as Roger Fitzalan). London, Davies, 1967.
A Place for the Wicked. London, Heinemann, and New York, Doubleday, 1968.
Bury Him among Kings. London, Heinemann, and New York, Doubleday, 1970.
Expressway (as Howard North). London, Collins, and New York, Simon and Schuster, 1973.
The Paragon. London, New English Library, 1975; as *Night Stop*, New York, Doubleday, 1975.
The Theta Syndrome. London, New English Library, and New York, Doubleday, 1977.
Blue Jay Summer. London, New English Library, and New York, Dell, 1977.
Seven Witnesses. London, Remploy, 1977.
The Sibling. London, New English Library, and Chicago, Playboy Press, 1979.

Novels

as T. Dudley-Smith *Over the Wall*.   London, Swan, 1943.
Double Who Double Crossed.   London, Swan, 1944.
Escape to Fear.   London, Swan, 1948.
Now Try the Morgue.   London, Swan, 1948.

Novels as Mansell Black

Dead on Course.   London, Hodder and Stoughton, 1951.
Sinister Cargo.   London, Hodder and Stoughton, 1951.
Shadow of Evil.   London, Hodder and Stoughton, 1953.
Steps in the Dark.   London, Hodder and Stoughton, 1954.

Novels as Warwick Scott

Image in the Dust.   London, Davies, 1951; as *Cockpit*, New York, Lion, 1953.
The Domesday Story.   London, Davies, 1952; as *Doomsday*, New York, Lion, 1953.
Naked Canvas.   London, Davies, 1954; New York, Popular Library, 1955.

Novels as Simon Rattray (series character: Hugo Bishop in all books; published as Adam
    Hall in US)

Knight Sinister.   London, Boardman, 1951; New York, Pyramid, 1971.
Queen in Danger.   London, Boardman, 1952; New York, Pyramid, 1971.
Bishop in Check.   London, Boardman, 1953; New York, Pyramid, 1971.
Dead Silence.   London, Boardman, 1954; as *Pawn in Jeopardy*, New York, Pyramid,
    1971.
Dead Circuit.   London, Boardman, 1955; as *Rook's Gambit*, New York, Pyramid,
    1972.
Dead Sequence.   London, Boardman, 1957.

Novels as Adam Hall (series character: Quiller in all books except *The Volcanoes of San
    Domingo*)

The Volcanoes of San Domingo.   London, Collins, 1963; New York, Simon and
    Schuster, 1964.
The Berlin Memorandum.   London, Collins, 1965; as *The Quiller Memorandum*, New
    York, Simon and Schuster, 1965; London, Collins, 1967.
The 9th Directive.   London, Heinemann, and New York, Simon and Schuster, 1966.
The Striker Portfolio.   London, Heinemann, and New York, Simon and Schuster, 1969.
The Warsaw Document.   New York, Doubleday, and London, Heinemann, 1970.
The Tango Briefing.   London, Collins, and New York, Doubleday, 1973.
The Mandarin Cypher.   London, Collins, and New York, Doubleday, 1975.
The Kobra Manifesto.   London, Collins, and New York, Doubleday, 1976.
The Sinkiang Executive.   London, Collins, and New York, Doubleday, 1978.
The Scorpion Signal.   London, Collins, and New York, Doubleday, 1979.

OTHER PUBLICATIONS

Novels (juvenile)

Into the Happy Glade (as T. Dudley-Smith).   London, Swan, 1943.
By a Silver Stream (as T. Dudley-Smith).   London, Swan, 1944.
Wumpus.   London, Swan, 1945.

Deep Wood.   London, Swan, 1945; New York, Longman, 1947.
Heather Hill.   London, Swan, 1946; New York, Longman, 1948.
More about Wumpus.   London, Swan, 1947.
The Island of the Pines.   London, Swan, 1948.
The Secret Travellers.   London, Swan, 1948.
Where's Wumpus?   London, Swan, 1948.
Badger's Beech.   London, Falcon Press, 1948; Nashville, Aurora, 1970.
The Wizard of the Wood.   London, Falcon Press, 1948.
Badger's Moon.   London, Falcon Press, 1949.
A Spy at Monk's Court (as Trevor Burgess).   London, Hutchinson, 1949.
Ants' Castle.   London, Falcon Press, 1949.
Mole's Castle.   London, Falcon Press, 1951.
Sweethallow Valley.   London, Falcon Press, 1951.
Challenge of the Firebrand.   London, Jenkins, 1951.
Secret Arena.   London, Jenkins, 1951.
The Racing Wraith (as Trevor Burgess).   London, Hutchinson, 1953.
Forbidden Kingdom.   London, Lutterworth Press, 1955.
Badger's Wood.   London, Heinemann, 1958; New York, Criterion, 1959.
The Crystal City.   London, Swan, 1959.
Green Glades.   London, Swan, 1959.
Squirrel's Island.   London, Swan, 1963.

Short Stories

Elleston Trevor Miscellany.   London, Swan, 1944.

Plays

The Last of the Daylight (produced Bromley, Kent, 1959).
Murder by All Means (produced Madrid, 1960; Farnham, Surrey, and London, 1961).
A Pinch of Purple (produced Bradford, 1971).
A Touch of Purple (produced Leatherhead, Surrey, and London, 1972).   London,
   French, 1973.
Just Before Dawn (produced London, 1972).

Screenplays: *Wings of Danger*, with John Gilling and Packham Webb, 1952.

Other

*Animal Life Stories: Rippleswim the Otter, Scamper-Foot the Pine Marten, Shadow the
   Fox.*   London, Swan, 3 vols., 1943–45.

Manuscript Collection: Mugar Memorial Library, Boston University.

*   *   *

With *The Quiller Memorandum*, for which he received an Edgar, Elleston Trevor, writing
under the pseudonym Adam Hall, initiated a series of espionage novels featuring Quiller, a
British "shadow executive." Quiller is employed by "the Bureau," a government agency
charged with such sensitive tasks that officially, at least, it does not exist. Quiller's
background – an infiltrator arranging escapes from Nazi concentration camps in World War
II – merely hints at the formidable array of specialized skills that his government still has need
of on occasion. A trouble shooter in situations where the expertise of MI5 and MI6, not to
mention the Foreign Office, is irrelevant, Quiller, we are told, is used only at the authorization
of the Prime Minister. In *The Quiller Memorandum*, he exposes a large, well-organized neo-

Nazi conspiracy based in Berlin. *The Striker Portfolio* finds him in Germany again, investigating a series of jet fighter crashes, evidently the result of sabotage despite the most elaborate security precautions. In *The Warsaw Document*, he wrecks a Russian plot to invade Warsaw using as a pretext fabricated evidence of a Western conspiracy to assist Polish dissidents. *The 9th Directive* shows him in Bangkok rescuing a kidnapped member of the British royal family. In *The Tango Briefing*, Quiller is parachuted into the Libyan desert with a small nuclear device to destroy some British-manufactured nerve gas aboard a crashed plane before Arab agents can get to it and embarrass the British by publicizing the existence of the gas. The automatic timing mechanism of the device is smashed during the drop, and for a time it looks as if Quiller will have to detonate the device – and himself in the process – before he devises a grisly but effective solution.

Hall's conception of Quiller, established in the first book and unchanged in its essentials in subsequent novels, offers relatively little scope for development, even by comparison with James Bond and Matt Helm – the fictional agents that he most closely resembles. It is this narrowness of concept that presumably led a reviewer to call for the pensioning off of Quiller after *The Kobra Manifesto*. Hall defines Quiller exclusively in terms of the knowledge and skills required for his exacting, dangerous work. Living only for the challenge of the mission, Quiller is shown to have no emotional or intellectual life independent of his work. Indeed, he apparently needs the pressures and dangers of the mission to confirm his very identity. Quiller's considerable, if specialized, knowledge of psychology, neurophysiology, and the processes of sleep and memory enhances his capacity for rational self-control under extreme stress. Each novel finds Quiller *in extremis*, observing with clinical, detached contempt his body's instinctual responses to mortal danger: "the organism had started panicking because some of the brain-think had filtered through and it was squealing to know what I intended to do about its survival and there wasn't an answer." This "I" – to the perfection of which Quiller has single-mindedly devoted himself – is as chilling a voice of disembodied rationality as contemporary espionage fiction affords. Add to this Quiller's irascibility, his humorlessness, his tendency to parade his expertise – and he is on the verge of becoming a bore. Objections to Quiller aside, however, Hall must be accounted a skillful practitioner of the fine art of creating suspense and a master of the "close focus" technique, as when, in *The Warsaw Document*, Quiller, hiding in a narrow broom closet, eludes a determined search by inching upward, feet braced against one wall, shoulders against the other, until he is above the level of the door. At this sort of thing, Hall has a sure touch and few peers.

—R. Gordon Kelly

TREVOR, Glen. Pseudonym for James Hilton. British. Born in Leigh, Lancashire, 9 September 1900. Educated at Leys School, Cambridge; Christ's College, Cambridge, B.A. (honours) in history. Columnist, *Irish Independent*, Dublin, in the 1920's. Settled in the United States in 1935. Recipient: Hawthornden Prize, 1934; Academy Award, 1943. *Died 20 December 1954.*

CRIME PUBLICATIONS

Novel

    Murder at School: A Detective Fantasia. London, Benn, 1931; as *Was It Murder?*, New York, Harper, 1933.

Uncollected Short Stories as James Hilton

"The Perfect Plan," in *Ellery Queen's Mystery Magazine* (New York), March 1946.
"The Mallet," in *To the Queen's Taste*, edited by Ellery Queen. Boston, Little Brown,
    1946; London, Faber, 1949.
"The King of the Bats," in *Ellery Queen's Mystery Magazine* (New York), March 1953.

OTHER PUBLICATIONS as James Hilton

Novels

Catherine Herself. London, Unwin, 1920.
Storm Passage. London, Unwin, 1922.
The Passionate Year. London, Butterworth, 1923; Boston, Little Brown, 1924.
The Dawn of Reckoning. London, Butterworth, 1925; n.p., Famous Books, 1937.
The Meadows of the Moon. London, Butterworth, 1926; Boston, Small Maynard,
    1927.
Terry. London, Butterworth, 1927.
The Silver Flame. London, Butterworth, 1928.
And Now Goodbye. London, Benn, 1931; New York, Morrow, 1932.
Contango. London, Benn, 1932; as *Ill Wind*, New York, Grosset and Dunlap, 1932.
Rage in Heaven. New York, King, 1932.
Knight Without Armour. London, Benn, 1933; as *Without Armor*, New York,
    Morrow, 1934.
Lost Horizon. London, Macmillan, and New York, Morrow, 1933.
Good-bye Mr. Chips. London, Hodder and Stoughton, and Boston, Little Brown, 1934.
We Are Not Alone. London, Macmillan, and Boston, Little Brown, 1937.
Random Harvest. London, Macmillan, and Boston, Little Brown, 1941.
The Story of Dr. Wassell. Boston, Little Brown, 1943; London, Macmillan, 1944.
So Well Remembered. Boston, Little Brown, 1945; London, Macmillan, 1947.
Nothing So Strange. Boston, Little Brown, 1947; London, Macmillan, 1948.
Morning Journey. London, Macmillan, and Boston, Little Brown, 1951.
Time and Time Again. London, Macmillan, and Boston, Little Brown, 1953.

Short Stories

To You, Mr. Chips. London, Hodder and Stoughton, 1938.
Twilight of the Wise. London, St. Hugh's Press, 1949.

Plays

Good-bye Mr. Chips, with Barbara Burnham, adaptation of the novel by Hilton
    (produced London, 1938). London, Hodder and Stoughton, 1938.
Mrs. Miniver, with others, in *Twenty Best Film Plays*, edited by John Gassner and
    Dudley Nichols. New York, Crown, 1943.
Shangri-La, with Jerome Lawrence and Robert E. Lee, music by Harry Warren,
    adaptation of the novel *Lost Horizon* by Hilton (produced New York, 1956). New
    York, Morris Music, 1956.

Screenplays: *Camille*, with Zoe Akins and Frances Marion, 1936; *We Are Not Alone*,
with Milton Krims, 1939; *The Tuttles of Tahiti*, with Lewis Meltzer and Robert Carson,
1942; *Mrs. Miniver*, with others, 1942; *Forever and a Day*, with others, 1944.

Other

Mr. Chips Looks at the World (lecture). Los Angeles, Modern Forum, 1939.
Addresses on the Present War and Our Hopes for the Future (radio talks). New York,
   CBS, 1943.
The Duke of Edinburgh. London, Muller, 1956; as *H.R.H.: The Story of Philip, Duke
   of Edinburgh*, Boston, Little Brown, 1956.

*   *   *

It has often been said that the English must be the only people in the world who are
obsessed by their schooldays, who carry the remembered pleasures and pains to the end of
their days, and who reproduce their memories in the form of histories, biographies, and
novels of a highly romantic or mysterious nature. Glen Trevor, in *Murder at School*, set his
murders at Oakington, one of those schools without any particular history or tradition but
still old enough to be able to provide the necessary discomforts to mould the character.

The school year of 1927–28 was a time when God was still an Englishman and the
Oakington murders were written from the viewpoint of the adults involved rather than the
boys. Two brothers, heirs to a fortune, die in what appear to be unfortunate accidents until it
is discovered that their housemaster will inherit their money. Very little ever seemed to be
accomplished in the way of lessons, so that when a master dies it is obviously not from
overwork. Some members of the staff might have felt at home in an Angela Brazil story; the
school padre remembered the 1914–18 War "as a sort of inter-school rugger-match on a
large scale" which must have been Great Fun as long as one was on the Winning Team.
When bodies began to drop in the most inconvenient places, an Old Boy (complete with Tie)
arrives on the scene to help the headmaster in all of his troubles.

Trevor wrote only one mystery but managed to produce a very neatly planned story
without detailed violence. *Murder at School* is not limp with Utopian emotions or rife with
those long-remembered resentments that sometimes dominate school-based stories. There is
merely mild amusement at the Public School system in the descriptions of this academy
famous for neither sports nor scholarship.

—Mary Groff

TRIPP, Miles (Barton). Also writes as Michael Brett. British. Born in Ganwick
Corner, Hertfordshire, 5 May 1923. Educated at Queen Elizabeth's Grammar School, Barnet,
Hertfordshire, 1933–41. Served in the Royal Air Force Bomber Command, 1942–46.
Married to Audrey Tripp; three children. Admitted as a solicitor, 1950: in private practice,
Stamford, Lincolnshire, 1950–52. Since 1953, Member of the Legal Staff, Charity
Commission, London; currently Deputy Charity Commissioner. Agent: A. D. Peters and
Company Ltd., 10 Buckingham Street, London WC2N 6BU, England.

CRIME PUBLICATIONS

Novels (series character: John Samson)

The Image of Man. London, Darwen Finlayson, 1955.
A Glass of Red Wine. London, Macdonald, 1960.

Kilo Forty.   London, Macmillan, 1963; New York, Holt Rinehart, 1964.
A Quartet of Three.   London, Macmillan, 1965.
The Chicken.   London, Macmillan, 1966; with *Zilla*, London, Pan, 1968.
One Is One.   London, Macmillan, 1968.
Malice and the Maternal Instinct.   London, Macmillan, 1969.
A Man Without Friends.   London, Macmillan, 1970.
Five Minutes with a Stranger.   London, Macmillan, 1971.
The Claws of God.   London, Macmillan, 1972.
Obsession (Samson).   London, Macmillan, 1973.
Woman at Risk.   London, Macmillan, 1974.
A Woman in Bed.   London, Macmillan, 1976.
The Once a Year Man (Samson).   London, Macmillan, 1977.
The Wife-Smuggler (Samson).   London, Macmillan, 1978.
Cruel Victim (Samson).   London, Macmillan, 1979.

Novels as Michael Brett (series character: Hugo Baron)

Diecast (Baron).   New York, Fawcett, 1963; London, Barker, 1964.
A Plague of Demons (Baron).   London, Barker, 1965.
A Cargo of Spent Evil (as John Michael Brett).   London, Barker, 1966.

Uncollected Short Stories

"A Remedy for Nerves," in *Winter's Crimes 1*, edited by George Hardinge.   London, Macmillan, 1969.
"Fixation," in *Winter's Crimes 3*, edited by George Hardinge.   London, Macmillan, 1971.
"A Lady from the Jungle," in *John Creasey's Mystery Bedside Book 1972*, edited by Herbert Harris.   London, Hodder and Stoughton, 1971.
"The Identity of His Father's Son," in *Winter's Crimes 6*, edited by George Hardinge.   London, Macmillan, 1974.
"Sister Nemesis," in *Winter's Crimes 8*, edited by Hilary Watson.   London, Macmillan, 1976.

OTHER PUBLICATIONS

Novels

Faith Is a Windsock.   London, Davies, 1952.
The Skin Dealer.   London, Macmillan, 1964; New York, Holt Rinehart, 1965.
The Fifth Point of the Compass.   London, Macmillan, 1967.

Play

Television Play: *A Man Without Friends*, from his own novel, 1972.

Other

The   Eighth   Passenger: A   Flight   of   Recollection   and   Discovery (autobiography).   London, Heinemann, 1969.

Miles Tripp comments:
As someone who would rather plant characters than clues, and would prefer that the story evolves through the characters rather than by their being shaped to fit the structure of a plot, I

naturally prefer psychology to technology and Simenon to either Christie or the imitators of Deighton. Although I write for my own pleasure, I also write in the hope that somewhere a reader will enjoy what I've written. I like to familiarize myself with a place before using it as a setting, but, apart from this, I have no rules, formulae, or special system.

*   *   *

Miles Tripp is an outstanding practitioner of the disturbing art of creating psychological suspense. Each novel features a different hero (or non-hero), but they are all flippant, cosmopolitan, British. In *A Man Without Friends* he writes about Marcus Wayne, a successful professional con-man who, among other things, practices graphology and enjoys high living. In *Woman at Risk* his protagonist is a barrister caught up in the murder of his mistress. The writing is brilliant and always witty: the reader does not so much ask himself "who done it?" as "who could have expected that to happen?" Edmund Crispin called Tripp an excellent writer, and he certainly gets no disagreement from me.

—Don Cole

TROY, Simon.   See WARRINER, Thurman.

TYRE, Nedra.   American.   Born in Offerman, Georgia.   Educated in public schools in Georgia; correspondence and extension courses, B.A.; Emory University, Atlanta, M.A.; Richmond School of Social Work, Virginia.   Worked as typist, sales clerk, library assistant, social worker, staff writer for social agencies, teacher of sociology at Richmond Professional Institute, Virginia.   Book reviewer, Richmond *News Leader* and Atlanta *Journal*.   Agent: Scott Meredith Literary Agency Inc., 845 Third Avenue, New York, New York 10022.   Address: 1118 Grove Avenue, Apartment 34, Richmond, Virginia 23220, U.S.A.

CRIME PUBLICATIONS

Novels

> *Mouse in Eternity.*   New York, Knopf, 1952; London, Macdonald, 1953; as *Death Is a Lover*, New York, Spivak, 1953.
> *Death of an Intruder.*   New York, Knopf, 1953; London, Collins, 1954.
> *Journey to Nowhere.*   New York, Knopf, and London, Collins, 1954.
> *Hall of Death.*   New York, Simon and Schuster, 1960; as *Reformatory Girls*, New York, Ace, 1962.
> *Everyone Suspect.*   New York, Macmillan, 1964; London, Gollancz, 1965.
> *Twice So Fair.*   New York, Random House, 1971.

Uncollected Short Stories

"Murder at the Poe Shrine," in *Ellery Queen's Mystery Magazine* (New York), September 1955.

"Tour de Couleur," in *Ellery Queen's Mystery Magazine* (New York), August 1956.

"Carnival Day," in *Ellery Queen's Thirteenth Annual.* New York, Random House, 1958; London, Collins, 1960.

"Reflections on Murder," in *Sleuth* (New York), December 1958.

"The Delicate Murderer," in *Ellery Queen's Mystery Magazine* (New York), November 1959.

"What Is Going to Happen," in *The Lethal Sex.* New York, Dell, 1959.

"The Gentle Miss Bluebeard," in *Alfred Hitchcock's Mystery Magazine* (North Palm Beach, Florida), November 1959.

"A Friendly Murder," in *Ellery Queen's Mystery Magazine* (New York), August 1961.

"Murder Between Friends," in *Alfred Hitchcock's Mystery Magazine* (North Palm Beach, Florida), August 1963.

"Typed for Murder," in *Signature* (New York), January 1967.

"A Case of Instant Detection," in *Ellery Queen's Mystery Magazine* (New York), May 1967.

"In the Fiction Alcove," in *Ellery Queen's Mystery Magazine* (New York), September 1967.

"Beyond the Wall," in *Alfred Hitchcock's Mystery Magazine* (North Palm Beach, Florida), June 1968.

"The Disappearance of Mrs. Standwick," in *Ellery Queen's Mystery Magazine* (New York), July 1968.

"The Attitude of Murder," in *Alfred Hitchcock's Mystery Magazine* (North Palm Beach, Florida), October 1969.

"Another Turn of the Screw," in *Ellery Queen's Grand Slam.* Cleveland, World, 1970; London, Gollancz, 1971.

"Recipe for a Happy Marriage," in *Ellery Queen's Mystery Magazine* (New York), March 1971.

"An Act of Deliverance," in *Ellery Queen's Mystery Magazine* (New York), August 1971.

"The Stranger Who Came Knocking," in *Ellery Queen's Mystery Magazine* (New York), June 1972.

"You Can't Trust Anyone," in *Ellery Queen's Mystery Magazine* (New York), June 1973.

"The Murder Game," in *Ellery Queen's Masters of Mystery.* New York, Davis, 1975.

"A Murder Is Arranged," in *Alfred Hitchcock's Mystery Magazine* (North Palm Beach, Florida), March 1975.

"A Nice Place to Stay," in *Ellery Queen's Magicians of Mystery.* New York, Davis, 1976.

"Killed by Kindness," in *Alfred Hitchcock's Tales to Keep You Spellbound*, edited by Eleanor Sullivan. New York, Davis, 1976.

"On Little Cat Feet," in *Ellery Queen's Mystery Magazine* (New York), February 1976.

"The Web," in *Mystery Monthly* (New York), October 1976.

"Cousin Anne," in *Mystery Monthly* (New York), February 1977.

"Accidental Widow," in *Alfred Hitchcock's Tales to Take Your Breath Away*, edited by Eleanor Sullivan. New York, Davis, 1977.

"The Dower Chest," in *Ellery Queen's Mystery Magazine* (New York), November 1977.

"Laughter Before Dying," in *Ellery Queen's Searches and Seizures.* New York, Davis, 1977.

"Daisies Deceive," in *Alfred Hitchcock's Tales to Scare You Stiff*, edited by Eleanor Sullivan. New York, Davis, 1978.

"Locks Won't Keep You Out," in *Ellery Queen's Napoleons of Mystery.* New York, Davis, 1978.

"Back for a Funeral," in *Ellery Queen's Mystery Magazine* (New York), October 1978.
"The More the Deadlier," in *Alfred Hitchcock's Mystery Magazine* (New York), October 1978.
"The Perfect Jewel," in *Ellery Queen's Mystery Magazine* (New York), June 1979.

OTHER PUBLICATIONS

Short Stories

Red Wine First. New York, Simon and Schuster, 1947.

*   *   *

It is inevitable that writers will draw upon their own past geographical and vocational backgrounds. Having been a social worker, Nedra Tyre has a special understanding of disadvantaged people. They are often potential victims, and she portrays them realistically and with considerable poignancy. Tyre victims are never merely life's losers; they are people with considerable inner resources, though unlucky.

She is particularly adept at describing the terrors of the elderly and lonely. *Death of an Intruder* has a seemingly simple plot regarding an old woman, living alone, whose house is "invaded" by another woman whom she cannot evict. One either dismisses it as unbelievable or one suspends disbelief and is carried along, finishing the book in one sitting and agreeing with Frances Crane who called it "superbly handled suspense." Two excellent short stories regarding the elderly are "Locks Won't Keep You Out," in which the mystery revolves around *what* it is that her protagonist is afraid of, and "On Little Cat Feet," in which an elderly woman, alone in an apartment house, is in deathly fear of a cat: she is a typical Tyre heroine, alone, poor, on foot, inevitably loaded down with groceries and library books.

Her old women do not accept their reduced circumstances lightly. Mary Allthorpe in "You Can't Trust Anyone" saves all year for her only pleasure, spring house tours in the South. On one of these crime enters her life. Widow Ellen Williams in "The Disappearance of Mr. Standwick" is travelling alone in Richmond when she calls a chance acquaintance and becomes involved in an unexpected adventure. Having lived most of her life in the South, Tyre is especially good at describing that area. While she doesn't write regional mysteries in the Faulknerian sense, she conveys how similar to the rest of the United States the new South has become, yet shows what it has retained to set it apart. A good example is "A Nice Place to Stay" regarding another character named Mrs. Williams.

Children are often as vulnerable as the old, and Tyre writes convincingly of them. Her novel *Hall of Death* is a fine mystery set at a Georgia reform school. "Carnival Day" is a heart-breaking story about a 12-year-old girl, whose parents are estranged, and her visit to an old-time Southern carnival. In "The Dower Chest" we see the terrors of apartment living and the city streets for Jenny, a bright little girl raised in the country, whose mother cannot meet her after school.

Tyre described the atmosphere and day-to-day operations of social work agencies in *Mouse in Eternity*. In "Another Turn of the Screw" she deals realistically with a work situation in a small bureaucracy, showing how a motive for murder can emerge from a supervisor-subordinate relationship. In "A Case of Instant Detection" a detective named Williams solves a murder committed while a film was shown in a sociology class.

Tyre's attachment to books (especially mysteries) is obvious. In "A Friendly Murder" Mary Williams (a name Tyre uses frequently) has her fateful meeting with a former Homicide Chief at the Public Library's Great Books Discussion Group. "In the Fiction Alcove" is set in a library in a large Georgia city while an ice storm paralyzes the city. Her devotion to literature (especially the work of Poe) is clear from one of her best short stories, the marvelously subtle "Tour de Couleur," and "Murder at the Poe Shrine" in which Miss Wilson, lecturer-guide-curator, solves a crime helped by knowledge of Poe.

In the appropriately named "Reflections on Murder" we have the archetypal Tyre heroine

– an independent woman who lives alone and reads mysteries as a hobby. In fact, the opening of this story is a brief essay on the genre. What happens when the heroine lets her hobby lead her to think about committing a murder is the crux of a highly unusual story from a highly unusual author.

—Marvin Lachman

UHNAK, Dorothy. American. Born in the Bronx, New York, in 1933. Educated at City College of New York, three years; John Jay College of Criminal Justice, degree c. 1970. Married; one daughter. Joined New York City Transit Police Department in 1953: Detective Second Grade, then Assistant to the Chief: Outstanding Police Duty Medal before leaving the force in 1967. Address: c/o Simon and Schuster, 1230 Avenue of the Americas, New York, New York 10020, U.S.A.

CRIME PUBLICATIONS

Novels (series character: Christie Opara)

The Bait (Opara). New York, Simon and Schuster, and London, Hodder and Stoughton, 1968.
The Witness (Opara). New York, Simon and Schuster, 1969; London, Hodder and Stoughton, 1970.
The Ledger (Opara). New York, Simon and Schuster, 1970; London, Hodder and Stoughton, 1971.
Law and Order. New York, Simon and Schuster, and London, Hodder and Stoughton, 1973.
The Investigation. New York, Simon and Schuster, 1977; London, Hodder and Stoughton, 1978.

OTHER PUBLICATIONS

Other

Policewoman: A Young Woman's Initiation into the Realities of Justice. New York, Simon and Schuster, 1964.

Manuscript Collection: Mugar Memorial Library, Boston University.

*   *   *

Dorothy Uhnak's credentials as a police novelist are impeccable. She served for 14 years with the New York City Transit Police, twelve of them as a detective. In 1964 she began to write of her experiences with a non-fiction account of her first years on the force. Policewoman has all Mrs. Uhnak's strengths and weaknesses as a writer. Her strengths include a good eye for the scenes and characters that bring a subject to life for the reader, and a copious, pounding style that forces the reader to be involved. Her weaknesses include this same style, which is capable of making even the obvious points three times. Like her nearest literary relative, Joseph Wambaugh, Uhnak is at pains to dispel the myths about police work that have been propagated in literature and on film. She makes the real pressures of police work clear: the struggle to develop the emotional shell that is absolutely necessary protection against constant exposure to the worst in human behavior, and the struggle to keep compassion and a modified idealism alive inside the shell. In *Policewoman*, and in all of her novels, there are scenes that justify every insistent adjective lavished on them. There is, for example, a retarded six-year-old who has been beaten to death by his grandmother. Despite the fact that the neighbors characterize him as the Dumb One, an unresponsive burden, all of his fingernails are bitten bloody. A scene such as this stops the reader's preconceived judgments cold.

Uhnak has improved steadily as a writer; *Law and Order* is perhaps her best book, and the recent *The Investigation* was a best-seller. *Law and Order* tells the story of three generations of the O'Malleys, an Irish Catholic family of policemen. Its argument is that New York's corrupt department cannot be reformed from the outside, only by insiders who know where all the bodies are buried and what happens if they are dug up and given a more appropriate funeral. Two episodes in the novel frame the inch-by-inch progress that Uhnak sees as the only kind of which humans are capable. At the beginning of the book, Sergeant O'Malley, violent and prejudiced, is killed in self-defense by a black prostitute whose pleas of illness he has ignored. She falls to her death moments afterward. O'Malley's grandson, 30 years later, has returned from Vietnam without prejudice, and with the knowledge of how to fight death. He gives the kiss of life to an injured black woman in the street. Both of these scenes ring with authenticity, as do Uhnak's portraits of the O'Malley wives and mothers, whose strength is narrow but very deep.

In all of Uhnak's work, there are impressive, unstereotyped portraits of women. *The Investigation* is held together by the slowly developed characterization of Kitty Keeler, a woman with beauty, intelligence, and Mafia connections, who may or may not have killed her two children. The character is based on a character from one of Uhnak's Christie Opara series, *The Ledger*. The earlier character, Elena Vargas, is presented as a woman trapped by her beauty, her innocence, and the color of her skin. Left with no socially acceptable way to achieve her ambitions, she chooses an alliance with a gangster who recognizes talent in her that respectable society is indifferent to. Kitty's story is essentially the same – only from a Mafia don did Kitty get, not just love, but recognition.

—Carol Cleveland

UNDERWOOD, Michael. Pseudonym for John Michael Evelyn. British. Born in Worthing, Sussex, 2 June 1916. Educated at Charterhouse School, Surrey; Christ Church, Oxford, 1935–38, M.A.; Grays Inn, London: called to the Bar, 1939. Served in the British Army, 1939–46: Major. Member of the Department of Public Prosecutions, London, 1946–76: Assistant Director, 1969–76; in grade Under-Secretary from 1972. Companion of the Bath, 1976. Agent: A. M. Heath and Company Ltd., 40–42 William IV Street, London WC2N 4DD. Address: 1 Riverbank, Datchet, Slough, Berkshire SL3 9BY, England.

CRIME PUBLICATIONS

Novels (series characters: Martin Ainsworth; Inspector/Superintendent Simon Manton)

Murder on Trial (Manton).   London, Hammond, 1954; New York, Washburn, 1958.

Murder Made Absolute (Manton). London, Hammond, 1955; New York, Washburn, 1957.
Death on Remand (Manton). London, Hammond, 1956.
False Witness (Manton). London, Hammond, 1957; New York, Walker, 1961.
Lawful Pursuit (Manton). London, Hammond, and New York, Doubleday, 1958.
Arm of the Law (Manton). London, Hammond, 1959.
Cause of Death (Manton). London, Hammond, 1960.
Death by Misadventure (Manton). London, Hammond, 1960.
Adam's Case (Manton). London, Hammond, and New York, Doubleday, 1961.
The Case Against Phillip Quest (Manton). London, Macdonald, 1962.
Girl Found Dead (Manton). London, Macdonald, 1963.
The Crime of Colin Wise (Manton). London, Macdonald, and New York, Doubleday, 1964.
The Unprofessional Spy (Ainsworth). London, Macdonald, and New York, Doubleday, 1964.
The Anxious Conspirator (Manton). London, Macdonald, and New York, Doubleday, 1965.
A Crime Apart. London, Macdonald, 1966.
The Man Who Died on Friday. London, Macdonald, 1967.
The Man Who Killed Too Soon. London, Macdonald, 1968.
The Shadow Game (Ainsworth). London, Macdonald, 1969.
The Silent Liars. London, Macmillan, and New York, Doubleday, 1970.
Shem's Demise. London, Macmillan, 1970.
A Trout in the Milk. London, Macmillan, 1971; New York, Walker, 1972.
Reward for a Defector. London, Macmillan, 1973; New York, St. Martin's Press, 1974.
A Pinch of Snuff. London, Macmillan, and New York, St. Martin's Press, 1974.
The Juror. London, Macmillan, and New York, St. Martin's Press, 1975.
Menaces, Menaces. London, Macmillan, and New York, St. Martin's Press, 1976.
Murder with Malice. London, Macmillan, and New York, St. Martin's Press, 1977.
The Fatal Trip. London, Macmillan, and New York, St. Martin's Press, 1977.
Crooked Wood. London, Macmillan, and New York, St. Martin's Press, 1978.
Anything but the Truth. London, Macmillan, 1978; New York, St. Martin's Press, 1979.
Smooth Justice. London, Macmillan, and New York, St. Martin's Press, 1979.
Victim of Circumstance. London, Macmillan, and New York, St. Martin's Press, 1980.

Uncollected Short Stories

"Operation Cash," in *Winter's Crimes 4*, edited by George Hardinge. London, Macmillan, 1972.
"Murder at St. Oswalds," in *Verdict of Thirteen: A Detection Club Anthology*, edited by Julian Symons. London, Faber, and New York, Harper, 1979.

Manuscript Collection: Mugar Memorial Library, Boston University.

Michael Underwood comments:
The common feature of all my books is a background of legal goings-on and court scenes and police (or private eye) investigation. The ingredients vary in proportion according to the

nature of the stories which range from detective novels to thrillers to spy books. All, however, are covered by the descriptive term of crime novel.

* * *

Michael Underwood is a crime writer who works largely by undramatic means. This might seem a contradiction. Crime, and especially murder, is at first blush a strongly dramatic affair. But it is so only at first blush. At the moment of a killing, though not always even then, there is drama. But often in real life it is momentary drama only. The whole process of a crime, both before that instant of drama and after it, is much more often tedious than high-coloured. And it is Underwood's great virtue − he is a lawyer and knows his facts − to convey, not perhaps the full tedium of a crime, but a good deal of its sober progress from point to point.

He does this whether he is describing the course of an investigation or, as he often does, the course of the legal process which is the true terminus of, say, an act of murder, though this is a part of the whole which in more crime books than not is simply omitted altogether. And Underwood's legal knowledge is used in such a way that his books differ even from those of that small section of the genre which does specialise in courtroom scenes. As often as not Underwood concentrates not on what happens in court, with all its slightly artificial dramatics, but on what happens outside the courtroom, in the Judge's chambers, in barristers' rooms, in perhaps the offices of the Director of Public Prosecutions.

And to his undramatic, factually correct, yet always truly fictional stories (always written with the reader in mind and not the actual circumstances of some tortuous real-life situation) he brings the quality of craftsmanship. To say of a book that it is written "with old-fashioned craftsmanship" is generally thought to be praising with faint damns. But craftsmanship is something that can be employed in any sort of book, whether action-packed or quiet, and which when it is absent can spoil to greater or less degree any book but a work of roaring genius. It is the unobtrusive making sure that everything fits, that nothing jars, that what is promised is present. And this Michael Underwood notably does.

It is a quality, too, which is likely to make an author's books progressively better as he learns what he does best, what it is sensible for him to eschew. And this, by and large, is true of the 30 books we have had from Underwood. Some, however, have stood out, generally those in which the plot has been more than usually ingenious. In general all his plots are, as one might expect, sufficient to the subject. But every now and again he has hit on one that works especially well. There was a short story (Underwood has not written many) based on a then perfectly possible way of defrauding banks with cheque cards. There was the superb puzzle, in *Menaces, Menaces*, which gave us a professional blackmailer safely in the cells during his Old Bailey trial when a demand for money was received bearing all the hallmarks of his particular modus operandi. How could he have been responsible? Or why was somebody imitating him so closely? And Underwood provided a thoroughly satisfactory explanation. There have been other books similarly intriguing and satisfying. They are peaks in a long range of solid hills.

—H. R. F. Keating

UPFIELD, Arthur W(illiam). Australian. Born in Gosport, Hampshire, England, 1 September 1888. Educated in public school, then apprenticed to a surveyor and estate agent; shipped by his father to Australia in 1911, where he worked as a cook, boundary rider, and itinerant worker. Served in the Australian Imperial Force, 1914–19. Married in 1915; one son. Worked as a private secretary in England, then returned to Australia as an itinerant trapper and miner until becoming a full-time writer. Headed Australian Geological Society expedition to northern and western Australia, 1948. *Died 13 February 1964.*

CRIME PUBLICATIONS

Novels (series character: Inspector Napoleon "Bony" Bonaparte)

The House of Cain. London, Hutchinson, 1928; New York, Dorrance, 1929.
The Barrakee Mystery (Bonaparte). London, Hutchinson, 1929; as *The Lure of the Bush*, New York, Doubleday, 1965.
The Beach of Atonement. London, Hutchinson, 1930.
The Sands of Windee (Bonaparte). London, Hutchinson, 1931.
A Royal Abduction. London, Hutchinson, 1932.
Gripped by Drought. London, Hutchinson, 1932.
Wings above the Diamantina (Bonaparte). Sydney, Angus and Robertson, 1936; as *Winged Mystery*, London, John Hamilton, 1937; as *Wings above the Claypan*, New York, Doubleday, 1943.
Mr. Jelly's Business (Bonaparte). Sydney, Angus and Robertson, 1937; London, John Hamilton, 1938; as *Murder Down Under*, New York, Doubleday, 1943.
Wind of Evil (Bonaparte). Sydney, Angus and Robertson, 1937; London, John Hamilton, 1939; New York, Doubleday, 1944.
The Bone Is Pointed (Bonaparte). Sydney, Angus and Robertson, 1938; London, John Hamilton, 1939; New York, Doubleday, 1947.
The Mystery of the Swordfish Reef (Bonaparte). Sydney, Angus and Robertson, 1939; New York, Doubleday, 1943; London, Heinemann, 1960.
Bushranger of the Skies (Bonaparte). Sydney, Angus and Robertson, 1940; New York, British Book Centre, 1963; as *No Footprints in the Bush*, New York, Doubleday, 1944; London, Penguin, 1950.
Death of a Swagman (Bonaparte). New York, Doubleday, 1945; London, Aldor, 1946.
The Devil's Steps (Bonaparte). New York, Doubleday, 1946; London, Aldor, 1948.
An Author Bites the Dust (Bonaparte). Sydney, Angus and Robertson, and New York, Doubleday, 1948.
The Mountains Have a Secret (Bonaparte). New York, Doubleday, 1948; London, Heinemann, 1952.
The Widows of Broome (Bonaparte). New York, Doubleday, 1950; London, Heinemann, 1951.
The Bachelors of Broken Hill (Bonaparte). New York, Doubleday, 1950; London, Heinemann, 1958.
The New Shoe (Bonaparte). New York, Doubleday, 1951; London, Heinemann, 1952.
Venom House (Bonaparte). New York, Doubleday, 1952; London, Heinemann, 1953.
Murder Must Wait (Bonaparte). London, Heinemann, and New York, Doubleday, 1953.
Death of a Lake (Bonaparte). London, Heinemann, and New York, Doubleday, 1954.
Sinister Stones (Bonaparte). New York, Doubleday, 1954; as *Cake in the Hatbox*, London, Heinemann, 1955.
The Battling Prophet (Bonaparte). London, Heinemann, 1956.
The Man of Two Tribes (Bonaparte). London, Heinemann, and New York, Doubleday, 1956.
Bony Buys a Woman. London, Heinemann, 1957; as *The Bushman Who Came Back*, New York, Doubleday, 1957.
Bony and the Black Virgin. London, Heinemann, 1959; New York, Collier, 1965.
Bony and the Mouse. London, Heinemann, 1959; as *Journey to the Hangman*, New York, Doubleday, 1959.

Bony and the Kelly Gang. London, Heinemann, 1960; as *Valley of Smugglers*, New York, Doubleday, 1960.

Bony and the White Savage. London, Heinemann, 1961; as *The White Savage*, New York, Doubleday, 1961.

The Will of the Tribe (Bonaparte). New York, Doubleday, 1962; London, Heinemann, 1963.

Madman's Bend (Bonaparte). London, Heinemann, 1963; as *The Body at Madman's Bend*, New York, Doubleday, 1963.

The Lake Frome Monster (Bonaparte; completed by J. L. Price and Dorothy Strange). London, Heinemann, 1966.

Bibliography: "The Novels of Arthur Upfield" by Betty Donaldson in *Armchair Detective* (White Bear Lake, Minnesota), November 1974.

* * *

Arthur Upfield's retentive mind must have casually stored away thousands of images during the 20 years he roamed over Australia working at one job after another, from opal gouger to boundary rider. In England as a teenager he had scribbled incessantly at unpublishable "Yellow Peril" manuscripts. Now an older friend was prodding him to put his talents as a writer to good use. This was probably at the back of his mind when he accepted a job as cook at the isolated Wheeler's Well in New South Wales. Settling down in the little iron-roofed pine-log hut, he rediscovered the satisfaction of writing. He realized it would be foolish to compete with Edgar Wallace or S. S. Van Dine, and decided to use the background and people of Australia to form the basis of his stories. He did this so well that his fictional homesteads can be fairly accurately placed on a map of Australia.

The Barrakee Mystery did not satisfy him even after it was rewritten; he set it aside and wrote a straight thriller, *The House of Cain*. One day Tracker Leon rode by Wheeler's Well and stopped to reminisce with Upfield about the five months they had ridden the dog-proof fence together. The half-caste was a delightful companion, intelligent and knowledgeable. Upfield was aware Leon had been born in North Queensland; his father was known to be white, his mother an aborigine who had been killed for breaking tribal law. He had received a good education and was a valued tracker attached to the Queensland Police. Leon suggested they should exchange some books before he continued his journey to Ivanhoe. As Upfield watched him ride off he came to a sudden decision: he would change the white detective in *The Barrakee Mystery* to one based on the half-caste. But what to call him? One of the books Tracker Leon had left him was Abbot's *Life of Napoleon Bonaparte*. That was it!

Of the 33 novels ultimately published, 29 had as the crime investigator Detective Inspector Napoleon Bonaparte of the Queensland Police. Upfield had created a vivid, totally believable character. Bony, as he prefers to be called, is an attractive, slender man with unexpectedly blue eyes in a smooth, dark face. His hair is well brushed, his nose straight; when he smiles he reveals regular white teeth. Normally a fastidious dresser, he can assume a very different character, drifting onto the scene of the crime as a swagman or horse-trainer with elastic-sided boots, a slightly dirty shirt, and old gabardine trousers. Bony obtained an M.A. degree at Brisbane University and married an educated half-caste, grey-eyed Marie; they have three sons, Charles, Bob, and Ed. He does not like to be hurried when on an investigation; he refers to himself as a tortoise, and objects so strenuously when his superiors try to turn him into a hare that he often resigns. Of course, he is always reinstated. He is considerate of the local police and, perhaps because he puts himself in the criminal's shoes, is never vindictive towards him. The "blacks" (aborigines) are very impressed when they see the initiation marks that have been made with a sharp flint on Bony's back and chest. In *The Sands of Windee* old Moongalliti examines the welts and, with his black eyes bulging, comments, "My, you beeg feller chief Nor' Queensland!"

Time is often the only ally that Bony has. He likes tough cases, those on which he can exercise his peculiar talents. Often a crime will be weeks or months old; there may be no body; time and weather may have conspired to cover up the clues; people may have forgotten what has happened. But by observing clues visible only to his sharp eyes (a turned pebble, a single hair caught on the bark of a tree, the behavior of an ant), by using his inherited aboriginal instincts and Western intelligence, by patiently jogging people's memories and just as patiently listening to what they have to say, Bony always solves the problem. Only once, after a beautiful woman had pleaded with him, did he not conclude a case by naming the murderer.

Upfield had a remarkable ability to describe the land and the people he grew to love so well. Each of his books has a different setting which Upfield exploited to the full, giving the reader a first-rate adventure story running parallel to the detective plot. *The Mystery of Swordfish Reef* is an exciting tale of big-game fishing in the Tasman Sea where Bony, battling a huge swordfish, describes his pulse as beating "like Thor's great hammer." *The Man of Two Tribes* is a story of survival in the vast, desolate Nullarbor Plain, the treeless expanse of sand and saltbush in southern Australia. *Bony and the Mouse* tells of a man going mad in a totally silent West Australian forest where nothing moves – no birds, no rabbits, no jerboa rats, no banded anteaters. *The New Shoe* contains an extraordinary description of an old craftsman painstakingly making a red-gum casket, which all but becomes Bony's coffin. *The Bone Is Pointed* is a chilling psychological thriller; our hero has to fight hard against *mauia*, one of the most potent forms of magic employed by aborigines against their enemies. The *Lake Frome Monster* was finished by J. L. Price and Dorothy Strange, using the copious notes left by Upfield on his death in 1964. The books in which the half-caste detective appears have been reprinted several times; the remaining four have long been out of print.

—Betty Donaldson

VANARDY, Varick. See **DEY, Frederic Van Rensselaer.**

VANCE, John Holbrook (Jack Vance). Also writes as Peter Held; John Holbrook; Ellery Queen; John Van See; Alan Wade. American. Born in San Francisco, California. Educated at the University of California, Berkeley, B.A. 1942. Married Norma Ingold in 1946; one son. Self-employed writer. Recipient: Mystery Writers of America Edgar Allan Poe Award, 1960; Hugo Award, 1963, 1967; Science Fiction Writers of America Nebula Award, 1966; Instructors of Science Fiction in Higher Education Jupiter Award, 1974. Agent: Kirby McCauley Ltd., 60 East 42nd Street, New York, New York, 10017. Address: 6383 Valley View Road, Oakland, California 94611, U.S.A.

CRIME PUBLICATIONS

Novels (series character: Sheriff Joe Bain)

Isle of Peril (as Alan Wade).   New York, Curl, 1957.
Take My Face (as Peter Held).   New York, Curl, 1957.
The Man in the Cage.   New York, Random House, 1960; London, Boardman, 1961.
The Fox Valley Murders (Bain).   Indianapolis, Bobbs Merrill, 1966; London, Hale, 1967.
The Pleasant Grove Murders (Bain).   Indianapolis, Bobbs Merrill, 1967; London, Hale, 1968.
The Deadly Isles.   Indianapolis, Bobbs Merrill, 1969; London, Hale, 1970.
Bad Ronald.   New York, Ballantine, 1973.
The House on Lily Street.   San Francisco, Underwood Miller, 1979.
The View from Chickweed's Window.   San Francisco, Underwood Miller, 1979.

Novels as Ellery Queen

The Four Johns.   New York, Pocket Books, 1964; as *Four Men Called John*, London, Gollancz, 1976.
A Room to Die In.   New York, Pocket Books, 1965.
The Madman Theory.   New York, Pocket Books, 1966.

Uncollected Short Story

"First Star I See Tonight" (as John Van See), in *Malcolm's Mystery Magazine* (New York), March 1954.

OTHER PUBLICATIONS

Novels

The Dying Earth.   New York, Curl, 1950.
The Space Pirate.   New York, Toby Press, 1953; as *The Five Gold Bands*, New York, Ace, 1963.
Vandals of the Void.   Philadelphia, Winston, 1953.
To Live Forever.   New York, Ballantine, 1956.
Big Planet.   New York, Bouregy, 1957; London, Hodder and Stoughton, 1977.
The Languages of Pao.   New York, Bouregy, 1958.
Slaves of the Klau.   New York, Ace, 1958.
The Dragon Masters.   New York, Ace, 1963; London, Dobson, 1965.
The Houses of Iszm and *Son of the Tree.*   New York, Ace, 1964.
The Star King.   New York, Berkley, 1964; London, Dobson, 1966.
The Killing Machine.   New York, Berkley, 1964; London, Dobson, 1967.
Monsters in Orbit.   New York, Ace, 1965; London, Dobson, 1977.
Space Opera.   New York, Pyramid, 1965.
The Blue World.   New York, Ballantine, 1966.
The Brains of Earth.   New York, Ace, 1966; London, Dobson, 1975.
The Last Castle.   New York, Ace, 1967.
The Palace of Love.   New York, Berkley, 1967; London, Dobson, 1968.
City of the Chasch.   New York, Ace, 1968; London, Dobson, 1975.
Emphyrio.   New York, Doubleday, 1969.
Servants of the Wankh.   New York, Ace, 1969; London, Dobson, 1975.
The Dirdir.   New York, Ace, 1969; London, Dobson, 1975.
The Pnume.   New York, Ace, 1970; London, Dobson, 1975.

The Anome. New York, Dell, 1973; London, Hodder and Stoughton, 1975.
The Brave Free Men. New York, Dell, 1973; London, Hodder and Stoughton, 1975.
Trullion: Alastor 2262. New York, Ballantine, 1973.
The Asutra. New York, Dell, 1974; London, Hodder and Stoughton, 1975.
The Gray Prince. Indianapolis, Bobbs Merrill, 1974; London, Hodder and Stoughton, 1976.
Marune: Alastor 933. New York, Ballantine, 1975.
Showboat World. New York, Pyramid, 1975; London, Hodder and Stoughton, 1977.
Maske: Thaery. New York, Berkley, 1976; London, Fontana, 1978.
Wyst: Alastor 1716. New York, Daw, 1978.
The Face. New York, Daw, 1979.

Short Stories

Future Tense. New York, Ballantine, 1964.
The World Between and Other Stories. New York, Ace, 1965.
The Eyes of the Overworld. New York, Ace, 1966.
The Many Worlds of Magnus Ridolph. New York, Ace, 1966; London, Dobson, 1977.
Eight Fantasms and Magics. New York, Collier, 1970.
The Worlds of Jack Vance. New York, Ace, 1973.
The Best of Jack Vance. New York, Pocket Books, 1976.
Green Magic. San Francisco, Underwood Miller, 1979.

Plays

Television Plays: *Captain Video* (6 episodes), 1952–53.

Bibliography: *Fantasms: A Bibliography of the Literature of Jack Vance* by Daniel J. H. Levack and Tim Underwood, San Francisco, Underwood Miller, 1978.

Manuscript Collection: Mugar Memorial Library, Boston University.

*   *   *

John Holbrook Vance was already famous as a writer of science fiction and fantastic adventure, under the shortened name Jack Vance, when he turned to mystery fiction. Much of his science fiction is built around pure crime story plots. Magnus Ridolph, created for a series of magazine stories in the late 1940's, is an interstellar trouble-shooter and con-man who redresses wrongs (for a fee) and even solves a murder. Six of his adventures were collected in book form as *The Many Worlds of Magnus Ridolph.* In *To Live Forever*, one of Vance's best novels, the murderer, Gavin Waylock, fights for survival in a highly structured society of the future. And in the series beginning with the novel *The Star King* a man hunts the five disguised non-humans who murdered his parents. These and other Jack Vance books are worth the attention of any reader who enjoys exotic adventure and strange locales.

In 1957 Vance's first contemporary mystery novel, *Isle of Peril*, was published under the pseudonym Alan Wade. This is the story of the violent events that occur when the owner of a small island sells parcels of land to a group of buyers who are not what they seem. A second pseudonymous mystery, *Take My Face* (by Peter Held), also appeared in 1957. Three years later Vance felt ready to put his own name on a mystery novel, and his confidence was justified: *The Man in the Cage*, a tale of intrigue and smuggling in Tangier, won an Edgar. In 1966, he published the first of two novels featuring Sheriff Joe Bain of San Rodrigo County, California. About *The Fox Valley Murders*, the critic Anthony Boucher said that the setting "is wonderfully real, and so is Sheriff Bain. A fresh kind of procedural story." *The Pleasant Grove Murders* was equally good. In *The Deadly Isles* the setting shifted to Tahiti and the South Seas for a more artificial and much less satisfying story. Vance was back in top form with *Bad Ronald*, a fascinating study of a young psychopath which manages to make incredible events convincing.

—R. E. Briney

VANCE, Louis Joseph. American. Born in Washington, D.C., 19 September 1879. Educated at Brooklyn Polytechnic Institute; Art Students' League, New York City. Married Nance Elizabeth Hodges in 1898 (separated); one son. Worked for public service corporation, New York, before becoming full-time writer. Published hundreds of short stories in popular magazines before the success of his mystery novels. *Died 16 December 1933.*

CRIME PUBLICATIONS

Novels (series character: Michael Lanyard, "The Lone Wolf")

> *Terence O'Rourke, Gentleman Adventurer.* New York, Wessels, 1905; London, Richards, 1906.
> *The Brass Bowl.* Indianapolis, Bobbs Merrill, and London, Richards, 1907.
> *The Black Bag.* Indianapolis, Bobbs Merrill, and London, Richards, 1908.
> *The Bronze Bell.* New York, Dodd Mead, and London, Richards, 1909.
> *The Pool of Flame.* New York, Dodd Mead, 1909; London, Richards, 1910.
> *Cynthia-of-the-Minute.* New York, Dodd Mead, and London, Richards, 1911.
> *The Bandbox.* Boston, Little Brown, and London, Richards, 1912.
> *The Destroying Angel.* Boston, Little Brown, 1912; London, Richards, 1913.
> *The Lone Wolf.* Boston, Little Brown, 1914; London, Nash, 1915.
> *Nobody.* New York, Doran, 1915; London, Hodder and Stoughton, 1916.
> *Sheep's Clothing.* Boston, Little Brown, 1915.
> *The False Faces* (Lanyard). New York, Doubleday, 1918; London, Skeffington, 1920.
> *The Dark Mirror.* New York, Doubleday, 1920; London, Hurst and Blackett, 1921.
> *Alias the Lone Wolf.* New York, Doubleday, and London, Hodder and Stoughton, 1921.
> *Red Masquerade* (Lanyard). New York, Doubleday, and London, Hodder and Stoughton, 1921.
> *Baroque.* New York, Dutton, and London, Hodder and Stoughton, 1923.
> *The Lone Wolf Returns.* New York, Dutton, 1923; London, Hodder and Stoughton, 1924.
> *The Dark Power.* London, Bles, 1925.
> *The Dead Ride Hard.* Philadelphia, Lippincott, 1926; London, Bles, 1927.
> *Lip Service.* London, Bles, 1928.
> *The Woman in the Shadow.* Philadelphia, Lippincott, 1930; London, Jarrolds, 1931.
> *The Lone Wolf's Son.* Philadelphia, Lippincott, 1931; London, Jarrolds, 1932.
> *The Trembling Flame.* Philadelphia, Lippincott, 1931; London, Jarrolds, 1932.
> *Detective.* Philadelphia, Lippincott, 1932; London, Jarrolds, 1933.
> *Encore the Lone Wolf.* Philadelphia, Lippincott, 1933; London, Jarrolds, 1934.
> *The Lone Wolf's Last Prowl.* Philadelphia, Lippincott, 1934; London, Jarrolds, 1935.
> *The Street of Strange Faces.* Philadelphia, Lippincott, and London, Jarrolds, 1934.

Uncollected Short Stories

"Old Man Menace," in *The Saint* (New York), May 1965.
"The White Terror," in *The Saint* (New York), August 1965.
"The Gulp Stream," in *The Saint* (New York), April 1966.
"The Flash," in *The Saint* (New York), September 1966.

OTHER PUBLICATIONS

Novels

The Private War. New York, Appleton, and London, Richards, 1906.
No Man's Land. New York, Dodd Mead, and London, Stevens and Brown, 1910.
The Fortune Hunter. New York, Dodd Mead, and London, Stevens and Brown, 1910.
Marrying Money (novelization of stage play *The Fortune Hunter*). London, Richards, 1911.
The Day of Days. Boston, Little Brown, 1913; London, Richards, 1914.
Joan Thursday. Boston, Little Brown, and London, Richards, 1913.
The Trey o' Hearts. New York, Grosset and Dunlap, 1914.
Bean Revel. London, Nash, 1920.
Linda Lee Incorporated. New York, Dutton, 1922.
Mrs. Paramour. New York, Dutton, 1924.
The Road to En-Dor. New York, Dutton, 1924.
White Fire. New York, Dutton, and London, Bles, 1926.
They Call It Love. Philadelphia, Lippincott, 1927.
Speaking of Women. Philadelphia, Lippincott, 1930; London, Jarrolds, 1932.

Plays

Screenplays: *Patria*, 1917; *The Lone Wolf's Daughter*, with Sig Herzig and Harry Revier, 1929.

*   *   *

Had Louis Joseph Vance not created Michael Lanyard, alias the Lone Wolf, it may be doubted if his work would be remembered. Inspired by, and following in the tradition of, Arsène Lupin, Lanyard is more human and introspective. He is (in Robert Sampson's phrase) a "bent hero," one of that breed who rid society of criminals by working from outside the law. The ethical position of the bent hero is shaky, but it is also part of a venerable tradition which may be traced to Robin Hood.

Vance's style is one of subdued sensationalism peppered with arcane words, but the serious tone and the glimpses of the Lone Wolf's mind at work make the most preposterous situations seem plausible. The Lone Wolf's world is free of that social festering and inarticulate horror that underlie the *Black Mask* style. Lanyard's origins are a mystery. He became a criminal willingly and just as willingly rejected that profession to prove himself worthy of a woman's trust. In *The False Faces* he pursues the murderer of his wife while gathering intelligence information for the Allies. In *Red Masquerade* he works for the British Secret Service to prevent the assassination of the King and the members of the Cabinet.

Vance may have thought little of his creation for he wrote only eight novels about Lanyard. The tradition of the noble outlaw which he kept alive certainly had a great influence on writers like Sapper and Leslie Charteris, however differently they reflect it.

—J. Randolph Cox

VAN DINE, S. S.   Pseudonym for Willard Huntington Wright.   American.   Born in Charlottesville, Virginia in 1888. Educated at St. Vincent College and Pomona College, California; Harvard University, Cambridge, Massachusetts; studied art in Munich and Paris. Married 1) Katharine Belle Boynton in 1907 (divorced, 1930); one daughter; 2) Eleanor Pulapaugh. Literary and Art Critic, Los Angeles *Times*, 1907; Editor-in-Chief, *Smart Set*, New York, 1912–14; Editor, *The International Studio*. Suffered a breakdown in 1923 and confined to bed for two years, when he began writing; screenwriter for Warner Brothers, 1931–32. *Died 11 April 1939.*

CRIME PUBLICATIONS

Novels (series character: Philo Vance in all books except *The President's Mystery Story*)

The Benson Murder Case.   New York, Scribner, and London, Benn, 1926.
The Canary Murder Case.   New York, Scribner, and London, Benn, 1927.
The Greene Murder Case.   New York, Scribner, and London, Benn, 1928.
The Bishop Murder Case.   New York, Scribner, and London, Cassell, 1929.
The Scarab Murder Case.   New York, Scribner, and London, Cassell, 1930.
The Kennel Murder Case.   New York, Scribner, and London, Cassell, 1933.
The Dragon Murder Case.   New York, Scribner, 1933; London, Cassell, 1934.
The Casino Murder Case.   New York, Scribner, and London, Cassell, 1934.
The Garden Murder Case.   New York, Scribner, and London, Cassell, 1935.
The President's Mystery Story, with others.   New York, Farrar and Rinehart, 1935.
The Kidnap Murder Case.   New York, Scribner, and London, Cassell, 1936.
The Gracie Allen Murder Case.   New York, Scribner, and London, Cassell, 1938; as
   The Smell of Murder, New York, Bantam, 1950.
The Winter Murder Case.   New York, Scribner, and London, Cassell, 1939.

Uncollected Short Stories

"The Scarlet Nemesis," in *Cosmopolitan* (New York), January 1929.
"A Murder in a Witches' Cauldron," in *Cosmopolitan* (New York), February 1929.
"The Man in the Blue Overcoat," in *Cosmopolitan* (New York), May 1929.
"Poison," in *Cosmopolitan* (New York), June 1929.
"The Almost Perfect Crime," in *Cosmopolitan* (New York), July 1929.
"The Inconvenient Husband," in *Cosmopolitan* (New York), August 1929.
"The Bonmartini Murder Case," in *Cosmopolitan* (New York), October 1929.
"Fool!" in *Cosmopolitan* (New York), January 1930.

OTHER PUBLICATIONS as Willard Huntington Wright

Novel

The Man of Promise.   New York, Lane, 1916.

Play

Screenplay: *The Canary Murder Case*, with others, 1929.

Other

Europe after 8:15, with H. L. Mencken and George Jean Nathan.   New York, Lane,
   1914.
Modern Painting: Its Tendency and Meaning.   New York, Lane, 1915.

What Nietzsche Taught. New York, Huebsch, 1915.
The Creative Will: Studies in the Philosophy and Syntax of Aesthetics. New York, Lane, 1916.
The Forum Exhibition of Modern American Painters, March Thirteenth to March Twenty-fifth, 1916. New York, Mitchell Kennerley, 1916.
Informing a Nation. New York, Dodd Mead, 1917.
Misinforming a Nation. New York, Huebsch, 1917.
The Future of Painting. New York, Huebsch, 1923.
"The Detective Novel," in *Scribner's* (New York), November 1926.
"Twenty Rules for Writing Detective Stories," in *American Magazine* (Springfield, Ohio), September 1928.
I Used to Be a Highbrow But Look at Me Now (as S. S. Van Dine). New York, Scribner, 1929.
"The Great Detective Stories," in *The Art of the Mystery Story: A Collection of Critical Essays*, edited by Howard Haycraft. New York, Simon and Schuster, 1946.

Editor, *The Great Modern French Stories.* New York, Boni and Liveright, 1917.
Editor, *The Great Detective Stories: A Chronological Anthology.* New York, Scribner, 1927.

Bibliography: "The Writings of Willard Huntington Wright" by Walter B. Crawford, in *Bulletin of Bibliography* (Westwood, Massachusetts), May–August 1963.

Manuscript Collection: Princeton University Library, New Jersey.

*   *   *

Willard Huntington Wright was a distinguished art critic, an editor from 1912–14 of *The Smart Set* magazine, a collaborator with H. L. Mencken and George Jean Nathan, the author of several books – including a devastating attack on the *Encyclopaedia Britannica*, *Misinforming a Nation* – a study of Nietzsche, several works on modern painting, and a novel, *The Man of Promise.* He had shown little interest in detective fiction when he was forced by overwork to take a long rest, during which he was forbidden to do any "serious" reading. In his long convalescence he read over 2,000 volumes of detective fiction and works on criminology, and applied to them the analytical methods of an art and literary critic. Out of this analysis came a quite prescriptive theory of detective fiction, later expressed in his introduction to the anthology *The Great Detective Stories* and his famous "Twenty Rules for Writing Detective Stories." In both he insisted that "The detective story is a kind of intellectual game ... a sporting event," with definite laws dealing with fair play and concentration on the puzzle. He excluded "love interest," elaborate characterization and description, and conspiracies, spies, political plots, and professional criminals.

Wright set about creating a set of detective plots according to these rules, submitted three of them to a publisher, and was given a contract. The first, *The Benson Murder Case*, with the amateur detective Philo Vance, appeared in 1926. It and its successor, *The Canary Murder Case*, revitalized the moribund detective story in America, attracted a new audience, and launched in America what Howard Haycraft has called "The Golden Age." Nine more Philo Vance novels followed before Wright's death in 1939, and a final work, in abbreviated second-draft form, *The Winter Murder Case*, appeared posthumously. Except for the unfortunate *Gracie Allen Murder Case*, their titles all have six letters. Wright declared that he would write only six S. S. Van Dine novels, saying that no one "has more than six good detective-novel ideas in his system," but the success of his first six Philo Vance novels with the critics, the reading public, and, above all, in motion picture versions, led him to continue. The last six, however, are markedly inferior to the first six, vindicating his initial judgment.

Despite the facts that the novels are written as though they were telling the inside story of actual celebrated cases – what Sutherland Scott calls "profound pseudo-realism" – and that the first two are, in fact, based on notorious murders (the Joseph Bowne Elwell case and the "Dot" King case), these stories are, as Van Dine's "Rules" would lead us to expect, tales resting primarily on elaborate and intricate plots, that, as Nicholas Blake said of John Dickson Carr's, "possess the mad logic and extravagance of a dream." This extravagance, intricacy, and unreality reach perhaps their highest expression in *The Bishop Murder Case*, in which a series of murders is based on the Mother Goose rhymes – Johnny Sprigg is shot through his wig, Humpty Dumpty is pushed from a wall, Cock Robin is killed by an arrow – and the clues include such intellectual matters as Ibsen's plays, chess moves, and mathematical theories. *The Green Murder Case*, with *The Bishop* and *The Scarab* one of Van Dine's best and his longest, devolves about a murderer who uses methods borrowed from – and recognized by Vance as being from – a German work on criminology.

The *deux ex machina*, Vance's phrase for the detective in his "Rules," is Philo Vance, who is a "young social aristocrat," an aesthete, an art critic, an expert on a wide range of esoteric subjects, an Oxford graduate, a dilettante, and an inveterate dropper of terminal g's. Vance, the friend of the New York District Attorney Markham, is an American equivalent of Lord Peter Wimsey and with many characteristics that remind us of H. C. Bailey's Reggie Fortune (Vance's cigarettes are Régie's), but he is even more clearly an idealized portrait of his author. Van Dine, Vance's attorney and constant companion, is the narrator of these novels, and he approaches Vance with a gravity appropriate for a diety, thus, perhaps, completing Wright's wish-fulfillment.

Vance's method is to apply a psychological understanding of people, as well as a wide-ranging knowledge, to the solution of his "cases." In actual fact, the plots almost always involve a series of murders and in a sense solve themselves by elimination. Vance's proof often rests on psychological evidence too slight to be the basis for an arrest, but Wright's Nietzschean attitudes make it possible for Vance to be on occasion executioner as well as detective, himself killing the murderer, as in *The Bishop* and *The Scarab*, or, more often, making the murderer's suicide possible. Although Vance aids his friend Markham in solving these cases, it is because they challenge him as intellectual puzzles; he has little interest in abstract justice and little respect for the law.

Two characteristic elements of the novels are extensive use of erudite footnotes and disquisitions on esoteric learning. In the early books, at least through *The Scarab Murder Case*, this learning and the footnotes, however pretentious, are integral to the plots and not only justified but entertaining. In the later books, like Vance's mannerisms, the erudition often seems added in undigested dollops and the pretensions of the notes become annoying. What once had amused and pleased became a source of irritation, resulting finally in Ogden Nash's couplet: "Philo Vance/Needs a kick in the pance."

Whether, had he lived, Wright could have adjusted to the changing tastes of his audience, no one knows. The early Ellery Queen novels, which certainly belong in the Van Dine tradition, gradually changed to very different kinds of books, but there is no evidence that Van Dine at the time of his death realized the need to change. These unchanged mannerisms and concepts have been costly to Van Dine's posthumous reputation, for they have prevented present day readers from discovering works which are, as Julian Symons says, "models of construction." Van Dine's place in the history of the American detective story is secure and important, but his place with contemporary readers is far lower than it deserves to be. As John Dickson Carr, a master of the same kind of plotting, said, Van Dine "juggled suspects with such dexterity, like twirling Indian-clubs, that we could only stare in admiration." Van Dine's world was remote from real life, but it was the place of delightfully intricate and challenging make-believe.

—C. Hugh Holman

VENNING, Michael. See RICE, Craig.

VICKERS, Roy C. Also wrote as David Durham; Sefton Kyle; John Spencer. British. Born in 1888(?). Educated at Charterhouse School, Surrey; Brasenose College, Oxford. Married Mary van Rossem; one son. Worked as a journalist and court reporter; Editor, *Novel Magazine*, London. *Died in 1965.*

CRIME PUBLICATIONS

Novels (series characters: Inspector Rason; Hugh Stanton; Jabez Winterbourne)

The Mystery of the Scented Death (Rason).   London, Jenkins, 1921.
The Vengeance of Henry Jarroman.   London, Jenkins, 1923.
Ishmael's Wife.   London, Jenkins, 1924.
A Murder for a Million.   London, Jenkins, 1924.
Four Past Four.   London, Jenkins, 1925; New York, Jefferson House, 1945.
His Other Wife.   London, Jenkins, 1926.
The Unforbidden Sin.   London, Jenkins, 1926.
The White Raven.   London, Jenkins, 1927.
The Radingham Mystery.   London, Jenkins, 1928.
A Girl of These Days.   London, Jenkins, 1929.
The Rose in the Dark.   London, Jenkins, 1930.
The Gold Game (Winterbourne).   London, Jenkins, 1930.
The Deputy for Cain.   London, Jenkins, 1931.
The Marriage for the Defence.   London, Jenkins, 1932.
The Whispering Death (as John Spencer).   London, Hodder and Stoughton, 1932; New York, Jefferson House, 1947.
Swell Garrick (as John Spencer).   London, Hodder and Stoughton, 1933.
Bardelow's Heir (Rason).   London, Jenkins, 1933.
Money Buys Everything (Rason).   London, Jenkins, 1934.
Kidnap Island (Rason).   London, Newnes, 1935.
Hide Those Diamonds! (Winterbourne).   London, Newnes, 1935.
The Man in the Red Mask.   London, Newnes, 1935.
Terror of Tongues! (Rason).   London, Newnes, 1937.
The Girl in the News.   London, Jenkins, 1937.
I'll Never Tell.   London, Jenkins, 1937.
The Enemy Within.   London, Jenkins, 1938.
The Life Between.   London, Jenkins, 1938.
Playgirl Wanted.   London, Jenkins, 1940.
She Walked in Fear (Rason).   London, Jenkins, 1940.
Brenda Gets Married.   London, Jenkins, 1941.
A Date with Danger.   London, Jenkins, 1942; New York, Vanguard Press, 1944.
War Bride.   London, Jenkins, 1942.
Six Came to Dinner (Stanton).   London, Jenkins, 1948.
Gold and Wine (Stanton).   London, Jenkins, 1949; New York, Walker, 1961.
Murder of a Snob.   London, Jenkins, 1949; New York, British Book Centre, 1958.
Murdering Mr. Velfrage.   London, Faber, 1950; as Maid to Murder, New York, Mill, 1950.

They Can't Hang Caroline (Stanton).   London, Jenkins, 1950.
The Sole Survivor, and The Kynsard Affair.   Roslyn, New York, Detective Book Club, 1951; London, Gollancz, 1952.
Murder in Two Flats (Stanton).   London, Jenkins, and New York, Mill, 1952.
Find the Innocent.   London, Jenkins, 1959.

Novels as David Durham

The Woman Accused.   London, Hodder and Stoughton, 1923.
Hounded Down.   London, Hodder and Stoughton, 1923.
The Pearl-Headed Pin.   London, Hodder and Stoughton, 1925.
The Forgotten Honeymoon.   London, Jenkins, 1935.
The Girl Who Dared.   London, Jenkins, 1938.
Against the Law.   London, Jenkins, 1939.

Novels as Sefton Kyle (series character: Inspector Rason)

The Man in the Shadow (Rason).   London, Jenkins, 1924.
Dead Man's Dower.   London, Jenkins, 1925.
Guilty, But −.   London, Jenkins, 1927.
The Hawk.   London, Jenkins, and New York, Dial Press, 1930.
The Vengeance of Mrs. Danvers.   London, Jenkins, 1932.
The Bloomsbury Treasure.   London, Jenkins, 1932.
Red Hair (Rason).   London, Jenkins, 1933.
The Life He Stole (Rason).   London, Jenkins, 1934.
The Man Without a Name.   London, Jenkins, 1935.
Silence.   London, Jenkins, 1935.
The Durand Case.   London, Jenkins, 1936.
Number Seventy-Three.   London, Jenkins, 1936.
The Body in the Safe (Rason).   London, Jenkins, 1937.
The Notorious Miss Walters.   London, Jenkins, 1937.
During His Majesty's Pleasure (Rason).   London, Jenkins, 1938.
Missing!   London, Jenkins, 1938.
Miss X.   London, Jenkins, 1939.
The Judge's Dilemma.   London, Jenkins, 1939.
The Shadow over Fairholme.   London, Jenkins, 1940.
The Girl Known as D 13.   London, Jenkins, 1940.
The Price of Silence.   London, Jenkins, 1942.
Love Was Married.   London, Jenkins, 1943.

Short Stories (series characters: Department of Dead Ends; Inspector Rason)

The Exploits of Fidelity Dove (Rason; as David Durham).   London, Hodder and Stoughton, 1924.
The Department of Dead Ends.   New York, Spivak, 1947; augmented edition, London, Faber, and Roslyn, New York, Detective Book Club, 1949.
Murder Will Out (Rason; Dead Ends).   London, Faber, 1950; Roslyn, New York, Detective Book Club, 1954.
Eight Murders in the Suburbs.   London, Jenkins, 1954; shortened version, as *Six Murders in the Suburbs*, Roslyn, New York, Detective Book Club, 1958.
Double Image and Other Stories.   London, Jenkins, and Roslyn, New York, Detective Book Club, 1955.
Seven Chose Murder (Rason; Dead Ends).   London, Jenkins, and Roslyn, New York, Detective Book Club, 1959.
Best Detective Stories (Rason; Dead Ends).   London, Faber, 1965.

OTHER PUBLICATIONS

Other

Lord Roberts: The Story of His Life.   London, Pearson, 1914.

Editor, Some Like Them Dead.   London, Hodder and Stoughton, 1960.
Editor, Crime Writers' Choice: The Fifth Anthology of the Crime Writers'
   Association.   London, Hodder and Stoughton, 1964.
Editor, Best Police Stories.   London, Faber, 1966.

*   *   *

The bibliography of Roy Vickers (who also wrote as Sefton Kyle, John Spencer, and David Durham) is not yet firm, since much of his work was pseudonymous and ephemeral, but he is known to have written more than 70 books of fiction.

Vickers's work up into World War II was primarily popular sensational fiction, occasionally topical (shopgirl romances, marital-law novels, depression stories, home-front novels), but more often concerned with crime, mystery, and/or detection. Most of this work attempted to follow market trends. His first novel in book form, The Mystery of the Scented Death, is in the manner of Sax Rohmer, while other novels are in the modes of Edgar Wallace, E. P. Oppenheim, and, occasionally, E. C. Bentley and Eric Ambler. Most of this earlier work is below the standard of his later short stories, but there are often rewarding elements that adumbrate his finer, more mature work. Sometimes there is a particularly intricate plot, as in Hounded Down, at other times highly imaginative "gimmicks" as in The Exploits of Fidelity Dove. More often, however, the outstanding element is in characterization, for example the Aunt of The Radingham Mystery or the ancient criminal Jabez Winterbourne who appears in The Gold Game and Hide Those Diamonds! Winterbourne is one of the finest criminal masterminds in the literature.

In 1935 there appeared in Fiction Parade "The Rubber Trumpet," the first of the short stories concerning the Department of Dead Ends. After a year or two, however, Vickers temporarily abandoned the series, and did not resume work on it until after the war. It is these later tales which unexpectedly revealed Vickers to be one of the finest British short story writers. Indeed, it has often been stated, with much truth, that the Department of Dead Ends stories were the best detective short stories of the 1940's. There are 38 stories in the series, with several others loosely connected with them. They are based on a (fictional) section of Scotland Yard, a storage place for the detritus of unsolved crimes. From this collection – murder weapons, clothing, toys found near the crime – solutions often emerge by chance. In this concept, it should be noted, Vickers breaks with the older theories of emergent justice (purposive fate, as with Wilkie Collins; hyper-rationalism, despite undercurrents of irrationality, as with Poe and Doyle; the scientific method, as with R. Austin Freeman) and sets up blind chance as the avenger of wrongs. The Department of Dead Ends stories are formally unusual in combining the techniques of factual crime writing and fiction. In essence they are capsulated novels, in which scores of life patterns appear in brief, offering a tragédie humaine of British society.

Vickers's later novels, while superior to his earlier work, are still not on the same level as his best short stories. Among his better novels may be listed Six Came to Dinner, despite an annoyingly jaunty playboy detective, Murdering Mr. Velfrage, with exceedingly skilled intricacies, and The Kynsard Affair, with many of the effects of the Department of Dead Ends.

—E. F. Bleiler

VIDAL, Gore. See **BOX, Edgar.**

VULLIAMY, C(olwyn) E(dward). Also wrote as Anthony Rolls. British. Born 20 June 1886. Studied art under Stanhope Forbes, Newlyn, Cornwall, 1910–13. Served in the King's Shropshire Light Infantry during World War I; joined Royal Welch Fusiliers, 1918: Camp Commandant of 28th Division Headquarters, and later Education Officer of the Division: Captain. Married Eileen Hynes in 1916 (died, 1943); one son and one daughter. Regular contributor to the *Spectator*, London. Fellow, Royal Society of Literature, and Royal Anthropological Society. *Died 4 September 1971.*

CRIME PUBLICATIONS

Novels

> *Don among the Dead Men.* London, Joseph, 1952.
> *Body in the Boudoir.* London, Joseph, 1956.
> *Cakes for Your Brithday.* London, Joseph, and New York, British Book Centre, 1959.
> *Justice for Judy.* London, Joseph, 1960.
> *Tea at the Abbey.* London, Joseph, 1961.
> *Floral Tribute.* London, Joseph, 1963.

Novels as Anthony Rolls

> *Lobelia Grove.* London, Bles, 1932.
> *The Vicar's Experiments.* London, Bles, 1932; as *Clerical Error*, Boston, Little Brown, 1932.
> *Family Matters.* London, Bles, 1933.
> *Scarweather.* London, Bles, 1934.

OTHER PUBLICATIONS

Novels

> *Fusilier Bluff: The Experiences of an Unprofessional Soldier in the Near East 1918–1919* (published anonymously). London, Bles, 1934.
> *Edwin and Eleanor: Family Documents 1854–56.* London, Joseph, 1945.
> *Henry Plumdew: His Memoirs, Experiences, and Opinions 1938–1948.* London, Joseph, 1950.
> *Jones: A Gentleman of Wales* (as Twm Teg). London, Chapman and Hall, 1954.
> *The Proud Walkers.* London, Chapman and Hall, 1955.

Other

> *Charles Kingsley and Christian Socialism.* London, Fabian Society, 1914.
> *Our Prehistoric Forerunners.* London, Lane, 1925.
> *Unknown Cornwall.* London, Lane, 1925.
> *Immortal Man: A Study of Funeral Customs and of Beliefs in Regard to the Nature and Fate of the Soul.* London, Methuen, 1926.

Voltaire. London, Bles, and New York, Dodd Mead, 1930.

The Archaeology of Middlesex and London. London, Methuen, 1930.

Rousseau. London, Bles, 1931; Port Washington, New York, Kennikat Press, 1972.

John Wesley. London, Bles, 1931.

James Boswell. London, Bles, 1932; Freeport, New York, Books for Libraries, 1971.

William Penn. London, Bles, 1933; New York, Scribner, 1934.

Judas Maccabaeus: A Study Based on Dr. Quarto Karadyne's Translation of the Ararat Codex (satire). London, Bles, 1934.

Aspasia: The Life and Letters of Mary Granville, Mrs. Delany, 1700–1788. London, Bles, 1935.

Mrs. Thrale of Streatham: Her Place in the Life of Dr. Samuel Johnson and in the Society of Her Time. London, Cape, 1936.

Royal George: A Study of George III. London, Cape, and New York, Appleton Century, 1937.

Outlanders: A Study of Imperial Expansion in South Africa, 1877–1902. London, Cape, 1938.

Crimea: The Campaign of 1854–56 with an Outline of Politics and a Study of the Royal Quartet. London, Cape, 1939.

Calico Pie: An Autobiography. London, Joseph, 1940.

A Short History of the Montagu-Puffins. London, Joseph, 1941.

The Polderoy Papers. London, Joseph, 1943.

Doctor Philligo: His Journal and Opinions. London, Joseph, 1944.

English Letter Writers. London, Collins, 1945.

Ursa Major: A Study of Dr. Johnson and His Friends. London, Joseph, 1946.

Man and the Atom: A Brief Account of the Human Dilemma. London, Joseph, 1947.

Byron, With a View of the Kingdom of Cant and a Dissection of the Byronic Ego. London, Joseph, 1948.

Prodwit's Guide to Writing. London, Joseph, 1949.

Rocking Horse Journey: Some Views of the British Character. London, Joseph, 1952.

The Onslow Family, 1528–1874, With Some Account of Their Times. London, Chapman and Hall, 1953.

Little Arthur's Guide to Humbug. London, Joseph, and New York, Eriksson-Taplinger, 1960.

Editor, *The Letters of the Tsar to the Tsaritsa 1914–1917*, translated by A. L. Hynes. London, Lane, and New York, Dodd Mead, 1929.

Editor, *The Red Archives: Russian State Papers and Other Documents 1915–1918*, translated by A. L. Hynes. London, Bles, 1929.

Editor, *The Anatomy of Satire: An Exhibition of Satirical Writing.* London, Joseph, 1950.

Translator, *The White Bull, with Saul and Various Short Pieces*, by Voltaire. London, Scholartis Press, 1929.

*   *   *

C. E. Vulliamy is little known as a mystery writer although he is a notable practitioner of the inverted form. He is also one of the oddest and most individual writers ever to write a mystery novel. His stinging wit and almost sublime sense of the absurd should give pause to anyone seeking out the origins of black humor.

Vulliamy's inverted tales are all cut to the same pattern. Usually a character will stumble upon what he thinks to be the perfect method of committing murder. The victims (and each book has more than one) are social parasites, often prone to malicious gossip, whose very existences cry out for extinction. The protagonist conceives and executes his first venture with perfect facility. Soon further crimes are contemplated, but his character begins a process of deterioration. Small mistakes are succeeded by larger blunders as the thin line between sanity and madness grows thinner. Fate intervenes, and the main character is apprehended by the police. A long and usually impressive trial scene follows. The verdict is always a gross miscarriage of justice, but fate once more assumes command, and straightens everything out with a massive dose of irony.

The stories are told with elegance, wit, and increasing amounts of pessimism and contempt for the fools that inhabit this planet. While Vulliamy's attitude toward mankind appears bleak, he does have the saving grace of being an accomplished and entertaining storyteller – especially in his best novels, *The Vicar's Experiments* and *Don among the Dead Men*.

—Charles Shibuk

WADE, Henry. Pseudonym for Henry Lancelot Aubrey-Fletcher, 6th Baronet. British. Born in Surrey, 10 September 1887. Educated at Eton College; New College, Oxford. Served in the First Battalion, Grenadier Guards, 1908–20, and fought in World War I: mentioned in despatched (twice); Distinguished Service Order; Croix de Guerre; also served in Grenadier Guards, 1940–45. Married 1) Mary Augusta Chilton in 1911 (died, 1963); four sons and one daughter; 2) Nancy Cecil Reynolds in 1965. Succeeded to the baronetcy, 1937. Justice of the Peace and County Alderman for Buckinghamshire; High Sheriff of Buckinghamshire, 1925. Lieutenant in the Body Guard of the Honorable Corps of Gentlemen-at-Arms, 1956–57. Commander, Royal Victorian Order. *Died 30 May 1969.*

CRIME PUBLICATIONS

Novels (series character: Chief Inspector Poole)

The Verdict of You All.   London, Constable, 1926; New York, Payson and Clarke, 1927.
The Missing Partners.   London, Constable, and New York, Payson and Clarke, 1928.
The Duke of York's Steps (Poole).   London, Constable, and New York, Payson and Clarke, 1929.
The Dying Alderman.   London, Constable, and New York, Brewer and Warren, 1930.
The Floating Admiral, with others.   London, Hodder and Stoughton, 1931; New York, Doubleday, 1932.
No Friendly Drop (Poole).   London, Constable, 1931; New York, Brewer Warren and Putnam, 1932; revised edition, Constable, 1932.
The Hanging Captain.   London, Constable, 1932; New York, Harcourt Brace, 1933.
Mist on the Saltings.   London, Constable, 1933.
Constable, Guard Thyself! (Poole).   London, Constable, 1934; Boston, Houghton Mifflin, 1935.
Heir Presumptive.   London, Constable, 1935; New York, Macmillan, 1953.
Bury Him Darkly (Poole).   London, Constable, 1936.
The High Sheriff.   London, Constable, 1937.
Released for Death.   London, Constable, 1938.
Lonely Magdalen (Poole).   London, Constable, 1940; revised edition, 1946.
New Graves at Great Norne.   London, Constable, 1947.
Diplomat's Folly.   London, Constable, 1951; New York, Macmillan, 1952.
Be Kind to the Killer.   London, Constable, 1952.

Too Soon to Die (Poole).   London, Constable, 1953; New York, Macmillan, 1954.
Gold Was Our Grave (Poole).   London, Constable, and New York, Macmillan, 1954.
A Dying Fall.   London, Constable, and New York, Macmillan, 1955.
The Litmore Snatch.   London, Constable, and New York, Macmillan, 1957.

Short Stories

Policeman's Lot.   London, Constable, 1933.
Here Comes the Copper.   London, Constable, 1938.

OTHER PUBLICATIONS

Other

A History of the Foot Guards to 1856 (as H. L. Aubrey-Fletcher).   London, Constable,
   1927.

*   *   *

Henry Wade was one of the really major figures of the Golden Age of the mystery story –
and thereafter – but, unfortunately, too few of his better novels and neither of his historically
important collections of short stories were published in America. This situation, combined
with a long period of critical neglect, gave Wade the status of an unknown master until the
late 1960's saw a long-overdue reassessment.

Wade was a practitioner of the school of modern British realism and a master of the police
novel. A staunch advocate of the classical detective story in its purest form, Wade also had
the ability to write inverted stories that bear comparison with the highest achievements in this
genre. Wade can best be compared to Freeman Wills Crofts in whose own demanding
tradition Wade ranked second to none. His police novels and inverted tales never quite
achieved the pinnacle of Crofts's *The Cask* or *The 12:30 from Croydon*, but his gifts for
characterization were deeper – especially in the inverted stories. His personal experiences as
Justice of the Peace lent depth to his depiction of the rural police. His strongly developed
sense of irony and his criticism of the legal system anticipated and influenced such writers as
Richard Hull, Cyril Hare, Henry Cecil, Raymond Postgate, Michael Underwood, and Roderic
Jeffries. He observed with precision the changing values of post-World War II England –
even more skilfully than did Agatha Christie – and he did more to explicate the psychology
and mores of the British people than any other writer in this genre.

Wade's earliest novels question the British legal system and its traditions. One of them, *The
Missing Partners*, details a potentially tragic miscarriage of justice. This novel is also Wade's
closest approximation of Crofts's style and method. *The Duke of York's Steps* was among the
most favorably reviewed books of the 1920's, and is usually cited in the older reference
works devoted to the genre. *The Dying Alderman*, with its dying message clue, is an advance
over his earlier work, and is written and plotted with great clarity and precision; it remains
surprisingly fresh today. *Mist on the Saltings* is a completely unexpected and unprecedented
work by Wade's or anyone else's standards. A partially inverted tale combined with a police
novel, this masterpiece boasts penetrating characterization, superb East Anglian marshland
atmosphere, and a powerful and deeply moving climax. Almost as good is *Heir Presumptive*
– a fully inverted tale about a man's efforts to kill several relatives in order to inherit a
fortune. Light in style and compulsively readable, its only drawback is that its ironic ending
can be rather too easily anticipated. This book was one of Wade's personal favorites, and the
deer-hunting scenes reflect his deep interest in the sport.

Wade stopped writing during the war and subsequent work indicates that this period and
its aftermath had a profound effect on his outlook. Few major writers of the Golden Age ever
staged a significant comeback as late as the 1950's. Wade did it by creating two masterpieces
with all his old skill and cunning, enriched by experience. *Too Soon to Die* was another

partially inverted murder tale about a family's attempt to evade exorbitant inheritance taxes. This gripping work shows that Wade continued to view his country's legal system with apprehension. *A Dying Fall* concerns the question of whether an unwanted wife's plunge from a balcony was suicide or murder. It combines Wade's best character delineation, a perceptive view of changing postwar values in England, and an ironic ending. This was Wade's last really major novel, a sublime and deeply personal work.

—Charles Shibuk

WADE, Robert. See **MILLER, Wade.**

WAINWRIGHT, John. Also writes as Jack Ripley. British. Born in Leeds, Yorkshire, 25 February 1921. Educated at elementary schools and studied at home; London University, external LL.B. 1956. Served as an Air Crew Gunner in the Royal Air Force, 1940–45. Married Avis Wainwright in 1942. Police Officer, West Riding Constabulary, Yorkshire, 1947–69. Since 1969, Columnist, *Northern Echo*, Darlington, County Durham. Agent: Campbell Thomson and McLaughlin Ltd., 31 Newington Green, London N16 9PU. Address: The Ridings, High Grantley, near Ripon, North Yorkshire, England.

CRIME PUBLICATIONS

Novels (series characters: Superintendent Gilliant; Chief Inspector Lennox; Superintendent Charles Ripley)

Death in a Sleeping City.   London, Collins, 1965.
Ten Steps to the Gallows.   London, Collins, 1965.
Evil Intent (Ripley).   London, Collins, 1966.
The Crystallised Carbon Pig (Gilliant).   London, Collins, 1966; New York, Walker, 1967.
Talent for Murder.   London, Collins, and New York, Walker, 1967.
The Worms Must Wait (Ripley).   London, Collins, 1967.
Web of Silence.   London, Collins, 1968.
Edge of Extinction.   London, Collins, 1968.
The Darkening Glass.   London, Collins, 1968.
The Take-Over Men.   London, Collins, 1969.
The Big Tickle.   London, Macmillan, 1969.
Freeze Thy Blood Less Coldly (Ripley).   London, Macmillan, 1970.
Prynter's Devil.   London, Macmillan, 1970.
The Last Buccaneer.   London, Macmillan, 1971.
Dig the Grave and Let Him Lie.   London, Macmillan, 1971.
Night Is a Time to Die.   London, Macmillan, 1972.
Requiem for a Loser (Gilliant).   London, Macmillan, 1972.

A Pride of Pigs. London, Macmillan, 1973.
High-Class Kill. London, Macmillan, 1973.
The Devil You Don't. London, Macmillan, 1973.
A Touch of Malice (Ripley). London, Macmillan, 1973.
The Evidence I Shall Give (Lennox). London, Macmillan, 1974.
Cause for a Killing. London, Macmillan, 1974.
Kill the Girls and Make Them Cry. London, Macmillan, 1974.
The Hard Hit (Ripley). London, Macmillan, 1974; New York, St. Martin's Press, 1975.
Square Dance (Lennox). London, Macmillan, and New York, St. Martin's Press, 1975.
Death of a Big Man (Ripley). London, Macmillan, and New York, St. Martin's Press, 1975.
Landscape with Violence (Gilliant). London, Macmillan, 1975; New York, St. Martin's Press, 1976.
Coppers Don't Cry. London, Macmillan, 1975.
Acquittal. London, Macmillan, and New York, St. Martin's Press, 1976.
Walther P.38. London, Macmillan, 1976.
Who Goes Next? London, Macmillan, and New York, St. Martin's Press, 1976.
The Bastard. London, Macmillan, and New York, St. Martin's Press, 1976.
Pool of Tears. London, Macmillan, and New York, St. Martin's Press, 1977.
A Nest of Rats. London, Macmillan, and New York, St. Martin's Press, 1977.
Do Nothin' till You Hear from Me. London, Macmillan, and New York, St. Martin's Press, 1977.
The Day of the Peppercorn Kill. London, Macmillan, 1977.
The Jury People. London, Macmillan, and New York, St. Martin's Press, 1978.
Thief of Time. London, Macmillan, and New York, St. Martin's Press, 1978.
Death Certificate. London, Macmillan, 1978.
A Ripple of Murders. London, Macmillan, 1978; New York, St. Martin's Press, 1979.
Brainwash. London, Macmillan, and New York, St. Martin's Press, 1979.
Duty Elsewhere. London, Macmillan, and New York, St. Martin's Press, 1979.
Tension. London, Macmillan, 1979.
The Reluctant Sleeper. London, Macmillan, 1979.
Home Is the Hunter, and The Big Kayo. London, Macmillan, 1979.
Take Murder.... London, Macmillan, 1979.

Novels as Jack Ripley (series character: John George Davis in all books)

Davis Doesn't Live Here Any More. London, Hamish Hamilton, 1971; New York, Doubleday, 1972.
The Pig Got Up and Slowly Walked Away. London, Hamish Hamilton, 1971.
My Word You Should Have Seen Us. London, Hamish Hamilton, 1972.
My God How the Money Rolls In. London, Hamish Hamilton, 1972.

Uncollected Short Stories

"The Man Who Grassed," in *Winter's Crimes 1*, edited by George Hardinge. London, Macmillan, 1969.
"Incident in Troletto," in *Winter's Crimes 4*, edited by George Hardinge. London, Macmillan, 1972.
"You Are Not Obliged to Say Anything," in *Winter's Crimes 6*, edited by George Hardinge. London, Macmillan, 1974.
"Rucker's New Year's Eve," in *Winter's Crimes 9*, edited by George Hardinge. London, Macmillan, 1977.

OTHER PUBLICATIONS

Plays

Radio Plays: *Death in a Sleeping City*, 1966; *Who Killed Emma Forcett?* (serial), 1967; *A Time for Despair*, 1967; *Hates Any Man?*, 1968; *Protection*, 1968.

Other

Shall I Be a Policeman? Exeter, Wheaton, 1967.
Guard Your Castle: A Plain Man's Guide to the Protection of His Home. London, Gentry Books, 1973.
Tail-End Charlie (war memoirs). London, Macmillan, 1978.

John Wainwright comments:

Despite this somewhat alarming list of books I find great difficulty in viewing myself as an "author." This, I think, is not unusual; for example, a bus driver rarely, if ever, consciously says to himself, "I'm a bus driver." The reality of authorship only comes home when an invitation is offered to attend some function *because* I happen to be an author. At that point a temporary world of unreality seems to take over, and it is a world of which I am not too fond. I like solitude and abhor any form of lionisation. The only product I (or any other writer of fiction) puts in the marketplace is an imagination. That I receive payment for that imagination never ceases to astound me. Of necessity I take my work seriously, but I never take myself seriously. I am a teller of tales. Nothing more. My first book, *Death in a Sleeping City*, was sent to an agent, and was accepted by an editor. That agent (John McLaughlin) and that editor (George Hardinge) still handle my work. They now handle it as my friends.

After writing, my chief interest is music. Good traditional jazz music and good symphony music. The stuff between – the Palm Court stuff – I find mildly annoying. I read a great deal but, unless a book is recommended to me, not crime stories. Of the present crime writers, le Carré tops my list of English crimesters, and McBain tops my list of American crimesters. As a personal opinion, I count *The Maltese Falcon* as the best crime novel ever written, and, after that, anything (everything) written by Chandler.

I was once asked what I would like to be if I wasn't an author. The answer I gave is a perfectly true answer. Dead!

*   *   *

One of the most versatile and prolific crime writers in Britain today, John Wainwright is primarily regarded as an exponent of the police procedural story. He normally concentrates upon one major case in each book, rather than following the classic police procedural format with a team of detectives handling a wide variety of cases simultaneously, is inclined towards presenting the extremes of criminal violence, and concentrates his analysis as much upon the actions of the criminals as upon those of the police.

In his first novel, *Death in a Sleeping City*, Wainwright skilfully portrayed the brutality of the professional criminal in a city in the north of England. It is a subject to which, with continual and ingenious variations, he has often returned. There can be little doubt that his own career as a police officer provided him with the ideal background for such novels. In *Death in a Sleeping City*, two Mafia gunmen have the temerity to kill on the "patch" of Detective Chief Superintendent Lewis; the dominant character of the book, Lewis is a man-hunting machine of calculating ruthlessness who treats criminals and his own men with equal contempt, and is described by a colleague as "the human equivalent to a killer-animal." Wainwright describes the chase in authentic detail as the police network swings into action, and he presents an enthralling glimpse into the relationships between the different kinds of police officers engaged in the investigation. He sets the stage with many of the characters who were to appear in subsequent books. There is Detective Inspector Raff, being trained in Lewis's methods and destined eventually to succeed him. There is Divisional Superintendent Collins, of the rimless spectacles and briar cigarette-holder, who enjoys the chase but hates the kill and is the complete antithesis of Lewis. "We are the scavengers, the disposers of offal," says Collins philosophically. "We clean the streets of their filth. We are, I suppose, glorified garbage collectors." Such men pursue the Mafia executioners through a series of murders, culminating in a trap which is sprung with a savagery rarely seen in English crime novels.

Time and again Wainwright returns to the horror of organised crime, pitting his police force against men who hold life cheaply and who are at war with law and order. The more domestic type of murder is not entirely neglected, but one senses that it plays only a small part in his scheme of things. He is more interested in the conflict between those who exist to protect society and those who would trample it to gain their own ends. He is also interested in the many conflicts among the policemen themselves. The established machinery is there to cope with any major investigation, but there is in Wainwright's books no archetypal policeman; his characters are presented in struggles of power and personality, which often hold more interest than the main story line. Sometimes the scene is the county area outside the city boundary – here we normally encounter Superintendent Ripley and his men – in books inclined toward the more classic type of detective fiction (e.g. *Dig the Grave and Let Him Lie*), although Ripley's men also perform well when facing the threat of urban violence spreading into the rural area (as in *Freeze Thy Blood Less Coldly*).

Of the police novels, arguably his major work is still *The Last Buccaneer*. Jules Morgan, obsessed with his supposed ancestor, the pirate Henry Morgan, plans the complete takeover and plunder of Wainwright's city. In this unusually long story, we follow the build-up as informers are eliminated and the gang is constructed by assembling top criminal brains and brawn, and we then switch from the police to the villains successively as the fatal day approaches in an atmosphere of almost unbearable suspense. From an early point in the book Jules Morgan's dream is taken over by the professional criminals with whom he has become associated – Wainwright's theme, that the amateur criminal who mixes with the real thing can expect nothing but an appalling fate, is one of which he is fond. Finally we witness a typical Wainwright holocaust, but one which he has never equalled for sheer carnage, as the organised forces remove any semblance of kid gloves and deal summarily with those attempting to hold the community to ransom.

It is difficult to do justice to Wainwright's many books; generalisation is unfair, for he has displayed such remarkable variety. His international thrillers (such as *The Crystallised Carbon Pig*, *Prynter's Devil*, and *Cause for a Killing*) are taut and realistically bloody evidence that his talent extends far beyond the confines of his city and county police forces, and his secret service men Jones and Dilton-Emmet rank high on the list of his numerous well-drawn characters. Occasionally Wainwright has turned to the more cerebral and classical detective problem, with the criminal revealed by the deductive Ripley (later to be tragically invalided, his bitterness revealing itself in the brilliant *Death of a Big Man*) or the academic Collins (most effectively in *Kill the Girls and Make Them Cry*). In *High-Class Kill*, he has even included a locked-room problem. Then again, he has successfully tried his hand at one-off studies of lone figures enmeshed in legal complexities of their own making – an alleged wife-murderer in *Acquittal*, a contract killer in *The Hard Hit*, a convicted but escaped murderer in *Thief of Time* – although it must be admitted that his forays into first-person narratives using the present tense are more irritating than effective.

Wainwright's greatest strength cannot really be pinpointed. The near-classical puzzle, the tough and realistic police story, the exploration of human relationships, and the psychological thriller are all represented in his impressive output. One has the strong feeling that his work will never grow stale.

—Melvyn Barnes

WALLACE, (Richard Horatio) Edgar. English. Born in Greenwich, London, 1 April 1875. Educated at St. Peter's School, London; Board School, Camberwell, London, to age 12. Served in the Royal West Kent Regiment in England, 1893–96, and in the Medical Staff Corps in South Africa, 1896–99; bought his discharge, 1899; served in the Lincoln's Inn branch of the Special Constabulary, and as a special interrogator for the War Office, during World War I. Married 1) Ivy Caldecott in 1901 (divorced, 1919), two daughters and two sons; 2) Violet King in 1921, one daughter. Worked in a printing firm, shoe shop, rubber factory, and as a merchant seaman, plasterer, and milk delivery boy, in London, 1886–91; South African Correspondent for Reuter's, 1899–1902, and the London *Daily Mail*, 1900–02; Editor, *Rand Daily News*, Johannesburg, 1902–03; returned to London: Reporter, *Daily Mail*, 1903–07, and *Standard*, 1910; Racing Editor, and later Editor, *The Week-End*, later *The Week-End Racing Supplement*, 1910–12; Racing Editor and Special Writer, *Evening News*, 1910–12; founded *Bibury's Weekly* and *R. E. Walton's Weekly*, both racing papers; Editor, *Ideas* and *The Story Journal*, 1913; Writer, and later Editor, *Town Topics*, 1913–16; regular contributor to the *Birmingham Post*, and *Thomson's Weekly News*, Dundee; Racing Columnist, *The Star*, 1927–32, and *Daily Mail*, 1930–32; Drama Critic, *Morning Post*, 1928; Founder, *The Bucks Mail*, 1930; Editor, *Sunday News*, 1931. Chairman of the Board of Directors, and film writer/director, British Lion Film Corporation. President, Press Club, London, 1923–24. *Died 10 February 1932.*

CRIME PUBLICATIONS

Novels (series characters: Detective Sergeant/Inspector Elk; Four Just Men; Superintendent Minter, The Sooper; J. G. Reeder; T. B. Smith)

The Four Just Men. London, Tallis Press, 1906; revised edition, 1906; revised edition, Sheffield, Weekly Telegraph, 1908; Boston, Small Maynard, 1920.
Angel Esquire. Bristol, Arrowsmith, and New York, Holt, 1908.
The Council of Justice (Just Men). London, Ward Lock, 1908.
Captain Tatham of Tatham Island. London, Gale and Polden, 1909; revised edition, as *The Island of Galloping Gold*, London, Newnes, 1916; as *Eve's Island*, Newnes, 1926.
The Nine Bears (Smith; Elk). London, Ward Lock, 1910; as *Silinski, Master Criminal*, Cleveland, World, 1930; as *The Cheaters*, London, Digit, 1964.
The Other Man. New York, Dodd Mead, 1911.
The Fourth Plague. London, Ward Lock, 1913; New York, Doubleday, 1930.
Grey Timothy. London, Ward Lock, 1913; as *Pallard the Punter*, 1914.
The River of Stars. London, Ward Lock, 1913.
The Man Who Bought London. London, Ward Lock, 1915.
The Melody of Death. Bristol, Arrowsmith, 1915; New York, Dial Press, 1927.
The Clue of the Twisted Candle. Boston, Small Maynard, 1916; London, Newnes, 1917.
A Debt Discharged. London, Ward Lock, 1916.
The Tomb of Ts'in. London, Ward Lock, 1916.
The Just Men of Cordova. London, Ward Lock, 1917.
Kate Plus Ten (Smith). London, Ward Lock, and Boston, Small Maynard, 1917.
The Secret House (Smith). London, Ward Lock, 1917; Boston, Small Maynard, 1919.
Down under Donovan. London, Ward Lock, 1918.
The Man Who Knew. Boston, Small Maynard, 1918; London, Newnes, 1919.
The Green Rust. London, Ward Lock, 1919; Boston, Small Maynard, 1920.
The Daffodil Mystery. London, Ward Lock, 1920; as *The Daffodil Murder*, Boston, Small Maynard, 1921.
Jack o' Judgment. London, Ward Lock, 1920; Boston, Small Maynard, 1921.
The Book of All Power. London, Ward Lock, 1921.

The Angel of Terror. Boston, Small Maynard, and London, Hodder and Stoughton, 1922; as *The Destroying Angel*, London, Pan, 1959.

Number Six. London, Newnes, 1922.

Captains of Souls. Boston, Small Maynard, 1922; London, Long, 1923.

The Crimson Circle. London, Hodder and Stoughton, 1922; New York, Doubleday, 1929.

The Flying Fifty-Five. London, Hutchinson, 1922.

Mr. Justice Maxell. London, Ward Lock, 1922.

The Valley of Ghosts. London, Odhams Press, 1922; Boston, Small Maynard, 1923.

The Clue of the New Pin. Boston, Small Maynard, and London, Hodder and Stoughton, 1923.

The Green Archer. London, Hodder and Stoughton, 1923; Boston, Small Maynard, 1924.

The Missing Million. London, Long, 1923; as *The Missing Millions*, Boston, Small Maynard, 1925.

The Dark Eyes of London. London, Ward Lock, 1924; New York, Doubleday, 1929.

Double Dan. London, Hodder and Stoughton, 1924; as *Diana of Kara-Kara*, Boston, Small Maynard, 1924.

The Face in the Night. London, Long, 1924; New York, Doubleday, 1929.

Room 13 (Reeder). London, Long, 1924.

Flat 2. New York, Garden City Publishing Company, 1924; revised edition, London, Long, 1927.

The Sinister Man. London, Hodder and Stoughton, 1924; Boston, Small Maynard, 1925.

The Three Oaks Mystery. London, Ward Lock, 1924.

Blue Hand. London, Ward Lock, 1925; Boston, Small Maynard, 1926.

The Daughters of the Night. London, Newnes, 1925.

The Fellowship of the Frog (Elk). London, Ward Lock, 1925; New York, Doubleday, 1928.

The Gaunt Stranger. London, Hodder and Stoughton, 1925; as *The Ringer*, New York, Doubleday, 1926.

The Hairy Arm. Boston, Small Maynard, 1925; as *The Avenger*, London, Long, 1926.

A King by Night. London, Long, 1925; New York, Doubleday, 1926.

The Strange Countess. London, Hodder and Stoughton, 1925; Boston, Small Maynard, 1926.

The Three Just Men. London, Hodder and Stoughton, 1925; New York, Doubleday, 1930.

Barbara on Her Own. London, Newnes, 1926.

The Black Abbot. London, Hodder and Stoughton, 1926; New York, Doubleday, 1927.

The Day of Uniting. London, Hodder and Stoughton, 1926; New York, Mystery League, 1930.

The Door with Seven Locks. London, Hodder and Stoughton, and New York, Doubleday, 1926.

The Joker (Elk). London, Hodder and Stoughton, 1926; as *The Colossus*, New York, Doubleday, 1932.

The Man from Morocco. London, Long, 1926; as *The Black*, New York, Doubleday, 1930.

The Million Dollar Story. London, Newnes, 1926.

The Northing Tramp. London, Hodder and Stoughton, 1926; New York, Doubleday, 1929; as *The Tramp*, London, Pan, 1965.

Penelope of the Polyantha. London, Hodder and Stoughton, 1926.

The Square Emerald. London, Hodder and Stoughton, 1926; as *The Girl from Scotland Yard*, New York, Doubleday, 1927.

The Terrible People. London, Hodder and Stoughton, and New York, Doubleday, 1926.

We Shall See! London, Hodder and Stoughton, 1926; as *The Gaol Breaker*, New York, Doubleday, 1931.

The Yellow Snake. London, Hodder and Stoughton, 1926.

Big Foot (Sooper). London, Long, 1927.

The Feathered Serpent. London, Hodder and Stoughton, 1927; New York, Doubleday, 1928.

The Forger. London, Hodder and Stoughton, 1927; as *The Clever One*, New York, Doubleday, 1928.

The Hand of Power. London, Long, 1927; New York, Mystery League, 1930.

The Man Who Was Nobody. London, Ward Lock, 1927.

The Ringer (novelization of stage play). London, Hodder and Stoughton, 1927.

The Squeaker. London, Hodder and Stoughton, 1927; as *The Squealer*, New York, Doubleday, 1928.

Terror Keep (Reeder). London, Hodder and Stoughton, and New York, Doubleday, 1927.

The Traitor's Gate. London, Hodder and Stoughton, and New York, Doubleday, 1927.

The Double. London, Hodder and Stoughton, and New York, Doubleday, 1928.

The Thief in the Night. London, Readers Library, 1928.

The Flying Squad. London, Hodder and Stoughton, 1928; New York, Doubleday, 1929.

The Gunner. London, Long, 1928; as *Gunman's Bluff*, New York, Doubleday, 1929.

The Twister (Elk). London, Long, 1928; New York, Doubleday, 1929.

The Golden Hades. London, Collins, 1929.

The Green Ribbon. London, Hutchinson, 1929; New York, Doubleday, 1930.

The India-Rubber Men (Elk). London, Hodder and Stoughton, 1929; New York, Doubleday, 1930.

The Terror. London, Detective Story Club, 1929.

The Calendar. London, Collins, 1930; New York, Doubleday, 1931.

The Clue of the Silver Key. London, Hodder and Stoughton, 1930; as *The Silver Key*, New York, Doubleday, 1930.

The Lady of Ascot. London, Hutchinson, 1930.

White Face (Elk). London, Hodder and Stoughton, 1930; New York, Doubleday, 1931.

On the Spot. London, Long, and New York, Doubleday, 1931.

The Coat of Arms. London, Hutchinson, 1931; as *The Arranways Mystery*, New York, Doubleday, 1932.

The Devil Man. London, Collins, and New York, Doubleday, 1931; as *The Life and Death of Charles Peace*, 1932.

The Man at the Carlton. London, Hodder and Stoughton, 1931; New York, Doubleday, 1932.

The Frightened Lady. London, Hodder and Stoughton, 1932; New York, Doubleday, 1933.

When the Gangs Came to London. London, Long, and New York, Doubleday, 1932.

Short Stories

Sanders of the River. London, Ward Lock, 1911; New York, Doubleday, 1930.

The People of the River. London, Ward Lock, 1912.

The Admirable Carfew. London, Ward Lock, 1914.

Bosambo of the River. London, Ward Lock, 1914.

Bones, Being Further Adventures in Mr. Commissioner Sanders' Country. London, Ward Lock, 1915.

The Keepers of the King's Peace. London, Ward Lock, 1917.

Lieutenant Bones. London, Ward Lock, 1918.

The Adventures of Heine. London, Ward Lock, 1919.

Bones in London. London, Ward Lock, 1921.

The Law of the Four Just Men. London, Hodder and Stoughton, 1921; as *Again the Three Just Men*, New York, Doubleday, 1933.

Sandi, The King-Maker. London, Ward Lock, 1922.

Bones of the River. London, Newnes, 1923.

Chick. London, Ward Lock, 1923.

Educated Evans. London, Webster, 1924.

The Mind of Mr. J. G. Reeder. London, Hodder and Stoughton, 1925; as *The Murder Book of Mr. J. G. Reeder*, New York, Doubleday, 1929.

More Educated Evans. London, Webster, 1926.

Mrs. William Jones and Bill. London, Newnes, 1926.

Sanders. London, Hodder and Stoughton, 1926; as *Mr. Commissioner Sanders*, New York, Doubleday, 1930.

The Brigand. London, Hodder and Stoughton, 1927.

Good Evans! London, Webster, 1927; as *The Educated Man – Good Evans!*, London, Collins, 1929.

The Mixer. London, Long, 1927.

Again Sanders. London, Hodder and Stoughton, 1928; New York, Doubleday, 1929.

Again the Three Just Men. London, Hodder and Stoughton, 1928; as *The Law of the Three Just Men*, New York, Doubleday, 1931; as *Again the Three*, London, Pan, 1968.

Elegant Edward. London, Readers Library, 1928.

The Orator. London, Hutchinson, 1928.

Again the Ringer. London, Hodder and Stoughton, 1929; as *The Ringer Returns*, New York, Doubleday, 1931.

Four Square Jane. London, Readers Library, 1929.

The Big Four. London, Readers Library, 1929.

The Black. London, Readers Library, 1929; augmented edition, London, Digit, 1962.

The Ghost of Down Hill (includes *The Queen of Sheba's Belt*). London, Readers Library, 1929.

The Cat Burglar. London, Newnes, 1929.

Circumstantial Evidence. London, Newnes, 1929; Cleveland, World, 1934.

Fighting Snub Reilly. London, Newnes, 1929; Cleveland, World, 1934.

The Governor of Chi-Foo. London, Newnes, 1929; Cleveland, World, 1934.

The Little Green Man. London, Collins, 1929.

Planetoid 127 (includes *The Sweizer Pump*). London, Readers Library, 1929.

The Prison-Breakers. London, Newnes, 1929.

Forty-Eight Short Stories. London, Newnes, 1929.

For Information Received. London, Newnes, 1929.

The Lady of Little Hell. London, Newnes, 1929.

The Lone House Mystery (Sooper). London, Collins, 1929.

Red Aces (Reeder). London, Hodder and Stoughton, 1929; New York, Doubleday, 1930.

The Reporter. London, Readers Library, 1929.

The Iron Grip. London, Readers Library, 1930.

Killer Kay. London, Newnes, 1930.

The Stretelli Case and Other Mystery Stories (omnibus). Cleveland, World, 1930.

The Lady Called Nita. London, Newnes, 1930.

The Guv'nor and Other Stories (Reeder). London, Collins, 1932; as *Mr. Reeder Returns*, New York, Doubleday, 1932; as *The Guv'nor and Mr. J. G. Reeder Returns*, Collins, 2 vols., 1933–34.

Sergeant Sir Peter. London, Chapman and Hall, 1932; as *Sergeant Dunn C.I.D.*, London, Digit, 1962.

The Steward. London, Collins, 1932.

The Last Adventure. London, Hutchinson, 1934.
The Woman from the East and Other Stories. London, Hutchinson, 1934.
Nig-Nog (omnibus). Cleveland, World, 1934.
The Undisclosed Client. London, Digit, 1962.
The Man Who Married His Cook and Other Stories. London, White Lion, 1976.

OTHER PUBLICATIONS

Novels

The Duke in the Suburbs. London, Ward Lock, 1909.
Private Selby. London, Ward Lock, 1912.
1925: The Story of a Fatal Peace. London, Newnes, 1915.
Those Folk of Bulboro. London, Ward Lock, 1918.
The Books of Bart. London, Ward Lock, 1923.
The Black Avons. London, Gill, 1925; as *How They Fared in the Times of the Tudors, Roundhead and Cavalier, From Waterloo to the Mutiny,* and *Europe in the Melting Pot,* 4 vols., 1925.

Short Stories

Smithy. London, Tallis Press, 1905; revised edition, as *Smithy, Not to Mention Nobby Clark and Spud Murphy,* London, Newnes, 1914.
Smithy Abroad: Barrack Room Sketches. London, Hulton, 1909.
Smithy's Friend Nobby. London, Town Topics, 1914; as *Nobby,* London, Newnes, 1916.
Tam o' the Scouts. London, Newnes, 1918; as *Tam of the Scoots,* Boston, Small Maynard, 1919; as *Tam,* Newnes, 1928.
Smithy and the Hun. London, Pearson, 1915.
The Fighting Scouts. London, Pearson, 1919.

Plays

An African Millionaire (produced South Africa, 1904). London, Davis Poynter, 1972.
The Forest of Happy Dreams (produced London, 1910; New York, 1914). Published in *One-act Play Parade,* London, Hodder and Stoughton, 1935.
Dolly Cutting Herself (produced London, 1911).
Sketches, in *Hullo, Ragtime* (produced London, 1912).
Sketches, in *Hullo, Tango!* (produced London, 1912).
Hello, Exchange! (sketch; produced London, 1913; as *The Switchboard,* produced New York, 1915).
The Manager's Dream (sketch; produced London, 1913).
Sketches, in *Business as Usual* (produced London, 1914).
The Whirligig (revue), with Wal Pink and Albert de Courville, music by Frederick Chappelle (produced London, 1919; as *Pins and Needles,* produced New York, 1922).
M'Lady (produced London, 1921).
The Whirl of the World (revue), with Albert de Courville and William K. Wells, music by Frederick Chappelle (produced London, 1924).
The Looking Glass (revue), with Albert de Courville, music by Frederick Chappelle (produced London, 1924).
The Ringer, adaptation of his own novel *The Gaunt Stranger* (produced London, 1926). London, Hodder and Stoughton, and New York, French, 1929.
The Mystery of Room 45 (produced London, 1926).
The Terror, adaptation of his own novel *Terror Keep* (produced Brighton and London, 1927). London, Hodder and Stoughton, 1929.

Double Dan, adaptation of his own novel (produced Blackpool and London, 1926).
A Perfect Gentleman (produced London, 1927).
The Yellow Mask, music by Vernon Duke, lyrics by Desmond Carter (produced Birmingham, 1927; London, 1928).
The Flying Squad, adaptation of his own novel (produced Oxford and London, 1928). London, Hodder and Stoughton, 1929.
The Man Who Changed His Name (produced London, 1928; New York, 1932). London, Hodder and Stoughton, 1929.
The Squeaker, adaptation of his own novel (produced London, 1928; as *Sign of the Leopard*, produced New York, 1928). London, Hodder and Stoughton, 1929.
The Lad (produced Wimbledon, 1928; London, 1929).
Persons Unknown (produced London, 1929).
The Calendar (also director: produced Manchester and London, 1929). London, French, 1932.
On the Spot (produced London and New York, 1930).
The Mouthpiece (produced London, 1930).
Smoky Cell (produced London, 1930).
Charles III, adaptation of a play by Curt Götz (produced London, 1931).
The Old Man (produced London, 1931).
The Case of the Frightened Lady (produced London, 1931). London, French, 1932; as *Criminal at Large* (produced New York, 1932), New York, French, 1934.
The Green Pack (produced London, 1932). London, French, 1933.

Screenplays: *Nurse and Martyr*, 1915; *The Ringer*, 1928; *Valley of the Ghosts*, 1928; *The Forger*, 1928; *Red Aces*, 1929; *The Squeaker*, 1930; *Should a Doctor Tell?*, 1930; *The Hound of the Baskervilles*, with V. Gareth Gundrey, 1931; *The Old Man*, 1931.

Verse

The Mission That Failed! A Tale of the Raid and Other Poems. Cape Town, Maskew Miller, 1898.
Nicholson's Nek. Cape Town, Eastern Press, 1900.
War! and Other Poems. Cape Town, Eastern Press, 1900.
Writ in Barracks. London, Methuen, 1900.

Other

Unofficial Despatches. London, Hutchinson, 1901.
Famous Scottish Regiments. London, Newnes, 1914.
Fieldmarshall Sir John French and His Campaigns. London, Newnes, 1914.
Heroes All: Gallant Deeds of the War. London, Newnes, 1914.
The Standard History of the War. London, Newnes, 4 vols., 1914–16.
War of the Nations, vols. 2–11. London, Newnes, 1914–19.
Kitchener's Army and the Territorial Forces: The Full Story of a Great Achievement. London, Newnes, 6 vols., 1915.
People: A Short Autobiography. London, Hodder and Stoughton, 1926; New York, Doubleday, 1929.
This England. London, Hodder and Stoughton, 1927.
My Hollywood Diary. London, Hutchinson, 1932.

Ghostwriter: *My Life*, by Evelyn Thaw, London, Long, 1914.

Theatrical Activities:
 Director: **Plays** – *The Calendar*, Manchester and London, 1929; *Brothers* by Herbert Ashton, Jr., London, 1929. **Films** – *Red Aces*, 1929; *The Squeaker*, 1930.

*   *   *

To this day the images conjured up by the name Edgar Wallace are of a frankly sensational nature – sinister cowled figures carrying swooning girls through shadowy corridors; bullets crashing through the windows of old manor houses; shrill cries of terror echoing through the murk of a dockside dawn – and it is often forgotten that this is merely the tip of a mammoth literary iceberg. He also wrote verse, essays, criticism, very good short stories, vast quantities of popular journalism, a 10-volume history of the Great War, various propaganda books, a number of highly successful plays, and ghosted at least three autobiographies – and it is this hugely diverse output that has undoubtedly done a great deal of harm to his latterday reputation. Nor has the frenetic pace at which he often worked helped matters. How could you take seriously a man who dashed off a play in four days and a novel over a weekend? Yet the play in question, *On the Spot*, is perhaps his most skilfully constructed drama, and the novel, *The Coat of Arms*, is certainly one of the tightest he ever plotted. Perhaps it is time, nearly 50 years after his death, for a serious reappraisal of his work, for much of what he wrote is by no means as trivial or as flawed as more recent commentators have maintained.

Certainly the flaws are there. Yet careless writing (name-changes half-way through a book) and glaring factual errors (he invariably confused carbon monoxide with carbon dioxide) are largely dismissed by the reader caught up in the headlong rush of the narrative. And although Wallace's world seems cliché-ridden, it must be remembered that the majority of the "clichés" were invented by him and only turned into clichés by later writers. The element of pure detection in his books is minimal, but then he was far more interested in thrilling situations than in the slow planting of clues. Nevertheless *The Four Just Men*, *The Clue of the New Pin*, *We Shall See!* and *Big Foot* all contain ingenious locked-room mysteries, and the unmasking of the villain in *The Crimson Circle*, *The Valley of Ghosts*, *A King by Night* and *The India-Rubber Men* still comes as a nicely-contrived shock (as does the "unmasking" in *Room 13* and *The Squeaker* of the hero).

Wallace was never afraid of experimenting, and some of his most fascinating books are those well outside his normal field. *Captains of Souls*, for instance, concerns the transference of souls, and is one of his best stories; the eminently readable straight novel *Those Folk of Bulboro* attacks organised religion; the "twin worlds" theme of *Planetoid 127* still holds up well today; and his Sanders of the River series (11 books in all) is surely a unique contribution to popular literature.

A strong thread of comedy runs throughout his books, and he had an instinctive feel for such low-life characters as garrulous charwomen and small-time burglars which was undoubtedly fostered by his upbringing in the slums of south-east London (his soldier-sketches – the Smithy books – epitomise the broader aspect of his comic genius). Yet his humour – as in *Double Dan* and *Barbara on Her Own* – could often rival that of his friend P. G. Wodehouse in its lightness of touch, and even, on occasion, become pure satire, as in *The Man Who Knew*, a splendid joke at the expense of detective-story conventions (and indeed of his own plot techniques).

His grasp of character exhibits itself most strongly in the various second-string detectives (mainly from Scotland Yard) that people his books and comment, like sardonic choruses, on the hero, heroine, main villain, life in general, and the thousand natural shocks their own flesh is heir to (usually rheumatism). Sergeant Totty, in the excellent *The Frightened Lady*, is a noteworthy character in this respect, but perhaps the best-remembered are the laconic Sooper (*Big Foot* and *The Lone House Mystery*) and the lugubrious Elk, whose wit is at its most mordant in *The Fellowship of the Frog* and *The Joker*. But probably Wallace's most famous character is J. G. Reeder, that uniquely English detective (vaguely connected with the Public Prosecutor's office) whose mind is definitely devious and whose meekness hides a wolfish ferocity when aroused. In many ways the Reeder books – *The Mind of Mr. J. G.*

Reeder, Terror Keep, Red Aces, and *The Guv'nor* – are Wallace's best endeavours in the field of pure detection, and undoubtedly the first book contains some of his best short stories.

To a certain extent Wallace was more convincing in the short story medium; certainly the compact format forced on him a self-discipline rarely to be found in the novels. His short stories are stunning examples of a lost art that flourished only during the inter-War years, when there were so many fiction magazines to nourish it: pithy, tightly-plotted, neatly-contrived, with twists in their tails even Ambrose Bierce and O. Henry would have applauded.

But it is still the thrillers – where nothing, except the hero (tough, tanned, and unfailingly cheerful) and the heroine (with her complexion of milk and roses, and nerves of steel), is as it seems to be – that grip the imagination and rivet the attention. How else could it be, when that sinister figure lurking just outside the street lamp's rays might possibly be a detective, and that benevolent old clergyman with the halo of white hair might well turn out to be a knife-wielding madman? In such a capricious world as this, it is surely satisfying to know, deep down, that after astounding revelation piled upon astounding revelation (and a thrilling chase) good will at last triumph over evil.

And although there is far more to Wallace, if you look for it, than the genre for which he is best remembered (and which he himself, almost single-handed, created), still he was above all an entertainer. "I write to amuse," he once said in an interview. As a summing-up of his creative talent – indeed, as an epitaph – this surely cannot be bettered.

—Christopher Lowder

WALLING, R(obert) A(lfred) J(ohn). British. Born in Exeter, Devon, 11 January 1869. Married Florence Victoria Greet in 1894 (died, 1948); two sons and one daughter. Journalist in Plymouth for many years: Editor, *Bicycling News*; Reporter, later Managing Editor, *Western Daily Mercury*; Editor, *Western Evening Herald*; Editor, later Managing Editor, *Western Independent*; Director, Whitfield and Newman. Magistrate in Plymouth from 1910; later Chairman of Justices and of the Licensing Bench. *Died 4 September 1949.*

CRIME PUBLICATIONS

Novels (series characters: Garstang; Philip Tolefree)

> *That Dinner-Party at Bardolph's.* London, Jarrolds, 1927; as *That Dinner at Bardolph's,* New York, Morrow, 1928.
> *The Strong Room.* London, Jarrolds, 1927.
> *Murder at the Keyhole.* London, Methuen, and New York, Morrow, 1929.
> *The Man with the Squeaky Voice.* London, Methuen, and New York, Morrow, 1930.
> *The Stroke of One* (Garstang). London, Methuen, and New York, Morrow, 1931.
> *The Fatal Five Minutes* (Tolefree). London, Hodder and Stoughton, and New York, Morrow, 1932.
> *Behind the Yellow Blind* (Garstang). London, Hodder and Stoughton, 1932; as *Murder at Midnight,* New York, Morrow, 1932.
> *Prove It, Mr. Tolefree.* New York, Morrow, 1933; as *The Tolliver Case,* London, Hodder and Stoughton, 1934.
> *Follow the Blue Car* (Tolefree). London, Hodder and Stoughton, 1933; as *In Time for Murder,* New York, Morrow, 1933.

Legacy of Death (Tolefree).   New York, Morrow, 1934; as *The Five Suspects*, London, Hodder and Stoughton, 1935.

VIII to IX (Tolefree).   London, Hodder and Stoughton, 1934; as *The Bachelor Flat Mystery*, New York, Morrow, 1934.

The Cat and the Corpse (Tolefree).   London, Hodder and Stoughton, 1935; as *The Corpse in the Green Pyjamas*, New York, Morrow, 1935.

The Corpse in the Coppice.   New York, Morrow, 1935; as *Mr. Tolefree's Reluctant Witnesses*, London, Hodder and Stoughton, 1936.

The Corpse with the Floating Foot (Tolefree).   New York, Morrow, 1936; as *The Mystery of Mr. Mock*, London, Hodder and Stoughton, 1937.

The Corpse in the Crimson Slippers (Tolefree).   London, Hodder and Stoughton, and New York, Morrow, 1936.

The Corpse with a Dirty Face (Tolefree).   London, Hodder and Stoughton, and New York, Morrow, 1936; as *The Crime in Cumberland Court*, Hodder and Stoughton, 1938.

Bury Him Deeper (Tolefree).   London, Hodder and Stoughton, 1937; as *Marooned with Murder*, New York, Morrow, 1937.

The Coroner Doubts (Tolefree).   London, Hodder and Stoughton, 1938; as *The Corpse with the Blue Cravat*, New York, Morrow, 1938.

More Than One Serpent (Tolefree).   London, Hodder and Stoughton, 1938; as *The Corpse with the Grimy Glove*, New York, Morrow, 1938.

Dust in the Vault (Tolefree).   London, Hodder and Stoughton, 1939; as *The Corpse with the Blistered Hand*, New York, Morrow, 1939.

They Liked Entwhistle (Tolefree).   London, Hodder and Stoughton, 1939; as *The Corpse with the Red-Headed Friend*, New York, Morrow, 1939.

Why Did Trethewy Die? (Tolefree).   London, Hodder and Stoughton, 1940; as *The Spider and the Fly*, New York, Morrow, 1940.

By Hook or by Crook (Tolefree).   London, Hodder and Stoughton, 1941; as *By Hook or Crook*, New York, Morrow, 1941.

Castle-Dinas (Tolefree).   London, Hodder and Stoughton, 1942; as *The Corpse with the Eerie Eye*, New York, Morrow, 1942.

The Doodled Asterisk (Tolefree).   London, Hodder and Stoughton, 1943; as *A Corpse by Any Other Name*, New York, Morrow, 1943.

A Corpse Without a Clue (Tolefree).   London, Hodder and Stoughton, and New York, Morrow, 1944.

The Late Unlamented (Tolefree).   London, Hodder and Stoughton, and New York, Morrow, 1948.

The Corpse with the Missing Watch (Tolefree).   New York, Morrow, 1949.

OTHER PUBLICATIONS

Short Stories

Flaunting Moll and Other Stories.   London, Harper, 1898.

Other

A Sea-Dog of Devon: A Life of Sir John Hawkins.   London, Cassell, and New York, Lane, 1907.

George Borrow: The Man and His Work.   London, Cassell, 1908.

Adventures of a Rubberneck.   Plymouth, Plymouth Press, 1932.

The Charm of Brittany.   London, Harrap, 1933.

The West Country.   London, Blackie, and New York, Morrow, 1935.

Green Hills of England.   London, Blackie, 1937; New York, Morrow, 1938.

The Story of Plymouth.   London, Westaway Books, and New York, Morrow, 1950.

Editor, *The Diaries of John Bright*.   London, Cassell, 1930.
Editor, *Plymouth*.   Plymouth, Incorporated Mercantile Association, 1930(?).

*   *   *

R. A. J. Walling's place in detective fiction is that of a competent practitioner of the British Golden Age novel. He broke little new ground and few traditions while writing numerous variations on the country-house puzzle. Occasionally his books looked like becoming spy thrillers or intrigue novels with threats of political terrors, but toward the end of these books he provided a solution with a personal motive or even an accident being the originating force.

That *Dinner-Party at Bardolph's*, Walling's first book, was typical of his early work. It deals with upper-class men (women have a very minor place in any of Walling's work) who are willing to withhold information or help someone they think is guilty simply because they feel it is the "fair-play" thing to do. Anything is acceptable if it avoids scandal or publicity. Those early books had a lightness and sense of humor that are absent from his work during the Depression and World War II eras. Throughout all his work Walling verges on the Had-I-But-Known style – opening chapters give hints of odd clues and horrible events that the characters would have done anything to avoid if they'd known what was coming. When those events are described in the narrative, they tend to be minor points or not nearly as thrilling or horrifying (by modern standards) as promised.

Philip Tolefree is the detective in most of Walling's books. Starting out as a private enquiry agent in non-criminal insurance matters, he takes on his first murder case in *The Fatal Five Minutes*. By the time of his last case, *The Corpse with the Missing Watch*, he has served in the Service, and is openly calling himself a detective, setting up a practice with another ex-Service agent. (It is never specified just what he did in the Service, it was all too secret and vital to national security.) Tolefree has his own Watson, James Farrar, who narrates the first stories, is dropped, and then appears as a character in later works. Tolefree is not a fair-play detective. He produces solutions that are, according to him, the "only" way the murder could have been done. How he reaches his conclusion is his own business. Thriller and puzzle elements are more important. The catchy *Corpse* titles in American editions of his work point up the sensational elements; but the titles are usually not descriptive of the plots. Like many traditional detectives, Tolefree occasionally lets the murderer go free (because it is more just than turning him in to the police); and sometimes murders are committed by accident. Characterization is limited and it is difficult to keep some of the characters clear. Troubled young lovers often muddy the waters. Continual discussion resolves all the problems and uncovers the villain. Violence is kept at a minimum, leaving alibis and time-sequence problems prominent.

While avoiding most of the excesses, Walling provides all the traditions and traits of the Golden Age, but falls short in his presentation of actual detection.

—Fred Dueren

WALSH, Thomas (Francis Morgan).   American.   Born in 1908. Educated at Columbia University, New York, B.A. 1933. Reporter, Baltimore *Sun*. Self-employed writer. Recipient: Mystery Writers of America Edgar Allan Poe Award, for novel, 1951, for short story, 1978. Address: 29 Bloomingdale Avenue, Saranac Lake, New York, U.S.A.

Crime Publications

Novels

Nightmare in Manhattan.   Boston, Little Brown, 1950; London, Hamish Hamilton, 1951.
The Night Watch.   Boston, Little Brown, and London, Hamish Hamilton, 1952.
The Dark Window.   Boston, Little Brown, and London, Hamish Hamilton, 1956.
Dangerous Passenger.   Boston, Little Brown, 1959.
The Eye of the Needle.   New York, Simon and Schuster, 1961; London, Cassell, 1962.
A Thief in the Night.   New York, Simon and Schuster, 1962; London, Cassell, 1963.
To Hide a Rogue.   New York, Simon and Schuster, 1964; London, Cassell, 1965.
The Tenth Point.   New York, Simon and Schuster, and London, Cassell, 1965.
The Resurrection Man.   New York, Simon and Schuster, 1966; London, Cassell, 1967.
The Face of the Enemy.   New York, Simon and Schuster, 1966; London, Cassell, 1968.
The Action of the Tiger.   New York, Simon and Schuster, 1968; London, Hale, 1969.

Uncollected Short Stories

"Guns of Gannett," in *Mystery League* (New York), December 1933.
"Alter Ego," in *A Century of Spy Stories*, edited by Dennis Wheatley.   London, Hutchinson, 1938.
"Live Bait," in *My Best Spy Story.*   London, Faber, 1938.
"Before the Act," in *Collier's* (Springfield, Ohio), 8 July 1939.
"Ed Mahoney's Boy," in *Collier's* (Springfield, Ohio), 10 February 1940.
"Mutton Dressed as Lamb," in *My Best Secret Service Story*, edited by A. D. Divine.   London, Faber, 1940.
"In Line of Duty," in *Collier's* (Springfield, Ohio), 8 February 1941.
"Stranger in the Park," in *Collier's* (Springfield, Ohio), 27 December 1941.
"A Name for Baby," in *Collier's* (Springfield, Ohio), 18 December 1943.
"Peaceful in the Country," in *Collier's* (Springfield, Ohio), 13 April 1946.
"Best Man," in *The Hard-Boiled Omnibus: Early Stories from Black Mask*, edited by Joseph T. Shaw.   New York, Simon and Schuster, 1946.
"Break-up," in *Murder: Plain and Fanciful*, edited by James Sandoe.   New York, Sheridan House, 1948.
"Hard Guy," in *Ellery Queen's Mystery Magazine* (New York), September 1948.
"Getaway Money," in *Ellery Queen's Mystery Magazine* (New York), November 1948.
"Sentence of Death," in *Best Detective Stories of the Year 1949*, edited by David Coxe Cooke.   New York, Dutton, 1949.
"Woman Expert," in *Ellery Queen's Mystery Magazine* (New York), May 1951.
"Girl in Car Thirty Two," in *Saturday Evening Post* (Philadelphia), 7 November 1953.
"The Night Calhoon Was Off Duty," in *Ellery Queen's Mystery Magazine* (New York), April 1954.
"The Blonde Nurse," in *Butcher, Baker, Murder-Maker.*   New York, Knopf, 1954.
"You Can't Change Sides," in *Ellery Queen's Mystery Magazine* (New York), February 1955.
"Will You Always Be Helping Me?" in *Ellery Queen's Mystery Magazine* (New York), January 1956.
"Women – Pests or Poison," in *Ellery Queen's Mystery Magazine* (New York), November 1956.
"I Killed John Harrington," in *For Love or Money*, edited by Dorothy Gardiner.   New York, Doubleday, 1957; London, Macdonald, 1959.
"Always Open and Shut," in *Ellery Queen's Mystery Magazine* (New York), February 1957.
"Murder on Order," in *Saturday Evening Post* (Philadelphia), 9 March 1957.

"Dear Lady," in *Ellery Queen's Mystery Magazine* (New York), March 1958.
"A Chump to Hold the Bag," in *Ellery Queen's Mystery Magazine* (New York), April 1958.
"Girl in Danger," in *Ellery Queen's Mystery Magazine* (New York), June 1958.
"Terror in His Heart," in *Ellery Queen's Mystery Magazine* (New York), August 1958.
"Cop on the Prowl," in *Ellery Queen's 13th Annual.* New York, Random House, 1958; London, Collins, 1960.
"The Second Chance," in *Ellery Queen's Mystery Magazine* (New York), January 1959.
"Always a Stranger," in *Ellery Queen's Mystery Magazine* (New York), September 1959.
"A Good Prospect," in *Anthology 1960*, edited by Ellery Queen. New York, Davis, 1960.
"Dangerous Bluff," in *Best Detective Stories of the Year*, edited by Brett Halliday. New York, Dutton, and London, Boardman, 1961.
"Three O'Clock Alarm" in *Ellery Queen's Mystery Magazine* (New York), December 1961.
"Homecoming," in *Ellery Queen's Mystery Magazine* (New York), December 1962.
"Callaghan in Buttons," in *Anthology 1964*, edited by Ellery Queen. New York, Davis, 1963.
"Danger in the Shadows," in *Anthology 1964 Mid-Year*, edited by Ellery Queen. New York, Davis, 1964.
"Enemy Agent," in *The Spy in the Shadows*, edited by Marvin Allen Karp. New York, Popular Library, 1965.
"Poor Little Rich Kid," in *Ellery Queen's Mystery Magazine* (New York), November 1967.
"Fall Guy," in *Ellery Queen's Mystery Magazine* (New York), September 1976.
"The Dead Past," in *Ellery Queen's Mystery Magazine* (New York), May 1977.
"The Killer Instinct," in *Ellery Queen's Mystery Magazine* (New York), July 1977.
"Mr. Bountiful," in *Ellery Queen's Mystery Magazine* (New York), August 1977.
"Chance after Chance," in *Ellery Queen's Mystery Magazine* (New York), November 1977.
"The Sacrificial Goat," in *Ellery Queen's Mystery Magazine* (New York), January 1978.
"Stakeout," in *Ellery Queen's Mystery Magazine* (New York), March 1978.
"The Closed Door," in *Ellery Queen's Mystery Magazine* (New York), May 1978.
"The Last of the Rossiters," in *Ellery Queen's Mystery Magazine* (New York), July 1978.
"Killer Bill," in *Ellery Queen's Mystery Magazine* (New York), September 1978.
"The Long Dark Street," in *Ellery Queen's Mystery Magazine* (New York), November 1978.
"The Stillness at 3:25," in *Ellery Queen's Mystery Magazine* (New York), February 1979.
"The Mayhew Job," in *Alfred Hitchcock's Mystery Magazine* (New York), July 1979.
"A Hell of a Cop," in *Ellery Queen's Mystery Magazine* (New York), August 1979.

Bibliography: "Department of Unknown Mystery Writers: Thomas Walsh" by Marvin Lachman in *Poisoned Pen* (Brooklyn), January–February 1979.

*   *   *

Thomas Walsh won his first Edgar in 1951 for his first novel, *Nightmare in Manhattan*. In 1978, he won his second, for the short story "Chance after Chance." In the 27 years between, Walsh has been writing steadily. There has been no better writer of the police story, and there has never been a better writer of the streets of New York.

Walsh had been a prolific short story writer before turning to the novel, and his brief experience as a newspaperman shows up in his fiction. His books have the visual and action qualities which stem from good reporting, and make good motion pictures. *Nightmare in Manhattan* (filmed as *Union Station*) is still considered one of the most successful of mysteries transferred to film. What Walsh called "Manhattan Depot" was quite evidently Grand Central Station, and the author explored its many warrens, and utilized its multiple levels and the confusing exits and entrances. This book was also one of the most successful of deadline stories, the tension stretched to high wire tightness with all action taking place within a 48-hour span.

Walsh's later work is as bright and vital as his early writing, seasoned now with the maturity of long experience. His books stand the true test of expertness: they can be read today not as dated material but with the same zest as when first published.

—Dorothy B. Hughes

WAMBAUGH, Joseph (Aloysius, Jr.). American. Born in East Pittsburgh, Pennsylvania, 22 January 1937. Educated at Chaffey College, Alta Loma, California, A.A. 1958; California State College, Los Angeles, B.A. 1960, M.A. 1968. Served in the United States Marine Corps, 1954–57. Married Dee Allsup in 1955; two children. Worked in the Los Angeles Police Department, 1960–74: Detective Sergeant. Since 1974, self-employed writer; creator and consultant for *Police Story* and *The Blue Knight* television series. Recipient: Mystery Writers of America Special Award, 1973. Address: P.O. Box 8657, San Marino, California 91108, U.S.A.

CRIME PUBLICATIONS

Novels

> *The New Centurions.* Boston, Little Brown, 1970; London, Joseph, 1971.
> *The Blue Knight.* Boston, Little Brown, 1972; London, Joseph, 1973.
> *The Onion Field.* New York, Delacorte Press, 1973; London, Weidenfield and Nicolson, 1974.
> *The Choirboys.* New York, Delacorte Press, 1975; London, Weidenfeld and Nicolson, 1976.
> *The Black Marble.* New York, Delacorte Press, and London, Weidenfeld and Nicolson, 1978.

OTHER PUBLICATIONS

Play

> Screenplay: *The Onion Field*, 1979.

*   *   *

Perhaps the first cop to write best-sellers, Joseph Wambaugh realistically portrays police activities in each of his works. *The New Centurions* and *The Blue Knight* adhere to the standard romance pattern, a dualistic view of man's environment as either paradisical or fallen, of man himself as either heroic or villainous. In *The Onion Field* and *The Choirboys* Wambaugh retains vestiges of the romance formula, but he treats it with tragic irony in *The Onion Field* and with gradually darkening comic irony in *The Choirboys*, his best work. *The*

Black Marble seems flawed by its juxtaposition of romantic love story, police procedural details, and psychological melodrama.

The New Centurions traces the careers of three policemen from their beginnings in the Los Angeles police academy in 1960 to the Watts riot of 1965, which symbolizes the chaos on which the centurions must impose order. Wambaugh correctly points out the insularity inherent in police work; policemen reject the weak and villainous in order to cope psychologically with the horrors such people perpetrate. The novel bears the characteristic stamp of many first works; though Wambaugh is self-consciously serious and prone to lecture, he creates sympathetic and recognizably human characters. While his centurions define themselves as agents of the law, his Blue Knight, a twenty-year veteran of the force, defines himself in terms of his own physical strength and his personal sense of what is good for the people on his beat. Unlike the new centurions, the Blue Knight sees himself as thwarted by the law. He will not allow himself any emotional involvement with others, choosing at the end of the novel not to retire, wed, and become a security officer but to remain on his beat. While he earns a measure of admiration for his courage, he seems primarily a pathetic figure, police work having isolated him from other people and also from the emotions of compassion and love.

Wambaugh carefully and with studied outrage examines the psychological effects of police work in *The Onion Field*, a "non-fiction novel" which delineates the mental collapse of Karl Hettinger after he and another policeman are surprised, disarmed, and kidnapped by two petty thieves who eventually murder Hettinger's partner. Hettinger flees, "escaping" into continual nightmares, impotence, kleptomania, and a series of trials, for the conviction of the murderers occurred before the Escobedo, Dorado, and Miranda decisions, and their death sentences pronounced before the Anderson decision abolished capital punishment in California. Wambaugh recounts each new trial in horrified detail, manipulating ironic parallels between the two policemen and the two murderers throughout. Here the law seems not merely to thwart the policemen but actually to favor the criminals.

Wambaugh also examines the psychic cost of police work in *The Choirboys*, but he does so with a broad and bawdy comic technique reminiscent of *Catch-22*. The novel includes a series of hilarious episodes depicting incompetent, high-ranking officers and alcoholic, claustrophobic, masochistic, sadistic, and vampiric policemen. Wambaugh intersperses accounts of the patrolmen's desperate shenanigans in MacArthur Park with more and more brutal accounts of criminal inhumanity, which the patrolmen are forced by their job to witness. The juxtaposition suggests how and why police work taints a cop's vision of others and of himself; it suggests as well how some policemen try to cope with horror. Wambaugh's control here – of episode, of character, and especially of tone – is remarkable.

The Black Marble is, therefore, something of a disappointment. Its hero, Valnikov, is a veteran cop like the Blue Knight. Like Hettinger and the choirboys, Valnikov has seen more than his share of cruelty and horror; the horror that causes him special anguish and that his partner, a policewoman/detective, helps him to purge, Wambaugh gradually reveals in the same way Joseph Heller reveals Snowden's secret in *Catch-22*. A dognapping provides the opportunity for some pointed satire of Pasadena, dogshows, and dogshow people. Valnikov's fight with the dognapper provides a realistic scene unlike most such fictional fare. The love affair of Valnikov and his partner ends the novel, happily, but rather patly.

—David K. Jeffrey

WARRINER, Thurman. Also writes as Simon Troy. British.

CRIME PUBLICATIONS

Novels (series character: Mr. Scotter in all books except *The Golden Lantern*)

> *Method in His Murder.*   London, Hodder and Stoughton, and New York, Macmillan, 1950.
> *Ducats in Her Coffin.*   London, Hodder and Stoughton, 1951.
> *Death's Dateless Night.*   London, Hodder and Stoughton, 1952.
> *The Doors of Sleep.*   London, Hodder and Stoughton, 1955.
> *Death's Bright Angel.*   London, Hodder and Stoughton, 1956.
> *She Died, Of Course.*   London, Hodder and Stoughton, 1958.
> *The Golden Lantern.*   London, Hodder and Stoughton, 1958.
> *Heavenly Bodies.*   London, Hodder and Stoughton, 1960.

Novels as Simon Troy (series character: Inspector Smith)

> *Road to Rhuine* (Smith).   London, Collins, and New York, Dodd Mead, 1952.
> *Half-Way to Murder.*   London, Gollancz, 1955.
> *Tonight and Tomorrow.*   London, Gollancz, 1957.
> *Drunkard's End.*   London, Gollancz, 1960; New York, Walker, 1961.
> *Second Cousin Removed* (Smith).   London, Gollancz, 1961; New York, Macmillan, 1962.
> *Waiting for Oliver.*   London, Gollancz, 1962; New York, Macmillan, 1963.
> *Don't Play with the Rough Boys* (Smith).   London, Gollancz, 1963; New York, Macmillan, 1964.
> *Cease upon the Midnight* (Smith).   London, Gollancz, 1964; New York, Macmillan, 1965.
> *No More A-Roving* (Smith).   London, Gollancz, 1965.
> *Sup with the Devil* (Smith).   London, Gollancz, 1967.
> *Swift to Its Close* (Smith).   London, Gollancz, and New York, Stein and Day, 1969.
> *Blind Man's Garden* (Smith).   London, Gollancz, 1970.

Uncollected Short Stories as Simon Troy

> "Once a Policeman," in *Ellery Queen's Mystery Magazine* (New York), October 1969.
> "The Liquidation File," in *Ellery Queen's Giants of Mystery.*   New York, Davis, 1976.

*   *   *

Good vs. evil and a seeming revolt against fundamentalist and fanatical religious groups are the sub-themes in many of the novels by Thurman Warriner. His hobbies – music, book collecting, and ecclesiastical architecture – provide interesting diversions for the unique and passionate characters which inhabit the pages of his books. Warriner's first book, *Method in His Murder*, is a tense psychological thriller, rich in English background and ecclesiastical history. The series heroes are Mr. Ambo, a very proper wealthy bachelor, Scotter, an outspoken, brash, private detective, and Archdeacon Toft, a devil-fearing man. The interaction and mixed dialogue of these diametrically opposed do-gooders add an amusing element to the suspenseful tales in which they are featured.

The author's best work, however, is that published as Simon Troy and starring the compassionate, steady, and insightful Inspector Smith. Heavy in suspense, characters, local color, and psychology, the Troy novels involve characters from every walk of life, from prostitutes to deacons, concert musicians to automobile salesmen, none of whom escapes the watchful eye of the determined and just Inspector Smith. The characters are presented in depth, the motives, psychological or otherwise, of the crimes are thoroughly explored, and the tension builds to a suspenseful climax.

—Mary Ann Grochowski

WATSON, Colin. British. Born in Croydon, Surrey, 1 February 1920. Educated at Whitgift School, Croydon, 1930–36. Married; two daughters and one son. Worked in advertising, London, 1936–38; journalist, 1938–40; worked for an engineering firm, 1940–45; leader-writer, Thomson Newspapers, 1952–60; worked for the BBC, Newcastle upon Tyne, 1957–60. Address: c/o Eyre Methuen Ltd., 11 New Fetter Lane, London EC4P 4EE, England.

CRIME PUBLICATIONS

Novels (series character: Inspector Purbright in all books except *Bump in the Night* and *The Puritan*)

Coffin, Scarcely Used. London, Eyre and Spottiswoode, 1958; New York, Putnam, 1967.
Bump in the Night. London, Eyre and Spottiswoode, 1960; New York, Walker, 1962.
Hopjoy Was Here. London, Eyre and Spottiswoode, 1962; New York, Walker, 1963.
The Puritan. London, Eyre and Spottiswoode, 1966.
Lonelyheart 4122. London, Eyre and Spottiswoode, and New York, Putnam, 1967.
Charity Ends at Home. London, Eyre and Spottiswoode, and New York, Putnam, 1968.
The Flaxborough Crab. London, Eyre and Spottiswoode, 1969; as *Just What the Doctor Ordered*, New York, Putnam, 1969.
Broomsticks over Flaxborough. London, Eyre Methuen, 1972; as *Kissing Covens*, New York, Putnam, 1972.
The Naked Nuns. London, Eyre Methuen, 1975; as *Six Nuns and a Shotgun*, New York, Putnam, 1975.
One Man's Meat. London, Eyre Methuen, 1977; as *It Shouldn't Happen to a Dog*, New York, Putnam, 1977.
Blue Murder. London, Eyre Methuen, 1979.

Uncollected Short Stories

"Return to Base," in *Ellery Queen's Mystery Magazine* (New York), June 1967.
"The Infallible Clock," in *Ellery Queen's Mystery Magazine* (New York), November 1967.
"The Harrowing of Henry Pygole," in *Winter's Crimes 6*, edited by George Hardinge. London, Macmillan, 1974.

OTHER PUBLICATIONS

Other

> *Snobbery with Violence: Crime Stories and Their Audience.* London, Eyre and
> Spottiswoode, 1971; New York, St. Martin's Press, 1972; revised edition, London,
> Eyre Methuen, 1979.
> "Interview with a Character," in *Murder Ink: The Mystery Reader's Companion*, edited
> by Dilys Winn. New York, Workman, 1977.
> "Mayhem Parva and Wicked Belgravia," in *Crime Writers*, edited by H. R. F.
> Keating. London, BBC Publications, 1978.

*   *   *

Snobbery with Violence, Colin Watson's study of 20th-century crime fiction, includes an acerbic chapter on the work of Agatha Christie; it is called "The Little World of Mayhem Parva" and it is sharply and wittily critical of those cloistered and sentimentalized villages in which Agatha Christie, like so many detective novelists of the 1920's and 1930's, loved to set her mysteries. Colin Watson's own amiable and extremely funny novels can be read as a dramatized version of this objection to Christie and her generation. Flaxborough, the East Anglian town that has been the setting for all Watson's novels, is the opposite of Mayhem Parva; Christie's villages are genteel, chaste, and picturesque; Flaxborough is vulgar and lively. Even to the admiring gaze of a visiting New York policeman it does not seem entirely picturesque: "A little town with the oldest jumble of housetops you ever saw and a pub and a church every twenty yards, and girls like flowers and very, very slow-moving old men with brick-coloured faces who looked as if they'd have to be hit by lightning before they'd die." In the words of a knowledgeable inhabitant, Flaxborough is "A high-spirited town.... Like Gomorrah."

Colin Watson has now published nine novels in the series, and Flaxborough has become an elaborate and solid creation. It is depicted with a sharply satirical eye (and ear) for the unpicturesque aspects of contemporary English life. Flaxborough abounds in streets like Abdication Avenue and in charities called Our Dumb Companions, the Barkers' League, the Dogs at Sea Society, the Canine Law Alliance, and Four Foot Haven. Watson delights in describing overstuffed middle-class interiors and overtended middle-class gardens: "He admired the Nymph's Grotto and the Merry Fisher Lad and the big model windmill, painted bright blue and red, with sails that really went round whenever the wind blew from Wanstead, and he recognized Maisie's handiwork in the Lord's Prayer done in musselshell mosaic around the concrete base of the bird table." He catalogues the possessions of the newly affluent in loving detail: in *The Naked Nuns*, for example, Arnold Hatch is the proud owner of a gadget that automatically closes his bedroom curtains and switches the light on at sunset, and of a car, a "Fairway Executive," fitted with a refrigerator, telephone, and duplicating machine.

As this eye for consumer goods would suggest, Watson has a special interest in the activities, whether dishonest or merely comic, of modern business. *Broomsticks over Flaxborough*, for example, includes a campaign for the detergent Lucillite ("Only Lucillite has saponified granules") run by a group of advertising men whose professional jargon is deftly captured: "Folk-fond – that's an image situation. But first things first. Before product acceptance, product *presentation*, right?" *The Naked Nuns* has a superbly funny account of a medieval banquet for coach parties and American tourists organized by the Floradora Club, complete with "capons" (badly cooked chickens), "wassail" (cheap wine), waitresses dressed as Nell Gwynne, and music provided by Roy Hubbard and the Rockadours. The neatly titled *One Man's Meat* deals with the tribulations encountered by the makers of Woof, a popular dog food.

Watson's portrait of the tawdry side of English provincial life is saved from bitterness by something rare in detective novels: a dirty sense of humour. He has an innocent love of bawdy jokes, bedroom farce, and rude words. Flaxborough at times resembles an animated seaside postcard. *The Flaxborough Crab*, for example, deals with the alarming effects of an improperly tested drug being dispensed by a local doctor: it converts harmless elderly men into enthusiastic but incompetent sex maniacs. The plot of *Coffin, Scarcely Used* turns on an elaborate conspiracy by which a doctor's surgery is used as a brothel. It comes as no surprise to learn that the Floradora Club in *The Naked Nuns* has a brothel at the back (the girls are all named after flowers), and that the witches coven in *Broomsticks over Flaxborough* is merely an excuse for various erotic goings-on.

In addition to the cast of sentimental animal lovers, drunken journalists, randy aldermen, and corrupt doctors, which changes from novel to novel, Watson uses a small group of recurrent characters. In this group the law is represented by Flaxborough's coroner, Mr. Albert Amblesby (once inadvertently described by a former mayor as one of "the venereal institutions of this ancient town"); his officer, Sergeant Malley; Dr. Heinemann, the pathologist; and Harcourt Chubb, the genteel and absent-minded Chief Constable. Most important are Inspector Purbright and his assistant, Detective Sergeant Sidney Love. Quiet, sensible, and with an air of deceptive amiability, Purbright is one of the more convincing detectives in recent fiction.

In his later work, though, Watson's interest seems to have been leaning more towards the criminals – more rogues than villains – who play minor but entertaining roles in his plots. The most important such figure – and probably Colin Watson's best comic creation – is Lucilla Edith Cavell Teatime, the genteel confidence lady. Miss Teatime combines apparent respectability (she is Secretary of the Flaxborough and Eastern Counties Charities Alliance) with a love of fraudulent schemes (for example, her plan in *The Flaxborough Crab* for selling chopped dandelions as a sexual stimulant called Samson's Salad) and a disconcertingly racy line in conversation: "To tell the truth, it is regarding the physical side of marriage that I have always been apprehensive.... There so seldom seems to be enough of it."

What happens to detection amid all this comedy? Inevitably it receives short shrift. Colin Watson's earliest books, *Coffin, Scarcely Used* and *Bump in the Night*, show his considerable skill in constructing intricate plots and allow Inspector Purbright to do some very creditable pieces of detection. But since then the comic element has predominated; the plots of the later novels are not slack or ill-constructed, but they are rarely the centre of either the reader's or the novelist's attention. There is no reason to regret this. There are many competent plotters among contemporary detective novelists, but there are few comic writers as energetic or entertaining as Colin Watson.

—Ian Ousby

WAUGH, Hillary (Baldwin). Also writes as Elissa Grandower; H. Baldwin Taylor; Harry Walker. American. Born in New Haven, Connecticut, 22 June 1920. Educated at Hillhouse High School, New Haven; Yale University, New Haven, B.A. 1942. Served as a Pilot in the United States Navy Air Corps, 1943–45: Lieutenant, J.G. Married Diana M. A. Taylor in 1951; two daughters and one son. Free-lance cartoonist and song writer; Teacher of mathematics and physics, Hamden Hall Country Day School, Connecticut, 1956–57; Editor of Branford *Review*, weekly newspaper, Connecticut, 1961–62; First Selectman, Town of Guilford, Connecticut, 1971–73. Past President, and currently Executive Vice-President, Mystery Writers of America. Agent: Ann Elmo Agency Inc., 60 East 42nd Street, New York, New York 10017. Address: 323 North River Street, Guilford, Connecticut 06437, U.S.A.

CRIME PUBLICATIONS

Novels (series characters: Chief Fred Fellows; Lieutenant Frank Sessions; Sheridan Wesley)

Madam Will Not Dine Tonight (Wesley). New York, Coward McCann, 1947; London, Boardman, 1949; as *If I Live to Dine*, Hasbrouck Heights, New Jersey, Graphic, 1949.
Hope to Die (Wesley). New York, Coward McCann, 1948; London, Boardman, 1949.
The Odds Run Out (Wesley). New York, Coward McCann, 1949; London, Boardman, 1950.
Last Seen Wearing.... New York, Doubleday, 1952; London, Gollancz, 1953.
A Rag and a Bone. New York, Doubleday, 1954; London, Foulsham, 1955.
The Case of the Missing Gardener (as Harry Walker). New York, Arcadia House, 1954.
Rich Man, Dead Man. New York, Doubleday, 1956; as *Rich Man, Murder*, London, Foulsham, 1956; as *The Case of the Brunette Bombshell*, New York, Fawcett, 1957.
The Eighth Mrs. Bluebeard. New York, Doubleday, 1958; London, Foulsham, 1959.
The Girl Who Cried Wolf. New York, Doubleday, 1958; London, Foulsham, 1960.
Sleep Long, My Love (Fellows). New York, Doubleday, 1959; London, Gollancz, 1960; as *Jigsaw*, London, Pan, 1962.
Road Block (Fellows). New York, Doubleday, 1960; London, Gollancz, 1961.
That Night It Rained (Fellows). New York, Doubleday, and London, Gollancz, 1961.
Murder on the Terrace. London, Foulsham, 1961.
The Late Mrs. D. (Fellows). New York, Doubleday, and London, Gollancz, 1962.
Born Victim (Fellows). New York, Doubleday, 1962; London, Gollancz, 1963.
Death and Circumstances (Fellows). New York, Doubleday, and London, Gollancz, 1963.
Prisoner's Plea (Fellows). New York, Doubleday, 1963; London, Gollancz, 1964.
The Missing Man (Fellows). New York, Doubleday, and London, Gollancz, 1964.
End of a Party (Fellows). New York, Doubleday, and London, Gollancz, 1965.
Girl on the Run. New York, Doubleday, 1965; London, Gollancz, 1966.
Pure Poison (Fellows). New York, Doubleday, 1966; London, Gollancz, 1967.
The Con Game (Fellows). New York, Doubleday, and London, Gollancz, 1968.
"30" Manhattan East (Sessions). New York, Doubleday, 1968; London, Gollancz, 1969.
Run When I Say Go. New York, Doubleday, and London, Gollancz, 1969.
The Young Prey (Sessions). New York, Doubleday, 1969; London, Gollancz, 1970.
Finish Me Off (Sessions). New York, Doubleday, 1970; London, Gollancz, 1971.
The Shadow Guest. New York, Doubleday, and London, Gollancz, 1971.
Parrish for the Defense. New York, Doubleday, 1974; London, Gollancz, 1975; as *Doctor on Trial*, New York, Dell, 1977.
A Bride for Hampton House. New York, Doubleday, 1975; London, Gollancz, 1976.
Madman at My Door. New York, Doubleday, 1978; London, Gollancz, 1979.

Novels as H. Baldwin Taylor (series character: David Halliday)

The Duplicate (Halliday). New York, Doubleday, 1964; London, Heinemann, 1965.
The Triumvirate (Halliday). New York, Doubleday, and London, Heinemann, 1966.
The Trouble with Tycoons. New York, Doubleday, 1967; as *The Missing Tycoon*, London, Hale, 1967.

Novels as Elissa Grandower (published as Hillary Waugh in UK)

Seaview Manor. New York, Doubleday, 1976; London, Gollancz, 1977.

The Summer at Raven's Roost. New York, Doubleday, 1976; London, Gollancz, 1978.

The Secret Room of Morgate House. New York, Doubleday, 1977; London, Gollancz, 1978.

Blackbourne Hall. New York, Doubleday, 1979.

Uncollected Short Stories

"Nothing But Human Nature," in *Murder Most Foul*, edited by Harold Q. Masur. New York, Walker, 1971.

"Galton and the Yelling Boys," in *Alfred Hitchcock's Tales to Scare You Stiff*, edited by Eleanor Sullivan. New York, Davis, 1978.

OTHER PUBLICATIONS

Other

"The Mystery Versus the Novel" and "The Police Procedural," in *The Mystery Story*, edited by John Ball. San Diego, University of California Extension, 1976.

Editor, *Merchants of Menace.* New York, Doubleday, 1969.

Hillary Waugh comments:

What does a writer say about his own work? I try to tell an interesting story about interesting people. I try to write it in such a way that the reader will forget he is reading and be totally unaware of my presence as the author. I try to put a little meat into my stories in hopes that the reader won't digest the book in a gulp and forget it, but will have something to chew on afterward. I would like my books to make the reader think, without the books telling him what to think. Lastly, I try to make sure that none of my books ever ends on an anti-climax. The tension should build to an explosion, not a let-down.

*   *   *

If Hillary Waugh had done nothing else than create the character of Chief Fred Fellows, he would hold an enviable place in the annals of detective fiction. Waugh has, however, another distinguished credit on his record: he wrote *Last Seen Wearing...*, widely regarded as one of the masterpieces of mystery-suspense fiction.

Unlike most writers of police fiction who set their stories in places like New York or Los Angeles, Waugh chose the small town of "Stockford," Connecticut, as the setting of the Fred Fellows series. Stockford is a rather ordinary town inhabited by conventional people, though it does have a delightfully high homicide rate.

Chief Fellows, a tobacco-chewing, story-telling folksy type who has problems with keeping his chest measurement greater than his waist measurement, may give a first impression of being the stereotyped rube cop, but that he most decidedly is not. Fellows knows police work, and although his methods are usually informal they are well organized and consistent with forensic science. In *Road Block*, for example, he can get an approximate fix on the robbers' hangout by figuring the mileage on a car that has been driven to that point, and in *The Con Game* he uses publicity to determine the whereabouts of a fugitive. Fellows also has the abilities of the police expert, however, as in *The Late Mrs. D.*, where he identifies some typing on the basis of very competent analysis of the idiosyncracies of the typeface used. Fellows is a strict chief (he chews out a patrolman for showing up with an unpolished button and chases a group of card-playing reporters out of headquarters), but he is a considerate officer who allows his men as much latitude as he can, and he is interested in justice to the extent that he once spent his vacation investigating the case of a condemned criminal who had appealed to him for help. In some ways Fellows is closer to the heroes of Great Policeman tradition of Inspector Maigret than to those of the police procedural novel. He is a believer in police teamwork, but more often than not the solutions to the mysteries come from the workings of his intelligence rather than lucky breaks or the legwork of his subordinates. On more than one occasion Fellows has solved the case only two-thirds of the way into the story and spends the rest of the time searching for confirmatory proof.

Before he began the Fellows series, Waugh wrote *Last Seen Wearing* ..., which Julian Symons selected for his list of the hundred greatest crime novels. Aspiring writers of fiction could profitably study the structure of this fine story, which is a model of sustained suspense. The tight form of the novel is shaped by a pure, uncluttered story-line, with no sub-plots and no spin-offs, no distraction of attention from the consuming problem presented at the beginning, repeatedly analyzed, and finally resolved without having been diluted or distorted. The most remarkable structural feature of the novel is that all the relevant facts (including a reasonably accurate speculation regarding the solution) are presented in the original definition of the problem, which occupies the first fourth of the book. From there on, the suspense is sustained by means of re-examination of the mystery from different points of view and by the growing intensity of excitement as various explanations are tested. False leads and false clues are not allowed to stand for more than two or three pages, and periods of confusion are of short duration. The first real break in the case does not come until halfway through the book.

Waugh is a practitioner of the well-made novel. Unlike many other writers of police procedural novels, he avoids multiple plots, and the mystery presented at the beginning of a story is the one solved at the conclusion. The typical Waugh story fits the classic pattern of detective fiction: the problem, the initial solution, the complication, the period of confusion, the dawning light, the solution, and the explanation.

Waugh's other series policeman is Detective Second Grade Frank Sessions of Homicide, Manhattan North. Although his sphere of operation is quite different from Fred Fellows's Stockford, Sessions shares with Fellows the mold of the Genteel Policeman, in that he is more like Ngaio Marsh's Roderick Alleyn than most of the other roughnecks of police fiction: dining with a young woman at a good French restaurant, Sessions is annoyed by her apparent impression that a policeman is out of his depth anywhere else than at a lunch counter. He is, also like Fellows, a real professional who deplores the lack of pride and enthusiasm among young cops and who feels frustrated when a rapist-murderer gets off free. Society is all wrong, Sessions believes, but the police have to keep on trying. Waugh has also written mysteries involving Sheridan Wesley and Philip Macadam, both standard private-eye types that might have come from the pages of Raymond Chandler. The stories are well plotted and the suspense strong, but they lack the freshness and originality of the Fred Fellows and Frank Sessions series.

Hillary Waugh has been a pioneer in the development of the police procedural story, along with Lawrence Treat and Maurice Procter. His main contribution to the craft has been his refusal to follow the formula adopted by most other writers, with the result that his police stories are less conventional and harder to imitate, depending more on sharp defintion than on multiplicity of involvements in the development of mystery and suspense.

—George N. Dove

WAYLAND, Patrick. Pseudonym for Richard O'Connor. Also wrote as Frank Archer; John Burke. American. Born in La Porte, Indiana, 10 March 1915. Educated in schools in Milwaukee, Wisconsin. Married Olga Derby in 1939. Actor; journalist in Chicago, New

Orleans, Boston, Washington, Los Angeles, and New York, 1936–57; after 1957, self-employed writer. *Died 15 February 1975.*

CRIME PUBLICATIONS

Novels (series character: Lloyd Nicolson in all books)

Counterstroke. New York, Doubleday, 1964; London, Hale, 1965.
Double Defector. New York, Doubleday, 1964; London, Hale, 1966.
The Waiting Game. New York, Doubleday, 1965; London, Hale, 1967.

Novels as Frank Archer (series character: Joe Delaney)

The Malabang Pearl (Delaney). New York, Doubleday, 1964; London, Hale, 1966.
Out of the Blue. New York, Doubleday, 1964; London, Hale, 1966.
The Widow Watchers. New York, Doubleday, 1965; London, Hale, 1967.
The Turquoise Spike (Delaney). New York, Fawcett, 1967; London, Jenkins, 1968.
The Naked Crusader. New York, Brandon, 1972.

OTHER PUBLICATIONS as Richard O'Connor

Novels

Company Q. New York, Doubleday, 1957; London, Redman, 1958.
Officers and Ladies. New York, Doubleday, 1958; London, Redman, 1960.
The Vandal. New York, Doubleday, 1960.

Other

Thomas: Rock of Chickamauga. New York, Prentice Hall, 1948.
Hood: Cavalier General. New York, Prentice Hall, 1949.
Sheridan: The Inevitable. Indianapolis, Bobbs Merrill, 1953.
High Jinks on the Klondike. Indianapolis, Bobbs Merrill, 1954; as *Gold, Dice, and Women*, London, Redman, 1956.
Guns of Chickamauga. New York, Doubleday, 1955.
Down to Eternity: How the Poor Edwardian and His World Died with the Titanic. New York, Fawcett, 1956; London, Fawcett, 1957.
Bat Masterson. New York, Doubleday, 1957; London, Redman, 1958.
Johnstown the Day the Dam Broke. Philadelphia, Lippincott, 1957; London, Redman, 1959.
Hell's Kitchen: The Roaring Days of New York's Wild West Side. Philadelphia, Lippincott, 1958.
Wild Bill Hickok. New York, Doubleday, 1959; London, Redman, 1960.
Pat Garrett: A Biography of the Famous Marshall and the Killer of Billy the Kid. New York, Doubleday, 1960.
Black Jack Pershing. New York, Doubleday, 1961.
Gould's Millions. New York, Doubleday, 1962.
The Scandalous Mr. Bennett. New York, Doubleday, 1962.
Courtroom Warrior: The Combative Career of William Travers Jerome. Boston, Little Brown, 1963.
Jack London: A Biography. Boston, Little Brown, 1964.
Bret Harte: A Biography. Boston, Little Brown, 1966.
Ambrose Bierce: A Biography. Boston, Little Brown, 1967.

The Lost Revolutionary: A Biography of John Reed, with Dale L. Walker.   New York,
Harcourt Brace, 1967.
Young Bat Masterson (juvenile).   New York, McGraw Hill, 1967.
Sitting Bull: War Chief of the Sioux (juvenile).   New York, McGraw Hill, 1968.
The German Americans: An Informal History.   Boston, Little Brown, 1968.
John Lloyd Stephen: Explorer of Lost Worlds.   New York, McGraw Hill, 1968.
Gentleman Johnny Burgoyne (juvenile).   New York, McGraw Hill, 1969.
The Common Sense of Tom Paine (juvenile).   New York, McGraw Hill, 1969.
Pacific Destiny: An Informal History of the U.S. in the Far East, 1776–1968.   Boston,
Little Brown, 1969.
Winged Legend: The Story of Amelia Earhart (as John Burke).   New York, Putnam,
1970.
The First Hurrah: A Biography of Alfred E. Smith.   New York, Putnam, 1970.
John Steinbeck (juvenile).   New York, McGraw Hill, 1970.
O. Henry: The Legendary Life of William S. Porter.   New York, Doubleday, 1970.
The Irish: Portrait of a People.   New York, Putnam, 1971.
The Oil Barons: Men of Greed and Grandeur.   Boston, Little Brown, 1971.
The Cactus Throne: The Tragedy of Maximillian and Carlotta.   New York, Putnam,
1971.
Ernest Hemingway (juvenile).   New York, McGraw Hill, 1971.
Sinclair Lewis (juvenile).   New York, McGraw Hill, 1971.
Buffalo Bill: The Noblest Whiteskin (as John Burke).   New York, Putnam, 1972.
*Duet in Drinks: The Flamboyant Saga of Lillian Russell and Diamond Jim Brady in
America's Gilded Age* (as John Burke).   New York, Putnam, 1972.
Iron Wheels and Broken Men: The Railroad Barons and the Plunder of the West.   New
York, Putnam, 1973.
The Spirit Soldiers: A Historical Narrative of the Boxer Rebellion.   New York, Putnam,
1973.
The Golden Summer: An Antic History of Newport.   New York, Putnam, 1974.
Heywood Broun: A Biography.   New York, Putnam, 1975.

Manuscript Collection: University of Maine Library, Orono.

*   *   *

Counterstroke, as well as being the title of one of Patrick Wayland's books, is also one of
those super-mysterious organisations that even the employees cannot understand. The agents
usually work alone, except in *The Waiting Game* which is an account of an attempted
defection by a 19-year-old Russian ballerina during an American tour. In this book Lloyd
Nicolson is forced, under protest, to work with Frank Thompson and he continues to have
sarcastic thoughts about him even to the end when rescued by his "assistant."

Nicolson is an ex-soldier who has been recruited by Counterstroke to do work that he
dislikes most heartily. His superior, Mr. Cramer, keeps him in line with various pressures and
semi-threats quite worthy of those dread Russians whom they regard as the enemy. Lloyd is
an expert at learning languages, he can be word-perfect in three months, and this to some
degree balances the disability of having an artificial leg. The enemy are always Perfect
Gentlemen and, while slugging and shooting it out, they never, never unstrap the leg while
they have him in their respective powers.

In *Counterstroke* the Chinese, by way of a change from the Russians, plan to dump one
billion dollars' worth of uncut heroin upon the United States. It will come in via Mexico at
the hands of various dirty-dealing Americans to whom cash is more viable than patriotism.
Nicolson seems to be able to operate efficiently with almost no food and very little sleep
which may be the reason why he is chosen and we are not. The theme in *Double Detector* is a
far, far sadder one for Nicolson. His close friend has crossed over and is willing to become a
traitor in order to see his East German wife once again. This is a most unhappy story taking

place in the dreary winter weather of the East Coast and Canada where the coldness of human intentions mixes equally with the weather.

It is a personal tragedy to lose any limb and insufficient attention is paid to the social and emotional problems Nicolson must face. An agent may be hard-boiled, but need he seem completely dead emotionally?

—Mary Groff

WEBB, Jack. Also writes as John Farr; Tex Grady. American. Born in Santa Monica, California, 2 April 1920. Educated at Belmont High School, Los Angeles, graduated 1938. Served in the United States Army Air Force, 1943–45. Married 1) the actress Julie London in 1947 (divorced), two children; 2) Dorothy Thompson in 1955 (divorced, 1957); 3) Jackie Loughery in 1958 (divorced, 1964). Worked in clothing store, 1938–42; announcer, disc-jockey, and actor, radio KGO, San Francisco, 1945–47; in radio in Hollywood, 1947–49; movie actor, 1950–61; radio and television producer; executive in charge of television production, Warner Brothers, 1963; created *Dragnet* radio series, 1949, and television version, 1951, 1967–70; created *Noah's Ark*, *True Series*, 1961, and *Adam-12*, 1968–71, for television; also television producer of *The D.A.*, 1971, *O'Hara, U.S. Treasury*, 1971, and *Emergency, Mobile One*, 1975. Recipient: Mystery Writers of America Edgar Allan Poe Award, for radio play, 1950, 1951; Emmy Award, for television series, 1955. Address: Universal City Studio, Universal City, California 91608, U.S.A.

CRIME PUBLICATIONS

Novels (series characters: Father Joseph Shanley and Sammy Golden in all books except
    One for My Dame and *Make My Bed Soon*)

    The Big Sin. New York, Rinehart, 1952; London, Boardman, 1953.
    The Naked Angel. New York, Rinehart, 1953; as *Such Women Are Dangerous*,
        London, Boardman, 1954.
    The Damned Lovely. New York, Rinehart, 1954; London, Boardman, 1955.
    The Broken Doll. New York, Rinehart, 1955; London, Boardman, 1956.
    The Bad Blonde. New York, Rinehart, 1956; London, Boardman, 1957.
    The Brass Halo. New York, Rinehart, 1957; London, Boardman, 1958.
    The Deadly Sex. New York, Rinehart, 1959; London, Boardman, 1960.
    The Delicate Darling. New York, Rinehart, 1959; London, Boardman, 1960.
    One for My Dame. New York, Holt Rinehart, 1961; London, Boardman, 1962.
    The Gilded Witch. Evanston, Illinois, Regency, and London, Boardman, 1963.
    Make My Bed Soon. New York, Holt Rinehart, 1963; London, Boardman, 1964.

Novels as John Farr

    Don't Feed the Animals. New York, Abelard Schuman, 1955; as *The Zoo Murders*,
        London, Foulsham, 1956; as *Naked Fear*, New York, Spivak, 1955.
    She Shark. New York, Ace, 1956.
    The Lady and the Snake. New York, Ace, 1957.
    The Deadly Combo. New York, Ace, 1958.

Uncollected Short Story

"Love Letter," in *Best Detective Stories of the Year 1975*, edited by Allen J. Hubin.   New York, Dutton, 1975.

OTHER PUBLICATIONS

Novel

High Mesa (as Tex Grady).   New York, Dutton, 1952; London, Foulsham, 1954.

Other

The Badge (on the Los Angeles Police Department).   Englewood Cliffs, New Jersey, Prentice Hall, 1958; London, W. H. Allen, 1959.

Theatrical Activities:

Director: **Films** – *Dragnet*, 1954; *Pete Kelly's Blues*, 1955; *The D.I.*, 1957; *30*, 1959; *The Last Time I Saw Archie*, 1961.

Actor: **Films** – *The Men*, 1950; *Sunset Boulevard*, 1950; *Dark City*, 1950; *The Halls of Montezuma*, 1951; *U.S.S. Teakettle*, 1951; *Appointment with Danger*, 1951; *Dragnet*, 1954; *Pete Kelly's Blues*, 1955; *The D.I.*, 1957; *30*, 1959; *The Last Time I Saw Archie*, 1961.

*   *   *

Jack Webb is best known for his television and film productions, particularly for *Dragnet* and *Pete Kelly's Blues*, but avid readers of crime fiction know him as the author of the Sammy Golden police novels. Golden is a homicide detective with the Los Angeles Police Department whose investigations bring him into cooperation with Father Joseph Shanley, a young priest whose church is in a poor Hispanic neighborhood. The resulting ethnic mix provides the series with a sensitivity to ethnic relationships and religious topicality that were unusual in the 1950's and early 1960's. The prose, however, sometimes runs to moralisms, the relationships among characters are not always convincing, and Webb must often strain credulity to allow his detective enough freedom for adventurous plots.

In *The Naked Angel* Golden finds himself pursued by his own department when he is framed by a murderer who runs a drugs and blackmail operation behind the façade of his used-car lot in Los Angeles. Father Shanley, who keeps a Father Brown next to his St. Augustine and teaches boxing to neighborhood youths, is kidnapped by the murderer and then captures him. In *The Damned Lovely* the two pursue the killer of a rabbi into a nearby oil town, where they expose corrupt police and capture the killer. Webb's non-fiction *The Badge* is a sympathetic portrayal of the workings of the Los Angeles Police Department, the source for much of his material.

—Larry N. Landrum

WEBB, Richard Wilson.   See **QUENTIN, Patrick.**

WEBSTER, Noah. See **KNOX, Bill.**

WELCOME, John. Pseudonym for John Needham Huggard Brennan. Irish. Born in Wexford, 22 June 1914. Educated at Sedbergh School, Yorkshire; Exeter College, B.A. in law 1936. Served in the Royal Artillery, 1940–42: Captain. Married Stella Peart in 1944; four daughters. Since 1945, Principal, Huggard and Brennan, solicitors, Wexford. Senior Steward, Irish National Steeplechase Committee, 1970. Agent: John Johnson, 45–47 Clerkenwell Green, London EC1R 0HT, England.

CRIME PUBLICATIONS

Novels (series character: Richard Graham in all books except *Stop at Nothing* and *Beware of Midnight*)

> *Run for Cover.* London, Faber, 1958; New York, Knopf, 1959.
> *Stop at Nothing.* London, Faber, 1959; New York, Knopf, 1960.
> *Beware of Midnight.* London, Faber, and New York, Knopf, 1961.
> *Hard to Handle.* London, Faber, 1964.
> *Wanted for Killing.* London, Faber, 1965; New York, Holt Rinehart, 1967.
> *Hell Is Where You Find It.* London, Faber, 1968.
> *On the Stretch.* London, Faber, 1969.
> *Go for Broke.* London, Faber, and New York, Walker, 1972.

OTHER PUBLICATIONS

Novels

> *Red Coats Galloping.* London, Constable, 1949.
> *Mr. Merston's Money.* London, Constable, 1951.
> *Mr. Merston's Hounds.* London, Jenkins, 1953.
> *Grand National.* London, Hamish Hamilton, 1976.
> *Bellary Bay.* London, Hamish Hamilton, and New York, Atheneum, 1979.

Other

> *The Cheltenham Gold Cup: The Story of a Great Steeplechase.* London, Constable, 1957; revised edition, London, Pelham, 1973.
> *Cheating at Cards: The Cases in Court.* London, Faber, 1963; as *Great Scandals of Cheating at Cards: Famous Court Cases*, New York, Horizon Press, 1964.
> *Fred Archer: His Life and Times.* London, Faber, 1967.
> *Neck or Nothing: The Extraordinary Life and Times of Bob Sievier.* London, Faber, 1970.
> *The Sporting Empress: The Story of Elizabeth of Austria and Bay Middleton.* London, Joseph, 1975.
> *A Light-Hearted Guide to British Racing.* London, Macdonald and Jane's, 1975.

> Editor, with V. R. Orchard, *Best Hunting Stories.* London, Faber, 1954.
> Editor, *Best Motoring Stories.* London, Faber, 1959.

Editor, *Best Secret Service Stories 1–2*.   London, Faber, 2 vols., 1960–65.
Editor, *Best Gambling Stories*.   London, Faber, 1961.
Editor, *Best Legal Stories 1–2*.   London, Faber, 2 vols., 1962–70.
Editor, *Best Crime Stories 1–3*.   London, Faber, 3 vols., 1964–68.
Editor, with Dick Francis, *Best Racing and Chasing Stories 1–2*.   London, Faber, 2 vols., 1966–69.
Editor, *Best Smuggling Stories*.   London, Faber, 1967.
Editor, *Best Spy Stories*.   London, Faber, 1967.
Editor, with Dick Francis, *The Racing Man's Bedside Book*.   London, Faber, 1969.
Editor, *Ten of the Best: Selected Short Stories*.   London, Faber, 1969.
Editor, *The Welcome Collection: Fourteen Racing Stories*.   London, Joseph, 1972.

*   *   *

John Welcome is important for his work in two different fields, as thriller-novelist and as anthology editor. His eight crime novels are pure-and-simple adventure-thrillers; they are briskly written and have a quick pace and a lighthearted narrative style. All except two feature the ex-amateur rider and sometime secret agent Richard Graham. Welcome always sets his thrillers in interesting locales, such as the Cote d'Azur, Provence, Corsica, or Corfu. His characters always belong to the devil-may-care smart sporting set – "the best people" – pursuing one another at breakneck speed in fast Bentley and Ferrari cars, gambling on fast horses, and dallying with fast women under the blue velvet night skies of the Mediterranean. Some of his anthologies cover the pastimes favoured by his fictional heroes.

—Herbert Harris

WELLS, Carolyn.   Also wrote as Rowland Wright.   American.   Born in Rahway, New Jersey, 18 June 1869. Educated in public schools and privately. Married Hadwin Houghton in 1918 (died, 1919). Deaf from the age of six. Librarian; then free-lance writer. Lived in New York City after 1919. *Died 26 March 1942.*

CRIME PUBLICATIONS

Novels (series characters: Kenneth Carlisle; Alan Ford; Lorimer Lane; Fleming Stone; Pennington Wise)

The Clue (Stone).   Philadelphia, Lippincott, 1909; London, Hodder and Stoughton, 1920.
The Gold Bag (Stone).   Philadelphia, Lippincott, 1911; London, Hodder and Stoughton, 1922.
A Chain of Evidence (Stone).   Philadelphia, Lippincott, 1912.
The Maxwell Mystery (Stone).   Philadelphia, Lippincott, 1913.
Anybody But Anne (Stone).   Philadelphia, Lippincott, 1914; London, Thompson, 1929.
The White Alley (Stone).   Philadelphia, Lippincott, 1915; London, Hodder and Stoughton, 1920.
The Bride of a Moment (Ford).   New York, Doran, 1916; London, Hodder and Stoughton, 1920.
The Curved Blades (Stone).   Philadelphia, Lippincott, 1916.

CRIME AND MYSTERY WRITERS

WELLS

Faulkner's Folly (Ford). New York, Doran, 1917.

The Mark of Cain (Stone). Philadelphia, Lippincott, 1917; London, Hodder and Stoughton, 1920.

The Room with the Tassels (Ford). New York, Doran, 1918.

Vicky Van (Stone). Philadelphia, Lippincott, 1918; London, Hodder and Stoughton, 1920; as *The Elusive Vicky Van*, London, Mellifont Press, 1934.

The Diamond Pin (Stone). Philadelphia, Lippincott, 1919.

The Man Who Fell Through the Earth (Wise). New York, Doran, 1919; London, Harrap, 1924.

In the Onyx Lobby (Wise). New York, Doran, and London, Hodder and Stoughton, 1920.

The Disappearance of Kimball Webb (as Rowland Wright). New York, Dodd Mead, 1920.

Raspberry Jam (Stone). Philadelphia, Lippincott, 1920.

The Come Back (Wise). New York, Doran, and London, Hodder and Stoughton, 1921.

The Luminous Face (Wise). New York, Doran, 1921.

The Mystery of the Sycamore (Stone). Philadelphia, Lippincott, 1921.

The Mystery Girl (Stone). Philadelphia, Lippincott, 1922.

The Vanishing of Betty Varian (Wise). New York, Doran, 1922; London, Collins, 1924.

The Affair at Flower Acres (Wise). New York, Doran, 1923.

Feathers Left Around (Stone). Philadelphia, Lippincott, 1923.

More Lives Than One (Lane). New York, Boni, 1923; London, Hutchinson, 1924.

Spooky Hollow (Stone). Philadelphia, Lippincott, 1923.

Wheels Within Wheels (Wise). New York, Doran, 1923.

The Fourteenth Key (Lane). New York, Putnam, 1924.

The Furthest Fury (Stone). Philadelphia, Lippincott, 1924.

The Moss Mystery. New York, Garden City Publishing Company, 1924.

Prillilgirl (Stone). Philadelphia, Lippincott, 1924.

Anything But the Truth (Stone). Philadelphia, Lippincott, 1925.

The Daughter of the House (Stone). Philadelphia, Lippincott, 1925.

Face Cards. New York, Putnam, 1925.

The Bronze Hand (Stone). Philadelphia, Lippincott, 1926.

The Red-Haired Girl (Stone). Philadelphia, Lippincott, 1926.

The Vanity Case. New York, Putnam, 1926.

All at Sea (Stone). Philadelphia, Lippincott, 1927; London, Thompson, 1929.

The Sixth Commandment. New York, Doran, 1927.

Where's Emily? (Stone). Philadelphia, Lippincott, 1927.

The Crime in the Crypt (Stone). Philadelphia, Lippincott, 1928.

Deep-Lake Mystery. New York, Doubleday, 1928.

The Tannahill Tangle (Stone). Philadelphia, Lippincott, 1928.

Sleeping Dogs (Carlisle). New York, Doubleday, 1929.

The Tapestry Room Murder (Stone). Philadelphia, Lippincott, 1929.

Triple Murder (Stone). Philadelphia, Lippincott, 1929.

The Doomed Five (Stone). Philadelphia, Lippincott, 1930.

The Doorstep Murders (Carlisle). New York, Doubleday, 1930.

The Ghosts' High Noon (Stone). Philadelphia, Lippincott, 1930.

Horror House (Stone). Philadelphia, Lippincott, 1931.

The Skeleton at the Feast (Carlisle). New York, Doubleday, 1931.

The Umbrella Murder (Stone). Philadelphia, Lippincott, 1931.

Fuller's Earth (Stone). Philadelphia, Lippincott, 1932.

The Roll-Top Desk Mystery (Stone). Philadelphia, Lippincott, 1932.

The Broken O (Stone). Philadelphia, Lippincott, 1933.

The Clue of the Eyelash (Stone). Philadelphia, Lippincott, and London, Laurie, 1933.

The Master Murderer (Stone). Philadelphia, Lippincott, 1933.

Eyes in the Wall (Stone).   Philadelphia, Lippincott, 1934.
In the Tiger's Cage (Stone).   Philadelphia, Lippincott, 1934.
The Visiting Villain (Stone).   Philadelphia, Lippincott, 1934.
The Beautiful Derelict (Stone).   Philadelphia, Lippincott, 1935.
For Goodness' Sake (Stone).   Philadelphia, Lippincott, 1935.
The Wooden Indian (Stone).   Philadelphia, Lippincott, 1935.
The Huddle (Stone).   Philadelphia, Lippincott, 1936.
Money Musk (Stone).   Philadelphia, Lippincott, 1936.
Murder in the Bookshop (Stone).   Philadelphia, Lippincott, 1936.
The Mystery of the Tarn (Stone).   Philadelphia, Lippincott, 1937.
The Radio Studio Murder (Stone).   Philadelphia, Lippincott, 1937.
Gilt-Edged Guilt (Stone).   Philadelphia, Lippincott, 1938.
The Killer (Stone).   Philadelphia, Lippincott, 1938.
The Missing Link (Stone).   Philadelphia, Lippincott, 1938.
Calling All Suspects (Stone).   Philadelphia, Lippincott, 1939.
Crime Tears On (Stone).   Philadelphia, Lippincott, 1939.
The Importance of Being Murdered (Stone).   Philadelphia, Lippincott, 1939.
Crime Incarnate (Stone).   Philadelphia, Lippincott, 1940.
Devil's Work (Stone).   Philadelphia, Lippincott, 1940.
Murder on Parade (Stone).   Philadelphia, Lippincott, 1940.
Murder Plus (Stone).   Philadelphia, Lippincott, 1940.
The Black Night Murders (Stone).   Philadelphia, Lippincott, 1941.
Murder at the Casino (Stone).   Philadelphia, Lippincott, 1941.
Murder Will In (Ford).   Philadelphia, Lippincott, 1942.
Who Killed Caldwell? (Stone).   Philadelphia, Lippincott, 1942.

Uncollected Short Stories

"Christabel's Crystal," in *The World's Best One Hundred Detective Stories*, edited by Eugene Thwing.   New York, Funk and Wagnalls, 10 vols., 1929.
"A Point of Testimony," in *Ellery Queen's Mystery Magazine* (New York), November 1942.
"The Adventure of the Clothes Line," in *The Misadventures of Sherlock Holmes*, edited by Ellery Queen.   Boston, Little Brown, 1944.
"The Shakespeare Title-Page Mystery," in *Ellery Queen's Mystery Magazine* (New York), September 1951.

OTHER PUBLICATIONS

Novels

Abeniki Caldwell.   New York, Russell, 1902.
The Gordon Elopement, with Harry Persons Taber.   New York, Doubleday, 1904.
Ptomaine Street: A Tale of Warble Petticoat.   Philadelphia, Lippincott, 1921.

Plays

Maid of Athens, adaptation of the operetta by Victor Leon, music by Franz Lehár (produced New York, 1914).
Jolly Plays for Holidays.   Boston, Baker, 1914.
The Meaning of Thanksgiving.   Philadelphia, Penn, 1922.
Queen Christmas.   Philadelphia, Penn, 1922.
The Sweet Girl Graduate.   Philadelphia, Penn, 1922.

Verse

Children of Our Town.   New York, Russell, 1902.
Folly for the Wise.   Indianapolis, Bobbs Merrill, 1904.
Rubáiyát of a Motor Car.   New York, Dodd Mead, 1906.
The Rubáiyát of a Bridge.   New York, Harper, 1909.
The Seven Ages of Childhood.   New York, Moffat Yard, 1909.

Other

The Story of Betty (juvenile).   New York, Century, 1899.
The Jingle Book.   New York, Macmillan, 1899.
Idle Idylls.   New York, Dodd Mead, 1900.
Folly in Fairyland.   Philadelphia, Altemus, and London, Kelly, 1901.
The Merry-Go-Round (juvenile).   New York, Russell, 1901.
Mother Goose's Menagerie (juvenile).   Boston, Noyes Platt, 1901.
Patty Fairfield (juvenile).   New York, Dodd Mead, 1901.
The Pete and Polly Stories (juvenile).   Chicago, McClurg, 1902.
A Phenomenal Fauna.   New York, Russell, 1902.
Eight Girls and a Dog (juvenile).   New York, Century, 1902.
Folly in the Forest.   Philadelphia, Altemus, 1902.
Trotty's Trip.   Philadelphia, Biddle, 1902.
The Bumblepuppy Book.   London, Isbister, 1903.
Patty at Home (juvenile).   New York, Dodd Mead, 1904.
In the Reign of Queen Dick (juvenile).   New York, Appleton, 1904.
The Staying Guests (juvenile).   New York, Century, 1904.
The Dorrance Domain (juvenile).   Boston, Wilde, 1905.
The Matrimonial Bureau, with Harry Persons Taber.   Boston, Houghton Mifflin, and
    London, Nash, 1905.
Patty in the City (juvenile).   New York, Dodd Mead, 1905.
At the Sign of the Sphinx.   New York, Duffield, 1906.
Dorrance Doings (juvenile).   Boston, Wilde, 1906.
The Emily Emmins Papers.   New York, Putnam, 1907.
Fluffy Ruffles (juvenile).   New York, Appleton, 1907.
Marjorie's Vacation (juvenile).   New York, Dodd Mead, 1907.
Rainy Day Diversions.   New York, Moffat Yard, 1907.
Patty in Paris (juvenile).   New York, Dodd Mead, 1907.
Patty's Friends (juvenile).   New York, Dodd Mead, 1908.
Patty's Summer Days (juvenile).   New York, Dodd Mead, 1908.
The Carolyn Wells Year Book of Old Favorites and New Fancies for 1909.   New York,
    Holt, 1908.
The Happy Chaps.   New York, Century, 1908.
Marjorie's Busy Days (juvenile).   New York, Dodd Mead, 1908.
Dick and Dolly (juvenile).   New York, Dodd Mead, 1909.
Marjorie's New Friend (juvenile).   New York, Dodd Mead, 1909.
Patty's Pleasure Trip (juvenile).   New York, Dodd Mead, 1909.
Pleasant Day Diversions.   New York, Moffat Yard, 1909.
Betty's Happy Year (juvenile).   New York, Century, 1910.
Dick and Dolly's Adventures (juvenile).   New York, Dodd Mead, 1910.
Marjorie in Command (juvenile).   New York, Dodd Mead, 1910.
Patty's Success (juvenile).   New York, Dodd Mead, 1910.
Marjorie's Maytime (juvenile).   New York, Dodd Mead, 1911.
Patty's Motor Car (juvenile).   New York, Dodd Mead, 1911.
Patty's Butterfly Days (juvenile).   New York, Dodd Mead, 1912.
The Lover's Baedeker and Guide to Arcady.   New York, Stokes, 1912.

Marjorie at Seacote (juvenile).   New York, Dodd Mead, 1912.

Christmas Carollin'.   New York, Bigelow, 1913.

The Eternal Feminine.   New York, Bigelow, 1913.

Girls and Gayety.   New York, Bigelow, 1913.

The Technique of the Mystery Story.   Springfield, Massachusetts, Home Correspondence School, 1913; revised edition, 1929.

Patty's Social Season (juvenile).   New York, Dodd Mead, 1913.

Pleasing Prose.   New York, Bigelow, 1913.

The Re-Echo Club.   New York, Bigelow, 1913.

Patty's Suitors (juvenile).   New York, Dodd Mead, 1914.

Two Little Women (juvenile).   New York, Dodd Mead, 1915.

Patty's Romance (juvenile).   New York, Dodd Mead, 1915.

Patty's Fortune (juvenile).   New York, Dodd Mead, 1916.

Two Little Women and Treasure House (juvenile).   New York, Dodd Mead, 1916.

Two Little Women on a Holiday (juvenile).   New York, Dodd Mead, 1917.

Baubles.   New York, Dodd Mead, 1917.

Doris of Dobbs Ferry (juvenile).   New York, Doran, 1917.

Patty Blossom (juvenile).   New York, Dodd Mead, 1917.

Patty-Bride (juvenile).   New York, Dodd Mead, 1918.

Patty and Azalea (juvenile).   New York, Dodd Mead, 1919.

A Concise Bibliography of the Works of Walt Whitman.   Boston, Houghton Mifflin, 1922.

Cross Word Puzzle Book.   New York, Putnam, 1924.

Book of American Limericks.   New York, Putnam, 1925.

A Book of Charades.   New York, Doran, 1927.

All for Fun: Brain Teasers.   New York, Day, 1933.

The Rest of My Life.   Philadelphia, Lippincott, 1937.

Editor, *A Nonsense* [*Parody, Satire, Whimsey, Vers de Société*] *Anthology.*   New York, Scribner, 5 vols., 1902–07.

Editor, *Such Nonsense.*   New York, Doran, 1918.

Editor, *The Book of Humorous Verse.*   New York, Doran, 1920; revised edition, 1936.

Editor, *An Outline of Humor.*   New York, Putnam, 1923.

Editor, *Ask Me a Question.*   Philadelphia, Winston, 1927.

Editor, *The World's Best Humor.*   New York, Boni, 1933.

Editor, *The Cat in Verse.*   Boston, Little Brown, 1935.

Editor, *American Detective Stories.*   New York, Oxford University Press, 1927.

Editor, *Best American Mystery Stories of the Year, Volume One* [and *Two*].   New York, Day, 2 vols., 1931–32.

*   *   *

Of Carolyn Wells it must be very nearly true to say that she never had an unpublished thought. An accomplished parodist, an indefatigable anthologist, a bibliographer and collector of Whitman, the author of a number of "society" novels of the Edwardian period, and the author of the first important critical work on detective fiction, she found time at last even to write her autobiography.

Her detective novels, inevitably, since she produced three or four a year from about 1915 to 1940, are written to a formula: the characters are brought before us, the conflicts suggested and the suspicions cast; the crime, invariably murder, and usually only one, is committed; the police and the amateurs are baffled; some five chapters before the end the professional detective is summoned, often by the chief suspect, often by a personal friend of the detective, for he is quite *persona grata* in the upper-class circles in which the novel almost always takes place; the detective explicates the case, with all in attendance, and the criminal often confirms his guilt with his suicide; the juvenile leads (one of them often a prime suspect), whose love has been secondary to the murder story, come together.

While Wells's grasp of plot construction is considerable, her gift for characterization is not, and even her detectives are personally unmemorable, partly because their late arrival gives us little opportunity to see their ratiocinative methods at work. Four of her detectives are worth special mention. Lorimer Lane, whose shrewdness is not evident in his bland, middle-aged reserve, may be seen to best advantage in *The Fourteenth Key*. Pennington (Penny) Wise and his rather bizarre young female assistant Zizi, who is generally shrewder than he, are best seen in *The Luminous Face*. Kenneth Carlisle, a movie actor turned detective, uses his acting ability for easier entrapment of criminals, best seen in *The Doorstep Murders* or *The Skeleton at the Feast*. By far the most prominent, Fleming Stone, "the great man," appeared first in a short story in 1906, and stayed with her to the end. But even Stone lacks character; it is often easier, in retrospect, to recall the plot of one of Wells's novels than to place the right detective in it. Two novels, however, in which Stone appears early enough for us to see something of his methods are *The Broken O* and *The Wooden Indian*.

In her 80 novels Wells uses a variety of backgrounds – the world of the theatre (*Prillilgirl*), the world of politics (*The Mystery of the Sycamore*), the academic world (*The Mystery Girl*) – yet none of these novels widens our understanding of these worlds. Her range of murder method is not wide: stabbing and shooting account for most of the deaths. She returned several times (*Raspberry Jam*, *Face Cards*, *The Daughter of the House*) to the locked room as the scene for her murder, and at least once (*The Tannahill Tangle*) set a double murder behind locked doors.

The device that Wells used most often is the change of identity. Substitutions spin the plot of *The Daughter of the House* and *The Fourteenth Key*. Two of her novels turn on the murderer's having a twin or double to provide him with an alibi. The theme is rather egregiously used in *Vicky Van*, in which the central character leads two different existences in adjoining houses. Wells does not probe the theme of identity change for psychological penetration, but neither does she ever fall back on the supernatural as explanation.

Carolyn Wells's novels make very entertaining reading, but they do not notably enlighten. *The Technique of the Mystery Story* deserves some homage as the first in its field, but its principal interest now is in its cataloguing of contemporary mystery writers, and its codification of rules for writing in the genre.

—Barrie Hayne

WELLS, Tobias.   See FORBES, Stanton.

WENTWORTH, Patricia.   Pseudonym for Dora Amy Elles. British.   Born in Mussoorie, India, in 1878. Educated privately and at Blackheath High School, London. Married 1) George Dillon (died, 1906), three stepsons; 2) George Oliver Turnbull in 1920, one daughter. Lived in Surrey after 1920. *Died 28 January 1961.*

CRIME PUBLICATIONS

Novels (series characters: Inspector Lamb; Maud Silver)

The Astonishing Adventure of Jane Smith. London, Melrose, and Boston, Small
   Maynard, 1923.
The Red Lacquer Case. London, Melrose, 1924; Boston, Small Maynard, 1925.
The Annam Jewel. London, Melrose, 1924; Boston, Small Maynard, 1925.
The Black Cabinet. London, Hodder and Stoughton, 1925; Boston, Small Maynard,
   1926.
The Dower House Mystery. London, Hodder and Stoughton, 1925; Boston, Small
   Maynard, 1926.
The Amazing Chance. London, Hodder and Stoughton, 1926; Philadelphia,
   Lippincott, 1927.
Anne Belinda. London, Hodder and Stoughton, 1927; Philadelphia, Lippincott, 1928.
Hue and Cry. London, Hodder and Stoughton, and Philadelphia, Lippincott, 1927.
Grey Mask (Silver). London, Hodder and Stoughton, 1928; Philadelphia, Lippincott,
   1929.
Will-o'-the-Wisp. London, Hodder and Stoughton, and Philadelphia, Lippincott,
   1928.
Fool Errant. London, Hodder and Stoughton, and Philadelphia, Lippincott, 1929.
Beggar's Choice. London, Hodder and Stoughton, 1930; Philadelphia, Lippincott,
   1931.
The Coldstone. London, Hodder and Stoughton, and Philadelphia, Lippincott, 1930.
Kingdom Lost. Philadelphia, Lippincott, 1930; London, Hodder and Stoughton, 1931.
Danger Calling. London, Hodder and Stoughton, and Philadelphia, Lippincott, 1931.
Nothing Venture. London, Cassell, and Philadelphia, Lippincott, 1932.
Red Danger. London, Cassell, 1932; as *Red Shadow*, Philadelphia, Lippincott, 1932.
Seven Green Stones. London, Cassell, 1933; as *Outrageous Fortune*, Philadelphia,
   Lippincott, 1933.
Walk with Care. London, Cassell, and Philadelphia, Lippincott, 1933.
Fear by Night. London, Hodder and Stoughton, and Philadelphia, Lippincott, 1934.
Devil-in-the-Dark. London, Hodder and Stoughton, 1934; as *Touch and Go*,
   Philadelphia, Lippincott, 1934.
Blindfold. London, Hodder and Stoughton, and Philadelphia, Lippincott, 1935.
Red Stefan. London, Hodder and Stoughton, and Philadelphia, Lippincott, 1935.
Hole and Corner. London, Hodder and Stoughton, and Philadelphia, Lippincott, 1936.
Dead or Alive. London, Hodder and Stoughton, and Philadelphia, Lippincott, 1936.
The Case Is Closed (Silver). London, Hodder and Stoughton, and Philadelphia,
   Lippincott, 1937.
Down Under. London, Hodder and Stoughton, and Philadelphia, Lippincott, 1937.
Mr. Zero. London, Hodder and Stoughton, and Philadelphia, Lippincott, 1938.
Run! London, Hodder and Stoughton, and Philadelphia, Lippincott, 1938.
The Blind Side. London, Hodder and Stoughton, and Philadelphia, Lippincott, 1939.
Lonesome Road (Silver). London, Hodder and Stoughton, and Philadelphia,
   Lippincott, 1939.
Who Pays the Piper? (Silver). London, Hodder and Stoughton, 1940; as *Account
   Rendered*, Philadelphia, Lippincott, 1940.
Rolling Stone. London, Hodder and Stoughton, and Philadelphia, Lippincott, 1940.
Unlawful Occasions. London, Hodder and Stoughton, 1941; as *Weekend with Death*,
   Philadelphia, Lippincott, 1941.
In the Balance (Silver). Philadelphia, Lippincott, 1941; as *Danger Point*, London,
   Hodder and Stoughton, 1942.
Pursuit of a Parcel. London, Hodder and Stoughton, and Philadelphia, Lippincott,
   1942.

The Chinese Shawl (Silver). London, Hodder and Stoughton, and Philadelphia, Lippincott, 1943.

Miss Silver Deals with Death. Philadelphia, Lippincott, 1943; as *Miss Silver Intervenes*, London, Hodder and Stoughton, 1944.

The Key (Silver). Philadelphia, Lippincott, 1944; London, Hodder and Stoughton, 1946.

The Clock Strikes Twelve (Silver). Philadelphia, Lippincott, 1944; London, Hodder and Stoughton, 1945.

She Came Back (Silver). Philadelphia, Lippincott, 1945; as *The Traveller Returns*, London, Hodder and Stoughton, 1948.

Silence in Court. Philadelphia, Lippincott, 1945; London, Hodder and Stoughton, 1947.

Pilgrim's Rest (Silver). Philadelphia, Lippincott, 1946; London, Hodder and Stoughton, 1948; as *Dark Threat*, New York, Popular Library, 1951.

Latter End (Silver). Philadelphia, Lippincott, 1947; London, Hodder and Stoughton, 1949.

Wicked Uncle (Silver). Philadelphia, Lippincott, 1947; as *Spotlight*, London, Hodder and Stoughton, 1949.

The Case of William Smith (Silver). Philadelphia, Lippincott, 1948; London, Hodder and Stoughton, 1950.

Eternity Ring (Silver). Philadelphia, Lippincott, 1948; London, Hodder and Stoughton, 1950.

Miss Silver Comes to Stay. Philadelphia, Lippincott, 1949; London, Hodder and Stoughton, 1951.

The Catherine Wheel (Silver). Philadelphia, Lippincott, 1949; London, Hodder and Stoughton, 1951.

The Brading Collection (Silver). Philadelphia, Lippincott, 1950; London, Hodder and Stoughton, 1952.

Through the Wall (Silver). Philadelphia, Lippincott, 1950; London, Hodder and Stoughton, 1952.

Anna, Where Are You? (Silver). Philadelphia, Lippincott, 1951; London, Hodder and Stoughton, 1953; as *Death at Deep End*, New York, Pyramid, 1963.

The Ivory Dagger (Silver). Philadelphia, Lippincott, 1951; London, Hodder and Stoughton, 1953.

The Watersplash (Silver). Philadelphia, Lippincott, 1951; London, Hodder and Stoughton, 1954.

Ladies' Bane (Silver). Philadelphia, Lippincott, 1952; London, Hodder and Stoughton, 1954.

Vanishing Point (Silver). Philadelphia, Lippincott, 1953; London, Hodder and Stoughton, 1955.

Out of the Past (Silver). Philadelphia, Lippincott, 1953; London, Hodder and Stoughton, 1955.

The Benevent Treasure (Silver). Philadelphia, Lippincott, 1954; London, Hodder and Stoughton, 1956.

The Silent Pool (Silver). Philadelphia, Lippincott, 1954; London, Hodder and Stoughton, 1956.

Poison in the Pen (Silver). Philadelphia, Lippincott, 1955; London, Hodder and Stoughton, 1957.

The Listening Eye (Silver). Philadelphia, Lippincott, 1955; London, Hodder and Stoughton, 1957.

The Gazebo (Silver). Philadelphia, Lippincott, 1956; London, Hodder and Stoughton, 1958; as *The Summerhouse*, New York, Pyramid, 1967.

The Fingerprint (Silver). Philadelphia, Lippincott, 1956; London, Hodder and Stoughton, 1959.

The Alington Inheritance (Silver). Philadelphia, Lippincott, 1958; London, Hodder and Stoughton, 1960.

The Girl in the Cellar (Silver). London, Hodder and Stoughton, 1961.

OTHER PUBLICATIONS

Novels

A Marriage under the Terror. London, Melrose, and New York, Putnam, 1910.
A Little More Than Kin. London, Melrose, 1911; as *More Than Kin*, New York, Putnam, 1911.
The Devil's Wind. London, Melrose, 1912.
The Fire Within. London, Melrose, 1913.
Simon Heriot. London, Melrose, 1914.
Queen Anne Is Dead. London, Melrose, 1915.

Verse

A Child's Rhyme Book. London, Melrose, 1910.
Beneath the Hunter's Moon: Poems. London, Hodder and Stoughton, 1945.
The Pool of Dreams: Poems. London, Hodder and Stoughton, 1953; Philadelphia, Lippincott, 1954.

Other

Earl or Chieftain? The Romance of Hugh O'Neill. Dublin, Catholic Truth Society of Ireland, 1919.

*   *   *

Although non-series mystery novels and a sequence of detective novels featuring the questionable competence of Inspector Lamb are included among Patricia Wentworth's dozens of contributions to the genre, she is best known for her enduring creation Miss Maud Silver whose career at a private detective agency after her retirement from the schoolroom spans 30 years.

Although Miss Silver is often compared with Christie's Miss Jane Marple, there is a major difference between the two. Unlike Miss Marple whose knowledge of her village is unparalleled and whose understanding of human nature is keen but whose status is always amateur, Miss Silver is a professional detective. She uses her drawing room as an office, having furnished it with a sensible desk; she undertakes cases for both friends and strangers; she is efficient and workmanlike in her investigations; most significantly she is paid for her work. Generally Miss Silver's clients are recommended by friends whom she has assisted in the past; her acquaintances seem to populate most of the English countryside and almost every book mentions previous cases she has solved. Even Miss Silver's relationship with the police is socially rather than professionally based; Frank Abbott is both friend, and, perhaps, surrogate nephew. Miss Silver's professional appearance is undercut by two features: her clothing and her knitting. In *The Gazebo* her dress is described as one forced upon undemanding elderly ladies by aggressive saleswomen; her spinster's hats – black felt in winter and black straw in summer – are noted in most volumes. The small, delicately colored children's garments which Miss Silver is usually knitting serve to diminish her professional threat and seem to suggest domestic comfort and safety to frightened clients or old-maid foolishness to unperceptive suspects.

Despite appearances, this detective carefully investigates background facts, interviews witnesses, tails questionable suspects, sidesteps the law to enter a locked house. She uncovers the truth and saves the innocent before the police have solved the case. Her clients are usually doubly innocent: first, they have not committed any crime or, usually, even any social solecism; second, they are quite young, often in love, and through naivety leave their actions open to misinterpretation by the cynical or the official. Always, they are from nice families, and Miss Silver's investigation both demonstrates their innocence of the crime and ensures that they continue to be regarded as ladies or gentlemen.

While Lewis Brading's security precautions for his jewel collection are unusual, other elements of *The Brading Collection*, a typical Silver story, conform to traditional demands. Greed and sexual attraction motivate several obvious suspects; love and suspicion vibrate between the young couple; past mistakes haunt the falsely accused. Miss Silver's detection, always undertaken to discover the truth and protect the innocent rather than to save a client, is juxtaposed with her moral lectures and Tennyson quotations. As expected, the good are rewarded with marriage and financial security; the wicked are punished with death – here, murder and suicide.

Wentworth's plotting is straightforward and classical; no accusation of bad faith can be leveled at her. The writing is clear-cut and competent; the details are reasonable. It is true that the novels are not of equal value, and after 40 cases Miss Silver's appeal wanes; however, the best of them, like *The Fingerprint*, *Grey Mask*, *The Brading Collection*, and *Poison in the Pen*, are dependable and engaging tales of detection.

—Kathleen G. Klein

WESTLAKE, Donald E(dwin). Also writes as Curt Clark; Tucker Coe; Timothy J. Culver; Richard Stark. American. Born in New York City, 12 July 1933. Served in the United States Air Force, 1954–56. Married 1) Nedra Henderson in 1957; 2) Sandra Kalb in 1967; four sons. Recipient: Mystery Writers of America Edgar Allan Poe Award, 1967. Agent: Paul R. Reynolds, Inc., 12 East 41st Street, New York, New York 10017, U.S.A.

Crime Publications

Novels (series characters: Dortmunder and others)

> *The Mercenaries.* New York, Random House, 1960; London, Boardman, 1961; as *The Smashers*, New York, Dell, 1962.
> *Killing Time.* New York, Random House, 1961; London, Boardman, 1962; as *The Operator*, New York, Dell, 1964.
> *361.* New York, Random House, and London, Boardman, 1962.
> *Killy.* New York, Random House, 1963; London, Boardman, 1964.
> *Pity Him Afterwards.* New York, Random House, 1964; London, Boardman, 1965.
> *The Fugitive Pigeon.* New York, Random House, 1965; London, Boardman, 1966.
> *The Busy Body.* New York, Random House, and London, Boardman, 1966.
> *The Spy in the Ointment.* New York, Random House, 1966; London, Beardman, 1967.
> *God Save the Mark.* New York, Random House, 1967; London, Joseph, 1968.
> *Who Stole Sassi Manoon?* New York, Random House, 1969; London, Hodder and Stoughton, 1971.
> *Somebody Owes Me Money.* New York, Random House, 1969; London, Hodder and Stoughton, 1970.
> *Up Your Banners.* New York, Macmillan, 1969; London, Hodder and Stoughton, 1971.
> *The Hot Rock* (Dortmunder). New York, Simon and Schuster, 1970; London, Hodder and Stoughton, 1971.

Adios, Scheherazade. New York, Simon and Schuster, 1970; London, Hodder and Stoughton, 1971.

Ex Officio (as Timothy J. Culver). New York, Evans, 1970.

I Gave at the Office. New York, Simon and Schuster, 1971; London, Hodder and Stoughton, 1972.

Bank Shot (Dortmunder). New York, Simon and Schuster, and London, Hodder and Stoughton, 1972.

Cops and Robbers. New York, Evans, and London, Hodder and Stoughton, 1972.

Help I Am Being Held Prisoner. New York, Evans, 1974; London, Hodder and Stoughton, 1975.

Jimmy the Kid (Dortmunder). New York, Evans, 1974; London, Hodder and Stoughton, 1975.

Two Much! New York, Evans, 1975; London, Hodder and Stoughton, 1976.

Brothers Keepers. New York, Evans, 1975; London, Hodder and Stoughton, 1977.

Dancing Aztecs. New York, Evans, 1976.

Enough. New York, Evans, 1977; London, Hodder and Stoughton, 1980.

Nobody's Perfect. New York, Evans, 1977; London, Hodder and Stoughton, 1978.

A New York Dance. London, Hodder and Stoughton, 1979.

Novels as Richard Stark (series characters: Alan Grofield; Parker)

The Hunter (Parker). New York, Pocket Books, 1962; as *Point Blank*, London, Hodder and Stoughton, 1967.

The Man with the Getaway Face (Parker). New York, Pocket Books, 1963; as *The Steel Hit*, London, Hodder and Stoughton, 1971.

The Outfit (Parker). New York, Pocket Books, 1963; London, Hodder and Stoughton, 1971.

The Mourner (Parker). New York, Pocket Books, 1963; London, Hodder and Stoughton, 1971.

The Score (Parker; Grofield). New York, Pocket Books, 1964; as *Killtown*, London, Hodder and Stoughton, 1971.

The Jugger (Parker). New York, Pocket Books, 1965; London, Hodder and Stoughton, 1971.

The Seventh (Parker). New York, Pocket Books, 1966; as *The Split*, London, Hodder and Stoughton, 1969.

The Handle (Parker; Grofield). New York, Pocket Books, 1966; as *Run Lethal*, London, Hodder and Stoughton, 1972.

The Rare Coin Score (Parker). New York, Fawcett, 1967; London, Hodder and Stoughton, 1968.

The Damsel (Grofield). New York, Macmillan, 1967; London, Hodder and Stoughton, 1968.

The Green Eagle Score (Parker). New York, Fawcett, 1967; London, Hodder and Stoughton, 1968.

The Black Ice Score (Parker). New York, Fawcett, 1968; London, Hodder and Stoughton, 1969.

The Dame (Parker). New York, Macmillan, and London, Hodder and Stoughton, 1969.

The Sour Lemon Score (Parker). New York, Fawcett, and London, Hodder and Stoughton, 1969.

The Blackbird (Grofield). New York, Macmillan, 1969; London, Hodder and Stoughton, 1970.

Deadly Edge (Parker). New York, Random House, 1971; London, Hodder and Stoughton, 1972.

Slayground (Parker). New York, Random House, 1971; London, Hodder and Stoughton, 1973.

Lemons Never Lie (Grofield).   Cleveland, World, 1971.
Plunder Squad (Parker).   New York, Random House, 1972; London, Hodder and Stoughton, 1974.
Butcher's Moon (Parker; Grofield).   New York, Random House, 1974; London, Hodder and Stoughton, 1977.

Novels as Tucker Coe (series character: Mitch Tobin in all books)

Kinds of Love, Kinds of Death.   New York, Random House, 1966; London, Souvenir Press, 1967.
Murder among Children.   New York, Random House, and London, Souvenir Press, 1968.
Wax Apple.   New York, Random House, 1970; London, Gollancz, 1973.
A Jade in Aries.   New York, Random House, 1971; London, Gollancz, 1973.
Don't Lie to Me.   New York, Random House, 1972; London, Gollancz, 1974.

Short Stories

The Curious Facts Preceding My Execution and Other Fictions.   New York, Random House, 1968.

Uncollected Short Stories

"The Ultimate Caper," in *New York Times Magazine*, 11 May 1975.
"Come Back, Come Back," in *Alfred Hitchcock's Tales to Scare You Stiff*, edited by Eleanor Sullivan.   New York, Davis, 1978.
"This Is Death," in *Ellery Queen's Mystery Magazine* (New York), November 1978.
"Mulligan Stew," in *Ellery Queen's Mystery Magazine* (New York), January 1979.

OTHER PUBLICATIONS

Novels

Anarchaos (as Curt Clark).   New York, Ace, 1967.
Gangway, with Brian Garfield.   New York, Evans, 1973.

Play

Screenplay: *Cops and Robbers*, 1972.

Other

Philip (juvenile).   New York, Crowell, 1967.
Under an English Heaven.   New York, Simon and Schuster, and London, Hodder and Stoughton, 1972.
"Hearing Voices in My Head," in *Murder Ink: The Mystery Reader's Companion*, edited by Dilys Winn.   New York, Workman, 1977.

Editor, with William Tenn, *Once Against the Law.*   New York, Macmillan, 1968.

Manuscript Collection: Mugar Memorial Library, Boston University.

Donald E. Westlake comments:
Being prolific is at once both delightful and embarrassing. As I go along from day to day, it

1465

doesn't *seem* to me I'm getting much accomplished, but on those rare occasions (such as the present one) when I tot it all up, there is rather a mess here.

When I began, 20 years ago, I scattered my shots in a variety of directions, only very gradually focusing my fire enough to be recognizably the same person over a span of time – a week, say. As the pseudonyms and the other genres have sloughed off I do seem to have dug myself a very specific niche – or grave – here on the dim moor of mystery fiction. My subject (unless I'm wrong about this) seems to be Bewilderment. Or don't you agree?

*   *   *

If there is a common thread running through most of Donald E. Westlake's extremely varied crime novels, it is that crime is no different from any other business enterprise and the intelligent professional criminal simply a form of the Organization Man. His earliest suspense novels under his own name, like *The Mercenaries*, dealt with the world of organized crime as seen from within, and did so with a rigor and objectivity worthy of Dashiell Hammett, so that Westlake quickly established himself as a master of what Anthony Boucher called "sustained narrative and observation within the framework of a self-consistent world, alien to law and convention."

In 1962 Westlake adopted the pseudonym of Richard Stark and published the first of many original paperback novels about a cold-blooded professional thief known only as Parker. *The Hunter*, in which we first meet Parker as he seeks revenge after being betrayed and left for dead by his ex-associates, was described by Boucher as "a harsh and frightening story of criminal warfare and vengeance ... written with economy, understatement and a deadly amoral objectivity." Several years later the book was freely adapted by director John Boorman into the finest *film noir* of the decade, *Point Blank* (1967), starring Lee Marvin. In the same year Westlake took Alan Grofield, one of the subordinate recurring characters in earlier Parker capers, and made him the protagonist of his own series. Grofield is not a full-time thief but robs banks and other institutions in order to support his less than scintillating career as a stage actor, and his adventures tend to be lighter in tone than Parker's. Westlake enjo s interweaving the exploits of his heist men in unusually striking ways. For instance, the first chapters of Grofield's third solo caper, *The Blackbird*, and of a later Parker book, *Slayground*, describe the same event – an armored car robbery that goes haywire – each from its protagonist's point of view, and the books then tell what happened to their respective characters after the auto smashup that ends the common experiences of the two thieves. Grofield is reunited with Parker in the last, longest and perhaps bloodiest of the Richard Stark novels, *Butcher's Moon*.

Meanwhile, after the first few works in the Hammett tradition, Westlake's novels under his own name, beginning with *The Fugitive Pigeon*, had mutated into wildly humorous farces populated by a succession of indolent young men, each wanting only to "do his own thing" but propelled willy nilly into unlikely dangers and intrigues. Thus is *The Spy in the Ointment* a Greenwich Village pacifist finds himself in a terrorist cell; in *God Save the Mark* the prime sucker for every con game in New York is sucked into a crime puzzle at once funnier and more dangerous than mere bunco; and in *Somebody Owes Me Money* a Runyonesque cabbie is trapped in the middle of a gang war. More recently Westlake has created a group of comic thieves led by the inept Dortmunder and given them a series of capers like the one described in *Bank Shot* in which they steal an entire bank located inside a mobile trailer home. These adventures are the light-hearted inversion of the dead serious crimes described in the Richard Stark novels; indeed in *Jimmy the Kid* the kidnap caper is inspired by the mush-witted thieves' reading of one of those very novels. Westlake's latest few books seem to dispense with the crime element almost completely, but *Two Much!*, in which a good-hearted amateur con man poses as twin brothers in order to marry each of two lovely and fabulously wealthy twin sisters, is as hilarious a comedy of suspense as one will find in the literature.

During the latter half of the 1960's Westlake adopted the pseudonym of Tucker Coe for five novels in the contemporary, disillusioned, minimally violent private-eye tradition of Ross Macdonald. The protagonist is Mitch Tobin, an ex-policeman who had been kicked off the

New York City force in disgrace because of the death of his squad-car partner while Tobin was in bed with a woman. Since then the guilt-wracked Tobin has buried himself in his Queens house, supported both financially and psychologically by his forgiving wife, unable to relate to his teen-age son, incapable of functioning in the outside world. In the first four of the five novels in which he appears, Tobin is interrupted in his self-made task of enclosing his Queens house with a high wall and, in the role of unofficial private investigator, is forced to enter the universe of some hated out-group which has constructed its own walls and which in other ways bears marked resemblances to himself. As he passes through the worlds of the professional criminal, the disaffected young, the mentally ill and the sexually different, he builds up a store of therapeutic experiences from which he slowly comes to realize that he is not unique in his isolation and guilt, and slowly begins to accept himself and return to the real world. The best novel in the series is *Wax Apple*, in which a psychiatrist hires Tobin to pose as an ex-mental patient and find out which resident in a "halfway house" is responsible for a series of vicious pranks. In Tobin's fifth and final case, *Don't Lie to Me*, he has obtained a private detective's license and is no longer obsessed with his wall.

Westlake's two decades in the field have established him as a skillful, prolific writer who is at home in a variety of criminous sub-genres and who adheres to no formula but readability. When the history of contemporary suspense fiction is compiled, he is likely to be recognized as one of its new masters.

—Francis M. Nevins, Jr.

WESTON, Carolyn. American.

Crime Publications

Novels (series characters: Casey Kellogg and Al Krug)

Tormented. New York, Surrey House, 1956.
Face of My Assassin, with Jan Huckins. New York, Random House, 1959.
Danju Gig. New York, Random House, 1969; as *Spy in Black*, London, Hale, 1972.
Poor, Poor Ophelia (Kellogg and Krug). New York, Random House, 1972; London, Gollancz, 1973.
Susannah Screaming (Kellogg and Krug). New York, Random House, 1975; London, Gollancz, 1976.
Rouse the Demon (Kellogg and Krug). New York, Random House, 1976; London, Gollancz, 1977.

*   *   *

After an inauspicious start, Carolyn Weston has had a small but increasingly mature output. Her first work (apart from an early paperback and a collaboration) is a cold war adventure novel, *Danju Gig*. This uninspired piece is strong on inappropriately "hip" dialogue and absurd stereotypes, and is weak on characterization, motivation, and credibility. The lifeless characters and the superficial plot might help an insomniac. Shad Smith, a black entertainer, and his Jewish PR man, Marty Brom, discover a Russian missile silo deep in the heart of Danju. After several assassination attempts, all ends well in a very hurried conclusion.

Weston's next book *Poor, Poor, Ophelia*, is a police procedural novel starring Santa Monica cop Casey Kellogg and his tougher, older partner Al Krug. Though the hip dialogue still abounds, and there is some problem with irrelevant and superfluous detail, this work is noticeably better than Weston's earlier novels. The characterizations, for example, are sharper and more complex; there is a believable contrast set up between the young, college-educated, liberal Kellogg and the older, conservative, irascible Krug. The plot, turning on the murder of Holly Berry and the attempted frame-up of David Farr, flows much more smoothly than *Danju Gig*. This novel became the pilot for the successful tv series, *The Streets of San Francisco*.

Susannah Screaming, the second Kellogg and Krug novel, is both unimaginative and formulaic. The dialogue and the narrative, however, are more natural than in Weston's previous works, there are occasional flashes of humor, and the characterization of Rees the parolee is strong. Weston's latest novel, *Rouse the Demon*, is her best so far. Another Kellogg and Krug story, this taut mystery of the murder of a hypno-therapist has a fast-paced narrative, carefully pruned detail, and at least one memorable character (Adrian Crewes). Interestingly, *Rouse the Demon* is also the *shortest* of the Kellogg and Krug works. Weston is learning.

—Donald J. Pattow

WHEATLEY, Dennis (Yates). British. Born in London, 8 January 1897. Educated at Dulwich College, London, 1908; H.M.S. Worcester, 1909–13; privately in Germany, 1913. Married 1) Nancy Robinson in 1923, one son; 2) Joan Gwendoline Johnstone in 1931. Served in the Royal Field Artillery, City of London Brigade, 1914–17; 36th Ulster Division, 1917–19 (invalided out); recommissioned in Royal Air Force Volunteer Reserve, 1939; Member, National Recruiting Panel, 1940–41; Member, Joint Planning Staff of War Cabinet, 1941–44; Wing Commander, 1944–45: United States Army Bronze Star. Joined his father's wine business, Wheatley and Son, London, 1914; worked in the business, 1919–26; sole owner, 1926–31. Editor, Dennis Wheatley's Library of the Occult, Sphere Books, London, from 1973 (over 40 volumes). Received Livery of Vintners' Company, 1918, and Distillers' Company, 1922. Fellow, Royal Society of Arts, and Royal Society of Literature. *Died 11 November 1977.*

CRIME PUBLICATIONS

Novels (series characters: Roger Brook; Julian Day; Molly Fountain; Duke de Richleau; Gregory Sallust)

The Forbidden Territory (Richleau). London, Hutchinson, and New York, Dutton, 1933.
Such Power Is Dangerous. London, Hutchinson, 1933.
Black August (Sallust). London, Hutchinson, and New York, Dutton, 1934.
The Fabulous Valley. London, Hutchinson, 1934.
The Devil Rides Out (Richleau). London, Hutchinson, 1934.
The Eunuch of Stamboul. London, Hutchinson, and Boston, Little Brown, 1935.

They Found Atlantis. London, Hutchinson, and Philadelphia, Lippincott, 1936.
Murder Off Miami. London, Hutchinson, 1936; as *File on Bolitho Blane*, New York, Morrow, 1936.
Contraband (Sallust). London, Hutchinson, 1936.
The Secret War. London, Hutchinson, 1937.
Who Killed Robert Prentice? London, Hutchinson, 1937; as *File on Robert Prentice*, New York, Greenberg, 1937.
Uncharted Seas. London, Hutchinson, 1938.
The Malinsay Massacre. London, Hutchinson, 1938.
The Golden Spaniard (Richleau). London, Hutchinson, 1938.
The Quest of Julian Day. London, Hutchinson, 1939.
Herewith the Clues! London, Hutchinson, 1939.
Sixty Days to Live. London, Hutchinson, 1939.
The Scarlet Imposter (Sallust). London, Hutchinson, 1940; New York, Macmillan, 1942.
Three Inquisitive People (Richleau). London, Hutchinson, 1940.
Faked Passports (Sallust). London, Hutchinson, 1940; New York, Macmillan, 1943.
The Black Baroness (Sallust). London, Hutchinson, 1940; London, Macmillan, 1942.
Strange Conflict (Richleau). London, Hutchinson, 1941.
The Sword of Fate (Day). London, Hutchinson, 1941; New York, Macmillan, 1944.
"V" for Vengeance (Sallust). London, Hutchinson, and New York, Macmillan, 1942.
The Man Who Missed the War. London, Hutchinson, 1945.
Codeword – Golden Fleece (Richleau). London, Hutchinson, 1946.
Come into My Parlour (Sallust). London, Hutchinson, 1946.
The Launching of Roger Brook. London, Hutchinson, 1947.
The Shadow of Tyburn Tree (Brook). London, Hutchinson, 1948; New York, Ballantine, 1973.
The Haunting of Toby Jugg. London, Hutchinson, 1948.
The Rising Storm (Brook). London, Hutchinson, 1949.
The Second Seal (Richleau). London, Hutchinson, 1950.
The Man Who Killed the King (Brook). London, Hutchinson, 1951; New York, Putnam, 1965.
Star of Ill-Omen. London, Hutchinson, 1952.
To the Devil – A Daughter (Fountain). London, Hutchinson, 1953.
Curtain of Fear. London, Hutchinson, 1953.
The Island Where Time Stands Still (Sallust). London, Hutchinson, 1954.
The Dark Secret of Josephine (Brook). London, Hutchinson, 1955.
The Ka of Gifford Hillary. London, Hutchinson, 1956.
The Prisoner in the Mask (Richleau). London, Hutchinson, 1957.
Traitors' Gate (Sallust). London, Hutchinson, 1958.
The Rape of Venice (Brook). London, Hutchinson, 1959.
The Satanist (Fountain). London, Hutchinson, 1960; New York, Ballantine, 1974.
Vendetta in Spain (Richleau). London, Hutchinson, 1961.
Mayhem in Greece. London, Hutchinson, 1962.
The Sultan's Daughter (Brook). London, Hutchinson, 1963.
Bill for the Use of a Body (Day). London, Hutchinson, 1964.
They Used Dark Forces (Sallust). London, Hutchinson, 1964.
Dangerous Inheritance (Richleau). London, Hutchinson, 1965.
The Wanton Princess (Brook). London, Hutchinson, 1966.
Unholy Crusade. London, Hutchinson, 1967.
The White Witch of the South Seas (Sallust). London, Hutchinson, 1968.
Evil in a Mask (Brook). London, Hutchinson, 1969.
Gateway to Hell (Richleau). London, Hutchinson, 1970; New York, Ballantine, 1973.
The Ravishing of Lady Mary Ware (Brook). London, Hutchinson, 1971.
The Strange Story of Linda Lee. London, Hutchinson, 1972.

The Irish Witch (Brook).   London, Hutchinson, 1973.
Desperate Measures (Brook).   London, Hutchinson, 1974.

Short Stories

Mediterranean Nights.   London, Hutchinson, 1942; revised edition, London, Arrow
   Books, 1963.
Gunmen, Gallants, and Ghosts.   London, Hutchinson, 1943; revised edition, London,
   Arrow Books, 1963.

OTHER PUBLICATIONS

Play

Screenplay: *An Englishman's Home (Madmen of Europe)*, with others, 1939.

Other

Old Rowley: A Private Life of Charles II.   London, Hutchinson, 1933; as *A Private Life
   of Charles II*, 1938.
Red Eagle: A Life of Marshal Voroshilov.   London, Hutchinson, 1937.
Invasion (war game).   London, Hutchinson, 1938.
Blockade (war game).   London, Hutchinson, 1939.
Total War.   London, Hutchinson, 1941.
The Seven Ages of Justerini's.   London, Riddle Books, 1949; revised edition, as
   1749–1965: The Eight Ages of Justerini's, Aylesbury, Buckinghamshire, Dolphin,
   1965.
Alibi (war game).   London, Geographia, 1951.
Stranger Than Fiction.   London, Hutchinson, 1959.
Saturdays with Bricks and Other Days under Shell-Fire.   London, Hutchinson, 1961.
The Devil and All His Works.   London, Hutchinson, and New York, American
   Heritage Press, 1971.
The Time Has Come (autobiography)
   The Young Man Said.   London, Hutchinson, 1977.
   Officer and Temporary Gentleman.   London, Hutchinson, 1978.
   Drink and Ink, edited by Anthony Lejeune.   London, Hutchinson, 1979.

Editor, *A Century of Horror Stories.*   London, Hutchinson, 1935; Freeport, New York,
   Books for Libraries, 1971; selection as *Quiver of Horror* and *Shafts of Fear*, London,
   Arrow Books, 2 vols., 1965; as *Tales of Strange Doings* and *Tales of Strange
   Happenings*, Hutchinson, 2 vols., 1968.
Editor, *A Century of Spy Stories.*   London, Hutchinson, 1938.

Bibliography: *Fyra Decennier med Dennis Wheatley: En Biografi & Bibliografi* by Iwan
Hedman and Jan Alexandersson, privately printed, 1963; revised edition, Strägnäs, Sweden,
DAST, 1973.

*   *   *

Dennis Wheatley was the master of the macabre to some, the creator (with Joe Links) of a
series of detective games, the "Crime Dossiers," to others. These were but a small part of his
output as the "Prince of Thriller Writers." In 40 years he produced over 60 books of
detection, adventure, romance, and fantasy; they sold over twenty million copies.

His characters believe in Britain and regret the passing of the Empire. Women generally
know their place, if not in the bed of the hero, then passing ammunition in battle. His heroes

are of the upper class (like the Duke de Richleau) or upper middle class (like Gregory Sallust) or rise to the upper class (like Roger Brook). When in *Dangerous Inheritance* Fleur Eaton declares herself a Socialist and shows an enlightened attitude about race, sex, and the underprivileged it is only partially a comment on the class consciousness of her father's generation. It also demonstrates the changes that have taken place in the world since de Richleau and Simon Aron set off into Soviet Russia to rescue Rex Van Ryn in the author's first published novel, *The Forbidden Territory*.

Wheatley's earliest books are fast-moving stories filled with good old-fashioned British ideals of fair play and sportsmanship sometimes making way for common sense in the face of death. His first written novel (not published for 10 years) *Three Inquisitive People* (1940) is actually a formal deductive story of murder. It is important because it is also the story of how his modern Musketeers (de Richleau, Simon Aron, Rex Van Ryn, and Richard Eaton) met. The murderer is obvious from the beginning, too many threads of the plot are inadequately tied together, and the last chapter is an anti-climax of maudlin sentiment, but there is a surprise or two.

As Wheatley developed he began to fill his books with digressions on economic theory, politics, and history, often in undigested helpings. Much of *They Used Dark Forces* is a combination of military strategy and Churchillian war memoirs and works to the detriment of the sweep of the plot. More interesting are the meals: details about what is served and with which wine, and descriptions of food down to the simplest meal of hot buttered toast and apple jelly. Wheatley's dialogue is often a sort of formal melodrama, not quite like ordinary speech. His Americans speak in the improbable accents found only in British fiction. Often his characters seem to be lecturing each other rather than responding, and Simon Aron's nasal negative, "ner," can be an irritant to the critical reader.

Though Wheatley became known for his stories of black magic (and followers of this sub-genre sought out his books) fewer than a dozen of the novels deal with that theme. His supernatural manifestations are often described in too much detail for them to be truly frightening; they could just as well have been replaced by gunmen or exotic villains. He comes closest to success in *The Haunting of Toby Jugg* and some of the short stories in *Gunmen, Gallants, and Ghosts*. His novels may be divided into six categories: black magic novels, adventure novels, and four sets of books with series characters: the Duke de Richleau, Gregory Sallust, Roger Brook, and Julian Day. Some of these were influenced by one of his own favorite writers, Alexandre Dumas.

The Richleau books take the Duke from age 18 in 1894 to his death in 1960 at 85. They were purposely based on Dumas's Musketeers cycle with the exiled monarchist (and his fondness for Hoyo de Monterrey cigars) in the role of Athos, the conservative Richard Eaton as d'Artagnan, Simon Aron (the Liberal Jew) as Aramis, and the Democratic American, Rex Van Ryn, as Porthos. Improbable as the stories may seem, they are entertaining and the characters are more vivid than others in the Wheatley world. *The Forbidden Territory* may have been inspired by John Buchan's *Greenmantle*, and almost matches that novel in excitement.

The first Gregory Sallust book, *Black August*, is a Wellsian view of England in the future during a Communist revolution. The Satanic looking cynical egoist, Sallust, is at his best, however, in the seven volumes about his wartime service as a British agent. He is sent by Sir Pellinore Gwaine-Cust (think of C. Aubrey Smith) behind German lines to help the German masses throw off the Nazi yoke. His major opponent is the chief of the Gestapo Foreign Department, Gruppenführer Grauber, and his major assistant is the beautiful Erika von Epp whom he marries at the end of the war. In *The Black Baroness* he thwarts a plan to kidnap the king of Norway, and in the last volume (*They Used Dark Forces*) he tries to defeat Hitler by recourse to occult means.

The Roger Brook novels are historical espionage and take Brook (as a special agent for Prime Minister William Pitt) into adventures throughout Europe, Asia, and the Americas between 1783 and 1815. Virtually every major historical event and person in that era is used by Wheatley in the series. The thread of plot that binds the books together is Roger's love for Georgina Thursby whom he wins and loses by turns. In the process he searches for the

Dauphin, brings Napoleon and Josephine together, foils a plot to assassinate the Emperor, and saves his own daughter from being sacrificed in a Black Mass on Walpurgis Night. While the plots may be impossibly melodramatic, the historical details are accurate and may be one of the reasons critics have given this series so much praise. The stories are told with such vigor that the reader is swept along and kept turning the page. Wheatley is not without a sense of humor as the scene in which Roger's wife, Mary, finds him in bed with Georgina in the final volume, *Desperate Measures*, shows.

The Julian Day trilogy is Wheatley's *Count of Monte Cristo*: a hero whose career has been ruined seeks revenge against those responsible.

While it's easy to fault Wheatley for archaic mannerisms and padded writing, there is no denying he has had an enormous readership around the world. He found that what the public wanted was what he enjoyed writing. A study of public taste could be based on his work.

—J. Randolph Cox

WHEELER, Hugh. See **QUENTIN, Patrick.**

WHITE, Ethel Lina. British. Born in Abergavenny, Monmouthshire, in 1887. Worked in the Ministry of Pensions, London. *Died in 1944.*

CRIME PUBLICATIONS

Novels

The Wish-Bone. London, Ward Lock, 1927.
'Twill Soon Be Dark. London, Ward Lock, 1929.
The Eternal Journey. London, Ward Lock, 1930.
Put Out the Light. London, Ward Lock, 1931; New York, Dial Press, 1933; as *Sinister Light*, New York, Paperback Library, 1966.
Fear Stalks the Village. London, Ward Lock, 1932; New York, Harper, 1942.
Some Must Watch. London, Ward Lock, 1933; New York, Harper, 1941; as *The Spiral Staircase*, Cleveland, World, 1946.
The First Time He Died. London, Collins, 1935.
Wax. London, Collins, and New York, Doubleday, 1935.
The Wheel Spins. London, Collins, and New York, Harper, 1936; as *The Lady Vanishes*, London, Collins, 1962.
The Elephant Never Forgets. London, Collins, 1937; New York, Harper, 1938.
The Third Eye. London, Collins, and New York, Harper, 1937.
Step in the Dark. London, Collins, 1938; New York, Harper, 1939.
While She Sleeps. London, Collins, and New York, Harper, 1940.
She Faded into Air. London, Collins, and New York, Harper, 1941.

Midnight House. London, Collins, 1942; as *Her Heart in Her Throat*, New York, Harper, 1942; as *The Unseen*, New York, Paperback Library, 1966.

The Man Who Loved Lions. London, Collins, 1943; as *The Man Who Was Not There*, New York, Harper, 1943.

They See in Darkness. London, Collins, 1944.

Uncollected Short Stories

"An Unlocked Window," in *My Best Mystery Story.* London, Faber, 1939.

"The Gilded Pupil," in *Detective Stories of Today*, edited by Raymond Postgate. London, Faber, 1940.

* * *

A writer with a Gothic touch, Ethel Lina White wrote about the defenceless female – whether the young rich girl needing protection from fortune hunters or the poor and underpaid governess or companion left to the torments that only spiteful employers can devise. They are wretched creatures trying to exist in gloomy situations, in decaying atmospheres full of unearthly threats, or earthly ones that are even worse, and trying bravely to cope with these real or imaginary terrors. The most horrifying story must surely be *Some Must Watch* (how many who saw the film, *The Spiral Staircase*, realise that the commonplace motive of the book was changed in the movie?). Not merely the loneliness of her life and the lack of family or a trustworthy friend, but also the total inability to communicate her fears, plunge the White heroine into situations that most sensible people would wish to avoid. Incidents remain unexplained that could have been resolved quite easily by a word to landlord, doctor, or police, but the word is unsaid, as a perverse sort of loyalty to someone or other must be upheld. So terrifying battles must be fought and won alone.

A feeling of the supernatural hangs over many of the books; a séance is used to predict disaster in *The Third Eye* and the terror is compounded by the use of a blinding night fog which makes an unfamiliar road look and feel even worse that it would on a dark, moonless night. Atmosphere is always used most effectively, whether in the musty and unused museum in *Wax* or the fearful obsession of a governess in *Midnight House.* In *Fear Stalks the Village* the terror is so widely spread over the community that it seems almost a resident.

The books are nearly always set in England, and there is usually a strong sense of property prevalent in them. A desperate need for a permanent home is felt by rich and poor alike; a home where the heart is in permanent residence, where a shelter may be taken from the world's critical eyes, and which serves as a place to hide during attacks of hysteria or demonic behaviour.

While romance frequently plays a part, and there is always a lingering belief in the benefits of true love, it does not dominate these books. The plots are based on a mighty sense of fortune, usually threatening. Threats play a strong part in the books, emotions seem to become characters, and the result is nearly always a very high level of tension.

—Mary Groff

WHITE, Jon (Ewbank) Manchip. British. Born in Cardiff, Glamorganshire, 22 June 1924. Educated at St. Catharine's College, Cambridge, 1942–43, 1946–50 (Open Exhibitioner in English Literature), M.A. (honours) in English, prehistoric archaeology, and oriental languages (Egyptology), and University Diploma in anthropology 1950. Served in the Royal

Navy and the Welsh Guards, 1942–46. Married Valerie Leighton in 1946; two children. Story Editor, BBC, London, 1950–51; Senior Executive Officer, British Foreign Service, London, 1952–56; free-lance writer, 1956–67: Scenario Editor, Hammer Films, London, 1956–57; Screenwriter, Samuel Bronston Productions, Paris and Madrid, 1960–64; Associate Professor of English, University of Texas, El Paso, 1967–77. Since 1977, Professor of English, University of Tennessee, Knoxville. Address: Department of English, University of Tennessee, Knoxville, Tennessee 37916, U.S.A.

CRIME PUBLICATIONS

Novels

> *Nightclimber.* London, Chatto and Windus, and New York, Morrow, 1968.
> *The Game of Troy.* London, Chatto and Windus, and New York, McKay, 1971.
> *The Garden Game.* London, Chatto and Windus, 1973; Indianapolis, Bobbs Merrill, 1974.
> *Send for Mr. Robinson.* New York, Pinnacle, and London, Panther, 1974.
> *The Moscow Papers.* Canoga Park, California, Major Books, 1979.

OTHER PUBLICATIONS

Novels

> *Mask of Dust.* London, Hodder and Stoughton, 1953; as *Last Race*, New York, Mill, 1953.
> *Build Us a Dam.* London, Hodder and Stoughton, 1955.
> *The Girl from Indiana.* London, Hodder and Stoughton, 1956.
> *No Home but Heaven.* London, Hodder and Stoughton, 1957.
> *The Mercenaries.* London, Long, 1958.
> *Hour of the Rat.* London, Hutchinson, 1962.
> *The Rose in the Brandy Glass.* London, Eyre and Spottiswoode, 1965.

Plays

> Screenplays: *Day of Grace*, with Francis Searle, 1957; *Man with a Dog*, 1958; *The Camp on Blood Island*, with Val Guest, 1958; *Mystery Submarine*, with Hugh Woodhouse and Bertram Ostrer, 1963; *Crack in the World*, 1965.

> Radio Plays: *Question of Honour*; *Apocalypse*; *Last Lap*; *The Circuit*; *Mustard Yellow*; *Wolf Pack*; *The Colonel*, 1960; *The Wages of Fear*, from novel by Georges Arnaud, 1961; *Souvenir*, 1962.

> Television Plays: *Chariot of Fire*, 1955; *Who Killed Menna Lorraine*, 1960; *Hour of the Rat*, 1961; *Witch Hunt*, 1967.

Verse

> *Dragon and Other Poems.* London, Fortune Press, 1943.
> *Salamander.* London, Fortune Press, 1946.
> *The Rout of San Romano.* Aldington, Kent, Hand and Flower Press, 1952.
> *The Mountain Lion.* London, Chatto and Windus, 1971.

Other

Ancient Egypt.   London, Wingate, 1952; New York, Crowell, 1953; revised edition, London, Allen and Unwin, and New York, Dover, 1970.

Anthropology.   London, English Universities Press, 1954; New York, Philosophical Library, 1955.

Marshal of France: The Life and Times of Maurice, Comte de Saxe.   London, Hamish Hamilton, and Chicago, Rand McNally, 1962.

Everyday Life in Ancient Egypt.   London, Batsford, 1963; New York, Putnam, 1964.

Diego Velazquez, Painter and Courtier.   London, Hamish Hamilton, and Chicago, Rand McNally, 1969.

The Land God Made in Anger: Reflections on a Journey Through South West Africa.   London, Allen and Unwin, and Chicago, Rand McNally, 1969.

Cortés and the Downfall of the Aztec Empire.   London, Hamish Hamilton, and New York, St. Martin's Press, 1971.

A World Elsewhere: One Man's Fascination with the American Southwest.   New York, Crowell, 1975; as *The Great American Desert*, London, Allen and Unwin, 1977.

Everyday Life of the North American Indian.   London, Batsford, 1979.

Editor, *Life in Ancient Egypt*, by Adolf Erman.   New York, Dover, 1971.

Editor, *The Tomb of Tutankhamen*, by Howard Carter.   New York, Dover, 1971.

Editor, *Manners and Customs of the Modern Egyptians*, by E. W. Lane.   New York, Dover, 1972.

Translator, *The Glory of Egypt*, by Samivel.   New York and London, Thames and Hudson, 1955.

Jon Manchip White comments:

My early fiction fell into the category of the conventional novel (though even then many critics noted that it possessed a strong streak of the bizarre). My books were primarily narratives with a straightforward realistic and social flavour. My later fiction, however, from *Nightclimber* onwards, falls into the more venerable category of the romance. That is, my more recent books are stories with a non-realistic, surrealist, or supra-realist basis: dramatic, highly-coloured, rooted not in reality but in fantasy, dreams, and nightmares.

What really occupies and amuses me nowadays is to devise an improbable or actually outrageous fundamental idea, and then, by treating it in a matter-of-fact manner, to induce my reader into being gripped by it and ultimately into accepting it, with an uneasy sensation, as something that might well have occurred. My masters in this field are such writers as Poe, Stevenson, d'Aurévilly, Kafka, Borges, Cortázar, Calvino, Mandiargues, and Greene in his "Entertainments." For me, to speak purely personally, this oblique and equivocal genre is for some reason more exciting and compelling than the mystery or detective story *pur sang*, which are securely anchored in reality. Perhaps my later fictions might be classed under some such label as "psychological thrillers" or even "psychic thrillers."

At any event, I like to call my "romances," of which it would be interesting to write increasingly extreme examples, my "Extravagant Tales." As I have said, they owe much of their inspiration to Poe and to what Stevenson was fond of referring to as his "crawlers" – stories to make the hair rise on the back of your neck.

*   *   *

Jon Manchip White is the author of strange, frightening, and (especially in his later fiction) gothic adventures. The settings stretch across several continents, sometimes in the same story, and generally are staged against dreamlike, outlandish backgrounds; his plots are charged with exciting and usually fantastic events; and instead of intricate designs his mysteries abound in brooding terrors. However, the most characteristic feature of White's tales is the middle-aged, courageous protagonist who must confront extreme obstacles to achieve his goals.

Mask of Dust, White's first novel, takes place in northern Italy, the setting of a spectacular international automobile race. The plot involves the dangers and thrills of the competition; its hero, a past champion and World War II fighter pilot now seeking a final triumph, must ultimately decide between his wife and the race. In *Hour of the Rat*, a senior civil servant feels driven to kill a Japanese industrialist whom he identifies, tentatively, as his persecutor in a prisoner of war camp. This protagonist resembles the heroes of *No Home but Heaven* and *The Mercenaries*, who must also conflict with their societies. In *The Rose in the Brandy Glass* the conflict is not so much the physical strife faced by most of White's protagonists, but the psychological and moral conflict of serious fiction: Retired Colonel Morrigan, refusing to compromise his integrity, struggles against the opportunity to share, dishonestly, in an inheritance.

Though exploited by corrupt and exorbitantly wealthy men, the protagonists of White's next three grotesque adventures risk their lives by clinging to their convictions. The hero of *Nightclimber*, White's most thrilling adventure novel, is an art historian who impulsively practices climbing tall urban buildings, a skill he perfected as a youth at Cambridge. In need of money, the protagonist accepts an offer from a decadent millionaire art collector to practice climbing an unknown thing in an unknown place. The novel's action takes place in several European cities, but its world is blurred by fantasy. White begins his story with images of the hero's frightening dream. And throughout the novel White juxtaposes the same images against the reality of the hero's escapade. Finally the brave historian, although not compelled to do so, makes the impossible leap across a huge gulf in the Cave of the Cyclops high in a Greek mountain. Later he miraculously drops onto the roof of the millionaire's headquarters and saves himself and a sexy middle-aged opera singer from the clutches of the Merganser Corporation.

As bizarre as the sides of the buildings and the mountain in the *Nightclimber*, the setting of the deadly encounter in *The Game of Troy* is a huge maze on a diabolical Texan's ranch. The hero, a successful architect, falls in love with and finally saves the life of a beautiful woman, the wife and the most valuable toy of the financial genius. Again White combines the actuality of the lovers' pending death with a nightmarish atmosphere: the vengeful husband traps, drugs, and finally hunts the protagonists through the winding corridors and the dead-ends of the architect's own elaborate contraption. In the last of his "extravagant tales," *The Garden Game*, White tells the story of how Major Morven Rickman, a "soldier-of-fortune," desperately tries to rescue his men from an evil group of tycoons who secretly entertain themselves by gambling on 20th-century gladiatorial combats. More than any other of his tales, this story contains characteristics of the gothic novel – the location of the pernicious games is a medieval schloss, complete with gloomy underground passages, dark staircases, and a mysterious tropical garden. Jon Manchip White's mysteries, particularly his later ones, are spellbinding adventures with seemingly super-human heroes who strive for their almost impossible conquests in progressively more ghastly situations.

—Frances D. McConachie

WHITE, Lionel. American. Born in Buffalo, New York, 9 July 1905. Served in the United States Army during World War II. Married Hedy White in 1970 (second marriage); one son. Journalist: reporter in Cleveland, New York, and other cities; Editor, *True* magazine, New York, 1935–36; publisher of several fact detective magazines in the 1940's.

Agent: Philip Spitzer, 11125 76th Avenue, Forest Hills, New York 11375; or, John Farquharson Ltd., 8 Bell Yard, London WC2A 2JU, England. Address: 13384 Contour Drive, Sherman Oaks, California 91423, U.S.A.

CRIME PUBLICATIONS

Novels

The Snatchers. New York, Fawcett, 1953; London, Miller, 1958.
To Find a Killer. New York, Dutton, 1954; London, Boardman, 1956; as *Before I Die*, New York, Tower, 1964.
Love Trap. New York, New American Library, 1955.
The Big Caper. New York, Fawcett, 1955; London, Fawcett, 1956.
Clean Break. New York, Dutton, and London, Boardman, 1955; as *The Killing*, New York, Tower, 1964.
Flight into Terror. New York, Dutton, 1955; London, Boardman, 1957.
Operation – Murder. New York, Fawcett, 1956; London, Fawcett, 1958.
The House Next Door. New York, Dutton, 1956; London, Boardman, 1958.
Right for Murder. London, Boardman, 1957.
Death Takes the Bus. New York, Fawcett, 1957; London, Fawcett, 1958.
Hostage for a Hood. New York, Fawcett, 1957; London, Fawcett, 1958.
Too Young to Die. New York, Fawcett, 1958; London, Fawcett, 1959.
Coffin for a Hood. New York, Fawcett, 1958; London, Fawcett, 1959.
Invitation to Violence. New York, Dutton, and London, Boardman, 1958.
The Merriweather File. New York, Dutton, 1959; London, Boardman, 1960.
Rafferty. New York, Dutton, 1959; London, Boardman, 1960.
Run, Killer, Run. New York, Avon, 1959.
Lament for a Virgin. New York, Fawcett, and London, Muller, 1960.
Steal Big. New York, Fawcett, 1960; London, Muller, 1961.
The Time of Terror. New York, Dutton, 1960; London, Boardman, 1961.
Marilyn K. Derby, Connecticut, Monarch, 1960.
A Grave Undertaking. New York, Dutton, 1961; London, Boardman, 1962.
A Death at Sea. New York, Dutton, 1961; London, Boardman, 1962.
Obsession. New York, Dutton, 1962; London, Boardman, 1963.
The Money Trap. New York, Dutton, 1963; London, Boardman, 1964.
The Ransomed Madonna. New York, Dutton, 1964; London, Boardman, 1965.
The House on K Street. New York, Dutton, 1965; London, Boardman, 1966.
A Party to Murder. New York, Fawcett, 1966; London, Jenkins, 1968.
The Night of the Rape. New York, Dutton, 1967; London, Hale, 1969.
The Crimshaw Memorandum. New York, Dutton, 1967; London, Macdonald, 1968.
Hijack. New York, Macfadden, 1969; London, Hale, 1970.
Death of a City. Indianapolis, Bobbs Merrill, 1970; London, Hale, 1972.
The Mexico Run. New York, Fawcett, 1974.
A Rich and Dangerous Game. New York, McKay, 1974.
Jailbreak. London, Hale, 1976.

OTHER PUBLICATIONS

Other

Protect Yourself, Your Family, and Your Property in an Unsafe World. Chatsworth, California, Books for Better Living, 1974.

Editor, with Philip C. Blackburn, *Logical Nonsense: Works, Now, for the First Time, Complete*, by Lewis Carroll. New York, Putnam, 1934.

Lionel White comments:
It's one way to make a living if you are too lazy to work or too incompetent to hold a job.

*   *   *

"Caper" novels, those dealing with the planning and execution of large-scale crimes, are a recognized sub-genre of mystery fiction. Lionel White, if he did not invent the caper story, is certainly one of the ablest practitioners in the field. He is at his best detailing the step-by-step planning of a crime, the crime itself, and its aftermath. He does so in a harsh, spare style that is hardly literary but which is well-suited to his subjects. Though such stories are primarily action-oriented, White is often surprisingly acute in revealing the psychology of his criminal characters as well as in itemizing the minutiae of their lives. Always in these books there is the feeling of suppressed violence, but when the expected violence does occur it is often so shocking that it takes the reader unaware and achieves an unpredictable effect. An example of this is the stunning scene in *Death Takes the Bus* in which a young girl is raped with a pistol barrel. Such a scene might strike some readers as sordid, but it tells a great deal about the kinds of people who live in the world of White's books.

White usually deals with standard capers: kidnapping in *The Snatchers*, a train robbery in *Operation – Murder*, a bus hijacking in *Death Takes the Bus*, a diamond heist in *Too Young to Die*, and a bank robbery in what may well be the definitive White book, *The Big Caper*. Rarely is any of the criminals arrested; but there is always retribution, never as a result of poor planning, but because of accidents, the little things that no amount of planning can take into account. Or sometimes the characters discover a tiny core of decency (or sentimentality) within themselves and bring about their own downfalls.

White does not always adhere to the caper formula. In *Lament for a Virgin*, for instance, he presents the familiar story of a man framed for murder in a small southern town and tells how an individual in such a spot manages to save himself. In a much later book, *The Mexico Run*, he describes the predicament of a young man involved in dope smuggling and murder. These books are entertaining but do not really represent White at the top of his form. One of his best books, *The House Next Door*, begins with a heist, but it is really a study of a small suburban community; the plot concerns an innocent man mistakenly jailed for murder. He can do nothing for himself, and even his lawyer believes him guilty. Only his wife comes to his defense and nearly loses her own life as one violent act begets another in what is almost a chain reaction. In *Rafferty* White tells the story of a Jimmy Hoffa-like labor leader and his rise to power. Such novels give White the opportunity to use a somewhat more refined style than in his paperback thrillers. He is also able to delve into the psychology of characters quite unlike the hardened criminals of his caper books.

White is rather neglected at present, but for unadorned action, suspense, and vigorous storytelling his novels have seldom been surpassed.

—Bill Crider

WHITECHURCH, Victor L(orenzo). British. Born 12 March 1868. Educated at Chichester Grammar School, Sussex; Chichester Theological College; Durham University, Licentiate of Theology. Married Florence Partridge; one daughter. Curate, Aston Clinton,

Buckinghamshire, 1891–94, and All Souls, Harlesden, London, 1894–96; Senior Curate, St. Luke's, Maidenhead, Berkshire, 1896–1904; Vicar, Blewbury, Berkshire, 1904–13; Diocesan Chaplain to the Bishop of Oxford, and Organising Secretary for Diocese of Oxford, Church of England Men's Society, 1913–14; Vicar of Aylesbury and Chaplain, Royal Buckinghamshire Hospital, 1914–23; Rural Dean, Aylesbury, 1919–31; Rector, Hartwell-with-Stone, Buckinghamshire, 1923–31. Editor, *The Chronicle of St. George* magazine, Chichester, 1891–92. Proctor in the Convocation of Canterbury for the Diocese of Oxford, and Member, Church Assembly, 1922–25. Honorary Canon, Christ Church, Oxford. *Died in May 1933.*

CRIME PUBLICATIONS

Novels

> *The Templeton Case.* London, Long, and New York, Clode, 1924.
> *The Crime at Diana's Pool.* London, Unwin, and New York, Duffield, 1927.
> *Shot on the Downs.* London, Unwin, 1927; New York, Duffield, 1928.
> *The Robbery at Rudwick House.* New York, Duffield, 1929.
> *Murder at the Pageant.* London, Collins, 1930; New York, Duffield, 1931.
> *The Floating Admiral*, with others. London, Hodder and Stoughton, 1931; New York, Doubleday, 1932.
> *Murder at the College.* London, Collins, 1932; as *Murder at Exbridge*, New York, Dodd Mead, 1932.

Short Stories

> *Thrilling Stories of the Railway.* London, Pearson, 1912.
> *The Adventures of Captain Ivan Koravitch.* Edinburgh, Blackwood, 1925.

OTHER PUBLICATIONS

Novels

> *The Course of Justice.* London, Isbister, 1903.
> *The Canon in Residence.* London, Unwin, 1904; New York, Baker and Taylor, 1911.
> *The Locum Tenens.* London, Unwin, 1906.
> *Concerning Himself: The Story of an Ordinary Man.* London, Unwin, 1909; New York, Baker and Taylor, 1911.
> *Off the Main Road: A Village Comedy.* London, Long, 1911.
> *Left in Charge.* London, Long, and New York, Doubleday, 1912.
> *A Downland Corner.* London, Unwin, 1912; New York, Holt, 1913.
> *Three Summers: A Romance.* London, Long, 1915.
> *If Riches Increase.* London, Long, 1923.
> *A Bishop Out of Residence.* London, Unwin, 1924.
> *Downland Echoes.* London, Unwin, 1924.
> *The Dean and Jecinora.* London, Unwin, and New York, Duffield, 1926.
> *Mixed Relations.* London, Benn, 1928.
> *First and Last.* London, Collins, 1929; New York, Duffield, 1930.
> *Mute Witnesses, Being Certain Annals of a Downland Village.* London, Benn, 1933.

Short Stories

> *The Canon's Dilemma and Other Stories.* London, Unwin, 1909.

Other

Parochial Processions: Their Value and Organisation.   London, S.P.C.K., 1917.
Concerning Right and Wrong: A Plain Man's Creed.   London, Faith Press, 1925.
The Truth in Christ Jesus.   London, Faith Press, 1927.

*   *   *

It wasn't until he was in his 40's that Victor L. Whitechurch, a remarkable English clergyman and honorary canon of Christ Church, Oxford, tried his hand at the intricate puzzles of the mystery story. Whitechurch had previously written numerous clerical romances, but his first collection of mystery stories, *Thrilling Stories of the Railway*, did not make its appearance until 1912; today it is considered one of the rarest books in the mystery genre. The book won a place in Ellery Queen's *Queen's Quorum* which only added to its desirability as a collector's item. The amusing hero of the book, Thorpe Hazell, is a railway detective, a health fanatic, a vegetarian, and a firm believer in physical exercise.

Between 1924 and his death in 1933 Whitechurch wrote six detective novels and a collection of short stories, *The Adventures of Captain Ivan Koravitch*. Whitechurch's unique method of plotting a mystery is outlined in the foreword to his masterpiece, *Shot on the Downs*. He states that he begins his mystery novels by describing the scene of the crime with no forethought to either plot or criminal, but then solves the crime by ordinary police methods. This contrasts to the usual method of plotting an ending first, and may account for the originality of Whitechurch's books.

—Mary Ann Grochowski

WHITFIELD, Raoul.   Also wrote as Ramon Decolta.   American.   Born in New York City in 1897; grew up in the Philippines. Served in the United States Army Air Corps in France during World War I. Newspaper reporter, then magazine writer. Travelled abroad and lived in Paris during the early 1930's; after 1934 illness curtailed his activity. *Died in 1945.*

Crime Publications

Novels

Green Ice.   New York, Knopf, 1930; as *The Green Ice Murders*, New York, Avon, 1947.
Death in a Bowl.   New York, Knopf, 1931.
The Virgin Kills.   New York, Knopf, 1932.

Uncollected Short Stories

"Scotty Troubles Trouble," in *Black Mask* (New York), March 1926.
"Roaring Death," in *Black Mask* (New York), August 1926.
"Flying Gold," in *Black Mask* (New York), September 1926.
"Delivered Goods," in *Black Mask* (New York), November 1926.

"Ten Hours," in *Black Mask* (New York), December 1926.
"Uneasy Money," in *Black Mask* (New York), January 1927.
"White Murder," in *Black Mask* (New York), February 1927.
"Sky-High Odds," in *Black Mask* (New York), March 1927.
"South of Savannah," in *Black Mask* (New York), May 1927.
"Bottled Death," in *Black Mask* (New York), June 1927.
"Live Men's Gold," in *Black Mask* (New York), August 1927.
"Sixty Minutes," in *Black Mask* (New York), October 1927.
"Red Pearls," in *Black Mask* (New York), November 1927.
"The Sky's the Limit," in *Black Mask* (New York), January 1928.
"Soft Goods," in *Black Mask* (New York), February 1928.
"Little Guns," in *Black Mask* (New York), April 1928.
"Black Murder," in *Black Mask* (New York), May 1928.
"First Blood," in *Black Mask* (New York), June 1928.
"Blue Murder," in *Black Mask* (New York), July 1928.
"High Death," in *Black Mask* (New York), August 1928.
"Red Wings," in *Black Mask* (New York), September 1928.
"Ghost Guns," in *Black Mask* (New York), October 1928.
"The Sky-Trap," in *Black Mask* (New York), November 1928.
"On the Spot," in *Black Mask* (New York), February 1929.
"Out of the Sky," in *Black Mask* (New York), March 1929.
"The Pay-Off," in *Black Mask* (New York), April 1929.
"High Odds," in *Black Mask* (New York), May 1929.
"Within the Circle," in *Black Mask* (New York), June 1929.
"The Carnival Kill," in *Black Mask* (New York), July 1929.
"River Street Death," in *Black Mask* (New York), August 1929.
"The Squeeze," in *Black Mask* (New York), September 1929.
"Sal the Dude," in *Black Mask* (New York), October 1929.
"Murder by Mistake," in *Black Mask* (New York), August 1930.
"Murder in the Ring," in *Black Mask* (New York), December 1930.
"About Kid Deth," in *Black Mask* (New York), February 1931.
"Face Powder," in *Black Mask* (New York), April 1931.
"Soft City," in *Black Mask* (New York), May 1931.
"For Sale – Murder," in *Black Mask* (New York), June 1931.
"The Sky Club Affair," in *Black Mask* (New York), August 1931.
"Red Terrace," in *Black Mask* (New York), September 1931.
"Steel Arena," in *Black Mask* (New York), October 1931.
"Van Cleve Calling," in *Black Mask* (New York), November 1931.
"Unfair Exchange," in *Black Mask* (New York), December 1931.
"Skyline Death," in *Black Mask* (New York), January 1932.
"Man Killer," in *Black Mask* (New York), April 1932.
"Walking Dynamite," in *Black Mask* (New York), May 1932.
"Blue Murder," in *Black Mask* (New York), September 1932.
"Dead Men Tell Tales," in *Black Mask* (New York), November 1932.
"Murder by Request," in *Black Mask* (New York), January 1933.
"Dark Death," in *Black Mask* (New York), August 1933.
"A Woman Can Kill," in *Black Mask* (New York), September 1933.
"Money Talk," in *Black Mask* (New York), October 1933.
"Not Tomorrow," in *Black Mask* (New York), November 1933.
"Murder Again," in *Black Mask* (New York), December 1933.
"High Murder," in *Black Mask* (New York), January 1934.
"Death on Fifth Avenue," in *Black Mask* (New York), February 1934.
"The Mystery of the Fan-Backed Chair," in *Hearst's International-Cosmopolitan* (New York), February 1935.
"The Great Black," in *Hearst's International-Cosmopolitan* (New York), August 1937.

"Inside Job," in *The Hard-Boiled Omnibus: Early Stories from Black Mask*, edited by
   Joseph T. Shaw.   New York, Simon and Schuster, 1946.
"Murder Is My Business," in *The Saint* (New York), March 1956.

Uncollected Short Stories as Ramon Decolta

"West of Guam," in *Black Mask* (New York), February 1930.
"Red Hemp," in *Black Mask* (New York), April 1930.
"Signals of Storm," in *Black Mask* (New York), June 1930.
"Enough Rope," in *Black Mask* (New York), July 1930.
"Nagasaki Bound," in *Black Mask* (New York), September 1930.
"Nagasaki Knives," in *Black Mask* (New York), October 1930.
"The Caleso Murders," in *Black Mask* (New York), December 1930.
"Silence House," in *Black Mask* (New York), January 1931.
"Diamonds of Dread," in *Black Mask* (New York), February 1931.
"The Man in White," in *Black Mask* (New York), March 1931.
"The Blind Chinese," in *Black Mask* (New York), April 1931.
"Red Dawn," in *Black Mask* (New York), May 1931.
"Blue Glass," in *Black Mask* (New York), July 1931.
"Diamonds of Death," in *Black Mask* (New York), August 1931.
"Shooting Gallery," in *Black Mask* (New York), October 1931.
"The Javenese Mask," in *Black Mask* (New York), December 1931.
"The Siamese Cat," in *Black Mask* (New York), April 1932.
"The Black Sampan," in *Black Mask* (New York), June 1932.
"Climbing Death," in *Black Mask* (New York), July 1932.
"The Magician Murder," in *Black Mask* (New York), November 1932.
"The Man from Shanghai," in *Black Mask* (New York), May 1933.
"The Amber Fan," in *Black Mask* (New York), July 1933.
"Death in the Pasig," in *The Hard-Boiled Omnibus: Early Stories from Black Mask*,
   edited by Joseph T. Shaw.   New York, Simon and Schuster, 1946.
"China Man" (as Raoul Whitfield), in *The Hardboiled Dicks*, edited by Ron
   Goulart.   Los Angeles, Sherbourne Press, 1965; London, Boardman, 1967.

OTHER PUBLICATIONS

Play

   Screenplay: *Private Detective 62*, 1933.

Other (juvenile)

   Wings of Gold.   New York, Knopf, 1930.
   Silver Wings.   New York, Knopf, 1930.
   Danger Zone.   New York, Knopf, 1931.
   Danger Circus.   New York, Knopf, 1933.

*   *   *

At his best, Raoul Whitfield was very good; at his weakest, infuriatingly bad. Today he is
little remembered. His short fiction is due a revival, especially the 24 stories in *Black Mask*
featuring Jo Gar, a Filipino private detective in Manila, and written under the pseudonym
Ramon Decolta (two stories about Gar also appeared in *Cosmopolitan*). For these stories
Whitfield drew on his intimate knowledge of the islands. Six of them, forming a "serial,"
were reprinted in *Ellery Queen's Mystery Magazine*. His other *Black Mask* stories vary in
quality, many of them stock action-pieces, the kind Joseph T. Shaw, the editor, was so fond

of. However, upon occasion Whitfield did first-rate work, e.g., "Murder by Mistake" and "Murder in the Ring"; the latter is his best story.

His novels fared well with critics and the public (he was at one time regarded as Hammett's peer), and still read well. *Green Ice* is a first-person narrative that concerns Mal Ourney, an ex-con just out of Sing Sing who goes after what he calls The Crime-Breeders, big-time hoods who prey on small-time crooks. In *Death in a Bowl* the Hollywood private dick Ben Jardinn solves the spectacular murder of conductor Hans Reiner during a concert in Hollywood Bowl. The plot is complicated but the pacing is excellent, and it is Whitfield's best novel. *The Virgin Kills* is his least satisfactory long work. *The Virgin* is a yacht; "kills" is a nominative plural, as in murders; and the setting is the annual Poughkeepsie Regatta on the Hudson River. Al Connors, a newspaperman, narrates.

—E. R. Hagemann

WHITNEY, Phyllis A(yame). American. Born in Yokohama, Japan, 9 September 1903. Educated at schools in Japan, China, the Philippines, Berkeley, California, San Antonio, Texas; graduated from high school in Chicago, 1924. Married 1) George Garner in 1925 (divorced, 1945); one daughter, 2) Lovell Jahnke in 1950 (died, 1973). Children's Book Editor, Chicago *Sun*, 1942–46, and Philadelphia *Inquirer*, 1946–48; Instructor in Juvenile Fiction Writing, Northwestern University, Evanston, Illinois, 1945–46, and New York University, 1947–58. Past President, Mystery Writers of America. Recipient: Youth Today Award, 1947; Mystery Writers of America Edgar Allan Poe Award, for juvenile, 1961, 1964. Agent: McIntosh and Otis Inc., 475 Fifth Avenue, New York, New York 10017, U.S.A.

CRIME PUBLICATIONS

Novels

> *Red Is for Murder.* Chicago, Ziff Davis, 1943; as *Red Carnelian*, New York, Paperback Library, 1968; London, Hodder and Stoughton, 1976.
> *The Quicksilver Pool.* New York, Appleton Century Crofts, 1955; London, Hodder and Stoughton, 1973.
> *The Trembling Hills.* New York, Appleton Century Crofts, 1956; London, Hodder and Stoughton, 1974.
> *Skye Cameron.* New York, Appleton Century Crofts, 1957; London, Hurst and Blackett, 1959.
> *The Moonflower.* New York, Appleton Century Crofts, 1958; as *The Mask and the Moonflower*, London, Hurst and Blackett, 1960.
> *Thunder Heights.* New York, Appleton Century Crofts, 1960; London, Hodder and Stoughton, 1973.
> *Blue Fire.* New York, Appleton Century Crofts, 1961; London, Hodder and Stoughton, 1962.
> *Window on the Square.* New York, Appleton Century Crofts, 1962; London, Hodder and Stoughton, 1969.
> *Seven Tears for Apollo.* New York, Appleton Century Crofts, 1963; London, Coronet, 1969.
> *Black Amber.* New York, Appleton Century Crofts, 1964; London, Hale, 1965.

Sea Jade. New York, Appleton Century Crofts, 1964; London, Hale, 1966.
Columbella. New York, Doubleday, 1966; London, Hale, 1967.
Silverhill. New York, Doubleday, 1967; London, Heinemann, 1968.
Hunter's Green. New York, Doubleday, 1968; London, Heinemann, 1969.
The Winter People. New York, Doubleday, 1969; London, Heinemann, 1970.
Lost Island. New York, Doubleday, 1970; London, Heinemann, 1971.
Listen for the Whisperer. New York, Doubleday, and London, Heinemann, 1972.
Snowfire. New York, Doubleday, and London, Heinemann, 1973.
The Turquoise Mask. New York, Doubleday, 1974; London, Heinemann, 1975.
Spindrift. New York, Doubleday, and London, Heinemann, 1975.
The Golden Unicorn. New York, Doubleday, 1976.
The Stone Bull. New York, Doubleday, and London, Heinemann, 1977.
The Glass Flame. New York, Doubleday, 1978; London, Heinemann, 1979.
Domino. New York, Doubleday, 1979.

OTHER PUBLICATIONS

Novels (juvenile)

A Place for Ann. Boston, Houghton Mifflin, 1941.
A Star for Ginny. Boston, Houghton Mifflin, 1942.
A Window for Julie. Boston, Houghton Mifflin, 1943.
The Silver Inkwell. Boston, Houghton Mifflin, 1945.
Willow Hill. New York, Reynal, 1947.
Ever After. Boston, Houghton Mifflin, 1948.
Mystery of the Gulls. Philadelphia, Westminster Press, 1949.
Linda's Homecoming. Philadelphia, McKay, 1950.
The Island of Dark Woods. Philadelphia, Westminster Press, 1951; as *Mystery of the Strange Traveler*, 1967.
Love Me, Love Me Not. Boston, Houghton Mifflin, 1952.
Mystery of the Black Diamonds. Philadelphia, Westminster Press, 1954; as *Black Diamonds*, Leicester, Brockhampton Press, 1957.
Step to the Music. New York, Crowell, 1953.
A Long Time Coming. Philadelphia, McKay, 1954.
Mystery on the Isle of Skye. Philadelphia, Westminster Press, 1955.
The Fire and the Gold. New York, Crowell, 1956.
The Highest Dream. Philadelphia, McKay, 1956.
Mystery of the Green Cat. Philadelphia, Westminster Press, 1957.
Secret of the Samurai Sword. Philadelphia, Westminster Press, 1958.
Creole Holiday. Philadelphia, Westminster Press, 1959.
Mystery of the Haunted Pool. Philadelphia, Westminster Press, 1960.
Secret of the Tiger's Eye. Philadelphia, Westminster Press, 1961.
Mystery of the Golden Horn. Philadelphia, Westminster Press, 1962.
Mystery of the Hidden Hand. Philadelphia, Westminster Press, 1963.
Secret of the Emerald Star. Philadelphia, Westminster Press, 1964.
Mystery of the Angry Idol. Philadelphia, Westminster Press, 1965.
Secret of the Spotted Shell. Philadelphia, Westminster Press, 1967.
Secret of Goblin Glen. Philadelphia, Westminster Press, 1968.
The Mystery of the Crimson Ghost. Philadelphia, Westminster Press, 1969.
Secret of the Missing Footprint. Philadelphia, Westminster Press, 1969.
The Vanishing Scarecrow. Philadelphia, Westminster Press, 1971.
Nobody Likes Trina. Philadelphia, Westminster Press, 1972.
Mystery of the Scowling Boy. Philadelphia, Westminster Press, 1973.
Secret of Haunted Mesa. Philadelphia, Westminster Press, 1975.
Secret of the Stone Face. Philadelphia, Westminster Press, 1977.

Other

Writing Juvenile Fiction. Boston, The Writer, 1947; revised edition, 1960.
Writing Juvenile Stories and Novels. Boston, The Writer, 1976.
"Gothic Mysteries," in The Mystery Story, edited by John Ball. San Diego, University
    of California Extension, 1976.
"Good Little Girls and Boys," in Murder Ink: The Mystery Reader's Companion, edited
    by Dilys Winn. New York, Workman, 1977.

Manuscript Collection: Mugar Memorial Library, Boston University.

*   *   *

Phyllis A. Whitney's long career of writing for young people and adults has produced
more than 50 novels, a number of articles on the writing of fiction, and two textbooks for
would-be writers of children's and young adult fiction. Her mysteries are novels of romantic
suspense, and she enjoys a large and faithful audience. Although she wrote her first adult
book, Red Is for Murder, in 1943, it was not until the publication of The Quicksilver Pool in
1955 that she began writing regularly for adults. Over the years, she has evolved a personal
type of romantic suspense novel, the family mystery, that she writes particularly well.

In most of Whitney's suspense novels, the crime has been committed some time before the
beginning of the book, but it has never been solved. A young woman, perhaps a long-lost
member of the family, returns home to find herself involved in events she does not
understand. Often her parents have left the family home because of the hidden events that her
presence brings forth once again. Alternatively, a young bride may find danger in her
husband's family home. In the more recent novels, Whitney has become more interested in
crime and detection. The mystery element of The Quicksilver Pool and The Trembling Hills is
not as central as it is in the later works in which there are murders to solve and villains to be
punished.

Setting is often highly significant in Whitney's work. Each research trip provides
background for a children's book as well as for a suspense novel. Blue Fire takes place in
South Africa; Black Amber, in Turkey; The Moonflower, in Japan (where she was born);
Hunter's Green, in a British country house; Columbella, in the Virgin Islands; Listen for the
Whisperer, in Norway. She also uses American settings if they are appropriate as places
where old families might have had their estates: the Georgia Sea Islands in Lost Island,
Newport in Spindrift, and the Catskills in The Stone Bull. A few of her novels are historical:
The Trembling Hills is set in San Francisco during the earthquake; Sea Jade and Window on
the Square, in 19th-century New England and New York City, respectively.

Almost all of her young heroines are searching for their own past, and the sense of identity
they gain from their fictional experiences involves personal growth and awareness as well as
solving the mystery of their past. Whitney often explores the mother-daughter relationship,
especially in her later fiction, as an integral part of the plot's development. Many of the
mothers in her works are beautiful women who are not nurturing toward their children;
some of them are the villains. The competition between mother and daughter is always a
central issue. In Columbella, the protagonist is hired as a companion-governess for a young
girl who has a sense of inferiority to her own mother, a situation also experienced by the
heroine. In Listen for the Whisperer, the heroine must resolve her ambiguous feelings about
her mother, a glamorous movie star who had left her and her father in order to further her
career. The Golden Unicorn has as its heroine an adopted child who wants to find her real
parents.

The villains in Whitney's novels are appropriate for family drama. They are ordinarily
motivated by a desire to avenge an imagined slight or to settle an old grievance or feud. The
female protagonist is in danger because of something she knows or something she represents
rather than for something she does. Since the source of evil is so ambiguous in Whitney's
novels, the atmosphere of suspense is both strong and diffuse. An aura of unease permeates

her books, promising excitement and mystery that become clearly delineated only at the end when villain, method, motive, and reward are all revealed at once.

Whitney's published commentary upon the writing of fiction reveals her seriousness about her art. Her work is formulaic, providing an expected and anticipated pleasure for her wide audience, but it is never off-hand or less than thoroughly professional. At her best, in *Window on the Square*, *Spindrift*, *Columbella*, *Hunter's Green*, and *Lost Island*, she is superb at evoking and sustaining complex and sophisticated terrors in a small domestic circle. Her characters are well drawn, convincingly motivated, and always interesting. While most of the well-known writers in the field of romantic suspense are British, Whitney has consistently written as well and as successfully as they, and she has found new ways to adapt the American landscape as background for her gothic fiction.

—Kay J. Mussell

WHITTINGTON, Harry. Also writes as Ashley Carter; Robert Hart Davis; Whit Harrison; Kel Holland; Harriet Kathryn Myers; Blaine Stevens; Clay Stuart; Harry White; Hallam Whitney. American. Born in Ocala, Florida, 4 February 1915. Educated in Florida public schools and extension and night classes. Served in the United States Navy, 1945–46: Petty Officer. Married Kathryn Odom in 1936; one daughter and one son. Copywriter, Griffith Advertising Agency, St. Petersburg, Florida, 1932–33; Assistant Manager and Advertising Manager, Capitol Theatre, St. Petersburg, 1933–34; Post Office Clerk, St. Petersburg, 1934–45; Editor, *Advocate*, St. Petersburg, 1938–45; free-lance writer, 1946–68; Editor, U.S. Department of Agriculture, 1968–75; since 1975, free-lance writer: author of many stories for King Features Syndicate, 1948–57, and *Man from U.N.C.L.E.*, *Dime Detective*, *Manhunt*, *Bluebook*, *Mantrap*. Agent: Anita Diamant, 51 East 42nd Street, New York, New York 10017; or, Mauri Grashin, 8730 Sunset Boulevard, Los Angeles, California 90069. Address: 1909 First Street, Indian Rocks Beach, Florida 33535, U.S.A.

CRIME PUBLICATIONS

Novels

    Slay Ride for a Lady. Kingston, New York, Quin, 1950.
    The Brass Monkey. Kingston, New York, Quin, 1951.
    Call Me Killer. Hasbrouck Heights, New Jersey, Graphic, 1951.
    Fires That Destroy. New York, Fawcett, 1951.
    The Lady Was a Tramp. Kingston, New York, Quin, 1951.
    Married to Murder. New York, Paperback Library, 1951.
    Murder Is My Mistress. Hasbrouck Heights, New Jersey, Graphic, 1951.
    Satan's Widow. New York, Paperback Library, 1951.
    Forever Evil. New York, Paperback Library, 1951.
    Swamp Kill (as Whit Harrison). New York, Paperback Library, 1951.
    Drawn to Evil. New York, Ace, 1952.
    Mourn the Hangman. Hasbrouck Heights, New Jersey, Graphic, 1952.
    Violent Night (as Whit Harrison). New York, Paperback Library, 1952.
    So Dead My Love! New York, Ace, 1953.
    Vengeful Sinner. New York, Croydon, 1953; as *Die, Lover*, New York, Avon, 1960.
    You'll Die Next! New York, Ace, 1954; London, Red Seal, 1959.

The Naked Jungle. New York, Ace, 1955.
One Got Away. New York, Ace, 1955.
Brute in Brass. New York, Fawcett, 1956; London, Red Seal, 1958.
Desire in the Dust. New York, Fawcett, 1956; London, Fawcett, 1957.
Humming Box. New York, Ace, 1956.
Saturday Night Town. New York, Fawcett, 1956; London, Fawcett, 1958.
A Woman on the Place. New York, Ace, 1956; London, Red Seal, 1960.
Across That River. New York, Ace, 1957.
Man in the Shadow (novelization of screenplay). New York, Avon, 1957.
One Deadly Dawn. New York, Ace, 1957.
Play for Keeps. New York and London, Abelard Schuman, 1957.
Temptations of Valerie (novelization of screenplay). New York, Avon, 1957.
Teen-Age Jungle. New York, Avon, 1958.
Web of Murder. New York, Fawcett, 1958; London, Fawcett, 1959.
Backwoods Tramp. New York, Fawcett, 1959; London, Muller, 1961.
Halfway to Hell. New York, Avon, 1959.
Strange Bargain. New York, Avon, 1959.
Strangers on Friday. New York and London, Abelard Schuman, 1959.
A Ticket to Hell. New York, Fawcett, 1959; London, Muller, 1960.
Connolly's Woman. New York, Fawcett, 1960; London, Muller, 1962.
The Devil Wears Wings. New York and London, Abelard Schuman, 1960.
Heat of Night. New York, Fawcett, 1960; London, Muller, 1961.
Hell Can Wait. New York, Fawcett, 1960; London, Muller, 1962.
A Night for Screaming. New York, Ace, 1960.
Nita's Place. New York, Pyramid, 1960.
Rebel Woman. New York, Avon, 1960.
Guerrilla Girls. New York, Pyramid, 1960; London, New English Library, 1970.
God's Back Was Turned. New York, Fawcett, 1961; London, Muller, 1962.
Journey into Violence. New York, Pyramid, 1961.
A Haven for the Damned. New York, Fawcett, 1962; London, Muller, 1963.
Hot as Fire, Cold as Ice. New York, Belmont, 1962.
69 Babylon Park. New York, Avon, 1962.
Don't Speak to Strange Girls. New York, Fawcett, and London, Muller, 1963.
The Doomsday Affair (novelization of tv play). New York, Ace, and London, New
    English Library, 1965.
Doomsday Mission. New York, Banner, 1967.
The Bitter Mission of Captain Burden. New York, Avon, 1968.

OTHER PUBLICATIONS

Novels

Vengeance Valley. New York, Phoenix, 1945; London, Ward Lock, 1947.
Cracker Girl. Beacon, New York, Beacon Signal, 1953.
Wild Oats. Beacon, New York, Beacon Signal, 1953.
Prime Sucker. Beacon, New York, Beacon Signal, 1953.
The Woman Is Mine. New York, Fawcett, 1953.
Saddle the Storm. New York, Fawcett, 1954; London, Fawcett, 1955.
Naked Island. New York, Ace, 1954.
Shadow at Noon (as Harry White). New York, Pyramid, 1955.
Mink. Paris, Gallimard, 1956.
Valerie. New York, Avon, 1957.
Star Lust. N.p., B and B Library, 1958.
Trouble Rides Tall. New York and London, Abelard Schuman, 1958.
Strictly for the Boys. N.p., Stanley, 1959.

Vengeance Is the Spur. New York and London, Abelard Schuman, 1960.
Young Nurses. New York, Pyramid, 1961.
Desert Stake-Out. New York, Fawcett, 1961; London, Muller, 1963.
Searching Rider. New York, Ace, 1961.
A Trap for Sam Dodge. New York, Ace, 1962.
Wild Sky. New York, Ace, 1962.
Cross the Red Creek. New York, Avon, 1962.
Small Town Nurse (as Harriet Kathryn Myers). New York, Ace, 1962.
Prodigal Nurse (as Harriet Kathryn Myers). New York, Ace, 1963.
Dry Gulch Town. New York, Ace, 1963.
The Fall of the Roman Empire (novelization of screenplay). New York, Fawcett, and
   London, Muller, 1964.
High Fury. New York, Ballantine, 1964.
Hangrope Town. New York, Ballantine, 1964.
His Brother's Wife (as Clay Stuart). Beacon, New York, Beacon Signal, 1964.
The Tempted (as Kel Holland). Beacon, New York, Beacon Signal, 1964.
Wild Lonesome. New York, Ballantine, 1965.
Valley of the Savage Men. New York, Ace, 1965.
Treachery Trail. Racine, Wisconsin, Whitman, 1968.
Smell of Jasmine. New York, Avon, 1968.
Charro. New York, Fawcett, 1969.
The Outlanders (as Blaine Stevens). New York, Harcourt Brace, 1979.

Novels as Whit Harrison

Body and Passion. New York, Paperback Library, 1951.
Nature Girl. New York, Popular Library, 1952.
Sailor's Weekend. New York, Popular Library, 1952.
Army Girl. New York, Popular Library, 1952.
Girl on Parole. New York, Popular Library, 1952.
Rapture Alley. New York, Popular Library, 1952.
Shanty Road. New York, Popular Library, 1953.
Strip the Town Naked. Beacon, New York, Beacon Signal, 1953.
Any Woman He Wanted. Beacon, New York, Beacon Signal, 1960.
A Woman Possessed. Beacon, New York, Beacon Signal, 1961.

Novels as Hallam Whitney

Backwoods Hussy. New York, Paperback Library, 1952.
Shack Road. New York, Paperback Library, 1953.
Sinners Club. New York, Paperback Library, 1953.
City Girl. New York, Paperback Library, 1953.
Backwoods Shack. New York, Paperback Library, 1954.
Wild Seed. New York, Ace, 1955.

Novels as Ashley Carter

Golden Stud, with Lance Horner. New York, Fawcett, 1975.
Master of Black Oaks. New York, Fawcett, 1976; London, W. H. Allen, 1977.
Sword of the Golden Stud. New York, Fawcett, 1977; London, W. H. Allen, 1978.
Secret of Blackoaks. New York, Fawcett, 1978.
Panama. New York, Fawcett, 1978; London, Pan, 1979.
Taproots of Falconhurst. New York, Fawcett, and London, W. H. Allen, 1979.

Plays

Screenplays: *Face of the Phantom*, 1960; *Pain and Pleasure*, 1965; *Strange Desires*, 1967; *Fireball Jungle*, 1968; *Island of Lost Women*, 1973.

Television Plays: *Lawman*, *The Alaskans*, and *The Dakotas* series.

Other

"The Paperback Original," in *The Mystery Writer's Handbook*, edited by Herbert Brean. New York, Harper, 1956.
"The Lucky Henchman of Joseph Peel," in *Quality of Murder*, edited by Anthony Boucher. New York, Dutton, 1962.
"The Key to Plotting," in *Writers' Digest* (Cincinnati), November 1972.

Theatrical Activities:
Director: **Film** – *Face of the Phantom*, 1960.

*   *   *

Of all the writers who specialized in soft-cover originals during the paperback boom of the 1950's, Harry Whittington was certainly the "king." Between 1951 and 1963 he published close to 50 crime novels in this medium, and at least 35 westerns and other genre fiction. Yet for all its prolificness, Whittington's work is inventive and of consistently high quality. His writing is crisp, with a good deal of emotional impact, and his characters, unlike those in so many soft-cover mysteries, are three-dimensional human beings instead of cardboard stereotypes. No less a critic than Anthony Boucher, writing in the New York *Times*, praised him as "one of the most versatile and satisfactory creators" of paperback suspense fiction.

Among Whittington's best works are *Fires That Destroy*, *Desire in the Dust*, *A Ticket to Hell*, *A Night for Screaming*, and *The Devil Wears Wings*. The last combines straight suspense with an in-depth psychological character study, and features a knowledgeable flying background and (as is the case in most of his crime novels) a vividly drawn Florida setting. Whittington has also written an excellent article on his speciality, "The Paperback Original," in *The Mystery Writer's Handbook*.

—Bill Pronzini

WIBBERLEY, Leonard.   See **HOLTON, Leonard.**

WIEGAND, William (George).   American.   Born in Detroit, Michigan, 11 June 1928. Educated at the University of Michigan, Ann Arbor (Intercollegiate Short Story Contest Prize, 1950), B.A. 1949, M.A. 1950; Stanford University, California, Ph.D. 1960. Briggs-Copeland Lecturer, Harvard University, Cambridge, Massachusetts, 1960–62; Lecturer in

English, Stanford University, 1964, 1969. Assistant Professor of English and Creative Writing, 1962–67, Associate Professor, 1967–72, and since 1972 Professor, San Francisco State University. Recipient: Mary Roberts Rinehart Award, 1950; San Francisco Foundation Joseph Henry Jackson Award, 1959. Address: Department of Creative Writing, San Francisco State University, 1600 Holloway Avenue, San Francisco, California 94132, U.S.A.

CRIME PUBLICATIONS

Novels

>*At Last, Mr. Tolliver.* New York, Rinehart, 1950; London, Hodder and Stoughton, 1951.
>*The Treatment Man.* New York, McGraw Hill, 1959; London, Muller, 1960.

OTHER PUBLICATIONS

Novel

>*The School of Soft Knocks.* Philadelphia, Lippincott, 1968.

Other

>Editor, with Richard Kraus, *Student's Choice.* Columbus, Ohio, Merrill, 1970.
>Editor, *In War Time*, by S. Weir Mitchell. New Haven, Connecticut, College and University Press, 1978.

William Wiegand comments:
Although I don't think of myself as primarily a detective story writer, both *The Treatment Man* and the book I'm working on now have some strange resemblances to detective fiction.

*   *   *

William Wiegand is a midwest American novelist whose first published work was a mystery novel, written when he was twenty-one years old, that won the first Mary Roberts Rinehart Award for detective fiction. *At Last, Mr. Tolliver* is a novel of considerable promise, narrating in a clear, straightforward style the story of Samuel Tolliver, a gentle and unassuming boarding house resident of somewhat mysterious antecedents, who finds himself deeply involved in the police investigation of the murder of a fellow boarder. Tolliver in the end has to solve the crime in order to exonerate himself. His character and background emerge slowly but effectively, and this constitutes the principal merit of the story, which is not long on conventional detection.

The Treatment Man was based on a prison uprising. (It, too, won a prize: the Joseph Henry Jackson Award.) Told from two perspectives – that of a convict and of a prison employee – it demonstrated once more the author's firm control of his material.

—Donald A. Yates

WIGG, T. I. G.   See McCUTCHAN, Philip.

WILCOX, Collin. Also writes as Carter Wick. American. Born in Detroit, Michigan, 21 September 1924. Educated at Antioch College, Yellow Springs, Ohio, B.A. Served in the United States Air Force: Private. Married Beverly Buchman in 1954 (divorced, 1964); two sons. Merchandise Manager, San Francisco Progress, 1949–50; Teacher at Town School, San Francisco, 1950–53; Partner, Amthor and Company, furniture store, San Francisco, 1953–55; Owner, Collin Wilcox Lamps, San Francisco, 1955–70. Since 1970, self-employed writer. Regional Vice-President, 1975, and Member, Board of Directors, 1976, Mystery Writers of America. Agent: Blassingame McCauley and Wood, 60 East 42nd Street, New York, New York 10017. Address: 4174 26th Street, San Francisco, California 94131, U.S.A.

CRIME PUBLICATIONS

Novels (series characters: Stephen Drake; Lieutenant Frank Hastings; Marshall McCloud)

The Black Door (Drake). New York, Dodd Mead, 1967; London, Cassell, 1968.
The Third Figure (Drake). New York, Dodd Mead, 1968; London, Hale, 1969.
The Lonely Hunter (Hastings). New York, Random House, 1969; London, Hale, 1971.
The Disappearance (Hastings). New York, Random House, 1970; London, Hale, 1971.
Dead Aim (Hastings). New York, Random House, 1971; London, Hale, 1973.
Hiding Place (Hastings). New York, Random House, 1973; London, Hale, 1974.
McCloud. New York, Award, 1973.
Long Way Down (Hastings). New York, Random House, 1974; London, Hale, 1975.
The New Mexico Connection (McCloud). New York, Award, and London, Tandem, 1974.
Aftershock (Hastings). New York, Random House, 1975; London, Hale, 1976.
The Faceless Man (as Carter Wick). New York, Saturday Review Press, 1975; London, Hamish Hamilton, 1976.
The Third Victim (Hastings). New York, Dell, 1976; London, Hale, 1977.
Doctor, Lawyer ... (Hastings). New York, Random House, 1977; London, Hale, 1978.
The Watcher (Hastings). New York, Random House, 1978; London, Hale, 1979.
Twospot, with Bill Pronzini. New York, Putnam, 1978.
Night Games (Hastings). New York, Random House, 1979.
Power Plays. New York, Random House, 1979.

OTHER PUBLICATIONS

Other

"Writing and Selling the Police Procedural Novel," in *The Writer* (Boston), January 1976.

Manuscript Collection: Mugar Memorial Library, Boston University.

Collin Wilcox comments:
Every game should have a gameplan. Since I published my first mystery novel, my plan has been to first establish an appealing detective hero, and then build a series around him. With that accomplished, my hero would be required to pay the bills while I ventured farther afield, into the "straight suspense" novels that can offer more challenge than the more formulaic detective story. With that plan in mind, I created Stephen Drake, a clairvoyant crime reporter. After two books, however, it was apparent that Stephen Drake couldn't pay his own way, much less finance excursions into other literary pastures. So I created Frank Hastings, a stubborn, honest, hard-working San Francisco homicide lieutenant. With Pete Friedman, his irascible co-lieutenant in homicide, Hastings has just wrapped up his tenth case. I hope he'll solve many more cases before he retires. Meanwhile, I've made two forays into straight suspense, one under the pseudonym Carter Wick. Neither of the two books has been very successful, but I'm glad I wrote them. I learned from the experience, and intend to continue learning. Like Hastings, I'm stubborn.

*   *   *

Since his first novel featuring Lieutenant Frank Hastings appeared in 1969, Collin Wilcox has achieved widespread recognition as a master of the contemporary police procedural. He is one of the few writers (Ed McBain is another) who has been able to combine the portrayal of investigative police work with incisive psychological and sociological examinations of the people who live, love, and die in a major metropolitan city.

Wilcox's first two novels, however, feature a wholly different kind of detective: Stephen Drake, a San Francisco newspaper reporter who has the gift of extrasensory perception. The first of these, *The Black Door*, relates the story of a double murder connected with a right-wing political group; the better of the two, *The Third Figure*, is about the mysterious slaying of an underworld crime czar. In both books Drake solves the cases through a nice balance of clue-gathering and clairvoyant insight.

But it was in *The Lonely Hunter* that Wilcox created Frank Hastings (then a sergeant on the San Francisco Homicide Squad) and began his climb into the front rank of mystery novelists. This is a tense and powerful story of murder and drug-dealing in the Haight-Ashbury hippie scene of the late 1960's, made intensely personal for Hastings by the fact that his own daughter, a runaway, is involved. Wilcox successfully uses this blend of straightforward police work and deep personal involvement in subsequent novels. *Aftershock* deals with a sadistic youth's campaign of terror against Hastings's girlfriend, Ann Haywood; *The Watcher* places both the lieutenant and his teen-age son in mortal danger in an isolated, rattlesnake-infested area of northern California – and offers in the bargain a strong study of father and son trying to bridge the generation gap. Other entries in the series, such as *Dead Aim*, *The Disappearance*, and *Long Way Down*, feature two or more cases on which Hastings is forced to work simultaneously. While each of these is first-rate, peopled with a rich cross-section of San Francisco's somewhat unique citizenry and lifestyles, they are perhaps less consummate than those books which focus on single cases. The three best of the series, *The Lonely Hunter*, *Aftershock*, and *Doctor, Lawyer ...* – the last a fine suspenseful story about an extortion plot against the city in which the Chief of Police is marked for death – are each single-case novels.

In addition to the Stephen Drake books, Wilcox has also written two other non-procedurals. *The Faceless Man* (as Carter Wick) is pure harrowing suspense involving drugs and a plot by a criminal psychopath to murder a small boy who witnessed a previous homicide. *The Third Victim* is a chilling and unnerving portrait of yet another kind of psychopathic personality.

—Bill Pronzini

WILLIAMS, Charles. American. Born in San Angelo, Texas, 13 August 1909. Educated in Brownsville High School, Texas, through tenth grade. Married Lasca Foster in 1939; one daughter. Radio Operator, United States Merchant Marine, 1929–39; Radio Inspector, Radiomarine Corporation, Galveston, Texas, 1939–42; Electronics Inspector, Puget Sound Navy Yard, Bremerton, Washington, 1942–46; Radio Inspector, Mackay Company, San Francisco, 1946–50. *Died in 1975.*

CRIME PUBLICATIONS

Novels

Hill Girl. New York, Fawcett, 1951; London, Red Seal, 1958.
Big City Girl. New York, Fawcett, 1951; London, Fawcett, 1953.
River Girl. New York, Fawcett, 1951; as *The Catfish Tangle*, London, Cassell, 1963.
Hell Hath No Fury. New York, Fawcett, 1953; London, Red Seal, 1958; as *The Hot Spot*, London, Cassell, 1965.
Nothing in Her Way. New York, Fawcett, 1953; London, Fawcett, 1954.
A Touch of Death. New York, Fawcett, 1954; London, Fawcett, 1955; as *Mix Yourself a Redhead*, London, Cassell, 1965.
Go Home, Stranger. New York, Fawcett, 1954; London, Red Seal, 1957.
Scorpion Reef. New York, Macmillan, 1955; London, Cassell, 1956; as *Gulf Coast Girl*, New York, Dell, 1956.
The Big Bite. New York, Dell, 1956; London, Cassell, 1957.
The Diamond Bikini. New York, Fawcett, 1956; London, Cassell, 1962.
Girl Out Back. New York, Dell, 1958; as *Operator*, London, Cassell, 1958.
Man on the Run. New York, Fawcett, 1958; as *Man in Motion*, London, Cassell, 1959.
Talk of the Town. New York, Dell, 1958; as *Stain of Suspicion*, London, Cassell, 1959.
All the Way. New York, Dell, 1958; as *The Concrete Flamingo*, London, Cassell, 1960.
Uncle Sagamore and His Girls. New York, Fawcett, 1959.
Aground. New York, Viking Press, 1960; London, Cassell, 1961.
The Sailcloth Shroud. New York, Viking Press, and London, Cassell, 1960.
Nude on Thin Ice. New York, Avon, 1961.
The Long Saturday Night. New York, Fawcett, 1962; London, Cassell, 1964.
Dead Calm. New York, Viking Press, 1963; London, Cassell, 1964.
The Wrong Venus. New York, New American Library, 1966; as *Don't Just Stand There*, London, Cassell, 1967.
And the Deep Blue Sea. New York, New American Library, 1971; London, Cassell, 1972.
Man on a Leash. New York, Putnam, 1973; London, Cassell, 1974.

OTHER PUBLICATIONS

Plays

Screenplays: *Les Félins (Joy House)*, with René Clement and Pascal Jardin 1964; *L'Arme à Gauche*, with Claude Sautet, 1965; *Don't Just Stand There*, 1968; *The Pink Jungle*, 1968.

*   *   *

The past and character constitute the mystery in the books of Charles Williams. For instance, the handsome young man in a dinghy, his boat adrift not far off, who seems mad with despair over the death of his fellow passengers, including his wife (*Dead Calm*); a good girl in town who seems as much a threat to the central character, a petty thief, as does a prostitute whose character and past are obvious (*Hell Hath No Fury*); the devastatingly beautiful Cathy Dunbar (central to Williams's plot) who is a clever bitch and a fallen angel besides (*Nothing in Her Way*); the strange girl first seen in a trance, apparent victim of a terrible plot, who blithely sets fire to the house and everything in it she owns (*A Touch of Death*).

His motto could be *cherchez la femme*, because most often the mystery is a woman. But sometimes the man who tells the story and runs into one of these amazing creatures has something to hide himself. The reader wants to know who did it, as well as what they'll do next, and that is not easy to predict. Williams rarely emphasizes detection, but is skilled at the contentions that make suspense, and a master at anticipating, outguessing, and surprising his reader. His most romantic novels are set at sea, for, like Conrad's, his characters handle themselves with more volition there than on land. The hero of two sea thrillers, *Aground* and *Dead Calm*, is the father of the more recent *Man on a Leash*, a tale set in Nevada and northern California. A man and a woman win out against the storms and waves, and best the human elements which take more than a compass to gauge. His best hero and heroine are in his sea thriller *Scorpion Reef*, with its compelling narrative, visual sensuality, and emulations of the plot twists of Joseph Conrad.

His novels include a series set in back-country bayou regions of the South. This recalls the characters of Erskine Caldwell and the milieus and style of some of the later books of James M. Cain. *Big City Girl* is about a scheming, profane villainess who manipulates the more naive hero and the more virtuous women with ease. More upbeat and entertaining than Caldwell's, the back-country novels are, nevertheless, sometimes more concerned with social forces than mystery and suspense.

Williams abstained from formula. Though his plots are often ingeniously devised, and his characterizations remarkably realized, Williams never gained the rank of a first-class thriller writer. There is an inconsistency of quality, especially in the later work, and pragmatic unconcern for value or morality in some of his work, with plot-ideas based on immoral or amoral premises. But he is a writer who seems at home with any new situation or idea. Every novel is different, from *And the Deep Blue Sea* with its large cast of characters seemingly bound for hell, held hostage aboard a ship with a burning cargo, to *Man on the Run* with the relationship of an innocent fugitive and the surprising owner of a house where he hides. His plots can take an astounding turn with the subtle wiggle of a walking girl's fingers, or the toss of a match when calm seems restored. Choosing one or another of the books of Charles Williams to read can be a highly unpredictable and entertaining experience.

—Newton Baird

WILLIAMS, Jay.   See **DELVING, Michael.**

WILLIAMS, (George) Valentine.   Also wrote as Douglas Valentine.   British.   Born 20 October 1883. Educated at Downside School; studied in Germany. Served as a Lieutenant in the Irish Guards, 1915: Military Cross (twice wounded); with the Guards Division Staff,

London, 1918–19; did confidential work for the Foreign Office, London, 1939–41, and at British Embassy, Washington, D.C., 1941–42; Member of the Political Warfare Department, Woburn Abbey, Bedfordshire, 1942–45. Married Alice Crawford. Sub-Editor, 1902–03, and Berlin Correspondent, 1904–09, Reuter's news agency; Journalist for the *Daily Mail*, London, from 1909: Paris Correspondent, 1909–13, Special Correspondent during Portuguese Revolution, 1910, reported Balkan War, 1913, first accredited correspondent to British General Headquarters, 1915, in charge of staff, Versailles Peace Conference, 1919, and later Foreign Editor; free-lance journalist in North Africa and United States during 1930's and 1940's. Chevalier, Order of the Crown of Belgium. *Died 20 November 1946.*

CRIME PUBLICATIONS

Novels (series characters: Dr. Adolph Grundt [Clubfoot]; Detective Sergeant Trevor Dene)

The Man with the Clubfoot (as Douglas Valentine). London, Jenkins, 1918; as Valentine Williams, New York, McBride, 1918.

The Secret Hand: Some Further Adventures by Desmond Okewood of the British Secret Service (as Douglas Valentine). London, Jenkins, 1918; as *Okewood of the Secret Service*, New York, McBride, 1919.

The Return of Clubfoot. London, Jenkins, 1922; as *Island Gold*, Boston, Houghton Mifflin, 1923.

The Yellow Streak. London, Jenkins, and Boston, Houghton Mifflin, 1922.

The Orange Divan. London, Jenkins, and Boston, Houghton Mifflin, 1923.

Clubfoot the Avenger. London, Jenkins, and Boston, Houghton Mifflin, 1924.

The Three of Clubs. London, Hodder and Stoughton, and Boston, Houghton Mifflin, 1924.

The Red Mass. London, Hodder and Stoughton, and Boston, Houghton Mifflin, 1925.

Mr. Ramosi. London, Hodder and Stoughton, and Boston, Houghton Mifflin, 1926.

The Pigeon House. London, Hodder and Stoughton, 1926; as *The Key Man*, Boston, Houghton Mifflin, 1926.

The Eye in Attendance (Dene). London, Hodder and Stoughton, and Boston, Houghton Mifflin, 1927.

The Crouching Beast (Clubfoot). London, Hodder and Stoughton, and Boston, Houghton Mifflin, 1928.

Mannequin. London, Hodder and Stoughton, 1930; as *The Mysterious Miss Morrisot*, Boston, Houghton Mifflin, 1930.

Death Answers the Bell (Dene). London, Hodder and Stoughton, 1931; Boston, Houghton Mifflin, 1932.

The Gold Comfit Box (Clubfoot). London, Hodder and Stoughton, 1932; as *The Mystery of the Gold Box*, Boston, Houghton Mifflin, 1932.

The Clock Ticks On (Dene). London, Hodder and Stoughton, and Boston, Houghton Mifflin, 1933.

Fog, with Dorothy Rice Sims. London, Hodder and Stoughton, and Boston, Houghton Mifflin, 1933.

The Portcullis Room. London, Hodder and Stoughton, and Boston, Houghton Mifflin, 1934.

Masks Off at Midnight (Dene). London, Hodder and Stoughton, and Boston, Houghton Mifflin, 1934.

The Clue of the Rising Moon (Dene). London, Hodder and Stoughton, and Boston, Houghton Mifflin, 1935.

Dead Man Manor. London, Hodder and Stoughton, and Boston, Houghton Mifflin, 1936.

The Spider's Touch (Clubfoot). London, Hodder and Stoughton, and Boston, Houghton Mifflin, 1936.

The Fox Prowls. London, Hodder and Stoughton, and Boston, Houghton Mifflin, 1939.
Double Death, with others. London, Gollancz, 1939.
Courier to Marrakesh (Clubfoot). London, Hodder and Stoughton, 1944; Boston, Houghton Mifflin, 1946.
Skeleton Out of the Cupboard. London, Hodder and Stoughton, 1946.

Short Stories

The Knife Behind the Curtain: Tales of Secret Service and Crime. London, Hodder and Stoughton, and Boston, Houghton Mifflin, 1930.
Mr. Treadgold Cuts In. London, Hodder and Stoughton, 1937; as *The Curiosity of Mr. Treadgold*, Boston, Houghton Mifflin, 1937.

OTHER PUBLICATIONS

Plays

Berlin, with Alice Crawford (produced New York, 1931; London, 1932).

Screenplay: *Land of Hope and Glory*, with Adrian Brunel, 1927.

Other

With Our Army in Flanders. London, Arnold, 1915.
Adventures of an Ensign (as Vedette). Edinburgh, Blackwood, 1917.
"Gaboriau: Father of Detective Novels," in *National Review* (London), December 1923.
The World of Action: The Autobiography of Valentine Williams. London, Hamish Hamilton, and Boston, Houghton Mifflin, 1938.

*   *   *

Journalist, actor, screenwriter, and mystery author, Valentine Williams produced more than 30 novels of espionage and suspense while also engaged in his many other occupations. Noteworthy among his non-fiction works is his comprehensive biographical and critical account of Emile Gaboriau, the French mystery author who wrote 21 massive novels in 13 years.

Williams's fictional works are primarily suspense or spy novels rather than detective novels, although he did create several notable characters. Dr. Adolph Grundt, known as Clubfoot, is a tempestuous German spy, simian in appearance and villainous in performance who first appeared in *The Man with the Clubfoot*, and appears in seven subsequent books. Trevor Dene, another series character, is a tawny-haired, bespectacled, young Detective Sergeant from Scotland Yard who has Holmesian powers of observation and deduction. He finds himself on a busman's holiday in the Adirondacks when a seeming suicide turns out to be murder in *The Clue of the Rising Moon* and again on Long Island in *Masks Off at Midnight* when a pageant is the scene of a homocide. Two other interesting characters are "The Fox," Baron Alexis De Bahl, in *The Fox Prowls* and Mr. Treadgold, a West End tailor and amateur detective, in *Dead Man Manor*.

—Mary Ann Grochowski

WILLIS, Ted (Edward Henry Willis; Baron Willis of Chislehurst). British. Born in Tottenham, Middlesex, 13 January 1918. Educated at state schools, including Tottenham Central School, 1923–33. Served in the Royal Fusiliers, 1940; Writer for the War Office and Ministry of Information. Married Audrey Hale in 1944; one son and one daughter. Artistic Director, Unity Theatre, London, 1945–48. Since 1967, Director, World Wide Pictures; Director, Capital Radio, London. Executive Member, League of Dramatists, London, 1948–74. Chairman, 1958–63, and President, 1963–68 and since 1976, Writers Guild of Great Britain; President, International Writers Guild, 1967–69. Since 1964, Governor, Churchill Theatre Trust, Bromley, Kent; Member of the Board of Governors, National Film School, London, 1970–73. Recipient: Berlin Festival Award, for screenplay, 1957; Edinburgh Festival Award; Writers Guild Award, 1964, 1967; Royal Society of Arts Silver Medal, 1967; Variety Guild of Great Britain Award, 1976. Fellow, Royal Society of Arts. Life Peer, 1963. Agent: Elaine Greene Ltd., 31 Newington Green, London, N16 9PU. Address: 5 Shepherds Green, Chislehurst, Kent BR7 6PB, England.

CRIME PUBLICATIONS

Novels (series character: George Dixon)

The Blue Lamp (Dixon). London, Convoy, 1950.
The Devil's Churchyard. London, Parrish, 1957.
Dixon of Dock Green: My Life, with Charles Hatton. London, Kimber, 1960.
Dixon of Dock Green: A Novel, with Paul Graham. London, Mayflower, 1961.
Death May Surprise Us. London, Macmillan, 1974; as *Westminster One*, New York, Putnam, 1975.
The Left-Handed Sleeper. London, Macmillan, 1975; New York, Putnam, 1976.
Man-Eater. London, Macmillan, 1976; New York, Morrow, 1977.
The Churchill Commando. London, Macmillan, and New York, Morrow, 1977.
The Buckingham Palace Connection. London, Macmillan, and New York, Morrow, 1978.
The Lions of Judah. London, Macmillan, 1979.

Uncollected Short Stories

"The Man from the White Mountains," in *Winter's Crimes 7*, edited by George Hardinge. London, Macmillan, 1975.
"Proof," in *Winter's Crimes 10*, edited by Hilary Watson. London, Macmillan, 1978.

OTHER PUBLICATIONS

Novel

Black Beauty. London, Hamlyn, 1972.

Plays

Sabotage (as John Bishop) (produced London, 1943).
Buster (produced London, 1943). London, Fore Publications, n.d.
All Change Here (produced London, 1944).
"God Bless the Guv'nor": A Moral Melodrama in Which the Twin Evils of Trades Unionism and Strong Drink Are Exposed, "After Mrs. Henry Wood" (produced London, 1945). London, New Theatre Publications, 1945.
The Yellow Star (also director: produced London, 1945).
What Happened to Love? (produced London, 1947).

No Trees in the Street (produced London, 1948).

The Lady Purrs (produced London, 1950). London, Deane, and Boston, Baker, 1950.

The Magnificent Moodies (produced London, 1952).

The Blue Lamp, with Jan Read (produced London, 1952).

A Kiss for Adele, with Talbot Rothwell, adaptation of the play by Barillet and Grédy (produced London, 1952).

Kid Kenyon Rides Again, with Allan Mackinnon (produced Bromley, Kent, 1954).

George Comes Home. London, French, 1955.

Doctor in the House, adaptation of the novel by Richard Gordon (produced London, 1956). London, Evans and New York, French 1957.

Woman in a Dressing Gown (televised, 1956). Included in *Woman in a Dressing Gown and Other Television Plays*, 1959; (revised version, produced Bromley, Kent, 1963; London, 1964); London, Evans, 1964.

The Young and the Guilty (televised, 1956). Included in *Woman in a Dressing Gown and Other Television Plays*, 1959.

Look in Any Window (televised, 1958). Included in *Woman in a Dressing Gown and Other Television Plays*, 1959.

Hot Summer Night (produced Bournemouth and London, 1958). London, French, 1959.

Woman in a Dressing Gown and Other Television Plays (includes *The Young and the Guilty* and *Look in Any Window*). London, Barrie and Rockliff, 1959.

Brothers-in-Law, with Henry Cecil, adaptation of the novel by Cecil (produced Wimbledon, Surrey, 1959). London, French, 1959.

When in Rome, with Ken Ferry, music by Kramer, lyrics by Eric Shaw, adaptation of a play by Garinei and Giovannini (produced Oxford and London, 1959).

The Eyes of Youth, adaptation of the novel *A Dread of Burning* by Rosemary Timperley (as *Fairwell Yesterday*, produced Worthing, Sussex, 1959; as *The Eyes of Youth*, produced Bournemouth, 1959). London, Evans, 1960.

Mother, adaptation of the novel by Gorky (produced Croydon, Surrey, 1961).

Doctor at Sea, adaptation of the novel by Richard Gordon (produced Bromley, Kent, 1961; London, 1966). London, Evans, and New York, French, 1961.

The Little Goldmine. London, French, 1962.

A Slow Roll of Drums (produced Bromley, Kent, 1964).

A Murder of Crows (produced Bromley, Kent, 1966).

The Ballad of Queenie Swann (televised, 1966; revised version, music by Dick Manning and Marvin Laird, lyrics by Ted Willis, produced Guildford, Surrey, 1967; as *Queenie*, produced London, 1967).

Dead on Saturday (produced Leatherhead, Surrey, 1972). London, Odanti Script Service, 1970.

Mr. Polly, music by Michael Begg and Ivor Slaney, lyrics by Willis, adaptation of the novel by H. G. Wells (produced Bromley, Kent, 1977).

Screenplays: *The Waves Roll On* (documentary), 1945; *Holiday Camp*, with others, 1947; *Good Time Girl*, with Muriel and Sydney Box, 1948; *A Boy, A Girl, and a Bike*, 1949; *The Huggetts Abroad*, with others, 1949; *The Undefeated* (documentary), 1950; *The Blue Lamp*, with others, 1950; *The Wallet*, 1952; *Top of the Form*, with John Paddy Carstairs and Patrick Kirwan, 1953; *Trouble in Store*, with John Paddy Carstairs and Maurice Cowan, 1953; *The Large Rope*, 1953; *One Good Turn*, with John Paddy Carstairs and Maurice Cowan, 1954; *Burnt Evidence*, 1954; *Up to His Neck*, with others, 1954; *It's Great to Be Young*, 1956; *The Skywalkers*, 1956; *Woman in a Dressing Gown*, 1957; *The Young and the Guilty*, 1958; *No Trees in the Street*, 1959; *Six Men and a Nightingale*, 1961; *Flame in the Streets*, 1961; *The Horsemasters*, 1961; *Bitter Harvest*, 1963; *Last Bus to Banjo Creek*, 1968; *Our Miss Fred*, 1972; and other documentaries.

Radio Plays: *Big Bertha*, 1962; *And No Birds Sing*, 1979.

Television Plays: *The Handlebar, The Pattern of Marriage, Big City, Dial 999, The Sullavan Brothers, Lifeline*, and *Taxi* series; *The Young and the Guilty*, 1956; *Woman in a Dressing Gown*, 1956; *Look in Any Window*, 1958; *Strictly for the Sparrows*, 1958; *Scent of Fear*, 1959; *Dixon of Dock Green* series, 1960 and later; *Days of Vengeance*, with Edward J. Mason, 1960; *Flowers of Evil* series, with Mason, 1961; *Outbreak of Murder*, with Mason; *Sergeant Cork* series, 1963; *The Four Seasons of Rosie Carr*, 1964; *Dream of a Summer Night*, 1965; *Mrs. Thursday* series, 1966; *The Ballad of Queenie Swann*, 1966; *Virgin of the Secret Service* series, 1968; *Crimes of Passion* series, 1970–72; *Copper's End* series, 1971; *Hunter's Walk* series, 1973, 1976; *Black Beauty* series, 1975; *Barney's Last Battle*, 1976; *Street Party*, 1977.

Other

Fighting Youth of Russia.   London, Russia Today Society, 1942.
The Devil's Churchyard (juvenile).   London, Parrish, 1957.
Seven Gates to Nowhere (juvenile).   London, Parrish, 1958.
Whatever Happened to Tom Mix? The Story of One of My Lives.   London, Cassell, 1970.

Theatrical Activities:

Director: **Plays** – Unity Theatre, London: *The Yellow Star*, 1945; *Boy Meets Girl* by Bella and Samuel Spewack, 1946; *All God's Chillun Got Wings* by Eugene O'Neill, 1946; *Golden Boy* by Clifford Odets, 1947; *Anna Christie* by Eugene O'Neill, 1947.

*   *   *

A late starter in the field of the crime novel, Ted Willis came to it with a considerable reputation in Britain both as a television writer (he was responsible for the creation of one of the best-loved characters on the small screen, the policeman Dixon of Dock Green) and as a playwright. The qualities he had shown in these pursuits, warmth, compassion, a feeling for the ordinary man, he brought to the crime novel.

But Ted Willis is also Lord Willis, a politically created Life Peer, a member of the Labour Party. And it was this aspect of his life that provided him with the setting for his first original novel, *Death May Surprise Us*, a story in which the Prime Minister of Great Britain is kidnapped. To it he brought his considerable knowledge of the everyday workings of politics, the little things, the day-to-day routine. And it was this accuracy of detail, a quality no doubt learnt in the making of television plays and series where in general an extremely lifelike surface is created, that gave to the book its distinctive quality. As a novel, however, it lacked the very quality spoken of in its title, surprise. Its people were inclined to behave in the expected way, lifelike though that was.

A year later he gave us *The Left-Handed Sleeper*, a novel on the fascinating subject of the sleeper spy, the man or woman left for years to build up a cover in a foreign country and then suddenly activated by a control in a distant and perhaps now largely forgotten homeland. To this he brought the same concentration on everyday detail that had given his first book its authenticity but now he seemingly felt more free to take risks with the characterisation, to create people who behaved occasionally in an unexpected way. And he concentrated a good deal of the book on the figure of the spy's wife (he has always been good at portraying women) with the result that you felt "Here is something that might have happened to me, or to my wife."

For his next book, *Man-Eater*, he deserted the world of Westminster and Whitehall to write something in the nature of a pure thriller. He took a very simple idea – two tigers escape into the English countryside – and he showed what the effects would be, in the likeliest manner. This was the "You are there" novel at its best. Then it was back to politics. But in an interestingly different way. *The Churchill Commando* is a sample of what might be called political action fiction, a genre comparable with science fiction in that it is always set in the future, though often in a pretty near future, and it creates a utopia (or a hell) there. There is quite a considerable British sub-industry in such crime books and Ted Willis's was a good example, a warning about the possible consequences of Britain's present actions. And, with his gift of giving life to the ordinary, it was highly effective as guesswork about the future. *The Buckingham Palace Connection* took yet another turn, a plunge back into the past with a conjecture about the fate of the children of the last Tsar. In one way it exemplifies to the full the Willis gift for making events seem as if they had happened to you: the narrator of the present-day outer story is a certain Life Peer called Lord Willis.

—H. R. F. Keating

WILLS, (Maitland) Cecil M(elville).   British.   Born in 1891.

CRIME PUBLICATIONS

Novels (series characters: Geoffrey Boscobell; Roger Ellerdine; Sylvester Pinkney)

Author in Distress (Boscobell).   London, Heritage, 1934; as *Number 18*, London, Lane, 1934.
Death at the Pelican (Boscobell).   London, Heritage, 1934.
Death Treads – (Boscobell).   London, Heritage, 1935.
Then Came the Police (Boscobell).   London, Heritage, 1935.
The Chamois Murder (Boscobell).   London, Heritage, 1935.
Fatal Accident (Boscobell).   London, Hodder and Stoughton, 1936.
Defeat of a Detective (Boscobell).   London, Hodder and Stoughton, 1936.
On the Night in Question (Boscobell).   London, Hodder and Stoughton, 1937.
A Body in the Dawn (Boscobell).   London, Hodder and Stoughton, 1938.
The Case of the Calabar Bean (Boscobell).   London, Hodder and Stoughton, 1939.
The Case of the R.E. Pipe (Boscobell, Ellerdine).   London, Hodder and Stoughton, 1940.
The Clue of the Lost Hour (Boscobell, Ellerdine).   London, Hodder and Stoughton, 1949.
The Clue of the Golden Ear-Ring (Boscobell, Ellerdine).   London, Hodder and Stoughton, 1950.
Who Killed Brother Treasurer? (Ellerdine).   London, Hodder and Stoughton, 1951.
What Say the Jury? (Ellerdine).   London, Hodder and Stoughton, 1951.
The Dead Voice (Ellerdine).   London, Hodder and Stoughton, 1952.
It Pays to Die (Ellerdine).   London, Hodder and Stoughton, 1953.
Death on the Line.   London, Hutchinson, 1954.
Death in the Dark (Ellerdine).   London, Hutchinson, 1955.
Midsummer Murder.   London, Hutchinson, 1956.
The Tiger Strikes Again (Ellerdine).   London, Hutchinson, 1957.
Mere Murder (Ellerdine).   London, Hale, 1958.
The Case of the Empty Beehive (Pinkney).   London, Hale, 1959.
Death of a Best Seller (Pinkney).   London, Hale, 1959.

The Colonel's Foxhound (Pinkney).   London, Hale, 1960.
Justice in Jeopardy (Ellerdine).   London, Hale, 1961.

*   *   *

Cecil M. Wills wrote numerous detective novels most of them featuring series detectives Geoffrey Boscobell or Roger Ellerdine. The early novels experiment with the incomparable Boscobell, who develops from an inexperienced but perceptive police sergeant to a skillful Scotland Yard superintendent. In the later novels, Ellerdine and his colleague Cherry Blossom replace Boscobell and exhibit more sleuthing powers than their predecessor. Wills frequently laces the mystery with political intrigue, particularly in his later books.

Boscobell's cunning, like that of Ellerdine and Blossom, increases as Wills's handling of the genre improves. In *Death at the Pelican* Boscobell uses his wits to escape murder and arrest his arch enemy, Theodore Edwards. In *The Chamois Murder* Boscobell, now a superintendent at Scotland Yard, foils the same nemesis by discovering, in a maze of false clues, that Edwards's partner committed burglary and murder; the partner, in his haste to provide an alibi, broadcast the Big Ben chimes three minutes early. The mechanics and motives of the crime and the method of solution are smooth and credible in the Boscobell mysteries, because, with each book, Wills extends the greed and refines the cunning of the nemesis to keep pace with the sharpening talents of the detective. Edwards is a worthy opponent who skillfully eludes the authorities throughout the novels. In *Death at the Pelican*, he causes nine days of wonder in the newspapers with a sensational escape from a police van which was taking him to trial. His disappearance in *The Chamois Murder*, in which he escapes detection for months by adopting the disguise of a baron, is even more startling. Though Edwards's identity is suspected, he is not apprehended until Boscobell discovers the mistake of the criminal's partner.

Wills's use of worthy opponents, slick detection, intricate plots, and ingenious murders culminates in the Ellerdine and Blossom mysteries. *The Tiger Strikes Again* features the impressive victory of this pair over the bizarre murderer Dr. Floyd Huish, the creator of a snake venom that destroys the most influential drug peddlers in London. Horatio Pinckney, in *The Colonel's Foxhound*, exhibits the same sleuthing prowess as Ellerdine and Blossom. Commissioned by a count to find some stolen treaty papers, Pinckney unearths a murder, discovers smuggled rubies and, with the help of the colonel's foxhound, restores the stolen papers. The book features a very intricate murder: the murderer removes a bullet from the victim and replaces it with one from another gun. The tightly-knit plot closes with the detective's personal comments; Wills often used this classic device – the detective's lengthy explanation and the criminal's confession – in his later books.

In his 30-year career Wills developed into a skillful writer: the increasing talents of his detectives correspond to his growing technical mastery of the genre.

—Donna Rose Casella Kern

WILMER, Dale.   See MILLER, Wade.

WILSON, Colin (Henry). British. Born in Leicester, 26 June 1931. Educated at Gateway Secondary Technical School, Leicester, 1942–47. Served in the Royal Air Force, 1949–50. Married 1) Dorothy Betty Troop in 1951 (marriage dissolved), one son; 2) Pamela Joy Stewart in 1960, two sons and one daughter. Laboratory Assistant, Gateway School, 1948–49; tax collector, Leicester and Rugby, 1949–50; labourer and hospital porter in London, 1951–53; salesman for the magazines *Paris Review* and *Merlin*, Paris, 1953. Full-time Writer since 1954. British Council Lecturer in Germany, 1957; Writer-in-Residence, Hollins College, Virginia, 1966–67; Visiting Professor, University of Washington, Seattle, 1968; Professor, Institute of the Mediterranean (Dowling College, New York), Majorca, 1969; Visiting Professor, Rutgers University, New Brunswick, New Jersey, 1974. Agent: David Bolt, Bolt and Watson Ltd., 8–12 Old Queen Street, Storey's Gate, London SW1H 9HP. Address: Tetherdown, Gorran Haven, Cornwall, England.

CRIME PUBLICATIONS

Novels

> *Ritual in the Dark.* London, Gollancz, and Boston, Houghton Mifflin, 1960.
> *Necessary Doubt.* London, Barker, and New York, Simon and Schuster, 1964.
> *The Glass Cage: An Unconventional Detective Story.* London, Barker, 1966; New York, Random House, 1967.
> *The Killer.* London, New English Library, 1970; as *Lingard*, New York, Crown, 1970.
> *The Schoolgirl Murder Case.* London, Hart Davis MacGibbon, and New York, Crown, 1974.

OTHER PUBLICATIONS

Novels

> *Adrift in Soho.* London, Gollancz, and Boston, Houghton Mifflin, 1961.
> *The World of Violence.* London, Gollancz, 1963; as *The Violent World of Hugh Greene*, Boston, Houghton Mifflin, 1963.
> *Man Without a Shadow: The Diary of an Existentialist.* London, Barker, 1963; as *The Sex Diary of Gerard Sorme*, New York, Dial Press, 1963.
> *The Mind Parasites.* London, Barker, and Sauk City, Wisconsin, Arkham House, 1967.
> *The Philosopher's Stone.* London, Barker, 1969; New York, Crown, 1971.
> *The God of the Labyrinth.* London, Hart Davis, 1970; as *The Hedonists*, New York, New American Library, 1971.
> *The Black Room.* London, Weidenfeld and Nicolson, 1971; New York, Pyramid, 1975.
> *The Space Vampires.* London, Hart Davis MacGibbon, and New York, Random House, 1976.

Short Story

> *The Return of Lloigor.* London, Village Press, 1974.

Plays

> *Viennese Interlude* (produced Scarborough, Yorkshire, and London, 1960).

Strindberg (as *Pictures in a Bath of Acid*, produced Leeds, Yorkshire, 1971; as *Strindberg: A Psychological Portrait*, produced New York, 1974; as *Strindberg: A Fool's Decision*, produced London, 1975). London, Calder and Boyars, 1970; New York, Random House, 1971.

Other

The Outsider. London, Gollancz, and Boston, Houghton Mifflin, 1956.

Religion and the Rebel. London, Gollancz, and Boston, Houghton Mifflin, 1957.

The Age of Defeat. London, Gollancz, 1959; as *The Stature of Man*, Boston, Houghton Mifflin, 1959.

Encyclopaedia of Murder, with Patricia Pitman. London, Barker, 1961; New York, Putnam, 1962.

The Strength to Dream: Literature and the Imagination. London, Gollancz, and Boston, Houghton Mifflin, 1962.

Origins of the Sexual Impulse. London, Barker, and New York, Putnam, 1963.

Rasputin and the Fall of the Romanovs. London, Barker, and New York, Farrar Straus, 1964.

Brandy of the Damned: Discoveries of a Musical Eclectic. London, Baker, 1964; as *Chords and Discords: Purely Personal Opinions on Music*, New York, Crown, 1966; augmented edition, as *Colin Wilson on Music*, London, Pan, 1967.

Beyond the Outsider: The Philosophy of the Future. London, Barker, and Boston, Houghton Mifflin, 1965.

Eagle and Earwig (essays). London, Baker, 1965.

Introduction to the New Existentialism. London, Hutchinson, 1966; Boston, Houghton Mifflin, 1967.

Sex and the Intelligent Teenager. London, Arrow, 1966; New York, Pyramid, 1968.

Voyage to a Beginning (autobiography). London, Cecil and Amelia Woolf, 1966; New York, Crown, 1969.

Bernard Shaw: A Reassessment. London, Hutchinson, and New York, Atheneum, 1969.

A Casebook of Murder. London, Frewin, 1969; New York, Cowles, 1970.

Poetry and Mysticism. San Francisco, City Lights, 1969; London, Hutchinson, 1970.

The Strange Genius of David Lindsay, with E. H. Visiak and J. B. Pick. London, Baker, 1970.

The Occult. New York, Random House, and London, Hodder and Stoughton, 1971.

New Pathways in Psychology: Maslow and the Post-Freudian Revolution. New York, Taplinger, and London, Gollancz, 1972.

Order of Assassins: The Psychology of Murder. London, Hart Davis, 1972.

L'Amour: The Ways of Love, photographs by Piero Rimaldi. New York, Crown, 1972.

Strange Powers. London, Latimer New Dimensions, 1973; New York, Random House, 1975.

Tree by Tolkien. London, Covent Garden Press-Inca Books, 1973; Santa Barbara, California, Capra Press, 1974.

Hermann Hesse. London, Village Press, and Philadelphia, Leaves of Grass Press, 1974.

Wilhelm Reich. London, Village Press, and Philadelphia, Leaves of Grass Press, 1974.

Jorge Luis Borges. London, Village Press, and Philadelphia, Leave of Grass Press, 1974.

A Book of Booze. London, Gollancz, 1974.

The Unexplained. Lake Oswego, Oregon, Lost Pleiade Press, 1975.

Mysterious Powers. London, Aldus, and Danbury, Connecticut, Danbury Press, 1975; as *They Had Strange Powers*, New York, Doubleday, 1975.

The Craft of the Novel. London, Gollancz, 1975.

Enigmas and Mysteries.　London, Aldus, and New York, Doubleday, 1976.
The Geller Phenomenon.　London, Aldus, 1976.
Mysteries: An Investigation into the Occult, The Paranormal and the Supernatural.　London, Hodder and Stoughton, and New York, Putnam, 1978.
Science Fiction as Existentialism.　Hayes, Middlesex, Bran's Head Books, 1978.

Editor, *Colin Wilson's Men of Mystery.*　London, W. H. Allen, 1977.
Editor, *Dark Dimensions: A Celebration of the Occult.*　New York, Everest House, 1978.

Bibliography: in *Colin Wilson* by John A. Weigel, New York, Twayne, 1975.

Manuscript Collection: University of Texas, Austin.

*　　*　　*

Colin Wilson is so much more than a writer of "mysteries" that his inclusion here might be equivocal if mystery writers had not recently become intellectually respectable. Wilson's first book, *The Outsider*, appeared in 1956 with a bang. Almost instantly an international best-seller, this compendium of learning later became controversial. Critics who at first had enthusiastically praised young Wilson as a prodigy of erudition reconsidered. After reading the work more carefully – or perhaps for the first time – many denounced him as a fraud.

Wilson, however, survived the attack on him and his first work. In fact, he flourished, establishing during the next two decades his professional competence as novelist, biographer, philosopher, and critic. In his crusade to defeat defeatism Wilson has not hesitated to mix genres, so that his novels are often didactic and his non-fiction anecdotal.

When read as Wilson intends them to be, his speculative fiction and so-called "crime novels" (Wilson's term) invite the reader to do much more than try to solve puzzles. Wilson makes no attempt to swindle the reader into vicarious thrills. He treats crime, for example, philosophically and esthetically. His killers are artists, and his detectives humanists. The "solution" is generally predictable because it is both logical and psychological. Wilson intends that killers, detectives, and readers all experience an epiphany. The victims, of course, are beyond redemption.

In *Ritual in the Dark* Wilson explores murder as a creative act. In *Necessary Doubt* the detective is an existentialist theologian who allows the criminal to escape at the end. In *The Glass Cage* the detective, an authority on the works of William Blake, is finally converted to the point of view of the killer. In *The Killer* the criminal is defended by the novelist as "not necessarily and completely wrong." In *The Schoolgirl Murder Case* the detective behaves much like a missionary. Wilson sees an affinity between detecting crimes and saving souls and thus Saltfleet in *The Schoolgirl Murder Case* is a new kind of detective, mixing mysticism and science. At one point he even consults a lady who specializes in psychic visions. Not surprisingly, her intuitions prove to be correct. It hardly seems to be playing the game fairly, however, to credit mystic events as equal to so-called real events in a hard-headed detective story. Yet Wilson may have found a new formula as viable for its genre as his new existentialism hopes to be for philosophy.

If Wilson shifts with the winds of opportunity it is because he is authentic enough to relate himself to humanity and its needs. Such awareness is indeed in danger of being mistrusted by skeptics not accustomed to dealing with a writer's work in terms of his intentions. Wilson addresses himself to strictly contemporary problems as he tries to penetrate the fog that for him obscures *real* reality. His methodology participates in his urgency, for his creed specifies that man is always more than any method. At times Wilson may be only absurdly heroic, in the sense of working against overwhelming odds; but he knows it more often than not and indulges in a minimum of despair and irony. Indeed, his urgency usually eradicates irony and discourages witty trivia as he fights the slackness which would follow an acceptance of despair as terminal. Determined to survive, he feels that, as the first new existentialist, he has earned the right to his optimism. Anyway, his ultimate wrongness or rightness may be insignificant when compared to the possible significance of his thrust and impact in nontechnical contexts.

Balanced, then, at the edge of mysticism in a universe which is obviously not governed by any of the old Sunday School gods, Wilson asks, as earnestly as Julian Huxley has, for religion without revelation. He would also develop a science without limitations on freedom. He urges man toward salvation by exhorting and stimulating him to see more, to hear more, to feel more, to touch more – that is, to apprehend what is *really* out there and what is *really* inside onself. The Outsider is invited to embrace the complete universe and to cure his outsiderism. Colin Wilson would have us save our souls!

—John A. Weigel

WITTING, Clifford. British. Born in London in 1907. Educated at Eltham College, London, 1916–24. Served as a bombardier in the Royal Artillery, 1942–44, and as a warrant officer in the Royal Army Ordnance Corps, 1944–46. Married Ellen Marjorie Steward in 1934; one daughter. Clerk, Lloyds Bank, London, 1924–42. Honorary Editor, *Old Elthamian*, London, from 1947. *Died.*

CRIME PUBLICATIONS

Novels (series characters: Sergeant/Inspector Peter Bradford; Inspector Harry Charlton)

Murder in Blue (Charlton).   London, Hodder and Stoughton, and New York, Scribner, 1937.
Midsummer Murder (Charlton).   London, Hodder and Stoughton, 1937.
The Case of the Michaelmas Goose (Charlton).   London, Hodder and Stoughton, 1938.
Catt Out of the Bag (Charlton).   London, Hodder and Stoughton, 1939.
Measure for Murder (Charlton).   London, Hodder and Stoughton, 1941; New York, Garland, 1976.
Subject: Murder (Charlton, Bradford).   London, Hodder and Stoughton, 1945.
Let X Be The Murderer (Charlton, Bradford).   London, Hodder and Stoughton, 1947.
Dead on Time (Charlton, Bradford).   London, Hodder and Stoughton, 1948.
A Bullet for Rhino (Charlton).   London, Hodder and Stoughton, 1950.
The Case of the Busy Bees (Charlton, Bradford).   London, Hodder and Stoughton, 1952.
Silence after Dinner (Charlton, Bradford).   London, Hodder and Stoughton, 1953.
Mischief in the Offing.   London, Hodder and Stoughton, 1958.
There Was a Crooked Man (Bradford).   London, Hodder and Stoughton, 1960; New York, British Book Centre, 1962.
Driven to Kill (Bradford).   London, Hodder and Stoughton, 1961.
Villainous Saltpetre.   London, Hodder and Stoughton, 1962.
Crime in Whispers (Bradford).   London, Hodder and Stoughton, 1964.

OTHER PUBLICATIONS

Plays

Screenplay: *Park Place (Norman Conquest)*, with others, 1953.

Television Plays: *Subject: Murder*, from his own novel, 1964; *The Quick One*, from a work by G. K. Chesterton, 1964.

Other

The Knights of St. Perran (juvenile).   London, University of London Press, 1948.
A Rotarian's Journal, Being the Record of the Adventures and Misadventures of an Obscure Member of a Great Fellowship.   Mitcham, Surrey, West Brothers, 1950.
The Facts of English, with Ronald Ridout.   London, Ginn, 1964; revised edition, London, Pan, 1973.
English Proverbs Explained, with Ronald Ridout.   London, Heinemann, 1967; New York, Barnes and Noble, 1968.

Editor, *The Uttermost Part of the Earth*, by E. Lucas Bridges.   London, Hodder and Stoughton, 1948.
Editor, *In the Land of Mao Tse-Tung*, by Carlo Suigo, translated by Muriel Currey.   London, Allen and Unwin, 1953.
Editor, *Raffles of the Eastern Isles*, by C. E. Wurtzburg.   London, Hodder and Stoughton, 1954.
Editor, *Kuwait and Her Neighbours*, by H. R. P. Dickson.   London, Allen and Unwin, 1956.
Editor, *The Unmarried Mother and Her Child*, by Virginia Wimperis.   London, Allen and Unwin, 1960.

*   *   *

Clifford Witting is a British author who is almost completely unknown in America. He wrote 16 detective novels of varying merit between his debut in 1937 and his final work in 1964. His masterpiece, *Measure for Murder*, was selected by Jacques Barzun and Wendell Hertig Taylor as one of the Fifty Classics of Crime Fiction 1900–1950.

Witting's first series character is the faceless Detective-Inspector Harry Charlton of the Lulverton CID, but he is eventually put out to pasture and replaced by his subordinate, Detective-Constable Peter Bradford, who achieves promotion to inspector. Witting's early work lacks distinction, but *Measure for Murder* is a complete reversal of form. Its prologue details the discovery of a murdered man, and then switches to a brilliant and gripping account of life in a theatrical troupe written by one of its members, Vaughan Tudor. When the manuscript ends the reader is jolted with the discovery that the sympathetic Tudor is the victim. Charlton's investigation follows. Witting's next novel *Subject: Murder* is almost as effective. It's narrated by Bradford, and tells about his army training experiences. It also contains clues that will help Charlton solve a murder that takes place in an army camp. The more conventional *Let X Be the Murderer* commences when a wealthy and aged knight seeks help from the police because he has been attacked in the middle of the night by a pair of luminous hands. Of Witting's subsequent books the best are *Dead on Time*, *A Bullet for Rhino*, and *There Was a Crooked Man*.

—Charles Shibuk

WOODS, Sara. Pseudonym for Sara Bowen-Judd, née Hutton. British. Born in Bradford, Yorkshire, 7 March 1922. Educated privately and at Convent of the Sacred Heart, Filey, Yorkshire, 1932–37. Married Anthony George Bowen-Judd in 1946. Worked in a bank and in a solicitor's office, London, during World War II; pig breeder, 1948–54; Assistant to Company Secretary, Rotol Ltd., Gloucester, 1954–58; Registrar, Saint Mary's University, Halifax, Nova Scotia, 1958–64. Address: 389 Dundas Street, Apartment N16–1, London, Ontario N6B 3L5, Canada.

Crime Publications

Novels (series character: Antony Maitland in all books)

Bloody Instructions. London, Collins, and New York, Harper, 1962.
Malice Domestic. London, Collins, 1962.
The Taste of Fears. London, Collins, 1963; as *The Third Encounter*, New York, Harper, 1963.
Error of the Moon. London, Collins, 1963.
Trusted Like the Fox. London, Collins, 1964; New York, Harper, 1965.
This Little Measure. London, Collins, 1964.
The Windy Side of the Law. London, Collins, and New York, Harper, 1965.
Though I Know She Lies. London, Collins, 1965; New York, Holt Rinehart, 1972.
Enter Certain Murderers. London, Collins, and New York, Harper, 1966.
Let's Choose Executors. London, Collins, 1966; New York, Harper, 1967.
The Case Is Altered. London, Collins, and New York, Harper, 1967.
And Shame the Devil. London, Collins, 1967; New York, Holt Rinehart, 1972.
Knives Have Edges. London, Collins, 1968; New York, Holt Rinehart, 1970.
Past Praying For. London, Collins, and New York, Harper, 1968.
Tarry and Be Hanged. London, Collins, 1969; New York, Holt Rinehart, 1971.
An Improbable Fiction. London, Collins, 1970; New York, Holt Rinehart, 1971.
Serpent's Tooth. London, Collins, 1971; New York, Holt Rinehart, 1973.
The Knavish Crows. London, Collins, 1971.
They Love Not Poison. London, Macmillan, and New York, Holt Rinehart, 1972.
Yet She Must Die. London, Macmillan, 1973; New York, Holt Rinehart, 1974.
Enter the Corpse. London, Macmillan, 1973; New York, Holt Rinehart, 1974.
Done to Death. London, Macmillan, 1974; New York, Holt Rinehart, 1975.
A Show of Violence. London, Macmillan, and New York, McKay, 1975.
My Life Is Done. London, Macmillan, 1975; New York, St. Martin's Press, 1976.
The Law's Delay. London, Macmillan, and New York, St. Martin's Press, 1977.
A Thief or Two. London, Macmillan, and New York, St. Martin's Press, 1977.
Exit Murderer. London, Macmillan, and New York, St. Martin's Press, 1978.
The Fatal Writ. London, Macmillan, and New York, St. Martin's Press, 1979.
Proceed to Judgment. London, Macmillan, and New York, St. Martin's Press, 1979.

Sara Woods comments:
I write crime novels with a legal background because the law has always interested me. To my great surprise, I have been complimented, occasionally, on my plots. This seems odd to me because my system is to take a situation, throw my characters in, and see what happens. You will gather from this that what I am most interested in is the development of character,

and I expect that is why I have chosen to write a series, with a group of the characters appearing in every book, and others merely reappearing from time to time.

*   *   *

Although born in England and educated in Yorkshire, Sara Woods did not begin writing until she moved to Nova Scotia; she is therefore often considered to be Canada's most successful detective fiction writer, although her novels are all set in England and owe more to the English tradition founded by Conan Doyle than to Canadian influences, criminal or otherwise. Woods worked in a solicitor's office, and her most successful novels are those in which her detective, the lawyer Antony Maitland, is active in the courtroom. *Trusted Like the Fox* is particularly effective in its presentation of courtroom scenes, and her first novel, *Bloody Instructions*, still has a freshness which later novels lack. Her production of Antony Maitland novels has been prodigious, but the strain of maintaining a serial detective in a form which offers little that is original becomes evident in such novels as *Enter the Corpse*, which can only be described as heavy going.

Woods has often been called an English Erle Stanley Gardner. This description is neither accurate nor just. Her plots, which are carefully controlled, are free of the atmosphere of artificial "courtroom tricks" – last-minute confessions, spectacular demonstrations, production of a "mystery witness" – which Gardner successfully exploited. Respect for the law is evident throughout, and Maitland's activities, though they could hardly be called realistic, are nevertheless more restrained than those of Perry Mason. Furthermore, although she is certainly prolific, Woods does not write as glibly as Gardner. She is always literate, though she never sacrifices the element of suspense, which is well-integrated into the ratiocinative atmosphere in which Maitland moves as a kind of legal "thinking machine." The title of each novel is a quotation from Shakespeare, a gimmick which affords more variety than many, and which is not employed in a self-conscious way.

The novels are in the style of the so-called "golden age" writers, with their insistence upon "the rules" of good construction. For example, romantic interest is conspicuous by its absence; the business of the books is detection, and this requires a single-minded concentration on details of the crime. Woods is "fair" to the reader, and it is actually possible to solve her crimes by using deductive methods. Furthermore, the presence of Scotland Yard, though it is, for the sake of verisimilitude, evident, is quite peripheral to the puzzle, for it is Antony Maitland who is the real detective. The crime is almost invariably murder, usually of a sensational or lurid nature, and Maitland, a figure of quiet domesticity, becomes involved in a series of suspenseful chases which culminate in the arrest of the guilty party.

Characterization is not Woods's strong point, which is, perhaps, the reason she chooses to concentrate on Maitland as her detective hero. In the context of the tradition of great eccentric detectives, he is a disappointment. Similarly, the secondary characters are often depicted as stereotypes: the grasping widow, the loyal secretary, etc. The chief interest for the reader lies in following an abstract problem from its initial presentation to its resolution. It is a characteristic of this kind of detective story that the characters tend to become pawns in a chess game which the reader plays in his head, and Woods is at a far remove from the sort of novelist who encourages total identification with her central character. Her literary antecedent is Agatha Christie rather than Mary Roberts Rinehart; and her puzzles, which are unveiled with just enough suspense to arouse our curiosity, are designed to baffle rather than to terrify.

—Joanne Harack Hayne

WOOLRICH, Cornell (George Hopley-). Also wrote as George Hopley; William Irish. American. Born in New York City in 1903; grew up in South America and New York City. Educated at Columbia University, New York. Married and separated. Recipient: Mystery Writers of America Edgar Allan Poe Award, for short story, 1948. *Died in 1968.*

CRIME PUBLICATIONS

Novels

    The Bride Wore Black.   New York, Simon and Schuster, 1940; London, Hale, 1942; as
      Beware the Lady, New York, Pyramid, 1953.
    The Black Curtain.   New York, Simon and Schuster, 1941; London, Macmillan, 1963.
    Black Alibi.   New York, Simon and Schuster, 1942; London, Hale, 1951.
    The Black Angel.   New York, Doubleday, 1943; London, Hale, 1949.
    The Black Path of Fear.   New York, Doubleday, 1944.
    Night Has a Thousand Eyes (as George Hopley).   New York, Farrar and Rinehart,
      1945; London, Penguin, 1949.
    Rendezvous in Black.   New York, Rinehart, 1948; London, Hale, 1950.
    Fright (as George Hopley).   New York, Rinehart, and London, Foulsham, 1950.
    Savage Bride.   New York, Fawcett, 1950.
    Death Is My Dancing Partner.   New York, Pyramid, 1959.
    The Doom Stone.   New York, Avon, 1960.

Novels as William Irish

    Phantom Lady.   Philadelphia, Lippincott, 1942; London, Hale, 1945.
    Deadline at Dawn.   Philadelphia, Lippincott, 1944; London, Hutchinson, 1947.
    Waltz into Darkness.   Philadelphia, Lippincott, 1947; London, Hutchinson, 1948.
    I Married a Dead Man.   Philadelphia, Lippincott, 1948; London, Hutchinson, 1950.
    You'll Never See Me Again.   New York, Dell, 1951.
    Strangler's Serenade.   New York, Rinehart, 1951; London, Hale, 1952.

Short Stories

    Nightmare.   New York, Dodd Mead, 1956.
    Violence.   New York, Dodd Mead, 1958.
    Hotel Room.   New York, Random House, 1958.
    Beyond the Night.   New York, Avon, 1959.
    The Ten Faces of Cornell Woolrich.   New York, Simon and Schuster, 1965; London,
      Boardman, 1966.
    The Dark Side of Love.   New York, Walker, 1965.
    Nightwebs, edited by Francis M. Nevins, Jr.   New York, Harper, 1971; London,
      Gollancz, 1973.
    Angels of Darkness.   New York, Mysterious Press, 1979.

Short Stories as William Irish

    I Wouldn't Be in Your Shoes.   Philadelphia, Lippincott, 1943; London, Hutchinson,
      1946; as *And So to Death*, New York, Spivak, 1944; as *Nightmare*, New York,
      Reader's Choice Library, 1950.
    After-Dinner Story.   Philadelphia, Lippincott, 1944; London, Hutchinson, 1947; as *Six
      Times Death*, New York, Popular Library, 1948.
    If I Should Die Before I Wake.   New York, Avon, 1945.
    The Dancing Detective.   Philadelphia, Lippincott, 1946; London, Hutchinson, 1948.

Borrowed Crimes. New York, Avon, 1946.
Dead Man Blues. Philadelphia, Lippincott, 1948; London, Hutchinson, 1950.
The Blue Ribbon. Philadelphia, Lippincott, 1949; London, Hutchinson, 1950; as
   Dilemma of the Dead Lady, Hasbrouck Heights, New Jersey, Graphic, 1950.
Somebody on the Phone. Philadelphia, Lippincott, 1950; as *The Night I Died*, London,
   Hutchinson, 1951; as *Deadly Night Call*, Hasbrouck Heights, New Jersey, Graphic,
   1951.
Six Nights of Mystery. New York, Popular Library, 1950.
Eyes That Watch You. New York, Rinehart, 1952.
Bluebeard's Seventh Wife. New York, Popular Library, 1952.
The Best of William Irish. Philadelphia, Lippincott, 1960.

Uncollected Short Stories

"Blonde Beauty Slain," in *Ellery Queen's Mystery Magazine* (New York), March 1959.
"Money Talks," in *Ellery Queen's Mystery Magazine* (New York), January 1962.
"The Poker Player's Wife," in *The Saint* (New York), October 1962.
"Story to Be Whispered," in *The Saint* (New York), May 1963.
"Steps ... Coming Near" (as William Irish), in *Ellery Queen's Mystery Magazine* (New
   York), April 1964.
"When Love Turns," in *Ellery Queen's Mystery Magazine* (New York), June 1964.
"Murder after Death," in *Ellery Queen's Mystery Magazine* (New York), December
   1964.
"It Only Takes a Minute to Die," in *Ellery Queen's Mystery Magazine* (New York), July
   1966.
"Divorce – New York Style," in *Ellery Queen's Mystery Magazine* (New York), June
   and July 1967.
"Intent to Kill," in *The Saint* (New York), September 1967.
"New York Blues," in *Ellery Queen's Mystery Magazine* (New York), December 1970.
"Death Between Dances," in *Ellery Queen's Mystery Magazine* (New York), October
   1978.

OTHER PUBLICATIONS

Novels

Cover Charge. New York, Boni and Liveright, 1926.
Children of the Ritz. New York, Boni and Liveright, 1927.
Times Square. New York, Liveright, 1929.
A Young Man's Heart. New York, Mason, 1930.
The Time of Her Life. New York, Liveright, 1931.
Manhattan Love Song. New York, Godwin, 1932.

Play

Screenplay: *The Return of the Whistler*, with Edward Bock and Maurice Tombragel,
   1948.

*   *   *

Cornell Woolrich was born in 1903 to parents whose marriage collapsed in his youth. The
experience of seeing Puccini's *Madame Butterfly* at age eight gave him a second intimation of
tragedy, and from the night three years later that he understood fully that someday he too,
like Cio-Cio-San, would have to die, he was haunted by a sense of doom that never left him.

He began writing fiction while at Columbia University, quitting in his junior year to pursue his dream of becoming another F. Scott Fitzgerald, and his first novel, *Cover Charge*, chronicles the lives and loves of the Jazz Age's gilded youth in the manner of his then literary idol. Following five more mainstream novels, a stint in Hollywood, a brief marriage, and many homosexual encounters, he returned to Manhattan. For the next quarter century he lived with his mother in a succession of residential hotels, going out only when it was absolutely essential, trapped in a bizarre love-hate relationship which dominated his external world just as the inner world of his fiction reflected in its tortured patterns the strangler grip in which his mother held him.

From 1934 until his death he wrote dozens of haunting stories of suspense, despair, and lost love, set in a universe controlled by diabolical powers who delight in savaging us. During the 1930's he wrote only for pulp magazines like *Black Mask* and *Detective Fiction Weekly*. His first suspense novel, *The Bride Wore Black*, launched his so-called Black Series which inspired the French *roman noir* and *film noir*. During the early 1940's he published superb novels under his own name and the pseudonyms William Irish (*Phantom Lady* and *Deadline at Dawn*) and George Hopley (*Night Has a Thousand Eyes*). Throughout the 1940's and 1950's numerous hardcover and paperback collections of Woolrich's short stories were issued, and many of his tales were adapted into movies and radio and television dramas, perhaps the best known Woolrich-based film being Alfred Hitchcock's *Rear Window*. Despite his overwhelming financial and critical success his personal situation remained wretched, and when his mother died in 1957 he cracked. From then until his own death in 1968 he lived alone, completing only a handful of final "tales of love and despair" but still gifted with the magic touch that could chill the reader's heart. One of his titles for an unwritten story captures his bleak philosophy: "First You Dream, Then You Die."

Although he wrote many types of stories, including quasi-police procedural novels, rapid-action whizbangs, and tales of the occult, Woolrich is best known as the master of pure suspense, evoking with awesome power and desperation of those who walk the city's darkened streets and the terror that lurks at noonday in commonplace settings. In his hands even such clichéd storylines as the race to save the innocent man from the electric chair and the amnesiac's search for his lost self resonate with human anguish. Woolrich's world is a feverish place where the prevailing emotions are loneliness and fear and the prevailing action a race against time and death, as in his suspense classics "Three O'Clock" and "Guillotine." His most characteristic detective stories end with our realization that no rational account of events is possible, and his suspense stories tend to close not with the dissipation of the terror but with its omnipresence.

The typical Woolrich settings are the seedy hotel, the cheap dance hall, the rundown movie house, and the precinct station backroom. The dominant reality in his world is the Depression, the Woolrich has no peers when it comes to describing a frightened little guy in a tiny apartment with no money, no job, a hungry wife and children, and anxiety eating him like a cancer. If a Woolrich protagonist is in love, the beloved is likely to vanish in such a way that the protagonist not only can't find her but can't convince anyone that she ever existed. Or, in another classic Woolrich situation, the protagonist comes to after a blackout (caused by amnesia, drugs, hypnosis, or whatever) and little by little becomes convinced that he committed a murder or other crime while out of himself. The police are rarely sympathetic, for they are the earthly counterparts of the malignant powers above and their primary function is to torment the helpless. All we can do about this nightmare world is to create, if we can, a few islands of love and trust to help us forget. But love dies while the lovers go on living, and Woolrich excels at showing the corrosion of a relationship between two people. Although he often wrote about the horrors both love and lovelessness can inspire, there are few irredeemably evil characters in his stories, for if any of his characters loves or needs love, or is at the brink of destruction, Woolrich identifies with him no matter what crimes he or she might also have committed. Technically many of his stories are awful, but like the playwrights of the absurd Woolrich knew that a senseless tale best mirrors a senseless universe. Some of his tales indeed end quite happily (usually thanks to outlandish coincidence), but there are no series characters in his work, and the reader can never know in advance whether a particular story of his will be light or dark – which is one reason why his stories are so hauntingly suspenseful.

Woolrich was the Poe of the twentieth century and the poet of its shadows. Trapped in a wretched psychological environment, understanding his own and everyone's trappedness, he took his decades of solitude and shaped them into the finest body of pure suspense literature ever written. He himself like Cio-Cio-San had to die, but the world he imagined will live.

—Francis M. Nevins, Jr.

WRIGHT, S. Fowler.   See FOWLER, Sydney.

WRIGHT, Willard Huntington.   See VAN DINE, S. S.

WYLIE, Philip.   See BALMER, Edwin.

WYND, Oswald.   See BLACK, Gavin.

X, Mr.   See HOCH, Edward D.

YORK, Andrew. Pseudonym for Christopher Robin Nicole; also writes as Robin Cade; Peter Grange; Mark Logan; Christina Nicholson. British. Born in Georgetown, British Guiana, now Guyana, 7 December 1930. Educated at Harrison College, Barbados; Queen's College, Guyana. Married Jean Barnett in 1951; two sons and two daughters. Clerk, Royal Bank of Canada, in the West Indies, 1947–56. Settled in Guernsey in 1957. Address: South Grange de Beauvoir, St. Peter Port, Guernsey, Channel Islands, United Kingdom.

CRIME PUBLICATIONS

Novels (series characters: Munroe Tallant; Jonas Wilde)

The Eliminator (Wilde). London, Hutchinson, 1966; Philadelphia, Lippincott, 1967.
The Co-Ordinator (Wilde). London, Hutchinson, and Philadelphia, Lippincott, 1967.
The Predator (Wilde). London, Hutchinson, and Philadelphia, Lippincott, 1968.
The Deviator (Wilde). London, Hutchinson, and Philadelphia, Lippincott, 1969.
The Dominator (Wilde). London, Hutchinson, 1969; New York, Lancer, 1971.
The Infiltrator (Wilde). London, Hutchinson, and New York, Doubleday, 1971.
The Expurgator (Wilde). London, Hutchinson, 1972; New York, Doubleday, 1973.
The Captivator (Wilde). London, Hutchinson, 1972; New York, Doubleday, 1974.
The Fear Dealers (as Robin Cade). London, Cassell, and New York, Simon and Schuster, 1974.
The Fascinator (Wilde). London, Hutchinson, and New York, Doubleday, 1975.
Dark Passage. New York, Doubleday, 1975; London, Hutchinson, 1976.
Tallant for Trouble. London, Hutchinson, and New York, Doubleday, 1977.
Tallant for Disaster. London, Hutchinson, and New York, Doubleday, 1978.

OTHER PUBLICATIONS

Novels as Christopher Nicole

Off White. London, Jarrolds, 1959.
Shadows in the Jungle. London, Jarrolds, 1961.
Ratoon. London, Jarrolds, and New York, St. Martin's Press, 1962.
Dark Noon. London, Jarrolds, 1963.
Amyot's Cry. London, Jarrolds, 1964.
Blood Amyot. London, Jarrolds, 1964.
The Amyot Crime. London, Jarrolds, 1965; New York, Bantam, 1974.
White Boy. London, Hutchinson, 1966.
King Creole (as Peter Grange). London, Jarrolds, 1966.
The Self-Lovers. London, Hutchinson, 1968.
The Devil's Emissary (as Peter Grange). London, Jarrolds, 1968.
The Thunder and the Shouting. London, Hutchinson, and New York, Doubleday, 1969.
The Tumult at the Gate (as Peter Grange). London, Jarrolds, 1970.
The Longest Pleasure. London, Hutchinson, 1970.
The Face of Evil. London, Hutchinson, 1971.
The Golden Goddess (as Peter Grange). London, Jarrolds, 1973.
Lord of the Golden Fan. London, Cassell, 1973.
Caribee. London, Cassell, and New York, St. Martin's Press, 1974.
The Devil's Own. London, Cassell, and New York, St. Martin's Press, 1975.
Mistress of Darkness. London, Cassell, and New York, St. Martin's Press, 1976.
Tricolour (as Mark Logan). London, Macmillan, and New York, St. Martin's Press, 1976.

Guillotine (as Mark Logan).   London, Macmillan, and New York, St. Martin's Press, 1976.

Black Dawn.   London, Cassell, and New York, St. Martin's Press, 1977.

The Power and the Passion (as Christina Nicholson).   London, Corgi, and New York, Coward McCann, 1977.

Sunset.   London, Cassell, and New York, St. Martin's Press, 1978.

Brumaire (as Mark Logan).   London, Wingate, and New York, St. Martin's Press, 1978.

The Savage Sands (as Christina Nicholson).   London, Corgi, and New York, Coward McCann, 1978.

The Secret Memoirs of Lord Byron.   Philadelphia, Lippincott, 1978; London, Joseph, 1979.

Other

West Indian Cricket (as Christopher Nicole).   London, Phoenix House, 1957.

The West Indies: Their People and History (as Christopher Nicole).   London, Hutchinson, 1965.

The Doom Fishermen (juvenile).   London, Hutchinson, 1969; as *Operation Destruct*, New York, Holt Rinehart, 1969.

Manhunt for a General (juvenile).   London, Hutchinson, 1970; as *Operation Manhunt*, New York, Holt Rinehart, 1970.

Where the Cavern Ends (juvenile).   London, Hutchinson, and New York, Holt Rinehart, 1971.

Appointment in Kiltone (juvenile).   London, Hutchinson, 1972; as *Operation Neptune*, New York, Holt Rinehart, 1972.

Introduction to Chess (as Christopher Nicole).   London, Corgi, 1973.

*   *   *

"He is the most dangerous man in the world." And the nine novels by Andrew York about this man, Jonas Wilde, the Eliminator, are to Ian Fleming's James Bond tales what a century ago the Martin Hewitt stories were to those about Sherlock Holmes: solid, if less spectacular stories modeled on a more famous hero whose popularity gave new life to an old form – in this case, the spy-adventure tale. Lacking the bizarre villains, tricky gadgets, and exotic color of far-off lands, the Wilde series has all the other characteristics of the Fleming formula: the secret agent authorized to kill, immensely attractive to women, and a connoisseur of wine and food, appearing in melodramatic fast-action adventures filled with violence and sex. Nevertheless, Wilde is no mere carbon copy; for example, he does not use a gun, killing with a karate blow behind the ear. Large chunks of the books are as exciting as anything in Fleming – see the scene from *The Co-Ordinator* in which Wilde is recognized in the midst of his enemies and forced to flee onto an ice-coated skyscraper ledge in a snow-storm – and grimly tries to carry out his assassination attempt by smashing through his victim's reinforced window before the arctic wind topples him from the high ledge.

But the novels as a whole never rise above these individual scenes, flawed by a fault the author is probably unaware of: though the telling is deadly serious, the plot line is often parody, a wild black humor blowing through it, as if the author were unconsciously laughing at the Fleming form. A few examples: in one novel Wilde is told by his superior that the people the Elimination Section has been killing are traitors; reassured, Wilde goes on his next mission – and discovers that his superior is in the pay of the Russians and that the Elimination Section, without knowing it, has been killing Britain's best citizens for months. In a black way, that's funny – the British spend months and millions creating the Section; the Russians spend five minutes to bribe one man – and get the entire Section working for them. In another novel Wilde has a slipped disc that throws his back out of joint and knocks him to the floor every time he tries a killing karate blow. In a third he seeks a multiple murderer, but discovers that *everyone* he investigates is guilty. In another, a group trying to assassinate an Arab prince orders Wilde to *protect* the prince in order to expose Wilde as an assassin – to make the prince's bodyguards so overconfident that perhaps the *next* attempt will succeed! A black mockery lies buried in these works. But that is the only major flaw in these well-written, suspenseful adventures; and Wilde remains, perhaps the best of all the men modeled on Ian Fleming's James Bond.

Recently York has struck out in a more original direction with a series of novels about Munroe Tallant, Police Chief of Grand Flamingo Island in the West Indies. Here his humor is conscious and intended, the native dialect authentic, and the setting so exotic – *Tallant for Disaster* deals with a tropical hurricane, sunken treasure ships centuries old, nude sunbathing beauties, and a vicious rape-murder – that it takes a while to realize that these works are really unusually colorful police procedural novels. Lighter in tone, better characterized, these novels are as a whole superior to the grimmer Wilde works and show a more individual future for York.

—Frank D. McSherry, Jr.

YORK, Jeremy. See **CREASEY, John.**

YORKE, Margaret. Pseudonym for Margaret Beda Nicholson, née Larminie. British. Born in Compton, Surrey, 30 January 1924. Educated at Prior's Field, Godalming, Surrey. Served in the Women's Royal Naval Service, 1942–45. Married Basil Nicholson in 1945 (divorced, 1957); one daughter and one son. Assistant Librarian, St. Hilda's College, Oxford, 1959–60; Library Assistant, Christ Church, Oxford, 1963–65. Vice-Chairman, 1978, and Chairman, 1979, Crime Writers Association. Agent: Curtis Brown Ltd., 1 Craven Hill, London W2 3EP. Address: Oriel Cottage, Long Crendon, Aylesbury, Buckinghamshire HP18 9AL, England.

CRIME PUBLICATIONS

Novels (series character: Patrick Grant)

> *Dead in the Morning* (Grant). London, Bles, 1970.
> *Silent Witness* (Grant). London, Bles, 1972; New York, Walker, 1973.
> *Grave Matters* (Grant). London, Bles, 1973.
> *Mortal Remains* (Grant). London, Bles, 1974.
> *No Medals for the Major.* London, Bles, 1974.
> *The Small Hours of the Morning.* London, Bles, and New York, Walker, 1975.
> *Cast for Death* (Grant). London, Hutchinson, and New York, Walker, 1976.
> *The Cost of Silence.* London, Hutchinson, and New York, Walker, 1977.

The Point of Murder. London, Hutchinson, 1978; as *The Come-On*, New York,
    Harper, 1979.
Death on Account. London, Hutchinson, 1979.

OTHER PUBLICATIONS

Novels

Summer Flight. London, Hale, 1957.
Pray, Love, Remember. London, Hale, 1958.
Christopher. London, Hale, 1959.
Deceiving Mirror. London, Hale, 1960.
The China Doll. London, Hale, 1961.
Once a Stranger. London, Hurst and Blackett, 1962.
The Birthday. London, Hurst and Blackett, 1963.
Full Circle. London, Hurst and Blackett, 1965.
No Fury. London, Hurst and Blackett, 1967.
The Apricot Bed. London, Hurst and Blackett, 1968.
The Limbo Ladies. London, Hurst and Blackett, 1969.

Other

"St. Mary Mead and Other Troubled Villages" and "Oxford vs. Cambridge: The Dark
    Blues Have the Most," in *Murder Ink: The Mystery Reader's Companion*, edited by
    Dilys Winn. New York, Workman, 1977.

Margaret Yorke comments:
    Writing about the hopes, fears, misunderstandings, and conflicts of ordinary people has
always interested me. My first 11 novels were family problem novels, but I was always
tempted to stir up their quiet plots with some violent action. With *Dead in the Morning* I
turned to crime fiction and began with the whodunit form because of the pattern already set
by successful women writers. The characters have always interested me more than the plots,
though I have enjoyed devising the puzzles. The idea for *No Medals for the Major* came to me
when I was thinking about how different we often feel inside from the face we present to the
world, and how an action, slight in itself, can have profound effects on other people whom
we may never meet. My recent novels have been about the victims of events over which they
have had no control: whydunits, and how it happened.

*   *   *

    Margaret Yorke has had, it may be said, two careers as a crime writer. She came to the
genre in any case from a different sort of fiction, the "problem" novel. But in crime she began
in a fairly conventional manner by inventing a series detective and writing a number of books
in which he featured. He was, however, a figure not of marked originality, a literary don (but
hadn't we had literary don detectives enough?), handsome (but if they weren't crazily
eccentric, they had to be handsome), and with the hero-like (but not strikingly memorable)
name of Patrick Grant. His adventures were apt to take him to only moderately exotic holiday
places. The books were better than the flat average of such work, but not outstanding.
    In 1974, however, Yorke decided to desert Grant for once. And she produced a memorable
book in, if one must categorise, the field of psychological suspense. But, though *No Medals for
the Major* had a death in it and puzzle too, it was not for the detection that it stood out. Its
excellence consisted in a fine portrait in depth of an unusual man, a retired Army major,
living in a village (social life very well described), lonely and awkward.
    Since this second, or third, debut she has done some fine work, while not altogether

abandoning her Patrick Grant books. There was *The Small Hours of the Morning* which took a slice of a small English town and ingeniously interwove the lives of a handful of its residents into a story that developed considerable tension. But it was again the portraits of ordinary people, a librarian, a dentist's assistant, a hire-car driver, that made the book so good. The people in it were each excellently real, with virtues and with faults, capable on occasion of fine, even noble, behaviour and equally capable of petty and mean actions. She showed here, for the first time I believe, an ability to deal with that trickiest of all hurdles for most writers, sexual relations. Indeed, it might be said to be a mark of a coming-of-age when a writer, however young or old in life, can tackle this subject in a manner that is neither frenziedly outspoken nor itchily modest. Yorke's level-headedness here is an enjoyment in itself. She showed it again notably in *The Point of Murder*.

The Cost of Silence is again set in a small town and we see a cross-section of its people, all portrayed with sympathetic understanding of weaknesses and strengths, though the picture of a young tearaway is perhaps not as successful as the others. One portrait stands out, though this time of a character in whom the unpleasant outweighs the pleasant – that of a fat and repulsive invalid wife, who nonetheless has her human side. The book is full of real people with real problems in a real world.

Such work is part of the considerable contribution which this distinctively female writer has to make to crime fiction as a whole.

—H. R. F. Keating

YUILL, P. B. Pseudonym for Gordon Williams and Terry Venables. British. **WILLIAMS, Gordon (Maclean):** Born in Paisley, Renfrewshire, 20 June 1939. Educated at John Neilson Institution, Paisley, Scottish Higher Leaving Certificate 1951. Served in the Royal Air Force for two years (national service). Married to Claerweh Williams; two daughters and one son. Reporter, feature writer, and sub-editor on newspapers and magazines in the 1960's. Lives in London. Agent: John Farquharson Ltd., Bell House, 8 Bell Yard, London WC2A 2JU, England. **VENABLES, Terry:** Manager, Crystal Palace football club, London.

CRIME PUBLICATIONS

Novels (series character: James Hazell)

The Bornless Keeper (by Williams). London, Macmillan, 1974; New York, Walker, 1975.
Hazell Plays Solomon. London, Macmillan, 1974; New York, Walker, 1975.
Hazell and the Three Card Trick. London, Macmillan, 1975; New York, Walker, 1976.
Hazell and the Menacing Jester. London, Macmillan, 1976.

Uncollected Short Stories

"You Make Your Own Luck" (by Williams), in *Winter's Crimes 6*, edited by George Hardinge. London, Macmillan, 1974.
"The Horseshoe Inn" (by Williams), in *Prevailing Spirits*, edited by Giles Gordon. London, Hamish Hamilton, 1976.

"Hazell and the Patriot," in *Winter's Crimes 9*, edited by George Hardinge.   London, Macmillan, 1977.

OTHER PUBLICATIONS by Gordon Williams

Novels

The Last Day of Lincoln Charles.   London, Secker and Warburg, 1965; New York, Stein and Day, 1966.
The Camp.   London, Secker and Warburg, and New York, Stein and Day, 1966.
The Man Who Had Power over Women.   London, Secker and Warburg, 1966; New York, Stein and Day, 1967.
From Scenes Like These.   London, Secker and Warburg, 1968; New York, Morrow, 1969.
The Siege of Trencher's Farm.   London, Secker and Warburg, and New York, Morrow, 1969.
The Upper Pleasure Garden.   London, Secker and Warburg, and New York, Morrow, 1970.
They Used to Play on Grass, with Terry Venables.   London, Hodder and Stoughton, 1971.
Walk, Don't Walk.   London, Hodder and Stoughton, and New York, St. Martin's Press, 1972.
Big Morning Blues.   London, Hodder and Stoughton, 1974.
The Duellists (novelization of screenplay).   London, Collins, 1977.
The Micronauts.   New York, Bantam, 1978.
The Microcolony.   New York, Bantam, 1979.

Gordon Williams comments:
 Hazell originated from an idea by Terry Venables for a story about switched babies, the private detective being only a useful story-teller. The character began to interest us while we were writing in tandem, and we began seeing Hazell as a suitable person to emulate in London terms the immortal Philip Marlowe. We produced three fairly successful books before Thames Television bought rights to the character, the result being a Hazell differing from the original in many matters of detail and spirit – largely disappointing in our opinions. In general terms Hazell represents our own joint attitude to the wonderful world of British snobbery.

*   *   *

 The name of P. B. Yuill, it is common knowledge, conceals two writers, the novelist Gordon Williams and the football club manager, Terry Venables. *The Bornless Keeper*, the first title to appear under the somewhat curious pseudonym, however, was exclusively a Williams work and as such, though it is an excellent crime story, full of genuine tension and one that looks at the world around it, really falls outside the canon.
 The canonical Yuill is concerned entirely with the adventures of a London private eye, name of Hazell. Hazell is an East Ender, telling his stories in genuine East End argot with flicks of rhyming slang ("Apples and pears" = stairs) and the hard rhythms that are typical of the area, and not all that easy to catch. He is tough, too, almost as much a criminal as the people he (on the whole) goes up against. And his knowledge of the dodges of the fly-boy world is extensive, as well as bearing all the signs of being accurate. But he is by no means a mere set of characteristics, surface true but stuck on to a dummy. He is underneath a recognisable human being, even a particularly warm one. Nor is the world in which Hazell operates simply a convenient setting for that particular sort of tale. It is the real world, the nerve-jangling metropolis of London where aspects of life that the Londoner daily

experiences, not the romantic or seamy bits that are encountered by only a few, play their real parts. And since it is the real world we are shown, our world with its faults, there is in the books an undertow of moral comment, not forced, certainly not laid on, but definitely there.

When Hazell goes out on an investigation the sort of place he is likely to find himself at is "Herbert Morrison House ... a twenty-storey block, shabby and rain-streaked, the walls thick with spray-on messages, nicknames, gang slogans, incurable optimism about West Ham football team." That's a real place where real people (and of the sort you don't too often find in crime books) live. In a similar way when Yuill portrays a bad man, such as "Moneybags" Beevers in *Hazell and the Menacing Jester*, although he is convincingly tough (as really tough and as really criminal as, on the other side of the Atlantic, are the hoods in the novels of George V. Higgins) he is also likely to be a person with whom in the end you sympathise, at least to the point of feeling you know what makes him tick.

It is, I suppose, no less than what one would expect of a novelist of the stature of Gordon Williams, author of *The Siege of Trencher's Farm* (filmed as *Straw Dogs*), itself a novel of suspense that only fails to qualify as a crime novel because it put what it had to say about violence before the mere build-up of tension. But the Yuill books are, quite definitely, as much written by the footballer as by the novel writer, and it is from the former, I suspect, that the unique flavour of Hazell comes, the sharply cheerful toughness.

—H. R. F. Keating

ZANGWILL, Israel. British. Born in the East End of London, 21 January 1864. Educated at schools in Plymouth and Bristol; Jews' Free School, Spitalfields, London; University of London, B.A. (honours). Married the writer Edith Ayrton in 1903; two sons and one daughter. Taught at the Jews' Free School, then worked as a journalist; edited the humorous periodical *Ariel*; writer from 1881. President, Jewish Territorial Organisation for the Settlement of Jews Within the British Empire, Jewish Historical Society, and Jewish Drama League. *Died 1 August 1926.*

CRIME PUBLICATIONS

Novel

    The Big Bow Mystery. London, Henry, 1892; Chicago, Rand McNally, 1895.

OTHER PUBLICATIONS

Novels

    The Premier and the Painter: A Fantastic Romance, with Louis Cowen (as J. Freeman Bell). London, Blackett, 1888; Chicago, Rand McNally, 1896.
    The Bachelors' Club. London, Henry, and New York, Brentano's, 1891.
    The Old Maids' Club. London, Heinemann, and New York, Tait, 1892.
    Merely Mary Ann. London, Tuck, 1893.
    Joseph the Dreamer. London, Heinemann, 1895.
    The Master. London, Heinemann, and New York, Harper, 1895.
    The Mantle of Elijah. London, Heinemann, and New York, Harper, 1900.

Jinny the Carrier: A Folk Comedy of Rural England. London, Heinemann, and New York, Macmillan, 1919.

Short Stories

Children of the Ghetto, Being Pictures of a Peculiar People. London, Heinemann, 3 vols., 1892; Philadelphia, Jewish Publication Society of America, 1892; vol. 2 of US edition reprinted as *Grandchildren of the Ghetto*, London, Dent, 1914.
Ghetto Tragedies. London, McClure, 1893; Philadelphia, Jewish Publication Society of America, n.d.
The King of Schnorrers: Grotesques and Fantasies. London, Heinemann, and New York, Macmillan, 1894.
The Celibates' Club, Being the United Stories of "The Bachelors' Club" and "The Old Maids' Club." London, Heinemann, 1898; New York, Macmillan, 1905.
Dreamers of the Ghetto. London, Heinemann, and New York, Macmillan, 1898.
They That Walk in Darkness: Ghetto Tragedies. London, Heinemann, and New York, Macmillan, 1899.
The Grey Wig: Stories and Novelettes. London, Heinemann, and New York, Macmillan, 1903.
Ghetto Comedies. London, Heinemann, and New York, Macmillan, 1907.

Plays

The Great Demonstration, with Louis Cowen (produced London, 1892). London, Capper and Newton, 1893.
Aladdin at Sea (produced Camborne, Cornwall, 1893).
The Lady Journalist (produced London, 1893).
Six Persons (produced London, 1893). London, French, 1899.
Threepenny Bits (produced Chatham, Kent, and London, 1895).
Children of the Ghetto, adaptation of his own novel (produced Deal, Kent, London, and New York, 1899).
The Moment of Death; or, The Never, Never Land (produced New York, 1900).
The Revolted Daughter (produced London, 1901).
Merely Mary Ann, adaptation of his own novel (produced New York, 1903; London, 1904). New York, Macmillan, and London, Heinemann, 1904.
The Serio-Comic Governess (produced New York, 1904). New York, Macmillan, 1904.
The Mantle of Elijah (produced New York, 1904).
The King of Schnorrers, adaptation of his own story (in Yiddish: produced New York, 1905).
Jinny the Carrier (produced Boston and New York, 1905).
Nurse Marjorie (produced New York, 1906).
The Melting-Pot (produced Washington, D.C., 1908; New York, 1909; London, 1912). New York, Macmillan, 1909; revised version, New York, Macmillan, and London, Heinemann, 1914.
The War God (produced London, 1911). London, Heinemann, 1911.
The Next Religion. London, Heinemann, and New York, Macmillan, 1912.
Plaster Saints: A High Comedy (produced London, 1914). London, Heinemann, 1914; New York, Macmillan, 1915.
The Moment Before: A Psychical Melodrama (produced Plymouth and London, 1916).
Too Much Money (produced Glasgow and London, 1918). London, Heinemann, 1924; New York, Macmillan, 1925.
The Cockpit. London, Heinemann, and New York, Macmillan, 1921.

We Moderns (produced Wilmington, Delaware, 1922; New York, 1923; Southport, Lancashire, and London, 1925). London, Heinemann, 1925; New York, Macmillan, 1926.

The Forcing House; or, The Cockpit Continued (produced London, 1926). London, Heinemann, and New York, Macmillan, 1923.

Verse

Blind Children. London, Heinemann, and New York, Funk and Wagnalls, 1903.

Other

Motza Kleis, with Louis Cowen (published anonymously). London, privately printed, 1882.

"A Doll's House" Repaired, with Eleanor Marx Aveling. London, The Authors, 1891.

Hebrew, Jew, Israelite. London, Jewish Chronicle, 1892.

The Position of Judaism. New York, privately printed, 1895.

Without Prejudice (essays). London, Unwin, and New York, Century, 1896.

The People's Saviour. New York, Harper, 1898.

The East African Question: Zionism and England's Offer. New York, Maccabbean Publishing Company, 1904.

What Is the ITO? London, Jewish Territorial Organization Offices, 1905.

A Land of Refuge. London, Jewish Territorial Organization Offices, 1907.

Talked Out! London, Women's Social and Political Union, 1907.

One and One Are Two. London, Women's Social and Political Union, 1907.

Old Fogeys and Old Bogeys (speech). London, Woman's Press, 1909.

The Lock on the Ladies. London, Women's Freedom League, 1909.

Report on the Purpose of Jewish Settlement in Cyrenaica. London, Jewish Territorial Organization Offices, 1909.

Be Fruitful and Multiply. London, Jewish Territorial Organization Offices, 1909.

Italian Fantasies. London, Heinemann, and New York, Macmillan, 1910.

Sword and Spirit. London, Jewish Territorial Organization Offices, 1910.

The Hithertos. London, Woman's Press, 1912.

The Problem of the Jewish Race. New York, Judaean Publishing Company, 1912.

Report of the Commission for Jewish Settlement in Angora. London, Jewish Territorial Organization Offices, 1913.

The War and the Women. New York, Metropolitan Magazine, 1915.

The War for the World (essays, includes verse). London, Heinemann, and New York, Macmillan, 1916.

The Principle of Nationalities (lecture). London, Watts, and New York, Macmillan, 1917.

The Service of the Synagogue, with Nina Davis Salaman and Elsie Davis. New York, Hebrew Publishing Company, 3 vols., 1917.

Chosen Peoples: The Hebraic Ideal "Versus" the Teutonic (lecture). London, Allen and Unwin, 1918; New York, Macmillan, 1919.

Hands Off Russia (speech). London, Workers' Socialist Federation, 1919.

The Jewish Pogroms in the Ukraine, with others. Washington, D.C., Friends of the Ukraine, 1919.

The Voice of Jerusalem. London, Heinemann, 1920; New York, Macmillan, 1921.

The Works, edited by A. A. Wolmark. New York, American Jewish Book Company, 14 vols., 1921; London, Globe, 14 vols., 1926.

Watchman, What of the Night? New York, American Jewish Congress, 1923.

Is the Ku Klux Klan Constructive or Destructive? A Debate Between Imperial Wizard Evans, Israel Zangwill, and Others. Gerard, Kansas, Haldeman Julius, 1924.

Now and Forever: A Conversation with Mr. Israel Zangwill on the Jew and the Future (interview with Samuel Roth). New York, McBride, 1925.
Our Own. New York, International Press, 1926.
Speeches, Articles, and Letters, edited by Maurice Simon. London, Soncino Press, 1937.
Zangwill in the Melting-Pot: Selections, edited by Elsie E. Morton. London, Harrap, n.d.; New York, Simmons, n.d.

Translator, *Selected Religious Poems of Ibn Gabirol, Solomon ben Judah, Known as Avicebron, 1020?–1070?,* edited by Israel Davidson. Philadelphia, Jewish Publication Society of America, 1923.

Bibliography: "Zangwill: A Selected Bibliography" by Annamarie Peterson in *Bulletin of Bibliography* (Boston), September–December 1961.

*   *   *

Israel Zangwill, the English author, journalist, and Zionist, made but a single contribution to the literature of detection, but it was a considerable one. Urged by the *London Star* in 1891 to submit a somewhat "more original piece of fiction," he complied with a story he had sketched out some time before. It had occurred to him that it would be a sensational literary challenge to "murder a man in a room to which there was no possible access." The ingenious solution almost immediately suggested itself to him and it was this tale that he submitted, in installments, to the *Star. The Big Bow Mystery* stands today as the first "locked room" mystery novelet, second in historical importance only to Poe's ground-breaking short story, "The Murders in the Rue Morgue" (1841).

Zangwill's narrative recounts with the flavor and a goodly measure of the style of Dickens an "impossible" murder in the Bow district of London. Retired police inspector Grodman is centrally involved in the discovery of the crime and in its subsequent investigation. In his egotism and masterful grasp of the mystery and all of its ramifications he strikingly resembles Sherlock Holmes, who at almost the same moment was being fleshed out in stories appearing in the *Strand Magazine. The Big Bow Mystery* is still eminently readable today, although its good-natured but not entirely gentle satire now seems more picturesque than it must have nearly a century ago. Zangwill worked in some amusing jibes at British politics, literary fashions, and the detective genre itself. However, none of this in any way diminishes the effect of the masterful plot and its extraordinary denouement.

—Donald A. Yates

NINETEENTH-CENTURY WRITERS

BRADDON, Mary Elizabeth (1835–1915). Also wrote as Babington White. British. Novels: *Lady Audley's Secret*, 1862; *Aurora Floyd*, 1863; *John Marchmont's Legacy*, 1863; *Eleanor's Victory*, 1863; *Henry Dunbar: The Story of an Outcast*, 1864; *Birds of Prey*, 1867; *Charlotte's Inheritance*, 1868; *Robert Ainsleigh*, 1872; *Lucius Davoren; or, Publicans and Sinners*, 1873; *The Cloven Foot*, 1879; *Wyllard's Weird*, 1885; *Thou Art the Man*, 1894; *Rough Justice*, 1898; *His Darling Sin*, 1899. Bibliography: in "The Novels of Mary Elizabeth Braddon: A Reappraisal of the Author of *Lady Audley's Secret*" (unpublished dissertation) by Benjamin M. Nyberg, Boulder, University of Colorado, 1965.

*   *   *

After deserting the stage, Miss Braddon in her twenties and thirties wrote popular fiction at frantic speed – under her own name and various pseudonyms – to save her lover, the Irish-born John Maxwell, from financial disaster. In later life the petite, cheerful author wrote in various genres, including novels of manners and historical fiction, and found time to edit Maxwell's magazine *Belgravia* and other publications. By far her most popular work, and one of her earliest, is *Lady Audley's Secret*. It is often deprecated as a "sensation novel," but Benjamin M. Nyberg remarks that in its depth of characterization and avoidance of a fairy-tale ending it is far superior to most works so designated. Nevertheless this eminently readable novel does include such features as bigamy, attempted murder, and madness. The amateur detective, Robert Audley, is particularly well drawn. Indeed, this work and the one that inspired it – Wilkie Collins's *The Woman in White* – are not only the earliest of all detective novels but two of the best. Her other good crime novels include *Aurora Floyd*, *John Marchmont's Legacy*, and the two-part story comprising *Birds of Prey* and *Charlotte's Inheritance*. Less recommended are *Henry Dunbar*, *Robert Ainsleigh*, and *Rough Justice*.

—Norman Donaldson

COLLINS, (William) Wilkie (1824–89). British. Novels: *Basil: A Story of Modern Life*, 1852; *Hide and Seek; or, The Mystery of Mary Grice*, 1854; *The Dead Secret*, 1857; *The Woman in White*, 1860; *No Name*, 1862; *Armadale*, 1866; *The Moonstone: A Romance*, 1868; *Man and Wife*, 1870; *The Law and the Lady*, 1875; *The Haunted Hotel: A Mystery of Modern Venice*, 1878; *I Say No*, 1884; *Little Novels*, 1887; *Blind Love*, completed by Walter Besant, 1890. Short Stories: *After Dark*, 1856; *The Queen of Hearts*, 1859; *Miss or Mrs.? And Other Stories in Outline*, 1873; *The Frozen Deep and Other Stories*, 1874; *Alicia Warlock, A Mystery and Other Stories*, 1875; *My Lady's Money*, 1878; *The Ghost's Touch and Other Stories*, 1885; *The Yellow Tiger and Other Tales*, 1924; *Tales of Suspense*, edited by Robert Ashley and Herbert van Thal, 1954. Plays: *No Name*, 1863; *Armadale*, 1866; *The Frozen Deep*, 1866; *The Woman in White*, 1871; *The Moonstone*, 1877.

*   *   *

Wilkie Collins is generally considered the greatest Victorian master of mystery fiction, and *The Moonstone* and *The Woman in White* are among the few works of the period that are still popularly read. Like most of the Victorians, however, Collins is now appreciated for only a small fragment of a very large corpus of work, and much of his better fiction lies unreprinted and unread. During his later years his reputation suffered greatly, and it is only recently that his greatness has been appreciated.

The Woman in White (serialized in Dickens's *All the Year Round* in 1859–60) made Collins a national figure. It was not only highly popular as fiction, but it became one of those odd works that have repercussions in the other arts. Collins's friends, if literary tradition is correct, recognized more than a story in the novel, for Collins is said to have met his long-time mistress, Caroline Graves, under the same circumstances as occur in the novel. This incident Collins combined with the history of a fraudulent inheritance, from Méjan's *Recueil des causes célèbres*, a large collection of factual crimes that he had picked up in France.

Outstanding among Collins's other work are the two great novels *Armadale* and *The Moonstone*. *Armadale*, the story of a criminal fraud and an attempted murder, is told in the framework of an unfolding prophetic dream. *The Moonstone*, the first significant detective novel in English, covers a spectacular theft, accompanied by somnambulism, clever scheming and a little Oriental magic.

While Collins wrote only a few stories that are detective fiction in the strict sense, many of his works describe crimes, upon which proto-detectives exercise themselves. In *Hide and Seek* Matt Marksman tries to find the seducer of his sister; in "The Diary of Anne Rodway" a working girl tries to identify the man who murdered her friend; in "The Yellow Tiger" a traveler becomes party to a scheme to force a confession from a murderer; and in *I Say No* and "The Story of the Sixth Poor Traveller" female proto-detectives perform elementary investigations. "The Girl at the Gate" is concerned with a poison plot, while "Miss or Mrs.?" tells of a hired assassination that miscarried. *Blind Love*, Collins's last, unfinished novel, returned to the theme of fraudulent death that he had used in *The Moonstone* and *The Haunted Hotel*, while *The Haunted Hotel* and "The Clergyman's Confession" combine crimes with supernatural manifestations.

Closer to the modern concept of a detective story (with reader participation in the mystery) are *The Moonstone*; *The Law and the Lady*, in which a female detective attempts to identify a murderer and break an alibi; and *My Lady's Money*, which features the eccentric private detective Old Sharon. In "A Marriage Tragedy" Mr. Dark first investigates a disappearance and then is confronted with one of the oldest crime plots, the blood-stained clothing without a corpse. "Who Killed Zebedee?" and "John Jasper's Ghost" are reminiscent of the form established by "Waters," while "Who Is the Thief?" parodies that same form. "A Stolen Letter" is an obvious rehash of Poe's "Purloined Letter."

Collins's greatest strength lay in the technical skill with which he treated his involved plots. Probably no other author in English literature has been as skilled in manipulating complex material into a consistent story and in inventing suspense devices to maintain reader interest. His occasional prolixity is more than counterbalanced by the painterly detail, fine characterizations, and overall ingenuity of his writing. His gifts, however, required space for their development, with the result that most of his short stories are not on the same level of quality as his better novels. Many of his short stories, too, align themselves more with the traditional proto-detective story than with the avant-garde forms of his day. While Collins was aware of the work of Poe and Gaboriau, he paid little heed to their contributions and worked in the mainstream of Victorian domestic and social fiction.

Many of the novels that we read today for mystery elements were originally written as novels of purpose. *The Dead Secret*, with its long search, and *No Name*, with its wonderful plots and counterplots, are really concerned with illegitimacy, while *Man and Wife*, which contains an excellent sealed-room murder situation, is really focused upon the intricacies of the marriage laws of the British Isles. Even deeper than social purpose, however, was Collins's preoccupation with Fate, not with the expected warp and weft, but with the strange lace knottings, crossed and tangled threads. Indeed, his interest did not lie in his characters themselves but in the cocoon around them. His fiction abounds with "coincidences," unusual parallelisms, and strange linkages. *Armadale*, "Percy and the Prophet," and *The Frozen Deep* are really stories of predestination, while the first version of *Basil* is obsessed with fate. Collins has often been criticized for such "illogical coincidence," but this is not a fair judgment. For Collins an involution of fate is not a cheap trick for effects, but is a study of the utterly unexpected, utterly irrational factor in life.

—E. F. Bleiler

DICKENS, Charles (John Huffam) (1812–70). British. Novels: *Oliver Twist; or, The Parish Boy's Progress*, 1838; *Barnaby Rudge: A Tale of the Riots of 'Eighty*, 1841; *Bleak House*, 1853; *Hunted Down*, 1859; *Great Expectations*, 1861; *Our Mutual Friend*, 1865; *The Mystery of Edwin Drood*, 1870. Sketches of police activity appear in *Household Words*, 1850–59, and *All the Year Round*, 1859–70, both edited by Dickens. Bibliography: *A Bibliography of the Periodical Works of Charles Dickens* by Thomas Hatton and Arthur H. Cleaver, London, Chapman, 1933.

*   *   *

Given his delight in complicated mysteries and startling denouements, his fascination with all forms of crime and punishment, and his love of novelty in an age when police detectives were still an innovation, it was inevitable that Dickens should have played an important role in shaping the development of the detective story in England.

Dickens made his first important contribution in a series of articles about the Detective Office in *Household Words*. Founded in 1842 and still employing only a small staff, the Office had received little attention and had, in fact, probably avoided publicity for fear of reawakening the traditional English antipathy to spies and detectives. But in Dickens it found an influential and energetic publicist. The policemen of Dickens's articles are ideal bureaucrats: efficient, resourceful, unflappable, and tireless in their service of the public good. At the same time they lead more raffish and adventurous lives than most bureaucrats do: they are expert at disguise and acting, and are ready to venture into those mysterious East End slums which most middle-class Victorians would have hesitated to enter.

Dickens's journalism about the police laid the groundwork for the portrait of Inspector Bucket in *Bleak House*. The book employs most of the familiar formulae of sensation fiction – missing wills, unacknowledged illegitimate children, mysterious pasts, violent deaths – and so affords considerable scope for the Inspector's activities. He crops up in most of the book's many plots and sub-plots before emerging, near the end, as a central figure in his investigation of the murder of the lawyer Tulkinghorn and his search for the missing Lady Dedlock. Like Inspector Field and the other policemen of the *Household Words* articles, Bucket conceals extraordinary qualities beneath an unassuming and respectable facade: he travels from place to place with an almost supernatural mobility, spans the social chasms that otherwise separate class from class, and sees with disturbing acuity into the hearts of his fellow-men.

Many of Bucket's qualities recur in the character of the imperturbable Inspector of *Our Mutual Friend* and in Sergeant Cuff of Wilkie Collins's *The Moonstone*. But Dickens's last contribution to detective fiction is of a different nature. *The Mystery of Edwin Drood*, the novel left half-finished at his death in 1870, concerns the disappearance of Edwin Drood (Dickens's projected titles carefully avoid mentioning the word "murder") amidst a host of sinister circumstances that seem to implicate his uncle, John Jasper. The book's fragmentary nature makes it tantalising and difficult to judge, but it still shows a careful dedication to the mechanics of the mystery plot and, in the figure of the complex and divided John Jasper, the beginnings of one of those studies in the tortured criminal that distinguish Dickens's later fiction.

—Ian Ousby

GODWIN, William (1756–1836). British. Novels: *Things as They Are; or, The Adventures of Caleb Williams*, 1794; *St. Leon: A Tale of the Sixteenth Century*, 1799.

*   *   *

William Godwin, pioneer anarchist and author of *Political Justice*, was also, in *Things as They Are; or, The Adventures of Caleb Williams*, the first British writer of consequence to use fiction as a vehicle for social criticism. *Caleb Williams*, as it is commonly known, was a popularization of ideas about the corrupting nature of power elaborated in *Political Justice*. It was also a political thriller and even a forerunner of the detective story in its strictest definition.

In *Caleb Williams* a wealthy and powerful landowner, Falkland, murders a neighbour and allows innocent men to be hanged because he cannot bear the shame of such a death. Falkland is a dual personality, a forerunner of Dr. Jekyll and Mr. Hyde, for he has endearing qualities of generosity and gentleness, and it is with horror that his devoted secretary, Caleb Williams, finds in an iron chest the evidence of his master's guilt. Caleb reveals his knowledge to Falkland, who threatens to accuse him of capital crimes if he reveals his discovery. Caleb flees, and, after many adventures, pursued by the law and subjected to relentless moral persecution by Falkland's agents, is driven to expose his master, who finally confesses. Here there is a Kafka-like inversion, for in confessing Falkland sheds his burden of guilt and Caleb assumes it, overwhelmed by remorse at having caused the downfall of a noble being culpable of a single great crime to which he was led by a false code of honour. *Caleb Williams* combines moral complexity, political lessons, and much suspenseful excitement.

The only other among Godwin's many novels that might be called a mystery is an occult tale, *St. Leon*, about an alchemist who gains wealth and immortality but finds that they bring him only sorrow and the world's enmity. The moral, close to Godwin's experience, is that whoever gains power through wisdom and uses it for the general good must expect misunderstanding and hatred. *St. Leon* is a less satisfying book than *Caleb Williams*, which, though its great popularity on publication has never revived, remains a minor classic.

—George Woodcock

LE FANU, (Joseph) Sheridan (1814–73). Irish. Novels: *The Cock and Anchor*, 1845; *The House by the Church-Yard*, 1863; *Wylder's Hand*, 1864; *Uncle Silas: A Tale of Bartram-Haugh*, 1864; *Guy Deverell*, 1865; *All in the Dark*, 1866; *The Tenants of Malory*, 1867; *A Lost Name*, 1868; *Haunted Lives*, 1868; *The Wyvern Mystery*, 1869; *Checkmate*, 1871; *The Rose and the Key*, 1871; *Willing to Die*, 1873; *The Purcell Papers*, 1880; *The Evil Guest*, 1895. Short Stories: *Ghost Stories and Tales of Mystery*, 1851; *Chronicles of Golden Friars*, 1871; *In a Glass Darkly*, 1872; *The Watcher and Other Weird Stories*, 1894; *Madam Crowl's Ghost and Other Tales of Mystery*, 1923.

*   *   *

"The Simenon of the peculiar" – properly qualified, this description (by V. S. Pritchett in *The Living Novel*) offers a useful corrective to the common misapprehension of Sheridan Le Fanu. This versatile writer though justifiably esteemed for his ghost stories, is all too often unrecognised as one of the founders of the mystery/detective novel and a continuing influence upon the genre.

An awareness of the history of the machinery of justice is evident in Le Fanu's work from start to close. In his first novel, *The Cock and Anchor*, modelled on Sir Walter Scott, the action develops out of the obstacles to crime control in early 18th-century Dublin ("with a most notoriously ineffective police"), whereas in the somewhat analogously disturbed conditions of Restoration Paris, the foolhardy protagonist of "The Room in The Dragon Volant" (1872) owes his "resurrection" largely to the vigilance of the Sûreté. Indeed, all his major novels display a significant element of detective interest: in *The House by the Church-Yard* the distinctive features of a footprint near the corpse are recorded and followed up despite the difficulties (caused by the poor communications of the time) in tracking down a wanted man, and the vital evidence of the murder weapon is appreciated; in *Uncle Silas* the scrutiny by the trustees of "waste" as well as the heiress's attempt to solve an ancient locked-room mystery further provoke the murderer to self-disclosure; in *Wylder's Hand* a comparison of calligraphy and post-marks reveals forgery pointing to homicide, and additionally "the antiseptic properties of that sort of soil" function in the denouement; Le Fanu's most innovative use of forensic science appears in *Checkmate* which deploys plastic surgery and medical records. Still further anticipation of developments in the genre is manifested by a characteristic of Le Fanu (predating Fortuné du Boisgobey's *Le Coup de Pouce* of 1875 by a decade) wherein the criminal mystery is not unravelled solely by the police or someone with particular skills in detection. There are a magistrate in *The House by the Church-Yard*, and an "ex-detective of the police office" in *Checkmate*, but generally solutions in Le Fanu's crime novels are the product of collective observation and reasoning, a plausible mixture of intelligence, miscalculation, and chance; women can be as alert as men, the search more intermittent than sustained.

Inevitably, with the swing of fashion such a realistic contribution came to be regarded as technically deficient by the standards of the classical detective story. Although in *Guy Deverell* readers are alerted to the possibility of secret passages, and the change in the appearance of a middle-aged man, insufficient warning about doubles is given in *Wylder's Hand*. Nor does Le Fanu concentrate upon the detective puzzle: the criminal is only one element in a complex social picture abundant with comedy, pathos, wisdom, and humanity. In all this Le Fanu much resembles Simenon, yet the operative word in Pritchett's comparison is "peculiar" – the occult significance of which cannot be neglected.

"The mind is a different organ by night and by day," and Le Fanu's psychological tensions arise from the thrilling balance he maintains between the natural and supernatural explanation, a poise dependent partly on structure, partly on style. Frequently an inset ghost story foreshadows the crime; this structural play upon the legal, religious, mental, and bodily implications of "possession" is akin to the puns and literary allusions typical of this writer. Apparently limpid in style, the novels are suffused with references to *Robinson Crusoe*, Scripture and Swedenborg, the Elizabethan and Jacobean dramatists, Milton and Bunyan, *The Arabian Nights*, Celtic lore as well as Radcliffe, all of which impart supernatural meaning even to mysteries that prove open to rational explanation – Le Fanu's basic image seems to be "*Paradise Lost*" and precariously "*Regained.*"

This spiritual message obviously distinguishes Le Fanu from Simenon. If they share a sombre understanding of the complexities that entrap not just victim and bereaved but also the criminal, the ultimate enigma recognized by the Irishman lies beyond the Belgian's tragic destiny, in a sense of "how microscopic are the beginnings of the Kingdom of God or of the mystery of iniquity in a human being's heart." So finally Le Fanu relates less to Simenon than to Chesterton, and especially, as *The Nine Tailors* avows, to Dorothy L. Sayers.

—Peter Caracciolo

POE, Edgar Allan (1809–1849).   American.   Fiction: *The Narrative of Arthur Gordon Pym of Nantucket*, 1838; "William Wilson," in *Tales of the Grotesque and Arabesque*, 1840; "The Murders in the Rue Morgue," in *The Prose Romances of Edgar Allan Poe*, 1843; "The Mystery of Marie Roget," "The Gold Bug," "The Black Cat," "The Purloined Letter," in *Tales*, 1845; "Thou Art the Man," in *The Works of the Late Edgar Allan Poe*, edited by Rufus Griswold, 1850–56. Bibliography: *Bibliography of the Writings of Edgar A. Poe* by John W. Robertson, privately printed, 1934.

*   *   *

The modern detective story begins with Edgar Allan Poe's "The Murders in the Rue Morgue" which appeared in *Graham's Magazine* in April 1841. Poe's achievement, however, was based on several decades of fiction written in England, Ireland, America, France, and Germany, with much of which he was acquainted. Before Poe there were mystery and detective stories of various sorts, and many of the motifs that we now consider important were in fairly common use in dozens of pre-Poe stories. These include the concept of describing a crime and its detection in fictional form, the frame-up, the conflict between official and private investigators, the impossible crime, the red herring solution, bizarre subject matter, criminological technicalities, the fictionalization of historical crimes, the sealed room, and the concept of the self-limited case.

Poe added at least seven new elements of overwhelming importance. These are the stooge narrator, the eccentric detective, the complete outsider as detective, the armchair detective, reader participation in a puzzle, ratiocination or precise analytical reasoning, and a calculus of probabilities as a tool for cutting through conflicting evidence. It should be noted that the technique of ratiocination – interpreting minor clues to arrive at a large result – appeared in Voltaire's *Zadig* and other earlier literature, but Poe's analytic reasoning is much broader in scope and is now first applied by a detective to a murder case.

A listing of motifs, however, cannot convey the magnitude of Poe's achievement, for most of the earlier detective literature is bumbling and inconsequential. Poe not only improved on such elements as he borrowed, but with his remarkable structural sense worked out a viable form that served as model for thousands of successors. For the first time there was a clear and concise statement of the problem, tabulation of the evidence, and a solution based on this evidence. For these reasons "The Murders in the Rue Morgue" is the single most important story in the history of the genre. In terms of immediate sources, the murderous orang-utan was probably suggested by the similar ape, Sylvan, in Walter Scott's *Count Robert of Paris*, although it is possible that a couple of factual incidents may have contributed to the idea. Poe's Paris was probably derived from the popular image of the Paris of the day: a strange dichotomy between a wild and wooly crime center where anything might happen and a citadel of suave refinement and sophistication. Paris, too, had long been renowned for the efficiency of its police system. While Vidocq's Paris has often been suggested as the prototype for Poe's, a stronger case can be made for Eugene Sue's.

"The Mystery of Marie Roget" (*Snowden's Lady's Companion*, 1842–43) marked a new venture: the use of a fictional model to solve a historical crime. Poe based his somewhat rambling "story" on the contemporary case of Mary Rogers, a handsome but loose tobacconist's clerk, whose murdered corpse was found in the Hudson. Using his "calculus of probabilities" Dupin sifted the evidence, and, in the version published in *Snowden's*, came to the conclusion that her lover, a naval officer, had murdered her. (An interruption in the publication was probably caused by news reports that a break was near in the case, and Poe did not wish to be caught wrong.) In the revised version of 1845, however, Poe also admitted the possibility that Mary Rogers had died as the result of an abortion. This was the leading contemporary theory of the crime, which remains unsolved. In "The Purloined Letter" (*The Gift* for 1845, probably published in October 1844) Dupin once again demonstrates his faculty of analysis. The accusation, often made, that Poe erred in placing the seal and the address of a letter on the same side of the paper, leads one to think that the critics have never seen an early 19th century letter. In addition to the three Dupin stories, Poe wrote a fourth detective story,

"Thou Art the Man!" (*Godey's Lady's Book*, November 1844). A parody of the crime story of the day, it fits the practice of William Leggett and William Gilmore Simms fairly closely, but Poe may well have had other authors in mind. It would be venturing too far to describe Poe's other stories that involve mystery in one form or another, but I might mention "The Gold Bug," in which the hero applies detectional analysis and cryptography; "William Wilson," murder and hypostatized personality fragments; "The Black Cat," murder and the irony of fate; and *The Narrative of Arthur Gordon Pym*, with cryptographic and mysterious elements that Poe left for the reader to work out for himself.

The recognition that Poe had created a new form was not immediate in the English-speaking world. In America his first disciple seems to have been John Babington Williams, M.D. (*Leaves from the Note-book of a New York Detective*, 1864–65), and in England the probably pseudonymous Andrew Forrester, Jr. (The British short detective story of the day evolved independently of Poe.) In France, however, Poe's work was recognized and rated highly, and Gaboriau, building upon Poe's foundation, created the modern detective novel.

—E. F. Bleiler

RICHMOND (anonymous author).   British.   Short Stories: *Richmond; or, Scenes from the Life of a Bow Street Runner*, 1827.

*   *   *

Richmond is the first collection of stories about a detective to be printed in the western world. It was published anonymously, and its authorship is unknown, although it has occasionally been attributed to either Thomas S. Surr or William Gaspey, popular novelists of the day. An analysis of its style, subject matter, and publishing circumstances, however, rules out both men as possible authors. (For details, see the edition by E. F. Bleiler, New York, Dover, 1976.)

A rambling novel, *Richmond* first describes the picaresque youth of Thomas Richmond, in which he is associated with various criminal types. About one third of the way through the book Richmond tires of his haphazard existence and joins the Bow Street Court in London as a Runner. Five of his cases then follow. Sometimes interlocked, they are concerned with kidnapping, smuggling, resurrection men, swindling, and general police work. They are all solved by rational, procedural means. There is some attempt at realism in characterizations, crimes, and background. The sources for *Richmond* were probably contemporary journalistic accounts of the Bow Street court and the exploits of historical Runners, but the author, who would seem to have been a young, inexperienced writer, had no real knowledge of the Bow Street operation. Where literary form was concerned, the author did not use contemporary models for treating crime fictionally (Godwin's *Caleb Williams*, certain crime-Gothic novels, the "frame plot"), but was probably aware of the then-popular linked occupational stories.

While *Richmond* is not a great work of art, it anticipates later developments clearly. It went without recognition in its day, however, and was apparently without historical influence, unless its basic concept influenced "Waters" some twenty years later.

—E. F. Bleiler

WATERS. Pseudonym for William Russell; also wrote as Inspector F; Lieutenant Robert Warneford, RN. British. Fiction: *Recollections of a Policeman*, 1852 (as *Recollections of a Detective Police-Officer*, 1856; *The Detective Officer and Other Tales*, 1878; *Recollections of a Detective*, 1887); *Leaves from the Diary of a Law Clerk*, 1857; *The Game of Life*, 1857 (as *Leonard Harlowe; or, The Game of Life*, 1862); *Recollections of a Sheriff's Officer*, 1860; *A Skeleton in Every House*, 1860; *The Experiences of a French Detective Officer Adapted from the Mss. of Theodore Duhamel*, 1861; *The Heir-at-Law and Other Tales*, 1861; *Experiences of a Real Detective* (as Inspector F.), 1862; *Undiscovered Crimes*, 1862; *Autobiography of an English Detective*, 1863; *Strange Stories of a Detective; or, Curiosities of Crime*, 1863; *Leaves from the Journal of a Custom-House Officer*, 1868; *The Valazy Family and Other Narratives*, 1869; *Mrs. Waldegrave's Will and Other Tales* (as Inspector F.), 1870.

*   *   *

Though there is no available biographical information on William Russell, who published most of his works under the pseudonym Waters, he is historically important as the first English writer of short detective fiction. In something of the manner of the pioneering French detective Eugène Vidocq, whose *Memoirs* (1829) presented as fact a considerably fictionized version of his sensational career, Russell wrote in the first person a series of stories, the first of which appeared in 1849, purporting to deal with cases on which he had worked as a London police official. His first collection appeared in New York in 1852 under the title *Recollections of a Policeman*; it was reprinted in London in 1856 as *Recollections of a Detective Police-Officer*. The popularity of Waters's books in this period – Poe's detective stories had preceded them by only a few years, and Wilkie Collins's major detective novels were not to come until the 1860's – showed the English public's eager interest in detective tales, gave rise to many imitations, and helped create a climate favorable to the appearance of Doyle's Sherlock Holmes stories in a later generation. Most of Waters's stories concentrate on the detective's often dangerous exploits in solving cases involving theft, forgery, murder, and the like, and thus exemplify, if in relatively crude ways, basic characteristics of detective fiction.

—Seymour Rudin

WOOD, Mrs. Henry (née Ellen Price) (1814–87). British. Novels: *East Lynne*, 1861; *The Channings*, 1862; *The Shadow of Ashlydyat*, 1863; *Trevlyn Hold; or, Squire Trevlyn's Heir*, 1864; *The Red Court Farm*, 1865; *Roland Yorke*, 1869; *Within the Maze*, 1872; *The Master of Greylands*, 1873. Short Stories: *Johnny Ludlow*, six series, 12 vols., 1874–99; *Told in the Twilight*, 1875.

*   *   *

In Mrs. Henry Wood's hundred or so stories (the count is not clear because of anonymous work and false attributions) murders, thefts, disappearances, and swindles appear frequently. They are often accompanied by detectives and detection. The second plot of her most famous work, *East Lynne*, for example, is an ingenious murder mystery superior to the sentimental first plot the Victorian stage treasured. Many of Mrs. Wood's novels are concerned with crime: *Trevlyn Hold*, disappearance and suspected murder; *The Master of Greylands*, murder with Gothic elements; *Within the Maze*, an escaped felon and Scotland Yard; *The Channings* and *Roland Yorke*, theft or embezzlement; *The Red Court Farm*, murder. Her short stories, in addition, are even more strongly concerned with crime and detection. About half of the stories in the Johnny Ludlow series deal with matters criminal and mysterious, and here the crime is central, without the distraction of concurrent plots.

Mrs. Wood was religious, a temperance enthusiast, and a moralist, and a strong element in her fiction is Victorian stability: rank, responsibility, harmony, morality. The life she evokes in well-plotted, detailed realism is now itself a fantasy world. This cosmos could be disturbed by the subtraction of a person, and much of Mrs. Wood's fiction is concerned with mysterious revenants (living or dead) who restore the original harmony. Crime, too, could shatter this crystalline world, but in a peculiar manner. Mrs. Wood cared little about the crime, nor did the detective process interest her greatly. When professional detectives appear, they are usually wrong. What really concerned Mrs. Wood was the impact of crime on the upper-middle-class social fabric and on the personalities of the suspects. These she analyzed in great detail.

Today Mrs. Wood is undeservedly forgotten. She was a skilled craftsman, despite sentimental quirks common to the period, and could produce good work when she wished. Her contemporaries rated her Johnny Ludlow stories highest, and in this I would concur.

—E. F. Bleiler

FOREIGN-LANGUAGE WRITERS

BORGES, Jorge Luis (1899–). Argentine. Fiction: *Ficciones*, 1962 (as *Fictions*, 1965); *Labyrinths*, 1962; *The Aleph and Other Stories*, 1970.

*   *   *

Jorge Luis Borges began to experiment tentatively in the 1930's with the short narrative tale, the genre in which he was to gain international acclaim. In the 1940's he initiated the slow, steady flow of short prose pieces that has continued for nearly 40 years, interrupted only briefly in the late 1950's when he became blind. His two most celebrated books – *Ficciones* (1944) and *El Aleph* (1949) were assembled from the earliest of these tales.

Borges's contributions to detective literature have been extensive and – foreseeably – singular. Most significant have been a handful of short stories – pre-eminent among them "Death and the Compass" – that have blended, in Borges's inimitable fashion, a popular form (the detective/crime short story) with perplexing metaphysical concepts. Borges's tale "The Garden of Forking Paths" has the form of a conventional spy story but in the end evokes a compelling metaphor of human existence. His fondness for detective fiction has been expressed in many ways. With his friend and collaborator Adolfo Bioy Casares, he published in 1942 a most unusual volume of detective short stories, *Seis problemas para don Isidro Parodi* [Six Problems for Don Isidro Parodi] and a short novelette *Un modelo para la muerte* [A Model for Death] (1946). Also with Bioy Casares he established in the mid-1940's a series of English and American detective novels in translation that has continued unbroken for more than 35 years. Again with Bioy Casares he has edited and helped to translate two anthologies of largely English and American detective short stories, which appeared in 1943 and 1956. He has clearly done more to promote the merits of the detective story than any other writer in the Spanish language.

—Donald A. Yates

BOULLE, Pierre (Francois Marie-Louis) (1912–). French. Novels: *Not the Glory*, 1955 (as *William Conrad*, 1955; *Spy Converted*, 1960); *Face of a Hero*, 1956 (as *Saving Face*, 1956); *White Man's Test*, 1956 (as *The Test*, 1957); *The Other Side of the Coin*, 1958; *S.O.P.H.I.A.*, 1959; *A Noble Profession*, 1960 (as *For a Noble Cause*, 1961); *The Executioner*, 1961 (as *The Chinese Executioner*, 1962); *The Photographer*, 1968 (as *An Impartial Eye*, 1968); *Ears of the Jungle*, 1972; *Desperate Games*, 1973; *The Virtues of Hell*, 1974. Short Stories: *Time Out of Mind and Other Stories*, 1966.

*   *   *

The French novelist Pierre Boulle is best known for his Far East adventures, including *S.O.P.H.I.A.* and *The Bridge on the River Kwai*, and his science fiction, including *The Planet of the Apes*.

Mystery elements common to much of Boulle's work are international intrigue, psychological suspense, ironic reversal, and surprise endings. *The Executioner*, set in pre-revolutionary China, explains why an executioner illegally poisons his victims rather than subject them to the elaborate ceremony preceding their legal beheading. *The Test* develops the tragic conflict of values resulting from the abduction of a young French girl from the Malay village and husband she has accepted to an alien European culture. In *The Other Side of the Coin* the American wife of a French rubber planter converts a beautiful Chinese communist guerrilla to capitalism, cosmetics, *haut couture*, and Christian love. The happy convert elopes with her benefactor's husband. "The Enigmatic Saint" gradually reveals the horrible motivation of the selfless benefactor of a medieval leper colony. In *The Photographer* a disabled war photographer discovers, then secretly aids, an assassination plot in order to create the perfect photograph of the event.

Boulle's subjects and settings often reflect his own experience as a rubber planter in Malaya, where he also served as a Free French agent during World War II. Boulle's exotic settings, obsessed characters, and carefully developed plots make his works, which usually make an ethical comment on society as a whole, an unusual treat for the mystery fan.

—Katherine Staples

BUTOR, Michel (Marie Francois) (1926–).   French.   Novel: *Passing Time*, 1960.

*   *   *

Jean-Pierre Attal, in an essay on Michel Butor's critical method, compares Butor to Hercule Poirot "who had little interest in signs, but much interest in criminal psychology." Attal also comments that one of the keenest pleasures for the reader of mystery novels is his surprise in learning the identity of the murderer. This importance of the denouement is also stressed by Robert Champigny in his study *What Will Have Happened* (1977), though he points out that some recent French novelists who incorporate mystery fiction elements into their narratives leave the crime unresolved and the identity of the criminal unconfirmed.

In fact, in *Passing Time*, Butor is more interested in following the signposts which may lead his amateur detective, Jacques Revel, to the uncovering and solving of an old crime, and the psychological elements are clouded by mystery and uncertainty. The narrative is preceded by a street map of the city of Bleston where the action takes place, though this simple, explicit chart is deceptive. The city itself is the chief obstacle to Revel's investigation, and the sooty, confusing streets of this English industrial town become the twisting detours of a labyrinth from which Revel extricates himself only by flight, his journey of discovery unfinished.

The novel is written in the form of a journal which retraces the various stages of Revel's investigation, but it becomes increasingly evident that the narrative is riddled with gaps. Vital information is being withheld from the reader in the selective entries, and, in the final entry, written as Revel is about to leave Bleston, he speaks of events which he had canceled until now. Revel, the detective, the relentless pursuer of the truth, is, in fact, also that mysterious arsonist whose activities have plagued the city. As the novelist burns the traditional structures of the detective novel, the principal character attempts to destroy the site of the crime he cannot solve, and the theoretical distinction between the detective and the criminal blurs in this expression of Revel's frustration and rage.

Passing Time is the only one of Butor's novels to deal specifically with the conventions of the genre, but each of his novels poses enigmas and refuses to solve them for the gratification of the reader. Some French critics have suggested – half-playfully, half-seriously – that the structures of mystery fiction underlie all narrative art. There may be some truth in this leveling of genre distinctions, and certainly Butor and other contemporary novelists, like criminals attacking the orderly structures of society, undermine the reader's confidence by attacking the conventions of the narrative. The reader, whose only crime is to seek escape from rather than a reflection of his own disharmonious existence, finds the curative powers of popular fiction turned to disruptive ends. But he may also reflect that the most popular of contemporary heroes, the private-eye and the urban precinct detective, have traditionally had a skeptical attitude about the apparently infallible powers of the classic fictional detective. As other contemporary structures fall apart, it should not be surprising that the open case file should become a feature of the detective novel. The novel, Butor seems to suggest, should pose dilemmas, not solve them, and it is ironically appropriate that the closed forms of the mystery novel should furnish the materials for that assault on conventions.

—Walter Albert

DÜRRENMATT, Friedrich (1921–). Swiss. Novels: *The Judge and His Hangman*, 1954 (as *End of the Game*, 1976); *The Pledge*, 1959; *A Dangerous Game*, 1960 (as *Traps*, 1960); *The Quarry*, 1962. Plays: *Fools Are Passing Through*, 1958 (as *The Marriage of Mr. Mississippi*, 1964); *The Visit*, 1958; *The Physicists*, 1963.

* * *

Inspired notably by Brecht, Kafka, and Wilder, but with an intellectual punch and theatrical drive altogether his own, Dürrenmatt hit the post-war German-speaking stage like a meteor and has left an indelible mark on the whole of contemporary drama. Particularly *The Marriage of Mr. Mississippi*, *The Visit*, and *The Physicists* include crimes dear to detectives. They are, however, incidental to perturbing explorations of the individual's helplessness and failure in uncontrollable conditions – of man in an environment governed by chance whose inexorable justice, if justice it is, is enigmatic. There are no solutions: "literature may not provide comfort" ("Conversation with Heinz Ludwig Arnold"). Yet the message of this brilliant and uncomfortable Swiss is not despair but humble persistence, tragicomedy his natural medium. It is also basic to detective fiction, of which Dürrenmatt is the first German-writing exponent to achieve international resonance. His novels, already classics, show an amazing but probably – for him – inevitable sweep through the genre.

Poirot's Christian name may seem a laughable incongruity; yet in his way he *is* a Hercules, not just in the pre-retirement *Labours*. In characteristic contrast, Marlowe decides "It wasn't a game for knights" (*The Big Sleep*); nevertheless, he is one, an authentic hero of our time. Wildly different, both their worlds allow attitudes and actions whose structures suggest these associations. Such figures and their adventures satisfy strong psychological needs (among them that for comfort) and can, when masterfully presented, hardly die, though they may date. Of this kind is Dürrenmatt's first novel, *The Judge and His Hangman*. Here Bärlach, detective Komissär at Berne, looks like a successfully transplanted version of the old bear, a Maigret Helveticus. Introduced, like many detectives, with a telescoped background, Bärlach is, however, not just old and famous, but about to retire, and he suffers from terminal cancer. Nevertheless he dominates all and duly gets his murderer (one of his subordinates), using him to "execute" a life-long adversary and master-criminal (Lupin and Carlos rolled in one) before chasing him into exile. Bärlach thus, again like many predecessors, arrogates the functions of justice, anticipating the four horrific old men in Dürrenmatt's kafkaesque novella *A Dangerous Game* (originally a radio play), linked to Bärlach also through the motif of hectic gluttony.

Things change in the immediate sequel, *The Quarry*. Bärlach, operated upon and hospitalised, tries to unmask a devil: a Swiss doctor now in a luxury clinic torturing and killing (through operations without anesthetic) the Rich as he did the Jews in a German extermination camp. Rumbling him by chance, Bärlach is recognised and destined to the same treatment. Utterly helpless, the weak old man awaits the hour of his martyrdom. He is saved (and the devil killed) by Gulliver, a new Ahasverus, who tells him: "Today one cannot fight evil on one's own, as the knights of yore went forth to combat some dragon.... You fool of a detective, time itself has shown you to be absurd." Besides the horrors of Nazism, influences like Dostoyevsky's "The Grand Inquisitor" and Kafka's "The Penal Colony" are visible. Bärlach, the hunter, has become the humiliated quarry whose supreme achievement is to meet with Christ-like silence the taunts of his tormentor, a voice of amoral, existential materialism. Bärlach had requested Dürer's picture "Knight, Death, and Devil" for his room. He is himself, Gulliver tells him, a "knight of the sad countenance" – a Don Quixote (and a staid variant of the grotesque Übelohe in *The Marriage of Mr. Mississippi*). A later radio play, *An Evening's Hour in Late Autumn*, cruelly if farcically repeats this juxtaposition of devil and knight, casting a sensational author in the role of the mass murderer committing his crimes in order to write about them, egged on by his readers, and a miserable sod of a retired accountant who has investigated him (and duly becomes his next victim) in the role of a Don Quixote.

After the detective, the genre itself is dispatched in *The Pledge* (subtitled "Requiem for the Detective Novel") on the grounds that it falsifies reality by giving it pattern and meaning. Dürrenmatt, in this chilling story of miscarried justice and the thwarted chase of a sex killer, has his cake (or rather chocolate truffles) *and* eats it. Chance disposes of the maniac, the truth comes too late for Matthäi, the detective who has gone mad over the business – but not for the reader. He remains, like Mohammed in Dürrenmatt's parable "Lecture on Justice and Right," the instructed observer.

—H. M. Klein

GABORIAU, Émile (1833–1873). French. Novels: *The Mystery of Orcival*, 1871 (as *Crime at Orcival*, 1952); *The Widow Lerouge*, 1873 (as *The Lerouge Case*, 1925); *The Clique of Gold*, 1874; *Within an Inch of His Life*, 1874 (as *In Peril of His Life*, 1883; *In Deadly Peril*, 1888); *Other People's Money*, 1875; *Marriage at a Venture*, 1879; *The Men of the Bureau*, 1880; *Monsieur Lecoq*, 1880 (part one: *Monsieur Lecoq: The Detective's Dilemma*, and *Monsieur Lecoq: The Detective's Triumph*, 1888; part two: *The Honor of the Name*, 1900); *The Count's Secret*, 1881 (as *The Count's Millions*, 1913; *Baron Trigault's Vengeance*, 1913); *The Slaves of Paris*, 1882 (part one: *Caught in the Net*, 1891; part two: *The Champdoce Mystery*, 1891); *Promise of Marriage*, 1883 (with *Marriage at a Venture* in *Marriage of Adventure*, 1921); *The Downward Path*, 1883; *File No. 113*, 1883 (as *Warrant No. 113*, 1884; *The Blackmailers*, 1907); *The Catastrophe*, 1885; *The Intrigues of a Prisoner*, 1885; *The Marquise de Brinvilliers*, 1886 (as *Marie de Brinvilliers*, 1888). Short Stories: *The Little Old Man of the Batignolles: A Chapter from a Detective's Memoirs*, 1880 (various reprints, as *Max's Marriage*, 1880; *A Beautiful Scourge*, 1883; *A Thousand Francs Reward*, 1887).

*   *   *

Historically Émile Gaboriau is second in importance only to Edgar Allan Poe. Poe crystallized the detective short story, and Gaboriau was the first to see clearly what was required of a longer form. He wrote the first novels in which the nature of the crime, the introduction and role of the detective, the extenders, the misdirections, the reader participation, and the solution are all carried through in the modern manner. It is also important to note that when the mainstream of modern detective fiction arose in England, it followed not the mode of the British Victorians like Collins, but that of Gaboriau.

In September 1865 Gaboriau's first detective novel, *L'Affaire Lerouge* (*The Widow Lerouge*) began to appear serially. In a curious parallel to Sherlock Holmes, however, it attracted little attention on first publication, but on reprint made its author world famous. It offered the consultant detective Tabaret, who had studied the literature of crime and worked by ratiocination, an opportunity to solve a very deceptive murder that is said to have been based on a contemporary crime. Six other works by Gaboriau are detective stories in the puristic sense. Three of these are built upon the ebullient personality of Lecoq of the Sûreté: *The Mystery of Orcival*, *File No. 113*, and *Monsieur Lecoq*. Separate are the novella *The Little Old Man of the Batignolles*, the short story "A Disappearance," and the novel *In Deadly Peril*. Several other novels are sensational social novels, although they contain mystery and crime elements in varying degree: *Caught in the Net* and *The Champdoce Mystery*, *The Count's Secret* and *Baron Trigault's Vengeance*, *The Clique of Gold*, and *Other People's Money*. A historical novel, *The Marquise de Brinvilliers*, is based loosely on the well-known factual crime.

Gaboriau considered himself a disciple of Poe's, and he united Poe's precision of form and concept of ratiocination with the sensational social novel of Balzac with its powerful emotional roots. Gaboriau, indeed, thought of himself as writing a new *comédie humaine*. Among the other sources which contributed to Gaboriau's crystallization were the French thriller of the day, particularly the work of his former employer, Paul Féval (who had previously unsuccessfully tried to imitate Poe); the strong French literature of factual crime; and the contemporary police blotter. Gaboriau attended the police courts and may have been the first writer of fiction to make a serious study of crime and criminology. As a result his work is a goldmine of information on legal and investigatory procedures.

From a literary point of view Gaboriau has been in eclipse for decades, but this is not just. He was a remarkable plotter, superior even to Collins, and a first-rate creator of criminalistic detail. His French is said to be brilliant stylistically, though he has been badly served in Victorian English translations. His largest weakness is in the creation of character; while the two detectives Tabaret and Lecoq are well drawn, the "romantic" characters, as has often been said, are cardboard. In terms of form perhaps his least valuable contribution has been the appending of second-rate historical romances to his detective stories to explain ultimate antecedents. In this he was followed by Doyle.

The individual novels have been variously estimated. Some critics have preferred *The Mystery of Orcival* or *File No. 113*, but this reviewer gives first preference to *Monsieur Lecoq*, Part One, and second to *The Widow Lerouge*.

—E. F. Bleiler

JAPRISOT, Sebastien (1931–). Pseudonym for Jean Baptiste Rossi. French. Novels: *The 10:30 from Marseilles*, 1963 (as *The Sleeping Car Murders*, 1967); *Trap for Cinderella*, 1964; *The Lady in the Car with Glasses and a Gun*, 1967; *Goodbye, Friend*, 1969.

*   *   *

Sebastien Japrisot's greatest talent lies in his ability to create fascinating, complex mysteries that keep the reader spellbound while trying to determine just what is going on. All four of his books are not merely escape stories but studies of personality and reality. The contradictions of what is and what appears to be are most blatant in *Trap for Cinderella* and *The Lady in the Car*. By carefully inflicting impossible situations and events on his characters, and telling their story by first-person narrative, he challenges the reader to find a way through the maze.

The 10:30 from Marseilles was Japrisot's first and most traditional novel. Using many of the techniques of the police procedural novel, he presents the problem of a girl killed on a train after it arrives in Paris. Routine questioning and locating of the co-passengers is interspaced with episodes about the passengers themselves. Japrisot avoids stereotyping the passengers by concentrating on each one, showing his vanities and fears – and then letting the murderer get to them before the police do. His inexperience as a crime writer shows in the visibility of the villain, and by having a rather improbable young boy solve the crime. But suspense, forward thrust, and reader-involvement make it an excellent working of a now common device.

A purely psychological tale based on a crime, *Trap for Cinderella* won the Grand Prix de la Littérature Policière. The exceedingly complex plot shoves the reader back and forth (as Michelle Isola is) between thinking Mi is a murderer or a victim. After recovering from disfiguring burns, Mi has lost her memory and doesn't know if she has been trying to kill her friend Do, or if she is, in fact, Do, who had killed Mi and taken her place. Ironic twists and snaps reinforce the searching-for-reality theme; the same events are told several times from different viewpoints. Each time a new factor is added to change the significance. *Trap for Cinderella* is also a good example of Japrisot's ability to handle potentially sensational material (lesbianism, rampant sex) in a reasonable way. These elements figure in all his books but never dominate them.

The reality theme is again brought forward in *The Lady in the Car*, also a prize-winner. At the beginning of the book, Dany Longo is on her way to the sea. An act of non-sensical, meaningless violence by an unseen man results in her hand being injured. From that point on she repeatedly meets impossibilities and craziness – everything she does seems to be a repeat performance; others recognize her and say she's been there earlier in the day. But Dany knows she hasn't been there before. An explanation does come, carrying the conclusion that although the world seems unreliable, there is a pattern, determined by chance, self-choice, and the acts of others.

Japrisot's last book, *Goodbye, Friend*, is a departure in style though it keeps many of the earlier themes. Dr. Barran returns from Vietnam and is asked to help replace some embezzled bonds in a vault. Of course the scheme goes wrong and Barran and a mercenary are trapped in a building, accused of theft and murder. Women are again the primary villains (amid hints of lesbianism) and a sense of fantastic impossibility (the world gone wrong) is a strong factor. Intentionally written in a movie scenario form, the book moves quickly, giving no time for thought or analysis along the way. But the end provides a last-paragraph twist (as in *Cinderella*) that shows how some events in the book were predictable.

—Fred Dueren

KIRST, Hans Hellmut (1914–).   German.   Novels: *The Night of the Generals*, 1963; *The Last Card*, 1967 (as *Death Plays the Last Card*, 1968); *Camp 7 Last Stop*, 1969; *Undercover Man*, 1970 (as *No Fatherland*, 1970); *Hero in the Tower*, 1972; *A Time for Scandal*, 1973 (as *Damned to Success*, 1973); *A Time for Truth*, 1974; *A Time for Payment*, 1976; *Nights of the Long Knives*, 1976; *Everything Has Its Price*, 1976; *The Twilight of the Generals*, 1979; *The Affairs of the Generals*, 1979.

*   *   *

One of the most successful of the post-war German novelists, Hans Hellmut Kirst is best known for his four "Gunner Asch" books, his novel *The Night of the Generals*, and for his satires of German army life. *The Night of the Generals* and *Nights of the Long Knives* might both be termed crime novels, particularly the former, which features an official detective. Both works make exciting and terrifying reading and, in the cynical detachment of their narrative method, represent the best technical achievements of recent European crime fiction.

However, Kirst's most significant contribution to the detective crime story is his "Munich Trilogy": *A Time for Scandal*, *A Time for Truth*, and *A Time for Payment*.

Featuring Detective-Inspector Keller of the Munich CID (who retires at the end of the first novel), the books are chronicles of crime, scandal, and corruption in high places in contemporary Germany. The novels are written with a kind of indifference; the narrative method involves the use of notebook and diary entries, newspaper reports, snatches of dialogue, and "straight" narration of events. The mood of the trilogy is thus starkly contemporary; the narration exposes the reader to a variety of interpretations or "filters" of events, while challenging him to put together a solution to the crime based upon "evidence" from a variety of predictable and unlikely sources. His stylistic originality places Kirst in the company of contemporary writers who have used the crime story to depict the paradoxes of modern urban life. Like the Swedes Sjöwall and Wahlöö, Kirst sees the official police as victims of the same mindless bureaucracy that has permeated civilian life, and like them, too, he is pessimistic about the possibility of social or legal reform. Finally, his passionate interest in social detail, and the combination of irony and compassion with which he records it, mark Kirst as a crime writer of a very high order.

Kirst has the distinction of having created perhaps the most memorable canine since *The Hound of the Baskervilles*. Anton the Newfoundland, who makes his appearance in *A Time for Scandal* and whose kidnapping is a central event in *A Time for Payment*, is one of the most endearing of fictional hounds. Endowed with a stoically loving personality, the dog is given to Detective-Inspector Keller by Harald Fein, an embattled but essentially decent architect-turned-businessman whom Keller saves from destruction. As Keller explains: "Anton has always known what it is to lead a dog's life − never abandoning hope of being loved unreservedly in spite of everything. Many people have never experienced such a hope and lots of them are forced to bury it still-born. They go on living, but what a life!" The first novel establishes the relationship between Keller and the dog, who becomes a symbol of integrity and hope in a sea of corruption. Keller's retirement from the CID allows him to employ methods, in the two subsequent novels, which would be unthinkable for the official force. Keller, then, forms a bridge between the professional detective of the *roman policier* and the more romantic private eye, with Anton as a combination partner and love interest.

A Time for Truth continues the examination of contemporary corruption by presenting the murder of journalist Heinz Horstmann. Predictably, the murder starts a chain of other crimes, from which none of the principal characters escapes unscathed (although two rival newspapers, demonstrating the power of the press, are able to establish a merger which protects the vested interests of each). The observation of contemporary life and morals is acute, the irony superbly controlled. In *A Time for Payment*, Kirst concludes his contemporary epic with a story of kidnapping, murder, student unrest, and grand larceny. The narration of this final volume is somewhat more straightforward than the others, with the journalistic interpolations less frequent, particularly at the beginning. Keller has now become a force unto himself, a giver of advice and director of a private machine of justice: "If a stranger received orders to contact Keller, no personal description was ever attempted. 'You'll know him by his dog' was enough of a clue." Although he receives an offer to return to the force, Keller prefers to continue alone. Our last view of him is on a park bench, with Anton at his feet.

—Joanne Harack Hayne

LEBLANC, Maurice (Marie Émile) (1864–1941). French. Novels: *Arsène Lupin*, with Edgar Jepson (novelization of play), 1909; *813*, 1910; *The Hollow Needle*, 1910; *The*

Frontier, 1912; *The Crystal Stopper*, 1913; *The Teeth of the Tiger*, 1914; *The Bomb-Shell*, 1916 (as *The Woman of Mystery*, 1916); *The Golden Triangle*, 1917; *Coffin Island*, 1920 (as *The Secret of Sarek*, 1920); *The Three Eyes*, 1921; *The Tremendous Event*, 1922; *Dorothy the Rope Dancer*, 1923 (as *The Secret Tomb*, 1923); *The Candlestick with Seven Branches*, 1925 (as *Memoirs of Arsène Lupin*, 1925); *The Girl with the Green Eyes*, 1927 (as *Arsène Lupin, Super-Sleuth*, 1927); *The Melamare Mystery*, 1930; *Man of Miracles*, 1931; *The Double Smile*, 1933 (as *The Woman with Two Smiles*, 1933); *From Midnight to Morning*, 1933; *The Return of Arsène Lupin*, 1933; *Wanton Venus*, 1935. Short Stories: *The Exploits of Arsène Lupin*, 1907; *Arsène Lupin Versus Holmlock Shears*, 1909 (as *The Blonde Lady*, 1910); *The Confessions of Arsène Lupin*, 1912; *The Eight Strokes of the Clock*, 1922; *Jim Barnett Intervenes*, 1928 (as *Arsène Lupin Intervenes*, 1929).

*　　*　　*

A law student, hack writer, crime reporter, and dramatist, Maurice Leblanc is best remembered as the author of the novels and stories featuring Arsène Lupin. Although he had enjoyed a prolific, if undistinguished, career as a writer for periodicals, it was not until 1906, when he was asked to write a crime story for a new journal, *Je Sais Tout*, that he produced the first Lupin adventure. *Arsène Lupin: Gentleman-Cambrioleur* was published a year later, and soon Lupin became a household word, not only in France, but around the world.

The origins of Arsène Lupin lie, first of all, in the Sherlock Holmes adventures and their inversion, the Raffles stories; and, second, in the tradition of rogue literature, a popular French example of which was Ponson de Terrail's *Rocambole* (1866). As to the first influence, Holmes appears in *Arsène Lupin Versus Holmlock Shears* and is badly outwitted by the sprightly Frenchman; and the "gentlemanly" Lupin is clearly a French version of the "amateur cracksman" who so alarmed Conan Doyle. Rocambole, the leader of a Paris street gang, a master of disguise and a flouter of bourgeois conventions (particularly as these are upheld by the police), was more a romantic adventurer than a detective/criminal. A further influence upon the creation of Lupin may be Gaboriau's Monsieur Lecoq; for, in his sardonic insistence that official detectives were merely thieves set to catch thieves, Gaboriau prepared the way for stories in which detective and criminal are one and the same. So clever is Lupin that he actually poses as Lenormand, chief of the Sûreté, and investigates the crimes committed by himself.

Most of the Lupin books cannot be considered detective fiction so much as burlesques of the form. Generally, the short stories are more successful than the full-length novels, in which the sense of frantic fun wears a bit thin. (Exceptions are *The Hollow Needle* and *813*, both of which contain some unusual features.) The rivalry between Lupin and Holmes is, to put it gently, sophomoric. The early short stories, however, can be read for sheer enjoyment of their farcical elements; and it is a tribute to Leblanc's creative energies that we are entirely engrossed by the "puzzles." We want to know how Lupin is going to escape from each new difficulty, and we side entirely with him because, unlike the fat bourgeois businessman from whom he steals works of art, or the dull-witted policemen who try to detect "by the book," Lupin exhibits a lively sense of the ridiculous, and so moves with ease from one cliff-hanging situation to another.

It is significant that murder rarely figures as the crime in a Lupin story. Lupin's criminal activities are almost never undertaken solely for personal gain. If he steals a painting, it is so that it may be genuinely appreciated. If he deliberately enchants a woman, it is because she is about to marry the wrong man. His disguises, so baffling to the police, are usually adopted for the sheer fun of the deception. Towards the end of his career, Lupin begins to work more and more in consort with the police – sometimes for reasons of his own, but often as a result of his idealism and sense of justice. Unfortunately, the feeling of fun so evident in the first volume of adventures is missing from those of the "reformed" Lupin.

Needless to say, deduction as a science plays little part in Lupin's methods; in this, he is at the opposite extreme from Gaboriau's Monsieur Lecoq. The mood of the stories is romantic, non-scientific, neo-gothic, and, above all, action-filled. They can, however, be read with enjoyment by the connoisseur of detective fiction – primarily as an antidote to those works which, in their insistence upon a rational explanation for all mysterious phenomena, take themselves – and the world – too seriously.

—Joanne Harack Hayne

LEROUX, Gaston (1868–1927).   French.   Novels: *The Mystery of the Yellow Room*, 1908 (as *Murder in the Bedroom*, 1945); *The Perfume of the Lady in Black*, 1909; *The Double Life*, 1909; *The Phantom of the Opera*, 1911; *The Man with the Black Feather*, 1912; *Balaoo*, 1913; *The Secret of the Night*, 1914; *The Bride of the Sun*, 1915; *The Man Who Came Back from the Dead*, 1916; *The Amazing Adventures of Carolus Herbert*, 1922; *The Floating Prison*, 1922 (as *Wolves of the Sea*, 1923); *Cheri-Bibi and Cecily*, 1923 (as *Missing Men*, 1923); *The Veiled Prisoner*, 1923; *Cheri-Bibi, Mystery Man*, 1924 (as *The Dark Road*, 1924); *The Dancing Girl*, 1924 (as *Nomads of the Night*, 1925); *The Burgled Heart*, 1925 (as *The New Terror*, 1926); *The Slave Bangle*, 1925 (as *The Phantom Clue*, 1926); *The Adventures of a Coquette*, 1926; *The Sleuth Hound*, 1926 (as *The Octopus of Paris*, 1927); *The Masked Man*, 1927; *The Son of Three Fathers*, 1927; *The New Idol*, 1928; *The Man of a Hundred Masks*, 1930 (as *The Man of a Hundred Faces*, 1930); *The Midnight Lady*, 1930; *The Haunted Chair*, 1931; *Lady Helena; or, The Mysterious Lady*, 1931; *The Missing Archduke*, 1931; *The Kiss That Killed*, 1934; *The Machine to Kill*, 1935.

*   *   *

Gaston Leroux enjoyed an adventurous life as a newspaper correspondent, lawyer, drama critic, legal chronicler, writer on hygiene, playwright, and world traveler which he imaginatively transformed into over 30 popular novels of mystery and detection. Best known for his novel *The Phantom of the Opera* Leroux was a *raconteur par excellence* who had a remarkable talent for telling a good – if somewhat incredible – story that engages and holds the reader's interest from first to last.

By general agreement, Leroux's *The Mystery of the Yellow Room* is considered the greatest masterpiece of French detective fiction. In this cleverly plotted novel structured around a *crime passionel* and a much-admired variation of the locked-room puzzle, Leroux established for all time the Least-Likely-Person element in detective fiction by making the "official" detective the culprit. To carry off his grand deception as well as to create rivalry between the professional detective and the amateur sleuth, Leroux introduced the 18-year-old Joseph Rouletabille, the first of the bright young reporters, who sees himself not as a policeman but as a journalist in the service of the truth. Rouletabille (so nicknamed for his bullet-shaped head) is blessed with ratiocinative powers and a devoted friend, Sainclair, who chronicles his adventures and serves as his perplexed Dr. Watson. Because it stretches coincidence beyond all credibility and has occasional moments of excessive melodrama, *The Mystery of the Yellow Room* ranks today among those classics of detective fiction that everyone "knows" but few have read.

—Arthur Nicholas Athanason

MONTEILHET, Hubert (1928–). French. Novels: *The Praying Mantises*, 1962 (as *Praying Mantis*, 1962); *Return from the Ashes*, 1963 (as *Phoenix from the Ashes*, 1963); *The Road to Hell*, 1964; *The Prisoner of Love*, 1965; *Cupid's Executioners*, 1967; *Murder at Leisure*, 1971; *A Perfect Crime, or Two*, 1971; *Murder at the Frankfurt Fair: A Wicked, Witty Novel about the Publishing of an International Bestseller*, 1976 (as *Dead Copy* ..., 1976).

*   *   *

Hubert Monteilhet, with no previous writing experience, chose to work in the detective novel where, according to his remarks in an interview published in the French edition of *Ellery Queen's Mystery Magazine* (No. 298), "the level was generally rather low and the slightest talent was more likely to be recognized."

His first novel, *The Praying Mantises*, was awarded the Grand Prix de Littérature Policière. A well-constructed and original plot based on the suspense novel, a pervasive, subtle humor, psychologically complex characters both cynical and detached, torn between greed and eroticism, were the ingredients which contributed to its success. In addition, the novel was distinguished by a consciously classical style which did not hesitate to use the imperfective subjunctive ostentatiously. These same elements, combined in similarly rigorous and virtuoso proportions, characterize all the early novels and, in particular, his masterpiece, *Return from the Ashes*. With his concern for approaching indirectly with a kind of mannered elegance and a taste for paradox certain moral and metaphysical problems, all these qualities were to make Monteilhet known as the Choderlos de Laclos of the detective novel. Subsequently, this subtle balance was very often disturbed either for eroticism, as the titles of certain novels suggest (*The Prisoner of Love, Cupid's Executioners*, and the untranslated *Pour Deux sous de Vertu*), or for an affected humor that becomes tedious (*The Road to Hell* and *Esprit, Es-Tu-La ?*). Yet Monteilhet occasionally rediscovered the vein of his first novels (as in *Murder at the Frankfurt Fair*) and succeeded in proving with *A Perfect Crime, or Two* that the theses of Thomas De Quincey on the art of crime are not without substance.

Monteilhet has defined himself as a writer of classical tastes: "By classical, I mean a permanent tendency of the mind to give precedence to order and reason over feeling. But in a classicism which seeks to be harmonious, reason must only win against madness by a fraction." His conception of the detective novel is also worth quoting: "As I understand it, the 'detective' novel is for the modern public what the tragedy was for the contemporaries of Pericles or Louis XIV."

—Jacques Baudou, translated by Walter Albert

ØRUM, Poul (1919–). Danish. Novels: *The Whipping Boy*, 1975 (as *Scapegoat*, 1975); *Nothing But the Truth*, 1976.

*   *   *

Detective Inspector Jonas Morck and his assistant Einarsen are the detectives in both of the translated novels by Poul Ørum. Morck is a happily married man of 47 and Einarsen is miserably wed to a successful business woman a few years his senior. His life is spent worrying about her real or imaginary affairs with other men while he is working in remote parts of Denmark. While Morck is a thoughtful, kindly man, Einarsen is just the opposite and the weak, the foolish, and the confused have a tough time at his hands during investigations.

In *The Whipping Boy* the murder victim is a 33-year-old nurse in Vesterso, a small resort that is closed for a good part of the year. The major suspect is a severely retarded kitchen hand, tall and strong but with the mind of a tiny child. He has been the butt of everybody's ill-humour since the day he was born, and it would seem quite natural that he might wish to wipe out a lifetime of bitterness by violence upon a woman. The boy also had a reputation of a peeping tom, but had never before tried sexually to molest anyone, except (possibly) a little slut also employed by the hotel. After the murderer has been arrested, it is still the scapegoat who suffers.

In *Nothing But the Truth* Jorgen Brehmer could be said to be the equal of Einarsen in both selfishness and cruelty. Possibly Brehmer might even be the more powerful in the small town that his family had controlled for so long; the local police did not care to be too openly critical of the man. A reporter on Brehmer's newspaper is murdered and the sordid personal lives of both the victim and the Brehmer family slowly emerges.

It is not just the themes that are so interesting in Poul Ørum's works. He also provides fascinating glimpses of a socialistic world that is not nearly so repressive as some of the spokesmen of capitalistic liberty wish us to believe.

—Mary Groff

ROBBE-GRILLET, Alain (1922–).   French.   Novels: *The Voyeur*, 1958; *Jealousy*, 1959; *In the Labyrinth*, 1960; *The Erasers*, 1964; *La Maison de rendez-vous*, 1966 (as *The House of Assignation*, 1970); *Project for a Revolution in New York*, 1972. Short Stories: *Snapshots*, 1968. Screenplay: *Last Year at Marienbad*, 1962.

*   *   *

If every detective story is an abstraction from the mundane mechanics of crime and punishment, Alain Robbe-Grillet goes one step further, abstracting the abstraction by making the *style* of detection his subject. Yet because of this deflection of interest from the what to the how of mystery, Robbe-Grillet's best results are two novels almost totally unlike formula narratives. In *Jealousy* and *In the Labyrinth*, the reader is freed to engage in pure search, undistracted by the appetites stimulated by mystery-reading: for rational detectives, clock-time discrepancies, conclusive solutions.

In the Labyrinth is Robbe-Grillet's nearest approach to the effect of Kafka. We do not feel obliged to discover anything in particular: we easily adopt the position of the investigator's superior in *The Erasers*, who "has stopped believing in the existence of any solution whatsoever." Instead, we search along with the soldier-protagonist, "attend" in terror and pity, the way we track the figures of tragedy. Similarly, *Jealousy* requires us *to be* jealous: any possible material corroboration of the narrator's obsession would be as nothing compared with the experience of suspicion itself.

Robbe-Grillet thus, at times, can make aesthetic concern for detection style as mode and for point-of-view technique compatible with his phenomenology. According to his *For a New Novel*, words represent mental acts of reciprocity with external reality. Things are inviolably separate from the fictional self yet possibly, *only* possibly, correlative to emotions and thoughts. For Mathias, the controlling consciousness in *The Voyeur*, the environment can reflect and even trigger sexual compulsions; but just as frequently the author can wring his fictive context of sea and rocks completely dry of human significance. So, whether the reader is the detective tracing the putative crime and criminal (*The Voyeur*) or a "Tiresias" accompanying the feverish searcher (*In the Labyrinth*, *Jealousy*), he must distinguish between described objects and events which mirror the central self's internal state, on the one hand –

they will be "clues" – and, on the other, the novelistic "reality," which is always impermeably "objectal." Such an exercise in the form of detection, while not detection itself, is what Robbe-Grillet substitutes for the hunting of catchable culprits in detective fiction proper.

Of his other works, *The Erasers*, most like a conventional mystery, is a deadpan parody of classical French tragedy in form (Beckett) and, in content and effect, a travesty of Sophocles, with its pseudo-solemn Oedipus references (Joyce). Robbe-Grillet's first "ciné-roman" is an ironic attempt to discover what happened "last year at Marienbad" by inventing it. The most romantic of Robbe-Grillet's artifacts, *Last Year at Marienbad* denies the past as determinant; thus it is intrinsically anti-detection. After *La Maison de rendez-vous*, a neat parody of the 1960's spy novel, comes the anti-politics of *Project for a Revolution in New York*, which is either a Swiftian satire on contemporary madness (with oddball SLA-type terrorists who are also their own detectives) or a post-modernist parody of de Sade for its own aesthetico-pornographic sake. As always, Robbe-Grillet's style is impeccably matter-of-fact, leaving one with the discomforting thought that our 1970's world is one in which anything can be imagined – a logical extension of a world in which nearly everything has been perpetrated. The surreal *Topologie d'une cité fantôme* continues the sado-erotic emphasis of *The Voyeur* and *Project* and retains the Robbe-Grilletian Ackroydian narrator (now a ritual slayer of "blond virgins and semi-virgins"). This latest novel also realizes Robbe-Grillet's conception of "generative fiction," first broached in 1963, in which the interest is "no longer in the thing described, but in the very movement of the description" (*For a New Novel*).

—John Snyder

SIMENON, Georges (1903–). Belgian. Novels featuring Inspector Jules Maigret: *The Strange Case of Peter the Lett*, 1933 (as *Maigret and the Enigmatic Lett*, 1963); *The Crime of Inspector Maigret*, 1933 (as *Maigret and the Hundred Gibbets*, 1963); *The Crossroads Murder*, 1933 (as *Maigret at the Crossroads*, 1963); *The Death of Monsieur Gallet*, 1933 (as *Maigret Stonewalled*, 1963); *Inspector Maigret Investigates* (omnibus), 1933; *Introducing Inspector Maigret* (omnibus), 1933; *The Crime at Lock 14*, *The Shadow in the Courtyard*, 1934 (as *Triumph of Inspector Maigret*, 1934; *Maigret Meets a Milord*, 1963; *Maigret Mystified*, 1964); *The Patience of Maigret* (novelets), 1939; *Maigret Abroad* (novelets), 1940; *Maigret to the Rescue* (novelets), 1940; *Maigret Travels South* (novelets), 1940; *Maigret Keeps a Rendezvous* (novelets), 1940; *Maigret and Monsieur Labbe* (novelets), 1941; *Maigret Sits It Out* (novelets), 1941; *Maigret on Holiday* (novelets), 1950; *No Vacation for Maigret*, 1953; *Maigret Right and Wrong* (novelets), 1954 (as *Inspector Maigret and the Strangled Stripper*, 1954); *Inspector Maigret and the Killers*, 1954 (as *Maigret and the Gangsters*, 1974); *Maigret and the Burglar's Wife*, 1955; *Maigret and the Dead Girl*, 1955; *Maigret in New York's Underworld*, 1955; *Maigret's Revolver*, 1956; *My Friend Maigret*, 1956 (as *The Methods of Maigret*, 1957); *Maigret Goes to School*, 1957; *Maigret's Little Joke*, 1957 (as *None of Maigret's Business*, 1958); *Maigret's First Case*, 1958; *Maigret and the Old Lady*, 1958; *Maigret and the Reluctant Witnesses*, 1959; *Maigret Has Scruples*, 1959; *Versus Inspector Maigret* (omnibus), 1960; *Madame Maigret's Own Case*, 1959 (as *Madame Maigret's Friend*, 1960); *Maigret Takes a Room*, 1960 (as *Maigret Rents a Room*, 1961); *Maigret Afraid*, 1961; *Maigret in Court*, 1961; *Maigret in Society*, 1962; *Maigret's Failure*, 1962; *Maigret's Memoirs*, 1963; *Maigret and the Lazy Burglar*, 1963; *Maigret's Special Murder*, 1964 (as *Maigret's Dead Man*, 1964); *Maigret and the Saturday Caller*, 1964; *Five Times Maigret* (omnibus), 1964; *Maigret Cinq* (omnibus), 1965; *Maigret Loses His Temper*, 1965; *Maigret Sets a Trap*, 1965; *Maigret on the Defensive*, 1966; *Maigret and the Headless Corpse*, 1967;

Maigret and the Nahour Case, 1967; *Maigret's Pickpocket*, 1968; *Maigret Has Doubts*, 1968; *Maigret and the Minister*, 1969 (as *Maigret and the Calame Report*, 1969); *Maigret Takes the Waters*, 1969 (as *Maigret in Vichy*, 1969); *Maigret Hesitates*, 1970; *Maigret's Boyhood Friend*, 1970; *Maigret and the Killer*, 1971; *Maigret and the Wine Merchant*, 1971; *Maigret and the Flea*, 1972 (as *Maigret and the Informer*, 1973); *Maigret and the Madwoman*, 1972; *A Maigret Quartet* (omnibus), 1972; *A Maigret Trio* (omnibus), 1973; *Maigret and Monsieur Charles*, 1973; *Maigret and the Dosser*, 1973 (as *Maigret and the Bum*, 1974); *Maigret and the Millionaires*, 1974; *Maigret and the Man on the Boulevard*, 1975 (as *Maigret and the Man on the Bench*, 1975); *Maigret and the Loner*, 1975; *Maigret and the Apparition*, 1975. Non-series novels: *The Disintegration of J.P.G.*, 1937; *In Two Latitudes* (novelets), 1942 (*Tropic Moon* reprinted, 1943); *The Man Who Watched the Trains Go By*, 1942; *Affairs of Destiny* (novelets), 1942; *Havoc by Accident* (novelets), 1943; *Escape in Vain* (novelets), 1943; *On the Danger Line* (novelets), 1944; *The Shadow Falls*, 1945; *Blind Alley*, 1946; *Lost Moorings* (novelets), 1946; *The First-Born*, 1947 (as *Magnet of Doom*, 1948); *Black Rain*, 1947; *Chit of a Girl* (novelets), 1949; *The Murderer, A Wife at Sea*, 1949; *Black Rain* (novelets), 1949; *The Snow Was Black*, 1950 (as *The Stain on the Snow*, 1953); *Poisoned Relations* (novelets), 1950; *Strange Inheritance*, 1950; *The Gendarme's Report, The Window over the Way*, 1951; *The Heart of a Man*, 1951; *Strangers in the House*, 1951; *Act of Passion*, 1952; *The Burgomaster of Furnes*, 1952; *The House by the Canal, The Ostenders*, 1952; *The Trial of Bebe Donge*, 1952; *Aunt Jeanne*, 1953; *The Girl in His Past*, 1953; *Satan's Children* (novelets), 1953 (*Four Days in a Lifetime* reprinted, 1977); *Ticket of Leave*, 1954; *Tidal Wave* (novelets), 1954 (*The Bottom of the Bottle* reprinted, 1977); *Violent Ends* (omnibus), 1954; *Across the Street*, 1954; *On Land and Sea* (as Victor Kosta; omnibus), 1954; *The Fugitive*, 1955 (as *Account Unsettled*, 1962); *Danger Ahead* (novelets), 1955; *The Magician, The Widow*, 1955; *Destinations* (novelets), 1955 (*Inquest on Bouvet* reprinted, 1958); *A Sense of Guilt* (novelets), 1955 (*Chez Krull* reprinted, 1974); *The Judge and the Hatter* (novelets), 1956 (*The Hatter's Phantoms* reprinted, 1976); *Sacrifice* (novelets), 1956; *The Witnesses, The Watchmaker*, 1956; *The Little Man from Archangel*, 1957; *The Stowaway*, 1957; *In Case of Emergency*, 1958; *The Son*, 1958; *The Negro*, 1959; *Striptease*, 1959; *Sunday*, 1960; *The Premier*, 1961; *The Fate of the Malous*, 1962; *The Iron Staircase*, 1963; *A New Lease of Life*, 1963; *The Patient*, 1963 (as *The Bells of Bicetre*, 1964); *The Train*, 1964; *Three Beds in Manhattan*, 1964; *The Door*, 1964; *The Accomplice* (novelets), 1964; *The Little Saint*, 1965; *The Man with the Little Dog*, 1965; *The Cat*, 1967; *The Confessional*, 1967; *Monsieur Monde Vanishes*, 1967; *The Old Man Dies*, 1967; *The Neighbors*, 1968 (as *The Move*, 1968); *Big Bob*, 1969; *The Prison*, 1969; *The Man on the Bench in the Barn*, 1969; *November*, 1970; *The Rich Man*, 1971; *Teddy Bear*, 1971; *The Disappearance of Odile*, 1972; *The Glass Cage*, 1973; *The Innocents*, 1973; *The Venice Train*, 1974; *The Others*, 1975; *Betty*, 1975. Short Stories: *The Short Cases of Inspector Maigret*, 1959. Bibliography: in *Simenon* by Bernard de Fallois, Paris, Gallimard, 1961; *Georges Simenon: A Checklist of His "Maigret" and Other Mystery Novels and Short Stories in French and in English Translations* by Trudee Young, Metuchen, New Jersey, Scarecrow Press, 1976.

* * *

Georges Simenon, one of the true giants of the novel, has earned through the fecundity of his imagination and his devotion to his craft the right to be termed a genius. Apparently equally indifferent to critical scorn or praise, impervious to the shifting currents of literary fashion, disdainful of pretentious philosophizing or didacticism, Simenon has resolutely gone his own way, followed his unique vision, creating a body of work with the power and inevitability of life itself. Like Balzac or Dickens or Faulkner, he has staked out his own bleak territory of the human heart, a world of passion and violence, suffering and disorder, over which broods the massive presence of his detective, Jules Maigret. One of the most important novelists of his time, and certainly one of the major figures in French literature, Simenon must also be considered one of the major writers of detective fiction; his detective stories belong among the finest examples of the genre and, like other great detective stories, deserve serious critical study.

Simenon's detective fiction, naturally, is as original and individual within its form as his other kinds of fiction are within the traditions of the "straight" novel. One of the tired truisms of critical study of the form asserts that the detective story could only flourish in Anglo-Saxon countries because of their early traditions of constitutional democracy; whether this statement is entirely true is open to question, but certainly the works of Simenon demonstrate that great detective fiction outside of the English-speaking world takes an entirely different direction, departing radically from the established conventions of the genre. Aside from the obligatory pattern of crime, mystery, and investigation, Simenon's novels bear almost no apparent relationship to any particular sub-genre of detective and mystery fiction, including the police procedural novel, which they superficially resemble. They are truly *sui generis*, properly deserving their own generic name, the "Maigret," after their unique protagonist.

Although Maigret is an official detective, he never solves his cases by means of the machinery available to him, the usual business of fingerprints and laboratory reports and minute examinations that constitute the work of policemen everywhere. On the other hand, he possesses none of the eccentric genius of the famous great detectives in the Sherlockian mold. His methods are peculiarly his own – he immerses himself in the ambience of criminal action, soaking up, spongelike, the quality and "feel" of the geography, the social class, the habits, the sights and sounds and smells, the daily life of the place, the region, the people who inhabit it. In the process he comes to find himself a part of the action, almost a character in his own case, as much a suspect as anyone he is investigating. As he comes to live in the world he examines, so too he comes to understand it; with that understanding, in a way that the reader can never really duplicate, appears the solution.

The famous method of Maigret seems compounded mostly out of the sympathetic human imagination; working without a great deal in the way of facts, clues, chains of evidence, it succeeds infallibly and its success always seems, when it comes, absolutely inevitable. The Maigrets often end with the detective regretting in some way his victory over the recalcitrant facts of life; because of his vast understanding of humanity, his chief emotion in discovering guilt is not a feeling of triumph but of pity. The generally misshapen or sordid or wasted lives he confronts evoke from him sorrow and compassion; he rediscovers for all his readers, over and over again, the terrible sadness of human pain, violence, suffering, and guilt, the dreadful knowledge of the motives for murder that reside in every human heart. The mysteries he solves seldom engage him so much as the endless puzzle of life that he must continually penetrate; his profession is a constant initiation into man's capacity to sin.

One of the most remarkable aspects of Maigret's reactions to the crimes he investigates is his vision of his task, what motivates him to be a detective. He does not see himself as an avenging angel, a bringer of justice, an official agent of his society, but instead, as he says in *Maigret's First Case*, as "a repairer of destinies." Maigret understands that his great talent for criminal investigation derives from his ability to live other people's lives; he also recognizes that with this faculty comes the responsibility of caring about the lives he recreates within himself. As he realizes, his task should really be like that of doctor or priest, to function as a sort of receptacle for the disease and corruption of humanity; like the doctor, he would like to cure his patients, like the priest, absolve them. In another book, he thinks of his ideal vocation as "a guide to the lost," and, like the psychoanalyst, he believes he can "bring a man face to face with his true self."

The unique quality of Maigret's character and the radical ideal of his detection indicate the originality of Simenon's work in mystery fiction. The conjunction of Simenon's sordid and frightening fictional world with the sympathetic omniscience of Maigret's methods has no parallel anywhere in the detective story. The absolute impersonality of the author in all of his novels helps to emphasize the importance of Maigret to the rest of his extraordinary body of work: the detective provides a view of the author and his attitudes toward his world and its people that appears nowhere else in Simenon. The detective seems to watch over the Simenon world, to act as guide, judge, even God for the people of that harsh continent that is everywhere and nowhere, except in the mind of its creator and within the human spirit – the country of sorrow that Simenon has made his own. The author's detective stories then, are important for themselves, for the genre, and for the rest of the Simenon canon; inevitably, they are important, too, for the study of literature anywhere.

—George Grella

---

van de WETERING, Janwillem (1931–).   Dutch.   Novels: *Outsider in Amsterdam*, 1974; *Tumbleweed*, 1974; *Corpse on the Dike*, 1975; *Death of a Hawker*, 1976; *The Japanese Corpse*, 1977; *The Blond Baboon*, 1978; *The Maine Massacre*, 1979.

*   *   *

Janwillem van de Wetering has endowed police fiction with a depth of meaning that would have been inconceivable in the early days of Sergeant Joe Friday. It is possible to read his stories on three distinct levels of meaning, which correspond to the levels of awareness of his three series characters.

First, there is the police-routine story with the customary mystery and solution, the questionings, pursuits, and arrests. The narrative fits the level of awareness of Adjutant Grijpstra, a very capable policeman who is also basically anti-intellectual and mentally a little dull. Grijpstra shares with many another fictional police detective the sorrows of an unsatisfying marriage and disappointing offspring.

The stories have another level, however: the world of dreams and symbolic actions, a level of reality-beyond-reality which often expresses itself in surrealistic images and relationships. This world corresponds to the level of awareness of Serjeant De Gier, who believes in a "miraculous surrealist world" and who has identified with his own subconscious to the extent that he can control some of his dreams with constructive results.

The highest level has implications that are almost cosmic in scope, the world of wisdom-beyond-wisdom. This is the level of awareness of the aged un-named commisaris, who has suffered much and learned much, who can feel himself close to the "terrible secret of life," and who can advise a young policeman not to be too logical because then he will never get beyond the surface of things. The commisaris has also attained a wisdom beyond surrealism, which he considers a meaningless term. In contrast to the erotic daydreams of Grijpstra and the controlled dreams of De Gier, the commisaris' dreams are seraphic, taking him to a level of awareness where he is neither asleep nor awake.

Van de Wetering employs a thematic device that is unique in police fiction, namely clusters of images that sharpen the tone of the novel and engender depth in the portrayal of character. In *Death of a Hawker*, for example, the associated images are repulsive: a trans-sexual policeman, snails, small toads that make a popping sound when the police car runs over them, a parrot that imitates a man vomiting, a disemboweled white rat. Collectively, these images underscore the basic nastiness of the situation and prepare the reader emotionally for the nightmare conclusion. Individually, they serve as mirrors of character for the people in the story: De Gier is repelled by "Elizabeth," the former policeman now living as a woman, but the commisaris likes and respects him; Grijpstra cringes at the sound of baby toads being run over, but the commisaris is undisturbed by them.

Most of this will go un-noticed by the typical mystery fan, except that the stories will seem a little odd, the police a little too amiable, the action a little too relaxed. To the perceptive reader, however, van de Wetering has demonstrated that the police procedural is an instrument capable of remarkable flexibility.

—George N. Dove

van GULIK, Robert H(ans) (1910–67).   Dutch.   Novels: *Dee Goong An* (novelets), 1949;
The Chinese Maze Murders (novelets), 1957; *The Chinese Bell Murders* (novelets), 1958; *The
Chinese Gold Murders* (novelets), 1959; *The Chinese Lake Murders* (novelets), 1960; *The Red
Pavilion* (novelets), 1961; *The Chinese Nail Murders* (novelets), 1961; *The Emperor's Pearl*
(novelets), 1963; *The Haunted Monastery* (novelets), 1963; *The Lacquer Screen* (novelets),
1963; *The Monkey and the Tiger* (novelets), 1965; *The Willow Pattern* (novelets), 1965;
Murder in Canton, 1966; *The Phantom of the Temple*, 1966; *Necklace and Calabash*, 1967;
Poets and Murder, 1968 (as *The Fox-Magic Murders*, 1973). Short Stories: *New Year's Eve in
Lan-Fang*, 1958; *Judge Dee at Work*, 1967.

*   *   *

Robert H. van Gulik, the Netherlands diplomat and renowned Sinologist, has been the
person most responsible for introducing the classical Chinese detective story to the West. His
first contribution was the *Dee Goong An*, a translation into English of large portions of the
anonymous 18th-century novel *Wu-ze-tian-si-da-qi-an*. This translation consisted of three
interlocked cases of the famous detective-magistrate Dee Jen-djieh (transliterated in *pinyin* as
Di Ren-jie). Although these cases were completely fictional, Di Ren-jie (630–700 A.D.) was a
historical figure who rose through the ranks of the Chinese civil service to become the
equivalent of Prime Minister to the Empress Wu. While Di had a significant place in Tang
history, he lived, oddly enough, in popular memory as the ideal district magistrate: honest,
fearless, righteous, highly intelligent, and remarkably gifted as a detective. Many folk plays
and short stories narrate feats of detection attributed to Di. The *Dee Goong An* made a stir in
many circles, for it was not only a fascinating work, but it revealed that China possessed a
more advanced and more sophisticated detective literature than had been supposed from the
rather trivial material that had hitherto been translated.

Van Gulik speculated that contemporary Chinese and Japanese readers might be interested
in modern versions of the classical form, and he decided to continue the Judge Dee stories. He
wrote two novels in English, *The Chinese Bell Murders* and *The Chinese Maze Murders*,
which were then translated into Japanese and published. It was soon recognized, however,
that the English texts had merits of their own and were too important to be used only as
translation sources. Van Gulik thereupon began a new series of Judge Dee mysteries aimed at
the western reader. All were first written in English, although some were first published in
Dutch. (For Netherlands newspapers he prepared 12 scripts for a cartoon series based on
Dee; the novel *The Phantom of the Temple* and several short stories were later adapted from
these scripts.) Van Gulik also wrote a thriller set in Amsterdam (*Een gegeven Dag, The Given
Day*), not published in English.

In his original fiction van Gulik took over the Judge Dee and associates (Ma Joong, Chiao
Tai, Sergeant Hoong) of the *Dee Goong An* without too much regard for the historical
Minister Di. While adhering to the common occidental practice of preparing a puzzle plot for
the reader (a technique not commonly used in the orient), van Gulik drew upon the
inexhaustible wealth of Chinese story for special motifs. He also used certain Chinese
structural devices in much of his work: a tripartite plot in which three seemingly independent
cases move along simultaneously and at times interlace, story frames, and occasional mildly
supernatural incidents. Dee was also portrayed as working within the historical
circumstances of Chinese administrative and criminal law, using techniques taken from
Chinese coroners' and magistrates' manuals. An erotic element in some of the novels,
however, is less traditional and presumably reflects van Gulik's own interests.

The Judge Dee stories are certainly the finest ethnographic detective novels in English.
They have been widely acclaimed for their originality, skilful plotting, and characterizations.
They are also fascinating for the vivid pictures they give of Chinese life, the details of which
are worked into the story without destroying narrative flow. This authentic China, however,
is not the Tang China of Di Ren-jie, but is essentially a generalized medieval China, such as
might have existed in Ming days, with an occasional Tang element. If van Gulik's work has a

flaw, apart from occasional sensationalism, it is in the author's English, which is not always perfectly idiomatic; but this situation varies from text to text.

Van Gulik's books usually contain short essays explaining the peculiarly Chinese aspects of his stories, while the *Dee Goong An* has extensive scholarly material on the Chinese detective story, criminology and jurisprudence. Van Gulik also translated a 13th-century collection of case histories and judicial decisions (*Parallel Cases from under the Peartree – Tang-yin-bi-shi*, 1956), which he occasionally used as a story source.

—E. F. Bleiler

WAHLÖÖ, Per (1926–75), and **Maj SJÖWALL** (1935–). Swedish. Novels in collaboration: *Roseanna*, 1967; *The Man on the Balcony*, 1968; *The Man Who Went Up in Smoke*, 1969; *The Laughing Policeman*, 1970; *The Fire Engine That Disappeared*, 1971; *Murder at the Savoy*, 1971; *The Abominable Man*, 1972; *The Locked Room*, 1973; *Cop Killer*, 1975; *The Terrorist*, 1977. Novels by Per Wahlöö: *The Assignment*, 1965; *Murder on the Thirty-First Floor*, 1966; *The Lorry*, 1968 (as *A Necessary Action*, 1969); *The Steel Spring*, 1970; *The Generals*, 1974.

*   *   *

In a 1966 essay Per Wahlöö stated the basis for the Martin Beck series he and Maj Sjöwall had started a year earlier. The series would consist of only ten novels. They chose the crime novel as a form because of its strong connection between people and society: it is impossible to be a lawbreaker – or a law enforcer – without a law, laid down and maintained by a society based upon certain political and economic realities and opinions. They wrote together, each writing alternate chapters after long research and detailed synopses. They were both communists, and the outspoken aim of their series was to "use the crime novel as a scalpel cutting open the belly of an ideologically pauperized and morally debatable so-called welfare state of the bourgeois type." The first two or three books would be almost totally apolitical; later ones would put down the mask and speak loud and clear.

Roseanna, *The Man Who Went Up in Smoke*, and *The Man on the Balcony*, thus, are straightforward procedural novels: a hard-working police team solving murders committed for private, and in two cases even pathological reasons holds center stage. They are better written, psychologically more complex, and more grimly realistic than most books in the type, but they keep inside the limits of good, serious entertainment.

Roseanna introduces Martin Beck, a laconic and competent detective with stomach pains, a failing marriage, and a quiet professionalism. He is surrounded by colleagues of the Stockholm Homicide Squad: the paunchy ex-paratrooper Lennart Kollberg, who hates violence and has a wider political, literary, and human outlook than his friend Beck; the big outspoken and impetuous Gunvald Larsson, a drop-out from high society; the small and careful Einar Rönn, who was born in, and forever longs to return to, the far north of Sweden; and last, but not least, the two patrolmen, Kristiansson and Kvant, recurrent comic characters with very little brain but quite a lot of brawn. *Roseanna* starts eight days after the nationalization of the Swedish police on 1 July 1964. The increasing replacement of common sense with weapons, gadgets, and a para-military organization following the take-over, the lack of backbone among the new, politically appointed leaders – these are prime targets for criticism throughout the series. The next two novels, *The Laughing Policeman* and *The Fire Engine That Disappeared*, begin to show the authors' intentions more clearly. In the first the motive for mass murder is the murderer's wish to keep his social position; in the second the

Beck team confront professional crime, up to then a rare phenomenon both in Swedish crime novels and Swedish reality. If the first criminals in the series were pathological, these two are grimly rational. They have chosen crime as a way of living in Swedish society.

The later novels often deal with crime *as* punishment. The business tycoon in *Murder at the Savoy* and the police superintendent who provides the title for *The Abominable Man* are murder victims, but there is little doubt that they are the real criminals, protected by their society, much more than the poor devils that pulled the triggers. *The Locked Room* has a superb John Dickson Carr-type puzzle, and much wild farce, but also bitterly points out that crimes against capital – like bank robberies – are considered by the ruling authorities much more serious than crimes against persons. *Cop Killer* lashes the press for its biased news and contrasts the professional common sense of the old-timers in the Beck team with the para-military battles against scared, lonely, young lawbreakers preferred by Beck's superiors. *The Terrorist* is the bitter, logical conclusion of the scalpel cut through the welfare state – a state so little worthy of its name that the murder of its symbolically responsible Prime Minister seems quite fair, even to the still apolitical Beck – and probably to most of the readers around the world.

Unlike most procedural series the Beck novels allow the main characters to grow older; more important and even more rare – to grow wiser, to develop and change views. Lennart Kollberg writes his resignation in *Cop Killer* because his qualities as a warm, thinking, feeling man are no longer of use to his society or his force. It is one of the authors' masterstrokes – and a proof of their ability to convince readers all over the world – when the resignation of a socialist detective for political reasons in a capitalistic state is a cause for regret both in Moscow and in New York, in Birmingham and in Belgrade. Beck stays on, but he has changed in the years since *Roseanna*. His career almost came to an end in *The Abominable Man* when he tried to carry the guilt of the whole force, and in *The Locked Room* he quietly and slowly reconsidered his life and his work. When we leave him in *The Terrorist* there is a Chairman Mao poster over his head. He didn't put it there, but he lets it stay up.

Wahlöö and Sjöwall's main contribution to the genre is their example of how a popular form can be used to distribute a new, complex – and in wide circles even unpopular – content. They have been misunderstood by some American critics with muddled politics who claimed that the series sharply criticized the socialist society of Sweden. They have been called simple communist propagandists. Both extremes are wrong. In writing a carefully planned and exceptionally well-executed series of police procedurals with socialist views, they have succeeded in a serious literary attempt to expand the borders of the detective story and use it to discuss and comment on a much wider and, in many ways, more criminal world.

—Bo Lundin

NOTES
ON
ADVISERS
AND
CONTRIBUTORS

ADEY, Alison Susan.   Civil Servant.   **Essay:** Emma Page.

ADEY, Robert C. S.   Customs Officer.   Author of reviews for *Cloak and Dagger* and *The Poisoned Pen*; "Behind a Victorian Locked Door", in *Antiquarian Book Monthly Review*, April 1975; and a forthcoming bibliography of impossible crime.   **Essay:** Peter Antony.

ADLEY, Derek.   Accountant.   Author of *The British Bibliography of Edgar Wallace*, 1969, *The Men Behind Boys' Fiction*, 1970, *The Saint and Leslie Charteris*, 1971, and *The World of Frank Richards*, 1975, all with W. O. G. Lofts; and numerous articles on children's literature, detective fiction, and films.   **Essays:** Roland Daniel; Max Pemberton (with W. O. G. Lofts).

ALBERT, Walter.   Associate Professor of French and Italian, University of Pittsburgh.   Author of articles in *Armchair Detective*, *Mystery Fancier*, *French Review*, *MLN*, and *Texas Studies in Literature and Language*; American correspondent and contributor to *Enigmatika*.   **Essays:** James Anderson; Michel Butor (appendix); Marion Randolph; translator of essay on Hubert Monteilhet (appendix).

ALDERSON, Martha.   Editor of elementary language arts textbooks, Webster Division, McGraw Hill Book Company.   **Essays** (with Neysa Chouteau): Dorothy Cameron Disney; Alistair MacLean.

ALDRICH, Pearl G.   Editorial Consultant; Editor and Publisher of *The Popular Culture Scholar*.   Author of *The Impact of Mass Media*, 1975, *Research Papers: A Manual for Beginners*, 1976, and the forthcoming book *Introducing Popular Culture*. Contributor to *Ms. Magazine*, *New Yorker*, *Armchair Detective*, *Journal of Popular Culture*, and Sunday Magazine of Philadelphia *Inquirer*. Teaches a course in mystery fiction.   **Essays:** Miriam Borgenicht; Heron Carvic; D. M. Devine; John Buxton Hilton.

ALLEY, Kenneth D.   Associate Professor of English, Western Illinois University, Macomb.   Author of "*High Sierra* – Swan Song for an Era," in *Journal of Popular Film*, 1976, and "*A Gun for Sale* – Graham Greene's Reflection of Moral Chaos," in *Essays in Literature*, 1978.   **Essay:** E. Richard Johnson.

ATHANASON, Arthur Nicholas.   Associate Professor of English, Michigan State University, East Lansing.   Author of "*The Mousetrap* Phenomenon," in *Armchair Detective*, 1979. Drama reviewer for *World Literature Today*.   **Essays:** Francis Beeding; Thomas Burke; Gaston Leroux (appendix).

BAIRD, Newton.   Partner in Talisman Press, Georgetown, California.   Co-Editor, *An Annotated Bibliography of California Fiction, 1664–1970*.   Author of numerous articles, including a long study of Fredric Brown, in *Armchair Detective*.   **Essays:** Fredric Brown; Michael Crichton; Joseph Hansen; Zelda Popkin; Charles Williams.

BAKERMAN, Jane S.   Associate Professor of English, Indiana State University, Terre Haute.   Adviser and contributor to *American Women Writers*, 1979.   Author of interviews with P. D. James, in *Armchair Detective*, Ruth Rendell, in *Mystery Nook*, and Daphne du Maurier, in *Writer's Yearbook*. Contributor and reviewer for those magazines and *Mystery Fancier*, *Cloak and Dagger*, and *The Poisoned Pen*.   **Essays:** Suzanne Blanc; Vera Caspary; Ursula Curtiss; Daphne du Maurier; Anthony Gilbert; Joseph Harrington; Elisabeth Sanxay Holding; Emma Lathen; Mary McMullen; Helen Reilly; Ruth Rendell.

BALL, John.   See his own entry.   **Essay:** Elliot Paul.

BANKS, Jeff.   Assistant Professor of English, Stephen F. Austin State University, Nacogdoches, Texas. Regular contributor to *Poisoned Pen*, *The Not-So-Private Eye*, and

Mystery Fancier, and has contributed articles to *Journal of Popular Culture* and *Armchair Detective*. **Essays:** Philip Atlee; George Baxt; Richard Condon; Donald Hamilton; Stephen Marlowe; Peter O'Donnell; Mickey Spillane.

BARNES, Melvyn. Borough Librarian and Arts Officer, Royal Borough of Kensington and Chelsea, London. Author of *Best Detective Fiction: A Guide from Godwin to the Present*, 1975, *Youth Library Work*, second edition, 1976, and "The Public Librarian of the Future," in *Prospects for British Librarianship*, 1976. Editor of the Remploy "Deerstalker" series of reprints of classic crime fiction. **Essays:** Frank Arthur; John Austwick; Marian Babson; Margot Bennett; Evelyn Berckman; Anthony Berkeley; Simon Brett; J. J. Connington; John Creasey; Freeman Wills Crofts; Francis Durbridge; Robert Finnegan; J. S. Fletcher; Leonard Gribble; Edward Grierson; Stanley Hyland; Philip MacDonald; Gil North; John Rhode; John Wainwright.

BAUDOU, Jacques. Film animator; Editor-in-chief of *Enigmatika* (Paris). Has written on le roman policier, Jules Verne, Jorge Luis Borges, and Maurice Renard. **Essay:** Hubert Monteilhet (appendix).

BECKER, Jens Peter. English Lecturer, University of Kiel, Germany. Author of *Der Englische Spionageroman*, 1973, and *Sherlock Holmes & Co.*, 1975, and Co-Author of *Der Detektivroman*, 1973 (revised edition, 1978), and *Der Detektiverzählung auf der Spur*, 1977. Has contributed many essays on English and American literature to quarterlies. **Essay:** Chester Himes.

BECKER, Mary Helen. Instructor of French, Madison Area Technical College, Wisconsin; Editor of *BREFF* (Bulletin de Récherches et d'Etudes Feministes Francophones). Author of essays on Proust, French women authors, and art, and translations from the Latin and French; Co-Author, *Ecrits de Femmes*, 1979. **Essays:** Pierre Audemars; John Boland; Herbert Brean; Janet Caird; Desmond Cory; L. P. Davies; Michael Delving; Margaret Erskine; Elizabeth Ferrars; Andrew Garve; Dorothy Gilman; Rosemary Harris; Patricia Highsmith; P. M. Hubbard; Alan Hunter; Elizabeth Lemarchand; Mabel Seeley; Van Siller; Phoebe Atwood Taylor.

BEDELL, Jeanne F. Assistant Professor of English, University of Missouri, Rolla. Author of essays on detective and espionage fiction, early modern British literature, and composition. **Essays:** G. D. H. and Margaret Cole; Bill Knox; Raymond Postgate.

BERGMAN, Carol Ann. Editor, Follett Publishing Company, Chicago. Contributor to *Contemporary Poets*. **Essay:** Brian Garfield.

BERTRAM, Manfred A. Senior English Master and Librarian, Christ's Church College, Christchurch, New Zealand. Formerly lecturer at Canterbury University. Author of short stories and poetry. **Essay:** Ngaio Marsh.

BLEILER, E. F. Editorial Consultant, Charles Scribner's Sons. Formerly Editor, Dover Publications. Has edited works by Ernest Bramah, R. Austin Freeman, Emile Gaboriau, Robert H. van Gulik, and Roy Vickers, and Dime Novelists and Victorian Sensational Novelists. Author of *The Checklist of Science-Fiction and Supernatural Fiction*, revised edition, 1978. **Essays:** Frederick Irving Anderson; Gelett Burgess; Wilkie Collins (appendix); Dick Donovan; Sydney Fowler; Jacques Futrelle; Emile Gaboriau (appendix); H. F. Heard; William Hope Hodgson; L. T. Meade; Arthur Morrison; Baroness Orczy; Edgar Allan Poe (appendix); Richmond (appendix); Basil Thomson; Robert H. van Gulik (appendix); Roy Vickers; Mrs. Henry Wood (appendix).

BLEILER, Ellen. Free-lance writer. **Essay:** Jessica Mann.

BREEN, Jon L. Librarian, Rio Hondo College, Whittier, California; Book reviewer ("The Jury Box"), *Ellery Queen's Mystery Magazine*. Author of 35 stories and critical works.

BRINEY, R. E. Professor of Mathematics and Chairman of Computer Science Department, Salem State College, Massachusetts; Editor, *Rohmer Review*. Contributor to *The Mystery Writer's Art*, 1971, *The Conan Grimoire*, 1971, and *The Mystery Story*, 1976; author of numerous articles and bibliographies for journals. Editor, *Master of Villainy: A Biography of Sax Rohmer*, 1972; Co-Editor, *Multiplying Villainies: Selected Mystery Criticism* by Anthony Boucher, 1973; Contributing Editor of *Encyclopedia of Mystery & Detection*, 1976. Member of the Board of *Views & Reviews*, 1972–75, and The Mystery Library. **Essays:** Robert Bloch; Anthony Boucher; John Dickson Carr; S. H. Courtier; August Derleth; Patrick Quentin; Sax Rohmer; John Holbrook Vance.

BROBERG, Jan. Critic since 1955; teacher since 1958; Editor of *Spektra Crime*. Has written five books about detective fiction, edited 12 collections of mystery short stories, and three books of essays about the genre; Co-Author of "Detective Fiction in Sweden" in *Armchair Detective*, October 1976. A founder of the Swedish Academy of Detection. **Essays:** Francis Clifford; Edmund Crispin; James McClure.

CAMPENNI, Frank. Member of the English Department, University of Wisconsin, Milwaukee. Author of reviews and articles. **Essays:** E. V. Cunningham; Ishmael Reed.

CARACCIOLO, Peter. Lecturer, Royal Holloway College, London University. Author of studies of Wilkie Collins, Conan Doyle, and *Wuthering Heights*; Science fiction reviewer for *The Tablet*, London. **Essay:** Sheridan Le Fanu (appendix).

CARPENTER, Richard C. Professor of English, Bowling Green State University, Ohio. Author of *Thomas Hardy*, 1964, and articles on Hawthorne, Conrad, Kay Boyle, and others. **Essays:** Ray Bradbury; Michael Collins; Eden Phillpotts.

CARTER, Steven. Assistant Professor of English, University of North Carolina, Wilmington; Co-Editor, *Tugboat Review*. Author of essays on Ross Macdonald, Ishmael Reed, and Julian Symons, and on science fiction writers. **Essay:** Mark McShane.

CAWELTI, John G. Professor of English, State University of New York at Albany. Author of *Apostles of the Self-Made Man*, 1965; *The Six-Gun Mystique*, 1971; *Adventure, Mystery, and Romance: Formula Stories as Art and Popular Culture*, 1976; and many essays on popular literature and culture.

CHOUTEAU, Neysa. Senior Editor, Webster Division, McGraw Hill Book Company. Author of programmed instruction series for industries and an arithmetic skills series. **Essays** (with Martha Alderson): Dorothy Cameron Disney; Alistair MacLean.

CLEVELAND, Carol. Free-lance writer. Contributor to *American Women Writers* and *The Academic American Encyclopedia*. **Essays:** Joan Aiken; Charlotte Armstrong; W. J. Burley; Amanda Cross; Dorothy Dunnett; Elizabeth Fenwick; Tim Heald; Tony Hillerman; Michael Z. Lewin; A. A. Milne; Anne Morice; Elizabeth Peters; Ross Thomas; Dorothy Uhnak.

COLE, Don. Radio and television personality, KFAB Broadcasting, Omaha, Nebraska. Regular reviewer for *Poisoned Pen* and radio interviewer. **Essays:** Brian Cooper; Miles Tripp.

COX, J. Randolph. Reference and Documents Librarian, St. Olaf College, Northfield, Minnesota. Author of bibliographies and studies of John Buchan, the Nick Carter authors, George Harmon Coxe, and others for *Dime Novel Roundup, Baker Street Journal, Edgar Wallace Newsletter, English Literature in Transition, Xenophile, Armchair Detective*, and other journals. **Essays:** George Harmon Coxe; Frederic Van Rensselaer Dey; Ron

Goulart; Berkeley Gray; Thomas W. Hanshew; Gavin Lyall; F. Van Wyck Mason; Craig Rice; Arthur Train; Louis Joseph Vance; Dennis Wheatley.

CRAIG, Patricia. Literary critic and reviewer. Author of *You're a Brick, Angela!*, 1976, *Women and Children First*, 1978, and a forthcoming study of fictional women detectives and spies titled *Sisters-in-Law*, all with Mary Cadogan; author of a forthcoming study of Ulster writing. Contributor to *New Statesman, Guardian, Books and Bookmen, Irish Press.* **Essays:** Gwendoline Butler; Joanna Cannan; Antonia Fraser.

CRIDER, Bill. Chairman of the Division of Humanities, Howard Payne University, Brownwood, Texas; Contributing Editor, *Paperback Quarterly*; publisher of *Macavity*, a fan magazine. Reviewer for journals on detective fiction; currently editing a study of publishing houses. **Essays:** Alan Caillou; Henry Klinger; Richard Sale; Lionel White.

CURJEL, Harald. Surgeon Captain, Royal Navy (retired). Member of the Sherlock Holmes Society of London and of two scion societies in America. **Essay:** Victor Bridges.

DENTON, Frank. Director of Instructional Resources, North Seattle Community College; Reviewer for Seattle *Times*; publisher of *Ash-Wing*, a science fiction magazine. **Essays:** John Blackburn; Victor Canning; Clive Egleton; Michael Gilbert; Hugh C. Rae.

DONALDSON, Betty. Free-lance writer. Author of "The Novels of Arthur Upfield" (bibliography) in *Armchair Detective*, 1974; co-author of *How Did They Die?*, 1979. **Essays:** Lillian Jackson Braun; Stephen Coulter; Julian Rathbone; Arthur Upfield.

DONALDSON, Norman. Senior Editor, Chemical Abstracts Service. Author of *Chemistry and Technology of Naphthalene Compounds*, 1958, and *In Search of Dr. Thorndyke*, 1971; co-author of *How Did They Die?*, 1979. Contributor to *Armchair Detective, Mystery and Detection Annual*, and *Thorndyke File.* **Essays:** E. F. Benson; Mary Elizabeth Braddon (appendix); Ernest Bramah; R. Austin Freeman; Ronald A. Knox

DOVE, George N. Dean (retired), College of Arts and Sciences, East Tennessee State University, Johnson City. Contributor to *The Reader's Encyclopedia*; author of series on the police procedural novel in *Armchair Detective*, the critical introduction to the Mystery Library edition of *Last Seen Wearing ...*, and works-in-progress on Ed McBain and the procedural novel. **Essays:** Rex Burns; Ed McBain; Maurice Procter; Lawrence Treat; Janwillem van de Wetering (appendix); Hillary Waugh.

DUEREN, Fred. Insurance Claims Supervisor; Conducts "Paper Crimes" column in *Armchair Detective* and contributes occasional essays. **Essays:** Harry Carmichael; Frances Crane; Sebastien Japrisot (appendix); Donald MacKenzie; Arthur Maling; Lenore Glen Offord; D. B. Olsen; Ludovic Peters; Evelyn Piper; Kelley Roos; Francis Selwyn; Jeremy Sturrock; R. A. J. Walling.

DUKE, Elizabeth F. Associate Professor of English, Virginia Commonwealth University, Richmond; Editor of Sunday Book Page in the Richmond *Times-Dispatch.* **Essays:** Manning Coles; Elizabeth Linington.

EMMONS, Jeanne Carter. Lecturer, Briar Cliff College, Sioux City, Iowa. **Essays:** Nigel Fitzgerald; Winston Graham.

EVANS, Elizabeth. Associate Professor of English, Georgia Institute of Technology, Atlanta. **Essay:** Helen MacInnes.

FRENCH, Larry L. Formerly General Counsel, Southern Illinois University,

Edwardsville; Publisher and Editor of *Notes for the Curious*, a John Dickson Carr Memorial Journal, and *SCHOOLAW*. Author of eight books on education law. Regular reviewer and contributer to journals on mystery fiction. Died in 1978. **Essays:** Lawrence G. Blochman; Nicholas Meyer.

GEHERIN, David J. Associate Professor of English, Eastern Michigan University, Ypsilanti. Author of essays on Ross Macdonald and "The Hardboiled Detective in the 70's: Some New Candidates"; the latter article, expanded, will appear as a book in 1980. **Essay:** John Gregory Dunne.

GILBERT, Elliot L. Professor of English, University of California, Davis. Editor of *The World of Mystery Fiction*, 1978. Member of the editorial board for The Mystery Library; his own fiction has appeared in *Ellery Queen's Mystery Magazine* and *Best Detective Stories of the Year 1970*. **Essay:** Joel Townsley Rogers.

GINDIN, James. Professor of English, University of Michigan, Ann Arbor. Author of *Postwar British Fiction*, 1962, *Harvest of a Quiet Eye: The Novel of Compassion*, 1971, and *The English Climate: An Excursion into a Biography of John Galsworthy*, 1979. **Essays:** Nicholas Blake; John D. MacDonald.

GOTTSCHALK, Jane. Professor of English, University of Wisconsin, Oshkosh. Author of essays on detective fiction for *Armchair Detective*; has been teaching a course in the subject since 1973. **Essays:** H. C. Bailey; Ruth Fenisong; Ellis Peters.

GRELLA, George. Associate Professor of English, University of Rochester. Author of studies of Ian Fleming, Ross Macdonald, and John le Carré for *New Republic*, essays on the formal detective novel and hard-boiled mystery fiction, and many other subjects. **Essays:** Kingsley Amis; W. R. Burnett; Len Deighton; Ian Fleming; Charles McCarry; Allan Prior; James Hall Roberts; Lawrence Sanders; Georges Simenon (appendix).

GRIMES, Larry E. Associate Professor of English and Director of Inter-disciplinary Studies, Bethany College, West Virginia. Has written for *Studies in Short Fiction*, *Journal of Popular Culture*, *Popular Culture Scholar*, *JDM Bibliophile*. **Essays:** Anna Clarke; S. B. Hough.

GROCHOWSKI, Mary Ann. Psychiatric Social Worker and owner of Suspense Unlimited Bookstore, West Allis, Wisconsin. Frequent contributor to journals and occasional reviewer of mystery fiction for Milwaukee *Journal*. **Essays:** Carol Carnac; James Hadley Chase; Octavus Roy Cohen; Marten Cumberland; Amber Dean; Dorothy Eden; Robert L. Fish; Hulbert Footner; John Godey; Simon Harvester; Clarence Budington Kelland; Constance and Gwyneth Little; Holly Roth; John Stephen Strange; Lee Thayer; Thurman Warriner; Victor L. Whitechurch; Valentine Williams.

GROFF, Mary. Free-lance writer. Specializes in articles on the English mystery, 1930–60, and contributes a feature to *Poisoned Pen* on adaptation of true crime to fiction. **Essays:** Charity Blackstock; Guy Cullingford; Katharine Farrer; Helen Nielsen; Poul Ørum (appendix); Robert Player; Shelley Smith; June Thomson; Glen Trevor; Patrick Wayland; Ethel Lina White.

HAGEMANN, E. R. Professor of Humanities, University of Louisville. Has written articles on Stephen Crane, J. W. De Forest, Ernest Hemingway, Henry James, B. Traven, and western American history, and on Paul Cain and Raoul Whitfield. **Essay:** Raoul Whitfield.

HARRIS, Herbert. See his own entry. **Essays:** Eric Bruton; John Bude; John Burke; Gwendoline Butler; Margaret Carr; Basil Copper; Frances Cowen; Rae Foley; Reg Gadney;

Margot Neville; Roger Ormerod; Rhona Petrie; E. and M. A. Radford; J. F. Straker; Margaret Summerton; John Welcome.

HARWOOD, John. Retired textile worker. Has written for *Rohmer Review, Mystery Reader's Newsletter,* and *Armchair Detective.* **Essay:** Arthur B. Reeve.

HAYNE, Barrie. Professor of English, Innis College, University of Toronto. Author of numerous papers for the Popular Culture Association. **Essays:** John Buchan; Alec Coppel; Miriam Allen deFord; Gerard Fairlie; Frances Noyes Hart; Fergus Hume; Cora Jarrett; Thomas Kyd; E. Phillips Oppenheim; Sapper; Helen Simpson and Clemence Dane; Carolyn Wells.

HAYNE, Joanne Harack. Co-ordinator, Programme Development, School of Continuing Studies, University of Toronto. Has taught courses regularly on the detective in literature and delivered papers on the subject for the Popular Culture Association. **Essays:** Christianna Brand; Lillian de la Torre; Mignon G. Eberhart; Helen Eustis; Reginald Hill; Hans Hellmut Kirst (appendix); Maurice Leblanc (appendix); Peter Lovesey; Mary Roberts Rinehart; Sara Woods.

HEILBRUN, Carolyn G. See her own entry as Amanda Cross. **Essay:** P. D. James.

HERGENHAN, L. T. Professor of English, University of Queensland, Brisbane; Editor, *Australian Literary Studies.*

HILL, Reginald. See his own entry. **Essays:** Desmond Bagley; Tony Kenrick; Michael Kenyon; Berkely Mather; Martin Russell.

HOCH, Edward D. See his own entry. **Essays:** William Brittain; John Collier; Dorothy Salisbury Davis; Stanley Ellin; Joyce Harrington; Michael Harrison; Ira Levin; Margaret Millar; Wade Miller; Bill Pronzini; S. S. Rafferty; Jack Ritchie.

HOLMAN, C. Hugh. See his own entry. **Essays:** William Faulkner; S. S. Van Dine.

HUBIN, Allen J. Manager, 3M Company; Founding Editor, *Armchair Detective,* since 1967. Author of *The Bibliography of Crime Fiction, 1749–1975,* 1979. Editor of six volumes of *Best Detective Stories of the Year,* 1970–1975, and *Best of the Best Detective Stories,* 1971. Conducted the weekly "Criminals at Large" column in the New York *Times,* 1968–1971.

HUGHES, Dorothy B. See her own entry. **Essays:** Gavin Black; John and Emery Bonett; Jon Cleary; Paul E. Erdman; Stanton Forbes; Sarah Gainham; Dorothy Gardiner; Arthur D. Goldstein; Matthew Head; Hammond Innes; Charlotte Jay; Brown Meggs; Gwen Moffat; Richard Martin Stern; Ernest Tidyman; Thomas Walsh.

IRELAND, Donald C. Assistant Headmaster of a boys' preparatory school and proprietor of A1 Crime Fiction in Sherborne, Dorset. Author of books on rugby, and contributor to *Armchair Detective.* **Essays:** Lionel Black; John G. Brandon; Roger Busby; Mark Corrigan; Hugh Desmond; W. Murdoch Duncan; T. C. H. Jacobs; Hamilton Jobson; Philip Loraine; Philip McCutchan; Ritchie Perry; Angus Ross; Jonathan Ross; Kenneth Royce; Douglas Rutherford.

JEFFARES, A. Norman. Professor of English Studies, University of Stirling; Chairman of the Literature Section, Scottish Arts Council. Has written extensively on William Butler Yeats and other Anglo-Irish writers, has edited *Restoration Comedy* (4 vols.) for the Folio Society, and also writes on American, commonwealth, and 18th-century English literature.   Editor of *Review of English Literature*; *Ariel: A Review of International English Literature*; *Writers and Critics* series; and *New Oxford English Series*.   **Essays:** Eric Ambler; Erskine Childers; Nicolas Freeling; Bram Stoker.

JEFFREY, David K.   Associate Professor of English, Auburn University, Alabama; Co-Editor, *Southern Humanities Review*. Author of many essays in scholarly journals.   **Essays:** Edward S. Aarons; Trevanian; Joseph Wambaugh.

JOYNER, Nancy C.   Professor of English, Western Carolina University, Cullowhee, North Carolina.   Author of *Edwin Arlington Robinson: A Reference Guide*, 1978; Contributor to *Great Writers of the English Language*.   **Essays:** C. Hugh Holman; Dorothy B. Hughes; Helen McCloy.

KEATING, H. R. F.   See his own entry.   **Essays:** Ted Allbeury; Margery Allingham; Agatha Christie; Lionel Davidson; Peter Dickinson; Arthur Conan Doyle; Ivor Drummond; Mary Fitt; Dick Francis; Dulcie Gray; William Haggard; Herbert Harris; E. W. Hornung; Mary Kelly; Ivy Litvinov; Laurence Meynell; Anthony Price; George Sims; Michael Underwood; Ted Willis; Margaret Yorke; P. B. Yuill.

KELLEY, George.   Business Consultant.   Regular contributor to journals on detective fiction; science fiction reviewer for *Paperback Quarterly*; Editor of *MAZES*, mystery fan magazine.   **Essays:** Gerald Kersh; Dan J. Marlowe.

KELLY, R. Gordon.   Associate Director of the American Studies Program, University of Maryland, College Park.   Author of *Mother Was a Lady: Self and Society in Selected American Children's Periodicals, 1865–1890*, 1974, and articles on literature and history and John D. MacDonald.   Contributor to *Twentieth-Century Children's Writers*.   **Essays:** Noel Behn; John Bingham; Peter Driscoll; Roger L. Simon; Elleston Trevor.

KENDLE, Burton.   Professor of English, Roosevelt University, Chicago.   Author of articles on D. H. Lawrence, John Cheever, William March, Tennessee Williams, and others.   Contributor to *Contemporary Novelists*, *Contemporary Poets*, and *Great Writers of the English Language*.   **Essays:** Roald Dahl; Robin Maugham; Joyce Porter.

KERN, Donna Rose Casella.   Graduate student in English, Michigan State University, East Lansing; Managing Editor, *The Gypsy Scholar*.   Contributor to *American Women Writers*.   **Essays:** A. E. Coppard; Max Murray; Bernard Newman; Cecil M. Wills.

KING, Daniel P.   Professor and Writer.   Regular reviewer for *World Literature Today*; contributes articles on criminology and criminal law to international jounals.   **Essays:** G. Belton Cobb; Macdonald Hastings; William Le Queux; Edgar Lustgarten; A. E. W. Mason; Nigel Morland.

KING, Margaret J.   Editor and Researcher, Humanist Center, Yellow Springs, Ohio.   Has written on the detective genre for *Antioch Review*, *Armchair Detective*, and *MELUS*; Contributor to *Women Writers of the World*.   **Essays:** John Ball; Earl Derr Biggers; A. H. Z. Carr; H. R. F. Keating; Harry Kemelman.

KLEIN, H. M.   Lecturer in Comparative Literature, University of East Anglia, Norwich.   Author of *Die Englische Komödie im 18. Jahrhundert* and a study of J. B. Priestley.   Editor and translator of English dramatic texts.   **Essays:** Friedrich Dürrenmatt (appendix); J. B. Priestley.

KLEIN, Kathleen G.   Assistant Professor of English, Indiana University/Purdue University, Indianapolis.   Author of articles for *Armchair Detective* and *American Women*

Writers; preparing a book on professional women detectives in fiction. **Essays:** Joan Fleming; Lucille Fletcher; Georgette Heyer; Lillian O'Donnell; Margaret Scherf; Josephine Tey; Patricia Wentworth.

LACHMAN, Marvin. Administrator, New York State Bureau of Disability Determinations, and free-lance writer. Senior Editor, *Encyclopedia of Mystery and Detection*, 1976; co-author, *Detectionary*, 1971. Author of continuing series on the American Regional Mystery and Sports and the Mystery Story in *Armchair Detective*; Conducts the column "It's about Crime" in *Mystery Fancier*. **Essays:** Ben Benson; Doris Miles Disney; Leslie Ford; James Holding; Sydney Horler; Ed Lacy; Hugh Pentecost; James Powell; Aaron Marc Stein; Nedra Tyre.

LAMMERS, Donald. Professor of History, Michigan State University, East Lansing; Member of the Editorial Board, *Albion*. Author of essays on Nevil Shute for *Journal of British Studies* and *Centennial Review*. **Essay:** Nevil Shute.

LANDRUM, Larry N. Associate Professor of English, Michigan State University, East Lansing. Co-Editor, *Dimensions of Detective Fiction*, 1976; Contributed "Guide to Detective Fiction" to *Handbook of American Popular Culture*, 1978; teaches courses in literature and popular culture. **Essays:** Frank Gruber; Ross Macdonald; Richard S. Prather; Jack Webb.

LOFTS, W. O. G. Advertising writer and rsearcher, and publisher's consultant. Author of *The British Bibliography of Edgar Wallace*, 1969, *The Men Behind Boys' Fiction*, 1970, *The Saint and Leslie Charteris*, 1971, and *The World of Frank Richards*, 1975, all with Derek Adley; and hundreds of articles on juvenile, detective, and other types of fiction. President, Cambridge Old Boys Book Club. **Essay** (with Derek Adley): Max Pemberton.

LOWDER, Christopher. Free-lance writer. Formerly on editorial staff of IPC Magazines, London. Wrote first published thriller, a Sexton Blake, at age of 19; currently writes pulp fiction and comicbooks under a variety of pseudonyms; author of critical articles on popular fiction and comicbook artists and authors. **Essays:** John Newton Chance; John Gardner; Edgar Wallace.

LUNDIN, Bo. Journalist and critic. Author of two studies of detective fiction: *Salongsbödlarna*, 1971, and *Spårhundarna*, 1973. Member of Swedish Academy of Detection. **Essays:** Leslie Charteris; Adam Diment; Per Wahlöö and Maj Sjöwall (appendix).

LYNDS, Dennis. See his own entry as Michael Collins. **Essays:** Brett Halliday; George V. Higgins.

MACDONALD, Andrew F. Specialist in Renaissance Drama, currently teaching international students, University of Texas, Austin. Author of articles on Ben Jonson, Shakespeare, English as a second language, teaching methods, and popular culture. **Essays:** Kenneth Benton; Frederick Forsyth.

MACDONALD, Virginia. Specialist in Renaissance Prose Fiction, English Department, University of Texas, Austin. Author of articles on Southwestern writers, popular culture, Shakespearian influences. **Essays:** Brian Cleeve; Pat Flower; Robert Harling; Shaun Herron; Stuart Jackman; Marie Belloc Lowndes.

MacDOUGALL, Susan B. Assistant Professor of English, University of Nevada, Reno. **Essays:** George Bellairs; The Gordons; Leonard Holton.

MAIO, Kathleen L. Librarian. Mystery Adviser for *Women and Literature*: *An*

Annotated Bibliography, third and fourth editions. Author of articles on women's mystery fiction in feminist and popular culture journals. **Essays:** Anne Hocking; Jean Potts.

MASSA, Ann. Lecturer in American Literature, University of Leeds. Author of *Vachel Lindsay: Fieldworker for the American Dream*, 1970, and *The American Novel Since 1945*, 1975; Co-Author of *American Literature, Nineteenth and Twentieth Centuries*, 1978. **Essays:** Nina Bawden; Ann Bridge; Elspeth Huxley; Robert Ludlum; T. S. Stribling.

McCAHERY, James R. Teacher of French and Romanian, Director of International Exchange Programs, Xavier High School, New York. Writes the continuing feature "Series Spotlight" for *The Not-So-Private Eye* and reviews for *Poisoned Pen*. Editor of the *Mystery Loves Company* fan magazine. **Essay:** Patricia McGerr.

McCONACHIE, Frances D. Teacher of Composition and Literature, DePaul University, Chicago. **Essays:** Henry Slesar; Jon Manchip White.

McSHERRY, Frank D., Jr. Commercial Artist and Writer. His most recent book jacket design was for the Mysterious Press edition of Cornell Woolrich's *Angels of Darkness*, 1978. Work in progress includes a study of the theory of criminal behavior. **Essays:** Jack Boyle; Andrew York.

MERTZ, Stephen. Free-lance writer. Has written on Michael Avallone for *Armchair Detective*, on Carroll John Daly for *Mystery Fancier*, and helped edit Don Pendleton's *The Executioner's War Book*, 1977. **Essays:** Willis Todhunter Ballard; Robert Leslie Bellem; Peter Cheyney; Frank Kane.

MEYERSON, Jeffrey. Editor and Publisher, *Poisoned Pen*, and mail-order book dealer. Has written for many of the other publications in the field. **Essays:** Thomas Gifford; Gregory Mcdonald.

MURRAY, Will. Free-lance writer; Vice-President and Editor, Odyssey Publications Inc.; Editor, *Duende*, a research journal on pulp magazines. Author of *The Duende History of The Shadow Magazine*, 1979, and Co-Author of *The Man Behind Doc Savage*, 1974. Regular contributor and interviewer for *Pulp* and *Xenophile*. **Essays:** Ken Crossen; Carroll John Daly; Lester Dent; Walter B. Gibson; Frederick Nebel; Frank L. Packard; Don Pendleton; R. T. M. Scott.

MUSSELL, Kay J. Director, American Studies Program, American University, Washington, D.C. Author of "Gothic Novels" for *Handbook of American Popular Culture*, 1978, "The Sexual Woman in Modern Gothic Fiction" for *Journal of Popular Culture*, 1975, and a forthcoming study of popular fictional formulas for women in America. **Essays:** Martha Albrand; Evelyn Anthony; Catherine Gaskin; Mary Stewart; Phyllis A. Whitney.

MUSTE, John M. Professor of English, Ohio State University, Columbus. Author of *Say That We Saw Spain Die*, 1966, and numerous essays on modern fiction. **Essays:** Bill S. Ballinger; Thomas B. Dewey.

NEVINS, Francis M., Jr. See his own entry. **Essays:** Cleve F. Adams; Michael Avallone; Edgar Box; Erle Stanley Gardner; Edward D. Hoch; Harry Stephen Keeler; John Lutz; Milton Propper; Ellery Queen; Donald E. Westlake; Cornell Woolrich.

NOLAN, William F. See his own entry. **Essays:** Steve Fisher; Ray Russell.

OCCHIOGROSSO, Frank. Associate Professor of English, Drew University, Madison,

New Jersey. Regular contributor and reviewer for *Armchair Detective*; has written on Dashiell Hammett for *New Republic*. **Essays:** Kenneth Fearing; Barry Perowne.

OUSBY, Ian. Associate Professor of English, University of Maryland, College Park. Author of *Bloodhounds of Heaven: The Detective in English Fiction from Godwin to Doyle*, 1976. **Essays:** Charles Dickens (appendix); Geoffrey Household; Christopher St. John Sprigg; Colin Watson.

PARKER, Robert B. See his own entry. **Essays:** Raymond Chandler; Dashiell Hammett.

PATTOW, Donald J. Professor of English, University of Wisconsin, Stevens Point. Teaches a course in mystery literature and contributes articles to the journals. **Essays:** Henry Cecil; Robert Eustace; Wallace Hildick; Richard Keverne; Carolyn Weston.

PIGGOTT, Stuart. Abercromby Professor of Archaeology, University of Edinburgh, now Emeritus. Author of numerous archaeological books and papers. **Essay:** Glyn Daniel.

PIKE, B. A. Teacher. Author of studies of Margery Allingham and Gladys Mitchell in *Armchair Detective*, contributions to *The Poisoned Pen*, an essay for *Scott: Modern Judgments*, 1968; creates crosswords for *The Listener*. **Essays:** Edward Candy; Beverley Nichols; John Trench.

PRONZINI, Bill. See his own entry. **Essays:** Gil Brewer; Frederick C. Davis; Bruno Fischer; Fletcher Flora; Geoffrey Homes; Day Keene; Harry Whittington; Collin Wilcox.

PRY, Elmer. Professor of English, DePaul University, Chicago. Author of essays on detective fiction for *Poe Studies*, *Armchair Detective*, and *WestAmerLit*, and other literary studies in *Style* and the *Literary Perspectives* series. **Essays:** Max Brand; Cornelius Hirschberg; Hugh Marlowe; Vincent Starrett.

RESTAINO, Katherine M. Dean, Saint Peter's College, Englewood Cliffs, New Jersey. Teacher of detective fiction and author of papers for Popular Culture Association. **Essays:** Samuel Fuller; Joseph Hayes; Norah Lofts; William P. McGivern.

RUDIN, Seymour. Professor of English, University of Massachusetts, Amherst; Member of Editorial Board and Performing Arts Critic, *Massachusetts Review*. Author of articles on theatre for *Commentary*, *Hudson Review*, and other journals; contributor of entries on detective fiction to *Encyclopedia International*, 1963. **Essays:** Jack Finney; Waters (appendix).

RUSSELL, Ray. See his own entry. **Essay:** William F. Nolan.

SALISKAS, Joan M. Member of the English Department, University of Illinois, Urbana. **Essay:** Brian Freemantle.

SCOTT, Art. Research Chemist; Editor of *Elementary, My Dear APA*, bi-monthly collection of mystery fan magazines, and publisher of *Shot Scott's Rap Sheet* for the series. **Essays:** Lawrence Block; Carter Brown; Richard Deming; David Dodge; William Campbell Gault; Henry Kane; Jonathan Latimer; James Leasor; Harold Q. Masur; Stuart Palmer; Bart Spicer.

SHIBUK, Charles. Free-lance writer. Senior Editor, *Encyclopedia of Mystery and Detection*, 1976; co-author, *Detectionary*, 1971; Columnist ("The Paperback Revolution") for *Armchair Detective* since 1967. **Essays:** Anthony Abbot; E. C. Bentley; Leo Bruce; Glyn

Carr; Elizabeth Daly; Val Gielgud; Bruce Graeme; Patrick Hamilton; Cyril Hare; Richard Hull; Jack Iams; Selwyn Jepson; Baynard H. Kendrick; C. Daly King; C. H. B. Kitchin; Paul McGuire; Patricia Moyes; C. E. Vulliamy; Henry Wade; Clifford Witting.

SLUNG, Michele. Free-lance writer. Editor, *Crime on Her Mind*, 1975; McKay-Washburn novels of suspense, 1975–77. Contributor to *The Mystery Story*, 1976; member of the Mystery Writers of America Awards Committee, and editor of a forthcoming MWA anthology. **Essays:** Anna Katharine Green; Michael Innes; Hilda Lawrence; Gladys Mitchell; Dorothy L. Sayers.

SMITH, Dwight C., Jr. Associate Professor, School of Criminal Justice, Rutgers University, New Brunswick, New Jersey. Author of *The Mafia Mystique*, 1975, and a study of the "Mafia" in contemporary fiction for *Italian Americana*, 1976. **Essay:** Ovid Demaris.

SNYDER, John. Associate Professor, Literature and Film, University of Houston, Clear Lake City. Author of *The Dear Love of Man: Tragic and Lyric Communion in Walt Whitman*, 1975, "The Spy Story as Modern Tragedy" in *Literature/Film Quarterly*, and other literary criticism. **Essays:** John le Carré; Alain Robbe-Grillet (appendix).

STAPLES, Katherine. Instructor in English, University of Texas, Austin. Translator of works by Henri Rousseau and of Arthur Rimbaud's *Les Illuminations*. **Essays:** Edwin Balmer and William MacHarg; Nicolas Bentley; Pierre Boulle (appendix); Lynn Brock; Jocelyn Davey; John P. Marquand.

STEDMAN, Jane W. Professor of English, Roosevelt University, Chicago. Author of *W. S. Gilbert*, 1979. Editor of *Gilbert Before Sullivan: Six Comic Plays*, 1967. Regular contributor to *Opera News* and to journals of Victorian studies. Originated and teaches a course in Literature and Aesthetics of Horror. **Essays:** Caryl Brahms; Shirley Jackson; F. Tennyson Jesse; Joseph Shearing.

STERN, Carol Simpson. Associate Professor, Department of Interpretation, Northwestern University, Evanston, Illinois. Research Consultant and Contributor, *English Literature in Transition*; Theatre and Book Reviewer for *Victorian Studies* and Chicago *Sun-Times*. Contributor to *Contemporary Poets* and *Contemporary Novelists*. **Essays:** Tom Ardies; June Drummond; John N. Iannuzzi; Roderic Jeffries; Arthur La Bern; Anthony Lejeune; Edmund McGirr.

TALBURT, Nancy Ellen. Professor of English and Assistant to the President, University of Arkansas, Fayetteville. Co-Editor of *A Mystery Reader*, 1975, and *The American Experience*, 1978. Author of articles on mystery fiction in journals and papers for the Popular Culture Association. **Essays:** Isaac Asimov; Josephine Bell; Phyllis Bentley; W. Somerset Maugham.

THOMPSON, George J. Associate Professor of English, Emporia State University, Kansas. Author of "The Problem of Moral Vision in Dashiell Hammett's Detective Novels," 5 installments in *Armchair Detective*, 1973–74. **Essays:** Francis M. Nevins, Jr.; Robert B. Parker.

TOWNSEND, Guy M. Journalist and Editor, Vevay Newspapers, Indiana; Editor and Publisher, *The Mystery Fancier*. Author of a study of Josephine Tey's treatment of Richard III. **Essays:** V. C. Clinton-Baddeley; Hildegarde Dolson; Richard and Frances Lockridge; Marco Page; Rex Stout.

WALL, Donald C. Professor of English, Eastern Washington University, Cheney. Author of a study of Apartheid in the fiction of James McClure; his own fiction has appeared in *Mike Shayne's Mystery Magazine*.   Chairman of the Mystery and Detective Program, Popular Culture Association Annual Meeting.   **Essay:** Joe Gores.

WASHBURNE, Carol.   Senior Editor, Elementary Language Arts, Webster Division, McGraw Hill Book Company.   Writes professionally for *Elementary English* and avocationally writes poetry.   **Essay:** Jean Stubbs.

WEAVER, William.   Critic and Translator.   Recipient of the National Book Award in the United States and the John Florio Prize in Great Britain, twice, for translations of contemporary Italian fiction.   Chief reviewer of crime fiction and music critic for *Financial Times*, London; critic for the *International Herald Tribune*.   **Essays:** Catherine Aird; Celia Fremlin; Roy Lewis.

WIEGEL, John A.   Professor of English, Miami University, Ohio.   Author of *Lawrence Durrell*, 1965, *Colin Wilson*, 1975, and *B. F. Skinner*, 1977.   **Essay:** Colin Wilson.

WHITLEY, John S.   Dean, School of English and American Studies, University of Sussex, Brighton.   Author of *William Golding: Lord of the Flies*, 1970, and *F. Scott Fitzgerald: The Great Gatsby*, 1970. Co-Editor of *Charles Dickens' American Notes*, 1972.   **Essays:** John Franklin Bardin; Andrew Bergman; James M. Cain; Derek Marlowe; Horace McCoy.

WOOD, Neville W.   Retired.   Collector of major Golden Age authors and Boys Weekly Publications.   Member, Sherlock Holmes Society of London.   **Essays:** Christopher Bush; A. Fielding; Milward Kennedy; Rufus King.

WOODCOCK, George.   Free-lance Writer, Lecturer, and Editor.   Author of verse (*Selected Poems*, 1967), plays, travel books, biographies, and works on history and politics; critical works include *William Godwin*, 1946, *The Incomparable Aphra*, 1948, *The Paradox of Oscar Wilde*, 1949, *The Crystal Spirit* (on Orwell), 1966, *Hugh MacLennan*, 1969, *Odysseus Ever Returning: Canadian Writers and Writing*, 1970, *Mordecai Richler*, 1970, *Dawn and the Darkest Hour* (on Aldous Huxley), 1972, *Herbert Read*, 1972, and *Thomas Merton*, 1978.   Editor of anthologies, and of works by Charles Lamb, Malcolm Lowry, Wyndham Lewis, and others.   **Essays:** Algernon Blackwood; G. K. Chesterton; Roy Fuller; William Godwin (appendix); Graham Greene; Julian Symons.

WORLEY, Joan Y.   Instructor of English, University of Oklahoma, Norman.   **Essay:** James Norman.

YATES, Donald A.   Professor of Latin American Literature, Michigan State University, East Lansing.   Editor of *Tales For a Rainy Night*, 1961; Editor and Translator of *Latin Blood*, 1972.   Collaborated in translating and editing *Labyrinths* by Jorge Luis Borges, 1962; has translated several Argentine detective novels, and published widely on Latin American fiction, the locked-room puzzle, and other literary topics; currently preparing a critical biography of Borges.   **Essays:** M. M'Donnell Bodkin; Jorge Luis Borges (appendix); H. C. Branson; Melville Davisson Post; Clayton Rawson; William Wiegand; Israel Zangwill.

WITHDRAWN